PIERS THE PLOWMAN

AND

RICHARD THE REDELESS

WILLIAM LANGLAND

THE VISION OF WILLIAM

CONCERNING

PIERS THE PLOWMAN

IN THREE PARALLEL TEXTS

TOGETHER WITH

RICHARD THE REDELESS

BY WILLIAM LANGLAND

(ABOUT 1362—1399 A.D.)

EDITED FROM NUMEROUS MANUSCRIPTS

WITH PREFACE, NOTES, AND A GLOSSARY

BY THE

REV. WALTER W. SKEAT, Litt. D., Ll.D.

VOL. I.—TEXT

OXFORD UNIVERSITY PRESS

OXFORD
UNIVERSITY PRESS

Great Clarendon Street, Oxford OX2 6DP

Oxford University Press is a department of the University of Oxford
It furthers the University's objective of excellence in research, scholarship,
and education by publishing worldwide in

Oxford New York

Athens Auckland Bangkok Bogotá Buenos Aires Cape Town
Chennai Dar es Salaam Delhi Florence Hong Kong Istanbul Karachi
Kolkata Kuala Lumpur Madrid Melbourne Mexico City Mumbai
Nairobi Paris São Paulo Singapore Taipei Tokyo Toronto Warsaw

and associated companies in Berlin Ibadan

Oxford is a registered trade mark of Oxford University Press
in the UK and in certain other countries

Published in the United States
by Oxford University Press Inc., New York

© Oxford University Press 1886

The moral rights of the author have been asserted
Database right Oxford University Press (maker)

Special edition for Sandpiper Books Ltd., 2001

All rights reserved. No part of this publication may be reproduced,
stored in a retrieval system, or transmitted, in any form or by any means,
without the prior permission in writing of Oxford University Press,
or as expressly permitted by law, or under terms agreed with the appropriate
reprographics rights organization. Enquiries concerning reproduction
outside the scope of the above should be sent to the Rights Department,
Oxford University Press, at the address above

You must not circulate this book in any other binding or cover
and you must impose this same condition on any acquirer

British Library Cataloguing in Publication Data

Data available

Library of Congress Cataloging in Publication Data

Data available

ISBN 0–19 811366–8 (Vol. 1)

1 3 5 7 9 10 8 6 4 2

Printed in Great Britain
on acid-free paper by
Biddles Ltd.,
Guildford & King's Lynn

CONTENTS OF VOLUME I.

			PAGE
EXPLANATION OF THE METHOD OF PRINTING THE TEXTS . .			1

PIERS THE PLOWMAN.

A. PROLOGUE;	B. PROLOGUE;	C. PASSUS I . .	2, 3
A. PASSUS I;	B. PASSUS I;	C. PASSUS II . .	20, 21
A. PASSUS II;	B. PASSUS II;	C. PASSUS III . .	40, 41
A. PASSUS III;	B. PASSUS III;	C. PASSUS IV . .	62, 63
A. PASSUS IV;	B. PASSUS IV;	C. PASSUS V . .	100, 101
		C. PASSUS VI . .	118
A. PASSUS V;	B. PASSUS V .	. . . . .	122
		C. PASSUS VII . .	131
		C. PASSUS VIII . .	167
A. PASSUS VI .	. . .	. . . .	180
A. PASSUS VII;	B. PASSUS VI;	C. PASSUS IX . .	192, 193
A. PASSUS VIII;	B. PASSUS VII;	C. PASSUS X . .	226, 227

VITA DE DO-WEL.

A. PASSUS IX;	B. PASSUS VIII;	C. PASSUS XI . .	252, 253
A. PASSUS X;	B. PASSUS IX .	. . . .	264
A. PASSUS XI;	B. PASSUS X;	C. PASSUS XII . .	284, 285
A. PASSUS XII	. . . .	. . . .	326
B. PASSUS XI;	C. PASSUS XII (*continued*)	. .	330, 331, 333
	C. PASSUS XIII	. . . . .	333
	C. PASSUS XIV	. . . .	352
B. PASSUS XII;	C. PASSUS XV	. . . . .	366, 367

CONTENTS.

		PAGE
B. Passus XIII;	C. Passus XVI	386, 387
B. Passus XIV		414
	C. Passus XVII	423

VITA DE DO-BET.[1]

B. Passus XV;	C. Passus XVII (*continued*)	436, 437
	C. Passus XVIII	453
B. Passus XVI;	C. Passus XIX	478, 479
B. Passus XVII;	C. Passus XX	498, 499
B. Passus XVIII;	C. Passus XXI	520, 521

VITA DE DO-BEST.

B. Passus XIX;	C. Passus XXII	550, 551
B. Passus XX;	C. Passus XXIII	578, 579

RICHARD THE REDELESS.

Prologue	603
Passus I	606
Passus II	609
Passus III	615
Passus IV	626

[1] In the C-text, the *Vita de Dobet* begins with Pass. xviii.

THE VISION OF WILLIAM

CONCERNING

PIERS THE PLOWMAN.

[IN the following pages all three versions of this Poem are exhibited in parallel texts. The A-text, or earliest version, appears at the upper part of the pages, as far as it goes. Being much shorter than the others, it disappears from the latter portion of the text.

The B-text, or second version, appears on the lower part of the left-hand pages; towards the end, it occupies the whole of each left-hand page.

The C-text, or latest version, appears on the lower part of the right-hand pages ; towards the end, it occupies the whole of each right-hand page.

The A-text is printed as it occurs in V = Vernon MS. (in the Bodleian Library). All deviations from V are shewn in the foot-notes, and are taken from other MSS., viz. T = Trin. Coll. Cam. R. 3. 14 ; H = Harl. 875, Brit. Museum ; U = Univ. Coll. Oxford ; H_2 = Harl. 6041 ; D = Douce 323 (Bodleian Library). V is imperfect, ending at Pass. XI. 180 ; the rest of this Passus is from T. Pass. XII is from MS. Rawl. Poet. 137, collated with U throughout lines 1-19 ; the rest of this Passus occurs in the Rawlinson MS. and in the Ingilby MS. *only.* Observe that the text in V abounds with *Southern* forms, due to the scribe.

The B-text is printed from L = MS. Laud 851 (Bodleian Library). All deviations from L are given in the foot-notes, and are taken from other MSS., viz. W = the MS. printed by Mr. Wright (Trin. Coll. Cam. B. 15. 17); O = Oriel 79 ; R = Rawl. Poet. 38 ; C = Camb. Univ. Lib. Dd. 1. 17 ; B = Bodley 814 ; C_2 = Camb. Univ. Lib. Ll. 4. 14 ; and Y = Mr. Yates Thompson's MS.

The C-text is printed from P = MS. Phillipps 8231. All deviations from P are shewn in the foot notes, many being mere corrections (due to collation) of defective spellings. The other MSS. are E = Laud 656 ; I = Ilchester MS. ; M = Museum MŠ. (Cotton, Vesp. B. 16) ; F = Camb. Univ. Lib. Ff. 5. 35 ; G = Camb. Univ. Lib. Dd. 3. 13 ; S = Corpus Christi Coll. Camb. 293 ; B = Bodley 814 ; K = (Kenelm) Digby 171 (Bodleian Library) ; T = Trin. Coll. Cam. R. 3. 14.]

Prologus.

IN a somer sesun · whon softe was the sonne,
I schop me in-to a schroud · a scheep as I were;
In habite of an hermite · vn-holy of werkes,
Wende I wydene in this world · wondres to here.   4
Bote in a Mayes morwnynge · on Maluerne hulles
Me bi-fel a ferly · a feyrie me thouhte;
I was weori of wandringe · and wente me to reste

INCIPIT LIBER DE PETRO PLOWMAN.

Prologus.

IN a somer seson · whan soft was the sonne,
I shope me in shroudes · as I a shepe were,
In habite as an heremite · vnholy of workes,
Went wyde in this world · wondres to here.   4
Ac on a May mornynge · on Maluerne hulles
Me byfel a ferly · of fairy me thou3te;
I was wery forwandred · and went me to reste
Vnder a brode banke · bi a bornes side,   8
And as I lay and lened · and loked in the wateres,
I slombred in a slepyng · it sweyued so merye.
Thanne gan I to meten · a merueilouse sweuene,
That I was in a wildernesse · wist I neuer where,   12
As I bihelde in-to the est · an hiegh to the sonne,
I seigh a toure on a toft · trielich ymaked;
A depe dale binethe · a dongeon there-inne,
With depe dyches and derke · and dredful of sight.   16
A faire felde ful of folke · fonde I there bytwene,
Of alle maner of men · the mene and the riche,
Worchyng and wandryng · as the worlde asketh.

A. 14. tri3ely T; triely U; wonderliche V H.   C. 2. me MFS; P *om.*

A. PROLOGUE. 8–19.   C. PASSUS I. 1–21.

Vndur a brod banke · bi a bourne syde,　　　　　　　8
And as I lay and leonede · and lokede on the watres,
I slumberde in a slepyng · hit sownede so murie.
　Thenne gon I meeten · a meruelous sweuene,
That I was in a wildernesse · wuste I neuer where,　　12
And as I beo-heold in-to the est · an-heiȝ to the sonne,
I sauh a tour on a toft · triȝely i-maket;
A deop dale bi-neothe · a dungun ther-inne,
With deop dich and derk · and dredful of siht.　　　16
　A feir feld ful of folk · fond I ther bi-twene,
Of alle maner of men · the mene and the riche,
Worchinge and wondringe · as the world asketh.

HIC INCIPIT VISIO WILLELMI DE PETRO PLOUHMAN.

PASSUS I.

IN a somere seyson · whan softe was the sonne,
　Y shop me in-to shrobbis · as y a shepherde were,
In abit as an ermite · vnholy of werkes,
Ich wente forth in the worlde · wonders to hure,　　4
And sawe meny cellis · and selcouthe thynges.
Ac on a May morwenyng · on Maluerne hulles
Me byfel for to slepe · for weyrynesse of wandryng;
And in a launde as ich lay · lenede ich and slepte,　　8
And merueylously me mette · as ich may ȝow telle;
Al the welthe of this worlde · and the woo bothe,
Wynkyng as it were · wyterly ich saw hyt,
Of tryuthe and of tricherye · of tresoun and of gyle,　　12
Al ich saw slepynge · as ich shal ȝow telle.
Esteward ich byhulde · after the sonne,
And sawe a toure, as ich trowede · truthe was ther-ynne;
Westwarde ich waitede · in a whyle after,　　　　16
And sawe a deep dale · deth, as ich lyuede,
Wonede in tho wones · and wyckede spiritus.
A fair feld, ful of folke · fonde ich ther bytwyne,
Alle manere of men · the mene and the ryche,　　　20
Worchynge and wandrynge · as the worlde asketh.

---

a MFSE; P *om.*　　4. worle P.　　16. wyle P.　　19. fol (*for* ful) P.

Summe putten hem to the plou3 · and pleiden hem ful seldene, 20
In eringe and in sowynge · swonken ful harde,
That monie of theos wasturs · in glotonye distruen.
   And summe putten hem to pruide · apparaylden hem ther-after,
In cuntinaunce of clothinge · queinteliche de-gyset; 24
To preyere and to penaunce · putten heom monye,
For loue of vr lord · liueden ful harde,
In hope for to haue · heuene-riche blisse;
As ancres and hermytes · that holdeth hem in heore celles, 28
Coueyte not in cuntre · to carien a-boute,
For non likerous lyflode · heore licam to plese.
   And summe chosen chaffare · to cheeuen the bettre,

Some putten hem to the plow · pleyed ful selde, 20
In settyng and in sowyng · swonken ful harde,
And wonnen that wastours · with glotonye destruyeth.
   And some putten hem to pruyde · apparailed hem there-after,
In contenaunce of clothyng · comen disgised. 24
   In prayers and in penance · putten hem manye,
Al for loue of owre lorde · lyueden ful streyte,
In hope forto haue · heueneriche blisse;
As ancres and heremites · that holden hem in here selles, 28
And coueiten nought in contre · to kairen aboute,
For no likerous liflode · her lykam to plese.
   And somme chosen chaffare · they cheuen the bettere,
As it semeth to owre sy3t · that suche men thryueth; 32
And somme murthes to make · as mynstralles conneth,
And geten gold with here glee · synneles, I leue.
Ac iapers and iangelers · Iudas chylderen,
Feynen hem fantasies · and foles hem maketh, 36
And han here witte at wille · to worche 3if thei sholde.
That Poule precheth of hem · I nel nought preue it here;
Qui turpiloquium loquitur · is Luciferes hyne.
   Bidders and beggeres · fast aboute 3ede, 40
With her belies and her bagges · of bred ful ycrammed;
Fayteden for here fode · fou3ten atte ale;
In glotonye, god it wote · gon hij to bedde,

A. 34. *This line is from* T; *also in* HUD; V *omits it.*   41. bratful T;
bretful H₂; bredful UD; faste VH.   B. 20. putten W; put L; *see* l. 23.
34. *Read* giltles, *as in* Text A.   39. is—hyne W; L *om.*   41. belies W;
bely L. bagges WCO; bagge L.   C. 22. pute P.   23. sawyng P.

As hit semeth to vre siht · that suche men scholden; 32
And summe murthhes to maken · as munstrals cunne,
And gete gold with here gle · giltles, I trowe.
  Bote iapers and iangelers · Iudas children,
Founden hem fantasyes · and fooles hem maaden, 36
And habbeth wit at heor wille · to worchen ȝif hem luste.
That Poul precheth of hem · I dar not preouen heere;
Qui loquitur turpiloquium · hee is Luciferes hyne.
  Bidders and beggers · faste a-boute eoden, 40
Til heor bagges and heore balies · weren bratful I-crommet;
Feyneden hem for heore foode · fouȝten atte alle;
In glotonye, God wot · gon heo to bedde,

Somme putte hem to plow · and pleiden ful seylde,
In settyng and in sowyng · swonken ful harde,
And wonne that thuse wasters · with glotenye destroyeth. 24
Somme putte hem to pruyde · and parailede hem ther-after,
In contenaunce and in clothynge · in meny kynne gyse;
In praiers and in penaunces · putten hem manye,
Al for the loue of oure lorde · lyueden ful harde, 28
In hope to haue a gode ende · and heuene-ryche blysse;
As ancres and eremites · that holden hem in hure cellys,
Coueytynge noȝt in contrees · to carien a-boute
For no lykerouse lyflode · hure lykame to plese. 32
And somme chosen cheffare · they cheuede the betere,
As hit semeth to oure syght · that soche men thryueth.
And somme murthes to make · as mynstrals conneth,
That wollen neyther swynke ne swete · bote swery grete othes, 36
And fynde vp foule fantesyes · and foles hem maken,
And hauen witte at wylle · to worche yf they wolde.
That Paul prechith of hem · prouen hit ich myghte,
Qui turpiloquium loquitur · ys Lucyfers knaue. 40
Bydders and beggers · faste a-boute ȝoden,
Tyl hure bagge and hure bely · were bretful ycrammyd,
Faytynge for hure fode · and fouhten atten ale.
In glotenye, god wot · goth they to bedde, 44

---

24. wit P.   distryeth P.   26. contenuance P.   28. lyueden ESM;
lyuend P.   29. goud (*for* gode) P.   33. cheffede P; cheued S.
42. bretful MFE; bredful P.   44. god wot MF; tho gomes PS.

6 A. PROLOGUE. 44–54.   B. PROLOGUE. 44–68.

And ryseth vp with ribaudye · this Roberdes knaues;   44
Sleep and sleuȝthe · suweth hem euere.
  Pilgrimes and palmers · plihten hem to-gederes
For to seche seint Ieme · and seintes at Roome;
Wenten forth in heore wey · with mony wyse tales,   48
And hedden leue to lyȝen · al heore lyf aftir.
Ermytes on an hep · with hokide staues,
Wenten to Walsyngham · & here wenchis aftir;
  Grete lobres and longe · that loth weore to swynke   52
Clotheden hem in copes · to beo knowen for bretheren;
And summe schopen hem to hermytes · heore ese to haue.

And risen with ribaudye · tho Roberdes knaues;   44
Slepe and sori sleuthe · seweth hem eure.
  Pilgrymes and palmers · pliȝted hem togidere
To seke seynt Iames · and seyntes in Rome.
Thei went forth in here wey · with many wise tales,   48
And hadden leue to lye · al here lyf after.
I seigh somme that seiden · thei had ysouȝt seyntes;
To eche a tale that thei tolde · here tonge was tempred to lye,
More than to sey soth · it semed bi here speche.   52
  Heremites on an heep · with hoked staues,
Wenten to Walsyngham · and here wenches after;
Grete lobyes and longe · that loth were to swynke,
Clotheden hem in copis · to ben knowen fram othere;   56
And shopen hem heremites · here ese to haue.
  I fonde there freris · alle the foure ordres,
Preched the peple · for profit of hem-seluen,
Glosed the gospel · as hem good lyked,   60
For coueitise of copis · construed it as thei wolde.
Many of this maistres freris · mowe clothen hem at lykyng,
For here money and marchandise · marchen togideres.
For sith charite hath be chapman · and chief to shryue lordes,
Many ferlis han fallen · in a fewe ȝeris.   65
But holychirche and hij · holde better togideres,
The moste myschief on molde · is mountyng wel faste.
  There preched a pardonere · as he a prest were,   68

A. 49. aftir THUD; tyme V.   50, 51. *These lines are from* TUH₂D; VH *omit them.*   54. hem THD; V *om.*   61. and THUD; V *om.*   B. 67.

A. PROLOGUE. 55–65. C. PASSUS I. 45–66.

I font there freres · all the foure ordres,
Prechinge the peple · for profyt of heore wombes,   56
Glosynge the gospel · as hem good liketh,
For couetyse of copes · construeth hit ille;
For monye of this maistres · mowen clothen hem at lyking,
For moneye and heore marchaundie · meeten ofte to-gedere. 60
Seththe charite hath be chapmon · and cheef to schriuen lordes,
Mony ferlyes han bi-falle · in a fewe ȝeres.
But holychirche bi-ginne · holde bet to-gedere,
The moste mischeef on molde · mounteth vp faste.   64
    Ther prechede a pardoner · as he a prest were,

And aryseth with ribaudrie · tho Roberdes knaues;
Slep and synful sleuthe · seweth suche euere.
Pylgrimis and palmers · plyȝhten hem to-gederes,
To seche seint Iame · and seyntys of Rome,   48
Wenten forth in hure way · with meny vn-wyse tales,
And hauen leue to lye · al hure lyf-time.
Eremytes on an hep · with hokede staues,
Wenten to Walsyngham · and hure wenches after;   52
Grete lobies and longe · that loth were to swynke,
Clothede hem in copis · to be knowe fro othere,
And made hem-selue eremytes · hure eise to haue.
Ich fond ther frerus · alle the foure ordres,   56
Prechynge the peple · for profit of the wombe,
And glosynge the godspel · as hem good lykede;
For couetise of copes · contrariede som doctors.
Meny of this maistres · of mendinant freres,   60
Hure monye and marchaundise · marchen to-gederes;
Ac sutth charite hath be chapman · and chef to shryue lordes,
Many ferlies han fallen · in a fewe ȝeres;
Bote holy churche and charite · choppe a-doun swich shryuers,
The moste myschif on molde · mounteth vp faste.   65
    Ther preched a pardoner · as he a prest were,

---

mychief L.   C. 45. wit P.   48. siche P.   49. wit P.   tales MF; tale PE.
53. that M; and P.   55. hem-silue P.   65. on IFS; of P.

And brou3t vp a bulle · with bisschopes seles,
And seide that him-self mihte · a-soylen hem alle
Of falsnesse and fastinge · and of vouwes I-broken. 68
The lewede men likede him wel · and leeueth his speche,
And comen vp knelynge · and cusseden his bulle;
He bonchede hem with his breuet · and blered heore ei3en,
And rauhte with his ragemon · ringes and broches. 72
Thus 3e 3iueth oure gold · glotonye to helpen,
And leueth hit to losels · that lecherie haunten.
Weore the bisschop i-blesset · and worth bothe his eres,

Brou3te forth a bulle · with bishopes seles,
And seide that hym-self my3te · assoilen hem alle
Of falshed of fastyng · of vowes ybroken.
 Lewed men leued hym wel · and lyked his wordes, 72
Comen vp knelyng · to kissen his bulles;
He bonched hem with his breuet · and blered here eyes,
And rau3te with his ragman · rynges and broches.
Thus they geuen here golde · glotones to kepe, 76
And leueth such loseles · that lecherye haunten.
Were the bischop yblissed · and worth bothe his eres,
His seel shulde nou3t be sent · to deceyue the peple.
Ac it is nau3t by the bischop · that the boy precheth, 80
For the parisch prest and the pardonere · parten the siluer,
That the poraille of the parisch · sholde haue 3if thei nere.
 Persones and parisch prestes · pleyned hem to the bischop,
That here parisshes were pore · sith the pestilence tyme, 84
To haue a lycence and a leue · at London to dwelle,
And syngen there for symonye · for siluer is swete.
 Bischopes and bachelers · bothe maistres and doctours,
That han cure vnder criste · and crounyng in tokne 88
And signe that thei sholden · shryuen here paroschienes,
Prechen and prey for hem · and the pore fede,
Liggen in London · in lenten, an elles.
Somme seruen the kyng · and his siluer tellen, 92
In cheker and in chancerye · chalengen his dettes
Of wardes and wardmotes · weyues and streyues.

 A. 81. tyme THUD; V *om.* C. 67. broute P. 68. my3the P.
72. breuet IM; bulles P. eyen FMS; eye P. 73. an (*for* and) P.

A. PROLOGUE. 76–83. C. PASSUS I. 67–92.

Heo scholde not beo so hardi · to deceyue so the peple. 76
Saue hit nis not bi the bisschop · that the boye precheth;
Bote the parisch prest and he · de-parte the seluer,
That haue schulde the pore parisschens · ȝif that heo ne weore.
 Persones and parisch prestes · playneth to heore bisschops, 80
That heore parisch hath ben pore · seththe the pestilence tyme,
And asketh leue and lycence · at Londun to dwelle,
To singe ther for simonye · for seluer is swete.

[*Compare* A. PROL. 90–95, p. 18.]

And brouȝte forth a bulle · with bisshopis seles,
And seide that hym-selue · myȝte asoilie hem alle   68
Of falsnesse of fastingés · of vowes to-broke.
Lewede men lyuede hym wel · and likeden hus wordes,
Comen and kneleden · to kyssen his bulles;
He blessede hem with hus breuet · and blerede hure eyen, 72
And raghte with hus rageman · rynges and broches.
Thus ȝe ȝeueth ȝoure golde · glotones to helpe,
And leneth it to loreles · that lecherie haunten.
Were the bisshop blessid · other worth bothe hus eren, 76
Hus sele sholde noȝt be sent · in deceit of the puple.
Ac it ys noȝt by the bysshop · that the boye precheth,
The parsheprest and the pardoner · parten the seluer,
That poore puple in parshes · sholde haue, yf thei ne were. 80
Persones and parsheprestes · pleynede to the bisshop,
That hure parshens ben poore · sitthe the pestelence tyme,
To haue licence and leue · in Londone to dwelle,
And synge ther for symonye · for seluer ys swete. 84
Bisshopes and bachilers · bothe maisters and doctors,
That han cure vnder cryst · and crownynge in tokne,
Ben chargid with holy churche · charyte to tulie,
That is, leel loue and lif · a-mong lered and lewed; 88
Thei lyen in Londone · in lentene, and elles.
Somme seruen the kynge · and hus seluer tellen,
In the chekkere and the chauncelrie · chalengynge hus dettes,
Of wardes and of wardemotes · wayues and strayues. 92

---

82. parshen P.   84. for IMF; the wyle P.   87. wit P.   89. lyen FS; leyen P.

10   B. PROLOGUE. 95-102.

[*Not in* **A**-*text.*]

And some seruen as seruantz · lordes and ladyes,
And in stede of stuwardes · sytten and demen.   96

[*Compare* **B**. x. 280-283.]

Here messe and here matynes · and many of here oures
Arn don vndeuoutlych; · drede is at the laste
Lest crist in consistorie · acorse ful manye.
I parceyued of the power · that Peter had to kepe,   100
To bynde and to vnbynde · as the boke telleth,
How he it left with loue · as owre lorde hight,

    B. 99. consistorie WCO ; constorie L.   C. 95. herde hit P.   97. broght I;
y-set P.   bounden P.   98. tol IMFS; tool P.   99. ther hangeth MFI;
hongeth there P.   100. wordle P.   104. world MF ; wolde P.   wryt IS ;
wry3t P.   105. the IMFS ; P *om*.   109. fore P.   118. For-thi FS ; For
thei P.   121. on SM ; in P.   *So in* l. 123.   130. hit lefte MF ; lofte P.

[*Not in* **A**-*text.*]

Somme aren as seneschals · and seruen othere lordes,
And ben in stede of stywardes · and sitten and demen.
Concience cam and acusede hem · and the comune hit herde,
And seide, 'ydolatrie ȝe soffren · in sondrye places menye,   96
And boxes ben broght forth · i-bounden with yre,
To vnder-take the tol · of vntrewe sacrifice.
In menynge of miracles · muche wex ther hangeth;
Al the world wot wel · hit myȝte nat be trywe: 100
Ac for it profitith ȝow to porswarde · ȝe prelates soffren
That lewede men in mysbylyue · leuen and deien.
Ich lyue wel, by oure lorde · for loue of ȝoure couetyse,
That al the world be the wors; · as holy wryt telleth   104
What cheste, and meschaunce · to the children of Israel,
Ful on hem that free were · thorwe two false preestes.
For the synne of Ophni · and of Finéés hus brother,
Thei were disconfit in bataille · and losten *Archa dei;*   108
And, for hure syre sauh hem syngen · and soffrede hem don ille,
And noȝt chased hem ther-of · and wolde noȝt rebukie hem,
A-non, as it was ytold hym · that the children of Israel
Weren disconfit in bataille · and *Archa dei* yloie,   112
And hus sones slayen · anon he ful for sorwe
Fro hus chaire thare he sat · and brak hus necke a-tweyne.
And al was for veniaunce · that he but noȝt hus children;
And for they were preestes · and men of holychurche,   116
God was wel the wrother · and tok the rathere veniaunce.
For-thi ich seȝe, ȝe preestes · and men of holychurche,
That soffren men do sacrifice · and worshepen maumettes,
And ȝe sholde be here fadres · and techen hem betere,   120
God shal take veniaunce · on alle swiche preestes
Wel harder and grettere · on suche shrewede faderes,
Than euere he dude on Ophni · and Finees, or on here fader,
For ȝoure shrewede suffraunce · and ȝoure owene synne.   124
Ȝoure masse and ȝoure matynes · and meny of ȝoure houres
Aren don vndeuotlich · drede ys at the laste
Leste crist in hus constorie · of ȝow a-corse menye.
Ich parceuede of the power · that peter hadde to kepe,   128
To bynden and vnbynden · as the boke telleth,
How he hit lefte with loue · as oure lorde wolde,

[*Not in* **A**-*text*.]

Amonges foure vertues · the best of alle vertues,
That cardinales ben called · and closyng ȝatis,   104
There crist is in kyngdome · to close and to shutte,
And to opne it to hem · and heuene blisse shewe.
Ac of the cardinales atte Courte · that cauȝt of that name,
And power presumed in hem · a pope to make,   108
To han that power that Peter hadde · inpugnen I nelle;
For in loue and letterure · the eleccioun bilongeth,
For-thi I can and can nauȝte · of courte speke more.
   Thanne come there a kyng · knyȝthod hym ladde,   112
Miȝt of the comunes · made hym to regne,
And thanne cam kynde wytte · and clerkes he made,
For to conseille the kyng · and the comune saue.
   The kyng and knyȝthode · and clergye bothe   116
Casten that the comune · shulde hem-self fynde.
   The comune contreued · of kynde witte craftes,
And for profit of alle the poeple · plowmen ordeygned,
To tilie and trauaile · as trewe lyf asketh.   120
The kynge and the comune · and kynde witte the thridde
Shope lawe and lewte · eche man to knowe his owne.
   Thanne loked vp a lunatik · a lene thing with-alle,
And knelyng to the kyng · clergealy he seyde;   124
'Crist kepe the, sire kyng · and thi kyngriche,
And leue the lede thi londe · so leute the louye,
And for thi riȝtful rewlyng · be rewarded in heuene!'
   And sithen in the eyre an hiegh · an angel of heuene   128
Lowed to speke in latyn— · for lewed men ne coude
Iangle ne iugge · that iustifie hem shulde,
But suffren and seruen— · for-thi seyde the angel,
'*Sum Rex, sum Princeps* · *neutrum fortasse deinceps ;—*   132
O qui iura regis · *Christi specialia regis,*
Hoc quod agas melius · *iustus es, esto pius !*
Nudum ius a te · *vestiri vult pietate ;*
Qualia vis metere · *talia grana sere.*   136
Si ius nudatur · *nudo de iure metatur.*
Si seritur pietas · *de pietate metas !*'

C. 134. cauȝt MFI; chaut P.   135. An (*for* And) P.   138. quaht P.
140. muche MF; meche P.   141. kynde; *miswritten* a kynde P.

[*Not in* **A**-*text*.]

Amonges foure vertues · most vertuose of vertues,
That cardinales ben callid · and closynde ȝates,   132
Ther crist is in kyngdome · to closye with heuene.
Ac of the cardinales at court · that cauȝt han such a name,
And power presumen in hem-self · a pope to make,
To haue the power that Peter hadde · repugnen ich nelle;   136
For in loue and in letterure · lith the grete eleccion;
Countrepleide it noȝt,' quath Conscience · 'for holy churches sake.'

Thanne cam ther a kyng · knyȝt-hod hym ladde,
The muche myȝte of the men · made hym to regne;   140
And thanne cam kynde witte · and clerkus he made,
And conscience and kynde wit · and knyȝt-hod to-gederes
Caste that the comune · sholde hure comunes fynde.
Kyndewit and the comune · contreuede alle craftes,   144
And for most profit to the puple · a plouh thei gonne make,
With leel labour to lyue · whyl lif and londe lasteth.
Than kynde wit to the kyng · and to the comune seide,

'Crist kep the, sire kyng · and thy kynryche,   148
And leue the lede so thy londe · that leaute the louye,
And for thy ryȝtful ruelyng · be rewardid in heuene.'

Conscience to cleregie · and to the kyng saide,
'*Sum rex, sum princeps · neutrum fortasse deinceps;*   152
O qui iura regis · christi specialia regis,
Hoc vt agas melius · iustus, et esto pius!
Nudum ius a te · vestiri vult pietate,
Qualia vis metere · talia grana sere;   156
Si seritur pietas · de pietate metas.'

---

145. profit FME; profytable P. 146. Wit P. wyl (*for* whyl) P. lif MFS;
lyue P. 148. sire MI; P *om.* 149. leue ISMFE; lyue P. 152. *neutrum*
ISMFE; miswritten *venturum* P.

[*Not in* **A**-*text.*]

Thanne greued hym a goliardeys · a glotoun of wordes,
And to the angel an hei3 · answered after,   140
'*Dum rex a regere · dicatur nomen habere,
Nomen habet sine re · nisi studet iura tenere.*'
And thanne gan alle the comune · crye in vers of latin,
To the kynges conseille · construe ho-so wolde—   144
'*Precepta Regis · sunt nobis vincula legis.*'
With that ran there a route · of ratones at ones,
And smale mys myd hem · mo then a thousande,
And comen to a conseille · for here comune profit;   148
For a cat of a courte · cam whan hym lyked,
And ouerlepe hem ly3tlich · and lau3te hem at his wille,
And pleyde with hem perilouslych · and possed hem aboute.
'For doute of dyuerse dredes · we dar nou3te wel loke;   152
And 3if we grucche of his gamen · he wil greue vs alle,
Cracche vs, or clowe vs · and in his cloches holde,
That vs lotheth the lyf · or he lete vs passe.
My3te we with any witte · his wille withstonde,   156
We my3te be lordes aloft · and lyuen at owre ese.'
  A raton of renon · most renable of tonge,
Seide for a souereygne · help to hym-selue;—
'I haue ysein segges,' quod he · 'in the cite of London   160
Beren bi3es ful bri3te · abouten here nekkes,
And some colers of crafty werk; · vncoupled thei wenden
Bothe in wareine and in waste · where hem leue lyketh;
And otherwhile thei aren elles-where · as I here telle.   164
Were there a belle on here bei3 · bi Iesu, as me thynketh,
Men my3te wite where thei went · and awei renne!
And ri3t so,' quod that ratoun · 'reson me sheweth,
To bugge a belle of brasse · or of bri3te syluer,   168
And knitten on a colere · for owre comune profit,
And hangen it vp-on the cattes hals · thanne here we mowen
Where he ritt or rest · or renneth to playe.
And 3if him list for to laike · thenne loke we mowen,   172

B. 140. answered CWO; answeres LR.   147. myd W; with L.   151.
(2*nd*) hem COR; LW *om.*   **C.** 159. Wer P.   160. atte GES; at the MF;
atte the P.   162. loue—lord SMFGI; oure lordes loue P.   lyppes MFGI;
lyppe P.   168. whan SMFE; wanne P.   169. ly3tlyiche P.   174. wit

[*Compare* **A**. PROL. 84–89; **B**. PROL. 210–215; p. 18.]

Conscience and the kyng · in-to the court wenten,
Where houede an hondred · in houes of silke,
Seriauntes hij semede · that seruen atte barre, 160
To plede for penyes · and poundes the lawe,
And nat for loue of oure lord · vnlose hure lyppes ones.
Thow my3t bet mete the myst · on Maluerne hulles,
Than gete a mom of hure mouth · til moneye be hem shewid.
Thanne ran ther a route · of ratones, as it were, 165
And smale mys with hem · mo than a thousand,
Come to on counsail · for hure comune profit;
For a cat of a court · cam whan hym lykyde, 168
And ouer-leep hem ly3tlyche · and lauhte hem at wille,
And pleide with hem periloslich · and putte hem ther hym lykyde:—
'And if we grucche of hys game · he wol greue ous sarrer,
To hus clees clawen ows · and in hys cloches holde, 172
That ous lotheth the lyf · er he lete ows passe.
My3te we with eny wyt · hus wil with-sette,
We my3te be lordes aloft · and lyue as vs luste.'
Tho saide a raton of renoun · most resonable of tonge, 176

'Ich haue yseie grete syres · in cytees and in tounes
Bere by3es of bry3t gold · al aboute hure neckes,
And colers of crafty werke · bothe kny3tes and squiers.

Were ther a belle on hure by3e · by Iesus, as me thynketh, 180
Men my3te wite wher thei wenten · and hure wey roume.
Ry3t so,' quath the raton · 'reison me shewith,
A belle to byggen of bras · other of bry3t seluer,
And knytte it on a coler · for oure comune profit, 184
And honge aboute the cattys hals · thanne hure we mowe
Wher he ryt other rest · other romyth to pleye.
And yf hym luste for to layke · thanne loke we mowe,

(*for* with) P. to with-sette PEFS; *but* MG *omit* to. 175. luste MF; lusten PES. 180. as SMFG; PE *om*. 181. wher M; wer PS. 186. Wher SGE; Wheþer MF; Wer P.

[*Not in* **A**-*text.*]

And peren in his presence · ther while hym plaie liketh,
And ȝif him wrattheth, be ywar · and his weye shonye.'
   Alle this route of ratones · to this reson thei assented.
Ac tho the belle was ybouȝt · and on the beiȝe hanged,   176
There ne was ratoun in alle the route · for alle the rewme of Fraunce,
That dorst haue ybounden the belle · aboute the cattis nekke,
Ne hangen it aboute the cattes hals · al Engelonde to wynne;
And helden hem vnhardy · and here conseille feble,   180
And leten here labour lost · and alle here longe studye.
   A mous that moche good · couthe, as me thouȝte,
Stroke forth sternly · and stode biforn hem alle,
And to the route of ratones · reherced these wordes;   184
'Thouȝ we culled the catte · ȝut sholde ther come another,
To cracchy vs and al owre kynde · thouȝ we crope vnder benches.
For-thi I conseille alle the comune · to lat the catte worthe,
And be we neuer so bolde · the belle hym to shewe;   188
For I herde my sire seyn · is seuene ȝere ypassed,
There the catte is a kitoun · the courte is ful elyng;
That witnisseth holiwrite · who-so wil it rede,
     Ve terre vbi puer rex est, &c.
For may no renke there rest haue · for ratones bi nyȝte;   192
The while he caccheth conynges · he coueite h nouȝt owre caroyne,
But fet hym al with venesoun · defame we hym neuere.
For better is a litel losse · than a longe sorwe,
The mase amonge vs alle · thouȝ we mysse a schrewe.   196
For many mannus malt · we mys wolde destruye,
And also ȝe route of ratones · rende mennes clothes,
Nere that cat of that courte · that can ȝow ouerlepe;
For had ȝe rattes ȝowre wille · ȝe couthe nouȝt reule ȝowre-selue.
I sey for me,' quod the mous · 'I se so mykel after,
Shal neuer the cat ne the kitoun · bi my conseille be greued,
Ne carpyng of this coler · that costed me neure.
And thouȝ it had coste me catel · biknowen it I nolde,   204
But suffre as hym-self wolde · to do as hym liketh,
Coupled and vncoupled · to cacche what thei mowe.
For-thi vche a wise wiȝte I warne · wite wel his owne.'—

B. 179. it WCRO; L *om.*   186. crope R; cropen WR; croupe L.

[*Not in* **A**-*text*.]

And appere in hus presence · whyle hym pleye lyketh,   188
And yf he wratthe, we mowe be war · and hus way roume.'
Al the route of ratons · to thys reison a-sentede,
Ac tho the belle was ybou3t · and on the by3e honged,
Ther was no raton of al the route · for al the reame of Fraunce,
That durste haue bounde the belle · a-boute the cattes necke,
Ne haue it hongid a-boute hus hals · al Engelond to wynne ;
And leten hure labour ylost · and al hure longe trauail.
A mous that muche good couthe · as me tho thou3te,   196
Strok forth sturneliche · and stod by-for hem alle,
And to the route of ratones · rehercede thuse wordes,
'Thauh we hadde ycullid the catte · 3ut sholde ther come another,
To cracchen ous and al oure kynde · thouh we crepe vnder benches.   200
For-thi ich consaile, for comune profit · lete the cat worthe,
And neuere be we so bold · the belle hym to shewe.
For ich hurde my syre sayn · seuen 3er passed,
"Ther the cat nys bote a kyton · the court is ful elynge ;"
Witnesse of holy wryt · who so can rede—   205
   Ue terre ubi puer est rex : Salamon.

Ich sigge it for me,' quath the mous · 'ich seo so muchel after,
Shal neuere the cat ne the kyton · by my consail, be greued,
Ne carpen of hure colers · that costide me neuere ;   208
And thauh it costned me catel · by-knowe ich ne wolde,
Bote soffren and sigge nouht · and so is the beste,
Tyl myschief amende hem · that meny men chasteth.
For meny mannys malt · we mys wolde distrye,   212
And 3e, route of ratons · of rest men a-wake,
Ne were the cat of the court · and 3onge kytones to-warde ;
For hadde 3e ratones 3oure reed · 3e couthe nat ruelie 3ow-selue.'

C. 188. whyle SE; wil P.   190. þe ratons PS; *but* MFGE *omit* þe.   191. ybou3th P.   on SMFG; P *om.*   193. þat durste MFS; þa þerste P.   194. engelonnd P.   196. þouthe P.   200. chracchen P.   201. For-þi F; For-þy SG; For þei P.   207. greuede P.   211. amenden P.   hem SMFE; hym P.   212. For SMFG; And PE.   mys MFG; myes P.

c

Ther houeth an hundret · in houues of selk, 84
Seriauns hit semeth · to seruen atte barre ;
Pleden for pons · and poundes the lawe,
Not for loue of vr lord · vn-loseth heore lippes ones.
Thow mihtest beter meten the myst · on Maluerne hulles, 88
Then geten a mom of heore mouth · til moneye weore schewed.
 I sauh ther bisschops bolde · and bachilers of diuyn
Bi-coome clerkes of a-counte · the kyng for to seruen;
Erchedekenes and deknes · that dignite hauen, 92
To preche the peple · and pore men to feede,
Beon lopen to londun · bi leue of heore bisschopes,
To ben clerkes of the kynges benche · the cuntre to schende.
 Barouns and burgeis · and bonde-men also 96

What this meteles bemeneth · ȝe men that be merye, 208
Deuine ȝe, for I ne dar · bi dere god in heuene!
 Ȝit houed there an hondreth · in houues of selke,
Seriaunts it semed · that serueden atte barre,
Plededen for penyes · and poundes the lawe, 212
And nouȝt for loue of owre lorde · vnlese here lippes onis.
Thow myȝtest better mete the myȝte · on Maluerne hulles,
Than gete a momme of here mouthe · but money were shewed.

[*Compare* B. PROL. 87–94 ; p. 8.]

 Barones an burgeis · and bonde-men als 216
I seiȝ in this assemble · as ȝe shul here after.
Baxsteres and brewesteres · and bocheres manye,
Wollewebsteres · and weueres of lynnen,
Taillours and tynkeres · and tolleres in marketes, 220
Masons and mynours · and many other craftes.
Of alkin libbyng laboreres · lopen forth somme,
As dykers and delueres · that doth here dedes ille,
And dryuen forth the longe day · with '*Dieu vous saue, Dame Emme!*' 224
Cokes and here knaues · crieden, 'hote pies, hote!
Gode gris and gees · gowe dyne, gowe!'
 Tauerners vn-til hem · tolde the same,
'White wyn of Oseye · and red wyn of Gascoigne, 228
Of the Ryne and of the Rochel · the roste to defye.'—
Al this seiȝ I slepyng · and seuene sythes more.

A. PROLOGUE. 97–109.   C. PASSUS I. 216–231.

I sauȝ in that semble · as ȝe schul heren her-aftur.
   Bakers, bochers · and breusters monye,
Wollene websteris · and weueris of lynen,
Taillours, tanneris · & tokkeris bothe,   100
Masons, minours · and mony other craftes,
Dykers, and deluers · that don heore dedes ille,
And driueth forth the longe day · with 'deu vous saue, dam Emme!'
   Cookes and heore knaues · cryen 'hote pies, hote!   104
Goode gees and grys · gowe dyne, gowe!'
Tauerners to hem · tolde the same tale
With good wyn of Gaskoyne · and wyn of Oseye,
Of Ruyn and of Rochel · the rost to defye.   108
Al this I sauȝ slepynge · & seue sithes more.

What this metals by-meneth · ȝe men that buth murye,   216
Diuine ȝe, for ich ne dar · by dere god almyȝty!

    [*Compare* C. I. 159–164; p. 15.]
    [*Compare* C. I. 85–92; p. 9.]

Ȝut mette me more · of mene and of ryche,
As barouns and burgeis · and bonde-men of throupes,
Al ich sauh slepyng · as ȝe shullen hure after;   220
Bothe bakers and brywers · bouchers and othere,
Webbesters and walkers · and wynners with handen,
As taylours and tanners · and tyliers of erthe,
As dikers and deluers · that don here dedes ille,   224
And dryueth forth hure daies · with '*deux saue dame Emme!*'
Kokes and here knaues · crieden 'hote pyes, hote!
Good goos and grys · go we dyne, gowe!'
Tauerners 'a tast for nouht' · tolden the same,   228
'Whit wyn of Oseye · and of Gascoyne,
Of the Ruele and of the Rochel wyn · the roste to defye.'
Al this ich sauh slepynge · and seuene sythes more.

        Explicit passus primus.

   A. 99, 100. *These two lines are from* TUD; V *omits* them.   105. gouwe V (*2nd time*).   108. ad (*for* and) V.   109. *This line is from* TUD; V *omits it.*   **B.** 215. monoy L.   224. longe WCO; dere L.   226. and WRO; a L.   **C.** 216. Wat P. but (*for* buth) P.   218. mete P.   222. an (*for 2nd* and) P.

PASSUS I.

Primus passus de visione.

WHAT this mountein be-meneth · and this derke dale,
And this feire feld, ful of folk · feire I schal ow schewe.
A louely ladi on leor · in linnene i-clothed,
Com a-doun from the clyf · and clepte me feire,   4
And seide, 'sone! slepest thou? · Sixt thou this peple
Al hou bisy thei ben · a-boute the mase?
The moste parti of the peple · that passeth nou on eorthe,

PASSUS I.

Passus Primus de visione.

WHAT this montaigne bymeneth · and the merke dale,
And the felde ful of folke · I shal ȝow faire schewe.
A loueli ladi of lere · in lynnen yclothed,
Come down fram a castel · and called me faire,   4
And seide, 'Sone, slepestow · sestow this poeple,
How bisi thei ben · abouten the mase?
The moste partie of this poeple · that passeth on this erthe,
Haue thei worschip in this worlde · thei wilne no better;   8
Of other heuene than here · holde thei no tale.'
  I was aferd of her face · theiȝ she faire were,
And seide, 'mercy, Madame · what is this to mene?'
'The toure vp the toft,' quod she · 'Treuthe is there-inne, 12
And wolde that ȝe wrouȝte · as his worde techeth;
For he is fader of feith · fourmed ȝow alle,
Bothe with fel and with face · and ȝaf ȝow fyue wittis
Forto worschip hym ther-with · the while that ȝe ben here. 16
And therfore he hyȝte the erthe · to help ȝow vchone
Of wollen, of lynnen · of lyflode at nede,
In mesurable manere · to make ȝow at ese;

A. 4. clyf UDH₂; loft VH; T kith.   9. holde TUD; ȝeueth V; ȝyue H.

Hauen heo worschupe in this world · kepe thei no betere;   8
Of other heuene then heer · holde thei no tale.'
Ich was a-ferd of hire face · thauh heo feir weore,
And seide, 'merci, ma dame · what is this to mene?'
'This tour and this toft,' quod heo · 'Treuthe is ther-inne,   12
And wolde that ȝe wrouȝten · as his word techeth;
For he is fader of fei · that formed ow alle
Bothe with fel and with face · and ȝaf ow fyue wittes,
Forte worschupen him therwith · while ȝe beoth heere.   16
And for he hihte the eorthe · to seruen ow vchone
Of wollene, of linnene · to lyflode at neode,
In mesurable maner · to maken ow at ese;

PASSUS II.

Incipit passus secundus.

WHAT the montayne by-meneth · and the merke dale,
And the feld ful of folke · ich shal ȝow fayre shewe.
A loueliche lady of lere · in lynnen y-clothid,
Cam doun fro that castel · and calde me by name,   4
And seide, 'Wille, slepest thow · syxt thow this puple,
How busy thai ben · a-boute the mase?
The most partie of the puple · that passeth on this erthe,
Haue thei worship in this worlde · thei willen no betere;   8
Of other heuene than here · thei holden no tale.'
Ich was aferd of hure face · thauh hue faire were,
And saide, 'mercy, ma dame · what may thys be to mene?'
'The tour vp-on toft,' quath hue · 'Treuthe ys ther-ynne,   12
And wolde that ȝe wrouhte · as hus word techeth.
For he is fader of faith · and formour of alle;
To be faith-ful to hym · he ȝaue ȝow fyue wittes
For to worshepen hym ther-with · while ȝe lyuen here.   16
Wherfore he het the elementes · to helpe ȝow alle tymes,
And brynge forth ȝoure bylyue · bothe lynnen and wollen,
And in mesure, thouh hit muche were · to make ȝow at ese.

---

16. therwith THU; V *om.*   C. 8. Haue IFEG; Haued P.   11. wat P.
16. wile P.   17. Werfore P.   elemens P.

And comaundet of his cortesye · in comune threo thinges;   20
Heore nomes beth neodful · and nempnen hem I thenke,
Bi rule and bi resun · rehersen hem her-aftur.
  That on clothing is · from chele ow to saue:
And that othur mete at meel · for meseise of thiseluen: 24
And drink whon thou druiȝest · but do hit not out of resun,
That thou worthe the worse · whon thou worche scholdest.
  For Lot in his lyf-dayes · for lyking of drinke,
Dude bi his douhtren · that the deuel louede,   28
Dilytede him in drinke · as the deuel wolde,

  And comaunded of his curteisye · in comune three thinges;   20
Arne none nedful but tho · and nempne hem I thinke,
And rekne hem bi resoun · reherce thow hem after.
That one is vesture · from chele the to saue,
And mete atte mele · for myseise of thi-selue,   24
And drynke whan thow dryest · ac do nouȝt out of resoun;
That thow worth the werse · whan thow worche shuldest.
  For Loth in his lifdayes · for likyng of drynke,
Dede bi his douȝtres · that the deuel lyked;   28
Delited hym in drynke · as the deuel wolde,
And lecherye hym lauȝt · and lay bi hem bothe;
And al he witt it wyn · that wikked dede.
    Inebriamus eum vino, dormiamusque cum eo,
    Vt seruare possimus de patre nostro semen.
Thorw wyn and thorw women · there was Loth acombred,   32
And there gat in glotonye · gerlis that were cherlis.
For-thi drede delitable drynke · and thow shalt do the bettere;
Mesure is medcyne · thouȝ thow moche ȝerne.
It is nauȝt al gode to the goste · that the gutte axeth,   36
Ne liflode to thi likam · that leef is to thi soule.
Leue not thi likam · for a lyer him techeth,
That is the wrecched worlde · wolde the bitraye.
For the fende and thi flesch · folweth the to-gidere,   40
This and that sueth thi soule · and seith it in thin herte;
And for thow sholdest ben ywar · I wisse the the beste.'

  A. 26. weore V; worthe THD.   33. ȝeore V; ȝerne THD.   **B.** 37,
38. LWC *wrongly omit from* that leef *to* likam; RO *supply the words*.   41.
sueth R; seest L; seeth WO; sees C.   **C.** 22. wer P.   23. Ther P.

And lecherie him lauhte · and lay bi hem bothe;
And al he witede hit wyn · that wikkede dede.
Dreede dilitable drinke · and thou schalt do the bettre; 32
Mesure is medicine · thauh thou muche ȝeorne.
Al nis not good to the gost · that the bodi lyketh,
Ne lyflode to the licam · that leof is to the soule.
    Leef not thi licam · for lyȝere him techeth, 36
That is the wikkede word · the to bi-traye.
For the fend and thi flesch · folewen to-gedere,
And schendeth thi soule · seo hit in thin herte;
And for thou scholdest beo war · I wisse the the bettre.' 40

He comaundid of his cortesye · in comune thre thynges, 20
Aren non nudful bote tho thre · nempnen hem ich thenke,
And rekene hem by rewe · reherce hem wher the lyketh.
The ferst of tho ys fode · and vesture the secounde,
And drynke that do the good · ac drynk nat oute of tyme. 24
Lo! Loth in hus lyue · thorw lecherouse drynke
Wikkydlich wroghte · and wratthede god al-myghty.
In hus dronkenesse a day · hus douhtres he dighte,
And lay by hem bothe · as the bok telleth. 28
In hus glotenie he by-gat · gerles that weren churles,
And al he wited the wyne · hus wikked dede.
    Inebriamus eum uino et dormiamus cum eo, ut seruare possimus
      de patre nostro semen . Genesis.
Thorgh wyn and thorw wommen · ther was Loth encombred;
For-thy dred dilitable drynke · bothe day and nyȝtes. 32
Mesure is medecyne · thauh thou muche wylne.
Al is noȝt good to the gost · that the gut asketh,
Ne liflode to the licame · that leof is to the saule;
Leue noȝt thy licame · for a lyere hym techeth, 36
That is the wrecchede worlde · that wolde the bygyle;
For the fend and thy flesch · folwen to-gederes,
And that seeth the saule · and seith hit the in herte,
And wisseth the to be ware · and what wolde the deceyuye.' 40

---

25. drenke P.   27. dronkenesse MI; dronknesse P.   29. he MFS; P *om.*
gerles I; gurles MG; P *om.*   wereren (*for* weren) P.   33. is a P; *the rest*
om. a.   34. gout P.   36. Leue FE; Leef IS; Lyef P.   39. seeþ EB;
seþ S; seyþ PG.   seith F; seiþ EB; seyþ SG; saith I; setth P.

'A madame, merci!' quath I · 'me liketh wel thi wordes.
Bote the moneye on this molde · that men so faste holden,
Tel me to whom that tresour appendeth?'
'Go to the gospel,' quath heo · 'that god seith himseluen,   44
Whon the peple him a-posede · with a peny in the temple,
ʒif heo schulden worschupe ther-with · Cesar heore kyng.
And he asked of hem · of whom spac the lettre,
And whom the ymage was lyk · that ther-inne stod.   48
  "Ceesar," thei seiden · "we seoth wel vchone."
    Reddite ergo que sunt cesaris cesari, et que sunt dei deo.
  "Thenne *Reddite*," quath God · "that to Cesar falleth,
Et que sunt dei deo · or elles do ʒe ille."

'Madame, mercy,' quod I · 'me liketh wel ʒowre wordes,
Ac the moneye of this molde · that men so faste holdeth,   44
Telle me to whom, Madame · that tresore appendeth?'
'Go to the gospel,' quod she · 'that god seide hym-seluen,
Tho the poeple hym apposed · with a peny in the temple,
Whether thei shulde ther-with · worschip the kyng Sesar.   48
And god axed of hem · of whome spake the lettre,
And the ymage ilyke · that there-inne stondeth?
"Cesaris," thei seide · "we sen hym wel vchone."
  "*Reddite Cesari*," quod god · "that *Cesari* bifalleth,   52
Et que sunt dei, deo · or elles ʒe done ille."
For riʒtful reson · shulde rewle ʒow alle,
And kynde witte be wardeyne · ʒowre welthe to kepe,
And tutour of ʒoure tresore · and take it ʒow at nede;   56
For housbonderye and hij · holden togideres.'
Thanne I frained hir faire · for hym that hir made,
'That dongeoun in the dale · that dredful is of siʒte,
What may it be to mene · ma-dame, I ʒow biseche?'   60
  'That is the castel of care · who-so cometh therinne
May banne that he borne was · to body or to soule.
Therinne wonieth a wiʒte · that wronge is yhote,
Fader of falshed · and founded it hym-selue.   64
Adam and Eue · he egged to ille,
Conseilled Caym · to kullen his brother;

A. 49. *Latin quotation from* H.   54. ʒow TH₂; ʒou HD; V *om.*   57.
doun V; dungeon TH₂D; *see* prol. 15.   62. it T; yt D; VH *om.*

A. PASSUS I. 52–64.   C. PASSUS II. 41–62.

For rihtfoliche resoun · schulde rulen ou alle,　　　52
And kuynde wit be wardeyn · oure weolthe to kepe,
And tour of vr tresour · to take hit ȝow at nede;
For husbondrie and he · holden to-gedere.'
　Thenne I fraynede hire feire · for him that hire made,　56
'That dungun in that deope dale · that dredful is of siht,
What may hit mene, madame · ich the bi-seche?'
　'That is the castel of care,' quod heo · 'hose cometh ther-inne,
Mai banne that he born was · to bodi or to soule.　　60
Ther-inne woneth a wiht · Wrong is i-hote,
Fader of falsness · he foundede it him-seluen;
Adam and Eue · he eggede to don ille;
Counseilede Caym · to cullen his brother;　　　　　　64

'A ma dame, mercy,' quath ich · 'me lyketh wel ȝoure wordes,
Ac the moneye of this molde · that men so faste kepeth,
Telle ȝe me now to wham · that tresour by-longeth?'
'Go to the gospel,' quath hue · 'and see what god sayde,　44
Whanne the puple aposed hym · of a peny in the temple,
And god askede of hem · whas was the coygne.

"Cesares," thei seiden · "sothliche we knowen."
"*Reddite Cesari*," seide God · "that to Cesar by-falleth,　48
Et que sunt dei, deo · other ellys ȝe don ille."
For ryhtfulliche reson · sholde ruele ȝow alle,
And kynde wit be wardeyn · ȝoure welthe to kepe,
And tutour of ȝowre tresoure · and take hit ȝow atte nede;　52
For hosboundrie and he · holdeth to-gederes.'
Ich fraynede hure faire tho · for hym that hure made,
'The dupe dale and durke · vn-semely to see to,
What may hit by-mene · madame, ich by-seche?'　　　56
'That is the castel of care · who-so cometh ther-ynne
May banne that he bore was · in body and in soule;
Ther-ynne wonyeth a wyȝt · that wrong is his name,
Fader of falshede · fond hit furst of alle;　　　　　60
Adam and Eue · he eggede to don ille,
Consailde Cayme · to cullen hus brother;

C. 45. Wanne P.　　52. hit MIG; PE *om.*　　61. egede P.

Iudas he iapede · with the Iewes seluer,
And on an ellerne treo · hongede him after.
He is a lettere of loue · and ly3eth hem alle
That trusteth in heor tresour · ther no truthe is inne.' 68
   Thenne hedde I wonder in my wit · what wommon hit weore,
That suche wyse wordes · of holy writ me schewede ;
And halsede hire in the hei3e nome · er heo theonne 3eode,
What heo weore witerly · that wissede me so feire. 72
'Holi churche icham,' quath heo · 'thou ouhtest me to knowe:
Ich the vndurfong furst · and thi feith the tau3te.
Thow brou3test me borwes · my biddyng to worche,
And to loue me leelly · while thi lyf durede.' 76

Iudas he iaped · with Iuwen siluer,
And sithen on an eller · honged hym after. 68
He is letter of loue · and lyeth hem alle,
That trusten on his tresor · bitrayeth he sonnest.'
   Thanne had I wonder in my witt · what womman it were
That such wise wordes · of holy writ shewed ; 72
And asked hir on the hie3e name · ar heo thennes 3eode,
What she were witterli · that wissed me so faire ?
   'Holicherche I am,' quod she · 'thow ou3test me to knowe,
I vnderfonge the firste · and the feyth tau3te, 76
And brou3test me borwes · my biddyng to fulfille,
And to loue me lelly · the while thi lyf dureth.'
   Thanne I courbed on my knees · and cryed hir of grace,
And preyed hir pitousely · prey for my synnes, 80
And also kenne me kyndeli · on criste to bileue,
That I mi3te worchen his wille · that wrou3te me to man ;
'Teche me to no tresore · but telle me this ilke,
How I may saue my soule · that seynt art yholden ?' 84
   'Whan alle tresores aren tried,' quod she · 'trewthe is the best ;
I do it on *deus caritas* · to deme the sothe ;
It is as derworth a drewery · as dere god hym-seluen.
Who-so is trewe of his tonge · and telleth none other, 88
And doth the werkis ther-with · and wilneth no man ille,

   A. 72. wisside TH₂ ; wysed D ; techeth V.   **B.** 81. kenne WCRO
kende L.   **C.** 64. An (*for* And) P.   65. ys a P ; MIFGSB *om*. a.   67.
his (*for* is) P.   69. wry3t P.   70. hals∍de MIFB ; hanslede P.   71. witterly

Thenne knelede I on my kneos · and cri3ed hire of grace,
And preiede hire pitously · to preye for vr sunnes,
And eke to teche me kuyndely · on crist to bi-leeue,
That Ich his wille mihte worche · that wrouhte me to mon.   80
'Tech me to no tresour · bote tel me this ilke,
Hou I may saue my soule · that seint art I-holde.'
'Whon alle tresour is I-tri3ed · treuthe is the beste;
I do hit on *Deus Caritas* · to deeme the sothe.   84
Hit is as derworthe a drurie · as deore god him-seluen.
For hose is trewe of his tonge · telleth not elles,
Doth his werkes ther-with · and doth no mon ille,

Iudas he by-iapede · thorgh Iewene seluer,
And afterward he heng hym · hye on an ellerne.   64
He ys lettare of loue · and lyeth alle tymes;
That tryst in erthely tresour . he by-traieth sonnest,
To en-combrye men with couetyse · that is hus kynde.,
Thanne hadde ich wonder in my wit · what womman hue were,
That suche wyse wordes · of holy wryt shewede;   69
And halsede hure on the heie name · er hue thennys wente,
What hue were witterly · that wissede me so and tauhte.
'Holychurche ich am,' quath hue · 'thow oghtest me to knawe;
Ich vnder-feng the formest · and fre man the made.
Thow broghtest me borwes · my byddyng to fulfille,   74
To leue on me and louye me · al thy lyf tyme.'
Thanne knelede ich on my knees · and criede hure of grace,
And preiede hure pytously · to preie for me to amende,
Al-so to kenne me kyndelich · on crist to by-leue,
'And teche me to no tresour · bote telle me thys ilke,
How ich may sauy my saule · that seynt art yholde.'   80
'Whanne alle tresours ben tried,' quath hue · 'treuthe is the beste;
Ich do hit on *Deus caritas* · to deme the sothe.
Hit is as derworthe a druwery · as dere god him-selue.
For he, is trewe of hus tonge · and of hus two handes,   84
And doth the werkes therwith · and wilneth no man ille,

IFEG; whiterly P.   72. to MIFSE; P *om.*   75. leue MIFSE; lyue P.
lyf SG; lif MFE; lyue P.   76. P *om.* and.   P *om.* of.   77. pytosly P.
78. by-lyue P.   80. ert P.   81. Qwenne P.   83. hem-selue P.   84. trywe
P; *but see* ll. 95, 96.

He is a-counted to the gospel · on grounde and on lofte,   88
And eke I-liknet to vr lord · bi seint Lucus wordes.
Clerkes that knowen hit · scholde techen hit aboute,
For Cristene and vn-cristene · him cleymeth vchone.
  Kynges and knihtes · scholde kepen hem bi reson,   92
And rihtfuliche raymen · the realmes a-bouten,
And take trespassours · and teiȝen hem faste,
Til treuthe hedde I-termynet · the trespas to the ende.
For Dauid, in his dayes · he dubbede knihtes,   96
Dude hem swere on heor swerd · to serue treuthe euere.
That is the perte profession · that a-pendeth to knihtes,

He is a god bi the gospel · agrounde and aloft,
And ylike to owre lorde . bi seynte Lukes wordes.
The clerkes that knoweth this · shulde kenne it aboute,   92
For cristene and vncristne · clameth it vchone.
  Kynges and kniȝtes · shulde kepe it bi resoun,
Riden and rappe down · in reumes aboute,
And taken *trangressores* · and tyen hem faste,   96
Til treuthe had ytermyned · her trespas to the ende.
And that is the professiqun appertly · that appendeth for knyȝtes,
And nouȝt to fasten a Fryday · in fyue score wynter;
But holden with him and with hir · that wolden al treuthe,   100
And neuer leue hem for loue · ne for lacchyng of syluer.
  For Dauid in his dayes · dubbed kniȝtes,
And did hem swere on here swerde · to serue trewthe euere ;
And who-so passed that poynte · was *apostata* in the ordre.   104
  But criste kingene kynge · kniȝted ten,
Cherubyn and seraphin · suche seuene and an-othre,
And ȝaf hem myȝte in his maieste · the muryer hem thouȝte ;
And ouer his mene meyne · made hem archangeles,   108
Tauȝte hem bi the Trinitee · treuthe to knowe,
To be buxome at his biddyng · he bad hem nouȝte elles.
  Lucifer with legiounes · lerned it in heuene,

  A. 94. teiȝen T ; tyen H₂; teyen D ; bynden V.   103. *This line, which
V omits, is a made up one from* H *and* U.   *The readings are* :—For crist
kynge of knyȝtus · knytted somtyme H ; And kyng, kyngene kyng · knyhtide
tene U ; And crist king of kinges · kniȝtide tene TH₂; and crist kyng of
knyȝtes · knyȝted ten D.   106. *From* TH₂UD ; V *omits this line.*   107.

And not to faste a Friday · in fyue score ʒeres,
But holden with hem and with heore · that asken the treuthe,
And leuen for no loue · ne lacching of ʒiftus;
And he that passeth that poynt · is a-postata in the ordre.
For crist, kyngene kyng · knyhtede tene,
Cherubin and Seraphin · an al the foure ordres,   104
And ʒaf hem maystrie and miht · in his maieste,
And ouer his meyne · made hem archaungelis,
And tauʒte hem thorw the Trinite · treuthe for to knowen,
And beo boxum at his biddynge · he bad hem not elles.   108
   Lucifer with legiouns · lerede hit in heuene;

He is a god by the gospel · and graunty may hele,
And like oure Lorde also · by seynt Lukys wordes.
Clerkus that knowen thys · shoulde kennen hit a-boute,   88
For cristene and vncristene · cleymen it echone.
Kynges and knyʒtes · shoulde kepen hit by reson,
Ryden and rappe a-doune · in reames a-boute,
And take trespassours · and tyen hem faste,   92
Til trewthe hadde ytermenyd · here trespas to the ende;
And holde with hym and with hure · that han trewe accion,
And for no lordene loue · leue the trewe partye.
Trewely to take · and treweliche to fyʒte,   96
Ys the profession and the pure ordre · that apendeth to knyʒtes;
Who-so passeth that poynt · ys apostata of knyʒt-hod.
For thei shoulde nat faste · ne for-bere sherte;
Bote feithfullich defende · and fyʒte for truthe,   100
And neuere leue for loue · in hope to lacche seluer.
Dauid by hus daies · dobbede knyʒtes,
And dude hem swerye on here swerde · to serue truthe euere.
Whanne god by-gan heuene · in that grete blysse,   104
He made knyʒtes in hus court · creatures ten,
Cherubin and seraphin · suche seuene and another;
Lucifer louelokest tho · ac lytel while it durede.
He was an archangel of heuene · on of godes knyʒtes;   108

hem THUD; V *om.*   B. 107. murger L.   C. 89. vncrestine P.
92. And I; And to PESG.   94. triwe P.   95. lordene I; lordes ME;
lordayne P.   96. fyʒete P; *see* l. 100.   97. pure MFESGB; poure PI.
98. Wo-so P.   aposteta P.   103. on MIFSGB; in P.   104. Wanne P.
106. P *om.* and.   107. wile P.   durede MIFSB; laste P.

He was louelokest of siht · aftur vr lord,
Til he brak boxumnes · thorw bost of him-seluen.
    Thene fel he with his felawes · and fendes bi-comen,   112
Out of heuene in-to helle · hobleden faste,
Summe in the eir, and summe in the eorthe · and summe in
    helle deope.
    Bote Lucifer louwest · liȝth of hem alle;

But for he brake buxumnesse · his blisse gan he tyne,   112
And fel fro that felawship · in a fendes liknes,
In-to a depe derke helle · to dwelle there for eure;
And mo thowsandes with him · than man couthe noumbre,
Lopen out with Lucifer · in lothelich forme,   116
For thei leueden vpon hym · that lyed in this manere:
    Ponam pedem in aquilone, et similis ero altissimo.

    And alle that hoped it miȝte be so · none heuene miȝte hem
    holde,
But fellen out in fendes liknesse · nyne dayes togideres,
Til god of his goodnesse · gan stable and stynte,   120
And garte the heuene to stekye · and stonden in quiete.

    Whan thise wikked went out · wonderwise thei fellen,
Somme in eyre, somme in erthe · and somme in helle depe;
Ac Lucifer lowest · lith of hem alle;   124
For pryde that he pult out · his peyne hath none ende;
And alle that worche with wronge · wenden hij shulle
After her deth day · and dwelle with that shrewe.
Ac tho that worche wel · as holiwritt telleth,   128
And enden as I ere seide · in treuthe, that is the best,
Mowe be siker that her soule · shal wende to heuene,
Ther treuthe is in Trinitee · and troneth hem alle.

  C. 113. on a-lofte P.   114. þan IB; To PEMFS.   116. sotthly P.
118. leue IFSEBG; loyne P.   120. fuel (*for* ful) P.   123. meuen E;

A. PASSUS I. 116–122.   C. PASSUS II. 109–134.   31

For pruide that he put out · his peyne hath non ende;   116
And alle that wrong worchen · wende thei schulen
After heore deth-day · and dwellen with that schrewe.
  Ac heo that worchen that word · that holi writ techeth,
And endeth as Ich er seide · in profitable werkes,   120
Mouwen be siker that heore soules · schullen to heuene,
Ther treuthe is in trinite · and corouneth hem alle.

He and other with hym · that hulde nou3t with treuthe,
Lopen out in lothliche forme · for hus false wille;
He hadde lust to be lyke · hus lord god almyghty.
  Ponam pedem meum in aquilone, et ero similis altissimo.
Lord! why wolde he tho · thulke wrechede Lucifer,   112
Lepen a-lofte · in the north syde
Than sitten in the sonne side · ther the day roweth?
Ne were it for northerne men · a-non ich wolde telle;
Ac ich wolle lacke no lyf' · quath that lady sothly;   116
'Hit is sykerer by southe · ther the sonne regneth
Than in the north by meny notes · no man leue other.
For thider as the fend flegh · hus fote for to sette,
Ther he failede and ful · and hus felawes alle;   120
And helle is ther he ys · and he ther ybounde.
Euene contrarie sitteth Criste · clerkus knowen the sothe;
  Dixit dominus domino meo, sede a dextris meis.
Ac of this matere no more · meuen ich nelle;
Hewes in the halyday · after hete wayten,   124
They care no3t thauh it be cold · knaues, when thei worchen.
In wonderwyse holy wryt · tellith how thei fullen;
Somme in erthe, somme in aier · somme in helle dupe,
Ac Lucifer lowest · lith of hem alle;   128
For prude that hym pokede · hus peyne hath no ende.
Alle that worchen that wikkede ys · wenden thei shulle
After hure deth-day · and dwelle ther wrong ys;
And alle that han wel y-wroght · wenden they shulle   132
Estwarde to heuene · euere to abyde,
Ther treuthe is, the trone · that trinite ynne sitteth.

---

meue PG.   124. Hewes I; Hewen B; Hynen M; *miswritten* He was P.
heten P.   125. wen P.

For I sigge sikerli · bi siht of the textes,
Whon alle tresor is I-tri3et · treuthe is the beste.   124
Lereth hit this lewed men · for lettrede hit knoweth,
That treuthe is tresour · triedest on eorthe.'
  'Yit haue I no kuynde knowing,' quod I · 'thou most teche
    me betere,
Bi what craft in my corps · hit cumseth, and where.'   128
  'Thou dotest daffe,' quath heo · 'dulle are thi wittes.'

For-thi I sey as I seide ere · bi si3te of thise textis,   132
Whan alle tresores arne ytried · treuthe is the beste.
Lereth it this lewde men · for lettred men it knowen,
That treuthe is tresore · the triest on erthe.'
  '3et haue I no kynde knowing,' quod I · '3et mote 3e kenne
    me better,   136
By what craft in my corps · it comseth and where.'
  'Thow doted daffe,' quod she · 'dulle arne thi wittes;
To litel latyn thow lernedest · lede, in thi 3outhe;
    Heu michi, quod sterilem duxi vitam iuuenilem!
It is a kynde knowyng,' quod he · 'that kenneth in thine herte
For to loùye thi lorde · leuer than thi-selue;
No dedly synne to do · dey thou3 thow sholdest:
This I trowe be treuthe; · who can teche the better,
Loke thow suffre hym to sey · and sithen lere it after.   144
For thus witnesseth his worde · worche thow there-after;
For trewthe telleth that loue · is triacle of heuene;
May no synne be on him sene · that vseth that spise,
And alle his werkes he wrou3te · with loue as him liste;   148
And lered it Moises for the leuest thing · and moste like to heuene,
And also the plente of pees · moste precious of vertues.
  For heuene my3te nou3te holden it · it was so heuy of hym-self,
Tyl it hadde of the erthe · yeten his fylle,   152
  And whan it haued of this folde · flesshe and blode taken,
Was neuere leef vpon lynde · li3ter ther-after,
And portatyf and persant · as the poynt of a nedle,
That my3te non armure it lette · ne none hei3 walles.   156

A. 137. preche it in THH₂D; prechet the V.   B. 139. The MSS. have
quia, not *quod*.   145. worche CO; worcheth L.   150. *Read* plante.
C. 136. Than S; That PMFIE.   138. wat P.   wheder I; whider B;

A. PASSUS I. 130–137. C. PASSUS II. 135–155.

Hit is a kuynde knowynge · that kenneth the in herte
For to loue thi louerd · leuere then thi-seluen;
No dedly sunne to do · dyʒe thauʒ thou scholdest.   132
This I trouwe beo treuthe! · hose con teche the betere,
Loke thou suffre him to seye · and seththe teche hit forthure!
For thus techeth us his word · (worch thou ther-aftur)
That loue is the leuest thing · that vr lord asketh,   136
And eke the playnt of pees; · preche it in thin harpe

Lere it thus lewede men · for lettrede hit knoweth,
Than treuthe and trewe loue · ys no tresour bettere.'   136
'Ich haue no kynde knowyng,' quath ich · 'ʒe mote kenne me
  bettere,
By what wey hit wexith · and wheder out of my menyng.'
' Thow dotede daffe,' quath hue · ' dulle aren thy wittes,
Ich leue thow lernedist to lyte · latyn in thy ʒowthe;   140
Heu michi, quod sterilem · duxi uitam iuuenilem!
Hit is a kynde knowyng · that kenneth in thyn herte
For to louye thy lord · leuest of alle,
And deye rathere than to do · eny dedlich synne;   144
  Melius est mori quam male uiuere.
And this ich trowe be treuthe · who so can teche the betere,
Loke thow soffrie hym to say · and so thow myght lerne.

For treuthe telleth that loue · ys tryacle for synne,
And most souereyne salue · for saule and for body.   148

Loue is the plonte of pees · and most preciouse of vertues;
For heuene holde hit ne myʒte · so heuy hit semede,
Til hit hadde on erthe · ʒoten hym-selue.
Was neuere lef vp-on lynde · lyghter ther-after,   152
As whanne hit hadde of the folde · flesch and blod ytake;
Tho was it portatyf and pershaunt · as the poynt of a nelde,
May non armure hit lette · nother hye walles;

---

whodur S; wider M; wonder P.   139. dolle P.   140. lyue P.   ʒoweþe P.
143. lauest P.   152. lygheter P.   153. wanne P.   folde IB; fold M;
flod PS.

Ther thou art murie at thi mete · whon me biddeth the ȝedde;
For bi kuynde knowynge in herte · comseth ther a fitte.
   That falleth to the fader · that formede vs alle.   140
He lokede on vs with loue · and lette his sone dye
Mekeliche for vre misdedes · forte amende vs alle.
And ȝit wolde he hem no wo · that wrouȝte him that pyne,
But mekeliche with mouthe · merci he by-souȝte,   144
To haue pite on that peple · that pynede him to dethe.
   Her thou miht seon ensaumple · in hymselfe one,

   For-thi is loue leder · of the lordes folke of heuene,
And a mene, as the maire is · bitwene the kyng and the comune;

Riȝt so is loue a ledere · and the lawe shapeth,
Vpon man for his mysdedes · the merciment he taxeth.   160
And for to knowe it kyndely · it comseth bi myght,
And in the herte, there is the heuede · and the heiȝ welle;
   For in kynde knowynge in herte · there a myȝte bigynneth.
And that falleth to the fader · that formed vs alle,   164
Loked on vs with loue · and lete his sone deye
Mekely for owre mysdedes · to amende vs alle;
And ȝet wolde he hem no woo · that wrouȝte hym that peyne,
But mekelich with mouthe · mercy he bisouȝte   168
To haue pite of that poeple · that peyned hym to deth.
   Here myȝtow see ensamples · in hym-selue one,
That he was miȝtful and meke · and mercy gan graunte
To hem that hongen him an heiȝ · and his herte thirled.   172
   For-thi I rede ȝow riche · haueth reuthe of the pouere;
Thouȝ ȝe be myȝtful to mote · beth meke in ȝowre werkes.
   For the same mesures that ȝe mete · amys other elles,
Ȝe shullen ben weyen ther-wyth · whan ȝe wende hennes;   176
      Eadem mensura qua mensi fueritis, remecietur vobis.
   For thouȝ ȝe be trewe of ȝowre tonge · and trewliche wynne,
And as chaste as a childe · that in cherche wepeth,

A. 139. comseth U; comsith T; cumse V.   142. misdede V; misdedis THUD.   143. wrouȝte THUD; wolde V.   146. hymselfe TUD; thi-self V.   149, 150. *These lines are from* THUD; V *has* For thi I rede the mihtful of mayn be meke of thi wordes. *The Latin quotation is in* H *only.*

A. PASSUS I. 147-154.   C. PASSUS II. 156-177.

Hou he was mihtful and meke · that merci gon graunte
To hem that heengen him hei3e · and his herte thurleden.   148
For-thi I rede the riche · haue reuthe on the pore ;
Thei3 3e ben mi3ty to mote · beth meke of 3our werkis ;
    Eadem mensura qua mensi fueritis, remecietur uobis ;
For the same mesure that 3e meten · a-mis other elles,
3e schul be weyen ther-with · whon 3e wenden hennes.   152
  For thau3 3e ben trewe of tonge · and treweliche winne,
And eke as chast as a child · that in chirche wepeth,

For-thy is loue ledere · of oure lordes folke in heuene,   156
And a mene, as the meyere is · by-twyne the kyng and the comune,
Ry3t so is loue a ledere · and the lawe shapeth ;
Vp man for hus mysdedes · the mercement he taxeth.
And for to knowe it kyndeliche · hit comseth by myghte,   160
In the herte, ther is the hefd · and the hye welle.
Of kynde knowyng in herte · ther comseth a myghte,
That falleth to the fader · that formede ous alle.
On ous he lokyde with loue . and let hus sone deye,   164
Meekliche for oure mysdedes · to amendy ous alle.
And 3ut wolde he hem no wo · that wroght hym al that tene,
Bote myldeliche with mouhte · mercy he by-souhte,
To haue pyte on that puple · that paynede hym to dethe.   168
  Her my3t thow see ensample · in hym-self one,
That he was myghtful and meke · and mercy gan graunte,
To hem that henge hym hye · and hus herte therlede.
For-thy ich rede 3ow ryche · haue reuthe of the poure ;
Thauh 3e be myghty to mote · beeth meke in 3oure workes ;
The same mesure that 3e meteth · amys other ellys,   174
3e shulleth be weyen ther-with · whanne 3e wenden hennes ;
    Eadem mensura qua mensi fueritis, remecietur uobis.
  Thauh 3e be trewe of 3oure tonge · and trewelich wynne,
And be as chast as a chyld · that nother chit ne fyghteth,   177

C. 157. P *om.* a.   158. shappeþ P.   163. to IFSGB ; in-to P.
166. teune P.   170. meuk P.   171. hym (*for* hem) P.   þorlede P.
173. meuk P.   175. wanne P.   *remicietur* P.   176. trywe P.
triwelich P.

Bote ȝe liuen trewely · and eke loue the pore,
And such good as god sent · treweliche parten,   156
Ȝe naue no more merit · in masse ne in houres
Then Malkyn of hire maydenhod · that no mon desyreth.
  For Iames the gentel · bond hit in his book,
That fey withouten fait · is febelore then nouȝt,   160
And ded as a dore-nayl · but the deede folewe.
Chastite withouten charite · (wite thou forsothe),
Is as lewed as a laumpe · that no liht is inne.
  Moni chapeleyns ben chast · but charite is aweye;   164
Beo no men hardore then thei · whon heo beoth avaunset;
Vn-kuynde to heore kun · and to alle cristene;

But if ȝe louen lelliche · and lene the poure,
Such good as god ȝow sent · godelich parteth,   180
Ȝe ne haue na more meryte · in masse ne in houres,
Than Malkyn of hire maydenhode · that no man desireth.
  For Iames the gentil · iugged in his bokes,
That faith with-oute the faite · is riȝte no thinge worthi,   184
And as ded as a dore-tre · but ȝif the dedes folwe;
    Fides sine operibus mortua est, &c.
For-thi chastite with-oute charite · worth cheyned in helle;
It is as lewed as a laumpe · that no liȝte is inne.
  Many chapeleynes arne chaste · ac charite is awey;   188
Aren no men auarousere than hij · whan thei ben auaunced;
Vnkynde to her kyn · and to alle cristene,
Chewen here charite · and chiden after more.
Such chastite with-outen charite · worth cheyned in helle!   192
  Many curatoures kepen hem · clene of here bodies,
Thei ben acombred with coueitise · thei konne nouȝt don it
     fram hem,
So harde hath auarice · yhasped hem togideres.
And that is no treuthe of the trinite · but treccherye of helle, 196
And lernyng to lewde men · the latter for to dele.
  For-thi this wordes · ben wryten in the gospel,
Date et dabitur vobis · for I dele ȝow alle.
And that is the lokke of loue · and lateth oute my grace,   200

    A. 160. V *misreads*: treuthe withouten fey.   *For* treuthe, D *has* fay, *and*
THU *have* feith. *For* fey, TH₂ *have* fait, *and* D *has* feet.   168. V *transposes*
chastite *and* charite; *see* l. 162.   176–185. *These lines are not in* V.   *Lines*

A. PASSUS I. 167–178. C. PASSUS II. 178–198.

Chewen heore charite · and chiden after more!
Such chastite withouten charite · worth claymed in helle!   168
   Curatours that schulden kepe hem · clene of heore bodies,
Thei beoth cumbred in care · and cunnen not out-crepe;
So harde heo beoth with auarice · i-haspet to-gedere.
That nis no treuthe of trinite · but tricherie of helle,   172
And a leornyng for lewed men · the latere forte dele.
   For theos beth wordes i-writen · in the ewangelye,
Date et dabitur vobis · for I dele ow alle
3oure grace and 3oure good happe · 3oure welthe for to wynne,
And therwith knoweth me kyndely · of that I 3ou sende.   177
That is the lok of loue · that letith out my grace

Bote yf 3e loue leelliche · and lene the poure,
Of such good as god sent · goodliche parte,
3e haue no more meryt · in masse ne in houres,   180
Than Malkyn of hure maidenhod · wham no man desireth.
   For Iamys the gentel · iuggeth in hus bokes,
That feith with-oute fet · ys febelere than nouht,
And ded as a dore-nayle · bote yf the dede folwe;   184
     Fides sine operibus mortua est.
Chastite with-oute charite · worth cheynid in helle;
Hit is as lewede as a lampe · that no lyght ys ynne.
   Meny chapelayns aren chast · ac charite hem faileth;
Aren none hardur ne hongryour · than men of holy churche,   188
Auerouse and euel-willed · whanne thei ben auaunsed,
And vnkynde to hure kyn · and to alle crystine;
Thei chewen here charite · and chiden after more;

And encombred with couetyse · thei conne nat out crepe,   192
So harde hath aueryce · hasped hem to-gederes.
And that ys no treuthe of the trinite · bote trecherie and synne,
And luther ensample, leue me · to the lewede puple.
   For thees aren wordes · wryten in the euangelye,   196
Date et dabitur uobis · for I dele 3ow alle.
And that is the lok of loue · that vnloseth grace,

176, 177 *are in* H *only; the rest are from* TDH₂.   B. 180. goed L.
C. 178. P *om.* 3e. lene to P; *but* MIFSGB *om.* to.   181. wam P.   182.
sugge{{ (*for* Iugge{{) P.   189. veuele (*for* euel) P.   wanne P.   193. to-
gedderes P.   197. P *om.* for I dele 3ow alle.

To counforte the carful · acumbrid with synne.
Loue is the leueste thinge · that our lord askith, 180
And eke the graith gate · that goth into heuene.
For-thi I seiȝe as I seide er · be siȝte of thise tixtes,

To conforte the careful · acombred with synne.
  Loue is leche of lyf · and nexte owre lorde selue,
And also the graith gate · that goth in-to heuene ;
For-thi I sey as I seide · ere by the textis, 204
Whan alle tresores ben ytryed · treuthe is the beste.
Now haue I tolde the what treuthe is · that no tresore is bettere,
I may no lenger lenge the with · now loke the owre lorde ! '

Whan alle tresouris arn triȝede · treuthe is the beste.   183
Now haue I tolde the what treuthe is · that no tresour is betere,
I may no lengere lenge · now loke the oure lord.'

That conforteth alle cristine · encombred with synne.
So loue ys lech of lyue · and lysse of alle peyne,   200
And the graffe of grace · and graythest wey to heuene.
For-thy ich may say, as ich seide · by syght of the tixt,
Whenne alle tresours ben tryed · treuth ys the best;
Loue it,' quath that lady · 'lette may ich no lengere   204
To lere the what loue ys' · and leue at me hue lauhte.

Explicit passus secundus.

C. 199. confortetth P.   200. pyne P.   201. an (*for* and) P.
grayþost P.   wey S; wei MF; way IB; P *om.*   203. Wenne P.
204. þe (*for* that) P.   205. wat P.   P *om.* me.

PASSUS II.

Passus secundus de visione.

YIT kneled I on my knees · and cried hire of grace,
And seide, 'merci, madame · for Maries loue of heuene
That bar the blisful barn · that bou3t vs on the roode,
Teche me the kuynde craft · forte knowe the False.' 4
'Loke on the lufthond,' quod heo · 'and seo wher he stondeth!

PASSUS II.

Passus secundus de visione, vt supra.

YET I courbed on my knees · and cryed hir of grace,
And seide, 'mercy, madame · for Marie loue of heuene,
That bar that blisful barne · that bou3te vs on the rode,
Kenne me bi somme crafte · to knowe the Fals.' 4
  'Loke vppon thi left half · and lo where he standeth,
Bothe Fals and Fauel · and here feres manye!'
  I loked on my left half · as the lady me taughte,
And was war of a womman · wortheli yclothed, 8
Purfiled with pelure · the finest vpon erthe,
Y-crounede with a corone · the kyng hath non better.
Fetislich hir fyngres · were fretted with golde wyre,
And there-on red rubyes · as red as any glede, 12
And diamantz of derrest pris · and double manere safferes,
Orientales and ewages · enuenymes to destroye.
  Hire robe was ful riche · of red scarlet engreyned,
With ribanes of red golde · and of riche stones; 16
Hire arraye me rauysshed · suche ricchesse saw I neuere;
I had wondre what she was · and whas wyf she were.
  'What is this womman,' quod I · 'so worthily atired?'
'That is Mede the mayde,' quod she · 'hath noyed me ful oft, 20

A. 5. he TUD; heo V.   C. 5. war P.   9. wommon P.   10. He
(*for* Hue); *see* l. 5.   wit P.   11. coronede P.   with FG; in PEMIS.

Bothe Fals and Fauuel · and al his hole meyne!'
I lokede on the luft half · as the ladi me tauhte;
Thenne was I war of a wommon · wonderliche clothed, 8
Purfylet with pelure · the ricchest vppon eorthe,
I-corouned with a coroune · the kyng hath no bettre;
Alle hir fyue fyngres · weore frettet with rynges,
Of the preciousest perre · that prince wered euere; 12
In red scarlet heo rod · i-rybaunt with gold;
Ther nis no qweene qweyntore · that quik is alyue.
  'What is this wommon,' quod I · 'thus wonderliche a-tyret?'
  'That is Meede the mayden,' quod heo · 'that hath me marred
    ofte, 16

PASSUS III.

Incipit passus tercius.

AND thanne ich knelede on my knees · and cryede to hure
    of grace,
And seide, 'mercy, madame · for Marye loue of heuene,
That bar that blessede barn · that boughte vs on the rode,
Kenne me by som craft · to knowe the false.' 4
'Loke vpon thy lyft half,' quath hue · 'lo whar he standith,
Bothe Fals and Fauel · and fykel-tonge Lyere,
And menye of hure maners · bothe men and wommen.'
Ich lokid on my lyft half · as the lady me tauhte, 8
And sauh a womman as yt were · wonderlich riche clothed.
Hue was purfild with peloure · non purere in erthe,
And coroned with a corone · the kynge hath no betere;
On alle hure fyue fyngres · rycheliche yrynged, 12
And ther-on rede rubies · and other riche stones.
Hure robe was ryccher · than ich rede couthe,
For to telle of hure atyre · no tyme haue ich nouth.
Hure a-raye with hure rychesse · rauesshede myn herte; 16
'Whas wyf hue were · and what was hure name,
Leue lady,' quath ich tho · 'layn nat yf ȝe knowen.'
'That ys Mede the mayde,' quath hue · 'that hath noyed me ofte,

---

16. wit P.   17. Was (*for* Whas) P.   18. Luue (*for* Leue) P.

And i-lakked my lore · to lordes aboute.
In the pope paleys heo is · as priue as my-seluen;
And so schulde heo nouȝt · for Wrong was hir syre;
Out of Wrong heo wox · to wrotherhele monye.   20
Ich ouhte ben herre then heo · I com of a bettre.
  To-morwe worth the mariage i-mad · of Meede and of Fals;

And ylakked my lemman · that Lewte is hoten,
And bilowen hire to lordes · that lawes han to kepe.
In the popis paleys · she is pryue as my-self,
But sothenesse wolde nouȝt so · for she is a bastarde.   24
  For Fals was hire fader · that hath a fykel tonge,
And neuere sothe seide · sithen he come to erthe.
  And Mede is manered after hym · riȝte as kynde axeth;
    Qualis pater, talis filius; bona arbor bonum fructum facit.

I auȝte ben herre than she · I cam of a better.   28
  Mi fader the grete god is · and grounde of alle graces,
O god with-oute gynnynge · and I his gode douȝter,
And hath ȝoue me mercy · to marye with my-self;
And what man be merciful · and lelly me loue,   32
Schal be my lorde and I his leef · in the heiȝe heuene.
  And what man taketh Mede · myne hed dar I legge,
That he shal lese for hir loue · a lappe of *caritatis.*
How construeth Dauid the kynge · of men that taketh mede, 36
And men of this molde · that meynteneth treuthe,
And how ȝe shal saue ȝow-self · the sauter bereth witnesse,
    Domine, quis habitabit in tabernaculo tuo, &c.
  And now worth this Mede ymaried · al to a mansed schrewe,
To one Fals Fikel-tonge · a fendes biȝete;   40
Fauel thorw his faire speche · hath this folke enchaunted,
And al is Lyeres ledyng · that she is thus ywedded.
  To-morwe worth ymade · the maydenes bruydale,
And there miȝte thow wite, if thow wolt · which thei ben alle   44

A. 20. Out of THUD; In-to V.   27. wyte THUD; seo V.   B. 27.
bona C; *bonus* LWO.   C. 20. lemmen P.   26. seilde P.   P *om.* if.
27. kynden P.   *Qualis* EFSB; *Talis* PIM.   30. herrer P.   a IFSB;

A. PASSUS II. 23–27. C. PASSUS III. 20–47. 43

Fauuel with feir speche · hath brou3t hem to-gedere,
And Gyle hath bi-gon hire so · heo graunteth al his wille; 24
And al is Li3eres ledynge · that heo leuen to-gedere.
   To-morwe worth the mariage i-mad · soth as I the telle,
That thou miht wyte, 3if thou wolt · whuche thei ben alle

And lowen vp-on my lemman · that Leaute ys hoten, 20
And lackyd hym to lordes · that lawes han to kepe,
In kynges court and in comune court · contrarieth my techynge.
In the popes paleys · hue is pryuy as my-selue,
Ac sothnesse wold no3t so · for hue is a bastarde; 24
On Fauel was hure fader · that hath a fykel tonge,
And selde soth seith · bote if he souche gyle;
And Mede ys manered after hym · as men of kynde karpen,
   Qualis pater, talis filius.
For shal neuere brere bere · beries as a vyne, 28
Ne on croked kene thorne · kynde fygys wexe;
   Bona arbor bonum fructum facit.
Ich ouhte be herre than hue · ich kam of a betere,
The fader that me forth brouhte · *filius dei* he hoteth,
That neuere lyede ne lauhwede · in al hus lyf-tyme. 32
Ich am hus dere douheter · duchesse of heuene;
What man that me louyeth · and my wille folweth,
Shal haue grace to good ynow · and a good ende;
And what man that loueth Mede · my lyf ich dar wedde, 36
He shal lese for hure loue · a lappe of trewe charite.
That most helpeth men to heuene · mede most letteth,
Ich do hit vpon Dauid · the doumbe wol no3t lye;
   Domine, quis habitabit in tabernaculo tuo, et cetera.
Dauid vn-doth hit hym-self · as the dumbe sheweth, 40
   Et super innocentem munera non accepit.
   To-morwe worth Mede wedded · to a mansed wrecche,
To on Fals Faithles · of the feendes kynne.
Fauel thorgh his flateryng speche · hath Mede foule enchantid,
And al is Lyers ledyng · that lady is thus ywedded. 44
Soffre now and thow shalt see · suche as ben apaiede,
That Mede ys thus ymaryed · to-morwe thow shalt aspie.
Know hym wel, yf thow kanst · and kep the fro hem alle

---

kynde PE.   33. dure (*for* dere) P.   36. wat P.   37. luse (*for* lese) P.
trywe P.   43. is (*for* his) P.

That longith to that lordschipe · the lasse and the more.   28
Know hem there ȝif thou canst · and kepe the fro hem alle,
ȝif thou wilnest to wone · with treuthe in his blisse;
Lerne his lawe that is so lele · and siththe teche it further.
I may no lengore lette · vr lord ich the bi-kenne;   32
And bi-come a good mon · for eny couetyse, ich rede.'
When heo was me fro · I loked and byhelde
Alle this riche retenaunce · that regneden with Fals
Weoren bede to the bruyt-ale · on bo two the sydes.   36
Sir Simonye is of-sent · to asseale the chartres,
That Fals othur Fauuel · bi eny fyn heolden,
And feffe Meede ther-with · in marriage for euere.

That longeth to that lordeship · the lasse and the more.
Knowe hem there if thow canst · and kepe thi tonge,
And lakke hem nouȝt, but lat hem worth · til lewte be iustice,
And haue powere to punyschen hem · thanne put forth thi resoun.
    Now I bikenne the Criste,' quod she · 'and his clene moder,   49
And lat no conscience acombre the · for coueitise of Mede.'
    Thus left me that lady · liggyng aslepe,
And how Mede was ymaried · in meteles me thouȝte;   52
That alle the riche retenauns · that regneth with the false
Were boden to the bridale · on bothe two sydes,
Of alle maner of men · the mene and the riche.
To marie this maydene · was many man assembled,   56
As of kniȝtes and of clerkis · and other comune poeple,
As sysours and sompnours · shireues and here clerkes,
Bedelles and bailliues · and brokoures of chaffare,
Forgoeres and vitaillers · and vokates of the arches;   60
I can nouȝt rekene the route · that ran aboute Mede.
    Ac Symonye and Cyuile · and sisoures of courtes
Were moste pryue with Mede · of any men, me thouȝte.
Ac Fauel was the first · that fette hire out of boure,   64
And as a brokour brouȝte hir · to be with Fals enioigned.
Whan Symonye and Cyuile · seiȝ here beire wille,
Thei assented for siluer · to sei as bothe wolde.

    A. 28-30. *These lines are from* UTH$_2$D; V *has only* l. 30, *thus*: Bote ȝif thow wilne to wone · with treuthe in his blisse.   **31.** *This line is in* H *only*.
34. *This line is in* H *only*.   **35.** retenaunce THUD; retenauntes V.   **38.**

A. PASSUS II. 40–51.   C. PASSUS III. 48–68.

Bote ther nas halle ne hous · that miht herborwe the peple,　40
That vche feld nas ful · of folk al a-boute.
　In middes on a mountayne · at midmorwe tyde
Was piht vp a pauilon · a proud for the nones;
And ten thousand of tentes . i-tilled be-sydes,　　　　　　44
For knihtes of cuntre · and comers aboute,
For sisours, for sumnors · for sullers, for buggers,
For lewede, for lerede · for laborers of thropes,
And for the flaterynge freeris · alle the foure orders,　　48
Alle to witnesse wel · what the writ wolde,
In what manere that Meede · in mariage was i-feffed;
To beo fastnet with Fals · the fyn was arered.

That louyeth hure lordsheps · lasse other more.　　　　　48

Lacke hem noȝt, bote lete hem worthe · tyl Leaute be iustice,
And haue power for to punyshe hem · then put forth thy reson
For ich by-kenne the Crist,' quath hue · ' and hus clene moder,
Encombre neuere thy conscience · for couetyse of Mede.'　52
　Thus left me that lady · lyggynge a slepe.
And ich sauh how Mede was maried · metyng as it were;
And al the riche retynaunce · that roteth hem on fals lyuynge
Were bede to that brudale · on bothe half the contreie,　56
Of many maner men · that were of Medes kunne;

Of knyȝtes, of clerkes · of other comune puple,
As sysours and somners · shereyues and here clerkes,
Budels and bailifs · and brokours of chaffare,　　　　　60
Forgoers and vytailers · and vokettus of the arches,
Ich kan noȝt rekenye the route · that ran a-boute Mede.
　Ac Symonye and Ciuile · and sisours of contreis
Were most pryuye with Mede · of eny men, me thouȝte.　64
Ac Fauel was the ferste · that fette hure out of chambre,
And as a brocour broghte hure forth · to be ioynid with Fals.
Whanne Symonye and Cyuyle · sauh here botheres wil,
Thay assented ther-to · at seluers praiere.　　　　　　68

---

fyn THUD; peyne V.　　48. *This line is in* H *only.*　　50. I-feffed H;
feffid TUD; V *om.*　　B. 59. chaffre L.　　C. 48. oþer þe more.　　61.
Forgoers IE; Vorgheours P.　　P *om.* the.　　64. wit P.　　me þouȝte
MFSBG; of þe route P.　　65. P *om.* out.　　66. wit P.　　67. Wanne P.

Thenne Fauuel fet hire forth · and to Fals taketh,　　　52
In forwarde that Falsnesse · schal fynden hire for euere,
To be boxum and boun · his biddyng to folfulle,
In bedde and at borde · boxum and hende,
And as sir Simonye wol sigge · to suwen his wille.　　　56
Now Simonye and Siuyle · stondeth forth bothe,
Vn-foldyng the feffement · that Falsnes made,
And thus bygonnen the gomes · and gradden wel hy3e :

Thanne lepe Lyer forth, and seide · 'lo here! a chartre,　　68
That Gyle with his gret othes · gaf hem togidere,'
And preide Cyuile to se · and Symonye to rede it.
Thanne Symonye and Cyuile · stonden forth bothe,
And vnfoldeth the feffement · that Fals hath ymaked,　　72
And thus bigynneth thes gomes · to greden ful hei3 :—

　　'*Sciant presentes et futuri, &c.*
Witeth and witnesseth · that wonieth vpon this erthe,
That Mede is y-maried · more for here goodis,
Than for ani vertue or fairenesse · or any free kynde.　　76
Falsenesse is faine of hire · for he wote hire riche ;
And Fauel with his fikel speche · feffeth bi this chartre
To be prynces in pryde · and pouerte to dispise,
To bakbite, and to bosten · and bere fals witnesse,　　80
To scorne and to scolde · and sclaundere to make,
Vnboxome and bolde · to breke the ten hestes ;—
　　And the erldome of enuye · and wratthe togideres,
With the chastelet of chest · and chateryng-oute-of-resoun,　84
The counte of coueitise · and alle the costes aboute,
That is, vsure and auarice · alle I hem graunte,
In bargaines and in brokages · with al the borghe of theft ;—
　　And al the lordeship of lecherye · in lenthe and in brede,　88
As in werkes and in wordes · and waitynges with eies,
And in wedes and in wisshynges · and with ydel thou3tes,
There as wille wolde · and werkmanship failleth.'

A. 56. to suwen HTH₂; to sewen D; schewen V.　　59. *From* HTUD;
V *omits this line.*　　**B.** 87. borgthe L.　　91. L *wrongly inserts* ne *before*
wolde.　　wermanship L.　　ʹ **C.** 72. stoden MFG ; stod P.　　73. vnfeeld P.
þat (*for* the) P.　　makede P.　　75. bylyuen P.　　78. shiche P.　　79. Witen I ;

A. PASSUS II. 60-66. C. PASSUS III. 69-96.

'Hit witen and witnessen · that woneth vppon eorthe,   60
That I, Fauuel, feffe Fals · to that mayden Meede,
To be present in pruyde · for pore or for riche,
With the erldam of envye · euer forto laste,
With alle the lordschupe · of lengthe and of brede,   64
With the kingdom of couetise · I croune hem to-gedere;
With the yle of vsure · and auarice the false,

Thenne leep Liere forth, and seide · 'lo! here a chartre,
That Gyle hath gyue to Falsnesse · and graunted to Mede,'
And preyth Cyuyle it to see · and Symonye it to rede.
Thanne Symonye and Cyuyle · stoden forth bothe,   72
And vnfeelde the feffement · that Fals hadde maked;
Thanne sayde Symonye · that Cyuyl it herde,
'Alle that louen and byleuen · vp lykyng of Mede,
Leueth hit leelly · thys worth hure laste mede,   76
That folwen Falnesse · Fauel, and Lyere,
And me, and swiche men · that after mede wayten.
    Sciant presentes et futuri : et cetera.
Witen alle and witnesen · that wonen here on erthe,
That Mede ys y-maried · more for hure richesse   80
Than for holynesse other hendenesse · other for hye kynde.
Falsnesse is fayne of hure · for he wot hure riche,
And Fauel hath with fals speche · feffed hem by this lettere
To be pryncs of prude · and pouerte to dispice,   84
To bakbyten and to bosten · and bere fals witnesse,
To scornie and to scolde · sclaundres to make,
Both vnbuxom and bold · to breke the ten hestes.
The erldom of enuye · and yre he hym graunteth,   88
With the castel of cheste · and chatering-out-of-reson;
The countee of couetise · he consenteth to bothe,
With vserye and auerice · and other false sleithes
In bargeyns and in brocages · with the borghe of thufthe, 92
And al the lordshep of lecherye · in lengthe and in brede,
As in workes and in wordes · and waitynges of eyes,
In wedes and in wisshynges · and with ydel thouhtes,
Ther that wil wolde · and werkmanshup faileth.   96

Wyten B; Wetyn P.   80. P *inserts* mechel *after* hure.   82. his (*for* is) P.
85. bagbyten P.   whitnesse P.   94. P *om.* 2nd and.   waitenges P.
95. P *om.* in.   wisshenges P.

Glotonye and grete othus · ich ȝiue hem i-feere,
With alle delytes and lustes · the deuel for to serue,   68
In al the seruyse of slouthe · I sese hem to-gedere:
   To habben and to holden · and al heore heyres aftur,
With the purtinaunce of purgatorie · in-to the pyne of helle:
Ȝeldynge for this thing · at the ȝeres ende,   72
Heore soules to Sathanas · to senden in-to pyne;
Ther to wonen with Wrong · whil god is in heuene.'
   In witnesse of whuche thing · Wrong was the furste,
Pers the pardoner · Paulynes doctor,   76

   Glotonye he gaf hem eke · and grete othes togydere,   92
And alday to drynke · at dyuerse tauernes,
And there to iangle and to iape · and iugge here euene cristene,
And in fastyng-dayes to frete · ar ful tyme were.
And thanne to sitten and soupen · til slepe hem assaille,   96
And breden as burgh-swyn · and bedden hem esily,
Tyl sleuth and slepe · slyken his sides;
And thanne wanhope to awake hym so · with no wille to amende,
For he leueth be lost · this is here last ende.   100
   And thei to haue and to holde · and here eyres after,
A dwellyng with the deuel · and dampned be for eure,
With al the purtenaunces of purgatorie · in-to the pyne of helle.
Ȝeldyng for this thinge · at one ȝeres ende,   104
Here soules to Sathan · to suffre with hym peynes,
And with him to wonye with wo · whil god is in heuene.
   In witnesse of which thing · Wronge was the first,
And Pieres the pardonere · of Paulynes doctrine,   108
Bette the bedel · of Bokyngham-shire,
Rainalde the reue · of Rotland sokene,
Munde the mellere · and many moo other.
'In the date of the deuel · this dede I assele,   112
Bi siȝte of sire Symonye · and Cyuyles leue.'
   Thenne tened hym Theologye · whan he this tale herde,
And seide to Cyuile · 'now sorwe mot thow haue,
Such weddynges to worche · to wratthe with Treuthe;   116
And ar this weddyng be wrouȝte · wo the bityde!

   A. 76. doctor TH₂; doctoure D; douhter V.   79. *From* HH₂; V *omits this line.*   85. wraththe THUD; teone V.   **B.** 97. bredun L.   116.

A. PASSUS II. 77–86.   C. PASSUS III. 97–119.

Bette the budul · of Bokynghames schire,
Rondulf the reue · of Rotelondes sokene,
Taberes and tomblers · and tapesters fele,
Monde the mulnere · and moni mo othure.   80
In the date of the deuel · the deede was a-selet,
Be siht of sir Symoni · and notaries signes.
    Then teonede him Teologye · whon he this tale herde,
And seide to Siuyle · 'serwe on thi lokkes,   84
Such weddyng to worche · to wraththe with Truthe;
And ar this weddyng beo wrou3t · wo the beo-tyde!

Glotenye he geueth hem · and grete othes to-gederes,
Al day to drynke · at dyuerse tauernes,
Ther to iangly and to iape · and iuge her emcristine,
And fastingdayes to frete · by-for noon, and drynke   100
With spicerie, spek ydelnesse · in veen speche, and spene,
And suwye forth swych felaushep · tyl thei ben fallen in slewthe,
And a-wake with wanhope · and no wil to amende,
For he leyueth be ylost · when he hus lyf leteth: 104
This lif to folwie Falsnesse · and folk that on hym leueth,
After hure deth a dwelling · day with-outen ende
In Luciferes lordshup · as thys lettere sheweth,
With al the portinaunce of purgatorye · and the payne of helle.' 108

In witnesse of this thyng · Wrong was the ferste,
And Peres the pardoner · of Paulynes queste,
Bette the budele · of Banneburies sokne,
Reynald the reue · and redyngkynges menye,   112
Munde the mylnere · and meny mo othere.
In the date of the deuel · this dede ys a-seled,
By syght of syre Symonye · and Cyuyles leue.
    Thanne tened hym Theologye · whenne he thys tale herde,
And seyde to syre Symonye · 'now sorwe mote thow haue,
Such a weddyng to worche · that wrathe myghte Treuthe. 118
And er this weddyng be wroughte · wo to al 3oure consail!

---

wendynges L.   C. 97. hym (*for* hem) P.   100. an (*for* and) P.
104. wen P.   105. lyueþ P.   106. P *om*. a.   112. and þe (*for* and) P.
116. tened IFS; tenede MG; tuemede (*sic*) P.   wenne P.   117. þow
mote P.   118. treuhþe P.

E

For Meede is a Iuweler · a mayden of goode,
God graunte vs to ȝiue hire · ther Treuthe wol a-signe.   88
And thou hast ȝiuen hire to a gilour · god ȝiue the serwe!
The tixt telleth not so · Treuthe wot the sothe;
   Dignus est operarius mercede sua;
Worthi is the werkmon · his hure to haue;
And thou hast feffet hire with Fals · fy on thi lawe!   92
   For lechours and lyȝers · lihtliche thou leeuest,
Simonie and thi-self · schenden holichirche;

For Mede is moylere · of Amendes engendred,
And god graunteth to gyf · Mede to Treuthe,
And thow hast gyuen hire to a gyloure · now god gyf the sorwe!
Thi tixt telleth the nouȝt so · Treuthe wote the sothe,   121
For *dignus est operarius* · his hyre to haue,
And thow hast fest hire to Fals · fy on thi lawe!
For al by lesynges thow lyuest · and lecherouse werkes,   124
Symonye and thi-self · schenden holicherche,

The notaries and ȝee · noyeth the peple,
ȝe shul abiggen it bothe · bi god that me made!
Wel ȝe witen, wernardes · but if ȝowre witte faille,   128
That Fals is faithlees · and fikel in his werkes,
And was a bastarde y-bore · of Belsabubbes kynne.
And Mede is moylere · a mayden of gode,
And myȝte kisse the kynge · for cosyn, an she wolde.   132
   For-thi worcheth bi wisdome · and bi witt also,

   A. 89. to THUD; V *om.*   95, 96. *From* H; V *omits both lines.*   97.
Nataries V.   **B.** 118. engendreth L.   **C.** 122. moder MIBG; dame

ȝe schule abygge it bothe · by god that me made,
At oo ȝeris ende · whan ȝe reken schul;   96
He and theose notaries · anuyȝen the peple.
For wel ȝe witen, wernardes! · but ȝif or wit fayle,
That Fals is a faytur · a faylere of werkes,
And a bastard i-boren · of Belsabubbes kunne.   100
And Meede is a Iuweler · a mayden ful gent;
Heo mihte cusse the kyng · for cosyn, ȝif heo schulde.
Worcheth bi wisdam · and bi wit aftur;

For Mede is moillere · Amendes was here dame;   120
Thouh Fals were hure fader · and Fykel-tonge hure syre,
Amendes was hure moder · by trewe mennes lokyng.
With-oute hure moder Amendes · Mede may noght be wedded,
For Treuth plyghte hure treuthe · to wedde on of hure douhteres,
And god grauntede it were so · so that no gyle were,   125
And thow hast ygeue hure as Gyle taughte · god ȝyue the sorwe!
For Cyuyl and thy selue . selde fulfilleth
That god wolde were ydo · with-oute som deceite.   128
Ich Theologie the tixt knowe · and trewe dome wytnesseth,
That Laurens the Leuite · lyggynge on the gredire,
Loked vp to oure lorde · and a-loud seide,
"God, of thy grace · heuene gates opene,   132
For ich, man, of thy mercy · mede haue deserued!"
And syththe man may an hey · mede of god deserue,
Hit semeth ful sothly · ryght so on erthe,
That Mede may be wedded · to no man bote to Treuthe; 136
And thow hast feffyd hure with Fals · fy on suche lawe!
For thorw lesynges ȝe lacchen · largeliche mede.
That ȝe nemeth and notaries · to nauht by-gynneth brynge
Holy churche, and charite · ȝe cheweth and deuoureth. 140
ȝe shulle a-bygge bothe · bote ȝe a-mende the sonnere.
For wel ȝe wyten, wernardes · as holy wryt telleth,
That Fals ys faithles · the fend ys hus syre,
And as a bastard ybore · byȝute was he neuere.   144
And Mede ys moillere · a maiden of goode,
Hue myghte cusse the kyng · as for hus kynswomman.
For-thy worcheth by wisdome · and by witte al-so,

PEFS.   mennes MI; men PEFS.   138. lacchen MIFS; lauhte P,

Ledeth hire to Londone · ther lawe is i-hondlet,   104
3if eny leute wol loken · that thei liggen to-gedere,
And 3if the Iustise wol Iugge hire · to be Ioynet with Fals.
3it be-war of the weddyng · for witti is Treuthe;
For Concience is of his counseil · and knoweth ou vchone;
And 3if he fynde such defaute · that 3e with Fals holden,   109
Hit schal bi-sitten oure soules · sore atte laste.'
Herto assentid Syuyle · but Symonye ne wolde
Tyle he had syluer · for his sawes and his selynge.   112
Then fet Fauel forth · floreynes i-nowe,
And bad Gyle go to · and 3yue gold aboute,
And namely to this notaries · that hem non lacked;

And ledeth hire to Londoun · there lawe is yshewed,
If any lawe wil loke · thei ligge togederes.
And thou3 Iustices iugge hir · to be ioigned with Fals,   136
3et beth war of weddyng · for witty is Truthe,
And Conscience is of his conseille · and knoweth 3ow vchone;
And if he fynde 3ow in defaute · and with the fals holde,
It shal bisitte 3owre soules · ful soure atte laste!'   140
    Here-to assenteth Cyuile · ac Symonye ne wolde,
Tyl he had siluer for his seruise · and also the notaries.
    Thanne fette Fauel forth · floreynes ynowe,
And bad Gyle to gyue · golde al aboute,   144
And namelich to the notaries · that hem none ne faille,
And feffe False-witnes · with floreines ynowe;
'For he may Mede amaistrye · and maken at my wille.'
    Tho this golde was gyue · grete was the thonkynge   148
To Fals and to Fauel · for her faire 3iftes,
And comen to conforte · fram care the Fals,
And seiden, 'certis, sire · cesse shal we neuere
Til Mede be thi wedded wyf · thorw wittis of vs alle.   152
For we haue Mede amaistried · with owre mery speche,
That she graunteth to gon · with a gode wille,
To Londoun, to loke · 3if that the lawe wolde
Iugge 3ow ioyntly · in ioye for euere.'   156
    Thanne was Falsenesse fayne · and Fauel as blithe,

    A. 108. of his counseil TUD; on of his V. 111-127. *From* H; *also*
(*except* l. 118) *in* TUD. V *omits these lines*. **C.** 148. londen P. wer P.

And feffe False-witnesse · with florens I-nowe, 116
For he may Mede a-maysteren · and make hir at his wylle;
For where falsenes is oft fownden · there feith fayleth.
Thoo the gold was 3ouen · grete were the thonkes
To False and to Fauel · for her feyre 3yftus. 120
Many comen, from care · to counforte the false,
And sworen on the hoolydom · that 'cesse schul we neuere
Or Mede be thi weddud wyf · thorou3 witte of vs alle.
For we han Mede a-maysterd · with oure myri wordis 124
That heo graunteth to goo · with a good wille,
To London, to loke · if the lawe wole
Iugge 3ou Ioyntely · to be Ioyned for euer.'
Thenne was Fals fayn · and Fauuel also blithe, 128

And ledeth hure to Londoun · wher lawe may declare, 148
Yf matrimoine may be · of Mede and of Falshede.
And thow iustices en-ioynen hem · thorgh iurers othes,
3ut be war of the weddyng · for wytty is Treuthe,
And Conscience is of hus consail · and knoweth 3ow alle; 152
And yf he fynde 3ow in defaute · and with the false holde,
Hit shal sitte 3oure soules · ful soure at the laste.'
Her-to a-sentyd Cyuyle · ac Symonie ne wolde,
Tyl he hadde seluer for the seel · and sygnes of notaries. 156
Tho fette Fauel forth · floreynes y-nowe,
And bad Gyle 'go gyue · gold al a-boute,
Nameliche, to notaries · that non of hem faille;
And feffe Falsnesse · with floreynes ynowe, 160
For he may Mede amaistren · with hus myry speche.'
Tho this gold was gyuen · gret was the thonkynge
That Fals and Fauel hadde · for here faire 3yftes,
And comen ful courteislich · to conforte the False. 164
Thei seide to hym softeliche · 'cesse shulle we neuere;
Til Mede be thy wedded wyf · we wolle nouht stynte.
For we han Mede a-maistrid · thorw oure myrye tonge,
That hue graunteth to go · with a good wille 168
To Londoun, and loke · yf lawe wol iuge;
To be maried for monye · Mede hath a-sented.'
Than was Fauel fayne · and Falsnesse blythe,

---

150. Iustices IFSE; Iustice PM.   151. wedyng P.   153. P *om.* and.
156. a (*for* and) P.   160. wit P.   169. londen P.

And lette sompne alle men · in cuntre a-boute,
To arayen hem redi · bothe burgeys and schirreues,
To weende with hem to Westmunster · to witnesse the deede.
 Thenne careden heo for caples · to carien hem thider ;   132
Bote Fauuel fette forth · foles of the beste,
And sette Meede on a schirreues bak · i-schood al newe,
And Fals on a sysoures backe · that softly trotted ;
(For falsnes aȝeyn the feith · sisoures he defouleth,   136
Thoruȝ comburance of couetyse · clymben aȝeyn truthe,
That the feith is defouled · and falsly defamed,
And falsnes is a lord i-woxe · and lyueth as hym lyketh) :
Fauel on a feyre speche · ful feyntly a-tyred ;   140
(For feire speche that is feithles · is falsnes brother ;

And leten sompne alle segges · in schires aboute,
And bad hem alle be bown · beggeres and othere,
To wenden wyth hem to Westmynstre · to witnesse this dede.   160
 Ac thanne cared thei for caplus · to kairen hem thider,
And Fauel fette forth thanne · folus ynowe ;
And sette Mede vpon a schyreue · shodde al newe,
And Fals sat on a sisoure · that softlich trotted,   164
And Fauel on a flaterere · fetislich atired.
 Tho haued notaries none · annoyed thei were,
For Symonye and Cyuile · shulde on hire fete gange.
 Ac thanne swore Symonye · and Cyuile bothe,   168
That sompnoures shulde be sadled · and serue hem vchone,
And lat apparaille this prouisoures · in palfreis wyse ;—
'Sire Symonye hym-seluen · shal sitte vpon here bakkes.
 Denes and suddenes · drawe ȝow togideres,   172
Erchdekenes and officiales · and alle ȝowre regystreres,
Lat sadel hem with siluer · owre synne to suffre,
As auoutrie and deuorses · and derne vsurye,
To bere bischopes aboute · abrode in visytynge.   176
 Paulynes pryues · for pleyntes in the consistorie,
Shul serue my-self · that Cyuile is nempned ;
And cartesadel the comissarie · owre carte shal he lede,
And fecchen vs vytailles · at *fornicatores*.   180

A. 135–143. *These lines are quoted from* H, *and those in parentheses occur in* H *only.* V *has only the one line—*And Fauuel on a Feir speche · Feyntliche atyret. T *and* D *have only the two lines—*

A. PASSUS II. 142-155.   C. PASSUS III. 172-191.   55

And thus sysoures ben sompned · the false to serue,
And feire-speche Fauel · that moche folke desceyueth).
   Thenne notaries none hors hedden · anuyed thei weore,   144
That Symonie and Siuile · schulden go on foote.
   Thenne seide Siuile · and swor bi the roode,
That sompnors schulde ben sadelet · and seruen hem vchone ;
'And lette apparayle prouisours · on palfreis wyse,   148
Sire Symonye hym-selfe · shal sitte on here bakkis,
And alle denes and sodenes · as destreres dihten,
For thei schullen beren bisschops · and bringen hem to reste.
   Paulines peple · for playntes in constorie   152
Schal seruen my-self · that Siuile hette;
Let cart-sadele vr commissarie · vr cart he schal drawe,
And fetten vr vitayles · of the fornicatours ;

And leten sompne alle segges · in eche syde a-boute,   172
And bed hem alle ben boun · beggeres and othere,
To wenden with hem to Westemynstre · hus weddyng to honoure.
Ac hakeneyes hadde thei none · bote hakeneyes to hyre ;
Thenne gan Gyle borwe hors · at meny grete maistres,   176
And shope that a shereyue · sholde bere Mede
Softliche in saumbury · fram syse to syse.
Fals and Fauel · sholde fecche forth sisours,
And ride on hem and on reues · ryght faste by Mede.   180
Symonye and Cyuyle · seiden and sworen
That prestes and prouisours · sholde prelates seruen,
'And ich my-self Cyuyle · and Symonye my felawe
Wollen ryden vp-on rectours · and riche men deuoutours,   184
And notories on persons · that permuten ofte,
And on poure prouysors · and on a-peles in the arches.
Somenours and southdenes · that *supersedeas* taketh,
On hem that louyeth lecherie · lepeth vp and rydeth,   188
On executores and suche men · cometh softliche after.
And let cople the comissarie · oure cart shal he drawe,
And fecche forth oure vitailes · of *fornicatores.*

    And fals sat on a sisour · þat softeliche trottide,
    And fauel vpon fair speche · fetisliche atirid.
U *has the same, omitting* sat ; H₂ *has also two similar lines.*   149. *From*
THUD; V *omits this line.*   B. 165. flatere L.   175. deuoses L.
C. 185. on IE ; and PMS.   186. in IE ; of MS ; on P.

And make Liȝere a long cart · to leden alle this othure 156
Fabulers and faytours · that on fote rennen.'
 Now Fals and Fauuel · fareth forth to-gedere,
And Meede in the middel · and al the meyne aftur.
I haue no tome to telle · the tayl that hem folweth, 160
Of so mony maner men · that on molde liuen.
 Bote Gyle was for-goere · and gyede hem alle.
Sothnesse sauh hem wel · and seide bote luyte,
Bote prikede on his palfrey · and passede hem alle, 164
And com to the kynges court · and Concience tolde,
And Concience to the kyng · carpede hit aftur.
 'Now be Crist,' quod the kyng · 'ȝif I mihte chacche
Fals othur Fauwel · or eny of his feeres, 168

 And maketh of Lyer a longe carte · to lede alle these othere,
As freres and faitours · that on here fete rennen.'
And thus Fals and Fauel · fareth forth togideres,
And Mede in the myddes · and alle thise men after. 184
I haue no tome to telle · the taille that hem folweth,
Of many maner man · that on this molde libbeth;
Ac Gyle was forgoer · and gyed hem alle.
 Sothenesse seiȝ hym wel · and seide but a litel, 188
And priked his palfrey · and passed hem alle,
And come to the kynges courte · and Conscience it tolde,
And Conscience to the kynge · carped it after.
 'Now by Cryst,' quod the kynge · 'and I cacche myȝte 192
Fals or Fauel · or any of his feres,
I wolde be wroke of tho wrecches · that worcheth so ille,
And don hem hange by the hals · and alle that hem meynteneth!
Shal neure man of molde · meynprise the leste, 196
But riȝte as the lawe wil loke · late falle on hem alle.'
 And comanded a constable · that come atte furst,
To 'attache tho tyrauntz · for eny thynge, I hote,
And fettereth fast Falsenesse · for enykynnes ȝiftes, 200
And gurdeth of Gyles hed · and lat hym go no furthere.

 And ȝif ȝe lacche Lyer · late hym nouȝt ascapen

A. 160. tome T; tyme for H; tunge UD; while V. 162. gyede TUD;

I wolde be wreken on this wrecches · that worchen so ille,
And don hem hongen bi the hals · and al that hem meyntenen;
Schal neuer mon vppon molde · meyntene the leste,
But riht as the lawe loketh · let fallen of hem alle.   172
   And comaunde the cunstable · that com at the furste,
To a-tache the traytours · for eny tresour,
Ich hote, ȝe fetere Fals faste · for eny kunnes ȝiftus,
And gurdeth of Gyles hed · let him go no forther;   176
And bringeth Meede to me · maugre hem alle.
   Symonye and Siuile · I seende hem to warne,
That holichirche for hem · worth harmet for euere.
And ȝif ȝe chacche Lyȝere · let him not a-skape,   180

Maketh of Lyer a lang cart · to lede alle these othere,   192
As fobbes and faitours · that on hure fet rennen.'
Thanne Fals and Fauel · ryden forth to-gederes,
And Mede in the myddes · and alle thuse men after.
Ich haue no tome to telle · the tail that hem folweth,   196
Of many manere men · for Medes sake sent after;
Ac gile was forgoere · to gyen al the puple,
For to wisse hem the weye · and with Mede a-byde.
Sothnesse seih hem alle · and seide bote a lytel,   200
And priked forth on pacience · and passede hem alle,
And cam to the kynges court; · to Conscience he tolde,
And Conscience to the kyng · carped it after.
'Now by Cryst,' quath the kyng · 'and ich cacche myghte   204
Fals other Fauel · other here felawe Lyere,
Ich wolde be wreke on tho wrecches · and on here werkus alle,
And do hem hongy by the hals · and alle that hem maynteneth,
Shal neuere man on this molde · maynpryse the leste,   208
But ryght as the lawe loketh · let falle on hem alle!'
He comaundyd a constable · that cam at the furste,
'Go atache tho tyrauns · for eny tresour, ich hote,
Let feterye fast Falsnesse · for eny kynnes ȝiftes,   212
And gurd of Gyles hefd · and lete hym go no wyddere,
And brynge Mede to me · maugre hem alle.
And if ȝe lacche Lyere · let hym nat a-skapie

---

gilede V.   171. man THD; non (*for* mon) V.   C. 192. þese F; þise I;
þes PS.   201. an P.   209. But MIF; And PES.

58 A. PASSUS II. 181-192. B. PASSUS II. 203-228.

To ben set on the pillori · for eny preyere;
I bydde thee awayte hem wele · let non of hem ascape.'
   Dreede at the dore stood · and the dune herde,
And wihtliche wente · to warne the False,   184
And bad him faste to fle · and his feeres eke.
Thenne Fals for fere · fleih to the freeres,
And Gyle doth him to go · a-gast for to dyȝe;
Bote marchaundes metten with him · and maaden him to abyden,
Bi-souȝten him in heore schoppes · to sullen heore ware,   189
Apparayleden him as a prentis · the peple for to serue.
Liȝtliche Lyȝere · leop a-wey thennes,
Lurkede thorw lones · to-logged of monye;   192

Er he be put on the pilorye · for eny preyere, I hote;
And bryngeth Mede to me · maugre hem alle.'   204
   Drede atte dore stode · and the dome herde,
And how the kynge comaunded · constables and seriantz,
Falsenesse and his felawschip · to fettren an to bynden.
Thanne Drede went wiȝtliche · and warned the Fals,   208
And bad hym flee for fere · and his felawes alle.
   Falsenesse for fere thanne · fleiȝ to the freres,
And Gyle doth hym to go · agast for to dye.
Ac marchantz mette with hym · and made hym abide,   212
And bishetten hym in here shope · to shewen here ware,
And apparailled hym as a prentice · the poeple to serue.
   Liȝtliche Lyer · lepe awey thanne,
Lorkynge thorw lanes · to-lugged of manye.   216
He was nawhere welcome · for his manye tales,
Ouer-al yhowted · and yhote trusse;
Tyl pardoneres haued pite · and pulled hym in-to house.
They wesshen hym and wyped hym · and wonden hym in cloutes,
And sente hym with seles · on sondayes to cherches,   221
And gaf pardoun for pens · poundmel aboute.
Thanne loured leches · and lettres thei sent,
That he sholde wonye with hem · wateres to loke.   224
Spiceres spoke with hym · to spien here ware,
For he couth of here craft · and knewe many gommes.
Ac mynstralles and messageres · mette with hym ones,
And helden hym an half-ȝere · and elleuene dayes.   228

    A. 182. *This line is in* H *only.*   200. wone THUD; ben V.   hem

He nas nouȝwher wel-come · for his mony tales,
Bote ouur-al i-hunted · and hote to trusse.   194
Pardoners hedden pite · and putten him to house,
Wosschen him and wrongen him · and wounden him in cloutes,
And senden him on Sonendayes · with seales to churches,   197
And ȝaf pardun for pons · poundmele a-boute.
  This leornden this leches · and lettres him senden
For to wone with hem · watres to loke.   200
Spicers speeken with him · to a-spien heore ware,
For he kennede him in heore craft · and kneuȝ mony gummes.
  Munstrals and messagers · metten with him ones,
And with-heolde him half a ȝer · and elleuene wykes.   204

Er he be put on the pullery · for eny preier, ich hote!'   216
  Drede stod at the dore · and al that duene herde,
What the kynges wil was · and wyghtlyche he wente,
And bad Falsnesse to flee · and hus feren alle.
Falsnesse for fere tho · flegh to the freres,   220
And Gyle dud hym to gon · agast for to deye;
Ac marchauns metten with hym · and made hym abyde,
And shutten hym in here shoppes · to shewen here ware,
And parailed hym lyke here prentys · the puple to seruen.   224
Lyghtliche Lyere · lep a-way thennes,
Lorkynge thorw lanes · to-logged of menye.
He was nawher welcome · for hus meny tales,
Ouer-al houted out · and yhote trusse,   228
Til pardoners hadden pitte · and pullede hym to house.
Thei woshe hym and wypede hym · and wonde hym in cloutes,
And sente hym on Sonnedayes · with seeles to churches,
And ȝaf pardon for pans · pound-meel a-boute.   232
Thanne lourede leches · and letters thei senten,
That Lyer shold wony with hem · waters to loke.
Spicers to hym speke · to aspie here ware,
For he can on here crafte · and knoweth meny gommes.   236
Ac mynstrales and messagers · mette with Lyere ones,
And with-helde hym half a ȝere · and elleue dayes.

THD; him V.   204. with-heode V.   B. 227. mynstalles L.   C. 216.
P *om.* the.   preior P.   218. whyghtlyche P.   220. P *om.* tho.   225. away
þo fro þennes P.   227. nawer wolcome P.   228. trosse P.   229. pollede P.
231. on MIFSG; in P.   232. ȝaf hym P.   for MIFSEG; of P.   235.
hem (*for* hym) P.   237. ones MIG; one P.

    Freres with feir speches · fetten him thennes;   205
For knowynge of comers · kepten him as a frere;
Bote he hath leue to lepen out · as ofte as him lyketh,
And is wel-come whon he wole · and woneth with hem ofte.

    Freres with faire speche · fetten hym thennes,
And for knowyng of comeres · coped hym as a frere.
Ac he hath leue to lepe out · as oft as hym liketh,
And is welcome whan he wil · and woneth wyth hem oft.   232

    Alle fledden for fere · and flowen in-to hernes,
Saue Mede the mayde · na mo durst abide.
Ac trewli to telle · she trembled for drede,
And ek wept and wronge · whan she was attached.   236

And alle fledden for fere · and flowen in-to huirnes;   209
Saue Meede the mayden · no mon dorste abyde;
But trewely to telle · heo tremblede for fere,
And eke wepte and wrong hire hondes · whon heo was a-tachet.

Ac Freres thorw fayre speche · fetten hym thennes;
For knowynge of comers · thei copyde hym as a frere;   240
Ac he hath leue to lepen out · as ofte as hym lyketh,
And ys welcome whanne he cometh · and woneth with hem ofte.
Symonye and Cyuyle · senten to Rome,
And putte hem thorw a-peles · in the popes grace.   244
Ac Conscience to the kyng · a-cusede hem bothe,
And seide, 'syre kyng, by Cryst · bote clerkus amende,
Thi kyngdom thorw here couetyse · wol out of kynde wende,
And holy churche thorw hem · worth harmed for euere.'   248
Alle fledden for fere · and flowen in-to hernes;
Saue Mede the mayde · no mo dorste a-byde.
Ac treweliche to telle · hue tremblede for fere,
And bothe wrang and wepte · whanne hue was a-tached.   252

Hic explicit passus iij^{us}.

C. 242. wolcome P.   wanne P.   247. weynde P; *see* C. iv. 19.   250.
þat (*for* the) P.   251. tryweliche P.   252. wanne P.   atachede P.

PASSUS III.

Passus Tercius de Visione.

NOW is Meede the mayden i-nomen · and no mo 'of hem alle,
With beodeles and baylyfs · i-brouht to the kyng.
The kyng clepet a clerke · (I knowe not his nome),
To take Meede the mayden · and maken hire at ese.   4
'Ichulle assayen hire my-self · and sothliche aposen

PASSUS III.

Passus tertius.

NOW is Mede the mayde · and namo of hem alle
With bedellus and with bayllyues · brou3t bifor the kyng.
The kyng called a clerke · can I nou3t his name,
To take Mede the mayde · and make hire at ese.   4
'I shal assaye hir my-self · and sothelich appose
What man of this molde · that hire were leueste.
And if she worche bi my witte · and my wille folwe,
I wil forgyue hir this gilte · so me god help!'   8
   Curteysliche the clerke thanne · as the kyng hight,
Toke Mede bi the middel · and brou3te hir in-to chaumbre,

And there was myrthe and mynstralcye · Mede to plese.
They that wonyeth in Westmynstre · worschiped hir alle;   12
Gentelliche with ioye · the iustices somme
Busked hem to the boure · there the birde dwelled,
To conforte hire kyndely · by clergise leue,
And seiden, 'mourne nought, Mede · ne make thow no sorwe,   16
For we wil wisse the kynge · and thi wey shape,
To be wedded at thi wille · and where the leue liketh,

A. 3. clerke THUD; cler V.   **B.** 17. wil R; wol W; L *om.*
C. 3. ys (*for* hys) P.   4. þat (*for* the) P.   6. Wat P.   7. mennes F;

A. PASSUS III. 6-17.   C. PASSUS IV. 1-19.

What mon in this world · that hire weore leouest.
And ȝif heo worche be my wit · and my wil folewe,
I schal for-ȝiue hire the gult · so me god helpe!'   8
   Corteisliche the clerk tho · as the kyng hihte,
Tok the mayden bi the middel · and brouhte hire to chaumbre.
   Ther was murthe and munstralsye · Meede with to plese;
Heo that woneth at Westmunstre · worschipeth hire alle.   12
   Gentiliche with Ioye · the Iustise soone
Busked him in-to the bour · ther the buyrde was inne,
Cumfortede hire kuyndely · and made hire good chere,
And seide, 'Mourne thou not, Meede, · ne make thou no serwe,
For we wolen wysen the kyng · and thi wey schapen,   17

PASSUS IV.

Incipit passus quartus.

NOW is Mede the mayde · and no mo of hem alle
   Thorw bedeles and bailifs · brouht by-fore the kynge.
The kyng kallid a clerk · ich can nouht hys name,
To take Mede the mayde · and make here at ese;   4
'Ich shal asaye hure my-self · and sothliche apose,
What man of thys worlde · that hure is leuest haue?
And yf hue wirche wisliche · by wys mennes counsail,
Ich wolle for-gyue hure alle hure gultes · so me god helpe!'   8
Cortesliche the clerk thenne · as the kynge hyghte,
Toke Mede by the myddel · and myldeliche here broughte
In-to boure with blysse · and by hure gan sitte.
Ther was myrthe and mynstralcy · Mede to plesen;   12
That wenden to Westmynstre · worshupde hure meny.
Gentelich with ioye · iustices somme
Buskede hem to the boure · ther this berde dwellyd,
Confortynge hure as thei couthe · by the clerkus leue,   16
And seyde, 'morne nat, Mede · ne make thow no sorwe;
For we wolle wisse the kyng · and thy wey shape
For to wende at thy wil · wher the luf lyketh,

---

men PEIS.   10. mydel P.   12. and MIFSE; of P.   17. ne MIF;
PES *om*.   18. shappe P.

A. PASSUS III. 18–29.   B. PASSUS III. 19–40.

For alle Concience craft · and casten, as I trouwe,
That thou schalt haue bothe my3t and maystrye · and make what the liketh
With the kynge and the comyns · and the courte bothe.'   20
   Mildeliche thenne Meede · merciede hem alle
Of heore grete goodnesse · and 3af hem vchone
Coupes of clene gold · and peces of seluer,
Rynges with rubyes · and richesses i-nouwe,   24
The leste man of here mayne · a mutoun of gold.
   Thenne lau3ten thei leue · this lordynges, at meede.
With that ther come clerkes · to cumforte the same:
'We biddeth the be blithe · for we beoth thin owne,   28
Forte worche thi wil · while vr lyf dureth.'

For al Conscience caste · or craft, as I trowe!'
   Mildeliche Mede thanne · mercyed hem alle   20
Of theire gret goodnesse · and gaf hem vchone
Coupes of clene golde · and coppis of siluer,
Rynges with rubies · and ricchesses manye,
The leste man of here meyne · a motoun of golde.   24
Thanne lau3te thei leue · this lordes, at Mede.
   With that comen clerkis · to conforte hir the same,
And beden hire be blithe · 'for we beth thine owne,
For to worche thi wille · the while thow my3te laste.'   28
Hendeliche heo thanne · bihight hem the same,
To 'loue 3ow lelli · and lordes to make,
And in the consistorie atte courte · do calle 3owre names ;
Shal no lewdnesse lette · the leode that I louye,   32
That he ne worth first auanced · for I am biknowen
There konnyng clerkes · shul clokke bihynde.'
   Thanne come there a confessoure · coped as a frere,
To Mede the mayde · he mellud this wordes,   36
And seide ful softly · in shrifte as it were,
'Thei3 lewed men and lered men · had leyne by the bothe,
And falsenesse haued yfolwed the · al this fyfty wyntre,
I shal assoille the my-selue · for a seme of whete,   40

A. 19, 20. *These lines are in* H *only*.   25. *From* THUD; V *omits this line*.   26. lau3ten HD; lau3te TU; tok V.   C. 20. a (*for* and) P.

A. PASSUS III. 30–41.   C. PASSUS IV. 20–42.

Hendeliche thenne heo · be-hihte hem the same,
To louen hem lelly · and lordes to maken,
And in constorie at court · to tellen heore names.   32
'Schal no lewednesse hem lette · the lewedeste that I loue
That he ne worth avaunset; · for icham i-knowe
Ther cunnynge clerkes · schul couche be-hynde.'
  Thenne com ther a confessour · i-copet as a frere;   36
To Meede the mayden · ful mekeliche he loutede,
And seide ful softely · in schrift as hit weore,
'Thauh lerede and lewede · hedden leyen bi the alle,
And thau3 Fals hedde folewed the · this fiftene winter,   40
I schal asoyle the my-self · for a summe of whete,

For alle Consciences cast · and craft, as ich trowe!'   20
  Mildeliche Mede tho · merciede hem alle
Of hure grete goudnesse · and gaf hem echone
Coupes of clene gold · and coppes of seluer,
Rynges with rubies · and other riche 3iftes,   24
The leste man of here meyne · a moton of golde.
Whenne thei had lauht here leue · at thys lady mede,
Thenne comen clerkus · to comfortye hure samen,
And beden here be blythe · 'for we ben thyn owne,   28
For to worche thy wil · the while we mowe dure.'
And Mede hendiliche · by-hyht hem the same,
To louen hem leellich · and lordes hem make,
'And porchace 3ow prouendres · while 3oure pans lasteth,   32
And bigge 3ow benefices · pluralite to haue,
And in constorie atte court · do calle 3oure names.
Shal no lewednesse lette · the clerk that ich louye,
That he ne worth ferst auanced · for ich am biknowe,   36
Ther connynge clerkus · shulleth clocke by-hynde.'
  Thenne com ther a confessour · coped as a frere,
To Mede that mayde · myldelich he sayde,
'Thauh lered men and lewede · had layen by the bothe,   40
And falshede yfounden the · al this fourty wynter,
Ich shal a-soily the my-selue · for a seem of whete,

---

25. man I; PEMFS *om.*   26. Wenne P.   28. owne FMS; owe PG.
29. wile P.   30. Ande P.   32. prouendres MIFSE; prouenders P.
wile P.   36. biknowe MIG; knowen P.   42. of MEFS; P *om.*

F

And eke be thi baude · and bere wel thin ernde
Among clerkes and knihtes · concience to falle.'
Thenne Meede for hire misdede · to that mon knelede,   44
And schrof hire of hir sunnes · schomeliche, I trouwe.
Heo tolde him a tale · and tok him a noble,
For to ben hire beode-mon · and hire baude after.
Thene he asoylede hire soone · and sith to hire seide,   48
'We han a wyndow in worching · wol stonden vs ful hei3e:

And also be thi bedeman · and bere wel thi message,
Amonges kni3tes and clerkis · conscience to torne.'
Thanne Mede for here mysdedes · to that man kneled,
And shroue hire of hire shrewednesse · shamelees, I trowe,   44
Tolde hym a tale · and toke hym a noble,
Forto ben hire bedeman · and hire brokour als.
Thanne he assoilled hir sone · and sithen he seyde,
'We han a wyndowe a wirchyng · wil sitten vs ful heigh :   48
Woldestow glase that gable · and graue there-inne thi name,
Siker sholde thi soule be · heuene to haue.'
'Wist I that,' quod that womman · 'I wolde nou3t spare
For to be 3owre frende, frere · and faille 3ow neure   52
Whil 3e loue lordes · that lechery haunteth,
And lakketh nou3t ladis · that loueth wel the same.
It is frelete of flesh · 3e fynde it in bokes,
And a course of kynde · wher-of we komen alle ;   56
Who may scape the sklaundre · the skathe is sone amended ;
It is synne of the seuene · sonnest relessed.
Haue mercy,' quod Mede · 'of men that it haunte,
And I shal keure 3owre kirke · 3owre cloystre do maken,   60
Wowes do whiten · and wyndowes glasen,
Do peynten and purtraye · and paye for the makynge,
That eury segge shal seyn · I am sustre of 3owre hous.'
Ac god to alle good folke · suche grauynge defendeth,   64
To writen in wyndowes · of here wel dedes,
On auenture pruyde be peynted there · and pompe of the worlde ;
For Crist knoweth thi conscience · and thi kynde wille,

A. 48. sith H ; sithen TU ; sethen D ; V *om.*   B. 48. ful WCRO ;
wel L.   58. the WO ; LC *om.*   61. whiten C ; whitten L.   C. 44.
kny3thes P.   45. man MIFSG ; frere P.   48. erende EI ; ernede P.

A. PASSUS III. 50-55. C. PASSUS IV. 43-71.

Woldustow glase the gable · and graue therinne thi nome,
Siker schulde thi soule ben · for to dwellen in heuene.'
'Wust I that,' quod the wommon · 'ther nis nouthur wyndou
    ne auter, 52
That I ne schulde maken othur mende · and my nome write,
That vche mon schulde seye · ich were suster of house.'
  Bote god to alle good folk · such grauynge defendet,

And ȝut be thy bedman · and brynge a-doun conscience
A-mong kynges and knyȝtes · and clerkus, if the lyke.' 44
  Thenne Mede for hure mysdedes · to this man knelyd,
Shrof hure of here synnes · shameles, y leyue,
Told hym a tale · and took hym a noble
For to be hure bedman · and bere wel hure erende, 48
Among knyȝtes and clerkus · conscience to turne.
  And he assoiled hure sone · and setthen he seide,
'We haue a wyndow a worchyng · wol stonden ous ful hye;
Wolde ȝe glase the gable · and graue ther ȝoure name, 52
In masse and in matyns · for Mede we shulleth synge
Solenliche and sothlich · as for a sustre of oure ordre.'
  Louelich that lady · lauhynge seyde,
'Ich shal be ȝoure frende, frere · and faille ȝow neuere, 56
The while ȝe louyeth thuse lordes · that lecherye haunten,
And lackieth noȝt thuse ladies · that louyeth the same.
Hit is bote frelete of flesch · ȝe fynden wel in bokis,
And a cours of kynde · wher-of we comen alle. 60
Ho may a-scapie the sclaundere · the scathe may sone be mendyd,
Hit ys synne as of seuene · non soner relesed.
  Haue mercy,' quath Mede · 'on men that hit haunten,
And ich shal keuery ȝoure kirke · and ȝoure cloistre maken, 64
Bothe wyndowes and wowes · ich wolle a-menden and glase,
And do peynten and portreyn · who paide for the makynge
That euery seg shal see, and seye · ich am sustre of ȝoure ordre.'
  Ac god to alle good folke · suche grauynge defendeth, 68
To wryten in wyndowes · of eny wel dedes,
Leste prude be peyntid there · and pompe of the worlde.
For god knoweth thy conscience · and thy kynde wille,

---

50. assoiled IFE; soiled P.   51. worcheng P.   57. wile P.   60. wer-of P.
62. relesede P.   64. ich E; i MIFSG; P om.   churche P.   66. wo P.

And seith, *Nesciat sinistra quid faciat dextera.*
Lete not thi luft hond · late ne rathe, 56
Beo war what thi riht hond · worcheth or deleth;
Bote parte hit so priueli · that pruide beo not seȝen
Nouther in siht, ne in soule · for god him-self knoweth
Ho is corteis, or kuynde · couetous, or elles. 60
 For-thi I lere ȝou, lordynges · such writynge ȝe leue,
To writen in wyndouwes · of ȝoure wel dedes,
Or to greden aftur godus folk · whon ȝe ȝiuen or doles;
Parauenture ȝe han · oure hure therfore here. 64
 For vr saueour hit seith · and him-seluen precheth,
  Amen dico vobis, receperunt mercedem suam;

And thi coste and thi coueitise · and who the catel ouȝte. 68
 For-thi I lere ȝow, lordes · leueth suche werkes,
To writen in wyndowes · of ȝowre wel dedes,
Or to greden after goddis men · whan ȝe delen doles;
An auenture ȝe han ȝowre hire here · and ȝoure heuene als; 72
  Nesciat sinistra quid faciat dextra.
Lat nouȝte thi left half · late ne rathe,
Wyte what thow worchest · with thi riȝt side;
For thus bit the gospel · gode men do here almesse.
 Meires and maceres · that menes ben bitwene 76
The kynge and the comune · to kepe the lawes,
To punyschen on pillories · and pynynge stoles
Brewesteres and bakesteres · bocheres and cokes;
For thise aren men on this molde · that moste harme worcheth 80
To the pore peple · that parcel-mele buggen.
 For they poysoun the peple · priueliche and oft,
Thei rychen thorw regraterye · and rentes hem buggen
With that the pore people · shulde put in here wombe; 84
For toke thei on trewly · thei tymbred nouȝt so heiȝe,
Ne bouȝte non burgages · be ȝe ful certeyne.

A. 66. *This line is in* H *only.*   72. percel-mel TUD; al schal V.
74. regatorie V.   **B.** 73. ne WCR; no LO.   **C.** 77. hure (*for* hue) P.

A. PASSUS III. 66-77.   C. PASSUS IV. 72-94.

Here forsothe thei fongen · her mede forth-with.
   Meires and maistres · and ȝe that beoth mene
Bitwene the kyng and the comuns · to kepe the lawes,   68
As to punisschen on pillories · or on pynnyng stoles
Brewesters, bakers · bochers and cookes;
For theose be men vppon molde · that most harm worchen,
To the pore people · that percel-mel buggen.   72
   Thei punisschen the peple · priueliche and ofte,
And recheth thorw regratorie · and rentes hem buggeth,
With that the pore people · schulde puten in heore wombe.
   For toke thei on trewely · thei timbrede not so hye,   76
Ne bouȝte none borgages · beo ȝe certeyne.

Thi cost and here couetyse · and who the catel ouhte.   72
For thy leue lordes loue · leueth suche wrytinges;
God in the gospel · such grauynge noȝt a-loweth,
   Nesciat sinistra quid faciat dextera.
Let nat thy lyft half · oure lord techeth,
Ywite what thow delest · with thy ryht syde.   76
   Ȝut Mede myldeliche · the meyre hue bysouhte—
Bothe shereues and seriauns · and suche as kepeth lawes
To punyshen on pillories · and on pynyng-stoles,
As bakers and brewers · bouchers and cokes—   80
(For thees men doth most harme · to the mene puple,
Richen thorw regratrye · and rentes hem byggen
With that the poure puple · sholde putten in hure womben;
For toke they on triweliche · they tymbrid nat so heye,   84
Nother bouhten hem burgages · be ȝe ful certayn:
Thei haue no pite of the puple · that parcel-mele mote biggen;
Thauh thei take hem vntydy thyng · thei hold hit no treson,
And thauh thei fulle nat ful · that for lawe is seled,   88
He gripeth ther-for as grete · as for the grete treuthe.
Meny sondry sorwes · in cytees fallen ofte,
Bothe thorw fuyr and flod · and al for false puple,
That by-gylen good men · and greueth hem wrongliche,
The whiche cryen on hure knees · that Crist hem auenge,
Here on thys erthe · other elles on helle,   94

---

83. Whit (*for* With) P.   86. pite MIFE; puteye P.   88. is seled MIFE;
y-seelde P.   90. cyte P; citees IFE.   93. wiche P.

70 **A.** PASSUS III. 78–83. **B.** PASSUS III. 87–95.

Bote Meede the mayden · the meir heo bi-sou3te,
Of alle suche sullers · seluer to taken,
Or presentes withouten pons · as peces of seluer,   80
Rynges with rubyes · the regratour to fauere.
'For my loue,' quod the ladi · 'loue hem wel vchone,
And soffre hem to sulle · sumdel a3eyn resoun.'

Ac Mede the mayde · the maire hath bisou3te,
Of alle suche sellers · syluer to take,   88
Or presentz with-oute pens · as peces of siluer,
Ringes or other ricchesse · the regrateres to maynetene.
'For my loue,' quod that lady · 'loue hem vchone,
And soffre hem to selle · somdele a3eins resoun.'   92
    Salamon the sage · a sarmoun he made,
For to amende maires · and men that kepen lawes,
And tolde hem this teme · that I telle thynke;
      *Ignis deuorabit tabernacula eorum qui libenter accipiunt
      munera, &c.*

    B. 95. thynko L.   **C.** 96. yueles E; hyueles P.   101. in þe (*for* þe) P.
103. men P; *see* l. 102.   105. ben; *suggested by* beth F; han be M (PEIS *om.*)   108. þynken P.   113. 3eftes P; *see* l. 117.   114. P *om.* 2*nd* a.
115. meyere P.   121. hue (*for* he) P.   123. wat P.

Bote Salamon the sage · a sarmoun he made, 84
To a-mende meires · and men that kepeth the lawe;
And tolde hem this teeme · that I wol telle nouthe:
> *Ignis deuorabit tabernacula eorum qui libenter accipiunt munera.*

That so by-gyleth hem of here good; · and god on hem sendeth
Feueres other fouler yueles · other fur on here houses,
Moreyne other othere meschaunce · and menye tyme hit falleth,
That innocence ys yherde · in heuene a-monge seyntes,
That louten for hem to oure lorde · and to oure lady bothe,
To graunten gylours on erthe · grace to amende, 100
And haue here penaunce on pure erthe · and no3t the pyne of helle.
And thenne falleth ther fur · on false menne houses,
And good menne for here gultes · gloweth on fuyr after.
Al thys haue we seyen · that som tyme thorw a brewere 104
Meny burgagys ben ybrent · and bodyes ther-ynne;
And thorw a candel, clomyng · in a corsed place,
Fel a-doun, and for-brende · forth al the rewe.
For-thy mayres that maken free men · me thynketh that thei ouhten 108
For to spure and aspye · for eny speche of seluer
What manere mester · other merchaundise he vsede,
Er he were vnder-fonge free · and felawe in 3oure rolles.
Hit ys no3t semly forsoth · in cyte ne in borwton, 112
That vsurers other regratours · for eny kynne 3yftes,
Be fraunchised for a free man · and haue a fals name)—
Ac Mede the mayde · the meyre hue by-souhte
Of alle suche sellers · suluer to take, 116
Other presentes with-oute pans · and other pryueye 3yftes,
And haue reuthe of the regratours · that han ryche hondes;
> *In quorum manibus iniquitates sunt: dextera eorum repleta est muneribus.*

'Loue hem for my loue' · quath this lady Mede,
'And soffre hem som tyme · to sulle a-3ens the lawe.' 120
Salamon the sage · a sarmon he made
In amendement of meyres · and othere stywardes,
And witnessyth what worth of hem · that wollen take mede:
> *Ignis deuorabit tabernacula eorum qui libenter accipiunt munera.*

Among this lewede men · this latin amounteth,
That fuir schal falle · and brenne atte laste 88
The houses and the homes · of hem that desyreth
For to haue ȝiftes · in ȝouthe or in elde.
Now beoth ȝe war, if ȝe wole · ȝe maysturs of the lawe; 91
For the sothe schale be souȝt of ȝoure soules · so me god helpe,
The suffraunce that ȝe suffre · such wrongus to be wrouȝt;
While the chaunce is in ȝoure choyse · cheose ȝe the best.
The king com from counseyl · and cleped aftur Meede,
And of-sente hire a-swithe · seriauns hire to fette, 96

Amonge this lettered ledes · this latyn is to mene, 96
That fyre shal falle, and brenne · al to blo askes
The houses and the homes · of hem that desireth
ȝiftes or ȝeresȝyues · bi-cause of here offices.
The kynge fro conseille cam · and called after Mede, 100
And ofsent hir alswythe · with seriauntes manye,
That brouȝten hir to bowre · with blisse and with ioye.
Curteisliche the kynge thanne · comsed to telle,
To Mede the mayde · melleth thise wordes : 104

'Vnwittily, womman ! · wrouȝte hastow oft,

Ac worse wrouȝtestow neure · than tho thow Fals toke.
But I forgyue the that gilte · and graunte the my grace ;
Hennes to thi deth day · do so namore ! 108

I haue a knyȝte, Conscience · cam late fro biȝunde ;
ȝif he wilneth the to wyf · wyltow hym haue ?'
'ȝe, lorde,' quod that lady · 'lorde forbede elles !

A. 91-94. *These lines are in* H *only*.   92. souȝte H.   98. *In* H *only*.
100. melis thise TH₂; moueth these U ; melodyes (*error for* meleth theose) V.
101. Unwittily ywys T ; Certis unwysely H ; Qweynteliche, quath the kyng V.
107. lord (2) TUD ; god V.   B. 97. brenne WCO; berne L.   98. that

And brou3te hire to boure · with blisse and with ioye;
With myrthe and with mynstrasye · thei pleseden hir ychoone.
Corteisliche the kyng · cumseth to telle,
To Meede the mayden · meleth theose wordes: 100
'Unwittily, ywys · wrouht hastou ofte;
Bote worse wrouhtest thou neuere · then whon thou Fals toke.
Ac I for3iue the this gult · and graunte the my grace;
Hennes to thi deth day · do so no more. 104
Ichaue a kniht hette Concience · com late from bi-3onde,
3if he wilne the to wyf · wolt thou him haue?'
'3e, lord,' quath that ladi · 'lord for-beode hit elles!

A-mong these lettrede lordes · this latyn ys to mene, 124
That fur shal falle and for-brenne · al to blewe askes
The houses and the homes · of hem that taken 3yftes.
 The kynge fram-consail cam · and callyd after Mede,
And sente for to see hure · ac ich say nat hym that ladde hure. 128
Corteisliche the kyng tho · as hus kynde wolde,
Lackede here a litel wyht · for that hue louede gyle,
And wilnede to be wedded · with-oute hys leue,
Tyl Treuth hadde tolde hure · a tokne fram hymselue; 132
And seyde, 'womman, vnwyttylich · wrou3t hast thow ofte;
Ich haue for-gyue the meny gultes · and my grace graunted
Bothe to the and to thyne · in hope thow sholdest a-mende;
And ay the lenger ich lete the go · the lasse treuthe ys with the;
For worsse wrouhtest thow neuere · than tho thow Fals toke.
3ut ich for-gyue the this gult · godes for-bode eny more
Thow tene me and Treuthe; · and thow mowe be y-take,
In the castel of Corf · ich shal do the close 140
Ther as an ancre · other in a wel wors wone,
And marre the with myschef · by seint Marye my lady,
That alle wommen wantowen · shulleth be war by the one,
And biterliche banne the · and alle that bereth thy name, 144
And teche the louye treuthe · and take consail of reson.
 Ich haue a kny3t, hatte Concience · cam late froo by3onde,
Yf he wilneth the to wyue · wolt thow hym haue?'
'3e, lord,' quath the lady · 'lord it me for-bede 148

WCRO; L om. 107. the (2) R; thee WO; L om. C. 124. these IFMS;
thes P. 130. litel EIFM; lyte P. 131. ys (for hys) P. 133. wommen
(wrongly) P. 139. tene me and IMFSG; tuene on P.

74   A. PASSUS III. 108–119.   B. PASSUS III. 112–134.

Bote ich holde me to oure heste · honge me sone!' 108
Thenne was Concience i-clepet · to comen and apeeren
To-fore the kyng and his counsel · clerkes and othure.
Kneolynge Concience · to the kyng loutede,
To wyte what his wille were · and what he do schulde.   112
'Woltou wedde this wommon,' quod the kyng · 'ȝif I wol assente?
Heo is fayn of thi felawschupe · for to beo thi make.'
'Nay,' quath Concience to the kyng · 'Crist hit me forbeode!
Er ich wedde such a wyf · wo me bi-tyde!   116
Heo is frele of hire flesch · fikel of hire tonge;
Heo maketh men misdo · moni score tymes;
In trust of hire tresour · teoneth ful monye.

But I be holely at ȝowre heste · lat hange me sone!'   112
And thanne was Conscience calde · to come and appiere
Bifor the kynge and his conseille · as clerkes and othere.
Knelynge Conscience · to the kynge louted,
To wite what his wille were · and what he do shulde.   116
'Woltow wedde this womman,' quod the kynge · ȝif I wil assente,
For she is fayne of thi felawship · for to be thi make?'
Quod Conscience to the kynge · 'Cryst it me forbede!
Ar I wedde suche a wyf · wo me bityde!   120
For she is frele of hir feith · fykel of here speche,
And maketh men mysdo · many score tymes;
Truste of hire tresore · trieth ful manye.
Wyues and widewes · wantounes she techeth,   124
And lereth hem leccherye · that loueth hire ȝiftes.
Ȝowre fadre she felled · thorw fals biheste,
And hath apoysounde popis · and peired holicherche;
Is nauȝt a better baude · bi-hym that me made,   128
Bitwene heuene and helle · in erthe though men souȝte!
For she is tikil of hire taile · talwis of hir tonge,
As comune as a cartwey · to eche a knaue that walketh,
To monkes, to mynstralles · to meseles in hegges.   132
Sisoures and sompnoures · suche men hir preiseth;
Shireues of shires · were shent ȝif she nere;

A. 112. *This line is from* H; TUD *have a similar line*; V *omits it.*
B. 127. and WRO; L *om.*   C. 149. holly IMFS; holiche P.   151. ys P.
154. wol IS; wolle P.   156. for-bude P; *see* l. 148.   160. he (*for* hue) P.

A. PASSUS III. 120–130.   C. PASSUS IV. 149–172.

Wyues and widewes · wantounesse heo techeth,   120
Lereth hem lecherie · that loueth hire ȝiftes;
Vr fader Adam heo falde · with feire biheste;
Apoysende popes · and peyreth holy chirche.
Ther nis no beter baude · (bi him that me made!)   124
Bitwene heuene and helle · in eorthe thauȝ men souhte.
Heo is tikel of hire tayl · talewys of hire tonge,
As comuyn as the cart-wei · to knaues and to alle;
To preostes, to minstrals · to mesels in hegges.   128
Sisours and sumpnours · suche men hire preisen;
Schirreues of schires · weore schent ȝif heo nere.

Bote ich be holly at thyn heste; · let honge me ellys!'
   Thenne was Conscience cald · to come and apeere
By-for the kyng and hys consail · as clerkus and othere.
Conscience knelynge · to the kyng loutede,   152
To wite what hus wil were · and what he do sholde.
   'Wolt thow wedde this maide · yf ich wol assente,
For hue ys fayne of thy felaushep · and for to be thy make?'
   Quath Conscience to the kynge · 'Crist it me for-bede!   156
Er ich wedde suche a wif · wo me by-tyde!
For hue ys freel of hure faith · and fikel of hure speche,
And maketh men mys-do · meny score tymes.
In trist of hure tresour · hue teneth ful menye;   160
Wyues and wodewes · wantownesse hue techeth,
And lereth hem to lecherie · that louyeth here ȝyftes.
Ȝoure fader hue felde · Fals and hue to-gederes;
Hue hath a-poisoned popes · hue apeireth holy churche;   164
Ys nauht a betere baude · by hym that me made!
By-twyne heuene and helle · alle erthe thauh me souhte.
For hue ys tykel of hure tail · talewys of tonge,
As comune as the cart-wey · to knaues and to alle,   168
To monkes and to alle men; · the meseles in heggys
Lyggeth by hure whenne hem lust · lered and lewed.
Sysours and somners · suche men hure preyseth,
Shereues of shires · were shent yf hue ne were.   172

---

teneþ IFME; tueneþ P.   164. a-poisened P.   167. talewys SI; talwys P.
170. wenne P.   172. Shereue P.

Heo doth men leosen heore lond · and heore lyues after,
And leteth passe prisons · and payeth for hem ofte.   132
Heo ȝeueth the iayler gold · and grotes to-gedere,
To vn-fetere the false · and fleo where hem lyketh.
Heo taketh the trewe bi the top · and tiȝeth him faste,
And hongeth him for hate · that harmede neuere.   136
Heo that ben curset in constorie · counteth hit not at a russche;
For heo copeth the comissarie · and coteth the clerkes;
Heo is asoyled as sone · as hire-self lyketh.
Heo may as muche do · in a mooneth ones,   140

For she doth men lese here londe · and here lyf bothe.
She leteth passe prisoneres · and payeth for hem ofte,   136
And gyueth the gailers golde · and grotes togideres,
To vnfettre the fals · fle where hym lyketh;
And taketh the trewe bi the toppe · and tieth hym faste,
And hangeth hym for hatred · that harme dede neure.   140
To be cursed in consistorie · she counteth nouȝte a russhe;
For she copeth the comissarie · and coteth his clerkis;
She is assoilled as sone · as hir-self liketh,
And may neiȝe as moche do · in a moneth one,   144
As ȝowre secret seel · in syx score dayes.
For she is priue with the pope · prouisoures it knoweth,
For sire symonye and hir-selue · seleth hire bulles.
She blesseth thise bisshopes · theiȝe they be lewed,   148
Prouendreth persones · and prestes meynteneth,
To haue lemmannes and lotebies · alle here lif-dayes,
And bringen forth barnes · aȝein forbode lawes.
There she is wel with the kynge · wo is the rewme,   152
For she is fauorable to the fals · and fouleth trewthe ofte.
Bi Iesu, with here ieweles · ȝowre iustices she shendeth,
And lith aȝein the lawe · and letteth hym the gate,
That feith may nouȝte haue his forth ·‿here floreines go so thikke.
She ledeth the lawe as hire list · and louedayes maketh,   157
And doth men lese thorw hire loue · that lawe myȝte wynne,
The mase for a mene man · thouȝ he mote hir eure.
Lawe is so lordeliche · and loth to make ende,   160

A. 141. ȝoure TH; vre V; the U.   C. 176. vnfetery E; vnfeterye P.
were P.   177. takeþ ME; take P.   178. him IMG; P om.   179.

A. PASSUS III. 141-149.   C. PASSUS IV. 173-199.

As ȝoure secre seal · in seuen score dayes.
Heo is priue with the pope · prouisours hit knowen;
Sir Simonie and hire-self · asselen the bulles;
Heo blessede the bisschopes · thouȝ that thei ben lewed.   144
   Prouendreres, persuns · preostes heo meynteneth,
To holde lemmons and lotebyes · al heor lyf-dayes,
And bringeth forth barnes · aȝeyn forbodene lawes.
Ther heo is wel with the kyng · wo is the reame!   148
For heo is fauerable to Fals · and fouleth Treuthe ofte.

For hue doth men lese here londe · and here lyf bothe;
Hue leteth passe prisoners · and paieth for hem ofte,
And geueth the gailer gold · and grotes to-gederes,
To vnfetery the false · and fle where hem lyketh;   176
And taketh trewe by the top · and tieth hem faste,
And hongeth him for haterede · that harmede neuere.
To be corsed in constorye · hue counteth nauht a rusche;
Hue copeth the comissarie · and coteth hus clerkus,   180
Hue is assoilid thus sone · as hure self lyketh.
Hue may ney as moche do · in a mounthe one
As ȝoure secret seel · in sexscore dayes.
Hue ys priuy with the pope · prouisours it knoweth,   184
For Symonye and hure-self · seeleth hure bulles.
   Hue blesseth thees byshopys · thauh thei be negh lewede,
Hue prouendreth persons · prestes hue menteyneth
To holde lemmanes and lotebyes · al here lif-dayes,   188
And bryngeth forth barnes · a-ȝens for-boden lawes;
Sunt infelices · quia matres sunt meretrices.
Ther hue ys wel wyth eny kynge · wo ys the reome,
For hue ys fauerable to Fals · that defouleth Treuthe.   192
   By Iesus, with hure iewels · the iustices hue shendeth;
Hue lyth a-ȝen the lawe · and letteth hym the gate,
That faith may nat haue hus forth · hure floreines goth so thycke;
And ledeth the lawe as hure lust · and louedayes maketh,   196
Thoruh which loueday ys lost · that leaute myȝte wynne,
The mase for a mene man · thauh he mote euere.
The lawe ys so lordlich · and loth to maken ende,

---

constarye P.   180. comessarie P.   181. asoilid P.   ase P.   self SMG;
lef P.   188. lemmenes P.   195. may IFMSG; ne may P.   197. wich P.
198. a IMFES; þe P.

Barouns and burgeis · heo bringeth to serwe,
Heo buggeth with heore Iuweles; · vr Iustises heo schendeth.
Heo lihth a3eyn the lawe · and letteth so faste,   152
That feith may not han his forth · hir florins gon so thikke.
Heo ledeth the lawe as hire luste · and loue-dayes maketh,
The mase for a mene mon · thau3 he mote euere.
Lawe is so lordlich · and loth to maken ende,   156
With-outen presentes or pons · heo pleseth ful fewe.
Clergye an couetise · heo coupleth to-gedere.
This is the lyf of the ladi · vr lord 3if hire serwe!   159
And alle that meynteneth hire · myschaunce hem bytide!

With-oute presentz or pens · she pleseth wel fewe.
  Barounes and burgeys · she bryngeth in sorwe,
And alle the comune in kare · that coueyten lyue in trewthe;

For clergye and coueitise · she coupleth togideres.   164
This is the lyf of that lady · now lorde 3if hir sorwe!
And alle that meynteneth here men · meschaunce hem bityde!
For pore men mowe haue no powere · to pleyne hem thou3
    thei smerte;
Suche a maistre is Mede · amonge men of gode.'   168
  Thanne morned Mede · and mened hire to the kynge,
To haue space to speke · spede if she my3te.
  The kynge graunted hir grace · with a gode wille;
'Excuse the, 3if thow canst · I can namore seggen,   172
For Conscience acuseth the · to congey the for euere.'
  'Nay, lorde,' quod that lady · 'leueth hym the worse,
Whan 3e wyten witterly · where the wronge liggeth;
There that myschief is grete · Mede may helpe.   176
And thow knowest, Conscience · I cam nou3t to chide,

A. 156. eende V.   160. myschaunce hem bytide HTUD; vr lord 3if hem care V.   161. the H; V *om*.   **C.** 200. Wit P.   202. P *om*. *2nd* in.   207. custemes P.   of IMFSE; and P.   þe IMFSE; þat P.   211. couetyce P;

For the pore may haue no pouwer · to playne, thau3 hem smerte,
Such a mayster is Meede · a-mong men of goode.'
 Thenne mornede Meede · and menede hire to the kyng
To haue space to speken · spede 3if heo mihte.   164
Thenne the kyng graunted hire grace · with a good wille:
'Excuse the, 3if thou const · I con no more seye;
For Concience hath a-cuiset the · to congeye for euere.'
'Nay, lord,' quath that ladi · 'leef him the worse   168
Whon 3e witen witerliche · wher the wrong lihth.
 Ther mischef is gret lord · Meede may helpe,
And thou knowest, Concience · I com not to chyde,

With-oute presentes other pans · hue pleseth ful fewe.   200
 Trewe burgeis and bonde · to nauht hue bringeth ofte,
And al the comune in care · and in couetyse;
Religion hue al to-reueth · and out of ruele to lybbe.
Ther nys cite vnder sonne · ne so riche reome   204
Ther hue ys loued and lete by · that last shal eny while,
With-oute werre other wo · other wicked lawes,
And customes of couetyse · the comune to distruye.
Vnsyttynge Suffraunce · hure suster, and hure-selue   208
Haue maked al-most · bote Marie the helpe,
That no lond loueth the · and 3ut leest thyn owene.
For Mede hath knyt clerkes · and couetyse to-geders,
That al the wit of this worlde · ys woxen in-to gyle.   212
Thus this lady ledeth thy londe · now lord 3eue hure sorwe!
For pore men der nat pleyne · ne here pleinte shewe,
Suche a maister ys Mede · a-mong men of goode.'
 Thanne mornede Mede · menyng hure to the kynge,   216
To haue space to speke · spede yf hue myghte.
The kyng graunted hure grace · with a good wyll;
'Excuse the yf thow canst · ich can no more seggen;
For Conscience acuseth the · to congie the for euere.'   220
'Nay, lord,' quath that lady · 'leyueth hym the werse,
When 3e wyten witerliche · in wham the wrong lyggeth.
Ther that myschief ys gret · Mede may helpen.
And that knoweth Conscience · ich cam no3t to chiden,   224

---

see l. 202. 212. whit P. 213. þy EG; þi IFMS; þys P. 218. wit P.
219. P *om*. the. 222. Wen P. wam P. 223. þat IMSEG; þe P.

Ne to depraue thi persone · with a proud herte. 172
Wel thou wost, Concience · (but ʒif thou wolt lyʒe),
Thow hast honged on my nekke · enleue tymes;
And eke i-gripen of my gold · and ʒiuen ther the lykede.
Whi thou wraththest the now · wonder me thinketh! 176

Ne depraue thi persone · with a proude herte.
Wel thow wost, wernard · but ʒif thow wolt gabbe,
Thow hast hanged on myne half · elleuene tymes, 180
And also griped my golde · gyue it where the liked;
And whi thow wratthest the now · wonder me thynketh.
ʒit I may as I myʒte · menske the with ʒiftes,
And mayntene thi manhode · more than thow knoweste. 184
Ac thow hast famed me foule · bifor the kynge here.
For kulled I neuere no kynge · ne conseilled ther-after,
Ne dede as thow demest · I do it on the kynge!

B. 187. it WRO; LC *om.*   C. 225. þi FME; þe P.   228. an (*for* and) P.   were P.   229. P *om.* the.   235. wer P.   236. P *om.* so.   240. felde IE; feld P.   241. houre P.   243. ys (*for* hys) P ; *and in* l. 251.   250. Wer P.   257. ycoronede P.

For ʒit I may as I mihte · menske the with ʒiftes,
Añd meyntene thi monhede · more then thou knowest,
And thou hast famed me foule · bifore the kyng heere.
For culde I neuere no kyng · ne counseilede ther-after ; 180
Ne dude I neuere as thou dust · I do hit on the kyng!

Ne to depraue thi persone · with a prout herte.
Wel thow wost wyterly · bote yf thow wolle gabbe,
Thow hast hanged on myn hals · elleuen tymes,
And al-so grypen of my gold · and gaf it where the lykede. 228
Why thow wratthest the now · wonder me thynketh,
ʒut ich may, as ich myghte · menske the with ʒyftes,
And menteyny thy manhod · more than thow knowest.

Ac thow hast famede me foule · by-fore the kynge here ; 232
For culde ich neuere no kyng · ne consailed so to done ;
Ac ich saued my-self · and sexty thousand lyues,
Bothe her and elles wher · in alle kynne londes.
Ac thow thy-self sothliche · ho so it segge dorste, 236
Hast arwed meny hardy men · that hadden wil to fyghte,
To brennen and to bruten · to bete a-doun strengthes.
In the contreis ther the kyng cam · conscience hym lette,
That he ne felde nat hus foes · tho fortune it wolde, 240
And as hus werdes were ordeined · by wil of oure lorde.
Caytiflyche thow, Conscience · consailedist the kyng leten
In hus enemys honde · hys heritage of Fraunce.
Vnconnyng ys that conscience · a kyngdome to sulle, 244
That ys conqueryd thorw comune helpe ; · a kyngdome other duche
May nat be sold sothly · so meny here part asken
Of folk that fauht ther-fore · and folwed the kynges wil.
The lest lad that longeth to hym · be the lond wonnen, 248
Loketh after lordshep · other othere large mede,
Wher-by he may as a man · for euere-more lyue after.
And that ys the kynde of a kyng · that conquereth of hys enemyes,
To helpe heyeliche al hus host · othere elles to graunte 252
Al that hus men mowen wynne · to do ther-myd here beste.
For-thy ich counsayle no kyng · eny counsayle aske
At Conscience, yf he coueyteth · to conquery a reome.
For sholde neuere Conscience · be my constable, 256
Were ich a kyng ycoroned · by Marye,' quath Mede,
'Ne be mareschal of my men · ther ich moste fyghte.

G

A. PASSUS III. 182-194.   B. PASSUS III. 188-213.

In Normandie nas he not · a-nuyȝed for my sake;
Ac thou thi-self sothliche · schomedest him there,
Creptest in-to a caban · for colde of thi nayles,   184
Wendest that wynter · wolde haue last euere,
And dreddest to haue ben ded · for a dim cloude,
And hastedest hamward · for hunger of thi wombe!
 Withouten pite, pilour! · pore men thou robbedest,   188
And beere heor bras on thi bac · to Caleys to sulle.
Ther I lafte wĩth my lord · his lyf forto saue,
Maade him murthe ful muche · mournynge to lete,
Battede hem on the bakkes · to bolden heore hertes,   192
Dude hem hoppe for hope · to haue me at wille.
Hedde I be marchal of his men · (bi Marie of heuene)!

In Normandye was he nouȝte · noyed for my sake;   188
Ac thow thi-self sothely · shamedest hym ofte,
Crope in-to a kaban · for colde of thi nailles,
Wendest that wyntre · wolde haue lasted euere,
And draddest to be ded · for a dym cloude,   192
And hiedest homeward · for hunger of thi wombe.
 With-out pite, piloure · pore men thow robbedest,
And bere here bras at thi bakke · to Caleys to selle.
There I lafte with my lorde · his lyf for to saue,   196
I made his men meri · and mornyng lette.
I batered hem on the bakke · and bolded here hertis,
And dede hem hoppe for hope · to haue me at wille.
Had I ben marschal of his men · (bi Marie of heuene)!   200
I durst haue leyde my lyf · and no lasse wedde,
He shulde haue be lorde of that londe · a lengthe and a brede,
And also kyng of that kitthe · his kynne for to helpe,
The leste brolle of his blode · a barounes pere!   204
 Cowardliche thow, Conscience · conseiledest hym thennes,
To leuen his lordeship · for a litel siluer,
That is the richest rewme · that reyne ouer houeth!
 It bicometh to a kynge · that kepeth a rewme,   208
To ȝiue mede to men · that mekelich hym serueth,
To alienes and to alle men · to honoure hem with ȝiftes;
Mede maketh hym biloued · and for a man holden.
Emperoures and erlis · and al manere lordes   212
For ȝiftes han ȝonge men · to renne and to ride.

I durste haue i-leid my lyf · and no lasse wed,
He hedde beo lord of that lond · in lenkthe and in brede;   196
And eke kyng of that cuththe · his cun for to helpe;
The leeste barn of his blod · a barouns pere.
  Sothliche, thou Concience · thou counseildest him thennes,
To leue that lordschupe · for a luitel seluer,   200
That is the riccheste reame · that reyn ouer houeth!
  Hit bicometh for a kyng · that kepeth a reame
To ȝiue meede to men · that mekeliche him seruen;
To aliens, to alle men · to honoure hem with ȝiftes.   204
Meede maketh him beo bilouet · and for a mon i-holden.
Emperours and eorles · and alle maner lordes
Thorw ȝiftes han ȝonge men · to renne and to ride.

Ac hadde ich, Mede, be hus mareschal · ouer hus men in Fraunce,
Ich dorst haue leid my lyue · and no lasse wedde,   260
He had be lord of that londe · in lengthe and in brede,
And al-so kyng of that cuth · hus kyn to haue holpen,
The leste brol of hus blod · a barones pere.
  Vnkyndely thow, Conscience · consailedest hym thennes,   264
To lete so hus lordshup · for a lytel moneye.
  Hyt by-cometh for a kyng · that shal kepe a reame,
To ȝeue men mede · that meklyche hym serueth,
To alienes, to alle men · to honoury hem with ȝyftes;   268
Mede maketh hym be by-loued · and for a man yholde.
Emperours and erles · and alle manere lordes
Thoruh ȝiftes hauen ȝemen · to rennen and to ryde.

C. 260. leid MFS; led P.   263. brol F; brolle I; brel P.   267.
mecklyche P.   268. ȝeftes P; *see* l. 162.   269. be IEFS; P *om.*   yholde
ES; yolde P.   271. ȝemen EFS; ȝemmen P.

G 2

The pope and his prelates · presentes vnderfongen, 208
And meedeth men hem-seluen · to meyntene heore lawes.
Seruauns for heore seruise · (ȝe seon wel the sothe),
Taketh meede of heore maystres · as thei mowen a-corde.
Beggers for heore biddyng · biddeth men meede; 212
Munstrals for heor murthe · meede thei asken.
The kyng meedeth his men · to maken pees in londe;
Men that knoweth clerkes · meede hem craueth.
Prestes that precheth · the peple to goode 216
Asketh meede and masse-pons · and heore mete eke.

The pope and alle prelatis · presentz vnderfongen,
And medeth men hem-seluen · to meyntene here lawes.
Seruauntz for her seruise · we seth wel the sothe, 216
Taken mede of here maistre · as thei mowe acorde.
Beggeres for here biddynge · bidden men mede;
Mynstralles for here murthe · mede thei aske.
The kynge hath mede of his men · to make pees in londe;
Men that teche chyldren · craue of hem mede. 221
Prestis that precheth the poeple · to gode, asken mede,
And masse-pans and here mete · at the mele-tymes.
Alkynnes crafty men · crauen mede for here prentis; 224
Marchauntz and mede · mote nede go togideres;
No wiȝte as I wene · with-oute mede may libbe.'
  Quod the kynge to Conscience · 'bi Criste! as me thynketh,
Mede is well worthi · the maistrye to haue!' 228
  'Nay,' quod Conscience to the kynge · and kneled to the erthe,
'There aren two manere of medes · my lorde, with ȝowre leue.
That one, god of his grace · graunteth in his blisse
To tho that wel worchen · whil thei ben here. 232
The prophete precheth ther-of · and put it in the sautere,
    Domine quis habitabit in tabernaculo tuo?

  A. 212. mede THD; mete V.   219. nede THUD; not V.   **B.** 227.
Quod WCRO; Quatȝ L.   **C.** 283. hue P.   285. Cryest P.   287.
P *om.* to þe kyng.   290. lyuen ISG; P *om.*   292. and IF; a PES.
298. whiterly P.   wer P.

Alle kunne craftes men · craueth meede for heore prentys;
Meede and marchaundie · mot nede go to-gedere.
Ther may no wiht, as I wene · with-outen meede libbe.' 220
   'Now,' quod the kyng to Concience · 'be Crist, as me thinketh,
Meede is worthi · muche maystrie to haue!'
   'Nay,' quod Concience to the kyng · and knelede to grounde;
'Ther beoth twey maner of meedes · my lord, bi thi leue. 224
That on, good god of his grace · ȝiueth, in his blisse,
To hem that wel worchen · whil that thei ben here.
   The prophete hit prechede · and put hit in the psauter,
      Qui peccuniam suam non dedit ad vsuram, &c.

The pope and alle prelates · presentes vnder-fongen, 272
And ȝeuen mede to men · to menteynye here lawes.
Seriauntes for here seruice · mede they asken,
And taken mede of here maistres · as thei mow a-corde.
Beggers and bedmen · crauen mede for here prayers. 276
Mynstrals for here mynstralcye · a mede thei asken.
Maistres that techen clerkes · crauen hure for mede.
Prestes that prechen · and the puple techen
Asken mede and masse-pans · and here mete bothe. 280
Alle kyne crafty men · crauen mede for here aprentys,
Marchaundise and mede · mote nedes go to-gederes.
Is no lede that leueth · that he ne loueth mede,
And glad for to grype hure · gret lord other poure.' 284
   Tho quath the kyng to Conscience · 'by Cryst, at my knowynge,
Mede ys worthy, me thynketh · the maistrye to haue.'
   'Nay,' quath Conscience to the kyng · 'clerkes wyten the sothe,
That Mede ys euermore · a meyntenour of gyle, 288
As the sauter sheweth · by suche as ȝeuen mede,
That vnlawfulliche lyuen · hauen large honden,
To ȝeue mede to men · more other lasse.
Ac ther ys mede and mercede · and bothe men demen 292
A desert for som doynge · derne other elles.
Mede meny tymes · men ȝeuen by-for the doynge;
And that ys nother reson ne ryht · ne no reame lawe
That eny man mede toke · bote he it myghte deserue, 296
And for to vndertake · to trauely for another,
And wot neuere witterly · wher he lyue so longe,
Ne haue hap to hus hele · mede to deseruen.

Tak no meede, mi lord · of men that beoth trewe; 228
Loue hem, and leeue hem · for vr lordes loue of heuene;
Godes meede and his merci · ther-with thou maiht winne.
Bote ther is a meede mesureles · that maystrie desyreth,
To meyntene misdoers · meede thei taken; 232
And therof seith the psauter · in the psalmes ende,
    In quorum manibus iniquitates sunt; dextera eorum repleta
        est muneribus;
That here riȝthond is hepid · ful of ȝeftis,
And heo that gripeth heore ȝiftus · (so me God helpe!)

"Lorde, who shal wonye in thi wones · and with thine holi seyntes,
Or resten on thi holy hilles?" · this asketh Dauid;
  And Dauyd assoileth it hym-self · as the sauter telleth, 236
    Qui ingreditur sine macula, et operatur iusticiam,
Tho that entren of o colour · and of on wille,
And han wrouȝte werkis · with riȝte and with reson;
And he that ne vseth nauȝte · the lyf of vsurye,
And enfourmeth pore men · and pursueth treuthe; 240
    Qui pecuniam suam non dedit ad vsuram, et munera super
        innocentem, &c.
And alle that helpeth the innocent · and halt with the riȝtful,
With-oute mede doth hem gode · and the trewthe helpeth—
Suche manere men, my lorde · shal haue this furst mede
Of god at a grete nede · whan thei gone hennes. 244
  There is an-other mede mesurelees · that maistres desireth;
To meyntene mysdoers · mede thei take;
And there-of seith the sauter · in a salmes ende,
    In quorum manibus iniquitates sunt, dextera eorum repleta
        est muneribus;
And he that gripeth her golde · so me god helpe! 248
Shal abie it bittere · or the boke lyeth!
  Prestes and persones · that plesynge desireth,
That taketh mede and mone · for messes that thei syngeth,
Taketh here mede here · as Mathew vs techeth; 252
    Amen, amen, receperunt mercedem suam.
That laboreres and lowe folke · taketh of her maistres,
It is no manere mede · but a mesurable hire.
  In marchandise is no mede · I may it wel a-vowe;
It is a permutacioun apertly · a penyworth for an othre. 256

A. PASSUS III. 236-243. C. PASSUS IV. 300-316.

Thei schullen a-bugge bitterly · or the bok ly3eth! 236
Preostes and persones · that plesyng desyreth,
And taketh meede and moneye · for massen that thei syngen,
Schullen han. meede in this molde · that Matheu hath i-grauntet;
    Amen dico vobis, receperunt mercedem suam.
That laborers and louh folk · taken of heore maystres, 240
Nis no maner meede · bote mesurable huyre.
In marchaundise nis no meede · I may' hit wel avoue;
Hit is a permutacion · a peni for another.

Ich halde hym ouer-hardy · other elles nouht trewe, 300
That *pre manibus* ys payed · other elles paye asketh.
Harlotes and hores · and al-so fals leches,
Thei asken hure huyre · er they hit haue deserued.
And gylours gyuen by-fore · and goode men at the ende, 304
When the dede ys ydo · and the day y-endyd.
And that ys, no mede · bote a mercede,
A maner dewe dette · for the doynge;
And bote if yt be payed prestliche · the payer is to blame, 308
As by the bok, that bit · no body to with-holde
The hure of hus hewe · ouer eue til a morwe:
    Non morabitur opus mercenarij tui apud te usque mane.
And ther is reson as a reue · rewarding treuthe,
And bothe the lord and the laborer · ben leelliche yserued. 312

The mede that meny prestes taketh · for masses that thei syngen,
    Amen, amen, Matheu seyth · *mercedem suam recipiunt.*
In marchaundise ys no mede · ich may it wel avowe;
Hit is a permutacion a-pertelich · o pene-worth for another. 316

A. 231. desyret V.   233. eende V.   234. *This line is in* H *only.*
B. 252. *receperunt* O; *recipiebant* LWCR.   **C.** 300. ouere P.   303. deseruede P.   307. dewe M; due S; diwe P.   309. wit-holde P. 310. hewe I; hywe P; hyne EFMS.   310. P om. *tui.*   313. prestes ME; prest P.

(NOT IN A-TEXT OR B-TEXT.)

[*Not in* A-*text.*]

[*Not in* B-*text.*]

C. 318. P *om.* or.   319. P *om.* and; *see* l. 320.   lege P; *see* l. 320.
322. þer-whit P.   323. P *om.* more.   326. erthe EIMFS; þe erthe P.
330. lyue SEI; leue P.   334. eeft P.   335. and IFG; a PEMS.   338. As MS; Ac PEIF.   341. ȝefte P.   342. P om. *nobis*.   344. Wat P.
347. fyndyng IMFSG; a fyndyng PE.   350. P *om.* a.

[*Not in* **A**-*text.*]

And thauh the kyng of hys cortesye · kaiser, other pope,
ȝeue lond other lordshup · or other large ȝiftes,
To here leele and lyge · loue ys the cause.
And yf the leelle and the lyge · be luther men after, 320
Bothe kyng and kayser · and the coroned pope
May desauowe that they dude · and douwe ther-with other,
And a-non by-nymen hym hit · and neuere more after
Nother thei ne here ayres · hardy to cleyme, 324
That kyng other cayser hym gaf · catel other rente.
For god gaf to Salamon · grace vp-on erthe,
Rychesse and reson · whyle he ryht lyuede,
And as sone as god seih · he suwed nouht hus wille, 328
He reuede hym of hys richesse · and of hus ryht mynde,
And soffrede hym lyue in mysbyleue · ich leyue he be in helle;
So that god geueth no thyng · that synne ne ys the glose.
And so ryght sothliche · may kyng and pope 332
Bothe gyue and grauntye · ther hus grace liketh,
And eft haue hit a-ȝeyn · of hem that don ille.
  Thus ys mede and mercede · as two manere relacions,
Rect and indyrect · rennynge bothe 336
On a sad and a syker · semblable to hym-selue—
As adiectif and substantyf · vnite asken,
Acordaunce in kynde · in cas and in numbre,
And ayther ys otheres help—· of hem cometh retribucion, 340
That ys the ȝifte that god ȝyueth · to alle leelle lyuynge,
Grace of good ende · and gret ioye after;
    Retribuere dignare, domine deus, omnibus nobis, et cetera.'
  Quath the kynge to Conscience · 'knowen ich wolde
What is relacion rect · and indyrect after, 344
And thanne adiectyf and substantif · for Englisch was it neuere.'
  'Relacion rect,' quath Conscience · 'ys a recorde of treuthe,
    Quia antelate rei est recordatiuum,
Folwyng and fyndyng out · the foundement of strenthe,
And styuelyche stonde forth · to strengthe of the foundement, 348
In kynde and in case · and in cours of noumbre;
As a leel laborer · that by-leuyth with hus maistre
In hus paye and in hys pyte · and in hus pure treuthe,
To paye hym yf he performeth · and haue pyte yf he faylleth, 352

[*Not in* A-*text.*]

[*Not in* B-*text.*]

C. 355. sustentif P. 356. P *om.* god. 357. triwc P. 358. in ys kynde P. 359. churche P. 361. sennes P. clansede P. 364. whit is P. 366. kyne P. 367. case MF ; cause PEISG. to MFG ; two PES. 368. wich P. 369. noȝt E ; nout M ; nat FSG ; not I ; noþer P. 370. for is P. 371. wo P. worliche P. 374. kyne P. 375. kynde P. 376. *This line is in* F *only.* 378. is P. 380. him MFS ; hem P.

[*Not in* **A**-*text.*]

And take hym for hus trauaile · al that treuthe wolde.
So of hol herte cometh hope · and hardy relacion
Seketh and suweth · hus substantif sauacion,
That ys god, the grounde of al · a graciouse antecedent. 356
And man ys relatif rect · yf he be ryht trewe;
He a-cordeth with Crist in kynde · *uerbum caro factum est*;
In case, *credere in ecclesia* · in holy kirke to byleyue;
In numbre, rotie and aryse · and remyssion to haue, 360
Of oure sory synnes · asoiled and clansed,
And lyue, as oure crede ous kenneth · with Crist withouten ende.
Thus is relacion rect · ryht as adiectif and substantif
A-cordeth in alle kyndes · with his antecedent. 364
Indirect thyng ys · as ho so coueited
Alle kynne kynde · to knowe and to folwe,
With-oute case to cacche to · and come to bothe numbres;
In which beth good and nat good · and graunte here nothers wil.
That is noȝt reisonable ne rect · to refusy my syres sorname,
Sitth y, his sone and seruaunt · suwe for his ryghte. 370
For who so wol haue to wyue · my worldliche daughter,
Ich wol feffe hym with hure fayre · and with hure foule taylende.
So indirect thyng ys · inliche to coueyte 373
To a-corde in alle kyndes · and in alle kynne numbre,
With-oute cost and care · in alle kynne trauaile,
With-oute resoun to rewarde · nauȝt recching of the peple. 376
Ac relacion rect · is a ryhtful custome,
As, a kyng to cleyme · the comune at his wille
To folwe hym, to fynde hym · and fecche at hem hus consail,
That here loue thus to him · thorw al the londe a-corde. 380
So comune cleymeth of a kyng · thre kynne thynges,
Lawe, loue, and leaute · and hym lord antecedent,
Bothe here hefd and here kyng · haldyng with no partie,
Bote stande as a stake · that styketh in a muyre 384
By-twyne two londes · for a trewe marke.
Ac the moste partie of the puple · pure indirect semeth,
For thei wilnen and wolde · as best were for hem-selue,
Thauh the kyng and the comune · al the cost hadde. 388
Al reson reproueth · such imparfit puple,
And halt hem vnstedefast · for hem lacketh case.

But raddest thou neuer *Regum* · thou recreiȝede meede,
Whi that veniaunce fel · on Saul and his children? 245
God sende to seie · bi Samuels mouthe,

Ac reddestow neuere *Regum* · thow recrayed Mede,
Whi the veniaunce fel · on Saul and on his children?
God sent to Saul · bi Samuel the prophete,
That Agage of Amaleke · and al his peple aftre 260
Shulde deye for a dede · that done had here eldres.

A. 244. thou TUD; that VH.   C. 391. As EIFS; Ac P.   393.
peccunie P.   399. no (*for* to) P.   401. churche P.   402. wen P.
403. sike EIG; asky P.   fore P.   arde P.   408. askyng IMSG; and

A. PASSUS III. 247–249. C. PASSUS IV. 391–419.   93

That Agag and Amalec · and al his peple aftur,
Schulden dye for a dede . that don hedde his eldren
A3eynes Israel and Aaron · and Moyses his brother.   249

As relatifs indirect · reccheth thei neuere
Of the cours of the case · so they cacche suluer,   392
Be the pecunie y-payed · thauh parties chide.
He that mede may lacche · maketh litel tale,
Nyme he a numbre · of nobles other of shullenges ;
How that clyentes a-corde · mede a-counteth lytel.   396
Ac adiectif and substantif · ys as ich er tolde,
That ys, vnyte, acordaunce · in case, gendre, and numbre ;
And ys to mene in oure mouth · more ne mynne,
Bote that alle manere men · wommen, and children,   400
Sholde conformye to on kynde · on holy kirke to by-leyue,
And coueite the case · when thei couthe vnderstonde,
To sike for hure synnes · and suffre harde penaunce,
For that ilke lordes loue · that for oure loue deyde,   404
And coueited oure kynde · and be cald in oure name,
    Deus homo,
And nymen hym into oure numbre · now and euere more ;
    Qui in caritate manet in deo manet, et deus in eo.
Thus is man and mankynde · in manere of a substantif,
As *hic et hec homo* · askyng an adiectif   408
Of thre trewe termysons · *trinitas unus deus;*
    Nominativo, pater et filius et spiritus sanctus.
  Ac ho so rat of *Regum* · rede me may of mede,
Hou hue Absolon · to hongynge brouhte ;
And sitthe, for Saul · sauede a kyng for mede   412
A-geyn godes comaundement · god toke suche veniaunce,
That Saul for that synne · and hus sone deyde,
And gaf the kyngdome to hus knaue · that kept sheep and lambren :
As men rat in *Regum* · after Ruth, of kynges,   416
Hou god sente to Saul · by Samuel the prophete,
That Agag of Amalek · and al hus lyge puple
Sholde deye delfulliche · for dedes of here eldren.

---

a kyng P.   409. trywe P.   416. As IMFG ; And P.   þat (*for* rat) P ;
see l. 410.   Ruth I ; reweþ P.

Samuel seide to Saul · God sendeth the and hoteth
To beo boxum and boun · his biddyng to worche;
'Wend thider with thin host · wymmen to culle,   252
Children and cheorles · chop hem to dethe,
Loke thow culle the kyng · coueyte not his goodes
For milions of moneye; · morther hem vchone.
Bernes and beestes · brenne hem al to askes.'   256
  And for he culde not the kyng · as Crist him-self hihte,
Coueytede feir catel · and culde not his beestes,

'For-thi,' seid Samuel to Saul · 'god hym-self hoteth
The, be boxome at his biddynge · his wille to fulfille:
Wende to Amalec with thyn oste · and what thow fyndest there,
    slee it;   264
Biernes and bestes · brenne hem to ded;
Wydwes and wyues · wommen and children,
Moebles and vnmoebles · and al that thow myȝte fynde,
Brenne it, bere it nouȝte awey · be it neuere so riche,   268
For mede ne for mone; · loke thow destruye it,
Spille it and spare it nouȝte · thow shalt spede the bettere.'
  And for he coueyted her catel · and the kynge spared,
Forbare hym and his bestes bothe · as the bible witnesseth,   272
Otherwyse than he was · warned of the prophete,
God seide to Samuel · that Saul shulde deye,
And al his sede for that synne · shenfullich ende.
Such a myschief mede made · Saul the kynge to haue,   276
That god hated hym for euere · and alle his eyres after.
The *culorum* of this cas · kepe I nouȝte to shewe;
An auenture it noyed men · none ende wil I make.
For so is this worlde went · with hem that han powere,   280
That who-so seyth hem sothes · is sonnest yblamed.
  I Conscience knowe this · for kynde witt me it tauȝte,
That resoun shal regne · and rewmes gouerne;
And riȝte as Agag hadde · happe shul somme.   284
Samuel shal sleen hym · and Saul shal be blamed,
And Dauid shal be diademed · and daunten hem alle,

   A. 250. seendeth V.   252. Weend V.   258. *Read* culde; kilde TUD;
slouh V; slow H.   260. Saul THUD; Samuel V.   264. clause TH₂;
VHU *om.*   265. *Read* nuyȝed; noiȝide T; noiede U; noyed D; *miswritten*

A. PASSUS III. 259-268.   C. PASSUS IV. 420-444.

Bote brouhte with him the beestes · as the bible telleth,
God sende to seye · that Saul schulde dye,   260
And al his seed for that sunne · schendfulliche ende.
Such a mischef meede · made the kyng to haue,
That god hatede him euere · and his heires after.
The *culorum* of this clause · kepe I not to schewe,   264
In auenture hit nuy3ed me · an ende wol I make:
  And riht as Agag hedde · hapne schulle summe;
Samuel schal slen him · and Saul schal be blamed,
Dauid schal ben dyademed · and daunten hem alle,   268

  'Saul,' quath Samuel · 'god hym-self hoteth   420
To be boxome at my bidding · hus bone to fulfylle.
Haste the with al thyn ost · to the lond of Amalek,
And al that lyueth in that londe · oure lord wol that thow slee hit,
Man, woman, and wif · child, widowe, and bestes;   424
Mebles and vnmebles · man and alle thynges,
Bren hit, ber nouht away · be hit neuere so riche,
For eny mede of moneye · al that thow myght spille;
Spar hit nat and thow · shalt spede the betere.'   428
  And for he coueited hyre catel · and the kyng spared,
For-bar hym and hus beste bestes · as the byble witnesseth,
Otherwise than god wolde · by warnyng of the prophete,
God seide to Samuel · that Saul sholde deye,   432
And al hus for that synne · and shendfulliche ende.
Thus was kyng Saul ouercome · for couetyse of mede,
That god hatid hym for euere · and alle hus ayres after.
The *culorum* of this cas · kepe ich nat to shewe,   436
An aunter hit nuyede me · non ende wol ich make.
For so ys the worlde went · with hem that han the power,
That he that seith most sothest · sonnest ys y-blamed.
  Ich Conscience knowe this · for kynde witt me tauhte,   440
That reson shal regne · and reames gouerne,
And ryht as Agag hadde · happen shulleth somme.
Samuel shal sle hym · and Saul shal be blamed,
And Dauid shal be diademyd · and daunten alle oure enemyes,   444

---

munged V.   267. blamet V.   C. 424. P *omits this line; it is from*
IMFSG.   430. whitnesseþ P.   438. hem IMFG; P *om.*   444. ande P.

And on Cristene kyng · kepen vs vchone.
Concience knoweth this ; · for kuynde wit me tauȝte
That resun schal regne · and reames gouerne ;
Schal no more Meede · be mayster vppon eorthe,   272
Bote loue and louhnesse · and leute to-gedere.
 And heo that trespasseth to trouthe · or doth aȝeyn his wille,
Leute schal don him lawe · or leosen his lyf elles.

And one Cristene kynge · kepen hem alle.
 Shal na more Mede · be maistre, as she is nouthe,   288
Ac loue and lowenesse · and lewte togederes,
Thise shul be maistres on molde · treuthe to saue.
 And who-so trespasseth ayein treuthe · or taketh aȝein his wille,
Leute shal don hym lawe · and no lyf elles.   292
Shal no seriaunt for here seruyse · were a silke howue,
Ne no pelure in his cloke · for pledyng atte barre.
Mede of mys-doeres · maketh many lordes,
And ouer lordes lawes · reuleth the rewmes.   296
 Ac kynde loue shal come ȝit · and conscience togideres,
And make of lawe a laborere · suche loue shal arise,
And such a pees amonge the peple · and a perfit trewthe,
That Iewes shal wene in here witte · and waxen wonder glade,
That Moises or Messie · be come in-to this erthe,   301
And haue wonder in here hertis · that men beth so trewe.
 Alle that bereth baslarde · brode swerde or launce,
Axe other hachet · or eny wepne ellis,   304
Shal be demed to the deth · but if he do it smythye
In-to sikul or to sithe · to schare or to kulter ;
 Conflabunt gladios suos in vomeres, &c. ;
Eche man to pleye with a plow · pykoys or spade,
Spynne, or sprede donge · or spille hym-self with sleuthe.   308
 Prestes and persones · with *placebo* to hunte,
And dyngen vpon Dauid · eche a day til eue.
Huntynge or haukynge · if any of hem vse,
His boste of his benefys · worth bynome hym after.   312
Shal neither kynge ne knyȝte · constable ne meire
Ouer-lede the comune · ne to the courte sompne,
Ne put hem in panel · to don hem pliȝte here treuthe,
But after the dede that is don · one dome shal rewarde,   316

   A. 280. Vnkuyndeesse (*sic*) V. 281. Ac TUD ; But H ; And V.

Schal no seriaunt for that seruise · were a selk houue, 276
Ne no ray robe · with riche pelure.
Meede of misdoers · maketh men so riche,
That lawe is lord i-waxen · and leute is pore.
Vnkuyndenesse is comaundour · and kuyndenesse is banescht.
Ac kuynde wit schal come ȝit . and concience to-gedere, 281
And make of lawe a laborer · such loue schal aryse!'

And on Cristene kyng · kepen ows echone.
Shal no Mede be maister · neuere more after,
Ac loue and louhnesse · and leaute to-gederes
Shullen be maistres on molde · trewe men to helpe; 448
And ho so taketh aȝen treuthe · other transuerseth aȝens reson,
Leaute shal do hym lawe · and no lif elles.
Shal no seriaunte for that seruyse · were a selk houe,
Ne pelour in hus paueylon · for pledyng at the barre. 452
Muchel yuel is thorw mede · meny tyme suffred,
And letteth the lawe · thorw here large ȝyftes.
Ac kynde loue shal come ȝut · and conscience to-gederes,
And make of lawe a laborer · suche loue shal aryse, 456
And such pees among the puple · and a parfyt treuthe,
That Iewes shal wene in here witt · and wexe so glade,
That here kyng be ycome · fro the court of heuene,
Moyses other Messias · that men be so trewe. 460
For alle that bereth baselardes · bryght swerde, other launce,
Axe, other acchett · other eny kynne wepne,
Shal be demed to the deth · bote yf he do hit smythie
In-to sykel other into sithe · to shar other to culter; 464
    Conflabunt gladios suos in uomeres, et lanceas suas in falces;
Ech man to pleye with a plouh · a pycoyse other a spade,
Spynnen, and spek of god · and spille no tyme:
Prestes and persons · *placebo* and *dirige*, 467
Here sauter and here seuene psalmis · for alle synful preyen.
Haukyng other hontyng · yf eny of hem hit vsie,
Shal lese ther-fore hus lyue-lode · and hus lif parauenture.
Shal nother kyng ne knyȝt · constable ne meyre
Ouer-cark the comune · ne to the court sompne, 472
Ne putte men in panell · ne do men plighte here treuthe;
Bote after the dede that ys ydo · the dome shal recorde,

B. 304. orther L.   C. 446. P. *om.* be maister.

[*Not in* **A**-*text.*]

Mercy or no mercy · as treuthe wil acorde.
Kynges courte and comune courte · consistorie and chapitele,
Al shal be but one courte · and one baroun be iustice;
Thanne worth Trewe-tonge, a tidy man · that tened me neuere.
Batailles shal non be · ne no man bere wepne,   321
And what smyth that ony smytheth · be smyte therwith to dethe,
    Non leuabit gens contra gentem gladium, &c.
And er this fortune falle · fynde men shal the worste,
By syx sonnes and a schippe · and half a shef of arwes;   324
And the myddel of a mone · shal make the Iewes to torne,
And saracenes for that siȝte · shulle synge *gloria in excelsis, &c.*,
For Makomet and Mede · myshappe shal that tyme;
    For, *melius est bonum nomen quam diuicie multe.*'
Also wroth as the wynde · wex Mede in a while,   328
'I can no Latyn,' quod she · ' clerkis wote the sothe.
Se what Salamon seith · in Sapience bokes,
That hij that ȝiueth ȝiftes · the victorie wynneth,
And moche worschip had ther-with · as holiwryt telleth,   332
    Honorem adquiret qui dat munera, &c.'
'I leue wel, lady,' quod Conscience · ' that thi Latyne be trewe;
Ac thow art like a lady · that redde a lessoun ones,
Was, *omnia probate* · and that plesed here herte,
For that lyne was no lenger · atte leues ende.   336
Had she loked that other half · and the lef torned,
She shulde haue founden fele wordis · folwyng therafter,
Quod bonum est tenete · treuthe that texte made!
And so ferde ȝe, madame! · ȝe couthe namore fynde,   340
Tho ȝe loked on Sapience · sittynge in ȝoure studie.
This tixte that ȝe han tolde · were gode for lordes,
Ac ȝow failled a cunnyng clerke · that couthe the lef haue torned!
And if ȝe seche Sapience eft · fynde shal ȝe that folweth,   344
A ful teneful tixte · to hem that taketh mede,
And that is, *animam autem aufert* · *accipientium, &c.*:
And that is the taille of the tixte · of that that ȝe schewed,
That theiȝe we wynne worschip · and with mede haue victorie,   348
The soule that the sonde taketh · bi so moche is bounde.'

    B. 322. smytheth WO; smithie R; smyteth LC.   337, 338. she WC;
sche RO; ȝe L.   C. 478. tydy ISG; trewe P.   tenede EG; tened IFM;

[*Not in* **A**-*text.*]

Mercy other no mercy · as most trewe a-corden.
Kynges court and comune court · constorie and chapitre, 476
Al shal be bote on court · and on berne be Iustice;
That worth Trewe-tunge, a tydy man · that tenede me neuere.
Batailles shulle neuere eft be · ne man bere eg-tool,
And yf eny man smythie hit · be smyte ther-with to dethe; 480
 Non leuabit gens contra gentem gladium, nec excercebuntur
 ultra ad prelium.
Ac er this fortune by-falle · fynde me shal the worste,
By syx sonnes and a ship · and half a shef of arwes.
And the myddell of a mone · shal makye the Iewes turne,
And sarasyns for that syght · shullen synge *credo in spiritum*
 sanctum. 484
For Makamed and Mede · shullen myshappen that tyme,
 For *melius est bonum nomen quam diuicie multe.*'
As wroth as the wynd · wex Mede ther-after—
'Lo what Salamon seith,' quath hue · 'in Sapience the byble,
"That ȝeueth ȝyftes, take ȝeme · the victorie he wynneth, 488
And moche worshep ther-with" · as holy writt telleth:
 Honorem acquirit qui dat munera.'
'Ich leue the, lady,' quath Conscience · 'for that Latyn is trewe :
Thow art lyke a lady · that a lesson radde,
Was, *omnia probate* · that plesed hure herte; 492
That leef was no lengere · and at the leues ende.
Ac hadde hue loked on the lift half · and the leef turned,
Hue sholde haue yfounde folwynge · fele wordes after,
 Quod bonum est tenete · a tyxte of treuthes makyng.
So he that secheth Sapience · fynde he shal that folweth
Tristilich a teneful tixt · to hem that taketh mede, 498
The whiche hatte, (as ich haue rad · and other that conne rede,)
 Animam aufert accipientium:
"Worshup he wynneth · that wol ȝeue mede,
Ac he that receyueth other recetteth hure · ys recettor of gyle."'
 Hic explicit passus quartus.

---

teunede P.   480. smyþen P; *see* l. 463.   482. shup P.   484. saresyns P.
486. waxe P.   490. leyue P.   for—trewe IMFSG; as holy wriȝt telleth P.
491. ert P.   492. þat IMFSG; wiche P.   493. leef IFSG; P *om*.   498.
teneful ISE; tuenful P.   500. hue (*for* he) P.

PASSUS IV.

Passus Quartus de Visione.

'SESETH,' seide the kyng · 'I suffre ȝou no more.
 Ȝe schulle sauȝtene forsothe · and serue me bothe.
Cusse hire,' quath the kyng · 'Concience, ich hote.'
'Nay, be Crist,' quod Concience · 'congeye me rather!   4
Bote Reson rede me ther-to · arst wol I dye!'

PASSUS IV.

Passus quartus de visione, vt supra.

'CESSETH,' seith the kynge · 'I suffre ȝow no lengere.
 Ȝe shal sauȝtne for sothe · and serue me bothe.
Kisse hir,' quod the kynge · 'Conscience, I hote.'
 'Nay, bi Criste,' quod Conscience · 'congeye me for euere!   4
But Resoun rede me ther-to · rather wil I deye!'
 'And I comaunde the,' quod the kynge · to Conscience thanne,
'Rape the to ride · and Resoun thow fecche;
Comaunde hym that he come · my conseille to here.   8
For he shal reule my rewme · and rede me the beste,
And acounte with the, Conscience · so me Cryst helpe,
How thow lernest the peple · the lered and the lewede.'
 'I am fayne of that forwarde' · seyde the freke thanne,   12
And ritt riȝte to Resoun · and rowneth in his ere,
And seide as the kynge badde · and sithen toke his leue.
 'I shal arraye me to ride,' quod Resoun · 'reste the a while'—
And called Catoun his knaue · curteise of speche,   16
And also Tomme Trewe-tonge- · telle-me-no-tales-
Ne-lesyng-to-lawȝe-of- · for-I-loued-hem-neuere—

A. 11. Crist T; god VHUD.   14. Reson THUD; Concience V.

'And I comaunde the,' quod the kyng · to Concience thenne,
'That thou rape the to ride · and Reson thou fette ;
Comaunde him that he come · my counseil to here.   8
For he schal reule my reame · and rede me the beste
Of Meede, and of other mo · and what mon schal hir wedde ;
And a-counte with Concience · so me Crist helpe!
How thou ledest my peple · lered and lewed.'   12
 'I am fayn of that foreward' · seide the freike thenne,
And rod riht to Reson · and rouned in his ere,
Seyde as the kyng sende · and seththe tok his leue.
 'I schal araye me to ride,' quod Reson · 'reste the a while'—   16
And clepte Caton his knaue · curteis of speche—

PASSUS V.

Incipit passus quintus.

'CESSETH,' saide the kyng · 'ich soffre ȝow no lenger ;
 ȝe shulleth sauhtne for sothe · and serue me bothe.
Kus hure,' quath the kyng · 'Conscience, ich hote.'
 'Nay, by Crist,' quath Conscience · 'conge me rather!   4
Bote Reson rede me ther-to · rather wol ich deye.'
 'And ich comaunde,' quath the kynge · to Conscience thenne,
'Rape the to ryde · and Reson that thow fecche ;
Comaunde hym that he come · my consail to hure,   8
For he shal rulye my reame · and rede me the beste,
Of Mede and of other mo · and what man shal hure wedde,
And a-counte with the, Conscience · so me Crist helpe,
How thow ledest my puple · lered and lewede.'   12
 'Ich am fayn of that forwarde · in fayth,' tho quath Conscience,
And rod forth to Reson · and rouned in hus ere,
And seide hym as the kyng saide · and sitthe tok hus leue.
 'Ich shal a-raye me to ryde,' quath Reson · 'rest thow a whyle:'—
And called Caton hus knaue · corteys of speche,   17
And al-so Tomme Trewe-tonge- · telle-me-no-tales-
Ne-lesynges-to-lauhen-of- · for-ich-louede-hit-neuere—

C. 7. Rape IMFSE ; Rappe P.   16. wyle P.   18. no MIFS ; none P.
19. lesenges P.

'Sette my sadel vppon Soffre- · til-I-seo-my-tyme,
And loke thou warroke him wel · with swithe feole gurthhes;
Hong on him an heui bridel · to bere his hed lowe,   20
ʒit wol he make moni a whi · er he come there.'
 Thenne Concience on his capul · carieth forth faste,
And Resun with him rideth · rappynge swithe;
Bote on a wayn Witty · and Wisdame i-feere   24

'And sette my sadel vppon Suffre- · til-I-se-my-tyme,
And lete warrok it wel · with Witty-wordes gerthes,   20
And hange on hym the heuy brydel · to holde his hed lowe,
For he wil make wehe · tweye er he be there.'
 Thanne Conscience vppon his caple · kaireth forth faste,
And Resoun with hym rit · rownynge togideres,   24
Whiche maistries Mede · maketh on this erthe.
 One Waryn Wisdom · and Witty his fere
Folwed hem faste · for thei haued to done
In the cheker and at the chauncerie · to be discharged of thinges;
And riden fast, for Resoun · shulde rede hem the beste,   29
For to saue hem, for siluer · fro shame and fram harmes.
 And Conscience knewe hem wel · thei loued coueitise,
And bad Resoun ride faste · and recche of her noither,   32
'There aren wiles in here wordes · and with Mede thei dwelleth;
There as wratthe and wranglyng is · there wynne thei siluer,
Ac there is loue and lewte · thei wil nouʒte come there;
  Contricio et infelicitas in vijs eorum, &c.
Thei ne gyueth nouʒte of god · one gose wynge,   36
  Non est timor dei ante oculos eorum.
For, wot god, thei wolde do more · for a dozeine chickenes,
Or as many capones · or for a seem of otes,
Than for loue of owre lorde · or alle hise leue seyntes.
For-thi, Resoun, lete hem ride · tho riche, bi hem-seluen,   40
For Conscience knoweth hem nouʒte · ne Cryst, as I trowe.'
 And thanne Resoun rode faste · the riʒte heiʒe gate,
As Conscience hym kenned · til thei come to the kynge.
 Curteisliche the kynge thanne · come aʒein Resoun,   44
And bitwene hym-self and his sone · sette hym on benche,

 A. 24. witty TH; wytty U; wyd V. B. 24. rit RO; rydes C; ritte L.
27. for thei WOB; L *om.* C. 21. worrok P. P *om.* the. 22. his

Folweden hem faste · for thei hedden to done
In esscheker and chauncelrie · to ben descharget of thinges;
And riden faste, for Reson · schulde reden hem the beste
For to sauen hem-self · from schome and from harme.   28
Bote Concience com arst · to court bi a myle,
And romede forth bi Reson · riht to the kyng.
   Corteisliche the kyng · thenne com to Resoun,
Bitwene himself and his sone · sette him on benche,   32

'And sette my sadel vppon Soffre- · til-ich-see-my-tyme,   20
Let warroke hym wel · with Avyse-the-by-fore,
For it is the wone of Wil · to wynse and to kyke;
Let peitrel hym and pole hym · with peyntede wittes.'
   Thenne Conscience on hus capel · comsed to prykie,   24
And Reson with hym ry3t · rounyng to-geders
Which a maister Mede was · a-mong poure and riche.
   Then Waryn Wysman · and Wyly-man his felawe
Fayn were to folwen hem · and fast ryden after,   28
To take red at Reson · that recorde sholde
By-fore the kyng and Conscience · yf thei couthen pleyne
On Wily-man and Wittiman · and Waryn Wrynge-lawe.
Ac Conscience knew hem wel · and carped to Reson: 32
'Here cometh,' quath Conscience · 'that couetyse seruen;
Ryd forth, syre Reson · and recche nat of here tales,
For ther wratthe and wranglyng ys · ther thei wolle a-byde;
Ac ther loue and leaute ys · hit lyketh nat here hertes: 36
    Contricio et infelicitas in uiis eorum, et uiam pacis non
    cognouerunt; non est timor dei ante oculos eorum.
Thei geueth no3t of good faith · god wot the sothe;
Thei wolde don for a dyner · other for a dosene capones
More than for oure lordes loue · other oure lady hus moder.'

Thanne Reson rod forth · and tok reward of no man,   40
And dude as Conscience kenned · til he the kyng mette.
   Corteslich the kyng then · cam and grette Reson,
And by-twene hymself and his sone · sette tho syre Reson,

(*for* is) P.   26. Wich P.   27. wily IFSE; wyle P.   31. williman P.
43. self IM; PEFS *om.*   is P.

And wordeden a gret while · wysliche to-gedere.
  Thene Pees com to parlement · and put vp a bille,
Hou that Wrong aȝeyn his wille · his wyf hedde i-take,
And hou he rauischede Rose · Reynaldes lemmon,   36
And Mergrete of hire maydenhod · maugre hire chekes.
'Bothe my gees and my grys · his gadelynges fetten ;
I dar not for dreede of hem · fihte ne chide.
He borwede of me bayȝard · and brouhte him neuer aȝeyn, 40
Ne no ferthing him fore · for nouȝt that I con plede.
He meynteneth his men · to morthere myn owne,

And wordeden wel wyseli · a gret while togideres.
  And thanne come Pees in-to parlement · and put forth a bille,
How Wronge aȝeines his wille · had his wyf taken,   48
And how he rauisshed Rose · Reginoldes loue,
And Margarete of hir maydenhode · maugre here chekis.
'Bothe my gees and my grys · his gadelynges feccheth ;
I dar nouȝte for fere of hym · fyȝte ne chyde.   52

He borwed of me bayard · he brouȝte hym home neure,
Ne no ferthynge ther-fore · for nauȝte I couthe plede.
He meyneteneth his men · to morther myne hewen,
Forstalleth my feyres · and fiȝteth in my chepynge,   56
And breketh vp my bernes dore · and bereth aweye my whete,
And taketh me but a taile · for ten quarteres of otes,
And ȝet he bet me ther-to · and lyth bi my mayde,
I nam nouȝte hardy for hym · vneth to loke.'   60
The kynge knewe he seide sothe · for Conscience hym tolde,
That Wronge was a wikked luft · and wrouȝte moche sorwe.
  Wronge was afered thanne · and Wisdome he souȝte   63
To make pees with his pens · and profered hym manye,
And seide, 'had I loue of my lorde thy kynge · litel wolde I recche,
Theiȝe Pees and his powere · pleyned hym eure !'   66

A. 36. hou THUD ; V om.   38. his THUD ; the V.   C. 44. wile P.
47. rauysede P.   49. gees IMEG ;· goos P.   52. wanne P.   seluer MG ;

Forstalleth my feire · fihteth in my chepynges,
Breketh vp my berne-dore · and bereth awei my whete,   44
And taketh me bote a tayle · of ten quarter oten;
And ȝit he bat me therto · and liȝth be my mayden.
I nam not so hardi for him · vp for to loke.'
The kyng kneuh he seide sooth · for Concience him tolde.   48
  Wrong was a-fert tho · and Wisdam souhte
To make his pees with pons · and proferde forth moneye,
And seide, 'Hedde I loue of the kyng · luite wolde I recche
Thauh Pees and his pouwer · playneden on me euere!'   52

And speken tho wise wordes · a long while to-gederes.   44
  Thenne cam Pees in-to parlement · and putte vp a bylle,
How that Wrong wilffullich · hadde hus wif for-leyen,
And how he rauyschede Rose · the riche wydewe, by nyghte,
And Margarete of here maidenhod · as he mette hure late.   48
'Bothe my gees and my grys · and my gras he taketh,
Ich dar nouht for his felaweshepe · in faith,' Pees seide,
'Bere sikerlich eny selúer · to seint Gyles doune;
He waiteth ful wel · whanne ich seluer take,   52
What wey ich wende · wel ȝerne he aspieth,
To robbe me and to ryfle me · yf ich ryde softe.
Ȝut he is bold for to borwe · and baddelich he payeth;
He borwede of me bayarde · and browte hym hom neuere,   56
Ne no ferthyng ther-fore · for nouht ich couthe plede.
He menteyneth hus men · to morthre myn hewes,
And for-stalleth myn faires · and fyghteth in my chepynges,
And breketh vp my bernes dore · and bereth away my whete,   60
And taketh me bote a taile · for ten quarters other twelue.
Ȝut he manasceth me and myne · and lyth by my mayde,
Ich am nouht hardy for hym · vnnethe to loke.'
The kyng knew that he seide soth · for Conscience hym tolde,
How Wronge was a wickede man · and moche wo wrouhte. 65
  Tho was Wrong a-fered · Wysdome he by-souhte;
On men of lawe Wrong lokede · and largelich hem profrede,
And for to haue of here help · handy-dandy payede.   68
'Had ich loue of the lorde · litel wolde ich recche
Of Pees and of hus power · thauh he pleynede euere!'

sulfere P.   56. P *om.* hom.   58. hywes P.   60. breke P.   wete P.
63. owneþe P.

Wisdam wente tho · and so dude Wit,
And for Wrong hedde i-do · so wikked a dede ;
And warnede Wrong tho · with such a wys tale ;
'Whose worcheth bi wil · wraththe maketh ofte ;   56
I sigge hit bi thi-seluen · thou schalt hit sone fynde.
Bote ȝif Meede make hit · thi mischef is vppe,
For bothe thi lyf and thi lond · liȝth in the kynges grace.'
    Wrong thenne vppon Wisdom · wepte to helpe,   60
Him for his handidandi · rediliche he payede.
Thene Wisdam and Wit · wente to-gedere,
And nomen Meede with hem · merci to wynne.
    Pees putte forth his hed · and his ponne blodi :   64
'Withouten gult, god wot · gat I this scathe.'

    Tho wan Wisdome · and sire Waryn the witty,
For that Wronge had ywrouȝt · so wikked a dede,   68
And warned Wronge tho · with such a wyse tale ;
'Who-so worcheth bi wille · wratthe maketh ofte ;
I seye it bi thi-self · thow shalt it wel fynde.
But if Mede it make ; thi myschief is vppe,   72
For bothe thi lyf and thy londe · lyth in his grace.'
    Thanne wowed Wronge · Wisdome ful ȝerne,
To make his pees with his pens · handi-dandi payed.
Wisdome and Witte thanne · wenten togideres,   76
And toke Mede myd hem · mercy to winne.
    Pees put forth his hed · and his panne blody ;
'Wyth-outen gilte, god it wote · gat I this skathe,
Conscience and the comune · knowen the sothe.'   80
    Ac Wisdom and Witt · were about faste
To ouercome the kyng · with catel, ȝif thei myȝte.
    The kynge swore, by Crist · and by his crowne bothe,
That Wronge for his werkis · sholde wo tholye,   84
And comaunded a constable · to casten hym in yrens,
'And late hym nouȝte this seuene ȝere · seen his feet ones.'
    'God wot,' quod Wysdom · 'that were nauȝte the beste ;
And he amendes mowe make · late meynprise hym haue ;   88
And be borwgh for his bale · and biggen hym bote,
And so amende that is mysdo · and euermore the bettere.'
    Witt acorded ther-with · and seide the same :

A. 60. Wrog V.   69. catel TUD ; meede VH.   B. 68. ywrouȝte L.

Concience and the kyng · knewen the sothe;
Wusten wel that Wrong · was a schrewe euere.
But Wisdam and Wit · weoren ȝeorne aboute faste   68
To ouercome the kyng . with catel ȝif heo mihten.
  The kyng swor tho bi Crist · and bi his coroune bothe,
That Wrong for his werkes · schulde wo thole,
And comaundede a constable · to casten him in irens;   72
'He ne schal this seuen ȝer · seon his feet ones.'
  'God wot,' quath Wisdam · 'that weore not the beste;
And he amendes make · let meynprise him haue;
And beo borw of his bale · and buggen him bote,   76
And a-menden his misdede . and euer-more the bettre.'
  Wit a-cordede herwith · and seide him the same :

Thoruh Wrong and hus werkes · ther was Mede yknowe,
For Wysdome and Wit tho · wenten to-gederes,   72
And toke Mede myd hem · mercy to wynne.
  Ȝut Pees putte forth hus hefd · and hus panne blody,
'With-oute gult, god wot · gat ich thys scathe;
Conscience knoweth hit wel · and alle the trewe comune.' 76
  Ac Wyles and Wit · weren a-boute faste
To ouercome the kynge · thorw catel, yf thei myghte.
  The kyng swor tho by Crist · and by his corone bothe,
That Wrong for hus workus · sholde wo tholie,   80
And comaundede a constable · to caste Wrong in yrenes,
Ther he ne sholde in seuen ȝere · see fet ne hondes.
  'God wot,' quath a wis on · 'that were nat the beste;
Yf he may amendes do · let meynpryse hym haue,   84
And be borw of hys bale · and byggen hym bote,
And a-mende that ys mys-do · and euere-more the betere.'
  Wit a-corded her-with · and witnessede the same;

C. 78. þorw *is miswritten* þow *in* P.   85. ys P.

'Hit is betere that boote · bale a-doun bringe
Then bale be beten · and boote neuer the better.'   80
    Thenne Meede meokede hire · and merci bi-souhte,
And profrede Pees a present · al of pure red gold:
'Haue this of me,' quod heo · 'to amende with thi scathe,
For ichul wage for Wrong · he wol do so no more.'   84
    Pees thenne pitously · preyede the kyng
To haue merci on that mon · that mis-dude him ofte:
'For he hath waget me a-mendes · as Wisdam him tauhte,
I forȝiue him that gult · with a good wille;   88
So that ȝe assented beo · I con no more sigge;
For Meede hath maad me amendes · I may no more aske.'

'Bettere is that bote · bale adoun brynge,   92
Than bale be ybette · and bote neuere the bettere.'
    And thanne gan Mede to mengen here · and mercy she bisought,
And profred Pees a present · al of pure golde:
'Haue this, man, of me,' quod she · 'to amende thi skathe,   96
For I wil wage for Wronge · he wil do so namore.'
    Pitously Pees thanne · prayed to the kynge
To haue mercy on that man · that mys-did hym so ofte:
'For he hath waged me wel · as Wysdome hym tauȝte,   100
And I forgyue hym that gilte · with a goode wille;
So that the kynge assent · I can seye no bettere;
For Mede hath made me amendes · I may namore axe.'
    'Nay,' quod the kynge tho · 'so me Cryst helpe!   104
Wronge wendeth nouȝte so awaye · arst wil I wite more;
For loupe he so liȝtly · laughen he wolde,
And efte the balder be · to bete myne hewen;
But Resoun haue reuthe on hym · he shal rest in my stokkes,
And that as lunge as he lyueth · but lowenesse hym borwe.'
    Somme men redde Resoun tho · to haue reuthe on that schrewe,
And for to conseille the kynge · and Conscience after,
That Mede moste be meynpernour · Resoun thei bisouȝte,   112
    'Rede me nouȝte,' quod Resoun · 'no reuthe to haue,
Til lordes and ladies · louien alle treuthe,
And haten al harlotrye · to heren it, or to mouthen it;
Tyl Pernelles purfil · be put in here hucche;   116

'Nay,' quod the kyng tho · 'so god ȝiue me blisse!
Wrong went not so awei · til ich wite more;   92
Lope he so lihtliche awei · lauȝwhen he wolde,
And eft be the baldore · forte beten myne hynen;
Bote Reson haue reuthe of him · he resteth in the stokkes
Also longe as I lyue · bote more loue hit make.'   96
  Thenne summe radde Reson · to haue reuthe of that schrewe,
And to counseile the kyng · and Concience bothe,
That Meede moste be meynpernour · Reson heo bi-souȝte.
  'Rede me not,' quod Reson · 'reuthe to haue,   100
Til lordes, and ladies · louen alle treuthe,
And Perneles porfyl · be put in heore whucche;

'Betere ys that bote · bale a-doun brynge,   88
Than bale be ybete · and bote neuere the betere.'
  Thanne gan Mede meken here · and mercy by-souhte,
And profrede Pees a present · al of pure golde;
'Haue this, man, of me,' quath hue · 'to amende thy scathe;
For ich wol wage for Wrong · he wol do so no more.'   93
  Pytouslich Pees tho · preyede the kyng
To haue mercy on that man · that meny tyme greuede hym—
'For he hath waged me wel · as Wisdome hym tauhte;   96
Mede hath mad myne amendes · ich may no more asken,
So alle myne claymes ben quyt · by so the kynge asente.'
  'Nay, by Crist,' quath the kynge · 'for Consciences sake,
Wrong goth nat so away · ar ich wite more;   100
Loupe he so lyghtlich · lauhen he wolde,
And eft be the boldere · to bete myne hewes;
Bote Reson haue reuthe of hym · he shal reste in stockes
As longe as ich lyue · for hus luther werkes.'   104
  Somme radde Reson tho · to haue reuthe on that shrewe,
And for to consail the kyng · on Conscience thei loked;
That Mede myghte be menepernour · reson thei by-souhte.
  'Red me nat,' quath Reson · 'no reuthe to haue,   108
Til lordes and ladies · louen alle treuthe,
And haten alle harlotrie · to huyren other to mouthen hit;
And Purneles porfil · be put in the whucche,

A. 94. hynen TUD; puple H; V *om*.   C. 89. ybete I; I-bete FS;
bete P.   90. muken P.   92. þus (*for* þis) P.   101. *After* lyghtlich P
inserts a-wey.   102. hewes I; hywes P; hynus FS.   111. wucche P.

Til children chereschinge · be chastet with ȝerdes,
Til harlotes holynesse · be holden for an hyne;   104
Til clerkes and knihtes · ben corteis of heore mouthes,
And haten to don heor harlotrie · and vsun hit no more;
Til prestes heore prechyng · preuen hit in hem-seluen,
And don hit in dede · to drawen vs to gode;   108
Til seint Iame beo i-souht · ther I schal a-signe,
And no man go to Galys · bote he go for euere;
And alle Rome-renners · for robbeours of bi-ȝonde
Bere no seluer ouer see · that bereth signe of the kyng,   112
Nouther grotes ne gold i-graue · with the kynges coroune,

And childryn cherissyng · be chastyng with ȝerdes;
And harlotes holynesse · be holden for an hyne;
Til clerken coueitise be · to clothe the pore and to fede,
And religious romares · *recordare* in here cloistres,   120
As seynt Benet hem bad · Bernarde and Fraunceys;
And til prechoures prechyng · be preued on hemseluen;
Tyl the kynges conseille · be the comune profyte;
Tyl bisschopes baiardes · ben beggeres chambres,   124
Here haukes and her houndes · helpe to pore religious;
And til seynt Iames be souȝte · there I shal assigne,

That no man go to Galis · but if he go for euere;
And alle Rome-renneres · for robberes of byȝonde   128
Bere no siluer ouer see · that signe of kynge sheweth,
Noyther graue ne vngraue · golde noither siluer,
Vppon forfeture of that fee · who so fynt hym at Douere,
But if it be marchaunt or his man · or messagere with letteres, 132

Prouysoure or prest · or penaunt for his synnes.
   And ȝet,' quod Resoun, 'bi the rode · I shal no reuthe haue,
While Mede hath the maistrye · in this moot-halle.
Ac I may shewe ensaumples · as I se other-while;   136
I sey it by my-self,' quod he · 'and it so were
That I were kynge with crowne · to kepen a rewme,
Shulde neuere wronge in this worlde · that I wite myȝte,
Ben vnpunisshed in my powere · for peril of my soule!   140

A. 119. *From* UT; VH *omit the line.*   B. 128. byȝende L.

A. PASSUS IV. 114-123.   C. PASSUS V. 112-137.   111

Vppon forfet of that fe · hose hit fynde at Douere,
Bote hit beo marchaund othur his men · or messager with lettres,
Or prouisours or preestes · that popes a-vaunset.   116
And ȝit,' quod Reson, 'bi the roode · I schal no reuthe haue,
While Meede hath eny maystrie   to mooten in this halle;
Ac y mai schewe ȝow ensamples · y seie be myselue.
For I sigge hit for my soule · and hit so weore   120
That ich weore kyng with croune · to kepen a reame,
Scholde neuer wrong in this world · that ich i-wite mihte,
Ben vn-punissched beo my pouwer · for peril of my soule!

And children cherissing · be chasted with ȝerdes,   112
And harlotes holynesse · be an hey ferye;
Til klerken couetise · be cloth for the poure,
Here pelure and here palfrayes · poure menne lyflode,
And religious out-ryders · reclused in here cloistres,   116
And be as Benit hem bad · Domenik and Fraunceis;
Tyl that lerede men lyue · as thei lere and techen,
And til the kynges consayl · be al comune profit;
Tyl bisshopes ben bakers · brewers and taylours,   120
For alle manere men · that thei fyndeth nedfol;
Tyl seynt Iame be souht · ther poure syke lyggen,
In prisons and in poore cotes · for pilgrymages to Rome,
So that non go to Galys · bote it be for euere;   124
And alle Rome-renners · for robbers in Fraunce
Bere no suluer ouer see · that kynges sygne sheweth,
Neither graue ne vngraue · of gold ne of suluer,
Vp forfeture of the fee · ho so fynt hym ouerwarde,   128
Bote it be marchaunt other hus man · other messager with
    lettres,
Prouisour other prest · other penaunt for hus synnes.
And ȝut,' quath Reson, 'by the rode · ich shall no reuthe haue,
Whyl Mede hath the maistrye · ther motyng is atte barre.   132
Ac ich may seye ensamples · as ich see othere;
Ich seye it for my-selue,' quath Reson · 'and hit so were,
That ich were kyng with corone · to kepe eny reame,
Shold neuere wronge in this worlde · that ich wite myghte,   136
Be vnpunysshed in my power · for peril of my soule,

C. 120. bisshepes P.   ben IM; be F; and P.   132. Wyl P.   his P.

Ne gete grace thorw ȝift · so me god helpe! 124
Ne for meede haue merci · but mekenesse hit make.
For *nullum malum* the mon mette · with *inpunitum*,
And bad *nullum bonum* · be *irremuneratum*.
Let thi clerk, sire kyng · construe this in Englisch; 128
And ȝif thou worchest hit in wit · ich wedde bothe myn eres,
That Lawe schal ben a laborer · and leden a-feld dounge,
And Loue schal leden thi lond · as the leof lyketh.'
Clerkes that were confessours · coupled hem to-gedere, 132

Ne gete my grace for giftes ·. so me God saue!
Ne for no mede haue mercy · but mekenesse it make.
For *nullum malum* the man · mette with *inpunitum*,
And badde *nullum bonum* · be *irremuneratum*. 144
Late ȝowre confessoure, sire kynge · construe this vnglosed;
And ȝif ȝe worken it in werke · I wedde myne eres,
That Lawe shal ben a laborere · and lede a-felde donge,
And Loue shal lede thi londe · as the lief lyketh!' 148
Clerkes that were confessoures · coupled hem togideres,
Alle to construe this clause · and for the kynges profit,
Ac nouȝte for conforte of the comune · ne for the kynges soule.
For I seiȝe Mede in the moot-halle · on men of lawe wynke, 152
And thei lawghyng lope to hire · and lafte Resoun manye.
Waryn Wisdome · wynked vppon Mede,
And seide, 'Madame, I am ȝowre man · what so my mouth
        Iangleth;
I falle in floreines,' quod that freke · 'an faile speche ofte.' 156
Alle riȝtful recorded · that Resoun treuthe tolde,
And Witt acorded ther-with · and comended his wordes,
And the moste peple in the halle · and manye of the grete,
And leten Mekenesse a maistre · and Mede a mansed schrewe.
Loue lete of hir liȝte · and Lewte ȝit lasse, 161
And seide it so heiȝe · that al the halle it herde,
'Who-so wilneth hir to wyf · for welth of her godis,
But he be knowe for a koke-wolde · kut of my nose!' 164
Mede mourned tho · and made heuy chere,
For the moste comune of that courte · called hire an hore.
Ac a sysoure and a sompnoure · sued hir faste,

A. 124. god THUD; gold V.   126. with TUD; with-outen V.

A. PASSUS IV. 133-140.   C. PASSUS V. 138-163.   113

Forte construe this clause · and distinkte hit after.
Whon Resun to this reynkes · rehersede theose wordes,
Nas non in that moot-halle · more ne lasse,   135
That ne held Reson a mayster tho · and Meede a muche wrecche.
Loue lette of Meede luite · and louh hire to scorn,
And seide hit so loude · that sothnesse hit herde,
'Hose wilneth hire to wyue · for weolthe of hire godes,
Bote he beo a cokewold i-kore · cut of bothe myn eres!'   140

Ne gete my grace thorw eny gyft · ne glosyng speche,
Ne thorw mede do mercy · by Marye of heuene!
For man, *nullum malum* · mette with *impunitum*,   140
And bad that *nullum bonum* · bee *irremuneratum*.
Lete thy confessour, syre kyng · construe this in English,
And ȝif ȝe worchen hit in werke · ich wedde bothe myn handes,
That lawe shal be a laborer · and lede a felde donge,   144
And loue shal lede thy land · as the leef lyketh.'
   Clerkus that were confessours · couplede hem to-gederes,
To construe this clause · kyndeliche what hit menede.

Mede in the mote-halle tho · on men of lawe gan wynke,   148
In sygne that thei sholde · with som sotel speche
Reherce tho a-non ryght · that myghte Reson stoppe.

   And alle ryghtful recordeden · that Reson treuthe seyde,
And Kynde Wit and Conscience · cortesliche thankede;   152
Reson for hus ryght speche · riche and poure hym louede,
And seiden, 'we seth wel · syre Reson, by thy wordes,
That meknesse worth mayster · ouer Mede atte laste.'
Loue let lyght of Mede · and Leaute ȝut lasse,   156
And cryed vp-on Conscience · the kynge hit myghte yhure,
'Who so wylneth hure to wyue · for welthe of hure goodes,
Bote he be knowe for cokewold · kut of my nose!'
   Mede mornede tho · and made heuy cheere,   160
For the comune called hure · queynte comune hore.
A sysour and a somner tho · softeliche forth ȝeden
With Mede the mayde · out of the mot-halle.

C. 143. worten (*error for* worchen) P.   145. leef MFSE; luf P.   147. wat P.   148. þe MFISE; þat P.   150. stope P.   161. called FSE; cald P.

I

114 A. PASSUS IV. 141–147. B. PASSUS IV. 168–191.

Was nouther Wisdam tho · ne Witti his feere,
That couthe warpen a word · to with-siggen Reson; 142
Bote stareden for studiing · and stooden as bestes.
   The kyng acordede, bi crist · to Resons connynge,
And rehersede that Reson hedde · rihtfoliche I-schewet:
'Bote hit is hard, be myn hed · herto hit bringe, 146
Al my lige leodes · to lede thus euene.'

And a schireues clerke · byschrewed al the route, 168
'For ofte haue I,' quod he · 'holpe ȝow atte barre,
And ȝit ȝeue ȝe me neuere · the worthe of a russhe.'
   The kynge called Conscience · and afterwardes Resoun,
And recorded that Resoun · had riȝtfullich schewed, 172
And modilich vppon Mede · with myȝte the kynge loked,
And gan wax wrothe with lawe · for Mede almoste had shent it,
And seide, 'thorw ȝowre lawe, as I leue · I lese many chetes;
Mede ouer-maistrieth lawe · and moche treuthe letteth. 176
Ac Resoun shal rekene with ȝow · ȝif I regne any while,
And deme ȝow, bi this day · as ȝe han deserued.
Mede shal nouȝte meynprise ȝow · bi the Marie of heuene!
I wil haue leute in lawe · and lete be al ȝowre Ianglyng, 180
And as moste folke witnesseth wel · wronge shal be demed.'
   Quod Conscience to the kynge · 'but the comune wil assent,
It is ful hard, bi myn hed · here-to to brynge it,
Alle ȝowre lige leodes · to lede thus euene.' 184
   'By hym that rauȝte on the rode' · quod Resoun to the kynge,
'But if I reule thus ȝowre rewme · rende out my guttes!
ȝif ȝe bidden buxomnes · be of myne assente.'
   'And I assent,' seith the kynge · 'by seynt Marie my lady,
Be my conseille comen · of clerkis and of erlis. 189
Ac redili, Resoun · thow shalt nouȝte ride fro me,
For as longe as I lyue · lete the I nelle.'

C. 167. modiliche MFSEG; myldeliche P.   169. Thorȝe P.   171. rekne (*for* rekene) I; rikene M; regne P.   wyle P.   174. ianglend P.

A. PASSUS IV. 148–154. C. PASSUS V. 164–192.

'Bi him that rauhte on the roode,' · quod Reson to the kyng,
'Bote I rule thus thi reame · rend out my ribbes!
ȝif hit beo so that boxumnesse · beo at myn assent.'   150
'Ich assente,' quod the kyng · 'bi seinte Marie mi ladi,
Beo my counseil i-come · of clerkes and of erles.
Bote rediliche, Reson · thou rydest not heonnes,
For as longe as I liue · lette the I nulle.'   154

A shereyues clerk cryede · 'a! *capiatis* Mede,   164
Et saluo custodias · sed non cum carceratis.
The kynge to his consail tho · tok Conscience and Reson,
And modiliche vp-on Mede · meny tyme lokede,
And lourede vp-on men of lawe · and lightliche seide,   168
'Thorȝ ȝoure lawe, ich leyue · ich lese menye escheytes;
Mede and men of ȝoure craft · muche treuthe letteth.
Ac Reson shal rekene with ȝow · yf ich regne eny whyle,
And deme ȝow, by thys day · as ȝe haue deseruyd.   172
Mede shal not meynprise ȝow · by Marye of heuene,
Ich wolle haue leaute for my lawe; · let be al ȝoure Ianglyng;
By leel men and lyf-holy · my lawe shal be demyd.'
Quath Conscience to the kynge · 'with-oute the commune help,
Hit is ful hard, by myn hefd · ther-to hit to brynge,
And alle ȝoure lege ledes · to lede thus euene.'   178
'By hym that rauhte on rode' · quath Reson to the kynge,
'Bote ich rewely thus alle reames · reueth me my syght;
And brynge alle men to bowe · with-oute byter wounde,
With-oute mercement other manslauht · amenden alle reames.
'Ich wolde hit were,' quath the kyng · 'wel al a-boute.
For-thy, Reson, redelyche · thow shalt nat ryden hennes,   184
Bote be my chyf chaunceler · in chekyr and in parlement,
And Conscience in alle my courtes · be as kynges Iustice."
'Ich a-sente," seyde Reson · 'by so thy-self y-huyre,
Audi alteram partem · a-mong aldermen and comuners;   188
And that vnsittynge Suffraunce · ne seele ȝoure pryueie letteres,
Ne sende *supersedeas* · bote ich asente,' quath Reson;
'And ich dar legge my lyf · that Loue wol lene the suluer,
To wage thyne, and help wynne · that thow wilnest after,   192

---

176. whith-oute P.   P *om.* the.   181. wonde P.   190. seynde P.   191.
þe IMFSE; þat P.

'Icham redi,' quod Reson · 'to reste with the euere; 155
So that Concience beo vr counseiler · kepe I no betere.'

'I am aredy,' quod Resoun · 'to reste with ȝow euere, 192
So Conscience be of owre conseille · I kepe no bettere.'
'And I graunt,' quod the kynge · 'goddes forbode it faile,
Als longe as owre lyf lasteth · lyue we togideres.' 195

'I graunte gladly,' quod the kyng · 'god forbeode he fayle;
And also longe as I lyue · leue we to-gedere.' 158

More than al thy marchauns · other thy mytrede bisshopes,
Other Lumbardes of Lukes · that lyuen by lone as Iewes.' 194
The kyng comaunded Conscience tho · to congie alle hus officers,
And receyuen tho that Reson louede; · and ry3t with that ich a-wakede. 196
Hic explicit passus quintus.

C. 196. wit P.

[*Not in* **A**-*text or* **B**-*text.*]

PASSUS VI.

Incipit passus sextus.

THUS ich a-waked, god wot · whanne ich wonede on
    Cornehulle,
Kytte and ich in a cote · clothed as a lollere,
And lytel y-lete by · leyue me for sothe,
Among lollares of London · and lewede heremytes;   4
For ich made of tho men · as reson me tauhte.
For as ich cam by Conscience · with Reson ich mette
In an hote heruest · whenne ich hadde myn hele,
And lymes to labore with · and louede wel fare,   8
And no dede to do · bote drynke and to slepe.
In hele and in vnite · on me aposede;
Romynge in remembraunce · thus Reson me aratede.
'Canstow seruen,' he seide · 'other syngen in a churche,   12
Other coke for my cokers · other to the cart picche,
Mowe other mowen · other make bond to sheues,
Repe other be a repereyue · and a-ryse erliche,
Other haue an horne and be haywarde · and liggen oute a
    nyghtes,   16
And kepe my corn in my croft · fro pykers and theeues?
Other shappe shon other clothes · other shep other kyn kepe,
Heggen other harwen · other swyn other gees dryue,
Other eny other kyns craft · that to the comune nedeth,   20
Hem that bedreden be · by-lyue to fynde?'
'Certes,' ich seyde · 'and so me god helpe,
Ich am to waik to worche · with sykel other with sythe,
And to long, leyf me · lowe for to stoupe,   24
To worchen as a workeman · eny whyle to dure.'

C. 1. wot god P.   wanne P.   3. And a lytel P.   y-lete IMSG; ich
let (*wrongly*) P.   6. wit P.   7. wenne P.   19. Eggen P.   20. oþer
MIFSG; P *om*.   nedeþ IME; nudeþ P.   25. wyle P.

C. PASSUS VI. 26–54.

[*Not in* A-*text or* B-*text; see* p. 118.]

'Thenne hauest thow londes to lyue by' · quath Reson,
  'other lynage riche
That fynden the thy fode? · for an ydel man thow semest,
A spendour that spende mot · other a spille-tyme,   28
Other beggest thy bylyue · a-boute at menne hacches,
Other faitest vp-on Frydays · other feste-dayes in churches,
The whiche is lollarene lyf · that lytel ys preysed,
Ther ryghtfulnesse rewardeth · ryght as men deserueth,   32
  Reddit unicuique iuxta opera sua.
Other thow art broke, so may be · in body other in membre,
Other ymaymed throw som mys-hap · wher-by thow my3t be
  excused?'
'Whanne ich 3ong was,' quath ich · 'meny 3er hennes,
My fader and my frendes · founden me to scole,   36
Tyl ich wiste wyterliche · what holy wryt menede,
And what is best for the body · as the bok telleth,
And sykerest for the soule · by so ich wolle continue.
And 3ut fond ich neuere in faith · sytthen my frendes deyden,
Lyf that me lyked · bote in thes longe clothes.   41
Yf ich by laboure sholde lyue · and lyflode deseruen,
That labour that ich lerned best · ther-with lyue ich sholde ;
  In eadem uocatione in qua uocati estis, manete.
And ich lyue in Londone · and on Londone bothe,   44
The lomes that ich laboure with · and lyflode deserue
Ys *pater-noster* and my prymer · *placebo* and *dirige*,
And my sauter som tyme · and my seuene psalmes.
Thus ich synge for hure soules · of suche as me helpen,   48
And tho that fynden me my fode · vouchen saf, ich trowe,
To be welcome whanne ich come · other-whyle in a monthe,
Now with hym and now with hure · and thus-gate ich begge
With-oute bagge other botel · bote my wombe one.   52
And al-so more-ouer · me thynketh, syre Reson,
Men sholde constreyne no clerke · to knauene werkes ;

C. 27. hydel P.   29. ate P.   31. wiche P.   33. ert P.   34. wer-by P.
35. Wanne P.   37, 38. wat P.   42. Hyf P.   43. þer-whit P. *in* M ;
the rest omit.   manete M ; *the rest omit.*   44. londone MSE ; londene P.
49. vochen P.   50. wolcome P.   wanne P.   wyle P.

[*Not in* **A**-*text or* **B**-*text.*]

For by lawe of *Leuitici* · that oure lord ordeynede,
Clerkes that aren crouned · of kynde vnderstondyng   56
Sholde nother swynke ne swete · ne swere at enquestes,
Ne fyghte in no vauntwarde · ne hus fo greue;
    Non reddas malum pro malo.
For it ben aires of heuene · alle that ben crounede,
And in queer and in kirkes · Cristes owene mynestres,   60
    Dominus pars hereditatis mee; & alibi: Clementia non constringit.
Hit by-cometh for clerkus · Crist for to seruen,
And knaues vncrouned · to cart and to worche.
For shold no clerk be crouned · bote yf he ycome were
Of franklens and free men · and of folke yweddede.   64
Bondmen and bastardes · and beggers children,
Thuse by-longeth to labour · and lordes kyn to seruen
Bothe god and good men · as here degree asketh;
Some to synge masses · other sitten and wryte,   68
Rede and receyue · that reson ouhte spende;
Ac sith bondemenne barnes · han be mad bisshopes,
And barnes bastardes · han ben archidekenes,
And sopers and here sones · for seluer han be knyghtes, 72
And lordene sones here laborers · and leid here rentes to wedde,
For the ryght of this reame · ryden a-ȝens oure enemys,
In confort of the comune · and the kynges worshep,
And monkes and moniales · that mendinauns sholden fynde, 76
Han mad here kyn knyghtes · and knyghtfees purchased,
Popes and patrones · poure gentil blod refuseth,
And taken Symondes sone · seyntewarie to kepe.
Lyf-holynesse and loue · han ben longe hennes,   80
And wole, til hit be wered out · or otherwise ychaunged.
For-thy rebuke me ryght nouht · Reson, ich ȝow praye;
For in my conscience ich knowe · what Crist wolde that ich wrouhte.

    C. 59. and alle P.   60. and—kirkes I; in churches P.   66. kyn to MF; children sholde P.   70. Ac IMSG; And P.   74. þis IMS; þes P.
77. purchase P.

[*Not in* A-*text or* B-*text; see* p. 120.]

Preyers of a parfyt man · and penaunce discret   84
Ys the leueste labour · that oure lord pleseth.
Non de solo,' ich seide · 'for sothe *uiuit homo*,
Nec in pane & pabulo · the *pater-noster* witnesseth;
Fiat uoluntas tua · fynt ous alle thynges.'   88
 Quath Conscience, 'by Crist · ich can nat see this lyeth;
Ac it semeth nouht parfytnesse · in cytees for to begge,
Bote he be obediencer · to pryour other to mynstre.'
 'That ys soth,' ich seide · 'and so ich by-knowe,   92
That ich haue tynt tyme · and tyme mysspended;
And 3ut, ich hope, as he · that ofte haueth chaffared,
That ay hath lost and lost · and atte laste hym happed
He bouhte suche a bargayn · he was the bet euere,   96
And sette hus lost at a lef · at the laste ende,
Suche a wynnynge hym warth · thorw wordes of hus grace;
     Simile est regnum celorum thesauro abscondito in agro, &
     cetera:
     Mulier que inuenit dragmam vnam, et cetera;
So hope ich to haue · of hym that is al-myghty
A gobet of hus grace · and bygynne a tyme,   100
That alle tymes of my tyme · to profit shal turne.'
 'Ich rede the,' quath Reson tho · 'rape the to by-gynne
The lyf that ys lowable · and leel to the soule'—
 '3e, and continue;' quath Conscience · and to the kirke ich wente.

And to the kirke gan ich go · god to honourie,   105
By-for the crois on my knees · knocked ich my brest,
Sykinge for my synnes · seggynge my *pater-noster*,
Wepyng and wailinge · tyl ich was a slepe.   108

[*Continued on* p. 123.]

C. 84. P *om.* a.   88. *tuas* P.   95. atte laste EIFS; at þe latiste P.
98. wyrdes P.   *vnam* M; P om.   104, 105. kirke IF; churche P.   107. sennes P.

PASSUS V.

Passus quintus de visione.

THE kyng and his knihtes · to the churche wenten
To heere matyns and masse · and to the mete aftur.
Thenne wakede I of my wink · me was wo with alle
That I nedde sadloker i-slept · and i-seȝe more.   4
Er I a furlong hedde i-fare · a feyntise me hente,
That forther mihti not a-fote · for defaute of sleep.
I sat softeliche a-doun · and seide my beo-leeue,

PASSUS V.

Passus quintus de Visione.

THE kyng and his ·knightes · to the kirke wente
To here matynes of the day · and the masse after.
Thanne waked I of my wynkynge · and wo was with-alle,
That I ne hadde sleped sadder · and yseiȝen more.   4
Ac er I hadde faren a fourlonge · feyntise me hente,
That I ne myȝte ferther a-foot · for defaute of slepynge;
And sat softly adown · and seide my bileue,
And so I babeled on my bedes · thei brouȝte me a-slepe.   8
  And thanne saw I moche more · than I bifore tolde,
For I say the felde ful of folke · that I bifore of seyde,
And how Resoun gan arrayen hym · alle the reume to preche,
And with a crosse afor the kynge · comsed thus to techen.   12
  He preued that thise pestilences · were for pure synne,
And the southwest wynde · on Saterday at euene
Was pertliche for pure pryde · and for no poynt elles.
Piries and plomtrees · were puffed to the erthe,   16
In ensample, ȝe segges · ȝe shulden do the bettere.
Beches and brode okes · were blowen to the grounde,
Torned vpward her tailles · in tokenynge of drede,
That dedly synne at domesday · shal fordon hem alle.   20

B. 13. were W; was LCRO.

And so I blaberde on my beodes · that brouhte me a-slepe. 8
Then sauh I muche more · then I beofore tolde,
For I sauh the feld ful of folk · that ich of bi-fore schewede,
And Concience with a crois · com for to preche.
He preide the peple · haue pite of hem-selue, 12
And preuede that this pestilences · weore for puire synne,
And this south-westerne wynt · on a Seterday at euen
Was a-perteliche for pruide · and for no poynt elles.
Piries and plomtres · weore passchet to the grounde, 16
In ensaumple to men · that we scholde do the bettre.
Beches and brode okes · weore blowen to the eorthe,
And turned vpward the tayl · in toknyng of drede
That dedly synne or domesday · schulde fordon hem alle. 20

[*Continued from* p. 121.]

Thenne mette me moche more · than ich by-fore tolde
Of the mater that ich mette fyrst · on Maluerne hulles.
Ich sauh the feld ful of folk · fram ende to other,
And Reson reuested · ry3t as a pope, 112
And Conscience his crocer · by-fore the kynge stande.
  Reson reuerentliche · by-for al the reame
Prechede, and prouede · that thuse pestilences
Was for pure synne · to punyshe the puple; 116
And the south-west wynd · on Saterday at eue
Was pertelich for prude · and for no poynt elles.
Piries and plomtrees · were poffed to the erthe
In ensample to syggen ous · we sholde do the betere; 120
Beches and brode okes · weren blowe to the grounde,
And turned vpward here tayl · in tokenynge of drede
That dedlich synne er domys day · shal for-do ous alle.

C. 109, 110. mete P.   111. to þe oþer P; *but* IMFSE *om.* þe.

Of this matere I mihte · momele ful longe,
Bote I sigge as I sauh · (so me god helpe)!
How Concience with a cros · comsede to preche.
He bad wastors go worche · what thei best couthe, 24
And wynne that thei wasteden · with sum maner craft.
He preiȝede Pernel · hire porfil to leue,
And kepen hit in hire cofre · for catel at neode.
Thomas he tauȝte · to take twey staues, 28

Of this matere I myȝte · mamely ful longe,
Ac I shal seye as I saw · so me god helpe!
How pertly afor the poeple · Resoun gan to preche.
He bad wastoure go worche · what he best couthe, 24
And wynnen his wastyng · with somme manere crafte.
And preyed Peronelle · her purfyle to lete,
And kepe it in hir cofre · for catel at hire nede.
Thomme Stowue he tauȝte · to take two staues, 28
And fecche Felice home · fro the wyuen pyne.
He warned Watt · his wyf was to blame,
That hire hed was worth halue a marke · his hode nouȝte
    worth a grote.
And bad Bette kut · a bow other tweyne, 32
And bete Betoun ther-with · but if she wolde worche.
And thanne he charged chapmen · to chasten her childeren;
Late no wynnynge hem forweny · whil thei be ȝonge,
Ne for no pouste of pestilence · plese hem nouȝte out of
    resoun. 36
' My syre seyde so to me · and so did my dame,
That the leuere childe · the more lore bihoueth,
And Salamon seide the same · that Sapience made,
    Qui parcit virge, odit filium.
The Englich of this latyn is · who-so wil it knowe, 40
Who-so spareth the sprynge · spilleth his children.'
And sithen he preyed prelatz · and prestes to-gideres,
'That ȝe prechen to the peple · preue it on ȝowre-seluen,
And doth it in dede · it shal drawe ȝow to good; 44
If ȝe lyuen as ȝe leren vs · we shal leue ȝow the bettere.'

A. 28. staues THU; stauenes V. **B.** 29. filice L.

And fette hom Felice · from wyuene pyne.
He warnede Watte · his wyf was to blame,
That hire hed was worth a mark · and his hod worth a grote.
He chargede chapmen · to chasten heore children;   32
Let hem wonte non eiȝe · while that thei ben ȝonge.
He preyede preestes · and prelates to-gedere,
That thei prechen the peple · to preuen hit in hem-seluen—
'And libben as ȝe lereth vs · we wolen loue ow the betere.'   36

Of this master ich myghte · momely ful longe,   124
Ac ich shal seye as ich seih · slepynge, as it were,
How Reson radde al the reame · ryght for to lyuen.
He bad wastours go worche · and wynne here sustinaunce
Thorw som trewe trauail · and no tyme spille.   128
He preide Purnele · here porfil to leue,
And kepe hit in here cofre · for catell at hure nede.
He tauhte Thomme Stowe · to take two staues,
And fecche Felice home · fram wyuen pyne.   132
He warnede Watte · hus wif was to blame,
For hure hefd was worth half mark · and hus hod nat a grote.
He bad Bette go kutte · a bowh other tweye,
And bete Beton ther-myd · bote hue wolde worche.   136
He charged chapmen · to chasten here children,
And lete no wynnynge for-wene hem · the while thei ben ȝonge;

For ho so spareth the spring · spilleth hus children;
And so wrot the wise · to wissen us alle,   140
   Qui parcit uirge, odit filium.

And sitthe he preide prelates · and prestes to-geders,
That hij precheth to the puple · prouen hit hem-selue;

'Lyue ȝe as ȝe lereth 'ous · we shulleth leyue ȝow the bettere.'

C. 124. ful IMFSEG; wel P.   130. nude P.   131. stowe E; stone P.
136. he (*for* hue) P.   138. wile P.   140. wisen hus P.

A. PASSUS V. 37–39.   B. PASSUS V. 46–48.

And seththe he radde religioun · the rule for to holde—
'Leste the kyng and his counseil · ȝor comunes apeire,
And beo stiward in oure stude · til ȝe be stouwet betere.   39

From   [Gregory the grete clerke · a good pope in his tyme
A. xi.   Of religioun the rewele · he reherside in his morals,
201–203.   And seide it in ensaumple · that thei shulde do the betere:

And sithen he radde religioun · here reule to holde—
'Leste the kynge and his conseille · ȝowre comunes appayre,
And ben stuwardes of ȝowre stedes · til ȝe be ruled bettre.'   48

       [Gregorie the grete clerke · and the goed pope   292
       Of religioun the reule · reherseth in his morales,
       And seyth it in ensaumple · for thei schulde do there-after,
       'Whenne fissches failen the flode · or the fresche water,
       Thei deyen for drouthe · whanne thei drie ligge;   296
       Riȝt so, quod Gregorie · religioun roileth,
       Sterueth and stynketh · and steleth lordes almesses,
       That oute of couent and cloystre · coueyten to libbe.'
       For if heuene be on this erthe · and ese to any soule,   300
       It is in cloistere or in scole · be many skilles I fynde;
       For in cloistre cometh no man · to chide ne to fiȝte,
       But alle is buxumnesse there and bokes · to rede and to lerne.
       In scole there is scorne · but if a clerke wil lerne,   304
From   And grete loue and lykynge · for eche of hem loueth other.
B. x.   Ac now is religioun a ryder · a rowmer bi stretes,
292–320.   A leder of louedayes · and a londe-bugger,
       A priker on a palfray · fro manere to manere,   308
       An heep of houndes at his ers · as he a lorde were.
       And but if his knaue knele · that shal his cuppe brynge,
       He loureth on hym and axeth hym · who tauȝte hym curteisye?
       Litel had lordes to done · to ȝyue londe fram her heires   312
       To religious, that haue no reuthe · though it reyne on her auteres.
       In many places ther hij persones ben · be hem-self at ese,
       Of the pore haue thei no pite · and that is her charite;
       Ac thei leten hem as lordes · her londe lith so brode.   316
       Ac there shal come a kyng · and confesse ȝow religiouses,
       And bete ȝow as the bible telleth · for brekynge of ȝowre reule,
       And amende monyales · monkes and chanouns,
       And putten hem to her penaunce · *ad pristinum statum ire*, 320

C. 144. P *om.* he.   145. apeyere P.   146. stewed F; stuede P; stuyd S; stywed G; stowed I.   149. wenne P.   150. dryen P.   154. in a cloistre P.   156. lykyng EIMF; lokynge P.   158. yholde EG; holde P.   159. *This line is from* MIFSG; P *om.*   160. to IM; in-to P.   162. but

	Whanne fisshes faile the flood · or the fresshe watir,	
	Thei diʒe for the drouʒte · whanne thei dreiʒe lengen;	
From	Riʒt so be religioun · it roileth and steruith,	206
A. xi.	That out of couent and cloistre · coueiten to libben.'	
204-210.	Ac now is religioun a ridere · and a rennere aboute,	
	A ledere of louedayes · and a lond-biggere,	
	Poperith on a palfrey · to toune and to toune.]	210

And sitthe he radde religion · here ruele to holde,   144
'Leste the kyng and hus consail · ʒoure comunes a-peyre,
And be stywardes of ʒoure stedes · til ʒe be stewed betere.
  Gregorie the grete clerk · gart write in bokes
The ruele of alle religious · ryghtful and obedient.   148
Right as fisshes in flod · whenne hem faileth water,
Deyen for drouthe · whenne thei drye liggen,
Ryght so religion · roteth and steruteh,
That out of couent and cloistre · coueyteth to dwelle.   152
For yf heuene be on thys erthe · other eny eyse for saule,
Hit is in cloistre other in scole · by meny skyles ich fynde.
For in cloistre cometh no man · to chide ne to fighte;
In scole ys loue and lownesse · and lykyng to lerne.   156
Ac meny day, men telleth · bothe monkes and chanouns
Han ride out of a-ray · here ruele vuel yholde,
Lederes of louedaies · and landes purchassed,
And priked a-boute on palfrais · fro places to maners,   160
An hepe of houndes at hus ers · as he a lord were;
And but hus knaue knele · that shal hus coppe holde,
He loketh al louryng · and 'lordein' hym calleth.
Lytel hadde lordes a-do · to ʒeue londe fro here aires   164
To religious, that han no reuthe · thauh hit reyne on here auters.
In places ther thei persons beth · by hem-self at ese,
Of the poure han thei no pyte · that is here pure charite.
ʒe leten ʒow alle as lordes · ʒoure londe lyth to brode.   168
Ac ʒut shal come a kyng · and confesse ʒow alle,
And bete ʒow, as the byble telleth · for brekyng of ʒoure reule,
And amende ʒow monkes · moniales, and chanons,
And putte ʒow to ʒoure penaunce · *ad pristinum statum ire.* 172

MFS; bit P.   163. loureng P.   lordein IME; lorden P.   165. religious IMFSE; religion P.   ryne P.   on IMFSG; in P.   167. his (*for* is) P. poure (*for* pure) P.

128   **A. PASSUS V. 40, 41.   B. PASSUS V. 49–60.**

And ȝe that secheth seynt Iame · and seintes at Roome,   40
Secheth seint Treuthe · for he may sauen ow alle;

From
B. x.
321–329.

And barounes with erles beten hem · thorugh *beatus virres* techynge,
That here barnes claymen · and blame ȝow foule:
   Hij in curribus, et hij in equis; ipsi obligati sunt, &c.
And thanne freres in here freitoure · shal fynden a keye ·
Of Constantynes coffres · in which is the catel   324
That Gregories god-children · han yuel dispended.
And thanne shal the abbot of Abyndoun · and alle his issu for euere
Haue a knokke of a kyng · and incurable the wounde.
That this worth soth, seke ȝe · that oft ouer-seˑ the bible:
   *Quomodo cessauit exactor, quieuit tributum; contriuit
   dominus baculum impiorum, et virgam dominancium
   cedencium plaga insanabili, &c.*
Ac ar that kynge come · Cayme shal awake.]   329

And sithen he conseilled the kynge · the comune to louye,
'It is thi tresore, if tresoun ne were · and triacle at thi nede.'

And sithen he prayed the pope · haue pite onˑ holicherche,
And er he gyue any grace · gouerne firste hym-selue.   52
  'And ȝe that han lawes to kepe · late treuthe be ȝowre
    coueytise,
More than golde or other gyftes · if ȝe wil god plese;
For who-so contrarieth treuthe · he telleth in the gospel,
That god knoweth hym nouȝte · ne no seynte of heuene,   56
   Amen dico vobis, nescio vos.
And ȝe that seke seynte Iames · and seintes of Rome,
Seketh seynt Treuthe · for he may saue ȝow alle;
Qui cum patre et filio · that feire hem bifalle
That suweth my sermon;' · and thus seyde Resoun.   60

C. 174. fretour P.   176. costantyn P.   177. ys (*for* hys) P.   178.
wonde P.   180. *Read* kirke.   190. he IMSEG; ȝe P.   hoþer P.
194. ouere.   199. Seicheþ P.

Qui cum patre et filio · feire mote you falle.'

And barons and here barnes · blame ʒow and reproue;
    *Hii in curribus et hi in equis: ipsi obligati sunt, et
    ceciderunt.*
Freres in here freitour · shulle fynde that tyme
Bred with-oute beggynge · to lyue by euere after,
And Constantyn shal be here cook · and couerer of here
    churche.   176
For the abbot of Engelonde · and the abbesse hys nece
Shullen haue a knok on here crounes · and in-curable the
    wounde;
    *Contriuit dominus baculum impiorum, uirgam domınancium,
    plaga in-sanabili.*
Ac er that kyng come · as cronycles me tolde,
Clerkus and holychurche · shal be clothed newe.   180
And sitthe he consailed the kyng · hus comune to louye;
For the comune ys the kynges tresour · conscience wot wel,
And al-so,' quath Reson · 'ich rede ʒow riche,
And comuners to a-corden · in alle kynne treuthe.   184
Let no kynne consail · ne couetyse ʒow departe,
That on wit and on wil · alle ʒoure wardes kepe.
Lo! in heuene an hy · was an holy comune,
Til Lucifer the lyere · leyued that hym-selue   188
Were wittyour and worthiour · than he that was hus maister.
Hold ʒow in vnite · and he that other wolde
Ys cause of alle combraunce · to confounde a reame.'
And sitthen he preide the pope · haue pyte of holy-churche,
And no grace to graunte · til good loue were   193
Among alle kynne kynges · ouer cristene puple:
'Comaunde that alle confessours · that eny kynge shryueth,
Enioynye hem pees for here penaunce · and perpetuel forʒeuenesse
Of alle manere acciouns · and eche man loue other.   197
And ʒe that secheth seint Iame · and seyntes of Rome,
Secheth seint Treuthe · in sauacion of ʒoure saules:
Qui cum patre et filio, · that faire hem by-falle   200
That suweth my sarmon' · and thus ended Reson.

    Hic explicit passus sextus.

A. PASSUS V. 43-48.   B. PASSUS V. 61-71.

Thenne ron Repentaunce · and rehersed this teeme,
And made William to weope · watur with his eȝen.   44
Pernel Proud-herte · platte hire to grounde,
And lay longe ar heo lokede · and to vr ladi criede,
And beo-hiȝte to him · that vs alle maade,
Heo wolde vn-souwen hire smok · and setten ther an here   48

Thanne ran Repentance · and reherced his teme,
And gert Wille to wepe · water with his eyen.

SUPERBIA.

Peronelle Proude-herte · platte hir to the erthe,
And lay longe ar she loked · and 'lorde, mercy!' cryed,   64
And byhiȝte to hym · that vs alle made,
She shulde vnsowen hir serke · and sette there an heyre
To affaiten hire flesshe · that fierce was to synne :
'Shal neuere heiȝe herte me hente · but holde me lowe,   68
And suffre to be myssayde— · and so did I neuere.
But now wil I meke me · and mercy biseche,
For al this I haue · hated in myne herte.'

C. N.B. *The errors in* P, *involving misuse of* h, *are henceforth silently corrected.*   6. vnsywe P.   8. heigh I; hy FS; hi M; myn P.   10. muke P.   21. and al my wit P.   vuel (*for* yuel) P; *see* l. 20.   22. P *om.* ich.

A. PASSUS V. 49–53. C. PASSUS VII. 1–26. 131

Forte fayten hire flesch · that frele was to synne:
'Schal neuer liht herte me hente · bote holde me lowe,
And suffre to beo mis-seid— · and so dude I neuere.
And nou I con wel meke me · and merci be-seche　52
Of al that ichaue i-had · envye in myn herte.'

PASSUS VII.

Incipit passus septimus.

WITH that ran Repentaunce · and reherced hus teme,
And made Wille to wepe · water with hus eyen.
Purnele Proute-herte · platte hure to the erthe,
Longe was er hue loked vp · and 'lord, mercy,' criede,　4
And by-highte to hym · that ous alle made,
Hue sholde vnsowen hure smok · and sette ther an heire,
To afaiten hure flesch · that fers was to synne.
'Shal neuere heigh herte me hente · bote holde me lowe,　8
And suffre to be myssaide · and so dude ich neuere.
Bote now wolle ich meke me · and mercy by-seche
Of alle that ich haue · yhated in myn herte.'
'Repente the,' quath Repentaunce · 'as Reson the tauhte,　12
And shryf the sharpliche · and shak of alle pruyde.'—

CONFESSIO SUPERBIE.

'Ich, Pruyde, pacientliche · penaunce ich aske;
For ich formest and ferst · to fader and to moder
Haue ybe vnboxome · ich biseche god of mercy;　16
And vnboxome ybe · nouht a-baissed to a-gulte
God and alle good men · so gret was myn herte;
In-obedient to holy churche · and to hem that ther seruen;
Demed for hure yuel vices · and excited othere　20
Thorw my word and my wit · hure yuel workes to shewe;
And scorned hem and othere · yf ich a skyle founde,
Lauhynge al a-loude · for lewede men sholde
Wene that ich were witty · and wyser than a-nothere;　24
Scorner and vnskilful · to hem that skil shewede,
In alle manere maners · my name to be yknowe;

K 2

[*Not in* **A**-*text.*]

From
B. xiii.
278-284.

[As in aparaile and in porte · proude amonges the peple,
Otherwyse than he hath · with herte or sy3te shewynge;
Hym willynge that alle men wende · he were that he is nou3te.
For-why he bosteth and braggeth · with many bolde othes, 281
And in-obedient to ben vndernome · of any lyf lyuynge,
And so syngulere by-hymself · as to sy3te of the poeple,
Was none suche as hym-self · ne none so pope-holy.] 284

From
B. xiii.
292-313.

[Wilnyng that men wende . his witte were the best, 292
Or for his crafty kunnynge · or of clerkes the wisest,
Or strengest on stede · or styuest vnder gurdel,
And louelokest to loken on · and lelest of werkes,
And non so holy as he · ne of lif clennere, 296
Or feyrest of feytures ' of fourme and of schafte,
And most sotyl of songe · other sleyest of hondes,
And large to lene · losse there-by to cacche;
And if he gyueth ou3te pore gomes · telle what he deleth; 300
Pore of possessioun · in purse and in coffre,
And as a lyon on to loke · and lordeliche of speche.
Baldest of beggeres · a bostour that nou3t hath,
In towne and in tauernes · tales to telle, 304
And segge thinge that he neuere seigh · and for soth sweren it;
Of dedes that he neuere dyd · demen and bosten,
And of werkes that he wel dyd · witnesse and seggen—
'Lo! if 3e leue me nou3t · or that I lye wenen, 308
Axeth at hym or at hym · and he 3ow can telle,
What I suffred and seighe · and some tymes hadde,
And what I couthe and knewe · and what kynne I come of.'
Al he wolde that men wiste · of werkes and of wordes, 312
Which my3te plese the peple · and praysen hymseluen:
*Si hominibus placerem, Christi seruus non essem;
Et alibi: nemo potest duobus dominis seruire.*]

C. 27. Semeng P.   32. Me wilnynge *must be right*; *cf.* Hym willnynge, *the reading of* R *for* Hym willynge *in* B. xiii. 280; *miswritten* Me wynnynge I; Me wilned PESG.   P *om*. as.   35. -nemynge P.   36. singeler P.
37. pope F; pop IMSG; pomp P.   38. in on M; on a P.   on anoþer P.
43. my stede P.   44. lykynggest P.   51. þouhte P.   58. and MF; and of IS; of P.   60. P *om*. be.

[*Not in* **A**-*text.*]

Semyng a souereyn on · wher-so me by-fulle
To telle eny tale · ich trowede me wiser 28
To carpen other to counsaile · than eny lered other lewede.
Prout of aparail · in porte amonge the puple
Other-wise than ich haue · with-ynne other with-oute,
Me wilnynge that men wende · ich were, as in aueyr, 32
Riche, and resonable · and ryghtful of lyuynge,
Bostynge and braggynge · wyth meny bolde othes,
Auauntyng vp-on my veine glorie · for eny vndernymynge;
And ȝut so synguler by my-self · as to sight of the puple, 36
Was non suche as my-self · ne non so pope-holy,
Som tyme in on secte · som tyme in another;
In alle kynne couetyse · contreuede how ich myghte
Be holde for holy · an hondred sithe, by that encheison; 40
Wilnede that men wende · my werkes were the beste,
And konnyngest of my craft · clerkes other othere,
And strengest vp-on stede · and styuest vnder gurdell,
And louelokest to loken on · and lykyngest a bedde; 44
And lykynge of such a lif · that no lawe preyseth,
Prout of my faire fetours · and for ich songe shulle.
And what ich gaf for godes loue · to god-sybbes ich tolde.
Thei to wene that ich were · wel holy and wel almesful, 48
And non so bold beggere · to bydden and craue;
Tales to telle · in tauernes and in stretes,
Thyng that neuere was thouht · and ȝut ich swor ich sauh hit,
And lyed on my lykame · and on my lyf bothe. 52
Of werkes that ich wel dude · wittnesse ich take,
And sygge to suche · that sytten me by-syde,
'Lo, yf ȝe leyue me nouht · other that ȝe wene ich lye,
Aske of hym other of hure · and thei conne ȝow telle 56
What ich soffrede and seih · and som tyme hadde,
And what ich knew and couthe · and what kyn ich kam of;'—
Al ich wolde that men wuste · when hit to pruyde sounede,
As to be preised a-mong the puple · thauh ich poure semede:
    Si hominibus placerem, Christi seruus non essem.
    Nemo potest duobus dominis seruire.'
'Now god of hus goodnesse · geue the grace to amende,' 61
Quath Repentaunce ryght with that; · and thenne roos Enuye.

A. PASSUS V. 54-63.   B. PASSUS V. 72-93.

Lechour seide 'allas!' · and to vr ladi criede
To maken him han merci · for his misdede,
Bitwene god almihti · and his pore soule,   56
With-that he schulde the Seterday · seuen ȝer after
Drinken bote with the doke · and dynen but ones.
Envye with heui herte · asket aftur schrift,
And gretliche his gultus · bi-ginneth to schewe.   60
As pale as a pelet · in a palesye he seemede,
I-clothed in a caurimauri · I couthe him not discreue;
A kertil and a courtepy · a knyf be his side;

LUXURIA.

Thanne Lecchoure seyde 'allas!' · and on owre lady he
    cryed,   72
To make mercy for his mis-dedes · bitwene god and his
    soule,
With that he shulde the Saterday · seuene ȝere there-after,
Drynke but myd the doke · and dyne but ones.

INUIDIA.

Enuye with heuy herte · asked after schrifte,   76
And carefullich *mea culpa* · he comsed to shewe.
He was as pale as a pelet · in the palsye he semed,
And clothed in a caurimaury · I couthe it nouȝte discreue;
In kirtel and kourteby · and a knyf bi his syde,   80
Of a freres frokke · were the forsleues.
And as a leke hadde yleye · longe in the sonne,
So loked he with lene chekes · lourynge foule.
His body was to-bolle for wratthe · that he bote his lippes,
And wryngynge he ȝede with the fiste · to wreke hymself he
    thouȝte   85
With werkes or with wordes · whan he seighe his tyme.
Eche a worde that he warpe · was of an addres tonge,
Of chydynge and of chalangynge · was his chief lyflode, 88
With bakbitynge and bismer · and beryng of fals witnesse;
This was al his curteisye · where that euere he shewed hym.
    'I wolde ben yshryue,' quod this schrewe · 'and I for shame
       durst;
I wolde be gladder, bi god · that Gybbe had meschaunce, 92
Than thouȝe I had this woke ywonne · a weye of Essex chese.

A. PASSUS V. 64–73.   C. PASSUS VII. 63–68.

Of a freris frokke · were the fore-sleuys.   64
As a leek that hedde i-leȝen · longe in the sonne,
So loked he with lene chekes ; · lourede he foule.
His bodi was bolled · for wraththe he bot his lippes.
Wrothliche he wrong his fust · he thouȝte him a-wreke   68
With werkes or with wordes · whon he seiȝ his tyme.
'Venim or vernisch · or vinegre, I trouwe,
Walleth in my wombe · or waxeth, ich wene.
I ne mihte mony day don · as a mon ouhte,   72
Such wynt in my wombe · waxeth, er I dyne.

From
C. vii.
170–174.

[Thenne seide Lecherie 'alas!' · and to oure lady cryede,
'Lady, to thy leue sone · lowte for me nouthe,
That he haue pyte on me putour · of hus pure grace and mercy,
With that ich shal,' quath that shrewe · 'Saterdayes, for thy loue,
Drynke bote with the douke · and dyne bote ones.]

CONFESSIO INUIDIE.

Enuye with heuy herte · asked after shrifte,
And criede '*mea culpa*' · corsynge alle hus enemys.   64
Hus clothes were of corsement · and of kene wordes ;

He wroth hus fust vp-on Wratthe · hadde he wysshes at wille,
Sholde no lyf lyuye · that on hus londe passede.

Chidynge and Ianglyng . that was hus chef lyflode,   68

A. 58. dyne TU ; eten VH ; *read* dynen.   63 64. *From* THU ; V *omits*
these lines.   73. dye (*for* dyne) V.   **B.** 76. scrifte L.   **C.** 68.
Ianglenge P.

Ichaue a neihȝebor me neih · I haue anuyȝed him ofte,
Ablamed him be-hynde his bak · to bringe him in disclaundre,
And peired him bi my pouwer · i-punissched him ful ofte,   76
Bi-lowen him to lordes · to make him leose seluer,
I-don his frendes ben his fon · with my false tonge;
His grase and his good hap · greueth me ful sore.
   Bitwene him and his meyne · ichaue i-mad wraththe,   80
Bothe his lyf and his leome · was lost thorw my tonge.
Whon I mette him in the market · that I most hate,
Ich heilede him as hendely · as I his frend weore.
He is douȝtiore then I · i dar non harm don him.   84
Bote hedde I maystrie and miht · I mortherde him for euere!
   Whon I come to the churche · and knele bi-fore the roode,

I haue a neighbore neyȝe me · I haue ennuyed hym ofte,
And lowen on hym to lordes · to don hym lese his siluer,
And made his frendes ben his foon · thorw my false tonge;   96
His grace and his good happes · greueth me ful sore.
Bitwene many and many · I make debate ofte,
That bothe lyf and lyme · is lost thorw my speche.
And whan I mete him in market · that I moste hate,   100
I hailse hym hendeliche · as I his frende were;
For he is douȝtier than I · I dar do non other.
Ac hadde I maystrye and myȝte · god wote my wille!
   And whan I come to the kirke · and sholde knele to the
      rode,   104
And preye for the poeple · as the prest techeth,
For pilgrimes and for palmers · for alle the poeple after,
Thanne I crye on my knees · that Cryste ȝif hem sorwe
That beren awey my bolle · and my broke schete.   108
   Awey fro the auter thanne · turne I myn eyghen,
And biholde how Eleyne · hath a newe cote;
I wisshe thanne it were myne · and al the webbe after.
And of mennes lesynge I laughe · that liketh myn herte;
And for her wynnynge I wepe · and waille the tyme,   113
And deme that hij don ille · there I do wel worse;
Who-so vndernymeth me here-of · I hate hym dedly after.
I wolde that vche a wyght · were my knaue,   116
For who-so hath more than I · that angreth me sore.
And thus I lyue louelees · lyke a luther dogge,

A. PASSUS V. 87–98. (NOT IN C-TEXT.) 137

And scholde preiȝe for the peple · as the prest vs techeth,
Thenne I crie vppon my knes · that Crist ȝiue hem serwe   88
That hath i-bore a-wei my bolle · and my brode schete.
   From the auter I turne · myn eiȝe, and bi-holde
Hou Heyne hath a newe cote · and his wyf another;
Thenne I wussche hit weore myn · and al the web aftur.   92
Of his leosinge I lauhwe · hit liketh me in myn herte;
Ac for his wynnynge I wepe · and weile the tyme.
   I deme men that don ille · and ȝit I do wel worse,
For I wolde that vch a wiht · in this world were mi knaue,   96
And who-so hath more thanne I · that angrith myn herte.
   Thus I liue loueles · lyk a luther dogge,

[*Not in* C-*text.*]

A. 83. as—frend THU; his frend as I V.   97. *From* THU; V *omits this line.*   B. 105. pople L; *see next line.*   108. beren W; baren C; bar L.

138   A. PASSUS V. 99–102.   B. PASSUS V. 119–130.

That al my breste bolleth · for bitter of my galle;
May no suger so swete · a-swagen hit vnnethe,   100
Ne no *diopendion* · dryue hit from myn herte;
ȝif schrift schulde hit thenne swopen out · a gret wonder hit were.'

That al my body bolneth · for bitter of my galle.

From B. xiii. 325–342.

[And blame men bihynde her bakke · and bydden hem meschaunce;
And that he wist bi Wille · tellen it Watte,
And that Watte wiste · Wille wiste it after,
And made of frendes foos · thorugh a false tonge,   328
'Or with myȝte of mouthe · or thorugh mannes strengthe
Auenge me fele tymes · other frete my-selue
Wyth-inne, as a shepster shere' · I-shrewed men and cursed!
   Cuius malediccione os plenum est, et amaritudine ;
   Sub lingua eius labor et dolor :
   Et alibi : filij hominum, dentes eorum arma et sagitte,
   Et lingua eorum gladius acutus :—
'There is no lyf that I louye · lastyng any while,   332
For tales that I telle · no man trusteth to me;
And whan I may nouȝt haue the maistrye · with malencolye I take,
That I cacche the crompe · the cardiacle some tyme,
Or an ague in suche an angre · and some tyme a feure,   336
That taketh me al a twelfmoneth · tyl that I dispyse
Lechecrafte of owre lorde · and leue on a wicche,
And segge, that no clerke ne can · ne Cryste, as I leue,
To the souter of Southwerke · or of Shordyche dame Emme! 340
And segge, that no goddes worde · gaf me neuere bote,
But thorw a charme had I chaunce · and my chief hele!']

I myȝte nouȝte eet many ȝeres · as a man ouȝte,   120
For enuye and yuel wille · is yuel to defye;
May no sugre ne swete thinge · asswage my swellynge,
Ne no *diapenidion* · dryue it fro myne herte,
Ne noyther schrifte ne shame · but ho-so schrape my mawe?'

'ȝus, redili,' quod Repentaunce · and radde hym to the beste,
'Sorwe of synnes · is sauacioun of soules.'

'I am sori,' quod that segge · 'I am but selde other,
And that maketh me thus megre · for I ne may me venge. 128
Amonges burgeyses haue I be · dwellynge at Londoun,
And gert bakbitinge be a brocoure · to blame mennes ware.

A. 102. schrit V.   C. 71. hit to wille P.   74. tymes IMSG;

A. PASSUS V. 103-106. C. PASSUS VII. 69-96.

'3us, rediliche,' quod Repentaunce · and radde him to goode,
'Serw for heore sunnes · saueth men ful monye.'   104
'Icham sori,' quod Envye · 'I ne am but seldene other,
And that maketh me so mad · for I ne may me venge.'

And blame men by-hynde hure bak · and bidde hem meschaunce.
Al that he wiste by Wylle · to Watkyn he told hit,
And that he wiste by Watkyn · tolde hit Wille after;
And made foos of frendes · thorw fals and fykel tonge :   72
'Other thorw myghte of mouthe · other thorw meny sleyghthes
Venged me fele tymes · other brend my-self with-ynne
Lyke a shappesters sheres · and shrewede myn emcristyne,
A3ens the consail of Crist · as clerkes fynden in bokes : 76
    *Cuius maledictione os plenum est et amaritudine et dolo : sub
    lingua eius labor et dolor.*
    *Filij hominum, dentes eorum arma et sagitte, et lingua eorum
    gladius acutus.*
Whenne ich ne may haue the maistrie · suche malancolie ich take,
That ich cacche the crampe · the cardiacle som tyme,
Other an ague in suche an angre · and som tyme a feuere,
That taketh me al a twelfmonthe · til that ich dispice   80
Leche-craft of oure lorde · and leyue on a wicche,
And sigge that no clerk can · ne Crist, as ich leyue,
To the souter of South-werk · such is hus 'grace.
For god, ne godes wordes · ne grace ne halp neuere,   84
Bote thorw a charme hadde ich a chaunce · and my chief hele.
  Ich myghte nat ete meny 3er · as a man auhte,
For enuye and vuel wil · ys vuel to defye.
May no suger ne swete thyng · a-swage my swellynges,   88
Ne dereworthe drynke · dryuen hit fro myn herte,
Neyther shame ne shrift · bote ho so shraped my mawe?'
  '3us, redilyche,' quath Repentaunce · 'and thow be ryght sory,
For thy synne soueraynliche · by-sechyng god of mercy.'   92
  'Ich am euere sory,' sayde Enuye · 'ich am bote selde other ;
That maketh me so megre · for ich ne may me auenge.
3ut am ich brocor of bakbytynge : and blame mennes ware
A-mong marchauns many tymes · nameliche in Londoun ;   96

---

tyme P.   *For* brend *read* fret.   76. P om. *et dolo*.   80. twelfmonnthe P.
95. baggebytynge P.

[*Not in* **A**-*text.*]

Whan he solde and I nou3te · thanne was I redy 131
To lye and to loure on my neighbore · and to lakke his chaffare.

I wil amende this, 3if I may · thorw my3te of God almy3ty.'

IRA.

Now awaketh Wratthe · with two whyte eyen,
And nyuelynge with the nose · and his nekke hangynge.
'I am Wrath,' quod he · 'I was sum tyme a frere, 136
And the couentes gardyner · for to graffe ympes;
On limitoures and listres · lesynges I ymped,
Tyl thei bere leues of low speche · lordes to plese,
And sithen thei blosmed obrode · in boure to here shriftes. 140
And now is fallen ther-of a frute · that folke han wel leuere
Schewen her schriftes to hem · than shryue hem to her persones.

And now persones han parceyued · that freres parte with hem,
Thise possessioneres preche · and depraue freres, 144
And freres fyndeth hem in defaute · as folke bereth witnes,
That whan thei preche the poeple · in many place aboute,
I, Wrath, walke with hem · and wisse hem of my bokes.
Thus thei speken of spiritualte · that eyther despiseth other, 148
Til thei be bothe beggers · and by my spiritualte libben,
Or elles alle riche · and riden aboute.
I, Wrath, rest neuere · that I ne moste folwe
This wykked folke · for suche is my grace. 152
I haue an aunte to nonne · and an abbesse bothe,
Hir were leuere swowe or swelte · than soeffre any peyne.

B. 143. han. W; L. *om.*   C. 111. me IMFEG; men P.   grucched

[*Not in* **A**-*text.*]

Whanne he solde and ich noght · thenne was ich a-redy
To lye and to loury · and to lacke myn neghebores,
Here werkes, here wordes · wher-so ich sete.
Now hit a-thynketh me in thouht · that euere ich so wrouhte;
Lord, er ich lyf lete · for loue of thy-selue, 101
Graunte me, goode lorde · grace of amendement.'

CONFESSIO IRE.

Thenne a-waked Wratthe · with to white eyen,
With a nyuylynge nose · nyppyng hus lyppes. 104
'Ich am Wratthe,' quath that wye · 'wol gladliche smyte
Bothe with ston and with staf · and stele vp-on myn enemy;
For to slee hym slehliche · slehthes ich by-thenke.
Thauh ich sytte thys seuen ʒer · ich sholde nat wel telle 108
The harme that ich haue idon · with hand and with tonge.
Vnpacient in alle penaunces · and pleyned, as hit were,
On god, whenne me greued ouht · and grucched of hus sonde,
As, som tyme in somer · and al-so in heruest, 112
Bote ich hadde wedir at my wil · ich wited god the cause,
In alle manere angres · that ich hadde other felede.
A-monges alle manere men · my dwellyng ys som tyme,
With lered and with lewede · that leef ben to hure 116
Harm of eny man · by-hynde other by-fore.
Freres folowen my vore · fele tyme and ofte,
And prouen vnparfit · prelates of holy churche;
And prelates pleynen of hem · for thei here parshenes shryuen
With-oute lycence and leue · and herby lyueth wratthe. 121
Thus thei speke and dispute · that eche dispiseth other.
Thus beggers and barouns · at debat aren ofte,
Til ich, Wratth, waxe an hyh · and walke with hem bothe; 124
Other til bothe be beggers · and by spiritualte lybben,
Or alle riche thus ride · rest shal ich nauht, Wratthe,
That ich ne mot folwy this folk · my fortune ys non other.
    Ich haue an aunte to a nunne · and to an abbodesse; 128
Hem were leuere swouny other swelte · than suffry eny peyne.

IES; grucche P.   114. In IMFSG; And P.   116. leef FS; lef E; luf P.
118. folowen E; folewen M; folwen I; flowen P.   129. sounye (*for* swouny) P.

[*Not in* **A**-*text*.]

    I haue be cook in hir kichyne · and the couent serued
Many monthes with hem · and with monkes bothe.   156
I was the priouresses potagere · and other poure ladyes,
And made hem ioutes of iangelynge · that dame Iohanne was
    a bastard,
And dame Clarice a kni3tes dou3ter · ac a kokewolde was hire
    syre,
And dame Peronelle a prestes file · priouresse worth she
    neuere,   160
For she had childe in chirityme · al owre chapitere it wiste.

    Of wykked wordes I, Wrath · here wortes i-made,
Til 'thow lixte' and 'thow lixte' · lopen oute at ones,
And eyther hitte other · vnder the cheke;   164
Hadde thei had knyues, bi Cryst · her eyther had killed other.
    Seynt Gregorie was a gode pope · and had a gode forwit,
That no priouresse were prest · for that he ordeigned.
Thei had thanne ben *infamis* the firste day · thei can so yuel
    hele conseille.   168

    Amonge monkes I mi3te be · ac many tyme I shonye;
For there ben many felle frekis · my feres to aspye,
Bothe prioure an supprioure · and owre *pater abbas;*
And if I telle any tales · thei taken hem togyderes,   172
And do me faste Frydayes · to bred and to water,
And am chalanged in the chapitelhous · as I a childe were,
And baleised on the bare ers · and no breche bitwene;
For-thi haue I no lykyng · with tho leodes to wonye.   176
I ete there vnthende fisshe · and fieble ale drynke;
Ac other while, whan wyn cometh · whan I drynke wyn at eue,
I haue a fluxe of a foule mouthe · wel fyue dayes after.

    C. 135. he (*for* hue) P; *see* l. 136.   138. lixt EIMFS; luxt P.   149.

[*Not in* **A**-*text.*]

Ich haue be cook in here kychene · and the couent serued
Meny monthes with hem · and with monkes bothe.
Ich was the prioresse potager · and other poure ladies,   132
And made here ioutes of iangles; · · 'dame Iohane was a bastarde,
And dame Clarice a knyghtes douhter · a cokewold was hure syre,
Dame Purnele a prestes file · prioresse worth hue neuere;
For hue hadde a childe in the chapon-cote · hue worth chalenged
    at eleccion.'   136
Thus thei sitte, tho sustres · som tyme, and disputen,
Til 'thow lixt' and 'thow lixt' · · be lady ouer hem alle;
And thenne a-wake ich, Wratthe · and wold be auenged.
Thanne ich crie and cracche · with my kene nailes,   140
Bothe byte and bete · and brynge forth suche thewes,
That alle ladies me lothen · that louen eny worschep.
Among wyues and wodewes · ich am ywoned sitte
Yparroked in puwes; · the person hit knoweth   144
How lytel ic louye · Letice at the style;
For hue hadde haly bred er ich · myn herte by-gan to chaunge.
After-ward after mete · hue and ich chidde,
And ich, Wratth, was war · and wroth on hem both,   148
Til aither cleped othere 'hore' · and of with the clothes,
Til bothe here heuedes were bar · and blody here chekes.

A-mong monkes myght ich be · ac meny tyme ich spare,
For ther beth meny felle frekus · myne afferes to aspye;   152
That ys, the priour and the suppriour · and oure *pater abbas.*
And yf ich telle eny tales · thei taken hem to-geders,
And don me faste Fridaies · to bred and to water.
ȝut am ich chalenged in chapitele-hous · as ich a childe were,
And baleysed on the bar ers · and no breche bytwyne.   157
Ich haue no lust, leyue me · to lenge a-mong monkes;
For hij eteth more fisch than flesh · and feble ale drynken.
Ac other-while whanne wyn cometh · and whenne ich drynke
    late,   160
Ich haue a flux of a foul mouth · wel fyf dayes after.

---

cleped—hore IMFSG; cliped oþere P.   157. in (*for* on) P.   159. drenken P; *see* l. 166.

[*Not in* **A**-*text.*]

Al the wikkednesse that I wote · bi any of owre bretheren 180
I couth it in owre cloistre · that al owre couent wote it.'
'Now repent the,' quod Repentaunce · 'and reherce thow
    neure
Conseille that thow cnowest · bi contenaunce ne bi riȝte;
And drynke nouȝte ouer delicatly · ne to depe noyther,   184
That thi wille bi cause ther-of · to wrath myȝte torne.
Esto sobrius,' he seyde · and assoilled me after,
And bad me wilne to wepe · my wikkednesse to amende.

From   [Thanne Lecchoure seyde 'allas!' · and on owre lady he cryed,
B. v.   To make mercy for his mis-dedes · bitwene god and his soule,
72-75   With that he shulde the Saterday · seuene ȝere there-after,
(p. 134).   Drynke but myd the doke · and dyne but ones.]

            [With lykyng of lecherye · as by lokyng of his eye.
            For vche a mayde that he mette · he made hir a signe
            Semynge to synne-ward · and some tyme he gan taste
From   Aboute the mouth, or bynethe · begynneth to grope,   347
B. xiii.   Tyl eytheres wille waxeth kene · and to the werke ȝeden,
344-352. As wel in fastyng-days and frydayes · and forboden nyȝtes;
            And as wel in Lente as oute of Lente · alle tymes ylyche,
            Suche werkes with hem · were neuer oute of sesoun;   351
            Tyl thei myȝte namore · and thanne had merye tales.]

C. 166. dupe P.   178. made to hure P.   182. as IE; and P.   194.
lecherous MF; lecherye P.

C. PASSUS VII. 162–195.

[*Compare* A. V. 54–58; p. 134.]

Al that ich wiste wickede · by eny of oure couent, 162
Ich cowede hit vp in oure cloistre · that al the couent wot hit.'
'Now repente the,' quath Repentaunce · 'and reherce neuere
What counsail that thow knowest · by contenaunce ne by speche.
And drynk nat ouer delicatliche · ne to depe neither, 166
That thy wil ne thy wit · to wratthe myghte turne.
Esto sobrius,' he seide · and a-soiled hym after,
And bad hym bidde to god · be hus help to amende. 169

CONFESSIO LUXURIE.

Thenne seide Lecherie 'alas!' · and to oure lady cryede,
'Lady, to thy leue sone · lowte for me nouthe,
That he haue pyte on me putour · of hus pure grace and
    mercy, 172
With that ich shal,' quath that shrewe · 'Saterdayes, for thy loue,
Drynke bote with the douke · and dyne bote ones.
Ich, gulty in gost · to god ich me shryue
As in lykynge of lecherie · my licames gultes, 176
In wordes, in wedes · in waitynge of eyen.
To eche maide that ich mette · ich made hure a sygne
Semynge to synne-warde · and somme gan ich taste
A-boute the mouthe, and by-nythe · by-gan ich to grope, 180
Til oure bothers wil was on; · to werke we 3eden
As wel fastyngdaies as Frydaies · and heye-feste euenes,
As luf in lente as oute of lente · alle tymes liche—
Suche werkus with ous · were neuere out of seson— 184
Til we myghte no more; · thanne hadde we murye tales
Of puterie and of paramours · and proueden thorw speches,
Handlynge and halsynge · and al-so thorw cussynge
Excitynge oure aither other · til oure olde synne; 188
Sotilede songes · and sende out olde baudes
For to wynne to my wil · wommen with gyle;
By sorcerye som tyme · and som tyme by maistrye.
Ich lay by the louelokeste · and loued hem neuere after. 192
Whenne ich was old and hor · and hadde lore that kynde,
Ich had lykynge to lauhe · of lecherous tales.
Now, lord, for thy leaute · of lechours haue mercy!'

L

Thenne com Couetyse · I couthe him not discreue,
So hungri and so holewe · sire Herui him loked. 108
He was bitel-brouwed · with twei blered ei3en,
And lyk a letherne pors · lullede his chekes;
In a toren tabart · of twelue wynter age;
But 3if a lous couthe lepe · I con hit not i-leue 112
Heo scholde wandre on that walk · hit was so thred-bare.
   'Ichaue ben couetous,' quod this caityf · 'I beknowe hit heere;
For sum tyme I seruede · Simme atte noke,

AUARICIA.

And thanne cam Coueytise · can I hym nou3te descryue 188
So hungriliche and holwe · sire Heruy hym loked.
He was bitelbrowed · and baberlipped also,
With two blered eyghen · as a blynde hagge;
And as a letheren purs · lolled his chekes, 192
Wel sydder than his chyn · thei chiueled for elde;
And as a bondman of his bacoun · his berde was bidraueled.
With an hode on his hed · a lousi hatte aboue,
And in a tauny tabarde · of twelue wynter age, 196
Al totorne and baudy · and ful of lys crepynge;
But if that a lous couthe · haue lopen the bettre,
She sholde nou3te haue walked on that welche · so was it thredebare.
   'I haue ben coueytouse,' quod this caityue · 'I biknowe it here; 200
For some tyme I serued · Symme atte stile,
And was his prentis ypli3te · his profit to wayte.
First I lerned to lye · a leef other tweyne,
Wikkedlich to weye · was my furst lessoun. 204
To Wy and to Wynchestre · I went to the faire,
With many manere marchandise · as my maistre me hi3te;
Ne had the grace of gyle · ygo amonge my ware,
It had be vnsolde this seuene 3ere · so me god helpe! 208
   Thanne drowe I me amonges draperes · my donet to lerne,
To drawe the lyser alonge · the lenger it semed;
Amonge the riche rayes . I rendred a lessoun,

B. 189. Heruy WO; Henri L.   C. 197. an (*for* and) P.   200. Wel

And was his pliht prentys · his profyt to loke. 116
Furst I leornede to ly3e · a lessun or tweyne,
And wikkedliche for to weie · was myn other lessun.
To Winchestre and to Wych · ich wente to the feire
With mony maner marchaundise · as my mayster hihte ; 120
Bote nedde the grace of gyle · i-gon a-mong my ware,
Hit hedde ben vn-sold this seuen 3er · so me god helpe !
Thenne I drou3 me a-mong this drapers · my donet to leorne,
To drawe the lyste wel along · the lengore hit semede ; 124
Among this riche rayes · lernde I a lessun,

CONFESSIO AUARICIE.

Thenne can Couetyse · ich can nat hym discryue, 196
So hongerliche and so holwe · Heruy hym-self lokede.
He was bytelbrowed and baberlupped · with two blery eyen,
And as a letherene pors · lollid hus chekus,
Wel sydder than hys chyn · ychiueled for elde : 200
As bondemenne bacon · hus berd was yshaue,
With hus hod on his heued · and hus hatte bothe ;
In a toren tabarde · of twelue wynter age ;

But 3if a lous couthe lepe · I leue hit, as y trowe, 204
He scholde not wandre on that welch · so was hit threde-bare.

'Ich haue be coueitous,' quath this caityf · 'ich byknow hit here.
For som tyme ich serued · Symme at the style,
And was his prentys yplyght · hus profyt to waite. 208
Furst ich lerned to lye · a lesyng other tweye ;
Wickedliche to weye · was my furst lesson.
To Wy and to Winchestre · ich wente to the faire
With many maner marchandises · as my maister heghte ; 212
Ne hadde the grace of gyle · gon among my ware,
Hit hadde ben vnsold thys seuen 3er · so me god helpe !
Ich drow me among drapers · my donet to lerne,
To drawe the lisure a-longe · the lenger it semed ; 216
Among the riche rayes · ich rendered a lesson,

IMFSEG ; Al P. 204, 205. *These lines are from* SIMFG ; P. *om.* 212.
P *om.* maner. maister MIFSEG ; maistres P.

148 A. PASSUS V. 126-135.   B. PASSUS V. 212-234.

Brochede hem with a pak-neelde · and pletede hem togedere,
Putte hem in a pressour · and pinnede hem ther-inne
Til ten ȝerdes other twelue · tolden out threttene.   128
  And my wyf at Westmunstre · that wollene cloth made,
Spak to the spinsters · for to spinne hit softe.
The pound that heo peysede by · peisede a quartrun more
Then myn auncel dude · whon I weyede treuthe.   132
  I bouhte hire barly · heo breuh hit to sulle;
Peni-ale and piriwhit · heo pourede to-gedere
For laborers and louh folk · that liuen be hem-seluen.

To broche hem with a pak-nedle · and plaited hem togyderes,
And put hem in a presse · and pynned hem therinne,   213
Tyl ten ȝerdes or twelue · hadde tolled out threttene.
  My wyf was a webbe · and wollen cloth made;
She spak to spynnesteres · to spynnen it oute.   216
Ac the pounde that she payed by · poised a quarteroun more
Than myne owne auncere · who-so weyȝed treuthe.
  I bouȝte hir barly-malte · she brewe it to selle,
Peny-ale and podyng-ale · she poured togideres   220
For laborers and for low folke; · that lay by hym-selue.
  The best ale lay in my boure · or in my bedchambre,
And who-so bummed ther-of · bouȝte it ther-after,
A galoun for a grote · god wote, no lesse;   224
And ȝit it cam in cupmel · this crafte my wyf vsed.
Rose the regratere · was hir riȝte name;
She hath holden hokkerye · al hire lyf-tyme.
  Ac I swere now, so the ik · that synne wil I lete,   228
And neuere wikkedliche weye · ne wikke chaffare vse,
But wenden to Walsyngham · and my wyf als,
And bidde the rode of Bromeholme · brynge me oute of dette.'
  'Repentedestow the euere,' quod Repentance · 'ne restitucioun
    madest?'   232
  'Ȝus, ones I was herberwed,' quod he · 'with an hep of
    chapmen,
I roos whan thei were arest · and yrifled here males.'

A. 131. by TU; VH *om.*   142. sothely HTU; V *om.*   **B.** 212.
pak-nedle WCO; bat-nedle L.   213. pynned C; pynnede O; pyned L.
214. hadde WOC; L *om.*   224. na L.   232. Repentedestow W;

A. PASSUS V. 136–145.   C. PASSUS VII. 218–236.

 The beste in the bed-chaumbre · lay bi the wowe,   136
Hose bummede therof · bouȝte hit ther-after,
A galoun for a grote · god wot, no lasse,
Whon hit com in cuppemel; · such craftes me vsede.
Rose the regratour · is hire rihte name;   140
Heo hath holden hoxtcrye · this elleuene wynter.
 Bote I swere nou sothely · that sunne wol I lete,
And neuere wikkedliche weye · ne fals chaffare vsen,
Bote weende to Walsyngham · and my wyf alse,   144
And bidde the rode of Bromholm · bringe me out of dette.'

To brochen hem with a batte-nelde · and bond hem togederes;
Ich putte hem in pressours · and pynned hem therynne,
Tyl ten ȝerdes other twelue · tilled out threttyne.   220
 My wif was a webbe · and wollen cloth made;
Hue spak to the spynnesters · to spynnen hit oute.
The pound that hue paiede hem by · peysed a quarter
More than myn auncel · whenne ich weied treuthe.   224
 Ich bouhte hure barliche · hue brew hit to selle,
Peny-ale and podyng-ale · hue pourede to-geders,
For laborers and lowe folke · that laye by hem-selue.
 The beste laye in my bour · and in my bed-chambre,   228
And who so bommede ther-of · he bouht yt ther-after,
A galon for a grote · and ȝut no grayth mesure,
Whanne it cam in coppe-mel; · this craft my wif vsede.
Rose the regratour · was hure ryght name;   232
Hue hath yholde hockerye · this eleuene wynter.'

 'Repentest thow neuere?' quath Repentaunce · 'ne restitucion
  madest?'
'Ȝus, ones,' quath he, 'ich was yherborwed · with an hep of
  chapmen;
Ich a-ros and rifled here males · whenne thei a reste were.' 236

Repentestow L. C. 220. ȝerdes IMFSE; ȝorde P. twlue (*sic*) P. 229.
P *om.* who. 233. þes (*for* þis) P. 235. hue (*for* he) P.

[*Not in* **A**-*text.*]

'That was no restitucioun,' quod Repentance · 'but a robberes thefte,
Thow haddest be better worthy · be hanged therfore 236
Than for al that · that thow hast here shewed.'
'I wende ryflynge were restitucioun,' quod he · 'for I lerned neuere rede on boke,
And I can no Frenche in feith · but of the ferthest ende of Norfolke.'
'Vsedestow euere vsurie,' quod Repentaunce · 'in alle thi lyf-tyme?' 240
'Nay, sothly,' he seyde · 'saue in my ȝouthe.
I lerned amonge Lumbardes · and Iewes a lessoun,
To wey pens with a peys · and pare the heuyest,
And lene it for loue of the crosse · to legge a wedde and lese it; 244
Suche dedes I did wryte · ȝif he his day breke.
I haue mo maneres thorw rerages · than thorw *miseretur et comodat.*
I haue lent lordes · and ladyes my chaffare,
And ben her brocour after · and bouȝte it my-self. 248
Eschaunges and cheuesances · with suche chaffare I dele,
And lene folke that lese wol · a lyppe at euery noble.
And with Lumbardes lettres · I ladde golde to Rome,
And toke it by taille here · and tolde hem there lasse.' 252
'Lentestow euere lordes · for loue of her mayntenaunce?'
'Ȝe, I haue lent lordes · loued me neuere after,
And haue ymade many a knyȝte · bothe mercere and drapere,
That payed neuere for his prentishode · nouȝte a peire gloues.' 256
'Hastow pite on pore men · that mote nedes borwe?'
'I haue as moche pite of pore men · as pedlere hath of cattes,
That wolde kille hem, yf he cacche hem myȝte · for coueitise of here skynnes.'
'Artow manlyche amonge thi neiȝbores · of thi mete and drynke?' 260
'I am holden,' quod he, 'as hende · as hounde is in kychyne,
Amonges my neighbores, namelich · such a name ich haue.'

[*Not in* **A**-*text.*]

'That was a reufol restitucion' · quath Repentaunce, 'for sothe;
Thow wolt hongy heye ther-fore · her other in helle!

Vsedest thow euere vserie · in al thy lyf-tyme?'
'Nay, sothliche,' he sayde · 'saf in my ȝouthe.   240
Ich lerned among Lumbardes · a lesson, and of Iewes,
To weie pans with a peis · and pared the heuyeste,
And lente for loue of the wed · the whiche ich let betere,
And more worth than the moneye · other men that ich lenede.

Ich lenede folk that lese wolde · a lippe in eche noble,   245
And with Lombardes letters · ich lenede gold at Rome;
So what bern of me borwed · he bouhte the tyme.'
'Lenedest thow euere to eny lorde · for loue of menteynaunce?'
  'Ich haue ylent to lordes and to ladies · that louede me neure
      after.   249
Ich haue mad meny a knyght · bote mercer and draper,
Payede neuere for here prentishode · nauht a payre gloues;
That chaffared with my chyuesaunce · cheuede selde after.' 252

B. 236. L *omits the former* be.   253. Lentestow; Lenestow L.   C. 240.
hue (*for* he) P.   250. P *om*. a.   251. payere P.

[*Not in* **A**-*text.*]

'Now god leue neure," quod Repentance · 'but thow repent
  the rather,
The grace on this grounde · thi good wel to bisette,   264
Ne thine ysue after the · haue Ioye of that thow wynnest,
Ne thi excecutours wel bisett · the siluer that thow hem leuest;
And that was wonne with wronge · with wikked men be des-
  pended.

From
B. xiii.
362–368.

[And menged his marchaundyse · and made a good moustre;—
The worste with-in was · a gret witte I lete hit;   363
And if my neighbore had any hyne · or any beste elles
More profitable than myne · many sleightes I made,
How I my3te haue it · al my witte I caste,   366
And but I it had by other waye · atte laste I stale it,
Or pryuiliche his purse shoke · vnpiked his lokkes.]

From
B. xiii.
371–375.

[3if I 3ede to the plow · I pynched so narwe,
That a fote-londe or a forwe · fecchen I wolde,   372
Of my nexte neighbore · nymen of his erthe;
And if I rope, ouer-reche · or 3af hem red that ropen
To seise to me with her sikel·that I ne sewe neure.]

From
B. xiii.
384–389.

[In halydayes at holicherche · whan ich herde masse,
Hadde I neuere wille, wot god · witterly to biseche
Mercye for my mysdedes · that I ne morned more   386
For losse of gode, leue me · than for my lykames giltes;
As, if I had dedly synne done · I dred nou3t that so sore
As when I lened and leued it lost · or longe ar it were payed.]

From
B. xiii.
392–399.

[And if I sent ouer see · my seruauntz to Bruges,   392
Or in-to Pruslonde my prentys · my profit to wayten,
To marchaunden with monoye · and maken her eschaunges,
Mi3te neuere me conforte · in the mene tyme
Noither messe ne matynes · ne none manere si3tes,   396
Ne neuere penaunce perfourned · ne *pater-noster* seyde,
That my mynde ne was more · on my gode, in a doute,
Than in the grace of god · and his grete helpes:
    Vbi thesaurus tuus, ibi et cor tuum.

C. 255. ayeres P.   265. oþer wey IMFSG; oþes a-way PE.

[*Not in* **A**-*text.*]

'Now redelich,' quath Repentaunce · 'and by the rode, ich leyue,
Shal neuere executor wel by-sette · the suluer that thow hym
    leuest,
Ne thyn ayres, as ich hope · haue ioye of that thow wan.
For the pope and alle hus penetauncers · power hem faylleth,
To a-soyle the of thy synnes · *sine restitutione;*   257
    Nunquam dimittitur peccatum, nisi restituatur ablatum.'
'With false wordes and wittes · ich haue wonne my goodes,
And with gyle and glosynge · gadered that ich haue,
Meddled my marchaundise · and mad a good moustre;   260
The werst lay with-ynne · a gret wit ich let hit.
And yf my neyhȝebore hadde an hyne · other eny best ellys
More profitable than myn · ich made meny wentes,
How ich myght haue hit · al my wit ich caste.   264
And bote ich hadde hit by other wey · atte laste ich stal hit,
Other pryuyliche hus pors shok · vnpiked hus lokes.
And yf ich ȝede to the plouh · ich pynchede on hus half-acre,
That a fot-londe other a forwe · fecchen ich wolde,   268
Of my neyhȝeboris next · nymen of hus erthe.
And yf y repe, ouere-reche · other ȝaf hem red that repen
To sese to me with here sykel : that ich sew neuere.
In halydayes at holy churche · whenne ich hurde messe,   272
Ich hadde neuere wil witerlich · to by-seche mercy
For my mysdedes · that ich ne mornede ofter
For lost of good, leyue me · then for lycames gultes.
Thauh ich dedliche synne dude · ich dradde hit nat so sore
As whenne ich lenede and leyuede hit lost · other longe er hit
    were paied.   277
And yf ich sente ouer see · my seruaunt to Brugges,
Other in-to Prus my prentys · my profit to a-waite,
To marchaunde with monye · and maken here eschaunge,   280
Myghte neuere man comforty me · in the meyn tyme,
Neither matyns ne masse · ne othere manere syghtes,
And neuere penaunse performede · ne *pater-noster* seyde,
That my mynde ne was · more in my goodes   284
Than in godes grace · and hus grete myghte.
    Ubi thesaurus tuus, ibi et cor tuum.'

273. P *om*. wil.   278. P *om*. ich.   285. P om. *et*.

[*Not in* **A**-*text.*]

For were I frere of that hous · there gode faith and charite is, 268
I nolde cope vs with thi catel · ne owre kyrke amende,
Ne haue a peny to my pitaunce · of thyne, bi my soule hele,
For the best boke in owre hous · thei3e brent golde were the leues,
And I wyst wytterly · thow were suche as thow tellest, 272
Or elles that I kouthe knowe it · by any kynnes wise.
Seruus es alterius · cum fercula pinguia queris,
Pane tuo pocius · vescere, liber eris.
Thow art an vnkynde creature · I can the nou3te assoille, 276
Til thow make restitucioun · and rekne with hem alle,
And sithen that resoun rolle it · in the regystre of heuene,
That thow hast made vche man good · I may the nou3te assoille;
 Non dimittitur peccatum · donec restituatur ablatum, etc.
For alle that haue of thi good · haue god my trouthe! 280
Ben holden at the heighe dome · to helpe the to restitue.

And who so leueth nou3te this be soth · loke in the sauter glose,
In *miserere mei deus* · ·where I mene treuthe,
 Ecce enim veritatem dilexisti, etc.
Shal neuere werkman in this worlde · thryue wyth that thow wynnest; 284
Cum sancto sanctus eris · construe me that on Englische.'
Thanne wex that shrewe in wanhope · and walde haue hanged him-self,
Ne hadde Repentaunce the rather · reconforted hym in this manere,
'Haue mercye in thi mynde · and with thi mouth bisech it, 288
For goddes mercye is more · than alle hise other werkes;
 Misericordia eius super omnia opera eius, etc.

From
B. v.
463–466.
[And 3ete wil I 3elde a3ein · if I so moche haue,
Al that I wikkedly wan · sithen I wytte hadde.
And though my liflode lakke · leten I nelle 465
That eche man ne shal haue his · ar I hennes wende.]

B. 272. tellest WCRO; telleth L.   273. *From* C; LWRO *omit this line.*
280. *For the former* haue, *as in* C, L *has* hath.   281. Ben WCO; Is L.

C. PASSUS VII. 286–315.

[*Compare* A. V. 236–239.]

'Now redeliche,' quath Repentaunce · 'ich haue reuthe of thy lyuynge.
Were ich a frere, in good faith · for al the gold on erthe
Ich nolde cope me with thy catell · ne oure kirke amende, 288
Ne take a meles mete of thyne · and myn herte hit wiste
That thow were such as thow seist ; · ich sholde rathere sterue:
  Melius est mori quam male uiuere.
Ich rede no faithful frere · at thy feste sytte ;
ʒut were me leuere, by oure lord · lyue by welle-carses 292
Than haue my fode and my fyndynge · of false menne wynnynges :
  Seruus es alterius · cum fercula pinguia queris,
  Pane tuo potius · uescere, liber eris.
Thow art an vnkynde creature · ich can the nat assoyle 296
Tyl thow haue ymad, by thy myght · to alle men restitucion ;
For alle that hauen of thy good · (haue god my treuthe !)
Beeth holden at the hye dome · to helpe the restitue.
The preest that thy tythe taketh · trowe ich non other, 300
Shal parte with the in purgatorie · and help paye thy dette,
Yf he wist thow were suche · when he reseyuyde thyn offrynge.
What lede leyueth that ich lye · loke in the sauter glosed
  On *ecce enim ueritatem dilexisti.*
Ther he shal wite witerliche · what vsure is to mene, 304
And what penaunce the prest shal haue · that prout is of thi tythes.
For an hore of hure ers-wynnynge · may hardiloker tythe
Than an erraunt vsurer · (haue god my treuthe !)
And erest shal come to heuene · by Cryst that me made !' 308
  Then was ther a Walishman · was wonderliche sory,
He highte 'ʒyuan ʒeld-aʒeyn- · if-ich-so-moche-haue,
Al that ich wickeddelich wan · sytthen ich wit hadde ;
And thauh my liflode lacke · leten ich nelle, 312
That ech man shal haue hus · er ich hennes wende.
For me ys leuere in this lif · as a lorel beggen,
Than in lysse to lyue · and lese lyf and soule.'

C. 288. kirke IMF ; churche P. 291. faitthful P. 292. carses EG ; carsus S ; cresses I ; carse P. 294. *fercucula* P. 296. ert P. 305. þi tiþus F ; his tiþes MS ; þe tethes P ; *read* þi tythes. 311. wit G ; witt E ; wyt S ; witte I ; hit PMF.

B. PASSUS V. 290-292.

From
A. v.
242-250.

[Robert the robbour · on *Reddite* he lokede,
And for ther nas not wher-with · he wepte ful sore.
But ȝit the sunfol schrewe · seide to him-seluen : 244
'Crist, that vppon Caluarie · on the cros diȝedest,
Tho Dismas my brother · bisouȝte the of grace,
And heddest merci of that mon · for *memento* sake,
Thi wille worth vppon me · as ich haue wel deseruet 248
To haue helle for euere · ȝif that hope neore.
So rewe on me, Robert · that no red haue,

From
B. v.
469-484.

[Robert the robbere · on *reddite* lokede, 469
And for ther was nouȝte wher-of · he wepe swithe sore.
Ac ȝet the synful schrewe · seyde to hym-selue,
'Cryst, that on Caluarye · vppon the crosse deydest, 472
Tho Dismas my brother · bisouȝte ȝow of grace,
And haddest mercy on that man · for *memento* sake,
So rewe on this robbere · that *reddere* ne haue,
Ne neuere wene to wynne · with crafte that I owe. 476
But for thi mykel mercy · mitigacioun I biseche ;
Ne dampne me nouȝte at domesday · for that I did so ille.'
What bifel of this feloun · I can nouȝte faire schewe,
Wel I wote he wepte faste · water with bothe his eyen, 480
And knowleched his gult · to Cryst ȝete eftsones,
That *penitencia* his pyke · he schulde polsche newe, . . .
For he had leyne bi *Latro* · Luciferes aunte.] 484

And al the wikkednesse in this worlde · that man myȝte worche or thynke,
Ne is no more to the mercye of god · than in the see a glede ;

Omnis iniquitas quantum ad misericordiam dei, est quasi sintilla in medio maris.

For-thi haue mercy in thi mynde · and marchandise, leue it, 292

B. 291. *quasi* WCOR ; L *om.*

C. PASSUS VII. 316-340.

From
A. v.
251-259.
> Ne neuere weene to wynne · for craft that I knowe.
> Bote for thi muchel merci ·· mitigacion I beseche ; 252
> Dampne me not on domes day · for I dude so ille.'
> Ak what fel of this feloun · I con not feire schewe,
> But wel ich wot he wepte fast · water with his eiȝen,
> And knouhlechede his gult · to Crist ȝit eft-sones, 256
> That *Penitencia* is pike · he schulde polissche newe,
> And lepe with him ouerlond · al his lyf-tyme,
> For he hath leiȝen bi *Latro* · Lucifers brother.]

Roberd the ryfeler · on *reddite* lokede, 316
And for ther was nat wher-with · he wepte ful sore;
And ȝut that synful shrewe · seide to heuene,
'Crist, that on Caluarye · on the croys deidest,
Tho Dismas my brother · by-souhte the of grace, 320
And haddest mercy on that man · for *memento* sake,
So rewe on me, Roberd · that *reddere* ne haue,
Ne neuere wene to wynne · with craft that ich knowe.
For thy muchel mercy · mytigacion ich by-seche, 324
Dampne me nouht at domys day · for that ich dude so ille.'
What by-fel of this felon · ich can nouht faire shewe ;
Wel ich wot he wepte faste · water with hus eyen,
And to Crist knowlechede · hus coupe ȝut eft-sone, 328
That penaunce hus pyk-staf · he wolde polische newe,
For he hadde leye by *Latro* · Lucifers aunte.
'By the rode,' quath Repentaunce · 'thow romest toward heuene,
By so that hit be in thyn herte · as ich hure thy tonge. 332
Trist in his mochel mercy · and ȝut myght thow be saued.
For al the wrecchednesse of this worlde · and wicked dedes
Fareth as a fonk of fuyr · that ful a-myde Temese,
And deide for a drop of water; · so doth alle synnes 336
Of alle manere men · that with good wille
Confessen hem and crien mercy · shullen neuere come in helle.
    Omnis iniquitas quoad misericordiam dei est quasi sintilla
      in medio maris.
Repente the anon,' quath Repentaunce · ryȝt so to the vsurer,
'And haue hus mercy in thy mynde · and marchaundise, leue
    hit; 340

C. 323. kowe (*for* knowe) P. 333. an P. 340. P *puts* haue *after* mynde.

158   A. PASSUS V. 146-152.   B. PASSUS V. 293-317.

 Nou ginneth the Gloton · for to go to schrifte,
And carieth him to chircheward · his schrift forte telle.
 Thenne Betun the breustere · bad him gode morwe, 148
And seththen heo asked of him · 'whoder that he wolde?'
 'To holi chirche,' quod he · 'for to here masse,
And seththen I-chule ben I-schriuen · and sunge no more.'
 'Ic haue good ale, gossib,' quod heo · 'Gloten, woltou asaye?'

 For thow hast no good grounde · to gete the with a wastel,
But if it were with thi tonge · or ellis with thi two hondes.
For the good that thow hast geten · bigan al with falsehede,
And as longe as thow lyuest ther-with · thow ȝeldest nouȝte, but
 borwest. 296
And if thow wite neuere to whiche · ne whom to restitue,
Bere it to the bisschop · and bidde hym of his grace,
Bisette it hym-selue · as best is for thi soule.
For he shal answere for the · at the heygh dome, 300
For the and for many mo · that man shal ȝif a rekenynge.
What he lerned ȝow in lente · leue thow none other,
And what he lent ȝow of owre lordes good · to lette ȝow fro
 synne.'

GULA.

 Now bigynneth glotoun · for to go to schrifte, 304
And kaires hym to-kirke-ward · his coupe to schewe.
 Ac Beton the brewestere · bad hym good morwe,
And axed of hym with that · whiderward he wolde.
 'To holi cherche,' quod he · 'forto here masse, 308
And sithen I wil be shryuen · and synne namore.'
 'I haue gode ale, gossib,' quod she · 'Glotown, wiltow assaye?'
'Hastow auȝte in thi purs · any hote spices?'
 'I haue peper and piones,' quod she · 'and a pounde of
 garlike, 312
A ferthyngworth of fenel-seed · for fastyngdayes.'
 Thanne goth Glotoun in · and grete othes after;
Cesse the souteresse · sat on the benche,
Watte the warner · and his wyf bothe, 316
Tymme the tynkere · and tweyne of his prentis,

 B. 312. she W; sche OR; he L. C. 343. bote þow P. 344. to
IMFSG; þow sholde P. 345. bid IMF; bidde E; bide P. 351.

A. PASSUS V. 153-160.   C. PASSUS VII. 341-364.   159

'Hastou ou3t i thi pors,' quod he · 'eny hote spices?'
'3e, Glotun, gossip,' quod heo · 'god wot, ful goode;
I haue peper and piane · and a pound of garlek,
A ferthing-worth of fenel-seed · for this fastyng dayes.'   156
  Thene geth Gloton in · and grete othus after;
Sesse the souters wyf · sat on the benche,
Watte the warinar · and his wyf bothe,
Tomkyn the tinkere · and tweyne of his knaues,   160

For thow hast no good, by good faith! · to bygge the with a wastell.
The good that thow hauest ygete · by-gan al with falshede;
As longe as thow lyuest ther-with · thow 3eldest nat, bote borw-
  est.
And yf thow wite neuere to wham · ne where to restitue,   344
Bere hit to the bischop · and bid hym of hus grace,
To by-setten hit hym-selue · as best be for thy soule;
For he shal answere for the · at the hye dome,
For the and for meny mo · that man shal 3eue rekenynge,   348
What he lerede 3ow to lyue with · and to lette 3ow fro thufthe.'

CONFESSIO GULE.

  Now by-gynneth Gloton · for to go to shryfte,
And kayres hym to-kirke-ward · hus coupe to shewe.
Fastyng on a Fryday · forth gan he wende   352
By Betone hous the brewestere · that bad hym good morwe,
And whederwarde he wolde · the brew-wif hym asked.
  'To holy churche,' quath he · 'for to hure masse,
And sitthen sitte and be yshriuen · and synwe namore.'   356
  'Ich haue good ale, godsyb · Gloton, wolt thow assaye?'
'What hauest thow,' quath he · 'eny hote spices?'
  'Ich haue piper and pionys · and a pound of garlik,
A ferthyng-worth of fynkelsede · for fastinge-daies.'   360
  Thenne goth Gloton yn · and grete othes after.
Sesse the sywestere · sat on the benche,
Watte the warynere · and hus wif dronke,
Thomme the tynkere · and tweye of hus knaues,   364

---

kirke IMF; churche P.   356. yschreuen P.   360. fertheng P.   361.
an (for and) P.

Hikke the hakeney mon · and Hogge the neldere,
Clarisse of Cokkes lone · and the clerk of the churche,
Sire Pers of Pridye · and Pernel of Flaundres,
Dauwe the disschere · and a doseyn othere.　　　　164
A ribibor, a ratoner · a rakere of Chepe,
A ropere, a redyng-kyng · and Rose the disschere,
Godfrei of Garlesschire · and Griffin the Walsche,
And of vp-holders an hep · erly bi the morwe　　　168
ʒiue the Gloton with good wille · good ale to honsel.
　　Thenne Clement the cobelere · caste of his cloke,
And atte newe feire · he leyde hire to sulle;
And Hikke the ostiler · hutte his hod aftur,　　　172

Hikke the hakeneyman · and Hughe the nedeler,
Clarice of Cokkeslane · and the clerke of the cherche,
Dawe the dykere · and a dozeine other;　　　　320
Sire Piers of Pridie · and Peronelle of Flaundres,
A ribibour, a ratonere · a rakyer of Chepe,
A ropere, a redyngkyng · and Rose the dissheres,
Godfrey of Garlekehithe · and Gryfin the Walshe,　324
And vpholderes an hepe · erly bi the morwe
Geuen glotoun with glad chere · good ale to hansel.

　　Clement the cobelere · cast of his cloke,
And atte new faire · he nempned it to selle;　　　328
Hikke the hakeneyman · hitte his hood after,
And badde Bette the bochere · ben on his side.
There were chapmen y-chose · this chaffare to preise;
Who-so haueth the hood · shuld haue amendes of the cloke. 332

　　Two risen vp in rape · and rouned togideres,
And preised these penyworthes · apart bi hem-selue;
Thei couth nouʒte bi her conscience · acorden in treuthe,
Tyl Robyn the ropere · arose bi the southe,　　　336
And nempned hym for a noumpere · that no debate nere,
For to trye this chaffare · bitwixen hem thre.
　　Hikke the hostellere · hadde the cloke,

A. 165. A TU; And V. a TU.; the V.　　182. *This line is in* H *only.*

A. PASSUS V. 173-183.   C. PASSUS VII. 365-389.   161

And bad Bette the bocher · ben on his bi-syde.
Ther weore chapmen i-chose · the chaffare to preise;
Hose hedde the hod · schulde haue amendes.
Thei risen vp raply · and rouneden to-gedere,   176
And preiseden the peniworthus · and parteden bi hemseluen;
Ther weoren othes an hep · hose that hit herde.
Thei couthe not bi heore concience · a-corde to-gedere,
Til Robyn the ropere · weore rad forte a-ryse,   180
And nempned for a noumpere · that no de-bat neore,
For he schulde preise the penyworthes · as hym good thou3t.
  Thenne Hikke the ostiler · hedde the cloke,

Hicke the hakeneyman · and Houwe the neldere,
Claryce of Cockeslane · the clerk of the churche,
Syre Peeres of Prydie · and Purnel of Flaundres,
An haywarde and an heremyte · the hangeman of Tyborne,   368
Dauwe the dykere · with a dosen harlotes
Of portours and of pykeporses · and pylede toth-drawers,
A rybibour and a ratoner · a rakere and hus knaue,
A ropere and a redyngkynge · and Rose the disshere,   372
Godefray the garlek-mongere · and Griffyn the Walish;
And of vp-holders an hep · erly by the morwe
Geuen Gloton with glad chere · good ale to hansele.
  Clemment the cobelere · cast of hus cloke,   376
And to the newe fayre · nempned hit to selle.
Hicke the hakeneyman · hitte hus hod after,
And bad Bette the bouchere · to be on hus syde.
Ther were chapmen y-chose · the chaffare to preise;   380
That he that hadde the hod · sholde nat habbe the cloke;
The betere thyng, by arbytours · sholde bote the werse.
Two rysen rapliche · and rounede to-geders,
And preysed the penyworthes · apart by hem-selue,   384
And ther were othes an hepe · for other sholde haue the werse.
Thei couthe nouht by here conscience · a-corde for treuthe,
Tyl Robyn the ropere · aryse thei bysouhte,
And nempned hym a nompeyr · that no debate were.   388
  Hicke the hakeneyman · hadde the cloke,

B. 338. *From* OC; L *omits this line.*   C. 365. P *om.* þe *after* Hicke.
370. pykeporeses P.   375. chire P.   377. nywe P.   379. þe IMFSE; P *om.*

M

In couenaunt that Clement · schulde the cuppe fulle,   184
And habbe Hikkes hod the ostiler · and hold him wel iseruet;
And he that repenteth rathest · schulde arysen aftur,
And greten sir Gloten · with a galun of ale.
   Ther was lauȝwhing and lotering · and 'let go the cuppe;'
Bargeyns and beuerages · bi-gonne to aryse,   189
And seeten so til euensong · and songen sum while,
Til Gloten hedde i-gloupet · a galoun and a gille.
He pissede a potel · in a *pater-noster*-while,   192
And bleuh the ronde ruwet · atte rugge-bones ende,
That alle that herde the horn · heolden heore neose after,

In couenaunte that Clement · shulde the cuppe fille,   340
And haue Hikkes hode hostellere · and holde hym yserued;
And who-so repented rathest · shulde arise after,
And grete sire Glotoun · with a galoun ale.
   There was laughyng and louryng · and 'let go the cuppe,' 344
And seten so til euensonge · and songen vmwhile,
Tyl Glotoun had y-globbed · a galoun an a Iille.
His guttis gunne to gothely · as two gredy sowes;
He pissed a potel · in a *pater-noster*-while,   348
And blew his rounde ruwet · at his rigge-bon ende,
That alle that herde that horne · held her nose after,
And wissheden it had be wexed · with a wispe of firses.
   He myȝte neither steppe ne stonde · er he his staffe hadde; 352
And thanne gan he go · liche a glewmannes bicche,
Somme tyme aside · and somme tyme arrere,
As who-so leyth lynes · forto lacche foules.
   And whan he drowgh to the dore · thanne dymmed his
      eighen,   356
He stumbled on the thresshewolde · an threwe to the erthe.
Clement the cobelere · cauȝte hym bi the myddel,
For to lifte hym alofte · and leyde him on his knowes;
Ac Glotoun was a gret cherle · and a grym in the liftynge, 360
And coughed vp a caudel · in Clementis lappe;

   A. 199. lacche TU; cacche VH.   2c2-207. *These lines are in* U *only*.
B. 347. gothely C; gotheli O; gothelen W; godly L.   357. stumbled
WCO; trembled L.   **C.** 400. rywett P. atte þe P.   401. þat G; þan P;
þe IMFE; his S.   402. þat hit hadde P.   403. stonnde P.   404. hue

And weschte that hit weore i-wipet · with a wesp of firsen.
He hedde no strengthe to stonde · til he his staf hedde; 196
Thenne gon he for to go · lyk a gleo-monnes bicche,
Sum tyme asyde · and sum tyme arere,
As hose leith lynes · to lacche with foules.
Whon he drouh to the dore · then dimmede his ei3en, 200
He thrompelde atte threxwolde · and threuh to the grounde.
Clement the coblere · cau3te Glotoun by the mydle,
And for to lyfte hym aloft · leide hym on his knees;
And Glotoun was a gret cherl · and grym in the lyftynge, 204
And cowhede vp a cawdel · in Clementis lappe,

In couenaunt that Clemment · sholde the coppe fylle,
And haue the hakeneymannes hod · and hold hym y-serued;
And who repentyde rathest · shold aryse after, 392
And grete syre Gloton · with a galon of ale.
Ther was lauhyng & lakeryng · and 'let go the coppe!'
Bargeynes and beuereges · by-gunne to aryse,
And setyn so til euesong rang · and songe vmbwhyle, 396
Til Gloton hadde yglobbed · a galon and a gylle.
Hus guttes gonne godely · as two gredy sowes;
He pissede a potell · in a *pater-noster*-while,
And blew hus rounde rewet · atte rygbones ende, 400
That alle that herde that horne · hulde here nose after,
And wusched hit hadde be wexed · with a wips of breres.
He myghte nother stappe ne stonde · tyl he a staf hadde.
Thanne gan he go · lyke a glemannes bycche, 404
Som tyme asyde · and som tyme a-rere,
As ho so laith lynes · for to lacche foules.
And whenne he drow to the dore · thanne dymmed hus eyen;
He thrumbled at the threshefold · and threw to the erthe. 408
Tho Clement the cobelere · cauhte hym by the mydel,
For to lyfte hym on loft · he leyde hym on hus knees;
Ac Gloton was a gret cherl · and gronyd in the liftynge,
And couhed vp a caudel · in Clementes lappe; 412

(*for* he) P. 405. P *om.* and. 408. thrumbled I; thromlide G; stomblede PE. þrew SIF; þreu P. 410. leyde I; leide MFG; ledde PES. 411. in IMSG; on P.

A. PASSUS V. 206-210.   B. PASSUS V. 362-380.

That the hungriest hound · of Hertforde schire
Ne durst lape of that laueyne · so vnloveli it smakith.
That with al the wo of this world · his wyf and his wenche   208
Beeren him hom to his bed · and brouhten him ther-inne.
And after al this surfet · an accesse he hedde,

Is non so hungri hounde · in Hertford schire
Durst lape of the leuynges · so vnlouely thei smau3te.
With al the wo of this worlde · his wyf and his wenche   364
Baren hym home to his bedde · and brou3te hym therinne.
And after al this excesse · he had an accidie,
That he slepe Saterday and Sonday · til sonne 3ede to reste.
Thanne waked he of his wynkyng · and wiped his eyghen;   368
The fyrste worde that he warpe · was, 'where is the bolle?'
His wif gan edwite hym tho · how wikkedlich he lyued,

And Repentance ri3te so · rebuked hym that tyme: 371
'As thow with wordes and werkes · hast wrou3te yuel in thi lyue,
Shryue the and be shamed ther-of · and shewe it with thi
    mouth.'
'I, Glotoun,' quod the gome · 'gylti me 3elde,
That I haue trespassed with my tonge · I can nou3te telle how
    ofte,
Sworen 'goddes soule' · and 'so god me help and halidom,'   376
There no nede ne was · nyne hundreth tymes;
And ouer-seye me at my sopere · and some tyme at nones,

From
B. xiii. [And more mete ete and dronke · then kende mi3t defie,]
404.

That I Glotoun girt it vp · er I hadde gone a myle,
And y-spilte that my3te be spared · and spended on somme
    hungrie;   380

A. 213. was TH; V *om*.   B. 370. wif WO; witte L.   C. 414.
þat IMFSEG; þe P.   417. excesse IMFSE; excessus P.   422. an (*for*

A. PASSUS V. 211–215.   C. PASSUS VII. 413–433.

That he slepte Seturday and Sonenday · til sonne wente to reste.
Thenne he wakede of his wynk · and wypede his ei3en ;   212
The furste word that he spac was · 'wher is the cuppe?'
His wyf warnede him tho · of wikkednesse and of sinne.
Thenne was he a-schomed, that schrewe · and schraped his eren,

---

Ys non so hongry hounde · in Hertforde-shire,
That thorst lape of that leuynge · so vnloueliche hit smauhte.
  With al the wo of the worlde · hus wif and hus wenche
Bere hym to hus bedde · and brouhte hym ther-ynne ;   416
And after al this excesse · he hadde an accidie,
He slep Saterday and Sonday · tyl sonne 3ede to reste.
Thenne awakyde he wel wan · and wolde haue ydronke ;
The ferst. word that he spak · was 'ho halt the bolle?'   420
Hus wif and hys inwit · edwited hym of hus synne ;
He wax a-shamed, that shrewe · and shrof hym al-so swithe
To Repentaunce ry3t thus ; · 'haue reuthe on me,' he seyde,
'Thow lord that on loft art · and alle lyues shope !   424
  To the, god, ich Gloton · gulty me 3elde
Of my trespas with tunge · ich can nauht telle how ofte,
Sworen 'thy saule and thy sydes' · and 'so help me, god
    almyghty !'
When that no ned was · meny tyme falsliche.   428
And ouer-sopede at my soper · and som tyme at nones

More than my kynde · myghte wel defye ;
And as an hounde that et gras · so gan ich to brake,
And spilde that ich spele myghte · ich can nouht speke for
    shame   432
The vylenye of my foule mouthe · and of my foule mawe.

---

and) P.   425. gulty ich me P.   427. P *om. 2nd* þy.   428. ned MS ; nede
IFE ; nud P.   431. ete P.   432. spele IFS ; spelide P.

And gon to grede grimliche · and gret deol to make 216
For his wikkede lyf · that he i-liued hedde.
'For hungur other for furst · I make myn a-vou,

Ouerdelicatly on fastyng-dayes · drunken and eten bothe,
And sat some tyme so longe there · that I slepe and ete at ones.
For loue of tales in tauernes · to drynke the more, I dyned,
And hyed to the mete er none · whan fastyng-dayes were.' 384
'This shewyng shrifte,' quod Repentance · 'shal be meryte
   to the.'
And thanne gan Glotoun grete · and gret doel to make
For his lither lyf · that he lyued hadde,
And avowed to fast— · 'for hunger or for thurst 388
Shal neuere fisshe on the Fryday · defien in my wombe,
Tyl Abstinence myn aunte · haue ȝiue me leue;
And ȝit haue I hated hir · al my lyf-tyme.'

ACCIDIA.

Thanne come Sleuthe al bislabered · with two slymy eiȝen : 392
'I most sitte,' seyde the segge · 'or elles shulde I nappe ;
I may nouȝte stonde ne stoupe · ne with-oute a stole knele.
Were I brouȝte abedde · but if my taille-ende it made,
Sholde no ryngynge do me ryse · ar I were rype to dyne.' 396
He bygan *benedicite* with a bolke · and his brest knocked,
And roxed and rored · and rutte atte laste.
'What! awake, renke!' quod Repentance · 'and rape the to
   shrifte.'
'If I shulde deye bi this day · me liste nouȝte to loke ; 400
I can nouȝte perfitly my *pater-noster* · as the prest it syngeth,
But I can rymes of Robyn Hood · and Randolf erle of Chestre,
Ac neither of owre lorde ne of owre lady · the leste that euere
   was made.
I haue made vowes fourty · and for-ȝete hem on the morne ;
I parfourned neure penaunce · as the prest me hiȝte, 405
Ne ryȝte sori for my synnes · ȝet was I neuere.
And ȝif I bidde any bedes · but if it be in wrath,
That I telle with my tonge · is two myle fro myne herte. 408

A. 219. fysch HTU ; V *om*. B. 388. to WCO ; L *om*.

Schal neuer fysch on Frydai · defyen in my mawe,
Er Abstinence myn aunte · haue i-ʒiue me leue; 220
And ʒit ichaue i-hated hire · al my lyf-tyme.'

On fastingdais by-fore none · ich fedde me with ale,
Out of reson, a-mong rybaudes · here rybaudrye to huyre.

Her-of, good god · graunte me forʒeuenesse, 436
Of al my luther lyuyng · in al my lyf-tyme.
   For ich a-vowe to verrey god · for honger other for thurste,
Shal neuere fish on Fryday · defye in my wombe,
Tyl Abstinence myn aunte · haue ʒeue me leue, 440
And ʒut haue ich hated hure · al my lyf-tyme.'
         Hic explicit passus septimus.

PASSUS VIII.

Incipit passus octauus.

CONFESSIO ACCIDIE.

THO cam Sleuthe al by-slobered · with two slymed eyen.
   'Ich most sitte to be shryuen,' quath he · 'or elles shal ich nappe.
Ich may nouht stonde ne stoupe · ne with-oute stoule knele.
Were ich brouhte in my bed · bote my taylende hit made, 4
Sholde no ryngynge do me ryse · tyl ich were rype to dyne.'
Benedicite he by-gan with a bolke · and hus brest knokede,
Rascled and remed · and routte at the laste.
'What a-wake, renk,' quath Repentaunce · 'rape the to shryfte!'
   'Sholde ich deye,' quath he, 'by this daye · ich drede me sore, 9
Ich can nouht parfytliche my *pater-noster* · as the prest hit seggeth.
Ich can rymes of Robyn Hode · and of Randolf, erl of Chestre,
Ac of oure lord ne of oure lady · the lest that euere was maked.
Ich haue a-vowed vowes fourty · and for-ʒut hem a morwe; 13
Ich parfourned neuere penaunce · that the preest me hihte,
Ne ryʒt sory for my synnes · ich sey neuere the tyme.
And ich bidde eny bedis · bote hit be in wratthe, 16
That ich telle with my tunge · ys ten myle fro my herte.

C. 1. to (*for* two) PM.   2. shryuen E; shryue P.   3. stonnde P.
9. me so sore P.

[*Not in* **A**-*text.*]

I am occupied eche day · haliday and other,
With ydel tales atte ale · and otherwhile in cherches;
Goddes peyne and his passioun · ful selde thynke I there-on.
 I visited neuere fieble men · ne fettered folke in puttes; 412
I haue leuere here an harlotrie · or a somer-game of souteres,
Or lesynges to laughe at · and belye my neighbore,
Than al that euere Marke made · Mathew, Iohn, and Lucas.
And vigilies and fastyng-dayes · alle thise late I passe, 416
And ligge abedde in lenten · an my lemman in myn armes,
Tyl matynes and masse be do · and thanne go to the freres;
Come I to *ite, missa est* · I holde me yserued.
I nam nouȝte shryuen some tyme · but if sekenesse it make, 420
Nouȝt tweies in two ȝere · and thanne vp gesse I schryue me.
 I haue be prest and parsoun · passynge thretti wynter,
ȝete can I neither solfe ne synge · he seyntes lyues rede,
But I can fynde in a felde · or in a fourlonge an hare, 424
Better than in *beatus vir* · or in *beati omnes*
Construe oon clause wel · and kenne it to my parochienes.
I can holde louedayes · and here a reues rekenynge,
Ac in canoun ne in the decretales · I can nouȝte rede a lyne.
ȝif I bigge and borwe it · but ȝif it be ytailled, 429
I forȝete it as ȝerne · and ȝif men me it axe
Sixe sithes or seuene · I forsake it with othes,
And thus tene I trewe men · ten hundreth tymes. 432
 And my seruauntz some tyme · her salarye is bihynde,
Reuthe is to here the rekenynge · whan we shal rede acomptes;
So with wikked wille and wraththe · my werkmen I paye.
ȝif any man doth me a benfait · or helpeth me at nede, 436
I am vnkynde aȝein his curteisye · and can nouȝte vnderstonde it;
For I haue and haue hadde · some dele haukes maneres,
I nam nouȝte lured with loue · but there ligge auȝte vnder the
  thombe.
 The kyndenesse that myne euene-cristene · kidde me fernyere,
Sixty sythes I, Sleuthe · haue forȝete it sith, 441

 B. 434. the WCO; L *om.* 440. fernyere WCR; ferne ȝer O; farnere L.
441. foȝete L. C. 21. viseted P. 22. harletrye P. 25. for-ȝete MSF;

[*Not in* **A**-*text.*]

Ich am ocupied eche day · haly day and other,
With ydel tales atte nale · and other-whyle in churches;
Godes pyne and hus passion · is pure selde in my thouhte. 20
Ich visited neuere feble man · ne feterid man in prisone;
Ich hadde leuere huyre of harlotrye · other of a lesyng to lauhen of,
Other lacke men, and lykne hem · in vnlykynge manere,
Than al that euere Marc made · Matheu, Iohan, other Lucas. 24
Vigilies and fastyngdayes · ich can for-ȝete hem alle.
Ich ligge a bedde in Lente · my lemman in myn armes,
Tyl matyns and messe be don · then haue ich a memorie atte freres.
Ich am nouht shryuen-som tyme · bote syknesse hit make, 28
Nouht twyes in ten ȝer · ȝut tel ich nauht the haluendele.
Ich haue be prest and person · passyng therty wintere,
Ȝut can ich nother solfye ne synge · ne a seyntes lyf rede.
Ac ich can fynde in a felde · and in a forlang an hare, 32
And holden a knyȝtes court · and a-counte with the reyue;
Ac ich can nouht constrye Catoun · ne clergialliche reden.
Yf ich bygge and borwe ouht · bote hit be y-tayled,
Ich for-ȝete hit as ȝerne · and yf eny man hit asketh, 36
Sixe sithe other seuene · ich for-sake hit with othes;
Thus haue ich tened trewe men · ten hondred tymes.
And som tyme my seruauns · here salarye is byhynde;
Reuthe ys to huyre the rekenyng · whenne we shulleth rede a-countes, 40
That with so wicked wil · my werkmen ich paye.
If eny man doth me a byn-fet · other helpeth me at nede,
Ich am vnkynde aȝeyns courtesye · ich can nat vnderstonde hit.
For ich haue and haue had · somdel haukes maneres, 44
Ich am nat lured with loue · bote ouht lygge vnder thombe.

The kyndenesse that myn emcristene · kydde me fern ȝere,
Syxty sithe ich sleuthe · haue for-ȝute hit sitthe.

---

for-ȝute P (*and in* l. 36). 26. lemman MIEF; lemen P. 34. catoun MI; canon PES. 36. P *om. 1st* hit. 38. tened MIES; tuned P. 39. salerye P. 42. nede IMFSE; nude P. 43. vnderstonnde P.

A. PASSUS V. 222-230.   B. PASSUS V. 442-466.

  Sleuthe for serwe · fel doun i-swowene,
Til *Vigilate* the veil · fette water at his ei3en,
And flatte on his face · and faste on him cri3ede, 224
And seide, 'war the for wonhope · that wol the bi-traye.
"Icham sori for my sunnes" · sei to thi-seluen,
And bet thi-self on the breste · and bidde god of grace,
For nis no gult her so gret · his merci nis wel more.' 228
  Thenne sat Sleuthe vp · and sikede sore,
And made a-vou bi-fore god · for his foule sleuthe;

In speche and in sparynge of speche · yspilte many a tyme
Bothe flesche and fissche · and many other vitailles;
Bothe bred and ale · butter, melke, and chese 444
Forsleuthed in my seruyse · til it my3te serue noman.
  I ran aboute in 3outhe · and 3af me nou3te to lerne,
And euere sith haue be beggere · for my foule sleuthe;
Heu michi, quod sterilem vitam duxi iuuenilem.' 448
  'Repentestow the nau3te?' quod Repentance · and ri3te with
   that he swowned,
Til *Vigilate* the veille · fette water at his ey3en,
And flatte it on his face · and faste on hym criede,
And seide, 'ware the fram wanhope · wolde the bitraye. 452
"I am sori for my synnes" · sey so to thi-selue,
And bete thi-selue on the breste · and bidde hym of grace;
For is no gult here so grete · that his goodnesse nys more.'
  Thanne sat Sleuthe vp · and seyned hym swithe, 456
And made avowe to-fore god · for his foule sleuthe,
Shal no Sondaye be this seuene 3ere · but sykenesse it lette,
That I ne shal do me er day · to the dere cherche,
And heren matines and masse · as I a monke were. 460
Shal none ale after mete · holde me thennes,
Tyl I haue euensonge herde · I behote to the rode.
And 3ete wil I 3elde a3ein · if I so moche haue,
Al that I wikkedly wan · sithen I wytte hadde. 464
  And though my liflode lakke · leten I nelle,
That eche man ne shal haue his · ar I hennes wende:

  A. 231. be TU; V *om.* 232. dore (*for* deore) V; dere T. **B.** 447. haue C; haue I WO; L *om.* 448. *quod* R; *quia* LWCO. **C.** 48. many FS; myn P; my E. 50. eche a P. 51. an (*for* and) P. 52. For-

A. PASSUS V. 231–239.   C. PASSUS VIII. 48–69.   171

'Schal no Sonenday be this seuen ȝer · (bote seknesse hit make),
That I ne schal do me ar day · to the deore churche,   232
And here matins and masse · as I a monk were.
    Schal non ale after mete · holde me thennes,
Til ichaue euensong herd · I beo-hote to the rode.
And ȝit I-chulle ȝelden aȝeyn · ȝif I so muche haue,   236
Al that I wikkedliche won · seththe I wit hade.
    And thauh my lyflode lakke · letten I nulle
That vche mon schal habben his · er ich henne wende :

In speche and in sparyng of speche · yspilt many tymes   48
Bothe flesh and eke fish ; · and vitaile ich kepte so longe,
Til eche lyf hit lothede · to lokye ther-on, other smylle hit ;
Bothe bred and ale · botere, melke, and chese
For-sleuthed in my seruice · and sette hous a fuyre,   52
And ȝede a-bowte in my ȝouthe · and ȝaf me to no thedom,
And sitthe a beggere haue y-be · for my foule sleuthe ;
Heu michi, quod sterilem · duxi uitam iuuenilem !'
    'Repente the,' quath Repentaunce · and ryȝt with that he
        swouned,   56
Til *Vigilate* the veille · vette water at hus eyen,
And flatte on hus face · and fast on hym criede,
And seide, ' war fro wanhope · that wol the by-traye.
" Ich am sory for my synnes " · seye to thy-selue,   60
And bet thy-selue on the brest · and bidde god of grace ;
For ther is no gilte so gret · that hus goodnesse ne ys more.
    Thanne sat Sleuthe vp · and seynede hym ofte,
And made a-vowe by-for god · for hus foule sleuthe,   64
' Shal no Soneday this seuene ȝer be · bote sycknesse hit make,
That ich ne shal do me or daye · to the dere churche,
And huyre matyns and masse · as ich a monke were.
Shal no ale after mete · holde me thennes,   68
Til ich haue hurd euesong · ich by-hote to the rode ! '

From C. vii. 310–313. (p. 155.)	[He highte ' ȝyuan ȝeld-aȝeyn· · if-ich-so-moche-haue, Al that ich wickeddelich wan · sytthen ich wit hadde ; And thauh my liflode lacke · leten ich nelle, 312 That ech man shal haue hus · er ich hennes wende.]

---

sleuthe P.   P *om.* and.   53. þedam P.   56. and MIF ; P *om.*   62.
is—gret I ; is gult noon so gret SG ; nys non so gret synne PE.   64. good
(*for* god) P.

172   A. PASSUS V. 240-249.   B. PASSUS V. 467-484.

And with the residue and the remenaunt · (bi the rode of
    Chester!)   240
I schal seche seynt Treuthe · er I seo Rome!'
Robert the robbour · on *Reddite* he lokede,
And for ther nas not wher-with · he wepte ful sore.
But ȝit the sunfol schrewe · seide to him-seluen :   244
'Crist, that vppon Caluarie · on the cros diȝedest,
Tho Dismas my brother · bi-souȝte the of grace,
And heddest merci of that mon · for *memento* sake,
Thi wille worth vppon me · as ich haue wel deseruet   248
To haue helle for euere · ȝif that hope neore.

And with the residue and the remenaunt · bi the rode of
    Chestre !
I shal seke treuthe arst · ar I se Rome!'   468
Robert the robbere · on *reddite* lokede,
And for ther was nouȝte wher-of · he wepe swithe sore.
Ac ȝet the synful shrewe · seyde to hym-selue,
'Cryst, that on Caluarye · vppon the crosse deydest,   472
Tho Dismas my brother · bisouȝte ȝow of grace,
And haddest mercy on that man · for *memento* sake,
So rewe on this robberè · that *reddere* ne haue,
Ne neuere wene to wynne · with crafte that I owe.   476
But for thi mykel mercy · mitigacioun I biseche;
Ne dampne me nouȝte at domesday · for that I did so ille.'
What bifel of this feloun · I can nouȝte faire schewe,
Wel I wote he wepte faste · water with bothe his eyen,   480
And knowleched his gult · to Cryst ȝete eftsones,
That *penitencia* his pyke · he shulde polsche newe,
And lepe with hym ouer londe · al his lyf-tyme,
For he had leyne bi *Latro* · Luciferes aunte.   484

From
B. xiii.
410-416.
|
[Which ben the braunches · that bryngeth a man to sleuth?
Is whanne a man morneth nouȝte for his mysdedes · ne maketh no
    sorwe,
Ac penaunce that the prest enioigneth · perfourneth yuel,
Doth none almes-dede · dret hym of no synne,   413
Lyueth aȝein the bileue · and no lawe holdeth ; . . .
And if he auȝte wole here · it is an harlotes tonge.

A. 257. pike he T ; pyke U ; prest V.   newe TU ; him newe V.

So rewe on me, Robert · that no red haue,
Ne neuere weene to wynne · for craft that I knowe.
Bote for thi muchel merci · mitigacion I be-seche;   252
Dampne me not on domes day · for I dude so ille.'
Ak what fel of this feloun · I con not feire schewe,
But wel ich wot he wepte faste · watur with his ei3en,
And knouhlechede his gult · to Crist 3it eft-sones,   256
That *Penitencia* is pike · he schulde polissche newe,
And lepe with him ouerlond · al his lyf-tyme,
For he hath lei3en bi *Latro* · Lucifers brother.

From C. vii. 316–330 (p. 157).

[Roberd the ryfeler · on *reddite* lokede,   316
And for ther was nat wher-with · he wepte ful sore;
And 3ut that synful shrewe · seide to heuene,
'Crist, that on Caluarye · on the croys deidest,
Tho Dismas my brother · by-souhte the of grace,   320
And haddest mercy on that man · for *memento* sake,
So rewe on me, Roberd · that *reddere* ne haue,
Ne neuere wene to wynne · with craft that ich knowe.
For thy muchel mercy · mytigacion ich by-seche,   324
Dampne me nouht at domys day · for that ich dude so ille.'
What by-fel of this felon · ich can nouht faire shewe;
Wel ich wot he wepte faste · water with hus eyen,
And to Crist knowlechede · hus coupe 3ut eft-sone,   328
That penaunce hus pyk-staf · he wolde polische newe,
For he hadde leye by *Latro* · Lucifers aunte.]

Ac whiche be the braunches · that bryngeth men to sleuthe?
Ys, whanne a man mourneth nat · for hus mysdedes;
The penaunce that the prest enioyneth · parfourneth vuele,   72
Doth non almys-dedes · and drat nat of synne,
Lyueth a3ens the by-leyue · and no lawe kepeth,
And hath no lykynge to lerne · ne of oure lord hure,
Bote harlotrie other horedom · other elles of som wynnyng.   76

[From B. PASSUS XIII. 417–445.]

[*Not in* A-*text.*]

From
B. xiii.
417–445.

Whan men carpeth of Cryst · or of clennesse of soule,
He wexeth wroth and wil nouȝt here · but wordes of myrthe.
Penaunce and pore men · and the passioun of seyntes
He hateth to here there-of · and alle that it telleth.   420
Thise ben the braunches, beth war · that bryngeth a man to
  wanhope!
Ȝe lordes and ladyes · and legates of holicherche,
That fedeth foles sages · flatereres and lyeres,
And han likynge to lythen hem · to do ȝow to lawghe;   424
  Ve vobis qui ridetis, &c.
And ȝiueth hem mete and mede · and pore men refuse,
In ȝowre deth-deyinge · I drede me ful sore,
Lest tho thre maner men · to moche sorwe ȝow brynge :
  Consentientes et agentes pari pena punientur.
Patriarkes and prophetes · and prechoures of goddes wordes   428
Sauen thorw her sarmoun · mannes soule fram helle ;
Riȝt so flatereres and foles · aren the fendes disciples,
To entice men thorw her tales · to synne and harlotrye.
Ac clerkes that knowen holywryt · shulde kenne lordes,   432
What Dauid seith of suche men · as the sauter telleth,
  Non habitabit in medio domus mee, qui facit superbiam et qui
    loquitur iniqua :
Shulde none harlote haue audience · in halle ne in chambres,
There wise men were · witnesseth goddes wordes;
Ne no mysproude man · amonges lordes ben allowed.   436
Clerkes and kniȝtes · welcometh kynges ministrales,
And for loue of the lorde · litheth hem at festes ;
Muche more, me thenketh · riche men schulde
Haue beggeres byfore hem · the whiche ben goddes ministrales, 440
As he seyth himself · seynt Iohan bereth witnesse :
  Qui vos spernit, me spernit.
Forthi I rede ȝow riche · reueles whan ȝe maketh
For to solace ȝoure soules · suche ministrales to haue ;
The pore, for a fol sage · syttynge at the heyȝ table,   444
And a lered man, to lere the · what oure lorde suffred

C. 79. and I; PMSEF *om*.   84. lawghe I; lawe P.   *quia lugebitis* E ;
PISM *om*.   91. harletrie P.   95. wise men IMSEF ; wysmen P.   96.

[*Not in* **A**-*text.*]

Whan men carpen of Cryst · other of clennesse of soule,
He wext wroth, and wol nat huyre · bote wordes of murthe.
Penaunce and poure men · and the passion of seyntes,
He hateth to huyre ther-of · and alle that ther-of carpen. 80
Thuse beth the braunches, be war · that bryngeth man to wan-
  hope.
ʒe lordes and ladyes · and legates of holy churche,
That feden fool sages · flaterers and lyers,
And han lykynge to lythen hem · in hope to do ʒow lawghe :
  Ve uobis qui ridetis, quia lugebitis, et cetera :
And ʒeueth suche mede and mete · and poure men refusen, 85
In ʒoure deth-deynge · ich drede me sore
Lest tho manere men · to moche sorwe ʒow brynge;
  As god wole; *Consencientes et agentes pari pena punientur.*
Patriarkes and prophetes · prechours of godes wordes 88
Sauen thorgh here sermons · mannes soule fro helle ;
Ryʒt so flaterers and foles · aren the fendes procuratores,
Entysen men thorgh here tales · to synne and to harlotrie.
Clerkus that knowen this · sholde kenne lordes, 92
What Dauid seide of suche men · as the sauter telleth,
  *Non habitabit in medio domus mee qui facit superbiam, qui
  loquitur iniqua.*
Sholde non harlot haue audience · in halle ne in chaumbre,
Ther that wise men were; · (witnesse of godes wordes),
Nother a mys-proud man · among lordes be a-lowed. 96
Clerkus and knyʒtes · welcometh kynges mynstrales,
And for loue of here lordes · lithen hem at festes ;
Muche more, me thenketh · riche men auhte
Haue beggers by-fore hem · whiche beth godes mynstrales, 100
As he seith hym-self · seynt Iohan bereth witnesse,
  Qui uos spernit, me eciam spernit.
Ther-for ich rede ʒow riche · reueles when ʒe maken
For to solace ʒoure soules · suche mynstrales to haue ;
The poure for a fol sage · syttynge at thy table, 104
With a lered man, to lere the · what oure lord suffrede

---

mys-prout P.   be MIF ; P *om.*   97. wolcomeþ P.   98. PE *om.* And.
104. fol MI ; foole E ; foul P ; *see* l. 83.

[*Not in* A-*text.*]

From
B xiii.
446–457.

For to saue thi soule · fram Sathan thin enemy,
And fithel the, without flaterynge · of gode Friday the storye;
And a blynd man for a bourdeoure · or a bedrede womman, 448
To crie a largesse by-for oure lorde · ȝoure good loos to schewe!
Thise thre maner ministrales · maketh a man to lawhe,
And, in his deth-deyinge · thei don him gret conforte,
That bi his lyue lythed hem · and loued hem to here. 452
Thise solaseth the soule · til hym-selue be-falle
In a wel gode hope, for he wrouȝte so · amonges worthi seyntes.
Ac flatereres and foles · thorw here foule wordes,
Leden tho that louen hem · to Luciferes feste, 456
With *turpiloquio*, a lay of sorwe · and Luciferes fithele.]

And thanne had Repentance reuthe · and redde hem alle to knele,
'For I shal biseche for al synful · owre saueoure of grace,
To amende vs of owre mysdedes · and do mercy to vs alle.
Now god,' quod he, 'that of thi goodnesse · gonne the worlde make, 488
And of nauȝte madest auȝte · and man moste liche to thi-selue,
And sithen suffredest for to synne · a sikenesse to vs alle,
And al for the best, as I bileue · what euere the boke telleth,
   O felix culpa! o necessarium peccatum Ade! &c.
For thourgh that synne thi sone · sent was to this erthe, 492
And bicam man of a mayde · mankynde to saue,
And madest thi-self with thi sone · and vs synful yliche,
   Faciamus hominem ad ymaginem et similitudinem nostram;
   Et alibi: qui manet in caritate, in deo manet, et deus in eo;
And sith with thi self sone · in owre sute deydest
On godefryday for mannes sake · at ful tyme of the daye, 496
There thi-self ne thi sone · no sorwe in deth feledest;
But in owre secte was the sorwe · and thi sone it ladde,
   Captiuam duxit captiuitatem.
The sonne for sorwe ther-of · les syȝte for a tyme

[*Not in* **A**-*Text.*]

For to sauy thy saule · fram Satan thyn enemye,
And fithele the, with-oute flateryng · of goode Fryday the geste,
And a blynde man for a bordiour · other a bedreden womman
To crye a largesse by-fore oure lorde · ȝoure goode loos to shewe. 109
Thuse thre manere mynstrales · maken a man to lauhe;
In hus deth-deynge · thei don hym gret comfort,
That by hus lyue litheth hem · and loueth hem to huyre. 112
Thuse solaceth the soule · til hym-self be-falle
In a wel good hope, for he wroghte so · a-mong worthy seyntes;
Ther flaterers and foles · with here foule wordes
Leden tho that lithen hem · to Luciferes feste, 116
With *turpiloquio*, a lay of sorwe · and Lucifers fithele,
To perpetuel peyne · other purgatorye as wykke;
For he litheth and loueth · that godes lawe despiceth;
  Qui histrionibus dat, demonibus sacrificat.
Tho was Repentaunce redy · and radde hem alle to knele,
'Ich shal by-seche for alle synfulle · oure sauyour of grace, 121
To a-menden ous of oure mysdedes · do mercy to ous alle.
God, of thy goodnesse · thow gonne the worlde make,
And of nouht madest ouht · and man lyke thi-selue, 124
Sitthe soffredest hym do synne · a syknesse to ous alle,
And for oure best, as ich by-leyue · what-euere the book telle;
  O felix culpa, o necessarium peccatum Ade!
For thorw that synne thy sone · sent was tyl erthe,
And by-cam man of a mayde · mankynde to a-mende, 128
And madest thi-selue with thy sone · oure soule and body lyche;
  Ego in patre, et pater in me est; et qui uidet me, patrem
  meum uidet.
And sitthe in oure secte · as hit semed, thow deydest,
On a Fryday, in forme of man · feledest oure sorwe;
  Captiuam duxit captiuitatem.
The sonne for sorwe ther-of · lees lyght for a tyme, 132

C. 107. fiþele EF; fitayle P. geste F; feste PEM; beste S. 112. *Read* liþeþ (*see* B-text); loueþ PEMS; leued I; leeueth F; *cf.* l. 119. 117. fitele P. 124. þe (*for* þi) P; see l. 60. 127. PE *om.* þat. 128. a IMF; PSE *om.* 129. þe (*for* þi) P. P *om. in* before *patre.* 130. secke P; *see* l. 137.

A thousent of men tho · throngen to-geders,　　260
Weopyng and weylyng · for heore wikkede dedes,

Aboute mydday whan most li3te is · and mele tyme of seintes;

Feddest with thi fresche blode · owre forfadres in derknesse, 501
　　Populus qui ambulabat in tenebris, vidit lucem magnam ;
And thorw the li3te that lepe oute of the · Lucifer was blent,
And blewe alle thi blissed · in-to the blisse of paradise.

The thrydde daye after · thow 3edest in owre sute,　　504
A synful Marie the seighe · ar seynte Marie thi dame,
And al to solace synful · thow suffredest it so were;
　　Non veni vocare iustos, set peccatores ad penitenciam.
And al that Marke hath ymade · Mathew, Iohan, and Lucas,
Of thyne dou3tiest dedes · were don in owre armes;　　508
　　Verbum caro factum est, et habitauit in nobis.
And bi so moche, me semeth · the sikerere we mowe
Bydde and biseche · if it be thi wille,
That art owre fader and owre brother · be merciable to vs,

And haue reuthe on thise ribaudes · that repente hem here sore,
That euere thei wratthed the in this worlde · in worde, thou3te,
　　or dedes.'　　513
　　Thanne hent Hope an horne · of *deus, tu conuersus viuificabis
　　　nos,*
And blew it with *beati quorum · remisse sunt iniquitates,*
That alle seyntes in heuene · songen at ones,　　516
　　*Homines et iumenta saluabis, quemadmodum multiplicasti
　　　misericordiam tuam, deus, etc.*
A thousand of men tho · thrungen togyderes;
Criede vpward to Cryst · and to his clene moder
To haue grace to go with hem · Treuthe to seke.

B. 514. *nos* R ; L *om.*

Cri3inge vpward to Crist · and to his clene moder
To haue grace to seche seint Treuthe · god leue thei so mote!

A-bowte midday whanne most lyght ys · and meeltyme of
  seyntes;
Feddest tho with thi fresshe blod · oure for-fadres in helle,
  Populus qui ambulabat in tenebris, lucem magnam uidit.
The lyght that lemed out of the · Lucifer hit blente,
And broughte thyne blessede fro thennes · in-to the blysse of
  heuene.   136
The thridde day ther-after · thow 3edest in oure secte;
A synful Marye the seyh · er seynt Marie thy moder,
And al to solace synful · thow soffredest hit so were;
  Non ueni uocare iustos, sed peccatores ad penitenciam.
And al that Marc hath ymad · Matheu, Iohan, and Lucas,   140
Of thyne douhtieste dedes · was don in oure secte;
  Uerbum caro factum est.
And by so moche hit semeth · the sykerloker we mowe
Bydde and by-seche the · yf hit be thy wil,
That art ferst oure fader · and of flessh oure brother,   144
And sitthen oure saueour · and seidest with thy tonge,
That what tyme we synful men · wolden be sory
For dedes that we han don ille · dampned sholde we be neuere,
Yff we knewelechid and cryde · Crist ther-of mercy;   148
  *Quandocumque ingemuerit peccator, omnes iniquitates eius
    non recordabor amplius.*
And for that mochel mercy · and Marie loue thy moder,
Haue reuthe of alle thuse rybaudes · that repenten hem sore,
That euere thei gulte a3ens the, god · in gost other in dede.'
Thenne hente Hope an horn · of *deus, tu conuersus uiuificabis
    nos,*   152
And blew hit with *beati quorum · remisse sunt iniquitates, et cetera,*
That alle seyntes with synful men · songen with Dauid,
  *Homines et iumenta saluabis, domine, quemadmodum multipli-
    casti misericordiam tuam, deus!*
A thousand of men tho · throngen to-gederes,
Cryyng vpward to Crist · and to hus clene moder,   156
To haue grace to go to Treuthe · god leyue that thei mote!

C. 133. P *om.* most.   141. in IMSFG; on PE; *see* l. 137.   144. ert
(*for* art) PE.

PASSUS VI.

Passus Sextus de visione, vt prius.

NOW riden this folk · and walken on fote
To seche that seint · in selcouthe londis.
Bote ther were fewe men so wys · that couthe the wei thider,
Bote bustelyng forth as bestes · ouer valeyes and hulles,   4
For while thei wente here owen wille · thei wente alle amys.
Til hit was late and longe · that thei a leod metten,
Apparayled as a palmere · in pilgrimes wedes.
He bar a bordun i-bounde · with a brod lyste,   8
In a wethe-bondes wyse · i-writhen aboute.
A bagge and a bolle · he bar bi his syde;

Ac there was wyȝte non so wys · the wey thider couthe, 520
But blustreden forth as bestes · ouer bankes and hilles,
Til late was and longe · that thei a lede mette,
Apparailled as a paynym · in pylgrymes wyse.
He bare a burdoun ybounde · with a brode liste,   524
In a withewyndes wise · ywounden aboute.
A bolle and a bagge · he bare by his syde;
An hundreth of ampulles · on his hatt seten,
Signes of Synay · and shelles of Galice;   528
And many a cruche on his cloke · and keyes of Rome,
And the vernicle bifore · for men shulde knowe,
And se bi his signes · whom he souȝte hadde.
    This folke frayned hym firste · fro whennes he come?   532
'Fram Synay,' he seyde · 'and fram owre lordes sepulcre;
In Bethleem and in Babiloyne · I haue ben in bothe,
In Ermonye, in Alisaundre · in many other places.
Ȝe may se bi my signes · that sitten on myn hatte,   536
That I haue walked ful wyde · in wete and in drye,
And souȝte gode seyntes · for my soules helth.'
    'Knowestow ouȝte a corseint · that men calle **Treuthe**?
Coudestow auȝte wissen vs the weye · where that wy dwelleth?' 540

A. 1, 2, 5. *These lines are in* H *only.*   6. hit H; V *om.*

A. PASSUS VI. 11-24. C. PASSUS VIII. 158-178.

An hundred of ampolles · on his hat seeten,
Signes of Synay . and schelles of Galys;   12
Moni cros on his cloke · and kei3es of Rome,
And the vernicle bi-fore · for men schulde him knowe,
And seo be his signes · whom he souht hedde.
  This folk fraynede him feire · from' whenne that he coome?
'From Synay,' he seide, · 'and from the sepulcre;
From Bethleem and Babiloyne · I haue ben in bothe,
In Ynde and in Assye · and in mony other places.
3e mouwe seo be my signes · that sitteth on myn hat,   20
That I haue walked ful wyde · in weete and in druye,
And souht goode seyntes · for my soule hele.'
  'Knowest thou ouht a corseynt · men calleth seynt Treuthe?
Const thou wissen vs the wey · wher that he dwelleth?'   24

Ac ther was weye non so wys · that the way thider couthe,
Bote blostrede forth as bestes · ouer baches and hulles,
Til late was and longe · that thei a lede mette,   160
A-paraild as a paynym · in pylgrymes wise.
He bar a bordon ybounde · with a brod lyste,
In a weythwynde wyse · ywrythe al aboute;
A bolle and a bagge · he bar by hus syde,   164
And an hondred hanypeles · on hus hatte seten,
Signes of Syse · and shilles of Galys,
And meny crouche on hus cloke · and keyes of Rome,
And the fernycle by-fore · for men sholde knowe,   168
And se by hus sygnes · wham he souht hadde.
  Thys folke frayned hym furst · fro whennes he come?
'Fro Sinay,' he sayde · 'and fro the sepulcre.
In Bethleem, in Babilonie · ich haue ybe bothe,   172
In Ermanie, in Alisaundre · and in Damascle,
3e may see by my synges · that sitten on my cappe,
Ich haue ysouht goode seyntes · for my soules helthe,
And walked ful wide · in wete and in drye.'   176
  'Knowst thow ou3t a cor-seynt,' quath ich · 'that men clepeth Treuthe?
Couthest thow wissen ous the way · whoder out treuthe wonycth?'

C. 169. And se IFS; As PE; *see* l. 174.   177. ou3t GS; au3t F; oght I; PE *om.*   core-seynt P.

'Nay, so god glade me!' · seide the gome thenne,
'Sauh I neuere palmere · with pyk ne with schrippe
Such a seint seche · bote now in this place.'
'Peter!' quod a plouȝ-mon · and putte forth his hed,　28
'I knowe him as kuyndeliche · as clerk doth his bokes;
Clene concience and wit · kende me to his place,
And dude enseure me seththe · to serue him for euere.
Bothe to sowen and to setten · while I swynke mihte,　32
I haue ben his felawe · this fiftene wynter;
Bothe i-sowed his seed · and suwed his beestes,
And eke i-kept his corn · i-caried hit to house,

'Nay, so me god helpe!' · seide the gome thanne,
'I seygh neuere palmere · with pike ne with scrippe
Axen after hym er · til now in this place.'

'Peter!' quod a plowman · and put forth his hed,　544
'I knowe hym as kyndely · as clerke doth his bokes;
Conscience and Kynde Witte · kenned me to his place,
And deden me suren hym sikerly · to serue hym for euere,
Bothe to sowe and to sette · the while I swynke myghte.　548
I haue ben his folwar · al this fifty wyntre;
Bothe ysowen his sede · and sued his bestes,
With-inne and with-outen · wayted his profyt.
I dyke and I delue · I do that treuthe hoteth;　552
Some tyme I sowe · and some tyme I thresche,
In tailoures crafte and tynkares crafte · what Treuthe can deuyse,
I weue an I wynde · and do what Treuthe hoteth.
For thouȝe I seye it my-self · I serue hym to paye.　556
Ich haue myn huire of hym wel · and otherwhiles more;
He is the prestest payer · that pore men knoweth;
He ne with-halt non hewe his hyre · that he ne hath it at euen.
He is as low as a lombe · and loueliche of speche,　560
And ȝif ȝe wilneth to wite · where that he dwelleth,
I shal wisse ȝow witterly · the weye to his place.'
'Ȝe, leue Pieres,' quod this pilgrymes · and profered hym huire
For to wende with hem · to Treuthes dwellyng-place.　564

A. 30. kende TU; tauȝte VH.　　B. 549. fifty WCO; fourty LR.

A. PASSUS VI. 36-46.   C. PASSUS VIII. 179-199.

I-dyket and i-doluen · i-don what he hihte,   36
With-innen and withouten · i-wayted his profyt;
Ther nis no laborer in this leod · that he loueth more,
For thauh I sigge hit my-self · I serue him to paye.
I haue myn hure of him wel · and otherwhile more;   40
He is the presteste payere · that pore men habbeth;
He with-halt non hyne his huire · that he hit nath at euen.
He is as louh as a lomb · louelich of speche,
And ȝif ȝe wolleth i-wite · wher that he dwelleth,   44
I wol wissen ow the wey · hom to his place.'
'Ye, leue Pers,' quod this palmers · and profreden him huire.

'Nay, so god me helpe' · seyde the gome thenne,
'Ich seyh neuere palmere · with pyk ne with scrippe   180
Asken after hym, er now · in thys ilke place.'

HIC PRIMO COMPARET PETRUS PLOUGHMAN.

' Peter !' quath a ploughman · and putte forth hus hefd,
'Ich knowe hym as kyndeliche · as clerkus don hure bokes.
Conscience and Kyndewit · kende me to hus place,   184
And maked me sykeren hym sitthen · to seruen hym for euere,
Bothe to sowe and to setten · the whyle ich swynke myghte,
With-ynne and with-oute · to wayten hus profyt.
Ich haue yben his folwer · al thes fourty wynter,   188
And serued Treuthe sothlyche · somdel to paye;
In alle kynne craftes · that he couthe deuyse
Profitable to the plouh · he putte me to lerne;
And thauh ich seye hit my-self · ich seruede hym to paye.   192
Ich haue myn hyre of hym wel · and other whyle more;
He ys the most prest paiere · that eny poure man knoweth.
He with-halt non hewe · hus hyre ouere euen;
He ys louh as a lombe · and leel of hus tonge,   196
And ho so wilneth to wyte · wher that Treuthe wonyeth,
Ich wol wissen ȝow wel · ryght to hus place.'
'Ȝe, leue Peers,' quath tho pylgrymes · and profrede Peers
   mede.

557. of hym R; L *om.*   C. 180. shrippe P.   183. Iich (*for* Ich) P.
185. seren (*for* seruen) P.   191. Prophitable P.   194. PE *om.* the.
195. hewe I; hywe P ; hyne EMSFG.

'Nai, bi the peril of my soule,' quod Pers · and bigon to swere,
'I nolde fonge a ferthing · for seynt Thomas schrine! 48
Treuthe wolde loue me the lasse · a gret while after!
  Bote ȝe that wendeth to him · this is the wei thider:
ȝe mote go thorw Mekenesse · bothe mon and wyf,
Til ȝe come in-to Concience · that Crist knowe the sothe 52
That ȝe loueth him leuere · then the lyf in oure hertes,
And thenne oure neihebors next · in none wyse apeire
Otherweys then thou woldest · men wrouȝten to thi-seluen.

'Nay, bi my soules helth,' quod Pieres · and gan forto swere,
'I nolde fange a ferthynge · for seynt Thomas shryne!
Treuthe wolde loue me the lasse · a longe tyme thereafter!

  Ac if ȝe wilneth to wende wel · this is the weye thider, 568
That I shal say to yow · and sette yow in the sothe.
ȝe mote go thourgh Mekenesse · bothe men and wyues,
Tyl ȝe come in-to Conscience · that Cryst wite the sothe,
That ȝe louen owre lorde god · leuest of alle thinges, 572

  And thanne ȝowre neighbores nexte · in non wise apeyre
Otherwyse than thow woldest · he wrouȝte to thi-selue.
  And so boweth forth bi a broke · Beth-buxum-of-speche,
Tyl ȝe fynden a forth · ȝowre-fadres-honoureth, 576
   Honora patrem et matrem, etc.
Wadeth in that water · and wascheth ȝow wel there;
And ȝe shul lepe the liȝtloker · al ȝowre lyf-tyme.
  And so shaltow se Swere-nouȝte- · but-if-it-be-for-nede-
And-namelich-an-ydel- · the-name-of-god-almyȝti. 580
    Thanne shaltow come by a crofte · but come thow nouȝte
       there-inne;
That crofte hat Coueyte-nouȝte- · mennes-catel-ne-her-wyues-
Ne-none-of-her-serauntes- · that-noyen-hem-myȝte;

A. 57. *From* UTD; V *omits this line.* **B.** 569. *From* CO; LWR *omit this line.* **C.** 200. pereil P. 212. And oþer-wyse PE; *but* IMFS *omit* And. 213. brok M; brook SF; bok P. 214. honourieþ P. 215.

So bouweth forth bi a brok · Beo-boxum-of-speche, 56
Forth til ȝe fynde a forde · ȝour-fadres-honoureth;
Wadeth in that water · wasscheth ow wel there,
And ȝe schul lepe the lihtloker · al oure lyf-tyme.
Sone schaltou thenne i-seo · Swere-not-but-thou-haue-neode-
And-nomeliche-in-idel- · the-nome-of-god-almihti.
Thenne schul ȝe come bi a croft · but cum ȝe not ther-inne;
The croft hette Coueyte-not- · mennes-catel-ne-heore-wyues-
Ne-non-of-heore-seruauns- · that-nuyȝen-hem-mihte; 64

'Nay, by the peril of my soule' · Peers gan swere, 200
'Ich nolde fonge a ferthing · for seynt Thomas shryne!
Were it told to Treuthe · that ich toke mede,
He wolde louye me the lasse · a longe tyme after.

ALTA UIA AD FIDELITATEM EST OBSERUATIO .X. PRECEPTORUM, UT
DICIT PETRUS PLOUHMAN.

Ac who so wol wende · ther as Treuthe dwelleth, 204
This ys the heye weye thyderwarde · wyteth wel the sothe.
ȝe most gon thorwe Meknesse · alle men and wommen,
Tyl ȝe come to Conscience · knowen of god selue,
That ȝe loue hym as lord · leelliche a-bouen alle; 208
That ys to seye sothliche · ȝe sholde rather deye
Than eny dedliche synne do · for drede other for preyere.
And thenne ȝoure neghebores next · in none wyse apeyre,
Other-wyse than ȝe wolde · thei wroughte ȝou alle tymes. 212
And so goth forth by the brok · a brygge as hit were,
Tyl ȝe fynde a forde · ȝoure-fadres-honoureth;
Wadeth wel in that water · and wascheth ȝow wel there,
And ȝe shulle lepe the lyghtloker · al ȝoure lyf-tyme; 216
    Honora patrem et matrem, et eris longeuus super terram.
Thanne shalt thow see Swery-nat- · bot-yt-be-for-nede-
Nameliche-an-ydel- · the-name-of-god-al-myghty.
Thanne shalt thow come by a croft · ac com thou nat ther-
    ynne,
The croft hatte Coueyte-nat- · mennes-catel-ne-here-wyues- 220
Ne-non-of-here-seruans- · that-nuyen-hem-myghte;

þe (*for* þat) P.   wasche PE.   217. see I; go by F; PEMS *omit*.   nude
(*for* nede) P.   219. PS *om.* thou.

186   A. PASSUS VI. 65–76.   B. PASSUS V. 584–606.

Loke thou breke no bouȝ there · but ȝif hit beo thin owne.
Twei stokkes ther stondeth · but stunt thou not there,
Thei hetten, Sle-not, Ne-stel-not · stryk forth bi hem bothe;
Lef hem on thi luft half · loke hem not aftur,   68
And hold wel thin haly-day · euere til euen.
Thenne schaltou blenchen at a brok · Ber-no-fals-witnesse,
He is frettet with-innen with floreyns · and othes wel monye;
Loke thou plokke no plonte ther · for peril of thi soule.   72
Thenne schaltou se Sei-soth- · so-hit-beo-to-done-
And-loke-that-thou-lyȝe-not- · for-no-monnes-bidyng.
Thenne schaltou come to a court · cleer as the sonne,
The mot is of Merci · the maner al abouten,   76

Loke ȝe breke no bowes there · but if it be ȝowre owne.   584
Two stokkes there stondeth · ac stynte ȝe nouȝte there,
They hatte Stele-nouȝte, Ne-slee-nouȝte · stryke forth by bothe;
And leue hem on thi left halfe · and loke nouȝte there-after;
And holde wel thyne haliday · heighe til euen.   588
Thanne shaltow blenche at a berghe · Bere-no-false-witnesse,
He is frithed in with floreines · and other fees many;
Loke thow plukke no plante there · for peril of thi soule.
Thanne shal ȝe se Sey-soth- · so-it-be-to-done-   592
In-no-manere-ellis-nauȝte- · for-no-mannes-biddynge.
Thanne shaltow come to a courte · as clere as the sonne,
The mote is of Mercy · the manere aboute,
And alle the wallis ben of Witte · to holden Wille oute;   596
And kerneled with Crystendome · man-kynde to saue,
Boterased with Bileue-so- · or-thow-beest-nouȝte-ysaued.
And alle the houses ben hiled · halles and chambres,
With no lede, but with Loue · and Lowe-speche-as-bretheren. 600
The brugge is of Bidde-wel- · the-bette-may-thow-spede;
Eche piler is of Penaunce · of preyeres to seyntes,
Of Almes-dedes ar the hokes · that the gates hangen on.
Grace hatte the gateward · a gode man for sothe,   604
Hys man hatte Amende-ȝow · for many man him knoweth;
Telleth hym this tokene · that Treuthe wite the sothe;

A. 73. se UD; V *om*.   B. 586. hatte CR; hatten O; hat L.   590.
fees WCR; foes L.   600. Wit L.   C. 222. ȝif SM; if IG; PEF *om*.
owne MSF; owe PE.   223. stynt ESF; stunt P.   228. friþed MIG;

A. PASSUS VI. 77–87.   C. PASSUS VIII. 222–245.

And alle the walles beth of Wit · to holde Wil theroute;
The carnels beth of Cristendam · the kuynde to saue,
Brutaget with the Bileeue · wher-thorw we moten· beo sauet.
Alle the houses beoth i-hulet · halles and chaumbres,   80
With no led, bote with Loue- · as-Bretheren-of-o-wombe.
The tour ther Treuthe is inne · i-set is aboue the sonne,
He may do with the day-sterre · what him deore lyketh;
Deth dar not do · thing that he defendeth.   84
Grace hette the ȝate-ward · a good mon forsothe,
His mon hette A-mende-thou · for mony men him knoweth;
Tel him this tokene · for Treuthe wot the sothe:

Loke thou bere nat there aweye · bote ȝif yt be thyn owne.
Two stockes ther stonden · ac stynt thow nouht there;
Thei hatte Stel-net and Slee-nat · stryk forth by hem bothe, 224
And leue hem in thy lift hand · and loke nouht therafter,
And hold wel thyn halyday · heye tyl euen.
Thenne shalt thou blenche at a bergh · Ber-no-fals-wytnesse,
He ys frithed yn with floreynes · and other fees menye,   228
Loke thow plocke ther no plaunte · for peryl of thy soule.
Thanne shalt thow see Seye-sothe- · so-hit-be-to-done-
In-no-manere-elles-nat- · for-no-mannes-preyere.
So shalt thow come to a court · as cleer so the sonne,   232
The mot ys of Mercy · in myddes the manere,
Al the wallynge ys of Wit · for Wil ne sholde hit wynne.
The kernels beth of Crystendome · that kynde to saue,
And boteraced with By-leyue-so- · other-thow-best-nat-saued.   236
Alle the houses beth heled · halles and chambres,
With no lede, bote with Loue · and with Leel-speche.
The barres aren of Buxumnesse · as bretheren of on wombe.
The brigge hatte Bid-wel- · the-bet-myght-thow-spede;   240
Eche pyler ys of Penaunce · and preyers to seyntes,
The hokes aren Almys-dedes · that the ȝates hongen on.
Grace hatte the gate-warde · a good man for sothe,
Hus man hatte Amende-ȝow · meny man hym knoweth.   244
Tel hym thys ilke tokne · 'Treuthe wot the sothe,

---

freþed P.   230. see I; go by F; PEMS *om.*   236. best IM; beest G;
worsthest (*sic*) P; worst ES.   239. breþeren IEF; breþres P.   240.
bregge (*for* brigge) P.   242. dedes IMEF; dede PS.

188 A. PASSUS VI. 88–96. B. PASSUS V. 607–625.

'I performede the penaunce · that the prest me en-ioynede; 88
I am sori for my sunnes · and so schal I euere
Whon I thenke ther-on · thau3 I weore a pope.'
Bidde A-mende-thou meken him · to his mayster ones,
To wynne vp the wiket-3at · that the wey schutte, 92
Tho that Adam and Eue · eeten heore bone;
For he hath the keye of the cliket · thau3 the kyng slepe.
And 3if Grace the graunte · to gon in in this wyse,
Thou schalt seo Treuthe him-self · sitten in thin herte. 96

'I parfourned the penaunce · the preest me enioyned,
And am ful sori for my synnes · and so I shal euere, 608
Whan I thinke there-on · theighe I were a pope.'
Biddeth Amende-3ow meke him · til his maistre ones,
To wayue vp the wiket · that the womman shette,
Tho Adam and Eue · eten apples vnrosted ; 612
    *Per Euam cunctis clausa est, et per Mariam virginem iterum
    patefacta est ;*
For he hath the keye and the cliket · thou3 the kyng slepe.
And if Grace graunte the · to go in in this wise,
Thow shalt see in thi-selue · Treuthe sitte in thine herte,
In a cheyne of charyte · as thow a childe were, 616
To suffre hym and segge nou3te · a3ein thi sires wille.

Ac bewar thanne of Wrath-the · that is a wikked shrewe,
He hath enuye to hym · that in thine herte sitteth ;
And pukketh forth pruyde · to prayse thi-seluen. 620
The boldnesse of thi bienfetes · maketh the blynde thanne,
And thanne worstow dryuen oute as dew · and the dore closed,
Kayed and cliketed · to kepe the with-outen ;
Happily an hundreth wyntre · ar thow eft entre. 624
Thus myght thow lesen his loue · to late wel by thi-selue,

  A. 91. Amende-thou; A-mende V ; *but see* l. 86. 98. that wykkide TUD ;
for he is a V. 99. in—sitteth TUD ; sitteth in thyn herte V. 103. kepe TD ;
holden V. **B**. 611. wayne *or* wayue. 612. *iterum* ; in R only. 613.
clikat L. 623. clikated L. **C**. 248. mekeþ M ; meek PS. 249. 3ates

Thenne loke that thou loue him wel · and his lawe holde;
Bote beo wel i-war of Wraththe · that wykkide schrewe,
For he hath envye to him · that in thyn herte sitteth;
And puiteth forth pruide · to preisen thi-seluen.   100
The boldnesse of thi benfes · blendeth thin eiȝen,
And so worthestou i-driuen out · and the dore i-closet,
I-keiȝet and i-kliketed · to kepe the ther-oute;
Hapliche, an hundred ȝer · er thou eft entre.   104
Thus maihtou leosen his loue · to leten wel bi thi-seluen,

Ich am sory for my synnes · and so shal ich euere,
And parfourne the penaunce · that the preest me highte.'
Rydeth to A-mende-ȝow · meketh ȝow to hus mayster Grace,
To openen and vndo · the hye ȝate of heuene,   249
That Adam and Eue · aȝens ous alle shutte :
    Per Euam ianua celi cunctis clausa est, et per Mariam
    uirginem iterum patefacta est.
A ful leel lady · vn-leek hure of grace ;
Hue hath a keye and a clyket · thauh the kynge slepe,   252
And may lede yn wham hue loueth · as here luf lyketh.
And yf Grace graunte the · to go yn in thys wise,
Thow shalt se Treuthe sytte · in thy selue herte,
And solace thy soule · and saue the fro pyne.   256
Al-so charge Charyte · a churche to make
In thyn hole herte · to herberghwen alle treuthe,
And fynde alle manere folke · fode to hure saules,
Yf loue and leaute · and owre lawe be trewe :   260
    Quodcumque petieritis in nomine meo, dabitur enim uobis.
Be war thenne of Wratthe · that wickede shrewe,
For he hath enuye to hym · that in thyn herte sytteth,
And poketh forth pruyde · to preysy thi-selue.
The boldnesse of thy bynfet · maketh the blynde thenne,   264
So worst thow dryuen out as deuh · and the dore closed,
Y-keyed and yclyketed · to close the with-oute,
Hapliche an hondred wynter · ar thow eft entrie.
Thus myght thou lese hus loue · to lete wel by thi-selue,   268

PEMS; *but* gate IF; *see* l. 251.   251. leel EMSFG; bel P.   vn-leek IS;
vnlek G; vn-lyke P; vnlocket M.   252. clykett P.   259. fode EMS;
foude P.   260. trywe P.   265. worst SM; worth PEIG.   266.
yclykeded P.   268. þe (*for* thi) PS.

Bote gete hit aȝeyn bi grace · and bi no ȝift elles.
Ak ther beoth seuen sustren · that seruen Treuthe euere,
And ben porters at posternes · that to the place longen.   108
That on hette Abstinence · and Humilitie a-nother,
Charite and Chastite · beoth tweyne ful choyse maidenes,
Pacience and Pees · muche peple helpen,
Largesse the ladi · ledeth in ful monye.   112
Bote hose is sib to this sustren · so me god helpe!
Is wonderliche wel-comen · and feire vnderfonge.
And bote ȝe ben sibbe · to summe of theos seuene,

And neuere happiliche efte entre · but grace thow haue.
Ac there aren seuene sustren · that seruen Treuthe euere,
And aren porteres of the posternes · that to the place longeth.   628
That one hat Abstenence · and Humilite an other,
Charite and Chastite · ben his chief maydenes,
Pacience and Pees · moche poeple thei helpeth,
Largenesse the lady · heo let in ful manye;   632
Heo hath hulpe a thousande oute · of the deueles ponfolde.
And who is sibbe to this seuene · so me god helpe!
He is wonderliche welcome · and faire vnderfongen.
And but-if ȝe be syb · to summe of thise seuene,   636
It is ful harde bi myne heued,' quod Peres · ' for any of ȝow alle
To geten ingonge at any gate there · but grace be the more.'
'Now, bi Cryst,' quod a cutpurs · 'I haue no kynne there!'
'Ne I,' quod an apewarde · ' bi auȝte that I knowe!'   640
'Wite god,' quod a wafrestre · 'wist I this for sothe,
Shulde I neuere ferthere a fote · for no freres prechynge.'
'Ȝus,' quod Pieres the plowman · and pukked hem alle to gode,
'Mercy is a maydene there · hath myȝte ouer hem alle;   644
And she is syb to alle synful · and her sone also;
And thoruȝe the helpe of hem two · (hope thow none other),
Thow myȝte gete grace there · bi so thow go bityme.'

A. 126. go TUD; come V.   B. 627. aren R; ar L; see l. 628.
C. 269. hit MSG; it I; PE om. gifte EI; gift M; gefte S; gyse P.
278-280. so me—seuene from SIMEG; P omits.   282. engang P.   287.

A. PASSUS VI. 116-126.   C. PASSUS VIII. 269-291.

Hit is ful hard, bi myn hed! · eny of ow alle   116
To gete in-goynge at that ȝat · bote grace beo the more.'
'Bi Crist,' quath a cutte-pors · 'I haue no kun there!'
'No,' quath an apeward · 'for nout that I knowe!'
'I-wis,' quath a waferer · 'wust I this for sothe,   120
Schulde I neuere forthere a fote · for no freres prechinge.'
'Ȝus,' quath Pers the plouȝ-mon · and prechede hire to goode,
'Merci is a mayden ther · and hath miht ouer hem alle;
Heo is sib to alle synful men · an hire sone alse;   124
And thorw the help of hem two · (hope thou non other),
Thou maiȝt gete grace ther · so that thou go bi-tyme.'

And geten hit a-geyn thorw grace · ac thorgh no gifte elles.
Ther ben seuene sustres · that seruen Treuthe euere,
And aren porters at posternes · that to the place longen;
That on hatte Abstinence · and Humilite another,   272
Charite and Chastite · ben hus chef maydenes,
Pacience and Pees · muche puple helpen,
Largenesse that lady · lat yn ful menye;
Non of hem alle · helpe may yn betere,   276
For hue paieth for prisons · in places and in peynes.
And ho is sybbe to thuse seuene · so me god helpe!
He is wondirlich welcome · and fayre vndirfonge.
Ho is not sib to these seuene · sothly to telle,   280
Hit is ful hard, by myn heued · eny of ȝou alle
To geten ingang at eny gate · bote grace be the more.'
'By Cryst,' quath a kitte-pors · 'ich haue no kyn there.'
'Ne ich,' quath an apewarde · 'by ouht that ich knowe!'   284
'Wyte god,' quath a wafrestre · 'wist ich the sothe,
Ich wolde no forther a fot · for no freres prechinge.'
'Ȝus,' quath Peers plouhman · and pokede hem alle to goode;
'Mercy is a mayde there · hath myght ouer hem alle;   288
And hue is sybbe to alle synful · and hure sone bothe.
And thorwe the help of hem two · hope thow non other,
Thow myght gete grace ther · so thow go by tyme.'

---

pokede EMSG; pukede P.   288. a EMIG; PS *om.*   290. two E;
tuo I; to PMS.

PASSUS VII.

Passus septimus de visione, vt prius.

'THIS weore a wikked wei · bote hose hedde a gyde,
That mihte folwen us vch a fote · forte that we come there.'

'By seynt Poule,' quod a pardonere · 'perauenture I be
nouȝte knowe there, 648
I wil go fecche my box with my breuettes · and a bulle with
bisshopes lettres!'
'By Cryst,' quod a comune womman · 'thi companye wil I
folwe,
Thow shalt sey I am thi sustre · I ne wot where thei bicome.'

PASSUS VI.

Passus Sextus.

'THIS were a wikked way · but who-so hadde a gyde
That wolde folwen us eche a fote;' · thus this folke hem
mened.

Quath Perkyn the plouman · 'bi seynt Peter of Rome,
I haue an half-acre to erye · bi the heighe way; 4
Hadde I eried this half-acre · and sowen it after,
I wolde wende with ȝow · and the way teche.'
'This were a longe lettynge' · quod a lady in a sklayre,
'What sholde we wommen · worche there-whiles?' 8

B. 3. Quatȝ L.   6. wolde WO; wil LR.   C. 294. nude (*for* nede) P.
296. greiþliche M; graithliche I; grettliche PESG.   301. syghit (*for* syghte) P.

Quath Perkyn the plou3mon · 'bi Peter the apostel,
I haue an half aker to herie · bi the hei3e weye; 4
Weore he wel i-eried · thenne with ou wolde I wende,
And wissen ou the rihte weye · til 3e founden Treuthe.'
'That weore a long lettynge' · quath a ladi in a skleir,
'What schul we wimmen · worche the while?' 8

'3e, villam emi,' quath on · 'and now most ich thudere, 292
To loke how me lyketh hit' · and tok hus leue at Peers.
Another a-non ryght · nede seyde he hadde
To folwen fif 3okes · 'for-thy me by-houeth
To gon with a good wil · and greithliche hem dryue; 296
For-thy ich praye 3ow, Peers · paraunter, yf 3e meteth
Treuthe, telleth to hym · that ich be excused.'
Thenne was ther on heihte Actif · an hosebounde he semed;
'Ich haue ywedded a wyf,' quath he · 'wel wantowen of maners;
Were ich seuenyght fro hure syghte · synnen hue wolde, 301
And loure on me and lyghtliche chide · and seye ich loue
    anothere.
For-thy, Peers plouhman · ich praye the telle hit Treuthe,
Ich may nat come for a Kytte · so hue cleueth on me;
    Vxorem duxi, et ideo non possum uenire.'
Quath Contemplacion, 'by Crist · thauh ich care suffre,
Famyn and defaute · folwen ich wolle Peers; 306
Ac the wey ys so wyckede · bote ho so hadde a gyde
That myght folwen ous ech fot · for drede of mys-tornynge.'
    Hic explicit passus octauus.

PASSUS IX.

Incipit passus Nonus.

THO seyde Perken plouhman · 'by seynt Peter of Rome,
Ich haue an half-acre to eren · by the hye weye.
Hadde ich ered that half-acre · and sowen hit after,
Ich wolde wende with 3ow · and the wey teche.' 4
    'That were a long lettynge' · quath a lady in a skleire,
'What sholde we wommen · worche the whiles?'

---

synnen M; syngun S; sinege G; seggen P.   304. cleueþ MISE; clyueþ P.
307. P *om. 2nd* so.   IX. 4. wit P.

O

194   A. PASSUS VII. 9-20.   B. PASSUS VI. 9-29.

'Summe schul souwe sakkes · for schedyng of whete,
And ȝe wyues that habbeth wolle · worcheth hit faste,
Spynneth it spedily · spareth noght ȝour fyngres,
Bote ȝif hit beo haly day · or elles holy euen.   12
Loketh forth or linnene · and labereth ther-on faste.
The neodi and the nakede · nym ȝeeme hou thei liggen,
And cast on hem clothes for colde · for so wolde treuthe;
For I schal lene hem lyflode · but ȝif the lond fayle,   16
As longe as I liue · for vr lordes loue of heuene.
And ȝe, loueli ladies · with oure longe fyngres,
That habbeth selk, and sendel · souweth, whon tyme is,
Chesybles for chapeleyns · and churches to honoure;   20

'Somme shal sowe the sakke,' quod Piers · 'for shedyng of
    the whete;
And ȝe, louely ladyes · with ȝoure longe fyngres,
That ȝe han silke and sendal · to sowe, whan tyme is,
Chesibles for chapelleynes · cherches to honoure.   12
Wyues and wydwes · wolle and flex spynneth,
Maketh cloth, I conseille ȝow · and kenneth so ȝowre douȝtres;
The nedy and the naked · nymmeth hede how hij liggeth.
And casteth hem clothes · for so comaundeth Treuthe.   16
For I shal lene hem lyflode · but ȝif the londe faille,
Flesshe and bred bothe · to riche and to pore,
As longe as I lyue · for the lordes loue of heuene.
And alle manere of men · that thorw mete and drynke lyb-
    beth,   20
Helpith hym to worche wiȝtliche · that wynneth ȝowre fode.'
'Bi Crist,' quod a knyȝte tho · 'he kenneth vs the best;
Ac on the teme trewly · tauȝte was I neuere.
Ac kenne me,' quod the knyȝte · 'and, bi Cryst, I wil assaye!' 24
'Bi seynt Poule,' quod Perkyn · 'ȝe profre ȝow so faire,
That I shal swynke and swete · and sowe for vs bothe,
And other laboures do for thi loue · al my lyf-tyme,
In couenaunt that thow kepe · holikirke and my-selue   28
Fro wastoures and fro wykked men · that this worlde struyeth.

A. 11. *From* UTH; V *omits this line.*   23. kennest HU; techest V.
25. kenne TU; tech V.   26. *This line is in* H *only.*   B. 9. (1*st*) the
WCRO; L *om.* C. 8. wete P. 9. wit P. 10. to sewen PE; MSG *om.* to.

A. PASSUS VII. 21–31.   C. PASSUS IX. 7–27.   195

And alle maner of men · that bi mete liuen,
Helpeth him worche wihtliche · that winneth oure fode.'
  'Bi Crist,' quath a kniht tho · 'thou kennest vs the beste!
Saue o tyme trewely · thus tauht was I neuere!   24
Bote kenne me,' quod the kniht · 'and I-chul conne erie;
I wol helpe thee to labore · whil my lyf lastith.'
  'Bi seint Peter,' quod Pers · 'for thou profrest the so lowe,
I schal swynken and sweten · and sowen for us bothe,   28
And eke labre for thi loue · al my lyf-tyme,
In couenaunt that thou kepe · holi chirche and my-seluen
From wastors and wikkede men · that wolden vs destruyen.

'Ich praye 3ow, for 3oure profit' · quath Peers to the ladyes,
'That somme sewe the sak · for shedynge of the whete :   8
And 3e worthly wommen · with 3oure longe fyngres,
That 3e on selke and sendel · sewen, whenne tyme ys,
Chesybles for chapelayns · churches to honoure.
Wyues and widowes · wolle and flax spynneth;   12
Conscience consaileth 3ow · cloth for to make
For profit of the poure · and plesaunce of 3ow-selue.
For ich shal lene hem lyflode · bote yf the lond faile,
As longe as ich lyue · for oure lordes loue in heuene.   16
And alle manere men · that by this molde buth susteyned,
Helpeth hem to worche wyghtly · that wynneth 3oure fode.'
  'By Cryst,' quath a kny3t tho · 'he kenneth ous the beste;
Ac on the teeme trewely · tauht was ich neuere;   20
Ich wolde ich couthe,' quath the kny3t · 'by Cryst and hus moder;
Ich wolde a-saye som tyme · for solas, as hit were.'
  'Sykerliche, syre kny3t' · seide Peers thenne,
'Ich shal swynke and swete · and sowe for us bothe,   24
And laboure for the while thou lyuest · al thy lyf-tyme,
In couenaunt that thou kepe · holy kirke and my-selue
Fro wastours and wyckede men · that this worlde struen.

---

wenne P.   11. honure P.   16. lyue IMSEG ; leue P.   18.
whyghtly P.   20. trywely P.   23. knyi3t P.   24. hus P.
25. lyuest EMS ; leuest P.   26. kirke I ; churche PEMS.   my EIG ;
me PMS.   27. Fro IMSG ; For PE.   this IMSE ; þus P.

O 2

And go thou hunte hardily · to hares and to foxes, 32
To beores and to bockes · that breketh menne hegges,
And fecche the hom faucuns · the foules to quelle;
For thei comen in-to my croft · and croppen my whete.'
    Ful curteisliche the kniht · conseiued theose wordes; 36
'Be my pouwer, pers · I plihte the my trouthe
To folfulle the foreward · while that I may stonde!'
    'But ȝit o poynt,' quod Pers · 'I preye the no more;
Loke thou teone no tenaunt · bote Treuthe wol assente: 40

And go hunte hardiliche · to hares and to foxes,
To bores and to brockes · that breketh adown myne hegges,
And go affaite the faucones · wilde foules to kille; 32
For suche cometh to my croft · and croppeth my whete.'
    Curteislich the knyȝte thanne · comsed thise wordes,
'By my power, Pieres,' quod he · 'I pliȝte the my treuthe
To fulfille this forward · thowȝ I fiȝte sholde; 36
Als longe as I lyue · I shal the mayntene.'
    'Ȝe, and ȝit a poynt,' quod Pieres · 'I preye ȝow of more;
Loke ȝe tene no tenaunt · but Treuthe wil assent.
And thowgh ȝe mowe amercy hem · late Mercy be taxoure, 40
And Mekenesse thi mayster · maugre Medes chekes,
And thowgh pore men profre ȝow · presentis and ȝiftis,
Nym it nauȝte, an auenture · ȝe mowe it nauȝte deserue;
For thow shalt ȝelde it aȝein · at one ȝeres ende, 44
In a ful perillous place · purgatorie it hatte.
And mysbede nouȝte thi bonde-men · the better may thow spede;
Thowgh he be thyn vnderlynge here · wel may happe in heuene,
That he worth worthier sette · and with more blisse, 48
Than thow, bot thou do bette · and lyue as thow shulde;
    Amice, ascende superius.
For in charnel atte chirche · cherles ben yuel to knowe,
Or a kniȝte fram a knaue there · knowe this in thin herte.
And that thow be trewe of thi tonge · and tales that thow hatie, 52
But if thei ben of wisdome or of witte · thi werkmen to chaste.
Holde with none harlotes · ne here nouȝte her tales,

B. 49. *From* C; LWRO *omit this line.*   **C.** 28. hardileche P.   32. knyitȝ (*for* knyȝt) P.   þes P.   35. ouere P.   36. tene IMSEG;

A. PASSUS VII. 41-48.   C. PASSUS IX. 28-50.   197

And ȝif pore men profreth ou · presentes or ȝiftes,
Taketh hem not, in auenture · ȝe mouwen hem not deseruen;
For thou schalt ȝelden hit a-ȝeyn · at one ȝeeres ende,
In a wel perilous place · that purgatorie hette.   44
And mis-beode thou not thi bonde-men · the beter thou schalt
    spede,
And that thi-self be trewe of tonge · and tales thou hate,
Bote hit beo wisdam or wit · thi werkmen to chaste.
Hold not thou with harlotes · here not heore tales,   48

And go honte hardiliche · to hares and to foxes,   28
To bores and to bockes · that breketh a-doune menne hegges;
And faite thy faucones · to culle wylde foules;
For thei comen to my croft · my corn to defoule.'
Corteysliche the knyȝt then · comsede these wordes;   32
' By my power, Peers · ich plyghte the my treuthe,
To defende the in faith · fyghte thauh ich sholde.'

' And ȝut on poynt,' quath Peers · 'ich praye ȝow ouermore;
Loke ȝe tene no tenaunt · bote yf Treuth wolle assente.   36
Whenne ȝe amercyn eny man · let Mercy be taxour,
And Meknesse thy maister · maugre Mede chekes.
Thauh poure men profre ȝou · presentes and ȝiftes,
Nym hit nat, an aunter · thow mowe hit nat deserue;   40
For thow shalt ȝulde, so may be · and somdel a-bygge.

Mys-beede nouht thy bondemen · the bet may thou spede;

Thauh he be here thyn vnderling · in heuene, paraunter,
He worth rather receyued · and reuerentloker sette;   44

    Amice, ascende superius.
At churche in the charnel · cheorles aren vuel to knowe,
Other a knyght fro a knaue · other a queyne fro a queene.
Hit by-cometh to a knyght · to be curteys and hende,
Trewe of hys tonge · tales loth to huyre,   48
Bote thei be of bounte · of batailes and of treuthe.
Hald nat of harlotes · huyre nat here tales,

---

tuene P.   37. Wenne P.   39. presantes P.   ȝeftes P.   42. boundemen P.
thou EMSG; þe P.

A. PASSUS VII. 49-59.   B. PASSUS VI. 55-77.

And nomeliche atte mete · suche men eschuwe,
For thei ben the deueles disours · I do the to vndurstonde.'
'Ich a-sente, be seint Iem!' · seide the kniht thenne,
'For to worche bi thi word · while my lyf dureth.'   52
   'And I schal a-paraile me,' quod Perkin · 'in pilgrimes wyse,
And wende with ou the rihte wei · til ȝe Treuthe fynde.'
He caste on his clothes · i-clouted and i-hole,
His cokeres and his coffus · for colde of his nayles,   56
He heng an hoper on his bac · in stude of a scrippe,
A busschel of bred-corn · he bringeth ther-inne :
'For I wol souwen hit my-self · and seththen with ou wende.

And nameliche atte mete · suche men eschue;
For it ben the deueles disoures · I do the to vnderstande.'   56
   'I assente, bi seynt Iame' · seyde the kniȝte thanne,
'Forto worche bi thi wordes · the while my lyf dureth.'
   'And I shal apparaille me,' quod Perkyn · 'in pilgrimes wise,
And wende with ȝow I wil · til we fynde Treuthe ;   60
And cast on me my clothes · yclouted and hole,
My cokeres and my coffes · for colde of my nailles,
And hange myn hoper at myn hals · in stede of a scrippe ;
A busshel of bredcorne · brynge me ther-inne ;   64
For I wil sowe it my-self · and sitthenes wil I wende
To pylgrymage as palmers don · pardoun forto haue.
Ac who so helpeth me to erie · or sowen here ar I wende,
Shal haue leue, bi owre lorde · to lese here in heruest,   68
And make hem mery there-mydde · maugre who-so bigruccheth it.
And alkyn crafty men · that konne lyuen in treuthe,
I shal fynden hem fode · that feithfulliche libbeth.
Saue Iakke the iogeloure · and Ionet of the stues,   72
And Danyel the dys-playere · and Denote the baude,
And frere the faytoure · and folke of his ordre,

And Robyn the rybaudoure · for his rusty wordes.
Treuthe tolde me ones · and bad me tellen it after,   76
Deleantur de libro viuentium · I shulde nouȝte dele with hem ;

A. 50. to THU ; V *om*.   68. I—hem T; V *om*.   C. 51. eschywe P.
53. kirke I ; churche PES.   57. wit P.   63. palmers EIS ; pilgrymes P.

A. PASSUS VII. 60–68.   C. PASSUS IX. 51–77.   199

For hose helpeth me to heren · or eny thing to swynken,   60
He schal haue, beo vr lord · the more huyre in heruest,
And make him murie with the corn · hose hit euere bigruccheth.
And alle kunnes craftus men · that cunne lyuen with treuthe,
I schal fynden hem heore fode · that feithfuliche lyuen;   64
Saue Iacke the iogelour · and Ionete of the stuyues,
And Robert the ribaudour · for his rousti wordes.
Treuthe tauhte hit me ones · and bad me telle hit forther,
Deleantur de libro · I ne shulde not dele with hem;   68

Nameliche atte mete · suche men eschewe;
Hit ben the deueles disours · to drawe men to synne.   52
Contreplede nat conscience · ne holy kirke ryghtes.'
'Ich assente, by seynt Gyle' · seyde the knyght thenne,
'For to worche by thy witt · and my wyf bothe.'
'Ich shal aparaile me,' quath Perkyn · 'in pylgrymes wyse,   56
And wende with alle tho · that wolle lyue in treuthe.'
He caste on hym hus clothes · of alle kynne craftes,
Hus cokeres and hus cuffes · as kynde witt hym tauhte,
And heng hus hoper on hus hals · in stede of a scrippe;   60
A boussel of bred-corn · brouht was ther-ynne.
'For ich wolle sowe hit my-self · and sitthe wol y-wende
To pylgrimages, as palmers don · pardon to wynne.
My plouh-fot shal be my pyk-staf · and picche a-two the rotes,*
And help my culter to kerue · and clanse the forwes.
And alle that helpen me to erye · other elles to weden,
Shal haue leue, by oure lorde · to go and glene after,
And make hym murye ther-myd · maugre ho by-grucche.   68
And alle kynne crafty men · that conne lyue in treuthe,
Ich shal fynde hem fode · that feythfullech lybben;
Saf Iack the iogelour · and Ionette of the styues,
And Danyel the dees-pleyere · and Denote the baude,   72
And al-so frere faytour · and folke of that ordre,
That lollers and loseles · for leel men halden,
And Robyn the rybaudour · for hus rusty wordes.
For Treuthe tolde me ones · and bade me telle hit forthere,   76
Deleantur de libro uiuencium · ich sholde nat dele with hem;

---

71. (1st) the IMG; P *om.*   72. denete P.   73. that IMSEG; þe P.   76.
me IMSEG; P *om.*   hit MS; P *om.*   * Cf. A. vii. 96; B. vi. 105; p. 202.

A. PASSUS VII. 69–76.   B. PASSUS VI. 78–93.

Holi churche is holden of hem · no tithe to taken;
   Et cum iustis non scribantur;
Thei ben a-scaped good thrift · god hem amende!'
Dame werche-whon-tyme-is · hette Pers wyf,
His douhter hette Do-riht-so- · or-thi-dame-wol-the-bete,   72
His sone hette Soffre-thi-souereyns- · for-to-han-heor-wille-
And-deeme-hem-not-for-ȝif-thou-do- · thou-schalt-hit-deore-abugge.
'Let god worthe with al · for so his woord techith;
For nou icham old and hor · and haue of myn owne,   76

For holicherche is hote of hem · no tythe to take,
   Quia cum iustis non scribantur;
They ben ascaped good auenture · now god hem amende!'
Dame Worche-whan-tyme-is · Pieres wyf hiȝte,   80
His douȝter hiȝte Do-riȝte-so- · or-thi-dame-shal-the-bete,
His sone hiȝte Suffre-thi-souereynes- · to-hauen-her-wille-
Deme-hem-nouȝte-for-if-thow-doste- · thow-shalt-it-dere-abugge.

'Late god yworth with al · for so his worde techeth;   84

For now I am olde and hore · and haue of myn owen,
To penaunce and to pilgrimage · I wil passe with thise other.
For-thi I wil, or I wende · do wryte my biqueste.

   In dei nomine, amen · I make it my-seluen.   88
He shal haue my soule · that best hath yserued it,
And fro the fende it defende · for so I bileue,
Til I come to his acountes · as my *credo* me telleth,
To haue a relees and a remissioun · on that rental I leue.   92
The kirke shal haue my caroigne · and kepe my bones;

   A. 71. werche THU; V *om.*   75. *From* THU; V *omits this line.*

A. PASSUS VII. 77–84. C. PASSUS IX. 78–100. 201

To penaunce and to pilgrimage · I wol passe with this othure.
For-thi I wole, ar I wende · write my testament.
   In dei nomine, amen · I make hit mi-seluen.
He schal haue my soule · that best hath deseruet,   80
And defende hit from the fend · for so I beo-leeue,
Til I come to myn a-countes · as my crede me telleth,
To ha reles and remission · on that rental I be-leeue.
The chirche schal haue my careyne · and kepe mi bones; 84

For holy churche hoteth · of hem to aske no tythe,
   Quia cum iustis non scribantur;
Thei ben ascaped good aunter · now god hem amende!'
Dame Worche-when-tyme-is · Peers wyf hyhte;   80
Hus douhter hihte Do-ryght-so- · other-thy-damme-shal-the-bete;
Hus sone hihte Suffre- · thy-souereynes-haue-here-wil-
Deme-hem-nouht-for-yf-thow-do- · thow-shalt-dere-abigge.
'Consaile nat the comune · the kyng to displese,   84
Ne hem that han lawes to loke · lacke hem nat, ich hote,
Let god worthe with al · as holy writ techeth;
   Super cathedram Moysi sedent, et cetera;
Maistres, as the meyres ben · and grete men senatours,
What thei comaunde as by the kyng · contrepleide hit neuere,
Al that they hoten, ich hote · heyliche, thow suffre hem; 89
By here warnyng and worchyng · worch thow ther-after;
   Omnia que dicunt, facite et seruate;
Ac after here doynge do thow nat · my dere sone,' quath Peers.
'For now ich am old and hor · and haue of myn owene, 92
To penaunces and to pilgrimages · ich wol passe with othere;
For-thi ich wolle, er ich wende · do wryten my byquyste.

       TESTAMENTUM PETRI PLOUHMAN.

   In dei nomine, amen · ich make hit my-self.
He shal haue my soule · that alle soules made,   96
And defende hit fro the feende · and so is my by-leyue,
Til ich come to hus acountes · as my crede telleth,
To haue remissioun and relees · on that rental ich leue.
The kirke shal haue my caroyne · and kepe my bones, 100

   C. 80. wen P.   81. heithe P; *see* l. 82.   89. they IES; þe P.   98, 99.
From IG; P *om*.   100. kirke IM; churche P.

A. PASSUS VII. 85-97.   B. PASSUS VI. 94-118.

For of my corn and catel · heo craueth the tithe.
I payede him prestly · for peril of my soule,
He is holden, ich hope · to haue me in muynde,
And munge me in his memorie · among alle Cristene.   88
   Mi wyf schal haue that I won · with treuthe, and no more,
And dele a-mong my frendes · and my deore children.
For thauh I dye this day · my dettes beoth i-quit;
I bar hom that I borwede · er I to bedde eode,   92
And with the residue and the remenaunt · by the rode of Chestre!
I wol worschupe ther-with · Treuthe in my lyue,
And ben his pilgrym atte plouȝ · for pore mennes sake.
Mi plouh-pote schal be my pyk · and posshen atte rootes,*   96
And helpe my coltre to kerue · and close the vorwes.'

For of my corne and catel · he craued the tythe.
I payed it hym prestly · for peril of my soule,
For-thy is he holden, I hope · to haue me in his masse,   96
And mengen in his memorye · amonge alle Crystene.
   My wyf shal haue of that I wan · with treuthe, and nomore,
And dele amonge my douȝtres · and my dere children.
For thowghe I deye to-daye · my dettes ar quitte,   100
I bare home that I borwed · ar I to bedde ȝede.
And with the residue and the remenaunte · bi the rode of
   Lukes!
I wil worschip ther-with · Treuthe bi my lyue,
And ben his pilgryme atte plow · for pore mennes sake.   104
My plow-fote shal be my pyk-staf · and picche atwo the rotes,*
And helpe my culter to kerue · and clense the forwes.'
   Now is Perkyn and his pilgrymes · to the plowe faren;
To erie this halue-acre · holpyn hym manye.   108
Dikeres and delueres · digged vp the balkes;
There-with was Perkyn apayed · and preysed hem faste.
Other werkeman there were · that wrouȝten ful ȝerne,
Eche man in his manere · made hym-self to done,   112
And some to plese Perkyn · piked vp the wedes.
   At heighe pryme Peres · lete the plowe stonde,
To ouersen hem hym-self · and who-so best wrouȝte,
He shulde be huyred ther-after · whan heruest-tyme come.   116
   And thanne seten somme · and songen atte nale,
And hulpen erie his half-acre · with 'how! trolliloli!'

A. PASSUS VII. 98–109. C. PASSUS IX. 101–123. 203

Now is Pers and the pilgrimes to the plouh i-fare;
To heren this half-acre · helpen him ful monye.
Dykers and deluers · dikeden vp the balkes; 100
Ther-with was Perkyn a-payed · and preisede hem ӡerne.
Othur werk-men ther weren · that wrouӡten ful monye,
Vche mon in his maner · made him to done;
And summe, to plese Perkyn · pykeden vp the weodes. 104
At heiӡ prime Perkyn · lette the plouӡ stonde,
While that he ouer-seӡe him-self · ho that best wrouhte;
He schulde ben huyred ther-aftur · whon heruest-tyme come.
Thenne seten summe · and songen atte ale, 108
And holpen him to herien · with 'hey! trolly-lolly!'

For of my corn and catel · he crauede my tythe.
Ich payed hit prestliche · for peril of my soule,
He is holdinge, ich hope · to haue me in hus masse,
And menge me in hus memorie · among alle Cristine. 104
My wyf shal haue of that ich wan · with treuthe, and no more,
And dele hit among my douhtres · and my dere children.
For thauh ich deyde thys day · my dettes ben quyted;
Ich bar hom that ich borwede · er ich to bedde ӡeode. 108
With the resydue and remenaunt · by the rode of Lukes,
Ich wolle worshupe ther-with · Treuthe al my lyf,
And be a pilgrym atte plouh · for profyt of poure and ryche.'
Now Perkyn with the pilgrimes · to the plouh is faren; 112
To eryen hus half-aker · holpen hym menye.
Dykers and deluers · diggeden vp the balkes;
Ther-with was Perkyn apayed · and paied wel here hyre.
Other werkmen ther were · that wrouhten ful ӡurne; 116
Eche man in hus manere · made hym-self to done;
And somme to plese Perkyn · pykede aweye the wedes.
Atte hye pryme Peers · let the plouh stonde,
And ouer-seyh hem hym-self · ho so best wrouhte, 120
He sholde be hyred ther-after · when heruest-tyme come.
Thenne seten some · and songen atten ale,
And holpen to erie this half-acre · with 'hoy! troly! lolly!'

---

* Cf. C. ix. 64; p. 199. **C.** 103. his (*for* is) P. 111. pulgrym P. 121. wen P.

'Now, be the prince of paradys' · quath Pers tho in wraththe,
'Bote ȝe rysen the rather · and rape ȝow to worche,
Schal no greyn that heer groweth · gladen ow at neode, 112
And thauh ȝe dyen for de-faute · the deuel haue that recche!'
Thenne weore the faytors a-ferd · and feynede hem blynde,
And summe leiden the legges a-liri · as suche losels cunne,
And playneden hem to pers · with suche pitouse wordes : 116
'We haue no lymes to labore with · vr lord we hit thonken,
Bote we preyeth for ou, Pers · and for oure plouh bothe,
That god for his grace · oure greyn multiplye,
And ȝelde ow for oure almus · that ȝe ȝiuen vs here! 120
For we mowe nouthur swynke ne swete · such seknes vs eileth.'

'Now, bi the peril of my soule!' quod Pieres · al in pure tene,
'But ȝe arise the rather · and rape ȝow to worche, 120
Shal no greyne that groweth · glade ȝow at nede ;
And though ȝe deye for dole · the deuel haue that reccheth!'
Tho were faitoures aferde · and feyned hem blynde,
Somme leyde here legges aliri · as suche loseles conneth, 124
And made her mone to Pieres · and preyde hym of grace :
'For we haue no lymes to laboure with · lorde, y-graced be ȝe !
Ac we preye for ȝow, Pieres · and for ȝowre plow bothe,
That god of his grace · ȝowre grayne multiplye, 128
And ȝelde ȝow of ȝowre almesse · that ȝe ȝiue vs here ;
For we may nouȝte swynke ne swete · suche sikenesse vs eyleth.'
'If it be soth,' quod Pieres, 'that ȝe seyne · I shal it sone asspye !
Ȝe ben wastoures, I wote wel · and Treuthe wote the sothe !
And I am his olde hyne · and hiȝte hym to warne 133
Which thei were in this worlde · his werkemen appeyred.
Ȝe wasten that men wynnen · with trauaille and with tene,
Ac Treuthe shal teche ȝow · his teme to dryue, 136
Or ȝe shal ete barly bred · and of the broke drynke.
But if he be blynde or broke-legged · or bolted with yrnes,
He shal ete whete bred · and drynke with my-selue,
Tyl god of his goodnesse · amendement hym sende. 140

A. 126. *Read* heren (*as in* 60, 99); eren T; swynken V. 133. *From* T ;
V *omits this line.* hem ; *miswritten* hym T. B. 138. (1*st*) or WCRO ;

'3if hit beo soth that 3e seyen,' quod Pers · 'sone I schal
  a-spye!
3e beoth wastors, I wot · and Treuthe wot the sothe!
Icham his holde hyne · and ou3te him to warne   124
Whuche wastors in world · his werk-men distruy3en.
3e eten that thei schulden eten · that heren for vs alle;
Bote Treuthe schal techen ow · his teeme for to dryue,
Bothe to sowen and to setten · and sauen his tilthe,   128
Gaste crowen from his corn · and kepen his beestes,
Or 3e schulle ete barly bred · and of the brok drynke.
Bote heo beo blynde or broke-schonket · or bedreden liggen,
Thei schul haue as good as I · so me god helpe,   132
Til god of his grace · gare hem to arise.

Quath Peers the plouhman · al in pure tene,   124
'Bote 3e aryse the rathere · and rape 3ow to worche,
Shal no greyn that here groweth · gladen 3ow at neede;
And thauh 3e deye for deul · the deuel haue that recche!'
Tho were faitours aferede · and feyned³ hem blynde,   128
And leyden here legges a-lyry · as suche lorelles conneth,
And maden here mone to Peers · how thei mowe nat worche:
'Ac we prayeth for 3ow, Peers · and for 3oure plouh bothe,
That god for hus grace · 3oure grayn multiplie,   132
And 3elde 3ow of 3oure almesse · that 3e 3euen us here.
We may nayther swynke ne swete · suche syknesse ous ayleth;
We haue none lymes to laborie with · lord god we thonketh.'

'3oure praiers,' quath Peers · 'and 3e parfit were,   136
Myght help, as ich hope; · ac hye Treuthe wolde
That no faiterye were founde · in folk that gon a-begged.
3e ben wastours, ich wot wel · that wasten and deuouren
That leel land-tylynge men · leelliche byswynken.   140
Ac Treuthe shal teche 3ow · hus teeme for to dryue,
Other 3e shulle ete barliche brede · and of the brok drynke,
Bote 3e be blynde other brokelegged · other bolted with yren.
Suche poure,' quath Peers · 'shullen partye with my goodes,
Bothe of my corn and of my cloth · to kepe hem fro defaute;

---

and L.   C. 125. aryse SIM; ryse P.   127. that IMSEG; þe P.   131.
fore (*2nd time*) P.   132. multeplie P.   133. 3ulde P.   3euene hus P.
140. leelleche P.   143, 144. wit P.

Ancres and hermytes · that holdeth hem in heore celles
Schulen habben of myn almus · al the while I liue,
I-nouh vche day at non · but no more til a morwe,   136
Leste the fend and heore flesch · fouleden heore soules;
Ones at noon is i-nou3 · that no werk ne vseth,
He abydeth wel the bet · that bommeth not to ofte.'   139
Thenne wastours gunne arise · and wolden han i-fouhte;

Ac 3e my3te trauaille as Treuthe wolde · and take mete and
    huyre
To kepe kyne in the felde · the corne fro the bestes,
Diken or deluen · or dyngen vppon sheues,
Or helpe make morter · or bere mukke a-felde.   144
In lecherye and in losengerye · 3e lyuen, and in sleuthe,
And al is thorw suffrance · that veniaunce 3ow ne taketh.
    Ac ancres and heremytes · that eten no3t but at nones,
And namore er morwe · myne almesse shul thei haue,   148
And of my catel to cope hem with · that han cloistres and
    cherches.
Ac Robert Renne-aboute · shal now3te haue of myne,
Ne posteles, but they preche conne · and haue powere of the
    bisschop;
They shal haue payne and potage · and make hem-self at
    ese,   152
For it is an vnresonable religioun · that hath ri3te nou3te of
    certeyne.'
    And thanne gan a wastoure to wrath hym · and wolde haue
    yfou3te,
And to Pieres the plowman · he profered his gloue;
A Brytonere, a braggere · a-bosted Pieres als,   156
And bad hym go pissen with his plow · for-pyned schrewe!
'Wiltow or neltow · we wil haue owre wille,
Of thi flowre and of thi flessche · fecche whan vs liketh,
And make vs murie ther-myde · maugre thi chekes!'   160
    Thanne Pieres the plowman · pleyned hym to the kny3te,
To kepe hym, as couenaunte was · fram cursed shrewes,
And fro this wastoures wolueskynnes · that maketh the worlde
    dere:

A. 141. one H; he TU; and V.   143. screwe V.   146. *From* UTH;

A. PASSUS VII. 141–149.   C. PASSUS IX. 146–158.

To Pers the plouh-mon · one profrede his gloue,
A Brutiner, a braggere · a-bostede him alse,
And bad go pisse him with his plouh · pillede schrewe!   143
'For we wolen habbe of thi flour · wol thou so nulle thou,
And of thi flesch fecche · whon that vs lyketh,
And make vs merye therwith · maugre thi chekes!'
Thenne Pers plouh-mon · playnede him to the kniht,
To kepen him, as couenaunt was · from cursede schrewes,   148
From wastors that wayten · winners to schende.

Ancres and heremites · that eten bote at nones,   146
And freres that flateren nat · and poure folke syke,
What! ich and myne · wolleth fynde hem that hem needeth.'

Thenne gan Wastour to wratth · and wolde haue fouhten, 149
And to Peers plouhman · proferede to fighte,

And bad hym 'go pisse with hus plouh · peyuesshe shrewe!'
A Brytonere com braggynge · a-bosted Peers al-so;   152
'Wolle thow, ne wolle thow · we wolleth habbe oure wil,
Bothe thy flour and thy flessh · fecchen when ous lyketh,
And make ous myrye ther-myd · maugre ho bygruccheth!'
Peers the plouhman tho · pleynede to the knyght,   156
To kepe hym and hus catel · as couenaunt was bytwyne hem:
'Awreke me of these wastours · that maken thys worlde dere;

V *omits the line.*   B. 147. no3t WCO; LR *om.*   C. 154. wen P.
158. worde P.

A. PASSUS VII. 150-159.   B. PASSUS VI. 164-183.

Curteisliche the kniht · as his kuynde wolde,
Warnede wastors · and wissede hem do betere; 151
'Or ȝe schul a-bugge hit bi the lawe · bi the ordre that I bere!'
'I was not wont to worche,' quod a wastour · 'ȝit wol I not
   biginne!'—
And lette luytel of the lawe · and lasse of the kniht,
And countede Pers at a peose · and his plouh bothe, 155
And manasede him and his men · whon that thei next metten.
'Nou be the peril of my soule,' · quath Pers the plouh-mon,
I schal a-peiren ow alle · for oure proude wordes!'
And hoped aftur Hunger tho · that herde him atte furste: 159

'For tho waste and wynnen nouȝte · and that ilke while 164
Worth neuere plente amonge the poeple · ther-while my plow
   liggeth.'
Curteisly the knyȝte thanne · as his kynde wolde,
Warned Wastoure · and wissed hym bettere, 167
'Or thow shalt abugge by the lawe · by the ordre that I bere!'
'I was nouȝt wont to worche,' quod Wastour · 'and now
   wil I nouȝt bigynne!'—
And lete liȝte of the lawe · and lasse of the knyȝte,
And sette Pieres at a pees · and his plow bothe,
And manaced Pieres and his men · ȝif thei mette eft sone. 172
'Now, by the peril of my soule!' quod Pieres · 'I shal
   apeyre ȝow alle!'
And houped after Hunger · that herd hym atte firste:
'A-wreke me of thise wastoures,' quod he · 'that this worlde
   schendeth!'
Hunger in haste tho · hent Wastour bi the mawe, 176
And wronge hym so bi the wombe · that bothe his eyen wattered;
He buffeted the Britoner · aboute the chekes,
That he loked like a lanterne · al his lyf after.
He bette hem so bothe · he barste nere here guttes; 180
Ne hadde Pieres with a pese-lof · preyed Hunger to cesse,
They hadde ben doluen bothe · ne deme thow non other.
'Suffre hem lyue,' he seyde · 'and lete hem ete with hogges,

A. 152. (1st) the THU; V om.   161. wastour THU; wastors V;
read wastor.   163. See l. 142.   bretoner TH; brytoner U; boye V.

A. PASSUS VII. 160–170.   C. PASSUS IX. 159–178.

'A-wrek me on this wastors,' quod Pers · 'that this world
   schendeth!' 160
Hongur in haste · hente Wastor bi the mawe,
And wrong him so be the wombe · that bothe his eȝen watreden,
And buffetede the Brutiner · aboute bothe his chekes;
He lokede lyk a lanterne · al his lyf after. 164
He beot so the boyes · he barst neih heore ribbes,
Nedde Pers with a peose-lof · i-preyed him to leue;
And with a benene bat · i-bot hem by-twene,
And hutte Hongur ther-with · a-midde bothe his lippes, 168
And he bledde in-to the bodiward · a bolleful of gruwel;
Nedde the fisicien furst · defendet him water

Thei counte nat of cursyng · ne holy kirke dreden;
Ther worth no plente,' quath Peers · 'and the plouh ligge.'
Curtesliche the knyght then · as hus kynde wolde, 161
Warned Wastour · and wissede hym betere,
'Other ich shal bete the by the law · and brynge the in stockes.'
'Ich was nat woned to wirche,' quath Wastour · 'and ich wolle
   nat now bygynne,' 164
And let lyght of the lawe · and lasse of the knyght,
And sette Peers at a pese · pleyne hym wher he wolde.
'Now, by Crist,' quath Peers · 'y shal apeyre ȝow alle!'
And hopede after Hunger · that herde him at the ferste. 168
'Ich praye the,' quath Peers tho · 'pur charite, sire Honger,
Awreke me of these wastours · for the knyght wol nat.'
Honger hente in haste · Wastour by the mawe,
And wrang hym by the wombe · that al waterede hus eyen.
He buffated the Brutener · a-boute the chekes, 173
That he loked lyk a lanterne · al hus lyf after.
He bet hem so bothe · he barst neih hure guttes,
Ne hadde Peers with a peese-lof · prayede hym by-leue. 176
'Honger, haue mercy of hem,' quath Peers · 'and let me ȝeue
   hem benes;
And that was bake for Bayarde · may be here bote.'

C. 159. kirke I; churche PES.   160. pleynte P.   164. wond P. to IMSG;
P om.   166. wer P.   168. him IMSG; P om.   170. þeese P.   176. wit P.
178. bayerde P.

P

A. PASSUS VII. 171-179.   B. PASSUS VI. 184-201.

To abate the barli-bred · and the benes i-grounde,
Thei hedden beo ded bi this day · and doluen al warm.   172
   Thenne faytors for fere · flowen to bernes,
And flapten on with fleiles · from morwe til euen,
That Honger nas not hardi · vp for to loke,
For a potful of peosun · that Pers hedde i-mad.   176
An hep of hermytes · henten heom spades,
And doluen drit and donge · to dutte Honger oute.
   Blynde and bedraden · weore botned a thousent,

Or elles benes and bren · ybaken togideres,   184
Or elles melke and mene ale' · thus preyed Pieres for hem.
   Faitoures for fere her-of · flowen in-to bernes,
And flapten on with flayles · fram morwe til euen,
That Hunger was nouȝt so hardy · on hem for to loke,   188
For a potful of peses · that Peres hadde ymaked.
An heep of heremites · henten hem spades,
And ketten here copes · and courtpies hem made,
And wenten as werkemen · with spades and with schoueles,   192
And doluen and dykeden · to dryue aweye hunger.
   Blynde and bedreden · were botened a thousande,
That seten to begge syluer · sone were thei heled.

For that was bake for Bayarde · was bote for many hungry,   196
And many a beggere for benes · buxome was to swynke,
And eche a pore man wel apayed · to haue pesen for his huyre,
And what Pieres preyed hem to do · as prest as a sperhauke.

And there-of was Peres proude · and put hem to werke,   200
And ȝaf hem mete as he myȝte aforth · and mesurable huyre.

  A. 186. Al THU; V *om*.   C. 180. whit P.   185. copes EIMS;
coppes P.   187. P *om*. hunger.   189. wit P.   191. of ESG; and P.

A. PASSUS VII. 180-188.   C. PASSUS IX. 179-204.   211

That ly3en for blynde · and for broke-legget   180
Vppon softe Sonenday · bi the hei3e weye;
Hungur hem helede · with an hot cake.
Lome mennes limes · weore lythet that tyme,
And bi-come knaues · to kepe Pers beestes,   184
And preyeden for charite · with Pers for to dwelle,
Al for couetyse of his corn · to caste a-wey Hunger.
Pers was proud ther-of · and put hem in offys,
And 3af hem mete and moneye · as thei mihte deseruen. 188

Tho were faitours a-fered · and flowen to Peersses bernes,
And flapten on with flailes · fro morwe til euene,   180
That Honger was nat hardy · on hem for to loke,
For a potful of potage · that Peersses wyf made.
An hep of eremites · henten hem spades,
Spitten and spradde donge · in despit of Hunger.   184
Thei coruen here copes · and courtepies hem made,
And wenten as workmen · to weden and mowen;
Al for drede of here deth · suche dyntes 3af Hunger.
Blynde and brokeleggede · he botnede a thousande,   188
And lame men he lechede · with longen of bestes.
Preestes and other peple · to Peers thei drowen,
And freres of alle fyue ordres · al for fere of Hunger.
For that that was bake for Bayarde · was bote for menye hungry,
Drosenes and dregges · drynke for menye beggeres.   193
Ther was no lad that lyuede · that ne lowede hym to Peers,
To be hus hole hewe · thauh he hadde no more
Bute lyf-lode for hus labour · and hus lone at nones.   196
Tho was Peers ful proude · and putte hem alle to werke,
In daubyng and in deluyng · in donge a-feld berynge,
In thresshynge, in thecchynge · in thwytynge of pynnes,
And alle kynne trewe craft · that man couthe deuyse.   200
Was no beggere so bolde · bote-yf he blynde were,
That dorst with-sitte that Peeres seyde · for fere of syre Hunger.
And Peers was proud ther-of · and putte hem alle to swynke,
And 3af hem mete and monye · as they myght deseruen.   204

---

193. drenke P.   194. P om. no; see l. 201.   195. hewe I; hywe P;
hyne EMSG.   202. wit-sitte P.   203. swynge P.

Thenne hedde Peers pite · and preiede Hunger to wende
Hom to his oune hurde · and holden him ther for euere.
   'And ȝit I preye the,' quod Pers · 'er thou passe henne,
Of bidders and of beggers · what is best to done?   192
I wot wel whon thou art i-went · thei wol worchen ful ille;
And mischef hit maketh · thei beoth so meke nouthe,
And for de-faute of foode · thus faste thei worchen;
And heo beoth my blodi bretheren · for god bouȝte vs alle. 196
Treuthe tauhte me ones · to louen hem vchone,
And helpen hem of alle thyng · aftur that hem neodeth.
   Ȝit wolde I witen ȝif thou wustest · what were the beste,

Thanne hadde Peres pite · and preyed Hunger to wende
Home in-to his owne erde · and holden hym there.

'For I am wel awroke now · of wastoures, thorw thi myȝte. 204
Ac I preye the, ar thow passe' · quod Pieres to Hunger,
'Of beggeres and of bidderes · what best be to done?
For I wote wel, be thow went · thei wil worche ful ille;
For myschief it maketh · thei beth so meke nouthe,   208
And for defaute of her fode · this folke is at my wille.

They are my blody bretheren,' quod Pieres · 'for god bouȝte
    vs alle;
Treuthe tauȝte me ones · to louye hem vchone,
And to helpen hem of alle thinge · ay as hem nedeth.   212
And now wolde I witen of the · what were the best,
And how I myȝte amaistrien hem · and make hem to worche.'
   'Here now,' quod Hunger · 'and holde it for a wisdome:
Bolde beggeres and bigge · that mowe her bred biswynke, 216
With houndes bred and hors bred · holde vp her hertis,
Abate hem with benes · for bollyng of her wombe;
And ȝif the gomes grucche · bidde hem go swynke,
And he shal soupe swettere · whan he it hath deseruid.   220
   And if thow fynde any freke · that fortune hath appeyred,
Or any maner fals men · fonde thow suche to cnowe;
Conforte hem with thi catel · for Crystes loue of heuene,

B. 206. to WCRO; L *om.*   214. An (*for* And) L.   223. hem RO;
hym LW.   C. 206. in IMSEG; on P.   216. wit P.   217. ben EM;

And hou I mihte a-maystren hem · and maken hem to worche.'
'Here nou,' quod Hunger · 'and holde hit for wisdam,   201
Bolde bidders and beggers · that mowen her mete biswinke,
With houndes bred and horse bred · hold vp heor hertes,
And bamme hem with bones · for bollyng of heore wombes;
And ȝif the gomes grucchen · bidde hem go swynke,   205
And thei schule soupe the swettore · whon thei han hit deseruet.
And ȝif thou fyndest eny freik · that fortune hath a-peiret
With fuir, or with fals folk · fonde suche to knowe;   208
Cumforte hem with thi catel · for Cristes loue of heuene,

Tho hadde Peers pite · of alle poure puple,
And bad Hunger in haste · hyhe out of contre
Home in-to his owen erthe · and halde hym ther euere—
'For ich am wel awreke · of wastours thorw thy myghte.   208
Ac ich praye the,' quath Peers · 'Hunger, er thow wende,
Of beggers and of bydders · what best be to done?
For ich wot wel, be thou went · worche thei wolle ful ylle;
Meschief hit maketh · thei ben so meke nouthe,   212
And for defaute this folke · folwen my hestes.
Hit is no thyng for loue · thei labour thus faste,
Bote for fere of famyn · in faith,' seide Peers;
'Ys no final loue with this folke · for al here faire speche;   216
And hit ben my blody brothren · for god bouhte vs alle.
Treuthe tauhte me ones · to louye hem echone,
And helpen hem of alle thyng · ay as hem nedeth.
Now wolde ich wite, or thow wentest · what were the beste,
How ich myghte a-maistren hem · to louye and laboure   221
For here lyflode; · lere me, syre Hunger.'
'Now herkne,' quath Hunger · 'and hold hit for a wysdome;
Bolde beggeres and bygge ' that mowe here bred byswynke,
With houndes bred and hors bred · hele hem when thei hungren,
And a-bane hem with benes · for bollynge of here wombe.
And yf the gromes grucche · bid hem go swynke,
And he shal soupe the swettere · when he hath deserued.   228
And yf thow fynde eny folke · wham false men han apaired,
Comforte hem with thy catel · for so comaundeth treuthe;

---

aren PG.   220. white P.   224. And bolde P; IMSEG *om*. And.   228.
wen P.   229. wam P.

214   A. PASSUS VII. 210–217.   B. PASSUS VI. 224–242.

Loue hem, and lene hem · so the lawe of kuynde wole.
And alle manere of men · that thou may3t aspye,
That neodi ben, or naket · and nou3t haue to spende,   212
With mete or with moneye · mak hem fare the betere,
Or with word or with werk · 'while that thou art here.
Mak the frendes ther-with · for so seint Matheu techeth,
    Facite vobis amicos de mammona iniquitatis.'
'I wolde not greue god,' quod Pers · 'for al the gold on
    ground;   216
Miht I sunneles don as thou seist?' · seide Pers thenne.

Loue hem and lene hem · so lawe of god techeth:—   224
    Alter alterius onera portate.
And alle maner of men · that thow my3te asspye,
That nedy ben, and nau3ty · helpe hem with thi godis,
Loue hem and lakke hem nou3te · late god take the veniaunce;
Theigh thei done yuel · late thow god y-worthe:—   228
    Michi vindictam, et ego retribuam.
And if thow wilt be graciouse to god · do as the gospel techeth,
And biloue the amonges low men · so shaltow lacche grace,
    Facile vobis amicos de mamona iniquitatis.'
'I wolde nou3t greue god,' quod Piers · 'for al the good on
    grounde;
Mi3te I synnelees do as thow seist?' · seyde Pieres thanne. 232
'3e, I bihote the,' quod Hunger · 'or ellis the bible lieth;
Go to Genesis the gyaunt · the engendroure of vs alle;
'*In sudore* and swynke · thow shalt thi mete tilye,
And laboure for thi lyflode' · and so owre lorde hy3te.   236
And Sapience seyth the same · I seigh it in the bible;
'*Piger pro frigore* · no felde nolde tilye,
And therfore he shal begge and bidde · and no man bete his
    hunger.'
Mathew with mannes face · mouthed thise wordes,   240
That *seruus nequam* had a nam · and for he wolde nou3te
    chaffare,
He had maugre of his maistre · for euermore after;

B. 228. y-worthe W; aworthe L.   229. wilt WCO; wil L.   230.
biloue WCO; bilow L.   C. 250. alowede P.

A. PASSUS VII. 218-227.   C. PASSUS IX. 231-251.   215

'ȝe, I be-hote the,' quod Hunger · 'or elles the bible lyȝeth;
Go to Genesis the Ieaunt · engendrure of vs alle;
In sudore and swynk · thou schalt thi mete tilie,   220
And labre for thi lyflode' · for so vr lord hiȝte.
And Sapiens seith the same · I saih hit in the bible;
'*Piger propter frigus* · no feld nolde he tilie,
He schal go bidde and begge · and no mon beete his hunger.'
Matheu the monnes face · he mommeth theose wordes,   225
'*Seruus nequam* hedde npnam · and for he nolde hit vsen,
He hedde maugre of his maister · euere more aftur;
    Auferte ab illo mnam, et date illi, etc.

Loue hem and lene hem · so lawe of kynde wolde;
    Alter alterius onera portate.
And alle manere men · that thow myght aspye   232
In meschief other in mal-ese · and thow mowe hem helpe,
Loke by thy lyf · let hem nouht for-fare.
Yf thow hast wonne ouht wickeliche · wisliche dispende hit;
    Facite uobis amicos de mammona iniquitatis.'
'Ich wolde nat greuye God,' quath Peers · 'for al the good
    on erthe;   236
Myghte ich synneles do as thou seist?' · seide Peers plouhman.
'ȝe, ich by-hote the,' quath Hunger · 'other elles the byble lyeth;
Go to oure by-gynnynge · tho god the worlde made,
As wise men han ywryte · and as wittnesseth *genesis*,   240
That seith, with swynke and with swot · and swetynge face
By-tulye and by-trauaile · treuly oure lyf-lode;
    In labore et sudore uultus tui uesceris pane tuo.
And Salamon the sage · with the same acordeth,
The slowe caytyf for colde · wolde no corn tulye;   244
In somere for hus slewthe · he shal haue defaute,
And gon abrybeth and beggen · and no man bete hus hunger.
    *Piger propter frigus noluit arare; mendicabit in hyeme et
    non dabitur ei.*
Matheu maketh mencion · of a man that lente
Hus seluer to thre manere men · and menynge that thei sholde
Chaffare and cheeue ther-with · in chele and in hete;   249
And he that best laborede · best was alowed,
And leders for here laborynge · ouere al the lordes goodes.

He bi-nom him his npnam · for he nolde not worche, 228
And ȝaf hit him in haste · that hedde ten bi-fore;
And seththen he thus seide · his seruauns hit herden,
He that hath schal haue · to helpe ther neod is,
And he that nouȝt hath, nouȝt schal haue · ne no mon him helpe; 232
And he that hopeth forte haue · hit him beo bi-reuet.'
For Kuynde Wit wolde · that vche mon wrouhte
With techinge or with tilynge · or trauaylynge of hondes,
Actyf lyf or contemplatyf · Crist wolde hit alse. 236
For so seith the sauter · in psalm of *beati omnes*,

And binam hym his mnam · for he ne wolde worche,
And ȝaf that mnam to hym · that ten mnames hadde, 244
And with that he seyde · that holicherche it herde,
'He that hath shal haue · and helpe there it nedeth,
And he that nouȝt hath, shal nouȝt haue · and no man hym helpe;
And that he weneth wel to haue · I wil it hym bireue.' 248
 Kynde witt wolde · that eche a wyght wrouȝte
Or in dykynge or in deluynge · or trauaillynge in preyeres,
Contemplatyf lyf or actyf lyf · Cryst wolde men wrouȝte.
The sauter seyth in the psalme · of *beati omnes*, 252
The freke that fedeth hym-self · with his feythful laboure,
He is blessed by the boke · in body and in soule:
 Labores manuum tuarum, etc.'

'Ȝet I prey ȝow,' quod Pieres · '*par charite*, and ȝe kunne
Eny leef of lechecraft · lere it me, my dere. 256
For somme of my seruauntz · and my-self bothe
Of al a wyke worche nouȝt · so owre wombe aketh.'
 'I wote wel,' quod Hunger · 'what sykenesse ȝow eyleth,
Ȝe han maunged ouer-moche · and that maketh ȝow grone. 260
Ac I hote the,' quod Hunger · 'as thow thyne hele wilnest,
That thow drynke no day · ar thow dyne somwhat.

A. 237. *The Latin is from* TH; V *om.*   **B.** 243. hym WCRO; L *om.*

Labores manuum tuarum quia manducabis, etc.
He that get his fode her · with trauaylinge in treuthe,
God ȝiueth him his blessyng · that his lyflode so swynketh.'
'Yit I preye the,' quod Pers · 'par charite, ȝif thou conne   240
Eny lyf of leche-craft · lere hit me, my deore.
For summe of my seruauns · beoth seke other-while,
Of alle the wike heo worcheth not · so heor wombe aketh.'
'I wot wel,' quod Hungur · 'what seknesse hem eileth,   244
Thei han i-maunget ouur muche · that maketh hem grone ofte.
Ac ich hote the,' quod Hungur · 'and thou thin hele wylne,
That thou drynke no dai · til thou haue dynet sumwhat;

Ac he that was a wrecche · and wolde nat trauayle,   252
The lord, for hus lacchesse · and hus luther sleuthe,
By-nom hym al that he hadde · and ȝaf hit to hus felawe
That leely hadde labored; · and thenne the lord seide,
'He that hath shal haue · and helpe ther hym lyketh;   256
And he that nauht haueth · he shal nauht haue,
And no man ȝut helpe hym; · . ꞏnd that he weneth haue,
Ich wolle hit hym by-reue · for ꞏ.ꞏs rechelesnesse.'
Lo! what the sauter seith · to swynkers with handes,   260
'Yblessed be alle tho · that here by-lyue byswynken
Thorw eny leel labour · as thorgh lymes and handes;'
    Labores manuum tuarum quia manducabis; beatus es, et
    bene tibi erit: et cetera.
These aren euydences,' quath Hunger · 'for hem that wolle
    nat swynken,
That here lyflode be lene · and lytel worth here clothes.'   264
'By Cryst,' quath Peers the plouhman tho · 'these prouerbes
    wolle ich shewe
To beggers, and to boyes · that loth ben to worche.
Ac ȝut ich praye ȝow,' quath Peers · 'pur charity, syre Hunger,
ȝyf ȝe can other knowe · eny kynne thynge of fysyk?   268
For some of my seruauns · and my-selue bothe,
Of alle a woke worchen nat · so oure wombe groneth.'
'Ich wot wel,' quath Hunger · 'what syknesse ȝow aileth;
ȝe haue manged ouere muche · that maketh ȝow be syke.   272

C. 261. here IG; he (*wrongly*) P.   byswynken EMG; swynken P.   262.
beatus—et cetera is in S only.   263, 265. Theese P.

Ete not, ich hote the · til hunger the take, 248
And sende the sum of his sauce · to sauer the the betere;
Keep sum til soper tyme · and sit thou not to longe,
A-rys vp ar appetyt · habbe i-ȝeten his fulle.
Let not sir Surfet · sitten at thi bord; 252
Loue him not, for he is a lechour · and likerous of tonge,
And aftur mony metes · his mawe is a-longet.
And ȝif thou diȝete the thus · I dar legge bothe myn eres,

Ete nouȝte, I hote the · ar hunger the take,
And sende the of his sauce · to sauoure with thi lippes; 264
And kepe some tyl soper-tyme · and sitte nouȝt to longe,
Arise vp ar appetit · haue eten his fulle.
Lat nouȝt sire Surfait · sitten at thi borde;
Leue him nouȝt, for he is lecherous · and likerous of tonge, 268
And after many manere metes · his maw is afyngred.

And ȝif thow diete the thus · I dar legge myne eres,
That Phisik shal his furred hodes · for his fode selle,
And his cloke of Calabre · with alle the knappes of golde, 272
And be fayne, bi my feith · his phisik to lete,
And lerne to laboure with londe · for lyflode is swete ;
For morthereres aren mony leches · lorde hem amende !
Thei do men deye thorw here drynkes · ar destinē it wolde.' 276
'By seynt Poule,' quod Pieres · 'thise aren profitable wordis!
Wende now, Hunger, whan thow wolt · that wel be thow euere
For this is a louely lessoun · lorde it the for-ȝelde!'

A. 250. sit TU; faste VH. 256. foode THU; lyflode V.   C. 274.
the IMG; P *om*.   276. *This line is from* MIG ; P *om*.   286. wit P.
295. to IM ; P *om*.   300. wenne P.

That Fisyk schal his forred hod · for his foode sulle, 256
And eke his cloke of Calabre · with knappes of gold,
And beo fayn, be my feith · his fisyk to lete,
And leorne to labre with lond · leste lyflode faile;
Ther beoth mo lyȝers then leches · vr lord hem amende! 260
Thei don men dyȝen thoruȝ heor drinke · er destenye wolde.'
  'Bi seint Poul!' quod Pers · 'theos beoth prophitable wordes!
This is a loueli lesson · vr lord hit the for-ȝelde!
Wend nou whon thi wille is · wel the beo for euere!' 264

Ac eet nat, ich hote · or hunger the take,
And sende the of hus sauce · to sauerie with thi lippes.
And kep som til soper-tyme · and sitte nauht to longe
At noon, ne at no time; · and nameliche at soper 276
Let nat syre Sorfait · sitten at thy borde,
And loke thow drynke no day · er thou dyne som-what.
Thenk that *Diues* for hus delicat lyf · to the deuel wente,
And Lazar, the lene beggere · that longed after cromes— 280
And ȝut had he hem nat · for ich Hunger culde hym—
And sitthe ich sauh hym sitte · as he a syre were,
At alle manere ese · in Abrahammes lappe.
And yf thow be of power · Peers, ich the rede, 284
Alle that greden at thy gate · for godes loue, after fode,
Parte with hem of thy payn · of potage other of souel,
Lene hem som of thy loof · thauh thou the lasse chewe.
And thauh lyers and lacchedrawers · and lolleres knocke, 288
Let hem abyde tyl the bord be drawe · ac bere hem none cromes,
Til alle thyn nedy neihebores · haue none ymaked.
  And yf thow dyght the thus · ich dar legge myn eres,
That Fysyk shal hus forrede hodes · for hus fode sulle, 292
And hus cloke of Calabre · for hus comunes legge,
And be fayn, by my faith · his fysyk to lete,
And lerne to labore with londe · leste lyflode hym faile.
Ther aren meny luthere leches · and leele leches fewe, 296
Thei don men deye thorgh here drynkes · er destyne hit wolde.'
  'By seynt Paul,' quath Peers tho · 'thou poyntest neih the treuthe,
And leelly seist, as ich leue · lord the for-ȝelde!
Wend now whenne thou wolt · and wel be thow euere, 300
For thow hast wel ywroke me · and also wel ytauht me.'

A. PASSUS VII. 265–278.   B. PASSUS VI. 280–304.

'I beo-hote the,' quod Hungur · 'heonnes nul I wende
Er I haue i-dynet bi this day · and i-dronke bothe.'
'I haue no peny,' quod Pers · 'poletes to bugge,
Nouther gees ne grys · bote twey grene cheeses,   268
And a fewe cruddes and craym · and a therf cake,
And a lof of benes and bren · i-bake for my children.
And I sigge, bi my soule · I haue no salt bacon,
Ne no cokeneyes, bi Crist · colopus to maken.   272
Bot I haue porettes and percyl · and moni colplontes,
And eke a cou, and a calf · and a cart-mare
To drawe a-feld my donge · whil the drouhthe lasteth.
Bi this lyflode I mot lyuen · til Lammasse tyme;   276
Bi that, ich hope forte haue · heruest in my croft;
Thenne may I dihte thi dyner · as the deore lyketh.'

'By-hote god,' quod Hunger · 'hennes ne wil I wende,   280
Til I haue dyned bi this day · and ydronke bothe.'
'I haue no peny,' quod Peres · 'poletes forto bigge,
Ne neyther gees ne grys · but two grene cheses,
A fewe cruddes and creem · and an hauer cake,   284
And two loues of benes and bran · y-bake for my fauntis.
And ȝet I sey, by my soule · I haue no salt bacoun,
Ne no kokeney, bi Cryst · coloppes forto maken.
Ac I haue percil and porettes · and many kole-plantes,   288
And eke a cow and a kalf · and a cart-mare
To drawe a-felde my donge · the while the drought lasteth.
And bi this lyflode we mot lyue · til Lammasse tyme;
And bi that, I hope to haue · heruest in my croft;   292
And thanne may I diȝte thi dyner · as me dere liketh.'
Alle the pore peple tho · pesecoddes fetten,
Benes and baken apples · thei brouȝte in her lappes,
Chibolles and cheruelles · and ripe chiries manye,   296
And profred Peres this present · to plese with hunger.
   Al Hunger eet in hast · and axed after more.
Thanne pore folke for fere · fedde Hunger ȝerne
With grene poret and pesen · to poysoun Hunger thei thouȝte.
By that it neighed nere heruest · newe corne cam to chepynge;
Thanne was folke fayne · and fedde Hunger with the best,   302
With good ale, as Glotoun tauȝte · and gerte Hunger go slepe.
   And tho wolde Wastour nouȝt werche · but wandren aboute,

A. PASSUS VII. 279-290. C. PASSUS IX. 302-326.

    Al the pore peple · pese-coddes fetten,
Bake benes in bred · thei brouhten in heor lappes,   280
Chibolles, cheef mete · and ripe chiries monye,
And proferde Pers this present · to plese with hungur.
    Honger eet this in haste · and asked aftur more.
Thenne this folk for fere · fetten him monye   284
Poretes, and peosen · for thei him plese wolden;
From that tyme that thulke weore eten · take he schulde his leue
Til hit to heruest hiȝede · that newe corn com to chepynge.
    Thenne was that folk fayn · and fedde Hunger ȝeorne   288
With good ale, and glotonye · and gart him to slepe.
And tho nolde the wastor worche · but wandren aboute,

'Ich by-hote the,' quath Hunger · 'that hennes nel ich wende
Er ich haue y-dyned by thys day · and y-dronke bothe!'
    'Ich haue no peny,' quath Peers · 'polettes for to bigge,   304
Nother goos nother grys · bote two grene cheses,
A fewe croddes and creyme · and a cake of otes,
And bred for my barnes · of benes and of peses.
And ȝut ich sey, by my saule · ich haue no salt bacon;   308
Nouht a cokeney, by Cryst · colhoppes to make.
Ac ich haue porett-plontes · perselye and scalones,
Chiboles and chiruylles · and chiries sam-rede,
And a cow with a calf · and a cart-mare,   312
To drawe a-feld my donge · the whyle drouth lasteth.
By this lyflode we mote lyue · tyl Lammasse tyme;
And by that, ich hope to haue · heruest in my crofte;
Thenne may I dyghte thy dyner · as me dere lyketh.'   316
    Alle the poure puple tho · peescoddes fetten;
Benes and baken apples · thei brouhte in here lappes,
And profrede Peers this present · to plese ther-with Hunger.
    Hunger eet al in haste · and askede after more;   320
Poure folke for fere tho · fedde Hunger ȝerne
With creym and with croddes · with carses and other herbes.
By that yt neihed heruest · and newe corn com to chepyng,
Thenne was this folke feyn · and fedde Hunger deynteuosliche,
And Gloton tho with good ale · gerte Hunger to slepe.   325
Tho wolde Wastour nat worche · bote wandrede aboute,

    C. 311. chirueylles P.   313. wyle P.   323. chipynge P.

Ne no beggere eten bred · that benes inne coome,
Bote coket and cler-matin · an of clene whete; 292
Ne non halfpeny ale · in none wyse drynke,
Bote of the beste and the brouneste · that brewesters sullen.
  Laborers that haue no lond · to liuen on bote heore honden,
Deyne not to dyne a day · niht-olde wortes. 296
Mai no peny-ale hem paye · ne no pece of bacun,
Bote hit weore fresch flesch · or elles fisch i-fri3et,
Bothe *chaud* and *pluschaud* · for chele of heore mawe.
  Bote he beo heihliche i-huret · elles wol he chide, 300

Ne no begger ete bred · that benes inne were, 305
But of coket or clerematyn · or elles of clene whete;
Ne none halpeny ale · in none wise drynke,
But of the best and of the brounest · that in borghe is to
    selle. 308
  Laboreres that haue no lande · to lyue on but her handes,
Deyned nou3t to dyne a-day · ny3t-olde wortes.
May no peny-ale hem paye · ne no pece of bakoun,
But if it be fresch flesch other fische · fryed other bake, 312
And that *chaude* or *plus chaud* · for chillyng of her mawe.
  And but-if he be heighlich huyred · ellis wil he chyde,
And that he was werkman wrou3t · waille the tyme,
A3eines Catones conseille · comseth he to Iangle:— 316
    Paupertatis onus pacienter ferre memento.
  He greueth hym a3eines god · and gruccheth a3eines resoun,
And thanne curseth he the kynge · and al his conseille after,
Suche lawes to loke · laboreres to greue.
  Ac whiles Hunger was her maister · there wolde none of hem
    chyde, 320
Ne stryue a3eines his statut · so sterneliche he loked.
  Ac I warne 3ow, werkemen · wynneth while 3e mowe,
For Hunger hiderward · hasteth hym faste,
He shal awake with water · wastoures to chaste. 324
Ar fyue 3ere be fulfilled · suche famyn shal aryse,
Thorwgh flodes and though foule wederes · frutes shul faille,
And so sayde Saturne · and sent 3ow to warne:

A. 305. statutes UH; statues V.   311. Saturne HU; Saturnes V.

That he was werkmon i-wrou3t • warie the tyme,
And corse 3erne the kyng • and al his counseil aftur,
Suche lawes to loke • laborers to chaste.

Ac while Hunger was mayster heer • wolde ther non chyde,
Ne striue a3eyn the statutes • so steorneliche he lokede.   305
I warne 3ou, alle werk-men • winneth while 3e mowe,
Hunger hiderward a3eyn • hi3eth him 3eorne.
He wole a-wake thorw watur • the wastours alle;   308
Er fyue 3er ben folfult • such famyn schal a-ryse,
Thorw flodes and foul weder • fruites schul fayle;
And so seith Saturne • and sent vs to warne.   311

Nother beggere eete bred • that benes were ynne,
Bote clerematyn and coket • and of clene whete;   328
Thei wolde non halpeny ale • in none wyse drynke,
Bote of the best and brounest • that brewesters sellen.
Laboreres that han no londe • to lyuen on bote here handes
Deyned noght to dyne a-day • nyght-olde wortes.   332
May no peny-ale hem paye • ne a pece of bacon,
Bote hit be freesch fleesch other fysch • fried other ybake,
And that *chaud* and *pluschaud* • for chillyng of here mawe.
Bote he be heyliche yhyred • elles wol he chide,   336
That he was a werkman ywroght • waryen the tyme;
Corteis Catones consail • comseth he by-grucche,
Paupertatis onus • pacienter ferre memento.

And thenne he corseth the kyng • and alle the kynges Iustices,
Suche lawes to lere • laborers to greue.   341
Ac while Hunger was here mayster • wolde non chide,
Ne stryue a-3ens the statute • he lokede so sturne.
Ac ich warne 3ow werkmen • wynne whyle 3e mowe,   344
For Hunger hyderwardes • hyeth hym faste;
He shal awake thorw water • wasters to chaste.
Ar fewe 3eres be fulfilled • famyne shal aryse,

And so seith *Saturnus* • and sent 3ow to warne.   348

B. 323. hideward L.   325. 3ere R; 3eer O; L *om.*   C. 332. noght I;
PEMG *om.*   342. wile P.   344. wyle P.   348. An P.

[*Not in* **A**-*text.*]

Whan ȝe se the sonne amys · and two monkes hedes, 328
And a mayde haue the maistrie · and multiplie bi eight,
Thanne shal Deth withdrawe · and Derthe be iustice,
And Dawe the dyker · deye for hunger,
But if god of his goodnesse · graunt vs a trewe. 332

[*Not in* **A**-*text.*]

Thorwe flodes and foule wederes · frutes shullen faile,
Pruyde and pestilences · shal muche puple fecche.
Thre shupes and a shaft · with an vm. folwyng,
Shal brynge bane and bataile · on bothe half the mone. 352
And thanne shal deth with-drawe · and derthe be Iustice,
And Dawe the deluere · deye for defaute,
Bote god of hus goodnesse · graunte ous a trewe. 355

Hic explicit passus nonus.

C. 350. pestelences P.   351. viij (*for* vm) I.

PASSUS VIII.

Passus octauus de visione, vt prius.

TREUTHE herde telle her-of · and to Pers sende,
To taken his teeme · and tilyen the eorthe;
And purchasede him a pardoun · *a pena et a culpa*
For him, and for his heires · euer-more aftur.   4
And bad holden hem at hom · and heren heore ley3es,
And al that euere hulpen him · to heren or to sowen,
Or eny maner mester · that mihte Pers helpen,

PASSUS VII.

Passus vij. de visione, vt supra.

TREUTHE herde telle her-of · and to Peres he sent,
To taken his teme · and tulyen the erthe,
And purchaced hym a pardoun · *a pena et a culpa*
For hym, and for his heires · for euermore after.   4
And bad hym holde hym at home · and eryen his leyes,
And alle that halpe hym to erie · to sette or to sowe,
Or any other myster · that my3te Pieres auaille,
Pardoun with Pieres plowman · treuthe hath ygraunted.   8
    Kynges and kny3tes · that kepen holycherche,
And ry3tfullych in reumes · reulen the peple,
Han pardoun thourgh purgatorie · to passe ful ly3tly,
With patriarkes and prophetes · in paradise to be felawes.   12
    Bisshopes yblessed · 3if thei ben as thei shulden,
Legistres of bothe the lawes · the lewed there-with to preche,
And in as moche as thei mowe · amende alle synful,
Aren peres with the apostles · this pardoun Piers sheweth,   16
And at the day of dome · atte heigh deyse to sytte.

B. 16. this WCO; thus LR.   C. 5. hym IG; P *om.*   7. myster MEG; meester P.   9. kirke I; churche PEG.   10. ryghtfulleche P.   18. custymes P.

A. PASSUS VIII. 8–19.   C. PASSUS X. 1–21.

Part in that pardoun · the pope hath i-graunted.   8
Kynges and knihtes · that kepen holi churche,
And rihtfuliche rulen · the reame and the peple,
Han pardoun thorw purgatorie · to passen ful sone,
With patriarkes in paradys · to pleyen ther-aftur.   12
Busschops that blessen · and bothe the lawes cunnen,
Loketh on that on lawe · and lereth men that other,
And bereth hem bothe on heore bac · as heore baner scheweth,
And precheth heore persouns · the peril of sunne,   16
Hou heore schabbede schep · schal heore wolle saue,
Han pardoun with the apostles · whon thei passen hennes,
And atte day of dom · with hem on deis setten.

PASSUS X.

Incipit passus decimus.

TREUTHE herde telle here-of · and to Peers sente
To take hus teeme · and tulye the erthe;
And purchased hym a pardon · *á pena et á culpa*,
For hym and for hus heyres · for euere to be asoiled;   4
And bad hym halde hym at home · and erye hus leyes,
And alle that hulpe hym to erye · to setten other to sawe,
Other eny manere myster · that myght Peers a-vayle,
Pardon with Peers plouhman · perpetual he graunteth.   8
Kynges and knyghtes · that holy kirke defenden,
And ryghtfulliche in reames · ruelen the comune,
Han pardon thorw purgatorie · to passy ful lyghtliche,
With patriarkes and prophetes · in paradyse to sitte.   12
Bisshopes yblessed · if thei ben as thei sholde,
Leel and ful of loue · and no lord dreden,
Merciable to meek · and mylde to the goode,
And bytynge on badde men · bote yf thei wolde amende,   16
And dredeth nat for no deth · to distruye, by here powere,
Lecherie a-mong lordes · and hure luther customes,
And sitthen lyue as thei lereth men · oure lord treuthe hem graunteth
To be peeres to a-posteles · alle puple to ruele,   20
And deme with hem at domes day · bothe quike and ded.

Marchauns in this margin · hedden mony ȝeres, 20
Bote non *a pena et a culpa* · the pope nolde hem graunte,
For thei holdeth not heore haly-day · as holy churche techeth,
And for thei sworen bi heore soule · —'so god hem moste helpe!'—
Aȝeyn heore clene concience · heore catel to sulle. 24
Bote vndur his secre seal · Treuthe sende a lettre,
And bad hem bugge boldely · what hem best lykede,
And seththen sullen hit a-ȝeyn · and saue the wynnynge,
And make *meson-deux* ther-with · meseyse to helpe, 28
And wikkede wones · wihtly to amende;
Beete brugges a-boute · that to-broke were,
Marie maydens · or maken hem nonnes;
Pore widewes that wolde beo · none wyues aftur, 32

Marchauntz in the margyne · hadden many ȝeres,
Ac none *a pena et a culpa* · the pope nolde hem graunte,
For thei holde nouȝt her halidayes · as holicherche techeth, 20
And for thei swere by her soule · and 'so god moste hem helpe,'
Aȝein clene conscience · her catel to selle.
Ac vnder his secret seel · Treuthe sent hem a lettre,
That they shulde bugge boldely · that hem best liked, 24
And sithenes selle it aȝein · and saue the wynnynge,
And amende *mesondieux* there-myde · and myseyse folke helpe,
And wikked wayes · wiȝtlich hem amende;
And do bote to brugges · that to-broke were, 28
Marien maydenes · or maken hem nonnes;
Pore peple and prisounes · fynden hem here fode,
And sette scoleres to scole · or to somme other craftes;
Releue religioun · and renten hem bettere;— 32
'And I shal sende ȝow my-selue · seynt Michel myn archangel,
That no deuel shal ȝow dere · ne fere ȝow in ȝowre deyinge,
And witen ȝow fro wanhope · if ȝe wil thus worche,
And sende ȝowre sowles in safte · to my seyntes in ioye.' 36
Thanne were marchauntz mery · many wepten for ioye,
And preyseden Pieres the plowman · that purchaced this bulle.
Men of lawe lest pardoun hadde · that pleteden for mede,

A. 20. Marchaus (*sic*) V.   28. *deux* T; *dieux* H; *deu* V.   45. loth H;

Fynde suche heore foode · for godes loue of heuene;
Sette scolers to scole · or to sum other craft,
Rule religion · and rente hem betere;
'And I schal sende ow my-self · seint Mihel myn aungel,   36
That no deuel schal ȝou dere · whon ȝe dye schulle,
That I ne schal sende ȝor soules · saaf in-to heuene,
And bi-foren the face of my fader · fourmen or seetes.
Vsure and auarice · and othes I defende,   40
That no gile go with ou · bote the grace of treuthe.'
  Thenne were marchaundes murie · thei wopen for ioye,
And ȝeeuen Wille for his writynge · wollene clothes;
For he copiede thus heore cause · thei couden him gret thonk.
Men of lawe hedden lest · for heo beoth loth   45

Marchans in the margine · hadden menye ȝeres,
Ac *á pena et á cúlpa* · Treuthe nolde hem graunte;   23
For thei holden nat here halydaies · as holychurche techeth,
And for thei swere by here saule · and 'so god me mote helpe!'
Aȝens clene conscience · for couetyse of wynnynge.
  Ac vnder his secre seel · Treuthe sente hem a lettere,
And bad hem bygge baldly · what hem best lykede,   28
And sitthen sellen hit a-ȝeyn · and saue the wynnynges,
Amenden *meson-dieux* ther-with · and myseyse men fynde,
And wikkede weyes · with here good amende,
And brygges to-broke · by the heye weyes   32
Amende in som manere wise · and maydenes helpen;
Poure puple bedredene · and prisones in stockes,
Fynde hem for godes loue · and fauntekynes to scole;
Releue religion · and renten hem bettere;   36
'And ich shal sende ȝow my-selue · seynt Michel myn angel,
That no deuel shal ȝow dere · ne despeir in ȝoure deyinge,
And sende ȝoure soules · ther ich my-self dwelle,
And there a-byde body and soule · in blisse for euere.'   40
  Tho were merchauns murye · somme wepte for ioye,
And preyde for Peers plouhman · that purchasede hem this bulle.
Alle the puple hadde pardon ynow · that parfytliche lyueden;
Men of lawe hadde lest · that loth were to plede,   44

---

lettered alle V.   B. 25. wynnyge L.   C. 27, 28. hym (*for* hem) P.
33. maydones P.   38. deyenge P.   40. þe (*for* there) P.

A. PASSUS VIII. 46–54.   B. PASSUS VII. 40–61.

To mote for mene men · but ȝif thei hadde money;
So seith the sauter · and Sapience bothe,
   Super innocentes munera non accipiunt.
   A regibus et princi-
      pibus erit merces eorum.
Of princes and prelatus · heor pencion schulde aryse,   48
And of the pore peple · no peneworth to take.
Ac he that spendeth his speche · and speketh for the pore
That is innocent and neodi · and no mon hath apeyret,
Cumforteth him in his caas · coueiteth not his goodes,   52
Bote for vr lordes loue · lawe for him scheweth,
Schal no deuel at his deth-day · deren him worth a myte,

For the sauter saueth hem nouȝte · such as taketh ȝiftes,   40
And namelich of innocentz · that none yuel ne kunneth;
   Super innocentem munera non accipies.
Pledoures shulde peynen hem · to plede for such, an helpe,
Princes and prelates · shulde paye for her trauaille;
   A regibus et pryncipibus erit merces eorum.
Ac many a Iustice an Iuroure · wolde for Iohan do more,   44
Than *pro dei pietate* · leue thow none other!
Ac he that spendeth his speche · and speketh for the pore
That is innocent and nedy · and no man appeireth,
Conforteth hym in that cas · with-oute coueytise of ȝiftes,   48
And scheweth lawe for owre lordes loue · as he it hath lerned,
Shal no deuel at his ded-day · deren hym a myȝte,
That he ne worth sauf and his sowle · the sauter bereth wit-
   nesse;
   Domine, quis habitabit in tabernaculo tuo, &c.
Ac to bugge water, ne wynde · ne witte, ne fyre the fierthe,   52
Thise foure the fader of heuene · made to this folde in comune;
Thise ben treuthes tresores · trewe folke to helpe,
That neuere shal wax ne wanye · with-oute god hym-selue.
Whan thei drawen on to deye · and indulgences wolde haue,
Her pardoun is ful petit · at her partyng hennes,   57
That any mede of mene men · for her motyng taketh.
Ȝe legistres and lawyeres · holdeth this for treuthe,
That, ȝif that I lye · Mathew is to blame,   60
For he bad me make ȝow this · and this prouerbe me tolde,
   Quodcumque vultis vt faciant vobis homines, facite eis.

A. PASSUS VIII. 55–63.   C. PASSUS X. 45–57.   231

That he ne worth siker saaf · and so seith the psauter,
Qui facit hec, non mouebitur in eternum.
Ac to bugge water, ne wynt · ne wit, (is the thridde),   56
Nolde neuer holy writ · god wot the sothe!
Theos threo for thralles · beo thriuen a-mong vs alle,
To waxen or to wonien · whether god lyketh,
His pardoun in purgatorie · is petit, I trouwe,   60
That eny meede of mene men · for motynge receyueth.
ӡe legistres and lawyers · ӡe witen wher I lyӡe;
Seththe ӡe seon that hit is so · serueth to the beste.

Bote thei *pre manibus* were payed · for pledyng atte barre.

Ac he that speneth hus speche · and speketh for the poure
That innocent and nedy is · and no man harme wolde,
And conforteth suche in eny cas · and coueyteth nat here ӡiftes,
And for the loue of oure lorde · lawe for hem .declareth,   49
Shal haue grace of god ynow · and a gret ioye after.
Beth ywar, ӡe wise men · and witty of the lawe ;

For whenne ӡe draweth to the deth · and indulgence wolde haue,
Hus pardon is ful petit · at hus partynge hennes,   53
That mede of mene men · for here motynge taketh.
For hit is symonye, to sulle · that send is of grace ;
That is, witt and water · wynd, and fuyr the furthe,   56
These foure sholden be fre · to alle folk that hit nedeth.

A. 46. *This line is in* H *only.*   47. V *omits all after* Regibus.   48. princes THU; parisches V.   55. *The Latin is in* H *only.*   56. (2*nd*) ne T; or H; V *om.*   C. 47. nedy IMEG; nudy P.   48. ӡeftes P.   51. wise men IMEG; wismen P.   52. wenne P.   57. nedeþ IME; needede P.

Libbinde laborers · that libben bi heore hondes,　　64
That treuliche taken · and treuliche tithen,
And liuen in loue and in lawe · for heore lowe hertes,
Hedde the same absolucion · that sent was to Pers.

Alle lybbyng laboreres · that lyuen with her hondes,
That trewlich taken · and trewlich wynnen,
And lyuen in loue and in lawe · for her lowe hertis,　　64
Haueth the same absolucioun · that sent was to Peres.
Beggeres ne bidderes · ne beth nouȝte in the bulle,
But if the suggestioun be soth · that shapeth hem to begge.
For he that beggeth or bit · but if he haue nede,　　68
He is fals with the fende · and defraudeth the nedy,
And also he bigileth the gyuere · ageines his wil.
For if he wist he were nouȝte nedy · he wolde ȝiue that an-other,
That were more nedy than he · so the nediest shuld be hulpe.　72
Catoun kenneth men thus · and the clerke of the stories,
Cui des, videto · is Catounes techynge,
And in the stories he techeth · to bistowe thyn almes;
　　Sit elemosina tua in manu tua, donec studes cui des.
Ac Gregori was a gode man · and bad vs gyuen alle　　76
That asketh, for his loue · that vs alle leneth:—
　　Non eligas cui miserearis, ne forte pretereas illum qui
　　meretur accipere. Quia incertum est pro quo Deo magis
　　placeas.
For wite ȝe neuere who is worthi · ac god wote who hath
　　nede,
In hym that taketh is the treccherye · if any tresoun wawe;
For he that ȝiueth, ȝeldeth · and ȝarketh hym to reste,　　80
And he that biddeth, borweth · and bryngeth hym-self in dette.
For beggeres borwen euermo · and her borghe is god almyȝti,
To ȝelden hem that ȝiueth hem · and ȝet vsure more:
　　Quare non dedisti peccuniam meam ad mensam, vt ego
　　veniens cum vsuris exegissem illam?
For-thi biddeth nouȝt, ȝe beggeres · but if ȝe haue gret nede;
For who-so hath to buggen hym bred · the boke bereth wit-
　　nesse,　　85
He hath ynough that hath bred ynough · though he haue nouȝt
　　elles:
　　Satis diues est, qui non indiget pane.

Bidders and beggers · beoth not in the bulle, 68
Bote the suggestion be soth · that schapeth hem to begge.
For he that beggeth or biddeth · bote he habbe neode,
He is fals with the fend · and defraudeth the neodi,
Aud eke gyleth the ȝiuere · al aȝeyn his wille. 72

Alle lybbynge laborours · that lyuen with here handes
Leelyche and lawefulliche · oure lord treuthe hem graunteth
Pardon perpetuel · ryght as Peers Plouhman. 60
Beggers and bydders · beth nat in that bulle
Bote the suggestion be soth · that shapeth hem to begge.
For he that beggeth other byddeth · bote yf he haue nede,
He ys fals and faitour · and defraudeth the nedy, 64
And also gyleth hym that gyueth · and taketh ageyns hus wyl.
For he that gyueth for godes loue · wolde nat gyue, hus thankus,
Bote ther he wyste hit were · wel gret neede to gyuen,
And most meritorie to men · that he ȝeueth for. 68
Caton a-cordeth ther-with · *cui des uideto;*

Wot no man, as ich wene · who is worthy to haue.

B. 75. L omits the former *tua*. 77. *Deo* W; *deum* L. 83. *exigissem*
CB; *exigerem* L. The MSS. omit *illam*. C. 58. laberours P. 59. lawe-
fulleche P. 61. þat IMEG; þe P. 62. sugestion P. shappeþ P. 63. (*2nd*)
he MI; þei P. 64. nedy IMEG; neede P. 68. mest P. fore P.

[*Not in* **A**-*text or* **B**-*text.*]

The most needy aren oure neighebores · and we nyme good hede,
As prisones in puttes · and poure folke in cotes, 72
Charged with children · and chef lordes rente,
That thei with spynnynge may spare · spenen hit in hous-hyre,
Bothe in mylk and in mele · to make with papelotes,
To a-glotye with here gurles · that greden after fode. 76
Al-so hem-selue · suffren muche hunger,
And wo in winter-tyme · with wakynge a nyghtes
To ryse to the ruel · to rocke the cradel,
Bothe to karde and to kembe · to clouten and to wasche, 80
To rubbe and to rely · russhes to pilie,
That reuthe is to rede · othere in ryme shewe
The wo of these women · that wonyeth in cotes;
And of meny other men · that muche wo suffren, 84
Bothe a-fyngrede and a-furst · to turne the fayre outwarde,
And beth abasshed for to begge · and wolle nat be aknowe
What hem needeth at here neihebores · at non and at euen.
This ich wot witerly · as the worlde techeth, 88
What other by-houeth · that hath meny children,
And hath no catel botè hus crafte · to clothy hem and to fede,
And fele to fonge ther-to · and fewe pans taketh.
Ther is payn and peny-ale · as for a pytaunce y-take, 92
Colde flessh and cold fyssh · for veneson ybake;
Frydayes and fastyng-dayes · a ferthyng-worth of muscles
Were a feste for suche folke · other so fele cockes.
These were almes, to helpe · that han suche charges, 96
And to comfortie such cotyers · and crokede men and blynde.
   Ac beggers with bagges · the whiche brewhouses ben here churches,
Bote thei be blynde other broke · other elles be syke,
Thauh he falle for defaute · that faiteth for hus lyf-lode, 100
Reccheth neuere, 3e ryche · thauh suche lorelles steruen.
For alle that han here hele · and here eyen syghte,
And lymes to laborye with · and lolleres lyf vsen,
Lyuen a-3ens godes lawe · and lore of holy churche. 104
   And 3ut arn ther other beggers · in hele, as hit semeth,

C. 74. wiþ MIG; P *om.* spenen E; spene IG; spynen P. 83. of IG;
þat P. þeese P. 86. aknowe MEG; yknowe P. 87. att P (1*st time*).
94. a IMEG; P *om.* 95. a folke P; *but* IMEG *omit* a. 116. wyght G;

C. PASSUS X. 106–136.

[*Not in* A-*text or* B-*text; see* p. 234.]

Ac hem wanteth here witt · men and women bothe,
The whiche aren lunatik lollers · and leperes a-boute,
And mad as the mone sitt · more other lasse. 108
Thei caren for no cold · ne counteth of no hete,
And arn meuynge after the mone · moneyles thei walke,
With a good wil, witlees · meny wyde contreys,
Ryght as Peter dude and Paul · saue that thei preche nat, 112
Ne myracles maken; "ac meny tymes hem happeth
To prophecien of the puple · pleyinge, as hit were,
And to oure sight, as hit semeth · suththe God hath the myghte
To ȝeuen eche a wyght wit · welthe, and his hele, 116
And suffreth suche so gon · hit semeth, to myn inwitt,
Hit arn as hus aposteles, suche puple · other as his priuye disciples.
For he sente hem forth seluerles · in a somer garnement,
With-oute bred and bagge · as the bok telleth, 120
 Quando misi uos sine pane et pera;
Barfot and bredles · beggeth thei of no man.
And thauh he mete with the meyre · amyddes the strete,
He reuerenceth hym ryght nouht · no rather than another;
 Neminem salutaueritis per uiam.
Suche manere of men · Matheu ous techeth, 124
We sholde haue hem to house · and help hem when thei come;
 Et egenos uagosque induc in domum tuam.
For hit aren murye-mouthede men · mynstrales of heuene,
And godes boyes, bordiours · as the bok telleth,
 Si quis uidetur sapiens, fiet stultus ut sit sapiens.
And alle manere mynstrales · men wot wel the sothe, 128
To vnder-fonge hem faire · by-falleth for the ryche,
For the lordes loue and ladies · that thei with lengen.
Men suffren al that suche seyn · and in solas taken,
And ȝut more to suche men · doth er thei passe, 132
Gyuen hem gyftes and gold · for grete lordes sake.
Ryght so, ȝe riche · rather ȝe sholde, for sothe,
Welcomen and worsshepen · and with ȝoure goode helpen 135
Godes mynstrales and hus messagers · and hus murye bordiours;

---

whiȝt E; whit P.   122. meyere P.   amyddes I; in-mydest P.   123.
salutaueritis EMG; *salutaueris* PI.   129. by-falleþ GE; by-falle P
135. Wolcomen P.   136. bordiours EI; burdiers (*see* l. 127).

Thei libben not in loue · ne no lawe holden;
Thei weddeth no wommon · that thei with deleth;

Late vsage be ȝowre solace · of seyntes lyues redynge,
The boke banneth beggarie · and blameth hem in this manere: 88
   Iunior fui, etenim senui; et non vidi iustum derelictum,
   nec semen eius querens panem.

For ȝe lyue in no loue · ne no lawe holde;
Many of ȝow ne wedde nouȝt · the wommen that ȝe with delen,
But as wilde bestis with wehe · worthen vppe and worchen,
And bryngeth forth barnes · that bastardes men calleth. 92

A. 73. not—ne UT; in no lawe · that V.   75. wilde—with TH; beestes

Bote as wilde beestes, with wo · worcheth to-gedere,
And bringeth forth barnes · that bastardes beon holden.   76

The whiche arn lunatik lollares · and leperes a-boute,
For vnder godes secre seel · here synnes ben ykeuered.
For thei bereth no bagges · ne none botels vnder clokes,
The whiche is lollaren lyf · and lewede eremytes,   140
That loken ful louheliche · to lacchen mennes almesse,
In hope to sitten at euen · by the hote coles,
Vnlouke hus legges abrod · other lygge at hus ese,
Reste hym, and roste hym · and his ryg turne,   144
Drynke drue and deepe · and drawe hym thanne to bedde;
And when hym lyketh and lust · hus leue ys to aryse;
When he ys rysen, rometh out · and ryght wel aspieth
Whar he may rathest haue a repast · other a rounde of bacon,
Suluer other sode mete · and som tyme bothe,   149
A loof other half a loof · other a lompe of chese;
And carieth it hom to hus cote · and cast him to lyue
In ydelnesse and in ese · and by others trauayle.   152
And what frek of thys folde · fisketh thus a-boute,
With a bagge at hus bak · a begeneldes wyse,
And can som manere craft · in cas he wolde hit vse,
Thorgh whiche craft he couthe · come to bred and to ale,   156
And ouer-more to an hater · to helye with hus bones,
And lyueth lyk a lollere · godes lawe hym dampneth.
'Lolleres lyuyng in sleuthe · and ouer-londe strykers
Beeth nat in this bulle,' quath Peers · 'til thei ben amendid,
Nother beggers that beggen · bote yf thei haue neede.   161
The bok blameth alle beggerye · and banneth in this manere,

  Iunior fui, etenim senui, non uidi iustum derelictum, nec
   semen eius querens panem; et alibi: Infirmata est
   uirtus mea in paupertate.

Hit needeth nauht nouthe · a-non for to preche,
And lere these lewede men · what thys Latyn meneth,   164
For hit blameth alle beggerie · be ȝe ful certeyn.
For thei lyue in no loue · ne no lawe thei holden;
Thei wedde non womon · that thei with delen,
Bringeth forth bastardes · beggers of kynde.   168

that V.   B. 88. *querens panem* OC; LWR *om.*   C. 138. ykeuerede P.
159. ouere-londe P.   166. ne IMEG; P *om.*

238   A. PASSUS VIII. 77-82.   B. PASSUS VII. 93-105.

Or his bac, or his bon · heo breketh in heore ȝouthe,
And goth, fayteth with heore fauntes · euer-more after.
Ther ben mo mis-happes amongus hem · hose taketh heede,
Then of alle othure men · that on molde wandren.   80
Thei that lyuen thus heore lyf · mouwe lothe the tyme,
That euere thei weore men i-wrouȝt · whon thei schul henne
    fare.

Or the bakke or some bone · he breketh in his ȝouthe,
And sitthe gon faiten with ȝoure fauntes · for euermore after.
There is moo mysshape peple · amonge thise beggeres,
Than of alle maner men · that on this molde walketh;   96
And thei that lyue thus here lyf · mowe lothe the tyme,
That euere he was man wrouȝt · whan he shal hennes fare.
   Ac olde men and hore · that helplees ben of strengthe,
And women with childe · that worche ne mowe,   100
Blynde and bedered · and broken here membres,

That taketh this myschief mekelych · as meseles and othere,
Han as pleyne pardoun · as the plowman hym-self;
For loue of her lowe hertis · owre lorde hath hem graunted 104
Here penaunce and her purgatorie · here on this erthe.

A. 78. fautes V.   88. loue of THU; V om.   B. 94. A (for And) L.
C. 171. messhapene P.   173. ȝe me PE; but MIG omit me.   175. heelples P.
181. men IMEG; P om.   182. pouerte IMEG; pourte P.   183, 192, &c;
þeese P.   185. pure IMFEG; poure P.   187. Only in IK; the rest omit

A. PASSUS VIII. 83-89.   C. PASSUS X. 169-196.

Bote olde men and hore · that helpes beoth of strengthe,
And wymmen with childe · that worchen ne mowen,   84
Blynde and bedreden · and broken heore membres,
That taken meschef mekeliche · as meseles or othere,
Han as pleyn pardoun · as the plouh-mon him-seluen;
For loue of heore lowe hertes · vr lord hath hem graunted   88
Heore penaunce and heore purgatorie · is her vppon eorthe.

Other the bak other som bon · thei breken of here children,
And gooth afaytyng with here fauntes · for euere-more after.
Ther arn mo misshapen · a-mong suche beggers,
Than of meny other men · that on this molde walken.   172
Tho that lyuen thus hure lyf · leyue ȝe non othere,
Thei han no part of pardon · of preyers, ne of penaunces.
  Ac olde men and hore · that helpes beeth and nedy,
And wommen with childe · that worche ne mowen,   176
Blynde men and bedreden · and broken in here membres,
And alle poure pacientes · a-payed of godes sonde,
As mesels and mendinauntes · men yfalle in myschef,
As prisons and pilgrimes · paraunter men yrobbed,   180
Other by-lowe thorwe luthere men · and lost here catel after,
Other thorgh fure other thorwe flood · falle to pouerte,
That taken these meschiefes meekliche · and myldliche at herte;
For loue of here lowe hertes · oure lord hath hem graunted
Here penaunce and here purgatorie · vp-on thys pure erthe, 185
And pardon with Peers Plouhman · *a pena et a culpa.*
And alle holy hermites · haue schal the same;
  Ac eremites that en-habiten · by the heye weyes,   188
And in borwes a-mong brewesters · and beggen in churches;—
Al that holy eremytes · hateden and despisede,
As rychesses and reuerences · and ryche mennes almesse,
These lolleres, lacchedraweres · lewede eremytes,   192
Coueyten the contrarie · as cotiers thei lybben.
For hit beth bote boyes · bollers atten ale,
Neyther of lynage, ne of lettrure; · ne lyf-holy as eremites,
That wonede whilom in wodes · with beres and lyones.   196

---

this line.   188. en-habiten hem PM ; *the rest omit* hem.   194. bollers IM ;
lollers (*wrongly*) PEFG.   195. Of lynguage of letture P; *but* I *inserts* Ney-
þer; *other* MSS. *have* Of lynage ne of lettrure.   196. whilom IMF; wyle P.

[*Not in* **A**-*text or* **B**-*text.*]

Some had lyf-lode of here lynage · and of no lyf elles;
And some lyuede by here lettrure · and labour of here hondes;
Somme hadde foreynes to frendes · that hem fode sente;
And bryddes brouhten to some bred · wherby thei lyueden.
Alle these holy eremytes · were of hye kynne, 201
For-soke londe and lordshep · and lykynges of the body.
Ac these eremytes that edefyen thus · by the hye weyes,
Whilom were workmen · webbes and taillours, 204
And carters knaues · and clerkus with-oute grace,
Helden ful hungry hous · and hadde much defaute,
Long labour and lyte wynnynge · and atte laste aspiden,
That faitours in frere clothynge · hadde fatte chekus. 208
For-thi lefte thei here laboure · these lewede knaues,
And clothed hem in copes · clerkus as hit were,
Other on of som ordre · othere elles a prophete;
A-ȝens the lawe he lyueth · yf Latyn be trewe; 212
Non licet uobis legem uoluntati, sed uoluntatem coniungere legi.
Now kyndeliche, by Crist · beth suche callyd 'lolleres,'
As by Englisch of oure eldres · of olde menne techynge.
He that lolleth is lame · other his leg out of ioynte,
Other meymed in som membre · for to meschief hit souneth.
And ryght so sothlyche · suche manere eremytes 217
Lollen aȝen the byleyue · and lawe of holy churche.
For holy churche hoteth · alle manere puple
Vnder obedience to bee · and buxum to the lawe. 220
Furst, religious, of religion · here ruele to holde,
And vnder obedience to be · by dayes and by nyghtes;
Lewede men to laborie; · and lordes to honte
In frythes and in forestes · for fox and other bestes 224
That in wilde wodes ben · and in wast places,
As wolues that wyryeth men · wommen and children;
And vp-on Sonedayes to cesse · godes seruyce to huyre,
Bothe matyns and messe · and, after mete, in churches 228

C. 204. Whilom IMGF; Wylen P. 206. Heelden P. ful IMFG;
PE *om*.   212. trewe IEF; trywe P.   215. of IEFG; of þe P.   223.
and MFG; PIE *om*.   226. wyrhyeþ P.   234. oþer E; or FG; P *om*.

C. PASSUS X. 229-261.

[*Not in* A-*text or* B-*text; see* p. 240.]

To huyre here euesong · euery man ouhte.
Thus it by-longeth for lorde · for lered, and lewede,
Eche halyday to huyre · hollyche the seruice,
Vigiles and fastyngdayes · forthere-more to knowe,   232
And fulfille tho fastynges · bote infirmite hit made,
Pouerte other othere penaunces · as pilgrymages and trauayles.
Vnder this obedience · arn we echone;
Who-so brekyth this, be wel war · bot yf he repente,   236
Amende hym and mercy aske · and meekliche hym shryue,
Ich drede me, and he deye · hit worth for dedlich synne
A-counted by-fore Crist · bote conscience excuse hym.
Loke now where these lolleres · and lewede eremytes,   240
Yf thei breke thys obedience · that ben so fer fro churche?
Wher see we hem on Sonedays · the seruyse to huyre,
As, matyns by the morwe? · tyl masse by-gynne,
Other Sonedays at euesonge · seo we wel fewe!   244
Othere labory for here liflode · as the lawe wolde?
Ac at mydday meel-tyme · ich mete with hem ofte,
Comynge in a cope · as he a clerke were;
A bacheler other a beaupere · best hym by-semeth;   248
And for the cloth that keuereth hym · cald is he a frere,
Wassheth and wypeth · and with the furste sitteth.
Ac while he wrought in thys worlde · and wan hus mete with treuthe,
He sat atte sydbenche · and secounde table;   252
Cam no wyn in hus wombe · thorw the weke longe,
Nother blankett in hus· bed · ne white bred by-fore hym.
The cause of al thys caitifte · cometh of meny bisshopes,
That suffren suche sottes · and othere synnes regne;   256
Certes, ho so thurste hit segge · *Symon quasi dormit;*
Vigilare were fairour · for thow hast gret charge.
For meny waker wolues · ben broke in-to foldes;
Thyne berkeres ben al blynde · that bryngeth forth thy lambren,
Dispergentur oues · thi dogge dar nat berke;   261

---

237. Amenden P.   240. were P.   241. fer IFG; PEM *om.*   244. wel EFG wol P.   245. here IMFEG; oure P.   247. Comynge MEFG; Conynge P.
249. he MEFIG; here P.   255. bisshepes P.   258. *Vigilare* IMFEG; *Vigilate* P.   261. beerke P.

'Pers,' quod a prest tho · 'thi pardon most I reden,
For I wol construe vch a clause · and knowen hit in Englisch.'
And Pers at his preyere · the pardon vnfoldeth,   92
And I bi-hynden hem bothe · bi-heold al the bulle.
In two lynes hit lay · and not a lettre more,
And was i-writen riht thus · in witnesse of treuthe:

'Pieres,' quod a prest tho · 'thi pardoun most I rede,
For I wil construe eche clause · and kenne it the on Engliche.'
And Pieres at his preyere · the pardoun vnfoldeth,   108
And I bihynde hem bothe · bihelde al the bulle.
Al in two lynes it lay · and nouȝt a leef more,
And was writen riȝt thus · in witnesse of treuthe :
  Et qui bona egerunt, ibunt in vitam eternam ;
  Qui vero mala, in ignem eternum.
'Peter!' quod the prest tho · 'I can no pardoun fynde,   112
But "Dowel, and haue wel · and god shal haue thi sowle,
And do yuel, and haue yuel · hope thow non other
But after thi ded-day · the deuel shal haue thi sowle!"'

B. 115. But WCO; That LR.

A. PASSUS VIII. 96-99.   C. PASSUS X. 262-291.   243

Et qui bona egerunt, ibunt in vitam eternam ;
Qui vero mala, in ignem eternum.

'Peter!' quod the preost tho · 'I con no pardoun fynde,   96
Bote "dowel, and haue wel · and god schal haue thi soule,
And do vuel, and haue vuel · hope thou non othur,
That aftur thi deth-day · to helle schaltou wende!"'

The tarre is vntydy · that to thyne sheep by-longeth,
Hure salue ys of *supersedeas* · in someneres boxes;
Thyne sheep are ner al shabbyd · the wolf shiteth woolle :   264
Sub molli pastore · lupus lanam cacat, et grex
In-custoditus · dilaceratur eo.
Hoow! hurde! wher is thyn hounde · and thyn hardy herte,
For to wyrie the wolf · that thy woolle fouleth?   268
Ich leyue, for thy lacchesse · thow leest meny wederes,
And ful meny fayre flus · falsliche wasshe!
When thy lord loketh to haue · a-louaunce for hus bestes,
And of the monye thow haddist ther-myd · hus meoble to saue,
And the woolle worth weye · woo ys the thenne!   273
Redde rationem uillicacionis tue · other in arerage falle!
Thyn hyre, hurde, as ich hope · hath nouht to quyty thy dette,
Ther as mede ne mercy · may nat a myte auayle,   276
Bote 'haue this for that · tho that thow toke
Mercy for mede · and my lawe breke,
Loke now for thi lacchesse · whether lawe wol the graunte
Purgatorie for thy paye · other perpetuel helle?'   280
For shal no pardoune praye for 3ow ther · nother princes letteres.'

'Peers,' quath a prest tho · 'thy pardoune most ich rede,
Ich can construen ech worde · and kenne hit the in Englishe.'
And Peers at hus preyere · the pardon vnfolded,   284
And ich by-hynde hem bothe · by-heeld al the bulle.
In two lynes hit lay · and no lettere more,
And was ywryte ryght thus · in witnesse of treuthe.
    Qui bona egerunt ibunt in uitam eternam :
    Qui uero mala, in ignem eternum.
'Peter!' quath the prest tho · 'ich can no pardon fynde,   288
Bote "do wel and haue wel · and god shal haue thy saule,
Do vuel and haue vuel · and hope thow non other
Bote he that vuel lyueth · vuel shal ende!"'

C. 274. in IMFEG ; P *om.*   275. Then (*for* Thyn) P.   281. 30we P.

R 2

And Pers, for puire teone · pollede hit a-sonder,   100
And siththe he seide to hem · these semely sawis,
   '*Si ambulauero in medio vmbre mortis, non timebo mala,*
    quoniam tu mecum es.
I schal sese of my sowynge,' quod Pers · 'and swynke not
   so harde,
Ne aboute my lyflode · so bisy beo no more!
Of preyere and of penaunce · my plouh schal ben heraftur,
And bi-loure that I beo-louh · er my lyf fayle.   105
The prophete his payn eet · in penaunce and wepyng;
As the psauter vs seith · so dude moni othere;
That loueth God lelly · his lyflode is wel muche: 108
   Fuerunt michi lacrime mee panes, die ac nocte.

And Pieres for pure tene · pulled it atweyne,   116
   And seyde, '*si ambulauero in medio vmbre mortis, non
    timebo mala; quoniam tu mecum es.*
I shal cessen of my sowyng,' quod Pieres · 'and swynk nouȝt
   so harde,
Ne about my bely-ioye · so bisi be namore!
Of preyers and of penaunce · my plow shal ben herafter,
And wepen whan I shulde slepe · though whete-bred me faille.
   The prophete his payn ete · in penaunce and in sorwe,   121
By that the sauter seith · so dede other manye;
That loueth god lelly · his lyflode is ful esy:
   Fuerunt michi lacrime mee panes die ac nocte.
   And, but if Luke lye · he lereth vs bi foules,   124
We shulde nouȝt be to bisy · aboute the worldes blisse;
Ne solliciti sitis · he seyth in the gospel,
And sheweth vs bi ensamples · vs selue to wisse.
The foules on the felde · who fynt hem mete at wynter?   128
Haue thei no gernere to go to · but god fynt hem alle.'
   'What!' quod the prest to Perkyn · 'Peter! as me thinketh,
Thow art lettred a litel · who lerned the on boke?'
   'Abstinence the abbesse,' quod Pieres · 'myne a. b. c. me
   tauȝte,   132
And Conscience come afterward · and kenned me moche more.'
   'Were thow a prest, Pieres,' quod he · 'thow miȝte preche
   where thow sholdest,
As deuynour in deuynyte · with *dixit insipiens* to thi teme.'

A. PASSUS VIII. 109–122. (NOT IN C-TEXT). 245

And bote ȝif Luke lyȝe · he lereth vs a-nother;
That to bisi we ne schulde beo · her vppon eorthe,
While we woneth in this world · to make vs wombe-ioye.
Ne *soliciti sitis* · he seith in his godspel, 112
And scheweth hit by ensaumple · vr soules to wisse.
The foules in the firmament · who fynt hem in winter?
Whon the forst freseth · foode hem bi-houeth;
Haue thei no gerner to go to · ȝit god fynt hem alle.' 116
'What?' quod the prest to Perkyn · 'Peter! as me thinketh,
Thow art lettret a luyte · ho lered the on boke?'
'Abstinence the abbesse · myn a-b-ce me tauȝte,
And Concience com aftur · and kennide me betere.' 120
'Weore thou a prest,' quod he · 'thou mihtest preche whon the luste,
Quoniam literaturam non cognoui · mihte be thy teeme!'

A. 101. *This line is in* H *only*; VTU *have* and seide, *at end of* l. 100.
V omits all after *timebo*. 106. prophete—eet U; prophetes peyneden hem V.
109. ȝif luke UT; luk H; the bok V. 114. who fynt THU (*see* l. 116);
heo feedeth V. 120. kennide TU; tauȝte VH. 122. thy HTU; my V.

'Lewede lorel!' quod he · 'luite lokestou on the bible,
On Salamones sawes · seldom thou bi-holdest;   124
Slynge awey these scorners, he seith · with here shrewid fliting,
For with hem redely · y kepe not to rest;
    Eice derisores et iurgia cum eis, ne crescant.'
The prest and Perkin tho · apposeden either other,
And thorw heore wordes I a-wok · and waitide aboute,   128
And sauh the sonne sitte south · euene that tyme.
Meteles and moneyeles · on Maluerne hulles,
Musyng on this meeteles · a myle-wei ich ȝeode.
Mony tyme this metels · han made me to studie   132
For Pers loue, the plouh-mon · ful pensyf in myn herte;

'Lewed lorel!' quod Pieres · 'litel lokestow on the bible, 136
On Salomones sawes · selden thow biholdest,
    Eice derisores et iurgia cum eis, ne crescant, &c.'
The prest and Perkyn · apposeden eyther other,
And I thorw here wordes a-woke · and waited aboute,
And seighe the sonne in the south · sitte that tyme, 140
Metelees and monelees · on Maluerne hulles,
Musyng on this meteles; · and my waye ich ȝede.
Many tyme this meteles · hath maked me to studye
Of that I seigh slepyng · if it so be myȝte,   144
And also for Peres the plowman · ful pensyf in herte,
And which a pardoun Peres hadde · alle the peple to conforte,
And how the prest impugned it · with two propre wordes.
Ac I haue no sauoure in songewarie · for I se it ofte faille;
Catoun and canonistres · conseilleth vs to leue   149
To sette sadnesse in songewarie · for, *sompnia ne cures.*
Ac for the boke bible · bereth witnesse,
How Danyel deuyned · the dremes of a kynge,   152
That was Nabugodonosor · nempned of clerkis.
Daniel seyde, 'sire kynge · thi dremeles bitokneth,
That vnkouth knyȝtes shul come · thi kyngdom to cleue;
Amonges lowere lordes · thi londe shal be departed.' 156
And as Danyel deuyned · in dede it felle after,
The kynge lese his lordship · and lower men it hadde.

    A. 124. seldom U; luitel V.   125, 126. *These lines are in* H *only.* For
Eice VTHU *have Ecce.* *ne crescant* TU; *nunc crescunt* V.   128. waitide

For that I sauh slepynge · ȝif hit so be mihte.
Bote Catoun construweth hit nay · an canonistres bothe,
And siggen bi hem-seluen · *sompnia ne cures*. 136
Ac for the bible · bereth witnesse hou
Daniel deuynede · the dremels of a kyng,
That Nabugodonosor · nempne these clerkes.
Daniel seide, 'sir kyng · thi sweuene is to mene, 140
That vnkouthe knihtes schul come · thi kingdam to clayme;
Among lower lordes · thi lond schal be departet.'
As Daniel diuinede · hit fel in dede after, 143
The kyng laste his lordschupe · and lasse men hit hadden.

The preest thus and Perkyn · of the pardon Iangled. 292
Throgh here wordes ich awook · and waitede aboute,
And seih the sonne in the south · sitte that tyme.
Meteles and moneyles · on Maluerne hulles,
Musynge on this meteles · a myle-wey ich ȝeode. 296
   And meny tymes this meteles · made me to studie
Of that ich seih slepynge · yf hit so be myghte,
And of Peers Plouhman · ful pensyf in herte,
And which a pardon Peers hadde · the puple to gladen, 300
And how the preest inpugned hit · thorwe two propre wordes.
Ac men setten nat by songewarie · men seen hit ofte faile,
Caton counteth hit at nouht · and canonistres at lasse.

Ac for the bok bible · bereth good wyttnesse, 304
How Daniel dyuinede · and vndude the dremeles
Of kyng Nabugodonosor · that no peer hadde,
And sitthe after to hus sones · seide hem what thei thouhte :—

THU; lokede V.   131. Musyng THU; Mony elynge V.   139. nempne—
clerkes UT; V *om*.   141. kindam V.   B. 137. *Eice* O; *Ecce* LWRC.   C.
296. þees P; *see* l. 297.   299. ful IFG; P *om*.   302. mei P (*for* 2*nd* men).

248 A. PASSUS VIII. 145-155. B. PASSUS VII. 159-178.

And Ioseph mette metels · ful meruilous alse,
How the sonne and the mone · and enleuene sterres
Falden bi-fore his feet · and heileden him alle.
'Beu fiz,' quod his fader · 'for defaute we schulle, 148
I my-self, and my sones · seche the for neode.'
Hit fel as the fader seide · in Pharaones tyme,
Ther Ioseph was Iustise · Egipte to kepen.
Al this maketh me · on metels to thenken 152
Mony tyme at midniht · whon men schulde slepe,
On Pers the plouh-mon · and whuch a pardoun he hedde,
And hou the preost inpugnede hit · al bi pure resoun,

And Ioseph mette merueillously · how the mone and the
    sonne,
And the elleuene sterres · hailsed hym alle. 160
Thanne Iacob iugged · Iosephes sweuene:
'Beau filtz,' quod his fader · 'for defaute we shullen,
I my-self and my sones · seche the for nede.'
It bifel as his fader seyde · in Pharaoes tyme, 164
That Ioseph was Iustice · Egipte to loken,
It bifel as his fader tolde · his frendes there hym souȝte.
And al this maketh me · on this meteles to thynke;
And how the prest preued · no pardoun to Dowel, 168
And demed that Dowel · indulgences passed,
Biennales and triennales · and bisschopes lettres,
And how Dowel at the day of dome · is dignelich vnderfongen,
And passeth al the pardoun · of seynt Petres cherche. 172

Now hath the pope powere · pardoun to graunte the peple
With-outen eny penaunce · to passen in-to heuene;
This is owre bileue · as lettered men vs techeth,
    Quodcumque ligaueris super terram, erit ligatum et in celis, &c.

And so I leue lelly · (lordes forbode ellis!) 176
That pardoun and penaunce · and preyeres don saue
Soules that haue synned · seuene sithes dedly.

    A. 153. men T; I VU.   C. 308. mette IMFEG; mete P.   312. þe
MFEG; P *om.* 313. pharaoes MFE; pharao hus P. 318. preeued P. 321.

A. PASSUS VIII. 156–165.   C. PASSUS X. 308–329.   249

And diuinede that Dowel · indulgence passede,   156
Bienals and trienals · and busschopes lettres.
Dowel on domesday · is digneliche i-preiset,
He passeth al the pardouns · of seint Petrus churche.
Now hath the pope pouwer · pardoun to graunte,   160
The peple with-oute penaunce · to passe to ioye.
This is a lef of vre bileeue · as lettret men vs techeth,
  Quodcunque ligaueris super terram, erit ligatum et in celis.
And so bileeue I lelly · (vr lord forbeode hit elles!)
That pardoun and penaunce · and preyers don sauen   164
Soules that han sunget · seuen sithes dedlich.

And Ioseph mette meruelousliche · how the mone and the sonne
And elleuene sterres · hailsede hym alle;   309
Thenne Iacob Iuged · Iosephes sweuene:
'*Beau fitz,*' quath the fader · 'we shulleth for defaute,
Ich my-self and my sones · seche the for neede;'   312
 Hit by-fel as the fader seide · in Pharaoes tyme,
That Ioseph was Iustice · Egipte to saue;
Hus eleuene brotheres · hym for neede souhte,
And hus fader Iacob · and al-so hus dame:—   316
Al this maketh me · on meteles to studie,
And how the preest preuede · no pardon to Do-wel;
And demede that Dowel · indulgences passede,
Byennals · and tryennals · and bisshopes letteres.   320
For ho so doth wel here · at the daye of dome
Worth faire vnderfonge · by-for god that tyme.
So Dowel passeth pardon · and pilgrimages to Rome;
ȝut hath the pope power · pardon to graunte   324
To puple, with-oute penaunce · to passen in-to Ioye,
As lettred men ous lereth · and lawe of holy churche:
  Quodcunque ligaueris super terram erit ligatum et in celis;
  Et quodcunque solueris super terram erit solutum et in celis.
And so ich by-leyue leelly · lordes forbode elles,
That pardon and penaunce · and preieres don saue   328
Saules that han synged · seuene sithes dedliche.

---

doþ wel MEFG; wel doþ P.   327. by-leue P (*elsewhere* by-leyue).   329.
Saules E; Soules MIFG; Saule P.   sithes IFG; sithe PE.

Bote trustene to trienals · treuly me thinketh
Is not so syker for the soule · sertes, as Do-wel.
For-thi I rede ȝow renkes · that riche ben on eorthe,   168
Vppon trust of oure tresour ; trienals to haue,
Beo ȝe neuer the baldore · to breke the ten hestes;
   And nomeliche, ȝe meires · and ȝe maister iuges,
That han the welthe of this world · for wyse men ben holden,
To purchasen pardoun · and the popes bulles.   173
At the dredful day of dom · ther dede schullen a-rysen,
And comen alle bi-fore Crist · and a-countes ȝelden,
How thou laddest thi lyf · and his lawe keptest,   176
What thou dudest day bi day · the doom the wol rehersen ;
A powhe-ful of pardoun ther · with prouincials lettres,

Ac to trust to thise triennales · trewly me thinketh,
Is nouȝt so syker for the soule · certis, as is Dowel.   180
   For-thi I rede ȝow, renkes · that riche ben on this erthe,
Vppon trust of ȝowre tresoure · triennales to haue,
Be ȝe neuere the balder · to breke the ten hestes;
And namelich, ȝe maistres · mayres and iugges,   184
That han the welthe of this worlde · and for wyse men ben holden,
To purchace ȝow pardoun · and the popis bulles.
At the dredeful dome · whan dede shullen rise,
And comen alle bifor Cryst · acountis to ȝelde,   188
How thow laddest thi lyf here · and his lawes keptest,
And how thow dedest day bi day · the dome wil reherce;
A poke-ful of pardoun there · ne prouinciales lettres,
Theigh ȝe be founde in the fraternete · of alle the foure ordres,   192
And haue indulgences double-folde · but if Dowel ȝow help,
I sette ȝowre patentes and ȝowre pardounz · at one pies hele!
For-thi I conseille alle Cristene · to crye god mercy,
And Marie his moder · be owre mene bitwene,   196
That god gyue vs grace here · ar we gone hennes,
Suche werkes to werche · while we ben here,
That after owre deth-day · Dowel reherce,
At the day of dome · we dede as he hiȝte.   200

   A. 187. Colophon *from* TUD; V *omits it*.   B. 183. ten CRO; x L.

A. PASSUS VIII. 179-187.   C. PASSUS X. 330-351.

Thauh thou be founden in fraternite · a-mong the foure ordres,
And habbe indulgence i-doubled · bote Dowel the helpe,   180
I nolde ȝeue for thi pardoun · one pye-hele!
Forthi I counseile alle Cristene · to crie Crist merci,
And Marie his moder · to beo mene bi-twene,
That god ȝiue vs grace · er we gon hennes,   184
Such werkes to worche · while that we ben here,
That aftur vr deth-day · Dowel reherce,
That atte day of dom · we duden as he us hiȝte.
    Explicit hic Visio Willelmi de Petro le Plouȝman. Eciam incipit Vita de Do-wel, Do-bet, et Do-best secundum wyt et resoun.

Ac to trysten vpon triennels · treweliche me thynketh
Ys nat so syker for the saule · certys, as ys Dowel.
  For-thi ich rede ȝow, renkes · that riche ben on thys erthe,
Vp trist of ȝoure tresour · tryennels to haue,   333
Be ȝe neuere the boldere · to breke the ten hestes;
And nameliche, ȝe maistres · meyres and Iuges,
That han the welthe of this worlde · and wise men ben holde,
To purchace ȝow pardon · and the popes bulles.   337
At the dredful day of dome · when dede men shullen ryse,
And comen alle by-fore Crist · a-countes to ȝelde,
Howe we ladde oure lyf here · and hus lawes kepte,   340
And how we dude day by day · the dome wol reherce.
A poke-ful of pardon there · ne prouincials letteres,
Thauh we be founde in fraternite · of alle fyue ordres,
And haue indulgences doblefolde · bote Dowel ous helpe,   344
Ich sette by pardon nat a peese · nother a pye-hele!
For-thi ich counsaile alle Cristine · to crye god mercy,
And Marye hus moder · be oure mene to hym,
That god ȝeue ous grace here · er we go hennes,   348
Suche workes to worche · whil we ben here,
That after oure deth-day · Dowel reherce
At the day of dome · we dude as he tauhte.—*Amen.*
    Hic explicit uisio Willelmi de Petro Plouhman.

---

187. dede WCR; ded L.   C. 330. apon (*for* vpon) P.   343. we IG;
he PMEF; *cf.* l. 344.   345. hele IMEG; hyle P.

PASSUS IX.

Incipit hic Dowel, Dobet, and Dobest.

THUS i-robed in russet · romed I a-boute
　Al a somer sesoun · for to seche Dowel,
And fraynide ful ofte · of folk that I mette
ʒif any wiʒt wiste · where Do-wel was at inne,　　　4
And what man he miʒte be · of many man I askide.

PASSUS VIII.

*Passus octauus de visione Petri Plowman.　Incipit Dowel, Dobet,
et Dobest.*

THUS yrobed in russet · I romed aboute
　Al a somer sesoun· · for to seke Dowel,
And frayned ful oft · of folke that I mette,
If ani wiʒte wiste · where Dowel was at inne,　　　4
And what man he miʒte be · of many man I axed.
　Was neuere wiʒte, as I went · that me wisse couthe
Where this lede lenged · lasse ne more;
Tyl it bifel on a Fryday · two freres I mette,　　　8
Maistres of the menoures · men of grete witte.
I hailsed hem hendely · as I hadde lerned,
And preyed hem par charitee · ar thei passed forther,
If thei knewe any contre · or costes, as thei went,　　12
Where that Dowel dwelleth · doth me to wytene.
　For thei ben men on this molde · that moste wyde walken,
And knowen contrees, and courtes · and many kynnes places,
Bothe prynces paleyses · and pore mennes cotes,　　16
And Do-wel and Do-yuel · where thei dwelle bothe.
　'Amonges vs,' quod the menours · 'that man is dwellynge,
And euere hath, as I hope · and euere shal here-after.'

A. 3. fraynide TH₂; askede V.　folk TUH₂; Men V.　4, 5. *These two
lines are from* T; *also in* UH₂; V *om.*　11. V *has* furre passede; passide
ferþere TUH₂.　12. V knewe, *and om.* any.　14. þe TH₂; a V.　**B.** 1.

A. PASSUS IX. 6–15.   C. PASSUS XI. 1–19.   253

Was neuer wiht as I wente · that me wisse couthe
Wher this ladde loggede · lasse ne more;
Til hit fel on a Friday · twei freres I mette,   8
Maistres of the menours · men of grete wittes.
Ich heilede hem hendeli · as ich hedde i-leorned,
And preiede hem, par charite · er thei passede furre,
'ʒif thei knewen any cuntre · or coostes a-boute   12
Wher that Dowel dwelleth · do me to wisse.'
'Mari,' quod the menour · 'a-mong vs he dwelleth,
And euer hath, as ich hope · and euer schal her-after.'

PASSUS XI.

Incipit uisio eiusdem Willelmi de Dowel.

THUS robed in russett · ich romede a-boute,
Al a somer seson · for to seke Dowel,
And frainede ful ofte · of folke that ich mette,
Yf eny wiht wist · wher Dowel was at ynne,   4
And what man he myghte be · of meny man ich askede.
 Was neuere wiht in this worlde · that wisse me couthe,
Wher that he longede · lasse ne more;
Til hit by-ful on a Frydaye · two freres ich mette,   8
Maisteres of the menours · men of grete witte.
Ich hailsede hem hendilyche · as ich hadde ylerned,
And prayede pur charite · ar thei passede forthere,
Yf thei knew eny contreie · other costes a-aboute,   12
Wher that Dowel dwelleth— · 'dere frendes, telleth me;
For ʒe aren men of thys molde · that most wide walken,
And knowen contreies and courtes · and menye kynne places,
Bothe princes paleis · and poure menne cotes,   16
And Dowel and Do-vuele · wher thei dwellen bothe.'
'Sothliche,' seide the frere · 'he soiourneth with ous freres,
And ay hath, as ich hope · and euer wol her-after.'

---

romed WCRO; rowmed L.   C. 3. And IMGF; P *om*.   4. with (*for* wiht) P. wer P.   9. þe IEF; PMS *om*. 10. ylernede P. 19. euer FGI; P *om*.

254   A. PASSUS IX. 16–24.   B. PASSUS VIII. 20–39.

'*Contra*,' quod I as a clerk · and comsede to dispuite,   16
'*Sepcies in die cadit iustus;*
Seue sithes a day, seith the bok · sungeth the rihtful mon;
And hose sungeth,' I seide · 'certes, as me thinketh,
That Dowel and Do-vuele · mowe not dwelle togedere.
Ergo, he nis not alwey · at hom among ow freres,   20
He is other while elles-wher · to wisse the peple.'
'I schal seie the, my sone' · seide the frere thenne,
'Hou seuen sithes the sadde mon · sungeth in a day;
Bi a forebisene,' seide the frere · 'I schal the feire schewe.   24

'*Contra*,' quod I as a clerke · and comsed to disputen,   20
And seide hem sothli, '*sepcies · in die cadit iustus;*

Seuene sythes, seith the boke · synneth the riȝtful.

And who-so synneth,' I seyde · 'doth yuel, as me thinketh,
And Dowel and Do-yuel · mow nouȝt dwelle togideres.   24
Ergo, he nys nauȝt alway · amonge ȝow freres;
He is otherwhile ellis-where · to wisse the peple.'
'I shal sey the, my sone' · seide the frere thanne,
'How seuene sithes the sadman · on the day synneth;   28
By a forbisene,' quod the frere · 'I shal the faire shewe.
 Lat brynge a man in a bote · amydde a brode water,
The wynde and the water · and the bote waggynge
Maketh the man many a tyme · to falle and to stonde;   32
For stonde he neuere so styf · he stombleth ȝif he moeue;

Ac ȝit is he sauf and sounde · and so hym bihoueth,
For ȝif he ne arise the rather · and rauȝte to the stiere,
The wynde wolde, wyth the water · the bote ouerthrowe;   36
And thanne were his lyf loste · thourgh lacchesse of hym-self.

And thus it falleth,' quod the frere · 'bi folke here on erthe;
The water is likned to the worlde · that wanyeth and wexeth,

A. 16. *Latin from* TUH₂; V *om.*   20. at hom TH₂; a tom V.
21. other TH₂; or V.   24. a forebisene TUH₂; ensaumple V.

Let bringe a mon in a bot · a-midde a brod water,
And the wint and the watur · and the waggyng of the bot
Maketh the mon mony tyme · to stomble and to falle;   27
(For stonde he neuere so stif · he stumbleth in the waggyng);
And ȝit he is saaf and sound · and so him bi-houeth;
For ȝif he ne rise the rather · and rauhte to the steorne,
The wynt wolde with the water · the bot ouer-throwe;   31
Ther weore the monnes lyf i-lost · thorw lachesse of himselue.
Riht thus hit fareth,' quod the frere · 'bi folk her on eorthe;
The watur is liknet to the world · that wonieth and waxeth;

'Contra,' quath ich as a clerke · and comsede to dispute,   20
And seide sothliche · '*septies in die cadit iustus*,
Fallynge fro ioye · Iesus wot the sothe !
"Seuene sythes," seith the bok · "syngeth day by day
The alther-ryghtfulleste renk · that regneth vpon erthe."   24
And ho so syngeth,' ich seide · 'certys, doth nat wel;
For ho so syngeth · sikerliche doth vuele,
And Do-wel and Do-vuele · may nat dwelle to-gederes.
Ergo, he ys nat al-way · at hom among ȝow Freres;   28
He is som while elles-wher · to wisse the puple.'
'Ich shal sei the, my sone,' · seide the frere thenne,
'How seuene sithes the sadde man · syngeth on the day.
By a forbusene,' quath the frere · 'ich shal the faire shewe.   32
Let brynge a man in a bot · in-myddes a brode water;
The wynde and the water · and waggynge of the bote
Maketh the man meny tyme · to stomble, yf he stande;
Stonde he neuere so styfliche · thorgh sterynge of the bote   36
He bendeth and boweth · the body is vnstable,
Ac ȝut he is saf and sounde; · so fareth hit by the ryghtful.
Thauh he falle, he falleth nat · bote as ho fulle in a bote,   39
That ay is saf and sounde · that sitteth with-ynne the borde.
So hit fareth,' quath the frere · 'by ryghtful mannes fallynge;
Thawe he thorgh fondinge falle · he falleth nat out of charite;
So dedliche synne doth he nat · for Dowel hym helpeth.
The water ys likned to the worlde · that wanyeth and wexeth;   44

---

32. lachesse TUH₂; sleuþe V.   B. 21. hem WCOB; L *om.*   C. 23. sythe P.
26. synegeþ P.   37. his (*for* is) P.   42. þorghe P.

The goodes in this world · ben lyk this grete wawes,
Riht as wyndes and watres · waleweth aboute.   36
The bot is liknet to the bodi · that brutel is of kuynde;
And thorw the fend and his flesch · and the false world
Sungeth the sadde mon · seuen sithes in the day.
But dedly sunne doth he not · for Dowel him helpeth,   40
That is, Charite the champion · cheef help aȝeyn sunne;
For he strengtheth the to stonde · he stureth thi soule,
That thauȝ thi bodi bouwe · as a bot in the water,
Euer is thi soule saaf · bote ȝif thi-self wolle.   44

The godis of this grounde aren like · to the grete wawes,   40
That as wyndes and wederes · walweth aboute.
The bote is likned to owre body · that brutel is of kynde,
That thorugh the fende and the flesshe · and the frele worlde
Synneth the sadman · a day, seuene sythes.   44
  Ac dedly synne doth he nouȝt · for Dowel hym kepith,
And that is Charite the champioun · chief help aȝein synne;
For he strengtheth man to stonde · and stereth mannes soule,
And thowgh thi body bow · as bote doth in the water,   48
Ay is thi soule sauf · but if thi-self wole
Do a dedly synne · and drenche so thi soule;
God wole suffre wel thi sleuthe · ȝif thy-self lyketh.
For he ȝaf the to ȝeresȝyue · to ȝeme wel thi-selue,   52
And that is witte and fre wille · to euery wyȝte a porcioun,
To fleghyng foules · to fisches & to bestes.
Ac man hath moste thereof · and moste is to blame,
But if he worche wel ther-with · as Dowel hym techeth.'   56
  'I haue no kynde knowyng,' quod I · 'to conceyue alle ȝowre
       wordes,
Ac if I may lyue and loke · I shal go lerne bettere.'
'I bikenne the Cryst,' quod he · 'that on the crosse deyde.'
And I seyde, 'the same · saue ȝow fro myschaunce,   60
And ȝiue ȝow grace on this grounde · good men to worthe.'
  And thus I went wide-where · walkyng myne one,
By a wilde wildernesse · and bi a wode-syde.
Blisse of tho briddes · abyde me made,   64

A. 47. þiself—maistrie TH₂; þou art þin owne mayster V.   50. þe TUH₂;
V om.   B. 43. (2nd) þe WCOB; þi LR.   49. if WCOB; LR om.   53.
a (for and) L.   59. quod he W; LCOB om.   64. abyde me made R;

Folewe thi flessches wil · and the fendes aftur,
And do dedlich sunne · and drenche thi-seluen,
God wol soffre the dye so · for thi-self hast the maistrie.'
  'I haue no kynde knowyng,' quod I · 'to conceyue thi wordes,
But ȝif I may liuen and loken · I schal go lerne betere.   49
I beo-take ȝou to crist · that on the crois diȝede.'
And thei seiden the same · 'God saue the from mischaunce,
And ȝiue the grace vppon grounde · in good lyf to ende.'   52
  Thus I wente wyden-wher · Dowel to seche;
And as I wente bi a wode · walkyng myn one,
Blisse of the briddes · made me to abyde,

The godes of this grounde aren lyke · to the grete wawes,
That as wyndes and wederes · walwen a-boute;
The bot ys lykned to oure body · that brotel ys of kynde,
That thorgh the fende and oure flesch · and this frele worlde   48
Syngeth seuene sithes · the saddest man on erthe,
And lyfholiest of lyf · that lyueth vnder the sonne.

  Ac free wil and free wit · folweth a man euere
To repenten and ryse · and rowen out of synne,   52
To contricion, to confession · til he come to hus ende.
Rather haue we no reste · til we restitue
Our lyf to oure lord god · for oure lykames gultes.'

  'Ich haue no kynde knowyng,' quath ich · 'to conceyue al thy
    speche,   56
Ac yf ich may lyue and loke · ich shal go lerne bettere.'
'Ich by-kenne the Crist,' quath he · 'that on the croice deide.'
And iche seide, 'the same · saue ȝow fro meschaunce,
And gyue me grace on this grounde · with good ende to deye.'   60
  Ich wente forth wyde-where · walkynge myn one,
In a wylde wyldernesse · by a wode-syde.
Blisse of the briddes · a-byde me made,

---

brouȝte me aslepe LWCOB; *cf.* l. 67.   **C.** 45. þis IMFEG; þe P.   46.
That I; For F; P *om.*   47. lycknede P; *see* l. 44.   49. Senegeþ P.
sithes IMFE; sithe P.   63. þe IMFG; P *om.*

258   A. PASSUS IX. 56-67.   B. PASSUS VIII. 65-87.

And vnder a lynde, vppon a launde · leonede I a stounde,   56
For to leorne the layes · that louely foules maden.
Blisse of the briddes · brou3ten me a slepe;
The meruiloste meetynge · mette I me thenne
That euere dremede driht · in drecchynge, I wene.   60
A muche mon, me thouhte · lyk to my-seluen,
Com and clepede me · be my kuynde nome.
'What art thou,' quod I · 'that my nome knowest?'
'That thow wost wel,' quod he · 'and no wi3t betere.'   64
'Wot I,' quod I, 'ho art thou?' · 'Thought,' seide he thenne,
'I haue suwed the this seuen 3er · se3e thou me no rathere?'
'Art thou Thou3t?' quod I tho · 'const thou me telle,

And vnder a lynde vppon a launde · lened I a stounde,
To lythe the layes · the louely foules made.
Murthe of her mouthes · made me there to slepe;
The merueillousest meteles · mette me thanne   68
That euer dremed wy3te · in worlde, as I wene.
A moche man, as me thou3te · and lyke to my-selue
Come and called me · by my kynde name.
'What artow,' quod I tho · 'that thow my name knowest?'   72
'That thow wost wel,' quod he · 'and no wy3te bettere.'
'Wote I what thow art?' · 'Thought,' seyde he thanne,
'I haue suwed the this seuene 3ere · sey thow me no rather?'
'Art thow Thought!' quod I tho · 'thou couthest me wisse   76
Where that Dowel dwelleth · and do me that to knowe?'
'Dowel and Dobet · and Dobest the thridde,' quod he,
'Aren three faire vertues · and beth nau3te fer to fynde.
Who-so is trewe of his tonge · and of his two handes,   80
And thorugh his laboure or thorugh his londe · his lyflode wynneth,
And is trusti of his tailende · taketh but his owne,
And is nou3t dronkenlew ne dedeignous · Dowel hym folweth.
Dobet doth ry3t thus · ac he doth moche more;   84
He is as low as a lombe · and loueliche of speche,
And helpeth alle men · after that hem nedeth;
The bagges and the bigurdeles · he hath to-broken hem alle,

A. 64. wi3t TUH₂; bodi V.   65. thought—þenne *from* U; V *has* þhou3te
I me seide I þenne.   66. V *om.* þou.   71. He (*for* Ho) V.   C. 69.

A. PASSUS IX. 68–79.   C. PASSUS XI. 64–85.

Wher that Dowel dwelleth · do me to wisse?'   68
'Dowel,' quod he, 'and Dobet · and Dobest the thridde
Beoth threo faire vertues · and beoth not fer to fynde.
Ho is meke of his mouth · mylde of his speche,
Trewe of his tonge · and of his two hondes,   72
And bi his labur or bi his lond · his lyflode wynneth,
And trusti of his taylende · taketh bote his owne,
And is not dronkeleuh ne deynous · Dowel him foleweth.
  Dobet doth thus · bote he doth muche more ;   76
He is as louh as a lomb · louelich of speche ;
While he hath ou3t of his owne · he helpeth ther neod is,
The bagges and the bi-gurdeles · he hath broken hem alle

And vnder lynde in a launde · lenede ich a stounde,   64
To lithen here laies · and here loueliche notes.
Murthe of here murye mouthes · made me to slepe ;
And merueilousliche me mette · a-myddes al that blisse.
  A muche man, me thouhte · lyke to my-selue,   68
Cam and callede me · by my kynde name.
'What art thow?' quath ich · 'that my name knowest?'
'That wost thou, Wille,' quath he · 'and no wight betere.'
  'Wot ich,' quath ich, 'ho art thow?' · 'Thouhte,' seide he
    thenne ;   72
'Ich haue the suwed this seue 3er · seih thou me no rather?'
  'Art thou Thouhte?' quath ich tho · 'thow couthest me wisse
Where that Dowel dwelleth · and do me to knowe?'
  'Dowel and Dobet,' quath he · 'and Dobest the thridde   76
Beth thre fayre vertues · and beeth nauht ferr to fynde.
Who-so is trewe of hys tonge · and of hus two handes,
And thorw leel labour lyueth · and loueth his emcristine,

And ther-to trewe of hus tail · and halt wel his handes,   80
Nouht dronkelewe ne deynous · Dowel hym folweth.
  Dobet doth al this · ac 3ut he doth more ;
He is lowe as a lombe · and loueliche of speche,
And helpeth herteliche alle men · of that he may aspare.   84
The bagges and the by-gurdeles · he hath to-broke hem alle,

---

kynde I ; ryhte PEFMG.   70, 72. ert P.   74. Ert P.   78. trywe P.
two EF ; to P.   79. þorwe P.   80. trywe P.

260   A. PASSUS IX. 80-91.   B. PASSUS VIII. 88-108.

That the Auerous hedde · or eny of his heires ;   80
And with Mammonas moneye · hath maked him frendes,
And is ronnen in-to religiun · and hath rendret the bible,
And precheth the peple · seint Poules wordes,
  Libenter sufferte.
"3e wyse, soffreth the vn-wyse · with ow for to libbe,"   84
And with glad wille doth hem good · for so god himself hi3te.
  Dobest is a-boue bothe · and bereth a busschopes cros,
Is hoket atte ende · to holden hem in good lyf.
A pyk is in that potent · to punge a-doun the wikkede,   88
That wayten eny wikkednesse · Dowel to teone.
And as Dowel and Dobet · duden hem to vnderstonde,
Thei han i-corouned a kyng · to kepen hem alle,

That the erl Auarous · helde, and his heires ;   88
And thus with Mammonaes moneie · he hath made hym frendes,
And is ronne in-to Religioun · and hath rendred the bible,
And precheth to the poeple · seynt Poules wordes,
  Libenter suffertis insipientes, cum sitis ipsi sapientes,
"And suffreth the vnwise · with 3ow for to libbe,"   92
And with gladde wille doth hem gode · for so god 3ow hoteth.
  Dobest is aboue bothe · and bereth a bisschopes crosse,
Is hoked on that one ende · to halie men fro helle.
A pyke is on that potente · to pulte adown the wikked,   96
That wayten any wikkednesse · Dowel to tene.
And Dowel and Dobet · amonges hem ordeigned
To croune one to be kynge · to reule hem bothe ;
That 3if Dowel or Dobet · did a3ein Dobest,   100
Thanne shal the kynge come · and casten hem in yrens,
And but if Dobest bede for hem · thei to be there for euere.

  Thus Dowel and Dobet · and Dobest the thridde,
Crouned one to be kynge · to kepen hem alle,   104
And to reule the Reume · bi her thre wittes,
And none other-wise · but as thei thre assented.'
  I thonked Thou3t tho · that he me thus tau3te;
' Ac 3ete sauoureth me nou3t thi seggyng · I coueite to lerne

---

   A. 87. hem U ; him V ; men TH$_2$.   88. in þat potent TH$_2$; V *has* in þe ende, *copied by mistake from* l. 87.   93. *This line is from* T ; *also in* UH$_2$; V *om.*   95. hem TUH$_2$; him V.   96. hem TUH$_2$; V *om.*   101. thou3t—that TH$_2$;

A. PASSUS IX. 92–103.   C. PASSUS XI. 86–108.

That ȝif Dowel or Dobet · dude aȝeyn Dobest,
And were vnbuxum at his biddinge · and bold to don ille,
Then schulde the kyng comen · and casten hem in prison,
And puiten hem ther in penaunce · with-outen pite or grace,
Bote ȝif Dobest beede for hem · a-byde ther for euere!   96
Thus Dowel and Dobet · and Dobest the thridde
Crounede on to beo kyng · and bi heor counseil worche,
And rule the reame · bi red of hem alle,
And otherwyse elles not · bute as thei threo assenten.'   100
I thonkede Thouȝt tho · that he me so tauȝte,
'But ȝit sauereth not me thi siggynge · so me God helpe,
More kuynde knowynge · I coueyte to here,

That the eorl Auerous · heeld, and hus eires;
And of Mammonaes moneye · mad hym meny frendes,
And is ronne in-to religion · and rendreth hus byble,   88
And precheth to the puple · seynt Poules wordes;
    Libenter suffertis insipientes, cum sitis ipsi sapientes ;
"Ȝe worldliche wyse · vnwyse that ȝe suffre,
Lene hem and loue hem" · this Latyn ys to mene.
Dobest bere sholde · the bisshopes croce,   92
And halye with the hoked ende · ille men to goode,
And with the pyk putte adoūne · *preuaricatores legis*,
Lordes that lyuen as hem lust · and no lawe a-counten;
For here mok and here meeble · suche men thynken   96
That no bisshop sholde · here byddinge with-sitte.
Ac Dobest sholde nat dreden hem · bote do as god hihte,
    Nolite timere eos qui possunt occidere corpus.
Thus Dowel and Dobet · diuinede, and Dobest,
And crounede on to be kyng · to culle with-oute synne   100
That wolde nat don as Dobest · diuinede and tauhte.
Thus Dowel and Dobet · and Dobest the thridde
Crounede on to be kyng · and kepen ous alle,
And reulen alle reaumes · by here thre wittes;   104
Bote other-wise ne elles nat · bote as thei three assented.'
Ich thonked Thouht tho · that he me so tauhte:
'Ȝut sauereth me nat thi sawe,' quath ich · 'so me Crist spede,
A more kynde knowyng · coueite ich to huyre   108

V *has* him feire · þo. B. 89. moneie WCOB; mone LR. 104. kepin L. C. 93.
þe IMFG; P *om*. 96. For IMFSG; Andfore P. 98. hem IMFSG; hym P.

A. PASSUS IX. 104-110.   B. PASSUS VIII. 109-126.

Hou Dowel and Dobet · and Dobest beth on eorthe.' 104
'But Wit con wisse the,' quod Thou3t · 'wher theos thre
    dwelleth,
Elles not no mon · that nou is alyue.
Thus Thou3t and I also · throly we eoden
Disputyng on Dowel · day aftur other, 108
And er we weoren war · with Wit conne we meeten.
He was long and lene · to loken on ful symple,

How Dowel, Dobet, and Dobest · don amonges the peple.' 109
'But Witte conne wisse the,' quod Thou3t · 'where tho thre
    dwelle;
Ellis wote I none that can · that now is alyue.'
Thou3te and I thus · thre days we 3eden, 112
Disputyng vppon Dowel · day after other,
And ar we were ywar · with Witte gan we mete.
He was longe and lene · liche to none other,
Was no pruyde on his apparaille · ne pouerte noyther, 116
Sadde of his semblaunt · and of soft chiere.
I dorste meue no matere · to make hym to Iangle,
But as I bad Thou3t tho · be mene bitwene,
And put forth somme purpos · to prouen his wittes, 120
What was Dowel fro Dobet · and Dobest fram hem bothe.
Thanne Thou3t in that tyme · seide thise wordes,
'Where Dowel, Dobet · and Dobest ben in londe,
Here is Wille wolde ywyte · yif Witte couthe teche hym, 124
And whether he be man or no man · this man fayne wolde
    aspye,
And worchen as thei thre wolde · this is his entente.'

A. 111. *This line is from* T; *also in* H₂; VU *om.*   114. But as I bad
þou3t þo · be mene betwene TH₂U; V *has* þou3t bad, *omitting* I.   118. hym
TH₂U; V *om.*   B. 125. L *om.* no.   C. 109. dobest MFS; ho dobest P;
who do best E; who doþ best I.   112. Thouth P.   118. dorste IS;

A. PASSUS IX. 111-118.   C. PASSUS XI. 109-126.

Was no pride on his apparail · ne no pouert nother,
Sad of his semblaunt · and of softe speche. 112
I durste meue no mateere · to make him to iangle,
Bote as I bad Thou3t tho · to beo mene bi-twene,
To putte forth sum purpos · to preuen his wittes.
Thenne Thou3t that tyme · seide theose wordes, 116
'Wher Dowel and Dobet · and Dobest beoth in londe,
Oure Wille wolde i-witen · 3if Wit couthe hym techen.'

Of Dowel and of Dobet · and Dobest of alle.'
'Bote Wit wolle the wisse,' quath Thouht · 'wher tho thre
    dwellen;
Elles know ich non that can · in none kynriche.'
Thouht and ich thus thre daies · to-gederes we 3eoden, 112
Disputynge vp Dowel · daye after othere;
And er we were ywar · with Wit gan we mete.
He was long and lene · lyke to non other,
Was no pruyde in hus aparail · ne pouerte nother; 116
Sad of hus semblant · with a softe speche.
Ich dorste meue no matere · to maken hym to Iangle,
Bote as ich bad Thouht tho · be mene by-twene,
And putte forth som purpos · to prouen hus wittes, 120
What Dowel was fro Dobet · and Dobest fro hem bothe.
Thenne Thouht in that tyme · seide these wordes,
'Wher Dowel and Dobet · and Dobest ben in londe
Her is on wolde wite · yf Wit couthe teche, 124
And what lyues thei lyuen · and what lawe thei vsen;
What thei drede and douten · dere syre, telleth.'[1]

---

durst FE; þurste P.   119, 122. thouth P.   120. proouen P.   122. þat
IMFSEG; þan P.   seide MFG; seede P.   þeese P.   123. Wher IMG;
War P.   been P.   126. an (*for* and) P.   douhten P.

[1] *The* Passus *is continued on* p. 265.

PASSUS X.

Passus primus de Dowel, &c.

'SIRE Dowel dwelleth,' quod Wit · 'not a day hennes,
In a castel, of Kuynde i-mad · of foure kunne thinges,
Of erthe and eir hit is mad · i-medelet to-gedere,
With wynt and with watur · ful wittiliche i-meint. 4
Cuynde hath closet ther-in · craftiliche with-alle,
A loueli lemmon · lyk to him-self,
Anima heo hette; · to hire hath envye

PASSUS IX.

Passus nonus de visione; et primus de Dowel.

'SIRE Dowel dwelleth,' quod Witte · 'nou3t a day hennes,
In a castel that Kynde made · of foure kynnes thinges;
Of erthe and eyre is it made · medled togideres,
With wynde and with water · witterly enioyned. 4
Kynde hath closed there-inne · craftily with-alle,
A lemman that he loueth · like to hym-selue,
Anima she hatte · ac Enuye hir hateth,
A proude pryker of Fraunce · *prynceps huius mundi*, 8
And wolde winne hir awey · with wyles, and he my3te.
Ac Kynde knoweth this wel · and kepeth hir the bettere,
And hath do hir with sire Dowel · is duke of this marches.
Dobet is hir damoisele · sire Doweles dou3ter, 12
To serue this lady lelly · bothe late and rathe.
Dobest is aboue bothe · a bisschopes pere;
That he bit, mote be do · he reuleth hem alle;
Anima that lady · is ladde bi his lerynge. 16
    Ac the constable of that castel · that kepeth al the wacche,
Is a wys kni3te with-al · sire Inwitte he hatte,
And hath fyue feyre sones · bi his first wyf;
Sire Sewel and Saywel · and Herewel the hende, 20

A. 6. to TUH₂; V *om.*   9. mihti V.   11, 12. Dowel—sire *from* U;

A. PASSUS X. 8–19.   C. PASSUS XI. 127–145.   265

A proud prikere of Fraunce · *princeps huius mundi*,   8
And wolde wynnen hire a-wei · with wiles ȝif he mihte.
Bote Kynde knoweth hit wel · and kepeth hire the betere,
And hath i-don hire to sire Dowel · duke of these marches.
Dobet is hire damysele · sire Doweles douȝter,   12
And serueth that ladi lelly · bothe late and rathe.
Thus Dowel and Dobet · and Dobest the thridde
Beoth maystres of this manere · that mayden to kepen.
But the cunstable of the castel · that kepeth hem alle,   16
Is a wys kniht with-alle · sire Inwit he hette,
And hath fyue feire sones · bi his furste wyf;
Sire Seowel and Seywel · and Herewel the hende,

[*This* Passus *is continued from* p. 263.]

'Syre Dowel dwelleth,' quath Wit · 'nat a daye hennes,
In a castel that Kynde made · of foure kyne thynges;   128
Of erthe, of aier yt is made · medled to-gederes,
With wynd and water · wittyliche en-ioyned.
Kynde hath closed ther-ynne · craftilyche with-alle
A lemman that he loueth wel · lyke to hym-selue;   132
Anima hue hatte · to hure hath enuye
A prout prikyere of Fraunce · *princeps huius mundi*,
And wolde wynne hure away · with wiles, yf he myghte.
And Kynde knoweth this wel · and kepeth hure the betere, 136
And dooth hure with syre Dowel · duk of thes marches.
Dobet ys here damsele · syre Doweles douhter,
To serue that lady leelly · bothe late and rathe.
Dobest ys a-boue bothe · a bisshopes peer,   140
And by hus lerynge is ladde · that ilke lady *Anima*.
 The constable of that castel · that kepeth hem alle
Is a wys knyght with-alle · syre Inwit he hatte;
And hath fyue faire sones · by hus furste wyf,   144
Syre Seewel, syre Seiwel · syre Huyrewel the hende,

V *om. by mistake, owing to repetition of* sire.   19. hende TUH₂; V *has* ende.
C. 130. en-ioynede P.

Sire Worche-wel-with-thin-hond · a wiht mon of strengthe, 20
And sire Godfrei Gowel · grete lordes alle.
Theose sixe ben i-set · to saue the castel;
To kepe this wommon · this wyse men ben charget,
Til that Kuynde come or sende · and kepe hire himseluen.' 24
'What calle ȝe the castel,' quod I · 'that Kuynde hath I-maket,
And what cunnes thing is Kuynde · con ȝe me telle?'
'Kuynde,' quath he, 'is creatour · of alle kunne beestes,
Fader and foormere · the furste of alle thing; 28

Sire Worche-wel-wyth-thine-hande · a wiȝte man of strengthe,
And sire Godfrey Gowel · gret lordes for sothe.
Thise fyue ben sette · to saue this lady *Anima,*
Tyl Kynde come or sende · to saue hir for euere.' 24
'What kynnes thyng is Kynde,' quod I · 'canstow me telle?'
'Kynde,' quod Witte, 'is a creatour · of alle kynnes thinges;
Fader and fourmour · of al that euere was maked;
And that is the gret god · that gynnynge had neuere, 28
Lorde of lyf and of lyȝte · of lysse and of peyne.
Angeles and al thing · aren at his wille.
Ac man is hym moste lyke · of marke and of schafte;
For thorugh the worde that he spake · wexen forth bestes, 32
 Dixit, et facta sunt;
And made man likkest · to hym-self one,
And Eue of his ribbe-bon · with-outen eny mene.
For he was synguler hym-self · and seyde *faciamus,*
As who seith, 'more mote here-to · than my worde one; 36
My myȝte mote helpe · now with my speche.'
Riȝte as a lorde sholde make lettres · and hym lakked parchemyn,
Though he couth write neuere so wel · ȝif he had no penne,
The lettres for al the lordship · I leue, were neuere ymaked. 40
  And so it semeth bi hym · as the bible telleth,
   There he seyde, *dixit, et facta sunt;*
He moste worche with his worde · and his witte shewe.
And in this manere was man made · thorugh myȝte of god almiȝti,
With his worde and werkemanschip · and with lyf to laste. 44
And thus god gaf hym a goost · of the godhed of heuene,
And of his grete grace · graunted hym blisse,
And that is lyf that ay shal last · to al his lynage after.

That is the grete god · that bigynnyng hedde neuere,
The lord of lyf and of liht · of lisse and of peyne.
Angeles and alle thing · arn at his wille,
Bote mon is him most lyk · of marke and of schap;   32
For with word that he warp · woxen forth beestes,
And alle thing at his wille · was wrouȝt with a speche,
Dixit et facta sunt;
Saue mon that he made · ymage to him-seluen,
Ȝaf him goost of his godhede · and grauntede him blisse,   36
Lyf that euer schal lasten · and al his lynage aftur.

Syre Worchewel with thyn hand · a wight man of strengthe,
And syre Godfaith Gowel · grete lordes alle.
These fyue ben ysett · for to sauye *Anima*,   148
Til Kynde come other sende · and kepe hure hym-self.'
 'What lyues thyng is Kynde?' quath ich · 'canst thow me telle?'
 'Kynde is a creator,' quath Wit · 'of alle kyne thynges,
Fader and formour · of al that forth groweth,   152
The whiche is god grettest · that gynnynge hadde neuere,
Lord of lyf and of lyght · of lysse and of payne.
Angeles and alle thyng · aren at hus wil;
Man is hym most lyk · of membres and of face,   156
And semblable in soule to god · bote yf synne hit make.

A. 27. ceatour V. bestis TU; V *has* best; *but see* l. 33.   30. lisse TH₂; blisse VU.   31. arn TUH₁; ben V.   **B.** 40. lettres O; lettre LWCRB.
47. his WR; LCOB *om.*   **C.** 149. seynde P.   150. canst FMS; can P.
151. a creator MS; creature P.

That is the castel that Kuynde made · *Caro* hit hette,
And is as muche to mene · as mon with a soule,
That he wrouhte with werk · and with word bothe;   40
Thorw miht of his maieste · mon was i-maket,
    Faciamus hominem ad ymaginem et similitudinem nostram.
Inwit and alle wittes · ben closet ther-inne,
For loue of that ladi · that Lyf is i-nempnet;
That is *Anima*, that ouer al · in the bodi wandureth,   44
But in the herte is hire hom · hiȝest of alle;
Heo is lyf and ledere · and a lemmon of heuene.
Inwit is the help · that *Anima* desyreth;

And that is the castel that Kynde made · *Caro* it hatte,   48
And is as moche to mene · as man with a soule;
And that he wrouȝt with werke · and with worde bothe,
Thorugh myȝte of the maieste · man was ymaked.

Inwit and alle wittes · closed ben ther-inne,   52
For loue of the lady *Anima* · that Lyf is ynempned;
Ouer al in mannes body · he walketh and wandreth,
Ac in the herte is hir home · and hir moste reste.
Ac Inwitte is in the hed · and to the herte he loketh,   56
What *Anima* is lief or loth · he lat hir at his wille;
For after the grace of god · the grettest is Inwitte.
Moche wo worth that man · that mys-reuleth his Inwitte,
And that be glotouns globbares · her god is her wombe;   60
    Quorum deus venter est.
For thei seruen Sathan · her soule shal he haue;
That liueth synful lyf here · her soule is liche the deuel.
And alle that lyuen good lyf · aren like god almiȝti,
    Qui manet in caritate, in deo manet, &c.
Allas! that drynke shal for-do · that god dere bouȝte,   64
And doth god forsaken hem · that he shope to his liknesse;
    *Amen dico vobis, nescio vos: et alibi: et dimisi eos
    secundum desideria eorum.*

   A. 41. *Faciamus—nostram*; from U.   50. is kept TU; he clepeþ V
(*mistake for* he kepeþ); *see* l. 16.   52. iþe siht · and bringeþ V; eiȝe-siȝt ·
and herynge TH₂; eye to sighte · and herynge U. *In* V, iþe *is probably*

After the grace of god · the gretteste is Inwit. 48
Inwit in the hed is · and helpeth the soule,
For thorw his connynge he kepeth · *Caro et Anima*
In rule and in reson · bote recheles hit make.
He eggeth the eiȝe-siht · and herynge to goode, 52
Of good speche and of cunnynge · he is the biginnere,
In monnes brayn he is most · and mihtiest to knowe,
Ther he is bremest · but ȝif blod hit make.
For whonne blod is bremore then brayn · then is Inwit i-bounde,
And eke wantoun and wylde · withouten eny resoun. 57

And as thow suxt the sonne · som tyme for cloudes
May nat shyne ne shewe · on shawes on erthe,
Right so letteth lecherie · and other luther synnes, 160
That god suweth nat synful men · and suffreth hem mysfare,
As somme hongen hem-self · and other while a-drencheth ;
God wol nat of hem wite · bote leteth hem yworthe,
As the sauter seith · by such synful shrewes, 164
  Et dimisi eos secundum desideria cordis eorum.
Loke! suche luther men · lome ben ryche
Of golde and of other good · ac godes grace hem faileth ;
For thei loueth and by-leyueth · al here lyf-tyme
More in catel than in Kynde · that alle kyne thynges wroghte, 168
The whiche is bothe loue and lyf · and lasteth withouten ende.
  Inwitt and alle wittes · closed ben ther-ynne ;
By loue and by leaute · ther-by lyueth *Anima*;
And Lyf lyueth by Inwitt · and lerynge of Kynde. 172
Inwitt is in the hefd · as *Anima* in the herte,
And muche wo worth hym · that Inwitt mys-speyneth.
For that is godes owen good · hus grace and hus tresoure,
That meny lede leeseth · thorw lykerouse drynke, 176
As Lot dude and Noe ; · and *Herodes* the daffe
Ȝaf hus douhter for a daunsyng · in a dissh the hefde
Of the blessyde baptiste · by-fore alle hus gustes.
Every man that hath Ynwitt · and hus hele bothe, 180
Hath tresour ynow in treuthe · to fynde with hym-selue.

---

written for iye *or* eiye.   C. 164. *desideria* IMFG ; *desiderium* P.   *cordis*
EF ; P *om*.   166. *This line is from* IMFSG ; PE *omit it*.   173.
P *om*. 2*nd* in.   177. an (*for* 2*nd* and) P.   178. P *om*. 1*st* a.

In ȝonge fauntes and fooles · with hem fayleth Inwit,
And eke in sottes thou miht seo · that sitteth atte ale ;
Thei heldeth ale in heore hed · til Inwit beo a-dreynt, 60
And ben brayn-wode as beestes · so heore blod waxeth.
  Thenne hath the pouke pouwer · sire *princeps huius mundi*,
Ouer suche maner men · miht in heore soules.
Bote in fauntes ne in fooles · the fend hath no miht 64
For no werk that thei worchen · wikked or elles ;

  Foles that fauten Inwitte · I fynde that holicherche
Shulde fynden hem that hem fauteth · and faderelees children ;
And wydwes that han nouȝte wher-with · to wynnen hem her
    fode, 68
Madde men, and maydenes · that helplees were ;
Alle thise lakken Inwitte · and lore bihoueth.
  Of this matere I myȝte · make a longe tale,
And fynde fele witnesses · amonges the foure doctours, 72
And that I lye nouȝt of that I lere the · Luke bereth witnesse.
  Godfader and godmoder · that sen her godchildren
At myseise and at mischief · and mowe hem amende,
Shal haue penaunce in purgatorie · but ȝif thei hem helpe. 76
For more bilongeth to the litel barne · ar he the lawe knowe,
Than nempnyng of a name · and he neuere the wiser !
Shulde no Crystene creature · crien atte ȝate,
Ne faille payn ne potage · and prelates did as thei shulden. 80
A Iuwe wolde nouȝte se a Iuwe · go Iangelyng for defaute,
For alle the moebles on this molde · and he amende it miȝte.
  Allas ! that a Cristene creature · shal be vnkynde til an other,
Sitthen Iuwes, that we Iugge · Iudas felawes, 84
Ayther of hem helpeth other · of that that hym nedeth.
Whi nel we Cristene · of Cristes good be as kynde
As Iuwes, that ben owre lores-men ? · shame to vs alle !
The comune for her vnkyndenesse · I drede me, shul abye. 88
  Bisschopes shul be blamed · for beggeres sake ;
He is worse than Iudas · that ȝiueth a Iaper siluer,
And biddeth the begger go · for his broke clothes :

> *Proditor est prelatus cum Iuda, qui patrimonium Christi
> minus distribuit : et alibi :*
> *Perniciosus dispensator est, qui res pauperum Christi inuti-
> liter consumit.*

A. PASSUS X. 66–73.   C. PASSUS XI. 182–184.   271

Bote the fadres and the frendes · for fauntes schul be blamet
Bote thei witen hem from wantounesse · whil that thei ben ȝonge.
And ȝif that thei ben pore or catelles · to kepen hem from ille,
Thenne is holy chirche a-signet · to helpen hem and sauen   69
From folyes, and fynden hem · til that thei ben wysore.
Bote vche wiȝt in this world · that hath wys vnderstondinge,
Is cheef souereyn of him-self · his soule for to ȝeme,   72
And cheuesschen him from charge · whon he childhode passeth,

Ac fauntekynes and fooles · the whiche fauten Inwitt,
Frendes schulden fynden hem · and fro folye kepe,
And holychurche helpe to · so sholde no man begge,   184

A. 59. sottes UTH$_2$; wrecches V.   61. ben TU; V om.   66. fauntes
TU; fautes V.   71. wiȝt T; wight U; mon V.   72. of H$_2$; ouer TU;
V om.   B. 67. fauteth RCOB; fauted LW.   83. crestene L.   C. 183.
schulden M; schold S; schal I; schulle G; schul F; suche PE.

Saue him-self from sunne · for so him bi-houeth;
For worche he wel other wrong · the wit is his oune.
Thene is Dowel a duyk · that distruieth vices,   76
And saueth the soule · that sunne hath no miht
To route ne to reste · ne to rooten in the herte;
And that is drede of god · for Dowel hit maketh,
Hit is biginnynge of goodnesse · god for to drede;   80
Salamon it seide · for a soth tale,
    Innicium sapiencie, timor domini.
For doute, men doth the bet; · Drede is such a mayster
That he maketh men meoke · and mylde of heore speche,
And alle kunne scolers · in scoles forte lerne;   84
Thenne is Dobet to beo war · for betynge of ȝerdes,
And therof seith the sauter · thi-seluen thou miht reden,
    Virga tua et baculus tuus, ipsa me consolata sunt.
Ac ȝif clene consience acorde · that thi-selfe dost wel,
Wilne thou neuere in this world · forte Dobetere;   88

He doth nouȝt wel that doth thus · ne drat nouȝt god almiȝty,
Ne loueth nouȝt Salamones sawes · that Sapience tauȝte;   93
    Inicium sapiencie, timor domini:
That dredeth god, he doth wel; · that dredeth hym for loue,
And nouȝt for drede of veniaunce · doth ther-fore the bettere;
He doth best, that with-draweth hym · by day and bi nyȝte   96
To spille any speche · or any space of tyme;
    Qui offendit in vno, in omnibus est reus.
Lesyng of tyme · treuthe wote the sothe!
Is moste yhated vp erthe · of hem that beth in heuene,
And sitthe to spille speche · that spyre is of grace,   100
And goddes gleman · and a game of heuene;
Wolde neuere the faithful fader · his fithel were vntempred,
Ne his gleman a gedelynge · a goer to tauernes!
    To alle trew tidy men · that trauaille desyren,   104
Owre lorde loueth hem and lent · loude other stille,
Grace to go to hem · and agon her lyflode;
    Inquirentes autem dominum non minuentur omni bono.

A. 81. *This line is from* T.   86. *et—sunt*; from TU; V om.   87.
This line is from T; V*ı has a corrupt line*, Bote clene concience acorde ·
bote þi-self Dowel.   88. *indicat hominem* TUH₂; V *indistinct.*   92. *Qui*

For, *Intencio indicat hominem.*
Bi counseil of Concience · a-cordynge with holy churche,
Loke thou wisse thi wit · and thi werkes aftur ;
For ȝif thou comest aȝein Concience · thou cumbrest thiseluen,
And so witnesseth godes word · and holiwrit bothe ; 92
    Qui agit contra conscientiam, edificat ad iehennam.
Bote ȝif thow worche bi godus word · I warne the for the beste,
What so men worden of the · wratthe the neuere ;
Catoun counseileth so · tak kepe of his teching,
    Cum recte viuas, ne cures verba malorum ;
Bote suffre and sitte stille · and sech thou no furre, 96
And beo glad of the grace · that god hath the i-sent ;
For ȝif thou cumse to clymbe · and coueyte herre,
Thou miht leose thi louhnesse · for a luitel pruyde.
I haue lerned how lewede men · han lered heore children, 100
That selden moseth the marbelston · that men ofte treden ;
  And riht so walkers · that walken a-bouten
From religion to religion · recheles ben thei euere.

Ne spille speche ne tyme · ne myspende neither
Meeble ne vnmeeble · mete nother drynke.
And thanne dude we alle wel · and ȝut wel bet to louye
Oure enemyes entyreliche · and help hem at here neede. 188
And ȝut were best to bee aboute · and brynge hit to hepe,
That alle londes loueden · and in on lawe by-leouede.
Bisshopes sholde be here-aboute · and brynge this to hepe,
For to leese there-fore here londe · and here lyf after. 192
The catel that Crist hadde · thre clothes hit were,
Ther-of was he ryfled · and robbed er he deyede ;
After that he les hus lyf · for lawe sholde loue wexe.
Prelates and preestes · and princes of holy churche 196
Sholde doute no deth · nother dere ȝeres,
To wenden as wyde · as the worlde were,
To tulien the erthe with tonge · and teche men to louye ;
For ho so loueth, leyue hit wel · god wol nat lete hym sterue 200
In myschef for lacke of mete · ne for myssynge of clothes ;
    Inquirentes autem dominum non minuentur omni bono.

—*iehennam* ; from U.   95. kepe UTH$_2$; hede V.   B. 97. *vno* WCOB ; *verbo* LR ; *see* B. xi. 301.   C. 190. loueden IMFE ; lyueden P.   an (*for* and) P.   194. he IMFEG ; P *om.* ryflede P.   199. eerthe P.

And men that cunne mony craftes · clergie hit telleth,   104
Thruft or theodam with hem · selden is i-seye;
    Qui circuit omne genus, nullius est generis.
Poul the apostel · in his pistel wrot
In ensaumple of suche · rennars a-boute,
And for wisdam is writen · as witnesseth clerkes,   108
    In ea vocacione qua vocati estis, in eadem permaneatis.
ȝif thou beo mon i-mariet · monk, othur chanoun,
Hold the stable and studefast · and strengthe thi-seluen
To beo blesset for thi beryng · ȝe, beggere thauh thou weore!
  Loke thou grucche not on god · thauȝ he the ȝeue luytel,   112
Beo payed with thi porcion · porore or ricchore.
Thus in drede lyth Dowel · and Dobet to soffren,
For thorw soffraunce seo thou miht · hou souereynes ariseth;
    Qui se humiliat, exaltabitur, &c.;
And so Ierede vs Luc · that lyȝede neuere.   116
And thus of drede and his dede · Dobest aryseth,.
Whuch is flour and fruit · i-fostred of bothe.
  Riht as the rose · that red is and swote,
Out of a ragged roote · and of rouwe breres   120
Springeth and spredeth · that spicers desyreth.
Or as whete out of a weod · waxeth vppon eorthe,
So Dobest out of Dowel · and Dobet doth springe

  Trewe wedded libbing folk · in this worlde is Dowel;   107
For thei mote worche and wynne · and the worlde susteyne.
For of her kynde thei come · that confessoures ben nempned,
Kynges and kniȝtes · kayseres and cherles,
Maydenes and martires · out of o man come.
The wyf was made the weye · for to help worche,   112
And thus was wedloke ywrouȝt · with a mene persone;
First bi the faderes wille · and the frendes conseille,
And sytthenes bi assent of hem-self · as thei two myȝte acorde.
And thus was wedloke ywrouȝt · and god hym-self it made;
In erthe the heuene is · hym-self was the witnesse.   117
  Ac fals folke faithlees · theues and lieres,
Wastoures and wrecches · out of wedloke, I trowe,
Conceyued ben in yuel tyme · as Caym was on Eue.   120
Of such synful shrewes · the sauter maketh mynde,
    Concepit in dolore, et peperit iniquitatem, &c. :

A. PASSUS X. 124-145.   C. PASSUS XI. 202-211.   275

A-mong men of this molde · that meke ben, or kuynde;   124
For loue of heore louhnesse · vr lord ʒiueth hem grace
Such werkes to worche · that he is with apayet.
Furst and foreward · to folk that ben i-weddet,
And libbeth as heore lawe wole · hit liketh God almihti;   128
For thorw wedlac the world stont · hose wol hit i-knowe.
Thei ben ricchest in reame · and the rote of Dowel;
For of heore kynde thei come · that confessours beth nempned,
Bothe maydens and martires · monkes and ancres,   132
Kynges and knihtes · and alle cunne clerkes,
Barouns and burgeis · and bonde men of tounes.
   Fals folk and feithles · theoues and lyʒers
Ben conseyuet in curset tyme · as Caym was on Eue,   136
After that Adam and Eue · hedden eten of the appel
Aʒeyn the heste of him · that hem of nouʒt made.
   An angel in haste · thennes hem tornde
In-to this wrecchede world · to wonen and to libben   140
In tene and in trauaile · to here lyues ende;
In that corsede constellacion · thei knewen to-gedere,
And brouʒten forth a barn · that muche bale wrouʒte.
   Caym men cleped him · in cursed tyme engendret,   144
And so seith the sauter · seo hit whon the liketh,
   Concepit in dolore, et peperit iniquitatem, &c.

Ho so lyueth in lawe · and in loue doth wel
As these weddid men · that this worlde susteynen?
For of here kynde thei come · confessours and martyres,   204
Patriarkes and prophetes · popes and maidenes.
For god seith hit hym-self · " shal neuere good appel
Thorw no sotel science · on sour stock growe;"
And hit ys no more to mene · bote men that buth bygetyn   208
Out of matrimonie nat moillere · mowe nat haue the grace
That leelle legitime · by lawe may cleyme.
And that my sawe be soth · the sauter bereth witnesse,
   Concepit in dolore, et peperit iniquitatem.

A. 105. *nullius—generis* U; V *om.*   108. *In—permaneatis* U; V *om.*
115. souereyn V; soueraynes TU. *exaltabitur, &c.* is from T.   124. molde TU;
world V.   132. an (*for* and) V.   141. *This line is from* U.   143. a barn TU;
barnes V.   wrouʒte TU; wrouʒten V; *cf. next line.*   145. *et—&c.* from T.
C. 203. theese P.   204. martyres MIFSG; maistres PE.   205. maidones P.
After l. 207, S *adds:* Nothur an a bytur brom · wex broune beryus.

T 2

And alle that come of that Caym · Crist hem hatede aftur,
And mony milions mo · of men and of wymmen
That of Seth and his suster · seththen forth coome ;   148
For thei marieden to corsed men · that comen of Caymes kuynde.
For alle that comen of that Caym · a-cursed thei weren,
And alle that couplede hem to that kun · Crist hem hatede dedliche.
Forthi he sende to Seth · and seide him bi an angel,   152
To kepe his cun from Caymes · that thei coupled not to-gedere.
And seththen Seth and his suster sed · weren spoused to Caymes,
A-ȝeyn godes heste · gurles thei geeten,
That god was wroth with heor werk · and suche wordes seide,
    Penitet me fecisse hominem ;
And is thus muche to mene · a-monges ȝou alle,   157
" That I makede mon · nou hit me for-thinketh ;"

And alle that come of that Caym · come to yuel ende.
For God sent to Seem · and seyde bi an angel,*   [*Cf. p. 279.]
" Thyne issue in thyne issue · I wil that thei be wedded,   124
And nouȝt thi kynde with Caymes · ycoupled ne yspoused."
Ȝet some, aȝein the sonde · of owre saueoure of heuene,
Caymes kynde and his kynde · coupled togideres,
Tyl god wratthed for her werkis · and suche a worde seyde,
" That I maked man · now it me athynketh ;"   129
    Penitet me fecisse hominem.
And come to Noe anon · and bad hym nouȝt lette :
" Swithe go shape a shippe · of shides and of bordes.
Thi-self and thi sones three . and sithen ȝowre wyues,   132
Buske ȝow to that bote · and bideth ȝe ther-inne,
Tyl fourty dayes be fulfilde · that the flode haue ywasshen
Clene awey the cursed blode · that Caym hath ymaked.
Bestes that now ben · shulle banne the tyme,   136
That euere that cursed Caym · come on this erthe ;
Alle shal deye for his dedes · bi dales and bi hulles,
And the foules that fleeghen · forth with other bestes,
Excepte oneliche · of eche kynde a couple,   140
That in thi shyngled shippe · shul ben ysaued."

A. 152. Seth ; V *has* Sem, *by mistake* ; *see* l. 148.   154. Seth ; Sem VT ;
see ll. 148, 152.   156. *fecisse—hominem* ; from TU ; V *om.*   163. þat ;
TH₂ *have* þat, *but omit* þe.   165. banne TUH₂ ; curse V.   **B.** 134. þe W ;

A. PASSUS X. 159-171.   C. PASSUS XI. 212-232.

And com to Noe anon · and bad him not lette
Swithe to schapen a schup · of schides and bordes; 160
Him-self and his sones thre · and seththen heore wyues,
Bringen hem to the bot · and byden ther-inne,
Til fourti dawes ben folfuld · that the flod haue i-wassche
Clene awey the cursede blod · that Caym hath i-maket. 164
"Beestes that now ben · mouwen banne the tyme
That euere that cursede Caym · com vppon eorthe;
Alle schulen dye for his dedes · bi dounes and hulles,
Bothe fisch and foules · forth with other beestes, 168
Out-taken eihte soules · and of vche beest a couple,
That in the schynglede schup · schullen ben i-saued;
Elles schal al dye · and to helle weende."

Caym the cursed creature · conceyued was in synne, 212
After that Adam and Eue · hadden ysynged;
With-oute repentaunce · of here rechelesnesse,
A rybaud thei engendrede · and a gome vnryghtful.
As an hewe that ereth nat · auntreth hym to sowe 216
On a leye-lond · a-ȝens hus lordes wille,
So was Caym conceyued · and so been cursed wrecches,
That lycame han a-ȝen the lawe · that oure lorde ordeynede.
Alle that come of Caym · caytyues were euere, 220
And for the synne of Caymes sed · seyde god to Noe,
  Penitet me fecisse hominem;
And bad shape hym a schip · of shides and of bordes,
"Thy-selue and thy sones three · and sitthen ȝoure wyues,
Buske ȝow to that bot · and a-bydeth ther-ynne 224
Tyl fourty dayes be fulfilled · and the flod haue wasshe
Clene away the cursede blod · that of Cayme ys spronge.
Bestes that now beeth · banne shulleth the tyme
That euere that cursed Cayme · cam on this erthe; 228
Alle shullen deye for hus dedes · by dales and hulles,
And the foules that flen · forth with othere bestes,
Except onliche · of eche kynde a peyre,
That in thy shynglede schip · with the shal be saued." 232

LCROB *om.*   139. forth CWROB; for L.   C. 214. rechilessnesse P.
216. hewe IG; hywe P.   222. schip IMFSG; shup P.   224. and IMF;
P *om.*   225. þe M; PEIFSG *om.*   232. schip MFS; shup P.

A. PASSUS X. 172-175.   B. PASSUS IX. 142-163.

Thus thorw cursede Caym · com care vppon alle;   172
For Seth and his suster children · spouseden either other,
A3eyn the lawe of vr lord · ly3en to-gedere,
And weoren maried at mischef · as men doth now heore
    children.

Here abou3te the barne · the belsyres gultes,
And alle for her forfadres · thei ferden the worse.
The gospel is here-ageine · in o degre, I fynde,   144
    *Filius non portabit iniquitatem patris, et pater non portabit
        iniquitatem filii, &c.*

Ac I fynde, if the fader · be false and a shrewe,
That somdel the sone · shal haue the sires tacches.
Impe on an ellerne · and if thine apple be swete,
Mochel merueile me thynketh · and more of a schrewe,   148
That bryngeth forth any barne · but if he be the same,
And haue a sauoure after the sire · selde seestow other;
    Numquam colligimus de spinis vuas, nec de tribulis fycus.
And thus thourw cursed Caym · cam care vppon erthe;
And al for thei wrou3t wedlokes · a3ein goddis wille.   152
For-thi haue thei maugre for here mariages · that marye so her
    childeren;
For some, as I se now · soth for to telle,
For coueitise of catel · vnkyndeliche ben wedded.
As careful concepcioun · cometh of suche mariages,   156
As bifel of the folke · that I bifore of tolde.
For goode shulde wedde goode · though hij no good hadde;
"I am *via et veritas*," seith Cryst · "I may auaunce alle."
    It is an oncomely couple · bi Cryst, as me thinketh,   160
To 3yuen a 3onge wenche · to an olde feble,
Or wedden any widwe · for welth of hir goodis,
That neuere shal barne bere · but if it be in armes!

A. 173. Seth; Sem VT; *see* l. 148.   B. 142. abou3te WCRB; abou3t L.
150. *colligimus* COB; *colligitur* LWR.   C. 233. aboute P.   235. *importabit* P.   *nec—filij*; *in* M *only*.   238. fore P.   (1*st*) þe EMFSG; P *om*.
248. engendrede P.   256. now EMIFS; P *om*.   257. chapman P.

For summme, as I seo nou · soth for to tellen, 176
For couetise of catel · vnkuyndeliche beoth maried,
And careful concepcion · cometh of such weddyng,
Also bifel of that folk · that I beo-fore schewede.
Hit is an vn-comely couple · be Cryst, as me thinketh, 180
To ȝeuen a ȝong wenche · to an old feble mon,
Or to wedden an old widewe · for weolthe of hire goodes,
That neuer schal child bere · bote hit beo in hire armes!

Here abouȝte the barn · hus belsires gultes,
And alle for here for-fadres · ferden the worse.
The godspel ys her-ageyn · as gomes may reden,
 *Filius non portabit iniquitatem patris, nec pater iniquitatem
 filij.*
Holy writ wittnesseth · that for no wickede dede 236
That the sire hym-self doth · by hus owene wil,
The sone for the syres synne · sholde nat be the werse.
West-mynster lawe, ich wot wel · worcheth the contrarie;
For thauh the fader be a frankelayne · and for a felon be
 hanged, 240
The heritage that the air sholde haue · ys at the kynges wille.
Ac the godspel ys a glose there · hudynge the greythe treuthe;
For god seide ensample · of suche manere isshue,
That kynde folweth kynde · and contrarieth neuere; 244
 *Nunquam colligunt de spinis vuas: et alibi, Bona arbor
 bonum fructum facit.*
Ac whi the worlde was a-drent · holy writ telleth,
Was for mariages of man-kynde · that men maden that tyme.
After that Caym the cursede · hadde culled Abel,
Seth, Adames sone · sitthen was engendred. 248
And god sente to Seth · so sone he was of age,* [*Cf. p. 276.]
That—for no kyne catel · ne no kyne byheste
Suffren hus seed seeden · with Caymes seed hus brother.
And for that Seth suffrede hit · god seide, "me forthynketh 252
That ich man made · othere matrimonye suffrede;
For good sholde wedden good · thauh thei no good hadde,
For ich am *uia et ueritas* · and may auaunce hem alle."
 Ac fewe folke now folweth this · for thei ȝeueth here children
For couetise of catel · and connynge chapmen; 257
Of kyn ne of kynredene · a-counteth men bote lytel.

In Ielesye Ioyeles · and Ianglynge in bedde 184
Mony peire seththen the pestilence · han pliht hem to-gedere;
The fruit that thei bringen forth · ben mony foule wordes,
Han thei none children bote chestes · and choppes hem bitwene.
Thauӡ thei don hem to Donmowe · but the deuel helpe 188
To folewen aftur the flucchen · fecche thei hit neuere;

Many a peire sithen the pestilence · han pliӡt hem togideres;
The fruit that thei brynge forth · aren foule wordes, 165
In Ialousye Ioyeles · and Ianglyng on bedde.
Haue thei no children but cheste · and choppyng hem bitwene.
And though thei don hem to Donmowe · but if the deuel help
To folwen after the flicche · fecche thei it neuere; 169
And but thei bothe be forsworne · that bacoun thei tyne.

For-thi I conseille alle Crystene · coueite nouӡt be wedded
For coueitise of catel · ne of kynrede riche. 172
Ac maydenes and maydenes · macche ӡow togideres,
Widwes and widwers · worcheth the same.
For no londes, but for loue · loke ӡe be wedded,
And thanne gete ӡe the grace of god · and good ynogh to lyue
  with. 176
And euery maner seculer · that may nouӡt continue,
Wysly go wedde · and war hym fro synne;
For leccherye in likyng · is lymeӡerde of helle.
Whiles thow art ӡonge · and thi wepne kene, 180
Wreke the with wyuynge · ӡif thow wilt ben excused.
Dum sis vir fortis · ne des tua robora scortis,
Scribitur in portis · meretrix est ianua mortis.

A. 188. donmowe—helpe, *from* U; V *has* done · al þat þei mowen; *where*
done *and* mowen *are corrupted from* donmowe.   190. that—tyne TUH$_2$;
and cursen that tyme V.   193. maidenis · macche ӡow ysamme T; V *has*
vnmaydens · clene ow save.   194. werchiþ riӡt T; V *has* worschupeþ.
B. 167. an (*for* and) L.   181. wilt O; wolt WCB; wil L.   **C.** 260.
ymanerede P.   yspronge EIMFSG; spronge P.   269. watel PE; walet IMF.
271. *This line is in* F *only*.   273. lelly SMG; sothliche PE.   281.
maidones P.   283. noobles P.   287. ert P.

Bote ȝif thei bothe ben forswore · that bacoun thei tyne.
    Forthi I counseile alle Cristene · coueite not ben i-weddet
For couetyse of catel · ne of kun riche ;   192
Bote maydens and maydens · maccheth ou ysamme,
Widewers and widewes · wercheth riȝt also,
And thenne glade ȝe god · that alle goodes sendeth !

Thauh hue be loueliche to loken on · and lofsom a bedde,
A mayde wel ymanered · of good men yspronge,   260
Bote hue haue eny other good · haue hure wol no ryche.
Ac let hure be vnloueliche · vnlofsom a bedde,
A bastarde, a bounde on · a begeneldes douhter,
That no curtesye can · bote let hure be knowe   264
For ryche other wel yrented · thauh hue reuely for elde,
Ther nys squier ne knyght · in contreye a-boute,
That he nel bowe to that bonde · to bede hure an hosebonde,
And wedden hure for hure welthe · and wisshen on the morwe
That hus wyf were wex · other a watel-ful of nobles.   269
In gelesie Ioye-less · and Ianglynge a bedde
Thei lyue here lif vnlouely · til deth hem departe.
    Meny peire sitthe the pestilence-tyme · han plight treuthe to
    louye,   272
Ac thei lyen lelly · here nother loueth othere.
The frut that thei bryngen forth · aren meny foule wordes;
Thei han no children bote cheste · and choppes hem by-twyne.
    Thauh thei don hem to Donemowe · bote the deuel hem helpe
To folwen for the flicche · feccheth thei hit neuere ;   277
Bote thei bothe be for-swore · that bacon thei tyne.
    For-thi ich counseile alle Crystine · coueite neuere be wedded
For couetise of catel · in no kynne wyse ;   280
Bote maydenes and maydenes · marieth ȝow to-gederes ;
And wydewers and wydewes · weddeth ayther othere,
And loke that loue be more the cause · than lond other nobles.
    And euerech manere seculer man · that may nat contynue,
Wisliche go wedde · and war the fro that synne   285
That lecherye is, a lykynge thyng · and lym-ȝerde of helle.
And whil thow art ȝong and ȝep · and thy wepne kene,
Awreke the therwith on wyuynge · for godes werk ich holde hit :
Dum sis uir fortis · ne des tua robora scortis,   289
Scribitur in portis · meretrix est ianua mortis.

For in vn-tyme treweli · bi-twene mon and wommon 196
Schulde no bed-bourde be · bote bothe weore clene
Of lyf and eke in loue · and in lawe alse.
That deede derne · do no mon scholde,
As is vset, bi-twene · sengle and sengle; 200
Seththen lawe hath i-loket · that vche mon haue a make
In mariage and matrimoyne · i-medlet to-gedere,
And worche that with his wyf · and with no wommon elles.
That other-gates ben i-geten · for gadelynges ben holden, 204

Whan 3e haue wyued, bewar · and worcheth in tyme; 184
Nou3t as Adam and Eue · whan Caym was engendred.
For in vntyme, trewli · bitwene man and womman,
Ne shulde no bourde on bedde be; · but-if thei bothe were clene
Bothe of lyf and of soule · and in parfyte charitee, 188
That ilke derne dede · do noman ne sholde.
And if thei leden thus her lyf · it liketh god almi3ti;
For he made wedloke firste · and him-self it seide;
    Bonum est vt vnusquisque vxorem suam habeat, propter for-
      nicacionem.
And thei that othergatis ben geten · for gedelynges ben holden,
As false folke fondelynges · faitoures and lyars; 193
Vngracious to gete goode · or loue of the poeple,
Wandren and wasten · what thei cacche mowe.
A3eines Dowel thei don yuel · and the deuel serue, 196
And after her deth-day · shulle dwelle with the same,
But god gyue hem grace here · hem-self to amende.
Dowel, my frende, is · to don as lawe techeth,
To loue thi frende and thi foo · leue me, that is Dobet. 200
To 3iuen and to 3emen · bothe 3onge and olde,
To helen and to helpen · is Dobest of alle.
And Dowel is to drede god · and Dobet to suffre,
And so cometh Dobest of bothe · and bryngeth adoun the mody,
And that is wikked Wille · that many werke shendeth, 205
And dryueth away Dowel · thorugh dedliche synnes.'

A. 204, 205. V *has only one line*, þat oþergates ben I-geten · ben fyndlynges and ly3ers; *I here follow* TUH₂. 213. werke H₂T; men V. **B.** 190.

That ben false folke and false heires · fyndlynges and ly3ers,
Vn-gracios to gete loue · or eni good elles,
Bote wandren as wolues · and wasten 3if thei mouwen.
A-3eyn Dowel thei don vuele · and the deuel plesen,   208
And aftur heore deth-day · schul dwelle with the schrewe,
Bute god 3iue hem grace · heer to a-mende.
Thenne is Dowel to dredren · and Dobet to suffren,
And so cometh Dobest aboute · and bringeth a-doun modi, 212
And that is wikkede Wil · that mony werke schendeth.'

3e that han wyues, beth war · worcheth nat out of tyme,
As Adam dude and Eue · as ich whil er tolde.   292

For sholde no bed-borde be · bote-yf thei bothe were

Clene of lyf and loue in saule · and in leel wedlok.
For that derne dede · do no man sholde
Bote wedded men with here wyues · as holy writ telleth;   296

    Bonum est ut unusquisque uxorem suam habeat, propter fornicacionem.

That othere-gates been gete · for gadelynges aren holde,
And fals folke and foundlynges · faitours and lyers,
Vngraciouse to gete good · othere good loue of puple,
A-waytynge and wastynge · al that thei cacche mowe;   300
A-3ens Dowel thei don vuele · and the deuel seruen,
And after here deth-daye · dwellen shulle in helle,
Bote god gyue hem grace · her goynge to amende.
And thus ys Dowel, my frend · to do as lawe techeth,   304
To louye and to lowe the · and no lyf to greue.
Ac to louye and to lene · leyf me, that is Dobet;
Ac to 3eue and to 3eme · bothe 3onge and olde,
Helen and helpen · is Dobest of all.   308
For the more a man may do · by so that he do hit,
The more is he worth and worthi · of wyse and goode ypreised.'
    Hic explicit passus primus de Dowel.

---

likeþ WOB; liked LR.   C. 291. beþ IMESG; ben P.   303. hem
IMFG; P *om.*   304. do IMSEG; day (*wrongly*) P.   309. Fore P.

PASSUS XI.

Passus secundus de Dowel, &c.

THENNE hedde Wit a wyf · was hoten dam Studie,
That lene was of lich · and of louh chere.
Heo was wonderliche wroth · that Wit me thus tauhte,
And al starinde dam Studie · steorneliche seide, 4
'Wel artou witti,' quod heo · 'wisdom to telle
To fayturs or to fooles · that frentik ben of wittes!'
And blamede him for his beere · and bad him beo stille

PASSUS X.

Passus decimus de visione, et secundus de Dowel.

THANNE hadde Witte a wyf · was hote dame Studye,
That lene was of lere · and of liche bothe.
She was wonderly wroth · that Witte me thus tau3te,
And al starynge dame Studye · sternelich seyde, 4
'Wel artow wyse,' quod she to Witte · · 'any wysdomes to telle
To flatereres or to folis · that frantyk ben of wittes!'
And blamed hym and banned hym · and badde hym be stylle,
With suche wise wordes · to wissen any sottes; 8
And seyde, '*noli mittere*, man · margerye-perlis
Amanges hogges, that han · hawes at wille.
Thei don but dryuele ther-on · draffe were hem leuere
Than al the precious perre · that in paradys wexeth. 12
I sey it bi suche,' quod she · 'that sheweth bi her werkes,
That hem were leuer londe · and lordship on erthe,
Or ricchesse or rentis · and reste at her wille,
Than alle the sothe sawes · that Salamon seyde euere. 16
 Wisdome and witte now · is nou3t worth a carse,
But if it be carded with coueytise · as clotheres kemben here wolle.
Who-so can contreue deceytes · and conspire wronges,
And lede forth a loue-day · to latte with treuthe; 20

A. 2. lene—lich TH₂; euer was i-liche V.   18. cardit TH₂; carket V.

With suche wyse wordes · to wisse eny fooles. 8
And seide, '*noli mittere* · margeri-perles
Among hogges that han · hawes at heore wille;
Thei don bot drauele theron · draf weore hem leuere
Then al the presciouse peerles · that in paradys waxen. 12
I sigge hit bi thulke,' quod heo · 'that bi heore werkes schewen
That hem weore leuere lond · and lordschupe on eorthe,
Richesse, rentes · or reste at heore wille
Then al the soth sawes · that Salamon seide euere. 16
Wisdam and wit nou · is not worth a russche
But hit beo cardet with couetise · as clothers doth heor wolle,
That conterfeteth disseites · and conspiret wronges,
And ledeth forth a loueday · to lette the trewthe; 20

PASSUS XII.

Incipit passus secundus de Dowel.

THENNE hadde Wit a wif · was hote dame Studie,
That ful lene lokede · and lif-holy semede;
Hue was wonderliche worth · that Wit so me tauhte.
Al starynge dame Studie · sterneliche seide, 4
'Wel art thow wys,' quath hue to Wit · 'suche wisdome to shewe
To eny fol other flaterere · other to frentik puple;'
And seide, '*nolite mittere*, 3e men · margerie-perles
A-monge hogges that hauen · hawes at wille; 8
Thei don bote dreuele theron · draf were hem leuere
Than al the preciouse perreye · that eny prince weldeth.
Ich segge hit by suche,' quath Studie · 'that shewen by here werkus,
Thei loueth lond and lordshup · and lykyng of body more 12
Than holynesse other hendenesse · other al that seintes techeth.
Wysdom and wit now · is nat worth a carse
Bote hit be carded with couetyse · as clothers kemben wolle.
Ho that can contreeue and caste · to deceyue the puple, 16
And lette with a loueday · treuthe, and by-gyle hym,

---

20. trewethe V.   B. 19. an (*for* and) L.   C. 4. staryenge P. sturneliche P.
5. (*2nd*) to IMFSEG; P *om.*   9. dreuelyn P.   12. Thei M; That PEIFSK.

That suche craftes cunnen · to counseil beoth i-clept,
And ben serued as syres · that serueth the deuel.
Iob the Ientel · in his Ieestes seide,
  *Quare via impiorum prosperatur, bene est omnibus qui praue
  et inique agunt?*
Ac he that holy writ hath · euer in his mouthe,   24

He that suche craftes can · to conseille is clepid;
Thei lede lordes with lesynges · and bilyeth treuthe.
Iob the gentel · in his gestes witnesseth,
That wikked men, thei welden · the welthe of this worlde,   24
And that thei ben lordes of eche a londe · that oute of lawe lib-
 beth;
  *Quare impij viuunt? bene est omnibus, qui preuaricantur et
  inique agunt?*
The sauter seyth the same · bi suche that don ille,
  *Ecce ipsi peccatores habundantes ; in seculo optinuerunt diui-
  cias.*
"Lo!" seith holy letterrure · "whiche lordes beth this shrewes!"
Thilke that god moste gyueth · leste good thei deleth,   28
And moste vnkynde to the comune · that moste catel weldeth;
  Que perfecisti, destruxerunt ; iustus autem quid fecit?
Harlotes for her harlotrye · may haue of her godis,
And Iaperes and Iogeloures · and Iangelers of gestes.
 Ac he that hath holy writte · ay in his mouth,   32
And can telle of Tobye · and of the twelue apostles,
Or prechen of the penaunce · that Pilat wrouȝt
To Iesu the gentil · that Iewes to-drowe :—
Litel is he loued · that suche a lessoun scheweth,   36
Or daunted or drawe forth · I do it on god hym-self!
 But tho that feynen hem folis · and with faityng libbeth,
Aȝein the lawe of owre lorde · and lyen on hem-selue,
Spitten and spewen · and speke foule wordes,   40
Drynken and dryuelen · and do men for to gape,
Lickne men and lye on hem · that leneth hem no ȝiftes,
Thei conne namore mynstralcye · ne musyke, men to glade,
Than Munde the mylnere · of *multa fecit deus!*   44

  B. 30. All the MSS. omit *quid fecit.*

A. PASSUS XI. 25-30. C. PASSUS XII. 18-34.

And con tellen of Tobie · and the twelfe apostles;
And prechen of the peuaunce · that Pilatus wrouhte
To Iesu the Ientil · that Iewes to-drowe
On cros vppon Caluarie · as clerkes vs telleth;— 28
Luytel is he loued or leten bi · that such a lessun redeth,
Or daunseled or drawen forth · this disours witen the sothe;

That can coueite and caste thus · aren cleped in-to counsail.
Qui sapiunt nugas · et crimina lege uocantur,
Qui recte sapiunt · lex iubet ire foras. 20
He is reuerenced and robed · that can robbe the peuple
Thorw fallas and false questes · and thorw fykel speche.
Iob the gentil and wys · in hus gestes wytnesseth
What shal worthe of suche · whenne thei lyf leten; 24
Ducunt in bonis dies suos, & in fine descendunt ad infernum.
The sauter seith the same · of alle suche ryche;
Ibunt in progenies patrum suorum, & usque in eternum non
uidebunt lumen:
Et alibi: Ecce ipsi peccatores, & cet.
"Lo!" holy lettrure seith · "whiche lordes been these shrewes!" 26
Tho that god most good gyueth · most greue ryght and
treuthe:
Que perfecisti, destruxerunt; iustus autem quid fecit?
And harlotes for hure harlotrie · aren holpen er nedy poure; 28
And that is no ryght ne reson · for rather men sholde
Help hem that hath nouht · than tho that han no neede.
Ac he that hath holy writ · aye in hus mouthe,
And can telle of Treuthe · and of the twelue apostels, 32
Other of the passion of Crist · other of purgatorie peynes,
Lytel is he a-lowed there-fore · among lordes at festes.

C. 18. coueite MEKG; coueyty P.   25. *progenies* EIF; *progenie* P.
26. thees P.   27. god IMFSKG; PE *om.*   *iustus—fecit; in* S *only.*
28. hure S; here IKG; P *om.* nudy P.   34. at IMFG; of P.

For ȝif harlotrie ne holpe hem the bet · (haue god my soule!)
More then musyk · or makyng of Crist, 32
Wolde neuer kyng ne kniht · ne canoun of seynt Pouleś
ȝeuen hem to heore ȝeres-ȝiue · the value of a grote!
Bote munstralsye and murthe · a-mong men is nouthe;
Lecherie and losengrie · and loseles tales, 36
And geten gold with grete othes · beoth gamus nou a dayes.
But ȝif thei carpen of Crist · (this clerkes and this lewede)
Atte mete in heor murthe · whon munstrals beoth stille, 39
Thenne telleth thei of the trinite · hou two slowen the thridde,
And bringeth forth ballede resouns · tak Bernard to witnesse,
And puyteth forth presumpciun · to preue the sothe.
Thus thei drauelen on heore deys · the deite to knowe,
And demeth god in-to the gorge · whon heore gottus follen. 44

Ne were here vyle harlotrye · haue god my treuthe,
Shulde neuere kyng ne kniȝt · ne chanoun of seynt Poules
ȝyue hem to her ȝeresȝiue · the ȝifte of a grote!
Ac murthe and mynstralcye · amonges men is nouthe 48
Leccherye, losengerye · and loseles tales;
Glotonye and grete othes · this murthe thei louieth.
Ac if thei carpen of Cryst · this clerkis and this lewed,
Atte mete in her murthes . whan mynstralles ben stille, 52
Thanne telleth thei of the trinite · a tale other tweyne,
And bringen forth a balled resoun · and taken Bernard to witnesse,
And putten forth a presumpsioun · to preue the sothe.
Thus thei dryuele at her deyse · the deite to knowe, 56
And gnawen god with the gorge · whan her gutte is fulle.
Ac the careful may crye · and carpen atte ȝate,
Bothe afyngred and a-thurst · and for chele quake;
Is none to nymen hym nere · his noye to amende, 60
But hoen on hym as an hounde · and hoten hym go thennes.
Litel loueth he that lorde · that lent hym al that blisse,
That thus parteth with the pore · a parcel whan hym nedeth.
Ne were mercy in mene men · more than in riche, 64
Mendinantz meteles · miȝte go to bedde.
God is moche in the gorge · of thise grete maystres,
Ac amonges mene men · his mercy and his werkis;
And so seith the sauter · I haue yseye it ofte, 68
Ecce audiuimus eam in Effrata, inuenimus eam in campis silue.

But carful mon may crien · and clepen atte ȝate
Bothe of hungur and of thurst · and for chele quake;   46
Nis no mon him neih · his nuy to amende,
Bote honesschen him as an hound · and hoten him go thennes!
Luyte loueth he that lord · that leneth him that blisse,   49
That thus parteth with the pore · a parcel whon him neodeth.
Neore merci in mene men · more then in riche,
With mony defauti meeles · mihte thei go to bedde.   52
God is muche in the gorge · of theose grete maystres,
Bote a-mong mene men · his merci and his werkes;
And so seith the psauter · sech hit in '*Memento*,'
    *Ecce audiuimus eam in Effrata, inuenimus eam in campis
    silue.*

Now is the manere atte mete · when mynstralles ben stylle,
The lewede a-ȝens the lered · the holy lore to dispute,   36
And tellen of the trinite · how two slowe the thridde,
And brynge forth ballede resones · and taken Bernarde to
    witnesse,
And putteth forth presompcions · to preouen the sothe.
Thus thei dreuelen atte deyes · the deyte to knowe,   40
And gnawen god with gorge · when here guttes fullen.
  Ac the carful mai crie · and quaken atte ȝate,
Bothe a-fyngred and a-furst · and for defaute spille,
Ys non so hende to haue hym yn · bote hote hym go ther
    god is!   44
Thenne semeth hit to my syght · to suche as so biddeth,
God is nat in that hom · ne hus help neither!
Lytel loueth he that lorde · that lente hym al that blisse,
That so parteth with the poure · a parcel, whenne hym nedeth.   48
Ne were mercy in mene men · more than in ryght ryche,
Meny time mendynans · myghte gon a-fyngred;
And so seith the sauter · ich sauh hit in *Memento,*
    *Ecce audiuimus eam (.i. caritatem) in Effrata; inuenimus
    eam in campis silue.*

A. 55. *eam* TUH₂; *eum* V.   C. 35. atte þe P.   47. al IMFSEKG; P *om.*

Clerkes and kete men · carpen of god ofte, 56
And han him muche in heore mouth · bote mene men in herte.

Clerkes and other kynnes men · carpen of god faste,
And haue hym moche in the mouthe · ac mene men in herte.

Freres and faitoures · han founde suche questiouns
To plese with proude men · sithen the pestilence tyme, 72
And prechen at seint Poules · for pure enuye of clerkis,
That folke is nouȝte fermed in the feith · ne fre of her goodes,
Ne sori for her synnes · so is pryde waxen 75
In religioun and in alle the rewme · amonges riche and pore,
That preyeres haue no power · the pestilence to lette.

And ȝette the wrecches of this worlde · is none ywar bi other,
Ne for drede of the deth · withdrawe nouȝt her pryde,
Ne beth plentyuous to the pore · as pure charite wolde, 80
But in gaynesse and in glotonye · for-glotten her goode hem-selue,
And breken nouȝte to the beggar · as the boke techeth,
Frange esurienti panem tuum, &c.

And the more he wynneth and welt · welthes and ricchesse,
And lordeth in londes · the lasse good he deleth. 84
Thobye telleth ȝow nouȝt so · take hede, ȝe riche,
How the boke bible · of hym bereth witnesse :
*Si tibi sit copia, habundanter tribue ; si autem exiguum,
illud impertiri stude libenter :—*
Who-so hath moche, spene manliche · so meneth Thobie,
And who-so litel weldeth · reule him ther-after ; 88

B. 70. hym WCROB; L *om.*   C. 55, 60. pestelences P.   56. *This*
line is from IKGSF ; *not in* PEM.   58. pryuyde P.   60. thees P.
62. deþe IMFSEK ; dyþe P.   63. þees P.   ywar IK ; whar P.   67.
Frange—tuam E ; *not in* P.   73. laste P.   80. *This line is in* I *only.*
83. lust MFSK ; loust P.

Freres and faytors · han founden suche questions   58
To plese with this proude men · seththe pestilence tyme;

Clerkus and knyghtes · carpen of god ofte,   52
And haueth hym muche in hure mouthe · ac mene men in herte.
Freres and faitours · han founde vp suche questiones
To plese with proute men · sitthe the pestilences,
And preching at seint Poules · in pure enuye of clerkes,   56
That folk is nouht ferm in the feith · ne free of here goodes,
Ne sory for here synnes; · so is pruyde en-hansed
In religion and al the reame · among ryche and poure,
That preyeres han no power · these pestilences to lette.   60
For god is def now a dayes · and deyneth nouht ous to huyre,
And good men for oure gultes · he al to-grynt to dethe;
And ȝut these wrecches of thys worlde · is non y-war by other,
Ne for drede of eny deth · with-draweth hem fro pruyde,   64
Ne parteth with the poure · as pure charyte wolde,
Bote in gayenesse and in glotenye · for-glotten here goodes,
And breketh nat here bred to the poure · as the book hoteth;
    Frange esurienti panem tuum; et egenos vagosque induc in domum tuam.
Ac the more he hath, and wynneth · the world at hus wylle,   68
And lordeth in leedes · the lasse good he deleth.
  Tobie tauhte nat so · taketh hede, ȝe ryche,
How he tolde in a tyme · and tauhte hus sone dele:
    Si tibi sit copia, abundanter tribue: si autem exiguum, illud impertiri libenter stude.
And this is no more to mene · bote "ho so muche good weldeth,   72
Be large ther-of while hit last · to leedes that been needy.
Yf thow haue lytel, leue sone · loke by thy lyue
Get the loue ther-with · thauh thou fare the werse."
Ac lust no lord ne lewed man · of suche lore nou to hure,   76
Bote lythen how they myghte lerne · lest good to spene.
And so lyuen lordes now · and leten hit a Dowel;
For is no wit worth now · bote hit of wynnynge soune,
And capped with clergie · to conspire wronge.   80
For-thi,' quath hue to Wit, 'be war · holy writ to shewe
Amonges hem that hauen · hawes atte wille,
The whiche is a lykynge and a lust · and loue of the worlde.'

Thei de-foulen vre fey · at festes ther thei sitten. 60
For nou is vche boye bold · brothel and other,
To talken of the trinite · to beon holden a syre,
And fyndeth forth fantasyes · vr feith to apeyre;
And eke de-fameth the fader · that vs alle made, 64
And craken aȝeyn the clergie · crabbede wordes.
"Whi wolde god vr saueour · suffre such a worm
In such a wrong wyse · the wommon to bi-gyle?

For we haue no lettre of owre lyf · how longe it shal dure.
Suche lessounes lordes shulde · louie to here,
And how he myȝte moste meyne · manliche fynde.
Nouȝt to fare as a fitheler or a frere · for to seke festes, 92
Homelich at other mennes houses · and hatyen her owne.
Elyng is the halle · vche daye in the wyke,
There the lorde ne the lady · liketh nouȝte to sytte.
Now hath vche riche a reule · to eten bi hym-selue 96
In a pryue parloure · for pore mennes sake,
Or in a chambre with a chymneye · and leue the chief halle,
That was made for meles · men to eten inne;
And al to spare to spille · that spende shal an other. 100
I haue yherde hiegh men · etyng atte table,
Carpen as thei clerkes were · of Cryste and of his miȝtes,
And leyden fautes vppon the fader · that fourmed vs alle,
And carpen aȝeine clerkes · crabbed wordes;— 104
"Whi wolde owre saueoure suffre · suche a worme in his blisse,
That bigyled the womman · and the man after,
Thorw whiche wyles and wordes · thei wenten to helle,
And al her sede for here synne · the same deth suffred? 108
Here lyeth ȝowre lore" · thise lordes gynneth dispute,
"Of that ȝe clerkes vs kenneth · of Cryst by the gospel;
Filius non portabit iniquitatem patris, &c.
Whi shulde we that now ben · for the werkes of Adam
Roten and to-rende? · resoun wolde it neuere; 112
Vnusquisque portabit onus suum, &c."
Suche motyues thei moeue · this maistres in her glorie,
And maken men in mysbileue · that muse moche on her wordes;
Ymaginatyf her-afterward · shal answere to ȝowre purpos.
Augustyne to suche argueres · he telleth hem this teme, 116
Non plus sapere quam oportet.

Bothe hir hosebonde and heo · to helle thorw him wenten, 68
And heore seed for that sunne · the same wo drien."
Suche motyues thei meuen · thei maistres in heor glorie,
And maketh men misbileeue · that musen on heore wordes.
But Austin the olde · for alle suche precheth, 72
And for suche tale-tellers · such a teeme scheweth,
Non plus sapere quam oportet sapere.

[*Not in* C-*text.*]

A. 61. an (*for* and) V. 71. musen on T ; leeuen in V. B. 93. houses
WCROB; house L.   107. wenten CRB ; went L.

This wilneth ȝe neuer to wite · whi that god wolde
Soffre Sathan · his sed to bi-gyle;
But leeueth on that lore · that lereth holichirche, 76
And preye him of pardoun · and penaunce in thi lyue,
And for his muchele merci · to amenden vs heere.
For alle that wilneth to wite · the weyes of god almihti,
I wolde his eȝe weore in his ers · and his heele aftur; 80
That euer eft wilneth to wite · whi that god wolde
Soffre Sathan · his seed to bi-gyle,
Or Iudas the Ieuȝ · Iesu bi-traye;
Al was as he wolde · lord, i-heried be thou! 84
And al worth as thou wolt · what so we tellen!

Wilneth neuere to wite · whi that god wolde
Suffre Sathan · his sede to bigyle,
Ac bileue lelly · in the lore of holicherche,
And preye hym of pardoun · and penaunce in thi lyue, 120
And for his moche mercye · to amende ȝow here.
For alle that wilneth to wyte · the weyes of god almiȝty,
I wolde his eye were in his ers · and his fynger after,
That euere wilneth to wite · whi that god wolde 124
Suffre Sathan · his sede to bigile,
Or Iudas to the Iuwes · Iesu bytraye.
Al was as thow wolde · lorde, yworschiped be thow,
And al worth as thow wolte · what so we dispute! 128
   And tho that vseth this hanelounes · to blende mennes wittes,
What is Dowel fro Dobet · now def mote he worthe,
(Sitthe he wilneth to wyte · whiche thei ben bothe),
But if he lyue in the lyf · that longeth to Dowel; 132
For I dar ben his bolde borgh · that Dobet wil he neuere,
Theigh Dobest drawe on hym · day after other.'
   And whan that Witte was ywar · what dame Studye tolde,
He bicome so confus · he couth nouȝte loke, 136
And as doumbe as deth · and drowe hym arrere;
And for no carpyng I couth after · ne knelyng to the grounde,
I myȝte gete no greyne · of his grete wittis,
But al laughyng he louted · and loked vppon Studye, 140
In signe that I shulde · biseche hir of grace.

A. 79. to wite þe UTH₂; two V; see ll. 73, 81, 88.   85. worþ TUH₂;
beo V.   86. my TH₂; me V.   88. siþen T; V *has* Sire.   93. mele

And nou cometh a conioun · and wolde cacchen of my wittes,
What is Dowel from Dobet! · nou daffe mot he worthe,
Sithen he wilneth to wite · whuche thei ben alle! 88
Bote he liue in the leste degre · that longeth to Dowel,
I dar ben his borw · that Dobet nul he neuere,
Thauȝ Dobest drawe on him · day aftur othur.'
And whon that Wit was i-war · hou his wyf tolde, 92
He bi-com so confoundet · he couthe not mele,
And as doumbe as a dore · drouȝ him asyde.
Bote for no craft that I couthe · ne knelyng to grounde,
I mihte gete no greyn · of his grete wittes, 96
But al lauȝwhinge he loutede · and lokede vppon Studie,
In signe that I schulde · bi-sechen hire of grace.

And whanne Wit was y-war · what Studie menede, 84
Ich myghte gete no greyn · of Wittes grete wittes,

Bote al lauhwynge he loutede · and loked vp-on Studie,
Semynge that ich sholde · by-sechen hure of grace.

TUHₐ; medle V.   96. his TUH₂; hire V.   B. 129. hauelounes L.
137. as WCROB; a L.   C. 84. y-war IK; whar P.   86. lotede P;
see l. 88.

And whon I wuste of his wil · to his wyf con I knele,
And seide, 'merci, madame, ȝoure mon schal I worthe,   100
To worchen ȝoure wille · while my lyf dureth;
Kenne me kuyndely · to knowen what is Dowel.'
  'For thi mekenesse, mon,' quod heo · 'and for thi milde speche,
I schal kenne the to my cosyn · that Clergye is i-hoten.   104
He hath wedded a wyf · with-inne this wikes sixe,
Is sib to the seuen ars · that Scripture is i-nempnet;
Thei two, as ich hope · after my be-sechyng,
Schul wisse the to Dowel · I dar vndertake.'   108
Thenne was I as fayn · as foul on feir morwen,
Gladdore then the gleo-mon is · of his grete ȝiftes,

And whan I was war of his wille · to his wyf gan I loute,
And seyde, 'mercy, madame · ȝowre man shal I worthe,
As longe as I lyue · bothe late and rathe,   144
Forto worche ȝowre wille · the while my lyf dureth,
With that ȝe kenne me kyndely · to knowe what is Dowel.'
  'For thi mekenesse, man,' quod she · 'and for thi mylde speche,
I shal kenne the to my cosyn · that Clergye is hoten.   148
He hath wedded a wyf · with-inne this syx monethes,
Is sybbe to the seuene artz · Scripture is hir name.
Thei two, as I hope · after my techyng,
Shullen wissen the to Dowel · I dar it vndertake.'   152
  Thanne was I also fayne · as foule of faire morwe,
And gladder than the gleman · that golde hath to ȝifte,
And axed hir the heighe weye · where that clergye dwelte,
'And telle me some token,' quod I · 'for tyme is that I wende.'   156
  'Axe the heighe waye,' quod she · 'hennes to Suffre-
Bothe-wel-and-wo · ȝif that thow wolt lerne,
And ryde forth by Ricchesse · ac rest thow nauȝt therinne,
For if thow couplest the ther-with · to Clergye comestow neuere.
And also the likerouse launde · that Leccherye hatte,   161
Leue hym on thi left halue · a large myle or more,
Tyl thow come to a courte · Kepe-wel-thi-tonge-
Fro-lesynges-and-lither-speche- · and-likerouse-drynkes.   164
  Thanne shaltow se Sobrete · and Symplete-of-speche,

A. 100. worþe TUH₂ beo V; *see* l. 85.   102. Kenne TUH₂; Teche V.

A. PASSUS XI. 111–121.   C. PASSUS XII. 88–110.

And askede hire the hei3e wey · wher Clergye dwelleth,
'And tel me sum tokne to him · for tyme is that I wende.' 112
'I schal teche the the hei3e wey,' quod heo · 'from hennes to Soffre-
Bothe-weole-and-wo · 3if that thou wolt leorne,
And ryd forth bi Richesse · reste the nou3t ther-inne;
For 3if thou couple the to him · to Clergie comestou neuere. 116
And eke the longe launde · that Lecherie hette,
Leue him on thi luft half · a large myle or more,
Forte thou come to a court · Kep-wel-thi-tonge-
From-lesynges-and-ly3eres-speche- · and-lykerous-drinke. 120
Thenne schaltou seo Sobre · and Symple-of-speche,

When ich was war of hus wille · to that womman ich loutede, 88
And seide, 'mercy, ma dame · 3oure man shal ich worthe
As longe as ich lyue · bothe late and rathe,
And for to worche 3oure wil · the while my lyf dureth,
With that 3e kenne me kyndeliche · to knowe what is Dowel.' 92
'For thi meeknesse,' quath hue · 'and for thi mylde speche,
Ich shal the kenne to Clergie · my cosyn, that knoweth
Alle kyne konnynges · and comsynges of Dowel,
Of Dobet and Dobest · for doctor he is yknowe, 96
And of Scripture the skylful · and scryuaynes were trewe.
For hue is sybbe to the seuen ars · and also my soster,
And Cleregies wedded wif · as wys as hym-selue
Of lore and of letterure · of lawe and of reson. 100
So with that that Cleregie can · and counsail of Scripture
Thow shalt conne and knowe · kyndeliche Dowel.'
Thenne was ich al so fayn · as foul of fair morwenynge,
Gladder than gleo-man · that gold hath to gyfte, 104
And asked of hure the heye way · wher that Cleregie dwelte—
'And tel me som tokne,' quath ich · 'for tyme is that ich wende.'
'Aske the heye wey,' quath hue · 'hennes to Suffre-
Bothe-wele-and-moche-wo · yf thow wolt lerne. 108
And ryd forth by Richesse · and rest nouht ther-ynne;
Yf thow coueite to be riche · to Cleregie comst thow neuere.

---

104. kenne TUH₂; teche V.   C. 91. duyreþ P.   97. skyful (*sic*) P.
trywe P.   102. kendeliche P.   110. coueite MFEK; coueity P.

That eche wy3t beo in wil · his wit the to schewe.
So schalt thou come to Clergye · that con mony thinges ;
Sei him this signe · that I sette him to scole,   124
And that I grette wel his wyf · for I wrot hire a bulle,
And sette hire to Sapience · and to hire psauter i-gloset.
  Lo! logyk I lered hire · and al the lawe after,
And alle musons in musyk · I made hire to knowe.   128
Plato the poyete · I put him furste to boke,
Aristotle and other mo · to arguen I tau3te ;
Gramer for gurles · I gon furste to write,
And beot hem with a baleys · but 3if thei wolde lernen.   132

That eche wi3te be in wille · his witte the to shewe,
And thus shaltow come to Clergye · that can many thinges.

  Saye hym this signe · I sette hym to scole,   168
And that I grete wel his wyf · for I wrote hir many bokes,
And sette hir to Sapience · and to the sauter glose.
  Logyke I lerned hir · and many other lawes,
And alle the musouns in musike · I made hir to knowe.   172
Plato the poete · I put hym fyrste to boke,
Aristotle and other moo · to argue I tau3te.
Grammer for gerles · I garte first wryte,
And bette hem with a baleis · but if thei wolde lerne.   176
Of alkinnes craftes · I contreued toles,
Of carpentrie, of kerueres · and compassed masouns,
And lerned hem leuel and lyne · though I loke dymme.
  Ac Theologie hath tened me · ten score tymes,   180
The more I muse there-inne · the mistier it semeth,
And the depper I deuyne · the derker me it thinketh ;
It is no science for sothe · forto sotyle inne ;
A ful lethy thinge it were · 3if that loue nere.   184
Ac for it let best by Loue · I loue it the bettre ;
For there that Loue is leder · ne lacked neuere grace.
Loke thow loue lelly · 3if the lyketh Dowel ;

A. 122. eche wy3t UTH₂; eueri mon V.   124. signe TUH₂; tokene V.
131. gurles H₂TU ; children V ; *see* Pass. x. 155. 134. kende TH₂; tau3te V.
137. muse TUH₂; studie V. mistlokere TU ; derkore V.   138. derkore
(*last note*); derkere T ; mistiloker V. 141. lat T ; V *om*. B. 169. grete

A. PASSUS XI. 133-143. C. PASSUS XII. 111-135.   299

Of alle maner craftus · I con counterfeten heor tooles,
Of carpunters and keruers; · I kende furst masouns,
And lered hem liuel and lyne · thau3 I loke dimme.
Bote Teologye hath teoned me · ten score tymes;   136
For the more I muse theron · the mistiloker hit semeth,
And the deppore I diuinede · the derkore me thou3te.
Hit is no science forsothe · to sotilen ther-inne,
Neore the loue that lyhth therinne · a lewed thing hit weore.   140
Bote for hit lat best bi Loue · I leeue hit the betere;
For that Loue is the lord · that lakkede neuer grace;
Leef wel ther-vppon · 3if thou thenke Dowel;

Bothe wommen and wyn · wratthe, yre, and slewthe,
Yf thow hem vse other haunte · haue god my treuthe !   112
To Clergie shult thow neuere come · ne knowe what ys Dowel.
Ac yf thou happe,' quath hue · 'that thow hitte on Clergie,
And hast vnderstondy̆ng · what he wolde mene,
Sey to hym thy-self · ouer-see my bokes,   116
And seye ich grette wel hus wif · ich wrot hure a byble,
And sette hure to Sapience · and to the sauter glosed.
Logyk ich lerede hure · and al the lawe after,
Alle the musons in musyk · ich made hure to knowe.   120
Plato the poete · ich putte hym ferst to booke,
Aristotle and othere · to arguen ich tauhte.
Grammere for gurles · ich gart furst wryte,
And bet hem with a baleyse · bote yf thei wolde lerne.   124
Of alle kyne craftes · ich contreeuede here tooles,
Of carpentrie, of kerueres · and contreeuede the compas,
And cast out by squire · bothe lyne and leuell.
Thus thorw my lore beth men ylered · thauh ich loke dymme.
Ac Theologie hath teened me · ten score tymes,   129
The more ich muse ther-on · the mystiloker hit semeth,
And the deppere ich deuyne · the derker me thynketh hit.
Hit is no science sothliche · bote a sothfast by-leyue;   132
Ac for hit lereth men to louye · ich by-leyue ther-on the bettere.
For Loue is a lykynge thyng · and loth for to greue;
Lerne for to louye · yf the lyke Dowel,

WCB; grette LRO. 172. muke (*for* musike) L. 174. Arestotle L.
C. 112. hem FS; hit PEIKG. 118. glosede P. 131. deerker P.
132. by-lyue P; *see* l. 133. 135. dowel IMFSK; to dowel PE; cf. l. 142.

For Dobet and Dobest · beoth drawen of Loue scole.   144
In other science hit seith · seo hit in Catoun,
    Qui simulat verbis, nec corde est fidus amicus,
    Tu quoque fac simile, sic ars deluditur arte.
But Theologie techeth not so · hose taketh kepe,
He kenneth us the contrarie · aȝeyn Catons wordes,
And biddeth vs ben as bretheren · and blessen vr enemys,   148
And louen hem that lyȝen on vs · lellyche at heor neode,
And do good aȝeyn vuel ; · god him-self hoteth,

For Dobet and Dobest · ben of Loues kynne.   188
In other science it seyth · I seigh it in Catoun,
    Qui simulat verbis, nec corde est fidus amicus,
    Tu quoque fac simile, sic ars deluditur arte.
Who-so gloseth as gylours don · go me to the same,   192
And so shaltow false folke · and faythlees bigyle,
This is Catounes kennyng · to clerkes that he lereth.
Ac Theologye techeth nouȝt so · who-so taketh ȝeme,
He kenneth vs the contrarye · aȝein Catones wordes ;   196
For he bit vs be as bretheren · and bidde for owre enemys,
And louen hem that lyen on vs · and lene hem whan hem nedeth,
And do good aȝeines yuel · god hym-self it hoteth,
    Dum tempus habemus, operemur bonum ad omnes, maxime
        autem ad domesticos fidei.
Poule preched the peple · that parfitnesse loued,   200
To do good for goddes loue · and gyuen men that asked,
And nameliche to suche · that sueth owre bileue.
And alle that lakketh vs or lyeth vs · owre lorde techeth vs to louye,
And nouȝt to greuen hem that greueth vs · god hym-self for-
    badde it,   204
    Michi vindictam, et ego retribuam.
For-thi loke thow louye · as longe as thow durest,
For is no science vnder sonne · so souereyne for the soule.
    Ac astronomye is an harde thynge · and yuel forto knowe,
Geometrie and geomesye · is ginful of speche ;   208
Who-so thenketh werche with tho two · thryueth ful late.
For sorcerye is the souereyne boke · that to the science longeth.
Ȝet ar there fybicches in forceres · of fele mennes makynge,
Experimentz of alkenamye · the poeple to deceyue,   212
If thow thinke to Dowel · dele ther-with neuere.

A. PASSUS XI. 151–159.   C. PASSUS XII. 136.

And seide hit him-self · in ensaumple for the beste,
Necesse est vt veniant scandala.
Bote astronomye is hard thing · and vuel to knowe,   152
Gemetrie and gemensye · is gynful of speche,
That worcheth with theose threo · thriueth he late,
For sorcerye is the souereyn bok · that to that science longith,
3et arn there febicchis of forellis · of mony mennes wittes,   156
Experimentis of alconomye · of Alberdes makynge;
Nigromancye and perimancie · the pouke to rise maketh;
3if thou thenche Dowel · dele with hem neuere.

For of Dobet and of Dobest · here doctor is dere Loue.'   136

A. 144. loue scole U; louis skile T; lore in scole V.   145. *fidus* TU;
fidelis V. *Tu—arte*; VTUH₂ *om., but given in* D.   147. kenniþ T; techeþ
V.   148. vs TUH₂; V *om.*   155, 156. bok—forellis *from* T; *also
in* UH₂; V *om.*   B. 189. seigh CWO; saye L. 190. *similat* L.   *nec* COB;
vel LW.   212. alkenamye WC; alkamye L.

A. PASSUS XI. 160–180.   B. PASSUS X. 214–229.

Alle theose sciences · siker, 1 my-seluen 160
Haue i-founded hem furst · folk to deceyue.
I be-take the to Crist,' quod heo · 'I con teche the no betere.'
I seide, 'graunt merci, madame' · and mekeliche hire grette,
And wente forth on my wei · withouten more lettynge, 164
And fond as heo fore-tolde · and forth gon I wende,
And ar I coome to Clergye · couthe I neuer stunte.
I grette the goode mon · as the gode wyf me tauȝte,
And afterward his wyf · I worschupet hem bothe, 168
And tolde hire the tokenes · that me i-tauȝt were.
Was neuer gome vppon grounde · seththen god made heuene,
Feirore vndurfonge · ne frendloker maad at ese,
Then I my-self sothli · so sone as heo wuste 172
That I was of Wittes hous · and with his wif dam Studie.
Curteisliche Clergye · clupte me and custe,
And asked hou Wit ferde · and eke his wyf Studie.
And I seide sothlyche · 'thei sende me hider 176
To leorne at ȝou Dowel · and Dobet after,
And setthen afturward to seo · sumwhat of Dobest.'
'Hit is a wel feir lyf,' quod heo · 'among the lewed peple,
Actif it is i-hoten · hosebondes hit vsen; 180

[*Here* MS. V *ends; the rest of the Passus is from* T.]

Alle thise sciences I my-self · sotiled and ordeyned,
And founded hem formest · folke to deceyue.
Telle Clergye thise tokenes · and Scripture after, 216
To conseille the kyndely · to knowe what is Dowel.'
I seide, 'graunt mercy, madame' · and mekeliche hir grette,
And went wiȝtlich awey · with-oute more lettynge.
And til I come to Clergye · I couthe neuere stynte. 220
And grette the good man · as Studye me tauȝte,
And afterwardes the wyf · and worshiped hem bothe,
And tolde hem the tokenes · that me tauȝte were. 223
Was neuere gome vppon this grounde · sith god made the worlde,
Fairer vnder-fongen · ne frendeloker at ese,
Than my-self sothly · sone so he wist
That I was of Wittis hous · and with his wyf dame Studye.
I seyde to hem sothely · that sent was I thider, 228
Dowel and Dobet · and Dobest to lerne.

Trewe tilieris on erthe · taillours and souteris,
And alle kyne crafty men · that cunne here foode wynne,
With any trewe trauaille · toille for here foode,
Diken or deluen · Do-wel it hatte. 184
To breke beggeris bred · and bakken hem with clothis,
Counforte the carful · that in castel ben fetterid,
And seken out the seke · and sende hem that hem nedith;
Obedient as bretheren · and sustren to othere; 188
Thus bed the Do-bet · so berith witnesse the sauter;
   Ecce quam bonum et quam iocundum, habitare, fratres, in vnum.
Sike with the sory · singe with the glade,
   Gaudere cum gaudentibus, et flere cum flentibus,
Dredles is Dobet · Dobest wot the sothe!
Sire Dobest hath benefices · so is he best worthi, 192
Be that god in the gospel · grauntith and techith;
   Qui facit et docuerit, magnus vocabitur in regno celorum.
Forthi is Dobest · a bisshopis pere,
Prince ouer godis peple · to prechen or to chaste.
Dobet doth ful wel · and dewid he is also, 196
And hath possessions and pluralites · for pore menis sake.
For mendynauntz at mischiefe · the men were dewid;
And that is riʒtful religioun · none renneris aboute,
Ne no leperis ouer lond · ladies to shryue. 200

Tho wente ich my way · with-oute more lettynge,
And to Clergie ich kam · as clerkes me seide.
And ich grette hym goodliche · and greithliche hym told,
How that Wit and hus wif · wissed me to hym, 140
To kenne and to knowe · kyndeliche Dowel.

A. 180. Actif it TUD; A lyf (*wrongly*) V.   191. *This line is from* MS.
Harl. 3954, fol. 122; TH₂UD *have only*, God wot, þis is dobet.   194. a UD;
TH₂ *om.*   B. 214. sciences WRB; science LO.   221. grette WCRO;
gret L.   C. 139. greiliche (*sic*) P.   141. kenne IMFS; kowe (*for*
knowe) P.

[*Not in* **A**-*text.*]

'It is a comune lyf,' quod Clergye · 'on holycherche to bileue,
With alle the artikles of the feithe · that falleth to be knowe.
And that is to bileue lelly · bothe lered and lewed, 232
On the grete god · that gynnying had neuere,
And on the sothfaste sone · that saued mankynde
Fro the dedly deth · and the deueles power,
Thorwgh the helpe of the holy goste · the whiche goste is of bothe;
Three propre persones · ac nou3t in plurel noumbre, 237
For al is but on god · and eche is god hym-selue;
    Deus pater, deus filius, deus spiritus sanctus;
God the fader, god the sone · god holigoste of bothe,
Maker of mankynde · and of bestes bothe. 240
  Austyn the olde · here-of he made bokes,
And hym-self ordeyned · to sadde vs in bileue.
Who was his autour? · alle the foure euangelistes; 243
And Cryst clepid hym-self so · the ewangelistes bereth witnesse :—
    Ego in patre et pater in me est; et, qui videt me, videt et patrem meum.
Alle the clerkes vnder Cryst · ne couthe this assoille,
But thus it bilongeth to bileue · to lewed that willen Dowel.
For had neuere freke fyne wytte · the feyth to dispute,
Ne man had no merite · my3te it ben yproued: 248
    Fides non habet meritum, vbi humana racio prebet experimentum.
  Thanne is Dobet to suffre · for thi soules helth,
Al that the boke bit · by holycherche techyng;
And that is—"man, bi thi mi3te · for mercies sake,
Loke thow worche it in werke · that thi worde sheweth; 252
Suche as thow semest in sy3te · be in assay y-founde;
    Appare quod es, vel esto quod appares:
And lat no body be · bi thi beryng bygyled,
But be suche in thi soule · as thow semest with-oute."
  Thanne is Dobest to be bolde · to blame the gylty, 256
Sithenes thow seest thi-self · as in soule clene;
Ac blame thow neuere body · and thow be blame-worthy:
    *Si culpare velis · culpabilis esse cauebis,
Dogma tuum sordet · cum te tua culpa remordet.* 260
God in the gospel · grymly repreueth

[*Not in* **A**-*text.*]

'By Cryst,' quath Clergie · 'yf thow coueyte Dowel,
Kep the ten commaundemens · and kep the fro synne;
And by-leyf leelly · how godes sone a-lyghte   144
On the mayde Marie · for mankynnes sake,
And by-cam man of that mayde · with-oute mannes kynde.
And al that holy churche · here-of can the lere,
By-leyf lelly there-on · and look thow do ther-after.   148

Her-of Austin the olde · made bokes and bokes;
Ho was hus autor · and him of god tauhte?
Patriarkes and prophetes · aposteles and angeles
And the holy trinite · to Austyn appeirede,   152
And he ous seide as he seih · and so ich by-leyue,
That he seih the syre and the sone · and seynte spirit togederes,
And alle thre bote on God · and her-of made he bokes,
3e, busiliche bokes; · ho beth hus wytnesses?   156
    Ego in patre et pater in me est; et qui me vidit, patrem
    meum uidit qui in celis est.
Alle the clerkes vnder Crist · ne couthe this asoile;
Bote thus by-longeth to by-leyue · alle that lyketh dowel.
For hadde neuere frek fyn wit · the faith to dispute,
Ne man myghte haue no merit ther-of · myghte hit be preoued;
    Fides non habet meritum, ubi humana racio prebet ex-
    perimentum.
Thus By-leyue and Leaute · and Loue is the thridde,   161
That maketh men to Dowel · Dobet, and Dobest.'

B. 237. propre R; *wrongly om. in* LWCOB.   C. 156. beþ IFKG; but
(*for* buth) P.   *me est* IM; P om. *est.*   160. preouede P.   *prebet ex-*
perimentum EMFS; *possidet dominium* (?) P.

x

[*Not in* **A**-*text.*]

Alle that lakken any lyf · and lakkes han hem-selue:
> *Quid consideras festucam in oculo fratris tui, trabem in oculo tuo non vides?*

Why meuestow thi mode · for a mote in thi brotheres eye,
Sithen a beem in thine owne · ablyndeth thi-selue? 264
> *Eice primo trabem de oculo tuo, etc.*,

Whiche letteth the to loke · lasse other more.
I rede eche a blynde bosarde · do bote to hym-selue;
For abbotes and for prioures · and for alle manere prelates,
As parsones and parisshe-prestes · that preche shulde and teche,
Alle manere men · to amenden by here my3te; 269
This tixte was tolde 3ow · to ben war, ar 3e tau3te,
That 3e were suche as 3e seyde · to salue with othere.
For goddis worde wolde nou3t be loste · for that worcheth euere,
If it auailled nou3t the comune · it my3te auaille 3owseluen. 273
 Ac it semeth now sothly · to the worldes syght,
That goddes worde worcheth nau3te · on lered ne on lewede,
But in suche a manere as Marke · meneth in the gospel, 276
> *Dum cecus ducit cecum, ambo in foueam cadunt.*

Lewed men may likne 3ow thus · that the beem lithe in 3owre eyghen,
And the festu is fallen · for 3owre defaute,
In alle manere men · thourgh mansed prestes.
The bible bereth witnesse · that alle the folke of Israel 280
Byttere abou3te the gultes · of two badde prestes,
Offyn and Fynes; · for her coueytise,
Archa dei myshapped · and Ely brake his nekke.
 For-thi, 3e corectoures, claweth her-on · and corecteth fyrst 3ow-seluen, 284
And thanne mowe 3e saufly seye · as Dauid made the sauter:
> *Existimasti inique quod ero tui similis: arguam te, et statuam contra faciem tuam.*

And thanne shal borel clerkes ben abasched · to blame 3ow or to greue,
And carpen nou3te as thei carpen now · and calle 3ow doumbe houndes, 287
> *Canes non valentes latrare,*

B. 262. *non vides* in R only.

[*Not in* A-*text.*]

[*Not in* C-*text*; *but compare* C. Pass. i. ll. 104–114 (p. 11), *with* B. Pass. x. ll. 280–283.]

Gregory the grete clerke · a good pope in his tyme,
Of religioun the rewele · he reherside in his morals,
And seide it in ensaumple · that thei shulde do the betere:
'Whanne fisshes faile the flood · or the fresshe watir,   204
Thei diȝe for the drouȝte · whanne thei dreiȝe lengen;

And drede to wratthe ȝow in any worde · ȝowre werkemanship
    to lette,   288
And be prestiore at ȝowre prayere · than for a pounde of nobles;
And al for ȝowre holynesse · haue ȝe this in herte.
    Amonges riȝtful religiouse · this reule schulde be holde;
Gregorie the grete clerke · and the goed pope   292
Of religioun the reule · reherseth in his morales,
And seyth it in ensaumple · for thei schulde do there-after,
'Whenne fissches failen the flode · or the fresche water,
Thei deyen for drouthe · whanne thei drie ligge;   296
Riȝt so, quod Gregorie · religioun roileth,
Sterueth and stynketh · and steleth lordes almesses,
That oute of couent and cloystre · coueyten to libbe.'
For if heuene be on this erthe · and ese to any soule,   300
It is in cloistere or in scole · be many skilles I fynde;
For in cloistre cometh no man · to chide ne to fiȝte,
But alle is buxumnesse there and bokes · to rede and to lerne.
    In scole there is scorne · but if a clerke wil lerne,   304
And grete loue and lykynge · for eche of hem loueth other.
Ac now is Religioun a ryder · a rowmer bi stretes,
A leder of louedayes · and a londe-bugger,
A priker on a palfray · fro manere to manere,   308
An heep of houndes at his ers · as he a lorde were.
And but if his knaue knele · that shal his cuppe brynge,
He loureth on hym and axeth hym · who tauȝte hym curteisye?
Litel had lordes to done · to ȝyue londe fram her heires   312
To religious, that haue no reuthe · though it reyne on here auteres!
    In many places ther hij persones ben · be hem-self at ese,
Of the pore haue thei no pite · and that is her charite;
Ac thei leten hem as lordes · her londe lith so brode.   316
    Ac there shal come a kyng · and confesse ȝow religiouses,
And bete ȝow, as the bible telleth · for brekynge of ȝowre reule,

---

A. 209. louedayes H₂; ladies TD; *see* l. 20.   B. 291—303. *These*

A. PASSUS XI. 206–210.

Riȝt so be religioun · it roileth and steruith,
That out of couent and cloistre · coueiten to libben.'
Ac now is Religioun a ridere · and a rennere aboute,   208
A ledere of louedayes · and a lond-biggere,
Poperith on a palfrey · to toune and to toune,

From
C. vi.
147–170
(p. 127).

[Gregorie the grete clerk · gart write in bokes   147
The ruele of alle religious · ryghtful and obedient.
Right as fisshes in flod · whenne hem faileth water,
Deyen for drouthe · whenne thei drye liggen,
Ryght so religion · roteth and sterueth,
That out of couent and cloistre · coueyteth to dwelle.   152
For yf heuene be on thys erthe · other eny eyse for saule,
Hit is in cloistre other in scole · by meny skyles ich fynde.
For in cloistre cometh no man · to chide ne to fighte;
In scole ys loue and lownesse · and lykyng to lerne.   156
Ac meny day, men telleth · bothe monkes and chanouns
Han ride out of a-ray · here ruele vuel yholde,
Lederes of louedaies · and landes purchassed,
And priked a-boute on palfrais · fro places to maners,   160
An hepe of houndes at hus ers · as he a lord were;
And but hus knaue knele · that shal hus coppe holde,
He loketh al louryng · and 'lordein' hym calleth.
Lytel hadde lordes a-do · to ȝeue londe fro here aires   164
To religious, that han no reuthe · thauh hit reyne on here auters.
In places ther thei persons beth · by hem-self at ese,
Of the poure han thei no pyte · that is here pure charite.
Ȝe leten ȝow alle as lordes · ȝoure londe lyth to brode.   168
Ac ȝꝫt shal come a kyng · and confesse ȝow alle,
And bete ȝow, as the byble telleth · for brekyng of ȝoure reule,

---

13 *lines are in* R *only*; *cf.* Text A *and* Text C.   302. no *from* Text C;
R *om.*   312. done RB; doñ L.

310 A. PASSUS XI. 211-215. B. PASSUS X. 319-331.

A bidowe or a baselard · he berith be his side;
Godis flessh and his fet · and hise fyue woundis 212
Arn more in his mynde · than the memorie of his foundours.
This is the lif of this lordis · that lyuen shulde with Do-bet,
And wel-a-wey wers · and I shulde al telle.

And amende monyales · monkes and chanouns,
And putten hem to her penaunce · *ad pristinum statum ire*, 320
And barounes with erles beten hem · thorugh *beatus-virres* techynge,
That here barnes claymen · and blame 30w foule:
    Hij in curribus et hij in equis; ipsi obligati sunt, etc.,
And thanne freres in here freitoure · shal fynden a keye
Of Costantynes coffres · in which is the catel 324
That Gregories god-children · han yuel dispended.
And thanne shal the abbot of Abyndoun · and alle his issu
    for euere
Haue a knokke of a kynge · and incurable the wounde. 327
    That this worth soth, seke 3e · that oft ouer-se the bible :
        Quomodo cessauit exactor, quieuit tributum ; contriuit dominus
            baculum impiorum,
        et virgam dominancium cedencium plaga insanabili, etc.
Ac ar that kynge come · Cayme shal awake. 329
Ac Dowel shal dyngen hym adoune · and destruyen his my3te.
'Thanne is Dowel and Dobet,' quod I · '*dominus* and kni3thode.

From
B. xi.
1-12.

[Thanne Scripture scorned me · and a skile tolde,
And lakked me in Latyne · and li3te by me she sette,
    And seyde, '*multi multa sciunt, et seipsos nesciunt.*'
Tho wepte I for wo · and wratth of her speche,
And in a wynkyng wratth · wex I aslepe. 4
A merueillouse meteles · mette me thanne,
That I was rauisshed ri3t there · and Fortune me fette,
And into the londe of Longynge · allone she me brou3te,
And in a myroure that hi3t Mydlerd · she mad me to biholde. 8
Sitthen she sayde to me · 'here my3tow se wondres,
And knowe that thou coueytest · and come ther-to, par aunter.'
Thenne hadde Fortune folwyng hir · two faire damoyseles,
Concupiscentia-carnis · men called the elder mayde, 12

B. 322. *et* WCROB; L *om.*   326. his WCROB; L *om.*   C. 163.

I wende that kinghed and kni3thed · and caiseris with erlis 216
Wern Do-wel and Do-bet · and Do-best of hem alle;
For I haue sei3e it my-selfe · and siththen red it aftir,
How Crist counseillith the comune · and kenneth hem this tale,
Super cathedram Moisi sederunt principes.
For-thi I wende that tho wyes · wern Do-best of alle!   220

From
C. vi.
171–180
(pp. 127,
129).

And amende 3ow monkes · moniales, and chanons,
And putte 3ow to 3oure penaunce · *ad pristinum statum ire.* 172
And barons and here barnes · blame 3ow and reproue;
 *Hii in curribus et hi in equis: ipsi obligati sunt, et
  ceciderunt.*
Freres in here freitour · shulle fynde that tyme
Bred with-oute beggynge · to lyue by euere after,
And Constantyn shal be here cook · and couerer of here churche.
For the abbot of Engelonde · and the abbesse hys nece   177
Shullen haue a knok on here crounes · and in-curable the wounde;
 *Contriuit dominus baculum impiorum, uirgam dominancium
  plaga in-sanabili.*
Ac er that kyng come · as cronycles me tolde,
Clerkus and holychurche · shal be clothed newe.]

Thanne Scripture scorned me · and many skyles shewede,
And contynaunce made to Clergie · to congie me, hit semede,
And lakkede me in Latyn · and lyght by me sette,   165
 And seide, '*multi multa sapiunt, et seipsos nesciunt.*'
Tho wepte ich for wo · and wrathede of here wordes,
And in a wynkynge ich worth · and wonderliche ich mette.
For ich was rauesched ryght ther; · Fortune me fette,   168
In-to the londe of longynge · and loue hue me brouhte,
And in a myrour, hihte Myddelerd · hue made me to loke,
And sutthe seide to me · 'her myghte thou see wondres,   171
And knowe that thow coueitest · and come ther-to, paraunter.'
 Thenne hadde Fortune folwynge hure · two faire maidenes,
Concupiscentia-carnis · me calde the eldere mayde,

þanne MF; þenne ISKG; The PE.   166. here I; hus P.   167. worth
MS; warth Pl.   an (*for* and) P.   mete P.   168. raueshede P.

312   A. PASSUS XI. 221, 222.   B. PASSUS X. 332-335.

I nile not scorne,' quod Scripture · 'but scryueyns liȝe;
Kinghod and kniȝthod · for auȝt I can aspie,   222

---

*From
B. xi.
13–35.*

And Couetyse-of-eyes · ycalled was that other;
Pryde-of-parfyte-lyuynge · pursued hem bothe,
And badde me, for my contenaunce · acounte Clergye liȝte.
Concupiscentia-carnis · colled me aboute the nekke,   16
And seyde, 'thou art ȝonge and ȝepe · and hast ȝeres ynowe
Forto lyue longe · and ladyes to louye.
And in this myroure thou myȝte se · myrthes ful manye,
That leden the wil to lykynge · al thi lyf-tyme.'   20
The secounde seide the same · 'I shal suwe thi wille;
Til thow be a lorde and haue londe · leten the I nelle,
That I ne shal folwe thi felawship · if Fortune it lyke.'
'He shal fynde me his frende' · quod Fortune therafter;   24
'The freke that folwed my wille · failled neuer blisse.'
Thanne was there one that hiȝte Elde · that heuy was of chere;
'Man,' quod he, 'if I mete with the · bi Marie of heuene,
Thou shalt fynde Fortune the faille · at thi moste nede,   28
And *Concupiscentia-carnis* · clene the forsake!
Bitterliche shaltow banne thanne · bothe dayes and niȝtes
Coueytise-of-eyghe · that euer thow hir knewe,
And Pryde-of-parfyt-lyuynge · to moche peril the brynge.'   32
'Ȝee, recche the neuere,' quod Recchelesnesse · stode forth in
    ragged clothes,
'Folwe forth that Fortune wole · thow hast wel fer til elde;
A man may stoupe tymes ynow · whan he shal tyne the croune!']

'I nel nouȝt scorne,' quod Scripture · 'but-if scryueynes lye;
Kynghod ne knyȝthod · by nauȝt I can awayte,   333
Helpeth nouȝt to heueneward · one heres ende,
Ne ricchesse riȝt nouȝt · ne reaute of lordes.

C. 176. me IMFSK; in PE.   179. ert P.   181. myȝt MESIK; myst P.
183. sewe MF; sywe P.   186. Hue (*for* He) P.   188. euy (*for* heuy) P.

Helpith nou3t to heuene · at one 3eris ende,
Ne richesse ne rentis · ne realte of lordis.   224

And Couetyse-of-eyen · ycald was that othere.
And Pruyde-of-parfit-lyuynge · pursewede me faste,   176
And bad me for my contynence · counte Clergies lore lyght.
Concupiscentia-carnis · comfortyde me in thys wyse,
And seide, 'thow art 3ong and 3ep · and hast 3eris ynowe
For to lyue longe · and ladyes to louye.   180
And in this mirour thow my3t see · murthes ful menye,
That lede the wol to lykynge · al thy lyf-tyme.'
The secounde mayde seide · 'ich shal sewe thi wil;
Til thow be a lord of londe · leten the ich nelle,   184
That ich ne shal folwie thy felaushupe · yf Fortune lyke.'
'He shal fynde me hus frende' · quath Fortune her-after;
'That man that me lyketh helpe · myghte nat myshappe.'
Thenne was ther on hiht Elde · that heuy was of chere;   188
'Man,' quath Elde, 'mete ich with the · by Marie of heuene!
Thou shalt fynde Fortune · faile at thy moste neede,
And *Concupiscentia-carnis* · clene the for-sake!
Byterliche shalt thow banne thenne · bothe dayes and nyghtes
Couetyse-of-eyen · that euere thow hure knewe,   193
And Pruyde-of-parfit-lyuynge · to muche peril the brynge.'
'3e, recche the neuere,' quath Rechelesnesse · stod forth in
    raggede clothes,
'Folwe forth that Fortune wol · thou hast ful fer to elde;   196
A man may stoupe tyme ynowe · when he shal tyne the corone!'
Syre Wanhope was sibbe to hym · as som men me tolde,
For Rechelesnesse in hus rybaudrie · ryht thus he seide,
'Go ich to helle, go ich to heuene · ich shal nouht go myn one!
Were hit al soth that 3e seyen · thou Scripture and Clergie,
Ich leyue neuere that lorde ne ladie · that lyueth her on erthe
Sholde sitte in godes sete · ne see god in hus blysse;   203
    *Ita impossibile est diuiti intrare in regnum celorum, sicut
    camelus foramen acus.*

---

189. mette P.   192. dayes IM; a daye PK.   195. recche IK; reccheþ PE
(*wrongly*).   196. feer P.   199. rybaurdrie P.   200. go (*before* myn)
IMFSGK; PE *om.*   202. eerthe P.

Poul prouith it is vnpossible · riche men in heuene,
Ac pore men in pacience · and penaunce togidere
Hauen eritage in heuene · ac riche men non.'—
'*Contra*,' quod I, 'be Crist! · that can I the wisse, 228
And prouen it be the pistil · that Petir is nempnid ;
  Qui crediderit et baptizatus fuerit, saluus erit.'
'That is *in extremis*,' quod Scripture · 'as Sarisines and Iewis
Mowe be sauid so · and so is oure beleue ;
That an vncristene in that cas · may cristene an hethene, 232
And for his lele beleue · whanne he his lif tyneth,
Haue eritage in heuene · as an hei3 Cristene.

Poule preueth it inpossible · riche men to haue heuene, 336
Salamon seith also · that syluer is worst to louye :
  Nichil iniquius quam amare peccuniam.
And Caton kenneth vs to coueiten it · nau3t but as nede techeth,
Dilige denarium, set parce dilige formam.
And patriarkes and prophetes · and poetes bothe 340
Wryten to wissen vs · to wilne no ricchesse,
And preyseden pouerte with pacience ; · the apostles bereth witnesse,
That thei han heritage in heuene · and bi trewe ri3te,
There riche men no ri3te may clayme · but of reuthe and grace.'
'*Contra*,' quod I, 'bi Cryste · that can I repreue, 345
And preue it bi Peter · and bi Poule bothe,
That is baptized beth sauf · be he riche or pore.'
'That is *in extremis*,' quod Scripture · 'amonges Saracenes
  and Iewes ; 348
Thei mowen be saued so · and that is owre byleue,
That an vncristene in that cas · may crysten an hethen,
And for his lele byleue · whan he the lyf tyneth,
Haue the heritage of heuene · as any man Crystene. 352
Ac Crysten men with-oute more · may nou3t come to heuene,
For that Cryst for Cristen men deyde · and confermed the lawe,
That who-so wolde and wylneth · with Cryste to aryse,
  Si cum Christo surrexistis, etc.,
He shulde louye and leue · and the lawe fulfille. 356
That is—"loue thi lorde god · leuest aboue alle,
And after, alle Crystene creatures · in comune, eche man other ; "
And thus bilongeth to louye · that leueth to be saued.
And but we do thus in dede · ar the daye of dome, 360

A. PASSUS XI. 235-242.

Ac Cristene men, god wot · comith not so to heuene;
For Cristene han a degre · and is the comune speche,   236
  Dilige deum, etc., et proximum tuum sicut teipsum.
Godis word witnessith we shuln ȝiue · and dele oure enemys,
And alle men that arn nedy · as pore men and suche,
  *Dum tempus est, operemur bonum ad omnes, maxime autem
    ad domesticos fidei.*
Alle kynne creatures · that to Crist beleuith
We be holde heiȝly · to herie and honoure,   240
And ȝiuen hem of oure good · as good as oure seluen,
And souereynliche to suche · that sewen oure beleue;

[*Not in* C-*text.*]

A. 232. That oon U; That arn TH₂; *read* That an.   238. as H₂U;
and T; D *om.*   B. 336. to WOB; LRC *om.*

A. PASSUS XI. 243-252.   B. PASSUS X. 361-386.

That is, iche Cristene man · be kynde to other,
And sithen hem to helpe · in hope hem to amende.   244
To harme hem ne slen hem · god hiȝte vs neuere;
For he seith it hym-selfe · in his ten hestis,
Non mecaberis, ne sle nouȝt · is the kynde Englissh,
    For, *Michi vindictam, et ego retribuam;*
I shal punisshen in purcatory · or in the put of helle   248
Eche man for his misdede · but mercy it make.'
'Ȝet am I neuere the ner · for nouȝt I haue walkid
To wyte what is Do-wel · witterly in herte;
For how I werche in this world · wrong other ellis,   252

It shal bisitten vs ful soure · the siluer that we kepen,
And owre bakkes that moth-eten be · and sen beggers go naked,
Or delyte in wyn and wylde foule · and wote any in defaute.
    For euery Cristene creature · shulde be kynde til other,   364
And sithen hethen to helpe · in hope of amendement.
God hoteth bothe heigh and lowe · that no man hurte other,
And seith, "slee nouȝt that semblable is · to myne owen liknesse,
But if I sende the sum tokne"; · and seith, *non mecaberis*,   368
Is, slee nouȝt, but suffre · and al for the beste.
    For, *Michi vindictam, et ego retribuam.*
"For I shal punysshen hem in purgatorie · or in the putte of helle,
Vche man for his mysdedes · but mercy it lette."'
    'This is a longe lessoun,' quod I · 'and litel am I the wyser;
Where Dowel is, or Dobet · derkelich ȝe shewen;   373
Many tales ȝe tellen · that Theologye lerneth;
And that I man made was · and my name yentred
In the legende of lyf · longe er I were,   376
Or elles vnwriten for somme wikkednesse · as holywrit wytnesseth,
    Nemo ascendit ad celum, nisi qui de celo descendit.
I leue it wel,' quod I, 'bi owre lorde · and on no letterure bettere.
For Salamon the sage · that Sapience tauȝte,
God gaf hym grace of witte · and alle his godes after,   380
To reule the reume · and riche to make;
He demed wel and wysely · as holy writte telleth.
Aristotle and he · who wissed men bettere?
Maistres that of goddis mercy · techen men and prechen,   384
Of here wordes thei wissen vs · for wisest as in here tyme,
And al holicherche · holdeth hem bothe ydampned!

A. PASSUS XI. 253–263.   C. PASSUS XII. 204–220.

I was markid, withoute mercy · and myn name entrid
In the legende of lif · longe er I were;
Or ellis vndir-writen for wykkid · as witnessith the gospel,
    Nemo ascendet ad celum nisi qui de celo descendit.
And I leue on oure lord · and on no lettrure betere;   256
For Salamon the sage · that Sapience made,
God ȝaf hym grace · and richesse to-gidere
For to reule his reaum · riȝt at his wille;
Dede he not wel and wisly · as holy chirche techith,   260
Bothe in werke and in woord · in world in his tyme?
Aristotle and he · who wrouȝte betere?
And al holy chirche · holden hem in helle!

For Clergie seith that he seih · in the seynt euangelie,   204
That ich man maked was · and my name y-entred
In the legende of lif · longe er ich were.
Predestinat thei prechen · prechours that this shewen,
Or prechen inparfit · ypult out of grace,   208
Vnwryten for som wikkednesse · as holy writ sheweth,
    Nemo ascendit in celum nisi qui de celo descendit.
Ich leyue hit wel, by oure lorde · and no lettrure bettere.
For Salomon the sage · that Sapience made,
God gaf hym grace of wit · and of good after,   212
Neuere to man so muche · that man can of telle,
To rewele alle reames · and ryche to make,
And deme wel and wislyche · wommen bereth witnesse;
    Non michi nec tibi, sed diuidatur.
Aristotle and he · hij tauhten men bothe;   216
Maisters that techen men · of godes muchel mercy
Witnessen that here wordes · and here werkes bothe
Weren wonder goode · and wise in here tyme,
And holychurche, as ich huyre · haldeth bothe in helle!   220

A. 247. *Non* UD; *ne* TH₂.   *mecaberis* (so in all MSS.)   252. wrong
UD; TH₂ *om.*   258. hym UD; hem TH₂.   **B.** 361. It WCROB; I L
(*line marked.*)   369. For—*retribuam* in R *only; cf.* Text A; *and see* l. 204.
377. *decendit* L.   381. *This line is in* R only.   **C.** 205. yentrede P.
207. Prodestinat P.   218. Whitnessen P.

And was there neuere in this world · to wysere of werkis;
For alle cunnynge clerkis · siththe Crist ȝede on erthe   265
Taken ensaumples of here sawis · in sarmonis that thei maken,
And be here werkis and here wordis · wissen vs to Dowel;

And if I shulde worke bi here werkes · to wynne me heuene,
That for her werkes and witte · now wonyeth in pyne,   388
Thanne wrouȝte I vnwysely · what-so euere ȝe preche.

Ac of fele witty in feith · litel ferly I haue,
Though her goste be vngraciouse · god for to plese.
For many men on this molde · more sette here hertis   392
In good than in god · for-thi hem grace failleth,
At here moste myschief · whan thei shal lyf lete.
As Salamon dede, and such other · that shewed gret wittes;
Ac her werkes, as holy wrytte seyth · was euere the contrarye.
For-thi wyse witted men · and wel ylettred clerkes,   397
As thei seyen hem-self · selden done ther-after,
   Super cathedram Moysy, etc.,
Ac I wene it worth of many · as was in Noes tyme,
Tho he shope that shippe · of shides and bordes;   400
Was neuere wriȝte saued that wrouȝt ther-on · ne other werkman elles,
But briddes and bestes · and the blissed Noe,
And his wyf with his sones · and also here wyues;
Of wriȝtes that it wrouȝte · was none of hem ysaued.   404
God leue it fare nouȝt so bi folke · that the feith techen
Of holicherche, that herberwe is · and goddes hous to saue,
And shelden vs fram shame ther-inne · as Noes shippe did bestes;
And men that maden it · amydde the flode adreynten.   408
The *culorum* of this clause · curatoures is to mene,
That ben carpenteres holykirke to make · for Crystes owne bestes,
   Homines et iumenta saluabıs, domine, etc.

B. 398. *cathedra* LWCB.   406. herberwe WCOB; heberwe L.   C. 232.
meste P.   236. Seilde P.   237. vntriwe P.   *sederunt*; in F only.   238.
Ac IMFKGS; And PE.   239. schip IMFSE; shup P.   240. writ P;

A. PASSUS XI. 268–270.   C. PASSUS XII. 221–250.   319

And ȝif I shal werke be here werkis · to wynne me heuene,   268
And for here werkis and for here wyt · wende to pyne,
Thanne wrouȝte I vnwisly · with alle the wyt that I lere!

Yf we sholden worchen after here workes · to wynnen ous heuene,
That for hure werkes and witt · wonyeth now in peyne,   222
Then wroghte we vnwisliche · for al ȝoure wyse techynge.
Ac ich countresegge the nat, Cleregie · ne thy connynge, Scripture;
That ho so doth by ȝoure doctrine · doth wel, ich leyue.   225
Ac me were leuere, by oure lorde · a lippe of godes grace
Than al the kynde witt that ȝe can bothe · and connynge of
    ȝoure bokes.
For of fele witty, in faith · litel ferly ich haue,   228
Thauh here gost be vngraciouse · god for to plese.
For meny men of this molde · setten more here herte
In worldliche good than in god · for-thy grace hem failleth.
At here moste meschef · mercy were the beste ;   232
And mercy of mercy · needes mot aryse,
As holy writ wittnesseth · godes word in the godspelle ;
    Eadem mensura qua mensi fueritis, remecietur uobis.
Ryght wel ywittede men · and wel lettred clerkes,
Selde arn thei seien · so lyue as thei lere ;   236
Witnesse on godes wordes · that was neuere vntrewe :
    Super cathedram Moysi sederunt, etc.
Ac ich wene hit worth of menye · as was in Noes tyme,
Tho that he shop the schip · of shides and of bordes,
Was neuere wright that ther-on wrouhte · ne workman y-saued,
Bote briddes and bestes · and the blessed Noe,   241
And hus wif with hus sones · and hus sones wyues ;
Of wrightes that hit wroughten · was non ysaued.
God leyue hit fare not so by folke · that the faith techen   244
Of holychurche, that sholde kepe · alle Cristine saules ;
For *archa Noe*, nymeth hede · ys no more to mene
Bote holychurche, herbergh · to alle that ben blessede.
The *culorum* of this clause · curatores ys to mene,   248
That ben carpenters vnder Criste · holy kirke to make
For lewede folke, godes foules · and hus free bestes ;
    Homines et iumenta saluabis, domine, etc.

see l. 243.   241. and the IMFSKG; þat the PE.   243. Of IMFSKG; And
PE.   246. nemeþ P.   248. cause P.   249. kirke I; churche P.

A Goode Friday, I fynde · a feloun was sauid
That hadde lyued al his lyf · with lesinges and theftis;   272
And for he kneu3 on the crois · and to Crist shref hym,
Sonnere hadde he saluacion · thanne seint Ion the baptist,
Ar Adam or Ysaye · or any of the prophetis,
That hadde leyn with Lucifer · manye longe 3eris;   276
A robbere hadde remission · rathere thanne thei alle,

At domes-day the diluuye worth · of deth and fyr at ones;
For-thi I conseil 3ow clerkes · of holy cherche the wri3tes,   412
Wercheth 3e werkes as 3e seen i-write · lest 3e worth nau3t ther-inne.
  On Gode Fridaye I fynde · a feloun was ysaued,
That had lyued al his lyf · with lesynges and with thefte;
And for he biknewe on the crosse · and to Cryste schrof hym,
He was sonnere saued · than seynt Iohan the baptiste,   417
And or Adam or Ysaye · or eny of the prophetes,
That hadde yleine with Lucyfer · many longe 3eres.
A robbere was yraunceouned · rather than thei alle,   420
With-outen any penaunce of purgatorie · to perpetuel blisse.
  Thanne Marye Magdaleyne · what womman dede worse?
Or who worse than Dauid · that Vries deth conspired?
Or Poule the apostle · that no pitee hadde,   424
Moche crystene kynde · to kylle to deth?
And now ben thise as souereynes · wyth seyntes in heuene,
Tho that wrou3te wikkedlokest · in worlde tho thei were.
And tho that wisely wordeden · and wryten many bokes   428
Of witte and of wisdome · with dampned soules wonye.
That Salamon seith, I trowe be soth · and certeyne of vs alle,
    Sunt iusti atque sapientes; et opera eorum in manu dei
      sunt, etc.;
There aren witty and wel-libbynge · ac her werkes ben yhudde
In the hondes of almi3ty god · and he wote the sothe   432
Wher for loue a man worth allowed there · and his lele werkes,
Or elles for his yuel wille · and enuye of herte,
And be allowed as he lyued so; · for bi lyther, men knoweth
      the gode;   435

A. 283. none U; non DH₂; now T.   285, 286. *These two lines are corruptly given in all the MSS. I correct them.*   B. 411, 413. *These lines are in R only. Cf.* C-Text.   diluuye, *from* MS. Camb. Univ. Lib. Ff. 5. 35; deluye R (*wrongly*).   fyr, *from* MS. Ff.; R *has* feer.   417. þe WCROB;

Withoute penaunce of purcatorie · to haue paradis for euere.
Thanne Marie the Maudeleyn · who miȝte do wers?
Or who dede wers thanne Dauid · that Vrie destroyede?   280
Or Poule the apostil · that no pite ne hadde,
Cristene kynde · to kille to dethe?
And arn none for sothe · souereynes in heuene,
As thise that wrouȝte wykkidly · in world whanne thei were.
And ȝet I forget ferthere · of fyue wyttis techinge,   285

At domes day a dyluuye worth · of deth and fuyr at ones;   251
Worcheth, ȝe wryghtes of holichurche · as holy writ techeth,
Lest ȝe be loste as the laborers were · that labored vnder Noe.
   A Goode Fryday, ich fynde · a felon was ysaued,
That vnlawefulliche hadde ylyued · al hus lyf-tyme;   255
And for he by-knew on the crois · and to Crist schrof hym,
He was sonnere ysaued · than seynt Iohan the Baptist,
And er Adam other Ysaie · other eny of the prophetes,
That hadden leye with Lucyfer · meny longe ȝeres.
A robber was y-raunsoned · rather than thei alle;   260
With-oute penaunce other passion · other eny other peyne
He passede forth pacientliche · to perpetuel blisse.
   Al-so Marie Magdelene · ho myghte do worsse
As in lykynge of lecherye · no lyf denyede?   264
And Dauid the douhty · that deuynede how Vrye
Mighte slilokeste be slayn · and sente hym to werre
Leelliche as by hus lok · with a lettere of gyle;   267
Paul the apostel, that no pite hadde · Cristene peuple to culle;
Now beeth these seintes, as men seyen · and souereynes in heuene,
Tho that worst wroghten · while thei weren here.
By that that Salamon seith · hit semeth that no wyght
Wot ho is worthi · for wele other for wicke,   272
Whether he is worthi to wele · other to wickede pyne:
   Sunt iusti atque sapientes, et opera eorum in manu dei sunt.
   Thus ich, Rechelesnesse, haue rad · registres and bokes,
And fond ich neuere, in faith · for to telle treuthe,

L *om.*   426. now WCOB; LR *om.*   430. *Sunt* R; *siue* LCOW.
C. 251. of fuyr P; *but* IMSKG *om.* of.   254. ysauede P.   256. schrof
EMIFS; schroue P.   261. With-outhe P.   264. denoyede P.   268.
crustene P.   269. þees P.   275. of treuthe P; *but* MFSEK *om.* of.

Y

That Clergie of Cristis mouth · comendit was euer;
For he seide it hym-selfe · to summe of his disciplis,
  Cum steteritis ante presides, nolite cogitare quid loquamini ;
And is as muche to mene · to men that ben lewid,   288
"Whether ʒe ben aposid of princes · or of prestis of the lawe,
For to answere hem · haue ʒe no doute;
For I shal graunte ʒow grace · of god that ʒe seruen,
The help of the holy gost · to answere hem at wille."   292
 The douʒtiest doctour · or dyuynour of the trinite,

And wherby wote men whiche is whyte · if alle thinge blake were,
And who were a gode man · but if there were some shrewe?
For-thi lyue we forth with lither men · I leue fewe ben gode.
For *qant* OPORTET *vyent en place · yl ny ad que* PATI,
And he that may al amende · haue mercy on vs alle!   440
For sothest worde that euere god seyde · was tho he seyde,
 nemo bonus.
 Clergye tho of Crystes mouth · commended was it litel,
For he seyde to seynt Peter · and to suche as he loued,
  Dum steteritis ante reges et presides, etc.;
"Though ʒe come bifor kynges · and clerkes of the lawe,   444
Beth nouʒte abasched · for I shal be in ʒoure mouthes,
And ʒyue ʒow witte at wille · and kunnynge to conclude
Hem alle that aʒeines ʒow · of Crystenedome disputen."
 Dauyd maketh mencioun · he spake amonges kynges,   448
And miʒte no kynge ouercome hym · as bi kunnyng of speche.
But witte ne wisdome · wan neuere the maystrye,
Whan man was at myschief · with-oute the more grace.
 The doughtiest doctour · and deuynoure of the trinitee,   452
Was Augustyn the olde · and heighest of the foure,
Sayde thus in a sarmoun · I seigh it writen ones,
  Ecce ipsi idioti rapiunt celum, vbi nos sapientes in inferno
   mergimur :
And is to mene to Englisshe men · more ne lasse,
"Aren none rather yrauysshed · fro the riʒte byleue   456
Than ar this cunnynge clerkes · that conne many bokes;
Ne none sonner saued · ne sadder of bileue,
Than plowmen and pastoures · and pore comune laboreres."

  A. 287. *Cum* U; *Dum* TH₂D; *quid loquamini* in U only.

A. PASSUS XI. 294-300. C. PASSUS XII. 276-293.

That Austyn the olde · and hi3este of the foure,
Seide this for a sarmoun · (so me god helpe!)
  Ecce ipsi ydioti rapiunt celum, vbi nos sapientes in infer-
    num mergemur;
And is to mene in oure mouth · more ne lesse,   296
"Arn none rathere yrauisshid · fro the ri3te beleue
Thanne arn thise grete clerkis · that conne many bokis;
Ne none sonnere ysauid · ne saddere of consience,
Thanne pore peple as plou3men · and pastours of bestis." 300

That Clergie of Cristes mouth · comended was euere.   276
For Crist seide to seintes · and to suche as he louede,
  Dum steteritis ante reges et presides, nolite cogitare quomodo
    aut quid loquamini, et cetera:
"Thauh 3e come by-fore kynges · and clerkes of the lawe,
Beeth nat a-ferd of that folke · for ich shal 3eue 3ow tonge,
Connynge and clergie · to conclude hem alle."   280
  Dauid maketh mencion · he spak among kynges,
And myghte no kynge hym ouer-come · as in connynge speche.
Sothly,' seide Rechelesnesse · 'ich see by menye euydences,
That nother wit ne wyghtnesse · wan neuere the maistrie 284
With-oute the grete gyfte of god · with hus grace and fortune.
  For he that most seih and seide · of the sothfast trinite
Was Austyn the olde · that euere man wiste.   287
He saide thus in hus sarmon · for ensample of grete clerkes,
  Ecce ipsi idioti rapiunt celum, vbi nos sapientes in inferno
    mergimur.
This is to mene no more · to men that ben lewede,
"Aren none rathere raueshed · fro the ryghte by-leyue
Cominliche than clerkes · most knowynge and connynge;
And none sonnere ysaued · ne saddere in the by-leyue 292
Than plouhmen and pastours · and poure comune peuple;'"

C. 277. *nolite, &c.* EFS; P *om.* 283. euedences P. 286. seith (*for* seih)
PEFKG; say S; si M; *see* l. 154.

Souteris and seweris · suche lewide Iottis
Percen with a *pater-noster* · the paleis of heuene,

Souteres and shepherdes · suche lewed Iottes 460
Percen with a *pater-noster* · the paleys of heuene,
And passen purgatorie penaunceles · at her hennes-partynge,
In-to the blisse of paradys · for her pure byleue,
That inparfitly here · knewe and eke lyued. 464
ȝee men knowe clerkes · that han cursed the tyme,
That euere thei couth or knewe more · than *credo in deum patrem ;*
And pryncipaly her *pater-noster* · many a persone hath wisshed.
I se ensamples my-self · and so may many an other, 468
That seruauntes that seruen lordes · selden falle in arrerage,
But tho that kepen the lordes catel · clerkes and reues.
Riȝt so lewed men · and of litel knowynge,
Selden falle thei so foule · and so fer in synne, 472
As clerkes of holikirke · that kepen Crystes tresore,
The which is mannes soule to saue · as god seith in the gospel:
Ite vos in vineam meam.' [1]

B. 460. shepherdes W; sheperdes L.

[[1] *For the continuation of the* B-*text, see* p. 330.]

A. PASSUS XI. 303.   C. PASSUS XII. 294-303.

Withoute penaunce, at here partynge · in-to heiȝe blisse!
  Breuis oracio penetrat celum.'

And lewede leele laborers · and land-tylynge peuple
Persen with a *pater-noster* · paradys other heuene,
Passinge purgatorie penaunceles · for here parfit by-leyue;   296
  Breuis oratio penetrat celum.

Selde falleth the seruant · so deepe in arerages
As doth the reyue other the conterroller · that rekene mot and
  a-counte
Of al that thei hauen had · of hym that is here maister.
Ac these lewede laborers · of lytel vnderstondynge   300
Selde fallen so foule · and so deepe in synne
As clerkes of holy churche · that kepen sholde and saue
Lewede men in good by-leyue · and lene hem at here neede.[1]

C. 297. arrirages P.   299. hadd P.   300. þees P.

[1 *For the continuation of the* C*-text, see* p. 331.]

PASSUS XII.

[*MS. Rawl. Poet.* 137; *fol.* 40. *Various Readings from* U. = Univ. Coll. Oxf., *and* Ing. = Ingilby MS.]

Passus tercius de Dowel.

'CRIST wot,' quod Clergie · 'knowe hit ȝif the lyke,
I haue do my deuer · the Dowel to teche;
And who-so coueyteth don betere · than the boke telleth,
He passeth the apostolis lyf · and put him to aungelys! 4
But I se now, as I seye · as me soth thinkyth,
The were lef to lerne · but loth for to stodie.
Thou woldest konne that I can · and carpen hit after,
Presumptuowsly, parauenture · a-pose so manye, 8
That hit myȝthe turne me to tene · and Theologie bothe.
ȝif I wiste witterly · thou woldest don ther-after,
Al that thou askest · a-soylen I wolde.'
Skornfully tho Scripture · set vp here browes, 12
And on Clergie criede · on Cristes holy name,
That he shewe me hit ne sholde · but ȝif I schriuen were
Of the kynde cardinal wit · and cristned in a font;—
And seyde hit so loude · that shame me thouȝte, 16
'That hit were bothe skathe · and sklaundre to holy cherche,
Sitthe Theologie the trewe · to tellen hit defendeth;
Dauid godes derling · defendyth hit al-so:
  Vidi preuaricantes et tabescebam:

[*Not in* **B***-text.*]

A. 3. coueite to don U; couetyth bene Ing. 4. U *om.* the. peryth (*for* put him) Ing. 5. thinkyth Ing.; thinkytȝ Rawl. 6. leue for to Ing. U *omits this line.* 9. it U; Rawl. Ing. *omit.* me Ing. U; Rawl. me*n* (*wrongly*). 12. tho Ing. U; þe Rawl. set vp here U; schet vp her Ing.; sherte vp his (!) Rawl. 13. cryede U; criyd Ing.; crieþ Rawl. 14. I schriuen Ing.; it stryf U; stryf Rawl. (*corruptly*). 15. U *om.* kynde. Ing. *om.* wit. 16. *For* hit U *has* it; Ing. Rawl. *om.* hit. thouȝthe Rawl. 17. Ing. U *om.* bothe. Ing. *inserts* al *before* holy. 18. that trewe is U; that true is Ing. (*for* the trewe). 19. preuaricantes Ing. U; preuaricationes Rawl. (*corruptly*). (U ends with the word *tabescebam,* which the author evidently construes as if it were *tacebam.*) 22. precheth Rawl.; preched Ing.

A. PASSUS XII. 20–46.

"I saw synful," he seyde · "ther-fore I seyde no-thing,"　20
Til tho wrecches ben in wil · here synne to lete.
And Poul precheth hit often · prestes hit redyn,
　Audiui archana uerba, que non licet homini loqui:
"I am not hardy," quod he · "that I herde with erys,
Telle hit with tounge · to synful wrecches."　24
And god graunted hit neuere · the gospel hit witnesseth,
In the passioun, whan Pilat · a-posed god al-myȝti,
And asked Iesu on hy · that herden hit an hundred,
"*Quid est ueritas?*" quod he · "verilyche tel vs;"　28
God gaf him non answere · but gan his tounge holde.
Riȝt so I rede,' quod she · 'rede thou no ferther;
Of that he wolde wite · wis him no betere.
For he cam not by cause · to lerne to Dowel,　32
But as he seyth, such I am · when he with me carpeth.'
And when Scripture the skolde · hadde this skile y-sheued,
Clergie in-to a caban · crepte anon after,
And drow the dore after him · and bad me go Dowel,　36
Or wycke, ȝif I wolde · whether me lyked!
　Than held I vp myn handes · to Scripture the wise,
To be hure man, ȝif I most · for euere-more after,
With that she wolde me wisse · wher the toun were,　40
That Kynde Wit the confessour · hure cosyn, was inne.
That lady than low · and lauȝte me in here armes,
And sayde, 'my cosyn Kynde Wit · knowen is wel wide,
And his loggyng is with Lyf · that lord is of erthe.　44
And ȝif thou desyre · with him for to a-byde,
I shal the wisse wynlyche · where that he dwelleth.'

[*Not in* C-*text.*]

---

archana uerba Ing.; *archane* Rawl. (*corruptly*).　23. Ing. *inserts* of *before* that.　24. wrecches Rawl.; schrewys Ing.　25. Ing. *om.* 1*st* hit.　26. whan Rawl.; how Ing.　26. -myȝthi Rawl.　27. that Rawl.; ther Ing.　30. red Rawl.; rede Ing. (*twice*).　31. wolde Rawl.; ȝernyth to Ing.　wis Rawl.; wysse Ing.　32. can nouth be cause Ing.　33. als ho Ing.; as he Rawl.; *read* as ho? Iangelyth Ing. (*for* carpeth).　34. thus wyt Rawl.; this scole Ing. (*read* this skile).　35. Ing. *om.* a. crepe Ing.　36. to Ing. (*for* after).　37. wykly Ing. qwethir that me Ing.　41. That Ing.; Rawl. *om.* the Ing.; hure Rawl. (*wrongly*). cosyn Rawl.; kynnysman Ing. 42. lowhe on me Ing. lauȝthe Rawl.; lawht Ing.　43. wel Rawl.; ful Ing. 44. his loggyng is Rawl.; is lyggyng Ing.　45. a-byde Rawl.; dwelle Ing. 46. wynlyche Ing.; Rawl. *om.*

A. PASSUS XII. 47-72.

And thanne I kneled on my knes · and kyste her wel sone,
And thanked hure a thousand sythes · with throbbant herte. 48
  She called [to ken] me · a clerioun that hy3te
Omnia-probate · a pore thing with-alle,
'Thou shalt wende with Wil,' quod she · 'whiles that him lykyth,
Til 3e come to the burghe · *quod-bonum-est-tenete*. 52
Ken him to my cosenes hous · that Kinde Wit hy3te,
Sey I sente him this segge · and that he shewe hym Dowel.'
  Thus we lau3te oure leue · lowtyng at onys,
And wente forth on my way · with *omnia-probate*, 56
And ere I cam to the court · *quod-bonum-est-tenete*,
Many ferlys me by-fel · in a fewe 3eris.
The fyrste ferly I fond · a-fyngrid me made;
As I 3ede thurgh 3outhe · a-3en prime dayes, 60
I stode stille in a stodie · and stared a-bowte;
'Al hayl,' quod on tho, and I answered 'welcome · and with
    whom be 3e?'
'I am dwellyng with Deth · and Hunger I hatte,
To Lyf in his lordshepe · longyth my weye, 64
To kyllyn him 3if I can · theigh Kynde Wit helpe;
I shal felle that freke · in a fewe dayes!'
'I wolde folwe the fayn,' quod I · 'but feyntise me henteth,
Me folweth such a feyntise · I may no ferther walke.' 68
'Go we forth,' quod the gome · 'I haue a gret boyste
At my bak, of broke bred · thi bely for to fylle;
A bagge ful, of a beggere · I bou3te hit at onys.'
Than maunged I with him · vp to the fulle, 72

[*Not in* B-*text.*]

A. 47. wel Rawl.; fete Ing. **48.** A thowsyng (*sic*) tymes I thankyd hire with throbbyng hert Ing. **49.** *I insert* to ken (*which both* MSS. *omit*) *to complete the sense and metre*. hy3t Rawl.; hite Ing. **51.** whiles that Rawl.; qwyl Ing. **52.** bowhe (*for* borowhe) Ing. **53.** hy3th Rawl.; hite Ing. **55.** lau3þe Rawl. (*read* lau3te); Ing. *om. this line.* **56.** And Rawl.; I Ing. on Rawl.; in Ing. **57.** And Rawl.; Ing. *om.* court Rawl.; cuntreyys Ing. **59.** a-fyngrid Rawl.; an hunger-it Ing. **60.** As I 3ede Rawl.; And I than Ing. 3owthe Ing.; *miswritten* 3ou · þe Rawl. **62.** and I answered Rawl.; I seyd Ing. **63.** hatte Rawl.; hyte Ing. **64.** in Rawl.; and Ing. longyth Ing.; longyt Rawl. **65.** *From* Ing.; Rawl. *omits. For* theigh, Ing. *has* thei (*badly*). **67.** quod I Ing.; Rawl. *om.* fentesye Rawl.; fayntys Ing.; *read* feyntise, *as in* A. v. 5, B. v. 5. hentith Ing.; hendeþ Rawl.; *read* henteth. **68.** fentyse Rawl.; fayntyse Ing.; *see above.* no ferther Rawl.; not forth Ing.

For myssyng of mete · no mesour I coude,
But ete as Hunger me hete · til my belly swellyd.
Ther bad me Hunger 'haue gode day!' · but I helde me stille;
For gronyng of my guttys · I durst gon no ferther.   76
With that cam a knaue · with a confessoures face,
Lene and rewlyche · with leggys ful smale.
He halsed me, and I · asked him after,
Of whennes that he were · and wheder that he wolde.   80
'With Deth I duelle,' quod he · 'dayes and ny3tes;
Mi name is Feuere; on the ferthe day · I am a-first euere;
I am messager of Deth · men haue I tweyne,
That on is called Cotidian · a courour of oure hous,   84
Tercian that other · trewe drinkeres bothe!
We han letteres of Lyf · he shal his lyf tyne;
Fro Deth, that is oure duk · swyche dedis we brynge.'
'My3te I so,' quod I, 'god wot · 3oure gates wolde I holden.'   88
'Nay, Wil!' quod that wy3t · 'wend thou no ferther,
But lyue as this lyf · is ordeyned for the;
Thou tomblest with a trepget · 3if thou my tras folwe;
And mannes merthe wrou3te no mor · than he deseruyth here,   92
Whil his lyf and his lykhame · lesten to-gedere.
And ther-fore do after Do-wel · whil thi dayes duren,
That thi play be plentevous · in paradys with aungelys!
Thou shalt be lau3t into ly3t · with loking of an eye,   96
So that thou werke the word · that holy wryt techeth,
And be prest to preyeres · and profitable werkes!'
Wille [wiste] thurgh in-wit · (thou wost wel the sothe!)

[*Not in* C-*text.*]

---

69. gome Ing.; gom Rawl.   70. Of battys and broken bred Ing.   Ing.
om. for.   71. bou3þe Rawl.; bowht Ing.   72. with him Ing.; wit Rawl.
to Ing.; at Rawl.   73. Rawl. *inserts* the *after* For.   74–76. *These three
lines are in* Ing. *only.*   78. *This line is in* Ing. *only.*   79. I haylsyd hym
hendely · and axid him after Ing.   80. when Rawl; qwennys Ing.; *read*
whennes.   82. a-threst Rawl.; athirst Ing.; *read* afirst.   83. masager
Rawl.; mensenger Ing.; *read* messager.   86. tyne Ing.; tyme (*wrongly*)
Rawl.   88. so Rawl.; *miswritten* se Ing. quod he (*obvious error for* quod I)
Ing.; Rawl. *om.*   MS. Ing. *ends with* l. 88.   88. My3th Rawl.; *read* My3te.
89. wy3th Rawl.; *read* wy3t.   92. wrou3th Rawl.   96. lau3th, ly3th Rawl.;
read lau3t, ly3t.   98–100. Unless the lines be spurious, these are the author's
own words; he kills himself off, by way of finishing his poem, but he lived to
rewrite it, nevertheless.   99. wiste *is supplied*; Rawl. *om.*

A. PASSUS XII. 100–103.   B. PASSUS XI. 1–25.

That this speche was spedelich · and sped him wel faste,   100
And wrou3te that here is wryten · and other werkes bothe
Of Peres the Plowman · and mechel puple al-so;
And whan this werk was wrou3t · ere Wille my3te a-spie,

[*Continued from* p. 324.]

PASSUS XI.

*Passus xj*ᵘˢ.

THANNE Scripture scorned me   and a skile tolde,
   And lakked me in Latyne · and li3te by me she sette,
And seyde, '*multi multa sciunt, et seipsos nesciunt.*'
Tho wepte I for wo · and wratth of her speche,
And in a wynkyng wratth · wex I aslepe.   4
A merueillouse meteles · mette me thanne,
That I was rauisshed ri3t there · and Fortune me fette,
And in-to the londe of Longynge · allone she me brou3te,
And in a myroure that hi3t Mydlerd · she mad me to biholde.
Sitthen she sayde to me · 'here my3tow se wondres,   9
And knowe that thow coueytest · and come ther-to, par aunter.'
   Thanne hadde Fortune folwyng hir · two faire damoyseles,
Concupiscencia-carnis · men called the elder mayde,   12
And Coueytise-of-eyes · ycalled was that other;
Pryde-of-parfyte-lyuynge · pursued hem bothe,
And badde me, for my contenaunce · acounte Clergye li3te.
   Concupiscencia-carnis · colled me aboute the nekke,   16
And seyde, 'thow art 3onge and 3epe · and hast 3eres ynowe,
Forto lyue longe · and ladyes to louye;
And in this myroure thow my3te se · myrthes ful manye,
That leden the wil to lykynge · al thi lyf-tyme.'   20
   The secounde seide the same · 'I shal suwe thi wille;
Til thow be a lorde and haue londe · leten the I nelle,
That I ne shal folwe thi felawship · if Fortune it lyke.'
'He shal fynde me his frende' · quod Fortune ther-after;   24
'The freke that folwed my wille · failled neuere blisse.'

A. 101. wrou3the Rawl. ; *read* wrou3te.   *This line means that, besides the* Vita de Dowel, Dobet, et Dobest, *the author wrote* Piers the Plowman.   After

A. PASSUS XII. 104, 105.   331

Deth delt him a dent · and drof him to the erthe,   104
And is closed vnder clom · Crist haue his soule!

Explicit Dowel.

[*Continued from* p. 325.]

Thanne Scripture scorned me · and many skyles shewede,
And contynaunce made to Clergie · to congie me, hit semede,
And lakkede me in Latyn · and lyght by me sette,   165
And seide, '*multi multa sapiunt, et seipsos nesciunt.*'
Tho wepte ich for wo · and wrathede of here wordes,
And in a wynkynge ich worth · and wonderliche ich mette.
For ich was raueshed ryght ther; · Fortune me fette,   168
In-to the londe of Longynge · and Loue hue me brouhte,
And in a myrour, hihte Myddelerd · hue made me to loke,
And sutthe seide to me · 'her myghte thou see wondres,   171
And knowe that thow coueitest · and come ther-to, paraunter.'
Thenne hadde Fortune folwynge hure · two faire maidenes,
Concupiscentia-carnis · me calde the eldere mayde,
And Couetyse-of-eyen · ycald was that othere.
And Pruyde-of-parfit-lyuynge · pursewede me faste,   176
And bad me for my contynence · counte Clergies lore lyght.
Concupiscentia-carnis · comfortyde me in thys wyse,
And seide, 'thow art ȝong and ȝep · and hast ȝeris ynowe
For to lyue longe · and ladyes to louye.   180
And in this mirour thow myȝt see · murthes ful menye,
That lede the wol to lykynge · al thy lyf-tyme.'
The secounde mayde seide · 'ich shal sewe thi wil;
Til thow be a lord of londe · leten the ich nelle,   184
That ich ne shal folwie thy felaushupe · yf Fortune lyke.'
'He shal fynde me hus frende' · quath Fortune her-after;
'That man that me lyketh helpe · myghte nat myshappe.'

From C. xii. 163-187 (p. 311).

---

line 105, twelve more lines are added by a certain Johan But, who mentions king Richard as being still alive.

Thanne was there one that hiȝte Elde · that heuy was of chere,
'Man,' quod he, 'if I mete with the · bi Marie of heuene,
Thow shalt fynde Fortune the faille · at thi moste nede,   28
And *Concupiscencia-carnis* · clene the forsake.
Bitterliche shaltow banne thanne · bothe dayes and niȝtes
Couetyse-of-eyghe · that euere thow hir knewe,
And Pryde-of-parfyt-lyuynge · to moche peril the brynge.'   32
 'Ȝee, recche the neuere,' quod Recchelesnes · stode forth in ragged clothes,
'Folwe forth that Fortune wole · thow hast wel fer til elde;
A man may stoupe tymes ynow · whan he shal tyne the croune.
 "*Homo proponit*," quod a poete · and Plato he hyght,   36
"And *deus disponit*," quod he · "lat god done his wille."
If Trewthe wil witnesse it be wel do · Fortune to folwe,
Concupiscencia-carnis · ne Coueityse-of-eyes
Ne shal nouȝt greue the gretly · ne bigyle the, but thow wolt.'
 'Ȝee, farewel, Phippe!' quod Fauntelte · and forth gan me drawe,   41
Til *Concupiscencia-carnis* · acorded alle my werkes.

 'Allas, eye!' quod Elde · and Holynesse bothe,
'That witte shal torne to wrecchednesse · for wille to haue his lykynge!'   44
Coueityse-of-eyghes · conforted me anon after,
And folwed me fourty wynter · and a fyfte more,
That of Dowel ne Dobet · no deyntee me ne thouȝte;
I had no lykynge, leue me if the leste · of hem auȝte to knowe.
 Coueytyse-of-eyes · cam ofter in mynde   49
Than Dowel or Dobet · amonge my dedes alle.
Coueytise-of-eyes · conforted me ofte,
And seyde, 'haue no conscience · how thow come to gode;
Go confesse the to sum frere · and shewe hym thi synnes.   53
For whiles Fortune is thi frende · freres wil the louye,

B. 53. þe RCB; þee WO; L *om.*

From C. xii. 188-197 (p. 313).

Thenne was ther on hiht Elde · that heuy was of chere ; 188
'Man,' quath Elde, 'mete ich with the · by Marie of heuene!
Thou shalt fynde Fortune · faile at thy moste neede,
And *Concupiscentia-carnis* · clene the for-sake!
Byterliche shalt thow banne thenne · bothe dayes and nyghtes
Couetyse-of-eyen · that euere thow hure knewe, 193
And Pruyde-of-parfit-lyuynge · to muche peril the brynge.'
'ȝe, recche the neuere,' quath Rechelesnesse · stod forth in raggede clothes,
'Folwe forth that Fortune wol · thou hast ful fer to elde ; 196
A man may stoupe tyme ynowe · when he shal tyne the corone!'

"*Homo proponit,*" quath a poete tho · and Plato he hihte, 304
"*Et deus disponit,*" quath he · "let god do hus wille."
Al that Treuthe a-tacheth · and testifieth for goode,
Thauh thei folwe that Fortune wole · no folie ich hit holde.
And *Concupiscentia-carnis* · shal the nat greue 308
Gretlich, ne by-gyly the · bote yf thy-self wolle.'
'ȝe, farewel, Fyppe!' quath Fauntelet · and forth gan me drawe,
Til *Concupiscentia-carnis* · a-corded to alle my werkes.
Of Dowel ne of Dobet · no deynte me thouhte, 312
Clergie and hus consail · ich countede ful lytel!

Hic explicit passus secundus de Dowel.

PASSUS XIII.

Incipit passus tercius de Dowel.

'ALAS, eye!' quath Elde · and Holynesse bothe,
'That wit shal turne to wrecchednesse · for welthe hath al hus wil!'
Couetise-of-eyen · confortede me after,

And seide, 'Rechelesnesse · recche the neuere! 4
By so thow riche were · haue thow no conscience
How that thow come to good ; · confesse the to som frere,
He shal a-soile the thus sone · how so thow euere wynne hit.
For while Fortune is thy frend · freres wollen the louye, 8

C. 304. a MFSEG ; þe P.   P. xiii. 7. so FTS ; P *om.*

And fecche the to her fraternite · and for the biseke
To her priour prouyncial · a pardoun forto haue, 56
And preyen for the, pol bi pol · ȝif thow be *pecuniosus.*'
  Set pena pecuniaria non sufficit pro spiritualibus delictis.
By wissynge of this wenche I wrouȝte · here wordes were so
  swete,
Tyl I forȝat ȝouthe · and ȝarn in-to elde.
And thanne was Fortune my foo · for al hir faire biheste, 60
And Pouerte pursued me · and put me lowe,
And tho fonde I the frere aferde · and flyttynge bothe,
Aȝeines owre firste forward · for I seyde I nolde
Be buryed at her hous · but at my parisshe cherche. 64
For I herde onys · how Conscience it tolde,
That there a man were crystened · by kynde he shulde be buryed,
Or where he were parisshene · riȝt there he shulde be grauen.
And for I seyde thus to freres · a fool thei me helden, 68
And loued me the lasse · for my lele speche.
Ac ȝet I cryed on my confessoure · that helde hym-self so
  kunnynge,
'By my feith, frere,' quod I · 'ȝe faren lyke thise woweres,
That wedde none wydwes · but forto welde here godis; 72
Riȝte so, by the rode · rouȝte ȝe neuere
Where my body were buryed · bi so ȝe hadde my siluer.
Ich haue moche merueille of ȝow · and so hath many an other,
Why ȝowre couent coueyteth · to confesse and to burye, 76
Rather than to baptise barnes · that ben catekumelynges.
Baptizyng and burying · bothe ben ful nedeful,
Ac moche more merytorie · me thynketh it is to baptize.
For a baptized man may · as maistres telleth, 80
Thorugh contricioun come · to the heigh heuene;
  Sola contricio delet peccatum.
Ac a barne with-oute bapteme · may nouȝt so be saued;
  Nisi quis renatus fuerit ex aqua, &c.;
Loke, ȝe lettred men · whether I lye or do nouȝte.'
And lewte loked on me · and I loured after. 84
'Wherfore lourestow?' quod Lewte · and loked on me harde,
'Ȝif I durste,' quod I, 'amonges men · this meteles auowe!'

B. 57. *peccuniosus* L.   *pecuniarea* L.   79. þynke L; þynkeþ WOR.
81. *delet peccatum* COB; *&c.* L.   82. *ex aqua, &c.* COB: L *om.*

And fastne the in here fraternite · and for the by-seche
To here priour prouincial · hus pardon to haue,
And praye for the, pol by pol · yf thow be pecunyous;
  Pena pecuniaria non sufficit, et cet.'
By wissynge of this wenche ich dude · hure wordes were so
  swete,   12
Til ich for-ȝat ȝouthe · and ȝorn in-to elde.
Thenne was Fortune my foo · for al here fayre by-heste,
And Pouerte pursuwede me · and putte me to be lowe,
And flittynge fond ich the frere · that me confessede,   16

And seide, 'he myghte me nat a-soile · bote ich suluer hadde
To restitue resonabliche · for al vnryghtful wynnynge.'
'Owh! how!' quath ich tho · and myn hefd waggede,
'By my faith, frere,' quath ich · 'ȝe fare lik the wouwere 20
That wilneth the wydewe · bote for to wedde here goodes.
Ryght so, by the rode,' quath ich · 'rouhte the neuere
Wher my body yburied were · by so ȝe hadde my goodes!'

Thanne lowh Leaute · for ich lourede on the frere;   24
'Whi lourest thow?' quath Leaute · 'leue syre,' ich seide,
'For this frere flaterede me · while he fond me riche;
Now ich am poure and penyles · at litel prys he set me:
Ich wolde hit were no synne,' ich seide · 'to seye that were
  treuthe.   28

C. 11. pecunyous EMFSK; pecunius P.   13. ȝorn TK; ȝorne P.   25.
leue EMSK; luue P.   26. thees (*for* this) P.

'ȝe, bi Peter and bi Poule,' quod he · 'and take hem bothe to
  witnesse,
    *Non oderis fratres secrete in corde tuo, set publice argue
      illos.*'
'Thei wol alleggen also,' quod I · 'and by the gospel preuen,
    Nolite iudicare quemquam.'
  'And wher-of serueth lawe,' quod Lewte · 'if no lyf ·vnder-
    toke it, 89
Falsenesse ne faytrye? · for sumwhat the apostle seyde,
    Non oderis fratrem.
And in the sauter also · seithe Dauid the prophete,
    Existimasti inique quod ero tui similis, &c.
It is *licitum* for lewed men · to segge the sothe, 92
If hem lyketh and leste · eche a lawe it graunteth,
Excepte persones and prestes · and prelates of holy cherche,
It falleth nouȝte for that folke · no tales to telle,
Though the tale were trewe · and it touched synne. 96
Thinge that al the worlde wote · wherfore shuldestow spare
To reden it in retoryke · to arate dedly synne?
Ac be neuere more the fyrste · the defaute to blame;
Thouȝe thow se yuel, sey it nouȝte fyrste · be sorye it nere
  amended. 100
No thinge that is pryue · publice thow it neuere,
Neyther for loue laude it nouȝt · ne lakke it for enuye;
    Parum lauda, vitupera parcius.'
  'He seith sothe,' quod Scripture tho · and skipte an heigh,
    and preched;
Ac the matere that she meued · if lewed men it knewe, 104
The lasse, as I leue · louyen it thei wolde.
This was her teme and her tyxte · I toke ful gode hede;
'*Multi* to a maungerye · and to the mete were sompned,
And whan the peple was plenere comen · the porter vnpynned
  the ȝate, 108
And plukked in *pauci* priueliche · and lete the remenaunt go
  rowme!'
Al for tene of her tyxte · trembled myn herte,
And in a were gan I waxe · and with my-self to dispute,

The sauter seith hit is no synne · for suche men as ben trewe
For to seggen as thei seen · and saue onliche prestes;
  *Existimasti inique quod ero tui similis; arguam te, & statuam
  contra faciem tuam.*
Thei wollen a-leggen al-so · and by the godspel preouen hit,
  Nolite iudicare quemquam.'
'Wher-of serueth lawe,' quath Leaute · 'and no lyf vndertoke
Falsnesse ne faiterie? · for som-what the apostel seide,   33
  Non oderis fratrem tuum secrete in corde tuo.
Thyng that al the worlde wot · where-fore sholdest thow spare
To rehercen hit by retoryk · to a-rate dedliche synne?
Ac be thow neuer the furste · the defaute to blame;   36
Thauh thow see, sey nat · som tyme, that is treuthe.
Thyng that wolde be pryue · publisshe thow hit neuere,
Nother for loue labbe hit out · ne lacke hit for non enuye;
  Parum lauda, uitupera parcius.'
'He seith soth,' quath Scripture tho · and skypte an hy,
  and prechede,   40
Ac the matere that hue meeuede · yf lewede men hit knewe,
The lasse, as ich leyue · louye thei wolde
The by-leyue of oure lorde · that lettrede men techen.
Of here teme and of here tales · ich took ful good hede;   44
Hue seide in here sarmon · selcouthe wordes :—
'*Multi* to a mangerie · and to the mete were sompned,
And whan the peuple was plener come · the porter vnpynnede
  the gate,
And plyghte in *pauci* pryueliche · and leet the remenant go rome.'
 Al for teene of here tixt · tremblede myn herte,   49
And in a weer gan ich wexe · and with my-selue to dispute

C. 33. *tuo* FST; P *om.*   40. tho ITSK; P *om.*   41. he (*for* hue,
wrongly) P; *cf.* ll. 49, 72.   45. He (*for* Hue); *see above.*

Whether I were chosen or nou3t chosen; · on Holicherche I
    thou3te,   112
That vnderfonge me atte fonte · for one of goddis chosen;
For Cryste cleped vs alle · come if we wolde,
Sarasenes and scismatikes · and so he dyd the Iewes,
    O vos omnes scicientes, venite, &c.;
And badde hem souke for synne · saufly at his breste,   116
And drynke bote for bale · brouke it who so my3te.
    'Thanne may alle Crystene come,' quod I · 'and cleyme
    there entre
By the blode that he bou3te vs with · and thorugh baptesme after,
    Qui crediderit & baptizatus fuerit, &c.
For though a Crystene man coueyted · his Crystenedome to reneye,
Ri3tfulliche to reneye · no resoun it wolde.   121
    For may no cherle chartre make · ne his catel selle
With-outen leue of his lorde · no lawe wil it graunte.
Ac he may renne in arrerage · and rowme so fro home,
And as a reneyed caityf · recchelesly gon aboute;   125
Ac Resoun shal rekne with hym · and rebuken hym at the laste,
And Conscience a-counte with hym · and casten hym in arrerage,
And putten hym after in a prisone · in purgatorie to brenne,
For his arrerages rewarden hym there · to the daye of dome,

But if Contricioun wol come · and crye, bi his lyue,   130
Mercy for his mysdedes · with mouth or with herte.'
    'That is soth,' seyde Scripture · 'may no synne lette
Mercy alle to amende · and mekenesse hir folwe,   133
For they beth as owre bokes telleth · aboue goddes werkes,
    Misericordia eius super omnia opera eius.'
    '3ee! baw for bokes!' quod one · was broken oute of helle,
Hi3te *Troianus*, had ben a trewe kny3te · toke witnesse at a pope,
How he was ded and dampned · to dwellen in pyne,   137
For an vncristene creature; · —'clerkis wyten the sothe,
That al the clergye vnder Cryste · ne mi3te me cracche fro helle,

But onliche loue and leaute · and my lawful domes.   140

    B. 126, 127. and rebuken—acounte with hym *in* R *only.*   128. hym
WROB; L *om.*   130. wel (*for* wol) L.   139. ne W; LCROB *om.*

Whether ich were chose other nat chose; · on Holy-churche ich thouhte,
That vnderfong me atte fount · for on of godes chosene. 52
'For Crist clepide ous alle · come yf we wolde,
Sarrasyns and scismatikes · and so he dude the Iewes,
And bad hem souken of hus brest · sauete for synne,
And drynke bote for bale · brouke hit ho so myghte; 56
O uos omnes sitientes, uenite ad aquas !
Thenne may alle Cristine come · and cleyme ther to entre
By that blod that he boughte ous with · and baptisme, as he tauhte,
Qui crediderit et baptizatus fuerit, saluus erit, & cetera.
For thauh a Crystine man coueytede · hus Crystendome to reneye,
Ryghtfulliche to reneye · no reson hit wolde. 60
For may no cherl a chartre make · ne hus catel selle
With-oute leue of the lorde · no lawe wolde hit graunte.
Ac he may renne in arerage · and rome fro home
As a recheles caitif · other reneyed, as hit semeth; 64
Ac Reson shal rekene with hym · and rebuke him atte laste,
And Conscience a-counte with hym · and caste him in arerages,
And putte hym thenne in prison · in purgatorie to brenne,
Rewardynge him ther for hus rechelesnesse · ryght to the day of dome, 68
Bote Contricion and Confession · crye, by hus lyue,
Mercy for hus mysdedes · with mouthe and with herte.'
'That is sothe,' seide Scripture · 'may no synne lette
Mercy, that hue nel al amende · yf meeknesse here folwe; 72
Thei bothe, as our bookes telleth · aren aboue godes werkes;
Misericordia eius super omnia opera eius.'
'Ye, baw for bookes!' quath on · was broken out of helle—
'Ich, *Troianus,* a trewe knyght · ich take witness of a pope,
How ich was ded, and dampned · to dwellen in helle 76
For an vncristene creature; · seynt Gregorie wot the sothe,
That al the Cristendome vnder Crist · ne myghte cracche me thennes,
Bote onliche loue and leaute · as in my lawes demynge!

C. 57. come IMTFS; P *om.*   58. *saluus erit* MFE; P *om.*   61. cheerl P.   62. With-ouhte P.   63. arerage KMS; arrirage P.   66. in MITSF; P *om.*   71. PE *insert* the *before* sothe.   73. beþe (*for* boþe) P.   75. P *om.* 2nd a.   78. cracche MFSEK; cacche P.

Gregorie wist this wel · and wilned to my soule
Sauacioun, for sothenesse · that he seigh in my werkes.
And, after that he wepte · and wilned me were graunted
Grace, wyth-outen any bede-byddynge · his bone was vnderfongen,
And I saued, as ȝe may se · with-oute syngyng of masses; 145
By loue, and by lernynge · of my lyuyng in treuthe,
Brouȝte me fro bitter peyne · there no biddyng myȝte.'
  'Lo, ȝe lordes, what leute did · by an emperoure of Rome,
That was an vncrystene creature · as clerkes fyndeth in bokes.
Nouȝt thorw preyere of a pope · but for his pure treuthe 150
Was that Sarasene saued · as seynt Gregorie bereth witnesse.
Wel ouȝte ȝe lordes, that lawes kepe · this lessoun to haue in
  mynde, 152
And on *Troianus* treuth to thenke · and do treuthe to the peple.
  This matir is merke for mani of ȝow · ac, men of holy cherche,
The Legende *Sanctorum* ȝow lereth · more larger than I ȝow telle!
Ac thus lele loue · and lyuynge in treuthe 156
Pulte oute of pyne · a paynym of Rome.
I-blessed be treuthe · that so brak helle-ȝates,
And saued the Sarasyn · fram Sathanas and his power,
There no clergie ne couthe · ne kunnynge of lawes. 160
Loue and leute · is a lele science;
For that is the boke blessed · of blisse and of ioye:—
God wrouȝt it and wrot hit · with his on fynger,
And toke it Moyses vpon the mount · alle men to lere. 164
  " Lawe with-outen loue," quod *Troianus* · " leye there a bene,
Or any science vnder sonne · the seuene artz and alle,
But if thei ben lerned for owre lordes loue · loste is alle the
  tyme : "—
For no cause to cacche siluer there-by · ne to be called a mayster,
But al for loue of owre lorde · and the bet to loue the peple. 169
For seynte Iohan seyde it · and soth aren his wordes,
  " *Qui non diligit, manet in morte*—
Who so loueth nouȝte, leue me · he lyueth in deth-deyinge"—
And that alle manere men · enemys and frendes, 172
Louen her eyther other · and lene hem as her-selue.
Who so leneth nouȝte, he loueth nouȝte · god wote the sothe,
And comaundeth eche creature · to confourme hym to louye,

B. 154—164. *These* 11 *lines are in* R *only.*

Gregore wiste this wel · and wilnede to my soule 80
Sauacion, for the sothness · that he seih in myn werkes;
And for he wilnede wepynge · that ich were saued,
God of hus goodnesse · seih hus grete wil;
With-oute moo bedes-byddyng · hus bone was vnderfonge, 84
And ich ysaued, as ȝe may see · with-oute syngynge of masse.
Loue, withoute leel by-leyue · and my lawe ryghtful
Sauede me Sarrasyn · soule and body bothe.'
'Lo, lordes! what Leaute dude · and leel dom y-used! 88

Wel auhte ȝe lordes that lawes kepen · this lesson to haue in mynde,
And on *Troianus* treuthe to thenke · alle tymes of ȝoure lyue,
And louye for ȝoure lordes loue · and do leaute euere more.

For lawe with-oute leaute · leye ther a bene! 92
Other eny science vnder sonne · the seuene ars and alle,
Bote loue and leaute hem lede · y-lost is al the tyme
Of hym that traueleth ther-on · bote treuthe be hus lyuynge.
Lo, loue and leaute · been oure lordes bookes, 96
And Cristes owen cleregie · he cam fro heuene to teche hit,
And sitthe seynt Iohan · seide hit of hus techynge;
  "*Qui non diligit, manet in morte:*"

C. 80. wist P.   86. with (*for* withoute) P.   94. hem METK; hym P.
95. hym SMFITK; hem PE.   98. hit is (*for* hit) P.

And souereynelyche pore poeple · and here ennemys after. 176
For hem that hateth vs · is owre meryte to louye,
And pore peple to plese; · here prayeres may vs helpe.
For owre ioye and owre hele · Iesu Cryst of heuene,
In a pore mannes apparaille · pursueth vs euere,   180
And loketh on vs in her liknesse · and that with louely chere,
To knowen vs by owre kynde herte · and castyng of owre eyen,
Whether we loue the lordes here · byfor owre lorde of blisse;
And exciteth vs bi the euangelye · that, when we maken festes,
We shulde nou3te clepe owre kynne ther-to · ne none kynnes riche;
  "*Cum facitis conuiuia, nolite inuitare amicos;*
Ac calleth the careful ther-to · the croked and the pore,   186
For 3owre frendes wil feden 3ow · and fonde 3ow to quite
3owre festynge and 3owre faire 3ifte; · vche frende quyteth so other.
Ac for the pore I shal paye · and pure wel quyte her trauaille,
That 3iueth hem mete or moneye · and loueth hem for my sake."
For the best ben somme riche · and somme beggers and pore.
For alle are we Crystes creatures · and of his coffres riche,
And bretheren as of o blode · as wel beggares as erles.   193
For on Caluarye of Crystes blode · Crystenedome gan sprynge,
And blody bretheren we bycome there · of o body ywonne,
As *quasi modo geniti* · and gentil men vche one,   196
No beggere ne boye amonges vs · but if it synne made;
  Qui facit peccatum, seruus est peccati, &c.
In the olde lawe · as holy lettre telleth,
Mennes sones · men called vs vchone,
Of Adames issue and Eue · ay til god-man deyde;   200
And after his resurreccioun · *Redemptor* was his name,
And we his bretheren, thourgh hym ybou3t · bothe riche and pore.
For-thi loue we as leue bretheren shal · and vche man laughe vp other,
And of that eche man may forbere · amende there it nedeth, 204
And euery man helpe other · for hennes shal we alle;
  Alter alterius onera portate.
And be we nou3te vnkynde of owre catel · ne of owre kunnynge neyther,
For noot no man how neighe it is · to be ynome fro bothe.
For-thi lakke no lyf other · though he more Latyne knowe, 208

  B. 183. Wherþer L. 207. noot O; not C; noet LR.

And nameliche poure peuple · here preiours may ous helpen;

For god, as the godspel seith · goth ay as in the poure,   100

And, as the euangelist wytnesseth · whan we maken festes,
We sholde nat clypie knyghtes ther-to · ne no kyne ryche;
   "*Cum facitis conuivium, nolite uocare amicos diuites, &c.;*
Ac calleth the carful ther-to · the crokede and the poure.
For eche frend fedeth other · and fondeth how he may quite 104
Meles and manshupes · eche a ryche man other;
Ac, for the poure may nat paye · ich wol paye my-self;
That louyeth and leneth hem · largeliche shal ich quite."

At Caluarie, of Cristes blood · Cristendome gan sprynge,   108
And blod-brethrene by-cam we ther · of on body wonne,
As *quasi modo geniti* · gentel men echone;
No begger ne boye among ous · bote yf synne hit make;
   Qui facit peccatum, seruus est peccati.
In the olde lawe, as the lettre telleth · menne sones me cald ous,
Of Adames ysshue and Eue · ay til god-man deide,   113
And after hus resureccion · *Redemptor* was hus name,
And we hus blody brethren · as wel beggers as lordes.
For-thy loue we as leue children · and lene hem that nedeth, 116

And euery man help other · for hennes shulleth we alle
To haue as we han deserued · as holychurche wittnesseth,
   *Et qui bona egerunt, ibunt in uitam eternam; qui vero
   mala, in ignem eternum.*

C. 102. *diuites* in E only.   111. PE *add* is *after* ous.   112. PEMK
om. 2nd the, *which* ITS *retain.*   113. Of MFSKT; And PE.   116. PE
om. we. nudeth (*for* nedeth) P.   118. *qui—eternum* in S only.

Ne vnder-nym nouȝte foule · for is none with-oute faute.
For what euere clerkis carpe · of Crystenedome or elles,
Cryst to a comune woman seyde · in comune at a feste,
That *fides sua* shulde sauen hir · and saluen hir of alle synnes. 212
Thanne is byleue a lele helpe · aboue logyke or lawe ;
Of logyke ne of lawe · in *Legenda Sanctorum*
Is litel allowaunce made · but if bileue hem helpe.
For it is ouerlonge ar logyke · any lessoun assoille, 216
And lawe is loth to louye · but if he lacche syluer.
Bothe logyke and lawe · that loueth nouȝte to lye,
I conseille alle Crystene · cleue nouȝte ther-on to sore.
For sum wordes I fynde ywryten · were of faithes techynge,
That saued synful men · as seynt Iohan bereth wytnesse ; 221
Eadem mensura qua mensi fueritis, remecietur vobis.
For-thi lerne we the lawe of loue · as owre lorde tauȝte,
And as seynte Gregory seide · for mannes soule helthe,
Melius est scrutari scelera nostra, quam naturas rerum.
Why I moue this matere · is moste for the pore, 224
For in her lyknesse owre lorde · ofte hath ben y-knowe.
Witnesse in the Paske-wyke · whan he ȝede to Emaus ;
Cleophas ne knewe hym nauȝte · that he Cryste were,
For his pore paraille · and pylgrymes wedes, 228
Tyl he blessed and brak · the bred that thei eten.
So bi his werkes thei wisten · that he was Iesus ;
Ac by clothyng thei knewe hym nouȝte · ne bi carpynge of tonge.
And al was in ensample · to vs synful here, 232
That we shulde be low · and loueliche of speche,
And apparaille vs nouȝte ouer proudly · for pylgrymes ar we alle ;
And in the apparaille of a pore man · and pilgrymes lyknesse
Many tyme god hath ben mette · amonge nedy peple, 236
There neuere segge hym seigh · in secte of the riche.
Seynt Iohan and other seyntes · were seyne in pore clothynge,
And as pore pilgrymes · preyed mennes godis.
Iesu Cryste on a Iewes douȝter alyȝte · gentil woman though she
were, 240
Was a pure pore mayde · and to a pore man wedded.
Martha on Marye Magdeleyne · an huge pleynte she made,
And to owre saueour self · seyde thise wordes,
*Domine, non est tibi cure quod soror mea reliquit me solam
ministrare, &c. ?*

For-thi lerne we lawe of loue · as oure lord tauhte;
The poure peuple faile we nat · whil eny peny ous lasteth. 120

For in here- liknesse oure lorde · lome hath be knowe;
Witnesse in the Paske-woke · when he ȝeode to Emaus;
Cleophas ne knew hym nat · that he Crist were,
For hus poure aparail · and pilgrimes clothes, 124
Til that he blessede here bred · and brak hit by-twyne hem.
So by hus werkes thei wiste · that he was Iesus;
Ac by hus clothing thei knewe hym nat · so caitifliche he ȝede.
   Al was ensample sothliche · to ous synful here, 128
We sholde be lowe and loueliche · and leel, eche man to other,
And pacient as pilgrimes · for pilgrimes arn we alle.
In the parail of a pilgrim · and in a poure liknesse
Holy seyntes hym seih · ac neuere in secte of riche. 132
   And seynte Marie hus moder · as Matheu bereth witnesse,
Was a pure poure mayde · and to a poure man ywedded.
Martha on Marie Magdalene · an huge pleynte hue made,
And to oure saueour selue · saide these wordes: 136
    Domine, non est tibi cure quod soror mea reliquit me solam
    ministrare?

B. 243. *sola* L.   C. 120. PE *om.* we.   131. licknesse P.   133. as
MFTSK; PE *om.*   135. PE *om.* hue.   136. *From* IKSTGM; PE *om.*
this line.

And hastiliche god answered · and eytheres wille folwed,   244
Bothe Marthaes and Maries · as Mathew bereth witnesse,
Ac pouerte god put bifore · and preysed it the bettre;
    Maria optimam partem elegit, que non auferetur ab ea.
And alle the wyse that euere were · by au3te I can aspye,
Preysen pouerte for best lyf · if pacience it folwe,   248
And bothe bettere and blisseder · by many folde than ricchesse.
Al though it be soure to suffre · there cometh swete after;
As on a walnot with-oute · is a bitter barke,
And after that bitter barke · (be the shelle aweye),   252
Is a kirnelle of conforte · kynde to restore;
So is, after, pouerte or penaunce · pacientlyche ytake.
For it maketh a man to haue mynde in gode · and a grete wille
To wepe and to wel bydde · wher-of wexeth mercy,   256
Of which Cryst is a kirnelle · to conforte the soule.
And wel sykerer he slepyth · the segge that is pore,
And lasse he dredeth deth · and in derke to be robbed,
Than he that is ri3te ryche · resoun bereth wytnesse;   260
    Pauper ego ludo, dum tu diues meditaris.
Al though Salamon seide · as folke seeth in the bible,
    Diuicias nec paupertates, &c.,
Wyser than Salamon was · bereth witnesse and tau3te,
That parfyte pouert was · no possessioun to haue,   264
And lyf moste lykynge to god · as Luke bereth witnesse,
    Si vis perfectus esse, vade & vende, &c.;
And is to mene to men · that on this molde lyuen,
Who so wil be pure parfyt · mote possessioun forsake,
Or selle it, as seith the boke · and the syluer dele   268
To beggeres that gone and begge · and bidden good for goddes
    loue.
For failled neuere man mete · that my3tful god serued;
    Non vidi iustum derelictum, nec semen eius querens panem;
As Dauid seith in the sauter · to suche that ben in wille
To serue god godeliche · ne greueth hym no penaunce,   272
    Nichil inpossibile volenti,
Ne lakketh neuere lyflode · lynnen ne wollen,
    Inquirentes autem dominum non minuentur omni bono.

B. 246. *auferetur—ea* COB; L om.   258. segge R; man LWCOB;
cf. l. 237.   270. *Non—panem* in O only.

And here aitheres wil · hasteliche god a-soilede,
And aitheres werkes and wil · ryght wel he alowede;
Ac god putte pouerte by-fore · and preouede hit for the bettere;
    Maria optimam partem elegit, que non aufereter ab ea.
And alle the wise that euere were · by ouht ich can aspie,
Preisede pouerte for beste · yf pacience hit folwe,   141
And bothe bettere and blessedere · by meny folde than richesse;
Thauh hit be sour to suffre · ther cometh a swete after.
As in a walnote, with-oute · ys a byter barke,   144
And after that biter barke · (be the shale aweye),
Ys a curnel of comfort · kynde to restorie;
So, after, pouerte and penaunce · pacientliche ytake,
Maketh man haue mynde in god · and hus mercy craue,   148

The whiche is curnel of comfort · for alle Cristene saules.
And wel sykerour he slepeth · the seg that is poure,
And lasse drat by daye · other in derk to be robbed,
Than he that ys ryht ryche · reson bereth wittnesse;   152
    Pauper ego ludo · dum tu diues meditaris.

Holichurche wittnesseth · "ho so for-saketh
Hus fader other hus frendes · fremde othere sibbe,
Other eny welthe in this worlde · hus wyf other hus children,
For the loue of oure lorde · loweth hym to be poure,   157
He shal haue an hundredfolde · of heuene-ryche blisse,
And lif lastyng for euere · by-fore oure lorde in heuene;
    Quicunque reliquerit patrem & matrem," &c.
Crist a-cordeth eft her-with · clerkes witen the sothe,   160
What god hym-self saide · to a seg that he louede;
"Yf the lyketh," quath god, "to lyue · the lif that is parfit,
Al that thow hast here · hasteliche go sulle hit;

C. 137. aithere (*for* aitheres) P; *see next line.*   147. ytake EIKST;
take P.   151. deerk P.   155. fremde MT; *miswritten* frende PEIFK.
159. *reliquerit* MFES; *relinquet* P.   160. whiten P.

If prestes weren parfyt · thei wolde no syluer take
For masses ne for matynes · nouȝte her mete of vsureres,
Ne neither kirtel ne cote · theigh they for colde shulde deye,
And thei her deuoir dede · as Dauid seith in the sauter,   277
    Iudica me, deus, et discerne causam meam.

[*Continued on* p. 356.]

B. 277. deuoir WCOB; deuor L.

C. PASSUS XIII. 164–195.

Ȝeue poure peuple the pans · ther-of porse thow none,   164
Ac ȝeue hem forth to poure folke · that for my loue hit asketh.
For-sake al and suwe me · and so is thi beste ;
   Si uis perfectus esse, uade & uende omnia que habes."
Thus consaileth Crist · in comun ous alle :—
" Ho so coueyteth to come · to my kynriche,   168
He mot for-sake hym-self · hus suster and hus brother,
And al that the worlde wolde · and my wil folwen,
   Nisi renunciaueritis omnibus que possidetis," &c.
Meny prouerbis ich myghte haue · of meny holy seyntes,
To testifie for treuthe · the tale that ich shewe,   172
And poetes to preouen hit · Porfirie and Plato ;
Aristotile, Ouidius · and elleuene hundred,
Tullius, Tholomeus · ich can nat telle here names,
Preouen pacient pouerte · pryns of alle vertues.   176
  And by the greyn that groweth · god ous alle techeth
Mischeifs on this molde · mekeliche to suffre :
   *Nisi granum frumenti cadens in terra mortuum fuerit,
   ipsum solum manet ;*
Bote yf the sed that sowen is · in the sloh sterue,
Shal neuere spir springen vp · ne spik on strawe curne ;   180
Sholde neuere whete wexe · bote whete fyrste deyde.
And other sedes al-so · in the same wyse,
That ben leide on louh erthe · ylore as hit were ;
And thorw the grete grace of god · of greyn ded in erthe   184
Atte laste launceth vp · wher-by we lyuen alle.
Ac seedes that been sowen · and mowe suffre wyntres,
Aren tydyour and tower · to mannes by-hofthe,
Than seedes that sowen beeth · and mowe nouht with forstes,
With wyndes ne with wederes · as in wynter-tyme ;   189
As, lynne-seed and lik-seed · and lente-seedes alle
Aren nouht so worthy as whete · ne so wel mowen
In the feld with the forst · and hit freese longe.   192
Ryght so, for sothe · that suffre may penaunces
Worth alowed of oure lorde · at here laste ende ;
And for here penaunce be preysed · as for a pure martir,

C. 166. *que habes* in S only.   170. *omnibus* EFS ; *omnia* PMIKT.
172. testefie P.   177. PE *om.* the.   178. *From* MIKTG ; PE *om. this line.*
179. that (*for* 1st the) P.   185. Atte the P. PE *om.* we.   188. forstes
EKG ; forste P.   195. PE *om.* a.

Other for a confessour ykud · that counteth nat a ruysshe   196
Fere, ne famyne · ne false menne tonges;
Bote as an hosebonde hopeth · after an hard wynter,
Yf god gyueth hym the lif · to haue a good heruest,
So preoueth these prophetes · that pacientliche suffreth.   200
Myschiefs and myshappes · and menye tribulacions
By-tokneth ful treweliche · in tyme comynge after
Murthe for hus mornynge · and that muche plente.
For Crist seide to hus seyntes · that for hus sake tholeden   204
Pouerte and penaunce · and persecucion of body,
Schullen haue more worschipe to wages · [and worthier ben yholde]
Than angeles—in here angre · on this wise hem grette,
 "*Tristitia uestra uertetur in gaudium :*
зoure sorwe in-to solas · shal turne atte laste,   208
And out of wo in-to wele · зoure wyrdes shul chaunge."
Ac who so redeth of the riche · the reuers he may fynde,
How god, as the godspel telleth · gyueth hem foul towname,
And that hus gost shal go · and hus good by-leue,   212
And asketh hym after · "ho shal hit haue,
The catel that he kepeth so · in coffres and in bernes?
And art so loth to leue · that leue shalt needes:
 O stulte, ista nocte anima tua egredietur ; que congregasti,
 cuius erunt ? Thesaurizat, & ignorat cui, &c.
An vnredy reue · thi residue shal spene,   216
That menye moththe was maister ynne · in a mynte-while;
Vp-holderes on the hul · shullen haue hit to selle."
   Lo, lo, lordes, lo · and ladies, taketh hede,
Hit lasteth nat longe · that is lycour swete,   220
As pees-coddes and pere-Ionettes · plomes and chiries!
That lyghtliche launceth vp · litel while dureth,
And that that rathest rypeth · roteth most saunest.
On fat londe and ful of donge · foulest wedes groweth;   224
Right so for sothe · suche that ben bysshopes,
Erles and archedekenes · and other ryche clerkes,

C. 200. these MKFS; thees P.   205. and MIFTSG; KPE *om.* (*twice*).
penaunce MIFTSG; penaunces PE.   206. Schullen—wages I (*the line being
imperfect; other copies omit the line*).   [and—yholde] *supplied from conjecture.*
207. Than I; Thanne T; PEKMS *om.*   210. P *om.* who. PE *om.* 1*st* the.
215. ert (*for* art) PEK.   *que—erunt* in E only.   *cui* in S only.   217.
PE *om.* maister.

C. PASSUS XIII. 227-248.

That chaffaren as chapmen · and chiden bote thei wynne,
And hauen the worlde at here wil · other-wyse to lyue.   228
Right as weodes wexen · in wose and in donge,
So of rychesse vpon richesse · arisen al vices.
Lo, lond ouere-layde · with marle and with donge,
Whete that wexeth ther-on · worth lygge ar hit ripe;   232
Right so, for sothe · for to sygge treuthe,
Ouer-plente pryde norssheth · ther pouerte destrueth hit.
   For, how hit euere be ywonne · bote hit be wel dispended,
Worldliche wele is wicked thynge · to hym that hit kepeth.   236
For yf he be fer ther-fro · ful ofte hath he drede
That fals folke fecche away · felonliche hus godes;
And ȝut more hit maketh men · meny tyme and ofte
To synegen, and to souchen · soteltees of gyle,   240
For couetyze of that catel · to culle hem that hit kepeth;
And so is meny man ymorthred · for hus money and goodes,
And tho that duden the dede · ydampned ther-fore after,
And he for hus harde holdynge · in helle, par aunter.   244
So couetise of catel · was combraunce to hem alle;
Lo, how pans purchasede · faire places and drede,
That rote is of robbers · the richesse with-ynne!
For he that gadereth so his good · god no-thyng preiseth.   248

Hic explicit passus iijus de dowel.

C. 230. arisen M; ariseth G; arist PEIKT (*badly*).   232. repe (*for*
ripe) P.   236. Worliche P.   242. men (*for* man) P.   247. PE *om.* of.
248. *In* M *only.*

PASSUS XIV.

Incipit passus quartus de Dowel.

A C wel worth Pouerte! · for he may walke vnrobbed
Among pilours in pees · yf pacience hym folwe.
Oure prynce Iesu pouerte chees · and hus aposteles alle,
And ay the lenger thei lyueden · the lasse good thei hadde; 4
    Tanquam nichil habentes, & omnia possidentes.
ȝut men rat that Abraam and Iob · were wonder ryche,
And out of numbre tho men · menye meobles hadden.
Abraam for al hus god · hadde muche teene,
In gret pouerte he was yput; · a pryns, as hit were, 8
By-nom hym ys housewif · and heeld here hym-self,
And Abraam nat hardy · ones to letten hym,
Ne for brightnesse of here beaute · here spouse to be by-knowe.
And for he suffrede and seide nouht · our iord sente tokne, 12
That the kynge cride · to Abraam mercy,
And deliuerede hym hus wif · with muche welthe after.
And also Iob the gentel · what Ioye hadde he on erthe,
How bittere he hit bouhte · as the book telleth! 16
And for he songe in hus sorwe · "*si bona accepimus a domino,
Dere-worthe dere god!* do we so *mala,*"
Al hus sorwe to solas · thorgh that songe turnede,
And Iob by-cam a Iolif man · and al hus Ioye newe. 20
Lo, how pacience in here pouerte · these patriarkes releuede,
And brouhte hem al aboue · that in bale rotede.
As greyn that lyth in the greot · and thorgh grace, atte laste,
Spryngeth vp and spredeth · so spedde the fader Abraam, 24
And al-so the gentel Iob; · here Ioie hath non ende.
    Ac leueth nouht, ȝe lewede men · that ich lacke richesse,
Thauh ich preise pouerte thus · and preoue hit by ensamples
Worthiour, as by holy writ · and wise philosopheres. 28
Bothe two beth goode · be ȝe ful certayn,
And lyues that our lorde loueth · and large weyes to heuene.

C. 1. vnrobbede P.   5. rat that MKT; ret that I; reedith that FG;
that of (*wrongly*) PE.   8. PE *om.* he.   17. *accepimus* MKFETG;
accipiam P.   29. beth ES; ben MIT; *miswritten* but P.

Ac the poure pacient · purgatorye passeth
Rathere than the ryche · thauh thei renne at ones. 32
For yf a marchaunt and a messager · metten to-gederes,
And scholde wenden o way · where both mosten reste,
And rekene byfore reson · a resonable acounte,
What one hath, what another hath · and what hy hadde bothe,
The marchante mote nede be lette · lengere then the messagere;
For the parcels of hus paper · and other pryuey dettes
Wol lette hym, as ich leyue · the lengthe of a myle.
The messager doth na more · bote with hus mouth telleth 40
Hus erande, and hus lettere sheweth · and is a-non delyuered.
And thauh thei wende by the wey · tho two to-gederes,
Thauh the messager make hus wey · a-mydde the whete,
Wole no wys man wroth be · ne hus wed take; 44
Ys non haiwarde yhote · hus wed for to take;
    Necessitas non habet legem.
Ac yf the marchaunt make hus way · ouere menne corne,
And the haywarde happe · with hym for to mete,
Other hus hatt other hus hode · othere elles hus gloues 48
The marchaunt mot for-go · other moneye of hus porse,
And ȝut be lett, as ich leyue · for the lawe asketh
Marchauns for here merchaundise · in meny place to tollen.
ȝut thauh thei wenden on way · as to Wynchestre fayre, 52
The marchaunt with hus marchaundise · may nat go so swithe
As the messager may · ne with so mochel ese.
For that on bereth bote a boxe · a breuet ther-ynne,
Ther the marchaunt ledeth a male · with meny kynne thynges,
And dredeth to be ded there-fore · and he in derke mete 57
With robbours and reuers · that riche men dispoilen;
Ther the messager is ay murye · hus mouthe ful of songes,
And leyueth for hus letteres · that no wight wol hym greue. 60
Ac ȝut, myghte the merchaunt · thorgh monye and other ȝiftes,
Haue hors and hardy men; · thauh he mette theoues,
Wolde non suche a-sailen hym · for hem that hym folweth,
As safliche passe as the messager · and as sone at hus hostil.

C. 35. acounte MIKF; acountes P. 40. P *om.* with. 41. erende IK; lettere PE. lettre KT; erande E; ernde P. 43. amyde P. 48. hode EK; hood ITFS; hed (!) P. 51. tollen TESG; tullen P. 58. P *inserts* with *before* reuers. 60. *For* wight *perhaps read* lede, *as in* T. 61. ȝeftes P.

ȝe wyten wel, ȝe wyse men · what this is to mene, 65
The marchaunt is no more to mene · bote men that ben ryche
Aren a-countable to Crist · and to the kyng of heuene,
That holden mote the heye weye · euene the ten hestes, 68
Bothe louye and lene · the leelle and the vnleelle,
And haue reuthe, and releue · with hus grete richesse,
By hus power, alle manere men · in meschief yfalle;
Fynde beggars bred · backes for the colde, 72
Tythen here goodes treweliche · a tol, as hit semeth,
That oure lord loketh after · of eche a lyf that wynneth
With-oute wyles other wrong · other wommen atte stuwes;
And ȝut more, to make pees · and quyte menne dettes, 76
Bothe spele and spare · to spene vpon the needful,
As Crist himself comaundeth · to alle Cristene peuple,
Alter alterius onera portate, et sic adimplebitis legem Christi.
The messagers aren the mendinans · that lyueth by menne almesse,
Beth nat ybounde as beth the riche · to bothe the two lawes, 80
To lene ne to lere · ne lentenes to faste,
And othere pryuey penaunces · the whiche the preest wot wel
That the lawe ȝeueth leue · suche lowe folke to be excused;
As, none tythes to tythen · ne clothe the nakede, 84
Ne in enquestes to come · ne *contumax*, thauh he worche
Haly day other holy eue · hus mete to deserue.
For yf he loueth and by-leyueth · as the lawe techeth,
Qui crediderit & baptizatus fuerit, saluus erit, &c.,
Telleth the lord a tale · as a trewe messager, 88
And sheweth by seel and sitthe by lettere · with what lord he dwelleth,
Knowelecheth hym Cristene · and of holy kirke by-leyue,
Ther is no lawe, as ich leyue · wol lette hym the gate,
Ther god is gatwarde hym-self · and eche a gome knoweth; 92
The porter of pure reuthe · may parforme the lawe,
In that he wilneth and wolde · ech wight as him-self.
For the wil is as muche worth · of a wrecche beggere,
As al that the ryche may reyme · and ryghtfulliche dele; 96

C. 68. PES *om.* 2*nd* the.   73. tryweliche P.   78. P *om.* him *in* himself.
et—christi in F only.   80. beeth P.   87. *saluus erit* MF; P *om.*
90. Knowelecheth KF; Kneweleche PE.   kirke I; churche PEFS.

C. PASSUS XIV. 97–100.

And as muche mede · for a myte that he offreth
As the riche man for al his moneye · and more, as by the
   godspel;
   *Amen dico uobis, quia hec uidua paupercula misit plus
   omnibus qui miserunt in gasophilacium ;*
So that poure pacient · is parfitest lif of alle,
And alle parfite preestes · to pouerte sholde drawe;   100

[*Continued on* p. 357.]

C. 98. is (*for* his) P.   *misit—omnibus* E.   *qui—gasophilacium* S.

[*Continued from* p. 348.]

Spera-in-deo speketh of prestes · that haue no spendyng-syluer,
That ʒif thei trauaille trewlich · and trusten in god almiʒti,
Hem shulde lakke no lyflode · noyther wollen ne lynnen.   280
And the title that ʒe take ordres by · telleth ʒe ben auaunced;
Thanne nedeth nouʒte ʒow to take syluer · for masses that ʒe syngen.
For he that toke ʒow ʒowre tytle · shulde take ʒow ʒowre wages,
Or the bisshop that blesseth ʒow · if that ʒe ben worthy.   284
    For made neuere kynge no knyʒte · but he hadde catel to spende,
As bifel for a kniʒte · or fonde hym for his strengthe;
It is a careful knyʒte · and of a caytyue kynges makynge,
That hath no londe ne lynage riche · ne good loos of his handes.
The same I segge for sothe · by alle suche prestes,   289
That han noyther kunnynge ne kynne · but a croune one,
And a tytle, a tale of nouʒte · to his lyflode at myschiefe,
He hath more bileue, as I leue · to lacche thorw his croune
Cure, than for konnyng · or—'knowen for clene of berynge.'
I haue wonder for why · and wher-fore the bisshop
Maketh suche prestes · that lewed men bytrayen.
    A chartre is chalengeable · byfor a chief iustice;   296
If false Latyne be in the lettre · the lawe it inpugneth,
Or peynted parenterlinarie · or parceles ouer-skipped;
The gome that gloseth so chartres · for a goky is holden.
So is it a goky, by god · that in his gospel failleth,   300
Or in masse or in matynes · maketh any defaute,
    Qui offendit in vno, in omnibus est reus, etc.
And also in the sauter · seyth Dauyd to ouerskippers,
    Psallite deo nostro, psallite; quoniam rex terre deus israel; psallite sapienter.
The bisshop shal be blamed · bifor god, as I leue,
That crouneth suche goddes kniʒtes · that conneth nouʒt *sapienter*
Synge ne psalmes rede · ne segge a messe of the day.   305
Ac neuer neyther is blamelees · the bisshop ne the chapleyne,
For her eyther is endited · and that of '*ignorancia Non excusat episcopos · nec idiotes prestes.*'   308

B. 281. ye WR; þei LCOB (*for 1st* ʒe).   285. no kynge no L.   294. for W; & L.   298. or W; LRCOB *om.*

[*Continued from* p. 355.]

For *spera-in-deo* speketh of prestes · that han no spendyng-seluer.
  That yf thay trauaile treweliche · and tristen in god almyghty,
Hem sholde neuere lackye lyflode · nother lynnen ne wollene.
  The title that ȝe taketh ȝoure ordres by · telleth ȝe beth
    auaunced,   104
And needeth nat to nyme seluer · for masses that ȝe syngen ;
For he that tok ȝow title · sholde take ȝow wages,
Other the bisshop that blessed ȝow · and enbaumede ȝoure fyngeres.
  For made neuere kyng knyght · bote he hadde catel to
    spene,
As by-fel for a knyght · other fond hym for hus strengthe ;   109
For hit is a carful knyght · and of a caitif kynges makynge,
That hath no londe ne lynage riche · ne good loos of hus hondes.
The same ich seye for sothe · by suche that ben preestes,   112
That han nother konnynge ne kyn · bote a corone one,
And a title, a tale of nouht · to hus liflode, as hit were.

Vuele ben thei suffred · suche that schenden masses
Throgh hure luther lyuynge · and lewede vnder-stondyng !   116
  A charter is chalangable · by-fore a chief Iustice,
Yf fals Latyn be in that lettere · the lawe hit enpugneth,
Other peynted par-entrelignarie · parcels ouer-skipped ;
The gome that so gloseth chartres · a goky he is yholden.
So is he a goky, by god · that in the godspel failleth,   121
In masse other in matynes · maketh eny defaute ;
  Qui offendit in uno, in omnibus est reus.
And ouer-skippers al-so · in the sauter seith Dauid,
  *Psallite deo nostro, psallite, quia rex terre deus ; psallite
    sapienter.*
The bishop shal be blamed · by-fore god, as ich leyue,   124
That coroneth suche clerkes · as for godes knyghtes,
That conneth nat *sapienter* · nother synge ne rede.
Ac neyther is al blameles · the bisshop ne the chapeleyn ;
For *ignorantia non excusat* · as ich haue herd in bookes.'— 128

C. 104, 106. titile P.   104. auaunced MT ; auaunsed IKEG ; amanced P.
114. titile P.   115. schenden EMS ; shynden P.   118. that lettere
MIKSEG ; the letteres P.   123. *psallite sapienter* M.

This lokynge on lewed prestes · hath don me lepe fram pouerte,
The whiche I preyse there pacyence is · more parfyt than ricchesse.'
Ac moche more in metynge thus · with me gan one dispute,
And slepynge I seigh al this · and sithen cam Kynde,   312
And nempned me by my name · and bad me nymen hede,
And thorw the wondres of this worlde · wytte for to take.
And on a mountaigne that Mydelerd hy3te · as me tho thou3te,
I was fette forth · by ensaumples to knowe,   316
Thorugh eche a creature and Kynde · my creatoure to louye.
I seigh the sonne and the see · and the sonde after,
And where that bryddes and bestes · by here makes thei 3eden,
Wylde wormes in wodes · and wonderful foules,   320
With flekked fetheres · and of fele coloures.
Man and his make · I my3te bothe byholde;
Pouerte and plente · bothe pees and werre,
Blisse and bale · bothe I seigh at ones,   324
And how men token mede · and mercy refused.

Resoune I seighe sothly · suen alle bestes
In etynge, in drynkynge · and in engendrynge of kynde;
And after course of concepcioun · none toke kepe of other,   328
As whan thei hadde ryde in rotey-tyme; · anon ri3te ther-after,
Males drowen hem to males · a mornynges bi hem-self,
And in euenynges also · 3ede males fro femeles.
There ne was cow ne cowkynde · that conceyued hadde,   332
That wolde belwe after boles · ne bore after sowe;
Bothe horse and houndes · and alle other bestes
Medled nou3te wyth here makes · that with fole were.

Briddes I bihelde · that in buskes made nestes;   336
Hadde neuere wye witte · to worche the leest.
I hadde wonder at whom · and where the pye lerned
To legge the stykkes · in whiche she leyeth and bredeth;
There nys wri3te as I wene · shulde worche hir neste to paye;
If any masoun made a molde ther-to · moche wonder it were.

B. 319. makes W; make LCRO; *see* l. 335.   331. 3ede R; 3e L.   339. leyeþ W; leythe L.

C. PASSUS XIV. 129-162.

Thus Rechelessnesse in a rage · a-resonede clergie,
And scornede Scripture · that meny skyles shewede,
Til that Kynde cam · Clergie to helpen,
And in the myrour of Myddel-erde · made hym eft to loke, 132
To knowe by ech creature · Kynde to louye.
And ich bowede my body · by-holdynge al a-boute,
And seih the sonne and the see · and the sand after,
Wher that briddes and bestes · by here makes ȝeden, 136
Wilde wormes in wodes · and wonderful foules
With fleckede fetheres · and of fele colours ;
Man and hus make · ich myghte see bothe,
Pouerte and plente · bothe pees and werre, 140
Blisse and biter bale · bothe ich seih at ones ;
And how that men mede token · and mercy refuseden.
  Reson ich seih sothliche · suwen alle bestes
In etynge, in drynkyng · in gendrynge of kynde ; 144
After cours of concepcion · non tok kepe of other
As when thei hadde ruteyed ; · a-non thei resten after.
Maules drowen hem to maules · on morwenynge by hem-self,
And femeles to femeles · herdeyed and drow. 148
Ther ne was kow ne kow-kynde · that conceyued hadde,
That wolde bere after bole · ne bor after sowe.
Ther was no kynne kynde · that conceyued hadde,
That ne lees the lykynge of lust · of flesch, as hit were, 152
Saue man and hus make ; · and ther-of me wondrede.
For out of reson thei ryde · and rechelesliche taken on,
As in durne dedes · bothe drynkynge and elles.
  Briddes ich by-helde · in bosshes maden nestes, 156
Hadde neuere weye wit · to worche the leste.
Ich hadde wonder at wham · and wher that the pye
Lernede legge styckes · that leyen in here neste ;
Ther is no wryght, as ich wene · sholde worche here nest to paye.
Yf eny mason therto · makede a molde 161
With alle here wyse castes · wonder me thynketh !

C. 132. mydel P. 136. ȝeeden P. 138. fetthers P. 143. sauh (*for* seih) P ; *see* ll. 135, 141. sotthliche P. 144. in (*before* drynkyng) KES ; and PTM. 150. wolde bere T ; wuld bere S ; beere P. 151. kynne MES ; kynde P. 152. lust MIKST ; loust P. 156. by-heelde P. neestes P. 158. wher · and at wham P (*only*) ; *the rest as in text*. 159. neste EIKSG ; neestes P ; *see next line*.

And ȝet me merueilled more · how many other briddes
Hudden and hileden · her egges ful derne
In mareys and mores · for men sholde hem nouȝt fynde,   344
And hudden here egges · whan thei there-fro wente,
For fere of other foules · and for wylde bestis.
And some troden her makes · and on trees bredden,
And brouȝten forth her bryddes so · al aboue the grounde;   348
And some bryddes at the bille · thorwgh brethynge conceyued;
And some kauked, I toke kepe · how pekokes bredden.
Moche merueilled me · what maister thei hadde,   351
And who tauȝte hem on trees · to tymbre so heighe,
There noither buirn ne beste · may her briddes rechen.
    And sythen I loked vpon the see · and so forth vpon the
        sterres,   354
Many selcouthes I seygh · ben nought to seye nouthe.
I seigh floures in the fritthe · and her faire coloures,
And how amonge the grene grasse · grewe so many hewes,
And somme soure and some swete · selcouthe me thouȝte;
Of her kynde and her coloure · to carpe it were to longe.
    Ac that moste moeued me · and my mode chaunged,   360
That Resoun rewarded · and reuled alle bestes,
Saue man and his make; · many tyme and ofte
No resoun hem folwed · and thanne I rebuked
Resoun, and riȝte · til hym-seluen I seyde,   364
'I haue wonder of the,' quod I · 'that witty art holden,
Why thow ne suwest man and his make · that no mysfait hem
        folwe?'

And Resoun arated me · and seyde, 'recche the neuere,   367

And ȝut ich meruaillede more · menye of tho bryddes
Hudden and heleden · durneliche here egges,   164
For no foul sholde hem fynde · bote hus fere and hym-self.
And some treden, ich tok kepe · and on trees bredden,
And brouhten forth here bryddes · al aboue the grounde.
In mareis and in mores · in myres and in wateres   168
Dompynges dyueden; · 'deere god,' ich sayde,
'Wher hadden these wilde suche witt · and at what scole?'
And whan the pocok caukede · ther-of ich took kepe,
How vn-corteisliche the cok · hus kynde forth strenede,   172
And ferliche hadde of hus fairnesse · and of hus foule ledene.

And siththe ich loked on the see · and so forth on the sterres,
Meny selcouth ich seih · aren nouht to seggen nouthe;
Ne what on floures in feldes · and of hure faire coloures,   176
How out of greot and of gras · grewe so meny huwes,
Somme soure and somme swete · selcouth me thouhte;
Of here kynde and of here colours · to carpen hit were to longe.

Ac that that moste meuede me · and my mod chaungede,   180
Was that ich seih Reson · suwen alle bestes
Saue man and mankynde; · meny tymes me thouhte,
Reson rewelede hem nat · nother riche ne poure.
Then ich aresonede Reson · and right til hym ich seide,   184
'Ich haue wonder in my witt · so wis as thow art holde,
Wher-for and why · so wide as thow regnest,
That thow ne ruelest rather · renkes than other beestes?
For ich see noone so ofte sorfeten · sothliche so mankynde;
In mete out of mesure · and meny tymes in drynke,   189
In wommen, in wedes · and in wordes bothe
Thei ouerdon hit day and nyght · and so doth noon othere.
Bestes ruwelen hem al by reson · and renkes ful fewe.   192
And ther-fore meruaileth me · for man, as in makynge,
Is most yliche the · in wit and in werkes,
Whi he ne loueth thy lore · and lyueth as thow techest?'
And Reson aresonede me · and seide, 'recche the neuere   196

C. 169. dyuyden P; dyuede IT; diuyde K.   170. these MKS; thees P.
172. hud (*for* hus) P.   strenede MIK; strende P.   173. ledene MKG;
leedene P.   175. ic (*for* ich) P; *see* l. 174.   176. P *om.* of.   178. sel-
couhth P.   180. moste I; most SKT; moost G; P *om.*   185. herte
(*for* art) P.   193. makynge KS; makyng ME; mankynde PG.   194.
His (*for* Is) P.   witt P.

Whi I suffre or nouȝt suffre · thi-self hast nouȝt to done; 368
Amende thow it, if thow myȝte · for my tyme is to abyde.
Suffraunce is a souereygne vertue · and a swyfte veniaunce.
Who suffreth more than god?' quod he · 'no gome, as I leue!
He miȝte amende in a minute-while · al that mys standeth, 372
Ac he suffreth for somme mannes good · and so is owre bettre.
Holy writ,' quod that weye · 'wisseth men to suffre;
    Propter deum subiecti estote omni creature.
Frenche men and fre men · affeyteth thus her childerne,
Bele vertue est soffrance · mal dire est petyt veniance, 376
Bien dire et bien soffrir · fait lui soffrant a bien venir.
For-thi I rede,' quod Reson · 'rewle thi tonge bettere,
And ar thow lakke eny lyf · loke if thow be to preyse!
For is no creature vnder Criste · can formen hym-seluen; 380
And if a man miȝte make · hym-self goed to the poeple,
Vch a lif wold be lakles · leue thow non other!
Ne thow schalt fynde but fewe · fayne for to here
Of here defautes foule · by-for hem rehersed. 384
    The wyse and the witty · wrote thus in the bible,
    De re que te non molestat, noli certare.
For be a man faire or foule · it falleth nouȝte for to lakke
The shappe ne the shafte · that god shope hym-selue;
For al that he did was wel ydo · as holywrit witnesseth, 388
    Et vidit deus cuncta que fecerat, et erant valde bona;
And badde euery creature · in his kynde encrees,
Al to murthe with man · that most woo tholye
In fondynge of the flesshe · and of the fende bothe.
For man was made of suche a matere · he may nouȝt wel astert
That ne some tymes hym bitit · to folwen his kynde; 393
Catoun acordeth there-with · *nemo sine crimine viuit.*'
    Tho cauȝte I coloure anon · and comsed to ben aschamed,
And awaked ther-with; · wo was me thanne 396
That I in meteles ne myȝte · more haue yknowen.
And thanne seyde I to my-self · and chidde that tyme;
'Now I wote what Dowel is,' quod I · 'by dere god, as me
    thinketh!'
And as I caste vp myn eyghen · one loked on me, and axed

B. 374—384. *These* 11 *lines are in* R *only.*   376. *pety* (for *petyt*) R.
379. my (*for* eny) R.   385. *noly* L.

Whi ich suffre other nat suffre : '—· ' certes,' ich seide, 197
' Ech a seg for hym-self · Salamon ous techeth;
    De re que te non molestat, noli certare.'
' Ho suffreth more than god ? ' quath he · ' no gome, as ich leyue !
He myght a-mende in a mynt-while · al that amys stondes ;
Ac he suffreth, in ensaumple · that we sholde alle suffren. 201
Ys no vertue so feyr · of value ne of profit,
As ys suffrance souereynliche · so hit be for godes loue.
And so witnesseth the wyse · and wysseth the Frenshe, 204
Bele uertue est suffraunce · mal dire est petite ueniaunce ;
Bien dire e bien suffrir · fait ly suffrable a bien uenir.
For-thi,' quath Reson, 'ich rede the · rewele thi tonge euere ;
And er thow lakke eny lyf · loke ho is to preise. 208
For is no creature vnder Cryst · that can hym-selue make ;
And yf Cristene creatures · couthen make hem-selue,
Eche lede wolde be lacles · leyf thow non othere !

Man was mad of suche matere · he may nat wel a-sterte 212
That som tymes hym tit · to folwen hus kynde;
Caton a-cordeth her-with · *nemo sine crimine uiuit.*'
   Tho cauhte ich colour a-non · and comsed to be ashamed,
And awaked ther-with ; · wo was me thenne, 216
That ich ne hadde ymet more · so murye as ich slepte,
And sayde a-non to my-self · ' slepynge, ich hadde grace
To wite what Dowel ys · ac wakynge neuere ! '

And thenne was ther a wiȝt · what he was ich nuste :— 220

C. 204. wittnesseth P.   206. *suffrer* PTMEG ; *suffrier* I ; read *suffrir*.
uenir IT ; *uener* PEG.   220. whiȝt P.

Of me, what thinge it were? · 'ywisse, sire,' I seide, 401
'To se moche and suffre more · certes,' quod I, 'is Dowel!'
'Haddestow suffred,' he seyde · 'slepyng tho thow were,
Thow sholdest haue knowen that Clergye can · and conceiued
    more thorugh Resoun ; 404
For Resoun wolde haue reherced the · ri3te as Clergye saide,
Ac for thine entermetyng · here artow forsake ;
    Philosophus esses, si tacuisses.
Adam, while he spak nou3t · had paradys at wille, 407
Ac whan he mameled aboute mete · and entermeted to knowe
The wisdom and the witte of god · he was put fram blisse ;
And ri3t so ferde Resoun bi the ; · thow with rude speche
Lakkedest, and losedest thinge · that longed nou3t to be done ;
Tho hadde he no lykynge · forto lere the more. 412
    Pruide now and presumpcioun · per-auenture, wole the appele,
That Clergye thi compaignye · ne kepeth nou3t to sue.
Shal neuere chalangynge ne chydynge · chaste a man so sone
As shal Shame, and shenden hym · and shape hym to amende.
For lat a dronken daffe · in a dyke falle, 417
Late hym ligge, loke nou3te on hym · til hym lest to ryse ;
For though Resoun rebuked hym thanne · reccheth he neuere,
Of clergie ne of his conseil · he counteth nou3t a rusche ; 420
To blame or for to bete hym thanne · it were but pure synne.
Ac whan Nede nymeth hym vp · for doute lest he sterue,
And Shame shrapeth his clothes · and his shynes wassheth,
Thanne wote the dronken daffe · wherfore he is to blame.'
    '3e seggen soth,' quod I · 'ich haue yseyne it ofte, 425
There smit no thinge so smerte · ne smelleth so soure,
As Shame, there he sheweth him · for euery man hym shonyeth !
Why 3e wisse me thus,' quod I · 'was for I rebuked Resoun.'
'Certes,' quod he, 'that is soth' · and shope hym for to
    walken ; 429
And I aros vp ri3t with that · and folwed hym after,
And preyed hym of his curteisye · to telle me his name.

B. 407. whhiles L.   419—421. reccheth—hym thanne *in* R *only*. R *has*
reccheth hym (*for* reccheth he), *and omits* To blame.   426. smitte L.

C. PASSUS XIV. 221–249.

'What ys Dowel?' quath that wi3t · 'y-wys, syre,' ich seyde,
'To see muche and suffren al · certes, syre, ys Dowel.'
  'Haddest thow suffred,' he seide · 'slepyng tho thow were,
Thow sholdest haue knowe that Cleregye can · and more con-
    ceyued thorwe Reson.   224
For Reson wolde haue reherced to the · ryght as Cleregie seide;
Ac for thyn entermetyng · her art thow for-sake :
    *Philosophus fuisses, si tacuisses; et alibi : Locutum me
    aliquando penituit, tacuisse nunquam.*
Adam, whiles he spak nat · hadde paradys at wylle ;   227
Ac whanne he mamelede a-boute mete · and musede for to knowe
The wisdome and the wit of god · he was putte out of blisse.
Ryght so ferde Reson by the · for thi rude speche,
And for thow woldest wyte why · of Resones pryuete.
  For pruyde and presompcion · of thy parfit lyuynge   232
Reson refusede the · and wolde nat reste with the,
Ne Cleregie of hus connynge · kepeth the nat shewe.
For shal neuere, er shame come · a shrewe wel be chasted.
For let a dronken daffe · in a diche falle,   236
Let hym lygge, lok nat on hym · til hym luste aryse ;
And thauh Reson rebuke hym thenne · reccheth he neuere,
Of clergie ne of kynde witt · counteth he nat a russhe :
To blame hym other to bete hym thenne · ich halde hit bote
    synne.   240
Ac when Neede nymeth hym vp · a-non he ys a-shamed,
And thenne wot he wher-fore · and whi he is to blame.'
  '3e seggeth soth, by my soule,' quath ich · 'ich haue seyen
    hit ofte,
Ther smyt no thynge so smerte · ne smelleth so foule   244
As Shame ; ther he sheweth hym · ech man shoneth hus
    companye.
Whi 3e worden to me thus · was for ich aresonede Reson.'
  '3e, certes,' quath he, 'that is soth' · and shop hym to walke ;
And ich a-roos vp ryght with that · and reuerencede hym fayre,
And yf hus wil were · he wolde hus name telle ?   249
    Hic explicit passus quartus de Dowel.

C. 223. suffrede P.   226. ert (*for* art) PE.   227. att P. 229. witt P.   237.
Let MKST ; Leet P.   on IKMST ; in PE.   238. rebuke IKMST ; rebuky P.
241. a-shamede P.   244. Ther IKMST ; Her PE.   248. ryght vp P.

PASSUS XII.

Passus duodecimus.

'I AM Ymagynatyf,' quod he · 'idel was I neuere,
Thou3e I sitte bi my-self · in sikenesse ne in helthe.
I haue folwed the in feithe · this fyue and fourty wyntre,
And many tymes haue moeued the · to thinke on thine ende, 4
And how fele fern3eres are faren · and so fewe to come,
And of thi wylde wantounesse · tho thow 3onge were,
To amende it in thi myddel age · lest mi3te the faylled
In thyne olde elde · that yuel can suffre 8
Pouerte or penaunce · or preyeres bidde;
   Si non in prima vigilia, nec in secunda, etc.
Amende the while thow my3te · thow hast ben warned ofte
With poustees of pestilences · with pouerte and with angres;
And with thi$e bitter baleyses · god beteth his dere childeren,
   Quem diligo, castigo.
And Dauid in the sauter seith · of suche that loueth Iesus, 13
   " *Virga tua et baculus tuus, ipsa me consolata sunt, &c.*
Al-though thow stryke me with thi staffe · with stikke or with 3erde,
It is but murth as for me · to amende my soule."
And thow medlest the with makynges · and my3test go sey thi
   sauter, 16
And bidde for hem that 3iueth the bred; · for there ar bokes ynowe
To telle men what Dowel is · Dobet, and Dobet bothe,
And prechoures to preue what it is · of many a peyre freres.'
I seigh wel he sayde me soth · and, somwhat me to excuse, 20
Seide, 'Catoun conforted his sone · that, clerke though he were,
To solacen hym sum tyme · as I do whan I make;
Interpone tuis interdum gaudia curis, etc.
And of holy men I herde,' quod I · 'how thei other-while 24
Pleyden, the parfiter to be · in many places.
Ac if there were any wight · that wolde me telle
What were Dowel and Dobet · and Dòbest atte laste,
Wolde I neuere do werke · but wende to holicherche, 28
And there bydde my bedes · but whan ich eet or slepe.'

B. 21. Seid L; Seide W.

PASSUS XV.

Incipit passus quintus de Dowel.

' ICH am Ymaginatif,' quath he · 'ydel was ich neuere,
Thauh ich sitte by my-self · suche is my grace;
Ich haue yfolwed the in faith · more than fourty wynter,
And wissede the ful ofte · what Dowel was to mene, 4
And counsailede the for Cristes sake · no creature to by-gyle,
Nother to lye nother to lacke · ne lere that is defendid,
Ne to spille speche · as to speke an ydel,
And no tyme to tyne · ne trewe thyng to teenen; 8
Lowe the to lyue forth · in the lawe of holychurche;
Thenne dost thow wel, with-oute drede · ho can do bet, no forse!
Clerkes that connen al · ich hope thei conne do bettere;
Ac hit suffiseth to be saued · and to be suche as ich tauhte. 12
Ac for to louye and lene · and lyue wel and by-leyue,
Ys ycallid *Caritas* · Kynde Loue in English;
And that is Dobet, yf eny suche be · a blessed man, that helpeth
That pees be and pacience · and poure with-oute defaute; 16
Beatius est dare quam petere.

C. 2. ich sitt E; i sitte MT; ysete P.   3. yfolwede P.   5. counsalede P.
8. tyne EMIKTS; tene P.   trywe P.   10. bett P.   13. an (*for 2nd*
and) P.   14. ycalid P.   16. That IMKST; And PE.

'Poule in his pistle,' quod he · 'preueth what is dowel; 30
    Fides, spes, caritas; et maior horum, etc.
Feith, hope, and charitee · and alle ben good,
And sauen men sundry tymes · ac none so sone as charite. 32
For he doth wel with-oute doute · that doth as lewte techeth;
That is, if thow be man maried · thi make thow louye,
And lyue forth as lawe wole · while ʒe lyuen bothe.
Riʒt so, if thow be religious · renne thow neuere ferther 36
To Rome ne to Rochemadore · but as thi reule techeth,
And holde the vnder obedyence · that heigh wey is to heuene.
    And if thow be mayden to marye · and miʒte wel contynue,
Seke thow neuere seynt forther · for no soule helthe. 40
For what made Lucyfer · to lese the heigh heuene,
Or Salamon his sapience · or Sampson his strengthe?
Iob the Iewe his ioye · dere he it abouʒte,
Arestotle and other mo · Ypocras, & Virgyle; 44
Alisaundre that al wan · elengelich ended.
Catel and kynde witte · was combraunce to hem alle.
Felyce hir fayrnesse · fel hir al to sklaundre;
And Rosamounde riʒt so · reufully bysette, 48
The bewte of hir body · in badnesse she dispended.
Of many suche I may rede · of men and of wommen,
That wyse wordes wolde shewe · and worche the contrarye,
    Sunt homines nequam bene de virtute loquentes. 52
    And riche renkes riʒt so · gaderen and sparen,
And tho men that thei moste haten · mynistren it atte laste;
And, for thei suffren & se · so many nedy folkes,
And loue hem nouʒt as owre lorde byt · lesen her soules;
    Date et dabitur vobis, etc.
So catel and kende wit · acombreth ful many; 57
Wo is hym that hem weldeth · but if he hem wel despende;
    Scientes et non facientes varijs flagellis vapulabunt;
Sapience, seith the boke · swelleth a mannes soule,
    Sapiencia inflat, etc.;
And ricchesse riʒt so · but if the rote be trewe; 60
Ac grace is a grasse ther-of · tho greuaunces to abate.
Ac grace ne groweth nouʒte · but amonges lowe;
Pacience and pouerte · the place is there it groweth,

B. 57-59. *These lines are in* R *only, and in* C-text.   58. wel M; wil R.

Ac catel and kynde witt · encombreth ful menye;
Woo is hym that hem weldeth · bote he hem wel dispeyne;
   Scientes et non facientes uariis flagellis uapulabunt.
Ac comunliche connynge · and vnkynde rychesse,
As, loreles to be lordes · and lewede men techeres,   20
And holy churche horen help · auerous and coueytous,
Droweth vp Dowel · and distruyeth Dobest.
Ac grace is a gras ther-fore · to don hem eft growe;
Ac grace groweth nat · til goode wil gynne reyne,   24
And wokie thorwe good werkes · wikkede hertes.

C. 18. hym (*for* hem) PE.   24. goode wil K; goode wille E; goud
wille S; god wol PI.

And in lele-lyuynge men · and in lyf-holy, 64
And thorugh the gyfte of the holygoste · as the gospel telleth,
    Spiritus vbi vult spirat, etc.
Clergye and Kynde Witte · comth of si3te and techynge,
As the boke bereth witnesse · to buirnes that can rede,
    Quod scimus, loquimur ; quod vidimus, testamur.
Of *quod scimus* cometh clergye · and connynge of heuene, 68
And of *quod vidimus* cometh kynde witte · of si3te of dyuerse peple.
Ac grace is a gyfte of god · and of gret loue spryngeth ;
Knewe neuere clerke how it cometh forth · ne kynde witte the weyes,
    Nescit aliquis vnde venit, aut quo vadit, etc.
Ac 3it is clergye to comende · and kynde witte bothe, 72
And namely clergye, for Crystes loue · that of clergye is rote.
For Moyses witnesseth that god wrote · for to wisse the peple,
In the olde lawe, as the lettre telleth · that was the lawe of Iewes,
That what woman were in auoutrie taken · were she riche or pore,
With stones men shulde hir stryke · and stone hir to deth. 77
A womman, as we fynden · was gulty of that dede,
Ac cryste of his curteisye · thorw clergye hir saued ;
For thorw carectus that Cryst wrot · the Iewes knewe hemseluen
Gultier as afor god · and gretter in synne
Than the woman that there was · and wenten awey for schame.
The clergye that there was · conforted the womman.
Holykirke knoweth this · that Crystes writyng saued ; 84
So clergye is conforte · to creatures that repenten,
And to mansed men · myschief at her ende.
    For goddes body my3te nou3te be · of þred, withouten clergye,
The which body is bothe · bote to the ri3tful, 88
And deth and dampnacioun · to hem that dyeth yuel.
As Crystes carecte conforted and bothe · coupable shewed
The womman that the Iewes brou3te · that Iesus thou3te to saue ;
    Nolite iudicare, et non iudicabimini, etc.
Ri3t so goddes body, bretheren · but it be worthily taken, 92
Dampneth vs atte daye of dome · as the carectes dede the iewes.
For-thi I conseille the for Cristes sake · Clergye that thow louye,
For Kynde Witte is of his kyn · and neighe cosynes bothe

B. 69. dyuese (*sic*) L.

C. PASSUS XV. 26-43.

Ac er suche a wil wexe · god hym-self worcheth,
And sent forth seint espirit · to don loue sprynge;
    Spiritus ubi uult spirat, et cetera.
So grace, with-oute grace · of god and of good werkes,   28
May nat bee, bee thow siker · thauh we bidde euere.
Cleregie cometh bote of siht · and kynde witt of sterres,
As to be bore other bygete · in suche constellacion,
That wit wexeth ther-of · and othere wyrdes bothe;   32
    Uultus huius seculi sunt subiecti uultibus celestibus.

So grace is a gyfte of god · and kynde witt a chaunce,
And cleregye and connyng · of kynde wittes techynge.

And ȝut is cleregie to comende · for Cristes loue, more
Than eny connynge of kynde witt · bote cleregie hit ruwele. 36
For Moyses wittnesseth that god wrot · in stoon with hus fynger,
Lawe of loue oure lorde wrot · longe er Crist were.

And Crist cam and confermede · and holy kirke made,
And in sond a sygne wrot · and seide to the Iewes,   40
'That seeth hym-self synneles · cesse nat, ich hote,
To stryke with stoon other with staf · this strompet to dethe;'
    Qui uestrum sine peccato est mittat in eam lapidem, & cetera.

For-thi ich consaile alle Cristene · cleregie to honoure;

C. 26. wil MKST; will wol P.   27. sent EKST; send PM.   32.
wyrdus S; wirdes K; wordes (*badly*) PEIT (*wyrdes* = destinies).   35. fore
P.   39. kirke I; churche PEFS.   42. strompett P.   *mittat—lapidem* in
E only.   43. consaily P; *see* l. 64.

To owre lorde, leue me; · for-thi loue hem, I rede;   96
For bothe ben as miroures · to amenden owre defautes,
And lederes for lewed men · and for lettred bothe.
For-thi lakke thow neuere logyke · lawe, ne his custumes,
Ne countreplede clerkes · I conseille the for eure.   100
For as a man may nou3t se · that mysseth his eyghen,
Namore can no klerke · but if he cau3t it first thorugh bokes.
Al-though men made bokes · god was the maistre,
And seynt spirit the saumplarye · and seide what men sholde
    write.   104
And ri3t as sy3te serueth a man · to se the heighe strete,
Ri3t so ledeth letterure · lewed men to resoun.
And as a blynde man in bataille · bereth wepne to fi3te,
And hath none happ with his axe · his enemye to hitte,   108
Namore kan a kynde-witted man · but clerkes hym teche,
Come for al his kynde witte · to Crystendome and be saued;
Whiche is the coffre of Crystes tresore · and clerkes kepe the
    keyes,
To vnlouken it at her lykynge · and to the lewed peple   112
3yue mercy for her mysdedes · if men it wole aske
Buxomelich and benygneliche · and bidden it of grace.
    Archa-dei in the olde lawe · Leuites it kepten;
Hadde neuere lewed man leue · to leggen honde on that chest,
But he were preste or prestes sone · patriarke or prophete.
    Saul, for he sacrifised · sorwe hym be-tydde,
And his sones al-so · for that synne myscheued,
And many mo other men · that were no Leuites,   120
That with *archa-dei* 3eden · in reuerence and in worchippe,
And leyden honde ther-on to liften it vp · and loren hir lif after.
For-thi I conseil alle creatures · no clergie to dispise,
Ne sette schort be here science · what so thei don hemselue.   124
Take we her wordes at worthe · for here witnesse be trewe,
And medle we nau3t muche with hem · to meuen any wrathe,
Lest cheste chafen vs · to choppe vche man other;
    Nolite tangere christos meos, etc.
    For Clergye is kepere · vnder Cryst of heuene;   128
Was there neuere no kny3te · but Clergye hym made.

B. 118–127. *These lines in* R *only and in* C-*text*.   126. medele we M;
ne medle we R.   127. chasen R; *see* C-text.

For as a man may nat seo · that mysseth hus eyen, 44
No more can no clerkes · bote if hit be of bookes.
And thauh men maden bokes · god was here maister,
And seynte spirit the saumplarie · and seide what men sholde wryte.
And ryght as syht serueth a man · to see the hye strete, 48
Ryght so lereth lettrure · lewede men to reson.
And as a blynde man in batayle · bereth wepne to fyghte,
And hath non hap with hus axe · hus enemy to hitte;
No more can a kynde-witted man · bote clerkes hym teche, 52
Come for alle hus kynde wyttes · thorwe Cristendom to be saued;
The whiche is cofre of Cristes tresour · and clerkes kepen the keyes,
To vnlouke hit at here lykynge · the lewede and lerede to helpe,
To 3eue mercy for mysdedes · yf men wolde hit aske 56
Buxumliche and benygneliche · and bydden hit of grace.
  Archa-dei in the olde lawe · Leuites hit kepten ;
Hadde neuere lewede man leue · to legge honde on that cheste,
Bote hit were preeste other preestes sone · patriarck other prophete.
  Saul, for he sacrifisede · sorwe hym by-tydde, 61
And hus sones for hus synnes · sorwe they hadden ;
And alle lewede that leyde hond theron · loren lyf after.
For-thy ich consaille alle creatures · no clerk to dispise, 64
Ne sette short by here science · what so thei don hemselue.
Take we here wordes a worth · for here wittnesses ben trewe,
And medle we nat moche with hem · to meeuen eny wratthe,
Leste cheste chaufe ous so · and choppe ech man othere ; 68
And do we as Dauid techeth · for doute of godes veniaunce ;
  Nolite tangere Cristos meos, &c.
For Cleregie is Cristes vikery · to conforte and to curen ;
Bothe lered and lewed were lost · yf cleregie ne were.

C. 45. if IKG ; 3if EMT ; P *om.*   53. sauede P.   59. on IMKT ;
in PES.   60. preestes PEIST ; prest MK.   63. *From* IKT ; *not in* P.
66. trywe P.

Ac Kynde Witte cometh · of alkynnes siȝtes,
Of bryddes and of bestes · of tastes of treuthe, and of deceytes.
Lyueres to-forn vs · vseden to marke 132
The selkouthes that thei seighen · her sones for to teche,

And helden it an heighe science · her wittes to knowe.
Ac thorugh her science sothely · was neuere no soule ysaued,
Ne brouȝte by her bokes · to blisse ne to ioye; 136
For alle her kynde knowynges · come but of dyuerse sightes.

Patriarkes and prophetes · repreued her science,
And seiden, her wordes ne her wisdomes · was but a folye;
As to the clergye of Cryst · counted it but a trufle; 140
 Sapiencia huius mundi, stulticia est apud deum.
For the heihe holigoste · heuene shal to-cleue,
And loue shal lepe out after · in-to this lowe erthe,
And clennesse shal cacchen it · and clerkes shullen it fynde;
 Pastores loquebantur ad inuicem.
He speketh there of riche men riȝt nouȝt · ne of riȝt witty,
Ne of lordes that were lewed men · but of the hexte lettred oute,
 Ibant magi ab oriente, etc.
If any frere were founde there · ich ȝif the fyue shillynges;
Ne in none beggares cote · was that barne borne,
But in a burgeys place · of Bethlem the best; 148
 Set non erat locus eis in diuersorio; et pauper non habet
 diuersorium.
To pastours and to poetes · appiered that aungel,
And bad hem go to Bethlem · goddis burth to honoure,
And songe a songe of solas · *gloria in excelsis deo!*
Riche men rutte tho · and in here reste were, 152
Tho it schon to the schepherdes · a schewer of blisse.

Clerkes knewe it wel · and comen with here presentz,
And deden her homage honourablely · to hym that was almyȝty.
Why I haue tolde the al this— · I toke ful gode hede 156
How thow contraryedest Clergye · with crabbed wordes,
"How that lewed men liȝtloker · than lettred were saued,

B. 139. was R; nas LWCROB; *but observe the alliteration.*   140. *est*
WCB; LRO *om.*   148. *eis* from the Vulgate; LCOB *om.*   152, 153.
These lines in R *only; and in* **C**-text.   153. þe M; R *om.*   156.
þe CRB; LW *om.*

Kynde-wittede men han · a cleregie by hem-selue ; 72
Of cloudes and of custumes · thei contreuede meny thynges,
And markede hit in here manere · and mused ther-on to knowe.
And of the selcouthes that thei seyen · here sones ther-of thei
 tauhte,
Thei helden hit for an hey science · here soteltes to knowe. 76
Ac thorw here science sothliche · was neuere soule ysaued,
Ne brouht thorwe here bokes · to blisse ne to ioye.
For al here kynde knowyng · cam bote of diuerse sightes
Of briddes and of bestes · of blisse and of sorwe. 80
 Patriarkes and prophetes · reprouede here science,
And seide here wordes and here wysdomes · ne was bote al
 folye ;
As to the cleregie of Cryst · thei countede hit bote a trufle ;
 Sapientia huius mundi stultitia est apud deum.
For the hye holygost · shall heuene to-cleue, 84
And loue shal leepe out after · in-to this lowe erthe,
And clannesse shal cacchen hit · and clerkes shullen hit fynde;
 Pastores loquebantur ad inuicem, et cet.
Hit speketh of riche men ryght nouht · ne of riche lordes,
Bote of clennesse and of clerkes · and kepers of bestes; 88
 Ibant magi ab oriente, ét cetera.
Yf eny frere were founde there · ich ȝeue the fyue shyllinges !
Nother in cote nother in caytyf hous · was Crist y-bore,
Bote in a burgeises hous · the beste of alle the toune.

 To pastours and to poetes · aperede the angel, 92
And bad hem go to Bedlehem · godes burthe to honoure,
And songen a song of solas · *Gloria in excelsis deo!*
Riche men routten tho · and in here reste were,
Tho hit shon to the shepehurdes · a shewere of blisse. 96
Clerkes knewen the comete · and comen with here presentes,
And dude here homage honorably · to hym that was almyghty.
Whi ich haue ytold the al this · ich took ful good hede,
How thow contrariedest Cleregie · with crabbede wordes, 100
That is, how lewede men and luthere · lyghtloker were saued

C. 75. selcouthes MEKSTG ; selcouthe P.   79. PE *insert* ne *before* cam.
80. PE *om.* 2nd of.   89. PE *om.* the.   94. songen M ; songe IT ; **syngen**
PEK.   101. lyghlokere P (*sic*). sauede P.

Than clerkes or kynde-witted men · of Crystene peple."
And thow seidest soth of somme · ac se in what manere :— 160
Take two stronge men · and in Themese caste hem,
And bothe naked as a nedle · her none sykerer than other,
That one hath connynge · and can swymmen and dyuen,
That other is lewed of that laboure · lerned neuere swymme;
Which trowestow of tho two · in Themese is in moste drede?
He that neuere ne dyued · ne nouȝt can of swymmynge,
Or the swymmere that is sauf · bi so hym-self lyke,
There his felaw flet forth · as the flode lyketh, 168
And is in drede to drenche · that neuere dede swymme?'
'That swymme can nouȝt,' I seide · 'it seemeth to my wittes.'
'Riȝt so,' quod the renke · 'resoun it sheweth,
That he that knoweth clergye · can sonner aryse 172
Out of synne and be sauf · though he synne ofte,
If hym lyketh and lest · than any lewed lelly.
For if the clerke be konnynge · he knoweth what is synne,
And how contricioun with-oute confessioun conforteth the soule,
As thow seest in the sauter · in psalme one or tweyne, 177
How contricioun is commended · for it caccheth awey synne;
    Beati quorum remisse sunt iniquitates, et quorum tecta sunt
       peccata, etc.
And this conforteth vch a clerke · and keuereth hym fram wanhope,
In which flode the fende · fondeth a man hardest; 180
There the lewed lith stille · and loketh after lente,
And hath no contricioun ar he come to shryfte · and thanne can
    he litel telle,
And as his lores-man leres hym · bileueth and troweth;
And that is after person or parisch prest · and, parauenture bothe
Vnconnynge to lere lewed men · as Luk bereth witnesse, 185
    Dum cecus ducit cecum, ambo in foueam cadunt.
Wo was hym marked · that wade mote with the lewed!
Wel may the barne blisse · that hym to boke sette;
That lyuynge after letterure · saued hym lyf and soule! 188
Dominus pars hereditatis mee · is a meri verset,
That has take fro Tybourne · twenti stronge theues;
There lewed theues ben lolled vp · loke how thei be saued!

B. 162. syker L; sikerer WCOB.   178. *peccata* in R only.   184.
bothe R; LWCB *om.*; cf. C-text.   185. *ambo in foueam* in OC₂ only;
cadunt I have supplied.

Than connynge clerkes · of kynde vnderstondyng ;
And thow seidest soth of somme · ac ich seye in what manere.
Take two stronge men · and in Temese cast hem,　　104
And bothe naked as a nelde · here nother heuyour than other ;
That on hath connynge · and can swimmen and dyuen,
That other is lewede of that labour · and lernede neuere swymme ;
Which is, trowest thow, of tho two · in Temese most in drede?'
　'He that can nat swymme,' ich seyde · 'hit semeth to alle
　　wittes.'　　109
'Ryght so,' quath that renke · 'reson hit sheweth,
That he that knoweth cleregie · can sonnere a-ryse
Out of synne, and be saf · thow he synegy ofte,　　112
If hym lyketh and lust · than eny lewede sothliche.
For yf the clerk be connynge · and knoweth what is synne,
And hou contricion with-oute confession · conforteth the soule,
As we seen in the sauter · in psalmes on other tweye,　　116
How contricion is comended · for hit caccheth a-wey synne,
　　*Beati quorum remisse sunt iniquitates, et quorum tecta sunt
　　　peccata, &c.:*
And that comforteth ech a clerk · and keuereth fro wanhope,
In whiche flood the feend · fondeth man hardest,
Ther the lewede lyeth stille · and loketh after lente,　　120
And hath no contricion · ar he come to shryfte ;
And than can he lytel telle · of on other of other,
Bote as his loresman lereth hym · he by-leyueth and troweth ;
And that is after person other pareshe-preest · and paraunter
　　bothe beth lewede　　124
For to lere lewede men · as Luc bereth wittnesse ;
　　Si cecus ducit cecum, ambo in foueam cadent:
For muche woo was hym marked · that wade shal with the
　　lewede.
　Wel may the barn blesse · that hym to book sette ;
That lyuynge after lettrure · sauede hym lyf and soule !　　128
Dominus pars hereditatis mee · ys a murye verset,
Hit hath ytake fro Tyborne · twenty stronge theeues ;
Ther lewede theeues ben lollid vp · loke how thei been sauede !

C. 104. two STG ; to PEMK.　　108. two STK ; to PEM.　　117. cac-
cheth MIKSG ; chacheth P.　　*et—peccata* E.　　118. a IKST ; PEMG *om.*
koeuereþ P.　　129. versett P.

The thef that had grace of god · on Gode Fryday as thow speke,
Was, for he ȝelte hym creaunt to Cryst on the crosse · and knew-
    leched hym gulty,   193
And grace axed of god · that to graunten it is redy
To hem that boxomeliche biddeth it · and ben in wille to
    amenden hem.
Ac though that thef had heuene · he hadde none heigh blisse,
As seynt Iohan and other seyntes · that asserued hadde bettere.
Riȝt as sum man ȝeue me mete · and sette me amydde the flore,
Ich haue mete more than ynough · ac nouȝt so moche worship
As tho that seten atte syde-table · or with the souereignes of
    the halle,   200
But sitte as a begger bordelees · bi my-self on the grounde.
So it fareth bi that feloun · that a Gode Fryday was saued;
He sit neither with seynt Iohan · Symonde, ne Iude,
Ne wyth maydenes ne with martires · confessoures ne wydwes,
But by hym-self as a soleyne · and serued on the erthe.   205
For he that is ones a thef · is euermore in daungere,
And as lawe lyketh · to lyue or to deye;
    De peccato propiciato, noli esse sine metu.
And forto seruen a seynt · and such a thef togyderes,   208
It were noyther resoun ne riȝt · to rewarde hem bothe aliche.
    And riȝt as *Troianus* the trewe knyȝt · tilde nouȝt depe in
    helle,
That owre lorde ne had hym liȝtlich oute · so leue I the thef be
    in heuene.   211
For he is in the lowest of heuene · if owre bileue be trewe,
And wel loselyche he lolleth there · by the lawe of holy-cherche,
    Quia reddit vnicuique iuxta opera sua, etc.
    And why that one thef on the crosse · creaunt hym ȝelt
Rather than that other thef · though thow wolde appose,   215
Alle the clerkes vnder Cryst · ne couthe the skil assoille;
    Quare placuit, quia voluit.
And so I sey by the · that sekest after the whyes,
And aresonedest Resoun · a rebukyng as it were,   218

B. 194. þat—is *from* W; and he is euer LCOB.   195. To hem *from* W.
LCROB *om.*   197. *In margin of* L—*in domo meo multe sunt mantiones.*
203. sit WC; sitte L.

The theef that hadde grace of god · a Goode Fryday, as thow
 toldest, 132
Was, for he ȝelde hym creaunt to Crist · and hus grace askede.
And god is ay gracious · to alle that gredeth to hym,
He wol no wickede man be lost · bote yf he wol hym-self;
 Nolo mortem peccatoris, sed ut magis conuertatur et uiuat.
And thauh the theef hadde heuene · he hadde non hye blisse
As seynt Iohan and other seyntes · that han a-serued bettere.
Ryght as som man ȝyueth me mete · and set me a-mydde the
 floor, 138
Ich haue mete more than ynowe · ac nat with so muche worshup
As tho that sytten at the syd-table · other with the souereynes
 in halle, 140
Bote, as a beggere, bordles · by my-self vpon the grounde.
So hit ferde by the felon · that a Goode Fryday was saued;
He sit nother with seynt Iohan · with Symon ne with Iude,
Ne with maydenes ne with martris · ne with mylde wydewes,
Bote as a soleyn by hym-self · and serued vp-on the grounde.
For he that ys ones a theef · is euere-more in daunger, 146
And as the lawe lyketh · to lyue other to deye,
 De peccato propiciato noli esse sine metu;
And for to seruen a seynt · and suche a theef to-gederes,
Hit were no reson ne ryght · to rewarde bothe yliche.
Ryȝt as *Traianus*, the trewe knyght · tulde nat deep in helle,
That oure lord ne hadde hym lyghtliche out · so leyueth of the
 theef in heuene.
For he ys in the lowest heuene · yf oure byleyue beo trewe, 152
And wel loseliche lolleth there · as by the lawe of holy-churche;
 Et reddet unicuique secundum opera sua.
Ac whi that one theef vp-on the croys · creaunt hym ȝelde
Rather than that other · thauh thou woldest apose,
Alle the clerkes vnder Crist · ne couthe thys asoile; 156
 Quare placuit, quia uoluit, etc.
And so ich seye by the · that sekest after weyes,
How creatures han kynde witt · and clerkes comen to bokes,

C. 133. ȝelde EIKG; ȝald T; ȝuld P. hem (*for* hym) P. **137.** a-seruede P.
138. sett P. **142.** sauede P. **143.** sit IMKSTG; sat P. **145.** seruede P.
149. yliche IKSEG; liche P. **150, 152.** trywe P. **153.** loseliche K;
losliche P; louslich E; loslich S; lifliche I; loueliche MT. *reddet* EIKMST;
reddit P. **154.** one I; o T; PEMSKG *om.* **158.** han IKG; and PEMS.

And of the floures in the fryth · and of her feire hewes,
Where-of thei cacche her coloures · so clere and so briȝte,   220
And willest of briddes and of bestes · and of hire bredyng to knowe,
Why somme be alowe and somme alofte · thi lykyng it were,
And of the stones and of the sterres · thow studyest, as I leue,
How euere beste or brydde · hath so breme wittes: 224
Clergye ne kynde witte · ne knewe neuere the cause,
Ac Kynde knoweth the cause hym-selue · and no creature elles.
He is the pyes patroun · and putteth it in hire ere,
That there the thorne is thikkest · to buylden and brede;
And Kynde kenned the pecok · to cauken in swich a kynde,
And kenned Adam · to knowe his pryue membres,   230
And tauȝte hym and Eue · to hylien hem with leues.
  Lewed men many tymes · maistres thei apposen,
Why Adam ne hiled nouȝte firste · his mouth that eet the apple,
Rather than his lykam a-low · lewed axen thus clerkes;   234
Kynde knoweth whi he dede so · ac no clerke elles.
Ac of briddes and of bestes · men by olde tyme
Ensamples token and termes · as telleth this poetes,
And that the fairest foule · foulest engendreth,   238
And feblest foule of flyght is · that fleegheth or swymmeth;
And that is the pekok·and the pohenne · proude riche men thei bitokneth,   240
For the pekok, and men pursue hym · may nouȝte fleighe heighe;
For the traillyng of his taille · ouertaken is he sone,
And his flesshe is foule flesshe · and his feet bothe,
And vnlouelich of ledene · and laith for to here.   244
  Riȝt so the riche · if he his ricchesse kepe,
And deleth it nouȝt tyl his deth-day · the taille of al sorwe.
Riȝt as the pennes of the pecok · peyneth hym in his fliȝte,
So is possessioun payne · of pens and of nobles   248
To alle hem that it holdeth · til her taille be plukked.
And though the riche repente thanne · and bīrewe the tyme,
That euere he gadered so grete · and gaf there of so litel,
Though he crye to Cryst thanne · with kene wille, I leue   252
His ledne be in owre lordes ere · lyke a pyes chiteryng.

B. 226. and WCOB; LR *om.*   247. peyneth WOB; payned LR.   253. chiteryng W; LCROB *om.*

And how the floures in the fritth · cometh to feyre hewes;
Was neuere creature vnder Cryst · that knew wel the bygynnynge
Bote Kynde, that contreeuede hit furst · of corteise wil.   161
He tauhte the tortle to trede · the pokok to cauke,
And Adam and Eue · and other bestes alle
A cantel of kynde witt · here kynde to saue.   164
Of good and of wikke · Kynde was the ferste,
He seih hit and suffrede hit · and seide hit bee sholde;
  Quia ipse dixit, et facta sunt ; ipse mandauit, et creata sunt.
Ac whi he wolde that wikkede were · ich wene and ich leyue,
Was neuere man vpon molde · that myghte hit aspye.   168

  Ac longe-lybbynge men · lyknede mennes lyuynge
To bryddes and to bestes · as here bokes telleth,
That the fayrest fowel · foulest engendreth,
And feblest fowel of flicht is · that fleeth othere swymmeth.   172
That is, the pokok and the popeiay · with here proude federes
By-tokneth ryght riche men · that regnen here on erthe.
For porsewe a pocok · other a pohen to cacche,
And haue hem in haste · at thyn owene wil;   176
For thei may nat fleo fer · ne ful hye nother,
For here fetheres that faire ben · to fle fer hem letteth.
Hus leedene is vnloueliche · and lothliche hus caroigne;
Ac for hus peyntede pennes · the pocok is honoured   180
More than for hus faire flesch · other for hus murye note.
Ryght so men reuerenceth more the ryche · for hus muche meeble
Than for the kyn that he cam of · other for hus kynde wittes.
Thus the poete preiseth · the pocok for hus federes,   184
And the riche for hus rentes · othere rychesse in hus schoppe.

C. 161. corteise ES; cortese K; curteis MI; korteis G; cortesie P.   172.
fleeth IM; fleth ET; flucht P.   173. pookoc P; pecok KTG.   withe P.
177. fer IMSTG; fur P.   178. fer IMSTG; feer P.   180. pennes IT;
fetheres PEMSKG (*badly*). his honourede P.   183. fore (*for* 2*nd* for) P.
185. fore P. schoppe EMKSG; sheepe P.

And whan his caroigne shal come · in caue to be buryed,
I leue it flaumbe ful foule · the folde al aboute,   255
And alle the other ther it lyth · enuenymeth thorgh his attere.
By the po feet is vnderstonde · as I haue lerned in Auynete,
Excecutoures, fals frendes · that fulfille nouȝt his wille
That was writen, and thei witnesse · to worche riȝt as it wolde.
Thus the poete preues that the pecok · for his fetheres is
       reuerenced,   260
Riȝt so is the riche · bi resoun of his godis.
   The larke, that is a lasse foule · is more louelich of ledne,
And wel awey of wenge · swifter than the pecok,
And of flesch, by fele folde · fatter and swetter.   264
To lowe-lybbyng men · the larke is resembled;
Arestotle the grete clerke · suche tales he telleth;
Thus he lykneth in his logyk · the leste foule oute.
And where he be sauf or nouȝt sauf · the sothe wote no clergye,
Ne of Sortes ne of Salamon · no scripture can telle.   269
Ac god is so good, I hope · that sitth he gaf hem wittis
To wissen vs weyes there-with · (that wissen vs to be saued,
And the better for her bokes) · to bidden we ben holden,   272
That god for his grace · gyue her soules reste;
For lettred men were lewed men ȝut · ne were lore of her bokes.'
   'Alle thise clerkes,' quod I tho · 'that on Cryst leuen,
Seggen in her sarmones · that noyther Sarasenes ne Iewes,
Ne no creature of Cristes lyknesse · with-outen Crystendome
       worth saued.'   277
   'Contra,' quod Ymagynatyf tho · and comsed for to loure,
       And seyde, 'saluabitur vix iustus in die iudicij.
Ergo saluabitur,' quod he · and seyde namore Latyne.
'Troianus was a trewe knyȝte · and toke neuere Cristendome,
And he is sauf, so seith the boke · and his soule in heuene.
For there is fullyng of fonte · and fullyng in blode-shedynge, 282
And thorugh fuire is fullyng · and that is ferme bileue;
       Aduenit ignis diuinus, non comburens, sed illuminans, etc.
   Ac trewth that trespassed neuere · ne transuersed aȝeines his
       lawe,   284
But lyueth as his lawe techeth ·' and leueth there be no bettere,
And if there were, he wolde amende · and in suche wille deyeth,

---

B. 256. enuenyméþ WCOB; enuenymed LR.   257. po feet WR; profeet (!) L.

The larke, that is a lasse fowel · is loueloker of lydene,
And swettur of sauour · and swyfter of wynge.
To lowe-lyuynge men · the larke is resembled,   188
And to leelle and to lyf-holy · that louen alle treuthe.
Thus Porfirie and Plato · and poetes menye
Lykneth in here logyk · the leeste fowel oute.
And whether hij be saf other nat saf · the sothe wot nat clergie,
Ne of Sortes, ne of Salamon · no scripture can telle   193
Whether thei be in helle other in heuene ; · other Aristotle the wise.
Ac god is so good, ich hope · sitthe he gaf hem wittes
To wissen ous weyes ther-with · that wenen to be saued,   196
And the bettere for here bookes— · to bidden we been holde
That god for hus grace · gyue here saules reste ;
For lettred men were but lewede men ȝut · ne were the lore
    of tho clerkes.'
'Alle these clerkes,' quath ich tho · 'that on Crist byleyuen,
Seggen in here sarmons · that nother Sarrasyns ne Iewes   201
With-oute baptisme, as by here bokes · beeth nat ysaued.'
'*Contra*,' quath Ymaginatif tho · and comsed to loure,
    And seide, '*uix saluabitur iustus in die iudicii*;
Ergo saluabitur,' quath he · and seide no more Latyn.   204
'Traianus was a trewe knyght · and took neuere Crystendome,
And he is saf, seith the bok · and his soule in heuene.
Ther is follyng of font · and follyng in blod-shedynge,
And thorw fuyr is follyng · and al is ferm by-leyue ;   208
    Aduenit ignis diuinus, non comburens sed illuminans.
Ac treuthe, that trespassede neuere · ne transuersede aȝens the
    lawe,
Bote lyuede as his lawe tauhte · and leyueth ther be no bettere,
And yf ther were, he wolde · and in suche a wil deyeth—   211

C. 192. wether P.   194. Wether P.   *After* l. 194 S *inserts these five
lines, which occur also in the* Duke of Westminster's MS. :—

  Iob was a paynym · and plesede god a prys,
  And aristele (*sic*) al-so · sewede þe same secte,
  And lad ful holy lyf · aftur lawe of kynde,
  Where-fore hit semeþ soþly · by sondry skylus to schewe
  Þat he is saf as was Iob · I can not seye þe soþe.
196. sauede P.   198. gyue MS ; ȝyue K ; ȝeue I ; ȝiue T ; gyf (*badly*) P.
200. theese P.   205. triwe P.   206. is (*for* his) P.   207. of (*for* in) P.
210. lyuede IT ; leuede MG ; leyuede P.   P *om.* his.   leyue (*for* leyueth) P.

Ne wolde neuere trewe god · but treuth were allowed;
And where it worth or worth nou3t · the bileue is grete of treuth, 288
And an hope hangyng ther-inne · to haue a mede for his treuthe.
> For, *Deus dicitur quasi dans vitam eternam suis, hoc est, fidelibus; et alibi;*
> *si ambulauero in medio vmbre mortis, etc.*

The glose graunteth vpon that vers · a gret mede to treuthe,
And witt and wisdome,' quod that wye · 'was somme tyme tresore,
To kepe with a comune · no katel was holde bettere, 292
And moche murth and manhod:'—and ri3t with that he vanesched.

B. 289. &c. CROB; LW. om.

Wolde neuere trewe god · bote trewe treuthe were a-lowed. 212
And where hit worth other nat worth · the by-leyue is gret of
   treuthe,
And hope hongeth ay ther-on · to haue that treuthe deserueth;
   Quia super pauca fidelis fuisti, supra multa te constituam:
And that is loue and large huyre · yf the lord be trewe,
And cortesie more than couenant was · what so clerkes carpen;
For al worth as god wole'— · and ther-with he vanshede. 217

Hic explicit passus quintus de Dowel.

C. 212. a-lowede P.

PASSUS XIII.

Passus terciodecimus.

AND I awaked there-with · witles nerehande,
And as a freke that fre were · forth gan I walke
In manere of a mendynaunt · many a ȝere after,
And of this metyng many tyme · moche thouȝt I hadde. 4
First, how Fortune me failled · at my moste nede,
And how that Elde manaced me · myȝt we euere meten;

And how that freris folwed · folke that was riche,
And folke that was pore · at litel prys thei sette, 8
And no corps in her kirkeȝerde · ne in her kyrke was buryed,
But quikke he biquethe hem auȝte · or shulde helpe quyte her dettes.

And how this coueitise ouercome · clerkes and prestes,
And how that lewed men ben ladde · but owre lorde hem helpe,
Thorugh vnkonnynge curatoures · to incurable peynes. 13
And how that Ymagynatyf · in dremeles me tolde,
Of Kynde and of his connynge · and how curteise he is to bestes,

And how louynge he is to bestes · on londe and on water; 16
Leueth he no lyf · lasse ne more;
The creatures that crepen · of Kynde ben engendred.
And sitthen how Ymagynatif seyde · *vix iustus saluabitur*,
And whan he had seyde so · how sodeynelich he passed. 20
I lay down longe in this thouȝte · and atte laste I slepte,
And, as Cryste wolde, there come Conscience · to conforte me that tyme,
And bad me come to his courte · with Clergye sholde I dyne.
And for Conscience of Clergye spake · I come wel the rather,

PASSUS XVI.

Incipit passus sextus de dowel.

AND ich awakede ther-with · wittlees ner hande;
As a frek that feye were · forth gan ich walke
In manere of a mendinaunt · meny ȝeres after.
And meny tyme of this meteles · muche thouhte ich hadde; 4
Furst, how Fortune me failede · at my moste neede,
And how Elde manacede me · so myghte happe,
That, yf ich lyuede longe · leue me by-hynde,
And vanshie alle myne vertues · and myne faire lockes. 8
And how that freres folweden · folk that was ryche,
And peuple that was poure · at lytel prys setten;
Ne corses of poure comune · in here kirke-ȝerd moste ligge,
Bote yf he quike by-quethe hem auht · other wolde helpe aquite
    here dettes. 12
And how this couetise ouer-cam · alle kynne sectes,
As wel lerede as lewede · and lord as the bonde.
And how that lewede men ben ladde · bote oure lord hem helpe,
Thorow vnconnynge curatours · to incurable peynes. 16
And how that Ymaginatif · in dremeles me tolde
Of Kynde and of hus connynge · and what connynge he ȝaf to
    bestes,
How louynge he is to eche lyf · a londe and a watere;
For alle he wisseth and ȝeueth wit · that walketh other crepeth.
And ich meruailede in herte · how Ymagynatif saide, 21
That *iustus* by-fore Iesu · *in die iudicii*
Non saluabitur · bote *uix* helpe;
And, whanne he hadde seide so · how sodeynlich he vanshede;
And so ich mused vpon this matere · that me luste to slepe. 25
    Thenne cam Conscience · and Cleregie after,
And beden me ryse and rome · for with Reson sholde ich dyne.
And ich a-ros and romed forth · with Reson we mette. 28

C. 6. so—happe IMKSG; so longe myghte ich happe PE. 7. lyuede IMKSTG; leuede P. 11. kirke IT; churche PES. 13. ow (*for* how) P. 17. that IKTG; P *om.* 19. is IMKSTG; was PE. 28. we EIMKSTG; ich P.

And there I say a maistre · what man he was I neste,　　25
That lowe louted · and loueliche to Scripture.
Conscience knewe hym wel · and welcomed hym faire;
Thei wesshen and wypeden · and wenten to the dyner.　　28
Ac Pacience in the paleis stode · in pilgrymes clothes,
And preyde mete for charite · for a pore heremyte.
　　Conscience called hym in · and curteisliche seide,
'Welcome, wye, go and wasshe · thow shalt sitte sone.'　　32
　　This maister was made sitte · as for the moste worthy,
And thanne Clergye and Conscience · and Pacience cam after.
Pacience and I · were put to be macches,
And seten by owre selue · at a syde-borde.　　36
　　Conscience called after mete · and thanne cam Scripture,
And serued hem thus sone · of sondry metes manye,
Of Austyn, of Ambrose · of alle the foure euangelistes;
　　　Edentes & bibentes que apud eos sunt.
Ac this maister ne his man · no manere flesshe eten,　　40
Ac thei ete mete of more coste · mortrewes and potages;
Of that men mys-wonne · thei made hem wel at ese.
Ac her sauce was ouer-soure · & vnsauourely grounde,
In a morter, *post-mortem* · of many bitter peyne,　　44
But if thei synge for tho soules · and wepe salt teres:
　　　Vos qui peccata hominum comeditis, nisi pro eis lacrimas et
　　　　orationes effunderitis, ea que in delicijs comeditis, in tor-
　　　　mentis euometis.
Conscience ful curteisly tho · comaunded Scripture
Bifor Pacience bred to brynge · and me that was his macche.
He sette a soure lof to-for vs · and seyde, '*agite penitenciam*,'
And sith he drough vs drynke · *diu-perseuerans.*　　49
'As longe,' quod I, 'as I lyue · and lycame may dure!'
'Here is propre seruice,' quod Pacience · 'ther fareth no prynce
　　bettere;'
And thanne he brouȝt vs forth a mees of other mete · of
　　Miserere-mei-deus ;　　52
And he brouȝte vs of *Beati-quorum* · of *Beatus-virres* makynge,
Et-quorum-tecta-sunt- · *peccata* in a disshe
Of derne shrifte, *Dixi* · and *confitebor tibi!*
'Brynge Pacience some pitaunce' · pryueliche quod Conscience;

B. 32. wye WO; wye (*altered to* wyel ȝe) L.　　49. *diu* OB; *dia* LWR.

We reuerencede Reson · and romed forth softeliche,
And mette with a mayster · a man ylike a frere.
Conscience knew hym wel · and welcomede hym fayre;
Thei wisshen and wypeden · and wenten to the dyner. 32
Pacience as a poure thyng cam · and preide mete for charite,
Ylike to Peers Plouhman · as he a palmere were,
Crauede and criede · for Cristes loue of heuene,
A meles mete for a poure man · other moneye, yf thei hadden.
Conscience knew hym wel · and welcomede hem alle; 37
Thei wisshen and wipeden · and wenten and setten.

The maister was made to sitte furst · as for the most worthy;
Reson stod and stihlede · as for stywarde of halle. 40
Pacience and ich weren · yput to be mettes,
And seten by ous selue · at a syd-table.

Cleregie calde after mete · and thenne cam Scripture,
And serued hem thus sone · of sondrie metes menie, 44
Of Austyn, of Ambrosie · of alle the foure euangelies,
Edentes et bibentes que apud illos sunt.
Ac of these metes this maister · myghte nat wel chewe;
For-thy he eet mete of more cost · mortrewes and potages.
Of that that men myswonne · thei maden hem wel at ese, 48
Ac here sauce was ouere-soure · and vnsauerliche grounde,
In a morter, *post-mortem* · of meny bitere peynes,
Bote yf thei synge for tho soules · and wepe salte teeres;
Uos qui peccata hominum comeditis, nisi pro eis lacrimas
effuderitis, ea que in delicijs comeditis; in tormentis euometis.
Thenne Reson radde · ryght a-non after, 52
That Conscience comaunde sholde · to do come Scripture,
And brynge bred for Pacience · bytynde apartie,
And to me that was hus mette tho · and other mete bothe.
He sette a soure loof · and seide, ' *agite penitentiam,*' 56
And sitthe he drow ous drynke · *diu-perseuerans,*
'As longe,' quath he, 'as the lyf · and the licame may dure.'
'This is a semeliche seruice!' · seide Pacience.

Thenne cam Contrition · that hadde coked for hem alle, 60

C. 32. wisshen T; wosshen P (*but see* l. 38).   34. he IMSTG; P *om.*
41. yputt P.   45. of EIKSG; and P.   46. thees P.   51. *euometis* ST;
en emergitis (!) P.   57. he IMKSTG; PE *om.*

And thanne had Pacience a pitaunce · *pro-hac-orabit-ad-te-omnis-*
    sanctus-in-tempore-oportuno ; 57
And Conscience conforted vs · and carped vs mery tales,
    Cor contritum et humiliatum, deus, non despicies.
Pacience was proude · of that propre seruice,
And made hym muirth with his mete · ac I morned euere, 60
For this doctoure on the heigh dese · dranke wyn so faste;
    Ve vobis qui potentes estis ad bibendum vinum !
He eet many sondry metes · mortrewes and puddynges,
Wombe-cloutes and wylde braune · & egges yfryed with grece.
Thanne seide I to my-self · so Pacience it herde, 64
'It is nou3t foure dayes that this freke · bifor the den of Poules,
Preched of penaunces · that Poule the apostle suffred,

In fame & frigore · and flappes of scourges; 67
    Ter cesus sum, et a iudeis quinquies quadragenas, &c.
Ac o worde thei ouerhuppen · at ech a tyme that thei preche,
That Poule in his pistel · to al the peple tolde;
    Periculum est in falsis fratribus.
Holywrit bit men be war · I wil nou3t write it here 70
On Englisch, an auenture · it sholde be reherced to ofte,
And greue there-with that good men ben · ac gramarienes shul rede;
    Vnusquisque a fratre se custodiat, quia, vt dicitur, periculum
    est in falsis fratribus.
Ac I wist neuere freke that as a frere 3ede · bifor men on
    Englisshe
Taken it for her teme · and telle it with-outen glosynge.
Thei prechen that penaunce · is profitable to the soule,
And what myschief and malese · Cryst for man tholed; 76

Ac this goddes gloton,' quod I · 'with his gret chekes,
Hath no pyte on vs pore · he perforneth yuel;
That he precheth he preueth nou3t' · to Pacience I tolde,
And wisshed witterly · with wille ful egre, 80
That disshes and dobleres · bifor this ilke doctour,
Were molten led in his maw · and Mahoun amyddes!

B. 58. *humilitatum* L.   81. and *miswritten* a *in* L.   82. molten
WCOB; moltoun L.

C. PASSUS XVI. 61-91.

And brouhte forth a pitaunce · was *pro-hac-orabit-omnis-sanctus-*
in-tempore-oportuno.
Conscience confortede ous · bothe Cleregie and Scripture,
  And seide, ' *cor contritum & humiliatum, deus, non despicies.*'
Pacience was wel apaied · of this propre seruyse,
And mad murye with this mete; · ac ich mournede euere,   64
For a doctor at the heye deys · drank wyn faste—
  Ue uobis qui potentes estis ad bibendum uinum—
And ete meny sondry metes · mortrews and poddynges,
Braun and blod of the goos · bacon and colhoppes.
Then seide ich to my-self · that Pacience hit hurde,   68
' ʒut is nat thre daies don · that this doctor prechede
At seint Paules by-for the peuple · what penaunce thei suffreden,
Alle that coueitede to come · to heuene hye ioye;
And how that Paul the apostle · what penaunce he tholede   72
For oure lordes loue · as holy lettrure telleth;
  In fame et frigore, etc.
Ac me wondreth in my witt · whi that thei ne preche,
As Paul the apostel prechede · to the peuple ofte,
  Periculum in falsis fratribus !
Holy writ bit men be war · and wisliche hem kepe,   76
That no fals frere · thorw flatrynge hem by-gyle ;
Ac me is loth, thow ich Latyn knowe · to lacky eny secte,
For alle we ben brethren · thauh we be diuersliche clothede.
Ac ich wiste neuere freek · that frere is ycalled   80
Of the fyue mendynauns · and made eny sarmon,
That took this for his teme · and told hit with-oute glose.
Thei prechen that penaunce · is profitable for the soule,
And what meschief and what mal ese · Crist for man tholede.
Ac this doctor and diuinour · and decretistre of canon,   85
And al-so a gnedy gloton · with to grete chekes,
Hath no pite on vs poure · he perfourneth vuele ;
That he precheth he proueth nat' · to Pacience ich tolde,   88
And wisshede witerliche · with a wil ful egre,
That in the mawe of that maister · alle tho metes were,
Disches and dobeleres · with alle the deyntes after !

C. 62. seide MIKSTG; seiden PE.   69. this IMESTG; thees P.   79.
breythrene P.   80. ycallede P.   82. fore P.   his IM ; here PETG.
85. thes (*for* this) P.   decretiste IMG ; decretestre P.   89. whisshede P.
91. wit (*for* with) P.

'I shal Iangle to this Iurdan · with his Iust wombe,
To telle me what penaunce is · of which he preched rather.'—
Pacience perceyued what I thou3t · and wynked on me to be stille,
And seyde, 'thow shalt se thus sone . whan he may no more,
He shal haue a penaunce in his paunche · and puffe at ech a worde,
And thanne shullen his guttis godele · and he shal galpen after;
For now he hath dronken so depe · he wil deuyne sone,   89
And preuen it by her Pocalips · and passioun of seynt Auereys,

That neither bacoun ne braune · blancmangere ne mortrewes
Is noither fisshe ne flesshe · but fode for a penaunte.   92
And thanne shal he testifye of a trinitee · and take his felawe to
    witnesse,
What he fonde in a freyel · after a freres lyuynge,
And but if the fyrst lyne be lesyng · leue me neuere after!
And thanne is tyme to take · and to appose this doctoure   96
Of Dowel and of Dobet · and if Dobest be any penaunce.'—
   And I sete stille, as Pacience seyde · and thus sone this doctour,
As rody as a rose · rubbed his chekes,
Coughed and carped · and Conscience hym herde,   100
And tolde hym of a trinite · and toward vs he loked.
'What is Dowel? sire doctour,' quod I · 'is Dowel any penaunce?'

'Dowel?' quod this doctour—· and toke the cuppe and dranke—
'Do non yuel to thine euenecrystene · nou3t by thi powere.'   104
   'By this day, sire doctour,' quod I · 'thanne be 3e nou3t in Dowel;
For 3e han harmed vs two : in that 3e eten the puddyng,
Mortrewes, and other mete · and we no morsel hade!
And if 3e fare so in 3owre fermorie · ferly me thinketh,   108
But chest be there charite shulde be · and 3onge childern dorste
    pleyne!
I wolde permute my penaunce with 3owre · for I am in poynte
    to Dowel!'
   Thanne Conscience curteisliche · a contenaunce he made,
And preynte vpon Pacience · to preie me to be stille,   112
And seyde hym-self, 'sire doctour · and it be 3owre wille,
What is Dowel and Dobet? · 3e deuynours knoweth.'

B. 91. blancmangere WCO; blaumanger *or* blanmanger L.   92. ne CROB; no L.   107. morsel WCB; mussel LRO.

'Ich shal Iangly to thys Iordan · with hus Iuste wombe,   92
And a-pose hym what penaunce is · and purgatorie on erthe,
And whi he lyueth nat as he lereth!' · 'let be,' quath Pacience,
And seide, 'thow shalt seo thus sone · whan he may na more,
He shal haue a penaunce in hus paunche · and puffe at eche
    worde;   96
Thenne shulleth his gottes godelen · and he by-gynne to galpe.
Now he hath dronke so depe · he wol deuiny sone,
And preouen it by here Apocalips · and by the passion of seint
    Aueray,
That nother bacon ne braun · blammanger ne mortreuus   100
Ys nother fissh ne flessh · bote fode for penauntes;
And take witnesse of the trinite · and take his felawe to wittnesse,
What he fond in a forel · of a freres lyuynge;
And bote the ferste leef be lesynge · leyf me neuere after!   104
And thenne is tyme to talke · and to apose this doctour
Of Dowel and of Dobet · and yf Dobet do eny penaunce.'
    Ich sat stille as Pàcience wolde · and thus sone this doctour,
As rody as a rose · roddede hus chekes,   108
Kowede and carpede · and Conscience hym herde,
And tolde of a trinite · and to-warde me he lokede.
'What is Dowel, sire doctour?' quath ich · 'is Dobet eny
    penaunce?'
'Dowel?' quath this doctour · and he drank after,   112
'Do thy neyhebore non harme · ne thy-selue nother,
Thanne dost thow wel and wisliche · ich dar hit wel a-vouwe.'
'Certes, sire,' thanne seide ich · 'hit semeth nat here,
In that ʒe parteth nat with ous poure · that ʒe passeth Dowel,
Nother louyeth as ʒe lereth · as oure lorde wolde,   117
    Et üisitavit et fecit redemptionem plebis sue israel.
And ʒe fare thus with ʒoure sike freres · ferly me thynketh,
Bote Dowel endite ʒow · *in die iudicii.*'
    Thenne Conscience ful curteisliche · a contenaunce he made,
And preynte vpon Pacience · to preye me be stille,   121
And seide hymself, 'syre doctour · by so hit be ʒoure wil,
What is Dowel and Dobet? · ʒe diuynours knoweth.'
'Ich haue seide,' seide the seg · 'y can seye no bettere,   124

C. 93. what IMETG; wich P.   97. he EM; PIT *om.*   102. is (*for
his*) P.   113. thy IEG; the P (*2nd time*).   119. endite IMT; endyty P.

'Dowel,' quod this doctour · 'do as clerkes techeth,
And Dobet is he that techeth · and trauailleth to teche other,
And Dobest doth hym-self so · as he seith and precheth:— 117
    Qui facit et docuerit, magnus vocabitur in regno celorum.'
'Now thow, Clergye,' quod Conscience · 'carpest what is Dowel.'
'I haue seuene sones,' he seyde · 'seruen in a castel,
There the lorde of Lyf wonyeth · to leren hym what is Dowel;
Til I se tho seuene · and my-self acorden, 121
I am vnhardy,' quod he · 'to any wy3t to preue it.
For one Pieres the Ploughman · hath inpugned vs alle,
And sette alle sciences at a soppe · saue loue one, 124
And no tixte ne taketh · to meyntene his cause,
But *dilige deum* · and *domine, quis habitabit, &c.*
And seith that Dowel and Dobet · aren two infinites,
Whiche infinites, with a feith · fynden oute Dobest, 128
Which shal saue mannes soule · thus seith Piers the Ploughman.

'I can nou3t her-on,' quod Conscience · 'ac I knowe wel Pieres;
He wil nou3t a3ein holy writ speken · I dar wel vndertake;
Thanne passe we ouer til Piers come · and preue this in dede.
Pacience hath be in many place · and perauntre cnoweth 133
That no clerke ne can · as Cryst bereth witnesse;
    Pacientes vincunt, &c.'
'At 3owre preyere,' quod Pacyence tho · 'so no man displese hym;
Disce,' quod he, '*doce* · *dilige inimicos.* 136
Disce, and Dowel · *doce,* and Dobet;
Dilige, and Dobest · thus tau3te me ones
A lemman that I loued · Loue was hir name.
"With wordes and with werkes," quod she · "and wille of thyne
    herte, 140
Thow loue lelly thi soule · al thi lyf-tyme;
And so thow lere the to louye · for the lordes loue of heuene,
Thine enemye in al wyse · euene-forth with thi-selue.
Cast coles on his hed · and al kynde speche, 144
Bothe with werkes and with wordes · fonde his loue to wynne;
And lay on hym thus with loue · til he laughe on the;
And but he bowe for this betyng · blynde mote he worthe!
Ac for to fare thus with thi frende · foly it were, 148
For he that loueth the lelly · lyte of thyne coueiteth.

B. 136. *In margin of* L—disce, doce, et dilige. 146. laughe C; laghe L.

Bote do as doctours telleth · for Dowel ich hit holde;   125
That traueileth to teche othere · for Dobet ich it holde;
And he that doth as he techeth · ich halde hit for a Dobest;
    Qui facit et docuerit, magnus uocabitur.'
'Now thow, Cleregie,' quath Conscience · 'carpe what is Dowel.'
'Haue me excused,' quath Cleregie · 'by Crist, bote in scole,
Shal no such motif be meued · for me, bote there,
For Peers loue the Plouhman · that enpugnede ones
Alle kyne konnynges · and alle kyne craftes,   132
Saue loue and leaute · and louhnesse of herte,
And no tixt taketh · to preoue this for trewe
Bote *dilige deum & proximum* · and *domine, quis habitabit in tabernaculo, &c.;*
And preoueth by pure skyle · inparfit alle thynges,   136
    Nemo bonus,
Bote leel loue and treuthe · that loth is to be yfounde.'

Quath Peers the Plouhman · '*pacientes uincunt.*
By-for perpetual pees · ich shal preoue that ich seide,
And a-vowe by-for god · and for-sake hit neuere,   140
That *disce, doce, dilige* · *deum* and thyn enemye;
Hertely thou hym helpe · emforth thy myȝt,
Cast hote coles on hus hefde · of alle kynde speche,
Fonde thorgh wit and with worde · hus loue for to wynne,   144
And ȝif hym eft and eft · euere at hus neede;
Conforte hym with thy catel · and with thy kynde speche,
And leye on hym thus with loue · tyl he lauhe on the;
And bote he bowe for this betynge · blynd mote he worthe!'
And whanne he hadde worded thus · wiste no man after,   149
Where Peers Plouhman by-cam · so prieueliche he wente.
And Reson ran after · and ryght with him ȝeode;
Saue Conscience and Cleregie · ich couthe no mo aspye.   152
And Pacience propreliche spak · tho Peers was thus passed,
'That loueth lelly,' quath he · 'bote lytel thyng coueyteth.

C. 129. me EIMTG; P *om.*   130. meeuede P.   139. preeouye P;
see l. 136.   143. hote EIMTG; oute P.   146. Conforte EG; Conforty P.
148. he IMTG; ȝe PM (1*st time*).   he IT; ich PE (2*nd time*).   149.
weste (*for* wiste) P.   151. and IMTG; P *om.*

Kynde loue coueiteth nouȝte • no catel but speche,
With half a laumpe lyne in latyne • *ex vi transicionis.*"
I bere there-inne aboute • fast ybounde Dowel,   152
In a signe of the Saterday • that sette firste the kalendare,
And al the witte of the Wednesday • of the nexte wyke after;
The myddel of the mone • is the miȝte of bothe.
And here-with am I welcome • there I haue it with me.'   156
  'Vndo it, late this doctour deme • if Dowel be therinne;
For, bi hym that me made • miȝte neuere pouerte,
Miseise, ne myschief • ne man with his tonge,
Colde, ne care • ne compaignye of theues,   160
Ne noither hete, ne haille • ne non helle pouke,
Ne noither fuire ne flode • ne fere of thine enemy
Tene the eny tyme • and thow take it with the;
  Caritas nichil timet.
And eek, haue god my soule! • and thow wilt it craue,   164
There nys neyther emperour ne emperesse • erl, kynge, ne baroun,
Pope, ne patriarch • that puyre reson ne schal make
The meyster of alle tho men • thoruȝ miȝt of this redeles;
Nouȝt thoruȝ wicche-craft, but thoruȝ wit • (and thow wilt thi-selue)
Do kynge and quene • and alle the comune after   169
Ȝyue the alle that thei may ȝiue • as for the best ȝemere,
And, as thou demest, wil thei do • alle here dayes after;
  Pacientes vincunt, &c.'
'It is but a *Dido*,' quod this doctour • 'a dysoures tale.   172
Al the witt of this worlde • and wiȝte mennes strengthe
Can nouȝt confourmen a pees • bytwene the pope and his enemys,
Ne bitwene two Cristene kynges • can no wiȝte pees make,
Profitable to ayther peple' • and put the table fro hym,   176
And toke Clergye and Conscience • to conseille, as it were,
That Pacience tho moste passe • for pilgrimes kunne wel lye.
  Ac Conscience carped loude • and curteislich seide,
'Frendes, fareth wel' • and faire spake to Clergye,   180
'For I wil go with this gome • if god wil ȝiue me grace,
And be pilgryme with Pacience • til I haue proued more.'
  'What?' quod Clergye to Conscience • 'ar ȝe coueitouse nouthe
After ȝeresȝyues or ȝiftes • or ȝernen to rede redeles?   184

B. 164–171. *These lines in* R *only; but cf.* C-*text.*   170. for þe; *such is my conjecture*; R *has* þe for.

Ich wolde, and ich will hadde · wynnen al Fraunce
With-oute bruting of burnes · other eny blod-sheding;   156
Ich take wittnesse,' quath he · 'at holy writ a partie;
   Pacientes uincunt.
For, by hym that me made! · my3te neuere pouerte,
Miseise, ne myschief · ne man with hus tonge
Tene the eny tyme · and thow take Pacience,   160
And bere hit in thy bosom · abowte wher thou wendest,
In the corner of a cart-whel · with a crowe croune.

Shal neuere burne be abaisshed · that hath this a-boute,
Neither hete ne hail · ne helle pouke hym greue,   164
Neither fuyr, nother flod · ne be a-fered of enemye;
   Caritas expellit omnem timorem;

Ther nis wyght in this worlde · that wolde the lette
To haue alle londes at thy lykyng · and the here lord make,
And maister of alle here meeble · and of here moneye after, 168
The kynge and alle the comune · and cleregie to the aloute
As for here lorde and ledere · and lyuen as thou techest.'

'This is a *Dido*,' quath this doctour · 'a disours tale!
Al the witt of this worlde · ne wyghte mennes strengthe   172
Can nat performen a pees · of the pope and of hus enemys

Profitable for bothe parties'— · and put the bord fram hym,
And tok Conscience and Cleregie · to counsel, as hit were.

  C. 155. adde P.   162. *From* IMETS; P *om. this line.*   171. *Dido*
MT; *Dydo* S; *dico* P.   172. wordle P.

I shal brynge ȝow a bible · a boke of the olde lawe,
And lere ȝow, if ȝow lyke · the leest poynte to knowe,
That Pacience the pilgryme · perfitly knewe neuere.'
 'Nay, bi Cryste,' quod Conscience to Clergye · 'god the forȝelde,
For al that Pacience me profreth · proude am I litel.   189
Ac the wille of the wye · and the wille of folke here
Hath moeued my mode · to mourne for my synnes.
The good wille of a wiȝte · was neure bouȝte to the fulle ; 192
For there nys no tresore therto · to a trewe wille.
Haued nouȝt Magdeleigne more · for a boxe of salue,
Than Zacheus for he seide · *dimidium bonorum meorum do pau-*
 peribus ?
And the pore widwe · for a peire of mytes,   196
Than alle tho that offreden · in-to *gazafilacium ?*'
 Thus curteislich Conscience · congeyde fyrst the frere,
And sithen softliche he seyde · in Clergyes ere,
'Me were leuer, by owre lorde · and I lyue shulde,   200
Haue pacience perfitlich · than half thy pakke of bokes!'
Clergye to Conscience · no congeye wolde take,
But seide ful sobreliche · 'thow shalt se the tyme,
Whan thow art wery for-walked · wilne me to consaille.' 204
 'That is soth,' seyde Conscience · 'so me god helpe !
If Pacience be owre partyng felawe · and pryue with vs bothe,
There nys wo in this worlde · that we ne shulde amende,
And confourmen kynges to pees · and al kynnes londes, 208
Sarasenes and Surre · and so forth alle the Iewes
Turne in-to the trewe feithe · and in-til one byleue.'
 'That is soth,' quod Clergye · 'I se what thow menest,
I shal dwelle as I do · my deuore to shewen,   212
And conformen fauntekynes · and other folke ylered,
Tyl Pacience haue preued the · and parfite the maked.'
 Conscience tho with Pacience passed · pilgrymes as it were.
Thanne had Pacience, as pylgrymes han · in his poke vittailles,
Sobrete, and symple-speche · and sothfaste-byleue,   217
To conforte hym and Conscience · if they come in place
There Vnkyndenesse and Coueytise is · hungrye contrees bothe.
 And as thei went by the weye · of Dowel thei carped; 220
Thei mette with a mynstral · as me tho thouȝte.

    B. 190. of WO ; LCRB *om.* (*2nd time*).

Ac ich took kepe how Conscience · congede sone this doctour,
And sitthe he seide to Cleregie · so that ich hit herde, 177
'By Cryst,' quath Conscience · 'Cleregie, ich wol nat lye,
Me were leuere, by oure lorde · and ich lyuye sholde,
Haue pacience parfitliche · than half thy pack of bokes! 180
Lettrure and longe studie · letteth ful menye,
That thei knoweth nat,' quath Conscience · 'what is kynde Pacience.
For-thi,' quath Conscience · 'Crist ich the by-teche,
With Pacience wol ich passe · parfitnesse to fynde.' 184

Thus thei wente forth here way · with gret wil ich folewede.
Thenne hadde Pacience, as pilgrimes hauen · in here poke vitailes,
Sobrete and symple-speche · and sothfast-byleyue, 187
To comforty hym and Conscience · yf thei come in place
Ther Vnkyndnesse and Couetyse ys · hongry contreis bothe.
And as thei wente by the wey · of Dowel gan thei carpe ; 190
Thei mette with a mynstral · as me tho thouhte.

C. 176. congede SG ; conged T ; conueide P.   184. Whit (*for* With) P.

Pacience apposed hym fyrste · and preyed hym he sholde hem telle
To Conscience, what crafte he couthe · an to what contree he wolde.
  'I am a mynstral,' quod that man · 'my name is *Actiua-vita* :
Alle ydel ich hatye · for of actyf is my name.   225
A wafrere, wil ȝe wite · and serue many lordes,
And fewe robes I fonge · or furred gounes.
Couthe I lye to do men laughe · thanne lacchen I shulde · 228
Other mantel or money · amonges lordes mynstralles.
Ac for I can noither tabre ne trompe · ne telle none gestes,
Farten, ne fythelen · at festes, ne harpen,
Iape ne Iogly · ne gentlych pype,   232
Ne noyther sailly ne saute · ne synge with the gyterne,
I haue none gode gyftes · of thise grete lordes,
For no bred that I brynge forth · saue a beneson on the Sonday,
Whan the prest preyeth the peple · her *pater-noster* to bidde
For Peres the Plowman · and that hym profite wayten.   237
And that am I, Actyf · that ydelnesse hatye,
For alle trewe trauaillours · and tilieres of the erthe ;
Fro Mychelmesse to Mychelmesse · I fynde hem with wafres. 240
  Beggeres and bidderes · of my bred crauen,
Faitoures and freres · and folke with brode crounes.
I fynde payne for the pope · and prouendre for his palfrey,
And I hadde neuere of hym · haue god my treuthe,   244
Noither prouendre ne parsonage · ȝut of the popis ȝifte,
Saue a pardoun with a peys of led · and two pollis amydde !
Hadde iche a clerke that couthe write · I wolde caste hym a bille,
That he sent me vnder his seel · a salue for the pestilence, 248
And that his blessyng and his bulles · bocches miȝte destroye :
    *In nomine meo demonia eicient, et super egros manus imponent,
       et bene habebunt.*
And thanne wolde I be prest to the peple · paste for to make,
And buxome and busy · aboute bred and drynke
For hym and for alle his · fonde I that his pardoun   252
Miȝte lechen a man · as I beleue it shulde.
For sith he hath the powere · that Peter hym-self hadde,

B. 249. *eicient* WCROB ; *eiciunt* L.   250. þe WCROB ; L *om*.

Pacience a-posed hym · and preide he sholde telle 192
What craft, that he couthe · and cortesly he seide,
'Ich am a mynstral,' quath this man · 'my name is *Activa-uita*,
Peers prentys the Plouhman · alle peuple to comfortye.'
'What manere mynstralcie · my dere frend,' quath Conscience, 196
'Hast thow vsed other haunted · al thy lyf-tyme?'
'Mynstralcie can ich nat muche · bote make men murye,
As a waffrer with waffres · and welcome godes gistes.
Of my labour thei lauhe · the lasse and the more. 200
The poure and the riche · y plese and payn fynde,
And fewe robis ich fonge · other forrede gounes.
Wolde ich lye and do men lauhe · thenne lacchen ich sholde
Mantels other moneye · a-mong lordes minstrales. 204
Ich can nat tabre ne trompe · ne telle faire gestes,
Farten, ne fithelen · at festes, ne harpen,
Iapen ne Iogelen · ne gentelliche pipe,
Nother sailen ne sautrien · ne singe with the giterne. 208
Ich haue none gode gyftes · of these grete lordes
For no bred that ich by-trauaile · to bryng by-fore lordes.
Ne were hit that the parishe · prayeth for me on Sonedayes,
Ich am sory that ich sew other sette · bote for my-self one.
Ac the prest and other peuple · prayeth for Peers Plouhman,
And for me, Actyf, hus man · that ydelnesse hate. 214
For lordes and lorelles · luthere and goode,
Fro Myhel-masse to Myhel-masse · ich fynde mete and drynke.
  Ich fynde payn for the pope · and praye hym ich wolde 217
That pestilences to pees · and to parfit loue turne.
For founde ich that hus blessing · and hus bulle myghte
Letten this luther eir · and lechen the syke— 220
As the booke bereth wittnesse · that he bere myghte
In hus mouth mercy · and amende vs alle,
   Super egros manus imponent, et bene se habebunt— *t*
Thenne wolde ich bee busy · and buxum to helpe
Eche kynne creature · that on Cryst by-leyueth. 224
For sutthe he hath the power · that seynt Peter hadde,

C. 194. thees (*for* this) P.   199. wolcome P.   gistes EMFS; gustes P.
206. fithelen IST; fithelyn P.   207. Iogelyn P.   209. goude (*for* gode) P.
210. bytrauaily P.   211. parishe I; parissh T; parshe P.   212. sew MS;
sewe P.   215. goude (*for* goode) P.   220. lechin P.   221. booke I;
boke S; book T; bookes P.

D d

He hath the potte with the salue · sothly, as me thinketh :
    Argentum et aurum non est mihi; quod autem habeo, hoc
    tibi do; in nomine domini, surge et ambula.
  Ac if miȝte of miracle hym faille · it is for men ben nouȝt
    worthy   256
To haue the grace of god · and no gylte of the pope.
For may no blyssyng done vs bote · but if we wil amende,
Ne mannes masse make pees · amonges Cristene peple,
Tyl pruyde be purelich fordo · and that thourgh payn defaute.
  For ar I haue bred of mele · ofte mote I swete.   261
And ar the comune haue corne ynough · many a colde mornynge;
So, ar my wafres ben ywrouȝt · moche wo I tholye.
  Alle Londoun I leue · liketh wel my wafres,   264
And lowren whan thei lakken hem— · it is nouȝt longe ypassed,
There was a carful comune · whan no carte come to toune
With bake bred fro Stretforth · tho gan beggeres wepe,
And werkmen were agaste a litel · this wil be thouȝte longe. 268
In the date of owre dryȝte · in a drye Apprile,
A thousande and thre hondreth · tweis thretty and ten,
My wafres there were gesen · whan Chichestre was maire.'
  I toke gode kepe, by Cryst · and Conscience bothe,   272
Of Haukyn the actyf man · and how he was y-clothed.
He hadde a cote of Crystendome · as holykirke bileueth,
Ac it was moled in many places · with many sondri plottes,
Of Pruyde here a plotte, and there a plotte · of vnboxome
    speche,   276
Of scornyng and of scoffyng · and of vnskilful berynge,
As in aparaille and in porte · proude amonges the peple,
Otherwyse than he hath · with herte or syȝte shewynge;   279
Hym willynge that alle men wende · he were that he is nouȝte.
For-why he bosteth and braggeth · with many bolde othes,
And in-obedient to ben vndernome · of any lyf lyuynge,
And so syngulere by hym-self · as to syȝte of the poeple,
Was none suche as hym-self · ne none so pope-holy,   284
Y-habited as an hermyte · an ordre by hym-selue,
Religioun sanz reule · and resonable obedience;
Lakkyng lettred men · and lewed men bothe,

B. 255. *hoc* RO; LCWB *om.*   265. hem WR; it LO.   267. bake R;
LWCOB *om.* (*but it improves the line*).   284. pope R; pompe L.

He hath pureliche the pot · with the same salue;
    Argentum et aurum non est michi ; quod autem habeo, hoc tibi do, etc.
Ac yf myghte of miracle hym faile · hit is for men beeth nat worthi
For to haue the grace of god · and no gult in the pope.   228
For may no blessynge do vs bote · bote yf we wol amende,
Ne mannes preier make pees · among Cristine peuple,
Til prude be pureliche for-do · and that thorw payn defaute;
    Ex habundantia panis et uini turpissimum peccatum aduenit.
Pure plente of payn · the peuple of Sodomye,   232
And reste and riche metes · rybaudes hem made.'

[*Continued on* p. 415; *compare* l. 232 *above with* l. 75 on p. 418.]

From C. vii. 30–40.

[Prout of aparail · in porte amonge the puple
Other-wise than ich haue · with-ynne other with-oute,
Me wilnynge that men wende · ich were, as in aueyr,   32
Riche, and resonable · and ryghtful of lyuynge,
Bostynge and braggynge · wyth meny bolde othes,
Auauntyng vp-on my veine glorie · for eny vndernymynge;
And ȝut so synguler by my-self · as to sight of the puple,   36
Was non suche as my-self · ne non so pope-holy,
Som tyme in on secte · som tyme in another;
In alle kynne couetyse · contreuede how ich myghte
Be holde for holy · an hondred sithe, by that encheison;   40

C. 228. good (*for* god) P.   230. preier F; preiere ME; preir P.

In lykyng of lele lyf · and a lyer in soule ;   288
With inwit and with outwitt · ymagenen and studye,
As best for his body be · to haue a badde name,
And entermeten hym ouer-al · ther he hath nouȝt to done,
Wilnyng that men wende · his witte were the best,   292
Or for his crafty kunnynge · or of clerkes the wisest,
Or strengest on stede · or styuest vnder gurdel,
And louelokest to loken on · and lelest of werkes,
And non so holy as he · ne of lif clennere,   296
Or feyrest of feytures · of fourme and of schafte,
And most sotyl of songe · other sleyest of hondes,
And large to lene · losse there-by to cacche ;
And if he gyueth ouȝte pore gomes · telle what he deleth ; 300
Pore of possessioun · in purse and in coffre,
And as a lyon on to loke · and lordeliche of speche.
Baldest of beggeres · a bostour that nouȝt hath,
In towne and in tauernes · tales to telle,   304
And segge thinge that he neuere seigh · and for soth sweren it ;
Of dedes that he neuere dyd · demen and bosten,
And of werkes that he wel dyd · witnesse and seggen—
'Lo! if ȝe leue me nouȝt · or that I lye wenen,   308
Axeth at hym or at hym · and he ȝow can telle,
What I suffred and seighe · and some tymes hadde,
And what I couth and knewe · and what kynne I come of.'
Al he wolde that men wiste · of werkes and of wordes,   312
Which myȝte plese the peple · and praysen hymseluen :
     Si hominibus placerem, Christi seruus non essem ;
     Et alibi : nemo potest duobus dominis seruire.
'Bi Criste,' quod Conscience tho · 'thi best cote, Haukyn,
Hath many moles and spottes · it moste ben ywasshe.'   315
'Ȝe, who so toke hede,' quod Haukyn · 'byhynde and bifore,
What on bakke and what on bodyhalf · and by the two sydes,
Men sholde fynde many frounces · and many foule plottes.'
  And he torned hym as tyte · and thanne toke I hede,
It was fouler by felefolde · than it firste semed.   320
It was bidropped with Wratthe · and wikked wille,
With Enuye and yuel speche · entysyng to fyȝte,

B. 293–299. *These lines in R only ; yet found in the* C-text *in a different part of the poem ; see* p. 405, ll. 42–46.

Wilnede that men wende · my werkes were the beste,
And konnyngest of my craft · clerkes other othere,
And strengest vp-on stede · and styuest vnder gurdell,
And louelokest to loken on · and lykyngest a bedde ; 44
And lykynge of such a lif · that no lawe preyseth,
Prout of my faire fetours · and for ich songe shulle.
And what ich gaf for godes loue · to god-sybbes ich tolde,
Thei to wene that ich were · wel holy and wel almesful, 48
And non so bold beggere · to bydden and craue ;
Tales to telle · in tauernes and in stretes,
Thyng thut neuere was thouht · and ʒut ich swor ich sauh hit,
And lyed on my lykame · and on my lyf bothe. 52
Of werkes that ich wel dude · wittnesse ich take,
And sygge to suche · that sytten me by-syde,
'Lo, yf ʒe leyue me nouht · other than ʒe wene ich lye,
Aske of hym other of hure · and thei conne ʒow telle 56
What ich soffrede and seih · and som tyme hadde,
And what ich knew and couthe · and what kyn ich kam of ;' —
Al ich wolde that men wuste · when hit to pruyde sounede,
As to be preised a-mong the puple · thauh ich poure semede :
  Si hominibus placerem, Christi seruus non essem.
  Nemo potest duobus dominis seruire.']

From
C. vij.
41–60.

Lyinge and laughynge · and leue tonge to chyde;
Al that he wist wykked · by any wiȝte, tellen it,   324
And blame men bihynde her bakke · and bydden hem meschaunce;
And that he wist bi Wille · tellen it Watte,
And that Watte wiste · Wille wiste it after,
And made of frendes foes · thorugh a false tonge,   328
'Or with myȝte of mouthe · or thorugh mannes strengthe
Auenge me fele tymes · other frete my-selue
Wyth-inne, as a shepster shere;' — · i-shrewed men and cursed!
> Cuius malediccione os plenum est, et amaritudine; sub lingua eius labor et dolor:
> Et alibi: filij hominum, dentes eorum arma et sagitte, et lingua eorum gladius acutus:—

'There is no lyf that I louye · lastyng any while,   332
For tales that I telle · no man trusteth to me,
And whan I may nouȝt haue the maistrye · with malencolye I take,
That I cacche the crompe · the cardiacle some tyme,
Or an ague in suche an angre · and some tyme a feure,   336
That taketh me al a twelf-moneth · tyl that I despyse
Lechecrafte of owre lorde · and leue on a wicche,
And segge, that no clerke ne can · ne Cryste, as I leue,
To the souter of Southwerke · or of Shordyche dame Emme!
And segge, that no goddes worde · gaf me neuere bote,   341
But thorw a charme had I chaunce · and my chief hele!'
I wayted wisloker · and thanne was it soiled
With lykyng of Lecherye · as by lokyng of his eye.   344
For vche a mayde that he mette · he made hir a signe
Semynge to-synne-ward · and some tyme he gan taste
Aboute the mouth, or bynethe · bygynneth to grope,
Tyl eytheres wille waxeth kene · and to the werke ȝeden,   348
As wel in fastyng-days and Frydayes · and forboden nyȝtes;
And as wel in Lente as oute of Lente · alle tymes ylyche,
Suche werkes with hem · were neuere oute of sesoun;
Tyl thei myȝte namore . and thanne had merye tales,   352
And how that lechoures louyen · lauȝen and iapen,
And of her harlotrye and horedome · in her elde tellen.

B. 338. of WCOB; or LR.   351. were WRCB; was L.   353. an L.

(NOT HERE IN C-TEXT.) 407

From
C. vii.
69–85.

[And blame men by-hynde hure bak · and bidde hem meschaunce.
Al that he wiste by Wylle · to Watkyn he told hit,
And that he wiste by Watkyn · tolde hit Wille after;
And made foos of frendes · thorw fals and fykel tonge :   72
'Other thorw myghte of mouthe ·' other thorw meny sleyghthes
Venged me fele tymes · other brend my-self with-ynne
Lyke a shappesters sheres · and shrewede myn emcristyne,
Aȝens the consail of Crist · as clerkes fynden in bokes :   76
   Cuius maledictione os plenum est et amaritudine et dolo :
   sub lingua eius labor et dolor.
   Filij hominum, dentes eorum arma et sagitte, et lingua
   eorum gladius acutus.
Whenne ich ne may haue the maistrie · suche malancolie ich take,
That ich cacche the crampe · the cardiacle som tyme,
Other an ague in suche an angre · and som tyme a feuere,
That taketh me al a twelfmonthe · til that ich dispice   80
Leche-craft of oure lorde · and leyue on a wicche,
And sigge that no clerk can · ne Crist, as ich leyue,
To the souter of South-werk · such is hus grace.
For god, ne godes wordes · ne grace ne halp neuere,   84
Bote thorw a charme hadde ich a chaunce · and my chief hele.]

From
C. vii.
175–188.

[Ich, gulty in gost · to god ich me shryue
As in lykynge of lecherie · my licames gultes,   176
In wordes, in wedes · in waitynge of eyen.
To eche maide that ich mette · ich made hure a sygne
Semynge to synne-warde · and somme gan ich taste
A-boute the mouthe, and by-nythe · by-gan ich to grope,   180
Til oure bothers wil was on ; · to werke we ȝeden
As wel fastyngdaies as Frydaies · and heye-feste euenes,
As luf in lente as oute of lente · alle tymes liche—
Suche werkus with ous · were neuere out of seson—   184
Til we myghte no more ; · thanne hadde we murye tales
Of puterie and of paramours · and proueden thorw speches,
Handlynge and halsynge · and al-so thorw cussynge
Excitynge oure aither other · til oure olde synne.]   188

Thanne Pacience parceyued · of poyntes of his cote,
Was colmy thorw Coueityse · and vnkynde desyrynge; 356
More to good than to god · the gome his loue caste,
And ymagyned how · he it my3te haue
With false mesures and mette · and with false witnesse;
Lened for loue of the wedde · and loth to do treuthe, 360
And awaited thorwgh which · wey to bigile,
And menged his marchaundyse · and made a gode moustre;—
'The worste with-in was · a gret witte I lete hit,
And if my neighbore had any hyne · or any beste elles, 364
More profitable than myne · many sleightes I made,
How I my3te haue it · al my witte I caste,
And but I it had by other waye · atte laste I stale it,
Or pryuiliche his purse shoke · vnpiked his lokkes, 368
Or by ny3t or by day · aboute was ich euere,
Thorwgh gyle to gadren · the good that ich haue.
3if I 3ede to the plow · I pynched so narwe,
That a fote-londe or a forwe · fecchen I wolde, 372
Of my nexte neighbore · nymen of his erthe;
And if I rope, ouer-reche · or 3af hem red that ropen,
To seise to me with her sykel · that I ne sewe neure.
And who so borwed of me · abou3te the tyme, 376
With presentes priueliche · or payed somme certeyne.
So, walde he or nou3t wolde he · wynnen I wolde;
And bothe to kyth and to kyn · vnkynde of that ich hadde.
And who so cheped my chaffare · chiden I wolde, 380
But he profred to paye · a peny or tweyne
More than it was worth · and 3et wolde I swere,
That it coste me moche more · swore manye othes.
In halydayes at holicherche · whan ich herde masse, 384
Hadde I neuere wille, wot god · witterly to biseche
Mercye for my mysdedes · that I ne morned more
For losse of gode, leue me · than for my lykames giltes;
As, if I had dedly synne done · I dred nou3t that so sore, 388
As when I lened and leued it lost · or longe ar it were payed.
So if I kydde any kyndenesse · myn euen-cristene to helpe,
Vpon a cruel coueityse · myn herte gan hange.

B. 355. LR om. 2nd of.   356. vkynde L.   374. I WCOB; L om.
376. borwed WR; borweth LCOB.   aboute LR; abou3te WOB.   385.
I WCOB; LR om.

[With false wordes and wittes · ich haue wonne my goodes,
And with gyle and glosynge · gadered that ich haue,
Meddled my marchaundise · and mad a good moustre ; 260
The werst lay with-ynne · a gret wit ich let hit.
And yf my neyhȝebore hadde an hyne · other eny best ellys
More profitable than myn · ich made meny wentes,
How ich myght haue hit · al my wit ich caste. 264
And bote ich hadde hit by other wey · atte laste ich stal hit,
Other pryuyliche hus pors shok · vnpiked hus lokes.

From C. vii. 258–277.

And yf ich ȝede to the plouh · ich pynchede on hus half-acre,
That a fot-londe other a forwe · fecchen ich wolde, 268
Of my neyhȝeboris next · nymen of hus erthe.
And yf y repe, ouere-reche · other ȝaf hem red that repen
To sese to me with here sykel · that ich sew neuere.
In halydayes at holy churche · whenne ich hurde messe, 272
Ich hadde neuere wil witerlich · to by-seche mercy
For my mysdedes · that ich ne mornede ofter
For lost of good, leyue me · then for lycames gultes.
Thauh ich dedliche synne dude · ich dradde hit nat so sore
As whenne ich lenede and leyuede hit lost · other longe er hit
  were paied. 277

And if I sent ouer see · my seruauntz to Bruges,   392
Or in-to Pruslonde my prentys · my profit to wayten,
To marchaunden with monoye · and maken her eschaunges,
Miȝte neuere me conforte · in the mene tyme,
Noither messe ne matynes · ne none manere siȝtes,   396
Ne neuere penaunce perfourned · ne *pater-noster* seyde,
That my mynde ne was more · on my gode, in a doute,
Than in the grace of god · and his grete helpes :
    Vbi thesaurus tuus, ibi et cor tuum.'
Ȝet the Glotoun with grete othes · his garnement hadde soyled,
And foule be-flobered it · as with fals speche ;   401
There no nede ne was · tok godes name an idel,
Swore there-by swithe ofte · and al by-swatte his cote.
And more mete ete and dronke · then kende miȝt defie—   404
'And kauȝte seknesse sum-tyme · for my sorfetes ofte ;
And thanne I dradde to deye · in dedlich synne'—
That in-to wanhope he worthe · and wende nauȝt to be saued,
The whiche is Sleuthe so slow · that may no slithes helpe it,
Ne no mercy amenden · the man that so deyeth.   409
    Which ben the braunches · that bryngeth a man to Sleuth ?
Is, whanne a man morneth nouȝte for his mysdedes · ne maketh
    no sorwe,
Ac penaunce that the prest enioigneth · perfourneth yuel, 412
Doth none almes-dede · dret hym of no synne,
Lyueth aȝein the bileue · and no lawe holdeth ;
Vch day is haliday with hym · or an heigh ferye ;
And if he auȝte wole here · it is an harlotes tonge.   416
Whan men carpeth of Cryst · or of clennesse of soule,
He wexeth wroth and wil nouȝte here · but wordes of myrthe.
Penaunce and pore men · and the passioun of seyntes
He hateth to here there-of · and alle that it telleth.   420
Thise ben the braunches, beth war · that bryngeth a man to
    wanhope !
Ȝe lordes and ladyes · and legates of holicherche,
That fedeth foles sages · flatereres and lyeres,
And han likynge to lythen hem · to do ȝow to lawghe ;   424
    Ve vobis qui ridetis, etc. :
And ȝiueth hem mete and mede · and pore men refuse,

B. 400–409. *In* R *only, and the text is corrupt.* 400. the *must be inserted* ; R *om.* garnement = garment, *miswritten* granement R. 402. tok *must be*

(NOT HERE IN C-TEXT.) 411

From
C. vii.
278–285.

And yf ich sente ouer see · my seruaunt to Brugges,
Other in-to Prus my prentys · my profit to a-waite,
To marchaunde with monye · and maken here eschaunge,   280
Myghte neuere man comforty me · in the meyn tyme,
Neither matyns ne masse · ne othere manere syghtes,
And neuere penaunse performede · ne *pater-noster* seyde,
That my mynde ne was · more in my goodes   284
Than in godes grace · and hus grete myghte.
  Ubi thesaurus tuus, ibi et cor tuum.']

From
C. vii.
425–433.

[To the, god, ich Gloton · gulty me зelde
Of my trespas with tunge · ich can nauht telle how ofte,
Sworen 'thy saule and thy sydes' · and 'so help me, god
  almyghty!'
When that no ned was · meny tyme falsliche.   428
And ouer-sopede at my soper · and som tyme at nones
More than my kynde · myghte wel defye;
And as an hounde that et gras · so gan ich to brake,
And spilde that ich spele myghte · ich can nouht speke for shame
The vylenye of my foule mouthe · and of my foule mawe.]   433

From
C. viii.
70–85.

[Ac whiche be the braunches · that bryngeth men to sleuthe?
Ys, whanne a man mourneth nat · for hus mysdedes;
The penaunce that the prest enioyneth ' parfourneth vuele,   72
Doth non almys-dedes · and drat nat of synne,
Lyueth aзens the by-leyue · and no lawe kepeth,
And hath no lykynge to lerne · ne of oure lord hure,
Bote harlotrie other horedom · other elles of som wynnyng.   76
Whan men carpen of Cryst ' other of clennesse of soule,
He wext wroth, and wol nat huyre · bote wordes of murthe.
Penaunce and poure men · and the passion of seyntes,
He hateth to huyre ther-of · and alle that ther-of carpen.   80
Thuse beth the braunches, be war · that bryngeth man to wan-
  hope.
Зe lordes and ladyes · and legates of holy churche,
That feden fool sages · flaterers and lyers,
And han lykynge to lythen hem · in hope to do зow lawghe:
  Ve uobis qui ridetis, quia lugebitis, et cetera:
And зeueth suche mede and mete · and poure men refusen,   85

---

inserted; R *om.*   407. worthe; *miswritten* wrathe R.   411. Is whanne
a man O; LRC *have the extraordinary false reading* His woman; *see* C-text.

In ȝowre deth-deyinge · I drede me ful sore,
Lest tho thre maner men · to moche sorwe ȝow brynge :
    Consencientes et agentes pari pena punientur.
Patriarkes and prophetes · and prechoures of goddes wordes 428
Sauen thorw her sarmoun · mannes soule fram helle ;
Riȝt so flatereres and foles · aren the fendes disciples,
To entice men thorw her tales · to synne and harlotrye.
Ac clerkes that knowen holywryt · shulde kenne lordes,   432
What Dauid seith of suche men · as the sauter telleth :
    *Non habitabit in medio domus mee, qui facit superbiam et
    qui loquitur iniqua :*
Shulde none harlote haue audience · in halle ne in chambres,
There wise men were · witnesseth goddes wordes ;
Ne no mysproude man · amonges lordes ben allowed.   436
  Clerkes and kniȝtes · welcometh kynges ministrales,
And for loue of the lorde · litheth hem at festes ;
Muche more, me thenketh · riche men schulde
Haue beggeres byfore hem · the whiche ben goddes ministrales,
As he seyth hym-self · seynt Iohan bereth witnesse :   441
    Qui vos spernit, me spernit.
For-thi I rede ȝow riche · reueles whan ȝe maketh
For to solace ȝoure soules · suche ministrales to haue ;
The pore, for a fol sage · syttynge at the heyȝ table,   444
And a lered man, to lere the · what oure lorde suffred,
For to saue thi soule · fram Sathan thin enemy,
And fithel the, with-out flaterynge · of gode Friday the storye ;
And a blynd man for a bourdeoure · or a bedrede womman,
To crie a largesse by-for oure lorde · ȝoure gode loos to schewe !
Thise thre maner ministrales · maketh a man to lawhe,
And, in his deth-deyinge · thei don him grete comforte,
That bi his lyue lythed hem · and loued hem to here.   452
Thise solaseth the soule · til hym-selue be-falle
In a wel gode hope, for he wrouȝte so · amonges worthi seyntes.
Ac flatereres and foles · thorw her foule wordes,
Leden tho that louen hem · to Luciferes feste,   456
With *turpiloquio*, a lay of sorwe · and Luciferes fithele.
  Thus Haukyn the actyf man · hadde ysoiled his cote,
Til Conscience acouped hym there-of · in a curteise manere,
Whi he ne hadde wasshen it · or wyped it with a brusshe. 460

(NOT HERE IN C-TEXT.) 413

In ʒoure deth-deynge · ich drede me sore
Lest tho manere men · to moche sorwe ʒow brynge;
    As god wole; *Consencientes et agentes pari pena punientur.*
Patriarkes and prophetes · prechours of godes wordes   88
Sauen thorgh here sermons · mannes soule fro helle;
Ryʒt so flaterers and foles · aren the fendes procuratores,
Entysen men thorgh here tales · to synne and to harlotrie.
Clerkus that knowen this · sholde kenne lordes,   92
What Dauid seide of suche men · as the sauter telleth,
    Non habitabit in medio domus mee qui facit superbiam,
    qui loquitur iniqua.
Sholde non harlot haue audience · in halle ne in chaumbre,
Ther that wise men were; · (witnesse of godes wordes),
Nother a mys-proud man · among lordes be a-lowed.   96
Clerkus and knyʒtes · welcometh kynges mynstrales,
And for loue of here lordes · lithen hem at festes;
Muche more, me thenketh · riche men auhte
Haue beggers by-fore hem · whiche beth godes mynstrales,   100
As he seith hym-self · seynt Iohan bereth witnesse,
    Qui uos spernit, me eciam spernit.
Ther-for ich rede ʒow riche · reueles when ʒe maken
For to solace ʒoure soules · suche mynstrales to haue;
The poure for a fol sage · syttynge at thy table,   104
With a lered man, to lere the · what oure lord suffrede
For to sauy thy saule · fram Satan thyn enemye,
And fithele the, with-oute flateryng · of goode Fryday the geste,
And a blynde man for a bordiour · other a bedreden womman,
To crye a largesse by-fore oure lorde · ʒoure goode loos to shewe.
Thuse thre manere mynstrales · maken a man to lauhe;   110
In hus deth-deynge · thei don hym gret comfort,
That by hus lyue litheth hem · and loueth hem to huyre.   112
Thuse solaceth the soule · til hym-self be-falle
In a wel good hope, for he wroghte so · a-mong worthy seyntes;
Ther flaterers and foles · with here foule wordes
Leden tho that lithen hem · to Luciferes feste,   116
With *turpiloquio*, a lay of sorwe · and Lucifers fithele,
To perpetual peyne · other purgatorye as wykke.]

From C. viii. 86–118.

B. 430. flateres L.   437–454. *These lines in* R *only*; *but found in* C-text.
454. gode; R *om.*   for—so; R *om*; *but cf.* C-text.   455. flateres (*for* flatereres) LR.

PASSUS XIV (DO-WEL VI).

Passus xiiij^{us}.

'I HAUE but one hool hatere,' quod Haukyn · 'I am the lasse
to blame
Though it be soiled and selde clene · I slepe there-inne on niȝtes;
And also I haue an houswyf · hewen and children—
    Vxorem duxy, et ideo non possum venire—
That wolen bymolen it many tyme · maugre my chekes!   4
It hath ben laued in lente · and oute of lente bothe,
With the sope of sykenesse · that seketh wonder depe,
And with the losse of catel · loth forto agulte
God or any gode man · bi auȝte that I wiste;   8
And was shryuen of the preste · that gaue me, for my synnes,
To penaunce pacyence · and pore men to fede,
Al for coueitise of my Crystenedome · in clennesse to kepen it.
And couthe I neuere, by Cryste · kepen it clene an houre,   12
That I ne soiled it with syȝte · or sum ydel speche,
Or thorugh werke or thorugh worde · or wille of myn herte,
That I ne flober it foule · fro morwe tyl eue.'
   'And I shal kenne the,' quod Conscience · 'of contricioun to
make,   16
That shal clawe thi cote · of alkynnes filthe,
    Cordis contricio, etc.: —
Dowel shal wasshen it and wryngen it · thorw a wys confessour,
    Oris confessio, etc.:—
Dobet shal beten it and bouken it · as briȝte as any scarlet,
And engreynen it with good wille · and goddes grace to amende the,
And sithen sende the to satisfaccioun · for to sowen it after,
    Satisfaccio dobest.
Shal neuere myste bimolen it · ne moth after biten it,
Ne fende ne false man · defoulen it in thi lyue;
Shall none heraude ne harpoure · haue a fairere garnement   24
Than Haukyn the actyf man · and thou do by my techyng;
Ne no mynstral be more worth · amonges pore and riche,
Than Haukynnes wyf the wafrere · with his *actiua-vita.*'

B. 1. hool WCOB; LR *om.*   18. shal W; schal O; LCRB *om.*

'Pees!' quath Pacience · 'ich praye the, syre Actyf!
For thauh neuere payn ne plough · ne potage were,

'And I shal purueye the paste,' quod Pacyence · 'though no
   plow erie,   28
And floure to fede folke with · as best be for the soule,
Though neuere greyne growed · ne grape vppon vyne.
Alle that lyueth and loketh · lyflode wolde I fynde,
And that ynough shal none faille · of thinge that hem nedeth.
We shulde nouȝt be to busy · a-bouten owre lyflode,   33
   *Ne solliciti sitis, etc.: volucres celi deus pascit, etc.: pacientes
   vincunt, etc.*'
Thanne laughed Haukyn a litel · and liȝtly gan swerye,
'Who so leueth ȝow, by owre lorde · I leue nouȝte he be
   blissed!'
'No,' quod Pacyence paciently · and out of his poke hente   36
Vitailles of grete vertues · for al manere bestes,
And seyde, 'lo! here lyflode ynough · if owre byleue be trewe!
For lente neuere was lyf · but lyflode were shapen,
Wher-of or wherfore · or where-by to lybbe.   40
   Firste the wylde worme · vnder weet erthe,
Fissch to lyue in the flode · and in the fyre the crykat,
The corlue by kynde of the eyre · moste clennest flessch of
   bryddes,
And bestes by grasse and by greyne · and by grene rotis,   44
In menynge that alle men · myȝte the same
Lyue thorw lele byleue · and loue, as god witnesseth;
      *Quodcumque pecieritis a patre in nomine meo, etc.: et
      alibi,
      Non in solo pane viuit homo, set in omni verbo, quod pro-
      cedit de ore dei.*'
But I loked what lyflode it was · that Pacience so preysed,
And thanne was it a pece of the *pater-noster* · *fiat voluntas tua*.
'Haue, Haukyn!' quod Pacyence · 'and ete this whan the
   hungreth,   49
Or whan thow clomsest for colde · or clyngest for drye.
Shal neuere gyues the greue · ne grete lordes wrath,
Prisone ne peyne · for—*pacientes vincunt*.   52
Bi so that thow be sobre · of syȝte and of tonge,
In etynge and in handlynge · and in alle thi fyue wittis,
Darstow neuere care for corne · ne lynnen cloth ne wollen,
Ne for drynke, ne deth drede · but deye as god lyketh,   56
Or thorw honger or thorw hete · at his wille be it;

Prude wolde putte hym-self forth · thauh no plouh erye. 236
Hit am ich that fynde alle folke · and fram hunger saue,
Thorgh the heye helpe of hym · that me hyder sente,

And seide, 'lo, here lyf-lode ynowe · yf oure by-leyue be trewe
For lent was ther neuere lyf · bote lyflode were yshape, 240
Wher-of othere wherfore · and wher-with to lyuen.
The worme that woneth vnder erthe · and in water fisshes,
The crykett by kynde of fur · and corlew by the wynde,
Bestes by gras and by greyn · and by grene rotes. 244
In menynge that alle men · myghte the same
Lyuen thorgh leell by-leyue · as oure lord wittnesseth,

> *Quodcunque petieritis patrem in nomine meo, dabitur enim uobis; et alibi:*
> *Non in solo pane uiuit homo, sed de omni verbo, quod procedit de ore dei.*

'Hast thow ay,' quath Actyf · 'suche mete with the?'
'ȝe,' quath Pacience, and hente · out of hus poke 248
A pece of the pater-noster · and profrede to vs alle.
And ich lustnede, and lokede · what lyflode hit were;
Thanne was hit *fiat-uoluntas-tua* · that sholde fynde vs alle.
'Haue, Actyf,' quath Pacience · 'and eet this when the hungreth,
Other whenne thow clomsest for colde · other clyngest for drouthe; 253
And shal neuere gyues the greue · ne grete lordes wratthe,
Pryson ne other payne · for—*pacientes uincunt;*
By so thow be sobre · of syght, and of tounge bothe, 256
In ondyng, in handlying · in alle thy fyue wittes,
That thow care for no corn · for cloth ne for drynke,
Ne deth drede, ne deuel · deye as god lyketh, 259
Whether thorw hunger other thorw hete · at hus wil be hit!'

C. 244. greyen (*for* greyn) P.   249. pece ITMFSE; pice P.

For if thou lyuest after his lore · the shorter lyf the better
Si quis amat Cristum · mundum non diligit istum.
For thorw his breth bestes wexen · and abrode ȝeden,
  Dixit et facta sunt, etc.:
Ergo thorw his breth mowen · men and bestes lyuen, 61
As holywrit witnesseth · whan men segge her graces,
  Aperis tu manum tuam, et imples omne animal benediccione.
It is founden that fourty wynter · folke lyued with-outen tulyinge,
And oute of the flynte spronge the flode · that folke and bestes
  dronke. 64
And in Elyes tyme · heuene was yclosed,
That no reyne ne rone; · thus rede men in bokes,
That many wyntres men lyueden · and no mete ne tulyeden.
Seuene slepe, as seith the boke · seuene hundreth wynter, 68
And lyueden with-oute lyflode · and atte laste thei woken,
And if men lyued as mesure wolde · shulde neuere more be
  defaute
Amonges Cristene creatures · if Crystes wordes ben trewe.
Ac vnkyndnesse *caristia* maketh · amonges Crystene peple, 72
And ouer-plente maketh pruyde · amonges pore and riche;
Ac mesure is so moche worth · it may nouȝte be to dere,
For the meschief and the meschaunce · amonges men of Sodome
Wex thorw plente of payn · and of pure sleuthe; 76
  Ociositas et habundancia panis peccatum turpissimum
  nutriuit.
For thei mesured nouȝt hem-self · of that thei ete and dronke,
Diden dedly synne · that the deuel lyked,
So vengeaunce fel vpon hem · for her vyle synnes;
Thei sonken in-to helle · tho citees vchone. 80
For-thi mesure we vs wel · and make owre faithe owre schel-
  troun,
And thorw faith cometh contricioun · conscience wote wel,
Whiche dryueth awey dedly synne · and doth it to be venial.
And though a man myȝte nouȝte speke · contricioun myȝte hym
  saue, 84
And brynge his soule to blisse · by so that feith bere witnesse,
That, whiles he lyued, he bileued · in the lore of holy-cherche;
Ergo contricioun, feith, and conscience · is kyndelich Dowel,

---

  B. 58. shorter WC; shotter L. 72. *caristia* RCOB; *carestia* L.

For yf thow lyuest after hus lore · the shorter lyf the betere ;
Si quis amat Christum · mundum non diligit istum,
Sed quasi fetorem · spernes illius amorem.
Thorgh hus breth bestes woxen · and a-brode ȝeden;   264
    Dixit et facta sunt.
Ergo thorw hus breth bestes lyuen · bothe men and fisshes,
As wytnesseth holy wryte · when we seyn oure graces,
    Aperis tu manum tuam, et imples omne animal benedictione.
Hit is founde that fourty wynter · folke leueden and nouht tylede,
And out of flent sprange the flod · that folke and bestes dronken.

And in Elyes time · heuene was yclosed,   269
That no reyne reynede · thus redeth men in bookes,
That menye wynter men lyueden · and of no mete telden.
Seuene slepen, as seith the book · more than syxty wynter,   272
Lyueden with-outen lyflode · and at the laste a-wakeden.
And yf men lyueden as mesure wolde · sholde neuere be defaute
Among Crysten creatures · yf Crystes worde be trewe ;
    Dabo tibi secundum peticionem tuam.'

[*See note on* p. 403.]

C. 263. *This line is in* E *only.*   266. breth ITS ; PEM *om.*   267. P *repeats* that.   268. P *om.* the.   272. slepen IMF ; slupen PE.   a (*for* as) P.
273. Leueden P ; *see* l. 274.   275. trywe P.

And surgienes for dedly synnes · whan shrifte of mouth failleth.
    Ac shrifte of mouth more worthy is · if man be inliche contrit;
For shrifte of mouth sleeth synne · be it neuere so dedly;   90
Per confessionem to a prest · *peccata occiduntur*,
There contricioun doth but dryueth it doun · in-to a venial synne,
As Dauid seith in the sauter · *et quorum tecta sunt peccata*.
Ac satisfaccioun seketh oute the rote · and bothe sleeth and
    voideth,
And, as it neuere had ybe · to nouȝt bryngeth dedly synne,
That it neuere eft is seen, ne sore · but semeth a wounde yheled.'
    'Where woneth Charite?' quod Haukyn · 'I wiste neuere
        in my lyue   97
Man that with hym spake · as wyde as I haue passed!'
    'There parfit treuthe and pouere herte is · and pacience
        of tonge,
There is Charitee, the chief chaumbrere · for god hymselue!'
    'Whether paciente pouerte,' quod Haukyn · 'be more
        plesaunte to owre driȝte   101
Than ricchesse riȝtfulliche ywonne · and resonablelich yspended?'
'Ȝe,' *quis est ille?*' quod Pacience · 'quik *laudabimus eum!*
Though men rede of richchesse · riȝt to the worldes ende,   104
I wist neuere renke that riche was · that whan he rekne sholde,
Whan it drow to his deth-day · that he ne dred hym sore,
And that atte rekenyng in arrerage fel · rather than oute of dette.
There the pore dar plede · and preue by pure resoun,   108
To haue allowaunce of his lorde · by the lawe he it cleymeth,
Ioye that neuere Ioye hadde · of riȝtful Iugge he axeth,
And seith, "lo! briddes and bestes · that no blisse ne knoweth,
And wilde wormes in wodes · thorw wyntres thow hem greuest,
And makest hem welnyegh meke · and mylde for defaute,   113
And after thow sendest hem somer · that is her souereigne Ioye,
And blisse to alle that ben · bothe wilde and tame.
Thanne may beggeres, as bestes · after bote waiten,   116
That al her lyf han lyued · in langour and in defaute.
But god sent hem some tyme · some manere Ioye,
Other here or elles where · kynde wolde it neuere;
For to wrotherhele was he wrouȝte · that neuere was Ioye shaped.
Angeles that in helle now ben · hadden Ioye some tyme,   121

        B. 89. inlich RO; iliche L.

'What is parfit Pacience?' · quath *Activa uita*. 276
'Meeknesse and mylde speche · and men of on wil,
The whiche wil loue ledeth · to oure lordes place;
And that is Charite, chaumpion · chief of alle vertues,
And that is poure pacient · alle perilis to suffre." 280
'Where pouerte and pacience · plese more god almyghty
Than do ryghtful richesse · and resonably to spende?'
'ȝe, *quis est ille?*' quath Pacience · 'quyk *laudabimus eum!*
Thauh men rede of riche · ryght to the worldes ende, 284
I wist neuere renke that riche was · that whan he rekne sholde,
And whan he drouh hym to the deth · that he ne dradde hym sarrer
Than eny poure pacient · and that preoue ich by reyson. 287
Hit are bote fewe folke of these riche · that ne falleth in arerage,
Thar the poure dar plede · and preoue by pure reysoune
To haue a-lowaunce of hus lorde; · by lawe he cleymeth Ioye,
That neuere Ioye hadde · of rightful Iuge he asketh; 291
And seith, "lo, briddes and bestes · that no blisse knoweth,
And wilde wormes in wodes · thorw wynter thow hem greuest,
And makest hem wel ney meek · and mylde for defaute;
After than thow sendest hem somere · that is here souereyn Ioye,
And blisse to alle that been · bothe wilde and tame. 296
Then may beggers, as bestes · after blysse asken,
That al here lif hauen lyued · in langour and defaute."
Bote god sende hem som tyme · of som manner Ioye,
Other heer other elles-wher · elles were it reuthe; 300
For to wrother-hele was he wrouȝt · that neuere was Ioye yshape.
Angeles that in helle now been · hadden som tyme Ioye,

C. 285. *This line is supplied from the* B-*text*, *to complete the sense; all the*
C-*text MSS. omit it.* 288. thees P. arirage P. 289. dar IMFSET; der P.
291. rightful IFST; ryght PE. 294. ney E; nei *or* ner P. 295. seyn-
dest P; *see* l. 299. here IST; hem P. 296. P *om.* that. 297. as ME;
and PST. 299. sum (1*st time*) T; PEMFS *om.* 301. wrouȝth P.

And *Diues* in deyntees lyued · and in *douce vye;*
Riȝte so resoun sheweth · that tho men that were riche,
And her makes also lyued · her lyf in murthe. 124
  Ac god is of a wonder wille · by that kynde witte sheweth,
To ȝiue many men his mercymonye · ar he it haue deserued.
Riȝt so fareth god by some riche · reuthe me it thinketh,
For thei han her hyre here · an heuene as it were, 128
And is gret lykyng to lyue · with-oute laboure of body;
And when he deyeth, ben disalowed · as Dauid seith in the sauter,
  Dormierunt, et nichil inuenerunt ;
And in an other stede also · *velud sompnum surgencium,*
  domine, in ciuitate tua, et ad nichilum rediges.
  Allas! that ricchesse shal reue · and robbe mannes soule 132
Fram the loue of owre lorde · at his laste ende!
Hewen that han her hyre afore · aren euermore nedy,
And selden deieth he out of dette · that dyneth ar he deserue it,
And til he haue done his deuor · and his dayes iourne. 136
For whan a werkman hath wrouȝte · thanne may men se the sothe,
What he were worthi for his werke · and what he hath deserued;
And nouȝt to fonge bifore · for drede of disalowynge.
So I segge by ȝow riche · it semeth nouȝt that ȝe shulle 140
Haue heuene in ȝowre here-beyng · and heuene her-after;
Riȝt as a seruaunt taketh his salarye bifore · and sitth wolde clayme
  more,
As he that none hadde · and hath huyre atte laste.
It may nouȝt be, ȝe riche men · or Matheu on god lyeth; 144
  De delicijs ad delicias, difficile est transire.
  Ac if ye riche haue reuthe · and rewarde wel the pore,
And lyuen as lawe techeth · done leute to alle,
Criste of his curteysie · shal conforte ȝow atte laste,
And rewarde alle dowble ricchesse · that reuful hertes habbeth.
And as an hyne that hadde his hyre · ar he bygonne, 149
And whan he hath done his deuor wel · men doth hym other bounte,
Ȝyueth hym a cote aboue his couenaunte · riȝte so Cryst ȝiueth
  heueue
Bothe to riche and to nouȝte riche · that rewfullich lybbeth; 152
And alle that done her deuor wel · han dowble hyre for her
  trauaille,
Here forȝyuenesse of her synnes · and heuene blisse after.

B. 144. *difficile* WCROB; *deficile* L.   145. ye WCROB; þe L.

And *Dives* in his deyntes lyuede · and in *douce uye;*
And now he buyeth hit ful bitere · he is a beggere of helle.

Many man hath hus Ioye here · for alle here wel dedes,   305
And lordes and ladyes ben callid · for leodes that thay haue,
And slepith, as hit semeth · and somere euere hem foleweth;
Whan deth a-waketh hem of here wele · that were here so ryche,
Than aren hit pure poure thynges · in purgatorie other in helle!
Dauid in the sauter · of suche maketh mynde,   310
    And seith, *dormierunt sompnum suum; et nichil inuenerunt*
    omnes uiri diuiciarum in manibus suis;
    Et alibi: Velut sompnum surgencium, et cet.

    Hic explicit passus sextus de Dowel.

PASSUS XVII. (DO-WEL VII.)

Incipit passus septimus.

ALAS! that Richesse shall reue · and robbe mannes soule
Fro the loue of oure lorde · at hus laste ende!
Thei that haue hure hyre by-fore · aren eueremore poure,
And shulle nat deye out of dette · to dyne er they deseruen hit.
When here deuer is don · and his daies iourne,   5
Then may men wite what he is worth · and what he hath deserued;
And nouht to fonge by-fore · for drede of disalouwynge.
So ich say by ʒow riche · hit semeth nat ʒe shulle   8
Haue two heuenes · for ʒoure her-beynge.

C. 303. lyuede TS; lyuynge PEMF.   306. an (*for* and) P.   309. haren P.
310. shuche P.   *sompnum suum* F (*only*).   *in—suis* E (*only*).
  Passus XVII. 1. richesse EMF; riche P.   2. Fro ETF; For PM.
6. white (*for* wite) P.   deseruede P.

Ac it nys but selde yseyn · as by holy seyntes bokes,
That god rewarded double reste · to any riche wye.   156
For moche murthe is amonges riche · as in mete and clothynge,
And moche murthe in Maye is · amonges wilde bestes,
And so forth whil somer lasteth · her solace dureth.
Ac beggeres aboute Midsomer · bredlees thei soupe,   160
And ȝit is wynter for hem worse · for wete-shodde thei gange,
A-fyrst sore and afyngred · and foule yrebuked,
And arated of riche men · that reuthe is to here.
Now, lorde, sende hem somer · and some manere Ioye,   164
Heuene after her hennes-goynge · that here han suche defaute!
For alle myȝtest thow haue made · none mener than other,
And yliche witty and wyse · if the wel hadde lyked.
And haue reuthe on thise riche men · that rewarde nouȝte thi
    prisoneres ;   168
Of the good that thow hem gyuest · *ingrati* ben manye ;
Ac, god, of thi goodnesse · gyue hem grace to amende.
For may no derth ben hem dere · drouth, ne weet,
Ne noyther hete ne haille · haue thei here hele,   172
Of that thei wilne and wolde · wanteth hem nouȝt here.
  Ac pore peple, thi prisoneres · lorde, in the put of myschief,
Conforte tho creatures · that moche care suffren
Thorw derth, thorw drouth · alle her dayes here,   176
Wo in wynter tymes · for wantyng of clothes,
And in somer tyme selde · soupen to the fulle ;
Comforte thi careful · Cryst, in thi ryche,
For how thow confortest alle creatures · clerkes bereth witnesse,
    Conuertimini ad me, et salui eritis :
Thus, *in genere* of his gentrice · Iesu Cryst seyde,   181
To robberes and to reueres · to riche and to pore.
Thow tauȝtest hem in the trinitee · to take baptesme,
And be clene thorw that crystennynge · of alle kynnes synnes ;
And if vs fel thorw folye · to falle in synne after,   185
Confessioun, and knowlechyng · and crauyng thi mercy
Shulde amende vs as many sithes · as man wolde desire.
Ac if the pouke wolde plede here-aȝeine · and punyssh vs in
    conscience,   188

B. 181. gentrice O; gentrise CB; gentries W; genitrice LR.   184. synnes RCO; synne WB; L *om.*   185. if WR; LCOB *om.*   186. knowleching CORB; knelechyng L.   188. pouke R; pope (!) LCWCOB; *see* l. 190.

Much myrthe is in May · a-monge wilde bestes,
And so forth whil somer lasteth · heore solace dureth ;
And muche myrthe a-monge riche men is · that han meoble
    ynow and heele.   12
Ac beggers a-boute Myd-somere · bredlees thei soupe,
And ȝut is wynter for hem wors · for wet-shood thei gangen,
A-furst and a-fyngred · and foule rebuked
Of these worlde-riche men · that reuthe hit is to huyre.   16
Now, lord, send hem somer som-tyme · to solace and to Ioye,
That al here lyf leden · in lowenesse and in pouerte !
For alle myghtest thow haue maked · men of grete welthe,
And liche witty and wys · and lyue with-oute neode ;   20
Ac for the beste, as ich hope · aren somme poure and some
    riche.
Ryght so haue reuthe of ous alle · that on the rode deydest,
And amende ous of thy mercy · and make ous alle meeke,
Louh and leel and louynge · and of herte poure ;   24
And send ous contricion · to clanse with oure soules,
And confession, to culle · alle kynne synnes,
And satisfaccion, the whiche fulfulleth · the fadres will of heuene.
And these been Dowel and Dobet · and Dobest of alle ;   28
Cordis contricio · cometh of sorwe in herte,
And *oris confessio* · that cometh of shrifte of mouthe,
And *operis satisfactio* · that for synnes payeth,
And for alle synnes · soueraynliche quiteth.   32
    Cordis contricio, oris confessio, operis satisfactio ;
These thre with-outen doute · tholen alle pouerte,
And lereth lewed and lered · heh and louh to knowe,
Ho that doth wel other bet · other best a-bouen alle ;
And holichurche and charite · here-of a chartere maden.   36

C. 11. forth ET ; fuith F ; fort P.   whil F ; while ET ; wil P.   13.
Ac F ; But T ; And PE.   14. whetshood P.   16. thes P.   wordle P.
19. myghtes P.   makede P.   20. and EFT ; an P.   21. as ETF ; P *om*.
22. roude P.   23. P *inserts* al *after* of.   33. Thees P.   whitouten P.

He shulde take the acquitance as quik · and to the qued schewe it,
    Pateat, etc., per passionem domini,
And putten of so the pouke · and preuen vs vnder borwe.
Ac the perchemyn of this patent · of pouerte be moste,
And of pure pacience · and parfit bileue.   192
Of pompe and of pruyde · the parchemyn decorreth,
And principaliche of alle peple · but thei be pore of herte.
Ellis is al an ydel · al that euere we writen,
Pater-nostres and penaunce · and pilgrimage to Rome.   196
But owre spences and spendynge · sprynge of a trewe wille,
Elles is al owre laboure loste; · lo! how men writeth
In fenestres atte freres · if fals be the foundement;
For-thi Crystene sholde ben in comune riche · none coueitouse
    for hym-selue.   200
    For seuene synnes that there ben · assaillen vs euere,
The fende folweth hem alle · and fondeth hem to helpe,
Ac with ricchesse that ribaude · rathest men bigyleth.
For there that richesse regneth · reuerence folweth,   204
And that is plesaunte to Pryde · in pore and in riche.
And the riche is reuerenced · by resoun of his richchesse,
There the pore is put bihynde · and par auenture can more
Of witte and of wysdom · that fer awey is better   208
Than ricchesse or reaute · and rather yherde in heuene.
For the riche hath moche to rekene · and riȝte softe walketh,
The heigh waye to-heuene-ward · oft ricchesse letteth,
    Ita inpossibile diuiti, etc.,
There the pore preseth bifor the riche · with a pakke at his rugge,
    Opera enim illorum sequuntur illos.
Batauntliche, as beggeres done · and baldeliche he craueth,   213
For his pouerte and his pacience · a perpetuel blisse;
    Beati pauperes, quoniam ipsorum est regnum celorum.
And Pryde in ricchesse regneth · rather than in pouerte,
Arst in the maister than in the man · some mansioun he hath.
Ac in pouerte there pacyence is · Pryde hath no myȝte,   217
Ne none of the seuene synnes · sitten ne mowe there longe,
Ne haue powere in pouerte · if pacyence it folwe.
For the pore is ay prest · to plese the riche,   220

B. 197. wille WCO; welle LRB.   211. *inpossibile* W; *possibile* LCROB.
212. *sequntur* LCRB.

Bote these thre that ich spak of · on domes day vs defenden,
Elles is in ydel · al oure lyuynge here,
Oure preyers and oure penaunce · and pilgrymages to Rome.
Bote oure spences and spending · sprynge of a trewe wille,   40
Elles is al oure labour lost; · lo, how men wryten
In fenestres at the freres · yf fals be the foundement!
For-thi Cristene men scholde been in comun riche · no couetise
   to hym-selue.
For seuene synnes that ther been · that assailen ous euere,
The fende folweth hem alle · and fondeth hem to helpe,   45
And with richesse tho ribaudes · rathest men by-gylen;
For ther that rychesse regneth · reuerences foleweth,
And that is plesaunt to Pruyde · in poure and in riche.   48
The ryche is yreuerenced · by reson of his richesse,
There the poure is yput by-hynde · and can parauntre more
Of wit and of wysedome · that fer wey is bettere
Than richesse other reaulte · and rather yhurde in heuene.   52
For the ryche hath muche to rekene · and ry3t softe walkith
The heye wey to-heuene-warde; · he halt hit nat ful euene;
There the poure presseth by-fore · with a pak at hus rygge,
   Opera enim illorum sequuntur illos.
Batauntlyche, as beggers don · and boldeliche he craueth,   56
For hus pouerte and pacience · perpetual Ioye.
Also Pruyde in richesse regneth · rather than in pouerte;
Other in the maister other in the man · som mancion he shewith.
Ac in pouerte ther pacience is · Pryude hath no my3te,   60
Ne non of the seuene synnes · sitte ne may ther longe,
Ne haue power in pouerte · yf pacience hit folewe.
For the poure is ay prest · to plese the riche,

C. 37. thes P.   vs TF; P *om.*   38. lyuynge ET; leuynge PF.   40.
trywe P.   49. is EFTG; P *om.* yreuerencede P.   is (*for* his) P.   51. wit FG;
witt E; whi3t P.   fer EFT; feer P.   52. an (*for* and) P.   53. ry3th P.
55. whit P.   *sequuntur* P.   60. my3ghte P.   61. ne may EF; may T;
no man (!) P.   63. prest EFTG; preest P.

And buxome at his byddyng · for his broke loues;
And buxomenesse and boste · aren euer-more at werre,
And ayther hateth other · in alle manere werkes.
  If Wratthe wrastel with the pore · he hath the worse ende;
For if they bothe pleyne · the pore is but fieble, 225
And if he chyde or chatre · hym chieueth the worse;
For loulich he loketh · and loueliche is his speche,
That mete or mone · of other men mote asken. 228
  And if Glotonie greue pouerte · he gadereth the lasse,
For his rentes ne wol nauȝte reche · no riche metes to bugge;
And thouȝ his glotonye be to gode ale · he goth to cold beddynge,
And his heued vn-heled · vn-esiliche i-wrye; 232
For whan he streyneth hym to streche · the strawe is his schetes;
So for his glotonie and his grete scleuthe · he hath a greuous penaunce,
That is welawo whan he waketh · and wepeth for colde,
And sum tyme for his synnes · so he is neuere murie, 236
Withoute mornynge amonge · and mischief to bote.
  And if Coueitise wolde cacche the pore · thei may nouȝt come togideres,
And by the nekke namely · her none may hente other.
For men knoweth wel that Coueitise · is of a kene wille, 240
And hath hondes and armes · of a longe lengthe.
And pouerte nis but a petit thinge · appereth nouȝt to his nauele,
And louely layke was it neuere · bitwene the longe and the shorte.
  And though Auarice wolde angre the pore · he hath but litel myȝte, 244
For pouerte hath but pokes · to putten in his godis,
There Auarice hath almaries · and yren-bounde coffres;
And whether be liȝter to breke? · lasse boste it maketh,
A beggeres bagge · than an yren-bounde coffre! 248
  Lecherye loueth hym nouȝt · for he ȝeueth but lytel syluer,
Ne doth hym nouȝte dyne delycatly · ne drynke wyn oft.
A strawe for the stuwes! · it stode nouȝt, I trowe,
Had thei no thyng but of pore men · her houses were vntyled!
  And though Sleuthe suwe pouerte · and serue nouȝt god to paye,

---

B. 227–237. *These lines are in* R *only.*   242. nauele WCR; naule L.
252. no thyng WCOB; none L. *For* vntyled, O *has* vnhiled (*perhaps better*).

And buxume at his biddyng · for hus breed and drynke; 64
And buxumnesse and bost · aren euere-more at wratthe,
And ayther hateth other · and mowen nat dwelle to-gederes.
Yf Wratthe wraxle with the poure · he hath the worsse ende ;
For yf thei bothe pleyne · the poure is bote fyble, 68
And yf he childe other chatere · hym chyuyth the worsse.
For loueliche he lokyth · and louh is hus speche,
That mete other moneye · of straunge men mote begge.
And yf Glotenye greue pouerte · he gadereth the lasse, 72
For hus rentes wol nat reche · ryche metes to bigge;
Thauh hus glotenye be of good ale · he goth to a cold beddyng,
And hus heued vn-heled · vneisyliche ywrye;
For when he streyneth hym to strecche · the straw is hus whitel; 76
So for hus glotonye and grete synne · he hath a greuous penaunce,

That is weylawey whan he awaketh · and wepeth for colde ;
So is he neuere more ful murye · so meschief hym folweth.

Thaugh Couetyce wolde with the poure wraxle · thei mai nat
    come to-gederis, 80
By the necke nameliche · her neither may henten other.
For men knoweth that Couetise · is of ful kene wil,
And hath hondes and armes · of a long lengthe,
And pouerte is a pety thyng · apereth nat to hus nauele; 84
A loueliche laik was hit neuere · by-twyne a long and a short.

Thauh Auarice wolde angrye pouerte · he hath bote lytel my3te ;

For pouerte hath bote pokes · to putten yn hus goodes,
Ther Auarice hath almaries · and yre-bounden cofres. 88
And whether be betere to breke · lasse boost hit maketh,
To breke a beggers bagge · than an yre-bounden cofre?
Lecherye loueth none poure · for he hath bote lytel seluer,
Ne doth men dyne dylicatliche · neyther drynk wyne ofte. 92
A straw for the stywes! · hy stod nat ful longe
And thay hadde non other haunt · bote of poure peple !
Thauh Slewthe suwe pouerte · and serue nat god to paye,

C. 64. is (*for* his) P.   68. pleyne FT; pleyn E; pleyen P.   his (*for*
is P.   80. whit (*for* with) P.   86, 88. auerice P.   my3the P.   88.
an (*for* and) P.

Mischief is his maister · and maketh hym to thynke, 254
That god is his grettest helpe · and no gome elles,
And his seruaunt, as he seith · and of his sute bothe. 256
And where he be or be nouȝte · he bereth the signe of pouerte,
And in that secte owre saueoure · saued al mankynde.
For-thi al pore that paciente is · may claymen and asken
After her endynge here · heuene-riche blisse. 260
Moche hardier may he axen · that here myȝte haue his wille
In londe and in lordship · and likynge of bodye,
And for goddis loue leueth al · and lyueth as a beggere;
And as a mayde for mannes loue · her moder forsaketh, 264
Hir fader and alle her frendes · and folweth hir make,

Moche is suche a mayde to louie · of hym that such one taketh,
More than a mayden is · that is maried thorw brokage, 267
As bi assent of sondry partyes · and syluer to bote,
More for coueitise of good · than kynde loue of bothe;—
So it fareth bi eche a persone · that possessioun forsaketh, 270
And put hym to be pacient · and pouerte weddeth,
The which is sybbe to god hym-self · and so to his seyntes.'
' Haue god my trouthe,' quod Haukyn · 'ȝe preyse faste Pouerte ;
What is Pouerte with pacience,' quod he · ' proprely to mene ? '

' *Paupertas*,' quod Pacience · ' *est odibile bonum,*
    Remocio curarum, possessio sine calumpnia, donum dei,
      sanitatis mater ;
    Absque solicitudine semita, sapiencie temperatrix, negocium
      sine dampno ;
    Incerta fortuna, absque solicitudine felicitas.'
' I can nouȝt construe al this,' quod Haukyn · 'ȝe moste kenne
    me this on Englisch.' 276
' In Englisch,' quod Pacyence, 'it is wel harde · wel to expounen;
Ac somdel I shal seyne it · by so thow vnderstonde.

(1) Pouerte is the first poynte · that Pryde moste hateth,
Thanne is it good by good skil · al that agasteth Pryde. 280

B. 263. an (*for* and) L.   276. me WR; L *om*.

Meschief is ay a mene · and maketh hym to thenke, 96
That god is hus grettest help · and no gome elles,
And he is seruaunt al-way, he seith · and of hus secte bothe.
And whether he be other be nat · he berith the sygne of pouerte,
And in that secte oure sauyour · sauede al mankynde. 100
For-thi alle poure that pacient is · of pure ryght may cleyme
After here endyng heere · heuene-riche blysse.
Much hardyloker may he aske · that her may haue hus will
In londe and in lordshepes · and lykynge of body, 104
And for goddes loue leueth al · and lyueth as a beggere.
As a mayde for a mannes loue · here moder for-saketh,
Hure fader and hure frendes · and gooth forth with hure para-
  mour;
Muche is suche a mayde to loue · of a man that suche on taketh
More than that maide is · that is ymaried by brocage, 109
As by asent of sondry bodyes · and seluer to bote,
More for couetice of catel · than kynde loue of the mariage.
So hit farith by ech a persone · that possession forsaketh, 112
And putteth hym to be pacient · and to pouerte hym weddeth,
The whyche is sibbe to Cryst self · and semblable bothe.'
  Quath Actyf tho al angryliche · and argueynge as hit were,
'What is Pouerte pacient?' quath he · 'ich praye that thou
  telle hit.' 116
'*Paupertas*,' quath Pacience · '*est odibile bonum,*
  Remocio curarum, possessio sine calumpnia, donum dei,
  sanitatis mater ;
  Absque solicitudine semita, sapiencie temperatrix, negocium
  sine dampno ;
  Incerta fortuna, absque solicitudine felicitas.'
'Ich can nat construen al this' · quath *Activa-uita.*
'Parfay,' quath Pacience · 'propreliche to telle
In English, hit is ful harde · ac somdel ich shal telle the. 120

DISTINCTIO PAUPERTATIS.

(1) Pouerte is the firste poynte · that Pruyde most hateth ;
"Thanne is pouerte good," quath Good Skyle · "thauh hit greue a
  lytel,

C. 97. god is EFTG ; good (*om.* is) P.   101. pure FG ; pur T ; poure
PE (*by confusion*).   102. Affter P.   104. lonnde P.   105. goddes EFT ;
godes G ; goodes P.   108. *of—taketh* EFG ; P *repeats* here moder for-saketh.

Ri3te as contricioun is confortable thinge · conscience wote
    wel,
And a sorwe of hym-self · and a solace to the sowle,
So pouerte propreliche · penaunce, and ioye,
Is to the body · pure spiritual helthe,   284
    Ergo paupertas est odibile bonum,
And contricioun confort · and *cura animarum.*
(2) Selde sit pouerte · the sothe to declare,
Or as Iustyce to Iugge men · enioigned is no pore,
Ne to be a maire aboue men · ne mynystre vnder kynges;
Selden is any pore yput · to punysshen any peple;   289
    Remocio curarum.
Ergo pouerte and pore men · perfornen the comaundement,
    Nolite iudicare quemquam.   The thridde:—
(3) Selde is any pore riche · but of ri3tful heritage;
Wynneth he nau3t with weghtes fals · ne with vnseled mesures,
Ne borweth of his neghbores · but that he may wel paye,   293
    Possessio sine calumpnia.
(4) The fierthe is a fortune · that florissheth the soule
Wyth sobrete fram al synne · and also 3it more;
It affaiteth the flesshe · fram folyes ful manye,   296
A collateral conforte · Crystes owne 3ifte,
    Donum dei.
(5) The fyfte is moder of helthe · a frende in alle fondynges,
And for the land euere a leche · a lemman of al clennesse,
    Sanitatis mater.
(6) The sexte is a path of pees · 3e, thorw the pas of Altoun
Pouerte my3te passe · with-oute peril of robbynge,   301
For there that pouerte passeth · pees folweth after,
And euere the lasse that he bereth · the hardyer he is of herte;
For-thi seith Seneca · *paupertas est absque solicitudine semita,*
And an hardy man of herte · amonge an hepe of theues;
    Cantabit pauper coram latrone viator.
(7) The seueneth is welle of wisdome · and fewe wordes sheweth,
For lordes alloweth hym litel · or lysteneth to his reson, 307
He tempreth the tonge to-treuthe-ward · and no tresore coueiteth ;
    Sapiencie temperatrix.

B. 286. sit WR; sitte LCO.   290. *The words* The thridde *are only a title to the next paragraph.*   305. *pauper* O; *paupertas* LWCRB (*badly*).

Al that may putten of Pruyde · in place ther he regneth."
Remocio curarum :—
(2) For selde sitt pouerte · the sothe to declare;   124
As a Iustice to Iuge men · men enioyneth ther-to no poure,
Ne to be a mayre ouere men · ne mynistre vnder kynges.
Selde is the poure yput · to punysshe eny peuple,
Ergo pouerte and poure men · parfournen the comaundement,
 Nolite iudicare quemquam.
 Possessio sine calumpnia :—
(3) Selde is the poure ryght riche · bote of hus riȝtful heritage,
He wynneth nat with wyghtes fals · ne with vnseled mesures,
Ne borweth of his neyghebore · bote that he may wel paye,
And lyghtly men leneth to fewe men · and men wene hym poure.
(4) The feorthe is a fortune · that florisshith the soule   133
With sobrete from alle synnes · and al-so ȝut more;
Hit defendeth the flessh · fro folyes ful menye :
And a collateral confort · Crystes owen sonde;   136
 Donum dei.
(5) Ȝut hit is moder of myȝt · and of mannes helthe,
And frende in alle fondynges · and of foule vueles leche,
 Sanitatis mater.
(6) The syxte, hit is a path of pees · ȝe, thorw the pas of Altoun
Pouerte myghte passe · with-oute peril of robbynge.   140
For ther as pouerte passeth · pees folweth commenliche,
And euere the lasse that eny lyf ledeth · the lyghter hus herte is there,
As he that wot neuere with wham · in nyghtes to mete;
 Paupertas est sine soliciludine semita : Seneca.
(7) The seuethe, hit is a welle of wysedome · and fewe wordes sheweth,   144
For lordes aloweth hym lytel · other leyth ere to hus reisone;
He tempreth hus tonge to-treuthe-ward · that no tresour coueyteth;
 Sapiencie temperatrix.

C. 124. selde EG; seilde P.   127. Selde ETG; Seilde P.   yput TG;
I-put F; pitt P; *see* l. 50.   129. Selde ETG; Seilde P.   riȝtful FT; ryght
PE.   130. whyghtes P.   131. is (*for* his) P.   132. lyghly (*by mistake*) P.
wene EFTG; P *om.*   134. from FT; aȝen E; whith P.   135. defendeth
FET; defendit P.   137. myȝth P.   altoun EF; haultone P.
143. nyȝtes E; niȝtes tyme T; myghtes P.   144. weelle P.

(8) The eigteth is a lele laborere · and loth to take more
Than he may wel deserue · in somer or in wynter,   310
And if he chaffareth, he chargeth no losse · mowe he charite
　　wynne ;
　　　　Negocium sine dampno.
(9) The nyneth is swete to the soule · no sugre is swettere ;
For pacyence is payn · for pouerte hym-selue,   313
And sobrete swete drynke · and good leche in sykenesse,
Thus lered me a lettred man · for owre lordes loue,
Seynt Austyn, a blissed lyf · with-outen bysynesse,   316
For body and for soule · *absque solicitudine felicitas.*
Now god, that al good gyueth · graunt his soule reste,
That thus fyrst wrote to wyssen men · what Pouerte was to mene ! '
　'Allas !' quod Haukyn the actyf man tho · 'that, after my
　　Crystendome,   320
I ne hadde ben den and doluen · for Doweles sake !
So harde it is,' quod Haukyn · 'to lyue and to do synne.
Synne suweth vs euere,' quod he · and sori gan wexe,
And wepte water with his eyghen · and weyled the tyme,   324
That euere he dede dede · that dere god displesed ;
Swowed and sobbed · and syked ful ofte,
That euere he hadde londe or lordship · lasse other more,
Or maystrye ouer any man · mo than of hym-self.   328
'I were nou3t worthy, wote god,' quod Haukyn · 'to were any
　　clothes,
Ne noyther sherte ne shone · saue for shame one,
To keure my caroigne,' quod he · and cryde mercye faste,
And wepte and weyled · and there-with I awaked.   332

B. 311. L *om. 1st* he.

(8) The eyhtethe, hit is a leel labour · and loth to take more.
Than he may sothliche deserue · in somer other in wynter; 148
And thauh he chaffare, he chargeth no los · mowe he charite wynne;
Negocium sine dampno.
(9) The nyethe, hit is swete to soules · is no suger swettere;
For pacience is hus paneter · and payn to pouerte fyndeth,
And sobrete ʒeueth here swete drynke · and solaceth here in alle angres. 152
Thus leryde me a lerede man · for oure lordes loue, seint Austyn,
That pure pouerte and pacience · was a louh lyuynge in erthe,
A blessid lyf with-oute busynesse · bote oneliche for the soule;
Absque solicitudine felicitas.
Now god that al thynge gyueth · graunte hus saule reste, 156
That wrot this to wisse men · what Pouerte was to mene!'

C. 150. (*2nd*) is T; ther is F; PEG *om.*   152. heere P (*twice*).

PASSUS XV (PROLOGUE TO DO-BET).

Passus xv^{us} : finit Dowel, et incipit Dobet.

A C after my wakyng · it was wonder longe,
Ar I couth kyndely · knowe what was Dowel.
And so my witte wex and wanyed · til I a fole were,
And somme lakked my lyf · allowed it fewe,   4
And leten me for a lorel · and loth to reuerencen
Lordes or ladyes · or any lyf elles,
As persones in pellure · with pendauntes of syluer;
To seriauntz ne to suche · seyde nouȝte ones,   8
"God loke ȝow, lordes!" · ne louted faire;
That folke helden me a fole · and in that folye I raued,
Tyl Resoun hadde reuthe on me · and rokked me aslepe,
Tyl I seigh, as it sorcerye were · a sotyl thinge with-al,   12
One with-outen tonge and teeth · tolde me whyder I shulde,
And wher-of I cam and of what kynde; · I coniured hym atte laste,
If he were Crystes creature · for Crystes loue me to tellen.
'I am Crystes creature,' quod he · 'and Crystene in many a place,   16
In Crystes courte i-knowe wel · and of his kynne a partye.
Is noyther Peter the porter · ne Poule with his fauchoune,
That wil defende me the dore · dynge ich neure so late.
At mydnyȝt, at mydday · my voice so is yknowe,   20
That eche a creature of his courte · welcometh me fayre.'
'What ar ȝe called,' quod I, 'in that courte · amonges Crystes peple?'
'The whiles I quykke the corps,' quod he · 'called am I *Anima* ;
And whan I wilne and wolde · *Animus* ich hatte ;   24
And for that I can and knowe · called am I *Mens* ;
And when I make mone to god · *Memoria* is my name ;
And when I deme domes · and do as treuthe techeth,

B. 5. me WRB; LCO *om.*   19. Tha (*for* That) L.

Thenne hadde Actyf a ledere · that heyhte *Liberum-arbitrium*,
That knewe Conscience ful wel · and Clergie bothe;
'He that hath londe and lordshep,' quath he · 'at the laste
ende   160
Shal be pourest of power · at hus partyng hennes.'
Thenne ich wondrede what he was · this *Liberum-arbitrium*,
And prayede Pacience · that ich a-pose hym moste.
And he suffrede me and seide · 'assay hus other name.'   164
'Leue *Liberum-arbitrium*,' quath ich · 'of what londe ar ye?
ʒif thow be Cristes creature · for Cristes loue, tel me.'
    'Ich am Cristes creature,' quath he · 'and Cristine in menye
    place,
And in Cristes court yknowe · and of hus kynne a partye; 168
Is nother Peter the porter · ne Paul with his fauchon,
That wolde defende me heuene dore · dynge ich neuere so
    late.
At myd-nyʒt, at mydday · my uoise is so yknowe,
That eche creature that loueth Criste · welcometh me faire.' 172
    'Wher-of serue ʒe?' ich seide · 'syre *Liberum-arbitrium*?'
'Of som tyme to fyghte,' quath he · 'falsnesse to destruye,
And som tyme to suffre · bothe sorwe and teene,
Layke other leue · at my lykynge chese,   176
To do wel other wikke · a wil with a reyson,
And may nat be with-oute a body · to bere me wher hym
    lyketh.'
'Thenne is that body bettere than thow,' quath ich · 'nay,'
    quath he, 'no betere;
Bote as a wode were a fure · thenne worchen thei bothe, 180
And ayther is otheres heete · and also of a wil;
And so is man that hath hus mynde · myd *Liberum-arbitrium*.
And the whyle ich quyke the cors · cald am ich *Anima;*
And whenne ich wilne other wolde · *Animus* ich hyhte,   184
And for that ich can and knowe · cald ich am "mannys Thouht;"
And whan ich make mone to god · *Memoria* ich hatte;
And when ich deme domes · and do as treuthe techeth,

C. 160. lonnde P.   162. thees (*for* this) P.   164. he MFTG; PE *om.*
171. nyʒth P.   172. wolcometh P.   177. wikke T; wicke EM; wike P.
180. thei M; PEFTG *om.*; *but it is well to keep it.*   183. cors TG; cours P;
corps M.

Thanne is *Racio* my riȝt name · Resoun an Englisshe;　28
And whan I fele that folke telleth · my firste name is *Sensus*,
And that is wytte and wisdome · the welle of alle craftes;
And whan I chalange or chalange nouȝte · chepe or refuse,
Thanne am I Conscience ycalde · goddis clerke and his notarie;
And whan I loue lelly · owre lorde and alle other,　33

Thanne is lele Loue my name · and in Latyn *Amor;*
And whan I flye fro the flesshe · and forsake the caroigne,
Thanne am I spirit specheles · and *Spiritus* thanne ich hatte.
Austyn and Ysodorus · ayther of hem bothe　37
Nempned me thus to name; · now thow myȝte chese,
How thow coueitest to calle me · now thow knowest alle my names.

> *Anima pro diuersis actionibus diuersa nomina sortitur : dum viuificat corpus, Anima est; dum vult, Animus est; dum scit, Mens est; dum recolit, Memoria est. Dum iudicat, Racio est; dum sentit, Sensus est; dum amat, Amor est; dum negat vel consentit, Consciencia est; dum spirat, Spiritus est.'*

'Ȝe ben as a bisshop,' quod I · al bourdynge that tyme,　40
'For bisshopes yblessed · thei bereth many names,
Presul and *pontifex* · and *metropolitanus*,
And other names an hepe · *episcopus* and *pastor*.'
'That is soth,' seyde he · 'now I se thi wille!　44
Thow woldest knowe and kunne · the cause of alle her names,

And of myne, if thow myȝtest · me thinketh by thi speche!'
'Ȝe, syre,' I seyde · 'by so no man were greued,
Alle the sciences vnder sonne · and alle the sotyle craftes　48
I wolde I knewe and couth · kyndely in myne herte!'
'Thanne artow inparfit,' quod he · 'and one of Prydes knyȝtes;

For such a luste and lykynge · Lucifer fel fram heuene:
> *Ponam pedem meum in aquilone, et similis ero altissimo.*

Then is *Racio* my ryhte name · "Reson" in Englissh;   188
And whenne ich fele that folke telleth · my furste name is *Sensus*,
And that is witte and wisedome · the welle of alle craftes;
And when ich chalange other nat chalange · chepe other refuse,
Thanne am ich *Conscientia* cald · godes clerk and hus notarie;
And when ich wol do other nat do · goode dedes other ille,   193
Then am ich *Liberum-arbitrium* · as lettrede men tellen;
And when ich loue leelly · oure lord and alle othere,
Then is "leel Loue" my name · in Latyn that is *Amor ;*   196
And when ich flee fro the body · and feye leue the caroygne,
Then am ich a spirit specheles · and *Spiritus* thenne ich hote.
Austyn and Ysidorus · ayther of hem bothe
Nempnede me this to name · thow now myght cheese   200
How thow coueitest to calle me · now knowest thow alle myne names.

> *Anima pro diuersis actionibus diuersa nomina sortitur ; dum uiuificat corpus, Anima est. dum uult, Animus est; dum recolit, Memoria est; dum iudicat, Racio est; dum sentit, Sensus est; dum amat, Amor est; dum declinat a malo ad bonum, Liberum arbitrium est; dum negat uel consentit, Consciencia est; dum spirat, Spiritus est.*

'3e ben as a bischop,' quath ich · al bordynge that tyme,
'For bischopes blessed · thei bereth meny names,
Presul and *pontifex* · and *metropolitanus*,   204
And other names an hepe · *episcopus* and *pastor.*'
'That is soth,' he seide · 'now ich seo thy wil
How thow woldest know and conne · the cause of alle here names,
And of myne, yf thow myghtest · me thynketh by thy speche!'   208
'3e, syre,' ich seyde, 'by so · that no man were a-greued,
Alle the science vnder sonne · and alle sotile craftes
Ich wolde ich knewe and couthe · kyndeliche in myn herte.'
'Thanne art thow inparfyt,' quath he · 'and on of Prydes knyghtes;   212
For suche a luste and lykynge · Lucifer fel fro heuene;

> *Ponam pedem meum in aquilone, et ero similis altissimo.*

C. 202. bischop EF; bihsshep P.   203. bischopes E; bihsshopes P.
209. a-greuede P.   212. art MFT; ert PEG. inparfy3t P.   213. louste P.
feel (*for* fel) P.

It were aȝeynes kynde,' quod he · 'and alkynnes resoun,   52
That any creature shulde kunne al · excepte Cryste one.
Aȝein such Salomon speketh · and dispiseth her wittes,
   And seith, *sicut qui mel comedit multum, non est ei bonum :*
   sic qui scrutator est maiestatis, opprimitur a gloria.
To Englisch-men this is to mene · that mowen speke and here,
The man that moche hony eteth · his mawe it engleymeth; 56
And the more that a man · of good mater hereth,
But he do ther-after · it doth hym double scathe :
Beatus est, seith seynt Bernard · *qui scripturas legit,*
Et verba vertit in opera · fullich to his powere.   60
Coueytise to kunne · and to knowe science
Pulte out of paradys · Adam and Eue ;
   Sciencie appetitus hominem inmortalitatis gloria spoliauit.
And riȝte as hony is yuel to defye · and engleymeth the mawe,
Riȝt so that thorw resoun · wolde the rote knowe   64
Of god and of his grete myȝtes · his graces it letteth.
For in the lykyng lith a pryde · and a lycames coueitise,
Aȝein Crystes conseille · and alle clerkes techyng,
   That is, *non plus sapere quam oportet sapere.*
Freres and fele other maistres · that to the lewed men prechen,
ȝe moeuen materes inmesurables · to tellen of the trinite, 69
That ofte tymes the lewed peple · of hir bileue douten.
Bettere byleue were mony · doctoures such techyng,
And tellen men of the ten comaundementz · and touchen the
  seuene synnes,   72
And of the braunches that burgeouneth of hem · and bryngeth
  men to helle,
And how that folke in folyes · myspenden her fyue wittes,
As wel freres as other folke · folilich spenen
In housyng, in haterynge · and in-to hiegh clergye shewynge,
More for pompe than for pure charite · the poeple wote the sothe
That I lye nouȝt, loo! · for lordes ȝe plesen,   78
And reuerencen the riche · the rather for her syluer ;
   Confundantur omnes qui adorant sculptilia ; et alibi :
   Vt quid diligitis vanitatem, et queritis mendacium?
Go to the glose of the verse · ȝe grete clerkes ;   80
If I lye on ȝow to my lewed witte · ledeth me to brennynge !

B. 62. *gloria* WO; *gloriam* LCRB.   79. *scultilia* L.

Hit were a-geyn kynde,' quath he · 'and alle kynne resoun
That eny creature sholde conne al · excepte Cryst one.
Aȝene alle suche Salamon speketh · and dispiseth here wittes, 216
    And seith, *sicut qui mel comedit multum, non ei bonum est :—*
        sic qui scrutator est magestatis, opprimetur a gloria.
To Englissh-men this is to mene · that mowen speke and huyre,
The man that muche hony eet · his mawe hit engleymeth:
The wyttiour that eny wight is · bote yf he worche ther-after,
The biterour he shal a-bygge · bote yf he wel worche; 220
Beatus, seith seynt Bernard · *qui scripturas legit,*
Et uerba uertit in opera · emforth his power.
Couetise to conne · and to knowe sciences
Putte oute of paradys · Adam and Eue; 224
    Sciencie appetitus hominem immortalitatis gloria spoliauit.
And ryght so as hony · is vuel to defie,
Ryght so sothly sciences · swelleth in a mannes saule,
And doth hym to be deynous · and deme that beth nat lerede;

Non plus sapere · seide the wyse, 228
Quam oportet sapere · lest synne of pruyde wexe.
Freres fele sithes · to the folke that thei prechen
Meuen motifs meny tymes · insolibles and fallaces,
That bothe lered and lewed · of here by-leyue douten; 232

To teche the ten commaundemens · were ten sithe bettere,

And how that folke folyliche · here fif wittes myspenden,
As wel freres as other folk · foliliche spenden
In housyng and in helyynge · in hih cleregie shewynge, 236
More for pomp and prude · as the peuple wot wel
That ich lye nat, loo · for lordes thei plesen,
And reuerenceth the ryche · the rather for here seluer,

C. 214. reisoune P. 216. MSS. *opprimatur*; but read *opprimetur*.
217. mene MFT; mete PE. 218. is (*for* his) P. 219. whyttiour P.
whight P. 220. wel M; wol PETG. 223. sciences EMTFG; science P;
see l. 226. 224. Pute P. *gloria* MFT; *gloriam* PEG. 234. that
EMFTG; the P. 235. folliliche P. 238. plesyn P.

For as it semeth, ȝe forsaketh · no mannes almesse,
Of vsureres, of hores · of auarous chapmen,
And louten to this lordes · that mowen lene ȝow nobles,   84
Aȝeine ȝowre reule and religioun · I take recorde at Iesus,
That seide to his disciples · *ne sitis personarum acceptores.*
  Of this matere I myȝte · make a longe bible,
Ac of curatoures of crystene peple · as clerkes bereth witnesse,
I shal tellen it for treuth sake · take hede who so lyketh!   89
As holynesse and honeste · oute of holicherche spredeth
Thorw lele libbyng men · that goddes lawe techen,
Riȝt so out of holicherche · alle yueles spredeth,   92
There inparfyt presthod is · prechoures and techeres.
And se it by ensample · in somer-tyme on trowes,
There somme bowes ben leued · and somme bereth none;
There is a myschief in the more · of suche manere bowes.   96
Riȝt so persones and prestes · and prechoures of holy cherche,
That aren rote of the riȝte faith · to reule the peple;
Ac there the rote is roten · reson wote the sothe,
Shal neure floure ne frute · ne faire leef be grene.   100
For-thi, wolde ȝe lettred leue · the leccherye of clothynge,
And be kynde, as bifel for clerkes · and curteise of Crystes goodes,
Trewe of ȝowre tonge · and of ȝowre taille bothe,
And hatien to here harlotrye · and nouȝt to vnderfonge   104
Tythes of vntrewe thinge · ytilied or chaffared,
Lothe were lewed men · but thei ȝowre lore folwed,
And amenden hem that mysdon · more for ȝowre ensamples,
Than forto prechen and preue it nouȝt · ypocrysie it semeth. 108
For ypocrysie in Latyn · is lykned to a dongehul,
That were bysnewed with snowe · and snakes wyth-inne;
Or to a wal that were whitlymed · and were foule wyth-inne.
Riȝt so many prestes · prechoures and prelates,   112
Ȝe aren enblaunched with *bele paroles* · and with clothes also,
Ac ȝowre werkes and ȝowre wordes there-vnder · aren ful vnlouelich.
    Iohannes Crysostomus · of clerkes speketh and prestes,
      Sicut de templo omne bonum progreditur, sic de templo omne
      malum procedit.

B. 90. honeste WCROB; honestete L.

A3ens the counsail of Cryst · as holy cleregye witnesseth; 240
    Ne sitis acceptores personarum.
Loo, what holy wryt wyttnesseth · of wikked techeres;
As holyness and honeste · out of holy churche
Spryngeth and spredeth · and enspireth the peuple
Thorgh parfit preest-hood · and prelates of holichurche, 244
Ryght so out of holychurche · al vuel spredeth,
Ther imparfit preest-hod is · prechours and techours.
And seo hit by ensample · of trees in somer-tyme,
Ther somme bowes bereth leues · and somme bereth none; 248
The bowes that bereth nat · and beeth nat grene-leuede,
Ther is a myschif in the more · of suche manere stockes.
Ryght so persones and preestes · and prechers of holy churche
Ys the rote of the ryght feithe · to reuwele the peuple; 252
Ac ther the rote is roten · reson wot the sothe,
Shal neuere floure ne frut wexe · ne fair leef be grene.
For wolde 3e letteride leue · the lecherie of clothinge,
And be courteis and kynde · of holykirke goodes, 256
Parte with the poure · and 3oure pruyde leue,
And therto trewe of 3oure tonge · and of 3oure tail also,
And haten harlotrie · and to vnderfonge the tythes
Of vserers and of hores · and of al vuel wynnynges, 260
Loth were lewede men · bote thei 3oure lore folweden,
And a-menden hem of here mysdedes · more for 3oure ensamples
Than for to preche and preuen hit nat; · ypocrisie hit semeth!
Ypocrisie is a braunche of pruyde · and most among clerkes, 264
And is ylikned in Latyn · to a lothliche dounghep,
That were by-snywe al with snow · and snakes with-ynne,
Or to a wal whit-lymed · and were blak with-inne.
Ry3t so meny preestes · prechours and prelates, 268
That beth enblaunched with *bele paroles* · and with *bele* clothes;
And as lambes thei loken · and lyuen as wolues.
Iohannes Crisostomus · karpeth thus of clerkes,
    *Sicut de templo omne bonum progreditur, sic de templo omne
    malum procedit.*

C. 240. whittnesseth P.   242. honeste EMFTG; honestete P.   246,
248, 250. Theer (*for* Ther) P.   252. (*2nd*) the MTF; PEG *om.*   ryghit P.
255. 3e MT; the PEG.   256. kirke T; churche P.   257. with the
EMFT; whithe P.   258. trywe P.   259. and MFTG; PE *om.*   265.
is MFT; PEG *om.*   267. *This line is in* T *only.*

*Si sacerdocium integrum fuerit, tota floret ecclesia ; si autem
coruptum fuerit, omnium fides marcida est.
Si sacerdocium fuerit in peccatis, totus populus conuertitur
ad peccandum.
Sicut cum videris arborem pallidam et marcidam, inteligis
quod vicium habet in radice,
Ita cum videris populum indisciplinatum et irreligiosum, sine
dubio sacerdocium eius non est sanum.*

If lewed men wist · what this Latyn meneth,   116
And who was myn auctor · moche wonder me thinketh,
But if many a prest bere · for here baselardes and here broches,
A peyre bedes in her hande · and a boke vnder her arme.
Sire Iohan and sire Geffray · hath a gerdel of syluer,   120
A basellarde, or a ballokknyf · with botones ouergylte.
Ac a portous that shulde be his plow · *placebo* to segge,
Hadde he neure seruyse to saue syluer ther-to · seith it with yvel
    wille!
Allas! ȝe lewed men · moche lese ȝe on prestes,   124
Ac thinge that wykkedlich is wonne · and with false sleigthes,
Wolde neuere witte of· witty god · but wikked men it hadde;
The which aren prestes inparfit · and prechoures after syluer,
Sectoures and sudenes · somnoures and her lemmannes.   128
This that with gyle was geten · vngraciouslich is spended;
So harlotes and hores · ar hulpen with such goodis,
And goddes folke for defaute ther-of · forfaren and spillen.
    Curatoures of holykirke · as clerkes that ben auerouse,   132
Liȝtlich that they leuen · loselles it habbeth,
Or dyeth intestate · and thanne the bisshop entreth,
And maketh murthe there-with · and his men bothe,
And seggen, "he was a nygarde · that no good myȝte aspare
To frende ne to fremmed · the fende haue his soule!   137
For a wrecched hous he helde · al his lyf tyme;
And that he spared and bispered · spene we in murthe."
By lered, by lewed · that loth is to spende,   140
Thus gone her godes · be the goste faren.
Ac for good men, god wote · gret dole men maken,
And bymeneth good mete-ȝyueres · and in mynde haueth,

B. 119. MS. O (*which in* l. 118 *has* heer *for* bere) *has a totally different
line here, viz.* Schulden go synge seruyseles · with sire philip the sparwe.
136. aspare WCRB; asspare L.

Si sacerdocium integrum fuerit, tota floret ecclesia ; si autem corruptum fuerit, omnium fides marcida est.
Si sacerdocium fuerit in peccatis, totus populus conuertitur ad peccandum.
Sicut cum uideris arborem pallidam et marcidam, intelligis quod uicium habet in radice,
Ita cum uideris populum indisciplinatum et irreligiosum, sine dubio sacerdocium eius non est sanum.

Alas! lewede men · muche leese ʒe that fynden 272
Vnkynde creatures · to beo kepers of ʒoure soules!
Ac thyng that wikkedliche is wonne · and with false sleithes,
Wolde neuere other-wise god · bote wicked men hit hadde,
As imparfit preestes · and prechers after seluer, 276
Secutours and sodenes · somners and here lemmannes;
And that with gyle was gete · vngraciousliche be dispended.

Curatours of holychurche · and clerkus that ben auarous,
Lightliche that thei leue · loseles hit deuouren. 280

Leyueth hit wel, lordes · bothe lered and lewede,
That thus goth here godes · atte laste ende,

C. 275. PE *insert* that *after* neuere.   279. auerous P.   280. deuouren EG ; deuoren P.

In prayers and in penaunces · and in parfyt charite.' 144
'What is Charite?' quod I tho · 'a childissh thinge,' he seide;
   '*Nisi efficiamini sicut paruuli, non intrabitis in regnum
    celorum;*
With-outen fauntelte or foly · a fre liberal wille.'
'Where shulde men fynde such a frende · with so fre an herte?
I haue lyued in londe,' quod I · 'my name is Longe Wille, 148
And fonde I neuere ful charite · bifore ne bihynde!
Men beth mercyable · to mendynantz and to pore,
And wolen lene there thei leue · lelly to ben payed.
  Ac charite that Poule preyseth best · and most plesaunte to
    owre saueoure, 152
    As, *non inflatur, non est ambiciosa, non querit que sua sunt*,
I seigh neuere such a man · so me god helpe,
That he ne wolde aske after his · and otherwhile coueyte
Thinge that neded hym nouȝt · and nyme it if he myȝte!
Clerkis kenne me that Cryst · is in alle places; 156
Ac I seygh hym neuere sothly · but as my-self in a miroure,
    Ita in enigmate, tunc facie ad faciem.
And so I trowe trewly · by that men telleth of charite,
It is nought championes fyȝte · ne chaffare, as I trowe.'
'Charite,' quod he, 'ne chaffareth nouȝte · ne chalengeth, ne
    craueth. 160
As proude of a peny · as of a pounde of golde,
And is as gladde of a goune · of a graye russet
As of a tunicle of Tarse · or of trye scarlet.
He is gladde with alle gladde · and good tyl alle wykked, 164
And leueth and loueth alle · that owre lorde made.

Curseth he no creature · ne he can bere no wratthe,
Ne no lykynge hath to lye · ne laughe men to scorne.
Al that men seith, he let it soth · and in solace taketh, 168
And alle manere meschiefs · in myldenesse he suffreth;
Coueiteth he none erthly good · but heuene-riche blisse.'

B. 152. *inflatur* WCROB; *inflatus* L. L om. *est.*   157. *Ita* COB;
It L.   164. tyl WCRO; ty L.

That lyuen a-ȝens holy lore : and the loue of charite.'

'Charite,' quath ich tho • 'that is a thing for sothe   284
That maistres comenden muche; • wher may hit be founde?
Ich haue lyued in London • meny longe ȝeres,
And founde ich neuere in faith • as freres hit precheth,
Charite, that chargeth nat • ne chit, thauh men greue hym, 288
As Paul in a pistele • of hym bereth witnesse;
   Non inflatur, non est ambiciosa, non querit que sua sunt.
Ich knew neuere, by Cryst • clerk nother lewede,
That he ne askede after hus • and other-whyle coueytede
Thyng that needede hym nat • and nyme hit, yf he myghte ! 292
For thoȝ men soȝt al sectes • of sustren and of bretheren,
And thow fynde hym, bote figuratifliche • a ferly me thinketh;
   Hic in enigmate, tunc facie ad faciem : —
And so ich trowe trewely • by that men tellen of Charite.'
  'Charite is a childish thing • as holichurche wittnesseth, 296
   *Nisi efficiamini sicut paruuli, non intrabitis in regnum
   celorum :*

DISTINCTIO CARITATIS.

As proud of a peny • as of a pounde of golde,
And al-so glad of a goune • of a grey russet
As of a cote of cammoka • other of clene scarlett.
He is glad with alle glade • as gurles that lauhen alle,   300
And sory when he seeth men sory • as thow seest children
Lauhen ther men lauhen • and loure ther men loureth.
And when a man swereth for soth • for soth he hit troweth;
He weneth that no wiȝt • wold lyghe and swere,   304
Ne that eny gome wolde gylen • other, ne greue,
For drede of god that is so good • and thus-gates ous techeth,
   Quodcunque uultis ut uobis faciant homines, facite eis.
He hath no lykynge to lauhe • ne lyghe, men to scorne;
Alle siknesses and sorwes • for solas he hem taketh,   308
And alle manere meschifs • as minstracie of heuene.

C. 283. That MFT; And PE.   286. aue (*for* haue) P.   lyuede P.   london
M; londoun F; lundoun T; londen PEG.   290. knew EMFG; knowe P.
clek P.   293. *From* EMFGT; P *om. this line.*   294. thow M; thou F;
PETG *om.*   296. *non—celorum* E.   *Distinctio, &c.* M.   302. an (*for*
and) P.   304. that MFT; nat PE.   whiȝt P.   306. gatis T (*read* gates);
PEMF *om.*   307. ne EMF; no P; ne to T.   lyhe P (*see* l. 304).   308. hem
MF; hit PET.

'Hath he any rentes or ricchesse · or any riche frendes?'
'Of rentes ne of ricchesse · ne reccheth he neuere.   172
For a frende that fyndeth hym · failled hym neuere at nede;
Fiat-voluntas tua · fynt hym euer-more.
And if he soupeth, ec̃. but a soppe · of *spera-in-deo*.
He can purtreye wel the *pater-noster* · and peynte it with *aues*,
And other-while is his wone · to wende in pilgrymage,   177
There pore men and prisones liggeth · her pardoun to hauɑ
Though he bere hem no bred · he bereth hem swetter lyflode,
Loueth hem as owre lorde biddeth · and loketh how thei fare.

And whan he is wery of that werke · thanne wil he some tyme
Labory in a lauendrye . wel the lengthe of a myle,   182
And ȝerne in-to ȝouthe · and ȝepliche speke
Pryde with al the appurtenaunce · and pakken hem togyderes,
And bouken hem at his brest · and beten hem clene,   185
And leggen on longe · with *laboraui-in-gemitu-meo*,
And with warme water at his eyghen · wasshen hem after.
And thanne he syngeth whan he doth so · and some tyme seith
    wepyng,   188
        Cor contritum et humiliatum, deus, non despicies.
'By Cryst, I wolde that I knewe hym,' quod I · 'no creature
    leuere!'
'With-outen helpe of Piers Plowman,' quod he · 'his persone
    seestow neuere.'
'Where clerkes knowen hym,' quod I · 'that kepen holykirke?'
    'Clerkes haue no knowyng,' quod he · 'but by werkes and
    bi wordes.   192
Ac Piers the Plowman · parceyueth more depper
What is the wille and wherfore · that many wyȝte suffreth,
        Et vidit deus cogitaciones eorum.
For there are ful proude-herted men · paciente of tonge,
And boxome as of berynge · to burgeys and to lordes,   196
And to pore peple · han peper in the nose,
And as a lyoun he loketh · there men lakketh his werkes.

For there ar beggeres and bidderes · bedemen as it were,
Loketh as lambren · and semen lyf-holy,   200
Ac it is more to haue her mete · with such an esy manere,

B. 175. eet R; eteth W; ette L.   194. What W; That LR; Wher COB.
199. bedemen WROB; bedmen LC.

Of deth ne of derthe · drad was he neuere,
Ne mysliked, thauh he loore · other lenede to that ilke
That neuere payed peny aȝe · in place there he borwede.' 312
'Who fyndeth hym his fode?' quath ich · 'other what frendes hath he,
Rentes other richesses · to releue hym at hus neode?'
'Of rentes ne of richesses,' quath he · 'reccheth he neuere,
A frend he hath that fynt him · that faileth him neuere. 316
On *Aperis-tu-manum* · alle thynge hym fyndeth;
Fiat-uoluntas-tua · festeth hym eche day.
And also he can clergie · *credo-in-deum-patrem*,
And portreieth wel the *pater-noster* · and peynteth hit with auees. 320
And other-while hus wone is · to wende in pilgrymages,
Ther poure men and prysouns beth · and payeth for here lyflode,
Clotheth hem and comforteth hem · and of Crist precheth hem,
What sorwes he suffrede · in ensample of ous alle, 324
That pouerte and pacience · parfitliche ytake
Ys muche merit to that man · that wel may suffren.
Whan he hath thus visited fetered folke · and other folke poure,
Then he ȝerneth in-to thouht · and ȝepliche he secheth 328
Pruyde, with alle the portinaunce · and packeth hem togederes,
And laueth hem in the lauandrie · *laboraui-in-gemitu-meo*,
And bouketh hem at hus brest · and beteth hit ofte,
And with warme water of hus eyen · woketh hit til hit white; 332
 Lauabis me, et super niuem dealbabor.
Thanne syngeth he whanne he so doth · and som tyme wepynge,
 Cor contritum et humiliatum, deus, non despicies.'
'Were ich with hym, by Crist,' quath ich · 'ich wolde neuere fro hym,
Thauh ich my by-lyue sholde begge · a-boute at menne hacches.
Wher clerkus knowe hym nat,' quath ich · 'that kepen holy-churche?' 336
'Peers the Plouman,' quath he · 'most parfitliche hym knoweth;
 Et uidit deus cogitationes eorum.

C. 316. *From* MFTG; PE *om. this line.*   320. wel MFTG; PE *om.*
327. visetid P.   331. beeteth P.   332. wharme P.   hit til hit M; hem til hit G; it til he F; hit he PT.

Than for penaunce and parfitnesse · the pouerte that such taketh.
There-fore by coloure ne by clergye · knowe shaltow hym neuere,
Noyther thorw wordes ne werkes · but thorw wille one.   204
And that knoweth no clerke · ne creature in erthe,
But Piers the Plowman · *Petrus, id est, Christus.*
For he ne is nou3te in lolleres · ne in lande-leperes hermytes,
Ne at ancres, there a box hangeth · alle suche thei faiten. 208
Fy on faitoures · and *in fautores suos!*
For charyte is goddis champioun · and as a good chylde hende,
And the meryest of mouth · at mete where he sitteth.
The loue that lith in his herte · maketh hym ly3te of speche,
And is companable and confortatyf · as Cryst bit hymselue, 213
  Nolite fieri sicut ypocrite, tristes, etc.
For I haue seyn hym in sylke · aud somme tyme in russet,
Bothe in grey and in grys · and in gulte herneys,
And as gladlich he it gaf · to gomes that it neded.   216
Edmonde and Edwarde · eyther were kynges,
And seyntes ysette · tyl charite hem folwed.
I haue seyne Charite also · syngen and reden,
Ryden and rennen · in ragged wedes,   220
Ac biddyng as beggeres · bihelde I hym neuere.
Ac in riche robes · rathest he walketh,
Ycalled and ycrimiled · and his crowne shaue,
And clenlich yclothed · in cipres and in Tartaryne.   224
And in a freres frokke · he was yfounde ones,
Ac it is ferre agoo · in seynt Fraunceys tyme;
In that secte sitthe · to selde hath he be knowen.
Riche men he recomendeth · and of her robes taketh,   228
That with-outen wyles · leden her lyues,
  Beatus est diues, qui, etc.
In kynges courte he cometh ofte · there the conseille is trewe,
Ac if coueityse be of the conseille · he wil nou3t come ther-inne.
In courte amonge Iaperes · he cometh but selde,   232
For braulyng and bakbytyng · and beryng of fals witnesse.
In the constorie bifor the comissarie · he cometh nou3t ful ofte,
For her lawe dureth ouer-longe · but if thei lacchen syluer;
And matrimoigne for monye · maken and vnmaken,   236

B. 213. companable RCO; compenable L.   224. *From* OCB; LWR *om. this line.*

By clothynge ne by karpinge · knowe shalt thou hym neuere, 338
Ac thorw werkes thou myght wite · wher forth he walketh;
    Operibus credite.

He is the muriest of mouthe · at metes ther he sitteth,

And compenable in companye · as Crist hym-self techeth,
    Nolite tristes fieri, sicut ypocrite.
Ich haue seyen hym my-self · som tyme in russett, 342
Bothe in greye and in grys · and in gylt harneys,
And al-so gladliche he gyueth · to gomes that hit needeth,
Eadmund and Edward · ayther were seyntes,
And chief charite with hem · and chast al here lyue, 346
Ich haue seyen Charite al-so · syngen and rede,
Ryden, and rennen · in raggede clothes,
Ac biddyng as a beggere · by-heold ich hym neuere,
Ac in riche robes · rathest he walketh, 350
Y-called and ycrymyled · and hus croune shaue.

And in a freres frocke · he was yfounde ones,
Ac it is fer and fele ʒeres · in Fraunceys tyme;
In that secte sitthe · to selde he hath be founde. 354
Riche men he comendeth · and of here robes taketh,
Of tho that leelliche lyuen · and louen and by-leyuen;
    Beatus est diues sine macula.
In kynges court he cometh · yf hus counsail be trewe;
Ac yf couetise be of hus counsail · he wol nat come ther-ynne.
Among the comunes in court · he cometh but selde, 359
For brawelynge and bacbytynge · and beryng of false wittnesse.
In constorie by-fore the comissarie · he cometh nat ful ofte,
For here lawe is ouere-longe · bote yf thei lacche seluer.

  C. 343. grys G; gris EFT; greys P.   352. a EMFTG; P *om.*   353.
fer FTG; feer P.   359. selde EMTG; seilde P.

And that conscience and Cryst · hath yknitte faste,
Thei vndon it vnworthily · tho doctours of lawe.
Amonges erchebischopes and other bischopes · and prelates of
　　holy cherche,
For to wonye with hem · his wone was sum tyme,　　　　240
And Cristes patrimonye to the pore · parcel-mel dele.
Ac auerice hath the keyes now · and kepeth for his kynnesmen,
And for his seketoures and his seruants · and somme for here
　　children.
　　Ac I ne lakke no lyf · but lorde, amende vs alle,　　　244
And gyue vs grace, good god · charite to folwe!
For who so my3te mete with hym · such maneres hym eyleth,
Noyther he blameth ne banneth · bosteth, ne prayseth,
Lakketh, ne loseth · ne loketh vp sterne;　　　　　　248
Craueth, ne coueiteth · ne crieth after more,
　　In pace in id-ipsum dormiam, etc.
The moste lyflode that he lyueth by · is loue in goddis passioun,
Noyther he biddeth, ne beggeth · ne borweth to 3elde;
Misdoth he no man · ne with his mouth greueth.　　　252
　　Amonges Cristene men · this myldnesse shulde laste;
In alle manere angres · haue this at herte—
That though thei suffred al this · god suffred for vs more,
In ensample we shulde do so · and take no veniaunce　　256
Of owre foes that doth vs falsenesse · that is owre fadres wille.
For wel may euery man wite · if god hadde wolde hymselue,
Sholde neuere Iudas ne Iuwe · haue Iesu don on rode,
Ne han martired Peter ne Poule · ne in prisoun holden.　　260
Ac he suffred in ensample · that we shulde suffre also,
And seide to suche that suffre wolde · that *pacientes vincunt*.
　　Verbi gratia,' quod he · 'and verrey ensamples manye,
In *Legenda Sanctorum* · the lyf of holy seyntes,　　　264
What penaunce and pouerte · and passioun thei suffred,
In hunger, in hete · in al manere angres.
Antony and Egidie · and other holi fadres
Woneden in wildernesse · amonge wilde bestes;　　　268
Monkes and mendynauntz · men bi hem-selue,
In spekes and in spelonkes · selden speken togideres.
Ac noyther Antony ne Egidy · ne hermite that tyme

　　B. 239-243.—*These lines are in* R *only.*　　270. an (*for* and) L.

With bisshopes he wolde beo · for beggers sake,
Ac auarice other-whiles · halt hym with-oute the gate.   364
Kynges and cardineles · knowen hym som tyme,
Ac thorw couetise and his consail · congeied is he ofte.
And ho so coueyteth to know hym · such a kynde hym folweth,
As ich tolde the with tonge · a lytel tyme passed;
For nother he beggeth, ne biddeth · ne borweth to ʒelde ;
He halt hit a nycete · and a foul shame   370
To beggen other to borwe · bote of god one ;
    Panem nostrum cotidianum da nobis hodie.'

Hic explicit passus septimus et ultimus de Dowel.

PASSUS XVIII.

Incipit passus primus de Dobet.

'THER is no suche,' ich seide · 'that som tyme ne borweth,
Other beggeth other byddeth · beo he ryche other poure,
And ʒut other-while wroth · with-oute eny synne.'
'Ho so is wroth and wolde be awreke · holi wryt,' quath he,
  'proueth   4
He passeth chief charite · if holichurche beo trewe ;
    Caritas omnia suffert.
Holy writ witnesseth · ther were suche eremites,
Solitarie by hem-self · and in here selles lyueden
With-oute borwynge other beggynge · bote of god one ;   8

C. 364. auerice P.   367. a MFT ; P *om*.   370. a nycete P ; T *has*
for a vice (*which seems better*).   371. da—*hodie* F (*only*).
    Passus XVIII. 5. hif P.   trywe P.   6. whitnesseþ P.

Of liouns ne of leoperdes · no lyflode ne toke,   272
But of foules that fleeth · thus fynt men in bokes.
Excepte that Egydie · after an hynde cryede,
And thorw the mylke of that mylde best · the man was susteyned;
And day by day had he hir nouȝt · his hunger forto slake,   276
But selden and sondrie tymes · as seith the boke and techeth.
  Antony a dayes · aboute none-tyme,
Had a bridde that brouȝte hym bred · that he by lyued;
And though the gome hadde a geste · god fonde hem bothe.   280
  Poule *primus heremita* · had parroked hym-selue,
That no man miȝte hym se · for mosse and for leues;
Foules hym fedde · fele wynteres with alle,
Til he founded freres · of Austines ordre.   284
Poule, after his prechyng · panyers he made,
And wan with his hondes · that his wombe neded.
Peter fisched for his fode · and his felawe Andrewe;
Some thei solde and some thei sothe · and so thei lyued bothe.
  And also Marie Magdeleyne · by mores lyued and dewes,   289
Ac moste thorw deuocioun · and mynde of god almiȝty.
  I shulde nouȝt this seuene dayes · seggen hem alle,
That lyueden thus for owre lordes loue · manye longe ȝeres.   292
  Ac there ne was lyoun ne leopart · that on laundes wenten,
Noyther bere, ne bor · ne other best wilde,
That ne fel to her feet · and fauned with the tailles.
And if thei couth han ycarped · by Cryst, as I trowe,   296
Thei wolde haue fedde that folke · bifor wilde foules.
For alle the curteisie that bestes kunne · thei kidde that folke ofte
In likkyng and in lowynge · there thei on laundes ȝede.
Ac god sent hem fode bi foules · and by no fierse bestes,   300
In menynge that meke thinge · mylde thinge shulde fede;
As who seith, religious · ryȝtful men shulde fynde,
And lawful men to lyf-holy men · lyflode brynge.

B. 276. And L; Ac R (*perhaps better*). 298, 299. *These lines are in R only.*

Excepte that Egidie · an hynde other-while
To hus selle selde cam · and suffrede to be melked.
Elles fouweles fedden hem · in frythes ther thei woneden,
Bothe Antonye and Erseny · and other mo fele. 12
Paul *primus heremita* · hadde parroked hym-selue,
That no man myghte se hym · for muche mos and leues;
Foweles hym fedde · yf frere Austyn be trewe;
For he ordeynede that ordre · other elles thei gabben. 16
Paul after his prechynge · panyeres he made,
And wan with hus hondes · al that hym neodyde.
Peter fysshed for hus fode · and hus fere Andreu;
Som thei solde, and som thei sode · and so thei leueden bothe.
Marie Magdalene · by mores leuede and dewes; 21
Loue and leel by-leyue · heeld lyf and soule to-gedere.
Maria Egyptiaca · eet in thyrty wynter
Bote thre lytel loues · and loue was her souel. 24
Ich can nat rekene hem ryght now · ne reherce here names,
That lyueden thus for oure lordes loude · meny longe ȝeres,
With-oute borwyng other beggyng · other the bok lyeth,
And woneden in wildernesse · a-mong wilde bestes; 28
Ac dorst no best byten hem · by daye ne by nyghte,
Bote myldeliche, whan thei metten · maden louh chere,
And feyre by-fore tho men · fauhnede with the tayles.
Ac bestes brouhte hem no mete · bot onliche the fouweles, 32
In tokenynge that trewe man · alle tymes sholde
Fynde honeste men and holy men · and other ryghtful peuple.
For wolde neuere feithful god · that freres and monkes token
Lyflode of luther wynnynges · in al here lif-tyme. 36
As wytnesseth holy writ · what Thobie seyde
To his wif, whan he was blynde · he herde a lamb blete;
'A! wyf! be war,' quath he · 'what ȝe haue here-ynne;
Lord leyue,' quath the lede · 'no stole thyng be here!' 40
Videte ne furtum sit: et alibi, melius est mori quam male uiuere.
This is no more to mene · bote men of holychurche
Sholde receyue ryght nauȝt · bot that ryght wolde,

C. 10. selde EMTG; seilde P.   16. gabben EMTG; gabbyn P.   17. is (*for* his) P.   30. chere EMT; chire P.   34. (1*st*) and MFTG; in PE. 35. god EMTGF; goud P.   37. writt P.   38. is (*for* his) P. he MFTG; PE *om*.   42. nauȝt MFT; nauth P.

And thanne wolde lordes and ladyes · be loth to agulte, 304
And to take of her tenauntz · more than treuth wolde,
Fonde thei that freres · wolde forsake her almesses,
And bidden hem bere it · there it was yborwed.
For we ben goddes foules · and abiden alwey, 308
Tyl briddes brynge vs · that we shulde lyue by.
For had ȝe potage and payn ynough · and peny-ale to drynke,
And a messe there-mydde · of o manere kynde,
Ȝe had riȝt ynough, ȝe religious · and so ȝowre reule me tolde:
   Nunquam, dicit Iob, rugiet onager cum herbam habuerit?
   aut mugiet bos cum ante plenum presepe steterit?
   Brutorum animalium natura te condempnat, quia cum eis
   pabulum commune sufficiat; ex adipe prodijt iniquitas tua.
If lewed men knewe this Latyn · thei wolde loke whom thei ȝeue,
And auyse hem bifore · a fyue dayes or sexe,
Or thei amortesed to monkes · or chanouns her rentes.
Allas! lordes and ladyes · lewed conseille haue ȝe 316
To ȝyue fram ȝowre eyres · that ȝowre ayeles ȝow lefte,
And ȝiueth to bidde for ȝow · to such that ben riche,
And ben founded and feffed eke · to bidde for other.
Who perfourneth this prophecye · of the peple that now lybbeth,
   Dispersit, dedit pauperibus, etc.?
If any peple perfourme that texte · it ar this pore freres! 321
For that thei beggen abouten · in buildynge thei spene,
And on hem-self sum · and such as ben her laboreres,
And of hem that habbeth thei taken · and ȝyue hem that ne habbeth.
 Ac clerkes and knyȝtes · and comuneres that ben riche, 325
Fele of ȝow fareth · as if I a forest hadde,
That were ful of faire trees · and I fonded and caste
How I myȝte mo ther-inne · amonges hem sette. 328
Riȝt so, ȝe riche · ȝe robeth that ben riche,
And helpeth hem that helpeth ȝow · and ȝiueth there no nede is.
As who so filled a tonne · of a fresshe ryuer,
And went forth with that water · to woke with Themese, 332
Riȝt so, ȝe riche · ȝe robeth and fedeth
Hem that han as ȝe han; · hem ȝe make at ese.
 Ac religious that riche ben · shulde rather feste beggeres
Than burgeys that riche ben · as the boke techeth; 336

B. 312. *onerger (by mistake)* L.

And refuse reuerences · and raueneres offrynges.
Thenne wolde lordes and ladies · be loth for to agulte,   44
And to take of here tenauns · more than treuthe wolde;
And marchauns merciable wolde be · and men of lawe bothe.
Wolde religiouse refuse · raueneres almesse,
Then grace sholde growe ʒut · and grene-leued wexe,   48
And Charite, that child is now · sholde chaufen of him-self,
And confortye alle Cristene · wold holykirke amende.
Iob the parfit patriark · this prouerbe wrot and tauhte,   51
To makye a man louye mesure · that monkes beeth and freres;

*Nunquam, dicit Iob, rugiet onager cum habuerit herbam,
aut mugiet bos cum ante plenum presepe steterit? Brutorum animalium natura te condempnat, quia cum pabulum sufficiat commune, ex adipe prodiit iniquitas.*

Yf lewede men knewe this Latyn · a litel thei wolde auisen hem
Er thei amorteisede eny more · for monkes other for chanons.
Alas! lordes and ladies · lewede counsail haue ʒe
That founded beth to fulle · to feffe suche and fede   56
With that ʒoure barnes and ʒoure blod · by goode lawe may cleyme!
For god bad hus blessede · as the book techeth,

Honora patrem et matrem, ut longeuus sis, etc.,

To helpe thy fader formest · by-fore freres and monkes,
And er prestes other pardoneres · other eny peuple elles.   60
Help thi kynne, Crist bit · for ther by-gynneth charite,
And afterwarde awaite · hoo hath moost neede,
And ther help yf thou hast · and that halde ich charite.

Loo! Laurence for hus largenesse! · as holy lore telleth,   64
That hus mede and hus man-hede · for euere-more shal laste;

Iusticia eius manet in eternum.

He gaf godes men godes goodes · and nat to grete lordes,
And fedde that a-fyngred were · and in defaute lyueden.   67
Ich dar nat carpe of clerkes now · that Cristes tresoure kepen,
That poure peuple by pure ryght · here part thei myghten aske;
Of that that holychurche · of the olde lawe cleymeth,
Priestes on aparail · and on Purnele spenen.   71

C. 49. him MF; heɱ PETG.   50. kirke T; churche PEFG.   55. ʒe MFTG; we P.   58. *ut—&c.* is in F only.   62. awhaite P.   66. (2nd) godes MG; goddes I; godis T; PE *om.*   68. dar IMFTG; der P.   70. þat þat MFITG; þat PE.

Quia sacrilegium est res pauperum non pauperibus dare.
Item, peccatoribus dare, est demonibus immolare.
Item, monache, si indiges et accipis, pocius das quam accipis.
Si autem non eges, et accipis, rapis.
Porro, non indiget monachus, si habeat quod nature sufficit.
For-thi I conseille alle Cristene · to confourmen hem to charite;
For charite with-oute chalengynge · vnchargeth the soule,
And many a prisone fram purgatorie · thorw his preyeres he delyuereth.
Ac there is a defaute in the folke · that the faith kepeth ; 340
Wherefore folke is the feblere · and nou3t ferme of bilieue.
As in Lussheborwes is a lyther alay · and 3et loketh he lyke a sterlynge,
The merke of that mone is good · ac the metal is fieble ;
And so it fareth by some folke now · thei han a faire speche,
Croune and Crystendome · the kynges merke of heuene, 345
Ac the metal, that is mannes soule · with synne is foule alayed ;
Bothe lettred and lewede · beth allayed now with synne,
That no lyf loueth other · ne owre lorde, as it semeth. 348
For thorw werre and wykked werkes · and wederes vnresonable,
Wederwise shipmen · and witti clerkes also
Han no bilieue to the lifte · ne to the lore of philosofres.
   Astrymyanes alday · in her arte faillen, 352
That whilum warned bifore · what shulde falle after.
Shipmen and shepherdes · that with shipp and shepe wenten,
Wisten by the walkene · what shulde bityde ;
As of wederes and wyndes · thei warned men ofte. 356
Tilieres that tiled the erthe · tolden her maistres,
By the sede that thei sewe · what thei selle mi3te,
And what to lene and what to lyue by · the londe was so trewe.
Now failleth the folke of the flode · and of the londe bothe,
Shepherdes and shipmen · and so do this tilieres ; 361
Noither thei kunneth ne knoweth · one cours bi-for another.
Astrymyanes also · aren at her wittes ende ;
Of that was calculed of the element · the contrarie thei fynde.

B. 339. delyuereth WOB; delyureth L.   354. sheperdes L.   359. what WCOB; LR *om.*   361. Sheperdes L.

C. PASSUS XVIII. 72–106.

Men may lykne letterid men · to a Lussheborgh, other werse,
And to a badde peny · with a good preynte.   73
For of muche moneye · the metal is ryght naught,
ȝut is the prente pure trewe · and parfitliche graue.
And so it fareth by false Cristine · here follouht is trewe,   76
Cristendome of holykirke · the kynges marke of heuene;
Ac the metal, that is mannes saule · of meny of these techeres
Is alayed with lecherie · and other lustes of synne,
That god coueiteth nat the coygne · that Crist hym-self prentede ;
And for synne of the soule · for-saketh hus owne coygne.   81
Thus are the lithere lykned · to Lussheborue sterlinges,
That faire by-fore folke · prechen and techen,
And worchen nat as thei fynden wryten · and wissen the peuple.
For what thorw werre and wrake · and wycked hyfdes,   85
May no preiour pees make · in no place, hit semeth ;
Lewede men hauen no by-leyue · so letterid men erren.
Neither the see ne the sande · ne the seed ȝeldeth   88
As thei woned were ; · in wham is defaute ?
Nat in god, that he nys good · and the grounde bothe ;
And the see and the seed · the sonne and the mone
Don her deuer day and nyȝt · and yf we duden also,   92
Ther sholde be plente and pees · perpetuel for euere.
Wederwise shupmen now · and other witty peuple
Han no by-leyue to the lyft · ne to the lood-sterre.
Astronomyens al day · in here art faillen,   96
That whilom warned men by-fore · what shoulde by-falle after.
Shupmen and shephurdes · by the séuen sterres
Wisten while and tolden · whenne hit shoulde reynen.
Tyliers that tyleden the erthe · tolden here maystres   100
By the seed that thei sewe · what thei shoulde notye,
And what lyue by and lene · the londe was so trewe.
Now failleth this folke · bothe sowers and shupmen,
Nother thei knoweth ne conneth · o cours by a-nother.   104
Astronomyens al-so · aren at here wittes end;
Of that was calculed of the clymat · the contrarye they fyndeth.

C. 72. luhssheborgh P.   75. an P.   76. triwe P.   77. kirke I; churche PEFG.   80. þe EMIFTG ; þat P.   preentede P.   81. þe EMIFTG ; P *om.*   82. luhssheborue P.   90. good IMFT; goud P.   92. nyȝth P.   94. Wederwise I ; Wonderwyse PEMFGT.   95. loodsterres P.   97. whilom IFTG; whilen PE.   102. whas P.

Gramer, the grounde of al · bigyleth now children; 365
For is none of this newe clerkes · who so nymeth hede,
That can versifye faire · ne formalich enditen;
Ne nou3t on amonge an hundreth · that an auctour can construe,
Ne rede a lettre in any langage · but in Latyn or in Englissh.
Go now to any degre · and but-if Gyle be mayster,
And Flaterere his felawe · vnder hym to fourmen,
Moche wonder me thynketh · amonges vs alle. 372
Doctoures of decres · and of diuinite maistres,
That shulde konne and knowe · alkynnes clergye,
And answere to argumentz · and also to a *quodlibet*,
(I dar nou3t seggen it for shame) · if suche weren apposed,
Thei shulde faillen in her philosofye · and in phisyk bothe. 377
Wher-fore I am afered · of folke of holikirke,
Lest thei ouerhuppen as other don · in offices and in houres.
Ac if thei ouerhuppe, as I hope nou3te · owre byleue suffiseth;
As clerkes in *Corpus-Christi* feste · singen and reden, 381
That *sola fides sufficit* · to saue with lewed peple.

Grammere, that grounde is of alle · by-gyleth now children;
For ther is nouthe non · who so nymeth hede,   108
That can versifie fayre · other formeliche endite,
Ne that can construen kyndeliche · that poetes maden.
Gowe now to eny degre · and, bote Gyle be halde a mayster,
And a flaterer for hus usshere · a ferliche me thynketh!   112
Doctours of decree · and of dyuyn maystres,
That shoulde the seuene ars conne · and a-soile *ad quodlibet*,
Bote thei faille in fylosophye ·—and filosophers lyueden,
And wolde wel examene hem—· wonder me thynketh!   116
Lord leyue that these preestes · leelly seyn here masses,
That thei ouerhuppe nat for hast! · as ich hope thei do nat,
Thogh hit suffise for oure sauacion · sothfast by-leyue;
As clerkus in *Corpus-Christi* feste · syngen and reden,   120
That *sola fides sufficit* · to saue with lewede peuple.
 Ac yf preestes do her deuer wel · we shullen do the bettere.
For Saresyns mowe be saued so · yf thei so by-leyuede,
In the lengthynge of here lyf · to leyue on holychurche.' 124
'What is holychurche, frend?' quoth ich · 'Charite,' he seyde,
'Lyf, and Loue, and Leaute · in o by-leyue and lawe,
A loue-knotte of leaute · and of leel by-leyue,
Alle kynne cristene · cleuynge on o wyl,   128
With-oute gyle and gabbynge · gyue and selle and lene.
Loue lawe with-oute leaute · lowable was it neuere;
God lereth no lyf to loue · with-oute leel cause:
Iewes, Gentiles, and Sarrasines · Iugen hem-selue   132
That leeliche thei by-leyuen · and ȝut here lawe dyuerseth;
And on god that al by-gan · with goode herte thei honoureth,
And either loueth, and bileuith · in on lord al-myȝti.
Ac oure lorde loueth no loue · bote lawe be the cause;   136
For lechours louen aȝen the lawe · and at the laste beeth dampned:
And theeues louen, and leaute haten · and at the laste beeth
    hanged:

C. 108. hede EMIT; hete P.   109. versifie IFT; uersie P.   112. hus-
shere P.   a FT; and PEI; MG *om*.   116. *This line is supplied from* M.
PEIFTG *omit*.   119. þogh I; þoȝ E; þowh F; þhaw M; That P.   suffise
EFT; suffice IG; suffuse P.   126. (3*rd*) and M; & oo F; a PEIG.   127.
A—knotte MFITG; And loue a knotte PE.   128. clyuynge P.   133.
dyuerseþ EMIFTG; dyuersen P.   135. *This line is from* M; *also in* IFGT;
PE *om*.   138. louen and T; louyen and I; PEMFG *om*.; *cf*. ll. 137, 139.

And so may Sarasenes be saued · scribes and Jewes;
Allas thanne! but owre loresmen · lyuen as thei leren vs,   384
And, for her lyuynge, that lewed men · be the lother god agulten.
For Sarasenes han somwhat · semynge to owre bileue,
For thei loue and bileue · in o persone almiȝty;
And we, lered and lewede · in on god bileueth.   388
Ac one Makometh, a man · in mysbileue
Brouȝte Sarasenes of Surre · and se in what manere.

B. 388. *After this* R *adds a line, which seems superfluous*—Cristene and vncristene · on one god bileueth.

And leelle men louen as lawe techeth · and loue ther-of aryseth,
The which is hefd of Charite · and hele of mannes soule. 140
*Dilige deum propter deum ; id propter ueritatem est. Et
inimicum tuum propter mandatum ; id propter legem est.
Et amicum propter amorem ; id est, propter caritatem.*
Loue god, for he is good · and grounde of alle treuthe;
Loue thyn enemy entyerly · godes heste to ful-fille ; 142
Loue thy frend that folweth thy wil · that is thy faire soule.
For whanne alle frendes faillen · and fleen a-wey in deiynge,
Then suweth the thy soule · to sorwe other to ioye,
And ay hopeth eft to be · with here bodye atte laste 146
In murthe other in mornynge · and neuere eft to departe.
And that is Charite, my leue childe · to be cher ouer thi soule;
Contrarie hure nauht, as in conscience · yf thou wolt come to
    heuene.'
'Wher Sarrasyns,' ich seyde · 'seo nat what is charite?' 150
'Hit may be that Sarrasyns hauen · a suche manere charite,
Louye, as by lawe of kynde · oure lord god al-myghty.
Hit is a kynde thyng, a creature · hus creatour to honoure ;
For ther is no man that mynde hath · that ne meoketh hym
    and by-secheth 154
To that lord that hym lyf lente · and lyflode him sendeth.
Ac meny manere men ther beoth · as Sarrasyns and Iewes,
Louyeth nat that lorde a-ryght · as by the Legende *Sanctorum*,
And lyuen oute of leel by-leyue · for thei leyue in a mene. 158
A man that hihte Makamede · for Messye thei hym heolde,
And after hus lerynge thei lyuen · and by lawe of kynde.
And when kynde hath hus cours · and no contrarye fyndeth,
Thenne is lawe lost · and lewete vnknowen. 162
Beaute saunz bounte · blessed was hit neuere,
Ne kynde *saunz cortesie* · in no contreye preysed.
Men fyndeth that Makamede · was a man ycrystned,
And a cardinal of court · a gret clerk with-alle, 166
And porsuede to haue be pope · pryns of holychurche;
And for he was lyke a Lussheborgh · ich leyue oure lord hym
    lette. 168

C. 143. (3*rd*) þy EIG ; þi MFT ; þe P. 150. Wher (*for* wheþer); *written*
Where IG; Whare F ; Were P ; Wheþer ET. 155. sendeþ EMFG ;
seyndeþ P. 162. vnknowyn P. 168. whas P. louhssheborgh P.

This Makometh was a Crystene man · and for he moste nou3te
    be a pope,
In-to Surre he sou3te · and thorw his sotil wittes   392
Daunted a dowue · and day and ny3te hir fedde;
The corne that she cropped · he caste it in his ere.
And if he amonge the people preched · or in places come,
Thanne wolde the coluer come · to the clerkes ere,   396
Menynge as after meet · thus Makometh hir enchaunted,
And dide folke thanne falle on knees · for he swore in his
    prechynge,
That the coluer that come so · come fram god of heuene
As messager to Makometh · men forto teche   400
And thus thorw wyles of his witte · and a whyte dowue,
Makometh in mysbileue · men and wommen brou3te,
That lered there and lewed 3it · lyuen on his lawes.
And sitth owre saueoure suffred · the Sarasenes so bigiled,
Thorw a crystene clerke · acursed in his soule;   405
Ac for drede of the deth · I dar nou3t telle treuthe,
How Englissh clerkes a coluer feden · that Coueityse hatte,
And ben manered after Makometh · that no man vseth treuth.
    Ancres and hermytes · and monkes and freres   409
Peren to apostles · thorw her parfit lyuynge.
Wolde neuere the faithful fader · that his ministres sholde
Of tyrauntz that teneth trewe men · taken any almesse,   412
But done as Antony did · Dominik and Frauncéys,
Benet and Bernarde · the which hem firste tau3te
To lyue bi litel and in lowe houses · by lele mennes almesse.
Grace sholde growe and be grene · thorw her good lyuynge,
And folkes sholde fynde · that ben in dyuerse sykenesse,   417
The better for her byddynges · in body and in soule.
Her preyeres and her penaunces · to pees shulde brynge
Alle that ben at debate · and bedemen were trewe;   420
    Petite et accipietis, etc.
Salt saueth catel · seggen this wyues;
    Vos estis sal terre, etc.
The heuedes of holicherche · and thei holy were,
Cryst calleth hem salt · for Crystene soules;
    Et si sal euanuerit, in quo salietur.

B. 398. A (*for* And) L.   411. ministres WC; minstres LR.

For-thi souhte he in-to Surrye · and sotiled hou he myghte
Beo mayster ouer alle tho men · and on this manere wroughte.
He endauntede a douue · day and nyght here fedde;
In aither of hus eris · pryueliche he hadde   172
Corn, that the coluer eet · when he cam in places.
And in what place he prechede · and the peuple tauhte,
Then sholde the coluere come · to the clerkes ere,
Menynge as after mete · thus Makamede here enchauntede. 176
And whan the coluer kam thus · thenne knelede the peuple,
For Makemede to men swor · 'hit was a messager of heuene,
And sothly god self · in suche a coluere lyknesse
Tolde hym and tauhte hym · hou to teche the peuple.'   180
Thus Makamede in mysbyleyue · man and womman brouhte,
And in hus lore thei leyuen ʒut · as wel lered as lewede.
And sutthe oure sauyour suffrede · suche a fals Crystine
Deceyue so Sarrasyns · sothly me thynketh,   184
Holy men, as ich hope · thorw help of the holy gost,
Sholde conuerten hem to Crist · and Cristendom to take.

C. 169. southte P.   sotiled I; sotilide T; sotelede G; sotelde M; sotile (*wrongly*) PE.   176. hus mete PE; *but* MIT *om.* hus.   177. knelede MIT; kneled F; knewele P.   186. (*2nd*) to IMFT; PEG *om.*

Ac fresshe flesshe other fisshe · whan it salt failleth, 424
It is vnsauory, for soth · ysothe or ybake.
So is mannes soule sothly · that seeth no good ensaumple
Of hem of holycherche · that the heigh weye shulde teche,
And be gyde, and go bifore · as a good baneoure, 428
And hardy hem that bihynde ben · and ȝiue hem good euydence.

Elleuene holy men · al the worlde torned
In-to lele byleue; · the liȝtloker, me thynketh,
Shulde al maner men · we han so manye maistres, 432
Prestes and prechoures · and a pope aboue,
That goddes salt shulde be · to saue mannes soule.

Al was hethenesse some tyme · Ingelond and Wales,
Til Gregory gerte clerkes · to go here and preche. 436
Austyn at Caunterbury · crystened the kynge,
And thorw myracles, as men may rede · al that marche he torned
To Cryst and to Crystendome · and crosse to honoure,
And fulled folke faste · and the faith tauȝte 440
More thorw miracles · than thorw moche prechynge,
As wel thorw his werkes · as with his holy wordes,
And seyde hem what fullynge · and faith was to mene.

Cloth that cometh fro the weuyng · is nouȝt comly to were,
Tyl it is fulled vnder fote · or in fullyng-stokkes, 445
Wasshen wel with water · and with taseles cracched,
Ytouked, and ytented · and vnder tailloures hande.
And so it fareth by a barne · that borne is of wombe, 448
Til it be crystened in Crystes name · and confermed of the bisshop,
It is hethene as to heueneward · and helpelees to the soule.

Hethene is to mene after heth · and vntiled erthe;
As in wilde wildernesse · wexeth wilde bestes, 452
Rude and vnresonable · rennenge with-out croperes.

Ȝe mynnen wel how Matheu seith · how a man made a feste;
He fedde hem with no venysoun · ne fesauntes ybake,
But with foules that fram hym nolde · but folwed his whistellynge;
Ecce altilia mea et omnia parata sunt, etc.;
And wyth calues flesshe he fedde · the folke that he loued. 457
The calfe bytokeneth clennesse · in hem that kepeth lawes.
For as the cow thorw kynde mylke · the calf norissheth til
  an oxe,

B. 453. croperes C; croperis B; cropers O; cropiers W; creperes L.
454. mynnen W; menen O; nymmen L (*wrongly*).

[*Not in* C-*Text.*]

So loue and lewte · lele men susteyneth, 460
And maydenes and mylde men · mercy desiren ;
Riȝt as the cow-calf · coueyteth swete mylke,
So don riȝtful men · mercy and treuthe.
[And by the hande-fedde foules · his folk vnderstonde, 464
That loth ben to louye · with-outen lernynge of ensaumples.
Riȝt as capones in a court · cometh to mennes whistlynge,
In menynge after mete · folweth men that whistlen,
Riȝt so rude men · that litel reson cunneth, 468
Louen and by-leuen · by lettred mennes doynges,
And by here wordes and werkes · wenen and trowen.
And, as tho foules to fynde · fode after whistlynge,
So hope thei to haue · heuene thoruȝ her whistlynge. 472
And by the man that made the feste · the mageste bymeneth ;
That is, god of his grace · gyueth al men blisse ;
With wederes and with wondres · he warneth vs with a whistlere,
Where that his wille is · to worschipen vs alle, 476
And feden vs and festen vs · for euere-more at ones.]
  Ac who beth that excuseth hem · that aren persounes and prestes,
That heuedes of holycherche ben · that han her wille here,
With-oute trauaille, the tithe del · that trewemen biswynkyn,
Thei wil be wroth for I write thus · ac to witnesse I take
Bothe Mathew and Marke · and *Memento-domine-Dauid ;* 482
  Ecce audiuimus eam in Effrata, etc.
What pope or prelate now · perfourneth that Cryst hiȝte,
  Ite in vniversum mundum et predicate, etc. ?
Allas ! that men so longe · on Makometh shulde byleue, 484
So many prelates to preche · as the pope maketh,
Of Nazareth, of Nynyue · of Neptalim, and Damaske,
That thei ne went as Cryst wisseth · sithen thei wilne a name,
To be pastours and preche · the passioun of Iesus, 488
And as hym-self seyde · so to lyue and deye ;
  Bonus pastor animam suam ponit, etc. ;
And seyde it in sauacioun · of Sarasenes and other.
For Crystene and vncristene · Cryst seide to prechoures,
  Ite vos in vineam meam.

B. 460. L *repeats* and. 464-477. *These lines are in* R *only.* 482.
Ecce—Effrata in R only. 487. wilne a R ; wil a L ; wille haue W ; wol
haue C ; wolen haue OB ; *but* R *is right.*

Alas! that men so longe · on Makamede by-leyuen,
So meny prelates to preche · as the pope maketh,   188
Of Nazareth, of Nynyve · of Neptalym, of Damaske,
That thei ne wendeth the wey · as holy writ biddeth,
Ite in universum mundum · sutthe ȝe wilneth the name
To be prelates, and preche · the passion of Iesus,   192
And as hym-self seyde · so lyue and deye;
    Bonus pastor animam suam ponit pro ouibus suis.

C. 188. prelates IFTG; priestes PE.   pope EMIFTG; peuple (!) P.
190. biddith P.

And sith that this Sarasenes · scribes, and Iuwes   492
Han a lippe of owre byleue · the liȝtloker, me thynketh,
Thei shulde torne, who so trauaille wolde · to teche hem of
    the trinite,
        Querite et inuenietis, etc.
It is reuth to rede · how riȝtwis men lyued,
How thei defouled her flessh · forsoke her owne wille,   496
Fer fro kitth and fro kynne · yuel-yclothed ȝeden,
Badly ybedded · no boke but conscience,
Ne no richchesse but the rode · to reioyse hem inne;
        Absit nobis gloriari, nisi in cruce domini nostri, etc.
And tho was plente and pees · amonges pore and riche;
And now is routhe to rede · how the red noble   501
Is reuerenced or the rode · receyued for the worthier
Than Crystes crosse, that ouer-cam · deth and dedly synne!
And now is werre and wo · and who so 'why' axeth,   504
For coueityse after crosse · the croune stant in golde.
Bothe riche and religious · that rode thei honoure,
That in grotes is ygraue · and in golde nobles.
For coueityse of that crosse · men of holykirke   508
Shul tourne as Templeres did · the tyme approcheth faste.
Wyte ȝe nouȝt, wyse men · how tho men honoured
More tresore than treuthe? · I dar nouȝt telle the sothe;
Resoun and riȝtful dome · tho religious demed.   512
Riȝt so, ȝe clerkes · for ȝowre coueityse, ar longe,
Shal thei demen *dos ecclesie* · and ȝowre pryde depose;
        Deposuit potentes de sede, etc.
Ȝif knyȝthod and kynde wytte · and comune conscience
Togideres loue lelly · leueth it wel, ȝe bisshopes,   516
The lordeship of londes · for euere shal ȝe lese,
And lyuen as *Leuitici* · as owre lorde ȝow techeth,
        Per primicias et decimas.
Whan Costantyn of curteysye · holykirke dowed
With londes and ledes · lordeshipes and rentes,   520
An angel men herde · an heigh at Rome crye,
'*Dos ecclesie* this day · hath ydronke venym,
And tho that han Petres powere · arn apoysoned alle.'
A medecyne mote ther-to · that may amende prelates,   524
That sholden preye for the pees; · possessioun hem letteth,

Hit is reuthe to rede · hou ryght holy men lyueden,
How thei defouleden here fleessh · for-soken here owen wil,
Fer fro kuth and fro kyn · vuel-clothed ȝeoden,   196
Baddeliche beddyd · no book bote here conscience,
Nother richesse bote the rode · to reioysen hem inne;
    Absit nobis gloriari nisi in cruce domini nostri Iesu Christi.
And tho was pees and plente · a-mong poure and riche;
And now is reuthe to rede · hou the rede noble   200
Ys yreuerenced by-fore the rode · and receyuyd for the worthier
To a-mende and to make · as with men of holichurche,
Than Cryst, other croys that ouercam · deth and dedly synne!
And now is werre and wo · and ho so 'whi' asketh,   204
For couetyse after a croys · the croune stant in golde.
Bothe riche and religiouse · that rode thei honouren
That in groetes is y-graue · and in gold nobles.
For couetyse of that croys · clerkes of holychurche   208
Schullen ouerturne as Templers duden · the tyme aprocheth faste.
Mynne ȝe nat, lettered men · hou tho men honourede
More tresour than treuthe? · ich dar nat telle the sothe
How tho corsede Crystine · catel and richesse worshepeden;
Reyson and riȝtful dome · the religious damnede.   213
Right so, ȝe clerkus, ȝoure couetise · er come ouht longe,
Shal dampne *dos ecclesie* · and depose ȝow for ȝoure pruyde;
    Deposuit potentes de sede.
Yf knyȝt-hod and kynde wit · and the comune and conscience
To-gederes louen leelliche · leyueth hit wel, bisshopes, 217
The lordshup of londes · leese ȝe shulle for euere,
And lyuen as *Leuitici* dude · and as our lord ȝow techeth,
    Per primicias et decimas.
Whenne Constantyn of hus cortesye · holykirke dowede   220
With londes and leedes · lordshepes and rentes,
An angel men hurde · an hih at Rome crye—
'*Dos ecclesie* this day · hath ydronke venym,
And tho that han Petres power · aren poysoned alle.'   224
A medecine moste ther-to · that myghte amende the prelates,
That sholden preye for the pees · and possession hem letteth;

  C. 196. Feer P.   198. reioyesen P.   *nobis* IG; *vobis* T; *nos* PEM.
211. þan IMETG; P *om.*   213. relious (*for* religious) P.   216. Hyf
(*for* Yf) P. knyȝtht P. whit (*for* wit) P. 218. þe EMITG; To (*wrongly*)
P. 220. kirke IT; churche PEFG.

Take her landes, ȝe lordes · and let hem lyue by dymes.

If possessioun be poysoun · and inparfit hem make,

Good were to dischargen hem · for holicherche sake, 528
And purgen hem of poysoun · or more perile falle.
   Ȝif presthod were parfit · the peple sholde amende,
That contrarien Crystes lawe · and Crystendome dispise.

For al paynymes prayeth · and parfitly bileueth 532
In the holy grete god · and his grace thei asken,
And make her mone to Makometh · her message to shewe.

B. 530. solde (*for* sholde) L.   532. paynymes WCROB; paynym L.

Taketh here londes, ȝe lordes · and leet hem lyue by dymes,
Yf ȝe kynges coueyten · in Cristene pees to lyuen.   228
For yf posession be poyson · and inparfyt hem make,
The heuedes of holychurche · and tho that be vnder hem,
Hit were charite to deschargen hem · for holychurches sake,
And purge hem of the olde poyson · ere more perel falle.   232
  For were preest-hod more parfyt · that is, the pope formest,
That with moneye menteyneth men · to werren vp-on cristine,
A-ȝens the lore of oure lorde · as seynt Luk wytnesseth,
    Michi uindictam, et ego retribuam, dicit dominus, &c.,
Hus prayers with hus pacience · to pees sholde brynge   236
Alle londes to loue · and that in a lytel tyme;
The pope with alle preestes · *pax-uobis* sholde make!
And take hede hou Makamede · thorwe a mylde doue,
He hald al Surrye as hym-self wolde · and Sarasyns in quyete;
Nouht thorw manslauht and mannes strengthe · Makamede hadde
    the mastrie,   241
Bote thorw pacience and pryuy gyle · he was prynce ouer hem
    alle.
In suche manere, me thynketh · moste the pope,
Prelates, and preestes · prayen and by-seche   244
Deuowtliche day and nyȝt · and with-drawe hem fro synne,
And crye to Crist that he wolde · hus coluere sende,
The whiche is the holy gost · that out of heuene descendede,
To make a perpetuel pees · by-twyne the prynce of heuene   248
And alle manere of men · that on this molde lybbeth.
Yf preest-hod were parfit and preyede thus · the peuple sholde
    amende,
That now contrarien Cristes lawes · and Cristendom despisen.
For sutthe that thes Sarasyns · scribes, and thes Iewes   252
Hauen a lippe of oure by-leyue · the lightloker, me thynketh,
Thei sholde turne, who so trauayle wolde · and of the Trinite
    techen hem.
For alle paynymes preyen · and parfitliche by-leyuen
In the grete heye god · and hus grace asken,   256
And maken here mone to Makamede · here message to shewe.

C. 229. inp*ar*fyȝt P.   232. oolde P.   233. p*ar*fyȝt P.   235. *et—&c.*
is in F only.   241. mannes I; manis T; PEMFG *om.*   244. Prelatis P.
246. seynde (*for* sende) P.   249. of MFT; P *om.*   254. who so IT;
þat PEMF.

Thus in a faith lyueth that folke · and in a false mene,   535
And that is routhe for ri3tful men · that in the rewme wonyen,
And a peril to the pope · and prelatis that he maketh,
That bere bisshopes names · of Bedleem and Babiloigne ;
[Whan the heye kynge of heuene · sent his sone to erthe,
Many miracles he wrou3te · man for to turne ;   540
In ensaumple that men schulde se · that by sadde resoun
Men mi3t nou3t be saued · but thoru3 mercy and grace,
And thoru3 penaunce and passion · and parfit bylef ;
And by-cam man of a mayde · and *metropolitanus*,   544
And baptised and bishoped · with the blode of his herte
Alle that wilned, and wolde · with inne-wit by-leue it.
Many a seint sytthen · hath soffred to deye,
Al for to enforme the faith · in fele contreyes deyeden,   548
In Ynde and in Alisaundre · in Ermonye and in Spayne,
In delfol deth deyeden · for there faith sake ;
In sauacion of the fayth · seynt Thomas was ymartired,
Amonges vn-kende Cristene · for Cristes loue he deyede,   552
And for the ri3t of al this reume · and al reumes Cristene.
Holy cherche is honoured · hey3liche thoru3 his deynge,
He is a forbysene to alle bishopes · and a bri3t myroure,
And souereyneliche to suche · that of Surrye bereth the name,]
That hippe aboute in Engelonde · to halwe mennes auteres,
And crepe amonges curatoures · and confessen ageyne the lawe,
    Nolite mittere falcem in messem alienam, etc.
Many man for Crystes loue · was martired in Romanye   559
Er any Crystendome was knowe there · or any crosse honoured.
  Euery bisshop that bereth crosse · by that he is holden,
Thorw his prouynce to passe · and to his peple to shewe hym,
Tellen hem and techen hem · on the trinite to bileue,
And feden hem with gostly fode · and nedy folke to fynden.
Ac Ysaie of 3ow speketh · and Osyas bothe,   565
That no man schuld be bischope · but if he hadde bothe,
Bodily fode and gostly fode · and gyue there it nedeth ;
    *In domo mea non est panis neque vestimentum, et ideo nolite
    constituere me regem.*

B. 539-556. *These lines, found in* R *only, properly belong to the* C-*text.*
543. R *has* byle *for* bylef, *by mistake.*   545. bischiued (*for* bishoped) R.
546. woled (*for* wolde) R.   558. and WR ; LCOB *om.*   560. Er W ;
Ar R ; Er ar LC.   564-567. *From* and nedy (564) *to* fode (567) *is in* R *only ;
omitted in* LWCOB, *probably owing to the repetition of* gostly fode.

Thus in a faith lyueth that folke · and in a false mene;
And that is reuthe for the ryghtful men · that in the reame wonyeth,
And perel for the prelates · that the pope maketh; 260
That bereth name of Neptalym · of Nynyue and of Damaske.
For when the holy kynge of heuene · sende hus sone to erthe,
Meny myracles he wrouhte · man for to turne,
In ensample that men · sholde seo by sad reyson, 264
That men myghte nat be sauede · bote thorw mercy and grace,
And thorw penaunce and passioun · and parfyt by-leyue;
And by-cam a man of a mayde · and *metropolitanus*,
And baptisede, and busshoppede · with the blode of hus herte
Alle that wilnede other wolde · with inwit by-leue hit. 269
Meny seint sitthe · suffrede deth al-so;
For to enforme the faithe · ful wyde-where deyden,
In Inde and in Alisaundrie · in Ermanye, in Spayne, 272
And fro mysbyleue · meny man turnede.
In sauacion of mannys saule · seynt Thomas of Caunterbury
Among vnkynde Cristene · in holychurche was sleye,
And alle. holychurche · honoured for that deyinge. 276
He is a forbusne to alle busshopes · and a bry3t myrour,
And souereyneliche to alle suche · that of Surrye bereth name;
And nat in Engelonde to huppe abowte · and halewen menne auters,
And crepe in a-monge curatours · and confessen a-3en the lawe;
Nolite mittere falcem in messem alienam. 280
Meny man for Crystes loue · was martred a-mong Romaynes
Er Cristendome were knowe ther · other eny croys honoured.
Eueriche busshope, by the lawe · sholde buxumliche wende,
And pacientliche, thorgh hus prouynce · and to hus peple hym shewe, 284
Feden hem and fillen hem · and fere hem fro synne;
In baculi forma · sit presul hec tibi norma,
Fer, trahe, punge gregem · seruando per omnia legem;
And enchaunte hem to charite · on holychurche to be-leyue. 288

C. 259. ryghtful IFT; ryght PE.   260. *This line is from* M; *also in* IFT; PE *omit.*   261. þat IMFT; And PE.   262. eerthe P.   266. parfy3t P.   268. an (*for* and) P.   269. inwit FG; inwhi3t P.   274. Cauntelbury P.   276. honourede P.   277. bry3the P.   279. engelounde P.   280. curatours MIFT; creatours PE.   confesson P.   *alienam messem* P.   282. wher (*for* were) P.   honourede P.   283. weynde P.   285. fillen M; follen I; fullen T; fulle FG; folwen PE.

Ozias seith for such · that syke ben and fieble,　　568
　　Inferte omnes decimas in oreum meum, vt sit cibus in domo mea.
Ac we Crystene creatures · that on the crosse byleuen,
Aren ferme as in the faith · goddes forbode elles!
And han clerkes to kepen vs ther-inne · and hem that shal
　　come after vs.
　　And Iewes lyuen in lele lawe · owre lorde wrote it hym-selue,
In stone, for it stydfast was · and stonde sholde eure—　　573
Dilige deum et proximum · is parfit Iewen lawe—
And toke it Moyses to teche men · til Messye come;
And on that lawe thei lyuen ȝit · and leten it the beste.　　576
　　And ȝit knewe thei Cryst · that Crystendome tauȝte,
For a parfit prophete · that moche peple saued
Of selcouth sores · thei seyen it ofte,
Bothe of myracles and meruailles · and how he men fested　580
With two fisshes and fyue loues · fyue thousande peple;
And bi that maungerye men miȝte wel se · that Messye he semed.
And whan he luft vp Lazar · that layde was in graue,
And vnder stone ded and stanke · with styf voys hym called,
　　Lazare, veni foras,
Dede hym rise and rowme · riȝt bifor the Iuwes.　　585
Ac thei seiden and sworen · with sorcerye he wrouȝte,
And studyeden to stroyen hym · and stroyden hemself;
And thorw his pacyence her powere · to pure nouȝt he brouȝte;
　　Pacientes vincunt.
Danyel of her vndoynge · deuyned and seyde,
　　Cum sanctus sanctorum veniat, cessabit vnxio vestra.
　　And ȝet wenen tho wrecches · that he were *pseudo-propheta*,
And that his lore be lesynges · and lakken it alle,　　591
And hopen that he be to come · that shal hem releue,
Moyses eft, or Messye · here maisteres ȝet deuyneth.
　　Ac Pharesewes and Sarasenes · Scribes and Grekis　　594
Aren folke of on faith · the fader god thei honouren;
And sitthen that the Sarasenes · and also the Iewes
Konne the firste clause of owre bileue · *Credo in deum patrem*
　　omnipotentem,
Prelates of Crystene prouynces · shulde preue, if thei myȝte,　598
Lere hem litlum and lytlum · *et in Iesum Christum filium,*

B. 568. *sit* O; LWCROB *om.*　　579. seyen RB; seyne L; seyn C.
581. an (*for* and) L.

C. PASSUS XVIII. 289-320. 477

For as the kynde is of a kny3t · other for a kynge to be take,
And among here enemys · in morteils bateles
To be culled and ouercome · the comune to defende;
So is the kynde of a curatour · for Cristes loue to preche,   292
And deye for hus dere children · to destroye dedly synne;
    Bonus pastor ;
And nameliche ther as lewede lyuen · and no lawe knowen.
Ac we Crystine conneth the lawe · and hauen of oure tounge
Busshopes and bookes · the byleyue to teche.   296
  Iuwes lyuen in the lawe · that oure lord tauhte,
Moyses to be maister ther-of · til Messie come,
And in that lawe thei leyue · and leten hit for the beste.
  And 3ut knewe thei Crist · that Cristendome tauhte,   300
And for a parfyt prophete · that muche peuple sauede,
And of selcouthe sores · sauede men ful ofte;
By the myracles that he made · Messie he semede,
Tho he lyfte vp Lazar · that leyde was in graue,   304
Quatriduanus cold · quik dude hym walke.
Iuwes seyden, that hit seyn · with sorcerie he wrouhte,
And stodieden hou to struyen him · and struyeden hem-selue,
And here power thourh hus pacience · to pure nouht brouhte.
  And 3ut thei seien sothliche · and so doth the Sarrasyns,   309
That Iesus was bote a Iogelour · a Iaper a-monge the comune,
And a sophistre of sorcerie · and *pseudo-propheta,*
And hus lore was lesynge · and lacken hit alle,   312
And hopen that he be to comynge · that shal hem releue;
Moyses other Makemede · here maistres deuineth;
And haueth suspecion to be saf · bothe Sarrasyns and Iewes,
Thorwe Moyses and Makamede · and myghte of god that mad al.
  Now sytthe that these Sarrasyns · and al-so the Iewes   317
Conne the ferste clause of oure by-leyue · *Credo in deum patrem,*
Prelates and preestes · sholde preoue, yf thei myghte,
Lere hem lytulum and lytulum · *et in Iesum Christum, filium*
    eius,   320

  C. 289. kny3th P.   290. And MIT; Al FG; PE *om.*   292. a curatour EMIF; creatour P.   293. destroye IMFT; distrye P.   295. comeþ (*for* conneþ) P.   300. knewe EMT; knowe PI.   303. myracles EIF; meracles P.   307. stodieden IT; fondeden PEM. him MF; hym T; hem PEIG.   308. brouhten (*for* brouhte) P.   309. 3ut MG; 3it IF; PE *om.* 317. theese P. an P.   320. *The first* lytulum *is miswritten* lytulhum *in* P.

Tyl thei couthe speke and spelle · *et in spiritum sanctum,* 600
And rendren it and recorden it · with *remissionem peccatorum,*
  Carnis resurreccionem, et vitam eternam. Amen.'

PASSUS XVI.

Passus xvj^{us}, et primus de Dobet.

'NOW faire falle ȝow!' quod I tho · 'for ȝowre faire shewynge,
For Haukynnes loue the actyf man · euere I shal ȝow louye;
Ac ȝet I am in a were · what charite is to mene.'
'It is a ful trye tree,' quod he · 'trewly to telle. 4
Mercy is the more ther-of · the myddel stokke is Reuthe.
The leues ben Lele-Wordes · the lawe of Holycherche,
The blosmes beth Boxome-Speche · and Benygne-Lokynge;
Pacience hatte the pure tre · and pore symple of herte, 8
And so, thorw god and thorw good men · groweth the frute Charite.'
'I wolde trauaille,' quod I, 'this tree to se · twenty hundreth myle,
And forto haue my fylle of that frute · forsake al other saulee.
Lorde,' quod I, 'if any wiȝte wyte · whider-oute it groweth?' 12
  'It groweth in a gardyne,' quod he · 'that god made hym-seluen,
Amyddes mannes body · the more is of that stokke;
Herte hatte the herber · that it in groweth,
And *Liberum-Arbitrium* · hath the londe to ferme, 16
Vnder Piers the Plowman · to pyken it and to weden it.'
'Piers the Plowman!' quod I tho · and al for pure ioye
That I herde nempne his name · anone I swouned after,
And laye longe in a lone dreme · and atte laste me thouȝte, 20
That Pieres the Plowman · al the place me shewed,
And bad me toten on the tree · on toppe and on rote.
With thre pyles was it vnder-piȝte · I perceyued it sone.
'Pieres,' quod I, 'I preye the · whi stonde thise piles here?' 24
  'For wyndes, wiltow wyte,' quod he · 'to witen it fram fallynge;
  Cum ceciderit iustus, non collidetur; quia Dominus supponit
    manum suam;

B. 11. saulee *is glossed by* edulium.   13. a WCROB; L *om.*   15. herber WCO; erber LR; herbergh B.

C. PASSUS XVIII. 321—XIX. 26.   479

Til thei couthe speke and spelle · *et in spiritum sanctum,*   321
Recorden hit and rendren hit · wyth *remissionem peccatorum,*
Carnis resurrectionem, et uitam eternam. Amen.'
Hic explicit passus primus de Dobet.

PASSUS XIX.

Hic incipit passus secundus de Dobet.

'LEUE *Liberum Arbitrium,*' quath ich · 'ich leyue, as ich hope,
Thou couthest telle and teche me · to Charite, ich leyue?'
Then louh *Liberum Arbitrium* · and ladde me forth with tales,
Til we comen in-to a contree · *Cor-hominis* hit hyhte,   4
Herber of alle pryuytees · and of holynesse.
Euene in the myddes · an ympe, as hit were,
That hihte *Ymago-dei* · graciousliche hit growede.   7
Thenne gan ich asken what hit hyhte · and he me sone tolde—
'The tree hihte Trewe-loue,' quath he · 'the trinite hit sette;
Thorgh louely lokynge hit lyueth · and launceth vp blossemes,
The whiche blosmes burnes · Benygne-speche callen;   11
And ther-of cometh a good frut · the which men callen Werkes
Of holynesse, of hendynesse · of help-hym-that-neodeth,
The whiche is callid *Caritas* · Cristes owen fode,
And solaceth alle soules · sorghful in purgatorie.'
'Now, certes,' ich seide · and sykede for ioye,   16
'Ich thonke ȝow a thowsend sythes · that ȝe me hider kende;
And suththen that ȝe fowche-saue · to seye me what hit hihte.'
And he thonked me tho · bote thenne took ich hede,   19
Hit hadde shoriers to shoue hit vp · thre shides of o lengthe,
And of o kynne colour · and o kynde, as me thouhte,
All thre yliche longe · and yliche large.
Muche meruailede me · on what more thei growede;
And efte askede of hym · of what wode thei were?   24
'Thees thre shoryeres,' quath he · 'that bereth vp this plonte,
Thei by-tokneth trewely · the Trinite of heuene;

C. 321. spelle MIT; spele PFG.   *et;* *miswritten* and P.
Passus XIX. 17. ȝow MIT; þe PEFG.   18. foweche P.   20. lengþye P.

And, in blowyng-tyme, abite the floures · but if this piles helpe.
The Worlde is a wykked wynde · to hem that wolden treuthe,
Coueityse cometh of that wynde · and crepeth amonge the leues,
And forfret neigh the frute · thorw many faire si3tes.   29
Thanne with the firste pyle I palle hym down · that is, *potencia-Dei-Patris*.
The Flesshe is a fel wynde · and in flourynge-tyme
Thorw lykyng and lustes · so loude he gynneth blowe,   32
That it norissheth nice si3tes · and some tyme wordes,
And wikked werkes ther-of · wormes of synne,
And forbiteth the blosmes · ri3t to the bare leues.
Thanne sette I to the secounde pile · *sapiencia-Dei-patris*,   36
That is, the passioun and the power · of owre prynce Iesu,
Thorw preyeres and thorw penaunces · and goddes passioun in mynde,
I saue it til I se it rypen · and somdel y-fruited.
And thanne fondeth the Fende · my fruit to destruye,   40
With alle the wyles that he can · and waggeth the rote,
And casteth vp to the croppe · vnkynde neighbores,
Bakbiteres breke-cheste · brawleres and chideres,
And leith a laddre there-to · of lesynges aren the ronges,   44
And feccheth away my floures sumtyme · afor bothe myn eyhen.
Ac *Liberum-Arbitrium* · letteth hym some tyme,
That is lieutenant to loken it wel · by leue of my-selue;

> *Videatis qui peccat in spiritum sanctum, nunquam remittetur, etc.;*
>
> *Hoc est idem, qui peccat per liberum arbitrium non repugnat.*

Ac whan the Fende and the Flesshe · forth with the Worlde 48
Manasen byhynde me · my fruit for to fecche,
Thanne *Liberum-Arbitrium* · laccheth the thridde plante,
And palleth adown the pouke · purelich thorw grace
And helpe of the holy goste · and thus haue I the maystrie.' 52
'Now faire falle 3ow, Pieres,' quod I · 'so faire 3e discryuen
The powere of this postes · and her propre my3te.
Ac I have thou3tes a threve · of this thre piles,
In what wode thei woxen · and where that thei growed;   56
For alle ar thei aliche longe · none lasse than other,
And to my mynde, as me thinketh · on o more thei growed,

B. 47. *repugnat* is written *repug'* or *repūg'* in the MSS.

C. PASSUS XIX. 27–59.

Thre persons in-departable · perpetuel were euere,
Of o wyl, of o wit · and here-with ich kepe   28
The frut of this faire tree · fro thre wykkede wyndes,
And fro fallyng of stok · hit faille nouht of hus myghte.
The Worlde is a wykkede wynde · to hem that wolde treuthe;
Covetyse cometh of that wynde · and *Caritas* hit abiteth;   32
And for-freteth that frut · with manye fayre syghtes;
And with the ferste plaunke ich palle hym doune · *Potencia-dei-patris*.
Thanne is Flessh a fel wynde · in flouryng-tyme;
Thorgh lecherie and lustes · so loude he gynneth blowe,   36
That hit norischeth nyce sy3tes · and som tyme wordes,
And menye wykkede wormes · workes of synne,
And al for-bit *Caritas* · to the bare stalke;
Thanne sette ich the secunde plaunke · *Sapiencia-dei-patris*,   40
The which is the passion and penaunce · and the parfytnesse of Iesus,
And ther-with ich warde hit other-whyle · til hit wexe rype.
Thenne fondeth the Feende · my frut to destruye,
And leith a laddere ther-to · of lesynges be the ronges;   44
With alle the wyles that he can · waggeth the roote
Thorw bak-byters and braweleres · and thorwe bolde chyderes,
And shaketh hit; ne were hit vnder-shored · certes hit sholde nat stande.
So these lourdeines litheren ther-to · that alle the leues fallen,   48
And feccheth a-way this frut som tyme · by-fore bothe myn eyen.
Thenne palle ich a-downe the pouke · with the thridde shoryere,
The whiche is *Spiritus-sanctus* · and soth-fast byleyue,
And that is grace of the Holy Gost; · and thus gat ich the mastrye.'   52
Ich totide vp-on that tree tho · and thenne tok ich hede,
Whether the frut were faire · other foul to loken on.
And the frut was wonder fair · non fairer beo myghte;
Ac in thre degrees hit grew · gret ferly me thouhte,   56
And askede tho 'yf hit were · al of on kynde?'
'3e, certes,' he seide · 'and sothliche thow leyue hit.
Hit is al of o kynde · and that shal ich prouen;

C. 31. wordle P.   32. *caritas* hit abiteþ ITG; hit beteþ *caritas* P.
35. fel MFTG; feel P.   37. norischeþ IEG; norceþ P.   43. fonndeþ P.
44. leithe P.   47. shorede P.   48. þees P.   54. wher (*for* were) P.

And of o gretnesse · and grene of greyne thei semen.'
'That is soth,' seide Pieres · 'so it may bifalle;   60
I shal telle the as tite · what this tree hatte.
The grounde there it groweth · Goodnesse it hiȝte,
And I haue tolde the what hiȝte the tree · the Trinite it meneth '—
And egrelich he loked on me · and ther-fore I spared   64
To asken hym any more ther-of · and badde hym ful fayre
To discreue the fruit · that so faire hangeth.

'Here now bineth,' quod he tho · 'if I nede hadde,
Matrymonye I may nyme · a moiste fruit with-alle.   68
Thanne contenence is nerre the croppe · as calewey bastarde,
Thanne bereth the croppe kynde fruite · and clenneste of alle,
Maydenhode, angeles peres · and rathest wole be ripe,
And swete with-oute swellyng · soure worth it neuere.'   72

B. 69. calewey O; caylewey R; **kaylewey W**; calawey Y; calwey L.

Ac somme ar swettere than some · and sonnere wollen rotye. 60
Men may seo on an appul-treo · meny tyme and ofte,
Of o kynne apples · aren nat yliche grete,
Ne of sewynge smale · ne of o swetnesse swete.
Tho that sitten in the sonne-syde · sonner aren rype, 64
Swettour and saueriour · and also more grettoure
Than tho that selde hauen the sonne · and sitten in the north-
    half;
And so hit fareth sothly · sone, by oure kynde.
Adam was as tree · and we aren as hus apples, 68
Somme of ows sothfast · and some variable,
Somme litel and some large · like apples of kynde.
As weddede men and wedewes · and ry3t worthy maidenes,
The whiche the *Seynt Esprit* seweth · the sonne of al heuene, 72
Conforteth hem in here continence · that lyuen in contemplacion,
As monkes and monyeles · men of holichurche;
These hauen hete of the Holi Gost · as crop of treo the sonne.
Wedewes and wedeweres · that here owen wil for-saken, 76
And chast leden here lyf · ys lyf of contemplacion,
And more lykyng to oure lorde · than lyue as kynde asketh,
And folwe that the flessh wole · and frut forth brynge,
That lettered men in here langage · *Actiua Uita* callen.' 80
'3e, syre,' ich seide, 'and sitthen · ther aren bote two lyues
That oure lorde a-loweth · as lered men ous techeth,
That is *Actiua Uita* · and *Uita Contemplatiua*,
Whi groweth this frut in thre degrees?' · 'for a good skyle,' he
    seide; 84
'Her by-neothe ich may nyme · yf ich neode hadde,
Matrimonye, a moiste frut · that multiplieth the peple.
Thenne a-boue is a betere frut · ac bothe two ben goode,
Wedewehode, more worthier · than wedlok, as in heuene. 88
Thanne is Virginite, more vertuous · and fairest as in heuene,
For that is euene with angeles · and angeles peer.
Hit was the furste frut · that the fader of heuene blessede,
And bad hit be of a bat of erthe · a man and a mayde; 92

C. 60. sannere P.　63. sewynge EIMT ; sywynge P.　o EIF ; PMT *om.*
66. þo MIFTG ; P *om.*　67. sotthly P. soone P.　71. ry3th P.　72.
seweþ MI ; sueth F ; PE *om.*　73. hem MEITF ; him P.　81. two FG ;
to PM.　85. habbe P.　86. multeplieþ P.　87. two ET ; to P.　·92.
P *om.* 1*st* of.

I prayed Pieres to pulle adown · an apple, and he wolde,
And suffre me to assaye · what sauoure it hadde.
And Pieres caste to the croppe · and thanne comsed it to crye,
And wagged Wydwehode · and it wepte after.   76
And whan it meued Matrimoigne · it made a foule noyse,
That I had reuth whan Piers rogged · it gradde so reufulliche.
For euere as thei dropped adown · the deuel was redy,
And gadred hem alle togideres · bothe grete and smale,   80
Adam and Abraham · and Ysay the prophete,
Sampson and Samuel · and seynt Iohan the baptiste;
Bar hem forth boldely · no body hym letted,
And made of holy men his horde · in *lymbo inferni*,   84
There is derkenesse and drede · and the deuel maister.
And Pieres for pure tene · that o pile he lauȝte,
And hitte after hym · happe how it myȝte,
Filius, bi the Fader wille · and frenesse of *Spiritus Sancti*,   88
To go robbe that raggeman · and reue the fruit fro hym.

And thanne spakke *Spiritus Sanctus* · in Gabrieles mouthe,
To a mayde that hiȝte Marye · a meke thinge with-alle,
'That one Iesus, a Iustice sone · moste Iouke in her chambre,

C. PASSUS XIX. 93-126.

In menynge that the faireste thyng · the furste thyng sholde honoure,
And the clennest creature · creatour ferste knowe.
In kynges court and knyghtes · the clennest men and fairest
Shullen serue for the lord selue · so fareth god almyghty.   96
Maidenes and marteres · ministred hym her in erthe,
And in heuene buth most pryue · and next hym by reson,
For the fairest frut · by-fore hym as of eorthe,
And swete with-oute swellinge · soure worth hit neuere.'   100
'This is a propre plonte,' quath ich · 'and pryueliche hit bloweth,
And bryngeth forth faire frut · folke of all nacion,
Bothe parfit and inparfit; · pure fayn ich wolde
A-saye what sauour hit hadde' · ich seide that tyme;   104
'Leue *Liberum-Arbitrium* · leet som lyf hit shake.'
A-non he het Elde · an hih for to clymbe,
And shaken hit sharply · the ripen sholden falle.
Elde clam towarde the crop · than comsede hit to crie;   108
He waggede Wedewehode · and hit wepte after;
He meuede Matrimonye · hit made a foule noyse.
For euere as Elde hadde eny doun · the deuel was wel redy,
And gederide hem alle to-gederis · bothe grete and smale,   112
Adam and Abraham · and Ysaye the prophete,
Sampson and Samuel · and seynt Iohan the baptist,
And bar hem forth baldely · no body tho hym lette,
And made of holy men hus horde · in *limbo inferni*,   116
Ther is derknesse and drede · and the deuel maister.
Thenne meuede hym mod · *in maiestate dei*,
That *Libera-Uoluntas-Dei* · lauhte the myddel shoriere,
And hitte after the fende · happe hou hit myghte.   120
Filius, by the faders wil · flegh with *Spiritus Sanctus*,
To ransake that rageman · and reue hym hus apples,
That fyrst man deceyuede · thorgh frut and false by-heste.
And thenne spake *Spiritus Sanctus* · in Gabrielis mouthe   124
To a mayde that hihte Marie · a meek thyng with alle,
That on Iesus, a Iustice sone · moste Iouken in hire chaumbre,

---

C. 101. plonte EFG; plante MIT; plente P. bloweþ P. 110. meeuede P. 116. P *ins.* doun *after* limbo; see B-text. 117. derknesse EMFT; deornesse (*sic*) P. 118. meouede P. 119. mydel P. 121. fleyght (*for* flegh) P. 122. þat EMFTG; þe P. 125. To a EMFTG; To þat P. P *om.* 2nd a.

Tyl *plenitudo temporis* · fully comen were,   93
That Pieres fruit floured · and fel to be ripe.
And thanne shulde Iesus Iuste there-fore · bi Iuggement of armes,
Whether shulde fonge the fruit · the fende or hymselue.'   96
The mayde myldeliche tho · the messager graunted,
And seyde hendelich to hym · 'lo me, his hande-mayden
For to worchen his wille · with-outen any synne;'
  Ecce ancilla domini; fiat michi secundum verbum tuum, etc.
And in the wombe of that wenche · was he fourty wokes,   100
Tyl he wex a faunt thorw her flesshe · and of fiʒtyng couthe,
To haue y-fouʒte with the fende · ar ful tyme come.
And Pieres the Plowman · parceyued plenere tyme,
And lered hym lechecrafte · his lyf for to saue,   104
That thowgh he were wounded with his enemye · to warisshe hym-self;
And did him assaye his surgerye · on hem that syke were,
Til he was parfit practisoure · if any peril felle,
And souʒte oute the syke · and synful bothe,   108
And salued syke and synful · bothe blynde and crokede,
And com'une wommen conuerted · and to good torned;
  Non est sanis opus medicus, set infirmis, etc.
Bothe meseles and mute · and in the menysoun blody,
Ofte he heled suche · he ne helde it for no maistrye,   112
Saue tho he leched Lazar · that hadde yleye in graue,
Quatriduanus quelt; · quykke did hym walke.
Ac as he made the maistrye · *mestus cepit esse*,
And wepte water with his eyghen · there seyen it manye.   116
Some that the siʒte seyen · saide that tyme,
That he was leche of lyf · and lorde of heigh heuene.
Iewes Iangeled there-aʒeyne · and Iugged lawes,
And seide he wrouʒte thorw wicchecrafte · and with the deueles miʒte,   120
  Demonium habes, etc.
'Thanne ar ʒe cherles,' quod Iesus · 'and ʒowre children bothe,
And Sathan ʒowre saueoure · ʒow-selue now ʒe witnessen.
For I haue saued ʒow-self,' seith Cryst · 'and ʒowre sones after,

---

  B. 96. fonge WO; fonde LCRB. 99. *secundum—tuum* is in B only.
107. if WCROBY; of L. felle CBY; fel O; fille W; fulle LR. 110.
infirmis O; the rest *in*'. 112. it WROB; LC *om*. 117. seyne L; *see last line.* 121. LWCY *corruptly have* ich *for* ihc (=iesus).

C. PASSUS XIX. 127–153. 487

Til *plenitudo temporis* · tyme ycome were,
That Elde felde efte that frut · other fulle to be rype, 128
That Iesus sholde Iuste ther-fore · in Iugement of armes,
Who sholde fecche this frut · the feend other Iesus self.
The maide myldeliche tho · the messager hue answerede,
And saide hendyliche to him · 'loo, me, hus handmayde, 132
For to worchen hus wil · with-oute eny synne;
    Ecce ancilla domini, fiat michi secundum verbum tuum,' etc.
And in the wombe of that wenche · he was fourty wokes,
And man by-cam of that mayde · to saue mankynde,
Byg and abydynge · and bold in hus barn-hede, 136
To hauen fouhten with the feende · ar ful tyme come.
Ac *Liberum-Arbitrium* · leche-crafte hym tauhte,
Til *plenitudo temporis* · hih tyme a-prochede,
That suche a surgeyn setthen · yseye was ther neuere, 140
Ne non so faithfol fysician; · for, alle that hym bysouhte,
He lechede hem of here langoure · lazars and blynde bothe;
    Ceci uident, claudi ambulant, leprosi mundantur:
And comune wymmen conuertede · and clansede hem of synne.

And he lyft vp Lazar · that lay in hus tombe, 144
Quatriduanus cold · quyke dude hym rome.
Ac er he made that miracle · *mestus cepit esse,*
And wepte water with hus eyen · the whi witen fewe.
Ac thoo that seyen that selcouth · seyden that tyme, 148
That he was god other godes sone · for that grete wonder.
And somme Iewes seiden · with sorcerie he wrouhte,
And thorwe the myghte of Mahon · and thorw mysbyleyue;
    Demonium habes.
'Thanne Sathan is ʒoure sauyour,' quath Iesus · 'and hath saued
    ʒow ofte; 152
Ac ich sauede ʒow sondry tymes · and also ich fedde ʒow

C. 127. ycome ETG; come P.   128. rype MFGT; rypy PE.   129.
in M; and PF; & by FG; & be in T.   133. *fiat—tuum* is in F only.
141. hym EMFGT; P *om.*   147. whiten P.   152. saveyour P. sauede P.
153. and MFTG; PE *om.*

ȝowre bodyes, ȝowre bestes · and blynde men holpen, 124
And fedde ȝow with fisshes · and with fyue loues,
And left baskettes ful of broke mete · bere awey who so wolde ;—'
And mysseide the Iewes manliche · and manaced hem to bete,
And knokked on hem with a corde · and caste adown her stalles,
That in cherche chaffareden · or chaungeden any moneye, 129
And seyde it in siȝte of hem alle · so that alle herden,
'I shal ouertourne this temple · and adown throwe,
And in thre dayes after · edifye it newe, 132
And make it as moche other more · in alle manere poyntes,
As euere it was, and as wyde · wher-fore I hote ȝow,
Of preyeres and of parfitnesse · this place that ȝe callen;
    Domus mea domus oracionis vocabitur.'
Enuye and yuel wille · was in the Iewes; 136
Thei casten and contreueden · to kulle hym whan thei miȝte,
Vche daye after other · 'theire tyme thei awaited.
Til it bifel on a Fryday · a litel bifore Paske,
The Thorsday byfore · there he made his maundee, 140
Sittyng atte sopere · he seide thise wordes—
'I am solde thorw one of ȝow · he shal the tyme rewe
That euere he his saueoure solde · for syluer or elles.'
    Iudas Iangeled there-aȝein · ac Iesus hym tolde, 144
It was hym-self sothely · and seide, '*tu dicis.*'
Thanne went forth that wikked man · and with the Iewes mette,
And tolde hem a tokne · how to knowe with Iesus,
And which tokne to this day · to moche is y-vsed, 148
That is, kissyng and faire contenaunce · and vnkynde wille;
And so was with Iudas tho · that Iesus bytrayed.
'*Aue, raby,*' quod that ribaude · and riȝt to hym he ȝede,
And kiste hym, to be cauȝt there-by · and kulled of the Iewes.
Thanne Iesus to Iudas · and to the Iewes seyde, 153
'Falsenesse I fynde · in thi faire speche,
And gyle in thi gladde chere · and galle is in thi lawghynge.
Thow shalt be myroure to manye · men to deceyue, 156
Ac the wors and thi wikkednesse · shal worth vpon thiselue;
    *Necesse est vt veniant scandala; ve homini illi per quem
    scandalum venit!*
Thow I bi tresoun be ytake · at ȝowre owne wille,

B. 139. bifor L.   145. hym-self WCROB; hym L.

With fisshes and with fyf loues · fyfe thousend at ones,
And ther-of lefte baskettes · ful of broke mete,
Broke bred, to beren hit · a-weye hoo so wolde. 156
Vnkynde and vnknowing!' quath Crist · and with a rop smot hem,
And ouer-turnede in the temple · here tables and here stalles,
And drof hem out alle · that ther bowten and solde,
    Eiecit ementes et vendentes de templo, etc.
And seide, 'this is an hous · of orisouns and of holynesse, 160
And whenne that my wil is · ich wol hit ouer-throwe,
And er thre dayes after · edefye hit newe;'
    Intra triduum reedificabo illud.
The Iewes tolden the Iustice · how that Iesus seyde; 163
Ac the ouerturnyng of the temple · by-tokned the resureccion.
Enuye and vuel will · ȝorn in the Iewes,
And porsuede hym pryueliche · and for pans hym bouhte,
    Ne forte tumultus fieret in populo,
Of Iudas the Iewe · Iesus owene disciple.
This by-fil on a Fryday · a litel by-fore Paske, 168
That Iudas and Iewes · Iesus thei mette.

'*Aue, rabbi,*' quath that ribaud · and right til hym he ȝede,.
And custe Iesus, to be knowe ther-by · and kauht of the Iewes.
Thanne Iesus to Iudas · and to the Iewes seyde, 172
'Falsnesse ich fynde · in thy faire speche,
And kene care in thy cossyngs · and combraunce to thiselue.
Thow shalt be myrour to menye · men to deceyue;
Wo to hem that thy wiles vsen · to the worldes ende! 176
    Ve homini illi per quem scandalum uenit.
Sitthe ich by treson am take · and to ȝoure wille, Iewes,

C. 159. *Eiecit,* &c. is in F only.   161. wol EG; wolde PT.   162. *Intra —illud* is in F only.   166. hym T; him MFI; hem PE.   171. kauhte P. 174. cossyns PE. þiselue EFT; þyselue IG; þe selue P.   176. wordles PG. 177. wille GT; wil F; wiles I; PE *om.*

Suffreth my postles in pays · and in pees gange.'
On a Thoresday in thesternesse · thus was he taken   160
Thorw Iudas and Iewes · Iesus was his name;
That on the Fryday folwynge · for mankynde sake
Iusted in Ierusalem · a Ioye to vs alle.
On crosse vpon Caluarye · Cryst toke the bataille,   164
Aȝeines deth and the deuel · destruyed her botheres myȝtes,
Deyde, and deth fordid · and daye of nyȝte made.
And I awaked there-with · and wyped myne eyghen,
And after Piers the Plowman · pryed and stared.   168
Estwarde and westwarde · I awayted after faste,
And ȝede forth as an ydiote · in contre to aspye
After Pieres the Plowman; · many a place I souȝte.
And thanne mette I with a man · a Mydlenten Sondaye,   172
As hore as an hawethorne · and Abraham he hiȝte.
I frayned hym first · fram whennes he come,
And of whennes he were · and whider that he thouȝte.

'I am Feith,' quod that freke · 'it falleth nouȝte to lye,   176
And of Abrahames hous · an heraud of armes.
I seke after a segge · that I seigh ones,
A ful bolde bacheler · I knewe hym by his blasen.'
'What bereth that buirn?' quod I tho · 'so blisse the bityde!'
'Thre leodes in o lith · non lenger than other,   181
Of one mochel and myȝte · in mesure and in lengthe;
That one doth, alle doth · and eche doth by his one.
The firste hath miȝte and maiestee · maker of alle thinges;   184
Pater is his propre name · a persone by hym-selue.
The secounde of that sire is · sothfastnesse, *Filius*,
Wardeyne of that witte hath · was euere with-oute gynnynge.
The thridde hatte the Holygoost · a persone by hym-selue,   188
The liȝte of alle that lyf hath · a londe and a watre,
Confortoure of creatures · of hym cometh al blisse.
So thre bilongeth for a lorde · that lordeship claymeth,
Myȝte, and a mene · to knowe his owne myȝte,   192
Of hym and of his seruaunt · and what thei suffre bothe.
So god that gynnyng hadde neure · but tho hym good thouȝte,
Sent forth his sone · as for seruaunt that tyme,
To occupien hym here · til issue were spronge,   196
That is, children of charite · and holicherche the moder.
Patriarkes and prophetes · and aposteles were the chyldren,

Suffreth myne apostles in pees · and in pees gangen;'
    Sinite hos abire, etc.
Thus Iewes to the Iustices · Iesus thei ladden.—
With muche noyse that nyght · ner frentik ich awakede,   180
In inwit and in alle wittes · after *Liberum-Arbitrium*
Ich waitede wyterly, ac ne wiste · whider he wente,
And thanne mette ich with a man · on Mydlentens Soneday,
As hor as an hawethorn · and Abraam he hihte.   184
'Of whennes art thow?' quath ich · and hendeliche hym grette.
'Ich am with faith,' quath that freek · 'hit falleth nat me to lye,
An heraude of armes · er eny lawe were.'
'What is hus conysaunce,' quath ich · 'in hus cote-armure?'   188
'Thre persones in o pensel,' quath he · 'departable from other;
O speche and o spirit · spryngeth out of alle,
Of o wit, of on wil · were neuere a-twynne;
And sondry to seo vpon · *solus deus* he hoteth.'   192
'Siththen thei ben surlepes,' quath ich · 'thei han sondry names.'
'That is soth,' saide he · 'the syre hatte *Pater*;
And the secunde is a sone · of the syre, *Filius*;
The thridde is that halt al · a thyng by hym-selue,   196
Holigost is hus name · and he is in alle.'
'This is merk thyng for me,' quath ich · 'and for meny other,
How o lord myghte lyue a thre · ich leyue hit nat,' ich seyde.

'Muse not to muche ther-on,' quath Faith · 'tyl thow more
    knowe,   200
Ac looke thow leyue hit leelly · al thy lyf-tyme,
That thre by-longeth to on lorde · that lygaunce cleymeth,
Mighte, and a mene · to seo hus owen mighte,   203
Of hym-self and of hus seruaunt · and what suffreth hem bothe.
God that gynnynge hadde neuere · bote tho hym gode thouhte,
Sente forth hus sone · as for seruaunt that tyme,
To okupien hym here · til issue were spronge,   207
The whiche aren children of charite · and holichurche the moder.
Patriarkes and prophetes · and apostles were the children;

C. 178. *Sinite—&c.* is in F only.   182. whider MFIT; weder P.   185. art MIFT; ert PEG.   187. And (*for* An) P.   193. surlepees (*for* surlepes) PE; surlep*us* F; surlepis T.   198. meerk P.   203. a MFTG; P *om.*   204. what MIFTG; PE *om.*

And Cryst and Crystenedome · and Crystene holycherche.
In menynge that man moste · on o god bileue,   200
And there hym lyked and loued · in thre persones hym shewed.
   And that it may be so and soth · manhode it sheweth,
Wedloke and widwehode · with virgynyte ynempned,
In toknynge of the Trinite · was taken oute of o man.   204
Adam owre aller fader · Eue was of hym-selue,
And the issue that thei hadde · it was of hem bothe,
And either is otheres Ioye · in thre sondry persones,
And in heuene and here · one syngulere name;   208
And thus is mankynde or manhede · of matrimoigne yspronge,
And bitokneth the Trinite · and trewe bileue.
Miȝte is matrimoigne · that multiplieth the erthe,
And bitokneth trewly · telle if I dorste,   212
Hym that firste fourmed al · the fader of heuene.
The sone, if I it durst seye · resembleth wel the wydwe,
   Deus meus, deus meus, vt quid dereliquisti me?
That is, creatour wex creature · to knowe what was bothe;
As widwe with-oute wedloke · was neure ȝete yseye,   216
Na more myȝte god be man · but if he moder hadde;
So wydwe with-oute wedloke · may nouȝte wel stande,
Ne matrimoigne with-oute moillerye · is nouȝt moche to preyse;
   Maledictus homo qui non reliquit semen in Israel, etc.
Thus in thre persones · is perfitliche manhede,   220
That is, man and his make · and moillere her children,
And is nouȝt but gendre of o generacioun · bifor Iesu Cryst in heuene,
So is the Fader forth with the Sone · and fre wille of bothe;
   Spiritus procedens a patre et filio;
Which is the Holygoste of alle · and alle is but o god.   224

B. 209. þus WCOBY; þis L.   213. Hym WO; He LCRBY.

And Crist and Cristendome · and Cristene holichurche
By-tokeneth the Trinite · and trewe by-leyue.
O god almyghty · that man made and wrouhte, 212
Semblable to hym-self · er eny synne were,
A thre he is ther he is · and hereof bereth wittnesse
The werkes that hym-self wrouhte · and this worlde bothe;
    *Celi enarrant gloriam dei, et opera manuum eius annunciat
       firmamentum.*
That he is thre persones departable · ich proue hit by man-
    kynde, 216
And o god almyghty · yf alle men beo of Adam.
Eue was of Adam · and out of hym ydrawe,
And Abel of hem bothe · and alle thre o kynde;
Ac these thre that ich carpe of · Adam, and Eue, 220
And Abel, here issue · aren bote on in man-hede.
Matrimonie with-oute moillere · is nat muche to preyse,
The bible bereth witnesse · a book of the olde lawe,
That a-corsed alle couples · that no kynde forth brouhte;
    Maledictus sit homo qui non reliquit semen in israel. 224
And a man with-oute a make · myghte nat wel of kynde
Multeplie, ne more-ouer · with-oute a make louye,
Ne with-oute a sowere be suche seede · this we seen alle.
Now go we to god-hede; · in god, Fader of heuene, 228
Was the Sone in hym-selue · in a *simile,* as Eue
Was, whanne god wolde · out of the wye y-drawe.
And as Abel of Adam · and of hus wif Eue
Sprang forth and spak · a spire of hem tweyne, 232
So out of the Syre and of the Sone · the *Seynt Espirit* of bothe
Ys, and ay was · and worth with-outen ende.
And as thre persones palpable · is pureliche bote o man-kynde,
The whiche is man and hus make · and moillere-is issue, 236
So is god godes sone · in thre persones the Trinite.
In matrimonie aren thre · and of o man cam alle thre,
And to godhede goth thre · and of o god is alle thre;
Loo, treys encountre treys,' quath he · 'in godhede and in man-
    hede.' 240

    C. 211. trywe P.   220. Ac M; And IFTG; As PE.   221. here EITG;
heer P; her F.   225. welle P.   228. go we TG; gowe I; goo wee P.
230. wye EG; wiȝ T; wy F; weye P.   232. spire EFT; spir P. tweyene P.
234. was T; weren PEMFG.

Thus in a somer I hym seigh · as I satte in my porche;

I ros vp and reuerenced hym · and ri3t faire hym grette;
Thre men to my sy3te · I made wel at ese,
Wesche her feet and wyped hem · and afterward thei eten   228
Calues flesshe and cakebrede · and knewe what I thou3te;
Ful trewe tokenes bitwene vs is · to telle whan me lyketh.
Firste he fonded me · if I loued bettere
Hym, or Ysaak myn ayre · the which he hi3te me kulle.   232
He wiste my wille by hym · he wil me it allowe,
I am ful syker in soule ther-of · and my sone bothe.
I circumcised my sone   sitthen for his sake;
My-self and my meyne · and alle that male were   236
Bledden blode for that lordes loue · and hope to blisse the tyme.
Myn affiaunce and my faith · is ferme in this bilieue;
For hym-self bihi3te to me · and to myne issue bothe
Londe and lordship · and lyf with-outen ende;   240
To me and to myn issue · more 3ete he me graunted,
Mercy for owre mysdedes · as many tyme as we asken;
    Quam olim Abrahe promisisti, et semini eius.
And sith he sent me to seye · I shoulde do sacrifise,
And done hym worshipe with bred · and with wyn bothe,   244
And called me the fote of his faith · his folke forto saue,
And defende hem fro the fende · folke that on me leueden.
Thus haue I ben his heraude · here and in helle,
And conforted many a careful · that after his comynge wayten.
And thus I seke hym,' he seide · 'for I herde seyne late   249
Of a barne that baptised hym · Iohan Baptiste was his name,
That to patriarkes and to prophetes · and to other peple in derknesse
Seyde that he seigh here · that sholde saue vs alle;   252
    Ecce agnus dei, etc.'
I hadde wonder of his wordes · and of his wyde clothes;
For in his bosome he bar a thyng · that he blissed euere.
And I loked on his lappe · a lazar lay there-inne

B. 249. herde WCROB; L *om.*

'Hauest thow seyen this?' ich seide · 'alle thre, and o god?'
'In a somer ich seyh hym,' quath he · 'as ich sat in my porche,
Where god cam goynge a-thre · ryght by my gate;
    Tres uidit et unum adorauit.
Ich ros vp and reuerencede god · and ryght fayre hym grette,
Wesh here feet, and wypede hem · and after thei eten,   244
And what ich thouhte and my wyf · he ous wel tolde.
He by-hihte ous issue and heir · and in oure olde age,
Ful trewe tokne by-twyne ous is · what tyme that ich mette hym;
How he fondede me ferst · my faire sone Ysaac,   249
To make sacrifice of hym · he het me, hym to honoure.
Ich with-sat nat hus heste · ich hope and by-leyue
Wher ich walke in this worlde · he wol hit me a-lowe.   252
Ich circumsysede my sone · and al-so, for hus sake,
My-self and my meyne · and alle that maule were
Bledden blod for that lordes loue · ich hope to blesse the tyme.
Myn affiaunce and my feith · is ferm in hus by-leyue;   256
For hym-self seide ich sholde haue · and myn issue bothe
Lond and lordshup ynow · and lyf with-outen ende.
To me and to myn issue · more he by-hihte,
Mercy for oure mysdedes · as meny tymes   260
As we wilnede and wolde · with mouth and herte asken.
And sitthen he sende me to sayn · and seide that ich sholde
Worshupen hym with wyn · and with bred bothe
At ones on an auter · in worshup of the Trinite,   264
And make sacrifice so · som-what hit by-tokneth;
Ich leyue that thilke lorde thenke · a newe lawe to make;
    Fiet unum ouile et unus pastor.
Thus haue ich beo hus heraude · her and in helle,   267
And comforted menye carful there · that after hus comyng loken.
For-thi ich seke him,' he seide · 'for seynt Iohan the baptist
Seide that he seih hym her · that sholde saue ous alle;
    Ecce agnus dei qui tollit peccata mundi.'
Thenne hadde ich wonder of hus wordes · and of hus wide
    clothes,
For in hus bosom he bar a thyng · and that he blessede ofte.   272
And ich loked in hus lappe · a lazar lay ther-ynne,

C. 248. mette EFG; mete PT.   252. wordle P.   256. in IFT; PE *om.*
270. saue IFTG; ioye PE.   *qui—mundi* is in F only.

Amonges patriarkes and profetes · pleyande togyderes.   256
'What awaytestow?' quod he · 'and what woldestow haue?'
'I wolde wyte,' quod I tho · 'what is in ȝowre lappe?'
'Loo!' quod he, and lete me se · 'lorde, mercy!' I seide,
'This is a present of moche prys · what prynce shal it haue?'
'It is a preciouse present,' quod he · 'ac the pouke it hath attached,   261
And me there-myde,' quod that man · 'may no wedde vs quite,
Ne no buyrn be owre borwgh · ne bryng vs fram his daungere;
Oute of the poukes pondfolde · no meynprise may vs fecche,
Tyl he come that I carpe of · Cryst is his name,   265
That shal delyure vs some daye · out of the deueles powere,
And bettere wedde for vs legge · than we ben alle worthy,
That is, lyf for lyf · or ligge thus euere   268
Lollynge in my lappe · tyl such a lorde vs fecche.'
'Allas!' I seyde, 'that synne · so longe shal lette
The myȝte of goddes mercy · that myȝt vs alle amende!'
I wepte for his wordes · with that sawe I an other   272
Rapelich renne forth; · the riȝte waye he went.
I affrayned hym fyrste · fram whennes he come,
And what he hiȝte and whider he wolde · and wightlich he tolde.

B. 260. a WCROB; L *om*.

With patriarkes and prophetes · pleiynge to-gederes.
'What waytest thow,' quath Faith · 'and what woldest thou haue?'
'Ich wolde wyte,' quath ich tho · 'what is in thy lappe?'   276
'Loo!' quath he, and leet me seo · 'lord, mercy!' ich seide,
'This is a present of muche prys · what pryns shal hit haue?'
'Hit is a preciouse present,' quath he · 'ac the pouke hit hath attached,
And me ther-with,' quath the wye · 'may no wed ous quite, 280
Ne no bern beo oure borghe · ne brynge ous out of daunger,
Fro the poukes poundfalde · no maynprise may ous fecche,
Til he come that ich carpe of · Crist is hus name,
That shal delyuery ous som day · out of the deueles powere, 284
And betere wed for ous wagen · than alle we beon worthi,
And that is, lif for lyf · other ligge thus euere,
Lollynge in my lappe thus · til such a lord ous fecche.'
'Alas!' ich seide, 'that synne · so longe shal lette   288
The myght of godes mercy · that myghte ous alle amende!'
And wepte for hus wordes; · with that ich seyh an other
Rappliche renne · the righte wey we wente;
And ich fraynede hym furst · fro whennes he come,   292
What he hihte, and whider he wolde · and wyghtliche he ous tolde.

Hic explicit passus secundus de Dobet.

C. 275. faiht P.   279. attachede P.   287. Lollynge IT; Longynge PEFG.   293. whider IT; whed*ur* F, whod*ere* E; woder P.

PASSUS XVII.

Passus xvij^{us}, *et secundus de Do-bet.*

'I AM *Spes*,' quod he, 'a spye · and spire after a kny3te,
That toke me a maundement · vpon the mounte of Synay,
To reule alle rewmes with ; · I bere the writte here.'

'Is it asseled?' I seyde · 'may men se thi lettres?'   4
'Nay,' he sayde, 'I seke hym · that hath the sele to kepe ;
And that is, crosse and Crystenedome · and Cryst there-on to hange.

And whan it is asseled so · I wote wel the sothe,
That Lucyferes lordeship · laste shal no lenger.'   8
'Late se thi lettres,' quod I · 'we mi3te the lawe knowe.'
Thanne plokked he forth a patent · a pece of an harde roche,
Wher-on were writen two wordes · on this wyse y-glosed,
 Dilige deum et proximum tuum, etc.
This was the tixte trewly · I toke ful gode 3eme ;   12
The glose was gloriousely writen · with a gilte penne,
 In hijs duobus mandatis tota lex pendet et prophetia.
'Ben here alle thi lordes lawes ?' quod I · '3e, leue me wel,'
 he seyde,
'And who so worcheth after this writte · I wil vndertaken,
Shal neuere deuel hym dere · ne deth in soule greue.   16
For though I seye it my-self · I haue saued with this charme
Of men and of wommen · many score thousandes.'
'He seith soth,' seyde this heraud · 'I haue yfounde it ofte ;
Lo here in my lappe · that leued on that charme,   20

Iosue and Iudith · and Iudas Macabeus,
3e, and sexty thousande bisyde forth · that ben nou3t seyen
 here.'

B. 11. were WCBY; weren O; was LR.   14. Ben WCBY; Been O;
Is LR.

PASSUS XX.

Hic incipit passus tercius de Dobet.

'ICH am *Spes*, a spye,' quath he · 'and spire after a knyght,
That tooke me a maundement · vp-on the mounte of Synay,
To ruele alle reames ther-with · in right and in reison.
Loo, here the lettere,' quath he · 'in Latyn and in Ebrew,   4
That ich seye is sothe · seo ho so lyketh.'
'Ys hit a-seled?' ich seyde · 'may men seo the letteres?'
'Nay,' he seyde, 'ich seke hym · that hath the seel to kepe,
The whiche is Criste and Cristendome · and a croys ther-on to
　　honge.   8
Were hit ther-with a-seeled · ich wote wel the sothe,
That Lucifers lordshup · ligge sholde ful lowe.'
'Leet se thi letteres,' quath ich · 'we myghte the lawe knowe.'
He plyghte forth a patente · a pece of an harde roche,   12
Wher-on was write two wordes · in this wise glosede;
　　Dilige deum et proximum tuum.
This was the tyxt treweliche · ich toke ful good gome ;
The glose gloryousliche was wryte · wyth a gylt penne ;
　　In his duobus mandatis pendet tota lex et prophete.
'Ys her al thy lordes lettere?' quath ich · '3e, leue me,' he
　　sayde,   16
'And ho so worcheth after this write · ich wol vnder-take,
Shal neuere deouel hym dere · ne deth in soule greue.
For thauh ich seye hit my-self · ich haue saued with this charme
Of men and of wymmen · meny score thousand.'   20
'He seith soth,' seide Faith · 'ich haue founde hit trewe.
Loo, her in my lappe,' quath Faith · 'that leyuede vp-on the
　　lettere,
Bothe Iosue and Iudith · and Iudas Makabeus,
And sixe thousand mo,' quath Faith · 'ich can nat seye here
　　names.'   24

C. 1. a spye IG ; a spie FT ; PE *om.*　spire T ; spere I ; spirr P.　3. in
(2) EIFT ; PG *om.*　6. a-selede P.　13. two ET ; to PFG.　*tuum* T ;
PEIG *om.*　14. treweliche P.　15. *&〰 prophete* EF ; PITG *om.*　16.
leue me he EIT ; leyf he me P.　24. seye F ; sei3e T ; seyn I ; telle PE.

'ȝowre wordes aren wonderful,' quod I tho · 'which of ȝow
   is trewest,
And lelest to leue on · for lyf and for soule?   24
Abraham seith that he seigh · holy the Trinite,
Thre persones in parcelles · departable fro other,
And alle thre but o god · thus Abraham me tauȝte,
And hath saued that bileued so · and sory for her synnes,   28
He can nouȝte segge the somme · and some aren in his lappe.
What neded it thanne · a newe lawe to bigynne,
Sith the fyrst sufficeth · to sauacioun and to blisse?   31
And now cometh *Spes*, and speketh · that hath aspied the lawe,
And telleth nouȝte of the Trinitee · that toke hym his lettres,
'To byleue and louye · in o lorde almyȝty,
And sitthe riȝt as my-self · so louye alle peple.'
The gome that goth with o staf · he semeth in gretter hele   36
Than he that goth with two staues · to syȝte of vs alle.
And riȝte so, by the rode! · resoun me sheweth,
It is lyȝter to lewed men · a lessoun to knowe,
Than for to techen hem two · and to harde to lerne the leest!
It is ful harde for any man · on Abraham byleue,   41
And welawey worse ȝit · for to loue a shrewe!
It is liȝter to leue · in thre louely persones
Than for to louye and leue · as wel lorelles as lele.   44
Go thi gate,' quod I to *Spes* · 'so me god helpe!
Tho that lerneth thi lawe · wil litel while vsen it!"
    And as we wenten thus in the weye · wordyng togyderes,
Thanne seye we a Samaritan · sittende on a mule,   48
Rydynge ful rapely · the riȝt weye we ȝeden,
Comynge fro a cuntre · that men called Ierico ;
To a Iustes in Iherusalem · he chaced awey faste.
Bothe the heraud and Hope · and he mette at ones   52
Where a man was wounded · and with theues taken.
He myȝte neither steppe ne stonde · ne stere fote ne handes,
Ne helpe hym-self sothely · for semiuyf he semed,
And as naked as a nedle · and none helpe aboute hym.   56
    Feith had first siȝte of hym · ac he flegh on syde,
And nolde nouȝt neighen hym · by nyne londes lengthe.
    Hope cam hippyng after · that hadde so ybosted,

'3oure wordes aren wonderful,' quath ich · 'wher eny of 3ow be
  trewe
And leel to be-leyuen on · for body other for soule?
Abraam seith that he seih · holiche the Trinite,
Thre persones parcel-mele · departable from other,   28
And alle thre bote o god; · thus Abraam bereth wittnesse,
And ysauede that by-leyueth so · and soty for here synnes,
He can no certayn summe telle · and somme aren in hus lappe.
What neodeth hit thanne · a newe lawe to brynge,   32
Sutthe the furste suffisede · so by-leyue and be ysaued?
And now cometh her this *Spes* · and hath aspied the lawe,
That of the Trinite ne telleth · ne taketh mo persones
To god-hede, bote o god · and o god almyghty,   36
The whiche alle men aren holde · ouere alle thyng to honoure;
And sitthe to loue and to leue · for that lordes sake
Alle manere of men · as muche as ous self.
And for to louye and to leyue · in o lord almyghty.   40
Hit is lyght for lewede · and for lerede bothe;
Ac for to by-leyue in o lorde · that lyueth in thre persones,
And lereth that we louye sholde · as wel lyeres as leele—
Go thy gat,' quath ich to *Spes* · 'so me god helpe,   44
Tho that leorneth thi lawe · wolle litel while hit vsen!'
  And as we wente in the way · thus wordyng of this matere,
Then seih we a Samaritan · cam syttynge on a mule,
Rydynge ful raply · the ryght way that we wente,   48
Comynge fram a contreie · that men callide Ierico,
To Iusten in Ierusalem · he Iacede awey ful faste.
Bothe Abraam and *Spes* · and he metten to-gederes
In a wilde wildernesse · wher theoues hadden bounde   52
A man, as me tho thouhte · to muche care thei brouhte.
For he ne myghte steppe ne stande · ne stere fot ne hondes,
Ne helpe hym-selue sothliche · for *semiuiuus* he semede,
And naked as a neelde · and non help aboute hym.   56
  Faith on hym hadde furst a sight · ac he fleih a-syde,
And wolde nat neyhle hym · by nyne londes lengthe.
  Hope cam hippyng after · that hadde so ybosted

C. 25. trywe P.   26. And al P; *but* EIFT *om.* al.   32. hit G; it IFT;
PE *om.*   33. ysauede P.   39. muche MFT; meche P.   44. to EMIFTG;
þo P.   46. wordyng of IMFTG; wondrynge in P.   51. and MIFTG;
adde (*sic*) P.

How he with Moyses maundement · hadde many men y-holpe;
Ac whan he hadde si3te of that segge · a-syde he gan hym drawe,
Dredfully, by this day! as duk · doth fram the faucoun.
    Ac so sone so the Samaritan · hadde si3te of this lede,
He li3te adown of lyard · and ladde hym in his hande,   64
And to the wye he went · his woundes to biholde,
And parceyued bi his pous · he was in peril to deye,
And but-if he hadde recourere the rather · that rise shulde he neure ;
And breyde to his boteles · and bothe he atamede;   68
Wyth wyn and with oyle · his woundes he wasshed,
Enbawmed hym and bonde his hed · and in his lappe hym layde,
And ladde hym so forth on lyard · to *lex-christi*, a graunge,
Wel six myle or seuene · biside the newe market;   72
Herberwed hym at an hostrye · and to the hostellere called,
And sayde, 'haue, kepe this man · til I come fro the Iustes,
And lo here syluer,' he seyde · 'for salue to his woundes.'
And he toke hym two pans · to lyflode as it were,   76
And seide, ' what he speneth more · I make the good here-after;
For I may nou3t lette,' quod that leode · and lyarde he bistrydeth,
And raped hym to-Iherusalem-ward · the ri3te waye to ryde.
    Faith folweth after faste · and fonded to mete hym,   80
And *Spes* spaklich hym spedde · spede if he my3te,
To ouertake hym and talke to hym · ar thei to toun come.
And whan I sey3 this, I soiourned nou3te · but shope me to renne,
And suwed that Samaritan · that was so ful of pite,   84
And graunted hym to ben his grome · 'gramercy,' he seyde,
'Ac thi frende and thi felawe,' quod he · 'thow fyndest me at nede.'
And I thanked hym tho · and sith I hym tolde,
How that Feith fleigh awey · and *Spes* his felaw bothe,   88
For si3te of the sorweful man · that robbed was with theues.
' Haue hem excused,' quod he · ' her help may litel auaille ;
May no medcyn on molde · the man to hele brynge,
Neither Feith ne fyn Hope · so festred ben his woundis,   92
With-out the blode of a barn · borne of a mayde.

    B. 68. *This line is in* R *only.*

Hou he with Moyses maundement · hade meny men holpen; 60
And whanne he hadde siht of this sike · asyde he gan drawe,
And dredfulliche with-drow hym · and dorste go no nerre.
Ac as sone so the Samaritan · hadde sighte of that syke,
He alyghte a-non of lyarde · and ladde hym in hus hondes, 64
And to this wye he wente · hus wondes to beholde.
He perceyuede by his pous · he was in peril to deye,
And bote he hadde recouer the rather · that rise sholde he neuere.

He vnbokelede hus boteles · and bothe he a-tamede; 68
With wyn and with oile · hus wondes he can lithe;
Enbaumede hym and bond hus heuede · and on bayarde hym sette,
And ledde hym forth to *lauacrum* · *lex-dei*, a graunge,
Is sixe myle other seuene · by-syde the newe markett, 72
And lefte hym there a lechinge · to lyuen if he myghte;
And took two pans to the hosteler · to take kepe to hym,
'And that goth mor for hus medicine · ich make the good aȝenwarde, 75
For ich may nat lette,' quath that lede · and lyarde he bystrydeth,

And rapede hym to ryde · the righte wey to Ierusalem.
Bothe Faith and hus felawe *Spes* · folweden faste after;

Ac ich suwede the Samaritan · and seide hou thei bothe
Weren afered, and flowen · fro the man y-wonded. 80
'Haue hem excused,' quath the Samaritan · 'here help wolde nat vaille,
Ne medecine vnder molde · the man to hele brynge,
Nother Faith ne fyn Hope · so festered aren hus wondes;
With-oute the blod of a barn · he beoth nouht ysaued, 84
The whiche barn mot neodes · be bore of a mayde,

C. 62. an (*for* and) P.   65. wye E; wy F; wiȝ T; weye P.   holde (*for* beholde) P.   76. ich E; i MIFT; P *om.* þat EIMFT; þe P.   80. y-wondede P·   84. a EIMFTG; þat P.

And be he bathed in that blode · baptised, as it were,
And thanne plastred with penaunce · and passioun of that babi,
He shulde stonde and steppe; · ac stalworth worth he neure,
Tyl he haue eten al the barn · and his blode ydronke.   97
For went neuere wy in this worlde · thorw that wildernesse,
That he ne was robbed or rifled · rode he there or ʒede,
Saue Faith, and his felaw · *Spes*, and my-selue,   100
And thi-self now, and such · as suwen owre werkis.
For outlawes in the wode · and vnder banke lotyeth,
And may vch man se · and gode merke take,
Who is bihynde and who bifore · and who ben on hors,   104
For he halt hym hardyer on horse · than he that is a fote.
For he seigh me, that am Samaritan · suwen Feith and his felaw
On my caple that hatte *Caro* · (of mankynde I toke it),
He was vnhardy, that harlot · and hudde hym *in inferno*.   108
Ac ar this day thre dayes · I dar vndertaken,
That he worth fettred, that feloune · fast with cheynes,
And neure eft greue grome · that goth this ilke gate;
    O mors, ero mors tua, etc.,
And thanne shal Feith be forester here · and in this frith walke,
And kennen out comune men · that knoweth nouʒte the contre,
Which is the weye that ich went · and wherforth to Iherusalem.
And Hope the hostelleres man shal be · there the man lith an
    helynge;
And alle that fieble and faynt be · that Faith may nouʒt teche,
Hope shal lede hem forth with loue · as his lettre telleth,   117
And hostel hem and hele · thorw holicherche bileue,
Tyl I haue salue for alle syke · and thanne shal I retourne,
And come aʒein bi this contree · and confort alle syke   120
That craueth it or coueiteth it · and cryeth there-after.
For the barne was born in Bethleem · that with his blode shal
    saue
Alle that lyueth in faith, and folweth · his felawes techynge.'
    'A! swete syre!' I seyde tho · 'wher shal I byleue,   124
As Feith and his felawe · enfourmed me bothe?
In thre persones departable · that perpetuel were euere,
And alle thre but o god · thus Abraham me tauʒte;—
And Hope afterwarde · he bad me to louye   128

    B. 111. *O—tua* in R only.   124. shal I YCB; I shal LWR.

And with the blod of that barn · embaumed and baptized.
And thauh he steppe and stande · right strong worth he neuere
Til he haue eten al that barn · and hus blod dronken,   88
And ȝut be plastred with pacience · when fondynges hym prykieth—
For wente neuere man this way · that he ne was here rifled,
Saue my-selue sothliche · and suche as ich louede—
And ȝut be-leyue leelly · vpon that litel baby,   92
That his likame schal lechen · atte laste ous alle.'

'A! syre,' ich seide · 'shul nat we by-leyue,
As Faith and hus felawe *Spes* · enformede me bothe,
In thre persones, a parceles · departable from other,   96
And all thre bote o god? · thus Abraham me tauhte.
And Hope afterwarde · of god more me tolde,

C. 86. embaumede P.   baptizede P.   88. heten (*for* eten) P.   89.
plastrede P.   90. man MIT; men PEF.   riflede P.   92. P *ins.* to
before beleyue.   93. schal EMIFG; P *om.*   94. weye (*for* we) P.

O god wyth al my good · and alle gomes after,
Louye hem lyke my-selue · ac owre lorde aboue alle.'
'After Abraham,' quod he · 'that heraud of armes,
Sette faste thi faith · and ferme bileue. 132
And, as Hope hi3te the · I hote that thow louye
Thyn euene-crystene euermore · euene-forth with thiself.
And if conscience carpe there-a3ein · or kynde witte oyther,
Or heretykes with argumentz · thin honde thow hem shewe ;
For god is after an hande · yhere now and knowe it.
   The fader was fyrst, as a fyst · with o fynger foldynge, 138
Tyl hym loued and lest · to vnlosen his fynger,
And profre it forth as with a paume · to what place it sholde.
The paume is purely the hande · and profreth forth the fyngres
To mynystre and to make · that my3te of hande knoweth,
And bitokneth trewly · telle who so liketh,
The holygost of heuene ; · he is as the paume. 144
The fyngres that fre ben · to folde and to serue,
Bitokneth sothly the sone · that sent was til erthe,
That toched and tasted · atte techynge of the paume
Seynt Marie a mayde · and mankynde lau3te ; 148
    Qui conceptus est de spiritu sancto, natus, etc.
The fader is thanne as a fust · with fynger to touche,
    Quia omnia traham ad me ipsum, etc.,
Al that the paume parceyueth · profitable to fele.
Thus ar thei alle but one · as it an hande were,
And thre sondry si3tes · in one shewynge. 152
The paume, for he putteth forth fyngres · and the fust bothe,
Ri3t so redily · reson it sheweth,
How he that is holygoste · sire and sone preueth.
And as the hande halt harde · and al thynge faste 156
Thorw foure fyngres and a thombe · forth with the paume,
Ri3te so the fader and the sone · and seynt spirit the thridde
Halt al the wyde worlde · with-in hem thre,
Bothe welkne and the wynde · water and erthe, 160
Heuene and helle · and al that there is inne.
Thus it is, nedeth no man · to trowe non other,
That thre thinges bilongeth · in owre lorde of heuene,
And aren serelepes by hem-self · asondry were neure, 164

B. 136. hem WR; hym LCR. 148. *natus* CBY; LWR *om.* 164. serelepes Y; serelopes W; *miswritten* serclepes L.

And lerede me for hus loue · to louye al man-kynde,
And hym abouen alle · and hem as my-selue ; 100
Nother lacky ne alose · ne leyue that ther were
Eny wickeder in this worlde · than y were myself,
And most imparfit of alle persones · and pacientliche suffre
Alle manere of men · and thauh ich myghte me venge, 104
I sholde tholie and thonken hem · that me vuel wolde.'
'He seide soth,' quath the Samaritan · 'and so ich rede the also.
And as Abraam the olde · of o god the taughte,
Loke thow louye and by-leyue · al thy lyf-tyme. 108
And if kynde witt carpe her-a3en · and other kynne thouhtes,
Other heretikes with argumens · thyn hond thou hem shewe!
  For god that al by-gan · in gynnynge of the worlde,
Ferde furst as a fust · and 3ut is, as ich leyue, 112
    Mundum pugillo continens,
As with a fust with o fynger · yfolde to-gederes,
Til hym liked and luste · to vnlose the fynger,
And profrede hit forth as with the paume · to what place it sholde.
The paume is the pith of the honde · and profreth forth the fyngres, 116
To mynystre and to make · that myght of hond knoweth,
And bytokneth trewely · telle ho so liketh,
The holy gost of heuene ; · he is as the paume.
The fyngres that freo beo · to folden and to clycchen 120
By-tokneth sothliche the sone · that sente was tyl erthe,
Touchede and tastede · at techynge of the paume,
Seynte Marie, a mayde · and mankynde lauhte ;
    Natus ex Maria uirgine.
The fader is thenne as the fust · with fynger and with paume,
To huden and to holde · as holy writ telleth ; 125
    Omnia traham ad me ipsum.
Al that the fynger gropeth · graythly he grypeth,
Bote yf that that he gropeth · greue the paume.
Thus are thei alle bote on · as hit an hande were, 128
A fust with a fynger · and a foll paume.

C. 102. wordle P.   107. tauhgte P.   117. mynestre P.   118. by-tockneþ P.   120. folden E ; folde MIFTG ; felden P.   121. sotthliche P.
125. wri3th (*for* writ) P.

Namore than myn hande may · meue with-outen fyngeres.
And as my fust is ful honde · yfolde togideres,
So is the fader a ful god · formeour and shepper,
  Tu fabricator omnium, etc.,
And al the my3te myd hym is · in makyng of thynges.　168
  The fyngres fourmen a ful hande · to purtreye or peynten
Keruynge and compassynge · as crafte of the fyngres;
Ri3t so is the sone · the science of the fader,
And ful god, as is the fader · no febler ne no better.　172
  The paume is purelich the hande · hath power bi hymselue,
Otherwyse than the wrythen fuste · or werkmanschip of fyngres;
For the paume hath powere · to put oute alle the ioyntes,
Anu to vnfolde the folden fuste · for hym it bilongeth;　176
And receyue that the fyngres recheth · and refuse bothe,
Whan he feleth the fust · and the fyngres wille.
So is the holygoste god · nother gretter ne lasse
Than is the sire and the sone · and in the same my3te,　180
And alle ar thei but o god · as is myn hande and my fyngres,
Vnfolden or folden · my fuste and myn paume,
Al is but an hande · how so I torne it.
  Ac who is herte in the hande · euene in the myddes,　184
He may receyue ri3t nou3te · resoun it sheweth;
For the fyngres, that folde shulde · and the fuste make,
For peyne of the paume ·· powere hem failleth
To clucche or to clawe · to clyppe or to holde.　188
Were the myddel of myn honde · ymaymed or yperssched,
I shulde receyue ri3te nou3te · of that I reche my3te.
Ac though my thombe and my fyngres · bothe were to-shullen,
And the myddel of myn hande · with-oute male ese,　192
In many kynnes maneres · I my3te my-self helpe,
Bothe meue and amende · though alle my fyngres oke.
Bi this skil, me thynketh · I se an euydence,
That who so synneth in the seynt spirit · assoilled worth he neure,
Noither here ne elles-where · as I herde telle,　197
  Qui peccat in spiritum sanctum, nunquam, etc.,
For he prikketh god as in the paume · that *peccat in spiritum sanctum.*

B. 176—178. for hym—fust and *is in* R *only.*　188. clucche WY; cluche R; clicche L.　195. þynketh WCYB; þynke L; *see* l. 278.　197, 198. *spiritu sancto* LWCYB; *spiritum sanctum* C₂. *nunquam* is in R only.

And as the fust is ful hand · yfolde to-gederes,
So is the fader a ful god · the furste of hem alle.
And as my fust is furst · er ich my fyngers shewe, 132
So is he fader and former · the furste of alle thynges;
 Tu fabricator omnium;
And alle the myghte with hym is · was, and worth euere.
 The fyngres is ful hand · for, failled thei here thombe,
Portrey ne peynte · parfitliche, ich leyue, 136
Sholde no wry3t worche · were he aweye.
Ry3t so, faillede the sone · the syre be ne myghte,
Ne holde, ne helpe · ne hente that he louede;
 Dextre dei tu digitus.
The paume is pureliche the honde · and hath power by hym-self,
Other-wise than the wrythen fust · other werkmanshup of fyngres.
For the paume hath power · to putten oute the Ioyntes,
And to vnfolde the fust · for hym hit bylongeth, 143
And receyuen that the fyngres rechen · and refuse, yf hym liketh,
Al that the fyngres and the fust · felen and touchen,
Beo he greued with here gripe · the holy gost let falle.
Thus is the holigost god · nother grettoure ne lasse 147
Thenne is the syre other the sone · and of the same myghte,
And alle thre nys bote o god · as my hand and my fyngres,
Vnfolde other yfolde · a fust-wyse other elles,
Al is hit bote on hand · hou so y turne hit.
 Ac ho so is hurt in the hand · euene in the myddes, 152
He may receyue ryght nouht · reson hit sheweth;
For the fyngeres that folde sholden · and the fust make,
For peyne of the paume · power hem failleth
To clucche other to clawe · to cluppe other to holde. 156
Were the myddel of myn hand · with-oute mal ese,
In menye kynne manere · ich myghte my-self helpe,
Bothe meue and amende · thauh alle my fyngres oken.
By this *simile,* he seide · 'ich seo an euidence, 160
That ho so synegeth in the *seynt espirit* · asoilled worth he neuere,
Nother her ne elles-wher · as ich herde telle;
 Qui peccat in spiritum sanctum neque remittetur ei, etc.
He priketh god as in the paume · that *peccat in spiritum sanctum.*

C. 130. yfoolde P.   133. an (*for* and) P.   137. wry3th P.   138.
Ry3ght P.   146. greueued P.   155. hem MIFG; hym PET.   161. as-
soillede P.   162. *neque—ei* is in F only.

For god the fader is as a fuste · the sone is as a fynger,   199
The holy goste of heuene · is, as it were, the pawme.
So who so synneth in seynt spirit · it semeth that he greueth
God, that he grypeth with · and wolde his grace quenche.
    And to a torche or a tapre · the Trinitee is lykned;
As wex and a weke · were twyned togideres,   204
And thanne a fyre flaumende · forth oute of bothe;
And as wex and weyke · and hote fyre togyderes
Fostren forth a flaumbe · and a feyre leye,
So doth the sire and the sone · and also *spiritus sanctus*   208
Fostren forth amonges folke · loue and bileue,
That alkyn Crystene · clenseth of synnes.
And as thow seest some tyme · sodeynliche a torche,
The blase there-of yblowe out · ȝet brenneth the weyke,   212
With-oute leye or liȝte · that the macche brenneth,
So is the holygost god · and grace with-oute mercy
To alle vnkynde creatures · that coueite to destruye
Lele loue other lyf · that owre lorde shapte.   216
And as glowande gledes · gladieth nouȝte this werkmen,
That worchen and waken · in wyntres niȝtes,
As doth a kex or a candel · that cauȝte hath fyre and blaseth,
Namore doth sire ne sone · ne seynt spirit togyderes,   220
Graunteth no grace · ne forȝifnesse of synnes,
Til the holi goste gynne · to glowe and to blase.
So that the holygoste · gloweth but as a glede,
Tyl that lele loue · ligge on hym and blowe,   224
And thanne flaumbeth he as fyre · on fader and on *filius*,
And melteth her myȝte in-to mercy · as men may se in wyntre
Ysekeles in eueses · thorw hete of the sonne,
Melteth in a mynut-while · to myst and to watre;   228
So grace of the holygoste · the grete myȝte of the Trinite
Melteth in-to mercy · to mercyable, and to non other.
And as wex with-outen more · on a warme glede
Wil brennen and blasen · be thei to-gyderes,   232
And solacen hem that may se · that sitten in derkenesse,

C. 167. queynche P.   168. likenede P.   169. were twyned I; were tweyned M; were twynnyd T; and warme fur (*by confusion with* l. 171) PEG. 171. and warm fuyr MG; and warme fur*e* I; were twynede P (*see* l. 169).

For the fader is as the fust · the sone is as the fyngres,   164
The holy gost of heuene · he is as the paume.
So ho so synegeth aȝens the *seynte espirit* · hit semeth that he
    greueth
God, ther he gripeth · and wolde hus grace quenche.
    For to a torche other to a taper · the Trinite is likened,   168
As wexe and a weke · were twyned to-gederes,
And fuyr flaumed · forth of hem bothe;
And as wex and weke · and warm fuyr to-gederes
Fostren forth a flaume · and a fayre lye,   172
That serueth these swynkeres · to seo by a nyghtes,
So doth the syre and the sone · and *seynt espirit* to-gederes,
Fostren forth a-mong folke · fyn loue and by-leyue,
That alle kynne Crystene · clanseth of synne.   176
And as thou suxt some tyme · sodenliche, of a torche
The blase beo blowen out · ȝut brenneth the weke,
With-outen lye and lyght · lith fuyr in the macche,
So is the holy gost god · and grace with-oute mercy   180
To alle vnkynde creatures · that coueyten to distruye
Leel lycame, and lif · that oure lorde shupte.
And as glowynge gledes · gladeth nat these workemen
That worchen and waken · in wynteres nyghtes,   184
As doth a kyx other a candele · that cauht hath fuyr, and blaseth,
No more doth the syre ne the sone · ne *seynte espirit* to-gederes
Graunten eny grace · ne for-gyuenesse of synnes,
Til the holy gost by-gynne · to glowen and blase.   188
So that the holy gost · gloweth bote as a glede,
Til that loue and by-leyue · leelliche to hym blowe.
Thenne flammeth he as fuyr · on fader and on *filius*,
And melteth myghte in-to mercy · as we may seo a wynter,
Isykles in euesynges · thorgh hete of the sonne   193
Melteth in a mynt-while · to myst and to water;
So grace of the holy gost · melteth al to mercy,
The grete myghte of the Trinite · to mercyable, and to none othere.
And as wex with-oute more · vpon a warm glede   197
Wol brennen and blasen · beo thei to-gyderes,
And solasen hem that mowe nat seon · syttyng in deorknesse,

---

179. lith IFMTG; lyght P.   183. glades P (*see* l. 189).   192. wey
(*for* we) P.

So wole the fader forȝif • folke of mylde hertes
That reufulliche repenten • and restitucioun make,
In as moche as thei mowen • amenden and payen.   236
And if it suffice nouȝte for assetz • that in suche a wille deyeth,
Mercy for his mekenesse • wil make good the remenaunte.
And as the weyke and fyre • wil make a warme flaumbe
For to myrthe men with • that in merke sitten,   240
So wil Cryst of his curteisye • and men crye hym mercy,
Bothe forȝiue and forȝete • and ȝet bidde for vs
To the fader of heuene • forȝyuenesse to haue.

   Ac hew fyre at a flynte • fowre hundreth wyntre,   244
Bot thow haue towe to take it with • tondre or broches,
Al thi laboure is loste • and al thi longe trauaille ;
For may no fyre flaumbe make • faille it his kynde.
So is the holy gost god • and grace with-outen mercy   248
To alle vnkynde creatures • Cryst hym-self witnesseth,
    Amen dico vobis, nescio vos, etc.
  Be vnkynde to thin euene-cristene • and al that thow canst bidden,
Delen and do penaunce • day and nyȝte euere,
And purchace al the pardoun • of Pampiloun and Rome,   252
And indulgences ynowe • and be *ingratus* to thi kynde,
The holy goste hereth the nouȝt • ne helpe may the by resoun ;
For vnkyndenesse quencheth hym • that he can nouȝte shyne,
Ne brenne ne blase clere • for blowynge of vnkyndenesse. 256
Poule the apostle • preueth whèr I lye,
    Si linguis hominum loquar, etc.
For-thy beth war, ȝe wyse men • that with the worlde deleth,
That riche ben and resoun knoweth • reuleth wel ȝowre soule.
Beth nouȝte vnkynde, I conseille ȝow • to ȝowre euene-crystene.
For many of ȝow riche men • bi my soule, men telleth,   261
Ȝe brenne, but ȝe blaseth nouȝte • that is a blynde bekene ;
    Non omnis qui dicit domine, domine, intrabit, etc.
  Diues deyed dampned • for his vnkyndenesse
Of his mete and his moneye • to men that it neded.   264

B. 258. worlde WCRYB ; wolde L.

C. 203. wile P. deyn P.   204. *From* I ; *also in* EMFTG ; P *omits this line.* 205. P *om.* as.   206. meerk P.   213. PE *ins.* no *before* flamme. 214. þe EMIFTG ; P *om.*   215. wittnesse P.   220. þe IMFTG ; PE *om.*

So wol the fader for-3yuen · folke of mylde hertes,   200
That rufulliche repenten · and restitucion maken,
In as muche as thei mowen · amenden and payen,
And yf hit sufficith nat for a-seth · that in suche wille deyen,
Mercy, for his mekenesse · wil make good the remenant.   204
And as the wicke and the warme fuyr · wol make a fayr flamme
For to murthen men with · that in merke sytten;
So wol Crist, of hus curtesye · and men crye hym mercy,
Bothe for-3euen and for-3uten · and 3ut bydde for ous   208
To the fader of heuene · for-3yuenesse to haue.

Ac hewe fuyr of a flynt · four hundred wynter;
Bote thou haue tache to take hit with · tunder and broches,
Al thy labour is lost · and al thy long trauayl;   212
For may no fuyr flamme make · faille hit hus kynde.
So is the holigost god · and grace with-oute mercy
To alle vnkynde creatures · as Crist hym-self wittnesseth;
  Amen dico uobis, nescio vos.
Beo vnkynde to thyn emcrystene · and al that thow canst bidde,
Dele and do penaunce · day and nyght euere,   217
And porchase al the pardoun · of Paumpelon and of Rome,
And indulgences ynowe · and be ingrat to thy kynde,
The holygost huyreth the nat · ne helpeth the, be thow certayn.
For vnkyndenesse quencheth hym · that he can nat shyne,   221
Ne brenne, ne blase cleer · for blowynge of vnkyndenesse.
Seynt Paul the apostel · proueth wher ich lye;
  Si linguis hominum loquar, etc.
For-thi beoth war, 3e wyse men · that with the worlde deleth,
That ryche beon and reson knowen · reuleth wel 3oure soule.
Beoth nat vnkynde, ich consaile 3ou · to 3oure emcristene.   226
For menye of 3ow ryche men · by my saule, ich lye nat,
3e brenneth, ac 3e blaseth nat · and that is a blynde bekne;
  Non omnis qui dicit michi domine, domine, intrabit in
  regnum celorum.
Mynne 3e nat, riche men · to which a meschaunce   229
That *Dives* deyed, and dampned was · for hus vnkyndenesse
Of hus mete and of hus moneye · to men that hit neodede?

---

221. queyncheþ P. can EIFT; ne can M; P *om.*   223. wer P.   224. wordle P.   227. 3ow IMFTG; PE *om.*   ryke (*for* ryche) P; *see* l. 225.
228. *michi* in F only.   230. was TG; is M; PEI *om.*

Vch a riche I rede · rewarde at hym take,
And gyueth ȝowre good to that god · that grace of ariseth.
For thei that ben vnkynde to his · hope I none other,
But thei dwelle there *Diues* is · dayes with-outen ende. 268
Thus is vnkyndenesse the contrarie · that quencheth, as it were,
The grace of the holy gooste · goddes owne kynde.
For that kynde dothe, vnkynde fordoth · as these cursed theues,
Vnkynde cristene men · for coueityse and enuye, 272
Sleeth a man for his moebles · wyth mouth or wyth handes.
For that the holygoste hath to kepe · tho harlotes destroyeth,
The which is lyf and loue · the leye of mannes bodye.
For euery manere good man · may be likned to a torche, 276
Or elles to a tapre · to reuerence the trinitee;
And who morthereth a good man · me thynketh, by myn inwyt,
He fordoth the leuest lyȝte · that owre lorde loueth.
    Ac ȝut in many mo maneres · men offenden the holy goste;
Ac this is the worste wyse · that any wiȝte myȝte 281

B. 267. þei WCBY; LR *om.*

C. PASSUS XX. 232-263.

ȝut wan he hit nat with wrang · ne with queynte sleythes,   232
Bote ryȝtfulliche, as men rat · al hus rychesse cam hym,
And on hym-self, seith the book · sotelede hou he myghte
Most lordliche lyuen · and leet hus lycame werie
Clothes of most cost · as clerkes bereth wittnesse;   236
    Epulabatur splendide, et induebatur bisso et purpura.
And for he was a nigard · to the neodful poure,
For godes treitour he is tolde · for al hus trewe catel,
And dampned is and dwelleth · with the deuel in helle.
Suththe he with-oute wiles wan · and wel myghte a-temye   240
Lordliche for to lyuen · and likyngliche be clothed,
And is in helle for al that · how wole riche nouthe
Excuse hem that beth vnkynde · and ȝut here catel wonne
With wiles and with luther wittes · and ȝut wollen nat atemye
To gon semliche ne sitte · sith holy writ techeth,   245
That that wikkedliche is wonne · to wasten hit, and to make frendes?
    Facite uobis amicos de mammona iniquitatis.
Eche a riche man, ich rede · reward her-of take,
And ȝeueth ȝoure good to that god · that grace of ariseth.   248
For ȝe that ben vnhende to hyse · hope ȝe none other,
Bote to dwelle ther *Dives* is · dayes with-outen ende.
Thus is vnkyndenesse kid · and aquencheth, as hit were,
The grace of the holygost · godes owene kynde;   252
For that that kynde doth · vnkynde for-doth.
Acorsede theoues, vnkynde Cristene men · for couetise and enuye
Sleeth a man for hus meobles · with mouth other with handes;
For that the holy gost hath to kepe · suche harlotes destruyen,
The whiche is lyf and loue · the lye of mannes body.   257
For euery maner good man · may be lykned to a torche,
Other elles to a taper · to reuerence with the trinite;
And ho so morthereth a good man · me thynketh, by myn in-witt,
He for-doth the light that oure lorde · loketh to haue worsshep of.
    And ȝut in mo maneres · men offendeth the holy gost;   262
Ac this is the worste wise · that eny wight myghte

C. 233. ryȝthfulliche P.   rat EMIT; *miswritten* þat P.   234. soutelede P.
240. whiles (*for* wiles) P.   245. sittþ P.   248. goud P.   251. kid T; PEMFI
om. aqueyncheþ P.   254. vnkende P; *but see* l. 253.   255. Sleehþ P.
meobles EF; mebles MIG; noebles P.   258. lycknede P.   259. to (1) EMFTG;
PI *om.*   260. morþrerþ P. goud P. by EIFG; be MT; in P.   263. whight P.

Synnen aȝein the seynt spirit · assenten to destruye,
For coueityse of any kynnes thinge · that Cryst dere bouȝte.
How myȝte he axe mercy · or any mercy hym helpe,   284
That wykkedlich and willefullich · wolde mercy anynte?
Innocence is nexte god · and nyȝte and day it crieth,
' Veniaunce, veniaunce · forȝiue be it neuere,
That shent vs and shadde owre blode · forshapte vs, as it were;
  Vindica sanguinem iustorum!'
Thus 'veniaunce, veniaunce' · verrey charite asketh;   289
And sith holicherche and charite · chargeth this so sore,
Leue I neure that owre lorde wil loue · that charite lakketh,
Ne haue pite for any preyere · there that he pleyneth.'   292
'I pose I hadde synned so · and shulde now deye,
And now am sory, that so · the seint spirit agulte,
Confesse me, and crye his grace · god, that al made,
And myldliche his mercy axe · myȝte I nouȝte be saued?'   296
'Ȝus,' seide the Samaritan · 'so wel thow myȝte repente,
That riȝtwisnesse thorw repentance · to reuthe myȝte torne.
Ac it is but selden yseye · there sothenesse bereth witnesse,
Any creature that is coupable · afor a kynges iustice,   300
Be raunsoned for his repentaunce · there alle resoun hym dampneth.
For there that partye pursueth · the pele is so huge,
That the kynge may do no mercy · til bothe men acorde,
And eyther haue equite · as holy writ telleth;   304
  Numquam dimittitur peccatum, donec restituatur ablatum.
Thus it fareth bi suche folke · that falsely al her lyues
Euel lyuen and leten nouȝte · til lyf hem forsake;
Drede of desperacion · dryueth a-weye thanne grace,
That mercy in her mynde · may nauȝt thanne falle;   308
Good hope, that helpe shulde · to wanhope torneth—
Nouȝt of the nounpowere of god · that he ne is myȝtful
To amende al that amys is · and his mercy grettere
Than alle owre wykked werkes · as holiwrit telleth,   312
  Misericordia eius super omnia opera eius.

B. 304. *donec* is in Y only; the two words following are supplied from Pass.
v. 279.   307, 308. *These lines are in R only.*

Synegen a-ȝens the *seynt espirit* · assenten to destruye, 264
For couetyse of eny kynne thyng · that Cryst dere boughte.
How myghte he aske mercy · other eny mercy hym defende,
That wikkidliche and wilfulliche · wolde mercy anyente?
Innocence is next god · and nyght and day hit cryeth, 268
'Veniaunce! venȝaunce! · for-ȝeue be hit neuere,
That shende ous and shadde oure blod · for-shupte ous, as hit semede;
  Vindica sanguinem iustorum!'
Thus 'veniaunce! veniaunce!' · verray charite asketh;
And suthen charite, that holychurche is · chargeth this so sore,
Leyue ich neuere that oure lorde · atte laste ende 273
Wol louye that lyf that loue · and leel charite destruyen.'
 'Ich pose ich hadde syneged so,' quath ich · 'and shold nouthe deye,
And now am ich sory that ich so · the *seynt espirit* agulte, 276
Confesse me and crye hus grace · god that al made,
And myldeliche hus mercy aske · myghte ich nat be saued?'
'Ȝus,' seide the Samaritan · 'so thou myghtest repente,
That ryghtwisnesse thorgh repentaunce · to reuthe myghte turne.
Ac hit is bote selde seyn · ther sothnesse bereth wittnesse 281
Eny creature be coupable · by-for a kynges Iustice,
Be yraunsoned for repentaunce · ther al reson hym dampneth.
Ther that partye porsueth · the apeel is so huge, 284
May no kynge mercy graunt · til bothe men a-corden,
That ayther partye haue equite · as holy writt witnesseth;
  Nunquam dimittitur peccatum, etc.
Thus hit fareth by suche folke · that folwen here owene wil,
That vuel lyuen and leten nat · til hem for-sake synne. 288
Drede of desperacion · thenne dryueth a-wey grace,
That mercy in here mynde · may nat thenne falle;
For good hope that hem helpe sholde · to wanhope turneth,
And nat of the nounpower of god · that he nys ful of myghte
To amenden al that amys is · and hus mercy grettour 293
Than alle oure wikkede werkus · as holy writ telleth,
  Misericordia eius super omnia opera eius.

C. 272. P ins. þat *before* charite.   276. PE *ins.* dude *after* so.   PE *ins.* to *before* agulte.   280. tow (*for* to) P.   281. seild P.   283. yraunsende P. 286. equite EITG; a quyte P.   witnesse P.   291. whamhope (*sic*) P. 292. nounpower F; noun-poer I; vnpower PE.

Ac, ar his riȝtwisnesse to reuthe tourne · some restitucioun
    bihoueth;
His sorwe is satisfaccioun · for hym that may nouȝte paye.
  Thre thinges there ben · that doth a man by strengthe
Forto fleen his owne hous · as holywryt sheweth.   316
That one is a wikked wyf · that wil nouȝt be chasted;
Her fiere fleeth fro hyr · for fere of her tonge.
And if his hous be vnhiled · and reyne on his bedde,
He seketh and seketh · til he slepe drye.   320
And whan smoke and smolder · smyt in his syȝte,
It doth hym worse than his wyf · or wete to slepe.
For smoke and smolder · smyteth in his eyen,
Til he be blere-nyed or blynde · and hors in the throte,   324
Cougheth, and curseth · that Cryst gyf hem sorwe
That sholde brynge in better wode · or blowe it til it brende.
  Thise thre that I telle of · ben thus to vnderstonde;
The wyf is owre wikked flesshe · that wil nouȝt be chasted,
For kynde cleueth on hym euere · to contrarie the soule.   329
And thowgh it falle, it fynt skiles · that frelete it made;
And that is liȝtly forȝeuen · and forȝeten bothe,
To man that mercy asketh · and amende thenketh.   332
The reyne that reyneth · there we reste sholde,
Ben sikenesses and sorwes · that we suffren oft,
As Powle the apostle · to the peple tauȝte,
    Virtus in infirmitate perficitur, etc.
And thowgh that men make · moche deol in her angre,   336
And ben inpacient in here penaunce · pure resoun knoweth,
That thei han cause to contrarie · by kynde of her sykenesse;
And liȝtlich owre lorde · at her lyues ende,
Hath mercy on suche men · that so yuel may suffre.   340
Ac the smoke and the smolder · that smyt in owre eyghen,
That is coueityse and vnkyndenesse · that quencheth goddes
    mercy.
For vnkyndenesse is the contrarie · of alkynnes resoun;
For there nys syke ne sori · ne non so moche wrecche,   344
That he ne may louye, and hym lyke · and lene of his herte
Good wille and good worde · bothe wisshen and willen

  B. 323. in WYB; LRC *om.*   330. þat WCRBY; þe L.   337. ben W;
be R; LCYB *om.*   346. Goed (*for* Good) L.

Ac er hus rightwisnesse to reuthe turne · restitucion hit maketh;
As sorwe of herte is satisfaccion · for suche as may nat paye.
  Ac thre thynges ther beoth · that doth a man to sterte   297
Out of his owene hous · as holy writ sheweth.
That on is a wikkede wif · that wol nat be chasted;
Hure fere fleeth fro huere · for fere of huere tounge.   300
And yf hus hous be vnheled · and reyne on hus bedde,
He seketh and seketh · til he slepe drye.
Ac when smoke and smorthre · smyt in hus eyen,
Hit doth hym wors than hus wyf · other wete to slepe.   304
For thorw smoke and smorthre · smerteth hus syghte,
Tyl he be bler-eyed other blynde · and the borre in hus throte,
Koweth and corseth · that Crist ȝyue hym sorwe
That sholde brynge yn bettere wode · other blowe til hit brente.
  These thre that ich telle of · thus beoth to vnderstonde;   309
The wif is oure wikkede fleshe · that wol nat be chasted,
For kynde clyueth on hym euere · to contrarie the soule.
And thauh he falle, he fynt skyles · that frelete hit made;   312
And that is lyghtliche for-ȝyue · and for-ȝute bothe
To man, that mercy asketh · and amende thenketh.
Ac the reyn that reyneth · ther we reste sholde,
Beoth syknesses and other sorwes · that we suffren ofte,   316
As seynt Paul the apostel · in hus pistles techeth,
    Virtus in infirmitate perficitur.
And thauh men maken · muche deol in here angre,
And beo inpacient in here penaunces · pure reson knoweth,
That thei han cause to contrarien · by kynde of here syknesse;
And lightliche oure lorde · at here lyues ende   321
Hath mercy of suche men · that vuel may suffrye.
Ac the smoke and the smorthre · that smyt in oure eyen,
That is couetise and vnkyndenesse · which quencheth godes mercy.
For vnkyndnesse is contrarie · of alle kynne reson;   325
For ther ne is syk ne sory · ne non so muche wrecche,
That he ne may louye, and hym lyke · and lene of hus herte
Good wil, good worde · bothe wusshen and wylnen   328

  C. 299. chastede P.   301. vnhelede P.   reyne EFTG; ryne PI; *see* l. 315.
on EMIFTG; in P.   302. til IFTG; er P.   304. whete P.   306. blereyde P.
308. bryngge P.   310. þat EMG; P *om.*   chastede P.   315. reyneþ EIFT;
ryneþ P.   316. ofte MFT; ouht P.   317. P ins. *Nam* before *Virtus*.
323. smyȝt P.   328. Goude P. goud P. whusshen P.

Alle manere men · mercy and for3ifnesse,
And louye hem liche hym-self · and his lyf amende.— 348
I may no lenger lette,' quod he · and lyarde he pryked,
And went away as wynde · and there-with I awaked.

PASSUS XVIII.

Passus xviij^{us}, et tercius de Dobet.

WOLLEWARD and wete-shoed · went I forth after,
As a reccheles renke · that of no wo reccheth,
And 3ede forth lyke a lorel · al my lyf-tyme,
Tyl I wex wery of the worlde · and wylned eft to slepe, 4
And lened me to a lenten · and longe tyme I slepte;
And of Crystes passioun and penaunce · the peple that of-rau3te,
Reste me there, and rutte faste · tyl *ramis-palmarum;*
Of gerlis and of *gloria laus* · gretly me dremed, 8
And how *osanna* by orgonye · olde folke songen.
One semblable to the Samaritan · and some-del to Piers the Plowman,
Barfote on an asse bakke · botelees cam prykye,
Wyth-oute spores other spere · spakliche he loked, 12
As is the kynde of a kyn3te · that cometh to be dubbed,
To geten hem gylte spores · or galoches ycouped.
Thanne was Faith in a fenestre · and cryde '*a! fili Dauid!*'
As doth an heraude of armes · whan auntrous cometh to iustes.
Olde Iuwes of Ierusalem · for Ioye thei songen, 17
Benedictus qui venit in nomine domini.
Thanne I frayned at Faith · what al that fare be-mente,
And who sholde Iouste in Iherusalem · 'Iesus,' he seyde,
'And fecche that the fende claymeth · Piers fruit the Plowman.'
'Is Piers in this place?' quod I · and he preynte on me, 21
'This Iesus of his gentrice · wole Iuste in Piers armes,
In his helme and in his haberioun · *humana natura;*
That Cryst be nou3t biknowe here · for *consummatus deus,* 24

B. 7. Reste WCOY; Rested LR.   11. prikye WO; prekie B; pryke LC.
16. auntrous RO; aunterous C; Auentrous W; aunt*ur*os L.   18. bemente
RO; bement L.   24. *consumatus* L.

Alle manere of men · mercy and for-ȝeuenesse, 329
And louye hem yliche hym-sylf · that hus lyf a-mende.
Ich may no lenger lette,' quath he · and lyarde he prykede,
And wente away as the wynde · and ther-with ich awakede.

Hic explicit passus tercius de Dobet.

PASSUS XXI.

Hic incipit passus quartus de Dobet.

WO-werie and wetschod · wente ich forth after,
As a recheles renke · that reccheth nat of sorwe,
And ȝeode forth lyke a lorell · al my lyf-tyme,
Til ich wax wery of this worlde · and wilnede efte to slepe, 4
And lenede me til lenten · and longe tyme ich slepte.
Of gurles and of *gloria laus* · gretliche me dremede,
And how *osanna* by orgone · olde folk songe.
On was semblable to the Samaritan · and somdel to Peers Plouhman,
Barfot on an asse bak · bootles cam prykye, 9
With-oute spores other spere · and sprakliche he lokede,
As is the kynde of a knyght · that cometh to be doubed,
To geten hus gilte spores · and galoches y-couped, 12
Then was Faith in a fenestre · and cryde, '*a! filij Dauid!*'
As doth an heraud of armes · when auntrous cometh to Iustes.
Olde Iewes of Ierusalem · for Ioye thei songen,
 Benedictus qui venit in nomine domini.
Thenne ich fraynede at Faith · 'what al that fare by-mente,
And ho sholde Iusten in Ierusalem?' · 'Iesus,' he seide, 17
'And fecche that the feond cleymeth · Peers frut the Plouhman.'
'Ys Peers in this place?' quath ich · and he preynkte vpon me,
'*Liberum-dei-arbitrium*,' quath he · 'for loue hath vndertake 20
That this Iesus of hus gentrise · shal Iouste in Peers armes,
In hus helme and in hus haberion · *humana natura;*
That Crist be nat knowe · for *consummatus deus*,

C. 1. wetschode P. 2. richeles P. 4. to IMFTG; PE *om.* 7. orgone F; orgene IT; orgne PE. folk FTG; men PEM. 12. y couped IMFT; y-coped PG. 14. auntres (*sic*) PEIMG; auntr*us* F; auntro*us* T. 16. fraynnede P. at IMFT; of G; PE *om.* 21. þis ME; þys G; þes P. genterise P. 22. in IMET; PFG *om.* 23. þa (*for* þat) P.

In Piers paltok the Plowman · this priker shal ryde;
For no dynte shal hym dere · as *in deitate patris.*'
'Who shal Iuste with Iesus?' quod I · 'Iuwes or scribes?'
'Nay,' quod he, 'the foule fende · and Fals-dome and Deth. 28
Deth seith he shal fordo · and adown brynge
Al that lyueth or loketh · in londe or in watere.
Lyf seyth that he likth · and leyth his lif to wedde,
That for al that Deth can do · with-in thre dayes, 32
To walke and fecche fro the fende · Piers fruite the Plowman,
And legge it there hym lyketh · and Lucifer bynde,
And forbete and adown brynge · bale and deth for euere:
 O mors, ero mors tua!
 Thanne cam *Pilatus* with moche peple · *sedens pro tribunali*,
To se how doughtilich Deth sholde do · and deme her botheres riȝte.
The Iuwes and the Iustice · aȝeine Iesu thei were, 38
And al her courte on hym cryde · *crucifige* sharpe.
Tho put hym forth a piloure · bifor Pilat, and seyde, 40
'This Iesus of owre Iewes temple · Iaped and dispised,
To fordone it on o day · and in thre dayes after
Edefye it eft newe · (here he stant that seyde it)
And ȝit maken it as moche · in al manere poyntes, 44
Bothe as longe and as large · bi loft and by grounde.'

'*Crucifige*,' quod a cacchepolle · 'I warante hym a wicche!'
'*Tolle, tolle!*' quod an other · and toke of kene thornes,
And bigan of kene thorne · a gerelande to make, 48
And sette it sore on his hed · and seyde in envye,
'*Aue, rabby!*' quod that ribaude · and threw redes at hym,
Nailled hym with thre nailles · naked on the rode,
And poysoun on a pole · thei put vp to his lippes, 52
And bede hym drynke his deth-yuel · his dayes were ydone.
'And ȝif that thow sotil be · help now thi-seluen,
If thow be Cryst, and kynges sone · come downe of the rode;

B. 35. and OY; LWCR *om.*   46. *Crufige* L.   47. o (*for* of) L.

In Peeres plates the Plouhman · this prykiere shal ryde; 24
For no dint shal hym dere · as *in deitate patris.*
'Ho shal Iouste with Iesus,' quath ich · 'Iewes, other scrybes?'
'Nay,' quath Faith, 'bote the feond · and Fals-dom-to-deye.
Deth seith he wol for-do · and a-doun brynge 28
Al that lyueth other loketh · a londe and a watere.
Lyf seith that he lyeth · and hath leyde hus lyf to wedde,
That for al that Deth can do · with-inne thre dayes,
To walke and fecche fro the feonde · Peers frut the Plouhman,
And legge hit ther hym lyketh · and Lucifer bynde, 33
And forbete and bringe adoun · bale and deth for euere;
 O mors, ero mors tua!'
Thenne cam *Pilatus* with muche peuple · *sedens pro tribunali*,
To seo hou douhtiliche Deth sholde do · and deme here beyer ryght.
The Iuwes and the Iustices · a3ens Iesus they were, 37
And alle the court cryede · '*crucifige*' lowde.
Thenne put hym forth a pelour · by-for Pilat, and seyde,
'Thys Iesus of oure Iuwen temple · Iapede and despisede, 40
To for-don hit on a day · and in thre dayes after
Edefien hit efte newe—· her he stant that seyde hit—
And 3ut make hit as muche · in alle manere poyntes,
Bothe as longe and as large · aloft and a-grounde, 44
And as wyde as hit euere was · this we witnessen alle.'
'*Crucifige*,' quath a kachepol · 'he can of wicche-crafte.'
'*Tolle, tolle*,' quath another · and toke of kene thornes,
And by-gan of a grene thorne · a garlaunde to make, 48
And sette hit sore on hus hefd · and suthe seyde in enuye,
'*Aue, rabbi*,' quath that ribaud · and reodes shotte at hus eyen:—
And nailede hym with thre nayles · naked on the rode,
And with a pole poyson · putten to hus lippes, 52
And beden hym drynke, hus deth to lette · and hus dayes lengthen;
And seide, 'yf he sothfast beo · he wol hym-self helpen;
And now, yf thow be Criste · godes sone of heuene,
Come a-doune of this rode · and thenne wol we leyue 56

C. 33. hit MG; it IFT; hym PE.   34. forbete MI; forbite PEFTG. and bringe adoun MFG; adoun and brynge PET.   and (3) MF; PEITG *om.* *ero—tua* EF; *tua ero mors* P.   36. deyme P.   38. lowede P.   39. forth IMFTG; PE *om.*   43. hit MEG; it IFT; P *om.*   45. whitnessen P.   49. on EMIFTG; in P.   50. rabbi M; rabi PITG.   and MEIFTG; a P.   53. beden IMT; bid PE.   54. sotthfast P.

Thanne shul we leue that Lyf the loueth · and wil nouȝt lete
    the deye!' 56
'*Consummatum est*,' quod Cryst · and comsed forto swowe
Pitousliche and pale · as a prisoun that deyeth;
The lorde of lyf and of liȝte · tho leyed his eyen togideres.
The daye for drede with-drowe · and derke bicam the sonne, 60
The wal wagged and clef · and al the worlde quaued.
Ded men for that dyne · come out of depe graues,
And tolde whi that tempest · so longe tyme dured.
'For a bitter bataille' · the ded bodye sayde; 64
'Lyf and Deth in this derknesse · her one fordoth her other;
Shal no wiȝte wite witterly · who shal haue the maystrye,
Er Sondey aboute sonne-rysynge' · and sank with that til erthe.
Some seyde that he was goddes sone · that so faire deyde, 68
    Vere filius dei erat iste, etc.
And somme saide he was a wicche · 'good is that we assaye,
Where he be ded or nouȝte ded · doun er he be taken.'
    Two theues also · tholed deth that tyme,
Vppon a crosse bisydes Cryst · so was the comune lawe. 72
A cacchepole cam forth · and craked bothe her legges,
And her armes after · of eyther of tho theues.
Ac was no boy so bolde · goddes body to touche;
For he was knyȝte and kynges sone · kynde forȝaf that tyme, 76
That non harlot were so hardy · to leyne hande vppon hym.
Ac there cam forth a knyȝte · with a kene spere ygrounde,
Hiȝte *Longeus*, as the lettre telleth · and longe had lore his siȝte.
Bifor Pilat and other peple · in the place he houed; 80
Maugre his many tethe · he was made that tyme
To take the spere in his honde · and Iusten with Iesus;
For alle thei were vnhardy · that houed on hors or stode,
To touche hym or to taste hym · or take hym down of rode. 84
But this blynde bacheler thanne · bar hym thorugh the herte;
The blode spronge down by the spere · and vnspered the kniȝtes
    eyen.
Thanne fel the knyȝte vpon knees · and cryed hym mercy—

That Lyf the louyeth · and wol nat lete the deye.'
'*Consummatum est*,' quath Crist · and comsede for to sounye
Pitousliche and paal · as prison that deyeth;
The lord of lyf and of light · tho leyde hus eyen togederes. 60
The day for drede ther-of with-drow · and deork by-cam the sonne;
The wal of the temple to-cleef · euene a two peces;
The hard roche al to-rof · and ryght derk nyght hit semede;
The erthe quook and quashte · as hit quyke were,   64
And dede men for that deon · comen oute of deope graues,
And tolden why that tempest · so longe tyme durede.
'For a byter bataile' · the dede bodye seyde,
'Lyf and Deth in this deorknesse · her on for-doth that other,
Ac shal no wiȝt wite witerliche · ho shal haue the mastrye, 69
Er Soneday, a-boute sonne-rysynge' · and sank with that til erthe.
Somme seiden he was godes sone · that so faire deyede;
    Vere filius dei erat iste:
Some seiden, 'he can of sorcerye · good is that we a-saye 72
Wher he be ded other nat ded · doun er he be take.'
  Two theoues ther wer · that tholeden deth that tyme
Vpon crois by-side Crist · so was the comune lawe.
Quikliche cam a cacchepol · and craked a-two here legges, 76
And here armes after · of euerich of tho theoues.
Ac ther was no boye so bolde · godes body to touche,
For he was knyght and kynges sone · kynde for-ȝaf that tyme
That no boye hadde hardinesse · hym to touche in deyinge. 80
Ac ther cam forth a blynde knyght · with a kene spere y-grounde,
Hihte *Longeus*, as the lettere telleth · and longe hadde lore hus sight.
By-fore Pilat and other peuple · in the place he houede.
Ac maugre hus meny teth · he was mad that tyme   84
To Iouste with Iesus · this blynde Iuwe *Longeus;*
For alle hij were vnhardy · that houede ther other stode,
To touche hym other to tryne hym · other to take hym doun
    and graue hym,   87
Bote this blynde bachelere · that bar hym thorw the herte;
The blood sprang doun by the sper · and vnsperrede the
    knyghtes eyen.
Tho fel the knyght vpon knees · and cryed Iesu mercy—

C. 62. pices P.   63. hit G; it IFT; PE *om.*   64. quashete P.   66. wy P.
69. wiȝt IF; wyȝt G; whit P.   81. a(2) IMT; PEFG *om.*   84. maugrey P.
90. fel MFTG; feol P.

'Aȝeyne my wille it was, lorde · to wownde ȝow so sore!'   88
He seighed and sayde · 'sore it me athynketh;
For the dede that I haue done · I do me in ȝowre grace;
Haue on me reuth, riȝtful Iesu!' · and right with that he wept.

Thanne gan Faith felly · the fals Iuwes dispise,   92
Called hem caytyues · acursed for euere,
For this foule vyleynye · 'veniaunce to ȝow alle!
To do the blynde bete hym ybounde · it was a boyes conseille.
Cursed caytyue! · kniȝthod was it neuere   96

To mysdo a ded body · by day or by nyȝte.
The gree ȝit hath he geten · for al his grete wounde.
For ȝowre champioun chiualer · chief knyȝt of ȝow alle,
Ȝelt hym recreaunt rennyng · riȝt at Iesus wille.   100
For be this derkenesse ydo · his deth worth avenged,
And ȝe, lordeynes, han ylost · for Lyf shal haue the maistrye,
And ȝowre fraunchise, that fre was · fallen is in thraldome,
And ȝe, cherles, and ȝowre children · chieue shal ȝe neure, 104
Ne haue lordship in londe · ne no londe tylye,
But al bareyne be · and vsurye vsen,
Which is lyf that owre lorde · in alle lawes acurseth.
Now ȝowre good dayes ar done · as Danyel prophecyed,   108
Whan Cryst cam, of her kyngdom · the croune shulde cesse;
    Cum veniat sanctus sanctorum, cessabit vnxio vestra.'
What for fere of this ferly · and of the fals Iuwes,
I drowe me in that derkenesse · to *decendit ad inferna.*
And there I sawe sothely · *secundum scripturas,*   112
Out of the west coste · a wenche, as me thouȝte,
Cam walkynge in the wey · to-helle-ward she loked.
Mercy hiȝt that mayde · a meke thynge with-alle,
A ful benygne buirde · and boxome of speche.   116
Her suster, as it semed · cam softly walkynge,
Euene out of the est · and westward she loked.
A ful comely creature · Treuth she hiȝte,

B. 109. of W; LRCOBY *om.*   cesse WCY; cece O; L *om.*

' A-ȝens my wil hit was,' quath he · ' that ich ȝow wonde made!'
He syghede and seide · ' sore hit me for-thynketh,   92
Of the dede that ich haue don · ich do me in ȝoure grace.
My londe and my lycame · at ȝoure lykynge taketh hit,
And haue mercy on me, ryghtful Iesu!' · and ryght with that he wepte.
   Thenne gan Faith foully · the false Iewes to despisen,   96
And calde hem ' caytifs a-corsed' · for this was a vil vilanye :—
' Veniaunce is to ȝou falle · that makede the blynde
Beten hym that was ded · hit was a boyes dede!'
Thus Faith bi-gon to fare · with the false Iewes—   100
' Corsede caityfs! · knyghthod was hit neuere
To bete a body ybounde · with eny briȝt wepne,
The gree ȝut hath he geten · for alle hus grete wondes.
For ȝoure champion chiualer · chief knyght of ȝow alle   104
ȝelt hym recreaunt rennynge · ryght at Iesus wil.
For beo this deorknesse ydo · Deth worth venkised,
And ȝe, lordlinges, han lost · for Lyf shal haue the maystrie,
And ȝoure fraunchise that freo was · fallen is to thraldom,   108
And alle ȝoure children cheorles · cheuen shulle thei neuere,
Ne haue lordshup in lond · nother lond tylie,
And as barayne beo · and by vsure libbe,
The whiche is lif that oure lorde · in alle lawes defendeth.   112
Now beoth ȝoure goode dayes don · as Daniel of ȝow telleth,
When Crist with crois ouercam · ȝoure kyngdom shal to-cleue ;
   Cum uenerit sanctus sanctorum, cessabit unctio uestra.'
   What for fere of this ferly · and of the false Iewes,
Ich drow in that deorknesse · to *descendit ad inferna,*   116
And ther ich seyh sothliche · *secundum scripturas,*
Out of the west, as it were · a wenche, as me thouhte,
Cam walkynge in the way · to-helleward hue lokede.
Mercy hihte that mayde · a mylde thyng with-alle,   120
And a ful benygne burde · and buxum of speche.
Heore sustre, as hit semede · cam softly walkynge
Euene out of the est · and westwarde hue thouhte,
A comely creature and clene · Treuthe hue hihte.   124

C. 95. and IFT; PEMG *om.*   100. *From* M; PEIFGT *omit this line.*
102. briȝth P.   104. campion P.   108. fraunchises P.   109. þe (*for*
thei) P.   118. weynche P.   119. he (*for* hue) P ; heo T; sche IM.   121.
benyngne P.   123. he (*for* hue) PFG; sche IMT.   124. heo (*for* hue) G ;
sheo P; sche IM; scheo F.

For the vertue that hir folwed · aferd was she neuere.　　120
Whan this maydenes mette · Mercy and Treuth,
Eyther axed other · of this grete wonder,
Of the dyne and of the derknesse · and how the daye rowed,
And which a liȝte and a leme · lay befor helle.　　124
'Ich haue ferly of this fare · in feith,' seyde Treuth,
'And am wendyng to wyte · what this wonder meneth.'
'Haue no merueille,' quod Mercy · 'myrthe it bytokneth.
A mayden that hatte Marye · and moder with-out felyng　　128
Of any kynnes creature · conceyued thorw speche
And grace of the holygoste ; · wex grete with childe ;
With-outen wem · in-to this worlde she brouȝt hym ;
And that my tale be trewe · I take god to witnesse.　　132
Sith this barn was bore · ben thritti wynter passed ;
Which deyde and deth tholed · this day aboute mydday.
And that is cause of this clips · that closeth now the sonne,
In menynge that man shal · fro merkenesse be drawe,　　136
The while this liȝte and this leme · shal Lucyfer ablende.
For patriarkes and prophetes · han preched her-of often,
That man shal man saue · thorw a maydenes helpe,
And that was tynt thorw tre · tree shal it wynne,　　140
And that deth doun brouȝte · deth shal releue.'
'That thow tellest,' quod Treuth · 'is but a tale of Waltrot!
For Adam and Eue · and Abraham with other,
Patriarkes and prophetes · that in peyne liggen,　　144
Leue thow neuere that ȝone liȝte · hem alofte brynge,
Ne haue hem out of helle · holde thi tonge, Mercy!
It is but a trufle that thow tellest · I, Treuth, wote the sothe.
For that is ones in helle · out cometh it neuere ;　　148
Iob the prophete, patriarke · reproueth thi sawes,
　　Quia in inferno nulla est redempcio.'
Thanne Mercy ful myldly · mouthed thise wordes,
'Thorw experience,' quod she · 'I hope thei shal be saued.
For venym for-doth venym · and that I proue by resoun.　　152
For of alle venymes · foulest is the scorpioun,
May no medcyne helpe · the place there he styngeth,

B. 146. helde (*for* holde) L.

For the vertue that here folwede · afered was hue neuere.
Whan theos maydenes metten · Mercy and Treuthe,
Ayther axed of other · of this grete wonder,
Of the deone and deorknesse · and how the day rowed, 128
And whiche a light and a leom · lay by-fore helle.
'Ich haue ferly of this fare · in faith,' seide Treuthe,
'And am wendyng to wyte · what this wonder meneth.'
'Haue no meruayle ther-of,' quath Mercy · 'murthe hit by-tokneth.
A mayde that hatte Marie · and moder with-oute felynge
Of eny kynde of creature · conceyuede thorw speche
And grace of the holygost · waxe gret with childe,
With-oute wommanes wem · in-to this worlde brouhte hym; 136
And that my tale is trewe · ich take god to witnesse.
Sutthen this barn was ybore · beoth thritty wynter passed,
Deyed and deth tholede · this day a-boute mydday;
That is the cause of this eclipse · that ouer-closeth now the sonne,
In menynge that man shal · fro meorknesse beo drawe, 141
The while this light and this leom · shal Lucifer a-blende.
For patriarkes and prophetes · han prechede her-of ofte,
That thyng that tynt was thorw treo · treo shal hit wynne, 144
And that that deth doun brouhte · deth shal releue.'
'That that thou tellest,' quath Treuthe · 'is bote a tale of Walterot!
For Adam and Eue · and Abraham with othere,
Patriarkes and prophetes · that in peyne liggen, 148
Leyf hit neuere that ȝon lyght · hem a-lofte brynge,
Ne haue hem out of helle; · hold thy tonge, Mercy,
Hit is trufle that thou tellest; · ich, Treuthe, wot the sothe,
That thyng that ones was in helle · out cometh hit neuere. 152
For Iob the parfit patriarke · repreoueth thy sawes,

Quia in inferno nulla est redempcio.'

Thenne Mercy ful myldeliche · mouthed thes wordes,
'Thorgh experience,' quath heo · 'ich hope thei shulle be sauede.
For venym for-doth venym · ther vecche ich euydence, 156
That Adam and Eue · haue shullen bote.
Of alle fretynge venymes · the vilest is the scorpion;
May no medecyne amende · the place ther he styngeth,

C. 125. he (*for* hue) PFT; sche IM; heo G.   128. roued PE; rouede
IG; rowide T.   129. P *ins.* wich *before* 2*nd* a.   136. wommanes FT;
womanes M; woman E; wommen P.   wordle PG.   137. trywe P.   142.
ableynde P.   149. ȝeon (*for* ȝon) P.

Tyl he be ded and do ther-to · the yuel he destroyeth,
The fyrst venymouste · thorw venym of hym-self.　　　156
So shal this deth for-do · I dar my lyf legge,
Al that Deth fordyd furste · thorw the deuelles entysynge;
And riȝt as thorw gyle · man was bigyled,
So shal grace that bigan · make a good sleighte;　　　160

　　Ars vt artem falleret.
Now suffre we,' seyde Treuth · 'I se, as me thinketh,
Out of the nippe of the north · nouȝt ful fer hennes,
Riȝtwisnesse come rennynge · reste we the while;
For he wote more than we · he was er we bothe.'　　　164
'That is soth,' seyde Mercy · 'and I se here bi southe,
Where Pees cometh playinge · in pacience yclothed;
Loue hath coueyted hir longe · leue I none other
But he sent hir some lettre · what this liȝte bymeneth,　　　168
That ouer-houeth helle thus; · she vs shal telle.'
Whan Pees, in pacience yclothed · approched nere hem tweyne,
Riȝtwisnesse her reuerenced · for her riche clothyng,
And preyed Pees to telle hir · to what place she wolde,　　　172
And in her gay garnementz · whom she grete thouȝte?
'My wille is to wende,' quod she · 'and welcome hem alle,
That many day myȝte I nouȝte se · for merkenesse of synne.
Adam and Eue · and other moo in helle,　　　176
Moyses and many mo · mercy shal haue;
And I shal daunce ther-to · do thow so, sustre!
For Iesus Iusted wel · Ioye bygynneth dawe;
　　Ad vesperum demorabitur fletus, et ad matutinum leticia.
Loue, that is my lemman · suche lettres me sente,　　　180
That Mercy, my sustre, and I · mankynde shulde saue;
And that god hath forgyuen · and graunted me, Pees, and Mercy,
To be mannes meynpernoure · for euere-more after.

B. 158. fordide W; dyd LCROB; *cf.* l. 343.

Til he be ded, ydo ther-to · and thenne hit destroieth 160
The ferst venemoste · thorgh vertu of hym-selue.
And so shal this deth for-do · ich dar my lyf legge,
Al that 'Deth and the deuel · dude formest to Eue.
Ryght as the gylour thorw gyle · by-gylede man formest, 164
So shal grace that al by-gan · make a good ende,
And by-gyle the gylour · and that is a good sleithe ;
     Ars ut artem falleret.'
' Now suffre we,' seide Treuthe · ' ich seo, as me thynketh,
Out of the nype of the north · nat ful fer hennes, 168
Ryghtwisnesse come rennynge ; · reste we the whyle ;
For hue wot more than we · hue was er we bothe.'
'.That is soth,' seide Mercy · ' and ich seo her by southe,
Wher cometh Pees pleyinge · in pacience yclothed; 172
Loue heore hath coueyted longe · leyue ich non other
Bote Loue haue sent heore som lettere · what this light bymeneth
That ouere-houeth helle thus ; · hue shal ous telle.'
   Whenne Pees, in pacience yclothed · aproched ayther other,
Ryghtwisnesse reuerencede Pees · in heore riche clothinge, 177
And prayede Pees to tellen huere · to what place hue wolde,
In heore gay garnemens · wham hue gladie thouhte?.
' My wil is to wende,' quath Pees · ' and wel-come hem alle,
That meny day myghte ich nat seo · for meorknesse of synne.
Adam and Eue · and other mo in helle,
Moyses and meny mo · mercy shullen synge;
And ich shal daunce ther-to · do al-so thow, suster! 184
For Iesus Iousted wel · Ioye by-gynneth to dawen;
    Ad uesperum demorabitur fletus, et ad matutinum leticia.
Loue that is my lemman · suche letteres me sente,
That Mercy my suster, and ich · mankynde shulde saue;
And that god hath for-gyue · and graunted to al mankynde,
Mercy, my suster, and me · to maynprise hem alle. 189
And Crist hath conuerted · the kynde of ryghtwisnesse
In-to pees and pyte · of hus pure grace.

C. 160. destroieþ MIF; distrieþ P.   162. dar EFIT; þar P.   168. feer
(*for* fer) P.   169. Rythwisnesse PM.   wyle P.   170. he PIFTG; *but
read* hue. P. *ins.* þan *after* er.   172. ycloþed EMITG; cloþed PF.   175.
he PIFTG; sche M; *read* hue.   176. ycloþed EMITG; cloþed PF.
178. heo F ; sche MI; she T ; he P; *read* hue.   179. heo FG ; sche MI ;
she T ; he P; *read* hue.   180. weynde P.   187. shulde M; scholde E ;
shullen PF ; schal ITG.

Lo! here the patent!' quod Pees · '*in pace in idipsum*— 184
And that this dede shal dure—· *dormiam et requiescam.*'
   'What, rauestow?' quod Riȝtwisnesse · 'or thow art riȝt dronke!

Leuestow that ȝonde liȝte · vnlouke myȝte helle,
And saue mannes soule? · sustre, wene it neure! 188
At the bygynnynge, god · gaf the dome hym-selue,
That Adam and Eue · and alle that hem suwed
Shulde deye doune riȝte · and dwelle in pyne after,
If that thei touched a tre · and the fruite eten. 192
Adam afterward · aȝeines his defence,
Frette of that fruit · and forsoke, as it were,
The loue of owre lorde · and his lore bothe,
And folwed that the fende tauȝte · and his felawes wille, 196
Aȝeines resoun, I, Riȝtwisnesse · recorde thus with treuth,
That her peyne be perpetuel · and no preyere hem helpe.
For-thi late hem chewe as thei chose · and chyde we nouȝt, sustres,
For it is botelees bale · the bite that thei eten.' 200
   'And I shal preue,' quod Pees · 'her peyne mote haue ende,
And wo in-to wel · mowe wende atte laste;
For had thei wist of no wo · wel had thei nouȝte knowen.
For no wiȝte wote what wel is · that neuere wo suffred, 204
Ne what is hote hunger · that had neuere defaute.

If no nyȝte ne were · no man, as I leue,
Shulde wite witterly · what day is to mene;

Shulde neuere riȝte riche man · that lyueth in reste and ese 208
Wyte what wo is · ne were the deth of kynde.
So god that bygan al · of his good wille
Bycam man of a mayde · mankynde to saue,
And suffred to be solde · to see the sorwe of deyinge, 212

B. 201. I WCOB; LR *om.*

Lo, here the patente!' quath Pees · '*in pace in idipsum*— 192
And that this dede shal dure—· *dormiam et requiescam.*'
   'Rauest thou?' quath Ryghtwisnesse · 'other thou art ryght dronke!
Leyuest thou that ȝon light · vnlouke myghte helle,
And saue mannes soule? · suster, wene hit neuere! 196
At the begynnynge of the worlde · god gaf the dom hymselue,
That Adam and Eue · and hus issue alle
Sholden deye doun-ryht · and dwelle in peyne euere,
Yf thei touchede the treo · and of the frut eten. 200
Adam afterwarde · a-ȝens hus defense,
Faste fret of that frut · and for-soke, as hit were,
The leel loue of oure lorde · and hus lore bothe,
And folwede that the feonde tauhte · and hus fleshes wil, 204
Aȝens reson and ryghtwysnesse; · recorde this with treuthe,
That here peyne is perpetuel · no preyere may hem helpe.
For-thi let hem chewe as thei chose · and chide we nat, susteres,
For hit is a botles bale · the byte that thei eten.' 208
   'And ich shal preye,' quath Pees · 'here peyne mote haue ende,
That here wo in-to wele · wende mote atte laste;
For hadde thei wist of no wo · wele hadde thei nat knowe;
For wot no wight what wele is · that neuere wo suffrede, 212
Ne what is hot hunger · that hadde neuere defaute.
Ho couthe kyndeliche · with colour discriue,
Yf alle the worlde were whit · other swan-whit alle thynges?
Yf no nyght ne were · no man, as ich leyue, 216
Sholde wite witerly · what day were to mene.
Ne hadde god suffred of som · other than hym-selue,
He hadde nat wist wyterly · whether deth wer soure other sweyte.
For sholde neuere right riche man · that lyueth in reste and hele
Ywyte what wo is · ne were the deth of kynde. 221
So god that al by-gan · of hus good wil
By-cam man of a mayde · mankynde to saue,
And suffrede to be solde · to seo the sorwe of deyynge, 224

   C. 193. *dormiam, &c.* is from EIMFTG; P *om.*   194. art IMFT; ert PEG.   204. sheshes (*for* fleshes) P.   209. P *ins.* an *before* ende.   210. atte þe (*for* atte, *wrongly*) P.   212. wight IFT; whit P.   214. wiþ T (*which seems the right reading*); wit P; wi*th*, *alt. to* whit E; white IF; whyȝt G; whijt M.   215. Hif (*for* Yf) P.   216. ne ITG; PEMF *om.* 217. whiterly P.   218. suffrede P.   219. weþer P.

The which vnknitteth al kare · and comsynge is of reste.
For til *modicum* mete with vs · I may it wel avowe,
Wote no wiȝte, as I wene · what is ynough to mene.
    For-thi god of his goodnesse · the fyrste gome Adam,   216
Sette hym in solace · and in souereigne myrthe;
And sith he suffred hym synne · sorwe to fele,
To wite what wel was · kyndelich to knowe it.
And after god auntred hym-self · and toke Adames kynde,   220
To wyte what he hath suffred · in thre sondri places,
Bothe in heuene, and in erthe · and now til helle he thynketh,
To wite what al wo is · that wote of al Ioye.

So it shal fare bi this folke; · her foly and her synne   224
Shall lere hem what langour is · and lisse with-outen ende.
Wote no wighte what werre is · there that pees regneth,
Ne what is witterly wel · til weyllowey hym teche.'
    Thanne was there a wiȝte · with two brode eyen,   228
Boke hiȝte that beupere · a bolde man of speche.
'By godes body,' quod this Boke · 'I wil bere witnesse,
That tho this barne was ybore · there blased a sterre,
That alle the wyse of this worlde · in o witte acordeden,   232
That such a barne was borne · in Bethleem citee,
That mannes soule sholde saue · and synne destroye.
And alle the elementz,' quod the Boke · 'her-of bereth witnesse.
That he was god that al wrouȝte · the walkene firste shewed;
Tho that weren in heuene · token *stella comata*,   237
And tendeden hir as a torche · to reuerence his birthe;
The lyȝte folwed the lorde · in-to the lowe erthe.
The water witnessed that he was god · for he went on it;   240
Peter the apostel · parceyued his gate,
And as he went on the water · wel hym knewe, and seyde,
    Iube me venire ad te super aquas.

B. 240. þe WRO; þat LCB.

The whiche vnknytteth alle care · and comsyng is of reste.
For til moreyne mete with ous · ich may hit wel a-vowe,
Ne wot no wight, as ich wene · what is ynowh to mene.
  For-thi god of hus goodnesse · the furst man Adam,   228
He sette hym in solace furst · and in souerayne murthe;
And sutthe suffrede hym to synege · sorwe to fele,
To wite ther-thorw what wele was · and kyndeliche to knowe.
And after auntrede god hym-self · and tok Adams kynde,   232
To wite what he hadde suffred · in thre sondry places,
Bothe in heuene and in erthe; · and now to helle he thenketh,
To wite what alle wo is · that wot of alle ioye;
  Omnia probate; quod bonum est tenete.
So shal hit fare by this folke · here folie and here synne   236
Shal lere hem what loue is · and lisse with-outen ende.
For wot no wight what werre is · ther as pees regneth,
Ne what is witerliche wele · til wele-a-way hym teche.'
  Thenne was ther a wight · with two brode eyen,   240
Book hihte that beau-pere · a bold man of speche.
'By godes body,' quath this Book · 'ich wole bere wyttnesse,
Tho this barn was ybore · ther blased a sterre,
That alle the wise of the worlde · in o wit a-cordede,   244
That suche a barn was ybore · in Bethleem the cyte,
That mannes soule sholde saue · and synne destruye.
And alle the elemens,' quath the Book · 'here-of bereth witnesse.
That he was. god that al wrouhte · the wolkene furst shewede;
Tho that weren in heuene · token *stella comata,*
And tenden hit as a torche · to reuerence hus burthe;   250
That light folwede the lorde · in-to the lowe erthe.
The water witnessede that he was god · for he wente on hym drye;
Peter the apostel · parceyuede hus gate,
And as he wente vpon the water · wel hym knewe, and seide,
Lord Crist, comaunde me · to come to the on watur;   255
  '*Domine, iube me uenire ad te super aquas.*'

C. 225. vnknettiþ T; vkny3teth (*sic*) I; vnknette M; vnknyt EF; vn-
knytte P; vn-knitte G; (*perhaps* vnknyt *is best, but this is the contracted form
of* vnknytteþ, *so that it is much the same*).   227. whight P.   228. goud-
nesse P.   231. white P. wat P.   232. tok MTG; touk P.   233. þre
IFTG; þe PE.   239. is IMFTG; PE *om.* whiterliche P.   240. whight P.
242. þis EMFTG; þes P.   244. acordede FG; acorde P.   247. whitnesse P.
249. þo EIMTG; To P.   252. whitnessed P. (2*na*) he IMFT; god PEG.
255. *This line is in* F *only.* super aquas EMF; PIT *om.*

And lo! how the sonne gan louke · her liȝte in her-self,
Whan she seye hym suffre · that sonne and se made! 244
The erthe for heuynesse · that he wolde suffre,
Quaked as quykke thinge · and al biquashte the roche!
Lo! helle miȝte nouȝte holde · but opened tho god tholed,
And lete oute Symondes sones · to seen hym hange on rode.

And now shal Lucifer leue it · thowgh hym loth thinke; 249
For *Gygas* the geaunt · with a gynne engyned
To breke and to bete doune · that ben aȝeines Iesus.

And I, Boke, wil be brent · but Iesus rise to lyue, 252
In alle myȝtes of man · and his moder gladye,
And conforte al his kynne · and out of care brynge,
And al the Iuwen Ioye · vnioignen and vnlouken;
And but thei reuerencen his rode · and his resurexioun, 256
And bileue on a newe lawe · be lost lyf and soule.'
    'Suffre we,' seide Treuth · 'I here and se bothe,
How a spirit speketh to helle · and bit vnspere the ȝatis;
        Attollite portas, etc.'
A voice loude in that liȝte · to Lucifer cryeth, 260
'Prynces of this place · vnpynneth and vnlouketh!
For here cometh with croune · that kynge is of glorie.'
Thanne syked Sathan · and seyde to hem alle,
'Suche a lyȝte, aȝeines owre leue · Lazar it fette; 264
Care and combraunce · is comen to vs alle.
If this kynge come in · mankynde wil he fecche,
And lede it ther hym lyketh · and lyȝtlych me bynde.
Patriarkes and prophetes · han parled her-of longe, 268
That such a lorde and a lyȝte · shulde lede hem alle hennes.'

B. 246. biquasht L.

Loo, how the sonne gan louke · hure light in huere-selue, 256
When hue sey hym suffry deth · that sonne and seo made!
Lo, the erthe for heuynesse · that he wolde deth suffre,
Quakede as quike thyng · and al to-quashte the roches!
Lo, helle myghte nat holde · bote openede, tho god deth tholede,
And let out Symondes sones · to se hym honge on rode, 261
  Non uisurum se mortem.
Now shal Lucifer leyue hit · thauh hym loth thynke;
For Iesus as a gyaunt · with a gyn cometh ȝonde,
To breken and to bete a-doun · alle that ben a-gayns hym, 264
And to haue out alle · of hem that hym liketh.
And ȝut ich, Book, wol beo brent · bote he arise to lyue,
And conforten al hus kyn · and out of care brynge,
And al the Iuwene Ioye · vnioynen, and vnlouken, 268
And bote thei reuerencen hus resurexion · and the rode honoure,
And by-leyue on a newe lawe · beo ylost lyf and soule!'
'Suffre we,' saide Treuthe · 'ich huyre and seo bothe
A spirit speke to helle · and bit vnsperre the ȝates; 272
  Attollite portas, principes, vestras; et eleuamini, porte eter-
   nales, etc.'
A voys loude in that light · to Lucifer seide,
'Princes of this palys · prest vndo the ȝates,
For here cometh with coroune · the kynge of alle glorie.'
Thenne syhede Satan · and seide to helle, 276
'Suche a light a-ȝeyns our leue · Lazar hit fette;
Colde care and combraunce · is come to ous alle.
Yf this kyng come yn · mankynde wol he fecche,
And leden hit ther Lazar is · and lightliche me bynde. 280
Patriarkes and prophetes · han parled her-of longe,
That suche a lorde and a lyght · shal leden hem alle hennes.
Ac rys vp Ragamoffyn · and reche me alle the barres
That Belial thy bel-syre · beot with thy damme, 284
And ich shal lette this lorde · and hus light stoppe;
Ar we thorw bryghtnesse be blent · barre we the ȝates.'

C. 257. he PEIFTG; heo M; *read* hue.   259. Quakede MEIFTG;
Quaquide P. to-quashete P.   262. lyue (*for* leyue) P.   263. ȝonde MF;
ȝont T; ȝeonde P.   268. vnioyenen P.   269. PG *ins.* yf *after* bote.
271. i MFT; we G; and PE; *read* ich.   279. þes (*for* þis) PG.   come
ITG; comeþ M; comen (*wrongly*) PF.   284. þy EIMFTG; þe P.   bel
IMG; beel PF.

'Lysteneth,' quod Lucifer · 'for I this lorde knowe,
Bothe this lorde and this liȝte; · is longe ago I knewe hym.
May no deth hym dere · ne no deueles queyntise,   272
And where he wil, is his waye; · ac war hym of the periles;
If he reue me my riȝte · he robbeth me by maistrye.
For by riȝt and bi resoun · tho renkes that ben here
Bodye and soule ben myne · bothe gode and ille.   276
For hym-self seyde · that sire is of heuene,
Ȝif Adam ete the apple · alle shulde deye,
And dwelle with vs deueles · this thretynge he made;

And he that sothenesse is · seyde thise wordes;   280

And sitthen I seised ·. seuene hundreth wyntre,
I leue that lawe nil nauȝte · lete hym the leest.'

'That is sothe,' seyde Sathan · 'but I me sore drede,
For thow gete hem with gyle · and his gardyne breke,   284

And in semblaunce of a serpent · sat on the appeltre,
And eggedest hem to ete · Eue by hir-selue,

Cheke we and cheyne we · and eche chyne stoppe,
That no light leope yn · at louer ne at loupe. 288
And thow, Astrot, hot out · and haue oute oure knaues,
Coltyng and al hus kynne · oure catel to saue.
Brynston boilaunt · brennyng out-casteth hit
Al hot on here heuedes · that entren ny the walles. 292
Setteth bowes of brake · and brasene gonnes,
And sheteth out shot ynowh · hus shultrom to blende.
Sette Mahon at the mangonel · and mulle-stones throweth,
With crokes and with kalketrappes · a-cloye we hem echone!'
   'Lusteneth,' quath Lucifer · 'for ich this lord knowe, 297
Bothe this lord and this lyght · is longe gon ich knew hym.
May no deth this lord dere · ne no deoueles queyntise,
And wher he wole, is hus wey; · ac war hym of the periles;
Yf he reue me of my ryght · he robbeth me by mastrie. 301
For by ryght and reson · the renkes that beon here
Body and soule beth myne · bothe good and ille.
For he hym-self hit seide · that syre is of helle, 304
That Adam and Eue · and al hus issue
Sholden deye with deol · and here dwelle euere,
Yf that thei touchede a treo · other toke ther-of an appel.
Thus this lorde of light · suche a lawe made, 308
And sitthe he is so leel a lorde · ich leyue that he wol nat
Reuen ous of oure ryght · sutthe reson hem dampned.
And sutthe we han beo sesed · seuene thowsend wynter,
And neuere was ther-aȝeyn · and now wolde by-gynne, 312
He were vnwrast of hus worde · that witnesse is of trewthe.'
'That is soth,' seide Satan · 'bote ich me sore doute,
For thow gete hem with gyle · and hus gardyn breke,
A-geyn hus loue and hus leue · on hus londe ȝeodest, 316
Nat in forme of a feonde · bote in forme of an addre,
And entisedest Eue · to ete by heore on,
   Ve soli!
And by-hihtest heore and hym · after to knowe,
As two godes, with god · bothe good and ille; 320
Thus with treison and with trecherie · thow troiledest hem bothe,

---

C. 288. leopen P.   289. oure IFTG; PE *om.*   292. on MFTG; in PE.
293. and EIMFTG; a P.   297. Lusteneþ M; Lustneþ G; Lusteth PE.
307. þat IMET; PFG *om.*   308. thees (*for* this) P.   313. treweþe P.
320. two ET; to PMFIG.

And toldest hir a tale · of tresoun were the wordes;
And so thow haddest hem oute · and hider atte laste.   288
It is nouȝte graythely geten · there gyle is the rote.'
'For god wil nouȝt be bigiled' · quod Gobelyn, 'ne bi-iaped;
We haue no trewe title to hem · for thorwgh tresoun were thei
    dampned.'   291
'Certes, I drede me,' quod the deuel · 'leste treuth wil hem fecche.

This thretty wynter, as I wene · hath he gone and preched;
I haue assailled hym with synne · and some tyme yasked
Where he were god or goddes sone? · he gaf me shorte answere.
And thus hath he trolled forth · this two and thretty wynter,

And whan I seighe it was so · slepyng, I went   297
To warne Pilates wyf · what dones man was Iesus;
For Iuwes hateden hym · and han done hym to deth.
I wolde haue lengthed his lyf · for I leued, ȝif he deyede,   300
That his soule wolde suffre · no synne in his syȝte.
For the body, whil it on bones ȝede · aboute was euere
To saue men fram synne · ȝif hem-self wolde.

And now I se where a soule · cometh hiderward seyllynge   304
With glorie and with grete liȝte · god it is, I wote wel.
I rede we flee,' quod he · 'faste alle hennes;
For vs were better nouȝte be · than biden his syȝte.
For thi lesynges, Lucifer · loste is al owre praye.   308
Firste thorw the we fellen · fro heuene so heiȝhe;
For we leued thi lesynges · we loupen oute alle with the,
And now for thi last lesynge · ylore we haue Adam,
And al owre lordeship, I leue · a londe and a water;   312
    Nunc princeps huius mundi eicietur foras.'

B. 310, 311. we loupen—lesynge *is in* R *only*.

And dudest hem breke here buxomnesse · thorw false by-heste;
Thus haddest thou hem oute · and hyder atte laste.
Hit is nat greythly getyn · ther gyle is the rote.' 324
'And god wol nat be by-gyled' · quath Gobelyn, 'ne by-Iaped;
We haue no trewe title to hem · for thi treison hit maketh.'
'For-thi ich drede me,' quath the deouel · 'lest treuthe wol hem fecche.
And as thow by-gyledest godes ymage · in goynge of an addre,
So hath god by-gyled ous alle · in goynge of a wye.' 329
'For god hath go,' quath Gobelyn · 'in a gome lyknesse
This thritty wynter, as ich wene · and went a-bowte and prechede. 331
Ich haue asailid hym with synne · and som tyme ich askede
Wher he were god other godes sone? · he gaf me short answere.
Thus hath he troiled · and trauailed in hus tyme
Forth like a tydy man · this two and thritty wyntere,
And whenne ich seih that hit was so · ich sotelide how ich myghte 336
Lette hem that louede hym nat · lest thei wolde hym martrye.
Ich wolde haue lengthed hus lyf · for ich leyuede, yf he deyede,
And hus soule huder come · he sholde shende ous alle.
The body, whyle hit on bones зede · a-boute was hit euere 340
To lere men to beo leel · eche man to louen other;
The whiche lif and lawe · be hit longe y-used,
Hit shal vndon ous deoueles · and doun brynge ous alle.'
'Now y seo wher hus soule · cometh seilinge hiderwardes 344
With glorie and with gret light · god hit is, ich wot wel.
Ich rede we fleo,' quath the feond · 'faste alle hennes;
For us were betere nat beo · than abyde in hus syghte.
For thi lesynges, Lucifer · we loste furst our Ioye, 348
And out of heuene hider · thi prude made ous falle;
For we leyuede on thy lesinges · ther losten we oure blysse.
And now, for a later lesynge · that thow lowe tyl Eue,
We han lost oure lordshep · a londe and in helle; 352
Nunc princeps huius mundi eicietur foras.'

C. 322. he (*for* here) P. 326. triwe P. 335. two EFT; to PMG.
336. hit MEG; it IFT; he P. 340. wyle P. зeden P. 342. yusede P.
343. don (*for* doun) P. 346. wey (*for* we) P. 347. hus (*for* us) P. 348.
lesynges IMFT; lesynge PEG; *see* l. 350. 350. lyuede P; *see* l. 338. oure
FTG; PE *om.*; *see* l. 348. 352. Whe (*for* We) P. lorshep P. *eicietur foras* in M only.

Efte the liȝte bad vnlouke · and Lucifer answered,
'What lorde artow?' quod Lucifer · '*quis est iste?*'
'*Rex glorie*' · the liȝte sone seide,
'And lorde of myȝte and of mayne · and al manere vertues;
    dominus virtutum;   316
Dukes of this dym place · anon vndo this ȝates,
That Cryst may come in · the kynges sone of heuene.'
And with that breth helle brake · with Beliales barres;
For any wye or warde · wide opene the ȝatis.   320
Patriarkes and prophetes · *populus in tenebris,*
Songen seynt Iohanes songe · '*ecce agnus dei.*'
Lucyfer loke ne myȝte · so lyȝte hym ableynte;
And tho that owre lorde loued · in-to his liȝte he lauȝte,   324
And seyde to Sathan, 'lo! here · my soule to amendes
For alle synneful soules · to saue tho that ben worthy.
Myne thei be and of me · I may the bette hem clayme.
Al-though resoun recorde · and riȝt of my-self,   328
That if thei ete the apple · alle shulde deye,
I bihyȝte hem nouȝt here · helle for euere.
For the dede that thei dede · thi deceyte it made;
With gyle thow hem gete · agayne al resoun.   332
For in my paleys, paradys · in persone of an addre,
Falseliche thow fettest there · thynge that I loued.
Thus ylyke a lusarde · with a lady visage,
Theuelich- thow me robbedest; · the olde lawe graunteth,   336
That gylours be bigiled · and that is gode resoun;

B. 324. lorde RWCOBY; L *om.*

Suththe that Satan · myssayde thus foule
Lucifer for hus lesynges · leyue ich non other,
Bote oure lord atte laste · lyeres here rebuke,   355
And wyte hem al the wrecchednesse · that wrouht is on erthe.
Beo yware, ʒe wise clerkes · and wytty men of lawe,
That ʒe be-leiʒe nat these lewed men · for atte laste Dauid
Witnesseth in hus wrytynge · what is lyeres mede;
    Odisti omnes qui operantur iniquitatem, et perdes omnes qui
     loquntur mendacium.
A lytel ich ouer-lep · for lesynges sake,   360
That ich ne segge as ich seih · suynge my teme!—
  For eft that light bad vnlouke · and Lucifer answerede,
'What lord art thu?' quath Lucifer; · a voys a-loud seyde,
'The lord of myght and of mayn · that made alle thynges. 364
Duke of this dymme place · a-non vndo the ʒates,
That Crist mowe comen in · the kynges sone of heuene.'
And with that breth helle brake · with alle Beliales barres;
For eny wye other warde · wyde openede the gates.   368
Patriarkes and prophetes · *populus in tenebris*,
Songen with seint Iohan · '*ecce agnus dei!*'
Lucifer loke ne myghte · so lyght him a-blente;
And tho that oure lord louede · with that lyght forth flowen. 372
'Lo, me her,' quath oure lorde · 'lyf and soule bothe,
For alle synful soules · to saue oure beyere ryght.
Myne thei were and of me · ich may the beter hem cleyme.
Al-thauh reson recorde · and ryght of my-selue,   376
That yf thei eten the appel · alle sholden deye,
Ich by-hihte hem nat here · helle for euere.
For the dedliche synne that thei duden · thi deceite hit made;
With gyle thow hem gete · ageyn alle reson.   380
For in my paleis paradis · in persone of an addere,
Falsliche thou fettest there · that me by-fel to loke,
By-glosedest hem and bygyledest hem · and my gardyn breke,
A-ʒeyns my loue and my leyue; · the olde lawe techeth,   384
That gylours be by-gylid · and in here gyle falle.

  C. 356. wyten P.   358. be-leiʒe T; by-gylie PE; bi-gile MG. þeos P.
P *om.* lewed.   359. Whitnesseþ P.   363. art IMFT; ert PEG.   364.
mayn MFTG; mayne IE; man P.   375. þei (*for* þe) P.   382. þou FG;
PEMIT *om.*   383. bygyledest G; bigilidest MIFT; gyledest PE.   385.
be EFTG; ben M; beþ P.

Dentem pro dente, et oculum pro oculo.
Ergo, soule shal soule quyte · and synne to synne wende,
And al that man hath mysdo · I, man, wyl amende.
Membre for membre · bi the olde lawe was amendes,   340
And lyf for lyf also · and by that lawe I clayme it,
Adam and al his issue · at my wille her-after.
And that deth in hem fordid · my deth shal releue,
And bothe quykke and quyte · that queynte was thorw synne;
And that grace gyle destruye · good feith it asketh.   345
So leue it nouȝte, Lucifer · aȝeine the lawe I fecche hem,
But bi riȝt and by resoun · raunceoun here my lyges :
    Non veni soluere legem, sed adimplere.
Thow fettest myne in my place · aȝeines al resoun,   348
Falseliche and felounelich; · gode faith me it tauȝte,
To recoure hem thorw raunceoun · and bi no resoun elles,
So that with gyle thow gete · thorw grace it is ywone.
Thow, Lucyfer, in lyknesse · of a luther addere,   352
Getest by gyle · tho that god loued;
And I, in lyknesse of a leode · that lorde am of heuene,
Graciousliche thi gyle haue quytte · go gyle aȝeine gyle!
And as Adam and alle · thorw a tre deyden,   356
Adam and alle thorwe a tree · shal torne aȝeine to lyue;
And gyle is bigyled · and in his gyle fallen :
    Et cecidit in foueam quam fecit.
Now bygynneth thi gyle · ageyne the to tourne,
And my grace to growe · ay gretter and wyder.   360
The bitternesse that thow hast browe · brouke it thi-seluen,
That art doctour of deth · drynke that thow madest!
   For I, that am lorde of lyf · loue is my drynke,
And for that drynke to-day · I deyde vpon erthe.   364
I fauȝte so, me threstes ȝet · for mannes soule sake;
May no drynke me moiste · ne my thruste slake,
Tyl the vendage falle · in the vale of Iosephath,
That I drynke riȝte ripe must · *resureccio mortuorum,*   368
And thanne shal I come as a kynge · crouned with angeles,
And han out of helle · alle mennes soules.
   Fendes and fendekynes · bifor me shulle stande,

And ho so hitteth out a mannes eye · other elles hus for-teth,
Othere eny manere membre · maymeth other hurteth,
The same sore shal he haue · that enye so smyteth ;   388
    Dentem pro dente, et oculum pro oculo.
So lyf shal lyf lete · ther lyf hath lyf anyented,
So that lyf quyte lyf · the olde lawe hit asketh.
Ergo, soule shal soule quyte · and synne to synne wende,
And al that man mys-dude · ich, man, to amenden hit ;   392
And that that deth for-dude · my deth to releuen,
Bothe aquyte and aquykye · that was aqueynt thorw synne ;
And gyle be by-gyled · thorgh grace atte laste,
    Ars ut artem falleret, etc.
So leyf hit nat, Lucifer · that ich a-ȝeyns the lawe   396
Fecche here eny synful soule · souereynliche by maistrie ;
Bot thorgh ryght and reson · raunson here myne lige ;
    Non ueni soluere legem, sed adimplere.
So that thorgh gyle was geten · thorwe grace is now y-wonne.
And as Adam and alle · thorw a treo deyden,   400
Adam and alle thorgh a treo · shal turne to lyue.
And now by-gynneth thi gyle · a-gayn on the turne,
And my grace to growe · ay wydder and wydder.
The biternesse that thow hast browe · now brouk hit thyself ;   404
That art doctour of deth · drynk that thow madest !
  For ich that am lord of lyf · loue is my drynke,
And for that drynke to-daye · deyede, as hit semede ;
Ac ich wol drynke of no dich · ne of no deop cleregie,   408
Bote of comune coppes · alle Cristene soules ;
Ac thi drynke worth deth · and deop helle thy bolle.
Ich fauht so, me fursteth ȝut · for mannes soule sake ;
    Sicio.
May no pyement ne pomade · ne presiouse drynkes   412
Moyste me to the fulle · ne my thurst slake,
Til the vendage valle · in the vale of Iosaphat,
And drynke ryght rype most · *resurreccio mortuorum.*
Then shal ich come as a kyng · with coroune and with angeles,
And haue out of helle · alle menne soules.   417
  Feondes and feondekenes · by-for me shullen stande,

C. 388. sore EIF ; sor MT ; for P.   389. P *om. 2nd* lyf.   393. my ITG ; ich PE.   405. art IMFT ; ert PEG.   414. valle P ; falle EIMFTG.

And be at my biddynge · where so eure me lyketh.   372
And to be merciable to man · thanne my kynde it asketh;
For we beth bretheren of blode · but nouȝte in baptesme alle.
Ac alle that beth myne hole bretheren · in blode and in baptesme,
Shal nouȝte be dampned to the deth · that is with-outen ende;
    Tibi soli peccaui, etc.
It is nouȝt vsed in erthe · to hangen a feloun   377
Ofter than ones · though he were a tretour.
And ȝif the kynge of that kyngedome · come in that tyme,
There the feloun thole sholde · deth or otherwys,   380
Lawe wolde, he ȝeue hym lyf · if he loked on hym.
And I, that am kynge of kynges · shal come suche a tyme,
There dome to the deth · dampneth al wikked;
And ȝif lawe wil I loke on hem · it lithe in my grace,   384
Whether thei deye or deye nouȝte · for that thei deden ille.
Be it any thinge abouȝt · the boldenesse of her synnes,
I may do mercy thorw riȝtwisnesse · and alle my wordes trewe.
And though holiwrit wil that I be wroke · of hem that deden ille,
    Nullum malum inpunitum, etc.,

Thei shul be clensed clereliche · and wasshen of her synnes   389
In my prisoun purgatorie · til *parce* it hote,
And my mercy shal be shewed · to manye of my bretheren.
For blode may suffre blode · bothe hungry and akale,   392
Ac blode may nouȝt se blode · blede, but hym rewe.'—
    Audiui archana verba, que non licet homini loqui.—
'Ac my riȝtwisnesse and riȝt · shal reulen al helle,
And mercy al mankynde · bifor me in heuene.
For I were an vnkynde kynge · but I my kynde holpe,   396
And namelich at such a nede · ther nedes helpe bihoueth;
    Non intres in iudicium cum seruo tuo, domine.
Thus bi lawe,' quod owre lorde · 'lede I wil fro hennes
Tho that me loued · and leued in my comynge.
And for thi lesynge, Lucifer · that thow lowe til Eue,   400

B. 386. abouȝte L.   397. *domine* is in O only.

And be at my byddyng · at blysse other at peyne.
Ac to beo merciable to man · thenne my kynde asketh;   420
For we beoth bretheren of blod · ac nat in baptisme alle.
Ac alle that beoth myn half-bretheren · in blod and in baptisme
Shal neuere eft in helle come · beo he ones oute;
  Tibi soli peccaui, et malum contra te feci, etc.
Hit is nat vsed on erthe · to honge eny felones   424
Ofter than ones · thauh thei weren treitours.
And yf the kyng of the kyngdom · come in the tyme
Ther a theof tholy sholde · deth other Iuwise,
Lawe wolde he ȝeue hym lyf · and he lokede on hym.   428
And ich, that am kynge ouer kynges · shal come suche a tyme,
Ther that dom to the deoth · dampneth alle wyckede;
And yf lawe wol ich loke on hem · hit lyth in my grace,
Whether thei deye other deye nat · dude thei neuere so ille.   432
Be hit eny thyng dere abouȝt · the boldness of here synne,
Ich may do mercy of my ryghtwisnesse · and alle myne wordes
  trewe.
For holy writ wole that ich be awreke · of hem that wrouhte ille;
  As, *nullum malum impunitum, et nullum bonum irremu-
  neratum.*
And so of alle wyckede · ich wolle here take veniaunce,   436
And ȝut my kynde, in my kene yre · shal contrarie my wil—
  *Domine, ne in furore tuo arguas me, neque in ira tuo
  corripias me—*
To beo merciable to menye · of my half-bretheren.
For blod may seo blood · bothe a-thurst and a-cale,
Ac blod may nat seo blod · blede, bote hym rewe.'—   440
  Audiui archana verba, que non licet homini loqui.—
'Ac my ryghtwisnesse and my right · shal regnen in helle,
And mercy and mankynde · by-for me in heuene.
For ich were an vnkynde kynge · bote ich my kyn holpe,
And nameliche at suche a neode · that neodes help asketh;   444
  Non intres in iudicium cum servo tuo, domine.
Thus by lawe,' quath oure lord · 'lede ich wol fro hennes
Alle that ich louye · and leyuede in my comynge.
Ac for the lesynge that thow, Lucifer · lowe til Eue,

C. 421. broþerne P (*and in* l. 422).   427. Iuwise EM; iewise IG; Iuwes P.
429. a kynge P; EIMFTG *omit* a.   PE *om.* a.   430. dampned P.   433.
dere abouȝt MFE; dure y-bouht P.   434. trywe P.   438. broþerne P.
443. holpe EIMFT; helpe P.

Thow shalt abye it bittre'— · and bonde hym with cheynes.

Astaroth and al the route · hidden hem in hernes,
They dorste nouȝte loke on owre lorde · the boldest of hem alle,
But leten hym lede forth what hym lyked · and lete what hym
    liste. 404
  Many hundreth of angeles · harpeden and songen,
        Culpat caro, purgat caro; regnat deus dei caro.
Thanne piped pees · of poysye a note,
'*Clarior est solito post maxima nebula phebus,*
Post inimicitias clarior est et amor. 408
After sharpe shoures,' quod Pees · 'moste shene is the sonne;
Is no weder warmer · than after watery cloudes.
Ne no loue leuere · ne leuer frendes,
Than after werre and wo · whan Loue and Pees be maistres. 412

Was neuere werre in this worlde · ne wykkednesse so kene,
That ne Loue, and hym luste · to laughynge ne brouȝte,
And Pees thorw pacience · alle perilles stopped.'
'Trewes,' quod Treuth · 'thow tellest vs soth, bi Iesus! 416
Clippe we in couenaunt · and vch of vs cusse other!'
'And lete no peple,' quod Pees · 'perceyue that we chydde!
For inpossible is no thyng · to hym that is almyȝty.'
'Thow seist soth,' seyde Ryȝtwisnesse · and reuerentlich hir
    kyste, 420
Pees, and Pees here · *per secula seculorum.*
        Misericordia et veritas obuiauerunt sibi; iusticia et pax
            osculate sunt.
Treuth tromped tho, and songe · '*Te deum laudamus*';
And thanne luted Loue · in a loude note,
        Ecce quam bonum et quam iocundum, etc.

Tyl the daye dawed · this damaiseles daunced, 424
That men rongen to the resurexioun · and riȝt with that I waked,
And called Kitte my wyf · and Kalote my douȝter—
'Ariseth and reuerenceth · goddes resurrexioun,
And crepeth to the crosse on knees · and kisseth it for a Iuwel!

B. 408. *clarior—amor* RCOBY; LW *om.*

Thow shalt abygge bitere,' quath god · and bond hym with
    cheynes. 448
Astrot and alle othere · hudden hem in heornes,
Thei dorst nat loken on oure lorde · the leste of hem alle,
Bote leten hym leden forth which hym luste · and leue whiche
    hym lykede.
Mony hundrede of aungelis · harpeden tho and songen, 452
    Culpat caro, purgat caro, regnat deus dei caro.
Thenne pipede Pees · of poetes a note,
'Clarior est solito · post maxima nebula phebus;
Post inimicitias · clarior est et amor.
After sharpest shoures,' quath Pees · 'most sheene is the sonne;
Ys no weder warmer · than after watery cloudes, 457
Nother loue leuere · ne leuere freondes,
Than after werre and wrake · whanne loue and pees beon
    maistres.
Was neuere werre in this worlde · ne wykkeder enuye, 460
That Loue, and hym luste · to lauhynge ne brouhte,
And Pees thorgh pacience · alle pereles stoppede.'
'Treuwes,' quath Treuthe · 'thou tellest soth, by Iesus!
Cluppe we in couenaunt · and ech of ous cusse other!' 464
'And leet no peuple,' quath Pees · 'parceyue that we chide!
For impossible is no thyng · to hym that is al-myghty.'
'Thow seist soth,' quath Ryghtwisnesse · and reuerentliche heo
    custe
Pees, and Pees heore · *per secula seculorum.* 468
    Misericordia et ueritas obuiauerunt sibi; iusticia et pax
    osculate sunt.
Treuthe trompede tho, and song · '*Te deum laudamus;*'
And then lutede Loue · in a lowd note,
    '*Ecce quam bonum et quam iocundum est habitare fratres*
    in unum!'
Tyl the day dawede · these damseles daunsede,
That men rang to the resurreccioun · and with that ich awakede,
And kallyd Kytte my wyf · and Kalote my doughter, 473
'A-rys, and go reuerence · godes resurreccioun,
And creop on kneos to the croys · and cusse hit for a Iuwel,

C. 449. Astrott P.   451. leten IE; leet F; let TG; leot P.   461. ne
EFT; PMI *om.*   462. *From* ITG; PEMF *omit this line.*

For goddes blissed body · it bar for owre bote, 429
And it afereth the fende · for suche is the my3te,
May no grysly gost · glyde there it shadweth!'

PASSUS XIX.

*Passus xix*ᵘˢ *; et explicit Dobet; et incipit Dobest.*

THUS I awaked and wrote · what I had dremed,
And di3te me derely · and dede me to cherche,
To here holy the masse · and to be houseled after.
In myddes of the masse · tho men 3ede to offrynge, 4
I fel eftsones a-slepe · and sodeynly me mette,
That Pieres the Plowman · was paynted al blody,
And come in with a crosse · bifor the comune peple,
And ri3te lyke in alle lymes · to owre lorde Iesu; 8
And thanne called I Conscience · to kenne me the sothe.
'Is this Iesus the Iuster?' quod I · 'that Iuwes did to deth?
Or it is Pieres the Plowman! · who paynted hym so rede?'
Quod Conscience, and kneled tho · 'thise aren Pieres armes, 12
His coloures and his cote-armure · ac he that cometh so blody
Is Cryst with his crosse · conqueroure of Crystene.'
  'Why calle 3e hym Cryst?' quod I · 'sithenes Iuwes calle hym Iesus?
Patriarkes and prophetes · prophecyed bifore, 16
That alkyn creatures · shulden knelen and bowen,
Anon as men nempned · the name of god Iesu.
Ergo is no name · to the name of Iesus,
Ne none so nedeful to nempne · by ny3te ne by daye. 20
For alle derke deuelles · aren adradde to heren it,
And synful aren solaced · and saued bi that name.
And 3e callen hym Cryst · for what cause, telleth me?

And ryghtfullokest a relyk · non riccher on erthe. 476
For godes blesside body · hit bar for oure bote,
And hit a-fereth the feonde · for such is the myghte,
May no grysliche gost · glyde ther hit shadeweth!' 479

Hic explicit passus quartus et ultimus de Dobet.

PASSUS XXII.

Hic incipit passus primus de Dobest.

THUS ich awakede and wrot · what ich hadde dremed,
And dyhte me derly · and dude me to churche,
To huyre holliche the masse · and be housled after.
In myddes of the masse · tho men ȝeden to offrynge, 4
Ich fel eft-sones a-slepe · and sodeynliche me mette,
That Peers the Plouhman · was peynted al blody,
And cam yn with a croys · by-fore the comune peuple,
And ryght like in alle lymes · to oure lord Iesu; 8
And thenne calde ich Conscience · to kenne me the sothe.
'Is this Iesus the Iouster?' quath ich · 'that Iuwes duden to dethe,
Other is hit Peers Plouhman? · ho peynted hym so rede?' 11
Quath Conscience, and kneolede tho · 'these aren Cristes armes,
Hus colours and hus cote-armure · and he that cometh so blody,
Hit is Crist with his crois · conquerour of Crystine.'
'Whi calle ȝe him Crist · siththen Iuwes cald hym Iesus?
Patriarkes and prophetes · propheciede by-fore, 16
That alle kynne creatures · sholden kneolen and bowen,
A-non as men nempned · the name of god Iesu.
Ergo is no name · to the name of Iesu,
Ne non so neodful to nempne · by nyghte ne by daye. 20
For alle deorke deoueles · dreden hit to huyre,
And synful ben solacede · and saued by that name.
And ȝe callen hym Crist · for what cause, telleth me?

C. 476. An (*for* And) P.
Passus XXII. 5. fel GT; ful M; felle EIS; feel P. 12. this (*for* these) P.
14. is (*for* his) P. 15. PE *ins.* þat *after* siþthen. 20. Ne IFGT; And PEM.

Is Cryst more of my3te · and more worthy name 24
Than Iesu or Iesus · that al owre Ioye come of?'
    'Thow knowest wel,' quod Conscience · 'and thow konne
        resoun,
That kny3te, kynge, conqueroure · may be o persone.
To be called a kni3te is faire · for men shal knele to hym; 28
To be called a kynge is fairer · for he may kny3tes make;
Ac to be conquerour called · that cometh of special grace,
And of hardynesse of herte · and of hendenesse bothe,
To make lordes of laddes · of londe that he wynneth, 32
And fre men foule thralles · that folweth nou3t his lawes.
The Iuwes, that were gentil-men · Iesu thei dispised,
Bothe his lore and his lawe · now ar thei lowe cherlis.
As wyde as the worlde is · wonyeth there none 36
But vnder tribut and taillage · as tykes and cherles.
And tho that bicome Crysten · by conseille of the baptiste,
Aren frankeleynes, fre men · thorw fullyng that thei toke,
And gentel-men with Iesu · for Iesus was yfulled, 40
And vppon Caluarye on crosse · ycrouned kynge of Iewes.
    It bicometh to a kynge · to kepe and to defende,
And conquerour of conquest · his lawes and his large.
And so dide Iesus the Iewes · he Iustified and tau3te hem 44
The lawe of lyf · that last shal euere;
And fended fram foule yueles · feueres and fluxes,
And fro fendes that in hem were · and fals bileue.
Tho was he Iesus of Iewes called · gentel prophete, 48
And kynge of her kyngdome · and croune bar of thornes.
And tho conquered he on crosse · as conquerour noble;
My3t no deth hym fordo · ne adown brynge,
That he ne aros and regned · and rauysshed helle. 52
And tho was he 'conquerour' called · of quikke and of ded;
For he 3af Adam and Eue · and other mo blisse,
That longe hadde leyne bifore · as Lucyferes cherles.

    And sith he 3af largely · alle his lele lyges 56

B. 40. yfulled WCY; yfolled L.   44. dide WCOBY; ded L.   47. were
WCBY; was L.

Is Crist more of myght · and more worthiere name 24
Than Iesu other Iesus · that al oure Ioy come of?'
'Thow knowest wel,' quath Conscience · 'and thow conne reson,
That knyght, kyng, conquerour · may be o persone.
To be cald a knyght is fair · for men shal to hym kneole; 28
To be cald a kyng is fairour · for he may knyghtes make;
And to be cald conquerour · that cometh of special grace,
Of hardynesse of heorte · and of hendeness bothe,
To make lordes of laddes · of londe that he wynneth, 32
And fre men foule thralles · that folwen nat hus lawes.
The Iuwes that weren gentel-men · Iesu thei dispiseden,
Bothe hus lore and hus lawe · now aren thei lowe cheorles.
As wide as the worlde is · wonyeth ther none 36
Bote vnder tribut and taillage · as tikes and cheorles.
And tho that by-comen Cristine · by consail of the baptist,
Aren frankelayns and freo · thorgh fullyng that thei toke,
And gentel-men with Iesu · for Iesus was yfulled, 40
And vp-on Caluarie on croys · y-crouned kyng of Iuwes.
  Hit by-cometh for a kyng · to kepen and defende,
And conquerour of hus conqueste · hus laies and hus large.
So dude Iesus the Iuwes · he Iustifiede and tauhte hem 44
The lawe of the lykyng lyf · that laste shal euere ;
And fendede hem fro foule vueles · feueres and fluxes,
And fro feondes that were in hem · and false by-leyue.
Tho was he Iesus of Iuwes cald · gentel prophete, 48
And kyng of here kyngdom · and corone bar of thornes.
And tho conquered he on croys · as conquerour noble ;
Myght no deth hym for-do · ne adoun brynge,
That he ne aros and regnede · and rauesshede helle ; 52
And tho was he 'conquerour' called · of quyke and of dede.
For he ȝaf Adam and Eue · and other mo blisse,
That longe hadde leye by-fore · as Luciferes cheorles;
And tok Lucifer the lothliche · that lorde was of helle, 56
And bond hym as he is bounde · with bondes of yren.
Ho was hardier than he? · hus heorte blode he shadde,
To maken alle folk freo · that folwen hus lawe.
  And sutthe he ȝaf largeliche · all hus leel lege 60

C. 31. boþe T ; *which* PEMFG *omit*.   41. on MIF ; with PET.   y-crouned
IF ; crouned EMT ; coronede P.   44. Iustefiede P.   60. ȝaf EFG ; ȝaue P ;
see l. 54.

Places in paradys · at her partynge hennes,
He may wel be called 'conquerour' · and that is Cryst to mene.
Ac the cause that he cometh thus · with crosse of his passioun,
Is to wissen vs there-wyth · that whan that we ben tempted,   60
Ther-with to fyȝte and fenden vs · fro fallyng in-to synne,
And se bi his sorwe · that who so loueth Ioye,
To penaunce and to pouerte · he moste putten hym-seluen,
And moche wo in this worlde · willen and suffren.   64
    Ac to carpe more of Cryst · and how he come to that name,
Faithly forto speke · his firste name was Iesus.
Tho he was borne in Bethleem · as the boke telleth,
And cam to take mankynde · kynges and aungeles   68
Reuerenced hym faire · with richesse of erthe.
Angeles out of heuene · come knelyng and songe,
    Gloria in excelsis deo, etc.
Kynges come after · kneled, and offred
Mirre and moche golde · with-outen mercy askynge,   72
Or any kynnes catel · but knowlechyng hym soeuereigne
Bothe of sonde, sonne, and see · and sithenes thei went
In-to her kyngene kyth · by conseille of angeles.
And there was that worde fulfilled · the which thow of speke;   76
    Omnia celestia, terrestria, flectantur in hoc nomine Iesu.
For alle the angeles of heuene · at his burth kneled,
And al the witte of the worlde · was in tho thre kynges;
Resoun and riȝtwisnesse · and reuth thei offred;
Wherfore and whi · wyse men that tyme,   80
Maistres and lettred men · *Magy* hem called.
That o kynge cam with resoun · keuered vnder sense.
The secounde kynge sitthe · sothliche offred
Riȝtwisnesse vnder red golde · resouns felawe.   84
Golde is likned to leute · that last shal euere,
And resoun to riche golde · to riȝte and to treuthe.
The thridde kynge tho cam · knelyng to Iesu,
And presented hym with pitee · apierynge by myrre;   88
For mirre is mercy to mene · and mylde speche of tonge.
Thre yliche honest thinges · was offred thus at ones,
Thorw thre kynne kynges · knelynge to Iesu.

B. 79. riȝtwisnesse WOY; riȝtfulnesse LCB; *see* l. 84.   90. was L; were WOY.

C. PASSUS XXII. 61–95.

Places in paradis · at here partyng hennes,
He may beo wel cald 'conquerour' · and that is Crist to mene.
Ac the cause whi he cometh thus · with croys and hus passion,
Ys, to wissen ous ther-wilh · that when we beo tempted, 64
Ther-with to fighten and fenden ous · fro fallyng in-to synne,
And seo by hus sorwe · that ho so loueth Ioye,
To penaunce and to pouerte · he mot putte hym-selue,
And muche wo in this worlde · wilnen and suffren. 68
 Ac to carpe more of Crist · and how he cam to that name,
Faithly for to speke · hus furste name was Iesus.
Tho he was bore in Bethleem · as the book telleth,
And cam to take mankynde · kynges and aungeles 72
Reuerencede hym ryght faire · with richesse of eorthe.
Aungeles of heuene comen · kneolede and songen,
 Gloria in excelsis deo.
Kynges comen after · kneolede and offride
Muche gold and murre · with-oute mercy askynge, 76
Other eny kynne catel · bote knewelechede hym souereyn
Bothe of sand, sonne, and see · and sitthen thei wente
In-to here kyngene kutthe · by counsail of aungeles,
And ther was that word fulfild · the which thou of speke; 80
 Omnia celestia, terrestria, flectantur in hoc nomine Iesu.
For alle the aungeles of heuene · at hus burthe kneolede,
And al the wit of the worlde · was in tho thre kynges;
Reson and ryghtwisnesse · and reuthe thei offrede;
Where-fore and whi · wise men that tyme, 84
Maistres and lettred men · *Magi* hem calde.
That on kynge cam with reson · ycouerid vnder sense;
The secounde kyng sitthen · sothliche he offrede
Ryghtwisnesse, vnder red gold · resones felawe. 88
Gold is likned to leaute · that laste shal euere,
And reson to ryche gold · to right and to treuthe.
The thridde kynge cam tho · and kneolede to Iesu,
And presentide hym with pite · aperynge by mirre; 92
For mirre is mercy to mene · and mylde speche of tonge.
Eorthliche honeste thynges · was offred thus at ones
Thorgh thre kynde kynges · kneolyng to Iesu.

 C. 73. Reuerencide P. 77. knewelichede P. 82. (1st) þe EMFGT; þat P.
83. ryghtwisnesse EMF; ryghtfulnesse PGT; *see* l. 88. 84. Werefore P.
89. licknede P.

Ac for alle thise preciouse presentz · owre lorde prynce Iesus   92
Was neyther kynge ne conquerour · til he gan to wexe
In the manere of a man · and that by moche sleight;
As it bicometh a conquerour · to konne many sleightes,
And many wyles and witte · that wil ben a leder;   96
And so did Iesu in his dayes · who so had tyme to telle it.
Sum tyme he suffred · and sum tyme he hydde hym;
And sum tyme he fauȝte faste · and fleigh otherwhile.
And some tyme he gaf good · and graunted hele bothe,   100
Lyf and lyme · as hym lyste, he wrought.
As kynde is of a conquerour · so comsed Iesu,
Tyl he had alle hem · that he for bledde.
  In his Iuuente this Iesus · atte Iuwen feste   104
Water in-to wyn tourned · as holy writ telleth,
And there bigan god · of his grace to Dowel.
For wyn is lykned to lawe · and lyf of holynesse;
And lawe lakked tho · for men loued nouȝt her enemys.   108
And Cryst conseilleth thus · and comaundeth bothe,
Bothe to lered and to lewed · to louye owre enemys.
So atte feste firste · as I bifore tolde,
Bygan god, of his grace · and goodnesse, to Dowel: 112
And tho was he cleped and called · nouȝt holy Cryst, but Iesu,
A faunt fyn, ful of witte · *filius Marie*.
For bifor his moder Marie · made he that wonder,
That she furste and formest · ferme shulde bilieue,   116
That he thorw grace was gete · and of no gome elles.
He wrouȝt that bi no witte · but thorw worde one,
After the kynde that he come of · there comsed he Dowel.
And whan he was woxen more · in his moder absence,   120
He made lame to lepe · and ȝaue liȝte to blynde,
And fedde with two fisshes · and with fyue loues
Sore afyngred folke · mo than fyue thousande.
Thus he conforted carful · and cauȝte a gretter name,   124
The whiche was Dobet · where that he went.
For defe thorw his doynges to here · and dombe speke he made,

---

B. 103. fore (*for* for) L.

Ac for alle thes preciose presentes · oure lord prince Iesus 96
Was nother kyng ne conquerour · til he comsede wexe
In the manere of a man · and that by muche sleithe;
As hit by-cometh for a conquerour · to conne menye sleithes,
And menye wiles and wyt · that wol be a ledere; 100
And so dude Iesus in hus dayes · ho so dorste tellen hit.
Som tyme he suffrede · and som tyme he hidde hym;
And som tyme he fauhte faste · and fleih other-while.
And som tyme he gaf good · and grauntede hele, 104
Bothe lyf and lyme · as hym luste, he wrouhte.
As kynde is of a conquerour · so comsede Iesus,
Til he hadde alle hem · that he for bledde.
  In hus Iuuente this Iesus · at the Iuwene feste 108
Turned water in-to wyn · as holy writ telleth,
And ther by-gan god of hus grace · gretliche to Dowel.
For wyn is lykned to lawe · and lyf-holynesse;
And lawe lackede tho · for men louede nat here enemys. 112
And Crist counsaileth thus · and comaundeth bothe
To lerede and to lewede · for to loue oure enemys.
So at that feste furst · as ich by-fore tolde,
By-gan god of hus grace · and of hus goodnesse to Do-wel; 116
And tho was he cleped and cald · nat onliche Crist, bote Iesu,
A fauntekyn ful of wytt · *filius Marie.*
For by-fore hus moder Marie · made he that wonder,
That sheo furst and formest · sholde ferme by-leyue, 120
That he thorgh grace was gete · and of no gome elles.
He wrouhte that by no wyt · bote by worde one,
After the kynde that he cam of · ther comsede he Dowel.
And whenne he was woxen more · in hus modres absence, 124
He made lame to leepe · and ȝaf light to blynd,
And fedde with two fisshes · and with fyue loues
Sore a-fyngred fele folke · mo than fyf thousand.
Thus he comfortede careful · and cauhte a grettere name, 128
The whiche was Dobet · wher that he wente.
For deue thorgh hus doynges · and dombe speke and herde,

C. 96. prince TGF; PEM *om.* 98. a EMFTG; P *om.* 104. he MFGT;
PE *om.* 106. kynde MFGT; PE *om.* 108. þe MF; PEGT *om.* 112.
enemys T; enemy*us* F; enmys M; enemy PEG; *see* l. 114. 116. to MTG;
PEF *om.* 117. cleped MEFT; clipede P. 125. PE *ins.* þe *after 2nd* to.
126. two EGT; to PMF. 127. Sore MFTG; So PE.

And alle he heled and halp · that hym of grace asked.
And tho was he called in contre · of the comune peple,   128
For the dedes that he did · *fili Dauid, Iesus!*
For Dauid was douȝtiest · of dedes in his tyme,
The berdes tho songe · *Saul interfecit mille, et Dauid decem milia;*
For-thi the contre there Iesu cam · called hym *fili Dauid,*   132
And nempned hym of Nazereth · and no man so worthi
To be kaisere or kynge · of the kyngedome of Iuda,
Ne ouer Iuwes Iustice · as Iesus was, hem thouȝte.
Where-of Caiphas hadde enuye · and other of the Iewes,   136
And forto done hym to deth · day and nyȝte thei casten;
Kulleden hym on crosse-wyse · at Caluarie on Fryday,
And sithen buryden his body · and beden that men sholde
Kepen it fro niȝt-comeres · with knyȝtes y-armed,   140
For no frendes shulde hym fecche · for prophetes hem tolde,
That that blessed body · of burieles shulde rise,
And gone in-to Galile · and gladen his apostles,
And his moder Marie; · thus men bifore demed.   144
The knyȝtes that kepten it · biknewe it hem-seluen,
That angeles and archangeles · ar the day spronge,
Come knelynge to the corps · and songen, '*Christus resurgens*'
Verrey man bifor hem alle · and forth with hem he ȝede.   148
The Iewes preyed hem pees · and bisouȝte the knyȝtes
Telle the comune that there cam · a compaignye of his apostoles,
And bywicched hem as thei woke · and awey stolen it.
Ac Marie Magdeleyne · mette hym bi the wey,   152
Goynge toward Galile · in godhed and manhed,
And lyues and lokynge · and she aloude cryde,
In eche a compaignye there she cam · '*Christus resurgens!*'
Thus cam it out that Cryst ouer-cam · rekeuered and lyued;   156
    Sic oportet Christum pati, et intrare, etc.;
For that that wommen witeth · may nouȝte wel be conseille!
Peter perceyued al this · and pursued after,
Bothe Iames and Iohan · Iesu for to seke,

B. 127. halpe L.   157. L *om. 2nd* þat.

And alle he heled and halp · that hym of grace askyde.
Tho he was callyd in the contreo · of the comune peuple, 132
For the dedes that he dude ·' *fili David, Iesus!*
For Dauid was the douhtiest · of dedus in hus tyme;
The buyrdes tho songen · *Saul interfecit mille, et Dauid decem milia;*
For-thi the contreye ther Iesu cam · cald hym *fili Dauid*, 136
Nempnede hym of Nazareth · and no man so worthi
To beo caiser other kyng · of the kyngdom of Iuda,
Ne ouer Iuwes Iustice · as Iesus was, hem thouhte.
Her-of had Cayfas enuye · and othere Iuwes, 140
And for to do hym to dethe · day and nyght thei casten,
And culled hym on croys-wyse · at Caluarye, on a Fryday,
And sutthen buriede hus body · and beden that men sholde
Kepen hit fro nyght-commeres · with knyghtes y-armed, 144
For no freonde sholde hit fecche · for prophetes hem tolde,
That that blessed body · of buriels sholde aryse,
And gon in-to Galile · and gladen hus apostoles,
And hus moder Marie; · thus me by-fore deuynede. 148
The knyghtes that kepten hit · by-knewen hem-selue,
That aungeles and archaungeles · ar the day spronge,
Comen kneolynge · to that corps, and songen,
'*Christus rex resurgens*' · and hit aros after, 152
Verrei man by-fore hem alle · and forth with hem ȝeode.
The Iuwes preyede hem of pees · and preyede tho knyghtes
Telle the comune, that ther cam · a companye of hus apostoles,
And by-wicched hem as thei woke · and a-way stelyn hit. 156
Ac Marie Magdalene · mette him by the weye,
Goynge to-ward Galile · in god-hede and man-hede,
And lyues and lokynge · and heo aloud cryede,
In eche companye ther heo cam · '*Christus resurgens*.' 160
Thus cam hit out that Crist ouer-cam · rekeouered, and lyuede;
Sic oportet Christum pati, et intrare gloriam suam,
For that that wommen witeth · may nat wel be consail!
Peter parceyuede al this · and porsuede after,
Bothe Iames and Iohan · Iesu to seke, 164

C. 135. þo EMG; so P. 139. was MFGT; PE *om.* 141. deþe EMG; diþe P. 146. buriels E; burielesse P. 150. and EFGTM; P *om.* 156. bywocched P. 157. him MFGT; hem PE. 161. leyuede P. 162. PFT *omit* 2nd þat; *found in* EMG.

Tadde and ten mo · with Thomas of Ynde.   160
And as alle thise wise wyes · weren togideres,
In an hous al bishette · and her dore ybarred,
Cryst cam in, and al closed · bothe dore and ʒates,
To Peter and to his aposteles · and seyde '*pax vobis!*'   164
And toke Thomas by the hande · and tauʒte hym to grope,'
And fele with his fyngres · his flesshelich herte.
Thomas touched it · and with his tonge seyde,
    '*Deus meus et dominus meus.*
Thow art my lorde, I bileue · god, lorde Iesu!   168
Thow deydest and deth tholedest · and deme shalt vs alle,
And now art lyuynge and lokynge · and laste shalt euere!'
Crist carped thanne · and curteislich seyde,
'Thomas, for thow trowest this · and trewliche bileuest it,   172
Blessed mote thow be · and be shalt for euere.
And blessed mote thei alle be · in body and in soule,
That neuere shal se me in siʒte · as thow doste nouthe,
And lellich bileuen al this · I loue hem and blesse hem;   176
    Beati qui non viderunt, et crediderunt, etc.'
And whan this dede was done · Dobest he tauʒte,
And ʒaf Pieres power · and pardoun he graunted
To alle manere men · mercy and forʒyfnes,
Hym myʒte men to assoille · of alle manere synnes,   180
In couenant that thei come · and knowleche to paye,
To Pieres pardon the Plowman · *redde quod debes.*
Thus hath Pieres powere · be his pardoun payed,
To bynde and to vnbynde · bothe here and elles-where,   184
And assoille men of alle synnes · saue of dette one.
Anone after an heigh · vp in-to heuene
He went, and wonyeth there · and wil come atte laste,
And rewarde hym riʒte wel · that *reddit quod debet*—   188
Payeth parfitly · as pure trewthe wolde.
And what persone payeth it nouʒt · punysshen he thinketh,
And demen hem at domes daye · bothe quikke and ded;
The gode to the godhede · and to grete Ioye,   192
And wikke to wonye · in wo with-outen ende.'

B. 176. *et crediderunt* COBY; LW *om.*   181. knewleche L.   184.
L *om.* where.   188. L *ins.* wil *after* And.

Taddee and ten mo · with Thomas of Ynde;
And as alle these wise wyes · weren to-gederes
In an hous al by-shutt · and here dore barred,
Crist cam yn, and al was closed · bothe dore and ȝates, 168
To Peter and to hus aposteles · and seyde, '*pax uobis!*'
And took Thomas by the hand · and tauhte hym to grope,
And fele with hus fyngres · hus fleshliche heorte.
Thomas touchede hit · and with hus tunge seyde, 172
  '*Dominus meus et deus meus,*
Thow art my lord, ich by-leyue · god, lord Iesu,
That deydest and deth tholedest · and deme shalt ous alle,
And now art lyuynge and lokynge · and laste shalt euere.'
Crist carpede thenne · and corteisliche seide, 176
'Thomas, for thou trowest this · and trewely by-leyuest hit,
Yblessed mote thou beo · and beo shalt for euere;
And blessed moten thei beo · in body and in soule,
That neuere shullen seo in syht · as thou seost nouthe, 180
And leelly by-leyuen al this · ich loue hem and blesse hem;
  Beati qui non uiderunt, et crediderunt.'
And when this dede was don · Dobest he thouhte,
And ȝaf Peers power · and pardon he grauntede
To alle manere of men · mercy and forȝyuenesse, 184
And ȝaf hym myghte to asoylye men · of alle manere synnes,
In couenaunt that thei come · and kneweliched to paye
To Peers pardon the Plouhman · *redde quod debes.*
Thus haueth Peers power · beo hus pardon payed, 188
To bynde and vnbynde · bothe here and elleswher,
And assoille of alle synnes · saue of dette one.
A-non after an hyh · vp in-to heuene
He wente, and woneth there · and wol come atte laste, 192
And rewardy him right wel · that *reddit quod debet,*
Payeth now parfitliche · as pure treuthe wolde.
And what persone payeth hit nat · punysshen he thenketh,
And demen hem at domesday · bothe quyke and dede; 196
The gode to the god-hede · and to grete Ioye,
And wyckede to wonye · in wo with-outen ende.'

C. 165. Taddee EM; Tadee PG.   166. as FMGT; PE *om.*   wyes FGT;
weyes P.   170. to grope EMFGT; þo grepe P.   173. art MFT; ert PEG.
184. an (*for* and) P.   187. þe T; PEMFG *om.*   189. elleswer P.   193.
him FT; hym G; hem PEM.   195. wat P.   196. hem EFG; hym PT.

Thus Conscience of Crist · and of the crosse carped,
And conseilled me to knele ther-to · and thanne come, me thou3te,
One *spiritus paraclitus* · to Pieres and to his felawes; 196
In lyknesse of a li3tnynge · he ly3te on hem alle,
And made hem konne and knowe · alkyn langages.
I wondred what that was · and wagged Conscience,
And was afered of the ly3te · for in fyres lyknesse 200
Spiritus paraclitus · ouer-spradde hem alle.
  Quod Conscience, and kneled · 'this is Crystes messager,
And cometh fro the grete god · and Grace is his name.
Knele now,' quod Conscience · 'and if thow canst synge, 204
Welcome hym and worshipe hym · with "*veni, creator spiritus.*"
Thanne songe I that songe · and so did many hundreth,
And cryden with Conscience · 'help vs, god of grace!'
And thanne bigan Grace · to go with Piers Plowman, 208
And conseilled hym and Conscience · the comune to sompne—
'For I wil dele to-daye · and dyuyde grace,
To alkynnes creatures · that kan her fyue wittes,
Tresore to lyue by · to her lyues ende, 212
And wepne to fy3te with · that wil neure faille.
For Antecryst and his · al the worlde shal greue,
And acombre the, Conscience · but if Cryst the helpe.
And fals prophetes fele · flatereres and glosers 216
Shullen come, and be curatoures · ouer kynges and erlis,
And Pryde shal be pope · prynce of holycherche,
Coueytyse and Vnkyndenesse · cardinales hym to lede.
For-thi,' quod Grace, 'er I go · I wil gyue 3ow tresore, 220
And wepne to fi3te with · whan Antecryst 3ow assailleth.'
And gaf eche man a grace · to gye with hym-seluen,
That ydelnesse encombre hym nou3t · envye, ne pryde,
  Diuisiones graciarum sunt, etc.
  Some he 3af wytte · with wordes to shewe, 224
Witte to wynne her lyflode with · as the worlde asketh,
As prechoures and prestes · and prentyces of lawe,
Thei lelly to lyue · by labour of tonge,
And bi witte to wissen other · as Grace hem wolde teche. 228

B. 211. kan L; han WCOYB.   226. prentyce L (*wrongly*).

Thus Conscience of Crist · and of the croys carpede,
And consailede me to kneole ther-to · and thenne cam, me thouhte, 200
On *spiritus paraclitus* · to Peers and to hus felawes,
In liknesse of a lyghtnynge · a-lyghte on hem alle,
And made hem conne and knowe · alle kynne languages.
Ich wondrede what that was · and waggede Conscience, 204
And was a-fered for the lyght · for in fuyres lyknesse
Spiritus paraclitus · ouer-spradde hem alle.
Quath Conscience tho, and kneolede · 'this is Cristes messager,
And cometh fro the grete god · Grace is hus name. 208
Kneole now,' quath Conscience · 'and yf thow conne synge,
Welcome hym and worshupe hym · with "*veni, creator spiritus*."'
And ich sang that song tho · and so dude meny hondred,
And cryden with Conscience · 'help ous, god of grace!' 212
Tho by-gan Grace · to go with Peers the Plouhman,
And consailede hym and Conscience · the comune to someny—
'For ich wolle dele to-day · and diuyde grace
To alle kynne creatures · that can hus fif wittes; 216
Tresour to lyue by · to here lyues ende,
And wepne to fight with · that wol neuere faille.
For Antecrist and hise · shal al the worlde greue,
And encombry the, Conscience · bote yf Crist the helpe. 220
And fele false prophetes · flaterers and glosers
Shullen come, and be curatours · ouer kynges and erles.
Thanne shal Pruyde be pope · and pryns of holychurche,
Couetise and Vnkyndenesse · cardinales hym to lede. 224
For-thi,' quath Grace, 'ar ich go · ich wole gyue ȝou tresour,
And wepne to fyghte with · whanne Antecrist ȝou assaileth.'
And gaf ech man a grace · to gye with hym-self,
That ydelnesse ne encombre hem nat · ne enuye, ne pruyde;
 Diuisiones graciarum sunt. 228
To somme men he ȝaf wit · with wordes to shewe,
To wynne with truthe · that the worlde asketh,
As preostes and prechours · and prentises of lawe,
Thei to lyue leelly · by labour of tounge, 232
And by wit to wyssen othere · as Grace wolde hem teche.

C. 202. licknesse P. lyghtynge PG.   203. conne EMG; come PT.
205. a-ferede P.   219. woidle P.   229. wiþ MEFT; PG *om*.

And some he kenned crafte · and kunnynge of sy3te,
With sellyng and buggynge · her bylyf to wynne,
And some he lered to laboure · a lele lyf and a trewe,
And somme he tau3te to tilie · to dyche and to thecche,   232
To wynne with her lyflode · by lore of his techynge.
And some to dyuyne and diuide · noumbres to kenne;
And some to compas craftily · and coloures to make;
And some to se and to saye · what shulde bifalle,   236
Bothe of wel and of wo · telle it or it felle,
As astronomyenes thorw astronomye · and philosophres wyse.
And some to ryde and to recoeure · that vnri3tfully was wonne;
He wissed hem wynne it a3eyne · thorw wightnesse of handes,
And fecchen it fro fals men · with Foluyles lawes.   241
And some he lered to lyue · in longynge to ben hennes,
In pouerte and in penaunce · to preye for alle Crystene.
And alle he lered to be lele · and eche a crafte loue other,   244
And forbad hem alle debate · that none were amonge hem.
'Thowgh some be clenner than somme · 3e se wel,' quod
    Grace,
'That he that vseth the fairest crafte · to the foulest I couth
    haue put hym,
Thinketh alle,' quod Grace · 'that grace cometh of my 3ifte;
Loke that none lakke other · but loueth alle as bretheren.   249
And who that moste maistries can · be myldest of berynge,
And crouneth Conscience kynge · and maketh Crafte 3owre
    stuward,
And after Craftes conseille · clotheth 3ow and fede.   252
For I make Pieres the Plowman · my procuratour and my reve,
And regystrere to receyue · *redde quod debes*.
My prowor and my plowman · Piers shal ben on erthe,
And for to tulye treuthe · a teme shal he haue.'   256
    Grace gaue Piers a teme · foure gret oxen;
That on was Luke, a large beste · and a lowe-chered,
And Marke, and Mathew the thrydde · myghty bestes bothe,
And Ioigned to hem one Iohan · most gentil of alle,   260
The prys nete of Piers plow · passyng alle other.

And somme he kende craftes · and connynge of syghte,
With syllynge and byggynge · here by-lyue to wynne.
And somme he lerede to laboure · a londe and a watere, 236
And lyue by that labour · a leel lyf and a trewe.
And somme he tauhte to tulye · to theche and to coke,
As here wit wold · when the tyme come.
And somme to dyuyne and dyuyde · numbres to kenne, 240
And craftely to compassen · and colours to make.
And somme to seo and to seye · what sholde by-falle
Bothe of wele and of wo · and be war by-fore,
As astronomyens thorw astronomye · and philosophers wise. 244
And somme to ryde and rekeuere · that vnryghtfulliche was wonne;
He wissede men wynnen hit aȝeyn · thorgh wyghtnesse of handes,
And fecchen hit fro false men · with Foleuyles lawes.
And somme he lerede to lyue · in longynge to be hennes, 248
In pouerte and in pacience · to preye for alle Crystyne.
And alle he lerede to beo leell · and eche a craft loue othere,
Nother bost ne debat · beo among hem alle.
'Thauh somme be clannere than some · ȝe seon wel,' quath Grace, 252
'That alle craft and connynge · cam of my ȝyfte.
Loke that non lacken other · bote louye as bretheren,
And he that most maistries can · beo myldest of berynge.
And coroneth Conscience kyng · and maketh Craft ȝowre stywarde, 256
And after Craftes consail · clotheth ȝow and fedeth.
For ich make Peers Plouhman · my procuratour and my reue,
And registrer to receyuen · *redde quod debes*.
My prower and my plouhman · Peers shal beo on erthe; 260
And for to tulye treuthe · a teome shal he haue.'
Grace gaf to Peers a teome · of foure grete oxen;
That on was Luc, a large beest · and a louh-chered,
Marc, and Matheu the thirde · myghty beestes bothe; 264
And Ioyned til hem on Iohan · most gentil of alle,
The prys neet of Peers plouh · passynge alle othere.

C. 234. PE *ins.* hem *after* kende.   237. 2*nd* a EMFGT; P *om.*   238. 1*st* to MFGT; PE *om.*   þeche E; þecche MT; teche PF.   241. craftely F; PEGT *om.*   248. lererede P.   252. clannore P.   254. broþrene P. 260. prower EG; prowour F; puruyour M; power P.   263. louh-chyrede P.

And Grace gaue Pieres · of his goodnesse, foure stottis,
Al that his oxen eryed · they to harwe after.
On hyȝte Austyne · and Ambrose an-other, 264
Gregori the grete clerke · and Ierome the gode;
Thise foure, the feithe to teche · folweth Pieres teme,
And harwed in an handwhile · al holy scripture,
Wyth two harwes that thei hadde · an olde and a newe, 268
  Id est, vetus testamentum et nouum.
And Grace gaue greynes · the cardynales vertues,
And sewe hem in mannes soule · and sithen he tolde her names.
Spiritus prudencie · the firste seed hyȝte,
And who so eet that · ymagyne he shulde, 272
Ar he did any dede · deuyse wel the ende;
And lerned men a ladel bugge · with a longe stele,
That cast for to kepe a crokke · to saue the fatte abouen.
  The secounde seed hiȝte · *spiritus temperancie.* 276
He that ete of that seed · hadde suche a kynde,
Shulde neuere mete ne mochel drynke · make hym to swelle,
Ne sholde no scorner ne scolde · oute of skyl hym brynge,
Ne wynnynge, ne welthe · of worldeliche ricchesse, 280
Waste worde of ydelnesse · ne wykked speche meue;
Shulde no curyous clothe · comen on hys rugge,
Ne no mete in his mouth · that maister Iohan spiced.
  The thridde seed that Pieres sewe · was *spiritus fortitudinis.*
And who so eet of that seed · hardy was eure 285
To suffre al that god sent · sykenesse and angres;
Myȝte no lesynge ne lyere · ne losse of worldely catel
Maken hym for any mournynge · that he nas merye in soule,
And bolde and abydynge · bismeres to suffre, 289
And playeth al with pacyence · *et parce michi, domine,*
And couered hym vnder conseille · of Catoun the wyse;
Esto forti animo, cum sis dampnatus inique. 292
  The fierthe seed that Pieres sewe · was *spiritus iusticie,*
And he that eet of that seed · shulde be euere trewe
With god, and nouȝt agast · but of gyle one.
For gyle goth so pryuely · that good faith other-while 296

B. 270. hem W; it LCOBY. 280. wordeliche L.

And sutthe Grace of hus goodnesse · gaf Peers foure stottes,
Al that hus oxen ereden · thei to harwen after. 268
On hihte Austyn · and Ambrosie another,
Gregori the grete clerk · and Ierom the goode.
Theose foure, the faith to teche · folwede Peers teom,
And harowede in an hand-whyle · al holy scripture, 272
With to eythes that thei hadden · an olde and a newe;
    Vetus testamentum et nouum.
And Grace gaf to Peers greynes · cardinales uertues,
And sewe hit in mannes soule · and sitthen he tolde here names.
Spiritus prudencie · the furste sed hihte; 276
That ho so eet that seed · ymagenye he sholde,
Er he dude eny dede · deuyse wel the ende;
And lerede men a ladel bygge · with a long stele,
That cast for to kele a crokke · and saue the fatte aboue. 280
    The secunde seed highte · *spiritus temperancie;*
He that eet of that seed · hadde suche a kynde,
Sholde neuere mete ne myschief · make hym to swelle;
Ne sholde no scornere · out of skyle hym brynge, 284
Nother wynnynge, ne welthe · of worldliche richesse,
Wast word, ne ydelnesse · ne wyckede speche meoue.
Sholde no curiouse clothe · come on hus rygge,
Nother mete in hus mouthe · that maister Iohan spicede. 288
    The thrydde seod that Peers sewe · was *spiritus fortitudinis;*
And ho so eet of that seed · hardy was he euere
To suffren al that god sente · syknesses and angres;
Myghte no lyere with lesynges · ne loos of worldly catell 292
Make hym for eny mournyng · that he ne was mury in soule,
And bold of a-bydyng · busemares to suffren,
And plede with pacience · and *parce michi, domine;*
And keouered hym vnder consail · of Caton the wise, 296
Esto forti animo · *cum sis dampnatus inique.*
    The furthe seed that Peers sewe · was *spiritus iusticie;*
And he that eet of that seed · sholde be euere trewe
With god, and nat a-gast · bote of gyle one. 300
For gyle goth so priuely · that good faithe other-whyle

C. 272. wyle PG.   277, 282. eet MFG; eete P.   283. to MFT;
PEG *om.*   285. wordliche P.   290. eet MFG; ete PE.   292. ne MFGT;
no PE. wordly PG.   298. *spiritus iusticie* EMFGT; P has a blank space.
299. euere M; euene PEGT. trywe P.   301. wyle P.

May nouȝte ben aspyed · for *spiritus iusticie*.
Spiritus iusticie · spareth nouȝte to spille
Hem that ben gulty · and forto correcte
The kynge, ȝif he falle · in gylte or in trespasse.   300
For counteth he no kynges wratthe · whan he in courte sitteth
To demen as a domes-man ; · adradde was he neure,
Noither of duke ne of deth · that he ne dede the lawe,
For present or for preyere · or any prynces lettres ;   304
He dede equite to alle · euene-forth his powere.
  Thise foure sedes Pieres sewe · and sitthe he did hem harwe
Wyth olde lawe and newe lawe · that loue myȝte wexe
Amonge the foure vertues · and vices destroye.   308
For comunelich in contrees · kammokes and wedes
Fouleth the fruite in the felde · there thei growe togyderes ;
And so don vices · vertues worthy.
Quod Piers, 'harweth alle that kunneth kynde witte · bi conseille
    of this doctours,   312
And tulyeth after her techynge · the cardinale vertues.'
'Aȝeines thi greynes,' quod Grace · 'bigynneth for to ripe,
Ordeigne the an hous, Piers · to herberwe in thi cornes.'
'By god ! Grace,' quod Piers · 'ȝe moten gyue tymbre,   316
And ordeyne that hous · ar ȝe hennes wende.'
And Grace gaue hym the crosse · with the croune of thornes,
That Cryst vpon Caluarye · for mankynde on pyned,
And of his baptesme and blode · that he bledde on rode   320
He made a maner morter · and Mercy it hiȝte.
And there-with Grace bigan · to make a good foundement,
And watteled it and walled it · with his peynes and his passioun,
And of al holywrit · he made a rofe after,   324
And called that hous Vnite · holicherche on Englisshe.
And whan this dede was done · Grace deuised
A carte, hyȝte Cristendome · to carye Pieres sheues ;
And gaf hym caples to his carte · Contricioun and Confessioun,
And made Presthode haywarde · the while hym-self went   329
As wyde as the worlde is · with Pieres to tulye treuthe.

B. 315. quod Piers L ; CBY *om.* quod.

May nat be aspied · thorw *spiritus iusticie.*
Spiritus iusticie · spareth nat to spille
Hem that beoth gulty · and for to corecte 304
The kyng, and the kyng falle · in eny thynge gulty.
For counteth he no kynges wraththe · when he in court sytteth
To deme as a domesman; · adrad was he neuere,
Nother of duk ne of deth · that he ne doth the lawe, 308
For present other for preyoure · othere eny princes letteres;
He dude equyte to alle · euene-forth hus knowynge.
  Theese foure seedes Peeres sewe · and sutthen he dude hem harwen
With olde lawe and newe lawe · that loue myghte wexe 312
Amonge these foure vertues · and vices destruyen.
For comunliche in contreies · cammokes and weodes
Fouleth the frut in the felde · ther thei growen to-gederes;
And so doth vices vertues · 'and for-thi,' quath Peers, 316
'Harweth alle that conneth kynde wit · by counsail of theose doctours,
And tulyeth after here techynge · the cardinale vertues.'
'Aȝeynst that thi greynes,' quath Grace · 'bygynneth to growe,
Ordeyne the an hous, Peers · to herberghen in thi cornes.' 320
'By god, Grace,' quath Peers · 'ȝe mote gyue me tymber,
And ordeyne that hous · er ȝe hennes wende.'
And Grace gaf hym the croys · with the corone of thornes,
That Crist vp-on Caluarie · for mankynde on peynede; 324
And of hus baptisme and blod · that he bledde on rode
He made a maner morter · and Mercy hit hihte.
And ther-with Grace by-gan · to make a good foundement,
And watelide hit and wallyde hit · with hus peynes and hus passion, 328
And of alle holy writt · he made a roof after,
And cald that hous Vnite · holychurche in Englishe.
And whanne this dede was don · Grace deuysede
A cart, hihte Cristendome · to carien home Peers sheues; 332
And gaf hym capeles to hus cart · Contricion with Confession,
And made Preosthood haiwarde · the while hym-self wente
As wide as the worlde is · with Peers to tulye treuthe,

C. 302. aspiede P. 312. newe EMFGT; with newe P. 316. an vertues PT; *but* EMFG *omit* an. 321. god MFGT; godes PE. 322. her (*for* er) P. wennde P. 324. one (*for* on) P. 334. wile P.

Now is Pieres to the plow · and Pruyde it aspyde,
And gadered hym a grete oest · to greuen he thinketh   332
Conscience and al Crystene · and cardinale vertues,
Blowe hem doune and breke hem · and bite atwo the mores;
And sente forth Surquydous · his seriaunt of armes,
And his spye Spille-loue · one Speke-yuel-byhynde.   336
Thise two come to Conscience · and to Crystene peple,
And tolde hem tydynges · 'that tyne thei shulde the sedes,
That Pieres there hadde ysowen · the cardynal vertues;
And Pieres berne worth broke · and thei that ben in Vnite   340
Shulle come out, and Conscience · and ȝowre two caples,
Confessioun and Contricioun · and ȝowre carte the Byleue
Shal be coloured so queyntly · and keuered vnder owre sophistrie,
That Conscience shal nouȝte · knowe by contricioun,   344
Ne by confessioun · who is Cristene or hethen,
Ne no maner marchaunt · that with moneye deleth,
Where he wynne wyth riȝte · with wronge, or with vsure.
With suche coloures and queyntise · cometh Pryde y-armed,
With the lorde that lyueth after · the luste of his body,   349
To wasten, on welfare · and on wykked kepynge,
Al the worlde in a while · thorw owre witte,' quod Pruyde.
  Quod Conscience to alle Crystene tho · 'my conseille is to wende   352
Hastiliche in-to Vnyte · 'and holde we vs there,
And preye we that a pees were · in Piers berne the Plowman.
For witterly I wote wel · we beth nouȝte of strengthe
To gone agayne Pryde · but Grace were with vs.'   356
And thanne cam Kynde Wytte · Conscience to teche,
And cryde and comaunded · al Crystene peple,
For to deluen a dyche · depe a-boute Vnite,
That holy-cherche stode in Vnite · as it a pyle were.   360
Conscience comaunded tho · al Crystene to delue,
And make a muche mote · that myȝte ben a strengthe,
To helpe holycherche · and hem that it kepeth.
Thanne alkyn Crystene · saue comune wommen,   364
Repenteden and refused synne · saue they one;
And fals men, flatereres · vsureres and theues,
Lyeres and questmongeres · that were forsworen ofte,

B. 344. conscioun (*for* conscience) L.   360. were COBY; L *om.*   366. flateres L.

And the londe of by-leyue · the lawe of holychurche. 336
Now is Peeres to the plouh; · Pruyde hit aspide,
And gadered hym a gret ost · greuen he thenketh
Conscience, and alle Cristene · and cardinale uertues,
To blowen hem doun and breken hem · and bite a-two the rotes;
And sente forth sourquidours · hus seriauns of armes, 341
And hus aspie Spille-loue · on Speke-vuel-by-hynde.
These to-comen to Conscience · and to Cristyne peuple,
And tolden hem tydynges · 'that tyne they sholde 344
The seedes that syre Peers sewe · the cardinale uertues;
And Peers bern worth to-broke · and thei that ben in Vnite
Shullen come out, and Conscience · and ȝowre two capeles,
Contricion and Confession · and ȝoure cart Bi-leyue 348
Shal be colered so queyntely · and keouered vnder oure sophistrie,
That Conscience shal nat · knowe by contricion,
Nother by confession · ho is Cristyne other hethene,
Ne no manere marchaunt · that with monye deleth, 352
Whether he wynne with right · with wrang, other with vsure.
With suche colour and queyntise · cometh Pruyde y-armed,
With the lord that lyueth after · the lust of hus bodye,
To wasten, in welfare · and in wickede kepynge, 356
Al the worlde in a while · thorugh oure wit,' quath Pruyde.
Quath Conscience to alle Crystyne tho · 'my consail is, we wende
Hastiliche in-to Vnite · and holde we ous there;
Preye we that a pees were · in Peers bern the Plouhman. 360
For wyterly ich wot wel · we beoth nat of strengthe
To go a-gayn Pruyde · bote Grace with ous were.'
And thenne cam Kynde Wit · Conscience to teche;
He criede, and comaundede · alle Cristyne people 364
To delue and dike a deop diche · al aboute Vnite,
That holychurche stod in holynesse · as hit were a pile.
Conscience comaundede tho · alle Crystyne to delue,
And make a muche mot · that myghte be a strengthe, 368
To helpe holychurche · and hem that hit kepeth.
Thenne alle kynne Crystyne · saue comune wommen,
Repentede and refusede synne · saue thei one;
And a sisour and a somenour · that weren for-swore ofte, 372

C. 340. a-two EFGT; a-to PS. 349. keouerede P. 353. Weder
(*for* Wheþer) P. 354. y-armed G; y-armyd ST; armede PE; *see* l. 144.
355. loust P. 372. a sisour MFSGT; assisour P.

Wytynge and willefully · with the false helden, 368
And for syluer were forswore · sothely thei wist it.
There nas no Crystene creature · that kynde witte hadde,
Saue schrewes one · suche as I spak of,
That he ne halpe a quantite · holynesse to wexe. 372
Somme thorw bedes-byddynge · and somme thorw pylgrymage,
And other pryue penaunce · and some thorw penyes-delynge.
And thanne welled water · for wikked werkes,
Egerlich ernynge · out of mennes eyen. 376
Clennesse of the comune · and clerkes clene lyuynge
Made Vnite holicherche · in holynesse to stonde.
'I care nouȝte,' quod Conscience · 'though Pryde come nouthe,
The lorde of luste shal be letted · al this lente, I hope. 380
Cometh,' quod Conscience · 'ȝe Cristene, and dyneth,
That han laboured lelly · al this lente-tyme.
Here is bred yblessed · and goddes body ther-vnder.
Grace thorw goddes worde · gaue Pieres power, 384
And myȝtes to maken it · and men to ete it after,
In helpe of her hele · onys in a moneth,
Or as ofte as they hadden nede · tho that hadde ypayed
To Pieres pardoun the Plowman · *redde quod debes.*' 388
'How?' quod al the comune · 'thow conseillest vs to ȝelde
Al that we owen any wyȝte · ar we go to housel?'
'That is my conseille,' quod Conscience · 'and cardynale vertues,
That vche man forȝyue other · and that wyl the *paternoster,* 392
    Et dimitte nobis debita nostra, etc.,
And so to ben assoilled · and sithen ben houseled.'
'ȝe, bawe!' quod a brewere · 'I wil nouȝt be reuled,
Bi Iesu! for al ȝowre Ianglynge · with *spiritus iusticie,*
Ne after Conscience, by Cryste · whil I can selle 396
Bothe dregges and draffe · and drawe it at on hole,
Thikke ale and thinne ale · for that is my kynde,
And nouȝte hakke after holynesse; · holde thi tonge, Conscience!
Of *spiritus iusticie* · thow spekest moche an ydel!' 400
'Caytyue,' quod Conscience · 'cursed wrecche!
Vnblessed artow, brewere · but if the god helpe;

B. 385. And W; LCOBY *om.*

Witynge and wilfulliche · with the false thei helden,
And for seluere were for-swore · sothly thei wisten hit.
Ther ne was Cristyne creature · that kynde wit hadde,
That he ne halp a quantyte · holynesse to wexe;   376
Some by bedes-byddyng · and somme by pilgrimages,
Other othere pryueie penaunces · and somme thorw pansdelynge.
And thenne water wellede · for wyckede werkes,
Egreliche ȝernynge · out of mennys eyen.   380
Clannesse of the comune · and clerkes clene lyuynge
Made Unite holychurche · in holynesse stonde.
'Ich care nat,' quath Conscience · 'thauh Pruyde come nouthe,
The lord of lust shal beo lett · al this lente, ich hope.   384
Cometh now,' quath Conscience · 'ȝe Cristyne, and dyneth,
That han labored leelly · al this lente-tyme.
Her is bred yblessid · and godes body ther-vnder.
Grace gaf thorw godes worde · to Peers Plouhman power   388
And myghte to maken hit · and men for to eten hit,
In help of here hele · ones in a monthe,
Other as ofte as thei hadde neode · thei that hadden payed
To Peers pardon the Plouhman · *redde quod debes*.'   392
'How?' quath alle the comune · 'consailest thou ous to ȝelde
Al that we owen eny wyght · er we go to housele?'
'That is my consail,' quath Conscience · 'and cardinale vertues,
That iche man forȝiue other · and that wile the pater-noster;
    Et dimitte nobis debita nostra, sicut et nos dimittimus, etc.,
And so to beo asoilled · and sytthen beo housled.'   397
'Ȝe, bawe!' quath a brewere · 'ich wol nat beo rueled,
By Iesu! for al ȝoure iangelynge · after *spiritus iusticie*,
Ne after Conscience, by Crist · for ich couthe selle   400
Bothe dregges and draf · and drawe at one hole
Thicke ale and thynne ale · and that is my kynde,
And nat to hacke after holynesse; · hold thy tonge, Conscience!
Of *spiritus iusticie* · thow spekest muche an ydel!'   404
'Caitif,' quath Conscience · 'corsede wreche!
Unblessed art thow, brewere · bote yf god the helpe;

C. 373. Whitynge P.   376. to MFSGT; PE *om.*   378. Oþe (*for* Oþer) P.   383. PEG *insert* now *after* nat.   384. loust P.   390. mounthe P.   392. þe FSTG; PEM *om.*   396. *From* T; *also in* MFSG; PE *omit this line*. dimittimus *is in* F *only*.   397. asoillede P.   398. ruelede P.   406. art MFST; ert PEG.

But thow lyue by lore · of *spiritus iusticie*,
The chief seed that Pieres sewe · ysaued worstow neure.   404
But Conscience the comune fede · and cardynale vertues,
Leue it wel thei ben loste · bothe lyf and soule.'
'Thanne is many man ylost' · quod a lewed vycory,
'I am a curatour of holykyrke · and come neure in my tyme
Man to me, that me couth telle · of cardinale vertues,   409
Or that acounted Conscience · at a cokkes fether or an hennes!
I knewe neure cardynal · that he ne cam fro the pope,
And we clerkes, whan they come · for her comunes payeth,   412
For her pelure and her palfreyes mete · and piloures that hem folweth.
The comune *clamat cotidie* · eche a man to other,
'The contre is the curseder · that cardynales come inne;
And there they ligge and lenge moste · lecherye there regneth :'—
For-thi,' quod this vicori · 'be verrey god, I wolde   417
That no cardynal come · amonge the comune peple,
But in her holynesse · holden hem stille
At Auynoun, amonge the Iuwes · *cum sancto sanctus eris, etc.*,
Or in Rome, as here rule wole · the reliques to kepe;   421
And thow, Conscience, in kynges courte · and shuldest neure come thennes,
And Grace, that thow gredest so of · gyour of alle clerkes,
And Pieres with his newe plow · and eke with his olde,   424
Emperour of al the worlde · that alle men were Cristene!
Inparfyt is that pope · that al peple shulde helpe,
And sendeth hem that sleeth suche · as he shulde saue;
And wel worth Piers the Plowman · that pursueth god in doynge,
Qui pluit super iustos · et iniustos at ones,   429
And sent the sonne to saue · a cursed mannes tilthe,
As bryȝte as to the best man · and to the beste woman.
Riȝte so Pieres the Plowman · peyneth hym to tulye   432
As wel for a wastour · and wenches of the stuwes,
As for hym-self and his seruauntz · saue he is firste yserued;
And trauailleth and tulyeth · for a tretour also sore
As for a trewe tydy man · al tymes ylyke.   436

B. 428. pursueth WCOBY; sueth L.

Bote thow lyue by the lore · of *spiritus iusticie*,
The chef seede that Peers sewe · saued worst thow neuere. 408
Bote Conscience the comune fede · and cardinale vertues,
Leyf hit wel, we beon lost · bothe lyf and soule.'
'Then is meny man ylost' · quath a lewede vicory;
'Ich am a curatoure of holykirke · and cam neuere in my tyme
Man to me, that couthe telle · of cardinale uertues, 413
Other that acountede Conscience · a cockes fether other an hennes!
Ich knew neuere cardinal · that he ne cam fro the pope,
And we clerkes, when thei cometh · for here comunes payeth,
For here pelure and palfrayes mete · and pylours that hem folwen.
The comune *clamat cotidie* · eche man to othere,
'The countrey is the corsedour · ther cardinales cometh ynne;
And ther thei liggen and lengen most · lecherie ther regneth:'—
For-thi,' quath this vicory · 'by verrai god, ich wolde 421
That no cardinal come · a-mong the comune peuple,
Bote in here holinesse · holden hem stille
At Auenoun, a-mong Iuwes · *cum sancto sanctus eris, etc.,* 424
Other in Rome, as here ruwele wolde · the relikes to kepe;
And thow, Conscience, in kynges court · and sholdest neuere
 come thennes,
And Grace, that thou so gredest of · were gyour of alle clerkes,
And Peers with hus newe plouh · and his olde bothe 428
Emperour of alle the worlde · that alle men were Crystyne!
Imparfit is the pope · that al the peuple sholde helpe,
And soudeth hem that sleeth · suche as he sholde saue;
Ac wel worthe Peers Plouhman · that porsueth god in doynge,
Qui pluit super iustos · *et iniustos* at ones, 433
And sent the sonne to saue · a corsed mannes tulthe,
As bryght as to the beste man · other to the beste womman.
Ryght so Peers Plouhman · peyneth hym to tulye 436
As wel for a wastour · other for a wenche atte stuwes,
As for hym-self and his seruauns · saue he is furst yserued;
So blessed beo Peers Plouhman · that peyneth hym to tulie,
And trauaileth and tuleth · for a tretour al-so sore 440
As for a trewe tydy man · alle tymes ylyke.

C. 412. kirke T; churche PEFSG. 420. liggyn P. 421. þeis (*for* þis) P. 423. holden EFG; heolden P. 426. come TG; go PEMFS.
441. triwe P. lyke P; y-liche STG; i-liche MF; *read* ylyke.

And worshiped be he that wrouȝte al · bothe good and wykke,
And suffreth that synful be · til some tyme that thei repente.
And god amende the pope · that pileth holykirke,
And cleymeth bifor the kynge · to be keper ouer Crystene, 440
And counteth nouȝt though Crystene · ben culled and robbed,
And fynt folke to fyȝte · and Cristene blode to spille,
Aȝeyne the olde lawe and newe lawe · as Luke ther-of witnesseth,
    Non occides: michi vindictam, etc.
It semeth, by so · hym-self hadde his wille, 444
That he ne reccheth riȝte nouȝte · of al the remenaunte.
And Cryst of his curteisye · the cardinales saue,
And tourne her witte to wisdome · and to wele of soule!
For the comune,' quod this curatour · 'counten ful litel 448
The conseille of Conscience · or cardinale vertues,
But if thei seiȝe as by syȝte · somwhat to wynnynge;
Of gyle ne of gabbynge · gyue thei neuere tale.
For *spiritus prudencie* · amonge the peple, is gyle, 452
And alle tho faire vertues · as vyces thei semeth;
Eche man sotileth a sleight · synne forto hyde,
And coloureth it for a kunnynge · and a clene lyuynge.'

    Thanne lough there a lorde · and 'by this liȝte,' sayde, 456
'I halde it ryȝte and resoun · of my reue to take
Al that myne auditour · or elles my stuwarde
Conseilleth me by her acounte · and my clerkes wrytynge.
With *spiritus intellectus* · they seke the reues rolles, 460
And with *spiritus fortitudinis* · fecche it I wole.'

    And thanne come there a kynge · and bi his croune seyde,
'I am kynge with croune · the comune to reule,
And holykirke and clergye · fro cursed men to defende. 464
And if me lakketh to lyue by · the lawe wil I take it,
There I may hastlokest it haue · for I am hed of lawe;
For ȝe ben but membres · and I aboue alle.
And sith I am ȝowre aller hed · I am ȝowre aller hele, 468
And holycherche chief help · and chiftaigne of the comune.
And what I take of ȝow two · I take it atte techynge

B. 444. hadd L.   450. seiȝe W; seigh C; seen O; sowe L.   456.
loughe L.   461. it WCOBY; L *om.*

And worsheped be he that wrouhte al · bothe good and wykke,
And suffreth hem that synful beon · til tyme that thei repenten.
And god amende the pope · that pileth holichurche,   444
And cleymeth by-fore the kyng · to beo kepere ouere Cristyne,
And counteth noȝt thauh Cristene men · be culled and robbed,
And fyndeth folke to fighte · and Cristene blod to spille,
Aȝeyn the lawe bothe old and newe · as Luk bereth wittnesse,
  Non occides: et alibi, Michi uindictam, et ego retribuam.
Sikerliche hit semeth, by so · hym-self hadde hus wil,   449
That he reccheth right nouht · of al the other remenaunt.
And Crist of hus cortesye · the cardinales saue,
And turne here wit to wisedom · and welthe for the soule! 452
For the comune,' quath this curatour · 'counten ful litel
The consail of Conscience · other cardinale uertues,
Bote hit soune as by syght · som what to wynnynge ;
Of gile ne of gabbynge · gyueth thei neuere tale.   456
For *spiritus prudencie* · among the peuple, is gyle,
And tho faire vertues · as vices thei hem semeth ;
Eche man soteleth a sleithe · synne for to huyde,
And coloreth hit for a connynge · and a clene lyuynge.'   460
  Then louh ther a lorde · and 'by this light!' seide,
'Ich halde hit right and reson · to take of my reeue
Al that myn auditour · other elles my stiwarde
Conseileth me by here a-counte · and my clerkes wrytynge. 464
With *spiritus intellectus* · thei toke the reeue-rolles,
And with *spiritus fortitudinis* · fecche hit, wol he, nul he.'
  Then cam ther a kynge · and by hus corone seide,
'Ich am a kyng with corone · the comune to reule,   468
And holychurch and clergie · fro corsede men to defenden.
And yf me lacketh to lyue by · the lawe wol that ich take
Ther ich may haue hit hastelokest · for ich am hefd of lawe,
And ȝe ben bote membrys · and ich a-boue alle.   472
Sitthen ich am ȝoure alre hefd · ich am ȝoure alre hele,
And holychurches chef help · and chefteyn of the comune.
And what ich take of ȝow two · ich take hit at techynge

C. 442. he MFSGT ; PE *om*.   443. suffreþ EMFGS; suffren P.   448.
nywe P.   *Et alibi* FS ; PEMTG *om*.   *et—retribuam* ST ; PEMFG *om*.   450.
he MSG ; hym PEF.   reccheþ MSFG ; rekeþ PE.   453. þes (*for* þis) P.
458. hem EMF ; hym P.   459. a EMFSGT ; P *om*. for MF ; PESGT *om*.

Of *spiritus iusticie* · for I iugge 3ow alle;
So I may baldely be houseled · for I borwe neuere, 472
Ne craue of my comune · but as my kynde asketh.'

'In condicioun,' quod Conscience · ' that thow konne defende
And rule thi rewme in resoun · ri3t wel, and in treuth,
Take thow may in resoun · as thi lawe asketh; 476
    Omnia tua sunt ad defendendum, set non ad depredandum ! '
The vyker hadde fer home · and faire tcke his leue,
And I awakned there-with · and wrote as me mette.

PASSUS XX.

Passus xx^{us} de visione, et primus de Dobest.

THANNE as I went by the way · whan I was thus awaked,
Heuy-chered I 3ede · and elynge in herte;
I ne wiste where to ete · ne at what place.
And it neighed nyeghe the none · and with Nede I mette, 4
That afronted me foule · and faitour me called.

' Coudestow nou3te excuse the · as dede the kynge and other,
That thow toke to thi bylyf · to clothes and to sustenance,
As by techynge and by tellynge · of *spiritus temperancie*, 8
And thow nome namore · than Nede the tau3te,
And Nede ne hath no lawe · ne neure shal falle in dette?
For thre thynges he taketh · his lyf forto saue, 11
That is, mete, whan men hym werneth · and he no moneye weldeth,
Ne wyght none wil ben his borwe · ne wedde hath none to legge.
And he cau3te in that cas · and come there-to by sleighte,
He synneth nou3te sothelich · that so wynneth his fode.
And though he come so to a clothe · and can no better cheuysaunce,

C. PASSUS XXII. 476—XXIII. 16.

Of *spiritus iusticie* · for ich Iugge ȝou alle; 476
So ich may baldely beo housled · for ich borwe neuere,
Ne craue of my comune · bote as my kynde asketh.'
'In condicion,' quath Conscience · 'that thou conne defende
And reule thy reame in reson · right wel, and in treuthe; 480
Than, that thow haue thyn askyng · as the lawe asketh;
    Omnia sunt tua ad defendendum, sed non ad deprehendendum!'
The vicory hadde fer hom · and faire tok hus leue,
And ich a-wakede ther-with · and wrot as me mette.

    Hic explicit passus primus de Dobest.

PASSUS XXIII.

    Hic incipit passus secundus de Dobest.

AND as ich wente by the waye · when ich was thus awaked,
Heuy-chered ich ȝeode · and elynge in heorte;
For ich ne wiste wher to ete · ne in what place.
And hit neyhede ny the noon · and with Neode ich mette, 4
That afrontede me foule · and faitour me calde.
'Couthest thou nat excuse the,' he seide · 'as dude the kyng
    and othere,
That thou toke to lyue by · to sustinaunce and clothes,
As by techinge and tellynge · of *spiritus temperancie*, 8
And that thow nome no more · than Neode the tauhte?
Neode hath no lawe · ne neuere shal falle in dette
For thre thynges that he taketh · hus lyf for to saue; 11
That is, mete, whanne men hym werneth · for he no monye weldeth,
And wot that non wol be hus borgh · nother hath wed to legge.
And he cacche in that cas · and come ther-to by sleithe,
Sotheliche he syneweth nat · that so wynneth hus fode.
And thauh he come so to a cloth · and can no betere cheuesaunce,

---

C. 476. Iugge MFST; Iuge PG. 477. houslede P. 480 P *om.* 2nd in.
482. vickery P; *see* l. 411. 483. mette EMSGT; mete P.
    Passus XXIII. 1. awakede P. 2. chered EMFG; chired P. 4. 'hit
SM; it FT; PEG *om.* 12. werneþ EMFSGT; wyrneþ P. 16. P *om.* a.

Nede anon riȝte · nymeth hym vnder meynpryse. 17
And if hym lyst for to lape · the lawe of kynde wolde
That he dronke at eche diche · ar he for thurste deyde.
So Nede, at grete nede · may nymen as for his owne, 20
Wyth-oute conseille of Conscience · or cardynale vertues,
So that he suwe and saue · *spiritus temperancie*.
For is no vertue by fer · to *spiritus temperancie*,
Neither *spiritus iusticie* · ne *spiritus fortitudinis*. 24
For *spiritus fortitudinis* · forfaiteth ful oft,
He shal do more than mesure · many tyme and ofte,
And bete men ouer bitter · and somme of hem to litel,
And greue men gretter · than goode faith it wolde. 28
And *spiritus iusticie* · shal iuggen, wolhe, nolhe,
After the kynges conseille · and the comune lyke.
And *spiritus prudencie* · in many a poynte shal faille
Of that he weneth wolde falle · if his wytte ne were. 32
Wenynge is no wysdome · ne wyse ymagynacioun,
Homo proponit et deus disponit · and gouerneth alle good vertues.
Ac Nede is next hym · for anon he meketh,
And as low as a lombe · for lakkyng of that hym nedeth. 36

Wyse men forsoke wele · for they wolde be nedy,
And woneden in wildernesse · and wolde nouȝte be riche.
And god al his grete Ioye · gostliche he left,
And cam and toke mankynde · and bycam nedy. 40
So nedy he was, as seyth the boke · in many sondry places,
That he seyde in his sorwe · on the selue rode,
"Bothe fox and foule · may fleighe to hole and crepe,
And the fisshe hath fyn · to flete with to reste, 44
There nede hath ynome me · that I mote nede abyde,
And suffre sorwes ful sowre · that shal to Ioye tourne."
For-thi be nouȝte abasshed · to bydde and to be nedy;
Syth he that wrouȝte al the worlde · was wilfullich nedy, 48
Ne neuer none so nedy · ne pouerere deyde.'
Whan Nede had vndernome me thus · anon I felle aslepe,

B. 47. byde L; bidde RCOB.

Neode nymeth hym a-non · vnder hus mayn-pryse. 17
And ȝif hym lust for to lape · the lawe of kynde wolde
That he dronk of eche a diche · er he deide for therste.
So Neode at grete neode · may nyme as for hus owene, 20
With-oute consail of Conscience · or cardinale uertues,
So that he suwe and saue · *spiritus temperancie.*
For is no vertue by-fore · to *spiritus temperancie,*
Nother *spiritus iusticie* · ne *spiritus fortitudinis.* 24
For *spiritus fortitudinis* · forfeteth ful ofte,
He shal do more than mesure · meny tyme and ofte,
And bete men ouere bittere · and som body to lyte,
And greue men grettour · than good faith wolde. 28
And *spiritus iusticie* · shal Iugen, wol he, nul he,
After the kynges counsaile · and the comune lyke.
And *spiritus prudencie* · in menye poynt shal fayle
Of that he weneth wolde falle · yf his wit ne were. 32
Wenynge is no wisedome · ne wys ymaginacion,
Homo proponit, deus disponit · god gouerneth alle goode vertues.
Next hym is Neode · for a-non he meoketh,
And is as louh as a lomb · for lackynge of that hym neodeth;
For Neode maketh neody · for neode louh-herted. 37
Filosofres for-soken welthe · for thei woide be neody,
And wonede wel elyngliche · and wolden nat be riche.
And god al hus grete ioye · gostliche he lefte, 40
And cam and took man-kynde · and by-cam ful neody.
He was so neody, seith the bok · in meny sondry places,
That he seide in hus sorwe · on the selue rode,
"Bothe fox and fowel · may fleo to hole and crepe, 44
And the fisshe hath fynnes · to flete with to reste,
Ther Neode hath ynome me so · that ich mot neode abyde,
And suffre sorwes soure · that shal to ioye turne."
For-thi beo nat a-basshed · to bydde and to beo neody, 48
Sithe he that wrouhte al the worlde · was wilfulliche neody;
Neuere non so neody · ne non so poure deyede.'
When Neode hadde vnder-nome me thus · a-non ich fel a-sleope,

---

C. 18. ȝif F; ȝeueþ (*wrongly*) PE.   27. bete EFST; beten M; bote P.
34. The MSS. *erroneously place the words* good vertues *at the beginning of*
l. 35.   36. þat hym GMFT; hym þat PES (*wrongly*).   46. abyde S;
abide MFT; byde PE.   48. abaihsshed P.   51. feol (*for* fel) P.

And mette ful merueillously · that, in mannes forme,
Antecryst cam thanne · and al the croppe of treuthe　　52
Torned it vp so doune · and ouertilte the rote,
And made fals sprynge and sprede · and spede mennes nedes;
In eche a contre there he cam · he cutte awey treuthe,
And gert gyle growe there · as he a god were.　　56
Freres folwed that fende · for he ȝaf hem copes,
And religiouse reuerenced hym · and rongen here belles,
And al the couent forth cam · to welcome that tyraunt,
And alle hise, as wel as hym · saue onlich folis;　　60
Which folis were wel leuer · to deye than to lyue
Lenger, sith leute · was so rebuked.
And a fals fende Antecriste · ouer alle folke regned;
And that were mylde men and holy · that no myschief dredden,
Defyed al falsenesse · and folke that it vsed;　　65
And what kynge that hem conforted · knowynge hem any while,
They cursed, and her conseille · were it clerke or lewed.

　　Antecriste hadde thus sone · hundredes at his banere,　　68
And Pryde it bare · boldely aboute,
With a lorde that lyueth · after lykynge of body,
That cam aȝein Conscience · that kepere was and gyoure
Ouer kynde Crystene · and cardynale vertues.　　72
'I conseille,' quod Conscience tho · 'cometh with me, ȝe foles,
In-to Vnyte holy-cherche · and holde we vs there,
And crye we to Kynde · that he come and defende vs,
Foles, fro this fendes lymes · for Piers loue the Plowman.　　76
And crye we to alle the comune · that thei come to Vnite,
And there abide and bikere · aȝein Beliales children.'

　　Kynd Conscience tho herde · and cam out of the planetes,
And sent forth his foreioures · feures and fluxes,　　80
Coughes, and cardiacles · crampes, and tothaches,
Rewmes, and radegoundes · and roynouse scalles,
Byles, and bocches · and brennyng agues;
Frenesyes, and foule yueles · forageres of kynde,　　84
Hadde yprykked and prayed · polles of peple,

B. 54. made R; LWCOB *om.*　　62. Lenger WCOB; Lengore L.　leute RB; lenten LWCO.

C. PASSUS XXIII. 52–86.

And mette ful merueilousliche · that, in a mannes forme,   52
Antecrist cam thenne · and al the crop of treuthe
Turned tyte vp-so-doun · and ouer-tilte the rote,
And made fals to springe and sprede · and spede menne neodes;
In eche contreie ther he cam · he cutte away treuthe,   56
And gert gyle growe ther · as he a god were.
Freres folweden that feonde · for he ʒaf hem copes,
And religiouse reuerencede hym · and rongen here belles;
Al the couent tho cam · to welcome that tyraunt,   60
And alle hise, as wel as hym · saue onliche fooles;
The whiche fooles weren · gladdere to deye
Than lyue lengoure, suthe leaute · was so rebuked.
And a fals feond Anticrist · ouer alle folke regnede,   64
That were mylde men and holye · that no meschief dradden,
Defieden al falsnesse · and folk that hit vsede;
And what kyng comfortede hem · knowynge here gyle,
Thei corsede, and here consail · were hit clerk other lewede. 68
 Anticrist thus sone hadde · hundredes at hus baner,
And Pruyde bar that baner · boldeliche aboute,
With a lorde that lyueth · after lykynge of hus body,
And cam a-ʒeyns Conscience · that keper was an gyour   72
Ouer kynde Cristyne · and cardinale uertues.
'Ich consail,' quath Conscience tho · 'cometh with me, ʒe fooles,
In-to Unite holichurche · and halde we ous there.
And crye we to Kynde · that he come and defende   76
Ous fooles fro the feondes lymes · for Peers loue the Plouhman.
And crye we on al the comune · that thei come to Unite,
Ther to abyde and bykere · aʒeyns Beliales children.'
 Kynde huyrde tho Conscience · and cam out of the planetes,
And sente forth his foreyours · feuers and fluxes,   81
Couhes, and cardiacles · crampes, and toth-aches,
Reumes, and radegoundes · and roynouse scabbes,
Bules, and bocches · and brennyng aguwes;   84
Frenesyes, and foule vueles · these foragers of kynde,
Hadden pryked and preyed · polles of people;

C. 54. tilte MFT; tilt P.   55. spede MFST; spedde PE.   58. he EMFST; ʒe P.   ʒaf EST; ʒaue P.   60. couant P.   wolcome P.   þat MFST; þe PE.   64. feon P; fend MT.   70. abouhte P.   81. foreyours EF; fereours (*for* foreours) P.   82. crampes MIF; claumpes PE.   86. prykede P.

That largelich a legioun · lese her lyf sone.
There was—'harrow and help! · here cometh Kynde,
With Deth that is dredful · to vndone vs alle!' 88
The lorde that lyued after lust · tho alowde cryde
After Conforte, a knyghte · to come and bere his banere.
'Al-arme! alarme!' quod that lorde · 'eche lyf kepe his owne!'
And thanne mette this men · ar mynstralles my3te pipe, 92
And ar heraudes of armes · hadden descreued lordes.

Elde the hore · he was in the vauntwarde,
And bare the banere bifor Deth · by ri3te he it claymed.
Kynde come after · with many kene sores, 96
As pokkes and pestilences · and moche poeple shente;
So Kynde thorw corupciouns · kulled ful manye.
Deth cam dryuende after · and al to doust passhed
Kynges and kny3tes · kayseres and popes; 100
Lered ne lewed · he let no man stonde,
That he hitte euene · that euere stired after.
Many a louely lady · and lemmanes of knyghtes
Swouned and swelted · for sorwe of Dethes dyntes. 104

Conscience of his curteisye · to Kynde he bisou3te
To cesse and suffre · and see where thei wolde
Leue Pryde pryuely · and be parfite Cristene.
And Kynde cessed tho · to se the peple amende. 108
Fortune gan flateren thenne · tho fewe that were alyue,
And byhight hem longe lyf · and Lecherye he sent
Amonges al manere men · wedded and vnwedded,
And gadered a gret hoste · al agayne Conscience. 112
This Lecherye leyde on · with a laughyng chiere,
And with pryue speche · and peynted wordes,
And armed hym in ydelnesse · and in hiegh berynge.
He bare a bowe in his hande · and manye blody arwes, 116
Weren fethered with faire biheste · and many a false truthe.
With his vntydy tales · he tened ful ofte
Conscience and his compaignye · of holicherche the techeres.

Thanne cam Coueityse · and caste how he my3te 120

Largeliche a legion · lees the lyf sone.
Ther was—'harow and help! · her cometh Kynde, 88
With Deth that is dredful · to vn-do ous alle!'
The lord that lyuede after lust · tho aloud criede
After Comfort, a knyght · to come and bere hus baner.
'Alarme! alarme!' quath that lorde · 'eche lyf kepe hus owene!'
Thenne mette these men · er mynstrales myghte pipe, 93
And er heraudes of armes · hadden discriued lordes.
Elde the hore · was in the vaunt-warde,
And bar the baner by-fore Deth · by right he hit claymede. 96
Kynde cam after hym · with menye kynne sores,
As pockes and pestilences · and muche people shente;
So Kynde thorgh corupcions · culde ful menye.
Deth cam dryuyng after · and al to douste paschte 100
Kynges and knyghtes · caysers and popes;
Lered ne lewide · he lefte no man stande;
That he hitte euene · sterede neuere after.
Many a louely lady · and here lemmanes knyghtes 104
Sounede and swelte · for sorwe of Dethes dyntes.
Conscience of hus cortesie · tho Kynde he by-souhte
To cessen and to suffren · and seo wher thei wolde
Leue pruyde pryuelich · and beo parfit Cristene. 108
And Kynde cessede tho · to seon the peuple amende.
Fortune gan flaterie thenne · thaym fewe that were a-lyue,
And by-hyght hem long lyf · and Lecherie he sente
Amonges alle manere men · wedded and vnwedded, 112
And gaderede a gret ost · al ageyn Conscience.
This Lecherie leyde on · with lauhynge chere,
And with pryuey speche · and peyntede wordes,
And armede hym in ydelnesse · and in hy beryng. 116
He bar a bowe in hus honde · and manye brode arwes,
Were fetherede with faire by-heste · and many a fals treuthe.
With vntidy tales · he teonede ful ofte
Conscience and hus companye · of holy churche the techers.
Thenne cam Couetise · and caste how he myghte 121

C. 90. loust P.   94. discriuede P.   96. þe MFST; a PE.   100.
dryuyng EMFS; dremend P.   paschte FS; passhte T; paihste P.   104.
louely EMFST; lofly P.   105. dyþes P.   111. hem MFST; hym PE.
112. vnweddede P.   114. leyde MFST; leyden PE. chere MFST; chire P.
116. in (1) EMFST; with P; *see* l. 123.   118. Where.   119. Whit P.

Ouercome Conscience · and cardynal vertues,
And armed hym in auaryce · and hungriliche lyued.
His wepne was al wiles · to wynnen and to hyden;
With glosynges and with gabbynges · he gyled the peple. 124
Symonye hym sente · to assaille Conscience,
And preched to the peple · and prelates thei hem maden,
To holden with Antecryste · her temperaltes to saue;
And come to the kynges conseille · as a kene baroun, 128
And kneled to Conscience · in courte afor hem alle,
And gart Gode-Feith flee · and Fals to abide,
And boldeliche bar adown · with many a bri3te noble
Moche of the witte and wisdome · of Westmynster halle. 132
He Iugged til a Iustice · and Iusted in his ere,
And ouertilte al his treuthe · with 'take-this-vp-amendement.'
And to the arches in haste · he 3ede anone after,
And torned ciuile in-to symonye · and sitthe he toke the official;
For a mantel of menyuere · he made lele matrimonye 137
Departen ar deth cam · and deuors shupte.
  'Allas!' quod Conscience, and cried tho · 'wolde Criste, of
     his grace,
That Coueityse were Cristene · that is so kene a fi3ter, 140
And bolde and bidyng · while his bagge lasteth!'
And thanne lowgh Lyf · and leet dagge his clothes,
And armed hym in haste · in harlotes wordes,
And helde Holynesse a Iape · and Hendenesse a wastour, 144
And lete Leute a cherle · and Lyer a fre man;
Conscience and conseille · he counted it a folye.
Thus relyed Lyf · for a litèl fortune,
And pryked forth with Pryde · preyseth he no vertue, 148
Ne careth nou3te how Kynde slow · and shal come atte laste,
And culle alle erthely creatures · saue Conscience one.
Lyf leep asyde · and lau3te hym a lemman,
'Heel and I,' quod he · 'and hieghnesse of herte 152
Shal do the nou3te drede · noyther Deth ne Elde,
And to for3ete sorwe · and 3yue nou3te of synne.'
This lyked Lyf · and his lemman Fortune,

B. 125. sent L.   137. mentel L.   138. deuors W; diuorce COB;
deuos L.   149. Ne WR; He CO; A (*sic*) L.   150. creature L.

Ouercome Conscience · and cardinale uertues,
And armed hym in auarice · and hungriliche lyuede.
Hus wepne was al wiles · to wynne and to huyden ; 124
With glosynges and with gabbyngs · he gylede the peuple.
Symonye hym sewede · to assaile Conscience,
And pressede on the pope · and prelates thei maden,
To holde with Antecrist · here temporalite to saue ; 128
And cam to kynges consail · as a kene baroun,
And knockede Conscience · in court by-fore hem alle,
And gerte Goode-Faith to flee · and Fals to a-byde,
And baldeliche bar adoun · with meny a bryght noble 132
Muche of the wit and wisdom · of Westmynster halle.
He Iogged til a Iustice · and Iousted in hus ere,
And ouertulte al hus treuthe · with 'tak-this-on-amendement.'
And to the arches in haste · he hyede a-non after, 136
And turnede cyuyle in-to symonye · and suth he tok the official ;
And for a menyuer mantel · he made leel matrimonye
Departe er deth come · and a deuors shupte.
   'Alas!' quath Conscience, and cride · 'wolde Crist, of hus
    grace, 140
That Couetise were Cristyne · that is so kene to fyghte,
And bold and abydynge · the while hus bagge lasteth!'
And thanne lowh loude Lyf · and let dagge hus clothes,
And armyd hym in haste · in harlotes wordes, 144
And held Holynesse a Iape · and Hendynesse a wastour,
And let Leaute a cherl · and Lyere a freo man ;
Conscience and consail · he countede hit a folye.
Thus relyede Lyf · for a litel fortune, 148
And pryketh forth with Pruyde · preyseth he no vertue,
Ne careth nouht hou Kynde slouh · and shal come atte laste,
And culle alle erthly creatures · saue Conscience one.
Lyf tho leep asyde · and lauhte hym a lemman, 152
'Hele and ich,' quath he · 'and hihnesse of herte
Shal do the nat drede · neither Deth ne Elde,
And to for-ȝete ȝouthe · and ȝyue nauht of synne.'
This likede Lyf · and Fortune hus lemman, 156

C. 125. Whith P. gabbyinges P. gylede S; gilide T; giled EF; gyleþ P.
126. sewede MFT; sywede P. 142. abydynge FS; byddynge P. þe MEF;
þy P. 143. lohw (for lowh) P. 146. chierl P. 147. hit a S; it a F;
hit ME; P om. 151. erthyly P. 155. to MFST; PE om. forȝute P.

And geten in her glorie · a gadelyng atte laste,   156
One that moche wo wrou3te · Sleuthe was his name.
Sleuthe wex wonder 3erne · and sone was of age,
And wedded one Wanhope · a wenche of the stuwes;
Her syre was a sysour · that neure swore treuthe,   160
One Thomme Two-tonge · ateynte at vch a queste.
This Sleuthe was war of werre · and a slynge made,
And threwe drede of dyspayre · a dozein myle aboute.
For care Conscience tho · cryed vpon Elde,   164
And bad hym fonde to fy3te · and afere Wanhope.
    And Elde hent good hope · and hastilich he shifte hym,
And wayued awey Wanhope · and with Lyf he fy3teth.
And Lyf fleigh for fere · to Fysyke after helpe,   168
And bisou3te hym of socoure · and of his salue hadde,
And gaf hym golde, good woon · that gladded his herte,
And thei gyuen hym agayne · a glasen houue.
Lyf leued that lechecrafte · lette shulde Elde,   172
And dryuen awey Deth · with dyas and dragges.
    And Elde auntred hym on Lyf · and atte laste he hitte
A fisicien with a forred hood · that he fel in a palsye,
And there deyed that doctour · ar thre dayes after.   176
'Now I see,' seyde Lyf · 'that surgerye ne fisyke
May nou3te a myte auaille · to medle a3ein Elde.'
And in hope of his hele · gode herte he hente,
And rode so to Reuel · a ryche place and a merye;   180
The companye of conforte · men cleped it sumtyme.
And Elde anone after me · and ouer myne heed 3ede,
And made me balled bifore · and bare on the croune,
So harde he 3ede ouer myn hed · it wil be seen eure.   184
'Sire euel-ytau3te Elde,' quod I · 'vnhende go with the!
Sith whanne was the way · ouer mennes hedes?
Haddestow be hende,' quod I · 'thow woldest haue asked leue!'
'3e! leue lordeyne!' quod he · and leyde on me with age, 188
And hitte me vnder the ere · vnethe may ich here;

B. 186. mennes WCROB; men L; *see* l. 286.

And geten in here glorie · a gadelyng atte laste,
On that muche wo wrouhte · Sleuthe was hus name.
Sleuthe wax wonder ȝerne · and sone was of age,
And wedded on Wanhope · a wenche of the stewes;   160
Here syre was a sysour · that neuere swor treuthe,
On Tomme Two-tounged · ateynt at eche enqueste.
This Sleuthe was sleyh of werre · and a slynge made,
And threw drede of dispayr · a doseyne myle a-boute.   164
For care Conscience tho · cryede vp-on Elde,
And bad hym fonde to fighte · and afere Wanhope.
   And Elde hente good hope · and hastiliche shrof hym,
And wayueth away Wanhope · and with Lyf he fighteth.   168
And Lif fleyh for fere · to Fisik after helpe,
And by-souhte hym of socour · and of his salue hadde,
And gaf hym gold, good won · that gladede here hertes,
And thei gauen hym agayn · a glasene houe.   172
Lyf leyuede that leche-craft · lette sholde Elde,
And to-dryue away Deth · with dyas and drogges.
   Elde auntred hym on Lyf · and atte laste he hitte
A fisician with a forrede hod · that he fel in a palsye,   176
And ther deiede that doctour · er thre dayes after.
'Now ich seo,' saide Lyf · 'that surgerye ne phisike
May nat a myte availle · to medlen a-ȝens Elde.'
And in hope of hus hele · good heorte he hente,   180
And rod so to Reuel · a ryche place and a murye;
The companye of comfort · men cleped hit som tyme.
And Elde hastede after hym · and ouer my hefde ȝeode,
And made me balled by-fore · and bar on the croune;   184
So harde he ȝeode ouer myn hefde · hit wol be sene euere.
'Syre vuel-ytauht Elde,' quath ich · 'vnhende go with the!
Suththe whanne was the hey wey · ouer menne hefdes?
Haddest thow be hende,' quath ich · 'thow woldest haue asked
   leue!'   188
'Ȝe! leue lordeyn!' quath he · and leyde on me with age,
And hitte me vnder the ere · vnnethe may ich huyre.

   C. 160. stywes P.   162. tomme MFS; Robert P.   163. Thes (*for*
This) P.   164. þrewe P.   165. þo MFT; PES *om*.   169. fleyht (*for*
fleyh) P.   fisik EMST; syke (*sic*) P.   170. his MFST; here PE.   171.
goud P.   172. gauyn P.   174. dyas and FS; dias and M; *miswritten*
dayes P.   182. clipid P.   184. ballide PT.   185. sene EMFST; syne P.
186. ytauhte P.   190. vnnyþe P.

He buffeted me aboute the mouthe · and bette out my tethe,

And gyued me in goutes · I may nouȝte go at large.
And of the wo that I was in · my wyf had reuthe, 192
And wisshed ful witterly · that I were in heuene.
For the lyme that she loued me fore · and leef was to fele,
On nyȝtes namely · whan we naked were,
I ne myght in no manere · maken it at hir wille, 196
So Elde and she sothly · hadden it forbeten.

And as I seet in this sorwe · I say how Kynde passed,
And Deth drowgh niegh me · for drede gan I quake,
And cried to Kynde · out of care me brynge. 200
'Loo! Elde the hoore · hath me biseye,
Awreke me, if ȝowre wille be · for I wolde ben hennes.'
'Ȝif thow wilt ben ywroken · wende in-to Vnite,
And holde the there eure · tyl I sende for the, 204
And loke thow conne somme crafte · ar thow come thennes.'
'Conseille me, Kynde,' quod I · 'what crafte is best to lerne?'

'Lerne to loue,' quod Kynde · 'and leue of alle othre.'
'How shal I come to catel so · to clothe me and to fede?' 208
'And thow loue lelly,' quod he · 'lakke shal the neure
Mete ne worldly wede · whil thi lyf lasteth.'
And there, by conseille of Kynde · I comsed to rowme
Thorw Contricioun and Confessioun · tyl I cam to Vnite; 212
And there was Conscience constable · Cristene to saue,
And biseged sothly · with seuene grete gyauntz,
That with Antecrist helden · hard aȝein Conscience.
Sleuth with his slynge · an hard saut he made, 216
Proude prestes come with hym · moo than a thousand,
In paltokes and pyked shoes · and pisseres longe knyues,
Comen aȝein Conscience; · with Coueityse thei helden.
'By Marie,' quod a mansed preste · of the marche of Yrlonde,

'I counte namore Conscience · bi so I cacche syluer, 221
Than I do to drynke · a drauȝte of good ale!'

B. 210. wordly L.

He boffatede me a-boute the mouthe · and bete oute my wang-
    teth,
And gyuede me with goutes · ich may nat go at large.   192
And of the wo that ich was yn · my wif hadde reuthe,
And wisshede wel witerlyche · that ich were in heuene.
For the lyme that she louede me for · and leef was to feele,
And a nyghtes nameliche · when we naked were,   196
Ich ne myghte in none manere · maken hit at heore wille,
So Elde and hue hit hadde · a-feynted and forbete.
    And as ich sat in this sorwe · ich sauh how Kynde passede,
And Deth drow neyghynge me · for drede gan ich quaken, 200
And criede carfully to Kynde · out of kare me brynge.
'Lo, hou Elde the hore · hath me byseye;
Awreke me, yf ȝoure wil beo · for ich wolde be hennes.'
'Yf thow wolt beo awreke · wende in-to Unite,   204
And hold the thare euere · til ich sende for the,
And loke thou conne som craft · er thou come thennes.'
'Consaileth me, Kynde,' quath ich · 'what crafte be best to
    leere?'
'Lerne to loue,' quath Kynde · 'and lef alle other thynges.' 208
'Hou shal ich come to catel so · to clothe me and to feode?'
'And thow loue leelliche · lacke shal the neuere
Wede ne worldlich mete · while thy lyf lasteth.'
And ich thorgh consail of Kynde · comsede to rome   212
Thorgh Contricion and Confession · til ich cam to Unite;
And ther was Conscience constable · Crystine to saue.
He was byseged sothliche · with seuene grete geauntes,
That with Antecrist helden · harde aȝeyns Conscience.   216
    Sleuthe with hus slynge · an hard saut he made.
Proude preostes cam with hym · passend an hundred;
In paltokes and pikede shoes · and pissares longe knyues,
Thei come aȝeyns Conscience; · with Couetise thei helden. 220
'By the Marie,' quath a mansed preest · was of the marche of
    Yrelonde,
'Ich counte Conscience no more · by so ich cacche seluer,
Than ich do to drynke · a drawt of good ale!'

C. 194. whiterlyche P.   195. þat MFS; PE *om.*   fore P.   196.
nyghȝtes P.   198. hue S; heo MF; he P.   a-feyntede P.   199. ich E;
y S; i FT; P *om.*   201. P *om.* out.   211. wordliche P.   215. bysegide P.
216. Aunticrist PS.   217. saut EFST; sauht P.   221. mansede P.

And so seide sexty · of the same contreye;
And shoten aȝein with shotte · many a shef of othes;   224
And brode hoked arwes · goddes herte, and his nayles,
And hadden almost Vnyte · and holynesse adowne.
   Conscience cryed, 'helpe · Clergye, or ellis I falle
Thorw inparfit prestes · and prelates of holicherche.'   228
Freres herden hym crye · and comen hym to helpe,
Ac for thei couth nouȝte wel her craft · Conscience forsoke hem.
Nede neghed tho nere · and Conscience he tolde
That thei come for coueityse · to haue cure of soules—   232
'And for thei arn poure, par auenture · for patrimoigne hem failleth,
Thei wil flatre, to fare wel · folke that ben riche;
And sithen thei chosen chele · and cheytif pouerte,
Lat hem chewe as thei chese · and charge hem with no cure!
For lomer he lyeth · that lyflode mote begge,   237
Than he that laboureth for lyflode · and leneth it beggeres.
And sithen freres forsoke · the felicite of erthe,
Lat hem be as beggeres · or lyue by angeles fode!'   240
   Conscience of this conseille tho · comsed forto laughe,
And curteislich conforted hem · and called in alle freres,
And seide, 'sires, sothly · welcome be ȝe alle
To Vnite and holicherche · ac on thyng I ȝow preye,   244
Holdeth ȝow in Vnyte · and haueth none envye
To lered ne to lewed · but lyueth after ȝowre rewle.
And I wil be ȝowre borghe · ȝe shal haue bred and clothes,
And other necessaries i-nowe · ȝow shal no thyng faille,   248
With that ȝe leue logyk · and lerneth for to louye.
For loue laft thei lordship · bothe londe and scole,
Frere Fraunceys and Dominyk · for loue to ben holy.
And if ȝe coueyteth cure · Kynde wil ȝow teche,   252
That in mesure god made · alle manere thynges,
And sette hem at a certeyne · and at a syker noumbre,
And nempned names newe · and noumbred the sterres;
   Qui numerat multitudinem stellarum, et omnibus eis nomina
      [*vocat*], *etc.*
Kynges and knyghtes · that kepen and defenden,   256

B. 235. cheytifte LR; cheitif C; chaytijf O.   242. curteilich L.   248.
I-nowe R; I-now C; ynowe WOB; anowe L.   254. hem W; it LCROB.
255. *nomina* CB; LWRO *om. vocat* is not in the MSS.

And so seide syxty · of the same countreo; 224
And shotten a3eyns hym with shot · many a schef of othes,
And brode-hokede arwes · godes herte, and hus nailes,
And hadde almost Vnite · and holychurche a-doune.
    Conscience cride, 'helpe · Cleregie, other ich falle 228
Thorgh imparfit preestes · and prelates of holychurche.'
Freres herde hym crie · and comen hym to helpe,
Ac for thei couthe nat wel here craft · Conscience for-soke hem.
Neode neyhede tho ner · to Conscience he tolde 232
That thei came for couetise · to haue cure of-soules—
'And for thei aren poure, paraunter · for patrimonye hem failleth,
Thei wolle flaterie to fare wel · to folke that ben riche.
And sitthen thei chosen chile · and chaytif pouerte, 236
Let hem chewe as thei chosen · and charge hem with no cure!
For lommere he lyeth · that liflode mote begge,
Than he that laboreth for lyflode · and leneth hit beggeres.
And sitthen freres for-soke · the felicite of erthe, 240
Lat hem be as beggers · other lyue by aungeles fode!'
    Conscience of this consail tho · comsede for to lauhe,
And cortesly confortid hem · and cald yn alle freres,
And seide, 'sires, sothly · wel-come be 3e alle 244
To Unite and to holichurche · ac o thing ich 3ow preye,
Holdeth 3ow in Unite · and haueth non enuye
To lerede ne to lewide · bote lyueth after 3oure reule.
And ich wol beo 3oure borw · 3e shulleth haue brede and clothes, 248
And other necessaries ynowh · 3ou shal no thyng lakke,
With that 3e leue logyk · and lerneth for to louye.
For loue lefte thei lordshupes · bothe londe and scole,
Frere Fraunceis and Domynyk · for loue to be holy. 252
And yf 3e coueiteth cure · Kynde wol 3ow telle,
That in mesure god made · alle manere thynges,
And sette hit at a sertayn · and at a syker numbre,
And nempnede hem names · and nombrede the sterres; 256
    Qui numerat multitudinem stellarum.
Kynges and knyghtes · that kepen and defenden,

C. 225. many—of EF; many a schef S; many shef of T; mony shef P.
226. harwes P; *see* l. 117.   236. chaitife M; chaitif T; cheityf S; caytif PE.
250. lernyeþ P.   253. 3e EMFST; he P.   255. a (1) EMFT; PS *om.*

Han officers vnder hem · and vch of hem certeyne;
And if thei wage men to werre · thei write hem in noumbre,
Or wil no tresorere hem paye · trauaille thei neure so sore.
Alle other in bataille · ben yholde bribours, 260
Pilours and pykehernois · in eche a place ycursed.
Monkes and monyals · and alle men of religioun
Her ordre and her reule wil · to han a certeyne noumbre.
Of lewed and of lered · the lawe wol and axeth 264
A certeyn for a certeyne · saue onelich of freres!
For-thi,' quod Conscience, 'by Cryst · kynde witte me telleth,
It is wikked to wage ȝow · ȝe wexeth out of noumbre!
Heuene hath euene noumbre · and helle is with-out noumbre;
For-thi I wolde witterly · that ȝe were in the registre, 269
And ȝowre noumbre vndre notaries sygne · and noyther mo ne lasse!'
Enuye herd this · and heet freres to go to scole,
And lerne logyk and lawe · and eke contemplacioun, 272
And preche men of Plato · and preue it by Seneca,
That alle thinges vnder heuene · ouȝte to ben in comune.
And ȝit he lyeth, as I leue · that to the lewed so precheth,
For god made to men a lawe · and Moyses it tauȝte, 276

Non concupisces rem proximi tui.

And euele is this yholde · in parisches of Engelonde,
For persones and parishprestes · that shulde the peple shryue,
Ben curatoures called · to knowe and to hele,
Alle that ben her parisshiens · penaunce to enioigne, 280
And shulden be ashamed in her shrifte; · ac shame maketh hem wende,
And fleen to the freres · as fals folke to Westmynstre,
That borweth and bereth it thider · and thanne biddeth frendes
ȝerne of forȝifnesse · or lenger ȝeres lone. 284
Ac whil he is in Westmynstre · he wil be bifore,
And make hym merye · with other mennes goodis.
And so it fareth with moche folke · that to the freres shryueth,
As sysours and excecutours · thei wil ȝyue the freres 288

B. 259. LWCROB *omit* Or, *but* Crowley *retains it.* WOB *surmount the difficulty by placing* l. 259 *after* l. 261.   270. notaries WCOB; notarie L.
284. lone O; loone WC; lene (*or* leue?) LR.   288. ȝyue þe WRO; ȝeue þe B; þe (*with* ue *above*) L.

Hauen officers vnder hem · and ech of hem a certayn; 258
And yf thei wage men to werre · thei wryten hem in numbre;
Wol no treserour take hem wages · trauayle thei neuere so sore,
Bote hij beon nempned in the numbre · of hem that ben ywaged.
Alle othere in bataille · beeth yholde brybours,
Pilours and pyke-herneys · in eche parshe a-corsede.
Monekes and monyales · and alle men of religion, 264
Here ordre and here ruele wol · to haue a certayn numbre.
Of lered and lewede · the lawe wole and asketh
A certayn for a certayn · saue onliche of freres!
For-thi,' quath Conscience, 'by Crist · kynde wit me telleth, 268
Hit is wickede to wage ȝou · ȝe wexeth oute of numbre!
Heuene haueth euene numbre · and helle is with-oute numbre;
For-thi ich wolde witerly · that ȝe were in registre,
And ȝoure numbre vnder notarie signe · and nother more ne lasse!'
  Enuye herde this · and het freres go to scole, 273
And lerne logik and lawe · and eke contemplacion,
And preche men of Plato · and prouen hit by Seneca,
That alle thyng vnder heuene · ouhte to beo in comune. 276
  He lyeth, as ich leyue · that to the lewede so precheth,
For god made to men a lawe · and Moyses hit tauhte,
  Non concupisces rem proximi tui.
And vuel is this yholde · in parshes of Yngelonde,
For persones and parshe-preestes · that sholde the peuple shryue,
And thei beon curatours cald · to knowe and to hele, 281
Alle that been here parshenes · penaunces to enioyne,
And beo ashamede in here shryft; · ac shame maketh hem wende,
And fleo to the freres · as fals folke to Westmynstre, 284
That borweth and bereth hit thuder · and thenne byddeth frendes
Ȝeorne of for-ȝeuenesse · other lenger ȝeres leue.
Ac while he is in Westmynstre · he wol be by-fore,
And maken hym myrie · with other menne goodes. 288
And so hit fareth by muche folke · that to freres hem shryueth,
As asisours and executours · thei shal ȝeue the freres

C. 262. yholde EST; yolde P.   269. wexeþ EFM; wexiþ T; wexit P.
271. whiterly P.   282. to enioyne MFS; enioyne T; enioyneþ P.   284.
þe EMST; P *om.*   290. asisours ES; asissours P; sisours MFT.   excecu-
tours P.

A parcel to preye for hem · and make hem-self myrye
With the residue and the remenaunt · that other men biswonke,
And suffre the ded in dette · to the day of dome.
 Enuye herfore · hated Conscience,   292
And freres to philosofye · he fonde hem to scole,
The while Coueytise and Vnkyndenesse · Conscience assailled.
In Vnite holycherche · Conscience helde hym,
And made Pees porter · to pynne the ʒates   296
Of alle taletellers · and tyterers in ydel.
Ypocrisye and he · an hard saut thei made.
Ypocrysie atte ʒate · hard gan fiʒte,
And wounded wel wykkedly · many a wise techer,   300
That with Conscience acorded · and cardinale vertues.
Conscience called a leche · that coude wel shryue,
'Go salue tho that syke ben · and thorw synne ywounded.'
Shrifte shope sharpe salue · and made men do penaunce   304
For her mysdedes · that thei wrouʒte hadden,
And that Piers were payed · *redde quod debes.*
 Somme lyked nouʒte this leche · and lettres thei sent,
ʒif any surgien were in the sege · that softer couth plastre.   308
Sire Lief-to-lyue-in-leccherye · lay there and groned;
For fastyng of a Fryday · he ferde as he wolde deye.
'Ther is a surgiene in this sege · that softe can handle,
And more of phisyke bi fer · and fairer he plastreth;   312
One frere Flaterere · is phisiciene and surgiene.'
Quod Contricioun to Conscience · 'do hym come to Vnyte,
For here is many a man · herte thorw Ypocrisie.'
'We han no nede,' quod Conscience · 'I wote no better leche

Than persoun or parissh-prest · penytancere or bisshop,   317
Saue Piers the Plowman · that hath powere ouer hem alle,
And indulgence may do · but if dette lette it.
I may wel suffre,' seyde Conscience · 'syn ʒe desiren,   320
That frere Flaterer be fette · and phisike ʒow syke.'
 The frere her-of herde · and hyed faste
To a lorde for a lettre · leue to haue to curen,
As a curatour he were · and cam with his lettres   324

B. 300. a WRB; LCO *om.* 303. and WR; LCOB *om.* 308. in R;
LWCOB *om.*; *see* l. 311. 311. softe WRCOB; soft L.

A parcel to preye for hem · and maken hem murye
With the remenant of the good · that other men byswonke, 292
And suffre the dede in dette · to the day of dome.
 Enuye here-fore · hatyde Conscience,
And freres to philosophie · he fond hem to scole,
The while Couetise and Vnkyndenesse · assailede Conscience.
In Vnite holichurche · Conscience held hym, 297
And made Pees portor · to pynne the ȝates.
Alle tale-tellours · and titereres in ydel,
Ypocrise and thei · an hard saut thei ȝeuen. 300
Ypocrise at the ȝate · harde gan fighte,
And wondede wel wickedly · meny a wys techere,
That with Conscience acordede · and cardinale uertues.
Conscience calde a leche · that couthe wel shryue, 304
To salue tho that sik were · and thorgh synne y-wonded.
Shruft shupte sharpe salue · and made men do penaunce
For here mysdedes · that thei wrouht hadde,
And that Peers pardoun were ypaied · *redde quod debes*. 308
 Some likede nat this leche · and lettres thei senten,
Yf eny surgeyn were in the sege · that softere couthe plastre.
Sire Lyf-to-lyue-in-lecherie · lay there and gronede;
For fastynge of a Friday · he ferde as he wolde deye. 312
'Ther is a surgen in the sege · that softe can handle,
And more of fisik by fer · and fairer he plastreth;
On frere Flaterere · is fisician and surgien.'
Quath Contricion to Conscience · 'do hym come to Unite, 316
For her is meny man · hurt thorgh Ypocrisye.'
'We haue no neode,' quath Conscience · 'ich wote no bettere
  leche
Than person other parshe-prest · penytancer other busshup,
Saue Peers the Plouhman · that hath powere ouere alle, 320
And indulgence may do · bote yf dette lette.
Ich may wel suffry,' quath Conscience · 'sutthe ȝe desiren
That frere Flaterere be fet · and fysyke ȝou syke.'
 The frere here-of herde · and hyede faste 324
To a lorde for a lettere · leue to haue to curen
As he a curatour were · and cam with hus letteres

C. 291. prarcel (*sic*) P. murye T; murie M; merye FS; murþe P. 300.
and (*for* an) P. saut ST; sawt F; swat (*sic*) PE. 314. fer MFT; feer P.
322. disyren P.

Baldly to the bisshop · and his brief hadde,
In contrees there he come in · confessiouns to here;
And cam there Conscience was · and knokked atte ȝate.
Pees vnpynned it · was porter of Vnyte, 328
And in haste asked · 'what his wille were?'
'In faith,' quod this frere · 'for profit and for helthe
Carpe I wolde with Contricioun · and therfore come I hider.'

'He is sike,' seide Pees · 'and so ar many other, 332
Ypocrisie hath herte hem · ful harde is if thei keure.'
'I am a surgien,' seide the segge · 'and salues can make;
Conscience knoweth me wel · and what I can do bothe.'
'I preye the,' quod Pees tho · 'ar thow passe ferther, 336
What hattestow? I preye the · hele nouȝte thi name.'
'Certes,' seyde his felow · 'sire *Penetrans-domos*.'
'Ȝe, go thi gate,' quod Pees · 'bi god, for al thi phisyk,
But thow conne somme crafte · thow comest nouȝt her-inne!
I knewe such one ones · nouȝte eighte wynter passed, 341
Come in thus ycoped · at a courte there I dwelt,
And was my lordes leche · and my ladyes bothe.
And at the last this limitour · tho my lorde was out, 344
He salued so owre wommen · til somme were with childe!'
Hende-speche het Pees · opene the ȝates—
'Late in the frere and his felawe · and make hem faire chere.
He may se and here · so it may bifalle, 348
That Lyf thorw his lore · shal leue Coueityse,
And be adradde of Deth · and with-drawe hym fram Pryde,
And acorde with Conscience · and kisse her either other.'

Thus thorw Hende-speche · entred the frere, 352
And cam in-to Conscience · and curteisly hym grette.
'Thow art welcome,' quod Conscience · 'canstow hele the syke?
Here is Contricioun,' quod Conscience · 'my cosyn, ywounded;
Conforte hym,' quod Conscience · 'and take kepe to his sores.
The plastres of the persoun · and poudres biten to sore, 357

Baldely to the bushope · and hus breef hadde,
In countreyes ther he cam · confessions to hure;   328
And cam ther Conscience was · and knockede atte ȝate.
Pees vnpynnede the dore · that was portour of Vnite,
And in hast he askede · 'what hus wil were?'
'In faith,' quath this frere · 'for profit and for helthe,   332
Carpe ich wolde with Contricion · and ther-fore cam ich hyder.'
'He is syke,' seide Pees · 'and so aren meny othere;
Ypocrisye hath hurt hem · ful hard is yf thei keuere.'
'Ich am a surgen,' seide the frere · 'and salues can ich make,
Conscience knoweth me wel · and what ich can don.'   337
'Ich preye the,' quath Pees tho · 'er thow passe forthere,
What hattest thow? ich praye the · hele nat thy name.'
'Certes,' seide his felawe · 'syre *Penetrans-domos*.'   340
'Ȝe, go thi gate,' quath Pees · 'by god, for al thy fysike,
Bote thow conne other craft · thou comest nat here-ynne!
Ich knew such on ones · nat eyhte wynter passede,
Cam yn thus y-coped · at a court there ich dwellede.   344
He was my lordes leche · and my ladies bothe,
And atte last this lymytour · tho my lord was oute,
He saluede so oure wommen · til somme were with childe!'
Hende-speche het Pees tho · opene the ȝates—   348
'Lat yn the frere and hus felawe · and make hem faire chere.
He may seo and huyre here · so may by-falle,
That Lyf thorgh hus lore · shal leue Couetise,   351
And to beo a-drad of Deth · and with-drawe hym fro Pruyde,
And acorde with Conscience · and cusse here aither othere.'
 Thus thorgh Hende-speche · entrede the frere,
And cam to Conscience · and corteisliche hym grette.   355
'Thou art welcome,' quath Conscience · 'canst thou hele syke?
Here is Contricion,' quath Conscience · 'my cosyn, ywonded;
Conforte hym,' quath Conscience · 'and take kepe to hus sores.
The plastres of the person · and the pouderes beoth to sore,

C. 331. askede MF; asked E; hesshede P.   335. þei EMFT; þey S; *miswritten* ȝe P.   337. done P.   339. þe EF; PMST *om.*   340. is (*for* his) P.   342. oþer MFS; any oþer E; eny PT.   344. y-copede P. 346. atte þe P. whas P.   347. where P.   349. And lat PE; *but* MFST *omit* And.   chere EMFST; chyre P.   356. art MFST; ert PE. wolcome P. 357. ywondede P.

He lat hem ligge ouerlonge · and loth is to chaunge hem;
Fro lenten to lenten · he lat his plastres bite.'
'That is ouerlonge,' quod this limitour · 'I leue I shal amende
    it;'—   360
And goth and gropeth Contricioun · and gaf hym a plastre
Of 'a pryue payement · and I shal praye for ȝow,
For alle that ȝe ben holde to · al my lyf-tyme,
And make ȝow, my lady · in masse and in matynes,   364
As freres of owre fraternite · for a litel syluer.'
Thus he goth and gadereth · and gloseth there he shryueth,
Tyl Contricioun hadde clene forȝeten · to crye and to wepe,
And wake for his wykked werkes · as he was wont to done.   368
For confort of his confessour · Contricioun he lafte,
That is the souereynest salue · for alkyn synnes.
  Sleuth seigh that · and so did Pryde,
And come with a kene wille · Conscience to assaille.   372
Conscience cryde eft · and bad Clergye help hym,
And also Contricioun · forto kepe the ȝate.
'He lith and dremeth,' seyde Pees · 'and so do many other;
The frere with his phisik · this folke hath enchaunted,   376
And plastred hem so esyly · thei drede no synne.'
'Bi Cryste,' quod Conscience tho · 'I wil bicome a pilgryme,
And walken as wyde · as al the worlde lasteth,
To seke Piers the Plowman · that Pryde may destruye,   380
And that freres hadde a fyndyng · that for nede flateren,
And contrepleteth me, Conscience; · now Kynde me auenge,
And sende me happe and hele · til I haue Piers the Plowman!'
And sitthe he gradde after grace · til I gan awake.   384

Explicit hic dialogus Petri Plowman.

B. 379. wordle L.

And lat hem lygge ouer-lange · and loth is to chaungen ; 360
Fro lente to lente · he let hus plastres byte.'
'That is ouerlonge,' quath this lymytour · 'ich leyue ich shal amende hit.'
He goth and gropeth Contrition · and gaf hym a plastre
Of 'a pryue payement · and ich shal preye for ȝow, 364
And for hem that ȝe aren holden to · al my lyf-tyme,
And make ȝow, my lady · in masse and in matynes,
As freres of oure fraternite · for a litel seluer.'
Thus he goth and gadereth · and gloseth ther he shryueth, 368
Til Contrition hadde clene for-ȝute · to crie and wepe and wake
For hus wickede werkes · as he was woned by-fore.
For comfort of hus confessour · Contricion he lefte,
That is the souereyne salue · for alle kynne synnes. 372
  Anon Sleuthe seih that · and so dude Pruyde,
And comen with a kene wil · Conscience to assaile.
Conscience criede eft · 'Cleregie, come help me!'
And bad Contricion to come · to helpe kepe the ȝate. 376
'He lith adreynt,' saide Pees · 'and so doth meny othere ;
The frere with hus fisik · this folke hath enchaunted,
And doth men drynke dwale · that men dredeth no synne.'
'By Crist,' quath Conscience tho · 'ich wol by-come a pilgryme,
And wenden as wide · as the worlde regneth, 381
To seke Peers the Plouhman · that Pruyde myghte destruye,
And that freres hadden a fyndynge · that for neode flateren,
And counterpleideth me, Conscience ; · nowe Kynde me a-venge,
And sende me hap and hele · til ich haue Peers Plouhman!'
And suthe he gradde after grace · til ich gan a-wake. 386

Hic explicit passus secundus de Dobest.

𝕰𝖝𝖕𝖑𝖎𝖈𝖎𝖙 𝖕𝖊𝖊𝖗𝖊𝖘 𝖕𝖑𝖔𝖚𝖍𝖊𝖒𝖆𝖓.

C. 361. byte T ; bite EMF ; byde PS. 362. lymytour EFT ; lymatour P.
363. and (1) EFS ; PMT *om.* 364. ȝowe P. 370. wonede P. 376. kepe EMST ; P *om.* 377. adreynt EMF ; adreynched P. 378. enchauntede P.
381. wordle P. 383. þat (1) EMFST ; þe P.

RICHARD THE REDELESS.

Prologus.

AND as I passid in my preiere · ther prestis were at messe,
In a blessid borugh · that Bristow is named,
In a temple of the trinite · the toune euen amyddis,
That Cristis chirche is cleped · amonge the comune peple,   4
Sodeynly ther sourdid · selcouthe thingis,
A grett wondir to wyse men · as it well my3th,
And dowtes ffor to deme · ffor drede comynge after.
So sore were the sawis · of bothe two sidis,   8
Of Richard that regned · so riche and so noble,
That whyle he werrid be west · on the wilde Yrisshe,
Henrri was entrid · on the est half,
Whom all the londe loued · in lengthe and in brede,   12
And ros with him rapely · to ri3tyn his wronge,
ffor he shullde hem serue · of the same after.
Thus tales me troblid · ffor they trewe were,
And amarride my mynde rith moche · and my wittis eke :   16
ffor it passid my parceit · and my preifis also,
How so wondirffull werkis · wolde haue an ende..
But in sothe whan they sembled · some dede repente,
As knowyn is in cumpas · of Cristen londis,   20
That rewthe was, if reson · ne had reffourmed
The myssecheff and the mysserule · that men tho in endurid.
I had pete of his passion · that prince was of Walis,
And eke oure crouned kynge · till Crist woll no lenger;   24
And as a lord to his liage · thou3 I lite hade,
All myn hoole herte was his · while he in helthe regnid.

---

10. MS. wyle.
12. *Cf.* He had be lord of þat *londe · in lengthe and in brede*; C. 4. 261.
13. *Cf.* Two *rysen rapliche* · and rounede to-geders; C. 7. 383.   MS. rosse
(*for* ros).   15. MS. where.   22. *For* endurid, *read* durede.

And ffor I wuste not witterly · what shulde ffall,
Whedir god wolde ȝeue him grace · sone to amende,   28
To be oure gioure aȝeyn · or graunte it another,
This made me to muse · many tyme and ofte,
For to written him a writte · to wissen him better,
And to meuve him of mysserewle · his mynde to reffresshe, 32
ffor to preise the prynce · that paradise made,
To ffullfill him with ffeith · and ffortune aboue,
And not to grucchen a grott · aȝeine godis sonde,
But mekely to suffre · what so him sente were.   36
And ȝif him list to loke · a leef other tweyne,
That made is to mende him · of his myssededis,
And to kepe him in confforte · in Crist and nouȝt ellis,
I wolde be gladde that his gost · myȝte glade be my wordis, 40
And grame if it greued him · be god that me bouȝte!
Ther nys no gouernour on the grounde · ne sholde gye him
   the better—
And euery Cristen kyng · that ony croune bereth,
So he were lerned on the langage · my lyff durst I wedde—
ȝif he waite well the wordis · and so werche therafter;   45
ffor all is tresour of the trinite · that turneth men to gode.
And as my body and my beste · ouȝte to be my liegis,
So rithffully be reson · my rede shulde also,   48
ffor to conceill, and I couthe · my kyng and the lordis;
And ther-ffor I ffondyd · with all my ffyue wyttis
To traueile on this tretis · to teche men ther-after
To be war of wylffulnesse · lest wondris arise.   52
And if it happe to ȝoure honde · beholde the book onys,

---

27. MS. wost; *but see* Pass. i. ll. 49 *and* 64, *below.*
30. *Cf. Musynge* on þis meteles · a myle-wey ich ȝeode;
  And *meny tymes* this meteles · *made me* to studie; C. 10. 296.
35. *Cf.* On *god,* whenne me greued ouht · and *grucched of hus sonde*;
                              C. 7. 111.
37. *Cf.* First I lerned to lye · *a leef other tweyne*; B. 5. 203.
43. MS. grounde (*an obvious error for* croune; *copied from* l. 42).
44. *Cf.* Ich dorst haue *leid my lyue* · and no lasse *wedde*; C. 4. 260.
46. *Cf.* Ther treuthe is, þe trone · þat *trinite* ynne sitteþ ..
  Than treuthe & trewe loue · ys no *tresour* bettere; C. 2. 134–136.
47. MS. oute.
48. *Cf.*—*bi Reson,* And *Rihtfuliche,* &c.; A. 1. 92, 93; *also,* For *ryhtfulliche reson*; C. 2. 50.   49. MS. couȝthe.
50. *For* ffondyd, MS. *has* ffordyd, *altered to* ffondyd. Mr. Wright *prints* ffordyd, *but see* B. 15. 327; *and cf.* C. 2. 15.

And redeth on him redely · rewis an hundrid,
And if ȝe sauere sum dell · se it fforth ouere,
ffor reson is no repreff · be the rode of Chester!   56
And if ȝe ffynde ffables · or ffoly ther-amonge,
Or ony ffantasie yffeyned · that no ffrute is in,
Lete ȝoure conceill corette it · and clerkis to-gedyr,
And amende that ys amysse · and make it more better: 60
ffor-ȝit it is secrette · and so it shall lenger,
Tyll wyser wittis · han waytid it ouere,
That it be lore laweffull · and lusty to here.
    ffor witterly, my will is · that it well liked   64
Ȝou and all ȝouris · and yonge men leueste,
To be-nyme hem her noyes · that neweth hem ofte.
ffor and they mvse theron · to the myddwardis,
They shall fynde ffele ffawtis · ffoure score and odde,   68
That youghthe weneth alwey · that it be witte euere.
And thouȝ that elde opyn it · other-while amonge,
And poure on it preuyly · and preue it well after,
And constrewe ich clause · with the *culorum*,   72
It shulde not apeire hem a peere · a prynce thouȝ he were,
Ne harme nother hurte · the hyghest of the rewme,
But to holde him in hele · and helpe all his ffrendis.
And if ony word write be · that wrothe make myghte   76
My souereyne, that suget · I shulde to be,
I put me in his power · and preie him, of grace,
To take the entent of my trouthe · that thouȝte non ylle.
ffor to wrath no wyght · be my wyll neuere,   80
As my soule be saff · ffrom synne at myn ende.
The story is of non estate · that stryuen with her lustus,
But tho that ffolwyn her fflessh · and here ffrelle thouȝtis;
So if my conceyll be clere · I can saie no more,   84
But ho be greued in his gost · gouerne him better,
And blame not the berne · that the book made,
But the wickyd will · and the werkis after.

---

55. Cf. ȝut sauereþ me nat þi sawe; C 11. 107.
56. Cf. bi þe rode of Chestre; B. 5. 467.
68. The MS. *omits* fynde.   69. MS. youghe.
72. Cf. þe *culorum* of þis *clause*; A. 3. 264; C. 12. 248.
78. Cf. Thenne knelede ich on my knees · and criede hure *of grace*,
    And *preide hure* pytously; C. 2. 76, 77.

And besieth him besely · to breden hem ffeedrin,
Tyll her ffre ffedris · be ffulliche y-pynned,   148
That they haue wynge at her wyll · to wonne vppon hille,
ffor venym on the valeye · hadde ffoule with hem ffare,
Tyll trouthe the triacle · telde somme her sothes.
   Thus baterid this bred · on busshes aboute,   152
And gaderid gomes on grene · ther as they walkyd,
That all the schroff and schroup · sondrid ffrom other.
He mellid so the matall · with the hand-molde,
That [they] lost [of their] lemes · the leuest that they had. 156
Thus ffoulyd this Faukyn · on ffyldis aboute,
And cauȝte of the kytes · a cartfull at ones,
That rentis and robis · with raveyn euere lauȝte.
Ȝit was not the Fawcon · ffull ffed at his likynge,   160
ffor it cam him not of kynde · kytes to loue.
Than bated he boldeliche · as a brid wolde,
To plewme on his pray · the pol ffro the nekk;
But the blernyed boynard · that his bagg stall,   164
Where purraile-is pulter · was pynnyd ffull ofte,
Made the Fawcon to ffloter · and fflussh ffor anger,
That the boy hadd be bounde · that the bagge kepte.
But sone ther-after · in a schorte tyme,   168
As ffortune ffolwith · ech ffode till his ende,
This lorell that ladde · this loby awey
Ouere ffrithe and fforde · ffor his ffals dedis,
Lyghte on the lordschepe · that to the brid longid,   172
And was ffelliche ylauȝte · and luggid ffull ylle,
And brouȝte to the brydd · and his blames rehersid
Preuyly at the parlement · amonge all the peple.
   Thus hawkyd this Egle · and houed aboue,   176
That, as god wolde · that gouerneth all thingis,
Ther nas kyte ne krowe · that kareyne hantid
That he ne [lauȝte] with his lynage · ne louyd ffull sone.
ffor wher so they fferde · be ffryth or be wones,   180
Was non of hem all · that him hide myȝth,

---

149. MS. heue (*for* haue).
151. *Cf.* For *treuthe* tellep þat loue · ys *tryacle* for synne; C. 2. 147.
156. MS. omits þey *and* of þeir.
158. MS. kuyttis, *with* kytes *written above; see* l. 161.
170. MS. hadde (*for* ladde).   179. MS. *omits* lauȝte.

Passus Primus.

NOW, Richard the redeles · reweth on ȝou-self,
That lawelesse leddyn ȝoure lyf · and ȝoure peple bothe;
ffor thoru the wyles and wronge · and wast in ȝoure tyme,
ȝe were lyghtlich y-lyfte · ffrom that ȝou leef thouȝte, 4
And ffrom ȝoure willffull werkis · ȝoure will was chaungid,
And rafte was ȝoure riott · and rest, ffor ȝoure daiez
Weren wikkid thoru ȝoure cursid counceill · ȝoure karis weren newed,
And coueitise hath crasid · ȝoure croune ffor euere! 8
Radix omnium malorum cupiditas.
Of alegeaunce now lerneth · a lesson other tweyne,
Wher-by it standith · and stablithe moste—
By drede, or be dyntis · or domes vntrewe,
Or by creaunce of coyne · ffor castes of gile, 12
By pillynge of ȝoure peple · ȝoure prynces to plese;
Or that ȝoure wylle were wrouȝte · thouȝ wisdom it nolde;—
Or be tallage of ȝoure townes · without ony werre,
By rewthles routus · that ryffled euere, 16
By preysinge of polaxis · that no pete hadde,
Or be dette ffor thi dees · deme as thou ffyndist;
Or be ledinge of lawe · with loue well ytemprid.
Though this be derklich endited · ffor a dull nolle, 20
Miche nede is it not · to mwse ther-on,
ffor as mad as I am · thouȝ I litill kunne,
I cowde it discryue · in a ffewe wordys;
ffor legiance without loue · litill thinge availith. 24
But graceles gostis · gylours of hem-self,
That neuere had harnesse · ne hayle-schouris,
But walwed in her willis · ffor-weyned in here youthe,
They sawe no manere siȝth · saff solas and ese, 28

---

9. *Cf.* Furst I *leornede* to lyȝe · *a lessun or tweyne*; A. 5. 117.
15. MS. towunes *or* townnes.
16. MS. routus, *altered to* routes, *unnecessarily.*
17. *Cf.* Or Poule þe apostle · *þat no pitee hadde*; B. 10. 424; C. 12. 268.
19. *Cf.* And *ledeþ þe lawe* as hure lust · and *louedayes* makeþ; C. 4. 196.
24. *Cf.* Lawe *with-outen loue* · leye þere a bene! B. 11. 165.
27. *Cf.* And lete no wynnynge *forwene* hem · *þe while þei ben ȝonge*; C. 6. 138.

And cowde no mysse amende · whan mysscheff was vp,
But sorwed ffor her lustus · of lordschipe they hadde,
And neuere ffor her trespas · oo tere wolde they lete!
ȝe come to ȝoure kyngdom · er ȝe ȝoure-self knewe,   32
Crouned with a croune · that kyng vnder heuene
Miȝte not a better · haue bouȝte, as I trowe;
So ffull was it ffilled · with vertuous stones,
With perlis of pris · to punnysshe the wrongis,   36
With rubies rede · the riȝth for to deme,
With gemmes and Iuellis · Ioyned to-gedir,
And pees amonge the peple · ffor peyne of thi lawis.
It was ffull goodeliche ygraue · with gold al aboute;   40
The braunchis aboue · boren grett charge;
With diamauntis derue · y-doutid of all
That wrouȝte ony wrake · within or withoute;
With lewte and loue · yloke to thi peeris,   44
And sapheris swete · that souȝte all wrongis,
Ypoudride wyth pete · ther it be ouȝte,
And traylid with trouthe · and treste al aboute;
ffor ony cristen kynge · a croune well ymakyd.   48
   But where this croune bicome · a clerk were that wuste;
But so as I can · declare it I thenke,
And nempne no name; · but tho that nest were,
ffull preuyly they pluckud · thy power awey,   52
And reden with realte · ȝoure rewme thoru-oute,
And as tyrauntis, of tiliers · token what hem liste,
And paide hem on her pannes · whan her penyes lacked.
ffor non of ȝoure peple · durste pleyne of here wrongis,   56
ffor drede of ȝoure dukys · and of here double harmes.
Men myȝtten as well haue huntyd · an hare with a tabre,

---

29. *Cf.* þi *myschief is vppe*; B. 4. 72.   30. MS. lordschpe.
33—37. *Cf.* And *coroned with a corone* · þe *kynge hath no betere* ; . . .
   And þer-on *rede rubies* · and oþer *riche stones* ; C. 3. 11, 13.
40. MS. abouȝte, *both here and in* ii. 2, 15, *and* 102. *Cf. gold al a-boute* ; C. 3. 158.
42, 45. *Cf.* And *diamantz* of derrest pris · and double manere *safferes* ; B. 2. 13; *see the whole passage.* MS. y-douutid.   43. MS. wroute.
44. *Cf.* Ac *loue* and louhnesse · and *leaute* to-gederes; C. 4. 447.
46. MS. Y-pouudride.   49. *Cf.* I *ne wot where* þei *bicome* ; B. 5. 651.
55. *Cf.* the account of how 'Pees' came by his '*panne* blody'; C. 5. 74.
56. *Cf.* For *pore men der nat pleyne* · ne here pleinte shewe; C. 4. 214; *see the whole passage.*

As aske ony mendis · ffor that thei mysdede,
Or of ony of her men · thou3 men wulde plete, 60
ffor all was ffelawis and ffelawschepe · that 3e with fferde,
And no soule persone · to punnyshe the wrongis;
And that maddid thi men · as thei nede muste.
ffor wo, they ne wuste · to whom ffor to pleyne. 64
ffor, as it is said · by elderne dawis,
'Ther gromes and the goodmen · beth all eliche grette,
Well wo beth the wones · and all that woneth ther-in!'
They ladde 3ou with loue · that 3oure lawe dradde, 68
To deme 3oure dukys myssdedis · so derue thei were.

 Thus was 3oure croune crasid · till he was cast newe,
Thoru partinge of 3oure powere · to 3oure paragals.
Thus lacchide they with laughinge · and lourid longe after, 72
But ffrist sawe they it not · ne youre-self nother;
ffor all was wisliche ywrou3te · as 3oure witte demed,
And no ffautis y-ffounde · till ffortune aperid.
But had 3oure croune be kepte · that comons it wiste, 76
Ther nadde morder ne mysscheff · be amonge the grette.
Thus 3oure cautell to the comoune · hath combred 3ou all,
That, but if god helpe · 3oure heruest is ynne.
Wyteth it not 3oure councelll · but wyteth it more 3oure-self, 80
The ffortune that ffallyn is · to ffeitheles peple;
And wayte well my wordis · and wrappe hem togedir,
And construwe thoru clergie · the clause in thin herte,
Of maters that I thenke · to meve ffor the best 84
ffor kyngis and kayseris · comynge here-after.

 Whane 3e were sette in 3oure se · as a sir aughte,
Ther carpinge comynliche · of conceill arisith,
The cheuyteyns cheef · that 3e chesse euere 88
Weren all to yonge of 3eris · to yeme swyche a rewme;
Other hobbis 3e hadden · of Hurlewaynis kynne,
Reffusynge the reule · of realles kynde.

---

67. MS. Woll.
72. *Cf.* þere was *laughyng* and *louryng*; B. 5. 344.   75. MS. fauutis.
80. *misspelt* Wytteth (*alt. to* Wyteth) *the first time, and* wyteh *the second time, in the* MS.
83. MS. *omits* þoru. *Cf. Clerkus* þat were confessours · couplede hem togederes *To construe this clause*; C. 5. 146, 147.
84. *Cf.* I dorste *meue* no *matere*; C. 11. 118.   85. MS. Kayseceris.

And whane ȝoure councceill I-knewe · ȝe come so at ones,　92
ffor to leue on her lore · and be led be hem,
ffor drede that they had · of demynge ther-after,
And ffor curinge of hem-self · cried on ȝou euere,
ffor to hente hele · of her owen greues,　96
More than ffor wurschepe · that they to ȝou owed,
They made ȝou to leue · that regne ȝe ne myȝte,
Withoute busshinge adoune · of all ȝoure best ffrendis,
Be a ffals colour · her caris to wayve,　100
And to holde hem in hele · if it happe myȝte.
 ffor trostith rith treuly · and in no tale better,
All that they moued · or mynged in that mater,
Was to be sure of hem-self · and siris to ben y-callid;　104
ffor that was all her werchinge · in worde and in dede.
But had ȝe do duly · and as a duke oughte,
The ffrist that ȝou fformed · to that ffals dede,
He shulde have hadde hongynge · on hie on the fforckis,　108
Thouȝ ȝoure brother y-born · had be the same.
Than wolde other boynardis · haue ben abasshyd
To haue meved ȝou to ony maters · that mysscheff had ben ynne.
But ffor ȝe cleued to knavis · in this cas I avowe,　112
That boldid thi burnes · to belde vppon sorowe,
And stirid ȝou stouttely · till ȝe stombled all.

Passus Secundus.

But moche now me merueilith · and well may I in sothe,
 Of ȝoure large leuerey · to leodis aboute,
That ȝe so goodliche ȝaf · but if gile letted,
As hertis y-heedyd · and hornyd of kynde,　4
So ryff as they ronne · ȝoure rewme thoru-oute,
That non at ȝoure nede · ȝoure name wolde nempne
In ffersnesse ne in ffoltheed · but ffaste ffle away-ward,
And some stode astonyed · and stared ffor drede,　8
ffor eye of the Egle · that oure helpe brouȝte.
And also in sothe · the seson was paste

---

98. MS. myste.　　　　　　　　　111. MS. myssheff.
Passus ii. 2. MS. abouȝte; *so also in* l. 15.　　9. MS. brouute.

RICHARD THE REDELESS: PASSUS II.

ffor hertis y-heedid · so hy and so noble
To make ony myrthe · ffor mowtynge that nyghed. 12
That bawtid ȝoure bestis · of here bolde chere;
They seuerid and sondrid · ffor somere hem ffaylid,
And ffowen in-to fforest · and ffeldis aboute,
All the hoole herde · that helde so to-gedir; 16
But ȝet they had hornes · half a ȝere after.
  Now liste me to lerne · ho me lere coude,
What kynnes conceyll · that the kyng had,
Or meued him most · to merke his liegis, 20
Or serue hem with signes · that swarmed so thikke
Thoru-oute his lond · in lengthe and in brede,
That ho so had hobblid · thoru holtes and tounes,
Or y-passid the patthis · ther the prynce dwellyd, 24
Of hertis or hyndis · on hassellis brestis,
Or some lordis leuere · that the lawe stried,
He shulde haue y-mette · mo than y-nowe.
ffor they acombrede the contre · and many curse seruid, 28
And carped to the comounes · with the kyngys mouthe,
Or with the lordis · ther they be-lefte were,
That no renke shulde rise · reson to schewe.
They plucked the plomayle · ffrom the pore skynnes, 32
And schewed her signes · ffor men shulde drede
To axe ony mendis · ffor her mys-dedis.
Thus leuerez ouere-loked · ȝoure liegis ichone;
ffor tho that had hertis · on hie on her brestis 36
ffor the more partie · I may well avowe,
They bare hem the bolder · ffor her gay broches,
And busshid with her brestis · and bare adoune the pouere,
Lieges that loued ȝou the lesse · ffor her [lither] dedis. 40
So, trouthe to telle · as toune-men said,
ffor on that ȝe merkyd · ȝe myssed ten schore
Of homeliche hertis · that the harme hente.
Thane was it ffoly · in ffeith, as me thynketh, 44
To sette siluer in signes · that of nouȝt serued.

---

16. to- *in* to-gedir *is supplied in the* MS. *in a later hand.*
17. a *is supplied in the* MS. *in a later hand;* cf. 'half *a* ȝere' in C. 3. 238.
25. MS, Or (*wrongly*).   35. MS. ichonne.
37. *Cf. ich may it wel avowe;* C. 4. 315.   40. MS. yuell (*for* lither).
45. *Cf.* Bere no *suluer* ouer see · that kynges *sygne* shewe þ; C. 5. 126.

I not what ȝou eylid · but if it ese were;
ffor ffrist at ȝoure anoyntynge · alle were ȝoure owene,
Bothe hertis and hyndis · and helde of non other;   48
No lede of ȝoure lond · but as a liege aughte,
Tyl ȝe, of ȝoure dulnesse · deseueraunce made,
Thoru ȝoure side signes · that shente all the browet,
And cast adoun the crokk · the colys amyd.   52
  Omne regnum in se diuisum desolabitur; luce xj°. c°.
Ȝit am I lewde · and litill good schewe,
To coueyte knowliche · of kyngis wittis,
Or wilne to witte · how was the mevynge,
That [ladde] ȝou to lykynge · ȝoure liegis to merke,   56
That loued ȝou full lelly · or leuerez beganne,
And as redy to ride · or renne at ȝoure heste,
As wyghte myghte wilne · wonnynge vppon erthe,
Tyll leuerez hem lette · and lordyns wrongis,   60
As ȝoure-self ffonde well · whane ffortune ȝou ffolwyd.
ffor whan ȝe list to lene · to ȝoure owen lymmes,
They were so ffeble and ffeynte · ffor ffaute of ȝoure lawe,
And so ffeble and wayke · wexe in the hammes,   64
That they had no myghte · to amende ȝoure greues,
Ne to bere byrthen · ȝoure banere to helpe.
But it longith to no liegeman · his lord to anoye,
Nother in werk ne in word · but if his witt ffayle.   68
"No, redely," quod Reson · "that reule I alowe;
Displese not thi demer · in dede ne in wordis,
But if the liste ffor to lede · thi lyf in dissese.
But ȝif god haue grauntyd the · grace ffor to knowe   72
Ony manere mysscheff · that myȝtte be amendyd,
Schewe that to thi souereyne · to schelde him ffrom harmes;
ffor, and he be blessid · the better the be-tydyth
In tyme ffor to telle him · ffor thi trewe herte."   76
  Now, ffor to telle trouthe · thus than me thynketh,

---

46. *Cf.* Ich *wot* wel, quath hunger · *what* syknesse ȝow aileþ; C. 9. 271.
52. *Cf.* þat cast for to kele a *crokke* · and saue the fatte aboue; C. 22. 280.
56. MS. *omits* ladde. 57. Cf. And to *loue* me *lelly*; B. 1. 78.
58. *Cf.* ȝemen · to *rennen* and to *ryde*; C. 4. 271.
61. ffolwyd; *the word* ffayled *is writen above, and is perhaps a better reading.*
63. MS. ffauȝte. 68. *Cf.* As *in workes* and *in wordes*; C. 3. 94.
69. *Cf.* Forþy, *reson, redelyche;* C. 5. 184.

That no manere meyntenour · shulde merkis bere,
Ne haue lordis leuere · the lawe to apeire,
Neither bragger ne boster · ffor no bremme wordis, 80
But ho so had kunnynge · and conscience bothe,
To stonde vnstombled · and stronge in his wittis,
Lele in his leuynge · leuyd be his owen,
That no manere mede · shulde make him wrye, 84
ffor to trien a trouthe · be-twynne two sidis,
And lette ffor no lordschep · the lawe to susteyne,
Whane the pore pleyned · that put were to wrongis.
And I were of conceill · by Crist that me bouȝte, 88
He shuld haue a signe · and sum-what be ȝere,
ffor to kepe his contre · in quiete and in reste.
This were a good grounde · so me god helpe!
And a trewe tente · to take and to ȝeue, 92
And ony lord of this londe · that leuerez vsith.
But how the gayes han y-gon · god wotte the sothe
Amonge myȝtfull men · alle these many ȝeris;
And, whedir the grounde of ȝifte · were good other ille, 96
Trouthe hathe determyned · the tente to the ende,
And reson hath rehersid · the resceyte of all.
Ȝit, I trowe, ȝoure entente · at the ffrist tyme,
Was, as I wene, ȝif I well thenke · in multitude of peple, 100
That ȝe were the more myȝtier · ffor the many signes
That ȝe and ȝoure seruauntis · aboute so thikke sowid;
And that they were more tristi · and trewer than other,
To loue ȝou ffor the leuere · that legeaunce stroied; 104
Or ellis ffor a skylle · that skathed ȝoure-self,
That comounes of contre · in costis aboute
Sholde knowe be hir quentise · that the kyng loued hem
ffor her priuy prynte · passinge another. 108
Ȝif that was ȝoure purpos · it passith my wittis
To deme discrecioun · of ȝoure well-doynge!
Thus were ȝe disceyued · thoru ȝoure duble hertis,
That neuere weren to truste · so god saue my soule! 112

---

80. *Cf.*—*braggynge · abosted*, &c.; C. 9. 152.
82. *Cf.* to *stomble*, yf he *stande;* C. 11. 35.   93. *For* And *read* For?
97. *Cf.* Til *trewþe hadde ytermenyd ·* here trespas to þe *ende;* C. 2. 93.
106. MS. abouȝte; *so also in* ll. 102, 152, 157, 182, 186. Cf. Yf þei knew eny *countreie ·* oþer *costes aboute;* C. 11. 12.

RICHARD THE REDELESS: PASSUS II.

But had the good Greehonde · be not agreued,
But cherischid as a cheffeteyne · and cheff of ȝoure lese,
Ȝe hadde had hertis ynowe at ȝoure wille · to go and to ride.
   And also in serteyne · the sothe ffor to telle,   116
I wondir not hyly · thouȝ heed-dere thou ffailid;
ffor litill on ȝoure lyf · the list ffor to rewe
On rascaile that rorid · with ribbis so lene,
ffor ffaute of her ffode · that fflatereris stelen,   120
And euere with here wylis and wast · ofte they hem anoyed,
That pouerte hem prickid · ffull preuyliche to pleyne,
But where, they ne wyste · ne ho it wolde amende!
Thus ȝe derid hem vnduly · with droppis of anger,   124
And stonyed hem with stormes · that stynted neuere,
But plucked and pulled hem · anon to the skynnes,
That the ffresinge ffrost · ffreted to here hertis.
So whanne ȝoure hauntelere dere · were all ytakyn,   128
Was non of the rasskayle · aredy ffull growe,
To bere ony bremme heed · as a best aughte,
So wyntris wedir · hem wessh with the snowis,
With many derke mystis · that maddid her eyne.   132
ffor well mowe ȝe wyttyn · and so mowe we all,
That harde is the somer · ther sonne schyneth neuere.
Ȝe ffostrid and ffodid · a ffewe of the best,
And leyde on hem lordschipe · aleyne vppon other,   136
And bereued the raskall · that rith wolde thei hadde,
And knewe not the caris · ne cursis that walkyd;
But mesure is a meri mene · thouȝ men moche yerne:—
    Deus exaudit clamorem pauperum, et iudicat causam eorum;
       Dauid in psalmis.
Thus be the rotus · ȝoure raskall endurid,   140
Tyll the blessid bredd · brodid his wyngis,
To couere hem ffrom colde · as his kynde wolde.
Rith as the hous-hennes · vppon londe hacchen,
And cherichen her chekonys · ffro chele of the wynter,   144
Ryth so the hende Egle · the heyere of hem all,
Hasteth him in heruest · to houyn his bryddis,

---

120. MS. ffauȝte. MS. fflateris.   128. MS. where.
139. *Mesure is* medcyne · *þouȝ þow moche ȝerne;* B. 1. 35; C. 2. 33.
142. Cf. *as hus kynde wolde;* C. 4. 129; and 9. 161.
145. MS. Eyere; *but see* iii. 74.

But cam with him a reclayme · ffro costis aboute,
And ffell with her ffetheris · fflat vppon the erthe,
As madde of her mynde · and mercy be-souȝte,   184
They myȝte not aschonne · the sorowe they had serued.
So lymed leues · were leyde all aboute,
And panteris preuyliche · pight vppon the grounde,
With grennes of good heere · that god him-self made,   188
That where so they walkid · they waltrid dounwardis;
And euere houed the Egle · on hie on the skyes,
And kenned clerliche · as his kynde axith,
Alle the preuy poyntis · that the pies wrouȝth.   192

Passus Tercius.

NOW leue we this beu brid · till I restore,
ffor mater that my mynde · is meued in now,
That whi the hie hertis · her hele so mysside,
That pasture axid · rith to here pure wombis;   4
I wolle schewe as I sawe · till I se better,
And if I walke out of the wey · I wolle me repente.
Now herkeneth, hende men · how that me thynkyth,
Sauynge souereynes · and sages avise,   8
That the moste myscheff · vppon molde on
Is demed the dede · y-do aȝeins kynde. ·
Ȝit clereth this clause · no-thinge my wittis,
With out more mater · what it mene wolde.   12
I mene of the hertis · that hautesse of ȝeris,
That pasture prikkyth · and her preuy age;
Whan they han hoblid on the holte · an hundrid of ȝeris,
That they ffeblen in ffleissh · in ffelle, and in bones, 16
Her kynde is to keuere · if they cacche myȝth
Adders that harmen · alle hende bestis;
Thoru busschis and bromes · this beste, of his kynde,
Secheth and sercheth · tho schrewed wormes,   20
That steleth on the stedis · to stynge hem to deth;

---

183. *Cf.* platte hure to þe erthe; C. 7. 3.
191. *Cf.* riȝte *as kynde axeth*; B. 2. 27.
Passus iii. 9. *Cf.* þe *moste myschif on molde* · mounteþ vp faste; C. 1. 65.
18. MS. armen, *with* h *supplied above the line.*

And whanne it happeth the herte · to hente the edder,
He putyth him to peyne · as his pray asketh,
And ffedith him on the venym · his ffelle to anewe, 24
To leue at more lykynge · a longe tyme after.
This is clergie, hir kynde · coltis nat to greue,
Ne to hurlle with haras · no Hors well atamed,
Ne to stryue with Swan · thouȝ it sholle werre, 28
Ne to bayten on the Bere · ne bynde him nother,
Ne to wilne to woo · that were hem ny sibbe,
Ne to liste ffor to loke · that her alie bledde;
This was aȝeins kynde · as clerkis me tolde: 32
 Propter ingratitudinem liber homo reuocatur in seruitutem,
  ut in stimulo compunccionis, et in lege ciuili.
And therffor the hertis · here hele so myssid,
And myȝte nat passe the poynte · of her prime age.
Now constrew ho so kunne · I can saie no more,
But ffare I wolle to the ffowle · that I beffore tolde. 36
 Off all billid breddis · that the bough spareth,
The propirte of partriche · to preise me lustith,
That in the somer seson · whane sittinge nyeth,
That ich ffoule with his ffere · ffolwith his kynde, 40
This brid be a bank · bildith his nest,
And heipeth his eiren · and hetith hem after.
And whane the dame hath ydo · that to the dede longith,
And hopith ffor to hacche · or heruest begynne, 44
Thanne cometh ther a congioun · with a grey cote,
As not of his nolle · as he the nest made,
Another proud partriche · and precyth to the nest,
And preuylich pirith · til the dame passe, 48
And sesith on his sete · with hir softe plumes,
And houeth the eyren · that the hue laide,
And with hir corps keuereth hem · till that they kenne,
And ffostrith and ffodith · till ffedris schewe, 52

---

23. *Cf. as* þe worlde *askeþ*; C. 1. 21. 25. *Cf. a longe tyme after;* C. 8. 203.
26. nat *above the line.* 27. MS. ne.
34. *Cf.* Whoso *passeþ* þat *poynt;* C. 2. 98.
39. *Cf.* In a *somer sesoun;* C. 1. 1.
41. *Cf.* Briddes I hihelde · þat in buskes made nestes; B. 11. 336; and compare the whole passage in B. 11. 318-353 with the context.
42. MS. heires, *which is obviously a blunder; for see* l. 50, *below. Heires* = heirs; but *eiren* = eggs.

And cotis of kynde · hem keuere all aboute.
But as sone as they styffe · and that they steppe kunne,
Than cometh and crieth · her owen kynde dame,
And they ffolwith the vois · at the ffrist note, 56
And leueth the lurker · that hem er ladde,
ffor the schrewe schrapid · to selde ffor her wombis,
That her lendys were lene · and leued with hunger.
But than the dewe dame · dineth hem swythe, 60
And ffostrith hem fforthe · till they ffle kunne.
  'What is this to mene, man?' · maiste thou axe,
'ffor it is derklich endited · ffor a dull panne;
Wherffore I wilne · ʒif it thi will were, 64
The partriche propurtes · by whom that thou menest?'
A! Hicke Heuyheed! · hard is thi nolle
To cacche ony kunnynge · but cautell bigynne!
Herdist thou not with eeris · how that I er tellde, 68
How the Egle in the est · entrid his owene,
And cried and clepid · after his owen kynde briddis,
That weren anoyed in his nest · and norished ffull ille,
And well ny yworewid · with a wronge leder? 72
But the nedy nestlingis · whan they the note herde
Of the hende Egle · the heyer of hem all,
Thei busked ffro the busches · and breris that hem noyed,
And burnisched her beekis · and bent to-him-wardis, 76
And ffolowid him ffersly · to ffighte ffor the wrongis;
They bablid with her billis · how thei bete were,
And tenyd with twiggis · two and twenty ʒeris.
Thus lafte they the leder · that hem wrong ladde, 80
And tymed no twynte · but tolled her cornes,
And gaderid the grotus · with gyle, as I trowe.
Than ffolwid they her ffre ffader · as good ffeith wolde,
That he hem ffede shulde · and ffostre fforther, 84
And bringe hem out of bondage · that they were brouʒth inne.
  Thanne sighed the swymmers · ffor the Swan ffailid,
And ffolwid this Faucoun · thoru ffeldus and tounes,
With many ffaire ffowle · thouʒ they ffeynte were, 88
And heuy ffor the hurte · that the Hors hadde.

---

53. MS. abouʒte.   62. *Cf. what is þis to mene;* B. I. 11.
    78. *Cf.* And so I *babeled* on my bedes; B. 5. 8.

618 RICHARD THE REDELESS: PASSUS III.

Ʒit they fferkyd hem fforth · as ffaste as they myʒte,
To haue the Egles helpe · of harme that they hadde;
ffor he was heed of hem all · and hieste of kynde,   92
To kepe the croune · as cronecle tellith.
He blythid the Beere · and his bond braste,
And lete him go at large · to lepe where he wolde.
But tho all the berlingis · brast out at ones,   96
As ffayne as the ffoule · that ffleith on the skyes
That bosse was vnbounde · and brouʒte to his owene.
They gaderid hem to-gedir · on a grette route,
To helpe the heeris · that had many wrongis;   100
They gaglide fforth on the grene · ffor they greued were,
That her ffrendis were ffalle · thoru ffelouns castis.
They mornyd ffor the morthir · of manffull knyʒtis,
That many a styff storme · with-stode ffor the comunes; 104
They monside the marchall · ffor his myssedede,
That euell coude his craft · whan he clothed the Stede.
And euere as they ffolwide · this Faucoun aboute,
At iche mevinge ffotte · venyaunce they asked   108
On all that assentid · to that synfull dede.

  Arere now to Richard · and reste here awhile,
ffor a preuy poynt · that persith my wittis.
Of ffautis I ffynde · that ffrist dede engendre   112
Cursidnesse and combraunce · amonge the yonge lordis,
And the wikkid werchinge · that walmed in her daies,
And ʒit woll here-after · but wisdome it lette.
That were a lord of lond · that lawe hathe in honde, 116
That to lyghtliche leueth · or lewte apere,
The tale of a trifflour · in turmentours wede,
That neuere reed good rewle · ne resons bookis!
ffor ben they rayed arith · they recchith no fforther, 120
But studieth all in stroutynge · and stireth amys euere;
ffor all his witte in his wede · ys wrappid ffor sothe,
More than in mater to amende · the peple that ben mys-led.

---

94. MS. brond; Mr Wright *prints* broud, *but surely it is merely* bond, *misspelt* brond *owing to the influence of the following word* braste.
97. MS. was (*for* as). Þanne was I *also fayne* · as *foule* of faire morwe; B. 10. 153; C. 12. 103.
98. MS. brouute.   99. MS. rouʒte.
105. MS. þe (*for* þey).   107. MS. abouʒte.   112. MS. ffauutis.
121. MS. strouutynge, *here and in* l. 134; *but see* l. 189.

ffor I say ffor my-self · and schewe, as me thynchith, 124
That ho is riall of his ray · that light reede him ffolwith;
3it swiche ffresshe ffoodis · beth ffeet in-to chambris,
And ffor her dignesse endauntid · of dullisshe nollis,
And, if thou well waite · of no wight ellis: 128
  Qui mollibus vestiuntur in domibus regum sunt : in euangelio.
Than waite mo wayes · how the while turneth
With gyuleris, Ioyffull · ffor here gery Iaces,
And ffor her wedis so wyde · wise beth y-holde;
They casteth hem to creaunce · the courte ffor to plese, 132
And hopen to be hied · in hast, yif they my3the,
Thoru swiche stif stroutynge · that stroyeth the rewme;
But here wey is all wronge · ther wisdom is ynned,
For they lepith als lyghtly · at the longe goynge, 136
Out of the domes carte · as he that throff neuere.
ffor they kepeth no coyne · that cometh to here hondis,
But chaunchyth it ffor cheynes · that in Chepe hangith,
And settith all her siluer · in seintis and hornes, 140
And ffor-doth the coyne · and many other craftis,
And maketh the peple ffor pens-lac · in pointe ffor to wepe;
And 3it they beth ytake fforth · and her tale leued,
And ffor her newe nysete · nexte to the lordis. 144
Now, be the lawe of Lydfford · in londe [and] in water
Thilke lewde ladde · ou3te euyll to thryue,
That hongith on his hippis · more than he wynneth,
And douteth no dette · so dukis hem preise, 148
But beggith and borwith · of burgeis in tounes
ffurris of ffoyne · and other ffelle-ware,
And not the better of a bene · thou3 they boru euere.
And, but if the slevis · slide on the erthe, 152
Thei woll be wroth as the wynde · and warie hem that it made;
And [but] 3if it were elbowis · adoun to the helis,
Or passing the knee · it was not acounted.

---

124. Cf. *Ich seye it for my-selue ;* C. 5. 134.
126. *Cf.* and *brou3te* hir *in-to chaumbre ;* B. 3. 10.
136. MS. But (*for* For); *wrongly repeated.* MS. lyghly.
140. MS. seimtis (*uncertain*). 142. MS. pephe.
145. MS. ne ; *read* and. 148. MS. dou3teth. 150. MS. whare.
153. *Cf.* As *wroth as þe wynd ;* C. 4. 486.
154. *Supply* but; *as in* l. 152.

And if Pernell preisid · the plytis bihynde, 156
The costis were acouñtid · paye whan he myȝth.
The leesinge so likyde · ladies and other,
That they Ioied of the Iette · and gyside hem ther-vnder;
And if Felice ffonde ony ffaute · thenne of the makynge, 160
Yt was y-sent sone · to shape of the newe.
But now ther is a gyse · the queyntest of all,
A wondir coriouse crafte · y-come now of late,
That men clepith kerving · the clothe all to pecis, 164
That seuene goode sowers · sixe wekes after
Moun not sett the seemes · ne sewe hem aȝeyn.
But ther is a proffit in that pride · that I preise euere.
ffor thei ffor the pesinge paieth · pens ten duble 168
That the clothe costened · the craft is so dere.
Now if I sothe shall saie · and shonne side tales,
Ther is as moche good witte · in swyche gomes nollis,
As thou shuldist mete of a myst · ffro morwe tyll euen! 172
Ȝit blame I no burne · to be, as him ouȝte,
In comliche clothinge · as his statt axith;
But to ledyn her lust · all here lyff-daies
In quentise of clothinge · ffor to queme sir pride, 176
And euere-more stroutynge · and no store kepe,
And iche day a newe deuyse · it dullith my wittis
That ony lord of a lond · shulde leue swiche thingis,
Or clepe to his conceill · swiche manere cotis, 180
That loueth more her lustis · than the lore of oure lord.
And if a lord his leuere · lyste ffor to ȝeue,
Ther may no gome ffor goodnesse · gette ther-of but lite,
ffor curtesie, ffor comlynesse · ne ffor his kynde herte, 184
But rather ffor his rancour · and rennynge ouere peple,
ffor braggynge and ffor bostynge · and beringe vppon oilles,
ffor cursidnes of conscience · and comynge to the assises.
This makyth men mysdo · more than ouȝte ellis, 188
And to stroute and to stare · and stryue aȝeyn vertu.

---

156. *Cf.* He preide *purnele* · here porfil to leue; C. 6. 129.
167. MS. aprffith (*sic*), *with* a profett *written above it.*
172. *Cf.* þow myȝt bet *mete þe myst* ; C. 1. 163.
176. *Cf.* In cuntinaunce *of cloþinge* · *queinteliche* de-gyset; A. pr. 24.
188. *Cf.* And *makeþ men mys-do* · meny score tymes; C. 4. 159.

So [be] clergie, the cause · comsith in grette,
Of all manere mysscheff · that men here vsyn.
ffor wolde they blame the burnes · that brouȝte newe gysis, 192
And dryue out the dagges · and all the Duche cotis,
And sette hem a-side · and scorte of hem telle,
And lete hem pleye in the porche · and presse non ynnere,
Ne no proude peniles · with his peynte sleve; 196
And eke repreue robbers · and riffleris of peple,
fflatereris and ffals men · that no ffeith vseth,
And alle deabolik doeris · dispise hem ichone,
And coile out the knyȝtys · that knowe well hem-self, 200
That were sad of her sawis · and suffre well coude,
And had traueilid in her tyme · and temprid hem-self,
And cherliche cheriche hem · as cheff in the halle,
ffor to ordeyne officeris · and all other thyngis; 204
Men shulde wete in a while · that the world wolde amende,
So vertue wolde fflowe · whan vicis were ebbid.

But now to the mater · that I be-ffore meved,
Of the gomes so gay · that grace hadde affendid, 208
And how stille that steddeffaste stode · amonge this reccheles peple,
That had awilled his wyll · as wisdom him taughte:
ffor he drough him to an herne · at the halle ende,
Well homelich yhelid · in an holsume gyse, 212
Not ouerelonge, but ordeyned · in the olde schappe,
With grette browis y-bente · and a berde eke,
And y-wounde in his wedis · as the wedir axith;
He wondrid in his wittis · as he well myȝthe, 216
That the hie housinge · herborowe ne myghte
Halfdell the houshould · but hales hem helped;
But ffor crafte that he coude · caste thenne or be-thenke,
He myȝte not wonne in the wones · ffor witt that he vsid; 220
But, aroutyd ffor his ray · and rebuked ofte,
He had leue of the lord · and of ladies alle,
ffor his good gouernaunce · to go or he drank!

---

190. MS. *omits* be. 193. *Cf.* let *dagge* hus cloþes; C. 23. 143.
198. MS. fflateris. 201. MS. couude. *So also in* l. 219.
217. MS. houusinge.
220. *Cf.* Lorde, who shal *wonye in* þi *wones;* B. 3. 234.
221. MS. arouutyd.

Ther was non of the mene · that they ne merueilid moche, 224
How he cam to the courte · and was not y-knowe;
But als sone as they wiste · that Witt was his name,
And that the kyng knewe him not · ne non of his kny3tis,
He was halowid and y-huntid · and y-hote trusse, 228
And his dwellinge ydemed · a bowe-drawte ffrom hem,
And ich man y-charchid · to schoppe at his croune,
3if he nyhed hem ony nere · than they had him nempned.
The portir with his pikis · tho put him vttere, 232
And warned him the wickett · while the wacche durid:
"Lete sle him!" quod the sleues · that slode vppon the erthe,
And alle the berdles burnes · bayed on him euere,
And schorned him, ffor his slaueyn · was of the olde schappe.
Thus Malaperte was my3tffull · and maister of hous, 237
And euere wandrid Wisdom · without the 3atis.
"By him that wrou3te this world!" · quod Wisdom in wrath,
"But 3if 3e woll sumtyme · I walke in amonge 3ou, 240
I shall fforbede 3ou burnes · the best on this erthe,
That is, gouernance of gettinge · and grace that him ffollwith;
ffor these two trewly · twynned 3et neuere."
And so it ffell on hem, in ffeith · ffor ffautis that they vsid, 244
That her grace was a-goo · ffor grucchinge chere,
ffor the wronge that they wrou3te · to Wisdom affore.
    ffor tristith, als trewly · as tyllinge us helpeth,
That iche rewme vndir roff · of the reyne-bowe 248
Sholde stable and stonde · be these thre degres:
By gouernaunce of grete · and of good age;
By styffnesse and strengthe · of steeris well y-yokyd,
That beth my3thffull men · of the mydill age; 252
And be laboreris of lond · that lyfflode ne ffayle.
Thanne wolde [right dome] reule · if reson were amongis us,
That ich leode lokide · what longid to his age,
And neuere ffor to passe more · oo poynt fforther, 256
To vsurpe the service · that to sages bilongith,

---

228. MS. y-hotte. *Cf.* Ouer-al houted out · *and yhote trusse;* C. 3. 228.
241. MS. burnesse. 244. MS. ffau3tis.
248. *Cf.* þe richest *rewme* · þat *reyne* ouer houeth; B. 3. 207.
249. *Cf.* gan *stable and stynte;* B. 1. 120.
253. *Cf.* And lerne to *labore with londe* · *lest lyflode hym faile;* C. 9. 295.
254. MS. *omits* right dome.

To be-come conselleris · er they kunne rede,
In schenshepe of souereynes · and shame at the last.
ffor it ffallith as well to ffodis · of four and twenty ȝeris,   260
Or yonge men of yistirday · to ȝeue good redis,
As be-cometh a kow · to hoppe in a cage!
It is not vnknowen · to kunnynge leodis,
That rewlers of rewmes · around all the erthe   264
Were not yffoundid · at the ffrist tyme
To leue al at likynge · and lust of the world,
But to laboure on the lawe · as lewde men on plowes,
And to merke meyntenourz · with maces ichonne,   268
And to strie strouters · that sterede aȝeine rithis,
And alle the myssedoers · that they myȝte ffynde,
To put hem in preson · a peere thouȝ he were;
And [not] to rewle as reremys · and rest on the daies,   272
And spende of the spicerie · more than it nedid,
Bothe wexe and wyn · in wast all aboute,
With deyntes y-doublid · and daunsinge to pipis,
In myrthe with moppis · myrrours of synne.   276
Ȝit fforbede I no burne · to be blithe sum while;
But all thinge hath tyme · ffor to tempre glees:
ffor caste all the countis · that the kyng holdith,
And loke how these lordis · loggen hem-self,   280
And euere shall thou ffynde · as ffer as thou walkiste,
That wisdom and ouere-wacche · wonneth ffer asundre;
But whane the gouernaunce goth thus · with tho the hous gie shulde,
And letith lyghte of the lawe · and lesse of the peple,   284
And herkeneth all to honour · and to ese eke,
And that ich wyght with his witte · waite on him euere,
To do hem reuerence aright · thouȝ the rigge brest,
This warmnesse in welth · with wy vppon erthe   288
Myȝte not longe dure · as doctourz us tellith.
ffor ho so thus leued · his lyff to the ende,
Euere wrappid in welle · and with no wo mette,

---

260. MS. *xxiiij*; to be read *four and twenty*, not *twenty-four*. Cf. l. 79, above.
272. MS. *om.* not.   274. MS. abouȝte.
282. MS. What, *probably* by mistake.
284. *Cf.* And *let lyght of þe lawe · and lasse of þe* knyght; C. 9. 165.

My3te seie that he sawe · that seie was neuere, 292
That heuene were vnhonge · out of the hookis,
And were boun at his bidding · 3if it be my3te!
But clerkis knew I non 3ete · that so coude rede
In bokis y-bounde · thou3 3e brou3te alle 296
That ony wy welldith · wonnynge vppon erthe;
ffor in well and in woo · the werld euere turneth,
3it ther is kew-kaw · thou3 he come late,
A new thing that noyeth · nedy men and other, 300
Whanne realles remeveth · and ridith thoru tounes,
And carieth ouere contre · ther comunes dwelleth,
To preson the pillourz · that ouere the pore renneth;
For that were euene in her weye · if they well ride. 304
  But 3it ther is a ffoule ffaute · that I ffynde ofte;
They prien affter presentis · or pleyntis ben y-clepid,
And abateth all the billis · of tho that nou3th bringith;
And ho so grucche or grone · a3eins her grette willes, 308
Mey lese her lyff lyghtly · and no lesse weddis.
Thus is the lawe louyd · thoru my3hty lordis willys,
That meyneteyne myssdoers · more than other peple.
ffor mayntenaunce many day · well more is the reuthe! 312
Hath y-had mo men · at mete and at melis,
Than ony cristen kynge · that 3e knewe euere;
ffor, as reson and rith · rehersid to me ones,
Tho ben men of this molde · that most harme worchen. 316
ffor chyders of Chester · were chose many daies
To ben of conceill ffor causis · that in the court hangid,
And pledid pipoudris · alle manere pleyntis.
They cared ffor no coyffes · that men of court vsyn, 320
But meved many maters · that man neuer thou3te,
And ffeyned ffalshed · till they a ffyne had,
And knewe no manere cause · as comunes tolde.
Thei had non other signe · to schewe the lawe 324
But a preuy pallette · her pannes to kepe,
To hille here lewde heed · in stede of an houe.

---

295. MS. kne. MS. couude.   305. MS. ffau3te.
309. *Cf.* Ich dorst haue leid *my lyue* · *and no lasse wedde*; C. 4. 260.
311. *Cf.* To *meyntene mysdoers* · Mede þei take; B. 3. 246.
316. *Cf.* For þise aren *men on þis molde* · *þat moste harme worcheth*; B. 3. 80.
317. MS. where.

They constrewed quarellis · to quenche the peple,
And pletid with pollaxis · and poyntis of swerdis,   328
And at the dome-ȝeuynge · drowe out the bladis,
And lente men leuere · of her longe battis.
They lacked alle vertues · that a Iuge shulde haue;
ffor, er a tale were ytolde · they wolde trie the harmes,   332
Without ony answere · but ho his lyf hatid.
And ho so pleyned to the prince · that pees shulde kepe,
Of these mystirmen · medlers of wrongis,
He was lyghtliche y-lauȝte · and y-luggyd of many,   336
And y-mummyd on the mouthe · and manaced to the deth.
They leid on thi leigis, Richard · lasshis y-now,
And drede neuere a dele · the dome of the lawe.
Ther nas rial of the rewme · that hem durste rebuke,   340
Ne Iuge, ne Iustice · that Iewis durste hem deme
ffor oute that thei toke · or trespassid to the peple.
This was a wondir world · ho so well lokyd,
That gromes ouere-grewe · so many grette maistris;   344
ffor this was the rewle in this rewme · while they here regnyd.

   Thouȝ I satte seuenenyght · and slepte ffull selde,
[I miȝte not reche redili · to rekene the nombre]
Of many mo wrongis · than I write coude;   348
ffor selde were the sergiauntis · souȝte ffor to plete,
Or ony prentise of courte · preied of his wittis,
The while the Degonys domes · weren so endauntid.
Tille oure sire in his see · aboue the seuene sterris,   352
Sawe the many mysscheuys · that these men dede,
And no mendis ymade · but menteyned euere
Of him that was hiest · y-holde for to kepe
His liegis in lawe · and so her loue gette.   356
He sente ffor his seruantis · that sembled many
Of baronys and baccheleris · with many briȝth helmes,
With the comunes [of] the contres · they cam all at ones;
And as a duke douȝty · in dedis of armes,   360
In full reall aray · he rood vppon hem euere,

---

336. MS. lyghliche. *Cf.* Lorkynge þorw lones · *to-logged of menye;* C. 3. 226.
347. *A line lost; supplied by guess.*   348. MS. Couude.
349. MS. serigauntis.   351. MS. dogonys; *see* l. 362, *below.*
352. *Cf.* by *the seuen sterres;* C. 18. 98.
354. MS. menteyne it, *absurdly.*

Tyll Degon and Dobyn · that mennys doris brastyn,
And were y-dubbid of a duke · ffor her while domes,
Awakyd ffor wecchis · and wast that they vsid,   364
And ffor her breme blastis · buffettis henten.
Than gan it to calme · and clere all aboute,
That iche man my3te · ho so mynde hadde,
Se, be the sonne · that so bri3te schewed,   368
The mone at the mydday · meve, and the sterris,
ffolwinge ffelouns · ffor her ffalse dedis,
Devourours of vetaile · that ffou3ten er thei paide.

Passus Quartus.

FOR where was euere ony cristen kynge · that 3e euere knewe,
That helde swiche an household · be the half-delle
As Richard in this rewme · thoru myserule of other,
That alle his ffynys ffor ffautis · ne his ffee-ffermes,   4
Ne ffor-ffeyturis ffele · that ffelle in his daies,
Ne the nownagis · that newed him euere,
As Marche and Moubray · and many mo other,
Ne alle the issues of court · that to the kyng longid,   8
Ne sellynge, that sowkid · siluer rith ffaste,
Ne alle the prophete of the lond · that the prince owed,
Whane the countis were caste · with the custum of wullus,
My3te not areche · ne his rent nother,   12
To paie the pore peple · that his puruyours toke,
Withoute preiere at a parlement · a poundage biside,
And a fifteneth · and a dyme eke,
And with-all the custum of the clothe · that cometh to ffayres?
And 3et, ne had creaunce icome · at the last ende,   17
With the comunes curse · that cleued on hem euere,
They had be drawe to the deuyll · ffor dette that they owed.
And whanne the reot and the reeuell · the rent thus passid,   20
And no thing y-lafte · but the bare baggis,
Than ffelle it afforse · to ffille hem a3eyne,
And ffeyned sum ffolie · that ffailid hem neuer,

---

364. MS. *wrongly inserts* And *at the beginning of this line.*
366. MS. abou3te.
Passus iv. 4. MS. ffau3tis.

And cast it be colis · with her conceill at euene, 24
To haue preuy parlement · for profit of hem-self,
And lete write writtis · all in wex closid,
ffor peeris and prelatis · that thei apere shuld,
And sente side sondis · to schreuys aboute, 28
To chese swiche cheualleris · as the charge wold,
To schewe ffor the schire · in company with the grete.
And whanne it drowe to the day · of the dede-doynge,
That souereynes were semblid · and the schire-knyʒtis, 32
Than, as her fforme is, ffrist · they begynne to declare
The cause of her comynge · and than the kyngis will.
    Comliche a clerk than · comsid the wordis,
And pronouncid the poyntis · aparte to hem alle, 36
And meved ffor money · more than ffor out ellis,
In glosinge of grette · lest greyues arise.
And whanne the tale was tolde · anon to the ende,
A-morwe thei must, affore mete · mete to-gedir, 40
The knyʒtis of the comunete · and carpe of the maters,
With citiseyns of shiris · y-sent ffor the same,
To reherse the articlis · and graunte all her askynge.
But ʒit ffor the manere · to make. men blynde, 44
Somme argued aʒein rith · then a good while,
And said, "we beth seruantis · and sallere ffongen,
And y-sent ffro the shiris · to shewe what hem greueth,
And to parle ffor her prophete · and passe no ffertthere, 48
And to graunte of her gold · to the grett wattis
By no manere wronge way · but if werre were;
And if we ben ffalls · to tho us here ffyndeth,
Euyll be we worthy · to welden oure hire." 52
Than satte summe · as siphre doth in awgrym,
That noteth a place · and no-thing availith;
And some had ysoupid · with Symond ouere euen,
And schewed ffor the schire · and here schew lost; 56
And somme were tituleris · and to the kyng wente,
And fformed him of foos · that good ffrendis weren,
That bablid ffor the best · and no blame serued
Of kynge ne conceyll · ne of the comunes nother, 60

---

    25. MS. pproffitt (*sic*).   28. MS. abouʒte.
    35. Cf. *Corteysliche* þe knyʒt þen · *comsede þese wordes;* C. 9. 32.

Ho so toke good kepe · to the *culorum*.
And somme slombrid and slepte · and said but a lite;
And somme mafflid with the mouth · and nyst what they mente;
And somme had hire · and helde ther-with euere,   64
And wolde no fforther affoot · ffor ffer of her maistris;
And some were so soleyne · and sad of her wittis,
That er they come to the clos · acombrid they were,
That thei the conclucioun than · constrewe ne couthe,   68
No burne of the benche · of borowe nother ellis,
So blynde and so ballid · and bare was the reson.
  And somme were so ffers · at the ffrist come,
That they bente on a bonet · and bare a topte saile   72
Affor the wynde ffresshely · to make a good ffare.
Than lay the lordis a-lee · with laste and with charge,
And bare aboute the barge · and blamed the maister,
That knewe not the kynde cours · that to the crafte longid,   76
And warned him wisely · of the wedir-side.
Thanne the maste in the myddis · at the monthe ende,
Bowid ffor brestynge · and brouȝte hem to lond;
ffor ne had thei striked a strake · and sterid hem the better,   80
And abated a bonet · or the blast come,
They had be throwe ouere the borde · backewarde ichonne.
And some were acombrid · with the conceill be-ffore,
And wiste well y-now · how it sholde ende,   84
Or some of the semble · shulde repente.
Some helde with the mo · how it euere wente,
And somme dede rith so · and wolld go no fforther.
Some parled as perte · as prouyd well after,   88
And clappid more ffor the coyne · that the kyng oweth hem
Thanne ffor comfforte of the comyne · that her cost paied,
And were be-hote hansell · if they helpe wold,
To be seruyd sekirly · of the same siluere.   92
And some dradde dukis · and Do-well ffor-soke; . . . .

---

61. For *culorum*, see C. 4. 436.
65. *Cf.* That I ne myȝte *ferther a-foot;* B. 5. 6.
70. *Cf.* And brynge forth *ballede resones;* C. 12. 38.
75. MS. abouȝte.   89. MS. owen.
93. *The rest of the page* (in the MS.) *is blank.*

END OF VOLUME I.

OTHER TITLES IN THIS HARDBACK REPRINT PROGRAMME FROM SANDPIPER BOOKS LTD (LONDON) AND POWELLS BOOKS (CHICAGO)

ISBN 0-19-	Author	Title
8264011	ALEXANDER Paul J.	The Patriarch Nicephorus of Constantinople
8143567	ALFÖLDI A.	The Conversion of Constantine and Pagan Rome
9241775	ALLEN T.W	Homeri Ilias (3 volumes)
6286409	ANDERSON George K.	The Literature of the Anglo-Saxons
8219601	ARNOLD Benjamin	German Knighthood
8208618	ARNOLD T.W.	The Caliphate
8144059	BAILEY Cyril	Lucretius: De Rerum Natura (3 volumes)
814167X	BARRETT W.S.	Euripides: Hippolytos
8228813	BARTLETT & MacKAY	Medieval Frontier Societies
8219733	BARTLETT Robert	Trial by Fire and Water
8118856	BENTLEY G.E.	William Blake's Writings (2 volumes)
8111010	BETHURUM Dorothy	Homilies of Wulfstan
8142765	BOLLING G. M.	External Evidence for Interpolation in Homer
814332X	BOLTON J.D.P.	Aristeas of Proconnesus
9240132	BOYLAN Patrick	Thoth, the Hermes of Egypt
8114222	BROOKS Kenneth R.	Andreas and the Fates of the Apostles
8214715	BUCKLER Georgina	Anna Comnena
8203543	BULL Marcus	Knightly Piety & Lay Response to the First Crusade
8216785	BUTLER Alfred J.	Arab Conquest of Egypt
8148046	CAMERON Alan	Circus Factions
8148054	CAMERON Alan	Porphyrius the Charioteer
8148348	CAMPBELL J.B.	The Emperor and the Roman Army 31 AD to 235
826643X	CHADWICK Henry	Priscillian of Avila
826447X	CHADWICK Henry	Boethius
8222025	COLGRAVE B. & MYNORS R.A.B.	Bede's Ecclesiastical History of the English People
8131658	COOK J.M.	The Troad
8219393	COWDREY H.E.J.	The Age of Abbot Desiderius
8644043	CRUM W.E.	Coptic Dictionary
8148992	DAVIES M.	Sophocles: Trachiniae
814153X	DODDS E.R.	Plato: Gorgias
825301X	DOWNER L.	Leges Henrici Primi
814346X	DRONKE Peter	Medieval Latin and the Rise of European Love-Lyric
8142749	DUNBABIN T.J.	The Western Greeks
8154372	FAULKNER R.O.	The Ancient Egyptian Pyramid Texts
8221541	FLANAGAN Marie Therese	Irish Society, Anglo-Norman Settlers, Angevin Kingship
8143109	FRAENKEL Edward	Horace
8142781	FRASER P.M.	Ptolemaic Alexandria (3 volumes)
8201540	GOLDBERG P.J.P.	Women, Work and Life Cycle in a Medieval Economy
8140215	GOTTSCHALK H.B.	Heraclides of Pontus
8266162	HANSON R.P.C.	Saint Patrick
8581351	HARRIS C.R.S	The Heart and Vascular System in Ancient Greek Medicine
8224354	HARRISS G.L.	King, Parliament and Public Finance in Medieval England to 1369
8581114	HEATH Sir Thomas	Aristarchus of Samos
8140444	HOLLIS A.S.	Callimachus: Hecale
8212968	HOLLISTER C. Warren	Anglo-Saxon Military Institutions
9244944	HOPKIN-JAMES L.J.	The Celtic Gospels
8226470	HOULDING J.A.	Fit for Service
2115480	HENRY Blanche	British Botanical and Horticultural Literature before 1800
8219523	HOUSLEY Norman	The Italian Crusades
8223129	HURNARD Naomi	The King's Pardon for Homicide – before AD 1307
9241783	HURRY Jamieson B.	Imhotep
8140401	HUTCHINSON G.O.	Hellenistic Poetry
9240140	JOACHIM H.H.	Aristotle: On Coming-to-be and Passing-away
9240094	JONES A.H.M	Cities of the Eastern Roman Provinces
8142560	JONES A.H.M.	The Greek City
8218354	JONES Michael	Ducal Brittany 1364–1399
8271484	KNOX & PELCZYNSKI	Hegel's Political Writings
8212755	LAWRENCE C.H.	St Edmund of Abingdon
8225253	LE PATOUREL John	The Norman Empire
8212720	LENNARD Reginald	Rural England 1086–1135
8212321	LEVISON W.	England and the Continent in the 8th century
8148224	LIEBESCHUETZ J.H.W.G.	Continuity and Change in Roman Religion
8143486	LINDSAY W.M.	Early Latin Verse
8141378	LOBEL Edgar & PAGE Sir Denys	Poetarum Lesbiorum Fragmenta
9240159	LOEW E.A.	The Beneventan Script
8115881	LOOMIS Roger Sherman	Arthurian Literature in the Middle Ages
8241445	LUKASIEWICZ, Jan	Aristotle's Syllogistic
8152442	MAAS P. & TRYPANIS C.A .	Sancti Romani Melodi Cantica
8113692	MANDEVILLE Bernard	The Fable of the Bees (2 volumes)
8142684	MARSDEN E.W.	Greek and Roman Artillery—Historical
8142692	MARSDEN E.W.	Greek and Roman Artillery—Technical
8148178	MATTHEWS John	Western Aristocracies and Imperial Court AD 364–425

ID	Author	Title
9240205	MAVROGORDATO John	Digenes Akrites
8223447	McFARLANE K.B.	Lancastrian Kings and Lollard Knights
8226578	McFARLANE K.B.	The Nobility of Later Medieval England
814296X	MEIGGS Russell	The Athenian Empire
8148100	MEIGGS Russell	Roman Ostia
8148402	MEIGGS Russell	Trees and Timber in the Ancient Mediterranean World
8141718	MERKELBACH R. & WEST M.L.	Fragmenta Hesiodea
8143362	MILLAR F.G.B.	Cassius Dio
8142641	MILLER J. Innes	The Spice Trade of the Roman Empire
8147813	MOORHEAD John	Theoderic in Italy
8264259	MOORMAN John	A History of the Franciscan Order
8181469	MORISON Stanley	Politics and Script
9240582	MUSURILLO H.	Acts of the Pagan Martyrs & Christian Martyrs (2 volumes)
9240213	MYRES J.L.	Herodotus The Father of History
9241791	NEWMAN W.L.	The Politics of Aristotle (4 volumes)
8219512	OBOLENSKY Dimitri	Six Byzantine Portraits
8270259	O'DONNELL J.J.	Augustine: Confessions (3 volumes)
263268X	OSLER Sir William	Bibliotheca Osleriana
8116020	OWEN A.L.	The Famous Druids
8131445	PALMER, L.R.	The Interpretation of Mycenaean Greek Texts
8143427	PFEIFFER R.	History of Classical Scholarship (volume 1)
8143648	PFEIFFER Rudolf	History of Classical Scholarship 1300–1850
8111649	PHEIFER J.D.	Old English Glosses in the Epinal-Erfurt Glossary
8142277	PICKARD–CAMBRIDGE A.W.	Dithyramb Tragedy and Comedy
8269765	PLATER & WHITE	Grammar of the Vulgate
8213891	PLUMMER Charles	Lives of Irish Saints (2 volumes)
820695X	POWICKE Michael	Military Obligation in Medieval England
8269684	POWICKE Sir Maurice	Stephen Langton
821460X	POWICKE Sir Maurice	The Christian Life in the Middle Ages
8225369	PRAWER Joshua	Crusader Institutions
8225571	PRAWER Joshua	The History of The Jews in the Latin Kingdom of Jerusalem
8143249	RABY F.J.E.	A History of Christian Latin Poetry
8143257	RABY F.J.E.	A History of Secular Latin Poetry in the Middle Ages (2 volumes)
8214316	RASHDALL & POWICKE	The Universities of Europe in the Middle Ages (3 volumes)
8154488	REYMOND E.A.E & BARNS J.W.B.	Four Martyrdoms from the Pierpont Morgan Coptic Codices
8148380	RICKMAN Geoffrey	The Corn Supply of Ancient Rome
8141556	ROSS Sir David	Aristotle: De Anima
8141076	ROSS Sir David	Aristotle: Metaphysics (2 volumes)
8141084	ROSS Sir David	Aristotle: Parva Naturalia
8141092	ROSS Sir David	Aristotle: Physics
9244952	ROSS Sir David	Aristotle: Prior and Posterior Analytics
8142307	ROSTOVTZEFF M.	Social and Economic History of the Hellenistic World (3 volumes)
8142315	ROSTOVTZEFF M.	Social and Economic History of the Roman Empire (2 volumes)
8264178	RUNCIMAN Sir Steven	The Eastern Schism
814833X	SALMON J.B.	Wealthy Corinth
8171587	SALZMAN L.F.	Building in England Down to 1540
8218362	SAYERS Jane E.	Papal Judges Delegate in the Province of Canterbury 1198–1254
8221657	SCHEIN Sylvia	Fideles Crucis
8148135	SHERWIN WHITE A.N.	The Roman Citizenship
825153X	SHERWIN WHITE A.N.	Roman Society and Roman Law in the New Testament
9240167	SINGER Charles	Galen: On Anatomical Procedures
8113927	SISAM, Kenneth	Studies in the History of Old English Literature
8113668	SKEAT Walter	Langland: The Vision of William Concerning Piers the Plowman (2 volumes)
8642040	SOUTER Alexander	A Glossary of Later Latin to 600 AD
8270011	SOUTER Alexander	Earliest Latin Commentaries on the Epistles of St Paul
8222254	SOUTHERN R.W.	Eadmer: Life of St. Anselm
8251408	SQUIBB G.	The High Court of Chivalry
8212011	STEVENSON & WHITELOCK	Asser's Life of King Alfred
8212011	SWEET Henry	A Second Anglo-Saxon Reader—Archaic and Dialectical
8143443	SYME Sir Ronald	Ammianus and the Historia Augusta
8148259	SYME Sir Ronald	History in Ovid
8143273	SYME Sir Ronald	Tacitus (2 volumes)
8142714	THOMPSON E.A.	The Goths in Spain
8200951	THOMPSON Sally	Women Religious
8142625	TURNER E.G.	Greek Papyri: An Introduction
924023X	WALBANK F.W.	Historical Commentary on Polybius (3 volumes)
8201745	WALKER Simon	The Lancastrian Affinity 1361–1399
8161115	WELLESZ Egon	A History of Byzantine Music and Hymnography
8140185	WEST M.L.	Greek Metre
8141696	WEST M.L.	Hesiod: Theogony
8148542	WEST M.L.	The Orphic Poems
8140053	WEST M.L.	Hesiod: Works & Days
8152663	WEST M.L.	Iambi et Elegi Gracci
9240221	WHEELWRIGHT Philip	Heraclitus
822799X	WHITBY M. & M.	The History of Theophylact Simocatta
8206186	WILLIAMSON, E.W.	Letters of Osbert of Clare
8208103	WILSON F.P.	Plague in Shakespeare's London
8247672	WOODHOUSE C.M.	Gemistos Plethon
8114877	WOOLF Rosemary	The English Religious Lyric in the Middle Ages
8119224	WRIGHT Joseph	Grammar of the Gothic Language

PIERS THE PLOWMAN

AND

RICHARD THE REDELESS

WILLIAM LANGLAND

THE VISION OF WILLIAM

CONCERNING

PIERS THE PLOWMAN

IN THREE PARALLEL TEXTS

TOGETHER WITH

RICHARD THE REDELESS

BY WILLIAM LANGLAND

(ABOUT 1362—1399 A.D.)

EDITED FROM NUMEROUS MANUSCRIPTS

WITH PREFACE, NOTES, AND A GLOSSARY

BY THE

REV. WALTER W. SKEAT, Litt.D., Ll.D.

VOL. II.—INTRODUCTION, NOTES, AND GLOSSARY

OXFORD UNIVERSITY PRESS

OXFORD
UNIVERSITY PRESS

Great Clarendon Street, Oxford OX2 6DP

Oxford University Press is a department of the University of Oxford
It furthers the University's objective of excellence in research, scholarship,
and education by publishing worldwide in

Oxford New York

Athens Auckland Bangkok Bogotá Buenos Aires Cape Town
Chennai Dar es Salaam Delhi Florence Hong Kong Istanbul Karachi
Kolkata Kuala Lumpur Madrid Melbourne Mexico City Mumbai
Nairobi Paris São Paulo Singapore Taipei Tokyo Toronto Warsaw

and associated companies in Berlin Ibadan

Oxford is a registered trade mark of Oxford University Press
in the UK and in certain other countries

Published in the United States
by Oxford University Press Inc., New York

© Oxford University Press 1886

The moral rights of the author have been asserted
Database right Oxford University Press (maker)

Special edition for Sandpiper Books Ltd., 2001

All rights reserved. No part of this publication may be reproduced,
stored in a retrieval system, or transmitted, in any form or by any means,
without the prior permission in writing of Oxford University Press,
or as expressly permitted by law, or under terms agreed with the appropriate
reprographics rights organization. Enquiries concerning reproduction
outside the scope of the above should be sent to the Rights Department,
Oxford University Press, at the address above

You must not circulate this book in any other binding or cover
and you must impose this same condition on any acquirer

British Library Cataloguing in Publication Data
Data available

Library of Congress Cataloging in Publication Data
Data available

ISBN 0–19 811366–8 (Vol. 2)

1 3 5 7 9 10 8 6 4 2

Printed in Great Britain
on acid-free paper by
Biddles Ltd.,
Guildford & King's Lynn

NOTE TO THIRD IMPRESSION.

THE edition of *Piers the Plowman* that Skeat completed nearly seventy years ago resulted in more attention being given to the poem than it had received for fully three hundred years. Since his edition was published manuscripts unknown to him have come to light, controversy over the authorship of the poem has flared up, and there has been much debate about its plan and intention. Skeat himself came to feel that his choice of the Vernon MS. as the basis for the 'A' text could be improved upon, and that there was no reason for supposing that the Laud MS. of the 'B' text was, as he once thought possible, the poet's autograph. Yet his work remains indispensable to serious students, whether their interests be literary or textual, historical or philological. Some of his interpretations might be re-phrased, but comparatively few have been questioned. His reproduction of MS. readings is almost always accurate; his decision to print the Laud MS. is approved by modern scholars; his conjectures as to dates of composition have given starting-points to recent investigators; and the challenge to his view that the three recensions were substantially the work of one man has been, in the opinion of most scholars, effectively answered. With the discovery in 1928 of another MS. of the fragment that Skeat called *Richard the Redeless* it has become difficult to accept his view that it was written by Langland; but the modern editors agree that 'there is undoubtedly a close connexion between the two poems'.[1]

The present reprint reproduces *verbatim* the edition of 1886; but a select bibliography, indicating the more important findings since his day, and the trend of recent discussion, has been added.

J. A. W. BENNETT.

[1] *See* Mum and the Sothsegger, edited from the manuscripts Camb. Univ. Ll. iv. 14 and Brit. Mus. Add. 41666 by Mabel Day and Robert Steele, 1936 (E.E.T.S. o.s. 199). The title is a variant of one in use in the sixteenth century.

CONTENTS OF VOLUME II.

INTRODUCTION: PAGE

§ 1. The three forms of the Poem vii
§ 2. Description of the A-text viii
§ 3. Date of the A-text (1362) ix
§ 4. Description of the B-text x
§ 5. Date of the B-text (1377) xi
§ 6. Description of the C-text (date about 1393) . . . xiv
§ 7. Additional passages in the C-text xv
§ 8. The form of the Poem xxi
§ 9. The meaning of 'Piers the Plowman' xxiv
§ 10. The Author's name xxvii
§ 11. The Author's life xxxii
§ 12. Criticisms on the Poem: by Isaac D'Israeli; Dr. Whitaker;
   Thomas Wright; the Hon. G. P. Marsh; Dean Milman . xxxviii
§ 13. Further observations liii
§ 14. Dialect of the Poem lvii
§ 15. Metre of the Poem lviii
§ 16. Manuscripts of the Poem lxi
§ 17. Classification and description of the MSS. . . . lxv
§ 18. Description of the printed editions lxxii
§ 19. Preface to 'Richard the Redeless' (1399) . . . lxxxii
§ 20. Argument to 'Piers the Plowman' (C-text) . . . lxxxvi
§ 21. Argument to 'Richard the Redeless' xci

BIBLIOGRAPHICAL NOTE xcv
NOTES TO PIERS THE PLOWMAN 1
NOTES TO RICHARD THE REDELESS 287
GLOSSARIAL INDEX 305
INDEX TO PROPER NAMES AND SUBJECTS 474

INTRODUCTION.

§ 1. THE THREE FORMS OF THE POEM.

IN 1866, now twenty years ago, I printed a short tract (no. 17 of the Original Series of the Early English Text Society) entitled 'Parallel Extracts from 29 MSS. of Piers Plowman, with comments, and a proposal for the Society's Three-text edition of the poem[1].' I believe I was the first to shew clearly, in this tract, that the number of distinct versions of the poem is really *three*, and not *two* only, as stated by Mr. T. Wright and others[2]. This truth had been suspected long ago by Mr. Price, who (in a note inserted in Warton's History of English Poetry, ed. 1840, ii. 63) expressly says—'from this manuscript [MS. Harl. 6041] it is evident that another and third version was once in circulation; and, if the first draught of the poem be still in existence, it is here perhaps that we may look for it. For in this, the narrative is considerably shortened; many passages of a decidedly episodic cast—such as the tale of the cat and the ratons, and the character of Wrath—are wholly omitted; others, which in the later versions are given with considerable detail of circumstance, are here but slightly sketched; and though evidently the text-book of Dr. Whitaker's and Crowley's versions, it may be said to agree with neither, but to alternate between the ancient and modern printed copies[3].' However, Mr. Wright took no notice of this remark, and even Dr. Morris, who in 1867 actually printed a considerable portion of the earliest version [A-text] for the first time[4], made no remark as to the peculiar contents of the MS. which he happened to follow. Hence my first care was to point out that there are really three distinct texts; and in order to save trouble in reference, I called the earliest of these the A-text, the second the B-text, and the latest the C-text; or otherwise, the "Vernon" text,

[1] This tract was reprinted, in an improved form, in 1886.
[2] Pref. to Wright's edition, 1856, p. xxxiii; pref. to Whitaker's edition, 1813, pp. xix, xxxi.
[3] By the 'ancient' copy is meant Crowley's, and by the 'modern,' Whitaker's edition.
[4] Specimens of Early English, Oxford, 1867; pp. 249-290.

the "Crowley" text, and the "Whitaker" text respectively. I shewed how to distinguish MSS. of one text from those of the others, and printed the same passage from twenty-nine different MSS., in the hope of obtaining further information. Since then, fresh MSS. have been found from time to time, and we now know of forty-five copies[1], mostly of the fourteenth and fifteenth centuries. A list of these is given further on.

§ 2. Description of the A-text.

The Vernon MS. (V.) is taken as the basis of the text, as far as l. 180 of Passus xi., where it unfortunately comes to an end, owing to a leaf having been cut out of the MS. The text of the rest of Passus xi., viz. ll. 181–303, is supplied from the Trinity MS. R. 3. 14 (T.). Pass. xii. (pp. 326–330) is supplied from MS. Rawlinson, Poet. 137, which is the only MS. containing the whole of this Passus. I give the various readings from the MS. in University College, Oxford (U.), which contains only the first 19 lines, and from the Ingilby MS. (Ing.), which contains lines 1–88, and actually supplies 5 new lines, viz. lines 65, 74–76, and 78. All three copies are inaccurate and unsatisfactory.

In editing the A-text, as printed from the Vernon MS. (throughout the Prologue, and Pass. i. 1 to xi. 180), the Trinity MS. (Pass. xi. 181–303), and the Rawlinson MS. (Pass. xii.), I have mended the text in a few places by help of the various readings obtained from a collation of other MSS.; see p. 1. Notice of all such alterations is given in the footnotes at the bottom of the page. Thus, in A. prol. 14 (p. 3) the word *triȝely* is from MS. T.; MS. V. has *wonderliche*, against the alliteration. The line A. prol. 34 (p. 5) is supplied from MS. T., being omitted in MS. V. altogether. All such alterations are fully described, and can be readily understood.

As the chief object of the present Parallel Edition of the three texts is to exhibit the corresponding passages of each at a glance, the A-text is, for convenience, printed on the upper half of every page, whilst the B-text occupies the lower part of the page on the left hand, and the C-text the lower part of the page on the right. Some-

---

[1] Even now, it would not surprise me if more copies should be found, though I hardly know where to look for them. There was once a *forty-sixth* copy, printed by Crowley in 1550, but now lost. Indeed, Crowley mentions a *forty-seventh*, marked with the date 1509. See p. lxxiii, note 3.

times, as at pp. 10, 11, the parallel passage is lacking in the A-text, in which case the words '*Not in A-text*' are printed in place of it. Moreover, as the A-text is much shorter than either of the others, it disappears after p. 331. The 12th Passus of the A-text is unique, and occupies pages 326-329 to the exclusion of the other texts, with six concluding lines on pp. 330, 331.

It is impossible to enumerate here the numberless variations between the three texts; though several of these are noticed further on. It may suffice to say here that the A-text, as being the earliest draught, is usually much briefer than the others, which were expanded from it. Yet there are passages where it is absolutely *fuller* than the others, especially in the course of A. Pass. x. Thus, at pp. 274, 275, where the B-text has 15 lines, and the C-text but 10, the corresponding passage in the A-text contains as many as 42 lines; of which at least lines 119-121 are prettily expressed, and might very well have been retained. The line A. x. 101 is another fine line that could ill be spared, though it was omitted by the author in revision. It is difficult to tell whether lines 99-105, at the end of A. Pass. xii., are genuine or not. If they are, then it is clear that the author merely wrote them by way of a temporary finish, and speaks of his death by anticipation; this is not unlikely. Otherwise, it is probable that he left this Passus incomplete, stopping at line 98, and that these lines were added by another hand, viz. by that of a certain John But, who in any case added twelve more worthless lines after line 105; see footnote to p. 330. Whichever of these suppositions be the true one, the author ultimately rejected the whole of A. Pass. xii., and began to rewrite the poem afresh, suppressing some of his old work, but adding much more that was new. See further below, in the account of the B-text.

§ 3. Date of the A-text (1362-3).

As to the date of the A-text, we are indebted to Tyrwhitt for having pointed out that the 'Southwestern wind on a Saturday at even,' mentioned near the beginning of Passus v., refers to the storm of wind which occurred on Jan. 15, 1362, which day was a Saturday[1]. There may have been more than one Saturday marked

---

[1] 'A. D. M.CCC.LXII.—XV die Januarii, *cira horam vesperarum*, ventus vehemens *notus Australis Africus* tantâ rabie erupt,' &c.; quoted by Tyrwhitt (in a note to the Advertisement of his Glossary to Chaucer), from the Continuator of Adam Murimuth, p. 115; cf. P. Pl., A. v. 14.

by a furious tempest, but the remark is rendered almost certainly true by observing that other indications in the poem point nearly to the same date, especially the allusion to the treaty of Bretigny in 1360, and to Edward's wars in Normandy[1]; as also the mention of the 'pestilence,' no doubt that of 1361[2]. These things put together leave no doubt that Tyrwhitt is right, and as the 'wind' is spoken of as being something very recent, the true date of the poem is doubtless 1362. But *how much* was then written? Not all certainly, possibly only the Vision of Piers Plowman, i.e. only the first eight Passus. The first few lines of the Vita de Dowel seem to imply that there was a *short* interval between the two poems, i.e. if we take them literally, and I can see no reason why we should not. This would assign the early part of 1362 as the date of the A-text of the Vision only, and the end of the same year or the beginning of 1363 as the date of Dowel. In all probability, the expansion of the poem into the form it assumes in Text B was not begun immediately, for it would obviously take some time and deliberation to render it nearly three times as long as at first, and to multiply the number of Latin quotations by *seven*. The latter fact, in particular, implies some considerable time spent in study.

§ 4. Description of the B-text.

The B-text is printed from MS. Laud Misc. 581 (L).; with improvements suggested by other MSS.; see p. 1. This version of the poem agrees very closely with that printed by Robert Crowley in 1550, and reprinted by Owen Rogers in 1561, from a very fair MS. which is no longer forthcoming. The text printed by Mr. Wright in 1842, and reprinted in 1856, is also of the B-type, but agrees somewhat more closely with Crowley's text than with the text as here printed. The MS. printed by Mr. Wright is denoted by the letter W. I may here remark that the MSS. of the B-text agree, in general, very closely, and that the number of various readings is small. Additional light upon this version of the poem can only be had from such MSS. as have not been fully collated. Of these, the most important are Y (Mr. Yates Thompson's MS.), already partially collated; and particularly MS.

---

[1] A. iii. 182; see Fabyan's Chronicles, p. 470.
[2] A. v. 13. There were *three* great pestilences, in 1349, 1361-2, and 1369; clearly, the *second* one is meant.

no. 129 formerly in the possession of Lord Ashburnham, but now in the British Museum and much more accessible. But I believe it will be found that this MS. agrees with the printed text so closely as to tell us very little beyond what we already know.

As to the general contents of the B-text, it is impossible to discuss at length all the alterations made in the preceding version (A-text). It must suffice to say that the suppressed passages were far exceeded in quantity by the numerous and long additions. Amongst *some* of the more remarkable of these are the following:

The introduction of a notice of the cardinal virtues, of a king to whom an angel gave words of advice in Latin, and of the fable of the rats who agreed to attempt to bell the cat, but were dissuaded from their purpose by a wise mouse (B. prol. 97–209); the assertion that Love is the treacle (or chief remedy) of heaven (B. i. 146–158); the father of Holychurch (B. ii. 29–38); the prophecy of a future reign of Peace, &c. (B. iii. 299–349); the introduction of the character of Wrath among the seven Deadly Sins (B. v. 134–187); the additional traits of the character of Avarice (B. v. 232–303); additional traits of the character of Gluttony (B. v. 371–385); and of Sloth (B. v. 392–448); the intercession of Repentance for the penitents (B. v. 485–516); a mysterious prophecy (B. vi. 328–332); advice of Cato and Gregory (B. vii. 71–88); the lord that lacked parchment (B. ix. 38–42); how idiots and others should be protected, &c. (B. ix. 59–92, 96–106, 113–117, 142–150, 177–185); of lying jesters, who know no music (B. x. 38–44); of the increase of pride and wealth (B. x. 73–100); of belief in the Trinity (B. x. 230–248); of Do-bet, Do-best, blind buzzards, and dumb dogs (B. x. 249–291); the prophecy of the king who shall reform religion, &c. (B. x. 309–331, 337–344, 357–363, 390–413, 428–441, 464–474). Here follows A. Pass. xii., which the B-text omits, but afterwards supplies a very long addition to the poem, viz. B. Pass. xi.–xx.

§ 5. DATE OF THE B-TEXT (1377).

We find, in B. xiii. 269–271, an allusion to 'a dry April' in the year 'a thousand and three hundred twice thirty and ten . . . when Chichester was mayor.' Some MSS., including that printed by Mr. Wright, read *twenty* for *thirty*, against the alliteration. But it is easily ascertained that John Chichester was elected mayor of London in October, 1369, and was still mayor in April, 1370. For example, in Riley's Memorials of London, p. 344, we find that 'on the 25th day of *April* in the year above-mentioned [1370] it was agreed by John de Chichestre, Mayor,' &c. It is singular that Fabyan gives most of the regnal years of Edward III. wrongly, because he accidentally omits the sixth year of Edward's reign altogether; and, being always afterwards a year wrong, seems to make Chichester mayor in 1368–9. This error is easily corrected, when once observed; and it is worth noticing that Fabyan says that (in the year which was *really* 1369) there was a third pestilence, and *excessive rain*, the result being a dearth in the year 1370, when wheat was sold at the excessive rate of 40*d.* the bushel. As our author is thus clearly right about the year of Chichester's mayoralty and the dearth, Fabyan's mention of the *previous* excessive rains render it probable that he is right also as to the drought in April. This being so, we see at once that the allusion in B. xiii. 269–271 indicates a date a few years later than 1370.

Again, Tyrwhitt[1] has shewn that the 'fable of the cat and the rattons' in the prologue can only refer to a period when the Black Prince was dead, and Richard had become the heir-apparent; for the fear was that the old king would be soon replaced by a child. The Black Prince died June 8, 1376, and the old king on June 21, 1377; so that the date of composition of the prologue to the B-text lies between these limits. Further, I think we must see that the curious passage about the coming of a time of universal jubilee (B. iii. 299–349) may well have been suggested by the very rare occurrence of the jubilee proclaimed in February, 1377, to celebrate the completion of Edward's fiftieth regnal year. All the conditions are satisfied if we date the beginning of the B-text in the earlier part of 1377; and, though it may not have been finished all at once, we may take the year 1377 as the best approximate date for the B-text generally.

There are two other allusions that require a short notice. There are several references to pestilences, and we know that the allusion to 'þise pestilences' in Pass. v. 13 (both in A-text and B-text) is to the pestilences of 1349 and 1362; but when 'the pestilence' is mentioned in B. xiii. 248 in close connection with a reference to the mayoralty of Chichester a few years previously, we may fairly conclude that the pestilence meant is that of 1376. Sometimes only three great pestilences are reckoned, viz. those of 1349, 1362, and 1369;

---

[1] Essay on Chaucer; note 57.

DATE OF THE B-TEXT (1377).

but some writers reckon a fourth, in 1376, and it seems to have been a severe one. Thus Fabyan says of it—'In this .1. yere [*read* xlix yere], fyl many wonderfull sykenesses amonge the people, whereof ye people dyed wonderly faste as well in Italye as in Englande; amonge the whiche dyed sir Edwarde called the lorde Spencer, a man of great fame, whose body was enteryd at Teukesbury. And for this mortalytie was so sharpe and sodayne, pope Gregory beforenamed graunted of his goodnesse to suche as were contrite and confessyd, clene remyssion of theyr synnes; the whiche indulgence contynued in Englande by the terme of .vi. monethes.'—Fabyan, ed. Ellis, p. 485. This grant of the pope's seems to be the very thing alluded to in the line discussed, and in l. 246 just above it, where Haukyn says that all that the pope sent him was 'a pardoun with a peys of led.'

The other allusion is in Pass. xv. 80, 81:

'Go to þe glose of þe verse · ʒe grete clerkes;
If I lye on ʒow to my lewed witte · ledeth me to brennynge!'

On this Dr. Whitaker remarks, at p. xxxii of his preface to the poem, that this is 'an allusion to the statute empowering the diocesan alone to commit heretics to the flames, which was enacted in the second of Henry Fourth.' I cannot admit this for a moment; it is contrary to all the other evidence, and it is almost certain that at least *some* of the MSS. which contain the passage are absolutely older than 1400. The fact is, that the famous statute of Henry IV. seems to be generally misunderstood. It did not in any way provide for the burning of heretics as a *new* remedy for heresy; it merely provided, as Mr. Arnold well points out[1], for the application of the remedy 'uberius et celerius.' It is easy, moreover, to shew how this was effected, viz. by empowering the *diocesan*, as Dr. Whitaker says, to act on his own responsibility. Before the passing of the statute, the punishment could be inflicted (and was inflicted) only by means, as it seemed to some, of an unnecessarily round-about procedure. If a bishop, as for instance the Bishop of Norwich in 1389, wished to burn a heretic, he had to go through the process of formally handing over the said heretic to the secular arm; and the secular arm could dispose of the criminal in any way that was deemed advisable. The statute did away with this troublesome necessity, and was passed, to use the very words of it, because the bishops 'per suam

---

[1] Introduction to Wyclif's Works, where this very question is discussed.

iurisdictionem spiritualem dictos perfidos et peruersos absque auxilio dictae maiestatis regiae sufficienter corrigere nequeunt.' The whole matter has been made clear to me by the kind help of C. H. Pearson, Esq., author of the Early and Middle Ages of England, who pointed out to me a decisive case in point, viz. the account given by Bracton of a man who, for the crime of wishing to marry a Jewess, was handed over to the secular arm and *burnt*, as early as in the reign of Henry III.[1] So that, as a net result, we find that the somewhat vague allusion to *burning* in the B-text, upon which Dr. Whitaker so confidently relied as proving that version of the poem to be later than 1401, proves no more than that it was later than the time of Henry III.; and, as to deciding between the claims of the B- and C-texts to priority, it proves just nothing at all; but rather did, in effect, induce Dr. Whitaker to decide wrongly.

§ 6. Description of the C-text.

The C-text, or latest version of the poem, is printed from the same MS. (Phillipps 8231) as that from which Dr. Whitaker's text was printed in 1813. Corrections are given from other MSS. of the same type; see vol. i. p. 1. The most valuable of the MSS. which I have *not* collated are MS. Dublin D. 4. 1, and the latter part of MS. Z. (Bodley 851). The C-text is a *second* revision of the poem, made by the author himself. On the whole, it is inferior to the B-text in general vigour and compactness. On the other hand, it is the fullest of the three texts, and the most carefully finished. It contains the author's last corrections after an attentive revision, and is evidently intended as a final form, requiring no further touches. This is best seen in the last two Passus. *At first sight*, they stand almost alike in the two latest texts; but closer inspection shews that the author has gone over them word by word, making a few slight but clear corrections here and there, down to the very end. Only the eighth line from the end (B. xx. 377, C. xxiii. 379) has been almost entirely recast, in

[1] Bracton's language is very explicit, and his authority is decisive. 'Cum autem clericus sic de crimine conuictus degradetur, non sequitur alia poena pro vno delicto, vel pluribus ante degradationem perpetratis. Satis enim sufficit ei pro poena degradatio, quae est magna capitis diminutio, nisi forte conuictus fuerit de apostasia, quia tunc primo degradetur, et postea *per manum laicalem comburatur*, secundum quod accidit in concilio Oxon., celebrato a bonae memoriae S. Cantuarien. Archiepiscopo, de quodam diacono qui se apostatauit pro quadam Iudea, qui cum esset per Episcopum degradatus, statim fuit igni traditus per manum laycalem.' Bracton, de Legibus Angliae, lib. iii. tract. ii. c. 9, ed. 1569, fol. 124.

ADDITIONS IN THE C-TEXT.

order to improve the alliteration. It is most satisfactory to perceive that the poet completed his revision with a high degree of care and attention, that he survived the work, and that in all probability he was satisfied with it, as there is no trace whatever of any later revision. If we prefer the B-text as a whole, we must never forget that the C-text is the best possible commentary upon it, and is often, indeed, much more, as it contains some additional passages which it would be a pity to have lost.

The date of the C-text is about 1393; see p. xxxiv.

§ 7. ADDITIONAL PASSAGES IN THE C-TEXT.

Most of the passages which are peculiar to the C-text will be found in the Notes to Mr. Wright's edition of Piers the Plowman; but as they are there printed in small type, it may be doubted whether they have received anything like the attention which they deserve. Moreover, they read much better in their right place, with their own proper context. These additional passages may sometimes be found by observing that the B-text on the opposite page often fails, thus presenting a blank space. To enumerate them all would be a long task, as the insertions are, occasionally, but one or two lines long; I here call attention to some of the more remarkable ones only.

Pass. i. 95–124. The author introduces Conscience as accusing the priests of idolatry or image-worship and of proclaiming false miracles; they are warned to take example from the evil fate of Hophni and Phineas.

Pass. ii. 108–125. Some curious observations on the fall of Lucifer, with speculations as to why he made his seat in the north (Isaiah xiv. 14).

Pass. iii. 28, 29. 'A briar cannot bear berries as a vine'; &c.

120–128. This passage is a good deal altered.

129–136. A curious allusion to the martyrdom of St. Lawrence, who is here said to have claimed heaven as his due, on account of his sufferings. See p. 36 in the Notes.

181–189. Civil and Simony are to ride on the backs of rectors, and notaries on the backs of parsons that permute often, &c.

243–248. A passage directed against appeals to the pope.

Pass. iv. 86–114. 'Regraters' or retail-dealers are pitiless, and expect full payment for short measure; they provoke God to send fevers and fire. Often fires happen in a town through the carelessness of brewers, or from a neglected candle. Surely mayors ought to enquire carefully into the characters of those whom they make free of a city.

140–145. Meed is threatened with imprisonment in Corfe Castle.

203–213. An important passage, addressed to Richard II., which helps us to fix the date of the C-text; see p. xxxiv.

236–258. Another important passage, on the duty of a king towards his people.

292–415. A passage of that subtle and simile-seeking character which was no doubt once highly esteemed, but to us seems tedious and puerile. The author undertakes to establish parallels between the two kinds of Meed and the two kinds of grammatical relation. In tone and style it is much like another tedious passage in which the mystery of the Trinity is exemplified by reference to a man's hand or to a blazing torch, which first appears in the B-text (xvii. 135–249). Any one who carefully compares these passages (i.e. if he thinks it worth his while) may easily see that the writer of one of them would be just the man to write the other. In other words, we cannot well put aside this passage as not genuine, because the author has already previously committed himself by penning a passage equally dull.

Pass. v. 50–55. Contains an allusion to St. Giles's down, Winchester, where a great fair used to be held.

187–196. An attack upon certain modes of injustice, and an allusion to the king's attempt to borrow money of the Lombards; cited and discussed in sect. 11 below; see p. xxxiv.

Pass. vi. 1–108. An autobiographical passage of great interest.

187–197. There was perfect unity in heaven till Lucifer rebelled; so also men who dislike unity cause trouble to a realm. The pope is entreated to have pity upon holy church.

Pass. vii. 14–29, 33–40. An amplification of the description of Pride.

65–68. An alteration in the description of Envy.

106–118, 143–150. An amplification of the description of Wrath. Note the allusion to *pews*, perhaps the earliest one in English literature.

176, 177; 190–195. An amplification of the description of Lechery.

258, 259; 291–293; 309–315; 331–333. On the sin of Avarice.

Pass. viii. 145–149. An addition to the prayer of Repentance.

ADDITIONS IN THE C-TEXT. xvii

257–260. God will 'charge Charity to make a church in thy heart, wherein to harbour truth'; &c.

292–306. Sinners begin with one accord to make excuse; one says, 'I have bought a farm'; another, 'I have bought five yoke of oxen;' a third, 'I have married a wife.'

Pass. ix. 136–138. 'Your prayers might help, if ye were perfect; but God wills that no deceit should be found in folk that go a-begging.'

198–202. Various kinds of agricultural work :—

> 'In daubing and in delving · in dung-afield-bearing,
> In threshing, in thatching · in thwiting[1] of pins,' &c.

279–290. The parable of Dives and Lazarus, and its moral.

350–352. The 'mysterious prophecy' here takes a new shape, as was remarked more than three hundred years ago by Crowley.

Pass. x. 71–280. Nearly all new, and very curious. The subjects are: the poor of London, poor lunatics, sham beggars and true ones, false hermits and true ones, 'lollers' and 'lolling' friars, and unfaithful pastors.

Pass. xi. 39, 40. When the righteous man sins, he falls only as a man who falls *within* a boat.

51–55. Free-will and Free-wit enable a man to row himself out of sin.

94–98. Bishops should take courage and dare to proceed against wealthy lords.

158–169; 175–181; 187–201. Sin hides God from man, whence arises despair. Wicked men believe more in wealth than in God. The folly of Lot, Noah, and Herod 'the daft,' who

> 'Gave his daughter for a dancing · in a dish the head
> Of the Blessed Baptist · before all his guests.'

We should love our enemies, and remember that the highest aim of man is to help in bringing about the Unity of Mankind, when all lands shall love each other, and believe in one law. Especially should this be the aim of bishops; &c.

208–210; 214–219. Illegitimate children. How Cain was conceived in sin.

239–244. A point of Westminster law.

> 'For though the father be a franklin · and for a felon be hanged,
> The heritage that the heir should have · is at the king's will;' &c.

[1] Whittling; i.e. pointing wooden pegs with a knife.

xviii ADDITIONS IN THE C-TEXT.

259–269. A rich man will not marry a pretty girl, if she be poor; but any squire or knight will marry the lowliest born, or the ugliest hag ever seen, if known to be rich or well-rented; and then wish, on the morrow,

'That his wife were wax · or a wattle-ful of nobles[1].'

309, 310. Two lines in William's best manner, such as should be engraved on the hearts of all true men :—

'For the more a man may do · *if only* he do it,
The more is he worth and worthy · of wise and good [men] praised.'

Ah! that admonitory clause—'by so þat he do hit!'

Pass. xii. 21–25. On successful cheats.

61, 62. 'For God is deaf now-a-days · and deigneth not to hear us,
And good men, for our guilts · he grindeth all to death.'

76–80. None now follow Tobit's counsel (Tobit iv. 9).

142–148; 161, 162. Various alterations are made here.

200–203; 224–227; 233, 234. Recklessness is introduced instead of the 'Loyalty' of the B-text; which involves several changes in the language.

Pass. xiii. 17, 18. William here reveals the plea which the friars put forward for not complying with the conditions of their letters of fraternity. They used to ask for an additional sum in order to enable them to *make restitution* for the evil winnings of their clients.

154–247. Nearly all new. William sings the praises of poverty, and likens all men to seeds sown in the ground. Those seeds are most worthy which can best stand the severest weather; so is it also with God's saints. Fruits that contain sweet juice will not keep long; so is it with those who are rich in this world only. Foulest weeds grow on the fattest lands; so likewise vices spring up out of riches. Wealth often excites the cupidity of robbers, who murder their victims; and so both murderers and murdered come to perdition.

Pass. xiv. 1–100. But Poverty may walk in peace, and fear no thieves. Abraham and Job were rich men, whom God tried and found patient. Yet Wealth is not evil in itself, though surely Poverty commonly reaches heaven the sooner. If a merchant and

[1] If his wife were turned to *wax*, she would be useful for making wax-candles for offering at the altar. A 'wateful' of nobles means a basketful of the coins so named.

a messenger go the same way, the former must needs be detained longest by his business at every resting-place. And whilst they are on the journey, the messenger may take a short cut across a wheatfield, as he is privileged to do; but if the merchant attempt to do the same, the hayward catches him and takes a pledge from him. If both go to the fair together, the merchant goes the slower, having more to carry; and goes with the heavier heart, having more to lose. Yet the merchant may reach his home safely at last. So likewise may rich and poor both reach heaven.

188–192. Men are more immoderate in their desires than any other animals.

Pass. xv. 3–27. Altered and abridged from the B-text.

30–32. A curious admission of the author's belief in astrology.

37–42; 72–74; 215, 216. Altered from the B-text.

Pass. xvi. 78, 79.

> 'It is loath to me, though I Latin know · to blame any sect,
> For all we are brethren · though we be diversely clothed.'

138; 149–152. In the B-text, a speech which is put into the mouth of Patience is now put into the mouth of Piers the Plowman, who is described as suddenly vanishing immediately after he has uttered it. The object is clearly to draw more attention to the opinions expressed in ll. 138–148; besides which, the emphatic direction that we are to love our enemies is very properly attributed to Piers the Plowman, i.e. to Jesus Christ.

154–157. Christian love and true Patience might win all France without bloodshed. L. 162 is a singular addition.

306–309. Rich men, after death, are often poor indeed.

Pass. xvii. 21–37. Altered and abridged from the B-text.

158–182. Altered from the B-text; with the substitution of Liberum-Arbitrium in the place of Reason.

Pass. xviii. 1–8; 12. Altered from the B-text.

37–40. A curious quotation from the Book of Tobit.

47–52. 'If religious [men] would refuse · the alms of raveners,
Then Grace would grow yet · and green-leaved wax,
And Charity, that is chilled now · should chafe of himself,
And comfort all Christians · if holy church would amend;' &c.

58–71. The poet drives home forcibly the doctrine that 'charity begins at home.'

82–93. Altered from the B-text.

ADDITIONS IN THE C-TEXT.

124–158. A discussion of the hope that Saracens and Jews may be saved.

233–249. The poet charges the pope, whose mission is peace, with maintaining war. He argues that the pope ought to promote Christianity by peaceful measures, just as Mahomet promoted his religion by means of a dove. The line

'Not through manslaughter and man's strength · had Mahomet the mastery'

involves an odd mistake, as the contrary fact is sufficiently notorious.

289–294. Just as a king's duty is to defend his people, fighting at their head at the risk of his life, so should a good pastor be ready to lay down his life for his flock.

Pass. xix. 4–30; 53–108; 118–120. Altered from the B-text. The two descriptions should be compared.

163, 164. 'The Jews told the justice · how that Jesus said [it];
But the over-turning of the temple · betokened the resurrection.'

228–234; 238–240. Adam, Eve, and Abel represent the Trinity. Eve was formed from Adam, and Abel proceeded from both.

Pass. xx. 232–246. An amplification of the parable of Dives. If Dives, who won his wealth *without* guile, was condemned, what will be the fate of those rich men who have won their wealth deceitfully? Make to yourselves friends with the mammon of unrighteousness, by spending your wealth wisely and liberally.

Pass. xxi. 214, 215; 218, 219. The fact that things can often be best perceived from observing their contrasts is here enforced.

283–296. This additional passage is a great curiosity; because, in representing Satan as opposing our Lord's entrance by the aid of *guns*, our author has anticipated Milton's use of them in Paradise Lost; vi. 470.

'But rise up, Ragamuffin · and reach me all the bars
That Belial, thy bel-sire · beat, with thy dam;
And I shall let[1] this lord · and His light stop!
Ere we through brightness be blinded · bar we the gates.
Check we and chain we · and each chink stop,
That no light leap in · at loover nor at loop-hole.
And thou, Ashtaroth, hoot out · and have out our knaves[2],
Colting, and all his kin · our chattels to save.

[1] i.e. hinder. [2] servants, lads.

> Brimstone boiling · burning out cast it
> All hot on their heads · that enter nigh the walls.
> Set bows of brake[1] · and brazen guns,
> And shoot out shot enough · His squadron to blind.
> Set Mahomet at the mangonel · and mill-stones throw ye,
> With crooks and with calthrops · clog[2] we them each one.'

319–322. Additional lines about the temptation of Adam and Eve.

329, 330; 334–337. Altered from B-text with additions.

353–361. A digression, for which the author apologizes, on the awful punishment that awaits liars.

386–388. The law requires an eye for an eye, and a tooth for a tooth.

Pass. xxii. This Passus contains eight new lines, viz. 56–59, 152, 237, 336, and 439. On the other hand, lines 247, 366, and 371 of B. xix. have disappeared.

Pass. xxiii. This Passus contains but two new lines, viz. 36 and 261. But there are several minute alterations, showing that the work of revision has been carried out to the very end of the poem.

§ 8. THE FORM OF THE POEM.

As the reader has sufficient material before him for forming his own opinion, I shall endeavour to touch very briefly upon the chief points of interest concerning Piers Plowman. I have no desire to urge my views upon the reader as regards doubtful points, and can readily understand that my statements, except as regards such simple matters of fact as are not liable to contradiction, may easily be of little worth.

We are sure, however, from the numerous MSS. still extant, that there are, broadly speaking, three distinct forms of the poem, the dates of which can be approximately ascertained; and we can now follow, line by line, the changes that were introduced in the two later versions by the process of revision. We also find that there are seven MSS. which contain a *mixture* of Texts; four of these combine a portion of the A-text with a portion of the C-text, the

---

[1] A 'brake' is an old term for various implements which permit great force to be employed; *bows of brake* almost certainly refer to such huge crossbows as those employed by the Genoese archers, which required a crank or winch to wind them up or 'set' them.

[2] Orig. *acloye*, i.e. *cloy*, clog, or impede. (But *cloy* and *clog* are unrelated words.)

junction being effected very unskilfully; whilst three combine a portion of the C-text with a portion of the B-text, and are so closely related that two of them are duplicates, and the third a later copy of them. But even this is not all. There are other MSS. which actually show the poem in intermediate stages. Thus MS. Harl. 3954 exhibits an *amplified* A-text, which at the beginning follows Type B, but towards the end approaches Type A. Unfortunately, this is a very poor and corrupt MS., but it suggests that the revision of the A-text may not have been accomplished all at once. I should say that the author commenced his first revision in the end of 1376 or the beginning of 1377, at which time he introduced the fable of the 'cat and rattons,' but did not finish it till the end of 1377 or later. The gradual growth of the C-text, or later revision, is still more clearly marked, and rests on better authority. The B-text was first *amplified* by the addition of numerous extra lines, as preserved in the remarkable MS. R. (Rawl. Poet. 38), which I should describe as being a copy of the B-text with later improvements and afterthoughts. These additional lines are all duly inserted in my edition of the B-text, but are absent from the edition by Mr. Wright. Strictly speaking, they should have been relegated to the foot-notes; but the advantage of having them in the text was too great to be lost, as they have sufficient authority, and are, to a great extent, preserved in the C-text as it finally appeared. There was even a second intermediate stage between the B- and C-texts. This is exhibited by the valuable and curious MS. I. (Ilchester MS.), which I should describe as being an earlier draught of the C-text. Nor are the various forms of the poem even thus exhausted, owing to the individual peculiarities of contents or arrangement of the various MSS. By selecting certain copies, we can detect the *ten* varieties of form which are enumerated below.

A. a. It is probable that the poem, in its *earliest* form of the A-text, terminated with Passus viii., since the Passus which I have, for convenience, called Pass. ix. really begins a new poem, viz. Vita de Dowel; see p. 252. Accordingly, two MSS., both imperfect, cease just before the end of Pass. viii. is reached. These are MS. H. (Harley 875) and the MS. in Lincoln's Inn.

A. b. Some MSS. comprise both the Visio de Petro Plowman (properly so called), and the Vita de Dowel; but omit the last Passus of Dowel, which I have called Pass. xii. Two of these appear to be complete at the end, viz. MS. D. (Douce 323) and MS.

THE FORM OF THE POEM.

A. (Ashmole 1468); but others are incomplete, viz. MS. V. (Vernon), which has lost a leaf, and the four MSS.[1] which exhibit a Mixed Text (A and C), and in which a portion of the C-text is tacked on to the end of A, Pass. xi.

A. c. Other MSS. contain Pass. xii., either wholly or in part. These are MS. Rawl. Poet. 137 (which is complete), the Ingilby MS., and MS. U. (University College)[2].

A. d. One MS. (Harl. 3954) exhibits an *amplified* A-text. Unfortunately, this MS. is almost certainly corrupt in many passages, so that its evidence is not of much value. The most remarkable point about it is its omission of Pass. xii.

B. a. We may here place the B-text in its commonest form, as it occurs in MS. L. (Laud Misc. 581), and as it was printed by Crowley and Wright.

B. b. The amplified B-text in MS. R. (Rawl. Poet. 38); see above, p. xxii.

C. a. Earliest draught of the C-text, in MS. I. (Ilchester MS.); see above, p. xxii.

C. b. The C-text in its usual form.

A. b. and **C. b.** Mixture of two texts in the same MS.; see the description of **A. b.** above.

C. b. and **B. a.** Mixture of two texts in the same MS.; as in MS. Additional 10574, and MS. Cotton, Calig. A. xi.; both in the British Museum.

Here are no less than ten forms of the poem; yet besides these, we have at least two copies which do not exactly resemble any of the rest. These are the partially corrupt copy in MS. XXVI. (Corp. Christi Coll. Oxon), and the ridiculously corrupted rubbish which appears in the earlier part of MS. Z. (Bodley 851), the very copy which contains a remarkably correct version of the *latter* part of the C-text. When all this is considered, it will be seen that it is quite impossible to tell the exact value of a MS. of Piers Plowman without at least a general examination of the whole of its contents. Lastly, the above classification of the MSS. (according to the *form* of the poem exhibited in them) does not wholly agree with the

---

[1] These are: MS. T. (Trinity College, Cambridge, R. 3. 14); Harl. 6041; Digby 145; and the Duke of Westminster's MS.

[2] MS. Dublin, D. 4. 12, is remarkably connected with this set, by the extraordinary way in which the subject-matter is transposed. But it ends at A. vii. 45, the rest being lost.

§ 9. THE MEANING OF 'PIERS THE PLOWMAN.'

classification given further on, where they are arranged according to the peculiarities of the various readings which they severally adopt.

In the excellent MS. Laud Misc. 581, from which the B-text of the poem is mainly printed, we find a title (now nearly illegible) expressed in the words—'Incipit Liber de Petro Plowman.' This title is applicable to the whole poem; and the same remark applies to the title in MS. Rawl. Poet. 137, which runs thus—'Hic incipit liber qui uocatur pers plowman : P*rologus*.' Sometimes, instead of 'Liber,' we find the term 'dialogus' or 'tractatus'; the former occurs in vol. i. p. 600, and the latter at the end of the MS. belonging to the Duke of Westminster. A closer examination shews that this 'Liber' is subdivided into two main parts. The title of the former is 'Visio Willelmi de Petro le Plowman'; while the title of the latter was, originally, 'Vita de Dowel, Dobet, et Dobest, secundum Wit et Resoun[1].' The former of these includes C. Pass. i.—x. (B. prol. and Pass. i.—vii.; A. prol. and Pass. i.—viii.). The latter part at first (i.e. in the A-text) included the remainder; but at a later period this remainder was split up into three distinct portions, called respectively 'Visio de Dowel,' 'Visio de Dobet,' and 'Visio de Dobest'; see vol. i. pp. 252, 253, 436, 453, 550, 551. We hence learn that 'Piers Plowman' is the subject of the book, the author's name being William. Unfortunately, when Crowley put out his edition in 1550, he translated the Latin *de* by 'of,' instead of 'concerning,' and gave the book the ambiguous title of 'The Vision of Pierce Plowman.' Hence careless readers at once jumped to the conclusion that Piers Plowman was the name of the *author*, not of the *subject*; and this mistake was even made by men of eminence, including Ridley, Churchyarde, Spenser, W. Webbe, F. Meres, Drayton, Hickes, and Byron[2]. There seems to be quite an attraction in this curious error; for it is still constantly made even by those who must to some extent have read the book; thus Mr. Bardsley, in

---

[1] See vol. i. p. 251.
[2] See Ridley, Works (Parker Society), p. 490; lines by Churchyarde in Skelton's Poems, ed. Dyce, vol. i. p. lxxviii; Spenser, Epilogue to the Shepheards Calender; Webbe, Discourse of English Poetrie, in Hazlewood's Ancient Critical Essays, ii. 33; F. Meres, in the same, ii. 149, 154; Drayton, Legend of Thomas Cromwell; Hickes, Thesaurus, i. 196; Moore, Life of Byron, under the date 1807.

his book on English Surnames, ed. 1873, p. 406, actually has the words—'Piers, in his Vision, says,' &c. We can say that such or such an expression occurs in the Faerie Queene or in Piers Plowman; but we ought not to talk of the Faerie Queene or of Piers Plowman as if they were English authors; nor is anything gained by so doing.

Even when this error is corrected, there still remains a slight ambiguity about the term, an ambiguity which is due to the author himself, and to the fragmentary character of his work. If we examine the earliest text of the poem, here called the A-text, we shall see at once that the author at first wrote three distinct Visions, viz. (1) the Vision of the Field full of Folk, of Holy Church, and of the Lady Meed; (2) the Vision of the Deadly Sins and of Piers Plowman; and (3) Vita de Dowel, Dobet, and Dobest. He afterwards called the whole work, in its earliest form, after his favourite character in it, conferring upon it the name of 'Liber de Petro Plowman.' In this earliest draught of the poem, his Plowman, commonly called Piers, is no more than the type of the ideal honest man, whom he represents as superintending farm-labourers in order to see that their work is done heartily and thoroughly, whilst at the same time he is so dear to God the Father on account of his unswerving integrity and faithfulness that he is actually qualified to guide the pilgrims who, with consciences fully quickened, have set off on a search for Truth, but can find no one else who knows the way to that unknown shrine. If we next examine the second text, here called the B-text, we shall find that the two first Visions are the same as before; but the former, Vita de Dowel, Dobet, and Dobest has dwindled down to a mere portion of a Vita de Dowel, and may now be called the Vision of Wit, Study, Clergy, and Scripture, though this is a change rather in the name than in the subject-matter [1]. But the work is now extended so as to include new visions; these are—(4) the Vision of Fortune, Nature, and Reason; (5) the Vision of Imaginative; (6) the Vision of Conscience, Patience, and Haukyn the Active-Man. Also, the Vita de Dobet[2], including (7) the Vision of the Soul and of the Tree of Charity; (8) the Vision of Faith, Hope, and Charity; (9) the Vision of the Triumph of Piers the Plowman. Also, the Vita de Dobest[3], including (10) the Vision of Grace; and (11) the Vision of Antichrist. In thus expanding his poem, William (naturally enough)

[1] See vol. i. pp. 252-324.   [2] Beginning on p. 436.
[3] Beginning on p. 550.

came to perceive more clearly that the true guide to God the Father, the true reformer of abuses, had already come to men in the person of Jesus, who must therefore be his true Piers. The first hint of this is given somewhat mysteriously in B. xiii. 123–132 (p. 394), with which compare C. xvi. 129–150 (p. 395). But shortly afterwards we are told explicitly who Piers really is. In B. xv. 190–206 (p. 448), when the dreamer is anxiously searching for the personification of Charity or Love, he is told that he can never see Charity without the help of Piers Plowman, who alone perceives the secret thoughts of men; in short, as he tells us, *Petrus est Christus*, i.e. Piers is Christ; see notes to C. xvii. 337 and B. xv. 206. In B. xvi. 17–53, Piers is seen by the dreamer in a vision, and almost immediately afterwards (B. xvi. 89) the same Piers is deputed by God the Father to do battle with the devil, and rescue from him certain fruit, i.e. the souls of righteous men then imprisoned *in limbo*. Hereupon Piers becomes incarnate in the form of Jesus (B. xvi. 94), and the dreamer beholds in succession (1) the preliminary Vision of Faith, Hope, and Charity, and (2) the Vision of the Triumph of Piers Plowman in the person of Jesus, who, after His crucifixion, descended into hell and brought thence the souls of the patriarchs, and afterwards arose from the dead (B. xix. 148) and ascended into heaven (B. xix. 186). He then deputed as his successor a new Piers, whose name was truly *Petrus*, or as we should now say, St. Peter the apostle (B. xix. 178, 196); and this Piers was again succeeded by the Popes of Rome, who were, in a spiritual sense, 'emperors of all the world' (B. xix. 425)[1]. And here William pauses to utter a reflection upon the very imperfect manner in which 'the pope' really represents the Son of God (B. xix. 426–434). The moral is one of the deepest importance for the history of mankind in all ages, and raises the very question which was of the most vital consequence in the progress of religious reformation. William goes to the root of the matter in thus endeavouring to make us see clearly that the popes were quite wrong in claiming to be merely the successors of St. Peter, inasmuch as St. Peter was, in himself and apart from Christ, of no account. They ought rather to have become the true successors of St. Peter's Master, who was the true *Petrus*, the very Rock upon which alone the church can abide firmly. It just made all the difference; for the spirit in which St. Peter acted was more than once at variance with the spirit of Jesus; and the history of the world would have been

[1] See note to C. xxii. 183.

very different if the popes had always acted as followers of the latter. This then is the meaning of Piers Plowman; in the earlier part of the poem, he is a blameless ploughman and a guide to men who are seeking the shrine of Truth, whilst in the latter part of it he is the blameless carpenter's son, who alone can shew us the Father. The ambiguity is surely not very great, and the reader who once apprehends this explanation will easily remember that the true Piers Plowman was certainly not a Middle-English author.

Our author can hardly be considered responsible for the meaning which was assigned to Piers Plowman by other English writers; yet it is worth while to add that the former part of his work was better known than the latter part, so that his readers almost unanimously took up his lower conception of the character. Thus it was that Piers Plowman became an accepted synonym for a plain man who makes it his business to act with integrity and to guide others to a knowledge of truth. Hence, in the Plowman's Tale (once wrongly attributed to Chaucer), and in Pierce the Ploughman's Crede[1], the person thus designated is merely an honest ploughman who knows his Creed and Paternoster better than the friars do; and much the same conception of the character appears in other works, such as the Praier and Complaynte of the Ploweman unto Christe, Pyers Plowmans Ex[h]ortation, and A goodlye Dialogue and Dysputacion between Pyers Ploweman and a Popish Preest.

§ 10. THE AUTHOR'S NAME.

The MSS. inform us, over and over again, that the author's Christian name, or at any rate his assumed Christian name, was William. This appears in two ways. First, the titles and colophons frequently call him *Willelmus*; see vol. i. pp. 3, 251, 253. Secondly, the author repeatedly calls himself Wille; see A. ix. 118, A. xii. 99, 103; B. v. 62, viii. 124; C. ii. 5, vii. 2, xi. 71; and, in one remarkable passage (B. xv. 148) he says—

'I haue lyued in londe, quod I · my name is longe wille,'

i.e. he calls himself Long Will, where 'long' means tall and alludes to his personal appearance; just as the poet Gascoigne was called 'Long George'; cf. note to C. xi. 68. Thirdly, we have the old

[1] I have endeavoured to show that these poems were both written by the same anonymous author; see my Introduction to Pierce the Ploughman's Crede (E. E. T. S.).

note in MS. Dublin D. 4. 1, that his name was William de Langland, and his father's name Stacy de Rokayle[1]; and an old note in one of the Ashburnham MSS. to the effect that 'Robert or william langland made pers ploughman.' The latter note cannot be right in suggesting the alternative name of Robert; and it is probable that this mistake arose from misreading 'i robed' (p. 252, l. 1) as 'I Rob*er*t.' However, John Bale gave him the name Robertus Langlande, as appears from a MS. note in his handwriting in the same Ashburnham MS.; see also his work on the Illustrious Writers of Great Britain[2]. Moreover, although Crowley printed his edition of Piers Plowman nine years earlier, I do not doubt that the unnamed person who gave him the same information was the same John Bale. Among the later authors who merely copy from Bale and Crowley we find Holinshed, Selden, J. Weever, David Buchanan (who coolly calls our author a native of Aberdeen !), Fuller, and Hearne. John Stow, confusing the mention of Malvern hills in the poem with the fact that there was a John of Malvern of some small note[3], boldly asserts, without a tittle of evidence, that the author's name was John Malverne, a fellow of Oriel College, Oxford ; and in this unwarrantable guess he is followed by Selden, who speaks doubtfully, and by Pits, who seems not to have doubted it at all; whilst Wood makes the singular statement that 'Robertus de Langland, Johan. Malverne

---

[1] The note runs thus, in a handwriting of the *fifteenth* century :—' Memorandum, quod Stacy de Rokayle, pater Willielmi de Langlond, qui Stacius fuit generosus, et morabatur in Schiptone under Whicwode, tenens domini le Spenser in comitatu Oxon., qui prædictus Willielmus fecit librum qui vocatur Perys Ploughman.' *Schiptone* is Shipton-under-Wychwood, 4 miles N. N. E. of Burford, Oxon. It is worthy of note that the poet himself tells us that, in his day, the son's surname was not necessarily the same as his father's. See note to C. iv. 369.

[2] 'Robertus Langelande, sacerdos, ut apparet, natus in comitatu Salopiæ, in villa vulgò dicta Mortymers Clibery, in terra lutea, octavo à Malvernis montibus milliario fuit. Num tamen eo in loco, incondito et agresti, in bonis litteris ad maturam ætatem usque informatus fuit, certò adfirmare non possum, &c. . . . . Illud veruntamen liquido constat, eum fuisse ex primis Joannis Wiclevi discipulis unum, &c. . . . Complevit suum opus anno domini 1369, dum Joannes Cicestrius Londini prætor esset.'—Balei, Script. Illustr. majoris Britanniæ, Cent. vi. p. 474. Basileæ, apud Oporinum, 1559.

[3] John de Malverne was prior of Worcester in 1395, and apparently died before 1415 ; see Wharton, Anglia Sacra, i. 549 ; Dugdale's Monasticon. A John Malvern wrote a continuation of Higden's Polychronicon ; C.C.C. MS. 197 ; see Appendix I to Higden's Polychronicon, ed. J. R. Lumby, vol. viii. pp. 355-406. A John Malvern was present at the examination of W. Thorpe in 1407; see Arber's English Garner, vi. 51.

THE AUTHOR'S NAME.

nonnullis appellatur.' We ought to set aside the names Robert and John, and be content with William; and in rejecting the name of John, we should reject the surname Malvern at the same time.

The author's surname is usually given as Langland, as we have seen. On the other hand, we have the curious note, in three of the C-text MSS., that the author's name was 'Willelmus W.'[1]; but the meaning of this 'W.' remains unknown[2]. A difficulty arises from the fact that, as Professor Pearson has pointed out to me, 'the only known family of Langlands has a very distinct history in connection with Somersetshire, Devonshire, and Dorsetshire, but never comes to view in the Midland Counties.' I find mention of Nicholas de Langgelonde and Radulphus de Langelande in the Wood MS. no. 1 (Bodleian Library), p. 195; Hugo de Langelonde, in Hearne's *Johannes Glastoniensis*, ii. 367, and other instances; especially in connection with the neighbourhood of East Brent, in Somersetshire, where there was a place specifically called Langlond; see Hearne (as above), ii. 323. See also MS. Addit. 5937, fol. 54 b, in the British Museum[3]. On account of this difficulty, Professor Pearson, in an article in the North British Review, April, 1870, p. 244, suggested that the surname Langley is more probable; and I here quote the most material part of his argument for the reader's convenience. 'The Langleys of Oxfordshire have not yet, we believe, found place in any county history. But their pedigree is abundantly proveable. They emerge into history with Thomas de Langley, who gives King John a hundred marks and a palfrey in 1213 to replace Thomas Fitzhugh in the guardianship of Wychwood Forest (*Rot. de Fin.* 485). From that time the Langleys, William, Thomas, John, John, and Thomas successively, were wardens of Wychwood, and owned land in Shipton-under-Wychwood as early as 1278, and as late as 1362 (*Rotul. Hundred.* ii. 729; *Inquis. post Mortem*, ii. 252). But the last Thomas died before the thirty-sixth year of Edward III., and was succeeded by his cousin and heir, Simon Verney (*Inquis. post Mortem*, ii. 252, 290).' This is sufficient to connect the name of Langley with Shipton, but does not fully solve the difficulty, as the

---

[1] In the Ilchester MS., at the end of Pass. x., we find—'Explicit visio Willelmi W. de Petro le Plowman.' So also in MS. Douce 104, fol. 39, back, and in MS. Digby 102, fol. 35.

[2] Professor Morley suggests that it means William of Wychwood. Observe that this 'W.' only occurs in the *latest* version.

[3] There was also a place called Langland near Whalley, in Lancashire; see The Coucher Book of Whalley (Chetham Soc.), ii. 527, iv. 1070.

poet probably did not belong to so good a family. He might, however, have been named from the hamlet of Langley, which is situate in the very parish of Shipton-under-Wychwood above mentioned. There is also another place named Langley, near Acton Burnel, in Shropshire; adjoining which is the hamlet of Ruckley or Rokele, which might be identified with *Rokayle*, the alleged surname of the poet's father. Professor Pearson continues :—'We find in Shropshire that younger members of the Burnel family were occasionally known as Burnels de Langley (*Inquis. post Mortem*, i. 12, 253); that there were other Langleys on the estate in the employ of the Burnel family; and that even the name of Rokeyle may be traced in one instance with high probability to the Welsh border (*Yearbook of 32 Edw. I. 298*).... A William de Langley was a tenant of William Burnel in 1228 (*Testa de Nevill*, 57). A Robert de Langley receives fifty marks due to Robert Burnel, afterwards Chancellor, in 1272 (*Exchequer Issues*, 87). A Robert de Langley was instituted clerk of *Rokesley* chapel some time between 1311 and 1349 (Eyton's *Shropshire*, vi. 147). Again, Henry de Rokesley and Richard de Waleys, whose name indicates a Welshman, both claimed to descend from Robert Paytevin; and one of the few Paytevins who can be traced was a follower of Roger de Mortimer, the lord of Cleobury Mortimer (*Parliamentary Writs*, iv. 1269). Seemingly therefore there were two families, one of Langley and one of Rokesle, who lived in adjoining hamlets, attached to the same manor, and of whom one was connected with the service of the Burnels, the other more remotely with the Mortimers, as being related to one of their dependants. Here then we perhaps get a clue to the poet's birth at Cleobury Mortimer, which was a possession of the Mortimers (*Inquis. post Mortem*, i. 190, ii. 224). It remains to explain the connection with Shipton-under-Wychwood. Edward Burnel (born 1287, died 1315) married Alicia, daughter of Hugh de Despenser, of whom we only know that she survived him (Eyton's *Shropshire*, vi. 135). And a Hugh de Despenser died in 1349, seized of the manor of Shipton-under-Wychwood (*Inquis. post Mortem*, ii. 160; Kennett's *Parochial Antiquities*, ii. 102). Now, whether the poet's ancestor was a Langley or a Rokesle, it seems easy from what has gone before to understand why he first held a farm under the Mortimers and afterwards under the Despensers. In fact, there was a group of great families connected by birth or position in Shropshire and Oxfordshire, and a group of small families who were naturally linked with their fortunes.'

From the above arguments we might be led to adopt, as a plausible theory, that the poet may have been named Langley from either of the above-mentioned hamlets, either that in Shropshire or that in Oxfordshire, since the family seems to have removed from one to the other. And if the reader finds the arguments convincing, he will be led to adopt Langley rather than Langland as the true name of the author. Yet I confess that I still hesitate as to whether we should do so; for it is very difficult, in such a case, to see how the traditional name of Langland came to be mentioned at all. It involves the unlikely substitution of the comparatively rare name of Langland[1] for a name which was much commoner and more widely spread; and this is a difficulty which I can hardly get over. In a matter so obscure, I now prefer to keep to the traditional name, though I confess that at one time I thought otherwise [2].

I think it worth while to point out a slight connection that exists between Wychwood and Malvern. When the poet talks of his having been put to school (C. vi. 36), and of his having received a clerical education, we may fancy him to have passed his early days in one of the priories at Malvern, either at the famous priory at Great Malvern, or at the lesser one at Little Malvern, which was considered as 'in one and inseparable body with the Church at Worcester' (Abingdon's Antiquities of Worcester Cathedral, p. 225). Now the Hugh le Despenser mentioned above as dying in 1349 (when William would be about seventeen years old), was son of the too famous Hugh le Despenser the younger (put to death Nov. 29, 1326), who had married Eleanor, sister and co-heir of Gilbert de Clare, earl of Gloucester[3], and by that marriage obtained the manor of Malvern, so that the manors of Malvern and Wychwood were in the hands of the same lord (see Sir H. Nicolas' Historic Peerage). In the Abbey Church (or more correctly, the Priory Church) at Great Malvern a large number of ornamental tiles still remain; some of these have armorial bearings depicted upon them, including those of Clare and Despenser. 'The arms of Clare, Despenser, and Beauchamp commemorate the lords of Malvern Chase, who, with others,

---

[1] There was a John Longland or Langland, who was bishop of Lincoln; born in 1473, died May 7, 1547. But instances of the name are very scarce, as will soon appear to any one who institutes the search.

[2] The remarkable line—'I haue lyued in *londe*, quod I · my name is *longe wille*' (B. xv. 148) contains *wille longelonde* backwards. Is this a mere chance?

[3] Another of his sisters founded Clare College, Cambridge, in 1326.

are reckoned among the chief benefactors of the Priory[1].' There is one ornament of this church too curious to be left without mention. We find in our poem (B. prol. 146; C. i. 165) the fable of the rats who proposed to 'bell the cat'; and in one of the monks' stalls is a 'miserere'-seat, ornamented with a grotesque carving which represents 'three mirthful rats hanging a cat[2].'

§ 11. The Author's Life.

Suppose it to appear, from what has been said above, that the author's name was William Langland; that he was born at Cleobury Mortimer, in Shropshire; and that his father was Stacy de Rokayle, who afterwards held a farm under one of the Despensers in the parish of Shipton-under-Wychwood in Oxfordshire[3]. From the expression that 'no clerk ought to receive the tonsure unless he be born of franklins and free men, and of wedded folk' (C. vi. 63), I should suppose that his father was a franklin, and that he was himself born in lawful wedlock[4]. At the time of writing the B-text (in 1377), he was (perhaps) 45 years old (B. xi. 46, xii. 3); this would fix the year of his birth about A. D. 1332. His father and his friends put him to school (possibly in the priory at Great Malvern), made a *clerk* or scholar of him, and taught him what holy writ meant (C. vi. 36, 37). He considered school to be 'a heaven upon earth' (B. x. 300), because in school 'all is obedience and books, reading and learning' (B. x. 303). In 1362, at the age of about thirty, he wrote the A-text of the poem, or at any rate the first part of it[5], without

[1] Cross's Handbook of Malvern, p. 86.

[2] The same, p. 91.

[3] About 4 miles from Burford, and not much more than 20 from Banbury. It is remarkable that William mentions 'the beadle of Banbury' with scorn, as if he had a grudge against him (C. iii. 111).

[4] M. Jusserand, in his Observations sur La Vision de Piers Plowman (Revue Critique, 1879), says that 'the contrary is the truth'; for which he relies upon the expression in C. ii. 73, where Holy-Church says to the poet, 'I received thee at the first, and made thee a free man'; so that he could not have been 'free' before. I believe that this objection can be met. The word 'free' here means *spiritually* free; for Holy-Church is referring to the time of the author's baptism in his infancy, as the context suggests; see also C. xiii. 52, 58, and p. xxxv, l. 17 (below). I do not think that a bondman's son could become a freeman by baptism only.

[5] The opening lines of A. Pass. ix. imply that a short interval took place between the composition of the preceding part of the poem and the latter part of it.

any thought (I should suppose) of continuing it at a later time. In this, he refers to Edward III. and his son the Black Prince (A. iv. 32); to the murder of Edward II. (A. iii. 180); to the great pestilences of 1348 and 1361, particularly the latter (A. prol. 81, v. 13, x. 185); to the treaty of Brétigny in 1360, and Edward's wars in Normandy (A. iii. 182-201, and notes, pp. 48, 49); and in particular, to the great storm of wind which took place on Saturday evening, Jan. 15, 1362 (A. v. 14, and note to C. vi. 117). This version of the poem he describes as having been partly composed in May (A. prol. 5) whilst wandering on the Malvern Hills [1], which are thrice mentioned in the part of the poem which is called the Vision of Piers Plowman in the most restricted sense, i.e. the Prologue and Pass. i.–viii. (see A. prol. 5, 88, viii. 130). In the Prologue to Do-wel, he describes himself as wandering about all the summer till he met with two Minorite friars on a certain Friday, and discoursed with them concerning Do-wel (A. ix. 8). It was probably not long after this that he went to reside in London, with which he already seems to have had some acquaintance [2]; there he lived in Cornhill, with his wife Kitte and his daughter Calote, for many long years (C. vi. 1, 2; xvii. 286; viii. 304 (and note); xxi. 473; B. xviii. 426).

In the early part of 1377 [3], he began to expand his poem into the B-text, wherein he alludes to the expected accession of Richard II. (B. prol. 190); to the jubilee (as I would suggest) in the last year of the reign of Edward III. (B. iii. 299, and note to C. iv. 456) [4]; to the battle of Creçy (B. xii. 107, and note to C. xv. 50); to the

---

[1] The poet mentions a broad bank by a bourn-side (A. prol. 8). I lately sought for this 'bourn,' and fully believe that I found the right place. But the bourn, though still running, is invisible; it is now carried *underground*, and supplies Great Malvern with water. It runs under St. Ann's Road, which now forms the regular approach from the neighbourhood of the priory church to the Hills. I was told that, before the bourn was carried underground, it came down the hill-side 'how it could'; and its course was evidently down the 'winding valley' between the North Hill and the Worcestershire Beacon. The local names 'Mill Lane' and 'Mill side' preserve traces of its former course below the church. The point is of much interest; for it goes far to prove that William ascended the hill from Great Malvern, and started from the priory. The 'broad bank' is the North Hill.

[2] Thus he mentions Cock Lane, Smithfield (A. v. 162); Cheapside (A. v. 165); the women of Flanders who haunted London (A. v. 163); Westminster (A. ii. 131, iii. 12).

[3] The Black Prince died June 8, 1376, when Richard became heir-apparent (see note to C. i. 165).

[4] In this note (sixth line), for 'then just begun' read 'soon expected to begin.'

fourth pestilence in 1376 (B. xiii. 248, and note to C. xvi. 220); and in particular, to the dearth in the dry month of April, 1370, when John Chichester was mayor of London (B. xiii. 271, and note, p. 203).

In the C-text, it is less easy to find clear instances of new allusions to the events of the period; but there is one passage in which the growing dislike of Englishmen to Richard II. is so plainly expressed that we may fairly suppose it to have been written after A.D. 1392. We find, in C. iv. 203-210, a complaint too plainly expressed to admit of any doubt as to the poet's feelings. He there tells the king, in the boldest language, that 'unseemly Tolerance (of evil men), which is own sister to Bribery, in combination with Bribery herself, have almost brought it about, except the Virgin Mary help thee, that *no land loveth thee, and least of all thine own land*.' Now, after Richard really took the government into his own hands in 1389, he was at first in considerable favour for some little time; but in 1392 there was a very great quarrel between himself and the Londoners, as related by Walsingham, and the feeling against him seems to have been very strong. The king's prodigality was beginning to make his exactions severely felt, and the quarrel turned, naturally enough, upon the question of money. Under the title 'De transgressionibus Londinensium, et ira Regis,' Walsingham (ed. Riley, ii. 207) relates the story thus. 'Sub eodem tempore, misit Rex ad cives Londiniarum, petens ab eis mutuo mille libras; cui procaciter, et ultra quam decuit, restiterunt, et pecuniam se non posse praestare petitam unanimiter affirmaverunt; sed et quemdam Lumbardum, volentem accommodare Regi dictam summam, male tractaverunt, verberaverunt, et paulo minus occiderunt.' This is the very story, I suppose, to which our author alludes in the passage—

> 'And ich dar legge my lyf · þat loue wol lene þe suluer,
> To wage thyne, and help wynne · þat þow wilnest after,
> More Jan al þy marchauns · oþer þy mytrede bisshopes,
> Oþer *lumbardes* of lukes · þat lyuen by lone as Iewes.'
>
> C. v. 191.

Here he tells the king that, if he wants money, he must not apply to the Lombards, but cultivate the love of his people. If this and the former allusion be considered, we may see grounds for placing the C-text later than 1392[1]. These are my reasons for selecting the

---

[1] Hardly in 1392; as the passage occurs also in the *early draught* of the C-text, in the Ilchester MS.; see p. xxiii.

year 1393 as a sufficiently approximate date, although I should not object to the opinion that the true date is later still. How it can be earlier, I cannot see; the long additional passage explaining the difference between Bribery and Wages (C. iv. 287–415) shews that this difference was considered as especially deserving of notice, and the whole tone of Pass. iv. indicates the poet's opinion as to the prevalence of gross misgovernment, which he here lays to the king's charge more directly than he had previously done. The very same tone is prevalent in the poem of 'Richard the Redeless,' the date of which is so clearly 1399. From all this it will be seen that, although the year 1393 is only assigned as a conjectural date, there are some good reasons for supposing that it is not far wrong. I believe that we may safely assume the dates 1393 and 1398 as the extreme limits between which the date of the C-text can vary.

M. Jusserand points out another probable allusion in C. vi. 63, where William says that no clerk ought to receive the tonsure unless he be the son of a free man; the idea of inserting this opinion may have been suggested by a petition of the commons in 1391, praying that entry into schools (which served to prepare for entry into the church) should be denied to the sons of bondmen (Rolls of Parliament, iii. 294). It is probable that William wrote the poem of Richard the Redeless[1] in September, 1399, at which time he was at Bristol. He was then probably about 67 years old, and he has a clear allusion to his old age; see Rich. iii. 260–262. Here we lose sight of him, and we must suppose him not to have long survived the end of the fourteenth century[2].

William has several allusions to his own tallness of stature (A. ix. 61; B. xv. 148; C. vi. 24). In one passage he tells us that he was loath to reverence lords and ladies, or persons dressed in fur or wearing silver pendants; he would never say 'God save you' to serjeants whom he met, for all of which proud behaviour, then very uncommon in a poor man, people looked upon him as a fool, and few approved of his mode of life (B. xv. 3–10). It requires no great stretch of imagination to picture to ourselves the tall gaunt figure of Long Will, in his long robes[3] and with his shaven head[4], striding along Cornhill, saluting no man by the way, minutely observant of

---

[1] I here assume that this poem is by the author of Piers Plowman, an assertion which is more particularly discussed below.
[2] The death of Chaucer took place in 1400 exactly.
[3] C. vi. 41.   [4] C. vi. 54, 56, 82.

the gay dresses¹ to which he paid no outward reverence. We should also observe his frequent allusions to lawyers, to the law-courts at Westminster, and to legal processes². He has a mock charter, beginning with the ordinary formula *Sciant presentes et futuri* (C. iii. 78); a form of making a will (C. ix. 95); and in one passage (C. xiv. 120) he speaks with such scorn of a man who draws up a charter badly, who interlines it or leaves out sentences, or puts false Latin into it, that we may fairly suppose him to have been conversant with the writing out of legal documents, and to have eked out his subsistence by the small sums received for doing so. Further, he tells us that no churl may make a charter (C. xiii. 61), and that a felon may not be twice hanged (C. xxi. 425); draws attention to a point of Westminster law (C. xi. 239); and talks of the bribery that was often effective in Westminster Hall, in the Court of Arches, and in procuring divorces (C. xxiii. 133, 136, 138). The various texts of the poem are so consistent, the revision is of so close and minute a character, and the numerous transpositions of the subject-matter in the latest version are managed with such skill, that we may well believe him to have been his own scribe in the first instance, though we cannot now certainly point to any MS. as an autograph. Nevertheless, the very neatly written MS. Laud 581 is so extremely correct as regards the sense, and is marked for correction on account of such minute errors, that, if it be not an autograph, he must at any rate have perused it, and its authority must be accepted in doubtful cases.

The author's exact condition in life remains somewhat uncertain. M. Jusserand seems to think that the passage in C. ii. 72–75 (cf. B. i. 75–78, A. i. 73–76), where Holy-Church claims the author as her true servant, proves that he was in the church; but I understand the matter quite differently, for it merely refers to his reception into the church by baptism, when he (to use his own words) 'brought her sureties to fulfil her bidding, and to believe in her and love her all his life-time;' or, as he again says in another passage, 'I thought upon Holy-Church, who received me *at the font* as one of God's chosen' (C. xiii. 51). The most explicit statements occur in C. vi. 1–101, where he tells us how he lived at one time in a cot on Cornhill, with his wife Kitte, clothed like a Loller, yet not much beloved by the Lollers of London, because he composed

---

[1] Rich. Redeless, iii. 152.
[2] C. i. 91; iii. 61, 148, 169, 174, 186; iv. 13, &c.

verses concerning them. Since his friends died, he had never found any mode of life that he cared to adopt, except that in long robes; the tools that he worked with and whereby he obtained his livelihood were the *pater-noster, placebo, dirige*, his psalter, and the seven psalms. He sung for the souls of such as had helped him to subsist, and went from house to house amongst such as were willing to give him an occasional meal, like a beggar who has no bag or bottle to carry about with him, but only his belly, as a receptacle for food. He claims exemption from manual labour because he is a tonsured clerk, who is exempted from toiling like a labourer, from swearing at inquests, and from fighting in the vanguard of an army; seeing that the prayers of a perfect man, and discreet penance[1], are the kinds of service that most please our Lord. It thus appears that he had received the tonsure, but probably had only taken minor orders, and, being a married man[2], was hardly in a position to rise in the church. He has many allusions to his poverty.

M. Jusserand points out that the poet seems to confess that he lived just such an idle and blameworthy life as did those against whom he directs his satire. He condemns those who went to live in London, in order 'to sing there for simony, for silver is sweet' (C. i. 84); yet he himself lived in London, and *upon* London, and sang for men's souls (C. vi. 44-48). He condemns beggars (C. ix. 124-128, 139, 158, &c.); yet he begged himself (C. vi. 51). He inveighs against 'great loobies and long, that loath were to work' (C. i. 53); yet he himself was 'too long to stoop low, or to work as a workman' (C. vi. 24). It is therefore fitting that he should remind men that they ought to practise what they preach (C. vi. 142); and that he should recognise the existence of men who 'could shew wise words, and yet work the contrary' (B. xii. 51). Nevertheless, I think we may see a wide difference between the vicars who had cure of souls, yet deserted their parishes in the time of trial, and the poor poet and student, who was fain to keep himself from starving by performing such duties as were most suitable for him; between the 'long loobies' who went on a pilgrimage to Walsingham as pretended hermits, and our Long Will, who had become so habituated

---

[1] There is a vein of satire running through all these remarks upon himself. Conscience, in fact, reproves him (C. vi. 89), and he admits the justice of the reproof.

[2] There was always more laxity in England (especially in the North) than on the continent, with respect to the celibacy of the clergy; see note to C. xi. 284.

to reading and learning that he was unfitted for working in the fields. We must not lay too much stress upon his confession, in his declining age, that he had often sadly misspent his time (C. vi. 93); many a man of active mind and contemplative habits is saddened by reflection upon his wasted opportunities. The man who composed Piers Plowman, and wrote it out himself, and subsequently revised it with great care, making numerous additions to it, and again wrote it out at least twice, not only proved his industry, but has left an enduring monument of a useful life.

§ 12. Criticisms on the Poem.

For the sake of completeness, I add a few selections from criticisms by various writers, but in an abbreviated form. The student who requires full information is referred to the works themselves.

BY ISAAC D'ISRAELI.

Isaac D'Israeli, in his Amenities of Literature, has an interesting article upon our author. He rightly censures the remark in Warton[1], that 'instead of availing himself of the rising and rapid improvements of the English language, Langland prefers and adopts the style of the Anglo-Saxon poets,' but is not happy in his own statement, that Langland 'avoided all exotic novelties in the energy of his Anglo-Saxon genius[2].' D'Israeli proceeds to discuss the poem, and has, among others, these remarks.

'Our author's indignant spirit, indeed, is vehemently democratic. He dared to write what many trembled to whisper. Genius reflects the suppressed feelings of its age . . . But our country priest, in his contemplative mood, was not less remarkable for his prudence than for his bold freedom, aware that the most corrupt would be the most vindictive . . . The sage, the satirist, and the seer (for prophet he proved to be), veiled his head in allegory; he published no other names than those of the virtues and vices; and to avoid personality, he contented himself with personification.

---

[1] Hist. Eng. Poetry, sect. viii.
[2] Our old critics generally go astray when they offer remarks upon the *language* of the Middle-English period, which they seldom understood. As a fact, Langland used the language of his neighbours, which abounded in words of French origin. See Marsh's Lectures, 1st Series, pp. 124, 168; and see p. xlix, note 1.

CRITICISMS ON THE POEM.

'A voluminous allegory is the rudest and the most insupportable of all poetic fictions; it originates in an early period of society—when its circles are contracted and isolated, and the poet is more conversant with the passions of mankind than with individuals. A genius of the highest order alone could lead us through a single perusal of such a poem, by the charm of vivifying details, which enable us to forget the allegory altogether . . . In such creative touches, the author of Piers Plowman displays pictures of domestic life with the minute fidelity of a Flemish painting; so veracious is his simplicity. He is a great satirist, touching with caustic invective or keen irony the public abuses and private vices; but in the depth of his emotions, and in the wildness of his imagination, he breaks forth in the solemn tones and with the sombre majesty of Dante.

'But this rude native genius was profound as he was sagacious; and his philosophy terminated in prophecy. At the era of the Reformation they were startled by the discovery of an unknown writer, who, two centuries preceding that awful change, had predicted *the fate of the religious houses from the hand of a king* (B. x. 327; p. 310). The visionary seer seems to have fallen on the principle which led Erasmus to predict that *those who were in power* would seize on the rich shrines, because *no other class of men* in society could mate with so mighty a body as the monks . . . .

'Why our rustic bard selected the character of a Ploughman as the personage adapted to convey to us his theological mysteries, we know not precisely to ascertain; but it probably occurred as a companion fitted to the humbler condition of the apostles themselves. Such however was the power of the genius of this writer, that his successors were content to look for no one of a higher class to personify their solemn themes. Hence we have the Creed of Pierce Ploughman, the Praier and Complaynte of the Plowman, the Plowman's Tale inserted in Chaucer's volume; all being equally directed against the vicious clergy of the day.'

BY DR. WHITAKER.

The most valuable passages in the Introduction to Dr. Whitaker's edition of Piers Plowman are those which relate to Langland himself and to the general character of his poem. Whether we entirely agree with him or not, these passages are certainly worthy of perusal, and I therefore reprint them here without further apology.

CRITICISMS ON THE POEM.

'During the reign of Edward the Third, one of the most splendid, but not the most refined in our annals, yet equally removed from both these extremes, arose in this country two poets, the writings of one of whom contributed to enlarge the minds, and of the other to improve the moral feelings of their contemporaries in a degree unfelt since the æras of the great Roman satirists. The first of these, a man of the world and a courtier, at once informed and delighted the higher orders by his original and lively portraits of human nature in every rank, and almost under every modification, while he prevented or perverted the proper effect of satire by the most licentious and obscene exhibitions. The latter, an obscure country priest, much addicted to solitary contemplation, but at the same time a keen and severe observer of human nature; well read in the scriptures and schoolmen, and intimately acquainted with the old language and poetry of his country, in an uncouth dialect and rugged metre, by his sarcastic and ironical vein of wit, his knowledge of low life, his solemnity on some occasions, his gaiety on others, his striking personifications, dark allusions, and rapid transitions, has contrived[1] to support and animate an allegory (the most insipid for the most part and tedious of all vehicles of instruction) through a bulky volume. By what inducement he was led to prefer this vehicle, it is not difficult to conjecture. From his subordinate station in the church, this free reprover of the higher ranks was exposed to all the severities of ecclesiastical discipline: and from the aristocratical temper of the times he was liable to be crushed by the civil power. Everything, therefore, of a personal nature was in common prudence to be avoided. The great were not then accustomed, as a licentious press has since disciplined them, to endure the freedoms of reprehension:—authority was, even when abused, sacred; and rank, when united with vice, was enabled to keep its partner in countenance. Above all, the great ecclesiastics were as vindictive as they were corrupt: and hence the satirist was compelled to shelter himself under the distant generalities of personification.

'But, unfortunately, by this means, whatever he gained in personal security, he lost in the point and distinctness of his satire. Mere personifications of virtues and vices, however skilfully and powerfully touched, are capable of few strokes: the quality is simple, but different individuals, who partake of it in a degree however preeminent, combine and modify it in such an infinite variety of ways,

---

[1] Printed 'continued'; but surely a misprint.

with other subordinate traits and features of character, that while the abstract property is one and the same, in its actual existence, as part of the moral nature of man, it is capable in skilful hands of infinite diversities of representation. It is indeed far from being necessary that the characters be real, but, for the purposes of satirical painting, they must be *persons*.

'From this uniformity of appearance in his abstract qualities the author has been betrayed, by the necessity of combination in some way or other, into the fault of mixing his personifications with each other; as, *ex. gr.* avarice and fraud, qualities which, though nearly akin, have no necessary co-existence[1]; and, for the same reason, wherever he deviates into personality, as in the coarse but striking scene of "Glutton's" Debauch, where the characters, though imaginary, are persons, not personifications, he paints with all the truth and distinctness of a Dutch master. . . . .

'Wherever born or bred, and by whatever name distinguished, the author of these Visions was an observer and a reflector of no common powers. I can conceive him (like his own visionary William[2]) to have been sometimes occupied in contemplative wanderings on the Malvern Hills, and dozing away a summer's noon among the bushes, while his waking thoughts were distorted into all the misshapen forms created by a dreaming fancy. Sometimes I can descry him taking his staff, and roaming far and wide in search of manners and characters; mingling with men of every accessible rank, and storing his memory with hints for future use. I next pursue him to his study, sedate and thoughtful, yet wildly inventive, digesting the first rude drafts of his Visions, and in successive transcriptions, as judgment matured, or invention declined, or as his observations were more extended, expanding or contracting, improving and sometimes perhaps debasing his original text[3]. The

---

[1] I believe this expresses a misapprehension. I suppose that the idea of connecting avarice and fraud is none of Langland's, but that he was merely following the conventional description of Avarice considered as one of the seven deadly sins. We find the same thing in Chaucer's Persones Tale:—' of avarice cometh eek lesynges, *thefte,* and fals witnesse and *fals othes* . . . . The synne of thefte is . . . . in borwyng of thin neighebores catelle in entent never to pay, and in semblable thinges.'

[2] His 'William' is not 'visionary' at all; it is simply and solely *his own name*.

[3] In spite of the fact that Dr. Whitaker did not perceive *which* was the oldest text, he yet here expresses the true state of the case with great clearness. Even

time of our author's death, and the place of his interment, are equally unknown, with almost every circumstance relating to him. His contemporaries, Chaucer and Gower, repose beneath magnificent tombs, but Langland (if such were really his name) has no other monument than that which, having framed for himself, he left to posterity to appropriate. . . . .

'The Reformers of the sixteenth century claimed as their own the Author of these Visions; but surely on no good grounds. That he believed and taught almost all the fundamental doctrines of Christianity has no tendency to prove him a Wickliffite or Lollard. The best and soundest members of the church of Rome have done the same. It is not defects but redundancies which we impute to them. Of the predestinarian principles afterwards professed by Wickliff, Langland seems to think with disapprobation; and when his visionary hero speaks of himself as belonging to the Lolleres, he evidently means, not the religious party distinguished by a similar name, but, in the usual strain of his irony, a company of idle wanderers[1]. Yet in the midst of darkness and spiritual slavery, his acute and penetrating understanding enabled him to discover the multiplied superstitions of the public service, the licentious abuse of pilgrimages, the immoral tendencies of indulgences, the bad effects upon the living of expiatory services for the dead, the inordinate wealth of the papacy, and the usurpations of the mendicant orders, both on the rights of the diocesans and of the parochial clergy. These abuses Langland, with many other good men who could endure to remain in the communion of the church of Rome, saw and deplored; but though he finally conducted his pilgrim out of the particular communion of Rome into the universal church, he permitted him to carry along with him too many remnants of his old faith, such as satisfaction for sin to be made by the sinner, together with the merit of works, and especially of voluntary poverty; but, above all, the worship of the cross; incumbrances with which the Lollards of his own, or the Protestants of a later age, would not willingly have received him as a proselyte.

the charge of 'debasing' the text may be sustained; there certainly seem to be several passages in which the C-text, by being altered, has been weakened. But other passages have been much improved.

[1] But it may also be said, that he tries to shew that the term *loller* might be applied with more fitness to others than the followers of Wyclif. Though not quite a Wycliffite, his sympathies were mostly with that party.

CRITICISMS ON THE POEM. xliii

'Neither was he an enemy to monastic institutions themselves: on the contrary, he appears to have sighed for the quiet and contemplative life of the cloister, could it have been restored to its primitive purity and order.

'On the nature and origin of civil society, as on most other subjects, he thought for himself; and, at a period when mankind had scarcely begun to speculate on such subjects at all, he boldly traced the source of kingly power to the will of the people, and considered government as instituted for the benefit of the governed. Indeed a strong democratic tendency may be discovered in many passages of his work. . . . .

'Crowley's editions of the Visions are printed from a MS. of late date[1] and little authority, in which the division of the passus is extremely confused, and the whole distribution of the work perplexed[2]. Still, it must be confessed, that, with the advantage of better MSS.[3], the investigation of the general plan of these Visions is not without its difficulties. The work is altogether the most obscure in the English language, both with respect to phraseology[4], to the immediate connection of the author's ideas, and to the leading divisions of the subject. . . . .

'All these varieties [of text], however, bear marks, not of the same spirit and genius only, but of the same peculiar and original manner, so that it is scarcely to be conceived that they are interpolations of successive transcribers. Whatever be the cause, however, it may confidently be affirmed, that the text of no ancient work whatever contains so many various readings, or differs so widely from itself.

'To account for this phenomenon, however, in the penury, or rather in the absence of original information relating to the author, we are at liberty to suppose that the first edition of his work appeared when he was a young man, and that he lived and continued

---

[1] 'He describes it as bearing date A.D. 1409. Advert. to ed. 1550.'—*Whitaker's note.* But this calmly begs the whole question. Crowley's words (to be found below, at p. lxxiii) distinctly imply that the date A.D. 1409 appeared in an 'auncient copye' which 'it chaunced him to se' rather than in the one which he chose to print from. Besides, the B-text was not written till A.D. 1377.

[2] All pure assertion and assumption. I find nothing of the kind.

[3] For 'better' read 'later,' rather; since the C-text is later than the B-text. Besides, Whitaker's 'MS. B' (Phillipps 8252) is really late, confused, and bad.

[4] Not often in *phraseology*; Langland is plain-spoken enough. The meanings of nearly all the harder words which he uses have been well ascertained.

in the habit of transcribing to extreme old age. But a man of *his* genius would not submit to the drudgery of mere transcription; his invention and judgment would always be at work; new abuses, and therefore new objects of satire, would emerge from time to time: and as a new language began to be spoken, he might, though unwillingly, be induced to adopt its modernisms, in order to make his work intelligible to a second or third generation of readers[1]. In this last respect, however, it is not improbable that his transcribers might use some freedoms; for while we deny them invention to add, we may at least allow them skill to translate[2]. . . . . .

'The writer of these Visions had the first, though perhaps not the most splendid, qualification of a moral poet, an acute moral sense, with a vehement indignation against the abuses of public and the vices of private life; to this was added a keen sarcastic humour, and a faculty of depicting the manners of low life with an exactness and felicity, which have never been surpassed, but by the great satirist of the present day[3]. His conscience appears to have held the torch to his understanding, rather than the reverse. He judges of actions by feelings, more than by induction. His casuistry is sometimes miserably perplexed, and his illustrations very unhappy. The first of these defects is to be ascribed to his acquaintance with the schoolmen, the second to his ignorance of classical antiquity; in his views of morality an understanding naturally perspicuous was clouded by the one, while in his powers of adorning a subject, a taste perhaps naturally coarse was left wholly unpolished by the other. He often sinks into imbecility[4], and not unfrequently spins out his thread of allegory into mere tenuity. But, on other occasions, when aroused by the subject, he has a wildness of imagination, which might have deserved to be illustrated by the pencil of Fuseli, and a sublimity (more especially when inspired by the great mysteries of revelation) which has not been surpassed by Cowper.

---

[1] This is rather a bold suggestion, but it deserves consideration. There certainly seem to be indications of avoidance of unusual words in the latest version. Thus, the word *trielich*, which occurs in B. prol. 14, is avoided by a change in the text; and 3*erne* in B. vi. 299 becomes *deynteuosliche* in C. ix. 324.

[2] Instances of such translation occur in MS. Harl. 2376, and elsewhere.

[3] A footnote explains that the reference is to 'Dr. Crabb.'

[4] Not 'often.' There is a long passage in C. iv. 336-409, which we should *now* call very stupid; it may once have been highly thought of.

'He had a smattering of French, but no Italian. I have endeavoured in vain to discover in these Visions any imitations of Dante, whose Inferno and Purgatorio, in some respects, resemble them. But the boldness of those works, which the familiarity of the Italians with the vices of their Popes rendered tolerable, and even popular, beyond the Alps, would have appalled the courage of a tramontane satirist, and shocked the feelings of his readers, in the fourteenth century.

'To the author of these Visions has been ascribed by some Protestant writers an higher inspiration than that of the muse, and his famous prediction of the fall of the religious houses has invested him with the more sacred character of a prophet[1]. . . . There is just enough in this celebrated prediction, compared with its supposed fulfilment, to excite a momentary surprise.

'The erudition of Langland, if such were really the author's name, besides his Saxon literature, consisted in a very familiar knowledge of the Vulgate, and the schoolmen: the first of which he appears to quote from memory, as he frequently deviates from the letter of that version. . . . His citations from the schoolmen I am unable to trace[2].'

BY THOMAS WRIGHT.

In the Introduction to Wright's edition, the editor considers the consecutive political and religious movements of the Middle Ages, and discusses the determination of the commons of England to obtain a redress of grievances.

'It is not to be supposed that all the other classes of society were hostile to the commons. The people, with the characteristic attachment of the Anglo-Saxons to the family of their princes, wished to believe that the king was always their friend[3], when not actuated by the counsels of his evil advisers; several of the most powerful barons stood forward as the champions of popular liberty; and many of the

---

[1] B. x. 317–327; cf. p. xxxix above.
[2] I have found many, but not all of these; see the Notes. Langland quotes the Creeds (B. x. 238, xvi. 223; C. iv. 409, 484, xviii. 318, xx. 123, xxi. 116); some Latin hymns (C. xviii. 121, xx. 112, 133, 139, xxi. 166, 452, xxii. 210); Dionysius Cato (A. x. 95; B. vii. 150, x. 190, 339, xii. 23; C. ix. 339, x. 69, xiv. 214, 226, xxii. 297); Isidore (C. xvii. 201); St. Bernard, St. Augustine, St. Gregory, St. Jerome, Boethius, Vincent of Beauvais; &c.
[3] Cf. P. Pl. C. i. 148–150; iv. 381; v. 166, 184.

monks quitted their monasteries to advocate the cause of the reformation. . . . . .

'The poem was given to the world under a name which could not fail to draw the attention of the people. Amid the oppressive injustice of the great and the vices of their idle retainers, the corruptions of the clergy, and the dishonesty which too frequently characterised the dealings of merchants and traders, the simple unsophisticated heart of the ploughman is held forth as the dwelling of virtue and truth. It was the ploughman, and not the pope with his proud hierarchy, who represented on earth the Saviour who had descended into this world as the son of the carpenter, who had lived a life of humility, who had wandered on foot or ridden on an ass. "While God wandered on earth," says one of the political songs[1] of the beginning of the fourteenth century, "what was the reason that He would not ride?" The answer expresses the whole force of the popular sentiment of the age: "because he would not have a retinue of greedy attendants by His side, in the shape of grooms and servants, to insult and oppress the peasantry." . . . . .

'It will be seen that the Latin poems attributed to Walter Mapes[2], and the collection of Political Songs[3], form an introduction to the Vision of Piers Plowman. It seems clear that the writer was well acquainted with the former[4], and that he not unfrequently imitates them. The Poem on the Evil Times of Edward II (in the Political Songs)[5] contains within a small compass all his chief points of accusation against the different orders of society. But a new mode of composition had been brought into fashion since the appearance of the famous Roman de la Rose, and the author makes his attacks less directly, under an allegorical clothing. The condition of society is revealed to the writer in a dream, as in the singular poem just mentioned, and in the still older satire, the *Apocalypsis Goliæ*[6]; but in Piers Plowman the allegory follows no systematic plot, it is rather a succession of pictures in which the allegorical painting sometimes disappears altogether, than a whole like the

---

[1] Political Songs, ed. Wright, p. 240.
[2] Edited by T. Wright for the Camden Society.
[3] Edited by the same, for the same.
[4] See notes to B. prol. 139 (p. 15), C. xv. 193, C. xvi. 99, C. xx. 297; and the notes at pp. 303, 366 of the Early English Text Society's edition.
[5] Quoted in notes to C. iv. 184, v. 46, vi. 118, vi. 157, ix. 292.
[6] See note to B. prol. 139 (p. 15). The opening lines of Piers Plowman resemble the beginning of the *Apocalypsis Goliæ*.

Roman de la Rose, and it is on that account less tedious to the modern reader; while the vigorous descriptions, the picturesque ideas, and numerous other beauties of different kinds, cause us to lose sight of the general defects of this class of writings . . . . . .

'The writer of Piers Plowman was neither a sower of sedition, nor one who would be characterised by his contemporaries as a heretic. The doctrines inculcated throughout the book are so far from democratic, that he constantly preaches the Christian doctrine of obedience to rulers. Yet its tendency to debase the great, and to raise the commons in public consideration, must have rendered it popular among the latter; and although no single doctrine of the popish religion is attacked, yet the unsparing manner in which the vices and corruptions of the church are laid open, must have helped in no small degree the cause of the Reformation. Of the ancient popularity of Piers Plowman we have a proof in the great number of copies which still exist[1], most of them written in the latter part of the fourteenth century[2]; and the circumstance that the MSS. are seldom executed in a superior style of writing, and scarcely ever ornamented with painted initial letters, may perhaps be taken as a proof that they were not written for the higher classes of society. From the time when it was published, the name of Piers Plowman became a favourite among the popular reformers . . . .

'The poem of Piers Plowman is peculiarly a national work. It is the most remarkable monument of the public spirit of our forefathers in the middle, or, as they are often termed, dark ages. It is a pure specimen of the English language, at a period when it had sustained few of the corruptions which have disfigured it since we have had writers of "grammars"; and in it we may study with advantage many of the difficulties of the language which these writers have misunderstood.'

BY THE HON. G. P. MARSH.

In Mr. Marsh's lectures on the Origin and History of the English Language, 8vo., 1862, p. 296, we read as follows :—

'Every great popular writer is, in a certain sense, a product of his country and his age, a reflection of the intellect, the moral sentiment,

---

[1] Viz. forty-five.

[2] Many of them belong rather to the fifteenth century; but some of the oldest have perished, as we can tell by the corrupt copies of them.

and the prevailing social opinions of his time. The author of Piers Ploughman, no doubt, embodied in a poetic dress just what millions felt, and perhaps hundreds had uttered in one fragmentary form or another. His poem as truly expressed the popular sentiment, on the subjects it discussed, as did the American Declaration of Independence the national thought and feeling on the relations between the Colonies and Great Britain. That remarkable document disclosed no previously unknown facts, advanced no new political opinions, proclaimed no sentiment not warranted by previous manifestations of popular doctrine and the popular will, employed perhaps even no new combination of words, in incorporating into one proclamation the general results to which the American head and heart had arrived. Nevertheless, Jefferson, who drafted it, is as much entitled to the credit of originality, as he who has best expressed the passions and emotions of men in the shifting scenes of the drama or of song.

'The Vision of Piers Ploughman thus derives its interest, not from the absolute novelty of its revelations, but partly from its literary form, partly from the moral and social bearings of its subject—the corruptions of the nobility and of the several departments of the government, the vices of the clergy and the abuses of the church—in short, from its connection with the actual life and opinion of its time, into which it gives us a clearer insight than many a laboured history. Its dialect, its tone, and its poetic dress alike conspired to secure to the Vision a wide circulation among the commonalty of the realm, and by formulating—to use a favourite word of the day—sentiments almost universally felt, though but dimly apprehended, it brought them into distinct consciousness, and thus prepared the English people for the reception of the seed, which the labours of Wycliffe and his associates were already sowing among them [1]. . . .

'The Vision of the Ploughman furnishes abundant evidence of the familiarity of its author with the Latin Scriptures, the writings of the fathers, and the commentaries of Romish expositors, but exhibits very few traces of a knowledge of Romance literature [2]. Still the proportion of Norman-French words, or at least of words which, though of Latin origin, are French in form, is quite as great as in

---

[1] In other words, Long Will was certainly a *prophet*, a speaker-out.
[2] He knew something of French, and quotes three French proverbs; see B. x. 439, C. xiv. 205, xviii. 163.

the works of Chaucer[1]. The familiar use of this mixed vocabulary, in a poem evidently intended for the popular ear, and composed by a writer who gives no other evidence of an acquaintance with the literature of France, would, were other proof wanting, tend strongly to confirm the opinion I have before advanced, that a large infusion of French words had been, not merely introduced into the literature, but already incorporated into the common language of England; and that only a very small proportion of those employed by the poets were first introduced by them.

'The poem, if not altogether original in conception, is abundantly so in treatment. The spirit it breathes, its imagery, the turn of thought, the style of illustration and argument it employs, are as remote as possible from the tone of Anglo-Saxon poetry, but exhibit the characteristic moral and mental traits of the Englishman, as clearly and unequivocally as the most national portions of the works of Chaucer or of any other native writer.

'The Vision has little unity of plan, and indeed—considered as a satire against many individual and not obviously connected abuses in church and state—it needed none. But its aim and purpose are one. It was not an expostulation with temporal and spiritual rulers, not an attempt to awaken their consciences or excite their sympathies, and thus induce them to repent of the sins and repair the wrongs they had committed; nor was it an attack upon the theology of the Church of Rome, or a revolutionary appeal to the passions of the multitude. It was a calm, allegorical exposition of the corruptions of the state, of the church, and of social life, designed, not to rouse the people to violent resistance or bloody vengeance, but to reveal to them the true causes of the evils under which they were suffering, and to secure the reformation of those grievous abuses, by a united exertion of the moral influence which generally accompanies the possession of superior physical strength.'

BY DEAN MILMAN.

In Dean Milman's History of Latin Christianity, vol. vi. p. 536 (ed. 1855), occurs the following excellent passage.

'Before Chaucer[2], even before Wycliffe, appeared with his rude

---

[1] The Prologue to Piers the Plowman and the first 420 lines of Chaucer's Prologue alike contain 88 per cent. of Anglo-Saxon words. See Marsh, Lectures on English, 1st Series, p. 124.

[2] Hardly 'before' Chaucer; the two writers were contemporaries.

satire, his uncouth alliterative verse, his homely sense, and independence of thought, the author of Piers Ploughman's Vision. This extraordinary manifestation of the religion, of the language, of the social and political notions, of the English character, of the condition, of the passions and feelings of rural and provincial England[1], commences, and with Chaucer and Wycliffe completes the revelation of this transition period, the reign of Edward III. Throughout its institutions, language, religious sentiment, Teutonism is now holding its first initiatory struggle with Latin Christianity. In Chaucer is heard a voice from the court, from the castle, from the city, from universal England. All orders of society live in his verse, with the truth and originality of individual being, yet each a type of every rank, class, every religious and social condition and pursuit. And there can be no doubt that his is a voice of freedom, of more or less covert hostility to the hierarchical system, though more playful and with a poet's genial appreciation of all which was true, healthful, and beautiful in the old faith. In Wycliffe is heard a voice from the University, from the seat of theology and scholastic philosophy, from the centre and stronghold of the hierarchy; a voice of revolt and defiance, taken up and echoed in the pulpit throughout the land against the sacerdotal domination. In the Vision of Piers Ploughman is heard a voice from the wild Malvern Hills, the voice, it should seem, of an humble parson, or secular priest. He has passed some years in London, but his home, his heart is among the poor rural population of central Mercian England. . . . . Whoever he was, he wrote in his provincial idiom, in a rhythm perhaps from the Anglo-Saxon times familiar to the popular ear; if it strengthened and deepened that feeling, no doubt the poem was the expression of a strong and wide-spread feeling. It is popular in a broader and lower sense than the mass of vernacular poetry in Germany and England. . . .

'The Visionary is no disciple, no precursor of Wycliffe in his broader religious views: the Loller of [the author of] Piers Ploughman is no Lollard; he applies the name as a term of reproach for a lazy indolent vagrant. The poet is no dreamy speculative theologian; he acquiesces seemingly with unquestioning faith in the Creed and in the usages of the Church. He is not profane but reverent as to the Virgin and the Saints. Pilgrimages, penances, oblations on the

---

[1] We may certainly say also—of the lower classes in the city of London.

altar, absolution, he does not reject, though they are all nought in comparison with holiness and charity ; on Transubstantiation and the Real Presence and the Sacraments he is almost silent [1], but his silence is that of submission, not of doubt. It is in his intense absorbing moral feeling that he is beyond his age: with him outward observances are but hollow shows, mockeries, hypocrisies without the inward power of religion. It is not so much in his keen cutting satire on all matters of the Church as his solemn installation of Reason and Conscience as the guides of the self-directed soul, that he is breaking the yoke of sacerdotal domination; in his constant appeal to the plainest, simplest Scriptural truths, as in themselves the whole of religion, he is a stern reformer. The sad serious Satirist, in his contemplation of the world around him, the wealth of the world and the woe, sees no hope, but in a new order of things, in which if the hierarchy shall subsist, it shall subsist in a form, with powers, in a spirit totally opposite to that which now rules mankind. The mysterious Piers the Ploughman seems to designate from what quarter that Reformer is to arise [2]. . . .

'With Wycliffe, with the spiritual Franciscans, Langland ascribes all the evils, social and religious, of the dreary world to the wealth of the Clergy, of the Monks, and the still more incongruous wealth of the Mendicants. With them, he asserts the right, the duty, the obligation of the temporal Sovereign to despoil the hierarchy of their corrupting and fatal riches . . . With the Fraticelli, to him the fatal gift of Constantine was the doom of true religion; with them he almost adores poverty, but it is industrious down-trodden rustic poverty ; not that of the impostor beggar, common in his days, and denounced as sternly as by the political economy of our own, still less of the religious mendicant. Both these are fiercely excluded from his all-embracing charity.

'Langland is Antipapal, yet he can admire an ideal Pope, a general pacificator, reconciling the Sovereigns of the world to universal amity. It is the actual Pope, the Pope of Avignon or

[1] But see C. xx. 82–88.
[2] A sentence here follows, which is based on a misconception. The phrase 'Peers pardon the Plouhman' (C. xxii. 187) involves a very curious grammatical construction (not uncommon in Early English), and signifies 'the pardon of (*or* given by) Piers the Ploughman.' But Dean Milman treats it as a *proper name*, 'Piers-Pardon-Ploughman,' which it cannot possibly be. Elsewhere we have 'Peers bern the plouhman,' meaning *Piers the Ploughman's barn* (C. xxii. 360).

of Rome, levying the wealth of the world to slay mankind, who is the subject of his bitter invective. The Cardinals he denounces with the same indignant scorn; but chiefly the Cardinal Legate, whom he has seen in England riding in his pride and pomp, with lewdness, rapacity, merciless extortion, insolence in his train. Above all, his hatred (it might seem that on this all honest English indignation was agreed) is against the Mendicant orders. Of the older monks there is almost total silence. For St. Benedict, for St. Dominic, for St. Francis he has the profoundest reverence. But it is against their degenerate sons that he arrays his allegorical Host; the Friars furnish every impersonated vice, are foes to every virtue; his bitterest satire, his keenest irony (and these weapons he wields with wonderful poetic force) are against their dissoluteness, their idleness, their pride, their rapacity, their arts, their lies, their hypocrisy, their delicate attire, their dainty feasts, their magnificent buildings, even their proud learning; above all their hardness, their pitilessness to the poor, their utter want of charity, which with Langland is the virtue of virtues.

'Against the clergy he is hardly less severe; he sternly condemns their dastardly desertion of their flocks, when during the great plague they crowded to London to live an idle life; that idle life he describes with singular spirit and zest. Yet he seems to recognise the Priesthood as of Divine institution. Against the whole host of officials, pardoners, summoners, Archdeacons, and their functionaries; against lawyers, civil as well as ecclesiastical, he is everywhere fiercely and contemptuously criminatory.

'His political views are remarkable. He has a notion of a king ruling in the affections of the people, with Reason for his chancellor, Conscience for his justiciary. On such a king the commonalty would cheerfully and amply bestow sufficient revenue for all the dignity of his office, and the exigencies of the state, even for his conquests. No doubt that commonalty would first have absorbed the wealth of the hierarchy. He is not absolutely superior to that hatred of the French, nor even to the ambition for the conquest of France engendered by Edward's wars and his victories. And yet his shrewd common sense cannot but see the injustice and cruelty of those aggressive and sanguinary wars.'

After some remarks upon the language and the allegory of the poem (some of which require to be slightly modified to make them absolutely accurate), and a slight sketch of the general plan of the poem considered as a whole, Dean Milman sums up the whole matter in the following just words :—

'The poet who could address such opinions, though wrapt up in prudent allegory, to the popular ear, to the ear of the peasantry of England; the people who could listen with delight to such strains, were far advanced towards a revolt from Latin Christianity. Truth, true religion, was not to be found with, it was not known by, Pope, Cardinals, Bishops, Clergy, Monks, Friars. It was to be sought by man himself, by the individual man, by the poorest man, under the sole guidance of Reason, Conscience, and of the Grace of God, vouchsafed directly, not through any intermediate human being, or even Sacrament, to the self-directing soul. If it yet respected all existing doctrines, it respected them not as resting on traditional or sacerdotal authority. There is a manifest appeal throughout, an unconscious installation of Scripture alone, as the ultimate judge; the test of everything is a moral and purely religious one, its agreement with holiness and charity.'

It should be remembered that several of the above remarks apply in particular to the C-text, which Dr. Milman seems to have examined the most attentively, doubtless because it is the longest and fullest.

§ 13. FURTHER OBSERVATIONS.

There are several points about the poem which render caution on the reader's part very necessary, if he would avoid being misled. One is, that the effect of its double revision has been to introduce apparent anachronisms. Thus, when the poet speaks of Reason being set on the bench between the king and his son (A. iv. 32), he referred originally to Edward III. and the Black Prince, as the remark was made in 1362; but when the line was allowed to stand without change in the later versions (B. iv. 45, C. v. 43), as occurring in a part of the poem which was not very much altered, the allusion was lost, and it must be taken merely as a general expression signifying that Reason was placed in a seat of dignity. The usual date assigned to the poem, 1362, is very misleading; for all depends upon which form of the poem is in question. It was in hand and subject to variation during at least twenty or thirty years, the date 1362 expressing merely the time of its commencement. Hence Langland was, in fact, very much more nearly contemporaneous

HISTORICAL ALLUSIONS.

with Chaucer than has been supposed, and cannot fairly be said to have preceded him. A comparison between these two great writers is very instructive; it is soon perceived that each was, in a great measure, the supplement of the other, notwithstanding the sentiments which they had in common.

Chaucer describes the rich much more fully than the poor, and shews the holiday-making, cheerful, genial phase of English life; but Langland pictures the homely poor in their ill-fed, hard-working condition, battling against hunger, famine, injustice, oppression, and all the stern realities and hardships that tried them as gold is tried in the fire. Chaucer's satire often raises a good-humoured laugh; but Langland's is that of a man who is constrained to speak out all the bitter truth, and it is as earnest as the cry of an injured man who appeals to heaven for redress.

The reader should beware also of being much influenced by the mention of the Malvern Hills. One great merit of the poem is, that it chiefly exhibits London life and London opinions, which are surely of more interest to us than those of Worcestershire. He does but mention Malvern three times, and those three passages may be found within the compass of the first eight Passus of Text A (prol. 5, 88; viii. 130). But how numerous are his allusions to London! He not only speaks of it several times, but he frequently mentions the law-courts of Westminster; he was familiar with Cornhill, Cheapside, Cock Lane in Smithfield, Shoreditch, Garlickhithe, Stratford, Tyburn, and Southwark, all of which he mentions in an off-hand manner[1]. He mentions no river but the Thames, which is with him simply synonymous with river; for in one passage he speaks of two men thrown into the Thames, and in another he says that rich men are wont to give presents to the rich, which is as superfluous as if one should fill a tun with water from a fresh river, and then pour it into the Thames to render it wetter[2]. To remember the London origin of a large portion of the poem is the true key to the right understanding of it.

It is impossible to give here an adequate sketch of that portion of English history which the poem illustrates, but it is very important that its close connection with history should be ever borne in mind. I will merely adduce one instance of this, one to which Mr. Wright has well drawn attention, and upon which I would lay even more stress than he has done. I allude to the rebellion under Wat Tyler.

---

[1] See Index to Proper Names, p. 474.   [2] B. xii. 161; xv. 332.

HISTORICAL ALLUSIONS.

It is most evident that Langland himself was intensely loyal; if he would not reverence men whom he saw going about in rich clothing, he had a most profound reverence and even affection for the king. In the Prologue to his poem upon Richard II., whom he rates soundly and spares not, he commences with words of most tender and even touching remonstrance; it evidently goes to his heart that he should be compelled by a sense of duty to administer a severe reproof to 'his sovereign, whose subject he ought to be [1].' He nowhere recommends or encourages revolutionary ideas, but the contrary, and he never could have intended his words to have roused the flame of rebellion. But the outspoken manner of them was just that which delighted the populace; his exaltation of the ploughman was gladly seized upon, and his bold words were perverted into watchwords of insurgency. He had but lately elaborated his second text of the poem, when John Balle, 'the crazy priest,' wrote the following remarkable letter to the commons of Essex.—'John Schep, som tyme Seynt Marie prest of ȝorke, and nowe of Colchestre, greteth welle Johan Nameles, and Johan the Mullere, and Johan Cartere, and biddeth hem that thei ware of gyle in borugh, and stondeth togiddir in Goddis name, and biddeth *Peres Plouȝman* go to his werke, and chastise welle Hobbe the robber, and taketh with ȝou Johan Trewman, and alle his felaws, and no mo, and loke schappe [2] ȝou to on heued, and no mo.

> Johan the Muller hath ygrownde smal, smal, smal;
> The Kyngis sone of hevene shalle paye for alle.
> Be ware or ye be wo,
> Knoweth ȝour frende fro ȝoure foo,
> Haveth ynowe, and seythe "Hoo"; [3]
> And *do welle* and *bettre*, and fleth synne,
> And seketh pees, and holde therynne;
> And so biddeth Johan Trewman and alle his felawes.'

For writing which, John Balle was drawn, hung, and quartered, July 15, 1381, just one month after Wat Tyler had been cut down by Sir William Walworth. See Thomæ Walsingham Historia Anglicana, ed. Riley, vol. ii. p. 33. The reader will remark the mention, not only of *Peres Plouȝman*, but of *dowelle* and *bettre*;

[1] Rich. the Redeless, prol. 77; see vol. i. p. 605.

[2] I.e. draw together under one leader; lit. look (that ye) shape you to one head. The double *p* in *schappe* is written (as not unusually) in an abbreviated form. It has been misread as *scharpe*, and some not very clever people have held it up as an example of the use of the phrase 'look sharp' in the fourteenth century.

[3] Say 'stop!' i. e. desist.

besides which, the name of *Schep* (i. e. shepherd), was probably adopted from the second line of the prologue[1], and the name of *Trewman* was possibly suggested by Langland's Tomme *Trew-tonge* (B. iv. 17)[2].

Dr. Whitaker suggested that the poem is not perfect; that it must have been designed to have a more satisfactory ending, and not one so suggestive of disappointment and gloom. I am convinced that this opinion is erroneous; not so much because all the MSS. have here the word *Explicit*, but from the very nature of the case. What other ending can there be? or rather, the end is not yet. We may be defeated, yet not cast down; we may be dying, and yet live. We are all still pilgrims upon earth. *That* is the truth which the author's mighty genius would impress upon us in his parting words. Just as the poet awakes in ecstasy at the end of the poem of Do-bet, where he dreams of that which has been already accomplished, so here he wakes in tears, at the thought of how much remains to be done. So far from ending carelessly, he seems to me to have ceased speaking at the right moment, and to have managed a very difficult matter with consummate skill. On this point Professor Morley has the following remarks, in his Illustrations of English Religion, p. 101.

'So ends the Vision, with no victory attained; a world at war, and a renewed cry for the grace of God, a new yearning to find Christ, and bring with him the day when wrongs and hatreds are no more. Though in its latest form somewhat encumbered by reiteration of truths deeply felt, the fourteenth century yielded no more fervent expression of the purest Christian labour to bring men to God. And while the poet dwells on love as the fulfilment of the law— a loyal not a lawless love—he is throughout uncompromising in requirement of a life spent in fit labour, a life of Duty[3]. The sin that he makes Pride's companion, in leading the assault on Conscience, is Sloth[4]. Every man has his work to do, that should be fruit of love to God and to his neighbour[5]. For omitted duties or committed wrongs there is, in Langland's system, no valid repentance that does not make a man do all he can to repair the omission, right the wrong. Langland lays fast hold of all the words of Christ,

---

[1] I.e. of Texts A and B; see note to C. i. 2.
[2] See Lives of English Popular Leaders in the Middle Ages; Tyler, Ball, and Oldcastle; by C. E. Maurice, London, 1873.
[3] C. xiii. 79, 96, 116–119.   [4] C. xxiii. 163.   [5] C. xix. 9–14.

and reads them into a Divine Law of Love and Duty. He is a Church Reformer in the truest sense, seeking to strengthen the hands of the clergy by amendment of the lives and characters of those who are untrue to their holy calling. The ideal of a Christian Life shines through his poem, while it paints with homely force the evils against which it is directed [1].'

§ 14. Dialect of the Poem.

There can be little doubt that the true dialect of the author is best represented by MSS. of the B-text, and that this dialect was mainly Midland, with occasional introduction of Southern forms. The A-text was printed from the Vernon MS., as this seemed to be the best MS., upon the whole; none of the MSS. of that text being very satisfactory. But the Vernon MS. differs in dialect from almost all other copies of the poem; the scribe, who has written out a large number of other poems also, has turned everything into the Southern dialect. The MSS. of the C-text are mostly in a Midland dialect, but it is remarkable that many of them frequently introduce Western forms, as if the author's copy had been multiplied at a time when he had returned to the West of England. There seems to be a slight tendency to use the plural indicative suffix -*eth* instead of -*en* (1) at the end of a line, (2) when the word *that* precedes. In the Parallel Extracts printed for the Early English Text Society, the form *beoþ* (or *beþ*) occurs in 4 MSS., after the word *that*, though nearly all the rest read *that ben* or *that be* (A. iii. 67); but in direct narration, as in l. 71, a large number of MSS. read *þes are*, or *þese arn*. The same line ends with *þat most harm werchiþ* (or *worcheþ*, &c.) in twelve instances; yet the usual suffix is -*en*, which occurs here in a large number of MSS., both after *that* and at the end of a line; so that the use of -*eth* is, to some extent, capricious [2]. A thorough investigation of the dialect would fill a small volume [3]. I will just note, as one point of

[1] There are excellent articles upon Piers the Plowman in the New Englander, April, 1875, and in the National Review, October, 1861.

[2] A similar mixture of forms appears in MS. Harl. 2253. See Altenglische Dichtungen des MS. Harl. 2253, mit Grammatik und Glossar herausgegeben von Dr. K. Böddeker. The excellent grammar prefixed to this work explains a large number of the forms that occur in Piers Plowman.

[3] See 'William Langland; a Grammatical Treatise;' by E. Bernard, Bonn, 1874; where the grammatical forms are collected.

interest, that there is a very late example of the suffix *-ene* to denote the genitive plural in the expression *kingene kynge*, i. e. king of kings, in B. i. 105; and a still later one in *Iuwene ioye*, i. e. joy of the Jews, C. xxi. 268. All the curious forms that are of any interest, such as *rat* for *redeth*, i. e. reads, are duly recorded, with copious references, in the Glossarial Index.

Dr. Morris points out that there are some traces of Northern influence, which may have been due to the West Midland dialect. Examples are: *she* for *heo* (B. i. 10); *aren* for *ben* or *beoþ*, which is particularly marked in B. ix. 30, where the alliteration depends upon the use of it; *merke* for *derke*, B. i. 1; *laike*, B. prol. 172; *alkin*, B. prol. 222; *gare*, with its pt. t. *garte, gerte* (see Glossary); *graith gate*, i. e. direct road, B. i. 203; *barne*, i. e. child, B. ii. 3; *whas*, whose, B. ii. 18; *tyne*, to lose (see Glossary); &c.

There are also some infinitives in *-ie* or *-ye*, which the West Midland and Southern dialects had in common. Examples are: *tilie*, B. pr. 120; *shonye*, B. pr. 174; *cracchy*, B. pr. 186; *stekye*, B. i. 121; *louye*, B. i. 141; &c. It would thus appear that the dialect of Piers Plowman differs from that of Chaucer in belonging to the West rather than to the East of England.

There is one error in syntax worthy of remark, because it occurs rather often; viz. that the author sometimes uses a singular verb with a plural noun, especially the verb *is* or *was*. A clear example is in B. v. 99.

There is also a peculiarity of spelling which is very noticeable, and is particularly common in the B-text, viz. the use of a *mute* final *e* to denote the fact that the preceding vowel is long; precisely as in modern English. Thus *schope* is written for *schoop*, B. prol. 2; *wote* for *woot* or *wot* (with long *o*), B. prol. 43. This use of the mute final *e* is very unfortunate, as it can only be distinguished from the fully pronounced *e* by a thorough study of Middle-English phonology and grammar.

§ 15. The Metre of the Poem.

The metre is that known as *alliterative*, the only metre which in the earliest times was employed in Anglo-Saxon poetry. It also resembles the older kind of alliterative poetry in being entirely without rime. Poems thus composed may be printed either in short

ALLITERATIVE METRE.

lines or long ones, as is most convenient. I have adopted the system of long lines, as Early English poems in this metre and of this period are invariably written in long lines in the MSS., except when written continuously, as we write prose[1]. Every long line is divided into two short lines or half-lines by a pause, the position of which is marked in the MSS. by a point (sometimes coloured red), or by a mark resembling an inverted semi-colon, or, very rarely, by a mark resembling a paragraph mark (¶) or inverted D (◖), coloured red and blue alternately. In some MSS., but these are generally inferior ones, the mark is entirely omitted. It is also not infrequently misplaced. In the present volume the position of the pause is denoted by a raised full-stop, and the reader will find that it almost invariably points out the right place for a slight rest in reading, and in very many places is equivalent to a comma in punctuation. If we employ the term '*strong* syllable' to denote those syllables which are most strongly accented and are of greatest weight and importance, and '*weak* syllable' to denote those having a slighter stress [2] or none at all, we may briefly state the chief rules of alliterative verse, as employed by our author and other writers of his time, in the following manner.

1. Each half-line contains two or more *strong* syllables, two being the original and normal number. More than two are often found in the first half-line, but less frequently in the second.

2. The initial-letters which are common to two or more of these strong syllables being called the *rime-letters*, each line should have two *rime-letters* in the first, and one in the second half. The two former are called *sub-letters*, the latter the *chief-letter*.

3. The chief-letter should begin the *former* of the two strong syllables in the second half-line. If the line contain only two rime-letters, it is because one of the sub-letters is dispensed with.

4. If the chief-letter be a consonant, the sub-letters should be the same consonant, or a consonant expressing the same sound. If a vowel, it is sufficient that the sub-letters be also vowels; they need not be the same, and in practice are generally different. If the chief-letter be a combination of consonants, such as *sp*, *ch*, *str*, and the like, the sub-letters frequently present the same combination, although the recurrence of the first letter only would be sufficient.

---

[1] So written in MS. Digby 102.
[2] The secondary or slighter accents are often difficult to determine.

These rules are exemplified by the opening lines of the prologue (B-text) :—

'In a *s*ómer *s*éson · whan *s*óft was the *s*ónnë[1],
I *sh*ópe me in *sh*róudës · as I a *sh*épe wérë,
In *h*ábite as an *h*éremite · vn*h*óly of wórkës,
*W*ent w*y*́de in this *w*órld · *w*óndres to hérë.
Ac on a *M*áy *m*órnynge · on *M*álueme húllës
Me by*f*él a *f*érly · of *f*áiry, me thóu3të;
I was *w*éry for*w*ándred · and *w*ént me to réstë
V'nder a *b*ródë *b*ánkë · bi a *b*órnës sídë,
And ás I *l*áy and *l*énëd · and *l*ókëd in þe wáteres,
I *sl*ómbred in a *sl*épyng · it *sw*éyued so mérye.'

Line 1 has *s* for its rime-letter; the sub-letters begin *somer* and *seson*; the chief-letter begins *soft*. The *s* beginning *sonne* may be regarded as superfluous and accidental.

Line 2 shews *sh* used as a rime-letter. The syllables marked with a diæresis are to be fully sounded, and counted as distinct syllables. The *e* at the end of *shope* merely shews that the preceding *o* is long, and is not syllabic.

Line 3 is tolerably regular; it reminds us that the *vn-* in *vnholy* is a mere prefix, and that the true base of the word is *holy*, beginning with *h*.

In line 4, the initial *W* in *Went* is superfluous.

In line 5, two strong syllables, viz. *May* and the first of *mornynge*, come together. This is rare, and not pleasing.

In line 6, *by-* in *byfel* is a mere prefix; and so is *for-* in *forwandred* in line 7.

In line 8, the *b* in *bi* is unnecessary to the alliteration.

In line 9, the secondary stress upon *as* is hardly inferior in strength to the stress upon the strong syllables.

In line 10, the chief-letter is *s*, but the sub-letters exhibit the combination *sl*.

The true swing and rhythm of the lines will soon be perceived. A few variations may be noticed.

(*a*) The chief-letter may begin the *second* strong syllable of the second half-line; as,—

'Vn*k*ýnde to her *k*ýn · and to állë *c*rístene;' B. i. 190.

(*b*) Sometimes there are two rime-letters in the second half-line,

---

[1] The secondary accents, for the greater clearness, are *not marked*. In l. 1, they probably fell upon the words *In* and *was*; in l. 2, upon *me* and *I*.

ACCOUNT OF THE MANUSCRIPTS. lxi

and one in the first. Such lines are rare; I give an example from the A-text of the poem, ii. 112:—

'Týle he had *s*ýluer · for his *s*áwes and his *s*élynge.'

(*c*) The chief-letter is sometimes omitted; but this is a great blemish. Thus, in l. 34 of the Prologue (B-text), nearly all the MSS. have *synneles*, instead of *giltles*, which is the reading of MS. R. 3. 14 in Trinity College, Cambridge.

(*d*) By a bold license, the rime-letter is sometimes found at the beginning of *weak* or subordinate syllables, as in the words *for*, *whil*, in the lines:—

'Þanne I *f*ráinëd hir *f*áirë · *f*or hým þat hir mádë;' B. i. 58.

'And *w*ith hím to *w*ónye *w*ith *w*ó · *w*hil gód is in héuene;' B. ii. 106.

These last examples are among the instances which go to shew that Langland was not very particular about his metre. He frequently neglects to observe the strict rules, and evidently considered metre of much less importance than the sense. These remarks may perhaps suffice, since, for more perfect specimens of alliterative verse, the poems of the Anglo-Saxon period should be particularly studied.

I gladly take advantage of the present opportunity to recommend the careful work of Dr. Rosenthal upon Middle-English Alliterative Verse, entitled—'Die alliterierende englische Langzeile im xiv. Jahrhundert; von F. Rosenthal. Halle; 1877.' This work is founded upon eight alliterative poems, all of which have been published for the Early English Text Society. At pp. 35–46 he gives comparative tables to all three texts of Piers Plowman, shewing all the instances in which the alliteration of the A-text varies from the normal form, and indicating at the same time the corresponding lines (if any) in texts B and C. The comparison is continued to the point where the A-text ceases, and accordingly ends with B. x. 474 and C. xii. 296. These tables have been reprinted, by the author's kind permission, in the General Preface to the Early English Text Society's edition of the poem.

§ 16. BRIEF ACCOUNT OF THE MANUSCRIPTS.

The seventeenth publication of the Early English Text Society was my edition of 'Parallel Extracts from twenty-nine manuscripts of Piers Plowman,' published with the view of obtaining further information about the MSS. and their contents. This led to further

lxii   NAMES OF THE MANUSCRIPTS.

discoveries, and enabled me, at a later time, to describe many more than those there noticed, and at the same time to do so more fully.

Owing to the finding of new MSS., the 'roman' numerals assigned by me to the MSS. do not strictly express the correct order, when we come to compare the MSS. in the exactest manner possible. I arrange them below in such a way as to shew which MSS. are most closely related to each other, but retain, for convenience, the 'roman' numerals which I at first assigned to them. Many of the MSS. are also indicated, in the footnotes, by capital letters; and I now give tables, shewing which MSS. the 'roman' numerals and the capital letters represent.

Roughly speaking, nos. I–XII and nos. XLIV, XLV belong to the A-text.

Nos. XIII–XXVIII belong to the B-text.

Nos. XXIX–XLIII belong to the C-Text.

But this is only a first approximation to the real values of the MSS., and is only assumed for convenience. As a fact, some MSS. are of a *mixed* character. There is a set in which the former part belongs to the A-text, and the latter to the C-text; and another set in which the former part belongs to the C-text, and the latter part to the B-text. We thus get a more exact classification, as follows:

A-text.   Nos. I. II. IV. VI. VII. VIII. IX. XI. XII. XLV. (*Ten.*)
B-text.   Nos. XIII. XIV. XV. XV* (i. e. the lost MS. printed by Crowley). XVI. XVII. XVIII. XIX. XX. XXI. XXII. XXVI. XXVII. XXVIII. (*Fourteen.*)
C-text.   Nos. XXIX. XXX. XXXI. XXXII. XXXIII. XXXIV. XXXV. XXXVI. XXXVII. XXXVIII. XXXIX. XL. XLI. XLII. XLIII. (*Fifteen.*)
Mixed text; A and C.   Nos. III. V. X. XLIV. (*Four.*)
Mixed text; C and B.   Nos. XXIII. XXIV. XXV. (*Three.*)

NAMES OF THE MSS., AS NUMBERED.

   I. Vernon MS., Bodleian Library.   (A-text.)
  II. Harleian MS., no. 875; British Museum.   (A-text.)
 III. MS. Trin. Coll. Cam. R. 3. 14.   (*Mixed;* A and C.)
  IV. Univ. College, Oxford.   (A-text.)
   V. Harleian MS., no. 6041; B. M.   (*Mixed;* A and C.)
  VI. MS. Douce 323; Bodleian Library.   (A-text.)
 VII. MS. Ashmole 1468, Bodl. Library.   (A-text.)
VIII. Lincoln's Inn, London.   (A-text.)
  IX. Harleian MS., no. 3954; B. M.   (A-text.)

NAMES OF THE MANUSCRIPTS.   lxiii

    X. MS. Digby 145, Bodl. Library. (*Mixed;* A and C.)
   XI. MS. Rawlinson, Poet. 137, Bodl. Library. (A-text.)
   XII. MS. Trin. Coll. Dublin, D. 4. 12. (A-text.)
  XIII. MS. Laud Misc. 581, Bodl. Library. (B-text.)
  XIV. MS. Rawlinson, Poet. 38, Bodl. Library; 4 leaves of which are bound up in MS. Lansdowne 398, in the British Museum. (B-text.)
   XV. MS. Trin. Coll. Cam. B. 15. 17. (B-text; printed by Wright.)
  XV*. MS. printed by Crowley. (*Lost.*)
  XVI. Mr. Yates Thompson's MS. (B-text.)
 XVII. Ashburnham MS. no. 129. (B-text.)
XVIII. Oriel College, Oxford. (B-text.)
  XIX. MS. Camb. Univ. Library, Ll. 4. 14. (B-text.)
  XX. Ashburnham MS. no. 130. (B-text.)
  XXI. MS. Camb. Univ. Library, Gg. 4. 31. (B-text.)
 XXII. MS. Camb. Univ. Library, Dd. 1. 17. (B-text.)
XXIII. MS. Bodley 814, Oxford. (*Mixed;* C and B.)
XXIV. MS. Additional 10574; B. M. (*Mixed;* C and B.)
 XXV. MS. Cotton, Calig. A. xi; B. M. (*Mixed;* C and B.)
XXVI. Corpus Christi College, Oxford. (B-text.)
XXVII. Caius College, Cambridge. (B-text.)
XXVIII. MS. Phillipps 8252; at Cheltenham. (B-text.)
XXIX. MS. Phillipps 8231. (C-text.)
 XXX. MS. Laud 656; Bodl. Library. (C-text.)
XXXI. MS. Bodley 851. (C-text.)
XXXII. The Earl of Ilchester's MS. (C-text.)
XXXIII. MS. Cotton, Vesp. B. xvi; B. M. (C-text.)
XXXIV. MS. Camb. Univ. Library, Ff. 5. 35. (C-text.)
XXXV. MS. Corpus Christi Coll. Cambridge, no. 293. (C-text.)
XXXVI. MS. Camb. Univ. Library, Dd. 3. 13. (C-text.)
XXXVII. MS. Digby 171, Bodl. Library. (C-text.)
XXXVIII. MS. Douce 104, Bodl. Library. (C-text.)
XXXIX. MS. Digby 102, Bodl. Library. (C-text.)
 XL. Harleian MS., no. 2376; B. M. (C-text.)
XLI. MS. Trin. Coll. Dublin, D. 4. 1. (C-text.)
XLII. Royal MS., 18. B. xvii; B. M. (C-text.)
XLIII. MS. Phillipps 9056. (C-text.)
XLIV. The Duke of Westminster's MS. (*Mixed;* A and C.)
 XLV. MS. belonging to Sir Henry Ingilby, of Ripley Castle, Yorkshire. (A-text.)

LETTERS DENOTING VARIOUS MSS.

Some of the above MSS. are denoted in the footnotes and elsewhere by letters. In the A-text, the letters employed are V, H, T, U, H2, and D. They denote the first six MSS. (I to VI) in the above list, and are chosen as representing the words Vernon, Harley, Trinity, University, Harley, and Douce.

In the B-text, the letters employed are L, R, W, Y, O, C2, C, and B. They denote MSS. XIII–XVI, XVIII, XIX, XXII, and XXIII in the above list, and are chosen as representing the words Laud, Rawlinson, Wright[1], Yates-Thompson, Oriel, Cambridge (no. 2), Cambridge, and Bodley.

In the C-text, the letters employed are P, E, I, M, F, S, G, and K. (Also B and T, which, as being *mixed* texts, have been already mentioned.) These letters denote MSS. XXIX, XXX, and XXXII–XXXVII in the above list. Most of them can be remembered by connecting them with the word they are meant to symbolise; but a few are arbitrarily chosen. Thus P, I, M, K represent, respectively, Phillipps, Ilchester, Museum[2], Kenelm-Digby. F represents MS. Ff. 5. 35 (Camb. Univ. Library). S is the *last* letter of Corpus. Only E (=Laud 656), and G (=Camb. Univ. Dd. 3. 13) have no symbolic meaning. I have also, in my larger edition, used A to denote MS. Ashmole, and Z to denote MS. Bodley 851. I had intended to use N to denote MS. Harl. 2376, but it was not worth collating.

The above letters, when arranged in alphabetical order, are as follows.

A. MS. Ashmole; no. VII. (A-text.)
B. Bodley 814; no. XXIII. (*Mixed;* C and B.)
C. Cambridge; no. XXII. (B-text.)
C2. Cambridge (later MS.); no. XIX. (B-text.)
D. Douce 323; no. VI. (A-text.)
E. Laud 656; no. XXX. (C-text.)
F. Ff. 5. 35, in Camb. Univ. Library; no. XXXIV. (C-text.)
G. Dd. 3. 13, in the same; no. XXXVI. (C-text.)
H. Harl. 875; no. II. (A-text.)
H2. Harl. 6041; no. V. (*Mixed;* A and C.)
I. Ilchester; no. XXXII. (C-text.)

---
[1] Because Mr. Thomas Wright printed this Trinity MS. *in extenso.*
[2] The only good example of the C-text in the (British) Museum.

CLASSIFICATION OF THE MSS. lxv

K. Kenelm-Digby 171; no. XXXVII. (C-text.)
L. Laud Misc. 581; no. XIII. (B-text.) *Adopted as the text.*
M. Museum MS.; Cott. Vesp. B. xvi; no. XXXIII. (C-text.)
N. HarleiaN MS. 2376; no. XL. (C-text.)
O. Oriel MS.; no XVIII. (B-text.)
P. Phillipps MS. 8231; no. XXIX. (C-text). *Adopted as the text.*
R. { Rawlinson MS. Poet. 38. } no. XIV. (B-text.)
   { Lansdowne 398. }
S. CorpuS MS., Camb.; no. XXXV. (C-text.)
T. Trinity MS. R. 3. 14; no. III. (*Mixed*; A and C.)
U. University Coll., Oxford; no. IV. (A-text.)
V. Vernon MS., Oxford; no. I. (A-text.) *Adopted as the text.*
W. MS. printed by Wright; no. XV. (B-text.)
Y. Mr. Yates Thompson's MS.; no. XVI. (B-text.)
Z. MS. Bodley 851; no. XXXI. (C-text.)

I may add that Whitaker printed his edition from MS. P.

§ 17. CLASSIFICATION AND DESCRIPTION OF THE MSS.

A classification of the MSS. has lately been made by Dr. Richard Kron, with the title 'William Langley's Buch von Peter dem Pflüger.' His results agree, in the main, with my own, but he has examined the less important MSS. with greater care than I gave to them, as my object was only to discover the value of such as were most worth collating. I therefore follow his classification as regards the groups of MSS. of a similar type.

Text A; group *a*: I. II. Group *b*: XI. IV. XLV. XII. Group *c*: III. V. XLIV. VIII. X. Group *d*: VI. IX. VII.

Text B; group *a*: XIII. XVII. XIV. Group *b*: XV. (and XV*), XXVII. XX. Group *c*: XVIII. XIX. XXI. XVI. Group *d*: XXVI. XXVIII. Group *e*: XXII. Group *f*: XXIII. XXIV. XXV.

Text C; group *a*: XXIX. XXX. XL. Group *b*: XXXII. XXXVIII. XXXIX. (*partly* III. V. XLIV. X; *also* XXIII. XXIV. XXV.) Group *c*: XXXI. Group *d*: XXXVII. XXXIII. XXXIV. Group *e*: XXXV. XLI. XXXVI. XLII. Group *f*(?): XLIII.

I now give very brief descriptions of the MSS., in the order indicated in the above groups.

I.—Text A; group *a*. Printed as the Text, as far as A. xi. 180. Denoted by **V**.

MS. Vernon, in the Bodleian Library, Oxford. The best text, but imperfect at the end. It occasionally omits necessary lines. The dialect in which the poem was first written has been *modified by a Southern scribe*; whence the numerous Southern forms. After A. xi. 180, a leaf has been cut out of the MS., so that all that follows is lost. The leaves are large, and the writing is in double columns, so that each leaf contains about 320 lines.

II.—Text A; group *a*. Denoted in the footnotes by **H**.

MS. Harley 875; in the British Museum. Imperfect, having lost vi. 52–vii. 2, and all after viii. 144. It contains some lines not found in other copies; and agrees more closely than any other copy with MS. I. above.

XI.—Text A; group *b*. The only copy which contains the whole of Passus xii., and from which the text of that Passus is (mainly) printed.

MS. Rawlinson, Poet. 137; in the Bodleian Library. Many of its readings resemble those of MS. IV.; and it retains the passage x. 205–xi. 47, which is wanting in that MS.

IV.—Text A; group *b*. Denoted in the footnotes by **U**.

MS. no. 45 in the library of University College, Oxford. Some of the text is transposed, just as in MS. XI. (above). It is also remarkable as containing the first 19 lines of Passus xii. Oddly enough, the same MS. also contains a fragment of a *different* A-text (Pass. ii. 1–23).

XLV.—Text A; group *b*.

MS. in the possession of Sir Henry Ingilby, of Ripley Castle, Yorkshire. Remarkable as containing a large portion (1–88) of Passus xii. Five of the lines in this portion occur in no other copy; these are lines 65, 74–76, and 78.

XII.—Text A; group *b*. Not collated.

MS. Dublin D. 4. 12. Imperfect; ending at A. vii. 45. Some of the text is transposed, nearly as in MSS. XI. and IV. It closely resembles these MSS.; but is much corrupted here and there, whilst *the dialect has been turned into Northumbrian*.

III.—*Mixed text*; partly Text A; group *c*. Used to form the Text in A. xi. 181–303. Denoted in the footnotes by **T**. Contains also a portion of the C-text, viz. C. xii. 297 to the end.

MS. R. 3. 14 in the library of Trinity College, Cambridge. Apparently the oldest MS. of this (the largest) group. This MS. contains the drawing which is given as a frontispiece to Mr. T. Wright's edition of Piers Plowman. It represents two men ploughing with two oxen; one man holds the plough, and the other a goad.

V.—*Mixed text*; partly Text A; group *c*. Denoted in the footnotes by **H 2**. It contains also a portion of the C-text, viz. C. xii. 297 to the end.

MS. Harl. 6041. This MS. is noticed by Warton, in his History of English Poetry: and his conjecture, that it belongs to the earliest class, is perfectly right. It resembles the MS. just above, but is of inferior value.

XLIV.—*Mixed text*; partly A-text (slightly amplified); group *c*. Contains also C. xiii. 1 to the end.

MS. in the possession of the Duke of Westminster. The scribe frequently omits lines, but he also *inserts* lines, most of which, strangely enough, really belong to the B-text. Many of the readings are peculiar and corrupt. It bears a *general* resemblance to MS. III.

VIII.—Text A; group *c*. Not collated.

MS. no. 150 in Lincoln's Inn. It contains only the Prologue and Passus i-viii. The readings frequently agree with those of MS. III, but many corruptions have been introduced by the scribe's excessive love of alliteration. It seems to have been partly written out from memory, odd half-lines being supplied from the scribe's own head.

X.—*Mixed text*; partly A-text, amplified; group *c*. Not collated.

MS. Digby 145, in the Bodleian Library, Oxford. This is an amplification of the A-text, as it contains the 'council of the rats,' belonging to the Prologue of the B-text. In this respect it resembles MS. IX (below). It also contains C. xii. 297 to the end. It is a poor copy.

VI.—Text A; group *d*. Denoted in the footnotes by **D**.

MS. Douce 323, in the Bodleian Library. It follows MS. III. rather closely, but is full of gross blunders. It contains the Prologue, and Passus i-xi. Some of the matter is transposed; thus, in Passus i, the order is thus: lines 1-79, 143-167, 80-127 (128-142 *omitted*), 143-end.

IX.—Text A, amplified; group *d*. Not collated.

MS. Harley 3954, in the British Museum. It contains the 'council of the rats,' belonging to the Prologue of the B-text, in which respect it resembles MS. X.; with other amplifications. It ends with Passus xi. Several passages appear to have been corrupted.

VII.—Text A; group *d*. Not collated.

MS. Ashmole 1468, in the Bodleian Library. Imperfect at the beginning; begins at A. i. 142, and ends with Passus xi. In some readings it agrees with the preceding.

XIII.—Text B; group *a*. MS. adopted as the basis of the text, and denoted by **L**.

MS. Laud Misc. 581, in the Bodleian Library. The best copy of the B-text, carefully and minutely corrected. I believe there is no reason why it may not be the author's autograph copy. Wherever a slight mistake is left in the text, there is a mark at the side to call attention to it. In any case, it is our best authority.

XVII.—Text B; group *a*. Not collated.

MS. Ashburnham 129, now in the British Museum. This MS. closely agrees with the foregoing. It retains the passage (B. xvi. 56–91) which MS. XXII. and others omit.

XIV.—Text B; group *a*. Denoted by **R**.

MS. Rawlinson, Poet. 38, in the Bodleian Library. Four leaves of this MS. are bound up in MS. Lansdowne 398, in the British Museum, and contain B. prol. 125–i. 137. The first, second, seventh, and eighth leaves are lost, as also 8 leaves which contained B. xviii. 411–xx. 27. It frequently omits lines; but it also contains 160 lines not in other MSS. of the B-text, and is really a copy of the B-text *with later improvements and after-thoughts*, at any rate as regards these additional passages. The additional lines are printed in this edition, and duly noticed in the footnotes. See especially B. xi. 374–384, 419–421; xii. 57–59, 118–127, 152, 153; xiii. 164–171, 293–299, 400–409, 437–454; xiv. 227–237; xv. 239–243, 298, 299, 464–477, 539–556; &c. These lines are not in Wright's edition.

XV.—Text B; group *b*. Denoted by **W**.

MS. marked B. 15. 17 in the library of Trinity College, Cambridge: and printed *in extenso* by Mr. Wright. A remarkably good MS., and but slightly inferior to MS. XIII. It omits, here and there, about a dozen lines. It contains the line B. xiii. 49, which was omitted in Wright's edition by accident.

XV*.—Text B; group *b*.

MS. printed by Crowley in 1550, and now lost. Its text resembles that of XV. very closely. In one passage (v. 166) it has a singular addition.

DESCRIPTION OF THE MSS.   lxix

> Saint gregory was a good pope, & had a good forwyt
> That no priores were priest, for y^t he prouided
> Lest happeli they had had no grace, to hold harlatri in,
> For they are ticle of her tonges, & muste al secretes tel.

The two last lines are in no other copy, yet they may be genuine. The word *harlatri* is used in the sense of 'a scurrilous tale,' as in B. v. 413.

XXVII.—Text B; group *b*. A mere transcript, and not a good one, of Rogers's edition of 1561.

MS. no. 201 in the library of Caius College, Cambridge. Worthless.

XX.—Text B; group *b*. Not collated.

MS. Ashburnham 130, now in the British Museum. A faulty copy, with attempted 'corrections,' which seem to have been taken from Crowley's printed edition. The same MS. contains also a *fragment* of Piers Plowman, viz. B. ii. 208–iii. 72, which is quite distinct (and different) from the complete copy.

XVIII.—Text B; group *c*. Denoted by **O**.

MS. no. 79 in the library of Oriel College, Oxford. A neat and good copy, with very regular grammatical forms, in the Midland dialect. Four leaves have been unfortunately lost; the missing passages are B. xvii. 96–340 and xix. 276–355. It contains one remarkable variation; see footnote to p. 444.

XIX.—Text B; group *c*. Denoted by **C 2**.

MS. Ll. 4. 14 in the Cambridge University Library. Apparently copied from the Oriel MS. when perfect, thus preserving the passages which are wanting in that MS. It also contains the line noticed in the footnote to p. 444. Very serviceable for filling up the gaps in the preceding MS.

This same MS. contains the *unique* copy of Richard the Redeless. The whole MS. is in the same handwriting.

XXI.—Text B; group *c*. Not collated.

MS. Gg. 4. 31 in the Cambridge University Library. A late and sometimes faulty copy from a fair text, which has many readings in common with the MS. next described.

XVI.—Text B; group *c*. Denoted by **Y**.

MS. in the possession of H. Yates Thompson, Esq. A fair text, which has furnished some useful readings.

XXVI.—Text B; group *d*. Not collated.

MS. no. 201 in the library of Corpus Christi College, Oxford. It contains several additional lines, which are often spurious. The method of division of the poem into Passus differs from that of every other MS.

XXVIII.—Text B; group *d*. Not collated.

MS. Phillipps 8252 (formerly MS. Heber 1088). A somewhat *mixed* text, chiefly of the B-type, with some additions from the C-text, quite unlike those in MS. XIV. Not of much value.

XXII.—Text B; group *e*. Denoted by **C**.

MS. Dd. 1. 17 in the Cambridge University Library. A remarkable text, with frequent examples of Northern forms. It omits several lines, especially the passage B. xvi. 56–91. Yet it is well worth consulting. I have admitted into the text a few additional lines from this MS. These are: B. v. 273, 338, 569; vi. 49; xv. 224. They are all explanatory, and help to make the sense clearer or fuller. But I fear that they are not genuine, and I now think that they should have been excluded.

XXIII.—*Mixed Text*; partly Text B, group *f*; and partly Text C, group *b*. Denoted by **B**.

MS. Bodley 814 (Oxford). A disappointing MS.; it presents a combination of texts, the point of junction being somewhere about l. 121 of Pass. ii. (B). Before that point, it resembles the C-text, but afterwards approaches the B-text, with which, soon after the beginning of Passus iii., it agrees very closely down to the end of the poem. Many of the readings are quite corrupt.

XXIV.—*Mixed Text*; partly Text B, group *f*; and partly Text C, group *b*.

MS. Additional 10574, in the British Museum. Imperfect at the end. A duplicate of the preceding MS.

XXV.—*Mixed Text*; partly Text B, group *f*; and partly Text C, group *b*.

MS. Cotton, Caligula A. xi.; in the British Museum. An exact copy of either XXIII. or XXIV.; probably of the former.

XXIX.—Text C; group *a*. Printed at length, and denoted by **P**.

MS. Phillipps 8231 (formerly Heber 973). Printed (not without many mistakes) by Dr. Whitaker, and now reprinted. The best MS. of the C-type, but not always correct. Several of the worst misspellings have been corrected, the false forms being relegated to the footnote. The commonest error consists in the confusion of initial *w* with initial *wh*. We also find *e* miswritten for *o*, and *o* for *e*. There is a tendency to the use of Western grammatical forms.

XXX.—Text C; group *a*. Denoted by **E**.

MS. Laud 656, in the Bodleian Library. A neat MS.; almost a duplicate of the preceding.

XL.—Text C; group *a*. Not collated.

MS. Harl. 2376, in the British Museum. A faulty copy, with numerous alterations for the worse.

XXXII.—Text C; group *b*. Denoted by **I**.

MS. belonging to the Earl of Ilchester. A curious, imperfect, yet important MS. The text has been made up from two imperfect texts, an A-text and a C-text; some of the matter comes twice over; several leaves have been lost; the remaining ones have been misnumbered, and then bound up in the wrong order. Partly injured by rats. In C. xiii. 206, where a line required to complete the sense occurs in this MS. only, the rats have eaten away the latter half of it! The C-text part of this MS. seems to be, as it were, an *earlier draught* of that text, with fewer alterations than in most of the other MSS.

XXXVIII.—Text C; group *b*. Not collated.

MS. Douce 104, in the Bodleian Library. It abounds with rudely drawn pictures. The text resembles that of the preceding, but it is of the C-type throughout.

XXXIX.—Text C; group *b*. Not collated.

MS. Digby 102, in the Bodleian Library. The poem is written as prose, to save space; but the divisions into lines and half-lines are marked. Imperfect at the beginning. Begins at C. iii. 156. Resembles the preceding.

⁎ To this group belong the MSS. containing a mixed Text; whether the mixture be with an A-type or a B-type. These MSS. have been already described, and are as follows. *Mixed*: A and C: MSS. III, V, XLIV, X (see pp. lxvi, lxvii). *Mixed*: B and C: MSS. XXIII, XXIV, XXV (see p. lxx).

XXXI.—Text C; group *c*. Not collated; denoted by **Z**.

MS. Bodley 851 (Oxford). The text is a mixed one, and in several hands. The former part is mere rubbish, written out from imperfect recollection. But the latter part, beginning with C. Pass. xi., exhibits a very fair text.

XXXVII.—Text C; group *d*, influenced by a MS. of group *b*. Denoted by **K**.

MS. Digby 171, in the Bodleian Library. A good MS. as far as it goes, but imperfect both at the beginning and end. Begins at C. iii. 217; ends at C. xvi. 65.

XXXIII.—Text C; group *d*. Denoted by **M**.

MS. Cotton, Vespasian B. xvi, in the British Museum. One leaf is missing, which contained C. xix. 245–xx. 30. Some of the subject-matter has been transposed in Passus xviii. It supplies an important line, completing a sentence, viz. C. xviii. 116.

XXXIV.—Text C; group *d*, influenced by a MS. of group *e*. Denoted by **F**.

MS. Ff. 5. 35 in the Cambridge University Library. Imperfect; the missing passages are C. viii. 265–x. 181, and C. xiv. 94–xvi. 178. It often resembles the preceding, but has some peculiar and faulty readings. (I have given a transcript of this MS. to the British Museum.)

XXXV.—Text C; group *e*. Denoted by **S**.

MS. no. 293 in the library of Corpus Christi College, Cambridge. Imperfect; having lost C. ix. 268–xi. 94, C. xvi. 80–156, the whole of Pass. xvii, xviii, xix, xx, and xxi, and xxii. 8–323. Yet the text is good.

XLI.—Text C; group *e*. Not collated.

MS. D. 4. 1 in the library of Trinity College, Dublin. Resembles the text in the preceding.

XXXVI.—Text C; group *e*. Denoted by **G**.

MS. Dd. 3. 13 in the Cambridge University Library. Resembles the text in MS. XXXV (above). Many single lines are omitted, as well as the following passages, viz.; i. 1–153, xiv. 227–xv. 40, xvi. 288–xvii. 41, and xxiii. 40–386.

XLII.—Text C; group *e*. Not collated.

MS. Bibl. Reg. 18. B. xvii. in the British Museum. Resembles the above.

XLIII. Text C; group *f* (?). Not collated.

MS. Phillipps 9056 (formerly MS. Heber 974). It has lost 42 lines at the end. A good deal spoiled by damp. Of the C-type; but its exact value is doubtful. It was probably never a good copy.

§ 18. DESCRIPTION OF THE PRINTED EDITIONS (B-TEXT).

Of the earliest printed editions by Robert Crowley, there are certainly three different impressions, all printed in one year, viz. in 1550.

(*a*) The first impression has on the title-page—'THE VISION of Pierce Plowman, now fyrste imprynted by Roberte Crowley, dwellyng

EDITIONS BY R. CROWLEY. lxxiii

in Ely rentes in Holburne. Anno Domini. 1505.[1] Cum priuilegio ad imprimendum solum.' It contains 117 leaves, not including the title or the leaf on which is the printer's address to the reader, or 119 leaves in all. The signature of Fol. cxvii. is Gg 1. Copies are rather scarce; there are, however, two in the British Museum, of which the one, on paper, was once the property of Thomas Tyrwhitt, and the other, on vellum, is in the Grenville collection. The most interesting part of it is Crowley's address, which is worth reprinting here. It is as follows.

'The Printer to the Reader.

BEynge desyerous to knowe the name of the Autoure of this most worthy worke (gentle reader) and the tyme of the writynge of the same : I did not onely gather togyther suche aunciente copies as I could come by, but also-consult such mē as I knew to be more exercised in the studie of antiquities, then I my selfe haue ben. And by some of them I haue learned that the Autour was named Roberte langelande, a Shropshere man borne in Cleybirie, aboute viii. myles from Maluerne hilles.[2]

For the time when it was written : it chaunced me to se an aunciente copye, in the later ende wherof was noted, that the same copye was written in the yere of oure Lorde .M.iiii.C. and nyne,[3] which was before thys presente yere, an hundred & xli. yeres. And in the seconde side of the .lxviii. leafe of thys printed copye, I finde mētion of a dere yere, that was in the yere of oure Lorde, M.iii. hundred and .L.[4] Iohn Chichester than beynge mayre of London. So that this I may be bold to reporte, that it was fyrste made and wrytten after the yeare of our lord .M.iii.C.L. and before the yere .M,iiiiC, and .ix which meane spase was .lix yeres. We may iustly cōiect therfore y^t it was firste written about two hundred yeres paste, in the tyme of Kynge Edwarde the thyrde. In whose tyme it pleased God to open the eyes of many to se hys truth,

---

[1] An evident mistake for 1550. Neither Lowndes nor Hazlitt seem to have observed this singular misprint; but see Ames, Typogr. Antiq. ii. 758.

[2] Without doubt, Crowley's authority was John Bale. I consider the distance from Cleobury Mortimer to the Malvern Hills to be rather a long 'eight miles.'

[3] An important statement, and a very probable one. MS. Douce 104 (C-type) is dated in the sixth year of Henry VI., i.e. 1427 or 1428.

[4] Crowley's MS. was wrong, Chichester was mayor in 1370. The right reading in B. xiii. 270 is 'twies *thretty* and ten'; but Crowley has *twenty* for *thretty* (30).

geuing them boldenes of herte, to open their mouthes and crye oute agaynste the worckes of darckenes, as did Iohn wicklefe, who also in those dayes translated the holye Bible into the Englishe tonge, and this writer who in reportynge certaine visions and dreames, that he fayned him selfe to haue dreamed: doeth moste christianlye enstruct the weake, and sharply rebuke the obstinate blynde. There is no maner of vice, that reigneth in anye estate of men, whiche this wryter hath not godly, learnedlye, and wittilye, rebuked. He wrote altogyther in miter; but not after ye maner of our rimers that write nowe adayes (for his verses ende not alike) but the nature of hys miter is, to haue thre wordes at the leaste in euery verse whiche beginne with some one letter. As for ensample, the firste two verses of the boke renne vpon .s. as thus.

> In a somer season whan sette[1] was the Sunne,
> I shope me into shrobbes, as I a shepe were.

The next runneth vpon .H. as thus.

> In habite as an Hermite vnholy of werckes. &c.

This thinge noted, the miter shal be very pleasaunt to read. The Englishe is according to the time it was written in, and the sence somewhat darcke, but not so harde, but that it may be vnderstande of suche as will not sticke to breake the shell of the nutte for the kernelles sake.

As for that is written in the .xxxvi. leafe of thys boke concernynge a dearth thē to come: is spokē by the knoweledge of astronomie as may wel be gathered bi that he saith, Saturne sente him to tell[2] And that whiche foloweth and geueth it the face of a prophecye: is lyke to be a thinge added of some other man than the fyrste autour. For diuerse copies haue it diuerslye. For where the copie that I folowe hath thus.

> And when you[3] se the sunne amisse, & two[4] monkes heades
> And a mayde haue the maistrye, and multiplie by eyght.[5]

[1] A convincing proof to me that Crowley's MS. had *softe*, which he misread. The old form of the past participle was *set*, not *sette*.

[2] See B. Pass. vi. 327–329; p. 222.

[3] Of course his MS. had *ye* in the *nominative*; accordingly, in the text itself, he printed *ye*.

[4] The second impression reads *thre* here, but both impressions read *two* in the passage as it stands in his text.

[5] In the text itself, the first impression has *eight*, but later impressions have *hight*.

Some other haue
Three shyppes and a shefe, wyth an eight folowynge
Shall brynge bale and battell, on both halfe the mone.[1]

Nowe for that whiche is written in the .l, leafe, cōcerning the suppression of Abbaies : the scripture there alledged, declareth it to be gathered of the iuste iudgment of god, whoe wyll not suffer abomination to raigne vnpunished.[2]

Loke not vpon this boke therfore, to talke of wonders paste or to come, but to amende thyne owne misse, which thou shalt fynd here moste charitably rebuked. The spirite of god gyue
the grace to walke in the waye of truthe,
to Gods glory, & thyne owne
soules healthe.
So be it.'

The first impression has a few marginal notes, but these are far less numerous than in the later impressions.

(*b*) The second and third impressions are both said to be 'nowe the seconde time imprinted,' so that it is not easy to say which was printed first, nor can we be quite sure that the copies are always bound up rightly. Indeed, it is clear that quires of one impression are sometimes supplemented by quires from the other. But it is certain that the true *second* impression is that which resembles the first most nearly, and the right title-page runs as follows :—' The vision of Pierce Plowman, nowe the seconde time imprinted by Roberte Crowley dwellynge in Elye rentes in Holburne. Whereunto are added certayne notes and cotations in the mergyne, geuynge light to the Reader, &c. .... Imprinted at London by Roberte Crowley, dwellyng in Elye rentes in Holburne. The yere of our Lord .M.D.L. Cum priuilegio ad imprimendum solum.' And on the last page, we find in the third line (Pass. xx. 381) the words *Fryers* and *finding*, as in the first impression, and the colophon begins with ' Imprinted.' There is a copy of this description in the British Museum, marked 1077 g 2, and another is in Heber's Catalogue; Part IX. no. 1717.

(*c*) In that which is really a *third* impression, the title-page is almost exactly the same, but the name of the printer is spelt 'Crowlye' where it first occurs. On the last page, we find *Friers*

---

[1] A clear proof that Crowley also had access to a MS. of the C-type : see C ix. 351 ; p. 225. It is odd that he noticed only this one variation.

[2] B. Pass. x. 317-327.

and *findinge* instead of *Fryers* and *finding*, and the colophon begins with 'Imprynted,' spelt with *y*. There is a copy of this description in the British Museum, marked 11623 *c*, and another in the library of King's College, Cambridge;[1] see also Heber's Catalogue; Part IX. no. 1716.

But all three impressions are much alike. The chief differences are, that the two later impressions have many more marginal notes, a few additional lines,[2] and also 6 extra leaves between the printer's preface and the poem itself, containing a brief argument or abstract of the prologue and of each of the Passus.[3] The first impression is the most correct; also the third impression is much less correct than the second, and considerably inferior to it.

(*d*) The next edition was by Owen Rogers, in 1561. The title is—'The Vision of Pierce Plowman, newlye imprynted after the authours olde copy, with a brefe summary of the principall matters set before euery part called Passus. Wherevnto is also annexed the Crede of Pierce Plowman, neuer imprinted with the booke before.[4] ¶ Imprynted at London, by Owen Rogers, dwellyng neare vnto great Saint Bartelmewes Gate, at the sygne of the spred Egle. ¶ The yere of our Lorde God, a thousand, fyue hundred, thre score and one. The .xxi. daye of the Moneth of Februarye. Cum priuilegio ad imprimendum solum.' This is a careless reprint of Crowley's *third* issue, and is almost worthless. It omits some lines, as e.g. Pass. i. 39, which Crowley retains. The 'Crede,' though mentioned in the title-page, is not always found in the volume.

(*e*) 'The vision and the creed of Piers Ploughman; newly imprinted.' Edited by Thomas Wright, M.A., F.S.A., &c. In two volumes. London: William Pickering. 12mo; 1842.

(*f*) The same; second and revised edition. London: J. R. Smith. 12mo; 1856.[5]

---

[1] I had a copy of my own (now given to the Cambridge University Library), which differs from the Museum copy in the title-page, and throughout quire D. This copy has a wrong title-page, but in quire D it is the B. M. copy that is at fault.

[2] Some (after B. prol. 215) are from an A-text, and some from a B-text not of group *a*. By observing these, and note 1 on the last page, we see that Crowley had access to *four MSS. at least.*

[3] The only thing that calls for remark here is that Crowley, in making an abstract of Pass. viii., identifies 'Pierce' with the dreamer, a blunder which has lasted ever since, and may last a long while yet.

[4] It had been imprinted by Wolfe in 1553, but not 'with the booke.'

[5] It may seem superfluous to say anything here concerning Mr. Wright's well-

THE LOST MANUSCRIPT.

Tyrwhitt has expressed an opinion (note 57 to Essay on the Language of Chaucer) that Crowley's edition was 'printed from so faulty and imperfect a MS. that the author, whoever he was, would find it difficult to recognize his own work.' On the other hand, Mr. Wright observes (Introd. to P. Pl. 2nd ed. p. xxxvi) that 'it is clear that Crowley had obtained an excellent manuscript.' Yet the two statements are easily reconciled, for the 'faultiness and imperfection' which Tyrwhitt justly attributes to Crowley's edition are clearly the result of his inability, in numerous instances, to read the text correctly. After collating Crowley's edition throughout (many of the results of which collation are given in my larger edition), it becomes manifest that the frequent blunders are Crowley's own, and his MS. must have been extremely good, even better at times, I venture to think, than the one which Mr. Wright has printed. For instance, it preserved prol. 170, ii. 186, v. 90, xviii. 361, xix. 86, and xx. 299, which MS. W. omits, although it had, in common with that MS., lost i. 145, xii. 105, and xv. 367. It is therefore to be regretted that Crowley's MS. has not yet been found.

In B. v. 167, his edition has *prouided*[1] instead of *ordeigned*; and after this line two new lines are introduced, which have been already once quoted at p. lxix above, viz.—

> Lest happeli they had had no grace, to hold harlatri in,
> For they are ticle of her tonges, & muste al secretes tel.

The two last lines are in no other copy, yet I do not think Crowley invented them, as there is no other instance, at least, of his having added to his text.[2] By this extra line, and by the list of lines above which it has preserved and lost, it may easily be identified, if found.[3]

Having had occasion to read Mr. Wright's *second* edition many times over, at the same time that I have been consulting the MS. which he used, I have observed a few trivial misprints, and I here give a list of them, rather for the sake of completeness than because

---

known and excellent edition; but it would hardly be just not to confess my *very great* obligations to it. Without its help my work would, at the least, have been doubled.

[1] This word *prouided* is perhaps a better reading than is furnished by any other copy. It keeps up the alliteration, and strikes one as being right.

[2] In three instances only, he falsifies his text of set purpose: viz. in vii. 156, xii. 87, and xiii. 159.

[3] Crowley has also two lines in Passus iii., viz. after l. 30 and l. 161 respectively, which appear nowhere else.

they are of any importance. I refer to the *lines*, as numbered in his editions, and mark with an asterisk those lines which are *correctly* printed in his *first* edition.

935*. Read *fructum.* 1341. For *pennes* read *thennes* (*þennes* in MS.). 1465. Insert *a* after *is.* 1957. Read *sergeant.* 2045. For *Leve* read *I leve.* 2257. For *nowe* read *mowe.* 2418. For *at* read *al.* 2505. For *the* read *ye.* 2701*. Read *herof.* 2865. Read *al to-torn.* 3233. Read *And.* 3383. Read *no gilt.* 3387. Read *avow* (MS. *auow*). 3522. After *tuam* add *deus.* 3555*. Read *Synay.* 3559. For *and* read *in.* 3619. For *helpe* read *helthe* (MS. *helþe*). 3807. After *in* insert *a.* 3949. Read *Quia.* 4008. For *his* read *this* (MS. *þis*). 4242. Read *portate.* 4272. Read *pro.* 4465*. For *her* read *her-of.* 5064. Read *is not dronkelewe.* 5108*. For *the* read *be.* 5158*. Read *is it.* 5384*. Read *minuentur.* 5553. For *or* read *on.* 5684*. Read *for.* 6168. Read *To salve* (MS. *to salue*). 6186. Read *mansede* (as directed in Mr. Wright's note). 6188. After *That* insert *al.* 6234. Read *Be hemself.* 6378. Read *gaf.* 6561. For *And* read *But.* 6654. For *and* read *quod.* 6667. For *Ne* read *No* (MS. *no*). 6781. Read *The defaute* (MS. *þe defaute*). 7134*. For *ne* read *no.* 7141. Read *discerne.* 7292. For *and* read *I.* 7625. Read *Nolite judicare, et non.* 8103*. Read *Edentes.* After l. 8127 (ending *pœnitentiam*) insert—And siththe he broughte us drynke *Dia perseverans.* [Compare B. xiii. 49.] 8776*. For *Of* read *Or* (MS. *or*). 8801*. For *Nor* read *For* (MS. *for*). 8915. Read *God or.* 8936. After *wasshen* insert *it.* 9192*. For *many* read *may.* 9207. Read *De deliciis.* 9566. Omit *no* after *do.* 10233*. Read *Founde.* 10265*. For *Fo* read *To* (MS. *to*). 10515. For *now* read *mow.* 11451*. Omit the third *to.* 12854*. Omit *the.* 13082. For *so* read *se.* 13946*. Read *And nede ne.* 13966. Read *So Nede at.* 14311*. For *hande* read *hadde.*

In most of the Latin quotations, Mr. Wright has purposely made the spelling conform with the usual mode, printing *sed* for *set, commodat* for *comodat, scintilla* for *sintilla,* and the like. There are also a few places where a question of editing arises. Thus, we should certainly read *bonched,* not *bouched* (147), *y-houted,* not *y-honted* (1318), *wyuen* not *wynen* (2530), *solue,* not *solne* (3319), *lenen,* not *leven* (3826), *lene,* not *leve* (4240), *meue,* not *mene* (5836), *meuestow,* not *menestow* (6149), *engreynen,* not *engreyven* (8941). The MS. can, of course be read either way. It is the old difficulty of having to decide between *n* and *u.*

EDITION BY DR. WHITAKER. lxxix

(g) The only edition of Piers the Plowman which exhibits the C-text is Dr. Whitaker's. The Title-page of the volume is as follows:—

'𝔙𝔦𝔰𝔦𝔬 𝔚𝔦𝔩𝔩𝔦 𝔡𝔢 𝔓𝔢𝔱𝔯𝔬 𝔓𝔩𝔬𝔲𝔥𝔪𝔞𝔫, 𝔍𝔱𝔢𝔪 𝔙𝔦𝔰𝔦𝔬𝔫𝔢𝔰 𝔢𝔧𝔲𝔰𝔡𝔢𝔪 𝔡𝔢 𝔇𝔬𝔴𝔢𝔩, 𝔇𝔬𝔟𝔢𝔱, 𝔢𝔱 𝔇𝔬𝔟𝔢𝔰𝔱. 𝔒𝔯 𝔗𝔥𝔢 𝔙𝔦𝔰𝔦𝔬𝔫 𝔬𝔣 𝔚𝔦𝔩𝔩𝔦𝔞𝔪 𝔠𝔬𝔫𝔠𝔢𝔯𝔫𝔦𝔫𝔤 𝔓𝔦𝔢𝔯𝔰 𝔓𝔩𝔬𝔲𝔥𝔪𝔞𝔫, 𝔞𝔫𝔡 𝔗𝔥𝔢 𝔙𝔦𝔰𝔦𝔬𝔫𝔰 𝔬𝔣 𝔱𝔥𝔢 𝔰𝔞𝔪𝔢 𝔠𝔬𝔫𝔠𝔢𝔯𝔫𝔦𝔫𝔤 𝔱𝔥𝔢 𝔒𝔯𝔦𝔤𝔦𝔫, 𝔓𝔯𝔬𝔤𝔯𝔢𝔰𝔰, 𝔞𝔫𝔡 𝔓𝔢𝔯𝔣𝔢𝔠𝔱𝔦𝔬𝔫 𝔬𝔣 𝔱𝔥𝔢 ℭ𝔥𝔯𝔦𝔰𝔱𝔦𝔞𝔫 𝔏𝔦𝔣𝔢. Ascribed to Robert Langland, a Secular Priest of the county of Salop; and written in, or immediately after, the year MCCCLXII. Printed from a MS. contemporary with the author, collated with two others of great antiquity, and exhibiting the original text; together with an introductory discourse, a perpetual commentary, annotations, and a glossary. By Thomas Dunham Whitaker, LL.D. F.S.A., Vicar of Whalley, and Rector of Heysham, in Lancashire. [Motto] Vatis hic noster in seculo suo doctissimus, et acerrimus morum vindex, clericis, quos in omnibus satyris, ipso summo pontifice non intacto perstringit; clericis inquam utriusque nominis, quid propter peccata eorum, hypocrisin, avaritiam, luxum, terrenorum cupidinem, defectum charitatis, beneficiorum et redituum abusum, desidiam et turpem gregum neglectum in postero tempore eventurum erat, prædixit. HICKES.[1]—London: printed for John Murray, Albemarle Street. MDCCCXIII.'[2]

The Dedication runs thus:—'To Richard Heber, Esq. of Hodnet, in the County of Salop, this edition of the first English Satirist, his old and spirited countryman, is inscribed,' &c., &c. The Contents of the book are: Introductory Discourse, pp. i–xlviii; Errata, p. xlix; additional Note, p. li; Text, in black letter, with Paraphrase below it, pp. 1–412 (pp. 265 and 266 being unrepresented, owing to a mistake in the pagination; since sheet Ll ends with p. 264, and sheet Mm begins with p. 267); Notes, pp. 1–18; Glossary, pp. 21–31. Printer's name, John Harding, St. John's Square, London.

It will be necessary to say a few words more upon the various parts of the book.[3]

---

[1] Hickesii Thesaurus, i. 107.

[2] Together with the particular copy of the work in my possession there came into my hands several additional particulars, including prospectus, printer's bills, &c. It thus appears that it was published by subscription, the number of subscribers (whose names are given) being two hundred, at five guineas apiece; increased to seven guineas for such copies as came into public sale. It was got up in so expensive a manner that the mere cost of printing, exclusive of woodcuts and binding, was £401 6s. 7d. It is of quarto size, and printed on very stout paper.

[3] The following mendacious and spiteful note upon Whitaker's edition appears

Title-page. This contains several errors. There is no reason for calling the author Robert, since he so often calls himself William. Again, the text written in or soon after A.D. 1362 was the A-text; the C-text must be some thirty years later. Consequently, Whitaker's edition does not exhibit 'the original text,' but the text as it stood after two recensions. Neither is Whitaker's text really 'collated' with two other MSS.; the readings cited in the Notes from his 'MS. B' are not more than fifty, and those from 'MS. C' not more than twenty.

Introductory Discourse. The general contents of this may be thus summarised. State of England in the reign of Edward III., pp. i, ii; Chaucer and Langland, pp. iii–v; Dialect of Langland is 'Mercno-Saxon,' pp. vi, vii; Alliterative poetry, pp. viii–x; Runic prosody, pp. xi, xii; Cædmon's metre, pp. xiii, xiv; Runic rhyme, p. xv; Ormulum and 'Moral Ode,' p. xvi; 'Pistill of Susan,' p. xvii; Langland not a Wickliffite, p. xviii; Date of Piers the Plowman, p. xix; Brief abstract of the Poem, pp. xx–xxx; MSS. of the Poem, pp. xxxi–xxxiii; Parallel Extracts from MS. A [Phillipps 8231], MS. B [Phillipps 8252],[1] MS. C [Oriel MS.],[2] and Crowley's print of 1550, the passage chosen being the description of Wrath [C. vii. 103–128],. pp. xxxiv, xxxv; Langland's powers as a satirist, pp. xxxvi–xxxix; Extreme obscurity of Langland's diction, p. xl; Concluding Remarks, p. xli; Testimonies of Authors concerning Langland, pp. xlii–xlviii; Errata, p. xlix; Note on the Ormulum and Jack Upland, p. li.

Of this discourse, there is not much that is still of value; the remarks on the Dialect have been superseded by the labours of Dr. Morris and others; those on Alliterative Poetry by Dr. Guest's History of English Rhythms, Mr. Sweet's Sketch of the History of

---

(as a quotation) in Lowndes, and has been reprinted in booksellers' catalogues over and over again, and will probably often be reprinted in the future whenever a copy of Crowley's edition occurs for sale. 'The value of the old editions is not at all lessened by the reprint of Dr. Whittaker (*sic*), as he carefully suppressed all the passages relating to the indecent lives and practices of the Romish clergy.' The fact is that Dr Whitaker suppressed nothing but a very few coarse lines which have no special reference to the 'Romish clergy.' Neither is the implied charge against Langland a fair one; he certainly would have had no sympathy with prurient hunters up of filth.

[1] The extract shows that this MS. is a mere jumble of texts, and almost without any value. See description of MS. XXVIII; p. lxx, l. 4.

[2] Whitaker's extract from this MS. (no. XVIII) contains many errors.

Anglo-Saxon Poetry, prefixed to Hazlitt's edition of Warton's English Poetry, my own Essay prefixed to vol. iii. of the edition of the Percy Folio MS. by Hales and Furnivall, &c.; whilst a great deal more than was known to Whitaker can be learnt from the since-published editions of the Ormulum, the Moral Ode, the Pistill of Susan, and the like. The *date* of the Poem he put down as 1362, though that is really the date of the A-text only; and, in considering his own text as of earlier date than Crowley's, he is now easily seen to have been wrong. His remarks on the extreme obscurity of Langland's diction are of a piece with his own evident difficulty in understanding it, and were caused, in a great measure, by his misreadings of the MS. The passages that are *really* obscure are singularly few. His concluding remarks contain the following interesting passage :—

'He [the editor] wishes to conciliate no favour to the work, by lamenting that it was undertaken in the languor of bad health, or that it was only prosecuted in the intervals of leisure which an active and occupied life allowed: both the facts, indeed, are true; but these, if likely to have injured the work in any material degree, were reasons why it ought not to have been begun; if otherwise, they will not contribute to lessen its actual defects. In short, he is ready to confess that, for the space of two years, it has received from him attention sufficient to have rescued it from very gross imperfections, and consequently, that its faults of this degree, whether more or fewer in number, are to be ascribed to a cause more humiliating than the indolence or carelessness of the editor.'

The marks of an evident anxiety to represent the MS. with extreme exactness are indeed most apparent on every page; how then are we to account for the frequent amazing variations from the true text of the old scribe? Only, I believe, by the old observation that the eye only sees that which it has been *trained* to see. It is clear that, as a scholar, he frequently misunderstood his author; and that, as a transcriber, he often failed in deciphering the not very difficult characters in which the MS. is written. The two causes together are quite sufficient to account for such mistakes as, despite all his care, are certainly to be found in his edition.

The most valuable passages in this Introductory Discourse have already been quoted above; see p. xxxix.

(*h*) The Early English Text Society's edition. Edited by the Rev. Walter W. Skeat. Part I. (A-text); 1867. Part II. (B-text); 1869. Part III. (C-text, together with Richard the Redeless, and the Crowned King); 1873. Part IV. § 1 (Notes); 1877. Part IV. § 2 (Glossary, Indices, and General Preface); 1884.

(*i*) The Vision of William concerning Piers the Plowman. B-text; Prologue and Pass. i.–vii. Oxford: at the Clarendon Press. First edition; 1869. Second edition; 1874. Third edition; 1879.

This small volume, being intended for beginners, contains the Vision concerning Piers Plowman only, exclusive of the additional poem entitled 'Do-wel, Do-bet, and Do-best.'

§ 19. RICHARD THE REDELESS.

This poem is now printed for the fourth time. It has already been twice printed by Mr. Wright, viz. for the Camden Society, 1838, and in 'Political Poems and Songs,' 1859, vol. i. p. 368, with the title of a 'Poem on the Deposition of Richard II.' The edition of 1838 is the one which I have most consulted, and is alone referred to in the Notes as 'Mr. Wright's edition.'

The third edition was edited by me for the Early English Text Society in 1873; and is here reprinted; together with the Notes, which have been slightly abridged.

I have purposely altered Mr. Wright's title, because it is somewhat misleading. It is clear from the internal evidence that the poem was written *before* Richard was formally deposed; whilst the title given by Mr. Wright is calculated to give the impression that it was written afterwards. The title 'Richard the Redeless' (i. e. Richard devoid of counsel) is simply taken from what is really the first line of the Poem, since the Prologue may be looked upon as a sort of preface. In that line—

'Now, Richard þe redeles · reweth on ȝou self'—

the poet very happily strikes the keynote of the whole poem, which is entirely concerned with the 'redeless' character of the king and his favourites.

The MS. from which the text is printed is, unfortunately, unique. It is MS. XIX. of the 'Piers Plowman' MSS., i. e. MS. Ll. 4. 14 in the Cambridge University Library. On observing the striking similarity between this MS. and the Oriel MS., I had at first a slight hope that some trace of another copy of the poem might appear in that MS. also, which is of earlier date. But the only trace discoverable is the somewhat significant one that a considerable number of leaves have been torn out of the MS., just where the poem

RICHARD THE REDELESS. lxxxiii

ought to have appeared. There remained therefore nothing to be done but to reproduce the text of the Cambridge MS. as carefully as possible, although it is, unfortunately, a rather late copy, written, perhaps, towards the middle of the fifteenth century. A few obvious corrections have been made, but the actual readings of the MS. have been always recorded in the footnotes in such cases. I have also carefully collated Mr. Wright's edition of 1838 with the MS., in order to correct the few errors which appear there. I have also inserted the five Latin quotations (viz. at i. 8; ii. 52, 139; iii. 32, 128) which Mr. Wright unfortunately omitted, owing to a peculiarity in the arrangement of the text by the scribe which requires careful attention, as will appear from the following explanation.

The copies of Piers the Plowman and of Richard the Redeless in MS. XIX. are in the same handwriting, and are similarly arranged; and this arrangement can only be rightly understood by examining the former carefully. By turning to it, we at once perceive that the scribe adopts the singular plan, apparent in no other copy of the poem, of writing the Latin quotations *in the margin* of the MS., instead of leaving them in their proper place in the text. They thus have the *appearance* of being supplementary, or added as a commentary; they look like detached annotations instead of forming an integral part of the text. Not observing this peculiarity, Mr. Wright unfortunately considered them as comments, and omits to mention any but one, which he quotes in his Preface with a misreading that led him to take a wrong view of the scribe's sentiments, as noted below, p. lxxxiv. If, however, these five quotations be considered, it will be seen that they all suit the context, and drop into their right places. Such appeals to Scripture or to the writings of 'clerks' are exactly in Langland's usual manner, and the quotations are to be ascribed to the author, and not to the scribe. There are, however, a few marginal notes *in a later hand*, such as 'Overwatchynge' against iii. 282; 'Kew-kaw' against iii. 299, and the like. But all these were written in many years afterwards, and have nothing to do with the original text except as valueless comments.

DATE OF RICHARD THE REDELESS (1399).

The internal evidence enables us to settle the date of the poem almost within a fortnight. Lines 23–29 in the Prologue shew clearly that it was written after Richard had been taken prisoner,

18, 1399, and before he had been formally deposed, Sept. 30 in the same year. Other indications of date are in the allusion to the execution of Lord Scrope at Bristol, July 29, and to the release of the Earl of Warwick, who almost immediately after is heard of at Newcastle-under-Lyne, August 25; see Notes to ii. 152 and iii. 94. Allowing a few days for news to travel, and observing the author's boldness in rebuking Richard, as if his chances of escape seemed but small, we see that the date is restricted very nearly to the first three weeks in September. We must therefore suppose it to have been partly written in September, 1399, without fear of error.

However, the course of events must have considerably interfered with the poet's plans, and it is almost certain that some lines were supplied at a later period. He begins by addressing the poem to Richard personally, whose hand he intended it to reach (prol. 53), declaring that he would not publish it till it had been approved of (prol. 61); but he afterwards declares that a day of reckoning had come, and that God had judged evil-doers and restored peace (iii. 352–371). I here throw out the suggestion for what it is worth, that the unfinished state of the existing copy of the poem may be due to the fact that the poem itself never *was* finished; that the course of events, in fact, cut it short in the middle. The news of Richard's formal deposition would naturally put an end to it.

Authorship of Richard the Redeless.

As to the authorship of the poem, I have not the slightest hesitation in ascribing it to William, the author of Piers the Plowman. That it must be his, and his only, was suggested to me years ago, on the first perusal of it; and after considering the question with the utmost care, from every point of view, not once only, but many times, I am not only entirely satisfied on this point in my own mind, but considerably surprised to think that there could ever have been a moment's doubt about it, or any place for a contrary opinion. Yet it is well known that Mr. Wright, though the editor both of Piers the Plowman and of the present poem, failed to see their common authorship, and has, indeed, given his opinion on the other side. But I have shewn (in my edition for the Early English Text Society) how he came to be misled upon this point; viz. by mistaking a quotation to be a scribe's comment, which really forms an integral part of the text; and by misreading and misconstruing that quotation.

I have shewn, further, that the internal evidence on this subject is fully sufficient; and the only argument I shall adduce here is by appealing to the evidence of originality in the poem of 'Richard.' An imitator of William might have copied his phrases, but how was he to attain to his genius? It is a great satisfaction to find, moreover, that William's power did not fail him in his old age. There are some passages in his last poem which exhibit him almost at his best. I shall merely give the references to some of these; the reader may then form his own opinion. See, e. g. Pass. i. 1–19; 25–59; ii. 162–167; 186–192; iii. 116–243; 324–337; 352–371; iv. 31–82. In particular, the passage iii. 116–189 is a well-wrought piece of lively and sustained satire, whilst the contrast between the fashionable courtiers and Wisdom in his homely garb 'of the old shape' (iii. 211–238) is excellent. The supposition of such passages being written by a poet of less power than William is like supposing that there may have been two Shakespeares. Few better things have ever been said than in his marvellous and bold substitution of the fashionable dresses of the courtiers for the courtiers themselves, as if the only part of the courtier that was worth mention was the dress which he wore. When Wisdom's life was threatened, it was not by creatures that could be called *men*, it was by the *sleeves themselves!* The severe and supreme contempt of the satire almost evaporates when we analyse it thus critically, but take the passage as it stands, and what could be better? Wisdom attempts to come near Richard's court, and what happens?

> He was hallooed [at] and hunted · and yhote truss[1],
> And his dwelling ydemed[2] · a bow-draught from them,
> And each man was charged · to chop at his crown,
> If he nighed them any nearer · than they had him named[3].
> The porter with his pikes · then put him outer,
> And warned[4] him the wicket · whilst the watch dured.
> 'Let's slay him!' quoth *the sleeves* · *that slid upon the earth*[5],
> And all the beardless burns[6] · bayed on him ever,
> And scorned him, for his slaveyn[7] · was of the old shape.
> Thus Malapert was mightful · and master of [the] house,
> And ever wandered Wisdom · without the gates.

Such was the end of Wisdom's attempt to insinuate himself into Richard's court.

[1] bidden to pack off.   [2] assigned.
[3] him nempned = named for him, assigned for him.
[4] forbade him, warned him away from.
[5] Alluding to the long sleeves then worn, which even trailed upon the ground.
[6] men.   [7] mantle, cloak.

Almost equally good is the description of the packed parliament of Sept. 1397, in iv. 31–82, which the reader may examine for himself. The vivid description of the members of parliament in iv. 53–73 may be applied, I fear, to some men of our own time; and well exemplifies the author's keenness of observation.

§ 20. ARGUMENT OF PIERS THE PLOWMAN. (TEXT C.)

As it is impossible to point out all the numerous variations between the three versions, and therefore difficult to exhibit an 'argument' which will fully represent them all, I here give the argument of the C-TEXT *only*, as being the longest and fullest. It must be borne in mind that this leaves passages entirely unaccounted for, especially the curious twelfth Passus of the A-text; but it will suffice to shew the general contents of the A-text.

N.B. The passages within square brackets are later additions, and are not found in the B-text.

The poem is distinctly divisible into two parts, the 'Vision of the Piers the Plowman,' and the 'Visions of Do-well, Do-bet, and Do-best.' Of these, the former is again divisible into two distinct visions, which may be called: (1) The Vision of the Field full of Folk, of Holy Church, and of Lady Meed, occupying Passus I.—V.; and (2) The Vision of the Seven Deadly Sins and of Piers the Plowman, occupying Passus VI.—X., preceded by a discourse between the author and Reason. The latter consists of three parts, viz. The Visions of Do-well, of Do-bet, and of Do-best. Passus I.—VII. of Do-well form Passus XI.—XVII. Passus I.—IV. of Do-bet form Passus XVIII.—XXI. Passus I. and II. of Do-best form Passus XXII. and XXIII. But some of these parts contain more than one vision, the number of visions in the whole poem amounting to *eleven*.

1. PIERS THE PLOWMAN.

I. VISION OF THE FIELD FULL OF FOLK, OF HOLY CHURCH, AND OF LADY MEED. *Passus I.* (B. *prol.*; A. *prol.*). The author describes how, weary of wandering, he sits down to rest upon the Malvern Hills, and there falls asleep and dreams. In his vision, the world and its people are represented to him by a field full of folk, busily engaged in their avocations. The field was situated between the tower of Truth, who is God the Father, and the deep dale which is the abode of the evil spirits. In it there were ploughmen and spendthrifts, anchorites, merchants, minstrels, beggars, pilgrims, hermits, friars, a pardoner with his bulls, and priests who had deserted their cures. [Conscience appears, and accuses the priests of permitting idolatry and the worship of images; warning them of the fate that befell Eli and his sons.] There was also a king, to whom Common-sense spake words of advice. Then was seen suddenly a rout of rats and mice, conspiring to bell the cat, from doing which they were dissuaded by a wise mouse. There were also barons, burgesses, tradesmen, labourers, and taverners touting for custom.

Passus II. (B. i.; A. i.). Presently, the poet sees a lovely lady, of whom he asks the meaning of the tower. She tells him it is the abode of the Creator, who provides men with the necessaries of life. The deep dale contains the castle of Care, where lives the Father of Falseness. He next asks her name, and she tell·

ARGUMENT OF PIERS THE PLOWMAN.

him she is Holy Church, and instructs him how great a treasure Truth is, how Lucifer fell through Pride, [with a passing remark on Lucifer's seat being in the North,] that Love is the treacle for sin, and that the way to heaven lies through Love.

Passus III. (B. ii.; A. ii.). He asks how he may know Falsehood. She bids him turn and see Falsehood and Flattery. Looking aside he sees, not them alone, but a woman in glorious apparel. He is told she is the Lady Meed (i. e. Reward) who is going to be married to Falsehood on the morrow. Holy Church then leaves him. The wedding is prepared, and Simony and Civil read a deed respecting the property with which Falsehood and Meed are to be endowed. Theology objects to the marriage, and disputes its legality, [referring to the Legend of St. Lawrence;] whereupon it is agreed that all must go to Westminster to have the question decided. All the parties ride off to London, Meed being mounted upon a sheriff and Falsehood upon a 'sisour.' Thus all come to the King's court, who vows that he will punish Falsehood and his crew if he can catch them. On hearing this, Liar flees to the friars, who pity him and house him for their own purposes.

Passus IV. (B. iii.; A. iii.). Lady Meed is arrested and brought before the king. The justices assure her all will go well. To seem righteous, she confesses and is shriven, offering to glaze a church window by way of amendment; and immediately afterwards, advises mayors and judges to take bribes. [Here the author takes occasion to warn all false dealers of the vengeance of God that awaits them.] The king proposes that Meed shall marry Conscience, and she is willing to do so; but Conscience refuses, and exposes her faults; [adding an attack upon the king (Richard II.) for his bad government.] She attempts to retaliate and to justify herself; but Conscience refutes her arguments. [Here a long and subtle passage is inserted in which the *two kinds* of Meed, viz. Lawful Wages and Rewards given for no good reason, are distinguished. An attempt is made to draw a parallel between them and the Direct and Indirect Relations in Grammar. Hire (i. e. Lawful Wages) resembles the Direct Relation, as when, e. g., an adjective agrees with its substantive in gender, case, and number. But Bribery or Needless Reward is like the Indirect Relation, in which there is no agreement in case.] Conscience then quotes the example of Saul to shew the evil of covetousness; and declares that Reason will one day reign upon earth, and punish all wrongdoers. Then shall men think that Messiah has come, and the reign of Peace shall begin. Conscience concludes by advising Meed always to read texts in connection with the context.

Passus V. (B. iv.; A. iv.). Acting upon the advice of Conscience, the king orders Reason to be sent for; who comes, accompanied by Wiseman and Wilyman. At this moment, Peace enters, with a complaint against Wrong. Wrong, knowing the complaint is true, gets Wisdom and Wit on his side by Meed's help, and offers to buy Peace off with a present. Reason, however, is firm and will shew no pity, but advises the king to act with strict justice. The king is convinced, and prays Reason to remain with him for ever after. [Reason reminds him that Love will give more money than the Lombards will lend him. The king dismisses all his corrupt officers.]

II. THE VISION OF THE SEVEN DEADLY SINS AND OF PIERS THE PLOWMAN. *Passus VI.* [This Passus opens with a curious and interesting discourse between Reason and the author, in the course of which the author refers to his own history and mode of life.] (B. v.; A. v.) The author goes to church, and soon falls asleep again, and has a second vision, in which he again sees the field full of folk, and

Reason preaching to the assembled people, reminding them that the late storm and pestilence were judgments of God. Here Reason introduces the remarkable prophecy that a king would come and reform religion, when the abbot of England should receive from him a knock, and incurable should be the wound.

Passus VII. Repentance seconds the efforts of Conscience, and many begin to repent. Of these the first is Pride, who makes a vow of humility. The second is Envy, who is described with much particularity, and who confesses his evil thoughts and his attempts to harm his neighbours. The third is Wrath, a friar, whose aunt was a nun, and who had been cook to a convent, and incited many to quarrel. The fourth is Luxury, who vows to drink only water. The fifth, Avarice, who confesses how he lied and cheated, and taught his wife to cheat; and, not understanding the word *restitution*, thought that it was another term for stealing. Robert the robber also repents, and prays earnestly for forgiveness. The sixth, Gluttony, who (on his way to church) is tempted into a beer-house, of the interior of which the author gives a life-like and perfect picture. He too repents, though not till he has first become completely drunk and afterwards felt the ill effects of drinking.

Passus VIII. The seventh is Sloth, a priest who knows rimes about Robin Hood better than his prayers, and can find a hare in a field more readily than he can read lives of saints. Repentance makes intercession for all the penitents. Then they all set out in search of Truth (A. vi.), but no one knows the way. Soon they meet with a palmer, who has met with many saints, but never with one named *Truth*. At this juncture Piers the Plowman 'put forth his head,' declaring that he knows Truth well, and will tell them the way, which he then describes. [Some of the sinners begin to make excuse.] The pilgrims think the way long, and want a guide.

Passus IX. (B. vi.; A. vii.). Piers says he will come himself and shew them, when he has ploughed his half-acre. Meanwhile, he gives good advice to rich ladies and to a knight. Before starting, Piers makes his will, and then sets all who come to him to hard work. Many shirk their work, but are reduced to subordination by the sharp treatment of Hunger. Next follow most curious and valuable passages respecting the diet of the poor, striking for higher wages, and the discontent caused by prosperity. A mysterious prophecy is appended.

Passus X. (B. vii.; A. viii.). At this time Truth (i.e. God the Father) sends Piers a bull of pardon, especially intended for kings, knights, bishops, and the labouring poor, and even for some lawyers and merchants, in a less degree. [Here is introduced a curious description of the poor of London, of 'lollers,' and of false hermits.] A priest disputes the validity of the pardon, and wants to read it. The dispute between this priest and Piers becomes so violent that the dreamer awakes, and the Poem of Piers the Plowman (properly so called) ends with a fine peroration on the small value of papal pardons, and the superiority of a righteous life over mere trust in indulgences, at the great Day of Doom.

2. Visio de Dowel.

III. The Vision of Wit, Study, Clergy, and Scripture. *Passus XI.* (B. viii.; A. ix.). In introducing a new poem, the 'Visio de Dowel,' the author begins by describing a dialogue that passed between himself and two Minorite friars concerning the doctrine of free-will. After this, he again falls asleep, and perceives in a dream a man named Thought. He asks Thought where Do-well, Do-bet, and Do-best live, and Thought gives him some account of these, but says that the best person to give him further information is Wit. After wandering for three days, the dreamer and Thought meet with Wit (B. ix.; A. x.). Wit tells the dreamer that Do-well dwells in a castle called *Caro*, wherein also is enclosed the Lady *Anima*, and they are guarded by the constable Inwit (Conscience), and his five sons (the senses). [Here follows a discourse upon the effect of Sin in hiding God from man], the duty of the church to protect idiots and helpless persons, [and upon the value of Love.] Next follow discussions upon the good that there is in well-assorted and lawful wedlock, and the evil of mercenary or ill-advised marriages, and of adulterous connections.

Passus XII. (B. x.; A. xi.). The dreamer applies to yet one more adviser, viz. Dame Study, the wife of Wit. She laments that wicked men most frequently obtain this world's wealth. She inveighs with great justice and force against the way in which shallow would-be theologians cavil about the mysterious things of God, and unworthily amuse themselves with vain quibbles. She laments the lack of charity, and the increase of pride. At last, she commends the dreamer to Clergy and Scripture, from whom he may hope to learn yet more. Accordingly, he seeks these, and receives some instruction from Clergy (B. xi.; A. xii.). Clergy's discourse is cut short by Scripture, who so scorns the poet that he weeps and falls into a new dream.

IV. THE VISION OF FORTUNE, NATURE, RECKLESSNESS, AND REASON. In a new vision, William sees Fortune, with her attendant damsels named Lust-of-the-flesh and Lust-of-the-eyes, who bid him rejoice in his youth. Here Recklessness is introduced, who discourses upon predestination in language similar to that in the conclusion of Pass. X. in the B-text.

Passus XIII. But at the approach of old age, William finds that the friars, once his friends, avoid him, because he wished to be buried in his parish church. Loyalty and Scripture give him good advice, and he is told why Trajan was released from hell. Recklessness cites Christ's example of humility, declares poverty to be like a walnut, enlarges upon the value of poverty, [compares men to various seeds and their vices to weeds, and declares that riches bring men to perdition.]

Passus XIV. [Here the praise of poverty is continued, with the examples of Job and Abraham. Recklessness narrates the parable of the merchant and the messenger, signifying the rich and the poor;] and concludes his harangue by saying that priests unfit for their office are as bad as a notary who knows not how to draw up a charter. William's dream continues, and he sees Nature, who shews him how all animals except man follow Reason. He asks why this is; Reason rebukes him, and he awakes.

V. THE VISION OF IMAGINATIVE. The dreamer beholds one who rebukes him for his impatience. He asks the stranger's name.

Passus XV. (B. xii.). The stranger says his name is Imaginative, exhorts him not to despise learning, instructs him as to the relative chances of salvation of the learned and the ignorant, and tells him why wealth is like a peacock's tail. After distinguishing between three kinds of baptism, Imaginative suddenly vanishes, upon which the dreamer awakes.

VI. THE VISION OF CONSCIENCE, PATIENCE, AND ACTIVA-VITA. *Passus XVI.* (B. xiii.). In the sixth vision, Conscience, Clergy, Patience, and the dreamer go to dine with Reason. At the high daïs is seated a doctor of the church, who astonishes all by his gluttony. After dinner, the doctor, being well primed with wine, is ready to expound theological subtleties. Conscience and Patience bid farewell to Clergy and Reason, and set out as pilgrims in company with the poet. Soon they meet with one Activa-Vita, who is a minstrel and seller of wafers (B. xiv.). Patience instructs Activa-Vita, and declares that beggars shall have joy hereafter.

Passus XVII. (B. xv.). Patience laments that riches should rob man's soul of God's love, praises poverty, and enumerates its nine advantages.

VII. THE VISION OF FREE-WILL AND OF THE TREE OF CHARITY. The poet next observes one Liberum-Arbitrium, who reproves him for presumption. William next inquires the nature of Charity, which Free-will defines.

3. VISIO DE DOBET.

Passus XVIII. Free-will quotes the Lives of the Saints, and shews that the friars are now far from being charitable. He alludes to the story of Mahomet's pet dove, to the fatal gift of Constantine, and to the miracles of Christ, ending with the charitable wish that Saracens and Jews may be saved.

Passus XIX. (B. xvi.). William is then shewn the tree upon which Charity grows, supported upon three props, the meaning of which is explained by Free-will. Next follows a part of the history of Christ, His incarnation, miracles, and betrayal by Judas Iscariot. At this point the dreamer suddenly awakes. In his anxious search after Free-will, he meets with Abraham or Faith.

VIII. THE VISION OF FAITH, HOPE, AND CHARITY. Faith (Abraham) explains how he became God's herald, and shews William the leper (Lazarus) lying in his lap.

Passus XX. (B. xvii.). Next William beholds *Spes*, or Hope, who, like Abraham, is in search of Piers. Spes and William journey towards Jerusalem, and behold a Samaritan riding near them. Soon they find a wounded man lying in the way. Faith and Hope pass by him, but the Good Samaritan (i. e. Charity or Christ Himself in the garb of Piers the Plowman) has compassion upon him, and takes care of him, leaving him at an inn called *Lex-Dei*. The Dreamer asks for instruction, and learns from the Samaritan how the Holy Trinity is symbolized by a man's hand, or by a blazing torch. The sin against the Holy Ghost is alluded to; also the three things which drive a man out of his own house. Once more the dreamer awakes.

IX. THE VISION OF THE TRIUMPH OF PIERS THE PLOWMAN. *Passus XXI.* (B. xviii.). This, the finest Passus in the whole poem, is entirely occupied with the history of Jesus. With growing power and vividness the poet describes the crucifixion, with the healing of Longeus, the struggle between Life and Death and between Light and Darkness, the meeting together of Mercy and Truth, Righteousness and Peace, whilst the Saviour rests in the grave; a triumphant description of His descent into hell, [where Satan attempts to oppose Him with 'brazen guns,'] and His victory over Satan and Lucifer, till the poet wakes in ecstasy, with the joyous peal of the bells ringing in his ears on the morning of Easter Day.

4. VISIO DE DOBEST.

X. THE VISION OF GRACE. *Passus XXII.* (B. xix.). But alas! the poem of Dobest reveals how far off the end yet is. The Saviour, having earned the names of Do-well, Do-bet, and Do-best, leaves earth, upon which Antichrist is soon to descend. Piers *henceforth* denotes the whole Christian body, upon whom Grace or the Holy Spirit bestows various gifts. Grace makes Piers His ploughman, and gives him four oxen (the four evangelists), and four 'stots' (the four chief Latin 'fathers'); also four seeds, which are the cardinal virtues. Pride and his host attack the Church of Unity. All men are invited by Conscience to partake of the eucharist, but an impenitent brewer refuses to do so, and an ignorant vicar reviles the cardinals whom the pope sends from Avignon. A lord and a king are introduced, who justify their own exactions. Then the dreamer awakes.

XI. THE VISION OF ANTICHRIST. *Passus XXIII.* (B. xx.). Before falling asleep once more, William encounters Need, who rebukes and instructs him. He then dreams once more how Antichrist assails the Church of Unity, which is defended by Conscience against Pride and all his host. Diseases assail all mankind; Death 'pashes' to the dust kings and knights, emperors and popes, and many a lovely lady. Life, with his mistress Fortune, indulges in all kinds of excesses. He becomes the father of Sloth, who marries Wanhope. Old-age appears as the enemy of Life. The dreamer takes refuge in the castle of Unity, which is beleaguered by many foes, especially by Sloth and Avarice. The friars craftily offer to aid Conscience. At last one Flattery, a friar, gains admission to the castle, offering to salve Conscience of all hurts with soothing but deadly remedies, till Conscience, hard beset by Pride and Sloth, cries out to Contrition to help him: but Contrition slumbers, benumbed by the deadly potions he has drunk. With a last effort Conscience arouses himself, and seizes his pilgrim's staff, determined to wander wide over the world till he shall find Piers the Plowman. Again the dreamer awakes, and here ceases the still unfinished history of the religious life of man.

§ 21. ARGUMENT OF RICHARD THE REDELESS.

Prologue[1]. And as I [i. e. the author of Piers the Plowman] was passing through Bristol, I came to Christ Church, where I heard strange news. For whilst king Richard was warring in the west against the wild Irish, Henry enered England on the east side, whom all the land loved, and rose with him to right his wrongs. For myself, I had pity upon our lawful king, and, not knowing what would be the end of the matter, determined to write him a poem of advice, recommending him to take God's visitation in patience. If it may please him to read over what I have written, I shall rejoice if it does him some good; and I will undertake to say that any prince in Christendom might learn from it, if he can understand English. If then, my liege, my book reaches your royal hand, deign to peruse it; for it shall not be published as yet, till wiser men have revised it. I hope it may profit both young and old; and if any word displeases my sovereign, I pray him not to mistake my good intentions towards him.

Passus I. Now, Richard the Redeless [counsel-less], have pity on yourself! Learn that allegiance is secured by conduct quite different from your own; not by exactions, robberies by your purveyors, or imposition of heavy taxes. Your courtiers are graceless 'ghosts,' that never wore armour nor felt a shower of hail. You came to your crown under most auspicious circumstances. Your crown was, as it were, adorned with pearls, rubies, gems, diamonds, and sapphires; it was powdered over with pity, and adorned with truth. But who can now tell what became of this crown? Your courtiers usurped the power that should have been yours; your people dared not complain. Men might as well have hunted a hare with a tabor, as have expected redress. Yet it was said of old time—'Where grooms and nobles are all equally great, wo be to that kingdom, and to all the

---

[1] The argument of the Prologue can only be well described by using the *first* person.

dwellers therein!' Thus was your crown broken, by the power you deputed to your favourites. Had it been preserved whole, we should not have heard of murders amongst the great. But your counsellors were young and giddy men, who selfishly misled you to their own advantage; they cajoled you into setting aside your true friends, and loving false deeds. Had you but done as a prince should do, you would have hung the first suggester of falsehood high upon the gallows, yea, though he had been your own brother. But you encouraged knaves, and this greatly emboldened them.

Passus II. The worst matter was, that you dispersed so widely your badges of the 'white hart.' The wearers of this badge, your retainers, ran rife throughout your realm. But some of them stood in awe of the Eagle [Bolingbroke]; and, moreover, the moulting-time of these harts was drawing nigh; it was nearly time for them to lose their horns. It amazes me to think that you should have suffered your harts [retainers] to be so numerous as to be a plague to your people. They skinned the poor mercilessly, and displayed their badges to silence complaints. So that, as the townspeople used to say, for every *hart* that you marked on a badge, you missed ten score of faithful *hearts* of subjects. These badges of yours spoilt all the broth, and upset the pot amongst the coals. Hence, when you wish to lean upon your limbs [the commons], they failed you. Though Reason warns me to speak respectfully, I must yet say that, in my opinion, no upstart of a retainer ought ever to wear a mark or badge; these should be reserved for good and great men, as, e. g., a just judge. I fear you have sought merely to multiply the number of your badge-wearers, and to attach them to yourself personally. Had the good Greyhound [the earl of Westmoreland] been cherished as a chieftain, you might have had 'white harts' enough in your service. But no wonder though 'head-deer' failed you, since you had no pity on the 'rascals' or lean deer. Meanwhile the Eagle [Bolingbroke] was fostering nestlings of his own, watching over them whilst their wings were growing. Then did this bird batter on the *bushes* [i.e. punish Bushy], and gather men as they walked on the *green* [i.e. seize and imprison Green], till all the 'scruff' and 'scrope' [an allusion to Scrope] was torn asunder. He so moulded the metal with his hand-mould, that these men lost the dearest limbs they had, viz. their heads. Even then this Falcon [also meaning Bolingbroke] was not fully fed. But the blear-eyed scoundrel who stole the *bag* [i.e. Bagot] made the Falcon flush for anger; and, ere long, this rascal was caught. Still the Eagle continued his hawking, till he had soon subdued every kite and crow. Many snares and gins were set in all directions, catching men wherever they went; and evermore the Eagle hovered on high, and clearly saw all the privy projects of the pies below.

Passus III. I return now from the Eagle, to speak once more of the harts, and how they came at last to misfortune. The worst of all faults are those committed against nature. Let me shew how this applies to the harts. When a hart comes to be a hundred years old, he adopts this plan for renewing his youth. It is his wont to catch and kill an adder, and to feed upon his venom, by which means he succeeds in renewing his skin[1]. It is natural, then, for the hart to prey upon the adder; but it is unnatural for him to attack a Colt [Thomas Fitz-alan], or a Horse [the earl of Arundel], or a Swan [the duke of Gloucester], or a Bear [the earl of Warwick]. It is therefore because of their unnatural conduct that the harts failed of success. Now hear the story of the partridge.[1] The partridge lays her eggs and sits upon them; but very soon another partridge comes and takes her place whilst

---

[1] These accounts of the habits of the hart and partridge express the received opinions of the period.

ARGUMENT OF RICHARD THE REDELESS.

she is off the nest, and hatches the young ones. Then the right mother-bird returns, and, at the sound of her call, the young birds desert the intruder and follow her. In like manner, when the Eagle returned to his young ones, they forsook the king who had oppressed them for two-and-twenty years, and returned to their true father. The Swan [the duke of Gloucester] had failed [was dead]; the Horse [the duke of Arundel] was sore hurt; but the Eagle released the bear [the earl of Warwick] and all his 'bearlings.' Then did they 'gaggle' on the *green* [i. e. attacked Green]; they cursed the Earl Marshal [the duke of Norfolk]; and followed the Eagle everywhere, ready for vengeance. To return to Richard and his misdeeds. One great fault amongst his courtiers was in the tyranny of fashion and the expense of dress. Such men keep no money that comes to them, yet they clip the king's coin and make it scarce. Except their sleeves slide upon the ground, they curse the robe-maker. They even follow a fashion which may be described as cutting the clothes to pieces, so that they have to pay for the piecing of the cloth together nearly twenty times the price of the cloth itself. Surely such followers of the fashion are not the men to be trusted. Yet we find that lords bestow liveries on such men, and choose them, not for any goodness or worth, but for their bragging and boasting. If lords would drive away the 'dagged' clothes and the 'Dutch' coats, and reprove robbers, and choose worthy men, the world would mend. Then I beheld how Wisdom presented himself at court, seeking admittance; wondering, as well he might, at the number of the household-retainers. But as soon as ever his true name became known, he was warned off the ground. 'Let's slay him,' quoth the sliding sleeves; and all the beardless boys mocked him. Then was Wisdom wroth, and said they should never win grace. Counsellors, Warriors, and Labourers are the true pillars of a realm; but lads of twenty-four years are not those whence Counsellors should be chosen. Rulers are chosen to uphold the law, not to spend the night in wakeful debauchery. But, fortunately, such misrule and riot cannot last for ever. Sooner or later comes a 'kew-kaw,' i. e. a change of fortune, when the robbers at last go to prison. Yet even then Bribery favours the bad, and mighty lords abet their evil followers. Fighting men from Chester pleaded in the courts in their own way, viz. with violence and intimidation; and those who dared to complain were in extreme danger. But at last the Lord of heaven arose in His righteous anger, summoned His archangels and angels, His barons and His bachelors, and rode against evil-doers in royal array. Then fell a deep calm, and the heavens waxed clear; and every man might see the moon move at midday, and the very stars pursuing after evil-doers.

Passus IV. Where was ever a king who kept so large a household as Richard did? So great were his expenses, that not even his unprecedented taxations could repay the poor for what his purveyors had exacted from them. But for credit, his men would have been drawn to the devil for the debts they owed. At last, when nothing was left but the bare bags, he determined to summon a submissive and corrupt parliament. When this venal assembly had come together, a clerk stood up, and asked them to vote supplies. Then some members pretended that they knew their duty, and made a shew as if they could not grant them; others sat in their places like mere ciphers; others were tale-bearers; others slumbered; others talked nonsense, or lost themselves in argument. Then there were others, newly elected, who were for dashing on at full sail; but the mast bent, and they were glad to strike sail to escape shipwreck. Some 'knew how it would all end;' others held always with the majority; whilst another set could talk of nothing but the money which the king owed to themselves. Others feared the lords, and forsook Do-well. [*Here the poem breaks off.*]

BIBLIOGRAPHICAL NOTE.

THE following bibliography, whilst intended to indicate the general direction of *Piers Plowman* studies since Skeat's day, and some of the materials now available, makes no claim to be exhaustive. It does not include unpublished dissertations or studies of particular passages —unless such studies bear on the work as a whole. When the substance of a work or article is incorporated in a later work by the same author, reference to the earlier work is not usually given.

A useful summary of views and investigations between the years 1886–1939 is to be found in 'The Present State of Piers Plowman Studies', by M. W. Bloomfield (Speculum, xiv. 215–32). Full bibliographical information is available in J. E. Wells, A Manual of the Writings in Middle English (and Supplements), and the annual volumes of The Year's Work in English Studies.

FACSIMILE

1936. Piers Plowman. The Huntington Library Manuscript (HM143) reproduced in photostat, with an introduction by R. W. Chambers and technical examination by R. B. Haselden and H. C. Schulz. San Marino.

EDITIONS

1928. The Vision of William Concerning Piers The Plowman . . . edited by W. W. Skeat (tenth edition of Prologue and Passus I–VII of B-text). Oxford.
Piers Plowman. Prologue and Passus I–VII, Text B, edited by J. F. Davis, revised by E. S. Olsewska (second edition). London.

1934. (For an edition of Passus III–V of the C-text *see* F. A. R. Carnegy, An Attempt to approach the C-text . . . *below*.)

1952. Piers the Plowman. A Critical Edition of the A-version, edited with Introduction, Notes and Glossary, by T. A. Knott and D. C. Fowler. Baltimore.

TRANSLATIONS

1905. The Vision of Piers the Plowman by William Langland done into modern English by The Rev. Professor Skeat (Prologue and Passus I–VII of B-text). London.
(Several other versions of this section have been published.)

1935. The Vision of Piers Plowman newly rendered into modern English by Henry W. Wells, with an Introduction by Nevill Coghill and Notes by the Translator. London (second edition, New York, 1945) (based on eclectic text).

1949. Visions from Piers Plowman taken from the Poem of William Langland and translated into modern English by Nevill Coghill. London. (B-text, with some omissions).

STUDIES OF THE TEXT AND COLLATIONS OF THE MSS.

1885. W. Kron, William Langley's Buch von Peter dem Pflüger. Göttingen.

1893. E. Teichmann, 'Zum Texte von William Langland's Vision', Anglia, xv. 223–60 (criticizes Skeat for rejecting certain readings).

1909. R. W. Chambers and J. H. G. Grattan, 'The Text of Piers Plowman', M.L.R. iv. 357–89 (chiefly concerning the A-text).

1911. R. W. Chambers, 'The Original Form of the A-text of Piers Plowman', M.L.R. vi. 302–23.

1915. T. A. Knott, 'An Essay toward the Critical Text of the A-version of Piers the Plowman', Modern Philology, xii. 389–421.

1916. R. W. Chambers, 'The Text of Piers Plowman: Critical Methods', M.L.R. xi. 257–75.

1918. Elsie Blackman, 'Notes on the B-text MSS. of Piers Plowman', Journal of English and Germanic Philology, xvii. 489–545.

1919. (R. W. Chambers in M.L.R. xiv. 129–51: *see below under* Authorship and Unity of the Text.)

1931. R. W. Chambers and J. H. G. Grattan, 'The Text of Piers Plowman', M.L.R. xxvi. 1–51.

1932. R. B. Haselden, 'The Fragment of Piers Plowman in Ashburnham No. cxxx', Modern Philology xxix. 391–4 (shows that the fragment was originally part of the complete text of the B-version found in this MS.; with facsimiles of pages from the fragment and the complete text).

1934. F. A. R. Carnegy, An Attempt to approach the C-text of Piers the Plowman. London (includes a critical edition of Passus III–V).

1935. R. W. Chambers, 'The Manuscripts of Piers Plowman in the Huntington Library, and Their Value for Fixing the Text of the Poem', Huntington Library Bulletin, No. 8, 1–27 (includes a study of the two MSS. of the B-text in the Library: HM 128 [formerly Ashburnham CXXX] and 114 [formerly

BIBLIOGRAPHICAL NOTE. xcvii

Phillipps 8252], and of the two MSS. of the C-text: 137 [formerly Phillipps 8231, Skeat's 'P'], and 143, which Chambers regarded as offering the best basis for a critical C-text. Some corrections of Skeat's readings of 'P', as far as Passus IX, are given in a footnote on p. 24).

1941. A. G. Mitchell, 'A Newly-discovered MS. of the C-text of Piers Plowman', M.L.R. xxxvi. 243-4. (The Sterling MS.: closely related to Skeat's 'V'.)

1941-2. R. W. Chambers, 'A Piers Plowman Manuscript', National Library of Wales Journal, ii. 42-43. (A note on NLW 733B— one of the composite MSS. in which the C-continuation was added to what was originally a copy of the A-text.)

1947. J. H. G. Grattan, 'The Text of Piers Plowman': A Newly discovered Manuscript and its Affinities', M.L.R. xlii. 1-8. (An account of the Chaderton MS., now in the University of Liverpool Library; it is another composite MS., in which part of C has been added to an A-text.)

J. H. G. Grattan, 'The Text of Piers Plowman: Critical Lucubrations with Special Reference to the Independent Substitution of Similars', Studies in Philology, xliv. 593-604.

1948. G. Kane, 'Piers Plowman: Problems and Methods of Editing the B-text', M.L.R. xliii. 1-25.

1948. J. A. W. Bennett, 'A New Collation of a Piers Plowman Manuscript', Medium Aevum, xvii. 21-31. (Contains corrections of Skeat's C-text from HM 137 ['P'] and (p. 22, n. 2) of Skeat's B-text from MS. Laud 581.)

1949. E. T. Donaldson, Piers Plowman, The C-text and Its Poet. New Haven. (Appendix A contains a table of all the known MSS. and a genealogy of the C-MSS.)

1950. G. Kane, 'Textual Criticism of Piers Plowman', Times Literary Supplement, 17 March, p. 176.

1951. D. C. Fowler, 'Contamination in Manuscripts of the A-text of Piers Plowman', P.M.L.A. lxvi. 495-504.

E. St. John Brooks, 'The Piers Plowman Manuscripts in Trinity College, Dublin', [D. 4. 1 and D. 4. 12] The Library, Fifth Series, Vol. VI, 141-53.

1952. T. A. Knott and D. C. Fowler, Piers Plowman. A Critical Edition of the A-version. . . . (See *under* Editions: pp. 22-28 contain a table of all known MSS. of the A-text, with brief descriptions and a classification.)

D. C. Fowler, 'The Relationship of the Three Texts of Piers the Plowman', Modern Philology, l. 5-22.

1953. E. T. Donaldson, 'The Texts of Piers Plowman: Scribes and Poets', Modern Philology, l. 269-73.

Authorship and Unity of the Text

1901. A. S. Jack, 'The Autobiographical Elements in Piers the Plowman', Journal of Germanic Philology, iii. 393–414.
1906. J. M. Manly, 'The Lost Leaf of Piers the Plowman', Modern Philology, iii. 359–66.
 H. Bradley, 'The Misplaced Leaf of Piers the Plowman', Athenæum, 21 April, p. 481.
1908. J. M. Manly, 'Piers Plowman and its Sequence', in The Cambridge History of English Literature, vol. ii (republished by the Early English Text Society, O.S. Extra Issue, 135 b).
1909. T. D. Hall, 'Was "Langland" the Author of the C-text of the Vision of Piers Plowman?', M.L.R. iv. 1–13. (Written, though not published, before Manly's chapter appeared, the article questions the authenticity of the C-text.)
1909.[1] J. J. Jusserand, 'Piers Plowman, the Work of One or of Five', Modern Philology, vi. 271–329.
 [1] J. M. Manly, 'The Authorship of Piers Plowman', Modern Philology, vii. 83–144.
1910.[1] J. J. Jusserand, 'Piers Plowman, ... A Reply', Modern Philology, vii. 289–326.
 T. D. Hall, 'The Misplaced Lines, Piers Plowman (A)', v. 236–41, Modern Philology, vii. 327–8.
 [1] R. W. Chambers, 'The Authorship of Piers Plowman', M.L.R. v. 1–32.
 G. C. Macaulay, 'The Name of the Author of Piers Plowman', M.L.R. v. 195–6 (argues for 'Robert' rather than 'William').
 H. Bradley, 'The Authorship of Piers the Plowman', M.L.R. v. 202–7 (republished by the Early English Text Society as O.S. extra volume 139 F).
 O. Mensendieck, 'Die Verfasserschaft der drei Texte des Piers the Plowman', Zeitschrift für Vergleichende Literaturgeschichte, xviii. 10–31.
 O. Mensendieck, 'The Authorship of Piers Plowman', Journal of English and Germanic Philology, ix. 404–20.
1912. G. C. Coulton, 'Piers Plowman, One or Five', M.L.R. vii. 102–4, 372–3.
1913–14. S. Moore, 'Studies in Piers the Plowman', Modern Philology, xi. 177–93, xii. 19–50.
1916–17. T. A. Knott, 'Observations on the Authorship of Piers The Plowman, A Reply to R. W. Chambers', Modern Philology, xiv. 531–57, xv. 23–41.

[1] Republished by the Early English Text Society as 'The Piers Plowman Controversy', 1910, O.S. Extra Issue 139 b, c, d, e.

1919. R. W. Chambers, 'The Three Texts of Piers Plowman, and their Grammatical Forms', M.L.R. xiv. 133–51.
1922. (*See* Mabel Day in M.L.R. xvii. 403–9, *under* Vocabulary and Verse-structure).
1928. Mabel Day, 'The Revisions of Piers Plowman', M.L.R. xxiii. 1–27 (argues in favour of multiple authorship).
A. H. Bright, New Light on Piers Plowman. London. (Preface by R. W. Chambers; attempts to reconstruct the poet's biography and suggests that the Vision of the Field of Folk took place near a field still called Longlands, near Ledbury (cf. A. T. Bannister, Times Literary Supplement, 7 Sept. 1922, p. 569. For a criticism *see* F. Krog, *Anglia*, lviii. 318–32.
1937. R. W. Chambers, 'Incoherencies in the A- and B-texts of Piers Plowman and their Bearing on the Authorship', London Medieval Studies, i. 27–39.
1943. M. W. Bloomfield, 'Was William Langland a Benedictine Monk?', Modern Language Quarterly, iv. 57–61.
1947. B. F. Huppé, 'The Authorship of the A and B texts of Piers Plowman', Speculum, xxii. 578–620.
1948 (for 1939). R. W. Chambers, 'Robert or William Longland?', London Medieval Studies, i. 430–62.
J. R. Hulbert, 'Piers the Plowman after Forty Years', Modern Philology, xlv. 215–25.
1950. H. Meroney, 'The Life and Death of Longe Wille', *ELH*, A Journal of English Literary History, xvii. 1–35.

DATE

1932. O. Carghill, 'The Date of the A-text of Piers Ploughman', P.M.L.A. xlvii. 354–62 (argues for 1376).
1935. N. K. Coghill, 'Two Notes on Piers Plowman. I. The Abbot of Abingdon and the Date of the C-text', Medium Ævum, iv. 83–89 (argues that the allusion in B. x. 327 was omitted in the C-text because such a reference would have been dangerous in 1394, when the abbot's tenants were resisting his alleged extortions).
1939. B. F. Huppé, 'The A-text of Piers Plowman and the Norman Wars', P.M.L.A. liv. 37–64 (argues in favour of a date later than 1373).
1941. B. F. Huppé, 'The Date of the B-text of Piers Plowman', Studies in Philology, xxxviii. 34–44 (maintains that it cannot have been completed before the autumn of 1378).
1943. J. A. W. Bennett, 'The Date of the A-text of Piers Plowman', P.M.L.A. lviii. 566–72 (modifies Huppé's argument and proposes a date *c.* 1370).

1943. A. Gwynn, 'The Date of the B-text of Piers Plowman', Review of English Studies, xix. 1–24 (claims that Passus XIII–XX were composed c. 1370–2).

1943. J. A. W. Bennett, 'The Date of the B-text of Piers Plowman', Medium Ævum, xii. 55–64 (further indications that it was not completed before 1378).

1949. B. F. Huppé, 'Piers Plowman: the Date of the B-text Reconsidered', Studies in Philology, xlvi. 6–13 (controverts Gwynn's arguments).

STUDIES BEARING ON THE POEM AS A WHOLE OR ON IMPORTANT ASPECTS OF IT

1894. J. J. Jusserand, Piers Plowman: a Contribution to the History of English Mysticism. London.
E. D. Hanscom, 'The Argument of The Vision of Piers Plowman', P.M.L.A. ix. 403–50.

1912. Dorothy L. Owen, Piers Plowman: A Comparison with ... French Allegories. London (second edition, 1915).

1914. H. S. V. Jones, 'Imaginatif in Piers Plowman', Journal of English and Germanic Philology, xiii. 583–8 (cf. O. Mensendieck, ib., ix. 404–20).

1924. R. W. Chambers, 'Long Will, Dante, and the Righteous Heathen', Essays and Studies by Members of the English Association, ix. 50–69. (See also T. P. Dunning, Medium Ævum, xii. 45.)

1929. H. W. Wells, 'The Construction of Piers Plowman', P.M.L.A. xliv. 123–40.

1932. H. W. Troyer, 'Who is Piers Plowman?' P.M.L.A. xlvii. 368–84.

1933. N. K. Coghill, 'The Character of Piers Plowman considered from the B-text', Medium Ævum, ii. 108–35 (*see also* his Introduction to the translation by Wells, 1935).
G. R. Owst, Literature and the Pulpit in Medieval England. Cambridge (*see* chap. ix).

1934. C. Dawson, 'The Vision of Piers Plowman': Part III of his Medieval Religion and other Essays. London.
F. A. R. Carnegy, The Relations between the Social and Divine Order in W. Langland's Vision of William concerning Piers the Plowman. Breslau.

1937. T. P. Dunning, Piers Plowman: An Interpretation of the A-text. London.

1938. H. W. Wells, 'The Philosophy of Piers Plowman', P.M.L.A. liii. 339–49.

1938. G. W. Stone, Jr., 'An Interpretation of the A-text of Piers Plowman', P.M.L.A. liii. 656–77.
Greta Hort, Piers Plowman and Contemporary Religious Thought. London, New York.
1939. R. W. Chambers, 'Piers Plowman: A Comparative Study': two essays in his 'Man's Unconquerable Mind: Studies of English Writers from Bede to . . . W. P. Ker'. London. (The first essay discusses the A-text, compares Piers Plowman and the Divine Comedy, and surveys Langland's fame in recent years; the second analyses the continuation of the poem as found in the B- and C-texts, and cites some parallels in later English poetry.)
1941. R. W. Chambers, 'Poets and their Critics: Langland and Milton' (Warton Lecture on English Poetry: Proceedings of British Academy, xxvii).
1945. N. K. Coghill, 'The Pardon of Piers Plowman' (Gollancz Memorial Lecture; Proceedings of British Academy, xxxi), for later discussions of the Pardon described in Passus (A) viii. 92 ff., see J. Lawlor, M.L.R. xlv (1950, 449–58) and R. W. Frank, jr., Speculum, xxvi (1951, 317–31).
1948. G. H. Gerould, 'The Structural Integrity of Piers Plowman B', Studies in Philology, xlv. 60–75.
1949. E. T. Donaldson, Piers Plowman. The C-text and its Poet. New Haven (a detailed and scholarly attempt to rehabilitate the C-text).
1950. J. A. W. Bennett, 'William Langland's World of Visions', The Listener, pp. 381–2.
1951. D. W. Robertson, Jr. and B. F. Huppé, Piers Plowman and Scriptural Tradition. Princeton.
G. Kane, 'The Vision of Piers Plowman', in his Middle English Literature (182–248). London.
1953. H. Maisack, William Langlands Verhältnis zum Zisterziensischen Mönchtum. Balingen.

VOCABULARY AND VERSE STRUCTURE

1889. K. Luick, 'Die englische Stabreimzeile. II. William Langley und seine Schule', Anglia, xi, 429–43.
1890. E. Teichmann, 'Zur Stabreimzeile in William Langland's Buch von Peter dem Pflüger', Anglia, xiii, 140–74.
1908. Mary Deakin, 'The Alliteration of Piers Plowman', M.L.R. iv. 478–83.
1910. Margaret Dobson, 'An Examination of the Vocabulary of the A-text of Piers the Plowman', Anglia, xxxiii, 391–6.

1914. K. Schumacher, 'Studien über den Stabreim in der mittelenglischen Alliterationsdichtung'. Bonner Studien zur englischen Philologie, Heft. xi.
1922. Mabel Day, 'Alliteration of the Versions of Piers Plowman in its bearing on their Authorship', M.L.R. xvii. 403–9.
1927. G. R. Stewart, Jr., 'The Meter of Piers Plowman', P.M.L.A. xlii. 113–28.
1930–5. J. P. Oakden, Alliterative Verse in Middle English. 2 vols., Manchester. (Vol. ii, c. 11 provides a list of alliterative phrases occurring in the poem.)
1937. H. Kittner, Studien zum Wortschatz William Langlands. Würzburg.

[M.L.R. = The Modern Language Review.
P.M.L.A. = Publications of the Modern Language Association of America].

NOTES

TO

PIERS THE PLOWMAN

*** The reader is requested to observe that the C-TEXT is made the *basis* of these notes; and, whenever a reference is given, it is to the C-text, unless the letter 'A' or 'B' be expressly prefixed. In such a case, 'B. 1. 6' (*or* 'B. i. 6') would mean Text B, Passus 1, line 6.

At the beginning of some notes the references to the other texts are supplied. Thus '1. (b. pr. 1; a. pr. 1)' is to be understood to mean that the lines corresponding to line 1 (of Passus I of the C-text) are B-text, prologue, l. 1, and A-text, prologue, l. 1. When there is *no* corresponding line in the A-text, the statement '*not in* a' is sometimes added; so likewise for the B-text. Whenever the letter *a* appears by itself within a square bracket, thus—[a], it is to be considered as an abbreviation for 'A-text;' so with the letters *b, c*.

Sometimes a note is given upon a passage in [a] or [b], when there is no corresponding line in [c]. In such a case, a line is prefixed to the reference. Thus the reference to the 7th line of the prologue of the B-text appears as '— (b. pr. 7; a. pr. 7).'

NOTES TO C. PASSUS I. (B. Prologue; A. Prologue.)

Passus signifies a portion or 'fytte' of a poem. In an entertainment given to Queen Elizabeth at Kenilworth, a minstrel, after singing a portion of a song, was instructed to make 'a pauz and a curtezy, for *primus passus*,' i.e. to signify that the first part was over. See Ritson's Metrical Romanceës, vol. i. p. ccxxii. Compare—' Thus passed is the *first pas* ' of this pris tale;' William of Palerne, l. 161.

N. B.—The References are to the C-text, except when A or B is expressly prefixed.

C. 1. 1. [**B.** prol. 1; **A.** prol. 1.] *softe*, mild, warm. Cf. 'as *soft* as air;' Ant. and Cleop., v. 2. 314.

2. *I shop me into shrobbis*, I betook me to the shrubs, i. e. to such shelter as shrubs afford; in other words, to an out-of-door life, independent of the shelter of a roof. The B-text has—*I shope me in shroudes*, i.e. I put myself into rough clothes, I put on rough clothes. The A-text has—*into a schroud*, i.e. into a rough outer garment. Cf. *shopen hem heremites*, arrayed themselves as hermits; B. prol. 57; A. prol. 54. *Shop*, lit. shaped; the phrase *I shop me* generally means *I got myself ready*, as in *he shop hym to walke*, he got ready to set off walking; Pass. xiv. l. 247. *As y a shepherde were*, as if I were a shepherd; referring (according to the context) either to the out-of-door life of the shepherd, or to his rough outer garments. Since *shepherd* is the reading of nearly all the MSS. of the C-text, it is clear that the word *shepe* (B-text), or *scheep* (A-text), has the same signification, viz. that of shepherd. In fact, John *Schep* (i.e. shepherd) was the assumed name of John Balle (Walsingham, ed. Riley, ii. 33); and in a rude hexameter, which gives the names of the leaders in Wat Tyler's rebellion, we have

'Jak *Chep*, Tronche, Jon Wrau, Thom Myllere, Tyler, Jak Strawe;'

where another reading for *Chep* is *Schep*. See Political Poems, ed. Wright, vol. i. p. 230. Again, in Lydgate's Chorl and Birde, pr. in Ashmole's Theatrum Chemicum, st. 48, p. 223, is the line—

'A *Chepys* Croke to the ys better than a Lance,'

i.e. a shepherd's crook would suit you better than a knight's spear. The word is still in use; see the entry '*Shep*, a shepherd' in Mr. Peacock's Glossary of Words used in Manley and Corringham (E. D. S.), with his examples. Some critics have rejected my explanation on the ground that *shep* is unknown! I may remind them that John Ball was a pastor rather than a sheep, and the example from Lydgate cannot be set aside. Let it be remembered that Chaucer has *hunte* for *hunter*, Kn. Ta. 1160; that *prisune* means *a prisoner*, Genesis and Exodus, ed. Morris, l. 2044; that *message* means *a messenger*, Chaucer's Man of Lawes Tale, l. 333, etc.; that *slep* means *a sleeper*, Ancren Riwle, p. 212; and observe the double use of *herd*, which does duty both for the A.S. *heord*, a flock, and A.S. *hyrde*, a guardian. The poet expressly tells us what his dress was like further on, where he describes himself as being 'thus robed in russett,' Pass. xi. l. 1. See note to that line.

3. *In abit as an ermite.* The simple shepherd's dress resembled that of a hermit. *Vnholy of werkes.* This Dr. Whitaker paraphrases by—'not like an anchorite who keeps his cell, but like one of those unholy hermits who wander about the world to hear and see wonders;' cf. l. 30 below, p. 5. Or it may simply be supposed to be inserted parenthetically, and to express the author's opinion of hermits in general; an opinion which he elsewhere repeats more than once. See particularly Pass. x. l. 203; and cf. note to l. 51 below.

5. 'And saw many cells, and various strange things.' The *cells* are the cells of the various religious houses which he visited; cf. Chaucer's Prol. l. 172, and see Cutts, Scenes and Characters of the Middle Ages,

p. 123. That the word should be spelt *selles* or *sellys* in some MSS. need not surprise us, since Dr. Morris prints *selle* in the very line of Chaucer to which I refer. I wish to add here, once for all, that it is unnecessary to refute, or even to mention, all the oddities of explanation that appear in Dr. Whitaker's notes. Here, for instance, he tells us that *cellis* ought to be *sellis*, inasmuch as it is 'pure Saxon, from *sellic*, wonderful;' but he omits to tell us how this compound adjective (*sél-líc*) could possibly produce the plural substantive *selles*. *Selcouthe* is from the A.S. *seld-cuð*, seldom known, strange, rare. It occurs again in Pass. xiv. ll. 175, 178. But I must beg leave to refer the reader, for the meanings of particular words, to the Glossary to this work, or to Dr. Stratmann's Old English Dictionary. It is needless to cite such references as may easily be found there; though, in the present instance, I will give them by way of example. *Selcouth* occurs (he tells us) in Layamon, l. 280; Genesis and Exodus, ed. Morris, l. 3972; Ancren Riwle, p. 8; Ormulum, l. 19217; King Alisaunder, ed. Weber, l. 154; William of Palerne, l. 2329; Prick of Conscience, l. 1518.

6. *Ac* is rightly translated by the *Bote* (= but) of the A-text. *May morwenyng;* the familiar expression *on a May morning* is almost equivalent to *once upon a time*. All readers of our early poets will remember the fondness which they exhibit for the month of May, especially when writing an exordium. Cf. Pass. xvii. l. 10.

Maluerne hulles, the Malvern hills in Worcestershire, on the border of Herefordshire. The poet mentions them thrice, viz. here, in l. 163 of this Passus (p. 15) and in Pass. x. 295. It may be that the first sketch of the poem was composed in that locality, but we must not be misled into supposing that the poem has much to do with Worcestershire. It is clear, both from very numerous allusions and from the whole tone of the poem, that the place which the poet knew best and most delighted to describe was the city of London. It cannot be too strongly impressed upon the reader (especially as the point has often been overlooked) that one great merit of the poem consists in its exhibition of *London* life and *London* opinions; and that to remember the *London* origin of, at any rate, the larger portion of the poem, is the true key to the right understanding of it. Though William is supposed to be bodily present on the Malvern hills, he is soon *fast asleep* there; and it is of the London world that he dreams.

7. *A ferly* [a, b, *not* c] means a wonder. Cf. 'And I will show you *ferlies* three;' Sir W. Scott: Ballad of Thomas the Rhymer. *Of fairy,* [a, b, *not* c] due to fairy contrivance. In William of Palerne (ed. Skeat), l. 230, we have the same expression *of feyrye* used to signify that a child is *of fairy origin*. On the word *fairy*, see Tyrwhitt's note to l. 6441 of the Canterbury Tales; and especially Keightley's Fairy Mythology, i. 12; ii. 239, 285. It is evident that the word is ultimately from the Latin *fatum;* whence Ital. *fatare*, to enchant; *fata* (probably short for *fatata*), a woman possessing supernatural power, a fay (Fr. *fée*). Cf. Span. *hada* or *hadada*, a fairy, witch; *hadado*, lucky; *hadador*, a sorcerer. It is worth remembering that the word *faerie* in Middle-English has three senses, none of them being equivalent to the

modern *fairy*. Thus it means (1) enchantment, as in the present passage;
cf. Ch. Squ. Tale, l. 201 ; (2) fairyland ; cf. Ch. Squ. Tale, l. 96 ; and note
the expression ' the contree of Fairye' in the Tale of Sir Thopas ; (3) the
people of fairyland (collectively) as in l. 3 of the Wyf of Bathes Tale. It is
used in the modern sense in Antony and Cleopatra, iv. 8. 12.

Me þouȝte; [a, b, *not* c] it seemed to me ; A.S. *me þuhte* (from *þincan*),
which is distinct from *þohte*, the past tense of *þencan*.

——(b. pr. 7 ; a. pr. 7.) *Forwandred*, tired out by wandering; the
A-text simply reads *of wandringe*. *Went me*, turned me, went ; to *wend*
originally meant to *turn*. *Me* is not here used as an 'ethic' dative,
as illustrated in Abbott's Shakespearian Grammar, 3rd ed. sect. 220.
We find the phrase '*wend þe* from wynne,' turn thyself from joy ;
Caedmon, ed. Thorpe, p. 56, l. 28. 'A! *wend te* awei!' ah! turn
thyself away ; Ancren Riwle, ed. Morton, p. 52. ' þus nou ssel eurich....
him-zelue wende,' thus now must every one turn himself; Ayenbite of
Inwyt, ed. Morris, p. 269, last line. And at p. 180 of the last-mentioned
work is a still clearer example—' ase þe wedercoc þet is ope þe steple, þet
him went mid eche wynde,' as the weathercock that is upon the steeple,
that turns itself with each wind. We have already had *shop me* (= betook
myself) in l. 2.

——(b. pr. 10 ; a. pr. 10.) *Sweyued so merye*, sounded so pleasantly.

14. 'I looked eastward, according to the position of the sun, i. e. towards
the sun ;' or [*as in* a, b] 'on high, towards the sun.' The poet, in his
vision, finds himself in a wilderness, that is, in the wide universe, with
power to survey a large part of it. On the East side he beholds a tower
which is the abode of Truth ; i. e. of God the Father, as is more particularly
explained in Pass. ii. 12 ; cf. viii. 232–279. To the West is a deep dale,
the residence of Death and of wicked spirits, containing [a, b, *not in* c]
a dungeon, which is elsewhere explained as being the castle of Care, and
the abode of Falsehood or Lucifer ; Pass. ii. 57. In the central space
between these is the 'fair field' of this world (Matt. xiii. 38). Thus the
poet beholds heaven before him, and the world beneath him, whilst hell
lies behind him.

It is most interesting to observe that this magnificent conception was
probably suggested to the poet by what he may have beheld on the
occasion of seeing some Morality performed. There are several passages,
especially in Passus xxi., which shew that he was quite familiar with the
pageants which were then so popular. In a Dissertation on Pageants, by
T. Sharp, there is an old drawing (an engraving of which is placed
opposite to p. 23) which excellently illustrates the present passage. We
learn from it that, in representing the Morality of the ' Castell of Perseuer-
aunce,' five scaffolds were erected for the purpose around an enclosed
central space. On the South, was ' caro skaffold,' the scaffold representing
the Fleshly nature of man ; on the West was ' mu*n*dus skaffold,' or the
scaffold representing the World ; on the North was ' Belyal skaffold,'
in allusion to the supposed abode of Lucifer in the North (see note to Pass.
ii. 113) ; on the North-east, ' Coveytyse skaffold,' or the abode of Avarice ;

and on the East 'deus skaffold,' or the abode of God. A careful examination of Mr. Sharp's work will render the whole matter sufficiently clear.

In the Chester Plays, ed. Wright, p. 10, the Creator is represented as saying—

'The worlde, that is bouth voyde and vayne,
I forme in the formacion,
With a *dongion of darckenes*,
Which never shall have endinge.'

21. *As the worlde asketh*, as the way of the world requires. In many other places, *aske* answers to our modern *require*. Cf. 'as matrymony askyth;' Myroure of our Lady, ed. Blunt, 1873, p. 192; and see Pass. ii. 34.

23. *Settyng*, planting [c, b]; *eringe*, ploughing [a]. *Swonken*, laboured. *Ful*, very; used like the German *viel*, though etymologically related to *voll*.

24. *That*, that which; 'and won that which these wasteful men expend in gluttony.'

26. *Contenaunce*, outward appearance. *Disgised* [b] *degyset* [a], decked out in strange guise. See a curious passage in Chaucer's Persones Tale (*de superbia*) about the 'strangeness and *disgisines*' of precious clothing. Cf. Knight de la Tour, ed. Wright, p. 64.

27. The A-text has *To* instead of *In;* the sense is the same.

28. *Ful harde*, very hardly, i. e. lived a very hard life. The B-text has *ful streyte*, very strictly. Observe that *-e* is a common adverbial ending.

29. *Heueneryche*, of the kingdom of heaven. This is an instance of a neuter noun forming the genitive case in *-e*. This genitive in *-e* is not common, except in the case of *feminine* nouns.

30. *Ancres*, anchorites. The word *ancre* is both masculine and feminine, as in the *Ancren Riwle*, i.e. the Rule of Anchoresses. See note to Pass. ix. 146.

31. *Carien*, wander, go up and down. The reader will observe that, as shewn by the reading of the B-text, the MSS. use *carien* and *cairen* as equivalent forms. The better form of the word is *cairen*. Compare examples of the use of Icel. *keyra* in Cleasby's Icel. Dict.; and, to the examples given by Stratmann s. v. *cairen*, add the following:—

'I am come hither a venterous Knight,
And *kayred* thorrow countrye farr;'
Percy Folio MS. ed. Hales and Furnivall, ii. 62. 116.
'Then I *kered* to a knight;'—id.; iii. 61. 118.

See also *keere, keered, kere*, and *kyreth* in the Glossary to the same work.

32. *For no*, etc., for (the sake of) any luxurious living, to please their body. Double negatives, like the *no* here following *noght*, are very common.

35. William speaks [b. 33, *not in* c] of the guiltless or honest minstrels, who played instruments merely to gain a livelihood; but this class of men had a bad name, and he proceeds to satirise the unscrupulous jesters and slanderers, whom *alone* he mentions in the C-text. The subject

C. PASS. I. 37. B. PROL. 35, 36. A. PROL. 35, 36.

of *minstrels* is very fully treated of in Ritson's Ancient Romances, vol. i, in Warton's History of English Poetry, Percy's Reliques, etc. See also Chambers' Book of Days, i. 430. Ritson tells us that the instruments they used were the harp, fiddle, bagpipe, pipe, tabour, cittern, hurdy-gurdy, bladder (or canister) and string, and, possibly, the Jew's-harp. The minstrels of King Edward III.'s household played the trumpet, cytole, pipe, tabret, clarion, and fiddle.

Another name for them is *gleemen*. *Jangelers, Jesters, Japers, Disours* (story-tellers), *Jougleors* or *Jugglers* (*joculatores*), all belong to the same fraternity. Cf. Pass. iii. 99. See also Tyrwhitt's note on Chaucer, Cant. Tales, 11453.

—— (b. pr. 35 ; a. pr. 35.) *Iapers*, jesters ; *Iangelers*, idle talkers, chatterers, babblers. Cotgrave gives—'*Iangler*, to jangle, prattle, tattle saucily or scurvily ; ' and—'*Jangleur*, m. a jangler, saucy pratler, scurvy tatler, scurrile jeaster.' See note to Pass. iii. 99. The phrase 'Judas's children' is equivalent to 'children of Satan,' the reference being to Judas Iscariot. See note to Pass. xi. 220; and cf. Pass. xix. 175, 176.

37. 'Invent foul fancies for themselves, and make fools of themselves, and (yet) have their wit at their will, (able) to work if they wished.' The sentence is elliptical, and incomplete ; we must mentally connect with the next line by saying—'*as for such fellows*, that which Paul preaches about them, I might (but will not) prove it (*or* adduce it) here ; (else might I be blameworthy myself, since) he who speaks slander is Lucifer's servant.' The text of S. Paul which William does *not* quote is *Qui non laborat, non manducet* (2 Thess. iii. 10), which is written in the margin of the Oriel (B-text) MS. The quotation *Qui, etc.*, is *not* from S. Paul, nor does William say that it is ; yet it has some resemblance to Eph. v. 4, Col. iii. 8.

41. *Yoden*, went ; equivalent to A.S. *ge-eodon*. The A-text has *eoden* (A.S. *eodon*) here, at least in the Vernon MS.

42. *Hure*, their. The bag or wallet was the beggar's inseparable companion, and was used for receiving the broken pieces of meat and bread bestowed upon him as alms. Cf. Pass. x. 120, 154. He also always carried a *bourdon*, or *staff*.

'That maketh beggares go with *bordon* and *bagges*.'

Song of the Husbandman ; see Polit. Songs (Camd. Soc. 1839), p. 150. See also Barclay's Ship of Fools, ed. Jamieson, i. 305.

Ycrammyd, crammed, the *y*- being the A.S. prefix *ge*-.

43. *Atten*, at the. It is also written *at the*, *at then*, or *atte;* and very frequently *atten ale* is written *atte nale*. In Chaucer's Cant. Tales, ed. Tyrwhitt, 6931, we find *at the nale ;* where most of the MSS. printed in the Six-text edition (Group D, l. 1349) have *atte nale*. So also *at the nende* for *at then end*. *Then* or *ten* is the dative of the article ; hence this corruption is generally found after a preposition. Another similar corruption is *the tone, the tother*, from *that one, that other ;* where the *t* is the sign of the neuter gender, as in *tha-t, i-t* ; compare the Latin *d* in *i-d, quo-d, illu-d*. *Ale* here means an *ale-house*, and such is the best interpretation of it in Launce's speech in Two Gent. of Verona, ii. 5. 61—'Thou hast

not so much charity in thee as to go *to the ale* with a Christian;' for only just above Launce says again—' If thou wilt, go with me *to the ale-house.*' See Staunton's Shakesp. vol. i. p. 43. Respecting *ale*, see Babees Book, ed. Furnivall, p. 208; Chambers' Book of Days, i. 637; Our English Home, p. 88.

44. The B-text has *hij* for *þey*; and [a] has *heo*. *Hij* is written for *hy*, a variation of *hi*, much as *ij* is written for *ii* or *y* in Dutch.

45. Compare
  'And ryght as *Robertes men* · raken [*wander*] aboute
  At feires & at ful ales · & fyllen the cuppe.'
        Pierce the Ploughmans Crede, l. 72.

' Robartes men, or Robertsmen, were a set of lawless vagabonds, notorious for their outrages when Piers Plowman was written. The statute of Edw. III. (an. reg. 5, c. xiv.) specifies " divers manslaughters, felonies, and robberies, done by people that be called *Roberdesmen, Wastours*, and *drawlacches.*" And the statute of Richard II. (an. reg. 7, c. v.) ordains, that the statute of King Edward concerning *Roberdesmen* and *drawlacches* should be rigorously observed. Sir Edward Coke (Instit. iii. 197) supposes them to have been originally the followers of *Robin Hood* in the reign of Richard I. See Blackstone's Comm. bk. iv. ch. 17.'—Warton's Hist. Eng. Poetry, vol. ii. p. 95, ed. 1840. William of Nassyngton says that they tried the latches of people's doors, contrived to get into houses, and then extorted money either by telling some lying tale or playing the bully. See Pass. viii. 11, and the confession of *Roberd the robber* in the B-text, Pass. v. 469. See also the description of the *wastour*, Pass. ix. 149; and of the *brytonere*, id. 152.

48. *Seint Iame*, i. e. Saint James or Santiago. His shrine at Compostella, in Galicia, was a famous place of pilgrimage; see Southey's poem of The Pilgrim to Compostella. Cf. Pass. v. 122. See a good popular account of him in Chambers' Book of Days, ii. 120 (July 25). A book called the Stacyons of Rome and The Pilgrims' Sea-voyage (ed. Furnivall, 1867, for the Early English Text Society) well illustrates this passage. Rome abounded with shrines at which several thousands of years of remission from purgatory could be obtained. The Sea-voyage is a satire upon the inconveniences of the pilgrimage to Compostella. For a note on *Palmer*, see Pass. viii. 162. For a good popular article on the Pilgrims of the Middle Ages, see pp. 157–194 of Scenes and Characters of the Middle Ages, by the Rev. E. L. Cutts. Out of the numerous allusions to Saint James in early writers, I select the following :—

  'At Rome sche hadde been, and at Boloyne,
  In Galice at seynt Iame, and at Coloyne;'
        Chaucer's Prol. 465.

Cf. Marco Polo, ed. Yule, ii. 259; Skelton, ed. Dyce, i. 106.

49. It is remarkable that the author should have changed the ironical expression *wyse tales* of the A-text and B-text into the more prosaic *unwyse tales* of the C-text. He seems to have wished to guard against all possibility of a mistake as to his real opinion.

50. That pilgrims were privileged to exaggerate pretty freely, seems to have been very generally understood. Thus in Trevisa's translation of Higden's Polychronicon, i. 225, we find a passing allusion to 'pilgrims and palmers, þat faste con liȝe.' And see Wordsworth's Eccl. Biog. 4th ed. i. 312.

51. See the chapter on Hermits in Cutts' Scenes and Characters of the Middle Ages, pp. 93-151. He rightly observes that the popular notion of a hermit, viz. that he lived altogether in retirement, is quite wrong as far as concerns England in the fourteenth century. A man could only become a hermit by consent of the bishop of the diocese, and he was admitted as hermit in a formal religious service. Mr. Cutts gives a summary of the service for habiting and blessing a hermit, from the Pontifical of Bishop Lacy of Exeter, of the fourteenth century; another account may be found in Lewis's Life of Bishop Pecock, ed. 1744, p. 94. Mr. Cutts observes that the hermit 'dressed in a robe very much like the robes of other religious orders; lived in a comfortable little house of stone or timber; often had estates, or a pension, for his maintenance, besides what charitable people were pleased to leave him in their wills, or to offer in their lifetime; he lived on bread and meat, and beer and wine, and had a chaplain to say daily prayers for him, and a servant or two to wait upon him; his hermitage was not always up in the lonely hills, or deep-buried in the shady forests—very often it was by the great high roads, and sometimes in the heart of great towns and cities.' The last assertion, strange as it may seem, is abundantly evident from a very extraordinary passage which appears in Piers the Plowman (in the C-Text *only*), viz. at Pass. x. 140-218. There was even a hermitage upon London wall; Riley's Memorials of London, p. 117. Compare also the description of 'an heap of hermits;' Pass. ix. 183; and the passage about hermits in Pass. xviii. 6-36.

52. Our Lady of Walsingham's shrine was much resorted to; its celebrity almost surpassed that of St. Thomas's shrine at Canterbury. In Blomefield's Norfolk we read that King Henry VIII. walked barefoot from Barsham to this shrine [no very great distance] and presented Our Lady with a necklace of great value. He also tells us that the common people had an idea that the Milky Way pointed towards Walsingham, and they called it *Walsingham-way* accordingly. It is remarkable that the Milky Way is, in Spain, called *the road to Santiago*; see Quart. Review, Oct. 1873; p. 464. The reason is obvious, viz. that the roads leading to such places of pilgrimage were as crowded with pilgrims as the Milky Way is with stars. It is impossible to cite all the numerous references to Walsingham. The best account is that given by Erasmus, in his Colloquy entitled Peregrinatio Religionis Ergo; an abstract of which will be found in Cutts' Scenes and Characters of the Middle Ages, p. 180. Quotations from the original will be found in the Percy Folio MS. iii. 465-471, in the essay prefixed to the ballad beginning—'As yee came ffrom the holy land Of *walsingham*;' to which the reader is particularly referred. See also Weever's Funeral Monuments, pp. 111, 131; Paston Letters, ed. Gairdner, i. 48. Ruins of the convent, with two wells called the 'wishing-wells,' are still to be seen at Old Walsing-

ham, Norfolk. The monastery was founded for Augustinian or Black Canons. See Chambers' Book of Days, i. 795, ii. 8, 174. The significance of the word *wenches* will best appear from the notice of the 'wenches' whom the Sompnour had 'at his retenue,' as described not far from the beginning of Chaucer's Freres Tale; or from the Examination of William Thorpe, in Foxe's Acts and Monuments, who told Archbishop Arundel—' I know well that when divers men and women will goe thus, after their owne wils and finding out, on pilgrimage, they will ordaine with them before, to have with them both men and women, that can well sing wanton songs.' And see Wyclif's Works, ed. Arnold, i. 83.

53. *Lobies*, loobies or lubbars; *longe*, tall. Compare the following curious example. 'Dauid with a mighty stroke of a stone out of a slyng hyt Goly on the heed; and leyd hym streyght alo*n*ge on the grounde, as *longe a lobour* as he was.' Horman's Vulgaria, leaf 269.

54. In Chaucer's Monkes Prologue, the *cope* is the mark of a *monk;* in Pierce the Ploughman's Crede, it is that of a *mendicant friar*. In Chaucer's Prologue, the Frere has a semi-cope. See also l. 59 below, and Pass. x. 210.

55. *And made hem-selue* is a sort of translation of the older phrase of the B-text, which has *And shopen hem*, i. e. and arrayed themselves as; see note to l. 2.

56. The four Orders of mendicant friars are severely satirized in The Ploughman's Crede; see notes in my edition on ll. 29, 486. They were the Carmelites (white friars), Augustines (Austin friars), Jacobins or Dominicans (black friars), and Minorites (gray friars). They are easily remembered by Wycliffe's jest upon them; for which see note to Pass. xi. 220.

58. To *glose* is to comment upon. The commentaries often strayed from and superseded the text. See Chaucer, Sompnoures Tale, l. 80. *As hem good lykede*, as it pleased them well. *Lykede* is very frequently thus employed as an impersonal verb. *Hem* is the dative case. *Good* is an adjective, but is used here with an adverbial force.

60. The B-text has *maistres freris*, master-friars; where the two nominatives plural are in apposition. *At lykyng* [b, a, *not* c], at their liking, as they like.

62. 'Since Love has turned pedlar.' This alludes to the money received by friars for hearing confessions. Besides this, the friars literally resembled pedlars when they carried about with them knives and pins to give away to women. See the description of the *Frere* in Chaucer's Prologue.

64. The three texts differ here, using different expressions for the same thought. The sense of the B-text is—' Except Holy Church and they [the friars] hold better together, the greatest mischief on earth will be increasing very fast.' The regular friars and secular clergy were so far from 'holding together,' that they quarrelled fiercely as to the right of hearing confessions. See Pass. vii. 120.

66. See Chaucer's description of a *Pardonere*, in his Prologue; and Massingberd's English Reformation, p. 127. For a passage on papal bulls, see Wyclif's Works, iii. 308.

69. *Of falsnesse of fastinges*, of breaking their vows of fasting. The first *of* belongs to *asoilie* or *assoilen*. The Vernon MS. of the A-text has *and fastinge*, as printed; but MSS. T. and U. have *of* for *and*, which is certainly better.

70. *Lewede*, unlearned; it exactly answers (in sense) to the modern adj. *lay*. *Lyuede hym wel*, believed him entirely.

72. The B-text and A-text have *He bonched*, etc.; lit. he banged them with his brevet, and bleared their eyes. We should now say, he thrust his brevet in their faces. The word is *bouched* in Mr. Wright's edition, but my collation of MSS. shews this to be an error; and, indeed, no such word as *bouch* exists. On the other hand, we find 'Bunchon, *tundo, trudo*,' in the Prompt. Parvulorum; Palsgrave gives—'To bounche or pusshe one; he buncheth me and beateth me, *il me pousse*.' Lydgate also, as quoted in Halliwell's Dictionary, s. v. Bonchen, has—'They bonchen theire brestis with fistes wondre soore;' MS. Ashmole 39, fol. 47; Skelton has—'With that he gaue her a *bounce*,' ed. Dyce, i. 158; and in Horman's Vulgaria, leaf 135, back, I find—'He came home with a face all to-bounced, Domum reuersus est facie contusa.'

To *blear one's eye* is a common phrase for to blind, delude, cajole. See Chaucer, C. T. 3863, 4047, 17201.

'Wyth fantasme, and fayrye,
 Thus sche *blerede hys yye*.'

Ly Beaus Disconus, l. 1432; Ritson's Met. Rom. vol. ii.

73. *Rageman*; properly a catalogue or roll of names; here applied to the charter or bull with numerous bishops' seals. Mr. Wright has a long note upon the word *Ragman-roll* at p. 81 of his Anecdota Literaria, 1844. He prints, at p. 83, a poem with the title of 'Ragman-roll,' from MS. Fairfax 16. There was even a game with this name, which is described in Wright's Homes of Other Days, p. 247. In imitation, probably, of the bull with many seals hanging from it, a parchment-roll was provided, on which were written verses descriptive of persons' characters; and against each verse was fastened a string. The parchment was rolled up, with the ends of the strings hanging out. The player chose one of the strings, and thus learnt his character. Gower alludes to this game, Conf. Amant. ed. Pauli, iii. 355. See also Skelton, Garlande of Laurell, l. 1490, and Dyce's note; P. Pl. Crede, l. 180; Cowel's Law Dictionary; Towneley Mysteries, p. 311; and Todd's Johnson, s. v. *rigmarole*. And see note to Pass. xix. 122.

Rings and *brooches* are often thus mentioned together. Near the end of the Pardoner's Tale, Chaucer makes the Pardoner ask the people to offer 'broches, spones, ringes.'

76. 'Were the bishop a truly holy man, or worth (i.e. fit to have) both his ears, his seal would not be sent (to the pardoner, for him) to deceive the people with.' The expression *blessid* is used by the poet to mean 'truly righteous' or 'truly holy,' as we learn from his use of it in Pass. x. 13, q. v. The phrase 'worth both his ears' is a satirical expression, signifying that the person spoken of is one to whom his ears are of some use, not one who turns a deaf ear to the complaints of the poor.

78. 'Yet it is not against the bishop that the young fellow preaches; for (often) the parish-priest and he (agree to) divide the money, which the poor people would else get.' Sometimes, instead of quarrelling (as described in Pass. vii. 120), the priest and pardoner compounded matters, and divided the spoil. Chaucer, however, in his Prologue, l. 704, makes the pardoner more than a match for the parson, and represents him as cheating both the parish-priest and his flock too. The phrase *noȝt by þe bysshop* might also be translated to mean 'not by the bishop's leave,' but the two preceding lines shew that the pardoner could easily obtain such leave. Hence we must consider it as spoken ironically, meaning— 'But you may be sure it is never against the bishop that he preaches.' The use of *by* in the sense of *against*, or *with reference to*, is common in Middle English. See 1 Cor. iv. 4, and the examples in Trench's Select Glossary and Eastwood and Wright's Bible Word-book.

80. *Yf þei ne were*, if they did not exist; we should now say, if it were not for them. It is a common Middle-English idiom.

82. *Pestelence tyme*. There were three great pestilences which were long remembered, viz. in 1348-9, 1361-2, and 1369; we may even count a fourth, in 1375-6. See note to Pass. vi. 115. The first was also called the *great* pestilence, and is probably here meant. In Pass. vi. 115, William speaks of *these pestilences*, with obvious reference to the *first and second* ones.

83. *To haue*, i.e. and petitioned the bishop that they might have. Cf. Chaucer, Prologue, where he says of the good parish priest,

'He sette not his benefice to huyre . . . .
And ran to *Londone*, unto seynte Poules,
To seeken him a chaunterie for soules.'

84. These chantry-priests, who 'sang for simony,' were sometimes called *annueleres*; see Chaucer, Chan. Yeom. Tale, l. 1. The little side-chapels, in which they sang their *annuels*, or anniversary masses for the dead, were called *chantries*, a name which still survives. See a curious note on the arrangements at St. Paul's Cathedral, in Dean Milman's History of Latin Christianity, vol. vi. p. 373, note *h*.

85. The whole of the passage in ll. 85-217 (b. pr. 87-209) is peculiar to the later texts of the poem, and is not found in the A-text, or earliest draught, with the exception of six lines, found in A. pr. 84-89. It is of much interest and importance, and refers entirely to *London*; it was probably inserted here, because London has just been mentioned.

86. *Crownynge*, i.e. the tonsure, which was a token of their clerical calling. Wyclif has the same expression; Wyclif's Works, ed. Arnold, iii. 447. On the tonsure, see Mrs. Jameson, Legends of Monastic Orders, p. xxxii. Mr. Peacock, in his notes to Myrc, p. 69, gives a long list of references.

89. 'Lie (i.e. lodge, dwell) in London during Lent, and at other times.'

90. *Tellen*, count. Formerly, the three principal courts of law, the

C. PASS. I. 93. B. PROL. 95. (NOT IN A.)

King's Bench, the Common Pleas, and the Exchequer, had a separate jurisdiction. The Exchequer decided only such cases as related to the collection of the revenue, and hence the ecclesiastics who held office in it are said here to *challenge* (i.e. to *claim*) the King's debts from the various *wards* or divisions of the city. The *wardmote* is the court, or *meeting*, held in each ward; see it fully described in the Liber Albus, p. 33. They also claimed for the King all *waifs* and *strays*, i.e. property without an owner and strayed cattle (as Mr. Wright explains it); but see *streyues* in the Glossary.

'Summe beth in ofice wid the king, and gaderen tresor to hepe,
And the fraunchise of holi cherche hii laten ligge slepe.'
Political Songs (Camd. Soc. 1839), p. 325.

We read also in the complaint of the Ploughman (Polit. Poems, i. 325), the following account of the ' canons seculer : '—

'They have great prebendes and dere,
Some two or three, and some mo;
A personage to ben a playing fere,
And yet they *serve the King also*,
And let to ferme all that fare
To whom that woll most give therefore;' etc.

Compare Wyclif's Works, iii. 215, 277, 335.

93. Wyclif complains in the same strain—'But our Priests ben so busie about wordlie [*worldly*] occupation, that they seemen better Baylifs or Reues, than ghostlie Priests of Jesu Christ.' Two Treatises against Friars, ed. James, p. 16. See also Wyclif's Works, ed. Arnold, iii. 277, 335. On the duties of a Treasurer, see the Babees Book, p. 318.

95-124. (*not in* b, a.) This curious passage is peculiar to the C-text. The Ilchester MS. is here fuller, and gives a part of what must have been the true form of lines 107-123, where the lack of alliteration shews that some corruption has crept into the text.

96. The sense of ll. 96-102 is—'Ye suffer idolatry in many different places, and boxes, bound with iron, are set forth, to receive the toll paid through such untrue sacrifice. In remembrance of miracles, much wax hangs there (at the shrine); all the world knows well that the stories told cannot be true. But ye prelates suffer laymen to live and die in such misbelief, because it is profitable to you to purseward.' The term *idolatry*, as applied to the worship of images, may be found in Wyclif; Works, ed. Arnold, iii. 462. On the next page we find—'hit semes that this offrynge to ymagis is a sotile caste of Anticriste and his clerkis, for to drawe almes fro pore men, and cumber worldly prestis with muck, that thai nouther know God ne hemselfe,' etc.; see also p. 293.

It is right to add that there is probably a special force in the epithet 'bound with iron' as regards the boxes mentioned in l. 97. It seems that such boxes were known to be meant for the reception of alms. This appears from a passage in Riley's Memorials of London, p. 586, where it is recorded how a certain William Derman was punished with the pillory because he 'pretended to be, and called himself, a domestic and serjeant of the House or Hospital [of Bedlem] aforesaid, for collecting alms and other works of charity for the said hospital. And so, under false colour, he walked about the city *with a box bound with iron*, ... and collected many alms therein.'

There is another allusion to these alms-boxes in B. xv. 208.

103. *Ich lyue wel*, I verily believe.

106. *Ful*, fell. The various readings are *fil* and *fel*.

109. *Syngen*, sin. This curious form of the verb occurs frequently in the C-text (MS. P); cf. A.S. *syngian*. The story of Hophni and Phinehas, alluded to in the B-text, x. 280-282 (p. 306) is, in the C-text, placed here, in the Prologue. Cf. 1 Sam. iv.

119. *Maumettes*, idols. Thus, in the Persones Tale (De Avaritia), Chaucer says—'an idolastre peraventure ne hath not but o *maumet* or two, and the avaricious man hath many; for certes, every florein in his coffre is his *maumet*.' The Old French *mahommet*, an idol, shews that the word is borrowed from the name of Mahomet. The false notion that the Mahometans were idolaters was very prevalent in the middle ages. Colonel Yule, in his edition of Marco Polo, vol. i. p. 174, quotes from Weber's Metrical Romances (vol. ii. p. 228) the following lines :—

'Kyrkes they made of crystene lawe,
And here *maumettes* lete downe drawe.'

He adds—'Don Quixote too, who ought to have known better, cites with admiration the feat of Rinaldo in carrying off, in spite of forty Moors, a golden image of Mahomed.' See also Selden, in his Table Talk, art. *Popery*. The word is not to be confused with *mammet*, a doll or puppet, as is often done.

125. (b. pr. 97.) *Houres*, i.e. canonical hours, prayers made at stated times in the day; see *Hours* in Hook's Church Dictionary, and the full account in the Ancren Riwle, p. 21. Cf. Pass. ii. 180.

126. *Drede ys*, there is a fear; it is to be feared.

127. *Constorie*, also spelt *Consistorie*, which is the fuller and more correct form; a church-council or assembly of prelates. It is here used of the Last Great Assembly held by Christ at the Day of Judgment. '*Consistory*, a word used to denote the Court Christian, or Spiritual Court. Every bishop has his consistory court, held before his chancellor or commissary, in his cathedral church, or other convenient place of his diocese, for ecclesiastical causes;' Hook's Church Dictionary. Cf. Pass. iv. 179, 476; also B. ii. 177.

131. I.e. Peter deputed the power of the Keys to the four cardinal virtues, viz. Prudence, Temperance, Fortitude, and Justice; see Pass. xxii. 274-310. The old English names are Sleight, Temperance, Strength, and Doom; see Ayenbite of Inwyt, p. 124, where we read further that—'Thise uour uirtues byeth y-cleped cardinals, uor thet hi byeth he*gh*est amang the uirtues, huer-of the yealde [*old*] filosofes speke. Vor be thise uour uirtues the man gouerneth himzelue ine thise wordle, as the apostles gouerneth holy cherche be his cardinals.' Compare Pass. xxii. 409-425, p. 575. So in Shakespeare, Henry VIII, iii. 3. 103—

'Upon my soul, two reverend *cardinal virtues*!
But *cardinal sins* and hollow hearts I fear ye.'

132. *Closynde ȝates*, closing gates. This is a sort of translation of the Latin *cardinalis*, which is derived from *cardo*, a hinge. The power of the keys is, as it were, made for the moment into a power of the hinges.

133. *Ther*, where. This sense of *there* should be carefully observed. Cf. l. 204 (b. pr. 190).

To closye with heuene, to close heaven with. The reader of Middle English must note, once for all, that the preposition *with* is commonly so placed as to follow its verb immediately. Thus, in the B-text, ii. 31, *to marye with myself* means 'to marry myself with;' and in the same, ii. 116, *to wratthe with treuthe* means 'whereby to make Truth angry;' both of those passages were altered in the C-text, as if to avoid the apparent ambiguity. So in Chaucer's Squire's Tale, l. 471, *to helen with your hurtes* means 'to heal your hurts with;' and in l. 641, *to helen with this hauk* means 'to heal this hawk with.' See also Pierce the Ploughman's Crede, l. 116, etc.

We may also note the occasional use of the infinitives in *-ye* or *-ie*; thus *to closye* is to close; so *asoilie*, in l. 68, and *rebukie* in l. 110 above; *cracchy*, B. prol. 186. It occurs also in the present tense, as in *louye*, i.e. may love, in l. 149 below.

134. *At court*, at the court of Rome. The B-text has *atte courte*, i.e. at the court. *Cauȝt han*, have caught; B-text, *cauȝt of*, i.e. received. The author revised his work in the minutest particulars, as is evident throughout. It is impossible to point out the extremely numerous variations, which the reader can only discover by a careful comparison of the texts.

—— (b. pr. 111.) I *can* speak more, for I have much I could say about them; yet I *cannot* speak more, out of reverence, for the power of electing a pope is a high and holy thing. Such seems to be William's meaning. Observe that the C-text has an entirely different and less ambiguous line, viz. l. 138.

139. (b. pr. 112.) Tyrwhitt rightly supposed that this part of the poem was written after the death of the Black Prince, when his son Richard was heir-apparent. This limits the date of composition of this portion (as it appears in the B-text) to the period between June 8, 1376, and June 21, 1377.

141. *Kynde witte* (a very common phrase in our author) is what we now call *common sense*.

143. 'Contrived that the commons should provide their provisions' [c]; *or*, 'Contrived that the commons should provide for themselves' [b]; where *themselves* appears to be equivalent to *all of them*.

144. *Alle craftes*, all handicrafts; the B-text has *Of kynde witte craftes*, handicrafts that could be pursued by help of common intelligence. Besides the king, knights, clergy, and commons, there was a fifth class, of ploughmen, etc., mere tillers of the soil, who were looked upon as inferior to the rest. The B-text is here more explicit.

C. PASS. I. 149. B. PROL. 123, 126. (NOT IN A.) 15

—— (b. pr. 123; *not in* c, a.) I have no doubt that the *lunatic* is
William himself. He is here expressing his favourite loyal hope that
the king may so govern as to be beloved by all loyal subjects. For the
use of *lunatic* there are three reasons : (1) it conveys a touch of satire,
as though it were a mad thing to hope for ; (2) a *lunatic* is privileged
to say strange things ; and (3) he expressly declares, at the beginning
of Pass. xv. (B-text), that people considered him a *fool*, and that he *raved*.
This opinion he bitterly adopts. He makes the lunatic, however, speak
clergealy, i. e. like a scholar.

The word *thing* does not necessarily imply contempt; it merely signifies
a creature, a person. Cf. 'For he was a ful dughti *thing* ;' Cursor Mundi
(Text C), l. 8182 ; ed. Morris.

149. *Leue*, grant. No two words have been more hopelessly confused
than *leue* and *lene*. See *Leue* in the Glossary. The line means—'And
grant thee to govern thy land, so that loyalty (i. e. thy lieges) may love thee.'

151. Conscience [*B-text*, the angel] condescends to speak, but only
in Latin, since common people ought not to be told how to justify them-
selves ; all who could not understand Latin or French had best suffer and
serve. The angel's reproof to the king is in Leonine or riming verses,
of which the first is a hexameter, and is put into the mouth of the king
himself. The remaining six [six in the B-text, but the C-text omits the
last but one of them] are alternate hexameters and pentameters, and
contain the angel's charge to the king. The verses may have been com-
posed by William himself, and may be thus translated :—

(You say) 'I am a king, I am a prince,' (but you will be) neither
    perhaps hereafter.
O thou who dost administer the special laws of Christ the King,
That thou mayst do this the better, as you are just, be merciful!
Naked justice requires to be clothed by thee with mercy;
Whatever crops thou wouldst reap, such be sure to sow.
If justice is stripped bare, let it be meted to thee of naked justice ;
If mercy is sown, mayest thou reap of mercy!

It may be added, that long pieces of advice to kings are common at
this period of English. Compare Gower's Confessio Amantis, lib. vii. ;
Occleve's poem, entitled De Regimine Principum ; and William's own
poem of Richard the Redeless.

—— (b. pr. 139 ; *not in* c, a.) *Goliardeys.* 'Un goliardois, Fr. ;
Goliardus, or *Goliardensis,* Lat. This jovial sect seems to have been
so called from Golias, the real or assumed name of a man of wit, toward
the end of the thirteenth century, who wrote the Apocalypsis Goliae,
and other pieces in burlesque Latin rimes, some of which have been
falsely attributed to Walter Map ... In several authors of the thirteenth
century, quoted by Du Cange, the *Goliardi* are classed with the *jocu-
latores et buffones.*'—Tyrwhitt ; note on l. 562 of Chaucer's Cant. Tales.
But it would appear that *Golias* is the sole invention of Walter Map,
and that the original 'Golias' poems are really his. He named his
imaginary Bishop Golias after the Philistine slain by David ; not without

some reference, perhaps, to the O. Fr. *goule*, Lat. *gula*, gluttony. Soon after, *Goliardus* meant a clerical buffoon; later still, it meant any *jougleur*, or any teller of ribald stories; in which sense it is used by Chaucer; Prologue, l. 560. 'A mynstralle, a *gulardous*' is mentioned in Rob. of Brunne, Handlyng Synne, l. 4704. See Morley's English Writers, vol. i. p. 586. William's *Goliardeys* is 'a glutton of words,' one full of long pieces which he could recite; cf. the Latin phrase *helluo librorum*. He is here made to quote, in an altered form, two lines which are also found as under :—

'O rex, si rex es, rege te, vel eris sine re, rex;
Nomen habes sine re, nisi te recteque regas, rex.'
Political Poems, ed. Wright, i. 278.

—— (b. pr. 143; *not in* c, a.) The commons are not supposed to have understood the angel's advice given in Latin, but they just knew as much as was good for them to know; they could just say—

'Precepta regis sunt nobis vincula legis.'

☞ **There is a slight alteration here in the C-text; for notes to B. prol. 146–191, see l. 165–205 below.**

159. (br. pr. 210; a. pr. 84; *see* p. 18.) Lines 159–164 (b. pr. 210–215, a. pr. 84–89) will be found in Texts A and B also (*see* p. 18); but it will be observed that this passage comes very much earlier in the C-text than in the B-text, having been transposed from its former place. The law-sergeants are here spoken of. 'Lawyers were originally priests and of course wore the tonsure; but when the clergy were forbidden to intermeddle with secular affairs, the lay lawyers continued the practice of shaving the head, and wore the coif for distinction's sake. It was at first made of linen, and afterwards of *white silk;*' British Costume, p. 126. It was a sort of skullcap; Strutt, Manners and Customs, iii. 76. And see Brand, Pop. Antiq. ed. Ellis, iii. 117, note. The white silk hoods are again alluded to in Pass. iv. l. 451.

161. (b. pr. 212; a. pr. 86; *see* p. 18.) *To plede*, to plead; the B-text has *plededen*, pleaded. This verb is derived from the O. Fr. *plet*, a plea, which is shortened from the Lat. *placitum*, an opinion. By the Statute of 36 Edw. III, c. 15 (A.D. 1362), it was enacted that pleadings should henceforward be conducted in English, but recorded in Latin. They were not *recorded* in English till the fourth year of George II.

The *penny* was an important coin in the time of Edward III.; but it should be observed that *any* coin, such as a florin, could be sometimes called a *penny*, in which case a *half-penny* would mean the half-florin, and a *farthing* (*fourth-ing*) the fourth part of the florin. See note to Pass. iii. 157. There is a satirical poem in praise of 'Sir Peny,' who was much sought after by all men, including lawyers. See Hazlitt, Early Popular Poetry, i. 165.

162. (b. pr. 213; a. pr. 87; *see* p. 18.) *Vnlose*, unclose, i. e. open; indeed, the Cotton MS. reads *open*. The A-text likewise has *vnloseþ*, unclose; but the B-text has *vnlese*, which is a bad spelling and should rather be *vnlose*.

163. (b. pr. 214; a. pr. 88; *see* p. 18.) 'Thou mightest better measure the mist on Malvern hills than get a *mum* out of their mouth, until money be exhibited to them.' A *mum* is anything approaching to a word, a *mumble;* as may be well illustrated from the Towneley Mysteries, p. 194, where we find the line—
'Though thi lyppus be stokyn [*tightly closed*], yit myght thou say *mom!*'
In the Merry Wives of Windsor, v. 2. 6, Slender says—'I come to her in white, and cry *mum!*' The whole of this passage is imitated by Lydgate in his London Lyckpeny; see Specimens of English, 1394–1579, ed. Skeat, p. 24.

☞ Observe the break here in the B-text; the transposed passage (see Note to C. 1. 159) ends here.

165. (b. pr. 146; *not in* a.) This well-known fable, of the rats and mice trying to hang a bell round the cat's neck, is nowhere so well told as here. Mr Wright says—'The fable is found in the old collection, in French verse of the fourteenth century, entitled Ysopet; and M. Robert has also printed a Latin metrical version of the story from a MS. of the same century. La Fontaine has given it among his fables.' It is a well-known story in Scottish history, that this fable was narrated by Lord Gray to the conspirators against the favourites of King James III., when Archibald, Earl of Angus, exclaimed, 'I am he who will bell the cat;' from which circumstance he obtained the name of Archibald Bell-the-Cat. In the present instance, the rats are the burgesses and more influential men among the commons; the mice, those of less importance. The cat is Edward III.; the kitten is his grandson Richard, then heir to the crown (1376–7).

Certainly Skelton had carefully read Piers the Plowman; and he too alludes to the fable in his Colin Clout, ll. 162–5 (ed. Dyce, i. 317).

The word *raton* is not uncommon; it is often called *rotten*, as in the line—' Here a *rotten*, here a mousse;' Chester Plays, ed. Wright, p. 51.

——— (b. pr. 152; *not in* c, a.) *Doute* in Middle English almost always means *fear*, as here. *Loke*, look about us; cf. l. 187 (b. pr. 172).

173. (b. pr. 155.) *Ous lotheth*, it loathes us, i. e. we loathe.

176. (b. pr. 158.) The reading *resonable* of the C-text makes it obvious that the form *renable* of the B-text is a mere contraction of the same word; MS. G. (C-text) has *resnable*. Chaucer has the same contracted form in the Freres Tale, l. 211—'And speke as *renably*, and faire, and wel.' Again, in Myrc's Duties of a Parish Priest (ed. Peacock, 1868), the Cotton MS. has '*renabulle* tonge' where the Douce MS. has 'resonable.' But it was often regarded as if formed from the verb *renne*, to run; hence it is still used in Norfolk in the form *runnable*; i. e. glib, loquacious. In the following it has, apparently, the older meaning:—

'Hir maners might no man amend;
Of tong she was *trew and renable*,
And of hir semblant soft and stabile.'
Ywaine and Gawaine, l. 208; in Ritson's Met. Rom., vol. i. p. 10.

C. PASS. I. 178. B. PROL. 159. (NOT IN A.)

—— (b. pr. 159.) 'Said, for a sovereign remedy for himself;' i. e. as far as himself was concerned. So again, in l. 206, the mouse says—'I sigge it for me,' I say it, as far as I am concerned. This line (b. pr. 159) was omitted in the revision, viz. in the C-text.

178. (b. pr. 161.) *Byȝes*, necklaces. *Colers of crafty werke*, collars of skilful workmanship; alluding to the gold chains, such as are still worn by sheriffs, etc.

—— (b. pr. 164.) 'And at other times they are elsewhere,' viz. away from London, living in retirement.

195. (b. pr. 181.) *Leten*, considered, esteemed; cf. B. iv. 160.

201. *Lete the cat worthe*, to let the cat be, to let it alone. Cf. Pass. iii. 49. *Worthe* is the A.S. *weorðan*, to be. When Alexander tamed Bucephalus, we read that

> 'Soone hee leapes on-loft · and *lete hym worthe*
> To fare as hym lyst faine · in feelde or in towne.'
> William of Palerne, etc.; ed. Skeat, 1867; p. 216.

203. (b. pr. 189.) [*Is*] *seuen ȝer passed*, [it is] seven years past, seven years ago.

204. The expressive word *elynge, elenge,* or *ellinge,* still common in Kent, includes the meanings *sad* and *solitary*. Henry VIII., in a letter to Anne Bullen, speaks of 'his *ellengness* since her departure;' Hearne's edition of Avesbury, p. 360. The word occurs again, Pass. xxiii. 2; and B. x. 94; and is used both by Chaucer and Occleve. See *Alange* in Murray's New Eng. Dictionary.

205. 'Uae tibi, terra, cuius rex puer est, et cuius principes mane comedunt;' Ecclesiastes x. 16.

When Robert Crowley reprinted *Piers Plowman*, in the time of *Edward VI.*, he added, for obvious reasons, this sidenote: 'Omnium doctissimorum suffragio, dicuntur hec de lassiuis, fatuis aut ineptis principibus, non de etate tenellis. Quasi dicat, ubi rex puerilis est.' (In this and other quotations, I follow the peculiar spellings of the originals. The use of *e* for *æ* in Latin words is very common.)

☞ A variation in the B-text here; for note to B. prol. 192, see note to l. 212.

207. (b. pr. 202; *not in* a.) Observe how *the cat* (Edw. III.) is here distinguished from *the kitten* (his grandson Richard).

208. *Ne carpen of*, nor shall men talk about. Supply *shal* from the line above. *Costide me neuere*, would never have cost *me* anything; for I would not have subscribed to it.

209. 'And, even if I *had* subscribed, I would not own it, but would submit and say nothing; and to do so is the best course.'

211. (*not in* b, a.) 'Till misfortune, that chastens many men, teaches them better.' The corresponding line (in position) in [b] is l. 206, expressed in totally different language.

212-215. (b. pr. 192-200; *not in* a.) The wise mouse here suggests that the rats want keeping in order themselves, and even mice have

C. PASS. I. 221. B. PROL. 218. A. PROL. 98. 19

been known to help themselves to people's malt. And (in the B-text, which is here fuller than the later one) he adds that the cat may sometimes be expected to go out catching rabbits, and meanwhile he will let the rats and mice alone. ' Better a little loss than a long sorrow ; (for there would, if the king died, be) confusion amongst us all, though we be rid of a tyrant.' William uses *the mase* (b. pr. 196) to mean *confusion, bewilderment;* and the whole line is explanatory of the ' long sorrow ' mentioned above.

The lines—' We mice (the lower order of commons) would eat up many men's malt, and ye rats (the burgesses) would wake men from their rest,' etc.—are almost prophetical. The rising of the peasantry under Wat Tyler took place but a short time after they were first written, viz. in June, 1381. No doubt our poet disapproved of the violence of that movement ; as is shewn by his curtailment of the passage in the C-text.

☞ A variation in the B-text here ; for notes to B. prol. 210–214, see notes to ll. 159–163 above, pp. 16, 17.

221. (b. pr. 218 ; a. pr. 98.) ' The trade of brewing was confined almost wholly to females, and was reckoned among the callings of low repute.'—Note to Liber Albus, ed. H. T. Riley ; p. 307. At p. 312 of the same we read, ' If any *brewer* or *brewster*,' etc. This accounts for the feminine termination in the form *brewesteres* [b]. So too we find *bakers* [c, a], but *baxsteres* [b], because baking also was to some extent in female hands. The retail-dealers or ' regratresses ' of bread were almost always females ; see Riley's Liber Albus, pp. 232, 309 ; and sometimes they baked their bread themselves ; Riley's Memorials of London, p. 324, note 1. See, however, the note to the next line here following—

222. *Wollewebsteres* [b], female weavers of woollen. But the distinction between *webbe*, a male weaver, and *webstere*, a female weaver, is not always made. Thus, in Pass. vii. 221 we find—

' My wif was a *webbe* · and wollen cloth made.'

And it may be admitted that the termination *-ster* (in A.S. a feminine one, as in modern *spinster*) does not seem to have been very carefully used at this period. On this point I beg leave to refer the reader to a passage, too long for quotation, in Marsh's Lectures on the English Language, ed. Smith, pp. 207, 208, 217. See also the remarks in Trench's English Past and Present, pp. 153-157 ; J. Grimm, Deutsche Grammatik, vol. ii. p. 134 ; vol. iii. p. 339 ; Koch, Engl. Gram., iii. 47. In Wright's Vocabularies, vol. i. p. 214, the words *baxter* and *brewster* are treated as masculine nouns, whilst, at p. 216 of the same, they are feminine.

—— (b. pr. 222.) ' Of labourers of every kind there leapt forth some.' For *alkin* we sometimes find *alle kyn, alle kynne, alles kinnes*, and even the odd form *alle skinnes*. The full form is *alles kynnes*, of every kind. It is in the genitive case ; see note to Pass. xi. 128. The word *labourers* in the Statutes of Edward III. is comprehensive, including masons, bricklayers, tilers, carpenters, ditchers, diggers, etc.

20   C. PASS. I. 223.   B. PROL. 220.   A. PROL. 100.

223. (b. pr. 220 ; a. pr. 100.) This line varies ; we find—'tailors and tanners, and tillers of earth' [c]; 'tailors and tinkers, and toll-takers in markets' [b]; 'tailors, tanners, and tuckers also' [a]. A *tucker*, now chiefly used as a proper name, is the same as a fuller of cloth ; and a *tucking-mill* means a fulling-mill for the felting of cloth.

225. *Deux saue dame Emme!* God save dame Emma! or *Dieu vous saue, dame Emme* [b, a]. Evidently the refrain of some low popular song. In B. xiii. 340 (p. 406), the poet speaks of ' dame Emme of Shoreditch,' which was a low locality.

227. 'Good geese and pigs! let's go and dine!' It was the practice thus to tout for custom, standing outside the shop-door. In the same way the taverners keep crying out, 'White wine! Red wine! A taste for nothing!' etc. Here again Lydgate copies from William; see Specimens of English, 1394-1579, ed. Skeat, pp. 25, 26.

229. White and red wines, chiefly imported from France, were common. Though *Osey* is said to come from Portugal in the first volume of Hackluyt's Voyages, p. 188, yet the name is certainly a corruption of *Alsace*. Thus *Ausoy* is written for Alsace frequently in the Romance of Partenay, and Roquefort explains the O.Fr. *Aussay* to mean *Alsatia*. The wines of Gascony, of the Rhine, and of Rochelle, need no explanation. In the C-text, l. 230, instead of a mention of the Rhine, as in the former versions, we find the readings *ruele, rule, ruel*, or *rewle*. The place meant is La Reole, above Bourdeaux, beside the river Garonne ; and the reference is to a kind of Bourdeaux wine.

The roste to defye, to digest the roast meat. This is well illustrated by the following oft-quoted passage :—

> 'Ye shall have rumney and malmesyne,
> Both ypocrasse, and vernage wyne,
> Mount rose and wyne of Greke,
> Both algrade, and respice eke,
> Antioche, and bastarde,
> Pyment also, and garnarde,
> Wyne of Greke, and muscadell,
> Both clarè, pyment, and *Rochell*;
> The reed your stomake *to defye*,
> And pottes of *Osey* set you by.'
>   Squyr of Lowe Degre ; Ritson's Met. Rom. iii. 176.

NOTES TO PASSUS II. (B. Passus I; A. Passus I.)

C. 2. 3. [B. 1. 3. A. 1. 3.] *A loueliche lady of lere*, i.e. *A lady, loueliche of lere*, A lady, lovely of countenance.

5. Here, for *sone* [b, a], the C-text has *Wille*, the poet's own name. For *slepest þou, syxt þow*, the B-text has *slepestow, sestow*, by a common habit. So in A.S., we find *scealtu* for *scealt þu*, i.e. shalt thou.

6. *Mase*, confused medley of people.
8. *Haue thei worship*, if they have honour.
9. *Thei holden no tale*, they kept no account, they regard not.
11. *What may thys be to mene*, what is the meaning of this? *To mene* takes the place of the A.S. *gerund*, where *to* is a preposition governing the dative case, and *mene* is for *mǣnanne*, a dative formed from the infinitive *mǣnan*, to mean. Thus *to mǣnanne* is, literally, *for a meaning*.
12. The tower is that mentioned in Pass. i. 15. *Truth* is here synonymous with the *Father of Faith*, i.e. God the Father and Creator.
15. *Fyue wittes*, five senses, viz. of hearing, sight, taste, smell, and touch. In Pass. xvi. 256 (p. 417) is the passage—

'Bi so thow be sobre · of syght and of tounge bothe,
In ondyng, in handlyng · in alle thy *fyue wittes*.'

20. *In comune thre thynges*, three things in common; viz. clothing, meat, and drink. 'The chief thing for life is water, and bread, and clothing, and an house to cover shame.' Ecclus. xxix. 21; cf. xxxix. 26. Cf. Spenser, F. Q., i. x. 37–39.

—— (b. 1. 24; a. 1. 24.) *For myseise*, as a remedy against disease or discomfort. This curious use of *for* is worth notice. It is sufficiently common.

—— (b. 1. 26; a. 1. 26.) *That thow worth*, so that thou become the worse for it. Cf. note to l. 185 below, p. 29.

25. (b. 1. 27; a. 1. 27.) Chaucer also cites this example of Lot, in the 23rd line of the Pardoner's Tale. And cf. B. Pass. xiv. 74–80 (p. 418).

** *For note to* b. 1. 31, *see note to* l. 30.

29. (b. l. 33; *not in* a.) The word *gerles* here refers to Lot's two sons, Moab and Ammon. There are several examples of the application of the word to the male sex. Thus, in the Coventry Mysteries, ed. Halliwell, p. 181, one of the Roman knights engaged in the Slaughter of the Innocents says—'Here *knave* gerlys I xal steke,' i.e. their knave-girls I shall pierce; and again, at p. 182, he says—'Upon my spere A *gerle* I bere;' whilst, at p. 186, we have the expression—'whan the *boys* sprawlyd at my sperys ende.' In Chaucer's Prologue, l. 664, the word *gurles* means young people; there is nothing to shew of which sex they were. See Trench, Select Glossary, s. v. *Girl*.

30. (b. 1. 31.) Gen. xix. 32. A large number of the Latin quotations with which the text is crowded, is taken from the Latin (Vulgate) version of the Bible. I indicate the references except in the case of some passages from the Gospels, etc., which are easily found.

** *For note to* b. 1. 33, *see note to* l. 29.

33. (b. 1. 35; a. 1. 33.) 'Moderation is a remedy, though thou mayst desire much;' or, 'mayst yearn for much [a, b].' This line reappears in Richard the Redeles, ii. 139, q. v. 'Mesure is a mery mene' is quoted as a proverb both by Skelton and Heywood.

34. This means—'Not all which the body desires is good for the soul, nor is all that is dear to the soul a source of life to the body. Believe not thy body, for a lying teacher instructs it, viz. this miserable world, which would fain betray thee.'

38. This passage bears an entirely different sense in the latest text from that which it has in the former ones. The C-text means—'For the fiend and thy flesh follow (i. e. persecute thee) together, whereas that protector (viz. Moderation) looks after thy soul, and whispers to thy heart, and instructs thee to beware, and (warns thee of) what would deceive thee.' The B-text means—'For the fiend and thy flesh follow thee together, and both *this* (i. e. the fiend) and *that* (i. e. thy flesh) pursue thy soul, and suggest evil to thy heart,' etc. The A-text means—'For the fiend and thy flesh follow together, and put thy soul to shame; behold it (i. e. an inclination to evil) in thine heart.' In no text is the sense very clear.

40. For *ware*, wary, the B-text has *ywar*. This is an instance of the prefix *y-*, the A. S. *ge-*, being prefixed to an adjective. It is the A. S. *gewær*, wary, cautious, from which the modern form *aware* (for *yware*) has been corrupted. *I wisse*, I teach, is to be distinguished from the adverb *I-wis*, certainly, which is only too often confounded with it; and both again are different from *I wot*, I know, and *I wist* (M. E. *wiste*), I knew, which are from the verb *to wit*.

45. *A posed hym of*, questioned him concerning; for *of*, Texts A and B have *with*. For *appose* in the sense of to question, to examine, see the quotations in Richardson.

48. 'Et ait illis Iesus; Cuius est imago haec, et superscriptio? Dicunt ei, Caesaris. Tunc ait illis: Reddite ergo quae sunt Caesaris, Caesari; et quae sunt Dei, Deo.' Matt. xxii. 20, 21 (Vulgate).

52. 'And (Common Sense should be) preserver of your treasure, and should bestow it on you in your need.' The reading *tour* (= tower) of the A-text is probably due to an error of the scribes; several A-text MSS. have the form *tutour*. If we retain *tour*, it must mean a safe place of custody. For the meaning of *take*, see note to Pass. iv. 47.

53. Here both C-text and A-text have *he*, referring to 'wit' (written *witte* in MS. H.), i. e. to Common Sense. But the B-text has *hij*, i. e. they, referring to Common Sense and Reason. *Husbandry* means economy, as in Shakespeare, Macbeth, ii. 1. 4, 'There's *husbandry* in heaven,' because no stars were out. The phrase *to hold* (i. e. keep) *together* has occurred before; B. prol. 66.

54. *For hym*, for the sake of Him who made her.

55. Here the poet asks the meaning of the 'deep dale,' with reference to that described in Pass. i. 17. In [b] and [a] he enquires about the 'dungeon in the dale,' on account of the difference of the wording of the original description. See B. pr. 15; A. pr. 15. The word *dungeon* does not appear in Pass. i. of the C-text, and is consequently omitted in the present passage.

60. *Fond hit*, found, or discovered it [c]; *founded it*, originated it [b, a]. Here *it* refers to *falsehood*, not to the *castle of care;* for, with our author, to *found* is to *originate*, not *to lay foundations*.

62. *Cayme*, Caim, i. e. Cain.

63. *Iewene*, of Jews. The gen. pl. ending is *-en* or *-ene;* see B. i. 105.

64. The idea that Judas hanged himself upon an *elder* occurs in Shakespeare, Love's Labour's Lost, v. 2. 610; and in Ben Jonson,—'He shall be your *Judas*, and you shall be his *elder-tree* to hang on;' Every Man out of Hum., iv. 4. See Nares. On the other hand, we read that 'the *Arbor Judæ* is thought to be that whereon Judas hanged himself, and not upon the *elder-tree*, as it is vulgarly said;' Gerrard's Herbal, ed. Johnson, p. 1428; quoted by Brand, Pop. Ant. iii. 283. Sir John Maundeville says that the very elder-tree was still in existence when he visited Jerusalem; see p. 93 of Halliwell's edition of Maundeville's Travels.

65. *Lettare*, preventer, hinderer, destroyer. *Lyeth hem* [b, a], lieth to them, deceives them.

66. *That*, those that.

71. *Wissede*, instructed. See note to l. 40 above, p. 22.

73. *Ich vnderfeng the*, I received thee, viz. at baptism. Hence the allusion to *borwes*, i. e. pledges, sureties, in the next line.

—— (b. I. 82; a. I. 80.) *Wroughte me to man*, shaped me so that I became a man. There are other instances of this phrase. Cf. B. i. 62.

79. (b. I. 83; a. I. 81.) *Teche me to*, direct me to. *Teach* is here used in its original sense, to indicate, point out by a *token* or sign; the A.S. *tǽcan* being cognate with the Greek δεικνύναι. *Thys ilke*, this same, this very thing. The word *tresour* alludes to l. 43; the dreamer now alters his question.

82. *Ich do hit on Deus caritas*, I appeal to the text *God is love* (1 John iv. 8) as my authority. Cf. *I do it on the kinge*, i. e. I appeal to the king; B. iii. 187.

84. The phrase *none other* [b] means—not otherwise (than the truth); and answers to *not elles* [a].

86. *By the gospel*, by what the gospel says. In the next line we are referred to St. Luke, that is, to the parable of the unjust steward, where those to whom are to be committed the 'true riches' are taught to be faithful in that which is least; Luke xvi. 10–13. See also Luke viii. 21.

89. 'Christians and heathens alike claim to learn the truth.'

92. *Trangressores* [b] is marked in the MSS. as a Latin word. Latin words are strongly underlined, frequently with a *red* stroke.

⁎ *For notes to* b. I. 98, 99, *and* a. I. 98, 99, *see note to* l. 97, *and the note next below it*.

94. (b. I. 100; a. I. 100.) *With hym and with hure*, with him and her, i. e. with every man and woman. Chaucer has the same expression—'Flemer of feendes out of him and here;' Man of Lawes Tale, l. 460.

97. (b. I. 98; a. I. 98.) *Apendeth to* [c, a], or *appendeth for* [b] signifies pertains to, belongs to.

—— (b. I. 99; a. I. 99.) *A Fryday*, one single Friday. *A Friday* generally means *on Friday*, but not here. Another reading is *o*, i. e. one.

⁎ *For note to* b. I. 102, a. I. 96, *see note to* line 102, p. 24.

98. (b. I. 104; a. I. 102.) An *apostata* was one who quitted his order

24   C. PASS. II. 99.   B. PASS. I. 102.   A. PASS. I. 96.

after he had completed the year of his noviciate. This is very clearly shewn by the following statement of a novice:—

   'Out of the ordre thof I be gone,
   Apostata ne am I none,
   Of *twelue* monethes me wanted *one*,
   And odde days nyen or ten.'
      Monumenta Franciscana, p. 606.

The writer of this was one who had been a novice in the order of St. Francis, but left it to become a Wycliffite. The form *apostata* occurs several times in Massinger; the plural form *apostataas* is used by Wyclif: see Wyclif's Works, ed. Arnold, iii. 368, 430, 476.

99. (*not in* b, a.) *Forbere sherte*, to go without a shirt. This was a form of penance. See note on *wolwarde* in C. xxi. 1.

102. (b. 1. 102; a. 1. 96.) *David, etc.* This may refer to 1 Sam. xxii. 2, to 1 Chron. xi. 1–3, or, still more probably, to 1 Chron. xii. 17, 18. When King Horn was dubbed a knight, as told in the romance of that name, he was girt with a sword, his spurs were fastened on him, and he was set upon a white steed. A few lines lower, at l. 105, we find Christ described as knighting the angels. *By hus daies*, i. e. in his time.

*** *For note* to b. 1. 104, a. 1. 102, *see note to* line 98 above, p. 23.

105. (b. 1. 105; a. 1. 103.) *Kyngene kynge* [b, a], king of kings. The genitive plural in *-ene* is from the A. S. ending *-ena*, as in *Witena gemóte*, meeting of wits (wise men). In like manner, we have *lordene*, i.e. of lords, in l. 95 above; and *Iewene*, of Jews, in l. 63. Wyclif says, in speaking of true religion, that—'Jesu Christ and his Apostles bene chiefe *knights* thereof, and after them holy Martirs and Confessours;' 'Two Treatises against Friers, ed. James, p. 19; reprinted in Wyclif's Works, ed. Arnold, iii. 367. The original sense of *knight* was *servant*. In the A.S. version of the Gospels, the disciples are called ' leorning-cnihtas.' Cp. Pass. ix. 47.

Ten; so in all the MSS., otherwise we might have expected *nine;* for the angels were generally distributed into three hierarchies of three orders each; first, seraphim, cherubim, and thrones; second, dominions, virtûes, and powers; third, principalities, archangels, and angels. William here enumerates the seraphim and cherubim, *seven such orders more*, and *one other*. But the *one other* is the order over which Lucifer presided, as implied by l. 107. This makes up the *ten* orders, as having been the *original* number. And that this is the true explanation is rendered certain by a passage in Early English Homilies, ed. Morris, 1868, p. 219, where the preacher enumerates the nine orders, and adds that the *tenth* order revolted and became evil; that the elder of the tenth order was called '*leoht berinde*,' i. e. light-bearing or Lucifer, who was beautifully formed, but who grew moody and said that he would sit in the *north part* of heaven, and be equal to the Almighty. For this sin he was driven out of heaven with his host. It must be added, that this *tenth* order was considered to rank altogether *above*, not *below*, the other nine; hence the Franciscan Friars used to call themselves the Seraphic Order, having installed their founder, St. Francis, '*above* the Seraphim, *upon the throne from which Lucifer fell.*'—See Southey's Book of the Church, ed. 1848, p. 182. A similar explanation is given in the Towneley Mysteries, p. 7 :—

> ' *Ten orders* in heven were,
> Of angels, that had offyce sere ;
> Of ich order, in thare degre,
> The ten parte felle downe with me [*i.e. with Lucifer*] ;
> For they held with me that tyde . . .
> God has maide man with his hend [*hands*]
> To have that blis withouten end,
> The *nine ordre* to fulfille
> That after us left, sich is his wille.'

Here the last two lines mean—' to make up a tenth order in addition to the nine that remained behind after us ; such is His will.' And in this case, the *tenth order* is mankind, and is reckoned as *below* the other nine ; Ps. viii. 5. See also Ælfric's Homilies, ed. Thorpe, i. 343 ; Cursor Mundi, ed. Morris, p. 32. The arrangement in nine orders was drawn up by St. Thomas Aquinas from the conceptions furnished by the pseudo-Dionysius. Cf. Spenser, F. Q., i. 12. 39 ; Dante, Paradiso, c. 28 ; Tasso, Gier. Lib., 18. 96; Milton, P. L., 5. 748; Peacock's edition of Myrc's Instructions to Parish Priests, l. 766, and note ¡ Warton's Hist. of Eng. Poetry, ed. Hazlitt, iii. 233, note 4; Milman, Hist. of Lat. Christ., vi. 409; Chester Plays, ed. Wright, p. 25 ; Ormulum, i. 34 ; and Chambers' Book of Days, i. 635. Allusions to this fall of Lucifer are very common; see Wycliffe's Two Treatises, p. 35 ; Ayenbite of Inwyt, ed. Morris, 1868, pp. 16, 182 ; Genesis and Exodus, ed. Morris, 1865, p. 3 ; Caedmon, ed. Thorpe, p. 18, etc. Chaucer's Monkes Tale begins with the Fall of Lucifer. See a long note by myself in Notes and Queries, 3rd S. xii. 110 ; and cf. next note.

111. (b. 1. 117 ; *not in* a.) **Ponam pedem**, etc. An inexact quotation from Isaiah xiv. 13, 14 : ' In caelum conscendam, super astra Dei exaltabo solium meum, sedebo in monte testamenti, in lateribus aquilonis. Ascendam super altitudinem nubium ; similis ero Altissimo.' It is curious that wherever the fall of Lucifer is mentioned, as in most of the places cited in the note above, there is often mention made also of Lucifer's sitting in the *north*. We find it even in Milton, P. L., v. 755-760 ; so also in Skelton's Colin Clout :—

> ' Some say ye sit in trones [thrones]
> Like princes *aquilonis*.'

In Chaucer's Freres Tale, l. 115, the fiend lives ' in the north contre.' In our C-text, ll. 112-118, William enquires *why* Lucifer chose the *north* side, but fears he shall offend *Northern men* if he says much about it. Yet he hints that the north is the place for cold and discomfort, and suitable enough for the fallen angel. A still more explicit explanation will be found in the Myrour of Our Lady, ed. Blunt, p. 189, where the writer is explaining the sense of the Latin hymn commencing—Caelestis erat curia. And, in the Icelandic Gylfaginning, we find—'niðr ok norðr liggr Helvegr,' i. e. downwards and *northwards* lieth the way to hell.

112-114. Here *wolde* ... *than* = chose ... rather than. Most of the MSS. give l. 114 in varying and corrupt forms.

114. *Ther the day roweth*, where the day beams. The very uncommon verb *rowen* means to beam, lit. to make or shew *rows* or streaks; it occurs again in Pass. xxi. 128. Cf. *day-rawe*, a day-streak, i. e. daybreak; see *Dayrawe* in Gloss. to Allit. Poems, ed. Morris (E. E. T. S.); also *dayerewe* in Stratmann, p. 119; and cf. 'rowes rede,' i. e. red streaks, in Proem to Chaucer's Complaint of Mars, l. 2. See the Glossary. By the expression *sonne side* is meant the *south*; see ll. 117, 122.

116. *Lacke no lyf*, blame no man. See *Lyf* in the Glossary.

118. *No man leue other*, let no one believe otherwise.

122. See Ps. cix. 1 in the Vulgate version; Ps. cx. 1, A. V.

—— (b. 1. 119; *not in* c, a.) *Nyne dayes*. So Milton—'Nine days they fell;' P. L., vi. 871; and so Hesiod (Theogony, 722) of the fall of the Titans.

127. (b. 1. 123; a. 1. 114.) Mr. Wright says—'In the Master of Oxford's Catechism, written early in the fifteenth century, and printed in Reliquiae Antiquae, vol. i. p. 231, we have the following question and answer—*C.* Where be the anjelles that God put out of heven, and bycam devilles? *M.* Som into hell, and som reyned in the skye, and som in the erth, and som in waters and in wodys.' This was an easy way of accounting for all classes of fairies, some of whom were supposed to be not malignant; for the fallen spirits were supposed to be not all equally wicked. The Rosicrucians, in like manner, placed the sylphs in the air, the gnomes in the earth, the salamanders in the fire, the nymphs in the water; and, as Pope says, in his Introduction to the Rape of the Lock—'The gnomes, or demons of the earth, delight in mischief; but the sylphs, whose habitation is the air, are the best-conditioned creatures imaginable.' Cf. Cursor Mundi, ed. Morris, ll. 491-496; Salomon and Saturn, ed. Kemble, p. 186; Myrour of Our Lady, ed. Blunt, p. 303.

129. *Hym pokede* [c], urged him on; *he pult out* [b] is the same as *he put out* [a]; i. e. he put forth, exhibited.

131. *Ther wrong ys*, where Wrong is, i. e. where Lucifer is [c]; *with that shrewe*, with that wicked one [b, a]. *Shrew* was used for wicked people of either sex; see Trench, Select Gloss.; and Myrc, ed. Peacock, p. 69.

133. The expression *eastward* [*not in* a, b] refers to the idea already expressed in Pass. i. 14, that the tower of Truth, or abode of the Trinity, is situated in the East.

—— (b. 1. 132; a. 1. 123.) The texts referred to are those cited above, viz. Reddite Caesari, etc. (l. 48), and Deus caritas (l. 82). This line (omitted here in the C-text) occurs again below; see l. 202, p. 39.

135. (b. 1. 134; a. 1. 125.) *Lere it þus lewede men* [c], teach it thus to unlearned men; or, *Lereth it this lewde men* [b, a], teach it to these unlearned men. To *lere* is to teach, *lerne* is to learn. *Lerne* sometimes

also means *to teach*, as in provincial English; and sometimes even *lere* is *to learn*, as in Chaucer. In German, the words *lehren* and *lernen* are fairly well distinguished. *This* and *thise* are both used as plurals of *this*. A *lewd* man means a lay-man, as distinguished from a *clerk* or scholar.

137. *Kynde knowing*, natural understanding; but in l. 142, the 'kynde knowyng' is identified with conscience.

138. 'In what manner it grows, and whither (i. e. in what way) it is out of my intelligence,' i. e. beyond my scope [c]; *or else*, 'By what contrivance (*or* power) it commences to exist in my body, and where it begins' [b, a].

141. I have not yet traced the original of this Latin rimed (or Leonine) hexameter. Perhaps William composed it for the occasion. It recurs in Pass. viii. l. 55; p. 171.

144. The Latin quotation is in [c] only. There is something like it in Pope Innocent's treatise De Contemptu Mundi, i. 24: 'Melius est ergo mori uitae quam uiuere morti.' But if we turn to Pass. xviii. 40, we see that the reference is really to the story of Tobit, who preferred death to reproach; 'expedit enim mihi mori magis quam uiuere;' Tobit iii. 6.

147. *Tryacle*, a sovereign remedy. '*Theriaca*, from which *treacle* is a corruption, is the name of a nostrum invented by Andromachus, who was physician to Nero;' Bacon's Advancement of Learning, ed. Wright; note at p. 296. See *Treacle* in my Etym. Dictionary. Cf. 'we kill the viper, and make a *treacle* of him;' Jeremy Taylor, vol. vi. p. 254. Again:—

'If poison chance to infest my soul in fight,
Thou art the *treacle* that must make me sound.'

Quarles' Emblems; Bk. v. Embl. 11.

Pliny has—'Fiant ex uipera pastilli, qui *theriaci* uocantur a Graecis;' Nat. Hist. lib. xxix. c. iv.; and, in lib. xx. c. xxiv., he gives a recipe for making a *theriacum*. See Southey's Common-Place Book, vol. ii. p. 599; Trench, English Past and Present; Trench, Select Glossary; etc. A full account of the history of this word is given by Professor Morley, at p. 21 of his Library of English Literature, with reference to the use of the word *triacle* in the old poem of The Land of Cokaygne, l. 84. The chief point to be observed is that it was considered to be an antidote against poisons, because it contained the flesh of vipers. Hence arose the saying that 'venom expels venom,' quoted by our author in Pass. xxi. 156, and further illustrated by him with reference to the scorpion. Professor Morley observes that—'since *triacle* was an electuary made with honey and tinged with saffron, the uncrystallisable syrup that drains from the sugar-refiner's mould had some resemblance to it, and inherited its name.' Cf. Rich. Redeles, ii. 151.

—— (b. l. 147.) *That spise*, that species, that kind of remedy for sin; referring to Love or Charity.

—— (b. l. 149.) *Lered it Moises*, taught it Moses; viz. in Deut. vi. 5, x. 12, etc.

149. (b. l. 150; a. l. 137.) *Plonte*, plant. By comparing the various MSS., it becomes clear that the right reading is *plonte*, *plante*, or *plaunte*;

and not *plente* = *plenty* [b], or *playnt* = *plaint* [a]. Cf. Isaiah liii. 2. *Prechet* [a] is put for *preche hit*, i.e. preach it, proclaim it.

150. (b. 1. 151; *not in* a.) *Hit*, sc. love; here used of the love of Christ, which heaven could not contain, till it had 'poured itself out upon the earth' [c], or till it had 'eaten its fill of the earth' [b], i. e. participated in the human nature by Incarnation. When it had taken flesh and blood, it became light as a linden-leaf, and piercing as a needle.

152. 'As light as linden' was an old proverb, of which several examples may be found. It occurs, e. g. in the Towneley Mysteries, p. 80; Joseph of Arimathie, ed. Skeat, l. 585; Skelton, Bowge of Courte, l. 231; and probably has reference to the lightness of the wood of the linden or lime-tree, which caused it to be much used for making shields. Thus the A.S. *lind* is frequently used in the sense of shield. In the present case, the proverb takes the form 'as light as a leaf upon a linden,' with reference to the ease with which the breeze stirs the leaves of that tree; and Chaucer has the very expression in the Envoy to his Clerkes Tale—' Be ay of chere as lyght as leef on lynde.'

—— (a. 1. 138; *not in* c, b.) 'Where thou art merry at thy meat, when men bid you play and sing.' This alludes to the very common custom of introducing music and singing at feasts. The guests not unfrequently took the harp as it was passed round, and displayed their skill. See Cutts, Scenes and Characters of the Middle Ages, p. 280.

Observe the use of the word *me* here; it is used as an impersonal pronoun, like the French *on*, and takes a verb in the singular number; see Glossary. The word *3edde* is the A.S. *giddian*. Cf. *yeddinges* in Ch. Prol. 237.

159. *The mercement he taxeth*, he imposes the fine. Blount, in his Law Dict., says—'There is a difference between *amerciaments* and *fines*: these [i. e. the latter], as they are taken for punishments, are punishments certain, which grow expressly from some statute; but amerciaments are arbitrarily imposed by affeerors.' See the whole of his article on *Amerciaments*. Cf.—'I soppose they wyl distreyn for the *mersymentes;*' Paston Letters, ed. Gairdner, i. 109. See Pass. ix. 37.

160. *To knowe it kyndely*, to understand it by natural reason; cf. ll. 137, 142. In Pass. xi. ll. 127-174 there is a description of the castle of *Caro* (man's body), which is guarded by the constable *Inwit* (conscience); and it is said of Inwit and of the five senses that—

'In the herte is hir home · and hir moste reste;' B. ix. 55.

163. *That falleth*, etc. That belongs to the Father; i. e. it is God the Father who implanted Conscience in man's heart.

166. *He*, sc. God the Son.

169. *One*, alone; dat. case of *on*, one, A.S. *án*.

175. *Eadem*, etc. Matthew vii. 2; Luke vi. 38. *Remecietur* is no misprint. Some Latin words are not always spelt alike in old MSS. Thus *scintilla* is frequently spelt *sintilla*, as in Pass. vii. 338, and *commodat* is spelt *comodat*, as in B. v. 246.

177. *That nother chit*, that neither chides. The expression *that in* *cherche wepeth* [b, a] probably refers to a chlld that is being baptized; baptism being often accompanied by tears on the part of the infant. The word *chast* here means innocent; and the application of the epithet to a child just baptized would be peculiarly appropriate.

178. *Bote yf,* unless. *Lene the poure* [c, b], lend to the poor; *loue the pore* [a], love the poor.

180. 'Ye have no more merit in the saying of mass or of the hours,' etc. The *hours* were the services said at stated times, viz. matins, prime, tierce, sext, nones, vespers, and compline.

181. The context shews that *Malkyn* is here equivalent to a wanton, but ugly slattern. 'There's more maids than Maukin' is quoted as a proverb in Camden's Remaines, ed. 1657, p. 304; see Hazlitt's Proverbs, p. 392. The nearest parallel passage in Chaucer is at the 30th line of the Man of Lawes Prologue; but the name *Malkin* is probably also used with some significance in the Miller's Tale; C. T. l. 4234, ed. Tyrwhitt. The word itself is the diminutive of the once common name Matilda; not of Mary. Hence we find, in the Prompt. Parv.—' Malkyne, or Mawt, propyr name, Molt, Mawde: *Matildis, Matilda.*' In provincial English *mawkin* denotes various things that are put to a servile purpose, as, e. g. a cloth used to sweep out an oven (Prompt. Parv.), or a scarecrow. In Scotland, it means a hare. See *Malkin, Mawkin* in Halliwell's Dictionary, and Bardsley's English Surnames, p. 64.

184. 'As dead as a door-nail' is still a common proverb; but there is an earlier instance of its use than in the present passage. It occurs twice in William of Palerne (ed. Skeat, ll. 628, 3396), which was written about A. D. 1350. Mr. Timbs, in his 'Things not generally known,' says that the door-nail meant in this proverb is the nail upon which, in old doors, the knocker strikes; and which may accordingly, I suppose, be considered as particularly dead owing to the number of blows which it receives; and the same explanation is given by Webster, but this is all mere guesswork. We find the proverb in Shakespeare—

'*Falstaff.* What, is the old king dead?
Pistol. As nail in door.'—2 K. Hen. IV. v. 3. 125.

It is certain, however, that the term *doornail* was also used more generally, viz. of the nails with which doors in the olden times were so plentifully studded; for they were sold by the thousand, as we learn from Riley's Memorials of London, p. 262; and Burton speaks of the milky way as 'that *via lactea,* or confused light of small stars, like so many nails in a door;' Anat. Mel., pt. 2. sec. 2. mem. 3. The B-text has *dore-tre,* i. e. door-post; *tree* being used here, as not unfrequently in our older authors, in the sense of timber or dead wood; cf. *rood-tree, axle-tree, boot-tree,* etc.; and see 'Specimens of English,' ed. Morris and Skeat, p. 239, l. 117.

The text referred to is—'Sicut enim corpus sine spiritu mortuum est, ita et fides sine operibus mortua est;' S. Jacob. ii. 26.

185. *Worth,* shall be; lit. becomes. Cf. *worst,* i. e. thou shalt be; Pass. viii. 265, p. 189.

186. Dan Michel, in his Ayenbite of Inwyt (ed. Morris, p. 233), says that virginity without love is as a lamp without oil, and refers to the Parable of the foolish virgins. No doubt William was likewise thinking of that parable in writing the present passage.

191. 'They chew up their charity (i. e. they eat up what they should give away), and then cry out for more.' This striking expression was copied by William's imitator, the author of Pierce the Ploughman's Crede ; see the *Crede*, ed. Skeat, l. 663.

192. *And encombred*, i. e. and, nevertheless, they are encumbered. For *encombred*, cf. Chaucer, Prol. 508.

195. 'And it is a bad example, believe me, to the laity' [c] ; or, 'And it is a lesson to the laity, to be all the later in giving alms,' i. e. to put off the giving away of alms [b, a]. We have *dele* in the same sense below (l. 197) in the phrase 'for I dele yow alle,' i. e. for it is I who distribute gifts to you all. For the use of *lewede*, cf. l. 135.

197. These words, '*date*, etc.,' begin the verse which has already been partially quoted above, at l. 175. See Luke vi. 38. In the A-text, the sense is :—'for I distribute to you all your grace and your good luck, to help you win your livelihood ; and do ye therefore, by alms-doing, acknowledge me by means of that which I send you, in a natural manner.'

198. The general sense in [b] is :—'and such alms-doing is like the lock (or, as we should now say, the *key*) of divine love, and lets out divine grace, that comforts all Christians that are oppressed with sin.'

200. 'Thus love is the physician of life, and relief of all pain, and the graft (engrafting) of grace, and the most direct way to heaven' [c] ; *or*, 'Love is the physician of life, and next our Lord himself, and also the direct way that leads to heaven' [b] ; *or*, 'Love is the dearest thing that our Lord requires (i. e. that which He most expects of us), and eke,' etc. [a].

201. The expression *graith gate* [b], meaning *direct way*, occurs in the History of Wallace, by Blind Harry, v. 135—

'For thair sloith-hund the *graith gate* till him yeid ; '

i. e. for their sleuth-hound went straight towards him.

203. Repeated from above ; see l. 81.

205. The Texts end the Passus differently ; the sense is either—'Love it, quoth that lady, for I may not stay longer to teach thee what love is ; and therewith she took leave of me' [c] ; or else, ' I may no longer stay with thee ; now may the Lord preserve thee' [b, a].

NOTES TO C. PASSUS III. (B. Pass. II ; A. Pass. II.)

2. (b. 2. 2 ; a. 2. 2.) *For marye loue of heuene*, for the love of Mary of heaven. In exactly the same way we have *of the lordes folke of heuene* = of the people of the Lord of heaven, B. i. 157 ; and *for the lordes loue of heuene*, B. vi. 19; in both of which places the C-text has *in heuene*, probably as being a clearer expression ; see C. ii. 156 ; ix. 16. Again we

C. PASS. III. 5, 6.   B. PASS. II. 5, 6.   A. PASS. II. 5, 6.   31

find *for crystes loue of heuene*, i. e. for the loue of Christ of (*or* in) heaven, B. vi. 223, where the C-text substitutes another phrase altogether.

5, 6. 'Look upon thy left hand; and see where he [Falsehood] stands; and not he only, but Favel [Flattery] also,' etc. The word *favel* here, signifying flattery (from Lat. *fabula*), must be carefully distinguished from the same word (from the German *falb*) as used to denote the colour (or the name) of a horse. Occleve, in his De Regimine Principum, ed. Wright, pp. 106, 111, fully describes *favelle* or flattery, and says—'In wrong preisyng is all his craft and arte.' Cf. Wiat's 2nd Satire, l. 67; Skelton, Bowge of Courte, l. 134. See Dyce's Skelton, i. 35; ii. 107, 264. Douce, in his Illustrations to Shakespeare, i. 475, rightly distinguishes between the two words, and correctly remarks that the phrase 'to curry favour,' originally 'to curry favel,' i. e. to groom a horse, is not connected with the word here used, but has reference to *favel* as denoting a yellow-coloured horse. The similarity of the words naturally drew them together, so that *to curry favel* easily took the sense of to flatter or cajole. See quotations for the phrase in Richardson and Nares, to which I can add the following:—

'Sche was a schrewe, as have y hele,
There sche *currayed favell* well.'
How a Merchant did his Wyfe betray, l. 203;
in Ritson's Ancient Popular Poetry.

And again—' Curryfauell, a flatterer, *estrille*;' Palsgrave.

9. *A womman*. Here William carefully describes the Lady Meed, who represents both Reward in general, and Bribery in particular; the various senses of *Meed* are explained in Pass. iv. 292-342. Female dress at this date was very extravagant, and we may compare with the text the following remarks in Lingard's History. 'Her head was encircled with a turban or covered with a species of mitre of enormous height, from the summit of which ribbons floated in the air like the streamers from the head of a mast. Her tunic was half of one colour, and half of another; a zone deeply embroidered, and richly ornamented with gold, confined her waist, and from it were suspended in front two daggers in their respective pouches;' vol. iv. p. 91. The present passage appears in the early text of 1362, otherwise William's description of Meed would have served admirably for the infamous Alice Perrers, who obtained a grant of Queen Philippa's jewels, and 'employed her influence to impede the due administration of justice in favour of those who had purchased her protection;' see Lingard, iv. 142. Indeed it is very likely that William perceived this likeness in first revising his poem, for the description of Meed's clothing was amplified in the B-text, and he *added* the *very* significant line,

'I had wondre *what she was* · and *whas wyf she were*.'

How Alice treated King Edward in his last illness is well known. Whitaker suggests that the Lady Meed is the original of Spenser's *Lady Munera;* see Spenser, F. Q., bk. v. c. ii. st. 9. Skelton, who borrowed several things from our author, did not forget to introduce 'mayden Meed' into his Ware the Hauke, l. 149. See also a curious passage, having a singular resemblance to the description given in the text, printed in Reliquiae Antiquae, vol. ii. p. 19, from a fragment in MS. E. D. N. no. 27, in the College of Arms.

10. *Purfild with peloure*, having her robe edged with fur. See Chaucer's Prologue, l. 193, and Morris' note. Compare—'The *purful* of the garment is to narowe ; *Segmentum* vestimenti est iusto angustius ; ' Hormanni Vulgaria, leaf 110 b. The laws about the kinds of furs to be worn by different ranks were very minute in their particulars ; see Memorials of London, ed. Riley, pp. 20, 153. Furred hoods, in particular, were much in fashion. Cf. Pass. vi. 129, 134.

—— (b. 2. 14 ; *not in* a.) *Enuenymes to destroye*. It was a common belief that precious stones could cure diseases, and that they were as antidotes against poisons. Thus ' Richard Preston, citizen and grocer, gave to the shrine of St. Erkenwald his *best sapphire stone*, for *curing of infirmities of the eyes*,' etc.; note in Milman's Lat. Christ., vi. 375 ; where Milman quotes from Dugdale, p. 21. See also Morte Arthure, ed. Brock, ll. 212–215 ; Ancren Riwle, pp. 134-136 ; Burton, Anat. Melan., pt. 2, sec. 4. m. 1. subsec. 4.

14. (b. 2. 15 ; a. 2. 13.) The word *engreyned* [b] means dyed in grain, i. e. dyed of a fast colour. The verb *engreynen*, to dye of a fast colour, occurs in B. xiv. 20 ; q. v. In Pierce the Ploughman's Crede, l. 230, a friar's kirtle is described as being of such fine texture (*ground*) that it would bear being dyed in grain. See the excellent note by Mr. Marsh, in his Lectures on the English Language (p. 55, ed. Smith), upon the signification of to *dye in grain*; and see *Greyn* in the Glossary to the Babees Book.

17. The force of ' *What* is this womman ' [b, a] is best given by the modern phrase ' *what sort of a* woman is this ? ' A similar use of *what* occurs in Layamon, l. 13844, where Hengist, before describing himself and his companions, says—' Ich þe wullen cuðen *what* cnihtes we beoð,' i. e. I will inform thee *what sort of knights* we are.

19. *Mede* is here used in the worse of the two senses above indicated, viz. in the sense of Bribery. We find a good example of this use in the Chronicle of London [ed. Nicolas], p. 13, where we are told that, in the twelfth year of Henry III., a common seal was granted to the city of London, and it was ordered that any one who shewed reesonable cause should be permitted to use it, ' and that no *mede* schulde be take no [*nor*] payed of eny man in no manner wyse for the said seall.'

> ' Many one for *mede* doþ ful euyl ;
> Me sey [*people say*] ofte—" *mede* ys þe deuyl." '
> Rob. of Brunne, Handlyng Synne, l. 8330.

Indeed, complaints of this character were, unfortunately, extremely common, and shew a disgraceful laxity of principle amongst advocates and judges at this period. See Political Songs, ed. Wright, pp. 197, 324.

20. *Leaute*, Loyalty. William arrays Love, Loyalty, Soothness, Reason, Conscience, Wisdom, and Wit on the one side, and Meed (daughter of Favel or False), Wrong, Favel or Flattery, Simony, Civil, Liar, and

Guile upon the other. Wisdom and Wit waver in their allegiance, but are won back again. The texts partially differ.

27. *As men of kynde karpen*, as men say concerning kinship—' Like father, like son.' The B-text has—*as kynde axeth*, as nature requires or provides; cf. Rich. Redeles, ii. 191. The text *bona arbor*, etc., is from Matt. vii. 17.

30. *Herre*, higher; other MSS. *heiere, hyur*, etc. With this form compare *ferre*, farther; Chaucer's Prol. 48; *derre*, dearer, Ch. Kn. Tale, 590; *nerre*, nearer, in the proverb—' Nere is my kyrtyl, but *nerre* is my smok;' Paston Letters, ed. Gairdner, i. 542.

—— (b. 2. 31; *not in* a.) *To marye with myself*; we should now arrange the words, *to marry myself with*; see note to Pass. i. 133, p. 14.

39. (b. 2. 38; *not in* a.) See Ps. xv. 1 (called Ps. xiv. in the Vulgate); also verse 5 of the same Psalm.

41. (b. 2. 39; *not in* a.) *Mansed*, cursed. Not *maused*, as in Wright's text. See the Glossary.

49. *Lete hem worthe*, etc.; let them be, till Loyalty be a justice or judge. Cf. note to Pass. i. 201, p. 18.

51. *Ich bykenne the Crist*, I commend thee to Christ; *Crist* is here in the dative case.

55. *Retynaunce*, retinue, suite of retainers; various readings *retenauns, retenauntes* (for *retenaunces*.) The word is rare, but is used by Gower (qu. in Halliwell), and in Wyclif's Works, ed. Arnold, iii. 478, where we have the plural *retenauncis*; (printed *retenauntis*, as it may have been written, owing to the confusion between *c* and *t*; though there are some misprints in this edition which cannot be laid upon the scribes.) Though the word is not easily to be found in the French Dictionaries, it presents no difficulty, being formed from *retenir*, just as *maintenance* is from *maintenir*.

56. (b. 2. 54; a. 2. 36.) *Brudale*, bride-ale or bridal. An *ale* means a feast merely. There were leet-ales, scot-ales, church-ales, clerk-ales, bid-ales, and bride-ales. At the *bride-ale*, moreover, the bride herself often brewed ale for her wedding-day, which her friends purchased at a high price, by way of assisting her and amusing themselves at the same time. See Brand's Popular Antiquities, ed. Ellis, ii. 144.

—— a. 2. 43 (*not in* c, b.) *A proud*, a proud one; a good illustration of *a fayr* as used by Chaucer, Prol. 165.

60. *Brokours.* In the reign of Edward I., a law was passed that 'no one shall be *broker*, but those who are admitted and sworn before the Mayor;' Liber Albus, ed. Riley, p. 505. The duties of the *bedel* are to be found in the same work, at p. 272. See note to line 111, p. 36.

63. In Passus xxiii., the church is described as assailed by numerous enemies. One is *Simony*, who causes good faith to flee away, and falseness to abide (xxiii. 131), and who boldly vanquishes much of the wit and wisdom of Westminster Hall by the use of many a bright noble. He is also there described as contriving divorces.

34   C. PASS. III. 66.   B. PASS. II. 65.   (A. II. 60.)

The exact signification of *sisour* does not seem quite certain, and perhaps it has not always the same meaning. The Low-Latin name was *assissores* or *assissiarii*, interpreted by Ducange to mean—' qui a principe vel a domino feudi delegati *assisias* tenent ;' whence Halliwell's explanation of *sisour* as a person deputed to hold assizes. Compare—

'Þys fals men, þat beyn *sysours*,
þat for hate a trewman wyl endyte,
And a þefe for syluer quyte ;'
          Robert of Brunne, Hand. Synne, 1335.

Mr. Furnivall's note says—' *Sysour*, an inquest-man at assizes. The *sisour* was really a juror, though differing greatly in functions and in position from what jurymen subsequently became; see Forsyth's Hist. of Trial by Jury.' In the Tale of Gamelyn, however, it is pretty clear that 'the xii *sisoures* þat weren on þe quest' (l. 871) were simply the twelve gentlemen of the jury, who were hired to give false judgment (l. 786). By *Cyuile* is meant a practitioner in the civil law.

66. *Brocour* is here used in the general sense of a contriver of bargains, a match-maker.

67. *Here boþeres wil* [c], or *here beire wille* [b], means 'the will of them both.'

79. The form of this mock charter may be compared with that of the charter whereby the Black Prince was invested, in 1362 (the very year in which William wrote the first version of his poem) with the principality of Aquitaine. It is given at length in Barnes's Life of Edward III.

81. *Hye kynde*, loftiness of nature, or perhaps simply high rank [c] ; *free kynde*, liberal nature, or perhaps gentle blood [b]. *Free* means both ' liberal ' and of ' high rank.'

83. *Feffed*, has granted ; or, as in [b], *Feffeth*, grants to them ; lit. *enfeoffs*, i. e. invests them with a fief or fee. In l. 160, *feffe* means simply *to fee*. See also l. 137. The Promptorium Parvulorum has—' Feffyd, *feofatus, feofactus*.' In Blount's Law Dictionary we find—'*Feofment* signifies *donationem feudi*, any gift or grant of any honours, castles, manors, messuages, lands, or other corporeal or immoveable things of like nature, to another in fee ; that is, to him and his heirs for ever ;' etc.

85. *To bakbyten*, to backbite or defame. See the quotations in Richardson, to which I may add—*Bacbitares* þe biteð oðre men bihinden ;' Ancren Riwle, p. 86 ; and see Rob. of Brunne, Hand. Synne, ll. 1514, 3538.

90. The expression *alle the costes about* [b] means—all the borders of it, all the neighbouring country ; cf. Matt. viii. 34. The expression *I croune hem togedere* [a] means—I invest them with conjointly, giving them a crown as the symbol of investiture.

92. In a note in his glossary, s. v. *brocage*, Mr. Wright explains the term to mean a treaty by a broker or agent, and adds—' It is particularly applied to treaties of marriage, brought about in this way. In the Romaunt of the Rose, l. 6971, Fals Semblant says—

" I entremete me of *brocages*,
I make pece and mariages."

C. PASS. III. 94. B. PASS. II. 89. (A. II. 72.)

So in the Miller's Tale (C. T. 3375) it is said of Absolon—
  "He woweth hire by menes and *brocage*,
  And swor he wolde ben hire owen page;"
that is, he wooed her by the agency of another person, whom he employed to persuade her to agree to his wishes.'
The borghe of thufthe, the borough of Theft.

94. *Waitynges of eyes*, watchings with the eyes, i. e. wanton looks, amorous glances. Cf. *after mede wayten*, i. e. look wistfully for some bribe, in l. 78 above.

96. 'Where the will is ready, but power fails.' Cf. Pass. vii. 184, 193.

99. *Iangly*, to gossip, to chatter idly. *Iape*, to mock, to gibe. See note to B. prol. 35 (p. 6), and compare the following.

'*Jangelyng* is whan a man spekith to moche biforn folk, and clappith as a mille, and taketh no keep [*heed*] what he saith;' Chaucer, Persones Tale, De Superbia. 'A philosophre saide, whan men askid him how men schulde plese the poeple, and he answerde, "do many goode werkes, and spek fewe *jangeles*." After this cometh the synne of *japers*, that ben the develes apes, for thay maken folk to laughen at her *japes* or *japerie*, as folk doon at the gaudes [*tricks*] of an ape; such *japes* defendith [*forbids*] seint Poule;' ibid., De Ira. In Horman's Vulgaria, leaf 76 *b*, we find—'He is a great iangler; *Impendio loquax*.' Many examples might be added. Cf. B. x. 31.

100. *Frete*, to eat, viz. before the proper time for eating arrived. See Pass. vii. 434.

104. It is necessary to remember that *he* and *hus* in this line are used vaguely and indefinitely, so that *he* is merely put for *such a one*. In the B-text, the apparent change from the plural to the singular, in *his* (l. 98) following upon *hem* (l. 97) is to be explained in a similar manner. There are many other similar examples in our author.

105. 'During this life to follow Falseness, and the folk that believe on him.'

106. Before *a dwelling*, i. e. a habitation, an abode, we must supply *he geueth hem*, from l. 97. In the B-text, it follows as an accusative case after the verbs *to have and to hold* in the preceding line.

—— (b. 2. 104.) *ʒeldyng*, giving up in return; cf. Pass. vii. 343. Compare the phrase—'to yield a crop;' Cymbeline, iv. 2. 180.

110. (b. 2. 108; a. 2. 76.) *Of paulynes queste* apparently means, belonging to the inquest or jury of Paulines; ·but in [b], the phrase is *of paulynes doctrine*, of the doctrine (or order) of the Paulines; and in [a] it is *Paulynes doctor*, a doctor of the Paulines. The name is not common, but I have observed the following uses of it. 'In the same yere [1310] began the ordre of *Paulyns*, that is to say 'Crowched Freres.''—A Chronicle of London (edited in 1827, and published by Longmans), p. 43. (But Matthew Paris says that the order of Crutched Friars came into England A.D. 1244). In a poem called the Image of Ypocrisie, written about A. D. 1533, a list is given of orders of *monks*, which includes the *Paulines*, the Antonines, Bernardines, Celestines, etc. And there were some hermits so named;

36   C. PASS. III. 111.   B. PASS. II. 109.   A. PASS. II. 77.

see the Pilgrim's Tale, l. 151, printed in App. I to Thynne's Animadversions, ed. Furnivall (Chaucer Society). See Mr. Furnivall's note at p. 141. The word *Paulynes* occurs again below, b. 2. 177 ; a. 2. 152 (*not in* c).

111. *Budele*. The oath of the Bedels is given at p. 272 of the Liber Albus. They were to suffer no persons of ill repute to dwell in the ward of which they were bedels, to return good men upon inquests, not to be regrators themselves, nor to suffer things to be sold secretly. It is remarkable that, in [c], William changed *Bokyngham-shire* (which was celebrated for thieves, see Hazlitt's Proverbs, p. 94) into '*Banbury soken.*' This may have been an intentional fling at the beadle of Banbury, with whom he may have quarrelled ; for it is to be noted that Banbury is at no great distance from Shipton-under-Wychwood, where William's father is said to have farmed land.

The word *soken*, or *soke*, as in *Hamsoken*, *Portsoken*, is sufficiently well-known as a law-term. It means (1) a privilege ; and (2) the district within which such a privilege or power is exercised. Chaucer (Reves Tale, C. T. 3985) uses *soken* of a miller's privilege of grinding corn within a particular district.

113. *Munde the miller* is mentioned again in B. x. 44, where the term denotes an ignorant fellow. Here it doubtless means a thief; cf. Chaucer, Prol. 562.

114. Skelton also has the remarkable expression 'in the deuylles date ;' Bowge of Courte, ll. 375, 455 ; Magnyfycence, ll. 954, 2198. But he may have copied it from William.

130. The word *leuita* in Low-Latin merely means *deacon* ; see Ducange. There were several saints named Lawrence, but *the deacon* is the one most famous and best known. His day is August 10, and a good account of him will be found in Chambers' Book of Days under that date ; vol. ii. p. 196. He suffered martyrdom at Rome about A.D. 257 or 259, by being broiled on a gridiron over a slow fire. The exact reference is to the account of St. Lawrence as given in the Aurea Legenda (cap. cxvii) :— ' Et gratias agens dixit, "gratias tibi ago, Domine, quia *ianuas tuas ingredi merui* ;" et sic spiritum emisit.'

142. The phrase *but if* [b, a] is practically *one* word, with the meaning *except, unless*. Chaucer has it also ; Cant. Tales, Group B, 2001, 3688 ; Group F, 687 ; etc.

143. The word *fikel* [b] is equivalent to *faithles* [c], or to *a faylere* [a]. The sense of *fikel* in Middle Eng. is not *changeable*, but *treacherous* ; see Pass. iv. 158. A good example of the word in the same sense occurs in Havelok, l. 1210.

151. *Wytty is treuthe*, wise is Truth. It must be remembered that Truth means God the Father, as in Pass. ii. 12.

154. *Bisitte* [b, a], or *sitte* [c], means—sit close to, press upon, oppress. *Ful soure* [c, b], very bitterly ; *sore* [a], sorely. In my edition of Chaucer's Prioresses Tale, etc. is a note to C. T. Group B, 2012, which I here reprint. ' Chaucer has here *Abyen it ful soure*, very bitterly shalt thou pay for it. There is a confusion between A. S. *súr*, sour, and A. S.

C. PASS. III. 157. B. PASS. II. 143. A. PASS. II. 113. 37

sár, sore, in this and in similar phrases; both were once used, but we should now use *sorely*, not *sourly*. In Laȝamon, l. 8158, we find "Þou salt it sore abugge," thou shalt sorely pay for it; on the other hand we find in P. Plowm. B. 2. 140—
"It shal bisitte ȝowre soules · ful *soure* atte laste."
So also in the C-text, though the A-text has *sore*. Note that, in another passage, P. Plowm. C. xxi. 448 (B. xviii. 401), the phrase is—"Thow shalt abygge *bitere*," thou shalt bitterly pay for it.'

157. *Floreynes*, florins; the name of which is derived from the city of Florence; indeed, we find the spelling *florences* three times in the Percy Folio MS., ed. Hales and Furnivall. We read in Fabyan (ed. Ellis, p. 455) under the year 1343—'In this yere also, kynge Edwarde made a coyne of fyne golde, and named it the *floryne*, that is to say, the peny of the value of vi*s*. viii*d*., the halfe peny of the value of iii*s*. iiii*d*., and the farthynge of the value of xx*d*., which coyne was ordeyned for his warris in Fraunce; for the golde thereof was not so fyne as was the noble, whiche he before in his xiiii. yere of his reygne had causyd to be coyned.' So in Thomas Walsingham, vol. i. p. 262, ed. Riley. The value of a *noble* was also 6*s*. 8*d*. See note to Pass. iv. 47, p. 41.

174. *Westemynstre*. William seems to have been very familiar with the courts of law at Westminster, as appears from the present and two following Passus. In Pass. xxiii. 284, we again find him speaking of the 'false folk' who repair 'to Westmynstre.' The number of statutes enacted there in the reign of Edward III. is considerable. See Liber Albus, p. 470.

175. Those who had horses could anticipate others at the court, by performing the journey more quickly, and they could thus obtain a first audience and administer a bribe. In a poem on The Evil Times of Edward II. we have—
' Coveytise *upon his hors* he wole *be sone there*,
And bringe the bishop silver, and rounen in his ere.'
Polit. Songs (Camd. Soc.), p. 326.
William, however, represents Meed as riding on the back of a sheriff, and makes False and Favel ride upon reeves, etc.; or, as in the B-text, which is differently expressed, he supposes sheriffs and sisours to serve for horses, puts saddles on the sompnours, and turns provisors into palfreys.

178. The curious word *saumbury* does not occur elsewhere, to my knowledge, in English literature. But it is easy to see what it means, and whence it was derived. A *saumbury* means, I suppose, a comfortable litter for a lady to ride upon, and is evidently closely connected with the old word *saumbue*, a saddle-cloth, which occurs in MS. Harl. 2252, fol. 115, as quoted in Halliwell's Dict. s. v. *Sambus*.
Turning to Roquefort's Glossaire, we find the following:—
'*Sambue*, housse d'une selle de cheval, harnois.
    Un palefrois bien enselez
    D'une moult riche *sambue*.—Roman de Merlin, MSS.'

'*Sambue*, sorte de char principalement à l'usage des dames, litière;' etc. Ducange has—'*Sambuca*, sella equestris ad mulierum usum;' which is merely a Latinised form of the original O. H. Ger. *sambuoh*, a litter (Schade).

Fram syse to syse, from one assize to another.

182. *Provisor* sometimes means a purveyor; but here has the usual sense in which it is employed in our statutes, viz. one that sued to the Court of Rome for a *provision*. A *provision* meant the providing of a bishop or any other person with an ecclesiastical living by the pope, before the death of the actual incumbent. The great abuses occasioned by this practice led to the enactment of the statutes of *Provisors* (25 Edw. III. c. vi., 27 Edw. III. c. i. § 1, and 38 Edw. III. c. i. § 4, and c. ii. § 1-4), wherein it was enacted that the bishop of Rome shall not present or collate to any bishopric or ecclesiastical benefice in England; and that whoever disturbs any patron in the presentation to a living, by virtue of a papal provision, such provisor shall pay fine and ransom to the king at his will; and be imprisoned till he renounces such provision, etc. See Blount's Law Dict., Wordsworth's Eccl. Biog. p. 145, and Blackstone's Comment. bk. iv. c. 8; also note on p. 47 below.

187. The curious form *southdenes* (*suddenes*, b; *sodenes*, a) is only a variation of *sub-deans*. In Robert of Brunne's Handlyng Synne, l. 1680, we have '*Suddekene*, or dekene hy,' where his French original has—'*Sodekene*, deakene, et presbiter.' Similarly, in a Poem on the Evil Times of Edward II., ed. Hardwick (Percy Society), stanza 66, the word *sub-bailiffs* takes the strange form *southbailys*. Respecting such forms as *supersedeas*, Pegge, in his Anecdotes of the English Language, p. 141, remarks—'Writs in law processes for the most part take their names from the cardinal *verb* on which their force turns, and which, from the tenor of them, is generally in the subjunctive mood, as being grammatically required by the context.... These being formerly in Latin, and issuing in the king's name, the proper officer was called upon in the second person of the singular number, after a short preamble,' etc. Hence *habeas, capias, supersedeas, fieri-facias*, and the like. A writ of *supersedeas* is, most often, a writ or command to suspend the powers of an officer in certain cases, or to stay proceedings.

—— (b. 2. 173-175.) 'As for archdeacons, etc., cause men to saddle them with silver, in order that they may permit our sin, whether it be adultery or divorces, or secret usury.'

—— (b. 2. 177.) *Paulynes pryues*. It may be that *pryues* is here the plural adjective, agreeing with *Paulynes*, as *French* adjectives not unfrequently take *s* in the plural. If so, the phrase means 'the confidential Paulines.' Otherwise, it must mean 'the confidential men of the Paulines' fraternity;' which comes to much the same thing. The MSS. of the A-class read *Paulines peple*, i. e. the people of the Paulines. Cf. note to line 110, above, p. 35.

191. This means—'And provide food for ourselves from (or at the expense of) adulterers.' The whole passage refers to the practice of

C. PASS. III. 196. B. PASS. II. 185. A. PASS. II. 160. 39

prosecuting or fining such victims as would prove most profitable. A parallel passage may be found in Chaucer's Prologue, ll. 649–665.

196. *Tome*, leisure. The adjective *toom* means empty, and neither word is to be confused with *time*.

204. *And*, if [c, b]; *ȝif* [a]. *And* is often written for *an*, if; and conversely, *an* is often written for the copulative conjunction *and*, as in B. ii. 207. The *two* forms are but *one* word; see Murray's New Eng. Dictionary.

208. *Maynpryse*, furnish bail, be security for. A person arrested for debt or any other personal action might find *mainprise* or bail, before the sheriffs or their clerks thereunto deputed. The person finding bail was called a *mainpernour*, lit. a taker by the hand, by metathesis from *mainpreneur*. See Liber Albus, p. 177; and cf. Pass. v. ll. 84 and 107. The finding of mainprise was used for screening rich offenders, and defeating the ends of justice.

212. *Eny kynnes yiftes*, gifts of any kind. *Eny kynnes* is the genitive singular, and is also spelt *enys kynnes*, or even assumes the odd form *any skynes;* as in MS. T [a].

216. *For eny preier*, in spite of any prayer. Cf. note to l. 240.

217. *Duene, dune*, din, noise [c, a]; *dome*, sentence, decision [b], as in Chaucer, Prol. 323.

221. *Dud hym to gon*, prepared himself to depart. The compassion shewn to Guile by merchants, and to Liar by pardoners, grocers, minstrels, and friars, is a brilliant touch of satire.

223. For pictures of London *shops*, see Chambers' Book of Days, i. 350.

226. 'Lurking through lanes, pulled about by many.' The word *lug* is especially used of pulling by the *lugs* or ears. '*Lugg*, to pull by the ears. 'I'll *lugg* thee, if thou do'st so;' *North;*' Pegge's Supplement to Grose's Prov. Dict. See Rich. Redeles, iii. 336.

228. 'Everywhere hooted (or hunted) away, and bidden to pack off.' *Ouer-al* is here just the German *überall*. Some MSS. favour the reading *hooted*, others *hunted;* it makes but little difference. See Rich. Redeles, iii. 228.

240. *For knowynge of comers*, to prevent recognition by visitors or strangers.

249. *Flowen into hernes*, fled away (or escaped) into corners or hiding-places.

252. *Atached*, taken prisoner. 'Persons attached on suspicion were in general allowed to go at large, in the interval before trial, upon surety or bail;' note to Liber Albus, p. 73; cf. pp. 77, 78, 88, 183, 349. See Pass. iv. 18, 19.

NOTES TO C. PASSUS IV. (B. Pass. III; A. Pass. III.)

13. *That*, i. e. they that, they who; cf. *they that* [b], *heo that* [a]. Many of the minor difficulties of construction can be at once solved by simple comparison of the three texts. It is therefore unnecessary to point them out in every case.

14. *Somme* (which is the reading of nearly all the MSS. of the B- and C-types) is simply the modern word *some*, but must be considered as partitive, and hence equivalent to *some of them*. The A-text simply has *soone*, i. e. soon.

20. *Consciences cast and craft*, Conscience's contrivance and art. In [b], the reading is *conscience*, which is merely another form of the genitive case. 'In O.E. of the 15th century, if the noun ended in a sibilant or was followed by a word beginning with a sibilant, the possessive sign was dropped; as, a *goose* egg, the *river* side;' Morris, Hist. Outlines of Eng. Accidence, p. 102. Hence the phrase 'for *conscience* sake,' Rom. xiii. 5; and the like.

23. The MSS. carefully distinguish between the spellings of the words *coupes* and *coppes* here; and for *coppes* we have, in [a], the reading *peces*. The words must, therefore, not be confused, if we can avoid it; and I think it possible that our author intended to make a distinction in sense between the French *coupe* and the A.S. *cuppa*, both borrowed from the same Latin word, viz. *cuppa*. *Coupe* may perhaps denote a vessel of large size, or a bowl; we find—'*Hec urna*, a cowpe; *Hic crater*, a pese;' Wright's Vocab., ed. Wülcker, col. 771. The form *coppe* or *cuppe* seems to have been chiefly used for a smaller drinking-vessel, containing enough for one person only; cf. Chaucer, Prol. 134, and note the following quotation. 'Some do vse to set before euerye man a lofe of bread, and *his cup*, and some vse the contrary;' Babees Book, p. 67. That this smaller cup was also called a *pece*, appears from the Promptorium Parvulorum, p. 388, where Mr. Way quotes the following :—'A pece of siluer or of metalle, *crater, cratera*.'—'*Crater, vas vinarium*, a pyece or wyne cuppe.'— '*Pece*, to drink in, *tasse*. Pece, a cuppe, *tasse, hanap*.' It was called *pece* to distinguish it from the *pot* or large flagon.

'A capone rosted broght she sone,
A clene klath, and brede tharone,
And a *pot* with riche wine,
And a *pece* to fil it yne.'

Ywaine and Gawin, l. 757 (Ritson's Met. Rom. i. 33). The phrase 'peces of siluer' occurs again below, in B. 3. 89.

25. *Moton*. 'Ye shall vnderstande that a *moton* is a coyne vsed in Fraunce and Brytaygne, and is of value, after the rate of sterlynge money, upon vs., or thereabout.'—Fabyan's Chronicles, ed. Ellis, p. 468. It was so called from its bearing an impression of a *lamb* (or *mutton*); on the other side was a figure of St. John the Baptist. In Cotgrave's French Dictionary, we find—'*Mouton à la grande laine*, a sheep well-woolled, or of great burthen; also, a coine of gold stamped on the one side with a sheep, on the other with a cross *fleury*, having at each angle a flower-deluce; John duke of Berry first caused it to be made about the year 1371.' Cotgrave, however, must here refer to a different coinage. They were really in use at an earlier period; as, at p. 297 of Memorials of London, ed. Riley, there is mention made (under date A.D. 1357) of a Teutonic knight, from whom some unknown thieves stole 400 golden shield-florins and *moutons d'or*, of the coinage of Philip and John, kings of France. Hence there is nothing strange in the use of the word in the A-text, written in 1362. The word is explained by Ducange, under its Low-Latin form *multo*.

26. *Had lauht here leue at*, had taken their leave of. *To lacche leue*, to take leave, is a common phrase. The author of the Alliterative 'Troy-Book,' ed. Panton and Donaldson, has a line almost identical with this one, as it stands in [b] and [a]. ' Than laght thai hor leue, tho lordes, in fere ; ' l. 9794.

The taking of bribes seems to have been a common failing with justices at this time. Compare—

' Hoc facit pecunia Quam omnis fere curia jam duxit in uxorem ;
Sunt justiciarii Quos favor et denarii alliciunt a jure.'

Polit. Songs (Camd. Soc.), p. 225 (cf. p. 226).

See also note above, Pass iii. 9, p. 31.

34. *Do calle*, cause to be called over. When the verb *do* is followed by an *active* verb in the infinitive mood, the latter is commonly best interpreted by giving it a *passive* signification. Thus, in l. 66 below, *do peynten and portreyn* is equivalent to 'cause it to be painted and pourtrayed.' So also *don saue* = cause to be saved, Pass. x. 328.

35. *Shal no lewednesse lette*, no ignorance shall hinder.

37. 'Where really skilful clerks shall limp along behind in the rear.' See *Clocke* in the Glossary.

38. *Frere*. Great sinners went to confession to a *friar* rather than to a parish-priest. Wyclif complains of this ; see Wyclif's Works, ed. Arnold, iii. 394 ; cf. pp. 377, 387. See Chaucer, Prol. 223.

47. *Took hym a noble*. Tyrwhitt remarks (note to Cant. Tales, 13852), that—'*to take*, in our old language, is also used for *to take to*, *to give*, as in l. 13334,

He *tok* me certain gold, I wot it wel.'

Whether the *noble* or *florin* was first coined, and what was the exact value of them, seem somewhat doubtful, unless we can depend upon the statement of Fabyan quoted above, Pass. iii. 157, and upon the following statement of the same, under the year 1339,—' In this yere also the kynge chaungyd his coyne, and made the noble & the half noble of the value of vi *s*. viii *d*., which at this day is worthe viii *s*. ix *d*. or x *d*., & the halfe noble after the rate, if they kepe the trewe weyght,' etc. There is a similar statement in A Chronicle of London, p. 57, under the 14th year of Edward III., which seems, as in Fabyan, to signify 1339 rather than 1340 : —' also the kyng made the coyne of goold : that is for to seyne, the *noble*, the half noble, and the ferthyng.' In the English Cyclopædia, under the heading *Coin*, we are told that—'it is from Edward III. that the series of English gold coins really commences, for no more occur till 1344, when that prince struck florins. The half and quarter-florin were struck at the same time. The florin was then to go for *six shillings*, though now it would be intrinsically worth nineteen. This coin being inconvenient, as forming no aliquot part of larger ideal denominations, seems to have been withdrawn.

C. PASS. IV. 51. B. PASS. III. 48. A. PASS. III. 49.

None have yet been found, but a few quarter-florins are preserved in cabinets, and one half-florin is known. In consequence, in the same year, the noble was published, of 6s. 8d. value, forming half a mark, then the most general idéal form of money. The obverse represents the king standing on a vessel, asserting the dominion of the sea. The noble was also attended by its half and quarter. This coin, sometimes called the *rose noble*, together with its divisions, continued the only gold coin, till the angels of Edward IV., 1465, and the angelets or half-angels, were substituted in their place. Henry V. is said to have diminished the noble, still making it go for its former value. Henry VI. restored it to its size, and caused it to pass for 10s., under the new name of ryal,' etc. William clearly intimates that *florins* were by no means scarce, and this seems at first sight to contradict that which has been said above. But the fact is simply, that most of the florins were coined abroad, chiefly at Florence; and it was ordered that florins de escu, and florins of Florence, should be current along with the sterlings, according to their value. Compare note to l. 25 (p. 40), where mention is made of the knight who lost 400 shield-florins (florins de escu) and moutons d'or. And see Ruding's Annals of the Coinage.

51. 'We have a window in working (i.e. being made), that will stand us very high,' i.e. that will cost us a large sum. For *stonden*, [b] has *sitten*, but the sense is the same. The practice of glazing windows is satirised also by William's imitator in the *Crede*, ll. 123-128. It was usual to introduce portraits or names of the benefactors in stained glass.

62. Lechery was one of the seven deadly sins. See Pass. vii. 170; and note to Pass. vii. 3.

67. The word *sustre* (sister) has a direct allusion to the letters of fraternity, by means of which any wealthy person could belong to a religious order of the mendicant friars. Cf. Pass. x. 342, 343; and xxiii. 367. See Massingberd, Eng. Reformation, p. 118.

71. *Thy kynde wille, (and) thi cost;* 'thy natural disposition, and thy expenses; as also their covetousness, and who really possessed the money' [c, b]; *or*, 'God knoweth who is courteous, or kind, or covetous, or otherwise' [a. 3. 59.]

—— (b. 3. 71.) *Or to greden after goddis men*, or to cry out for God's men, i.e. to send for the friars.

—— (b. 3. 75.) 'For thus the Gospel bids good men give their alms.' *Bit* is for *biddeth;* so also *rat* = readeth, Pass. iv. 410; *rit* = rideth, B. iv. 13; *halt* = holdeth, B. iii. 241; etc.

79. *Pillories*. Under the xvth year of Edward IV., Fabyan tells us that— 'this yere this mayer [Robert Basset, salter] dyd sharpe correccion vpon bakers for makynge of lyght brede, in so muche that he sette dyuerse vpon the pyllory, ... and a woman named Agnes Deyntie was also there punysshed for sellyng of false myngyd [mixed] butter.' In Riley's Memorials of London, there is frequent mention of the punishment of the pillory for various offences, chiefly for fraudulent practices. Thus, in A.D. 1316, two bakers were so punished for making bread 'of false, putrid, and rotten

C. PASS. IV. 82. B. PASS. III. 80. A. PASS. III. 71.

materials; through which, persons who bought such bread were deceived, and might be killed,' p. 121. In A.D. 1387, a baker's servant was put on the pillory for inserting a piece of iron into a loaf, in order to make it seem of full weight; p. 498. Others were so punished for enhancing the price of wheat, pp. 314, 317; for selling putrid meat or carrion, pp. 240, 266, 271, 328, etc.; for selling sacks of charcoal of short measure, p. 446; etc. Sometimes fraudulent bakers were drawn upon a hurdle; ibid. pp. 119, 120, 122, 423.

Pynyng-stoles, stools of punishment, also called *cucking-stools*. The *cucking-stool* was a seat of ignominy; see Chambers' Book of Days, i. 211.—'In Scotland, an ale-wife who exhibited bad drink to the public was put upon the *Cock-stule*, and the ale, like such relics of John Girder's feast as were totally uneatable (see Bride of Lammermoor) was given to the poor folk.' It was different from the *ducking-stool*, which was a punishment for scolds. See Brand; Popular Antiquities, iii. 102 (note), and 103. Brand seems to confound the two. Cf. note to Pass. v. 122.

—— (b. 3. 80.) This line recurs in Rich. Redeles, iii. 316.

—— (b. 3. 81.) *Parcel-mele*, by small parcels, i.e. retail.

82. *Regratrye*, selling by retail. The wholesale dealer was called an *Engrosser* (whence our *grocer*), because he sold in the *gross* or *great* piece. The retail dealer was called a *Regrater* or *Regrateress*; cf. ll. 113, 118, and Pass. vii. 232. In Riley's translation of the Liber Albus, p. 232, we read—'No baker shall give unto the *regratresses* the six-pence on Monday morning by way of hansel-money, or the three-pence on Friday for curtesy-money; but, after the ancient manner, let him give thirteen articles of bread for twelve.' It is worth while to add, that this last passage explains clearly the meaning of the common expression, *a baker's dozen*—meaning *thirteen*. The bakers did not sell the bread to the public, but to the regratresses, or women who took the bread round to each customer's door. The regratress's profit came from the fact that, according to 'the ancient manner,' she received 13 *loaves at the price of* 12 from the baker, and sold them *separately* to various customers afterwards at a price which was duly regulated and might not be exceeded. The frauds and adulterations of the *regraters* were a constant source of annoyance, and were frequently complained of.

84. 'For, if they had made their profits honestly, they would not have built (houses for themselves) so loftily; nor could they have bought for themselves such tenements; be ye full sure of it.'

Wyclif has similar remarks upon this subject; see Works, ed. Arnold, iii. 334.

87. 'Though they deliver to them a dishonest quantity, they consider it as no fraud; and, though they do not fill up to the top the measure that has been sealed according to law, they grasp as much money for it as they would do for the full true measure.' The allusion is to the sealing or marking of measures, to insure their being true. Thus it was ordered, 'that no brewster or taverner shall sell from henceforth by any measure but the gallon, pottle, and quart; and that these shall be sealed

with the seal of the Alderman; and that the tun of the brewster shall be of 150 gallons, and be sealed with such seal of the Alderman;' etc. etc. Liber Albus, ed. Riley, p. 233.

93. Compare a similar passage in Pass. xx. 268–271.

106. In 1276, a fire occurred in the city because a man left a candle burning and fell asleep; Riley's Mem. of London, p. 8; cf. p. 46.

108. In a Charter of Edward the Second, we find it ordered 'that an inhabitant [of the city of London], and especially an Englishman by birth, a trader of a certain mistery or craft, shall not be admitted to the freedom of the city aforesaid except upon the security of six reputable men, of such certain mistery or craft,' etc.; Liber Albus, ed. Riley, p. 127; see also pp. 388, 425. It is clear, from William's complaint, that men who had enriched themselves contrived to obtain the freedom of the city without too close enquiry as to the manner in which their wealth had been acquired.

117. *Presentes.* Presents made, not in money, but in silver cups, etc. See note to l. 23, p. 40. For the text *in quorum*, etc., see Ps. xxv. 10 (Vulgate); xxvi. 10 (A. V.).

—— (b. 3. 90.) To *maintain* was to aid and abet others in wrong-doing, by supplying them with money or exerting influence in their behalf. It was a recognized law term; and Blount observes that—'there lies a writ against a man for this offence, called a Writ of Maintenance. See Coke on Littleton, fol. 368 b.' Cf. Paston Letters, ed. Gairdner, i. 145, 151; Wyclif's Works, ed. Arnold, iii. 322; and see ll. 231, 288, below.

123. The quotation is not from Solomon, but from Job xv. 34 :—'fire shall consume the tabernacles of bribery.' Mr. Kemble justly points out that this is one of the numerous instances in which wise sayings were commonly attributed to Solomon, whether they were his or not. See Salomon and Saturn, ed. Kemble, p. 108.

125. The sense of *blewe* in this passage is livid, dull gray; cf. Icel. *blár*, livid, whence M. E. *blo*, as in [b]. So in the Towneley Mysteries, p. 224, we have 'as *blo* as led,' as livid as lead. Compare our phrase— 'to beat black and *blue*.' The form *blewe* is French.

—— (b. 3. 99.) *Yeresyyues*, lit. year-gifts. ' *Yeresgive* is a toll or fine taken by the king's officers on a person's entering an office; or rather, a sum of money or bribe, given to them to connive at extortion or other offences in him that gives it; see Chart. Hen. II.; fourth Chart. Hen. III.; and ninth Chart. Hen. III.;' Privilegia Londini, by W. Bohun, of the Middle Temple, 1723; quoted in Notes and Queries, 4th Ser. iv. 560. This definition perfectly suits the present passage, but we may fairly assume, from the form of the word, that it once meant an *annual* donation (like the modern Christmas box), generally given, it would appear, upon New Year's day. It came to be so troublesome that we find special exemptions from it, as in the following :—' Also, that the city of London shall be quit of Brudtol, and Childewite, and *Yeresgive*, and Scot-ale;' Liber Albus, ed. Riley, pp. 117, 138.

C. PASS. IV. 127. B. PASS. III. 100. A. PASS. III. 95. 45

Palsgrave has—'Newe-yeres gifte, *estrayne*;' and Cotgrave—'*Estreine*, f. a New-years Gift, or Present; also, a Handsell.'

127. *The kynge.* Richard II. had ascended the throne when the second revision of the poem was made, but the description was originally intended for Edward III., for whom it is much more suitable.

129. *As hus kynde wolde*, as his nature disposed him. See Pass. ix. 161, and Rich. Redeles, ii. 142.

138. The C-text varies here somewhat. The sense (of that text) is—'Yet I forgive thee this offence; it is God's forbidding (i. e. may God forbid) that thou vex me and Truth any more; if thou mayst be taken (in such an offence), I shall cause thee to be enclosed in Corfe castle, as if you were an anchorite there, or in some much worse abode;' etc. Corfe Castle (*not mentioned in* b, a) is well described in Timbs's Abbeys, Castles, and Ancient Halls of England, vol. ii. pp. 371–376. The allusion is doubtless significant. It was in Corfe Castle that Edward II. was confined in 1327, before his removal thence to Bristol, and finally to Berkeley. Again, the use of the word anchorite may refer to the curious story of the hermit Peter, who prophesied evil to king John, for which he was 'committed to prison within the castle of Corf; [and,] when the day by him prefixed came without any other notable damage unto king John, he was by the kings commandement drawne from the said castell into the towne of Warham, and there hanged, togither with his sonne;' Holinshed's Chronicle, sub anno 1213. See Shakespeare's King John, iv. 2. 147, and Mr. Staunton's note upon the passage. There is, too, a grim humour in the words 'oþer in a wel wors wone;' for Mr. Timbs quotes from Dr. Maton's Observations, vol. i. p. 12, the following remarks upon Corfe Castle. 'We could not view without horror the dungeons which remain in some of the towers; they recalled to our memory the truly diabolical cruelty of king John, by whose order 22 prisoners, confined in them, were starved to death.'

163. In the expression *your father*, the person really referred to (in the original draft of the poem) was Edward II., the father of Edward III., who was upon the throne at the time when the A-text was composed. It is true that the reading of the Vernon MS., adopted as the *basis* of the A-text, is—'Vr fader Adam heo falde,' i. e. she overthrew (lit. felled) our father Adam; but the various readings in the MSS. shew that such a reading is a mere mistake on the part of the scribe of that MS., since *Adam* does not appear in any other MS. whatever. The matter is put beyond doubt by the words in Meed's reply, where she says (A. iii. 180, 181) that 'she never did kill any king, nor gave counsel to that effect; that she never did what Conscience accused her of, and that she appealed to the king himself as witness.' The really remarkable point is that the poet, in his last revision, should have allowed this expression to stand; but we may note that the latter part of the line is altered in [c], and the new line is not inapplicable to the Black Prince, whose troubles arose from the failure of Don Pedro to supply him with the money which he had promised. There are, however, several such apparent inconsis-

46   C. PASS. IV. 164.   B. PASS. III. 127.   A. PASS. III. 123.

tencies, shewing that, much as the poet altered his work in revision, there were some passages which—probably because they were too well known to his readers—he did not feel wholly at liberty to interfere with. In such cases we must compare all three texts together.

164. 'She (i.e. Meed or Bribery) hath poisoned popes, and she impairs holy church.' The reader need not suppose that the allusion here is any actual poisoning of any special pope; it is probably only a brief mode of reference to the famous saying attributed to an angel—'This day is *poison* shed abroad upon the church.' See note to Pass. xviii. 220 for further information. However pope Benedict XI., who died in 1304, is said to have been poisoned.

167. *Talewys*, full of tales, loquacious, addicted to talebearing, slanderous. As Dr. Stratmann gives no instance of the use of this word except by our poet, I add a few by way of illustration.

'And sone, thy tong thou kepe also,
And be not *tale-wyse* be no way;'
How the Wise Man taught his Son, l. 33;
in Ritson's Anc. Pop. Poetry.
'[Be not] to toilose, ne to *talewijs*, for temperaunce is best;'
Babees Book, p. 12.

See Mr. Furnivall's Glossary to the Babees Book for other examples. The word *tale*, in Middle English, commonly has a bad sense, and signifies a lie, or something near it; see l. 47 above; and cf. Pass. i. 49.

171. *Sysours;* see note to Pass. iii. 63, p. 34. A *sompnour, somner,* or *summoner* was an officer who summoned delinquents to appear in an ecclesiastical court. See the description of the Sompnour in Chaucer's Prol., and in the Prologue to the Freres Tale. Cf. also Wyclif, Works, ed. Arnold, iii. 320.

175. *Grotes*, lit. great coins, because, until they were coined, there was no silver coin larger than the penny. Cf. Du. *groot*, Fr. *gros*. 'In this yere [1349] the kynge caused to be coyned grotes and halfe grotes, the whiche lacked of the weyghte of his former coyne, ii *s*. vi *d*. in a *li*. [*libra*, pound] Troy.'—Fabyan, p. 461. The *groat* should have been equal to four silver pennies, but was only equal to about three and a half. A drawing of one may be seen in Knight's Pictorial Hist. England, i. 837.

177. 'And she seizes true men [the true man, *a, b*] by the top,' i.e. by the head. See Halliwell, who quotes—'Thou take hym by the toppe and I by the tayle;' Chester Plays, ii. 176.

183. Compare the following extract from Wyclif's Works, ed. Arnold, iii. 307. 'And whanne many londis schulde falle into the kyngis hondis, bi eschet or othere juste menes, thes worldly clerkis and veyn religious *meden* gretly the kyngis officeris and men of lawe, to forbarre the kyngis right, and maken hemself lordis wrongfully. And thus bi the kyngis goodis thei maken his officeris and lege men to forswere hem [*themselves*], and defraude here lege lord. . . . Also many worldly peyntid clerkis geten the *kyngis seel*, hym out-wittynge, and senden to Rome for beneficis moche gold; and whanne the king sendith his *privey seel* for to avaunce goode

C. PASS. IV. 184. B. PASS. III. 146. A. PASS. III. 142. 47

clerkis, and able bothe of good lif and gret cunnyng to reule, thei bryngen forth hereby many worldly wrecchis, unable to reule o soule for defaute of kunnyng and good lyvyng, and thus *vsen the kyngis seel* ayenst Goddis honour and the kyngis, and profit of Cristene peple, where the kyng undirstondith [*supposes*] to do wel bi here suggestion.'

184. *Provisors.* A writ summoning one to appear for contempt of the sovereign was called *præmunire*, from its first word. 'Numerous statutes have defined what shall be such a contempt as amounts to a præmunire. Most of the earlier are directed against *provisors*, as they were called, or persons who purchased from Rome provisions for holding abbeys or priories, etc., before those benefices were vacant (25 Edw. III., Stat. 5, c. 22. Stat. 6), or for exemption from obedience to their proper ordinary (2 Hen. IV. c. 3), or bulls for exemption from tithes,' etc.—English Cyclopædia, s. v. Præmunire. Massingberd's Engl. Ref. p. 238. See note to Pass. iii. 182, p. 38.

Complaints of bribery at the court of Rome were common. A Poem on the Evil Times of Edward II. says :—

'Voiz of clerk is sielde [*seldom*] i-herd at the court of Rome,
Ne were he nevere swich a clerk, *silverles if he come ;*'
Polit. Songs, ed. Wright, p. 324.

185. See the passages upon Simony in Wyclif's Works, ed. Arnold, iii. 226, 278–287, and 488. Wyclif's definition of it is—'For whoevere cometh to presthod or benefice by yifte of money-worth, bi preiere or servyce, cometh in by *symonye*, as Seynt Gregoir and the lawe techeth.'

188. The word *loteby*, meaning paramour or concubine, was used of both sexes. See Halliwell's Dictionary; Robert of Brunne, Handl. Synne, l. 1732; and cf. the following :—

'Now am I younge, stoute, and bolde, . . .
Now frere menour, now jacobin,
And with me folwith my *loteby*
To don me solace and company ;' Rom. Rose, 6339—

where, in the French original, we find the word to be *compaigne*.

'She stal awai, mididone,
And wente to here *lotebi*;' Seven Sages, ed. Weber, l. 1443.

194. 'She lieth against the law, and hindereth it (in its) way.' *Gate* = way, as in B. i. 203.

195. 'So that the truth cannot find its way out,' i. e. cannot appear. Here *forth* = means of progress, way forward.

196. *Louedayes.* Love-day, 'commonly meant a law-day, a day set apart for a leet or manorial court, a day of final *concord* and *reconciliation* :' [as we read in the Coventry Mysteries, p. 111 :]—

'Now is the *love-day* mad of us fowre fynially,
Now may we leve in pes as we were wonte.'

'Hock-day was usually set apart for a love-day, law-day, or court-leet.'— Timbs' Nooks and Corners of English Life, pp. 224, 228. [Hock-day was the second Tuesday after Easter.] William uses the term again, B. v. 427, and it occurs in Chaucer, Prol., l. 258. It was so called because the object was the amicable settlement of differences ; but it is clear, from our author, that on such occasions much injustice was frequently done to the poor. This is remarkably confirmed by a passage in Riley's Memorials of London, p. 173, where it was ordered (A.D. 1329)—'that no one of the City . . shall go out of this city, to maintain [i. e. unjustly abet] parties, such as taking seisins, or holding *days of love*, or making other congregations within the city or without, in 'disturbance of the peace of our Lord the king, or in affray of the people, and to the scandal of the city.' See also p. 158, where a day of love was appointed at St. Paul's church, to settle a trade dispute by arbitration. Cf. Tyrwhitt's note to Chaucer, Prol. 260; Wyclif's Works, ed. Arnold, iii. 322; Paston Letters, ed. Gairdner, i. 496; and Titus Andronicus, i. 1. 491.

198. (cf. a. 3. 155.) *The mase*, etc. 'It is bewilderment for a poor man, though he plead (here) ever.' Some MSS. have *plede* instead of *mote;* and both [a] and [c] omit *hir*, which is also spelt *here, heer*, in the MSS., and means 'here.' The word *mote* is not common as a *verb*, but we find it in Robert of Brunne's Handlyng Synne, l. 9803, with the gloss *plete* written above it ; a clear proof that *plead* was the sense intended by it.

—— (b. 3. 164.) *Clergye* most frequently means *learning*, as opposed to *lewdness*, ignorance. It probably means so here, as bribery makes clever men covetous.

222. (b. 3. 175.) It is a mark of respect for Meed to address the king in the plural number, and a mark of familiarity or contempt to address Conscience in the singular. This distinction is very carefully observed by our author, by Chaucer, and by the author of William of Palerne. See Abbott, Shakesp. Grammar, 3rd edit. art. 231.

227. The reading is either—*hanged on myn hals*, hung upon my neck [c] ; or *hanged on myne half* [b], i.e. hung upon my side, clung to my party. The word is *never* here written *hals* [neck] in MSS. of the B-class, although curiously enough, the Vernon MS. has *nekke*.

230. *Yut ich may*, etc. 'Yet I may perhaps, as far as I might have the power, honour thee with gifts.' In Cursor Mundi, ed. Morris, l. 109, two MSS. have the word *menske* where the other two have *worschipe*.

233. Meed here repudiates the charge made against her, and appeals to the king himself. It is singular that this passage, which originally referred to Edward II., should have been retained in the C-text ; but, upon this point, consult the note to l. 163, p. 45. Compare also the next note.

—— (b. 3. 188.) This alludes to Edward's wars in Normandy, and, in particular, to the treaty sealed at Bretigny, near Chartres, on the 8th of May, 1360. Edward renounced his claim to the crown of France, and his claim to Normandy, Anjou, Touraine, and Maine, and restored all his conquests except Calais and Guisnes ; but reserved Poitou, Guienne, and the county of Ponthieu. The dauphin agreed to pay for the ransom of his father King John, the sum of 3,000,000 scutes (*escus*) or crowns of gold. See Lingard, iv. 118 ; Thomas Walsingham, i. 290; Fabyan, p. 471. The sufferings of the English in their previous retreat from Paris to Bretagne were very great, and they encountered a most dreadful tempest near

C. PASS. IV. 245. B. PASS. III. 200. A. PASS. III. 184. 49

Chartres, with violent wind and heavy hail. Hence the allusions in the text to the cold, to the lengthening out of winter till May, to the dim cloud, and to the famine from which the army suffered. 'It is to be noted,' says Stow, 'that the 14 day of April, and the morrow after Easter Day (1360), King Edward with his host lay before the city of Paris; which day was full dark of mist and hail, and so bitter cold, that many men died on their horsebacks with the cold; wherefore unto this day it hath been called the *Black Monday*.' Meed suggests that, instead of exacting money, Edward should have foregone it, or even have paid some, to secure to himself the kingdom of France. The articles agreed to at Bretigny were never fulfilled; Lingard, iv. 130. In the C-text, this passage is much altered.

245. I here note that Walsingham (ed. Riley, ii. 170) says that, in the year 1387, a French messenger was caught, on whom was found a compact, by which the king of France was to buy Calais and the adjacent country from Richard.

—— (b. 3. 190.) *For colde*, i.e. keep off the cold. See note to Pass. ix. 59.

248. Cf. Pass. xxii. 32.

259. (b. 3. 200.) *Mareschal.* 'When the king summoned his military tenants, the earl constable and earl mareschal held the principal command under the sovereign; but in armies raised by contract, he appointed two or more mareschals, whose duty it was to array the forces and to direct their movements.'—Lingard, iv. 190. The word occurs in the Crowned King, l. 102.

263. The sense of *brol* is a brat; the reading in [a] is *barn*. We find— 'a beggers *brol*,' P. Pl. Crede, 745; 'Al bot the wrech *brol* that is of Adamis blode;' Reliq. Antiq. ii. 177; 'Belial *brolles*,' i.e. children of Belial; Wyclif, iii. 238.

—— (b. 3. 220.) The two earlier versions here differ remarkably; and, in the last revision, the line was cut out. In [a], we have—'the king pays or rewards his men to keep peace in the land;' but in [b] it runs—'the king receives tribute from his men, to keep peace,' etc. The discrepancy is best explained by rejecting the reading of the Vernon MS. (taken as the basis of the A-text), and substituting for it the reading of U (the MS. in University College, Oxford), which agrees with the B-text exactly.

281. (b. 3. 224.) *Alle kyne crafty men*, skilled workers (craftsmen) of every kind. *Alle kyne* is here a corrupter form of *alle kynes* or *alkynnes*, a genitive case; see the B-text; and cf. note to Pass. xi. 128.

290. 'They that live in an unlawful manner have liberal hands for giving bribes.' The Latin original is quoted in [b]. *Large* in Middle-English often means *liberal;* cf. the sb. *largesse*, and see l. 454 below.

292. In the two first texts, Conscience here distinguishes between the two meanings of Meed, viz. (1) divine reward, shewn by God towards well-doers, and (2) corruption or bribery. (For the Latin quotations, see Ps. xv.) In the C-text, Conscience enters into a new and elaborate distinction between Meed (or reward, or prepayment, or bribe), and Mercede (or wages due for work actually done). The long illustration from grammar

in ll. 335-409 is barely intelligible, and very dull; yet it may very well have given great satisfaction to some of his readers, who delighted in such subtilties. A similarly elaborated passage occurs in Pass. xx. 111–122.

301. The phrase *prae manu* in Latin sometimes means in hand, in readiness. By *prae manibus* the poet evidently means payment in advance, prepayment before the work is done; see the four lines following, and cf. Pass. x. 45, where the phrase recurs.

309. 'According to the Bible, that bids that no one shall withhold the hire of his servant over the evening till the next morning;' cf. Levit. xix. 13.

—— (b. 3. 236.) *Assoileth it*, solves the question; see Ps. xv. 2.

—— (b. 3. 237.) *Of o colour*, of one colour, pure, spotless.

—— (b. 3. 240.) The quotation ends—*innocentem non accepit;* Ps. xv. 5.

330. (*not in* b, a.) This belief, that Solomon is still left in hell, is repeated at Pass. xii. 220. See note to that line.

331. This singular line means, as it stands—'So that God giveth nothing (to any man), but sin is a comment upon it;' which may be explained as signifying that God gives things to men with a clause of revocation; and the comment or explanation of the text is given by the word *sin;* i.e. sin against Him revokes the promise. But when we remember that the 'glose,' or comment on a text, was commonly in Latin, it is clear that the true reading is not the *English* word 'synne,' as in the MSS., but the *Latin* word 'sin;' a theory which is sufficiently proved by the fact that the excellent Ilchester MS. has the reading 'si,' and the same reading is found in MS. Digby 102; so that the right reading is—'that *si* [or *sin*] ne is the glose.' We thus get the very simple sense —'So that God giveth nothing without an *if;*' which is unquestionably what is intended. The use of *sin* may be illustrated by the parable of the unfruitful tree:—'et siquidem fecerit fructum; *sin* autem, in futurum succides eam;' Luc. xiii. 9.

337. 'In a settled and secure (or regular) manner, agreeing with themselves (according to rule).' The reader must puzzle out this passage for himself if he cares to read it. Some lines are very curious; e. g. ll. 369, 370; 381-385.

342. The quotation is part of a Latin grace, which is printed at p. 390 of the Babees Book, and runs thus:—' Retribuere dignare, Domine Deus, omnibus nobis bona facientibus, propter nomen sanctum tuum, uitam eternam; Amen.' This agrees with William's loose translation in the three lines above.

358. Quoted from John i. 14. The quotation at l. 406 is from 1 Jo. iv. 16.

368. 'In which are good and bad; and to grant the will of neither of them.'

369. This is interesting evidence, that it was then beginning to be considered right for a son to bear the same surname as his father.

372. It is well to remember that *taylende* does not mean *tail-end* (as in

MS. F), but *tallying*, reckoning, enumeration or computation of property. Blount, in his Law Dictionary, explains that *tail* is a term used of fee (or property) that is not fee simple, being not in the owner's free power to dispose of. *Fayre* means 'honestly come by,' and *foule* the reverse.

410. 416. (b. 3. 257; a. 3. 244.) *Rat*, reads; contracted from *redeth*; it occurs again in Pass. xiv. 5, where MS. P wrongly has *that of* instead of *rat that*. It occurs also in Polit. Songs, ed. Wright, p. 327, l. 88; and (in the form *ret*) in Old Eng. Homilies, ed Morris, 1. Ser. 125. *Regum*, the book *of Kings*; i. e. the first two books, generally called the books of Samuel. See 2 Sam. xviii. ; 1 Sam. xv.

—— (b. 3. 258.) There is no apparent alliteration, but Langland considers *v* and *f* to answer to one another, as in Pass. iii. 61, so that *veniaunce* rimes to *fel*.

419. (b. 3. 261.) See Exod. xvii. 8 for the sin of Amalek.

420. *Hoteth to be boxome*, bids (thee) be obedient.

425. The word *mebles*, i. e. moveables, meant not only corn, cattle, and merchandise, but money, fuel, furniture, and wearing apparel; Lingard Hist. Eng. iv. 174. '*Movable good*, as cuppe, or chalice, mytir, bacul [staff]; or *unmovable good*, as hous, feeld, wode;' Pecock's Repressor, ii. 386.

437. 'In case it should annoy me [men *in* b], I make *no* ending, i. e. draw no conclusion; but the A-text has—'I will make an end,' i. e. say no more.

442. *Somme*, to some whom I will not specify; dat. plural, used indefinitely. See note to l. 14 of this Passus, p. 40.

450. 'Loyalty, and no one else, shall execute the law upon him, [b, c];' *or*, 'Loyalty shall execute the law upon him, or else he shall lose his life' [a]. See *Lyf* or *Lif* in the Glossary.

—— (b. 3. 295.) 'Meed, from amongst misdoers, makes many lords, and rules the realms so as to supersede the lord's laws' [b]; *or*, 'Meed, from amongst misdoers, makes men so rich, that (corrupt) Law is become lord, and Loyalty is poor' [a].

451. *Selk houe*, (white) silk hood. Cf. note to Pass. i. 159, p. 16.

456. With this line Pass. iii., in the A-text, abruptly terminates. The admirable addition here made was suggested, I feel confident, by the recent proclamation of a *jubilee*, in the last year of Edward III. (Feb. 1377), proclaimed because the king had attained the *fiftieth* year of his reign; Lingard, iv. 146. Taking his cue from this, the poet hopes the reign of Richard II, soon expected to begin, may usher in a new era of perfect peace; but, in ll. 481-5, he suddenly prophecies that certain rather unlikely events will first happen, thus revealing his fear that no such good time was at hand.

The above suggestion is fully confirmed by a passage in John of Bridlington's pretended prophecies, bk. iii. c. viii., where the jubilee of Edward III. is described in the lines—

'Pacis erunt dies, belli terrore remoto,' etc.;

and the writer, in his commentary, takes great care to explain that the *jubilee* means the 50th year of Edward's *reign*, not of his *life*.

461. *Baselardes.* 'Temp. Rich. II., civilians wore swords called *baselards* or *badelaires*. Example; monument of a civilian, King's Sombourne Church, Hants, 1380.'—Godwin's Handbook of English Archaeology, p. 261. ' The *baselard* was of two kinds, straight and curved . . . By Statute 12 Rich. II., c. vi., it was provided that—" null servant de husbandrie ou laborer ne servant de artificer ne de vitailler porte desore enavant *baslard*, dagger, nespee [*nor sword*] sur forfaiture dicelle." Priests were strictly inhibited from wearing this instrument of war, but the rule was constantly broken.' —Note by Peacock to Myrc's Instructions for Parish Priests (Early English Text Society); p. 67. In Wright's Essays, ii. 269, will be found a Ballad on the Baselard, printed from a Sloane MS. It shews that the weapon had a red sheath, a twisted haft, a silver chape or plate at the end of it, etc. The frequent enactments against the wearing of weapons by civilians, etc., in the reigns of Edward III. and Richard II., shew how often this law was disregarded. See Liber Albus, pp. 335, 554, 555. The word occurs again in B. xv. 121.

464. See note to l. 480 below.

465. The Old French *picois*, signifying a mattock or pick-axe, has given rise to the tautological form *pick-axe* which we now employ; the modern form is a mere clever corruption, due to the foreign form of the old termination, and is not to be found in our older authors. In the Prompt. Parv. we have ' Pykeys, mattokke;' in Riley's Memorials of London, p. 284, there is mention of '5 pikeyses;' in the Paston Letters, ed. Gairdner, i. 106, ' pikoys' is used as a plural; and Robert of Brunne, in his Handlyng Synne, ll. 940–1, remarks :—

'Mattok is a pykeys,
Or a pyke, as sum men seys.'

467. To hunt (not with hounds, but) with *placebo* [b] means to be diligent in singing *placebo*, i. e. in saying the Office for the Dead. In B. xv. 122, we find the author speaking of saying *placebo*.

The *placebo* was an antiphon in the Office for the Dead at Vespers, which began—' *Placebo* domino in regione uiuentium ' (Ps. cxvi. 9, or cxiv. 9 in the Vulgate). Our word *dirge* is a contraction of *dirige*, as here used. This word begins the antiphon ' Dirige, Dominus meus, in conspectu tuo uitam meam' (cf. Ps. v. 8), used in the first nocturn at matins, in the Office for the Dead. For further illustration, see Mr Way's note to *Dyryge* in the Promptorium; Mr Arnold's note to Wyclif's Works, iii. 374; Dr Rock's Church of our Fathers, iii. 123; and Ancren Riwle, p. 22.

To sing *placebo* came to be used in a humorous sense, viz. to flatter. ' Flattereres ben the deueles chapeleyns, that singen ay *Placebo* ;' Chaucer, Pers. Tale, De Ira. Hence the name *Placebo* for a flattering character in the Merchauntes Tale. Cf. Ayenbyte of Inwyt, ed. Morris, p. 60; Dyce's Skelton, ii. 121.

468. 'And pray, saying their Psalter and Seven Psalms, for all sinful people.' The Seven Psalms are the seven penitential psalms, viz. Pss. 6, 32, 38, 51, 102, 130, 143; all of which are now appointed to be read on Ash Wednesday.

C. PASS. IV. 468. B. PASS. III. 310. (NOT IN A.) 53

—— (b. 3. 310.) To 'ding upon David' means to practice singing the Psalms repeatedly. In some verses in MS. Arundel 292, fol. 71 verso, printed in Reliq. Antiq. i. 292, we have the very expression:—
'I donke vpon David til my tonge talmes;'
i. e. till my tongue fails me; cf. Du. *talmen*, to loiter, be idle.

474. (b. 3. 316.) *After the dede*, according to the deed.

480. Isaiah ii. 4: 'Et iudicabit gentes, et arguet populos multos: et conflabunt gladios suos in uomeres, et lanceas suas in falces: non leuabit gens contra gentem gladium, nec exercebuntur ultra ad praelium.'

481. Fanciful prophecies were then in vogue; see those of John of Bridlington, in Political Poems, ed. Wright, vol. i. William has another similar one at the end of Pass. ix. This present one merely vaguely hints at a final time when Jews and Mahometans shall be converted. Line 483 is sufficiently clear. The 'middle of a moon' (cf. B. xiii. 155) means the full moon, and, in particular, the Paschal full moon; whilst 'to torne' means 'to be converted.' The sense is, accordingly, that 'the Paschal full moon (with the events of the crucifixion) shall cause the Jews to be converted to Christianity; and next, at the sight of their conversion, Saracens also shall declare their belief in the Holy Ghost; for both Mohammed and Meed shall then meet with ill-success.' Compare Pass. xviii. ll. 317–322.

The mention of 'six suns' in l. 482 is no doubt an allusion to the portents supposed to have been seen in the sky on various occasions; cf. 3 Henry VI., Act ii. sc. 1. l. 25—
'Dazzle mine eyes, or do I see *three suns?*' etc.

485. (b. 3. 327; *not in* A.) See Prov. xxii. 1.

486. 'As wrath as the wind,' i. e. as angry as a boisterous wind, is evidently a proverbial expression. Our author has it again in Rich. Redeles, iii. 153.

487. The quotation is not from the book of Wisdom, but from Prov. xxii. 9. Meed quotes only *half* of it, for which Conscience reproves her, and quotes the rest, l. 499. The full verse is—' Uictoriam et honorem acquiret qui dat munera; animam autem aufert accipientium.'

492. The lady read but *half* the text. It is—'Omnia autem probate, quod bonum est tenete,' 1 Thess. v. 21.

—— (b. 3. 342.) *Were gode*, would be good.

497. (b. 3. 344.) 'So he that refers to Wisdom' or rather to Proverbs [c]; *or*, 'And if ye refer again to Wisdom,' [b].

500. 'He wins worship, who is willing to give a reward, but he that receives or accepts it is a receiver of guile' [c]; *or*, 'But though, by giving a reward, we win worship and obtain a victory, yet the soul that receives the present, is to that extent under an obligation' [b]. Both of these are comments upon the text in the note to l. 487.

NOTES TO PASSUS V. (B. Passus IV; A. Passus IV.)

2. (b. 4. 2; a. 4. 2.) *Sauhtne*, be reconciled. I would call attention to the letter *n* in this word. In Moeso-Gothic, verbs in *-nan* have a passive signification; thus *fulljan* means *to fill*, but *fullnan* means *to become full*. According to this analogy, we find the A.S. *sehtian* or *sahtlian* = to make peace, to reconcile others; but *sahtnan* (if such a form were to occur, and it no doubt once existed) would mean to become at peace, to be reconciled. The word is therefore correctly spelt here, and has the sense of to become at peace, be reconciled. See *sauhten, sahtlien, sahtnien* in Stratmann; and add to the examples there given, the references—Gamelyn, l. 150; Cursor Mundi, l. 16; Pricke of Conscience, l. 1470.

17. *Caton his knaue.* Cato his servant. The servant of Reason is no doubt here called Cato but of respect for Dionysius Cato, whom our author often quotes; see note to Pass. ix. 338. In the next line we may have mention of Tom True-tongue, an imaginary name which has occurred before, iv. 478; and elsewhere we have mention of an opposite character, viz. Tom Two-tongued, xxiii. 162. Here, however, the name is lengthened out into a whole sentence. For similar long names, not unlike those of Puritan times, see l. 20 below; ix. 80, 81, 82, 83.

19. *Lesynges*, leasings, lies, idle tales to laugh at. Compare:—

'Trofels [*trifles*] sal i yow nane tell,
Ne *lesinges* forto ger [*make*] yow lagh.'

Ywaine and Gawaine, l. 150 (Ritson's Met. Rom.)

20. Here Reason tells his servant Cato to put a saddle upon Patience or Sufferance (represented here as a horse), and further to restrain it with the girth called Advise-thee-beforehand [c], *or* Wittyword [b], because it is the habit of Will (the horse's temper) to wince and kick, and to shew signs of impatience. The word *warroke* is very rare, but appears again in Mr Wright's Volume of Vocabularies, 1st Series, p. 154. To *make wehe* (b. 4. 22) is to make a neighing sound, to neigh; *wehe* being, like the Welsh *wihi*, an imitation of that sound. Chaucer uses the word in his Reves Tale (C. T. l. 4064). In the Ayenbite of Inwyt also (ed. Morris, 1868, p. 204) is a similar passage. 'Thanne the bodiliche wyttes byeth ase thet hors thet yernth wyth-oute bridle zuo thet hit deth falle his lhord. Ac the herte chaste ham of-halt mid the bridle of skele;' i. e. then the bodily wits are as the horse that runneth without bridle, so that it causes its lord to fall. But the chaste heart restrains them with the bridle of reason. Cf. James i. 26; iii. 2. 3. In the Trial of Treasure (in Dodsley's Old Plays, ed. Hazlitt, iii. 297), we have the very same idea. The character named Inclination is led in 'in his bridle, shackled,' and begins a speech with, '*We-he! he! he! he!* ware the horse-heels, I say; I would the rein were loose, that I might run away.'

26. *Which*, what sort of, what kind of; a common meaning of *which*, especially before *a*. Cf. notes to Pass. iii. 17, x. 300.

27. *Waryn*, also spelt Guarin, or Guerine, was once a common and popular Christian name; see Bardsley's English Surnames, p. 24.

36. (b. 4. 35; *not in* a.) See. Ps. xiii. 7 (Vulgate).

43. *His sone*, Edward the Black Prince, a great favourite with the people. He did not leave England to take possession of Acquitaine till Feb 2. 1363. William having once inserted this in the earliest version of his poem, does not seem to have thought it worth while to alter it, as he retains the expression *his sone* even in [c]. Cf. note to l. 171, p. 59.

45. *Putte vp a bylle* [c, a] ; *Put forth a bille* [b] ; The former is the more usual expression, as in Fabyan's Chronicles [1410-11] :—'The commons of this lande *put vp a bylle* vnto the kyng,' etc. The sense is—brought forward a petition. Compare Paston Letters, i. 151, 153.

With respect to this appeal of Peace to the king, see the scene in Sir F. Palgrave's Merchant and Friar, p. 242, where a maiden appeals to the king, saying—'from our Lord the King, he who wears the English-Saxon crown, and who hath sworn to observe the good laws of the Confessor, do I now demand that even justice which hath been refused to me at home.' And see p. 238 of the same work.

46. *Wrong* is a representative of the oppressive tribe known as *the king's purveyors*. The peasantry often complained of them bitterly, accusing them of taking things by violence ; see note to. l. 61. In the poem of King Edward and the Shepherd (printed by Hartshorne in his Ancient Metrical Tales) is the following :—

> 'I hade catell, now have I non ;
> Thay take my bestis, and don thaim slon,
> And payen but a *stick of tre* . . . .
> Thai take geese, capons, and henne,
> And alle that ever thei may with renne,
> And reves us our catell . . . .
> Thei toke my hennes and my geese,
> And my schepe with all the fleese,
> And ladde them forth away.'

So in Political Songs (Camd. Soc. 1839), p. 186—
> 'Est vitii signum pro victu solvere *lignum*.'

So in God spede the Plough, printed at the end of Pierce the Ploughman's Crede, ed. Skeat, 1867, p. 70.

A long complaint against these purveyors will be found in the Towneley Mysteries, at p. 99. A very similar complaint appears in Robert of Brunne's Handlyng Synne, ll. 7420-3.

To add to the troubles of the peasantry, they were liable to be imposed upon by *false* purveyors, mere imposters who wished to practise extortion ; see Riley's Memorials of London, p. 645.

51. St. Giles's down is near Winchester ; see note to Pass. vii. 211.

58. To *maintain* was the technical term for to aid and abet in wrong-doing ; cf. iii. 207, iv. 187, etc. See note to B. iii. 90. *Hewes*, domestics ; A. S. *hiwan*, domestics, servants ; Whitaker took it to mean *ewes!* The A-text has *owne*, i. e. own people, but some MSS. have *hynen*, i. e. hinds.

59. 'He forestalls (my sales) at fairs.' To *forestall* was to buy up goods before they had been exposed in the market. It was strictly discouraged ; see Liber Albus, ed. Riley, p. 172 ; and Memorials of London, ed. Riley, pp. 83, 387.

61. *And taketh me*, etc.; and gives me a tally (and nothing else) for ten or twelve quarters (of oats). The statements in the note to l. 46 were often true in *two* senses; the peasants were paid (1) by a wooden tally, and (2) by a beating, as William says in the following line, as it stands in [b] and [a]. An exchequer-tally was an account of a sum lent to the Government. The tally itself was a rod of hazel, one of a pair that *tallied*, with notches on it to indicate the sum lent. It was not easy to realize this sum afterwards. Cf. Chaucer, Prol. 570:—

'For whether that he payde, or *took by taille*.'

And Jack Cade says to Lord Say (2 Hen. VI. iv. 7. 38) that ' our forefathers had no other books but the score and the tally.' The tally is still used to some extent both in England and France.

68. It is clear that *handy-dandy* in this passage means a covert bribe or present, as, for instance, a bag conveyed to the judge's hand which he was to open at leisure, when he would find the contents satisfactory. The explanation in Halliwell's Dictionary is as follows :—'*Handydandy*. A game thus played by two children. One puts something secretly, as a small pebble, into one hand, and with clenched fists he whirls his hands round each other, crying, "Handy-spandy, Jack-a-dandy, which good hand will you have?" The other guesses or touches one ; if right, he wins its contents ; if wrong, he loses an equivalent.' For a somewhat fuller notice, see Halliwell's Popular Rhymes and Nursery Tales, 1849, p. 116. The explanation in Brand (Pop. Antiq. ed. Ellis, ii. 420) is rather confused. Douce, in his Illustrations of Shakespeare, ii. 167, quotes from a tract—'as men play with little children at *handye-dandye, which hand will you have*, when they are disposed to keep any thinge from them ;' but it should be added that the game is then almost sure to end in the child's receiving a present. Florio, in his Ital. Dictionary, 1598, has :—' Bazzicchiare, to shake betweene two hands ; to play *handy-dandy*.' In King Lear, iv. 6. 157, the word seems to mean simply—guess which you please. Shakespeare says—'See how yond justice rails upon yond simple thief! Hark in thine ear: change places, and, *handy-dandy*, which is the justice, which is the thief?'

—— (b. 4. 72.) *But if Mede*, etc.; 'unless Meed cause it to be otherwise, thy misfortune is aloft.' William often uses *make it* in the sense of to bring it about, to cause it to be so; cf. C. ix. 212. But when the words *it make* are preceded by *but*, they mean 'cause it to be otherwise ;' cf. viii. 28. *Myschief* commonly signifies mishap or ill-luck in Middle-English; cf. ix. 212, 233. *Vppe* is here an adverb, signifying on high, aloft, in the ascendant.

—— (b. 4. 73.) *Lyth in his grace*. Offenders convicted of great crimes were put *in the king's grace*, who could hang them and confiscate their property, unless he were pleased to shew mercy. Sometimes he was satisfied with exacting a heavy fine ; cf. ll. 88-90 (B-text).

82. (b. 4. 86.) *Seuen yere*, seven years ; put for a long, but indefinite period. So again in Pass. vii. 214, xi. 73.

C. PASS. V. 85. (NOT IN B.) (NOT IN A.)

85. 'And (let the meinpernour) be pledge for his misfortune, and buy a remedy for him.' See note to Pass. iii. 208, and cf. l. 173 below. This is one of the numerous passages in which *bale* and *boot* (woe and advantage) are opposed to each other.

104. Note the three different endings of the line. *For his luther werkes*, for his evil deeds [c]; *but lowenesse hym borwe*, unless Humility (or Submission) go bail for him [b]; *bote more loue hit make*, unless a greater degree of love cause it to be otherwise [a]; where *make* is used as in b. 4. 72, c. viii. 28.

107. *Menepernour*, i. e. *mainpreneur*, taker by the hand, a surety; see note to iii. 208.

110. *Harlotrie*, ribaldry, buffoonery, jesters' tales. Cf. Chaucer, Prol. l. 561. See note to l. 113 below, and to viii. 22, p. 95.

111. *Purnele* or *Peronelle* (from Petronilla) was a proverbial name for a gaily dressed bold-faced woman; it would be long before she put away her finery in a box. This line is almost repeated in Pass. vi. 129; see also Rich. Redeles, iii. 156. May 31 was dedicated to S. Petronilla the Virgin. She was supposed to be able to cure the quartan ague; Chambers' Book of Days, ii. 389. The name, once common, now scarcely survives except as a surname, in the form Parnell; see Bardsley's English Surnames, p. 56. A *hutch* was the usual name for a clothes-box, such as was often placed at the foot of a bed; see Our English Home, p. 101. Pictures of *hutches* are given in Wright's Homes of Other Days, at pp. 274, 275, 276, 279. It also signified boxes of another kind; thus Palsgrave has—'Byn, to kepe breed or corne, *huche*.' 'Hutche or whyche, *Cista, archa*;' Prompt. Parv.; see Way's note.

112. *And children*, etc.; and the cherishing of children be chastised with rods [c, a]; *or*, and the cherishing of children be, that they be chastised with rods [b]. *To cherish* is to cocker, spoil. *Children* is the genitive plural, like *klerken* in l. 114.

113. *Harlotes*, ribalds, jesters, buffoons; it is applied to both sexes, but much more commonly to *males* in Middle English. In a note to the Canterbury Tales, l. 649, Tyrwhitt remarks that, in l. 6068 of the Romaunt of the Rose, the expression 'king of harlotes' is a translation of the French *roy de ribaulx*. Mr Wright, in speaking of the same passage, viz. the description of the Sompnour in Chaucer's Prologue, says—'this passage gives us a remarkable trait of the character of the ribald, or harlot, who formed a peculiar class of Middle-age society. Among some old glosses in the Reliquiae Antiquae, vol. i. p. 7, we find " *scurra*, a harlotte." In the Coventry Mystery of the Woman taken in Adultery, it is the young man who is caught with the woman, and not the woman herself, who is stigmatised as a harlot.' In Riley's Memorials of London, p. 474, a man is said to have spoken against the lord mayor, and to have 'asserted the said mayor to be a false scoundrel or *harlot*.' See also Mr Wright's remarks on the word *ribald* in his Political Songs, p. 369. The sense is—'And till the holiness of harlots be (observed as) a high holiday.' *Ferye* is the Latin *feria*; and *an* is the indefinite article. All

doubt about the meaning is removed by the fortunate circumstance that the expression 'an heigh ferye' occurs again in B. xiii. 415, where the sense is obvious. The reading of [b] and [a] is to the same effect, but very differently expressed. There, the sense is—'And till the holiness of harlots be considered as of small value, i. e. as of common occurrence;' the *literal* sense being—'be considered as worth a hind.' The value of a hind or farm-labourer (*hyne*) was not considered as very great; indeed the Rawlinson MS. (R) writes *nauȝte* in place of the 'an hyne' of other B-text MSS.

116. 'And till religious men, fond of riding about, be shut up in their cloisters' [c]; *or*, 'And till religious men, fond of roaming, say *recordare* in their cloisters.' The word *religious* means one of a religious order, a monk or a friar. The words *outrider* [c] and *roamer* [b] refer to the use of horses by such men, and to their fondness for pilgrimages; see B. x. 306—313. *Recordare* is the first word of a mass for avoiding sudden death, appointed by Pope Clement at Avignon, the recital of which secured to the hearers 260 days' indulgence. This is best shewn by the following rubric from the Sarum Missal, 1532; fol. lij. 'Missa pro mortalitate evitanda, quam dominus papa clemens fecit et constituit in collegio, cum omnibus cardinalibus; et concessit omnibus penitentibus vere contritis et confessis sequentem missam audientibus. cclx. dies indulgentie . . . . . et eis mors subitanea nocere non poterit; et hoc est certum et approbatum in auinione et in partibus circumuicinis.' Then follows—'*Officium*. Recordare domine, testamenti tui, et dic angelo percutienti, cesset iam manus tua:' etc.

By Clement must be meant Clement V., who removed the papal see to Avignon in 1309, and died in 1314. It was he who first made public sale of indulgences in 1313, and whose decretals and constitutions were known as the *Clementines*.

117. Saint Benedict, founder of the Benedictine order of Monks, was born about A.D. 480, and died about A.D. 542. Saint Dominic (A.D. 1170 -1221) founded the order of Dominican or Black Friars. Saint Bernard, of Cistercium or Citeaux, near Chalons, better known as S. Bernard of Clairvaux, founded the order of Cistercians or Bernardines; he was born A.D. 1091, died 1153. S. Francis of Assisi, founder of the Franciscan order of friars or Friars Minorites, was born 1182, died 1226.

120. 'Till bishops be as bakers, brewers, and tailors,' i.e. till bishops provide bread, ale, and clothing for the needy' [c] *or*, as in [b], 'Till bishops' horses be turned into beggars' chambers;' i.e. till the money spent by bishops on horses go to furnish rooms for beggars. *Bayard* [b] was a common name for a horse; originally, for a horse of a bay colour. 'As bold as blind Bayard' was an old proverb, which occurs in Chaucer, near the end of the Chan. Yem. Tale; in Lydgate's Warres of Troy, Book V; and in Skelton, ed. Dyce, i. 123, l. 101.

122. The reading in [b] and [a] is—*There I shal assigne*, where I (Reason) shall ordain. There is no need to go to Gallicia.

In the C-text, Reason *does* assign places to find S. James in; viz. *prisons*,

C. PASS. V. 125. B. PASS. IV. 156. (NOT IN A.) 59

poor cottages, and *sick-rooms.* By '*for* pilgrymages' in l. 123 we must understand '*instead of* pilgrimages.'

125. *Rome-renners*, runners to Rome. 'And (until) all Rome-runners bear no silver over sea that bears the image of the king, for the sake of enriching robbers that dwell in France [c]; *or*, beyond sea' [b, a]. Part of the procurator's oath to the English king was—'that he would not send money out of the kingdom without the royal license.'—Lingard, iv. 205. In 1376, the commons presented a petition to the pope, stating that the taxes paid yearly by them to the pope amounted to five times the royal revenue. 'In the reign of Henry III., the Italians, who were beneficed here, drew from England more than thrice the amount of the king's revenues, fleecing by means of priests, who were aliens also, the flock which they never fed.'—Southey; Book of the Church. p. 187 (6th ed., 1848). Cf. Milman, Hist. Latin Christianity, vi. 111. Perhaps it is proper to add that by the words *in France* our poet refers to the papal residence at Avignon; cf. Pass. xxii. 424. Fabyan says that, in 1365, Peter's pence were commanded to be no more gathered, but he adds—' neuerthelesse at this present tyme [Henry VII.] they be gaderyd in sondry shyres of Englande;' p. 477.

128. 'On penalty of forfeiting that property, in case any one finds him ready to cross over' [c]; *or*, 'finds him (*or* it) at Dover' [b, a]. *Ho so* = whoso, whosoever; i. e. in case any one. *Ouerwarde* = in the direction of (crossing) over. *At Dover* refers to the then existing law—'that no pilgrim should pass out of the realm, to parts beyond the seas, but only *at Dover*, on pain of a year's imprisonment;' Ruding's Annals of the Coinage, 3rd ed. 1840, vol i. p. 211.

140. 'For the man named *nullum malum* met with one called *inpunitum*,' etc. This is merely a way of introducing the words in italics. The quotation is repeated in Pass. xxi., at l. 435. It is taken from the following:—' Ipse est iudex iustus . . . qui nullum malum praeterit impunitum, nullum bonum irremuneratum;' Pope Innocent; De Contemptu Mundi, lib. iii. cap. 15.

—— (b. 4. 156.) *I falle in*, I fall amongst, I meet with. Warin Wisdom used to meet with a florin (of course by mere accident), and suddenly find himself unable to plead.

169. See the passage from Wyclif's Works, iii. 307, quoted in the note to Pass. iv. 183, p. 46.

171. The remark 'yf iche regne eny whyle' seems merely expletive, signifying only 'if I continue in power;' cf. l. 104 above. In the B-text, it may have referred to the great age of Edward III.

176. *Withoute the comune help*, unless the commons help me [c] : *but the comune wil assent*, unless the commons will assent [b].

—— (b. 4. 189.) *Be my conseille comen*, when my council is come. The Trinity MS. (printed by Mr Wright) has *By my counseil commune*, by my common council; which is certainly a corrupt reading.

189. *Vnsittynge suffraunce*, unbecoming tolerance; i. e. fraudulent connivance. See the phrase again in Pass. iv. 208.

190. See note to Pass. iii. 187, p. 38.

194. *Lukes,* Lucca; see note to Pass. ix. 109. In 1392, the Londoners severely beat a Lombard who offered a loan to the king; Walsingham, ed. Riley, ii. 207.

NOTES TO PASSUS VI.

1. (*not in* b, a.) Lines 1-108 are peculiar to the C-text, and are of great interest, being to some extent autobiographical. Here William tells us of his life in Cornhill, where he lived, clothed like a loller, with his wife Kit and his daughter Calote (mentioned in Pass. xxi. 473), yet not much liked by the lollers and hermits around him. He then describes his own laziness in amusing terms.

Perhaps I ought to remark here that there is no particular difficulty about his statement that he was married. See Milman, Hist. of Lat. Christianity, ed. 1855, v. 72; vi. 101.

2. *Lollere.* Though much has been written on this important word, the history of it has not been very well made out; chiefly, I think, because the passages concerning it in Piers the Plowman have not been sufficiently observed. The standard passage upon it will be found in Pass. x. 98-254, every word of which requires careful reading. The word occurs there several times; see ll. 103, 107, 137, 140, 158, 192, 213; cf. also ll. 215, 218. See also l. 31 of the present Passus. It occurs also in Chaucer, at the eleventh line after the conclusion of the Man of Lawes Tale (Group B, l. 1173, in the Six-text Edition), and I quote here, for the reader's convenience, my note upon that line at p. 141 of the Prioresses and other Tales, Oxford, 1874.

' The reader will not clearly understand this word till he distinguishes between the Latin *lollardus* and the English *loller,* two words of different origin which were *purposely* confounded in the time of Wyclif. The Latin *Lollardus* had been in use before Wyclif. Ducange quotes from Johannes Hocsemius, who says, under the date 1309—" Eodem anno quidam hypocritae gyrovagi, qui *Lollardi,* sive Deum laudantes, vocabantur, per Hannoniam et Brabantiam quasdam mulieres nobiles deceperunt.' He adds that Trithemius says in his Chronicle, under the year 1315—" ita appellatos a Gualtero Lolhard, Germano quodam"; [but the reference may be wrong; see Maitland, Essay on Lollards.] Kilian, in his Dictionary of Old Dutch, says—" Lollaerd, mussitator, mussitabundus;" i. e. a mumbler of prayers. This gives two etymologies for *Lollardus.* Being thus already in use as a term of reproach, it was applied to the followers of Wyclif, as we learn from Thomas Walsingham, who says, under the year 1377—" Hi uocabantur a uulgo *Lollardi,* incedentes nudis pedibus;" and again, " Lollardi sequaces Joannis Wyclif." But the Old English *loller* (from the verb *to loll*) meant simply a lounger, an idle vagabond, as is abundantly clear from a notable passage in Piers the Plowman, C-text (ed. Skeat), x. 213-218; where William tells us plainly :—

"Now kyndeliche, by crist · beþ suche callyd *lolleres*,
As by englisch of oure eldres · of old menne techynge.
He that *lolleþ* is lame · oþer his leg out of ioynte," etc.
This will explain how it was that when the Wycliffites were called lollers, they sometimes turned round, and said their opponents were the *true* lollers, the *true* idle fellows. [Here was inserted a wrong reference; but I believe the foregoing statement to be correct.]

'Here were already two (if not three) words confused, but this was not all. By a bad pun, the Latin *lolium*, tares, was connected with *Lollard*, so that we find in Political Poems, l. 232, the following:—

"Lollardi sunt zizania,
Spinae, uepres, ac *lollia*,
Quae uastant hortum uineae."

This obviously led to allusions to the Parable of the Tares, and fully accounts for the punning allusion to cockle, i.e. tares, in [Chaucer, Group B.] l. 1183. Mr Jephson observes that *lolium* is used in the Vulgate Version, Matt. xiii. 25; but this is a mistake, as the word there used is *zizania*. Gower, Prol. to Conf. Amant., speaks of—

"This newe secte of *lollardie*,
And also many an heresie."

Also in book V.—

"Be war that thou be not oppressed
With anticristes *lollardie*," etc.

The reader should observe that William elsewhere uses the phrase *to be lolled up* (lit. to be made to dangle about) as a euphemism for *to be hung*; Pass. xv. 131. Also, in P. Pl. Crede, l. 532, to *loll* means to accuse of heresy; see my note to that line. See also Knyghton, ed. Twysden, col. 2706; Hardwick's Glos. to Elmham, Hist. Monast. Cant.; Pecock's Repressor, pp. 128, 654; Pict. Hist. of England, ii. 140; Prompt. Parv., p. 311, note 3; Mosheim, Eccl. Hist. iii. 355.

3. *Lytel y-lete by*, lightly esteemed. Cf. note to Rich. Redeles, iii. 284.

5. 'For I composed verses about those men, as Reason taught me.' To *make* is to write verses, to compose, and a poet was called a *maker*. See fuller remarks upon these words in the note to B. xii. 16.

6. 'For, as I passed by Conscience, I met with Reason.' The allusion is to his vision of Conscience in the last Passus; still, he is here in a waking dream only, and represents himself as again beholding this creature of his imagination; passing by him indeed, but only to meet another phantom, with whom he converses. The dialogue is really carried on between William's carnal and spiritual natures, between his flesh and his spirit.

10. 'Being in health (of body), and in soundness or unity (of mind), a certain being thus cross-examined me.'

13. *Coke* = (1) to cook; (2) to put hay into cocks. A *coker* sometimes means a reaper (Halliwell), but the explanation that it formerly meant a charcoal-burner is not satisfactory. Richardson quotes the following. 'Bee it also prouided, that this act, nor anything therein contained doe in

any wise extende to any *cockers* of haruest folkes that trauaile into anie countrie of this realme for haruest worke, either corne haruest, or hay haruest, if they doe worke and labour accordingly;' Rastall, Statutes; Vagabonds, etc., p. 474. The context shews that the sense is—'Or put hay into cocks for my harvestmen.'

14. The first *mowe* signifies to mow hay; the second (also spelt *mouwen, muwe, mywen*) means to put into a mow, to stack.

16. *Haywarde*. See Mr Way's note to this word in the Promptorium Parvulorum. 'The *heyward*,' he says, 'was the keeper of cattle in a common field, who prevented trespass on the cultivated ground.' In fact the word signifies a *hedge-warden*, one whose duty it was to see that the cattle were kept within their proper boundaries. In the Romance of Alexander, ed. Weber, l. 5754, we have—

'In tyme of heruest mery it is ynough,
Peres and apples hongeth on bough;
The hayward bloweth mery his horne,
In eueryche felde ripe is corne.'

See also Bardsley's English Surnames, p. 198; Wyclif's Works, i. 104; and see further remarks in the note to Pass. xiv. 45. Cf. Pass. xxii. 334.

20, 21. 'Or a craft of any other kind, such as is necessary for the community, in order to provide sustenance for them that are bed-ridden.' This recognises the duty of the young to provide for the aged and infirm.

24. *To long*, i.e. too long in the back or legs, too tall. Occleve says the very same of himself; De Regim. Principum, ed. Wright, p. 36:—

'With ploughe kan I not medle, ne with harwe,
Ne wote nat what lond goode is for what corne;
And for to lade a carte or fille a barwe,
To whiche I never used was a-forne.
My bak unbuxom hathe suche thynge forsworne,' etc.

By *unbuxom* is meant here unbending, stiff, not lissome. Our author alludes, doubtless, to his own nickname of 'Long Will'; see B. xv. 148. For *long* in the sense of *tall*, see Pass. i. 53.

32. See Ps. lxi. 13 (Vulgate).

33. *Broke* means having broken bones, or some permanent injury; cf. ix. 143; x. 99, 169–172.

36. 'My father and my friends found means to send me to school.' To *find* is to *provide for*. Cf. Chaucer's Prol. 301, 302.

39. *By so*, provided that I will continue in well-doing.

41. *Longe clothes*. This refers to the dress which he wore as being one of the secular clergy. On this subject, see Cutts's Scenes and Characters of the Middle Ages, pp. 241–244. For the quotation, see 1 Cor. vii. 20.

44. 'I live *in* London, and *upon* London,' i.e. upon the work which London affords. He was one of the 'great crowd of priests who gained a livelihood by taking temporary engagements to say masses for the souls of the departed.' See Cutts's Scenes and Characters of the Middle Ages, p. 207; also pp. 201, 202.

46. *Primer;* a book of elementary religious instruction. The word

occurs in the fifth stanza of Chaucer's Prioresses Tale, and in the Promptorium Parvulorum, A.D. 1440. 'My *primer* clothed with purpill damaske' occurs in a will dated 1493; Cullum's Hist. of Hawsted, 2nd ed. p. 137. Sir John Cullum's note says—'The primer contained a collection of prayers, psalms, hymns, etc., in Latin and English; retained with alteration, after the Reformation. Brit. Top. vol. ii. p. 323.'

We are told that souls may be helped out of purgatory 'as to lernyd men, as bi masses singyng, saing of sawters, *placebo*, and *dirige*, commendacions, .vij. psalmes, and the .xv. psalmes, with the letenye, bi almesdede and bi pilgrimage: and also bi lewid men with the paternoster, the ave Maria, and the crede, almesdede, fastyng, and pilgrimage, and bi many other good dedis;' Vision of William Staunton, 1409; MS. Reg. 17 B 43; quoted in St Patrick's Purgatory, by T. Wright, p. 149. For *placebo* and *dirige*, see note to Pass. iv. 467, p. 52.

47. *Sauter*, psalter. *Seven psalmes;* see note to Pass. iv. 468, p. 52.

52. 'I have no bag (for victuals), nor bottle (for drink), but only my belly (wherein to bestow food).' This accurate description of his mode of obtaining a livelihood is very interesting.

56. *Crouned*, crowned (with the tonsure). See note to Pass. i. 86, p. 11. The opposite expression, 'uncrowned,' occurs in l. 62 below.

58. See 1 Thess. v. 15; Levit. xix. 18. Also (l. 60) Ps. xv. 5 (Vulgate).

59. *It ben aires*, they are heirs. This is the usual idiom of the period. Cf. 'hit are bote fewe folke;' Pass. xvi. 288; 'than aren hit pure poure thynges;' Pass. xvi. 309; also 'hit am I;' Chaucer, C. T. 3764.

79. 'And choose Simon's son to keep the sanctuary.' The phrase 'Simon's son' means the son of Simon Magus, i.e. one who has been guilty of Simony, or one whose wealth was his only recommendation. See Pass. x. 257; and note to Rich. Redeles, iv. 55. It is an expression resembling that of 'Judas' children'; B. prol. 35.

88. *Fynt ous alle þynges*, provides us with all things; cf. B. vii. 121–129; and B. xiv. 48. See Matt. iv. 4; vi. 10.

89. 'I can not see that this applies.' The word *lyeth* here means *applies, is to the point*. Conscience tells him that his remarks are not quite to the point; and, in the next line, uses the word 'parfytnesse' with reference to the word 'parfyt' in l. 84.

101, 102. 'And to enter upon a period that will turn all the periods of my life to profit.' See Matt. xiii. 44; Luke xv. 9.

109. Here begins the Second Vision, which may be called the Vision of the Seven Deadly Sins and of Piers the Plowman; the subject of the First Vision having been the Field Full of Folk, Holy Church, and the Lady Meed. This second Vision begins with the same scene as the First, viz. the scene of the Field Full of Folk (l. 111), only that now Reason and Conscience appear in the King's presence, and Reason preaches a sermon before the assembled multitude. (N.B. In [a], it is *Conscience* who is the preacher.)

115. *These Pestilences.* There were three (some reckon four) terrible pestilences at this period, which were long remembered, and proved such

scourges that the land was left partly untilled, causing severe famines to
ensue. They took place in 1348 and 1349, 1361 and 1362, and 1369; a
fourth was in 1375 and 1376. The *two first* are really the ones alluded
to, the A-text having been written before the third took place. The first
of them is computed to have begun at varying dates. Mr Wright gives
an extract from a register of the Abbey of Gloucester (MS. Cotton, Domit.
A. viii., fol. 124) to this effect—' Anno Domini m^o. ccc^o. xlviij^o., anno vero
regni regis Edwardi III post conquestum xxxij^o., incepit magna pestilentia
in Anglia, ita quod *vix tertia pars* hominum remansit;' and he adds—
' This pestilence, known as the *black plague*, [or *black death*] ravaged most
parts of Europe, and is said to have carried off in general about two-
thirds of the people. It was the pestilence which gave rise to the
Decamerone of Boccaccio. For an interesting account of it, see Michelet's
Hist. de France, iii. 342-349.' See also the marvellous description of it
by Boccaccio himself. Lingard says that it reached Dorchester in August,
and London in September, 1348. Fabyan says it began in August,
1348. Sir H. Nicolas, in The Chronology of History, p. 345, says it
began May 31, 1349, which is surely the wrong year. A fuller account is
given in Prof. Thorold Rogers' Hist. of Agricult. and Prices in England,
i. 294, who says—' The Black Death appeared at Avignon in Jan. 1348,
visited Florence by the middle of April, and had thoroughly penetrated
France and Germany by August. It entered Poland in 1349, reached
Sweden in the winter of that year, and Norway, by infection from England,
at about the same time.'. . . ' On the 1st Aug. 1348, the disease appeared
in the seaport towns of Dorsetshire, and travelled slowly westwards and
northwards . . to Bristol. . . . The plague continued to Oxford, and . .
reached London by the 1st of November. It appeared in Norwich on the
1st of January [1349], and then spread northwards.' It terminated on the
29th September, 1349. The *second* pestilence is the one to which William
more immediately alludes. It lasted from August 15, 1361, to May 3,
1362 ; See Sir H. Nicolas, as above. Some records are dated from the
times of these plagues. Allusions to them as God's punishments for sin
are common in the writers of the period. See the next note.

117. *Southwest wynd.* Tyrwhitt first pointed out that this is an allusion
to the violent tempest of wind on Jan. 15, 1362, which was a *Saturday*.
He refers to the mention of it by Thorn, Decem Script. col. 2122 ; by
Walsingham (see Riley's edition, vol. i. p. 296) ; and by the Continuator
of Adam Murimuth, p. 115. The last notice is the most exact. 'A.D.
m.ccc.lxii, xv die Januarii, *circa horam uesperarum*, uentus uehemens *notus
Australis Africus* tantâ rabie erupit,' etc. Walsingham calls it *nothus
Auster Africus.* It is alluded to by many other chroniclers also. Fabyan
says, p. 475—' In this xxxvii yere, vpon the daye of seynt Mauryce, or the
xv daye of Januarii, blewe so excedynge a wynde that the lyke therof was nat
seen many years passed. This began *about euynsong tyme* in the *South*,'
etc. He says it lasted for five days. We find the same notice again in A
Chronicle of London, p. 65, where it is said to have taken place, in the year
1361 on ' seynt Maurys day.' This means the same year (viz. 1361-2), which

was called 1361 during the months of January and February, and 1362 afterwards; according to the old reckoning. Fabyan wrongly calls it the day of St. Maurice; the 15th of Jan. is the day of St. *Maur*, a disciple of St. Bennet. It is noticed again in Hardyng's Chronicles, ed. Ellis, 1812, p. 330; in Riley's Memorials of London, p. 308; and in the Eulogium Historiarum, ed. Haydon, iii. 229. Blomefield tells us that it blew down the spire of Norwich Cathedral. It will be observed that the second great pestilence was prevailing at the time. Compare the prophecies of John of Bridlington, printed in Wright's Political Poems, lib. iii. capp. 10, 11.

118. These judgments (as they seemed to be) were looked upon as due to *Pride*, because it was the chief and most pernicious of the seven deadly sins; see Pass. vii. 3. Cf. Political Songs, ed. Wright, p. 344.

127. Compare Pass. i. 24; ix. 139-176.

129. Compare note to Pass. v. 111, p. 57; and see vii. 3.

131. *Thomme Stowe*, &c. A difficult passage. Whitaker has *Stone* and *wynen*, and explains it—'He taught Thom. Stone to take two sticks, and fetch home Felice, his spouse, from drinking wine.' This does not explain *pyne*. The MSS. have *Stowue, stouue, Stowe, of stowe;* in the Trinity MS. (R. 3. 14) the other word is clearly *wyuene;* whilst MS. Laud 656 has the unmistakable form *wyfen;* and Whitaker himself notes that MS. Phillipps 8252 has the form *wyvyn*. Like *kyngene, clerken,* it is a genitive plural, and as *pyne* invariably means punishment, *wyuen pyne* is only one more allusion to the *women's punishment*, the *cucking-stool*. I suppose the sentence to mean that *Tom Stowe*, who had neglected his wife and let her get into bad ways, or who had allowed her to be punished as a scold, had much better fetch her home than leave her exposed to public derision. Such an errand would require a strong arm, and two staves would be very useful in dispersing the crowd. I do not think it is meant that he is to beat *her*, for then *one* would have sufficed; nor would Reason give such bad advice.

133. *Watte*, the contraction of *Water*, which was another form of *Walter*, and by no means uncommon. Cf. 'nout Willam (*sic*) ne *Water;*' Ancren Riwle, p. 340; cf. Shak., 2 Hen. VI. iv. 1. 35.

134. Nothing so invited satire as the head-dresses of the females. Chaucer makes the wife of Bath's to have weighed *ten pounds!* The hair was generally enveloped in a caul of net-work of gold, which fitted close to both sides of the face. Thus, in the *Crede*, we read of 'great-headed queans, *with gold by the eyes,*' l. 84.

Even as early as in the reign of Edw. I., we find that only ladies of the upper class were permitted to wear furred hoods; Liber Albus, p. 584.

135. *Bette* was a male name, and has already been applied to a beadle; Pass. iii. 111. It was a mere variation of *Bat*, a shortened form of Bartholomew; see Bardsley's English Surnames, p. 72. Of course *bad* means 'commanded'; Mr. Bardsley seems to have taken it to be an adjective!

136. *Beton* was a female name, as shewn by the context, and by Paŝs. vii. 353. It was a pet name for Beatrice; see Bardsley's English Surnames, p. 58 and Index. Beton was probably Bette's daughter.

138. *Wynnynge* means success in business, gain by trading. *Forwene* means to spoil by over-indulgence (lit. to *for-wean*, i. e. to wean amiss), and is well illustrated by the following quotation. 'De unwise man & *forwened* child habbeð boðe on lage; for þat hie habben willeð boðe here wil;' i.e. the unwise man and the spoilt child have both one law (custom); for they both desire to have their will; Old Eng. Homilies (2nd Series), ed. Morris, p. 41. Cf. A. S. *forwened*, proud, i. e. spoilt, over-indulged; and see Rich. Redeles, i. 27, where William says of King Richard's courtiers that they 'walwed in her willis *forweyned* in here youthe.' The advice is addressed to the chapmen or traders, and means—'let no success in your business induce you to spoil your children in their infancy.' In the A-text, the line means—'let them lack no awe, whilst they are young.' In the next line (of the B-text only) the advice is continued thus :— 'nor (allow yourselves) to please them unreasonably, on account of any virulence (lit. power) of a pestilence.' It is worth observing that ll. 36-41 of the B-text do not appear in [a]; and consequently, by the time they were added, both the third and fourth pestilences, viz. of 1369 and 1375, had taken place. Hence there was additional reason to fear that the anxiety to rear children would lead to excessive indulgence to them.

——— (b. 5. 38.) *The leuere childe*, etc.; 'to the dearer child, the more teaching is necessary.' This was a common proverb, as pointed out by Mr. Wright, and is found in the proverbs of Hendyng, written about 1300 —'*Luef child lore byhoueth*, Quoth Hendyng.' See Specimens of Early English, ed. Morris and Skeat, p. 36; or Reliq. Antiq. i. p. 110; and cf. Hazlitt's Early Pop. Poetry, vol. i. p. 191. The original source is Prov. xiii. 24—'Qui parcit uirgæ, odit filium suum; qui autem diligit illum, instanter erudit.'

142. *That hij preche*, that which they preach. Cf. B. iv. 122.

144. *Religion*, religious orders, as in Pass. x. 36. *Religious* is used in the same sense four lines below. *Religiuns* is used in the sense of 'religious communities;' Ancren Riwle, p. 24.

146. This idea is enlarged upon in ll. 147-178 below; and this is doubtless the reason why the latter passage, which in the B-text was in a different place (viz. in the tenth Passus) was shifted so as to occupy its present position.

☞ Note the sudden leap here, from B. 5. 48 (A. 5. 39) to B. 10. 292 (A. 11. 201). The passages in small type appear again in their proper places; see p. 308 of the text.

147. The passage contained in ll. 147-180 answers to B. x. 292-329, and a part of it answers also to A. xi. 201-210. It is, in fact, the first of the passages *inserted* in the C-text from a later portion of the A- and B-texts. It is now made to form a part of Reason's sermon, instead of part of Scripture's discourse. It shortens the latter, and comes in much more

C. PASS. VI. 151. (B. PASS. X. 297. A. PASS. XI. 206.) 67

naturally as a part of the former. The change is a considerable improvement, and skilfully managed.

Lines 291–303 of the B-text are found in one MS. only (MS. R.).

By 'Gregory the great clerk' is meant pope Gregory I., surnamed the Great, born about A.D. 544, died A.D. 604. But it would be no easy task to find the passage referred to. Tyrwhitt, in a note to l. 179 of the Prologue to the Canterbury Tales, says, 'the text alluded to is attributed by Gratian, *Decret.* P. ii. Cau. xvi. Q. 1. c. viii. to a Pope Eugenius—" Sicut piscis sine aqua caret uita, ita sine monasterio monachus."' William quotes it from his 'morales' [b], i. e. from the 'Moralium Libri xxxiv,' one of the most important of Gregory's works. The phrase 'Gregori the grete clerk' occurs again in Pass. xxii. 270; q. v. In Kingsley's The Hermits, p. 74, a quotation is given from the life of St. Antony by Athanasius, published by Heschelius in 1611, in which monks who stay away from their retreats are likened to fishes upon dry land.

151. *Roteþ and sterueth*, becomes rotten and dies. In [a] and [b] we find *roileth*, the meaning of which, in this passage, is (probably)—wanders about, ranges about restlessly. It is clear that there are at least two distinct words which assume the form *roil*. Mr. Wedgwood rightly points out the distinction between the verb to *roil* or *rile* in the sense of to disturb, trouble, vex, and the same verb in the sense of to range about restlessly. Mr. Atkinson, in his Cleveland Glossary, gives '*Roil*, v. n. to romp or play boisterously, to make a petty disturbance by riotous play,' and connects this with Icel. *rugl* or *ruglan*, disturbance, and *rugla*, to disturb; after which he cites the present passage of Piers the Plowman. This is, I suspect, a mistake; since the Cleveland verb is evidently *roil*, to disturb, and is connected with *rollick*. We should rather take notice of the following passages, as being more to the point.

In Chaucer's Wife of Bath's Prologue, Six-text, D. l. 653, we have—

'Man shal not suffre his wyf go roule aboute—'

where, for *roule*, the Lansdowne MS. has *roile*.

Roile is used in the sense of to wander about in Holinshed's Chronicles, vol. ii. p. 21, col. 2. We find in the Prompt. Parv. p. 436—'Roytyn, or gon ydel a-bowte, roytyn or *roylyn*, or gone ydyl abowte, *vagor, discurro.*' In Levins' Manipulus Vocabulorum, we have 'to *Royle* abroad, *diuagari;*' ed. Wheatley, p. 214, l. 43. In Harman's Caveat (ed. Furnivall, p. 31) we read of rascals that 'wyll wander,' of whom he says again—' These vnrewly rascales, in their *roylynge*, disperse themselues into seuerall companyes,' etc. Compare also—'he will not wander nor *royle* so farre aboute;' Turberville, Book of Venerie, ed. 1575, p. 141. And again— '*royling* aboute in ydlenes;' Sir T. More, Dialogue concerning Heresies, ed. 1557, p. 194, col. 2.

It is remarkable that there is also a pair of substantives which take the same form, and are respectively connected with the pair of verbs already mentioned. Thus *roil*, in the sense of a romp, a hoyden, a big ungainly woman, may be referred to the verb *roil*, to disturb, to romp; whilst, in connection with the verb *roil*, to wander loosely about, we find the sub-

68 C. PASS. VI. 157. (B. PASS. X. 306. A. PASS. XI. 208.)

stantive *roil* applied to a staggering, stumbling, and tired horse. I give two examples of the latter.
    'But sure that horse which tyreth like a *roile*,' etc.
    Gascoigne's Complaint of Phylomene (qu. by Richardson).
'For it hath ben often tymes sene that by the good swimming of horse many men haue ben saued; and, contrary wise, by a timorouse *royle*, where the water hath vneth come to his bely, his legges hath foltred [*faltered, given way*]: wherby many a good and propre man hath perisshed;' Sir T. Elyot: The Governour, Book I. ch. 17; ed. 1531. See also a passage from Heywood quoted in Dyce's Skelton, ii. 379.
    I conclude, then, that the sense of *roileth* in this passage is 'plays the vagabond;' in allusion to the habits of the mendicant friars.
    157-161. 'The bishops and abbots of the middle ages hunted with great state, having a large train of retainers and servants; and some of them are recorded for their skill in this fashionable pursuit. Walter, bp. of Rochester, who lived in the 13th century, was an excellent hunter, and so fond of the sport, that at the age of fourscore he made hunting his sole employment, to the total neglect of the duties of his office. (P. Blensensis, Epist. lvi. p. 81.) In the succeeding century an abbot of Leicester surpassed all the sportsmen of the time in the art of hare-hunting (Knyghton, apud Decem Scriptores, p. 263); and, even when these dignitaries were travelling from place to place, upon affairs of business, they usually had both hounds and hawks in their train. Fitzstephen assures us, that Th. à Becket, being sent as ambassador from Henry the Second to the court of France, assumed a state of a secular potentate; and took with him dogs and hawks of various sorts, such as were used by kings and princes (Stephanid. vit. S. Thom.);' Strutt's Sports and Pastimes, ed. Hone, p. 11. See also Warton, Hist. Eng. Poet. ed. 1840, ii. 57; Polit. Songs, ed. Wright, p. 327; Rob. of Brunne, Hand. Synne, 3086-9; Wyclif's Works, ed. Arnold, iii. 520.
    See also The Ploughman's Tale, in Wright's Political Poems, i. 307, 334, especially noting the lines where the author says it is not right

       'That a man should a monke "lord" call
        Ne serve on knees, as a king'—

which hints at the same practice as is mentioned in our text, l. 162.
    159. For *lovedays*, see note to Pass. iv. 196, p. 47.
    160. The verb to *prike*, meaning to ride about, is the verb usually employed by the poets and ballad-writers.

    'The tanner seyde—"what manner man are ye?"
    'A *preker abowt*,' seyd the kyng, "in manye a contre."'
        The King and the Barker; in Hazlitt's Early Pop. Poetry, i. 5.
The word *poperith* [a] is of extremely rare occurrence; I know of no other instance of its use.
    164. 'Little had lords to do;' i. e. lords might have found something better to do. The form *a-do* is doubtless short for *at do*, as proved by the instances in Mätzner's Engl. Gramm. vol. iii. p. 58; the word *at* being (as

C. PASS. VI. 165. (B. PASS. X. 313. NOT IN A.) 69

in Icelandic) the usual sign of an infinitive of purpose. Hence, for *a-do* [c], we find *to done* in [b].

165. The sense is—'to men belonging to religious orders, who do not care though the rain falls on their altars;' i.e. who do not even attempt to repair the roofs of their churches, though the rain falls on the altar itself. This passage is cleared up by the following words of Wyclif. 'Also freris bylden mony grete chirchis and costily waste housis, and cloystris as hit were castels . . . where-thorw parische chirchis . . . ben payred [*impaired*], and in mony placis undone . . . For, by þis new housinge of freris, þof hit rayne on þo auter of þo parische churche, þo blynde puple is so disseyved þat þei wil raþer gif to waste housis of freris þen to parische chirchis,' etc.; Works, ed. Arnold, iii. 380. Cf. l. 176 below.

166. 'That is, where they have vicars of their own body, residing on their appropriated benefices;' Whitaker.

169. This famous prediction, so curiously fulfilled in the time of Henry the Eighth, was certainly written before the event, as Warton remarks, being found in MSS. written before A. D. 1400. It was merely due to the prevalent views as to the supreme power of the king; see Gower's Confessio Amantis, ed. Pauli, iii. 381; and cf. Pass. i. 148-157; iii. 245-248; iv. 381-385; v. 166-175; etc. Wyclif was of the like opinion. 'For siþ clerkis ben lege men to kingis in whos landis þei ben inne, kyngis han power of God to punische hem in Goddis cause, boþe in bodi and in catel;' Works, ed. Arnold, ii. 88.

171. Ducange gives *monialis* with sense of 'a nun;' and *moniale*, 'a nunnery.' For an explanation of *canon*, see the word in Hook's Church Dictionary. 'Regular canons were such as lived under a rule, that is, a code of laws published by the founder of that order. They were a less strict sort of religious than the monks, but lived together under one roof, had a common dormitory and refectory, and were obliged to observe the statutes of their order;' etc., etc. See Wyclif's Works, i. 216; iii. 345; Wright's Political Songs, notes on p. 372.

172. I do not know whence the Latin phrase is taken. The nearest Biblical passage is in Levit. xxv. 10:—'Reuertetur homo ad possessionem suam, et unusquisque rediet ad familiam pristinam;' which has reference to the year of jubilee. This may be the passage intended; cf. Pass. iv. 455-480, and the note to iv. 456, p. 51. Cf. Jerem. vi. 16.

—— (b. 10. 321.) *Beatus vir* means the first Psalm, so called from the first two words. The 'teaching' is that of the 6th verse—'the way of the ungodly shall perish.'

173. The Latin version has—'Hi in curribus, et hi in equis: nos autem in nomine Domini Dei nostri inuocabimus. Ipsi obligati sunt, et ceciderunt: nos autem surreximus et erecti sumus;' Ps. xix. 8, 9 (Vulgate). Cf. Psalm xx. 7, 8, in the A. V. The allusion is to the use of *horses* by the monks; see note to l. 157, p. 68.

174-176. The two texts vary very much here. The sense is—'Friars shall, in that day, find bread in their refectory without having to beg for it, sufficient for them to live upon for ever after ; and Constantine shall be their cook, and the coverer (*or* recoverer) of their church' [c] ; *or*—'And then shall friars find in their refectory a key of Constantine's coffers, wherein is the property that Gregory's spiritual children have spent so ill' [b]. The word *freitour*, corrupted to *fratery* or *fratry*, is used by Tyndal to signify a refectory (Tyndal's works, Parker Society, ii. 98) ; and described in a note to Grindal (Works, Park. Soc. 272, *note*). Mr. Cutts says—'it would answer to the great chamber of mediæval houses, and in some respects to the Combination-room of modern colleges ;' Scenes and Characters of the Middle Ages, p. 80. It was not necessarily the common hall, but might be a separate room ; and it would appear probable, from some quotations given in Fosbroke's Antiquities, that the monks dined in the *freitour* on *feast-days*, which is probably the reason for the use of the word in this place. Cf. Pierce the Ploughman's Crede, ll. 203, 212, 220, 284, 701 ; Bale's Kynge Johan, p. 27 ; Wright's Polit. Songs, p. 331 ; St. Brandan, p. 13 ; Wyclif's Works, i. 292. Halliwell refers also to Davies' Ancient Rites, 1672, pp. 7, 124, 126. '*Freytowre*, refectorium ;' Prompt. Parv. 'A *frayter* or place to eate meate in, refectorium ;' Withal's Dict., ed. 1608, p. 250. The original form was the O. Fr. *refretoir*, from Lat. *refectorium*.

The allusion to Constantine is explained in the note to xviii. 220, q. v.

The word *couerer* may either mean 'one who covers ;' i. e. one who provides or mends a roof, in allusion to l. 165 ; or it may mean 'one who recovers or restores,' since *keuere* or *couere* is sometimes thus used ; Will. of Palerne, 1521. By 'Gregory's god-children' is meant the monks of England, because the monastic state was introduced into England by St. Augustine, who was sent hither by Pope Gregory the Great, A.D. 596.

Our author seems to be looking forward to a time when the friars should be supported by some kind of regular endowment, under state control. This was a strange remedy to suggest, but he seems to have thought any plan better than their subsistence upon alms.

177. The 'abbot of England' [c] is a less happy phrase than the 'abbot of Abingdon' [b]. Mr. Wright says—'There was a very ancient and famous abbey at Abingdon in Berkshire. Geoffrey of Monmouth was abbot there. It was the house into which the monks, strictly so called, were first introduced in England, and is, therefore, very properly introduced as the representative of English monachism.' An excellent account of the Abbey of Abingdon will be found in Timbs's Abbeys and Castles of England, ii. 197–199.

178. *On here crounes*, on their shaven crowns ; alluding to the tonsure, as usual. This is a poor and unlucky alteration, since the B-text has *of a kynge*. However, the C-text has the word *kyng* in the line following. For the Latin, see Isaiah xiv. 4, 5, 6.

181–197. Much altered from B. v. 49–56, and not found in [a]. The advice to the king and nobles to cherish the commons is lengthened, and made more emphatic, ll. 183–191 being new. Four lines are added

C. PASS. VI. 185. B. PASS. V. 57. A. PASS. V. 40.

in the advice to the pope; ll. 194-197. But the advice to the lawyers is omitted.

185, 186. 'Let not counsel of any kind, nor any avarice part you; so that one understanding and one will may keep all that you have the charge of.'

198. Here all three texts once more come together. The poet advises those who had been wont to go on pilgrimage to Compostella or to Rome to try and find out the way to *Saint Truth*. This subject, of performing a pilgrimage to the shrine of Truth, is taken up again at Pass. viii. 155-181; see especially viii. 157, 177. By *Saint Truth* is here meant the Truth of the Divine Nature.

200. A usual ending of a homily was—'Qui cum patre et spiritu sancto uiuit et regnat per omnia secula seculorum. Amen;' Old Eng. Homilies, ed. Morris, ii. 115. In the present case, we have to substitute *filio* for *spiritu sancto*. Cf. Chaucer, Somp. Tale, l. 26.

NOTES TO PASSUS VII.

1. 'Then ran Repentance, and repeated his (i. e. Reason's) theme, and made Will weep water with his eyes.' *Will* means the author himself, who elsewhere calls himself Will in the same off-hand manner. Cf. Pass. ii. 5; xi. 71; also B. 8. 124; 15. 148; and A. 12. 51, 84, 94. Cf. also—'wepte water with his eyghen;' B. 14. 324.

3. Here begins the Confession of the Seven Deadly Sins. Few subjects are more common in our old authors than this one, of the Seven Deadly Sins. See, for instance, Chaucer's Persones Tale, *passim*; Ælfric's Homilies, ed. Thorpe, ii. 219; Wyclif's Works, iii. 225; the Ancren Riwle, ed. Morton, pp. 198-204; Religious Pieces (ed. Perry, E. E. T. S.), pp. 11, 22; Dan Michel's Ayenbite of Inwyt, ed. Morris, p. 16; the Calendar of Shepherds, chapter viii., as described in Warton's Hist. Eng. Poetry, ed. 1840, ii. 387; Political, Religious, and Love Poems, ed. Furnivall, p. 215; Hymns to the Virgin and Christ, ed. Furnivall, p. 62; Spenser's Faerie Queene, bk. i. c. 4; etc., etc. In the Ancren Riwle each of these sins is represented by some animal; so that we have (1) the Lion of Pride; (2) the Nedder (or Adder) of Envy; (3) the Unicorn of Wrath; (4) the Scorpion of Lechery; (5) the Fox of Avarice; (6) the Sow of Gluttony; and (7) the Bear of Sloth. Our author was probably aware of these symbols, for he says of a *proud* man that he was 'as a *lyon* on to loke,' B. 13. 302; of *Envy*, that he had an *adder's* tongue, B. 5. 87; and, in describing *Gluttony*, he speaks of 'two greedy *sows*,' vii. 398.

The following is a list of the sins, with their Latin and Middle-English names, in the order in which they occur in the C-text of Piers the Plowman. (N.B. By 'A. R.' is meant the Ancren Riwle, p. 276; and by 'A. I.' the Ayenbite of Inwyt, p. 159.)

1. *Superbia* (Pride); prude, A. R.; prede, A. I.
2. *Inuidia* (Envy); onde, A. R.; enuie, A. I.
3. *Ira* (Anger); wreȝȝe, A. R.; felhede, *or* hate, A. I.
4. *Luxuria* (Lechery); lecherie, A. R. and A. I.
5. *Auaritia* (Covetousness); coueitise, P. Pl.; giscunge, A. R.; auarice, *or* couaytyse, *or* scarsnesse, A. I.
6. *Gula* (Gluttony); giuernesse, A. R.; glotounye, A. I.
7. *Accidia* (Sloth); slouhȝe, A. R.; onlosthede, *or* slacnesse, A. I.

The following is a list of their opposites or remedies:
1. *Humilitas* (Humility); edmodnesse, A. R.; boȝsamnesse, A. I.
2. *Caritas* (Charity, Love); luue, A. R.; loue, A. I.
3. *Patientia* (Patience); þolemodnesse, A. R.; mildnesse, A. I.
4. *Castitas* (Chastity); chastete, A. I.
5. *Eleemosyna* (Bounty); largesse, A. I.
6. *Abstinentia* (Abstinence); sobrete, A. I.
7. *Uigilantia* (Business); gostlich gledscipe, A. R.; prouesse, A. I.

All of these remedies are mentioned in Pass. viii. 272-275, with the exception that 'pees' is put in the place of Business or Watchfulness.

Of all the seven sins, Pride is considered as the chief, and the root and spring of all the rest. It is expressed in Shakespeare by *ambition;*—

'Cromwell, I charge thee, fling away *ambition;*
By that sin fell the angels.'—Henry VIII. iii. 2. 441.

Cf. note to Pass. ii. 105. It is singular that it is the only vice which William personifies by a female. He doubtless does so with particular reference to extravagance in dress, to repress which a special Statute was passed in 1363; see Lingard, iv. 91 (*note*). In the C-text, however, is a long additional passage (ll. 14-60), in which the confession of Pernel Proud-heart is supplemented by that of a male example of Pride. Cf. Pass. xxii. 337.

6. *An heire*, i.e. a hair-shirt. It is said of a good widow, that 'she made greate abstynence, and wered the *hayre* vpon the wednesday and vpon the fryday;' Knight de la Tour, ed. Wright, p. 193. The same is said of Saint Cecilia in Chaucer, Cant. Ta. 15601; and of the Lady Margaret; Memoir of Margaret, Countess of Richmond and Derby, by C. H. Cooper, p. 76.

14. In revising his work for the last time, William made one considerable alteration in the plan of his work. The fact is that, in his B-text, the poet did, to some extent, enlarge upon the favourite and common subject of the Seven Deadly Sins *twice over;* once in the proper place (B. Pass. V.), and a second time, in describing the character of Haukyn, the active man (B. Pass. XIII). But, on revising his work, he saw how much could be gained by combining the two sets of descriptions in one, and at the same time making a few alterations and additions. Accordingly, the description of Haukyn's *pride* (B. 13. 278-313) was so placed as to form a part of the allegorical character of Pride (C. vii. 30-60). The result is that the poet now gives us *two* examples of Pride;

one, Pernel Proud-heart, a *female* character, ll. 3-13; and a second, named simply Pride, a *male* character, ll. 14-60.

16. *Vnboxome*, disobedient. The right word, because *buxomnesse*, i. e. obedience or humility, was considered as the opposite virtue to pride; see note to l. 3. Cf. l. 19.

20. *Demed*, i. e. I judged others; the nominative *I* must be supplied. So also before *scorned* in l. 22.

27. 'Seeming to be a sovereign (*or* principal) one, wheresoever it befell me (*or* fell to my lot) to tell any tale, I believed myself wiser in speaking or in counselling than any one else, whether clerk or layman.'

30. Here begins the supplementary passage, introduced into this place from what was the description of Haukyn in [b].

31. (b. 13. 279.) *Ich haue*, I possess. His apparel was more costly than his property warranted.

32. (b. 13. 280.) *Me wilnynge*, myself desiring; *hym willynge* [b], himself desiring. This is a remnant of the A. S. idiom, according to which two ablatives or datives could be used together like the Latin ablative absolute; see Vernon's A. S. Grammar, p. 75. *Aueyr* = Fr. *avoir*, i. e. property. See *Avere*, *Avoir* in Halliwell. This line is partly repeated at l. 41.

35. (cf. b. 13. 282.) *For eny vndernymynge*, in spite of any reproof. This use of *for* is not uncommon; cf. Mätzner, Engl. Gramm. vol. ii. pt. i. p. 444.

37. (b. 13. 284.) *Pope-holy*, lit. holy as the pope; but used to mean hypocritical. This odd word is fully illustrated in Dyce's Skelton, ii. 230. The word occurs four times in Skelton, i. 209, l. 24; 216, l. 247; 240, l. 472; 386, l. 612; in Barclay, Ship of Fooles, fol. 57, ed. 1570 (*or* ed. Jamieson, i. 154); Polit. Poems, ed. Wright, ii. 251.

—— (b. 13. 291.) 'And especially to intermeddle, where he has nothing to do with the matter.'

46. (cf. b. 13. 298.) *And for ich songe shulle*, and because I sang shrilly. *Shill* or *shull* for *shrill* is not uncommon.

—— (b. 13. 299.) That is, he was in the habit of boasting ' at he was liberal in lending money, though he knew he should lose it.

58. (b. 13. 311.) 'And what I knew and was capable of, and of what kin I came.'

59. (cf. b. 13. 312.) *When hit to pruyde sounede*, when it tended to my pride, when it contributed to make me proud. This use of *sounen* is common; see, e.g. Chaucer's Prologue, l. 307; Cant. Tales, Group B. 3157, 3348; F. 517.

60. (cf. b. 13. 313.) See Galat. i. 10; Mat. vi. 24.

62. (cf. b. 13. 314.) In the account of the Confession of the Seven Deadly Sins, the confessor is Repentance; in that of the Confession of Haukyn (B. xiii), the confessor is Conscience. In the revised account (C. vii), only the name of Repentance is retained.

☞ For notes to B. v. 72-75 (A. v. 54-58), see l. 170 below, p. 81.

74   C. PASS. VII. 63. B. PASS. V. 76. A. PASS. V. 59.

63. (b. 5. 76; a. 5. 59.) The reader should compare William's descriptions of Envy, etc., with the descriptions in Dunbar's Dance of the S̩even Deadly Sins, and in Spenser's Faerie Queene, bk. i. canto iv. Skelton probably copied hence some of his traits of Envy in his Philip the Sparowe, ll. 905-948. But the famous description of Envy is in Ovid; Metam. ii. 775—

'Pallor in ore sedet; macies in corpore toto,' etc.
See also Chaucer's Persones Tale; and, in particular, consult Burtǫn's Anatomy of Melancholy, pt. 1, sec. 2. mem. 3. subsec. 7.

64. *Mea culpa*. The form of confession contained the words—'Peccaui nimis cogitatione, locutione, et opere : *mea culpa*.' See Proctor on the Common Prayer, p. 193.

—— (b. 5. 78.) A *pelet* was a pellet or ball used as a war-missile; see Chaucer, House of Fame, iii. 553. As these were commonly made of stone, the comparison 'pale as a pellet' is perfectly natural and intelligible.

—— (b. 5. 79.) *Caurimaury*, evidently the name of some coarse rough material; see the Glossary. It is worth observing that in Prof. Rogers's Hist. of Agriculture and Prices in England, vol. ii. p. 536, there is a mention of the buying of a material called *Taursmaurs* (together with Persetum and Camelot, i. e. perse and camelet) in the year 1287. I much suspect that this is a misprint for *Caursmaurs*, as the letters *c* and *t* are often written alike in old MSS.

—— (b. 5. 80.) *Kirtel*, a kind of under-jacket, worn beneath the jacket or *kourteby*. The very various explanations given are due to the fact that the word was loosely used. A *full kirtle* was a jacket and petticoat; a *half kirtle* was either one or the other; and the term *kirtle* alone could signify any one of the three. The context must always be considered. See Gifford's note to Cynthia's Revels (Johnson's Works, ii. 260), quoted in Dyce's Skelton, ii. 149; my note to P. Pl. Crede, l. 229; Strutt, Dress and Habits, p. 349.

—— (b. 5. 87.) Possibly an allusion, as already hinted, to the adder as the emblem of Envy. Cf. Ps. cxl. 3; Rom. iii. 13.

—— —— (a. 5. 70.) The odd reading *vernisch* (varnish) is inferior to that of *verious* (T) or *vergeous* (U). In former times, *verjuice* was used as a sauce with boiled capon, crab, goose, &c. See *Verjuice* in the Index to the Babees Book.

—— —— (a. 5. 71.) *Walleth*, creates nausea. Cf. '*Walsh*, insipid' in Atkinson's Cleveland Glossary; '*Wallowish*, nauseous' in Halliwell. The various readings give *walewith*, *walweth*, which shew that is not the more usual verb *wallen*, to boil, here, though the sense is much the same.

—— (b. 5. 89.) The word *back-biting* is rather old. We find it in the Ancren Riwle, p. 82; and at p. 86, we read that '*Bacbitares*, þe biteð oðre men bihinden, beoð of two maneres;' and it is explained that there are two kinds of them, those who openly speak evil of others, and those who pretend to be friendly. Chaucer, in his description of Envy (Persones Tale), describes five kinds of 'backbytyng.'

—— (b. 5. 91.) *Gybbe*, Gib; short for Gilbert, whence Gibbs, Gibson, Gibbons, Gipps, etc. A *Gib-cat* means a male-cat; we now say a Tom-Cat. See *Gib-cat* in Nares.

—— (b. 5. 93.) Palsgrave has 'Wey of chese, *maige*.' There is a peculiar force in the mention of *Essex*, because the Essex 'wey' was of unusual weight. In Arnold's Chronicle, ed. 1811, p. 263, the Suffolk wey is 2 cwt. 32 lbs.; but the Essex wey is 3 cwt.

—— (b. 5. 94.) *Ennuyed*, annoyed; various readings *anoyed*, *ennyed*, *enuyed*. The alliteration shews that the word is really *ennuyed*, annoyed, not *enuyed*, envied.

—— (b. 5. 95.) 'And lied against him to lords, to make him lose his money.' Cf. Rom. Rose, 6940.

—— (b. 5. 101.) *Hailse hym hendeliche*, greet him courteously; cf. Pass. x. 309. Tyrwhitt (note to C. T. 13575) is wrong in not distinguishing between *hailsen*, to salute, greet (Icel. *heilsa*, to say *hail* to one, to greet), and *halsen*, to embrace, and sometimes to beseech (A. S. *healsian*, to take round the neck). But Palsgrave makes the distinction correctly, giving ' I *haylse* or greete, *Ie salue*,' and 'I *halse* one, I take hym aboute the necke, *Iaccole;*' p. 577. See *halch* in Gloss. to Percy Folio MS.; *hailsen* in Gloss. to The Destruction of Troy, ed. Panton and Donaldson; and *halsynge* in l. 187 below.

—— (b. 5. 107.) 'Christ give them sorrow;' a form of cursing; repeated in Pass. xx. 307. The 'bowl' and the 'broken (i. e. torn or ragged) sheet' were things of small value, yet Envy could not refrain from cursing the thief. The bowl was probably a wooden one, used to contain scraps of broken victuals. It was also used for washing out-of-doors, and was thus easily lost. It also meant a large drinking-cup; see note to l. 420, p. 93.

The expression '*broken* sheet' sounds odd, but it is a provincial expression. Grose, in his Provincial Glossary, ed. 1790, has—'*Break*, to break, to tear. *Hampshire*. In this county *break* is used for *tear*, and *tear* for *break;* as " I have *a-torn* my best decanter or china dish;" " I have *a-broke* my fine cambrick apron."' So also we find mention of a '*broken* surplice, with manye an hole ;' Test. of Love, pt. ii, in Chaucer's Works, etc., ed. 1561, fol. ccxcvi, col. 2.

—— (b. 5. 110.) In [b] it is *Eleyne* [Ellen], a female, who has the new coat; in [a] it is *Heyne*, a male. The coat was an article of female as well as of male attire; see Solomon's Song, v. 3.

—— (b. 5. 111.) *And al þe webbe after*, and (I wish that) the whole piece of cloth (from which the coat was cut) was mine too.

—— (b. 5. 112.) *Of*, at. *Liketh*, pleases. Chaucer says of envy that it is 'sorwe of other mennes prosperite ; and, after the word of seint Austyn, it is sorwe of other mennes wele, and joye of other mennes harm.'

—— (b. 5. 114.) 'And I judge that they do ill, where I do much worse.'

—— (b. 5. 115.) 'Whoever reproves me for it.' Mr. Wright mis-

76   C. PASS. VII. 69.   B. PASS. V. 119.   A. PASS. V. 99.

interprets *vndernymeth* in his Glossary. Pecock, in his Repressor, uses the word often. He begins that work with ' *Vndirnyme* thou,' etc. as a translation of the Lat. 'argue' in 2 Tim. iv. 2. It is very common in Wyclif's Bible, with the sense of ' to reprove,' ' to blame.'

—— (b. 5. 119.) *Bitter*, bitternesse. ' Thanne cometh eek *bitterness* of herte, through which *bitternesse* every good deede of his neighebore seemeth to him *bitter* and unsavery ;' Chaucer; Persones Tale, De Inuidia.

☞ Here there is a sudden leap, from B. 5. 119 to B. 13. 325.

69. (b. 13. 325.) Here, again, the description of Haukyn's envy [b] is shifted so as to form part of the Confession of Envy ; see note to l. 14 above, p. 72.

70. (b. 13. 326.) *By*, concerning, with reference to.

74. (b. 13. 330.) The right reading is not *brend*, but *fret*, of which *vrede, vride*, in some MSS., are variations or corruptions. *Fret* is the past tense, as in xxi. 202, being often used as a strong verb in Middle-English ; see examples in Stratmann, who gives the forms *freet, frat, fret*. The comparison is excellent. Envy fretted himself internally, just as the inner edges of a tailor's pair of shears grate against each other when used.

75. (b. 13. 331.) A *shappester* or *shepster* was a female cutter-out or *shaper* of garments, and not a female sheep-shearer, as suggested by Mr. Wright, and asserted by Mr. Timbs, in Nooks and Corners of Old England, p. 229. ' *Shepster* is *shapester*, one who *shapes*, forms, or cuts out linen garments, as appears from Palsgrave, v. *Schepstarre*, and Nares, v. *Shepster;*' Student's Manual of the English Language, by G. P. Marsh, ed. Smith, p. 217. The word is not in the original edition of Nares, but in the later edition by Wright and Halliwell, where two good illustrations are given. ' A sempster or *shepster*, sutrix ;' Withal's Dict. ed. 1608, p. 146 ; and—' Mabyll the *shepster* chevissheth her [*performs her work*] right well ; she maketh surplys, shertes, breeches, keverchiffs, and all that may be wrought of lynnen cloth ;' Caxton's Boke for Travellers. Elyot also renders *sarcinatrix* by ' a *shepster*, a seamester.' See Notes and Queries, 1 S. i. 356.

76. (b. 13. 331.) Ps. x. 7 ; Ps. lvi. 5 (Vulgate).

—— (b. 13. 332.) *Lyf* means here a living person, a man, as elsewhere.

78. (b. 13. 335.) *Crompe*, cramp ; see xxiii. 82. For this affliction the common remedy was the charm called a cramp-ring, i. e. a ring blessed by the king upon Good Friday, and worn by the sufferer; see Chambers, Book of Days, i. 418. For *cardiacle*, see note to Pass. xxiii. 82.

81. (b. 13. 338.) The word *witch* was formerly used of both sexes. See the quotations in Trench's Select Glossary.

83. (b. 13. 340.) Nothing more is known of the cobbler of Southwark, or dame Emma of Shoreditch, who were probably famous in their own day. They were evidently dealers in sorcery and charms for diseases. Cf. note to Pass. i. 225, p. 20.

☞ Here ends the second insertion from B. Pass. xiii.

86. Agrees with B. 5. 120 and A. 5. 72. At l. 88, the agreement is with B., 5. 122 and A. 5. 100.

87. (b. 5. 121. 'Envy and ill-will are difficult things to digest.' There are other examples of the use of the singular verb with a pair of nominatives ; see B. 5. 99.

88. This question is addressed by Envy to his confessor, Repentance. 'Cannot any sugar or sweet thing (be found to) assuage my swellings, nor any valuable medicine (*or* expectorant, *b*, *a*) drive it out of my heart, nor any shame or confession (relieve me), except one were (actually) to scrape my maw ? ' A forcible way of expressing the question —' can none but the most violent measures relieve my moral sickness ? ' *Diapenidion* answers almost exactly to the modern barley-sugar, being a kind of sweet stuff twisted into a thread, and used to relieve coughs, etc. The prefix *dia* is explained by Cotgrave as 'tearme set before medicinall confections or electuaries, that were devised by the Greeks.' Hence Life is said to 'drive away death with *dias* and drugs ; ' xxiii. 174 (see note). The termination *penidion* means a little twist (of thread, originally), being a diminutive of the Greek πήνη, a thread. This *penidion* became *pénide* in French, and *pennet* in English, according to Cotgrave's explanation, who says—' *Penide*, f. a pennet ; the little wreath of sugar taken in a cold.' See Dict. Universel des Sciences ; Paris, 3rd ed. 1857 ; par M.-N. Bouillet ; Notes and Queries, 4 S. vi. 202. I am indebted for the explanation of this word to Professsor Morley.

Compare—' certes, than is loue the medicyn that casteth out the venym of envye fro mannes hert ; ' Chaucer's Pers. Tale ; Rem. cont. Invidiam.

93. 'I *am* sorry ; I am but seldom otherwise.' Surely a clever rejoinder.

96. *Nameliche*, especially. Note the mention of London, and that this passage is not in [a]. There is but little mention of London in [a] ; probably because the author was not much acquainted with it in 1362. The C-text (l. 95) has—'I am a broker of back-biting ; ' but the B-text (l. 130) means—' I caused detraction to be made by means of a broker, to find fault with other men's ware.' That is, he employed brokers to depreciate his neighbour's goods ; *be*=by. The oath of the brokers is given at p. 273 of the Liber Albus. On *backbiting*, see note to B. 5. 89 above, p. 74.

103. *Ira*. Curiously enough, William entirely omitted this vice in his earliest version. Seeing his mistake, he elaborated the character with great care. He makes Wrath to have been a *friar*, the nephew of an abbess ; he was first employed as gardener to the convent, and afterwards as cook in the kitchen ; but, in [c], the mention of gardening is omitted. William doubtless refers to the terrible wrath then displayed by the secular clergy against the friars, and by the friars against them, and even by one order of friars against another.

113. 'Unless I had weather to suit me, I blamed God as the cause of it.' Compare l. 111 with Rich. Redeles, prol. 35.

114. *Angres*, afflictions, troubles, crosses.

78   C. PASS. VII. 118.   B. PASS. V. 143.   (NOT IN A.)

118. *Vore*, a southern form of *fore*, means a course, a track. Cf. 'heo nomen heore *vore*,' they took their course, Layamon, l. 13667 ; ' so forleost þe hund his *fore*,' so the dog loses his track ; Owl and Nightingale, l. 815 (or 817).

119. 'And prove the prelates to be imperfect.' Cf. B. 5. 145.

120. 'And prelates complain of them, because they (the friars) shrive their parishioners.' Cf. B. 5. 142. 'For comynly, if þer be any cursid iurour, extorsioner, or avoutrer [*adulterer*], he wil not be schryven at his owne curat, bot go to a flatryng frere, þat wil asoyle him falsely for a litel money by ȝeere, þof he be not in wille to make restitucioun and leeve his cursid synne;' Wyclif's Works, ed. Arnold, iii. 394. See also Crede, l. 468 ; Chaucer, Prol. 218, etc. And see below, Pass. xxiii. 323-367.

―― (b. 5. 138-150.) A slightly difficult, but important passage. It means—' I (continually) grafted lying tales upon *limitors* and *lectors*, till they bare leaves of servile speech, to flatter lords with, and afterwards they blossomed abroad in (my lady's) bower, to hear confessions. And now there is fallen therefrom a fruit, so that folk would much rather shew their schrifts to *them*, than shrive themselves to their own parsons. And now that the parsons have found out that friars share (the profits of confession) with them, these *possessioners* preach (to the people) and calumniate the friars ; and the friars (on the other hand) find *them* to be in fault, as people bear witness, (and say) that when they preach to the people, in many places around (it will be found) that I, i. e. Wrath, go with them, and teach them out of my books. Thus both parties talk about spiritual power, so that each despises the other, till either they are both beggars, and live by the spiritual authority which I give them, or else they are all rich, and ride about (like rich people). I Wrath never rest from following about the wicked folk—for such is my grace.' Wrath here insinuates that the quarrel generally terminates in one of two ways ; either the secular clergy turn beggars like the friars, or the friars obtain wealth enough to buy horses like the secular clergy. The quarrel was, as to which should hear confessions.

―― (b. 5. 138.) *Limitours* were members of a convent to whom a certain limited district was assigned to beg in, in order that, each mendicant having a certain round to make, no family might be left unsolicited. Bread, bacon, cheese, logs of wood, etc., were often ready for the limitour when he called. See Massingberd's Eng. Reformation, p. 110 ; Chaucer, Prol., l. 209 ; and Somp. Tale, l. 3.

Listres are *lectors*. This is ascertained by the following entry in the Promptorium Parvulorum, A.D. 1440. ' *Lyysterre* [*various readings* lystyr, lystore, listyr] *Lector*.' The editor, Mr. Way, says this is 'the *reader*, who occupied the second place in the holy orders of the Church.' By *second* place is meant second in ascending order. But I am told, on excellent authority, that *lector* means rather a lecturer, or occasional preacher, which gives the right sense. Mr. Wright's explanation of *lister* is wrong, and the absurd guess by Mr. Cutts is worse. It answers to an O. F. *listre*,

C. PASS. VII. 125. B. PASS. V. 144. (NOT IN A.) 79

a variant of *litre*, which is the F. form of Lat. nom. *lector.* See *Limiters* and *Lectors* in the Index to the Parker Soc. publications.

—— (b. 5. 144.) *Possessioneres ;* see Chaucer's Sompnoures Tale, l. 14. Tyrwhitt says—'An invidious name for such religious communities as were endowed with lands. The Mendicant orders professed to live entirely upon alms.' Mr. Wright says—'the regular orders of monks, who possessed landed property and enjoyed rich revenues,' etc. But it is clear that, in the present passage, a *possessioner* means one of the *beneficed clergy*, as the word *persones* is used as an equivalent. And it is worth remarking, that this same explanation will suit the context in Chaucer's Sompnoures Tale much better than if we suppose *monks* to be intended. Observe, for instance, l. 19:—

'Nought for to holde a *prest* jolif and gay;'

and, farther on, the friar says,—

'These curates ben ful negligent and slowe;'
'This every lewed *vicary* or *persoun*
Can say, how ire engendreth homicyde,' etc.

Nothing can give us so clear an idea of a friar as the commencement of this tale of Chaucer's.

In other passages, *possessioners* is used more generally, and it could be applied either to the *monks*, who possessed property in common, or to the *parochial clergy*, who possessed it as laymen did; as pointed out in the note to Bell's Chaucer, iii. 104.

125. It is clear that *spiritualte* here means spiritual power, authority, or rank.

129. *Hem* (or *hir*) *were leuere*, it were liefer to them (or to her); i. e. they (or she) had rather swoon or die. See Chaucer, Prol. 293.

133. 'And made them broths of various scandals.' Compare—'then serue potage, as wortes, *Iowtes*, or browes, with befe, motton, or vele;' Babees Book, p. 274. Mr. Furnivall says (ib. p. 287)—'These are broths of beef or fish boiled with chopped herbs and bread; Household Ordinances, p. 461. Others are made "with swete almond mylke," *ib*. See "Joutus de Almonde," p. 15, *Liber Cure ;* also pp. 47, 48.' See '*Jowtys*, potage,' in Prompt. Parv.; Mandeville's Travels, ed. Halliwell, p. 58; Gower, ed. Pauli, iii. 161, 162.

Chaucer likewise reproves 'jangling' near the end of his 'De Ira' in the Persones Tale ; cf. note to B. prol. 35, p. 6.

135. *A prestes file*, a priest's concubine, as Mr. Wright suggests in his Glossary, such being a meaning of the French *fille*. So in Rob. of Brunne, Handl. Synne, 4540, we find—'For to rage wyth ylka *fyle*.' See *File* and *Fyllok* in Halliwell's Dictionary.

136. *In the chapon-cote*, in the hen-house [c]; *in chiritime*, at cherry-time [b]. 'In some counties cherry-fairs are frequently held in the cherry-orchards. They are the resort of the gay and thoughtless, and as such frequently metaphorically alluded to by the early writers. Thus Occleve, De Regim. Princ. ed. Wright, p. 47—"This lyf, my sone, is but

a *chery-feyre;*"' Brand, Pop. Antiq., ed. Ellis, ii. 457. See *Cherry-fair* in Halliwell's Dictionary; Skelton, ed. Dyce, ii. 85.

——— (b. 5. 162.) *I-made* (written *made* in WCB) is the first person of the past tense, which is sometimes found with the prefix *I-* (A.S. *ge-*). The sense is—I, Wrath, fed them with wicked words; lit. I prepared their vegetables with wicked words. There is clearly a pun here, in the contrast of *words* with *worts*. Fluellen makes the same pun.

138. (b. 5. 163.) *Thow lixt*, thou liest. Cf. Crede, 542.

——— (b. 5. 165.) *Her eyther*, each of them. *Other*, the other.

——— (b. 5. 166.) *Seynt Gregorie*. 'It appears that some Abbesses did at one time attempt to hear the confessions of their Nuns, and to exercise some other smaller parts of the clerical function; but this practice, I apprehend, was soon stopped by Gregory IX., who has forbidden it in the strongest terms.—Decretal. l. v. tit. 38. c. x.;' Tyrwhitt, Introd. Discourse to Cant. Tales, note 7. Tyrwhitt gives the Latin text of the Decretal.

——— (b. 5. 167.) *Were prest*, should be a priest, i.e. should hear confessions.

——— (b. 5. 168.) *Infamis;* so in the MSS. It is put for the nom. plural. Cf. Pass. xxii. 162.

144. 'Imparked in pews;' i.e. fenced in by the pew as a park is fenced in by palings; see xviii. 13. This is said to be the earliest passage in which the word *pew* occurs. It also supports the supposition that pews were originally for women only. See note to Peacock's edition of Myrc, p. 74; and see *Pews* in Index to Parker Soc. publications.

145. 'How little I love Letice at-the-Style.' Letice is Lat. Lætitia. From 'at-the-style' comes the name Styles; see Bardsley's Eng. Surnames, pp. 85, 90. See l. 207.

146. 'Because she received the holy bread before me, my heart began to change (towards her).' On the difference between 'holy-bread' and the eucharistic wafer, see Peacock's edition of Myrc, p. 89; and cf. note to Pass. xvi. 210.

149. 'Till each called the other a whore, and (it was) off with their clothes;' i.e. with their outer garments, and hoods, which they tore off each other's backs and heads.

154. *Thei taken hem togeders*, they take counsel together; viz. as to what punishment they shall assign to me.

156. *Chapitele-house*, chapter-house. See the chapter-house described in Cutts's Scenes and Characters of the Middle Ages, p. 79. 'If any had a complaint to make against any brother, it was here made and adjudged. Convent business was also here transacted.'

157. *Baleysed*, punished with a *baleis* or rod; see Pass. xii. 124. The Prompt. Parv. has—'Baleys, *virga*.' Mr. Way's note is—'Hereafter occurs in the Promptorium "ȝerde, baleys, *virga*." *Virga* is rendered "a ȝerde or a rodde," Med. and Ort. Voc.; and such the *baleys* seem to have been, and not a besom, *balai*, in the present sense of the word. Matthew Paris (ed. Wats, p. 848) relates that in 1252 a person came to perform penance at St. Albans, "ferens in manu virgam quam vulgariter *baleis* appellamus,"

with which he was disciplined by each of the brethren. Wats, in the Glossary, observes, " Ita Norfolcienses mei vocant virgam majorem, et ex pluribus longioribus viminibus ; qualibus utuntur pædagogi severiores in scholis." . . . Forby does not notice it; but the verb to *balase* occurs amongst the provincialisms of Shropshire.' See Miss Jackson's Shropshire Word-book. The quotation from Matthew Paris is given at length in Warton, Hist. Eng. Poetry, ed. 1840, ii. 82, note 53, from which we further learn that the culprit was 'vestibus spoliatus,' and that the discipline was administered *in the chapter-house.*

159. *Feble*, weak, thin, poor, watery. In the Praier and Complaynte of the Ploweman (Harl. Misc. vi. 112), the poor man is said to have '*febele* mete, and *febele* drink, and *feble* clothinge.' Cf. Havelok, 323.

168, 169. The words *me* and *my* in [b] are evident blunders, but are found in most of the MSS. of that type ; perhaps in all. Yet Crowley has *hym* and *his*, and probably followed his copy. In the C-text, the author has altered them to *hym* and *hus* (= his). By *he*, is meant Repentance ; by *hym*, Wrath. ' Esto sobrius ' refers to the text ' Sobrii estote,' 1 Pet. v. 8.

☞ In the earlier texts, the description of Luxuria comes sooner; at B. 5. 72 (A. 5. 54). For note to B. 5. 188 (A. 5. 107) see note to C. 7. 196, just below.

170. In the two earlier texts, the confession of Luxury is very short. The poet's chief warning is there directed against getting drunk upón a Saturday, when work was over sooner than on other days, as it was the eve of Sunday. The votive mass of the Virgin Mary was said upon Saturday, and hence, in her honour, ' there arose a custom, amid all ranks, of vowing to keep, for a certain length of time, a rigid fast each Saturday;' Rock, Church of Our Fathers, iii. 281.

174. To 'drink with the duck' is to drink water, as a duck does.

☞ Here comes in the third insertion from B. (13. 344-352).

196. (b. 5. 188.) The vice of Avarice is discussed in Burton, Anat. of Melancholy, pt. 1. sec. 2. mem. 3. subsec. 12. Cf. Pass. xvii. 80 ; xxiii. 121.

197. *Heruy*, Harvey. Skelton has the same name for a covetous man.
'And *Haruy* Hafter, that well coude picke a male.'

Skelton, ed. Dyce, i. 35.

198. *Bytelbrowed*, having beetling or prominent brows. This rather scarce word occurs in The Destruction of Troy, ed. Panton and Donaldson, l. 3824, and in A Balade Pleasaunte, stanza 3 (Chaucer's Works, ed. 1561, fol. 344). ' The *beetled browes* signifieth malice, cruelty, letchery, and envy ;' Shepherdes Kalender, sig. P 2. See also Rom. and Juliet, i. 4. 32.

199. 'And like a leathern purse his cheeks flapped about ; (they were) even longer than (i. e. hung down lower than) his chin, and they trembled with age.'

201. ' His beard was shaven like bondmen's bacon ' [c] ; i. e. cut off in rather a ragged manner : *or*, ' His beard was beslobbered, as a bondman's

82 C. PASS. VII. 203. B. PASS. V. 196. A. PASS. V. 111.

is with bacon' [b]. Warton notes numerous examples of *menne* as the form of the genitive plural, e.g. Pass. iv. 102, v. 115, vi. 29, vii. 293, ix. 29, x. 214, etc. ; the very word *bondmenne* occurs again, vi. 70. The form *mennes* also occurs, as in viii. 220.

203. In Chaucer's Prologue, l. 541, the *tabard* is the dress of the ploughman. In a poem printed in Reliq. Antiq. i. 62, it is used of a poor man's upper garment. In the Coventry Mysteries, p. 244, Annas is represented as a bishop, in a scarlet gown, over which is 'a blew *tabbard* furryd with whyte.' In Sharp's Dissertation on Pageants, p. 28, a similar garment, used for a bishop in a mistery, is called a '*taberd* of scarlet.' See also Dyce's Skelton, ii. 283 ; Ducange, s. v. *Tabartum ;* Strutt's Dress and Habits, ii. 301 ; Riley, Mem. of London, p. 5, note 6 ; etc. Dresses of a *tawny* colour (see B-text) were used by minstrels ; see Cutts, Scenes and Characters of the Middle Ages, p. 305. Jews also used to wear orange-tawny bonnets, and hence Avarice is rightly fitted with ' a tawny tabard ;' for 'usurers should have orange-tawney bonnets, because they do Judaize ;' Bacon's Essays, 41.

—— (b. 5. 197.) Compare Chaucer's Chan. Yem. Prol. l. 82—' It is al baudy and to-tore also.' *Baudy* means dirty.

204. Hazlitt, in his Book of Proverbs, p. 216, has—' If a louse miss its footing on his coat, 'twill be sure to break its neck.' And Palsgrave has —' He hath made my gowne so bare that a lowse can get no holde on it ;' ed. 1852, p. 620.

205. The word *welch* is plainly written in most of the MSS. of [c] and [b]. In MS. L [b] it may be read either *welche* or *welthe*, and I thought at one time that the reading *welþe* of MS. W. decided the question in the latter direction. However, MS. R [b] has the spelling *welsch*, which is equally good evidence on the other side, and *t* is constantly written for *c*. MS. T [a] has *walsshe scarlet*, i. e. Welch scarlet, and this gives the most likely solution of the word. It is probable that *welche* means Welsh flannel, and that *Walsshe scarlet* is red flannel. The Vernon MS. has *walk*, i. e. thing to walk on.

207. *Symme at the Style* [c, b] ; *Simme atte noke*, i. e. Sim at the oak [a]. On these and similar names, see Bardsley's English Surnames, pp. 85-90. The form 'atte noke' is for ' atten oke,' i.e. *at then oke*, where *then* is a later form of *tham* (A. S. þæm), the old dative sing. of the def. article, as explained in the note to Pass. i. 43. In the name Atterbury, it is interesting to notice that the *feminine* form of the article is preserved. If we had to write ' at the town ' in Anglo-Saxon, we should put *at thære byrig*, because the sb. *burh* (our *borough*) becomes *byrig* (our *bury*) in the dative case ; and, as it is a feminine noun, it takes the feminine dative article, viz. *thære*. The form Attenborough is later, and due to a change of gender of the substantive. Besides *atte noke*, we even find *atte norcharde* (i. e. *at then orcharde*), whence the name *Norchard ;* so also *Nash* from *ash*, *Nalder* from *alder*, *Nelmes* from *elms*, *Novene* from *oven ;* Bardsley's Eng. Surnames, p. 86.

209. We have here three different equivalent expressions, viz. 'a leasing

(i.e. a lie) or two' [c]; 'a leaf or two' [b]; 'a lesson or two' [a]. The expression 'a leaf or two' is to be explained by observing that, in the next line, Avarice talks of his *lesson*, and of learning his *Donet* or primer in l. 215. In like manner, still keeping up the allusion to reading, he learns to lie just a leaf or two, i.e. as much as would fill a couple of leaves. All ambiguity is removed by the parallel passage in Richard the Redeles, Prol. 37—

'ȝif him list to loke · *a leef other tweyne.*'

Note also 'a lesson other tweyne;' id. i. 9.

211. *Wy* is Weyhill, near Andover in Hampshire. Weyhill fair is a famous one to this day, and lasts eight days. The fair for horses and sheep is on Oct. 10; that for cheese, hops, and general wares, on Oct. 11, and the six days following. 'The tolls derived from the sheep-fair form part of the stipend of the rector of Weyhill;' *Standard* newspaper, Oct. 11, 1870. Warton has a long note upon fairs, which should be consulted; see Hist. Eng. Poetry, ed. 1840, ii. 55; ed. 1871, ii. 259. 'One of the chief of them,' he says, 'seems to have been that of St Giles's hill or down near Winchester, to which our poet here refers. It was instituted, and given as a kind of revenue to the bishop of Winchester, by William the Conqueror, who by his charter permitted it to continue for three days.... In the fair, several streets were formed, assigned to the sale of different commodities; and called the Drapery, the Pottery, the Spicery, etc.' Fairs long continued to be the principal marts for purchasing necessaries in large quantities. Winchester fair is mentioned in the Liber Albus, p. 201. Compare the description of Stourbridge fair (near Cambridge) in Prof. Rogers's Hist. of Agriculture and Prices in England, i. 141.

213. 'The grace (or favour) of guile' is a satirical expression. We speak rather of 'the grace of God.'

214. *Thys seuen yer*, these seven years, i.e. a long but indefinite period. Cf. 'That is the best dance without a pipe That I saw *this seven year;*' The Four Elements, in Old Plays, ed. Hazlitt, i. 47; also Much Ado about Nothing, iii. 3. 134, etc. And see Pass. i. 203, v. 82, xi. 73.

215. *Donet*, primer. 'Properly a Grammar, from *Ælius Donatus*, the Grammarian.... Among the books written by bishop Pecock, there is the *Donat* into Christian religion, and the Folower to the *Donat.*'—Warton's Hist. Eng. Poet. ii. 56, ed. 1840. See also the note in Dyce's Skelton, ii. 343; Gloss. to Chaucer; *Donat* in Cotgrave; and Prompt. Parv. p. 126.

216. In 1353, statutes were passed regulating the length and breadth of cloth.—Thom. Walsingham, ed. Riley, i. 277.

217. *Rayes*, striped cloths. *Ray* means properly a *ray, streak, stripe;* but it was commonly used in the above sense. It was enacted—'that cloths of *ray* shall be 28 ells in length, measured by the *list* [edge], and 5 quarters in width.'—Liber Albus, p. 631. 'A long gown of *raye*' occurs in Lydgate's London Lyckpeny; see Specimens of English, 1394–1579, ed. Skeat, p. 25. The Latin name for striped cloth was *radiatus;* see Prof. Rogers's Hist. of Agriculture and Prices in England, i. 577.

218. *To brochen*, etc. ;—'To pierce them with a packing-needle, and I fastened them together; and then I put them in a press, and penned them fast in it,' etc.

221. *Webbe* (A.S. *webba*) is a male weaver in Chaucer, Prol. 362; the fem. is both *webbe* (A.S. *webbe* in Beowulf, ed. Grein, l. 1942) and *webster*. Observe *spynnesters*, i. e. female spinners, in the next line; and cf. note to Pass. i. 222, p. 19.

223. *The pound*, etc. She paid the people whom she employed by the pound, and used too heavy a weight; thus cheating them of their dues.

224. *Auncel*, a kind of balance, perhaps the Danish steelyard. Blount tells us, in his Law-Dictionary, that, 'because there was wont to be great deceit [in its use], it was forbidden, 23 Edw. 3, Stat. 5. cap. 9; 34 ejusdem, cap. 5; and 8 Hen. 6, cap. 5. . . . By a Constitution made by Henry Chicheley, Archbishop of Canterbury, Anno 1430—Pro abolitione ponderis vocati *le auncel-weight*, seu *scheft* [shift], seu *pounder*, etc., doloso quodam stateræ genere; qui utitur, excommunicandus.' In A. D. 1356, we find 'one balance, called an *auncere*,' valued at 12*d.*; and '2 balances, called *aunceres*,' valued at 6*s.*; see Riley's Memorials of London, p. 283. We also find mention of 'Thomas le Aunseremaker' in Riley's Memorials of London, pref. p. xxii; cf. Bardsley's Eng. Surnames, p. 359.

226. *Peny-ale* is common ale, thin ale, as is certain from its being spoken of as a most meagre drink, suitable for strict-living friars, in B. 15. 310. *Podyng-ale* (*puddyng-ale* in Trin. MS.) was probably named from its being thick like *pudding*. Thus in Pass. xxii. 402, a fraudulent brewer boasts of drawing *thick ale* and *thin ale* out of one hole in a cask. The penny-ale was sold at *a penny a gallon*, but the best ale at 4*d*.

227. In [a], the reading *liuen be hemseluen* of course means 'live by themselves.' But in [b] the reading is *lay by hymselue*, where *hymselue* probably refers to the *ale*; see the next line, and note the common use of *hym* for *it*. Indeed, Crowley has the reading *it-selfe*. In [c], however, the reading returns to *hemselue*, and the sense is the same as in [a].

231. *In coppemel*, by cups at a time. She knew better than to measure it in a gallon measure. Concerning ale measures, see Liber Albus, p. 233.

233. *Hockerye*, i. e. the retail trade. A *huckster* was one who retailed ale, etc. from door to door. 'Item, that no *brewer* or *brewster* sell any manner of *ale* unto any *huckster*,' etc.—Liber Albus, p. 312. And again —'that no *hucstere* shall sell ale;' Riley's Memorials of London, p. 347. *Huckster* is generally applied, in the City books, to females only.

—— (b. 5. 228.) *So the ik*, so may I thrive [b]; *sothely*, soothly, verily [a].

—— (b. 5. 230.) *Walsyngham*. See note to Pass. i. 52, p. 5.

—— (b. 5. 231.) *Rode of Bromeholme*, cross of Bromholm in Norfolk. In A Chronicle of London, p. 10, we find, anno 1224 [rather 1223 or 1222] 'the emperour Baldewyn, which whanne he wente to bataile to fyghte with

C. PASS. VII. 234. B. PASS. V. 232. (NOT IN A.) 85

Godes enemyes, he hadde a croos boren before hym, whiche crosse seynt Eleyne made of the crosse that Cryst deyde upon; and there was an Englyssh prest that tyme with hym that was called Sir Hughe, and he was borne in Norfolke, the whiche prest broughte the same crosse to Bromholm in Norfolke.' Mr. Wright refers to Matthew Paris (p. 268); and adds—'In the MS. Chronicle of Barthol. de Cotton, it is recorded at the date 1223—Eo tempore Peregrinatio de Bromholm incepit.' Hence Avarice could visit Our Lady of Walsingham, and the piece of the true cross at Bromholm in one journey, and pray to be brought out of debt by having his cheating tricks forgiven him. It is interesting to remember that Bromholm priory was within a mile of Paston hall, the residence of the Paston family. See Paston Letters, ed. Gairdner, pref. p. xxv. The story of the finding of the True Cross by Helen, mother of Constantine, is well known. Cf. Chaucer, Reves Tale, 366; Pardoneres Tale, 489.

*** 234–309. (b. 5. 232–289.) *Not found in the* A-text.

——— (b. 5. 238.) He pretends that he thought *restitution* was the French for *robbery*. *Rifle* was used in a stronger sense then that it is now. Cf. 'he had called him a malefactor, and common *rifler;*' Riley's Memorials of London, p. 208. Norfolk is evidently considered as one of the least refined parts of the island, being in an out-of-the-way corner; and we are to infer that French was almost unknown there. The common proverb—'Jack would be a gentleman if he could speak French'—shews that the common people had much difficulty in learning it. Trevisa fixes the date 1385 as the year, *just before* which children began to learn to translate Latin into *English* instead of *French*, as formerly. See Warton, Hist. Eng. Poetry, ed. 1840, i. 5; Dyce's Skelton, ii. 93.

239. *Vserie*, usury. 'All usury was prohibited as a sin by the Canon Law;' Southey, Book of the Church, p. 187.

241. *Lumbardes and Jewes*. 'A set of *Lombards* established themselves here, in connexion with the legates, to advance money upon all sums due to the Pope, for which they exacted the most exorbitant usury,' etc.—Southey, *as above*. Cf. Pass. v. 194; Chaucer, Schipm. Tale, l. 367; Polit. Poems, ed. Wright, ii. 184; and see *Lumber* in Trench's Select Glossary. The Jews were constantly accused of being the offenders, whenever clipped coin was found, which was very often. See the chapter on 'Jews in England' in Annals of England, p. 162.

243. 'And lent (the light coin) for love of the pledge, which I set more store by and considered more valuable than the money or the men to whom I lent it.' The B-text is more awkward, because it involves a change in the subject of the sentence. However, it certainly means—'and lend it for love of the cross, (for the borrower) to give me a pledge and lose it,' where the latter 'it' refers to the pledge; cf. B. 13. 360. The key to the passage is to remember that borrowers often gave pledges of much value. Owing to a positive want of money, 'Christians did not feel any scruple in parting with their most valued treasures, and giving them as pledges to the Jews for a loan of money when they were in need of it. This plan of lending on pledge, or usury, belonged specially to the Jews in Europe during

the Middle Ages;' P. Lacroix, Manners, Customs, and Dress during the Middle Ages, p. 451. Sir John Maundeville says that a King of France bought the crown of thorns, spear, and one of the nails used at the Crucifixion, from the Jews, 'to whom the Emperour had *leyde hem to wedde*, for a gret summe of sylvre.' *For love of the cross* is a clever pun, as *cross* refers frequently to the cross on the back of old coins, and was a slang name for a coin, as in Shakespeare; 2 Hen. IV. i. 2. 253; see note to Pass. xviii. 200. *Cross-and-pile* is the old name for *heads and tails*. It is clear enough what Avarice did: he first clipped coins and then lent them, taking a pledge which he hoped would not be redeemed.

—— (b. 5. 246.) Compare—'Iucundus homo qui *miseretur et commodat*, disponet sermones suos in iudicio.' Ps. cxii. 5 (cxi. 5, Vulgate). Avarice obtained more manors through his customers being in arrears of payment, than he could have obtained by practising liberality. *Maneres* is spelt *manoirs* in MS. W.

—— (b. 5. 249.) In an ordinance against usurers (38 Edw. III.) we find that certain persons exerted themselves to maintain usury—'which kind of contract, the more subtly to deceive the people, they call *exchange* or *chevisance*, whereas it might more truly be called *mescheaunce* (wickedness);' Liber Albus, p. 319, and see p. 344. Cotgrave has—'*Chevissance*, f: an agreement or composition made; an end or order set down, between a creditor and debtour.' Cf. Chaucer, Prol. 282.

250. (b. 5. 255.) Avarice, in his dealings with knights, used to buy silk and cloth from them at a sufficiently cheap rate; and he now ironically calls his customers mercers and drapers, who never paid anything for their apprenticeship.

—— (b. 5. 261.) 'As courteous as a dog in a kitchen.' This alludes to an old ironical proverb, which appears in French in the form—'Chen en cosyn [*cuisine*] compaignie ne desire;' in Latin in the form—'Dum canis os rodit, sociari pluribus odit;' and in Middle English—'Wil the hund gnaȝh bon, i-fere neld he non;' i. e. while the hound gnaws a bone, companion would he none. See Wright's Essays, i. 149.

—— (b. 5. 263.) The third word in the line may be either *leue* or *lene*. The distinction is, that *leue* means grant or permit, followed by a clause; but *lene* means grant or give (lit. lend), followed by an accusative case. By this test, we should read *lene* (and not *leue*, as printed), because the phrase is *lene þe grace*, i. e. give thee grace. *In the present case*, however, it looks as if the poet really began the sentence with *god leue* (a common expression), and afterwards finished the sentence another way; i. e. he seems to have meant—'God grant never, unless thou the sooner repent, for thee (to have) grace upon this earth to employ thy property well.'

253. The arrangement here is rather hard to follow. Line 253 really answers to B. 5. 263; l. 254 to B. 5. 266; l. 255 to B. 5. 265. Next, ll. 256 –259 are new, but include a Latin quotation following after B. 5. 279. Then comes the passage in ll. 260-285, borrowed from B. 13. 362-399; whilst, at l. 287, the author returns to B. 5. 268.

257. (cf. b. 5. 279.) 'Si enim res aliena, propter quam peccatum est, cum reddi possit, non redditur, non agitur pænitentia, sed fingitur; si autem ueraciter agitur, non remittetur peccatum, nisi restituatur ablatum; sed, ut dixi, cum restitui potest;' S. Augustini Epist. cliii., sect. 20; Opera, ed. Migne, ii. 662.

☞ **Here come in passages from B. 13. 362–399.**

260. (b. 13. 362.) 'I mixed my wares, and made a good shew; the worst (of them) lay hidden within; I considered it a fine trick.'

267. (b. 13. 371.) *Half-acre* was a colloquial term for a small lot of ground; cf. Pass. ix. 2, 3.

270. (b. 13. 374.) 'And if I reaped, I would over-reach (i. e. reach over into my neighbour's ground), or gave counsel to them that reaped,' etc. Mr. Wright reminds us that, in olden times, 'the corn-lands were not so universally hedged as at present, and that the portions belonging to different persons were separated only by a narrow furrow, as is still the case in some of the uninclosed lands in Cambridgeshire.' We find a similar allusion in Robert of Brunne, Handlyng Synne, ll. 2445–8.

278. (b. 13. 392.) 'Bruges was the great mart of continental commerce during the 13th, 14th, and 15th centuries.'—Wright.

279. (b. 13. 393.) *Prus*, Prussia. As early as in the reign of Henry III. we find that the import-due 'for one hundred stockfish imported from Pruz' was 'one farthing;' Liber Albus, p. 209. See the account 'Of the commoditees of Pruse' in Polit. Poems, ed. Wright, ii. 169. Mr. Wright remarks that 'Prussia was then the farthest country in the interior of Europe with which a regular trade was carried on by the English merchants.' The present passage implies that it was carried on at some risk.

285. (b. 13. 399.) Mat. vi. 21.

☞ **Here ends the fourth insertion from B. Pass. xiii.**

290. The Latin quotation has occurred before; see note to Pass. ii. 144, p. 27. And it occurs again; see note to Pass. xviii. 40.

294. 'Thou art the slave of another, when thou seekest after dainty dishes; feed rather upon bread of thine own, and thou wilt be a free man.' I have not succeeded in tracing the source of this quotation.

297. *By þy myght*, according to thine ability. After this line two lines of the B-text (ll. 278, 279) have been dropped, but the Latin quotation following them has been preserved at an earlier place. See note to l. 257, at the top of this page.

301. *Parte with þe*, share with thee; according to the principle of the proverb, that the receiver is as bad as the thief. See the parallel passage in Pass. xviii. 41–50.

303. By the 'sauter-glose' is meant the gloss or commentary upon the Psalter. The Glosa Ordinaria upon the verse here referred to contains a remark from Augustine—'Sic misericordias dat, vt seruet ueritatem; vt nec peccata sint impunita eius cui ignoscit.' This is probably what the poet had in mind. Ps. li. (l. in the Vulgate) is called *Miserere mei Deus* from the three first words in it. In verse 6 (8 in the Vulgate) we find—'Ecce enim ueritatem dilexisti: incerta et occulta sapientiae tuae manifestasti mihi.' St. Augustine's own comment on the text is— 'Impunita peccata etiam eorum quibus ignoscis non reliquisti. *Ueritatem dilexisti;* id est, sic misericordiam prærogasti, vt seruares et ueritatem;' Opera, ed. Migne, iv. 592.

—— (b. 5. 285.) Ps. xviii. 25 (xvii. 26 in the Vulgate) has—'Cum sancto sanctus eris, et cum uiro innocente innocens eris.' Cf. Pass. xxii. 424.

—— (b. 5. 289.) The Latin quotation is not quite exact. 'Suauis Dominus uniuersis: et miserationes eius super omnia opera eius.' Ps. cxliv. 9, Vulgate.

309. The first line of this passage has been curiously altered. We find in [a] and [b]—'And yet I will pay back again, if I have so much (as will suffice for it), all that I have wrongfully acquired ever since I had knowledge (of things);'—and this forms part of the Confession of Sloth. But in [c] we are introduced to a new penitent, a companion of Avarice, who was a Welshman, and bore the singular name of Evan Pay-again-if-I-have-enough-all-that-I-wrongfully-acquired-since-I-had-knowledge, etc., etc. The name 'yevan' (as it is spelt in MSS. I, F, M, and S) is clearly the Welsh Evan, i. e. John. His long surname is similar to others that our author uses elsewhere; see Pass. v. 18, ix. 80–83.

—— (b. 5. 467, p. 172 of the text.) *The rode of chestre,* the cross or rood at Chester. Mr. Wright quotes from Pennant's Tour in Wales (edit. 1778, p. 191), to shew that a famous cross once stood in a spot formerly known as the *Rood-eye,* i. e. Rood-Island, but now known only by the corrupted name of *Roodee,* and used as a race-course. (See, on this corruption, my note in Notes and Queries, 4 S. iii. 228.) Cf. Rich. Redeles, prol. 56.

316. *Ryfeler* in [c] is equivalent to *robbere* in [b] and [a]. We have already had the verb *rifle* in the sense of to rob; l. 236 above. As for *robber,* the similarity of the word to *Robert* early gave rise to a pun, whereby *Robert* came to be used as an equivalent for *thief.* Thus in Political Songs, ed. Wright, p. 49, occurs the expression—'per *Robert, robber* designatur.' And see Polit. Poems, ed. Wright, p. 354, l. 4 from bottom. See also the note to Pass. i. 45, p. 7.

Reddite; i. e. the text—'Reddite ergo omnibus debita;' Rom. xiii. 7.

317. 'And, because there was nothing wherewith (to make restitution), he wept very sorely.' *Wher-of* [b] = *wher-with* [c, a].

320. In the apocryphal gospel of Nicodemus, the name of the penitent thief is *Dismas* or *Dimas,* and that of the other thief, *Gestas.* See Cowper's Apocryphal Gospels, pp. 246, 364, 426; Cov. Myst. p. 316. Other names for them are Titus and Dumachus, as in Longfellow's Golden Legend.

321. The allusion is to the words of the thief—'Domine, *memento* me, cum ueneris in regnum tuum;' Luke xxiii. 42.

It is well worth notice that the penitent thief is spoken of, in [b], under the heading 'Accidia;' but, in [c], under 'Confessio Auaricie.' The former is the right place. His repentance was the stock example of an argument against Wanhope, as resulting from Sloth. See Pass. viii. 59.

322. *Reddere ne haue,* have no means wherewith to make restitution

C. PASS. VII. 323. B. PASS. V. 476. A. PASS. V. 251.

[c, b] ; *no red haue,* have no guidance [a]. *Red* is for *rede,* i. e. counsel, good advice from others.

323. 'Nor ever expect to earn enough, by any craft that I know' [c] ; *or,* 'on account of any craft that I know' [a] ; *or,* 'by help of any handicraft, the amount that I owe' [b]. *Craft* is here used in a good sense, viz. that of skill in trade, as we use *handicraft.* The word *owe* [b] has two senses in Middle-English ; (1) to possess, and (2) to owe in the modern sense. To obviate confusion, the scribe of MS. L has written *debeo* above the word.

329. 'That he would polish anew his pike-staff, called Penance (*or* Penitence [b. a]) ;' to which [a] and [b] add—'and by help of it leap over the land (i. e. be a pilgrim) all his life-time.' A pilgrim always carried a staff, generally with a spike at the end, whence it was called a pike-staff. It was also called a *bordoun,* as in viii. 162. A *land-leper* or *land-loper* was a vulgar name for a pilgrim, the word *leap* meaning to *run,* like the German *laufen.* Thus Cotgrave has—'*Villotier,* m. : A vagabond, *land-loper,* earth-planet, continuall gadder from towne to towne.' The word *hym* (b. 5. 483 ; a. 5. 258) has reference to the pike-staff. Cf. viii. 180.

330. 'Because he had associated with *Latro,* who was Lucifer's aunt' [c, b] ; *or* 'Lucifer's brother' [a]. The word *latro* refers to the expression in Luke xxiii. 39—' Unus autem de his qui pendebant *latronibus.*'

☞ **End of the transposed portion of B and A : return to B. 5. 290, and (at 1. 350) to A. 5. 146.**

338. (b. 5. 291.) There is a parallel passage in Hampole's Pricke of Conscience, ll. 6311-6319 :—

> 'For the mercy of God es swa mykel here,
> And reches over alle, bathe far and nere,
> That alle the syn that a man may do,
> It myght sleken, and mare thar-to.
> And thar-for says *Saynt Austyn* thus,
> A gude worde that may comfort us :
> *Sicut scintilla ignis in medio maris,*
> *ita omnis impietas viri ad misericordiam Dei.*
> "Als a litel spark of fire," says he,
> "In mydward the mykel se,
> Right swa alle a mans wykkednes
> Un-to the mercy of God es."'—(Ed. Morris, p. 171.)

A similar quotation from Saint Augustine, with a list of venial sins, will be found in Chaucer, Pers. Tale, near the end of *pars secunda penitentiæ.*

The nearest passage to this which I have yet found is the following :—
' Tanquam unda misericordiæ peccati ignis exstinguitur.'—S. August. in Ps. cxliii. 2 (Vulgate).

341. *To bygge the with a wastell,* to buy thee a cake with. See note to Pass. i. 133, p. 14.

349. *Lerede yow to lyue with,* taught you to live upon [c]; *Lent yow of owre lordes good,* lent (i. e. gave) you, of our Lord's wealth; i. e. spiritual strength [b].

359. *Pionys,* seeds of the pæony. They were used as a medicine, but sometimes also as a spice, as here. See note in Liber Albus, p. 197.

360. *Fastinge-daies.* We learn from l. 352 that the circumstances here described took place on a *Friday,* a fitting day for Glutton to go to church and confess. Cf. also ll. 434, 439. The scene here described with such vivid dramatic power took place, it is evident, in some large ale-house in London, not very far from Cock Lane, Smithfield (l. 366), from Cheapside (b. 5. 322), and from Garlickhithe (b. 5. 324). It was also very near a *church* (ll. 355, 366). At one time I supposed that the 'Boar's Head,' in Eastcheap, immortalized by Shakespeare, might have been the very tavern here meant; but the Boar's Head is not mentioned as being a tavern till 1537, and the localities mentioned point rather to Cheapside, with its famous Bow church; Chambers, Book of Days, i. 301. Moreover, William lived at one time in *Cornhill,* which is close by. See Pass. vi. 1, and cf. note to l. 366 below. In any case, Glutton is the Sir John Falstaff of the scene.

Respecting fennel, Lydgate says, in his Prologue to the Siege of Thebes,
'But toward night, eate some fenell rede,
Annis, comin, or coriander sede.'

362. Here we find the forms *sywestere* (sewster, needlewoman) in [c], and *souteresse* (female shoemaker) in [b], where [a] has *souters wyf. Sesse* or *Cesse* is *Cis,* the short for Cicely, i. e. Cecilia.

365. A hackney-man was one who let out horses on hire; the term occurs A.D. 1308, in Riley's Memorials of London, p. 63.

366. Women of ill repute might be put in the pillory; and if so, they were afterwards to be led 'through Chepe and Newgate, to *Cokkeslane,* there to take up their abode.'—Liber Albus, p. 395. Cock Lane, West Smithfield, has been lately rebuilt. See also note to l. 367. The church may have been Bow church; see note to l. 360. Or again, it may have been St Peter's in Cornhill, since that church was emphatically *the* church, and its rector had precedence of all others; see Memorials of London, ed. Riley, p. 653.

367. *Syre Peeres,* Sir Piers. Observing Chaucer's line in the Prol. to the Non. Pr. Tale—

'Wherfor, *sir* monk, or dan *Piers* by your name'—

and remembering that *Sir* was, at that date, the usual title of a monk or priest, we may feel sure that the same is intended here. The word *prydie* occurs nowhere else, and may be a mere name; but I strongly suspect that (like most things in our author) it has some definite meaning. I would therefore suggest that it is put for *prie-dieu,* which means a sort of fald-stool; and is, accordingly, a hint at the proper duties of Sir Piers. But here, by a severe stroke of satire, this ecclesiastic, who should be praying to God, is found on a tavern-bench, beside Pernel of Flanders, about the significance of whose name there is no doubt whatever. The reader who

C. PASS. VII. 368. B. PASS. V. 320. A. PASS. V. 164.   91

will turn to Riley's Memorials of London, p. 535, will find, in the Regulation as to street-walkers by night, who were especially 'Flemish women,' that they were forbidden 'to lodge in the city, or in the suburbs thereof, by night or by day; but they are to keep themselves to the places thereunto assigned, that is to say, to the stews on the other side of Thames, and *Cokkeslane;* on pain of losing and forfeiting the upper garment that she shall be wearing, together with the hood, every time that any one of them shall be found doing to the contrary of this proclamation.' This explains, at the same time, the allusion to Cock Lane in the line above, and agrees with the following list of the characteristics of London, as given in MS. Trin. Coll. O. 9. 38, printed in Reliq. Antiq. ii. 178.

'Haec sunt Londonis, pira, pomaque, regia thronus,
Chepp-stupha, *coklana,* dolum, leo, verbaque vana.'

The name *Purnel* or *Pernel* has been commented on above, in the note to Pass. v. 111, p. 57; see also note to Pass. xviii. 71.

368. *Tyborne,* Tyburn. Executions were formerly very frequent. See Knight's Pop. Hist. Eng. VII. chap. vi.; Butler's Hudibras, I. ii. 532; Dr. Johnson's poem of London, l. 238, with the note on it in Hales's Longer English Poems, 1872, p. 313. Tyburn was afterwards called Westbourn; its site varied (see Hales), but one position of it is still marked, at the junction of Edgeware Road and Oxford Street. There seems to have been another place of execution, in the parish of St Thomas-a-Waterings, in Southwark, called, by way of distinction, Tyburn *of Kent;* see Pegge's Kenticisms, ed. Skeat, Proverb 11.

369. *Dauwe* is for *Davie* or *David.* Cf. 'When *Dauie Diker* diggs and dallies not;' Gascoigne's Steel Glas, 1078; in Specimens of English, 1394–1579, ed. Skeat, p. 322. Hence the names Dawson, Dawkes, Dawkins, Dakin (for Dawkin), Dawes, etc. For *diker,* i.e. ditcher, the Vernon MS. has *disschere,* i.e. a maker of metal dishes; but some other MSS. of the A-text (as T and U) have the reading *dykere,* which is certainly correct. The word *disschere* comes in more fitly a few lines further down, viz. in l. 372 (b. 5. 323; a. 5. 166). Mr Bardsley, in his English Surnames, p. 349, remarks that the 'disher' all but invariably worked in pewter, and quotes the names of John le Discher, Robert le Disshere, and Margaret la Disheress.

371. *Rakere,* or *Rakyer of Chepe,* a scavenger of West Cheap, or Cheapside. The word *rakyer,* i.e. a raker or street-sweeper, occurs in a Proclamation made in the 31st year of Edw. III. See Riley's Memorials of London, pp. 67, 299, 522, and Liber Albus, p. 289.

372. A *roper* means a ropemaker; the phrase 'corder or roper' occurs A.D. 1310, in Riley's Memorials of London; where mention is also made of a 'roperie' or rope-walk, situate in the parish of Allhallows' the Great, Thames Street. Palsgrave has 'Ropar, a ropemaker, *cordier,*' and Levins has 'Roper, *restio.*'

373. *Garlekhithe* [b] is near Vintry Ward. Stow says—'There is the parish church of St. James, called at Garlick-hithe, or Garlick-hive; for that of old time, on the bank of the river Thames, near to this church,

C. PASS. VII. 375.   B. PASS. V. 326.   A. PASS. V. 169.

garlick was usually sold;' Survey of London, ed. 1842, p. 93. The next landing-place, westward, is Queen Hithe. See Smith's English Gilds, p. 1.

It has been suggested that *Griffin* is an allusion to the Griffin (Griffin to the vulgar eye, though Cockatrice in the Heralds' office), which was emblazoned on the ancient shield of the principality of Wales.—Notes and Queries, 3rd S. xii. 513. The Harleian MS. 875 (A-text) has *Gruffith*, i.e. Griffith, a common Welsh name.

375. *To hansele*, as a bribe, i.e. to propitiate him. On this word, see the article in Halliwell's Dictionary, and cf. Brand's Pop. Antiq. ed. Ellis, iii. 262. It occurs again in Rich. the Redeles, iv. 91.

377. *To þe newe fayre*, or *Atte new faire*, at the new fair. There is a reference here to an old game or custom of barter called in Teutonic law-books the *Freimarkt*. It seems that Hikke chose Bette to be his deputy. Then Bette and one appointed by Clement tried to make a bargain, but could not settle it till Robyn was called in as umpire, by whose decision Clement and Hikke had to abide. Hikke obtained the cloak, which was the better article, and Clement was allowed to fill up his cup at Hikke's expense (l. 390). If either drew back, he was to be fined a gallon of ale. See the article on this subject in Englische Studien, v. 150. In fact, 'to chaffer at the new fair' became a proverbial phrase for to exchange, as is clear from a passage in Wyclif's Works, iii. 167. Compare Rob. of Brunne, Hand. Synne, ll. 5977-5980—

'For men þat loue to do gylerye,
At þe alehous make þey marchaundye,
To loke 3yf þey kunne com wyþynne,
Here negheburs þyng falsly to wynne.'

383. *Rapliche* [c, a], quickly; *in rape* [b], in haste. To the examples in Stratmann add—'He ros vp *raply;*' Arthur, ed. Furnivall, (E. E. T. S.) 1864, l. 87; and Rich. Redeles, pr. 13.

394. In a tavern-song in Ritson's Ancient Songs, i. 138, we find—

'And lette the cuppe goo route,
Good gosyp.'

Compare Gower's Conf. Amant. ed. Pauli, vol. iii., where we find at p. 13—

'Some laugh and some loure;'

and at p. 3—

'With drie mouth he sterte him up,
And saith—"now *baillez ça* the cuppe."'

397. *Yglobbed*, gulped down, swallowed. In Smith's Eng. Gilds, p. 59, we find that an alderman of the Gild of St. John the Baptist, in Lynn, was allowed the extraordinary quantity of *two* gallons of ale, and every brother *or sister* that was sick 'in tyme of drynkyn' was to have 'a potel.' A *pottle* (see l. 399) is two quarts, or half a gallon; a *gill* is a quarter of a pint, or the thirty-second part of a gallon.

398. To *godely, gothely*, or *gothelen*, is to rumble. The word is very rare, but may be found three times at p. 135 of Popular Treatises on Science, ed. Wright, where it is used of the rumbling sound of thunder.

C. PASS. VII. 402. B. PASS. V. 351. A. PASS. V. 195. 93

It is probably much the same word as that used at p. 66 of the Ayenbite of Inwyt, where it is said of slanderers or railers that 'þe on godeleþ þanne oþrene,' i.e. the one rails at the other. Cf. Icel. *gutla*, to gurgle. It occurs again in Pass. xvi. 97.

402. *Wexed* [c, b], waxed, or stopped up; *I-wipet* [a], wiped. The word 'waxed' is here used merely in jest : to *wax* meant to stop tight, to stop up ' as tight as wax,' because wax was sometimes used for that purpose. See the Romans of Partenay, ed. Skeat, l. 2817. *Wips* is an old spelling of *wisp*, like *crips* for *crisp*, or *waps* for *wasp*. Cf. 'Wyspe, *torques, torquillus;*' Prompt. Parv. It means a little twist of straw, as fully explained in Brand's Popular Antiq., ed. Ellis, iii. 396.

404. Gleemen were sometimes blind in former times, as now, and were led, in like manner, by a dog who consulted only his own ideas as to the course to be taken. See Ritson, Met. Rom. i. ccxiv.

405. We find in the Tale of Beryn—
'Sometyme thou wilt avaunte [*go in front*], and sometyme arere.'

406. ' Like one who lays nets, to catch birds with.'

408. *Thrumbled* [c] or *thrompelde* [a] obviously has the sense of *stumbled* [b]. Shakespeare (3 Hen. VI. iv. 7. 11) has—
'For many men that stumble at the threshold
Are well foretold that danger lurks within '—
on which Douce (Illustrations of Shak. ii. 30) remarks—' To understand this phrase rightly, it must be remembered that some of the old thresholds or steps under the door were, like the hearths, raised a little, so that a person might stumble over them unless proper care were taken.'

420. *Ho halt* [c], who holds? i.e. who detains? *Bolle* signified not only a bowl, but a capacious cup; hence the reading *cuppe* [a]. Cf. ' Twelve hanaps of gold, called *bolles ;*' Riley's Mem. of Lond. p. 429. Hence the term *boller* for a deep drinker, as in Pass. x. 194.

421. ' His wife and his conscience reproved him for his sin' [c]. Some MSS. of [b] have *wit*, i.e. his common sense ; others have *wif*, as in [a].

424. ' Thou, O Lord, who art aloft, and didst shape (or create) all creatures.' *Lyf*, creature, as elsewhere in our author.

427. Hard swearing was extremely common ; see Chaucer, Pard. Tale, C. T. 12565 ; also the discussion in the Shipm. Prol. ; and Pers. Tale, *De Ira*.

☞ Here is a very short digression to B. 13. 404.

430. (cf. b. 13. 404.) Here our author takes a few expressions from the Confession of Haukyn in B. 13. 404, 405. The line means—' More than my natural constitution could well digest' [c] ; *or*, 'And ate more meat and drank more than his natural constitution could digest' [b]. See note to Pass. i. 229, p. 20.

431. (cf. b. 13. 405.) 'And, like a dog that eats grass, I began to vomit.' *Et* is for *eteth*, 3 p. s. pr. tense. From *brake* comes *parbreak*, used by Spenser, F. Q. i. 1. 20.

94   C. PASS. VII. 432. B. PASS. V. 380. (NOT IN A.)

432. (b. 5. 380.) 'And wasted that which I might have spared (or saved;') the B-text being the more explicit. The word *spele*, to spare, is rare ; but see Pass. xiv. 77, and the three other examples in Stratmann.

NOTES TO C. PASSUS VIII.
(B. Pass. V. 392–VI. 2; A. Pass. V. 222–VII. 2; with an insertion from B. XIII. 410–457.)

4. 'If I am once in bed, no ringing (of the church bell) shall make me get up till I am ready for dinner, unless some call of nature renders it necessary.' In this passage ' tail-end ' [b] is simply used for ' tail ; ' in [c], as in other passages, *tailende* may mean reckoning by tally, or money affairs, from the verb *tailen ;* see, e.g. B. 8. 82 (A. 9. 74), and note to iv. 372, p. 50; and cf. *ytayled* in l. 35 below (C-text). *Hit made* = should cause it ; so in l. 28 below, we have 'bote syknesse hit make.'
Compare Towneley Myst. p. 314.

7. *Rascled* [c] ; *roxed* [b], stretched himself. *Rox* is much the same as the Lowland Scotch *rax*, to stretch, which is, indeed, only a form of *reach*. *Rasclen* is a secondary verb, derived from *rax*, and perhaps influenced in form by the A.S. *wraxlian*, to wrestle. We find in Layamon's Brut, ed. Madden, l. 25991—

'And seoððen he gon ramien · and raxlede swiðe,
& adun lai bi þan fure · & his leomen strahte;'

which Sir F. Madden interprets by—'and afterwards he gan to roar, and vociferated much, and down lay by the fire, and stretched his limbs.' But surely *raxlede* means 'stretched himself' in this passage also. The explanation is found in Levins' Manipulus Vocabulum, ed. Wheatley, which has—'Raskle, *pandiculari*,' col. 35 ; and again—' Ruskle, *pandiculari*,' col. 194. So also *I raxled* = I stretched myself, roused myself ; Allit. Poems, ed. Morris, A. 1174.

Remed [c], either 'cried out,' or 'stretched himself ;' *rored* [b], roared. Observe that *ramien* occurs in the passage from Layamon just quoted. Compare the description of Sloth given by Robert of Brunne, Handlyng Synne, ll. 4258–60, 4280–2 ; also 4244–6—

'Whan he heryþ a bel ryng. . . . .
þan begynneþ he to klawe and to *raske*.'

11. This seems to be the earliest mention of Robin Hood. The next earliest is in Wyntoun's Chronicle, written about A.D. 1420, where Little John is also mentioned. But Mr. Wright thinks that one of the extant Robin-Hood ballads is really of the date of Edward II. See his Essays on England in the Middle Ages, ii. 174. '*Randolf, erl of chestre*, might be the Randulph or Randle, Earl of Chester, who lived in Stephen's time,' and was earl from A.D. 1128 to 1153 ; but the reference is rather, as Ritson

C. PASS. VIII. 14. B. PASS. V. 405. (NOT IN A.)

supposed, to his grandson of the same name, who married no less exalted a personage than Constance, widow of Geoffrey Plantagenet, and mother of Prince Arthur ; and who was earl from 1181 to 1231 or 1232. When this Randle was besieged by the Welsh in Rhuddlan castle, he was released by a *rabble of minstrels*, led by Roger Lacy (see Ritson's Ancient Songs vol. i. pp. vii. and xlvi., and Percy's Essay on the Ancient Minstrels) ; and, since some privileges were conferred on the minstrels in consequence of this exploit, the least they could do in return would be to make ' rymes ' concerning him. See the Percy Folio MS., 1867 ; vol. i. p. 258. Concerning Robin Hood, see also Chambers, Book of Days, ii. 606, and i. 580. The ' Robin-Hood games ' were held on May 1.

The expression 'a ryme (*or* geste, *or* tale) of Robin Hood' came to mean, proverbially, any idle story. See two examples of this in Barclay, Ship of Fools, ed. Jamieson, ii. 155, 331.

14. See Chaucer's Pers. Tale, *de Accidiâ*.

19. *Atte nale*, at the ale-house ; see note to Pass. i. 43, p. 6. We here read that Sloth, who was a priest (see l. 30) used to resort to the ale-house like the ' Sir Piers ' mentioned in Pass. vii. 367 ; and even ventured to talk scandal in the church itself. Barclay is explicit in his denunciation of the latter practice, which was carried to a shameless extent ; see his Ship of Fools ; ed. Jamieson. ii. 155.

22. *Harlotrie*, a scurrilous tale. In a MS. Glossary printed in Reliq. Antiq. i. 7, we find—' *Scurra*, a harlotte ; ' and '*Scurrilitas*, a harlotrye.'

Somer-game of souteres, a summer game played by shoemakers. A *summer-game* is probably the same as *summering*, a rural sport at Midsummer. See Nares, who refers to Brand's Pop. Antiq. i. 240 (4to ed.) ; Strutt's Sports and Pastimes, p. xxvi. ; and Mr Markland's Essay on the Chester Mysteries, in the 3rd vol. of Malone's Shakespeare, p. 525, ed. Boswell. Nares also quotes an extract about ' May-games, wakes, *summerings*, and rush-bearings.' The great day was on St. John the Baptist's eve, i. e. June 23, or Midsummer eve. The games themselves answered to what we now call 'athletic sports ; ' and it was usual to conclude them with large bonfires. I add a few illustrative quotations, some of which shew that these games were not always very respectably conducted.

> ' Another Romayn told he me by name,
> That, for his wyf was at a *someres game*,
> Without his witing, he forsook hire eke.'
> Chaucer ; Wyf of Bathes Prologue.

> ' Daunces, karols, *somour-games*,
> Of many swych come many shames.'
> Rob. of Brunne, Hand. Synne, l. 4684.

See also Strutt, Sports and Pastimes, p. 317, who refers to Bourne's Antiq. vol. ix. c. 27 ; and to verses on Midsummer Eve by Barnaby Googe. Cf. Harman's Caveat, ed. Furnivall, p. 47 ; Stowe, Survey of London (folio, 1633), pp. 84, 85 ; and the description of the Cotswold games at Whitsuntide in Chambers, Book of Days, i. 714.

25. *Late I passe* [b], I let pass, I pay no heed to. Cf. Chaucer, Prol. 175.

27. Cf. Shakesp. Hen. VIII. iii. 2. 294. The latter part of the line in [c] seems to mean—'then I have mention made of me at the friars' convent,' i. e. by the friars. The word *memorie* means 'mention' here; see Cotgrave. Sloth was mentioned by name by the friars in their prayers, because he had bought from them a letter of fraternity. See Wyclif's Treatise 'Of Lettris of Fraternite,' where we read—'þei graunten letters of bretherhed under her comyne seele, þat her breþer schal have part of alle her gode dedes, bothe *in lif* and in deth, and rekkenen mony werkes;' Works, ed. Arnold, iii. 420. I suppose the word *memorie* more often bears the signification of commemoration or service for the dead. Compare—

> 'Their pennie Masses, and their Complynes meete,
> Their Diriges, their Trentals, and their shrifts,
> Their *memories*, their singings, and their gifts.'
> Spenser; Moth. Hub. Tale, 452.

—— (b. 5. 419; *not in* a.) *Ite, missa est;* the concluding words of the service of the mass.

28. *Bote syknesse hit make*, unless sickness causes it (to be so); i. e. unless an attack of illness frightens me into confession. See this expression repeated in l. 65 below; and cf. note to l. 4 above, p. 94.

29. 'Yet I tell not the half (of my sins)' [c]; 'and then I shrive myself by guess' [b], i. e. I mention sins at random when I cannot call them to mind.

31. *Solfye*, i. e. *sol-fa*. To *sol-fa* is to practise singing the scale of notes. See a poem on Learning to Sing. pr. in Reliq. Antiq. i. 292—'I *solfe* and singge after,' etc.; and see *solfa* in the Index to Dyce's edition of Skelton.

—— (b. 5. 425.) *Beatus vir*, Ps. i. or cxii. *Beati omnes*, Ps. cxxviii. Wyclif speaks of 'unable curatis, þat kunnen not the ten comaundementes, ne rede her sauter;' Works, iii. 277. It was not uncommon for a man to know the whole Psalter by heart; Rock, Church of Our Fathers, iii. 5.

34. *Catoun*, Cato; see note to Pass. ix. 338.

—— (b. 5. 428.) *Canoun*, the canon of the mass; see the Glossary. *Decretales*, Decretals; a collection of popes' edicts and decrees of councils, forming a part of the canon-law. Five books of them were collected by Gregory IX., 1227; and a sixth by Boniface VIII., in 1297. See *Decretals* in Haydn's Dict. of Dates.

35. 'If I buy and give a pledge for anything, then, unless it be marked on a tally,' etc. The B-text means—'If I buy (anything) and give a pledge for it (without paying down the money), then,' etc.; the general sense being the same.

45. I. e. unless something eatable is held in the hand. We may compare the proverbial phrase used by Chaucer (C. T. 4132, 5997)—

> .   'With empty hand men may no haukes tulle;'

52. *Forsleuthed*, wasted by idle carelessness. *And sette hous a fuyre*, and set the house on fire (by my carelessness).

55. A Leonine hexameter; I do not know from whom it is quoted.

57. *Vigilate* refers to Mk. xiii. 37—'Quod autem uobis dico : omnibus dico : Vigilate.' *Veille*, probably 'watcher;' the reading *wakere* occurs in MS. H [a].

59. *War fro wanhope*, beware of despair. This is an allusion to the usual supposed result of Sloth ; see l. 81 below, and observe how Chaucer, in his Persones Tale (*de Accidiâ*), describes the result of Sloth in the words—'Now cometh wanhope, that is, despair of the mercy of God,' etc. So also in Rob. of Brunne, Hand. Synne, l. 5171 ; Ayenbite of Inwyt, ed. Morris, p. 34.

Wolde [b], who would, *or* which would ; the relative being omitted.

61. In Hampole's Prick of Conscience, ed. Morris, ll. 3398-3411, the ten things that destroy venial sins are holy water, almsdeeds, fasting, the sacrament, the Pater Noster, shrift, the bishop's blessing, the priest's blessing, *knocking upon the breast as practised by a meek man*, and extreme unction. *Bidde god of grace*, pray to God for His grace ; cf. l. 121 below.

65. *Bote sycknesse hit make* [c, a], unless sickness cause it (to be otherwise), unless sickness be the cause ; *but sykenesse it lette* [b], unless sickness prevent it.

☞ Observe the break here; for notes to B. 5. 463-484 (A. 5. 236-259) see above, notes to C. 7. 309, etc., on pp. 88, 89.

70. (b. 13. 410.) *Braunches*, branches ; the usual theological term for the subdivisions of a subject. See Chaucer's Persones Tale, De Septem Peccatis Mortalibus ; Ayenbite of Inwyt, p. 31, l. 6, and p. 33.

In the English translation of Calendrier des Bergers (Shepherd's Calendar), ed. 1656, sig. D 6, and sig. E 6, we find—'The first great branch of the tree of vicis is pride, and he hath xvii branches growin[g] out of him,' etc. And again—'Here endeth the branches and small spraies of the sinne of Wrath, and hereafter followeth the xvii. branches of Sloth, as, Evill thought, Annoy of wealth, readinesse to evill, Pusillanimity, Evill will, breaking vowes, Impenitence, Infidelity, Ignorance, Vain Sorrow, slowly (*sic*), evill hope, Curiosity, Idlenesse, Evagation, letting to do good, Desolation.'

83. (b. 13. 423.) *Fool sages*, foolish wise men ; alluding to the jesters, who were professed fools, yet often made sensible remarks. See l. 104 below. See Luke vi. 25.

87. (b. 13. 427.) The Latin is perhaps not so much a quotation as a maxim of law. Richardson (s. v. *Consense*) quotes—'But whosoeuer was the manqueller of this holy man, it shall appere, that both the murtherer and the *consenter* had condigne and not vndeserved punishment, for their bloudye stroke and butcherly act.'—Hall, Edw. iv. an. 10.

93. (b. 13. 433.) See Ps. c. 7 (Vulgate).

97. (b. 13. 437.) Strutt, in his Sports and Pastimes, p. 177, gives several examples of the amounts of money paid to minstrels, such as the following, for example. 'At the marriage of Elizabeth, daughter of Edward I., to John, Earl of Holland, every *king's minstrel* received 40 shillings.'

98 C. PASS. VIII. 101. (B. PASS. XIII. 441. NOT IN A.)

Compare Froissart's account of the rewards given to minstrels by Gaston de Foix; vol. iv. cap. 41.

101. (b. 13. 441.) See Luke x. 16.

107. (b. 13. 447.) 'And fiddle for thee the story of Good Friday;' i.e. and, instead of having a fiddler to play to you, let a learned man recite the events of the crucifixion.

109. 'To cry before our Lord for a *largesse*, in order to shew your excellent praise.' To 'cry largesse' is to ask for a bounty, and is a common phrase. The term is still used in some parts by gleaners, who cry 'largesse!' when they see a stranger passing by. I heard it thus used near Hunstanton, in Norfolk, in 1873. The use of the word obviously originated in a desire to propitiate the Norman nobles by addressing them in French.

112. *By hus lyue*, during his lifetime. *Litheth hem*, listens to them [c]; *lythed hem*, listened to them [b].

117. 'With their evil-speaking, which is a song of sorrow, and the very fiddle of Lucifer;' meaning that evil-speaking, such as was indulged in by flatterers and jesters, leads men to destruction. Cf. Pass. i. 40. For *lay*, MS. W. wrongly has *lady*.

☞ **Here ends the inserted passage from B. Pass. xiii.**

119. Here *that* is put for *them that*. 'For he listens to and loves them that despise God's law.' The Latin quotation much resembles that quoted at B. 15. 336; see note to that line.

120. Here Repentance is personified, as in Pass. vii. 1, 12, 62, 331, 423; he is the priest to whom the various penitents make their confession. 'Then was Repentance ready, and advised them all to kneel, and said—"I shall beseech, on the part of all sinners, that our Saviour will shew them His grace."' To *beseech of* is to *beseech for*, to beg to obtain. Cf. to *bidde god of grace*, i.e. to pray to God for His grace, in l. 61 above.

126. *Ade*, written for *Adæ*, i.e. of Adam. The Bishop of Chester has kindly pointed out to me that this is taken from a passage in the Sarum Missal, viz. from the Canticle 'Exultet' sung upon Holy Saturday (Easter Eve) at the blessing of the Paschal candle:—'O certe necessarium Ade peccatum et nostru*m*; q*uod* Christi morte deletum est. O felix culpa, que talem ac tantum meruit habere redemptorem.' So in Wyclif's Works, ed. Arnold, i. 321.

129. 'And madest Thyself, together with Thy Son, like unto our soul and body' [c]; *or*, 'and us sinful men alike' [b]. The sense is clearer than the construction. Cf. b. 5. 495. See John xiv. 9, 10.

130. *Thi self sone* [b], Thy Son Himself. *In oure secte* [c]; *in owre sute* [b]. It makes no difference, since *secta* (from Lat. *sequi*) meant, in mediæval Latin, either the right of prosecuting an action at law or the *suit* or action itself; where *suit* is from the Fr. *suivre*, the equivalent of *sequi*. And again, *secta* meant a *suit* of clothes, and such is the meaning here. We should now say—'in our *flesh*.' Cf. ll. 137, 141. 'There were also at least two *qualities of cloth*, the *secta generosorum*, and the *secta valettorum*, the

C. PASS. VIII. 133.   B. PASS. V. 498.   A. PASS. V. 260.   99

distinction being so marked that I have felt myself able to draw up a table which shall contain both qualities;' Hist. Agric. in England, by J. E. T. Rogers, i. 578. *Secta* even means a *suite* or set of people; cf. 'and thereupon he produced his *suit*.'—Liber Albus, p. 342; where the Latin has *sectam*, i. e. his set of witnesses. For the quotation, see Eph. iv. 8.

—— (b. 5. 498.) *It ladde*, led it (i. e. the sorrow) captive. See Eph. iv. 8, Ps. lxviii. 18.

133. *Meel-tyme of seyntes*, meal-time of saints. This expression seems to be a figurative one, having reference to the time of the crucifixion, when Christ's blood was shed upon the cross. It can hardly refer directly to the sacrifice of the mass, because that was more usually celebrated at an earlier hour of the day; see Rock, Church of Our Fathers, iii. pt. 2. 43. It has also been suggested that there is reference here to Canticles i. 7, q. v. I prefer to take it in connection with the succeeding context, and to suppose that the poet is speaking of the crucifixion as having been a time of refreshment to our forefathers who sat in darkness; the force of which reference can only be understood by readers who are familiar with the apocryphal gospel of Nicodemus.

The quotation from Isaiah ix. 2 is explained in the apocryphal Gospel of Nicodemus with reference to the 'Harrowing of Hell,' i. e. the descent of Christ into hell to fetch out the souls of the patriarchs. See the whole account, as there narrated; and cf. Pass. xxi. 369.

135. Compare this with the account given of the Harrowing of Hell in Pass. xxi. This line, e. g., nearly agrees with Pass. xxi. 371; and the expression *blewe* (b. 5. 503) is explained by þat breþ in Pass. xxi. 367.

137. *In oure secte*, in our *suit*, i. e. in a human body; see note to l. 130. The reference is to the Resurrection. With l. 139, cf. Matt. ix. 13.

140. *Ymad*, composed, narrated. To *make* is to compose, especially in verse; but here it is applied to prose writings. See John i. 18.

141. *In owre armes* [b], in our armour, or in arms marked with our device: a phrase taken from the terms of a tournament. See Pass. xxi. 21.

149. 'And because of that great mercy, and for the love of Mary thy mother.' The construction is explained in the note to Pass. xvi. 131. The quotation is from Jerem. xxxi. 34.

150. *Rybaudes*, ribalds. See a long note in Political Songs, ed. Wright, 1839, p. 369. It was chiefly applied to the lower class of retainers, who could be relied on to do the lord's dirty work. See also Ducange, s. v. *ribaldus* and *goliardiæ*. Cf. Pass. ix. 75.

152. *Hente*, seized. In Ps. lxxi. 20, we find 'thou shalt quicken me again,' but the Vulgate has the past tense instead of the future 'conversus vivificasti me.'

153. Ps. xxxii. (xxxi. in the Vulgate) begins with—'Beati quorum remissae sunt iniquitates, et quorum tecta sunt peccata.' The next quotation is from Ps. xxxv. 7 (Vulgate).

155. Here the three texts agree once more. It is probable that the first two lines of A. Passus VI. (found in H only) are spurious. Yet they are useful for connecting the sense with the lines preceding.

157. *God leyue that thei mote*, God grant that they might do so [c, also a] ; *treuthe to seke*, to seek Truth [b]. The A-text has *leue ;* see note to B. 5. 263, on p. 86.

161. *Paynym*, pagan, Saracen (because of his foreign appearance) is the reading of [c] and [b] ; but [a] has *Palmere*. This excellent description of a Palmer should be noted. Mr. Wright aptly draws attention to a similar description in Sir Walter Scott's Marmion, canto i. st. 23, 27. Instead of quoting these familiar lines, I give Sir Walter Scott's note— ' A *Palmer*, opposed to a *pilgrim*, was one who made it his sole business to visit different holy shrines ; travelling incessantly, and subsisting by charity : whereas the Pilgrim retired to his usual home and occupations when he had paid his devotions at the particular spot which was the object of his pilgrimage.' In the notes to Bell's edition of Chaucer, this statement is challenged, and it is asserted that a *palmer* meant a pilgrim to the Holy Land *only*, but many passages shew that it was often used in a much wider signification, and I see no good reason for altering Sir Walter's definition, which seems to have been copied from Speght. Mr. Cutts, in his Scenes and Characters of the Middle Ages, which the reader should consult, says (at p. 167)—'When the pilgrim reached the Holy Land, and had visited the usual round of the holy places, he became entitled to wear the palm in token of his accomplishment of that great pilgrimage ; and from that badge he derived the name of Palmer.' And this, no doubt, is the true explanation, viz. that a palmer was one who made it his business to go on pilgrimages, and that he earned his standing as a professional pilgrim by going to the Holy Land.

162. *Bordon*, a staff ; not a burden, as erroneously explained by Fosbrooke. The list may have been wound round it for use in case of accident. King Horn, when disguised as a palmer, carried a 'burdon' and a 'scrippe ;' K. Horn, ed. Lumby, l. 1061.

163. ' Wound round and round it, after the manner of a climbing plant.' The *withiewind* was a name for the wild convolvulus. Cotgrave has— ' *Liseron*, m. Withiwind, Bindweed, Ropeweed, Hedge-bells.' And Minsheu says—' Woodbinde, binde-weede, or *withiewinde*, because it windes about other plantes.' Cf. A. S. *wiðwinde*, convolvulus or bindweed.

164. The *bowl* and *bag* were invariably carried, the former to drink out of, the latter to hold scraps of meat and bread. See Cutts, Scenes and Characters of the Middle Ages, p. 174.

165. The *ampullæ* were little phials, containing holy water or oil. They were generally made of lead or pewter, nearly flat, and stamped with a device denoting the shrine whence they were brought. ' The chief sign of the Canterbury pilgrimage was an ampul (*ampulla*, a flask) ; we are told all about its origin and meaning by Abbot Benedict, who wrote a book on the Miracles of St. Thomas ;' Cutts, as above, p. 170. A drawing of one is given on the next page of the same work.

Dr. Rock (Church of Our Fathers, iii. 423–442) has some remarks on this passage which should be consulted ; but I unhesitatingly reject his

C. PASS. VIII. 166. B. PASS. V. 528. A. PASS. VI. 12. 101

clumsy punctuation of this line, which raises more difficulties than it solves. The 'hundred' of ampuls is simply a poetic exaggeration which can mislead no one. In the story of The Pardonere and the Tapstere, it is said of the Canterbury pilgrims, that—'they set their signys upon their hedes, and som oppon their cappe.'

166. On pilgrims' *signs*, see Chambers, Book of Days, i. 338. 'Besides the ordinary insignia of pilgrimage, every pilgrimage had its special *signs*, which the pilgrim on his return wore conspicuously upon his hat or his scrip, or hanging round his neck, in token that he had accomplished that particular pilgrimage;' Cutts, Scenes and Characters of the Middle Ages, p. 167; which see. Thus the *ampullæ* were the special signs of the Canterbury pilgrimage; the scallop-shell was the sign of the pilgrimage to Compostella; whilst the signs of the Roman pilgrimage were a badge with the effigies of St. Peter and St. Paul, the cross-keys or 'keyes of rome' (l. 167), and the vernicle (l. 168). The proper sign of the pilgrimage to the Holy Land was the cross or 'crouche' (l. 167); this 'was formed of two strips of coloured cloth sewn upon the shoulder of the robe;' Cutts, as above, p. 167.

Syse [c] certainly means Assisi, in Umbria, the place of birth and death of the celebrated St. Francis, founder of the Franciscan order of friars. Plenary indulgence was granted to all pilgrims who visited the church of St. Mary of Angels at Assisi on a particular day of the year. See the life of St. Francis in Sir Jas. Stephen's Essays in Eccl. Biog. (4th ed.), p. 85. The B-text and A-text have the reading *Sinai;* with reference to the convent of St. Katharine there. *Shilles of galys*, shells of Gallicia. See the legend of the scallop-shell of St. James of Compostella in Cutts, as above, p. 169. Cf. Pass. i. 48; v. 124.

168. The *vernicle*, as worn by pilgrims, was a copy of the handkerchief of St. Veronica, which was miraculously impressed with the features of our Lord. 'Inter has feminas una fuit Bernice, sive Veronice, vulgo Veronica, qui sudarium Christo exhibens, ut faciem sudore et sanguine madentem abstergeret, ab eo illud recepit, cum impressa in illo eiusdem Christi effigie, ut habet Christiana traditio;' Cornelius a Lapide, in St. Matt. xxvii. 32. This is one of the numerous cases in which a legend has been invented to explain a name. Bernice, Berenice, or Veronica, was the traditional name of the woman who was cured of an issue of blood, the name having been suggested by the actual mention of a Bernice in the Acts of the Apostles. Ere long, it was popularly explained as being equivalent to the words *vera icon*, i.e. true likeness inscribed under the celebrated portrait of Christ impressed upon a handkerchief, and preserved in St. Peter's Church at Rome. Copies of this portrait were called *Veronicæ* or *Veroniculæ*, whence the English name *vernicles*. See the Legends of the Holy Rood, ed. Morris, pp. 170, 171 (where two old drawings of the vernicle are reproduced); Mrs. Jameson's Sacred and Legendary Art, ii. 269-271; Chambers, Book of Days, i. 100.

171. Pilgrims to *Sinai* used to visit the convent of St. Catharine, with its various relics; see Maundeville's Travels, ed. Halliwell, p. 59. Also,

102 **C. PASS. VIII. 172. B. PASS. V. 534. A. PASS. VI. 18.**

at p. 74 of the same, we read that 'when men comen to Jerusalem, here first pilgrymage is to the chirche of the *Holy Sepulcre*, where oure Lord was buryed.' See Maundeville's description of it.

172. The numerous sights at *Bethlehem* are described by Maundeville, ed. Halliwell, pp. 70-72. Concerning *Babylon*, see the same work, pp. 56, 57.

173. *Ermanie*, Armenia. *Alisaundre*, Alexandria. *Damascle* (better spelt *Damaske*), Damascus. The curious form *Assye* in the A-text (Vernon MS.) is probably only another spelling of *Assisi;* see note to l. 166 above.

By going to *Armenia*, the pilgrim could see Noah's ark, as asserted in Heywood's *Four P's;* see Hazlitt's Old Plays, i. 334, note 5. *Alexandria* was much used as a port of arrival for pilgrims. Moreover, 'in that cytee was seynte Kateryne beheded,' etc.; Maundeville's Travels, p. 55. *Damascus* was considered as having been the scene of the Creation of Adam; see Chaucer's Monkes Tale.

177. *Corseynt* is for O. French *cors seint*, i.e. *corps saint*, holy body; and hence, a saint or sainted person.

'And hys ymage ful feyre depeynte,
 Ry3t as he were a *cors seynt;*' Rob. of Brunne, Hand. Synne, 8739.

182. *Peter!* i.e. by St. Peter. This is a very common exclamation, of which there are several instances. See e.g. Chaucer's House of Fame, ii. 526, in Morris's edition; where Tyrwhitt's edition has *Parde*. Innocent III. used to swear by St. Peter; see Southey's Book of the Church, p. 156. Compare also Pass. ix. 1.

As to the duties of a ploughman, here described in ll. 186-192 (b. 5. 548-556), we should compare the poem of How the Plowman lerned his Paternoster, printed in Hazlitt's Early Popular Poetry, vol. i., and in Reliq. Antiq. i. 43.

The character of PIERS THE PLOWMAN is here introduced for the first time. When all the penitents and searchers after Truth are at fault, when even a palmer declares he never heard of any saint of that name, the homely ploughman steps forward, declaring that he knows Truth well. It was his own conscience and native common sense that led him to this knowledge. We may *here* take Piers as the type of Honesty, not without remembering that the poet *afterwards* identifies him with the truest of all Teachers of men, our Lord Christ Jesus; see Pass. xxi. 19-24.

192. Cf. also l. 189. *To paye*, lit. to (his) pleasure, i.e. to His satisfaction. By Truth is meant God the Father. *Paye* is not here equivalent to *pay* in the modern sense, notwithstanding the occurrence of *hyre* (hire) in the next line.

195. ' He does not withhold wages from any servant beyond the evening,' i.e. till next day. See Pass. iv. 310.

201. *For seynt Thomas shryne*, for all the wealth on St. Thomas' shrine at Canterbury. A description of this shrine, when in its glory, is given by Erasmus, Colloq. *Peregrinatio Religionis ergo.*

204. Piers here directs the pilgrims how to reach Paradise. There are

C. PASS. VIII. 208. B. PASS. V. 572. A. PASS. VI. 53.

several points of resemblance between the rest of this Passus and a French poem by Rutebuef, and we may fairly infer, both from this and other passages, that William was acquainted with Rutebuef's writings. The particular poem here, to some extent, followed is 'La Voie de Paradis, ou, ci commence La Voie d'umilitei,' printed in Œuvres de Rutebuef, ed. Jubinal, ii. 24-55. See also another poem 'La Voie de Paradis,' in the same volume, p. 227. Rutebuef, in his turn, imitated a similar poem by his predecessor Raoul de Houdaing, a poet of the 13th century.

208. (b. 5. 572; a. 6. 53.) The way to Truth lies through the love of God and of our neighbour, i. e. through the ten commandments, most of which are named below, viz. the fifth in l. 214, the third in l. 217, the tenth in l. 220, the eighth and sixth in l. 224, the fourth in l. 226, and the ninth in l. 227. See Exod. xx. 12, etc.

217. *Swery-nat*, etc.; swear not unless it be necessary, and, in particular, (swear not) idly by the name of God Almighty. The whole phrase forms, in William's allegorical language, the name of a place.

226. Robert of Brunne, in his Handlyng Synne, l. 801, says—

'The þryd commaundement yn owre lay
Ys—holde weyl þyn halyday.'

He explains that this means that we are to keep holy the Sunday, but he further proceeds to argue in favour of the Saturday half-holiday. Cf. note to Pass. vii. 170, p. 81.

227. *Blenche*, turn aside. So, in the Tale of Beryn—

'And when thou approchist and art the castell nygh,
Blench fro the brode gate, and enter thow nat there.'

Bergh, a hill; corrupted in several MSS. to *borgh*, a borough. In [a] we find the reading *brok*, a brook, with alternative readings *bourne* or *bak* (beck, stream), and *berwe*, another form of *bergh*.

228. *Frithed in*, enclosed by a wood, wooded thickly round. A *frith* is a wood surrounded by a fence or hedge; see *Frith* in my Dict. The line means—'It (i. e. the hill of Bear-no-false-witness) is hedged round by florins and many other fees;' i. e. by the bribes which tempt man to break the ninth commandment.

232. This description of Truth's abode may have been partly imitated from the French poem Le Chastel d'Amour, by Bishop Grosteste, translated under the title of the Castle of Love. See 'Castel off Loue,' ed. Weymouth, p. 31; whence I quote the following lines:—

'On trusti roche heo [i. e. the castle] stondeþ faste,
And wiþ depe diches beþ bi-caste.
And þe carnels so stondeþ vp-riht,
Wel i-planed and feir i-diht.
Seue barbicans þer beoþ i-wrouht;
With gret ginne al bi-þouht,
And euerichon haþ ȝat and tour;
þer neuer ne fayleþ socour.'

See also note to l. 270, p. 105.

235. *Kernels*, battlements; spelt *kirnels* in Cursor Mundi, 9901, and

carnels in the Castle of Love; see note to l. 232. The O.Fr. *crenel* had two senses, viz. (1) a battlement; and (2) a loophole. It comes to much the same thing, as the battlements have embrasures between them. Cf. Lat. *crena*, a notch, whence Lat. *crenellus*, O.Fr. *crenel;* cf. Eng. *cranny*. We often find that, in olden times, the barons obtained leave to *crenellate*, or fortify, their castles. In the Ancren Riwle, p. 62, we have—'þe *kerneaus* of þe castel beoð hire huses þurles;' i.e. the loopholes of the castle are the windows of their houses.

236. *Boteraced*, buttressed. In MS. B (Bodley 841) of the B-text, we have *bretaskid;* in MS. Vernon (A-text) we have *brutaget*, and in MS. U (Univ. Coll. Oxford, A-text) we have *briteschid*. These words signify 'provided with a *bretage* or *bretische*,' i.e. with a parapet. Colonel Yule, in his edition of Marco Polo, i. 302, says—'*Bretesche*, *Bertisca* (whence *brattice*, and *bartizan*) was a term applied to any boarded structure of defence or attack, but especially to the timber parapets and roofs often placed on the top of the flanking-towers in mediæval fortifications; and their use quite explains the sort of structure here intended;' viz. in Marco Polo's Travels, bk. ii. cap. iv.

249. 'To open and undo' [c]; 'to lift up the wicket' [b, a]. The reading *wynne vp* [a] presents no difficulty; it means to get up or lift up by force; compare the Lowland Scotch use of the verb *win*. The word in [b] may be read either as *wayne* or as *wayue*, but *wayue* is better. With *wayue* compare—'*wafte* he vpon his wyndowe' (he waved open his window), Allit. Poems, ed. Morris, B. 453; and cf. Icel. *veifa*, to wave. We find *wayne* in the Destruction of Troy, ed. Panton and Donaldson (E. E. T. S.); but I think it should be *wayue*.

250. Note the various readings—'shut against us all' [c]; 'ate unroasted apples' [b]; 'ate their bane' [a]. The Latin quotation is thus Englished in MS. Harl. 7322, fol. 143:—

'þe ȝates of parais · þoruth eue weren iloken,
And þoruth oure swete ladi · Aȝein hui beoþ noupe open.'

Political, Rel., and Love Poems, ed. Furnivall, p. 230.
Compare also the following:—
'Paradise yettis all opin be throu the'—
where *the* = *thee*, the person addressed being the Virgin Mary; see Morris's edition of Chaucer, vol. vi. p. 310. Compare too An Old English Miscellany, ed. Morris, p. 194; Legends of the Holy Rood, ed. Morris, p. 205 (where *keiþed* should be *keiyed*). In the Anglo-Saxon version of Ælfric's Homily on the Assumption of the Virgin, ed. Thorpe, i. 446, we have a passage which the editor translates by—'Through our old mother Eve the gate of heaven's kingdom was closed against us, and again, through Mary it is opened to us, by which she herself has this day gloriously entered.' This homily is imitated from Jerome's epistle to Paula and Eustochium, but the only similar passages which I can find there are the following:—'Ac per hoc, quicquid maledictionis infusa est per Euam, totum abstulit benedictio Mariae;' and again—'Quapropter gaudete, gaudete, inquam,

C. PASS. VIII. 251. B. PASS. V. 622. A. PASS. VI. 102. 105

quia uobis uia patefacta est caelorum;' Opera S. Hieronymi, ed. Migne, vol. 11, col. 127 and col. 141. But I suspect that these are the original passages whence were derived, not only the sentence quoted by our author, but other similar allusions.

251. *Vnleek hure*, unlocked it; (*hure* = her, i.e. the gate; other MSS. have *hire, hit, it*). *Of grace*, by her grace, as a favour.

260. (*not in* b, a.) See John xvi. 23.

265. *Worst þow*, thou shalt be; also written *worstow* [b], and *worþestou* [a]. *Dryuen out as deuh*, driven forth and dispersed like dew. See Hosea xiii. 3.

268. *To lete wel by thiselue*, to think much of thyself; cf. l. 263. *Lette* is a misprint for *lete*.

270. *Seuene sustres*, seven sisters. To counteract the seven deadly sins, seven Christian virtues were enumerated by early theologians. See note to C. vii. 3, p. 71. Cf. Castle of Love, ed. Weymouth, p. 39. Sometimes the number of the seven guardians was made up in another way, viz. by adding the three chief spiritual virtues, Faith, Hope, and Charity, to the four cardinal ones, viz. Prudence, Temperance, Justice, and Fortitude.

It is probable that the idea of this passage is a very old one. There is something very like it in Hermas, Pastor, bk. iii. similitude ix. v. 140 (ed. Hone), in Hone's Apocryphal Gospels.

277. 'For she pays for (i.e. ransoms) prisoners in places and in pains.' See *Prison* in the Glossary.

282. *Bote grace be the more*, unless mercy be extended.

283. *Kitte-pors*, thief. On cut-purses, see Chambers, Book of Days, ii. 669.

285. *Wyte God*, God defend (us); an old oath, from the verb *witen* in the sense of defend, guard. It occurs in the French Romance of King Horn, MS. Harl. 527, fol. 72 b, col. 2—'Ben iurez *Wite God* kant auerez beu tant,' i.e. you freely swear 'God defend us,' when you shall have drunk so much. It is quite different from the more common expression 'God wot,' i.e. God knows.

Wafrestre, a female seller of wafers; see note to Pass. xvi. 199.

288. *Mercy* is here the Virgin Mary. Cf. Cursor Mundi, l. 10062.

—— (b. 5. 651.) 'Thou shalt say I am thy sister; I know not where they have gone to;' or, 'what has become of them.' *Bicome* is the past tense pl., and the phrase *wher þei bicome*, is like the modern—'where they can have got to;' or, 'what has become (*or* come) of them.' The best illustration of this is from the romance of Joseph of Arimathie, ed. Skeat, l. 607, where the white knight is described as vanishing from sight, in consequence of which the spectators wonder 'where þe white kniht *bi-com*,' i.e. where he had gone to, or what had become of him.

292. *Villam emi*, I have bought a farm, etc.; St. Luke xiv. 18–20.

299. 'Then was there one named Active, he seemed to be a husband.' Here *husband* may mean husbandman, but I think it is to be taken literally in this passage. Cf. Pass. xvi. 194–233.

301. *Synnen*, sin, is the right reading; it means to sin against the seventh commandment.

304. *For a kytte*, because of a Kit, i.e. because of a wife. *Kit* was no doubt a common name enough; but the point of the allusion is to be found in the fact that it was the name of the poets *own* wife; see Pass. vi. 2; xxi. 473.

305. 'Though I may suffer tribulation.'

307. 'But the way is so bad, unless one were to have a guide.' Cf. *wikkede weyes* in Pass. x. 31.

The two last lines of this Passus (in the C-text) are at the beginning of a new Passus in the two older texts.

308. *Ech fot*, i.e. every step of the way.

NOTES TO C. PASSUS IX. (B. Pass. VI.; A. Pass. VII.)

N.B. The two first lines of B. Pass. vi. and A. Pass. vii. belong to C. Pass. viii.

C. ix. l. [B. vi. 3; A. vii. 3.] *Perken*, i.e. Peterkin, the diminutive of Peter; hence the names Perkins, Parkinson, etc.; cf. l. 112 below. Concerning the oath by St. Peter, see note to Pass. viii. 182, p. 102.

2. *An half-acre*, i.e. a small piece of ground. This term was used generally, without *special* reference to the exact size of the field. *Eren*, to plough; as in Deut. xxi. 4; 1 Sam. viii. 12; Is. xxx. 24. See Wright's Bible Word-book; and cf. Pass. xxii. 268. It is often wrongly said to be 'derived' from the Lat. *arare*, but it is merely *cognate* with it.

8. *For shedynge*, i.e. to prevent the shedding or spilling of wheat; alluding to the loss of grain when sacks are badly sewn or are out of repair. Cf. *for colde*, B. 6. 62, commented on in the note to l. 59 below, p. 108.

11. Compare Ancren Riwle, p. 421—'Make no purses, to gain friends therewith, nor blodbendes of silk; but shape, and sew, and mend church vestments and poor people's clothes.' For a full description of a chasuble, often ornamented with 'a mass of rich golden needlework,' see Rock, Church of our Fathers, i. 314—371.

15. 'For I shall give them (the poor) their sustenance, unless the land fail to yield produce;' i.e. as long as I can afford it: with a reference to the frequent dearths that happened about this time.

16. *For oure lordes loue in (of) heuene;* for love of our Lord in heaven. Observe the difference of arrangement, especially when *of* is used, as in [b, a]. So, in Chaucer, *the Grekis hors Sinon*, is *the horse of Sinon the Greek;* see other instances in the note to Pass. xvi. 131. Cf. b. 6. 223 below.

26. Lord Cobham, speaking of the duties of knights, said—'In knight-

C. PASS. IX. 29. B. PASS. VI. 31. A. PASS. VII. 33. 107

hood are all they which beare sword by law of office. These should defend God's lawes, and see that the gospell were purely taught, conforming their lives to the same, and secluding all false preachers . . . . They ought also to preserve God's people from oppressors, tyrants, and thieves; to see the Clergy supported, so long as they teach purely, pray rightly, and minister the sacraments freely;' Wordsworth's Eccl. Biog. i. 362. The context of Cobham's speech shews that he was following the old threefold division of the church into the Oratores (priests), Bellatores (warriors), and Laboratores (commons); and he had no doubt learnt this from Wyclif, who has very similar expressions. See Wyclif's Works, ed. Arnold, iii. 130, 131, 145, 206.

29. *Bockes*, bucks [c, a]; *brockes*, badgers [b]. See *Brock* in Halliwell's Dict., and *Brok* in Prompt. Parv. A badger had three names, viz. a *bawsin*, a *brock*, and a *gray;* Juliana Berners, Book of St. Alban's, sig. D. vi.; Dyce's Skelton, ii. 303.

30. 'And tame thy falcons' [c]; 'And go and tame for thyself falcons' [b]; 'And fetch home for thyself falcons' [a].

32. Compare Rich. Redeles, iv. 35.

36. Probably borrowed from Wyclif; compare his Works, ed. Arnold, iii. 206.

37. 'When you fine any man, let Mercy be the assessor of the fine;' i. e. let the fine be a light one. The next line means—'and let Meekness be your master (i. e. rule over you), in spite of all that Meed can do. The expression 'maugre mede chekes,' lit. in spite of Meed's cheeks, is to the same effect as the modern expression 'in spite of his teeth.' Cf. Chaucer's use of 'maugre hir heed;' Kn. Tale, 311, 1760.

40. 'Take it (i. e. the present) not, in case you may not be deserving of it; for you will have to repay it, it may be, and to pay somewhat dearly for it.' The end of the latter line slightly varies in [b] and [a]. The line following, having reference to purgatory, does not appear in the C-text.

42. See a tale about a Knight and a Bondman in Robert of Brunne, Handl. Synne, 8671, seqq. Cf. Luke xiv. 10.

45. *Vuel to knowe*, hard to discern; just as *vuel to defye* means hard to digest; Pass. vii. 87. The idea is, that all are equal in the grave.

46. The last part of the line varies in [b]. In [c] it means—'or a *quean* from a *queen*.' We make a difference of spelling in these words, but they are, of course, mere doublets, and both mean 'woman.' It is obviously impossible to tell which is which; nor is it material.

47. A knight was, above all things, expected to be courteous and true; cf. Chaucer, Prol. 46; Sq. Tale, 95.

50. *Hold nat of* is the same as *holde with none* [b], or *hold not þou with* [a]; i. e. do not encourage.

Harlotes, ribalds; a term here applied to tellers of loose stories, whence our author calls them 'the devil's *disours*,' i.e. the devil's story-tellers. They held forth in the hall 'atte mete,' whilst their employers were eating. They were *men*, as said in l. 51; see also note to Pass. v. 113, p. 57. Cf.

108   C. PASS. IX. 54.   B PASS. VI. 57.   A. PASS. VII. 51.

Pass. xvi. 171; see *Diseur* in Cotgrave; and *disour* in Gower, Conf. Amantis, ed. Pauli, iii. 167.

54. *Seynt Gyle*, saint Giles or Ægidius. His day was Sept. 1; see an account of him in Chambers' Book of Days, ii. 296; and see note to B. 15. 267. In [b] and [a] the knight swears by saint James.

59. Halliwell explains *Cockers* 'as a kind of rustic high shoes, or half-boots, fastened with laces or buttons. Old stockings without feet are also so called.' Probably it means old stockings without feet, worn as gaiters. Jamieson tells us that coarse stockings without feet are called *hoggers* in Ross-shire. Compare the ballad of Dowsabell in Percy's Reliques, written by Drayton; where *cockers* seems to mean buskins or gaiters:—

'His mittens were of bauzens [*badger's*] skinne,
His *cockers* were of cordiwin [*Cordovan leather*],
His hood of miniveere.'

For colde [b, a] means—as a protection against cold. A good parallel instance of this use of *for* occurs in Chaucer's Sir Thopas, 'for percinge of his herte;' C. T. Group B., l. 2052. See also B. 1. 24.

60. *Hoper*, a seed-basket. 'Vas cum quo seminatores seminant, a sedelepe or a hopere;' MS. Gloss., pr. in Rel. Antiq. i. 7. It was also called a *seed-leep*, a *cob*, or a *seed-cob*. The 'hoper' here mentioned held a bushel.

61. In his Glossary of certain Lincolnshire words (Eng. Dial. Soc.) Mr. Peacock has—'*Breadcorn*, corn to be ground into *breadmeal* (i. e. flour with only a portion of the bran taken out, from which brown bread is made); not to be used for finer purposes. It is a common custom of farmers, when they engage a bailiff, to give him a certain sum of money per annum, and to allow him also his *bread-corn*, at 40s. per quarter.' In this case, Piers uses some of this for sowing.

68. *Maugre ho by-grucche*, in spite of him that grumbles. See the variations in [b] and [a].

71. *Iogelour*, juggler; Lat. *ioculator*. See Tyrwhitt's note to Chaucer, C. T. l. 11453. Ritson, Metrical Romances, i. pp. clix, ccv of Preface, insists that *jougleour* ought never to be misspelt *jongleur*, as is often done; but this is a question of chronology, the form *jongleur* being the later one; see *Iougleur* and *Iongleur* in Cotgrave. See also Warton, Hist. Eng. Poet. ed. 1840, i. 82; ii. 10, 168. There is an old play called Jack Juggler; see Dodsley's Old Plays, ed. Hazlitt, vol. ii. The expression 'And ye Janettes of the stewys' occurs in the Towneley Mysteries, p. 314.

77. 'Deleantur de libro uiuentium, et cum iustis non scribantur,' Ps. lxviii. 29 (Vulgate). William interprets the last part of the quotation to mean, that churchmen ought not to receive tithes from such people. Cf. Pass. vii. 306. On the subject of *tithes*, see Wordsworth, Eccl. Biog. i. 319.

79. *Thei ben ascaped*, etc. Dr. Whitaker paraphrases this by—'they have escaped payment by good luck'—which is probably right. For *aunter*, the Vernon MS. reads *thrift*, success.

84. Here Piers again begins speaking. In [b], he begins at l. 84; in [a], at l. 75.

86. *Let god worthe*, may God be with all, etc. See Matt. xxiii. 2.

90. Dr. Whitaker rightly suggests that all the MSS. are wrong here. It is obvious that *worchyng* is an error for *wording*, or for some equivalent expression; for see l. 91. Cf. Matt. xxiii. 3.

95. Lines 95-111 contain Piers' *biqueste*, i. e. his will. It begins with a common formula—*In dei nomine*. He bequeaths his soul to his Maker, his body to the church to which he paid tithes, his money to his wife and children. Whitaker remarks upon this passage—'To commit the soul to Him who made it, was, in the course of a century and a half after this time, accounted so heretical, that the church would not have kept the testator's bones. For this very offence, and for omitting the names of the Virgin Mary and other saints, as joint legatees, the body of a Mr. Tracy was dug up out of his grave.' See Tracie's will in Massingberd, Eng. Ref. p. 165; also in Chambers, Book of Days, ii. 429.

101. The word *he* clearly refers, as in l. 103, to the *persona ecclesiae*, the parson. The Vernon MS. has *heo*, the feminine form, with reference to the word *chirche* preceding it.

103. Instead of *holden* [b, a], we find in [c] the form *holdinge*. This represents a common corruption, which appears also in *beholding*, as used for *beholden* by Shakespeare and others. See Rich. III., ii. 1. 129; Jul. Caesar, iii. 2. 70; and Abbott, Shak. Grammar, 3rd. ed. sect. 372.

104. 'And mention me in his commemoration.' See note to Pass. viii. 27, p. 96.

109. For *Lukes*, MSS. of the A-type have *Chestre*; cf. B. 5. 467, and the note on p. 88. *Lukes* is Lucca (as in Pass. v. 194), formerly also spelt *Luca*, where there was a famous cross. *Luke* (for Lucca) occurs in Jewel's works, ii. 917 (Parker Soc.).

—— (b. 6. 105.) 'My plough-foot shall be my pike-staff, and pick (peck, or pierce) in two the roots' [b] 'My plough-put shall be my pike, and push at the roots' [a]. To understand this, it must be remembered that the pike-staff (or pike) means the pilgrim's spiked staff, as explained in note to Pass. vii. 329. Piers says that, instead of carrying a pike-staff like a pilgrim, he will make good use of his plough-foot, so as to push aside or pierce through the roots that are in the soil. In [a], the reading is *plouh-pote* (i. e. plough-put), where *pote* is used in the sense of something to poke or push with; see '*Pote*, (1) to push, or kick; (2) a broad piece of wood used by thatchers to open the old thatch and *thrust in* the new straw,' in Halliwell; cf. *puten*, to push, in Stratmann. The parts of a plough, according to Gervase Markham's Complete Husbandman (quoted in Prof. Rogers' Hist. Agric. in England, i. 534), are (1) the plough-beam; (2) the skeath; (3) the plough's principal hale, on the left; (4) the plough-head; (5) the plough-spindles; (6) the right-hand hale; (7) the plough-rest; (8) the shelboard; (9) the coulter; (10) the share; (11) the plough-foot. The plough-foot is explained to be 'an iron implement, passed through a mortise-hole, and fastened at the farther end of the beam by a

110 **C. PASS. IX. 112. B. PASS, VI. 107. A. PASS. VII. 98.**

wedge or two, so that the husbandman may, at his discretion, set it higher or lower; the use being to give the plough earth, or put it from the earth, for the more it is driven downward the more it raises the beam from the ground, and makes the beam forsake the earth; and the more it is driven upward, the more it lets down the beam, and makes the irons bite the ground.' It was also called a *plough-shoe*, or *ferripedalis;* id. p. 537. A similar definition of a plough-foot, as being 'a staye to order of what depenes the ploughe shall go,' is given in Fitzherbert's Boke of Husbandry, fol. 2, back. In a modern plough, small wheels are generally used instead of it.

In the A-text, MS. H (Harleian 875) reads *plowbat*. I suppose the *plowbat* is not the same as the *ploughfoot*, but is rather to be identified with the *ploughstaff* or *ploughpaddle*, which was no fixed part of the plough at all, but a sort of paddle sometimes used for cleaning a plough, or clearing it of weeds, or for breaking very large clods. This is alluded to by Strutt, Manners and Customs, ii. 12.

112. *Perkyn*, little Piers or Peter; the same as Peterkin. It is merely a familiar term for Piers in this passage, as in l. 1.

119. *Hye pryme*. This expression occurs in a poem by Lydgate, which is better known, perhaps, than any other of his, named 'The London Lickpeny:'

'Then to Westmynster gate I presently went,
When the sonn was at *hyghe pryme*.'—MS. Harl. 367.

It seems to mean, when *prime was ended*, and it certainly marks the first break in the day's work. Cotgrave explains *prime* as the first hour of the 'artificial day' (or day according to the sun) which begins at about 8 in winter, 4 in summer, and at 6 only at the equinoxes; but Mr. Brae, in his edition of Chaucer's Astrolabe, pp. 90-101, makes it clear that, in Chaucer's time, the word was not used with reference to the artificial day, but with reference to the 'natural day,' or day as marked by a clock. Again, some explain *prime* to be the *fourth part* of the natural day, viz. from 6 o'clock till 9 A.M.; see Tyrwhitt's note, Cant. Tales, l. 3904. Others again explain *prime* to mean 6 A.M. It is easy to reconcile these variations by supposing that reference was made sometimes to the *beginning*, sometimes to the *end* of the period from 6 to 9, or again, sometimes to the *whole* of that period. By putting together the various passages where Chaucer uses the word *prime*, I have shewn, in my edition of Chaucer's Astrolabe, p. lxii., that the term was commonly used in the sense suggested by Tyrwhitt, viz. as denoting the period from 6 to 9 A.M.; but, when restricted to a particular moment, it meant the *end* of that period, or 9 A.M. only. It was probably to avoid the usual vagueness in the use of the word that the phrase *high prime* is here employed; since the latter clearly means that the period of prime was ended, or that it was 9 o'clock exactly. In like manner I should explain Chaucer's *fully pryme*, in Sir Thopas; Cant. Tales, Group B. 2015; whilst in the Squyeres Tale, l. 360, the expression *pryme large* may very well mean a little past the hour of prime, a little past nine; in which case we must suppose that Chaucer is mentioning the very latest

C. PASS. IX. 122. B. PASS. VI. 117. A. PASS. VII. 108. 111

hour for rising, even after a night of unusual revelry. Mr. Dyce says—'concerning this word see Du Cange's Gloss. in Prima and Horae Canonicae, Tyrwhitt's Gloss. to Canterbury Tales, Sibbald's Gloss. to Chron. of Scot. Poetry, and Sir F. Madden's Gloss. to Syr Gawayne.'

It is clear from ll. 120 and 121, that Piers was a 'head harvest-man.' See Knight's Pictorial Hist. of England, i. 840; the notice of the 'head-reaper' in Cullum's History of Hawsted; and a good article on the duties of a ploughman in Chambers' Book of Days, i. 96.

122. *Atte nale* [b] = *atten ale* [c], or *at then ale*, i.e. at the ale.

123. *Hoy troly lolly* is the burden of a song, answering nearly to the modern *tol de rol*. In Ritson's Ancient Songs, vol. ii. p. 7, is a song, with a burden of *trolly loley* occurring at every third line; whilst in Hickscorner (Dodsley's Old Plays, ed. Hazlitt, i. 179) we find the same exclamation of *hey, troly, loly*. And Skelton (ed. Dyce, i. 15) says—

'Wyth *hey troly loly, lo*, whip here, Jak.'

Here is meant, that all which some of the men did towards ploughing the half-acre was to sit and sing choruses over their cups.

127. *Haue that recche*, take him who cares. *Recche* = may reck, as appears from the reading *reccheth*, i. e. recketh, in [b].

128. 'Then were *faitours* afraid;' see the remarks on *faitours* in the note to l. 179 below, where the former half of this line is repeated.

See also Pass. x. 61-218, and notes to Pass. ix. 188, x. 169.

138. *Gon abegged*, go a-begging. This construction was first, I believe, explained by myself, in my preface to the C-text, p. lxxxvii (E. E. T. S. edition), which see. I have there said that *gon abegged* is a corruption of the older reading *gon abeggeth* in the Ilchester MS. The *-ed* is a corruption of *-eth*, answering to the A.S. suffix *-að* or *-oð*, used in what are called verbal substantives, i. e. substantives derived from verbs. Thus, in Robert of Gloucester (in Specimens of English, Part ii., ed. Morris and Skeat, p. 14) we find—

'As he rod *an honte*þ · & par-auntre is hors spurnde'—

i. e. as he rode *a-hunting*, and his horse accidentally stumbled.

There is another example of this construction only a few lines further on, viz. in l. 246 (C-text), where we have 'gon abrybeþ' in two MSS. but 'gon abribed (*or* abribid)' in two others; and where the Ilchester MS. even has—'And gon abribeth and abeggeth.'

When once the ending *-ed* was thus sometimes used in place of the uncommon ending *-eth*, it was easily perpetuated, on account of its coincidence in form with that of the past participle. It was used, in particular, with the verb *to go*. I give four clear examples of it in Chaucer and Gower.

In the Wyf of Bathes Prologue (Cant. Tales, ed. Tyrwhitt, l. 5936) we have the expression *gon a caterwawed*, which clearly means 'to go a-caterwauling.'

In the Pardoneres Tale, Group C. l. 406 (ed. Tyrwhitt, 12340), we have the expression *gon a blakeberied*, which simply means go a-blackberrying, i. e. go where they list. Tyrwhitt gave up this expression as inexplicable, but it is really very simple when the right key is thus applied to it.

So in Gower's Confessio Amantis, bk. i, to 'ryde amayed' means 'to ride a-Maying,' for we are expressly told that the month was May.

And in Conf. Amant. bk. vi. we read of a priest who is drunk, and 'goth astrayed,' i. e. goes wandering about.

Here are seven examples of this construction. I leave it to the reader to find more.

146. *Ancres and hermits.* See notes to Pass. i. 30, 51; pp. 5, 8. And see the Reply of Friar Daw Topias, in Polit. Poems, ed. Wright, ii. 64.

It is certain that *nones* originally meant about three o'clock in the afternoon, though it was afterwards shifted so as to mean midday, our modern *noon.* There seem to have been two principal meal-times, viz. dinner at about nine or ten A.M., and supper at about five or six P.M.; cf. ll. 275, 278. See Wright's Hist. of Domestic Manners, p. 155. We have reference to two meals in the day in Pass. vii. 429 (see note to that line), and in l. 434 Glutton is made to confess that he had wrongly eaten, on fasting-days, 'before none;' cf. Pass. iii. 100. The question of the time meant in this passage is not easy to settle. Taken in connection with the passages just referred to, and remembering the use of 'none' in other passages, I think that the hour meant is what we now call noon, viz. 12 o'clock; and that we are to understand the anchorites and hermits as having but *one* meal; that meal being taken at the hour of twelve, because the 'dinner-time' was at 12 instead of 9 on fasting-days. In Our English Home, p. 34, we read—'In the rules for the regulation of the household of the Princess Cecil, mother of Edward the fourth, it is laid down, that upon ordinary days dinner was to be held at eleven, but upon fasting-days at twelve.' So in The Myrour of Our Lady, ed. Blunt, p. 15, we read—'At houre of tyerse [here 9 A.M.] labourers desyre to haue theyr dyner.... At houre of none the sonne is hiest.' The hours varied at different dates, but, in our author's time, dinner and supper were the only meals.

In Riley's Memorials of London, p. 265, note 7, we learn that certain donations for drink to workmen are called in the Letter-book G, fol. iv. (27 Edw. III.), *nonechenche.* This is the modern *nuncheon;* and the spelling shews that the derivation is from *none,* noon, and *schenche,* a pouring out or dispensing of drink, from A.S. *scencan,* to pour out drink, to 'skink.' Similarly, the prov. E. *nammut,* luncheon, is *noon-meat.*

—— (b.6. 151.) The word *posteles* is only another spelling of *apostles,* and is not to be confused with *postills,* i. e. commentaries. Crowley actually has the reading *apostles;* and perhaps it is to the point to observe that the word *apostle* is written *postuli* in Icelandic. We have here possibly an allusion to Wyclif's 'poor priests,' as they were called; cf. Massingberd's English Reformation, p. 133. In any case, the word is clearly used with the sense of 'preachers.'

158. *Wolveskynnes* [b], of the kind or nature of a wolf. Cf. P. Ploughman's Crede, l. 459.

160. 'There will be no plenty, quoth Piers, if the plough lie idle' [c]; 'Shall never any plenty be among the people, whilst my plough lies idle' [b].

C. PASS. IX. 165. B. PASS. VI. 170. A. PASS. VII. 154. 113

165. Cf. Rich. Redeles, iii. 284.

166. *Sette peers at a pese*, accounted Piers at the value of a pea; i.e. set him at naught. The form *pese* or *pees* (Lat. *pisum*) is quite correct; the plural is *pesen* or *peses*; see ll. 176, 307; and A. 7. 176. The *singular* form *pea* really exhibits as great a blunder as if we were to develop *chee* as the singular of *cheese;* yet it is not a solitary instance, since we have 'that heathen Chinee' as a formation from *Chinese, cherry* from *cherris* (Lat. *cerasus*), *sherry* from *sherris* (Span. *Xeres*), etc.; see an article on the words Chinee, Maltee, Portuguee, Yankee, Pea, Cherry, Sherry, and Shay, by Danby P. Fry, Esq.; Phil. Soc. Trans. 1873-4, p. 253.

168. 'And whooped after (i.e. called loudly for) Hunger, who heard him at the (very) first.' The reader should notice that *hunger* has here a very strong meaning, and is nearly equivalent to *famine*. See Trench, Select Glossary, s. v. *Hunger*.

174. The phrase 'lene as lanterne' occurs in an alliterative poem on the Destruction of Jerusalem, MS. Laud 656, fol. 16 *b*, l. 8 from bottom of the leaf. The expression in the text, 'lyk a lanterne,' is very graphic. The effect of Hunger's attack upon the Britoner was such that one could see through him.

179. *Faitours* has occurred before, Pass. iii. 193, ix. 128; it is equivalent to lying vagabonds, or canting rogues. The following extract is from The Athenaeum of Feb. 27, 1869. 'In a MS. of the early part of the fifteenth century—William of Nassington's translation of John Waldby's treatise on the Paternoster, etc.—we find an earlier notice than we had expected of shamming beggars in England. Their trade must have been a well-known one, as they had a special name—*Faytours*—slugs or lazy scoundrels:—

"*ffaytours* wynnes mete and moné
Of þaim þat has mercy and pyte;
ffore lyther whyles cane þai fynde,
To make þaim seme crokede and blynde,
Ore seke, or mysays, to mennes syght;
So cane þai þaire lymes dyght,
ffor men suld þaim mysays deme;
Bote þai are noght swilke als þai seme."'

185. 'They cut their copes, and made them into jackets.' The cope was 'a kind of cloak worn during divine service by the clergy. It reaches from the neck nearly to the feet, and is open in the front, except at the top, where it is united by a band or clasp;' Hook's Church Dictionary. The clergy were specially distinguished by the use of such 'long clothes,' as William calls them; see Pass. vi. 41. But long clothes were unsuited for hard manual labour, and are therefore here described as being cut short. Cf. Strutt, Manners and Customs, ii. 85; and see *courtepy* in Chaucer's Prol. 290.

188. *Bedreden* [b], bedridden; see the Glossary. 'Also freris seyn in dede, þat hit is medeful to leeve þe comaundement of Crist, of gyvynge of almes to pore feble men, to pore croked men, to pore blynde men, and to *bedraden* men, and gif þis almes to ypocritis, þat feynen hem holy and

nedy;' Wyclif's Works, iii. 372. *He botnede*, he cured [c]; *were botened*, were cured [b]. The word *botnede* is not very correctly used. The right distinction is that *boten* means to better, to cure, but *botnen* is to become better, to recover, to be cured, according to the analogy of Gothic verbs ending in -*nan*: but such a difference is seldom made at this date.

191. This mention of *five* orders of friars is very remarkable, and is peculiar to MSS. of the C-class. It occurs again in Pass. x. 343, and xvi. 81. In most other passages we have mention of *four* orders only; see note to Pass. i. 56, p. 9. The *fifth* order was that of the Crutched Friars, and the mention of them is an indication, probably, of the date of this latest version of the poem; but, unfortunately, it does not afford a clue that can be worked out. 'Confluxerant in aedes quatuor ordines Mendicantium; his adjunxit sese *quintus Cruciferorum*, adversus hunc, ceu nothum, quatuor illi magno tumulto coorti sunt; rogabant ubi vidissent unquam plaustrum quinque rotarum;' etc. Erasmus, Funus, Colloq. ii. 59.

192. *Bayarde*, a common name for a horse; used by Chaucer, Gower, and Skelton. William refers to the custom of giving horses *bread* to eat, as is still common on the continent. Cf. l. 225. A statute of Edw. III. orders—that horsebread be made only of beans and peas, without other mixture. Sometimes poor people had no better fare. In Gammer Gurton's Needle, Act i. sc. 2, Hodge says he has had nothing to eat the whole day 'save this pece of dry horsbred.'

207. *Erthe* [c]; *erde* [b]; *hurde* [a]. The best reading is *erde*, A.S. *earde*. The sense is well illustrated by the A.S. version of St. Luke iv. 23—'dó hér on þínum *earde*,' etc., i. e. do here in thy *country*.

216. *Final*, complete, full, perfect. Gower has the expression 'final pees,' i. e. perfect peace, in the Prologue to his Confessio Amantis; ed. Pauli, i. 36. Whitaker misprints it *smal*, and explains 'no smal' as 'little,' simply ignoring the negative.

217. *Hit ben* [c] is the common phrase, and is equivalent to *They are* [b] or *heo beoþ* [a]; cf. l. 52. *Blody broþren*, brethren by blood or birth; the sense is obvious, but this use of *bloody* is extremely rare. Compare—'*Bloody*, well-bred, coming of a good stock. " He comes of a *bloody* stock; that's why he's good to poor folks;"' Peacock's Linc. Gloss. (E. D. S.).

221. After the pestilence of 1349, there was a want of labourers. Edward published a proclamation, compelling men and women, in good health, and under sixty years of age, to work at stated wages. But it was evaded, and, in harvest-time especially, exorbitant wages were both demanded and given. See Lingard, Hist. Eng. (3rd ed.), iv. 89; Th. Walsingham, ed. Riley, i. 276, 277; and Liber Albus, pp. 584, 634.

225. *Houndes bred*. The Prioresse in Chaucer (Prol. 147) fed her hounds with 'wastel breed.' Cf. Percy Household Book, p. 353.

226. *Abane hem*, give them disease, lit. poison them [c]; *Abate hem*, reduce them, keep them thin [b]; *bamme hem*, cozen them [a]. *For bollynge of here wombe*, to prevent swelling of their bellies, to keep them from growing fat. On this use of *for*, see notes to ll. 8 and 59, pp. 106, 108. Cf. 'Bean-belly Leicestershire,' in Hazlitt's Eng. Proverbs, p. 81.

C. PASS. IX. 231. B. PASS. VI. 224. A. PASS. VII. 210.

231. *Lene hem*, give to them ; lit. lend to them. Cf. Gal. vi. 2.

233. ' In misfortune or disease, if thou canst help them' [c].
Naughty [b], having naught.

> 'She had an idea from the very sound
> That people *with naught* were *naughty.*'
> Hood ; Miss Kilmansegg.

—— (b. 6. 228.) *Late god yworthe*, let God alone ; see note to Pass. i. 201. *Michi vindicta*, etc. ; Rom. xii. 19. *Vindictam* is the reading of the MSS., both here and in B. x. 369, and, though the Vulgate has *Mihi vindicta*, yet the same reading—*mihi vindictam*—will be found in the Ancren Riwle, pp. 184, 286 ; at p. 178 of Old Eng. Homilies, 2nd Series, ed. Morris ; and at p. 112 of Albertani Brixiensis Liber Consolationis, ed. Thor Sundby. So that we should not be warranted in making the ' correction.'

246. ' Propter frigus piger arare noluit ; mendicabit ergo aestate, et non dabitur illi ;' Prov. xx. 4. The quotation above is from Gen. iii. 19. *Sapience* (b. 6. 237) means the book of Wisdom ; William frequently refers to the wrong book of the Bible for his quotations. In [c], the MSS. mostly read *hyeme* for *estate*. However, *estate* is right, and the reading *hyeme* is an adaptation, to suit our own climate. On the word *abrybeþ* [c], see note to l. 138 above, p. 111.

247. *With mannes face* [b, a]. An allusion to a common representation of the evangelists, which likens Matthew to a *man*, Mark to a *lion*, Luke to a *bull*, and John to an *eagle*: cf. Ezekiel i. 10, Rev. iv. 7. Sometimes the arrangement varied ; see the Ormulum, vol. i. p. 201. Of course *face* has no special force here ; yet it is rather curious that we find in one case, and in addition to the usual symbol of St. Matthew, a *man's head*. A striking example of this occurs in the splendid Lindisfarne MS. of the Gospels (MS. Cotton, Nero D. 4), where St Matthew is depicted writing, with a man's head peering at him from behind a curtain.

—— (b. 6. 241.) *Nam*, a mina. It is glossed in the Laud MS. by the words—'a besaunt ;' and in the Vernon MS. [a] by the word 'talentum.' Wyclif's version has 'besaunt' in Luke xix. 16. The parable occurs both in Matt. xxv. and Luke xix. ; but the use of the word *nam* shews that our author was thinking rather of St. Luke's account, where the word μνᾶ is used, from the Hebrew *maneh*. See the article on *Weights* in Smith's Bible Dictionary. In l. 243 [b], we have the better spelling *mnam*. For the value of a *besant*, see Ormulum, ed. White, ii. 390.

—— (b. 6. 251.) Richard Rolle de Hampole, amongst others, carefully distinguishes between *active life*, or *bodily* service of God, and *contemplative life* or *ghostly* (i. e. spiritual) service. See his prose treatises, ed. Perry (E. E. T. S. 1866), p. 19 ; and see p. xi. of Mr. Perry's preface.

The distinction between these two kinds of life seems to have been founded upon St. James's epistle, especially (I suppose) the last verse of the first chapter.

C. PASS. IX. 283. B. PASS. VI. 252. A. PASS. VII. 237.

The two kinds of life are typified by Martha and Mary, Peter and John, and Rachel and Leah.

—— (b. 6. 252.) 'Beati omnes, qui timent Dominum; qui ambulant in uiis eius. Labores manuum tuarum quia manducabis; beatus es, et bene tibi erit.' Ps. cxxvii. 1, 2 (Vulgate). See the quotation at l. 262 [c].

—— (b. 6. 269.) *Afyngred*, greatly hungry. It is corrupted from the A.S. pp. *of-hyngred*, very hungry. The word occurs in the Vox and Wolf, in Hazlitt's Early Popular Poetry, vol. i. p. 58; Polit. Songs, ed. Wright, p. 342, l. 418; and in a note on 'The Tale of the Basyn and the Frere and the Boy;' (Pickering, 1836.) In [a] we have the equivalent word *a-longet* = *of-longet*, i. e. filled with longing, very greedy.

283. See the Parable of Dives in Pass. xx. 229-246, and the mention of Lazarus 'in Abraham's lap' in Pass. xix. 273.

286. On *souel*, see note to B. xvi. 11.

288. *Lacchedrawers*, thieves; also called *drawlacches*. See note to Pass. i. 45, p. 7. *Lolleres*, vagabonds; see note to Pass. x. 213, p. 126.

289. *Tyl the bord be drawe*, till the table be removed. The 'board' or table was laid upon trestles, and removed after meals; see Our English Home, p. 30.

290. *None*, the noon-tide meal; cf. note to l. 146 above, p. 112.

292. (b. 6. 271.) Ef.

'And ȝit ther is another craft that toucheth the clergie,
That ben thise false fisiciens that helpen men to die.'
Polit. Songs (Camd. Soc.), p. 333.

See Chaucer's Prologue, 'll. 411-444, and the description of physicians in Barclay's Ship of Fools, ed. Jamieson, i. 263.

293. A 'cloke of calabre' means a cloak trimmed with Calabrian fur. In the Coventry Mysteries, p. 242, we read—'Here colere splayed, and furryd with ermyn, *calabere*, or satan.' Calabre was a *grey* fur, the belly of which was *black*.—Riley, Memorials of London, pp. 329, 331.

295. Cf. Rich. Redeles, iii. 253.

304. 'In the parish of Hawsted, Suffolk, the allowance of food to the labourer in harvest was, two herrings per day, milk from the manor dairy to make cheese, and a loaf of bread, of which fifteen were made from a bushel of wheat. Messes of potage made their frequent appearance at the rustic board.'—Knight, Pict. Hist. England, i. 839. Mr. Knight obtained this information from the Rev. Sir John Cullum's History of Hawsted, which gives a great number of exact and curious details concerning the farm-life of the period at which our author wrote.

A certain passage in the Chester Plays (ed. Wright, p. 123) was evidently intended to describe and record the usual food of shepherds. See Harrison, Description of England (bk. ii. ch. 13); Andrew Boorde's Introduction of Knowledge, ed. Furnivall, especially pp. 258-282.

C. PASS. IX. 305.   B. PASS. VI. 283.   A. PASS. VII. 268.   117

With respect to the *prices* of provisions, some idea may be gained from those mentioned in Memorials of London, ed. Riley, p. 312, viz.:— 'best goose, 6*d*.; best sucking-pig, 8*d*.; best capon, 6*d*.; a hen, 4*d*.; best rabbit, 4*d*.; a roast goose, 7*d*.;' etc. This was in the year 1363. The reader may find most minute details in the History of Prices and Agriculture in England, by J. E. T. Rogers.

305. *Grys*, pig; see Pass. i. 227. *Green cheses*, i.e. fresh cheeses; see A. Boorde (as above), p. 226; and cf. The complaint of Scotland, ed. Murray, pp. 42, 43.

306. *A cake of otes*, an oat-cake [c]; *an hauer cake*, an oaten cake [b]; *a therf cake*, an unleavened cake [a]. 'Panis sine fermento, *therf breed*;' MS. Glos. pr. in Rel. Antiq. i. 6. 'Thei make the sacrament of *therf breed*;' Maundeville's Travels, ed. Halliwell, p. 121. And see Wyclif's Works, ii. 287.

309. We find mention of 'colopys of venyson' and 'colopes of the wyld dere' in Hazlitt's Early Pop. Poetry, vol. i. pp. 24, 28. Brand says, 'Slices of this kind of meat (i.e. salted and dried) are to this day termed *collops* in the north, whereas they are called *steaks* when cut off from fresh or unsalted flesh.'—Pop. Antiq. vol. i. p. 62. Cf. Pass. xvi. 67; and see *Riblette* in Cotgrave.

311. From this passage, and the frequent allusions to *cherry-fairs* in our old authors (see note to Pass. vii. 136), it is clear that cherries were a common fruit. Gough wrongly supposed that cherries were at this time unknown in England.

314. *Lammasse*, i.e. Loaf-mass, Aug. 1. In Anglo-Saxon times, a *loaf* was offered on this day, as an offering of first-fruits. See Chambers' Book of Days, ii. 154.

328. 'Panis de *coket*' is mentioned in a MS. of Jesus Coll. Oxford, 1 Arch. i. 29, fol. 268, as being slightly inferior to *wastel* bread. See the whole passage, now printed in Munimenta Academica, ed. Anstey, i. 180. The fine kinds of white bread were called simnel bread or *pain demaigne*, wastel bread, coket, clere matyn, and manchet bread. The common kinds of brown bread were tourte, trete, and bis. Cf. Riley, Memorials of London, p. 644; Chambers' Book of Days, i. 119; Strutt, Manners and Customs, iii. 57; Liber Albus (*Cocket* and *Bread* in the Index).

329. *Halpeny ale*; i.e. ale at a half-penny per gallon.

336. As to the high wages of labourers, see note to l. 221 above, p. 114. The statutes concerning them are alluded to in l. 341 below.

338. Dionysius Cato is the name commonly assigned to the author of a Latin work in four books, entitled Dionysii Catonis Disticha de Moribus ad Filium. The real author is unknown, but the work may perhaps be referred to the fourth century. It was very popular, both in Latin, and in English and French versions. William here quotes part of the 21st distich of the first book, which runs thus:—

'Infantem nudum quum te natura crearit,
Paupertatis onus patienter ferre memento.'

346. *Water*, i.e. floods; cf. l. 349.

348. Great disasters were often attributed to the malign influence of the planet Saturn. Besides this, great foresight was attributed to the god Saturn. This is very well illustrated by Chaucer's Knightes Tale, ll. 1585-1620. We may note also the following passage in the Commentary to book iii. c. xi. of the prophecies of John of Bridlington (ed. Wright). 'Primo est notandum, quod Saturnus est stella maxima nociva terræ et inductiva pestilenciarum ; unde, secundum Misaelem, Saturnus est planeta malevolus, frigidus, siccus, ponderosus, et nocturnus ; et, secundum Catholicon, in iudiciis signat moerorem et tristitiam.' It may be added that this remark was made with especial reference to the pestilence of 1361-2, and was the expression of the generally received opinion. Mr. Wright, in his Preface to Piers Plowman, p. xii., says, 'This terrible calamity [the Black Death of 1349] was said by the astrologers to have been brought about by an extraordinary conjunction of Saturn with the other planets, which happened scarcely once in a thousand years.' So also in the Shepheard's Kalender, ed. 1656, fol. O 1 :—'Saturne is the highest planet of all the seven ; . . . he giveth all the great *colds* and *waters;*. . .When he reigneth, there is much theft used, and little charity . . . and old folk shall be very sickly, many diseases shall reigne among the people, etc. . . . This planet is cause of hasty death,' etc.

In the A-text (earliest version), the Passus ends with this line. Ll. 349-355 (b. 328-332) were added afterwards ; wherein William imitates, not perhaps without ridicule, the mysterious prophecies which were then popular ; such as, for instance, the prophecies of John of Bridlington. Lines 351, 352, are, of course, inexplicable (cf. Pass. iv. 481-483) ; but the rest is clear enough. By *deth* is meant such a great pestilence as that which earned the name of the Black Death, and which was sometimes called simply 'the dethe,' as in Political, Religious, and Love Poems, ed. Furnivall, p. 98, l. 153. 'The pestilence shall withdraw, Famine shall then be the judge, and Dawe the ditcher (cf. Pass. vii. 369) shall die for hunger, unless God, of His goodness, grant us a truce.'

NOTES TO C. PASSUS X. (B. Pass. VII.; A. Pass. VIII.)

C. 10. 1. (B. 7. 1 ; A. 8. 1.) It has already been explained that *Truth* signifies God the Father. Cf. Pass. ii. 12 ; viii. 204 ; and see ll. 27, 37 below.

3. *A pena et culpa.* On this expression Mr. Arnold remarks (note to Wyclif's Works, i. 136)—'The ordinary indulgence absolved *poena, sed non culpa.* In theory, the guilt of sins, and the *eternal* punishment due to them, were remitted in the sacrament of penance ; it was the temporal punishment only, the *poena*, which the indulgence professed to remit, in whole or in part. But it is well known that, during the 14th and 15th centuries, a great laxity prevailed, if not in the actual wording of indulgences, at any rate in the language of those to whom their distribution was entrusted.' See also vol. iii. p. 362 of the same work. In l. 23 below, it clearly means *plenary* remission.

—— (b. 7. 14.) *Bothe the lawes*, i. e. our duty towards God, and towards our neighbours.

—— (a. 8. 17.) See a similar passage in ll. 264-268 of this Passus; C-text, p. 243.

17. *By here powere*, as far as lies in their power; a not uncommon phrase. We must not make the mistake of supposing *by* to signify *by means of* in this passage. Cf. note to Pass. vii. 297, p. 87.

21. 'And, together with them, to judge both quick and dead at doomsday' [c]; 'And at the day of doom, to sit at the high daïs' [b]; *or*, 'to sit with them at the daïs' [a]. Tyrwhitt, in a long note on Chaucer, Prol. 372, gives an account of the word daïs, in which he seems to have been misled by a false etymology. The daïs was, in fact, the table *itself* (Lat. *discus*), and the high daïs was the high table at the upper end of the hall. In later times, the name was transferred, sometimes to the platform on which the table stood, and sometimes to the canopy overhanging the table. See Cotgrave.

22. *Menye yeres*, i. e. many years' remission of purgatory.

30. *Mesondieux*, put for *maisons de dieu*, houses of God. A hospital was called a *maison-dieu* or *masondewe;* see Halliwell.

31. *Wikkede weyes*, i.e. bad roads [c, b]; *wikkede wones*, bad dwellings, ruinous cottages [a]. Cf. Pass. viii. 307. *With here good*, i. e. with their property or wealth.

32. The making and repairing of bridges was an excellent work of charity. Wyclif notices it; Works, iii. 283. See Rock, Church of Our Fathers, iii. 201, 202.

33. In the ordinances of the Gild of the Palmers, at Ludlow, we find provision for making a contribution out of the common chest, to enable any good poor girl of the gild 'either to go into a religious house or to marry, whichever she wishes to do;' English Gilds, ed. Toulmin Smith, p. 194. Dr. Rock, in his Church of Our Fathers, gives other examples; vol. iii. pp. 35, 53.

35. *Fauntekynes (scoleres) to scole.* To pay for the education of poor scholars, especially at Oxford, was justly esteemed an excellent form of charity. Cf. Chaucer, Prol. 301, 302; God Spede the Plough, 75.

38. To understand this passage, we must remember that it was the common belief that a dying man saw devils all around him, seeking to terrify him and make him despair. This is most clearly shewn by a passage in Hampole's Pricke of Conscience, ed. Morris, ll. 2220-2231, etc. In old woodcuts, it is not uncommon to see representations of devils gathering round the bed of a dying man; see, e. g. Wright's Hist. of Caricature, p. 68. It was thought that 'unto Michael alone belonged the office of leading each soul from earth to the judgment-seat of Christ;' Rock, Church of Our Fathers, iii. 149; see also p. 210. Cf. Rev. xii. 7, 8.

—— (a. 8. 39.) 'And form (i.e. prepare) your seats before the face of My Father.' Here *Truth* is, for the moment, identified with Christ instead of with God the Father, as elsewhere. The reference is obviously to John xiv. 2, 3.

—— (a. 8. 43.) 'And gave Will, for his writing, some woollen clothes; and, because he thus copied out the clause for them, they gave him many thanks.' For *Cause* (Vernon MS.), the reading *clause* (in MSS. T., U., H.) is a great improvement.

This interesting variation affords us yet one more instance in which the author mentions himself by name. He represents himself as writing out a new form of indulgence, coming (not from the Pope, but) from God Himself; and this new form was received with delight by the merchants. We also see that our author was sometimes employed as a scribe, and that he received payment in clothes instead of money from some of his employers.

45. (cf. b. 7. 39.) *Pre manibus*, in advance. See Pass. iv. 301, and the note, p. 50.

—— (b. 7. 41.) 'Qui pecuniam suam non dedit ad usuram, et munera super innocentem non accepit ;' Ps. xiv. 5 (Vulgate). The first verse of the same Psalm, which in English Bibles is Ps. xv., is quoted below, at l. 51 [b].

—— (b. 7. 43.) I do not know the source of this quotation. It somewhat resembles Ecclus. xxxviii. 2—'A Deo est enim omnis medela, et a rege accipiet donationem.'

(b. 7. 44.) Johan was probably some unscrupulous fellow of middle rank, and we should get very good sense by supposing that he was a cook like the 'master Johan' mentioned in Pass. xxii. 288, whose crowning merit was that he could make spiced meat acceptably.

—— (b. 7. 50.) 'No devil, at his deathday, shall harm him a mite, so that he will not be safe, and his soul too.' *Worth* is here a verb. The construction is awkward to express. Cf. note to l. 38 above.

52. (b. 7. 56.) *3e* [c] refers to the *wise men* (l. 51) ; and, similarly, *thei* [b] refers to the *legistres and lawyeres*, mentioned in l. 59 [b].

53. *Hus* [c] = *his* [a] is used generally, and is equivalent to *her* = their [b]. *Partynge hennes*, departure hence, i. e. death.

55. 'For it is simony to sell that which is sent (us) by grace ; that is to say, wit, and water, and wind, and fire, which is the fourth thing,' etc. [c]. 'But to buy water, nor wind, nor wit, nor fire, which is the fourth thing, *is a thing which Holy Writ never permitted*' [b]; where the words in italics are supplied from [a], to complete the sense, and *ne* (nor) would be better expressed in modern English by 'or.' Again— 'But to buy water, nor wind, nor wit (which is the third thing) Holy Writ never permitted ; God knows the truth' [a]. The constructions are awkward, but the sense is clear. *Wit* here takes the place of *earth*, along with three of the four elements ; and the meaning is—'Human intelligence is a gift of God, like three at least of the four elements,

C. PASS. X. 58. B. PASS. VII. 62. A. PASS. VIII. 64. 121

and is free for all men to profit by. Just as we should accord the free use of fire, water, and air to all men, so should we help them with our counsel and advice.' Our author is merely insisting that one form of charity (and a very good form of it) is to give sound advice and kindly counsel *even* to those who cannot afford to pay for it. One gross form of cruelty practised by some lawyers was to exact from a poor man all he could afford to pay, and then to pay no attention whatever to his case.

In the A-text, we have but *three* things mentioned, viz. wit, water, and wind. In l. 58 [a], they are called 'thralls,' i. e. servants, or things which are at all men's service.

*** For notes to B. 7. 56, 57 (A. 8. 60), see notes to ll. 52, 53, p. 120.

58. *With* [c, b] = *bi* [a], by means of ; cf. Pass. ix. 331.

66. *Hus thankus*, of his own choice, of his own free will : lit. of his thank. It is a very old phrase, and occurs twice in Chaucer's Knightes Tale ; ll. 768, 1249.

69. *Caton*, Cato. See note to Pass. ix. 338, p. 117. Prefixed to Cato's Distiches are some 'Breves sententiae,' of which the twenty-third consists only of the words—*Cui des, videto.* Mr. Wright says that by *the clerk of the stories* [b] is meant Peter Comestor (died A.D. 1198), to whom Lydgate, in his Minor Poems (p. 102, ed. Halliwell), gives the title of *maister of storyes;* and I find him mentioned again, by the same title in Pecock's Repressor, ii. 529 ; cf. i. 17. For some account of him, see Nouvelle Biographie Générale, tom. xi. col. 332; Paris, 1855. The title *clerk of stories* would then refer to the Historia Scholastica, of which Peter Comestor was the author. The Historia Scholastica is an account of all the chief events recorded in the Old and New Testaments, with additions from profane authors ; and, since it is composed of many parts, to each of which the title *historia* is given (as, e. g. Historia Libri Genesis, Historia Euangelica, etc.), it would naturally be called 'stories' in English. The passage which our author had in his mind was the following passage in Comestor's Historia Libri Tobie :— ' De substantia tua fac elemosynas, quia elemosyna ab omni peccata liberat, et magnum prestat fiduciam coram deo omnibus facientibus eam ;' which is abridged from Tobit iv. 7-11. In Pass. xviii. 40, our author quotes a passage from Tobit ii. 21, which is also in Comestor ; see the note to that passage.

—— (b. 7. 76.) Gregory the Great was pope from A. D. 590 to 604. But the quotation is really from the following :—' Ne eligas cui bene facias. . . . Incertum est enim quod opus magis placeat Deo ;' S. Eusebii Hieronymi Comment. in Ecclesiasten, cap. xi. 6; vol. 23, col. 1103, of Migne's edition : and see the text itself, viz. Eccles. xi. 6. Instead of 'Gregory,' William should have said 'Jerome,' who also was one of the four chief ' Latin Fathers ;' see Pass. xxii. 269, 270.

—— (b. 7. 85.) *Hath to buggen hym bred*, hath (enough) to buy himself bread. For the quotation at l. 83, see Luke xix. 23.

—— (b. 7. 86.) This quotation is not from the Bible. The original passage is—'Satis diues, qui pane non indiget. Nimium potens est, qui seruire non cogitur;' S. Hieronymi Epist. cxxv. ed. Migne, vol. i. col. 1085.

71. *And we nyme*, if we take. *And* (= if) occurs in all the best MSS.

72. *Prisones*, prisoners; as explained in the note to Pass. i. 2 (p. 2); so also in l. 180 below. *Puttes*, pits, i. e. dungeons.

74. 'That which, by their spinning, they manage to save up, that they spend in house-rent.' *Hit* is the antecedent to *That*.

75. 'Both in milk and meal, to make messes of porridge with, to satisfy their children with, that cry for food.' Here we note the peculiar situation of the preposition *with* (see note to Pass. i. 133); and the use of *gurles* for children of either sex (see note to Pass. ii. 29). *Papelote* is a sort of porridge, made with meal and milk, and used as food for children.

79. *Ruel* is the Fr. *ruelle*, a little street, or lane. Cotgrave has,—'la ruelle du lict, the space between the bed and the wall;' and this is the sense here, with reference to the place where the cradle was placed. See Wright's Homes of Other Days, p. 412, where we find the remark—'the space thus left between the bed and the curtains was perhaps what was originally called in French the *ruelle* (lit. the "little street") of the bed, a term which was afterwards given to the space between the curtains of the bed and the wall.' Cf. 'such a woman! I had rather see her *ruelle* than the palace of Louis le Grand;' Farquhar, Constant Couple, i. 1.

80, 81. 'Both to card and comb, to patch (or mend) and to wash, to rub and to reel, and to peel rushes.' The operations of carding and combing wool are well understood. To 'reel' means to wind the yarn or thread from the spindle upon a reel; see 'Relyn wyth a reêle, *Alabrizo*,' Prompt. Parv. p. 429; and '*Devider*, to wind (as yarn, etc.), to reele;' Cotgrave. The peeling of rushes was for the purpose of making rushlights for use in the long winter evenings; see Notes and Queries, 4 S. iii. 552, iv. 43. Palsgrave has—'I pyll rysshes, *Ie pille des ioncz*. In wynter tyme good houswyues pyll risshes to burne in stede of candles, *en hyuer les bonnes mesnaigieres pillent des ioncz pour les brusler en lieu de chandelles.*'

85. *Afyngrede and afurst*, hungry and thirsty; see note to B. vi. 269, p. 116. *To turne the fayre outwarde*, to keep up appearances, to keep up a look of respectability; a truly expressive phrase. This description of the struggling life of the honest well-conducted poor is in William's best manner, and is of undying interest.

91. 'And (there are) many to grasp thereat (i. e. at his earnings), and he receives but few pence (for his work).' The poor man has many mouths to feed with his small and hardly earned wages.

92. 'There bread and penny-ale (we should now say "small beer") are accepted in place of a pittance.' In other words, they are glad to get a piece of bread and some common ale as a friar is to receive 'a good pittaunce,' to use Chaucer's expression (Prologue to Cant. Tales, l. 224). The modern sense of *pittance* is misleading; it was a really good thing, and Tyrwhitt well remarks, in his Glossary, that it meant 'an extraor-

C. PASS. X. 98. (NOT IN B.) (NOT IN A.)

dinary allowance of victuals, given to monastics in addition to their usual commons.' See *Pictantia* in Ducange.

Thus this line runs exactly parallel to ll. 93-95, which tell us that 'cold flesh and cold fish are, in their eyes, as good as roast venison; and, on Fridays and fasting-days, a farthing's worth of mussels, or as many cockles, would be quite a feast for such folks.' In 1390, mussels were sold at 8 bushels for 5*d*.; Hist. Agric. and Prices in England, by J. E. Thorold Rogers, ii. 558. At this rate, a farthing's worth would be more than 12 quarts; a sufficient quantity.

98. 'But beggars with bags—which brewhouses are their churches.' This remarkable use of *which* is still common in London, as is well known.

103. *Lolleres lyf*, the life of a vagabond. The word *loller* occurs frequently in this passage; see note to l. 213, p. 126.

108. 'And more or less mad, according as the moon sits;' i. e. according to the moon's phases; see *Lunacy* in Webster's Dictionary. So in l. 110 below, the phrase 'after the mone' means 'according to the moon.'

118. 'They are like His apostles.' This singular belief, that idiots were more or less inspired, was no doubt common at a time when the 'fool' was an established attendant at great men's tables. Dean Ramsay, in his Anecdotes of Scottish Life, chap. vi., gives many curious anecdotes of idiot wit, and says that "many odd sayings which emanated from the parish idiots *were traditionary in country localities*." See Luke, xxii. 35 for the quotation at l. 120.

122. William tells us that he was himself considered as a lunatic by some, because he did not reverently salute persons of authority whom he met in the streets. See B. Pass. xv. 5-10. Cf. Luke, x. 4; Matt. x. 42, xxv. 35; Isaiah, lviii. 7.

127. *Boyes*, servants, followers; not here used in a bad sense, as is often the case elsewhere. *Bordiours*, jesters: Fr. *bourdeurs* (Cotgrave); see l. 136. See 1 Cor. iii. 18.

129. 'To receive them liberally is the duty of the rich.' It was a point of courtesy to be liberal to the minstrels. Cf. Pass. viii. 97; also B. xiii. 227, xiv. 24.

131. 'Men allow all that such men say to pass, and consider it as entertaining.'

140. 'Which is the life of lollers, and of ignorant hermits.' *Lollaren* is the genitive plural; cf. *kingene*, B. i. 105; *klerken*, C. v. 114. See note to l. 213, p. 126.

153. *Fisketh*, wanders, roams.

This scarce word occurs in Sir Gawayne and the Grene Knight, ed. Morris, l. 1704; Prompt. Parv., p. 162; Tusser, Five Hundred Points, etc., ed. Mavor, p. 286; Whitgift's Works, i. 528; and see Nares, Palsgrave, and Miss Jackson's Shropshire Wordbook.

'*Fieska*, to *fisk* the tail about; to *fisk* up and down;' Swedish Dictionary, by J. Serenius.

124   C. PASS. X. 154.   B. PASS. VII. 91.   A. PASS. VIII. 75.

'*Fjeska*, v. n. to fidge, to fidget, to *fisk* :' Swed. Dict. (Tauchnitz).

154. *A begeneldes wyse*, in the guise of a beggar. The word *begeneld* does not seem to occur elsewhere, but we may compare it with the form *beggilde*, which occurs in two MSS. as a various reading for *beggares*, in the following extract :—' Hit is *beggares* rihte uorte beren *bagge on bac*, and burgeises for to beren purses ;' Ancren Riwle, ed. Morton, p. 168. It thus appears that *begeneld*, *beggild*, and *beggare* are nearly equivalent forms ; *beggilde* (with -*e* suffixed) being either a genitive plural or a genitive sing. *feminine*. In fact -*ild* is a fem. suffix, by analogy with A. S. fem. names ending in -*hild*. The *bag* was the beggar's constant appendage ; see note to Pass. i. 42, p. 6.

157. 'And moreover to a garment, to cover his bones with.'

162. *The bok*, the Bible ; Ps. xxxvi. 25 (Vulg.) ; xxx. 11 (Vulg.)

—— (b. 7. 91.) *With wehe*, with a neighing noise, as explained in the note to Pass. v. 20, and with reference to Jer. v. 8. Probably *wo* in [a] has a similar meaning.

168. *Beggers of kynde*, beggars by nature, 'born beggars,' as we should say. In [b] and [a] we have a different reading.

169. In [b], the word *he* is used quite indefinitely, so that *he* = one of you; cf. *heo* = they [a]. Neither in [a] or [b] is it made quite clear whether the breaking of the child's bone is accidental or not ; but in [c] we find an explicit statement that there were parents so detestably wicked as to break a bone of one of their own children, in order to appeal more powerfully to the sympathy of those from whom they begged. The same statement occurs in Barclay's Ship of Fools, ed. Jamieson, i. 304. Many of the cripples, however, were merely lazy tramps who shammed lameness ; see the chapter on Gipsies, Tramps, and Beggars in P. Lacroix, Manners, Customs, and Dress during the Middle Ages, especially the pictures of the sham lame beggars, p. 469 ; and see p. 471. Compare Burns' poem of The Jolly Beggars. Cf. Pass. ix. 138.

170. *Gooth afaytyng*, they go abegging [c] ; *gon faiten*, ye go and beg [b] ; *goth fayteth*, they go and beg [a]. If the reader considers the seven instances of the construction explained in the note to Pass. ix. 138 (p. 111), he may perhaps see reason for thinking that the original reading in this passage was *goth a-fayteth*, of which the recorded readings are modifications.

—— (b. 7. 98.) *Man wrought*, created as a man [b]; *men i-wrouȝt*, created as men [a]. *Hennes fare*, depart hence ; i. e. die ; cf. l. 53 above.

177. *Bedreden.* Dr. Rock (Church of Our Fathers, iii. 34) gives many instances of bequests to bed-ridden poor people.

178. *Apayed of godes sonde*, resigned to God's visitation.

179. *Mesels*, lepers. In a note to Amis and Amiloun, l. 1259, Mr. Weber says—'About the time this story was originally invented, the loathsome disease of leprosy was in full force. According to Le Grand (Fabliaux, vol. v. p. 138), it was imported into France during the period of the first and second race of kings, by trade from Egypt, Palestine, and Syria. . . . They were expelled from all intercourse with men, banished to small huts by the side of the highways, and furnished with a gray mantle, a cap, and a wallet. They were obliged to give warning to the approaching traveller by their clapper-dish;' Weber's Metrical Romances, iii. 365. The famous Robert Bruce died of leprosy in 1329. In 1346, an ordinance was made to exclude lepers from the City of London; Riley's Memorials of London, p. 230.

188. I beg leave to refer the reader to Cutts' Scenes and Characters of the Middle Ages, which contains four chapters on the Hermits and Recluses of those times. The present passage (ll. 188-211) is quoted and commented upon at pp. 100, 101; and again, at pp. 95, 97, 102, the author cites, in illustration, Pass. i. 1-4 (which is compared with xi. 1, 2), Pass. i. 27-32, 51, 53-55; ix. 146, 147; and B. xv. 267-273. See the note to Pass. i. 51. See also Mrs. Jameson's Sacred and Legendary Art, Malory's Morte Darthur, bk. xii. c. 3, bk. xiii. c. 16, bk. xv. c. 4, bk. xvi. c. 3-6, bk. xviii. c. 22, bk. xxi. c. 10; Spenser's Faerie Queene, i. 1. 29-35; art. *Hermitages* in English Cyclopaedia (Supplement to 'Arts and Sciences'), etc.

190. The construction is awkward, but the sense readily appears by taking 'þe contrarie' in l. 193 as an adverbial phrase, with the force of 'contrariwise.' There is a pause at the end of l. 189, and 'These lolleres' is in apposition with the 'eremites' in l. 188. The sense is—'These lollers, etc., contrariwise covet all that the old holy hermits hated and despised, viz. riches, and reverences, and rich men's alms.' The passage seems to have been written in hot haste, under the influence of strong feelings of indignation. It is clear that the 'lollers' did not covet the contrary of riches, but the contrary of what holy hermits hated. There is no real difficulty here; the grammatical construction is certainly awkward, but the language strong and intelligible.

194. Here *boyes* is used contemptuously, as it probably is in Pass. i. 78, and not as in l. 127 above. *Bollers*, drunkards, men who were too fond of the *bolle* (bowl). Cf. 'Thise cokkers [cockfighters] and thise *bollars;*' Towneley Myst. p. 242.

195. *Lyf-holy*, holy of life. Mr. Way seldom made a mistake, but he misunderstood and misprinted this word. At p. 303 of his edition of the Promptorium Parvulorum, read 'LYYF-HOLY, *Devotus, sanctus.*'

196. See Pass. xviii. 6-8, and 28-31.

197. 'Some received their sustenance from their relatives, and from no one else.' Here *lyf* = a person, man; as in other passages.

200. See the same statement in Pass. xviii. 11.

203. 'Many of the hermitages were erected along the great highways of the country, and especially at bridges and fords, apparently with the express view of their being serviceable to travellers;' Cutts, Scenes and Characters, p. 103. Hence the knights-errant, in the Morte Darthur, frequently come to a hermitage, and pass a night there; see note to l. 188.

204. That the ranks of the monks and friars were recruited from amongst the very poorest of the working classes is notorious. See P. Pl. Crede, 744-753; Plowman's Tale, pt. iii.

211. 'Or one of some order (of friars), or else a prophet.' *Prophet* is

probably here synonymous with *hermit*, as Mr. Cutts suggests; otherwise, it refers to the privileged idiots who are described as prophesying in l. 114. See note to l. 118 above, p. 123.

212. The Latin means—'It is not lawful for you to conform the law to your will, but it is for you to conform your will to the law.' I do not know whence it is quoted.

213. *Kyndeliche*, naturally, properly, rightly. The argument is that the term *loller* as a term of reproach may be rightly applied to these false hermits. A man who lolls about must be one who is lame or maimed; for 'it hints at some accident;' l. 216. Just so do these hermits 'loll' against right belief and law, offering but a lame and maimed obedience to the ordinances of the church. William proceeds to shew this by an enquiry into their conduct, and lays stress upon the word 'obedience,' which occurs four times, viz. in ll. 220, 222, 235, 241.

This passage throws much light upon the word *loller*. It proves beyond all doubt that the true sense of the word, in 'englisch of oure eldres,' was one who lolls about, or, in other words, a lazy vagabond. Moreover, our English word, though purposely confused with the Low-Latin term *lollardus*, originally existed independently of it. To make the confusion still greater, the Latin term *lollardus* and the Old English *loller* were mixed up with jests about *lolia*, or tares, which the Wycliffites were accused of sowing amongst the good wheat of the church's doctrines. For further information, see note to Pass. vi. 2, p. 60. Cf. Pass. vii. 199; xv. 153; and P. Pl. Crede, 224. And see the note to l. 218 below.

216. 'Or maimed in some member; for it hints at (lit. sounds like) some accident.' *Meschief* means some mischance or accident, as in l. 179 above. For *souneth*, cf. Chaucer, Prol. 307, etc.

218. *Lollen*, i. e. offend by disobedience; see note to Pass. vi. 2. The sense is greatly cleared up by the extra line preceding this in a fragment found in the Ilchester MS., viz.—

'So þise lewed lollers · as lame men þey walken.'

226. This is evidence that wolves were still found in England at this period, though probably only 'in waste places.'

228. For *mete*, the reading *noon* occurs in a fragment printed in Pref. III (C-text), p. xxxvi (E. E. T. S. edition). Cf. the expression 'at mydday meel-tyme,' l. 246; and see Pass. vii. 429, 434; and note to Pass. ix. 146, p. 112. In this passage, our author is expressly speaking of Sunday.

233. 'And fulfil those fasts, unless infirmity has caused it to be otherwise.' This curious use of *make* occurs several times; cf. Pass. viii. 4, 28, 65.

238. *And*, if. *Worth*, will be.

240. *Where*, whether. In l. 242, it may mean either *whether* or *where;* probably the latter.

243. All the MSS. read *As*, signifying 'as for instance;' cf. Pass. i. 223. We might think that '*At* matyns' would be a simpler reading, but it would be quite a mistake to substitute a modern idiom for an old one against all authority.

249. The conduct of a friar at table is described at length in Pass. xvi. 30–175, q. v. Cf. P. Pl. Crede, 760–774.

251. *In this worlde,* at a worldly occupation.

257. 'Certainly, if one durst say so, Simon is as it were asleep; it were better for thee to keep watch, for thou hast a heavy responsibility.' The allusion is to Mark, xiv. 37, 38—'Et ait Petro, Simon, dormis? non potuisti una hora uigilare? Uigilate et orate,' etc. William here addresses a bishop, whom he calls Simon, as being a successor of Simon Peter. Cf. Rich. Redeles, iv. 55, and the note.

260. 'Thy barkers (i. e. dogs) that conduct thy lambs are all blind.' Suggested by Isaiah, lvi. 10—'Speculatores eius caeci omnes, nescierunt uniuersi: canes muti, non ualentes latrare.' In the next line the quotation is from Zech. xiii. 7—'Percute pastorem, et dispergentur oues.'

262. Every shepherd used to carry a tar-box, called a *tarre-boyste* in the Chester Plays, p. 121, or a *terre-powghe* (tar-pouch) in P. Pl. Crede, l. 618. It held a salve containing tar, which was used for anointing sores in sheep. See note to l. 264 below.

263. 'Their salve (i. e. the sheep's salve) is made of *supersedeas,* and (carried about) in sompnours' boxes.' That is, all the healing which the sheep receive is that they are smothered with writs of *supersedeas,* at the pleasure of meddling sompnours. See note to Pass. iii. 187, p. 38. The word *boxes* refers to the shepherds' tar-boxes; see note above.

264. *Ner al shabbyd,* nearly all scabby. 'Among the diseases peculiar to sheep, the *scab* is very frequently mentioned . . . . It was discovered that tar . . . was a specific for the complaint. . . . It is clear that the remedy was mixed with butter or lard, and then rubbed in.'—Hist. of Agriculture and Prices in England, by J. E. Thorold Rogers, vol. i. p. 31.

265. Chaucer seems to allude to the same passage in his Doctoures Tale, where he says—

'Under a shepherd softe and negligent
The wolf hath many a sheep and lamb to-rent.'

In his edition of Salomon and Saturn, at p. 63, Kemble quotes the Old French form of the proverb thus :—'a mol pasteur lou lui chie laine;' cf. p. 54, prov. 76, where *non* must be struck out.

273. 'And (when) the wool shall be weighed, wo is thee then!' The reference is to the day of judgment.

275. *Hope,* expect, fear. So also *hope thow,* i. e. expect, in l. 290.

277. Here *toke* = didst bestow; cf. note to Pass. iv. 47. The sense is— 'But (thou wilt hear a voice, saying)—receive this (punishment) in return for that (conduct); when (i. e. since) thou didst bestow indulgence for hire, and didst break my law,' etc.

288. (b. 7. 112.) *Peter!* i. e. by Saint Peter; as before. See Matt. xxv. 46.

—— (b. 7. 120.) 'And I will weep when I should sleep, though wheaten bread fail me (in consequence of my watching)' [b]; 'And I will look loweringly upon that whereon I formerly smiled, ere my life fail' [a].

—— (b. 7. 121.) *His payn ete,* ate his bread; see Ps. xli. 4 (Vulg.).

—— (b. 7. 122.) 'According to what the Psalter says, so did many others as well.' Cf. 'Multae tribulationes iustorum;' Ps. xxxiii. 20 (Vulgate).

—— (b. 7. 123.) 'He that truly loves God, his sustenance is very easily procured' [b]; *or*, 'is very considerable' [a]. The text alluded to here is certainly Ps. xxxiii. 11 (Vulgate), quoted a little further on, in Pass. xi. 201.

—— (b. 7. 124.) *Luke*. But the reference is really to Mat. vi. 25. In another place, William makes just the reverse error; see note to B. vi. 241.

—— (b. 7. 125.) This line recurs, very slightly altered from its form in [b]; see B. xiv. 33, with the same reference to Mat. vi. 25.

—— (b. 7. 128.) 'The birds in the field, who supplies them with food in winter? Though they have no garner to go to, yet God provides for them all.' *Fynt*, findeth, provides for, as in Pass. vi. 88; so *fynde* in xvi. 251.

—— (b. 7. 135.) The priest contemptuously suggests that Piers might *suitably* take for his text either 'The *fool* hath spoken,' Ps. xiv. 1 or xiii. 1, Vulgate [b]; or else 'Quia literaturam non cognoui' (Ps. lxx. 15, Vulg.), i.e. for I know no learning [a]. The corresponding verse in the English version in the latter instance is quite differently expressed, being 'for I know not the numbers thereof;' Ps. lxxi. 15.

—— (b. 7. 136.) *Lewed lorel*, ignorant reprobate. Chaucer translates 'perditissimum quemque' in Boethius, De Cons. Phil. Lib. i. pr. 4, by 'euery lorel;' see Morris's edition, p. 21. It is also spelt *losel;* thus in P. Pl. Crede, l. 750, we have 'losells,' but in l. 755 the word is 'lorels.' In the 'Glosse' to Spenser's Shep. Kal. (July) is the odd explanation— 'Lorrell, a losell;' shewing that *lorel* was then looked upon as the older form. The Prompt. Parv. has—'Lorel or losel, *lurco;*' see Way's note.

—— (a. 8. 125, 126.) These lines are probably spurious, and introduced in the Harleian MS. as a translation of the Latin quotation from Prov. xxii. 10. They mean—'Cast out these scorners with their cursed scolding, for I do not readily consent (*or* care) to dwell with them.'

—— (b. 7. 137.) I have elsewhere remarked that *Eice* is the usual spelling of *Ejice* in MSS. of the fourteenth century; and it is probably quite correct. Nearly all the MSS. wrongly read *Ecce*, as in Crowley's edition. The quotation is from Prov. xxii. 10—'Eice derisorem, et exibit cum eo iurgium, cessabuntque causae et contumeliae.'

295. (b. 7. 141.) *Meteles*, meat-less, without food; as in The Frere and the Boy, l. 151, in Ritson, Anc. Pop. Poetry. It is a totally different word from the *meteles* in the next line, which signifies *a dream*. In this line we have the third and last reference to the Malvern hills; see Pass. i. 6, 163.

300. *Which a*, what sort of a. This is the usual idiom; cf. Ch. Knyghtes Tale, 1817. See note to Pass. v. 26, p. 54.

302. *Setten nat by songewarie*, value not the interpretation of dreams. A Metrical Treatise on Dreams (MS. Harl. 2253, fol. 119) is printed in Reliq. Antiq. i. 261. There is a chapter on Dreams in Brand, Pop. Antiq. ed. Ellis, iii. 127; and see some curious examples of dreams

in Chambers, Book of Days, i. 276, 394, 617 ; ii. 188. The cock in Chaucer's Nonne Prestes Tale discourses eloquently upon this subject.

303. *Caton*, i. e. Dionysius Cato ; cf. note to Pass. ix. 338. The quotation is from the following :—

'Somnia ne cures, nam mens humana quod optans [*vel* optat],
Dum uigilat, sperat, per somnum cernit id ipsum.'

Dion. Cato ; Distich. ii. 31.

This Chaucer (Non. Pr. Ta. 121) translates by ' ne do no fors of dremes.'

306. The Vulgate has the spelling *Nabuchodonosor*, but the spelling *Nabugodonosor* is found in the MSS. of Chaucer, Wyclif, and Gower ; the A.V. has Nebuchadnezzar. The reference is properly to Dan. ii. 39, but it is tolerably clear that our author, in his two earlier versions, was really thinking of Belshazzar and the handwriting on the wall ; Dan. v. 28. In the latest version, he seems to have partly perceived his mistake, as he leaves out five or six lines, and inserts l. 307 in place of them. It is remarkable that this new line does not much mend the matter, as the poet inadvertently writes the plural for the singular. He should have written *sone, him*, and *he*, instead of *sones, hem*, and *thei*.

—— (b. 7. 158.) The best reading is *lees* (as in MSS. W, O, and B) ; it means 'lost.' The same spelling occurs in Joseph of Arimathie, ed. Skeat, l. 125 ; and in Seven Sages, ed. Wright, l. 3425.

309. *Hailsede*, saluted ; cf. B. v. 101. See Gen. xxxvii. 9, 10.

311. *Beau fitz*, fair son. This is a singular version of the story ; for the Bible-account shews that Jacob hardly expected the dream to be fulfilled.

319. *Indulgences*. ' When indulgences came to be sold, the pope made them a part of his ordinary revenue, and according to the usual way in those, and even in much later times, of farming the revenue, he let them out usually to the Dominican friars ;' Massingberd, Hist. Ref. p. 126. Wyclif declared them to be futile ; Works, i. 60 ; iii. 256, 362, 459.

320. Wyclif (Works, iii. 398) uses the word *quienals*, on which Mr. Arnold has the note—' *Quienal* seems to be a corruption of *quinquennale*, by which was meant an arrangement for saying mass for a departed soul during the period of five years. *Triennale* (Engl. *trinal* or *trienal*) and *annuale* are similar arrangements for three years or one year.' To which may be added, that *biennale* was a similar arrangement for the space of two years. The most common word of this description was *trental*, which meant the saying of thirty masses for the dead, usually on thirty different days. See the curious poem of ' St. Gregory's Trental,' pr. in Polit. Relig. and Love Poems, ed. Furnivall, pp. 83-92. ' A trental of masses used to be offered up for almost every one on the burial-day ;' Rock, Church of Our Fathers, ii. 504 (note).

322. *Worth faire vnderfonge*, will be well received [c] ; *is dignelich vnderfongen*, is worthily received [b]; *is digneliche ipreiset*, is worthily praised [a]. By *dowel* [a, b] is meant ' do-well,' i. e. doing well, or the doing of good works. See note to l. 351 below. Compare Pass. xvii. 37-39.

324. In the Prick of Conscience, ed. Morris, pp. 104, 105, we find an explanation of 'pardon;' that it is a remission of pain, and a part of the treasure of holy church, gathered together by the merits of the saints. The pope (says Richard Rolle) bears the keys of this treasure, and is God's vicar on earth, having, by succession, the power of the keys as delivered to St. Peter (Matt. xvi. 19); and not only the pope, but every bishop (though in a less degree) has the power of granting pardon. This throws some light upon the 'bishops' letters' mentioned in l. 320.

342. *Poke-ful*, pouch-ful, a bagful or sackful. *Prouincials letteres*, provincial letters, or letters provincial. We frequently find, in Middle English, that an adjective of Romance origin takes an -*s* (or -*es*) in the plural; indeed, we have already had an instance of this in the case of the word *cardinales*, Pass. i. 132. Dr. Morris draws attention to this in his Hist. Outlines of English Accidence, p. 104, sect. 105; but he adds the restriction, that the adjective is then placed after its substantive, of which he gives several examples. Such is certainly the usual arrangement, but there are a few exceptions, as in the present instance. A very clear example occurs in Chaucer's Treatise on the Astrolabe (ed. Skeat). In pt. 1, sect. 5, l. 7, the four quarters of the firmament are called the 'four principals plages,' but in pt. 2, sect. 31, l. 10, they are called the 'four plages principalx.' Again, in pt. 1, sect. 16, l. 8, we find 'lettres capitals,' but in pt. 2, sect. 3, l. 20, we have 'capitalles lettres.' See also Note to Pass. xiv. 128. The 'provincial letters' referred to are evidently letters of fraternity granted by a *provincial*, which was a name given to the monastic superior, who had the direction of all the religious houses of the same fraternity in a given district termed the *province* of that order. See the term 'priour prouincial' in Pass. xiii. 10.

343. Here is another allusion to the 'letters of fraternity.' Wealthy people could, by means of these charters of fraternization, granted to them on the payment of so much money, become entitled to the prayers, masses, and merits of the order to which they thus belonged. Cf. Pass. iv. 67, xiii. 9, xxiii. 367. The present passage shews that the same rich man could belong to all the orders of friars at once; as is shewn also by the friar's remonstrance in Chaucer's Sompn. Tale,

'What nedeth you diuerse freres to seche?'

For 'fyue orders' the earlier texts have 'foure ordres.' On this variation, see note to Pass. ix. 191, p. 114. and cf. Pass. xvi. 81.

345. 'I value not the pardon at the value of a pea, or of a pie-heel.' What a *pie-heel* means in this place it is not quite easy to say, nor is it of much importance, as it is obviously something of small value. I think it means a pie-crust, since *heel* is used provincially to mean the rind of cheese or the crust of bread; see *Heel* in Halliwell, and in Miss Jackson's Shropsh. Word-book. Burns has *kebbuck-heel*, the remaining part of a cheese, in his Holy Fair.

350. 'That, after our death-day, Do-well may declare, at the day

C. PASS. X. 351. B. PASS. VII. 200. A. PASS. VIII. 187.

of doom, that we did as he bade us.' Here Do-well is personified, as in l. 344.

351. Here terminates that part of the poem which is properly called the Vision of Piers the Plowman.

It is quite clear that William had intended to wind up his poem here by discoursing on the excellencies of Doing Well; and, in this concluding passage, the word *Do-wel* accordingly occurs four times (ll. 319, 331, 344, 350), without any hint of Doing Better or Doing Best. But an afterthought suggested that Do-well, if supplemented by Do-bet and Do-best, deserved that much more should be said about it ; and that, in fact, here was matter for a whole new poem. The opening lines of A. Pass. ix (which, it should be remembered, is only a *prologue*, and therefore, like the first prologue, much shorter than the other Passus) seem to indicate a short lapse of time between the conclusion of one poem and the commencement of the other. The poet's adventure with the two Minorite friars may possibly have had some foundation in fact; at any rate, it is very naturally inserted, and serves admirably to introduce a new Vision.

In the C-text, all the Prologues are done away with, and Passus XI. is lengthened out till it is very nearly of the same length as Passus XII.

NOTES TO C. PASSUS XI. (B. Pass. VIII., IX. ; A. Pass. IX., X.)

1. (b. 8. 1 ; a. 9. 1.) *Thus robed in russett.* MS. 201 in Corpus Christi College, Oxford, has two spurious lines at the commencement of this Passus, and begins thus :—

    And wanne y awaked was · y wondred were y were,
    Til þat y be-þowhte me · what þyng y dremede,
    & y-Robet in russet · gan rome a-bowhte.

The scribe seems to have meant us to read '& y, Robert, in russet,' as he writes the word ' Robt,' with a stroke through the *b*. It is easy to see how such a misreading may have given rise to the fiction that the author's name was *Robert*, as stated in a note in MS. Ashburnham 130.

All three texts agree in making the Vision of Do-well begin here. We also see that the author's original idea was to consider this Passus as an *introductory* one, or a mere Prologue ; and this is why Passus IX. of the A-text and Passus VIII. of the B-text are both rather short ; the former containing but 118, and the latter but 126 lines. But, in the C-text, he gave up the idea of introductory Prologues, which occasioned two alterations. The former was, that he called the opening Passus of the whole poem by the name of *Passus I.*, instead of by the name of *Prologus*. The latter was, that, being no longer bound to the idea of inserting an introductory Prologue at the beginning of the poem of Do-well, he more than doubled the length of the present Passus, by putting Passus VIII. and IX. of the B-text together, and writing some new lines. Thus it came about that the divisions of the poem are much less distinctly marked in the C-text, and we may consider the whole work, in that form, as *continuous*, viz. from Pass. I. (the first) to Pass. XXIII. (the last).

A long passage, beginning with the first line of the present Passus, is quoted, with notes, in Warton's Hist. of Eng. Poetry, ed. 1840, vol. ii. pp. 45 and 66; ed. 1871, vol. ii. p. 251. The notes in the edition of 1840 are not much to be trusted.

Russet was a name given to a coarse woollen cloth, of a reddish brown colour. '*Russet, birrus* or *burreau* [or *borel*], *cordetum*, and *sarcilis* are quoted by the indefatigable Strutt, as coarse woollen cloths used for the garments of the lower orders during the thirteenth century;' British Costume, p. 120. Russet was the usual colour of hermits' robes; Cutts, Scenes and Characters of the Middle Ages, p. 97. We learn from the short poem on Arther, ed. Furnivall (E. E. T. S. 1864), l. 582, that a 'russet cote' was the outer dress of a nun. In an Act passed in 1363, to restrict the dress of the peasantry, it was ordered that all people not possessing 40 shillings' worth of goods and chattels 'ne usent nule manere de drap, si noun blanket et *russet* laune de xii*d*,' i. e. shall not wear any manner of cloth, except blanket and russet wool of twelvepence; Stat. Realm, i. 381; see Bardsley's Eng. Surnames, p. 394; Our English Home, p. 108. To be 'clad in russet' became an almost proverbial phrase for wearing homely garments; see Pass. xvii. 298, 342. Lastly, russet was especially used by shepherds, and this is what our author chiefly refers to in the present passage, since he tells us that he was arrayed like a shepherd; cf. note to Pass. i. 2.

2. *Al a somer seson*, all the summer; alluding to the Visions which he saw 'on a May morning,' Pass. i. 6; B. v. 9. In the two earlier texts, the poet sees two visions in one morning (B. i. 6; v. 9), and wakes at noon (B. vii. 140); after which he here describes himself as wandering about all the succeeding summer. In the C-text, a long interval occurs between those two visions, during which the poet talks with Reason 'in a hot harvest;' Pass. vi. 7.

4. 'If any one knew where Do-well lodged, and what sort of a personage he might be, I enquired of many a man.' For *what* = what sort of a, cf. note to Pass. iii. 17, p. 32. The notion of *Do-well* was suggested by the 'two lines' of which 'the pardon of Piers the Plowman consisted;' see Pass. x. 286, 289. The poet having once learnt that Do-well leads to life eternal, dwells upon the idea (see Pass. x. 318, 319, 321, 323, 331, 344, 350), and now determines to find out what Do-well is, and where he resides.

8. *Two freres*, two friars. The friars often went about in pairs. See Chaucer, Sompn. Tale, l. 32.

9. 'Masters of the Minorites;' i. e. masters, or men of superior learning, belonging to the order of the Minorites or Grey Friars. There is, too, a special force in the word *Maisteres*, as it signifies that these two Minorites were both 'masters of divinity,' a title much coveted by some of the order, who wore caps to signify that they had obtained it, as explained in Wyclif's Works, iii. 376. See note to Pass. xvi. 30.

13. The words *doth me to wytene*, i. e. cause me to know [b], must be supposed to be uttered by William to the Minorites.

20. *Contra*, i. e. I dispute that. The author speaks 'as a clerk,' uses a Latin word common in the schools.

21. The full text is—'Septies enim cadit justus, et resurget: impii autem corruent in malum;' Prov. xxiv. 16. But, for *enim*, our author has *in die;* and the same reading is quoted in Hampole's Pricke of Conscience, l. 3432; ed. Morris, p. 94.

32. *A forbusene*, an example, similitude; i. e. parable; cf. Pass. xviii. 277. The following parable, of the man in the wagging boat, is well illustrated by the curious book called the Shepherds Kalender. In an edition printed in 1656, at signature H 6, there is a picture of a man in a ship, steering with a paddle; behind him is portrayed a demon, who tries to rock the boat; in front of him, above, is God the Father (or perhaps Christ), who encourages him to proceed. The text has—'Chap. XIII. Hereafter followeth of the man in the Ship, that sheweth the unstablenesse of the world.' The idea here referred to (suggested by 1 Pet. iii. 20, 21) is the very common one to which an allusion may be found in our Baptismal Service—'that he . . . may be received into the ark of Christ's Church; and . . . may so pass the waves of this troublesome world,' etc. In Ælfric's Homilies, ed. Thorpe, ii. 385, this similitude is attributed to St. Augustine. Accordingly, we find in his works the source of all these allusions, in the words—'Interea nauis portans discipulos, i. e. ecclesia, fluctuat et quatitur tempestatibus tentationum; et non quiescit uentus contrarius, i. e. aduersarius ei diabolus, et impedire nititur ne perueniat ad quietem,' etc.; S. Aug. Sermo lxxv. cap. iii, ed. Migne, v. 475. See other passages from the fathers cited in Trench on the Miracles, 6th ed., pp. 148, 149.

34. In a MS. Glossary, printed in Reliq. Antiq. i. 6, we find—'*vacillare*, to wagge, *sicut navis in aqua*.'

35. 'Causes the man often to stumble, if he stands up' [c]; *or*, 'to fall, and again to stand up' [b]; *or*, 'to stumble and fall' [a]. Mr. Wright well shews that the reading of the B-text, though rather awkward, is not wrong; 'to falle and to stonde' means 'to fall, and again to rise,' and is justified by the text quoted in the note to l. 21—'cadit iustus, *et resurget*.' See note to l. 52 below.

42. *Fondinge*, temptation; not 'folly,' as in Whitaker.

46. 'That move about (or fluctuate), just as the winds and storms do.'

—— (b. 8. 52.) 'For He (God) gave thee, as a year's-gift, the means of taking good care of yourself; that is, (He gave you) instinct and free will, to every creature a portion.' Here *to yres3yue* means, by way of present, or as a free gift. For *yres3yue*, see note to B. iii. 99, p. 44.

52. Compare Chaucer, Pers. Tale (near beginning)—'But natheles, men shulde hope that, at euery tyme that man falleth, be it neuer so ofte, that he may aryse through penaunce, if he haue grace: but certain, it is gret doute.'

134 C. PASS. XI. 54. B. PASS. VIII. 58. A. PASS. IX. 49.

54. *Rather*, sooner; referring to *ende* in the previous line. 'Sooner than our death, we have no rest.'

57. In Warton's Hist. E. P. ed. 1840, ii. 68, it is pointed out that William here uses 'one of those primitive figures which are common to the poetry of every country;' and the following parallel is quoted from Homer, Il. i. 88:—

Οὖτις, ἐμεῦ ζῶντος καὶ ἐπὶ χθονὶ δερκομένοιο,
Σοὶ κοίλης παρὰ νηυσὶ βαρείας χεῖρας ἐποίσει.

It occurs elsewhere in our poem. Cf. 'Al þat *lyueth* other *loketh*,' xxi. 29; 'And *lyues* and *lokynge*,' xxii. 159; 'And now art *lyuynge* and *lokynge*,' xxii. 175. The phrase clearly means—'if I may live and have the use of my faculties.'

58. *Ich bykenne the Crist*, I commit thee to Christ; and the same is the sense of *I beo-take you to crist* [a]; see Pass. iii. 51.

61. *Walkynge myn one*, walking alone, walking by myself. The reading of MS. F [c], is *al myn oone*. I will merely observe here, in passing, that all who are really conversant with Middle-English MSS. must be well aware that the word *alone* is constantly written *al one*, and that the insertion of a word like *myn* between *al* and *one* is sufficiently common, so that there can be no doubt about the derivation of the mod. Eng. *alone* from *al* (all) and *one*. See examples under *án* in Grein and Stratmann; and under *one* in Gloss. to Will. of Palerne, where we find *al himself one*, l. 3316; *himself one*, l. 657; *bi hereself one*, l. 3101; *him one*, ll. 17, 4112; etc.

68. *A muche man*, i. e. a big or tall man. In the legend of St. Christopher, who was of gigantic stature, we read that people were afraid of him because 'he was so *moche*;' Early Eng. Poems and Lives of Saints, ed. Furnivall, p. 63, l. 128. We may draw the conclusion that the poet was himself of large stature (cf. Pass. vi. 24); whence his nickname of 'Long Will,' B. xv. 148. We learn from l. 72 that the stranger whom the poet meets is named Thought; and he is, in fact, merely William's double, the personification of his own contemplative power, who had 'followed him about these seven years,' and was therefore like himself in all respects.

69. *By my kynde name*, by my right name, the name to which I was accustomed. He called him 'Wille;' see l. 71. The same name occurs elsewhere, as in A. xii. 94; B. v. 62, viii. 124, xv. 148; C. ii. 5, etc.

73. 'I have followed thee these seven years; sawest thou me no sooner?' Of course 'these seven years' is mere indefinite expression, signifying a long while; see notes to Pass. v. 82; vii. 214.

80. *Trewe of hus tail*, true in his reckoning;— i.e. careful never to defraud. *Tail* (French *taille*) here means *a tally;* in [b] and [a] we have *tailende*, i. e. tallying, or reckoning kept by a tally. *Halt wel his handes*, restrains well his hands, i. e. 'keeps them from picking and stealing.'

84. 'And helps all men heartily, out of that which he has to spare' [c]; 'And helps all men, according to what is lacking to them' [b].

85. *Bygurdeles*, purses; so called because they used to hang at the girdle. The word occurs in the A.S. version of Matt. x. 9. Hence arose the name of *cut-purse*, which, in our days, has given place to *pick-pocket*.

To-broke, broken them in twain, destroyed them.

86. 'Which the earl named Avarous (i. e. avaricious one) and his heirs had possession of.' The Vernon MS. omits the word *Erl;* but it might have been inserted in [a] on the authority of the other MSS., which rightly omit the words *eny of.* Read, in [a], the line thus—
Þat þe Erl Auerous · hedde, or his heires.

87. 'And has made for himself many friends, by means of the money of Mammon.' Our author seems to take Mammon to be a man's name ; cf. Mat. vi. 24. His use of the word *of* here is an excellent illustration of the language of our Authorised Version in Luke xvi. 9 ; where also *of* = by means of (as in the Revised Version). The Greek has—ἐκ τοῦ μαμωνᾶ τῆς ἀδικίας ; the Latin Vulgate has—' de mammona iniquitatis.'

88. *Is ronne into religion* probably means—'has entered into the ministry,' or 'has entered the service of Christ.' The word *religion* was frequently used to signify a religious order, as in Wyclif's Works, iii. 437, l. 8 ; and the word *religious* was applied to any one who had entered a religious order. Cotgrave gives 'a religious house' as one of the meanings of *religion* in French. But it is difficult to imagine that our author should so deliberately recommend entry into a religious house, unless perhaps it were a house for *monks*, and not for *friars*. We must also bear in mind that Wyclif was at great pains to extend the meaning of the word *religion* beyond its old narrow limits. His tract on the Fifty Heresies of Friars begins with a protest upon this very point. He says—'First, freris seyn þat her religioun, founden of synful men, is more perfite þen þat religion or ordir þe whiche Crist hymself made. . . . Cristen men sey þat þe *religion and ordir* þat Crist made for his disciplis and *prestes*, is moste perfite, moste esy, and moste siker ;' Works, iii. 367. Again, in Pass. xviii. l. 47, we find *religiouse* used quite generally, as equivalent to *men of holy churche* in l. 41 above. Whence it is clear that, whilst the words *religion* and *order* were considered as nearly synonymous, they were understood by the Wycliffites as at least including secular priests, and need not be so restricted in their sense as would at first sight appear.

Rendreþ, translates [c] ; *hath rendred*, has translated [b, a]. In reading this line, the reader is sure to be reminded of Wyclif; yet the expression occurs in the A-text, written A.D. 1362 ; whilst the Wycliffite translation of the Bible does not appear to have been completed till about 1380. But the apparent inconsistency is easily removed by observing that our author has probably no distinct reference to Wyclif in particular, but rather to the *idea* of which Wyclif's work was the successful realisation. He is praising the conduct of those who were persuaded that a translation of the Bible was necessary ; and we may readily suppose that, even as early as 1360, many were in the habit of translating portions of the Bible for the use of the unlearned in a more systematic way than it had been done before. The Wycliffite version itself was not the work of a short period only, nor of one man. Our extant Early English homilies

136 C. PASS. XI. 90. B. PASS. VIII. 92. A. PASS. IX. 84.

shew that, whilst the preachers invariably quoted the Latin version of the Bible, they commonly gave a translation of the passage at the same time. Neither were metrical English versions of parts of the Bible at all uncommon at an early period. The reader who wishes for further information should consult the admirable Preface to the Wycliffite Versions, by Sir F. Madden and Mr. Forshall.

One conclusion may be drawn, at any rate, with much confidence. If the word *religion* in this line is to be taken (which I doubt) in its strictest sense of 'religious order,' then there can be no reference here to Wyclif, the enemy of all monks and friars.

90. It will be observed that William mistranslates the Latin text (2 Cor. xi. 19), taking *suffertis* as if it were in the imperative mood. It is not, however, so much a mistranslation as due to a variation of reading, since the MSS. of the A-text actually have *sufferte*.

92. *Croce*, crosier [c]; badly spelt *crosse* or *cros* [b, a]. William goes on to describe the bishop's crosier as furnished with a hook at the upper end, and a spike at the lower. The 17th line of Chaucer's Freres Tale alludes to a bishop catching offenders 'with his crook.' So here the bishop is described as drawing men to good life by the hook of the crosier, whilst he strikes down hardened transgressors with the spike. *Croce* means a crook, and is a different word from *cross;* see *Croce* in Prompt. Parv., p. 103, and note 5, *which consult*. On the bishop's crosier, see Rock, Church of Our Fathers, ii. 181-198.

94. *Potent*, properly a crutch, but here used as a synonym for crosier. 'Potent, or crotche. *Podium*,' Prompt. Parv. Way's note says—'"*Potence*, a gibbit; also a crutch for a lame man;" Cotgrave. See Ducange, v. *Potentia*. Chaucer termed the "tipped staf," carried by the itinerant limitour, a "potent;" Sompn. Tale, 7358. Cf. R. of Rose, 368, 7417; Vision of P. Ploughman (ed. Wright), 5092.' A cross-potent, in heraldry, signifies a cross whose arms have ends shaped like a crutch.

95. This line is in explanation of the words *preuaricatores legis*, i.e. wilful evaders or misinterpreters of the law. It means—'Lords who live as it pleases them, and respect no law.'

96. 'Such men (i.e. the lords mentioned above) think that, because of their muck (i.e. wealth) and their movable property, no bishop ought to oppose their request (*or*, their command).' For the text, see Matt. x. 28.

110. 'Only Wit will teach thee' [c]; *or*, 'can teach thee' [b, a].

112. The curious word *þroly* occurs only in the Vernon MS. [a]. It means quickly, earnestly; see William of Palerne, 612, 3518; Joseph of Arimathie, 91; and Stratmann's Dictionary. I draw attention to it because I think it will be found that the A-text contains several provincial words which were afterwards eliminated in order to make the poem more widely understood. William's residence in London enabled him to realise that some of the words of his native county were not known there.

118. 'I durst propose no subject, to make him talk freely, but only so far as I then besought Thought to be a mediator between us, and to propose some matter to test his abilities.'

124. *Here is on*, here is one [c] ; *Here is wille*, here is Will [b] ; *Oure wille*, Our Will [a.] The phrase 'our Will' is still in use in Shropshire ; it is a formula used by relatives of the person spoken of.

127. (b. 9. 1 ; a. 10. 1.) *Nat a daye hennes*, not a day's journey from this place.

128. 'In a castle that Nature made, out of things of four kinds.' Properly *kyne* (*kynnes*, b) is a genitive case singular in form, though oddly used with the numeral *four ;* see *cyn* in Grein's A.S. Dictionary. Indeed, we find in some MSS. the curious form *foure skynnes*, a variation of *foures kynnes*. Compare—'Clerkes and other kynnes men,' i. e. clerks and men of another sort, B. x. 69. The awkwardness of the phrase led to the dropping of the genitive sign (-*s*), and people came to regard the words as to be construed in the order in which they stood. Hence we no longer say 'things of four kinds,' but 'four kinds of things.' It is remarkable that, in some instances, the B-text preserves the genitive suffix, where the C-text drops it. Thus we have—none kynnes riche, B. xi. 185; no kyne ryche, C. xiii. 102 ; any kynnes catel, B. xix. 73 ; eny kynne catel, C. xxii. 77 ; many kynnes maneres, B. xvii. 193 ; menye kynne manere, C. xx. 158. Cf. alkin, B. prol. 222 ; alle kynne, C. ix. 69. We find also—þre kynne kynges, B. xix. 91 ; any kynnes wise, B. v. 273.

There is a note upon the word *kynnes* or *cunnes* in Weymouth's edition of the Castle of Love, p. 40, where several examples will be found. In Laȝamon, for instance, we have—on aiȝes cunnes wisan, iii. 23 ; monies kunnes folc, i. 73 ; a summes kunnes wisen, i. 168 ; on ælches cunnes wise, i. 344 ; anes kunnes iweden, iii. 207. So also 'alkyns trees,' Allit. Morte Arthur, ed. Brock, 3244 ; 'what kyns schappe ;' Rob. of Brunne's Chron. prol. l. 155. Other forms are—moni kunne, allirkin, this kin, what kin, etc. Several good examples will be found in the Cursor Mundi, as 'sumkins,' 115 ; 'tuinkyn,' 512 ; 'serekin,' 1016, etc.

The idea intended in this passage is the following. 'Sir Dowel' is the type of perfect humanity, afterwards exemplified in the person of Christ. This humanity or human nature dwells in a castle, that is, in the body or in the flesh, as is explained in B. ix. 48 (*not in* c), where the name of the castle is said to be *Caro*. Moreover, this body is formed of four things, i. e. of the four elements.

The notion of the four elements being earth, air, fire, and water, is alluded to by Ovid, Metamorphoseon, lib. i. 26-31 ; but William either took it from Peter Comestor's account of the Creation, or simply adopted it as being familiar to every physician of the day who had studied (as all did) the works of Galen. See the life of Galenus in the English Cyclopaedia. Dr. White, in a note to the Ormulum, ii. 406, quotes a passage from St. Augustine, where he says it is notorious that man's body is composed of the four elements—'notissima enim sunt quatuor primordia quibus corpus constat ;' Serm. li. De Concord. Matth. et Luc. § 34. In the same passage St. Augustine reminds us that there are four parts of the world, meaning the four quarters of the compass. In English we find very frequent allusions to these elements ; see the Anglo-Saxon Exameron,

138   C. PASS. XI. 130. B. PASS. IX. 4. A. PASS. X. 4.

p. 22 (ed. Norman); an Anglo-Saxon Manual of Astronomy, printed in Wright's Popular Treatises on Science, p. 17; Ormulum, ll. 17605-17608; Cursor Mundi, ed. Morris, pp. 28, 38, etc. The four 'humours' or 'complexions' of men were connected by Galen with the four elements. Those of a *sanguine* temperament have an excess of *blood*, due to *air*; those of a phlegmatic temperament, an excess of phlegm, or *water*; those of a melancholy temperament, an excess of the dull *earth*; and lastly, those of a choleric temperament, an excess of *fire*. Nares well refers us to Twelfth Night, ii. 3. 10; Julius Cæsar, v. 5. 73; Ant. and Cleop., v. 2. 292; Shak. Sonnets, 44 and 45, etc.

The remark of St. Augustine, that there are *four* elements as there are *four* quarters of the world, will explain an otherwise obscure passage in Solomon and Saturn, ed. Kemble, p. 178. 'Tell me, whence Adam's name was formed? I tell thee, of four stars. Tell me, what they are called? I tell thee, *Arthox, Dux, Arótholem, Minsymbrie*.' Cf. Reliquiae Antiquae, i. 288. The simple solution is that we have here corrupted forms of the Greek words for East, West, North, and South, viz. *anatole, dusis, arctos, mesembria;* as is fully proved in a note to Dr. White's edition of the Ormulum, vol. ii. p. 425. And this completely explains a passage in the Cursor Mundi, ed. Morris, p. 42, which is otherwise unintelligible. Throughout the account of Dowel, William is partly following the traditional explanation concerning man's body, as being guarded by Conscience, and served by the Five Wits. See the Homily entitled Soul's Ward, in Early English Homilies, ed. Morris, i. 244; Pricke of Conscience, pp. 157, 158.

130. It is very remarkable that William gives the names of the four elements as earth, air, *wind*, and water; putting *wind* in the place of *fire*. Whitaker coolly proposed to turn *eyre* into *fyre*, not observing that the MSS. all agree. Price (in Warton) says it is a mistake, due to the exigencies of alliteration, and calls attention to the mention of 'wit, water, wind, and fire' in Pass. x. 56. I do not think it is a mistake at all, but a deliberate statement; and that some plain distinction between *air* and *wind* was intended. William must have been thinking of some explanation similar to that given in the Cursor Mundi, ed. Morris, p. 38; where, after telling us that Adam was made of the four elements (l. 518), we find, at l. 539—

'þe ouer *fir* gis man his sight,
þat ouer *air*, of hering might;
þis vnder *wynd* him gis his aand,
þe *erth*, þe tast, to fele and faand.'

Here is a clear distinction between the 'upper air' and the 'under (or lower) wind;' and we may, accordingly, consider that William means by 'wind' that which we call *air*, but by 'air' that which is expressed by the Latin *aër*, which he confuses with *aether*, and this again with *fire*. Indeed, we find him elsewhere describing the four elements as being *welkin, wind, water*, and *earth;* B. xvii. 160. It is surely best to suppose that the text is uncorrupt. It is, moreover, remarkable that, in Sanskrit

C. PASS. XI. 133. B. PASS. IX. 7. A. PASS. X. 7. 139

literature, *five* elements (or *Bhûtas*) are enumerated, viz. fire, water, earth, *air, and æther;* see Benfey's Sansk. Dict. p. 658, col. 2.

133. *Anima*, the soul; which is described as placed within the body by Nature, and as being a 'lemman' or favourite, whom Nature loves. Similarly, in the Pricke of Conscience, l. 5797, the soul is described as being God's daughter who is 'leve and dere' to Him.

To hure hath enuye, etc., i. e. the Prince of this world has envy (or feels spite) towards her. Cf. Pass. viii. 262.

134. 'A proud pricker (or horseman) of France, viz. the Prince of this World.' To *prick* is to spur, to ride; see Spenser, F. Q. i. 1. 1. Dr. Whitaker calls attention to this instance of 'ancient national prejudice; for this proud pricker of France is the devil.' See a similar insinuation in All's Well, iv. 5. 40. The expression *princeps huius mundi* is from St. John xvi. 11; Vulgate version. Mr. Wright remarks that 'until the fifteenth century there appears to have been a strong prejudice among the lower orders against horses and horsemen; their name was connected with oppressors and foreigners.' This he exemplifies by a quotation from his edition of Political Songs, p. 240.

137. *Dooth hure*, places her [c]; *hath do hir*, hath placed her [b, a]. *Thes marches*, these borders, these parts. *Is duke*, who is duke [b]; the relative being omitted, as is frequently the case. Cf. *Is* (= which is), B. x. 369; *Was* (= who was), B. x. 453.

143. *Inwit*, Conscience. Cf. the 'Ayenbite of Inwyt,' i.e. Remorse (lit. Again-biting) of Conscience; the name of a treatise by Dan Michel of Northgate, written A. D. 1340. Conscience is represented as the keeper of the castle of man's body.

146. Here William makes the five sons of Conscience to be See-well, Say-well, Hear-well, Work-well, and Goodfaith Go-well. This is a deviation from the original idea, which made the five guardians to be the Five Wits or Five Senses (cf. l. 170); as is (by the way) so admirably illustrated in Bunyan's allegory of the Holy War. See Ancren Riwle, ed. Morton, p. 48. So also in the Sermon called Sawles Warde, in Old Eng. Homilies, ed. Morris, Ser. i. p. 245, the servants of Wit are said to be the five wits. Cf. Prov. iv. 23; and see B. xiv. 54, and the note to Pass. ii. 15, p. 21.

150. *What lyues þyng*, what thing alive, i.e. what living thing [c]; *What kynnes thyng*, a thing of what kind, i. e. what kind of thing [b, a]. For the phrase *what kynnes*, see note to l. 128 above. The word *lyues*, properly the gen. case of *lyf* (life), is often used adverbially, in the sense of alive; and here, it is boldly used as an adjective, as in Pass. xxii. 159, q. v. It occurs in at least five MSS. of the C-text spelt *lyues, lyuus, leuys*; and I can well believe that it was the author's own substitution, notwithstanding that it detracts from the alliteration, as to which he is often extremely indifferent.

151. *Kind*, i.e. Nature, is here explained to mean the God of nature, or the First Person of the Trinity. Cf. l. 168.

155. Observe the use of (the Northern) *aren* here. It is the author's own word; for the whole stress of the alliteration falls upon the initial *a*.

—— (b. 9. 32.) Compare B. xiv. 60. See Ps. cxlviii. 5 (Vulgate).

—— (b. 9. 35.) 'God was singular (i.e. sole) by Himself; and yet He said *faciamus*;' i.e. He used the plural number. See the account of the Creation in Peter Comestor's Historia Scholastica; and see Gen. i. 26.

—— (b. 9. 38.) 'Just as if a lord had to write a letter, and could get no parchment—though he could write never so well, yet, if he had no pen—the letter, I believe, would never be written, for all the lord's ability.' In this curious illustration of the Trinity, the Father is signified by the ability to write, and the other two Persons by the pen and parchment. The word *lettres* (like Lat. *literae*) has a singular sense.

157. *Bote yf synne hit make*, unless sin cause it (to be otherwise). Cf. Pass. viii. 4, 8, 65; x. 233.

163. 'God will not know of (regard) them, but lets them be (lets them alone), as the Psalter says with regard to such sinful wretches.' See Ps. lxxx. 13 (Vulgate). For *by* (= with regard to), see note to Pass. i. 78.

168. *Kynde*, the God of nature; see note to l. 151.

170. 'Conscience and all the (five) senses are enclosed therein.' Here the word *therein* must be referred back to 'þat castel,' in l. 142. The fact is that the author, in revising the text for the last time, inadvertently omitted the line which contains the true antecedent to *therein*; that line being B. ix. 48 (A. x. 38).

—— (b. 9. 54.) *He* [b] is for *heo*, and means *she*; see *hir* in the next line, and *heo* in A. x. 46. But in B. ix. 56, the same form (*he*) is masculine.

173. (b. 9. 55). The B-text means—'But in the heart is her home, and her chief abode. But Conscience is in the head, and looks after (i.e. watches over) the heart; and, at his will, he assents to whatever is pleasing or displeasing to the Soul.' This notion, that *anima* or 'life' is in the heart, is derived from the text already cited in the note to l. 146, viz. Prov. iv. 23—' Keep thy heart with all diligence; for out of it are the issues of life.'

Here, again, we see the influence of Galen's doctrines. 'He divided the functions into three great classes. The *vital* functions are those whose continuance is essential to life; the *animal* are those which are perceived, and for the most part are *subject to the will*; whilst the *natural* are performed without consciousness or control. He then assumed certain abstract principles upon which these functions were supposed to depend. He conceived the first to have their seat in the *heart*, the second in the *brain*, and the third in the *liver*;' Eng. Cyclopaedia, s. v. Galenus.

—— (a. 10. 55.) 'There is he (i. e. Conscience) most active, unless blood cause it (to be otherwise); for when blood (i. e. animal passion) is more active (*or* fiercer) than the brain, then Conscience is fettered, and becomes also wanton and wild, and devoid of reason.' This alludes to the idea in the last note, of the difference between the Brain, the Blood, and the Heart, considered as residences of the Soul.

174. 'And great woe will be to him, who misspends (*or* misrules, *b*) his Conscience.' William proceeds to cite the examples of Lot, as in

C. PASS. XI. 181.   B. PASS. IX. 63.   A. PASS. X. 62.   141

Pass. ii. 25 ; of Noah (see Gen. ix. 21) ; and of Herod, whom Chaucer couples with Lot in a similar manner in his Pardoner's Tale.

——— (b. 9. 63.) The introduction of the text 'Qui manet in caritate' (1 John iv. 16) appears the more natural when we remember that it was commonly repeated in the Graces before and after meat. See Babees Book, ed. Furnivall, p. 382; and cf. Pass. xvi. 266.

——— (b. 9. 64, 65.) 'Allas! that drink shall destroy them that God redeemed at a dear price; and that it causes God to forsake them that He created in His likeness!' See Matt. xxv. 12 ; Ps. lxxx. 13 (Vulgate).

181. (*not in* b, a.) *To fynde with hym-selue*, to provide for himself therewith.

——— (a. 10. 62.) 'Sir Prince of this world' is the devil, as already explained ; see note to l. 134. The same is therefore the meaning of 'þe Pouke ;' cf. B. xiv. 190; C. xix. 50. See note to Pass. xvi. 164.

——— (a. 10. 73–75.) 'And keep himself clear from all imputation, when he grows beyond childhood, and save himself from sin, as is his duty; for, whether he work well or ill, the blame is his own.' *Wit* = *wyte*, blame. It is spelt *wyte* in MS. U.

——— (b. 9. 70.) 'All these lack responsibility, and teaching is necessary (for them).' Cf. B. v. 38.

——— (b. 9. 72.) The 'four doctors' are St. Gregory, St. Jerome, St. Augustine, and St. Ambrose. See Pass. xxii. 269, note.

——— (b. 9. 80.) 'Nor lack bread nor pottage, if prelates did as they ought.' *And* = *an*, if. So also in l. 82 [b].

——— (b. 9. 84.) 'Since Jews, whom we esteem as comrades of Judas.' Cf. B. prol. 35 ; and see note to l. 220, p. 143.

——— (b. 9. 86.) 'Why will not we Christians be as charitable with Christ's property as Jews, who are our teachers, are (with theirs)? Shame upon us all! The commons, for their uncharitableness, I fear, shall pay the penalty.'

——— (b. 9. 91.) *Broke*, torn ; as in B. v. 108; see note at p. 75. The Latin quotations may be compared with those in B. xv. 336. I cannot find the exact words here quoted, but the reference may be to the following passage in the Compendium by Peter Cantor, cap. xlvii. in vol. 205 of Migne's Patrologiae Cursus Completus, at col. 135 : 'Sic dantibus objici potest, quod similes sunt Judae . . . quanto magis furtum et sacrilegium committit, qui patrimonium crucifixi, pauperibus erogandum, non dico ad horam, dat carni et sanguini, sed officium dispensandi res pauperum, dum vixerit, nepoti committit.' And again, at col. 150: 'Malum est indignis de patrimonio Christi dare, periculosum est, de illis dispensatores rerum pauperum constituere.' For '*minus* distribuit,' Mr. Wright wrongly reads '*mimis* distribuit.'

——— (a. 10. 78.) *Route*, to slumber, lit. to snore; *reste*, to take rest, remain ; *rooten*, to take root.

——— (b. 9. 92.) *Drat* = *dredeth*, which actually occurs in l. 94 [b].

——— (b. 9. 93.) 'Nor loves the sayings of Solomon, who taught wisdom.'

142   C. PASS. XI. 189. B. PASS. IX. 105. A. PASS. X. 82.

We find the saying four times. Ps. cx. 10 (Vulg.); Ecclus. i. 16; Prov. i. 7; Prov. ix. 10. The text quoted at l. 97 [b] is James ii. 10.

—— (a. 10. 82.) 'For fear, men do better,' etc.

—— (a. 10. 92.) Observe the distinction between 'God's word' and 'holy writ;' by the latter is meant the works of the fathers of the church. I do not know whence the quotation is taken. The reference to the Bible may be to Heb. x. 26, 27.

—— (a. 10. 95; *not in* c, b.) *Catoun*, Dionysius Cato. The passage is—
    'Cum recte uiuas, ne cures uerba malorum,
      Arbitrium non est nostri, quid quisque loquatur.'
                                            Distich. liber iii. dist. 3.

—— (a. 10. 98.) *Coueyte herre*, covet to climb still higher. Cf. *furre* = further, in l. 96 [a].

—— (a. 10. 101.) *Selden moseth*, seldom becomes moss-covered. See Ray's Proverbs, under 'A rolling Stone gathers no moss.'

—— (b. 9. 105.) *Lent* = *leneth*, i.e. lends, gives, grants. *Loude other stille*, whether loudly or silently; a proverbial phrase, formerly very common, signifying 'under all circumstances,' or 'at all times,' 'always.' See *Loud-and-still* in Halliwell.

—— (b. 9. 106.) I. e. 'our Lord grants grace, to enter into them, (helping them) to obtain their livelihood.' See Ps. xxxiii. 11 (Vulgate).

189. 'And it would be still best of all to be busy about (this endeavour), and to effect this one result, viz. that all lands should love (one another), and should believe in one law.' To *bringe to hepe* means to put into one heap, to collect into one result. We find *to hepe* used in the sense of *together*, or *in one*, by Chaucer, in his translation of Boethius, ed. Morris, p. 140; Troil. and Cress., iii. 1764 (ed. Tyrwhitt); Treatise on the Astrolabe, ed. Skeat, part 1, sect. 14. See also l. 191 below.

193. The expression 'thre clothes,' i. e. three pieces of cloth, is merely indefinite. The fullest account is that in St. John xix. 23, 24, which says there were four soldiers, who cast lots for His coat, but divided the rest of His garments amongst them by rending them.

195. 'After that, He lost his life, in order that law should increase to love,' i. e. that the dispensation of the Law should give way to the greater dispensation of the Gospel of love.

201. See Ps. xxxiii. 11 (Vulgate).

—— (a. 10. 115.) 'For thou mayst see how sovereigns arise (i. e. how men come to power) by means of patience.' See Luke xiv. 11.

—— (a. 10. 117.) 'Thus Do-best arises out of the dread of God (which is Do-wel), and out of its effect on the conduct (which is Do-bet); and hence it is like flower and fruit, being fostered by them both.' William then proceeds to say that the red and sweet rose, much prized by spice-sellers (and representing Do-best), springs out of a ragged root (Do-well) and rough briars (Do-bet). Cf. Myrour of our Lady, ed. Blunt, p. 283.

—— (b. 9. 117.) 'The heaven (of wedlock) is upon earth; God Himself was the witness.' The reference in the words 'God Himself was the witness' is to the marriage at Cana; John ii. 2.

C. PASS. XI. 206. B. PASS. IX. 120. A. PASS. X. 136. 143

206. The reference is to Matt. vii. 18. Cf. Pass. iii. 29; xi. 244; xix. 61-70.

209. To obtain the full sense, the word *of* must be understood as repeated before *moillere*, which William uses in the sense of 'lawful wife;' see Pass. xix. 222, 236. Thus the line means—'Out of wedlock, not by a lawful wife.' For the quotation, see Ps. vii. 15 (Vulgate).

212. Mr. Wright's note is—'According to a very curious legend, which was popular in the middle ages, Cain was born during the period of penitence and fasting to which our first parents were condemned for their breach of obedience.' Peter Comestor says—'Adam cognouit vxorem suam, sed non in paradiso, sed iam reus et eiectus.'

220. The notion that Cain's children were exceedingly wicked is frequently alluded to in the middle ages; insomuch that 'to be of Cain's kin' or 'to be of Judas' kin' was a proverbial expression equivalent to the Scriptural expression 'sons of Belial.' The usual spelling of *Cain* was *Caym* or *Caim*, which enable Wyclif to say that the friars were denoted by the word *Caim*, since the four orders of them were the Carmelites, Augustines, Jacobins, and Minorites, the initials of which compose that word. See my note to P. Plowm. Crede, l. 486.

⁎ *For note to* b. 9. 123 (a. 10. 152), *see note to l*. 249 below.

222. Compare with this the descriptions of the ark in Allit. Poems, ed. Morris, B. 309-344; Genesis and Exodus, ed. Morris, 561-574; Cursor Mundi, ed. Morris, 1664-1722; Chester Plays, ed. Wright, p. 243.

232. The word *scingles* occurs in the Land of Cokaygne, l. 57, and King Alisaunder, ed. Weber, l. 2210. '*Scingles*, wooden tiles, for which those of clay were afterwards substituted. Those ships in which the edges of the planks cover each other like tiles, and which we now ... call *clinkerbuilt* vessels, were formerly called *shingled ships*, as in P. Plowman;' Ellis, Specimens of Early Poets, i. 87. '*Shyngles*, hyllyng of an house;' Palsgrave. '*Shyngle*, whyche be tyles of woode suche as churches and steples be covered wyth, *scandulæ*;' Huloet. See Levins, Manip. Vocab.; Prompt. Parv., p. 446.

233. 'Here the son paid the penalty for the sins of his ancestor.'

235. The word 'godspel' is a mistake; see Ezek. xviii. 20.

—— (b. 9. 146.) Compare—'Sith all children be *tached* with euill manners;' Batman on Bartholome, lib. vi. c. 6. See *Tache* in Halliwell.

240. The attainder of felony caused 'corruption of blood;' i.e. the felon's goods were escheated to the feudal lord instead of going to his heirs. See *Felony*, and *Corruption of Blood*, in Blount's Law Dictionary.

244. See Matt. vii. 16, 17.

249. William may have derived this command of God to Seth from Peter Comestor, who follows Methodius; Hist. Schol. Genesis, cap. xxxi. A similar account, also attributed to Methodius, and perhaps merely borrowed from Comestor, appears in The Story of Genesis and Exodus, ed. Morris, ll. 517-554.

144   C. PASS. XI. 254.   B. PASS. IX. 158.   A. PASS. X. 180.

In most MSS. of the B-text, (ix. 123), and some of those of the A-text, (x. 154), the name *Seth* is miswritten *Sem* or *Seem*, i. e. Shem; which was a more familiar name.

254. 'For good men should wed good women, though they should have no goods;' i. e. though they be poor. In MS. L., the first *good* is glossed by *boni*, the second by *bonas*.

—— (b. 9. 160.) See Wyclif's Works, iii. 191. Compare the chapter in Barclay's Ship of Fools (ed. Jamieson, i. 247) entitled—'Of yonge folys that take olde wymen to theyr wyues for theyr ryches.' See note to l. 272 below.

—— (b. 9. 163.) 'Who shall never bear a child, except it be (by carrying it) in her arms.' A pun on the two senses of *to bear*.

263. *A bounde on*, a bound one, i. e. one who is a bond-woman. In l. 267, we have the spelling *that bonde*. For the word *begeneldes*, see Pass. x. 154, and the note on p. 124 above.

269. The wish here alluded to, that an ugly bride might be turned into wax, is easily explained. Wax was much used for churches, to which it was frequently offered, and was very costly. It was also usual to offer as much wax as was *equivalent to the weight of the person* in whose behalf it was given; hence it was easy to find a use even for a large quantity of it.

271. 'They live their life in an unloving manner, till death parts them.' It is interesting to remember that the phrase 'til deth us departe' (altered in 1661 to 'till death us *do* part') was formerly used in the Marriage-Service, even at an early period.

272. Mr. Wright (note to l. 5507 of his edition) quotes a passage from the Continuator of William de Nangis (in Dacherii Spicileg. iii. 110, ed. 1723) which gives a very different account of the results of the hasty marriages which followed upon the great pestilence; but the remarks refer to the continent. He says that many twins, and sometimes three at a birth, were born, and that few women were barren. He complains, however, of a great increase in iniquity and ignorance. See Wyclif's discourse Of Weddid Men and Wifis in his Works, ed. Arnold, vol. iii. pp. 188-201; especially p. 191. The great pestilence was that of 1369; see note to Pass. vi. 115, p. 63.

275. 'They have no children except strife, and exchanges (of reproaches) between them.' That is, the sole result of their marriage is continual quarreling.

276. *Don hem*, do themselves; i. e. betake themselves, go.

In the present passage we have the earliest known allusion to the singular custom known as that of 'the Dunmow flitch of Bacon.' The custom was—'that if any pair could, after a twelvemonth of matrimony, come forward, and make oath at Dunmow [co. Essex] that, during the whole time, they had never had a quarrel, never regretted their marriage, and, if again open to an engagement, would make exactly that they had made, they should be rewarded with a flitch of Bacon;' Chambers, Book of Days, i. 749; which see for a good article on the subject.

C. PASS. XI. 278. B. PASS. IX. 170. A. PASS. X. 190. 145

See also Eastern England, by Walter White, vol. ii. p. 225 ; Halliwell's Dictionary, s. v. *Dunmow.*

278. 'Unless they are both forsworn (i. e. forswear themselves), they lose the bacon.'

281. Here *maydenes* is used of both sexes ; *maydenes and maydenes* = bachelors and spinsters. We find something like this in Chaucer, Cant. Tales, 3227-3230; see Tyrwhitt's note to C. T. 3227.

284. The allusion is obviously to the advice of St. Paul—' Quod si non se continent, nubant. Melius est enim nubere, quam uri ; ' ad Corinth. i. 7. 9. At l. 296, William quotes 1 Cor. vii. 2. The expression 'euerech manere seculer man' was, no doubt, intended to include the secular clergy ; and the passage is important, as shewing that many were of opinion that the secular clergy, at least, should be allowed lawfully to marry. In his Notes to Myrc, Mr. Peacock says, at p. 66, that in 1450, ' the Church of England had long refused its sanction to the marriage of persons in holy orders. Though it was contrary to the theory of the Western Church from very early days, there is the most positive evidence that, before the Norman conquest, English priests were frequently married. In the North of England, celibacy was the exception rather than the rule. A clerical family, whose pedigree has been compiled by Mr. Raine (Priory of Hexham, Surtees Soc., vol. i. p. li.) held the office of Priest of Hexham from father to son for several generations.' See Ælfric's Homilies, ed. Thorpe, ii. 95. Wyclif's Works, ed. Arnold, iii. 190 ; Massingberd's History of the Reformation, pp. 81, 242. Compare Chaucer's statement in Cant. Tales, l. 3941—'The persone of the toun hire father was.'

286. *A lykynge thyng,* a pleasant (or enticing) thing [c] ; *in likyng,* in sensual pleasure [b]. *Lymyerde,* lime-rod or lime-twig ; in allusion to the twig covered with birdlime by which birds are sometimes caught. Cf. the Ploughman's Crede, l. 564.

287. ʒ*ep,* active, vigorous [c] ; omitted here in [b], though it occurs in B. xi. 17. See ʒ*eap* in Stratmann, and *Yep* in Halliwell.

289. (b. 9. 182 ; *not in* a.) John of Bridlington, whose Latin verses are printed in Polit. Poems, ed. Wright, vol. i., has the two lines following :—

' Dedita gens scortis morietur fulmine sortis,
 Scribitur in portis, meretrix est ianua mortis ; ' p. 159.

These are Leonine verses, and probably at one time well known, as these citations seem to shew. Cf. Prov. vii. 27.

291. Compare Old Eng. Homilies, ed. Morris, Ser. 1, p. 133 ; Ælfric's Homilies, ed. Thorpe, ii. 94 ; Ayenbite of Inwyt, ed. Morris, p. 224. *Out of tyme,* at an unseasonable time. In l. 186 [b] = 196 [a], we have the curious equivalent phrase *in vntyme,* i.e. at an unseasonable time, as in Rob. of Brunne, Handlyng Synne, l. 2965. And see Ratis Raving, book iii. l. 187 ; also p. 18, l. 590.

304. 'And so, my friend, Do-well is to do what the law ordains' [c, b] ; and [c] adds—' to love and to humble thyself, and to grieve no one.'

—— (b. 9. 204.) 'And so Do-best comes from both (the others), and

146   C. PASS. XII. 2.   B. PASS. X. 2.   A. PASS. XI. 2.

subdues the obstinate (nature of man), that is to say, the wicked self-will that spoils many a (good) work.'

NOTES TO C. PASSUS XII. (B. Pass. X—XI. 42; A. Pass. XI.)

2. (b. 10. 2; a. 11. 2.) 'Who looked very lean, and appeared austere' [c]; 'Who was lean in face, and in body too' [b]; 'Who was lean of body, and of humble look' [a]. *Lere* commonly means complexion, face, look; see *hleor* in Stratmann. As regards *liche*, see *lic* and *liche* in Stratmann, who attempts a distinction between these forms. In this view, *lic* or *lich* = A.S. *lic*, a corpse, a body, whilst *liche* = A.S. *lica*, likeness, form. If this be correct, we have here the former of these words. The term *lic* or *lich* is often understood of a dead body, or corpse, as in *lich-gate*, and in Chaucer's *liche-wake*, Kn. Ta. 2100; but instances are not wanting in which it is applied to the living form. Thus in Kyng Alisaunder, ed. Weber, l. 3482, we have—'The armure he dude on his *liche*,' i. e. on his body. Corresponding to the A.S. *lica*, we have 'inn an manness *like*,' in the form of a man, Ormulum, 5813; 'ine the *liche* of man;' Shoreham's Poems, ed. Wright, p. 20, l. 3.

—— (b. 10. 7.) *And banned him*, and severely rebuked him [b]; *for his beere*, for his noisiness, or loudness of speech [a].

7. 'Nolite dare sanctum canibus, neque mittatis *margaritas* uestras ante porcos,' Matt. vii. 6; where the Greek text has μαργαρίτας. The expression 'margery-pearl' is therefore a reduplicated one; it occurs again in Palsgrave, who has—'Margery-perle, *nacle*.' See also Wyclif's description of *margarites;* Works, i. 286.

8. Repeated below (see l. 82); where 'haws' are explained to mean pleasure and love of the world.

9. 'Draff would be more acceptable to them.' In Skelton's Elinor Rummyng, ll. 170, 171, we have:—

'Get me a staffe,
The swyne eate my *draffe*.'

Mr. Dyce seems uncertain whether it means a coarse liquor, i. e. hogwash, or brewers' grains. It is a general term for refuse, and also bears the meaning of husks and chaff, the refuse of thrashed corn; which may be intended here. See Mr. Way's note on 'Draffe' in the Prompt. Parv.; where he cites Chaucer's 'Why shuld I sowen *draf* out of my fist' (Persones Prol.), and the expression '*draf*-sak' in the Reve's Tale. 'Still swine eat all the draff' is a common proverb, and is cited by Shakespeare; Merry Wives, iv. 2. 105.

10. 'Than all the precious stones, that any prince is master of' [c]; *or*, 'that grow in Paradise' [b]; *or*, 'pearls, that grow in Paradise' [a]. The allusion to *Paradise* is readily understood by referring to Gen. ii. 12. Note also the old belief, that stones could *grow*.

14. *Nat worth a carse,* not worth a cress [c, b]; not worth a rush [a]. Chaucer has—'ne raught he not a *kers;*' C. T. 3754. And in Allit. Poems, ed. Morris, A. 343, we have—'For anger gayneȝ the not a *cresse,*' i.e. avails thee not a cress. A 'cress' means a plant of cress (not necessarily water-cress, as some say), i.e. a thing of small value. Hence, by an odd corruption, the modern expression—'not worth a *curse.*' Chaucer has several equivalent expressions, as, e.g. 'Ne sette I nought the mountance of a *tare;*' Kn. Tale, 712.

15. 'Unless it be carded by means of Covetousness, just as clothiers comb wool.' The sense is, that Wisdom and Intelligence are not now esteemed when rightly employed; to be appreciated, they must suffer themselves to be 'dressed' over by the workings of Avarice, so that they may be employed to deceive, cajole, and beguile; see l. 80 below. The simile is an excellent one when its force is perceived. We may put it more shortly thus. Ability, to be appreciated in these days, must allow itself to be 'dressed' by Avarice, as wool is when it is carded. In Horman's Vulgaria, leaf 149, back, is the expression—'I can bothe carde wolle and kembe it, Noui lanam et carminare et pectere.' And see note to B. xv. 446.

17. 'And hinder truth, and beguile it, by means of a love-day' [c]; 'And preside over a love-day, to hinder truth thereby' [b]; 'And presides over a love-day, to hinder truth thereby' [a]. For *love-day,* see note to Pass. iv. 196, p. 47.

19, 20. '·They who understand trifles and slanders are called in (to help) by the law; but the law bids them to be off, who are truly wise.' I do not know the source of this quotation.

22. *Fallas,* trickery, deceit. It occurs in the Tale of Beryn.

'But now shull ye here the most sotill *fallace,*
That ever man wrought till other, and highest trechery.'

Again, in the Testament of Love, book ii. (near the end), we find—'Mylke of *fallas* is venym of disceite.' '*Fallace* is as who seye gyle;' Rob. of Brunne, Handl. Synne, l. 2782. *Fallaces* is used as a plural adjective in Pass. xvii. 231.

24, 25. See Job, xxi. 13. Also Ps. xlviii. 20 (Vulgate).

26, 27. These two lines are a loose translation of the text above, quoted at length in [b]. The A. V. has—'Behold, these are the ungodly, who prosper in the world; they increase in riches;' Ps. lxxiii. 12 (lxxii. in the Vulgate).

28. 'And ribalds, for the sake of their ribaldry, are helped (with gifts) before the needy poor' [c]; 'Ribalds, for their ribaldry, may receive of their goods' [b]; i.e. may receive presents out of the wealth of the wicked. See note to Pass. v. 113, p. 57.

32. *Tobye,* i.e. Tobit [b, a]; see l. 70 below, and cf. Pass. xviii. 37.

34. *Alowed,* praised [c]; *loued,* loved [b]; *loued or leten bi,* loved or esteemed [a]. *He* = such a one.

—— (b. 10. 42.) 'Liken men (to various objects of ridicule), and lie against them that give them no gifts.' To *liken* is to compare; in this case, for the purpose of exciting ridicule. See B. x. 277.

—— (b. 10. 44.) 'Munde the miller' has been mentioned before; see note to Pass. iii. 113, p. 36. I regret to say that I know no more than Munde did what is the precise reference in the words *multa fecit Deus;* unless it be to Ps. xxxix. 6—'Multa fecisti tu, Domine Deus,' etc.

—— (a. 11. 32.) *Makyng of Crist*, the composing of verses concerning Christ.

—— (b. 10. 47.) *Yeresyiue*, year's-gift; see notes to B. iii. 99, B. viii. 52.

35. 'When the minstrels are silent.' The minstrels played to the guests during the feasts in the great halls; and, whenever they paused for a while, the time was often filled up, as we are told here, by jesting disputes on very sacred subjects. See more on this subject below, B. x. 92-134, C. xvi. 194-210.

38. *Ballede resones*, bald reasons. The expression occurs again in Richard Redeles, iv. 70, which is more explicit, viz. :—

'So blynde and so *ballid* · and bare was the reson.'

Chaucer has the same spelling—'His heed was *balled;*' Prol. 198. Our author has it also, with reference to the head; see Pass. xxiii. 184. There is no difficulty in the expression, and Hotspur's celebrated speech has something very like it; 1 Hen. IV., i. 3. 65—

'This *bald* unjointed chat of his, my lord,
I answer'd indirectly, as I said.'

'They take Bernard to witness;' i. e. they quote from St. Bernard such passages as they think will suit their arguments. It is easy to wrest the sense of passages in argument, so that we need not be surprised at finding (as Price, in Warton, remarks) that 'the abbot of Clairvaux was a zealous opponent of the scholastic subtleties satirized in the text.'

40. *Atte deyes*, at the daïs or high table; see note to Pass. x. 21, p. 119.

41. 'And gnaw God with their throat (defame Him with their words), when their bellies are full.' A forcibly indignant rebuke. Cf. B. x. 66.

42. Compare Rob. of Brunne's Handlyng Synne, ll. 6896-6900.

43. The alliteration is made by the treble recurrence of *f*. Hence the spellings *afyngred* and *afurst*, as in [c], are the best. These are, however, corruptions of *of-hyngred* and *of-thurst*, i. e. exceedingly plagued by hunger and thirst. The word *afyngred* has occurred before; see B. vi. 269, and the note (p. 116); cf. also l. 50 below. And the whole phrase occurs again; see Pass. xvii. 15.

With *afurst*, compare *of-thurste*, King Horn, 1120; *hof-thurst*, Vox and Wolf, 273; *of-thurst*, Ancren Riwle, p. 240; *afurst*, Joseph of Arimathie, ed. Skeat, l. 553.

44. 'There is no one so generous as to have him indoors, but he bids him go where God is,' i. e. to heaven [c]; 'There is no one to take him near himself, to remedy his annoyance (*or* suffering); but only to cry ho! upon him, as at a dog, and bid him go thence' [b]; 'There is no man nigh him, to remedy his suffering; but only to chase him away like a dog,' etc.; [a]. The words *hoen, honesschen* may be either in the

infinitive mood, or in the pres. pl. indicative, with the word *they* understood; it matters little which. *Hoen* is to cry ho! to hoot at; see *Howen, How, Hoo, Ho,* in Halliwell's Dict. Cf. note to Pass. iii. 228, p. 39.

Honesschen is spelt *honysche* in MS. U, and *hunsen* in MS. T (both A-text); we find also the pp. *honsched,* in the phrase '*honsched* as an hounde,' A. ii. 194 (MS. H). The lit. sense is 'to disgrace,' hence to treat with contumely; from *honiss-*, stem of the pres. part. of O. F. *honir,* to disgrace, put to shame; cf. '*honi* soit qui mal y pense.' Hence may be explained two passages in the Allit. Romance of Alexander, ll. 3004 and 3792, which have never been explained till now. In the first passage we are told that Alexander tried to cross a frozen river, when the ice gave way, the result being that

'His hors it *hunyschist* [*sic;* an error for *hunyschit*] for euire · & he wit*h* hard schapid;'

i.e. it put to shame (did away with) his horse for ever, and he himself hardly escaped.

In the other passage we are told that it was so h'ot in the month of August, when Alexander went against the Indian king Porus, that it made an end of some of his soldiers, oppressed as they were with their armour.

'Sum in þair*e* harnais for hete · was [*sic*] *honest* for euir*e*;'

i.e. some of them, in their armour, owing to the heat, where shamed (or disabled) for ever.

51. By *memento* is meant Ps. cxxxi., beginning with 'Memento, Domine, David, et omnis mansuetudinis eius;' the sixth verse being—'Ecce audiuimus eam in Ephratah,' etc. The word *eam* refers to the ark of the covenant; but our author, by inserting the gloss 'i. [=id est] caritatem' intends us to understand it as referring to Christian love. He seems to take the whole verse as signifying—'we can most easily find Christian charity amongst the poor, and in country-places.'

52. 'Clerks and knights' [c]; 'Clerks and men of another kind,' i.e. clerks and others [b]; 'Clerks and intelligent men' [a]. The word *kete* seems to signify keen of wits, acute, in this passage; see the note upon it in my glossary to William of Palerne.

56. Note this allusion to the preaching of the friars at St. Paul's; see it again, Pass. xvi. 70. The preaching-place was in the open air, at St. Paul's Cross. Latimer preached there in fine weather, and in the 'Shrouds,' a place of shelter, in less favourable weather.

63. 'And yet, as for these wretches who are devoted to this world, not one of them takes warning by the other.'

64. An instance of the minute care with which the text was revised. The C-text has *eny deth,* a general expression; but [b] has *the deth,* i.e. the great pestilence emphatically called 'the Death;' see note to Pass. ix. 348, p. 118. The expression was made more general because that event was, at the time of the second revision, less recent. Similarly, in ll. 55, 60, we have the plural *pestilences,* where the B-text has the singular.

65. 'Nor share their goods with the poor' [c]; 'Nor are bountiful to the poor' [b].

67. It is worth observing that this quotation from Isaiah (lviii. 7) was a familiar one, because it was repeated in the Latin grace on fish-days during Lent; see Babees Boke, ed. Furnivall, p. 383.

68. The reading *hath* [c] is not so good as *welt* [b]. *Welt* is equivalent to *weldeth*, which actually occurs just below, l. 72, and in B. x. 88; the sense is wields, commands, makes use of; see l. 12 above, and B. x. 24, 29. These contracted forms of the 3rd pers. sing. pres. indicative are very common; just above we have *to-grynt* for *to-gryndeth*, l. 62; and just below, *lust* for *lusteth*, l. 76.

69. 'And (the more he) is landlord of tenements, the less property he gives away.' The word *leedes*, often used by Robert of Brunne in the sense of *tenements*, or *rents*, is really the same word as *leedes* in the commoner sense of *men*; which, curiously enough, occurs almost immediately below, in l. 73. It probably meant at first serfs sold with the land, and secondly holdings in general.

74. 'If thou have but little, dear son, take care, by thy manner of life, to get love thereby, though thou fare the worse for it.' The sense of B. x. 88 is much the same—'And who-so commands but little, let him rule himself accordingly.' From Tobit iv. 9.

79. 'For no intelligence is esteemed now, unless it tend to gain.' Compare Chaucer, Prol. 275, and see note to l. 15 above, p. 147.

80. 'And (unless it be) capped with learning, in order to plot wrongdoing.' The word 'capped' refers to the caps worn by masters of divinity, as a mark of their degree; see note to Pass. xi. 9, p. 132.

——— (b. 10. 91.) 'And how he might, in a hospitable manner, provide for the greatest number of people.' *Manliche*, hospitable, has occurred before; B. v. 260. *Fynde*, to provide for, has occurred several times; see, e. g., B. vii. 128. *Meyne* is spelt *meynee* in MS. W, and is the usual word for 'household.'

——— (b. 10. 92.) An allusion to the 'feast-finding minstrels,' as Shakespeare calls them; Lucrece, 817. The friars were equally celebrated for haunting the feasts of the rich; see Pass. xvi. 30, 47.

——— (b. 10. 94.) 'Dull is the hall, every day of the week, where neither the lord nor lady likes to sit.' See note on *elyng*, Pass. i. 204, p. 18.

I here transcribe Mr. Wright's excellent note upon the present passage. 'This is a curious illustration of contemporary manners. The *hall* was the apartment in which originally the lord of the household and the male portion of the family passed their time when at home, and where they lived in a manner in public. The chambers were only used for sleeping, and as places of retirement for the ladies, and had, at first, no fire-places (*chymenees*), which were added, in course of time, for their comfort.

'The *parlour* was an apartment introduced also at a comparatively late period, and was, as its name indicates, a place for private conferences or conversation. As society advanced in refinement, people sought to live less and less in public, and the heads of the household gradually deserted the hall, except on special occasions, and lived more in the parlour and in the " chambre with a chymenee." With the absence of the lord from the hall, its festive character and indiscriminate hospitality began to diminish; and the popular agitators declaimed against this as an unmistakeable sign of the debasement of the times.'

Observe that the word *chymneye* (l. 98) means properly a fireplace at this period, in accordance with its derivation from the Lat. *caminus*. Cf. '*chimney's* length' in L' Allegro, l. 111; 'the *chimney* is south the chamber;' Cymbeline, ii. 4. 80. Harrison, in his Description of England, p. 212, says—' Now have we manie *chimnies*, and yet our tenderlings complaine of rheumes, catarrhs, and poses [*colds in the head*]; then had we none but *reredosses*, and our heads did never ake.' See Halliwell's Dict., who gives this quotation s. v. *reredosse*, which he explains as an open firehearth.

—— (b. 10. 100.) ' And all in order to refrain from expending that which another will spend afterwards.' Many misers leave their money to spendthrift heirs.

—— (b. 10. 105.) ' Why was our Saviour pleased to suffer such a serpent to enter His (place of) bliss,' i. e. the garden of Eden? Observe the use of *worm* for a large serpent; cf. Ant. and Cleopatra, v. 2, and see Pass. xiv. 137 (C-text).

—— (b. 10. 110, 112.) See Ezek. xviii. 20; Gal. vi. 5.

—— (b. 10. 115.) This is a very curious allusion; the author is referring, by anticipation, to a later passage of his poem. The speaker in this passage is Dame Study; she is addressing the poet himself, and says— ' One named Imaginative shall, hereafter, give an answer to your question.' The *question* is about Do-well, etc., and is proposed in C. xi. 121 (being expressly called a *purpos* in the preceding line). The *answer* is actually given, as Dame Study promised, by one Imaginative, in C. xv. 1–22. See B. viii. 120, 121; xi. 399–402; xii. 1, 26, 30.

—— (b. 10. 116.) Perhaps our author refers to the following passage in St. Augustine: ' Unde aliquid sapere quam res se habet, humana tentatio est. Nimis autem amando sententiam suam, uel inuidendo melioribus, usque ad praecidendae communionis et condendi schismatis vel haeresis sacrilegium peruenire, diabolica praesumptio est. In nullo autem aliter sapere quam res se habet, angelica perfectio est;' De Baptismo, contra Donatistas, lib. 2, cap. 5. See also St. Jerome's commentary on the text cited, viz. Rom. xii. 3.

—— (b. 10. 120.) Here *penance* is considered as a gift of God's grace. The line means—' But pray to Him for (the graces of) pardon and penance, during your life.'

—— (b. 10. 128.) *Worth*, shall be; as opposed to *was*.

—— (a. 11. 86.) Compare Rich. Redeles, iii. 45 :—

' Thanne cometh ther a *congioun* · with a grey cote.'

Spelt *cangun* in Hali Meidenhad, ed. Cockayne, p. 33. In Mr. Cockayne's Glossary is the following explanation :—' *Cangun*, a broad short built man.' ' *Congeon*, one of low stature, or a dwarf;' Bailey

C. PASS. XII. 94. B. PASS. X. 129. A. PASS. XI. 105.

(1759). 'The cammede *kongons* cryen after col, col, And blowen here bellewys that al here brayn brestes,' the crooked *conguns* cry after coal, coal, And blow their bellows till their brains crack ; Reliq. Antiq. i. 240. It occurs four times in the Chester Plays, spelt *congeon, counjon, congion.* It is plain that *conioun* is used as a term of contempt.

—— (b. 10. 129.) 'And those that use these wiles, to blind men's wits.' The term *hanelon* is used in the same sense in Peter Langtoft, ed. Hearne, p. 308 ;—' with *hanelon* [not *hauelon*] tham led,' he led them with guile. In Sir Gawayn and the Grene Knyght, l. 1708, it is said of a fox that he '*Hamlounez*, & herkenez · bi heggez ful ofte ;' i. e. he winds about, and often listens beside hedges. Sir F. Madden refers to the Boke of St. Albans, fol. e6, back.

> 'And iff yowre houndys at a chase · renne ther ye hunt,
> And the beest begynne to renne · as herttis be wont,
> Or for to *hanylon*, as doos · the fox with his gyle,
> Or for to crosse, as the roo · dooth oder-while.'

Also to the older treatise of Twety, MS. Cotton, Vesp. A. xii., fol. 6, b— '*Sohow* goth to alle maner of chases . . but if yowre houndes renne to one chace, that is to seye, rusest, or *hamylone*, or croisethe, or dwelle,' etc.

Hence it is clear that the sb. *hanilon* means the winding course or wile of a fox, and the vb. means to wind about in order to beguile. Cf. '*Hannicrochemens*, subtilties, intanglements.'—Cotgrave.

94-98. This passage is rather hazy in [c], having been altered without sufficient heed to the context. In [b] it means—'He hath wedded a wife, within the last six months, who is akin to the Seven Arts ; Scripture is her name.' In [c] the word *scripture* is either governed by *comsynges*, i. e. beginnings, sources ; or perhaps a better sense is obtained by supplying *is* before *of scripture*, so that the sentence will mean—'I will recommend you to Clergy, my cousin, who knows all the arts and beginnings of Do-well, Do-bet, and Do-best; for he is celebrated as a doctor (*or*, teacher) ; and he is the skilful (one) in Scripture, if only scriveners would be correct.' *And* (in l. 97) = *an*, if; *were* = would be, as often elsewhere. See note to B. x. 332 below; p. 158.

The *seven arts* or *seven sciences* were contained in the so-called trivium and quadrivium. The trivium contained grammar, logic (or dialectics), and rhetoric; the quadrivium, music, arithmetic, geometry, and astronomy ; according to the mnemonic lines :—

> *Gram.* loquitur; *Dia.* vera docet; *Rhet.* verba colorat.
> *Mus.* canit ; *Ar.* numerat; *Geo.* ponderat; *Ast.* colit astra.

See a somewhat lengthy note upon the subject in Marco Polo, ed. Yule, i. 13 ; Hallam's Introd. to the Lit. of Europe, i. 3 (ed. 1860), etc. Logic is alluded to in l. 119, Music in l. 120, Grammar in l. 122, and Geometry in l. 127.

Our poet expressly mentions the 'seven arts' below; Pass. xiii. 93 (b. 11. 166).

C. PASS. XII. 103. B. PASS. X. 153. A. PASS. XI. 109. 153

103. *Foul*, bird. 'As glad as a bird is of a fine morning' is the meaning of the proverbial expression here used. It was once quite a common proverb. See Chaucer, Kn. Ta. 1579; and Shipm. Tale, 51.

104. *To gyfte*, for a gift, as a gift [c, b].

107. This passage is in much the same strain as one in Pass. viii. 204-234 ; q. v.

118. *Sapience*, the book of Wisdom. *Sauter glosed*, the Psalter with a commentary or gloss, such as that by Nicholas de Lyra. It is Dame Study (see l. 86) who is the speaker ; she taught men the seven sciences; see note to l. 94.

120. *Musons*, measures. The etymology is easier than the exact use of it. It is the F. *moison*, from Lat. acc. *mensionem*, a measuring. Cotgrave has—'*Moyson*, size, bignesse, quantity, full length.' Roquefort gives— '*Muison*, mesure ;' but adds a false etymology. Burguy has—'*moison*, mesure, forme; de *mensio*.' In a Poem on Learning to Sing, printed in Reliquiae Antiq., i. 292, we find a definition of it :—

'Qwan ilke note til other lepes, and makes hem a sawt,
That we calles a *moyson* in gesolreutz en hawt.'

Here 'a sawt,' i. e. a leap, is printed 'a-sawt,' as if it meant 'assault;' and *gesolreutz* is printed *gesolrentz*, which makes no sense. It plainly means G-sol-re-ut (all musical terms) with z added to denote the plural; and 'en hawt' is the French *en haut*.

On application to Mr. Chappell, I received from him the following explanation, which he kindly gave me at once :—

'The meaning of "measures" is the time and rhythm of *mensurable* music, as opposed to plain chant, which was *immensurable*. The measures were denoted by signs at the commencement, which were puzzling to learn. A circle meant "perfect" or triple time; a semi-circle "imperfect" or common time. To these were added bars (1, 2, or 3) across certain lines of the staff, and the meaning depended upon which of the lines were thus crossed. They denoted whether the *mode* was major or minor, and the "probation" or division into minims. For a printed book in which to see them exemplified, refer to Piero Aron's "Toscanello in Musica," fol. Vineggia, 1539.

'There are two G-sol-re-uts in the Guidonian scale, therefore the upper one was distinguished as G-sol-re-ut *the haut*. A third G in the scale was the lowest note, called Gamma-ut, or gamut, written Γ. Thus G-sol-re-ut *the haut* is the mark of the *treble clef* (now a corruption of the letter G), in which all music for women and boys was written; and I understand the quotation from Reliquiae Antiquae to mean—"That (skipping music) we call a *measure* (or mensurable music)," fit for a boy's voice (and not for a man's). [Give us the *tenor* to hold on with, whilst they *skip*.] The tenor did not then mean a high-voice part, but rather the low one that held on the plain chant, while higher voices made "division" or variation upon it.'

Since *muson* meant measure, it was easily extended to signify measurement or dimension. Thus, in Riley's Memorials of London, p. 563, anno

1406, mention is made of some boxes, that might be made 'of nine diffcrent dimensions [orig. *mewsons*] in length, and breadth, and depth within.'

123. *Gurles*, children; boys rather than girls; see note to Pass. ii. 29, p. 21, and cf. A. 10. 155.

124. *Baleyse*, a rod; see note to Pass. vii. 157, p. 80.

133. 'But because it teaches men to love, I believe in it the more'.[c]; 'But because it sets the highest value on love, I love it the more' [b]; *or*, 'I believe it the more' [a].

—— (b. 10. 189.) *Catoun*, Dionysius Cato; see his Disticha, lib. i. 26. For *simile*, another reading is *simules*, for the improvement of the prosody. Cf. Pass. xxi. 166.

—— (b. 10. 192.) 'Whoever speaks fairly (yet deceitfully), as flatterers do, let (each) one resort to the same (plan).' This line and the next is a translation of the two Latin Lines above. The expression *go me* is for *go men*, i.e. let one go, or resort to. The shortened form *me* for *men* occurs but seldom in Piers the Plowman; other instances are in C. xii. 174; xiii. 112. It is well-known that *me* or *men* was used in Middle English (properly with a singular verb) with the force of the Fr. *on*. See Morris's Hist. Accidence, p. 143; and p. 144, note 1. Sir F. Madden remarks, in his edition of Layamon, iii. 455, note to l. 2124—'*me* is used in Layamon as *man* or *mon* in A.S., and as *on* in French. The same form occurs in the Sax. Chron. anno 1137, and often afterwards, and in the poem of the Grave, in Thorpe's Analecta, p. 142.' The verb *go* is in the 3 p. s. imperative. The most remarkable point about this passage is the late date of this use of *me*, which is more usually found in the twelfth and thirteenth centuries. Still, it occurs in Trevisa, A.D. 1387; see Specimens of English, 1298-1393, ed. Morris and Skeat, p. 236, l. 15. Cf. the form *go we* = let us go; Pass. i. 227.

—— (b. 10. 199.) See Gal. vi. 10.

—— (b. 10. 204.) For a note upon 'Michi vindictam,' see note to B. vi. 228, on p. 115.

—— (b. 10. 208.) 'Geometry and geomancy are guileful of speech,' i.e. full of deceit in the terms employed by their professors. *Geomesye* should rather be *geomensye;* see A-text, l. 153. For further remarks, see note to A. xi. 158, p. 155.

—— (b. 10. 211.) 'Yet are there contrivances (?) in caskets of many men's making' [b]; 'Yet are there contrivances (?) of boxes, of many men's inventions' [a]. The word *fybicches, febicchis, fibeches*, or *febucches*, is plainly written in the MSS., but I cannot trace any such word in English, French, or Scandinavian. I cannot even feel sure of the meaning; perhaps 'contrivances' or 'cheating tricks' suits the context; or it may have been a technical name for some compound substance employed by sorcerers and pretenders to witchcraft. A *forcer* is a casket or coffer; a *forel* is a box, or chest, or case; both these words are well illustrated by Mr. Way. See his notes to the Prompt. Parv. p. 170, note 2, and p. 171, note 2. *Forel* is the mod. Fr. *fourreau*, a sheath, case, scabbard.

(NOT IN C.) B. PASS. X. 212. A. PASS. XI. 157.   155

—— (b. 10. 212.) *Alkenamye*, alchemy. The various spellings are *alkenamye, alkenemye, alconomye, alknamye*, and, in one MS. only, *alkamye*. It is clear that William meant the word to be spelt as above; but for what reason does not appear. Roquefort gives the Old Fr. as *alkemie, alquemie, arquemie*. *Of Alberdes making*, of Albert's doing. The allusion is to the celebrated Albertus Magnus (died A.D. 1280), whose attainments were of the most varied kind, and who was ranked with Roger Bacon and Raymond Lully as an authority upon the occult sciences; see Warton, Hist. E. P. ed. 1840, ii. 337.

—— (a. 11. 158.) *Nigromancye*, necromancy. Archbishop Trench, in his English Past and Present, 4th ed., p. 244, has a note upon this word, which should be consulted. He rightly tells us, that 'the Latin mediæval writers, whose Greek was either little or none, spelt the word *nigromantia*, as if its first syllables had been Latin.' Hence, he says, the origin of the term 'the *Black* Art' as applied to necromancy. Just as necromancy signifies divination by means of the dead (cf. 1 Sam. xxviii. 8; Lucan, Pharsalia, vi. 720-830), so pyromancy (here spelt *perimancie*) signifies divination by means of fire; and *geomancy*, divination by means of the earth. See these and similar terms in Brand's Pop. Antiq. ed. Ellis, iii. 329; and Burton's Anat. of Melancholy. See the quotations in Richardson, s. v. *Necromancy*. Compare also—'that horrible swering of adiuration and coniuracion, as don thise false enchauntours and *nigromancers* in basins full of water, or in a bright swerd, in a cercle, or in a fire, or in a sholder-bone of a sheep.... What say we of hem that beleuen on diuinales, as by flight or by noise of briddes or of bestes, or by sorte of *geomancie*, by dremes, by chirking of dores, or craking of houses, by gnawing of rattes, and swiche maner wrecchednesse?' Chaucer, Pers. Tale, *De Ira*.

The pouke to rise maketh, cause the devil to rise, raise the devil; a result commonly supposed, in former times, to be within the power of magic; see 2 Hen. VI., i. 4. 24; 1 Hen. VI., v. 3. 2; and Marlowe's Doctor Faustus. On the word *pouke*, see note to Pass. xvi. 164.

—— (a. 11. 180.) 'It (i.e. the life) is called the Active life; husbandmen lead it, and all other true tillers upon earth; tailors and cobblers, and craftsmen of every kind, that know how to earn their food, or to toil for it with any true labour, or to ditch or dig; (such a life) is called Do-well.' Line 185 begins the account of Do-bet, which commands men to feed and clothe the poor, etc.

—— (a. 11. 189, 190, 193.) See Ps. cxxxii. 1 (Vulg.); Rom. xii. 15; Matt. v. 19.

—— (a. 11. 198.) 'For the sake of beggars who have fallen into misfortune were such men endowed.'

—— (b. 10. 230.) Here the word *It* refers to Do-well. 'Do-well is a common mode of life, quoth Clergy, viz. to believe in holy church,' [b]; 'Do-well is a very upright life, quoth she, among the common people,' [a]; p. 302. The definitions of Do-well in the two texts vary considerably. In [b], it is made to depend upon orthodox belief in the Trinity; but in [a], it is identified with the Active Life, according to the favourite

C. PASS. XII. 157. B. PASS. X. 238. (NOT IN A.)

distinction between the Active Life and the Contemplative one; see Pass. xvi. 194, and B. vi. 251.

—— (b. 10. 238.) The Latin line 'Deus pater,' etc. is quoted from the Athanasian Creed. The next quotation is from John, xiv. 9, 10.

157. (b. 10. 245.) 'Not all the clerks under Christ could explain this; but thus it behoves all to believe who approve of Do-well' [c]; *or*, 'but thus it behoves all the unlearned, who desire to Do Well, to believe' [b].

159. (b. 10. 247.) 'For, had no man ever a subtle wit, to dispute against the faith, no man could have any merit in faith, if it could all be proved.' Line 160 is, however, merely a translation of the Latin sentence following, which means—'Faith has no good desert, where the human reason supplies proof.' The sentence is from S. Gregorii xl. Homil. in Evang. lib. ii. homil. xxvi.; in St. Gregory's Works, ed. Migne, vol. 2, col. 1197; where we find—'Sed sciendum nobis est quod divina operatio, si ratione comprehenditur, non est admirabilis; nec fides humana habet meritum cui humana ratio praebet experimentum.' This is frequently quoted by our old authors. See Occleve, De Regim. Princ. ed. Wright, p. 13; Reliq. Antiq., i. 127, 207.

—— (b. 10. 253.) 'Be found, upon trial, to be in reality such as thou seemest to be. Appear what like thou art, or be what thou appearest.' I do not know whence this is quoted.

—— (b. 10. 259.) 'If thou wouldst blame, take heed not to be blameworthy; for thine instruction is contemptible, when thine own fault makes thee feel remorse.' I do not know the source of these lines; the rime in the latter shews them to be of no very early date.

—— (b. 10. 262.) 'All that blame any person, and have defects themselves.' *Lyf* = person.

—— (b. 10. 263.) 'Why excitest thou thy wrath because of a mote,' etc. *Meuestow* = *meuest thou*, movest thou. Chaucer quotes the same text (Matt. vii. 3) at the end of the Reeve's Prologue; see also Pierce the Pl. Crede, ll. 141, 142.

—— (b. 10. 266.) 'I advise every blind buzzard to amend himself.' A *buzzard* here means a worthless fellow. It is properly the name of an inferior kind of hawk, useless for hawking; as in the Romaunt of the Rose, l. 4031:— 'More pity that the eagle should be mewed,
  While kites and *buzzards* prey at liberty.'
                                                         Rich. III., i. 1. 132.

—— (b. 10. 271.) 'That ye should be such as ye spoke of, in order to heal others with.' *To salue with othere* = *to salve othere with*, to heal (or anoint) others with. Compare Chaucer's Sq. Tale, 639.

—— (b. 10. 276.) *Marke* is an error of the author's; he means *Matthew*. See Matt. xv. 14; and Luke, vi. 39.

—— (b. 10. 277.) 'Unlearned men may make this comparison about you; that the beam lies in your eyes, and the mote, through your defect, is fallen into the eyes of men of every kind, by means of cursed priests.' *Festu* is the right word here; see 'Quid consideras *festucam*,' etc. at l. 262 above. 'Festue to spell with, *festeu;*' Palsgrave.

—— (b. 10. 281.) 'Bitterly paid for the sins,' etc. This reference to Hophni and Phineas was afterwards introduced into the C-text, at greater length, but near the beginning of the poem. See Pass. i. 105-123.

—— (b. 10. 284.) 'Therefore, ye correctors, seize hold of this advice, and first correct yourselves.'

—— (b. 10. 285.) The text 'Existimasti, etc.' (Ps. xlix. 21, Vulgate) is quoted again below; C. xiii. 30.

—— (b. 10. 286.) *Borel clerkes* no doubt means, as Tyrwhitt suggested, lay-clerks, i. e. learned laymen, laymen who could read. *Borel* was a coarse cloth of a brown colour; see *Burellus* in Ducange, and *bureau* in Cotgrave. Hence the phrases—*a borel man*, a plain man; Chaucer, C. T. 11028; *borel folk*, lay people, id. 7453; *borel men*, laymen, id. 13961. The next quotation is from Isaiah, lvi. 10.

Here comes a passage (B. x. 292-329, A. xi. 201-210), which has already occurred; see Notes to Pass. vi. 147-179, pp. 66-70; to which add the following.

—— (b. 10. 321, 322.) See Ps. i. 6; Ps. xix. 8, 9 (Vulgate), xx. 7, 8 (A.V.).

—— (b. 10. 328.) See Isaiah, xiv. 4, 5, 6.

Next comes the passage in A. xi. 211-220, B. x. 330, 331, upon which I give the notes here following.

—— (a. 11. 211.) *Bidowe*, a curved dagger. Ducange gives '*Bidubium*, ferramentum rusticum, i. q. *falcastrum;*' and '*Dubio*, instrumentum incurvum.' The *falcastrum* was a sickle at the end of a long pole, used for cutting brushwood. Soldiers armed with weapons resembling it were called in Old French *bidaux* (Roquefort); and Roquefort also gives us —'*Bedoil*, sorte d'arme, courbée comme une serpe.' The prefix *bi* probably meant that the weapon was double-edged; and it is clear, that in the present case, the handle was a short one. The word *baselard* has been already explained; see note to Pass. iv. 461, on p. 52.

—— (a. 11. 212.) The reference here is to the horrible oaths in which even the 'religious' indulged; cf. Chaucer's Pard. Tale, and Pers. Tale, *De Ira*.

—— (b. 10. 330.) The word *dominus*, here used merely for the alliteration, is exactly equivalent to *kinghed* (i. e. the kingly estate) in A. xi. 216, q. v.

—— (a. 11. 215.) 'And even a great deal worse, if I were to tell everything.' For the quotation at l. 219, see Matt. xxiii. 2.

Next we return to C. xii. 163, where there is again a transposition of the B-text; see B. xi. 1.

163. *Many skyles*, many reasons [c]; *a skile*, a reason [b]. This answers to A. xii. 12, but the resemblance here to the A-text is so slight that A. Pass. xii. will be considered, by itself, further on.

164. 'And made a gesture to (*or*, gave a look at) Clergy, to dismiss me, as it seemed.'

165. 'And blamed me in Latin, and set light by me,' i.e. lightly esteemed

158 C. PASS. XII. 167. (B. PASS. XI. 4.) A. PASS. XI. 221.

me. The quotation is from the first words of Cogitationes Piissimae de cognitione humanae conditionis, cap. i., wrongly attributed to St. Bernard; see St. Bernard's Works, ed. 1839, vol. ii. p. 660.

167. 'And I fell (lit. became) into a sleepiness, and wonderfully I dreamt' [c]; 'And, in a sleepy sullenness, I fell asleep' [b]. The word *wynkyng* is an adjective in [b], but a substantive in [c]. It means *sleepy*, or *sleepiness*. Dr. Morris translates 'lokinge withuten *winkunge*' by 'sight without *sleepiness*;' Old Eng. Homilies, 1 Series, p. 144.

170. 'And she caused me to gaze into a mirror, named Middle-earth;' i. e. upon the mirror of the World; wherein he would behold all the world's delights; see l. 181. Poets seem to have been fond of the notion of seeing things in a mirror; we have the Mirror for Magistrates, Gascoigne's Steel Glass (or Mirror), the magic mirror in Chaucer's Squire's Tale, etc.

173. William really introduces us to *three* persons; the two damsels who accompany Fortune, and who personate the Lust-of-the-Flesh and the Lust-of-the-Eyes, and a third personage named the Pride-of-Life; according to a common exposition of the three kinds of temptation addressed to our Lord.

188. 'Then there was one named Old-age, who was mournful of look.' Cf. *heuy-chered*, downcast; Pass. xxiii. 2.

194. Before *brynge* supply the word *shal* (see *shalt* in l. 192). 'And Pride-of-perfect-life shall bring thee to much peril.'

195. *Stod*, i. e. who stood; the relative is omitted. In the B-text, Recklessness only speaks eight lines, and soon after we have a long discourse by Loyalty, beginning at B. xi. 148, and ending at l. 308. In the C-text, that discourse is delivered by Recklessness, ll. 200–309, a change which necessitated several modifications in the wording.

197. *The corone*, the crown of hair left on the head of those who had received the tonsure; see note to Pass. i. 86, p. 11. *To tyne the corone*, i. e. to lose the crown, was to lose this hair; in other words, to become wholly bald, through the effect of age. Recklessness advises the poet to amuse himself while he may, and not to bend his back by stooping to do hard labour (cf. Pass. vi. 24); for, when he goes bald, and grows old, he will stoop easily enough then; in allusion to another common effect of age. There is a slight variation between *tyme ynowe*, i. e. time enough, soon enough [c], and *tymes ynow*, i. e. times enough, often enough [b].

The poet clearly implies, in this passage, that he had *himself* received the tonsure.

200. *Go ich*, whether I go. *Myn one*, by myself, alone.

203. See Matt. xix. 24.

Here is a return to the original order; beginning with B. x. 332; A. xi. 221.

—— (b. 10. 332.) 'I will not speak scornfully, quoth Scripture, unless scriveners lie.' This expression (which somewhat resembles C. xii. 97) means that the writings of divines will not be found to use scoffing language, unless scribes wilfully corrupt their meaning. Before the invention of

(NOT IN C.) B. PASS. X. 334. A. PASS. XI. 223. 159

printing, the author was much at the mercy of the scrivener whom he employed; as Chaucer's Lines to Adam Scrivener plainly shew.

—— (b. 10. 334.) 'Help (men) not heavenward (to the extent of) a hair's end' [b]; *or*, 'at the end of a whole year' [a]. The former expression denotes a very *small quantity*; the latter, a *large* space of *time*.

—— (b. 10. 337.) See Ecclesiasticus, x. 10.

—— (b. 10. 339.) Dionysius Cato, Distich. lib. iv. dist. 4, has—

'Dilige denarî, sed parce dilige, formam;
Quem nemo sanctus nec honestus captat ab aere.'

Our MSS., however, read *denarium*. *Set* for *sed* is common.

Perhaps our author sometimes quoted Cato at second-hand; his selections from that author resemble those in Vincent of Beauvais, Spec. Hist. v. 108-110; and Vincent has likewise the reading *denarium*.

—— (b. 10. 344.) 'Where rich men may claim no right (of entrance), except by (God's) mercy and grace' [b]. Remember *there* = where.

—— (b. 10. 346.) 'And prove it both by Peter and Paul.' William does not make this good; for he really refers to Mark, xvi. 16; see [a]. Perhaps he was thinking also of 1 Pet. iii. 21; Eph. v. 26, 27.

—— (b. 10. 348.) 'That text refers to extreme cases; such as the baptism of Saracens or Jews.' The words *in extremis* probably refer to the case of people lying at the point of death. See the next note.

—— (b. 10. 350.) 'That even an infidel (*or* pagan) in that case (i.e. in a case of extreme need) may baptize a heathen; and he (i.e. the baptized person) may, for his true belief, when he loses his life, have the inheritance of heaven, just like any other baptized person.' This seems a little startling at first, but William had doubtless good authority for his statement. Professor Pearson, whom I consulted about this question, at once gave me the following quotations. At the council of Florence, in 1438, it was ruled as follows. 'In casu autem necessitatis non solum sacerdos vel diaconus sed etiam laicus vel mulier, imo *paganus et hereticus* baptizare potest, dummodo formam servet ecclesiae et facere intendat quod facit ecclesia;' Eugenius ad Armenos; Concilia, Tom. 33, p. 575 (ed. Paris). 'Casus. *Paganus* quidam baptizavit hominem in forma ecclesiae; quare quaesitum fuit, quid erat faciendum. Et respondit Isidorus, quod Papa non attendit baptizantem hominem, sed Dei virtutem in baptismo.'—Gratiani Decreta; De Baptismo, pars iii. distinctio 4, col. 2073, ed. Antverpiae, 1573.

See also Hook's Church Dictionary, art. *Baptism, Lay;* William de Shoreham, ed. Wright, p. 12; Myrc's Instructions for Parish Priests, ed. Peacock, p. 5. Compare B. xi. 82; xv. 448-550; 490, 491; 594, 595.

—— (b. 10. 355.) The text is—' Igitur, si consurrexistis cum Christo, quae sursum sunt quaerite, ubi Christus est in dextera Dei sedens;' Coloss. iii. 1.

—— (b. 10. 356.) 'He should love and believe, and fulfil the law.' *Leue* = believe; see l. 359, which means—'And thus it behoves him to love, who believes he is saved.'

—— (b. 10. 361.) 'It shall oppress us very bitterly, (viz. such wealth as is in) the silver that we hoard, and our clothes that are moth-eaten (by being stored away), while we see beggars go naked; or if we delight in wine and wild fowl, and know any to be in want.' *Bisitten* = to sit close to, oppress; from *sitten*, to sit, to fit closely. *Soure* = sourly, bitterly; see note to Pass. iii. 154, p. 36. The expression *moth-eaten* refers to Matt. vi. 19.

The word *bakkes* is glossed by *panni* in MS. L. A *bakke* had two senses: (1) the human back; and (2) a covering for the back; somewhat as when we speak of the *arm* of a coat, or the *leg* of a pair of trousers. The latter odd use of the word appears in Chaucer, Group G, l. 881, Six-text edition, where five MSS. have *bak*, whilst the Ellesmere MS. alone reads *bratt*. The passage is in the Canon's Yeoman's Prologue (l. 328), and, in the Hengwrt MS., is as follows:—

'So semeth it; for, ne had thei but a shete
Which [that] thei myghte wrappe hem in a nyght,
And a *bak* to walken in[ne] by day-light,
They wolde hem selle, and spenden on the craft.'

Bratt = Welsh *brat*, a clout, a rag, etc.; and Chaucer clearly means, by *bak*, some kind of course cloak or mantle. William, however, uses it of a rich man's dress. We may hence conclude that it was a general term; and probably the nearest modern equivalent is the word *cloak*; which will suit both passages. I may observe that *bakke* has yet a third sense in Middle-English, viz. the animal commonly called a *bat*; for this, see Halliwell's Dictionary.

From the sb. *bak*, a cloak, was formed the verb *bakken*, to clothe with a mantle, which occurs in A. xi. 185, q. v.

—— (b. 10. 368, 369.) *But if*, unless. Here our author commits a very curious mistake; he actually quotes *non mecaberis* for the purpose of translating it by 'slay not.' I fear we must lay the mistake upon William himself, as it stands the same in so many MSS. of both the A-type and B-type. Mr. Wright's note really goes to prove that such odd mistakes may easily occur. He says—'A mistake in the original MS. for *necaberis*, as it is rightly printed in Crowley's edition.' But we know that it is *not* 'rightly printed;' for the reason that *necare* is not a deponent verb, and *non necaberis* = 'thou shalt not *be killed*.' A better suggestion is the *non necabis* of the Oriel MS.; but the Vulgate version has 'non occides.' Obviously, the right explanation is, that the author, at the moment of composing, thought of the *words* of what is now the 7th commandment whilst thinking of the *meaning* of the one preceding it. In these cases, the text is likely to be right.

—— (b. 10. 371.) *But mercy it lette*, unless Mercy hinder it [b]; *but mercy it make*, unless Mercy cause it to be otherwise [a].

206. *Legende of lif*, the Book of Life; see Rev. xx. 12, 15. Referring to the doctrine of predestination.

208. 'Or else they preach (that their hearers are) imperfect, and thrust out from grace.' *Ypult*, thrust; lit. put.

209. *Vnwryten*, not written down [c, b]; *vndirwriten for wykkid*, written (*or* marked) under as being wicked [a]. See John iii. 13.

215. 'And to judge well and wisely, as women bear witness' [c]; 'He judged well and wisely, as Holy Writ tells' [b]; 'Did he not well and wisely, as Holy Church tells?' [a]. Alluding to the famous judgment of Solomon; whence the expression—'as women bear witness,' because he decided the dispute between them. The text quoted in [c] is from the saying of the woman who was in the wrong—'Nec mihi, nec tibi sit; sed diuidatur;' 1 Kings iii. 26.

220. Aristotle was supposed to be in hell for lack of baptism. But Dante places him in the first circle, or place of least punishment; see Inferno, iv. 131. It seems to have been a general belief that Solomon also was condemned to hell; but Dante (Parad. x. 110) speaks of it as being a disputed point.

230. *Men of this molde* = men of this earth or world; the B-text reads *men on this molde*, men upon this earth; which comes to the same thing. The phrase is common.

232. This means that if we wish for mercy ourselves, we must shew mercy to others; then our mercifulness will win for us God's compassion.

239. See Pass. xi. 222. For preceding quotations, see Matt. vii. 2, xxiii. 2.

244. 'God grant that it may not be so with them that teach the faith.'

245. In [c], the word *churche* should be *kirke*, to suit the alliteration; see l. 249. Our author uses either form; for in Pass. xiii. 51, we must have the form *churche*. The Ilchester MS., which has *kirke* in l. 249, is deficient here, which was my sole reason for not venturing on the emendation.

247. *Herbergh*, a harbour, a safe shelter. The phrase 'the ark of Christ's church' occurs in our Baptismal Service; it was suggested by 1 Pet. iii. 20, 21. Compare note to Pass. xi. 32, p. 133.

248. 'The end of this clause (*or* argument) has reference to curators (*or* curates).' In other words, the sequel of my argument refers to men who have cure of souls, whom I liken to the carpenters or 'wrights' who assisted Noah in making the ark. See Ps. xxxv. 7 (Vulgate).

251. 'At doom's day there shall be a flood of death and fire at once.' *Dyluuye* = Lat. *diluuium*, the deluge. That is, the world was once destroyed by a deluge of water; it shall hereafter be destroyed by a deluge of deadly fire. See 2 Pet. iii. 10.

252. In [b], the sense is—'Work ye such works as ye see recommended in writing, less ye be not found therein;' where by 'therein' is meant 'in holy church,' in the ark of safety.

256. *Byknew on*, acknowledged. *Byknowe* = to confess; Pass. i. 209; Pass. vii. 206. Hence *byknew on* = confessed in, i. e. confessed belief in, acknowledged. The penitent thief is here said to have been saved before John the Baptist and others, because it was said to him—'To-day shalt thou be with Me in paradise;' and it was believed that when Christ had descended into hell, fetching thence the souls of John the Baptist, of Adam, Isaiah, and other saints, He led them to Paradise, when they found that

162 C. PASS. XII. 260. B. PASS. X. 420. A. PASS. XI. 277.

the penitent thief had already obtained entrance there. Such is the account given in the apocryphal gospel of Nicodemus. Cf. Pass. xxi. 369, 370.

260. *Rather*, sooner; solely with reference to *time*. Cf. *sonnere* in l. 257.

263. The Gospels merely say of Mary Magdalene—'out of whom went seven devils;' Luke viii. 2; Mark xvi. 9. There is not a word to connect her with the account in the preceding chapter of St. Luke, viz. Luke vii. 37-50. We are quite at liberty to reject the once prevalent notion, which has found its way even into our Bibles, viz. in the heading to Luke vii., where we read—'Mary Magdalene anointeth Christ's feet.' But it is very clear that our author took Mary Magdalene to have been the same with 'the woman that was a sinner;' hence it is that he says—'who could have done worse in fondness for lechery, for she refused no man.' The spelling *maudeleyn* in [a] is worthy of notice; it shews that the pronunciation of the word as *Maudlin* is of early date.

265. *Vrye*, Uriah. See 2 Sam. xi. 14, 15. The C-text means—'who devised how Uriah might be most slily slain, and sent him to war, truly, as to all appearance, but provided with a deceitful letter.' *As by hus lok* = to judge by his (David's) look.

—— (b. 10. 431.) Translated from Eccles. ix. 1—'Sunt iusti atque sapientes, et opera eorum in manu dei; et tamen nescit homo, utrum amore an odio dignus sit.' *Wel-libbynge*, living a good life; a translation of 'iusti.'

—— (b. 10. 433.) 'Whether a man shall be esteemed there for his love and his true deeds, or whether he shall be esteemed for his ill will and envy of heart, in accordance with the way in which he lived; for, by (observing) the bad, men discern the good.'

273. The quotation is from Eccles. ix. 1. Cf. b. 10. 431.

275. 'And, in faith, to tell the truth, I never found that learning was ever commended by the mouth of Christ' [c]; 'And moreover I further forget [i. e. cannot remember], as far as the teaching of my five wits goes, that learning,' etc. [a]. The B-text has but *one* line (10. 442), viz. 'Learning was then little commended by Christ's mouth.'

—— (b. 10. 438.) 'Therefore let us continue to live with wicked men (*or*, as wicked men do); I believe few are good.' This is not a very proper sentiment; but it is hardly William's own. He is following up a particular line of argument, which, in the C-text, he puts into the mouth of *Recklessness*.

—— (b. 10. 439.) 'For when the word "must" comes forward, there is nothing for it but to suffer.' A proverbial expression; we now say—'What can't be cured, must be endured.' The mixture of Latin and Old French is curious. The spelling *qant* for *quant* was common; see Burguy's Glossaire. *Ny* was written for *n'y*. *Ad* should rather be *at*, the old spelling of the 3rd pers. sing. indic. of *avoir; at* being for *habet*. It is now written *a*, except in the phrase *y at il*, which is ridiculously written *y a-t-il*, as if the *t* belonged to nothing. Indeed, many still believe that the *t* is 'inserted for euphony,' though why a *t* is more 'euphonious' than another letter, they cannot tell us. The whole line becomes, in modern spelling—For, 'quand *oportet* vient en place, il n'y a que *pati*.' See a similar French proverb in Pass. xiv. 205, 206.

In a short poem on Grammatical Rules, printed in Reliquiae Antiquae, ii. 14, we find the proverb again in the form following:—

'And, when *oportet* cums in .plas,
Thou knawys *miserere* has no gras.'

277. The quotation is from Mark xiii. 9, 11.

280. *Conclude*, refute [c, b]; *answere*, reply to [a]. In the Examination of W. Thorpe, printed in Wordsworth's Eccl. Biog. i. 266, we read—'In all those temptations Christ *concluded* the fiend, and withstood him.' Cf. Ps. cxviii. 46 (Vulgate).

287. *That euere man wiste*, that ever man knew [c]; and highest of the four [b, a]. By 'the four' is meant the four chief 'Latin Fathers;' see Pass. xxii. 269, and the note.

288. St. Augustine did not say this 'in a sermon,' but in his Confessions. The passage runs thus—'Surgunt indocti et coelum rapiunt, et nos cum doctrinis nostris sine corde, ecce ubi uolutamur in carne et sanguine;' S. Aug. Confess. Lib. viii. c. 8; ed. Migne, vol. 32, col. 757. Cf. Mat. xi. 12; xxi. 31. The spelling *idioti* occurs in several MSS., and Ducange gives *idiotus* as well as *idiota*. See *Idiot* in Trench's Select Glossary. The Greek ἰδιώτης meant a private person, one not in public life; and secondly, an uneducated person. It is used here in the latter sense. Thus—'images be the laymen's books, and pictures are the Scripture of *idiots* and simple persons;' Homilies: Against Perils of Idolatry.

294. 'And ignorant true-hearted labourers and land-tilling people' [c]; 'Cobblers and shepherds [*or* sewers, i. e. men who sew, *A-text*], such ignorant fellows' [b]. The word *soware* is given as a variation of 'sewstare or sowstare, *sutrix*' in the Prompt. Parv. We have had the verb *sewen*, to sew, in Pass. ix. 8, 10. Thus *souter* (= Lat. *sutor*) is equivalent to *sewer* (from A.S. *séowian*).

295. *Persen*, pierce, force their way into; cf. Mat. xi. 12. *A paternoster*, just one short prayer.

Dr. Rock says—'That the souls of the good are carried to heaven instantly after death, is a truth expressed repeatedly in our old literature;' Church of Our Fathers, iii. 204.

Here ends A. Pass. xi. For notes to A. Pass. xii., see p. 164.

298. *The reyue*. Comp. Chaucer, Prol. 587–622, especially l. 602—

'Ther couthe no man bringe him in arrerage.'

302. 'As clerks of holy church, who ought to keep and save unlearned people in true belief, and give them (things) in their need' [c]; 'As clerks of holy church, who keep Christ's treasure, that is to say, man's soul, in order to save it,' etc. [b]. Cf. B. xv. 491.

Here ends B. Pass. x. For notes to B. xi. 1–35, see notes to ll. 163–197 above, pp. 157, 158.

NOTES TO A. PASSUS XII; (NOT IN C, B.)

1. This twelfth Passus is very scarce. Of ll. 1–19 there are but three copies extant, of ll. 20–88 but two, and of the remainder, but one. If ll. 99–103 are not William's, I suppose they are John But's, who certainly added twelve lines after l. 105.; see footnote to p. 331 of the text.

6. 'It would please you to learn, but displease you to study;' i.e. you do not mind learning when you can be *told* a thing, but you are too lazy to find out *by yourself*. This state of mind is still common.

7. 'You would like to know all that I know, so as to be able to retail it to others.'

8. 'In order, perhaps, to question so many people in a presumptuous manner, that it might turn to harm as regards me, and as regards Theology also. If I knew for certain that you would do according to my teaching, I would explain all you ask me.'

14, 15. 'That he should not shew it me, unless I should be shriven by natural chief Wisdom, and christened in a font.' Somewhat obscure.

18. *Defendeth*, forbids; as in C. iv. 68 (B. iii. 64; A. iii. 55).

19. 'Vidi praeuaricantes, et tabescebam: quia eloquia tua non costodierunt;' Ps. cxviii. 158 (Vulgate). It is clear that William translates *tabescebam* as if it were *tacebam*; see l. 20.

22. See 2 Cor. xii. 4.

28. 'What is truth? said jesting Pilate, and would not stay for an answer;' Bacon's Essays, i. William, on the other hand, suggests that Christ did not deem Pilate deserving of an answer.

33. Alluding to A. xi. 286, where William says that Christ never commended 'Clergy;' accordingly, Clergy now retorts, saying ironically, 'I am such as he says,' i.e. I am not to be commended; and declines to say more.

34. *This skile y-sheued*, shewed (me) this reason.

35. This resembles the line—
Creptest into a caban · for colde of thi nayles; A. iii. 184.

39. 'To be her servant, if I might, for ever after.' We often find *moste* = might; thus *myghte* (C. v. 107) is written for *moste* (B. iv. 112; A. iv. 99).

40. *With that*, on the condition that. *Me wisse*, instruct me. *Were*, might be, was.

42. *Low*, laughed. *Lauȝthe* (Rawl. MS.), written for *laughte*, i.e. caught, seized; see ll. 55, 96.

49. 'She called, to shew me the way, a young chorister named *omniaprobate*.' *Clerioun* is Chaucer's *clergeon*, Cant. Tales, Group B. 1693; see my note on the line, in The Prioresses Tale, etc., ed. for the Clarendon Press. 'Omnia probate; quod bonum est tenete;' 1 Thess. v. 21.

55. *Laughte oure leue*, took our leave; cf. A. iii. 26.

58. This line has occurred before; A. Prol. 62 (B. Prol. 65; C. i. 63).

59. *A-fyngrid* = *of-hungred*, extremely hungry. Cf. l. 63.

67. *Henteth,* seizeth. Cf.—' a feyntise me hente,' A. v. 5, 6.
80. 'Whence he had come, and whither he meant to go.'
82. 'My name is Fever ; on the fourth day I am always thirsty.' An allusion to the so-called quartan fever, which 'grieueth from the fourth daye to the fourth daye ;' see Batman upon Bartholome, lib. vii. c. 40— 'Of the feauer quartane, his signes and remedies.'
So also *quotidian* is a daily fever ; and *tertian* one that recurs every third day. See ll. 84 and 85.
86. *Letteres of lyf,* i. e. a letter belonging to Life, directed to Life, or (as we should now say) a letter *for* Life. Fever is bringing a letter from his master Death, to tell Life that he must die ; cf. C. xxiii. 168–179. *Letteres* = a letter ; see note to B. ix. 38, p. 140.
88. 'If I might do so, God knows I should like to go your way ;' i. e. to accompany you. Here the Ingilby MS. suddenly ends.
91. 'Thou wilt tumble as if caught in a pit-fall, if thou follow my track.' *Tomblest* is the present used for the future, as in Anglo-Saxon. *Trepget* is the Fr. *trebuchet,* from the O. Fr. *tresbucher,* to overthrow. Cotgrave gives—' *Trebuchet,* m. a pit-fall for birds ; a pit, with a trap-door, for wild beasts ; also, a pair of gold weights ; also, an old fashioned engine of wood, from which great and battering stones were most violently thrown.' Halliwell gives the spelling *trepeget.* For ' *Trase* (1) a trace, path ; (2) a track,' see Halliwell.
92. *Wrouȝþ* (in MS.) is certainly a mistake for *worth,* which the scribe might not have understood, as it is a rather uncommon word. *Worth* = shall be ; see the Glossary. The reading *wrouȝþ* is impossible, because the future tense is absolutely required. The sense is—' man's joy shall be no greater than he deserves (by his life) here.'
96. *Lauȝth* (in MS.) is for *laught,* caught, taken up. *Lyȝth* = light, i. e. heaven. *Loking of an eye,* glance of an eye ; i. e. in the twinkling of an eye ; cf. 1 Cor. xv. 52.
99. The sense is—'Will (the author) knew by intuition—thou knowest well the truth—that this speech was immediate, and made great haste, and wrought that which is here written, and other works too, concerning Piers the Plowman,' etc. If ll. 99–103 are genuine, then we must regard the mention of his death as a mere flourish ; but they are probably spurious, and added by one John But, who avowedly added some lines at the end of the copy in the Rawlinson MS., in the course of which he mentions Rich. II. as being still alive. If so, then they express John But's belief that the author was dead, as to which he must have been (at the time) mistaken. Possibly the author's *real* name and position were no better known in his own time than they are now.

☞ Here the A-text ends ; the notes pass on to C. xii. 304.

304. ' Homo proponit, sed Deus disponit ;' De Imitatione Christi, lib. i. c. 19. The proverb is quoted again, Pass. xxiii. 34. The attribution of it to Plato is probably a mistake ; the obvious source of it is—' Cor hominis disponit uiam suam ; sed Domini est dirigere gressus eius ;' Prov. xvi. 9.
310. ' " Yea, farewell, Phip ! " quoth Childishness.' Here *fauntelet* =

C. PASS. XIII. 1. B. PASS. XI. 43.

a little child [c], which is equivalent in sense to *fauntelte* = childishness [b]. Childishness is here introduced in opposition to Elde (old age), l. 188. Elde gives the poet good advice, but Recklessness (l. 195) and Childishness tell him to despise that advice, which, for a time, he does. Moreover, Childishness dismisses the good advice of Elde in the most flippant and contemptuous manner, viz. by the expression—'Well, farewell, Phip [sparrow]!' i.e. good bye to you, be off! you may go! Compare the phrase—'Go farewell, feldefare!' in the Romaunt of the Rose, 5513, which must be considered in connection with its context; see also Chaucer's Troilus and Cress. iii. 861—'The harme is done, and farewel feldefare.' So also in the Cant. Tales—

And *farewel*, al the reuel is ago; l. 11516.

The pot to-breketh, and *farewel*, al is go; l. 16376.

By consulting all these passages, it will be found that 'farewel' was used much as we should use the phrase—' it's all over, and it's of no good to talk about it.' ' Farewel, feldefare' was marked by Tyrwhitt as a phrase not understood by him, but it is clearly an ironical way of dismissing a profitless or unpleasant subject. The fieldfare visits England in the winter, from November to April; its departure is therefore observed with pleasure, as a sign of the beginning of milder weather. See Hazlitt's Eng. Prov. p. 128.

Fyppe or *phippe* is for *Phip*, the contracted form of Philip; see note to B. xv. 119.

NOTES TO C. PASSUS XIII. (B. Pass. XI. 43-277.)

The references within a parenthesis refer to the B-text.

13. 1. (11. 43.) *Eye*, an interjection denoting astonishment, answering nearly to our 'eh!' It is spelt *ey* in Tyrwhitt's Chaucer, C. T. 3766, 10165. Cf. G. *ei*.

2. (11. 44.) *For welthe*, etc.; because Wealth does all that he pleases [c]; but in [b] we have—*for wille to haue his lykynge*, in order for Will to have his pleasure. And here *Will* may either denote the mind's desire, or the poet himself, with reference to his name of ' Will.' The latter interpretation suits the context very well; see *me* in l. 41, *my* in l. 42, and *me* again in l. 45 of the B-text.

—— (11. 46.) *Wynter*, years. It is well known that our ancestors commonly calculated by *winters*, as being, to them, the most serious part of the year to provide for. See numberless instances in the Anglo-Saxon Chronicle.

And a fyfte more, and a fifth (year) besides. That is, the poet was 45 years old, as he again tells us in B. xii. 3. Taking A. D. 1377 as the date of the B-text (see Pref. B. pp. ii–v), we thus get A. D. 1332 as the year of his birth.

Observe that the next line (l. 47) of [b] corresponds to C. xii. 312.

4. (11. 52.) In the C-text, we must suppose that Lust-of-the-Eyes addresses Recklessness in l. 4, but in l. 5 turns to the poet and addresses him in a like strain. William has, at the moment, identified his opinions with those of Recklessness, whose arguments he for the time adopts. See the speeches of Recklessness in C. xii. 195-197, 200-309, and observe that he is mentioned by name in C. xii. 274 and 283. The B-text is clearer, because no mention is made of Recklessness after l. 40.

6. (11. 52.) Here, to *come to good* means to arrive at the possession of property, to acquire wealth. *Morally* speaking, it would be a 'going to the bad.' With reference to confession to *friars*, see notes to Pass. iv. 38, p. 41, and vii. 120, p. 78.

9. *Fraternite.* This alludes to the 'letters of fraternity' or 'provincial letters.' See notes to Pass. iv. 67; x. 342, 343; pp. 42, 130.

11. *Pol by pol*, head by head; i.e. severally, separately. Each sinner who had made the proper payment would have a separate mass said for his benefit.

21. 'That desireth the widow, only to be married to her wealth' [c]; 'That marry no widows, except in order to command (*lit.* wield) their goods' [b]. We frequently find similiar charges against the friars. See Polit. Poems, ed. Wright, pp. 331, 332; Jack Upland, sectt. 16, 17; Wyclif's Works, iii. 374.

—— (11. 77.) *Catekumelynges*, i.e. catechumens. In Hook's Church Dictionary we find—'*Catechumens;* a name given, in the first ages of Christianity, to the Jews or Gentiles who were being prepared and instructed to receive baptism,' etc. See the whole article.

—— (11. 81.) I do not know where to find the quotation 'sola contritio,' etc. Chaucer has the same remark. 'I say that contrition sometime delivereth man fro sinne,' etc.; Pers. Tale, Prima Pars Penitentiae. Cf. Ps. xxxii. 5; 1 John i. 9.

—— (11. 82.) See B. xv. 448-450, and note to B. x. 350. See John iii. 5.

24. Love and Loyalty are mentioned, as persons, in Pass. v. 36, 156; since which we have had no more mention of them. In this line Loyalty is suddenly brought before us again, without any introduction. 'Then laughed Loyalty, because I frowned upon the friar' [c]; *or*, 'And Loyalty looked on me, and I frowned afterwards' [b].

30. The expression *and saue onliche prestes* means that the only exception to the duty of publicly rebuking sinners is in the case of priests who have learnt the existence of sins in the course of confessions made to them. See note below, to B. xi. 92, p. 168. Cf. Ps. xlix. 21 (Vulgate).

—— (11. 87.) It would not be very easy to support the duty, of rebuking sinning brethren publicly, from St. Peter's epistles, but our author may have been thinking rather of certain passages in those of St. Paul; especially Gal. ii. 11, 1 Tim. v. 20, Titus i. 13, ii. 15. Or, indeed, the reference to St. Peter may very easily point to St. Paul's open rebuke of him; Gal. ii. 11. The text 'non oderis' is from Levit. xix. 17—'Non oderis fratrem tuum in corde tuo, sed publice argue eum, ne habeas super illo peccatum.'

It is particularly to be noted that there is a pun upon the word *fratres*. Literally, it means *brethren*, but our author tells us plainly that it also means *friars ;* see note to Pass. xvi. 75, and observe l. 90 [b] below.

31. Here William uses the counter argument. 'But they (the friars) will quote a text to a different effect, viz. Mat. vii. 1.'

32. Loyalty replies—'Of what use then were the law, if no man ever reproved falsehood and deceit? Surely it was for some good reason that the apostle said *non oderis fratrem*.'

Lyf, a living person, a man. *Vndertoke*, rebuked, reproved. This sense is required by the context, and is justified by our author's use of *vndernymeth* in the same sense, that of *reproveth*, in B. v. 115; since *nyme* and *take* are words of the same power and sense.

William is verbally wrong in using the word 'apostle' here, since the text occurs in Levit. xix. 17, as above noted; but perhaps he considered that St. Paul practically quoted that text in 1 Tim. v. 20, which bears the very same sense, though worded differently.

—— (11. 92.) *Licitum*, permitted. The argument is—every law permits laymen to speak the truth openly in all cases; but parsons and priests must not utter 'tales,' i.e. matters recounted to them in confession. At first sight, this looks like an argument in favour of the supposition that the author was himself a layman; but it is clearly meant that the clergy were *likewise* permitted to speak freely, with the sole exception that they must not utter sins admitted to them in the confessional. And the reader will further observe the advice in ll. 36-39, and the argument, in l. 34, that the misdeeds of the friars were *so notorious* that it could not be wrong to speak against them. We must not lay stress upon the *three lines* in B. xi. 92-94, apart from their context, but fairly read and ponder the *whole* of that Text.

—— (11. 96.) *And*, if. 'Even though the recital were true, if it touched upon sinful conduct.'

46. The Vulgate version has—'*Multi* enim sunt uocati, *pauci* uero electi;' Mat. xxii. 1-13.

Mangerie, a feast; lit. an eating. Wyclif uses the very same word with respect to this same parable of the Great Supper; Works, i. 4. The word occurs at least thrice in the Tale of Gamelyn; ll. 345, 434, 464.

51. Holy-church, it may be remembered, was introduced as a person in Pass. ii. 72, and was made to say, in the next line—

'Ich *vnderfeng* þe formest · and fre man þe made.'

With respect to ll. 53-73, Whitaker remarks—'the best theology of modern times will scarcely furnish a better refutation of the doctrine of absolute election and reprobation, than this admirable passage.' For the quotations, see Isaiah lv. 1; Mat. xvi. 16.

61. This is one of the frequent allusions which shew that William was familiar with legal matters. The reference is to the legal condition of 'villeins,' which is illustrated by Littleton's Book of Tenures, sect. 172-208. There were two principal classes of villeins, viz. 'villeins in gross,' who

were of the lowest class, and could be sold by their lords; and a rather higher class, named 'villeins regardant,' here referred to, who were attached to the soil, and specially engaged in agriculture. 'These were in a better condition than villeins in gross, were allowed many indulgences, and even, in some cases, a limited kind of property; yet the law held that the person and property of the villein belonged entirely to his lord, the rule being the same as that in the Roman law, that whatever was acquired through the slave was acquired by the lord;' English Cyclopaedia, Arts and Sciences, s. v. Villein. See also Bruce, ed. Skeat, i. 229-274.

73. See Ps. cxliv. 9 (Vulgate).

74. *Baw*, an expression of great contempt, used again in Pass. xxii. 398. It is clearly the word which is spelt *buf* in Chaucer's Sompnours Tale, Group D, l. 1934; and it was obviously intended to express contempt. Cf. Mod. E. *bah!*

75. *Troianus* means Trajan. In B. xi. 155, we are expressly referred to the Legenda Sanctorum for the story; see Caxton's translation of the Golden Legend, fol. lxxxvii. Bacon alludes to it in his Advancement of Learning, ed. W. Aldis Wright, pp. 54, 55, in these words:—' On the other side, how much Trajan's virtue and government was admired and renowned, surely no testimony of grave and faithful history doth more lively set forth, than that legend tale of Gregorius Magnus, bishop of Rome, who was noted for the extreme hatred he bare towards all heathen excellency; and yet he is reported, out of the love and estimation of Trajan's moral virtues, to have made unto God passionate and fervent prayers for the delivery of his soul out of hell; and to have obtained, with a caveat that he should make no more such petitions.' Mr. W. A. Wright adds a note—' This story is told of Gregory the Great in his life by Paulus Diaconus, c. 27, and in that by Joannes Diaconus, lib. ii. c. 44; and is referred to by Joannes Damascenus, De iis qui in Fide Dormierunt, c. 16.'

87. *Sarrasyn*, Saracen, i. e. unbeliever, idolater. In B. xi. 157, he is called a 'paynym of Rome.' The terms Saracen and Pagan were often used as synonymous with Mahommedan, and it was a universal belief with Christians in the middle ages that Mahommedans were idolaters. Cf. Pass. iv. 484, xviii. 123, 132, 150–186.

—— (11. 147.) *There no biddyng myghte*, where no prayer could do so. Trajan could not have been released by prayers offered in the usual manner; only by a special grace. For *there = where*, cf. B. xi. 160 below.

88. Let the reader observe the inverted comma at the beginning of this line. In the B-text the speech is spoken by Loyalty, and extends to 163 lines, ending with l. 310. In the C-text, it is spoken by Recklessness, and consists of no less than 288 lines, ending with C. xiv. 128.

'See, ye lords, what Loyalty effected, and true judgment as practised by him' [c]; 'See, ye lords, what Loyalty did with respect to an emperor of Rome.' On this use of *by*, see note to Pass. i. 78, p. 11.

—— (11. 164.) 'And gave it to Moses on the mount, to teach all men.' See the note on *took;* Pass. iv. 47; p. 41.

92. 'As for Law without Loyalty (i. e. Truth), stake but a bean on it!'

[c]; 'As for Law without Love, saith Trajan, stake but a bean on it' [b]. William is fond of this theme; cf. Pass. iv. 447-450, v. 144, 145, 156, etc.

93. *Seuene ars*, seven arts; see note to Pass. xii. 98, p. 152.

98. See 1 John iii. 14 (Vulgate).

—— (11. 173.) 'Should each of them love the other, and lend to them (*or* give to them) as they would to themselves.' *Lene*, lend, give; not *leue*, believe, as that would make nonsense.

—— (11. 180.) Surely a beautiful line; cf. Mat. xxv. 40. See C. xii. 121 below.

103. *Carful*, full of care, wretched; cf. Pass. xii. 42, and see Luke xiv. 12.

105. *Manshupes*, courtesies, honours, compliments. In the Ormulum, l. 19014, *mannshipe* means dignity. In Layamon, *monscipe* occurs repeatedly; and Sir F. Madden remarks (vol. iii. p. 439)—'This word does not occur in Bosworth's A. S. Dictionary, although it is difficult to suppose it did not exist. It is used very frequently in both texts of Layamon, and its usual meaning undoubtedly is *honor, worship, dignity*.' It is clear that, in the present passage, the sense is nearly that of the Lowland-Scotch *mensk* or *mense* (which see in Jamieson), from the A.S. *mennisc*, humane.

106. In [c], *for* is a conjunction, meaning *because*; in [b], it is the common preposition.

107. *That*, those who [c]; who [b].

109. *Blod-breþrene*, brethren by blood; written *blody bretheren* in [b]. See l. 115 below, and the phrase *bretheren as of o blode* in B. xi. 193; and see note to Pass. ix. 217; p. 114.

110. *Quasi modo geniti* was a familiar phrase, and used as a name for Low Sunday, or the octave of Easter, because, in the Sarum Missal, the Office for that day begins with the text 1 Pet. ii. 2; viz. 'quasi modo geniti infantes, rationabile sine dolo lac concupiscite.' The Duke of Westminster's MS. adds *infantes*.

111. *Bote yf synne hit make*, unless sin cause it to be so [c]; *or*, unless sin caused it to be so [b]; cf. Pass. viii. 4, 28, 65. See John viii. 34.

112. *Me*, i. e. men, people; the usual indefinite pronoun, common in Middle-English. See Morris, Outlines of Eng. Accidence, p. 144, note 1. Thus *me calde vs* = we were called. The B-text has the form *men*. See note to B. x. 192, p. 154.

Considering that William had no access to a concordance, he is remarkably correct in his argument. The phrase 'children of men' occurs 19 times in the Old Testament, but, in the New, not at all; whilst 'children of God' occurs 10 times in the New Testament, but not once in the Old.

116. 'Therefore let us love (one another) as dear children, and give to them that need' [c]; 'Therefore let us love as dear brethren ought to do, and let each man smile upon another; and, out of what each man can spare, let him give help where it is necessary' [b].

117. 'For we shall all (depart) hence.' See Gal. vi. 2.

—— (11. 207.) 'For no man knows how nigh is the time for him to be taken away from both (property and skill). Therefore let no living being

C. PASS. XIII. 137. B. PASS. XI. 216.

blame another, though he know more Latin, nor repròve him foully, since there is none faultless.'

—— (11. 216.) 'For it is very long before logic can explain thoroughly a moral discourse.' *Lessoun* seems to mean a 'lesson' taken out of the Legenda Sanctorum. To *assoille* is to resolve, explain, answer, satisfy, etc.; lit. to absolve; see *asoilede* in C. xiii. 137 below.

137. 'And God quickly made answer with respect to the desire of each of them' [c]; 'And God quickly answered, and followed (i.e. acceded to) the wish of each' [b]. See Luke x. 40, 42.

—— (11. 245.) *Mathew.* A mistake; St. Matthew does not mention them; see Luke x. 40-42.

146. *Kynde*, natural vigour. In The Book of Quinte Essence, ed. Furnivall, p. 1, we have the expression—' how þat olde men, and feble in *kynde*, myȝte be *restorid*.' It is rather odd that so much virtue should here be attributed to walnuts, but it was no doubt a common belief. It is sufficiently verified by the words of Andrew Boorde, in his Introduction of Knowledge, ed. Furnivall, p. 283; where, speaking 'of nuttes, great and smale,' he says—' The *walnut* and the banocke be of one operacyon. They be tarde and slow of digestyon, yet they doth *comforte the brayn if the pyth or skyn be pylled of, and than they be nutrytyue.* Fylberdes be better than hasell nuttes; yf they be newe, and taken from the tree, *and the skyn or the pyth pulled of, they be nutrytyue, & doth increase fatnes.'* A *banocke*, by the way, is the West-of-England *bannut.* Halliwell says— the growing tree is called a *bannut* tree, but the converted timber *walnut.*' An explanation given me in Shropshire affords a further light. I was told that a *bannut* was the ordinary walnut such as is commonly seen there, but a *walnut* was a similar nut of a larger size, imported from abroad, in accordance with the well-known derivation of the word.

151. *Drat*, a contracted form of *dredeth* [b].

—— (11. 262.) *Salamon.* But, strictly speaking, the text (Prov. xxx. 8) is not Solomon's; it occurs in the proverbs of Agur, son of Jakeh; Prov. xxx. 1.

—— (11. 265.) The text in St. Luke is—'Adhuc unum tibi deest: omnia quaecunque habes uende, et da pauperibus;' Lu. xviii. 22. William really quotes the parallel passage, in Mat. xix. 21. He seems to have observed the mistake, as it does not appear in the C-text.

—— (11. 270.) See Ps. xxxvi. 25 (Vulgate); Mat. xvii. 20; Ps. xxxiii. 11 (Vulgate).

—— (11. 277.) *And thei her deuoir dede*, if they did their duty. William refers us to Ps. xlii. 1 (Vulgate), i.e. to Ps. xliii. 1 (A. V.), which does not seem to be much connected with the subject. But no doubt he meant us to consider the general tenor of the whole Psalm, which has language suitable for priests in verses 3 and 4, and breathes the true spirit of reliance upon God's protecting care.

☞ A long insertion here in the C-text; B. 11. 278 corresponds to C. xiv. 101.

159, 166, 170. Mat. xix. 29, 21; Luke xiv. 33.

173. (*not in* b.) *Poetes.* The poets (or rather authors) here mentioned are merely named at random, just as in Pass. xv. 190. It would be useless to point out what these authors have really said in praise of poverty. Consult Burton's Anatomy of Melancholy.

Porfirie of course represents the celebrated Greek philosopher Porphyrius (died A.D. 306), many of whose works are extant.

175. *Tullius*, i. e. M. Tullius Cicero. *Tholomeus*, i. e. Ptolemaeus the astronomer (floruit A.D. 130–160), author of the Almagest, etc. Chaucer (C. T. 5906) cites a passage which may very well be the one here intended.

179, 180. Cf. John xii. 24. 'Unless the seed that is sown die in the slough (*or* mould), no blade will ever spring up, nor any ear of corn harden to grain upon the straw.' Palsgrave has—'*Spyre* of corne, *barbe du ble*.' '*Spyre* of corne or herbe, *Hastula;*' Prompt. Parv. *Spike* is the Lat. *spica*, an ear of corn ; cf. Icel. *spik*, a spike, a sprig. To *curne* is to form grain, to granulate ; cf. G. *körnen* ; see Rob. of Gl., ed. Hearne, p. 490.

187. 'Are more seasonable and hardier (lit. tougher) for man's behoof.' William's father is said to have been a farmer ; and this is one of the innumerable passages that prove him to have been qualified to sing of 'The Plowman.'

188. Observe *with* = against, as in l. 192. *Mowe nouht*, may not endure, cannot hold out.

192. 'Cannot so well hold out against the frost, in the open field, if it freeze long.'

193, 194. *That*, they that. *Worth alowed of*, will be approved by. The whole passage is good.

204–207. This passage is the only incomplete one in the C-text. Line 206 is from the Ilchester MS., and is incomplete because the rats have eaten the end of it. The missing portion must have been like what I have supplied within square brackets. The sense is—'For Christ said to His saints, that for His sake suffered poverty, penance, and persecution of body, (they) shall have the more honour for their reward, and be esteemed more worthy than angels ; in their affliction, He greeted them in this wise, viz. your sorrow shall be turned into joy.' It deserves to be particularly noted that, in our author, as in Hampole, the word *anger* means *affliction* or *distress*, and just answers to the Latin *tristitia*. See John xvi. 20.

209. *Wyrdes*, weirds, fates, destinies.

211. *Foul towname*, evil 'to-name,' evil nickname; alluding to the word *stulte* below. Stratmann gives three examples of *toname*, as meaning *cognomen;* viz. Wycl. Ecclus. xlvii. 19 ; Manning, l. 7000 ; Layamon, l. 9383.

212. 'And that his spirit shall depart hence, and his wealth remain behind.' See *bilæfen* in Stratmann.

215. Here the person is changed, from the third to the second. 'Thou that art so loath to leave that which thou must needs leave.' See Luke xii. 20. The whole text in Ps. xxxviii. 7 (Vulgate) is—'Thesaurizat, et ignorat cui congregabit ea.'

216, 217. *Unredy*, void of counsel, improvident. Æthelred was named the Unready because he was void of counsel and imprudent; from A.S. *unrǽd*, bad advice. The sense is—'an improvident reeve shall spend what thou leavest; (he shall spend) in a moment that (wealth) in which many a moth was master;' i.e. in which many a moth revelled. Cf. B. x. 362. *Mynte-while*, a moment; this form is clearly due to the confusion between *mite* and *minute*, on which see Way's note to 'Mynute, myte, minutum' in Prompt. Parv. p. 340. See also Pass. xiv. 200, where the B-text (xi. 372) has *minute-while*. It must be remembered, too, that *mites* are called *mints* in the West of England.

218. *Vpholderes*, dealers in second-hand articles, as in Pass. vii. 374; the Duke of Westminster's MS. has *Vpholsters*. *The hul*, the hill; which, beyond all doubt, means Cornhill; cf. Pass. vi. 1; Liber Albus, p. 624.

221. *Pees-coddes*, pods of peas. *Pere-ionettes*, evidently pears that were soon ripe. 'In *July* come . . . early peares, and plummes in fruit, *ginnitings*, quadlins;' Bacon, Essay 46. The *genniting* is an early apple. Cotgrave has—' Pomme de S. Jean, S. John's apple, a kind of a soon-ripe sweeting;' and again—'Hastiveau, a hasting apple or peare;' and— ' Hastivel, as Hastiveau; or, a soon-ripe apple, called the St. John's apple' P. Lacroix (Manners, Customs, etc. during the Middle Ages, p. 116) tells us that, in the 13th century, one of the best esteemed pears was the *hastiveau*, which was 'an early sort, and no doubt the golden pear now called St. Jean.' I have no doubt that the term *ionette* (and probably *genniting*) is ultimately derived from *Jean*, and that the reference is to St. John's day, June 24. Cf. F. *Jeannot* (O.F. *Jeannet*) as a diminutive of *Jean*.

222. 'Soon ripe, soon rotten;' Heywood's Proverbs.

224. ' Most subject is the fattest soil to weeds;' 2 Hen. IV. iv. 4, 54.

229. *Wose*, i. e. ooze, slime, mud. It occurs in the Tale of Beryn, ed. Furnivall, l. 1742. And see Prompt. Parv., p. 532, note 3.

230. ' So out of riches, (heaped) upon riches, arise all vices.'

232. *Worth lygge*, will lie down; will be 'laid' by its own over-weight.

244. *Hus harde holdynge*, his close keeping (of his wealth), his parsimonious grasping, his 'closefistedness.'

246. ' See how money has (often) purchased both fair mansions and, at the same time, terror; money, which is the root of robbers; I mean, the riches that is kept within-doors.' The sense is clear, but the construction is very awkward. A *place* often means a manor-house or squire's mansion, as in Chaucer's Sir Thopas, first stanza. Money is called the 'root' of robbers, as being productive of robbery.

NOTES TO PASSUS XIV. (B. Pass. XI. 278—END.)

Lines 1–100 are peculiar to the C-text.

1. 'But well may it be for poverty.' *Wel worth*, well be it, is the opposite of *wo worth*, which is much more common. Cf. 'O *well* is thee;' Ps. cxxviii. 2 (Pr. Book).

4. See 2 Cor. vi. 10.

5. *Men rat*, people read, one reads. *Men*, being indefinite, takes the singular verb. *Rat* is short for *redeth*, as in Pass. iv. 410, 416.

10. Understand *was*. 'And Abraham (was) not bold enough once to hinder him.' See Gen. xx.

18. *Do we so mala*, let us also receive evil. See Job ii. 10.

23. *Thorgh grace*, by God's favour, or blessing.

45. This is interesting testimony. It shews that messengers were sometimes privileged, and might take a short cut without trespass. It also shews that the hayward, in case of trespass, used to exact a pledge (such as a hat, or a pair of gloves, see l. 48 below) from the trespasser. A similar allusion occurs in a burlesque song about the Man in the Moon, of whom it is said that—

> 'He hath hewe sumwher a burthen of brere,
> Tharefore *sum hayward hath taken ys wed;*'
>   Ritson's Ancient Songs, i. 69.

In this case, the allusion is to committing trespass for the purpose of cutting some briars for fuel.

'Necessity has no law;' quoted as 'Need hath no law' in Pass. xxiii. 10. Skelton, in his Colin Clout, ll. 864, 865, says—

> 'But it is an olde sayd sawe,
> That nede hath no lawe.'

The same form occurs in Heywood; and see Ray's Proverbs.

52. Winchester fair. See note to Pass. vii. 211, p. 83.

55. *Breuet*, a letter or note. Cotgrave has —'*Brevet*, m.: a briefe, note, breviate, little writing,' etc. See Hist. Agriculture in England, by J. E. T. Rogers, i. 666, for examples of messengers being sent with a scroll. He observes—'Parchment, though not very cheap, was quite within the use of most persons of any substance. The letter was written on a slip of this material, a narrow piece being cut half way through at the bottom to which the seal was annexed, and the whole rolled round and tied with thread, or in some cases silk.' In the present passage, the letter is described as enclosed in a box.

69. 'Both to love, and to give alms (lit. lend) to the true and the false.'

71. *By hus power*, as far as lies in his power.

72. *Backes*, clothes for the back, cloaks; see B. x. 362, and the note, p. 160. *For the colde*, as a protection against the cold; see B. vi. 62.

73. 'Truly to pay tithes of their property; which tithe, as it seems, is a sort of toll (or payment) which our Lord expects from every living creature that makes money without fraud or wrong-dealing, or without keeping women in brothels (as the brothel-keepers do).'

Loketh after, looks for, expects to have. *Lyf*, creature. But our author remarks that men ought not to presume to offer tithes of gains that they have obtained by fraudulent means, neither ought brothel-keepers to offer of the money paid them by those who lodge with them. See Pass. vii. 287-308.

77. *Spele*, to spare, hoard ; see Pass. vii. 432.

78. See Galat. vi. 8.

80. *The two lawes*, i.e. the duty to God and to our neighbour. William means that the poor beggars could not carry out some parts of these duties, especially the giving of alms, the imparting of instruction, and fasting during Lent. They could not clothe the naked, they were excused from paying tithes and serving on inquests, and they were permitted to work on saints'-days and vigils to earn food.

85. *Contumax*, contumacious, a despiser of authority. '*Contumax* is he that thurgh his indignation is ayenst euery auctoritee or power of hem that ben his soueraines ;' Chaucer, Pers. Tale, *De Superbia.* With l. 87, cf. Mark xvi. 16.

90. 'Cc fesses himself to be a Christian, and of holy-church's belief.'

91. 'There is no law, in my belief, that will hinder him in his way, where God is the porter Himself, and knows every one (who enters). The Porter, out of pure compassion, may fulfil the law (by admitting him), inasmuch as he (the poor beggar) desires (to do) and would (do) to each man as to himself.' It is clear from what follows that *he* (l. 94) refers to the beggar, not to the porter.

96. *Reyme*, grasp at, reach after, acquire. Such I take to be the sense of this difficult word. Halliwell gives '*Rame*, to reach, or stretch after.' 'To rame, *pandiculor* ;' Coles' Dict. ; and again, '*Rame*, to rob or plunder. Lincolnshire ;' also, '*Ream*, to hold out the hand for taking or receiving ; North.' So in Polit. Songs, ed. Wright, p. 150—

'Thus me pileth the pore and pyketh ful clene,
The ryche *raymeth* withouten eny ryght.'

98. See Mark xii. 43 ; Luke xxi. 3.

101. This is an obvious and interesting allusion to Wyclif's so-called 'Poor Priests.' See Wyclif's Works, i. 63, 176, 177 ; iii. 272, 293, etc. By 'Spera-in-deo' is meant part of Ps. xxxvi (Vulgate) or Ps. xxxvii (A.V.) ; the third verse of which is—'Spera in Domino, et fac bonitatem ; et inhabita terram, et pasceris in diuitiis eius.' The whole of the rest of the psalm, verses 4-40, is full of encouragement to well-doers.

104. 'The title (of 'priest') by which you take orders proclaims that you are advanced,' i.e. are set in authority. The very word *priest* or *presbyter*, i.e. elder, entitles the man who bears the name to some respect.

106. *Tok*, gave ; as elsewhere. 'He that gave you the title should give you your wages ; or else the bishop should do so who ordained you, and anointed your fingers.' In l. 106, the person intended by *he* is probably the pope himself, as is suggested by his being likened to a king in l. 108.

112. *By*, with reference to ; as elsewhere.

113. 'Who have neither skill nor relationship (to great men), but only the tonsure, and the title of priest, a thing of no account, to live upon, as it were.' *Corone* means the tonsure; see l. 125, and cf. Pass. i. 86, and the Note. *A tale of nouht*, a reckoning of no value, a thing of no account; because the title, though in some degree a sign of rank (see l. 104), is often slightly esteemed, and does not go for much in the way of supporting the man who bears it.

118. 'If false Latin be in that document, the law impugns it.' This clearly shews, I think, that William had often drawn up, or at least copied out, legal documents.

119. *Peynted parentrelignarie*, 'i. e. interlined; for I cannot think that mere interlineary flourishes would vitiate a charter ;' Whitaker.

122. See James ii. 10.

123. The advice of David is contained in the word *sapienter;* or, in our English version, 'sing ye praises *with understanding;*' Ps. xlvii. 7. William is declaiming against 'ouerskippers,' or those who skipped over passages in reciting masses or other services. In Reliq. Antiq. i. 90, there is a distich which is remarkable for preserving the epithets bestowed on those who either *mumbled, skipped,* or *leaped over* the Psalms in chanting :—

'Ecclesiae sunt tres qui servitium male fallunt;
Momyllers, forscyppers, ovrelepers, non bene psallunt.'

Compare also Rel. Ant. i. 290 ; Poems of Walter Mapes, ed. Wright, p. 148. Palsgrave has—'I *Ouerhyppe* a thyng in redyng or suche lyke, *Ie trespasse:* you haue *ouer-hypped* a lyne, *vous auez trespasse vne ligne.*' See *ouerhuppen* in B. xiii. 68.

125. *Coroneþ*, marks with the tonsure, shaves in a priestly manner. See note to l. 113, and compare—

'With *croune* and berde al fresh and newe yshaue.'
Chaucer ; C. T. 13239.

The term *knightes* is correctly used, since it meant servants. Cf. A.S. *leorning-cniht*, a disciple, lit. a learning-servant. Mr. Cutts, in his Scenes and Characters of the Middle Ages, p. 247, quotes this passage, and reminds us that priests commonly had the title of *Sir*, which is another reason for the use of the term *knight*.

128. 'For either of them is indicted, and that by reason of the statement, that ignorance does not excuse bishops, nor unlearned priests' [b]. The word *idiotes* is here used as an adjective, with the French plural ending. Cf. *cardinales*, Pass. i. 132; *prouincials*, Pass. x. 342, and the note, p. 130.

With respect to the word *idiot*, see note to Pass. xii. 288, p. 163.

With this line is concluded the long speech which, in [c], is spoken by Recklessness, and begins at xiii. 88. In [b], it ends two lines further on, and is spoken by Loyalty, who begins at B. xi. 148.

150. *Bere*, make a noise, low [c]; *belwe*, bellow [b].

156. Compare Bacon's Advancement of Learning, ed. W. Aldis Wright,

p. 151—'Quis psittaco docuit suum χαῖρε? . . . Who taught the bee to sail through such a vast sea of air, and to find the way from a field in flower a great way off to her hive?' Mr. Thomas Wright aptly quotes a favourite passage from Hurdis's Poems:—

> 'But most of all it wins my admiration
> To view the structure of this little work,
> A bird's nest. Mark it well, within, without;
> No tool had he that wrought, no knife to cut,
> No nail to fix, no bodkin to insert,
> No glue to join. His little beak was all.
> And yet how neatly finished!' etc.

161. 'If any mason were to make a mould for it with all her (the pie's) wise contrivances, it seems to me a wonder!' See remarks on the magpie's nest in The Architecture of Birds, p. 325.

169. *Dompynges* (spelt *doppynges* in MS. E), is clearly only another name for the *dab-chick*, called by Drayton 'the diving *dobchick*,' Polyolbion, s. 25. We also find *didapper*, spelt *dive-dapper* by Middleton; see Nares. Halliwell gives *dopchicken* as the Lincolnshire name. In the Prompt. Parv. p. 127, we have the entry—'Doppar, or dydoppar, watyr-byrde. *Mergulus*,' immediately followed by 'Doppynge,' left unexplained, as meaning the same. Cf. A.S. *dopened, dopfugel, doppettan*.

—— (11. 349.) This curious idea was derived from Aristotle. 'The pregnancy and conception of barren eggs is quick in most birds, as in the partridge . . . for if the hen stands in the way of the *breath* of the male she conceives, and immediately becomes of no use for fowling;' Arist. Hist. of Animals, bk. vi. c. ii. § 9; tr. by Creswell (Bohn's Library).

171. Cotgrave gives—'*Cauquer*, to tread a hen, as a cock doth;' and Palsgrave—'I trede, as a cocke dothe an henne, *Ie cauque*.' It is the Lat. *calcare*.

181. 'Was the fact that I saw Reason follow all animals' [c]; 'Because Reason regarded and ruled all animals' [b]. Observe *rewarded* for 'regarded.'

192. *Reason*. 'He should have said by *instinct*, which would have removed the difficulty;' Whitaker.

197. The B-text means—'Why I suffer (it to be so), or suffer it not; thou thyself hast naught to do (with it). Amend it if thou canst, for *my* time is to be waited for. Patience is a sovereign virtue, and is (really) a swift vengeance.' The apparent paradox in the last line is an evident reference to Luke xviii. 7.

198. See Ecclus. xi. 9.

199. 'Who is more long-suffering than God? quoth he; no one, as I believe.'

—— (b. 11. 374.) See 1 Pet. ii. 13.

204. 'And so the wise man witnesseth, and so the French proverb instructs us' [c]; 'French men and free men thus train their children' [b]. The conjunction of 'Frenchmen' with 'free men' is striking, and points to the French-speaking habits of the upper classes. Observe how

'freo man' is opposed to 'cherl;' Pass. xxiii. 146. *Affeyteth* means literally *tame*, and was used, in French, with respect to hawks; it here means *train, tutor*, or *discipline*. For the opinion of 'the wise man,' see Eccles. vii. 8.

* 205. 'A fair virtue is Patience; evil speaking is a petty vengeance. To speak well of others and to endure things patiently make the patient man come to a good end.' These two lines are really four short lines, in rime. The word *suffrable* is rare, and less intelligible than the form *soffrant* of the B-text, which I have adopted in the above translation. The form *ly* or *li* (better than *lui*) was used in Old French as an article; see Burguy's Grammaire, I. 46, 53.

Chaucer has some lines much resembling ll. 202-208 of the present passage; see his Frankeleyn's Tale, C. T. 11085-11092—

'Patience is an hey vertue certein,' etc.

211. 'Each man would be blameless, believe thou none otherwise!' With *lacles*, blameless, cf. *lakke*, to blame, in l. 208.

—— (11. 389.) 'And bade every created thing multiply according to its kind, and all to please man with, who must endure wo, through the temptation of the flesh and of the fiend also.'

213. *Tit*, for *tideth* [c]; *bitit*, for *bitideth* [b]; i.e. it betides or happens to him.

214. From Dionysius Cato, Distichorum liber, i. 5 :—

'Si uitam inspicias, hominum si denique mores,
Cum culpant alios, nemo sine crimine uiuit.'

Cf. Horace, lib. i. Serm. Sat. iii. 23.

216. (11. 396.) *And awaked.* Here ends the Fourth Vision.

217. (11. 397.) Whitaker refers us to a similar passage in the Tempest, iii. 2. 149.

220. 'And then there appeared a wight, who he was I knew not' [c]; 'And, as I lifted up mine eyes, one looked at me, and asked me' [b]. The stranger's name is Imaginative; Pass. xv. 1. Here, in fact, begins the Fifth Vision, or the Vision of Imaginative; ending, in both texts, at the conclusion of the Passus next following.

226. *Entermetyng*, intermeddling, with reference to the text Ecclus. xi. 9, quoted at l. 198 above. See the verb *entermeted* in l. 408 of the B-text. Cotgrave has—'*S'entremettre de*, to meddle, or deal with, to thrust himself into.' In Pecock's Repressor, i. 145, we have—'Who euer schewith him lewid ... he is worthi to be forbode fro *entermeting* with the Bible in eny party ther-of.' The quotation 'philosophus esses, si tacuisses' is from Boethius, de Cons. Phil. lib. ii. prosa 7; see Chaucer's translation of Boethius, ed. Morris, p. 59. Compare Prov. xvii. 28, x. 19; Dion. Cato, lib. i. dist. 3, 12; Monumenta Franciscana, p. 600.

228. *Mamelede aboute mete*, prated about food, viz. the forbidden fruit. Cf. *mamely*, B. v. 21; and Milton, P. L. ix. 921.

234. 'Nor doth Clergy at all care to shew thee (some) of his cunning' [c]: 'That Clergy careth not to follow thy company' [b].

235. Cf.—'Uerecundia pars est magna penitentiae;' quoted from St. Augustine in the Ancren Riwle, p. 331.

247. 'Yea, certainly, that is true; and he got ready to set off walking.' See note to Pass. i. 2. Cf. *shope her*, Gower, C.A. iii. 62.

NOTES TO C. PASSUS XV. (B. Pass. XII.)

1. By *ymaginatyf* is represented what we should call Imagination or Fancy. William means, in particular, *his own* power of Imagination; see l. 3. Line 2 describes Imagination as a lonely power, ever busy; *to which* [b] *adds*—in all states of health. And see note to B. x. 115, on p. 151, which accounts for the introduction of Imaginative in the present passage.

3. This is an important line, as fixing the poet's age. In the B-text, he is 45, in the year 1377, and so born about 1332. In the C-text, William has altered it to the purposely vague form 'more than forty years.'

7. 'Nor to waste speech, as, e. g., by speaking idly.'

9. 'Humble thyself to continue to live,' etc.

—— (12. 9.) See Luke xii. 38.

—— (12. 12.) See Prov. iii. 12; Rev. iii. 19.

—— (12. 14.) This is rather a singular interpretation of 'thy rod and thy staff, they comfort me;' Ps. xxiii. 4. William takes it to mean that God's corrections turn to consolations.

—— (12. 16.) *Makynges*, poems; so *make*, to write poetry, to compose, in l. 22 below; and in C. Pass. vi. 5. See Trench, Select Glossary, s. v. *Make*. One of the earliest instances of the use of *makyere* in the sense of 'author' occurs in the Kentish Ayenbyte of Inwyt, ed. Morris, p. 269; written A. D. 1340. The A. S. *scóp* and O. H. G. *scof* mean a 'shaper.' The German *dichter* means an 'arranger;' the Fr. *trouvère*, Provençal *troubadour*, and Ital. *trovatore* mean a 'finder.' With the expression *sey thi sauter*, compare C. Pass. vi. 45-52.

—— (12. 19.) *Peyre freres*, pair of friars. *Peyre* often means a set; but here *pair*. The friars often went about in pairs; see Ch. Somp. Ta. l. 32, and cf. C. Pass. xi. 8. For the omission of the word *of* after *peyre*, cf. 'a peyre tables' in Chaucer's Astrolabe, ed. Skeat, ii. 40. 18.

—— (12. 21.) *His sone*. The title of Cato's book is Dionysii Catonis Disticha de Moribus *ad Filium*.

—— (12. 23.) The quotation is from Distich. iii. 7 :—
 'Interpone tuis interdum gaudia curis,
 Ut possis animo quemuis sufferre laborem.'

—— (12. 30.) See 1 Cor. xiii. 13.

—— (12. 37.) *Rochemadore*. Roquemadour or Roquemadou (Rupes Amatoris) is said to be a town in Guienne, on the river Dordogne, formerly called also Rocamacorus or Rochemindour. See the Knight de la Tour-Landry, ed. Wright, p. 70, and his note at p. 213.

'The Virgin of Rocamadour was famous as early as the eighth century, for, if tradition is to be believed, Charlemagne and his brave followers came to pay it homage on their return from an expedition against the Gascons; and the sword of Roland, deposited as an offering upon the altar of the chapel of St. Michael, is still [1874] to be seen. Around this sanctuary, dedicated to the Virgin, were seventeen chapels hewn *in the rock* [note the name of the place]; they were dedicated to Jesus Christ, to the Twelve Apostles, to St. John the Baptist, to St. Anne, to St. Michael, and to *St. Amadour*, whose hermitage was here, and who had no doubt brought from the East the black Virgin who has been venerated there for twelve or fifteen centuries.'—Lacroix, Military and Religious Life in the Middle Ages, p. 388.

—— (12. 39.) This line is very difficult. It seems that *mayden to marye* must be an expression meaning 'a maiden as regards marriage,' i. e. unmarried; and the rest of the line then means—'and mightest well continue (such).' That it was so understood is rendered probable by the reading *contene* (i. e. contain) of the Oriel MS., just as two MSS. have *conteyne* for *contynue* in C. Pass. xi. 284, which see. Though the author speaks strongly in favour of marriage in Pass. xi. 281-288, he yet puts the unmarried life above it, as in Pass. xix. 89, 90. I think this is, accordingly, the right interpretation; and agree with Mr. Wright in placing no comma after *mayden*.

—— (12. 41.) William is arguing in praise of Loyalty or obedience. Lucifer fell through pride and consequent disobedience; see note to Pass. ii. 105, p. 24. Solomon and Samson were disloyal to chastity.

—— (12. 43.) 'Job the Jew bought his joy very dearly;' or, 'paid dearly for his prosperity.' William here really changes his subject. Having mentioned the examples of Lucifer, Solomon, and Samson, he proceeds to adduce further examples of such as fell from great prosperity into subsequent adversity. This was a favourite theme with the writers of the time, as exemplified by Boccaccio's De Casibus Virorum Illustrium, Chaucer's Monkes Tale, and Lydgate's Falls of Princes.

—— (12. 44.) Mr. Wright has a note here which I quote. 'These three names were the great representatives of ancient science and literature in the middle ages. Aristotle represented philosophy, in its most general sense; Virgil represented literature in general, and more particularly the ancient writers who formed the *grammar* course of scholastic learning, whether verse or prose; Ypocras, or Hippocrates, represented medicine. They are here introduced to illustrate the fact that men of science and learning, as well as warriors and rich men, experience the vicissitudes of fortune.' It remains, however, to be explained in what sense these three worthies experienced adversity. This is not to be explained from the history of their lives on earth, but by the universal belief of the time that their souls were lost, as was also that of Solomon; see this expressly declared in Pass. xii. 211-220. The spelling *ypocras*, for Hippocrates, occurs in some MSS. of Chaucer, Prol. 431. There is a legend concerning him, which brings him to an evil end, in The Seven Sages, ed. Wright, 1046–1153 (cf. Introd. pp. lviii, lx.); see also Weber's Metrical Romances, iii. 41, 77, 368. Virgil was chiefly celebrated, in the middle ages, as having been a great magician, who, according to Vincent of Beauvais, fabricated certain magical statues at Rome.

—— (12. 45.) *Elengelich*, sadly, miserably; see note to Pass. i. 204. Alexander's sad and early death is well described by Plutarch. Most likely William adopted the current notion that Alexander died by poison, as told, e. g., in the Romance of Alexander, ed. Weber, ll. 7850–7893.

—— (12. 46.) 'Wealth and natural intelligence became a source of ruin to them all.' In all the above examples, their fall was due either to riches or to pride of knowledge. This remark shews that William adopted the legendary tales about Hippocrates and Virgil that have been indicated above. Strict grammar would require the use of *or*, not *and*, in this line. See nearly the same expression below, C. xv. 17; B. xii. 57.

—— (12. 47.) *Felyce hir fayrnesse.* For remarks on this use of *hir*, see note to Pass. xix. 236. 'Felice's fairness became altogether a disgrace to her.' It is probable that we have here a reference to some particular version of the famous romance of Guy of Warwick. See the Percy Folio MS., ed. Hales and Furnivall, ii. 509, 515. Note particularly the quotation at the latter reference, viz.—' Dame *Felys*, daughter and heire to Erle Rohand, for her beauty called *Felyse belle*, or *Felys the faire* by true enheritance, was countesse of Warwyke, and lady and wyfe to the most victoriouse Knight, Sir Guy ; ... but when they wer wedded and been but a litle season togither, he departed from her to her greate hevynes, and never was conversaunt with her after, to her vnderstandinge ;' etc. The conduct of dame Felice had been disdainful ; and, when Sir Guy quitted her at the end of the fortieth day, she must have felt it as a great disgrace. Her fairness had but brought slander and scandal upon her. She even thought of suicide.

—— (12. 48.) 'And Rosamund, in like manner, pitiably bestowed herself,' i. e. sacrificed herself. The word *bysette* is properly active, meaning to employ, as in C. vii. 254 ; we must supply *her*, i. e. herself. The name of Rosamund is but too notorious. A very curious account of her is given in The French Chronicle of London, ed. G. J. Aungier, for the Camden Society, 1844.

—— (12. 52.) I do not know whence this is quoted. It is not in Cato's Distiches. For the quotation at l. 56, see Luke vi. 38.

17. Nearly repeated from above; B. xii. 46.

18. (12. 58.) See Luke xii. 47, 48 ; 1 Cor. viii. 1.

—— (12. 60.) *But if the rote be trewe*, unless the root (or foundation) of it be true; i. e. unless the wealth be acquired by perfectly just and fair means. Otherwise, the wealth is rather 'a root of robbers,' i. e. productive of thieves ; because what has been untruly obtained deserves to be untruly taken away ; see Pass. xiii. 247, and the note, p. 173.

20, 21. These two lines are parenthetical, and explanatory of the expression *vnkynde rychesse*, which means wealth unnaturally acquired, wrongful gains. They mean—'As, for instance, when abandoned wretches come to be lords, and ignorant men set up as teachers, and holy church becomes a giver to harlots and is avaricious and covetous.' *Horen* is the genitive plural.

23. There is a pun here on the words *grace* and *grass*, which must have been pronounced very much the same at this period. The latter is used, in this passage, in the sense of *a herb of healing virtue*, as in William of Palerne, ed. Skeat, ll. 636, 644, 799, 1030. Compare the pun by which *rue*, to repent, caused the herb *rue* to be called the 'herb of grace;' Hamlet, iv. 5. 181.

24. 'Till good-will begin to rain (upon it)' [c]; 'but amongst the humble' [b].

25. *Wokie*, soften, moisten. The sense is, that grace is like a healing herb; but it grows not till good-will rains upon it, and moistens (*or* softens) men's wicked hearts by means of good works. Halliwell gives '*wokey*, moist, sappy,' as a Durham word; also '*Weaky*, moist, watery. *North*.' Cf. A. S. *wácian*, to weaken; G. *weichen*, to soak, to macerate.

27. (12. 65, 67, 71.) See John iii. 8, 11.

40. The *sygne* [c], or *carectus*, i. e. characters [b], has reference to the words written by Christ upon the ground; John viii. 7. See this illustrated in the Coventry Mysteries, ed. Halliwell, pp. 220, 221, where Christ is represented as writing upon the ground the sins of the accusers. St. Augustine says (Homil. on St. John vi. 6) that Christ, by writing on the ground, signified that he was the Lawgiver; it was to remind the Jews that The Law had at first been written on tables of stone; and this reminded the Pharisees of the Law, and how *each one ought to judge himself*. It is clear that William was thinking of this interpretation, since he refers to the Law of Moses just above. It is also easy to see how St. Augustine's remark was changed into the statement that Christ wrote each man's *sins* upon the ground.

The word *sygne* (*carectus*, b) is curious. It seems to indicate that Christ's words upon the ground were supposed to have been denoted rather by special characters or signs than by ordinary letters. See the Chapter on 'Characts' in Brand's Popular Antiquities (ed. Ellis, iii. 319), shewing that Gower uses *carect* in the sense of a charm—'With his *carect* would him enchaunt;' Conf. Amant. bk. i. See also *Caractes* in Halliwell's Dictionary.

50. It seems reasonable to suppose that this comparison of an untaught man to a 'blind man in battle' may have been suggested by the well-known yet unusual instance of such an occurrence at the battle of Creçy, A. D. 1346, in which the blind king of Bohemia was slain. See Froissart, Chron., bk. i. c. 129.

65. 'Nor think lightly of their science, whatever they do themselves.'

66. 'Let us take their words at their (true) worth, for their witnesses are true.'

68. 'Lest strife should thus enrage us, and each man should aim blows at another.' Cf. *choppe adoun*, strike down, Pass. i. 64. With l. 69, cf. Ps. civ. 15 (Vulgate).

83. See 1 Cor. iii. 19. For the texts below, cf. Luke ii. 15, Matt. ii. 1.

88. 'But of cleanness and of clerks, and keepers of beasts' [c]; 'Nor of lords that were ignorant men, but of the most learned men existing' (lit. the highest lettered men out) [b]. This use of *oute* with a superlative is very remarkable; we can still say 'the last thing *out*.' It occurs again below; xv. 191.

91. This seems a strange version of the Bible narrative in Luke ii. 7. But the notion would hardly be one which William invented; I have no doubt he merely adopted some opinion which he had met with. Thus Peter Comestor writes—'Ingressi vero magi *domum* [cf. Matt. ii. 11] quam *diuersorium* lucas nominat.' This plainly shews how the notion might arise. The Magi entered a *house;* this house was wrongly identified with the *inn;* and the *inn* was imagined to be the best house in the town. See Dict. of the Bible, s. v. *Inn*.

92. *Poetes.* This idea was possibly founded upon the words of St. Luke, that 'the shepherds returned, glorifying and praising God.' We are reminded of Cædmon, the neatherd and poet.

96. *Tho*, when. *Hit*, i. e. 'the glory of the Lord;' Luke ii. 9. *Shewere*, a 'shewer,' i.e. a revealer or discloser. *Shewere* is the usual Middle-English word for *a mirror;* see the examples in Stratmann, of which I here cite a few. '*Shewers, Sheweres*, mirrors, Exod. xxxviii. 8; Is. iii. 23;' Wycliffite Glossary. So also—' ase ine *scheauwere*,' as in a mirror; Ancren Riwle, p. 92; 'ane sseawere,' a mirror, Ayenbyte of Inwyt, ed. Morris, p. 84.

97. *Clerkes*, learned men, viz. the Magi. *Comete;* see note to Pass. xxi. 243.

100. *Crabbede*, harsh, cross, peevish. The reference is to Pass. xii. 275–303; B. x. 442–474. In the B-text, the poet speaks the 'crabbed words' himself; see B. x. 372. In the C-text, they are put into the mouth of Recklessness (see xii. 200), who is the poet's confidential friend and adviser for the time being.

104. The illustration here given is imitated from Boëthius, lib. 4, pr. 2. See Chaucer's translation, ed. Morris, p. 114, ll. 9–16.

Temese, the Thames. This use of the name of a river (without the definite article preceding it) is still common in many parts of England, and sounds well; it seems to add to the dignity of the river. In Shropshire they talk of 'Severn.'

105. 'And both naked as a needle, neither of them heavier than the other;' where, for 'heavier,' the B-text has *sykerer*, i. e. safer, or in a less dangerous position. This proverbial expression occurs in the form 'naked as nedel,' in MS. Laud 656, fol. 6 b, line 2.

117. See Ps. xxxi. 1 (Vulgate); xxxii. 1 (A.V.).

120. *Loketh after lente*, waits for Lent.

124. *After*, according to, according to the instructions of. Observe the distinction here between a parson and a parish-priest. The former was properly a rector, the latter might be a vicar or perpetual curate. See *Parson* in Hook's Church Dictionary. William is here very severe upon their frequent ignorance.

125. *Luk*, Luke. See Luke vi. 39; but William's words are somewhat nearer to Matt. xv. 14.

126. 'For much woe was marked out (allotted) to him that has to wade with the ignorant.' The image refers to a man who employs a guide to conduct him over a ford, and finds that he is unacquainted with the depth of the stream.

127. 'Well may the child bless him that set him to his book,' i. e. taught him to read. *That* = him that.

128. *After letterure*, according to written precepts.

129. '*Verset*, a versicle, or short verse;' Cotgrave.

The allusion is to the 'benefit of clergy,' and to the 'neckverse.' Such allusions are very numerous. Thus, in Marlowe's Jew of Malta, A. iv. sc. 4, we have—'within forty foot of the gallows, conning his neck-verse.' A note on the passage, in Cunningham's edition, says—'The words used by a criminal to establish his right to " benefit of clergy." The fifty-first Psalm was generally selected, and the opening words *Miserere mei Deus* came to be considered the neck-verse, *par excellence*. The ceremony was not abolished till the reign of Queen Anne.' In Hudibras, part iii. c. 1, we find—

'And if they cannot read one verse
I' th' psalms, must sing it, and that's worse.'

'In Hudibras's days,' observes Dr. Grey, 'they used to sing a psalm at the gallows; and therefore he that, by not being able to *read* a verse in the Psalms, was condemned to be hanged, must *sing*, or at least hear a verse sung, under the gallows before he was turned off. This custom arose from the practice of what was called benefit of clergy. In the times when book-learning was a rare accomplishment, a person who was tried for any capital crime, except treason or sacrilege, might obtain an acquittal by "praying his clergy;" the meaning of which was, to call for a Latin Bible, and read a passage in it, generally selected from the Psalms. If he exhibited this capacity, he was saved as a person of learning, who might be useful to the state; if he could not read, however, he was hanged. Hence the common saying among the people, that if they could not read their neck-verse at sessions, they must sing it at the gallows.' See a very graphic description of such an ordeal in Sir F. Palgrave's Merchant and Friar, at p. 175. The benefit merely saved the man's life; he could still be subjected to fine or imprisonment; see ll. 146, 147 below. It is clear from the present passage that *Dominus pars hereditatis* (Ps. xv. 5, Vulgate), was also in use as a neck-verse in the time of Richard II. as well as *Miserere mei*.

131. 'Where ignorant thieves are hung, see how they (the clerks) are saved!'

133. *Yelde hym creaunt*, yielded himself as a believer. The more

usual phrase is exemplified in *yelt him recreaunt*, yields himself as a coward, which occurs in Pass. xxi. 105. The form *yelde* is here weak, but the verb was originally a strong one.

135. The quotation is inexact. The Vulgate has — 'nolo mortem impii, sed ut conuertatur impius a uia sua et uiuat;' Ezek. xxxiii. 11.

136. That there are degrees of bliss in heaven has been at all times a prevalent belief. See Dante's Divina Commedia; Ayenbyte of Inwyt, ed. Morris, p. 267; Hampole's Pricke of Conscience, l. 7876. Cf. Matt. v. 19; xi. 11; xviii; 2 Cor. xii. 2; etc.

138. In like manner King Horn, when disguised, enters the hall, and sits upon the ground like a beggar. See King Horn, ed. Lumby, ll. 1115-1133. The 'sovereigns of the hall' were those who sat at the high table, generally raised upon a daïs.

145. *A soleyn*, a solitary person. *Soleyn* is our modern *sullen*; see examples in Stratmann; to which add—'In *solein* place by my-selue;' Gower, Conf. Amant. iii. 6.

146. See note to l. 129 above. The quotation is from Ecclus. v. 5— 'De propitiato peccato noli esse sine metu, neque adicias peccatum super peccatum.'

150. See the note to Pass. xiii. 75. *Tulde*, dwelt; lit. pitched his tent. The verb is *telden*, to pitch a tent, which see in Stratmann. It is a derivative of A. S. *teld*, a tent.

153. See Ps. lxi. 13 (Vulgate); Matt. xvi. 27.

156. Cf. Ps. cxxxiv. 6 (Vulgate) : ' Omnia quaecunque uoluit, Dominus fecit in caelo, in terra, in mari, et in omnibus abyssis.' See the ' Thyrde Lesson' in the Monday service used by the nuns of Sion, in the Myrour of our Lady, ed. Blunt, p. 182, and Peter Comestor's Historia Scolastica, at the end of cap. xxiv.

157. *By thee*, with respect to thee. *Weyes*, ways [c] ; *the whyes*, the reasons why, lit. the why's [b].

158. See Pass. xiv. 170-193.

—— (12. 228.) ' The nest [of the magpie] is usually placed conspicuous enough, either in the middle of some hawthorn bush, or on the top of some high tree. The place, however, is always found difficult of access, for the tree pitched upon generally grows in some thick hedgerow, fenced by brambles at the root, or sometimes one of the higher bushes is fixed upon for the purpose;' Goldsmith's Animated Nature, iii. 170. ' Its nest, well fortified with blackthorn twigs, is a curiosity;' Eng. Cyclopædia, s. v. Corvidæ; Pica caudata. Cf. note to Pass. xiv. 156, p. 176.

166. See Ps. cxlviii. 5 (Vulgate).

171. ' That the fairest bird (i. e. the peacock) engenders in the foulest manner.' Cf. Pass. xiv. 171-173.

179. See the description of the peacock's long tail, ugly feet, and harsh cry in Laurence Andrewe's Noble Life, cap. xci, quoted in The Babees Boke, ed. Furnivall, p. 219. Though the flesh is here called 'foul flesh' [b], or 'loathsome' [c], peacock was, as Mr. Wright remarks, a celebrated dish at table. See also the note to l. 184 below.

184. *The poete*, the author, the writer. William would have called a poet a *maker* (see note to B. xii. 16); he uses *poet* to denote any writer, whether in prose or verse, as when he speaks of Plato as being such (Pass. xii. 304), or Cicero and Aristotle (Pass. xiii. 173-175 ; and see l. 190 below). In the present passage, the writer meant is Aristotle ; see below, B. xii. 266. Thus in Batman vpon Bartholome, lib. xii. c. 31, we read—' And Aristotle sayth, that the Pecocke hath an vnstedfast and euill-shapen head, as it were the head of a serpent, and with a crest. And he hath a simple pace, and small necke and areared, and a blew breast, and a taile ful of bewty, distinguished on high with wonderful fairnesse ; and he hath foulest feet and riueled [*wrinkled*]. And he wondereth of the fairenesse of his fethers, and areareth them vp, as it were a circle about his head ; and then he looketh to the foulenesse of his feete, and lyke as he wer ashamed, he letteth his fethers fall sodeinlye : and all the taile downeward, as though he tooke no heed of the fairenesse of his fethers : and he hath an horrible voice.'

The original passage in Aristotle, Hist. of Animals, bk. vi. cap. 9, says but little about the peacock's tail or feet. Cf. note to l. 179 above. See also Holland's tr. of Pliny, bk. x. c. 20 ; quoted by Richardson (s. v. *Peacock*).

—— (12. 253.) *Chiteryng*, chattering, chirping. In Trevisa's translation of Higden's Polychronicon, i. 239, the word is used of the note of the starling—' With mouth than *chetereth* the stare.' And in the Ancren Riwle, p. 152—' Sparuwe is a *cheaterinde* bird ; *cheatereth* euer ant chirmeth.' Chaucer has—' As eny swalwe *chiteryng* on a berne,' Milleres Tale, l. 72 (C. T. 3258 ; Harl. MS.). Palsgrave has—' I *chytter*, I make a charme as a flocke of small byrdes do whan they be together, *Ie iargonne*.' Two more examples are in Halliwell's Dict. s. v. *Chitre*.

—— (12. 255.) *Flaumbe;* 3 p. s. subj. used with a future sense. ' I believe it will contaminate very foully all the earth around it.' *Flaumbe* is the same word as *flame*, from the O.Fr. *flamber*, to blaze, burn, throw out flames. It is here curiously used in the sense to spread a taint, to contaminate. The same verb occurs, in a neuter sense, in MS. Laud 656, fol. 4 b, where we have—

' A flauo*ur flambe*þ þ*er*-fro · þey felleden h*i*t alle ; '

i. e. a scent is exhaled from it, they all perceived it. In the same MS., fol. 10, we have the verb in its usual sense—

' Quarels *flambande* of fure · flowen out harde ; '

i. e. crossbow-bolts, blazing with fire, flew out fast. The connection in idea is easily perceived ; a burning piece of wood emits blaze, smoke, heat, and smell, all at once. So the Lat. *flagrare* is to burn, to glow ; but its derivative is the Fr. *flairer*, to scent ; cf. *flayre*, a sweet smell, in Hampole's Pricke of Conscience, l. 9017.

—— (12. 257.) ' By the peacock's feet is meant,' etc. *Auynete*, a certain collection of fables. Mr. Wright says—' In the fourteenth and fifteenth centuries, as any grammar was called a *Donet* [see note to Pass.

C. PASS. XV. 190. B. PASS. XII. 258.

vii. 215] because the treatise of Donatus was the main foundation of them all, so, from Æsop and Avianus, from whom the materials were taken, any collection of fables was called an *Avionet* or an *Esopet.* The title of one of these collections in a MS. of the Bibl. du Roi at Paris is—Compilacio Ysopi alata cum Avionetto, cum quibusdam addicionibus et moralitatibus. (Robert, *Fabl. Inéd. Essay*, p. clxv.) Perhaps the reference in the present case is to the fable of the Peacock who complained of his voice, the 39th in the collection which M. Robert calls *Ysopet.*

Avianus flourished about the fourth century, and wrote 42 Æsopic fables in Latin elegiac verse, of no great merit.

—— (12. 258.) Robert of Brunne (Handlyng Synne, ll. 6259-6264) says—

'Of alle fals þat beryn name
Fals executours are moste to blame,' etc.

190. The authors Porphyry and Plato are cited at random, as in Pass. xii. 304; xiii. 173. It is hopeless to verify such references; the names are merely introduced as a sort of flourish. The alliteration has, for once, much to do with the selection of the names; like *poet*, they begin with *p*. In the B-text, the author referred to is Aristotle; see next note.

—— (12. 266.) I doubt if the comparison of poor men to larks is to be found in Aristotle; see his Hist. of Animals, for a description of the lark.

Aristotle is here called 'the great clerk.' The real reason of the great influence of Aristotle's writings from the eleventh to the sixteenth centuries is pointed out in Milman's Hist. of Lat. Christianity, vi. 443; he was regarded as 'the teacher of logic, the master of dialectics.' Observe the occurrence of *logyk* in the next line.

191. 'The least bird existing;' a hyperbolical expression. On *oute*, see note to l. 88 above.

192. See this discussed in Pass. xii. 216-223.

193. (12. 269.) *Sortes* is a mere corruption of Socrates, as Mr. Wright supposes. His reference to Walter Map's Poems, p. 251, is much to the point. The passage is—

'Adest ei bajulus cui nomen Gnato,
Praecedebat logicum gressu fatigato,
Dorso ferens sarcinam ventre tensam lato,
Plenam vestro dogmate, *o Sortes et Plato!*'

Gower (C. A. iii. 366) says—'*Sortes* and Plato with him come.' *Sortes* means Socrates in A. Neckam, de Naturis Rerum, ed. Wright, p. 289.

Speaking of logic, Barclay (in his Ship of Fools, ed. Jamieson, i. 144) says—

'Now Sortes *currit*, now is in hand Plato.'

There is no allusion here to the mode of divination known as *sortes sanctorum* (see Ducange), which I mention only that it may not be supposed that I have overlooked that supposition. In fact the context shews that Sortes is a man's name.

204. The right quotation is—'Et si iustus uix saluabitur, impius et peccator ubi parebunt?' 1 Pet. iv. 18. William lays a stress upon *uix*, and says—'since the just man shall *scarcely* be saved, it follows that he *shall* be saved.' See Pass. xvi. 23, and the note, (p. 189), for a still clearer statement of the same opinion. For the story of Trajan, see Pass. xiii. 75, and the note, p. 169.

207. *Follyng*, baptism. See Matt. iii. 11; Acts ii. 3.

208. Compare—'Ignis enim triplicem uim habet, scilicet, illuminandi, calefaciendi, consumendi,' etc.; Old Eng. Homilies, ed. Morris, ii. 118.

209. *Treuthe* here signifies a true man, a righteous man; see *he* in l. 211. *Transuersede*, transgressed, lit. traversed. See *Traverser* in Cotgrave.

210. 'But (ever) lived as his own law taught (him), and believes there is no better (law); and if there were (a better law made known to him), he would (have kept it), and in such a desire dieth—surely the true God would never (permit) but that (such) true truth were commended. And whether it shall be so or shall not be so, the faith of the true man is great; and a hope ever depends upon that faith, that he shall have what he deserves.' In [b], l. 286, the reading is—'he would amend;' and in l. 289—'to have a reward for his truth.' The sentence is terse and elliptical, but the sense is clear; the argument is that of St. Paul, in Rom. ii. 13-15.

The first quotation in [b] probably refers to John xvii. 2—'Sicut dedisti ei potestatem omnis carnis, ut omne quod dedisti ei, det eis uitam aeternam.'

The second quotation is from Ps. xxii. 4 (Vulgate)—'Nam, et si ambulauero in medio umbrae mortis, non timebo mala: quoniam tu mecum es.' The rest of the verse has been already quoted above; B. xii. 13.

214. See Matt. xxv. 23.

216. 'And a present beyond what was agreed for, whatever clerks may say.' Cf. Pass. iv. 317.

217. 'For all shall be as God will.' Cf. l. 213 above.

—— (12. 290.) 'The gloss on that verse grants a large reward to true men.' See note to l. 209 above for the sense of *treuthe* here, and note to l. 210 for the whole verse from Psalm xxii. The Glosa Ordinaria contains the following remark on the words *mecum es*. 'I.e. in corde per fidem, vt post umbram mortis ego tecum sim.' This shews that the 'meed' spoken of is, that true men shall dwell with God hereafter.

—— (12. 292.) 'To keep (*or* maintain) a community with; no (sort of) wealth was considered better.'

Here ends the Fifth Vision, or the Vision of Imaginative. The Sixth Vision follows almost immediately.

NOTES TO C. PASSUS XVI. (B. Pass. XIII–XIV. 131.)

2. (13. 2.) *Feye*, fated to die [c] ; *fre*, at liberty [b]. A remarkable variation.

3. *Mendinaunt*, mendicant friar. The spelling is peculiar, but is the same in all the MSS. ; see also l. 81 below, and Pass. xiv. 79. In the Sixtext edition of Chaucer, Group D, l. 1906, the first five MSS. have the readings *mendynantz, mendynauntis, mendinantz*, and *mendenauntz*. The word occurs also in Pierce the Plowman's Crede, l. 66, where it is spelt *mendynauns*.

Meny ȝeres after. This expression may, after all, mean nothing. At the same time, we know that the recensions of the poem occupied many years, and it is quite possible that the expression is literally true. If so, some time must have elapsed between the first composition of Passus XV. and of Passus XVI., i.e. between Passus XII. and XIII. of the B-text. See note to l. 173 below, p. 198.

5. Here our author recapitulates a part of the Vision of Do-wel. The references are to Pass. xiii. 14–27, 233–247, xiv. 112–128, xv. 120–126, 157–168, 203–217.

7. There is an awkward change of construction here; the word *þat* should be followed by a subjunctive mood, but *leue* is the infinitive, governed by *manacede*, whilst *vanshie* appears to be used as a transitive verb. Thus the sense is—'And how Old-age threatened me, (that) it might so happen, that, if I lived long—(he threatened, I say,) to leave me behind, and to consume all my powers, and my fair locks.'

23. See the note to Pass. xv. 204. The expression here used in the C-text, viz. 'but *vix* help,' refers to a curious popular exposition which, as Wyclif informs us, was then current. His words are—'And, *as men seien*, in this word " unneþe shal þe just man be saved," is menyd þis word Iesus, whoso coude undirstonde it. For in þis word VIX ben but þree lettris, V, and I, and X. And V bitokeneþ fyue ; I betokeneth Iesus ; and X bitokeneþ Crist. [Cf. Gk. Χριστός.] And so þis resoun seiþ þat þe just man shal be saved by þe V woundis of Iesus Crist oure Lord.'—Works, i. 337.

26. Here begins the Sixth Vision, viz. of Conscience, Patience, and Activa-Vita (called Haukyn the Active Man in the B-text). It properly terminates at Pass. xvii. 157 (or at the end of B. xiv.).

27. In [c], William dines with Conscience, Clergy, Reason, and Patience ; in [b], Reason is omitted.

—— (13. 24.) 'And because Conscience spake of Clergy, I came all the sooner.'

30. *What man he was I neste*, I knew not what sort of a man he was [b]. But the C-text is more explicit, saying—'a man like a friar.'

Mayster means a master of divinity; in l. 65 he is called a *doctor;* see note to that line. Compare—

'And also þis myster men ben *maysters* icalled;'
Pierce Pl. Crede, l. 574; cf. l. 838.
'No *maister*, sir (quod he), but seruitour,
Though I haue had in scole such honour;'
Ch. Sompnoures Tale, l. 485.

So too in the Complaint of the Ploughman, in Political Poems, ed. Wright, i. 337; and see Pass. xi. 9, and the note. Accordingly, Mr. Wright notes that the word *maister* 'was generally used in the scholastic ages in a restricted sense, to signify one who had taken his degree in the schools—a master of arts.' In Jack Upland, we find the question—'why make ye so many *maisters* among you [friars], sith it is against the teaching of Christ and his apostles?'

40. *Stihlede,* arranged every thing, set all in order. Other MSS. have stithlede (M), stihȝlede (K), stiȝtlide (T); stiȝlede (G). It is commonly spelt with *t* after the *h*, as in P. Pl. Crede, l. 315; see further examples in Stratmann.

41. *Mettes,* companions at table [c]; *macches*, mates [b]. The same variation occurs below, in l. 55 (b. 13. 47). With the former cf. A. S. '*gemettan*, comestores,' in Bosworth and Toller's A. S. Dictionary; and with the latter cf. A. S. *gemæcca*, a companion, a wife.

43. *Calde after*, called for, expressed a wish for.

45. See Luke x. 7. The dishes have very singular names; see especially l. 61, and B. xiii. 52–55. The guests have before them, for their consumption, portions of the writings of the fathers and various texts of Scripture, and even the drink was called *diu-perseuerans*. The friar turned away from these uninviting viands, and regaled himself with 'meat of more cost;' but even so, he did not quite escape. The sauce which he chose had been made from ingredients ground in a mortar named *post-mortem*, which is a way of saying that after death he would suffer for his gluttony.

The use of such names for the dishes is an important matter, as we are able to tell whence William derived the idea of describing so strange a feast. Warton (Hist. E. P. ed. Hazlitt, ii. 263) has noted William's obligations, in another passage, to Huon de Meri's Tornoiment de l'Antichrist. In this poem, now printed by P. Tarbé, in his Poètes de Champagne, xv. 13, is a description of a feast in which the dishes are named after various *sins;* and the author says—

'De divers mès, de divers vins
Fumes plenièrement servi.
Et sachiez bien qu'oncques ni vi
Fèves et pois, oes ne harenc;
Tuz les mès Raoul de Hodenc
Eumes sans faire riot.'

I. e. we had plenty of different dishes and wines; but we did not have beans and peas, nor goose, nor herring, but all the dishes described by

Raoul de Hodenc. This shews that Huon de Meri himself borrowed the idea, viz. from Le Songe d'Enfer of Raoul de Houdans (or Hodenc), also printed by M. Tarbé in the same volume, pp. 134-148. See also the description of the Abbot of Gloucester's Feast in Reliq. Antiq., i. 140.

47. (13. 41.) *Mortrewes and potages;* and in l. 66 we have *mortrews and poddynges.*

The making of *mortrewes* was one of the qualifications of Chaucer's Cook; Prol. 386: see Tyrwhitt's note on the line.

See Prompt. Parv., p. 13, note 1; p. 70, note 5; p. 344, note 2; also Babees Book, pp. 151, 170, 172; a Recipe for 'mortrewes de chare' in Liber Cure Cocorum, p. 9; 'of fysche,' p. 19; etc.

48. 'They made themselves well at ease with that which men had won amiss,' i. e. gained by cheating.

50. The whole expression, from *post-mortem* down to *teeres*, is the allegorical name of the mortar. This name signifies—'after death they shall suffer many bitter pains, unless they sing for those souls and weep salt tears for them.' The expression *tho soules* means the souls of the men who had 'mis-won' their wealth. The passage requires to be pondered before its full sense is perceived; yet a little thought will shew that it is of some satirical force. The friars (he would say) fared sumptuously, paying for their rich fare with the money which wealthy cheats had left to them when in present fear of death; but they must bear in mind that they will suffer bitterly hereafter for their gluttony, unless they actually perform that which they have solemnly engaged to do, viz. sing masses for the souls of such wealthy persons. Hence the aptness of the Latin quotation (the source of which I know not) which signifies—'Ye who feast upon the sins of men, unless ye pour out tears on their behalf, ye shall vomit up those meats amid torments which ye feast upon amid pleasures.'

57. 'And then he drew for us a drink, the name of which was *Long-enduring*.' This line was omitted in Mr. Wright's edition by mere accident; it is in the MS. which he used. The allusion is to the text, Matt. x. 22. See Matt. iii. 2 for the quotation in l. 56.

58. *Quod I* [b], changed to *quath he* [c]; an improvement. In the B-text, it looks like a poor joke, as if the author expresses his readiness to drink as long as he lives.

61, 62. See Ps. xxxi. 6; l. 19.

65. See Isaiah v. 22. *A doctor* [c]; *this doctor* [b]. Note that the word *a* is not indefinite here; it is the same idiom as we should still use if we were to say—'I was sorry to see a doctor drink wine so fast.' *For* = because; and assigns the reason of William's mourning. See þis *doctor* in l. 69, and again in l. 85. In l. 90 he is called *that master;* he is, in fact, the friar who sat at the head of the table (ll. 30, 39).

——(13. 63.) *Wombe-cloutes*, tripes; lit. belly-rags. Halliwell notes that it is explained by *omentum* in the Nominale MS.

70. The friar preached 'at St. Paul's' [c]; or 'before the dean of St.

Paul's' [b]. Latimer preached his famous Sermon on the Ploughers, 18 Jan. 1549, in the 'shrowds' of St. Paul's, having previously preached at St. Paul's Cross, Jan. 1, 1548. See note to Pass. xii. 56, p. 149.

73. (13. 67.) See 2 Cor. xi. 24, 25, 27.

—— (13. 68.) *Ouerhuppen*, hop over, skip over, omit; see note to Pass. xiv. 123, p. 176.

75. 'Peril among false brethren,' 2 Cor. xi. 26. I have already noted the pun upon 'brethren' and 'friars;' see note to B. xi. 87; pp. 167, 168. The jest is a venerable one.

81. *Fyue mendynauns*, five mendicant orders; see notes to l. 3 above, p. 189, and to Pass. ix. 191, p. 114.

85. *Decretistre of canon*, student of the decretals and canon law. Ducange gives—'*Decretista*, qui studet in decretis. *Magistri decretistae*, professores juris canonici.' See B. v. 428, and the note (p. 96). The odd termination *-istre* occurs again in Chaucer's *diuinistre*, C. T. 2813; but it is a mere corruption of Lat. *-ista*, by confusion with *-is-ter*.

86. *Gnedy*, niggardly [c]; *goddes*, God's (ironically) [b]. *Gnedy* is connected with A. S. *gnéðen*, moderate (Bosworth), and A. S. *gnéað*, sparing (Grein); see *gnede* in Glossary to Havelok, and in Halliwell.

91. *Dobeleres*, platters. William wishes the doctor, who had so greedily swallowed all the eatables, had swallowed dishes and platters too! '*Dobeler*, vesselle; *Parapses;*' Prompt. Parv.; see Way's note.

—— (13. 82.) In the B-text, William wishes that the plates and dishes had turned to molten lead within the glutton's stomach. Cf. Ancren Riwle, p. 216; Hampoles Pricke of Conscience, l. 9433. The expression 'and Mahoun amyddes' is equivalent to 'and the devil in the midst of them.' *Mahoun* is Mahomet, often used as a name for an idol, and idols were supposed to be tenanted by devils. See note to Pass. i. 119, p. 13; and cf. Joseph of Arimathie, ed. Skeat, ll. 373-402.

92. (13. 83.) 'I shall argue with this chamber-pot, with his bottle-like belly.'

Jordan is used both by Chaucer and Shakespeare, and is fully explained in the Prompt. Parv., p. 267, note 1. Considering the connection, I think there can be no doubt that the word *Iuste* is not to be explained as *just* (which would make poor sense), and still less as a tournament (which is Mr. Wright's solution, making no sense at all); but is the word *juste*, in its signification of flagon, bottle, or wine-jar. The Prompt. Parv. has—'*Iuste*, potte, *Oenoforum, justa;*' see Way's note. Ducange has—'*Iusta demesuralis*, seu *tertiera*, mensura uini aliquantulum maior consueta quae monachis *in festis solemnioribus* dabatur.' Halliwell explains *Juste* as 'a kind of vessel with a wide body and long straight neck.' The word is happily employed. The Trinity MS. (C-text) has the adjectival form *iusty*, i. e. like a *juste*.

—— (13. 85.) The alliteration suggests that the word *wynked* (so in all the MSS.) is miswritten for the unusual word *preynte*, which occurs just below, in C. xvi. 121, B. xiii. 112. See note to l. 121 below.

C. PASS. XVI. 95. B. PASS. XIII. 86.

95. *May na more*, can do no more, can eat and drink no longer; cf. *til we myghte no more*, C. vii. 185; B. xiii. 352.

97. *Godelen*, rumble; see note to Pass. vii. 398, p. 92.

99. *Here apocalips*, their Apocalypse. The use of the word *their* is most significant; the reference is not to St. John, but to the Apocalypse of the gluttons, i. e. to the Apocalipsis Goliæ by Walter Mapes, a sort of parody upon St. John, the argument of which may be read in Morley's Eng. Writers, i. 587–590. The following extract from that argument will fully explain the allusion. 'Then I read of the Morals and the Deeds of Abbots, who declare by their base shaving, vile habit, and watery eyes, that they scorn delights and carry contrite hearts; but whose throats when they dine are open sepulchres, whose stomachs are whirlpools, and their fingers rakes ... As pye with pye, parrot with parrot, the brothers chatter and feed, eat till their jaws swell, drink till there is a deluge in their stomachs.' See the Latin Poems of Walter Mapes, ed. Wright, Camden Society, 1841.

The next reference is bitterly satirical, if, as I suppose, it relates to an instance of extreme and rigid abstinence. There is no saint named *Averey* or *Averay;* the word is possibly a corruption of *Aurea*. The day of St. Aurea is Oct. 4; and, according to Vincent of Beauvais, Spec. Hist. lib. 23, cap. lxx, St. Aurea drank only such drink as she could distil from cinders, but there was one rash sister who doubted the fact, and was consequently punished by palsy.

But seeing that the context asserts that delicate meats are proper food for a penitent, it is better to take the name to refer to St. *Avoya* (Lat. *Advisa*), who was fed with delicately white and sweet bread from heaven; see Dr. Brewer's Dict. of Miracles, p. 14.

100. *Blammanger* is Chaucer's *blancmanger*, Prol. 389. Tyrwhitt, in his Glossary, remarks that it 'seems to have been a very different dish in the time of Chaucer, from that which is now called by the same name. There is a receipt for making it in MS. Harl. 4016. One of the ingredients is "the brawne of a capon, tesed small."' Mr. Furnivall says—'*Blanchmanger*, a made dish of Cream, Eggs, and Sugar, put into an open puff paste bottom, with a loose cover.' He also quotes— '*Blamanger* is a Capon roast, or boile, minced small, planched (*sic*) Almonds beaten to paste, Cream, Eggs, Grated Bread, Sugar and Spices boiled to a pap.—R. Holme.' See Babees Book, p. 217; and the Glossary to that volume.

103. (13. 94.) 'What he (i. e. his fellow) really found in a case, belonging to a friar's living,' i. e. provisions [c]; *or*, 'What he really found in a basket, according to a friar's living' [b]. The meaning is that the doctor was ready to bring forward his companion as a witness; and the said companion was ready to state what very poor fare he had often found in a poor friar's provision-box.

Forel has been explained above; see note to B. x. 211, p. 154; it means a case, sheath, box, scabbard, and sometimes a book-cover; see Prompt. Parv.

Freyel is the Low-Latin *fraelum*, a rush-basket or mat-basket, especially used for containing figs and raisins. See 'Frayle of frute, *Palata, carica*' in Prompt. Parv., and Mr. Way's note. In Kennett's Parochial Antiquities, the glossary has—'*Frayle*, a basket in which figs are brought from Spain and other parts.' Palsgrave has—'Frayle for fygges, *cabas, cabache.*' See *cabas, cabasser* in Cotgrave.

Of means 'belonging to' [c]; *after* means 'in accordance with' [b].

112. 'This portrait of gluttony and hypocrisy combined, is in Langland's best manner, strong and indignant. There is genuine humour in this line; the doctor, beginning to discourse on good works, only utters a single word before he interrupts the sentence to drink;' Whitaker's note. Cowper has hit off the very same trait, in his poem on Hope :—

'The Christian hope is—Waiter, draw the cork—
If I mistake not—Blockhead, with a fork!' etc.

113. 'Do no evil to thy fellow-Christian, that is, not as far as your power goes' [b]. *By þi powere*, to the extent of your power; a common phrase.

—— (13. 107.) *Morsel* is the better spelling; the reading *mussel* points a provincial pronunciation, which may still be heard, though *mossel* (*in glossic*—mos'l) is more common.

118. See Luke i. 68. 'If ye so treat your sick friars, it seems to me a wonder unless Do-well accuses you in the day of judgment' [c]; 'And if ye act thus in your infirmary, it seems to me a wonder unless strife exists where love ought rather to exist, if only young children dared complain' [b]. This speech was obviously a very bold one, because Conscience immediately advises him to be silent. I cannot help thinking that strange rumours were afloat as to the treatment of sick friars by their companions, as shewn by the very curious passage in P. Pl. Crede, l. 614; see my note on the line. It was clearly a sore subject with the doctor.

Compare also Wycliff's charge against the friars, that they imprisoned, and even tortured, members of their own order; Works, iii. 383.

121. *Preynte*, winked. Just as Chaucer has *spreynd*, from *springen*, to sprinkle, so *preynte* is from the verb *prinken*. The traces of this word are slight. Halliwell gives '*Prink*, to look at, to gaze upon. *West.*' It is not to be confused with *prink* or *prick*, used in the same sense as *prank*, to trim. Cf. note to B. xiii. 85, just above, p. 192.

125. Crowley inserts *is* before *do* in [b]. It is required for the sense, but is omitted in all the MSS. With l. 127 cf. Matt. v. 19.

129. Clergy, having heard the doctor's very correct explanation, declines to explain the matter himself in a scholastic manner, on the ground that he is not now in the schools, and chiefly because of his love for Piers the Plowman (Christ). The doctor's explanation was just; for, though acting as a sinner, he could talk as a saint. Accordingly, Clergy declines to explain the matter scholastically, but at the same time hints that there is a higher law—the law of Love, the law taught by Christ—which excels all the teaching of the schools.

—— (13. 119.) *Seuene sones.* Clergy's seven sons are the seven sciences, as Crowley rightly observes here in a sidenote. Still, William is hardly consistent with himself, since in B. x. 150 (q. v.) he says that the Seven Sciences are *relations* merely of Scripture, who is Clergy's wife. He now calls them *sons.*

131. 'For love of Piers the Plowman, who once impugned sciences and crafts of every kind except love, loyalty, and humility' [c]; 'For a certain Piers the Plowman hath impugned us all, and counted all sciences as worth a mere sop, except Love only' [b].

Note the construction in 'peers loue þe plouhman,' repeated in xxiii. 77. We have it again in 'peers prentys þe plouhman,' i. e. the apprentice of Piers the Plowman, xvi. 195; in 'peers pardon þe plouhman,' i. e. the pardon of Piers the Plowman, xxii. 187, 392; and in 'peers bern þe plouhman,' i. e. the barn of Piers the Plowman, xxii. 360. So Chaucer, Sq. Ta. 209, has 'the Grekes hors Sinon,' i. e. the horse of Sinon the Greek; and in a note to that line I have given other instances of this common idiom.

135, 136. See Matt. xxii. 37, 39; Ps. xiv. 1 (Vulgate); Mark x. 18.

138. The saying *patientes vincunt* is attributed to Piers the Plowman in [c], and to Christ in [b], shewing that the immediate reference is to the Gospels. Yet they contain no such words, though fairly expressing the sense of Matt. x. 22—'qui autem perseuerauerit usque in finem, hic saluus erit.' A more usual form of the proverb is—'uincit qui patitur;' see Hazlitt's Eng. Proverbs, pp. 175, 450.

I suspect that William was thinking of the words of Dionysius Cato, who, in his Breves Sententiæ, gives the advice—'Parentes patientia uince;' Sent. xl. And again, in his Distiches, lib. i. 38, he says—

'Quem superare potes, interdum uince ferendo,
Maxima enim morum semper patientia uirtus.'

Cf. Virgil, Æn. v. 710; Ovid, Art. Am. ii. 197, Am. iii. 11. 7, Am. i. 2. 10. Compare also Chaucer's Frank. Ta., 45-47—

'Patience is a hy vertue certein,
For it venquisheth, as thise clerkes seyn,
Thinges that rigour neuer sholde atteine.'

And again, in Old Eng. Homilies, ed. Morris, 2nd Ser., p. 80, we have what looks very like a new version of Cato, viz.—'Quém superare nequis, patienter uince ferendo.'

By comparing the two texts, we see that Piers the Plowman is already, at this point, identified with Christ; and the reader should bear in mind that this identification is adhered to, for the most part, throughout nearly all the remainder of the poem. In the C-text, Christ himself here appears upon the scene, unannounced, at this line; and after speaking but one sentence, again vanishes; see l. 150. In the B-text, the sentence is attributed to Love, who was beloved by Patience.

143. 'Cast upon his head the hot coals of all kind speech.' See Rom. xii. 20; Prov. xxv. 22; a passage which is usually explained as having

reference to the melting of metals by fire, and to the melting of an enemy's heart by kindness. See Ancren Riwle, p. 407.

148. 'Unless he become obedient through this sort of beating, may he become blind!' *Bowe* has reference to the common word *buxom* (lit. *bow-some*), which means obedient.

150. *Where he by-cam*, where he had gone to; see note to B. v. 651, p. 105.

155. 'I would (i. e. I could) easily, if I had the will, conquer all France without destruction of men or any bloodshed; I take to my witness a portion of holy writ—"the patient conquer."' See note to l. 138 above, p. 195.

—— (13. 150.) 'Natural affection covets nothing (from thee) but speech,' i.e. asks only for kind words from thee.

—— (13. 151.) This line is a complete riddle. I merely offer a wild guess at the sense of it. Suppose 'a lamp-line in Latin' to be a Latin inscription on such a lamp as was often kept burning in old churches; as when, e. g. J. Cowper, A. D. 1503, provided for finding 'a lampe before the roode in the cherche of Hawsted;' see Sir J. Cullum, Hist. of Hawsted, p. 17. Suppose such an inscription to have been a verse from the Bible expressive of good-will, as, e.g. 'Gloria in altissimis Deo, et in terra pax hominibus bonae uoluntatis,' Lu. ii. 14; a verse which is still not seldom seen inscribed within a church. Then the sentence might mean—'Natural affection expects from you no wealthy gift, but only kindly words; it expects merely some kindly expression, such as *pax hominibus*.' This still leaves *ex vi transicionis* unexplained; nor can I explain it.

—— (13. 152.) Here are riddles upon riddles; the passage is purposely obscure, though no doubt contemporary readers understood it. In the first place, the word *there-inne* refers to nothing that has preceded; but we can explain it. It is clear, from l. 157 [b], that Patience is here supposed to hold up a bundle before the company, and to say—'See! herein I have Do-well, fast tied up.' Moreover, the bundle is clearly supposed to contain *Caritas*, or Charity; see ll. 163, 164. This explains why Patience says, in l. 156—'and herewith I am welcome, wherever I have it with me.' The general solution of the riddle (it is called *redeles* in l. 167), is Charity, exercised with Patience. Hence, in ll. 153-155, we are told that Charity 'is betokened by the Saturday that first set the calendar, and by the signification (wit) of the Wednesday of the week next after it; the full moon being that which causes the might of both.' Now the full moon is the Paschal full moon, as in a former enigmatic passage; see note to Pass. iv. 481, p. 53. Mr. A. P. Cooke has sent me the following suggestion. 'The sign of the Saturday seems to me to mean Holy Baptism, the font having anciently been hallowed on Easter Eve. The epistle of Easter Wednesday was Acts iii. 12-19, and so the wit of this day may be Repentance; the force of both Baptism and Repentance depending upon the Cross, which was set up in the middle of the Paschal month.' I certainly think that the Saturday can be no other than Holy Saturday, or Easter Eve. And it may well have been said to have set first the Calendar; for, Adam having been created on Friday (cf. Salomon and Saturn, ed. Kemble, p. 198) the Saturday was to him the first complete day, and the first Sabbath. Besides, there was an idea that the particular Saturday which was the first Sabbath was nearly at the Paschal season; since it was supposed that the world was created at the time of the vernal equinox. Compare—

'Swylce eác rímcræftige
On þá ylcan tíd emniht healdað,
Forþan wealdend god worhte æt frymðe,
On þá sylfan dæge sunnan and mónan.'
                           Menologium, ed. Grein, l. 44.

I. e. 'as also the clever calculators consider the equinox to be at that same season, because God the Ruler created, at the beginning, on that very day both sun and moon.' The chief things in connection with Saturday are Holy Baptism, wherein the font 'denoteth the holy sepulchre' (Old Eng. Homilies, ed. Morris, 2nd Ser., p. 94), and the Assumption of the Virgin; see Myrour of Our Lady, ed. Blunt, p. 257. The Wednesday service was sometimes connected with the birth of the Virgin and with her Conception; 'thus in the feastes of the Concepcyon and of the Natyuyte of oure lady, ye saye the story of the wednesday;' Myr. of Our Lady, p. 277. Again, we learn from the same volume, pp. 212, 213, that the Incarnation was particularly celebrated in the Wednesday service, with special reference to 'charyte' or divine Love. The fact that the word 'charyte' occurs so repeatedly in the 'thyrde lesson' of this Wednesday service surely points to the right solution. I therefore agree with Mr. Cooke in explaining the 'sign of the Saturday' as Holy Baptism, but prefer to interpret the 'wit of the Wednesday' as meaning the Incarnation; and I would refer to the Myrour of Our Lady (q. v.) in support of this view.

That the passage has, at any rate, a general reference to the great events of Christianity, cannot admit of any doubt. From Christ it is that we learn the lessons of Love and Patience.

162. This odd line is probably genuine, as it is preserved in five MSS. out of seven. It probably alludes to some saying which has not been preserved. A friend suggests that a cart-wheel has *no* corner, so that the expression is a jesting one, implying that to carry charity always with one is not so very easy. Perhaps this is meant.

164. *Helle pouke*, goblin of hell; *helle* being the genitive case. In other passages, e.g. in Pass. xix. 282 (which compare with l. 284), the word *pouke* means the devil. It is the same word as Puck, but used here in a bad sense. Cf. Icel. *púki*, the devil, commonly with the notion of a wee devil, an imp; Dan. *pokker*, the devil; Welsh *pwca*, or *pwci*, hobgoblin, fiend; Gaelic *bocan*, a hobgoblin, a spectre; cf. the name Pug in Ben Jonson's 'The Devil is an Ass.'

Puck is often identified with Robin Goodfellow; see Hazlitt, Fairy Tales, etc., p. 33. Cf. Spenser, *Epithalamion*, l. 341. The Herefordshire form of the word is *Pout;* see Sir G. C. Lewis's Herefordshire Glossary. Professor Morley, in his Library of English Lit., p. 234, has a note on the word. Some of the etymological remarks of various writers upon this word seem to me of extremely doubtful value.

For further examples of the use of the word, see *Puck* and *Pouke* in Nares. The form *pouke* first appears, perhaps, in l. 566 of Richard Coer de Lion, in Weber's Met. Rom., ii. 25.

—— (13. 170.) 'To give all that they can give to thee, as being the best guardian.' This makes good sense, and is no doubt right, though the MS. transposes *the* and *for.*

165. See 1 John iv. 18.

171. *Dido,* a tale of Dido ; an old tale known to every *disour* or story-teller ; nothing new.

173. This line stands nearly the same in both texts. The expression here used is hardly strong enough for us to be sure that the reference is to the famous Schism of the Popes, Sept. 20, 1378. If, on the contrary, the reference be to that event, it only proves that the B-text was in hand for some time, having been commenced in 1377. See note to l. 3 above, p. 189.

—— (13. 175.) This line, be it noted, was omitted in the C-text, no doubt because the allusion was to an event that was then too far in the past. A truce had been concluded with France in 1389, to last till 1392 ; it was renewed in 1392, to last till 1393, and a four years' truce was again concluded on May 27, 1394. This truce was firmly established by Richard's marriage with Isabella of France, Oct. 31, 1396. The conclusion is that the C-text was written *after* 1389, as was certainly the case.

Gower, writing in 1393, says in his Prologue to the Confessio Amantis—

> 'But whyle the lawe is reuled so
> That clerkes to the werre intende,
> I not how that they sholde amende
> The woful worlde in other thinges
> To make pees betwen the kinges
> After the lawe of charitee,
> Whiche is the propre duetee
> Belongend unto the presthode.'

In the B-text, commenced in 1377, the allusion is clearly to such events as are recorded in the following quotations.

'1372. This same yere ... too cardinalx wete sent fro the pope to entrete for the pees betwen the two reaumes ;' A Chronicle of London, p. 69.

'1374. In this yere, at the town of Bruges in Flaundres, was tretyd upon diverses articles hangyng betwen the pope and kyng Edward. Also the same yere was treted at Bruges for the pees betwen the too reaumes ;' id. p. 70.

'Edward [in 1374] obtained a truce ... The pope continually exhorted the kings to convert the truce into a peace ; but their resentments were too violent, their pretensions too high, to allow of any adjustment;' Lingard, Hist. Eng., iv. 140.

174. *Put the bord fram him;* 'that is, pushed away the table in a passion, which accounts for the following reflection, on the want of patience in learned men.'—Whitaker. For *bord*, [b] has *table*.

—— (13. 178.) Cf. Pass. i. 50, and the note, p. 8.

—— (13. 184.) *Yeresyyues*, new year's gifts. They were given both *by* the sovereign, and *to* him; see Brand, Pop. Antiq., ed. Ellis, i. 14. They were also given to secure favours; see note to B. iii. 99, p. 44.

—— (13. 204.) *Forwalked*, tired out with walking; cf. *forwandred*, B. prol. 7. *Wilne me to consaille*, to desire to have me to counsel you, i. e. when you will be glad to ask my counsel. *Wilne* seems to be in the infinitive mood, governed by the sentence 'thou shalt see the time.'

—— (13. 209.) *Surre*, Syria; cf. the form *Surrye* in the first line of Chaucer's Man of Lawes Tale. *Forth*, by way of continuance; it is the positive degree of *further*. William looked forward to a time when Saracens and Jews should all be converted to Christianity; see Pass. iv. 458, 484; xviii. 317.

191. The description here given of a minstrel should be noted. See note to Pass. i. 35, and cf. Pass. viii. 82–119. Mr. Wright refers us, for a sketch of such a character, to Shaw's Dresses and Decorations of the Middle Ages, the Introduction to Percy's Reliques, and Chappell's History of National Airs. I have already referred to Ritson's Ancient Romances, and Warton's Hist. of Eng. Poetry. See also Ritson's Ancient Songs, p. xvi, where he reminds us that they were commonly classed with vagabonds.

194. *Actiua uita*, Active life. See note to B. vi. 251, p. 115. ' This is clepid actif liif, whanne men travailen for worldli goodis, and kepen hem in rightwisnesse;' Wyclif, Works, i. 384. It will be seen, however, that the minstrel here described was very far from being an honest man, and was hardly justified in giving himself so honest a name.

195. *Peers prentys the plouhman*, an apprentice of Piers the Plowman; i. e. a true servant of Christ; see note to l. 131, p. 195. But the minstrel's claim to this character was of the slightest; it turns out that his sole point of connection with a religious life was that he made or sold wafers for holy use!

199. *Godes gistes*, God's guests; i. e. guests at the Table of the Lord, communicants. A *waferer* answers very nearly to what we now call a *confectioner;* see Our English Home, pp. 70–72. They sold ornamented cakes and eucharistic wafers. See Bardsley's English Surnames, p. 324 ; cf. Chaucer, C. T. 3379, 12413.

The fem. form *wafrestre* has already occurred; see Pass. viii. 285.

202. Robes and furred gowns were common gifts to minstrels, from the great men before whom they exhibited; see B. xiv. 24 ; and cf. C. Pass. viii. 82–109. Some minstrels were not itinerant, but were retained by rich men as jesters; these are the 'lords' minstrels' mentioned in l. 204.

205. *Tabre*, play upon the tabor; *trompe*, play upon the trumpet. 'In a poem against the growing taste for the tabor, printed in M. Jubinal's volume entitled Jougleurs et Trouvères, the low state into which the minstrel's art had fallen is ascribed to a growing love for instruments of an undignified character, such as the *tabor*, which is said to have been brought to us from the Arabs, and the *pipe;*' Homes of Other Days, by T. Wright, p. 200. See the whole passage; also p. 209. 'Dost thou live by thy *tabor?*' Twelfth Night, Act iii. sc. 1. See also Spenser, Shep. Kal. May, l. 22; Rob. of Brunne, Handlyng Synne, l. 8993. Small drums were known to the Egyptians; Chappell, Hist. of Music, i. 292.

Gestes, tales, romances. See Warton, Hist. Eng. Poetry, ed. Hazlitt, ii. 85, note.

206. This passage is sufficiently exemplified by comparison with a note which Warton prefers 'to give in Latin;' see his Hist. Eng. Poetry, ed. 1840, ii. 393, note *w*; or ed. 1871, iii. 162, note 3; cf. Ritson, Met. Rom., vol. i. p. clxxxi. I have little doubt that William had himself witnessed the Coventry Mysteries, and is here alluding to them; see Halliwell's edition of the Cov. Myst., pp. 21, 29.

Fithelen, play the fiddle. See the picture of the Anglo-Saxon *fithele* in Wright's Homes of Other Days, p. 46; also Wackerbath's Account of Anglo-Saxon Music; Strutt's Sports and Pastimes; Hart's History of the Violin.

207. *Iapen*, play tricks, act as buffoon. 'Summe iuglers beoð þet ne kunnen seruen of none oþer gleo buten makien cheres, and wrenchen mis hore muð, and schulen mid hore eien;' i.e. there be some jugglers that know no other way of causing fun except to make faces, and distort their mouth, and scowl with their eyes; Ancren Riwle, p. 210.

208. *Sailen*, dance; *sautrien*, play on the psaltery [c]; *saute*, leap, bound [b]. Cf. Rom. of the Rose, l. 769:—

'There was many a timbestere,
And *sailours*, that I dar wel swere
Couthe hir craft ful parfitly;'

where *sailours* means *dancers*, whatever may be the sense of the disputed word *timbestere*, which I should suppose to mean a female player upon the timbrel or tambourine; see *Timbre* in Burguy's Glossaire, and observe the use of *tymbres* for 'timbrels' in Kyng Alisaunder, ed. Weber, l. 191. Cotgrave gives—'*Saillir*, to go out, issue forth; appear above, stand out beyond others; also, to leap, jump, bound, skip, hop.' *Giterne*, a kind of guitar, used (as says the text) to accompany the voice in singing. Cf. Chaucer, C. T. 3333, 3363, 4394; and see *Gittern* in Halliwell and Prompt. Parv.; also *Gittern* and *Citterne* in Nares. The Duke of Westminster's MS. has—Ne citalon ne gitaron ne synge wiþ þe crowþe.

209. Concerning gifts to minstrels, cf. notes to Pass. viii. 97; x. 129; xvi. 202; and to B. xiv. 24; pp. 97, 123, 199, 205.

210. In the B-text, at least, there is surely an allusion here to the *holy-bread*, i.e. 'ordinary leavened bread cut into small pieces, blessed, and given to the people;' as explained in the note to Peacock's edition of Myrc's Instructions to Parish Priests, p. 89; q. v. Cf. Pass. vii. 146.

213. *Peers plouhman* seems to be used here in the sense of the Church of Christ upon earth, as in Pass. xxii. We still use a Prayer for the Church Militant.

And that hym profite wayten, and them that look after profit for him [b].

216. From Michaelmas to Michaelmas, i.e. from year to year, year by year. We may suppose that the waferer in our text found it convenient, accordingly, to keep his accounts from one Michaelmas to another. The Chamberlain of London, for example, who is the treasurer of the corporation, seems to have made up his accounts from Michaelmas to Michaelmas, since we learn that he was expected to 'give in his account each year, between the Feasts of Saint Michael and of Saint Simon and St. Jude, 28 October;' Liber Albus, ed. Riley, p. 42. The accounts of farm-bailiffs were kept from Michaelmas to Michaelmas; see Cullum's Hist. of Hawsted. And see Chambers, Book of Days, ii. 389.

—— (13. 242.) *With brode crounes,* i. e. wearing the tonsure, as in other passages.

217. The expression 'provender for his palfrey' [b] alludes to the custom of giving bread to horses; see Pass. ix. 225. The statement that the waferer provided 'bread for the pope' is to be taken in a satirical sense. It clearly alludes, I think, to the money contributed to the Pope under the name of Peter's-pence; see note to Pass. v. 125, p. 59. Thus the waferer complains that, though he has contributed to the support of the pope, the pope has done nothing for *him;* and, in the B-text, by a play upon the word *prouendre,* he says that, whilst he has provided provender (horse-bread) for the pope's palfrey, the pope has found no provender (or *prebend*) for himself in return.

—— (13. 246.) All that he had ever received was a pardon with a leaden weight on it, bearing two heads in the middle of it. Mr. Wright remarks that 'the papal bulls, etc., had seals of lead, instead of wax.' The very name *bull* (from *bulla,* a leaden seal) reminds us of this. See *Bulls* in Hook's Church Dictionary.

The two 'polls' or heads are those of St. Peter and St. Paul. The *bulla* was round and flat, like a coin, and bore impressions on both sides. An example of one (used by Pope Boniface VIII) is figured at p. 273 of Lacroix' Military and Religious Life of the Middle Ages. On the one side is the inscription 'BONIFATIVS PP: VIII;' on the other are the heads of St. Peter and St. Paul, marked 'S. PE.' and 'S. PA.' respectively. Three similar *bullæ,* of Urban III., Gregory XII., and Leo II. respectively, are engraved in the Engl. Cyclop. Arts and Sciences, Supplement, p. 387; s. v. *Bulla.*

—— (13. 247.) 'Had I a clerk that could write, I would send him in a petition.' The waferer could not write himself, and seems to have had a difficulty in finding a professional scribe. A *bylle* is a petition; see note to Pass. v. 45; p. 55.

C. PASS. XVI. 220. B. PASS. XIII. 260.

220, 221. *Founde ich*, if I could find, if I found. *Letten this luther eir*, put a stop to this pestilential air. This must refer to some pestilence that was prevailing at the time, and I have supposed that the date of the C-text is about A.D. 1393. A glance at Haydn's Dictionary of Dates, s.v. *Plague*, will shew that the so-called four great pestilences of 1349, 1362, 1369, and 1376 were not the only ones; such plagues were of constant recurrence. Some, for instance, give the name of *fourth* pestilence to that of 1383; and 30,000 people died in London of a pestilence in 1407. In the B-text, the allusion is clearly to the pestilence of 1376, as shewn by comparison with the note to b. 13, 270, pp. 203, 204.

Whitaker remarks that—'the irony of these lines is exquisite. If, saith the poet, the promise of miraculous gifts of healing bestowed on the Apostles is not extended to their successor the pope, the reason is, because mankind are unworthy of such a blessing, for in another essential circumstance, the pope exactly resembles his first predecessor, St. Peter—"Silver and gold hath he none." The whole account of Active Life, and of the indisposition of the great to reward useful services, while they pay liberally for mere entertainment, is excellent.'

I suppose Whitaker means that the resemblance of the Pope to St. Peter in the matter of poverty is an ironical expression, the actual fact being that he was notoriously wealthy. In the life of Thomas Aquinas in the Encyclopædia Britannica, there is an anecdote which is exactly to the point. 'Aquinas found the Holy Father [Innocent IV.] seated by a table covered with piles of indulgence-money. "You see," said the Pontiff, "the church is no longer in the days when she could say—Silver and gold have I none." "True, holy Father," said Aquinas, "and she is as little able to say to the sick of the palsy—Rise up and walk."'

I would add that the notion of trying to buy a 'salve for the pestilence' from the pope was a fine idea for an unscrupulous quack. If Haukyn the waferer could have obtained it, beyond all doubt he would have made a good thing of it. But even this idea was surpassed by that of the quack, who, according to Horace Walpole, sold pills 'as good against an earthquake;' see Chambers, Book of Days, i. 233.

222, 226. See Mark xvi. 18; Acts iii. 6.

231. 'Till pride be entirely destroyed, and that (will be) through lack of bread.' The pestilences produced famines, which were considered as God's judgments against pride; see Pass. vi. 115–118.

—— (13. 267.) *Stretforth*, Stratford; Chaucer's 'Stratford-atte-Bowe.' Here lived numerous bakers, who supplied some part of London with bread. In Riley's Memorials of London, p. 291, we read that, in 1356, carts bringing wheat and flour from Stratford to the City, had to pay 3*d.* per week; also that, in 1310, and again in 1316, some of the Stratford bread was seized, as being short of weight; id. pp. 71, 121.

But the most explicit note is that in Stowe's Survey of London, p. 159, who refers to the very passage in our text. Stowe's remarks are as follows:—'And because I have here before spoken of the bread-carts

(NOT IN C.) B. PASS. XIII. 268.

comming from Stratford at the Bow, ye shall understand that of olde time the bakers of breade at Stratford were allowed to bring dayly (except the Sabbaoth and principall feasts) diverse long cartes laden with bread, the same being two ounces in the pennie wheate-loafe heavier than the penny wheate-loafe baked in the citie, the same to be solde in Cheape, three or foure carts standing there, betweene Gutherans lane and Fausters lane ende, one cart on Cornehill, by the conduit, and one other in Grasse streete. ... Moreover in the 44. of Edward the third, John Chichester being maior of London, I read in the visions of Pierce Plowman, a booke so called, as followeth. "There was a careful commune when no cart came to towne with baked bread from Stratford: tho gan beggers weepe, and workemen were agast a little, this will be thought long, in the date of our Drite, in a drie Averell, a thousand and three hundred, twise thirtie and ten," etc. ... These bakers of Stratford left serving of this citie, I know not uppon what occasion, about 30 yeares since' [i.e. about 1570].

—— (13. 268.) 'And workmen were somewhat terrified; this will be long remembered.' Here *thoughte* is used in the sense of *thought on;* which is, indeed, the reading of the Bodley MS.

—— (13. 269.) Mr. Wright, misled by the reading of the Trinity MS., identifies this mention of 'a dry April' with Fabyan's mention of 'the drie sommer' in the 27th year of Edward the third; but the year really meant here is 1370, as in the text, and that there was 'a dry April' in that year is rendered exceedingly probable by the mention by Fabyan of 'excessyvenes of rayne' in the previous autumn of 1369. That there was an extraordinary dearth in 1370, Fabyan expressly testifies; wheat, he tells us, sold at xl*d.* a bushel. No wonder that 'the commons were filled with anxiety, and the workmen were a little aghast,' as described in ll. 266, 267. See the next note.

—— (13. 270.) 'My cakes were scarce there, when Chichester was mayor.'

Gesen, scarce, rare. *Geason* occurs in this sense in Jewel's Works, iv. 723; and (spelt *geson*) in the same, iii. 622 (Parker Society). See five more examples in Halliwell, s. vv. *Geason, Geson.* For early examples of it, see *gǽsne* in Grein's A. S. Dictionary.

An apparent difficulty about this date is due to Fabyan's curious error of omitting all mention of the sixth year of Edward III, and by his confusion of the regnal year (beginning Jan. 25) with the year of the mayor of London (beginning Oct. 28). Our author, as might be expected, is perfectly correct. Chichester was elected in 1369 (probably in October) and was still mayor in 1370. In Riley's Memorials of London, p. 344, we find 'Afterwards, on the 25th day of April in the year above-mentioned [1370], it was agreed by John de Chichestre, Mayor,' etc. It is important to insist upon this, because the MS. followed by Mr. Wright, in company with many inferior ones, has the corrupt reading 'twice *twenty* and ten.' But MSS. L. and R. set us right, and it is easily ascertained that Chichester was mayor in 1369-70, and was never re-elected. Stowe and other old writers have the right date. See the quotation from Stowe in note to l. 267.

Another result is, that Stowe did not follow *any of the printed copies*, but some MS.; and if he obtained his information from any of the sources now extant, it was from MS. R.

There are several notices of John de Chichestre in Riley's Memorials of London. It appears that he was a goldsmith, and a wealthy man. His year lasted from Oct. 28, 1369, to Oct. 27, 1370; and he was still alive in 1376 (p. 404). He is noticed also in A Chronicle of London, p. 68, in the words :—'John Chichestre, mayor, goldsmyth. In this yere was so gret derthe of corne in Engelond that a busshell of whete was worth xld.'

☞ **Here is a break. Some portions of the B-text have already appeared at an earlier place in the C-text, and have been already commented on; see pp. 73, 76, 81, 87, 93, 97, 98. The notes here following refer to B. xiv. 1-131, and to C. xvi. 232-310.**

—— (14. 1.) *Hatere*, garment. This word is miswritten as *batere* in the Assumpcioun de notre Dame, l. 149, printed in King Horn, ed. Lumby, p. 48; see Mr. Lumby's note at p. 121. See several examples in Stratmann, s. v. *hatre*, to which add Rob. of Brunne, Chron., ed. Hearne, i. 204. See *haterynge* below, B. xv. 76. 'The cloak, robe, or gown of the day was often the coverlet at night;' and again—'Shirts were, in fact, such valuable articles, that ... we find them not unfrequently ... devised by will;' Hist. of Agriculture and Prices in England, by J. E. Thorold Rogers, i. 120, and 66.

—— (14. 2.) 'I sleep in it at night.' This may mean that Haukyn used his garment at night as a coverlet. If it is to be taken literally, it is somewhat at variance with the usual custom, which was, as Mr. Wright remarks, for all classes of society to go to bed quite naked; as said in Pass. xxiii. 196. The reader may look at Plates XIV, XV, and XVI in the Babees Book. See also *Naked-bed* in Nares; Our English Home, p. 92; Chambers, Book of Days, ii. 232. With l. 3, cf. Luke xiv. 20.

—— (14. 5.) 'It has been washed both during Lent, and out of Lent.' The whole passage is a kind of parable. Haukyn's one garment symbolises the carnal nature of man, which requires shrift in the same way that a garment needs to be washed. He has been shriven, he tells us, both in Lent and out of it; he has been washed with the soap of sickness, and purified by the loss of worldly wealth. See this idea worked out in an old sermon on Shrift in Old English Homilies, ed. Morris, 2nd Ser. p. 56. Cf. Isaiah i. 16, 18. 'Omnia confessione lavantur;' Ancren Riwle, p. 300. A 'washing-day' in olden times was a great event.

—— (14. 15.) *Flober*, sully, dirty; see *beflobered* above, B. xiii. 401. Cf.—'*Flop*, a mass of thin mud;' Barnes, Dorsetsh. Glossary.

—— (14. 16.) *Contrition* was divided into three parts or acts, viz. contrition of heart, confession of mouth, and satisfaction of deed; see

Pass. xvii. 25-32. The penitent is to be sorry in thought, word, and deed; to feel sorrow, to express it, and to prove it by doing penance, or by making restitution. The whole of the Persones Tale is really upon this subject of Shrift. So likewise in Old Eng. Homilies, ed. Morris, 1st Ser. pp. 49, 51—'Cordis contritione moritur peccatum, oris confessione defertur ad tumulum, operis satisfactione tumulatur in perpetuum;' which resembles the quotation below, B. xiv. 91. Such is the usual formula; thus we find in Peter Cantor, ed. Migne, Cursus Patrologicus, vol. 205, col. 342—'Post confessionem cordis sequitur de confessione oris. Est enim triplex confessio; cordis, . . . oris, et operis.' See Polit. Rel. and Love Poems, ed. Furnivall, p. 218; Ancren Riwle, pp. 299-348; Barclay, Ship of Fools, ed. Jamieson, i. 196, and the article *Penance* in the Index to the Parker Society's publications.

—— (14. 19.) 'Do-bet shall beat and buck it.' 'I Bucke lynen clothes to scoure of their fylthe, & make them whyte, *Ie bue;*' Palsgrave. '*Buée*, lie wherewith clothes are scowred; also, a buck of clothes;'— '*Buer*, to wash a buck; to scowre with lie;' Cotgrave. To *buck* is to cleanse clothes by steeping them in lye; see *Buck* in Webster, Nares, Halliwell, Wedgwood, and Richardson. See *bouketh* in Pass. xvii. 331. The various processes are accurately described. First of all, some of the dirt is to be 'clawed' or scraped off; next, Do-well is to wash the garment and wring it, so as to remove such part of the dirt as could be easily removed by water; next, Do-bet is to beat it thoroughly with a washing-beetle and then to soak it in lye, so as to restore its original colour; it was then to be re-dyed in grain, for which purpose (if not before) it would be taken to pieces; after which, Do-best was to sew it all together again, and it would be as good as new.

—— (14. 20.) *Engreynen it*, dye it in grain, i.e. of a fast colour. See note to C. iii. 14, and cf. note to Chaucer, C. T. Group B, l. 1917, in my edition of The Prioresses Tale, etc. (Clar. Press).

—— (14. 24.) Heralds and harpers often had *new* garments given them; see notes above, C. xvi. 202, 209; pp. 199, 200.

—— (14. 27.) 'Than the wife of Haukyn the waferer;' see note to C. xvi. 131, p. 195.

232-236. Lines 232, 233 (on p. 403) have some resemblance to B. xiv. 75, 76 (p. 418); and l. 236 has the same ending as B. xiv. 28. See note below, to B. xiv. 76, p. 207. Cf. Ezek. xvi. 49.

—— (14. 33.) This line closely resembles B. vii. 125, 126.

240. The sense is much the same as that of the proverb—'God never sendeth mouth but he sendeth meat' (Heywood); on which Ray well remarks—'This proverb is much in the mouth of poor people, who get children, but take no care to maintain them. Rather it intimates, that God never sends children, but he gives the parents the means of providing for them.'

243. The cricket is here said to live in the fire. Usually, this fabulous story is spoken of the salamander, called *Grylio* in the Bestiary of Philip de Thaun; see Wright's Popular Treatises on Science, p. 97, and Ayen-

bite of Inwyt, ed. Morris, p. 167 (near the bottom). The cricket's Latin name was *gryllus;* hence, possibly, a confusion between the animals. Indeed, we find in the Prompt. Parv. the entry—'*Crykette,* salamandra, crillus, grillus.' Still, the notion of a cricket living in the fire is the more reasonable, on account of its partiality for the domestic hearth.

Our author seems to assert here that the curlew lived upon air, a fable generally told of the chameleon. 'The food of this well-known and wary bird (*Numenius arquatus*), which is called in Scotland the Whaup, consists of earth-worms, slugs, small testaceans, and insects;' Eng. Cycl. Nat. Hist. art. Scolopacidæ, p. 718. However, Gower (Conf. Amant. bk. vi.) has the lines—

> 'And, as the plover doth of the eire,
> I liue, and am in good espeire,' etc.

And P. Lacroix, in his Manners, Customs, etc. during the Middle Ages, p. 132, quotes from an old author the statement that 'plovers feed on air.'

246. See John xiv. 13; Matt. iv. 4.

251. *Fynde vs alle,* provide for us all. Cf. Matt. vi. 10.

253. *Clomsest for colde,* art benumbed with cold. Cf. Du. *kleumen,* to be benumbed with cold; *kleumer,* a chilly person; *kleumsch,* chilly. Ray has—'*Clumps, Clumpst,* idle, lazy, unhandy; *Lincolnshire* . . . *Clumpst* with cold, i. e. benummed;' also—'*Clussumed;* as, "a *clussum'd* hand," a clumsie hand. *Cheshire.*' The sense of Mid. Eng. *clomsen* is, I suppose, *to become torpid,* or *useless,* especially from the effect of cold, with ultimate reference to the verb *clemmen,* to pinch. Hence, I should translate—'He is outher *clomsed,* or wode' in the Pricke of Conscience, l. 1651, by 'he is either stupefied or mad.' And I should suppose the quotation given in Dr. Morris's Glos. to Pr. of Cons., p. 287, from the Gospel of Nichodemus, fol. 213, viz. 'we er *clomsed* gret and smalle,' to mean 'we are stupefied, great and small;' for it is an expression used by the fiends to express their state of amazement and confusion at Christ's approach. A person is *clumsy* who has no more use of his fingers than if they were benumbed. Surely, too, '*clumsid* hondis' in Wyclif, Isaiah xxxv. 3, means 'clumsy or weak hands,' rather than 'unloosed,' as in the Wycl. Glos.; and answers equally well to the Lat. *dissolutas.* See *Acomelyd* in Prompt. Parv., and Way's note; and especially *Comelyd* in the same, with Way's note; pp. 6, note 3, and 88, note 6.

Clyngest for drouthe, art pined with thirst; see *clingen* and *clengen* in Stratmann. Shakespeare has—'Till famine *cling* thee,' i. e. pine thee, shrivel thee up; Macb. v. 5. 40.

257. *Ondyng,* smelling [c]; *etynge,* eating [b]. *Fyue wittes,* five senses; the B-text, by the repetition of idea in *tonge* and *etynge,* mentions but three of them; the revised C-text mentions all but the sense of hearing. See note to Pass. ii. 15, p. 21. The true sense of *onding* is 'breathing;' see '*Ondyn* or brethyn, *aspiro, anelo,*' in Prompt. Parv.,

p. 364, and Way's excellent note. Here it is used of sniffing, or drawing in the breath in the act of smelling.

263. This line is found in one MS. only. I cannot trace the origin of these Leonine verses; William may have composed them himself.

266. (14. 62.) Whoever will turn to the Babees Book, ed. Furnivall, pp. 382, 386, will see at once that the text 'Aperis tu manum tuam' was repeated daily in saying grace, and was therefore very familiar to every one. It is well worth noting that William has quoted several texts which were used in graces, viz. 'Qui in caritate,' etc., Pass. iv. 406; 'Frange esurienti,' etc., Pass. xii. 67; 'Dispersit, dedit pauperibus,' etc., B. xv. 320; 'Iustitia eius manet,' etc., Pass. xviii. 65. See also Pass. iv. 342.

267. This of course refers to the forty years' wandering of the Israelites in the wilderness, and to the issue of water from the smitten rock; Numb. xx. 11; Deut. viii. 15.

269. *Elyes*, Elias's, Elijah's. See James v. 17: 1 Kings xvii. 1.

270. *Reynede*, rained [c]; *rone*, rained [b]. The use of the strong preterite of this verb is very rare; cf. *roon*, Trevisa, ii. 239.

271. *Wynter*, years; according to the usual A. S. idiom. *Of no mete telden*, made account of no food, i.e. made no special provision [c]; *no mete ne tulyeden*, earned no food by tilling the ground [b]. *Telden* is from *tellen*; various readings include *tolden*, *toolden*.

272. *The book* is the Legenda Aurea of Jacobus de Voragine. The allusion is to the common legend of the Seven Sleepers of Ephesus, told at length in the Legenda Aurea, in Gregory of Tours, De Gloria Martyrum, i. 9; and in Baring Gould's Curious Myths of the Middle Ages, Ser. i. p. 88. The day on which they are commemorated is July 27, and the supposed date of their 'sleep' is A.D. 250.

In the B-text, they are said to have slept for 700 years; in [c], for more than 60 years; Jacobus de Voragine says 360 years, though he also says it was from the time of the Decian persecution (A.D. 250) to the 30th year of Theodosius II (A.D. 432), less than 200 years. The common account says their sleep was from A.D. 250 to A.D. 479, a period of 229 years. Theodosius died A.D. 450. In no way can the chronology be brought right.

275. Cf. Ps. xxxvi. 4.

—— (14. 72.) 'But dearth causes unkindness.' *Caristia* is here the nominative case, and the reading *caristiam* is wrong. The word was in common use in the 14th century. We find the entry 'magna caristia ferri' four times, under the dates, 1353, 1354, 1355, and 1371, in Prof. J. E. Thorold Rogers, Hist. of Agric. and Prices in England, ii. 607. William refers to *mesure* (moderation) as being the priceless mean between dearth and plenty.

—— (14. 76.) The Latin quotation here is differently worded from that at C. xvi. 231. It resembles a sentence in Peter Cantor, ed. Migne, col. 331—'Et abundantia panis causa fuit peccati Sodomorum;' see also col. 333. So also in the Ancren Riwle, p. 422—'Of idelnesse awakeneð muchel flesshes fondunge. Iniquitas Sodome saturitas panis et ocium.' And again—'haec [Sodoma] propter abundantiam panis, et per luxuriae magnitudinem excessit modum libidinis;' S. Hieronymi Dialogus adv. Pelagianos, lib. i. sect. 17; ed. Migne, t. ii. col. 511. The ultimate reference is clearly to Ezek. xvi. 49.

—— (14. 80.) 'They sunk into hell, those cities, each one of them.' This was the accepted account; see Mandeville, ed. Halliwell, p. 101; Allit. Poems, ed. Morris, B. 968.

—— (14. 81.) 'Therefore let us act with great moderation, and make our faith our defence.' William uses the word in the old sense; cf. A.S. *scyld-truma*, a strong shield, lit. a troop-shield. Note that William's use of the word exactly accounts for our word *shelter*, which I take to be a mere corruption of *sheltrom* or *sheltron*.

—— (14. 91.) Here William again recognises the three acts of Shrift, mentioned in note above, B. xiv. 16. He here says,—*Contrition of heart* merely turns a deadly sin into a venial one; but *confession of mouth* slays the sin; and thirdly, *satisfaction of deed* removes and puts away the slain sin, as if it had never been.

283. *Ye*, yea, is used in expressing mere assent, like the modern *aye*. See note on *ʒis* in Glos. to Will. of Palerne. The question (in ll. 281, 282) is put in such a form as to suggest that the patient endurance of poverty is not more meritorious than a rightful expenditure of wealth. To which the reply is—'Aye, but *who* is that righteous rich man? Only point him out, and we will soon praise him!'

299. *Bote*, unless. *Sende*, may send [c]; *sent*, sendeth [b].

301. 'For he was wrought to evil fortune, who was never created for joy;' or perhaps, 'for whom joy was never prepared.' The curious expression *to wrotherhele* is composed of the preposition *to*, followed by *wrother*, the dat. fem. of *wroth*, and the dat. of the fem. sb. *hele* (A. S. *hǽlu*). *Hele* means *health, condition,* as usual; *wroth* means angry, and hence *bad, evil*. The suffix -*er* corresponds to the A. S. dat. fem. adjectival suffix -*re*. Instances occur in Layamon, l. 29556; Rob. of Glouc., ed. Hearne, pp. 143, 164; Rob. of Brunne, pp. 104, 201, 221; Squire of Lowe Degree, ap. Ritson, iii. 157; Old Eng. Misc., ed. Morris, p. 148. The opposite expression, *to goder hele*, with the sense of 'fortunately,' is also common, and exhibits the same dat. fem. suffix.

303. *Douce uye*, luxurious life; Fr. *douce vie*. Luke xvi. 19.

304. *Buyeth hit ful bitere*, pays very dearly for it.

306. *Leodes*, tenements, possessions. The phrase 'londes and leedes' occurs in Will. of Palerne, l. 4001; frag. of Alisaunder (in the same volume), l. 12.

307. Here the life of the rich is likened to a pleasant slumber, with dreams of perpetual summer, from which death is the harsh awakening.

309. *Than aren hit*, lit. then are it, i.e. then are they. The usual idiom; see note to Pass. vi. 59, p. 63.

310. See Ps. lxxv. 6, lxxii. 20 (Vulgate); Ps. lxxvi. 5, lxxiii. 20 (A. V.).

NOTES TO C. PASSUS XVII. (B. XIV. 132—XV. 252.)

2. (14. 133.) *At hus laste ende*, at his death; referring to *mannes* in l. l.
5. *Deuer*, duty; F. *devoir*. This word seems only to occur in the phrase 'to do one's dever,' i. e. to do one's duty. Examples are—
'Doth now your deuoir, yonge knyghtes proude;' Kn. Tale, 1740.
'And doth nought but his deuer;' Will. of Palerne, l. 474; cf. ll. 520, 2546. So also in the allit. Morte Arthure, l. 1940; Troy-Book, l. 797.

At a later period, this word was confused with its derivative *endeavour*, and to 'do one's dever' came to signify to do one's endeavour, to do one's best at anything. In this sense it is used in Shropshire to this day, and in the West of Scotland, as noted in Jamieson and by Mr. Donaldson in his note to the Troy-Book, at p. 475. I am of opinion, however, that this latter sense is *not the right one* in the Troy-Book, nor elsewhere in Middle English.

Daies iourne, i. e. day's work, day's task. Hence our word *journeyman*. William little thought that *day* and *journey* are from the same root, and that he was repeating the same idea!

This passage should be compared with Pass. iv. 294–305.

8. *By*, with reference to. *Hit semeth nat*, it befits not, it is not seemly.
—— (14. 148.) 'And reward with double riches all that have pitying hearts.' So *rewarde wel* = pay good wages, in B. xiv. 145, just above; and see ll. 153, 154 below.
—— (14. 152.) *Rewfullich lybbeth*, live a life of compassion, live mercifully. Cf. the expression 'reuful hertes' just above, l. 148.

13. The best time for the poor was, no doubt, harvest-time; see Pass. ix. 323. Compare Chaucer's Prologue to the Man of Law's Tale.

14. *Wet-shood*, wet-shoe'd, with wet shoes, wet-footed. See note to Pass. xxi. 1, p. 247.

15. *Afurst and afyngred*, oppressed by thirst and hunger; see note to Pass. xii. 43 (p. 148), and to B. vi. 269 (p. 116).

20. 'And all equally intelligent and wise, and (have made them to) live without penury' [c]; *or*, 'if it had well pleased Thee' [b].

21. 'But it is all for the best, as I hope, that some are poor and some rich.'

25. See note to B. xiv. 91, p. 208. *To clanse with oure soules*, to cleanse our souls with; the usual idiom.

27. *The fadres will of heuene*, the will of the Father in heaven; see note above to Pass. xvi. 131; p. 195.

29. See note to B. xiv. 91, p. 208.
—— (14. 171.) 'For no dearth, nor drought, nor (excessive) wet can be any injury to them;' viz. to the wealthy. *Dere* is here a substantive; see several instances in Stratmann.
—— (14. 172.) *Haue thei here hele*, if they have their health.
—— (14. 179.) *Thi careful*, Thy people who are full of care and misery.

See *care* = misery in l. 175 above; and see *careful* in Wright's Bible Word-book and Trench's Select Glossary. See Isaiah xxx. 15.

—— (14. 181.) *In genere of his gentrice*, in the nature of [i. e. by reason of] His gentle birth, *or* humanity. *Gentrise* is gentleness or nobility of birth or disposition; it occurs in l. 52 of the later life of St. Juliana.

Cf. *genterie* and *gentillesse*, as explained in the Wyf of Bathes Tale.

—— (14. 188.) 'But if the devil would plead against this,' etc. *The pouke* has been explained before; see note to Pass. xvi. 164, p. 197. It is very remarkable that nearly all the scribes have strangely inserted the word *pope* instead of *pouke*. However, MS. R. has the right reading, and in l. 190- the word has not been thus altered.

—— (14. 189.) *He*, i. e. Christ; cf. ll. 179, 181. *As quik*, as quickly as possible, immediately. We have the very same idiom in the phrase *as tyte* B. xiii. 319; xvi. 61. In Cambridgeshire, the ordinary phrase 'very hot' is expressed by '*as hot as hot*,' or sometimes (but more rarely) by '*as hot*' alone; and the same with other adjectives and adverbs.

The qued, the Evil One.

—— (14. 190.) 'And so put off (repel) the devil, and prove us to be under a security.' The passion of Christ is the pledge of Redemption.

—— (14. 191.) *Be moste*, ought to be, lit. must be. *Moste* is dissyllabic, and thus the rhythm of the line is preserved. *Be* is the infinitive mood.

—— (14. 193.) *Decorreth*, departs; *of*, from. Mätzner refers *decorreth* to the O. F. *decorre;* Cotgrave gives *decourir* only in the senses 'to run down, to haste, or hye apace.' The line seems to signify 'the record departs from pomp and pride (i. e. has nothing to do with them), and especially from all but the lowly.'

37. *Bote*, unless, except. Cf. Pass. x. 338-345.

41, 42. 'Lo! how men write upon the windows in the friars' chapels! if the foundation be false (it is all in vain).' Mr. Wright remarks—'Both in the Vision of Piers Ploughman and in the Creed, there are frequent expressions of indignation at the extravagant expenditure in painting the windows of the abbeys and churches. It must not be forgotten that, a little later, the same feeling as that exhibited in these satires led to the destruction of many of the noblest monuments of medieval art.' See P. Pl. Crede, ll. 120-129, 162, 175, 206, and cf. Pass. iv. 64-74 above.

44. *Seuene synnes*, the Seven Deadly Sins, so fully described above; see note to Pass. vii. 3, p. 71.

46. *With richesse*, by means of riches. It is not meant that Riches is a sin, but that it is the allurement to it; indeed, to all the Seven Sins, as is more particularly explained below. *Tho ribaudes*, those evil ones, i. e. the Seven Sins, [c]; *that ribaude*, that Evil One [b]. The sense is—'and those evil ones [*or*, that Evil One] soonest beguile men by means of riches.'

50. *Can more*, knows more.

54. *Heye wey*, high road. The quotation in [b] is intended to refer to Matt. xix. 23—'quia diues difficile intrabit in regnum caelorum.' The next quotation is from Rev. xiv. 13.

56. *Batauntlyche*, hastily; or rather, with noisy and eager haste. This is rather a clumsy compound, and does not appear to occur elsewhere. *Bataunt* is the O. Fr. *batant*, properly the pres. part. of *batre* or *battre*, to beat. Burguy has—'Batre, Battre, de *batuere ; venir batant*, ii. 376 [i. e. vol. ii. p. 376 of Burguy's Grammaire de la Langue d'oïl]; *tot batant*, battant, tout courant, en toute hâte.' Cotgrave has—'*Batant*, beating, battering, thrashing. *Il arriua tout batant*, he came very hastily... *Il les chassa tout batant*, he pursued them very hard.' Thus *batant* clearly refers to the noisy and eager way in which beggars beset and clamour round an almsgiver, thronging and pushing against one another.

58. William now discusses the enticements of Riches to the Seven Sins. *Pride* is discussed in ll. 58-66; *Wrath*, ll. 67-71; *Gluttony*, ll. 72-79; *Avarice*, ll. 80-90; *Lechery*, ll. 91-94; *Sloth*, ll. 95-105. There does not seem to be any mention of *Envy*, unless it be in ll. 69-71; but perhaps it would not have been easy to shew that the poor are more free from this vice than the rich.

59. This line is slightly, but remarkably, varied in the two texts. In [b], William says of Pride, that 'he hath some dwelling rather in the master than in the man.' Afterwards, calling to mind the arrogant manners of the retainers in a great household, who were themselves well-fed and well clothed, he altered it to—'Either in the master or in the man he shews some abiding.'

70-79. (14. 227-237.) Only found in one MS. of the B-text.

76. This line is an allusion to an old proverb, quoted by Mr. Riley (Memorials of London, p. 8, note 4) from the Book of Husbandry, attributed to Robert Grosteste, bp. of Lincoln :—' Whoso streket his fot forthere than the whitel will reche, he schal streken in the straw,' i. e. he that stretches his foot further than the blanket, will stretch into the straw. In fact, as Mr. Riley remarks, 'the bed of those days, among the humbler people, was nothing but a whitel, or blanket, thrown upon a heap of straw.' Hence William says that the poor man, stretching himself, finds that part of his blanket [*or* of his sheets, b] is nothing but straw. The words *whitel* (A. S. *hwitel*) and *blanket* are equivalent, and refer to the *white* colour of the material.

77. Compare—'The king of gluttony hath no jollity, There [i. e. where] poverty is pight;' The World and the Child, in Hazlitt's Old Plays, i. 249.

81. *Nameliche*, especially. *Her neither*, neither of them [c]; *her none*, neither (lit. none) of them [b].

84. *Apereth nat*, etc., and hardly comes up to (reaches to) his navel.

85. *A loueliche laik*, a good struggle, a satisfactory bout, good sport.

89. 'And which of the two is easier to break open? which is it that makes less noise?' *or* 'it makes less noise' [b]. '*Boost*, a noise; a provincial word still familiar [1813] in the Midland counties;' Whitaker.

93. *A straw for*, i. e. small indeed would be the value of. *Hy stod nat*, they would not stand, would not exist. *Stod* is here in the subjunctive mood.

94. 'If they had no other use but by poor people' [c]; *or*, 'If they received nothing except from poor men, their houses would be roofless' [b]. In the latter case, for *untyled*, i. e. without a tiled roof, the Oriel MS. has the good reading *vnhiled*, uncovered.

96. *Meschief*, adversity. *Mene*, mean, instrument [c]; *his maister*, his teacher [b].

98. *Secte*, retinue, train, company of followers. The form *sute* [b] has the same sense; see note to Pass. viii. 130, p. 98, which closely resembles l. 100 in the present passage. Note that *secte*, in l. 100, has rather the sense of *suit* or apparel.

106. As a maiden who quits her home to be honourably married to the man of her choice, so (says our author) are those who forsake wealth for the love of Christ. This is little else than an inversion of St. Paul's simile in Eph. v. 25, as if he had said—'wives, love your husbands, even as the church also loveth Christ.' There is also, of course, a reference to Matt. xix. 29; and any weakness in our author's argument really rests upon the question 'as to whether those who, in his time, embraced voluntary poverty, did so in such a manner as truly to fulfil the intention of that text.'

108. The sense is—'greatly ought such a maiden to be loved by him that marries one of her character.'

109. *Brocage*, treaty by an agent. 'He woeth hire by menes and *brocage*;' Ch. C. T. 3375. Cf. Rom. of the Rose, 6971.

112. For *persone*, Crowley's text has *parson*. Such is the meaning intended here; see note to B. v. 144, p. 79.

114. *Semblable bothe*, like Him also [c]; *so to his seyntes*, and likewise to His saints [b].

117. Very near the end of the Wyf of Bathes Tale is this passage—

> 'Pourete is hateful good; and, as I gesse,
> A ful gret bringer out of bisynesse;
> A gret amender eek of sapience
> To him that taketh it in patience;
> Pouerte is this, although it seme elenge,
> Possessioun that no wight wol chalenge.'

In the margin of the Ellesmere MS. is the note:—'Secundus Philosophus. Paupertas est odibile bonum, sanitatis mater, curarum remocio, sapientie reparatrix, possessio sine calumpnia.' It will be seen that Chaucer's lines are a mere paraphrase of this, with the omission of 'sanitatis mater.' Tyrwhitt's note is—'In this commendation of Poverty, our author seems plainly to have had in view the following passage of a fabulous conference between the emperor Adrian and Secundus the philosopher, reported by Vincent of Beauvais, *Speculum Historiale*, lib. x. cap. 71. "Quid est Paupertas? Obidile bonum; sanitatis mater; remotio curarum; sapientiae repertrix; negotium sine damno; possessio absque calumnia; sine sollicitudine felicitas." What Vincent has there published appears to have been extracted from a larger collection of *Gnomae* under the name of Secundus, which are still extant in Greek and in Latin. See Fabric. Bib. Gr., l. vi. c. x. and MS. Harl. 399. The author of *Pierce Ploughman* has quoted and paraphrased the same passage.' In an edition of Vincent, printed in 1624, the reading 'temperatrix' occurs instead of 'repertrix,' exactly as in our text. None of the versions include the clause 'donum dei,' for which see the note to l. 136 below.

120. (14. 277.) *By so*, provided that [b].

128. The 'commandment' is in Matt. vii. 1—'Nolite iudicare, ut non iudicemini.'

130. *Vnseled*, unsealed. Gallons, pottles, and quarts, used by brewsters and taverners, were to be 'sealed with the seal of the Aldermen;' Liber Albus, p. 233. Cf. note to Pass. iv. 87, p. 43.

136. *Sonde*, sending, gift [c]; *yifte*, gift [b]. The clause 'Donum dei' is not contained in the sentence from Secundus, as given by Vincent of Beauvais. In speaking of poverty, Burton observes—'Though it be *donum dei*, a blessed estate, the way to heaven, as Chrysostome calls it\ (Comment. ad Hebraeos), *God's gift*, the mother of modesty, and much to be preferred before riches,' etc.; Anatomy of Melancholy, pt. 1, sec. 2, mem. 4, subsec. 6. The passage in Chrysostom occurs in his Commentary on the Epistle to the Hebrews, cap. x. homil. 18, sec. 3 (ed. Migne); where we find—'Tantum bonum est paupertas; est enim quaedam deductio ad caelum, unctio athletica, magna quaedam et admirabilis exercitatio, portus tranquillus.' I do not find the actual words 'donum Dei,' but just above, sec. 2, St. Chrysostom says—' diuitiae et paupertas sunt a Domino.'

139. *Altoun*, Alton in Hampshire; not Halton, in Cheshire, as suggested by Whitaker. All the MSS., except P., have the reading *altoun* or *alton*, without initial *h*. This point was completely cleared up by a discussion in Notes and Queries; see N. and Q., 3rd Ser., xii. 373, 468, 4th Ser., i. 277, 464. In the course of this correspondence, W. H. R. M. cited the following extract from p. 107 of the late T. Hudson Turner's Account of Domestic Architecture of the Thirteenth Century. 'The wooded pass of Alton, on the borders of Surrey and Hampshire, which was not disafforested until the end of Henry's reign, was a favourite ambush for outlaws, who there awaited the merchants and their trains of sumpterhorses travelling to or from Winchester: even in the fourteenth century the wardens of the great fair of St. Giles, held in that city, paid five mounted sergeant-at-arms to keep the *pass of Alton* during the continuance of the fair, "according to custom."' W. Chapman says— 'The district (of Alton) is known to have been for a very long period the resort of robbers. There is a spot in the parish of Bentley, and close to the forest of Alice Holt, to which the word 'pass' would not be inapplicable; but it is more than probable that the word is used in the sense of road or passage, as ordinarily applied at the present day,' etc.

The above explanation, I may add, is made quite certain by William's allusions to Winchester fair; see Pass. vii. 211, xiv. 52, and especially the parallel passage to the present one in Pass. v. 51–54, where Peace is described as being robbed on his way to St. Giles's down, whereon Winchester Fair was held.

C. PASS. XVII. 143. B. PASS. XIV. 304.

143. I do not see why reference is here made to Seneca, as the quotation given is a part of the longer one at l. 117. Perhaps the name of Seneca was added by the scribes, because his name occurs in the parallel passage in Chaucer (note to l. 117 above)—

'Glad pouerte is an honest thing certeyn;
This wol Senek and othere clerkes seyn.'

Here the allusion is to a passage in Seneca's second Epistle, where he professes to quote Epicurus—' Honesta (inquit) res est laeta paupertas. Illa vero non est paupertas, si laeta est. Non qui parum habet sed qui plus cupit, pauper est.'

Similar sentiments may be found frequently in Seneca. See his Letters (Epist. iv, xvii, lxxx.)

—— (14. 305.) The quotation is from Juvenal, Sat. x. 22. The second word in the line should, of course, be *uacuus*, but most MSS. have *paupertas*. I have adopted the reading *pauper* of the Oriel MS. because it scans, and comes nearer to the true reading.

Chaucer, in his Wyf of Bathes Tale (Group D, l. 1191), alludes to the same passage.

151. *Paneter*, keeper of the pantry. From the Lat. *panis*, Fr. *pain*, are derived from the F. *panetier* and *paneterie*, respectively explained by Cotgrave to mean 'a pantler' and 'a pantry.' The keeper of the pantry was, at a later period, generally called a *pantler;* sometimes a *panterer* (see Halliwell), with an unnecessary reduplication of the last syllable. The B-text has *payn*, i.e. bread.

153. The B-text is rather obscure. It is easily made out, however, by comparing it with the C-text, which shows that *Seynt austin* is a nominative case, in apposition with *a lettred man*. The reference to Saint Augustine probably means no more than that similar praise of poverty is to be found in his writings; as e. g. in his De Civitate Dei, lib. iv. c. 3 (Opera, ed. Migne, vii. 114).

—— (14. 322.) *Harde* here means wretched, miserable, perilous. The general sense is—'So miserable (*or* perilous) is it to continue in sin, and yet sin pursueth us ever.'

—— (14. 325.) *Dede dede*, did deed; three MSS. read *dide* for the first *dede*.

—— (14. 328.) 'Or master over any man more than over himself.' Cf. Prov. xvi. 32.

—— (14. 332.) Here ends the Sixth Vision, as clearly marked in [b].

—— (15. 1.) Here, in [b], begins the poem of Do-bet; but, in [c], it does not begin till farther on, at Pass. xviii. 1.

158. (*see* 15. 12.) Here begins the Seventh Vision, which may be called the Vision of *Anima* and of the Tree of Charity [b], or that of *Liberum Arbitrium* (Free Will) and of the Tree of Charity [c]. The various names of *Anima* (as given in the quotation at l. 201) are considered in the C-text as various names of *Liberum Arbitrium*. See note to l. 201.

169. St. Peter is generally represented with a key or keys, in allusion to Matt. xvi. 19; St. Paul is generally represented with a sword.

179. No doubt this refers to the favourite poem, perhaps by Walter Map, called Dialogus inter Corpus et Animam ; see Mr. Wright's edition of Mapes (Camden Soc.), pp. 95, 321, 334 ; Mätzner's Altenglische Sprachproben, i. 92. In the course of this Dialogue the question is debated, whether the Body or the Soul has the higher authority, and each accuses the other of causing their common misery. Our poet likens them to a piece of wood on fire. The Body is the wood, the Soul the flame ; and the two together contribute to the burning.

183. For an account of these various names, see the Latin quotation at l. 201, and the note to that line.

186. 'And when I make my moan (i. e. complain) to God, I am called Memory.' The expression *maden mone* has occurred before, Pass. ix. 130. The author seems to have misunderstood the Latin original— 'dum recolit, memoria est.' I suppose that *recolit* here means remembers, recollects ; but William has either taken it in another sense, or adopted another reading, or else has varied the phrase to suit the requirements of alliteration.

191. 'And when I claim or claim not, buy or refuse to buy.' The reader will miss the sense unless he remembers the old sense of *challenge*.

193, 194. These two lines do not appear in the B-text ; neither do we find there the corresponding Latin clause (dum declinat a malo ad bonum, liberum arbitrium est). Still it is evident that William attached much importance to this inserted clause, as he now makes *Liberum Arbitrium* to be the principal name of the Soul.

201. In l. 199 we are referred to St. Augustine and Isidore as authorities for the Latin quotation here given. It is to be found in Isidore, Etymologiarum Liber xi [not xl. as in Mr. Wright's note], cap. 1 ; also in his Differentiarum Liber ii. cap. 29. Mr. Wright adds—'They are repeated by Alcuin, De Anim. Rat. N. x. p. 149—' *Animus* est, dum vivificat ; dum contemplatur, *spiritus* est ; dum sentit, *sensus* est ; dum sapit, *animus* est ; dum intelligit, *mens* est ; dum discernit, *ratio* est ; dum consentit, *voluntas* est ; dum recordatur, *memoria* est.' See Political, Religious, and Love Poems, ed. Furnivall, p. 37.

Between the quotations as given in [b] and [c] there are two variations. The first is that [c] omits the clause ' dum scit, mens est.' This omission must have been a mere accident, as the translation of the clause is retained in l. 185. The other is that [c] inserts the clause ' dum declinat a malo ad bonum, liberum arbitrium est,' which is translated in ll. 193, 194, whilst at the same time the name of the allegorical personage seen in the vision is changed from *Anima* to *Liberum Arbitrium.* There seems to be small reason for this change, which is no improvement. It is hard to see how all these various names can be applied to Free Will.

It is clear from Drayton's Works that he had read William's Vision, and it is very likely that it was from this very passage that he derived his Sonnet to the Soul.

In Hickscorner (Hazlitt's Old Plays, i. 154) Free Will is introduced as one of the personages, and is made to describe himself.

213. Isaiah xiv. 14; see note to Pass. ii. 111, p. 25.

216. This saying (from Prov. xxv. 27) is attributed to Solomon in Prov. xxv. 1. The B-text has the reading *opprimitur*, the C-text *opprimatur*; but the ordinary reading of the Vulgate is *opprimetur*. Chaucer quotes this saying in his tale of Melibeus. Cf. Hampole's English prose Treatises, ed. Perry, 1866 (E. E. T. S.), p. 42: 'For the wyse man saise thus; *Scrutator maiestatis opprimetur a gloria;* that es to say, Raunsaker of the myghte of Godd and of His maieste withowttene gret clennes and meknes sall be ouerlayed and oppresside of hymselfe.'

220. 'The more dearly he shall pay for it, unless he act rightly.' On the phrase *abygge bitere*, see note to Pass. xxi. 448.

221. The following passage from St. Bernard has nearly the same force as the expression in the text, though differently worded. 'Ut opera tua uerbis concinant, immo uerba operibus, ut cures uidelicet plus facere quam docere;' S. Bernardi Epistolæ; Epist. cci. vol. i. p. 370 (ed. Migne).

224. See Pass. xiv. 227-229.

225. *Vuel to defie*, difficult to digest. See Pass. i. 230.

227. *Deynous*, disdainful, contemptuous. *Deme that*, judge them that. *That* is often used for *he that* or *they that*. Cf. Rom. xii. 3.

231. *Meuen*, discuss; lit. move. Both in [b] and [c] we have examples of French plural adjectives terminating in *s;* cf. Pass. xviii. 290. Thus *materes inmesurables* [b] means immeasurable or infinite subjects; and *motifs insolibles* [c] means insoluble questions or problems. *Fallaces* may be construed either as an adjective or a substantive. If the former, the sense is 'insoluble and fallacious problems.' If the latter, it is 'insoluble problems and falsehoods.' The former is better. For *fallas*, when used as a substantive, see note to Pass. xii. 22, p. 147.

—— (15. 71.) 'It were better for many doctors to abandon such teaching.' *Byleue* sometimes means to leave off, abandon, quit, forsake; as in the first line of a poem on the Birth of Jesus, printed in Altenglische Legenden, ed. Horstmann:—'Of joie and blisse is al my song, kare to *bileue;*' p. 64.

—— (15. 73.) The Seven Deadly Sins were supposed to have several off-shoots or branches. See Chaucer, Persones Tale, De Septem Peccatis mortalibus. See note above, to Pass. viii. 70, p. 97.

234. *Fif wittes*, five senses; see note to Pass. ii. 15, p. 21.

—— (15. 80.) *Glose*, the comment. Perhaps the allusion is to St. Augustine, in Psalm iv. 3 (Opera, v. iv. col. 79, ed. Migne):—'Utquid ergo temporalium rerum amore detinemini? utquid tanquam prima, extrema sectamini? ... Cupitis enim permanere uobiscum quae omnia transeunt tanquam umbra.' For the quotations, see Ps. xcvi. 7, iv. 3 (Vulg.).

—— (15. 81.) 'If I lie against you, as far as my ignorant wit is concerned, lead me to the burning.' This interesting passage has a clear allusion to the burning of heretics. The common opinion, that no man was burnt for his religion in England before 1401, can be proved to be wrong: see Wyclif's Works, ed. Arnold, Introd. p. x); so that the present allusion does not in any way contradict the date 1377, which I have assigned for the composition of the B-text.

240. It is difficult to find in the gospels the words here quoted. William was probably thinking of the first verse of the second chapter of St. James; see also Deut. i. 17; xvi. 19; Levit. xix. 15; Prov. xxiv. 23; Ecclus. xlii. 1. Or perhaps the text in Luke xiv. 12 may be meant, owing to the mention of 'the rich' in l. 239.

—— (15. 89.) This line might be considered as the poet's own motto. It exactly expresses the spirit in which he wrote.

250. 'There is a disease in the root of such kind of stems;' *or* 'of boughs' [b]. *More*, a root, is still in use, especially in Hampshire, and was used by one of the witnesses in the Tichborne Trial, to the perplexity of judge and jury. See Pass. xviii. 21, and the note, p. 224.

Hence the 'myschif in the more' comes to the same thing as 'the rote is roten' in l. 253.

264. In the Ayenbite of Inwyt, ed. Morris, p. 25, Hypocrisy is called the Sixth Bough of Pride. Chaucer (Persones Tale, De Superbia) enumerates 'inobedience, avaunting, *ipocrisie*, despit, arrogance,' etc., among the 'twigges and harmes that comen of pride.'

265. *In latyn*. Mr. Wright remarks—'The monks had collections of comparisons, similitudes, proverbs, etc., to be introduced in their sermons, and even when preaching in English they generally quoted them in Latin. This I suppose to be the meaning of the expression here.'

Chaucer has a passage closely resembling this, Sq. Tale, Group F, 512 –520, where he compares a 'ypocrite' to a serpent hidden under flowers, or to a fair tomb above a corpse. See Matt. xxiii. 27; Acts xxiii. 3.

271. The passage here attributed to St. John Chrysostom is not to be found in his genuine works. It occurs in the 38th of a set of Homilies on the Gospel of St. Matthew, a work of an uncertain author, sometimes called 'Opus Imperfectum' from its incomplete state, and printed in some editions of St. Chrysostom's works as an Appendix to his Homilies on St. Matthew. The text commented on is contained in Matt. xxi. 12–20, and the comment is as follows. 'Nam sicut de templo omne bonum egreditur, sic et de templo omne malum procedit . . . Sic si aliquis Christianorum peccauerit, non omnino peccant et sacerdotes; si autem et sacerdotes fuerint in peccatis, totus populus conuertitur in peccandum. Uidit arborem pallentibus foliis marcidam, et intellexit studiosus agricola, quia laesuram in radicibus haberet. Nam uere quemadmodum cum uideris arborem pallentibus foliis, marcidam intelligis, quia aliquam culpam habet circa radicem: ita cum uideris populum indisciplinatum et irreligiosum, sine dubio cognosce, quia sacerdotium eius non est sanum;' Incerti authoris Hom. 38 in Matt. ex cap. xxi; in S. Chrysost. Op., Parisiis, 1570, tom. ii. col. 877. It is obvious that William's quotation was made from memory.

It is clear, too, that the author of the Opus Imperfectum was thinking of Isaiah xxiv. 2— ' Ut populus, sic sacerdos.'

—— (15. 118.) *But if*, except, unless. *Bere*, were to bear ; past tense, subjunctive mood. The sense is—' I should be very much surprised unless many priests were to carry a set of beads in their hand and a book under their arm, instead of their baselards and their brooches.' See note to l. 121.

—— (15. 119.) *A peyre bedes*, a set of beads ; see Chaucer, Prol. 159. A *pair* (from Lat. *par*) is often used of a set of things of *equal* size. Thus 'a pair of stairs' is a flight of stairs ; and 'a pair of cards' is a pack of cards ; see Nares and Halliwell.

Observe the curious variation here in the Oriel MS., which also has *heer* for *bere* in the line above, giving the sense—' unless many priests here, instead of (having) their baselards and their brooches, should go and sing, where there is no service, along with Sir Philip the sparrow.' That is, they would be turned out of their employment as priests, and be obliged to sing out of doors with the sparrows.

The epithet ' sir ' is playfully applied to the sparrow as if he too were a priest, and could sing mass. Skelton's poem on ' Phyllyp Sparowe' shews clearly that Philip or Phip was a name for a pet sparrow, probably because it somewhat resembles the bird's chirp. Cf. Lat. *pipire*, to chirp. Thus Legonidec, in his Dictionary of Breton words, has—*Filip*, s. m. passereau ou moineau, oiseau. Ce nom est une onomatopée, étant formé de l'imitation du cri de l'oiseau qu'il désigne. On le nomme aussi *chilip* et *golven*.' So in Shakespeare's King John, i. 1. 231, we find—' Good leave, good Philip ; ' with the answer—' Philip! sparrow.' See Pass. xii. 310, and the note, p. 166.

—— (15. 120.) 'Sir John and Sir Geoffrey.' The title ' sir ' was the common title of respect, chiefly used in the three instances of ' sir king,' ' sir knight,' and ' sir priest,' as noted by Bradford, vol. i. p. 589 (Parker Society). Priests especially were so called ; Bradford, vol. ii. p. 7, note. See further under ' Sir ' in the Parker Society's Index. From the same Index, we learn that ' Sir John ' was a familiar title for a priest ; Bradford, i. 71, 589, ii. 120, 313 ; Cranmer, ii. 306 ; Latimer, i. 317 ; Ridley, 104; Tyndale, i. 146, 277, ii. 239, etc. See also Chaucer, Group B. 4000, and my note in The Prioresses Tale, etc. (Clarendon Press.) Of course, John is a very common name. We may also infer from the present passage that *Geoffrey* was also formerly a common name, which is the fact. Cf. note to Pass. xiv. 125, p. 176.

—— (15. 121.) *Basellarde*, a kind of sword, which priests were particularly forbidden to wear, an injunction which they commonly disregarded. Compare Ploughman's Tale ; in Polit. Poems, ed. Wright, i. 331 ; Polit. Songs, ed. Wright, p. 328. See note to Pass. iv. 461, p. 52.

Ballokknyf, probably a large knife, such as were worn suspended from the girdle ; cf. note to Pass. xxiii. 219. *With botones ouergylte*, with gilt studs on the handle or sheath. Cf. Chaucer, Prol. 366. The two following items are taken from an inventory of Sir John Fastolf, A.D.

1459; Paston Letters, ed. Gairdner, i. 478, 488. 'Item, j. bollok-hafted dager, harnesyd wyth sylver, and j. chape thertoo.' 'Item, iij. kneyves in a scheythe, the haftys of every withe naylys gilt.'

—— (15. 122.) *Portous*, a breviary. Also spelt *portasse*, *portesse*, *poortos*, *portous*, etc., all from O. F. *porte-hors* = Lat. *portiforium*, which see in Ducange. 'Poortos, booke, *portiforium*, *breviarium*;' Prompt. Parv. 'The *Portous*, or Breviary, contained whatever was to be said by all beneficed clerks, and those in holy orders, either in choir, or privately by themselves, as they recited their daily canonical hours; no musical notation was put into these books.'—Rock, Church of Our Fathers, v. iii. pt. 2, p. 212; see also v. iii. pt. 1, p. 55. The expression 'a breviary that should be his plough for saying *placebo*' means that he should be diligent in using the breviary. There is a parallel passage in Pass. iv. 467; see the note to that line, p. 52, and cf. Wyclif's Works, iii. 374, note.

The passage means—'but, as for a breviary that should be his plough to say *placebo* with, unless he had some service (to say) in order to save some silver in addition, he says it with an ill will.' The priests used to continue to say *Placebo*, and *Dirige* and masses all through the month following a funeral; Rock, Church of Our Fathers, ii. 516. They said these with a better will when well paid, or when money was left for additional masses.

Dirige came to mean the morning-service for the dead, *Placebo* the evening-service, and *Requiem* the mass for the same; see Rock, Church of our Fathers, ii. 502, 503.

272. *Leese ye*, ye lose [c]; *lese ye on*, ye lose by, spend on [b]. *Fynden*, provide for.

277. *Sodenes*, sub-deans; see note to Pass. iii. 187, p. 38.

278. See a similar description of the evil ways of some priests in Old Eng. Homilies, ed. Morris, 2nd Ser., p. 162.

280. 'That which they leave, profligates readily devour it' [c]; *or*, 'get it' [b].

—— (15. 141.) 'Thus depart their goods, when the spirit has fled.'

284. (15. 145.) The B-text says—'What is charity? said I. A childlike thing, said he; a free liberal will, free from puerility and folly.' The corresponding line in [c] is really l. 296.

286. 'I have lived in London many long years' [c]; 'I have lived in the country, quoth I, my name is Long Will' [b]. This is an important line, in both versions. We hence learn that the author lived at first in the country, and then a long while in London, and that he was commonly known by the name of Long Will, obviously with reference to his tallness of stature; cf. note to Pass. xi. 68, p. 134. The poet Gascoigne, a tall man, was commonly called 'Long George.'

—— (15. 151.) 'And will lend (*or* give) where they expect to be faithfully repaid.'

289, 292, 296. See 1 Cor. xiii. 4, 5, 12; Matt. xviii. 3.

291. *Hus* [c] = *his* [b]. *Askede after hus*, asked for his dues.

295. *By that*, with reference to what people say about charity.

298. *Russet* was the name of a coarse and common cloth; see l. 342 below, and note to Pass. xi. 1, p. 131.

299. *Cammoka.* Halliwell has—'*Camaca,* a kind of silk or rich cloth. Curtains were often made of this material. See the Squyr of Lowe Degre, 835; Test. Vetust. p. 14; Coventry Mysteries, p. 163.' Migne's edition of Ducange has—'*Camoca,* panni serici vel pretiosioris species; étoffe fine de poil de chameau ou de chèvre sauvage; olim *camocas*' [i.e. O. Fr. *camocas*]. And see Roquefort.

Tarse [b] was the name of a kind of silken stuff formerly much esteemed, and said to have come from a country called *Tharsia* adjoining Cathay (China). See Chaucer, Kn. Ta., 1302. Ducange explains *Tarsicus* as 'panni preciosioris species,' and quotes (says Mr. Wright) a visitation of the treasury of St. Paul's, London, in 1295, where there is mention of 'Tunica et dalmatica de panno Indico Tarsico besantato de auro,' and of a 'casula de panno Tarsico.' Roquefort gives '*Tartaire,* sorte d'étoffe de Tartarie;' and if *Tars* be the same as *Tartarie* (as stated in Migne's edition of Ducange), then *Tharsia* is merely another name for *Tartary,* which is very probable. Further, as the people of Tartary were called, in Old French, *Tartarins* (see Roquefort), it is clear that the O. Fr. *Tartaire* is the same as *Tartarin,* defined by Halliwell to be 'a kind of silk.' The only difficulty caused by this identification is that it is not at first clear why the word *tarse* should be used here, whilst in B. xv. 224 (just below) we have *tartaryne.* The most probable explanation of the difference is to suppose that the latter line (omitted in the three best MSS. and in Crowley's edition) is spurious, in which case it is easy to see that *tartaryne* was suggested by the mention of *tarse,* and is, in fact a gloss upon it. See also British Costume, p. 105, note.

In his edition of Marco Polo (i. 259), Col. Yule, speaking of the cloths called *nakh* and *nasij,* says—'these stuffs, or such as these were, I believe, what the medieval writers called *Tartary cloth,* not because they were made in Tartary, but because they were brought from China and its borders through the Tartar dominions. Dante alludes to the supposed skill of the Turks and Tartars in weaving gorgeous stuffs (*Inf.* xvii. 17); and see Mandeville's Travels, pp. 175, 247.'

Trye [b] means *choice;* and the allusion is, of course, to robes of expensive material and splendid colour.

—— (15. 165.) *Leueth,* believes; answering to *let it soth,* considers it true, in l. 168 [b].

306. See Matt. vii. 12.

317. 'One named "Thou-openest-thine-hand" provides all things for him.' Compare Pass. xvi. 266, and see note to that line; p. 207.

318. Compare Pass. xvi. 251 (b. 14. 48).

321. The reader must not for a moment suppose that William here commends pilgrimages. The next line tells us that he only means such pilgrimages as conduct the charitable man to the cottages of the poor and to prisons. See the parallel passage, Pass. v. 122, 123; and see l. 327 below.

328. 'Then he enters (lit. runs) into thoughtfulness (*or* anxiety), and eagerly seeks out Pride, with all its appurtenances, and packs them up together, and (afterwards) washes them in the laundry called *Laboraui* (Ps. vi. 7, Vulgate), and soaks them in his breast, and often beats it, and with warm tears he moistens it till it becomes white' [c]. The passage is, of course, highly figurative. Charity is represented as first visiting the poor people and wretched prisoners, with the hope of alleviating their sufferings. This done, the charitable man turns his thoughts inward. Having helped others, he has more leisure for self-examination. He becomes anxious for himself; he collects all his proud feelings, and cleanses them by the groanings of prayer. He 'buck-washes' them, or cleanses yet more thoroughly, within his own breast, which he beats in self-condemnation. With tears of contrition he washes his breast white, and becomes whiter than snow. Cf. Ps. l. 9, 19 (Vulgate).

The B-text runs differently, viz.—' He will labour in a laundry nearly the length of a mile [i.e. for a third of an hour], and enter into the thoughts of his youth (lit. run into youth), and eagerly address Pride, with all its appurtenances, and pack them together, and soak them in his breast, and beat them clean, and lay upon them (i. e. labour upon them) long with *Laboraui* (i. e. penitential groans), and afterwards wash them with tears.' Here the word *them* represents proud thoughts and feelings.

The word ȝ*erne*, meaning here to run, hasten, must not be confounded with ȝ*erne*, to desire. William uses the latter in B. i. 35, as equivalent to *wylne* in C. ii. 33. But the sense is settled here by the expression 'ȝorn into elde,' Pass. xiii. 13; and we certainly have ȝ*ernynge* for running in Pass. xxii. 380. Several examples of ȝ*erne*, to run (A.S. *yrnan*) may be found in the Glossary to the Ayenbite of Inwyt. William also uses the form *rennen*, Pass. xvii. 348; he simply adopts that form which best suits the alliteration at the moment.

The word ȝ*outhe* (B. 15. 183) was ill-chosen; accordingly, in [c], the poet gave up the alliteration for the sake of the better word *pouht*, meaning inward care, anxiety. He also changed the inexpressive *speke* into the more intelligible *secheth*. See note to B. 14. 19, p. 205.

336. *Wher*, whether; the usual contraction. It is equivalent to—' is it the case that?'

337. Here *Piers the Plowman* is completely identified with *Jesus Christ*; cf. B. 15. 206. See Matt. ix. 4, Luke xi. 17; also John x. 38, Matt. vi. 16.

—— (15. 197.) *Han peper in the nose*, conduct themselves superciliously. To 'have pepper in the nose' is to take offence, to be angry; see the examples in Halliwell; Cotgrave, s. v. *Chevre*; 1 Henry IV, i. 3. 41.

—— (15. 198.) *As a lyoun*, i.e. proudly; see B. 13. 302, and note to Pass. vii. 3, p. 71. *There*, where, when.

—— (15. 206.) See note to l. 337, just above. The text is misquoted; it is—' petra autem erat Christus;' 1 Cor. x. 4. It has evidently been taken in connection with Matt. xvi. 18—'tu es Petrus, et super hanc petram,' etc. Whence *Piers* = *Petrus* = *petra* = *Christus*.

—— (15. 207.) *Landeleperes hermytes*, vagabond hermits ; observe the nominatives in apposition.

—— (15. 208.) *At ancres*, among anchorites. *Box*, an alms-box ; see note to Pass. i. 96, p. 12.

—— (15 209.) 'Fie upon hypocrites, and upon them that favour them !'

343. 'Both in (sober) grey and in (costly) fur, and in gilt armour.' Charity is found among all classes.

345. *Seyntes*, saints [c] ; *kynges*, kings [b]. They were both. The reference is, of course, to St. Edmund, the martyr, king of East Anglia, died Nov. 20, 870, and to St. Edward the Confessor, died Jan. 5, 1066, whose shrine is in Westminster Abbey. See Chambers, Book of Days, i. 54.

347. 'Sing and read ;' i. e. discharge the duties of a priest.

350. *Rathest*, soonest.

351. 'Wearing a cap and with anointed hair, and having his crown shaven.' The 'kelle' or caul was chiefly used with reference to the ornamental network worn over the hair by women ; but it sometimes meant, as here, a man's cap. Another instance of this is in Chaucer, Troil. and Cress. iii. 775 (ed. Tyrwhitt), or iii. 727 (ed. Morris). The right reading in that line is—'And maken hym a howue aboue a calle,' i. e. *a hood over a cap*. The person here spoken of as an embodiment of Charity seems to be meant for a rich ecclesiastic, of a kindly and liberal nature.

—— (15. 224.) This line, being found in only a few MSS. of the B-class, is probably spurious ; still it is in keeping with the context. See the note to l. 299 above, p. 220.

353. St. Francis, the founder of the Franciscan or Grey Friars, or Minorites, was *himself* held in great reverence, though his followers were, in course of time, so much disliked. See P. Pl. Crede, 511. And see below, B. 15. 413.

355. 'He commends rich men and receives robes (i. e. presents) from them, of such as live truly, and love and believe' [c] ; *or*, 'of such as lead guileless lives' [b]. See Ecclus. xxxi. 8.

—— (15. 237.) *That*, that which, viz. marriage.

—— (15. 244.) 'But I blame nobody.' *Lyf*, a living being.

—— (15. 249.) See Ps. iv. 9.

NOTES TO C. PASSUS XVIII. (B. XV. 253–601.)

5. (*not in* b.) See 1 Cor. xiii. 7.

—— (15. 254.) *Angres*, afflictions, trials ; see C. xiii. 207, and the note.

—— (15. 258.) 'For every one may well know, that, if God Himself had so willed, neither Judas nor any Jew could have placed Jesus on the cross.'

—— (15. 264.) The reference is probably to the Aurea Legenda of Jacobus de Voragine, but there are numerous other collections. Ælfric's

Homilies, ed. Thorpe, i. 545, mentions a book called Uitae Patrum. See the note on Lives of Saints in Warton, Hist. Eng. Poetry, ed. 1871, ii. 58.

—— (15. 267 ; *cf.* c. 18. 12.) St. Anthony, reputed as one of the first of anchorites, and the founder of Monachism, was born in Egypt, about A.D. 251, or later, and died Jan. 17, 356. His day is Jan. 17, and an excellent account of him may be found in Chambers, Book of Days, i. 124, 126. He was the first to live a solitary life in a desert, but his mode of life was soon imitated by multitudes. St. Ægidius, better known as St. Giles, died about 700 ; his day is Sept. 1. ' Giles, or Ægidius, a very eminent saint of the seventh century, is believed to have been a Greek who migrated to France, ... [and settled] in a hermitage, first in one of the deserts near the mouth of the Rhone, finally in a forest in the diocese of Nismes. ... There is a romantic story of his being partly indebted for his subsistence to a Heaven-directed hind, which came daily to give him its milk ; ' Chambers, Book of Days, ii. 296 ; cf Brewer, Dict. of Miracles, p. 360.

St. Arsenius [c] was, says Mr. Wright, ' a noble Roman who, at the end of the fourth century, retired to Egypt to live the life of an anchorite in the desert.' He died July 19, 449 ; his day is July 19. See further in the note to l. 17 below, p. 224.

—— (15. 268.) This line corresponds to C. xviii. 28.

—— (15. 270.) *Spekes an spelonkes*, caves and caverns. The word *speke* probably occurs nowhere else as an English word, and does not appear in any Glossary, to my knowledge. If it were not for the context, it were hard to guess the sense. However, it is clear that *spelonke* is the Lat. *spelunca*, from which it follows that *speke* is the Lat. *specus*. William, though probably the only author who uses *speke*, is not the only author to use *spelonke*. The phrase ' double *spelunke*, or double cave ' occurs in Mandeville's Travels, ed. Halliwell, p. 66. ' Who knoweth not that our recluses have grates of yron in their *speluncȝes* and dennes?' Reliques of Rome, by T. Becon, 1563. fol. 53 ; quoted in Rock, Ch. of Our Fathers, iii. 118. Cf. also—' *Spelonque* ; f. A hole in a rock ; a wild beast's den ; ' Cotgrave.

8. Nearly repeated from C. xvii. 371.

—— (15. 273.) *Foules that fleeth*, birds that fly. So in Ælfric's Homilies, ed. Thorpe, i. 547, we are told that some saints were served by angels, some by *birds*. See note to B. 15. 279 below.

9. (15. 274.) For this story of the hind, see note to B. 15. 267 above.

—— (15. 279.) Mr. Wright observes that this story does not occur in the usual accounts of St. Anthony. The fact is that our poet has made a slight mistake. In the next line he says—'and though the man had a guest, God provided for them both.' He is right as to St. Anthony and St. Paul being fed by a bird, but it was St. Anthony who was the *guest*, and St. Paul the hermit who was the *host*. The story is, in fact, to be found in the life of St. Paul. See Vita S. Pauli, cap. 10 ; in S. Hieronymi Opera, ed. Migne, vol. ii. ; and see the next note.

13. St. Paul (of Thebes) is here called the first hermit. He and St. Anthony were the first to lead a heremitic life ; and St. Jerome calls the

former the *author* of that mode of life, the latter its *illustrator*—'huius uitae auctor Paulus, illustrator etiam Antonius;' Epist. 22, ad Eustochium, cap. 16. During the persecution under Decius, Paul fled to a desert on the East of the Nile, and there became the founder of the anchorites or solitary hermits. 'Paulus *primus eremita* semper ieiunauit, quousque de caelis sibi panis mitteretur, qui duplicatus est cum ad eum ueniret Antoninus' (*sic*); Peter Cantor, ed. Migne, col. 328. See Mrs. Jameson's Sacred and Legendary Art, ii. 368; Kingsley's The Hermits; Vita S. Pauli, by St. Jerome (Opera, ed. Migne ii.) He died A.D. 342; and his day is Jan. 15.

Parroked, enclosed; lit. imparked; see Pass. vii. 144.

15. *Frere austyn*, Augustine the friar. A general term for the Augustine or Austin Friars; see B-text. The four orders of friars fiercely disputed as to the priority of their respective foundations, and each sought to shew that their order was older than the rest. The Austin friars took their name from the celebrated St. Augustine of Hippo; but, to prove their antiquity, maintained that their order was really due to St. Paul, the *first* hermit; see this claim asserted by an Austin friar in P. Pl. Crede, ll. 306–317. But even this was outdone; for the Carmelites said their order dated from the time *of the prophet Elijah!* See P. Pl. Crede, note to ll. 29, and 48.

17. *Panyeres*, baskets. The word is curiously chosen, as St. Paul was a tent-maker; Acts xviii. 3. Yet Chaucer seems to have the same idea—

'I wol nat do no labour with my hondes,
Ne make *baskettes*, and lyue thereby . . .
I wol non of the *apostles* counterfete.'
Prol. to Pardoneres Tale.

However, it was St. Paul who set the example of labouring with his hands; and, in imitation of him, we find an early example of *basket-making* by St. Arsenius. See Mrs. Jameson's Sacred and Legendary Art, 3rd ed. p. 757.

19. St. Peter and St. Andrew were fishers; Matt. iv. 18.

21. 'Mary Magdalen lived by roots (to eat) and dews (to drink).' See the note to Pass. xvii. 250, p. 217.

The notion that St. Mary Magdalen and Mary, the sister of Lazarus, were one and the same person is almost wholly unfounded, and indeed repulsive; but, in olden times, it was almost universal. See, *Mary Magdalene* in The Concise Dictionary of the Bible, ed. W. Smith, p. 521. Tradition relates that St. Mary Magdalen found her way to the South of Gaul, and retired to a solitary life in a desert not far from Marseilles. See Mrs. Jameson's Sacred and Legendary Art, i. 337; Chambers, Book of Days, ii. 101. Her day is July 22.

23. 'Sancta Maria Aegyptiaca quadraginta annis uixit de duobus panibus et radicibus;' Peter Cantor, ed. Migne, col. 328. The usual day assigned to St. Mary of Egypt (S. Maria Egyptiaca) is April 9. She is said to have lived in the fifth century. Chaucer alludes to her in the Man of Lawes Tale (Group B. 500).

24. 'Love was her relish.' See note to B. xvi. 11, p. 235.

28. This line corresponds to B. 15. 268.

31. Wild beasts are not uncommonly represented in early art as associating with the saints on friendly terms. Compare the story of Daniel in the lion's den, from which many other similar accounts may have been imitated; St. Jerome is often represented with a lion beside him.

33. (15. 301.) *Trewe man*, a truthful man [c]; *meke þinge*, a meek creature [b]. Birds, being supposed to be milder by nature than beasts, are here taken to represent the better class of men. The idea of the excellence of birds seems to have been due to the expression 'uolucres coeli,' the birds of *heaven*, in Matt. viii. 20. Cf. B. 15. 308.

34. *Fynde*, provide for, support. The B-text means—'as if one should say that just men ought to provide for men of religious orders.'

40. The story in the book of Tobit is that Tobit's wife Anna, in receiving wages for some work done, received also a present of a kid from her employers. Tobit was blind; but, hearing the kid's cry, thought that it must have been stolen, and compelled his wife to restore it, not believing her account of it. His words were—'*Uidete, ne forte furtiuus sit;* reddite eum dominis suis, quia non licet nobis aut edere ex furto aliquid, aut contingere;' Tob. ii. 21 (Vulgate); ii. 13 (A. V.). Upon this, his wife taunts him; whereupon, being grieved, he laments his fate in being reproached, concluding with the words—'*expedit enim mihi mori magis quam uiuere;*' Tob. iii. 6.

William gives both quotations inexactly; the latter is an improvement on the original. He has quoted it twice before; see Pass. ii. 144, and the note, p. 27; also Pass. vii. 290.

In the edition of Batman vpon Bartholome, printed at London by Thomas East in 1582, the colophon contains the motto—'Mieulx vault movrir en vertu que vivre en honte;' shewing that the phrase was a proverbial one.

41. The meaning is clear enough. Just as Tobit, being blind, thought himself in danger of having stolen goods brought into his house, so the clergy and other religious, being blind sometimes to the faults of the rich, were in danger of receiving from them things which had been stolen from the poor. In the B-text the advice is particularly given to the friars (15. 306). See the parallel passage in Pass. vii. 300-302.

49. *Child*, i. e. chilled; MSS. M. and F. have *cold*. *Chaufen*, grow warm.

—— (15. 306.) *Fonde thei*, if they found.

—— (15. 310.) *Peny ale*, common ale. See note to Pass. vii. 226, p. 84.

52. *Mesure*, moderation. The first part of the quotation is from Job vi. 5; the last part is probably from some comment on that text. There is something like it in the following: 'Uel ipsa uos bruta animalia doceant, quae quando necessariis abundant, neque rugiunt, neque mugiunt;' S. Brunonis Episcopi Signiensis Exp. in Job vi. 5.

54. *Amorteisede*, granted in mortmain. Cotgrave gives, as one of the

meanings of F. *amortir*, 'to grant, alien, or pass away, in mortmain.' See Blount's Nomolexicon.

56. The B-text means—'and are (regularly) founded and endowed in order to pray for others.' In the C-text the construction is inverted, the last half of the line coming first in the sense. The sense is—'to endow and feed such as are already fully founded, (to endow them, I say,) with the money that your children and kindred may lawfully claim.'

64. *Largenesse*, liberality. The story of St. Lawrence is that, by command of Bishop Xystus, he distributed to the poor all the wealth which was at that time in the treasury of the church of Rome. The emperor, attempting to seize these treasures, was told by St. Lawrence that he should see the wealth of the church; and the saint then pointed to the poor of Rome, as being the true treasures of the Christian community. On this the emperor revenged himself by commanding that St. Lawrence should be roasted to death. See the note to Pass. iii. 130, p. 36.

65. See Ps. cx. 3 (Vulgate); cxi. 3 (A.V.).

66. 'He (Lawrence) gave God's goods (i.e. the treasures of the church) to God's men (i.e. to the poor).'

71. *Purnele*, a common female name; hence, a concubine.

—— (15. 329.) *Robeth*, robe, clothe, give rich clothes to; and so in l. 333.

—— (15. 332.) *To woke with themese*, to moisten the Thames with. It is common to find *with* in this close conjunction with the verb. The word *woke* presents more difficulty; it is discussed above, in the note to Pass. xv. 25, p. 182. Hazlitt's collection of Proverbs has—'To cast water into the sea, *or*, into the Thames.' Ray's comment is—'that is, to give to them who had plenty before; which, notwithstanding, is the dole general of the world. Lumen soli mutuari, etc.'

—— (15. 336.) 'Sacrilegium est res pauperum dare non pauperibus;' Peter Cantor, ed. Migne, cap. 47. 'Maximum periculum est de patrimonio Christi pauperibus non dare;' id. 'Pars sacrilegii est rem pauperum dare non pauperibus;' S. Hieron. Epist. 66. § 8. 'Res pauperum non pauperibus dare, par sacrilegio crimen esse dignoscitur;' Gaufrid. Abb. Declam. ex Bernard. (inter S. Bernardi Opera, tom. ii. p. 612. 'Paria sunt et dare peccatoribus, et immolare demonibus;' Pet. Cantor, cap. 47. 'Paria sunt histrionibus dare, et daemonibus immolare;' id.; quoted, but inexactly, from St. Jerome.

Peter Cantor, cap. 48, also quotes from St. Jerome the words—'O monache, si indiges et accipis, potius das quam accipis; si non indiges et accipis, rapis, quia distribuenda pauperibus tibi usurpas.'

See also Wyclif's Works, iii. 473, note. Cf. 1 Tim. vi. 8.

—— (15. 339.) *Prisone*, prisoner, see Pass. x. 34; xxi. 59, etc.

72. *Lussheborgh*, a light coin. They were spurious coins imported into England from Luxembourg, whence the name. See Liber Albus, ed. Riley, p. 495; Blount's Nomolexicon. The spelling *Lusscheburghe* is used to denote the town of Luxemburg in the Allit. Morte Arthure, ed. Brock, l. 2388.

77. 'The mark of the king of heaven.' That is, the cross made in baptism. *Croune*, the tonsure [b].

78. It is well to note that *of* [c] means *by;* i.e. the metal, man's soul, is by many of these teachers alloyed, etc.

98. *Shephurdes.* See a curious passage in the Complaynt of Scotlande, ed. Murray, pp. 46, 47, on the indebtedness of the science of astronomy to Shepherds. The Calendrier des Bergers deals with astronomy. So in the English translation—'Thus endeth the Astrology of Shepheards, with the knowledge that they have of the stars, planets, and movings of the skies;' Sheph. Kal., ed. 1656, sig. A 4, back. And again, at chap. xxxi—'Here followeth the Shepheards Astrology.' William again mentions the 'seven stars' in Rich. Redeles, iii. 352; he means the *seven planets*, not Charles's Wain or the Pleiades, as in later English.

99. On weather omens, see the chapter so headed in Brand, Pop. Antiq., ed. Ellis, iii. 241.

103. By comparing the texts, we see that 'the folk of the flood' are sailors, and 'the folk of the land' are sowers or husbandmen. Wyclif has a similar lament; Works, iii. 416.

106. *Clymat*, latitude [c]; *element*, air [b]. A *climate* was, at this time, a region of the earth between certain parallels of latitude. See *Climate* and *Element* in Trench's Select Glossary; and my note on *climates* in Chaucer's Treatise on the Astrolabe, Part ii., sect. 39, l. 19; ed. Skeat, p. 85.

107. Grammar was considered as the first of the 'seven arts,' and as the foundation of the rest; see Pass. xii. 98, 122. *Bygyleth*, deceives, perplexes, leads astray.

—— (15. 369.) This is an important line. It shews how common was some knowledge of Latin, and in what high esteem French was held. It is also remarkable as being omitted in the C-text; possibly because French was going out of fashion.

111. *Gowe*, let us go; see note to Pass. i. 227, p. 20.

114. *Seuene ars*, the 'seven arts;' see note to Pass. xii. 94, p. 152. *Asoile ad quodlibet*, answer to any question, generally.

115, 116. 'Unless they should fail in philosophy—that is to say, if there were any philosophers in existence who would carefully examine them—I should be much surprised' [c]. *Apposed*, questioned [b].

118. *Ouerhuppe*, skip over parts of the service; see note to Pass. xiv. 123, p. 176.

120. The feast of Corpus Christi was held on the Thursday after Trinity Sunday, in memory, as was supposed, of the miraculous confirmation of the doctrine of transubstantiation under Pope Urban IV.; it was instituted between 1262 and 1264, and confirmed by the council of Vienne in 1311. It was the favourite day for acting miracle-plays and mysteries, as is well known. See *Corpus Christi* in Nares.

121. William is quite right in referring us to the service for Corpus

Christi day. In the Breviary, 'in festo Corporis Christi,' will be found the hymn beginning—'Pange, lingua, gloriosi ;' and the fourth stanza has—'Ad firmandum cor sincerum *Sola fides sufficit.*'

To saue with lewede peuple, to save ignorant people with.

130. 'The law of love without loyalty (or sincerity) was never praise-worthy.' Here 'loue lawe,' lit. law of love, means law founded upon love. The expression is an awkward one, and would be obscure but for the expression in l. 136, where mention is made of 'love that has law for a cause,' i. e. an orderly love, a love founded on law, one that is in accord with God's will. Thus the general sense is—'God does not approve of law, even if founded on love, if loyalty (or truth) be excluded from it. He teaches none to love without a true cause. Jews, Gentiles, and Saracens, suppose that they believe truly, and honour, love, and believe in one God alike ; but their law is different,' etc. (Here William probably uses 'Gentiles' as meaning other than Christians.) 'But our Lord approves of no love but what is founded on law,' etc. The whole passage is one of those uninteresting specimens of subtlety into which our author sometimes sinks. The Latin quotation at l. 140 is the best guide to the sense of this passage.

In the phrase 'loue lawe,' *loue* must be a genitive case ; the infinitive mood takes (generally) the form *louye*.

148. This line is a repetition of l. 143, and has the same sense. William says that true Charity is to be *cher*, i. e. fond, concerning one's own soul ; i. e. so to love one's own eternal welfare as to avoid sin and be kind to all. I have no doubt that he has hêre used the wrong word ; he meant to have said *chary*, i. e. to be chary (anxious, careful) over one's soul. He evidently took *chary* to be a corruption of the F. *cher*, and thought it would be more correct to use the F. form. Unluckily, *chary* has nothing to do with *cher*, being the A. S. *cearig*, careful, from *cearu* or *caru*, care, anxiety.

150. *Wher*, whether, whether is it the case that.

153. 'It is a natural thing for a creature to honour his Creator.'

157. *As by*, according to. They love not God with that love of which we read in the Legend of the Saints ; i. e. in the Golden Legend.

158. 'They live not in a true belief, for they believe in a (merely human) mediator.'

167. *Porsuede*, endeavoured. *Moste noughte be*, might not be, could not attain to being [b. 15. 391]. The true account of the career of Mohammed was very imperfectly known at this time in England. The phrase 'souhte in-to surrye' (l. 169), lit. made his way to Syria, probably refers to the famous Hegira, or flight from Mecca to Medina, July 15, 622.

The use of the words 'pope' and 'cardinal' seems strange here, but is justified by the current opinion of the time. This will best appear from Mr. Wright's excellent note, which I here transcribe.

'This account of Mohammed was the one most popularly current in the middle ages. According to Hildebert, who wro a life of the pseudo-prophet in Latin verse in the 12th century, Mohammed was a

Christian, skilled in magical arts, who, on the death of the patriarch of Jerusalem, aspired to succeed him:—
  'Tunc exaltari magus hic et *pontificari*
  Affectans auide.'
His intrigues being discovered, the emperor drives him away, and in revenge he goes and founds a new sect. The story of the pigeon, which is not in Hildebert, is found in Vincent of Beauvais, Spec. Hist. lib. xxiii. c. 40.'

168. *A lussheborgh;* see note to l. 72 above.

171. *Endauntede a douue,* tamed a dove. This story is from Vincent of Beauvais, as stated in the note to l. 167. See Andrew Boorde, Introduction of Knowledge, c. 37; 1st Pt. of Hen. VI, i. 2. 140.

—— (15. 413.) *Antony,* the hermit; see note on p. 223. *Dominik,* of Castile, the founder of the Dominican or Black Friars, also known as the Friars Preachers or Jacobins; born April 5, 1170, died Aug. 6, 1221. His day is Aug. 4. See Mrs. Jameson's Legends of the Monastic Orders, p. 227; Chambers, Book of Days, ii. 169. *Francis,* of Assisi, founder of the Franciscan friars, or Minorites; see Mrs. Jameson's Legends of the Monastic Orders; Chambers, Book of Days, ii. 413. His day is Oct. 4. Cf. note to Pass. v. 117, p. 58.

—— (15. 414.) *Benet and Bernarde;* see note to Pass. v. 117, p. 58.

—— (15. 420.) *And,* if. And so in l. 422 [b]. See Matt. vii. 7; v. 13.

—— (15. 430.) Alluding to the eleven apostles. William forgets St. Matthias.

—— (15. 436.) *Gregory,* the Great, born 544, died Mar. 12, 604. See Chambers, Book of Days, i. 361, 679; and note to Pass. vi. 147, p. 67. His day is March 12.

—— (15. 437.) St. Augustine, the famous missionary to England, died about 607. His day is May 26. See Chambers, Book of Days, i. 681.

—— (15. 445.) *Fulled.* The note, by Dr. White, to the Ormulum, ii. 626, is wrong. *Fulled* is from A. S. *fullian,* to baptize, cleanse; not a Teutonic word, but due to Lat. *fullo.*

The operation which is now generally understood by *fulling* is a very different one. It is a process of beating the wool so as to felt it together; and it happens that the name of this 'process (formerly more often called *tucking*) is also connected with the Lat. *fullo.*

William mentions two ways in which the *cleansing* process was formerly effected. Sometimes it was 'fulled under foot,' by being trodden upon, much as when Scotch washerwomen wash clothes by stamping upon them with naked feet; or, at other times, thoroughly cleansed in some sort of frame which he appears to denote by ' fulling-stock;' and which, moreover, must have materially differed from what is now called a fulling-stock, as employed in the modern process of felting. Perhaps the comma at the end of l. 445 may be left out. Then ll. 445 and 446 mean—'till it is cleansed under foot, or well washed with water in fulling-stocks, and afterwards scratched over with teazles.'

—— (15. 446.) *Taseles,* teasles. A reference to the Engl. Cyclopædia will best explain this. 'In the fulled state the cloth presents a woolly and rough appearance, to improve which it goes through the processes of *teazling* or *raising*, and *shearing* or *cutting*. The object of the first is to raise the ends of the fibres above the surface, and of the second to cut them off to a uniform level. The raising of the fibres is effected by thistle-heads, teazling-cards, or wire brushes. Teazles are the seed-pods of the *dipsacus fullonum*, having small hooked points on their surfaces. They were formerly used in the cloth manufacture thus. A number of them were put into a small frame with handles, so as to form a kind of curry-comb; and this was worked by two men over the surface of the cloth, which was suspended horizontally. . . . . In some machines the teazling-points are made of wire, to obviate the waste of 3000 natural teazles, which takes place in the dressing of one piece of cloth.' It will be observed that William alludes to this process a little too early. The cloth was not teazled till it had been 'tucked' (i. e. fulled) and 'tented;' see the next note.

'*Dipsacus Fullonum* is the Clothier's Teazel, a plant with large heads of flowers, which are imbedded in stiff, hooked bracts. These heads are set in frames and used in the dressing of broad-cloth, the hooks catching up and removing all loose particles of wool, but giving way when held fast by the substance of the cloth;' Rev. C. A. Johns, Flowers of the Field, p. 314.

—— (15. 447.) *Ytouked*, tucked or thickened; this is the process which is *now* called *fulling;* see note to l. 445 above, p. 229. Hence the name of *Tucker*.

Ytented, stretched on tenter-hooks. This process, strictly speaking, precedes that of tucking. ' After the second scouring, it is carried 'to the drying-room, or the tenter-ground, where it is stretched out by means of hooks on rails, and allowed to dry in a smooth and extended state;' Engl. Cycl., as above. After the tenting, it is picked over, fulled or tucked, teazled, sheared, brushed, and then finally smoothed; till it comes at last 'under the tailor's hand.'

—— (15. 451.) *Hethene*, heathen. This derivation of *heathen* from *heath* is correct; cf. Lat. *paganus*, from *pagus*, a village.

—— (15. 455.) *Fesauntes*, pheasants. Mr. Wright remarks—'The pheasant was formerly held in the same honour as the peacock, and was served at table in the same manner. It was considered one of the most precious dishes. See Le Grand d'Aussy, Hist. de la Vie privée des François, ii. 19.' See Babees Book, ed. Furnivall, p. 278.

—— (15. 456.) *Fram hym nolde*, would not go away from him; i. e. were tame. See note to l. 467 [b] below. See Matt. xxii. 4.

—— (15. 458.) The calf was a clean animal; Lev. xi. 3. See a some-what similar passage in the Ormulum, ll. 1220–1249.

—— (15. 467.) This refers to the art of calling birds by the use of a pipe. Cf. the anonymous Testament of Love, book ii, fol. 297, col. 2; appended to Chaucer's Works, ed. 1561.

At p. 212 of Lacroix (Manners, Customs, and Dress during the Middle

Ages), there is an excellent illustration of 'Bird-piping, or the manner of catching birds by piping.'

Observe that ll. 464-477 are preserved *only* in the Rawlinson MS.

——(15. 472.) The word *whistlynge* at the end of this line may have been wrongly repeated; we should rather read *techynge*.

The general sense is—just as fowls are allured by whistling, so ignorant men are attracted heavenwards by wise teachers.

—— (15. 473.) The nominative to *bymeneth* is *matheu* in l. 454. 'And, by the man who made a feast [Matt. xxii] he signifies the majesty (of God).'

—— (15. 475.) 'By His tempests and His wonders He warns us, as by means of a whistler, wherever it is His will to honour us all, and to feed and feast us at the same time, for evermore.'

—— (15. 476.) *Worschipen*, to honour, shew regard to. We could hardly have a clearer instance of the difference between the old and modern senses of this word; for God is here said to 'worship' men. So in Wyclif's translation of John xii. 26—'If ony man serve me, my fadir schal *worschip* him.' See *Worship* in Trench's Select Glossary.

—— (15. 478.) The argument goes back to l. 433, and the first part of this line is best taken interrogatively. 'And who are they that excuse themselves (from attempting the work of conversion)? They are the parsons and priests.'

—— (15. 479.) *Han her wille*, obtain their wish, get what they want, viz. their tithes.

—— (15. 482.) William's argument still refers to the conversion of the heathen, as in ll. 430-443. He therefore appeals to *Mathew*, i. e. Matt. xxviii. 19, and to *Marke*, i. e. Mark xvi. 15 (quoted below). He also refers to the psalm beginning with 'Memento, domine, Dauid,' i. e. Ps. cxxxi. in the Vulgate version; the 6th verse being—'Ecce audiuimus eam in Ephrata; inuenimus eam in campis siluae,' which has already been quoted before; see note to Pass. xii. 51, p. 149. In that former place, *eam* is interpreted to mean *caritatem*, i. e. Christian love. So here, William clearly interprets the verse as meaning that Christian love is to be met with in unexpected places, from which he infers the duty of preaching to the heathen.

189. See l. 538 [b] below for the mention of bishops of Bethlehem and Babylon. The pope used to appoint titular bishops *in partibus infidelium*, who were never intended to reside in their dioceses. The famous Bedlam hospital for the insane owes its name to a similar circumstance. It was originally known as St. Mary's of Bethlehem, and was 'founded by Stephen Fitzmary, in 1247, for the pious purpose of sheltering and entertaining the *bishop of Bethlehem* whenever he should be in London;' De Vere, Studies in English, p. 211. It was afterwards granted by Henry VIII., in 1545, to the city of London, and became a hospital for the reception of lunatics. Mention is made of a 'Bishop of Bedlem' in 1298; Riley's Memorials of London, p. 39. Whitaker well remarks, that 'these bishops in partibus, most of whom were abbots and priors, living at ease in the lazy plenty of

their own well-endowed houses, were of all men least qualified for missionaries, and would be least inclined to hearken to this call of residence.'

191, 193, 198. See Mark xvi. 15; John x. 11; Gal. vi. 14.

—— (15. 489, 490, 494.) See John x. 11; Matt. xx. 4; vii. 7.

200. *Red noble*, the gold coin so called. On the noble, see note to Pass. iv. 47, p. 41. There is an allusion here to the cross on the reverse of the coin; whence 'rode' in ll. 201, 206, and 'croys' in ll. 203, 205, 208. The same pun has occurred before, B. 5. 244, and is very common in old authors. Many examples are cited in Warton, Hist. Eng. Poetry, ed. Hazlitt, iii. 278, note 7.

205. (15. 505.) 'The answer is—because of greediness after the cross, the crown stands (i.e. is shewn) in the gold.' Men, covetous only of that *cross* which appears on money, are best satisfied with that *crown* which is seen on gold. Cf. note to Pass. xviii. 77, p. 227. Perhaps we may go so far as to see a reference here to the proverb—'no cross, no crown.' If so, we may suppose William to say that, in order to accommodate the seekers after the cross on a piece of money, the crown (on the king's head) is placed upon the coin also; so that they who have the cross, have the crown too.

I do not think *crown* is here to be taken in the sense of a piece of money. The English crowns only began with Henry VIII.; and the foreign *écus* were called 'sheeldes' in English, as in Chaucer's Prologue, l. 278.

209. *Ouerturne*, perish, be suppressed [c]; *tourne*, change their lives, be converted; see l. 254 below [c]. The allusion is to the suppression of the order of the Templars, which was still fresh in men's memories at that time. See Haydn, Dict. of Dates. There is an excellent article (with a list of books) on the Templars in the Engl. Cyclopædia, Div. Arts and Sciences, viii. 125.

215. *Demen*, judge, condemn [b]. *Dos ecclesie*, the endowment of the church; see l. 223 below. See Luke i. 52.

219. *Leuitici*, the Levites; cf. Deut. xii. 6 :—' Et offeretis in loco illo holocausta et uictimas uestras, *decimas et primitias* manuum uestrarum,' etc.

220. This story is thus alluded to in Pecock's Repressor, p. 323. 'It is fablid to be trewe, that whanne greet Constantine the Emperour was baptisid of Siluester Pope, and hadde endewid [*endowed*] Siluester Pope with greet plente of londis of the empire, a voice of an aungel was herd in the eir, seiyng thus: "In this dai venom is hildid [*poured*] into the chirche of God." Wherfore the seid endewing bi immovable godis to the clergie is vnvertuose and yuel.' Pecock gives this as a favourite story of the Lollards, and argues against the conclusion drawn from it by them; see Prof. Babington's note.

See also Wyclif's Works, ed. Arnold, iii. 341, 477; in the former of which the voice is that of a 'fend' or fiend, in the latter that of an 'aungel.' Further remarks on the story occur in Prof. Babington's edition of Pecock's Repressor, in the Addenda, vol. ii. p. 699.

It is to be suspected that not only is the story of the angel's voice a fabrication, but also that upon which it was founded, viz. the pretended gift of the Lateran by Constantine to Sylvester. Massingberd (Eng. Ref., p. 53) remarks—'It was believed in the middle ages that the emperor Constantine had given the Bishop of Rome his territory in Italy; though there was no truth in it, and no proof that there was any lordship belonging to the see before the age of Charlemagne.' There is actually a representation, in one of the grand frescoes in the Vatican, of Constantine bestowing the city of Rome upon pope Sylvester, A.D. 385; the date being as imaginary as the circumstance. See Mrs. Jameson's Sacred and Legendary Art, 3rd ed. pp. 687, 692.

The death of Wyclif upon St. Sylvester's day (Dec. 31, 1384) was interpreted as a judgment upon him for having defamed that pope.

227. *Dymes*, tithes. Palsgrave has—' Dyme, tythe, *disme*.' The term *dyme* was applied not only to the tithes due to the clergy, but to the tenths paid to a king by his subjects, or to a feudal lord by his vassals.

Wyclif appealed in strong terms to the temporal lords to take away from the clergy all superfluous wealth; Works, iii. 478, 479. He constantly maintained that tithes and offerings were amply sufficient for the maintenance of priests; Works, i. 199; see also i. 147, 282; iii. 513.

234. (*not in* b.) This allusion has some bearing on the date of the C-text. The chronology is as follows :

Death of Gregory XI., and schism of the Popes, 1378.

The popes elected were Urban VI., recognised in England ; and Clement VII., anti-pope, recognised in France. Urban VI. died in 1389.

Boniface XI. was elected in 1389. Benedict, called the XIII., succeeded Clement as anti-pope in 1394.

In 1379, Urban proclaimed a crusade against the anti-pope, and 'took into his pay the mercenary troop called the company of St. George;' Engl. Cyclopædia.

In any case, the present passage should be compared with Wyclif's Tract De Pontificum Romanorum Schismate, whose remarks on the bull of pope Urban, granting indulgences for the crusade against the anti-pope, seem to be here, to some extent, followed. See Wyclif's Works, iii. 244, 246. The date of Wyclif's tract appears to be 1382.

235. Not in Luke ; see Rom. xii. 19; Deut. xxxii. 35.

241. (*not in* b.) This assertion, that Mohammed's success was not achieved by the sword, is remarkable for its wide deviation from the truth.

252-254. These lines correspond to B. 15. 492-494 (p. 470).

258. *In a false mene*, in a false mediator; see *mene* in Pass. x. 347, as compared with B. 7. 196. Dr. Stratmann oddly assigns to this word (in this passage) the sense of moan or complaint.

261. See note above, to l. 189, on p. 231.

267. (15. 544.) *Metropolitanus* was formerly commonly used as synonymous with *archiepiscopus;* see Ducange. It here seems to mean 'chief bishop' of all the world ; Jerusalem being the original Christian metropolis.

274. St. Thomas of Canterbury, i.e. Thomas Becket, the most famous of English saints. He was canonized in 1221, but at the Reformation his shrine was dismantled, and the very name of the saint erased from the calendar. So stringent were the orders to demolish the records of his name, that not even the MSS. of Piers the Plowman have escaped. This line is much defaced in MSS. M and I (C-text) and in MS. R (B-text).

276. 'And all holy church (was) honoured on account of that death;' [c]; 'Holy church is highly honoured through his death' [b].

277. *Forbusne*, example, pattern; in Pass. xi. 32, it means an example or parable.

278. *Surrye*, Syria. This looks like a pointed personal allusion.

279. *Huppe abowte*, dance about, skip from place to place. *Hoppen* commonly means to dance in Middle English; indeed, a dance is still called a *hop* in jocular speech. *Halewen menne auters*, to consecrate men's altars. The allusion is to the very lucrative way in which titular bishops could employ themselves, by consecrating churches, etc., and by ordaining priests. See A Supplicacyon for the Beggers, by Simon Fish; ed. Furnivall (E. E. T. S.), p. 2; Wyclif, Works, i. 282; and P. Plowm. Crede, l. 356.

280. *Aȝen þe lawe*, against the law; i.e. contrary to the precept in the Mosaic law—'thou shalt not move a sickle into thy neighbour's standing corn;' Deut. xxiii. 25. Cf. note to Pass. vii. 120, p. 78.

281. *Among romaynes*, among the Romans [c]; *in Romanye*, in Romania [b]. Romania, according to Ducange, was sometimes used merely to signify Roman territory; and such, according to our author's own interpretation, is the meaning here. St. Paul and St. Peter both suffered at Rome, before Christianity was triumphant there. The argument is, that missionaries must expect persecution, but ought not therefore to flinch from their duties.

286. It would be difficult to trace whence these Leonine verses are derived; indeed, William may himself have composed them. The sense is—'In the shape of the crosier be this rule (evident) to thee, O bishop; bear, lead, goad on the flock, preserving the law in all cases.' *Presul* is the vocative case; it often means a bishop (Ducange). The allusion is to the bishop's staff or crosier; see note to Pass. xi. 92, p. 136.

—— (15. 565.) *Ysaie*, Isaiah iii. 7. *Osyas*, Hosea; the second quotation, however, is from Malachi, iii. 10.

—— (15. 574.) 'Love God and thy neighbour.' See Luke x. 27.

—— (15. 575.) *Toke it moyses*, delivered it to Moses; see note to Pass. iv. 47, p. 41; and cf. C. xx. 2, 74.

305. *Quatriduanus*, four days dead. 'Domine, iam fetet, *quatriduanus* est enim;' Jo. xi. 39.

—— (15. 589.) See Daniel ix. 24, 26.

313. *Hopen*, expect. 'It signifies the mere expectation of a future event, whether good or evil;'—Tyrwhitt's note to Chaucer, C. T. 4027.

See *Hope* in Nares, who cites the story of the Tanner of Tamworth (from Puttenham's Arte of Poesie, bk. iii. c. 22, ed. Arber, p. 263), who said—'I hope I shall be hanged to-morrow.'

To comynge, to come; a corruption of the old gerundial form *to comenne*, A. S. *tó cumenne*. 'Eart þu ðe to *cumenne* eart,' art thou he that is to come? Luke vii. 20.

315. 'And have the expectation that they will be saved.'

319. 'Prelates and priests (*or*, prelates of Christian provinces, b) should endeavour, if they could, gradually to teach them the other clauses.'

320. *Lytulum and lytulum*, by littles and littles, gradually. Cf. *litlum and litlum*, gradually, Gen. xl. 10 (A. S. version).

NOTES TO C. PASSUS XIX. (B. Pass. XVI.)

19. 3. *Ladde—tales*, conducted me on my way, instructing me with tales as we went.

4. *Cor-hominis*, the heart of man; called 'herte' in B. 16. 15. Man's heart is here likened to a garden in which the tree of Charity grows.

5. *Herber*, garden; Lat. *herbarium*, O. Fr. *herbier;* spelt *erber* in some MSS. of B-text.

6. *Ympe*, a graft, shoot, scion; but here used of a sapling or young tree. This tree, growing in Man's Heart, is called *Imago-Dei* (God's Image), otherwise 'Trewe-loue,' otherwise Patience [b]; its fruit is Charity, and it is supported on three props representing the three Persons of the Trinity. The blossoms of this tree are Kind Speech. In the B-text, its root is Mercy, its stem is Ruth or Pity, and its leaves are the words that compose the Law of Holy Church.

The introduction of the three props betokening the Trinity (see ll. 20-26) shews that William had in his mind the old Legend of the Holy Rood, which tells us how the tree of which Christ's cross was made grew up from three stems, one of cedar, one of cypress, and one of pine. See Cursor Mundi, ll. 1417-1432, 6341-6343, 8005-8050, 8905-8976, 16547-16576, etc.; Legends of the Holy Rood, pp. 62-86, especially pp. 29, 77.

—— (16. 11.) *Saulee* (also spelt *saule, soule, saulees*) is rightly glossed by *edulium* in MS. Laud 581. See *Sool* in Halliwell. *Souel* occurs in Wyclif's Works, i. 63, where it is misprinted *sonel;* also in Pass. ix. 286 above.

—— (16. 25.) *For wyndes*, against winds. *To witen it*, to keep it. See Ps. xxxvi. 24 (Vulgate); xxxvii. 24 (A.V.).

—— (16. 26.) *Abite*, they bite (i. e. nip) the blossoms. The word *they* must be understood before *abite;* with reference to the winds.

The 'three wicked winds' (c. 19. 29) are explained to mean the World, the Flesh, and the Devil. See The Myrour of Our Lady, p. 189.

32. 'Avarice comes from (is produced by) that wind (viz. the World), and it nips Charity' [c]; *or* 'and creeps among the leaves' [b].

34. 'And with the first plank (*or* pile, b), which is the power of God the Father, I beat him down.' The verb *palle* is very rare, but occurs in Joseph of Arimathea, ed. Skeat, 499, where it is said of a warrior that he 'proude doun *pallede*,' i. e. beat down the proud ones. The derivation may have been from the Latin *palus*, a stake, whence O. Fr. *pal*, a great stick, Eng. *pale;* in which case *palle* would mean to beat with such a stick.

44. 'And lays a ladder against it, the rungs of which consist of lies.'

45. *Waggeth the roote*, violently shakes the lower part of the trunk; as men do who try to shake fruit off a tree.

46. *Thorw*, by means of [c]. But in [b], the image is bolder. The devil is represented as throwing things up into the top of the tree of Charity, to knock the fruit down. (For *croppe* = top, see note to b. 16. 69.) The things which he thus throws up are very remarkable; they are not ordinary sticks or brick-bats, but unkind neighbours, backbiters, brawlers, and chiders. The word *breke-cheste* (written *breke þe cheste* in the Trinity MS.) is evidently used as an epithet of *backbiters*. I am satisfied that it does not refer, as might appear at first sight, to any breaking open of chests or boxes. *Cheste* means here, as in several other passages (see Glossary), strife, dispute, quarrelling; compare Chaucer's Persones Tale, *De Ira*, where 'the sinne of contumelie or strife and *cheste*' is spoken of not long before we are told that 'homicide is also by *backbiting*.' Whatever difficulty there may be in this epithet resides in the word *breke* rather than in *cheste*. We commonly speak of *breaking* the law, i. e. of offending against what is right; but *break* is also used in the sense of to vent, as in 'to *break* one's mind,' i.e. to declare it; 'to *break* a jest,' i.e. to utter a jest. See Todd's Johnson, ed. 1827; s. v. *Break*, in senses 13, 14, 23, 41. So here *breke-cheste* means, literally, an utterer of strife or debate, a venter of quarrelsome humour; or, since it is used as an adjective, we may equate it with 'strife-venting,' or, in more familiar language, 'mischief-making.' Thus *bakbiters breke-cheste* (or *breke the cheste*) simply means 'mischief-making backbiters.' Such men are the very ones to destroy neighbourly charity; cf. Prov. xvii. 14. That this is really the sense is, in my opinion, proved by comparing the parallel passage in B. xiii. 108, 109—

'And if ȝe fare so in ȝowre fermorie · ferly me þinketh
But *chest* be þere *charite shulde be* · & ȝonge childern dorste pleyne!'

I. e. 'and if ye go on like this in your infirmary, it seems to me a very strange thing if strife does not arise where charity ought rather to be found, if indeed young children might dare to utter complaints.'

—— (16. 46.) *Letteth hym some tyme*, resists him for a while. So also *lette* = resist, hinder, in l. 288 [c] below.

—— (16. 47.) *Loken*, look to, guard; cf. B. i. 207. The second Latin sentence signifies—'This means the same as—he that sins by his own free will does not resist sin.' Perhaps the reference is to Heb. xii. 4.

—— (16. 55.) 'But I have a multitude of thoughts concerning these three supports.'

60. Compare Pass. xiii. 220–223.

C. PASS. XIX. 63. B. PASS. XVI. 69.

63. 'Nor gradually small, nor with one sweetness sweet.' *Of sewynge*, in regular order, in perfect gradation or succession; from the verb *sewe*, or *sue*, to follow; see l. 72 below. The word *suant*, regular, is still used in Devonshire; see *souant*, in Glos. B. 6, published by the Eng. Dialect Society.

78. 'And more pleasing to our Lord than to live as nature suggests.'

82. The Active Life and Contemplative Life are frequently contrasted in old authors. See notes to Pass. xvi. 194, and to B. vi. 251; pp. 199, 115.

84. *For a good skyle*, for a good reason. The three degrees or qualities of the fruit are explained to mean married life, widowhood, and virginity. This classification is clearly founded on Rev. xiv. 4, 5, and 1 Tim. v. 3-14. Cf. Wyclif, Works, iii. 190; Ælfric's Homilies, ed. Thorpe, ii. 94.

—— (16. 69.) 'Then continence is nearer the top, like a bastard sweet pear.' *Crop*=top; Chaucer's Kn. Tale, 674, and the 7th line of the Prologue. Cf. mod. E. *crop* as a verb.

Caleweis (plural) occurs in the Romaunt of the Rose, 7093, where the original has—'La poire du *caillouel*,' l. 12189 (Roquefort), or l. 12468 (Tyrwhitt). Roquefort and Burguy give wrong etymologies. Cotgrave has—'*Caillouet*, the name of a very sweet pear.' It is clear that William meant a pear of this description, sweet and good to eat, and presumably soft, and not, as Roquefort absurdly suggests, one so stony as not to be fit for anything till cooked. The etymology is really very simple, but to be found in a very different direction. Lacroix, in his Manners, Customs, and Dress during the Middle Ages, p. 116, says—'Of pears, the most esteemed in the 13th century were the *hastiveau*, . . . the *caillou* or *chaillou*, a hard [?] pear, which came from Cailloux in Burgundy.' Yet even here the epithet 'hard' lingers, in accordance with Roquefort's suggestion. To me, it is clear that the hardness resided, not in the *pear*, but in the *soil* of Cailloux, which may very easily and reasonably have taken its name from the Fr. *caillou*, a flint.

Mr. Furnivall sends me the following note, which seems conclusive. '*Chaillous*, poires de Cailloux en Bourgogne;' indeed, 'Poires de Chaillou' occurs as a street-cry: see *Les Crieries de Paris*, par Guillaume de la Villeneuve (end of 13th century); in Fabliaux et Contes, publiées par Barbazan, ed. Méon, 1808, ii. 279, l. 48.

The identity of *calewey* with the Fr. *caillouet* was pointed out by Herbert Coleridge, Phil. Soc. Trans. 1859, p. 72.

Why the epithet *bastard* was applied to this pear, I cannot say. Perhaps it may mean grafted, or cultivated. See *Bastardiere* in Cotgrave.

93. *Faireste þyng*, fairest work of creation, man; answering to *clennest creature* in the next line. So also *the furste þyng* must mean the Great First Cause, answering to *creatour* in the next line. See ll. 95-100.

97. *Hym*, to Christ; alluding to Luke viii. 3; xxiii. 56.

105. (*not in* b.) 'Dear Free-Will, let somebody shake it.' See *Lyf* in the Glossary.

107. *Ripen*, ripe ones; most MSS. have *ripe*. The retention of the final *n* is remarkable; it is the true old A. S. plural of the definite form of the adjective; þe *ripen* = A. S. þá rípan.

108. 'Old-Age climbed towards the top,' etc. [c]; 'And Piers threw things towards the top,' etc. [b].

111. 'For ever, as soon as Old-Age had cast any down' [c]; 'For ever, as they dropped down' [b]. The idea is, that the inhabitants of the tree retain life as long as they remain on it; but, by the attacks of Old Age, one after another drops off. Cf. Merch. of Venice, iv. 1. 115.

116. *In Limbo inferni*, in the verge of hell. 'A *limbo* large and broad;' Paradise Lost, iii. 495. *Limbus patrum* was the name given to the supposed outermost circle of hell; from Lat. *limbus*, a border, hem of a garment. The souls of the olden patriarchs were detained here till the descent of Christ into hell, when He released them, and led them to heaven. See Pass. xxi. 279-282, 451.

118. 'Then anger arose (bestirred itself) in the Majesty of God, so that God's Free-will seized the middle prop (the symbol of Christ), and hit after (i. e. struck in the direction of) the fiend, let the blow fall where it might,' or at hap-hazard.

122. *Rageman* or *raggeman*, in this passage, means the devil. In Pass. i. 73 (see the note to that line) it means a papal bull. The fact is, that in Pass. i. it is a familiar abbreviation for *ragman-roll*, i. e. the devil's roll or the craven's roll, but in the present passage we have the word in its original form and sense. The best spelling is *ragman*, as in MS. Y [b], and the true sense seems to be a craven, a coward. Cf. Icel. *ragr*, craven, cowardly; *ragmenni*, a craven person; *ragmennska*, cowardice. To call a person *ragr* was to offer him a great insult. Thus *rag* means cowardly; whence *ragman* (1) a craven, (2) the devil: whence again *ragmanroll*, (1) the craven's roll (which gives us the reason *why* the Scotch called the deeds of allegiance to Edward I. by that name); (2) a deed with seals, such as a papal bull, sometimes called *ragman* for the sake of brevity; (3) a game in which a roll was used, with strings supplying the place of the seals; (4) a long list or catalogue of names, as in P. Pl. Crede, 180 (unless it is there applied to the maker of such a list); (5) an unintelligible or tedious story, a sense preserved in the modern *rigmarole*. See note to Pass. i. 73, p. 10; also *Ragman* in Halliwell's Dictionary.

126. *Iouken*, sleep, rest, slumber. This word, borrowed from the O. Fr. *jouchier*, F. *jucher*, is very rare in English. I believe it only occurs as a term in hawking. A hawk that went to roost was said to *jouke*. In the Termys of Haukyng, as given in the Boke of St. Albans, fol. a 6, we are told that it is proper to say 'that your hauke *Ioukith*, and not slepith.' See *Jucher* in Cotgrave.

127. (16. 93.) *Plenitudo temporis*, the fulness of time; Gal. iv. 4. See l. 139 below.

The narrative, up to l. 179, is full of allusions to the Gospels, but can so easily be followed that I need not point them out.

C. PASS. XIX. 165. B. PASS. XVI. 136.   239

165. 3*orn*, ran; i.e. pervaded their minds, occupied their thoughts [c]; *was*, were [b]. In both texts, the verb is in the singular number.

166. *Porsuede*, they pursued. Supply *they*; cf. B-text.

168. *Paske*, the Passover. Used by Wyclif, Matt. xxvi. 1.

—— (16. 140.) *There*, where. *Made his maundee*, i. e. washed His disciples' feet. 'The Thursday before Easter is called *Maundy Thursday, dies mandati*, a name derived from the ancient custom of washing the feet of the poor on this day, and singing at the same time the anthem—"Mandatum novum," etc.; John xiii. 34... The notion was, that the washing of the feet was a fulfilling of this command; and it is so called in the rubric, *conveniunt clerici ad faciendum mandatum*. This rite, called *mandatum* or *lavipedium*, is of great antiquity, both in the Eastern and Western Church. During the middle ages, it was not only customary in monasteries, but with bishops, nobles, and even sovereigns, to wash the feet of the poor, and to distribute alms;' Humphry on the Common Prayer, p. 179. See also *Maundy* in my Etym. Dict. The popular derivation from *maund*, a basket, is utterly wrong.

178. (16. 159.) *Pees* [c] and *pays* [b] are merely different spellings of the same word, from O. Fr. *pais*, Lat. *pacem*, peace. The repetition of the words is a defect in the line, but we must remember that the two clauses are quite distinct. The line means—'Let my apostles remain undisturbed, and let them depart peaceably;' or, more briefly—'Let my apostles alone, and let them go in peace.'

—— (16. 165.) *Her botheres myghtes*, the powers of them both. *Her* = A. S. *hira*, of them. *Botheres* (also spelt *bother, beire*, see footnote) is the genitive plural. Cf. Pass. iii. 67; xxi. 374.

—— (16. 166.) 'Died, and destroyed death, and turned night into day.' The last expression is explained by Pass. xxi. 129, 185, 369, 371, 454.

180. (16. 167.) Here the poet again awakes, and the Seventh Vision terminates. Immediately afterwards, the Eighth Vision begins (at l. 183), being the Vision of Faith, Hope, and Charity. The poet awakes when the Vision ends; see Pass. xx. 332.

183. *Mydlentens Soneday*, Mid-lent Sunday; i. e. the fourth Sunday in Lent; Wheatley on the Common Prayer, p. 227.

188. (cf. 16. 180.) 'What is his cognisance, as shewn on his coat-of-arms' [c]; *or*, 'What (coat-of-arms) does that man bear? quoth I then; (tell me) so may bliss betide you!' [b]. The person meant is Christ, or Piers the Plowman as he is called just above in the B-text (l. 171).'

199. 'How one lord might live in three; I believe it not, I said.' *A þre*, in three, occurs again in l. 214 below, which means 'he is in three where he is.'

215. See Ps. xix. 1; *or* xviii. 1 (Vulgate).

218. (cf. 16. 205.) 'Eve was of Adam, and taken out of him, and Abel proceeded from both; and all three are one nature' [c]. 'Adam (was) the father of us all, Eve proceeded from him, and their issue was of them both; and each of them is the delight of the other, though in three separate

persons' [b]. St. Augustine, De Trinitate, lib. xii. c. 5 (Opera, ed. Migne, viii. 1000) mentions this comparison of the Trinity to husband, wife, and offspring; but he does not think it a good illustration.

224. This text is not from the Bible, but from the apocryphal gospel of the Nativity of Mary, to be found in the *Aurea Legenda*, very near the beginning. Compare the Cursor Mundi, l. 10265.

The idea was no doubt founded on Gen. xxx. 23; 1 Sam. i. 6; Luke i. 25.

236. *Moillere-is issue*, the wife's offspring [c]; the wife's children [b]. *Moillere* is Old French. Burguy gives—'*Moilier, moillier, muillier, muller, mouillier*, femme, épouse: *mulier*.' The ending *-is* (written a little apart from the word) is the suffix of the genitive case; and we may note here how completely words of foreign origin were subjected to English grammar. The plan of writing the suffix a little apart from the word is not particularly uncommon in old MSS. Thus *sone-is* is put for *sones* = son's, in the Romans of Partenay, ed. Skeat, p. 9, l. 28. It also happens that *is* is often written for *his*, as in William of Palerne, ll. 8, 69, 181, etc. Hence arose, by a curious confusion, such substitutions as *egle hys* for *egles* (eagle's); as in Specimens of English, 1298-1393, ed. Morris and Skeat, sect. xviii. *a*. l. 96, and the note. But besides this, the use of *his*, after a *proper name*, sprang up *independently*, for the sake of convenience of expression, as is apparent from the later text of Layamon; *in which case* it is not to be regarded as a mere mistake, but rather as an intentional periphrasis. See Sir F. Madden's Glossarial Remarks on Layamon, l. 1459; and an article in the Cambridge Philological Museum, vol. ii. p. 245. At a later period, the frequent use of *his* further suggested the use of *her* after feminine nouns, especially when proper names; see an example of this in the present poem, viz. *Felyce hir fayrnesse*, B. xii. 47. In the present passage, we have an excellent example of its use after an ordinary substantive, since the Laud MS. (B-text) has *moillere her*, as printed; though five MSS. omit the *her*. Lastly, the error arose, and is still current, of looking upon *his* as the *real origin* of the suffix of the genitive case, according to which odd notion *his* itself must be short for *he + his*, which again must be short for *he + he + his*, and so on, ad infinitum! Of course, such an explanation fails also in such words as *queen's, woman's*, and the like, and is inadmissible in Latin and German; so that it may safely be dismissed. With Eng. *fish's*, for example, from A.S. *fisc-es*, compare Ger. *fisch-es*, Mœso-Goth. *fisk-is*, Old Frisian *fisk-is* or *fisk-es*, Icel. *fisk-s*, Lat. *pisc-is*.

242. Compare Cursor Mundi, ll. 2703-2712; Maundeville's Travels, p. 66. The account followed seems to be that in Peter Comestor's Historia Scholastica, who says—'Apparuit dominus Abrae in conualle mambre. Cumque eleuasset oculos, *vidit tres* viros: et occurrens illis, *vnum* ex eis *adorauit*.' The three angels have generally been regarded as a symbol of the Trinity; hence the expression in the text—'Where God came, going in three.' But note the use of *he* (i.e. Christ) in l. 246. See Dict. of the Bible, s. v. *Angels*.

—— (16. 229.) *Calues flesshe;* see Gen. xviii. 7, 8.
253. *My sone,* i.e. Ishmael; Gen. xvii. 23.
257. Cf. Gen. xii. 2; xiii. 16; xv. 5-16; xviii. 17, 18; Rom. iv. 13; Gal. iii. 8, 9; Luke i. 55.
263. William was thinking of Melchizedek's offering of bread and wine; see Gen. xiv. 18. We are also told that Abraham built altars; Gen. xii. 7, 8; xiii. 18. Beyond this, there is no warrant for the expressions in the text. It is easy to see that William perceived, in the mention of 'bread and wine' (Gen. xiv. 18), a token of the Holy Eucharist.
266. 'I believe that that Lord is thinking of making a new law.' *Thenke* is the 3rd pers. sing. of the pres. subjunctive. See John x. 16.
267. (16. 247.) Abraham was God's herald here on earth, as being 'the father of all them that believe;' Rom. iv. 11; cf. Gal. iii. 8. He is also called God's herald in hell, viz. in one version of the Apocryphal Gospel of Nicodemus; see Cowper's Apoc. Gospels, p. 301. Cf. note to l. 116 above.
270. See John i. 29.
273. *Lazar,* a leper. Lepers were so named after Lazarus. Here, however, the reference is to no other than Lazarus himself, who is here said to be·in Abraham's lap; as in Luke xvi. 22. See *Lazarus* in Dict. of the Bible.
286. *Or ligge,* or he must lie.
291. 'Quickly run the very way we went' [c]; 'Quickly run forth; he went the same way' [b]. Or the line in [b] may mean—'Quickly run forth the very way he (Abraham) went;' which comes to the same thing.
The new object in William's vision is *Spes,* or Hope; see Pass. xx. 1.

NOTES TO C. PASSUS XX. (B. Pass. XVII.)

C. 20. 1. (B. 17. 1.) *Spes,* Hope; the expectation of the Messiah's coming. Hence he is called 'a spy,' i.e. a scout. *Spire after,* enquire about, seek information concerning. *Knyght,* i.e. Christ; see l. 8.
2. *Tooke,* gave; as in l. 74 below. *Maundement,* commandment, i.e. the Mosaic law; see l. 60 below.
4. *Latyn,* the Vulgate version. *Ebrew,* the Hebrew original.
7. *Nay;* i.e. it is *not* sealed. The Law was to be fulfilled by the death of Christ, and its spirit confirmed by the giving of 'a new commandment.'
8. Observe how the texts differ by transposing the words *criste* and *croys.* The B-text describes the seal as representing the cross and Christendom (i.e. baptism?) and the figure of Christ hanging upon the cross. In the C-text, it would seem that Christ is the keeper of the seal, Christendom the seal itself, and the cross the impression upon it;

in which case the words 'there-on to hang' refer to the seal with its impress, since the old seals hung down from the deeds to which they were attached.

10. 'That Lucifer's dominion would lie full low' [c]; *or*, 'shall last no longer' [b]. The death of Christ destroyed Lucifer's power.

12. '*Letters patent* are writings, sealed with the Great Seal of England, whereby a man is enabled to do or enjoy that which otherwise of himself he could not. *Anno* 19 *Hen.* 7, *cap.* 7. And they are so called, because they are *open*, ready to be shewed for confirmation of the authority thereby given;' Blount's Law Dictionary. Thus a *patent* is like what we should now call a *license*.

A pece of an harde roche; alluding to the tables of stone on which the Mosaic law was written.

13. *Wordes*, i. e. precepts. *Glosede*, glossed, explained; see l. 15. The text at l. 15 is Matt. xxii. 40.

18. 'No devil shall harm him.' See Pass. x. 38, note, p. 119.

21. 'Faith' [c]; 'this herald' [b]. See Pass. xix. 267, note, p. 241.

22. *In my lappe;* see Pass. xix. 273, note, p. 241. *That leyuede*, them that believed; cf. l. 30.

23. See the apocryphal books of Judith and the Maccabees.

25. *Wher eny of ȝow*, whether either of you? i. e. can it be that either of you? [c]; see [b].

27. *Abraham;* see Pass. xix. 242.

30. 'And (hath) saved (them) that so believed, and (are) sorry for their sins.'

33. 'So to believe and be saved' [c]; 'for salvation and bliss' [b].

42, 43. The texts differ not only in language, but in argument. 'But to believe in one Lord that dwells in Three Persons, and who moreover teaches us that we ought to love liars as much as true men' [c]. 'It is easier to believe in Three lovely Persons than to love and believe rascals as much as true men' [b]. The passage is badly altered, and becomes inconsistent in [c]. Instead of declaring, as in [b], that Hope's law is harder than Abraham's, the author rather clumsily attributes to Hope an opinion which is a mixture of the two laws.

47. *Samaritan.* This is the Good Samaritan of St. Luke's parable. He here appears as the representative of *Charity*, since we have been already introduced to Faith and Hope. He is, in the C-text, little more than a mere abstraction, and not, as in the B-text, Christ himself veiled in human flesh by the Incarnation. Towards the end of the Passus, Charity degenerates into an uninteresting instructor in dogmatic theology.

49. St. Luke represents the unfortunate traveller as going *towards* Jericho. William here supposes the Samaritan to be coming *from* it, and to meet him. Cf. Old Eng. Homilies, ed. Morris, 1st ser. pp. 78-85, in a homily 'De Natali Domini;' Wyclif's Works, i. 33; and cf. note to l. 57 below.

50. The Samaritan is characteristically represented as going to Jeru-

salem for the purpose of taking part in a tournament. *Iacede away*, jounced along, jaunced along. '*Jounce*, to bounce, thump, and jolt, as rough riders are wont to do;' Forby. Cf. Shakespeare's '*jauncing* Bolingbroke;' Richard II. v. 5. 94; see *janser* in Cotgrave. The Prompt. Parv. has—'Iowncynge, or grete vngentylle mevynge, *Strepitus*.' At first, the poet wrote *chaced* [b]; in [c], he ventured on what seems to be a (partially) coined word, to make the alliteration more exact.

55. *Semiuiuus*, half alive; Luke x. 30 (Vulgate).

56. The proverb 'as naked as a needle' has occurred before; Pass. xv. 105; see note.

57. Here William identifies the 'priest' of the parable with Faith or Abraham; the Levite, with Hope; and the Samaritan, with Charity. But he merely followed the received interpretation.

58. (17. 58.) *Nyne londes lengthe*, the distance of the breadth of nine ridges in a field. See *Land* in Halliwell.

62. (17. 62.) *Dredfulliche*, in great terror. Observe the reading of [b]—'as the (wild) duck does from the falcon.'

64. *Lyarde*, a common name for a horse, properly of a gray colour; see '*liart, liarde*, gris, gris-pommelé,' in Burguy, which corresponds clearly to Chaucer's 'pomely gray;' Prol. l. 616. 'Thou shalt ride sporeles [spur-less] o thy *lyard;*' Ballad on Rich. of Almaigne (Harl. MS. 2253), in Percy's Reliques. See *Liard* in Halliwell; Tyrwhitt's note to Cant. Tales, l. 7145; Richard Coer de Lion, l. 2330, and note in Weber's Met. Rom. iii. 355; Burns, Holy Fair, st. 2.

67. 'And unless he had a recovery very soon, he would never rise again.'

68. *Vnbokeled*, unbuckled, undid [c], as in Chaucer, Pers. Prol. 26; *breyde*, hastened [b]. *Atamede*, broached; see Prompt. Parv. p. 16.

70. *Bayarde*, properly a bay horse [c]. As the same animal is called *lyarde* only six lines above, and again in six lines below, we see that both terms were used in a general sense. The B-text has—'and laid him in his lap.'

71. *Lauacrum*, a bath, in allusion to the baptismal font. William here, however, makes 'Lauacrum Lex Dei' the name of a grange [c]; called 'Lex Christi' in [b]. The grange represents the church of Christ. 'What is this inn? It is holy church;' Old Eng. Hom., ed. Morris, 1st ser. i. 84.

Graunge, a grange, a farm-house; especially a lone farm-house with its barns, stables, etc. Very common.

72. Introduced to express the solitary character of the grange. *Besyde*, i. e. away from. *Newe markett*, market-town.

74. 'And gave two pence to the inn-keeper, to take care of him' [c]; 'and gave him two pence, for his nourishment, as it were' [b]. The pence were *silver* pennies; see line above in [b].

75. *That goth mor*, whatever more is required [c]; *he speneth more*, he spends more [b]. *Make the good*, make good to you, will repay you.

—— (17. 81.) *Spaklich*, nimbly; see Pass. xxi. 10, and the note.

—— (17. 85.) 'And offered to become his servant.'

88. An allusion to the Sacrament of the Lord's Supper.

89. *And ȝut*, etc., and moreover be plaistered with Patience, when temptations assail him [c]. Alluding probably to the proverb—'Patience is a plaister,' i.e. is an excellent remedy. Hazlitt gives it in the form—'Patience is a plaister for all sores.'

90. *Rifled*, robbed; i.e. deprived of grace by the assaults of the world, the flesh, and the devil. 'These three, like three robbers, fight against each believing man as long as we wander in the wilderness of this world;' Old Eng. Homilies, ed. Morris, 1st ser. 242. In [c], ll. 90, 91 are parenthetical.

—— (17. 102.) *Lotyeth*, lurk. The word *lotynge* in Chaucer (Group G. 186) is glossed by *latitantem* or *latitans* in four MSS.

—— (17. 107.) 'On my horse called Flesh.' Compare—'Then he [the Samaritan] brought him on his own beast, that is, a rude mare; which denoteth our vile flesh whensoever we have made the body subject to the soul;' Old Eng. Hom., ed. Morris, i. 84.

—— (17. 108.) *Vnhardy*, timid, fearful; alluding to Satan. *Harlot*, knave; see Trench's Select Glossary, and note to Pass. v. 113, p. 57.

—— (17. 109.) *Thre dayes;* alluding to the texts Matt. xxvii. 63, Mark viii. 31. The text at l. 111 is Hosea xiii. 14.

94. *Shul nat we*, are we not to? [c]. *Wher shal I*, whether shall I, am I to? [b].

96. *A parceles*, in separate parts, i.e. Persons [c]. See l. 28 above.

101. *Nother lacky ne alose*, neither to blame nor praise.

110. This supposed proof of the Trinity, from a fancied analogy with the fist, palm, and fingers of the hand, was no doubt borrowed from an older source; but I am unable to point it out.

112. *Ferde furst*, fared first, acted first. *And ȝut is*, and still is like one.

'The line 'mundum pugillo continens' is the third line of the third stanza of the hymn 'Quem terra, pontus, sidera,' given in the Roman Breviary at Matins in the Office of the Blessed Virgin. See Daniel's Thesaur. Hymnolog. i. 172. The idea is taken from Isaiah xl. 12.

125. (17. 149.) See John xii. 32.

—— (17. 160.) 'Both sky and wind, water and earth.' See note to Pass. xi. 130, p. 138.

—— (17. 164.) *Serelepes*, separately, an adverb; as in the Ormulum, ed. White, p. 15, l. 513; p. 17, l. 573.

133. *Shepper*, creator [b]. 'The line "Tu fabricator omnium" is the first line of the second stanza of the hymn "Jesu saluator saeculi." It appears in the office for Compline of the Salisbury Breviary, or of the Aberdeen Breviary;' note communicated by Rev. J. A. Smith.

139. The Latin line here quoted is the 10th line of the very well-known hymn beginning—'Ueni Creator Spiritus.' See Daniel, Thesaur. Hymnolog. i. 213.

146. *Beo he*, if he be. *Let falle*, lets (it) fall, referring to *al þat* in

the preceding line. *Let* is the 3 p. s. present, contracted from *leteth*, as in B. xv. 168. The sense is made a little clearer by altering the comma after *liketh* in l. 144 to a semi-colon.

159. *Oken*, ached ; a strong past tense. Cf. *oc*, Layamon, l. 6707.

162. See Mark iii. 29.

168. The Trinity was often likened to the sun ; as in Cursor Mundi, l. 291. The same is said in Ælfric's Homilies, ed. Thorpe, i. 283 (cf. i. 279) in a sermon De Fide Catholica. This is probably from St. Augustine, who says—'Ignis, splendor, et calor simul atque inseparabilia, nec distincte, sed aequaliter habitant unam lucernam, et una Trinitas Deus simul non potest inhabitare animam humanam?' S. Aug. Sermo de Quarta Feria, cap. vi ; ed. Migne, vi. 692. And again—'Ecce in igne quaedam tria conspicimus ; ignem, splendorem et calorem ; et cum sint tria, unum lumen est.... Et haec non confuse unum sunt, nec disiuncte tria, sed cum unum sint, tria sunt.... Nam cum ad ignem refers ustionem, ibi operatur et splendor et calor ;' etc. S. Aug. De Symbolo Sermo ad Catechumenos, cap. ix. ed. Migne, vi. 659: cf. 692.

But the following quotation comes still closer to our text. 'For in the tapre be three things, the matter, and use, and disposition and shape ; and the matter is treble, as Isidore saith, the waxe, wike, and fire. The wike is made of hempe thrid, and the ground and fundament of the taper ; and the waxe compasseth the wike, and findeth [*provides for, sustains*] and nourisheth the fire, that is lyght, and is end and complement of either. For it worketh in the waxe and in the wike, and turneth them into his owne likenes ; and things of diuers kinde haue within themselues wonderfull and most couenable vnitye ;' Batman upon Bartholomè, lib. xix. cap. 62. This chapter is headed 'De Cereo,' with a reference to Isidore, lib. xx ; but Isidore merely says—'Cereus per derivationem a *cera* nomen habet, ex quo formatur ;' S. Isidori Hispalensis episcopi Etymologiarum, lib. xx. c. 10.

A *torch* was a large twisted wreath of tow, or a twisted candle. '*Torche*, Cereus ;' Prompt. Parv.

179. 'Without flame and light, if fire lies (remains) in the match' [c] ; *or*, 'that burns away the match' [b].

180. This line and the next are (nearly) repeated below ; see l. 214 (b. 17. 248).

194. Compare—'Lacrima compassionis est tepida sicut aqua nivis, quae defluit ad calorem solis ;' Old Eng. Hom., ed. Morris, ii. 150.

203. *Aseth* [c] ; *assetz* [b,] i. e. assets. The spelling *aseth* or *asseth* is the usual one. See *Assets* in Murray's New E. Dictionary.

214. (17. 248.) Repeated from above ; see l. 180. For the text, see Matt. xxv. 12.

216. *Beo*, i. e. if thou be. It is a supposition, not a command ; cf. note to l. 146 above, p. 244.

218. *Paumpelon*, Pampeluna, the old capital of the kingdom of Navarre.

223. *Wher*, whether. See 1 Cor. xiii. 1.

228. *Blynde*, invisible, useless. See Matt. vii. 21.

232. Such was no doubt the usual view taken of the character of Dives. See Wyclif's Works, i. 3. Cf. Luke xvi. 19.

240, 244. *Atemye*, attain. This curious spelling is borne out by the frequent occurrence of *manteme* or *manteym* in Lowland Scotch, where we should now write *maintain*. Thus Barbour has *manteym*, Bruce, x. 779; *manteyme*, xi. 318, 401; etc.

247. *Reward*, regard. 'Take note of this' [c]; 'pay regard to him' [b].

249. *Hyse*, His (i. e. God's) servants; the final *e* denoting a plural; however [b] has *his*. *Hope*, expect; see note to Pass. xviii. 313.

251. *Kid*, manifested, made known [c].

259. 'To reverence the Trinity therewith.' A taper represents the Trinity, and similarly good men may be represented by so excellent a symbol.

270. For *ours* [c] read *ous*, us. See Rev. vi. 10.

274. *Lyf*, man; as elsewhere. 'Will love that man who destroys love and true charity.' Here *destruyen* is the author's slip for *destruyeth*, due to the verb being near to *two* objective cases. Such slips are common in English authors.

275. *Ich pose*, I put the case. *Shold nouthe deye*, had now to die, were now about to die.

284. *Ther þat partye porsueth*, where the (injured) party prosecutes. *Apeel*, appeal, accusation; spelt *pele* [b], which is miswritten *peple* in several MSS.; see footnote in [b]. See *Appeal* in Blount's Law Dictionary, and in the New Eng. Dictionary by Dr. Murray.

286. This quotation has occurred before; see note to Pass. vii. 257.

288. *Til hem forsake synne*, till sin at last leaves them, viz. at death [c]; till life leaves them [b]. This rather curious use of *forsake* is exactly parallel to the expression in the last line of Chaucer's Doctours Tale :—'Forsaketh sinne, or [*ere*] sinne yow forsake.'

Chaucer repeats the expression near the beginning of his Persones Tale.

292. 'Not through the non-power (i. e. lack of power) of God.' *Noun-power* is opposed to *power* in Chaucer's translation of Boëthius, ed. Morris, p. 75. So too—'there as lacketh his power, his *nonpower* entereth;' Testament of Love, book ii.; ed. 1561, fol. ccc. back, col. 2. See Ps. cxliv. 9 (Vulgate).

295. *Restitucion hit maketh*, restitution causes it, *or* is the cause, viz. of God's justice turning to mercy [c]; 'some restitution is necessary' [b].

297. Perhaps the original form of this commonly quoted proverb is this :—'Tria sunt enim quae non sinunt hominem in domo permanere: fumus, stillicidium, et mala uxor;' Innocens Papa, de Contemptu Mundi, i. 18. It is a mere compilation from Prov. x. 26, xix. 13, and xxvii. 15. Chaucer refers to it in his Tale of Melibeus, Prol. to Wif of Bathes Tale, and Pers. Tale, *De Ira;* see also Kemble's Solomon and Saturn, pp. 43, 53, 63; Walter Mapes, ed. Wright, p. 83; etc.

304. *Wors to slepe*, to sleep worse, i. e. less. To understand this, we must remember the pungent effects of the smoke of imperfectly dried

wood in houses with no proper chimney; see the effects described in
l. 306.

306. *Bler-eyed*, blear-eyed [c]; *blere-nyed* [b]. The prefixing of an
n is common in English, and is probably due in some cases to the *n* in
the word *an*, as in *a newt* for *an ewt*. At any rate we find *neyes* for
eyes, as when a bear is described 'with his two pinke *neyes*' in a quo-
tation given in Jesse's History of the British Dog, vol. ii. Halliwell's
Dict. gives *nall*, an awl, etc. On the other hand, we have *napron* for
apron, etc.

307. 'Coughs, and curses (saying) may Christ give them sorrow.'
Cf. B. v. 107.

312. 'And though it (lit. he, i.e. the flesh) fall into sin, it discovers
reasons (excuses), as, e.g. that frailty caused it to fall.'

317. *Pistles*, epistles. See 2 Cor. xii. 9.

327. 'But he may love, if it please him, and lend good will and a good
word out of his heart, both to wish and desire mercy and forgiveness for
all conditions of men.'

NOTES TO C. PASSUS XXI. (B. Pass. XVIII.)

N.B. This is, upon the whole, at once the best written and the most
interesting Passus in the whole poem. The subject is the death, descent
into hell, and resurrection of the Saviour of mankind.

The three chief sources of the subject-matter are (1) the Gospel
narratives; (2) Grostête's Castel of Love; and (3) the apocryphal
Gospel of Nicodemus, especially as cited in the chapter De Resurrectione
Domini of the Aurea Legenda of Jacobus a Voragine. These sources
will be commented on more particularly in their due places.

Besides these, the author constantly shews that he had in his mind
some actual representation of the circumstances; so that the reader
must throughout consult The Coventry Mysteries.

1. 'Wo-weary and wet-shod' [c]; 'Woolward and wet-shod' [b].
'*Wetshod*, with water in the shoes. "Are you not *wetshod?*" have
not your shoes taken in water?'—Marshall's Glossary of Yorkshire
Words, 2nd ed. 1796. In Oxfordshire it is pronounced *Watcherd* [woch
urd], and used correctly by many who have no idea of what are the
component parts of the word. The opposite form, *dryshod*, is better
known; see Isaiah xi. 15. The corresponding Icelandic word is *skóvátr*,
lit. shoe-wet.

Wolleward [b] is thus explained by Palsgrave. '*Wolwarde*, without
any lynnen nexte ones body. *Sans chemyse.*' The sense of the word
is clearly—with wool next to one's body, or, *literally*, with the body
towards wool. It is well discussed and explained by Nares, who says—
'Dressed in wool only, without linen, often enjoined in times of super-

stition, by way of penance.' See Love's Labour Lost, v. 2. 717, and the five other examples which Nares cites. See also Hampole's Pricke of Conscience, l. 3512; Pierce the Ploughman's Crede, l. 788; and *Woolward* in my Etym. Dict. and in the Supplement (2nd ed.).

A similar penance was the custom of wearing a hair-shirt; see note to Pass. vii. 6, p. 72.

4. *Eft to slepe*, to sleep again.

Here begins the Ninth Vision, or the Vision of the Triumph of Piers the Plowman, which extends to the end of the Passus in each Text.

5. 'And leant about (idled about) till Lent-time' [c]; *or*, 'till a Lent-time' [b]. The phrase is not very clear. *Lenede me* (lit. leant myself) probably means leant about or idled about; much as the verb to *loll* meant the same thing; cf. Pass. x. 215, 218. Cf. *reste me* in l. 7 [b].

—— (18. 6, 7.) These two lines are very awkward. They are almost certainly misplaced, and should follow l. 8; yet all the MSS. agree. As they stand, we must at any rate understand (from l. 3) the words—'And *I dreamt* of Christ's passion and penance,' etc.

Of-rauȝte, reached to, extended to. The sense is—'And I dreamt of Christ's passion and penance, that extended to the people;' with reference to the *effects* of the Passion. *Of-rauȝte* is the past tense of *ofrechen*, to reach to; of which see examples in Stratmann.

Reste me, rested myself; *reste* is the past tense, as in Layamon, l. 3511. *And rutte faste*, and snored fast, slept heavily. *Tyl ramis palmarum*, till Palm Sunday (came).

Palm Sunday was often called *dominica palmarum*, or more commonly *in ramis palmarum*. See Procter's History of the Book of Common Prayer, 3rd ed. p. 279; also cap. ccxvii. in the Legenda Aurea, ed. Grässe, 2nd ed., headed—'De dominica in ramis palmarum.'

6. 'I dreamt much about children and *gloria laus*.' *Gurles* here means children of both sexes, as opposed to *olde folk* in the next line; cf. notes to Pass. ii. 29, xii. 123. The allusion is to the children who, on Palm Sunday, used to sing a hymn in honour of Jesus, beginning with the words 'Gloria, laus.' An account of the Palm Sunday procession is given in Pecock's Repressor, i. 203, 269; see also Chambers, Book of Days, i. 395; Rock, Church of Our Fathers, iii. pt. 2, pp. 68, 227, 231; Brand's Pop. Antiquities, etc.

See also the Coventry Mystery of the Entry into Jerusalem; ed. Halliwell, p. 256; York Plays, p. 201.

7. 'And how the old folk sang Hosanna to instruments of music,' *or*, 'to the organ.' *Orgone* [c] or *orgonye* [b] answers to the Lat. *organa*, of which it is a mere corruption. *Organum* signified any mechanical instrument, and, in particular, an instrument of music; see Chappell, Hist. of Music, i. 327. 'What we now call *an organ* was formerly styled *the organs;* and, so low as the last century, *a pair of organs;*' Pegge, Anecdotes of the English Language, ed. 1844, p. 122. (Of course *a pair* here means *a set*, referring to the set of pipes; cf. 'a paire of bedes' for a set of them, and *a pair of stairs* for a flight of them.) Similarly, a single clavichord was called a 'payre of clauycordys;' Skelton, ed. Dyce, ii. 94.

8. *On was*, one who was [c]. Christ is here represented as riding into Jerusalem, and is said to be like the Good Samaritan described in Pass. xx. 63-77. He is also like Piers Plowman, as being the personification of Human Nature; see ll. 21-24 below.

9. *Bootles*, without boots. Such is the sense really intended here; cf. 1. Hen. IV. iii. 1. 66, 67. *Cam prykye*, came riding; lit. came to ride.

10. *Sprakliche*, sprightly, lively [c]; and it is probable that *spakliche* [b] is really the same word, with the *r* dropped. In fact, MS. R. (B-text) reads *spracliche*. The dropping of *r* is remarkably shewn in the common word *to speak*, which ought, of course, to be *spreak*, as it is from the A.S. *sprecan;* cf. G. *sprechen*, Du. *spreken*. The word *sprakliche* seems to be Scandinavian; cf. Icel. *sprækr*, *sprækligr*, sprightly; *sparkr*, lively. It is found, however, in English dialects where the Scandinavian element is small. Thus, in Akermann's Wiltshire Glossary, we have—'*Sprack*, lively, active, intelligent. "A *sprack* un," a lively one.' Halliwell also gives—'*Sprag*, the same as *Sprack*, quick, lively, active. *West*.' Our common word *spark*, in the sense of a gay fellow, is also merely the Icel. *sparkr*. *Spakliche* may be the same word, and, if so, is quite a different word from the adverb formed from the Middle English *spak*, mild, tame, borrowed from the Icel. *spakr*, quiet, gentle.

11. The comparison of Christ to a knight is most curious, and is kept up throughout the Passus. The idea is old enough. See The Ancren Riwle, p. 390.

12. It is well known that three very essential ceremonies were the dubbing the new-made knight with the flat of a sword, the girding on of a sword, and the buckling on of spurs; as humorously described in Don Quixote, ch. iii. Hence the phrase 'to win one's spurs.' But the last part of this line is extremely obscure, though I think *galoches y-couped* must mean shoes cut down, alluding to some peculiarity in the make of the shoe as used by knights. I do not agree with Mr. Halliwell in his explanation of this passage under *Coppid*. No doubt *coppid* means *peaked;* but the word *here* used is not *coppid*, peaked, but *couped*, cut; and the passage that really throws most light on our text is one in the Romaunt of the Rose (l. 842), where Mirth is described as attired in a most elegant suit of clothes—

> 'And shode he was with great maistrie,
> With shoone *decoped*, and with lace.'

Here 'shoone decoped' can only mean 'shoes cut down;' for the French prefix *de-* will not sort well with *coppid*, from the Welsh and the A. S. *cop*. Cotgrave gives—'Decoupé, cut down, cut off; pared, or cut away; slit, sliced.' Hence the reference is not at all to the *peaks* of the shoes, but to the fashion of slashing or slitting them by way of ornament, just as Chaucer (C. T. 3318) describes the clerk Absolon as having 'Poules windowes coruen on his shoos;' and just as Hamlet speaks of 'razed shoes;' Act iii. sc. 2. Cf. *couped shon*, Torrent of Portugal, 193 [page 51].

As to *galoches*, we learn from Cotgrave that, in his time, the term was restricted to wooden clogs, but Way's note (Prompt. Parv. p. 184) clearly shews that the term was also formerly used of the expensive shoes worn by the upper classes.

I conclude, then, that the allusion is to such fashionably slashed or 'rased' shoes as were only worn by knights or those of still higher rank.

Our author alludes to the peaked shoes also, but it is *in another passage;* see 'pikede shoes,' Pass. xxiii. 219.

13. Alluding to Matt. xxi. 9—'Hosanna filio David,' etc.

14. The allusion is to the proclamation by the heralds of the names and titles of the knights who come to the tournament. Cf. Rich. II. i. 3. 104.

Auntres in MS. P. is certainly a mere misspelling of *auntrous* [b]; and the footnotes to the B-text shew that *auntrous* means *adventurous*, as usual in other authors. The substantive *knights* is understood, and the word *auntrous* means, accordingly, 'adventurous knights;' or, as they were sometimes called, 'knights adventurers.' Chaucer's Sir Topas was one of these:—

'And for he was a knyght *auntrous*,
He nolde slepen in noon hous,
But liggen in his hoode.'

The word *auntres* means *adventures*, and would make nonsense. MS. T (C-text, footnote) has the right reading.

15. See Matt. xxi. 9.

18. 'And fetch that which the fiend claims, viz. the fruit of Piers the Plowman.' The reference is to Pass. xix. 55–123, particularly to ll. 111, 122. Mankind are the apples of the tree of Charity, stolen by Satan and hid in hell, whence Christ recovered them by assuming the form of Piers Plowman, i.e. by His Incarnation and subsequent Passion.

19. *Preynkte*, gazed, looked; see Pass. xvi. 121, and note, p. 194. '*Prink*, to look at; to gaze upon. *West;*' Hall. Dict.

21. *Of his gentrise*, as consistent with his noble birth. See Pass. xv. 90, 91.

In peers armes, in Piers' coat-armour, i.e. with the coat of arms which would indicate Piers. The next line explains clearly what is meant by Piers the Plowman in this Passus. It means Mankind, or Human Nature in its highest form; and Christ assumed Piers' armour by His Incarnation.

24. *Plates*, plate-armour [c]; *paltok*, a kind of jacket [b]. 'Habent etiam aliud indumentum sericum quod vulgo dicitur *paltok;* et si bene disponeretur, potius ad cultum ecclesiasticum cederet quam ad terrenum; unde dicitur in Libris Regum quod Salamon in tota vita sua talibus non est usus;' Eulogium Historiarum, ed. Haydon, iii. 230. This passage is cited in Camden's Remaines, and thence again by Strutt, Manners and Customs, ii. 84. Observe that our author elsewhere speaks of *paltokes* as being worn by priests; Pass. xxiii. 219. We find 'Paltok. *Baltheus*' in the Prompt. Parv. p. 380, on which see Way's long illustrative note.

28. This and the subsequent lines clearly suggested the beautiful poem

entitled Death and Liffe, printed in the Percy Folio MS., ed. Hales and Furnivall, p. 56, with an Introduction by myself (p. 49), in which I have discussed the points of resemblance between that poem and our text.

34. 'And beat thoroughly and bring down (to destruction) sorrow and death for ever.' In the B-text, supply the marks of quotation after *tua*, at the end of the Latin text. See Hosea xiii. 14.

35. 'Sedente autem illo pro tribunali,' etc.; Matt. xxvii. 19.

36. *And deme here beyer ryght*, and adjudge the right of them both; cf. l. 374. *Beyer* [c] and *botheres* [b] are different forms of the genitive case of *both*. *Beyer* and *beire* are from the A.S. gen. pl. *begra; botheres* is formed from *bother* (Icel. *báðir*, gen. *báðra*), by the unnecessary addition of *-es*.

46. *Wicchecrafte*. This was probably suggested by a passage in the Apocryphal Gospel of Nicodemus; see Cowper's translation of the Apocryphal Gospels, p. 270—'And the Jews said, he is a *magician*, and therefore he doeth these things;' and again, at p. 272—'us, who know well that he is a *magician*.' See also John xix. 15; York Plays, p. 329.

50. Suggested by Matt. xxvii. 29, 30—'posuerunt . . . arundinem in dextera eius. Et genu flexo ante eum, illudebant ei dicentes: *Aue rex Iudæorum*. Et expuentes in eum, *acceperunt arundinem, et percutiebant caput eius*.' But the poet has translated this in a very odd way.

51. *Thre nayles*. A long essay might be written on the wholly unimportant question whether *three* nails or *four* were used in the Crucifixion. 'St. Cyprian, St. Augustine, St. Gregory of Tours, and Pope Innocent III., as also Rufinus, and Theodoret, reckon *four* nails;' F. C. H., in N. and Q., 3rd S. iii. 392. The *three* nails are mentioned by St. Gregory Nazianzen; by Nonnus (Greek poet, fifth century); in the Ancren Riwle, p. 391; Polit. Rel. and Love Poems, ed. Furnivall, p. 111; Coventry Mysteries, ed. Halliwell, p. 315; etc. And see Godwin's Archæological Handbook, p. 270.

Naked; see Pass. xi. 193. So in the Ancren Riwle, p. 260; Legends of the Holy Rood, ed. Morris, p. 200.

53. There is a most remarkable variation here; in the B-text, Christ is said to be asked to drink, to *shorten* his life; in the C-text, to *lengthen* it. See Smith's Dict. of the Bible, art. *Gall*.

57. *That lyf the louyeth*, that Life loves thee; see l. 30 above.

59. A magnificent line; there are many passages of real power and sublimity in this Passus.

Prison, a prisoner; as elsewhere. In the English version of the Castel of Love, ed. Weymouth, ll. 330-334, we actually find *prisoun* = a prisoner, and *prison* = a prison, in the same passage; so too in Gen. and Exodus, ed. Morris, 2040, 2044. Cf. Mid. Eng. *message*, a messenger.

61. Compare Legends of Holy Rood, ed. Morris, p. 144; Towneley Mysteries, p. 255.

79. *Kynde forȝaf*, nature granted. *Kynde*, lit. Nature, here means the God of Nature, the Creator, as in Pass. xi. 128. *For-ȝaf* is here merely the intensive of *ȝaf*, and means 'fully gave,' or 'fully granted.' This

sense is unusual, but we may compare the A. S. *forgeafe* = Lat. *dedisti;* Gen. iii. 12. And see l. 188 below.

82. This story is from the Aurea Legenda, cap. xlvii. Longinus was a blind centurion, who pierced the side of Christ; when drops of the Sacred Blood cured his infirmity. The day of St. Longinus is Mar. 15; see Chambers, Book of Days. The name *Longinus* is most likely derived from λόγχη, a lance, the word used in John xix. 34; and the legend was easily developed from St. John's narrative. The name Longinus first appears in the Apoc. Gospel of Nicodemus. Allusions to it are very common.

83. *Houede*, waited in readiness; see *hovin* in Stratmann. Cf. 'where that she *hoved* and abode;' Gower, Conf. Amant. iii. 63. Cf. *ouer-houeth* in l. 175 below.

87. *Tryne*, to touch [c]; *taste*, to handle [b]. The verb *tryne*, to touch, is exceedingly rare; I can only find one other clear example. One is— 'þat non *trinde* the tres,' that none should touch the trees; Alexander and Dindimus, l. 132. Somewhat like it is the A. S. *tringan*, to touch, which is also rare. In Spelman's edition of the A. S. Psalms (Ps. ciii. 33), *qui tangit montes* is glossed by *se hrynð muntas;* and, for *hrynð*, the various readings are *gehrinð* and *tringað*. Possibly also *be-trende* = touched, in Altenglische Legenden, ed. Horstmann, p. 127, l. 491. N.B. This verb is not to be confused with *trinen*, to step, go (see Stratmann), from the Danish *trine*, to step. Perhaps *trinen* = A. S. *æthrinan*.

Taste is best explained from Cotgrave, who gives—' *Taster*, to taste, or take an essay of; also, to handle, feele, touch, or grope for.'

89. A similar miracle is told in the Life of St. Christopher, l. 219, in Lives of Saints, ed. Furnivall.

90. This is the usual form of the story. Thus, in the Coventry Mysteries, p. 335, after Longinus (or Longeus) has smitten Christ, 'he fallyth downe on his knees.' Then he says—

> 'Now, good lord, fforgyf me that,
> That I to the now don have;
> For I dede I wyst not what—
> The Jewys of myn ignorans dede me rave.
> Mercy! Mercy! Mercy! I crye.'

So too in the Towneley Mysteries, p. 231; York Plays, p. 368.

97. See remarks on *Caitiff* in Trench's Select Glossary.

103. *The gree*, the prize, the honour of the day; as Tyrwhitt explains it in a note to C. T. 2735 (Kn. Ta. 1875). ' *To win the gre* is a common Scottish phrase still used to express " to be victor," " to win the prize," " to come off first," " to excel all competitors," note to the allit. Troy-book, ed. Panton and Donaldson, p. 483.

105. ȝelt, yields; pres. tense. 'Yields himself recreant' (i.e. acknowledges himself defeated). *Rennyng*, whilst running his course (in the tilt). Cf.—'Sothly, he that despeireth is like the coward campioun

recreaunt, that seith *recreaunt* withoute neede;' Chaucer, Pers. Tale, *De Accidia*.

107. *Lordlinges*, sirs; cf. *lordings* in Chaucer. The B-text has the term of reproach, *lordeynes*, i.e. clowns, blockheads; see *Lourdin* and *Lourdaut* in Cotgrave. The derivation is, of course, from F. *lourd*, Lat. *luridus*, though Bailey oddly equates it to *Lord Dane*!

108. On *thraldom*, see Barbour's Bruce, ed. Skeat, i. 225-274; Cursor Mundi, ll. 9483-9492.

111. It was believed that *usury* was a very wicked thing in any form; see note to Pass. vii. 239, p. 85.

114. *To-cleue*, split or fall asunder; see Dan. ix. 24.

116. Perhaps there is an allusion here to the services called *in tenebris*, respecting which Strutt (Manners and Customs, iii. 174) quotes from a MS. to the effect that, three days before Easter, 'holy chirch usith theise three daies to say service in the euene tyde, *in the derknesse;* wherefore it is callid with you *Tenebris*, that is, darkness.'

118. Lines 118-128 are quoted in Warton, Hist. Eng. Poetry, ii. 262, ed. 1871; ii. 85, ed. 1840.

Mercy comes from the West, Truth from the East, Righteousness from the North, and Peace from the South. That is, the actors were to come from the four different quarters, and meet in the middle of the open space which served for a stage. See note to Pass. i. 14.

119. Here *he* [c] = *heo* or *hue*, she; cf. *she* in [b]. So in ll. 178, 179. *To helleward*, in the direction of hell; i.e. (as the context shews) eastward. Now this is expressly contrary to the description in Pass. i. 16, where the abode of Death is in the West; see note to Pass. i. 14. I explain it thus. The scenes are quite different; and the reference is, not to the Eastern and Western quarters of the world, but to the Eastern and Western ends of the space on which the actors moved in the Mysteries. This will readily suggest that whilst, in the Mystery of the Creation, it would be convenient and appropriate to place the throne of God in the East, it would be equally convenient (appropriateness not being considered) to represent Christ's triumph over Satan in the same position. The reason for it was that the same wooden platform, of which the upper stage supported the divine throne, served, in its lowest or lower stage, as a place of resort for the demons. A well-made platform had three stages or stories, the upmost representing heaven, the middle one the world, whilst the lowest, more or less concealed by curtains, served as a 'green-room' for actors, and for the resort of the demons. A hole in the side of this lowest stage was called the mouth of hell, out of which fire and smoke sometimes issued, mingled with the cries of the lost. See all this described in Chambers, Book of Days, i. 634; and in Sharp's Dissertation on Pageants, especially p. 23.

120. *Mercy*. The passages relating to Mercy, Truth, Justice, and Peace (ll. 120-239 and 453-471) are imitated from Bp. Robert Grosteste's Chastel d'Amour, and are to be compared with that poem, or with the English version called The Castel of Love, edited from the Vernon MS.

by Dr. Weymouth for the Philological Society, 1864; pp. 13-24; also with The Parable of a King and his Four Daughters, introduced into the Cursor Mundi, ed. Morris, pp. 548-560, ll. 9517-9752.

The whole parable is obviously founded on a single verse in Psalm lxxxv. 10 (lxxxiv. 11 in the Vulgate), viz.—' Misericordia et ueritas obuiauerunt sibi : iustitia et pax osculatae sunt.'

128. *Rowed*, began to beam, began to dawn; see note to Pass. ii. 114, p. 26; and cf. 'And whan the day began to *rowe;*' Gower, Conf. Amantis, bk. iii ; ed. Chalmers, p. 80, col. 2. And again—' Qwen the *day-raw* rase,' when the day-dawn rose ; Alexander, ed. Stevenson, l. 392. *Rowes* (= rays) occurs in Wright's Vocabularies, i. 167.

140. *Clips* [b] is a shortened form of *eclipse* [c]. 'This was the greattest *clypse*,' etc.; Hormanni Vulgaria, leaf 100.

For remarks on the 'eclipse' at the Crucifixion, see Wyclif's Works, ii. 51, and the note ; Smith's Dict. of the Bible, art. *Eclipse*.

144. This was a favourite theme. On the notion, that the timber of the true cross was derived from the pippins of the apple-tree that caused the Fall of Man, were founded the curious legends concerning the true cross; see Dr. Morris's introduction to his edition of The Legends of the Holy Rood. See also the note to l. 400 below.

145. *Releue*, lift up again ; from Lat. *releuare*.

146. *A tale of walterot*, an idle tale, an unmeaning story, a piece of absurdity. The better spelling seems to be *waltrot* [b]; see the footnotes. If we transpose the word, we obtain *trotwal*, and it is, at any rate, worth remarking that *troteuale* occurs, in the very same sense, four times in Robert of Brunne's Handling Synne, ll. 47, 5971, 8080, 9244; see Halliwell's Dictionary, s. v. *Trotevale*. The *sense* of the phrase is obvious, being equivalent to *trufle* (a trifle) in l. 151 below.

I can even adduce plausible etymologies. *Waltrot* may easily have been imported, through the O. French, from O. H. German. Schade (s.v. *Thruðr*) gives an O. H. G. name *Waledrudis*, where *-drudis* is allied to O. H. G. *trúta*, modern provincial G. *trute*, a witch. The O. H. G. *trúta* was a night-hag or nightmare ; see *Trud* in Schmeller's Bayerisches Wörterbuch, ed. 1869, iii. 649; and see *drude* in Grimm's Ger. Dict. Further, the O. H. G. *trúta* is the Icel. *þrúðr;* and *trotevale* is a French rendering of Icel. *þrúðvaldr*, which represents no less a personage than the mighty Thor, here degraded into the symbol of an idle tale. In this case, the ending *-valdr* is connected with Icel. *valda*, to rule, E. *wield*. See *þrúðr* and *þróttr* in the Icel. Dictionary ; *Thruðr* in Schade's O. H. G. Dictionary.

147. It was the almost universal belief that Adam and all his descendants (with the exception of Enoch, Elijah, and the penitent thief) descended into hell, and there remained till Christ fetched them thence after His crucifixion. See particularly the chapter De Resurrectione Domini (cap. liv.) of the Aurea Legenda. Cf. Early Eng. Homilies, i. 236, 130.

153. The reference is to Job vii. 9—' Sicut consumitur nubes, et pertransit ; sic qui descenderit ad inferos, non ascendet.'

156. 'Because venom destroys venom, for that I fetch evidence' [c]. 'For venom destroys venom, and that I prove by reason' [b]. Cf. the proverb—Like cures like.

158. The notion that a dead scorpion is a remedy for a scorpion's sting is to be found in Bartholomæus de Proprietatibus Rerum; lib. 18, c. 98, De Scorpione. Compare—'*Lezard Chalcidique*, A spotted Lizard which is very venomous, and yet, taken in drink, healeth the hurt he did;' Cotgrave's F. Dict. Also—' the scorpion's sting, which being full of poyson, is a remedy for poyson;' Lily's Euphues, ed. Arber, p. 411. Cf. note to Pass. ii. 147.

166. The line 'Ars ut artem falleret' occurs in the third stanza of the hymn 'Pange, lingua, gloriosi;' see Daniel, Thesaurus Hymnologicus, i. 164. Cf. ' Fallite fallentes,' Ovid, de Arte Amat. i. 645.

'For often he that wol begile
Is guiled with the same guile,
And thus the guiler is beguiled.'
Gower, Conf. Amant. bk. vi (ed. Chalmers, p. 194, col. 2).

· ' Begiled is the giler thanne.'—Rom. of the Rose, l. 5762.

' A gilour shal himself begiled be.'—Ch. Cant. Tales, l. 4319. Cf. Ps. vii. 16; ix. 15.

178. *He wolde*, she wished to go; where *he*=she, as in l. 119 above. Cf. A. xii. 80, and the note, p. 165.

179. *Wham he gladie thouhte*, whom she intended to gladden [c]; whom she intended to greet [b].

185. *For*, because. *Iousted*, jousted; cf. ll. 21, 103.

188. *Forgyue*, fully granted; cf. *forȝaf* in l. 79, and the note. 'And granted to all mankind, (for) Mercy my sister and myself to bail them all' [c]; 'and granted to me, Peace, and to Mercy, (for us) to be man's *mainpreneurs* for evermore hereafter' [b]. See notes to Pass. iii. 208; v. 107, pp. 39, 57.

192, 193. *Patente;* see note to Pass. xx. 12, p. 242. *This dede shal dure*, this (legal) deed shall last good. The Latin words form fragments of the whole text, which is:—' In pace in idipsum dormiam, et requiescam;' Ps. iv. 9.

199. See note to l. 147 above; and cf. Pass. xix. 111–117.

201. *Hus defense*, the prohibition laid upon him. See *Defence* in Trench's Select Glossary.

202. *Fret*, ate. Cf. ' a moth *fretting* a garment;' Ps. xxxix. 12 (Prayer-Book); see *Fret* in Trench's Select Glossary.

217. 'Should know assuredly what day is to mean,' i.e. what the meaning of ' day ' is. Supply a full stop (which has dropped out) at the end of the line in the C-text.

221. *The deth of kynde*, death from natural causes.

225. ' Which unknits all care, and is the commencing of rest.' A line even finer than Shakespeare's—' Sleep, that knits up the ravelled sleave of care;' Macb. ii. 2. 37.

226. *Moreyne*, a murrain [c]; an improvement upon *modicum*, i.e. a moderate quantity, short allowance [b].

235. The Latin text, in [c] only, is from 1 Thess. v. 21, and has been quoted already; Pass. iv. 492, 496.

239. 'Till wellaway teach him;' till he learns experience of suffering, which causes him to cry *well-away*.

241. 'That *beau-père* was called Book.' Cotgrave notes that *Beau père* is 'the title of a Frier which is a confessor.'

243. A comet was called *stella comata* (see l. 249) and, in English, a *blazing star*. 'The blasynge starre is now gone. *Cometes iam excessit;*' Hormanni Vulgaria, leaf 99, back. On the wonderful appearances at Christ's birth, see Cowper's Introd. to the Apoc. Gospels, p. xxxiii.; Peter Comestor's Historica Scholastica; Ælfric's Homilies, ed. Thorpe, i. 109, 229; Aurea Legenda, cap. xiv., De Epiphania Domini; Smith's Dict. of the Bible, art. 'Star of the Wise Men;' etc. The passages in Ælfric bear a considerable general resemblance to the text.

256. 'Lo! how the sun did lock (shut up) her light within herself.' An extremely interesting example of the use of *sonne* as a feminine noun. The A. S. *sunne* is feminine. Chaucer (C. T. 1497) calls the sun *Phebus*, and accordingly makes it masculine.

259. *Quike*, alive, living. 'And wholly shattered in twain the rocks' [c]; *or* 'the rock' [b]. We find 'quaschyn, or brysyn, or cruschyn, *briso, quasso;*' Prompt. Parv. p. 419; and, on the same page, 'quaschyn, or daschyn, or fordon, *quasso, casso.*'

261. *Symondes sons*, the sons of Simeon; where Simeon is the 'just and devout' man mentioned in St. Luke ii. 25, 26. The reference is to the Apocryphal Gospel of Nicodemus, which is the foundation of all the numerous representations in ancient Mysteries of the scene known as the 'Harrowing of Hell,' a phrase denoting the removal thence of the souls of the righteous when Christ descended thither. The story of the Gospel of Nicodemus is very important for the understanding of many passages in Early English, and should be consulted. There is an epitome of it in the Legenda Aurea, cap. liv., which our author seems to have followed.

There are very frequent allusions to this striking narrative of the Harrowing of Hell in our old authors, which are too numerous to be mentioned here. A good account of the influence of the Gospel of Nicodemus upon European literature will be found in a handy volume of 101 pages, entitled—'Das Evangelium Nicodemi in der Abendländischen Literatur; nebst drei Excursen über Joseph von Arimathia als apostel Englands, das Drama "harrowing of Hell," und Jehan Michel's passion Christi;' von Dr. Richard Paul Wülcker, Paderborn, 1872.

263. The expression 'Jesus as a giant' [c] explains the obscure phrase '*gigas* the giant' [b]. The reference, in the first instance, was either to the very common legend of St. Christopher, or to Samson, who, by carrying off the gates of Gaza, was a type of Christ's breaking the gates of hell; Ælfric's Homilies, i. 227.

272. *Bit vnsperre*, bids unbar. See Ps. xxiii. 9 (Vulgate).

276. *To helle*, to hell; a translation of the Lat. '*Sathan Dixit ad inferum*' in the Gospel of Nicodemus. But [b] has merely *to hem alle*.

277. *Lazar hit fette*, it (sc. the light) fetched Lazarus away; see note to l. 261.

278. *Combraunce*, trouble, misfortune; it occurs three times in The Destruction of Troy, ed. Panton and Donaldson.

280. *Hit*, i. e. mankind. *Ther lazar is*, where Lazarus is [c].

283. Mr. Halliwell, in his Dictionary, remarks that *Ragamofin* is a name of a demon in some of the old mysteries. It has since passed into a sort of familiar slang term for any one poorly clad. The demons, it may be observed, took the comic parts in the old mysteries, and were therefore sometimes fitted with odd names.

In the Towneley Mysteries, p. 246, we have the names *Astarot*, Anaballe, Berith, and Belyalle. Mr. Wright notes that the name *Astaroth*, 'as given to one of the devils, occurs in a curious list of actors in the Miracle Play of St. Martin, given by M. Jubinal, in the preface to his Mystères Inédits, vol. ii. p. ix. It is similarly used in the Miracle Play of the Martyrdom of St. Peter and St. Paul, [ed.] Jubinal, ib. vol. i. p. 69.' He also notes its occurrence in the Towneley Mysteries. In the King of Tars, ed. Ritson, it is the name of an idol. It occurs in our poem *twice;* see ll. 289, 449.

287. *Cheke we*, let us check; i. e. interrupt his course. I believe this to be a very early example of the use of this word as a *verb*. As a *substantive*, it occurs in Rob. of Brunne; see Richardson's Dictionary.

Chyne, a chink; A. S. *cíne*. It is used by Wyclif and Mandeville; see Stratmann. In the Romance of Partenay, ed. Skeat, 4343, we have the expression—'in a *chine* of the roch,' i. e. rock. It is still in common use in the Isle of Wight for a cleft in a cliff.

288. *Louer*, a loover. 'A *loouer* or tunnell in the roof or top of a great hall to avoid smoke, *Fumarium, spiramentum;*' Baret. '*Louer* of a hall, esclère;' Palsgrave. See *Louver* in my Etym. Dictionary.

Loupe, a loop-hole. '*Loupe* in a towne-wall or castell, *creneau;*' Palsgrave.

289. *Astrot*, Ashtaroth; see l. 449, and note to l. 283. *Hot out*, hoot out, cry aloud; various readings, *hote, hoot. Haue oute,*.i. e. fetch out.

293. *Bowes of brake*, bows with a rack or winch; an allusion to crossbows of the largest size and strongest tension. Pictures of these cross-bows in the hands of Genoese and other archers are not uncommon; see Fairholt, Costume in England, pp. 175, 176; Johnes's Froissart, i. 165; Knight's Old England, i. 225, fig. 872. In the allit. Troy-book, ed. Panton and Donaldson, p. 186, l. 5728, the Greeks attack the Trojans—

'With ablastis also [thai] atlet to shote,
With *big bowes of brake* bykrit full hard.'

The note to the line gives three explanations, the first and third of which I reject without hesitation, but the second is correct, viz. that the *brake* was the crank or handle which the soldier worked when using the bow. The old word *brake* was *a general name for any mechanical contrivance*, especially a lever, *that enabled great force to be used.* Hence it means (1) a pump-handle; (2) a flax-dresser's instrument; (3) a twitch for horses; (4) a sort of rack, or instrument of torture; (5) a frame for confining vicious horses when being shod, etc. ; see *Brake* in Halliwell. The word is Old Low German, and probably some of the contrivances came from the Netherlands. Cf. Du. *braak*, a brake ; *vlasbraak*, a flax-dresser's brake. The derivation of the sb. is ultimately from Du. *breken* (O. Du. *braken*), to break ; cognate with A. S. *brecan*. Cf. O. Du. *brake*, a fetter for the neck, an instrument of torture ; and see *Brake* in Richardson.

Lydgate tells us, in his Siege of Thebes, part iii, that Tydeus was shot by one of the defenders of the city by a bolt from a bow of brake. An iron-headed ·' quarrel,' shot from a bow of brake, was the most fatal weapon known in the olden times, before the invention of gunpowder; and even, perhaps, for some time afterwards.

Brasene gonnes. Observe that this mention of guns is not in the B-text (1377). *Gonne* was used of a machine for casting stones, but here it is *brazen*. In Chaucer's House of Fame, iii. 553 (written about 1384 ?), a *gonne* is discharged by gunpowder. An early mention of cannon is in Barbour's Bruce, written in 1375. See my note to The Bruce, bk. xix. l. 399.

294. *Shultrom*, squadron; also spelt *shiltrum*, and by Barbour *childrome* or *cheldrome*. It is a corruption of the A. S. *scyld-truma*, lit. a troop-shield, and hence an armed company or battalion of soldiers. The word occurs frequently in Barbour's Bruce ; and see other examples in Stratmann, s. v. *schild*.

I may add that Satan here expresses his belief that Christ was accompanied by a host of angels. We may impute this false impression to his fears. Angels are first mentioned in l. 452.

295. *Mangonel*, a large engine for throwing heavy stones, etc. See the detailed descriptions of various engines in Col. Yule's edition of Marco Polo, ii. 122.

296. *Crokes*, hooks ; especially such hooks as were fastened on to the end of a long pole, and could be used as grappling-irons, for annoying assailants, removing scaling-ladders, and the like.

Kalketrappes, calthrops or caltrops; defined by Webster as 'an instrument with four iron points [fastened to a ball] so disposed that, three of them being on the ground, the other projects upward. They are scattered on the ground where an enemy's cavalry are to pass, to impede their progress by endangering the horse's feet.' 'Caltrap of yryn, fote hurtynge, *hamus ;*' Prompt. Parv., p. 59 ; on which see Mr. Way's note. See *Calthrop* in my Etym. Dictionary.

297. Lucifer is here made quite a different personage from Satan; cf. ll. 353, 354. Satan is the Prince or Duke of Death, but Lucifer is the Prince of Hell, called in the Latin 'inferus ; ' see note to l. 276 above, and cf. l. 273. Cf. Cursor Mundi, p. 1030 ; Town. Myst., p. 246. However, our author has paid small regard to the account in the Gospel of Nicodemus, and has put some of the speeches into the wrong mouths. The reference to Lazarus in l. 277 should not have been made by Satan, but by Lucifer; and in l. 315 we have a complete confusion, because the Temptation is there ascribed, not to Satan, but to Lucifer; see note to that line,

below. Wyclif speaks of the 'pride of Lucifer and cruelte of Sathanas;' Works, iii. 296.

298. *Is longe gon*, it is long ago since I (first) knew him. For *gon* [c], the B-text has *ago*.

302. 'By right and reason.' See the reasoning below, in ll. 376-403. Cf. Cursor Mundi, p. 246.

311. 'And since we have been seised (of them) for 7000 years' [c]; 'And since I possessed (them) for 700 years' [b]. The reading *I seised* [b] is very awkward; but the various readings are no better. The best emendation is the author's own, as given in [c]. The alteration from 700 to 7000 is an improvement, as coming nearer to the supposed length of the period indicated. The use of the number *seven* is merely to render the time rather indefinite, according to the author's practice elsewhere; see the notes on the indefinite expression *seven yere* in Pass. v. 82, p. 56, and vii. 214, p. 83.

The supposed period during which the patriarchs remained in hell was, according to the Gospel of Nicodemus, 5500 years. In the Knight de la Tour, p. 59, the term is said to be 5000 years. In the Coventry Mysteries, p. 105, the time from the Creation to the birth of Christ is said to be 4604 years. In the Towneley Mysteries, p. 244, the term is 4600 years. In the Deuelis Perlament, l. 324, Lucifer says he has dwelt in hell for more than 4000 years; Hymns to the Virgin and Christ, ed. Furnivall, p. 51. So also in the Ancren Riwle, p. 54.

315. 'Because thou obtainedst them by guile, and didst break into his garden.' Here the Temptation of man is ascribed to Lucifer, which makes much confusion, because in ll. 297, 302, Lucifer is made the same with the Prince of Hell; see note to l. 297 above. The Temptation should have been ascribed to Satan, who is called 'the deouel' in l. 327.

In the Deuelis Perlament (Hymns to the Virgin and Christ, ed. Furnivall, p. 50), the Temptation of man is ascribed, as here, to Lucifer; but then Satan, Lucifer, and Hell are made into *three* separate persons.

318. *By heore on*, alone by herself; equivalent to the expression *by hir-selue* [b]. The text alluded to is—'Si unus ceciderit, ab altero fulcietur; uæ soli: quia cum ceciderit, non habet subleuantem se;' Eccles. iv. 10.

321. *Troiledest*, didst deceive, didst bewitch. The word is very rare; but Burguy gives '*troiller*, *truiller*, ensorceler, charmer, tromper; de l'ancien norois *trölla*, enchanter.' Though rare in French or English, it is common enough in the Scandinavian languages. Cf. Icel. *trylla*, to enchant, charm, fascinate; Dan. *trylleri*, magic, etc.; all derived from the Icel. *troll*, Dan. *trold*, a goblin.

325. I quote here Mr. Wright's note. 'Goblin is a name still applied to a devil. It belongs properly to a being of the old Teutonic popular mythology, a hob-goblin, the "lubber-fiend" of the poet [Milton, *L'Allegro*], and seems to be identical with the German *kobold*. See Grimm, Deutsche Mythologie, p. 286.' *Gobelin* occurs as the name of one of the shepherds in the Mystery of the Nativity, printed by M. Jubinal in his Mystères

Inédits, vol. ii. p. 71. It occurs as the name of a devil in a song of the commencement of the 14th century, in Polit. Songs, p. 238—

'Sathanas huere syre seyde on his sawe,
    Gobelyn made is gerner of gromene mawe.'

Cf. note to l. 283, p. 257.

326. *Hit maketh*, causes it to be so, brings about this result [c]. On this curious phrase, see note to Pass. viii. 28, p. 96.

334. The words *troiled* [c] and *trolled* [b] are altogether different. The C-text means—'Thus hath he deceived (me), and laboured continually, during his lifetime, like a careful man, for these 32 years;' where *tydy* means orderly, careful (lit. timely), as in Pass. iv. 478. The B-text means—'And thus hath he rolled on (i. e. continued) for these 32 years;' where *troll* is used in a neuter sense, though it is the same word as when we speak of *trolling* a hoop. 'Tryllyn, or trollyn, *volvo;*' Prompt. Parv. The word *troiled* [c] has been explained in the note to l. 321 just above. But it is very probable that the reading *troiled* in *this* passage is a mere mistake of the scribes, due to the use of *troiledest* just above, and a far better reading would be to retain the *trolled* of the B-text. It will be observed that there was no chance of confusion in the B-text, because the line containing *troiledest* does not appear there.

The 'two and thirty years' refers to the length of Christ's life.

—— (18. 298.) 'To warn Pilate's wife, what manner of man Jesus was.' The mention of Pilate's wife in Matt. xxvii. 19 easily led on to the idea of an old legend, that the dream of Pilate's wife was caused by a demon, who endeavoured to defer the death of Christ and the consequent defeat of Satan. (This is clearly the idea intended in the C-text, ll. 336-339.) See the Coventry Mysteries, pp. 308, 309; York Plays, p. 277.

The phrase *what dones man*, i. e. a man of what make, is very singular and rare. Here *dones* is the pp. *don*, made, used as a substantive, and even taking a genitive suffix, such as we see in the phrase *what kynnes man;* see the account of *kynnes* in the note to Pass. xi. 128, p. 187. Mr. W. Aldis Wright has kindly given me another instance of the use of this word. In Hearne's edition of Rob. of Gloucester, p. 112, is the line—'He askede, wat God and wat þing Mercurius was.' The Trinity MS. has, in this passage, the reading—'He axede what *Idone* god,' etc.; and the Digby MS. has 'what man*ere* god.' I have also myself found two more examples of this word; both in the Alexander fragment, which I have called Alexander and Dindimus, ll. 222, 999.

340. *On bones ȝede*, went about with its bones, i. e. went about alive. Cf. Luke xxiv. 39.

344. This is a beautiful conception, and well expressed; the bright soul of Christ is seen sailing towards the dark abode of the demons, with even and majestic motion. Compare the appearance of *Anima Christi* in the Coventry Mysteries, p. 330. Mr. Wright bids us observe a similar excellent use of the word *sailing* by Milton, Sams. Agon., 713.

348. (18. 308.) *Lesynges*, lies; translated by Lat. *mendacia* in a marginal note in MS. M. See next note.

351. *Lowe*, liedst, didst lie [c]; cf. l. 447 below. 'The *lesynge* was when he sayde to Eue that they shulde not dye, though they eate of that fruyte;' Myrour of Our Lady, ed. Blunt, p. 204. 'Leesynge, or lyynge, or gabbynge, *mendacium;*' Prompt. Parv., p. 298; and see Way's note.

352. 'In land (i. e. earth) and in hell' [c]; 'on land and on water' [b]. See John xii. 31.

353–361. A mere digression on lying, to be considered as within a parenthesis, as the author himself tells us. In l. 358, *beleiȝe* means belie, deceive. In l. 361, *suynge my teme* = pursuing my theme or discourse. The text is from Ps. v. 7 (Vulgate).

362. Here the account follows the usual narrative rather closely; see note to l. 261. Compare also Cursor Mundi, p. 1036; Cov. Mysteries; The Deuelis Perlament (Hymns to the Virgin, ed. Furnivall), p. 49, etc. *Eft*, again, a second time; see l. 272 above.

367. Cf. Castel of Love, ed. Weymouth, p. 64—

'Helle ȝates he al to-breek,
And to-daschte al þe fendes ek,' etc.

368. 'For all that any wight or gate-warden could do.'

369. The Latin phrases 'populus in tenebris' and 'ecce agnus dei' are used because they are cited in the Gospel of Nicodemus.

372. (18. 324.) 'With that light flew forth' [c]; cf. *flowen* in Pass. iii. 249. 'He caught up into His light' [b]; with which cf. A. xii. 96, and the note, p. 165.

'Descendit ad inferna, ut Adam protoplastum, et Patriarchas, et Prophetas, omnesque iustos, qui pro originali peccato ibidem detinebantur, liberaret;' Sermo de Symbolo, cap. vii.; App. to S. August. Op. vi. col. 1194, ed. Migne.

374. 'To preserve the right (i. e. just claim) of us both' [c]. On the word *beyere*, see note to l. 36 above, p. 251.

The argument which follows is to shew that the claim of Satan to the soul of man has been satisfied, and that Christ has established a newer and better claim. No doubt our author has here again followed Grosteste; see Castel of Love, ed. Weymouth, pp. 51–54. Also the Towneley Mysteries, p. 250.

379. *Hit made*, caused it, brought it about; cf. l. 326.

382. 'Falsely thou didst fetch there (i. e. thence) that which it was my part to guard' [c]; *or*, 'the thing that I loved' [b].

—— (18. 335.) 'Thus like a lizard (serpent), with a lady's face.' The words *lizard* and *lady* refer to the fact that the serpent who tempted Eve was sometimes represented with short feet, like a lizard or crocodile, and the face of a young maiden. Even when the feet do not appear, the face is commonly retained, as in the representation in the chapter-house of Salisbury cathedral. See the woodcut in Wright's Hist. of Caricature, p. 73. Compare the Chester Plays, ed. Wright, p. 26; Coventry Mysteries, p. 29; the allit. Destruction of Troy, ed. Panton and Donaldson, p. 144, l. 4451; Chaucer, Man of Lawes Tale, Group B, l. 360, which see. One authority for the notion is Peter Comestor, who says, in his Historia Libri Genesis, that Satan 'elegit quoddam genus serpentis (vt ait Beda) *virgineum vultum* habens.'

385. See note to l. 166 above. And cf. l. 395 below.

388. *Enye*, any one; acc. case. See Exod. xxi. 24.

389. *Lyf* is used over and over again by our author to signify *a living person*, a man; see the Glossary. In this passage it is used both in this and in the more usual sense; so that, though the text has a puzzling appearance, it is easy enough to any one familiar with the rest of the poem. The sense is—' So must a (living) man lose his life, whenever that (living) man has destroyed the life of another; so that life may pay for life, as the old law demands.'

392. *Ich man to amenden hit*, I, in my nature of Man, (am ready) to amend it. But the B-text is better.

394. *Aquykye*, quicken, make alive again. Cf.—' For to *quykee* in hem the mynde and remembraunce of the biforeseid thingis;' Pecock's Repressor, i. 237. 'Quyknyn, quykyn, *vegeto, vivifico;*' Prompt. Parv., p. 421.

398. *Myne lige*, my liege servants; see Matt. v. 17.

—— (18. 355.) 'Let guile go against guile.' This helps to illustrate the difficult expression explained in the note to B. x. 192, p. 154.

400. In the Legenda Aurea, cap. liii. (De Passione Domini), ed. Grässe, 2nd ed., p. 229, we have—'quia sicut Adam deceptus fuit in ligno, ita Christus passus fuit in ligno. In quadam hystoria Graecorum dicitur, *quod in eodem.*' The last statement is very curious; cf. note to l. 144 above. Cf. the Towneley Mysteries, p. 72.

404. *Brouk*, enjoy; lit. brook. 'As I brew, so must I needs drink;' proverb, in Camden's Remaines, 1614. In French, 'Avallez ce que vous avez brassé.' Cf. 'Suilk als þai brued, now ha þai dronken;' Cursor Mundi, l. 2848.

'And who so wicked ale breweth,
　　Ful ofte he mote the werse drinke;' Gower, Conf. Amant., bk. iii.

409. The idea is a good one, when once apprehended. Christ says that *His* drink is *love;* and this He will drink (i.e. receive) not from any deep source, nor from the learned only, but from all true Christian souls, which are to Him as homely vessels containing it. The metaphor is strikingly original, characteristic, and beautiful. Lines 408–410 are not in the B-text, and distinctly shew that the power of the poet had not failed him, at the time of the last revision of his poem.

411. The alliteration is not apparent in [b]; but at once appears in [c], which shews that the author pronounced *thirst* as *first;* just as in the phrase 'afurst and afyngred;' Pass. xvii. 15. See John xix. 28.

412. 'Pymente, drynke, *pigmentum, nectar, mellicratum;*' Prompt. Parv., p. 399; see Way's note; also Halliwell's Dictionary, s. v. *Piment*, and the note in The Babees Book, ed. Furnivall, p. 203.

Pomade was, as its name implies, made of apples, and therefore a kind of cider. See *Pomade* in Roquefort, and *Pomata* in Ducange. Our *pomatum* was also so called because formerly made from apples; but its use is very different.

414. 'Till the vintage fall (i. e. take place) in the vale of Jehoshaphat, and I drink the right ripe must, the resurrection of the dead.' This is an extension of the idea commented on in the note to l. 409.

Vendage answers to the Low Lat. *vindagia*, another form of *vindemia*, whence the Fr. *vendange* or *vendenge*, which see in Cotgrave.

The valley of Jehoshaphat is here supposed to be the future scene of the resurrection of mankind, an idea derived from Joel iii. 2, 12, 13. It is a name now given to the deep ravine between Jerusalem and the Mount of Olives, formerly called Kidron or Cedron. See Smith's Dict. of the Bible, art. *Jehoshaphat*, q. v. See Maundeville's Travels, ed. Halliwell, pp. 95, 114; Cov. Mysteries, p. 393; Ælfric's Homilies, ed. Thorpe, i. 441; Wyclif's Works, ii. 405.

418. *Feondekenes*, fiendkins, little fiends; a coined word.

423. *Beo he*, if he be. See Ps. l. 6 (Vulgate).

425. *Ofter þan ones*, more than once. This expression looks at first as if the author were speaking ironically; but our author is always so serious and explicit upon points of law, of which he shews a special knowledge, that we must accept his words literally as a remarkable testimony to the fact that, if hanging was improperly performed, it was usual to respite the criminal, and the more so, if the king happened to be near enough to be applied to personally for a pardon. A most interesting paper concerning cases of imperfect hanging, entitled 'Hanging from a historical and physiological point of view,' was contributed to the Medical Times and Gazette of June 10, 1871, p. 669, in which the present passage was cited and numerous illustrations given. One of these is as follows. In 1363, as is related by Henry of Knighton, in his Chronicle of English History, col. 2627 :—'Walter Wynkeburn having been hanged at Leicester, after having been taken down from the gallows as a dead man, was being carried to the cemetery to be buried, but began to revive in the cart. To this man King Edward [III.] granted pardon in Leicester Abbey, and gave him a Charter of pardon, thus saying in my [Knighton's] hearing:—Deus tibi dedit uitam, et nos dabimus tibi cartam.'

This instance is most remarkable, and can hardly be other than the very one of which William was thinking. It occurred in 1363, and, as he intimates, the king happened to be at the very place where the execution took place, and spoke to the criminal personally.

Other remarkable cases of resuscitation occurred later, such as that of Anne Greene, about 1650; see Plot's Natural Hist. of Oxfordshire, p. 197; Derham's Physico-Theology, 3rd ed., 1714, p. 157; Gent. Magazine, vol. lxx.; Knight's Book of Table-talk, 1836, i. 236; Plot's Nat. Hist. of Staffordshire, p. 292. Three persons, all tailors, escaped from the gallows at Cork between 1755 and 1766; the Cork Remembrancer, by Edwards, p. 214. The Scottish law permits but one hanging, as in the case of Margaret Dickinson, 1728; see The Newgate Calendar, vol. ii. p. 233. Compare Scott's Heart of Mid Lothian, ch. iii. The law in England, however, seems to have changed completely since the olden times, since Blackstone says expressly that 'if the criminal be not thoroughly killed, the officer of the sheriff must hang him again.'

433. 'If the boldest of their sins be at all dearly paid for;' i.e. if I have adequately suffered for their sins. See note to l. 448.

435. As to the Latin quotation here, see note to Pass. v. 140, p. 59. For the next quotation, see Ps. xxxvii, 1 (Vulgate).

—— (18. 390.) *Til parce it hote*, till the word 'Spare-thou' command it (to be otherwise); i.e. till the word *parce* be the signal of their release. *It hote* is a similar phrase to *it make;* see Pass. viii. 28. See Mr. Wright's work on St. Patrick's Purgatory.

439. *Blood* here signifies kinship, relationship ; or rather the personification of kinship, i.e. a relative; see l. 421. The sense is, that one relative can bear to see another thirsty or chilly, but will pity him if he is actually wounded and bleeding.

Athurst = A. S. *of-þyrsted*, very thirsty (Cædmon, ed. Thorpe, p. 3, l. 7).

Similarly, *acale* is probably an old pp. (of the strong form) allied to the verb *akelen* (Court of Love, l. 1076), and signifies very chilled, extremely cold. Cf. Icel. *kala*, to cool, of which the pp. is *kalinn*. Three other examples of *acale* occur in Seven Sages, ed. Weber, p. 59, l. 1512; Gower, Conf. Amant., iii. 296, 303.

440. *Bote hym rewe*, without feeling pity. See 2 Cor. xii. 4.

444. *Neodes*, of necessity. See Ps. cxiii. 2 (Vulgate).

448. 'Thou shalt bitterly pay for it.' Cf. Pass. xvii. 220. 'Ne ec ne scule ȝe nefre ufel don þet e hit ne sculen mid uuele bitter abuggen,' nor yet shall ye ever do any evil without bitterly expiating it; Old Eng. Homilies, ed. Morris, i. 41.

There is a curious picture of Christ holding Death in chains in P. Lacroix, Military and Religious Life in the Middle Ages, p. 449.

449. *Astrot* [c]; *Astaroth* [b]; i.e. Ashtoreth, or Astarte. Ashṭoreth was symbolised by the moon, but answers rather to Venus. See Smith's Dict. of the Bible, s. v. See l. 289, and note to l. 283.

452. Suggested by Ps. xlvii. 5 (xlvi. 6, Vulgate)—'Ascendit Deus in iubilo, et Dominus in uoce tubae.' So in Old Eng. Homilies, ii. 114, the sentence 'etiam in sono tubae, prout regem decet, ascendit' is explained to signify Christ's reception into heaven at His ascension.

The Latin quotation forms 2 lines, viz. the 3rd and 4th lines of the 4th stanza of the hymn beginning 'Aeterne rex altissime,' used in the Office of the Ascension at Matins, in the Roman Breviary. *Culpat* is not used in its (active) sense, but in the (neuter) Low-Latin sense; see '*Culpare*, delinquere' in Ducange. Hence the lines mean—'The flesh sins, the flesh redeems from sin, the flesh reigns as God of God.'

454. One of these lines is quoted by Matthew Paris. The word *nebula* is an odd one, but stands the same in all the MSS.; *nubila* may have been intended. The idea is common, and agrees with our proverbs—'After a storm comes a calm' (Camden's Remaines); and 'After black clouds, clear weather' (Heywood's Proverbs). So also in

C. PASS. XXI. 461. B. PASS. XVIII. 414. 265

the Test. of Love, book i.; ed. 1561, fol. cclxxxx. col. i.; Tale of Beryn, ed. Furnivall, l. 3955; Tobit iii. 22 (Vulgate)—a text which is quoted and translated in the Ancren Riwle, p. 376. Cf. Ovid, Trist., ii. 141-150; Boethius, De Consol. Philosophiæ, lib. iii. met. 1.

461. 'But Love, if it pleased him, could turn it to laughter.'

467, 468. The B-text means—'Thou sayest true, said Righteousness, and reverently kissed her (that is to say) Peace, and Peace (kissed) her; for ever and ever.' The MSS. of the B-text all agree in the reading *hir;* but the reading *heo* of the C-text is a very great improvement, and the sentence then becomes simple enough, viz.—' and reverently she kissed Peace, and Peace (kissed) her.' See Ps. lxxxiv. 11 (Vulgate).

470. *Lutede*, played the lute. See Ps. cxxxii. 1 (Vulgate).

472. On the ringing of bells on Easter morn, see Rock, Church of Our Fathers, iii. pt. 2, p. 251; Wordsworth, Eccl. Biography, i. 617.

473. *Kitte;* mentioned again as the poet's wife in Pass. vi. 2; see also Pass. viii. 304, and the note, p. 106.

Calot was a rather common name; and not a very reputable one. See *Callot* in Nares.

475. 'Creeping to the cross' was an old ceremony of penance; see Nares, s. v. *Cross*. Also Ratis Raving, ed. Lumby, note on p. 128. It was most often practised on Good Friday; see Old Eng. Homilies, ed. Morris, ii. 94, l. 9; Pecock's Repressor, i. 267, 270; Rock, Church of Our Fathers, iii. pt. 2, p. 241; Calfhill's Works, p. 100 (Parker Society); Parker Society's Index, s. v. *Cross;* Brand, Popular Antiquities, ed. Ellis, i. 153; etc. The extract from Pecock (i. 270) explains also the allusion to kissing the cross. He says—'But so it is, that to the crosse on Good Fridai men comen in louȝest wise, creeping on alle her knees, and to this crosse in so lowȝe and deuout maner they offren, and the feet of thilk cross thei in deuoutist maner kissen.' The injunction in Ratis Raving, l. 2793—'Nocht our oft creip the cross on kneis' shews that the penance was also performed at other times.

478. The supposed power of the cross over evil spirits is notorious. See Legends of the Holy Rood, ed. Morris, pp. 160, 169. A striking example is in Massinger's Virgin Martyr, Act v. sc. 1, where the demon Harpax, at the sight of a cross made of flowers, exclaims—'Oh! I am tortured!'

NOTES TO C. PASSUS XXII. (B. Pass. XIX.)

(The two texts differ but slightly throughout this Passus.)

22. 1. (19. 1.) Here ends the Ninth Vision; see note to l. 5.

3. *To be housled*, to receive the Holy Communion; cf. ll. 394, 397, 476 below. According to Pass. xxi. 472, the time indicated is Easter day, on which this duty was especially practised. See Rock, Church of Our Fathers, iii. pt. 2, p. 169, where this passage is quoted. He remarks that

pilgrims were commonly *houselled* before setting off on their pilgrimage; and describes the *houselling* of King Henry VII. at his coronation. See also Nares's Glossary; note in Peacock's edition of Myrk, p. 69; and note to l. 390 below.

5. Here begins the Tenth Vision, or the Vision of Grace.

7. In pictures representing Christ after His resurrection, He is commonly represented as bearing a long but light cross, with a banner. This is called the cross of the resurrection. See Rock, Church of Our Fathers, iii. pt. 2, p. 226. Cf. l. 14.

11. It is strange that the B-text MSS. nearly all agree in reading *Or it is*. Clearly, *Other is hit*, as in [c], is far better.

14. It is clear from l. 62 that our author, who was unacquainted with Greek, supposed that the word *Christ* signified 'conquerour.' On this supposed sense of the word the whole argument depends. A similar example occurs much earlier, in an Anglo-Saxon gloss of the *Quicunque Vult*, where the phrase 'Domini nostri Jesu *Christi*' is rendered by 'drihtnes ure hælendes *cinges;*' see Swainson, on the Nicene and Apostles' Creeds, p. 487, note 1. And the same appears even more clearly in the Lindisfarne MS. containing the Northumbrian version of the Gospels, where the Latin *christum* is glossed by 'crist vel ðone cynig,' i.e. Christ or the king; St. John ix. 22. The same supposed sense of the word *Christ* seems to be hinted at in the Chester Plays, ed. Wright, p. 105.

54. That is according to the Gospel of Nicodemus, Christ, by the 'harrowing of hell,' delivered the souls of Adam and Eve and others from the place of torment by His descent into it. See Pass. xxi. 451.

Other mo, to others besides; as in Pass. v. 10. So also *ten mo*, ten others, in l. 165 below.

62. 'And that is the meaning of " Christ."' See note to l. 14.

75. *Kinges*, the Three Kings. The Magi were called the Three Kings. See the Aurea Legenda, cap. xiv., *De Epiphania Domini.*

A long note upon them will be found in Marco Polo, ed. Yule, i. 78. There is a long legend about them, in English prose, quoted from MS. Harl. 1704, appended to Wright's edition of the Chester Plays, pp. 266–304. See also Brand's Popular Antiquities, ed. Ellis, i. 21; Maundeville's Travels, ed. Halliwell, p. 70; Peter Comestor's Historia Scholastica ; Chambers, Book of Days, i. 61 ; Dict. of the Bible, art. *Magi;* etc.

Chrysostom says that the gold, myrrh, and frankincense were mystic gifts, indicating that Christ was King, Man, and God ; our author interprets them as signifying righteousness, ruth, and reason respectively. See notes below.

80. *Of speke*, spakest of. See Phil. ii. 10.

86. 'The first king came, offering Reason, signified by incense.' Incense was often considered as a symbol of prayer, and hence, according to Chrysostom, it indicated that Christ was God. As it was used by the priests, it was by some taken to refer to Christ's priesthood.

A reference to the Old Kentish Sermons, in An Old Eng. Miscellany, ed.

Morris, p. 27, will show that the preachers were accustomed to exhort their hearers to offer to Christ gold, and frankincense, and myrrh, as the Magi did; and, in doing this, they gave new interpretations to those symbols. Our author has likewise, in his turn, attempted equally fanciful interpretations, with small success. In fact, he contradicts himself flatly; compare l. 86 with l. 90.

He seems to mean this. They offered Christ *incense*, meaning thereby a submission to Him of their reasonable service, and as expressing their belief in the reasonableness of His authority. They offered *gold*, signifying (1) the kingly justice (observe that 'rightwiseness' translates the Lat. *iustitia*, Pass. xxi. 169), which was 'reason's fellow,' inasmuch as kingly justice and reasonable commands should always be closely allied, in accordance with the burden of our author's song throughout Pass. v, especially in ll. 184–186; and also signifying (2) lealty, or fidelity in a subject. (Line 90 is altogether out of place, and due to some confusion of mind.) Lastly, they offered *myrrh*, signifying pity, ruth, or mercy in the king, and mildness of speech in the subject as well as in the king. The political meaning seems to be that a king should be reasonable, just, and mild; and that the subject should be free, loyal, and respectful.

93. Myrrh is more commonly interpreted in connection with death, because it was used in embalming the dead; see Cursor Mundi, l. 11504, where it is interpreted as pointing to Christ's mortality as a Man.

'Sacred gifts of mystic meaning:
 Incense doth their God disclose;
 Gold the King of Kings proclaimeth,
  Myrrh His *sepulchre* foreshews.'
   Hymns Ancient and Modern :—'*Earth has many a noble city.*'

99. This was strikingly exhibited in the life of Robert Bruce; we might almost imagine a reference to him here.

134. *Of dedus*, for his deeds, in his deeds; see 1 Sam. xviii. 7.

138. *Caiser*, emperor. It occurs again in Pass. xxiii. 101, and in Richard Redeles, i. 85.

146. *Of buriels*, from the sepulchre. Like *hidels, metels*, etc., *buriels* is in the singular number, being the A. S. *byrgels*, a tomb. Wyclif wrongly supposed it to be a plural, and invented the false forms *buriel*, which he uses in Mark vi. 29, and *biriel*, in Matt. xxvii. 60, etc.; see *burȝels* in Stratmann, and note to Group G, l. 186, in Chaucer's Man of Lawes Tale, etc. (Clarendon Press edition).

151. Alluding to the account in Matt. xxviii. 2. See Rock, Church of Our Fathers, iii. pt. 2, p. 253.

159. *Lyues and lokynge*, alive and looking round Him. See l. 175 below, and note to Pass. xi. 57, p. 134. The adverbial form *lyues* occurs five times in Havelok the Dane, ll. 509, 1003, 1307, 1919, 2854.

161. *Cam hit out*, it happened. See Luke xxiv. 46.

165. *Tadde*, Thaddæus. *Thomas of ynde*, Thomas of India. See Wyclif's Works, i. 153, and note; Marco Polo, ed. Yule, ii. 293, where Col. Yule

remarks that 'the tradition of Thomas's preaching in India is very old, so old that it is, probably, in its simple form true.' St. Jerome accepts the tradition; Sci. Hieron. Epist. lix. *ad Marcellam*. It is mentioned in the Apocryphal Acts of the Apostles, and by Gregory of Tours. 'The little town where the body of St. Thomas lay was Mailapúr, the name of which is still applied to a suburb of Madras about three and a half miles south of Fort George;' note in Marco Polo, ed. Yule, ii. 292. It is the fact that there is a community called 'the Christians of St. Thomas' at this very day, and that the tradition is well known at Madras. See also Smith's Dict. of the Bible, art. *Thomas*. And see John xx. 28, 29.

183. Here, and in l. 201, *peers* means St. Peter. In l. 188 it means St. Peter's successors, the bishops; and, in particular, the Pope.

186, 187. 'Provided that they should come, and acknowledge, in a satisfactory manner, their trust in the pardon of Piers the Plowman, which contains the words—"pay what thou owest."' *Kneweliched*, should acknowledge, is the past tense subjunctive; the B-text has the present tense. *To paye* means 'so as to please God;' cf. *to paye* as used in Pass. viii. 189, 192. *Peers pardon the plouhman* means 'the pardon of Piers the Plowman,' just as *peers bern the plouhman* means 'the barn of Piers the Plowman' in l. 360 and in Pass. xxiii. 77. This idiom has been already explained; see note to Pass. xvi. 131, p. 195; but has been singularly misunderstood by Dean Milman, in the useful summary of 'Piers the Plowman' in his History of Latin Christianity.

By the words 'redde quod debes' our author expresses his belief that a pardon is of none effect unless the culprit does what he can to make restitution; cf. Pass. vii. 316, 322; and see l. 193 below. Lines 186, 187 recur below, slightly varied; see ll. 391, 392.

201. *Paraclitus*, Paraclete, Comforter; see Acts ii. 1-4.

204. *Waggede conscience*, nudged Conscience; gave him a hint that he should explain it to me. See l. 207.

210. *Veni*, etc. The first line of the hymn at vespers, on the feast of Pentecost. It is mentioned in our Prayer-book still, in the rubrics to the Ordering of Priests and the Consecration of Bishops. See Rock, Church of Our Fathers, iii. pt. 2, p. 256.

213. Here Grace is the Holy Ghost, and Piers the Plowman is still Christ; the latter title not being used of Christ's deputed successors till l. 258 below, though the name of *peers* has been once so used above, in l. 188. See note to l. 183.

216. *Hus* [c] is used indefinitely, like our 'one's;' but the reading *her* [b] is certainly simpler. *Can*, knows how to control, has full possession of. The alliteration shews this to be the right reading, but it is a very forced expression, so that we need not wonder that most of the scribes turned it into *han* [b, footnote]. Thus the line means :—'To creatures of every kind, if one knows how to use one's five wits' [c]; *or*—'To creatures of every kind, that possess their five wits' [b]. On *five wits*, see note to Pass. ii. 15, p. 21.

227. *To gye with hymself*, to guide himself with, to rule his conduct by.

This (to us) odd position of *with* is the usual fourteenth-century idiom. See note to Pass. i. 133, p. 14.

229. See 1 Cor. xii. 4. The gifts of the Holy Spirit were sometimes reckoned as being seven in number. Our author, however, simply enumerates different professions and handicrafts.

235. ' To gain their livelihood by selling and buying.'

238. *To coke*, to put hay into cocks ; see note to Pass. vi. 13, p. 61. The present passage helps us to the meaning of the word, as it is here said to be an operation connected with tillage. The B-text reads *dyche*, to ditch.

247. If the context be carefully considered, I think it plain that our author is here commending that stern and rough mode of redressing justice which is sometimes practised by honest men in violent times, to the sudden confusion of oppressors who have made themselves intolerable. Thus ' foleuyles lawes' are laws of the character of Lynch laws, and were (similarly) so named, I presume, from some now forgotten worthy, who used to take a short course with men convicted of oppression or knavery. The word *foleuyles* (also spelt *foleviles*, *foluyles*) can hardly be other than a proper name, spelt (as usual in MSS.) with a small letter. We should now spell such a name Folville or Fouville. This seems to me the most likely solution. If the reader is pleased to take *Folville* as the name of a place, it will then mean ' silly town,' and the name may have been fictitious. It is remarkable that, in the Tale of Beryn, there is a description of a ' false town ' with very peculiar laws. But whatever solution be chosen, the general sense of the passage is sufficiently clear.

—— (19. 247.) It is almost a pity that the author left out this line in revision. The miller should bear in mind that the chimney-sweep's calling is as irreproachable (morally) as his own.

260. *Prower*, purveyor, provider of necessaries. The word occurs in Pecock's Repressor, p. 467, and is explained to mean ' purueier,' p. 468. Mr. Wright's Glossary wrongly has—' *Prowor*, a priest ; ' which is copied into Halliwell's Dictionary. Roquefort is, I think, quite wrong also. In fact, we have in *prowor* only another form of *purveyor*, without any difference in the sense ; the interpretation ' purveyor' is the very thing which the context requires, and has the express authority of Pecock.

262. In the History of Hawsted, by Sir J. Cullum, 2nd ed., p. 216, we are told that, in Suffolk, in the 14th century, oxen were as much used as horses ; and, in ploughing heavy land, would go forward where horses would stop.

The oxen here signify the Four Evangelists. The idea was easily suggested by the fact that St. Luke is commonly symbolised by an ox.

267. *Stottes*, bullocks. This sense best suits the context. It is sometimes disputed whether *stot* means a bullock or a stallion ; but it is clear that it has *both* meanings ; indeed, it has a third meaning, since it also represents our modern *stoat*. The sense of bullock is still preserved in the North, though the term is also applied to an old ox ; see Atkinson's Cleveland Glossary. Cf. ' Stotte, *boveau ;*' Palsgrave. ' Aythor cow or *stott ;* '

Towneley Mysteries, p. 112. Icel. *stútr*, a bull; Swed. *stut*, a bullock; Dan. *stud*, an ox, a bullock. The sense of stallion or young horse is equally certain; we have Chaucer's Reve mounted on a 'ful good stot;' Prol. l. 617. 'Stot, hors, *caballus;*' Prompt. Parv. '*Stottus*, equus admissarius;' Ducange. Ger. *stute*, a mare; *stuterei*, a stud of horses. Cf. our *stud*, and Dan. *stodhest*, a stallion; O. H. Ger. *stuot, stuat*, a stud of brood-horses. The connection between *stoat* and the two senses of *stot* may perhaps be accounted for by supposing the original sense of the word to be connected with breeding.

268. 'All that his oxen ploughed, they (were) to harrow afterwards.'

269. This refers to the four chief Latin fathers, St. Jerome, St. Gregory, St. Ambrose, and St. Augustine. See Mrs. Jameson's Sacred and Legendary Art, 3rd ed., p. 281.

272. *Hand-whyle*, a very short space of time. Stratmann gives four examples, to which I add—'Herkinys now a *hondqwile* of a hegh cas;' allit. Troy-book, ed. Panton and Donaldson, l. 7346. In this line, *harowede* (lit. harrowed) means *went over, commented upon*.

273. *Eythes* [c] has the same sense as *harwes* [b], viz. harrows. The word is rare, but easily accounted for, as it is the A. S. *egeðe*, a rake, a harrow, cognate with the O. H. Ger. *agide, egida, ekitha*, Mod. Ger. *egge*, a harrow.

The two harrows symbolise the Old and New Testaments.

274. *Cardinales virtues,* cardinal (or chief) virtues. On the construction, see note to Pass. x. 342, p. 130. On the Four Virtues, see note to Pass. i. 131, p. 13.

279. *Stele*, a handle; cf. Chaucer, C. T. Group A. 3785. 'Steal, s. the *steal* of any thing, i.e. manubrium, the handle; or pediculus, the foot-stalk;' Ray's South and East-Country Words. The line means— 'and taught men to buy a ladle with a long handle.' See next note.

280. *Cast*, short for *casteth*, i.e. intends. *Kele*, to cool [c]; *kepe*, to pay heed to [b]. This line throws some light on the expression to 'keel the pot,' in the Song at the end of Love's Labour's Lost. The remarks in Nares and Halliwell are just, that the word simply means to *cool*, or *keep cool*, and not to scum. In Glossary B. 1, published by the Eng. Dialect Society, we have—'*Keel*, to keep the pot from boiling over; North of England.' The operation really intended is that the cook shall watch the pot, and gently stir it when it seems likely to boil over. The watching is denoted by *kepe* [b]; the gentle stirring by *kele* [c]. The latter is merely the A. S. *célan*, to cool, and is rather common; see *kelen* in Stratmann, and note—'Kelyn, or make colde, *frigefacio;*' Prompt. Parv. Hence the reference to Prudence in ll. 279, 280 means—'And taught men to buy a ladle with a long handle, whoever intends to stir (*or* watch) a pot, and to preserve the fat that floats on the top.' The illustration from Marston, given by Nares, is very much to the point:—'Faith, Doricus, thy brain boils; *keel* it, *keel* it, or all the fat's in the fire.'

288. *Maister Iohan*, master John. Merely a contemptuous name for a cook; much as we might now say 'Mister Jack.'

294. *Of abydyng*, in sufferance, in patience [c]; *and abydynge*, and patient [b].

297. Quoted from Dionysius Cato, Distich., ii. 14—
'Esto animo forti, quum sis damnatus inique,
Nemo diu gaudet, qui iudice uincit iniquo.'
Another reading is *forti animo*, as in the text.

305. *And*, if [c]; *ʒif*, if [b]. 'If the king happen to be in any respect guilty' [c].

307. *Domesman*, judge; lit. man of doom. Chaucer translates *censor* in Boethius, lib. ii. met. 6, by this word, saying of Nero—'he was so hard-herted that he myʒte ben *domesman* or *Iuge* of hire dede beaute;' ed. Morris, p. 55.

314. Skelton has 'crokyd as a *camoke*;' ed. Dyce, i. 117; where a *cammock* means a crooked piece of timber, a bent stick, from the Celtic (Welsh and Gaelic) *cam*, crooked; so also in Lily's Euphues, ed. Arber, p. 408. But in the present passage the *cammock* is the troublesome weed called the rest-harrow (short for *arrest-harrow*), or *Ononis arvensis;* called the *cammock*, doubtless, from its crooked and tough roots. Cotgrave has —'*Arreste-bœuf*, the herb Rest-harrow, petty whinne, grand-furze, Cammocke.'

317. 'Harrow all such as have natural ability by means of the counsel of these Doctors (of the church), and cultivate (in them) the cardinal virtues according to their teaching.'

320. 'To stow thy corn in.' *Cornes* is often used to signify *corn* in Middle-English. It occurs, for example, in Chaucer's account of Samson in The Monkes Tale; in Spec. of English, pt. ii., ed. Morris and Skeat, p. 70, l. 39; and in Wyclif's Works, ed. Arnold, iii. 329, where it is misprinted *corves*.

324. *That ... on peynede = on whiche ... peynede*, i.e. on which Christ suffered pain. The form *pyned* [b] is perhaps better, being the older English word.

330. The house of Unity denotes Holy Church. Compare—'þe þridde onhede [*one-hood, unity*] is of þe chirche, and of her partis, oon in God;' Wyclif's Works, ed. Arnold, i. 403.

335. Here *peers* (Piers) is at last completely transferred from its reference to Christ, so as to mean His faithful pastors and teachers. Grace (i.e. the Holy Ghost) accompanies these wherever they go, in order 'to till truth,' i.e. to spread the truth of the Christian faith.

337. Cf. Pass. ix. 112. The description of Pride's attack upon the church is more fully given in Pass. xxiii. 70. See note to Pass. xxiii. 69.

340. *Rotes* [c] and *mores* [b] have the same sense, viz. roots. See note to Pass. xviii. 21, p. 224.

341. *Sourquidours*, proud or arrogant men [c]; *surquidous*, an arrogant man, but used as a proper name [b]. *Surquidours* would answer to a French form *sorcuideurs*, and *surquidous* to *sorcuideux*, both from the Old Fr. *sorcuider*, to presume, to be arrogant, to think too much of oneself; from Lat. *super-cogitare*.

343. *To-comen*, approached [c]; *two come*, two came [b]. The change from *two come* was made necessary by the changes in the two preceding lines.

360. 'Let us pray that there might be peace in Piers the Plowman's barn,' i.e. in the church. And see note to l. 187 above.

366. 'That Holy Church might stand in Holiness, as if it were a peel,' i.e. a fort [c]; *or*, 'that Holy Church might stand in Unity,' etc. [b]. Holy Church (or Unity) is here represented as being a castle. Holiness (see l. 382) is the moat that protects it, the water that fills the moat being derived from the tears of penitents. The Christians dig a deep ditch round Holy Church or Unity, so that the structure is plainly seen to resemble a *pile*, i.e. a fort. *Pile* is the Lat. *pila*, a pillar, dam, or pier. 'Pyle, of a bryggys fote, or other byggynge [i.e. building], *pila;*' Prompt. Parv., p. 398. 'Pere, or pyle of a brygge or other fundament, *pila;*' id. p. 394. Cf. 'saxea pila' in Æneid, ix. 711. But in this passage it seems to mean 'fort,' like the North of England *peel*.

380. *Egrelich*, bitterly, rather than quickly. Such is the usual old sense, as when we find 'esill [i.e. vinegar] strong and *egre*' in the Romaunt of the Rose, l. 147. See *Eager* in Trench's Select Glossary.

ȝ*ernynge* [c] = *ernynge* [b], i.e. running; from A.S. *ge-yrnan* or *yrnan*, to run.

390. The author of the Ancren Riwle (at p. 412) recommends that the laity should not receive the Holy Communion oftener than 15 times in a year at the most. Queen Elizabeth of York, wife of Henry VII., seems to have communicated thrice in the year, on Easter-day, All Saints'-day, and Christmas-day; see the Layfolk's Mass-book, ed. Simmons, p. 239. Chaucer says *once* a year at least—' and certes ones a yere at the leste wey it is lawful to be houseled, for sothely ones a yere alle thinges in the erthe renoulen' [*renew themselves*]; Pers. Tale, at the end of Remedium Luxuriæ. Robert of Brunne says the same, Handl. Synne, ll. 10298–10301.

391, 392. 'Or as often they should have need, that is to say, those who had (duly) paid according to the pardon of Piers the Plowman (which expresses the condition),—"pay what thou owest."' See note to l. 187; and cf. ll. 193, 259.

395. 'Such (said Conscience) is my counsel, and such is also the counsel of the Cardinal Virtues.' Cf. Matt. vi. 12.

398. *Bawe*, an interjection of contempt; see note to Pass. xiii. 74.

402. *Thicke ale;* see note to Pass. vii. 226, p. 84.

403. *Hacke*, to hoe, to grub about, to toil. This is, of course, spoken contemptuously, and must have been suggested by the preceding allegory, in which Holiness has been described as the ditch or moat which protects the castle of Unity or Holy Church; see ll. 376, 382. The word is expressive, and well chosen; cf. Dan. *hakke*, Swed. *hacka*, a hoe; and cf. '*Hack*, a strong pick-axe, or hoe,' Halliwell; also '*Hack*, to stammer; to cough faintly and frequently; to labour severely and indefatigably; to chop with a knife; to break the clods of earth after ploughing;' id.

Mr. Wright has rather missed the figure intended, and explains it by 'to follow, or run after; to cut along after,' where the 'cut along' is not an explanation, but a misleading play upon words, introducing an unauthorised guess. Mr. Halliwell has copied this in his Dictionary, s. v. *Hakke*, but *minus* the 'cut along.'

408. *Worst thow* [c], or *worstow* [b], thou shalt be. Here *worst* is for *worthest*, from the verb *worthen*, to become.

412. *Curatoure*, curate. 'Rector, vicar, every one having *cure* of souls, was a "curate" once. Thus "bishops and *curates*" in the Liturgy;' Trench's Select Glossary, p. 57; which see for examples.

419. Wordsworth (Eccl. Biography, 4th ed., i. 569, 570) cites these lines in illustration of the duke of Suffolk's words, aimed at Wolsey and Campeggio:—'It was never merry in Englande while we had any cardinalls amongst us.'

424. *Auenoun*, Avignon; the place where the pope's court was. Avignon, in the S. E. of France, was 'ceded by Philip III. to the pope in 1273. The papal seat was removed by Clement V. to Avignon in 1309. In 1348 Clement VI. purchased the sovereignty from Jane, countess of Provence and queen of Naples. In 1408, the French, wearied of the schism, expelled Benedict XIII., and Avignon ceased to be the seat of the papacy;' Haydn's Dict. of Dates. 'With the English court these Popes of Avignon were deservedly unpopular; they were governed by French influence, and often thwarted, as far as they could, the designs of England against France;' Massingberd's Hist. of Eng. Reform., p. 49. See also the note to l. 430.

The Jews were no doubt very useful in finding money for the popes at Avignon; and it is recorded that Clement VI. (A.D. 1342–1352) forbad any persecution of the Jews there; Hist. of Prices and Agric. in England, by J. E. T. Rogers, i. 297.

The expression—'with the holy thou shalt be holy' (Ps. xvii. 26, Vulgate, xviii. 26, A. V.), is of course ironical; and refers to an implied association of the cardinals with the Jews.

425. 'To keep the relics.' The cardinals always bore the title of some church within the city of Rome; and all the churches contained relics. See Engl. Cyclop., art. *Cardinals;* and The Stations of Rome, ed. Furnivall (E. E. T. S.).

427. In [c] *And* means *if;* but in [b] it means *and*. Hence the sense is—'If Grace, that thou sayst so much about, were the guide of all clerks' [c]; *or*, 'And Grace, that thou sayst so much about, should be the guide of all clerks' [b]. Respecting Conscience at the king's court, see Pass. iv. 156, etc.

430. It is difficult to find in our author any very clear allusion to the famous schism of the popes in 1378, and perhaps he was intentionally rather cautious upon that subject; unlike Wyclif, who was glad to speak of it. Still there is possibly an allusion to it here, and in ll. 446, 447 [b. 19. 441, 442] below. 'Imperfect is the pope, who ought to assist all people,

and pays [*or* sends out, *b*] them who slay such as he ought to save.' See note to l. 447.

431. *Soudeth*, pays [c]; *sendeth*, sends out [b]. The change is curious; MS. M. has *sowdeth*. The verb *souden* is formed from the sb. *soud*, pay, as 'in sowd,' i.e. in pay, Mandeville's Travels, p. 155; quoted in Halliwell to illustrate '*Soudes*, wages.' Cotgrave has—'*Sould*, souldiers' lendings, intertainment, or pay; an old word.' Ducange has—'*Solidare* (1) confirmare, asserere; (2) firmare, munire; (3) stipendium praebere.' Thus the Low Lat. *solidare* answers both to the verb *souden* in the text, and to the Eng. *solder*, to fasten, in which the *l* is dropped in ordinary pronunciation. And we may note a similar dropping of the *l* in the derived word *sowdears*, i.e. hirelings, soldiers (see *Sowdears* in Halliwell), and in the common pronunciation, *sodgers*, of the same word. See also note to l. 447.

432. *Wel worthe;* see note to Pass. xiv. 1. *Porsueth*, follows, imitates. See Matt. v. 45.

434. *Sent*, short for *sendeth*, sends; the present tense.

436. Here Piers the Plowman is completely identified with the agriculturist, with sole reference to ordinary agricultural work, as in Pass. ix. 112–121. Cf. Gascoigne's Steel Glas, ll. 1017–1050; in Spec. of English, 1394–1579, ed. Skeat, p. 320.

443. *Suffreth*, bears with; as when we say of God, that He is 'long-suffering.'

447. *Fyndeth*, provides with necessaries, provides for; not very different in sense from *soudeth*, pays, in l. 431; see the Glossary. It is not clear whether the allusion is to the crusades which the popes encouraged, or to the blood shed in the war which took place between the partisans of pope and anti-pope. If the latter, the B-text (A.D. 1377) can hardly have been completed till the end of 1378. The English took the side of Urban VI., the pope of Rome, as against Clement VII., the anti-pope of Avignon.

I find two passages in Wyclif in which he inveighs against the pope as an encourager of war; see his Works, iii. 140, 330.

448. *Luk*, St. Luke. St. Luke 'bears witness' by quoting the words of the 'old law.' *Non occides* occurs in Luke xviii. 20 (Vulgate), and in Exod. xx. 13. And see Heb. x. 30.

455. *But hit soune*, unless it tend [c]; *But if þei seiȝe*, unless they should see [b]; where *seiȝe* is the past tense subjunctive. The alteration is very striking. It looks as if our author had (before revising his poem) become acquainted with Chaucer's Prologue—' Sownynge alway thencrees of his winninge;' l. 275. In fact, he could hardly have done otherwise, as his C-text was not written till A.D. 1393 at the earliest.

456. 'Of guile and of lying they make no account;' i.e. they do not hesitate to deceive.

465. (19. 460.) Whitaker remarks—'These Reeve-Rolls, of which I have seen some, little later than our author's time, consisted, for one year, of several sheets stitched together, and contained very curious and minute details of all the receipts and expenses of these officers. There was more order and exactness in the economy of our old nobility than we are apt to imagine.'

466. 'And with the spirit of Strength I fetch it, whether the reeve likes it, or not' [c]; *or*, 'I will fetch it' [b]. Compare Rob. of Brunne, Handl. Synne, l. 4416.

467. *By hus croune*, with reference to his crown. See note (on *by*) to Pass. i. 78, p. 11.

471. *Hastelokest*, most hastily, soonest; cf. *wisloker*, more certainly, more carefully, B. xiii. 343. Cf. the form *hardyloker*, C. 17. 103. The suffix *-loker* (for *-liker*) answers to the modern suffix *-lier*.

473. *Youre alre hefd*, the head of you all. *Youre alre hele*, the health (or safety) of you all. In l. 390 above, *hele* signifies salvation.

481. '*Then* (I grant) that thou mayest have what thou askest for, as the law requires,' [c]; 'Thou mayest take in reason,' etc. [b]. The change is very significant; the king is no longer to *take*, but to *ask for* what he wants. Richard II. was rapidly falling into disgrace.

I do not know whence the Latin quotation is taken. It looks like a maxim which William had picked up in the law-courts at Westminster.

482. *Hadde fer hom*, had far (to go to get) home.

483. *As me mette*, as I dreamed. Here ends the Tenth Vision, or the Vision of Grace.

NOTES TO C. PASSUS XXIII. (B. Pass. XX.)

23. 2. *Elynge*, sad, solitary; see note to Pass. i. 204, p. 18. And see l. 39 below.

4. 'And I met with Need.' The poet more than once thus describes himself as meeting with allegorical personages during his waking moments. Thus, in Pass. vi. 6, he meets with Reason. The last Vision does not really begin till l. 51 below. See note to l. 51.

7. 'That you took (things) to live upon, for your food and clothing.'

10. Alluding to the proverb—'Necessitas non habet legem.' See note to Pass. xiv. 45, p. 174.

11. The three necessary things are meat, drink, and clothing; see note to Pass. ii. 20, p. 21. See a curious passage in the Romaunt of the Rose, ll. 6717-6760, on the conditions which render begging allowable.

12. 'That is, (firstly) meat, when people refuse to give it him because he possesses no money.'

14. *And*, if. *Cacche*, take [c]; *caughte*, were to take [b].

21. For the counsel of Conscience, see Pass. xxii. 383-397. For the Cardinal Virtues, see Pass. xxii. 274-310.

22. 'Provided that he follow and preserve the spirit of Moderation.'

34. See Pass. xii. 304, and the note, p. 165.

35. 'Next him is Need.' That is, the highest virtue is that of Temperance or Moderation, and the next thing that controls a man's actions is Necessity, which is subordinate to Temperance, but to no other Virtue.

37. 'For Need makes needy men humble, on account of their wants.'

43. 'On the cross itself.' A singular mistake; the saying belongs to a much earlier period of our Lord's life.

46. 'Whereas Necessity has so seized me that I must needs stay,' etc.

49. *Wilfulliche*, willingly, by choice. The usual old sense of *wilful* is *voluntary*. The sense of the word is remarkably shewn in Batman vppon Bartholomè, lib. 7, cap. 13:—'A Cramp is a violent shrinking of sinewes, taking aweye and hindering *wilfull* moouing,' i. e. voluntary motion. See Trench's Select Glossary, s. v. *Wilful;* Richardson's Dictionary, s. v. *Wilfully;* etc.

50. See Pass. xi. 193, 194.

51. Here begins the Eleventh (and last) Vision, or the Vision of Antichrist.

53. *Antecrist*, Antichrist. 'It is not improbable that Langland here had his eye on the old French *Roman d'Antechrist*, a poem written by Huon de Meri, about the year 1228. The author of this piece supposes that Antichrist is on earth, that he visits every profession and order of life, and finds numerous partisans. The Vices arrange themselves under the banner of Antichrist, and the Virtues under that of Christ. These two armies at length come to an engagement, and the battle ends to the honour of the Virtues, and the total defeat of the Vices..... The title of Huon de Meri's poem deserves notice. It is [*Le*] *Turnoyement de l'Antechrist.....* The author appears to have been a monk of St. Germain des Pres, near Paris. This allegory is much like that which we find in the old dramatic Moralities. The theology of the middle ages abounded with conjectures and controversies concerning Antichrist, who at a very early period was commonly believed to be the Roman pontiff. See this topic discussed with singular penetration and perspicuity by Dr. Hurd, in Twelve Sermons Introductory to the Study of the Prophecies, 1772, p. 206, seq.'—Warton, Hist. Eng. Poetry, ed. 1840, ii. 60 ; or ed. 1871, ii. 263. Mr. Wright has also given some account of de Meri's poem in his St. Patrick's Purgatory, pp. 113, 114. It is printed at length in P. Tarbè's Poètes de Champagne, vol. xv. A comparison of it with our text shews no close resemblance of language, but only a certain similarity of ideas.

Wyclif compared the pope to Antichrist more than once; see his Works, i. 138, ii. 394, iii. 341.

54. *Tyte*, quickly [c]; ingeniously substituted for *it* [b].

69. Pride, as the chief of the Seven Deadly Sins, is rightly made to bear Antichrist's banner. Cf. Pass. xxii. 337; also Robert of Brunne's Handlyng Synne, l. 3406.

71. *A lorde;* this is the personification of Lechery. See ll. 90, 114 ; and cf. Pass. vii. 170.

75. Unity or Holy-church is the castle into which the followers of Conscience retreat ; see Pass. xxii. 359. This is well illustrated by the fine illuminated picture called The Fortress of Faith, copied from a miniature of the 15th century, at p. 408 of Military and Religious Life in the Middle Ages, by P. Lacroix. 'The fortress, besieged by the impious and the heretics, is defended by the Pope, the bishops, the monks, and the doctors, who are the Chevaliers of the Faith.'

I may remark that the author of The Reply of Friar Daw Topias (printed in Political Poems, ed. Wright, vol. ii. pp. 57, 58) seems to have read our author's account of Antichrist's battle-array carefully. He thus addresses the Wycliffites—

'It ar ȝe that stonden bifore in Anticristis vanwarde,
And in the myddil and in the rerewarde ful bigly enbatailid;
The devel is ȝour duke, and pride berith the baner,' etc.

76. *Kynde*, Nature. Conscience supposes that Nature, for love of Piers the Plowman, will assist men against spiritual foes. But the result is represented as being very different; for Nature also becomes man's enemy, afflicting him with various bodily diseases; see l. 80. Yet Nature is, at last, man's true friend; see l. 109.

80. Nature is represented as coming 'out of the planets,' because diseases were supposed to be due to planetary influence. 'Whan the planetes ben vnder thilke signes, thei causen vs by hir influence operaciouns and effectes lik to the operaciouns of bestes;' Chaucer, Astrolabie, pt. i. sect. 21, l. 41. Warton well compares the catalogue of diseases here given with that in Milton, Paradise Lost, xi. 474.

82. *Cardiacles*, spasms of the heart. The word has already occurred in Pass. vii. 78. It occurs also in Chaucer's Pardoner's Prologue; in the Prologue to the Tale of Beryn, ed. Furnivall, l. 493; etc. Cotgrave gives, as one of the meanings of Fr. *cardiaque*—'a consumption, and continuall sweat, by the indisposition of the heart, and parts about it.' Batman vppon Bartholomè, lib. 7. cap. 13, has a chapter 'Of the Crampe;' and lib. 7. cap. 32 is 'Of heart-quaking, and the disease *cardiacle*.' Ducange has—'*Cordiacus*, (1) qui patitur morbum cordis; (2) morbus ipse.'

Cramps could be cured, it was supposed, by the use of cramp-rings; see note to Pass. vii. 78, p. 76.

83. *Reumes*, rheums, colds and catarrhs. *Radegoundes*, running sores; especially used of sore eyes. The word is, apparently, compounded of *reed*, red, and *gound* (A.S. *gund*), matter of a sore. The A.S. *gund* occurs, for example, in the compound *healsgund*, scrofula, lit. neck-sore. The fourth chapter of part 1 of the A.S. Leechdoms has a title beginning 'Læce-cræftas wiþ healsgunde,' i. e. remedies against scrofula; Wanley's Catalogue of A.S. MSS. p. 176. The Prompt. Parv., p. 206, has—'Gownde of the eye, *ridda, albugo;*' on which Way notes—'Skinner gives the word *gound* as used very commonly in Lincolnshire, signifying the running or impure secretion of the eyes. It occurs in the glosses on G. de Biblesworth, Arundel MS. 220, fol. 297 b—"*Vostre regardz est gracious* (louelik), *Mes vos oeyz sunt saciouz* (gundy); *Des oeez outez la sacye* (þe gunde), *E de nees la rupye* (þe maldrope)." Bp. Kennett, in his glossarial collection, Lansd. MS. 1033, has the following note: "Gunded eyes, Westm. Goundy,

filthy like running sores, Gower. Gunny eyes, Yorksh. Dial." A. S. *gund*, pus, sanies. Skelton describes the "eyen gowndye" of Elynour Rumming.' See Dyce's Skelton, i. 96, l. 34, and the note; also the Prompt. Parv., p. 426; and Way's note. In the modern word *red-gum*, the latter element is an ingenious substitution for the A. S. *gund*, which has become obsolete.

The spelling *radegoundes* in the MSS. of both texts and generally elsewhere makes it very probable that the word was sometimes corrupted in yet another way; viz. by confusion with a proper name, that of St. Radegund. Nothing was more common than to suppose that certain saints could cure certain sores; see the list of saints and ailments in Chambers, Book of Days, ii. 389. St. Radegund, the wife of Lothaire I. of France, died Aug. 13, 587. Her life is in the Aurea Legenda, ed. Grässe, cap. ccxl. (otherwise 211); and see Fabyan's Chronicle, ed. Ellis, p. 79. Her skill in performing miracles is dilated upon in the Knight of Latour Landry, ed. Wright, p. 114, where her name is oddly corrupted into 'seint Aragon that was quene of Fraunce.'

92. *Alarme*, to arms! The early use of this word is remarkable.

Lyf, a living wight, as frequently before. There is, too, a play upon the word. *Eche lyf kepe hus owene* (*lyf*), let each living wight save his own (life).

100. This is one of the finest passages in the poem. In modern spelling it is—

> 'Death came driving after, and all to dust pashed
> Kings and knights, kaisers and popes;
> Learned nor lewd, he left no man to stand;
> They that he hit evenly stirred never after.
> Many a lovely lady and their lemans, knights,
> Swooned and swelted, for sorrow of death's dints.'

109. 'And Nature ceased (her plagues) then, to see the people amend.' This passage is ironical; for, as Mr. Wright well remarks, 'the allusion is to the dissipation of manners which followed the pestilence.' Cf. Pass. xi. 272. And see note to l. 150 below.

114. The author once more recurs to the favourite topic of the Seven Deadly Sins (cf. Pass. vii.), and mentions Lechery in l. 114, Avarice in l. 121, and Sloth in ll. 159, 217; having already mentioned Pride in l. 70. See also l. 215, where the 'Sins' are called 'geauntes.'

126. 'Simony followed him' [c]; 'Simony sent him,' i.e. Avarice [b]. See Chaucer's remarks on simony in his Pers. Tale, *De Auaritia;* and cf. Pass. iii. 72, 181.

127. 'Pressed on the pope,' i.e. used his influence with the pope [c]; 'Preached to the people' [b]. A remarkable variation.

130. 'And beat Conscience' [c]; 'And submitted (hypocritically) to Conscience' [b]. Another striking change in tone.

133. 'The law-courts have been held at Westminster from the earliest Anglo-Norman times, it being the king's chief palace;' Wright's note. Cf. Pass. iii. 174.

134. This is a humorous allusion to a sort of mock tournament. Simony runs a tilt at the justice's ear, and by a crafty whisper of a bribe overturns all his ideas of truth and justice. He accompanies his offer of money with the words—'take this [deed, and at the same time this money] on amendment;' meaning, 'surely you can amend this.' *Iogged til*, jogged on towards, rode leisurely towards; with a glance at the use of *jog* in the sense of to nudge a half-sleeping man. Compare the remark in Barclay's Ship of Fools, ed. Jamieson, i. 25, 'That aungels worke wonders in westmynster hall.' *Aungels* or *angels* are the gold coins so called.

136. 'The court of the arches was a very ancient consistory court of the archbishop of Canterbury, held at Bow Church in London, which was called St. Mary de Arcubus or St. Mary le Bow, from the circumstance of its having been built on arches;' Wright's note. Cf. Pass. iii. 61, 186.

137. 'And turned Civil (the civil law) into Simony,' i.e. made it subservient to simoniacal purposes; cf. Pass. iii. 71, 127, 183. *He tok*, he gave to, i.e. gave some bribe to; in other words, he bribed. See *tok* as used in Pass. iv. 47, and the note thereon, at p. 41.

139. An allusion to the (old) form of words in the Marriage Service— 'till death us *depart*,' i.e. separate us; now altered to 'do part.'

143. *Lowh*, laughed. *Lyf*, Life. It must be carefully noticed that the poet here describes, by the name of Life, a man of fashion of the period. *Let dagge his clothes*, caused his clothes to be 'dagged,' i.e. curiously cut. See Rich. Redeles, iii. 193; and the well-known passage from Chaucer's Persones Tale on the 'superfluite of clotheynge.' In the Prompt. Parv., p. 111, we have—'Dagge of clothe, *fractillus;*' and, at p. 255—'Iagge or dagge of a garment, *fractillus;*' see Way's notes on these words. The fashion of jagging, or cutting in slits, the borders of garments was much in vogue at this period, and indeed for some time afterwards, as may be seen in any work on costume. It was a favourite subject for satire.

146. *Let*, considered; 'considered Loyalty as but a churl,' i.e. a slave.

148. 'Thus Life rallied (i.e. became presumptuous) because of a little good fortune.' Cf. note to l. 109 above.

150. The Black Death was followed by a singular recklessness of conduct on the part of the survivors; 'in the same way as the surviving inhabitants of Lisbon became more dissolute after their earthquake, and the Athenians after the plague by which their city was afflicted; see Thucydides, bk. ii.'—Dunlop's Hist. of Fiction, on the Decameron of Boccaccio. See the remarks of Warton on this subject; Hist. Eng. Poetry, ed. 1871, ii. 355.

154. 'Shall cause thee not to fear either death or old age.' Life is addressing Fortune.

155. *Yyue nauht of*, care nothing about; i.e. be reckless as to.

160. *Wanhope*, despair. William makes Wanhope the spouse of Sloth, because they were considered to be in close relationship. In Chaucer's Pers. Tale, *De Accidia*, we find—' Now cometh *wanhope*, that is, despeir of the mercy of God ... Which dampnable sinne, if it continue unto his end, it is cleped the sinne of [i. e. against] the holy gost.' Cf. Pass. viii. 81. The Dutch form, *wanhoop*, is still in use.

162. 'One Tom Two-tongued, attainted at each inquest.' This Tom Two-tongued (*or* Two-tongue, *b*) is the opposite of Tom True-tongue, mentioned in Pass. v. 18.

167. Here Elde (Old Age), who had formerly fought under Death's banner on the side of the Vices, is now shriven, and takes the side of the Virtues, though still fighting against Life. The poet has rather clumsily used *good hope* in this line in its usual sense, whilst *wanhope* in the next line is a personification. Thus the line means—'And Old Age laid hold of good hope, and hastily shrove himself' [c] ; *or*, 'hastily he shifted his ground' [b]. Cf. 'good heorte he hente,' i. e. he plucked up courage, in l. 180 below.

169. 'Life fled for fear to Physic for help.' Cf. Pass. ix. 292.

170. 'And besought him for aid, and had some of his salve.'

171. *Good won*, a good quantity. 'Woone, or grete plente, *copia*, *habundancia*;' Prompt. Parv., p. 532, and see Way's note. The word is not uncommon ; see *wân* in Stratmann.

172. 'And they gave him in return a glass cap ;' lit. a glass hood. The sense of this phrase is 'an imaginary protection ;' something that seemed a defence, but was really frail and inefficient. The expression is ironical, and was probably proverbial, much as we speak of living 'in glass houses.' There are at least two other examples of its use. In the Debate between the Soul and Body, printed in Mätzner's Alteng. Sprachproben, i. 98, the Soul reproaches the body, saying—

'That thou louedest me thouȝ lete,
And madest me an *houue of glas*;
I dide al that the was sete,
And thou my traytor euer was.'

I. e. Thou didst pretend that thou lovedst me ; and thou madest me a glass hood ; I did all that was sweet to thee, and thou wast ever a traitor to me. (In this passage the Vernon MS. reads *swete* for *sete*.) Here the phrase 'madest me a glass hood' obviously means 'didst lull me into a state of false security.'

Again, in a passage in Chaucer (first explained by myself), viz. in Troilus and Cressida, v. 469, Fortune is said to have an intention of deluding Troilus ; or, as the poet puts it—'Fortune his *howue* intended bet *to glase*,' i. e. Fortune intended to *glaze his hood* still better for him, i. e. to make a still greater fool of him.

We may also note another passage in Chaucer's Troil. and Cress., bk. ii. l. 867 (Aldine edition, vol. iv. p. 188), where there is an allusion to a similar proverb :—

'And forthy, who that hath an hede of verre
Fro caste of stones war him in the werre.'

I. e. And therefore, let him who has a *head of glass* beware of the casting of great stones in war.

See also my note on *vitremyte*, in Chaucer's Cant. Tales, B. 3562 in the Clarendon Press edition of Chaucer's Prioresses Tale, etc.

Glasen is the adj. from *glas*. In the Praier and Complaint of the Ploughman, printed in the Harleian Miscellany, vi. 103, we read of 'greet stonen houses full of *glasene* windowes.'

173. 'Life believed that medical skill would stop (*or* delay) Old Age.'

174. *To-dryue*, drive away; infin. mood. *Dyas and drogges*, remedies and drugs. The word *dia* has been already explained in the note to Pass. vii. 88, p. 77; which see. I may add that Burton, in his Anatomy of Melancholy, pt. 2, sect. 4, mem. 1, subsect. 5, mentions various conserves and confections, some hot, such as 'diambra, diamargaritum calidum, dianthus, diamoschum dulce, ... diagalinga, diacyminum, dianisum, diatrion piperion,' etc. The term *diachylon* is still in use.

Dragges (drugs) were used by Chaucer's Doctor of Phisik; Prologue, 426.

175. *Auntred hym on*, adventured himself against; a term of the tournament.

176. *Forrede*, furred; see Pass. ix. 292.

183. There is here a singular and sudden change. Old Age, hasting after Life, encounters the poet on his way. As a result, we hear no more about Life, but the poet contents himself with narrating the result of his own *personal* encounter with Old Age. Old Age begins by passing over the poet's head, rendering him bald.

186. *Vuel-ytauht*, evil taught, ill-instructed. *Vnhende*, ill manners go with thee; lit. let ill-mannered fellows go with thee: see l. 188.

189. *3e*, yea, to be sure! an ironical form of assent. *Leue lordeyn*, dear sluggard! 'Lurdayne, *lourdault*;' Palsgrave.

196. *Naked*. See note to B. xiv. 2, p. 204. See some curious verses on Old Age, printed in Reliq. Antiq., ii. 210.

203. *Hennes*, hence, i.e. out of this life; see Pass. x. 53, 348.

204. *Unite*, Unity or Holy Church, the castle of Conscience; see Pass. xxii. 330.

210. *And*, if. *Lacke þe*, fail thee.

215. *Geauntes*, giants; i.e. the Seven Deadly Sins; see note to l. 114 above.

219. *Paltokes*, cloaks; see note to Pass. xxi. 24, p. 250. *Pikede shoes*, peaked shoes; see note to Pass. xxi. 12, p. 249.

Pissares. In the Phil. Soc. Trans. for 1859, p. 72, two guesses are made as to the sense of this word. First, that it is a corruption of *pistor*, a baker, which is plainly incredible; and secondly, that it means a fisherman, from the O. Fr. *pischer*, to fish (Roquefort), which is equally stupid. William knew perfectly well how to say *bakere* or *fisher* without turning the words into *false* Old French. Surely the word expresses exactly what the sound tells us, and is equivalent to a familiar Biblical expression for 'every male;' 1 Kings xiv. 10; xvi. 11. It was, I suppose, a cant term, or nickname, given neither to *bakers* nor *fisher-*

men, but (as the context requires) to *soldiers* or *armed retainers*, notable in those days for coarse insolence. The fault of the priests here inveighed against is that they wore 'long knives' or swords like soldiers. The knife itself had what was probably a cant name; see B. xv. 121. I do not think there need be much difficulty here.

221. *Mansed*, cursed; see note to Pass. iii. 41, p. 33. *Was*, who was.

223. Compare the expression—'An 'twere not as good a deed as drink;' 1 Henry IV., ii. 1. 33; 2. 23.

225. *Othes*. It is remarkable that the horrible swearing then so prevalent is here charged upon the Irish priests. Wyclif refers to 'comyn swereris by Goddis herte, bonys, nailis, and sidis, and oþere membris;' Works, iii. 332. Chaucer says—'For Cristes sake, swere not so sinnefully, in dismembring of Crist, by soule, herte, bones, and body;' Pers. Tale, *De Ira*.

228. The rest of this Passus, from this point to the end, has been paraphrased by Drayton, in his Legend of Thomas Cromwell, Earl of Essex. He makes the usual stupid blunder of taking Piers the Plowman to be the name of the *author*.

232. *Neode*, Need, Poverty; who appeared at the beginning of the Passus; ll. 4-50.

236. *Chile*, chilliness, cold; as in B. i. 23.

237. *Chewe*, eat, feed. Cf. Pass. ii. 191; and note to xxi. 404, p. 262.

238. *Lommere he lyeth*, he tells lies oftener. The word *lomere* [b] is glossed, in the B-text, by *sæpius*, shewing that it was obsolescent. For examples of *lome*, i. e. often, see Stratmann.

252. Francis and Dominick were respectively the founders of the Grey and Black Friars. See notes to B. xv. 413, and to Pass. v. 117.

256. See Ps. cxlvi. 4 (Vulgate); cxlvii. 4 (A. V.).

261. Lines 37 and 261 are peculiar to the C-text.

262. *Brybours*, robbers; such is the old sense of the word. See Marsh's Lectures on the Eng. Language, repr. in Smith's Manual of Eng. Language, p. 169; also *Bribe* in Trench's Select Glossary.

263. *Pilours*, strippers of the dead; Ch. Kn. Tale, l. 149. *Pykeherneys*, plunderers of armour, men who stole armour (formerly called *harness*) from the slain in battle. In the Towneley Mysteries, *Pikeharnes* is the name given to Cain's serving-boy. Cf. *picker* in the sense of thief.

265. *A certayn numbre*, a fixed number. For example, the charter of foundation of Sion Monastery ordained that the establishment should consist of 60 nuns, including the abbess, and of 25 religious men; Myrour of Our Lady, ed. Blunt, Pref. p. xvi. A common number in a religious house was 13, in remembrance of our Lord and his apostles; see Chaucer, C. T. 7841; Chambers, Book of Days, i. 104.

269. *Oute of numbre*. Chaucer, in his Wyf of Bathes Tale, l. 12, declares that the friars were 'As thikke as motes in the sonne-beme,' and that their omnipresence had driven away all the fairies. Wyclif

says that 'not two hundrid ȝeere agone þer was no frere ... And now ben *mony thousande* of freris in Englond;' Works, iii. 400.

270. *Euene numbre;* an allusion to Rev. vii. 4-8. But the next verse (Rev. vii. 9) tells us differently. The statement that 'hell is without number' is an allusion to Job x. 22—'terram miseriae et tenebrarum, ubi umbra mortis, et *nullus ordo*, sed sempiternus horror inhabitat.' This is referred to again in Chaucer's Pers. Tale (Prima Pars Penitentiae), where he says—'And eke Job seith, that in helle is non ordre of rule. And al be it so, that God hath create al thing in right ordre, and nothing withouten ordre, but alle thinges ben ordred and numbred, yet natheles they that ben dampned ben nothing in ordre, ne hold non ordre.'

Cf. the Reply of Friar Daw Topias (pr. in Polit. Poems, ii. 105).

275. Whitaker remarks here:—'The introduction of heathen morality is an old evil in Christian pulpits. On this subject the old and modern bard sympathise with each other:—

"How oft, when Paul hath given us a text,
    Do Epictetus, Plato, Tully preach."—COWPER.'

277. Observe this emphatic renunciation, on the poet's part, of the principles of communism. It is clear that he protests here against the scandalous, yet not unnatural, use that had been made of his poem by John Ball and other such preachers; and here plainly disavows all sympathy with unprincipled and thoughtless rioters. See Exod. xx. 17.

284. 'Shame makes men flee to the friars,' instead of going to be shriven by their own parish priest. See note to Pass. vii. 120, p. 78.

William says of the 'fals folke' that they borrow money, and take it to Westminster, viz. to bribe the judges with (see ll. 131-139 above); and then they earnestly beg their friends to forgive the debt, or grant them a longer time for repayment. Yet whilst they are in Westminster, they make merry with the officials, whom they treat with the borrowed money. Similarly, he says, executors give some of the deceased man's money to the friars; and having done this, they safely appropriate the remainder.

293. 'And leave the dead man (still) in debt, till doomsday.' The friars and executors shared the money, whilst the creditors remained unpaid.

299. *Titereres in ydel*, tattlers in an idle manner, idle tattlers. The Prompt. Parv. has—'Tateryn, or iaueryn, or speke wythe-owte resone, or iangelyn, chateryn, iaberyn, *garrio, blatero*.' The word *titeren* is related to *tateren* just as *tittle* is to *tattle*, and expresses the same thing in a less degree or more suppressed manner. To *tittle* is *to tattle secretly*, and so to *titter* is here to *tatter* in a subdued manner. In modern English, to *titter* means to giggle, to laugh in a subdued manner.

304. It has been remarked that William seems to have been somewhat indebted to Huon de Meri for his description of Antichrist's army; see note to l. 53 above. It is probable that he has here also taken a few

ideas from that poem. Compare the following passage, printed in the Poètes de Champagne, ed. P. Tarbé, vol. xv. p. 91—

> 'Lors me semont Conpunccion
> Et Dévocion sa cosine
> Que j'alasse querre medicine . . . . .
> Dont ma Dame Confession
> Une merveilleuse oncion
> Me fist; et tant s'umelia
> Qu'ele meismes me lia
> Sor mes plaies molt doucement.'

See also ll. 356–361 below.

308. 'And (took care) that Piers' pardon was paid, (according to the precept)—"pay what thou owest."' See Pass. xxii. 187, 193.

320. Here Piers the Plowman is Christ, the true Head of the Church, having power to grant indulgences to all who have paid their debts, i.e. who have tried to perform all duties.

324. The whole description of friar Flatterer in ll. 324–372 is in the poet's best manner.

335. *Ful hard;* 'it is a very unlikely thing that they will recover.'

340. Alluding to the text—'Ex his enim sunt, qui *penetrant domos*, et captiuas ducunt mulierculas oneratas peccatis, quae ducuntur uariis desideriis;' 2 Tim. iii. 6.

351, 352. 'That Life [the man of fashion, *note to l.* 143] shall, through his teaching, give up Avarice, and (cease) to be afraid of Death;' etc.

353. 'And agree with Conscience, and either (i.e. each) of them kiss the other.'

359. Plaisters were much in use; see note to Pass. xx. 89, p. 244. Whitaker observes upon this line—'There is an impropriety in this; it was not the part of Conscience to complain that the parish-priest was too severe a confessor.'

367. One more allusion to the 'letters of fraternity;' see notes to Pass. iv. 67, and Pass. x. 343, pp. 42, 130.

378. 'Flatereres ben the deueles *enchauntours*, for thei maken a man wenen himself be like that he is nought like . . . . Flattreres ben the deueles chapeleynes, that euer singen *Placebo;*' Chaucer, Pers. Tale, *De Ira.*

379. In the B-text, the author has omitted the alliteration; in the C-text, he has completely amended the line.

Dwale, an opiate, a sleeping-draught. Chaucer, in his Milleres Tale, says of the tired household that they 'needed no *dwale;*' Cant. Tales, ed. Tyrwhitt, l. 4159. The Prompt. Parv. has—'Dwale, herbe, *morella somnifera, morella mortifera;*' and see Way's note, p. 134. Mr. Way says that Chaucer 'makes repeated allusion to the somniferous qualities of the nightshade, or dwale, the *Atropa belladonna.*' I only know of *one* allusion in Chaucer, viz. the one just cited. The word occurs again, however, in the Court of Love, l. 998, a poem once strangely attributed to Chaucer. Johns, in his Flowers of the Field, says—'*Atropa bella-donna* (Deadly Nightshade, Dwale). . . . Buchanan relates that the Scots mixed the juice of Belladonna with the bread and drink, with which by their truce they were supposed to supply the Danes, which so intoxicated them, that the Scots killed the greater part of Sweno's army while asleep.'

Dwale, something *stupefying* or *causing delirium*, being connected with the A. S. *dwolung*, dotage, *dwala*, an error, *gedwola*, an error, *gedwolman*, an impostor, *gedwolsum*, erroneous, *gedwælan*, to deceive, *dwelian* or *dwolian*, to err, also to deceive; with the Dutch *dwalen*, to err, *dwaaltuin*, a labyrinth, *dwaallicht*, a will-of-the-wisp; Dan. *dvale*, a trance, torpor, stupor, *dvale-drik*, a soporific (dwale-drink); O. H. G. *twalmgetrank*, a soporific (dwale-drink); *twalm*, enchantment. It is allied to E. *dull* and *dwell*.

There is a remarkable passage in the A. S. poem of St. Andrew (ed. Grein, l. 33) which is worth quoting in connection with the present passage:—

'Syððan him gebléondan bitere tósomne
drýas þurh *dwolcræft* drync unheórne
se onwende gewit, wera ingeþanc.'

I. e. 'Then they blended for them bitterly together,
These magicians, by magic art, a horrible drink
Which perverted the wit, the mind of the men.'

383. *Hadden*, might have; subj. mood. *Fyndynge*, provision. On which Pecock, in his Repressor, ed. Babington, ii. 390, remarks—'this word *fynding*, forto speke of such *fynding* as is mynystring of costis and expensis and other necessarie or profitable thingis into that a certeyn deede be doon and executid'—which is sufficient to shew that it properly means 'provision for all necessary purposes only.'

386. *Gradde*, cried aloud; from A. S. *grǽdan*, to cry out. *After grace*, for God's favour.

Here the poem ends. Conscience, hard beset by Pride and Sloth, has besought Contrition to come and help him; but Contrition slumbers, benumbed by the deadly potion with which the flattering friar has enchanted him. With a last effort Conscience arouses himself, and seizes his pilgrim's staff, determined to wander wide over the world till he shall find Piers the Plowman, the true Saviour of mankind. His last loud cry for God's help awakes the sleeper from his Vision.

Dr. Whitaker suggested that the poem is not perfect; that it must have been designed to have a more satisfactory ending, and not one so suggestive of disappointment and gloom. I am convinced that this opinion is erroneous; not so much from the fact that nearly all the MSS. have here the word *Explicit*, as from the very nature of the case. What other ending can there be? or rather, the end is not yet. We may be defeated, yet not cast down; we may be dying, and behold, we live. We are all still pilgrims upon earth. *This* is the truth which the author's mighty genius would impress upon us in his parting words.

Just as the poet awakes in ecstacy at the end of the poem of Dobet, where he dreams of that which has been already accomplished, so here he is awoke by the cry of Conscience for help, and is silent at the thought of how much remains to be done. So far from ending carelessly, he seems to me to have ceased speaking at the right moment, and to have managed a very difficult matter with consummate skill.

NOTES

TO

'RICHARD THE REDELESS.'

NOTES TO THE PROLOGUE.

THE parallel passages in the Vision are cited in the footnotes, which see.

2. *Bristow*, Bristol. It was from Bristol that Richard set sail for Ireland, and it was there that Henry gave one of the first proofs of his power, by the execution of Lord Scrope and others; see note to Pass. ii. 152 below.

3, 4. An allusion to the Church of the Holy Trinity, described in Barrett's Bristol, p. 464. It was in the very centre of the old town, at one of the corners where the four principal streets, High Street, Broad Street, Corn Street, and Wine Street met. See a plan of Bristol in 1479 in Ricart's Kalendar, edited by Miss L. T. Smith for the Camden Society, p. 10.

10. *wild Yrisshe*. This was a common phrase, and occurs several times in a poem entitled—'Of the commodities of Irelonde, and policye and kepynge therof, and conquerynge of *wylde Iryshe*.' See Polit. Poems, ed. Wright, ii. 185. See also the French Chronicle of the Betrayal and Death of Richard II., ed. B. Williams, p. 171; Spenser, View of the State of Ireland; and A. Borde's Introduction of Knowledge, ed. Furnivall, pp. 132, 334.

11. *On the est halfe*, on the Eastern side of England, viz. near Ravenspurgh in Yorkshire, where Henry landed on the 4th of July, 1399. (This is a fresh proof, were any needed, of the absurdity of Froissart's statement as to the landing of Henry at Plymouth.) Richard returned from Ireland to England about the 25th of July, landing (as it would appear) at Harlech. See note to Shakespeare's Rich. II., ed. Clark and Wright, Act iii. Sc. 2. The French Chronicle edited by Mr. B. Williams gives this date as August 13, which seems far more likely; for else we have to suppose that Henry took several weeks to find Richard, which is improbable.

5. *sourdid*, arose; from O.F. *sourdre*, Lat. *surgere;* it occurs in Chaucer.

NOTES TO RICHARD THE REDELESS: PROLOGUE.

8. 'So violent (or angry) were the sayings on both sides.' No doubt much partisanship was displayed, and great differences of opinion arose.

14. *serue* commonly means to *deserve;* but here it is, 'that he should serve them the same,' viz. by righting *their* wrongs.

17. Observe the author's uncertainty as to the end of it all; cf. ll. 24, 27.

19. 'Some repented;' i.e. those who had applauded Henry's acts at Bristol began to turn again to Richard. L. 21 means that they expressed their opinion 'that it was a pity the king's reason had not enabled him to reform the misrule from which the country suffered.'

22. *in endurid*, continued in. Read *in durede; endurid* is a mere gloss upon *durede*, and makes the line halt.

33. *preise*, praise. I think *preie* (pray) would be better.

37. 'And if it please him to peruse a leaf or two (of this treatise), that is written to amend him.'

41. *grame*, (I would) be sorry, be vexed.

42. The sense passes on to l. 45, ll. 43 and 44 being parenthetical. 'Every prince might learn from my words; yea, every Christian king that wears a crown might do so, if he only could read English.'

47. *my beste*, i.e. the best I have.

49. *and I couthe*, i.e. if I could, if I knew how.

53. *ʒoure*, i.e. the *king's* hand. Sovereigns were addressed as *ye;* equals as *thou*. So *ʒe* is used below; and hence also the use of the *plural* imperative *redeth*.

54. *rewis an hundrid*, a hundred rows or lines.

61. 'For at present it is secret, and so it shall remain some time longer, till wiser men have looked it over.' The author's intention was to get some friend to correct it before it should be presented to the king. But the course of events defeated his wishes.

66. 'To take away their *ennui*, that so often bores them.' For young people to be soon 'bored' is nothing new.

69. 'Since youth always supposes it [i.e. fault-finding, criticism] to be (a proof of) wisdom.'

72. *with the culorum*, with the sequel thereof; see Glossary.

73. 'It would not hurt them a whit.' *A peere* means *a pear*, i.e. to the extent of the value of a pear; just as we say not worth a *kerse*, i.e. a blade of grass; for which phrase see P. Pl. B. x. 17. The expression 'not worth a pere' occurs in Morte Arthure, Bk. xv. Cap. vi.; Globe edition, p. 377.

80. *be*, the subjunctive or imperative mood; 'may it never be my will.' So in l. 85, *ho be* is 'whosoever may be.'

82. Probably a direct allusion to the 'Vision;' particularly to the strife between Poverty and the Seven Deadly Sins in C. Pass. xvii. 58, etc.

NOTES TO PASSUS I.

1. *Richard the redeles*, i. e. devoid of counsel. Such is also the true meaning of the title *Unready* as applied to Æthelred; see Freeman, Old Eng. Hist. for Children, p. 190. Cf. note above to Prol. l. 53.

2. *leddyn*, for *ledden*, 2 p. pl.; used with a double meaning; viz. *led* your life and *ruled* your people.

4. *y-lyfte*, lifted, removed. Mr. Wright prints *y-lyste*, with the explanation 'listed, taken;' which I do not understand, unless it means that *listed* is put for *enlisted*. But this would hardly be the language of the fourteenth century.

11. An enumeration of things that do *not* promote allegiance amongst subjects, viz. dread or awe, blows, unjust judgments, bad coinage, pillage of the people, self-will of the king, taxes imposed in time of peace and exacted by ruthless plunderers.

17. Here *preysinge* obviously means *appraising*, as in C. 7. 384; *of* means *by means of;* and *polaxis* is put for the men who used them, viz. the king's officers; see Pass. iii. 328. They appraised the goods of the king's subjects at whatever value was most convenient.

18. 'Or whether by the debts thou contractest in dice-playing, judge as thou findeſt it.' The verb *deme* governs l. 10 and all that follows. The change from *you* to *thou* is remarkable, and probably due to the mention of dice-playing, which is charged upon the king as being a *personal* vice.

19. 'Or by right guidance of the law, justly tempered with love.' Cf. l. 24 below.

25. *gostis*, spirits. An allusion to the king's favourites, such as De Vere and De la Pole.

26. 'That never wore armour, nor (felt) showers of hail.'

30. 'They mourned over the pleasures of lordship which they once had; but never let fall one tear for their sinś.'

42. *y-doutid of*, feared by. See the parallel passages in A. 2. 10–14; B. 2. 10–17; C. 3. 11–16. In l. 44, *yloke* means *locked, joined*.

47. *traylid*, fenced round; cf. *trellis. treste*, trust.

51. *nest*, nighest. The allusion is probably to the extreme intimacy between the king and his favourites, the 'graceless ghosts' mentioned in l. 25 above.

54. *of tiliers*, from husbandmen. Compare C. 5. 45–65.

57. De Vere was Duke of Ireland; and De la Pole Earl of Suffolk. Though the latter was but an Earl, he is probably alluded to. Three other of 'Richard's dukes' were the Dukes of Albemarle, Surrey, and Exeter. Lingard says that, in 1397, Richard 'created his two cousins of Derby and Rutland, Dukes of Hereford and Albemarle; his two uterine brothers, the Earls of Kent and Huntingdon, Dukes of Surrey and Exeter;' etc. Albemarle is Shakespeare's Aumerle, who was devoted to Richard; and the Dukes of Surrey and Exeter were put to death by Henry IV.

58. We find in Hazlitt's English Proverbs the four following—'Drumming is not the way to catch a hare;'—'It is a mad hare that will be caught with a tabor;'—'Men catch not a hare with the sound of a drum;' and—'You may catch a hare with a tabor as soon.' So also in Political Poems, ed. Wright, ii. 219, we find—'Men with a tabour may lyghtly cacche an hare.' It must have been a common phrase. Strutt gives a drawing of a hare beating a tabor, copied from a MS. See Strutt, Sports and Pastimes, 2nd ed. 1810, p. 220; and cf. Ben Jonson's Bartholomew Fair, A. v. sc. 3.

66. This saying was attributed to Beda. See An Old Eng. Miscel. ed. Morris, p. 185.

77. The 'murder' was that of the Duke of Gloucester, who was put to death at Calais in 1397, probably by the king's order. The 'mischief' or evil fortune was that of the Dukes of Norfolk and Hereford, whom Richard had banished, of the Archbishop of Canterbury (Thomas Arundel), and of the Earls of Arundel and Warwick.

79. *is ynne;* i.e. is already gathered. In other words, 'you need not expect further help.'

80. 'Blame not your council, but rather yourself for it, viz. for the fact that ill fortune has befallen the faithless.'

90. *hobbis*, clowns. So also *hoball*, a clownish lout, in Roister Doister, iii. 3. 18; *hobbadehoy*, etc. Mr. Wright gives the following note on *Hurlewayn*. ' The only other instance of this word that I have observed in Early English poetry, occurs in the prologue to the Tale of Beryn, printed at the end of Urry's Chaucer:

"As Hurlewaynes meyne in every hegge that rapes."

'*Hurlewaynes meyné* is the *Maisnie Hellequin* of old French popular superstition, in Latin *familia Harlequini*. The name is spelt in different ways, Hellequin, Herlequin, Henequin, etc. The legend was, that Charles the Fifth of France, and his men, who fell all in a great battle, were condemned for their crimes to wander over the world on horseback, constantly employed in fighting battles. Some derived the name from that of the Emperor; Charles quint, Charlequin, Herlequin, Hellequin. Of course this derivation is wrong, and the legend a fabrication of later date, to explain it. See Grimm's Mythologie, p. 527; Le Roux de Lincy's Livre des Legendes, p. 148–150, 240–245; and Michel's Benôit, vol. ii. p. 336, where in a note is given a most extraordinary story about them. See also Paulin Paris's Catalogue of the French Manuscripts of the Bibliothèque du Roi, vol. i. p. 322–325.'

A similar phrase is *Kaymes kin*, i.e. Cain's kin, concerning which see Havelok, l. 2045 and the note.

96. ' To get a remedy of their own grievances.'

99, 100. *busshinge*, pushing, butting; with a jesting reference to Bushy; see note to Pass. ii. 152. *fals colour*, false pretence; as in Acts xxvii. 30. This *false colour* was *Green;* see Pass. ii. 153. *wayve*, remove.

107, 108. *ȝou formed*, instigated you. *fforckis*, gallows.

110. Halliwell gives '*Boinard*, a low person, a term of reproach,' with a reference to Wright's Anecdota Literaria, p. 9. This merely shews

that it occurs in l. 288 of the story called 'Dame Siriz,' which is there printed at length. The line runs—' Be stille, boinard ;' which is equivalent to 'hold your tongue, stupid !' See Pass. ii. l. 164.

113. *belde*, grow strong, wax bold ; *to belde vppon sorowe*, to strengthen themselves at the expense of those on whom they brought misery.

NOTES TO PASSUS II.

2. The key to the whole passage at the beginning of this Passus is to observe that the author is inveighing against the king's servants, and in particular against their wearing of badges. *Livery (leuerey* in line 2, *leuere* in l. 26) is used here in the particular sense of *uniform*, though it also meant a grant or allowance to servants of a more general kind ; as when, for instance, Spenser defines it as an 'allowaunce of horse-meate, as they commonly use the woord in stabling, as to keepe horses at liverye ;' View of the State of Ireland, Globe edition, p. 623. The author complains that the king had *marked* his servants (l. 20) with badges or 'signes' (l. 21), which were made of silver (l. 45) and which bore the image of a *hart* (l. 4). The whole passage is aptly illustrated by the following remarks. ' The *White Hart* was the favourite badge of Richard II. At a tournament held in Smithfield in 1390, in honour of the Count of St. Pol, Count of Luxemburg, and the Count of Ostrevant, eldest son of Albert, Count of Holland and Zealand, who had been elected members of the garter, " all the kynges house were of one sute ; theyr cotys, theyr armys, theyr sheldes, and theyr trappours were browdrid all with *whyte hertys*, with crownes of gold about their neck, and cheynes of gold hanging thereon, which *hertys* was the *kynges leverye* that he gaf to *lordes, ladyes, knyghtes, and squyers*, to knowe his household people from others ;" Caxton's Chronicle at the end of Polychronicon, lib. ult. chap. vi.'—The History of Signboards, by Larwood and Hotten, p. 112. This tournament is described by Froissart, Chron. Bk. iv. c. 23. Richard probably took this badge from the cognisance of his mother, the 'fair maid of Kent,' which was a white hind. See Mrs. Palliser's Historic Devices, p. 363.

Lingard's remarks are also very applicable here. Speaking of the Statutes passed at the beginning of the reign of Henry IV., he says—' A fourth forbade, under the heaviest penalties, any person besides the king to give liveries to his retainers. These badges had long been one of the principal expedients by which the great lords were enabled to increase their power, and to maintain their quarrels. Whoever wore the livery was bound in honour to espouse the cause of the donor ; and it was worn not only by those who had received fees, or were engaged in actual services, but by as many as were willing to accept it as an honour, or in token of friendship, or with a view to future emolument.' Lingard's reference is to Rot. Parl. iii. 428, 442 ; Stat. 1 Hen. IV. c. 10, 14.

Richard's badges or cognisances were the white hart kneeling, collared and chained, Or ; the sun in splendour ; the pod of the *planta genistæ*, or broom ; and branches of rosemary. The white falcon has also been attributed to him, but Mr B. Williams supposes this to have really belonged to Queen Isabel, as it certainly was her device. See Williment's Regal Heraldry, pp. 20, 23.

7. *ffoltheed*, folly. See *folte*, a fool, in Prompt. Parv.

9. *eye*, awe, dread. That the *Eagle* means Bolingbroke is placed beyond all doubt by Pass. iii. l. 69. An eagle was one of the numerous badges of his grandfather Edward III.

12. *ffor mowtynge*, because of the moulting season that was drawing near. The moulting time for a hart is when it sheds its horns, i.e. the spring, as Lord Surrey says, in his well-known sonnet on Spring—

'The hart hath hong his olde hed on the pale.'

But the author merely means that the horns were past their prime; the summer was indeed over (l. 14), yet the harts contrived to retain their horns for another half-year (l. 17); i.e. till the next spring.

13. *bawtid*, probably only a variation of *batid*, i.e. abated, diminished the courage of. Cf. 'Batyn, or abaten of weyte or mesure. *Subtraho;*' Prompt. Parv.

25. The simple correction *Of* for *Or* at once gives good sense. The *Of* became *Or*, because it had *Or* both above and below it. It means 'whoever went much about would soon see more than enough of harts and hinds on retainers' breasts, or else the livery of some lord who destroyed the law.' *Hassell* I suppose to be some kind of retainer; it is an O. French form of the Low Lat. *haistaldi*, i.e. 'qui in praediis dominorum mansiones habent et glebæ sunt addicti; idem q. *Coloni, Hospites, Manentes, Rustici*, etc.;'—Du Cange. From O. Sax. *hagastald* (A. S. *hægsteald*).

28. *seruid*, deserved; so also in iv. 59.

36. *hertis*, harts, i.e. on the *signes* or badges. But in l. 43, it has both meanings, viz. *harts* and *hearts*. 'For every *hart* which you marked on a badge, you lost ten score of loyāl *hearts*.' I believe there is also a play upon the word *mark*, which sometimes signifies to *hit, succeed in hitting* (as in Pass. iii. 268), and is here opposed to *miss*. This smart saying is attributed to the *townmen*, as being sharper than *countrymen*.

40. For *yuell* read *lither*, obviously the right word. See the Glossary.

51. *side* means wide or large; see Glossary. These badges 'spoilt all the broth, and upset the pot among the coals.'

57. *or leuerez beganne*, before these liveries came into use.

62. *lymmes*, limbs; i.e. the commons.

78. *meyntenour*, a technical term for one who abets another in wrongdoing, and supports him in defeating justice; see C. 4. 288.

83. *leuynge*, living. *leuyd be*, believed by, trusted by.

89. *He*, such a one; referring to *ho so* in l. 81.

92. *tente*, intent, purpose; but (both here and in l. 97) it is used rather with the sense of *argument, ground, reason*. *to take and to ȝeue*, for granting and giving. Observe that *to take* commonly means to *bestow*, as in C. 2. 52, etc.

93. This line is unconnected with the context. Perhaps for *And* we may read *For*. But, more probably, a line has been lost before it.

94. *gayes*, ornaments; a *gay* signifies anything gaudy or gay, as a highly coloured child's picture, or a fine piece of clothing. See Nares' Glossary, ed. Halliwell and Wright. It here refers to the badges and privileges already spoken of.

96. This means, that Truth has decided whether the ground of giving these badges was good or bad.

107. *quentise*, quaintness of dress, uniform.

113. *greehonde*, greyhound. Mr. Wright suggests the Earl of Dorset (John Beaufort), as the badge of the Beauforts was a greyhound; but he was of no great mark. In this difficulty, Mr G. E. Adams, Somerset Herald, has kindly suggested the solution—'Why should not the greyhound stand for Ralph Neville, created Earl of Westmoreland by Richard II., and of his Privy Council, Constable of the Tower of London, etc.? He was one of those who greatly contributed to raise Henry to the throne. In Surtees' Durham, vol. i. plate 8, are two seals of the Earls of Westmoreland supported by *greyhounds*. The supporters granted to Elizabeth Widville were a lion (of March), and a *greyhound;* which latter Sandford says was in allusion to the supporters of the Nevilles, from whom Edward's mother was descended.' Besides, he may easily have taken the badge of the greyhound from his alliance with the Beauforts. In the Annals of England, p. 216, note k, we read—'Ralph, lord Neville, had been created Earl of Westmoreland by Richard II., ... but he was the *brother-in-law* of Henry of Lancaster, and rendered him most essential service *against* his benefactor. He married, for his second wife, *Joan Beaufort, daughter of John of Gaunt.*'

117. *heed-dere*, head-deer, principal deer, i. e. chief men; cf. l. 128.

118. 'For little, during your life, it pleased you to have pity on the inferior sort of deer.' A *rascal* was a lean deer, fit neither for hunting nor eating. So also in l. 129.

123. 'But where (to complain) they knew not.'

128. *hauntelere dere*, antlered deer; cf. l. 117.

139. 'Moderation is a good mean, though men desire a great deal.' 'Mesure is a mery mene' was a proverb, and is quoted by Skelton in his Magnificence, l. 385. Mr Dyce says—'Heywood in his Epigrammes vpon Prouerbs has ten on "Measure is a mery meane";' and Mr Hazlitt quotes from Heywood's Proverbs, ed. 1562, the couplet—

'Measure is a merry mean, as this doth shew,
Not too high for the pye, nor too low for the crow.'

140. *be the rotus endurid*, lived upon roots.

145. *heyere*, exalter; from *hey*, high. See iii. 74.

147. *ffeedrin*, feathers, a Southern form; but in the next line we find *ffedris*.

148. *y-pynned*, furnished with *pens* or *quills*.

150. 'For poison, in the valley, would have suited them ill.' Here

venym probably means merely *close air;* and hence, metaphorically, various slanders and false reports. See the line following.

151. 'Till Truth, the remedy (for slander), told her true tales to some.'

152-154. A clear allusion to *Bushy, Green,* and *Scrope.* 'Thus this bird battered the *Bushes* around, and gathered up men as they walked on the *Green,* till all the "scruff" and *Scrope* parted asunder.' *Scruff* means *rubbish,* or a very common kind of fuel. Blount gives '*Scruff,* a kind of fuel which poor people, when firing is dear, gather up at ebbing water in the bottom of the Thames at London, and consists of coal, little sticks, cockleshels, and the like.' Halliwell also gives '*Shruff,* light rubbish wood; any short dry stuff used for fuel.' *Schroup* is merely a slightly disguised spelling of *Scrope.* The author intimates that *scruff* and *scrope* were much the same thing, and proceeds to say—'He so mixed the metal with the hand-mould, (i.e. so moulded events) that they lost, of their limbs, the dearest that they had,' i.e. their heads. Sir John Bushy was speaker of the House of Commons in 1394. Sir Henry Green was son of the Sir Henry Green, who had been Justice of the King's Bench in the reign of Edward III. Bolingbroke had been joined by the Duke of York, whom Richard had left behind as Regent of England during his own absence in Ireland, and their united forces appeared before Bristol on Monday the 28th of July, or, in the words of Holinshed—'the foresayd Dukes with their power, wente towardes Bristow, where at their comming, they shewed themselues before the towne and Castell, beeing an huge multitude of people. There were enclosed within the Castell, the Lord Wil. *Scrope* Erle of Wiltshire, and Treasorer of Englande, Sir Henry *Greene,* and Sir John *Busshy* knightes, who prepared to make resistance, but when it would not preuayle, they were taken, and brought forth bound as prisoners into the Campe, before the Duke of Lancaster;' p. 1106. They were tried and beheaded the following day, Tuesday, July 29. See another allusion to Bushy in Pass. iii. 75, and to Green in Pass. iii. 101. And see, in particular, the curious song on King Richard's Ministers, in Mr. Wright's edition of 'Political Poems,' which contains such expressions as—

> 'There is a *busch* that is forgrowe,
> Crop it welle, and holde it lowe,
>   Or elles hit wolle be wilde;
> The long gras that is so *grene*
> Hit most be mowe, and raked clene,
>   Forgrowe hit hath the fellde,' etc., etc.

Also, the expression, 'Aquila dux,' descriptive of Henry, p. 368; with many other allusions of a similar kind.

157. *ffoulyd,* went a-fowling, i.e. bird catching. The *Falcon* here is the same as the *Eagle* (see l. 176), i.e. Henry; but there may be an allusion to his junction with the Duke of York, whose badge was a *falcon* and fetterlock. It was also a badge of Edward III.

159. *robis,* robes, rich clothing.

NOTES TO RICHARD THE REDELESS: PASSUS II. 295

162. *bated*, strove to fly, fluttered. Nares says—'a term in falconry; to flutter the wings as preparing for flight, particularly at the sight of prey; probably for *battre*, Fr.

" That with the wind
Bated, like eagles having newly bathed;" 1 Hen. IV. 4. i.

[where it means fluttered to shake off the wet]. The true meaning of the word is beautifully exemplified in the following passage of Bacon: "wherein (viz. in matters of business) I would to God that I were hooded, that I saw less; or that I could perform more; for now I am like a hawk that *bates*, when I see occasion of service; but cannot fly because I am tyed to another's fist;" *Letter* ii.'

163. *plewme*, to pluck off the feathers of the prey; see Nares. This the Eagle did so fiercely as to sever the poll (or head) from the neck. Cf. note to l. 152.

164. *bler-nyed*, for *blear-eyed*. So also *pink nyez* for small eyes, quoted from Laneham in Nares, s. v. *Pink eyne. boynard;* see i. 110. The line means 'the blear-eyed scoundrel who stole his bag;' where *his* refers to the 'pray,' i.e. to Scrope, then treasurer of England. There is here an allusion to Sir William Bagot, Sheriff of Leicestershire, 6 and 7 Richard II. The account in the present poem certainly implies that Bagot set out with Lord Scrope and the rest for Bristol, though he saved his life by leaving them and escaping to Ireland before Henry's arrival there; cf. Shakespeare's Rich. II. Act ii. sc. 2. He was, however, caught at last, and severely reproved. He seems to have diverted attention from himself by accusing the Duke of Aumerle, against whom a 'bill' drawn up by Bagot was read in Parliament on Thursday, Oct. 16. Bagot survived till the year 1407. This furnishes a key to this somewhat difficult passage, in which the author partly reverts to the events *before* Scrope's execution, and of which the general sense is:—' The eagle was striving to seize his prey (Lord Scrope), that he might rend his head off; but the blear-eyed scoundrel (Bagot) who had stolen the treasurer's bag, in which the spoils of the poor were often fastened tightly, made the falcon angry, and anxious that Bagot should be bound. But soon after, this wretch (*lorell*, viz. Bagot) who had led away this looby (Scrope) all the way over forest and ford, fell, on account of his false deeds, into the domain belonging to Henry, and was caught and brought before him and publicly reproved.' In the Political Poems, ed. Wright, are several allusions to the 'bagge,' i.e. Bagot. The feeling against them may be gathered from Holinshed, who says (p. 1102)—' The common brute ranne, that the kyng had sette to ferme the realme of England vnto Sir William Scrope Earl of Wiltshire, and then treasurer of Englande, to Sir John Bushy, Syr John Bagot, and sir Henry Greene Knights.'

165. 'Wherein the very rags of the poor were often penned or fastened.' *Purraile-is* is the gen. case of O. Eng. *poraille*, poor people. *Pulter* probably answers to the Swed. *paltor*, rags, and the Scottish *peltrie;* we still use the adjective *paltry*, from the same root.

296 NOTES TO RICHARD THE REDELESS: PASSUS III.

169. *ffode*, man, person; cf. *ffodis* in Pass. iii. l. 260.
179. *louyd* = *lowyd*, i. e. lowered, put down; as in iii. 310, q. v.
182. *reclayme*, a call to return, a term in falconry. See Strutt's Sports and Pastimes.
186. *lymed leues*, leaves covered with bird-lime.

NOTES TO PASSUS III.

1. *beu brid*, fine bird; i. e. Henry. *restore* governs *that whi* in l. 3; it means 'establish that reason why;' i. e. make good my assertions.
10. *aȝeins kinde*, contrary to nature's laws.
13. *hertis*, harts; referring back to ii. 4.
17. *Her kynde*, their natural habit. *to keuere*, to recover; i. e. to regain the strength which they had when in their prime. The story of the hart, in the old Bestiaries, is that, when he grows old, he seeks out an adder and swallows it; but, the adder's poison causing him to burn, he rushes to the water and drinks plentifully, so rendering the venom harmless; after which he sheds his horns, and renews his strength. See An Old Eng. Miscellany, ed. Morris, pp. 10 and 205; Wright's Popular Treatises on Science, p. 86; Altenglische Sprachproben, ed. Mätzner, i. 55; and the *Physiologus* of Thetbaldus, in Latin verse, printed among the works of Hildebert (fol. Paris, 1708, p. 1174). Mr. Wright quotes, from the prose Latin Bestiarius, the following. '*De cervo*. Dicuntur etiam nongentos vivere annos, atque cum infirmitate vel senectute deficere senserint, spiritu narium serpentes de cavernis suis extrahunt, et superata eorum pernicie veneni pabulo reparantur;' MS. Reg. 12. C. 19.

The story also occurs in Pliny; see Holland's translation, Book viii. c. 33. Hence the device of a stag, attacked by serpents, fleeing to a fountain; see Mrs. Palliser's Historic Badges, p. 46.

23. *peyne*, death. *as his pray asketh*, as his prey (i. e. the necessity of swallowing his prey) requires.
26. 'Now this is the nature of learning,' i. e. the natural thing for learned men to do. An awkward expression, and I suspect the reading is corrupt; I would read—'This is *clerlie* hir kynde,' i. e. this is evidently their natural habit; see note to l. 190 below. At any rate, the sense is that the harts should have attacked venomous adders, and not colts, horses, swans, or bears.

The *horse* is Richard Fitz-alan, Earl of Arundel, beheaded on Tower-hill A. D. 1397; the *colt*, his son Thomas, who fled to join Henry, and was one of the small company who landed with him at Ravenspurgh; the *swan*, Thomas, Duke of Gloucester, Richard's uncle, so treacherously murdered by his orders at Calais, about the same time that Arundel was beheaded; and the *bear*, Thomas Beauchamp, Earl of Warwick, seized with Arundel by Richard's orders, and banished by him for life to the Isle of Man, though afterwards released by Henry. They were named from their badges, the *white horse* being that of Arundel, the *swan* that of the Duke of Gloucester, which he had adopted from his father Edward III., who sometimes used it;

NOTES TO RICHARD THE REDELESS: PASSUS III.

and the *black bear* that of the Earl of Warwick. See Political Songs, ed. Wright, vol. i. p. 419.

27. *hurlle with haras*, persecute with annoyance.

28. *sholle werre*, shall war, i. e. attack.

32. Mr. C. H. Pearson sends me the very passages from the civil law which are here referred to. In the Codex, lib. vi. tit. 7. § 2, we find—'Si manumissus *ingratus* circa patronum suum exstiterit. . . . a patrono *rursus sub imperio ditioneque mittatur*,' etc. And again, in the Codex, lib. vi. tit. 7. § 4, there is a similar passage.

38. Mr. Wright quotes the story of the partridge from the Latin Bestiary, MS. Reg. 12. C. 19, fol. 53.—'*De perdice*. Phisiologus dicit satis astutum esse perdicem, quia aliena ova diripit. . . . Adeo autem fraudulenta, ut alterius perdicis ova diripiens fovet. Sed fraus fructum non habet. Nam pulli, cum vocem propriae genitricis audierunt, naturali quodam instinctu hanc quae eos fovit relinquunt, et ad eam quae eos genuit revertuntur.' See also Wright's Popular Treatises on Science, p. 108; and Alex. Neckam, de Naturis Rerum, ed. Wright, lib. i. c. 44 (taken from Cassiodorus). The notion that one partridge will steal and hatch the eggs of another seems to have been known even to the Orientals; hence the expression in Jeremiah xvii. 11—'As the partridge sitteth on eggs, and hatcheth them not.'

42. *eiren*, eggs. So in Wyclif's Works, ed. Arnold, iii. 157, and not 'heirs,' as the editor explains it. See l. 50 below.

45. *congioun*. Mr. Wright prints *cougioun*. Halliwell gives '*Conjoun*, a coward,' without reference or authority. But in the Chester Plays, ed. Wright, we find 'thou caitiffe, thou *congeon!*' p. 40; 'that vile *counjon*,' p. 177; 'suche a *congeon*,' p. 178; and a soldier appointed to slay the Innocents says, 'With this speare I thinke to assaie To kille manye a smalle *congion*,' p. 179.

46. *not of his nolle*, smooth (lit. closely cropped) of his head; cf. *notheed* in Chaucer; and see l. 66. *as he the nest made*, as if he had made the nest himself. The forms *his* and *he* should obviously be *hir* and *hue* (she).

50. *hue*, she; þe *hue*, the 'she'-bird.

51. *kenne*, generate, come to life; cf. *kindle*, to bring forth young.

58. *schrapid*, scraped up the ground (for food for them).

59. *leued*, i. e. they lived.

79. *two and twenty;* from 1377 to 1399.

81. *tymed*, (perhaps) delayed, put off for a time; but this is improbable. It is much more likely to be an error for *tyned*, i. e. lost. *no twynte*, not a jot. Mr. Wright cites a passage from the Prol. to Beryn, l. 433—'So he that payd for all in-feer had nat a *twynt;*' Urry's Chaucer, p. 598.

86. *swan;* the Duke of Gloucester, as before. So the *hors* is again the Earl of Arundel, in l. 89.

90. *fferkyd hem forth*, proceeded.

94. *beere*, the Bear, the Earl of Warwick, whom Henry released. 'When the Duke of Lancaster had imprisoned him [Richard] and those of his council in the Tower, the first thing he did was to recal the

Earl of Warwick from his banishment, and to give him his liberty;' Froissart's Chronicles, bk. iv. c. 114. But it appears that Henry, with his usual promptness, had already taken upon himself to set Warwick at liberty, though he did not obtain the consent of parliament till afterwards. In fact, Warwick met Richard at Newcastle-under-Lyne about the 25th of August; see The French Chronicle, ed. B. Williams, p. 212; note 2.

98. *bosse*, lit. an excrescence, hump. The reason for such an appellation does not appear, unless it merely means 'that great one.' Cf. *boss*, a large marble. Or perhaps 'master;' see *Boss* (Du. *baas*) in Webster.

101. 'They cackled or complained against the *green;*' i.e. Sir Henry Green, as before.

105. *monside*, cursed; miswritten for *mansid*, or another spelling of it.

106. 'Who ill knew his business, when he bandaged (lit. clothed) the Steed:' The Earl-marshal was Thomas De Mowbray, Duke of Norfolk, son-in-law to the Earl of Arundel. The latter was executed by Richard's orders; and, as Froissart tells us, the Earl-marshal actually bandaged his father-in-law's eyes at the execution; see Froissart, bk. iv. c. 92. Such was, at any rate, the common story, as given also by Walsingham. But Lingard (referring to Rot. Parl. iii. 374–377, 435) shews that it cannot be true, as the Earl-marshal was not present, the lord Morley being his lieutenant on the occasion. This is why the poet says Mowbray knew his craft ill; for the office of a marshal (lit. servant of the horse) is to attend to the wants of a horse, not to bandage its eyes. For *cloþed*, Mr. Wright prints *cloped*, which he explains by *clipped*. But there is no fault in clipping a horse; nor is there such a verb as *clope*.

114. *walmed*, boiled up; A. S. *wylm*, a boiling.

116. *That were*, That would be, indeed! Ironical.

118. Cf. 'Hii ben degised as *turmentours* that comen from clerkes plei;' Polit. Songs, ed. Wright, p. 336. Mr. Wright's note says—'Men who have performed the part of devils, or tormentors, in the miracle-plays, which were performed by the clerks.' This is just what is here meant.

121. *stroutynge*, exactly the modern 'swelling about.' Cf. '*Strowtyn*, or bocyn out. *Turgeo;*' Prompt. Parv.

126. *ffeet;* for *fet*, fetched.

127. *endauntid*, respected, made much of.

128. 'And, if you take good notice, by nobody else.'

129. 'Then observe in more (i.e. other) ways how the time goes.'

130. *gery*, changeable, ever-changing, as in Chaucer; see also Dyce's ed. of Skelton, ii. 206. *Iaces*, fringes or ribands. Cf. '*Jace*, a kind of fringe. *Devon;*' Halliwell. A hawk's *jesses* were thin strips of leather, silk, or riband.

132. *creaunce*, credit. The line probably means—'They go upon credit.'

136. 'For they leap as lightly out of the doom-cart, at their long

NOTES TO RICHARD THE REDELESS: PASSUS III.

journey, as a wretch that never was successful.' The 'longe goynge' here signifies death upon the gallows.

139. *chaunchyth*, for *chaungyth*, change ; so also *y-charchid* for *y-chargid* in l. 230. *cheynes*, chains of gold, ornaments that are exposed for sale in Cheapside.

140. *seintis*, girdles ; but the word is indistinctly written in the MS. The line perhaps means—'And use all their silver for ornamenting girdles or drinking-horns.'

141. *for-doth*, spoil, clip. Hence the *pens-lac*, or lack of money, in l. 142.

145. *Lidford*, in Devon. The proverb, as given by Fuller, is—
'First hang and draw,
Then hear the cause by Lydford law.'
A curious vindication of this kind of justice, commencing with the lines
"I oft have heard of Lydford law,
How in the morn they hang and draw,
And sit in judgment after'—
is ascribed to Wm. Browne, the author of Britannia's Pastorals. It is printed entire in Chambers' Book of Days, ii. 327, with the explanation that—' Lydford itself is the chief town of the Stannaries, and the proverb probably was levelled at the summary decisions of the Stannary courts which, under a Charter of Edward I., had sole jurisdiction of all cases in which the natives were concerned, that did not affect land, life, or limb.'

152. The whole passage is best illustrated from Chaucer's Persones Tale, where we read—'As to the firste synne, that is in superfluite of clotheynge, which that makid is so dere, to harm of the poeple, not oonly the cost of embrowdyng, the deguyse, endentyng or barryng, owndyng, palyng or bendyng, and semblable waste of cloth in vanite ; but ther is also costlewe furring in here gownes, so mochil pounsing of chiseles to make holes, so moche *daggyng* [see l. 193] of scheris ; with the superfluite in lengthe of the forsaide gownes, traylinge in the donge and in the myre, on hors and eek on foote, as wel of man as of womman, that al thilke traylyng is verraily (as in effect) wasted, consumed, thredbare, and rotyn with donge, rather than it is yeven to the pore,' etc.; Chaucer's Works, ed. Morris, iii. 296. See also a note in Dyce's ed. of Skelton, ii. 248.

156. *pernell*, Purnel (short for Petronilla), a common female name, particularly used of a woman of loose character. Another such name was *Felice*, which is used in l. 160.

159. *Iette*, another spelling (as Tyrwhitt notes) of *get*, used by Chaucer (Prol. l. 684) to mean *fashion*. Tyrwhitt quotes an apposite passage from Occleve's De Regimine Principum—
'Also ther is another *newe gette*,
All foule waste of cloth and excessif.'

168. 'For they pay for the piecing together of it twenty times the cost of the cloth itself; so dear is the workmanship.'

186. *beringe vppon oilles*, the use of flattery ; see *Oilles* in the Glossary. Perhaps *vppon* should be altered to *vp of*.

VOL. II.   T

190. 'So, as we learn, the cause begins amongst the great,' etc. Very awkward; and probably, just as in l. 26 above, *clergie* is miswritten for *clerlie*. We then should have—'So evidently the cause of all evil begins amongst the great;' which is doubtless the sense intended.

209. *þat steddeffaste*, that steadfast one. The poet does not *at first* say whom he means; but he is really drawing a picture of 'Wit,' i. e. Wisdom, who is supposed to come to the king's court, and look about him with wonder at all that goes on there. Hence *awilled his wyll* in l. 210 must mean—'controlled his will,' or 'gained mastery over his will,' and could rule himself wisely. The key is given in ll. 226, 238.

228. *halowid*, hallooed at. *yhote trusse*, bidden to pack off.

230. *schoppe*, for *choppe*, i. e. *chop*, hit. Cf.

      'And gunne *choppen* al aboute
      Every man vpon the *crowne;*'
            Chaucer; Hous of Fame, iii. 734, 735.

236. *slaueyn*, mantle; see Halliwell.

242. *gouernance of gettinge*, lit. moderation in getting, i. e. a just mode of getting money, by imposing moderate taxes; a proceeding which will win *grace*, i. e. favour. In l. 250 *gouernaunce* means government, counsel. There is an allusion to an old proverb, given by Dr. Morris in his Glossary to Chaucer's Prologue (l. 281). 'Grace groweth after [i. e. according to] governance.'

249. The 'three degrees' or ranks were, in olden times, the *Oratores*, (here Counsellors), l. 250; *Bellatores* (Warriors), ll. 251, 252; and *Laboratores* (Labourers), l. 253.

259. *schenshepe*, for *schendship*, i. e. ruin.

265. 'Were not created (or elected) at the first.'

268. 'To mark "maintainers" with maces;' i. e. to beat them; in contradistinction to the marking with badges mentioned above.

272. The word *not* has been dropped, making nonsense of the whole. Restore it, and we have—'And not to rule like bats (awake only at night), and rest all day,' etc. See l. 277.

276. *moppis*, fools, apes; cf. *moppe*, foolish, Seven Sages, ed. Weber, l. 1414.

282. *ouere-wacche*, the being awake too late at night.

284. *letith lyghte of*, despises. The nominative is *the king*, understood.

287. 'To do them right reverence, though his back break,' viz. with stooping. We ought to read *hem* for *him* in l. 286, or else *him* for *hem* here.

288. 'This glow of wealth may not last long with any mortal wight.'

299. *kew-kaw*, a sudden change, a subversion; see *kew* in Jamieson.

302. *carieth*, another form of *caireth*, wander; see C. 1. 31.

303. 'To imprison the robbers that over-run the poor.'

307. 'And put down (refuse) all the complaints.'

310. *louyd*, for *lowyd*, i. e. brought low; as in ii. 179. Compare all this with C. 4. 156-319.

315. 'For, as reason and justice once told me.' The use of *me* here is most important, for the author immediately goes on to cite a line from Piers the Plowman, thus directly implying that he wrote that poem also.

317. *chiders of chester*, wranglers from Chester, who took part with the king. Lingard says that the king's body-guard of archers had been 'levied in the county of Chester.' In fact, one of Richard's titles was *Earl of Chester*, a title which he received from Edward III.; and he afterwards created himself *prince of Chester*. He had the special reason for assuming this title, that he wished to ingratiate himself with the people of that county. This we are expressly told in the following note, printed in Polit. Poems, ed. Wright, i. 461: 'Anno regis Ricardi xxj. incipiente, rex assumpsit sibi nomen principis Cestriae, *ob amorem populi Cestriae*, in parliamento, ubi novi domini creantur, scilicet Henricus comes Derby in ducem Herefordiae,' etc. In MS. Harl. 1989, a rising of *Cheshire men* in favour of Richard is recorded as taking place immediately after his return from Ireland; see Appendix C to the Chronicque de la Traison et Mort de Richart, ed. Williams. Walsingham (ed. Riley, ii. 225) refers to the 'satis feralis turba Cestrensium, armata securibus, gladiis, arcubus et sagittis.' See also Grafton's Chronicle, i. 464, 468; Hardyng's Chronicle, cap. cxcii. Grafton says: 'Those Cheshire men ... accompted the king *to be as their felowe;*' (see Pass. i. l. 66).

319. *pipoudris*, i.e. in the court of Pie-Poudre; the summary court formerly held at fairs, and so called from the dusty feet (*pieds poudreux*) of those present.

320. *coyffes*, coifs such as were worn by the sergeants-at-law; cf. B. prol. 210; and see *houe*, i.e. a hood, in l. 326.

325. *pallette*, a leather head-piece, which served them instead of a coif or hood, and helped to keep their brain-pans safe; see note in Way's Prompt. Parv. p. 378. To *hille* is to cover.

330. 'And gave men the free experience of their long staves.' To *lend leverè* is to *deliver blows;* see Wm. of Palerne, ed. Skeat; ll. 1233, 3822.

341. *Iustice*, a justice, i.e. an administrator of justice; but *Iewis* (Lat. *judicium*) is justice itself, i.e. the sentence of the law.

347. Here a line has evidently dropped out; we want one like the one supplied by guess.

350. 'Or any apprentice of the court asked to employ his wits.'

351. *Degon* is clearly a term of contempt; see note to l. 362 below. The word *endauntid*, made much of, has already occurred, l. 127 above.

352. 'Till our Lord, in His seat above the seven stars,' i.e. the seven planets; as in the fragment A. of the Alexander Romance, l. 630. God's throne was thought to be beyond the sphere of Saturn, the outermost planet. Cf. Milton, P. L. iii. 481. At a later time, the 'seven stars',meant the Pleiades.

354. *meynteyned of him*, upheld or abetted by him. The MS. reading (see foot-note) is an obvious error.

357. *He*, i.e. the Lord. His servants, 'the barons and bachelors in

bright helms,' are the angels, accompanied by whom 'He rode in full royal array.' A striking and curious passage.

362. *degon and dobyn*, evidently Diggon and Dobbin, both common names for country bumpkins, here used in contempt of the upstarts who used to burst in men's doors and rob them. Spenser introduces *Diggon* and *Hobbinol* into his Shepherdes Kalender for September.

363. *while domys*, occasional (or temporary) sentences.

364. *Awakyd*, awoke to a sense of their folly, on account of their night-wakes and wastefulness. *wecches*, wakes, revels.

366. *it*, viz. the sky, the heavens.

NOTES TO PASSUS IV.

Lines 1–16 form one long interrogatory sentence.

6. *nownagis*, nonages, minorities ; *newed*, renewed, i. e. renewed his funds. It is clear from this that, when a nobleman succeeded to a title while in his minority, the king had a share of the estate.

7. *marche and moubray*. Mr. Wright says the reference is to—' Roger de Mortimer, fourth Earl of March, who was committed in ward to the Earl of Arundel. John de Mowbray and Thomas de Mowbray both succeeded to the title while in their minority in this reign.'

10, 11. *prophete*, profit ; as in l. 48. *countis*, accounts. *wullus*, wools.

12. 'Might not go far enough, even with the addition of his rent, to repay the poor for that which his purveyors took from them.'

15. *fifteneth*, fifteenth. *dyme*, a tenth ; Lat. *decima*.

The tenths and fifteenths were granted by distinct classes. See Hallam, Middle Ages, iii. 54 ; 7th ed. Lingard says—' Richard had previously demanded an aid of the commons ; and on the fourth day (i. e. Jan. 31, 1398) they voted him, with the assent of the lords, *a tenth and a half, and a fifteenth and a half;* and in addition, as if they sought to make him independent of parliament, granted him the tax on wool, wool-fells, and hides, not for a short and determinate period as usual, but for the whole term of his natural life (Rot. Parl. iii. 368).' This is clearly the very occasion to which our author is referring.

17. *creaunce*, the credit-system. It means that the court-revellers spent so much that they would have been utterly ruined by debt if they had not paid some of it by promises only.

20. *reot*, riot ; the expenses of revelry.

24–30. This probably has a special reference to the compliant parliament which met in Sept. 1397, concerning which Fabyan complains that the king would not be controlled in the election of sheriffs, and that 'where before times the king of England used to send commissioners unto burgesses of cities and towns, to choose for their free liberty such knights of the shire as they thought most useful for the common weal of the said shire and land, now King Richard would appoint the persons, and will them for to choose such as then he named.' Lines 28-30 particularly refer to these sheriffs.

24. *colis*, falsehoods, deceits, stratagems. Very rare; but it occurs in Gascoigne's Steel Glas, l. 1114—
   'Nor colour crafte by swearing precious *coles*.'

See Specimens of English, A.D. 1394-1579; ed. Skeat, p. 323. Cf. *col-fox* crafty fox, in Chaucer; and see note by M. R. in Notes and Queries, Fourth Series, iv. 358.

38. 'In deceiving the great, lest grievances arise.'

45. 'Some argued *against* the king's right of taxation; but this was merely a blind.'

49. *wattis*, wights, people. In the Coventry Mysteries (ed. Halliwell, p. 294), a messenger, speaking of Christ just after His capture, says—
   'ȝe xal fynde hym a strawnge *watt*.'

And in the Towneley Mysteries (Surtees Society), p. 8, Cain's serving lad says of himself—
   'Gedlinges, I am a fulle gret *wat*.'

53. 'Some sat, like a cipher in arithmetic, that marks a place, though of no intrinsic value.' So also in Crowley's Select Works, ed. J. M. Cowper, p. 73—
   'And at the last thou shalt be founde
   To occupye a place only
   As do in A[u]g[r]ime ziphres rounde,
   And to hynder learnyng greatlye.'

The old copy of Crowley, having the misspelling *Agime* for *Augrime*, looks hardly explicable at first sight; and Mr Cowper does not explain it.

55. *Symond*, Simon. I have no doubt that 'to sup with Simon' means here to sup with ecclesiastics, to share in the revels which some churchmen indulged in. *Simon* means Simon Peter, and is used elsewhere by the author as a general name for the clergy; see C. 10. 257, and cf. Mark xiv. 37.

57. *tituleris*, tattlers, tale-bearers. 'These went to the king, and informed him of foes, who were really friends and spoke for the best, and deserved no blame at all.'

63. *mafflid*, mumbled, spoke indistinctly.

66. This alludes to the logic-splitters.

72. *bente on a bonet*, spread an extra sail. To *bend* a sail is to fasten it to its yard or stay. A *bonnet* is an addition to a sail, or an additional part laced to the foot of a sail. *topte sail*, a top-sail.

74. *laste*, burden; cf. G. *last*, a load. *charge*, a heavy weight. It seems to refer to the trimming of the vessel.

75. If *bare aboute* is the modern *put about*, it means 'altered the course of;' an explanation which suits well with l. 76.

77. This seems to mean that the lords lay comfortably sheltered on the lee-side, and warned the steersman as to what was going on on the weather-

side ; doing so, probably, by guess. Yet the line is rather obscure. The result was that the mast bent, and nearly broke (l. 79) ; and if they had not taken in the additional sails in time, they would have fallen overboard owing to the lurching of the vessel.

86. *the mo*, the majority.

89. *clappid*, clattered, spoke loudly. Some, instead of looking after the money due to the commons, asked for what the king owed *themselves*, and so far succeeded that they were promised an earnest of money (*hansell*) if they would help the king; for they should be helped to some of the same silver as he received himself.

93. 'And some forsook well-doing, because they feared the great.' An obvious allusion to the author's poem of Do-well.

It is reasonable to suppose that the present poem was never finished. The course of events at the time was so rapid as soon to supersede all conjecture and good advice.

GLOSSARIAL INDEX.

WHEN numbers are used without any symbol preceding them, the reference is to the Passus and Line of the C-text. References to the B-text or A-text invariably have ' b.' or ' a.' prefixed to the numbers. References to Richard the Redeles have ' R.' prefixed. References to the *prologue* to the A-text or B-text are indicated by ' pr.'
References to which ' *n* ' is subjoined are to words occurring, not in the text, but in the various readings in the foot-notes.
Besides the abbreviations *s.*, *adj.*, *adv.*, for *substantive, adjective, adverb*, &c., the following are used in a special sense :—*v.*, a verb in the infinitive mood ; *pr, s.*, present tense, 3rd person singular ; *pr. pl.*, present tense, 3rd person plural ; *pt. s.*, past tense, 3rd person singular ; *pt. pl.*, past tense, 3rd person plural. Other persons are denoted by the figures 1 or 2.
The etymology of words is given occasionally, in the case of the more difficult words. Languages are cited in the usual manner, as O.F. for Old French, A.S. for Anglo-Saxon, and the like.
My former Glossary (published for the Early English Text Society) is on a larger scale. Space has been saved, in the present Glossary, by giving but few references for common words, and by the omission of some words (such as *Abbesse*, an abbess) of which the sense is obvious.
When the modern English form is noted (as e, g. mod. E, *abash*, under Abasched), the etymology is to be found in my Etymological Dictionary. References to ' notes ' are to the Notes in the present volume.
Proper Names will not be found *here*, but in the separate Index.

A, *adj*. one, a single, 2. 27 ; b. 1. 99 ; b. 17. 39 ; one and the same, 17. 181. And see note to a. 2. 43, p. 33.

A, *prep*. on, in, 20. 192, 21. 62, 21. 352, 22. 236 ; on, 15. 142 ; during, b. 11. 330 ; A bedde, in bed, 8. 26 ; A day, in the day, 9. 332 ; A fure, on fire, 17. 180 ; A fuyre, a-fire, 8. 52 ; A morwe, on the morrow, 4. 310 ; A nyghtes, by night, 10. 78 ; A parceles, in separate parts, severally, 20. 96 ; A reste, in rest, asleep, 7. 237 ; A slepe, asleep, 3. 53 ; A þre, *adv.* in three (persons), 19. 199 ; A worth, according to their worth, 15. 66.

A, *prep*. of, a. pr. 6 ; *a feyrie* = of fairy origin. See note to 1. 7, p. 3.

A, *interj*. ah ! 2. 41, 5. 164.

A-bane, *imper. s.* give them disease, 9. 226. See note, p. 114.

Abasched, *pp*. abashed, alarmed, b. 10. 445 ; ashamed, b. 10. 286 ; Abasshyd, deterred, R. 1. 110 ; Abaisshed, ashamed, 16. 163 ; Abaissed, 7. 17. Mod. E. *abash.*

Abate, *v*. soften, assuage, b. 12. 61 ;

soften, moisten, a. 7. 171 ; Abateth, *pr. pl*. put down, refuse, set aside, R. 3. 307 ; Abated, *pp.* lowered, R. 4. 81 ; Abate, *imp. s.* reduce, keep under, b. 6. 218.

Abbodesse, an abbess, 7. 128.

A-b-ce, *s*. alphabet, a. 8. 119 ; A-b-c, b. 7. 132. See Cath. Angl. p. 1, n. 7.

Abedde, in bed, b. 5. 395. See **A,** *prep.*

A-begged, *in phr*. gon abegged = go a-begging, 9. 138. See note, p. 111.

Abie, *v*. pay for, atone for, b. 3. 249. See **Abugge.**

Abiggen, *v.* pay for, b. 2, 127. See **Abugge.**

Abit, dress, 1. 3. Lit. habit.

Abite, *pr. pl.* they (i. e. the winds) bite off, nip off, b. 16. 26 ; Abiteþ, *pr. s.* bites off, nips, 19. 32. A. S. *ábítan.*

Ablamed, *pp.* blamed, a. 5. 75.

Ablende, *v.* blind, b. 18. 137 ; Ableynte, *pt. s.* b. 18. 323 ; Ablente, 21. 371. See below.

Ablyndeth, *pr. s.* blinds, b. 10. 264.

GLOSSARIAL INDEX.

A-bosted, *pt. s.* boasted against, defied in a bragging manner, 9. 152, b. 6. 156. Cf. E. *boast.*

A-bouen, *prep.* above, before, higher than, 8. 208, 17. 35; Aboue, b. 9. 14.

A-boute, *prep.* about, round, 1. 193; Abouten, b. 1. 6.

A-boute, *adv.* around, 11. 266; everywhere, a. 8. 30; employed about, in a busy state, b. 13. 369.

Abouȝte. See **Abugge.**

A-brode, *adv.* abroad, 16. 264; about, b. 14.60; Abrod, widely apart, 10. 143.

Abrybeþ; gon abrybeþ = go a-begging, 9. 246. See note to 9. 138, p. 111. '*Briber,* to beg his bread;' Cotgrave.

Abugge, *v.* atone for, pay for, suffer for (a thing), b. 6. 83, 168; a. 3. 236, a. 7. 74, 152; Abouȝte, *pt. s.* 11. 233, b. 9. 142, b. 12. 43, b. 13. 376; Abouȝte, *pt. pl.* b. 10. 281; Abouȝt, *pp.* paid for, 21. 433. See also **Abye, Abygge, Abie, Abigge.** A. S. *dbycgan*; corrupted to *abide* in the 16th century.

A-bydyng, *s.* patience, endurance, 22. 294.

Abydynge, *pres. part.* enduring, persevering, persistent, 19. 136, 23. 143; b. 19. 289.

Abye, *v.* suffer, atone, atone for, pay for, b. 9. 88, b. 18. 401. See **Abie, Abugge.**

A-bygge, *v.* pay dearly for, suffer for (a thing), 3. 141, 9. 41, 17. 220, 21. 448. See **Abigge, Abugge.**

Ac, *conj.* but, 1. 62, 191; 2. 42, 4. 115, 10. 330. A. S. *ac,* Goth. *ak.* See also **Ak.**

A-cale, *pp.* chilled, very cold, 21. 439, p. 264. Cf. Icel. *kalinn,* pp. of *kala,* to cool. See note. And see **Akale.**

Accesse, *s.* an attack of sickness, esp. of fever, a. 5. 210. See *Axes* in Cathol. Anglicum.

Acchett, hatchet, axe, 4. 462.

Accidie, *s.* a fit of sluggishness, fit of sloth, 7. 417; b. 5. 366. Lat. *accidia.*

Accombreth. See **Acombre.**

A-cloye, *imper.* 1 *pl.* let us embarrass, encumber, 21. 296. Orig. to lame a horse by driving a nail into his foot in shoeing. '*Enclouer vn cheval,* to prick a horses foot in the shooing;' Cotgrave. See *Acloyde* in Gloss. to Fitzherbert's Husbandry (E. D. S.).

Acombre, *v.* trouble, vex, hinder, clog, encumber, b. 2. 50, b. 19. 215; Acombreth, *pr. pl.* are a hindrance to,

b. 12. 57; Acombrede, *pt. pl.* encumbered, plagued, R. 2. 28; Acombred, *pp.* overcome, overwhelmed, b. 1. 32; b. 1. 194; Acombrid, R. 4. 67. See *encombrer* in Cotgrave; and Prompt. Parv. p. 6, n. 4.

Acordaunce, concord, agreement, 4. 339, 398.

Acorden, *v.* agree, b. 5. 335, b. 13. 121; Acorde, *v.* 4. 275, 374, 380; to grant, b. 3. 317; Acordeth, *pr. s.* 4. 358, 364, 9. 243; A-corden, *pr. pl.* agree, come to an agreement, 20. 285; Acorde, *pr. s. subj.* a. 10. 87; *pr. pl. subj.* b. 17. 303; Acordede, *pt. s.* held with, 23. 303; agreed, a. 4. 78; Acorded, *pt. s.* agreed, 12. 311; agreed to, b. 11. 42; Acordeden, *pt. pl.* agreed, b. 18. 232; Acordede, united, 21. 244; A-cordynge, *pres. part.* agreeing, a. 10. 89.

A-corse, *pr. s. subj.* should curse, 1. 127, b. pr. 99; Acorsed, *pt. s.* 19. 224; Acorsed, *pp.* accursed, 21. 97. From A.S. *corsian,* to curse.

A-corsede, accursed, 20. 254, 23. 263. Pl. of *acorsed,* pp. of the verb above.

A-counte, *v.* go through accounts, reckon up, 8. 33, 13. 66; give account, 12. 298; esteem, think of, b. 11. 15; A-counteþ, *pr. s.* cares, 4. 396; Acounteþ, *pr. pl.* esteem, 11. 258; Acountede, *pt. s.* counted, valued, 22. 414; A-counted, *pp.* counted, reckoned, 10. 239; considered, a. 1. 88; thought anything of, R. 3. 155; Acountid, *pp.* counted, R. 3. 157.

A-couped, *pt. s.* blamed, accused, b. 13. 459. '*Encoulper,* to appeach, accuse, blame for;' Cotgrave. See **Coupe,** and see note to the line.

A-day, lit. on or in the day, hence, at morn, b. 6. 310. See **A,** *prep.*

Addre, serpent, 21. 317, 328; Adders, *pl.* R. 3. 18.

Adiectif, adjective, 4. 338.

A-do, to do, 6. 164. (Put for *at do,* where *at* is the sign of the infinitive or gerund in Northern English.) See note on p. 68.

Adoune, *adv.* down, 9. 29, 11. 94, 23. 227, b. 10. 330, R. 2. 39; *also* Adoun, Adowne, Adown. A. S. *of dúne,* lit. off the down or hill.

Adrad, *pp. as adj.* afraid, greatly afraid, 22. 307, 23. 352; Adradde, *pl.* b. 19. 21. A.S. *ádrǽdan,* to dread greatly.

A-drencheþ, *pr. pl.* drown (themselves), 11. 162; Adreynten, *pt. pl.* were drowned, b. 10. 408; Adreynt, *pp.* a.

GLOSSARIAL INDEX.

10. 60; drenched (with physic), 23. 377; A-drent, *pp.* drowned, 11. 245. A.S. *ádrencan.*
Afaiten, *v.* to tame, 7. 7; Affaiten, b. 5. 37; Affaiteth, *pr. s.* restrains, b. 14. 296; Affeyteth, *pr. pl.* train, b. 11. 375; Affaite þe, tame for thyself, b. 6. 32. '*Affaiter,* as *Affaicter,* to trim, trick, deck, ... also to tame, reclaim;' Cotgrave. See note to b. 11. 375, on p. 178, line 1.
Afaytyng, a-begging, 10. 170. Put for *a faytyng,* where *a* = on. See A, *prep.*; and see **Faiten.**
A-felde, *adv.* to the field, a-field, 5. 144; Afeld, 9. 198.
Afere, *v.* frighten away, 23. 166; b. 20. 165; Afereth, *pr. s.* frightens, drives away, 21. 478, b. 18. 430; A-fered, *pp.* seized with fear, 5. 66; afraid, frightened, 9. 179, 16. 165, 20. 80, 21. 125; Aferede, *pp. pl.* 9. 128; Aferd, *pp.* 2. 10, 12. 279; Afert, a. 4. 49; Aferde, *pp. pl.* b. 6. 123. A.S. *áfǽran,* to terrify.
A-feynted, *pp.* enfeebled, 23. 198.
Affaiten. See **Afaiten.**
Affendid, *pp.* offended, R. 3. 208.
Afferes, *pl.* affairs, business, doings, 7. 152.
Affeyteth. See **Afaiten.**
Afflaunce, reliance, trust, 19. 256.
Affoot. See **Afote.**
Affor. See **Afore.**
Afforse, *adv.* perforce, R. 4. 22. '*A force,* with much indeavour;' Cotgrave.
Affrayned, 1 *pt. s.* asked, b. 16. 274. See **Frained.**
Afore, *adv.* before, b. 14. 134; Affore, R. 3. 246; Afor, *prep.* b. 5. 12, b. 16. 45; in the sight of, b. 12. 81; Affor, *prep.* before, R. 4. 73.
Aforth, *v.* afford, b. 6. 201. A.S. *forð-ian,* to further aid, advance, perform. Hence mod. E. *afford.*
A-fote, *adv.* afoot, a. 5. 6; Afoot, b. 5. 6; Affoot, R. 4. 65.
Afrontede, *pt. s.* addressed, confronted, accosted, 23. 5.
After, *prep.* according to, like to, like, 3. 27, 4. 272; Aftur, a. 7. 198; After, according to (the position of), 1. 14; in accordance with, b. 12. 188, b. 13. 94; for, 15. 120; After the dede, according to the deed, 4. 474; After person, according to the parson's instructions, 15. 124.
After, *adv.* after, secondly, b. 10. 358; Aftur, a. 8. 4.

Afurst. See **Afyrst.**
A-fyngred, *pp. as adj.* exceedingly hungry, oppressed by hunger, 12. 43, 50; 17. 15, 18. 67; b. 6. 269; A-fyngrid, a. 12. 59; Afyngrede, *pp. pl.* exceedingly hungry, 10. 85. Put for *of-hyngred,* from A.S. *ofhyngrian (of-hingrian),* to be excessively hungry. See **Afyrst,** and note to b. 6. 269.
Afyrst, *pp. as adj.* athirst, very thirsty, oppressed by thirst, b. 14. 162; Afurst, 10. 85, 12. 43, 17. 15. A.S. *of þyrst, (of þirst, of þirsted),* pp. very thirsty. See above, and note to 12. 43.
Agasteth, *pr. s.* frightens, drives away, b. 14. 280; Agast, *pp.* afraid, terrified, in fear, 3. 221, 22. 300; Agaste, *pl.* b. 13. 268. A.S. *gǽstan,* to terrify.
Agayn, Ageyn, Agayns. See **Aȝein, Aȝeines.**
A-glotye, *v.* satisfy, fill, 10. 76. Cf. E. *glut.*
Agon, *v.* obtain, b. 9. 106. Cf. A.S. *ágangan,* to require; Genesis ix. 5.
A-goo, *pp.* gone, departed, R. 3. 245. E. *ago.*
A-greued, *pp.* annoyed, troubled, vexed, 17. 209, R. 2. 113.
A-grounde, *adv.* on the ground, 21. 44: on this earth, b. 1. 60.
Agulten, *v.* to offend against. offend, b. 15. 385; Agulte, 7. 17, b. 14. 7; commit sin, be guilty, 18. 44; Agulte, 1 *pt. s.* offended against, 20. 276, b. 17. 294. A.S. *ágyltan.*
Aier, air, 2. 127, 11. 129. See **Eir.**
Air, heir, 11. 241; Aires, *pl.* 6. 59. See **Eir, Ayre.**
Aither, *pron.* either. Here aiþeres, of each of them, 13. 137, 138; Aiþer oþere, each other, 23. 353; Oure aiþer oþer = each of us (exciting) the other, 7. 188. See **Ayþer.**
Ak, *conj.* but, a. 5. 254. See **Ac.**
Akale, *pp.* chilled, b. 18. 392. See **Acale.**
Aker, acre, 9. 113, a. 7. 4.
Aknowe, *pp.*; Be aknowe = acknowledge, confess, 10. 86. A.S. *oncná-wan* to acknowledge.
Al, *adv.* altogether, 2. 30; entirely, wholly, b. 1. 31; Al a = the whole of a, b. 6. 258; Al day, continually, 18. 96; Al so, as, 12. 103.
Alarme, *interj.* to arms, 23. 92. E. *alarm;* see note.
Alay, alloy, b. 15. 342.
Alayed, *pp.* alloyed, 18. 79, b. 15. 346. From O.F. *aleier* (later *aloyer*), Lat. *alligare,* to combine.

Alconomye, alchemy, a. 11. 157. See **Alkenamye**.
Alday, *adv.* continually, b. 15. 352. See **Al**.
Ale, *s.* ale, 7. 159; ale-house, 1. 43, 9. 122, 10. 194; Alle (*better* Ale), ale, i.e. a feast or ale-house, a. pr. 42.
A-lee, *adv.* on the lee, to leeward, R. 4. 74.
A-leggen, *v.* allege, 13. 31; Alleggen, declare, b. 11. 88; A-legged, *pp.* a. 12. 102.
Aleyne (?), R. 2. 136. Perhaps for *aleid* = *on-leid*, laid upon ; hence *aleyne vppon oþer* = one laid upon another. *Lein* (lain) and *leid* (laid) are frequently confused. Or perhaps read *a leen*, i.e. one gift (lit. loan) upon another.
Aliche, *adv.* alike, b. 12. 209, b. 16. 57.
Alie, ally, R. 3. 31.
Aliri, *adv.* across (said of the legs), b. 6. 124, a. 7. 115. Cf. 'And fond hir liggyng *lirylong*,' i.e. and found her lying with her legs stretched out; Pardoner and Tapster, 310, in the Tale of Betyn, ed. Furnivall. From the A.S. *lira*, the flesh, muscles, esp. used for the fleshy parts of the leg, as in *spær-lira*, the calf of the leg, occurring as a gloss to *sura* in Wright, A.S. Vocab. i. 44, where we also find 'Pulpa, vel viscum, *lira*,' and 'Nates, *ears-lyre*.' It is the same word as the Platt-Deutsch *lurre*, the loin, thigh, in the Bremen Wörterbuch. Hence *a-liri* = with the calf of one leg resting on the shin of the other. At least, such seems to be the sense intended. See **A-lyry**.
Alkamye, alchemy, b. 10. 212 (Laud MS.). See also **Alkenamye**, and note.
Alkenamye, alchemy, b. 10. 212. See **Alconomye**, **Alkamye**. '*Alcanamye*, corinthium, elixer;' Cath. Angl.
Alkynnes, of every kind; Of alkinnes craftes = of crafts of every kind, b. 10. 177; Of alkynnes siȝtes = of sights of every kind, b. 12. 130; Of alkynnes filthe = from filth of every kind, b. 14. 17; Alkynnes resoun, reason of every kind, b. 15. 52, b. 17. 343; Alkynnes creatures, creatures of every kind, b. 19. 211; Alkynnes crafty men, craftsmen of every kind, b. 3. 224. Also contracted to Alkyn, *as in* Alkyn crafty men = craftsmen of every kind, b. 6. 70; Alkin libbyng laboreres = living labourers of all kinds, i.e. all kinds of labourers alive, b. pr. 222.

Alle; *for* **Ale**, q. v.
Alleggen. See **Aleggen**.
Aller, of all; ȝowre aller, of you all, b. 19. 468; Owre aller, of us all, b. 16. 205. A.S. *ealra*, gen. pl. of *eall*, all. See **Alre**.
Allowaunce, praise, approval, estimation, b. 11. 215, b. 14. 109.
Allowe, *v.* praise, b. 16. 233; *pr. pl.* praise, b. 14. 307; Allowed, *pt. pl.* praised, b. 15. 4; Allowed, *pp.* praised, approved, b. 10. 433, 435. '*Allouer*, to allow, advow, approve, like well of;' Cotgrave. See also **Alowe**.
Almaries, *pl.* aumbries, ambries, places for keeping things, cupboards, 17. 88. See *Ambry* in my Etym. Dict.
Almesful, *adj.* charitable, 7. 48.
Almesse, alms, charity, 9. 133, 10. 141; **Almus**, a. 7. 120, 135; Almes, b. 7. 75; Almesses, *pl.* alms, b. 10. 298; presents received as alms, b. 15. 306. A.S. *ælmesse*, from Lat. *eleemosyna*.
Alofte, *adv.* on high, aloft, high up, up, in elevation, 1. 175, b. 12. 222; Aloft, 21. 44.
A-longet, *pp.* filled with longing, greedy, a. 7. 254. See note, p. 116, l. 11.
Alose, *v.* praise highly, 20. 101. '*Los*, laud, praise;' Cotgrave.
A-louance, profit, lit. hire, 10. 271. From F. *louer*, to hire, Lat. *locare*.
Aloute, *v.* bow, bow down, 16. 169. See **Loute**.
A-lowaunce, praise, approval, 16. 290. See **Allowe**.
A-lowe, *v.* commend, praise (for it), 19. 252; I *pr. s.* I approve of, R. 2. 69; Aloweþ, *pr. s.* approves of, 4. 74; commends, 19. 82; Alowede, *pt. s.* praised, commended, 13. 138; Allowed, *pp.* praised, 8. 96. See **Allowe**.
Alowe, *adv.* low down, b. 12. 222; Alow, b. 12. 234.
Alre, *adj. gen. pl.* of all, 22. 473. See **Aller**.
Al-so, Also, *adv. and conj.* as, 17. 298, 22. 440; also, likewise, 21. 184; Alse, a. 5. 144; Als, also, b. 3. 72; as, b. 4. 195.
Alswythe, *adv.* as quickly as might be, b. 3. 101. From *als*, as, and *swithe*, quickly.
Alþer-ryghtfulleste, *adj. sup.* most righteous of all, 11. 24.
A-lyghte, *pt. s.* descended, 12. 144; dismounted, 20. 64; alighted, settled, 22. 202.
A-lyry, *adv.* 9. 129. See **Aliri**.
Alyue, *adv.* alive, living, b. 8. 111, a. 2. 14.

GLOSSARIAL INDEX. 309

Amaistren, *v.* have power over, control, compel, keep in subjection, 3. 161, 9. 221; Amaystren, a. 7. 200; Amaysteren, a. 2. 117; Amaistrye, to teach, instruct, govern, manage, control, b. 2. 147; Amaistrien, b. 6. 214; A-maistrid, *pp.* mastered, got the power over, 3. 167; Amaysterd, a. 2. 144. '*Maistrier*, to master, govern, rule, sway, &c.;' Cotgrave. Cf. Shropshire *amaister*, to teach. 'An old man near Leintwardine, speaking of his schoolmaster, said, 'E used to *amaister* me, Sir.'—Shrop. Wordbook.

Amanced, *pp.* excommunicated (*a wrong reading*), 14. 104 *n.* See **Mansed.**

Amarride, *pt. pl.* disturbed, vexed, R. pr. 16.

Amende, *v.* amend, grow better, 2. 77; to make amends or restitution, 20. 314; amend, aid, better, repair, b. 10. 121; reform, b. 10. 319; remedy, b. 10. 60; Amenden, *v.* b. 10. 269; Amendy, *ger.* to correct, 2. 165; Amenden, *pr. pl.* make amends, 20. 202.

Amendes, *pl.* satisfaction, amends, 3. 120, 5. 84. To amendes = as satisfaction for, b. 18. 325; Myne amendes = satisfaction to me, 5. 97.

Amercy, *v.* to amerce, fine, b. 6. 40; Amercyn, 2 *pr. pl.* fine, 9. 37.

Amonge, *adv.* at times, b. 14. 237; Oþerwhile amonge, at odd times, occasionally, R. pr. 70.

Amonges, *prep.* amongst, 1. 131; Amongus, a. 8. 79; Amongis, R. 3. 254.

Amorteisede, *pt. pl.* granted in mortmain, 18. 54; Amortesed, b. 15. 315. See note, p. 225.

A-morwe, *adv.* on the morrow, next morning, 8. 13, R. 4. 40.

Amounteþ, *pr. s.* amounteth to, signifies, a. 3. 87.

Ampulles, *pl.* ampullae, small phials for holy water, b. 5. 527; Ampolles, a. 6. 11. See note, p. 100; and see **Hanypeles.**

Amydde, *prep.* amidst, in the middle of, b. 8. 30; through the midst of, 14. 43.

A-myddes, *prep.* amidst, 11. 67.

Amyddes, *adv.* in the middle, b. 13. 82.

An, *conj.* and, 23. 72; b. 7. 44. Short for *and.*

An, *conj.* if, b. 2. 132.

An, *adj.* one, b. 17. 183; An othre, one other, another, b. 1. 106 (see note).

An, *prep.* on, upon, 5. 113; in, b. 15. 28; An auenture = in case, lest by chance, b. 3. 72; An hy, on high, 6. 187; An hih, 19. 106; An hiegh, b. pr. 13; An ydel = idly, in an idle manner, b. 5. 580; = in vain, uselessly, 15. 7. A.S. *an, on,* on, in.

Ancre, an anchoress, 4. 141; Ancres, *pl.* anchorites, 1. 30, 9. 146. A.S. *ancra,* an anchorite, Lat. *anachoreta.*

And, *conj.* if, 3, 204, 7. 289, &c.

Anewe, *v.* renew, R. 3. 24.

Angre, ill-temper, vexation, 7. 79; trouble, suffering, misery, 13. 207; violence, b. 13. 336; trial, affliction, b. 17. 336; Angres, *pl.* troubles, sufferings, 7. 114; afflictions, b. 12. 11. (Seldom used in the modern sense.)

Angre, *v.* annoy, injure, b. 14. 244; Angrye, *v.* 17. 86; Angreth, *pr. s.* makes angry, b. 5. 117. Icel. *angra.*

An-heiȝ, *adv.* on high, a. pr. 13. See **An,** *prep.*

Anon, *adv.* immediately, soon, 1. 111, 2. 115; presently, soon, b. 9. 130; presently, soon after, 4. 323. A:S. *on án,* in one, i. e. in a moment.

Anoye, *v.* vex, R. 2. 67; Anoyed, *pt. pl.* annoyed, R. 3. 71. See **Anuyed.**

Anuyed, *pp.* vexed, displeased, a. 2. 144; Anuyȝed, a. 3. 182, a. 5. 74; Anuyȝen, *pr. pl.* annoy, trouble, a. 2. 97. See **Anoye.**

Any þinge, in any respect, at all, b. 18. 386.

Anyente, *v.* destroy, annihilate, 20. 267; Anyented, *pp.* 21. 389. '*Aneantir*, to abrogate, annichilate;' Cotgrave. (*Anentesch* is from the F. base *aneantiss-.*)

Apaied. See **Apayed.**

Apaired. See **Apeire.**

Aparail, dress, apparel, 7. 30, 11. 116; Aparaille, b. 13. 278; Apparaille, b. 8. 116; Apparail, a. 9. 111. See **Parail.**

Aparaile, *v.* dress, prepare, a. 7. 53; A-paraild, *pp.* dressed, 8. 161; Apparaille, *v.* a. 2. 170, b. 6. 59; Apparayle, *v.* a. 2. 148. See **Parailede.**

Apartie, *adv.* apart, 16. 54; Aparte, separately, R. 4. 36.

Apayed, *pp.* pleased, 9. 115; b. 6. 110, 198; a. 7. 101; contented, 10. 178; With apayet = pleased with, a. 10. 126; Apaied, *pp.* pleased, 16. 63; Apaiede, *pp. pl.* pleased, 3. 45. O.F. *apaier,* to appease, from Lat. *pacare.*

Apeel, appeal, accusation, 20. 284; see note, p. 246. See **Apeles.**

GLOSSARIAL INDEX.

Apeere, *v.* appear, 4. 150; Apeeren, *v.* a. 3. 109.
Apeire, *v.* harm, injure, R. pr. 73; a. 6. 54; impair, R. 2. 79; Apeiren, a. 7. 158; Apeyre, injure, damage, 8. 211; punish, 9. 167; Apeireþ, *pr. s.* harms, injures, 4. 164; Appeireth, b. 7. 47; Apeyre, 2 *pr. pl. subj.* b. 5. 573; Apeyre, *pr. pl. subj.* diminish, 6. 145; Appayre, *pr. pl. subj.* b. 5. 47; Apeire, a. 5. 38; Appeyred, *pt. pl.* b. 6. 134; Apaired, *pp.* injured, 9. 229; Appeyred, *pp.* b. 6. 221. Cf. E. *impair.* *Apeire* answers to a Low Lat. form **adpeiorare,* from *peius,* worse.
A-peles, *pl.* appeals, 3. 186, 244. See **Apeel.**
Apendeþ, *pr. s.* belongs, is proper to, 2. 97; Appendeth, *pr. s.* b. 1. 45. '*Appendre,* ... to depend on, hang by, appertaine;' Cot.
A-pertelich, *adv.* openly, plainly, 4. 316; Aperteliche, evidently, a. 5. 15.
Apewarde, keeper of apes, 8. 284.
Apeyre. See **Apeire.**
A-poisoned, *pp.* poisoned, 4. 164; Apoysoned, infected, b. 15. 523.
Apose, *v.* question, ask, 4, 5, 15. 155, 16. 93, 17. 163; Aposen, examine verbally, a. 3. 5; oppose in disputation, a. 12. 8; Appose, question, ask, examine, b. 3. 5, b. 12. 215; Apposen, *pr. pl.* ask, question, b. 12. 232; Aposede, *pt. s.* questioned, cross-examined, 6. 10; Aposed, *pt. s.* 16. 192; *pt. pl.* 2. 45; Apposed, *pt. s.* b. 1. 47, b. 13. 222; Apposeden, *pt. pl.* disputed, argued, b. 7. 138; Aposid, *pp.* a. 11. 289; Apposed, *pp.* b. 15. 376.
Apostata, apostate, 2. 98.
Apparaille. See **Aparail.**
Appeireth, Appeyred. See **Apeire.**
Appele, *v.* accuse, b. 11. 413.
Appendeth. See **Apendeþ.**
Appose. See **Apose.**
Aprentys, *pl.* apprentices, 4. 281. See **Prentys.**
Aprocheþ, *pr. s.* approaches, 18. 209; Aproched, *pt. s.* 21. 176.
Aquencheþ, *pr. s.* quenches, 20. 251; Aqueynt, *pp.* quenched, destroyed, 21. 394. A.S. *ácwencan.*
Aquite, *v.* pay, pay off, 16. 12; Aquyte, *v.* redeem, 21. 394.
Aquykye, *v.* quicken, make alive again, 21. 394.
Ar, *adv. and conj.* before, ere, 8. 267, 9. 347, 11. 11, 13. 232. A S. *ǽr.*
Ar, are; It ar þis=it is these, b. 15. 321.

A-rate, *v.* correct, rebuke, reprove, 13. 35, b. 11. 98; Aratede, *pt. s.* reproached, 6. 11; Arated, blamed, b. 11. 367; Arated, *pp.* rated, abused, b. 14. 163. Cf. E. *rate,* to scold.
Arbytours, *pl.* arbitrators, 7. 382.
Arches, *pl.* court of Arches, 23. 136, b. 2. 60, b. 20. 135. See note, p. 279.
Areche, *v.* reach, R. 5. 12. A.S. *árǽcan.*
A-redy, *adj.* ready, 7. 97, b. 4. 192.
Aredy, *adv.* ready, already, R. 2. 129.
Aren, *pr. pl.* are, 1. 126, 2. 139. See **Arn, Ar.**
Arerage, arrears, debt, 10. 274, 13. 63, Arrerage, b. 10. 469; Arerages, *pl.* 12. 297. '*Arrerage, Arrierage,* an arrerage, the rest, or the remainder of a paiment, that which was left unpaid, or behind;' Cotgrave.
A-rere, *adv.* backwards, 7. 405; Arrere, b. 5. 354; *used as imper. pl.* return, R. 3. 110.
Arered, *pp.* raised, levied, a. 2. 51.
A-resonede, *pt. s.* argued with, 14. 129; 1 *pt. s.* 14. 184; Aresonedest, 2 *pt. s.* didst argue with, b. 12. 218. '*Araisonner,* to reason, conferre, talke, discourse with;' Cotgrave.
Arest, at rest; lit. *on* rest, b. 5. 234.
Arith, *adv.* rightly, R. 3. 120.
Armes, *pl.* arms (weapons), 19. 187; heraldic arms, insignia, 22. 12; coatarmour, b. 5. 508 (in owre armes = with our device upon His coat of arms).
Arn, *pr. pl.* are, 10. 105, 110.
Aroutyd, *pp.* driven out of the assembly, R. 3. 221. From the sb. *rout.*
Arrerage. See **Arerage.**
Arrere. See **Arere.**
Ars, *pl.* arts, 12. 98. See **Artz.**
Arst, *adv. superl.* first, b. 4. 105; sooner, b. 14. 216. A.S. *ǽrest,* superl. of *ǽr.*
Artow, *for* art thou, thou art, b. 5. 260, b. 8. 72.
Artz, *pl.* arts, sciences, b. 10. 150. See **Ars.**
Arwed, *pp.* rendered slothful, made cowardly, 4. 237. A.S. *eargian,* to be slothful; from *earg,* inert. See Cath. Angl. p. 12, *n.* 4.
Arwes, *pl.* arrows, 4. 482, 23. 117, 226.
As, *conj.* as if, a. 5. 233, R. 3. 46; *used pleonastically,* 12. 282, 14. 28; As by = to judge by, according to, 12. 265, 18. 157; As quik, very quickly, b. 24. 189; As tyte, at once, quickly, b. 13. 319.
Asailen. See **Assaile.**

GLOSSARIAL INDEX.   311

Asaye. See **Assaye.**
A-scapie, *v.* escape, 4. 61; Ascapen, b. 2. 202; Ascaped, *pp.* 9. 79; escaped (hence, separated from), a. 7. 70. See **Askapie.**
A-schomed, *pp.* ashamed, a. 5. 215.
Aschonne, *v.* shun, avoid, R. 2. 185.
Asele. See **Assele.**
Aserued. See **Asserue.**
A-seth, *s.* satisfaction, 20. 203. See note, and Cath. Angl. p. 13, *n.* 6.
Asisours, *pl.* jurors, 23. 290. From F. *assise,* 'an assize or sessions;' Cot. See **Sisour.**
A-skapie, *v.* escape, 3. 215; A-skape, a. 2. 180. See **Ascapie.**
Asken, *v.* ask, 19. 261; Askeþ, *pr. s.* requires, 1. 21, 4. 301, 6. 67, 22. 478; R. 3. 23 (see the note); Askiþ, *pr. s.* requires, a. 1. 180; Asken, *pr. pl.* ask, require, a. 1. 100; demand, 4. 246. See **Axe.**
Askes, *pl.* ashes, 4. 125. A.S. *asce,* pl. *ascan.*
Askyng, *s.* request, 22, 480.
A-slepe, asleep, b. 2. 51.
Asoile. See **Assoille.**
Asondry, *adv.* separate, b. 17. 164.
Aspare, *v.* spare, afford, 11. 84.
Aspie, *v.* look at, see, discover, spy, 3. 46, 235; 13. 140; Aspien, to look after, mind, a. 2. 201; Aspye, to spy out, b. 5. 170; Aspied, *pp.* examined, 20. 34; seen, 22. 302.
Aspie, *s.* a spy, 22. 342.
Assaile, *v.* assail, attack, 23. 374; A-sailen, 14. 63; Asailid, *pp.* tempted, 21. 332.
Assay, the trial, proof, b. 10. 253.
Assaye, *v.* try, examine, 7. 357; taste, try, b. 16. 74; practise, b. 16. 106; endeavour, b. 6. 24; Assayen, examine, a. 3. 5; Asaye, *v.* try, examine, 4. 5, 9. 22; try (it), a. 5. 152; Assaye, 1 *pr. pl.* try, prove (it), b. 18. 69; Assay, *imp. s.* try, ask, 17. 164. E. *essay.*
Assele, 1 *pr. s.* I seal, b. 2, 112; Asselen, *pr. pl.* seal, a. 3. 143; A-seled, *pp.* 3. 113, 20. 6; A-seeled, 20. 9; A-selet, sealed, signed, a. 2. 81. From O.F. *seël,* Lat. *sigillum.*
Asserued, *pp.* deserved, b. 12. 197; A-serued, *pp.* 15. 137.
Assetz, satisfaction, b. 17. 237. O.F. *assez,* enough, Lat. *ad satis.*
Assises, *s. pl.* assizes, R. 3. 187.
Assoille, *v.* explain, solve, b. 10. 245, b. 12. 216; absolve, pardon, 22. 190, b. 5. 276, b. 19. 180, 185; Assoyle, absolve, 7. 296; Assoile, b. 3. 40; As-soilen, b. pr. 70; Asoile, *v.* answer, solve, explain, 12. 157; absolve, 13. 7; Asoily, 4. 42; Asoilie, 1. 68; A-soylye, 22. 185; Asoyle, absolve, a. 3. 41; Asoylen, absolve, a. pr. 67; Assoilled, *pp.* forgiven, absolved, b. 3. 143. O.F. *assoiler,* Lat. *ab-soluere.*
A-sterte, *v.* escape, avoid, 14. 212; A-stert, b. 11. 392. Lit. to *start* from, or away from.
Astonyed, *pp.* astonied, R. 2. 8.
Astronomyens, *pl.* astronomers, 18. 96; 22. 244; Astrymyanes, b. 15. 352.
A-swage, *v.* assuage, soften, 7. 88.
A-swiþe, *for* As swiþe, *adv.* as quickly as possible, a. 3. 96.
At, *prep.* of, 2. 205, b. 3. 25, b. 13. 309; of, from, 3. 176, 4. 379; according to, 4. 285; amongst, b. 15. 208; in, b. 7. 128.
At ones, *adv. phr.* at once, b. 11. 324; together, b. 5. 163.
Atache, *v.* to attach, arrest, a. 2. 174; Attache, b. 2. 199; Atacheþ, *pr. s.* as *pl.* cling to, cleave to (*governing treuthe*), 12. 306 (see the next line); Attached, *pt. s.* laid claim to, b. 16. 261; Attached, *pp.* claimed, 19. 279; arrested, b. 2. 236; A-tached, *pp.* arrested, 3. 252; Atachet, a. 2. 212; Atache, *imp. s.* arrest, 3. 211. E. *attach.*
Atamede, *pt. s.* broached, opened (a vessel), 20. 68, b. 17. 68. '*Attamyn* a wesselle wyth drynke, abbrochyn, *Attamino, depleo;*' Prompt. Parv. From an O.F. form *atamer* = Lat. *attami-nare;* but the usual F. form is *enta-mer* (see Cotgrave) = Lat. *intaminare.*
Atamed, *pp.* tamed, R. 3. 27.
Atemye, *v.* attain, 20. 240. 244.
Ateynt, *pp.* attainted, accused, 23. 162; Ateynte, b. 20. 161. '*Attaint,* raught, or attained unto . . . tainted, attainted, convicted, appeached, accused of, charged with;" Cot.
Aþurst, *pp. as adj.* athirst, very thirsty, 21. 439, b. 10. 59. See **Afyrst.**
Athynkeþ, *impers. pr. s.* grieves, repents, 7. 100, b. 18. 89. A.S. *of-þyncan.*
Attache. See **Atache.**
Atte, *put for* at te (=the), at the, 1. 160, 4. 34, &c.; Atten, at the, 1. 43, 9. 122.
Attere, venom, poison, b. 12. 256. A.S. *átor, áttor,* venom.
Atweyne, in two, 1. 114, b. 7. 116. Lit. ' on twain.'

GLOSSARIAL INDEX.

A-two, *adv.* asunder, apart, in two, 9. 64, 21. 76.
A-twynne, *adv.* apart, separated, 19. 191. Cf. Icel. *tvinnr,* two and two.
Auaile, *v.* avail, be useful for, be of advantage to, assist, help; Auaille, b. 7. 7, 10. 273; Auayle, 10. 276; A-vayle, 10. 7; Availith, *pr. s.* is worth, R. 1. 24, R. 4. 54; Auailled, *pt. s.* helped, b. 10. 273. '*Avaylyn,* or profytyn, *Valeo, prosum*;' Prompt. Parv.
Auarous, *adj.* miserly, avaricious, 17. 279; used as a personification of Avarice, b. 8. 88; Auerous, covetous, 11. 86; Auerouse, 2. 189.
Auarousere, *adj. comp. pl.* more avaricious, b. 1. 189.
Auaunce, *v.* advance, promote, 11. 255, b. 9. 159; Avaunset, *pt. pl.* have promoted, raised to the rank, a. 4. 116; Auaunced, *pp.* promoted, advanced, placed in authority, 14. 104; Auaunsed, 2. 189; Avaunset, a. 1. 165; Auanced, 4. 36.
Auauntying, *pres. part.* vaunting, boasting, 7. 35.
Auctour, author, b. 15. 368.
Audience, hearing, 8. 94.
Auditour, auditor of accounts, 22. 463.
Auenture, *s.* chance; Good auenture = by good luck, b. 6. 79; An auenture = lest perchance, b. 3. 72; In auenture = in case, a. 7. 42; lest perchance, a. 3. 265; On auenture = in case, b. 3. 66. See **Aunter.**
Auerous. See **Auarous.**
Aues, *pl.* Aves, prayers beginning with *Ave, Maria,* b. 15. 176.
Aueyr, wealth, property, 7. 32. O.F. *aveir, avoir,* to have, used as sb. with the sense of 'property.' See **Avere, Avoir** in Halliwell.
Auhte, *pt. s.* ought, 7. 86; Aughte, R. 2. 49. See **Auȝte.**
Avise, *s.* advice, R. 3. 8.
Auisen, *v. refl.* look round them, think, reflect, 18. 53. See **Auyse.**
Auncel, a steel-yard, weighing machine, 7. 224; Auncere, b. 5. 218. See Murray's New English Dictionary.
Aungel, angel, b. 12. 149; Aungeles, *gen. pl.* of angels, 23. 241.
Aunter, *s.* adventure, fortune, luck; Good aunter = by good luck, peradventure, 9. 79; An aunter, in case, lest perchance, 4. 437, 9. 40. See **Auenture.**
Auntrep, *pr. s. refl.* adventures (himself), ventures, 11. 216; Auntrede,

pt. s. ventured, 21. 232; Auntred, b. 18. 220; Auntred, *pt. s. refl.* ventured (with *on* = against), 23. 175. See above.
Auntres, *pl.* adventurers, 21. 14. Probably an error for Auntrous.
Auntrous, *adj. as sb. pl.* adventurous knights, b. 18. 16.
Auoutrie, adultery, b. 2. 175, b. 12. 76. O. F. *avouterie, avulterie,* from Lat. *adulterium.*
Avowe, *v.* declare, assert, avouch, maintain, 4. 315, 16. 140, 21. 226; Auouwe, 16. 114; Auoue, a. 3. 242; Avowe, 1 *p. s. pr.* avouch, R. 1. 112. O. F. *avouer,* later *advouer,* 'to advow, avouch, . . warrant, authorize,' &c.; Cotgrave. From Lat. *aduocare.*
A-vowe, 1 *pr. s.* make a vow, vow, 7. 438; Avowed, *pt. s.* made a vow, b. 5. 388; A-vowed, *pp.* 8. 13. Distinct from the above. See below.
Auowe, *s.* vow, b. 5. 547; '*Auowe,* Votum'; Prompt. Parv.
Auter, altar, 19. 264; Auteres, *pl.* b. 10. 313; Auters, 6. 165. O.F. *alter, auter, autel,* from Lat. *altare.*
Autor, authority, teacher (lit. author), 12. 150; Autowr, b. 10. 243.
Auyse, *v. refl.* consider, b. 15. 314; Avyse þe byfore = take advice beforehand, 5. 21. See **Auisen.**
Auȝt, *as adv.,* at all, b. 5. 311, 540.
Auȝte, 1 *pt. s.* I ought, b. 2. 28. See **Auhte.**
Awaite, *v.* watch for, 18. 62; Awayte, espy, b. 10. 333; guard, keep (in prison), a. 2. 182; Awaytestow, 2 *pr. s.* art thou looking at, b. 10. 257; Awayted, 1 *pt. s.* watched, searched, b. 16. 169.
A-wake, *v.* awake, arouse, 1. 213; Awakyd, *pt. pl.* awoke (to a sense of their folly), R. 3. 364.
Away-ward, *adv.* away, R. 2. 7.
Awgrym, *s.* arithmetic, R. 4. 53. '*Awgrym, Algorismus*'; Prompt. Parv.
Awilled, *pp.* willed, R. 3. 210.
A-wreke, *v.* avenge, a. 5. 68; Awreke, *pp.* 9. 208, 18. 4; Awroke, *pp.* b. 6. 204; Awreke, *imp. s.* 9. 158; satisfy, 11. 288; Awrek, revenge, a. 7. 160. A.S. *áwrecan.*
Axe, *v.* ask, b. 4. 102, b. 17. 284, R. 2. 34; Axen, *v.* b. 5. 543, b. 14. 261; Axeth, *pr. s.* requires, asks, claims, b. 10. 311, b. 14. 110; Axith, *pr. s.* requires, R. 3. 215; demands, R. 3. 174; Axen, *pr. pl.* ask, b. 12. 234; Axe, *pr. pl. subj.* b. 5. 430; Axed, 1

pt. s. I asked, b. 10. 155; Axid, *pt. pl.* required, R. 3. 4; Axe, *imp. s.* b. 10. 157; Axeth, *imper. pl.* ask, b. 13. 309.

Ay, *adv.* always, ever, continually, 6. 95, 11. 19; Aye, 12. 31.

Ayeles, *pl.* grandfathers, ancestors, b. 15. 317. O.F. *aiel,* Ital. *avolo;* from Lat. *auus.*

Ayre, heir, b. 16. 232; Ayres, *pl.* 4. 324, 435. See Air.

Ayþer, *pron.* either, each, each (of them), 4. 340, 17. 199; Ayþer oþer, each the other, each other, 11. 282, 17. 66. See Aither.

Aȝe, *adv.* again, back, 17. 312; Aȝein, b. 6. 44. See below.

Aȝein, *prep.* against, contrary to, b. 3. 155, 291; in return for, b. 5. 437; Aȝeyn, 22. 448; in return for, a. 11. 150; Aȝeine, b. 10. 104; Aȝene, 17. 216; Aȝen, 10. 218; Ageyn, 21. 380; Agayne, b. 19. 356; Come aȝein = came to meet, b. 4. 44.

Aȝeines, *prep.* against, contrary to, b. 4. 48; in opposition to, b. 9. 196; in return for, b. 10. 199; Aȝeynes, against, contrary to, b. 15. 52; Aȝeyns, contrary to, 21. 277; Aȝeins, b. 3. 92; Aȝens, against, 8. 151, 11. 217; A-gayns, 21. 264. E. *agains-t.*

Aȝeines, *conj.* against the time that, before the time that, b. 19. 314; Aȝeynst, 22. 319.

Aȝenwarde, *adv.* again, in return, 20. 75.

Aȝeyn, Aȝen. See Aȝein.

Aȝeynes, Aȝens. See Aȝeines, *prep.*

Aȝeynst. See Aȝeines, *conj.*

Babeled, 1 *pt. s.* babbled, muttered, b. 5. 8; Bablid, *pt. pl.* talked, chattered, R. 3. 78.

Baberlupped, *adj.* thick-lipped, 7. 198; Baberlipped, b. 5. 190.

Bacheler, novice in arts, one who is initiated, 10. 248; novice in arms, young knight, b. 16. 179; Bachelere, 21. 88; Bachelers, *pl.* bachelors, young men, b. pr. 87; Bachilers, 1. 85; Baccheleris, R. 3. 358. A *bachelor* was a novice in arms or arts.

Baches, *pl.* valleys, 8. 159. See *bæch* in Stratmann.

Backes, *pl.* See Bakkes.

Bad, (1) begged; (2) bade. See Bidde and Bede.

Badde peny, bad penny, counterfeit coin, 18. 73.

Baddelich, *adv.* badly, poorly, ill, 5. 55; Baddeliche, 18. 197.

Bagge, *s.* bag, pouch, purse, 1. 42, 6. 52; Bagg (with an allusion to Bagot, see the note), R. 2. 164; Bagges, *pl.* 11. 85.

Baiardes. See Bayarde.

Bakbite, *v.* backbite, slander, defame, b. 2. 80; Bakbyten, 3. 85.

Baken, *pp.* baked, 9. 318, b. 6. 295; Bake, 9. 178, 192; b. 6. 196. A.S. *bacen,* pp.

Bakesteres, *pl.* (female) bakers, b. 3. 79; Baxteres, b. pr. 218. A.S. *bœcestre,* a woman who bakes.

Bakken, *v.* cover their backs, clothe, a. 11. 185. See Bakkes.

Bakkes, *pl.* clothes (glossed *panni*), b. 10. 362; Backes, 14. 72. Lit. clothes for the *back,* cloaks; see note, p. 160. And see above.

Balder, *adj. comp.* bolder, more daring, b. 4. 107; Baldore, a. 4. 94.

Baldly, *adv.* boldly, 10. 28, b. 20. 325; Baldely, 19. 115; confidently, without hesitation, 22. 477.

Bale, sorrow, misfortune, misery, trouble, mischief; (also) wrong, harm, injury, destruction, 5. 85, 88, 89; 13. 56, 21. 33. A.S. *bealu, bealo.*

Baleyse, *s.* rod, stick, instrument of punishment, 12. 124; Baleis, b. 10. 176; Baleyses, *pl.* rods, b. 12. 12. See note to 7. 157, p. 80; and Prompt. Parv.

Baleysed, *pp.* flogged, beaten, whipped, 7. 157. Still in use in Shropshire; see Miss Jackson's Wordbook.

Balies, *s. pl.* bellies, a. pr. 41. See Bely.

Balkes, *s. pl.* ridges of land left unploughed, balks, 9. 114; b. 6. 109. A.S. *balca.* See *Balk* in Halliwell.

Balled, *adj.* bald, 23. 184, b. 20. 183; (metaphorically, as applied to a reason) bald, trite, worn out, insufficient, b. 10. 54; Ballid, R. 4. 70; Ballede, *pl.* 12. 38.

Ballokknyf, a kind of large knife worn suspended from the girdle, b. 15. 121. See note, p. 218.

Bamme, *imp. s.* cozen (?); or fill (?), feed (?), a. 7. 204. Prob. from M. E. *baumen,* to anoint, grease, lit. to cover with balm. The sense would thus be 'grease,' in a jocular sense. See *bame* in Halliwell, and *bawm* in Evans, Leicest. Glossary.

Baneoure, standard bearer, b. 15. 428. '*Banyowre,* or bannerberere;' Prompt. Parv.

GLOSSARIAL INDEX.

Baner, banner, flag, a. 8. 15; Banere, b. 20. 68, 95.
Banne, *v.* curse, 2. 58, 4. 144; Banneth, *pr. s.* curses, 10. 162; prohibits severely, b. 7. 88; Banned, *pt. s.* severely rebuked him, b. 10. 7.
Bar, *pt. s.* bore. See Bere.
Bar, *adj.* bare, stripped of hair, 7. 150; naked, 7. 157; Bare, naked, b. 5. 175; bald, 23. 184; Bare, empty, R. 4. 21; bare, trite, R. 4. 70.
Barge, *s.* ship, R. 4. 75.
Barke, husk, outer skin (of a walnut), 13. 144.
Barliche, barley, 7. 225.
Barliche, *adj.* made of barley, 9. 142.
Barn, child, 3. 3, 11. 233, 15. 127, 20. 84, 21. 243; Barne, b. 2. 3, b. 9. 142; man, b. 16. 250; Barnes, *pl.* children, 4. 189, 6. 70; Barnes bastardes = bastard children (where *bastardes* is used as a pl. adj.), 6. 71. A.S. *bearn.*
Barn-hede, childhood, manhood, 19. 136.
Barre, bar (in the legal sense, in the phr. *atte barre* = at the bar), 1. 160, 4. 452; Barres, *pl.* bars, bolts, 8. 239, 21. 283.
Barre, *imper.* 1 *pl.* let us bar, let us fasten, 21. 286.
Barst, *pt. s.* burst, broke, 9. 175; Barste, b. 6. 180. A.S. *bærst,* pt. t. of *berstan.*
Baselard, a kind of long dagger or short sword, suspended from the girdle, a. 11. 211; Basellarde, b. 15. 121; Baslard, b. 3. 303; Baselardes, *pl.* 4. 461, b. 15. 118. See note, p. 52.
Bat, in the double sense of 'bat' or 'mass,' a. 7. 167; Bat of erþe = mass or lump of earth (cf. E. *brick-bat*), 19. 92; Battis, *pl.* bats, i. e. staves, R. 3. 330; Battys, small pieces of broken meat, a. 12. 70 (Ingilby MS.).
Bat, *pr. s.* beats. See Bete.
Bataille, battle, 1. 108, b. 12. 107; contest, b. 16. 164; Bataile, warfare, 9. 352.
Batauntliche, *adv.* hastily, eagerly, b. 14. 213; Batauntlyche, 17. 56. F. *tout batant,* very hastily; Cotgrave. See note, p. 211.
Bated, *pt. s.* fluttered, R. 2. 162. See the note. A term in hawking; cf. O.F. *batre,* to beat.
Baterid, *pt. s.* beat, R. 2. 152; Batered, 1 *pt. s.* patted, b. 3. 198. Cf. O.F. *batre,* to beat; and see **Battide.**
Batte-nelde, large needle, packing-needle, 7. 218; Batnedle, b. 5. 212 *n.*

Used as equivalent to *paknelde, packenedle.*
Battide, 1 *pt. s.* patted, a. 3. 192. See **Baterid.**
Baude, bawd, 4. 165, 9. 72.
Baudy, *adj.* dirty, b. 5. 197. Cf. W. *baw,* dirty, *bawaidd,* dirty.
Baxteres. See **Bakesteres.**
Baw (an exclamation of contempt), bah! 13. 74; Bawe, 22. 398. See note, p. 169.
Bawtid, *pt. s.* (*for* Bated), abated, R. 2. 13. See note, p. 292.
Bayarde, a horse, properly a bay horse, 9. 192, 20. 70; b. 6. 196; Bayard, b. 4. 53; Bay3ard, a. 4. 40; Baiardes,*pl.* b. 4. 124. From F. *bai,* Lat. *badius,* bay-coloured.
Bayed, *pt. pl.* bayed, R. 3. 235.
Bayten, *v.* (with *on*), bait, attack, R. 3. 29. E. *bait.*
Be-, *prefix.* See Beo-, Bi-, By-.
Be, *prep.* by, b. 5. 130, R. 2. 140, 180; beside, with, a. 4. 46; concerning, of, b. 12. 124; on (the), R. pr. 10; with reference to, a. 4. 119; Be þat, according to that, a. 11. 193; Be clergie, as found out by learning (conjectural reading), R. 3. 190; Beo, by, according to, a. 4. 123. A.S. *be.*
Be, *v.* be, b. pr. 79, &c.; Be moste = must be, b. 14. 191; Ben, *v.* a. 2. 21; Beth, *pr. s.* is, b. 10. 347; Beth, 1 *pr. pl.* b. 3. 27; Ben, 2 *pr. pl.* b. 6. 132; Beþ, Beth,*pr. pl.* 6. 166; Buth, 11. 208, 19. 98; Ben, *pr. pl.* 2. 81, 21. 264; It ben = they are, b. 6. 56; Beest, 2 *pr. s.* (*with fut. sense*), shalt be, b. 5. 598; Best, 8. 236; Be, 1 *pr. s. subj.* may be, 8. 298; Be,*pr. s. subj.* may be, b. 14. 247; Be he, let him be, b. 10. 347; when (the life) is, b. 15. 141; if (my council) be, b. 4. 189; Be þow, if thou be, b. 6. 207; Be, *pp.* been, 13. 121; become, 1. 62; Beth, *imp. pl.* 10. 51, b. 2. 137; Be we, let us be, b. pr. 188. See Beeþ, Beo, Aren, Was, Were.
Beau fitz, fair son, 10. 311. F. *beau fils* (O.F. *fiz*). See Beu.
Beaupere, father, elder, reverend father, 10. 248, 21. 241. See note, p. 256; and Cath. Angl. p. 27, note 4.
Beaute, beauty, 14. 11; Bewte, b. 12. 49.
Beches, *pl.* beech-trees, 6. 121.
Bed, Bede. See Bede, Bidde.
Bed-bourde, bed-play, marriage, a. 10. 197; Bed-borde, 11. 293. See **Bourde.**

GLOSSARIAL INDEX. 315

Bedden hem, v. repose, rest in bed, b. 2. 97.
Beddyd, provided with a bed, 18. 197.
Beddyng, bed, 17. 74.
Bede, v. to offer, 11. 267; Bed, *pt. s.* bade, has ordered, a. 11. 189; Bad, *pt. s.* bade, ordered, 5. 117, 141; Beden, *pt. pl.* bade, 4. 28, 16. 27; Bede, b. 18. 53; Bed, *pt. pl.* 3. 173; Bede, *pp.* bidden, invited, 3. 56; Boden, *pp.* b. 2. 54. A.S. *béodan.* Confused with Bidden, to pray. See **Bit, Biddeth.**
Bede, prayer, b. 11. 144; Beodes, *pl.* a. 5. 8; Bedes byddyng = praying of prayers, bidding of beads, 13. 84; Bydde my bedes, bid my beads, b. 12. 29; Bidde any bedes, pray any prayers, 8. 16; Babeled on my bedes = muttered my prayers over, b. 5. 8. A.S. *bed, gebed,* a prayer. To *bid one's beads* is, properly speaking, to *pray one's prayers;* but the name *beads* was afterwards transferred to the balls strung upon a string, by which the prayers were counted off. See **Bedes.**
Bedel, a beadle, apparitor, or summoner, b. 2. 109; Bedeles, *pl.* 4. 2; O.F. *bedel (bedeau* in Cotgrave).
Bedeman, one who prays for another for money, a beadsman, b. 3. 41, 46; Bedman, 4. 43, 48; Bedemen, *pl.* b. 15. 199; Bedmen, 4. 276.
Bedered. See **Bedreden.**
Bedes, beads; Peyre bedes, set of beads, b. 15. 119. See **Bede.**
Bedes-byddynge, bidding of beads, b. 19. 373; Bedes-byddyng, 13. 84. See **Bede.**
Bedreden, *adj.* bedridden, 6. 21, 8. 108, 10. 177; Bedredene, *pl.* 10. 34; Bedrede, b. 13. 448; Bedraden, a. 7. 179; Bedered, b. 7. 101. See Cath. Angl. pp. xxix, 25.
Beede, *pt. s. subj.* should intreat, beg, a. 9. 96. See **Bidde.**
Beekis, *s. pl.* beaks, R. 3. 76.
Beere, *s.* noisiness, noisy behaviour, a. 11. 7. See **Bere,** v. to low as a cow. A.S. *gebǽru,* demeanour, noise, clamour; M.E. *bere* (Stratmann).
Beere, 2 *pt. s.* didst bear away, carry off, a. 3. 189; Beeren, *pt. pl.* bore, carried, a. 5. 209. See **Bere.**
Bees, Beest. See **Be,** v.
Beest, beast, animal, 22. 263; Best, R. 2. 130; Beestes, *pl.* 22. 264; a. 3. 256; Bestes, *pl.* 4. 424.
Beete, relieve, repair. See **Bete.**

Beeþ, *pr. pl.* are, 7. 299; *imp. pl.* be, 2. 172. See **Be.**
Be-falle, *pr. s. subj.* fall, b. 13. 453.
Be-flobered, *pp.* muddied, made dirty, b. 13. 401. See **Flober.**
Begeneldes, *gen. sing.* beggar's, 10. 154, 11. 263. See note, p. 124.
Beggerye, *s.* begging, 10. 162.
Behote, 1 *pr. s.* vow, promise, b. 5. 462; Beohote, a. 5. 235; Behihte, *pt. s.* promised, a. 3. 30; Beohi3te, *pt. s.* a. 5. 47; Behote, *pp.* R. 4. 91. A.S. *behátan.* See **Bihote.**
Beire, *gen. pl.* of both, b. 2. 66. See **Beyer.** A.S. *begra,* gen. pl. of *bá,* both.
Bei3, a metal ornament for the neck, collar of bright metal, b. pr. 165, 176; Bi3es, *pl.* b. pr. 161. And see **By3e.** A.S. *béah,* any circular metal ornament, as a ring, bracelet, collar, crown.
Bekne, *s.* beacon, 20. 228; Bekene, 17. 262.
Beknowe, 1 *pr. s.* acknowledge, a. 5. 114.
Bele, *adj. pl.* good, fair, b. 15. 113. O.F. *bel,* F. *beau.* See **Beu.**
Belde, v. grow bold (?), R. 1. 113. See note. Cf. A.S. *byldan,* to embolden, M.E. *belden,* (Stratmann, p. 51).
Belefte, *pp.* left, R. 2. 30. See *biláfen,* to remain, in Stratmann, p. 63.
Be-lei3e, 2 *pr. pl. subj.* belie, tell lies to, 21. 358. See **Bily̨eþ.**
Belsyre, grandfather, 21. 284; Belsires, *gen. sing.* ancestor's, 11. 233. 'Bellsyre, Auus;' Cath. Angl. p. 27.
Belwe, v. bellow, b. 11. 333.
Bely, *s.* belly, 1. 42; b. pr. 41.
Bely-ioye, appetite, delight in food, lit. belly-joy, b. 7. 118.
Belye, v. to lie against, belie, slander, b. 5. 414; Be-lei3e, 2 *pr. pl. subj.* belie, tell lies to, 21. 358. See **Bily̨eþ.**
Bemeneth, *pr. s.* means, signifies, b. pr. 208; a. 1. 1; Bemente, *pt. s.* signified, b. 18. 18. See **By-meneþ.**
Ben. See **Be.**
Bene, bean, 13. 92; R. 3. 151; Benes, *pl.* 9. 177, 226, 307, 327.
Benefys, benefice, b. 3. 312; Benefices, *pl.* benefices, 4. 33; possessions, a. 11. 192.
Benene, *adj.* made of beans, a. 7. 167.
Beneson, *s.* blessing, b. 13. 235.
Benfait, a benefit, kind deed, b. 5. 436; Benfes, *pl.* good deeds, a. 6. 101; F. *bienfait.* See **Bienfetes, Bynfet.**

VOL. II. U

316   GLOSSARIAL INDEX.

Bente, *pt. pl.* fastened, R. 4. 72. Used in a nautical sense, as in modern English.
Benygneliche, *adv.* with good will, 15. 57; gently, mildly, b. 12. 114.
Benyme, *v.* take away from, R. pr. 66. A.S. *beniman.*
Beo-, *prefix.* See **Be-, Bi-, By-**.
Beo, *prep.* by, according to, a. 4. 123. See **Be**.
Beo, *v.* be, a. 8. 32; *ger.* to be, a. 9. 98; *imp. pl.* a. 8. 170; *pr. pl. subj.* 19. 217; Beoþ, *pr. s. as fut.* will be, 20. 84; *pl.* shall be, a. 7. 91; *imp. pl.* be, 20. 224, 226; *pr. pl.* are, a. 1. 16; Beo, *pr. pl.* a. 8. 58; Beon, *pr. pl.* are, 21. 302; 1 *pr. pl.* 19. 285; 2 *pr. pl.* 20. 225.
Beodeles, *s. pl.* beadles, a. 3. 2. See **Bedel**.
Beodeman, *s.* beadsman, one who prays for another for money, a. 3. 47. See **Bedeman**.
Beodes, *s. pl.* prayers, a. 5. 8. See **Bede**.
Beofore, *adv.* before, a. 5. 9.
Beoheold, 1 *p. s. pr.* beheld, a. pr. 13. See **Bihelde**.
Beohiȝte, Beohote. See **Behote**.
Beoleeue, *s.* belief, creed, a. 5. 7. See **Bileue**.
Beo-louh, *pt. s.* 1 *p.* smiled at, a. 8. 105. Lit. laughed at; *louh* is the pt. t. of *laȝen,* to laugh.
Beores, *pl.* bears, a. 7. 33. See **Bere,** *s*.
Beot, *pt. s.* beat, hammered out, 21. 284; buffeted, a. 7. 165; 1 *pt. s.* corrected, a. 11. 132. See **Bete**.
Beo-take, 1 *pr. s.* commend, a. 9. 50. See **Betake**.
Berde, fair maid, lit. bride, 4. 15; Berdes, damsels, *pl.* b. 19. 131. See **Birde**.
Berde, *s.* beard, b. 5. 194; R. 3. 214.
Berdles, *adj.* beardless, R. 3. 235.
Bere, *v.* bear, carry, 11. 92, b. 3. 268; wear, 1. 178; Beren, a. 2. 151; Bereþ, *pr. s.* bears, 19. 223; Beriþ, *pr. s.* a. 11. 189; Bereth, *pr. pl.* bear, 20. 236; Bar, *pt. s.* bore, carried, 8. 162; pierced, 21. 88; thrust, 23. 132; Bar, 1 *pt. s.* a. 7. 92; Bere, 2 *pt. s.* didst bear, b. 3. 195; Bere, *pt. pl.* carried, 7. 416; Baren, *pt. pl.* b. 5. 108; Bare, *pt. pl.* turned, put (about), R. 4. 75; Ber, *imper. s.* bear, carry, 4. 426; Bereth, *imp. pl.* a. 8. 15; Bere, *pt. pl. subj.* b. 5. 139 See **Bore**.
Bere, *v.* low (as a cow), 14. 150. See *beren,* to cry out, in Stratmann.

Bere, *s.* bear, R. 3. 29; Beres, *pl.* 10. 196.
Bereued, 2 *pt. pl.* didst bereave, R. 2. 137. See **Bireue**.
Bergh, hill, 8. 227; Berghe, b. 5. 589. A.S. *beorg.*
Beries, *pl.* berries, grapes, 3. 28; Beryus, 11. 207 *n.*
Berke, *v.* bark, 10. 261.
Berkeres, barking-dogs, watch-dogs, 10. 260.
Berlingis, *s. pl.* little bears, cubs, R. 3. 96.
Bern, *s.* barn, 22. 346, 360; Berne, b. 19. 340; Bernes, *pl.* 9. 179; Bernes dore = barn-door, 5. 60.
Bern, man, 7. 247, 19. 281; Berne, 4. 477, R. pr. 86; Bernes, *pl.* men, a. 3. 256; Biernes, *pl.* b. 3. 265. See **Burn**. A.S. *beorn.*
Berne-dore, barn-door, a. 4. 44.
Beryng, *s.* bearing, manners, conduct, mien, 23. 116; Berynge, 22. 255.
Besely, *adv.* busily, R. 2. 147. See **Bisy**.
Besieth, *pr. s.* busies, R. 2. 147. See **Bisy**.
Best, 2 *pr. s. as fut.* shalt be, 8. 236. See **Be**.
Beste, *adj.* best, a. 2. 133; *as sb.* best, best part (of me), R. pr. 47; To þe beste = for the best purpose, as well as possible, a. 8. 63; Best, greatest benefit, advantage, 8. 126; best thing, R. 3. 241.
Bestes, beasts. See **Beest**.
Bet, *adj.* better, richer, 6. 96. Properly the adverbial form; see below.
Bet, *adv.* better, 8. 240, 9. 42, 15. 10; more easily, 1. 163; *ill spelt* Bette, b. 5. 601. A.S. *bet.*
Betake, 1 *pr. s.* commend, a. 11. 162; Beotake, a. 9. 50. Cf. A.S. *betǽcan,* to shew, commit, deliver. See **Byteche**.
Bete, *v.* beat, knock, 21. 264; punish, correct, chastise, 9. 163, 23. 27; Beten, *v.* strike, beat, 21. 99; beat, correct, b. 10. 321, b. 14. 19; Bet, *pr. s.* beats, b. 4. 59; Bat, *pr. s.* beats, assaults, (*short for* Beteþ), a. 4. 46; Bette, *pt. s.* beat, b. 6. 180; 1 *pt. s.* b. 10. 176; But, *pt. s.* chastised, 1. 115; Bet, 1 *pt. s.* beat, chastised, 12. 124; Bete, *pp.* R. 3. 78; Bet, *imp. s.* beat, 8. 61; smite, a. 5. 227. See also **Beot**.
Bete, *v.* to better, remedy, b. 6. 239; relieve, 9. 246; Beete, *v.* help (or abate), a. 7. 224; repair, a. 8. 30. A.S. *bétan,* to profit; from *bót.*

GLOSSARIAL INDEX. 317

Betere, *adj. comp.* better, 19. 285; Bettere, 2. 136; More better, R. pr. 60.
Betere, *adv.* better, 1. 120; Bettre, more highly, b. 11. 246.
Beth. See **Be**.
Be-þenke, *v.* bethink, think of, R. 3. 219. See **By-þenke**.
Bette. See **Bet**.
Bettre. See **Betere**, *adv.*
Be-twynne, *prep.* between, R. 2. 85.
Betydde, *pt. s.* befell, happened to, b. 12. 118. See **Bitit, Bytydde**.
Betynge, *s.* beating, attack, chastisement, 16. 148.
Beu, *adj.* beautiful, fine, R. 3. 1. And see **Beau fitz, Bele**.
Beuerages, *s. pl.* beverages, i. e. drinkings, a. 5. 189.
Bewar, *imper. pl.* beware, be careful, b. 9. 184. Put for *be war*.
Bewte. See **Beaute**.
Beyer, *adj.* of both; Here beyer, of both of them, 21. 36; Oure beyere, of us both, 21. 374. See **Beire**.
Bi-, *prefix.* See **Be-, Beo-, By-**.
Bi, *prep.* by, through, b. 4. 134: with, b. 1. 28; past, a. 11. 115; commensurately with, a. 5. 76; according to, in accordance with, b. 4. 70, b. 10. 251; during, in, b. 13. 452; with reference to, with respect to, with regard to, b. 4. 71, b. 5. 180, b. 8. 38; Bi so, provided that, b. 5. 647; Bi so þat, provided that, so long as, b. 14. 53; Bi my lyue, throughout my lifetime, b. 6. 103; By þat, by that, by that time, b. 6. 292, 301; By þe bischop (b. pr. 80) may mean either with reference to the bishop, or with the bishop's permission. See also **By**.
Bible, *s.* Bible, b. 8. 90; book, b. 15. 87. See **Byble**.
Bicomeþ, *pr. s.* is becoming, befits, b. 3. 208; Bicome,*pt. s.* became, b. 10. 136; went to, R. 1. 49; Bicomen, *pt. pl.* (they) became, a. 1. 112; Bicome, *pt. pl.* have gone to, b. 5. 651. Cf. G. *beikommen*, to reach to. See **Bycome**.
Bidde, *v.* pray, beg, ask for, 7. 169, 20. 216; b. 5. 231, b. 6. 239; Bidden, *v.* b. 12. 114, b. 17. 250; Biddeth, *pr. s.* asks, a. 1. 138; begs, b. 7. 81; Bidde, 1 *pr. s.* pray, bid (beads), 8. 16; Bit (*for* Biddeth), *pr. s.* begs, b. 7. 68; Bidden, *pr. pl.* beg, ask for, solicit, b. 3. 218; Biddeþ,*pr.pl.* a. 3. 212; Bidde, 1 *pr. pl.* pray, 15. 29; Bidde, *imp. s.* pray, b. 5. 454; Bidde of = pray for, a. 5. 227; Bid, *imp. s.* 8. 240; Biddeth, *imp. pl.* b. 5. 610, b. 7. 84; Bad, *pt. s.*

prayed, 23. 376; Bad, 1 *pt. s.* begged, asked, prayed, a. 9. 114; Bede, *pt. s. subj.* should intercede, b. 8. 102. A.S. *biddan*, to pray. pt. t. *bæd.* Confused with Bede, to bid, to offer, q. v. And see **Bydden**.
Bidderes, *pl.* beggars, b. 6. 206, b. 7. 66, b. 13. 241; Bidders, *pl.* b. pr. 40; a. pr. 40. See **Bidde and Bydders**.
Biddeth, *pr. s.* orders, commands, b. 3. 75; Biddeþ, *pr. pl.* bid, 12. 45. And see **Bit**. (Due to confusion between Bidde and Bede.)
Biddyng, *pres. pt.* begging, 17. 349. See **Bidde**.
Biddyng, *s.* praying, prayer, b. 11. 147; Biddynge, b. 3. 218 (the line means—"beggars ask men for money for their prayers to God for their benefactors"). See **Bidde, Byddyng**.
Biden, *v.* await, b. 18. 307; Bideth, *imp. pl.* remain, abide, b. 9. 133. A.S. *bídan.* See **Byden**.
Bidowe, *s.* a curved dagger, a. 11. 211. See note, p. 157.
Bidraueled, *pp.* slobbered, covered with grease, b. 5. 194. Cf. A.S. *drabbe*, dregs: Low G. *drabbelen*, to slobber.
Bidropped, *pp.* spotted, b. 13. 321.
Bidyng, *pres. pt.* abiding, enduring, b. 20. 141.
Bienals. See **Biennales**.
Bienfetes, *pl.* good deeds, b. 5. 621 (where it refers to presumption due to trusting to one's own good deeds). See **Benfait**.
Biennales, *pl.* masses said for a period of two years, b. 7. 170; Byennals, 10. 320; Bienals, a. 8. 157. See note.
Biernes, *pl.* men, b. 3. 265. See **Bern**.
Bifalleth, *pr. s.* belongs, b. 1. 52; Bifel, *pt. s.* happened, b. 5. 479, b. 7. 164; was proper, became, b. 11. 286; happened, came, a. 10. 179; Bifalle, *pr. s. subj.* may happen, b. 5. 59; Bifalle, *pp.* befallen, happened, a. pr. 62. See **Befalle, Byfalle**.
Bifore, *adv.* in front, before, b. 13. 316. See **Beofore, Byfore**.
Biforen, *prep.* before. a. 8. 39; Biforn, b. pr. 183; Bifor, b. 7. 188. See **Byfor**.
Bigge, *v.* buy, 4. 33; b. 6. 282; Biggen, *v.* b. 4. 89; Bigge, 1 *pr. s.* b. 5. 429; Bouhte, *pt. s.* 6. 96, 7. 225; a. 5. 133; paid for, suffered for, 14. 16; Boughte, *pt. s.* redeemed, 3. 3; Bouhte, 9. 217; Bouȝte,*pt. s.* b. 2. 3, b. 3. 86; redeemed, R. pr. 14; Bouȝt,*pt. s.* a. 2. 3; Bouȝþe, 1 *pt. s.* bought, a. 12. 70; Bouhte, *pt. pl.* 19. 166; Bouhten, *pt. pl. subj.*

U 2

GLOSSARIAL INDEX.

would have bought, 4; 85 Bouȝte, *pp.* b. 13. 192. A.S. *bycgan.* See **Bugge, Bygge.**
Biggere, *s.* buyer, a. 11. 209.
Bigile, *v.* beguile, deceive, b. 10. 118, 125; Bigileth, *pr. s.* b. 7. 70; Bigiled, *pp.* b. 18. 290. See **Bigyle, Bygyle.**
Bi-gon, *pt. s.* began, 21. 100; Bigonne, *pt. pl.* a. 5. 189. See **Bygan.**
Bi-gon, *pp.* persuaded, deceived (lit. gone about), a. 2. 24. A.S. *begán,* to go about, commit.
Bi-gruccheth, *pr. s.* begrudges, repines at, murmurs at (it), b. 6. 69. See **Bygrucche.**
Bigurdeles, *pl.* purses, b. 8. 87. A.S. *bigyrdel,* a purse, because worn '*by* the *girdle.*' See **By-gurdeles,** and the note, p. 134.
Bi-gyle, *v.* deceive, a. 11. 67, 75, 82. See **Bigile.**
Bihelde, 1 *pt. s.* beheld, saw, b. 7. 109; Bi-heold, a. 8. 93; Beoheold, a. pr. 13.
Biheste, *s.* promise, b. 3. 126, b. 11. 60; behest, promise, a. 3. 122. A.S. *beháes,* a vow. See **Byheste.**
Bihote, 1 *pr. s.* promise, vow, b. 6. 233; Bihiȝte, *pt. s.* b. 16. 239; Bihight, b. 3. 29; Bihyȝte, b. 18. 330. See **Behote, Byhote.**
Bihyȝte, 1 *pt. s.* promised, b. 18. 330. See **Bihote.**
Bi-iaped, *pp.* mocked, b. 18. 290. See **By-Iapede.**
Bikenne, 1 *pr. s.* commend, commit, b. 2. 49, b. 8. 59. See **Kenne, Bykenne.**
Bikere, *v.* fight, contend, lit. bicker, b. 20. 78. See **Bykere.**
Biknowen, *v.* acknowledge, confess, b. pr. 204; Biknowe, 1 *pr. s.* b. 5. 200; Biknewe, *pt. s.* b. 10. 416; *pt. pl.* b. 19. 145; Biknowen, *pp.* well known, favourably received, b. 3. 33; Biknowe, *pp.* known, acknowledged, 4. 36; b. 18. 24. See **Byknowe.**
Bildith, *pr. s.* builds, R. 3. 41.
Bileue, *imper. pl.* believe, trust, b. 10. 119; Bileeue, *v.* a. 1. 79; Beo-leeue, 1 *pr. s.* a. 7. 81.
Bileue, *s.* belief, creed, b. 5. 7, b. 7. 175, b. 10. 202; Bileeue, a. 6. 79. A.S. *geléafa.* See **Beoleeue, Byleue.**
Bille, petition, b. 4. 47, b. 13. 247; Billis, *pl.* complaints, R. 3. 307. See **Bylle.**
Bille, beak, bill, b. 11. 349.
Billid, *pp.* beaked, having bills, R. 3. 37.
Bilongeth, *impers. pr. s.* it behoves, b.

10. 246, 359; *pr. pl.* belong, b. 16. 191. See **By-longeþ.**
Biloue þe, *imp. s.* make thyself beloved, b. 6. 230; Biloued, *pp.* beloved, b. 3. 211.
Bi-loure, *v.* lower at, look sullenly at, a. 8. 105.
Bilyeth, *pr. pl.* lie against, b. 10. 22; Bilowen, *pp.* lied against, accused falsely, b. 2. 22; a. 5. 77. See **Belye.**
Bimolen, *v.* soil, sully, b. 14. 22. From A.S. *mál,* a spot, E. *mole.*
Binam, *pt. s.* took away from, b. 6. 243; Binom, *pt. s.* a. 7. 228. See **By-nymen.** A.S. *beniman.*
Bineth, *adv.* beneath, b. 16. 67; Bineoþe, a. pr. 15; Bineoþe, 19. 85.
Biqueste, bequest, will, b. 6. 87. See **Byquyste.**
Biquethe, *pt. s. subj.* should have bequeathed, b. 13. 10. See **By-quethe.**
Birde, *s.* lady, b. 3. 14. See **Berde, Buirde, Burde.** The same word as E. *bride.*
Bireue, *v.* bereave, take away by force, b. 6. 248; Bireuet, *pp.* taken away, a. 7. 233. See **Bereued, Byreue.** A.S. *beréafian.*
Birewe, *pr. pl.* rue, lament, b. 12. 250.
Bisechen, *v.* beg, beseech, ask, a. 11. 98; Biseche, *v.* b. 10. 141; Biseke, *v.* pray, b. 11. 55; Bisouȝten, *pt. pl.* a. 2. 189. See **Bysechen.**
Biseged, *pp.* besieged, b. 20. 214.
Bisette, *v.* employ, bestow, b. 5. 264, 299; By-sette. 7. 254. See **By-sette.** A.S. *bisettan,* orig. to set round.
Biseye, *pp.* visited, b. 20. 201. See **Byseye.** A.S. *beséon,* to look round, behold, regard.
Bishetten, *pt. pl.* shut, b. 2. 213; Bishette, *pp.* shut up, with closed doors, b. 19. 162. From A.S. *scyttan,* to shut.
Bishoped, *pt. s.* confirmed, b. 15. 545.
Bisitten, *v.* oppress, press on, beset, harass, encumber, b. 10. 361; a. 2. 110. A.S. *bisittan,* to beset.
Bislabered, *pp.* beslobbered, bedabbled, dirty, b. 5. 392. See **By-slobered.** Cf. E. *slabber, slobber.*
Bismer, *s.* calumny, reproach, reviling, b. 5. 89; Bismeres, *pl.* b. 19. 289. A.S. *bismer,* insult, lit. a 'besmearing.'
Bisouȝten. See **Bisechen.**
Bispered, *pt. s.* locked up, b. 15. 139. A.S. *sparrian,* to shut up.
Biswinke, *v.* labour for, gain by work, a. 7. 202; Biswynke, *v.* b. 6. 216;

GLOSSARIAL INDEX. 319

Biswynkyn, *pr. pl.* b. 15. 480; Biswonke, *pt. pl.* b. 20. 290. See Byswynke. A.S. *beswincan.*
Bisy, *adj.* busy, b. 7. 125; Bisi, b. 7. 118, a. 8. 110.
Bi-syde, *adv. used as sb.*; On his bisyde, on his side, on his behalf, a. 5. 173.
Bit, *pr. s.* begs, b. 7. 68. See Bidde.
Bit, *pr. s.* (*for* Biddeth), bids, orders, 4. 309, 16. 76, 18. 61, 21. 272. (Due to confusion of Bidde and Bede.)
Bitelbrowed, *adj.* with beetling or overhanging brows, b. 5. 190; Bitelbrouwed, a. 5. 109; Bytelbrowed, 7. 198. See note, p. 81.
Biten, *v.* bite, b. 14. 22; Bote, *pt. s.* bit, b. 5. 84; Bot, a. 5. 67. See Byte.
Bitere, *adv.* bitterly, dearly, 16. 304; Bittere, sharply, bitterly, 23. 27. See Byttere.
Biterliche, *adv.* bitterly, sorely, 4. 144; Byterliche, 12. 192.
Biterour, *adv.*·more dearly, 17. 220.
Bitit (*for* Bitideth), *impers. pr. s.* it happens, it befals, b. 11. 393.
Bi-traye, *v.* betray, a. 5. 225. See Bytraye.
Bitter, *s.* bitterness, b. 5. 119; a. 5. 99. See note, p. 76, l. 5.
Bitwene, *adv.* between, b. 8. 119, b. 9. 167. See By-twyne.
Bitwixen, *prep.* amongst, b. 5. 338.
Bi-tyme, *adv.* in time, betimes, soon, b. 5. 647.
Biȝes. See Beiȝ.
Biȝete, *s.* offspring, b. 2. 40. See Biȝute.
Bi-ȝonde, *adv.* beyond, a. 3. 105; across, i. e. over sea, a. 4. 111; Biȝunde, b. 3. 109; Byȝonde, 4. 146.
Biȝute, *pp.* begotten, 3. 144.
Blaberde, *pt. s.* babbled, mumbled over, a. 5. 8. Dan. *blabbre,* to gabble.
Bladis, *s. pl.* blades, sword-blades, R. 3. 329.
Blake, *adj.* black, b. 10. 436.
Blameles, free from blame, 14. 127.
Blamet, *pp.* blamed, a. 10. 66.
Blammanger, a dish somewhat like a cheesecake, 16. 100; Blancmangere, b. 13. 91. See note; and Cath. Angl. p. 34, *n.* 3.
Blase, *s.* flame, blaze, 20. 178.
Blase, *v.* blaze, flame, burn brightly, 20. 188; Blasen, *v.* 20. 198; Blaseth, *pr. s.* 20. 185; Blaseþ, 2 *pr. pl.* 20. 228; Blased, *pt. s.* shone brightly, 21. 243.
Blasen, *s.* blazon, coat of arms, b. 16. 179.

Blast, *s.* blast, R. 4. 81; Blastis, *pl.* tumults, R. 3. 365.
Blede, *v.* be shed, bleed, 21. 439; Bledden, *pt. pl.* bled, shed, 19. 255; Bledde, *pt. s. subj.* should bleed, R. 3. 31.
Blenche, *v.* blench, flinch, (hence) turn aside, 8. 227. See note, p. 103.
Blende, *v.* blind, 21. 294, b. 10. 129; Blendeþ, *pr. s.* a. 6. 101; Blente, *pt. s.* 8. 135; Blent, *pp.* 21. 286, b. 5. 502. A.S. *blendan.*
Blerede, *pt. s.* made dim, cast a mist over, bedimmed, 1. 72; dimmed, b. 5. 191. Cf. Swed. *plira,* Dan. *plire,* to blink. See note, p. 10.
Bler-eyed, *adj.* blear-eyed, 20. 306; Blere-nyed, b. 17. 324; Blernyed, R. 2. 164. See note, p. 295.
Blery, *adj.* bleared, 7. 198. See above.
Blessen, *v.* to bless, a. 11. 148; Blessede, *pt. s.* blessed, (perhaps) signed with the cross, 19. 272; Blessed, *pt. s.* b. 11. 229; Blessid, *pp.* consecrated, R. 2. 75.
Blete, *v.* bleat, 18. 38.
Bleuh, *pt. s.* blew, sounded, a. 5. 193. See Blowen.
Blewe, *adj.* livid, ash-coloured, 4. 125. See Blo; and see note, p. 44.
Blisful, *adj.* blissful, blessed, a. 2. 3; full of happiness (which He bestows upon others), b. 2. 3.
Blisse, *s.* pleasure, happiness, b. 8. 64, b. 11. 324; a. 3. 97, a. 9. 55; place of bliss, as *in his blisse*=to enter His paradise, b. 10. 105. See Blys.
Blisse, *v.* bless, b. 12. 187, b. 16. 237; Blissed, *pp as adj.* blessed, b. 5. 503, b. 10. 402, b. 14. 35. (Due to confusion of A.S. *blissian* with *blétsian.*) See Blessen.
Blisseder, *adj. compar.* more blessed, b. 11. 249. '*Blyssyd,* beatus;' Cath. Angl.
Bliþe, *adj.* glad, pleased, a. 2. 128; Blithe, merry, R. 3. 277. See Blythe.
Blo, *adj.* livid, ash-coloured, b. 3. 97. Icel. *blár,* livid.
Blod, blood, 19. 255, 20. 270; family, race, kin, lineage, 4. 263, 6. 78; Blode, b. 9. 135. See also 21. 439, and the note, p. 264.
Blod-breþrene, *pl.* brethren of one blood, 13. 109.
Blody, *adj.* covered with blood, 5. 74, 7. 150; by blood, of one blood, related, 9. 217, 13. 115; Blodi, a. 7. 196. See note to 9. 217.
Blosmed, *pt. pl.* blossomed, b. 5. 140.

320 GLOSSARIAL INDEX.

Blosmes, *pl.* blossoms, 19. 11; Blossemes, 19. 10.
Blostrede, *pt. pl.* wandered blindly about, blundered, stumbled about, 8. 159; Blustreden, b. 5. 521. Cf. '*blustreden* as blynde' = wandered about like blind people, Allit. Poems, B. 886.
Blowen, *v.* blow (as wind), 22. 340; Blew, *pt. s.* b. 5. 515; Blowen, *pp.* blown, b. 5. 18. And see **Bleuh**. A.S. *bláwan*.
Blowyng-tyme, rough weather, storm, b. 16. 26. Compare the preceding line; else it may mean 'time of blossoming.'
Blysse, bliss, happiness, 1. 29; Blys, a. 12. 112. See **Blisse**.
Blythe, *adj.* cheerful, merry, glad, pleased, 3. 171, 4. 28. See **Bliþe**.
Bo, *adj.* both, a. 2. 36. A.S. *bá*.
Boeches, *pl.* tumours, boils, swellings, 23. 84, b. 13. 249. E. *botch = boss*. 'Bohche, botche, *Ulcus*;' Prompt. Parv.
Bocher, *s.* butcher, a. 5. 173; Bochere, b. 5. 330; Bochers, *pl.* a. pr. 98; Bocheres, *pl.* b. pr. 218. See **Bouchere**.
Bockes, *pl.* bucks, 9. 29.
Boden, *pp.* bidden, invited, b. 2. 54. See **Bede,** *v.*
Bodiward, inwards, within the body, a. 7. 169.
Body, *s.* person, b. 10. 258: *som body,* some people, 23. 27; Bodi, body, a. 5. 67; Bodies, *pl.* a. 1. 169.
Bodyhalf, the front part (of a dress), b. 13. 317.
Boffatede, *pt. s.* buffeted, struck, 23. 191. See **Buffated**.
Boilaunt, *pres. part.* boiling, 21. 291. O.F. *boillant,* pres. part.
Bok, book (Bible), 2. 28, 10. 120; Boke, 1. 129; Bokis, *pl.* 4. 59. A.S. *bóc*.
Bolden, *v.* embolden, cheer up, a. 3. 192; Boldid, *pt. s.* emboldened, R. 1. 113; Bolded, 1 *pt. s.* b. 3. 198.
Bole, bull, 14. 150; Boles, *pl.* b. 11. 333. Icel. *boli*.
Bolke, *s.* belch, eructation, 8. 6. 'To belche, belke, or bolke, *ructare*;' Cath. Angl.
Bolle, cup, bowl, 7. 420, 8. 164, 21. 410. A.S. *bolla*. See note, p. 93.
Bolleful, *s.* bowlful, a. 7. 168.
Bollers, *pl.* drunkards, 10. 194. Lit. 'bowlers'; see note.
Bolleþ, *pr. s.* swells, a. 5. 99; Bolled,

pp. swollen, a. 5. 67. See **Bolneþ**. Cf. Exod. ix. 31.
Bollynge, *s.* swelling, 9. 226. (For bollynge = to prevent swelling.)
Bolneþ, *pr. s.* swells, b. 5. 119. See Cath. Angl. p. 36, n. 6.
Bolted; bolted with yren = supported with iron fastenings, 9. 143. The allusion is to the strengthening of weak limbs by the use of iron supports.
Bommeþ, *pr. s.* tastes, drinks, a. 7. 139; Bommede, *pt. s.* tasted, drank, 7. 229. See **Bummede**.
Bonched, *pt. s.* struck, smote, lit. banged, knocked, b. pr. 74; Du. *bonken,* to knock, rap. See note to 1. 72; and see **Bunchiþ**.
Bond, *s.* bond, band, 6. 14, R. 3. 94. See *Bond* in Shropsh. Wordbook.
Bond, *pt. s.* bound, 21. 448, 22. 57; bound up, 20. 70; enclosed, a. 1. 159; 1 *pt. s.* fastened, 7. 218.
Bondage, *s.* bondage, servitude, R. 3. 85.
Bonde, *s.* bond-woman, servant-maid, 11. 267. '*Bonde,* as a man or woman, *Servus, Serva*;' Prompt. Parv.
Bonde, *pl.* bondmen, i. e. husbandmen, 4. 201. A.S. *bonda,* borrowed from Icel. *bóndi,* short for *búandi,* a peasant, tiller of the soil.
Bondman, *s.* a husbandman, labourer, tiller of the soil, b. 5. 194; Bondemen, *pl.* 1. 219, 9. 42; Bondemenne, *gen. pl.* of bondmen, of husbandmen, 6. 70, 7. 201. See above.
Bone, petition, prayer, request, 4. 421, 13. 84. E. *boon*.
Bone, *s.* bane, poison, a. 6. 93. See *bane* in Prompt. Parv.
Bones, *s. pl.* bones. On bones = with its bones, 21. 340. See note.
Bonet, *s.* additional sail, or additional part of a sail, R. 4. 72, 81. See Cath. Angl. p. 36, n. 10.
Boost, noise, 17. 89; Boste, b. 14. 227. See note, and see **Boste**.
Bootles, *adj.* boot-less, without boots, 21. 9. See the note.
Bor, boar, 14. 150; Bore, b. 11. 333; Bores, *pl.* wild boars, 9. 29.
Bord, board, table, 9. 289, 16. 174; Borde, *dat.* 9. 277, b. 6. 267; side-timbers, side of a boat, 11. 40; Oure þe borde = overboard, R. 4. 82; Bordes, *pl.* boards, planks, 11. 222. A.S. *bord*. See notes, pp. 116, 199.
Bordiour, jester, 8. 108; Bordiours, *pl.* 10. 127, 136. '*Bourdeur,* a mocker,

GLOSSARIAL INDEX.

jeaster, cogger, liar, foister, guller of people;' Cotgrave. See **Bourdeoure**.
Bordles, *adj.* without a seat at the table, 15. 141. See **Bord**.
Bordon, pilgrim's staff, 8. 162. F. *bourdon*. See note. p. 100.
Bordynge, *pres. pt.* joking, jesting, 17. 202. See **Bourdynge**.
Bore, boar. See **Bor**.
Bore, *pp.* born, 2. 58. See **Bere**.
Borel, *adj.* lay, b. 10. 286. See note. So Gower calls himself '*a borel clerke*'; C. A. i. 5.
Borgages. See **Burgages**.
Borgh, *s.* bail, surety, pledge, 23. 13; b. 10. 133; Borghe, 19. 281; Borw, 23. 248; Borw of=security for, 5. 85; Borwe, b. 14. 190; Borwgh, b. 4. 89; Borwes, *pl.* sureties, sponsors, 2. 74. A.S. *borh*, a pledge.
Borghe, borough, town, 3. 92, b. 2. 87; Borugh, R. pr. 2; Borowe, R. 4. 69; Borwes, *pl.* 10. 189. A.S. *burh*.
Bornes. See **Bourne**.
Borre, *s.* þurr, huskiness, 20. 306.
Borwe, *v.* to borrow, 3. 176. 5. 55, 17. 371; Borwe, 1 *pr. s.* borrow, give security for, 8. 35, 22. 477; Borwest, 2 *pr. s.* 7. 343; Borweth, *pr. s.* borrows, 18. 1; Berwith, R. 3. 149; Borweþ, *pr. pl.* 23. 285; Borwen, b. 7. 82; Boru, R. 3. 151; Borwede, *pt. s.* borrowed, 5. 56; Borwed, b. 4. 53; Borwede, 1 *pt. s.* 9. 108, a. 7. 92; Borwe, *pr. s. subj.* give security for, b. 4. 109.
Borwton, borough, lit. borough-town, 4. 112.
Bosarde, buzzard, worthless fellow, b. 10. 266. See note, p. 156.
Bosome, bosom, b. 16. 254.
Bosse, *s.* master, lord (?), R. 3. 98. Cf. Du. *baas*, a master, now used in America in the form *boss*. It is difficult to see how it can mean a *boss* (excrescence). See note.
Bosshes. See **Busehes**.
Bost, boasting, blustering, arrogance, 17. 65, 22. 251; Boste, b. 14. 222.
Boste, noise, b. 14. 247. The same word as the above. See **Boost**.
Bosten, *v.* to boast, 3. 85; Bosteth, *pr. s.* b. 13. 281; Bostynge, *pres. part.* boasting, 7. 34.
Bostour, boaster, bragger, b. 13. 303; Boster, R. 2. 80.
Bot, boat, ship, ark, 11. 33, 47; Bote, b. 8. 31; Bote, *dat.* 11. 34, 36.
Bot, *pt. s.* bit, a. 5. 67. See **Biten**.
Bote, *s.* help, aid, benefit, good, advantage, remedy, relief, 5. 85, 88, 89; 9. 178, 192; 13. 56, 16. 229, 21. 157, 477; Bote, advantage, reward, recompense, b. 14. 116; To bote=to boot, in addition, 17. 110. A.S. *bót*.
Bote, *v.* make up the difference, give up something to make things equal, 7. 380. From the sb.
Bote, *conj.* except, unless, 1. 64, 3. 141, 4. 149, 8. 16, 10. 62; if—not, 21. 266; Bot, unless, b. 17. 245; Bote yf, *conj.* unless, 2. 178, 9. 15, 10. 63; Bote þer=except where, 10. 67. See **But**.
Bote, *adv.* but, only, 1. 204, 4. 477.
Bote, *pt. s.* bit, b. 5. 84. See **Biten**.
Botel, bottle, 6. 52; Boteles, *pl.* 20. 68; Botels, 10. 139.
Botelees. See **Botless**.
Boteles, *adj.* without boots, b. 18. 11. See **Bootles**.
Botened. See **Botnede**.
Boteraced, furnished with buttresses, buttressed, 8. 236.
Botere, butter, 8. 51.
Botless, *adj.* incurable, irremediable, 21. 208; Botelees, b. 18. 200. From *bote*, sb.
Botnede, *pt. s.* helped, cured, 9. 188; Botned, *pp.* restored, assisted, a. 7. 179; Botened, *pp.* b. 6. 194. Cf. Goth. *gabatnan*, to profit.
Bope, *adj.* both, 11. 18 *n.* 20. 285; Her botheres=of them both, 3. 67, b. 16. 165, b. 18. 37; Oure boþers=of us both, 7. 181. Icel. *báðir*, both.
Bothe, *adv.* also, at the same time, b. 12. 90. 95.
Botones, *pl.* buttons, b. 15. 121.
Bouchere, butcher, 7. 379; Bouchers, *pl. l.* 221. See **Bocher**.
Boughte, **Bouhte**. See **Bigge**.
Bouken, *v.* cleanse with lye, b. 14. 19, b. 15. 185; Boukeþ, *pr. s.* cleanses, 17. 331. Cf. E. *buckwash*. See note, p. 205.
Boun, *adj.* ready, 3. 173; willing, a. 2. 54; obedient, R. 3. 294; Bown, ready, b. 2. 159. Icel. *búinn*, pp. of *búa*, to prepare.
Bounde, *pp.* bound, i. e. servile, 11. 263. See note.
Bounte, goodness, 9. 49; reward, b. 14. 150.
Bour, *s.* inner room, esp. a lady's chamber or 'bower,' 7. 228, a. 3. 14; Boure, 4. 11, 15; b. 2. 64; Bowre, b. 3. 102. A.S. *búr*.
Bourde, play, sport, b. 9. 187. '*Bourdes*, scoffs, jeasts;' Cotgrave.

GLOSSARIAL INDEX.

Bourdeoure, jester, b. 13. 448. See **Bordiour.**
Bourdynge, *pr. pt.* joking, jesting, b. 15. 40. See **Bordynge.** '*Bourder*, to toy, trifle, dally, bourd or jeast with;' Cotgrave.
Bourne, *s.* stream, brook, a. pr. 8; Bornes, *gen.* b. pr. 8. A.S. *burna.*
Boussel, bushel, 6. 61. See **Busschel.**
Bouwe, *pr. s. subj.* bow, bend, give way, a. 9. 43; Bouweþ, *imp. pl.* bend or direct your course, a. 6. 56. See **Bowe.**
Bouȝ, *s.* bough, a. 6. 65; Bow, b. 5. 32; Bowh, branch, 6. 135; Bowes, *pl.* 17. 248.
Bouȝte, Bouȝþe. See **Bigge.**
Bow, Bowh, bough. See **Bouȝ.**
Bowe, *v.* bow, 11. 267; become obedient, submit, 5. 181; Bowen, *v.* bow, 22. 17; Bowe, *pr. s. subj.* bend, give way, submit, 16. 148; Bow, *pr. s. subj.* may incline, lean aside, b. 8. 48; Bowede, 1 *pt. s.* bowed, bent, 14. 134; Bowid, *pt. s.* R. 4. 79; Boweth, *imp. pl.* bend, turn, b. 5. 575. And see **Bouwe.**
Bowe-drawte, *s.* bowshot, R. 3. 229.
Bowten, *pt. pl.* bought, 19. 159. See **Bigge.**
Boxomeliche, *adv.* obediently, humbly, b. 12. 195.
Boxum, *adj.* obedient, humble, a. 1. 108; Boxome, b. 3. 263; gentle, b. 18. 116. See **Buxome.**
Boxumnesse, *s.* obedience, a. 4. 150; Boxumnes, a. 1. 111. See above.
Boye, man, knave, young man, lad, servant, 1. 78, 13. 111, 21. 78, 80; Boyes, *pl.* servants, followers, 9. 266, 10. 127, 194; Boyes, *gen.* boy's, young man's, knave's, 21. 99. It implies contempt rather than youth.
Boynard, scoundrel, fool, R. 2. 164; Boynardis, *pl.* R. 1. 110. See note, p. 290. O.F. *buinard* (Mätzner); *buisnart,* foolish (Roquefort).
Boyste, *s.* box, a. 12. 68. O.F. *boiste,* F. *boîte.*
Brak, broke, See **Breke.**
Brake, *v.* vomit, 7. 431. 'Brakyn, *Vomo;*' Prompt. Parv. '*Braken,* to vomit;' Hexham's Dutch Dict.
Brake, in phr. *bowes of brake,* bows worked with a winch, 21. 293. See the note, p. 257.
Bras, brass, 1. 183; money, a. 3. 189.
Brast, burst. See **Bresten.**
Bratful. See **Bretful.**

Braun, brawn, boar's flesh, 16. 67, 100; Braune, b. 13. 63, 91.
Braunches, *pl.* branches, twigs, i. e. various ways, b. 13. 410 (see note); Braunchis, branching ornaments, R. 1. 41.
Brayn-wode, *adj.* brain-mad, mad, a. 10. 61.
Breche, breeches, 7. 157, b. 5. 175.
Bred, bread, food, 6. 175, b. 11. 229, b. 15. 179.
Bred, bird. See **Brid.**
Bred-corn, corn of which to make bread, 9. 61; Bred-corne, b. 6. 64. See note, p. 108.
Brede, breadth, 3. 93, 4. 261; R. pr. 12, R. 2. 22. A.S. *brǽdu.*
Breden, *v.* breed, engender, b. 2. 97; cause to grow, R. 2. 147; Bredeth, *pr. s.* breeds, brings forth young, b. 11. 339; Bredden, *pt. pl.* bred, 14. 166.
Bredles, *adj.* without food, 10. 121; Bredlees, 17. 13.
Bredyng, *s.* breeding, b. 12. 221.
Breef, brief, written authority, 23. 327. See **Breuet.**
Breke, *v.* to break open, break, b. 7. 183; Breken, *v.* 21. 264, 22. 340; Brekyþ, *pr. s.* transgresses, 10. 236; Breken, *pr. pl.* distribute, b. 10. 82; Breketh, *pr. pl.* break, b. 6. 31, Breke, 2 *pl. pr. subj.* b. 5. 584; Brak, *pt. s.* broke, 1. 114; burst, b. 11. 158; distributed, 13. 125; Brake, *pt. s.* broke, b. 10. 283; Breke, 2 *pt. s.* didst break, 10. 278, 21. 383; Breke, *pt. s. subj.* should break, should miss, b. 5. 245; Broke, *pp.* broken, 19. 155; b. 14. 221; torn, b. 5. 108; maimed, with a broken limb, 6. 33, 10. 99.
Breke-cheste, *s. as adj.* brawling, strife-causing, b. 16. 43. See note.
Brekynge, *s.* breach, b. 10. 318.
Breme, *adj.* vigorous, strong, b. 12. 224; furious, R. 3. 365; Bremme, proud, R. 2. 130; *pl.* furious, R. 2. 80. A.S. *bréme,* famous.
Bremest, *adj. superl.* strongest, most powerful, most active, a. 10. 55.
Bremore, *adj. comp.* more powerful, more active, a. 10. 56. See **Breme.**
Bren, *s.* bran, b. 6. 184. The usual M.E. form; O.F. *bren.*
Brennen, *v.* burn, 4. 238, 20. 198; Brenne, *v.* 13. 67, b. 3. 97; Brenneþ, *pr. s.* 20. 178; Brenneþ, 2 *pr. pl.* burn, 20. 228; Brente, *pt. s.* 20. 308; Brende, b. 17. 326; Brend, 1 *pt. s.* burnt, consumed, wore away, 7. 74; Brent, *pp.* burnt, 21. 266; Brent gold, i. e. very

GLOSSARIAL INDEX. 323

bright gold, b. 5. 271; Brennyng, *pres. pt.* burning, 21. 291; Bren, *imper. s.* burn, 4. 426; Brenne, b. 3. 265. Icel. *brenna.*
Brennynge, *s.* burning, the stake, b. 15. 81.
Brere, briar, bramble, 3. 28; Breres, *pl.* 7. 402; Breris, R. 3. 75.
Breste, *s.* breast, a. 5. 99, 228.
Bresten, *v.* burst, break in pieces; Brest, *pr. s. subj.* break, R. 3. 287; burst, R. 3. 94; Brastyn, *pt. pl.* burst, R. 3. 362. A.S. *berstan.*
Brestynge, *s.* breaking, R. 4. 79.
Bretful, *adv.* brimful, full to the brim, 1. 42, a. pr. 41 *n*; Bratful, a. pr. 41; Bredful, a. pr. 41 *n.* Swed. *bräddful,* brimful, from *brädd,* a brim.
Brethynge, *s.* breath, b. 11. 349.
Breuet, letter of indulgence, note, 1. 72, 14. 55; Breuettes, *pl.* b. 5. 649. Dimin. of Breef, q. v.
Brew, *pt. s.* brewed, 7. 225; Breuh, a. 5. 133. See **Browe.**
Brewestere, female brewer, ale-wife, 7. 353; Brewesteres, *pl.* 10. 189, b. pr. 218; Brewesters, *pl.* 9. 330; Breusters, *pl.* a. pr. 98.
Brew-wif, brewster, ale-wife, 7. 354.
Breyde, *pt. s.* he hastened, b. 17. 68. A.S. *bregdan,* Icel. *bregða.*
Bribours, *pl.* robbers, b. 20. 260; Brybours, 23. 262. See Prompt. Parv.
Brid, bird, R. 2. 162, R. 3. 1; Bridde, b. 15. 279; Bred, R. 2. 152; Bredd, R. 2. 141; Briddes, *pl.* birds, 11. 63, 14. 156; Breddis, R. 3. 37. See **Bryddes.** A.S. *bridd.*
Bridale, bridal, b. 2. 54; Bruydale, b. 2. 43; Brudale, 3. 56. See **Bruydale.**
Brigge, bridge, 8. 240; Brygge, 8. 213; Brygges, *pl.* 10. 32. See **Brugge.** A.S. *brycg.*
Britoner, an inhabitant of Brittany, a Frenchman, used as a term of reproach, b. 6. 178; Brytonere, b. 6. 156. See **Brutiner.**
Brocage, treaty by an agent, bargain, agency, 17. 109; Brokage, b. 14. 267; Brocages, *pl.* dealings, commissions, 3. 92. See note, p. 34.
Brochen, *v.* fasten together, stitch loosely together, 7. 218; Brochede, 1 *pt. s.* a. 5. 126. '*Brocher,* to stitch grossely, to set or sowe with great stitches;' Cotgrave.
Broches, *pl.* brooches, 1. 73; b. 15. 118; R. 2. 38; *also* matches, 20. 211. Cf. F. *brochard, brochette,* a wooden peg (Cotgrave).

Brockes, *pl.* badgers, b. 6. 31.
Brocour, broker, bargain-maker, agent, 3. 66; Brokour, b. 2. 65; Brocor, 7. 95; Brokours, *pl.* 3. 60. See notes.
Brod, *adj.* broad, wide, 8. 162; a. 6. 8; Brode, *pl.* thick, 6. 121; wide open, 21. 240; broad, 23. 117; b. 13. 242, b. 18. 228.
Brode, *adv.* widely, 6. 168.
Brode-hokede, *adj.* with broad barbs, 23. 226.
Brodid, *pt. s.* expanded, R. 2. 141. Lit. 'made broad.'
Brok, brook, stream, 8. 213, 9. 142; Broke, b. 6. 137.
Brokage. See **Brocage.**
Brokelegged, *adj.* with a broken leg, 9. 143; Broke-legget, a. 7. 180; Brokeleggede, *pl.* 9. 188.
Broke-schonket, *adj.* broken-shanked, broken-legged, a. 7. 131.
Brokours. See **Brocour.**
Brol, child, brat, 4. 263; Brolle, b 3. 204. See note. In Prompt. Parv. p. 50, we find: 'Breyel [*for* breþel?], *Brollus, brolla, miserculus.*'
Brom, *s.* broom, 11. 207 *n*; Bromes, *pl.* R. 3. 19.
Brotel, *adj.* brittle, fragile, 11. 47. See **Brutel.**
Broþel, *adj.* worthless (fellow), wretch, a. 11. 61. From A.S. *broð-en,* pp. of *bréoðan,* to ruin. The word occurs in Skelton's Magnificence, l. 2132, on which Dyce notes that it 'was formerly applied as a term of reproach to the worthless of either sex.' See also the Coventry Mysteries, ed. Halliwell, pp. 217, 308.
Brouke, *pr. s. subj.* enjoy, receive, 13. 56; Brouk, *imp. s.* 21. 404. A.S. *brúcan.*
Brounest, *adj. superl.* brownest, darkest, 9. 330.
Brouȝten, *pt. pl.* (for *pt. s.*), put, a. 9. 58.
Browe, *pp.* brewed, 21. 404. See note, p. 262. And see **Brew.**
Browet, *s.* pottage, R. 2. 51. '*Brouët,* potage, or broth;' Cotgrave.
Brudale, bridale, 3. 56. See **Bridale.**
Brugge, bridge, b. 7. 601; Brugges, *pl.* b. 7. 28. See **Brigge.**
Brutaget, *pp.* supported, buttressed, a. 6. 79. See note to 8. 236. p. 104.
Brutel, *adj.* frail, b. 8. 42; Brotel, 11. 47. From A.S. *bréotan,* to break.
Bruten, *ger.* to break in pieces, 4. 238. A.S. *brytan,* to break.

Brutiner, *s.* an inhabitant of Brittany, a swaggerer, a. 7. 142. See **Britoner.**
Bruting, *s.* destruction, 16. 156. See **Bruten.**
Bruydale, *s.* bride-ale, wedding-feast, now corrupted into *bridal,* b. 2. 43. See **Bridale.**
Brybours, *pl.* robbers, 23. 262. See **Bribours.** See note, p. 282.
Bryddes, *pl.* birds, 10. 200, 14. 163; young birds, nestlings, 14. 167, R. 2. 146. See **Brid.**
Brygge. See **Brigge.**
Brynston, brimstone, 21. 291. Cf. Icel. *brennistein,* brimstone.
Brytonere. See **Britoner.**
Brywers, *pl.* brewers, 1. 221.
Budele, beadle, officer, 3. 111; Budul, a. 2. 77; Budels, *pl.* 3. 60. A. S. *bydel;* distinct from (yet cognate with) Bedel, q. v.
Buffated, *pt. s.* buffeted, beat, hit, 9. 173; Buffeted, b. 20. 190. See **Boffatede.**
Bugge, *v.* buy, b. pr. 168, b. 7. 24, b. 14. 230; Buggen, v. buy, procure, b. 7. 85; Buggeþ, *pr. s.* buys, bribes, a. 3. 151; Buggen, *pr. pl.* b. 3. 81; Buggeþ,*pr.pl.* a. 3. 74. A.S. *bycgan.* See **Bigge.**
Buggers, *s. pl.* buyers, a. 2. 46.
Buggynge, *s.* buying, b. 19. 230. See **Byggynge.**
Buirde, maid, b. 18. 116. A.S. *brýd.* See **Birde.**
Buirn, man, b. 11. 353, .b. 16. 180; Buyrn, b. 16. 263; Buirnes, *pl.* men, b. 12. 67. See **Burn.**
Bules, *pl.* boils, 23. 84; Byles, b. 20. 83. A.S. *býle.*
Bulle, bull, papal rescript, 1. 67; 10. 42, 61, 285; Bulles, *pl.* 1. 71, 4. 185, 10. 337. L. *bulla,* a boss of metal, the seal of a bull.
Bummede, *pt. s.* tasted, took a draught, a. 5. 137; Bummed, *pt. s.* b. 5. 223. Prov. E. *bum,* drink, *bumpsy,* tipsy, See **Bommeþ.**
Burde, lady, 21. 121. A.S. *brýd,* a bride. See also **Berde, Birde, Buirde, Buyrde.**
Burdoun. See **Bordon.**
Burgages, *pl.* tenements, 4. 85, b. 3. 86; Burgagys, 4. 105; Borgages, a. 3. 77. Properly tenements in a town; from F. *bourg,* a town. ' *Bourgage,* a township ... also, a tenure in *Burgage,* held either of the King (as in our Bourough English) or of other lords of the burough, and subject to no other then the customarie and accustomed rents and services thereof;' Cotgrave.
Burgeis, *pl.* citizens, townspeople, 1. 219, 4. 201; R. 3. 149; Burgeys, b. 15. 196; Burgeyses, b. 5. 129; Burgeises,*gen.sing.*townsman's, citizen's, 15. 91; Burgeys, *gen. sing.* b. 12. 148.
Burgeouneth, *pr. pl.* bud, shoot, b. 15. 73.
Burgh-swyn, *pl.* town-pigs, b. 2. 97.
Buriede, *pt. pl.* buried, 22. 143; Buryden, b. 19. 139.
Buriels, grave, sepulchre, 22. 146; Burieles, b. 19. 142. A.S. *byrgels.*
Burn, man; Burne, 16. 163; R. 3. 173; Burnes, *pl.* 16. 156, 19. 11; R. 1. 113, R. 3. 192. See also **Bern, Buirn.**
Burpe, Burthe, birth, 15. 93, 21. 250, 22. 81; Burth, b. 12. 150.
Busches, *s. pl.* bushes (with an allusion to Bushy,) R. 3. 75; Bosshes, 14. 156. See **Buskes, Busshes.**
Busemares, *pl.* disgraces, 22. 294. See **Bismer.**
Busiliche, *adv.* studiously, earnestly, 12. 156.
Busked him, *pt. s.* prepared himself to go, repaired, went, a. 3. 14; Buskede hem, *pt. pl.* hurried, went, 4. 15; Busked, *pt. pl.* started, hurried, R. 3. 75; Buske, *imp. pl.* hasten, make ready, 11. 224. Icel. *búask,* to prepare oneself, reflexive form of *búa,* to prepare.
Buskes, bushes, b. 11. 336. See **Busches.**
Busschel, *s.* bushel, a. 7. 58. See **Boussel.**
Busshes, *pl.* bushes, R. 2. 152; Busschis, R. 3. 17. See **Busches, Buskes.**
Busshid, *pt. pl.* pushed, butted, R. 2. 39. Cf. O. Du. *buysschen,* to strike (Hexham).
Busshinge, *s.* pushing, butting (with punning allusion to *Bushy*), R. 1. 99. See above.
Busshope, bishop, 18. 283; Busshup, 23. 319; Busshopes, *pl.* 18. 277; Busschopes, *pl.* a. 8. 13; Busschopes, *gen. sing.* a bishop's, a. 9. 86; Busschopes, *gen. pl.* a. 8. 157. See **Bischop.**
Busshoppede, *pt. s.* confirmed, lit. ' bishopped,' 18. 268. ' I *bysshop* a chylde, as a bysshop dothe whan he confermeth hym;' Palsgrave.
Bustelyng, *pr. pt.* bustling (prob. put for *pr. pl.*), a. 6. 4.
But, *conj.* unless, except, b. 3. 112, b.

GLOSSARIAL INDEX. 325

6. 120; But if, *conj.* unless, except, b. 3. 305, b. 5. 420; if . . . not, a. 11. 132; But ʒif, unless, a. 7. 16. See **Bote**.

But, *pt. s.* beat, chastised, 1. 115. See **Bete**.

Buth, *pr. pl.* are, 11. 208, 19. 98; Buþ, 9. 17. See **Be**.

Buxum, *adj.* obedient, 10. 220; ready, willing, 16. 223; courteous, complaisant, a. 6. 56; mild, gentle, 21. 121; Buxome, obedient, humble, b. 1. 110; obliging, ready, b. 13. 251; Buxume, willing, 17. 64. See **Boxum**.

Buxumliche, *adv.* obediently, humbly, 15. 57; willingly, 18. 283; Buxomelich, b. 12. 114.

Buxumnesse, obedience, readiness, 8. 239, 17. 65; Buxomnesse, 21. 322, b. 14. 222; Buxomnes, b. 4. 187. See **Buxum**.

Buyeþ, *pr. s.* pays for, 16. 304. See **Bigge, Bugge**.

Buylden, *v.* build its nest, b. 12. 228.

Buyrde, *s.* lady, a. 3. 14; Buyrdes, *pl.* maidens, damsels, 22. 135. See **Burde**.

By-, *prefix.* See **Be-, Beo-, Bi-**.

By, *prep.* in, during, 2. 102, 8. 112; beside, 14. 136; in the cáse of, for, b. 11. 148; as regards, b. 12. 217; of, with respect, 15. 65; of, about, concerning, b.11.289; according to, as far as is in, *or* lies in (*or* lay in), after, 7. 297, 10. 17, 14. 71; after, b. 14. 25; By þys day = for this day, 9. 303; with reference to, 4. 289, 11. 164; R. 3. 65; with reference to (*or* by permission of, 1. 78; with reference to, against (the character of), 7. 70. And see **Bi**.

By so, provided that, 5. 98, 13. 5; By so þat, provided that, 17. 209; By so þat, in proportion as, 11. 309.

Bycome, *v.* become, 23. 380; Bycomeþ, is becoming, befits, 4. 266, 6. 61; Bycam, *pt. s.* became, was made, 8. 128, 19. 135; went, was gone to, 16. 150; By-comen, *pt. pl.* became, 22. 38; Bycome, 1 *pt. pl.* we became, were made, b. 11. 195; Bycam, 1 *pt. pl.* were made, 13. 109. See **Bicomeþ**.

Bydden, *v.* beg, pray, 7. 49; Bydde, *v.* 20. 208; Bydde my bedes = say my prayers, b. 12. 29; Byddeþ, *pr. s.* begs, asks alms, 10. 63; Byddeþ (with *of*), *pr. pl.* pray (for), 23. 285. See **Bidde**.

Bydders, *s. pl.* beggars, 1. 41, 9. 210, 10. 61. See **Bidderes**.

Byddyng, *s.* praying, bidding; Bedes byddyng = bidding of beads, praying of prayers, 13. 84, 22. 377; Byddynges, prayers, b. 15. 418. See **Biddyng**.

Byddyng, *s.* bidding, orders, command, request, 2. 74, 21. 419; Byddinge, 11. 97. See **Biddyng**.

Byden, *v.* remain, bide, a. 10. 162.

Byennals, *pl.* masses said for two years, 10. 320. See **Biennales**.

By-falle, *v.* happen, befall, 22. 242, 23. 350; By-falleþ, *pr. s.* befals, is due, 2. 48; By-falle, *pr. s. subj.* may befal, 6. 200; Byfel, *pt. s.* befell, fell to, 1. 7, 7. 326; By-fil, *pt. s.* happened, 19. 168; Byful, 11. 8; Byfel me = happened to me, b. pr. 6; Byfulle, *impers. pt. s. subj.* it might happen to, might befall, 7. 27. See **Befalle, Bifalleth**.

By-fore, *adv.* beforehand, 22. 16. See **Bifore**.

Byg, great, mighty, 19. 136. See **Bygge**.

By-gan, *pt. s.* began, 7. 342; gave beginning to, created, 2. 104, 20. 111, 21. 222; Bygunne, *pt. pl.* began, 7. 395; Bygonnen, *pt. pl.* a. 2. 59; Bygonne, *pt. s. subj.* should begin, were to begin (work), b. 14. 149. See **Bigon**.

By-gat, *pt. s.* begat, 2. 29; Bygete, *pp.* begotten, 15. 31; Bygetyn, 11. 208.

Bygge, *adj. pl.* big, strong, 9. 224. See **Byg**.

Byggen, *v.* to buy, 1. 183; Bygge, *v.* 10. 28; Bygge þe with a wastell = buy thyself a cake with, 7. 341; Byggen, *pr. pl.* buy, produce, 4. 82. See **Bigge**.

Byggynge, *s.* buying, 22. 235. See **Buggynge**.

By-glosedest, 2 *pt. s.* didst deceive, 21. 383.

Bygonne, Bygunne. See **Bygan**.

By-grucche, *v.* to grumble at, 9. 338; Bygruccheþ, *pr. s.* grumbles, finds fault, 9. 155; *pr. s. subj.* may grumble, 9. 68. See **Bigruccheth**.

By-gurdeles, *s. pl.* purses, 11. 85; see note. See **Bigurdeles**.

Bygyle, *v.* deceive, beguile, 2. 37, 15. 5, 21. 166; Bygyly, *v.* 12. 309; Bygylede, *pt. s.* 21. 164; Bygyledest, 2 *pt. s.* didst beguile, 21. 328, 383; Bygyled, *pp.* deceived, cheated, 21. 325, 329; Bygylid, *pp.* 21. 385; Bygylen, *pr. pl.* 17. 46. See **Bigile, Bigyle**.

By-gynnynge, *s.* beginning, 15. 160;

GLOSSARIAL INDEX.

creation, the book of Genesis, 9. 239. See **Bigynnyng**.
Byheste, promise, 11. 250, 13. 14, 19. 123, 21. 322, 23. 118. See **Biheste**.
By-hofthe, s. behoof, advantage, use, 13. 187. O. Fries. *bihofte*. See **Byhoueþ**.
By-hote, 1 *pr. s.* promise, vow, 8. 69; assure, 9. 238, 302; By-hihte, *pt. s.* promised, 19. 259; By-highte, 7. 5; Byhight, *pt. s.* promised, b. 20. 110; Byhiȝte, *pt. s.* vowed, b. 5. 65; By-hyht, *pt. s.* 4. 30; By-hihte, 1 *pt. s.* promised, 21. 378; Byhote god=I vow to God, b. 6. 280. See **Bihote**.
By-houeþ, *impers. pr*, it behoves, is necessary, 8. 295; is the fate of, 10. 89. See **Bihoueth**.
By-hyht, *pt. s.* promised, 4. 30. See **By-hote**.
By-Iapede, *pt. s.* deceived, cheated, 2. 63; By-Iaped, *pp.* mocked, 21. 325. See **Bi-iaped**.
By-kenne, 1 *pr. s.* I commend, commit, 3. 51, 11. 58; see note. See **Bikenne**.
Bykere, *v.* fight, bicker, 23. 79. See **Bikere**.
By-knowe, *v.* acknowledge, confess, 1. 209; 1 *pr. s.* 6. 92; By-know, 1 *pr. s.* 7. 206; By-knew, *pt. s.* (with *on*), confessed, acknowledged (his guilt), 12. 256 (see note); By-knewen, *pt. pl.* acknowledged, 22. 149; Byknowe, *pp.* acknowledged (to be), 14. 11. See **Biknowen**.
Byles, *pl.* boils, b. 20. 83. See **Bules**. A.S. *býle*.
By-leue, s. belief, faith, creed, 22. 336; By-leyue, 8. 74, 9. 97. See **Bileue**.
By-leue, *v.* leave off, cease, desist, 9. 176; remain behind (*or* leave behind), 13. 212 (see note); Byleue, *v.* to leave, give up; the line means, 'it were better for many doctors to give up such teaching,' b. 15. 71. Properly *intransitive*, but it seems to be used transitively; see *bilǽfen* in Stratmann.
By-leyue, 1 *pr. s.* I believe, 12. 133; By-leyueþ, *pr. pl.* believe, trust, 11. 107; By-leyue, *pr. pl.* 21. 270; By-leyuest, 2 *pr. s.* 2. 177; By-leouede, *pt. pl.* believed, 11. 190; By-leyf, *imp. s.* believe, 12. 144, 148. See **Bileue**.
Bylle, a petition, 5. 45. See note, p. 55.
Bylongeþ, *pr. s.* belongs, pertains, 2. 43, 20. 143; is proper for, 6. 66. See **Bilongeth**.
By-lowe, *pp.* lied against, slandered, 10. 181. See **Belye**, **Bilyeþ**.

Bylyf, belief, b. 19. 230. See **Byleue**.
Bylyue, livelihood, means of living, sustenance, 2. 18, 6. 21. A.S. *bigleofa*, food.
By-meneþ, *pr. s.* means, signifies, betokens, 1. 216, 2. 1, 21. 174; Bymente, *pt. s.* 21. 16. See **Bemeneth**.
Bymeneth, *pr. pl.* lament, bemoan, b. 15. 143. A.S. *bimǽnan*.
Bymolen, *v.* bespot, sully, b. 14. 4. From A.S. *mâl*, a mole, spot, mark.
By-neoþe, *adv.* beneath, 19. 85; By-nythe, 7. 180. See **Bineth**.
Byn-fet, benefit, kindness, goodness to others, 8. 42, 264. See **Benfait**.
By-nymen, *v.* deprive, take away again, 4. 323; By-nom, *pt. s.* took away from, 9. 254, 14. 9; Worth by-nome hym=shall be taken away from him, b. 3. 312. See **Binam**.
By-nythe, *adv.* beneath, below, 7. 180. See **By-neoþe**.
By-quethe, *pr. s. subj.* bequeath, 16. 12. See **Biquethe**.
Byquyste, *s.* will, bequest, 9. 94. See **Biqueste**.
By-reue, *v.* deprive, take away, 9. 259. See **Bireue**.
Byrthen, *s.* burden, R. 2. 66.
Byschrewed, *pt. s.* cursed, b. 4. 168.
By-sechen, *v.* beseech, beg, ask, 12. 87; By-seche, *v.* beg, pray, 13. 9; By-souhte, *pt. s.* besought, 4. 77, 5. 66; By-seke, *imp. s.* intercede, a. 12. 111. See **Bisechen**.
By-sette, *v.* employ, lay out, bestow, dispose of, 7. 254; By-setten, *v.* 7. 346; Bysette, *pt. s.* bestowed (herself), b. 12. 48 (see the note, p. 181). See **Bisette**.
Byseye, *pp.* sought me out, treated, visited, 23. 202. (Mätzner translates it by *hat mich heimgesucht*.) See **Biseye**. A.S. *bisegen*, pp. of *biséon*, to regard.
By-shutt, *pp.* shut, barred, 22. 167.
By-slobered, *pp.* bedabbled, dirtied, slobbered over, 8. 1. See **Bislabered**.
Bysnewed, *pp.* covered with snow, b. 15. 110; By-snywe, *pp.* 17. 266.
Bystrydeþ, *pr. s.* bestrides, mounts, 20. 76. See **Bistrode**.
By-swatte, *pt. s.* covered with sweat, b. 13. 403.
Byswynke, *v.* work for, earn by labour, 9. 224; Byswynken, *pr. pl.* work at, labour on, 9. 140; Byswynken, 2 *pr. pl.* labour for, earn by labour, 9. 261; By-swonke, *pp.* earned by labour, worked for, 23. 292. See **Biswinke**.

GLOSSARIAL INDEX. 327

Bysynesse, care, anxiety, b. 14. 316.
Byt (*for* Biddeth), *pr. s.* bids, b. 12. 56. See **Bit** = bids.
Byte, *v.* bite, take effect, 23. 361; Bytynde, *pres. pt.* eating, 16. 54. See **Biten.**
Byte, *s.* bite, morsel, 21. 208.
By-teche, 1 *pr. s.* commend, 16. 183. A.S. *betǽcan,* to deliver.
Bytelbrowed, *adj.* with prominent brows, 7. 198. See **Bitelbrowed.**
Byter, *adj.* bitter, sharp, 5. 181, 21. 67. See **Bitere.**
By-þenke, 1 *pr. s.* bethink myself of, 7. 107. See **Be-þenke.**
By-trauaile, 1 *pr. s,* labour for, 16. 210; 1 *pr. pl. as fut.* we shall labour for, 9. 242.
Byttere, *adv.* dearly, bitterly, b. 10. 281. See **Bitere.**
By-tulye, 1 *pr. pl. as fut.* we shall cultivate the ground for, 9. 242. See **Tulien.**
By-twyne, *prep.* between, 4. 384; amongst, 13. 125. See **Bitwene.**
Bytwyne, *adv.* between, 1. 19.
By-tydde, *pt. s.* befell, happened, 15. 61. See **Betide.**
Bytynge, *adj.* sharp, severe, 10. 16.
By-wicched, *pt. pl.* bewitched, charmed to sleep, 22. 156.
Byȝe, necklace, collar, 1. 180; Byȝes, *pl.* 1. 178. See **Beiȝ.**
Byȝonde, *adv.* beyond, abroad, over sea, 4. 146. See **Biȝonde.**
Byȝute, *pp.* begotten, 3. 144. See **Biȝute.**

Caas, *s.* case, misfortune, a. 8. 52. See **Cas.**
Caban, *s.* cabin, a. 12. 35. 'A Caban of cuke, *capana*;' Cath. Angl. See **Kaban.**
Cacchen, *v.* catch, seize, 15. 86; find out, a. 11. 86; gain, get, b. 11. 168; *ger.* to catch hold, depend (on), 4. 367; Caccheþ, *pr. s.* drives, 15. 117; snatches, takes, b. 12. 178; Cacche, *pr. pl.* receive, b. 12. 220; Cacche, *pr. s. subj.* take, seize, obtain, 23. 14; *pr. pl. subj.* 4. 392; Cauhte, *pt. s.* caught, 7. 409; gained, 22. 128; Cauȝte, *pt. s.* caught, R. 2. 158; Kauȝte, 1 *pt. s.* b. 13. 405; Kauht, *pp.* captured, taken, 19. 171; Cauht, *pp.* caught, 20. 185. See **Chacche.**
Cacchepol, officer, 21. 76. '*Cahchpolle,* or pety seriawnte;' Prompt. Parv. See **Kachepol.**
Caiser, emperor, 22. 138; Caiseris, *pl.*

a. 11. 216. See **Kaiser, Cayser.** From Lat. *Cæsar*.
Caitif, *s.* wretch, 13. 64; Caityue, b. 5. 200; Caityf, vagabond, b. 11. 125, a. 5. 114. O.F. *caitif, chetif,* from Lat. *captiuus.*
Caitif, *adj.* wretched, poor, 14. 110. See **Caytyf, Chaytif.**
Caitifliche, *adv.* wretchedly, in a humble manner, 13. 127.
Caitifte, vileness, 10. 255. O.F. *caitivete, chaitivete* (Mätzner).
Cake, *s.* cake, loaf, 9. 306. Cf. prov. E. *cake* of bread.
Cakebrede, bread in the form of a cake, b. 16. 229.
Calabre, Calabrian fur, 9. 293. See note, p. 116.
Calculed, *pp.* calculated, 18. 106.
Calewey, pears of Cailloux, b. 16. 69. See note, p. 237.
Calfe, calf, b. 15. 458; Calues, *gen.* calf's, b. 15. 457.
Calme, *v.* grow calm, R. 3. 366.
Cam. See **Comen.**
Cammoka, a kind of rich stuff, 17. 299. See note, p. 220. From Pers. *kimkhá,* damask silk.
Cammokes, *pl.* plants of the rest-harrow, 22. 314. See note, p. 271.
Can, Canstow. See **Conne.**
Canonistres, *pl.* divines, men skilled in canon-law or ecclesiastical law, 10. 303. '*Canoniste,* a Canonist, or Professor of, or Practiser in, the Canon Law;' Cotgrave.
Canoun, canon of the mass, b. 5. 428. The part of the Mass called Canon Missæ.
Cantel, little bit, 15. 164. O.F. *cantel,* whence F. *canteau, chanteau,* 'a corner-peece'; Cotgrave. See Cath. Angl. p. 53, n. 4.
Capel, horse, 5. 24; Capul, a. 4. 22; Caple, b. 4. 23; Capeles, *pl.* 22. 333, 347; Caples, *pl.* b. 2. 161. O. Icel. *kapall,* Làt. *caballus.*
Capped, *pp.* capped, completed, finished off, 12. 80. See note.
Carded, *pp.* carded, 12. 15. See **Karde.**
Cardiacle, pain in the heart, disease or spasm of the heart, 7. 78; Cardiacles, *pl.* 23. 82. See note, p. 277, and Cath. Angl. p. 54, n. 5.
Cardinale, *adj.* cardinal, chief, 22. 318; chief, supreme, a. 12. 15; Cardinales, *pl.* 1. 132, 22. 274.
Care, woe, anxiety, trouble, misery, 8. 305, b. 14. 175; Caris, *pl.* troubles, R. 1. 100. See **Kare.**

Carecte, sign, character, letter, b. 12. 90; Carectes, *pl.* b. 12. 80, 93. '*Caracte* in pricke song, *minime* ;' Palsgrave. And see *Caractes* in Halliwell.

Careden, *pt. pl.* wanted, wished, were anxious, a. 2. 132.

Careful, *adj.* full of care, anxious, troubled, wretched, miserable, poor, b. 9. 156, b. 10. 58; Carful, 12. 42, 13. 303, 14. 110. See note to b. 14. 179.

Carefullich, *adv.* anxiously, mournfully, b. 5. 77; Carfully, 23. 201.

Carien, *v.* (1) carry, 22. 335, a. 2. 132; (2) go, wander, roam, 1. 31, a. pr. 29; Carieþ him = betakes himself, a. 5. 147; Carieth, *pr. pl.* wander, R. 3. 302.

Caristia, dearth, b. 14. 72. See note.

Carket, *pp.* afflicted (*but an error for* Carded), a. 11. 18 *n.*

Carnels, *s. pl.* battlements, a. 6. 78. See **Kernels**.

Caro, flesh, the body, b. 9. 48.

Caroigne, carcase, body, b. 6. 93, b. 12. 254; flesh, 15. 179; Caroygne, corpse, 17. 197; Caroyne, body, b. pr. 193; body, flesh, 9. 100; Careyne, flesh, a. 7. 84; Kareyne, carrion, R. 2. 178. O.F. *caroigne*, F. *charogne*, E. *carrion.*

Carpen, *v.* talk, chatter, speak, tell, 7. 29, 14. 179; Ne carpen = nor (shall I) speak, 1. 208; Carpe, *v.* talk, 23. 333, R. 4. 41; speak, b. 19. 65; Carpe, 1 *pr. s.* speak, 19. 220, 283; Carpen, *pr. pl.* talk, speak, chatter, 8. 77, 12. 52; Carpeth, *pr. pl.* b. 13. 417; Carpe, *pr. s. subj.* talk, argue, 20. 109; *pr. pl. subj.* may say, b. 11. 120; Carpede, *pt. s.* spoke, said, 22. 176, 199; chattered, 16. 109; Carped, *pt. s.* talked, b. 13. 100; told, 3. 203; spoke, b. 13. 179; Carped, *pt. pl.* talked, b. 13. 220, R. 2. 29. See **Karpeþ**. '*Carpyn*, or talkyn, *Fabulor* ;' Prompt. Parv.

Carpinge, *s.* talk, R. 1. 87; Carpynge, talking, speech, b. 11. 231; Carpyng, b. pr. 203; talk, b. 10. 138. See **Karpinge**.

Carse, *s.* cress, a thing of no value, 12. 14; Carses, *pl.* cresses, 9. 322. See note, p. 147. A.S. *cerse, cærse*, cress.

Cart, *v.* drive carts, 6. 63.

Cartfull, cartful, R. 2. 158.

Cartsadele, *v.* harness, yoke, a. 2. 154; Cartesadel, *imp. s.* b. 2. 179. A *cartsaddle* is the small saddle put on the back of a draught-horse when harnessed ; see Cath. Angl. p. 55, n. 2.

Cart-whel, cart-wheel, 16. 162.

Cas, case, instance, circumstance, 4. 436, 10. 48, 23. 14; case (in grammar), 4. 339; Case, case (in grammar), 4. 349; Cas, mishap,' misfortune, b. 7. 48. See **Caas**.

Cast, contrivance, 4. 20; Castes, *pl.* 14. 162; Castis, *pl.* R. 3. 102; Conscience caste = Conscience's device, b. 3. 19. From the verb *casten.*

Casten, *v.* cast, a. 9. 94; contrive, a. 3. 18; Caste, *v.* plan, contrive, 12. 16, 18; R. 3. 219; send, b. 13. 247; Cast, *pr. s.* (*for* Casteth), intends, 10. 151, 22. 280; Casteth, *pr. pl.* devise, R. 3. 132; Caste, *pt. s.* cast, a. 5. 170; planned, schemed, devised, 23. 121; Cast, *pt. s.* R. 4. 24; purposed, b. 19. 275; Caste, 1 *pt. s.* contrived, b. 15. 327; exercised (my wit), 7. 264; Casten, *pt. pl.* devised, plotted, 22. 141; Caste, *pt. pl.* determined, 1. 143; Cast, *pp.* cast, melted and cast in a mould, R. 1. 70; Caste, *imp. s.* consider, R. 3. 279; Cast, *imp. s.* cast, put, a. 7. 15. Icel. *kasta.*

Catekumelynges, *pl.* catechumens, b. 11. 77. See note, p. 167.

Catel, property, goods, wealth, 1. 209, 4. 72, 5. 78, 8. 221, 9. 101; Catell, 6. 130, 7. 288. And see **Katel**.

Catelles, *adj.* without property, a. 10. 68.

Caudel, mess, 7. 412. See Cath. Angl. p. 56, n. 2.

Caue, tomb, grave, b. 12. 254.

Cauke, *v.* to tread, breed, 15. 162; Cauken, b. 12. 229; Caukede, *pt. s.* 14. 171; Kauked, *pt. pl.* b. 11. 350. O.F. *cauquer*, Lat. *calcare.*

Caurimaury, the name of a coarse rough material, b. 5. 79; Caurimauri, a. 5. 62. In Pierce the Ploughman's Crede, the ploughman is miserably clad : 'His cote was of a cloute · that *cary* was y-called.' In Skelton's Elynour Rummyng, some slatterns are thus spoken of—'Some loke strawry, Some *cawry mawry* ;' l. 149. Halliwell also refers (s. v. *Cary*) to Collier's Memoirs of Alleyn, p. 21.

Causis, *pl.* trials at law, R. 3. 318.

Cautell, craftiness, wiliness, R. 1. 78; wariness, precaution, R. 3. 67. See Prompt. Parv.

Cayser, emperor, 4. 325; Caysers, *pl.* 23. 101. See **Caiser**.

GLOSSARIAL INDEX. 329

Caytiflyche, *adv.* meanly, 4. 242. See **Caitifliche.**
Caytyf, *s.* wretch, low fellow, miserable creature, 9. 244; Caytifs, *pl.* 21. 97; Caytyues, 220. See **Caitif.**
Caytyf, *adj.* wretched, poor, 15. 90; Caytyue, b. 11. 287. See **Caitif.**
Certayn, *adj. as sb.* certain (number), fixed number, 23. 258, 267.
Certes, *adv.* certainly, assuredly, 6. 22, 14. 197, 23. 340; Certis, b. 2. 151; Certys, 10. 331.
Cessen, *v.* cease, leave off. 23. 107; b. 7. 117; Cesse, *v.* 3. 165; Cesse, 3 *imper. s.* cease, 15. 41; Cesseþ, *imp. pl.* cease, be still, 5. 1.
Chacche, *v.* catch, a. 2. 167; Chacche, 2 *pr. pl.* a. 2. 180. See **Cacche.**
Chaced, *pt. s.* hurried, b. 17. 51.
Chafen, *pr. pl. subj.* should excite (apparently used with a nom. singular), b. 12. 127. Read *chafe*; see **Chaufen.**
Chaffare, merchandise, goods, ware, 3. 60, 7. 380; Cheffare, 1. 33.
Chaffare, *v.* make a bargain, deal, trade, 9. 249; Chaffareth, *pr. s.* b. 14. 311; Chaffaren, *pr. pl.* 13. 227; Chaffare, *pr. s. subj.* trade, 17. 149; Chaffared, *pt. pl.* 7. 252; Chaffared, *pp.* bargained, 6. 94; gained in trade, b. 15. 105.
Chalengeth, *pr. s.* claims as a due, b. 15. 160; Chalange, 1 *pr. s.* claim, 17. 191; Chalengen, *pr. pl.* claim, b. pr. 93; Chalengynge, *pres. part.* claiming, demanding, 1. 91; Chalenged, *pp.* arraigned, accused, 7. 136, 156; Chalanged, *pp.* b. 5. 174. See Prompt. Parv.
Chalengynge, *s.* contradiction, b. 15. 338; Chalangynge, accusing, b. 5. 88, b. 11. 415.
Chanoun, *s.* canon, b. 10. 46, a. 10. 109; Chanouns, *pl.* 6. 157; Chanons, *pl.* 6. 171.
Chapitele-hous, *s.* chapter-house, 7. 156; Chapitel-hous, b. 5. 174.
Chapitre, chapter (of a religious house), 4. 476; Chapitere, b. 5. 161; Chapitele, b. 3. 318.
Chapman, trader, merchant, 1. 62; Chapmon, a. pr. 61; Chapmen, *pl.* merchants, tradesmen, 6. 137; b. 5. 34, 233, 331.
Chapon-cote, hen-house, 7. 136. Lit. 'capon-cote.'
Charge, *s.* responsibility, 10. 258; blame, imputation, a. 10. 73; weight, R. 1. 41; burden, duty, R. 4. 29; cargo, R. 4. 74.

Charge hem, *v.* burden themselves, b. 20. 236; Chargeþ, *pr. s.* is burdened with, 17. 149; feels overburdened, grieves as if burdened, cares, 17. 288; loads, burdens with a penalty, 20. 272; accounts (it as), b. 14. 311; Chargeth, *pr. pl.* insist upon, b. 17. 290; Chargede, *pt. s.* charged, a. 5. 32; Chargid, *pp.* charged, entrusted, 1. 87; Charget, *pp.* a. 10. 23.
Charnel, charnel-house, 9. 45.
Chartre, charter, contract, deed, 3. 69; Chartres, *pl.* b. 11. 299.
Chastelet, *s.* little castle, domain, b. 2. 84.
Chasten, *v.* punish, chastise, correct, 6. 137; Chaste, *v.* 9. 346, b. 6. 53, b. 11. 415; Chasteþ, *pr. pl.* correct, chasten, 1. 211; Chasted, *pt. s.* corrected, chastised, 1. 110; Chasted, *pp.* 5. 112, 14. 235; Chastet, a. 4. 103. O. F. *chastier*, from Lat. *castigare*. See Cath. Angl. p. 60.
Chastyng, *s.* chastisement, b. 4. 117.
Chatere, *pr. s. subj.* chatter, argue, 17. 69; Chatre, b. 14. 226.
Chatering, *s.* chattering, 3. 89.
Chaude, Chaud, *adj.* hot, b. 6. 313; *plus chaud* = hotter, very hot, b. 6. 313. F. *chaud.*
Chaufen, *v.* become warm, 18. 49; Chaufe, *pr. s. subj.* excite, enrage, chafe, 15. 68. E. *chafe.*
Chaumbrere, chamberlain, b. 14. 100.
Chaunce, good fortune, b. 13. 342; alternative of fortune, a. 3. 94.
Chaunceler, chancellor, 5. 185.
Chauncelrie, chancery, chancellor's court, 1. 91, a. 4. 26.
Chaunchyth, *pr. pl.* change, R. 3. 139. Put for *chaungyth.*
Chaytif, *adj.* low, mean, 23. 236. See **Caitif.**
Cheeif-mete, *s.* lit. chief meat, a. 7. 281. Other MSS. have *chiriuellis* or *cheruelys*, i. e. chervils; also *chesteyns*, i. e. chestnuts.
Cheere, countenance, looks, mien, 5. 160. See **Chere.**
Chees, *pt. s.* chose, 14. 3. See **Chese.**
Cheeue, *v.* prosper, make gain, 9. 249; Cheeuen, *v.* succeed, a. pr. 31. See **Cheuen.**
Chef, *adj.* chief, principal, 1. 62; Chef lordes, landlords, 10. 73; Cheff, R. 2. 114; Chyf, 5. 185.
Cheffare. See **Chaffare.**
Chefteyn, chief, leader, 22. 474; Cheffeteyne, prince, R. 2. 114.
Chekè, *imper.* 1 *pl.* let us stop up, lit. check, 21. 287.

Cheker, *s.* exchequer, b. pr. 93; Chekkere, 1. 91; Chekyr, 5. 185.
Chekonys, *pl.* chickens, R. 2. 144.
Chele, *s.* cold, chill, 9. 249; b. 1. 23; b. 10. 59; R. 2. 144; For chele = to prevent a chill, a. 7. 299. A.S. *céle,* cold, *sb.*
Cheorles, *pl.* labourers, churls, servants, 9. 45, 21. 109. See **Cherl.**
Cheose, *imp. pl.* choose, a. 3. 94. See **Chese.**
Chepe, *s.* Cheapside (in London), b. 5. 322.
Chepe, 1 *pr. s.* buy, bargain, 17. 191; Cheped, *pt. s.* bargained for, b. 13. 380.
Chepyng, market, 9. 323; Chepynge, b. 4. 56; Chepynges, *pl.* bargainings, 5. 59.
Cher, *adj.* dear; Cher ouer = careful of, 18. 148.
Chere, face, appearance, mien, 7. 375, 12. 188; Cheere, 5. 160. E. *cheer.* See **Chiere.**
Cherissing, *s.* cherishing, over-indulgence, 5. 112; Cherissyng, b. 4. 117; Chereschunge, a. 4. 103.
Cherl, churl, serf, peasant, 7. 413, 13. 61; Cherle, b. 11. 122; ill-mannered fellow, b. 5. 360; Cherles, *pl.* churls, b. 6. 50; Cherlis, b. 19. 35; ill-behaved fellows, b. 1. 33. A.S. *ceorl.* See **Cheorles, Churles.**
Cherliche, *adv.* dearly, R. 3. 203.
Cheruelles, *pl.* chervils, b. 6. 296. See **Chiruylles.**
Chese, *v.* choose, 17. 176; b. 15. 38; R. 4. 29; Chees, 14. 3; Chese, *pt. pl.* b. 20. 236; Chesse, 2 *pt. pl.* R. 1. 88. See **Cheose.**
Chesibles, *pl.* chasubles, b. 6. 12. See **Chesybles.**
Cheste, *s.* strife, quarrelling, 1. 105, 3. 89; Chest, b. 2. 84; Chestes, *pl.* strifes, quarrels, a. 10. 187. A.S. *céast.*
Cheste, chest, ark, 15. 59.
Chesybles, *pl.* chasubles, 9. 11. See **Chesibles.** See note, p. 106.
Chetes, *s. pl.* escheats, property reverting to the king, b. 4. 175.
Cheuen, *v.* prosper, 21. 109; Cheuen, *pr. pl.* thrive, b. pr. 31; Cheuede, *pt. pl.* prospered, throve, 1. 33, 7. 252. Short for *acheue.* See Prompt. Parv. p. 73, n. 7. See **Cheeue, Chieue.**
Cheuesaunce, *s.* agreement, bargain, 23. 16; Cheuesances, *pl.* agreements about the loan of money, b. 5. 249.

The *cheuesaunce* or exchange refers to the system whereby the laws against usury were evaded. See note, p. 86.
Cheuesschen, *v.* keep clear, guard, save, a. 10. 73. Cf. *chewyse* = save, in Morte Arthure, l. 1750; and see Mätzner, p. 569.
Chewe, *v.* chew, eat, devour, 16. 46, 21. 207; Cheweþ, 2 *pr. pl.* eat up, 3. 140; Chewen, *pr. pl.* 2. 191.
Cheyne, *imper.* 1 *pl.* let us place chains (upon the gates), 21. 287; Cheynid, *pp.* chained, 2. 185.
Cheytif, *adj.* low, mean, wretched, b. 20. 235. See **Caitif.**
Chiboles, *pl.* small onions, 9. 311. F. *ciboule,* Lat. *cæpulla.*
Chiden, *v.* quarrel, chide, 4. 224; abuse, b. 13. 380; Chiden, *pr. pl.* cry out, ask noisily, 2. 191; Chide, *pr. pl. subj.* may cry out, may find fault, 4. 393; Chidde, 1 *pt. s.* blamed, b. 11. 398; Chidynge, *pres. pt.* quarrelling, 7. 68. See **Chyde, Chit.**
Chiere, looks, mien, b. 8. 117, b. 20. 113. See **Chere.**
Chieue, *v.* thrive, prosper, b. 18. 104; Chieueth, *impers. pr. s.* it succeeds, results, turns out, b. 14. 226. See **Cheuen.**
Chiftaigne, chief, head, b. 19. 469.
Child, *pp.* chilled, 18. 49.
Chile, *s.* cold, 23. 236. See **Chele.**
Chillyng, *s.* chilling, 9. 335. (For *chillyng* = against chilling, to prevent chilling.)
Chircheward, *adv.* towards the church, a. 5. 147.
Chiries, *pl.* cherries, 9. 311, 13. 221.
Chirityme, cherry-time, time of gathering cherries, b. 5. 161. See note.
Chiruylles, *pl.* pot-herbs, chervils, 9. 311. See **Cheruelles.**
Chit, *pr. s.* chides, 2. 177, 17. 288. See **Chiden.**
Chiteryng, *s.* chattering, twittering, b. 12. 253. See note, p. 186.
Chiualer, *s.* knight, 21. 104.
Chiueled, *pt. s.* shivered, trembled, b. 5. 193. 'Chyueryng, as one dothe for colde;' Palsgrave.
Choppe, *v.* strike, b. 12. 127; *pr. s. subj.* knock, 1. 64; strike, 15. 68; Chop, *imp. s.* hew, a. 3. 253.
Choppes, *s. pl.* blows, knocks, disputes, 11. 275, a. 10. 187.
Choppyng, *s.* exchange (of abuse), b. 9. 167.
Choyse, *s.* choice, a. 3. 94.
Choyse, *adj.* choice, a. 6. 110.

GLOSSARIAL INDEX. 331

Churles, *pl.* labourers, servants, 2. 29. See **Cherl.**
Chyde, *v.* find fault, b. 13. 323; complain, a. 7. 303; *pr. s. subj.* quarrel, dispute, b. 14. 226; Chydde, 1 *pt. pl.* chid, disputed, b. 18. 418. See **Chiden.**
Chyderes, *pl.* quarrelsome persons, 19. 46; Chyders, brawlers, R. 3. 317.
Chydynge, *s.* fault-finding, b. 11. 415.
Chyuesaunce, an agreement for borrowing money, 7. 252. See **Cheuesaunce.**
Chyf, *adj.* chief, principal, 5. 185. See **Chef.**
Chymneye, hearth, fire-place, b. 10. 98. See note, p. 151.
Chyne, chink, crevice, 21. 287. A.S. *cinu.* See note, p. 257.
Chyuyþ, *pr. s. impers.* befalls, happens, 17. 69. See **Cheuen.**
Cipres, *s.* fine gauze, b. 15. 224. Cotgrave translates *Crespe* by 'cipres, cob-web lawn.'
Circumsysede, 1 *pt. s.* circumcised, 19. 253; Circumcised, b. 16. 235.
Citees, *pl.* cities, b. 14. 80.
Citiseyns, *s. pl.* citizens, R. 4. 42.
Clam. See **Clymbe.**
Clameþ, *pr. pl.* proclaim, publish, cry aloud, b. 1. 93. See **Clayme.**
Clannere, *adj.* cleaner, 22. 252.
Clannesse, cleanness, purity, pure life, 15. 86, 22. 381.
Clanse, *v.* purify, clear, cleanse, 9. 65; Clanse with oure soules = cleanse our souls with, 17. 25; Clanseþ, *pr. pl.* 20. 176; Clansede, *pt. s.* cleansed, purified, 19. 143; Clansed, *pp.* 4. 361.
Clappid, *pt. pl.* clattered, spoke loudly, R. 4. 89.
Clause, *s.* clause, sentence, tale, a. 3. 264, R. pr. 72.
Clawen, *v.* claw, seize, catch hold of, 1. 172; Clawe, *v.* 20. 156; grip, b. 17. 188; scrape, cleanse by scraping, b. 14. 17; Claweth, *imper. pl.* seize hold of, b. 10. 284. '*Claw*, to seize hold of, to snatch at;' Shropsh. Word-book.
Clayme, *v.* claim, b. 10. 344, b. 14. 142; Claymen, *pr. pl.* b. 10. 322; Claymede, *pt. s.* 23. 96; Claymed, *pp.* a. 1. 168. See **Cleyme, Clameþ.**
Claymes, *pl.* claims, 5. 98.
Cleer, *adj.* bright, clear, 8. 232.
Cleer, *adv.* brightly, 20. 222.
Clees, *pl.* claws, 1. 172.
Clef, *pt. s.* was rent, b. 18. 61. See **Cleue** (to divide).
Clene, *adj.* sinless, pure, upright, 3. 51, 8. 156, 22. 381, 460.

Clene, *adv.* clean, completely, quite, b. 9. 135, a. 10. 164.
Clennesse, cleanness, purity, 15. 88; Of al clennesse = who is all purity, b. 14. 299.
Clepe, *v.* call, invite, b. 11. 185; Clepeþ, *pr. s.* call, 8. 177; a. 9. 62; Cleped, *pt. s.* called, 7. 149; invited, b. 11, 114; Clepide, *pt. s.* called, 13. 53; Clepid, *pt. s.* R. 3. 70; Clepte, *pt. s.* a. 1. 4; summoned, a. 4. 17; Cleped, *pt. pl.* called, 23. 182, a. 10. 144; Cleped, *pp.* called, named, 22. 117; summoned, 12. 18; Clepid, b. 10. 21. A.S. *cleopian, clipian,* to call. See **Clypie.**
Clere, *v.* grow clear, R. 3. 366.
Clerematyn, *s.* a kind of fine bread, 9. 328. Cf. O.F. *cler,* clear, *matin,* morning; it was probably used for breakfast.
Clergialliche, *adv.* in a clerkly manner, like a clerk, scholarly, 8. 34; Clergealy, b. pr. 124.
Clergie, prob. an error for *clerlie,* clearly, R. 3. 26. See the note.
Clergye, *s.* learning (sometimes personified), b. 3. 164, b. 10. 148, 442, b. 15. 76; (esp. writing,) b. 12. 72; learned men, men of letters, b. pr. 116; Clergie, 22. 469; Cleregie, 12. 101; Clergies, *gen.* Learning's, 12. 99; Clergise, *gen.* b. 3. 15. See note to b. 3. 164, p. 48.
Clerioun, *s.* young scholar, chorister, a. 12. 49. See my note to Chaucer, Cant. Tales, Group B, l. 1693.
Clerke, *s.* clerk, student, man of learning, b. 3. 3, b. 7. 73; a. 3. 3; Clerk, 4. 3, R. 4. 35; Clerkes, *pl.* clerks, scholars, b. pr. 114; Clerkis, *pl.* b. 10. 73; Clerkus, *pl.* 2. 88, 122; Clerken, *gen. pl.* b. 4. 119. See **Klerke.**
Cleue, *v.* to cleave, be attached, b. 11. 219; Cleueþ, *pr. s.* clings to, 8. 304; Cleued, *pt. s.* stuck, R. 4. 18; Cleved, 2 *pt. pl.* cleaved, clung, R. 1. 112; Cleuynge, *pres. pt.* 18. 128.
Cleue, *v.* to cleave, divide, b. 7. 155; Clef, *pt. s.* was rent, b. 18. 61.
Cleyme, *v.* claim, 4. 324, 11. 210; Cleymeþ, *pr. s.* 4. 381, 16. 290; Cleymen, *pr. pl.* claim, 2. 89; Him cleymeþ = claim it, claim to know it (read *it* for *him,* as in other MSS.), a. 1. 91. See **Clayme, Clameþ.**
Cliket, *s.* a kind of lock or fastening, b. 5. 613; Clyket, 8. 252. Miss Jackson thus explains it in her Shropshire Word-book. 'An iron link is attached to the gate by means of a staple; this

VOL. II.   x

GLOSSARIAL INDEX.

link is terminated by a short hasp-like bolt. On the gate-post is an iron plate, having in it a kind of key-hole, into which the before-mentioned bolt fits, much after the manner of the fastening of a trunk, thus securing the gate.' From F. *cliquet*, which Cotgrave explains as 'the ring, knocker, or hammer of a doore;' from the verb *cliquer*, to click or snap, a word of imitative origin. The Welsh *clicied*, a door-latch, is borrowed from the West of England *clicket*, not *vice versâ*. The M.E. *cliket* also means a kind of latch-key, as in Chaucer, C. T. 9990. See Cath. Angl. p. 66; Mandeville's Trav. p. 210. ' *Hoc clitorium*, a clekyt;' Wright's Voc. i. 237.

Cliketed, *pp.* fastened with a 'cliket' or catch, b. 5. 623. See above.

Clippe, 1 *pl. imper.* let us embrace, b. 18. 417. See **Clyppe, Cluppe.**

Clips, eclipse, b. 18. 135. See note.

Cloches, *pl.* claws, talons, clutches, 1. 172. Also spelt *cloke, clouche*; see Mätzner.

Clocke, *v.* limp, hobble, 4. 37; Clokke, b. 3. 34. F. *cloquer, clocher*, 'to limp, or hault;' Cotgrave.

Clom, *s.* clay, a. 12. 100. A.S. *clam*, clay.

Clomsest, 2 *pr. s.* art benumbed, 16. 253; b. 14. 50. See note; and Cath. Angl. p. 69, n. 4; Prompt. Parv. p. 6, n. 3.

Clomyng, *pres. part.* guttering (as a candle), 4. 106. ' *Clome*, to gutter, as a candle; *North*;' Halliwell.

Clos, *s.* close, conclusion, R. 4. 67.

Close, *v.* to enclose; Do the close = cause thee to be enclosed, 4. 140; Closye with heuene = to enclose heaven with, 1. 133; Closed, *pp.* enclosed, 11. 131; shut up, b. 9. 5; buried, a. 12. 100; Closid, *pp.* enclosed, R. 4. 26; Closynde, *pres. part.* closing, 1. 132.

Clop, *s.* cloth, 9. 13; piece of clothing, 23. 16; Cloþe, cloth, R. 4. 16; clothing, dress, 22. 287; Cloþes, *pl.* clothes, dress, 19. 271; pieces of cloth, 11. 193.

Cloþed, *pt. s.* put a cloth upon, blindfolded, R. 3. 106; Cloþede, *pt. pl.* clothed, 1. 54.

Cloþers, *pl.* cloth-makers, 12. 15, a. 11. 18; Clotheres, b. 10. 18.

Clothynge, *s.* clothing, dress, b. 11. 238.

Clouten, *ger.* to patch, 10. 80. See below.

Cloutes, *pl.* rags, patches, patched clothes, 3. 230. A.S. *clút*, a clout, patch.

Clowe, *v.* claw, scratch, b. pr. 154. See Mätzner, s. v. *clawen*. See **Clawen.**

Clucche, *v.* grasp, clutch, seize, 20. 156, b. 17. 188.

Cluppe, *v.* clip, clasp, 20. 156; Cluppe we, let us embrace, 21. 464; Clupte, *pt. s.* embraced, a. 11. 174. See **Clippe, Clyppe.**

Clycchen, *v.* clutch, grasp, 20. 120. See **Clucche.**

Clyket. See **Cliket.**

Clymat, latitude, 18. 106. See note.

Clymbe, *v.* to climb, a. 10. 98; Clam, *pt. s.* 19. 108.

Clyngest, 2 *pr. s.* art pined, art parched, 16. 253. See note, p. 206.

Clypie, *v.* call, invite, 13. 102. See **Clepe.**

Clyppe, *v.* catch hold of, grasp, b. 17. 188. See **Clippe.**

Cobelere, cobbler, 7. 376, 409.

Cockes, *gen.* cock's, 22. 414.

Cockes, *pl.* cockles, shell-fish, 10. 95. W. *cocs*, cockles.

Coffes, *pl.* cuffs, b. 6. 62. See **Cuffes.**

Cofre, coffer, chest, 6. 130, 17. 90; keeper, 15. 54; Coffre, keeper b. 12. 111; coffer, b. 14. 248; Cofres, *pl.* 17. 88; Coffres, *pl.* coffers, treasures, 13. 214. O.F. *cofre*, Lat. *cophinus*, Gk. κόφινος.

Coile, *v.* choose, R. 3. 200. E. *cull*, from O.F. *coillir, cuillir*.

Cok, cock, male bird, 14. 172; Cockes, *gen.* cock's, 22. 414.

Coke, *v.* put hay into cocks, 6. 13, 22. 238. See note, p. 61.

Coked, *pp.* cooked, 16. 60.

Cokeney, cook's assistant, scullion, inferior cook, 9. 309; Cokeneyes, *pl.* scullions, a. 7. 272. I have now no doubt at all that this difficult word (whence mod. E. *cockney*) answers to an O.F. *coquine* = Low Lat. *coquinatus*, from *coquinare*, to cook, serve as scullion, a derivative of Lat. *coquina*. It is easily seen how *coquinatus* might mean either (1) a person connected with the kitchen, as in M.E. *cokeney*, a scullion; (2) a child brought up in the kitchen, or pampered by servants, as in E. *cockney*, often used in this sense; and (3) a hanger-on to a kitchen, or pilfering rogue, whence F. *coquin*, as in Cotgrave.

Cokeres, *pl.* a kind of half-boots or gaiters, 9. 59. See note, and Prompt. Parv. p. 84, n. 6. A.S. *cocer*, a sheath.

Cokers, *pl.* men employed in putting hay

GLOSSARIAL INDEX. 333

into cocks, harvest-men, 6. 13. See note, p. 61.

Coket, a kind of fine bread, so named from the stamp upon it, 9. 328. See note, p. 117. *Cocket*, in the Liber Albus, p. 40, means a stamp or seal.

Cokewold, cuckold, 5. 159, 7. 134; Kokewolde, b. 4 164, b. 5. 159. See Cath. Angl. p. 85, n. 6.

Coles, *pl.* coals, fire, 10. 142; Colys, R. 2. 52.

Colhoppes; see Coloppes.

Colis, *s. pl.* deceits, falsehoods, stratagems, R. 4. 24. See note, p. 153.

Collateral, *adj.* additional, helpful, 17. 136.

Colled, *pt. s.* took round the neck, embraced, b. 11. 16. From O.F. *col*, the neck.

Colmy, *adj.* smutty, grimy, dirty, b. 13. 356. See note. 'Culme of a smeke [smoke], *fuligo*;' Prompt. Parv. 'Coom, dust, dirt; *North*;' Halliwell.

Coloppes, *s. pl.* collops, b. 6. 287; Colhoppes, 9. 309, 16. 67. *Collops* are slices of meat, beaten and then cooked. Ihre gives the O.Swed. *kollops*, which he explains as 'edulii genus, confectum ex carnis segmentis, tudite lignea probe contusis et maceratis.' Cf. Swed. *klappa*, Du. *kloppen*, to beat. See note, p. 117; and Cath. Angl. p. 72, n. 4.

Colour, colour, 21. 214; appearance, b. 15. 203; colour, cloke, pretence, 22. 354, R. 1. 100. Cf. Acts xxvii. 30.

Coloureth, *pr. s.* disguises, b. 19. 455; Colereþ, 22. 460; Colored, *pp.* 22. 349.

Col-plontes, *pl.* cabbages, a. 7. 273.

Coltre, coulter, a. 7. 97. See Culter.

Coluer, dove, pigeon, 18. 173, 177; Coluere, 18. 175. E. *culver*.

Comaundement, command, 4. 413.

Combraunce, encumbrance; hence, trouble, confusion, sorrow, 6. 191, 19. 174, 21. 278; hindrance, 13. 245; vexatious conduct, R. 3. 113; Comburance, a. 2. 137. See note, p. 257.

Combred, *pp.* encumbered, ruined, R. 1. 78. See Cumbrest.

Comburance, *s.* encumbrance, a. 2. 137. See Combraunce.

Come, *s.* coming, R. 4. 71.

Comen, *v.* come, b. 7. 188; Comestow (*for* Comest þou), thou comest, thou wilt come, b. 10. 160; Come, 2 *pr. s. subj.* mayst come, b. 11. 52; arrive, reach, 13. 6; Cam, *pt. s.* came, 1. 139, 4. 239; Com, *pt. s.* 9. 152; Come, *pt. s.* 22. 25; Cam him of kynde = came to him by nature, R. 2. 161; Come, *pt. pl.* b. 19. 70; agreed, 1. 167; Comen, *pt. pl.* b. 2. 150; Comen, *pp.* come, b. 4. 189; Com, *imp. s.* enter, pass, 8. 219. See Comst, Comth.

Comende, *v.* to be commended, 15. 35; Comenden, *pr. pl.* praise, 17. 285; Comended, *pp.* commended, praised, 12. 276.

Comers, *pl.* strangers, visitors, passers-by, 3. 240. Cf. A.S. *cuma*, a comer, stranger, guest.

Comforty, *v.* cheer, comfort, 7. 281, 16. 188; Comfortye, 16. 195; Comfortie, *ger.* 10. 97.

Cominliche, *adv.* generally, 12. 291.

Comissarie, commissary, 3. 190, 4. 180, 17. 361. '*Commissary*, an officer of the bishop, who exercises spiritual jurisdiction in places of the diocese so far distant from the episcopal see, that the chancellor cannot call the people to the bishop's principal consistory court. without putting them to inconvenience;' Ogilvie, Imperial Dict.

Comliche, *adv.* becomingly, eloquently, R. 4. 35.

Comly, *adj.* comely, fit, 15. 444; Comliche, R. 3. 174.

Comlynesse, *s.* comeliness, R. 3. 184.

Commaundemens, *pl.* commandments, 12. 143.

Commenliche, *adv.* generally, 17. 141.

Commissarie, *s.* commissary, a. 2. 154. See Comissarie.

Compaignye, company, b. 13. 160; company, R. 4. 30.

Companable, *adj.* agreeable in company, pleasant, b. 15. 213; Compenable, 17. 341.

Compas, compass, compasses for measuring, 12. 126.

Compassen, *v.* contrive, plan, 22. 241; Compas, measure with compasses, b. 19. 235; Compassed, 1 *pt. s.* provided with compasses, b. 10. 178 (see c. 12. 126).

Comseth, *pr. s.* commences, begins, 9. 338; Comseþ, *pr. s.* 2. 160; Comsith, R. 3. 190; Comsed, *pt. s.* began, 5. 24, 15. 203; Comsede, *pt. s.* 19. 108, 21. 58, 22. 97; Comsed, 1 *pt. s.* 14. 215; Comsede, 1 *pt. s.* I began, 11. 20. From O.F. *comencer*.

Comst, 2 *pr. as fut. s.* wilt come, 12. 110. See Comen.

334   GLOSSARIAL INDEX.

Comsyng, *s.* commencing, beginning, 20. 225; Comsynges, *pl.* 12. 95.
Comth, *pr. pl.* come, spring, b. 11. 66. See **Comen.**
Comune, *adj.* common, 21. 75, 409; b. pr. 148; common, low, 22. 370; of the people, of the commons, 3. 22, 4. 245; In comune = in public, publicly, b. 11. 211; Comuyn, common, a. 3. 127; Comune wymmen, *pl.* prostitutes, 19. 143.
Comune, *s.* commons, common people, commonwealth, community, 1. 95, 4. 202; Comunes, *pl.* the commons, b. pr. 113; Comunes, *pl.* provisions, 'commons,' 1. 143, 22. 416.
Comuners, *pl.* commoners, the commonalty, 5. 188, 6. 184.
Comunete, *s.* community, R. 4. 41.
Comunliche, *adv.* commonly, generally, 15. 19; frequently, 22. 314; Comynliche, R. 1. 87.
Comyns, *s. pl.* commons, a. 3. 20. See **Comune.**
Con, can. See **Conne.**
Conceill, *s.* council, R. 3. 180, 318; Conceyll, R. 4. 60.
Conceyue, *v.* understand, 11. 56; Conceyuede, *pt. s.* conceived, 21. 134; Conceyued, *pp.* conceived, b. 9. 120.
Conclude, *v.* refute, 12. 280, b. 10. 446. See note, p. 163.
Conferme, *v.* strengthen; Confermed, *pt. s.* confirmed, b. 10. 354; Confermede, *pt. s.* 15. 39; Confermed, *pp.* 15. 449.
Conformye, *v.* conform, 4. 401. See **Confourmen.**
Confort, *s.* comfort, 17. 136; Confforte, R. pr. 39; Conforte, consolation, b. 13. 541; strengthening, b. 11. 253.
Confortatyf, *adj.* cheering, b. 15. 213.
Conforten, *v.* cheer, comfort, 21. 267; Conforte, *v.* comfort, strengthen, cheer, b. 1. 201; Confortye, *v.* comfort, 18. 50; Conforted, *pt. s.* encouraged, cheered, b. 11. 45; Confortede, *pt. s.* comforted, 13. 3; Confortid, cheered, 23. 243; Conforte, *imp. s.* b. 6. 223. See **Counforte.**
Confourmen, *v.* establish, make, b. 13. 174; Confourme, *v.* adapt, join, b. 11. 175; Conformye, *v.* conform, 4. 401.
Confus, *adj.* confused, b. 10. 136.
Congey, *v.* bid farewell to, dismiss, get rid of, b. 3. 173; Congeye, a. 3. 167; Congie, *v.* 4. 220, 5. 195; Congeyde, *pt. s.* took leave of, b. 13. 198; Congede, *pt. s.* took leave of, 16. 176;

Congeied, *pp.* dismissed, 17. 366; Conge, *imper. s.* dismiss, 5. 4; Congeye me = say farewell to me, dismiss me, b. 4. 4. O. F. *congier,* Ital. *congedare,* to dismiss.
Congeye, *s.* farewell, b. 13. 202. See above.
Congioun, *s.* coward, caitiff, R. 3. 45; Conioun, stupid fellow, a. 11. 86. See notes, pp. 151, 297.
Conjured, I *pt. s.* begged, b. 15. 14.
Conne, *v.* understand, know, 12. 102; learn, a. 7. 25; Can, I *pr. s.* know, understand, 4. 3, 8. 10; Con, I *pr. s.* can, am able, a. 4. 41; *as* I *pt. s.* did, a. 11. 99; Const, 2 *pr. s.* canst, a. 6. 24; art able, a. 3. 166; Can, *pr. s.* knows, 13. 101; Can on = is skilled in, 3. 236; Can of = is skilled in, 21. 46, 72; Can = can use, has the use of, 22. 216: Con, *pr. s.* can, is able to, b. pr. 199; knows how to, a. 9. 105; Canstow = canst thou, 6. 12, b. 20, 354; Conneþ, *pr. s.* know, understand, 14. 126; know how, can, 1. 35; b. pr. 33; Connen, *pr. pl.* know, 15. 11; Conne, *pr. pl.* know, understand, b. 10. 43; can, know how to, 2. 192, 15. 11; *as pt. pl.* did, a. 9. 109; Conne, 2 *pr. s. subj.* knowest, understandest, 22. 26; canst, 22. 479; learn, 23. 206, 342; can, b. 8. 110; Coude, *pt. s.* knew, R. 3. 106; I *pt. s.* knew, a. 12. 72; Coudestow, couldst thou, b. 5. 540; Couden, *pt. pl.* returned, gave, lit. knew, a. 8. 44; Coude, *pt. pl.* could, b. pr. 129; Couth, I *pt. s.* knew, b. 15. 49; could, b. 15. 2; was capable of, b. 13. 311; Couthest, 2 *pt. s.* couldest, 11. 74, 23. 6; Couth, Couthe, *pt. s.* could, 11. 6; knew, 1. 196, 8. 158; Couthen, *pt. pl.* could, 14. 210; Couthe, *pt. pl.* could, b. 10. 245; understood, knew, 23. 231; Couth, *pt. pl.* knew, b. 10. 466. A.S. *cunnan.* See **Konne.**
Connynge, *s.* learning, knowledge, wit, 12. 224, 14. 234. See **Konnyng, Kunnynge.**
Consail, council, 5. 166; advice, 22. 38; a secret, 22. 162; Conseille, advice, counsel, b. pr. 202; council, b. pr. 148; consultation, b. 10. 21. See **Counsail.**
Conscience, *gen.* conscience's, b. 3. 19.
Conseille, *v.* advise, b. 10. 217; Consaile, I *pr. s.* 1. 201; Consailest, 2 *pr. s.* 22. 393; Conseileþ, *pr. s.* 22. 464; Consailede, *pt. s.* advised, 22. 200; Consailedist, 2 *pt. s.* 4. 242;

GLOSSARIAL INDEX. 335

Consaileþ, *imper. pl.* 23. 207. See Counsaile.
Conselleris, *s. pl.* counsellors, R. 3. 258. See Counseiler.
Consenteþ, *pr. s.* agrees (to give), 3. 90.
Conseyuet, *pp.* conceived, a. 10. 136.
Consistorie, consistory, i. e. the ecclesiastical court of an archbishop, bishop, or commissary, b. pr. 99. See Constorie. See note, p. 13.
Conspired, *pt. s.* plotted, b. 10. 423.
Const. See Conne.
Constorie, consistory, 1. 127, 4. 34, 476; 17. 361; Constorye, 4. 179. See Consistorie (of which it is a shortened form).
Construen, *v.* construe, read, explain, interpret, 10. 283, 17. 118, 18. 110; Construe, *v.* 5. 142; b. pr. 144; Constrewe, R. 4. 68; Constrye, 8. 34; Construweþ, *pr. s.* explains, a. 8. 135; Construeþ, *pr. pl.* a. pr. 58; Constrewe, *pr. s. subj.* R. pr. 72; Constrewed, *pt. pl.* made, R. 3. 327; Constrwe, *imp. s.* R. 1. 83; Constrew, 3 *imp. s.* let him explain, R. 3. 35. 'To constru, *exponere, construere, commentari;*' Cath. Angl.
Contemplacion, contemplative life, 19. 73.
Contenaunce, look, gesture, 16. 120; b. 13. 111; outward appearance, 1. 26; favour (as opposed to *right*), b. 5. 183. See Contynaunce.
Contene, *v.* contain, b. 12. 39. See note.
Conterfeteþ, *pr. s.* counterfeits, a. 11. 19. See Counterfeten.
Conterroller, controller, steward, accountant, 12. 298.
Continence, self-restraint, 19. 73; Contynence, 12. 177.
Continue, *v.* continue (so), remain chaste, b. 9. 177; Contynue, 11. 284. Another reading is *contene*, i. e. contain, be continent.
Contra, on the other side, i. e. I deny that, b. 8. 20.
Contrarie, *s.* contrary, a. 11. 147.
Contrarie, *v.* oppose, 20. 311, 21. 437; b. 17. 329; Contrarien, *v.* grumble, 20. 320; Contrarieþ. *pr. s.* opposes, 3. 22; is contrary, 11. 244; Contrarien, *pr. pl.* oppose, act contrary to, b. 15. 531; Contrariedest, 2 *pt. s.* didst oppose, 15. 100; Contrariede, *pt. pl.* opposed, contradicted, 1. 59; Contrarie, *imp. s.* oppose, 18. 149.
Contreie, country, 11. 12; Contreye, 22. 136; Contreo, 22. 132; Contree,

b. 13. 223; Contreies, *pl.* 22. 314; Contreis, 16. 189; Contreys, 10. 111; Contrees, 1. 31; districts, b. 13. 219. See Countreo, Cuntre.
Contreplede, *imper. pl.* contradict, oppose, 9. 53; Contrepleide, 9. 88; Contrepleteth, *pr. pl.* plead against, oppose, b. 20. 382. See Counterpleideþ.
Contreue, *v.* contrive, find out, b. 10. 19; Contreeue, *v.* plan, 12. 16; Contreued, *pt. s.* devised, b. pr. 118; Contreeuede, planned, 15. 161; Contreued, 1 *pt. s.* invented, b. 10. 177; Contreuede, 1 *pt. s.* contrived, 7. 39; Contreeuede, 1 *pt. s.* planned, 12. 125; Contreuede, *pt. pl.* found out, 1. 144, 15. 73; Contreueden, *pt. pl.* b. 16. 137.
Contumax, *adj.* contumacious, 14. 85. See note.
Contynaunce, gesture, 12. 164. See Contenaunce.
Contynence, self-restraint, 12. 177. See Continence.
Contynue; see Continue.
Conuerten, *v. refl.* turn (themselves), 18. 186; Conuerted, *pp.* converted, 21. 190.
Conynges, *pl.* conies, rabbits, b. pr. 193.
Conysaunce, mark, 19. 188.
Coome, *pt. s. subj.* came, a. 6. 16; 1 *pt. s.* came, a. 11. 166; *pt. pl.* a. 7. 291; sprang, a. 10. 148. See Comen.
Coostes, *s. pl.* districts, a. 9. 12. See Costes.
Cope, *v.* cover with a cope, provide a cope for, 7. 288, b. 5. 269; Copeþ, *pr. s.* clothes in a cope, provides with a cope, 4. 180; Copyde, *pt. pl.* dressed in a cope, 3. 240; Coped, b. 2. 230; Coped, *pp. as adj.* dressed in a cope, 4. 38.
Copes, *s. pl.* copes, capes or cloaks used by friars, 1. 59, 9. 185; Copis, *pl.* 1. 54. See note, p. 113.
Cople, *v.* to yoke; Lete cople = cause to be yoked, 3. 190.
Coppe, cup, 6. 162, 7. 390; Coppes, *pl.* 4. 23; Coppis, *pl.* b. 3. 22.
Coppe-mel, *adv.* cup by cup, in portions of a cupful at a time, 7. 231. Cf. E. *piece-meal;* and A.S. *mǽlum,* in parts, in pieces.
Corette, *v.* correct, R. pr. 59. Prob. miswritten for *corecte.*
Coriouse, *adj.* curious, R. 3. 163.
Corlew, curlew, 16. 243.
Corner, 16. 162. (The line is obscure;

336   GLOSSARIAL INDEX.

perhaps ' the corner of a cart-wheel '
is a sarcastic expression for ' nowhere.'
A circle has *no* corner).
Cornes, *pl.* corn, grain, 22. 320. See
note.
Corone, crown, coronet, 3. 11, 5. 79,
135; hair left by the tonsure, 12. 197,
14. 113; Coroune, 21. 275. See
Croune.
Coroneþ, *pr. s.* marks with the tonsure.
14. 125; Corouneþ, *pr. s.* crowns, a.
1. 122; Coroneþ, *imper. pl.* crown,
22. 256; Coroned, *pp.* 3. 11, 4. 321.
Corps, corpse, dead body, 22. 151;
living body, b. 1. 137, b. 15. 23;
living body, 17. 183; Corses, *pl.*
corpses, 16. 11.
Corse, *v.* curse, a. 7. 302; Corseþ, *pr.
s.* 9. 340; Corsede, *pt. pl.* 23. 68;
Corsed, *pp.* 4. 179; Corsynge, *pres.
pt.* 7. 64. A.S. *corsian.* See **Curset**.
Corsed, *pp. as adj.* cursed, wicked, 4.
106, 22. 434; Corsede, inauspicious,
a. 10. 142; Corsede, *pl.* 18. 212, 21.
101, 22. 469.
Corsedour, *adj.* worse, more cursed, 22.
419; Curseder, b. 19. 415.
Corsement, *s.* cursing, curses, 7. 65.
Corseynt, a holy person, saint, 8. 177;
Corseint, b. 5. 539. Lit. ' holy body.'
Cf. Morte Arthure, 1164; Chaucer's
Dream, 942. See note, p. 102.
Cortesye, kindness, condescension, 2.
20, 4. 317; Cortesie, 15. 216. See
Curtesye.
Corteys, *adj.* courteous, 5. 17; Corteis,
a. 3. 60. See **Curteis**.
Corteysliche, *adv.* courteously, polite-
ly, 9. 32; Corteisliche, 23. 355;
gently, 22. 176; Cortesliche, 4. 9:
Cortesly, courteously, kindly, 16. 193.
See **Curteisliche**.
Coruen, *pt. pl.* cut up, cut away, 9. 185.
Lit. ' carved.'
Corupcions, *pl.* sores, illnesses, 23. 99.
Cosenes, *gen.* cousin's, a. 12. 53.
Cossyngs, *pl.* kisses, 19. 174. A.S. *coss*,
a kiss. See **Kussyng, Cussynge**.
Costed, *pt. s.* cost, b. pr. 203; Costide,
pt. s. 1. 208; Costed, *pp.* b. pr. 204.
Costes, *s. pl.* coasts, districts, regions,
11. 12; Costis, R. 2. 106, R. 3.
157.
Costned, *pt. s.* cost, 1. 209; Costened,
pt. s. R. 3. 169. See examples in
Mätzner.
Cosyn, cousin, relative, 12. 94, 23. 357;
Cosynes, *pl.* b. 12. 95.
Cote, cottage, cot, 6. 2, 10. 151; Cotes,
pl. 5. 123, 10. 72.

Cote, *s.* coat, b. 11. 276, b. 13. 314;
R. 3. 45; Cotis, *pl.* R. 3. 53, 180.
Cote-armure, coat-armour, coat-of-
arms, 19. 188, 22. 13, b. 19. 13.
Coteþ, *pr. s.* coats, provides with coats,
4. 180, b. 3. 142, a. 3. 138.
Cotidian, *adj.* quotidian, i. e. quotidian
or daily fever, a. 12. 84.
Cotiers, *pl.* cotters, cottagers, 10. 193;
Cotyers, 10. 97.
Couche, *pr. pl.* lie, lie down apart, i. e.
be left in the lurch, a. 3. 35. Other
MSS. have *clokke*, i. e. hobble, limp.
Coude, Couden, Coudestow. See
Conne.
Coueiten, *v.* covet, desire eagerly, b.
10. 338; Coueite, *v.* b. 9. 171; Cou-
eyte, *v.* a. 10. 98; Coueite, 1 *pr. s.*
desire, am anxious, 11. 108; Coueyte,
1 *pr. s.* a. 9. 103; Coueitest, 2 *pr. s.*
b. 15. 39; Coueytest, 2 *pr. s.* desirest,
b. 11. 10; Coueiteth, *pr. s.* covets, a.
8. 52; Coueyteþ, *pr. s.* desires greatly,
4. 255; Coueiteþ, 2 *pr. pl.* covet, de-
sire, 23. 253; Coueiten, *pr. pl.* are
eager, a. 11. 207; Coueyten, *pr. pl.*
10. 193, b. 10. 299; Coueyted, *pt. s.*
desired, was eager, b. 11. 120; Cou-
eited, *pt. s. subj.* should desire, 4.
365; Coueyted, *pp.* coveted, desired,
21. 173; Coueyte, *imp. s.* a. 3. 254;
imp. pl. 8. 220.
Coueitise, greed, avarice, b. pr. 61;
Coueityse, b. 13. 391; Coueytise, b.
10. 18. See **Couetise**.
Coueitouse, *adj.* covetous, b. 11. 183:
Coueytous, 15. 21.
Couenaunt, bargain, agreement, con-
dition, 7. 390, 9. 26, 21. 264; Couen-
aunte, b. 14. 151; Couenant, 15. 216,
a. 7. 30.
Couent, convent, 6. 152, 7. 130, 23.
60; Couentes, *gen.* convent's, b. 5. 137.
O.F. *covent* (as in *Covent* Garden.)
Couerer, recoverer, restorer, reformer,
6. 176. See note, p. 70.
Couetise, greed, covetousness, avarice,
desire, 1. 59, 3. 90; Couetyse, 1. 103,
7. 39; Couetyce, 17. 80; Couetyze,
13. 241. See **Coueitise**.
Couhed, *pt. s.* coughed, 7. 412. See
Cowhede.
Counforte, *v.* comfort, cheer, encou-
rage, a. 1. 179, a. 2. 121. See **Con-
forten**.
Counsail, counsel, advice, 22. 79, 317;
Counseil, a. 2. 108.
Counsaile, 1 *pr. s.* counsel, advise, 10.
346; Counseile, 11. 279, a. 8. 182;
Counsaileþ, *pr. s.* 22. 113; Counseil-

GLOSSARIAL INDEX. 337

ede, 1 *pt. s.* counselled, advised, plotted, a. 3. 180; Counseildest, 2 *pt. s.* didst counsel, a. 3. 199. See Conseille.

Counte, *v.* account; Counteþ, *pr. s.* values, cares, 13. 196, 22. 306; Counten, *pr. pl.* value, 22. 453; Counteþ, *pr. pl.* account, a. 3. 137; Countede, 1 *pt. s.* reckoned, esteemed, 12. 313.

Counterfeten, *v.* imitate, a. 11. 133. See Conterfeteþ.

Counterpleideþ, *pr. pl.* plead against, argue against, 23. 384; Counterpleide, *imp. s.* oppose, 1. 138; Counterplede, contradict, b. 12. 100. See Contreplede.

Countis, *s. pl.* accounts, R. 3. 279, R. 4. 11.

Countreo, country, 23. 224. See Contreie.

Countresegge, 1 *pr. s.* contradict, 12. 224. Lit. ' counter-say.'

Coupable, *adj.* culpable, guilty, 20. 282, b. 12. 90. F. *coupable.*

Coupe, fault, sin, guilt, 7. 328, 351; b. 5. 305. O.F. *colpe* (Burguy); Lat. *culpa.*

Coupes, cups, bowls, 4. 23. 'Cowpe, *cupa;*' Cath. Angl. See note, p. 40.

Coupleþ, *pr. s.* couples, joins, links, fastens, b. 3. 164; Couplest, 2 *pr. s.* joinest, b. 10. 160; Coupled hem = joined themselves, b. 4. 149; Couplede hem = joined themselves, 5. 146; Coupled and vncoupled = whether held in or free, b. pr. 206.

Courbed, 1 *pt. s.* bent, bowed, knelt, b. 1. 79, b. 2. 1. O.F. *courber;* Lat. *curuare.*

Courour, *s.* courier, a. 12. 84.

Courte, *s.* court, court of a mansion, b. 5. 594; Courte, enclosure, b. 10. 163; yard, b. 15. 466; Courtes, *pl.* courts (of mansions), 11. 15.

Courteislich, *adv.* courteously, 3. 164. See Corteysliche.

Courtepy, *s.* short coat or cloak, cape, a. 5. 63; Courtepies, *pl.* 9. 185; Courtpies, b. 6. 191. Du. *kort*, short, *pije*, rough coat (whence E. *peajacket*). Cf. Goth. *paida*, a coat. ' *Hoc epitogium*, cowrteby;' Wright's Voc. i. 196, col. 2.

Couth, Couthest, Couth. See Conne.

Couth, 1 *pr. s.* make known, proclaim, b. 5. 181. Cf. A.S. *cýðan*, to make known, from *cúð*, known.

Cowhede, *pt. s.* coughed, (with *vp*), a. 5. 205; Cowede, 1 *pt. s.* (with *vp*), brought up, made public (lit. coughed up), 7. 163. See Couhed, Koweþ.

Cowkynde, anything of the nature of cows, b. 11. 332.

Coyffes, *s. pl.* coifs, R 3. 320.

Coygne, coin, 2. 46; Coyne, R. 3. 138, R. 4. 89.

Crabbed, *adj.* angry, cross, peevish, perverse, b. 10. 104, b. 12. 157; Crabbede, 15. 100.

Cracchen, *v.* scratch, claw, 1. 200; Cracche, *v.* b. pr. 154; clutch, 13. 78, b. 11. 139; Cracchy, *v.* claw, b. pr. 186; Cracche, 1 *pr. s.* scratch, 7. 140; Cracched, *pp.* scratched, carded, b. 15. 346.

Craft, *s.* way, skill, art, knowledge, 3. 4; b. 3. 19; power, contrivance, b. 1. 137, a. 1. 128; Craft, handicraft, trade, 22. 250; Crafte, trade, b. 13. 223; Craftes, *pl.* arts, trades, 12. 125, 17. 190; Craftus, *pl.* a. 11. 133; Craftis, *pl.* wiles, R. 3. 141.

Crafte, *s.* craft, vessel, R. 4. 76.

Crafty, *adj.* cunning, skilful, skilled in handicrafts, 1. 179. 4. 281; belonging to a craft or trade, b. 3. 224, b. 6. 70.

Craken, *v.* talk, chatter, murmur, grumble, a. 11. 65; Craked, *pt. s.* cracked, broke, 21. 76; b. 18. 73. ' Crake, to murmur, grumble;' Shropsh. Wordbook.

Crasid, *pp.* crazed, broken, cracked, R. 1. 8, R. 1. 70.

Craue, *v.* seek, pray for, beg, ask for, ask, b. 13. 164; Craueþ, *pr. s.* b. 15. 160; Craue, 1 *pr. s.* 22. 478; Crauede, *pt. s.* asked, desired, 9. 101.

Craym, *s.* cream, a. 7. 269.

Creaunce,*s.* borrowing, system of credit, R. 1. 12, R. 4. 17; Casten hem to creaunce = try to get credit, R. 3. 132. See notes, pp. 298, 302.

Creaunt, believer, 15. 133, 154, b. 12. 193; (as a) believer, b. 12. 214.

Credo, the creed, b. 6. 91.

Crepe, *v.* creep, 23. 44; Crepen, *pr. pl.* b. 13. 18; Creptest, 2 *pt. s.* didst creep, a. 3. 184; Crope, didst creep, b. 3. 190; Crepte, *pt. s.* a. 12. 35; Crepe, 1 *pr. pl. subj.* may creep, creep, 1. 200; Crope, 1 *pt. pl. subj.* were to creep, b. pr. 186; Creop, *imper. s.* creep, 21. 475; Crepeth, *imp. pl.* b. 18. 428.

Creym, cream, 9. 322; Creyme, 9. 306; Craym, a. 7. 269.

Cristendome, Christian religion, Christianity, 19. 210, 20. 8; Cristendam, a. 6. 78. See Crystendome. 'A cry-

stendam, *baptismus, baptisma, christianitas, cristianismus;* Cath. Angl.
Cristene, *adj.* Christian, 19. 210, 20. 254, 21. 409; Cristene, *adj. pl.* Christian (men), 2. 89, 4. 445; Cristine, Christians, 9. 104. See **Crystene.**
Cristene, *v.* baptise, a. 11. 232; Cristned, *pp.* christened, i.e. one who is just christened, a mere infant, a. 12. 15.
Croce, crosier, 11. 92. O.F. *croce,* 'a crosier, a bishop's staff;' Cotgrave.
Crocer, bearer of a crosier, 6. 113.
Croddes, *pl.* curds, 9. 306, 322; Cruddes, b. 6. 284. See **Cruddes.**
Croft, *s.* field, enclosure, 6. 17, 8. 219, 220; 9. 31.
Crois, cross, 6. 106, 12. 256, 21. 75.
Croked, *adj.* crooked, twisted, 3. 29; deformed, b. 11. 186; Crokede, *pl.* crooked, 10. 97, 13. 103.
Crokes, *pl.* crooks, hooks, 21. 296.
Crokke, pot, crock, pitcher, 22. 280; Crokk, R. 2. 52.
Cromes, *pl.* crumbs, 9. 280, 289.
Crompe, cramp, b. 13. 335.
Crop, top, upper part of a tree, 19. 75, 108; Croppe, b. 16. 42. A.S. *cropp, croppa,* a sprout, shoot.
Crope. See **Crepe.**
Croperes, *pl.* harness on the hinder part of a horse, cruppers, b. 15. 453.
Croppen, *pr. pl.* eat, devour, a. 7. 35; Cropped, *pt. s.* ate, b. 15. 394. Properly, to bite off the *crop* or top of growing wheat.
Cros, *s.* cross, a. 5. 23, 245.
Crouche, a cross, 8. 167.
Croune, crown of the head (alluding to the crown of hair left after receiving the tonsure), 23. 184; R. 3. 230; the tonsure or crown of hair itself, b. 11. 35; (sense obscure), 16. 162; Crounes, *pl.* crowns, heads (esp. those that have been tonsured), 6. 178. See **Corone.**
Croune, *ger.* to crown, b. 8. 99; Crouneth, *pr. s.* marks with the tonsure, b. 11. 304; Crounede, *pt. pl.* crowned, 11. 100; Crouned, *pp.* shorn in the shape of a crown, having received the tonsure, 6. 56, 63.
Crowe, crow (?), crow's (?), 16. 162.
Crowen, *s. pl.* crows, a. 7. 129.
Crownynge, *s.* the tonsure, 1. 86; Crounyng, b. pr. 88.
Croys, cross, 7. 319. See **Crois.**
Croys-wyse, *adv.* (with *on*), by way of crucifixion, 22. 142.
Cruche, cross, sign or mark of a cross, b. 5. 529. See **Crouche.**

Cruddes, *pl.* curds, b. 6. 284. See **Croddes.**
Crykett, cricket, 16. 243.
Crysten, *v.* baptise, b. 10. 350.
Crystendome, Christendom, the Christian religion, 8. 235; baptism, 13. 59; Crystenedome, b. 10. 447; baptism, b. 11. 120. See **Cristendome.**
Crystene, *adj.* Christian, b. 10. 425, b. 15. 88; Christian people, b. 9. 171, b. 11. 118; Crystine, Christians, 2. 190.
Crystennynge, *s.* baptism, christening, b. 14. 184.
Cuffes, *pl.* cuffs, 9. 59. See **Coffes.**
Cullen, *v.* to kill, slay, destroy, 2. 62, a. 1. 64; Culle, *v.* 9. 30, 11. 100, 12. 268; Culde, *pt. s.* killed, slew, 23. 99; 1 *pt. s.* 4. 233, 9. 281; Culled, *pt. pl.* 22. 142; Culled, 1 *pt. pl. subj.* should kill, b. pr. 185; Culled, *pp.* 11. 247, 18. 291. See **Kullen, Kylle.**
Culorum, end, conclusion, 4. 436, 12. 248, b. 3. 278, b. 10. 409, a. 3. 264, R. pr. 72, R. 4. 61. This word is short for *seculorum,* in the phrase *in secula seculorum,* for ever and ever, common at the *end* of sermons and prayers, and especially of anthems. Hence it came to mean end or conclusion.
Culter, coulter, 4. 464, 9. 65. See **Coltre.**
Cumbrest, 2. *pr. s.* injurest, a. 10. 91; Cumbred, *pp.* encumbered, a. 1. 170. See **Combre.**
Cumpas, *s.* compass, circumference, R. pr. 20.
Cumseth, *pr. s.* commenceth, begins, a. 1. 128, 139, a. 3. 39; Cumse, 2 *pr. s. subj.* commence, a. 10. 98. See **Comseth.**
Cun, *s.* kin, race, family, a. 3. 197, a. 10. 153; What cunnes þing = a thing of whut kind, a. 10. 26. See **Kun.**
Cunnen, *pr. pl.* can, a. 1. 170; know, a. 8. 13; Cunneth, *pr. pl.* know, b. 15. 468; Cunne, *pr. pl.* know how (to), a. pr. 33, a. 7. 115; know, a. 10. 104. See **Conne.**
Cunnynge, *adj.* cunning, a. 3. 35; wise, a. 11. 265.
Cuntinaunce, *s.* appearance, outward show, a. pr. 24. See **Contenaunce.**
Cuntre, *s.* country, district, a. pr. 95, a. 2. 129. See **Contreie.**
Cuppe, *s.* cup, b. 10. 310, b. 13. 103, a. 5. 184. See **Coppe.**
Cuppemel, *adv.* by cupfuls, a. 5. 139; Cupmel, b. 5. 225.

GLOSSARIAL INDEX. 339

Curatour, curate, priest, one who has cure of souls, 18. 292, 22. 453; Curatours, *pl.* 16. 16, 17. 279; Curatoures, *pl.* curates, b. 1. 193, b. 10. 409; Curatores, 12. 248. See note, p. 273.

Cure, a charge, cure of souls, 1. 86, 23. 233, 237, 253; b. pr. 88.

Curen, *v.* cure, heal, 15. 70, 23. 325.

Curinge, *s.* healing, aid, R. 1. 95.

Curne, *v.* form into grain, 13. 180. See note. Formed (as if from an A.S. *cyrnan**) from *corn*, sb. See below. Cf. G. *körnen*.

Curnel, kernel, 13. 146, 149. A.S. *cyrnel;* from *corn*. See **Kirnelle**.

Curseder, more accursed, b. 19. 415. See **Corsedour**.

Cursidnesse, *s.* wickedness, mischievous behaviour, R. 3. 113; Cursidnes, R. 3. 187.

Cursyng, *s.* cursing, excommunication, 9. 159.

Curteis, *adj.* courteous, a. 3. 17; Curteys, 9. 47; Curteise, loving, b. 13. 15. See **Corteys**.

Curteisliche, *adj.* courteously, kindly, 16. 120, b. 3. 103; Curtesliche, 9. 161. See **Corteysliche**.

Curtesye, courtesy, manners, 11. 264; kindness, 20. 207; Curtesie, courtesy, R. 3. 184; Curteisye, kindness, b. 1. 20; compassion, b. 12. 79; behaviour, manners, b. 10. 311. See **Cortesye**.

Cusse, *v.* kiss, embrace, 3. 146, 23. 353; a. 2. 102; Custe, *pt. s.* 19. 171, 21. 467; kissed (me), a. 11. 174; Cusse, *imp. s.* 21. 475, a. 4. 3. A.S. *cyssan ;* from *coss*.

Cussynge, *s.* kissing, 7. 187. See **Cossyngs, Kussyng**.

Custum, *s.* custom, toll, R. 4. 11; Custumes, *pl.* observances, 15. 73, b. 12. 99.

Cut, *imper. s.* cut, a. 4. 140.

Cuth, race, people, 4. 262; Cuþþe, a. 3. 197. E. *kith*.

Cutpurs, *s.* cutpurse, thief, b. 5. 639; Cutte-pors, a. 6. 118.

Cuynde, *s.* nature, a. 10. 5. See **Kuynde**.

Daffe, fool, idiot, dolt, 2. 139, 11. 177, 14. 236, b. 1. 138, b. 11. 417, 424; a. 1. 129, a. 11. 87. Cf. Shropshire *daffish*, shy, bashful (Jackson).

Dagge, *v.* to cut at the edges; Let dagge = caused to be cut at the edges, 23. 143; Leet dagge, b. 20. 142. See below.

Dagges, *s. pl.* jagged edges, curious ornaments of garments, R. 3. 193. See note to l. 152, p. 299.

Daies, *s. pl.* days; *on þe daies*, all day, in the daytime, R. 3. 272. See **Reremys**.

Dale, *s.* dale, 2. 1.

Dame, dame, mother, 3. 120, 10. 316; female, R. 3. 43; mother, R. 3. 55; Dam, mother, dame, a. 11. 1; Damme, 21. 284.

Damesele, damsel, maid, attendant, 11. 138; Damoisele, b. 9. 12; Damysele, a. 10. 12; Damoyseles, *pl.* maidens, b. 11. 11; Damseles, 21. 471.

Dampne, *v.* condemn, 18. 215; Dampneþ, *pr. s.* 10. 158, 20. 283, 21. 430; Dampned, *pt. s.* 21. 310; Dampned, *pp.* damned, condemned, 8. 147, 20. 230; Dampne, *imp. s.* 7. 325. O. F. *damner*.

Dar, *pr. s.* dare, 10. 261, 16. 289; 1 *pr. s.* 1. 217, 3. 36; Darstow = darest thou, b. 14. 55; Dorste, *pt. s.* dared, durst, 3. 250, 20. 62; 1 *pt. s.* 11, 118; *pt. s. subj.* would dare, 4. 236; *pt. pl.* dared, b. 13. 109. See **Der**. A.S. *dear*, pt. t. *dorste*.

Daubyng, *s.* plastering, 9. 198.

Daunce, *v.* dance, 21. 184.

Daunger, danger, 15. 146; Daungere, power to harm, b. 16. 263.

Daunseled, *pp.* cherished, made much of, a. 11. 30. This very rare word is the frequentative of *daunsen*, to fondle, cherish, also a very rare word. In Wyclif, Isaiah lxvi. 12, 13, we find *daunsen*, as another form of *daunten*, in the sense of cherish or fondle; cf. 'to *dawnte*, or to *cherys*, blanditractare ;' Cath. Angl. See below.

Daunten, *v.* daunt, tame, subdue, 4. 444; Daunted, *pt. s.* tamed, b. 15. 393; Daunted, *pp.* made much of, b. 10. 37. Cf. Shropshire *daunted*, shy, timid (Jackson).

Dawen, *v.* dawn, 21. 185; Dawe, *v.* b. 18. 179; Dawede, *pt. s.* 21. 471. A.S. *dagian*, to become day; from *dæg*, day.

Dawes, *pl.* days, a. 10. 163; Dawis, R. 1. 65. A.S. *dagas*, pl. of *dæg*.

Day, *s.* a day's journey, b. 9. 1; a. 10. 1; Daye, 11. 127; Day bi day = day by day, a. 8. 177; Day after other, one day after another, ceaselessly, b. 10. 134; Dayes, *pl.* days, a. 1. 96; Dayes, *gen. sing. as adv.* by day, 12. 192.

Daysterre, *s.* day-star, a. 6. 83.

Debat, strife, dissension, disagreement, 7. 123, 22. 251; Debate, b. 5. 98, 337.
Decorreth, *pr. s.* departs (*of* = from), b. 14. 193. Mätzner offers as an explanation, 'ablaufen, zu Ende gehen, schwinden.' This he attributes to the O.F. *decorre, decourre;* Cotgrave gives *decourir*, but only in the senses ' to run down, to haste, or hye apace; also, to purge downwards.' Taking *decorreth of* to mean ' flows away from, recedes from, glides away from, departs from,' the line signifies, ' the record departs from pomp and pride (has nothing to do with them), and especially from every one but the lowly.'
Decretistre, lawyer, one learned in ecclesiastical law, 16. 85.
Ded, *pp. as adj.* dead, 10. 21, 21. 73; Dede, *pl.* 10. 338, 22. 196; the dead, b. 7. 187.
Ded, *s.* death, b. 3. 265. Cf. Swed. *död*, Dan. *död*.
Ded-day, *s.* death-day, b. 7. 50, 115.
Dede, deed, 2. 30, 2. 184; fact, a. 8. 143; performance, a. 10. 17; charter, 3. 113; In dede = indeed, b. 10. 360; Dedes, *pl.* miracles, 22. 133; legal documents, a. 12. 82; Dedus, *pl.* deeds, 22. 134.
Dede, *pt. s.* did. See **Do**.
Dede-doynge, *s.* deed, R. 4. 31.
Dedeignous, *adj.* proud, conceited, disdainful, b. 8. 83. ' *Desdaigneux*, disdainful, scornful;' Cotgrave. See **Deynous**.
Dedliche, *adj.* deadly, mortal, 11. 43, 21. 379; Dedlich, 2. 144, 6. 123; Dedly, b. 10. 235.
Dedliche, *adv.* mortally, 10. 329; Sunget dedlich = sinned mortally, committed deadly sin, a. 8. 165.
Deeme. See **Demen**.
Dees, *s. pl.* dice, R. 1. 18.
Dees-pleyere, dice-player, dicer, 9. 72; . Dysplayere, b. 6. 73.
Def, *adj.* deaf, 12. 61, b. 10. 130; Deue, *pl.* deaf (men), 22. 130.
De-fameþ, *pr. s.* defames, a. 11. 64; Defamed, *pp.* a. 2. 138.
Defaute, *s.* default, want, lack, b. 13. 260, b. 14. 70, 113, b. 15. 131, b. 18. 205; lack, want, need, poverty, 16. 274, 294, 21. 213; b. 9. 81, b. 10. 363; default, deficiency, famine, 3. 153, 8. 306; fault, defect, 13. 36; fault, mistake, 14. 122; Defautes, *pl.* faults, failings, b. 11. 384; In defaute

= in fault, b. 2. 139; For defaute = for want, for need, b. 5. 6, b. 6. 209. ' A defaute, *defectus;*' Cath. Angl.
Defauti, *adj.* scanty, a. 11. 52.
Defence, prohibition, b. 18. 193. See **Defense**.
Defenden, *v.* protect, defend, 22. 469; Defende, *v.* defend, 20. 266; forbid, 17. 170; Defendeþ, *pr. s.* forbids, 4. 68, 21. 112; Defendyþ, a. 12. 19; Defende, 1 *pr. s.* forbid, a. 8. 40; Defendet, *pt. s.* forbade, a. 3. 55; Defendid, *pp.* forbidden, 15. 6.
Defense, prohibition, 21. 201; Defence, b. 18. 193. See note, p. 255.
Defie, *v.* be digested, *also* digest, 17. 225, b. 13. 404; Defye, *v.* 1. 230, 7. 87, 430, 439; Defyen, *v.* a. 5. 219; Defien, b. 5. 389; Defieden, *pt. pl.* defied, 23. 66. O.F. *deffier*, to distrust; whence M.E. *defien*, to renounce, reject, defy, also, to digest. See note, p. 20.
Defoule, *v.* damage, spoil, 9. 31 ; Defoulen, *v.* dirty, defile, b. 14. 23 ; Defouleþ, *pr. s.* tramples on, treads under foot, oppresses, 4. 192, a. 2. 136; Defoulen, *pr. pl.* trample on, a. 11. 60; Defouleden, *pt. pl.* trampled on, subdued, 18. 195; Defouled, subdued, b. 15. 496; Defouled, *pp.* trampled on, a. 2. 138. ' *Defouler*, to tread or trample on, also, to rebuke, reproach ;' Cotgrave. The sense of ' defile ' is due to confusion with A.S. *fýlan*, to befoul, from *fúl*, foul. ' Defowled, *maculatus ;*' Cath. Angl.
Degiset, *pp.* disguised, apparelled, a. pr. 24. See **Disgisid**.
Deide, Deiede. See **Deye**.
Deis, *s.* daïs, higher seat, a. 8. 19. See **Deys**.
Deiynge, *s.* death, 18. 144. See **Deyinge**.
Dele, *s.* bit, R. 3. 339; Some dele = partly, b. 5. 438. See **Dell**.
Dele, *v.* deal, distribute, share, distribute alms, give, 9. 106, 12. 71, 14. 96, 22. 215 ; deal, have intercourse with, 9. 77; divide, b. 11. 268; Dele, 1 *pr. s.* give, share, impart, 2. 197 ; Delest, 2 *pr. s.* distributest, 4. 76; Deleþ, *pr. s.* trades, deals, 22. 352 ; distributes, shares, b. 10. 84; gives, a. 3. 57 ; Deleþ, 2 *pr. pl.* deal, 20. 224; Delen, 2 *pr. pl.* deal, b. 3. 71, b. 7. 90; Deleth, *pr. pl.* distribute, share, b. 10. 28; Delen, *pr. pl.* have intercourse with, 10. 167 ; Dele, *imp. s.* deal, have dealings, a. 11. 159 ,

GLOSSARIAL INDEX 341

Delt, *pt. s.* dealt, a. 12. 99. A.S. *dǽlan.*
Delfol, *adj.* doleful, miserable, b. 15. 550. O.F. *deol, doel,* mourning; see Dole.
Delfulliche, *adv.* miserably, 4. 419. See above.
Delicatliche, *adv.* luxuriously, daintily, 7. 166.
Delitable, *adj.* delightful, pleasant, nice, b. 1. 34. See Dilitable.
Delited, *pt. s.* delighted, pleased, b. 1. 29; Dilytede, a. 1. 29. 'To delite, *delectare;*' Cath. Angl.
Dell, part; Sum dell = in some measure, R. pr. 55. See Dele.
Delt. See Dele.
Deluen, *v.* dig, b. 6. 143; Delue, *v.* 22. 365, 367; Delue, 1 *pr. s.* b. 5. 552; Deluen, *pr. pl.* a. 11. 184; Doluen, *pt. pl.* dug, b. 6. 193; Doluen, *pp.* buried, b. 6. 182. A.S. *delfan.*
Deluere, *s.* digger, ditcher, one who works with the spade, 9. 354; Delueres, *pl.* b. pr. 223.
Deluyng, *s.* digging, 9. 198; Deluynge, b. 6. 250.
Delycatly, *adv.* luxuriously, daintily, b. 14. 250. See Delicatliche.
Delynge, *s.* distribution, b. 19. 374. See Dele.
Delytes, *s. pl.* delights, a. 2. 68.
Delyuery, *v.* deliver, 19. 284; Delyuered, *pp.* free of his business, 14. 41.
Demen, *v.* deem, think, suppose, judge, 22. 196; condemn, b. 15. 514; give an opinion, b. 13. 306; Deme, *v.* judge, 2. 82, 17. 227; suppose, R. pr. 7; decide, 21. 36; adjudge, decree, R. 3. 341; sentence, 5. 172; sit in judgment, 10. 21; Deeme, *v.* judge, decide, a. 1. 84; Deme, 1 *pr. s.* judge, b. 5. 114; consider, a. 5. 95; Demest, 2 *pr. s.* judgest, givest sentence, b. 13. 171; Demeþ, *pr. pl.* judge, a. 11. 44; Demen, *pr. pl.* pronounce judgments, 1. 94; consider, 4. 291; Demed, *pt. s.* decided, b. 7. 169; judged, ruled, b. 10. 382; Demede, 1 *pt. s.* judged, concluded, 10. 319; Demed, 1 *pt. s.* judged, 7. 20; condemned, b. 15. 512; Demed, *pp.* sentenced, 4. 463; condemned, b. 4. 181; Demyd, *pp.* administered, 5. 175; Deme, *imp. s.* judge, 9. 83, R. 1. 18; Deeme, a. 7. 74. A.S. *déman;* from *dóm.*
Demer, *s.* judge, R. 7. 70.
Demynge, *s.* judgment, 13. 79, R. 1. 94.

Den, *s.* dean, b. 13. 65; Denes, *pl.* a. 2. 150.
Dene, noise, din, 3. 217; Deone, 21. 128; Deon, 21. 65. See Dyne. A.S. *dyn, dyne.*
Dent, *s.* dent, blow, a. 12. 99.
Denyede, *pt. s.* refused, rejected, 12. 264.
Deol, sorrow, pain, 21. 306; lamentation, 20. 318, b. 17. 336, a. 5. 216; Deul, 9. 127. O.F. *deol,* mod. F. *deuil.* See Dole.
Deone, Deon. See Dene, din.
Deop, *adj.* deep, 21. 408.
Deore, *adv.* See Dere.
Deork. See Derk.
Deorknesse, *s.* darkness, 20. 199, 21. 68, 106.
Deop, death, 21. 430. See Dep.
Deouel. See Deuel.
Departable, *adj.* able to be separated, distinct, separable, 19. 189, 216; 20. 28. 'Departiabylle, *diuisibilis;*' Cath. Angl.
Departe, *v.* part, separate, divide, 6. 185; Departe, *pr. pl.* part, share, a. pr. 78; Departe, *pr. s. subj.* separates, 11. 271; Departed, *pp.* divided, parted, b. 7. 156.
Depe, *adv.* deeply, 7. 166, b. 13. 89, b. 14. 6. See Deop.
Depose, *v.* put down, b. 15. 514.
Depper, *adv.* more deeply, more closely, b. 10. 182, b. 15. 193; Deppere, 12. 131; Deppore, a. 11. 138. See Deop.
Depraue, *v.* slander, defame, depreciate, 4. 225; *pr. pl.* b. 5. 144.
Der, *pr. pl.* dare, 4. 214. See Dar.
Dere, *v.* hurt, harm, injure, 10. 38, 20. 18, 21. 25, 299; Deren, *v.* b. 7. 50; Derid, 2 *pt. pl.* harmed, injured, R. 2. 124. A.S. *derian;* from *daru,* sb.
Dere, *s.* hurt, injury, b. 14. 171. See note, p. 209. A.S. *daru.*
Dere, *adj.* dear, 8. 66, b. 14. 325; expensive, R. 3. 169.
Dere, *adv.* dearly, 9. 316; Deore, especially, a. 6. 83; well, a. 7. 278; Me dere liketh = it dearly pleases me, I like best, b. 6. 293.
Dere-worthe. See Derworthe.
Derk, *adj.* dark, 21. 63; Deork, darkened, 21. 61; Derke, *def.* a. 1. 1; Durke, 2. 55; Derke, *pl.* b. pr. 16; Deorke, *pl.* black, 22. 21.
Derke, *s.* the dark, darkness, 14. 57; night, b. 11. 259.
Derker, *adj. comp.* darker, 12. 131;

Derkore, *adv. comp.* more darkly, a. 11. 138.
Derklich, *adv.* darkly, mysteriously, R. 1. 20; Derkelich, b. 10. 373.
Derling, *s.* darling, a. 12. 19.
Derly, *adv.* neatly (lit. dearly, in a costly way), 22. 2.
Derne, *adj.* secret, 4. 293, 11. 295, b. 2. 175, b. 9. 189, b. 13. 55, a. 10. 199; Durne, secret, 14. 155. A.S. *dyrne.* See **Derue.**
Derne, *adv.* secretly, b. 11. 343. See above.
Derrest, *adj. sup.* dearest, most valuable, b. 2. 13.
Derth, dearth, famine, b. 14. 171, 176; Derthe, 9. 353.
Derue. Perhaps we should read *derue,* good, excellent, in R. 1. 42; and *derue,* bold, audacious, in R. 1. 69. If so, *derue* is the pl. of *derf,* strong, bold. In R. 1. 42, it may mean excellent, i. e. rare.
Derworthe, *adj.* precious, 2. 83, a. 1. 85; Derworth, b. 1. 87; Dereworthe, 7. 89, 14. 18.
Desauowe, *v,* disavow, revoke, 4. 322.
Deschargen. See **Dischargen.**
Descreued. See **Discreue.**
Dese, daïs, table, b. 13. 61. See **Deys.**
Desert, *s.* thing due, thing earned, 4. 293.
Deseruen, *v.* earn, deserve, 6. 42, 9. 204; *ger.* 4. 299; *v.* a. 7. 42, 188; Deserue, *v.* 3. 134; Deseruyþ, *pr. s.* deserveth, a. 12. 92; Deseruen, *pr. pl.* earn, 17. 4; Deserue, *pr. s. subj.* may earn, has earned, b. 14. 135; Deserued, *pp.* deserved, earned, 3. 133; Derseruet, *pp.* a. 5. 248, a. 7. 80.
Deseueraunce, *s.* separation, R. 2. 50.
Despeir, *v.* make to despair, 10. 38.
Despende, *pr. s. subj.* spend, use, b. 12. 58; Despended, *pp.* spent, b. 5. 267. See **Dispended.**
Desperacion, despair, b. 17. 307.
Despit, *s.* spite, 9. 184.
Destine, *s.* destiny, fate, b. 6. 276; Destyne, 9. 297.
Destreres, *pl.* horses, chargers, a. 2. 150. O.F. *destrier,* Lat. *dextrarius.* '*Destrier,* a steed, a great horse;' Cotgrave.
Destruyen, *v.* destroy, 22. 313; Destruye, *v.* 17. 174, 19. 43; Destrueþ, *pr. s.* destroys, 13. 234; Destroieþ, *pr. s.* 21. 160; Destroyeth, *pr. pl.* waste, 1. 24; Destruyen, *pr. pl.* 20.

256; Destruye, 2 *pr. subj.* destroy, b. 3. 269. See **Distruye.**
Desyrynge, *s.* desire; vnkynde desyrynge = unnatural affection, b. 13. 356.
Determyned, *pp.* decided, R. 2. 97.
Deþ, death, 1. 17, 4. 463; Deth, b. 10. 79; To deþe = to death, 2. 168; Deþes, *gen. sing.* death's, 23. 105.
Deþ-day, death-day, death, 2. 131, 10. 350; Deþ-daye, 11. 302. See **Dedday.**
Deþ-deynge, *s.* hour of death, lit. death-dying, 8. 86; Deth-deyinge, b. 11. 171.
Deth-yuel, death-drink, b. 18. 53.
Dette, debt, 4. 307, 10. 275; R. 4. 19; Dettes, *pl.* 1. 91.
Deu, *s.* God (F. *dieu*) a. pr. 103.
Deue, *adj. pl.* deaf (men), 22. 130. See **Def.**
Deuel, devil, 3. 113, 9. 127, 10. 38; Dcoucl, 20. 18, 21. 327; Deueles, *gen.* devil's, 9. 52; Deoueles, *gen.* 21. 299; Deoueles, *pl.* devils, imps, 21. 343.
Deuer, *s.* endeavour, duty, task, 17. 5, 18. 92; a. 12. 2. F. *devoir.* See **Deuor.**
Deuh, dew, 8. 265. See note.
Deuiny, *v.* explain, 16. 98; Deuyne, *v.* interpret, b. 13. 89; Deuyne, 1 *pr. s.* guess at, search into, examine, 12. 131; Deuineþ, *pr. pl.* suppose, 18. 314; Deuynede, *pt. s.* explained, a. 8. 138; contrived, 12. 265; prophesied, 22. 148; Deuine 3e, *imp. pl.* do ye explain, b. pr. 209; Deuyned, *pt. s.* b. 7. 152. See **Diuine, Dyuyne.**
Deul, grief, sorrow, dool, 9. 127. See **Deol, Dole.**
Deuor, duty, b. 14. 136; Deuore, b. 13. 212; Deuoir, b. 11. 277. See **Deuer.**
Deuors, divorce, 23. 139, b. 20. 138 (where it seems to be plural); Deuorses, *pl.* b. 2. 175.
Deuoutours, *pl.* adulterers, 3. 184. Also spelt *deuoutrours,* viz. in MS. E. *Devoterer* occurs in this sense in Becon's Works, i. 450 (Parker Society). The more usual form is *avoutrer.*
Deuyne. See **Deuiny.**
Deuynour, interpreter, explainer, teacher, b. 7. 135; Deuynoure, b. 10. 452; Deuynours, *pl.* commentators, b. 13. 114. See **Diuinour.**
Deuyse, *v.* point out, 8. 190; think on, consider, 22. 278; Deuysede, *pt. s.* planned, devised, 22. 331.

GLOSSARIAL INDEX. 343

Deuyse, *s.* device, R. 3. 178.
Dewe, *adj.* due, owing, 4. 307; due, natural, real, R. 3. 60.
Dewid, *pp.* endowed, a. 11. 196.
Deye, *v.* die, perish, 2. 144, 3. 221, 4. 432, 11. 60; Dey, *v.* b. 1. 142; Deyeþ, *pr. s.* 15. 211; Deieth, *pr. s.* dies, b. 14. 135; Deyen, *pr. pl.* b. 10. 296; Deien, *pr. pl.* 1. 102; Deidest, 2 *pt. s.* didst die, 7. 319; Deydest, 2 *pt. s.* 22. 174; Deyede, *pt. s.* 11. 194; Deiede, 23. 177; Deyed, *pt. s.* 20. 139; Deyde, *pt. s.* b. 10. 354; Deide, *pt. s.* 11. 58, 23. 19; perished, 7. 336; Deyeden, *pt. pl.* suffered death, b. 15. 548; Deyden, *pt. pl.* died, 6. 40; Deye, 2 *pr. pl. subj.* b. 6. 122. Icel. *deyja*. See **Diȝe, Dye, Dyȝe.**
Deyes, daïs, high table, 12. 40; Deis, a. 8. 19; Dese, b. 13. 61; Deyse, b. 7. 17. O.F. *deis, dais,* Lat. *discus.* See note to 10. 21. See **Deys.**
Deyinge, *s.* dying, death, 10. 38, 18. 276; Deiynge, 18. 144; Deyynge, 20. 224. See **Deþ-deynge.**
Deyne, *pr. pl.* deign, a. 7. 296; Deyneþ, *pr. s.* 12. 61; Deyned, *pt. pl.* 9. 332, b. 6. 310.
Deynous, *adj.* proud, conceited, disdainful, 11. 81. 17. 227. A corruption of Dedeignous, q. v. See Cath. Angl. p. 95, n. 4.
Deynte, *s.* importance. 12. 312; Deyntee, value, b. 11. 47; Deyntes, *pl,* dainties, sweetmeats, 16. 91; luxuries, 16. 303, R. 3. 275; Deyntees, *pl.* b. 14. 122. O.F. *deintet,* Lat. acc. *dignitatem.*
Deynteuosliche, *adv.* daintily, luxuriously, 9. 324.
Deys, *s.* dais, upper table, high table in hall, 16. 65, a. 11. 43; Deyse, b. 7. 17; Deis, a. 8. 19. See **Deyes, Dese.**
Deyynge, *s.* dying, death, 20. 224.
Diademyd, *pp.* crowned, 4. 444, b. 3. 286; Dyademed, a. 3. 268.
Diamauntis, *s. pl.* diamonds, R. 1. 42; Diamantz, *pl.* b. 2. 13.
Diapenidion, *s.* a remedy, b. 5. 123; Diopendion, a. 5. 101. See note, p. 77.
Diche, ditch, 14. 236, 22. 365; channel of water, 21. 408.
Did. See **Don.**
Dido, a tale of Dido, a thrice-told tale, an old story, 16. 171, b. 13. 172. The story of Dido was very well known. It was indeed a common 'disours tale,' as the text has it.

Diete þe, 2 *pr. s. subj.* diet thyself, b. 6. 270. See **Diȝete.**
Diggeden, *pt. pl.* digged, dug, 9. 114. See **Dike.**
Dighte, *pt. s.* handled, 2. 27; Dihten, *v.* prepare, make ready, a. 2. 150; Dihte, *v.* a. 7. 278; Dyghte, *v.* prepare, 9. 316; Dyght, 2 *pr. s. subj.* conduct, 9. 291; Dyhte, 1 *pt. s. refl.* dressed myself, 22. 2. See **Diȝte.** A.S. *dihtan.*
Dignelich, *adv.* worthily, nobly, honourably, b. 7. 171. F. *digne,* Lat. *dignus.*
Dignesse, *s.* haughtiness, R. 3. 127.
Dihte, Dihten. See **Dighte.**
Dike, *v.* dig (esp. to dig a ditch), 22. 365; Diken, *v.* b. 6. 143; Dyke, 1 *pr. s.* b. 5. 552; Diken, *pr. pl.* a. 11. 184; Dikeden, *pt. pl.* dug, a. 7. 100; Dykeden, b. 6. 193. A.S. *dician.*
Dikers, *pl.* ditchers, 1. 224; Dikeres, b. 6. 109. See **Dykere.**
Dilitable. *adj* pleasant (lit. delightful), 2. 32. See **Delitable.**
Diluuye, deluge, b. 10. 411; Dyluuye, 12. 251. Lat. *diluuium.*
Dilytede, *pt. s.* delighted, a. 1. 29. See **Delited.**
Dimmede, *pt. pl.* became dim, a. 5. 200; Dymmed, *pt. pl.* 7. 407.
Dineth, *pr. s.* feeds, R. 3. 60. See **Dynen.**
Dint, blow, 21. 25. See **Dynt.**
Diopendion, See **Diapenidion.**
Dirige, dirge, 4. 467. See note.
Disalouwynge, *s.* disapproval, 17. 7; Disalowynge. b. 14. 139.
Disalowed, *pp.* not approved of, b. 14. 130.
Dischargen, *v.* unload, relieve, b. 15. 528; Deschargen, *v.* 18. 231; Descharget, *pp.* discharged, dispatched, a. 4. 26.
Disclaundre, *s.* evil fame, disrespect, a. 5. 75. Lit. *dis-slander,* where the prefix is intensive.
Disconfit, *pp.* discomfited, defeated, 1. 108, 112.
Discret, *adj.* proper, suitable, 6. 84.
Discreue, *v.* describe, b. 5. 79, b. 16. 66; Descriue, describe, draw, 21. 214; Discryue, describe, 7. 196; Descreued, *pp.* described, b. 20. 93; Discriued, *pp.* named, described, 23. 94.
Disgisid, *pp.* tricked out, finely dressed, b. pr. 24. See **Degiset.**
Disours, *gen.* romance-singer's, storyteller's, 16. 171; Dysoures, b. 13. 172; Disours, *pl.* professional story-

GLOSSARIAL INDEX.

tellers, minstrels, 9. 52; Disoures, b. 6. 56. O.F. *diseor*, a tale-teller, from *dire*, Lat. *dicere*. See *Dysowre* in Prompt. Parv.
Dispended, *pp.* spent, 13. 235, 17. 278; b. 10. 325; misused, b. 12. 49; Dispende, *imper. s.* spend, use, 9. 235; Dispeyne, *pr. s. subj.* spend, lay out, 15. 18. See **Despende.**
Dispise, *v.* despise, 15. 64, R. 3. 199; Dispice, *v.* 3. 84; Dispice, 1 *pr. s.* 7. 80; Dispiseþ, *pr. s.* despises, 17. 216; Dispiseden, *pt. pl.* 22. 34; Despisede, 10. 190.
Dispoilen, *pr. pl.* rob, plunder, 14. 58.
Dispute, v. to argue, 11. 20: Dispuite, a. 9. 16; Disputen, *pr. pl.* argue, 7. 137.
Disschere. See **Disshere.**
Dissese, *s.* lack of ease, misery, R. 2. 71.
Disshere, dish-maker, dish-seller, 7. 372; Disschere, dish-seller, a. 5. 166; Dissheres, *s.* female dish-seller, b. 5. 323. 'John le Disshere' is mentioned (A.D. 1304) in Memorials of London, ed. Riley, p. 54. (In a. 5. 164, read *dykere,* i. e. ditcher.) See note to 7. 369.
Distinkte, *pt. pl.* distinguished, explained, a. 4. 133.
Distruye, *v.* put down, put an end to, 10. 17; Distrye, *v.* destroy, 1. 212; Distruyeþ, *pr. s.* destroys, 15. 22; Distruȝen, *pr. pl.* a. 7. 125; Distruen, a. pr. 22. See **Destruyen.**
Diues, the rich man in the parable, b. 14. 122.
Diuine, *imper. pl.* guess, explain, 1. 217; Diuinede, *pt. s.* interpreted, a. 8. 143, 156; 1 *pt. s.* explored, a. 11. 138; *pt. pl.* determined, 11. 99, 101. See **Dyuyne, Deuiny.**
Diuinour, interpreter, commentator, 16. 85; Diuynours, *pl.* 16. 123. See **Deuynour, Dyuynour.**
Diuyde, *v.* share, 22. 215. See **Dyuyde.**
Diuyn, *s.* divinity, a. pr. 90. See **Dyuyn.**
Diȝe, *pr. pl.* die, perish, a. 11. 205; Diȝede, *pt. s.* a. 9. 50; Diȝedest, 2 *pt. s.* didst die, a. 5. 245. See **Deye.**
Diȝete, 2 *pr. s. subj.* diet, a. 7. 255. See **Diete.**
Diȝte, *v.* dight, prepare, make ready, b. 6. 293; Diȝte, 1 *pt. s.* prepared, dressed, b. 19. 2. See **Diȝhte.**
Do. See **Don.**
Dobbede, *pt. s.* dubbed, created, 2. 102; Doubed, 21. 11. See **Dubbede.**
Dobeleres. See **Dobleres.**

Dobest, Do-best, 11. 76; to do best, 22. 182.
Dobet, Do-better, 11. 76, 22. 129; Dobetere, a. 10. 88. See **Bet.**
Doblefold, *adv.* two-fold, 10. 344.
Dobleres, *pl.* platters, b. 13. 81; Dobleres, 16. 91. See note, p. 192.
Doctour, doctor, teacher, a. 11. 293; b. 10. 452; Doctoure, b. 13. 61; Doctours, *pl.* learned men, 22. 317.
Doel, *s.* lamentation, b. 5. 386. See **Dole.**
Doeris, *s. pl.* doers, R. 3. 199.
Dogge, dog, 10. 261.
Doke, *s.* duck, b. 5. 75; Douke, 7. 174; Duk, b. 17. 62.
Dole, *s.* dool, lamentation, grief, sorrow, b. 6. 122; b. 15. 142; Doel, b. 5. 386. See **Deol, Deul.**
Doles, *s. pl.* portions, alms, a. 3. 63.
Doluen. See **Deluen.**
Dombe, *adj. pl.* dumb (men), 22. 130. See **Doumbe.**
Dome, doom, judgment, sentence, 4. 474, 7. 299, 10. 321; Dom, 13. 88, 21. 27; a. 8. 19, 174; Domys, *gen. sing.* of doom, judgment, 6. 123, 7. 325; Domes day, day of judgment, 10. 21; Domes carte, doom-cart, cart in which a criminal is carried to execution, R. 3. 137; Domes, *pl.* sentences, judgments, decisions, b. 15. 27.
Domesday, day of judgment, doomsday, 22. 196 (cf. 12. 251); b. 5. 20, b. 10. 411, a. 5. 20, 253.
Domes-man, dooms-man, judge, 22. 307. See note.
Dome-ȝeuynge, *s.* judgment, decision (lit. doom-giving), R. 3. 329.
Dompynges, *pl.* dab-chicks, diving birds, 14. 169. See note.
Don, *v.* do, cause, 15. 23, 27; a. 1. 63; Don him lawe = execute law upon him, a. 3. 275; Done, *v.* do, effect, b. 11. 37; Done, *ger.* to do, 4. 233; Do, *v.* do, cause, make, 8. 5, 11. 75; Do come = cause to come, 16. 53; Do me = take, betake myself, 8. 66; Do, 1 *pr. s.* place, put, 21. 93; make, cause, a. 7. 50; I do it on = I lay it upon, I appeal to, I refer it to, I call to witness concerning it, 2. 82, 3. 39, b. 1. 86, b. 3. 187, b. 10. 37; Don, *pr. pl.* do, act, b. 8. 109, b. 10. 11; cause, a. 8. 164; *refl.* betake themselves, go, 11. 276; a. 10. 188; Do, *pr. pl.* cause, b. 10. 41; Done, *pr. pl.* do, act, practise, b. 10. 398; fulfil, b. 14. 153; Done, 2 *pr. pl.* do, b. 14. 146; Don, *pr. pl. subj.* they may

GLOSSARIAL INDEX. 345

betake (themselves), b. 9. 168; Dede, *pt. s.* did, b. 1. 28; Dede dede = did a deed, b. 14, 325; Dude, *pt. s.* did, made, 1. 123, &c.; caused, made, 19. 145; Dude me = I betook myself, 22. 2; Dud, *pt. s.* prepared, 3. 221; Dudest, 2 *pt. s.* didst cause, 21. 322; Duden, 1 *pt. pl.* did, a. 8. 127; Dude, *pt. pl.* 23. 6; Duden, *pt. pl.* put, 22. 10; committed, 21. 379; Dede, *pt. pl.* b. 7. 122; Deden, b. 5. 547; b. 18. 388; R. 3. 112; Dude, *pt. pl. subj.* should act, a. 9. 92; Doth, *imp. pl.* b. 5. 44; Don, *pp.* caused, made, done, b. 11. 309; Do, *pp.* applied, b. 18. 155; done, b. 11. 38, R. 1. 106; Do hir with = hath given her in charge to, b. 9. 11. Used in many phrases; as, Do maken = I cause to be made, b. 3. 60; Do peynten — cause to be painted, b. 3. 62; Don saue = cause to be saved, b. 7. 177; Don hym lese = cause him to lose, b. 5. 95; Do men deye = cause men to die, b. 6. 276.
Dones, *gen.*; What dones = of what sort, b. 18. 298. See note. So also *wat done man* = what sort of man, Sir Ferumbras, 3445 (where the reading is quite correct).
Donet, grammar, primer, elementary instruction, 7. 215. See note.
Donge, dung, manure, 5. 145, 9. 184, 198; Dounge, a. 4. 130.
Dongehul, dunghill, b. 15. 109.
Dongeon, dungeon, b. pr. 15; Dongeoun, b. 1. 59; Dungun, a. pr. 15, a. 1. 57. The *donjon, dongeon,* or keep-tower, is the principal tower in a castle; in the lower part of it prisoners were often confined, whence our *dungeon.* See *Dungeon* in my Etym. Dict.
Doob, *pr. s.* entrusts, places, 11. 137. See Don.
Dore, door, 3. 217, 7. 407; entrance, b. 15. 19; Doris, *pl.* R. 3. 362.
Dore-nayl, *s.* door-nail, 2. 184. See note.
Dore-tre, the wooden bar of a door, b. 1. 185. Mätzner explains it as 'door-post;' whilst the mod. Swed. *dörrträ,* Dan. *dörtræ,* mean 'lintel.' But a passage in Havelok (l. 1806) makes it clear that the *doretre* was *the barre of the dore,* i. e. the large wooden bar or beam formerly used to fasten a door, and reaching right across it, being slipped through staples in the door-posts.
Dorste. See Dar.

Dosen, dozen, 7. 369; Dosene, 5. 38; Doseyn, a. 5. 164; Doseyne, 23. 164; Dozein, b. 20. 163.
Doted, *adj.* foolish, doting, b. 1. 138; Dotede, 2. 139. Cf. F. *radoter,* to dote.
Dotest, *adj. supèrl.* most doting, stupidest, a. 1. 129. See above.
Dop, *pr. s.* doeth, does, 2. 85; causes, 4. 173, &c.; *pl.* cause, 20. 297, 304; *imp. pl.* cause, b. 8. 13. See Don.
Doubed, *pp.* dubbed, 21. 11. See Dobbede.
Douce, *adj.* pleasant, luxurious, b. 14. 122. F. *douce,* fem. of *doux.*
Douhter, daughter, 9. 81, 11. 138, a. 7. 72; Douheter, 3. 33; Doughter, 21. 473; Douȝter, b. 2. 30, b. 11. 240; Douhtres, *pl.* daughters, 2. 27; Douȝ-tres, b. 6. 99. A.S. *dóhtor.*
Douhtiest, *adj.* mightiest, most valiant, 22. 134; Douhtieste, *pl.* noblest, 8. 141; Doughtiest, greatest, b. 10. 452; Douȝtiest, mightiest, a. 11. 293.
Douhtiliche, *adv.* doughtily, 21. 36; Doughtilich, b. 18. 37.
Douhty, *adj.* valiant, 12. 265; Douȝty, R. 3. 360.
Douke, duck, 7. 174. See Doke.
Doumbe, *adj.* dumb, 3. 39; b. 10. 137; a. 11. 94; þe doumbe = the dumb one, i. e. a *book,* 3. 39. See Dombe.
Doun, *adv.* down, 21. 73, 87.
Doun, *s.* down, hill; Doune, *dat.* 5. 51; Dounes, *pl.* hills, a. 10. 167. A.S. *dún.*
Dounghep, dungheap, 17. 265.
Doun-riht, *adv.* quite, entirely, 21. 199.
Doust, dust, powder, b. 20. 99; Douste, *dat.* 23. 100.
Doute, *v.* fear, 11. 197; 1 *pr. s.* 21. 314; Douteth, *pr. s.* R. 3. 148; Douten, *pr. pl.* 11. 126; doubt, are in doubt, b. 15. 70.
Doute, *s.* fear, 15. 69. See Dowtes.
Douue, dove, 18. 171; Dowue, b. 15. 393, 401.
Douwe, *v.* endow, 4. 322; Dowede, *pt. s.* 18. 220; Dowed, *pt. s.* b. 15. 519.
Douȝter. See Douhter.
Douȝtiest. See Douhtiest.
Douȝtiore, *adj. comp.* doughtier, stronger, a. 5. 84.
Douȝty, *adj.* doughty, R. 3. 360. See Douhty,
Do-vuele, Do-evil, Do-ill, 11. 17, 27.
Dowble, *adj.* double, b. 18. 148.
Dowed. See Douwe.
Dowel, *s.* a well-doing, 10. 318, 319;

GLOSSARIAL INDEX.

12. 78, 22. 110; **Doweles**, *gen.* Dowell's, b. 9. 12, b. 14. 321.
Dowtes, *pl.* doubts, fears, R. pr. 7. See **Doute**.
Dowue, dove, b. 15. 393, 401. See **Douue**.
Doynge, *s.* deed, thing done, action, actions, 4. 293, 294; 9. 91.
Dozein, dozen, b. 20. 163. See **Dosen**.
Drad, *pp. as adj.* afraid, 17. 310.
Dradde. See **Drede**.
Draf, refuse, grains, hog's-wash, 12. 9, 22. 401; Draffe, b. 10. 11, b. 19. 397. See note, p. 146.
Dragges, *pl.* comfits, b. 20. 173. Cf. Chaucer, Prol. 246. '*Dragée*, a kind of disgestive powder, usually prescribed unto weak stomacks after meat;' Cotgrave. From Gk. τράγημα.
Drat. See **Dreden**.
Drauele. See **Dreuele**.
Drauȝte, draught, b. 20. 222. See **Drawt**.
Drawen, *v.* draw, a. 4. 108; Drawe, *v.* a. 2. 154; Drough, *pt. s.* drew, b. 13. 49; Drouh, *pt. s.* drew near, 16. 286; a. 5. 200; Drouȝ, *pt. s.* moved, drew, a. 11. 94; 1 *pt. s.* I drew, a. 5. 123; Drowgh, *pt. s.* drew, b. 20. 199; drew near, b. 5. 356; Drow, *pt. s.* drew, 16. 57, 23. 200; drew near, approached, b. 14. 106; drew, shut, a. 12. 36; Drowe, *pt. s.* drew, R. 4. 31; Drowe hym arere = drew back, retreated, b. 10. 137; Drow, 1 *pt. s.* drew back, 21. 116; Drow, 1 *pt. s.* drew, betook (me), 7. 215; *pt. s.* drew (nigh), 7. 407; Drowe, 1 *pt. s.* withdrew, b. 18. 111; *refl.* drew myself, went amongst, b. 5. 209; Drowen, *pt. pl.* drew, came, 9. 190; *refl.* betook themselves, attached themselves, 14. 147; Drow, *pt. pl.* 14. 148; Drowe, *pt. pl.* R. 3. 329; Drawen, *pp.* drawn, a. 11. 144; Drawen forþ, *pp.* brought forward, advanced, praised, a. 11. 30; Drawe, *pp.* drawn, withdrawn, 21. 141. A.S. *dragan*.
Drawt, 23. 223. See **Drauȝte**.
Drecchynge, *s.* disturbance caused by dreams, excitement of dreams, a. 9. 60. Cf. Chaucer, C. T. 16372. A.S. *dreccan*, to vex.
Drede, *s.* dread, fear, 3. 217, 6. 122; a. 10. 79, 81. See **Dreede**.
Drede, *v.* be afraid, fear, dread, b. 10. 288; Dreden, *ger.* a. 10. 211; 1 *pr. s.* 8. 59; *refl.* 21. 327; Dreden, *pr. pl.* 9. 159, 22. 21; Drat, *pr. s.* (*for* Dredeth), dreads, fears, 8. 73, 13. 151;

Dret, b. 13. 413; Dradde, 1 *pt. s.* dreaded, feared, 7. 276; *pt. s.* 16. 286; Draddest, 2 *pt. s.* didst fear, b. 3. 192; Dradde, *pt. pl.* R. 1. 68; Dradden, 23. 65; Dreddest, 2 *pt. s.* didst 'dread, a. 3. 186; Dred, *pt. s.* was afraid, b. 14. 106; Dred, *imp. s.* dread, avoid, 2. 32. A.S. *drǽdan*.
Dredfulliche, *adv.* in alarm, in terror, 20. 62; Dredfully, b. 17. 62.
Dredles, *adv.* doubtless, without doubt, a. 11. 191.
Dreede, *s.* dread, a. 2. 183. See **Drede**.
Dregges, *pl.* dregs, 9. 193, 22. 401.
Dreiȝe, *adj. pl.* on dry land, out of the water, a. 11. 205. See **Drie**, **Drye**.
Dremede, 1 *pt. s. refl.* dreamt, 21. 6; *pt. s.* a. 9. 60; Dremed, *pp.* 22. 1.
Dremels, *s.* dream, vision, a. 8. 138; Dremeles, 10. 305, 16. 17. The usual M.E. form is *dreme* (see below); *dremels* is formed from *drem-en* with the suffix -*els*, in imitation of *met-els*, a dream. See **Metels**.
Drenche, *v.* be drowned, b. 12. 169; *imp. s.* drown, b. 8. 50, a. 9. 46.
Dret, *pr. s.* (*for* Dredeth), dreads, b. 13. 413. See **Drede**.
Dreuele, *v.* drivel, slobber (*also*, metaphorically), chatter, talk foolishly, 12. 9; Drauele, *v.* a. 11. 11; Dreuelen, *pr. pl.* drivel, chatter, talk foolishly, 12. 40; Drauelen, a. 11. 43. See **Dryuele**.
Drewery. See **Druerie**.
Drie, *adj. pl.* dry, out of the water, b. 10. 296; Dreiȝe, a. 11. 205.
Drien, *pr. pl.* suffer, endure, a. 11. 69. A.S. *dréogan*; Lowl. Sc. *dree*.
Driht, *s.* man, a. 9. 60. Here used to denote a single individual; but the A.S. *dryht* properly means a company, host, multitude.
Drinken, *v.* drink, a. 5. 58; Dronk, *pt. s.* drank, 23. 19; Dronke, *pt. pl.* b. 14. 64; Dronken, *pt. pl.* 16. 268; Dronken, *pp.* (*often as adj.*) drunk, drunken, 14. 236.
Drit, *s.* dung, manure, a. 7. 178. Icel. *dritr*, mod. E. *dirt*.
Driueþ, *pr. pl.* drive; Driueþ forþ = pass away (the time), a. pr. 103. See **Dryue**.
Driȝte, Lord, b. 14. 101. A.S. *dryhten*, a lord, the Lord; the final *n* being dropped. See **Dryȝte**.
Drof. See **Dryue**.
Drogges, *pl.* drugs, 23. 174

GLOSSARIAL INDEX. 347

Dronke, Dronken. See **Drinken.**
Dronkelewe, *adj.* given to drink, 11. 81; Dronkeleuh, a. 9. 75; Dronkenlewe, b. 8. 83.
Drosenes, dregs, lees that sink to the bottom, 9. 193. A.S. *drosna, drosne,* pl. dregs; from *dréosan.*
Drough, Drouh. See **Drawen.**
Drouhþe, *s.* drought, a. 7. 275; Drouthe, 6. 150; thirst, 16. 253; Drouth, drought, 9. 313. See **Drouȝte.**
Drouȝ. See **Drawen.**
Drouȝte, *s.* drought, a. 11. 205. See **Drouhþe.**
Drow, Drowen. See **Drawen.**
Droweþ, *pr. pl.* dry (up), 15. 22.
Drue, dry; Drynke drue = drain the pot, 10. 145. See **Drye.**
Drurie, *s.* precious thing, treasure, object of affection, a. 1. 85; Druwery, 2. 83; Drewery, b. 1. 87. O.F. *druerie,* affection, *drut,* a lover; from O.H.G. *trut, drut,* beloved (G. *traut*).
Druiȝest, 2 *p. s. pr.* art dry, art thirsty, a. 1. 25. See **Droweþ.**
Drye, *adj.* dry, 6. 150, b. 13. 269; Druye, *adj. as s.* dry weather, dry places, a. 6. 21; Drye, thirst, drought, b. 14. 50.
Dryest, 2 *pr. s.* art dry, art thirsty, b. 1. 25.
Drynkynge, *s.* drinking, b. 11. 327.
Dryue, *v.* drive, a. 5. 101; Dryueþ, *pr. s.* 20. 289, b. 9. 206; presses, b. 14. 92; *pr. pl.* pass, spend, 1. 225; Drof, *pt. s.* drove, 19. 159; thrust, a. 12. 104; Dryuyng, *pres. pt.* driving, dashing, 23. 100; Dryuende, *pres. pt.* driving, b. 20. 99. See **Driueþ.**
Dryuele, drivel, b. 10. 11; Dryuele, *pr. pl.* drivel, prate, talk nonsense, b. 10. 56; Dryuelen, *pr. pl.* b. 10. 41. See **Dreuely.**
Dryȝte, *s.* Lord, b. 13. 269. See **Driȝte.**
Dubbede, *pt. s.* dubbed, created (knights), a. 1. 96; Dubbed, *pp.* b. 18. 13. See **Dobbede.**
Duche, duchy, 4. 245.
Duchesse, duchess, 3. 33.
Dude, Dudest. See **Don.**
Duelle, 1 *pr. s.* dwell, a. 12. 76.
Duk, duke, lord, 11. 137; chief, master, a. 12. 87; Duke, a. 10. 11; leader, R. 1. 106; prince, lord, 21. 365; Duyk, a. 10. 76; Dukys, *pl.* R. 1. 57; *gen. pl.* R. 1. 69.
Duk, duck, b. 17. 62. See **Doke.**
Dullisshe, *adj.* dull, R. 3. 127.
Dullith, *pr. s.* dulls, R. 3. 178.
Dulnesse, stupidity, R. 2. 50.

Dune, *s.* noise, din, a. 2. 183. See **Dene.**
Dungun. See **Dongeon.**
Dupe, *adj.* deep, 2. 55, 127. See **Deop.**
Dure, *v.* last, continue, endure, 6. 25, 16. 58; live, 4. 29; endure, b. 10. 89; Durest, 2 *pr. s.* livest, b. 10. 205; Dureþ, *pr. s.* lasts, endures, 12. 91; *pr. s. as fut.* shall last, b. 10. 145; Duren, *pr. pl.* endure, last, a. 12. 94; Durede, *pt. s.* lasted, continued, 2. 107, 21. 66; Durid, R. 3. 233.
Durke, *adj.* dark, 2. 55. See **Derk.**
Durne, *adj.* secret, 14. 155. See **Derne.**
Durneliche, *adv.* secretly, in secret places, 14. 164. See **Derne.**
Dust, 2 *p. s. pr.* dost, actest, a. 3. 181.
Dutte, *v.* shut (out), drive (out), a. 7. 178. A.S. *dyttan,* to close, shut out.
Duyk, *s.* duke, lord, a. 10. 76. See **Duk.**
Dwale, an opiate, 23. 379. See note.
Dwelling, *s.* a dwelling, habitation, 3. 106.
Dyademed, *pp.* crowned, a. 3. 268. See **Diademyd.**
Dyas, *pl.* remedies, medicines, 23. 174. See note, p. 281.
Dyche, *s.* ditch, b. 19. 359.
Dye, *v.* die, a. 1. 141, a. 8. 37.
Dyght, Dyhte. See **Dighte.**
Dyke, ditch, b. 11. 417.
Dyke, Dykeden. See **Dike,** *v.*
Dykere, ditcher, 7. 369, b. 5. 320; Dyker, b. 6. 331; Dykers, *pl.* 9. 114.
Dylicatliche, *adv.* daintily, luxuriously, 17. 92. See **Delicatliche.**
Dyluuye, deluge, 12. 251. See **Diluuye.**
Dym. See **Dymme.**
Dyme, *s.* tenth (as a tax), R. 4. 15; Dymes, *pl.* tithes, 18. 227.
Dymme, *adj.* dim, dark, dismal, 21. 365; dull of sight, 12. 128; Dym, dim, b. 18. 317.
Dymmed, *pt. pl.* became dim, 7. 407, b. 5. 356. See **Dimmede.**
Dyne, din, b. 18. 62, 123. See **Dene.**
Dynen, *v.* dine, a. 5. 58; Dyneth, *pr. s.* b. 14. 135; Dyneþ, *imp. pl.* dine ye, 22. 385. See **Dineth.**
Dyner, dinner, 5. 38, 9. 316.
Dyngen, *v.* knock, beat, b. 10. 330; strike violently (as with a flail), b. 6. 143; to keep pounding away, b. 3. 310; Dynge, 1 *pr. s. subj.* though I knock, 17. 170, b. 15. 19. Cf. Swed. *dänga,* Dan. *dænge,* to bang, hit violently.
Dynt, *s.* blow; Dynte, b. 18. 26; Dyntes, *pl.* blows, 23. 105, b. 20. 104; strokes,

VOL. II.   Y

GLOSSARIAL INDEX.

9. 187; Dyntis, *pl.* blows, R. 1. 11. See **Dint**. A.S. *dynt*, a blow.

Dysoures, romance-singers, b. 13. 172. See **Disours**.

Dys-playere, dice-player, gambler, b. 6. 73. See **Dees-pleyere**.

Dyuen, *v.* dive, 15. 106, b. 12. 163; Dyueden, *pt. pl.* dived, plunged into water, 14. 169.

Dyuerseþ, *pr. s.* is different, varies, 18. 133.

Dyuyde, *v.* divide, analyse, 22. 240. See **Diuyde**.

Dyuyn, *s.* divinity, 18. 113. See **Diuyn**.

Dyuyne, *v.* explain, 22. 240. See **Diuine**.

Dyuynour, *s.* interpreter, commentator, a. 11. 293. See **Diuinour**.

Dyʒe, *v.* die, a. 1. 132, a. 2. 187. See **Deye**.

Ebbid, *pp.* ebbed, R. 3. 206.

Ebrew, Hebrew, 20. 4.

Eche, *adj.* each, every, b. 9. 140; Eche a = every, 20. 247.

Echone, each one, 2. 89, 4. 22, 445. From Eche and On (= one).

Edder, *s.* adder, R. 3. 22.

Edefien, *v.* build, build up, 21. 42; Edefye, 19. 162; Edefyen, *pr. pl.* build their hermitages, 10. 203.

Edwite, *v.* rebuke, reprove, reproach, b. 5. 370; Edwited, *pt. pl.* rebuked, reproved, 7. 421. A.S. *ed-wítan*, to reproach; from *ed*, again, *wítan*, to blame. Cf. A.S. *æt-wítan*, whence E. *twit*.

Eek, *adv.* also, moreover, b. 13. 164. See **Ek**.

Eende, *s.* end, a. 3. 233. See **Ende**.

Eeris, *s. pl.* ears, R. 3. 68. See **Ere**.

Eet. See **Eten**.

Eft, *adv.* again, 4. 334, 5. 102, 8. 267, 13. 160, 14. 132; Efte, 21. 4, 42. A.S. *eft*, again.

Eft-sones, *adv.* soon after, again, 22. 5, b. 5. 481, b. 19. 5; Eftsone, 7. 328, b. 6. 172. A.S. *eft-sóna*, soon after, again.

Egges, *pl.* eggs, 14. 164, b. 11. 343, 345, b. 13. 63.

Eggeþ, *pr. s.* incites, a. 10. 52; Eggede, *pt. s.* incited, egged on, instigated, 2. 61; Egged, *pt. s.* b. 1. 65; Eggedest, 2 *pt. s.* didst urge, b. 18. 286. Icel. *eggja*, to incite; from Icel. *egg*, edge.

Egle, eagle, R. 2. 9, 176; R. 3. 69.

Egre, *adj.* eager, hearty, 16. 89.

Egreliche, *adv.* eagerly, sharply, bitterly, 22. 380; Egrelich, eagerly, b. 16. 64; Egerlich, bitterly, b. 19. 376. See note, p. 272.

Eg-tool, edged-tool, weapon, 4. 479.

Eighen, eyes. See **Eʒe**.

Eigteth, *num. adj.* eighth, b. 14. 309. See **Eyhteþe**.

Eileþ, *pr. s.* ails, afflicts, a. 7. 121, 244. See **Eyleth**.

Eir, air, 16. 220. See **Eyre**, **Aier**.

Eiren, *s. pl.* eggs, R. 3. 42. Formed by adding *-n* (for *-en*) to *eire* = A.S. *ǽgru*, pl. of *ǽg*, an egg.

Eires, *s. pl.* heirs, 11. 86. See **Eyres**.

Eise, ease, comfort, 1. 55. See **Eyse**, **Ese**.

Eiþer, each, the one; Eiþer oþer = each with the other, each other, a. 8. 127. See **Eyther**.

Eiʒe, *s.* awe, respect, a. 5. 33. See note, p. 66. A.S. *ege*, *ǽge*, *eige*, awe, dread. See **Eye**.

Eiʒen, eyes. See **Eʒe**.

Eiʒe-siht, eye-sight, sight, a. 10. 52.

Ek, *adv.* also, moreover, besides, b. 2. 236; Eke, b. 2. 92, a. 1. 137, a. 2. 185; Eek, b. 13. 164. A.S. *éac*.

Elde, *s.* old age, age, 7. 200, 11. 265, 23. 95. A.S. *yldo*, *yldu*; from *eald*, old.

Elderne, *sb. pl. gen.* ancestors', R. 1. 65. See **Eldres**.

Eldres, *pl.* elders, forefathers, ancestors, 10. 214, b. 3. 261; Eldren, *pl.* 4. 419, a. 3. 248.

Element, sky, b. 15. 364; Elementes, *pl.* elements, 2. 17; Elementz, *pl.* b. 18. 235; Elemens, *pl.* 21. 247. See note, p. 277. *Element* still means air or sky in the dialect of Essex.

Elengelich, *adv.* sadly, miserably, b. 12. 45; Elyngliche, 23. 39. See **Elynge**.

Eliche, *adv.* alike, R. 1. 66.

Ellerne, elder-tree, 2. 64, b. 9. 147; Eller, b. 1. 68. A.S. *ellen*. Still called *ellern* in Shropshire.

Elles, *adv.* at other times, 1. 89; b. pr. 91; otherwise, 4. 293, 10. 327, 17. 38; else, b. 15. 6, a. 7. 12; otherwise (than the truth), a. 1. 86 (cf. l. 108 below); Otherwyse elles not = in no other way, a. 9. 100; Ellis, otherwise, b. 6. 233; Ellys, else, 2. 49. A.S. *elles*.

Elles-wher, *adv.* elsewhere, 16. 300, 20. 162; Elliswhere, b. 8. 26.

Elleue, eleven, 3. 238; Eleuene, 10. 315. See **Enleuene**.

Elynge, *adj.* miserable, wretched, 1. 204, 23. 2, b. 20. 2; Elyng, b.

GLOSSARIAL INDEX. 349

pr. 100, b. 10. 94. See note, p. 18. In a note to his Sprachproben, 1. 148, Mätzner shews that the sense is rather 'miserable' than 'lonely' in most of the passages where it occurs. It is properly the A.S. *ælenge*, protracted, tedious; but was probably confused with A.S. *ellend*, foreign, hence exiled, lonely. See **Alange** in Murray's New Eng. Dict.

Elyngliche. See **Elengelich.**

Embaumede, *pt. s.* anointed, 20. 70; Embaumed, *pp.* 20. 86. See **Enbaumede.**

Emcristene, fellow-Christian, 20. 226; Emcrystene, 20. 216; Emcristine, fellow-Christian, 8. 46, 11. 79; Emcristyne, 7. 75; Emcristine, *pl.* fellow-Christians. Short for Euencristene, q. v. Cf. Shropshire *eme*, direct, near, said of a road; where *eme* is merely a contraction of *even*.

Emforth, *prep.* in proportion to, 16. 142. Short for Euenforth, q. v.

Emperour, emperor, b. 13. 165.

Enbaumede, *pt. s.* anointed, 14. 107; Enbawmed, b. 17. 70. See **Embaumede.**

Enblaunched. *pp.* whitened, made outwardly fair, 17. 269.

Enchaunte, *v.* enchant, charm, 18. 288; Enchauntede, *pt. s.* 18. 176; Enchaunted, *pt. s.* b. 15. ;97; Enchaunted, *pp.* bewitched, enchanted, 23. 378.

Encheison, reason, 7. 40. A variation of M.E. *acheison;* from O.F. *acheison,* occasion, reason, from Lat. acc. *occasionem.*

Encombry, *v.* annoy, trouble, 22. 220; Encombrye, ruin, 2. 67; Encombreþ, *pr. pl.* encumber, 15. 17; Encombre, *pr. s. subj.* trouble, 22. 228; Encombred, *pp.* troubled, 2. 192; ruined, 2. 31.

Encountre, *pr. pl.* meet, 19. 240.

Endauntede, *pt. s.* tamed, 18. 171; Endauntid, *pp.* respected, held in reverence, made much of, R. 3. 127, 351. See **Daunten.**

Ende, last end, death, b. 12. 86; Eende, end, a. 3. 233.

Enditen, *v.* compose a letter, b. 15. 367; Endite, *v.* 18. 109; Endite, *pr. s. subj.* indict, 16. 119; Edited, *pp.* indicted, accused, b. 11. 307; composed, written, R. 1. 20, R. 3. 63.

Endurid, *pt. pl.* remained, R. pr. 22; survived, R. 2. 140.

Endynge, *s.* death, end, b. 14. 260. See **Ende.**

Enforme, *v.* establish, teach, b. 15. 548; teach, 18. 271; Enfourmeth, *pr. s.* teaches, b. 3. 240; Enformede, *pt. pl.* taught, 20. 95; Enfourmed, *pt. s.* informed, b. 17. 125.

Engendreþ, *pr. s.* breeds, begets, 15. 171, b. 12. 238; Engendrede, *pt. pl.* begat, 11. 215; Engendred, *pp.* 11. 248; Engendret, *pp.* a. 10. 144.

Engendrure, engendering, beginning, a. 7. 219 (with an allusion to the sense of *Genesis*).

Engenderynge, *s.* engendering, procreation, b. 11. 327.

Engleymeþ, *pr. s.* makes clammy, cloys, chokes, 17. 218. 'Gleymyn, or yngleymyn, *visco, invisco;*' Prompt. Parv. 'Gleyme, *limus, gluten, glucium;*' id. Cf. A.S. *ge-lám,* i.e. *lám,* loam, clay, preceded by *ge-*.

Englisch, *adj.* English; On Englisch, in the English language, b. 13. 71; In Englisch, in English, a. 8. 91; Englissh, the English translation, a. 11. 247; Englisshe, *pl.* b. 10. 455.

Engreynen, *v.* dye in grain, b. 14. 20; Engreyned, *pp.* dyed in grain, or of a fast colour, b. 2. 15. See notes, pp. 32, 205.

Engyned, *pt. s.* contrived, b. 18. 250. From M.E. *engin.*

En-habiten, *pr. pl.* live, dwell, 10. 188.

En-hansed, *pp.* advanced, increased, 12. 58.

Enioyneþ, *pr. s.* enjoins, 8. 72, b. 13. 412; En-ioynen, *pr. pl.* enjoin, bid (them do so), 3. 150; Enioynye, *pr. pl. subj.* enjoin, 6. 196; En-ioynede, *pt. s.* a. 6. 88; Enioyned, *pt. s.* imposed, b. 5. 607; En-ioyned, *pp.* joined, joined together, 11. 130; Enioigned, *pp.* joined, b. 2. 65; commanded, b. 14. 287.

Enleuene, eleven, a. 8. 146; Enleue, a. 3. 174. A.S. *endleofan, endlufon.* See **Elleue.**

Ennuyed, *pp.* annoyed, b. 5. 94. 'Ennuyer, to annoy, vex, trouble;' Cotgrave. See note, p. 75.

Enpugneþ, *pr. s.* impugns, invalidates, 14. 118; Enpugnede, *pt. s.* challenged, impugned, 16. 131.

Enqueste, inquest, 23. 162; Enquestes, *pl.* 6. 57, 14. 85.

Ensample, example, 2. 169, 195; 6. 120, 11. 243; Ensaumple, 14. 201; b. 10. 294; Ensamples, *pl.* instances,

examples, 5. 133, b. 1. 170, b. 10. 468;
Ensaumples, *pl.* b. 4. 136.
Enseure, *v.* insure, engage, a. 6. 31.
Enspireþ, *pr. s.* inspires, 17. 243.
Entente, intent, intention, b. 8. 126, R.
2. 99; Entent, R. pr. 79.
Entermeten, *v.* meddle, interfere, b. 13.
291; Entermeted, *pt. s.* interfered, b.
11. 408. '*S'entremettre*, to meddle
or deal with;' Cotgrave.
Entermetyng, *s.* meddling, interfering,
14. 226, b. 11. 406. See above.
Entre, *v.* enter, 13. 57; Entren, *pr. pl.*
enter, come, 21. 292; Entrie, 2 *pr. s.
subj.* mayest enter, 8. 267; Entrid,
pp. inserted, a. 11. 253.
Entre, *s.* admission, b. 11. 118.
Entyreliche, *adv.* heartily, 11. 188;
Entyerly, 18. 142.
Entysyng, *s.* temptation, enticement, b.
13. 322; Entysynge, b. 18. 158.
Enuenymes, *pl.* poisons, b. 2. 14.
Enuenymeþ, *pr. s. as fut.* will envenom,
poison, b. 12. 256.
Eny, *adj.* any, 2. 144, 3. 211, 4. 69;
Enye, 21. 388; Eni, a. 10. 206.
Enykynnes, of any kind; Enykynnes
ȝiftes = gifts of any kind, b. 2. 200.
Eode, 1 *p. s. pt.* went, a. 7. 92; Eoden,
pt. pl. went, a pr. 40; 1 *pt. pl.* went,
proceeded, a. 9. 107. A.S. *eode*, went.
Eorl, earl, 11. 86; Eorles, *pl.* a. 3. 206.
A.S. *eorl.* See Erl.
Eorþe, *s.* earth, a. 1. 7; ground, a. 8. 2,
89, 110; Erthe, b. 12. 205.
Equite, justice, 20. 286; b. 17. 304;
Equyte, 22. 310.
Er, *conj.* before, 1. 173, 2. 70, 3. 119.
See Ar.
Er, *adv.* before, b. 18. 164; before,
formerly, a. 1. 120; R. 3. 68.
Erande, errand, message, 14. 41;
Erende, 4. 48; Ernde, a. 3. 42.
Erchebischopes, *s. pl.* archbishops, b.
15. 239.
Erchedekenes, *s. pl.* archdeacons, b. 2.
173, a. pr. 92.
Erde, *dat.* (*from nom.* Erd), habitation,
home, b. 6. 202. A.S. *eard*, native soil.
Ere, ear, 5. 14, 17. 145, 23. 134; Eres,
pl. 9. 291; Eris, *pl.* 18. 172; Eren, *pl.*
1. 76; Eeris, R. 3. 68.
Eremites, *s. pl.* hermits, 1. 30, 9. 183;
Eremytes, 10. 140. See Ermite.
Eren, *v.* to plough, 9. 2; Erie, *v.* 9. 123,
b. 6. 67; *pr. s. subj.* b. 14. 28; Ereþ,
pr. s. 11. 216; Ereden, *pt. pl.* ploughed,
22. 268; Ered, *pp.* 9. 3; Eried, *pp.* b.
6. 5. A.S. *erian,* Goth. *arjan.* See
Eryen.

Erende, errand, message, 4. 48. See
Erande, Ernde.
Erest, *adv.* soonest, 7. 308. A.S. *ǽrest.*
Ergo, therefore, b. 8. 25, b. 18. 338.
Eringe, *s.* ploughing, a. pr. 21.
Eritage, heritage, a. 11. 227, 234.
Erl, earl, 8. 11, b. 8. 88; Erles, *pl.* 4.
270, b. 10. 321; Erlis, *pl.* b. 19. 217.
See Eorl.
Erldom, earldom, 3. 88.
Erliche, *adv.* early, 6. 15.
Ermite, hermit, 1. 3; Ermytes, *pl.* a.
pr. 50. See Eremites.
Ernde, errand, a. 3. 42. See Erande,
Erende.
Ernynge, *pr. pt.* running, b. 19. 376.
Erraunt, *adj.* common, arrant, 7. 307.
Cf. ' an outlawe, or a thef *erraunt*,'
i.e. arrant thief, Chaucer, C.T. 17156.
' *Errant*, wandring, . . vagabond;'
Cotgrave. Hence mod. E. *arrant*,
with *ar* for *er* as in *parson* for *person*,
&c. The account of *arrant* in my
Etym. Dict. (1st ed.) is a mistaken
one.
Ers, fundament, 7. 157; tail, back, 6.
161, b. 10. 309.
Ers-wynnynge, *s.* trade of her body, 7.
306.
Ert, 2 *pr. s.* art, 2. 80 *n*, 11. 287 *n*.
Erthe, earth, ground, b. 12. 205. See
Eorþe.
Erthly, *adj.* earthly, 23. 151.
Eryen, *v.* plough, 9. 113; Erye, *v.* 9. 66,
10. 5; Erye, *pr. s. subj.* 16. 236;
Eryed, *pt. pl.* b. 19. 263. See Eren.
Erys, *pl.* ears, a. 12. 23. See Ere.
Eschaunge, *s.* exchange, barter, 7. 280;
Eschaunges, *pl.* b. 5. 249.
Escheytes, *pl.* escheats, forfeitures, 5.
169.
Eschewe, *imp. s.* eschew, avoid, 9. 51;
Eschue, b. 6. 55; Eschuwe, a. 7. 49.
Ese, ease, comfort, 2. 19, 10. 143, 152;
14. 54; R. 3. 285; luxuriousness, R.
2. 46. See Eise, Eyse.
Espirit, spirit; *Seint espirit,* Holy
Spirit, 15. 27.
Esscheker, *s.* the exchequer, a. 4. 26.
See Cheker.
Est, East, 21. 123, b. 18. 118; Est half
= east side, R. pr. 11.
Estate, *s.* rank, class (of men), R. pr.
82.
Estwarde, *adv.* towards the east, 2. 133;
Esteward, 1. 14.
Esy, *adj.* easy, b. 7. 123, b. 15. 201.
Eten, *v.* eat, 22. 389; take meals, b. 10.
96; Ete, *v.* 23. 3; Eet, *v.* b. 5. 120;
Eteth, *pr. s.* b. 15. 56; Eet, *pr. s.* (*for*

GLOSSARIAL INDEX.

Eteth), 17. 218; Et, *pr. s.* 7. 431;
Ette, *pr. s.* he eats, b. 15. 175 (*a bad
spelling*) ; Eten, *pr. pl.* 9. 146 ; Eet, *pt.
s.* ate, 16. 47 ; Ete, *pt. s.* b. 7. 121 ;
Eten, *pt. pl.* 19. 245, b. 11. 229 ; 2 *pt.
pl.* b. 13. 106; Eten, *pp.* eaten, 20. 88;
Etyng, *pr. pt.* b. 10. 101 ; Eet, *imper.
s.* 9. 273.
Etynge, *s.* eating, b. 11. 327.
Euangelie, gospel, 12. 204 ; Euangelye,
2. 196 ; Euangelies, *pl.* 16. 45.
Euangelistes, evangelists, b. 10. 243,
b. 13. 39.
Euel-willed, *adj.* evil-disposed, 2. 189.
Eue, *s.* eve, evening, 4. 310.
Euel-ytauȝte, *pp.* ill-taught, unmannerly, b. 20. 185.
Euen, *s.* even, evening, 10. 87, 142 ;
Ouere euen = the evening before,
overnight, R. 4. 55 ; Euene, *dat.* 9.
181 ; Euenes, *pl.* eves, 7. 182.
Euen-cristene, fellow-Christian, b. 13.
390; Euene-crystene, b. 2. 94, b. 5.
440. Cf. A.S. *efenbisceop*, a co-bishop ;
and Swed. *jämn-christen*, fellow-
Christian (where Swed. *jämn* = A.S.
efen). See Emcristene.
Euene, *adj.* even, 23. 270.
Euene, *adv.* evenly, exactly, 2. 122, 20.
152 ; just, a. 8. 129; fairly, 5. 178 ;
even so, a. 4. 147 ; Euen, exactly, R.
pr. 3.
Euene-forth, *adv.* equally ; Euene-forth
with = equally with, equally as, b 13.
143, b. 17. 134. See below.
Euene-forth, *prep.* according to, to the
extent of, 22. 310, b. 19. 305. See
Emforth. So also ' *emforth* my
might ;' Chaucer, C.T. 2237 ; Leg. of
Good Women, 2128.
Euensong, *s.* evensong, a. 5. 190 ; Euen-
songe, b. 5. 345, 462. See Euesong.
Euenynges, *pl.* evenings, b. 11. 331.
Euerich, *pron.* each, 21. 77 ; Eury, b. 3.
63. (Mod. E. *every*.)
Euer-more, *adv.* evermore, a. 8. 78 ;
Euermo, b. 7. 82.
Eueses, *pl.* the eaves, (*or* eaveses, *since*
eaves *is singular*), b. 17. 227. Pl. of
euese = A.S. *efese, efes*, eaves. See
Euesynges.
Euesong, evensong, 7. 396.
Euesynges, *pl.* eaves, 20. 193. Cf. prov.
E. *aisings*, the eaves ; also M.E. *eues-
unge*, a clipping, Ancren Riwle, p.
398 ; and *euesing* in Levins. See
Eueses.
Eure, *adv.* ever, for ever, b. 15. 573.
Euydence, *s.* proof, 21. 156, b. 17. 195;

Euydences, *pl.* proofs, 12. 283 ; examples, instances, 9. 263.
Ewages, *pl.* beryls, b. 2. 14. *Ewage*
answers to Lat. *aquaticus*, and obviously here denotes some precious
stone. Marsh says it is the green
beryl, called by jewellers *aqua marina*,
with reference to its clear colour. In
Holland's Pliny, bk. 37, c. 5, we
read that, of beryls, 'those are best
esteemed which carry a sea-water
green, and resemble the greennesse of
the sea when it is cleare.' The beryl
is sometimes blueish. I find mention
of the *blewe ewage* in A Ballade of our
Lady, pr. in Chaucer's Works, ed.
1561, fol. 329, back. And see *aigage*
in Godefroy.
Excepte þat, except that, 18. 9.
Exciteth, *pr. s.* urges, b. 11. 184.
Executor, an executor, 7. 254 ; Executores, *pl.* 3. 189 ; Executours, 23.
290.
Experimentz, experiments, b. 10. 212 ;
Experimentis, a. 11. 157.
Expounen, *v.* to explain, expound, b.
14. 277.
Eye, *interject.* eh ! alas ! 13. 1. Cf. G.
ei.
Eye, *s.* awe, dread, R. 2. 9. A.S. *ege*.
See Eiȝe.
Eyen, *pl.* eyes, 7. 2, 177 ; 15. 44, 19.
147 ; Eyghen, b. 5. 109, 191. See
Eȝe. A.S. *éagan*, pl. of *éage*.
Eyhteþe, *num. adj.* eighth, 17. 147.
See Eigteth.
Eyleth, *pr. s.* ails, troubles, vexes, b.
6. 130, 259 ; *pr. pl.* affect, b. 15.
246; Eylid, *pt. s. impers.* ailed, R. 2.
46. See Eileþ.
Eyre, *s.* air, b. pr. 128, b. 1. 123, b. 9.
3, b. 14. 43. See Eir.
Eyres, *pl.* heirs, b. 2. 101, b. 3. 277, b.
15. 317. See Eires.
Eyse, ease, comfort, 6. 153. See Eise,
Ese.
Eyther, *adj.* each ; Her eyther other,
each of them the other, b. 11. 173;
and see b. 5. 148, 164; Eytheres, *gen.
s.* of each of them, b. 11. 244, b. 13.
348. See Eiþer.
Eythes, *pl.* harrows, 22. 273. A.S.
egeðe, a rake, harrow ; cf. O.H.G.
egida, mod. G. *egge*, harrow.
Eȝe, *s.* eye, a. 11. 80 ; Eȝen, *pl.* eyne,
eyes, a. 5. 44 ; Eyghen, *pl.* b. 5. 109,
191 ; Eyghe, *pl.* b. 11. 31 ; Eyghes,
b. 11. 45 ; Eiȝen, a. pr. 71, a. 5. 200.
See Eyen.

GLOSSARIAL INDEX.

Fabulers, *pl.* liars, story-tellers, a. 2. 157. Lat. *fabula*, a tale.
Fader, father, b. 1. 14, a. 8. 39, a. 10. 28; Fadre, b. 3. 126; Faderes, *pl.* 1. 122; Fadres, *pl.* fathers, a. 10. 66; instructors, 1. 119. A.S. *fæder*.
Faderlees, *adj.* fatherless, b. 9. 67.
Faille, *v.* fail, 22. 218; want, lack, b. 9. 80; Failleþ, *pr. pl.* fails, 20. 155; Faille, *pr. pl.* come short, fail to receive, 3. 159; Failen, *pr. pl.* want, are deprived of, lack, b. 10. 295; Faile, a. 11. 204; Faille, *pr. s. subj.* if it fail of, 20. 213; Failede, *pt. s.* failed, 2. 120; Failled, lacked, failed to gain, b. 11. 25; Faillede, *subj.* were absent, 20. 138; Failled, *pt. pl. subj.* lacked, wanted, 20. 135; Failid, 2 *pt. s. subj.* shouldst lack, R. 2. 117. See **Faylere**.
Faire, *s.* fair, market, 7. 211; Faires, *pl.* 5. 59. See **Fayre**.
Faire, *adv.* fairly, 6. 200; well, kindly, 10. 322; fairly, plainly, 11. 32; nobly, 21. 71. See **Fayre**.
Fairer, *adv.* more kindly, b. 10. 225.
Fairour, *adj. comp.* nobler, more honourable, 22. 29; better, more profitable, 10. 258.
Fairy, *s.* enchantment, b. pr. 6. See **Feyrie**.
Fait, *s.* action done, deed, a. 1. 160; Faite, b. 1. 184. F. *fait*, Lat. *factum*.
Faite, *imp. s.* tame, 9. 30. Short for Afaite, q.v. And see **Fayten**.
Faiten, *v.* beg, beg under false pretences, b. 7. 94; Faitest, 2 *pr. s.* beggest, 6. 30; Faiteþ, *pr. s.* begs, 10. 100; Faiten, *pr. pl.* use false pretences, are deceivers, b. 15. 208. Coined from F. *fait*, act, deed; thus the sense was, originally, to adopt an act, to pretend to a deed. See **Faiterie**, **Faitour**, the latter of which may have at once suggested the verb. See **Fayteþ**.
Faiterie, deceit, imposture, 13. 33; Faiterye, 9. 138. See above; and see **Faytrye**.
Faithly, *adv.* faithfully, truly, 22. 70, b. 19. 66.
Faitour, pretender, vagabond, impostor, deceiver, 10. 64, 23. 5, b. 20. 5; Faitours, *pl.* lying vagabonds, impostors, cheating beggars, 3. 193, 9. 128, 10. 208, 11. 298; Faitoures, b. 6. 123. O.F. *faiteor*, a maker, answering to Lat. acc. *factorem*. Factor had the sense of agent; hence that of contriver. See **Faiten**, **Faytour**; also note, p. 113.
Faityng, *s.* lying, deceit, b. 10. 38. See above.
Fallaces, *adj. pl.* fallacious, deceitful, 17. 231. (Or sb. pl. = deceits.) See note; and see below.
Fallas, *s.* deceit, deception, 12. 22. '*Fallace*, a fallacy, guile, deceit, crafty trick;' Cotgrave. See note; and see above.
Fallen, *v.* fall, a. 2. 172; befal, a. 5. 42; *v. trans.* to cause to fall, fell, overthrow, a. 3. 43; Fall, *v.* happen, R. pr. 27; Falleþ, *pr. s.* falls, a. 1. 140; Falleþ, *pr. s.* falls, belongs, 2. 163; happens, 4. 97, b. 8. 38; Falleth, *pr. pl.* are proper, b. 10. 231; Falle, 1 *pr. s.* I fall (amongst), I light (upon), b. 4. 156; Falle, *pr. s. subj.* happen, come to pass, b. 3. 323; Falde, *pt. s.* caused to fall, a. 3. 122; Falden, *pt. pl.* fell, a. 7. 147; Fallyn, *pp.* fallen, happened, R. 1. 81; Fallen, *pp.* b. pr. 65; Falle, 3 *p. imp. s.* befall, b. 16. 1; Falleth, *pr. s. impers.* befalls, befits, becomes, suits, b. 11. 95, 386; b. 16. 176; Fel, *pt. s.* fell, 21. 90; befel, a. 5. 254, a. 8. 143; turned out, became, b. 12. 47; Felle, *pt. s.* happened, b. 7. 157; was necessary, R. 4. 22; Fellen, *pt. pl.* fell, b. 1. 119; Ful, *pt. s.* fell, 1. 113, 2. 120; Fullen, *pt. pl.* fell, 2. 126; Fulle, *pt. s. subj.* should fall, 11. 39; should happen, 19. 128.
Fals, *adj.* false, 3. 42; *as sb.* falsehood, 3. 6; *def. form*, þe false, a. 9. 38; falsehood, 3. 4; Fals, *pl.* false men, b. 3. 138.
Falshed, *s.* falsehood, b. pr. 71, b. 1. 64; Falshede, 2. 60, 4. 41.
Falsliche, *adv.* falsely, deceitfully, ill, 7. 428, 10. 270, 21. 382.
Falsnesse, *s.* deceit, 19. 173, a. pr. 68. See **Falshed**.
Famede, *pp.* defamed, slandered, 4. 232. Probably short for *defamed*. See Cath. Angl. p. 122, n. 1.
Fange, *v.* take, receive, b. 5. 566. See **Fonge**. Cf. A.S *fón*, to take, catch, pt. t. *feng*, pp. *fangen*.
Fantasie, *s.* fancy, R. pr. 58; Fantasies, *pl.* silly inventions, b. pr. 36; Fantasyes, *pl.* fancies, a. 11. 63.
Fare, *v.* fare, go, a. 8. 82; depart, b. 7. 98; return, R. 3. 36; act, 21. 100; happen, 21. 236; Wel fare = to fare well, 6. 8; Fareþ, *pr. s.* fares, is, 20.

GLOSSARIAL INDEX. 353

287; fares, b. 13. 51; happens, a. 9. 33; Fareth, *impers. pr. s.* fares, is, happens, 11. 38, 41; Fare, *pr. s. subj.* happen, 12. 244; Fareþ, *pr. pl.* are, lit. go, 7. 335; travel, fare, b. 2. 183; go, a. 2. 158; Fare, 2 *pr. pl.* fare, are treated, b. 13. 108; Faren, 2 *pr. pl.* act, b. 11. 71; Faren, *pp.* gone, passed, 9. 112; Fare, *pp.* suited, R. 2. 150; Fareth, *imp. pl.* fare, speed ye, b. 13. 180.
Fare, *s.* doing, business, proceeding, 21. 16, 130; course, R. 4. 73.
Farten, *v.* break wind, 16. 206.
Faste, *v.* fast, a. 1. 99.
Faste, *adv.* fast, quickly, readily, soon, 1. 41, b. 10. 69; earnestly, a. 5. 224; diligently, a. 7. 13.
Fastingdaies, *pl.* fast-days, 7. 431; Fastyngdaies, 7. 182; Fastyngdayes, 8. 25.
Fastinges, *s. pl.* fastings, fasts, 1. 69; Fastynges, days of fasting, 10. 233. See above.
Fastne, *v.* join, attach, lit. fasten, 13. 9; Fastnet, *pp.* united (in marriage), a. 2. 51.
Fat, *adj.* rich, 13. 224; Fatte, *pl.* fat, 10. 208.
Fatte, *s.* fat, 22. 280, b. 19. 275.
Fauchon, falchion, sword, 17. 169.
Faucoun, falcon, b. 17. 62, R. 3. 87; Faucones, *pl.* falcons, 9. 30; Faucuns, a. 7. 34. See **Faukyn.**
Fauel, *s.* the impersonification of Flattery or Deceit, 3. 6, 24, 43; Fauuel, a. 2. 6, 158. O.F. *favele.* Lat. *fabella,* idle discourse; from Lat. *fabula.* See note, p. 31.
Fauht, Fauhte. See **Fighten.**
Fauhnede. See **Fauned.**
Faukyn, falcon, R. 2. 157. See **Faucoun.**
Fauned, *pt. pl.* fawned, b. 15. 295; Fauhnede, 18. 31. See **Fayn.**
Faunt, infant, child, b. 16. 101, b. 19. 114; Fauntes, *pl.* 10. 170; b. 7. 94; Fauntis, b. 6. 285. Merely a shortened form of *infant.* Cf. Ital. *fante,* boy, man, *fantino,* little child, &c. So also Roquefort gives O.F. *fant* = *enfant.*
Fauntekyn, child, 22. 118; Fauntekynes, *pl.* children, 10. 35. Dimin. of *faunt.*
Fauntelet, *s.* Infancy, lit. a little infant, 12. 310. See below.
Fauntelte, childishness, b. 11. 41, b. 15. 146. See note, p. 165, last line.
Faute, fault, b. 11. 209; lack, want, R. 2. 63, 120; Fautes, *pl.* faults, b. 10. 103; Fautis, R. 3. 112; Fawtis, R. pr. 68. ' Fawte, or defawte, *defectus;*' Prompt. Parv.
Fauten, *pr. pl.* fail in, are without, are wanting in, 11. 182, b. 9. 66; Fauteth, b. 9. 67.
Fauuel. See **Fauel.**
Fauȝte. See **Fighten.**
Fawtis, *s. pl.* defects, faults, R. pr. 68. See **Faute.**
Fayle, *v.* fail, 23. 31; Fayleþ, *pr. s.* is wanting, a. 10. 58; Faylled, *pt. s.* failed, b. 12. 7.
Faylere, *s.* one who fails to perform a duty, a non-performer, a. 2. 99.
Fayn, *adj.* fain, glad, pleased, 5. 13, 12. 103.
Fayne, *adv.* gladly, b. 8. 125; Fayn, a. 12. 67.
Fayre, *s.* fair, market, 7. 377.
Fayre, *adj.* fair, just, coming by good means, 4. 372; *as sb.* fair (side), 10. 85. See **Faire.**
Fayre, *adv.* fairly, plainly, 2. 2.
Fayrnesse, beauty, fairness, b. 12. 47.
Fayten, *v.* to tame, mortify, a. 5. 49. O.F. *afaiter,* to prepare, from Lat. *affectare.* See **Faite, Afaiten.**
Fayteþ, *pr. pl.* beg, wander like beggars, a. 8. 78; Fayteden, *pt. pl.* made pretence, shammed, begged deceitfully, b. pr. 42. See **Faiten.**
Faytour, lying vagabond, impostor, 9. 73; Faytur, a. 2. 99; Faytoure, b. 6. 74; Faytours, *pl.* a. 2. 157 = Faytors, *pl.* a. 7. 173, a. 11. 58; Fayturs, a. 11. 6. See **Faitour.**
Faytrye, fraud, deceit, b. 11. 90. See **Faiterie.**
Faytynge, *pres. part.* telling lying tales, feigning, shamming, 1. 43. See **Faiten.**
Fe, *s.* property, a. 4. 114. See **Fee.**
Febicchis, contrivances (?), a. 11. 156. See note, p. 154, Rietz gives Swed. dial. *febba, fibba,* to be boastful, thoughtless, or awkward, *febbla,* to trip, *fipla,* to be awkward, words allied to the Icel. *fipla,* to touch, to finger, all words of difficult origin. These words (if connected) point to the sense ' awkward contrivances,' or ' clumsy tricks.' Cf. b. 10. 211.
Feble, *adj.* feeble, a. 10. 181; weak, poor, 7. 159. See **Fieble.**
Feblen, *pr. pl.* grow feeble, R. 3. 16.
Fecchen, *v.* abstract, steal, take away, 7. 268, 9. 154; take away, recover, 22. 247; Fecche, *v.* take, bear away,

21. 279; take, fetch away, 6. 132, 19. 282, b. 2. 180, b. 5. 29; bring back, 21. 18; bring, 3. 191, b. 11. 55; obtain, 4. 379; Feccheþ, *pr. pl.* bring back, 11. 277; Feccheth, steal, b. 4. 51; Fecche, bring home, a. 10. 189; Fecche, 2 *pr. s. subj.* fetch, bring, 5. 7. A.S. *feccan.* Compare **Fetten.**
Feden, 2 *pr. pl.* feed, support, 8. 83; Fedde, 1 *pt. s.* fed, 7. 434.
Federes, *pl.* feathers, 15. 173, 184; Fedris, R. 2. 148, R. 3. 52; Feedrin, R. 2. 147 (cf. the pl. *uetheren* in the Ayenbite of Inwyt, p. 270). See **Fether.**
Fee, property, 5. 128. See **Fe.**
Feedrin, *pl.* feathers, R. 2. 147. See **Federes.**
Fee-fermes, *pl.* fee-farms, rented farms, R. 4. 4.
Feende, fiend, devil, 9. 97.
Feere, *s.* companion, mate, a. 4. 141; Feeres, *pl.* a. 2. 168, 185. See **Fere.**
Feet, *pp.* fetched, R. 3. 126. See **Fetten.**
Feffe, *v.* endow, 3. 160, 4. 372, 18. 56; fee, b. 2. 146; Feffe, 1 *pr. s.* endow, a. 2. 61; Feffeth, *pr. s.* endows, b. 2. 78; Feffed, *pp.* endowed, dowered, 3. 83, 137, b. 15. 319. ' *Fieffer,* to infeoffe, to grant, pass, alien a *fief,* or an inheritance in fee ;' Cotgrave.
Feffement, deed of gift, or of endowment, 3. 73. See above.
Fei, faith, a. 1. 14. See **Fey.**
Feir, *adj.* fair, a. 3. 258, a. 11. 179; flattering, a. 2. 23. See **Fayre.**
Feire, *s.* fair, market, a. 5. 119, 171; chance of selling, a. 4. 43. See **Fayre, Feyre.**
Feire, *adv.* fairly, kindly, a. 6. 114; clearly, a. 9. 24; fortunately, b. 5. 59, a. 5. 42; in order, a. 1. 2. See **Fayre.**
Feirore, *adv. comp.* more kindly, a. 11. 176.
Fel, fell, befel. See **Fallen.**
Fel, *s.* skin, a. 1. 15; Felle, R. 3. 16, 24. A.S. *fell,* Lat. *pellis,* a skin; E. *fell-monger,* a dealer in hides.
Fel, *adj.* fell, fierce, b. 16. 31; Felle, *pl.* cruel, 7. 152, b. 5. 170. See Cath. Angl. p. 126, n. 4.
Felawe, *s.* mate, companion, 3. 183, 205; partner, b. 15. 287; Felaw, b. 12. 168; Felawes, *pl.* companions, 22. 201; fellows, a. 1. 112; Felawis, companions, R. 1. 61.
Felawschipe, *s.* fellowship, a. 3. 114;

Felawship, society, b. 1. 113; Felawschepe, R. 1. 61; Felaweshepe, crew, 5. 50.
Feld, field, 1. 19, 2. 2, 6. 111.
Felde, *pt. s.* of Felle, q. v.
Fele, *adj.* many, 4. 495, 7. 74, 10. 91, 14. 138, 22. 127, 221. Fele folde = many times, b. 12. 264. A.S. *fela.* See **Feole.**
Fele, *v.* feel, experience, 21. 230, 22. 171; 1 *pr. s.* observe, b. 15. 29; Felen, *pr. pl.* feel, touch, 20. 145; Felede, 1 *pt. s,* felt, experienced, 7. 114; Feledest, 2 *pt. s.* didst feel, 8. 131, b. 5. 497.
Felefolde, many times, b. 13. 320. See **Fele,** *adj.*
Felicite, happiness, 23. 240.
Felle, *s.* skin, coat, R. 3. 16, 24. See **Fel,**
Felle, *v.* fell, defeat, kill, a. 12. 66; Felde, *pt. s.* felled, ruined, 4. 163, 240; Felde, *pt. s. subj.* should knock down, 19. 128. A.S. *fellan.*
Felle, *adj. pl.* violent, cruel, 7. 152; b. 5. 170. See **Fel.**
Felle-ware, *s.* skin-ware, fur, R. 3. 150. See **Fel,** *sb.*
Felliche, *adv.* felly, cruelly, R. 2. 173; Felly, fiercely, b. 18. 92. See **Fel.**
Feloun, *s.* felon, criminal, b. 10. 414; Felon, 7. 326; Felones, *pl.* criminals, 21. 424; Felouns, *gen. pl.* R. 3. 102.
Felounelich, *adv.* like a felon, b. 18. 349; Felonliche, wickedly, wrongfully, 13. 238.
Felynge, *s.* touch, 21. 133.
Femeles, *pl.* females, 14. 148.
Fend, fiend, devil, 2. 38, 3. 143; Fende, 11. 48, b. 1. 40, b. 8. 43; Fendes, *gen. sing.* fiend's, B. 90; Fendes, *pl.* a. 1. 112. See **Feond.**
Fendekynes, *pl.* little fiends, b. 18. 371. See **Feondekenes.**
Fenden, *v.* defend, 22. 65, b. 16. 61; Fendede, *pt. s.* 22. 46; Fended, b. 19. 46. Short for **Defenden.**
Fenel-seed, *s.* fennel-seed, b. 5. 313. ' The fruit, or, in common language, the seeds, are carminative, and frequently employed in medicine ;' Imperial Dict. They were used as a spice, to put into drinks.
Fenestre, window, 21. 13; Fenestres, *pl.* 17. 42. O.F. *fenestre,* Lat. *fenestra.*
Fentesye, *s.* faintness, a. 12. 67 *n*; better Fentyse, a. 12. 68. See **Feyntise.**
Feole, *adj.* many, a. 4. 19. See **Fele.**
Feond, *s.* fiend, devil, 21. 18, 27, 346;

GLOSSARIAL INDEX. 355

Feondes, *pl.* 21. 418. See **Fend, Feende.**
Feondekenes, *pl.* little fiends, 21. 418. See **Fendekynes.**
Feorthe, *num. adj.* fourth, 17. 133; Ferþe, a. 12. 82.
Fer, *adj.* far, distant, b. 8. 79, b. 15. 497; a. 9. 70. See **Ferr.**
Fer, *adv.* far, a long way, 10. 241, 22. 482, b. 11. 34; long time, 12. 196; Fer home = far (to go) home, b. 19. 477; Fer awey = far away, very much, b. 14. 208.
Fer, *s.* fear, R. 4. 65. See **Fere.**
Ferde, *pt. s.* fared, seemed, 20. 112, b. 20. 310; acted, 14. 230, b. 11. 410; went on, 23. 312; prospered, did, a. 11. 176; Ferden, *pt. pl.* fared, 11. 234, b. 9. 143; Ferde, went, R, 2. 180; Ferde, 2 *pt. pl.* fared, R. 1. 61; 2 *pt. pl. subj.* ye would have fared, ye would fare, b. 3. 340. A.S. *féran*, to go; der. from *fōr*, pt. t. of *faran.*
Fere, partner, mate, companion, 14. 165, 18. 19, 20. 300; Feren, *pl.* companions, 3. 219: Feres, *pl.* b. 2. 6. A.S. *geféra*, a travelling companion, from *fōr*, pt. t. of *faran.*
Fere, *s.* fear, 9. 191, 20. 300.
Fere, *v.* frighten, terrify, 18. 285, b. 7. 34. A.S. *fǣran.*
Fere, fire, 13. 197. See **Fur.**
Ferkyd, *pt. pl. refl.* proceeded, R. 3. 90. (See examples of M.E. *ferken* in Mätzner, where this passage is cited.)
Ferly, *adj.* wonderful, 16. 118. A.S. *fǣrlic*, sudden, from *fǣr*, fear, sudden danger; cf. Du. *vaarlijk*, quickly, G. *gefährlich*, dangerous.
Ferly, *s.* wonder, a wonder, 12. 228, 19. 56, 21. 115, 130; Ferliche, wonder, 14. 173; Ferlies, *pl.* wonders, marvels, 1. 63; Ferlyes, a. pr. 62; Ferlis, b. pr. 65. From **Ferly,** adj. (above). See note, p. 3.
Ferm, *adj.* firm, stedfast, 12. 57.
Ferme, *adv.* firmly, 22. 120.
Fermed, *pp.* firmly established, confirmed, b. 10. 74.
Fermes, *s. pl.* farms, R. 4. 4. See **Fee-fermes.**
Fermorie, infirmary, b. 13, 108. 'A fermory, *infirmarium*;' Cath. Angl.
Fern, *adj.* old; Fern ȝere = of old years, long ago, 8. 46. A.S. *fyrn*, Goth. *fairnis*, old. See below.
Fernyere, *adv.* formerly, b. 5. 440.
Fernȝeres, *pl.* old years, past years, b. 12. 5. See **Fern.**

Fernycle, vernicle, 8. 168. See note, p. 101.
Ferr, *adj.* far, 11. 77. See **Fer.**
Fers, *adj.* violent, fierce, 7. 7.
Fersly. *adv.* fiercely, R. 3. 77.
Fersnesse, *s.* fierceness, boldness, R. 2. 7.
Ferst, *num. adj.* first, 2. 23; former, 21. 161; *adv.* first of all, 8. 144; in the first place, 7. 15; At þe ferste = immediately, 9. 168. See **Furste.**
Ferþe, *adj.* fourth, a. 12. 82. See **Feorthe, Fierthe.**
Ferthere, *adv.* further, a. 11. 285.
Ferthing, a farthing, 8. 201.
Ferthyng-worth, farthing's-worth, 7. 360, 10. 94.
Ferye, holiday, 5. 113; Be an hey ferye = be (especially observed) as a high holiday or chief festival; Heigh ferye, high festival, b. 13. 415. F. *ferie*, Lat. *feria.* 'Feries, holy-daies,' &c.; Cotgrave.
Fesauntes, *pl.* pheasants, b. 15. 455.
Fest. *pp.* fastened, joined, b. 2. 123. (The readings vary; the A-text MSS. have *feffet, festnyd, fastnid;* the B-text MSS. have *fest, fast.*) See Cath. Angl. p. 128, n. 5.
Feste, feast, 8. 116, 22. 108, 115; Festes, *pl.* 12. 34.
Feste-dayes, *s. pl.* feast-days, 6. 30.
Festen, *v.* feast, b. 15. 477; Feste, b. 15. 335; Festeþ, *pr. s.* entertains, 17. 318.
Festered, *pp.* festered, corrupted, 20. 83; Festred, b. 17. 92.
Festu, mote, b. 10. 278. Cf. Shropshire *fescue*, a pointer used in teaching children to read. See note, p. 156.
Festynge, *s.* feasts, b. 11. 188.
Fet *pr. s.* fetches, leads, conducts, a. 2. 52; Fet, *pt. s.* fetched, a. 2. 113: *pp.* 23. 323. See **Fetten.**
Fet, *pt. pl.* feet, 3. 193, 5. 82.
Fet, action, deed, works, 2. 183. See **Feet.**
Fet, *pr. s.* (*short for* Fedeþ), feeds, b. pr. 194.
Feterye, *v.* fetter; Let feterye = cause to be fettered, 3. 212; Fetere, 2 *pl. pr. subj.* ye may fetter, a. 2. 175; Feterid, *pp.* fettered, bound, 8. 21.
Fether, feather, 22. 414; Fetheris, *pl.* b. 11. 321. See **Federes.**
Fetherede, *adj. pl.* feathered, 23. 118; Fethered, b. 20. 117.
Fetislich, *adv.* nicely, neatly, handsomely, b. 2. 11, 165. O.F. *faitis,*

GLOSSARIAL INDEX.

Lat. *factitius.* See *faictis* in Cotgrave.
Fetours, *pl.* features, 7. 46; Feytures, b. 13. 297.
Fetten, *v.* fetch, a. 2. 155; Fette, a. 3. 96; Fette, *pr. s. subj.* fetch, bring, a. 4. 7; *pt. s.* a. 5. 223; brought, 3. 65, b. 2. 162, a. 2. 133; produced, b. 5. 450; took away, 21. 277, b. 11. 6; took, 12. 168; *ill spelt* Fet, a. 2. 113; Fettest, 2 *pt. s.* didst fetch away, 21. 382, b. 18. 334; Fetten, *pt. pl.* fetched, brought, brought away, 3. 239, 9. 317; Fetten, *pr. pl.* fetch, steal, a. 4. 38; Fet, *pp.* 23. 323; *ill spelt* Fette, b. 11. 316. A.S. *fettan, fetian.* See **Fecchen.**
Fettren, *v.* to fetter, b. 2. 207.
Feuere, *s.* fever, 7. 79, a. 12. 82; Feure, b. 13. 336.
Fey, *s.* faith, religion, belief, a. 1. 160, a. 11. 60. See **Fei.**
Feye, *adj.* fated to die, 16. 2; Fey, dead, 17. 197. A.S. *fǽge,* Icel. *feigr.*
Feynen, *pr. pl.* feign, pretend, b. 10. 38; Feynen hem = imagine for themselves, b. pr. 36; Feynede, *pt. pl.* feigned, pretended, 9. 128, a. 7. 114.
Feynte, *adj. pl.* faint, R. 2. 63.
Feyntise, *s.* faintness, attack of weakness, b. 5. 5. The O.F. *feintise* means properly dissembling, feigning, but also cowardice; hence the present sense.
Feyntly, *adv.* falsely, hence in a pretentious manner, a. 2. 140. (But the reading is probably false; read *fetisly.*)
Feyre, *adj.* fair, b. 9. 19.
Feyres, *pl.* fairs, markets, b. 4. 56. See **Feire.**
Feyrest, *adj.* fairest, most handsome, b. 13. 297.
Feyrie, *s.*; A feyrie = of feyrie, i.e. of fairy origin, a strange thing, a. pr. 6. See **Fere.**
Feyth, *s.* faith, belief, b. 10. 247.
Feytures, features, b. 13. 297. See **Fetours.**
ff.—*For words beginning with* ff, *see under* F (*the single letter*).
Fieble, *adj.* helpless, weak, b. 5. 177, 412. See **Feble** ; and note, p. 81.
Fiere, partner, consort, b. 17. 318. See **Fere.**
Fierse, *adj.* fierce, b. 15. 300. See **Fers.**
Fierthe, *ord. adj.* fourth, b. 7. 52, b. 14. 294. See **Ferþe, Feorthe.**
Fif, *num.* five, 8. 295, 22. 216.
Fifteneth, *adj. num. as sb.* fifteenth, fifteenth part (as a tax), R. 4. 15. See note.
Fighten, *v.* fight, struggle, 22. 65; Fihte, *v.* fight, make opposition, a. 4. 39; Fauht, 1 *pt. s.* fought, 21. 411; Fauȝte, 1 *pt. s.* b. 18. 365; Fauhte, *pt. s.* 22. 103; Fauht, *pt. pl.* (or *s.*), 4. 247; Fouhten, *pt. pl.* fought, 9. 149; quarrelled, 1. 43.
Fikel, *adj.* fickle, inconstant, 4. 158. See **Fykel** ; and note to 3. 143.
File, concubine, 7. 135. '*Fille,* a daughter; also, a maid, lass, wench;' Cotgrave.
Final, *adj.* complete, perfect, real, 9. 216. See note.
Firses, *pl.* pieces of a furze-bush, b. 5. 351 ; Firsen, a. 5. 195.
Fisch, fish, 7. 159.
Fisician, physician, 23. 176, 315.
Fisik, physic, medicine, 23. 169, 314, 378 ; Fisyk, a. 7. 256.
Fiskeþ, *pr. s.* wanders, roams, 10. 153. See note; also Cotgrave, s.v. *Coquette.* Cf. Shropshire *fisk,* to wander idly.
Fithel, fiddle, b. 9. 102. A.S. *fiðele,* from Low Lat. *uidula,* a viol.
Fiþelen, *v.* play on the fiddle, 16. 206. See **Fythelen** ; and note, p. 200.
Fitheler, fiddler, b. 10. 92.
Fitte, *s.* a fitt or canto of a ballad, a. 1. 139. A.S. *fit, fitt,* a song, *fittan,* to sing, dispute.
Fiz, *s.* son, a. 8. 148; Fitz, 10. 311. O.F. *fiz,* Lat. *filius.* The *tz* is due to the old sound of O.F. *z* (*ts*).
Flamme, *s.* flame, blaze, 20. 205. See **Flaume.**
Flammeþ, *pr. s.* flames, 20. 191.
Flappes, *pl.* strokes, b. 13. 67.
Flapten, *pt. pl.* flapped, struck, 9. 180. Cf. O.F. *frapper;* Du. *flap,* a stroke, blow.
Flat, *adv.* flat, R. 2. 183.
Flateren, *v.* flatter, b. 20. 109; Flaterie, *v.* 23. 110.
Flaterere, flatterer, 12. 6, 23. 315, 325 ; Flaterers, *pl.* 22. 221.
Flaterynge, *v.* flattery, b. 13. 447 ; Flatrynge, 16. 77.
Flatte, *pt. s.* dashed, cast quickly, 8. 58. Cf. O.F. *flat,* a blow, *flatir,* to dash.
Flaumbe, *pr. s. subj. as fut.* it will exhale, spread a bad odour, b. 12. 255. See note, where I have made it transitive; but *folde* may be governed by *aboute;* thus it may mean—' it will exhale an ill scent all about the ground.' See note, p. 186.
Flaume, flame, 20. 172.

GLOSSARIAL INDEX. 357

Flaumed, *pt. s.* flamed, 20. 170; Flaumende, *pr. pl.* flaming, b. 17. 205; Flaumbeþ, *pr. s.* bursts into flame, b. 17. 225. See **Flammeþ**.
Flax, 9. 12. See **Flex**.
Flayles, *pl.* flails, b. 6. 187.
Fle, *v.* flee, a. 2. 185; fly, R. 3. 61.
Fleckede, *adj. pl.* spotted, speckled, 14. 138. Icel. *flekkr*, a spot.
Fleen, *v.* fly from, avoid, b. 17. 316; Fleo, *v.* fly, 15. 177, 23. 44; flee, a. 3. 134; Fleighe, *v.* flee, b. 20. 43; fly, b. 12. 241; Fleghyng, *pres. pt.* flying, b. 8. 54; Fleeþ, *pr. s.* flies, 15. 172; Flen, *pr. pl.* fly, 11. 230; Fleeth, *pr. pl.* b. 15. 273; Fleeghen, *pr. pl.* b. 9. 139; Fleo, 1 *pr. pl. subj.* flee, 21. 346; Fleigh, *pt. s.* fled, hurried, b. 17. 88; Flegh, fled, flew, hastened, 2. 119, 3. 220, 19. 121; Fleih, *pt. s.* fled, flew, hurried, 20. 57, 22. 103; Fleyh, *pt. s.* fled, 23. 169; Fleiȝ, *pt. s.* fled, b. 2. 210; Flowen, *pt. pl.* flew, escaped, fled, 3. 249, 9. 179, 20. 80; Fledden, *pt. pl.* 3. 249. This difficult verb is a result of the mixture of A.S. *fléon* (strong verb) with a weak verb answering to Icel. *flýja*.
Fleessh, flesh, body, 18. 195.
Fleeth, Flegh, Fleighe, Fleiȝ. See **Fleen**.
Fleiles, *s. pl.* flails, a. 7. 174.
Flekked, *adj.* spotted, b. 11. 321.
Flen, Fleo. See **Fleen**.
Flent, rock, 16. 268. See **Flynt**.
Flessh, flesh, a. 11. 212; natural desire, 2. 38, 4. 59; Of flessh = according to the flesh, 8. 144; Flesche, the flesh, b. 3. 55; Fleshes, *gen.* flesh's, 21. 204.
Flete, *v.* swim, float, 23. 45, b. 20. 44; Flet, *pr. s.* floats, is carried along, b. 12. 168. A.S. *fléotan*, to float, swim.
Fleyh, fled. See **Fleen**.
Flex, flax, b. 6. 13; Flax, 9. 12.
Flicche, flitch, 11. 277. See **Flucchen**. A.S. *flicce*.
Fliting, *s.* quarrelling, a. 8. 125. A.S. *flítan*, to chide.
Flittynge, *pres. pt.* moving away, removing himself, skulking, 13. 16. See **Flyttynge**.
Flober, 1 *pr. s.* dirty, soil, b. 14. 15. Cf. Beflobered; and see note to b. 14. 15, p. 204.
Flod, flood, overflow of a river, 6. 149; deluge, a. 10. 163; stream, b. 10. 295; Flodes, *pl.* floods, 9. 349.
Floreines, *pl.* florins, 4. 195; b. 2. 143.
Florissiþ, *pr. s.* makes to prosper, causes to flourish, preserves, 17. 133; Florissheth, b. 14. 294.
Floter, *v.* flutter, R. 2. 166.
Floured, *pt. s.* flowered, b. 16. 94.
Floures, *pl.* flowers, 14. 176.
Flouryng-tyme, time of flowering, 19. 35.
Flowen. See **Fleen**.
Flucchen, *s.* flitch of bacon, a. 10. 189. See **Flicche**. (The final *n* properly denotes the plural, but here represents the A.S. stem *fliccan*; cf. E. *bracken*.) Cf. Shropshire *flitchen*, a flitch of bacon, pl. *flitchens*.
Flus, fleece, 10. 270.
Flussh, *v.* fly about quickly, R. 2. 166. See Mätzner.
Flux, running, flow, 7. 161.
Flynt, flint, rock, 20. 210.
Flyttynge, *pr. pt.* moving away, removing himself, b. 11. 62.
Fo, foe, 6. 58; Fon, *pl.* foes, a. 5. 78; Foon, b. 5. 96.
Fobbes, *pl.* cheats, 3. 193. Such seems to be the meaning here; in the Prompt. Parv. we find, '*Foppe*, idem quod *Folet*; fatuellus, stolidus, follus.' Thus the lit. sense is fools, stupid fellows, dupes. Cf. '*Fub*, to put off, to deceive;' also '*Fobbed*, disappointed, *North*;' in Halliwell.
Fode, food, victuals, 1. 43, 2. 23.
Fode, *s.* person, being, R. 2. 169; Fodis, *pl.* lads, R. 3. 260. See **Foodis**; and numerous examples in Mätzner.
Fodith, *pr. s.* feedeth, R. 3. 52; Fodid, 2 *pt. pl.* didst nourish, R. 2. 135.
Fol, *s.* fool, 12. 6; b. 13. 444; Fole, b. 15. 3; Foles, *pl.* 1. 37; Folis, b. 10. 6. The expression *fol sage*, 8. 104, or *fool sage*, 8. 83, means a sage fool, or licensed jester. The note explains *fool sages* by 'foolish wise men,' but it would appear that it is *fol*, not *sage*, which was accounted as the sb. in this phrase; see **Sage**.
Folde, fold, enclosure, 2. 153; Foldes, *pl.* sheep-folds, 10. 259.
Folde, earth, ground, b. 12. 255; world, b. 7. 53. A.S. *folde*.
Folde, times, fold, b. 11. 249.
Folde, *v.* shut, close, 20. 154; shut, b. 17. 176.
Fole, foal, young, b. 11. 335.
Foleuyles, 22. 247; Foluyles, b. 19. 241. See the note, p. 269.
Folewe, *v.* follow, a. 3. 7; Folewen, *v.* try for, a. 10. 189; Foleweþ, *pr. s.* follows, attends, 16. 307.

GLOSSARIAL INDEX.

Folfulle, *v.* fulfil, do, a. 2. 54, a. 7. 38 ; Folfuld, *pp.* fulfilled, completed, a. 10. 163.
Folie, folly, 21. 236 ; Folye, 11. 183 ; Foly, b. 13. 148 ; Folyes, *pl.* b. 15. 74.
Foliliche, *adv.* foolishly, 17. 235.
Folk, people, 4. 247.
Foll, *adj.* full, complete, 20. 129.
Follen, *pr. pl.* are full, a. 11. 44.
Follouht, baptism, 18. 76. A.S. *fulluht, fulwiht,* baptism.
Follyng, *s.* baptism, 15. 207, 208.
Foltheed, *s.* folly, R. 2. 7. From *folet, folt,* dimin. of *fol.*
Folwen, *v.* follow, attend to, accompany, try for, 8. 295, 14. 213 ; Folwie, 3. 105, 12. 185 ; Folwy, *v.* follow, 7. 127 ; Folweþ, *pr. s.* 3. 34 ; Folwith, *pr. s.* R. 3. 40 ; Folweþ, *pr. pl.* incite, 11. 51 ; Folwen, *pr. pl.* follow, 20. 287, 22. 59 ; observe, 22. 33 ; attend to, 9. 213 ; Folwed, *pt. s.* acceded to, b. 11. 244 ; Folwyd, R. 2. 61 ; Folwynge, *pres. part.* following, coming after, 4. 495 ; next after, b. 16. 162 ; attending, 12. 173.
Folwer, follower, 8. 188 ; Folwar, b. 5. 549.
Fon, *s. pl.* foes, a. 5. 78. See **Fo.**
Fond, Fonde, found. See **Fynden.**
Fonde, *v.* try, endeavour, 23. 166 ; Fondeth, *pr. s.* 13. 104, 17. 45 ; tries, tempts, 15. 119 ; b. 12. 180 ; Fondede, *pt. s.* tried, proved, 19. 249 ; Fonded, *pt. s.* b. 16. 231 ; Fonded, 1 *pt. s.* endeavoured, b. 15. 327 ; Fondyd, 1 *pt. s.* R. pr. 50 ; Fonde, *imp. s.* endeavour, 16. 144, b. 6. 222. A.S. *fandian,* to seek, try to find ; from *fand,* pt. t. of *findan.*
Fondelynges, *pl.* foundlings, b. 9. 193. See **Foundlynges.**
Fondinge, *s.* temptation, 11. 42 ; Fondynge, b. 11. 391.
Fonge, *v.* take, accept, 8. 201, a. 6. 48 ; grasp, seize, 10. 91 ; receive, 17. 7 ; Fonge, 1 *pr. s.* receive, 16. 202 ; Fongen, *pr. pl.* receive, a. 3. 66. Cf. A.S. *fón,* pt. t. *féng,* pp. *fangen,* to receive. See **Fange.**
Fonk, spark, 7. 335. Dan. *funke.*
Font, 1 *p. s. pt.* found, a. pr. 55.
Foo, foe, enemy, 13. 14 ; Foos, *pl.* 7. 72.
Foodis, *pl.* lads, R. 3. 126. See **Fode.**
Fool, fool, b. 11. 68 ; Fooles, *pl.* a. 10. 58, 64 ; (ironically), 23. 61, 62 ; Fool sage, licensed jester, 8. 83. See **Fol.**
Foormere, *s.* creator, a. 10. 28.
For, *prep.* for fear of, to prevent, against, 3. 240, 9. 8, b. 1. 24, b. 3. 190, b. 6. 9 ; b. 16. 25 ; to keep off, a. 7. 15 ; in spite of, 3. 211, 216 ; 7. 35 ; by, for the sake of, 2. 54 ; as, 20. 238 ; As for = as was proper for, as being, b. 13. 33. See **Fore.**
For, *conj.* because, 1. 116, 4. 412, 11. 234, 15. 133 ; in order that, 14. 165, a. 6. 14, R. pr. 14.
Forbede, *v.* forbid, R. 3. 241 ; Forbede, 1 *pr. s.* R. 3. 277 ; Forbede, *pr. s. subj.* 4. 148, 156 ; Forbeode, *pr. s. subj.* a. 3. 107 ; For-badde, *pt. s.* has forbidden, b. 10. 204 ; For-boden, *pp.* 4. 189 ; For-bodene, *pp. pl.* a. 3. 147 ; For-bode, *pp.* b. 3. 151. In the last two instances *forbode lawes* (or *forbodene lawes*) is incorrectly used to mean 'laws that forbid it.'
For-bere, *v.* forbear to wear, go without, 2. 99 ; spare, afford, b. 11. 204 ; For-bar, *pt. s.* spared, forbore (to kill), 4. 430.
Forbete, *v.* beat thoroughly, 21. 33 ; beat down, b. 18. 35 ; Forbeten, *pp.* enfeebled, b. 20. 197.
Forbiteth, *pr. s.* eats away, b. 16. 35 ; For-bit, 19. 39.
For-bode, *s.* forbidding ; Godes forbode = may it be the forbidding of God, i.e. God forbid, 4. 138 ; Goddes forbode elles = it is God's prohibition that it should be otherwise, b. 15. 570 ; Lordes forbode = it is the Lord's forbidding, i. e. the Lord forbid, 10. 327. Cf. b. 4. 194, b. 7. 176. Palsgrave (p. 548) has : 'I fende to Goddes forbode it shulde be so, *a Dieu ne playse quaynsi il aduiengne.*' A.S. *forbod,* prohibition.
For-brenne, *v.* utterly burn, burn up, 4. 125 ; Forbrende, *pt. s.* utterly burnt, 4. 107.
Forbusne (*better* Forbusen), pattern, example, 18. 277 ; Forbusene, *dat.* parable, 11. 32 ; Forbysene, example, b. 15. 555. A.S. *forebysn.*
Forceres, *pl.* caskets, b. 10. 211. ' *Forchier, Forcier, Forsier,* cassette, écrin, coffre-fort ; en bas Latin, *forsarius* ;' Roquefort.
Forckis, *s. pl.* gallows, R. 1. 108.
Forde, ford, 8. 214, R. 2. 171.
For-don, *v.* destroy, 21. 41, b. 5. 20, a. 5. 20 ; For-do, *v.* 6. 123, 21. 28, 162 ; For-doþ, *pr. s.* undoes, destroys, 20. 253, 261 ; b. 18. 152 ; unmakes, b. 17. 271 ; *pr. pl.* destroy, spoil, clip, R. 3. 141 ; For-dude, *pt. s.* destroyed, 21. 393 ; Fordid, *pt. s.* b. 16. 166 ; Fordo, *pp.* 16. 231, b. 13. 260. A.S. *fordón.*

GLOSSARIAL INDEX. 359

Fore bledde, bled for, b. 19. 103. See **For.**
Forebisene, s. example, similitude, parable, a. 9. 24. See **Forbusne.**
Foreioures, pl. messengers, foragers, b. 20. 80. '*Fourrier,* an harbinger;' Cotgrave. See **Foreyours.**
Forel, chest, box, 16. 103; Forellis, pl. caskets, boxes, a. 11. 156. See note, p. 154; and Prompt. Parv. p. 171, note 2.
Fore-sleuys, s. pl. fore-sleeves, fronts of the sleeves, a. 5. 64.
Foreward, s. agreement, promise, a. 4. 13, a. 7. 38. See **Forward.** A.S. *foreweard.*
Foreward, adv. first, to begin with, foremost, a. 10. 127.
Foreynes, pl. adj. as sb. strangers, 10. 199.
Foreyours, pl. foragers, 23. 81.
For-fadres, pl. forefathers, ancestors, 8. 134, 11. 234.
Forfaiteth, pr. s. offends, b. 20. 25. See **Forfeteþ.**
For-fare, v. perish, 9, 234; Forfaren, pr. pl. are ruined, fare ill, b. 15. 131. A.S. *forfaran.*
Forfet, s. forfeit, a. 4. 114.
Forfeteþ, pr. s. fails, 23. 25.
Forfeture, forfeiture, 5. 128.
Forfreteþ, pr. s. eats away, 19. 33; Forfret, pr. s. nips, b. 16. 29.
For-glotten, pr. pl. waste in gluttony, devour, swallow, 12. 66.
Forgoere, guide, fore-goer, avauntcourier, harbinger, 3. 198; Forgoers, pl. 3. 61; Forgoeres, b. 2. 60. A *foregoer* or *harbinger* was a man sent on in front of a lord in his progress, to provide lodgings and provisions for him and his followers.
Forlang, furrow, 8. 32. See **Furlong.**
For-leyen, pp. lain with wrongfully, 5. 46.
Formalich, adv. in proper manner, correctly, b. 15. 367; Formeliche, 18. 109.
Formen, v. make, form, b. 11. 380; Formed, pt. s. persuaded, R. 1. 107; Formed, pt. pl. informed, R. 4. 58. (In R. it is short for *informed.*)
Formest, adv. at the first, first, first of all, 2. 73, 7. 15, 18. 59.
Formour, creator, maker, 2. 14, 11. 152; Former, 20. 133.
Fornicatores, pl. fornicators, b. 2. 180. (A Latin form.)
For-pyned, pp. pinched with hunger, famished, wretched, b. 6. 157. Cf. Chaucer, Prol. 205.

Forred, furred, b. 20. 175; a. 7. 256; pl. 9. 292.
For-sake, v. deny, 16. 140; 1 pr. s. 8. 37; For-sakeþ, pr. s. denies, rejects, 18. 81; Forsaketh, 2 pr. pl. refuse, b. 15. 82; Forsoke, pt. s. 21. 202, 23. 231; For-soken, pt. pl. forsook, gave up, 23. 38; For-sake, pp. forsaken, 14. 226.
Forse, matter, consequence; No forse = it matters not, 15. 10.
Forshapte, pt. s. unmade, b. 17. 288.
For-shupte, pt. s. mis-created, 20. 270.
For-sleuthed, pp. wasted by carelessness, spoilt, 8. 52.
Forst, frost, 13. 192; Forstes, pl. 13. 188.
For-stalleþ, pr. s. forestalls, 5. 59. See note, p. 55.
For-swore, pp. forsworn, perjured, 22. 372; Forsworen, b. 19. 367.
Forte, for to, in order to, to, a. 1. 173. a. 2. 4; Forto, b. 10. 145.
Forte, conj. until, a. 11. 119; Forte þat, until, a. 7. 2.
For-teþ, pl. fore-teeth, front-teeth, 21. 386.
Forþ, adv. forth, 22. 153; throughout, 4. 107, 21. 335; henceforth, b. 10. 438; finally, b. 13. 209; further, R. pr. 55.
Forth, s. (1) ford, b. 5. 576; (2) course, free course, 4. 195.
Forþere, adv. further, hence, 9. 76, 11. 11; a. 6. 121 (*understand* go); Forther, b. 8. 11.
For-þi, conj. therefore, 1. 118, 13. 119, 19. 269, 20. 224; wherefore, 6. 82. A.S. *for þý.*
For-þynkeþ, impers. pr. s. (it) repents, 11. 252, 21. 92.
For-walked, pp. tired out with walking, b. 13. 204.
Forwandred, pp. tired out with wandering, b. pr. 7.
Forward, s. agreement, bargain, b. 6. 36, b. 11. 63. See Foreward, which is a better spelling.
Forwe, furrow, 7. 268; the width of a furrow, b. 13. 372; Forwes, pl. 9. 65, b. 6. 106.
Forweny, v. spoil by indulgence (lit. for-wean), b. 5. 35; Forwene, v. 6. 138; Forweyned, pp. pampered, R. 1. 27. See note, p. 66.
For-why, conj. wherefore, b. 13. 281.
Forwit, s. forewit, forethought, foreknowledge, b. 5. 166.
Forȝelde, pr. s. subj. repay, requite, 9. 299, b. 6. 279, b. 13. 188.

For-ȝete, v. forget, 23. 155; For-ȝuten, v. 20. 208; For-ȝat, 1 pt. s. 13. 13, b. 11. 59; Forȝeten, pp. b. 17. 331; For-ȝute, pp. forgotten, 8. 47, 20. 313.
For-ȝiue, v. forgive, a. 3. 8; Forȝeuen, v. 20. 208; For-ȝaf, pt. s. gave freely, granted, 21. 79; Forȝeuen, pp. forgiven, b. 17. 331; Forȝiue, b. 17. 287.
For-ȝyuenesse, forgiveness, 20. 209, 22. 184.
Fostren, pr. pl. (with prep. forth), support, produce, 20. 172, 175; b. 17. 207; Fostrith, pr. s. cherishes, R. 3. 52; Fostrid, 2 pt. pl. as sing. didst cherish, R. 2. 135.
Fot, foot, 20. 54; A fot, a-foot, 8. 286; Fot londe = a foot of land, 7. 268; Fote, foot, 2. 119; support, basis, b. 16. 245.
Foul, s. fowl, bird, 12. 103; Foules, birds, 7. 406; Fouweles, 18. 11. See Fowel.
Foule, adj. foul, sinful, wicked, a. 5. 230; miserable, low, 22. 33; ill-gotten, 4. 372.
Foule, adv. shamefully, foully, 3. 43, 4. 232; wickedly, b. 10. 472; rudely, 21. 353, b. 3. 185; ill, R. 2. 150.
Fouler, adj. comp. dirtier, b. 13. 320.
Foulest, adv. in the most foul manner, b. 12. 238.
Fouleþ, pr. s. destroys, spoils, 10. 268; reviles, b. 3. 153, a. 3. 149; Fouleþ, pr. pl. foul, make foul, defile, 22. 315; Fouleden, pt. pl. subj. should defile, a. 7. 137.
Foully, adv. shamefully, 21. 96.
Foulyd, pt. s. went a-fowling, R. 2. 157. See Foul.
Foundede, pt. s. founded, set on foot, a. 1. 62; Founded, 1 pt. s. founded, b. 10. 215.
Foundement, foundation, 4. 347, 17. 42, 22. 327.
Foundlynges, s. pl. foundlings, 11. 298.
Foundours, s. pl. founders, a. 11. 213.
Fount, font, 13. 52.
Fourlonge, furlong, b. 5. 5, 424. See Forlang.
Fourmen, v. form, prepare, a. 8. 39. Fourmed, pt. s. formed, created, b. 1. 14.
Fourmour, former, creator, b. 9. 27. See Formour.
Fowche-saue, 2 pr. s. subj. vouchsafe, deign, 19. 18.
Fowel, fowl, bird, 15. 171; Fowle, R. 3. 36. See Foul.
Foyne, s. marten, R. 3. 150. 'Fouine,

Fouinne, the Foine, wood-martin, or beech-martin;' Cotgrave.
Frainede, 1 pt. s. asked, enquired, 11. 3; Frained, b. 1. 58; Fraynede, 2. 54, 19. 292, 21. 16; Frayned, b. 5. 532, b. 8. 3; Fraynide, a. 9. 3; Fraynede, pt. s. a. 6. 6; Frayned, 8. 170. A.S. frignan.
Fram, from, 8. 106, 16. 237.
Frankelayne, franklin, freeholder, 11. 240; Frankelayns, pl. 22. 39; Frankelens, 6. 64.
Fraternite, s. brotherhood, society, esp. religious brotherhood. 10. 343, 13. 9, 23. 367.
Fraunchise, freedom, 21. 108.
Fraunchised, pp. enfranchised, made freemen, 4. 114.
Frayel, basket; Freyel, b. 13. 94. See note, p. 194.
Frayned. See Frainede.
Fre, adj. free, 2. 73; freeborn, 22. 33; generous, bountiful, charitable, b. 10. 74; Free, charitable, 12. 57. See Freo. See note to 3. 81, p. 34.
Freek, s. man, 16. 80, 19. 186.
Freel, adj. frail, fickle, 4. 158.
Freese, pr. s. subj. freezes, 13. 192. See Freseþ.
Freik, man, a. 7. 207; Freike, fellow, a. 4. 13. See Freek, Frek.
Freitour, refectory, 6. 174; Freitoure, b. 10. 323. O.F. refretoir (Roquefort); Low. Lat. refectorium. The loss of re- was probably due to confusion with frater. See note, p. 70.
Frek, man, creature, fellow, 10. 153, 12. 159, 16. 2; Freke, b. 4. 12, 156; Frekus, pl. fellows, 7. 152. A.S. freca, one who is bold, a hero. See Freek, Freik.
Frele, adj. frail, fickle, liable to err, 11. 48, b. 3. 121. See Freel.
Frelete, frailty, 4. 59, 20. 312.
Fremde, pl. strangers, not of kin, 13. 155; Fremmed, s. a stranger, b. 15. 137. A.S. fremede, fremde, strange.
Frendloker, adv. in a more friendly manner, a. 11. 171.
Frenesse, liberality, grace, b. 16. 88.
Frenesyes, pl. frenzies, fits of madness, 23. 85, b. 20. 84.
Frentik, adj. mad, 12. 6, 19. 179; silly, a. 11. 6.
Freo, adj. free, 20. 120, 21. 108.
Freonde, friend, 22. 145.
Frere, friar, 4. 38, 11. 18; Frere, gen. of a friar, 10. 208; Freres, gen. friar's, b. 5. 81; Freres, pl. 11. 8, b. 2. 182; Frerus, 1. 56; Freris, b. pr. 58. O.F. frere.
Freseþ, pr. s. freezes, a. 8. 115; Fre-

GLOSSARIAL INDEX. 361

singe, *pr. pt.* freezing, R. 2. 127;
Freese, *pr. s. subj.* 13. 192.
Frete, *v.* eat, devour, 3. 100, b. 2. 95;
1 *pr. s.* I fret, vex, b. 13. 330; Fret,
pt. s. ate, 21. 202 ; Frette, *pt. s.* b. 18.
194; Freted, *pt. s.* R. 2. 127. A.S.
fretan, pt. t. *frǣt.*
Fretted, *pp.* adorned, b. 2. 11; Frettet,
a. 2. 11 ; provided, a. 6. 71. A.S.
frǣtwian, to adorn; *frǣtu,* an ornament.
Fretynge, *pres. pt. as adj.* destructive,
21. 158. See **Frete.**
Freyel, basket, b. 13. 94. See **Frayel.**
Frist, *adj. superl.* first, R. 1. 107, R. 2.
99, R. 3. 56 ; *adv.* first, at first, R. 1.
73, R. 4. 33.
Fritth, forest, wood, plantation, 15.
159; b. 17, 112 ; Frithe, R. 2. 171 ;
Fritthe, b. 11. 356. W. *fridd* is
prob. borrowed from Middle English
frith, which was probably orig. the
same word as A.S. *frið,* peace (hence,
a protected or enclosed space). See
Mätzner. See **Fryth.**
Friped, *pp.* enclosed, 8. 228 ; b. 5. 590.
See above.
Fro, *prep.* from, 1. 54 ; off, 1. 114 ;
Froo, from, 4. 146.
Froo, *prep.* from, 4. 146. See **Fro.**
Frounces, *pl.* wrinkles, folds, b. 13.
318. O.F. *fronce,* from *froncer,* verb.
Frut, fruit, 21. 18, 32 ; children, 11.
274 ; Frute, R. pr. 58 ; Fruit, a. 10.
186; Frutes, *pl.* 9. 349.
Fryth, wood, plantation, b. 12. 219, R.
2. 180. See **Fritth.**
Fuir, *s.* fire, a. 3. 88 ; Fuire, b. 12. 283.
See **Fur.**
Ful, *adj.* full, very, a. 3. 157.
Ful, *adv.* very, 1. 22, b. pr. 20.
Ful, Fullen, fell. See **Fallen.**
Fulfulleþ, *pr. s.* fulfils, 17. 27 ; Fulfild,
pp. 22. 80.
Fulle, full ; To the fulle = to their
satisfaction, b. 14. 178.
Fulle, *s.* fill, b. 6. 266.
Fulle, *v.* fill, a. 5. 184 ; Fulle, *pr. pl.
subj.* 4. 88.
Fulled, *pp.* fulled, cleansed, b. 15. 445 ;
pt. s. baptised, b. 15. 440. A.S.
fullian. See note, p. 229.
Fullyng, *s.* baptism, 22. 39 ; Fullynge,
b. 15. 443. See **Fulled.**
Fullyng-stokkes, *pl.* fulling-frames, b.
15. 445.
Fur, fire, 4. 96, 102, 125 ; Fure, 10.
182. A.S. *fýr.*
Furre, *adv. comp.* further, a. 9. 11, a.
10. 96.

Furst, *s.* thirst, a. 5. 218.
Furst, *adv.* first, 2. 60, 7. 209.
Furste, *adj.* first, 11. 144 ; Furste, *pl.*
chief, first (men), 10. 250.
Fursteþ ; Me fursteþ = I am thirsty, 21.
411. See **Furst,** *sb.*
Furthe, *ord. adj.* fourth, 10. 56.
Fust, fist, 7. 66, 20. 112.
Fust-wyse, *adv.* ; A fust-wyse = in the
form of a fist, 20. 150.
Fuyr, fire, 4. 91, 7. 335, 10. 56; Fuy-
res, *gen.* of fire, 22. 205. See **Fuir,
Fur.**
Fybicches, *pl.* contrivances (?), b. 10.
211. See **Febicchis** ; and note.
Fyble, *adj.* feeble, weak, 17. 68.
Fyfte, *adj.* fifth, 14. 298, b. 11. 46.
Still pron. *fift* in Shropshire.
Fygys, *pl.* figs, 3. 29.
Fykel, *adj.* fickle, false, 3. 25, 7. 72 ;
deceitful, 12. 22. See **Fikel.**
Fyn, *adj.* fine, good, 20. 83 ; clever,
subtle, 12. 159.
Fyn, *s.* fin, b. 20. 44 ; Fynnes, *pl.* 23.
45.
Fyn, *s.* fine, fee, a. 2. 38, 51.
Fynden, *v.* find, b. 7. 30 ; provide,
provide for, b. 9. 67, b. 15. 564, a. 2.
53. a. 7. 64; support, a. 10. 70;
Fynde, *v.* 8. 32, a. 8. 96 ; procure, a.
8. 33 ; provide for, 4. 379 ; To fynde
with hym selue = to find (food) for
himself with, 11. 181 ; Fynde, 1 *pr. s.*
provide, find (in), b. 13. 240 ; Fyndeþ,
pr. s. supports, maintains, 22. 447 ;
Fynt, *pr. s.* (*for* Fyndeth), finds, 5.
128, 20. 312 ; Fynt men = people find,
b. 15. 273 ; Fynt, provides for, 17.
316, b. 19. 442 ; supplies, 6. 88 ;
feeds, b. 15. 174 ; Fynden, 2 *pr. pl.*
find, see, 4. 59 ; Fond, 1 *pt. s.* I found,
12. 275 ; found, met, 1. 56 ; Fonde,
1 *pt. s.* 1. 19, b. 11. 62 ; Fond, *pt. s.*
found, discovered, 2. 60 ; chose, 14.
109 ; provided for, 23. 295 ; Fonde,
pt. s. found, b. 13. 94; chose, b. 11.
186 ; Fonde, 1 *pt. s. subj.* if I found,
b. 13. 252 ; Founde, if I found, were
I to discover, 16. 219 ; Founden, *pt.
pl.* provided for, found the money for,
6. 36 ; invented (for themselves), a.
pr. 36 ; Fonde, *pr. pl. subj.* if they
found, b. 15. 306 ; Fonde, 2 *pl. pt.*
found, experienced, R. 2. 61.
Fyndynge, *s.* support, living, maintenance, 7. 293 ; provision, 23. 283.
Fyne, *adj.* subtle, b. 10. 247. See **Fyn.**
Fynkelsede, fennel-seed, 7. 360. Lat.
fœniculum.
Fynys, *s. pl.* fines, R. 4. 4.

GLOSSARIAL INDEX.

Fyr, *s.* fire, b. 10. 411; Fyre, b. 14. 42. See **Fur, Fuir.**
Fysch, fish, 9. 334.
Fysshed, *pt. s.* fished, 18. 19.
Fysyk, medicine, 9. 268, 294; a physician (lit. Physic), 9. 292.
Fysyke, *pr. s. subj.* administer physic to, 23. 323.
Fythelen, *v.* play the fiddle, b. 13. 231. See **Fiþelen.**
Fyue, *num.* five, 10. 343.
Fyȝte, *s.* fight, contest, b. 15. 159.

Gabbe, *v.* lie, 4. 226, b. 3. 179; Gabben, *pr. pl.* 18. 16. Icel. *gabba,* to delude, mock.
Gabbynge, *s.* lying, 22. 456; deceit, 18. 129, b. 19. 451.
Gable, gable-end of a church, b. 3. 49.
Gadelyng, vagabond, 23. 157; Gadelynges, *pl.* 11. 297; associates, fellows, men, b. 4. 51. A.S. *gædeling,* a companion. See **Gedelynge.**
Gadereþ, *pr. s.* collects (money), 23. 368; Gaderen, *pr. pl.* heap up (wealth), b. 12. 53; Gaderede, *pt. s.* gathered, 23. 113.
Gaf. See **Gyue.**
Gaglide, *pt. pl.* cackled, R. 3. 101.
Gailer, gaoler, 4. 175.
Galle, *s.* gall, bile, anger, b. 5. 119, a. 5. 99; malice, b. 16. 155.
Galoches, *pl.* shoes, 21. 12. See note.
Galon, gallon, 7. 230; Galoun, b. 5. 224; Galoun ale = gallon of ale, b. 5. 343.
Galpen, *v.* yawn, b. 13. 88; Galpe, 16. 97. See Chaucer, Sq. Tale, 350, 354.
Gamen, play, b. pr. 153; Gamus, *pl.* games, a. 11. 37. A.S. *gamen,* a game.
Gan, *pt. s.* did (*used as a mere auxiliary verb*), 20. 61; 1 *pt. s.* b. 10. 142; Gan, 1 *pt. pl.* did, 11. 114. See **Ginneþ.**
Gangen, *v.* go, depart, 19. 178; Gange, b. 2, 167; Gangen, *pr. pl.* go, walk, 17. 14; Gange, b. 14. 161. A.S. *gangan, gán.*
Garlaunde, garland, crown, 21. 48.
Garlek-mongere, garlick-dealer, 7. 373.
Garlesschire, *pr. n.* Garlick-shire, i.e. Garlickhithe, a. 5. 167.
Garlik, garlick, 7. 359.
Garnement, garment, dress, 10. 119, b. 13. 400; Garnemens, *pl.* clothes, 21. 179.
Gart, 1 *pt. s.* caused, 12. 123; Garte, 1 *pt. s.* b. 10. 175; Gart, *pt. s.* caused,

made, 6. 147, b. 20. 130; *pt. s.* b. 1. 121. Icel. *göra,* Swed. *göra,* Dan. *gjöre,* to cause. See **Gerte.**
Gaste, *v.* frighten, chase, drive, a. 7. 129. Cf. E. *a-ghast.*
Gat, *pt. s.* begat, b. 1. 33.
Gate, *s.* way, road, 14. 91, 23. 341, b. 1. 203; course, going, walking, 21. 253; Gat, way, road, 20. 44; Heiȝe gate = high road, b. 4. 42;' Graith gate = direct road or way, b. 1. 203; Gates, *gen.* way; ȝoure gates = your way, in the same direction as you take, a. 12. 88.
Gate-ward, porter, gate-keeper, 8. 243, b. 5. 604.
Gayenesse, pleasure, merriment, 12. 66; Gaynesse, b. 10. 81.
Gayes, *s. pl.* gay clothes, ornaments, R. 2. 94. See note.
Gazafilacium, the treasury, b. 13. 197. Gk. γαζαφυλάκιον.
Geauntes, *pl.* giants, 23. 215.
Gedelynge, vagabond, b. 9. 103; Gedelynges, *pl.* b. 9. 192. See **Gadelyng.**
Gederide, *pt. s.* gathered, 19. 112.
Geeten, *pt. pl.* begat, a. 10. 155.
Gemensye, *s.* geomancy, a. 11. 153. See note, p. 155.
Gemetrie, *s.* geometry, a. 11. 153.
Gendrynge, *s.* begetting, 14. 144.
Genere, the nature (abl. of Lat. *genus*), b. 14. 181.
Gent. *adj.* noble, nobly-born, a. 2. 101. O.F. *gent,* from Lat. *genitus,* i.e. well-born.
Gentel-men, free men, 22. 34, 40.
Gentil, *adj.* noble, 6. 78, 22, 265; of noble family, b. 11. 240; Gentel, noble, free, gentle, 2. 182, 13. 110; patient, b. 10. 23. See **Ientel.**
Gentrice, noble birth, b. 18. 22; humanity, b. 14. 181; Gentrise, noble nature, 21. 21. O.F. *genterise,* later form of *gentilise,* sb.; from *gentil,* adj.
Geomesye, geomancy, b. 10. 208. See **Gemensye.**
Gerdel, *s.* girdle, b. 15. 120.
Gerelande, garland, b. 18. 48.
Gerles, *pl.* children, 2. 29; Gerlis, b. 1. 33. The term is applicable to either sex; note, p. 21. See **Gurles.**
Gerner, *s.* garner, barn. a. 8. 116; Gernere, b. 7. 129.
Gerte, *pt. s.* caused, 9. 325; made, 23. 131; Gert, 23. 57; Gert, *pp.* b. 5. 130. See **Gart.**
Gerthes, *pl.* girths; Witty wordes

GLOSSARIAL INDEX. 363

girthes = the girths of wise speech, b. 4. 20; Gurþes, a. 4. 19.
Gery, *adj.* changeful, R. 3. 130. See Chaucer; and Dyce's Skelton, ii. 206. Cf. Lat. *gyrus.*
Gesen, *adj.* scarce, rare, b. 13. 271. A.S. *gǽsne;* see note.
Geste, guest, companion, b. 15. 280.
Geste, story, account, 8. 107; Gestes, *pl.* stories, romances, history, 12. 23, 16. 205; Ieestes, a. 11. 23. O.F. *geste,* Lat. neut. pl. *gesta.*
Geten, *v.* gain, receive, 21. 12; recover, 8. 269; Gete, *v.* get, obtain, find, 8. 291, 12. 85; Get, *pr. s.* gets, a. 7. 238; Gete, *pr. for fut. pl.* ye will obtain, ye will gain, b. 9. 176; Gete, 2 *pt. s.* didst gain, didst get, 21. 315, 380; Gat, *pt. s.* begat, b. 1. 33; 1 *pt. s.* got, b. 4. 79; Geten, *pt. pl.* begat, 23. 157; Gete, *pp.* got, gained, 17. 278; begotten, 11. 297, 22. 121; Igeten, *pp.* a. 10. 204.
Geþ, *pr. s.* goeth, goes, a. 5. 157.
Geueþ, *pr. pl.* give; Geueþ no3t of = care not for, 5. 37.
Gie, *v.* guide, rule, R. 3. 283.
Gile, deceit, fraud, 22. 456.
Gille, *s.* gill, a quarter of a pint, a. 5. 191. See Gylle, Iille.
Gilour, *s.* deceiver, a. 2. 89.
Ginful, *adj.* treacherous, guileful, b. 10. 208. From *gin,* sb. a snare; see Gyn.
Ginneþ, *pr. s.* begins, a. 5. 146; Gynneth, *pr. pl.* begin, b. 10. 109; Gynne, *pr. s. subj.* begin, 15. 24, b. 17. 222; Gon, 1 *pt. s.* began, a. 11. 131; did, a. pr. 11; *pt. s.* did, a. 1. 147; Gonne, 2 *pt. s.* begannest, didst begin, b. 5. 488; Gonne, *pt. pl.* did, 1. 145; began, 7. 398; Gunne, *pt. pl.* began, did, a. 7. 140. A.S. *ginnan.* See Gan.
Gioure, *sb.* guide, leader, R. pr. 29. See Gyen.
Girt, 1 *pt. s.* cast, threw, b. 5. 379. Properly pt. t. of *girden, gurden,* to strike. See Gurd.
Gistes, *pl.* guests, 16. 199.
Giterne, guitar, gittern, 16. 208.
Gladen, *v.* gladden, cheer, delight, 10. 300; Glade, *v.* b. 6. 121; Gladie, *v.* 21. 179; Glade, *v.* rejoice, be cheered, R. pr. 40; Glade, 2 *pr. pl.* please, a. 10. 195; Gladeþ, *pr. pl.* cheer, 20. 183; Gladieth, *pr. pl.* b. 17. 217; Glade, *pr. s. subj.* make glad, a. 6. 25.
Glase, *v.* glaze, find the cost of glazing, furnish with glass, 4. 52, 65; Glasen, *v.* b. 3. 61.
Glasene, made of glass, 23. 172.
Gle, *s.* glee, singing, a. pr. 34; Glees, *pl.* joys, R. 3. 278.
Glede, live coal, glowing coal, spark, 20. 189, 197; Gledes, *pl.* 20. 183. A S. *gléd;* from *glówan.*
Gleo-man, glee-man, minstrel, 12. 104; Gleo-mon, a. 11. 110; Gleomonnes, *gen.* minstrel's, a. 5. 197.
Globbares, *pl.* gluttons, b. 9. 60.
Glose, gloss, commentary, comment, explanation, 11. 242, 20. 15, b. 5. 282. O.F. *glose,* L. *glossa,* Gk. γλῶσσα.
Gloseþ, *pr. s.* explains, comments, 14. 120; expresses, gives meaning to, b. 11. 299; flatters, deceives, 23. 368; Glosynge, *pres. part.* explaining, 1. 58; Glosinge, deceiving, R. 4. 38; Glosed, *pt. pl.* commented on, made glosses on, b. pr. 60; Glosed, *pp.* glossed, commented on, 7. 303; Glosede, *pp. pl.* explained, 20. 13.
Glosers, *pl.* deceivers, 22. 221.
Glosyng, *adj.* flattering, 5. 137.
Glosynge, *s.* interpreting falsely, glossing over, b. 13. 74; flattery, 7. 259; Glosynges, *pl.* deceits, 23. 125. See Glose.
Gloton, glutton, 7. 350, 9. 325; Glotoun, b. 6. 303; Glotown, b. 5. 310; Glotones, *pl.* 1. 74. b. pr. 76.
Glotonye, gluttony, b. 10. 81, a. 2. 67; Glotonie, b. 14, 229.
Gnedy, *adj.* miserly, niggardly, sparing, 16. 86. See *gnede* in Havelok, 97. A.S. *gnéað, gnéð,* sparing, stingy.
Go, *v.* walk, R. 2. 115; depart, R. 3. 223; Go at large = walk about freely, 23. 192; Goo, *v.* proceed, a. 2. 125; Go slepe = go and sleep, b. 6. 303; Go swynke = go and work, b. 6. 219; Go me to = let one go to, let one examine (where *me* = man, one), b. 10. 192; Go gyle aʒeine gyle = let guile be opposed to guile, b. 18. 355; Go ich = whether I go, 12. 200; Go, *pp.* gone, 21. 330.
Gobet, morsel, small portion, 6. 100. Lit. 'mouthful.'
God-children, children spiritually, b. 9. 74, b. 10. 325.
Gode, *adj.* good, happy, 1. 29; *pl.* 22. 197; Goed, b. 10. 292.
Gode, *s.* kindness, b. 8. 93; To gode = to good conduct, b. 3. 222.
Gode, *s.* goods, property, wealth, b. 2. 131; Goed, b. 1. 180; Godes, *pl.*

VOL. II. Z

GLOSSARIAL INDEX.

wealth, 11. 45, b. 15. 141; Godis, *pl.* goods, b. 8. 40, b. 10. 30.
Godelen, *v.* rumble, 16. 97; Godele, b. 13. 88; Godely, 7. 398. See Gopelen; and note, p. 92.
Godeliche, *adv.* religiously, truly, b. 11. 272; Godelich, kindly, liberally, b. 1. 180; Goodliche, 2. 179.
God-man, He who was God and Man, 13, 113, b. 11. 200.
Godspel, gospel, 1. 58, 11. 235.
Godsyb, gossip, friend, 7. 357; Godsybbes, *pl.* 7. 47.
Goky, *s.* fool, stupid fellow, 14. 120, 121; b. 11. 299. Mod. E. *gawky.*
Goliardeys, *s.* a buffoon, b. pr. 139. See note, p. 15.
Gome, man, creature, person, 8. 179, 11. 215, 14. 199, 17. 97, 22. 121; Gom, *s.* a man, a. 12. 69 *n*; Gome, *gen. sing.* man's, 21. 330 (A.S. *guman,* gen. of *guma,* man); Gomes, *pl.* men, 11. 235, 17. 344; Gomes, *pl. gen.* men's, R. 3. 171. A.S. *guma,* Lat. *homo.*
Gome, *s.* notice, heed, 20. 14. Icel. *gaumr,* heed.
Gommes, gums, kinds of gum (used generally for spices), 3. 236.
Gon, *v.* move, go, walk, 20. 245, b. 2. 154; *pr. pl.* b. pr. 43, b. 7. 94; Gone, *pr. pl.* b. 3. 244; go about, b. 11. 269; go, are spent, b. 15. 141; Gon, *pp.* gone, past, 21. 298; Goth, *pr. s.* goes, b. 5. 314; Goþ mor = is spent over and above, 20. 75; Goth, *pr. pl.* go, 1. 44.
Gon, Gonne. See **Ginneþ.**
Gonnes, *pl.* guns, 21. 293.
Good, *s.* goods, property, money, wealth, 2. 179, 7. 275; Goodes, *pl.* 7. 284.
Good, *adv.* well; Good likeþ = best pleases (them), a. pr. 57.
Goodmen, *s. pl.* men of substance, R. 1. 66.
Goost, spirit, soul, b. 9. 45.
Gorge, *s.* throat, 12. 41.
Gose, *gen. sing.* goose's, b. 4. 36; Gees, *pl.* 5. 49, 6. 19.
Gossip, *s.* gossip, neighbour, friend, a. 5. 154; Gossib, b. 5. 310.
Gost, spirit, 2. 34, 7. 175; mind, R. pr. 85; Goste, soul, b. 1. 36; spirit, b. 10. 236, 391; life, b. 15. 141; Gostis, *pl.* spirits, i.e. men, R. 1. 25.
Gothely, *v.* rumble, b. 5. 347. Cf. Icel. *gutla,* to gurgle. See **Godelen.**
Gottes, *pl.* guts, 16. 97; Gottus, bellies, a, 11. 44. See **Gut.**
Gouernance, *s.* government, R. 3. 250;
behaviour, R. 3. 223; Gouernance of gettinge = mode of getting money, by imposing moderate taxes, R. 3. 242.
Goune, gown, 17. 298; Gounes, *pl.* 16. 202.
Goutes, attacks of gout, 23. 192.
Gowe, let us go; Gowe dyne = let us go and dine, 1. 227; let us go (to examine), 18. 111.
Gowel, Go-well, 11. 147.
Goynge, *s.* manner, gait, 21. 328; Longe goynge = long departure, long journey, i. e. death upon the gallows, R. 3. 136.
Grace, favour, R. 3. 242; Of grace = as a favour, b. 12. 114; Graces, *pl.* graces (after meat), 16. 266.
Gradde. See **Greden.**
Graffe, *s.* graft, engrafting, 2. 201.
Graffe, *v.* to graft, b. 5. 137.
Graith, *adj.* direct, b. 1. 203. Icel. *greiðr,* ready; cf. G. *gerade,* direct. See **Grayþ;** and note, p. 30.
Grame, *v.* be sorry, be vexed, R. pr. 41. A.S. *gramian.*
Gramercy, many thanks, b. 17. 85. F. *grand merci.*
Gras, healing herb, 15. 23.
Graue, *v.* engrave, have inscribed, 4. 52 (in allusion to the engraving of a name on a brass plate beneath a stained window); bury, 21. 87; interred, b. 11. 67; Graue, *pp.* stamped, engraven, 5. 127.
Graunge, farm-house, grange, 20. 71. See note, p. 243.
Graunt, *adj.* great; Graunt mercy = many thanks, b. 10. 218.
Grauntye, *v.* grant, give, 4. 333; Graunty, *v.* 2. 86; Graunte, *v.* a. 1. 147; Graunteþ, *pr. s.* agrees, consents, 3. 168; allows, b. 11. 93; Grauntiþ, *pr. s.* grants, a. 11. 193; Graunten, *pr. pl.* grant, 20. 187; Grauntede, *pt. s.* granted, allowed, 3. 125; Graunted, 1 *pt. s.* offered, b. 17. 85.
Grauynge, *s.* engraving (of a name on a plate beneath a window), *or* painting (of a window), 4. 68.
Grayþ, *adj.* true, exact, 7. 230; Grayþest, most direct, 2. 201. See **Graith.**
Graythly, *adv.* readily, quickly, easily, 20. 126; Gŕaythely, duly, b. 18. 289. See **Graith.**
Grece, grease, b. 13. 63.
Greden, *v.* to cry aloud, b. 2. 73, a. 3. 59; Greden after = cry out for, send for, b. 3. 71; Grede, *v.* lament, a. 5. 216; Gredest, 2 *pr. s.* talkest, 22. 427, b. 19. 423; Greden, *pr. pl.* cry, 10. 76;

GLOSSARIAL INDEX. 365

beg, 9. 285; Gredeþ, *pr. pl.* cry, 15. 134; Gradde, *pt. s.* cried aloud, cried out, 23. 386; Gradden, *pt. pl.* proclaimed, a. 2. 59. A.S. *grædan*, to cry aloud.
Gredire, gridiron, 3. 130.
Gree, *s.* prize, 21. 103. O.F. *gre, gret*, pleasure, recompense; Lat. *gratum*.
Greehonde, greyhound, R. 2. 113.
Greipliche, *adv.* readily, quickly, 8. 296, 12. 139. See Graith, Graythly.
Grene, *adj.* green, fresh, 21. 48; *pl.* new, 9. 305.
Grene, *s.* green, common (but with allusion to Green), R. 2. 153, R. 3. 101.
Grennes, *pl.* springes, snares, R. 2. 188. A.S. *grin*, a snare, gin.
Greot, gravel, earth, mould, lit. grit, 14. 23, 177. A.S. *gréot*.
Gret, *adj.* great, b. 15. 142; Grete, *pl.* great men, R. 3. 250; Grette, R. 3. 190.
Grete, *v.* weep, b. 5. 386. A.S. *grǽtan*.
Greten, *v.* greet, welcome, a. 5. 187; Grete, 1 *pr. s.* b. 10. 169; Grette, 1 *pt. s.* saluted, greeted, accosted, 12. 139, 19. 244; treated, a. 11. 125; sent a salutation to, 12. 117; Grette, *pt. s.* addressed, saluted, greeted, 5. 42, 13. 207. A S. *grétan*.
Gretliche, *adv.* greatly, exceedingly, much, 21. 6, 22. 110.
Grettoure, *adj. comp.* greater, 20. 147; larger, 19. 65.
Greuaunces, *pl.* pains, b. 12. 61.
Greuen, *v.* grieve, annoy, vex, trouble, 22. 338, b. 10. 204; Greue, *v.* 12. 134; annoy, harass, 23. 28; Greuye, *v.* offend, 9. 236; Greuest, 2 *pr. s.* troublest, b. 14. 112; Greueth, *pr. s.* grieves, annoys, b. 11. 272; Greueth hym = vexes himself, becomes angry, b. 6. 317; Greueþ, *pr. pl.* trouble, vex, 4. 92; annoy, b. 10. 204; Greue, *pr. pl.* wrong, 12. 27; Greue, *pr. s. subj.* annoy, trouble, 20. 127; Greuede, *pt. s.* injured, 5. 95; Greued, *pt. s.* vexed, troubled, 7. 111; Greued hym = grew angry, b. pr. 139; Greued, *pp.* troubled, 1. 207; injured, b. 15. 47.
Greues, *s. pl.* griefs, grievances, R. 1. 96; Greyues, R. 4. 38.
Greye, *s.* gray clothing, 17. 343.
Greyn, *s.* grain, corn, 9. 126, 13. 177; grain, least bit, particle, 12. 85; Greyne, grain, colour, b. 16. 59 (see note to 3. 14); Greynes, *pl.* seed-corn, 22. 274.
Greys, *s.* fur, 17. 343. See Grys.

Greythe, *adj.* ready, plain, 11. 242. See Graith, Grayp.
Greythly, *adv.* readily, well, 21. 324.
Greyues; see Greues.
Grimliche, *adv.* dreadfully, exceedingly, a. 5. 216. See Grymly.
Gripe, *s.* grasp, 20. 146.
Gripeth, *pr. s.* takes hold, grasps, 20. 167; grasps, demands, 4. 89, b. 3. 248; Grypeþ, *pr. s.* grasps, 20. 127; Gripeþ, *pr. pl.* take, receive, a. 3. 235; Grypen, *pp.* grasped, received, 4. 228; Griped, *pp.* clutched, b. 3. 181. A.S. *grípan*.
Gris, *pl.* little pigs, pigs, b. pr. 226; Grys, 1. 227, 5. 49. Icel. *gríss*, Swed. *gris*, a pig.
Grome, groom, man, lad, servant, b. 17. 85, 111; Gromes, *pl.* 9. 227, R. 1. 66, R. 3. 344.
Grone, *v.* groan, a. 7. 245; Groneþ, *pr. s.* is ill, 9. 270; Gronede, *pt. s.* groaned, 23. 311.
Grope, *v.* feel, handle, touch, 7. 180, 22. 170; Gropeþ, *pr. s.* feels, tries by touch, 23. 363; touches, 20. 126.
Grote, a groat, 6. 134, 7. 230; Grott, groat, morsel, R. pr. 35; Grotes, *pl.* 4. 175, 18. 207.
Grounde, *pp.* pounded, b. 13. 43.
Growede, *pt. pl.* b. 16. 56; Growe, *pp.* grown, R. 2. 129. (The pp. is strong.)
Grucchen, *v.* grumble, R. pr. 35; Grucche, *v.* a. 10. 112; Gruccheth, *pr. s.* murmurs, b. 6. 317; Grucche, 1 *pr. pl. subj.* murmur, 1. 171; Grucche, *pr. pl.* grumble, find fault, 9. 227, R. 3. 308; Grucchen, *pr. pl.* a. 7. 205; Grucched, 1 *pt. s.* grumbled, repined, 7. 111; Grucchinge, *pres. pt.* grumbling, grudging, R. 3. 245. O.F. *grocer*, to murmur.
Gruwel, *s.* gruel, a. 7. 169.
Grym, *adj.* heavy, b. 5. 360.
Grymly, *adv.* heavily, b. 10. 261.
Grype, *v.* grasp, receive, 4. 284.
Grys, *s.* fur (properly the fur of the grey squirrel), b. 15. 215. See Greys. F. *gris*, gray.
Grys, pigs. See Gris.
Gult, fault, offence, guilt, sin, crime, 4. 138, 5. 75; Gultes, *pl.* crimes, sins, 4. 8, 7. 176, 11. 55.
Gulte, *pt. pl.* offended. committed sin, 8. 151. Cf. A.S. *ágyltan*.
Gulte, *adj.* gilt, b. 15. 215.
Gultier, *adj. comp.* more guilty, b. 12. 81.
Gulty, *adj.* guilty, 7. 175, 425; convicted, b. 12. 78.

Z 2

GLOSSARIAL INDEX.

Gunne, *pt pl.* began, a. 7. 140.
Gurd, *imper. s.* strike, 3. 213; Gurdeth of, *imp. pl.* strike off, b. 2. 201. See Girt.
Gurdel; Vnder gurdel = beneath the girdle, in the loins, b. 13. 294; Vnder gurdell, 7. 43.
Gurles, *pl.* children (of either sex), 10. 76, 12. 123. See Gerles.
Gurþes, *s. pl.* girths, a. 4. 19. See Gerthes.
Gustes, *s. pl.* guests, 11. 179. See Gistes.
Gut, gut, belly, 2. 34; Guttes, *pl.* 7. 398; Guttis, *pl.* b. 5. 347. See Gottes.
Gyaunt, giant, 21. 263; Gyauntz, *pl.* b. 20. 214. See Geauntes.
Gyde, *s.* guide, 8. 307.
Gyen, *v.* guide, direct, 3. 198; Gye, *v.* guide, govern, R. pr. 42; rule (his conduct), 22. 227; To gye with hymseluen = to guide his conduct by, b. 19. 222; Gyede, *pt. s.* guided, a. 2. 162. O.F. *guier, guider.* See Gie.
Gyf, give. See Gyue.
Gyfte, gift; To gyfte = as a gift, 12. 104. See ȝift.
Gyle, *s.* deceit, fraud, 1. 12. (Sometimes used as a proper name.)
Gyleþ, *pr. s.* deceives, beguiles, defrauds, 10. 65.
Gylle, gill, quarter of a pint, 7. 397.
Gylour, deceiver, 21. 164, 166; Gylours, *pl.* 4. 100, 304, 21. 385. See Gilour.
Gylt, gilt, 17. 343. 20. 15. See Gulte.
Gylte, fault, b. 13. 257. See Gult.
Gylty, *adj.* guilty (folk), b. 10. 256. See Gulty.
Gyn, engine, 21. 263.
Gynful, *adj.* guileful, deceitful, a. 11. 153. See above.
Gynneþ, Gynne. See Ginneþ.
Gynnynge, *s.* beginning, 11. 153, 19. 205, 20. 111.
Gyour, *s.* guide, leader, 22. 427, 23. 72, b. 19. 423. See Gyen.
Gyse, manner, fashion, 1. 26, R. 3. 162, 212.
Gyside, *pt pl.* disguised, R. 3. 159.
Gyterne, a kind of guitar, b. 13. 233. See Giterne.
Gyue, *v.* give, 22. 225; Gyueth, *pr. s.* grants, b. 10. 28; Gyueþ, *pr. pl.* render, 22. 456; Gyue, *pr. s. subj.* give, b. 7. 197; Gyf, (may he) give, b. 2. 120; Gaf, *pt. s.* gave, 15. 195, 18. 66; delivered, 21. 197; returned, 21. 333; Gyue, *pp.* given, b. 2. 148. See Geueþ, ȝiuen.

Gyuede, *pt. s.* fettered, bound, lamed, 23. 192; Gyued, *pt. s.* b. 20. 191. See Gyues.
Gyues, *s. pl.* gyves, fetters, 16. 254, b. 14. 51.
Gyuleris, *s. pl.* beguilers, R. 3. 130. See Gylour.

Ha, have. See Haue.
Habbeth, Habbe. See Haue.
Haberion, habergeon, coat of mail, 21. 22; Haberioun, b. 18. 23.
Hacche, *v.* hatch, R. 3. 44; Hacchen, *pr. pl.* R. 2. 143.
Hacches, *pl.* hatches, half-doors, buttery-doors, 6. 29, 17. 335.
Hacke. See Hakke.
Hagge, *s.* hag, b. 5. 191.
Hailse, 1 *pr. s.* salute, greet, b. 5. 101; Hailsede, 1 *pt. s.* saluted, 11. 10; Hailsed, 1 *pt. s.* b. 8. 10; Hailsede, *pt. pl.* reverenced, saluted, 10. 309; Hailsed, *pt. pl.* b. 7. 160. Icel. *heilsa,* to hail, salute; Swed. *helsa.* See note to b. 5. 101; p. 75.
Haiwarde. See Haywarde.
Hakeneyes, *pl.* horses, 3. 175.
Hakeneyman, *s.* horse-dealer, esp. one who used to let out horses for hire, 7. 365, 378, 389; Hakeneymannes, *gen. sing.* of the horse-dealer, 7. 391.
Hakke, *v.* hack, hoe; hence, grub, toil, b. 19. 399; Hacke, *v.* 22. 403.
Halde, *v.* keep, 9. 207; Holden, *v.* keep, a. 8. 5; Holde hym = to stay, remain, b. 7. 5; Holden hym, b. 6. 202; Halde, 1 *pr. s.* hold, consider, esteem, 4. 300, 14. 240, 16. 127; Haldeþ, *pr. s.* considers, 12. 220; Holdeth, b. 10. 386; Holdith, *pr. s.* maintains, R. 3. 279; Halt, *pr. s.* holds, 19. 196, b. 3. 241; keeps, 7. 420, 11. 80; considers, 4. 390; bears, b. 17. 105; Holdeþ, *pr. pl.* keep, a. 7. 134; Holden, confine, 1. 30; Holden tale = take account, 2. 9; Holde tale, b. 1. 9; Hald, *pt. s.* held, 18. 240; Helde, *pt. s.* considered, b. 11. 70; held, kept fast hold of, 11. 86; Helden, considered, b. 11. 68; Helde of = depended upon, R. 2. 48; Heeld kept, 18. 22; Hulde, *pt. pl.* kept, 2. 109; stopped, 7. 401; Hold, respect, a. 6. 69; Holdeþ, *imp. pl.* keep, 23. 246; Holdeth, hold, b. 7. 59; Halde, *pp.* considered, 18. 111; Holden, *pp.* held, bound, 23. 365; b. 12. 272, b. 15. 561, a. 7. 69; considered (to

GLOSSARIAL INDEX. 367

be), b. 4. 118; Holde, *pp.* bound, 15. 197; considered (to be), 10. 336, 11. 297; observed, b. 10. 291; Haldyng, *pres. part.* holding, siding, 4. 383; Holdinge, *pp.* (*for* Holden), bound, 9. 103. A.S. *healdan.*
Hales, *s. pl.* tents, R. 3. 218. '*Hale* in a felde for men, *tref;*' Palsgrave. '*Tabernaculum*, a pauilion, tente, or *hale;*' Cooper's Thesaurus. See Cath. Angl.
Halewen, *ger.* hallow, consecrate, 18. 279. See Halwe.
Half, *s.* side, part, 3. 5, 4. 75, b. 2. 5; Halue, b. 10. 162.
Half acre, small piece of land, 7. 267, 9. 2. See note, p. 87.
Half-delle, *s.* half, R. 4. 2; Halfdell þe=half of the, R. 3. 218. Lit. 'half-deal.' See Haluendele.
Haliday. See Halyday.
Halidom, *s.* holy relics, b. 5. 376. From Icel. *helgir dómar*, relics of saints, saintly relics, *helgidómr*, sanctuary; the primary meaning of *dómr* being *doom.*
Halie, *v.* drag back, pull, hale, b. 8. 95; Halye, 11. 93.
Halowid, *pp.* hallooed at, shouted at, R. 3. 228.
Halp. See Helpen.
Halpeny, at a half-penny a gallon, 9. 329. See note to 7. 226.
Hals, *s.* neck, 1. 185, 3. 207, 4. 227, 9. 60. A.S. *heals.*
Halsede, 1 *pt. s.* besought, conjured, 2. 70, a. 1. 71; Halsed, *pt. s.* embraced, a. 12. 79. A.S. *healsian*, to embrace, beseech; from *heals*, neck.
Halsynge, *s.* embracing, 7. 187.
Halt, *pr. s.* holds. See Halde.
Halue, *adj.* half, b. 5. 31, b. 6. 108.
Halue, *s.* See Half.
Haluendele, half part, half, 8. 29. See Halfdelle.
Halwe, *ger.* to consecrate, b. 15. 557. See Halewen.
Haly, *adj.* holy, 14. 86; Haly bred, holy bread, 7. 146. See note to Pass. 16. 210.
Halyday, holiday (*also written* Haly day), 2. 124, 10. 231; Haliday, b. 5. 588; Halydayes, *pl.* holidays, 7. 272.
Halye, *v.* haul, drag, 11. 93.
Hamward, *adv.* homeward, a. 3. 187.
Han. See Haue.
Handen, *pl.* hands, i. e. manual labour, 1. 222. See Hond.
Handidandi. See Handydandy.

Hand-molde, hand-mould, R. 2. 155. See note.
Hand-whyle, *s.* short time, short space of time, 22. 272.
Handy-dandy, a secret bribe, 5. 68; Handidandi, b. 4. 75. Lit. a juggling trick with the hands. See note. The word is merely a reduplicated form of *hand*, used to call attention to the closed hand when containing something of a nature to be guessed at. Hence *dandy*, used alone, came to be a slang name for the hand, as in 'tip us your *dandy*,' i. e. shake hands.
Hanelounes, *pl.* wiles, tricks, b. 10. 129. See note, p. 152.
Hange, *v.* depend, b. 13. 391; Heng, *pt. s.* hung, suspended, 9. 60; hanged, hung, 2. 64; Heengen, *pt. pl.* hanged, a. 1. 148; Hangid, *pt. pl.* waited for trial, R. 3. 218; Hanged, *pp.* hung, hanged, 11. 240; Hangyng, *pr. pt.* attached, hanging, b. 12. 289. (The strong intransitive verb and the weak transitive verb are here mixed up, as in modern English.) See Hongen.
Hansele, *s.* an earnest (of good fellowship), a treat, 7. 375; Hansell, earnest money, R. 4. 91. See note, p. 92.
Hanted, *pt. s.* frequented, sought after, R. 2. 178. Mod. E. *haunt.*
Hanypeles, *pl.* ampullæ, little phials, 8. 165. See Ampulles.
Hap, *s.* luck, fortune, success, 4. 299, 15. 51, 23. 385; Happes, *pl.* successes, b. 5. 97.
Hapliche, *adv.* haply, perhaps, 8. 267, a. 6. 104.
Hapne, *v.* happen, a. 3. 266.
Happe, *v.* happen, b. 3. 284, b. 6. 47; Happe, *pres. s. subj.* happen, R. pr. 53; Happe how it my3te=at haphazard. b. 16. 87; Happed, *impers. pt. s.* has happened to, 6. 95.
Haras, *s.* harassment, annoyance, R. 3. 27.
Harde, *adj.* close, parsimonious, 13. 244; sore, disastrous, b. 14. 322.
Harde, *adv.* sternly, b. 11. 85; hard. a. 8. 102; Ful harde=with great difficulty, b. 20. 233.
Hardier, *adj.* bolder, 22. 58.
Hardier, *adv.* more boldly, b. 14. 261.
Hardiliche, *adv.* boldly, 9. 28, b. 6. 30; Hardily, vigorously, a. 7. 32.
Hardiloker, *adv.* more boldly, 7. 306; Hardyloker, 17. 103.
Hardinesse, *s.* daring, boldness, 21. 80; Hardynesse, 22. 31.

Hardy, *adj.* bold, daring, brave, 4. 324, 14. 10, b. 14. 305.
Hardy, *v.* encourage, b. 15. 429.
Harlot, *s.* scurrilous person, ribald, buffoon, teller of ribald stories (used, apparently, of men only), 8. 94; Harlotes, *gen. sing.* ribald's, 23. 144; Harlotes, *pl.* 4. 302, 7. 369; rascals, wicked men, 20. 256. See note, p. 57. Cf. '*Scurra*, a harlotte;' Reliq. Antiq. i. 7.
Harlotrie, profligacy, ribaldry, dissipation, 5. 110, 8. 76, 91; a scurrilous tale, b. 5. 413; Harlotrye, profligacy, ribald stories, 8. 22, b. 4. 115. Cf. '*Scurrilitas*, harlotrye;' Reliq. Antiq. i. 7.
Harneys, armour, 17. 343; Harnesse, R. 1. 26. See **Herneys.**
Harow, *interj.* harow! alas! 23. 88; Harrow, b. 20. 87.
Harowede, *pt. pl.* harrowed, i. e. glossed or commented upon (metaphorically), 22. 272. See **Harwen.**
Harpen, *v.* play on the harp, 16. 206, b. 13. 231; Harpeden, *pt. pl.* 21. 452.
Harpoure, minstrel, b. 14. 24.
Harwen, *v.* harrow, 6. 19, 22. 268, 311; Harweþ, *imp. pl.* harrow, 22. 317.
Hasped, *pp.* joined, fastened (as with a hasp), 2. 193.
Hassellis, *z. pl. gen.* of retainers, R. 2. 25. Obviously a French spelling of O.H.G. *heistalde* or *hagestalt,* mod. G. *hagestolz,* a bachelor, cognate with A. S. *hago-steald, hæg-steald, hehsteald,* an unmarried person, young warrior, young man. For the O.H.G. forms, see Schade. Cf. Low Lat. *haistaldi, hestaldi,* retainers.
Hastelokest, *adv. sup.* soonest, 22. 471; Hastlokest, b. 19. 466.
Hastou, Hastow. See **Haue.**
Hat, *s.* hat, a. 6. 11. 20.
Hat, *pr. s.* is named, is called, b. 5. 582, 629. A.S. *hátan,* to be called, 3 pr. s. *hátte ;* but confused with A.S. *hátan,* to command, 3 pr. s. *hát.* See **Hatte.**
Hater, *s.* dress, suit of clothes, 10. 157; Hatere, b. 14. 1. See **Haterynge,** below; *hatre* in Stratmann; and see note, p. 204.
Haterynge, *s.* dress, b. 15. 76. See **Hater.**
Hatien, *v.* hate, b. 15. 104; Hatyen, b. 10. 93; Hatie, 2 *pr. s. subj.* b. 6. 52; Haten, *pr. pl. subj.* hate, 5. 110; Hatede, *pt. s.* hated, a. 10. 146.

Hatte, 1 *pr. s.* I am called, 17. 186, b. 15. 24, a. 12. 63; Hattest, 2 *pr. s.* art named, 23. 339; Hattestow (*for* Hattest thou), art thou called, b. 20. 337; Hatte, *pr. s.* is named, 8. 220, 243; That hatte=who is named, 4. 146; Hatte, *pt. s.* was called, was named, 21. 133; Hatte, *pt. pl.* are named, 8. 224. See **Hat, Heihte,**
Hette. A.S. *hátan,* to be called, pr. and pt. *hátte.* The present form answers to Goth. *haitada,* I am called; see John xi. 16 in Gothic.
Haue, *v.* have; Habbe, *v.* 7. 381; Habben and holden=have and hold, a. 2. 70; Han, *v.* have, a. 3. 239; take, b. 18. 370; Ha, *v.* a. 7. 83; Hauest, 2 *pr. s.* hast, 19. 241; Hastou (*for* Hast thou), a. 3. 101; Hastow, b. 3. 105; Habbeth, *pr. pl.* have, b. 14. 148, a. pr. 37; get, b. 15. 133; Han, *pr. pl.* have, 1. 134, 19. 193; Haueth, b. 7. 65; Habbe, *pr. s. subj.* a. 8. 70; Haue, *pr. s. subj.* bring, lead, fetch, 21. 150; may (God) have, b. 13. 164; Haue, *pr. s. subj.* if they have, provided they have, 2. 8; Hadde, 1 *pt. s.* had, 11. 10; Haddest, 2 *pt. s.* didst have, 7. 321; Haddestow, hadst thou, b. 11. 403; Hadde, *pt. s.* experienced, b. 3. 284; Haued, b. 3. 39; Hedde, *pt. s.* had, a. 1. 69; possessed, a. 9. 80; if I had, a. 3. 194; Hedden, *pt. pl.* had, a. 2. 144; Hedden, a. 8. 20; Haued, b. 2. 166, 219; Haue, *imper. s.* take, receive, b. 14. 49; Haueþ, *imp. pl.* have, feel, 23. 246.
Hauer, *s. as adj.* oaten, made of oats, b. 6. 284. Du. *haver,* G. *hafer,* oats.
Haunt, *s.* use, custom, 17. 94.
Hauntelere dere, antlered deer, R. 2. 128 (cf. l. 117).
Haunten, *pr. pl.* practise, use, 1. 75, 4. 57, 63; b. pr. 77; a. pr. 74; Haunteþ, b. 3. 53; Haunte, 2 *pr. s. subj.* practise, art addicted to, 12. 112; Haunted, *pp.* practised, 16. 197.
Hautesse, *s.* length, lit. height, R. 3. 13.
Hawes, *pl.* haws, fruit of the hawthorn, 12. 8, 82; b. 16. 10.
Hayward, a hedge-warden; overseer, cattle-keeper, 6. 16, 7. 368, 14. 47; Haiwarde, 14. 45, 22. 334. From A.S. *hege,* hedge, and *weard*; see note, p. 62. In Wright's Vocab. i. 278, col. 1, we find '*Hic inclusarius,* a hayward.'
He, *pron.* it, a. 7. 5; she, b. 1. 140

GLOSSARIAL INDEX. 369

(= A.S. *héo*); used indefinitely, in the sense *one of you*, b. 6. 138.
Hed, head. See Heued.
Hedde, had. See Haue.
Hede, heed, notice, b. 11. 106.
Heed-dere, head deer, chief deer, R. 2. 117.
Heedis, heads. See Heued.
Heeld, kept. See Halde.
Heele, health. See Hele.
Heengen. See Hange.
Heep, number, crowd, b. pr. 53.
Heer, *adv.* here, in this world, a. 1. 9, a. 10. 210. See Her.
Heere, *s.* hair, R. 2. 188. See Heres.
Heeris, *s. pl.* heirs, R. 3. 100. See Heires.
Heet, *pt. s.* bade, b. 20. 271. See Hoten.
Hefd, head. See Heued.
Hegges, *pl.* hedges, 9. 29, b. 3. 132, b. 6. 31; Heggys, 4. 169.
Heghte, *pt. s.* ordered, bade, 7. 212. See Hoten.
Heigh, *adj.* high, b. 10. 366, b. 11. 81; proud, 7. 8; An heigh = on high, b. 15. 521; Heighe, high, b. 6. 4, 114; chief, principal, b. 12. 105; noble, b. 12. 134; direct, b. 10. 155; Heie, sacred, 2. 70; Heiȝ, high, b. 1. 162; full, a. 7. 105, a. 11. 234; Heiȝe, a. 1. 71, a. 7. 4; direct, b. 4. 42; heavenly, a. 11. 303; Heh, 17. 34; Hey, 5. 113; large, 3. 134; Hey way, highway, 23. 187; An heiȝ, on high, a. *pr.* 13; Heye way, highway, 12. 105; Heye weyes, highways, 10. 32, 188; Heyȝ table = high table, b. 13. 444.
Heighe, *adv.* highly, especially, b. 5. 588; Heiȝe, dearly, a. 3. 49; loudly, b. 4. 162. See Heye.
Heihliche, *adv.* at a high price, a. 7. 300. A.S. *héahlíce*, highly.
Heihte, *pt. s.* was named, 8. 299. See Hatte.
Heilede, 1 *pt. s.* saluted, greeted, a. 5. 83, a. 9. 10.
Heipeth, *pr. s.* heaps, R. 3. 42.
Heire, *s.* hair-cloth, hair-shirt, 7. 6; Heyre, b. 5. 66. See note, p. 72.
Heires, *pl.* heirs, children, b. 8. 88; Heyres, 10. 4, a. 2. 70.
Heiȝ, Heiȝe. See Heigh, Heighe.
Heiȝly, *adv.* with much respect, a. 11. 240. See Heyliche.
Heh, *adj.* high, 17. 34. See Heigh.
Helde. See Halde.
Heldeþ, *pr. pl.* pour, a. 10. 60. A.S. *heldan*, *hyldan*, to incline (hence, to pour out).

Hele, health, safety, prosperity, 4. 299, 6. 7, 7. 85, 10. 102, 11. 180; salvation, 22. 390; a. 6. 22; remedy, b. 13. 342; Soule hele = soul's health, b. 5. 270; Heele, health, 17. 12. A.S. *hælu*.
Hele; *in phr.* pye hele (*or* heele, *or* hyle), 10. 345; pies hele (*v. r.* pese hule), b. 7. 194. See note. The most likely sense is, I think, 'a remaining piece of a pie,' or else, 'a piecrust.' I have already referred to Halliwell, who gives *heel* as meaning the rind of cheese, or the crust of bread; but more light is thrown on the word by the Shropshire *heel*, as to which I copy the following from Miss Jackson's Word-book. '*Heel*, the top crust of a loaf cut off, or the bottom crust remaining. Burns has *kebbuckheel*, i. e. the remaining part of a cheese, in his Holy Fair.' Perhaps the original sense was 'cover,' hence 'rind' or 'crust,' from the verb *hele*, to cover, below.
Hele, *v.* hide, conceal, b. 5. 168; Heleden, *pt. pl.* covered, concealed, 14. 164; Hele, *imp. s.* hide, 23. 339; Heled, *pp.* covered, roofed, 8. 237. A.S. *helan*. See Helye.
Helen, *v.* heal, b. 9. 202; Helede, *pt. s.* a. 7. 182.
Helis, *s. pl.* heels, R. 3. 154.
Helle, *s.* hell, 4. 330; Helle, *gen.* of hell, b. 11. 158.
Helleward, *adv.* (with *to*), towards hell, 21. 119.
Helpen, *v.*; Helpen of = help with, provide with, a. 7. 198; Halp, *pt. s.* helped, 7. 84, 22. 131, 376; Halpe, *pt. s.* b. 19. 127; Holpe, *pt. s.* a. 11. 31; Holpen, *pt. pl.* helped, 9. 113; Hulpen, *pt. pl.* b. 6. 118, a. 8. 6; Holpyn, *pt. pl.* b. 6. 108; Halpe, b. 7. 6; Holpe, 1 *pt. s. subj.* were to help, b. 18. 396; Hulpe, *pt. pl. subj.* would help, 10. 6; Holpen, *pp.* helped, assisted, 12. 28; Hulpen, b. 15. 130; Holpe, b. 4. 169; Hulpe, b. 5. 633; Helpeþ, *imp. pl.* help, a. 7. 22.
Helthe, *s.* healing, 23. 332; salvation, b. 11. 223, b. 12. 40; Helth, safety, b. 10. 249.
Helye, *v.* to cover; To helye with hus bones = to cover his bones with, 10. 157. See Hele, *v.*
Helynge, *s.* healing; An helynge = a-healing, b. 17. 115.
Helyynge, *s.* dress, covering, 17. 236. See Helye.
Hem, *pron. dat.* to them, them, b. 3.

370 **GLOSSARIAL INDEX.**

345, b. 6. 16, b. 8. 93; *acc.* them, 1. 30, 20. 105; Heom, *acc.* themselves, a. pr. 25.

Hem-seluen, themselves, b. pr. 59, b. 3. 215; **Hem-selue,** 1. 55; Hem-self, 18. 7, R. 3. 200.

Hende, *adj.* courteous, polite, kind, 9. 47, 11. 145, 12. 44, 23. 188; noble, R. 3. 18, 74. A.S. *gehende,* near (from *hand*).

Hendeliche, *adv.* courteously, 19. 185, b. 3. 29; Hendelich, b. 16. 98; Hendely, b. 8. 10; Hendiliche, kindly, 4. 30; Hendilyche, 11. 10; Hendyliche, 19. 132. See above.

Hendenesse, *s.* kindness, courteousness, courtesy, gentleness, 3. 81, 12. 13; Hendeness. 22. 31; Hendynesse, 19. 13. See **Hende.**

Hende-speche, mildness of speech, 23. 348.

Hendeþ, *pr. s.* seizes, a. 12. 67 *n.* Put *for* henteþ (*spelt* hentiþ *in the* Ingilby MS.); see **Henten.**

Heng, Hengen. See **Hange.**

Hennes, *adv.* hence, 2. 175, 5. 184; from this spot, b. 9. 1; away from here, 23. 203; out of this present life, b. 19. 242, a. 1. 152; (go) hence, b. 11. 205; Henne, hence, a. 7. 191; Heonnes, a. 4. 153. See note to b. 7. 98, p. 124.

Hennes-goynge, *s.* departure hence, i. e. death, b. 14. 165.

Henten, *v.* seize, catch hold of, 17. 81; Hente, *v.* seize, grasp, take possession of, get, 7. 8, 20. 139, b. 5. 68; Hente, *pt. s.* caught, seized, took, 8. 152, 9. 171, 23. 167; Hent, *pt. s.* b. 6. 176; Henten, *pt. pl.* seized (for themselves), 9. 183; Henten hem = caught hold of for themselves, seized, b. 6. 190; received, R. 3. 365; Hente, *pt. pl.* received, took, R. 2. 43. A.S. *hentan.*

Heo, *pron.* she, b. 1. 73, b. 3. 29, b. 5. 632. A.S. *héo.*

Heo, *pron.* they, a. pr. 43, a. 1. 8.

Heom, themselves. See **Hem.**

Heonnes, hence. See **Hennes.**

Heore, *pron. pers.* her, 21. 172.

Heore, *pron. poss.* her, 21. 122; By here one = by herself alone, 21. 318.

Heore, *pron. poss.* their, 17. 11; a. pr. 28; to their, a. 8. 16; Heor, a. 1. 19. A.S. *heora,* of them.

Heornes. See **Herne.**

Heorte. See **Herte.**

Hep, number, crowd (lit. heap), 1. 51, 7. 235, 9. 183; Heep, b. pr. 53; Hepe, heap, great number, quantity, 7. 385,

17. 205; To hepe = into a heap, hence, to a result, to pass, 11. 189, 191. In Chaucer's treatise on the Astrolabie, *to hepe* means into one, tightly together, together; see note to 11. 189, p. 142.

Hepid, *pp.* heaped full, a. 3. 234.

Her, *adv.* here, 19. 267; Lo me her = see me here, 21. 373.

Her, of them, their. See **Here.**

Her-ageyn, against this, 11. 235. See **Her-aȝen, Here-ageine.**

Heraude, herald, 19. 187, 267; Heraudes, *pl.* 23. 94.

Her-aȝen, *adv.* in opposition to this, 20. 109. See **Her-ageyn.**

Herber, garden, 19. 5. Lat. *herbarium;* O.F. *herbier,* given in Littré.

Herbergh, harbour, place of refuge, 12. 247; Herberwe, b. 10. 406.

Herberghen, *v.* harbour, lodge, stow, find room for, 22. 320; Herberghwen, *v.* 8. 258; Herberwe, *v.* b. 19. 317; Herborowe, *v.* R. 3. 217; Herborwe, *v.* a. 2. 40; Herberwed, *pt. s.* b. 17. 73; *pp.* b. 5. 233.

Her-beynge, *s.* residence here (in this world), 17. 9. See **Here-beyng.**

Herde, *s.* herd, flock, R. 2. 16.

Herdeyed, *pt. pl.* collected, flocked, lit. formed into a herd, 14. 148.

Here, *pron.* of them, 11. 273; Her, 17. 81; Her eyther = either of them, both of them, b. 11. 307; Her one = one of them; Her other = the other of them, b. 18. 65; Her none = neither of them, b. 12. 162.

Here, *poss. pron.* their, 1. 123, 12. 136, 19. 158, 20. 135.

Here, *v.* to hear, listen to, b. 10. 90, b. 12. 244; Hereth, *pr. s.* b. 15. 57; Herde, *pt. s.* 3. 217, 9. 168; Herden, *pt. pl.* heard, a. 7. 230.

Here, *s.* hair-cloth, *hence,* a hair shirt, a. 5. 48. See **Heire.**

Here, *adv.* in this world, b. 7. 105.

Here-aboute, *adv.* about this, (employed) on this, 11. 191.

Here-ageine, against this, opposed to this, b. 9. 144; Here-aȝeine, b. 14. 188. See **Her-ageyn.**

Here-beyng, *s.* life here, present life, b. 14. 141. See **Her-beynge.**

Here-fore, *adv.* for this, 23. 294.

Heremyte, hermit, 7. 368, b. 13. 30; Heremytes, *pl.* 6. 4.

Heren (*miswritten for* Eren), *v.* to ear, plough, till, a. 7. 60.

Heres, *gen. s.* hair's, b. 10. 334. A.S. *hǽr.* See **Heere.**

GLOSSARIAL INDEX. 371

Herewel, Hear-well, b. 9. 20.
Herfore, *adv.* for this reason, b. 20. 291.
Herie, *v.* to praise, a. 11. 240.
Herien, *v.* (*for* Erien), to plough, a. 7. 109. See **Heren**.
Herkne, *imper. s.* hearken, 9. 223; Herkeneth, *pr. s.* R. 3. 285.
Herne, *s.* corner, nook, R. 3. 211; Hernes, *pl.* 3. 249, b. 2. 233; Heornes, corners, hiding-places, 21. 449. See **Huirnes**. A.S. *hyrne*, corner, from *horn*.
Herneys, armour, b. 15. 215.
Her-of, *adv.* of this, 22. 140.
Herre, *adj. comp.* higher, superior, 3. 30, b. 2. 28, a. 2. 21.
Herre, *adv.* higher, more highly, a. 10. 98. See note, p. 142.
Herte, heart, 11. 173, b. 15. 49; Heorte, 22. 31; Hertes, *pl.* hearts, a. 8. 66.
Herte, *s.* hart, R. 3. 22; Hertis, *pl.* harts (alluding to the badges of the White Hart granted by Richard II. to his retainers), R. 2. 4, 36, 115; R. 3. 3.
Herte, *pp.* hurt, injured, b. 17. 184, b. 20. 315.
Herteliche, *adv.* heartily, willingly, 11. 84.
Heruest, harvest, harvest-time, 6. 7, 7. 112; autumn, R. 2. 146.
Hesshede, *pt. s.* asked, 23. 331 *n.* See **Asken**.
Heste, order, bidding, command, behest, 4. 149, 19. 251, b. 3. 112; Hestes, *pl.* orders, commands, commandments, 3. 87, 9. 213, 10. 334. A.S. *hǽs,* (with added *t*).
Het, bade. See **Hoten**.
Hete, *s.* heat, warmth, 2. 124, 9. 249, 10. 109, 20. 193.
Hethene, *adj.* heathen, infidel, 23. 351, b. 15. 450; *as sb.* Hethen, b. 10. 350; Heþene, a. 11. 232; Hethen, *adj. pl.* heathen (men), b. 10. 365.
Hethenesse, *s.* heathendom, pagan country, b. 15. 435.
Hetith, *pr. s.* heats, hatches, R. 3. 42.
Hette, 1 *pr. s.* am named, a. 2. 153; *pr. s.* is named, a. 6. 63, a. 7. 44; Hetten, *pr. pl.* are named, a. 6. 67; Hette, *pt. s.* was named, called, a. 7. 72; *pt. s.* (who is) named, a. 3. 105. See **Hatte**, **Hote**.
Heued, head, 7. 202, 8. 281; Heuede, 20. 70; Hefd, 2. 161; Hefde, 11. 178, 16. 143; Hed, a. 2. 176, a. 6. 28; Heuedes, *pl.* 7. 150, 18. 230, 21.

292; Hefdes, *pl.* 23. 187. A.S. *héafod*.
Heuene, heaven, 2. 9, a. 1. 109, a. 2. 2, 74; *gen. sing.* of heaven, b. pr. 106, b. 14. 154.
Heuene-ryche, *gen. sing.* of the kingdom of heaven, 1. 29; Heuene-riche, b. pr. 27, b. 14. 260. A.S. *heofonríce*.
Heueneward, *adv.* (with *to*), towards heaven, b. 10. 334; To heueneward = as regards heaven, b. 15. 450.
Heuy, *adj.* heavy, 2. 150; mournful, 12. 188.
Heuy-chered, *adj.* sad, cast-down, with mournful looks, 23. 2.
Heuynesse, sorrow, 21. 258.
Hewe, *imper. s.* knock, strike, 20. 210; Hew, b. 17. 244.
Hewe, servant, labourer, 4. 310, 8. 195; Hewen, *pl.* b. 4. 55; Hewes, *pl.* 2. 124. A.S. *híwan,* pl. domestic servants.
Hewes, *pl.* hues, colours, 15. 159; b. 11. 357.
Hexte, *adj. superl.* highest, b. 12. 145.
Hey, high. See **Heigh**.
Heye, *adv.* highly, i.e. completely, 8. 226. See **Heighe**.
Heye-feste, high festival, 7. 182.
Heyere, *s.* exalter (lit. one who makes high), R. 2. 145, R. 3. 74.
Heyhte, *pt. s.* was named, 17. 158. See **Hette**, **Hatte**.
Heyliche, *adv.* highly, at high wages, 9. 336; earnestly, 9. 89; Heyeliche, nobly, 4. 252.
Heyne, *s.* a proper name, a. 5. 91. Cf. G. *Hans*.
Heyre, hair-shirt. See **Heire**.
Heyres. See **Heires**.
Hey3, *adj.* high, chief; Hey3 table = high table, b. 13. 444.
Hey3liche, *adv.* highly, b. 15. 554. See **Heihliche**.
Hider, *adv.* hither, a. 11. 176. See **Huder**, **Hyder**.
Hiderwardes, *adv.* hitherwards, 21. 344. See **Hyderwardes**.
Hie; On hie = on high, R. 1. 108. See **Heigh**.
Hiedest, 2 *pt. s.* didst hasten, b. 3. 193; Hied, *pp.* sped, R. 3. 132. See **Hyeþ**.
Hiegh, *adj.* high, noble, great, b. 10. 101, b. 15. 76. See **Heigh**.
Hieste, *adj. superl.* highest, R. 3. 92.
Highte, bade. See **Hihte**.
Highte, was named. See **Hihte**.
Hihnesse, highness, courage, 23. 153.
Hihte, *pt. s.* ordered, bade, commanded, 8. 14, 11. 98; Highte, 8. 247;

GLOSSARIAL INDEX.

Hight, *pt. s.* b. pr. 102. See Hoten, Hiȝte.
Hihte, *pt. s.* (which) was called, named, 12. 170; was named, 12. 304; 19. 7; Highte, *pt. s.* was named, 7. 310; Hiht, *pp.* named, 12. 188. See Hatte, Hette, Hiȝte.
Hij, *pron.* they, 1. 160, 6. 142, 12. 216, 15. 192. A.S. *hig.*
Hille, *v.* cover, R. 3. 326; Hiled, *pt. s.* b. 12. 233; Hileden, *pt. pl.* b. 11. 343; Hiled, *pp.* roofed, b. 5. 599. Icel. *hylja,* to cover. See Hele.
Hippe, *pr. pl.* hop, skip, b. 15. 557; Hippyng, *pres. pt.* leaping, skipping, 20. 59, b. 17. 59. See Huppe, Hoppe.
Hir, *poss. pron.* their, b. 15. 70. See Here.
Hir, *pron. fem.* her, b. 11. 11; it, a. 5. 171 : Hire to goode = for her good, a. 6. 122. See Here.
Hise, *pron. pl.* his (followers), 22. 219, 23. 61. See Hyse.
Hit, *pron.* it, 19. 216, 279; Hit are = they are, 16. 288; Hit = for it, a. 7. 117. A.S. *hit.*
Hitteþ, *pr. s.* knocks, 21. 386; Hitte, *pt. s.* struck, hit, 19. 120, 23. 103; touched, 7. 378; flung down, b. 5. 329; Hitte, 2 *pr. s. subj.* meet with, chance upon, 12. 114. See Hutte.
Hiȝeste, *adj. superl.* highest, greatest, a. 11. 294.
Hiȝeþ, *pr. s. refl.* hies, hurries himself, a. 7. 307; *pt. s.* Hiȝede, hastened, came near to, a. 7. 287. See Hyeþ.
Hiȝte, *pt. s.* commanded, b. 5. 206, b. 7. 200; promised, a. 7. 221; Hight, bade, b. pr. 102; Hiȝte (*for* Hiȝt), *pp.* bidden, b. 6. 133. See Hote, Hyȝte, Hihte.
Hiȝte, *pt. s.* was named, b. 6. 80, 81; Hiȝt, b. 11. 8. See Hihte, Hatte.
Ho, *pron.* who, which man, 22. 351, a. 3. 60; (*interrogatively*), 11. 72, 12. 150; one who, whoso, whoever, 4. 61, 8. 278, 11. 39; Ho so, one who, 7. 406; if any one, 4. 365; one, 8. 307; whoever, whosoever, 10. 257, 20. 5; Ho þat, whoever, 12. 16. (Never used as a *simple* relative, as in modern English.) See Ho-so.
Hobbis, *pl.* clowns, louts, R. 1. 90. '*Hob*, a country clown : it is the short for Robert;' Halliwell.
Hobleden, *pt. pl.* hobbled, limped, a. 1. 113; Hoblid, *pp.* R. 3. 15; Hobblid, *pp.* gone, travelled, R. 2. 23.

Cf. Du. *hobbelen,* to jolt about, to stammer.
Hockerye, retail dealing, 7. 233. See Hokkerye.
Hod, *s.* hood, 6. 134, 7. 202, 378; Hode, 14. 48, b. 5. 31, 195; Hodes, *pl.* hoods, 9. 292. See Hood.
Hoen, *pr. pl.* cry ho! shout at, b. 10. 61. See note to 12. 44, p. 148.
Hoked, *adj.* crooked, curved, furnished with a hook at the upper end, 11. 93; Hokede, 1. 51; Hokide, a. pr. 50.
Hokes, *pl.* hooks, hinges, b. 5. 603, 8. 242. See Hookis.
Hokkerye, *s.* retail dealing, b. 5. 227; Hockerye, 7. 233. Lit. 'hawker-y.' See note, p. 84.
Hol, *adj.* whole, entire, true, 4. 354; Hole, 8. 258, 9. 195; Hole, *adj. pl.* entire, i.e. neatly mended up, b. 6. 61. A.S. *hál.*
Holde, *adj.* (*for* Olde), old, a. 7. 124.
Holden, Holt. See Halde.
Hole, whole. See Hol.
Holely, wholly. See Holliche.
Holiche, *adv.* wholly, altogether, 20. 27. See Holliche.
Holigost, Holy Ghost, 19. 197, 20. 147, b. 10. 239.
Holliche, *adv.* wholly, fully, completely, entirely, 22. 3; Holly, 4. 149; Holiche, altogether, 20. 27; Holy, b. 19. 3.
Holpe, Holpen, Holpyn. See Helpen.
Holsume, *adj.* wholesome, R. 3. 212.
Holte, *s.* wood, R. 3. 15; Holtes, *pl.* R. 2. 23. A.S. *holt.*
Holwe, *adj.* hollow-cheeked, 7. 197, b. 5. 189.
Holy, *adv.* entirely, b. 19. 3. See Holliche.
Hom, house, lit. home, 12. 46; home, a. 8. 5; *as adv.* home, back, 5. 56, 22. 482; At hom = at home, a. 9. 20; Homes, *pl.* homes, a. 3. 89.
Homelich, *adv.* from house to house, making themselves at home, b. 10. 93; in a homely way, R. 3. 212.
Homeliche, *adj.* homely, clownish, R. 2. 43.
Hond, hand, 20. 110; Honden, *pl.* 4. 290, a. 7. 295; Hondes, 4. 118, 5. 82.
Hondred, hundred, 22. 211; Hondreth, b. pr. 210, b. 13. 270.
Honesschen, *v.* to drive away, as one chases out a dog, a. 11. 48. See note, p. 149. From *honiss-,* stem of the pres. part. of O.F. *honir,* later *honnir,* 'to reproach, disgrace, dishonour, de-

GLOSSARIAL INDEX. 373

fame, shame, revile'; Cotgrave. Of Teut. origin; cf. G. *hohn*, and Goth. *hauns*, vile.

Honest, *adj.* honourable, valuable, b. 19. 90.

Hongen, *v.* to hang, be hanged. a. 2. 170; Honge, *v.* 1. 185, 4. 149, 20. 8; Hongy, *v.* be hanged, 7. 238; Do hongy = cause to be hanged, 3. 207; Hongeþ, *pr. s.* hangs, depends, 15. 214; hangs, executes, 4. 178; Hongith, *pr. s.* hangs, suspends, puts, R. 3. 147; Hongen, *pr. pl.* hang, 11. 162; Hongede hym = hanged himself, a. 1. 66; Hongen, *pt. pl.* crucified, b. 1. 172; Hongid, *pp.* hung, suspended, 1. 194; Honged, 1. 191; Honge, *imp. s.* hang, a. 3. 108; Hong, *imp. s.* hang, place, a. 4. 20. The weak transitive verb and strong intransitive are mixed up. See **Hange**.

Honger, hunger, 7. 438, 9. 169.

Hongerliche, *adj.* hungry-looking, 7. 197.

Hongynge, *s.* hanging, 4. 411, R. 1. 108.

Honsel, *s.* gift; To honsel = as a gift, a. 5. 169. See **Hansele**.

Honte, *v.* hunt, 9. 28, 10. 223.

Hontyng, *s.* hunting, 4. 469.

Hony, honey, 17. 218, 225.

Hookis, *s. pl.* hooks, R. 3. 293. See **Hokes**.

Hool, *adj.* whole, untorn, b. 14. 1; Hoole, whole, R. pr. 26.

Hoolydom, *s.* sacred relics, a. 2. 122.

Hoow, ho! 10. 267. See **How**.

Hope, *s.* expectation, a. 3. 193.

Hope, 1 *pr. s.* expect, fear, 10. 275, b. 10. 151; Hopeþ, *pr. s.* expects, 18. 146; Hopen, *pr. pl.* expect, 18. 313; Hope, *imp. s.* expect, look for, a. 6. 125. See note, p. 234.

Hopede, called out. See **Houped**.

Hoper, seed-basket, 9. 60. See note.

Hoppe, *v.* dance, a. 3. 193, R. 3. 262. See **Huppe**, **Hippe**.

Hor, *adj.* white-haired, hoary-headed, 7. 193, 9. 92; Hore, 10. 175, 23. 95. A.S. *hár*.

Horde, hoard, gathering, 19. 116.

Hore, whore. 5. 161; Hores, *pl.* 4. 302; Horen, *gen. pl.* of harlots, 15. 21. Icel. *hóra*.

Horedom, unclean life, whoredom, 8. 76, b. 13. 354.

Hornyd, *pp.* provided with horns, R. 2. 4.

Hors, *pl.* horses, 3. 176, 14. 62; Horse, *pl.* b. 11. 334. A.S. pl. *hors*.

Hors-bred, horse-bread, 9. 225. See note, p. 114.

Hosboundrie, economy, prosperity, 2. 53. See **Husbondrie**.

Hose, whoso. See **Ho-so**.

Hosebonde, husband, 11. 267; Hosebonde, farmer, 13. 198; Hosebondes, *pl.* husbandmen, farmers, a. 11. 180. See note to 8. 299, p. 105.

Ho-so, whoso, b. pr. 144; Hose, whoso, whoever, a. 1. 86.

Host, host, army, 4. 252.

Hostel, *v.* provide with lodging, b. 17. 118.

Hosteler, inn-keeper, 20. 74; Hostellere, b. 5. 339. From b. 5. 329, it appears that a *hosteler* also let horses for hire. Cf. Mod. E. *ostler*.

Hostil, inn, 14. 64.

Hostrye, hostelry, inn, b. 17. 73.

Hot, *imper. s.* hoot, cry, 21. 289. (Hot out = cry aloud.)

Hote, 1 *pr. s.* am called, 17. 198; Hoteþ, *pr. s.* is named, 3. 31; Hoten, *pp.* named, called, 3. 20; Hote, *pp.* named, 12. 1. See **Hat**, **Hatte**, **Heihte**, **Hette**, **Hihte**, **Hiȝte**, **Hyȝte**.

Hoten, *v.* bid, order, command, a. 11. 48; Hote, 1 *pr. s.* 3. 211, 216; Hoteþ, *pr. s.* bids, 4. 420, 9. 78, 10. 219; Hote, *pr. s.* (*for* Hoot, short *for* Hoteth), bids, 12. 44; Hoten, *pr. pl.* bid, 9. 89; Hote, *pr. s. subj.* bid (it be so), b. 18. 390 (see note); Het, *pt. s.* commanded, 2. 17, 23. 273; Hote, *pp.* bidden, b. 6. 78. See **Heet**, **Heghte**, **Hiȝte**, **Hyȝte**. A.S. *hátan*.

Hou, *adv.* how, 4. 411, 20. 60.

Houe, hood, cap, 4. 451; Houes, *pl.* 1. 159. A.S. *húfe*, a mitre, cap. See **Houue**; and see note to 23. 172, where *glasen houe* is explained.

Houed, Houeth. See **Houyn**.

Houped, *pt. s.* whooped, called out, shouted, b. 6. 174; Hopede, 9. 168.

Houres, the 'hours' of the breviary, services, 1. 125, 2. 180.

Housbonderye, *s.* economy, b. 1. 57. See **Hosboundrie**.

Housele, the Holy Communion, 22. 393. A.S. *húsel*.

Houseled, *pp.* housled; Be houseled = to receive the holy communion, b. 19. 3; Housled, 22. 3. See note, p. 265.

Hous-hyre, house-rent, 10. 74.

Housyng, *s.* building houses, 17. 265. b. 15. 76.

GLOSSARIAL INDEX.

Houted, *pp.* hooted at, 3. 228.
Houue, hood, coif, a. 3. 276; Houues, *pl.* b. pr. 210. See **Houe.**
Houyn, *v.* hover over, R. 2. 146; Houeþ, *pr. s.* hovers, dwells, b. 3. 207; hovers over, R. 3. 50; *pr. pl.* hover about, wait about, a. pr. 84; Houede, *pt. s.* waited, 21. 83; Houed, b. pr. 210; Houyd, *pt. s.* hovered, dwelt hovering, R. 2. 176; Houede, *pt. pl.* waited, 21. 86; Houed, *pt. pl.* b. 18. 83; Houvede, *pt. pl.* waited about, 1. 159. Cf. E. *hover.* See note, p. 252.
How, *interj.* ho! 13. 19.
Howue, *s.* hood, b. 3. 293. See **Houe.**
Hoxterye, *s.* huckstery, retail dealing, a. 5. 141. See **Hokkerye.**
Hoy! troly! lolly! a burden of a popular song, 9. 123. See note.
Hucche, hutch, b. 4. 116. A *hutch* was an iron-bound clothes-box common in bedrooms. From O.F. *huche,* a hutch (Cotgrave); from Low Lat. *hutica,* a word probably of Teutonic origin. See note to 5. 111, p. 57.
Huden, *v.* hide, 20. 125; Hudde, *pt. s.* hid, b. 17. 108; Hudden, *pt. pl.* 14. 164, 21. 449; Hudynge, *pres. pt.* hiding, 11. 242. See **Huyden.** A.S. *hýdan.*
Huder, *adv.* hither, here, 21. 339. See **Hider, Hyder.**
Hue, *pron.* she, 2. 10, 12; 4. 155; *s.* the 'she'-bird, R. 3. 50. See **Heo.**
Huere, *pron. poss.* her, 20. 300; *pron. pers* 21. 178. See **Hure.**
Huere selue, herself, 21. 256.
Huire, *s.* hire, a. 6. 46; b. 5. 557; Huyre, b. 6. 141. See **Hure.**
Huirnes, *pl.* corners, a. 2. 209. See **Herne.**
Hul, *s.* hill, i.e. Cornhill, 13. 218 (see note); Hulles, *pl.* hills, 1. 6, 163; 6. 110. A.S. *hyll.*
Hulde. See **Halde.**
Hule, *s.* husk, shell; Pese hule, shell of a pea; a various reading for *pies hele,* in b. 7. 194.
Hulpe, Hulpen. See **Helpen.**
Hungreþ, *pr. s. impers.* hunger comes to (thee), 16. 252; Hungren, *pr. pl.* are hungry, 9. 225.
Huppe, *v.* hop, skip, dance, run, 18. 279. See **Hoppe, Hippe.**
Hurde, *s.* dwelling, abode, a. 7. 190. (*A bad reading for* Erd = A.S. *eard,* abode.)
Hurde, herd, i.e. shepherd, 10. 267, 275.

Hure, *v.* hear, 1. 4, 185, 220; Hurde, 1 *pt. s.* heard, 1. 203; Hurd, *pp.* 8. 69. See **Here.**
Hure, *s.* hire, pay, reward, wages, 4. 278, 310; Huire, b. 5. 557. See **Huyre, Huire.**
Hure, *pron. pers.* her, 11. 133, a. 12. 48; *dat.* to her, 4. 6; it (lit. her), 8. 251. See **Huere, Here.**
Hure, *pron. poss.* her, 20. 300; (*used of* the sun) 21. 256.
Hure, *poss. pron.* their, 1. 32.
Hurlle, *v.* hurtle, push with horns, R. 3. 27.
Hus, *pron.* his, 1. 27, 4. 252; *indefinitely* = their, 10. 53 (see note); his own, 17. 291.
Husbondrie, *s.* thriftiness, a. 1. 55; Hosboundrie, 2. 53. See note, p. 22.
Hutte, *pt. s.* hit, struck, a. 7. 168; threw, cast, a. 5. 172. See **Hitte.**
Huyden, *v.* hide, conceal, 23. 124; Huyde, *v.* 22. 459. See **Huden.**
Huyre, *s.* hire, pay, wages, 4. 303, 15. 215. See **Hure, Huire.**
Huyred, *pp.* hired, engaged, b. 6. 314, a. 7. 107.
Huyren, *v.* hear, listen to, 5. 110; Huyre, *v.* 8. 22, 9. 48, 10. 227; Huyre, 1 *pr. s.* hear, 12. 220; Huyreþ, *pr. s.* hears, listens to, 20. 220; Huyrde, *pt. s.* heard, 23. 80.
Huyrewel, Hear-well, 11. 145.
Hy, *adj.* high, proud, 23. 46; On hy = aloud, in a loud tone, a. 12. 27. See **Heigh, Hiegh.**
Hy, *pron.* they, 14. 36, 17. 93. See **Hij.**
Hyder, *adv.* hither, 16. 238, 21. 323, 23. 333. See **Hider, Huder.**
Hyderwardes, *adv.* hitherwards, 9. 345. See **Hiderwardes.**
Hyeþ, *pr. s. refl.* hurries himself, hies him, 9. 345; Hyede, *pt. s.* hied, hastened, 23. 136. See **Hiedest, Hiȝeth, Hyhe.**
Hyfdes, *pl.* heads, 18. 85. See **Heued.**
Hyght, *pt. s.* bade, ordered, 4. 9. See **Hihte.**
Hyght, was named. See **Hyhte.**
Hyh; An hyh, on high, i.e. loud and violent, 7. 124; on high, 22. 191. See **Hy.**
Hyhe, *v.* hasten, hie, 9. 206. See **Hyeþ.**
Hyhte, 1 *pr. s.* am called, 17. 184; *pt. s.* was called, was named, 19. 4, 8; Hyght, b. 11. 36. See **Hihte.**
Hylien, *v.* cover, b. 12. 231. See **Hille, Hele.**

GLOSSARIAL INDEX. 375

Hyly, *adv.* greatly, R. 2. 117.
Hym, him; Hym willynge, *dat.* he himself desiring, b. 13. 280 (see note to 7. 32); Hym and hure=him and her, every man and woman (see note, p. 23), 2. 94.
Hynde, hind, doe, 18. 9, b. 15. 274; Hyndis, *pl.* R. 2. 25.
Hyne, *s.* hind, i. e. servant, labourer, 7. 262, b. pr. 39, b. 6. 133; For an hyne=as a thing of small value, lit. at the value of a servant, b. 4. 118 (see note); Hynen, *pl.* hinds, peasants, labourers. Mod. E. *hind.*
Hyse, *pron. poss. pl.* his creatures, 20. 249. See **Hise.**
Hy3e, *adv.* loudly, with a loud voice, a. 2. 59. See **Hy, Hyh.**
Hy3te, *pt. s.* was named, was called, b. 11. 315; Hy3t, a. 12. 49; Hy3th, *pr. s.* is called, a. 12. 53. See **Hihte, Hyhte, Hote.**
Hy3te, *pt. s.* bade, commanded, b. 1, 17, b. 6. 236. See **Hihte.**

J is written like **I** in the MSS.; hence *Iangle* is for *Jangle,* &c.
I-, *prefix chiefly used with the pp. of verbs.* For *further examples, see* **Y-**.
I, *prep.* in, a. 5. 153.
Iacede, *pt. s.* jogged, 20. 50. See note, p. 243.
Iaces, *s. pl.* fringes, ribands, R. 3. 130. See note.
Iangelers, *pl.* chatterers, story-tellers, b. pr. 35, b. 10. 31, a. pr. 35. See **Iangle.**
Iangle, *v.* gossip, chatter idly, prate, talk freely, argue, 3. 99, 11. 118; Iangly, *v.* talk, argue, 16. 92; Iangled, *pt. s.* quarrelled, argued, 10. 292; Iangeled, *pt. s.* argued, b. 16. 144; murmured, b. 16. 119; Ianglyng, *pres. part.* quarrelling, disputing, 7. 68; Ianglyng, *pr. part.* chattering, begging, b. 9. 81. O.F. *jangler,* to jest; from a Teutonic root; cf. Du. *janken,* to howl. See note, p. 35.
Iangles, *pl.* quarrels, 7. 133.
Ianglynge, *s.* quarrelling, jangling, chattering, 11. 270; Ianglyng, 5. 174; Iangelynge, 22. 399.
Iape, *s.* joke, mockery, jest, 23. 145.
Iapen, *v.* jest, mock, play tricks, act the buffoon, 16. 207; Iape, *v.* jest, 3. 99; act the buffoon, b. 13. 232; Iapede, *pt. s.* mocked, 21. 40; cheat-ed, a. 1. 65; Iaped, *pt. s.* cheated, b. 1. 67; jested, b. 18. 41. Cf. F. *japper,* to bark, yelp.
Iaper, jester, buffoon, 18. 310; Iaperes, *pl.* jesters, b. 10. 31; Iapers, *pl.* b. pr. 35, a. pr. 35.
Iayler, *s.* jailor, a. 3. 133.
I-bake, *pp.* baked, a. 7. 270.
Ibore, *pp.* borne, carried, a. 5. 89; I-boren, born, sprung, a. 2. 100. See **Y-bore.**
I-bot, *pt. s.* beat, a. 7. 167.
I-bounden, *pp.* bound, 1. 97; I-bounde, a. 6. 8, a. 10. 56.
Ibroken, *pp.* broken, a. pr. 68.
I-brouht, *pp.* brought, a. 3. 2.
I-caried, *pp.* carried, a. 6. 35.
Ich, *pron.* I, 1. 4, 2. 41, 4. 134, 8. 177. See **Ik, Y.**
Icham, *for* Ich am, I am, a. 1. 73.
Ichaue, *for* Ich haue, I have, a. 5. 152, 221.
Iche, *adj.* each, every, 22. 396, a. 11. 243; Ich, each, R. 3. 40.
Ichone, *pron.* each one, R. 2. 35; Ichonne, R. 3. 268.
I-chose, *pp.* chosen, a. 5. 174. See **Ychose.**
Ichulle (*for* Ich wulle), I will, a. 3. 5; Ichule, I will, a. 5. 151; Ichul, a. 4. 84.
Iclepet, *pp.* called, a. 3. 109; Iclept, a. 11. 21. See **Y-clepid.**
I-clouted, *pp.* patched, a. 7. 55. See **Yclouted.**
Icopet, *adj.* dressed in a cope, a. 3. 36. See **Y-coped.**
I-corouned, *pp.* crowned, a. 2. 10, a. 9. 91. See **Ycoroned.**
Icrommet, *pp.* crammed, a. pr. 41.
Idel, *adj.* idle, b. 12. 1; In idel=in vain, a. 6. 61.
Idiotes, *adj.* unlearned, ignorant (priests), b. 11. 308. See note, p. 176.
Idoluen, *pp.* delved, dug, a. 6. 36.
Idon, *pp.* done, 7. 109, a. 6. 36; made, a. 5. 78; given in charge, committed, a. 10. 11.
Idyket, *pp.* ditched, a. 6. 36.
Ieaunt, *s.* giant, a. 7. 219.
Ieestes, *s. pl.* history, sayings, a. 11. 23. See **Geste.**
I-eried, *pp.* ploughed, a. 7. 5.
Iette, *s.* fashion, R. 3. 159. See note. O.F. *get,* F. *jet;* from Lat. *iactus.* See below.
Ieu3, Jew, a. 11. 83. See below.
Iewes, *pl.* Jews, b. 10. 35, 348; Iewene, *gen. pl.* of Jews, 2. 63.
Iewis, *s.* judgment, the sentence of the law, R. 3. 341. See **Iuwise.**

I-fare, *pp.* fared, gone, a. 5. 5, a. 7. 98. A.S. *gefaren,* pp. of *faran.*

I-feere, *adv.* together, a. 2. 67, a. 4. 24. Usually *in fere* = in company; from A.S. *féra,* a companion.

I-feffed, *pp.* endowed, a. 2. 50. See **Feffe.**

I-fostred, *pp.* nourished, a. 10. 118.

I-founded, *pp.* invented, lit. founded, appointed, a. 11. 161. See **Y-ffoundid.**

Igeten, *pp.* begotten, a. 10. 204. See **Geten, Ygete.**

I-gloset, *pp.* glossed, furnished with commentaries, a. 11. 126. See **Glosep, Yglosed.**

I-gloupet,*pp.* swallowed, gulped down, a. 5. 191. See **Yglobbed.**

I-graue, *pp.* engraved, stamped in the mint, a. 4. 113. See **Graue.**

I-graunted, *pp.* granted, a. 8. 8; Igrauntet, assigned, a. 3. 239.

I-gripen, *pp.* grasped, snatched, seized, a. 3. 175. See **Gripeth.**

Ihaspet, *pp.* hasped, clasped, fastened, a. 1. 171.

I-heried, *pp.* praised, a. 11. 84. A.S. *herian,* to praise.

I-holde, *pp.* held, considered; þat seint art I-holde = thou that art considered to be a saint, a. 1. 82; I-holden, *pp.* a. 3. 205. A.S. *geholden,* pp. of *healdan.*

I-hole, *adj. pl.* whole, i.e. mended up, a. 7. 55. A.S. *gehál.* See **Hole,** *adj.*

I-hondlet, *pp.* handled, treated, dispensed, a. 2. 104.

I-hoten, *pp.* called, named, a. 11. 104, 180; Ihote, a. 1. 61. See **Hat, Y-hote.**

I-hulet, *pp.* roofed, a. 6. 80. Icel. *hylja,* to cover.

Ihuret, *pp.* hired, paid with wages, a. 7. 300. See **Huyre, Yhyred.**

Iille, a gill, b. 5. 346. See **Gille.**

Ik, *pron.* I, b. 5. 228. A.S. *ic.*

I-keiȝet, *pp.* keyed, i.e. locked, a. 6. 103. See **Y-keyed.**

I-kliketed,*pp.* fastened, a. 6. 103. See **Cliket.**

I-knewe, *pt. s.* knew, R. 1. 92; I-knowe, *pp.* known, b. 15. 17, a. 3. 34. See **Yknowen.**

I-kore, *pp.* chosen as, picked out as, a. 4. 140. A.S. *gecoren,* pp. of *céosan,* to choose.

I-lakked, *pp.* blamed, found fault with, a. 2. 17. See **Lakke.**

I-leid, *pp.* laid, staked, a. 3. 195.

Ileiȝen, *pp.* lien, lain, been laid, a. 5. 65. A.S. *gelegen,* pp. of *licgan,* to lie. See **Yleine.**

I-leorned, *pp.* learnt, been taught, a. 9. 10.

Ileue, *v.* to believe, a. 5. 112. A.S. *gelýfan,* to believe.

Ilke, *adj.* same, 4. 404, 11. 141; very, 8. 141, 245; very thing, 2. 79.

Ille, *adj. pl.* wicked, 11. 93.

Ille, *adv.* ill, b. 10. 26. See **Ylle.**

I-loket, *pp.* taken care, ordained, decided (lit. 'looked,' i. e. looked to), a. 10. 201.

Ilyke, *adj.* like, b. 1. 50. A.S. *gelíc.* See **Iliche.**

I-made, 1 *pt. s.* made, b. 5. 162; Imad, *pp.* a. 10. 2; celebrated, a. 2. 22; I-maket, *pp.* a. pr. 14. See **Ymad.**

Imaunget, *pp.* eaten, a. 7. 245. F. *manger.*

I-medlet, *pp.* mingled, joined, a. 10. 202; Imedelet, a. 10. 3. See **Ymedeled.**

I-meint, *pp.* prepared, mingled, a. 10. 4. A.S. *gemenged,* pp. of *mengan,* to mix.

Imparfit, *adj.* unjust, unfair, 4. 389. See **Inparfit.**

Impe, *imper. s.* graft, b. 9. 147. See **Ymped.**

Impugneth, *pr. s.* impugns, calls in question, b. 11. 297; Impugned, *pt. s.* b. 7. 147; *pp.* accused, b. 13. 123. See **Inpugnen.**

In, *prep.* on, 22. 479.

In-departable, *adj.* indivisible, 19. 27.

I-nempnet, *pp.* named, called, a. 10. 43, a. 11. 106. See **Ynempned.**

Infamis, old Lat. pl. for *infames,* censured (but prob. here simply misused for *infames*), b. 5. 168. *Infamia* was a note of censure, involving certain disabilities.

Ingang, *s.* ingoing, entrance, admission, ingress, 8. 282; Ingonge, b. 5. 638.

In-goynge *s.* entrance, admission, a. 6. 117. See **Ingang.**

Ingrat, *adj.* ungrateful, unkind, 20. 219.

Ingratus, unkind, b. 17. 253; *Ingrati,* pl. ungrateful, b. 14. 169.

Inliche, *adv.* inwardly, in heart, 4. 373; b. 14. 89.

Inmesurables, *adj. pl.* infinite, b. 15. 69.

In-myddes, *prep.* into the midst of, 11. 33.

Inne, *adv.* within, in, b. 6. 305; a. 1. 163; therein, b. 10. 99; in, at home, a. 12. 41; into, R. 3. 85.

GLOSSARIAL INDEX. 377

Inne, *s. dat.* dwelling, residence; At inne=in (his) abode, in residence, b. 8. 4. See **Ynne.**
Inne-wit; see **Inwit.**
Innocentz, *pl. as sb.* innocent people, prob. children, b. 7. 41.
In-obedient, *adj.* disobedient, 7. 19, b. 13. 282.
Inomen, *pp.* taken, a. 3. 1. A.S. *genumen,* pp. of *niman,* to take. See **Nym.**
I-nouh, *adj.* enough, a. 7. 136; Inouwe, *pl.* a. 3. 24; Inowe, *pl.* b. 20. 248. A.S. *genóh,* pl. *genóge.*
Inpacient, impatient, 20. 319.
Inparfit, *adj.* imperfect, 12. 208, 16. 136; Inparfyt, 17. 212; faulty, b. 15. 93. See **Imparfit.**
Inparfitly, *adv.* not in a perfect manner, b. 10. 464.
Inpossible, *adj.* impossible, b. 10. 336, b. 18. 419.
Inpugnen, *v.* impugn, gainsay, b. pr. 109; Inpugned, *pt. s.* found fault with, 10. 301. See **Impugneth.**
Insolibles, *adj. pl.* insoluble, 17. 231.
In-stude, *adv.* instead of, in the place of, a. 7. 57.
In-til, *prep.* into, b. 13. 210.
Into, *prep.* within, a. 11. 44.
Inwit, inward knowledge, i.e. conscience, 7. 421, 11. 143, 18. 269; Inwitt, 11. 170; understanding, intelligence, 10. 117; Inwitte, b. 9. 18; Innewit, b. 15. 546. See note, p. 139.
Iogelen, *v.* play juggler's tricks, 16. 207; Iogly, *v.* b. 13. 232.
Iogelour, buffoon, juggler, 9. 71, 18. 310; Iogeloure, b. 6. 72; Iogeloures, *pl.* b. 10. 31. O.F. *jougleor, jogleor* = Lat. *ioculatorem.* See note, p. 108.
Iogged, *pt. s.* jogged, went hastily, 23. 134; Iugged, b. 20. 133.
Iogly, *v.* juggle, b. 13. 232. See **Iogelen.**
Ioied, *pt. pl.* rejoiced, R. 3. 159.
Iolif, *adj.* joyful, 14. 20.
Iordan, chamber-pot, 16. 92 (spoken contemptuously of a glutton); Iurdan, b. 13. 83. See note, p. 192.
Iottes, *pl.* peasants, low people, men of small intelligence, b. 10. 460; Iottis, a. 11. 301. Cf. *jolt-head,* Two Gent. of Verona, III. i. 290.
Iouken, *v.* rest, slumber, 19. 126; Iouke, b. 16. 92. See note, p. 238.
'*Ioucher, Iucher,* to roost, or pearch;' Cotgrave.
Iourne, day's work, 17. 5.
Iouste, *v.* tilt, joust, 21. 21, 26. 85;

Iousted, *pt. s.* tilted, 21. 185. O.F. *iouster,* Low Lat. *iuxtare.*
Iouster, jouster, champion, 22. 10. See above.
Ioutes, *pl.* broths, pottages, 6. 133, b. 5. 158. '*Iowtys,* potage, *Brassica, juta;*' Prompt. Parv.; see Way's note. And see note, p. 79.
Ioye-less, *adj.* joy-less, miserable, 11. 270; Ioyeles, b. 9. 166.
Ioyntely, *adv.* in union, together, a. 2 127.
I-preiset, *pp.* esteemed, a. 8. 158. See **Ypreised.**
I-punissched, *pp.* punished, a. 5. 76.
I-quit, *pp.* paid, a. 7. 91.
Irens, *s. pl.* irons, chains, fetters, a. 4. 72. See **Yren.**
I-robed, *pp.* robed, dressed, a. 9. 1. See **Yrobed.**
I-rybaunt, *pp.* embroidered with rows, lit. with ribbons (of gold lace or precious stones), a. 2. 13.
Is, *used for* are, b. 16. 230.
Is, *put for* -es, *the termination of the gen. case,* a. 5. 257.
I-schewet, *pp.* showed, a. 4. 145.
I-schood, *pp.* shod, a. 2. 134.
I-schriuen, *pp.* shriven, a. 5. 151.
I-seo, *v.* see, a. 6. 60; I-seye, *pp.* seen, found, a. 10. 105; Iseȝe, *pp.* a. 5. 4. A.S. *geséon.*
I-seruet, *pp.* served, well served, suited, a. 5. 185. See **Y-serued.**
Iset, *pp.* set, placed, a. 6. 82.
I-seye, *pp.* seen, found, a. 10. 105. See **I-seo.**
Iseȝe, *pp.* seen, a. 5. 4. See **I-seo.**
I-shrewed, *pp.* cursed, b. 13. 331.
I-slept, *pp.* slept, a. 5. 4.
I-souht, *pp.* sought, a. 4. 109. See **Ysouht.**
I-sowed, *pp.* sown, a. 6. 34. See **Ysowen.**
Issue, *s.* issue, progeny, offspring, 19. 221; Issu, b. 10. 326; Isshue, 11. 243; Issues, *pl.* issues, out-goings, R. 4. 8. See **Ysshue.**
I-swowene, *pp.* in a swoon, a. 5. 222. A.S. *geswógen;* see *Swoon* in my Etym. Dict.
Isykles, *pl.* icicles, 20. 193. A.S. *ísgicel.* See *Ikyl* in Prompt. Parv. '*Ickles, stiriæ;*' Levins.
It, *pron.* it, i.e. the sky, the heavens, R. 3. 366.
It ben=they are, *or* it is, 6. 59.
Itermynet, *pp.* decided upon, adjudged, a. 1. 95. See **Ytermyned.**
I-tilled, *pp.* set up, pitched, a. 2. 44.

Put for *itilded* = *itelded*, set up or spread out, as a tent; from A.S. *teld*, a tent.
Itriȝed, *pp.* tried, a. 1. 83; I-triȝet, a. 1. 124. See Ytried.
Iuellis, *s. pl.* jewels, R. 1. 38.
Iuge, *s.* judge, 16. 291; Iuges, *pl.* 10. 335; Iugges, *pl.* b. 7. 184.
Iugen, *v.* be judge, 23. 29; Iuge, *v.* decide, decree, 3. 169; Iugge, *v.* adjudge, order, a. 2. 106, 127; judge, b. pr. 130; Iugge, 1 *pr. s.* judge, rule, 22. 476; judge to be, b. 9. 84; Iuggeþ, *pr. s.* declares, decides, 2. 182; Iuged, *pt. s.* determined, 10. 310; Iugged, *pt. s.* b. 7. 161.
Iugged, *pt. s.* jogged, rode hastily, b. 20. 133. See Iogged.
Iurdan, a chamber-pot, jordan, a term of contempt, b. 13. 83. See Iordan.
Iurers, *gen. pl.* jurors', 3. 150.
Iuste, *adj.* swollen, like a *juste* or bottle, bottle-like, 16. 92; Iust, b. 13. 83. See the note. p. 192.
Iusten, *v.* joust, contend in a tournament, 20. 50; Iuste, *v.* 19. 129; Iusted, *pt. s.* b. 16. 163.
Iuster, jouster, b. 19. 10.
Iustes, *pl.* jousts, tournaments, tournament, 21. 14, b. 17. 51.
Iustice, *s.* judge, magistrate, 19. 163, 22. 139; Iustise, a. 2. 106.
Iustiflede, *pt. s.* approved, 22. 44.
Iuuente, *s.* youth, 22. 108. O.F. *jovente*, youth (Burguy).
Iuwe, Jew, 21. 85; Iuwes, *pl.* b. 10. 126; Iuwene, *gen. pl.* of Jews, 21. 268; Iuwen, *gen. pl.* of the Jews, b. 1. 67, b. 15. 574. See Iuwen.
Iuwel, jewel, 21. 475; treasure, b. 18. 428; Iuweles, a. 3. 151; Iuellis, R. 1. 38.
Iuweler, *s.* one who possesses jewels, a wealthy person, a. 2. 87. Lit. 'jeweller.'
Iuwen, *adj.* (or *gen. pl.*) Jewish, *or* of Jews, 21. 40. See Iuwe. (If it is the gen. pl., then *oure Iuwen* = of us Jews.)
Iuwise, *s.* judgment, sentence of death, 21. 427; Lewis, R. 3. 341. O.F. *juise* = Lat. *iudicium*.
I-war, *adj.* wary, aware, a. 6. 98, a. 11. 92. A.S. *gewær*. See Ywar.
I-waxen, *pp.* become, grown, a. 3. 279; I-woxe, a. 2. 139.
I-wayted, *pp.* watched after, taken heed of, a. 6. 37.
I-went, *pp.* went, gone, a. 7. 193.

Iwis, *adv.* verily, a. 6. 120. A.S. *gewis*, *adv.* verily.
I-witen, *v.* know, learn, 'a. 9. 118; I-wite, *v.* know, discover, a. 4. 122; know, a. 6. 44. A.S. *gewitan*, to understand. See Ywite.
I-woxe. See I-waxen.
I-wriþen, *pp.* twisted, entwined, a. 6. 9. A.S. *gewriðen*, pp. of *wriðan*.
I-writen, *pp.* written, a. 1. 174; I-write, b. 10. 413; Y-wryten, b. 11. 220; Y-wryte, 9. 240. A.S. *gewriten*, pp. of *writan*.
I-wrouȝt, *pp.* made, created, a. 8. 82. A.S. *geworht*, pp. of *wyrcan*. See Ywrouȝt.
I-wrye, *pp.* twisted, b. 14. 232. See Ywrye.
Iȝeten, *pp.* eaten, a. 7. 251. A.S. *ge-eten*, eaten. In the South of England, the people say, 'I have *a-yeat* an apple.' See Yeten.
I-ȝiue, *pp.* given, a. 5. 220. See ȝiuen.

Kaban, cabin, b. 3. 190. See Caban.
Kachepol, officer, catch-poll, 21. 46. See Cacchepol.
Kairen, *v.* to go about, b. pr. 29; *pr. s.* Kaireth, goes, b. 4. 23; Kaires hym = goes, betakes himself, b. 5. 385 (cf. 7. 351); Kairen hem, *v.* betake themselves, b. 2. 161. Confused with *carien* in some MSS.
Kaiser, Emperor, 4. 317; Kaisere, b. 19. 134. See Caiser, Kayser.
Kalendare, calendar, b. 13. 153.
Kalketrappes, *pl.* calthrops, caltraps, 21. 296. See the note.
Kallyd, 1 *pt. s.* called, 21. 473.
Kam, 1 *pt. s.* came, 12. 138; am descended, 3. 30, 7. 58. See Comen.
Kammokes, *s. pl.* the plants called rest-harrow, b. 19. 309. See Cammokes.
Karde, *ger.* card wool, 10. 80. See Carded.
Kare, anxiety, b. 18. 213; care, trouble, 23. 201; Karis, *pl.* cares, R. 1. 7. See Care.
Kareyne, carrion, R. 2. 178. See Caroigne.
Karpeþ, *pr. s.* speaks, 17. 271; Karpen, *pr. pl.* say, 3. 27. See Carpen.
Karpinge, *s.* talking, talk, 17. 338. See Carpinge.
Katel, property, wealth, b. 12. 292. See Catel.
Kauht. See Cacchen.

GLOSSARIAL INDEX. 379

Kauked. See **Cauke.**
Kauȝte. See **Cacchen.**
Kayed, *pp.* fastened with a key, b. 5. 623.
Kayres, *pr. s.* (with *hym*), betakes himself, goes, 7. 351; see **Kairen.**
Kayser, emperor, 4. 321; Kayseres, *pl.* b. 9. 110; Kayseris, *pl.* R. 1. 85. See **Caiser.**
Keiȝes, *s. pl.* keys, a. 6. 13.
Kele, *v.* cool, 22. 280. A.S. *célan.*
Kembe, *ger.* comb wool, 10. 80; Kemben, *pr. pl.* 12. 15, b. 10. 18. A.S. *cemban;* from *camb*, a comb.
Kende, *s.* nature, natural powers, b. 13. 404. See **Kynde.**
Kene, *adj.* sharp, keen, 3. 29, 7. 140; bitter, 7. 65; fierce, bold, 23. 129, 141.
Kenne, *gen. pl.*; Alle kenne = of all kinds, a. 12. 105. A.S. *cynna,* gen. pl. of *cynn.* See **Kun.**
Kenne, *v.* tell, teach, shew, 2. 78, 137; shew, introduce, b. 10. 148; direct, 12. 94; explain, 10. 283; b. 5. 246; proclaim, 2. 88; make (it) known, b. 1. 92; know, 12. 141; Ken, to shew, guide, a. 12. 49; Kennest, 2 *pr. s.* teachest, a. 7. 23; Kenneth, *pr. s.* teaches, 4. 362, 9. 19; Kenneth, 2 *pr. pl.* teach, b. 10. 110; Kenne, *pr. pl.* teach, tell, b. 15. 156; Kenne, 2 *pr. s. subj.* teach, shew, b. 10. 146; Kenne, 2 *pr. pl. subj.* teach, 12. 92; Kennide, *pt. s.* taught, informed, a. 8. 120; Kenned, *pt. s.* guided, b. 4. 43; taught, 5. 41, b. 7. 133; Kende, *pt. s.* taught, 22. 234; shewed (me) the way, a. 6. 30; Kennede him = instructed himself, was learned, a. 2. 202; Kende, 1 *pt. s.* taught, a. 11. 134; 2 *pt. pl.* taught the way, 19. 17; *pt. pl.* shewed the way, 8. 184; Kenned, *pt. pl.* guided, b. 5. 546; Kenne, *imp. s.* teach, 3. 4, b. 2. 4; Kenneth, *imp. pl.* teach, b. 6. 14. Icel. *kenna,* to teach, to know; Goth. *kannjan,* to make known.
Kenne, *pr. pl.* produce chickens, R. 3. 51. A.S. *cennan,* to generate, beget.
Kennyng, *s.* instruction, lesson, b. 10. 194.
Keouered, *pt. s.* covered, sheltered, 22. 296; *pp.* covered up, hidden, 22. 349. See **Keuery.**
Kepen, *v.* protect, guard, take care of, 11. 103, 22. 42; observe, keep, 2. 90; Kepen hem = govern themselves, a. 1. 92; Kepe, *v.* rule, govern, 5. 135; support, keep, b. 12. 292; take care of, b. 19. 275; Kepe, 1 *pr. s.* care, care for, desire, b. 3. 278, b. 4. 193;

Kepeþ, *pr. s.* cares, 14. 234; will care, b. 11. 414; Kepith, *pr. s.* sustains, b. 8. 45; Kepen, *pr. pl.* watch over, a. 8. 9; Kepe no betere = regard nothing further, a. 1. 8; Kep, *pr. s. subj.* may keep, 1. 148; Kepten, *pt. pl.* kept, guarded, 15. 58, 22. 149; Kep, *imp. s.* keep, 3. 47; observe, 12. 143.
Kepe, *s.* care, attention, notice, heed, 14. 145, 20. 74.
Keper, keeper, guardian, 23. 72; Kepere, 22. 445.
Kepynge, *s.* living, 22. 356. Cf. the Cambridge use of *keep* in the sense of live or lodge.
Kerneled, *pp.* furnished with battlements, crenellated, b. 5. 597.
Kernels, *pl.* battlements, 8. 235. O.F. *crenel* (later *creneau*), a battlement, dimin. of O.F. *cren, cran,* a notch, Lat. *crena.* See note, p. 103.
Kertil, *s.* under-jacket, a. 5. 63. See **Kirtel.**
Kerue, *v.* carve, i.e. cut, 9. 65, b. 6. 106, a. 7. 97.
Kerueres, *pl.* carvers, sculptors, 12. 126; Keruers, a. 11. 134.
Keruynge, *s.* carving, sculpturing, b. 17. 170; Kerving, cutting, slashing, R. 3. 164.
Kete, *adj.* intelligent, sharp, keen-witted, a. 11. 56. Cf. Icel. *kátr,* joyful, *kæti,* joy. See Mätzner, and Gloss. to Will. of Palerne.
Ketten, *pt. pl.* cut, b. 6. 191.
Keuery, *v.* (1) cover, roof in, 4. 64; Keure, *v.* cover, b. 3. 60; (2) Keuere, *v.* recover, R. 3. 17; Keure, *v.* recover, b. 20. 333; Keuereþ, *pr. s.* (1) covers, 10. 249; protects, b. 12. 179; (2) recovers, 15. 118; Keuere, *pr. pl.* recover, 23. 335; Keuered, *pp.* (1) covered, hidden, 22. 86, b. 19. 82, 343. The 2nd meaning (*recover*) occurs in Chaucer, Troilus, i. 918, and in Will. of Palerne. And see **Keouered.**
Kew-kaw, *s.* sudden change, subversion, R. 3. 299. In Ayrshire, *kew* means 'an overset'; Jamieson.
Kex, dried hemlock-stalk used for a torch, a kind of rushlight, b. 17. 219; Kyx, 20. 185. See Prompt. Parv. p. 277, n. 4, and Wright's Vocab. i. 157. '*Kex,* a stem of the hemlock or cowparsley;' Gloss. to Barnes, Dorsetsh. Poems. W. *cecys,* s. pl. hollow stalks, hemlock; cf. W. *cegid,* Lat. *cicuta,* hemlock. '
Keye, *s.* key, b. 10. 323.

VOL. II.   A a

GLOSSARIAL INDEX.

Kidde, *pt. s.* shewed, b. 5. 440; *pt. pl.* b. 15. 298; Kydde, *pt. s.* shewed, 8. 46; 1 *pt. s.* b. 13. 390; Kid, *pp.* made known, manifested, 20. 251. A.S. *cydde*, pt. t. of *cýðan*, to make known.
Kille, *ger.* to smite, a. 11. 282. See **Cullen**.
Kingene; see **Kyngene**.
Kinghed, *s.* kingship, a. 11. 216; Kinghod, a. 11. 222.
Kirke, church, 4. 64, 6. 104.
Kirke-ȝerd, church-yard, 16. 11; Kirkeȝerde, b. 13. 9.
Kirnelle, kernel, b. 11. 253, 257. See **Curnel**.
Kirtel, kirtle, under-jacket, b. 5. 80, b. 11. 276. See note, p. 74.
Kisseth; see **Kyssen**.
Kith, Kitth. See **Kyth**.
Kitoun, *s.* kitten, b. pr. 190; Kyton, 1. 204, 207; Kytones, *pl.* 1. 214.
Kitte-pors, cut-purse, thief, 8. 283. See **Cutpurs**.
Klerken, *gen. pl.* of clerks, 5. 114.
Knappes, *pl.* knops, knobs, buttons, b. 6. 272, a. 7. 257.
Knaue, servant, 1. 40, 4. 415, 5. 17, 9. 46, b. 4. 14; fellow, a. 12. 71; Knaues, *pl.* 1. 45, 2. 125; Knauene, *gen. pl.* knaves'; Knauene werkes = work suited for serving-men, 6. 54.
Knawe, *v.* know, 2. 72.
Knelyng, *s.* kneeling, bending, b. 10. 138, a. 11. 95.
Kneolen, *v.* kneel, 22. 17; Kneole, 22. 28, 200; Kneolede, *pt. s.* knelt, 22. 12, 91; Knelede, 1 *pt. s.* I kneeled, 3. 1; Kneleden, *pt. pl.* 1. 71; Kneolede, 22. 74, 81; Kneolynge, *pres. pt.* 21. 151.
Knewleched, *pt. s.* confessed, acknowledged, b. 12. 193; Knewelechede, *pt. pl.* acknowledged, 22. 77; Knewelechid, 1 *pt. pl.* 8. 148; Knewliched, *pt. pl. subj.* should acknowledge, 22. 186. See **Knowleche**.
Knihtes, *s. pl.* knights, a. 1. 92; Kniȝtes, servants, b. 11. 304; Knyȝtes, followers, b. 15. 50. See note, p. 176.
Knockede, *pt. pl.* struck, 23. 130.
Knouhlechede, *pt. s.* acknowledged, confessed, a. 5. 256.
Knowen, *v.* know, 4. 343; Kneuh, a. 4. 48; Knewe, *pt. s.* knew, understood, b. 13. 187; Kneuȝ, a. 2. 202; acknowledged, a. 11. 273 (see note); 2 *pt. s.* knewest, b. 11. 31; Knewen, *pt. pl.* knew, a. 9. 12; Knowe, *pp.* known, 1. 54; Knowen, *pp.* a. 12. 43; Knoweþ, *imp. pl.* know ye; Knoweþ of = acknowledge, give (me) thanks for, a. 1. 177.
Knowes, knees, b. 5. 359.
Knowing, *s.* understanding, a. 1. 127; Knowyng, knowledge, 11. 108; understanding, 11. 56; Knowynge, knowledge, 22. 310; understanding, 4. 285; recognition, *as in* For knowynge of = to prevent recognition by, 3. 240; Knowynges, *pl.* sciences, various kinds of knowledge, b. 12. 137.
Knowleche, *pr. pl.* acknowledge, b. 19. 181; Knowelecheþ, *pr. s.* acknowledges, 14. 90; Knowlechede, *pt. s.* 7. 328; Knowleched, *pt. s.* confessed, b. 5. 481; Knowlechyng, *pres. pt.* b. 19. 73. See **Knewleched, Knouhlechede**.
Knowliche, *s.* knowledge, R. 2. 54.
Knyghtfees, the incomes of knights, 6. 77.
Knyghthod, a knight's act, 21. 101.
Knyhtide, *pt. s.* knighted, a. 1. 103.
Kokeney. See **Cokeney**.
Kokewolde. See **Cokewold**.
Koleplantes, *pl.* cole-worts, cabbages, b. 6. 288. See **Colplontes**.
Konne, *v.* learn, a. 12. 7; Kunne, *v.* know, b. 15. 53; learn, b. 15. 45; Kunne, 1 *pr. s.* know, R. 1. 22; Konne, *pr. pl.* can, know how to, b. 6. 70; Kunne, *pr. pl.* know how, b. 13. 178; Kunneth, *pr. pl.* know, b. 7. 41; Kunne, *pr. s. subj.* can, R. 3. 35.
Konnyng, knowledge, b. 11. 293; Konnynge, learning, 14. 113; Konnynges, *pl.* knowledge, sciences, 12. 95.
Kourteby, b. 5. 80. See **Courtepy**.
Koweþ, *pr. s.* coughs, 20. 307; Kowede, *pt. s.* 16. 109. See **Cowhede**.
Kullen, *v.* kill, b. 166; Kulle, *ger.* to kill, b. 16. 137; Kulled, put to death, b. 16. 152. See **Cullen**.
Kulter, coulter, b. 3. 306. See **Culter, Coltre**.
Kun, *s.* kin, kindred, a. 1. 166; race, a. 10. 151; kin, relative, a. 6. 118; Kunne, *dat.* kin, family, race, 3. 57; Kynne, *dat.* kin, family, b. 15. 17; Kynne, *acc.* (*pl.*?), kindred, family, b. 11. 185, 290; Kunnes, *gen.* of kind, (*in various phrases as*) Eny kunnes ȝiftus = gifts of any kind, a. 2. 175; Alle kunnes = of every kind, a. 7. 63; Of alle kynnes = of every kind, b. 14. 184; Any kynnes catel = property of any kind, b. 19. 73; None kynnes = of no kind, b. 11. 185; Many kynnes = of many a kind, b. 8. 15; What

GLOSSARIAL INDEX. 381

kynnes conceyll = advice of what sort, i.e. what 'sort of advice, R. 2. 19; What kynnes thyng = a thing of what kind, b. 9. 25; Of foure kynnes þinges = of things of four kinds, b. 9. 2; Kunne, *gen. pl. (as in)* Alle kunne = of all kinds, a. 3. 218; Alle kunne beestes = beasts of all kinds, a. 10. 27; Foure kunne þinges = things of four kinds, a. 10. 2, 27; No kyne catel = property of no sort, 11. 250; Of foure kyne þynges = of things of four kinds, 11. 128; No kyne = of no kind, 13. 102; Alle kyne = of every kind, a. 11. 182; þre kynne kynges = kings of three kinds (*or*, of three races), b. 19. 91; Thre kynne þynges = things of three kinds, 4. 381; Alle kynne = of all kinds, a. 11. 238; Alle kynne kynde = methods of every kind, 4. 366; Meny kynne = of many kinds, 1. 26, 11. 15, 14. 56; Kynne, *sing.* (*put for* Kynnes, *gen.*), *as in* Eny kynne þynge = a thing of any kind, i. e. any sort of, 9. 268; Oþer kynne = of another kind, 20. 109. A.S. *cynn*, kind, race. The mod. E. idiom is different; we do not say *a thing of any kind*, but *any kind of thing*. See Cun; and note to 11. 128, p. 137.

Kunne, Kunneth. See **Konne.**
Kuth, Kutthe. See **Kyth.**
Kuynde, Kuyndeliche. See **Kynde, Kyndeliche.**
Kydde, *pt. s.* showed, 8. 46; 1 *pt. s.* b. 13. 390. See **Kidde.**
Kyke, *ger.* to kick, 5. 22.
Kyn, kine, 6. 18; Kyne, b. 6. 142.
Kynde, *s.* nature, 3. 27, 4. 251; gender, 4. 339, 358; kind, people, a. 11. 282; kindred, 20. 219; children, young, b. 11. 327; kind, race, b. pr. 186; natural disposition, b. 2. 27; natural strength, 13. 146, b. 11. 253; natural desire, 9. 78; natural issue, 19. 224; (natural) seed, 14. 172; Kuynde, nature, a. 7. 150, a. 9. 37; race, mankind, a. 6. 78; Of kynde = by nature, 10. 168, 11. 47; Kyndes, *pl.* manners, ways, 4. 364, 374. A.S. *cynd.* See **Kende.**
Kynde, *adj.* natural, 3. 29, 11. 56, 12. 227; b. 11. 182; correct, a. 11. 247; proper, own, 11. 69; instinctive, b. 8. 57; usual, b. 8. 71; Kuynde, natural, a. 3. 270; usual, a. 9. 62, 103; innate, a. 2. 4; Kynde wit = common sense, 2. 51; Kuynde wit, a. 1. 53; Kynde knowyng = natural knowledge, 2. 137; Kuynde knowing = natural understanding, conscience, a. 1. 127. A.S. *cynde.* See **Kende.**
Kyndeliche, *adv.* naturally, 2. 160, 8. 183, 12. 102; kindly, 2. 78; properly, 10. 213; intimately, 12. 92; in ordinary language, i.e. in plain English, 5. 147; Kyndelich, naturally, b. 14. 87; intimately, b. 1. 81, b. 5. 545; kindly, b. 3. 15; Kuyndeliche, intimately, a. 6. 29.
Kynde-witted, *adj.* naturally clever, 15. 52.
Kyne. See **Kun.**
Kyngene, *gen. pl.* of kings, 22. 79; Kingene, b. 1. 105. The suffix *-ene* is a survival of the A.S. *gen. pl.* suffix *-ena* of the weak declension.
Kynghod, kingly estate, b. 10. 333.
Kynne, Kynnes. See **Kun.**
Kyngriche. See **Kynriche.**
Kynredene, *s.* kindred, 11. 258; Kynrede, b. 9. 172. A.S. *cynn*, kin; with suffix *-ræden.*
Kynriche, *s.* kingdom, 11. 111, 13. 168; Kynryche, 1. 148.
Kyssen, *ger.* kiss, 1. 71; Kyste, *pt. s.* kissed, b. 18. 420; Kyste, 1 *pt. s.* a. 12. 47; Kisseth, *imp. pl.* b. 18. 428. A.S. *cyssan;* from *coss*, a kiss.
Kyth, family, relatives, kindred, b. 13. 379; Kyth, country, b. 19. 75; Kitth, b. 15. 497; Kitthe, b. 3. 305; Kuth, kith, friends, 18. 196; Kutthe, country, 22. 79.
Kyton. See **Kitoun.**
Kytte, Kit (*proper name*), used as a general name for a bride, it being the name of the author's own wife, 8. 304; cf. 6. 2, 21. 473.
Kyx, rush-light, 20. 185. See **Kex.**

Labbe, *imp. s.* talk, speak, prate about, 13. 39. Cf. 'a *labbing* shrewe,' Chaucer, C. T. 10,302 (Squires Prologue); '*labbyng* tonge'; Romans of Partenay, 3751. Cf. Skt. *lap,* to speak.
Laborie, *v.* labour, work, 9. 135; Labory, b. 15. 182; Laboure, R. 3. 267; Labre, a. 7. 29; Labereþ, *imp. pl.* a. 7. 13.
Lac, *v.* lack, R. 3. 142. See **Lakke.**
Lacchedrawers, *pl.* thieves, burglars, 9. 288, 10. 192. Lit. latch-drawers, i. e. lifters of the latch, men who sneak into houses; see note to 1. 45, p. 7.
Lacchen, *v.* catch, gain, obtain, 10. 141, 16. 203; receive, b. 13. 228; Lacche, *v.* catch, gain, receive, take, 2. 101, 4. 394; Laccheth, *pr. s.* seizes,

A a 2

b. 16. 50; Lacchen, *pr. pl.* gain, get, receive, b. 15. 235; Lacche, 17. 362; Lacchen, 2 *pr. pl.* ye gain, get, 3. 138; Lacche, 3. 215; Lacche, *pr. s. subj.* receive, b. 11. 217; 2 *pr. s. subj.* catch, b. 2. 202; Lauhte, *pt. s.* caught, took, seized, 1. 169, 2. 205, 19. 119, 20. 123, 23. 152; took (to himself), practised, a. 1. 30; Lauȝte, *pt. s.* took, seized, caught, b. pr. 150, b. 16. 86; took upon him, b. 17. 148; Lauȝthe, seized, a. 12. 55 *n.*; Lauȝt hym, took to himself, practised, b. 1. 30; Lauȝþe, 1 *pt. pl.* took, a. 12. 55; Lauȝten, *pt. pl.* took; Lauȝten leue at = took leave of, a. 3. 25; Lauȝte, *pt. pl.* seized, R. 2. 159; Lacchide, *pt. pl.* took, received, grasped, R. 1. 72; Lauht, *pp.* taken, 4. 26; Lauȝth, *pp.* caught, snatched away, a. 12. 96 *n.* A.S. *læccan, ge-læccan.* 'Latchyd, *arreptus*;' Prompt. Parv.

Lacchesse, *s.* laziness, remissness, negligence, 9. 253, 10. 269, 279; b. 8. 37; Lachesse, a. 9. 32. From O.F. *lasche*, slack (Cotgrave); Roquefort gives *lachesse*. See *Latchesse* in the Prompt. Parv.

Lacching, *s.* taking, receiving, a. 1. 101. A.S. *læccan*, to seize.

Lacke, &c. See Lakke, &c.

Lacles. See Lakles.

Lad, Ladde. See Leden.

Lady, *gen.* lady's, b. 18. 335; Ladi, lady, a. 3. 32.

Lafte, left, remained. See Leue, to leave.

Laies, *pl.* laws, 22. 43. Cf. *lay* = law, religious profession, Chaucer, C. T. 4796. O.F. *lei*.

Laies, lays. See Lay, *s.*

Laik, game, sport, trial of strength, 17. 85. Icel. *leikr*, play.

Laike, *v.* play, sport, b. pr. 172. Icel. *leika*, to play. See Layke.

Laith, *adj.* hateful, b. 12. 244. Icel. *leiðr*, loathed, hateful. See Loth.

Laith, *pr. s.* lays, is setting, 7. 406. See Leyn.

Lakeryng, *s.* chiding, (?), 7. 394. The B-text has *louryng*. It seems to be from a vb. *lakeren*, frequentative of *lakken*, to blame; the sense is, accordingly, 'reproaching continually.' See below.

Lakke, *v.* blame, find fault with, b. 5. 132; Lacke, v. 2. 116, 7. 98, 8. 23; Lacky, *v.* 16. 78, 20. 101; Lacke, 1 *pr. s.* find fault with, blame, 14. 26; Lakketh, *pr. s.* blames, b. 15. 248, b.

17. 291; Lackieþ, 2 *pr. pl.* blame, find fault with, 4. 58; Lakkeþ, b. 3. 54; Lakketh, *pr. pl.* b. 10. 203, b. 15. 198; Lakken, b. 10. 262; Lacken, 18. 312; Lakke, 2 *pr. s. subj.* blame, find fault with, 14. 208; *pr. s. subj.* 22. 254; Lakkede, *pt. s.* blamed, reproved, 12. 165; Lackede, 4. 130; Lakked, b. 11. 2; Lakkedest, 2 *pt. s.* didst find fault, b. 11. 411; Lakked, *pt. pl.* blamed, found fault with, b. 15. 4; Lackyd, *pp.* blamed, found fault with, 3. 21; Lakke, *imper. s.* find fault with, b. 2. 47; Lakkyng. *pr. pt.* blaming, b. 13. 287. O. Fries. *lakia*, Du. *laken*, to blame.

Lakke, *v.* lack, fail, be wanting, 23. 249, b. 11. 280; Lackye, *v.* 14. 103; Lakketh, *pr. s.* is wanting, fails, b. 11. 273; etc.

Lakkes, *pl.* faults, b. 10. 262. O. Du. *lack, lacke*, vituperation, blaming, or vice (Hexham). 'Lak, or defawte, *defectus, defeccio*;' Prompt. Parv.

Lakles, *adj.* faultless, b. 11. 382; Lacles, 14. 211. See above.

Lambren, *pl.* lambs, 4. 414, 10. 260.

Lammase, Lammas, the first of August, 9. 314. See note, p. 117.

Lande-leperes, *pl.* vagabond hermits, b. 15. 207. See note to 7. 329.

Land-tylynge, *adj.* land-cultivating, farming, 9. 140, 12. 194.

Langoure, pain, suffering, illness, 19. 142; Langour, 16. 298.

Lape, *v.* lap, lap up, drink, 7. 414, 23. 18, b. 5. 363.

Lappe, lap, bosom, 7. 412, 9. 283, 19. 273; *hence*, a portion, share (*orig.* flap or skirt of a garment), 3. 37; Lappes, *pl.* laps, skirts, 9. 318. A.S. *læppa*, a flap or loose border or fold of a garment, also the lap.

Large, *adj.* liberal, generous, 4. 290, 12. 73; wide, broad, full, b. 10. 162; as *sb.* bounty, liberality, 22. 43, b. 19. 43.

Largeliche, *adv.* largely, freely, bountifully, 3. 138, 13. 107; quite, fully, 23. 87.

Largenesse, bounty, liberality, 8. 275; bounty, 18. 64.

Larger, *adv.* more fully, b. 11. 155.

Largesse, largess, bounty, 8. 109; a largess, b. 13. 449. '*Largesse*, bounty, liberality;' Cotgrave. See note.

Larke, lark (bird), 15. 186.

Lasse, *adj. comp.* less, 12. 69, 20. 147, b. 2. 45; lower, a. 8. 144; smaller, b. 12. 262.

GLOSSARIAL INDEX. 383

Lasse, *adv.* less, 3. 48, 9. 165.
Lasshis, *s. pl.* lashes, stripes, R. 3. 338.
Laste, *v.* last, endure, 22. 45, 89, a. 2. 63; Last, *v.* 4. 205; Lastiþ, *pr. s.* lasts, a. 7. 26; Lastyng, *pr. pt.* enduring, keeping it up, b. 13. 332; Last, *pp.* lasted, a. 3. 185. See **Lesten.**
Laste, *pt. s.* lost (or perhaps for *lafte,* left), a. 8. 144.
Laste, *s.* ballast, R. 4. 74. A.S. *hlæst,* a load.
Lat, *pr. s.* leads (if contracted for *ledyth*); or permits, allows (if for *leteth*), b. 9. 57.
Lat, let, lets. See **Leten.**
Latere, *comp.* more slowly, less diligently, a. 1. 173; Latter, b. 1. 197.
Latte, *v.* hinder, impede, b. 10. 20. See **Letten.**
Latter. See **Late,** *adv.*
Lauandrie, laundry, 17. 330.
Laude, *imper. s.* praise, b. 11. 102.
Laueþ, *pr. s.* washes, 17. 330; Laued, *pp.* washed, b. 14. 5. F. *laver.*
Laueyne, *s.* mess, slop, a. 5. 207. *Laueyne* is probably equivalent to O.F. *lavange* (also *lavaille, lavasse*), a sudden gush or flow of water, an avalanche of snow; Roquefort. A more exact equivalent occurs in the Ital. *lavana* (also *lavaglie, lavaccia*), explained by Torriano (ed. 1688) as meaning 'all manner of soapsuds or soapwater, dish-water, hog's draff, swine's wash.' This is certainly what is here meant.
Lauhen, *v.* laugh, 5. 101, 8. 22, 17. 302; To lauhen of = to laugh at, 5. 19; Lauhe, *v.* 7. 194, 8. 110, 16. 203, 23. 242; Laughe, *v.* b. 11. 203; Lawȝe of = to laugh at, b. 4. 18; etc.
Lauhte, took. See **Lacchen.**
Lauhyng, *s.* laughter, 7. 394; Laughynge, mockery, b. 13. 323.
Laumpe, lamp, b. 13. 151.
Launce, lance, 4. 461.
Launceþ, *pr. s.* shooteth, springeth; Launceþ vp, springs up, 13. 185, 222; shoots forth, 19. 10.
Launde, glade, lawn, meadow, 1. 8, 11. 64; Laundes, *pl.* b. 15. 293, 299. See Cath. Angl. p. 210, n. 6.
Lauȝte. See **Lacchen.**
Lay, *s.* lay, song, 8. 117; Layes, *pl.* b. 8. 66.
Layke, *v.* play, sport, 1. 187, 17. 176. See **Laike.**
Layke, *s.* struggle, contest, sport, b. 14. 243. See **Laik.**

Layn, *imper. s.* conceal, hide, 3. 18. Icel. *leyna,* to conceal.
Lazar, leper, 19. 273; Lazars, *pl.* 19. 142. The name is taken from the story of Lazarus.
Leaute, *s.* loyalty, good faith, 1. 149, 3. 20, 4. 197, 5. 36.
Leche, leech, physician, 17. 138, 23. 304; b. 1. 202.
Leche-craft, medical skill, 7. 81, 23. 173, b. 6. 256, a. 7. 241.
Lechen, *v.* heal, restore, 16. 220, 20. 93, b. 13. 253; Lechede, *pt. s.* healed, cured, 9. 189.
Lechours, *pl.* lechers, dissolute persons, 7. 195, a. 2. 93.
Lechinge, *s.*; A lechinge = during recovery, 20. 73.
Led, *s.* lead (metal), b. 13. 82.
Lede, man, person, creature, 4. 283, 7. 303, 11. 176, 14. 211, 18. 40, 20. 76; Ledes, *pl.* subjects, 5. 178; Leedes, 12. 73. A.S. *léod,* people. See **Leod, Ledes.**
Lede, *s.* lead, 8. 238. See **Led.**
Leden, *v.* lead, conduct, guide, 21. 280, 282; Lede, *v.* lead, conduct, guide, 8. 253, 22. 224; carry, 5. 144; govern, 1. 149, 4. 148; Lede forth = preside at, b. 10. 20; to draw (a cart), b. 2. 179; Ledest, 2 *pr. s.* guidest, rulest, 5. 12; Ledeþ, *pr. s.* carries, 14. 56; sways, a. 3. 154; Ledeþ forþ = presides over, a. 11. 20; Laddest, 2 *pt. s.* didst lead, b. 7. 189; a. 8. 176; Ladde, *pt. s.* led, conducted, 1. 138, 4. 128, Ladde, 1 *pt. pl.* led, spent, 10. 339; Ladden, *pt. pl.* 19. 179; Ladde, guided, R. 1. 68; Leddyn, 2 *pt. pl.* R. 1. 2; Ladde, *pp.* led, 11. 141; induced, b. 13. 12; Ledeth, *imp. pl.* conduct, b. 2. 134, a. 2. 104.
Ledene, *s.* voice, language, cry, 14. 173; Ledne, b. 12. 253, 262; Leedene, 15. 179. See **Ludene.** A.S. *léden, léden,* voice, language, which is merely an A.S. rendering of the word *Latinum* or *Latinus.*
Ledes, *pl.* tenements, b. 15. 520; Leedes, 12. 69, 18. 221. The word *ledes* = tenements, may be the same word as *ledes* = men. It prob. meant at one time the labourers belonging to an estate. See **Lede, Leod.**
Ledinge, *s.* leading, conducting, administering, R. 1. 19; Ledyng, plan, management, 3. 44, b. 2. 42; Ledynge, a. 2. 25.
Leedene; see **Ledene.**

Leedes, men. See **Lede**.
Leedes, tenements. See **Ledes**.
Leef, *adj.* lief, willing, pleased, glad, 7. 116, 23. 195; dear, R. 1. 4; Lef, pleasant, a. 12. 6; Leue, dear, 3. 18, 4. 73, 7. 140, 23. 189, a. 6. 46; (ironically), b. 20. 188; willing, b. 13. 323; *voc.* dear, 19. 1. See **Leof**. **Lief**.
Leef, *adv.* dearly, 5. 145. See **Lief**, **Leue**, **Luf**.
Leef, believe. See **Leue**.
Leef, *s.* leaf (of a tree), b. 15. 100; leaf (of a book), page, 4. 493, 16. 104, R. pr. 37; bit, piece, small portion, b. 6. 256, b. 7. 110 (cf. b. 5. 203); Lef, leaf, 2. 152; leaf of a book, b. 3. 337; a thing of no value, 6. 97; portion, part, a. 8. 162; Leues, *gen.* leaf's, 4. 493, b. 3. 336; Leues, *pl.* leaves, b. 12. 231.
Leel, *adj.* true, loyal, faithful, upright, honest, 1. 88, 146; 4. 350, 8. 196, 9. 262, 10. 14; Leelle, *pl.* 14. 69; real, 11. 210; loyal (subjects), 4. 319: Leele, *pl.* upright men, 20. 43; Lele, true, b. 11. 69; noble, honourable, a. 2. 31; Lele, *pl.* b. 10. 433. O.F. *leal*, loyal.
Leeliche, *adv.* loyally, 23. 210; Leelliche, verily, 20. 190; faithfully, 2. 178; honourably, in all truth, 12. 267; Leelly, truly, faithfully, 3. 76; steadfastly, 12. 144; Leely, faithfully, 9. 255; Lelliche, b. 1. 179; Lelly, truly, 11. 273, b. 1. 78; faithfully, 12. 148, b. 9. 13; Lewed lelly =truly ignorant, b. 12. 174; Lelli, truly, b. 3. 30.
Leel-speche, true speech, 8. 238.
Leere, learn. See **Leren**.
Leese, lose; Lees, lost. See **Lesen**.
Leesynge, *s.* wastefulness, R. 3. 158. The M.E. *lesing* has four senses: (1) loss, waste; (2) lying; (3) loosing; (4) gleaning.
Leet, let. See **Leten**.
Leeue, believe. See **Leue**.
Leeue, *pl.* dear. See **Leef**.
Lef, leave. See **Leue**.
Lef, *adj.* See **Leef**, *adj.*
Lefte, left, remained. See **Leue**.
Lege, *adj.* loyal, true, liege, 5. 178; *adj. pl. as sb.* lieges, true subjects, 22. 60.
Legende, *s.* writing; hence, book, 12. 206.
Leggen, *v.* lay, place, b. 12. 116; lay (upon), labour (on), b. 15. 186; Legge, *v.* lay, place, deposit, 14. 159,

15. 59; lay aside, part with, 9. 293; lay, stake, pledge, wager, 5. 191, 9. 291; Leiþ, *pr. s.* is laying, a. 5. 199; Leid, *pp.* laid, placed, 6. 73; wagered, 4. 260. A.S. *lecgan*. See **Leyn**.
Legiaunce, *s.* allegiance, R. 1. 24; Legeaunce, R. 2. 104.
Legistres, *pl.* legists, advocates, men skilled in the law, b. 7. 14, 59; a. 8. 62. O.F. *legistre, legiste*, 'avocat, procureur, jurisconsulte, docteur en loix;' Roquefort. Lat. *legista*.
Leigis, liege men, R. 3. 338.
Lei3en, lain. See **Liggen**.
Lele, *adj.* See **Leel**.
Lelest, *adj. sup.* truest, b. 17. 24; most faithful, b. 13. 295. See **Leel**.
Leme, light, glow, brightness, b. 18. 124. A.S. *léoma*.
Lemed, *pt. s.* shone, 8. 135; see above.
Lemes, *pl.* limbs, R. 2. 156. See note. See **Leome**.
Lemman, *s.* sweetheart, lover (used of both sexes), 11. 132, 21. 186, 23. 152, 156; favourite, beloved one, b. 14. 299; mistress, 3. 20, 8. 26; Lemmon, sweetheart, a. 4. 36; Lemmanes, *pl.* sweethearts, 17. 277; mistresses, b. 3. 150; Lemmons, *pl.* concubines, a. 3. 146. Contracted from A.S. *leóf man*, dear man; *man* being used of either sex.
Lendys, *s. pl.* loins, R. 3. 59. A.S. *lendenu*, pl. the loins.
Lene, *v.* lean, depend (on), R. 2. 62; Lenede, 1 *pt. s.* reclined, 1. 8, 11. 64; leant, 21. 5; Lened, 1 *pt. s.* lay down, b. 8. 65; Lened, 1 *pt. s. refl.* leant myself, reposed, b. 18. 5. See **Leonede**.
Lene, *v.* giue (lit. lend), give to, 5. 191, 9. 15, 12. 303; Lene, 1 *pr. s.* lend, b. 5. 250; Leneth, *pr. s.* giveth, 13. 107; Lent (*for* Lendeth), b. 9. 105; Leneþ, 2 *pr. pl.* give, 1. 75; Lene 2 *pr. pl.* 2. 178; Leneth, *pr. pl.* give, bestow, b. 10. 42; Lenede, 1 *pt. s.* lent, 7. 244; Lened, 1 *pt. s.* lent, b. 13. 389; made loans, b. 13. 360; Lentestow, 2 *pt. s.* didst thou lend, b. 5. 253; Lente, *pt. s.* gave, 12. 47; gave, dealt out, R. 3. 330; Lent, *pt. s.* gave, b. 5. 203; granted, b. 10. 62; Lent, *pp.* given, 16. 240; Lene, *imp. s.* give, 9. 231; lend to, a. 7. 210; Lene, *imp. pl.* lend to, 11. 91. A.S. *lǽnan*, mod. E. *lend*.
Lenge, *v.* to linger, remain, dwell, tarry, 7. 158, b. 1. 207, a. 1. 185; Lengen, *pr. pl.* remain, reside, are

GLOSSARIAL INDEX.

kept, 10. 130; Lenged, *pt. s.* tarried, b. 8. 7.
Lengere, *adj.* longer, 4. 493; Lenger, b. 3. 336, b. 5. 210.
Lengere, *adv. compar.* longer, 2. 204, a. 1. 185; Lenger, 4. 136.
Lengthed, *pp.* lengthened, prolonged, 21. 338.
Lente, Lestestow. See **Lenen.**
Lenten, Lent-time, the season of Lent, 1. 89, b. pr. 91; Lentenes, *pl.* (during) periods of Lent, 14. 81.
Lente-seedes, *pl.* Lent-seeds, i.e. seeds sown in spring, 13. 190. '*Lent-grain,* barley, oats, and pease (but not wheat);' Shropsh. Wordbook.
Leod, *s.* man, a. 6. 6; Leode, man, b. 3. 32, b. 17. 78; person, R. 3. 255; Leodes, *pl.* men, persons, people, b. 4. 184, b. 16. 181; Leodis, *pl.* men, persons, R. 2. 2. See **Lede.**
Leod, *s.* tenement, a. 6. 38; Leodes, *pl.* possessions, 16. 306 (see note). See **Ledes.**
Leof, *adj.* dear, pleasing, 2. 35.
Leom, light, brightness, 21. 129, 142. See **Leme.**
Leome, *s.* limb, body, a. 5. 81. See **Lemes.**
Leonede, 1 *pt. s.* leaned, reclined, a. pr. 9. See **Lene.**
Leop, Leope. See **Lepen.**
Leopart, leopard, b. 15. 293.
Leor, face. See **Lere.**
Leorne. See **Lerne.**
Leornyng, *s.* teaching, instruction, lesson, a. 1. 173. See **Lerynge.**
Leosen. See **Lesen.**
Leosinge, *s.* losing, loss, a. 5. 93. See **Lesen.**
Leouest, *adj.* liefest, dearest, a. 3. 6. See **Leef.**
Lepen, *v.* leap, run, 2. 113, 3. 41, a. 2. 207; Lepe, *v.* 7. 204, 8. 216; digress, b. 11. 309; Leepe, *v.* 15. 85; Leope, *pr. s. subj.* leap, dart, 21. 288; Leep, *pt. s.* leapt, 23. 152; Leop, ran, a. 2. 192; Lep, ran, 3. 225; Lepe, *pt. s.* b. 2. 68. See **Lope, Loupe.**
Leperes, *pl.* runners, wanderers, 10. 107, 137.
Lere, face, complexion, 2. 3; b. 10. 2; Leor, a. 1. 3. A.S. *hleor.*
Lered, *adj.* learned, educated (*usually in the pl.*=learned men) 1. 88, 7. 29, 10. 230. Orig. pp. of Leren.
Leren, *v.* teach, b. 13. 120; Lere, *v.* 15. 6, 21. 237; shew, b. 11. 164; learn (improperly used), a. 11. 270; teach, tell, R. 2. 18; Leere, *v.* learn (in phr. *to leere* = for teaching, for learning), 23. 207; Lere, 1 *pr. s.* teach, b. 3. 69; Lereþ, *pr. s.* teaches, 4. 162, 15. 49; *as fut.* will teach, b. 11. 155; Leres, *pr. s.* teaches, b. 12. 183; Lereþ, 2 *pr. pl.* 6. 143, a. 5. 36; Leren, b. 5. 45; Lereþ, *pr. pl.* teach, 10. 19; Lere, 12. 236; Lerede, *pt. s.* taught, 7. 348, 20. 99; learnt, a. 1. 109 (other MSS. *lernyd*); Leryde, *pt. s.* taught, 17. 153; Lered, b. 16. 104; Lere, *imper. s.* teach, 2. 135, 9. 222; Lere þe = teach thyself, b. 13. 142; Lereþ, *imp. pl.* teach, b. 1. 134; Lereþ hit þis = teach it to these, a. 1. 125; Lered, *pp.* taught, a. 10. 100. A.S. *léran,* to teach.
Lerne, *v.* learn, 2. 146, a. 9. 49; Leorne, a. 9. 57; Lernest, 2 *pr. s.* teachest, b. 4. 11; Lerneth, *pr. s.* teaches, b. 10. 374; Lerneþ, 2 *pr. pl.* learn, 23. 250; Leorneþ, *pr. pl.* 20. 45; Lerned, 1 *pt. s.* learnt, 6. 43, b. 5. 203; taught the use of, b. 10. 179; Lernedest, 2 *pt. s.* b. 1. 139; Lerned, *pt. s.* taught, b. 5. 302; Leornden, *pt. pl.* discovered, a. 2. 199; Lerned, *pp.* learnt, been taught, b. 8. 10; learnt, b. 11. 167; instructed, R. pr. 44; Lerne, 1 *imper. pl.* let us learn, b. 11. 222; Lerneth, *imp. pl.* learn, R. 1. 9. See below. The senses of *learn* and *teach* are confused; see **Leren.**
Lerynge, *s.* teaching, instruction, 11. 141, 172; 18. 160; b. 9. 16.
Lese, *s.* leash (properly a set of *three*), R. 2. 114.
Lese, *ger.* to glean, b. 6. 68. Shropshire *lease.*
Lesen, *v.* lose, forfeit, b. 5. 625; Lese, *v.* 3. 37; Leese, *v.* 11. 192; Leosen, *v.* a. 3. 131, 275; a. 6. 105; Leose, *v.* a. 5. 77; Leest (*for* Lesest), 2 *pr. s.* 10. 269; Leeseþ, *pr. s.* loses, 11. 176; Leese, 2 *pr. pl.* 17. 272; Lesen, *pr. pl.* they lose, b. 12. 56; Lese, *pr. pl.* lose, waste (see the note to 17. 272); Lees, *pt. s.* lost, gave up, 8. 132, 14. 152; Les, 11. 195; Lese, b. 7. 158; Lese, *pt. pl.* lost, b. 20. 86. See **Loren, Loore.** A.S. *léosan,* pt. t. *léas.*
Lest, *impers. pr. s.* it pleases, b. 11. 418, b. 12. 174; *pt. s.* it pleased (him), b. 17. 139; Leste, *pr. s. subj.* it please, b. 11. 48. See **Liste.**
Leste, *adj.* least, 4. 25.
Leste, *conj.* lest, a. 5. 38.
Lesten, *pr. pl.* last, hold, a. 12. 93. See **Laste.**

Lesyng, *s.* lie, lying tale, leasing, lying, 7. 209, 8. 22; Lesynge, 16. 104; Leesynge, deceitfulness, R. 3. 158; Lesynges, *pl.* lies, deceits, 3. 138, 5. 19; Lesinges, lies, a. 11. 272. A.S. *léasung,* lying; from *léas,* loose, false.

Lesyng, *s.* loss, waste, b. 9. 98; Lesynge, loss, b. 5. 112. See **Lesen**.

Lete, *v.* (1) to let, permit, allow, 21. 57; Lat worþe = let be, let alone, b. pr. 187; Leteþ, *pr. s.* allows, lets, 4. 174, b. 3. 136; Letiþ, a. 1. 78; Lat (*for* Leteþ), lets, allows, 8. 275, b. 20. 358; Leet, *pt. s.* let, allowed, 13. 48, 19. 277; Let, *pt. s.* 2. 164; Lete, *pt. s.* b. 1. 165; Leten, *pt. pl.* let, allowed, b. 18. 404; Lete, *pr. s. subj.* let, b. pr. 155; Lat, *imper. s.* let, allow, b. 2. 47; Late, b. 4. 86; Leet, 19. 105; Leten, *v.* (2) leave, desert, 12. 184; leave, 4. 242; cease, 7. 312; cease (from evil), b. 17. 306; Lete, *v.* leave, forsake, lose, forego, give up, 4. 265, 9. 294; let fall, R. 1. 31; Leteth, *pr. s.* leaves, 3. 104; Leten, *pr. pl.* leave off, 20. 288; give up, 12. 24;—(3) to cause; Leten, *pt. pl.* caused; Leten sompne = caused to be summoned, 3. 172; Lete write = had (writs) written, R. 4. 26; Let, *imp. s.*; Let brynge = cause to be brought, 11. 33; a. 9. 25; Lat hange me = cause me to be hanged, b. 3. 112; Lete warrok it = cause it to be girt, b. 4. 20;—Leten, *v.* (4) think, consider, a. 6. 105; Late wel by = set store by, b. 5. 625; Let, *pr. s.* considers, believes, b. 15. 168; Let best by = thinks most highly of, b. 10. 185; Let wel bi = esteems, a. 11. 41; Letith lyghte of = despises, R. 3. 284; Leten, 2 *pr. pl. reflex.* esteem, consider yourselves, 6. 168; Leten, *pr. pl.* consider, hold, 18. 299; Leten hem = behave (as), b. 10. 316; Let, 1 *pt. s.* considered, esteemed, 7. 243; Lete, 1 *pt. s.* b. 13. 363; Lete, *pt. s.* accounted, b. 20. 145; Lette, cared, thought, a. 7. 154; Let, *pt. s.* considered, 23. 146; Let lyght = thought little, 5. 156; Lete liȝte, b. 4. 161; Leten, *pt. pl.* they considered, 1. 195; Leten bi = esteemed, a. 11. 29; Lete by, 4. 205. A.S. *lǽtan*.

Lethy, *adj.* idle, useless, b. 10. 184. Cf. O. Fries. *letheg, ledich,* Du. *ledig,* empty, idle.

Lette, *pt. s.* caused; Lette sompne = caused to be summoned, a. 2. 129; Lette, *imp. s.*; Lette apparayle = cause to be apparelled, a. 2. 148; Let cardsadele = cause to be harnessed, a. 2. 154. See **Leten** (3).

Letten, *v.* let, i.e. hinder, prevent, 14. 10, 16. 220; Lette, *v.* stop, hinder, impede, prevent, delay, 2. 155, 4. 35; restrain, b. 5. 303; delay, remain, tarry, wait, 2. 204, 20. 76; cease, R. 2. 86; Lete, prevent, a. 3. 191; Letteth, *pr. s.* hinders, 4. 454, 11. 160; makes difficulties, a. 3. 152; Letteþ, *pr. pl.* prevent, hinder, 15. 178; Letted, *pt. s.* prevented, b. 16. 83; hindered, R. 2. 3; put a stop to, b. 3. 197; Lette, *pt. s.* hindered, 19. 115; *pt. pl.* R. 2. 60; Lette, *pr. s. subj.* prevent, b. 5. 458; b. 10. 371; hinder, stop, R. 3. 115; Letted, *pp.* hindered, b. 19. 380; Lette, *pp.* 14. 37; Lett, *pp.* 22. 384. See **Latte**. A.S. *lettan,* Du. *letten*.

Lettere, *s.* hinderer, a. 1. 67; Letter, b. 1. 69; Lettare, 2. 65. See **Letten**.

Letterure. See **Lettrure**.

Lettre, *s.* letter, a. 8. 25, 94; covenant, agreement, b. 10. 89; writ, b. 11. 198; Lettere, letter, 20. 4, 22; Lettres, *pl.* letters, 5. 129, a. 2. 199, a. 4. 115; a letter, b. 9. 38, 39; Letteres of = letters concerning, a. 12. 86.

Lettred, *adj.* educated, learned, 10. 326, 12. 235, 15. 199; Lettret, a. 8. 118, 162; Lettrede, *adj. pl.* educated (men), 2. 135, 4. 124; Letteride, 17. 255.

Lettrure, doctrine, learning, education, 10. 195, 198, 12. 210; scripture, 12. 26; Letterure, learning, 1. 137, 12. 100; scripture, b. 10. 27; writing, b. 10. 378.

Lettynge, *s.* delay, hindrance, 9. 5, 12. 137. See **Letten**.

Leue, *v.* believe, 2. 75, 95; 20. 38, b. 5. 45, b. 10. 356; Leue, 1 *pr. s.* I believe, 2. 140; Leue wel = I fully believe, b. 3. 333; Leeue, 1 *pr. s.* a. 11. 141; Leeuest, 2 *pr. s.* trustest, a. 2. 93; Leuestow, believest thou, b. 18. 187; Leueth, *pr. s.* believes, trusts, b. 2. 101, b. 10. 359; Leue, 2 *pr. pl.* believe, b. 13. 308; Leuen, *pr. pl.* b. 12. 275; Leue, think, b. 15. 151; Leueth, believe, b. pr. 77; Leeueþ, a pr. 69; Leued, 1 *pt. s.* believed, b. 13. 389; Leueden, *pt. pl.* b. 1. 117; Leuyd, *pp.* R. 2. 83; Leue, *imper. s.* trust, believe, 2. 36, 195; Leeue, trust to, a. 3. 29; Leef, *imp. s.* a. 1. 36, a. 3. 168, a. 11. 143; Leue, *imper. s.* 3 *p.* let (him) believe, 2. 118;

GLOSSARIAL INDEX.

Leueþ, *imp. pl.* 14. 26; Leeueþ, a. 11. 76. See **Leyue, Lyue.** A.S. *geliefan, gelýfan.*

Leue, *pr. s. subj.* grant, may he grant, 1. 149, b. pr. 126, a. 5. 263. See **Leyue.** (Only used in the phrase *God leue* or *Christ leue*, i.e. may God (or Christ) grant.) A. S. *lýfan*, to allow; from *léaf*, leave, permission; see **Leue,** *sb.* On the distinction between *leue* and *lene*, see note to b. 5. 263, p. 86.

Leue, *v.* leave, desert, give up, abandon, 13. 215, b. 1. 101; desist, a. 7. 166; lose, 4. 470; Chese layke oþer leue = choose to play or to leave it alone, 17. 176; Leueth, *pr. s.* leaves, deserts, forsakes, b. 13. 17; Leuen, *pr. pl.* leave, b. 15. 133; Leueþ, *pr. pl.* a. pr. 74; Leue, *pr. pl. subj.* omit, a. 3. 61; Lafte, 1 *pt. s.* remained, stayed behind, a. 3. 190 (other MSS. have *lefte*); Lefte, *pt. s.* left, 1. 130, 23. 102; Lefte, *pt. pl.* remained, 19. 155; Lafte, *pt. pl.* left, b. 4. 153, R. 3. 80; Laft, *pt. pl.* left, b. 20. 250; Leue, *imp. s.* leave, b. 10. 162; Leue of, *imp. s.* leave off, b. 20. 207; Lef, leave, give up, 23. 208; Leueþ, *imper. pl.* forsake, give up, 4. 73. A.S. *læfan.*

Leue, *v.* live, R. 3. 25, 266; Leuen, *pr. pl.* 1. 102; Leueden, *pt. pl.* 16. 267; Leued, *pt. pl.* R. 3. 59; Leue, 1 *pl. imp.* let (us) live, a. 4. 158. See **Libbe.**

Leue, *s.* leave, permission, 1. 50, 83; 7. 121, 440; leave, farewell, 2. 205; extension of time, 23. 286. A.S. *léaf*, leave.

Leue, *adj.* dear. See **Leef.**

Leue, *adv.* dearly, b. pr. 163, b. 3. 18. See **Leef, Leuere, Leuest.**

Leuell, *s.* use of the level, 12. 127. See **Liuel.**

Leuere, *adj. comp.* dearer, preferable, 12. 9, 21. 458; Leuer, b. 10. 14. See **Leef.**

Leuere, *adv. comp.* sooner, rather, 7. 129; more dearly, a. 1. 131; more dearly, b. 1. 141; Were wel leuer = it would be dearer (for them), they would rather, b. 20. 61. See **Leef,** *adj.,* **Leue,** *adv.*

Leuere, *s.* delivery, experience, R. 3. 330; livery, R. 2. 26, 79, 104, R. 3. 182; Leuerey, delivery, grant, R. 2. 2; Leuerez, *pl.* liveries, badges, R. 2. 35, 57, 93. Mod. E. *livery*, short for *delivery.*

Leues, *gen.* leaf's, 4. 493.

Leuest, *adj.* dearest, 4. 6, a. 1. 136; chief, b. 10. 357; .best, R. 2. 156; Leueste, *adj.* most pleasing, 6. 85; dearest, a. 1. 180. See **Leef.**

Leuest, *adv.* most dearly, especially, b. 5. 572; Leueste, R. pr. 65.

Leuite, deacon (lit. Levite), 3. 130.

Leute, fidelity, loyalty, b. pr. 126, b. 11. 148; uprightness, true dealing, b. 14. 146; Lewte, loyalty, truth, obedience to law, b. pr. 122, b. 2. 21.

Leuynge, *s.* life, R. 2. 83.

Leuynges, *pl.* leavings, b. 5. 363.

Lewed, *adj.* ignorant, uneducated, 1. 88, 21. 358, b. 7. 136; worthless, useless, b. 1. 187, a. 1. 163; Lewde, *adj.* ignorant, R. 2. 53; Lewede, *adj.* worthless, 2. 186; ignorant, a. 8. 123; *pl.* ignorant, 1. 70, 2. 135; Lewide, 23. 102, 247; Lewid, a. 11. 288. A.S. *lǽwed;* E. *lewd,* but not in the modern sense.

Lewedeste, *adj. superl.* most ignorant, a. 3. 33.

Lewednesse, ignorance, 4. 35.

Lewte. See **Leute.**

Leyde, laid. See **Leyn.**

Leye, *s.* flame, b. 17. 207, 213. A.S. *líg, lýg,* a flame.

Leye, Leyen. See **Ligge.**

Leye-lond, lea-land, 11. 217.

Leyes, *pl.* fields, leas, 10. 5.

Leyn, *v.* lay; Leyne, *ger.* to lay, b. 18. 77; Leyeþ, *pr. s.* lays (her eggs), b. 11. 339; Laith, *pr. s.* lays, is setting, 7. 406; Leyth, *pr. pl.* turn, apply, 17. 145; **Leyde,** *pt. s.* laid, placed, b. 5. 359; put, a. 5. 171; Leyed, *pt. s.* laid, b. 18. 59; Leyde on, *pt. s.* pressed forward, 23. 114; Leyden, *pt. pl.* laid, placed, 9. 129; Leyde, *pt. pl.* b. 6. 124; Leyde, *pp.* laid, placed, 21. 30; Leye, *imp. s.* lay, stake, wager, *as in* Leye þer a bene = stake (but) a bean upon it, 13. 92; Lay on, *imp. s.* attack, b. 13. 146. See **Leggen.**

Leyue, *v.* believe, trust, 21. 262; 1 *pr. s.* (I) believe, 4. 46, 330; Leyuest, 2 *pr. s.* believest, 21. 195; Leyueth, *pr. s.* believes, supposes, 3. 104; Leyuede, 1 *pt. s.* 21. 338; *pt. s.* 23. 173; Leyf, *imp. s.* believe, trust, 6. 24, 11. 306; Leyue, 6. 3; Leyueþ, *imp. pl.* believe, 4. 221. See **Leue.**

Leyue, *pr. s. subj. as imper.* grant, 8. 157, 12. 244, 18. 40. See **Leue.** (Only in the phrase *God leyue* or *Lord leyue.*)

Liage, *s.* liege (servant), R. pr. 25. Apparently an error for Liege, q. v.

Libben, *ger.* to live, a. 11. 207; *ger.* b. 8. 92; Libbe, *v.* 21. 111; Libbeth, *pr. pl.* live, b. 2. 186; Libben, *pr. pl.* b. 5. 149; Libbing, *pr. pt.* living, b. 9. 107; Libbyng, b. pr. 222; *pr. pt. as adj.* b. 15. 91; Lybbyng, b. 7. 62. See **Lybbe**.

Licame, body, 2. 35, 16. 58; Licam, a. pr. 30; Likame, 20. 93; Licames, *gen.* of the body, 7. 176. A.S. *líc-hama*. See **Likame, Lykame, Lycame**.

Lich, *s.* body, a. 11. 2; Liche, b. 10. 2. A.S. *líc*. See note, p. 146.

Liche, *adj.* like, resembling, b. 5. 353, 489. See **Lyche**.

Liche, *adv.* alike, 7. 183, 17. 20.

Licitum, pp. allowed, allowable, b. 11. 92.

Lickne, *pr. pl.* liken, compare, disparage by comparison, b. 10. 42; see note, p. 147. See **Likne**.

Lief, *adj.* fain, glad, b. 20. 309. See **Leef**.

Lief, *adv.* dearly; þe lief likeþ = it dearly pleases thee, i.e. you like best, b. 4. 148. See **Leef**.

Liege, *s.* subject, liege man, R. 2. 49; Liegis, *gen. sing.* liege lord's, R. pr. 47; Liegis, *pl.* subjects, R. 2. 20. See **Lige**.

Liegeman, *s.* subject, R. 2. 67.

Lieutenant, lieutenant, b. 16. 47.

Lif, way of living, 21. 112. See **Lyf**.

Lif, man, living creature, 4. 450. See **Lyf**.

Lif-dayes, *pl.* life, days of their life, 4. 188; days of his life, b. 1. 27.

Lif-holy, *adj.* holy of life, 12. 2. See **Lyf-holy**.

Liflode, *s.* support of life, sustenance, means of living, food, 2. 35, 7. 312. A.S. *líf-láde*, corrupted to *livelihood* in modern English. See **Lyflode**. ' A *lyuelade*, victus;' Cath. Angl.

Lift, *adj.* left, 4. 494, 8. 225. See **Luft, Lyft**.

Lifte, sky, b. 15. 351. See **Lyft**.

Lige, *adj.* liege, loyal, b. 4. 184, a. 4. 147; *as sb. pl.* liege servants, 21. 398. See **Liege, Lyge**.

Liggen, *v.* lie, remain, 6. 16, a. 2. 105; Ligge, *v.* 19. 286; rest, 15. 11; Ligge, 1 *pr. s.* 8. 26; Liggeþ, *pr. s.* lies, is, b. 3. 175; Lith, *pr. s.* lies, 1. 137; remains, resides, b. 12. 181; reaches, b. 10. 316; lies ill, 23. 377; Lith. *pr. s.* lies, *put for subj.* if there lie or remain, 20. 179; Lithe, *pr. s.* lies, resides, b. 10. 277, b. 18. 384;

Liggen, *pr. pl.* lie, 6. 150; reside, 22. 420; Ligge, *pr. pl.* lie, remain, b. 10. 296; Liggeth, lie, are lying, b. 15. 178; lie (down to rest), b. 6. 15; Ligge, *pr. s. subj.* lies idle, 9. 160; lie, dwell, be, b. 5. 439, b. 17. 224; *pr. pl. subj.* may lie, b. 2. 135: Lay, 1 *pt. s.* lay, 1. 8; Lay bi = lay with, b. 1. 30; Leyen, *pt. pl.* lay, 14. 159; Leyen, *pp.* lain, a. 3. 39; Leyn, remained, a. 11. 276; Leiȝen, lain, a. 5. 259; Leye, *pp.* lain, been, 12. 259, 22. 55; Leye by = lain with, 7. 330; Layen, 4. 40; Liggyng, *pres. pt.* b. 2. 51. See **Lyeþ, Lygge**. A.S. *licgan*.

Lightliche, *adv.* easily, 5. 168. See **Lihtliche, Lyghtliche**.

Lightloker, *adv.* more readily, 18. 253. See **Lihtloker, Lyghtloker**.

Lihþ, *pr. s.* lies, tells lies, a. 3. 152, 169. See **Liȝen**.

Lihtliche, *adv.* easily, a. 2. 93, a. 4. 93. See **Lightliche**.

Lihtloker, *comp. adv.* more lightly, a. 6. 59. See **Lightloker**.

Likame, body, 20. 93; Likam, b. 1. 37. See **Licame**.

Likerous, *adj.* lecherous, dainty, luxurious, b. pr. 30, b. 6. 268; Likerouse, b. 10. 161, 164. See **Lykerous**.

Likeþ, *pr. s. impers.* pleases, b. 1. 43, b. 2. 231; Liked, *pt. s. subj.* should please, R. pr. 64; Lyked, b. pr. 60, 149. See **Lykeþ**.

Likne, *v.* compare, b. 10. 277; Likened, *pp.* likened, like, 20. 168; Liknet, a. 9. 34; Likned, 11. 44. See **Lickne, Lykne**.

Lik-seed, leek-seed, 13. 190.

Likth, *pr. s.* lies, tells lies, b. 18. 31. See **Liȝen**.

Likyng, *s.* sensual pleasure, b. 9. 179; fondness, b. 1. 27; Likynge, R. 3. 266. See **Lykynge**.

Likyngliche, *adv.* according to (his) pleasure, 20. 241.

Limes, *s. pl.* limbs, a. 7. 183. A.S. *lim*. See **Leome, Lemes, Lyme**.

Limitour, licensed begging friar, b. 20. 344; Limitoures, *pl.* b. 5. 138. See note, p. 78. See **Lymytour**.

Lippe, morsel, portion, part, bit, 7. 245, 12. 226. See **Lappe, Lyppe**.

Lisse, *s.* joy, happiness, 21. 237; a. 10. 30. See Gloss. to Will. of Palerne; and see **Lysse**. A.S. *liss, líðs*, tranquillity, from *líðe*, lithe, gentle.

Liste, *v.* desire, R. 3. 31; List, *pr. s. impers.* it pleases, b. pr. 172; Liste,

pr. s. subj. may please, R. 2. 71 ; Liste, *pt. s.* it pleased, b. 1. 148 ; List, *pt. s.* it pleased, R. 2. 118 ; List, 2 *pt. pl.* were pleased, R. 2. 62 ; Liste, *pt. s. subj.* it would please, b. 5. 400. See Lest, Lyste. A.S. *lystan*, to please.
Listres, *pl.* lectors, b. 5. 138. See note, p. 78. O.F. *listre*, variant of *litre* = Lat. *lector*. The *lector* here means a lecturer or preacher; not the *lector* of the Minor Orders.
Lisure, list, edge of cloth, 7. 216. ' *Lisiere*, the list of cloth, or of stuffe;' Cotgrave. See Lyser.
Lite, *adj.* little, R. 4. 62. See Lyte. A.S. *lyt*.
Lite, *s.* little, R. pr. 25.
Litel, *adj.* little, 4. 394, b. 10. 88. See Luitel.
Lith, *pr. s.* lies, dwells, b. 1. 124, &c. See Liggen.
Lith, *pr. s.* lies, tells lies, b. 3. 155. See Liȝen.
Lith, *s.* limb, member, i. e. body, b. 16. 181.
Lithen, *v.* to listen to, 11. 65 ; Litheth, *pr. s.* listens, 8. 112 ; *pr. pl.* listen to, b. 13. 438 ; Lithen, *pr. pl.* listen, 8. 98. Icel. *hlýða*, to listen.
Liþer, *adj.* wicked, bad, defective, vicious, b. 5. 387, b. 10. 164 ; Lithere, *pl.* 18. 82. See Luther, Lyther.
Litheren, *pr. pl.* sling ; Litheren þer-to = sling at it, cast stones at it, 19. 48. The verb is formed from A.S. *liðere*, a sling (Leo).
Litlum and lytlum, *adv.* by degrees, by little and little, b. 15. 599. See Lytulum. A.S. *lytlum, by* little, dat. of *lytel*, little ; *litlum and litlum*, A.S. version of Gen. xl. 10.
Liuel, *s.* the level, the use of the level, a. 11. 135. O.F. *livel ;* see *level* in Skeat's Etym. Dict.
Lixt, 2 *pr. s.* liest, tellest lies, 7. 138 ; Lixte, b. 5. 163. See note, p. 80. See below.
Liȝen, *v.* lie, tell lies ; Lixt, 2 *pr. s.* 7. 138 ; Lixte, b. 5. 163 ; Lihþ, *pr. s.* a. 3. 152, 169 ; Likth, *pr. s.* b. 18. 31 ; Lith, *pr. s.* b. 3. 155. See Lyȝen, Lowe, Lye.
Liȝere, *s.* liar, a. 2. 156.
Liȝte, *adv.* lightly, b. 4. 161.
Liȝter, *adj.* easier, b. 14. 247.
Liȝtlich, *adv.* easily, b. 15. 133 ; Liȝtly, readily, b. 14. 34. See Lyȝtliche.
Liȝtloker, *adv.* more easily, more readily, b. 5. 578. See Lihtloker.
Liȝtnynge, flame, b. 19. 197.

Liȝþ, *pr. s.* lies, a. 1. 115.
Lobres, *pl.* lubbers, a. pr. 52. Cf. Du. *lobbes*, a booby. See note, p. 9.
Loby; looby, lubber, R. 2. 170 ; Lobyes, b. pr. 55. See above.
Lockes. See Lokkes.
Lof, loaf, b. 13. 48 ; Loues, *pl.* b. 6. 285. See Loof, Loue.
Lofsom, *adj.* loveable, 11. 259. A.S. *lufsum*.
Loft, *sb.* height ; On loft = aloft, up, 7. 410, 424 ; On lofte, a. 1. 88 ; Bi loft = on high, above, b. 18. 45. A.S. *lyft*, air.
Loggen, *pr. pl.* lodge, R. 3. 280 ; Loggede, *pt. s.* lodged, dwelt, a. 9. 7.
Loggyng, *s.* lodging, a. 12. 44.
Lok, *s.* look, looks, mien, 12. 267.
Lok, *s.* lock, fastening of a door ; *hence*, key, 2. 198 ; Lokke, b. 1. 200 ; Lokkes, *pl.* locks (of a box), b. 13. 368 ; Lokes, locks, 7. 266.
Loken, *v.* look to, watch over, b. 16. 47 ; look, see, have my sight, a. 9. 49 (see note) ; look after, guard, b. 7. 165 ; provide (lit. look to it), b. 2. 135 ; Loke, *v.* look, see, 11. 57, b. 10. 265 ; look about me, 5. 63, b. 4. 60 ; look after, a. 5. 116 ; enforce, a. 7. 303 ; attend to, 9. 85 ; examine, a. 2. 200 ; look over, peruse, inspect, b. 2. 224, R. pr. 37 ; see, find out, b. pr. 172, b. 2. 155 ; look on, behold, b. 1. 187 ; observe, 3. 234 ; expect, look for, provide for (the result), R. 3. 31 ; Lokye, *v.* look, 8. 50 ; Loke, 1 *pr. s.* look, seem, a. 11. 135 ; Lokestou, 2 *p. s. pr.* lookest thou, a. 8. 123 ; Lokeþ after, expects (to have), 4. 249 ; waits for, b. 12. 181 ; Loketh, *pr. s.* expects, 10. 271, 20. 261 ; looks, sees (the light), 21. 29 ; looks about, b. 18. 30 ; takes care, b. 15. 180 ; decides, a. 2. 172 ; Loken, *pr. pl.* look, 10. 141 ; wait, 19. 268 ; Loketh, *pr. pl.* have the use of their sight, b. 14. 31 ; Lokeþ, *pr. pl.* inspect, prepare, a. 7. 13 ; Loke, *pr. s. subj.* look to, watch over, guard, b. 1. 207, b. 15. 9 ; Lokid, 3. 8 ; Loked, *pt. s.* looked, 3. 131, b. 6. 321 ; Hym lokyd = seemed, b. 5. 189 ; Him loked, a. 5. 108 ; Lokyde, *pt. s.* looked, gazed, 2. 164 ; Lokide, attended to, R. 3. 255 ; Lokynge, *pr. pt.* looking about, 22. 159, 175 ; b. 19. 154, 170 ; Loke, *imp. s.* look, 3. 5, 10. 240 ; see to it, take care, b. 3. 269, b. 10. 205 ; Loketh, *imp. pl.* look, a. 8. 14 ; Loke, *imp. pl.* see, take care, b. 9. 175. A.S. *lócian*.

Lokkes, *pl.* locks of hair; *hence,* head, a. 2. 84; Lockes, hair, 16. 8.

Lokynge, *s.* looking (to), referring (to), glancing (at), b. 11. 309; look, glance, b. 13. 344; Loking, *s.* glance (of the eye), twinkling (of an eye), a. 12. 96.

Lollere, *s.* loller, idle vagabond, 6. 2, 10. 158; Lolleres, *pl.* 10. 192, 213, 240; Lollares, 6. 4, 10. 137; Lollers, 9. 74, 10. 107; Lollarene, *gen. pl.* of lollers, 6. 31; Lollaren, *gen. pl.* 10. 140; Lolleres, *gen. pl.* 10. 103. See note to 10. 213.

Lolleþ, *pr. s.* lolls, limps about, lounges, rests, 10. 215, 15. 153; Lollen, *pr. pl.* offend against, 10. 218 (prob. with reference to the sb. *lollere*); Lolled, *pt. s.* wagged, b. 5. 192; Lollid, *pt. pl.* flapped, 7. 199; Lollid vp = hung up, made to swing about, 15. 131; Lollynge, *pr. pt.* lolling, lying, 19. 287. The senses of *offending* and *lying* are due to the sb. *lollere.*

Lomb, lamb, 23. 36.

Lome, *adj.* lame, a. 7. 183.

Lome, *adv.* often, frequently, 11. 165, 13. 121, 17. 97; Lomer, *adv. comp.* (*glossed* sepius), more often, b. 20. 237. A.S. *gelóme.*

Lomes, *pl.* tools, 6. 45. A.S. *gelóman,* pl. utensils, tools.

Lompe, lump, 10. 150.

Lond, land, country, 4. 210; Londe, *gen.* of a ridge in a field, b. 13. 372 (unless *fote-londe* here, and *fot-londe* in c. 7. 268, be a compound sb., like E. *headland,* Shropsh. *adla̦nd*); Londes, *pl.* lands, estates, b. 9. 175; Londes, *gen. pl.* ridges in a field, 20. 58. 'Land,' that part of ground between the furrows in a ploughed field;' Halliwell.

Londe-bugger, land-buyer, b. 10. 307.

Lone, *adj.* lone, b. 16. 20.

Lone, loan, lending, 5. 194.

Lone, *s.* lane, a. 5. 162.

Long, *adj.* tall, a. 9. 110; Longe Wille, the author's name, b. 15. 148; Longe, *pl.* tall, 1. 53. See notes to 1. 53, and 17. 286.

Longe-lybbynge, *adj. pl.* long-living, long-lived, 15. 169.

Longen, *pl.* lungs, 9. 189.

Longeþ, *pr. s.* belongs, a. 11. 89; Longiþ, a. 11. 155; Longyt, *for* Longyth (as in the Ingilby MS.), *pr. s.* belongs, a. 12. 64; Longeþ, *pr. s.* belongs, is attached, 4. 248; Longith, *pr. s. impers.* it suits, R. 2. 67; Longeth, *pr. pl.* belong, b. 2. 49; Longen,

pr. pl. belong, 8. 271, a. 6. 108; Longith, are attached to or connected with, a. 2. 28; Longede, *pt. s.* resided, 11. 7; Longed, *pt. s.* was proper for, was fit, b. 11. 411; longed, desired, 9. 280; Longid, *pt. s.* belonged, R. 2. 172. A.S. *langian.*

Lood-sterre, lode-star, pole-star, 18. 95.

Loof, loaf, 9. 287, 10. 150.

Loore, *pt. s. subj.* lost, 17. 311. See **Lesen.**

Loos, loss, 22. 292. See **Los.**

Loos, *s.* praise, fame, report, 8. 109, 14. 111. O.F. *los,* Lat. *laus.*

Lope, *pt. s.* leaped, ran away, escaped, a. 4. 93; Lope, *pt. pl.* ran, b. 4. 153; Lopen, *pt. pl.* leapt, ran, 2. 110; Lopen, *pp.* ran away, b. 5. 198. See **Lepen.**

Lordein, sluggard, vagabond, lazy rascal, 6. 163; Lordeyn, 23. 189; Lordeyne, b. 20. 188; *pl.* villains, b. 18. 102. O.F. *lourdein* (Roquefort); see *lourd, lourdaut, lourdin,* in Cotgrave. See **Lurdeyn, Lourdeines.**

Lordene, *gen. pl.* of lords, 2. 95, 6. 73.

Lordeþ, *pr. s.* is lord, plays the lord, 12. 69.

Lordliche, *adv.* nobly, luxuriously, 20. 235, 241.

Lordynges, *s. pl.* lordlings, little lords, a contemptuous expression, a. 3. 26. It is often used for our modern *sirs,* without any contempt being implied. See below.

Lordyns, *s. gen. pl.* of little lords, R. 2. 60. Put for *lordynges;* see above.

Lore, instruction, teaching, 10. 104, 12. 128; learning, doctrine, a. 11. 76, R. 1. 93.

Lore, *pp.* See **Loren.**

Lorel, an abandoned fellow, lazy vagabond, worthless fellow, 7. 314, b. 7. 136; Lorell, wretch, 21. 3, R. 2. 170; Loreles, *pl.* 1. 75, 15. 20; Lorelles, 9. 129. See **Losel,** and note, p. 128.

Loren, *pt. pl.* lost, 15. 63, b. 12. 122; Lore, *pp.* 7. 193, 21. 82; been deprived of, b. 18. 79. See **Lesen.**

Loresman, teacher, instructor, 15. 123; Loresmen, *pl.* b. 9. 87.

Lorkynge, *pres. part.* lurking, 3. 226.

Lorn. See **Loren.**

Los, *s.* loss, 17. 149. See **Loos.**

Losedest. See **Losen.**

Losel, *s.* wretch, profligate fellow, vagabond; Loseles, *pl.* vagabonds, 9. 74, 17. 280; Losels, a. pr. 74; Loselles,

GLOSSARIAL INDEX. 391

b. 15. 133; **Loseles,** *gen. pl.* vagabonds', b. 10. 49. See **Lorel.**
Loseliche, *adv.* loosely, freely, at ease, 15. 153. The various readings give the former syllable as *los-, lose-, loose-, lous-, lowse-,* which make the identification with mod. E. *loose* certain. It is, accordingly, so explained in Stratmann.
Losen, *v.* praise; **Loseth,** *pr. s.* praises, b. 15. 248; **Losedest,** 2 *pt. s.* didst praise, b. 11. 411. See **Loos.**
Losengerye, *s.* flattery, lying, b. 6. 145; Losengrie, a. 11. 36. Cf. O. F. *losengier,* 'a flatterer, cogger, beguiler;' Cotgrave.
Lotebyes, *s. pl.* concubines, 4. 188, a. 3. 146; Lotebies, b. 3. 150. See note.
Lotering, *s.* cunning, dealing (?), a. 5. 188. Sense uncertain; perhaps allied to A.S. *lot,* deceit, *lotwrenc,* cunning, hypocrisy (Bosworth). Cf. **Lotyeth.**
Loth, *adj.* unwilling, loath, 1. 53, 4. 199, 9. 266. See **Laith.**
Loþe, *v.* loathe, hate, a. 8. 81; Loþeth, *pr. s. impers.* it loathes, disgusts; Ous loþeth, we loathe, 1. 173; Loþen, *pr. pl.* loathe, 7. 142; Loþede, *pt. s.* 8. 50.
Lother, *adj.* more unwilling, b. 15. 385.
Lopliche, *adj.* loathsome, disgusting, vile, 2. 110, 15. 179; Lothelich, b. 1. 116.
Lotyeth, *pr. pl.* lurk, b. 17. 102. See note, p. 244. A.S. *lutian,* to lurk.
Loude, *adv.* loudly, aloud, 23. 143; Loude other stille=loud or still, i. e. under all circumstances, b. 9. 105; see note, p. 142.
Loue, loaf, 9. 196; Loues, *pl.* 19. 154. See **Lof, Loof.**
Loue-day, a love-day, day for the settlement of disputes by arbitration, 4. 197, 12. 17; Louedayes, *pl.* 4. 196; Louedaies, 6. 159. See note, p. 47.
Loueles, *adj. or adv.* loveless, without love, a. 5. 98.
Loueliche, *adj.* lovely, handsome, pleasant, agreeable, amiable, 2. 3, 11. 65, 83, 259; affable, a. 9. 77; pleasant, b. 12. 262.
Loueliche, *adv.* becomingly, b. 13. 26.
Loueloker, *adj. comp.* sweeter, pleasanter, 15. 186.
Louelokest, *adj.* the handsomest (lit. loveliest), 2. 107, 7. 44, b. 13. 295; Louelokeste, 7. 192.
Louer, loover, louvre, 21. 288. The derivation is *certainly* from the F. *l'ouvert.* See note.

Louerd, *s.* lord, a. 1. 131.
Loues, *pl.* See **Loue.**
Louh, *pt. s.* laughed, 19. 3, 22. 461, a. 4. 137; Loughe, b. 19. 456. See **Lauhen, Lowh.**
Louh, *adj.* lowly, meek, humble, 8. 196, 17. 24, 154; quiet, a. 11. 2; low, common, poor, a. 3. 240; low, deep, 13. 183.
Louh-chered, having a meek look, 22. 263. See **Lowe-chered.**
Loueliche, *adv.* lowly, humbly, 10. 141. See **Loulich.**
Louh-herted, *adj.* humble, 23. 37.
Louhnesse, lowliness, meekness, humility, 4. 447, 16. 133.
Louke, *v.* lock, shut up, b. 18. 243. See **Lowke.** A.S. *lúcan,* to lock, enclose.
Loulich, *adj.* lowly, b. 14. 227. See **Louheliche.**
Loupe, loop-hole, 21. 288; see note.
Loupe, *pt. s.* escaped, b. 4. 106; Loupen, 1 *pt. pl.* leapt, fled, b. 18. 310; Loupe, *pt. s. subj.* if (he) escaped, were (he) to escape, 5. 101. See **Lepen.**
Lourdeines, *pl.* vagabonds, 19. 48. See **Lordein.**
Loure, *v.* scowl, frown, look sullen, 8. 302, 15. 203, 17. 302; Loury, *v.* 7. 98; Lourest, 2 *pr. s.* frownest, 13. 25; Lourestow (*for* Lourest thou), dost thou look angrily, b. 11. 85; Loureth, *pr. s.* scowls, b. 10. 311; Loureþ, *pr. pl.* look gloomy, 17. 302; Lourede, 1 *pt. s.* I frowned, 13. 24; Lourede, *pt. s.* looked angrily, 5. 168; Lourede, *pt. pl.* looked discontented, frowned, 3. 233; Loured, b. 2. 223; Lourid, scowled, looked sad, R. 1. 72; Lourynge, *pres. pt.* b. 5. 83. Mod. E. *lower* (better *lour*). See **Lowren.**
Louryng, *s.* frowning, scowling, b. 5. 344. See above.
Lous, louse, 7. 204. With the text cf. '*louse's-lather,* the ladder-like breach made in knitting by dropping a stitch;' Shropsh. Glossary.
Loute, *v.* bow, b. 10. 142; Louten, 2 *pr. pl.* are humble, b. 15. 84; Louten, *pr. pl.* kneel, pray, 4. 98; Loutede, *pt. s.* bowed, made obeisance, 4. 152, 12. 86; bowed low, a. 3. 37; Louted, *pt. s.* b. 3. 115. See **Lowtyng.** A.S. *hlútan,* to bow.
Louwest, *adj. superl.* lowest, a. 1. 115.
Louyen, *v.* love, b. 11. 105; Louye, *v.* 6. 181; Louie, *v.* be pleased, b. 10. 90; To louie=to be loved, b. 14. 266; Louyeth, *pr. s.* 13. 107, 21. 57;

Louyeþ, 2 *pr. pl.* love, 16. 117;
Louieth, *pr. pl.* b. 10. 50'; Louye, 2
pr. s. subj. love, b. 12. 94; Louye, *pr.
s. subj.* may love, 1. 149; Louye,
imper. s. love, b. 12. 34. A.S. *lufian*.
Louyd (*for* **Lowyd**), *pt. s.* put down,
brought low, R. 2. 179; *pp.* brought
low, R. 3. 310. See **Lowe**, *v.*
Louynge, *adj.* loving, b. 13. 16.
Low, *adj.* humble, meek, lowly, b. 8.85;
Lowe, *adj. pl.* humble, meek, 10. 184.
Low, *pt. s.* laughed, a. 12. 42. See
Lauhen, **Lowh**.
Lowable, *adj.* praiseworthy, commendable, 6. 103, 18. 130. Short for
allowable.
Lowe, *adv.* lowly, humbly, b. 12. 265;
low, b. 11. 61 (where it is perhaps an
adjective, as in the C-text).
Lowe, *v. refl.* humble thyself, 11. 305;
humbles, 13. 157; Lowede, *pt. s.*
humbled, 9. 194; Lowed, stooped, b.
pr. 129; Lowe þe, *imp. s.* humble
thyself, 15. 9. From *low*, adj.
Lowe, 2 *pt. s.* didst lie, didst tell falsely,
21. 351, 447; didst speak falsely, b.
18. 400; Lowen vpon = lied against,
3. 20 ; Lowen on = lied against, b. 5.
95. A.S. *léogan*, to lie, pp. *logen*.
See **Liȝen**.
Lowe-chered, *adj.* mild-faced, having
a meek look, b. 19. 258. See **Louhchered.**
Lowe-lyuynge, *adj.* lowly, humble, 15.
188.
Lower, *adj. compar.* lower, inferior, a.
8. 142.
Lowh, *pt. s.* laughed, 13. 24, 23. 143.
See **Lauhen**, **Louh**.
Lowke, *v.* shut up, lock up, 21. 256.
See **Louke**.
Lowren, *pr. pl.* look cross, b. 13. 265.
See **Loure**.
Lowtyng, *pres. part.* bowing, a. 12. 55;
Lowte, *imper. s.* bend the knees, bow,
7. 171. See **Loute**.
Lowynge, *s.* humbling themselves, submissiveness, b. 15. 299. [It can
hardly mean *lowing* as a cow.]
Luf, *adv.* dearly, 4. 19, 8. 253; willingly,
7. 183. See **Leef**.
Luft, *adj.* left (hand), a. 2. 7, a. 3. 56;
left (side), a. 6. 68.
Luft, *s.* worthless fellow, weak creature,
wretch, b. 4. 62. From the adj. *luft*
(above), worthless, weak, left. See
Left in my Etym. Dict.
Luft, *pt. s.* raised, lifted, b. 15. 583.
Icel. *lypta* (for *lyfta*), to lift.
Lufthond, *s.* left hand, a. 2. 5.

Luggid, *pp.* pulled about, R. 2. 173.
See note to 3. 226.
Luite, *adv.* little. a. 4. 51; lightly, a. 4.
137 ; seldom, a. 8. 123. See **Lite**,
Luyte.
Luitel, *adj.* little, a. 3. 200.
Lullede, *pt. pl.* flapped about, wagged,
a. 5. 110. See **Lolleþ**.
Lured, *pp.* allured, caught, 8. 45.
Lurkede, *pt. s.* lurked, a. 2. 192.˙ See
Cath. Angl. p. 224.
Lurker, *s.* intruder, R. 3. 57.
Lusarde (lizard), serpent, b. 18. 335.
Lussheborgh, a light coin (lit. a coin
of Luxembourg), 18. 72; Lussheborue, *adj.* counterfeit, 18.82; Lussheborwes, *pl.* counterfeit money, light
coin of Luxembourg, b. 15. 342. See
note, p. 226.
Lust, a desire, pleasure, fancy, 2. 111,
R. 3. 175, 266.
Lust, *pr. s.* (*for* **Lusteth**), desires, is
willing, 12. 76; *pr. s. impers.* it
pleases, 4. 170, 10. 146 ; Luste, *pr. s.
impers.* it pleases (her), a. 3. 154;
Luste, *pr. s. subj.* may please, 14. 237;
Luste, *pr. s. impers.* it pleased, 20.
114, 21. 451 ; Hem luste = it pleased
them, a. pr. 37 ; Luste, *impers. pt. s.
subj.* it should please, 1. 175. A.S.
lystan; from *lust.*
Lustnede, 1 *pt. s.* listened, 16. 250;
Lusteneþ, *imp. pl.* 21. 297.
Lusteth, *imper. pl.* listen, 21. 297 *n.*
Lusty, *adj.* pleasant, profitable, R. pr.
63.
Lutede, *pt. s.* played on a lute, 21. 470.
Luther, *adj.* wicked, evil, false, bad,
treacherous, 2. 195, 4. 320, 5. 104, 7.
437, 9. 253, 10. 18, 11. 160, 20. 244;
bad, pestilent, 16. 220; ill-tempered, a.
5. 98 ; Luthere, *pl.* 9. 296. See **Liþer**.
A.S. *lýðre*, bad (Grein).
Luyte, *adj.* little, a. 2. 163; *as sb.* a
little, a. 7. 118. See **Luite**.
Luytel, *adj.* little, a. 10. 112. See
Luitel.
Lyard, horse, b. 17. 64, 71; Lyarde,
20. 64, 76, 331. See note, p. 243.
Lybbe, *v.* to live, 4. 203 ; Lybbeth, *pr.
pl.* 18. 249; Lybben, *pr. pl.* 7. 125, 9.
70; Lybbynge, *pres. part.* living, 10.
58. See **Libben**, **Lyuen**.
Lycame, body, 11. 219, 20. 182, 21.
94 ; Lycames, *gen. sing.* of the body,
7. 275. See **Licame**, **Likame**.
Lycence, *s.* licence, 7. 121.
Lyche, *adj.* like, 8. 129. See **Liche**.
Lycour, juice, 13. 220.
Lydene, voice, 15. 186. See **Ledene**

GLOSSARIAL INDEX. 393

Lye, s. flame, glow, 20. 172, 179, 257.
A.S. *líg*, a flame (Grein).
Lye, I *pr. s.* lie, tell lies, 20. 223, 227;
Lye, *pr. pl.* b. 10. 42, 332; Lyeth,
pr. pl. tell lies about, slander, b. 10.
203; Lyede, *pt. s.* deceived, 3. 32.
See **Liȝen, Lowe, Lyghe.**
Lyere, liar, 2. 36, 3. 6, 225.
Lyeþ, *pr. s.* applies (lit. lies), 6. 89.
See **Liggen**; and the note, p. 63.
Lyf (1), life (sometimes personified), 21.
30, b. 1. 202, b. 9.188. See **Lif, Lyue.**
Lyf (2), living creature, living person,
creature, man, 2. 116, 7. 67, 8. 50,
11. 305, 12. 264, 13. 32, 14. 74, 19.
105, 20. 274. A peculiar use of the
word above. It occurs again, in this
sense, in the Kingis Quair, st. 31; and
in Gower, C. A. i. 362, l. 15. See **Lif.**
Lyf (put for *leef*), *s.* leaf, small piece of
instruction, short lesson, a. 7. 241.
See **Leef.**
Lyfholiest, *adj. sup.* most upright of
life, 11. 50.
Lyf-holy, *adj.* religious, devout, holy
of life, 5. 175, 10. 195. See note, p. 125.
Lyf-holynesse, holiness of life, 6. 80,
22. 111.
Lyflode, means of life, livelihood, food,
viands, 1. 32, 5. 115, 6. 42, 7. 68. See
Liflode.
Lyft, *adj.* left, 3. 5, 4. 75. See **Lift, Luft.**
Lyft, sky, 18. 95. See **Luft, Lifte.**
Lyft, *pt. s.* lifted, 19. 144.
Lygaunce, loyalty, allegiance, 19. 202.
Lyge, *adj.* liege, liege (men), liege
(subjects), 4. 319, 320, 418; Lyges,
pl. as sb. lieges, subjects, servants, b.
18. 347. See **Lige.**
Lygge, *v.* lie, remain, recline, be laid,
10. 143, 13. 232; Lyggen, *pr. pl.* lie,
4. 170, 5. 122; Lyggynge, *pres. part.*
lying, 3. 53, 130. See **Liggen.**
Lyghe, *v.* lie, tell lies, 17. 304. See
Lye, Liȝen.
Lyghte, *pt. s.* alighted, R. 2. 172. See
Lyȝte.
Lyghtliche, *adv.* lightly, easily, readily, 3. 225, 8. 302, 10. 11.
Lyghtloker, *adv.* more lightly, readily,
easily, 8. 216, 15. 101. See **Lightloker.**
Lyghtnynge, *s.* flame, 22. 202.
Lyhþ, *pr. s.* lies, exists, a. 11. 140. See
Liggen.
Lyinge, *s.* lying, b. 13. 323.
Lykame, body, 1. 32, 7. 52; Lykam,
b. 12. 234; Lykhame, a. 12. 93;
Lykames, *gen.* body's, 11. 55; of
my body, b. 13. 387. See **Licame.**

Lykerous, *adj.* luxurious, dainty, lecherous, a. 11. 120.
Lykeþ, *pr. s. impers.* it pleases, 12.
187, b. 8. 51; Lykeþ, *pr. pl.* please,
2. 41; Lykede, *pt. s. impers.* it pleased,
1. 58; Lykyde, 1. 168; Lyked, *pt. s.*
pleased, 6. 41; Lyke, *pr. s. subj.*
please, 23. 30; Lyke, *pr. s. subj.
impers.* it please, 20. 327. See
Likeþ.
Lykne, *v.* compare, liken, 8. 23; Lykneth, *pr. s.* b. 12. 267; Lyknede, *pt.
pl.* compared, likened, 15. 169; Lykned, *pp.* 11. 47. See **Likne.**
Lyknesse, likeness, 21. 330.
Lykyng, *adj.* pleasing, 22. 45; Lykynge, 11. 286.
Lykynge, *s.* liking, desire, pleasure,
wish, 12. 182, 14. 152.
Lykyngest, *adj.* most pleasing, 7.
44.
Lymé, limb, 23. 195, b. 5. 99, b. 19.
101; Lymes, *pl.* 6. 8, 9. 135; Feondes lymes, limbs of the fiend, 23. 77,
b. 20. 76; Lymmes, *pl.* limbs, R. 2.
62. See **Limes.**
Lymed, *pp.* covered with bird-lime, R.
2. 186.
Lymytour, authorised beggar, 23. 346,
362. See **Limitour.**
Lym-ȝerde, limed-twig, snare, 11. 286;
Lymeȝerde, b. 9. 179. See note.
Lynage, family, descent, lineage, parentage, 6. 26, 14. 111; good family,
10. 195, 197.
Lynde, lime-tree, linden-tree, 2. 152,
11. 64. A.S. *lind.*
Lyne, line, 12. 127; cord for measuring, a. 11. 135; Lynes, *pl.* lines, 10.
286; snares for birds, 7. 406.
Lynne-seed, lin-seed, i.e. flax-seed,
13. 190.
Lyppe, *s.* a portion, part, b. 5. 250.
See **Lippe.**
Lyser, *s.* list, edge of cloth, b. 5. 210.
See **Lisure.**
Lysse, comfort, happiness, 7. 315;
relief, 2. 200. See **Lisse.**
Lyste, *pr. s. subj.* please, R. 3. 182.
See **Liste.**
Lyste, *s.* list, edge of a piece of cloth,
a. 5. 124; strip of cloth, 8. 162. See
Liste.
Lyte, *adj.* little, 10. 207, b. 13. 149.
See **Lite.**
Lyte, *adv.* (or *adj.*) little, 2. 140; *adv.*
23. 27. See **Lite.**
Lyth, *pr. s.* lies, 4. 193; rests, 21. 431;
consists, a. 10. 114. See **Liggen.**
Lyþen, *v.* hear, listen to, 8. 84, b. 13.

GLOSSARIAL INDEX.

424; Lythe, *ger.* b. 8. 66; Lythen, *pr. pl.* listen, are anxious to hear, 12. 77; Lythed, *pt. s.* has listened, b. 13. 452. See **Lithen**.
Lyther, *adj.* false, bad, evil, b. 10. 435, b. 15. 342. See **Luther**.
Lyþet, *pp.* rendered lithe or active, a. 7. 183.
Lytulum, *adv.* by little; *lytulum and lytulum*, gradually, 18. 320. See **Litlum**.
Lyue, *dat.* life, 1. 25; In my lyue = during my life, a. 7. 94; By hus lyue, during his lifetime, 13. 69; By thy lyue, during thy life, 12. 74. See **Lyf**, which is the *nom.* case.
Lyue, 1 *pr. s.* believe, 1. 103; Lyuede, 1 *pt. s.* believed, thought, 1. 17; Lyuede hym wel, *pt. pl.* entirely believed him, 1. 70. See **Leue**.
Lyue-lode, livelihood, means of living, 4. 470. See **Lyflode**.
Lyuen, *v.* live, 20. 73, 235; Lyuye, *v.* 7. 67; Lyueþ, *pr. s.* passes his life, a. 2. 139; Lyueden, *pt. pl.* lived, passed their lives, 1. 28, 16. 271; Lyue, 1 *pl. imp.* let us live, b. 10. 438; Lyueþ, *imp. pl.* live, 23. 247; Lyuynge, *pr. pt.* living, alive, 22. 175. See **Lybbe, Libben**.
Lyueres, men who lived, lit. livers, b. 12. 132.
Lyues, *adv.* alive, i. e. living, 11, 150, 22. 159. See note, p. 134. Cf. 'Right as a *lyues* creature;' Gower, C. A. ii. 14, l. 16. A.S. *lífes*, gen. of *líf*, life, used adverbially.
Lyuynge, *s.* living, life, b. 11. 14, 156; food, provisions, 16. 103; Lyuyng, way of life, 7. 437; After a freres lyuynge = according to a friar's way of living or diet, b. 13. 94.
Ly3en, *v.* lie, tell lies, a. pr. 49; Ly3eþ, *pr. s.* deceives, a. 1. 67; Ly3e. *pr. s. subj.* lie, speak falsely, a. 8. 109; Ly3en on = lie against, a. 11. 149. See **Li3en**.
Ly3en, *pt. pl.* lay, a. 10. 174. (Not a good form; prob. for Ley3en or Le3en.) See **Liggen**.
Ly3ere, *s.* a liar, a. 1. 36.
Ly3te, *pt. s.* alighted, settled, b. 19. 197. See **Li3te, Lyghte**.
Ly3tliche, *adv.* easily, 1. 169. See **Li3tlich**.

Maad. See **Maken**.
Macche, match (for helping to strike a light), 20. 179.

Macche, mate, companion, b. 13. 47; Macches, *pl.* b. 13. 35. A.S. *gemæcca*.
Macche, *imper. pl.* match, mate, b. 9. 173; Maccheth, a. 10. 193.
Maceres, *s. pl.* mace-bearers, officers of the courts of justice, b. 3. 76.
Maces, *s. pl.* maces, R. 3. 268.
Ma dame, madam, 12. 89.
Maddid, *pt. s.* maddened, R. 1. 63; *pt. pl.* bewildered, R. 2. 132.
Made. See **Maken**.
Mafflid, *pt. pl.* mumbled, spoke indistinctly, R. 4. 63. Cf. 'he wot nou3t what he *maffleþ*;' Trevisa. ii. 91. O. Du. *maffelen*, to stammer (Hexham); North of Eng. *maffle*.
Mai. See **Mowe**.
Maidenhod, maidenhead, virginity, 2. 181, 5. 48. See **Maydenhod**.
Maiht, Maihtou. See **Myghte**.
Maire, mayor, magistrate, authority, lord mayor (of London), b. 3. 87, b. 13. 271. See **Meires**.
Maiste, 2 *pr. s.* mayest, R. 3. 62. See **Mowe**.
Maister, master, 4. 215, 446, 6. 189; captain of a ship, R. 4. 75; Maistre, 4. 350; Maistres, *pl.* masters, lords, 4. 275; masters, doctors, learned men, b. 10. 113, 384; superiors, b. 8. 9; Maisters, 1. 85; Maisteres, 11. 9 (see note). See **Maystres**.
Maistrie, mastery, superior power, force, 21. 301, 397, a. 9. 47; dominion, sway, b. 6. 329; victory, 12. 284; Maistrye, mastery, victory, supremacy, 4. 286, 5. 132; force, 7. 191; chief authority, b. 13. 334; great achievement, b. 16. 112; Maistries, *pl.* arts, sciences, 22. 255; masterful deeds, b. 4. 25. See **Maystrie, Mastrye**.
Mai3t, *pr. s.* mayst, a. 6. 126. See **Mowe**.
Make, *s.* partner, consort, mate, 4. 155, 14. 139, 19. 225, 226, 236; Makes, *pl.* mates, partners, 14. 136, b. 11. 319, 335. Icel. *maki*.
Maken, *v.* make, 22. 59, 389; Make, *v.* make, a. 2. 117; compose, write, b. 7. 61; Makye, *v.* cause, make, 4. 483; Make, 1 *pr. s.* compose verses, b. 12. 22; Makeþ, *pr. s.* makes, considers, 4. 394; Makeþ hit, causes it (to be so), 21. 326; Maken, *pr. pl.* make, 20. 201; Make, *pr. s. subj.* cause, bring (it) about, 8. 28; cause it (to be otherwise), 11. 157; Made, 1. *pt. s.* composed poetry, 6. 5; Maade, 1 *pt. s.* I made, a. 3. 191;

GLOSSARIAL INDEX.   395

Made, *pt. s.* composed, b. 5. 415; made him, set himself, a. 7. 103; caused (it), b. 17. 330; did, performed, 19. 146; Maden, *pt. pl.* made, induced, 23. 127; built, 14. 156; wrote, composed, have written, 18. 110; Made, *pt. s. subj.* had made, R. 3. 46 (see the note); Maad, *pp.* a. 4. 90; Maked, *pp.* made, b. 7. 143. See note to b. 12. 16, p. 179.

Makyng, *s.* composing verses, a. 11. 32; Makynge, making, R. 3. 160; Makynge, feature, 14. 193; Makynges, *pl.* verse-making, b. 12. 16 (see note).

Malaperte, *s.* jackanapes, R. 3. 237.

Male, portmanteau, bag, wallet, 14. 56; Males, *pl.* 7. 236. F. *malle*, E. *mail-bag*. See Cath. Angl. p. 226, n. 5.

Mal-ese, *s.* discomfort, pain, injury, 9. 233, 16. 84, 20. 157. Lit. 'ill ease.'

Malkyn, *s.* (*proper name*) Malkin, i.e. Maud-kin, dimin. of Maud; used in the sense of a common woman, a kitchen-wench, 2. 181. See note.

Mamely, *v.* mumble, prate, b. 5. 21; Mamelede, *pt. s.* 14. 228. See Mommeþ, Momely.

Man, servant, man, b. 13. 40, b. 14. 216; Mannes, *gen. sing.* man's, 20. 257, 22. 275; Mannes, *gen. pl.* men's, 11. 41.

Manasceþ, *pr. s.* threatens, 5. 62; Manasen, *pr. pl.* b. 16. 49; Manacede, *pt. s.* threatened, 16. 6; Manaced, *pp.* menaced, R. 3. 337.

Manere, manor, estate, 8. 233, b. 5. 595, b. 10. 308; Maner, a. 6. 76; Maners, *pl.* 6. 160; Maneres, *pl.* b. 5. 246.

Manere, kind, sort, 1. 20; way, a. 2. 50; (used without *of* following), 3. 197, 4. 110, 9. 283, 21. 43, 367; Maner, 3. 57; Maners, *pl.* manners, habits, customs, 3. 7.

Manered, *pp.* mannered, disposed, endued with manners, 3. 27.

Manfful, *adj.* manly, R. 3. 103.

Manged, *pp.* eaten, 9. 272; Maunged, b. 6. 260.

Mangerie, feast (lit. an eating), 13. 46. See *Mangerie* in Cotgrave. See **Maungerye**; and note, p. 168.

Mangonel, catapult, engine for casting stones, &c., 21. 295. '*Mangonneau*, an old-fashioned sling, or engine, whereout stones, old iron, and great arrowes were violently darted;' Cotgrave.

Man-hede, manhood, nature of man, 19. 221, 240; manliness, uprightness, 18. 65; Manhod, b. 12. 293.

Manliche, *adj.* manly, humane, charitable, hospitable, b. 5. 260.

Manliche, *adv.* hospitably, generously, b. 10. 87, 91; manfully, b. 16. 127.

Mansed, *pp. as adj.* cursed, excommunicated, 3. 41, 23. 221. A very corrupt form; short for *amansed = amansumed*, from the pp. of A.S. *ámǽnsumian*, to excommunicate, from A.S. *mǽne = gemǽne*, common. We find *mannsenn* in the Ormulum, 10522. See **Monside**.

Manshupes, *s. pl.* courtesies, compliments, entertainments, 13. 105. See note.

Manslauht, slaughter, bloodshed, 5. 182, 18. 241.

Marbelston, *s.* stone (lit. marblestone), a. 10. 101.

Marchal. See **Marschal**.

Marchaunt, merchant, 14. 33; Marchante, 14. 37; Marchaundes, *s. pl.* merchants, a. 2. 188; Marchauns, *pl.* 3. 222, 5. 193; Marchans, 10. 22.

Marchaunden, *v.* trade, b. 13. 394; Marchaunde, *v.* 7. 280.

Marchaundise, goods, merchandise, 1. 61, 4. 282, 14. 53; Marchaundyse, b. 13. 362; Marchaundie, a. pr. 60; trade, business, a. 3. 219.

Marche, boundary, border, district, province, 23. 221; Marches, *pl.* 11. 137.

Marchen, *pr. pl.* march, go, 1. 61.

Mareis, *s.* marsh-land, 14. 168. '*Marais*, a marsh, or fenne;' Cotgrave.

Mareschal. See **Marschal**.

Margerie-perles, *pl.* pearls, 12. 7; Margerye-perle, b. 10. 9. '*Marguerite*, a (Margarite) pearl;' Cotgrave. See note, p. 146.

Marieth, *imp. pl.* marry, 11. 281.

Mark, mark (coin), 6. 134. The value of a mark was 13*s*. 4*d*.

Marke, land-mark, 4. 385; feature, b. 9. 31, a. 10. 32.

Marke, *v.* observe, b. 12. 132; Marked, *pp.* marked out, allotted, 15. 126; Markid, *pp.* noted down, a. 11. 253.

Marre, *v.* destroy, ruin, 4. 142; Marred, *pp.* injured, a. 2. 16.

Marschal, marshal, b. 3. 200; Marchal, a. 3. 194; Marchall, R. 3. 105; Mareschal, 4. 258, 259.

VOL. II.   B b

Martrye, *v.* martyr, slay, 21. 337; Martired, *pp.* b. 15. 260.
Marye, *pr. pl.* marry, give in marriage, b. 9. 153.
Masager, *s.* messenger, a. 12. 83 *n.* See **Messager.**
Mase, confused medley of people, 2. 6; confusion, bewilderment, 4. 198, b. pr. 196, b. 3. 159.
Masoun, mason, b. 11. 341.
Masse, mass, 1. 125, 2. 180; Massen, *pl.* a. 3. 238.
Masse-pans, money paid for the saying of masses, lit. mass-pence, 4. 280.
Mastrye, mastery, 19. 52, 21. 69. See **Maistrie.**
Matall, metal, R. 2. 155.
Matere, *s.* matter, subject, 2. 123, b. 8. 118, b. 11. 224; substance, b. 11. 392; Mater, matter, subject, 6. 110, 124; Mateere, a. 9. 113; Maters, *pl.* R. 1. 84.
Matynes, *pl.* matins, 1. 125, 23. 366; Matyns, 8. 27, 10. 228.
Maugre, *s.* displeasure, punishment, b. 9. 153, a. 7. 227; ill-will, b. 6. 242. F. *mal gré.*
Maugre, *prep.* in spite of, 3. 214, 9. 39. 68, 155, 21. 84.
Maule, *adj.* male, 19. 254; Maules, *pl.* 14. 147.
Maumettes, *pl.* idols, 1. 119. See note.
Maundee, maundy, i.e. washing of the disciples' feet, b. 16. 140. See note.
Maundement, commandment, 20. 2, 60; b. 17. 2, 60.
Maunged, 1 *pt. s.* ate, a. 12. 72; *pp.* eaten, b. 6. 260. See **Manged.**
Maungerye, feeding, meal, feast, b. 11. 107, b. 15. 582. See **Mangerie.**
Mawe, maw, stomach, 7. 90, 9. 170, 335; Maw, b. 13. 82.
May, May (the month), 1. 6.
Mayde, maid, 3. 19, 5. 62. See **Maide.**
Mayden, *s.* maiden, a. 3. 1; Maydenes, *pl.* 8. 273; unmarried persons of both sexes, bachelors and spinsters, b. 9. 173.
Maydenhod, *s.* maidenhood, virginity, a. 1. 158.
Maymeþ, *pr. s.* maims, 21. 387.
Mayn, *s.* power, might, 21.364; Mayne, b. 18. 315.
Maynprise, *s.* bail, security, 19. 282; Mayn-pryse, 23. 17. See below.
Maynprise, *v.* bail out, 21. 189; Maynpryse, *v.* 3. 208. See note, p. 39.
Mayntenaunce, *s.* maintenance, abetting of misdoers, b. 5. 253, R. 3. 312.

Mayntene, *v.* support, abet, b. 3. 90, 184, b. 6. 37; Maynteneþ, *pr. pl.* 3. 207. See note to b. 3. 90.
Mayre, *s.* mayor, magistrate, 17. 126. See **Maire.**
Maystres, *pl.* masters, lords, b. 10. 66; Maysturs, a. 3. 91. See **Maister.**
Maystrie, mastery, 21. 107; power, authority, dominion, a. 1. 105, a. 3. 222; Maystrye, authority, mastery, full power, b. 14. 328; victory, b. 10. 450. See **Maistrie.**
Me, *pron. indef.* people, one, 4. 166, 410, 481, 12. 174, 13. 112, 22. 148, b. 10. 192, a. 1. 138, a. 5. 139. See note to b. 10. 192. *Me* is short for *men,* which is not the plural of *man,* but a weakened form of the word *man* itself. It is used exactly as the G. *man.* See **Men.**
Mebles, moveables, moveable property, 4. 425. See **Moebles, Meoble, Meeble;** and note, p. 51.
Mechel, *adj.* many, a. 12. 102.
Meddled. See **Medlen.**
Mede, bribery, R. 2. 84; (personified), 3. 19, 27; reward, bribe (sometimes in a good sense), 8. 202; Mede, *gen.* meed's, 9. 38; Meede, reward, a. 8. 61; bribery, a. 3. 1. See note to 4. 292, p. 49.
Medeth, *pr. s.* rewards, pays, b. 3. 215; Meedeþ, *pr. pl.* reward, a. 3. 209.
Medlen, *v.* meddle, interfere, engage, fight, 23. 179; Medle, *v.* fight, b. 20. 178; Medlest, 2 *pr. s.* dabblest, meddlest, b. 12. 16; Meddled, 1 *pt. s.* mixed, 7. 260; Medled, *pt. pl.* mixed, b. 11. 335; Medle, 1 *pr. pl. imper.* (let us) meddle, 15. 67, b. 12. 126; Medled, *pp.* mingled, 11. 129. See **Mellid.** O.F. *medler, mesler,* to mix.
Medlers, *pl.* meddlers, R. 3. 335.
Meeble, movable property, 11. 96, 186; 15. 182, 16. 168. See **Moebles, Mebles, Meoble.**
Meede. See **Mede.**
Meedeþ. See **Medeth.**
Meekliche, meekly, 2. 165.
Meeles. See **Meles.**
Meel-tyme, meal-time, 8. 133.
Meenes, Meeneth. See **Mene,** *v.*
Mees; mess, dish, b. 13. 52. O.F. *mes,* lit. a thing sent; from Lat. *missus.* See **Messe.**
Meeteles. See **Metels.**
Meeten, Meetynge. See **Meten, Metyng.**
Meeuen. See **Meuen.**

GLOSSARIAL INDEX. 397

Megre, *adj.* thin, 7. 94.
Meires, *pl.* mayors, magistrates, a. 3. 67. See **Maire, Mayre**.
Meke, *adj.* meek, lowly, 2. 170.
Meken, *v.* humble, render meek, 5. 90; Meke', *v.* 7. 10; Meketh, *pr. s.* becomes humble, b. 20. 35; Mekeþ, *imper. pl.* humble (yourselves), 8. 248. See **Meokeþ**.
Meklyche, *adv.* lowly, humbly, 4. 267; Mekeliche, 13. 178.
Meknesse, humility, meekness, 5. 155; Mekenesse, 20. 204.
Mele, meal, ground corn, 10. 75.
Mele, *v.* speak, a. 11. 93; Meleþ, *pr. s.* a. 3. 100; Melleth, *pr. s.* b. 3. 104; Mellud, *pt. s.* b. 3. 36. Icel. *mæla*, to speak.
Meles, *gen. sing.* of a meal; Meles mete, food taken at a meal, 7. 289; for a meal, 16. 36; Meles, *pl.* meals, 13. 105; Meeles, a. 11. 52; Melis, R. 3. 313.
Melke, milk, 8. 51, b. 5. 444.
Melked, *pp.* milked, 18. 10.
Mellere, miller, b. 2. 111.
Melleth, Mellud. See **Mele**, *v.*
Mellid, *pt. s.* mixed, R. 2. 155. (Put for *medlid.*) See **Medlen**. See Cath. Angl. p. 233, n. 5.
Membre, limb, member, 6. 33; Membres, *pl.* 10. 177.
Memorie, memory, remembrance, 8. 27, 9. 104. See note, p. 96.
Men, *indef. pron.* a man, one, people, 14. 5, b. 11. 12, 199. See **Me**.
Men, *pl.* men, 1. 20, &c. See **Menne**.
Mendinant, mendicant, beggar (orig. a mendicant friar), 1. 60; Mendinaunt, 16. 3; Mendynaunt, b. 13. 3; Mendinauntes, *pl.* poor persons, 10. 179; Mendinauns, 6. 76; Mendinans, 14. 79; Mendinantz, b. 10. 65; Mendynauns, *pl.* mendicant friars, 16. 81; Mendynans, beggars, 12. 50; Mendynantz, b. 15. 150; Mendynauntz, a. 11. 198. See note, p. 189.
Mendis, *s. pl.* amends, R. 1. 59.
Mene, *adj.* mean, common, poor, 1. 20, 4. 81; Mene, common (people), 1. 218; Mene ale=common ale, b. 6. 185. A.S. *gemǽne*, common.
Mene, *adj.* mean, middle, b. 9. 113; in an intermediate position, a. 3. 67; as *sb.* instrument, means, 17. 96; mean, intermediate between extremes, R. 2. 139. And see below.
Mene, *s.* mediator, 2. 157, 10. 347, 11. 119, 18. 158; Menes, *pl.* b. 3. 76. F. *moyen*. Stratmann's explanation of *mene*=moan, prayer, in b. 15. 535, I believe to be wrong. It means 'mediator.'
Mene, *ger.* to signify; *chiefly in the phrase* is to mene=is to signify, signifies, 2. 11, 4. 124, 399; Mene, 1 *pr. s.* mean, *hence* tell, b. 5. 283; Menest, 2 *pr. s.* meanest, b. 13. 211; Meneþ, *pr. s.* signifies, means, 21. 131; Menede, *pt. s.* signified, meant, 6. 37, 12. 84; Mente, *pt. pl.* R. 4. 63; Menynge, *pr. pt.* intending, seeking, 18. 176, b. 15. 397.
Mene (*for* Meyne), *s.* household, R. 3. 224. See **Meyne**.
Menede, *pt. s. refl.* bemoaned herself, complained, a. 3. 163; Mened, b. 3. 169; *pt. pl.* b. 6. 2; Menyng, *pres. pt.* complaining, 4. 216. A.S. *mǽnan*, to make moan.
Menepernour, surety, bail, 5. 107. See note; and see **Meynpernour**.
Mener, *adj. comp.* more mean, lowlier, b. 14. 166.
Menged, *pt. s.* mixed, mingled, b. 13. 362. A.S. *mencgan*. See Cath. Angl. p. 234, n. 1.
Mengen, *v.* to commemorate, mention, b. 6. 97; Menge, *v.* 9. 104; Mengen here, remember herself, take counsel with herself, reflect, b. 4. 94. A.S. *mynegian*, *myngian*, to admonish. See **Munge**; and see *munegen* in Stratmann.
Menne, *gen. pl.* of men, men's, 4. 102, 103, 9. 29, 11. 16; Mennes, 10. 141, 16. 172; Mennys, 22. 380; Menis, a. 11. 197. See note to 7. 201.
Menour, *s.* Minorite (friar), a. 9. 14; Menours, *pl.* 11. 9, a. 9. 9. See **Minours**.
Menske, *v.* honour, 4. 230. See note, and note to 13. 105. Coined from the sb. *mensk*, honour, which was orig. an adj. meaning humane.
Menteyny, *v.* maintain, support, abet, 4. 231; Menteyneþ, *pr. s.* 4. 187, 5. 58. See note to 5. 58.
Meny, *adj.* many, 1. 26, 19. 260.
Menyng, meaning; *hence* intelligence, understanding, 2. 138; Menynge, intention, endeavour, b. 15. 467; signification, token, 1. 99, 16. 245, 21. 141.
Menyng, complaining. See **Menede**.
Menynge, intending. See **Mene**, *v.*
Menysoun, flux, b. 16. 111. '*Menison, menisoun, menoison;* on appeloit ainsi la maladie, la dysenterie, le dévoiement, le flux de ventre, dont

B b 2

GLOSSARIAL INDEX.

l'armée de S. Louis fut attaquée;'
Roquefort. From Lat. acc. *minutionem*; *minutio sanguinis*, bloodletting (White). See further in Cath. Angl.

Menyuer, *s.* fur, miniver, 23. 138. '*Menu ver*, the furre minever, also, the beast that bears it;' Cotgrave. From *menu*, small, and *vair*, the name of a fur (Lat. *uarius*).

Meoble, property, goods, properly *moveable* property, 10. 272; Meobles, *pl.* moveables, property, 14. 6, 17. 12; Moebles, b. 3. 267; Mebles, 4. 425. F. *meubles*; the diphthong *oe* or *eo* represents the sound of F. *eu*; cf. mod. E. *people* = *peuple* (O.F. *people, poeple*). See **Mebles**.

Meoke, *adj.* meek, a. 10. 83. See **Meke**.

Meokeþ, *pr. s.* humbles (himself), 18. 154, 23. 35; Meokede, *pt. s.* a. 4. 81. See **Meken**.

Meorknesse, darkness, 21. 141, 181. See **Merkenesse**.

Meoue, *v.* move, excite, 22. 286. See **Meuen**.

Mercede, due reward, proper pay, 4. 291, 306. From Lat. acc. *mercedem*.

Mercement, fine, penalty, 2. 159, 5. 182; Merciment, b. 1. 160. See note, p. 28. 'A mercyment, *amerciamentum, misericordia*;' Cath. Angl.

Merciable, *adj.* merciful, compassionate, kind, 10. 15, 18. 46, 21. 420, 438.

Merciede, *pt s.* thanked, 4.21; Mercyed, b. 3. 20. F. *merci*, thanks.

Merciment. See **Mercement**.

Mercy, thanks, 2. 41, b. 10. 218; (your) pardon, b. 1. 11; Merci, mercy, a. 1. 144; Mercye, mercy, b. 14. 331.

Mercyed. See **Merciede**.

Mercymonye, reward, pay, recompence, allowance. b. 14. 126.

Meri, *adj.* cheerful, fortunate, b. 12. 189.

Merit, *s.* merit, a. 1. 157.

Meritorie, *adj.* necessary, suitable, 10. 68.

Merke, *s.* mark, heed, b. 17. 103; mark, stamp, b. 15. 343; Merkis, *pl.* badges, R. 2. 78.

Merke, *v.* mark, R. 2. 20, 56; mark, strike, R. 3. 268; Merkyd, 2 *pt. pl.* marked, R. 2. 42.

Merke, *adj.* dark, murky, 2. 1, b. 1. 1; mysterious, b. 11. 154; Merk, 19. 198. A.S. *myrce*.

Merke, *s.* darkness, 20. 206.

Merkenesse, darkness, b. 18. 175. See **Meorknesse**.

Merþe, *s.* mirth, a. 12. 92.

Meruayle, marvel, wonder, 21. 132; Merueile, b. 9. 148.

Merueilith, *pr. s. impers.* it makes (me) wonder, R. 2. 1; Merueilled, *impers. pt. s.* caused (me) to wonder, surprised (me), b. 11. 342; Merueilid, *pt. pl.* marvelled, R. 3. 224.

Merueillouse, *adj.* marvellous, wonderful, b. 11. 5.

Merueillousest, *adj. superl.* most wonderful, b. 8. 68.

Merueilousliche, *adv.* wonderfully, 11. 67.

Meruiloste, *adj. superl.* most wonderful, a. 9. 69.

Merytorye, *adj.* meritorious, b. 11. 79.

Meschaunce, misfortune, evil fate, harm, ruin, 1. 105, 4. 97, 7. 69, 11. 59, 20. 229.

Meschef, trouble, discomfort, misfortune, 9. 212, 233, 14. 71; Meschef, 12. 232; Meschiefs, *pl.* misfortunes, b. 15. 169; Meschiefes, 10. 183; Meschifs, 17. 309. See **Mischief**.

Meseise, *s.* misease, discomfort; For meseise = to prevent discomfort, a. 1. 24; Meseyse, illness, a. 8. 28. See **Miseise, Myseise**.

Meseles, *pl.* lepers, 4. 169, b. 3. 132; Mesels, 10. 179, a. 3. 128. O.F. *mesel*, a leper, Low. Lat. *misellus*, dimin. of *miser*. (Not to be confused with E. *measles*.) See note, p. 124.

Meson-deu, *s.* a hospital, a. 8. 28; Meson-dieux, *pl.* 10. 30. See note; and Cath. Angl. p. 229, n. 8.

Messager, messenger, 14. 33, 43; 22. 207; Messagers, *pl.* 3. 237; Messageres, *pl.* b. 2. 27. See **Masager**.

Messe, mess, dish of food, b. 15. 311. See **Mees**.

Messe, mass, 10. 228; Messes, *pl.* b. 3. 251. See **Masse**.

Mester, art, trade, occupation, 4. 110. O. F. *mestier*, F. *métier*, Lat. *ministerium*. See **Mystermen**.

Mesurable, *adj.* reasonable, fair, b. 1. 19, b. 3. 254.

Mesure, measure, moderation, 2. 33, 174, 16. 274; reason, b. 14. 70; Mesures, *pl.* measures, b. 14. 292.

Mesure, *pr. subj.* 1 *pl.* let us moderate, let us regulate, b. 14. 81.

Metals. See **Metels**.

Mete, meat, food, 4. 280, 20. 231, 22. 283; meat, meals, dinner, supper, 13.

GLOSSARIAL INDEX. 399

46, b. 10. 52; Metes, *pl.* kinds of food, b. 13. 38.
Mete, *v.* meet, b. 8. 114; 1 *pr. s.* b. 11. 27; Meteþ, 2 *pr. pl.* meet with, 8. 297; Mette, 1 *pt. s.* met, met with, 11. 3, 19. 183, 23. 4; Metten, *pt. pl.* met, 14. 33, 20. 51; Mette, 19. 169, 23. 93; Mette, *pp.* met, found, b. 11. 236.
Meteles, *adj.* without food, 10. 295; Metelees, b. 7. 141.
Metels, *s.* dream, vision, a. 8. 132, 145, 152; Metals, 1. 216; Meteles, 10. 296, 317; Meeteles, a. 8. 131. Formed with A.S. suffix -*els* (= -*el-sa*,* a *singular* suffix) from M.E. *meten*, to dream. See **Meten.**
Meten, *v.* mete, measure, a. pr. 88; Mete, *v.* 1. 163; Meteþ, 2 *pr. pl.* measure with, 2. 174; Mete, 2 *pr. pl.* b. 1. 175; Meten, 2 *pr. pl.* a. 1. 151.
Meten, *v.* dream, b. pr. 11; Meeten, a. pr. 11; Mette, 1 *pt. s.* dreamt, 6. 110, 12. 167, 23. 52; Mette, *pt. s.* dreamt, 10. 308; *impers.* Me mette = I dreamt, 1. 9, 6. 109, 11. 67; Metyng, *pres. pt.* dreaming, 3. 54. A.S. *mǽtan*, to dream.
Mete-ȝyueres, *pl.* meat-givers, charitable persons, b. 15. 143.
Metropolitanus, metropolitan bishop, 18. 267. See note.
Mette, met. See **Mete.**
Mette, *s.* companion at dinner, 16. 55; Mettes, *pl.* 16. 41. A.S. *gemettan*, pl. men who partake of a common meal; Ælfric's Homilies, ed. Thorpe, ii. 282.
Mette, *dat.* measure, b. 13. 359. A.S. *gemet*, a measure.
Metyng, *s.* a dream, dreaming, b. 13. 4; Metynge, b. 11. 311; Meetynge, a. 9. 59.
Meuen, *v.* speak, argue (lit. move), 2. 123; stir up, cause, arouse, excite, b. 12. 126; Meeuen, *v.* 15. 67; Meue, *v.* move, 20. 159; propose, start, suggest, 11. 118; Meoue, *v.* 22. 286; Meuve, *v.* R. pr. 32; Meve, move, suggest, R. 1. 84, R. 3. 367; Meuestow, 2 *pr. s. for* Meuest thou, raisest, excitest, b. 10. 263; Meuen, *pr. pl.* propose, raise, suggest, 17. 231; Meuede, *pt. s.* moved, shook gently, 19. 110; surprised, 14. 180; Meued, *pt. s.* incited, R. 2. 20; proposed, b. 11. 104; Meved, moved, R. 3. 207; Meeuede, *pt. s.* proposed, started, 13. 41; *pt. pl.* suggested, R. 3. 321; Meuynge, *pres. pt.* moving, wandering, 10. 110; Mevinge, *pres. pt.* moving, R. 3. 108; Meued, *pp.* moved, R. 3. 2; discussed, 16. 130; Meved, *pp.* incited, R. 1. 111. See **Moeue.**
Mevynge, *s.* instigation, R. 2. 55.
Meymed, *adj.* maimed, 10. 216.
Meyn, *adj.* mean (intermediate), 7. 281. See **Mene,** *adj.*
Meyne, train, retinue, household, 4. 25, 19. 254. O.F. *maisnee*, household; from Low. Lat. *mansionata*, a derivative of *mansio*.
Meynpernour, *s.* bail, security (lit. a taker by the hand), b. 4. 112, b. 18. 183. See **Menepernour.**
Meynprise, *s.* bail, surety (lit. a taking by the hand), b. 2. 196, b. 4. 88; Meynpryse, 5. 84.
Meynprise, *v.* bail, be surety for, 5. 173.
Meyntene, *v.* support, back up, abet, b. 3. 246; support, prove, b. 13. 125; Meynteynye, *v.* support, maintain, 4. 273; Meynteyneþ, *pr. s.* maintains, abets, b. 3. 149; Meynteneþ, a. 4. 42; Meyntenen, *pr. pl.* a. 2. 170; Meynteyne, *pr. pl.* maintain, R. 3. 311; Meynteneth, *pr. pl.* b. 3. 166; Meynteyned, *pp.* aided, abetted, R. 3. 354. See note to b. 3. 90, p. 44.
Meyntenour, supporter, maintainer, abettor, 4. 288; Meyntenourz, *pl.* R. 3. 268.
Meyre, mayor, magistrate, 4. 77, 115, 471; Meyres, *pl.* 10. 335. See **Meires.**
Meyster, master, b. 13. 167. See **Maister.**
Middel, *s.* middle, a. 2. 159; waist, a. 3. 10.
Middes, *only in phr.* In middes, in the midst, a. 2. 42. See **Myddes.**
Midmorwe, *s.* mid-morning, a. 2. 42.
Miht, *s.* might, a. 1. 105; mastery, a. 10. 63. See **Miȝtes, Myghte.**
Mihtful, *adj.* powerful, a. 1. 147. See **Miȝtful, Myghtful.**
Mihti, *for* Miht I, might I, i.e. might I go, a. 5. 6; *for* Mihte, *pt. s.* might, a. 10. 9.
Ministred, *pt. pl.* served, 19. 97.
Minours, *s. pl.* Minorite friars, a. pr. 101. See **Menour.**
Minstracie, minstrelsy, 17. 309.
Minstrales, *pl.* minstrels, 16. 204. See **Mynstral.**
Mirour, mirror, 12. 181.
Mirre, myrrh, 22. 92, 93; Myrre, b. 19. 88. See **Murre.**
Misbeode, *imp. s.* injure, a. 7. 45. See **Mysbede.** A.S. *misbéodan*.

Misbileeue, *v.* disbelieve, a. 11. 71.
Mischief, adversity, misfortune, ill luck, b. 14. 254; Mischef, a. 3. 262; At meschef = with ill results, a. 10. 75. See **Meschief, Myschief**.
Misdede, *s.* misdeed, a. 3. 44; Misdedes, *pl.* a. 1. 142. See **Mysdedes**.
Misdo, *v.* do amiss *or* evil, err, a. 3. 118; Misdoth, *pr. s.* cheats, acts dishonestly towards, b. 15. 252; Misdude him = injured him, a. 4. 86. See **Mysdo**.
Miseise, trouble, grief, 16. 159. See **Myseise, Meseise**.
Misseid, *pp.* slandered, a. 5. 51.
Mistier, *adj. comp.* more mystic, more mysterious, b. 10. 181; Mistiloker, a. 11. 137; Mystiloker, 12. 130. In this instance, the adj. *misty* is short for *mystic*, not derived from the sb. *mist*. The Prompt. Parv. gives '*mysty*, misticus,' as distinct from '*mysty*, nebulosus.'
Mitigacion, *s.* compassion, mercy, a. 5. 252. See **Mytigacion**.
Miʒtes, *pl.* powers, miracles, b. 10. 102. See **Miht**.
Miʒtful, *adj.* mighty, b. 1. 171. See **Mihtful, Myʒtful**.
Miʒty, *adj.* mighty, great, a. 1. 150.
Mnam, *s.* a 'mina,' talent (a Greek coin), b. 6. 243; Mnames, *pl.* b. 6. 244. See note, p. 115.
Mo, *adj.* more (in number), others, others besides, 1. 166, 3. 250, 4. 1, 10. 171; Moo, b. 10. 174; more, 13. 84. (It can almost always be explained by 'more in number,' or 'besides.' It refers to number, not to size.)
Mo, *adv.* more, b. 14. 328.
Mo, *s.* majority, R. 4. 86.
Moche, *adj.* much, b. 9. 49; great, exceeding, b. 10. 121; tall, big, b. 8. 70. See **Muche**.
Moche, *adv.* greatly, exceedingly, b. 17. 344; often, b. 10. 66.
Mochel, *adj.* great, exceeding, 7. 333, 8. 149; much, b. 19. 278. See **Muchel**.
Mochel, *s.* greatness, size, b. 16. 182.
Mod, anger, 19. 118; temper, mood, mind, 14. 180; Mode, anger, b. 10. 263; thought, b. 11. 360.
Moder, mother, 3. 51, 122; Moder, *gen.* mother's, b. 19. 120; Modres, *gen.* 22. 124.
Modiliche, *adv.* angrily, 5. 167; Modilich, b. 4. 173.

Mody, *adj.* obstinate, proud, b. 9. 204; Modi, the obstinate (person), a. 10. 212.
Moebles, *pl.* property, goods (lit. moveables), b. 3. 267, b. 9. 82. See **Mebles, Meoble**.
Moeue, *pr. s. subj.* move, stir, b. 8. 33; Moeuen, 2 *pr. pl.* bring forward, discuss, b. 15. 69; Moeue, *pr. pl.* raise, use, b. 10. 113; Moeued, *pt. s.* moved, surprised, b. 11. 360; Moeued, *pp.* moved, excited, b. 13. 291; urged, b. 12. 4. See **Meuen**.
Moillere, woman (usually a wife), 3. 120, 145; a (lawful) wife, 11. 209, 19. 222; the woman, b. 16. 221; Moillere-is, *gen.* wife's, 19. 236. See note to 19. 236.
Moillerye, womankind, b. 16. 219.
Moiste, *v.* moisten, slake, b. 18. 366. See **Moyste**.
Mok, filthy lucre (lit. muck), 11. 96.
Molde, earth (lit. mould), 1. 65, 2. 42, 3. 208; On molde = on the earth, in the world, 1. 65; Of this molde, of this earth, R. 3. 216. See note to 12. 230.
Molde, mould, model, pattern, 14. 161.
Moled, *adj.* spotted, stained, b. 13. 275. From A.S. *mál*, a mark. Hence *iron-mould*, orig. *iron-mole*, i. e. iron-stain.
Moles, *pl.* spots, stains, b. 13. 315. A.S. *mál*.
Molten, *pp.* melted, b. 13. 82.
Mom, mum, a slight sound made with closed lips, 1. 164; Momme, b. pr. 215. E. *mum*; cf. E. *mumble*, M.E. *mummyn*, to be mute, Prompt. Parv. See note, p. 17.
Momely, *v.* chatter, babble, prate, 6. 124; Momele, *v. a.* 5. 21. E. *mumble*. See **Mommeþ, Mamely**.
Mommeþ, *pr. s.* mouths, utters, a. 7. 225. See **Mom**.
Mon, *s.* man, a. 1. 80; Monnes, *gen.* man's, a. 10. 54.
Mone, moon, 10. 108, 110, 308; lunation, month, 4. 483.
Mone, *s.* moan, complaint; *only in the phr.* make mone = make complaint, pray, 9. 130, 17. 186.
Mone, money, *adj.* moneyless, b. 7. 141. See **Moneye**.
Monekes, *pl.* monks, 23. 264.
Monelees, *adj.* moneyless, b. 7. 141. See **Moneyeles**.
Monethes, *pl.* months, b. 10. 149. See **Monþe, Mooneþ**.
Moneye, money, 2. 42, 4. 265; Moneie,

GLOSSARIAL INDEX. 401

b. 8. 89; **Money,** a. 8. 46; Monye, 1. 61·; Mony, R. 4. 37; Monoye, b. 13. 394; Mone, b. 14. 228.
Moneyeles, *adj.* moneyless, penniless, a. 8. 130; Moneyles, 10. 110, 295; Monelees, b. 7. 141.
Monhede, manhood, a. 3. 178.
Moniales, *pl.* nuns, 6. 76, 171; Monyales, 23. 264; Monyals, b. 20. 262; Monyeles, 19. 74. See note, p. 69. '*Moniale, f.* a nun'; Cotgrave.
Monoye. See **Moneye.**
Monside, *pt. pl.* cursed, R. 3. 105. See **Mansed.**
Monþe, *s.* month, R. 4. 78. See **Moneþ.**
Monye, *adj.* many, a. 5. 104; Mony, b. 15. 71; Moni, a. 2. 80.
Moo. See **Mo.**
Mooneþ, month, a. 3. 140. See **Moneþ.** A. S. *mónað.*
Mooten, *v.* argue, plead, a. 4. 118. See **Mote.**
Moot-halle, *s.* meeting-hall, court, b. 4. 135. A. S. *mót,* a meeting.
Moppis, *s. pl.* fools, apes, R. 3. 276. Cf. Du. *moppen,* to pout, and E. *mope.* In the Seven Sages, ed. Weber, l. 1414, we find 'a *moppe* wild,' i. e. a wild foolish person; and, 2 lines lower, it is said of the same person, that he was '*moppe* and nice,' i. e. apish and foolish.
Mor, *adv.* more, 20. 75.
Morales, The '*xxxiv Libri Moralium*' of Pope Gregory, b. 10. 293. See note, p. 67.
Morder, *s.* R. 1. 77. See **Morthir.**
More, *adj. comp.* greater, 8. 62, b. 16. 133, R. 237.
More, root, 17. 250, 19. 23; b. 15. 96, b. 16. 5, 14, 58; Mores, *pl.* roots, 18. 21. Cf. A. S. *wealmora,* a parsnep, lit. 'foreign root'; Skt. *múla,* a root. See note to 18. 21.
Mores, *pl.* moors, heaths, 14. 168, b. 11. 344.
Moreyne, murrain, 4. 97, 21. 226.
Morne, *imper. s.* grieve, mourn, 4. 17; Mornede, *pt. s.* lamented, 4. 216; Mornyd, *pt. pl.* R. 3. 103. See **Mourneþ.**
Mornynge, mourning, grief, 13. 203, 18. 147.
Mornynges, *pl.* the mornings, b. 11. 330.
Morsel, *s.* morsel, bit, b. 13. 107. See note.
Morteils, *adj. pl.* mortal, deadly, 18. 290.

Morter, mortar, 16. 50, 22. 326, b. 13. 44.
Morþere, *ger.* to murder, slay, a. 4. 42; Morthre, *ger.* 5. 58; Morther, b. 4. 55; Morþereþ, *pr. s.* 20. 260, b. 17. 278; Morþerde, 1 *pt. s. subj.* would have murdered, a. 5. 85; Morþer, *imp. s.* slay, a. 3. 255. Cf. Goth. *maurthrjan,* to murder.
Morthereres, *pl.* murderers, b. 6. 275.
Morthir, *s.* murder, R. 3. 103. See **Morder.**
Mortrewes, *pl.* messes of pounded meat, &c., 16. 47, b. 13. 41, 62; Mortrews, 16. 66; Mortreuus, 16. 100. See the note, p. 191.
Morwe, the morning, morrow, 4. 310, 9. 180; Morwen, a. 11. 109.
Morwenyng, morning, 1. 6; Morwenynge, 12. 103; Morwnynge, a. pr. 6.
Mos, moss, 18. 14.
Moseþ, *pr. s.* becomes mossy, a. 10. 101.
Most, *adj. sup.* greatest, 20. 236; chief, 1. 65, b. 9. 55; Moste commune, greatest part of the commons, majority of the commons, b. 4. 166.
Moste, Most. See **Mot.**
Mot, 1 *pr. s.* may, 7. 127; Mote, 2 *pr. s.* mayest, 3. 117, 22. 178; Mot, *pr. s.* must, 6. 28; Mote, *pr. s.* may, 21. 209, 210; must, 17. 71, 23. 238; may, b. 13. 147; must be used, b. 15. 524; More mote here-to = more must (be used) for this, b. 9. 36; Mote = may it, a. 5. 42; Moten, *pr. pl.* may, 22. 179, a. 6. 79; Mote, might, 8. 157; may, a. 5. 263; Mot, must, a. 3. 219; Moste, 1 *pt. s.* might, 17. 163; Most, 1 *pt. s.* might, a. 12. 39; Moste, *pt. s.* must, b. 9. 42; must be used, 18. 225; might, a. 4. 99; might, b. 15. 391; ought, b. 13. 315; Be moste = must be, b. 14. 191; Most, must, 21. 415; 1 *pt. s.* must, ought to go, 8. 292. A. S. *mót,* pt. t. *móste.*
Mot, *s.* moat, 8. 233, 22. 368. O. F. *mote.*
Mote, *s.* mote, b. 10. 263.
Mote, *v.* to plead, dispute, discuss a law-case, b. 1. 174, a. 1. 150; Mote, *pr. s. subj.* may plead, may argue, 4. 198 (see note). From A. S. *mót,* a meeting, assembly. See **Mooten.**
Mot-halle, court-house, 5. 163; Motehalle, 5. 148. From A. S. *mót,* meeting, assembly.
Motif, motion, question, 16. 130; Motifs, *pl.* subjects, 17. 231; Mo-

GLOSSARIAL INDEX.

tyues, motions, propositions, b. 10. 113; arguments, a. 11. 70.
Moton, a gold coin, 4. 25. Lit. 'mutton,' or sheep. See note.
Motynge, pleading, discussion, 10. 54; Motyng, 5. 132.
Moue, 1 *pr. s.* mention, bring forward (lit. move), b. 11. 224. See **Meuen, Moeue**.
Moun, *pr. pl.* may, R. 3. 166. See **Mowe**.
Mounteþ, *pr. s.* mounts; Mounteþ up = increases, 1. 65.
Mounthe, month, 4. 182. See **Moneþ**.
Mous, mouse, 1. 196; Mys, *pl.* 1. 166, 212.
Moustre, show, appearance (lit. muster), 7. 260.
Mouthen, *v.* speak, utter, talk about, 5. 110; Mouthed, *pt. s.* spoke, uttered, 21. 154.
Mouwe, may. See **Mowe**.
Mowe, *pr. s.* may, 21. 366; Mai, a. 4. 119; Mowen, *pr. pl.* may, can, 4. 253; may endure, 13. 191; Mouwen, *pr. pl. a.* 7. 42; Mouwe, a. 8. 81; Mowe, 1 *pr. pl.* may, 8. 142; are able, 9. 344; Mowe, *pr. pl.* may, can, 11. 209; Mow, b. 8. 24.
Mowen, *v.* mow, 9. 186; Mowe, 6. 14. See note to 6. 14.
Mowen, *v.* put hay into mows or heaps, 6. 14. See note.
Mowtynge, *s.* moulting-season, R. 2. 12. See note, p. 292.
Moylere, woman, lady, b. 2. 118, 131. See **Moillere**.
Moyste, *v.* quench thirst, 21. 413. See **Moiste**.
Muche, *adj.* great, 1. 140; exceeding, a. 4. 136; tall, big, 11. 68. See **Moche**. See note to 11. 68.
Muchel, *adj.* much, great, exceeding, 4. 453; much, 1. 206. See **Mochel**.
Muirth, joy, enjoyment, b. 13. 60. See **Murthe**.
Mulle-stones, *pl.* mill-stones, 21. 295.
Mulnere, *s.* miller, a. 2. 80. A.S. *myln*, a mill; from Lat. *molina*. See **Mylnere**.
Multi, *adj.* many, b. 11. 107.
Munge, *v.* remember, keep in mind, a. 7. 88. See **Mengen**.
Munstrals, *pl.* minstrels, a. pr. 33, a. 2. 203. See **Mynstral**.
Munstralsye, minstrelsy, a. 11. 35.
Muriest, *adj.* merriest, 17. 340.
Murre, myrrh, 22. 76. See **Mirre**.
Murthe, mirth, joy, 11. 66, 21. 132, 229; game, a. 3. 191; Murth, b. 12.

15; Murthes, *pl.* mirths, amusements. 1. 35. See **Myrthe, Muirth**.
Murthen, *v.* cheer, make merry, 20. 206; please, gratify, b. 11. 390. See **Myrthe**.
Mury, *adj.* merry, happy, 22. 293; Murye, glad, blithe, 7. 185, 9. 67; keen, 1. 216; Murie, merry, b. 14. 236. See **Myry**.
Murye, *adv.* pleasantly, 14. 217.
Muryer, *adj.* merrier, pleasanter, b. 1. 107.
Muscles, *pl.* mussels, shell-fish, 10. 94.
Muse, *v.* ponder, R. pr. 30; 1 *pr. s.* muse, reflect, 12. 130; Musen, *pr. pl.* a. 11. 71; Muse, b. 10. 114; Mvse, *pr. pl. subj.* muse, R. pr. 67; Musede, *pt. s.* thought, 14. 228; Mused, *pt. pl.* 15. 74; Musynge, *pres. part.* musing, 10. 296. See **Mwse**.
Musons, *pl.* measures, 12. 120. See note. O. F. *moison*, from Lat. *mensionem*.
Mussel, a morsel, b. 13. 107 *n.* See **Morsel**.
Must, *s.* must, new wine (also, a drink made with honey), b. 18. 368. See Prompt. Parv.
Mute, *adj. pl.* mutes, dumb (men), b. 16. 111.
Mutoun, *s.* a gold coin called a 'mutton' or sheep, a. 3. 25. See **Moton**.
Muynde, *s.* remembrance, a. 7. 87. See **Mynde**.
Mwse, *v.* muse, ponder, R. 1. 21. See **Muse**.
Mychelmesse, Michaelmass, b. 13. 240. See **Myhelmasse**.
Myd, *prep.* with, 5. 73, 17. 182. A.S. *mid*.
Mydday, *adj.* of noon, 10. 246.
Myddelerd, earth (lit. middle-yard), 12. 170; Myddel-erde, 14. 132. See **Mydelerd**.
Myddell, *s.* middle, 4. 483; Myddel, waist, 4. 10; Mydle, waist, a. 5. 202; Mydel, 7. 409.
Myddes, middle; *only in phr.* In þe myddes = in the midst, 3. 195; In þe myddis, R. 4. 78; In myddes, 22. 4; In middes, a. 2. 42.
Myddwardis, middle; To the m., to the very middle, R. pr. 67.
Mydelerd, middle-earth, the world, b. 11. 315; Mydlerd, b. 11. 8. See **Myddelerd**.
Mydlentens, *gen.* of Mid-lent, 19. 183.
Myghte, *pt. s.* could, 7. 403; Maiht, 2 *pt. s.* mightest, a. 3. 230; Maihtou,

GLOSSARIAL INDEX. 403

mightest thou, a. 6. 105. See **My3te, Mowe.**
Myghtful, *adj.* powerful, 2. 170. See **Mihtful, Mi3tful, My3tful.**
Myhel-masse, Michaelmas, 16. 216. See **Mychelmesse.**
Mykel, *adj.* great, b. 5. 477; much, b. pr. 201. See **Mekel.**
Mylde, *adj.* lowly, b. 10. 147.
Myldeliche, *adv.* meekly, 2. 167. See **Mildeliche.**
Myldenesse, patience, b. 15. 169.
Myldest, *adj.* meekest, 22. 255.
Myle, mile, b. 10. 162; Myle, *pl.* miles, 8. 17, 23. 164.
Myle-wey, distance of a mile, 10. 296.
Mylnere, miller, 3. 113, b. 10. 44. See **Mulnere.**
Myn, *pron. pcss.* my, 19. 257; Myn one = by myself, alone, 11. 61, 12. 200. See note, p. 134.
Mynde, *s.* mind, a. 11. 213; memory, b. 11. 49; mention, 16. 310; remembrance, b. 11. 152, 255.
Mynge, *v.* remember, make mention; Mynged, *pt. pl.* thought upon, R. 1. 103. A.S. *mynegian.* See **Mengen, Munge.**
Mynistren, *pr. pl.* spend, b. 12. 54.
Mynne, less, 4, 399. Icel. *minni,* less.
Mynne, 2 *pr. pl.* remember, 18. 210, 20. 229. A.S. *mynian,* to admonish.
Mynours, *pl.* diggers in mines, b. pr. 221.
Mynstral, minstrel, 16. 191, 194.
Mynstralcie, music, minstrelsy, 16. 196, 198; Mynstracie, a. 3. 98.
Mynstre, a minster, 6. 91.
Mynt-while, a moment, very short space of time, 14. 200, 20. 194; Mynte-while, 13. 217; Mynut-while, moment, b. 17. 228. See note, p. 173.
Mynystre, *v.* minister, handle, b. 17. 142.
Myrour, mirror, 12. 170, 14. 132; example, 19. 175; Myroure, b. 11. 8; Myrrours, *s. pl.* mirrors, R. 3. 276. See **Mirour.**
Myrthe, mirth, 4. 12; Myrthes, *pl.* pleasures, b. 11. 19. See **Murthe.**
Myrthe, *gen.* to cheer, b. 17. 240. See **Murthen.**
Myry, *adj.* merry, flattering, 3. 161; Myrye, 3. 167, 9. 155; Myri, pleasing, a. 2. 124. See **Mury.**
Mys, *pl.* mice, 1. 166, 212. See **Mous.**
Mys, *adv.* amiss, b. 11. 372.
Mys-bede, *imper. pl.* injure, harm, 9. 42. See **Misbeode.**
Mysbileue, *s.* misbelief, false belief,

false faith, b. 10. 114; Mysbyleue, 4. 330; Mysbyleyue, false belief, 18. 181.
Myschaunce, *s.* mischance, mishap, misfortune, evil, b. 8. 60. See **Mischaunce, Meschaunce.**
Myscheued, *pt. pl.* met with misfortune, b. 12. 119. Cf. 'mischefyd, *erumpnatus*;' Cath. Angl.
Myschief, misfortune, suffering, ruin, 1. 211, 4. 223; Myschef, 4. 142; Myschif, 1. 65; At myschiefe = in case of misfortune, b. 11. 291. See **Mischief, Meschief.**
Mysdedes, *pl.* offences, misdeeds, 2. 159. See **Misdede.**
Mys-do, *v.* do wrong, do amiss, offend, transgress, 4. 159; maltreat, b. 18. 97; Mysdon, *pr. pl.* do wrong, b. 15. 107; Mysdid, *pt. s.* injured, b. 4. 99; Mys-dude, *pt. s.* did amiss, 21. 392; Mysdo, *pp.* done amiss, b. 4. 90. See **Misdo.**
Myseise, trouble, pain, discomfort, b. 1. 24, b. 9. 75. See **Miseise.**
Myselue, myself, 21. 376.
Myserule, *s.* misrule, R. 4. 3.
Myseyse, *adj.* troubled, unfortunate, wretched, 10. 30.
Mysfait, misdeed, b. 11. 366.
Mysfare, *v.* to miscarry, meet with misfortune, 11. 161.
Mys-hap, mishap, misfortune, 6. 34. See **Mishappes.**
Myshappen, *v.* meet with misfortune, 4. 485; Myshapped, *pt. s.* met with a mishap, b. 10. 283.
Mysled, *pp.* misled, R. 3. 123.
Mysliked, *pt. s.* was displeased, 17. 311.
Myster, occupation, employment, 10. 7. See **Mester.**
Myspende (*for* Mysspende), *v.* misspend, waste, 11. 185; Mys-speyneþ, *pr. s.* misspends, misuses, abuses, 11. 174; Myspenden, *pr. pl.* misuse, waste, 17. 234; Mysspended, *pp.* wasted, 6. 93.
Mys-proud, *adj.* vain, 8. 96.
Mys-reuleth, *pr. s.* mis-governs, b. 9. 59.
Myssayde, *pt. s.* abused, rebuked, 21. 353; Myssaide, *pp.* slandered, 7. 9. See **Mysseide.**
Mysscheff, *s.* mischief, ill doing, R. 1. 111; Myssecheff, disaster, R. pr. 22.
Mysse. *s.* fault, R. 1. 29.
Mysseide, *pt. s.* argued against, b. 16. 127. See **Myssayde!**
Myssep, *pr. s.* is without, is deprived

of, 15. 44; **Mysside**, *pt. pl.* missed, R. 3. 3; Myssed, 2 *pt. pl.* R. 2. 42.
Mysshape, *pp. as adj.* mis-shapen, deformed, b. 7. 95. See **Misshapen**.
Mysspendeþ. See **Myspende**.
Myssynge, *s.* lack, want, 11. 201; Myssyng, a. 12. 73.
Myst, *s.* mist, fog, 20. 194; Mystis, *pl.* fogs, R. 2. 132.
Mystiloker, *adj. comp.* mistier, more confused, 12. 130. See **Mistier**.
Mystirmen, *s. pl.* men of a trade or 'mistery,' R. 3. 335. See **Mister, Mester**.
Mys-tornynge, *s.* going astray, wandering from the path, turning aside, 8. 308.
Myswonne, *pt. pl.* gained dishonestly, got by cheating, 16. 48.
Myte, mite, 10. 276, 14. 97, 23. 179; A myte = in the least, a. 8. 54; Mytes, *pl.* half-farthings, b. 13. 196.
Mytigacion, mercy, 7. 324. See **Mitigacion**.
Mytrede, *adj. pl.* mitred, 5. 193.
Myȝte, 1 *pt. s.* might, could, b. 9. 71; Myȝt, 2 *pt. s. as pr.* mayest, canst, 12. 181; Myȝte, mayest, b. 12. 10; mightest, b. 11. 19; Myȝtow, mayest thou, b. 11. 9; Myȝte, *pt. s.* might, could, b. 9. 9; Myȝthe, a. 12. 9; Myȝth, 1 *pt. s. subj.* might, a. 12. 88. See **Mowe**.
Myȝtful, *adj.* able, b. 17. 310; almighty, b. 11. 270; powerful, b. 1. 174; Myȝtfull, mighty, R. 2. 95. See **Miȝtful**.

Na, *adv.* no, 14. 40, 16. 95. Only in the phr. *na mo* or *na more*. See **Namore**.
Nai, *adv.* nay, a. 6. 47. See **Nay**.
Naked, *adj.* naked, 21. 51; Naked as a neelde (needle), 20. 56.
Nale, the ale-house; Atte nale = Atten ale (*at þen ale*), at the ale-house, 8. 19. See note to 1. 43.
Nam (*for* Ne am), am not, b. 5. 420.
Nam, b. 6. 241. See **Mnam**.
Nameliche, *adv.* especially, 3. 159, 7. 96, 9. 276; Namelich, b. 7. 41, 184. Cf. G. *namentlich*.
Namore, *adv.* no more, b. 3. 108, b. 12. 102, 279. See **Na**.
Nappe, *v.* sleep, fall asleep, 8. 2.
Narwe, *adv.* closely, narrowly, b. 13. 371.
Nas (*for* Ne was), was not, a. 2. 40, a. 3. 182, R. 3. 340.
Nat, *adv.* not, 1. 162, 3. 18, 19. 251.

Naþ (*for* Ne haþ), hath not, a. 6. 42.
Naue (*for* Ne haue), have not, a. 1. 157.
Nauele, *s.* navel, 17. 84; Naule, b. 14. 242.
Nauht, *adj.* valueless, 18. 74.
Nauȝt, *adv.* not, b. pr. 80; Nauȝte, b. 8. 79; Nauȝt but, only, b. 10. 338.
Nauȝty, *adj.* having nothing, very poor, b. 6. 226. See note.
Nay, *adv.* negatively, in the negative, a. 8. 135. See **Nai**.
Ne, *adv. and conj.* nor, not; not, 1. 217; not (*doubled*), b. 18. 414; nor, 4. 399, 11. 7; Ne were = were it not, 16. 211; were it not for, 1. 214. A.S. *ne*.
Nedde (*for* Ne hadde), had not, a. 5. 4, a. 7. 166.
Nede, need, necessity, b. 20. 4; Nedes, *pl.* b. 20. 54. See **Neode**.
Nede, *adv.* needs, necessarily, 14. 37, b. 3. 225. See **Nedes**.
Nedeler, *s.* needle-seller, b. 5. 318. See **Neldere**.
Nedes, *adv.* necessarily, b. 3. 257. See **Nede, Needes, Neodes**.
Nedeþ, *pr. s. impers.* there is need, 12. 48, b. 10. 63; Nediþ, is needful to, a. 11. 187; Neded, *impers. pt. s.* was necessary, b. 15. 155; Neodyde, *pt. s. impers.* was necessary, 18. 18; Neodede, *pt. pl.* needed, 20. 231; Nedid, *pt. s.* needed, R. 3. 273. See **Needede, Neodeþ**.
Nedfol, *adj.* needy, indigent, 5. 121. See **Neodful**. 'Nedeful, *necessarius*;' Cath. Angl.
Nedle, needle, b. 1. 155; Naked as a nedle, b. 12. 162. See **Nedele, Neelde, Nelde**.
Nedy, *adj.* poor, needy, 10. 47, b. 11. 236. See **Neody**.
Needede, *pt. s.* was needful, 17. 292. See **Nedeþ**.
Needes, *adv.* necessarily, 13. 215. See **Nedes**.
Neelde, needle, 20. 56. See **Nedle, Nelde**.
Neet (animal), neat, ox, 22. 266. See **Nete**.
Negh, *adv.* nearly, almost, nigh, 4. 186. See **Neih**.
Neghebores, *pl.* neighbours, 7. 98, 8. 24. See **Neihebores**.
Neghed, *pt. s.* approached, b. 20. 231. See **Neighen**.
Neighe, *adj.* nigh, near, b. 11. 207; nearly connected, b. 12. 95.
Neighen, *v.* approach, b. 17. 58; Neighed, *pt. s.* drew near, approached,

b. 6. 301; Neihed, *pt. s.* approached,
9. 323; Neghed, b. 20. 231. See
Nyeth, Nyghed, Neyhede.
Neih, *adv.* nigh, 9. 175; almost, a. 7.
165; Neiȝe, nearly, b. 3. 144. See
Negh.
Neih, *prep.* near, nigh to, 9. 298.
Neihebores, *pl.* neighbours, 9. 290, 10.
87; Neihebors, a. 6. 54; Neighebores, 10. 71. See **Neghebores, Neyhebore.**
Nel, 1 *pr. s.* (I) will not, 9. 302; Nelle,
1 *pr. s.* 12. 184; Nel (= Ne wil), will
not, 11. 267; Nelle (= Ne wille), will
not, 1. 136, 2. 123; Neltow, 2 *pr. s.*
thou wilt not, b. 6. 158. See **Nile,
Nul.** A.S. *nyllan;* cf. Lat. *nolle.*
Nelde, needle, 2. 154, 15. 105; Neelde,
20. 56. See **Nedle.** Shropshire *nild.*
Neldere, needle-seller, 7. 365, a. 5. 161.
See **Nedeler.**
Nemeþ, 2 *pr. pl.* take, receive, 3. 139.
See **Nymen.**
Nempnen, *v.* name, 2. 21; Nempne, *v.*
name, b. 1. 21, b. 16. 19; utter, 2.
20; Nempne, 1 *p. s. pr.* name, R. 1.
51; *pr. pl.* name, call, a. 8. 139;
Nempnede, *pt. s.* named, called, 17.
200; gave (names), 23. 256; Nempned, 7. 377, 388; Nempned, *pt. pl.*
named, mentioned, 22. 18; Nempned,
pp. named, mentioned, 23. 261; called,
named, b. 2. 178, b. 7. 153; appointed,
R. 3. 231. A.S. *nemnan.*
Nempnyng, *s.* naming, calling, b. 9.
78.
Neode, *s.* need, 22. 391, 23. 4, 20; time
of need, 21. 444; Neodes, *pl.* necessities, wants, 23. 55. See **Nede.**
Neodes, *adv.* needs, necessarily, 20. 85,
21. 444. See **Nedes.**
Neodeþ, *impers. pr. s.* needs it, there is
need, 20. 32. See **Nedeþ.**
Neodful, *adj.* necessary, 22. 20; needy,
20. 237. See **Nedfol.**
Neody, *adj.* needy, 23. 37; Neodi, a. 7.
14, 212.
Neore (*for* Ne weore), *pt. s. subj.* were
not, a. 5. 249; were there not, a. 11.
51; should not be, a. 5. 181. See
Nere.
Ner, *adv.* nearly, almost, 10. 264.
Ner, *adv. comp.* nearer, 23. 232; Nere,
b. 20. 231.
Nere (*for* Ne were), *pt. s. subj.* were
not, did not exist, b. 3. 134, b. 10.
184. See **Nam, Neore.**
Ner-hande, *adv.* nearly, 16. 1.
Nerre, *adj. comp.* nearer, b. 16. 69;
Ner, a. 11. 250. Cf. note to 3. 30.

Nest, *adj. superl.* next, nearest, R. 1.
51.
Neste (*for* Ne wiste), 1 *pt. s.* did not
know, was ignorant, b. 13. 25.
Nestes, *pl.* nests, 14. 156.
Nete, ox, b. 19. 261. See **Neet.**
Newe, *adj.* new; Of þe newe, anew, R.
3. 161; Nywe, new, 22. 273.
Newe, *adv.* anew, 19. 162.
Newed, *pt. pl.* recruited his purse, R.
4. 6; Newed, *pp.* renewed, R. 1. 17.
See note to R. 4. 6.
Neweth, *pr. pl.* annoy, R. pr. 66. See
Noyen.
Nexte, *adj. superl.* nearest, b. 13. 373;
next to, 20. 268.
Ney, *adv.* nigh, nearly, 4. 182, 16. 294.
See **Neyȝe, Ny.**
Neyhebore, neighbour, 16. 113; Neyhȝebore, 7. 262; Neyhȝeboris, *pl.* 7.
269. See **Neihebores, Neghebores.**
Neyhede, *pt. s.* approached, was near,
23. 4, 232; Neyghynge, *pres. pt.* approaching, 23. 200.
Neyhle, *v.* approach, 20. 58. Cf. A.S.
néahlǽcan, to approach.
Neyȝe, *prep.* nigh, b. 5. 94. See **Ney.**
Nice, *adj.* foolish, b. 16. 33. See
Nyce.
Nigard, miser, 20. 237.
Nigromancye, *s.* necromancy, a. 11.
158. See note.
Niht-olde, *adj.* a night old, a little
stale, a. 7. 296. See **Nyght-old,
Nyȝt-olde.**
Nile, 1 *pr. s.* will not, a. 11. 221; Nil,
pr. s.; Nil nauȝt, will not (with
double negative), b. 18. 282. See
Nel, Nul.
Nippe, *s.* cold region, place of extreme
cold, b. 18. 162. See **Nype** (where
another possible meaning is given).
Nis (*for* Ne is), is not, a. pr. 77, a. 1.
34. See **Nys.**
Niȝt-comeres, *pl.* men who might come
at night, b. 19. 140. See **Nyghtcommeres.**
Niȝtes, *adv.* at night, b. 11. 30.
No þyng, not at all, by no means, 9.
214.
Noble, noble, gold coin, 4. 47, 7. 245;
Nobles, *pl.* 4. 395. Its value was 6s.
8d. See note, p. 41.
Noet, *pr. s.* knows not; Noet no man
= no man knows (with double negative), b. 11. 207. See **Not.**
Noither, *pron.* neither; Of her noither
= of neither of them, b. 4. 32.
Noither, *conj.* neither, b. 13. 92; nor,
b. 4. 130. See **Noyther.**

GLOSSARIAL INDEX.

Noke; Atte noke = atten oke, at the oak, a. 5. 115. See note, p. 82.
Nolde, 1 *pt. s.* would not, 8. 201; *pt. s.* b. 6. 238, a. 7. 290; desired (it) not, R. 1. 14; *pt. pl.* would not, 10. 23; Nolde, *pt. pl.* would not (go), b. 15 456.
Nolle, *s.* head, pate, R. 1. 20; Nollis, *pl.* R. 3. 127. A.S. *hnol, hnoll,* vertex.
Nombrede, *pt. s.* numbered, 23. 256. F. *nombrer.*
Nome, *s.* name, a. 1. 71; Nomes, *pl.* names, a. 1. 21.
Nome, 2 *pt. s.* didst take, 23. 9; Nomen, *pt. pl.* took, a. 4. 63. See **Nymen**.
Nomeliche, *adv.* especially, a. 6. 61. See **Nameliche**.
Nompeyr, umpire, 7. 388. See **Noumpere**; and see *Umpire* in my Etym. Dict.
Non, *adj.* none, not any, 4. 437, 8. 73; None, no, 8. 211; none, b. 8. 111; Her none = not one (neither) of them, b. 14. 239.
None, noon, 7. 434; Non, 10. 87; a meal so called, orig. the noon-tide meal, 9. 290. See **Nones, Noon**.
Nones, nones, a meal-time so called, 7. 429, 9. 146. See note, p. 112.
Nones, *in phr.* for þe nones = for þen ones, i.e. for the once, for the occasion, a. 2. 43. Here þen stands for þám, dat. of the def. article. Palsgrave (p. 865) translates *for the nones* by F. *a propos.*
None-tyme, noontide, b. 15. 278.
Nonne, *s.* nun, b. 5. 153; Nonnes, *pl.* b. 7. 29.
Noon, noon, 9. 276. See **None**.
Norischeþ, *pr. s.* nourishes, 19. 37; Norssheþ, encourages, 13. 234.
North-half, north side, 19. 66.
Nose, nose, 5. 149.
Not (*for* Ne wot), *pr. s.* knows not, a. 9. 106; 1 *pr. s.* know not, R. 2. 46. A.S. *nát*, short for *ne wát*. See **Noet, Nuste, Nyst**.
Not, *adj.* closely cropped, smooth-pated, R. 3. 46. Cf. *not-heed* in Chaucer, Prol. 109.
Notarie, notary, scribe, 17. 192; Notaries, *gen.* notary's, b. 20. 270; Notarie, *gen.* notary's, 23. 272; Notaries, *pl.* notaries, 3. 139, 159; a. 2. 82; Notories, 3. 185.
Note, song, 21. 453; note, b. 18. 407 Notes, *pl.* notes (of music), 11. 65; points, degrees, 2. 118.
Noteth, *pr. s.* denotes, R. 4. 54.
Noþer, *pron.* neither; Here noþer =

neither of them, 11. 273; Here noþers will = the will of neither of them, 4. 368.
Noþer, *conj. and adv.* neither, 11. 116, 22. 97; nor, 2. 155; Noþer—ne, neither—nor, 17. 169.
Notye, *v.* gain, receive, have for their use, 18. 101. A.S. *notian*, to use.
Nou a dayes, now-a-days, a. 11. 37.
Nouht, nothing, 1. 210; Nout, a. 6. 119.
Nouht, *adv.* not, 11. 81; Nought, b. pr. 29. See **Nouȝt, Nauȝt**.
Noumbre, number, 4. 349.
Noumpere, *s.* umpire, arbitrator, b. 5. 337. See **Nompeyr**.
Nounpower, want of power, 20. 292; Nounpowere, b. 17. 310. For *nonpower*; see note.
Nouthe, *adv.* now, 7. 171, 10. 163; Nouth, 3. 15. A.S. *nú þá*, just now.
Nouþur, *conj.* neither, a. 3. 52; Nouþur .. ne, neither .. nor, a. 7. 121.
Nouȝt, *adv.* not, b. pr. 79; Nouȝte, b. 6. 130. See **Nauȝt, Nouht**.
Now, *adv.* now that, b. 5. 143.
Nownages, *s. pl.* minorities (lit. non-ages), R. 4. 6.
Noye, suffering, b. 10. 60; Noyes, *s. pl.* R. pr. 66. Short for *annoyes* = annoyances. See **Nuy**.
Noyen, *v.* annoy, injure, harm, b. 5. 583; Noyed, *pt. pl.* R. 3. 75; Noyed, *pp.* troubled, injured, 3. 19. Short for *annoyen*, mod. E. *annoy*. See **Nuyen, Neweth**.
Noyther, *conj.* neither, b. 4. 130; *adv.* b. 5. 184; Noyther .. ne, *conjs.* neither .. nor, b. 15. 18; Ne .. noyther, nor .. either, b. 18. 116. See **Noither, Nouþur**.
Npnam, *s.* a mina, a. 7. 226.
Nudful, *adj.* needful, necessary, 2. 21. See **Nedfol**.
Nul, *pr. s.* will not, wishes not, 22. 466, 23. 29; Nulle, will not, a. 4. 154; Wol þou so nulle þou = whether thou wilt or not, a. 7. 144. See **Nel, Nile**.
Numbres, *pl.* arithmetic, 22. 240. See **Noumbre**.
Nuste, 1 *pt. s.* knew not, 14. 220. For Ne wuste, wist not. See **Not, Nyst**.
Nuy, *s.* hurt, grief, a. 11. 47. See **Noye**.
Nuyen, *v.* annoy, 8. 221; Nuyȝen, hurt, a. 6. 64; Nuyede, *pt. s. subj.* should injure, 4. 437; Nuyȝed, should vex, a. 3. 265. See **Noyen**.
Ny, *adv.* nearly, R. 3. 30.
Ny, *prep.* near to, 21. 292, 23. 4.

GLOSSARIAL INDEX.   407

Nyce, *adj.* foolish, 19. 37. See **Nice.**
Nycete, *s.* foolishness, folly, 17. 370; Nysete, R. 3. 144.
Nyeth, *pr. s.* draws near, approaches, R. 3. 39. See **Neighen.**
Nyethe, *num. adj.* ninth, 17. 150. A.S. *nigoda.* See **Nyneth.**
Nygarde, miser, b. 15. 136.
Nyghed, *pt. s.* drew nigh, R. 2. 12. See **Neighen.**
Nyght-commeres, *pl.* comers by night, 22. 144. See **Niʒt-comeres.**
Nyghtes, *adv.* by night, 12. 192; A nyghtes = by night, 20. 173. See **Nyʒtes.**
Nyght-old, *adj.* one day old (lit. one night old), 9. 332. See **Niht-olde.**
Nyhed, *pt. s.* approached, R. 3. 231. See **Neighen.**
Nymen, *v.* take, receive, 4. 406, 7. 269, b. 10. 60; Nyme, *v.* take, 14. 105; have, b. 15. 68; Nymeþ, *pr. s.* takes, 14. 241, 18. 108; lifts, b. 11. 422; Nemeþ, 2 *pr. pl.* take, receive, 3. 139; Nyme, 1 *pr. pl.* take, 10. 71; Nyme, *pr. s. subj.* may take, will take, 17. 292; if he receive, if he take, 4. 395; Nome, 2 *pt. s.* didst take, 23. 9; Nomen, *pt. pl.* took, a. 4. 63; Nym, *imp. s.* take, accept, 9. 40; Nymmeth, *imp. pl.* b. 6. 15. A.S. *niman,* to take; cf. G. *nehmen.*
Nyne, *num.* nine, 20. 58.
Nyneth, *num. adj.* ninth, b. 14. 312. See **Nyethe.**
Nype, a place of piercing cold, 21. 168; Nippe, b. 18. 162. Lit. *nip;* cf. ' It is a *nipping* and an eager air;' Hamlet, i. 4. 2. See Nippe; and see below. (Such I suspect to be the simple meaning. If anything else is intended, perhaps the sense is ' peak ' or ' hill-top.') Such a word occurs in the Norweg. *knippa,* a knoll, hill-top (Aasen); Swed. dial, *knippa,* a knoll, acclivity, hill; *knip,* a crag (Rietz); Icel. *gnípa,* a peak.
Nyppyng, *pres. part.* biting, 7. 104.
Nys (*for* Ne ys), is not, 20. 292; Nys bote = is only, 1. 204. See **Nis.**
Nysete, *s.* daintiness, folly, R. 3. 144. See **Nycete.**
Nyst, *pt. pl.* knew. not, R. 4. 63. *For* ne wiste; see **Nuste.**
Nyuylynge, *pres. part.* snivelling, 7. 104. Cf. M.E. *neesen* = sneeze.
Nyʒtes, *adv.* by night, a. 12. 81. See **Nyghtes.**
Nyʒt-olde, *adj. pl.* not freshly gathered, 6. b. 310. See **Niht-olde.**

O, *adj.* one, 4. 316, 18. 104, 19. 189; a single, b. 9. 111; the same, 14. 34; one and the same, b. 16. 58; That o = the one, the first, b. 19. 82. See **On, Oo.**
Obediencer, a certain officer in a monastery, 6. 91. ' *Obédienciaire,* religieux qui desservoit un bénéfice par ordre de son supérieur; officier de chapitre qui faisoit les distributions manuelles aux chanoines présens au chœur;' Roquefort. ' *Obedianciers,* foure church-officers, viz. a Deane, Archdeacon, Almner, and Sexton;' Cotgrave. ' *Obedientiarius,* qui vel aliquod in monasterio officium exercet, vel qui in cellam et prioratum mittitur, eamque procurat;' Ducange.
Obrode, *adv.* abroad, b. 5. 140. For *on brode,* lit. on (the) broad.
Occupien hym, *ger.* to employ himself, dwell, b. 16. 196; Ocupied, *pp.* occupied, engaged, 8. 18. See **Okupien.**
Oest, host, company, b. 19. 332. See **Ost.**
·**Of,** *prep.* according to, 23. 275; with regard to, 13. 100; about, a. 11. 32; at, 16. 200; by, 17. 16, 18. 78, 19. 171; by means of, 11. 87; for, 3. 1, 12. 87; for, addressed to, a. 12. 86; in return for, b. 6. 129; from, 4. 344; at the hands of, b. 13. 234; from, out of, 1, 213; in, a. 3. 119; some of, 7. 298, b. 20. 169; Of þe same = in the same way, R. pr. 14; Of more = besides, b. 6. 38.
Of, *adv.* off, a. 4. 140.
Offices, *pl.* church services, b. 15. 379.
Official, person in office, officer, 23, 137; ' *Official,* an Officiall, a Commissary, or Chancelor, to a Bishop,' &c.; Cotgrave.
Offys, *s.* office, a. 7. 187; Offices, *pl.* church services, b. 15. 379.
Of-rauʒte, *pt. pl.* reached, extended to, b. 18. 6. Cf. *ofreche* = overtake, Will. of Palerne, 3874; = attain, reach, King Horn, 1283.
Of-sente, *pt. s.* sent for, sent after, a. 3. 96; Of-sent, *pp.* sent for, a. 2. 37.
Oghtest, 2 *pt. s.* oughtest, 2. 72. See **Owe.**
Oilles, *pl.* oils, hence, flattery; Beringe vppon oilles = the use of flattery, lit. 'the bearing of oil upon (a great man);' R. 3. 186. Perhaps *vppon* is an error for *vp* (up) or *vp of* (up of). This very curious phrase is illustrated in N. and Q. 6. S. i. 75,

118, 203. We find 'hilde vp þe kynges oyl,' lit. held up the king's oil, flattered or abetted him; Trevisa, iii. 447; 'holden up his oile' = approve of what he (a king) says, Gower, ed. Pauli, iii. 159; 'to bere up oile' = to say he (Ahab) was in the right, id. iii. 172; in all the passages it has reference to a king whose opinions are upheld by flatterers. Again, Ps. cxli. 5 has, in the Vulgate, 'Oleum autem peccatoris non impinguet caput meum;' which Wyclif translates 'the oyle of a synner [shal] make not fat myn heed;' and Bellarmine's commentary has — 'Significat blandiloquentiam adulatoris.' In Cath. Angl. p. 120, *fagynge* is explained by 'blanditia, .. adulacio, .. *oleum*, ut in psalmo, *oleum autem peccatoris,*' &c. Mr. Marshall (in N. and Q.) says that 'oleum ore ferre' is noticed as a proverb in *Adagia*, p. 28, fol., Typ. Wechel, 1629. Cf. mod. E. 'to butter a person.'

Oken, *pt. pl.* ached, 20. 159. See note. A.S. *acan*, to vex, ache.

Okes, *pl.* oak-trees, 6. 120.

Okupien, *v.* employ (himself), dwell, 19. 207. See Occupien.

On, *prep.* in, b. 7. 107; On the day, a-day, 11. 31; On peynede = suffered upon, 22. 324; at, during, b. 14. 2; against, b. 14. 144; On auenture = in case, b. 3. 66.

On, *adj.* one, 1. 167, 4. 401; alone, 21. 318; a certain, 3. 25, 42; *as sb.* one, a certain one, a. 12. 62; one, man, person, 5. 83; þat on, the one, a. 8. 14. See O, One.

Oncomely, *adj.* unseemly, b. 9. 160.

On-crosse-wyse, by crucifixion, b. 19. 138.

Ondyng, *s.* smelling, 16. 257. See note, p. 206. Icel. *anda*, to breathe.

One, *adj.* alone, 2. 169, 4. 143; in particular, a. 1. 146; Myn one, by myself, a. 9. 54; By his one, by himself, b. 16. 183. And see One.

Ones, *adv.* once, 1. 162, 7. 235; Onis, b. pr. 213; Onys, b. 11. 65; At ones = at once, 19. 154.

Onliche, *adv.* only, 11. 331, 13. 30; Oneliche, 17. 155.

On-syde, *adv.* aside, b. 17. 57.

Oo, one, a single, a. 2. 96. See O, On.

Openen, *v.* open, undo, 8. 249; Opyn, *pr. s. subj.* R. pr. 70.

Or, *conj. and adv.* ere, before, b. pr. 155, b. 6. 87, b. 10. 418. See Ar.

Or, *prep.* before, 8. 66, a. 5. 20; in preference to, b. 15. 502.

Or, *conj.* either, a. 8. 77; Or while = other while, i.e. at times, sometimes, a. 9. 21.

Or, *pron.* your, a. 2. 97.

Ordeyne, *v.* ordain, appoint, R. 3. 204; Ordeyned, 1 *pt. s.* arranged, ordained, b. 10. 214; set, applied, b. 19. 242; Ordeynede, *pt. s.* ordained, 6. 55; established, 18. 16; Ordeigned, *pt. s.* ordained, b. 5. 167; Ordeygned, b. pr. 119; Ordeigned, *pt. pl.* ordained, arranged, b. 8. 98; arranged, R. 3. 213; Ordeyne, *imp. s.* make ready, 22. 320, 322.

Ordre, order, rank, 2. 97; a whole order, b. 13. 285; Ordres, orders (of friars), 1. 56, 9. 191; holy orders, b. 11. 281.

Orgone, *s.* organ; Bi orgone = to the sound of the organ, 21. 7. See note.

Orientales, *pl.* sapphires, b. 2. 14. 'The precious stones called by lapidaries *Oriental Ruby*, *Oriental Topaz*, *Oriental Amethyst*, and *Oriental Emerald*, are red, yellow, violet, and green sapphires, distinguished from the other gems of the same name which have not the prefix *oriental*, by their greatly superior hardness, and greater specific gravity;' Engl. Cyclop. s.v. Adamantine Spar.

Orisouns, *pl.* prayers, 19. 160.

Ost, host, company, army, 4. 422, 22. 338; Oest, b. 19. 332.

Ostiler, innkeeper, or probably ostler, a. 5. 172.

Otes, oats, 9. 306; Oten, *gen. pl.* of oats, a. 4. 45. A.S. *áta*, gen. pl. *átena*.

Oþer, *conj.* or, 1. 76, 12. 6; Oþur, a. 2, 38; Oþer .. oþer, either .. or, 16. 300. And see Oþure.

Oþer, *adv.* otherwise, 2. 118.

Oþer, second. See Oþure.

Oþere-gates, *adv.* otherwise, 11. 297.

Oþerweys, *adv.* otherwise, a. 6. 55.

Oþer-while, *adv.* at times, sometimes, occasionally, 7. 160, 22. 103; Oþerwhyle, 6. 50; Oþerwhiles, 17. 364.

Oþes, *pl.* oaths, 1. 36, 3. 97; Oþus, a. 2. 67.

Oþure, *adj.* other, a. 8. 80; Oþer, second, a. 5. 118; Oþeres, *gen.* the other's, 4. 340; of the other, b. 16. 207; Oþere, *pl.* others, 22. 233.

Ou, *pron.* you, a. 1. 52, a. 2. 108. See 30u, Ow.

Ouer, *prep.* over, i.e. beyond, 4. 310; Ouer-al, *adv.* everywhere, 3. 228; es-

GLOSSARIAL INDEX.   409

pecially, b. 13. 291. 'Ouer alle, *passim.*' Cath. Angl.
Ouer-cark, *v.* trouble, harass, overcharge, 4. 472. (The mod. E. *cark* is a mere variant of *charge,* i. e. burden.)
Ouer-closeþ, *pr. s.* overshadows, covers, 21. 140.
Ouercome, *v.* surpass, b. 10. 449; Ouercam, *pt. s.* overcame, 21. 114; came over, spread over, 16. 13; Ouercome, *pt. s.* overpowered, b. 13. 11.
Ouerdon, *pr. pl.* act to excess, 14. 191.
Ouere- (*in compounds*); see **Ouer-**.
Ouergrewe, *pt. pl.* surpassed, R. 3. 344.
Ouer-hardy, *adj.* too daring, too bold, 4. 300.
Ouer-houeþ, *pr. s.* hovers over, hangs over, b. 18. 169; Ouere-houeþ, 21. 175. Cf. E. *hover.*
Ouerhuppen, *pr. pl.* skip over, omit, miss words in reading, b. 13. 68, b. 15. 379; Ouerhuppe, b. 15. 380; *pr. pl. subj.* 18. 118. See **Huppen.**
Ouer-lange, *adv.* over-long, too lo ig, 23. 360.
Ouere-layde, *pp.* covered, 13. 231.
Ouerlede, *v.* domineer over, b. 3. 314.
Ouerlepe, *v.* overtake by running, outrun, catch, b. pr. 199; Ouerlep, 1 *pt. s.* have digressed, 21. 360; Ouer-leep, *pt. s.* ran faster than, overtook by running, outran, 1. 169.
Ouere-loked, *pt. pl.* looked down upon, despised, R. 2. 35.
Ouer-londe, *adv.* over the country, about the country, 10. 159.
Ouere-longe, *adj.* over long, too tedious, 17. 362; very long, b. 11. 216. See **Ouerlange.**
Ouermaistrith, *pr. s.* overmasters, b. 4. 176.
Ouermore, *adv.* in addition, 9. 35.
Ouer-plente, superfluity, 13. 234.
Ouer-reche, *v.* reach over to that belonging to another, eneroach, b. 13. 374; Ouere-reche, 7. 270.
Ouersen, *v.* oversee, b. 6. 115; Ouerse, 2 *pr. pl.* overlook, peruse, b. 10. 328; Ouer-seyh, *pt. s.* superintended, 9. 120; Ouer-seȝe, a. 7. 106; Ouerseye (me), *pp.* overseen, i.e. forgotten (myself), b. 5. 378; Ouersee, *imp. s.* examine, 2. 116. Cf. '*Yvrognet,* somewhat drunken, *overseen* ;' Cotgrave.
Ouer-skipped, *pp.* omitted, 14. 119.
Ouer-skippers, *pl.* skippers, priests who omit passages in reading, 14. 123. See note.

Ouer-sopede, 1 *pt. s.* ate too much, took too much supper, 7. 429.
Ouer-spradde, *pt. s.* covered, overshadowed, lit. spread over, 22. 206.
Ouertake, *v.* overtake, b. 17. 82.
Ouertulte, *pt. s.* upset, overturned, lit. tilted over, 23. 135; Ouer-tilte, 23. 54. See *tilt* (2) in my Etym. Dict.
Ouere-wacche, *s.* over-watching, being awake too late at night, R. 3. 282.
Ouerwarde, *adv.* in the direction of crossing over, about to cross (the Channel), 5. 128.
Ouht, everything, each thing, 8. 124; somewhat, something, 8. 45. See **Out.**
Ouhte, Ouhtest. See **Owen.**
Oune, *adj.* own, a. 10. 75. See **Owen.**
Oure, *pron.* your, a. pr. 73. See **Ou** = you.
Oures, *pl.* 'hours' of the breviary, b. pr. 97.
Ous, *pron.* us, ourselves, 1. 173, 11. 18. See **Ows.**
Out, *pron.* aught, anything, R. 4. 37; Oute, R. 3. 342. See **Ouht.**
Oute, *adv.* out, in existence; þe leeste fowel oute = the smallest bird in existence, 15. 191, b. 12. 267; þe hexte lettred oute = the most learned in existence, b. 12. 267. (This curious use of *out* is still common.)
Out-ryders, *pl.* riders about, 5. 116.
Out-taken, *prep.* except, save, a. 10. 169.
Outwitt, the faculty of observation, b. 13. 289. Cf. **Inwit.**
Ouȝt, aught, anything, a. 9. 78. See **Ouht.**
Ouȝt, *adv.* at all, a. 5. 153.
Ow, *pron.* you, a. 1. 2. See **Ou.**
Owe, 1 *pr. s.* owe (glossed in the MS. by *debeo*), b. 5. 476; Owen, 1 *pr. pl.* owe, 22. 393; Ouhte, 1 *pt. s.* ought, 3. 30; should, a. 2. 21; Ouhtest, 2. *pt. s.* oughtest, a. 1. 73; Ouhte, *pt. s.* ought, 6. 69, 23. 276; owned, possessed, 4. 72. A. S. *āgan*; pr. s. *ic āh*; pt. s. *ic āhte*. See **Oghtest.**
Owen, *adj.* own, b. 10. 367; Owene, 1. 124; *pl.* own possessions, 9. 92.
Owh, *interject.* oh! 13. 19.
Owre, *pron.* our, b. 8. 42; Owre bettre = our best plan, b. 11. 173.
Ows, *pron.* us, 1. 172; Ous, 1. 173.
Oxe, ox, b. 15. 459.
Oyther, *conj.* either, b. 17. 135.

Paal, *adj.* pale, 21. 59; Pale, b. 5. 78.

GLOSSARIAL INDEX.

Pacient, *adj. as sb.,* patient, meek (man), 14. 31 : Pacientes, *pl.* patient sufferers, 10. 178.
Packeþ, *pr. s.* packs, 17. 329. See **Pakken.**
Paiere, payer, 8. 194.
Paieþ, *pr. s.* pays the ransom for, 8. 277. See **Paye.**
Pak, small bundle, 17. 55.
Pakken, *v.* pack, b. 15. 184.
Pakneelde, *s.* packing-needle, a large needle, such as is used for sewing up packages, a. 5. 126; Paknedle, b. 5. 212. Cf. Du. *naald,* a needle. See **Batte-nelde.**
Paleis, palace, 21. 381 ; Paleys, 3. 23 ; Palys, 21. 274; Paleis, *pl.* 11. 16; Paleyses, *pl.* b. 8. 16.
Palfrey, *s.* palfrey, nag, b. 2. 189, b. 13. 243 ; Palfrayes, *gen. pl.* riding-horses, 22. 417.
Palle, 1 *pr. s.* beat, strike, knock, 19. 34, 50; Palleth, *pr. s.* b. 16. 51. Perhaps from F. *pale,* a pale, stick ; see note, p. 236.
Pallette, *s.* head-piece, R. 3. 325. '*Palet,* armowre for the heed, *Pelliris, galerus;'* Prompt. Parv. See Way's note. O. F. *palet,* a sort of head-piece ; Roquefort.
Palpable, *adj.* evident, 19. 235.
Paltok, jacket, b. 18. 25 ; Paltokes, *pl.* 23. 219. See note to 21. 24; and *paletot* in my Etym. Dict.
Panell, the jury-list or panel, 4. 472. 'The *pannel* of a jury is the slip of parchment on which the names of the jurors are written ;' Wedgwood.
Paneter, keeper of a pantry, 17. 151. See note.
Panne, skull, brain-pan, 5. 74 ; Ponne, a. 4. 64 ; Pannes, *pl.* skulls, heads, R. 1. 55.
Pans, *pl.* pence, money, 3. 232. See **Pens, Pons.**
Pans-delynge, *s.* distribution of money, almsgiving, 22. 378. See above.
Panteris, *pl.* snares for birds, R. 2. 187. See *painter* in my Etym. Dict.
Panyeres, *pl.* baskets (panniers), 18. 17. See note.
Papelotes, *pl.* messes of porridge, made with meal and milk, 10. 75. 'Paplote, *papatum;'* Cathol. Angl.
Par, *prep.* for, for the sake of, a. 9. 11. O. F. *par,* Lat. *per.*
Par charitee, *phrase,* for the love of God), b. 8. 11.
Paragals, *pl.* companions, R. 1. 71. A *paragal* (O. F. *paragel,* later *parageau*) is properly 'a younger brother, who by partition enjoys part of the land descended from his ancestor ;' Cotgrave. This explains the bitter satire of the text, where Richard is accused of sharing his power and wealth with dissipated courtiers, who are his *paragels,* i. e. like younger brothers admitted to an equal share of the realm with himself.
Parail, apparel, dress, 13. 121 ; Paraille, b. 11. 228. See **Aparail.**
Parailede, *pt. pl.* arrayed, apparelled, 1. 25 ; Parailed, 3. 224. See **Aparaile.**
Paramour, lover, 17. 107 ; Paramours, *pl.* concubines, 7. 186.
Paraunter, *adv.* perchance, peradventure, 8. 297, 9. 43 ; Parauntre, 17. 50; Parauenture, b. 12. 184. O.F. *par auenture,* by chance.
Parce, spare, i.e. the command to spare, b. 18. 390. Lat. *parce.*
Parceit, *sb.* power of perception, R. pr. 17. From O. F. *parceit* (not found), answering to Lat. *perceptum.*
Parcel, part, share, portion, little bit, 12. 48, 23. 291 ; Parcels, *pl.* parts, 14. 119; particulars, 14. 38; Parceles, *pl.* parts, b. 11. 298 ; separate parts, 20. 96.
Parcel-mele, *adv.* separately, bit by bit, 20. 28 ; by small parcels, by retail, 4. 86. Cf. **Poundmeel.**
Parceyue, *v.* perceive, 21. 465 ; Parceyueth, *pr. s.* looks, sees, b. 15. 193 ; Parceuede, 1 *pt. s.* 1. 128 ; Parceyuede, *pt. s.* 21. 253.
Parchemyn, parchment, b. 9. 38 ; (parchment) deed, b. 14. 193.
Pardoner, a seller of pardons, 1. 66, 3. 110.
Pardoun, pardon, 20. 218.
Pare, *v.* pare, cut down, b. 5. 243 ; Pared, 1 *pt. s.* clipped, pared, 7. 242. F. *parer.*
Par-entrelignarie, *adv.* in an interlined manner, with interlineations, 14. 119. See note.
Parfay, by my faith, 17. 119. O. F. *par fei.*
Parfit, *adj.* perfect, upright, 12. 296, 21. 153 ; pure, b. 15. 144 ; Parfyte, b. 9. 188.
Parfiter, *adj. comp.* more perfect, b. 12. 25.
Parfitest, *adj. sup.* most perfect, 14. 99.
Parfitliche, *adv.* perfectly, truly, 16. 180, 17. 325.
Parfitnesse, perfectness, perfection, 16.

GLOSSARIAL INDEX. 411

184, b. 10. 200; uprightness, b. 15. 202.
Parfourne, *v.* perform, fulfil, 8. 247; Parfourneþ, *pr. s.* 8. 72; Parfournen, *pr. pl.* 17. 128; Parfourned, 1 *pt. s.* 8. 14. See **Performen.** O. F. *parfournir* (Cotgrave); E. *perform.*
Parisshene, a parishioner, b. 11. 67; Parisschens, *pl.* a. pr. 79; Parisshiens, b. 20. 280; Parshens, 1. 82. F. *paroissien.* See **Paroschienes.** 'A parischen, *parochianus;*' Cath. Angl.
Parle, *v.* speak, talk, R. 4. 48; Parled, *pt. pl.* R. 4. 88.
Parloure, room, b. 10. 97. See note.
Paroles, pl. words, b. 15. 113.
Paroschienes, *pl.* parishioners, b. pr. 89. See **Parisshene.**
Parroked, *pp.* enclosed, shut in, 18. 13. Lit. 'imparked;' from A. S. *pearroc,* mod. E. *paddock,* enclosure.
Parshe, *s.* parish, 23. 263.
Parshens. See **Parisshene.**
Parsonage, benefice, b. 13. 245.
Parsones, parsons, b. 10. 268. See **Persone.**
Parte, *v.* share, have a part, 7. 301, 17. 257; Partye, 9. 144; Parteth, *pr. s.* shares, b. 10. 63; Parteþ, 2 *pr. pl.* share, 16. 116; Parte, 2 *pr. pl.* impart, 2. 179; Parten, 2 *pr. pl.* a. 1. 156; Parteth, *pr. pl.* share, 12. 65; Parten, *pr. pl.* 1. 79; Parteden, *pt. pl.* settled the shares, divided (the value of the articles), a. 5. 177; Parte, *imp. s.* share, give away, bestow, 9. 286.
Parti, Partie. See **Partye.**
Partinge, *s.* imparting, R. 1. 71. See **Partynge.**
Partriche, partridge, R. 3. 38 (see note).
Partye, *v.* share, have a part, 9. 144. See **Parte.**
Partye, *s.* party (in a lawsuit), 20. 284, 286; b. 17. 302; A partye = partly, 17. 168, b. 15. 17; Partie, part, portion, 2. 7, 4. 386; part, passage, 16. 157; Parti, part, a. 1. 7; More partie = most part, R. 2. 37; Partyes, *pl.* persons, b. 14. 268.
Partynge, *s.* departing, departure, 10. 53; Here hennes partynge = their departure hence, death, a. 11. 303; Partyng, departure, 22. 61; Partinge, imparting, R. 1. 71.
Pas, *s.* pass, 17. 139, b. 14. 300.
Paschte, *pt. s.* dashed, pounded, 23. 100. See *Pash* in my Etym. Dict.
Paske, Easter, 13. 122; Paske week, Easter week, b. 11. 226.
Passe, *v.* pass, escape, 4. 174; pass, a.

3. 132; pass on, b 13. 178; Passy, *v.* pass, 10. 11; Passeþ, *pr. s.* passes, oversteps, 2. 98; goes beyond, 18. 5; surpasses, a. 12. 4; Passith, *pr. s.* surpasses, R. 2. 109; Passeþ, *pr. pl.* live, pass their lives, 2. 7; Passid, 1 *pt. s.* passed, went, R. pr. 1; Passede, *pt. s.* walked, 7. 67; surpassed, 10. 319; Passed, passed out of sight, b. 13. 20; Passid, surpassed, R. pr. 17; Passede, *pt. pl.* passed on, went, 11. 11; Passid, surpassed, R. 4. 20; Passed, *pp.* past, 1. 203; Passede, *pp. pl.* past, ago, 23. 343; Passynge, *pr. pt.* surpassing, 22. 266; Passinge, surpassing, R. 2. 108; Passend, *as prep.* passing, beyond, more than, 23. 218.
Passhed, *pt. s.* dashed, b. 20. 99. See **Paschte.**
Passion, suffering, 8. 20, 79.
Paste, paste, pastry, b. 13. 250.
Pastours, *pl.* shepherds, herdsmen, 12. 293, b. 12. 149.
Patent, *s.* letter patent, open deed, indulgence, pardon, b. 14. 191, b. 17. 10; Patente, 20. 12; Patentes, *pl.* letters patent, letters of privilege (so called because open to the inspection of all men), b. 7. 194. See note, p. 242.
Paternoster-while, the time taken to say a pater-noster, short time, b. 5. 348. 'But a Pater noster whyle, *que tant quon die sa pate nostre ;*' Palsgrave, p. 854. Cf. note to 12. 295.
Paþ, path, 17. 139; Patthis, *pl.* roads, R. 2. 24.
Pauci, a few, b. 11. 109.
Pauilon, *s.* pavilion, tent, a. 2. 43; Paueylon, (lawyer's) coif, 4. 452. See *papillon* in Cotgrave and Littré.
Paume, palm (of the hand), 20. 115.
Paunche, stomach, 16. 96.
Paye, *v.* please, satisfy, 9. 333; Payeth, *pr. s.* pays, 22. 194; makes satisfaction, 17. 31; Paieth, *pr. s.* pays the ransom for, 8. 277; Paye, *imp. s.* let him pay, 8. 157.
Paye, *s.* satisfaction; To paye, to his satisfaction, 8. 189, 192; satisfactorily, 14. 160. See note to 8. 192.
Payere, *s.* payer, a. 6. 41.
Payn, bread, food, 9. 286, 10. 92, 16. 201, 217; Payne, b. 6. 152; Payn defaute, lack of bread, 16. 231.
Paynede, *pt. pl.* tortured, 2. 168.
Paynym, *s.* pagan, Saracen, heathen, gentile, 8. 161, b. 5. 523; Paynymes, *pl.* 18. 255. (A false use; the true orig. sense was *paganism,* heathendom.)
Pays, peace, b. 16. 159. See note.

VOL. II.   C C

Pece, *s.* piece, 9. 333, 20. 12; Peces, *pl.* pieces, 21. 62; Peces, *pl.* small drinking-cups, cups, b. 3. 89. '*Pece*, a cuppe, *tasse*;' Palsgrave. 'Pece, cuppe, *Crater*;' Prompt. Parv.

Pecok, *s.* peacock, b. 12. 229.

Pecunie, money, 4. 393.

Pecuniosus, *adj.* a moneyed (man), b. 11. 57; rich, moneyed, 13. 11.

Peer, *s.* peer, rival, 10. 306, 11. 140; Peere, nobleman, R. 3. 271; Peeres, *pl.* companions, 10. 20; Peeris, nobles, R. 1. 44. See **Pere**.

Peere, *s.* a pear, the value of a pear, R. pr. 73. So in Sir Ferumbras, l. 5722. See note.

Peerles, *s. pl.* pearls, a. 11. 12. See **Perlis**.

Pees, *s.* peace, 2. 149, 4. 457, 5. 45; silence, 16. 234. And see note to b. 16. 159.

Pees, *s.* a pea (*sing.*), a thing of no value, b. 6. 171.

Peescoddes, *pl.* peas-cods, pea-shells, pea-pods, 9. 317. See **Pesecoddes**.

Peese-lof, loaf made of pease, 9. 176. See **Peselof**.

Peire, *s.* pair, couple, 11. 272. See **Peyre**.

Peired, *pp.* injured, b. 3. 127. See **Apeire**; and **Peyrep**.

Peis, *s.* weight, 7. 242. O.F. *peis, pois,* F. *poids*. See **Peys**.

Peitrel, *v.* put breast-armour upon (said of a horse), 5. 23. Eng. *poitrel*, from O.F. *peitrel, poitrel,* Lat. *pectorale,* that which covers the breast. 'A patrelle, *pectorale*'; Cath. Angl.

Pekokes, peacocks, b. 11. 350. See **Pokok**.

Pele, appeal, accusation, b. 17. 302. See **Apeel**.

Pelet, *s.* pellet, stone-ball, b. 5. 78. Pellets were stone-balls used as missiles, and were naturally of a pale white colour. 'A *pelet* of stone or lede;' Cath. Angl.

Pelour, accuser, lit. appealer or appellant, 21. 39.

Pelure, *s.* fur, 22. 417, b. 2. 9, b. 3. 294; Peloure, 3. 10; Pelour, 4. 452; Pellure, b. 15. 7. O.F. *pelure*, fur; from Lat. *pellis*.

Penaunce, suffering, punishment, penance, 4. 101, 6. 84, 196; Penaunces, *pl.* 1. 27.

Penaunceles, *adj.* without performing penance, without suffering punishment, 12. 296.

Penaunt, one undergoing penance, penitent, 5. 130; Penauntes, *pl.* persons undergoing penance, 16. 101. See **Penytancer**.

Pencion, *s.* payment, reward, a. 8. 48.

Pendauntes, *pl.* hanging ornaments of a belt, b. 15. 7.

Peneworth; see **Penyworthes**.

Penne, pen, 20. 15; Pennes, *pl.* feathers, 15. 180.

Pens, *pl.* pence, b. 2. 222, b. 3. 161; *gen. pl.* of pence, R. 3. 142. See **Pans, Peny**.

Pensel, banner, pennon, 19. 189. Cf. O.F. *penoncel* (Roquefort), *pennoncel* Cotgrave), a little pennon; also (says Roquefort), a standard, ensign, or banner, particularly of bachelors-in-arms, and sometimes of squires. In the present instance it is used in much the same sense as shield in heraldry. 'Pensell, a lytel baner;' Palsgrave.

Pensyf, *adj.* thoughtful, 19. 299.

Pensyf, *adv.* thoughtfully, a. 8. 133.

Peny, penny, 2. 45, 9. 304; Penyes, *pl.* pence, money, 1. 161. See **Pens, Pans**.

Peny-ale, poor, common ale (at a penny a gallon), 7. 226, 10. 92; Peni-ale, a. 5. 134. See note, p. 84.

Penytancer, confessor, one who imposes a penance, 23. 319; Penetauncers, *pl.* 7. 256.

Penyworthes, goods, lit. pennyworths, 7. 284; Peniworþus, a. 5. 177.

Peose, *s.* pea, a. 7. 155; Peose lof, loaf made of peas, a. 7. 166; Peosen, *pl.* peas, a. 7. 285. See **Pees, Pese**. The pl. *peasen* is still in use in Shropshire.

Peper, pepper, b. 15. 197. 'Least [lest] you gentlewomen shoulde *take pepper in the nose*, when I put but salte to your mouthes;' Lyly, Euphues, ed. Arber, p. 375. And see note.

Peple, *s.* people, a. 1. 5, a. 8. 10; followers, a. 2. 152.

Perauenture, *adv.* perhaps, 4. 470.

Percel-mel, *adv.* by retail, in parcels at a time, a. 3. 72. See **Parcelmele**.

Percen, *pr. pl.* pierce, force a way into, b. 10. 461. See **Persen**.

Perchemyn, parchment, b. 14. 191. See **Parchemyn**.

Percil, parsley, b. 6. 288. F. *persil*, from Gk. πετροσέλινον. See **Perselye**.

Pere, *s.* equal, peer, 4. 263, b. 3. 204; match, a. 3. 198; Peres, *pl.* equals, b. 7. 16. See **Peer**.

GLOSSARIAL INDEX. 413

Pere-Ionettes, *pl.* early-ripe pears, 13. 221. See note.
Peren, *v.* appear, b. pr. 173. See **Apere.**
Peren, *pr. pl.* become peers, are as equals, b. 15. 410; Peryth to aungelys, is a peer to angels, ranks with angels, a. 12. 4 (Ingilby M.S.).
Performen, *v.* make, bring about, 16. 173; Perfourneþ, *pr. s.* acts, 16. 87; performs, b. 13. 412; Perforneth, does, b. 13. 78. See **Parfourne.**
Periloslich, *adv.* dangerously, 1. 170.
Perilous, dangerous, a. 7. 44.
Perimancie, *s.* pyromancy, divination by fire, a. 11. 158. See note.
Perlis, *pl.* pearls, b. 10. 9.
Permutacion, exchange, 4. 316.
Permute, *v.* exchange, b. 13. 110; Permuten, *pr. pl.* change, exchange, i.e. exchange livings, 3. 185.
Perreye, *s.* jewelry, precious stones, 12. 10; Perre, b. 10. 12. F. *pierrerie,* from *pierre.*
Persant, *pres. pt.* piercing, b. 1. 155. See **Persen.**
Perselye, parsley, 9. 310. See **Percil.**
Persen, *pr. pl.* pierce, effect an entrance into, 12. 295; Persith, *pr. s.* pierceth, R. 3. 11; Pershaunt, *pres. pt.* 2. 154. See **Percen.** See note, p. 163.
Persone, person, 4. 225; form, 21. 381; parson, priest, 7. 144; Persones, *pl.* parsons, 1. 81, 23. 280. See **Parsones.**
Perte, *adj.* apert, manifest, obvious, a. 1. 98. See **Apert.**
Perte, *adv.* openly, R. 4. 88.
Pertelich, *adv.* plainly, evidently, 6. 116; Pertliche, b. 5. 15; Pertly, b. 5. 23. See **Apertelich.**
Peryth. See **Peren.**
Pese, *s.* a pea, a thing of no value, 9. 166; Peses, *pl.* peas, 9. 307; Pesen, b. 6. 198. See **Pees, Peose;** and see note, p. 113.
Pesecoddes, *pl.* pea-pods, pea-shells with the peas in them (peas were often boiled in the shells), b. 6. 294. See **Peescoddes.** 'A peyscodde, *siliqua;*' Cath. Angl.
Pese-lof, loaf made from peas, b. 6. 181. See **Peeselof.**
Pesen, Peses. See **Pese.**
Pesinge, *s.* piecing, joining, R. 3. 168.
Pestilence-tyme, time of the plague, 11. 272.
Pete, *s.* pity, R. pr. 23.
Peter! *interj.* by saint Peter! b. 5. 544, b. 7. 112, 130.

Petit, *adj.* little, small, 10. 53, b. 7. 57.
Peuple, people, persons, 12. 21.
Peyne, pain, 20. 155, 21. 206; Peynes, *pl.* sufferings, 22. 328; penalties, 8. 277.
Peyneþ, *pr. s. refl.* exerts (himself), 22. 436; *pr. pl.* trouble, encumber, b. 12. 247; Peynen hem, take pains, b. 7. 42; Peynede, *pt. s.* suffered pain, 22. 324.
Peynte, *v.* paint, 20. 136; illuminate, decorate with painting, b. 15. 176; Peynten, b. 3. 62; Do peynten= cause to be painted, 4. 66 (see note to 4. 34); Peynted, *pt. s.* stained, coloured, 22. 11; Peynted, *pp.* written, b. 11. 298; coloured, stained, 22. 6; disguised, flattering, b. 20. 114; Peynte, painted, R. 3. 196; Peyntede, *pp. pl.* painted, 5. 23.
Peyre, *s.* pair, couple, 11. 231; set, b. 15. 119. See note, p. 218. See **Peire.**
Peyreþ, *pres. s.* impairs, injures, a. 3. 123. See **Peired.**
Peys, *s.* weight, lump, b. 13. 246; weight, b. 5. 243. See **Peis.**
Peysed, *pt. s.* weighed, 7. 223; Peysede, a. 5. 131. See **Peis.**
Peyuesshe, *adj.* ill-tempered, peevish, 9. 151.
Phippe, a pet name for a sparrow, b. 11. 41. See note, p. 218.
Piane, *s.* peony-seeds, a. 5. 155. See **Piones.**
Picche, *v.* throw, pitch (hay), 6. 13; pick, cut, divide with a sharp point, 9. 64. See **Piht;** and see *Pitch* in Shropsh. Wordbook.
Pies hele, (probably) remnant of a pie-crust, b. 7. 194 (see note); Pies, *pl.* pies, pasties, a. pr. 104.
Pies, *pl.* magpies, R. 2. 192.
Piht, *pp.* pitched, fixed, a. 2. 43; Pight, *pp.* pitched, placed, R. 2. 187. Pp. of *picchen.*
Pike, *s.* staff (furnished with a spike), a. 5. 257; Pikis, pikes, R. 3. 232.
Piked, *pt. pl.* picked as with a sharp instrument, hoed (as we should now say), b. 6. 113. See **Picche.**
Pikede, *adj. pl.* peaked, 23. 219. Cf. note.
Pile, pile, foundation (as of a fort or strong building), 22. 366; prop, b. 16. 36, 86. See **Pyle.** See the note; and cf. Lowl. Sc. *peel,* a small fort.
Pileþ, *pr. s.* robs, pillages, 22. 444, b. 19. 439. O.F. *piller,* to rob. See **Piloure.**
Pilie, *ger.* to peel, 10. 81.

C C 2

GLOSSARIAL INDEX.

Pillede, *adj.* bald-headed, a. 7. 143. See **Pylede**. Cf. '*peeled* priest' in Shakespeare, 1 Hen. VI. i. 3. 30. See *peel* in my Etym. Dict.

Pillynge, *s.* robbery, R. 1. 13.

Piloure, robber (i.e. pillager), stripper or despoiler of the dead, b. 3. 194, b. 18. 40; Piloures. *pl.* b. 19. 413; Pilours, 14. 2, 23. 263; Pillourz, R. 3. 303. O.F. *piller*, to rob. See *Pilleur* in Cotgrave.

Pinnede, 1 *pt. s.* penned, fastened tightly, a. 5. 127. See **Pynne**.

Pionys, seeds of the pæony, 7. 359. See note. ' A pyon, *pionia, herba est;*' Cath. Angl. See **Piane**.

Pipe, *v.* pipe, play the pipe, b. 20. 92 ; Pipede, *pt. s.* played, 21. 453.

Piper, pepper, 7. 359.

Pipis, *s. pl.* pipes, fifes, R. 3. 275.

Pipoudris, *s. pl.* cases in the court of pie-powder, R. 3. 319. See note.

Piries, *pl.* pear-trees, 6. 119. A.S. *pirige*, a pear-tree ; from Lat. *pyrus*.

Pirith, *pr. s.* peers, watches, R. 3. 48.

Piriwhit, *s.* some common kind of perry (lit. white perry), a. 5. 134. ' Pirrey, Pirre, *piretum, est potus factus de piris;*' Cath. Angl.

Pissares, *gen. pl.* soldiers', ruffians', 23. 219. See note.

Pistle, epistle, b. 12. 30; Pistele, 17. 289 ; Pistles. *pl.* epistles, 20. 317.

Pitaunce, provision, share, portion, dole, 16. 61, b. 5. 270. See note to 10. 92. See **Pytaunce**.

Pite, *s.* pity, mercy, 22. 92, a. 1. 145 ; Pitee, b. 10. 424. See **Pete**.

Piþ, *s.* pith, strength, stay, chief support, 20. 116.

Pitouse, *adj.* piteous, a. 7. 116.

Pitousliche, *adj.* pitiable, 21. 59.

Pitously, *adv.* piteously, a. 1. 78.

Place, *s.* dwelling, abode, a. 6. 45 ; Places, *pl.* mansions, 13. 246. See note, p. 173.

Placebo, 4. 467, b. 15. 122. See notes.

Plastre, *v.* lay on a plaister, 23. 310 ; Plastreþ, *pr. s.* lays on a plaister, 23. 314; Plastred, *pp.* covered with a healing plaister, 20. 89 (see note).

Plates, *pl.* armour, plate-armour, 21. 24.

Platte, *pt. s. reflex.* threw himself flat, 7. 3 ; threw herself flat, b. 5. 63. F. *plat*, Swed. *platt*, flat.

Plaunke, plank, pole, 19. 34, 40.

Play, *s.* pleasure, a. 12. 95.

Playne, *v.* complain, a. 3. 161 ; Playneþ, *pr. pl.* a. pr. 80 ; Playnede, *pt. s.* a. 7. 147 ; Playneden, *pt. pl.* accused, a. 4. 42 ; *refl.* complained, a. 7. 116. See **Pleyne**.

Playnt, *s.* plant, growing shrub, a. 1. 137. Badly spelt; other MSS. have *plante, plonte, plaunte*. (*Playnt* should mean complaint.)

Playntes, *s. pl.* plaints, complaints, a. 2. 152. See **Pleyntes**.

Plede, *v.* plead, bring a complaint, 1. 161, 10. 44, 22. 295 ; Plededen, *pt. pl.* pleaded, b. pr. 212; Pleteden, b. 7. 39; Pledid, R. 3. 319. See Plete ; and see note, p. 16.

Pleide, *pt. s.* amused himself, 1. 170 ; Pleiden, *pt. pl.* played, amused themselves, 1. 22 ; Pleyed, b. pr. 20; Pleiden hem, amused themselves, a. pr. 20 ; Pleiynge, *pr. pt.* playing, 19. 274. See **Pleye**.

Pleinte, plaint, complaint, 4. 214. See **Pleynte**.

Plenere, *adj.* full, b. 16. 103. From Lat. *plenus*.

Plenere, *adv.* in full numbers, fully, b. 11. 108 ; Plener, 13. 47.

Plentevous, *adj.* plenteous, abundant, a. 12. 95 ; Plenteuous, generous, openhanded, b. 10. 80.

Plesaunce, pleasure, 9. 14.

Plesaunte, *adj.* pleasing, b. 14. 101.

Plese, *v.* please, b. 10. 72, a. 3. 11 ; Plesen, 2 *pr. pl.* court, b. 15. 78 ; *pr. pl.* a. 10. 209; Plesed, *pt. s.* pleased, 4. 492 ; Pleseden, *pt. pl.* amused, a. 3. 98.

Plesyng, *s.* pleasure, gratification, a. 3. 237.

Plete, *v.* plead, R. 1. 60, R. 3. 349 ; Pleteden, *pt. pl.* pleaded, b. 7. 39 ; Pletid, R. 3. 328. O.F. *plait*, from Lat. *placitum*. See **Plede**.

Pletede, 1 *pt. s.* plaited, folded up, a. 5. 126. See Cath. Angl.

Plewme, *ger.* plume, i. e. to pluck feathers off the neck, R. 2. 163. See the note.

Pleye, *v.* to play, 1. 188, 4. 465 ; Pleyen, *ger.* amuse themselves, a. 8. 12 ; Pleyinge, *pres. part.* playing, amusing themselves, 10. 114; Pleyande, *pres. pt.* playing, b. 16. 256. See **Pleide**.

Pleyn, *adj.* full, complete, a. 8. 87 ; Pleyne, b. 7. 103. F. *plein*, L. *plenus*.

Pleyne, *v.* complain, plead, 4. 214, b. 13. 109, R. 1. 56 ; Pleyne hem, b. 3. 167 ; Pleyneth, *pr. s.* complains, b. 17. 292 ; Pleynen, *pr. pl.* complain, 7. 120 ; Pleyne, plead, b. 14. 225 ;

GLOSSARIAL INDEX. 415

Pleyned, 1 *pt. s.* complained, 7. 110;
Pleyned hym, b. 6. 161; Pleynede,
pt. pl. complained, 1. 81; Pleyned
hem, b. pr. 83; Pleyne, *pr. s. subj. as
imp.* let him complain, 9. 166. See
Playne.
Pleynte, *s.* complaint, 13. 135; Pleyn-
tes, *pl.* pleas, b. 2. 177. See **Playnte.**
Plihte, 1 *pr. s.* pledge, plight, a. 7. 37;
Plihten, *pr. pl.* agree, a. pr. 46; Pliht,
pp. pledged, a. 5. 116; plighted, be-
trothed, a. 10. 185. See **Plyghte.**
Plocke, *imper. s.* pluck, 8. 229; Plokke,
a. 6. 72; Plokked, *pt. s.* pulled, drew,
b. 17. 10. See **Plukked, Plyghte.**
Plomayle, *s.* plumage, R. 2. 32. F.
plumail, ' a plume of feathers, a goose-
wing, or duster of feathers ;' Cotgrave.
Plomes, *pl.* plums, 13. 221.
Plomtrees, *pl.* plum-trees, 6. 119.
Plonte, plant, 2. 149, 19. 25. See note.
Plotte, a patch, b. 13. 276; Plottes,
patches, b. 13. 275.
Plouh, plough, 1. 145, 4. 465.
Plouh-fot, plough-foot, 9. 64. See
note, p. 109; and see Fitzherbert's
Book of Husbandry, § 3, l. 38.
Plouhman, ploughman, 8. 182, 287;
10. 299; Peers prentys þe plouhman
=apprentice of Piers Plowman, 16.
195; Plouhmen, *pl.* ploughmen, 12.
293.
Plouh-pote, *s.* plough-put, a. 7. 96.
See note to b. 6. 105. Whether it is
identical with the 'plough-foot' or
not, is not quite clear.
Plouȝmon, *s.* ploughman, a. 6. 28.
Plow, plough, b. 15. 122.
Plowman, *s.* ploughman, a. 12. 102.
See **Plouhman.**
Plukked, *pt. s.* pulled, drew, b. 11. 109;
Plucked, *pt. pl.* plucked, R. 2. 32;
Plukked, *pp.* plucked out, b. 12. 249.
See **Plocke, Plyghte.**
Pluralite, pluralities, 4. 33; Pluralites,
pl. (many) endowments, a. 11. 197.
Pluschaud, adj. very hot, a. 7. 299.
F. *plus chaud.*
Plyghte, 1 *pr. s.* pledge, 9. 33; Plyghte,
pt. s. pledged, 3. 123; Plyȝhten, *pt. pl.*
agreed, 1. 47. See **Plihte.**
Plyghte, *pt. s.* plucked, 20. 12; drew
quickly, 13. 48. Used as pt. t. of
Plocke, q. v.
Plytis, *s. pl.* plaits, folds, R. 3. 156.
Po, *gen.* peacock's, b. 12. 257. A.S.
pawe, Lat. *pauo.*
Pocalips, Apocalypse, b. 13. 90.
Pockes, *pl.* pustules; *hence,* small pox,
23. 98. See **Pokkes.**

Pocok, peacock, 14. 171 See **Pekok,
Pokok,** and **Po.**
Poddynges, *pl.* puddings, 16. 66.
Podyng-ale, thick ale, lit. pudding-ale,
7. 226.
Poeple, people, b. 1. 5. See **Puple.**
Poffed, *pp.* blown, puffed, 6. 119. See
Puffe.
Pohen, pea-hen, 15. 175; Pohenne, b.
12. 240. See **Pocok.**
Pointe : In pointe ffor, at the point of,
ready to, R. 3. 142.
Poised, *pt. s.* weighed, b. 5. 117. See
Peis.
Poke, bag, pouch, pocket, 16. 186, 248;
Pokes, *pl.* 17. 87. See **Powke.**
Poke-ful, bag-ful, sack-ful, 10. 342.
Pokep, *pr. s.* presses, pushes, puts, 8.
263 ; Pokede, *pt. s.* urged on, incited,
2. 129, 8. 287. See **Pukketh.**
Pokkes, *pl.* pocks, small pox, b. 20. 97;
Pockes, 23. 98.
Pokok, peacock, 15. 162, 173. See
Pocok.
Pol, poll, head, R. 2. 163; Pol by pol,
head by head, one by one, 13. 11 (see
note, p. 167); Polles, *pl.* heads, 23.
86; Pollis, b. 13. 246 (see note).
Polaxis, *s. pl.* pole-axes, hence, men
carrying pole-axes, R. 1. 17; Poll-axis,
pole-axes, R. 3. 328.
Pole, *v.* put a guard or martingale upon
his head (said of a vicious horse), 5.
23. From the sb. *poll,* head; cf. Pei-
trel. (Such seems to be the sense in-
tended; the Ilchester MS. has *pul* =
pull.)
Polettes, *pl.* chickens, pullets, 9. 304;
Poletes, b. 6. 282.
Polische, *v.* polish, 7. 329; Polsche, b.
5. 42.
Pollede, *pt. s.* pulled, tore, a. 8. 100.
See **Pul.**
Pomade, cider, 21. 412. Lit. 'drink
made from apples ;' from Lat. *pomum.*
See note.
Pondfolde, pound, pinfold, b. 16. 264;
Ponfolde, b. 5. 663. From A.S. *pund,*
sb. *pyndan,* vb. See **Poundfalde.**
Ponne, *s.* brain-pan, skull, a. 4. 64.
See **Panne.**
Pons, *pl.* pence, money, a. pr. 86. See
Pans, Pens.
Pontifex, pontiff, b. 15. 42.
Pope, *s.* pope, a. 6. 90; Popes, *gen.*
pope's, 3. 23; Pope, *gen.* pope's, a.
2. 18. For this last form cf. A.S.
pápan, gen. of *pápa,* pope.
Pope-holy, holy as a pope, hypocritical,
7. 37. See note.

GLOSSARIAL INDEX.

Popeiay, parrot, popinjay, 15. 173.
Poperiþ, *pr. s.* trots, ambles, a. 11. 210. Frequentative of *pop*, to bob, to move quickly. Not found elsewhere.
Poraille, *s.* the poor people, b. pr. 82. O.F. *pouraille* (Roquefort).
Porchace, *v.* to procure, provide, 4. 32; Porchase, *imp. s.* purchase, buy, 20. 218. See **Purchace**.
Pore, *adj.* poor, 4. 214; *as sb.* poor man, b. 10. 63.
Poret, *s.* young onion, kind of leek, b. 6. 300; Porettes, *pl.* b. 6. 288. O.F. *poret;* cf. F. *porreau*.
Porett-plontes, leeks, pot-herbs, 9. 310. See above.
Porfil, trimming or edges of clothes, esp. fur-trimmings, 5. 111. See **Purfil**.
Porore, *adj. comp.* poorer, a. 10. 113.
Porse, purse, 14. 49; Pors, 7. 199, 266; a. 5. 110.
Porse, *imp. s.* put into a purse, pocket up, 13. 164. See above.
Porsueþ, *pr. s.* follows, 22. 432; prosecutes (at law), 20. 284; Porsuede, *pt. s.* followed, 22. 163; endeavoured, 18. 167; *pt. pl.* pursued, 19. 166. See **Pursueth**.
Porswarde, *adv.* purseward; To porswarde, as regards your purses, 1. 101.
Portatyf, *adj.* easily carried, light, 2. 154, b. 1. 155.
Porte, bearing, conduct, 7. 30.
Portinaunce, belongings, appurtenances, 3. 108, 17. 329. See **Appurtenaunces** and **Purtinaunce**.
Portous, a breviary, b. 15. 122. Put for *portehors*, i. e. 'carry abroad,' a F. substitution for Lat. *portiforium*. See note.
Portrey, *v.* pourtray, draw, delineate, 20. 136; Do portreyn = cause to be covered with pictures or drawings, 4. 66; Portreieþ, *pr. s.* draws, writes, 17. 320. See **Purtraye**.
Pose, 1 *pr. s.* suppose, put the case, 20. 275. F. *poser*.
Possed. See **Posshen**.
Possessioneres, *pl.* possessioners, beneficed clergy, b. 5. 144. See note.
Possessioun, possessions, property, endowment, b. 11. 264.
Posshen, *v.* push, a 7. 96; Possed, pushed, tossed, b. pr. 151. See *Posson* in Prompt. Parv. Shropshire *poss*. F. *pousser*, Lat. *pulsare*.
Postles, *pl.* apostles, b. 16. 159; Posteles, preachers, b. 6. 151 (see note).
Potage, pottage, soup, 9. 182, 286.

Potager, pottage-maker, 6. 132.
Potel, *s.* pottle (two quarts), b. 5. 348; Potell, 7. 399. See note to 7. 397.
Potent, *s.* staff, a. 9. 88. See note to 11. 94.
Pouere, *adj.* poor, b. 1. 173. See **Poure**.
Pouerere, *adj.* more poor, poorer, b. 20. 49.
Pouerte, poverty, 10. 182, 234; meanness, shabbiness, 11. 116; Pouert, poverty, b. 11. 264; meanness, a. 9. 111.
Pouke, devil, demon, goblin, imp, 16. 164, 19. 50, 279; Poukes, *gen.* devil's, 19. 282. Icel. *púki*. See note, p. 197. A common word in Ireland, esp. in the West, in such phrases as—' What the *puck* are you doing?'
Poundfalde, pound, prison, pinfold, 19. 282. See **Pondfolde**, **Ponfold**. Cf. Shropsh. *pounded*, pent up.
Pound-meel, *adv.* by pounds at a time, 3. 232. Cf. **Parcelmele**.
Poure, *adj.* poor, 2. 172, 6. 78; poor people, 20. 237. (I suppose that *poure=povre*, rather than that *ou* is a diphthong.) See **Pouere**.
Poure, *pr. s. subj.* pore, R. pr. 71.
Pourede, *pt. s.* poured, 7. 226.
Pous, pulse, 20. 66.
Pouste, power, dominion, b. 5. 36; Poustees, *pl.* violent attacks, b. 12. 11. O. F. *poeste*, from Lat. *potestas*.
Pouwer, *s.* power, a. 3. 161; authority, a. 8. 160.
Powke, *s.* bag, pouch, a. 8. 178. See **Poke**.
Poynt, *s.* point, 2. 98, 6. 118, 9. 35; reason, a. 5. 15; Poynte, b. 13. 110; matter, b. 14. 279; Poyntes, *pl.* points, respects, 21. 43.
Poyntest, 2 *pr. s.* pointest, 9. 298.
Poyson, poison, 21. 52.
Poysye, poetry, b. 18. 406.
Practisoure, practitioner, b. 16. 107.
Pray, *s.* prey, R. 2. 163.
Prayed, *pp.* preyed upon, b. 20. 85.
Pre manibus, in advance, 4. 301. See note, p. 50.
Prechen, *v.* preach, b. 10. 34; Preche, *v.* 23. 275; preaches to, a. 9. 83; Prechiþ, *pr. s.* preaches, speaks, 1. 39; Prechede, *pt. s.* preached, 6. 115, 21. 331; Prechede, *pp.* declared, spoken, 21. 143; Prechynge, *pres. part.* preaching to, addressing, 1. 57; Prechet (*for* Preche it), preach it, proclaim it, a. 1. 137 (other MSS. have *preche it*).
Preciousest, *adj. superl.* most precious, a. 2. 12.

GLOSSARIAL INDEX.

Preest-hood, priesthood, 17. 244. See **Prest-hod**.
Preier, prayer, 16. 230 ; Preiere, R. pr. 1.
Preifis, *sb. pl.* experiences, lit. proofs, R. pr. 17.
Preise, *v.* appraise, value, 7. 380 ; Preiseden, *pt. pl.* a. 5. 177. See below.
Preisen, *v.* praise, a. 6. 100 ; Preise, R. 3. 38 ; *pr. pl.* R. 3. 148 ; Preysed, *pt. s.* b. 6. 110 ; Preyseden, *pt. pl.* b. 7. 38. See above, and see **Preyse**.
Prente, impression, stamp, 18. 75. See **Preynte**.
Prentede, *pt. s.* stamped, marked, 18. 80. See **Preynte**.
Prentishode, apprenticeship, 7. 251.
Prentys, apprentice, pupil, 3. 224, 7. 208 ; Prentise, R. 3. 350 ; *pl.* apprentices, b. 3. 224, b. 5. 317 ; Prentys, *pl.* a. 3. 218 ; Preyntyces, *pl.* students, novices, b. 19. 226. See **Aprentys**.
Preosthood, priesthood, 22. 334.
Preouen, *v.* prove, test, 12. 39, 13. 31 ; Preoued, *pp.* 12..160. See **Preuen**.
Present, gift, bribe, 22. 309.
Present, *adj.* present, i. e. conspicuous in men's presence, publicly seen, a. 2. 62.
Presentide, *pt. s.* presented, 22. 92.
Presompcion, presumption, arrogance, 14. 232 ; Presumpsioun, assumption, assumed argument, supposition, b. 10. 55 ; Presompcions, *pl.* suppositions, 12. 39.
Preson, *s.* prison, R. 3. 271.
Preson, *v.* imprison, R. 3. 303.
Presse, *v.* press, R. 3. 195 ; Preseth, *pr. s.* presses, pushes, b. 14. 212.
Pressour, press for cloth, a. 5. 127 ; Pressours, *pl.* 7. 219. See Cath. Angl.
Prest, priest, 1. 66, 5. 130 ; Preste, priest, b. 12. 117 ; Prestes, priest's, 7. 135 ; Prestes, *pl.* a. 4. 107.
Prest, *adj.* ready, quick, 8. 194, 17. 63. O. F. *prest*, F. *prêt*.
Prest, *adv.* quickly, immediately, 21. 274. See above.
Prestest, *adj. sup.* readiest, b. 5. 558.
Prestiore, *adj. comp.* more ready, b. 10. 289.
Presthod, priesthood, priests, b. 15. 93. See **Preosthood**.
Prestliche, *adv.* readily, quickly, 4. 308, 9. 102.
Presul, bishop, b. 15. 42 ; *voc.* O bishop, 18. 286. Lat. *præsul*. See note, p. 234.

Presumen, *pr. pl.* presume on, assume, 1. 135.
Preuaricatores, pl. evaders, 11. 94. See note to 11. 95.
Preuen, *v.* prove, test, b. 11. 88 ; Preue, *v.* prove, b. 5. 43 ; endeavour, b. 15. 598 ; prove by practice, b. 15. 108 ; Preueth, *pr. s.* proves, b. 10. 336 ; declares plainly, b. 12. 30 ; proves to be, b. 17. 155 ; practises, b. 13. 79 ; Preue, *pr. s. subj.* prove, test, R. pr. 71 ; Preuede, *pt. s.* proved, 10. 318 ; Preued, b. 7. 168. See **Preouen**.
Preuy, *adj.* privy, R. 3. 111, 325.
Preuyliche, *adv.* secretly, R. 2. 122.
Preyed, *pp.* preyed upon, 23. 86.
Preyen, *v.* pray, b. 11. 57 ; Preye, 1 *pr. s.* pray, a. 7. 39 ; Preyþ, *pr. s.* begs, prays, 3. 71 ; Preyen, *pr. pl. as fut.* shall say in prayer, 4. 468 ; Preiede, 1 *pt. s.* prayed, begged, 2. 77, a. 9. 11 ; Preiȝede, *pt. s.* a. 5. 26 ; Preyede, *pt. pl.* (*with* of = for), prayed, begged, 22. 154 ; Preied of, *pp.* asked for, R. 3. 350 ; Preye of, *imp. pl.* prey for, b. 10. 120.
Preyere, prayer, request, 8. 210, 21. 206 ; Preyoure, 22. 309 ; Preyeres, *pl.* 12. 60. See **Preier**.
Preynte, *pt. s.* winked, glanced, 16. 121, b. 13. 112, b. 18. 21 ; Preynkte, 21. 19. See Sir Ferumbras, ll. 1238, 1365 ; and Glossary. And see note to 16. 121, p. 194. The infin. is *prinken*.
Preynte, impress, stamp, 18. 73. See **Prente**. Short for *empreynte*, i. e. imprint.
Preyse, *ger.* to praise, i. e. worthy of praise, b. 11. 379 ; Preysy, *v.* praise, 8. 263 ; Preyseþ, *pr. s.* approves of, praises, 7. 45 ; Preyseþ, *pr. pl.* 4. 171 ; Preysen, *pr. pl.* b. 11. 248 ; Preyseden, *pt. pl.* b. 10. 342. See **Preisen**.
Preysed, *pt. pl.* appraised, valued, 7. 384. See above.
Preysinge, *s.* appraising, R. 1. 17. See **Preisen**.
Prickid, *pt. s.* incited, R. 2. 122. See **Prikeþ**.
Prien, *pr. pl.* pry, seek, R. 3. 306 ; Pryed, 1 *pt. s.* b. 16. 168. See Cath. Angl. p. 291, n. 4.
Prikeþ, *pr. s.* pricks, wounds, 20. 163 ; Prikkyth, excites, stimulates, R. 3. 14 ; Prikede, *pt. s.* spurred, 21. 331, a. 2. 164 ; Priked, rode fast, 3. 201 ; Pricked, *pp.* ridden, 6. 160. See **Prykie** ; and note, p. 68.
Prikyere, rider, horseman, 11. 134 ;

418   GLOSSARIAL INDEX.

Prikere, a. 10. 8; Priker, b. 10. 308. See **Prykiere**.
Prime, *adj.* prime, vigorous, a. 12. 60, R. 3. 34.
Prime, *s.* prime; Hei3 prime, high prime, i. e. about 9 A.M., a. 7. 105. See note, p. 110.
Princeps huius mundi, prince of this world, 11. 134.
Priour, prior, 13. 10; ·Pryour, 6. 91.
Pris, *s.* price, value, b. 2. 13.
Prison, *s.* prisoner, 21. 59; Prisoun, b. 18. 58; Prisone, b. 15. 339; Prisons, *pl.* prisoners, captives, 8. 277; Prisones, *pl.* prisoners, 10. 34, 72; Prisounes, b. 7. 30. O.F. *prison*, a prisoner. See note, p. 251.
Prisoneres, *pl.* prisoners, captives, b. 3. 136, b. 14. 168, 174.
Priueliche, *adv.* privily. quietly, secretly, 16. 150, b. 11. 109; Priuely, 22. 301. See **Pryueliche**.
Priuy, *adj.* secret, special, R. 2. 108; Priuye, intimate, close, 10. 118; Priue, intimate, familiar, a. 2. 18. See **Pryue**.
Procuratour, proctor, agent, 22. 258, Procuratores, *pl.* 8. 90.
Profrest, 2 *pr. s.* offerest, a. 7. 27; Profreth, *pr. s.* offers, b. 13. 189; puts (forward), 20. 116: Profreþ. *pr. pl.* offer, a. 7. 41; Profre, *pr. pl.* 9. 39; Profrede, *pt. s.* offered, 5. 91, 16. 249; held, 20. 115; Proffrede, *pt. s.* offered (gifts), 5. 67; Profred, b. 13. 381; Profrede, *pt. pl.* offered, 8. 199. Shropsh. *proffer*, to offer.
Prophete. *s.* profit, R. 4. 10, 48.
Prophitable, *adj.* profitable, a. 7. 262.
Propirte, *s.* property, R. 3. 38; Propurtes, *pl.* R. 3. 65.
Propre, *adj.* separate, distinct, b. 10. 237; fine, goodly, b. 13. 51.
Propreliche, *adv.* suitably, with propriety, 16 153; properly, 17. 119; really, b. 14. 283; Proprely, exactly, b. 14. 274.
Propurtes. See **Propirte**.
Proud, *adj.* proud, a. 7. 187; a proud one, a. 2. 43; Prout, 4. 225, 7. 30, 46, 305.
Proud-herte   See **Proute-herte**.
Prouen, *v.* prove, try, test, 1. 39, 11. 120, 19. 59, 23. 275; Proue, 1 *pr. s.* prove, 19. 216; Prouyd, *pt. s.* proved, R. 4. 88; Proueden, 1 *pt. pl.* tried, attempted sin, b. 7. 186. See **Preuen**.
Prouendre, food, fodder, b. 13. 243. '*Prouende*. pabulum;' Levins.
Prouendreres, *pl* men who hold prebends, a. 3. 45. See below; and Cath Angl. p. 292.
Prouendres, *pl.* prebends, 4. 32. O.F. *provendre*, 'bénéfice ecclesiastique;' Roquefort. From Lat. *præbenda*, a ration, allowance, which became O.F. *provende*, and then *provendre*, with excrescent *r*. Cf. E *provender*, which is the same word.
Prouendreþ, *pr. s* maintains, supports, provides with prebends, 4. 187. From *prouendre*, sb.
Prouincials, *adj. pl.* provincial, 10. 342. See note.
Prouisours, *pl.* provisors. i. e. persons named by the pope to a living not vacant, 3. 182, 4. 184. See notes.
Prout; *see* **Proud**.
Proute-herte, *adj.* proud of heart, 7. 3; Proude-herte, b. 5. 63; Proudherte. a. 5. 45.
Prower, *s.* purveyor, provider, 22. 260; Prowor, b. 19. 255. See note.
Prude, *s.* pride, 2. 129, 6. 118; Pruide, a. pr. 23; Pruyde, 1. 25; show, pomp, 11. 116.
Prydie, 7. 367. See note.
Pryed, 1 *pt. s.* pried, b. 16. 168. See **Prien**.
Prykie, *v.* to spur away, ride fast, 5. 24; Cam prykye, came riding, 21. 9 (see note); Prykeþ, *pr. s.* rides, 23. 149; Prykieþ, *pr. pl.* stir, incite, 20. 89; Pryked, *pt. s.* spurred, b. 17. 349; Pryked. *pp.* pricked, wounded, 23. 86. See **Prikeþ**.
Prykiere, rider, horseman, 21. 24; Pryker, b. 9. 8. See **Prikyere**.
Pryme, prime, nine o'clock A.M., 9. 119. See **Prime**.
Prymer, a book of elementary religious instruction, 6. 46. See note.
Prynte, mark; Priuy prynte, special mark of distinction (viz. a badge), R. 2. 108
Prys, *s.* price, value, 16. 10, 19. 278. See **Pris**.
Prys, *adj.* prize, chief, 22. 266.
Prysouns, *pl.* prisoners, 17. 322. See **Prison**.
Pryue, *adj.* private, secret, 13. 38, 23. 364; closely connected, familiar, intimate, 19. 98; Pryueie, private, secret, 5. 189; Pryueye, 4. 117; Pryuey, 14. 38; Pryuy, intimate, friendly, 3. 23; Pryues, *pl. as sb.* secret friends b. 2. 177. See **Priuy**.
Pryueliche, *adv.* secretly, 13. 48, 18. 172. See **Priueliche**.
Pryuete, secrets, secret counsel (lit.

GLOSSARIAL INDEX. 419

privity), 14. 231; Pryuytees, *pl.* secrets, 19 5.
Psauter, *s.* psalter, psalms, a. 3. 227; the psalmist, a. 8. 55, 107. See **Sauter.**
Puffe, *v.* puff, breathe hard, blow, 16. 96. See **Poffed.**
Puire, *adj.* pure, mere, a. 5. 13, a. 8. 100. See **Pure.**
Puiten, *v.* put, place, a 9. 95; Puiteþ, *pr. s.* puts, a. 6. 100; Puyteth, *pr. pl.* put, a. 11. 42.
Pukketh. *pr. s.* pokes, pushes, puts, b. 5. 620; Pukked, *pt. s.* incited, b. 5. 643. See **Pokeþ.**
Pul. *v.* pull (?). (prob. a misreading in MS. I.; see Pole); Pulled, 2 *pt. pl.* didst pull, didst pluck (off their feathers), R. 2. 126. See **Pollede.** 'To pulle byrdes, *deplumare;*' Cath. Angl.
Pullory, *s.* pillory, 3.-216.
Pulte, *v.* to push, beat, strike, b. 8. 96; Pulte, *pt. s.* pushed, drove, put, b. 15. 62; pulled, put, b. 11. 157; Pult, put, b. 1. 125. From Lat. *pultare*, frequent. of *pellere.* See **Putten.**
Pulter, rags, R. 2. 165. Cf. Swed. *paltor*, rags, and E. *paltry.* See note.
Punge, *v.* push, drive (lit. goad), a. 9. 88. A.S. *pyngan*, borrowed from Lat. *pungere*, to prick.
Fuple, people, 1. 77. See **Poeple.**
Pur, *prep.* (F. *pour*), for, 9. 169, 267; for the sake of, 11. 11.
Purchace, *v.* purchase, 10 337; Purchasede, *pt. s.* obtained, provided, a. 8. 3. See **Porchace.**
Pure, *adj.* pure, perfect, true, 12. 65; very, 10. 185; mere, 4. 101; alone, 6. 116. See **Puyre, Puire.**
Pure, *adv.* purely, 19. 103; quite, b. 11. 267; very, 8. 20.
Pureliche, *adv.* quite, surely, wholly, 16. 226, 231; simply, 19. 235; Purelich, completely, b. 13. 260.
Purfil, the furred trimming of a dress, b. 4. 116; Purfyle, b. 5. 26. See **Porfil,** and note to 3. 10. F. *pourfiler*, to work on an edge, embroider with thread, adorn; cf. E. *profile.* See below.
Purfild, *pp.* having her robe edged with fur, 3. 10. '*Pourfiler d'or*, to purfle, tinsell, or overcast with gold thread, &c.;' Cotgrave. See above, and note.
Purnele, a concubine, 18. 71. From the common female name *Purnele* or *Pernel;* see note to 5. 111.

Purpos, *s.* purpose, i.e. proposition, 11. 120. See note to b. 10. 115.
Purraile-is, *gen. sing.* (*for* Porailles), of the poor people, R. 2. 165. See **Poraille.**
Pursueth, *pr. s.* follows, b. 11. 180, b. 19. 428; prosecutes, b. 17. 502; Pursuwede, *pt s.* followed, attended, 13. 15; Pursued, followed, b. 11. 14. See **Porsueþ.**
Purtinaunce, *s.* belongings, a. 2. 71; Purtenaunces, *pl.* b. 2. 103. See **Portinaunce.**
Purtraye, *v.* pourtray, draw, b. 3. 62; write, b. 15. 176. See **Portrey.**
Purueye, *v.* provide, supply with, b. 14. 28.
Put, pit, b. 14. 174; Puttes, *pl.* pits, dungeons, 10. 72. See **Putte.**
Puterie. lechery, debauchery, 7. 186. F *puterie* (Cotgrave).
Putour, whoremonger, 7. 172. See above; and cf. F. *putier* (Cotgrave).
Putte, pit, b. 10. 370. Dat. of Put (above).
Putten, *v.* put, 20. 142; set, b. 10. 320; Putteth, *pr. s.* puts, b. 12. 227; Put, *pr. s.* (*short for* Putteth), puts, a. 12. 4; prepares, b.14. 271; Putten, *pr. pl.* put, b. 10. 55; Putte, *pt. s.* put, a. 6. 28; Putte vp, *pt. s.* brought forward (said of a petition), 5. 45; Putten, *pt. pl.* put, placed, 21. 52; Putte, set, 1. 22; Put, *pp.* pushed, b. 14. 207. See **Pulte.**
Puyre, *adj.* pure, clear, b. 13. 166. See **Pure.**
Puwes, *pl.* pews, 7. 144.
Puyteth, *pr. pl.* put, a. 11. 42. See **Puiten, Putten.**
Pycoyse, pickaxe, 4. 465. O.F. *pikois, piquois*, from *pic*, a pike; the E. *pickaxe* is a corrupted form of this M.E. word. See note.
Pye, magpie, 14. 158; Pyes, *gen.* magpie's, b. 12. 227, 253.
Pye, pie; Pye-hele, pie-crust, 10. 345. See note.
Pyement, spiced drink, 21. 412. 'Pyment, drynke, *pigmentum;*' Prompt. Parv.
Pyk, spiked end, point, spike, 11. 94; Pyke, b. 8. 96; Pyk, pike-staff, 8. 180.
Pyked *pp.* peaked, b. 20. 218.
Pyke-herneys, *pl.* plunderers of armour, 23 263. From *pyken*, to pick, steal. and *herneis*, harness, armour. See note.
Pyken *v.* to pick up, hoe, b. 16. 17; Pykeden, *pt. pl.* a. 7. 104.

GLOSSARIAL INDEX.

Pykeporses, pickpockets, lit. pick-purses, 7. 370.
Pykers, pickers, thieves, 6. 17. See note to 23. 263.
Pykoys. See **Pycoyse**.
Pyk-staf, pike-staff, staff furnished with a spike, 7. 329. See **Pyk**.
Pyle, firm foundation, b. 19. 360; Pyles, *pl.* piles, props, b. 16. 23. From F. *pile* = Lat. *pīla*, a stone pier, &c. See **Pile**.
Pylede, *adj. pl.* bald, 7. 370. See *Pilled* in Halliwell; and see **Pillede** above.
Pyler, pillar, 8. 241.
Pylours, *pt.* thieves, robbers, 22. 417. See **Piloure**.
Pynchede, 1 *pt. s.* pinched a piece out, encroached, 7. 267.
Pyne, pain, punishment, suffering, 4. 101, 6. 132, 8. 20. See note, p. 65.
Pynede, *pt. s.* tormented, a. 1. 145; suffered, b. 19. 319. A.S. *pínan*, from *pín*, sb. See above.
Pynne, *v.* bar, bolt, fasten, 23. 298, b. 20. 297; Pynned, 1 *pt. s.* fastened, 7. 219; Pynnyd, *pp.* fastened in, R. 2. 165. See **Pinnede**.
Pynnes, *pl.* pins, pegs, 9. 199.
Pynyng-stoles, stools of punishment, cucking-stools, 4. 79. See note.
Pype, *v.* play on the pipe, b. 13. 232. See **Pipe**.
Pytouslich, *adv.* piteously, 5. 94; Pytously, 2. 77. See **Pitously**.

Quaken, *v.* shiver, tremble with cold, 12. 42; quake, shake, 23. 200; Quake, *v.* quake, shiver, a. 11. 46; Quakede, *pt. s.* quaked, shook, 21. 259; Quook, 21. 64.
Quarters, quarters (of wheat), 5. 61.
Quartrun, *s.* a quarter, a. 5. 131. The form *quarteroun* is in Mandeville, ed. Halliwell, p. 301.
Quashte, *pt. s.* trembled, shook, 21. 64. *Quasser*, the same as *casser*, 'to breake, burst, crash in pieces, quash asunder;' Cotgrave.
Quaþ, 1 *pt. s.* (1) said, 11. 20; Quaþ, *pt. s.* said, quoth, 1. 182, 2. 12; Quatʒ, *pr. s.* quoth, b. 6. 3; Quod, a. 2. 5; Quod, *pt. pl.* R. 3. 234.
Quatriduanus, adj. for four days, b. 16. 114.
Quaued, *pt. s.* quaked, shook, b. 18. 61. '*Quavyn*, as myre, *tremo;*' Prompt. Parv.
Qued, the Evil One, b. 14. 189. See *cwed* in Stratmann. Cf. O Du. *quaedt*,

'bad, malicious, perverse;' *quade*, 'ill, evill, bad, naughty, or wicked;' Hexham. Mod. Du. *kwaad*, bad; *kwade*, the devil. It occurs as late as in Skelton, ed. Dyce, i. 168, l. 4.
Queer, the choir, 6. 60.
Queinteliche, *adv.* curiously, a. pr. 24. See **Queyntely**.
Quelle, *v.* kill, a. 7. 34; Quelt, dead, b. 16. 114. A.S. *cwellan*.
Queme, *v.* please, R. 3. 176. A.S. *cweman*.
Quenche, *v.* quench, destroy, 20. 167; oppress, R. 3. 327; Quencheþ, *pr. s.* 20. 221, 324; Queynte, *pp.* killed, b. 18. 344.
Quentise, quaint array, R. 2. 107; fashion, R. 3. 176. See **Queyntise**, **Qweyntore**.
Queste, inquest, jury, 3. 110, b. 20. 161; Questes, *pl.* inquiries, 12. 22.
Questmongeres, *pl.* men who made a business of conducting inquests, b. 19. 367. The word occurs in Pecock's Repressor.
Queyne, common woman, quean, 9. 46. A.S. *cwén*. See note.
Queynte, *adj.* well-known, notorious, 5. 161; *pl.* cunning, 20. 232. See **Qweyntore**.
Queynte; see **Quenche**.
Queyntely, *adv.* curiously, strangely, 22. 349; Queyntly, cunningly, b. 19. 343.
Queyntest, *adj. superl.* most curious, R. 3. 162.
Queyntise, cunning, art, craft, 21. 299, 22. 354. See **Quentise**. '*Cointise*, quaintnesse, comptnesse, neatness, trimnesse;' Cotgrave. '*Qventyse*, or sleythe, *astucia, calliditas;*' Prompt. Parv.
Quik, *adj.* alive, 18. 305; living, a. 2. 14; Quikke, while living, in his lifetime, b. 13. 10; Quike, *adj.* (while alive, 16. 12; live, 21. 259; *pl.* living, 10. 21. See **Quyke**.
Quik, *adv.* quickly; As quik, as quickly as possible, at once, b. 14. 189. See **Quyk**.
Quite, *v.* requite, repay, 13. 104, 107; ransom, 19. 280; acquit, b. 16. 262; Quiteþ, *pr. s.* pays, makes amends, 17. 32.
Quod. See **Quaþ**.
Quodlibet, anything you please, any proposed subject, b. 15. 375.
Quook, *pt. s.* quaked, shook, 21. 64. See **Quaken**.
Quyk, *adv.* quickly, soon, 16. 283. See **Quik**.

GLOSSARIAL INDEX. 421

Quyke, *adj.* quick, living, alive, 19. 145, 21. 64; *pl.* 22. 196; Quykke, b. 16. 114. See **Quik.**

Quykke, *v.* revive, b. 18. 344; Quykke, 1 *pr. s.* animate, b. 15. 23; Quyke, 17. 183. Pecock has *quykee.*

Quyte, *v.* pay, settle, 14. 76; requite, b. 11. 189; Quyty, *v.* satisfy, 10. 275; make satisfaction for, b. 18. 338, 344; Quyteth, *pr. s.* repays, requites, b. 11. 188; Quyte, *pr. s. subj.* pay for, 21. 390; Quyted, *pp.* settled, satisfied, 9. 107; Quyt, settled, 5. 98; Quytte, *pp.* requited, repaid, b. 18. 355. See **Quite.**

Qweyntore, *adj. comp.* more adorned, more tricked up, a. 2. 14. '*Coint,* quaint, compt, neat, fine, . . . tricked up ;' Cotgrave.

Radde, *pt. s.* advised, counselled, exhorted, 5. 105, 6. 126, 8. 120 ; proposed, 16.-52; *pt. pl.* advised, a. 4. 97 ; Rad, *pp.* advised, bidden, chosen, a. 5. 180. A.S. *rǽdan,* to advise, also to read ; see below.

Radde, *pt. s.* read, 4. 491 ; Raddest, 2 *p.* hast thou read, a. 3. 244 ; Rad, *pp.* read, 4. 499, 12. 274. See **Reden.**

Radegowndes, *pl.* running sores, esp. sores in the eyes, 'redgum,' 23. 83. See the note.

Rafte, *pp.* reft, taken away, R. 1. 6. See **Reuen.**

Rageman, (1) the devil, 19. 122; Raggeman, b. 16. 89; (2) a papal bull, 1. 73; Ragemon, a. pr. 72 ; Ragman, b. pr. 75. See notes, pp. 10, 238.

Ragged, ragged, b. 11. 33 ; rough, a. 10. 120.

Raghte, *pt. s.* reached, seized, 1. 73. See **Rauhte, Rau3te.**

Rakere, scavenger, lit. raker, 7. 371 ; Rakyer, b. 5. 322. See note.

Ramis Palmarum, Palm-Sunday, b. 18. 7.

Ransake, *v.* despoil, 19. 122.

Rape, *s.* haste, b. 5. 333. See below. 'Rape, or haste;' Prompt. Parv.

Rape, *imp. s. reflex.* hurry thyself, hasten, make haste, 5. 7, 6. 102, 8. 8; 2 *pr. pl. subj.* 9. 125; Rapede, *pt. s. refl.* hastened, 20. 77 ; Raped, b. 17. 79. Icel. *hrapa,* to hasten. 'Rapyn, or hastyn ;' Prompt. Parv.

Rapelich, *adv.* hastily, quickly, b. 16. 273; Rapely, b. 17. 49, R. pr. 13. See **Rape, Rapliche.**

Rapliche, *adv.* quickly, hastily, 7. 383 ; Raply, 20. 48. See **Rapeliche, Rappliche.**

Rappe, *v.* hasten, hurry ; Rappe adoune, hurry along, ride quickly (throughout), 2. 91 ; Rappynge, *pres. part.* hurrying, hasting, a. 4. 23. See **Rapliche, Rape.**

Rappliche, *adv.* hastily, 19. 291. See **Rapliche.**

Rascaile, rascal deer, lean deer, R. 2. 119; Rasskayle, R. 2. 129.

Rascled, *pt. s.* stretched himself, 8. 7. Frequentative of *rax,* to stretch. See note.

Rat, *pr. s.* (*for* Redeth), reads, 4. 410, 416 ; Men rat, people read, 14. 5, 20. 233. See **Reden**; and see note, p. 51.

Rathe, *adv.* early, soon, 11. 139, 12. 90. A.S. *hraðe,* quickly.

Raþer, *adv.* sooner, rather, 5. 5, 9. 44, 10. 123; more quickly, more readily, b. 10. 456 ; earlier, beforehand, b. 13. 84; The raþer, very soon, 20. 67 ; Raþere, sooner, 1. 117, 2. 144. See above.

Rathest, *adv. superl.* soonest, 7. 392, 10. 148, 13. 223. See **Rathe.**

Raton, a rat, b. pr. 158; Ratoun, b. pr. 167; Ratones, *pl.* 1. 165, 198, 215; b. pr. 146. F. *raton ;* cf. Span. *raton.* See note, p. 17. '*Hic rato,* raton ;' Wright's Vocab. i. 187; '*Hic sorex,* a raton ;' ibid. 220.

Ratoner, ratcatcher, 7. 371, a. 5. 165 ; Ratonere, b. 5. 322.

Raueneres, *gen. pl.* robbers, 18. 43, 47. From the verb *to ravin;* formed from O.F. *ravine,* sb. = Lat. *rapina,* plunder ; see **Raveyn.**

Rauesshede. See **Rauischede.**

Rauest, 2 *pr. s.* dost thou rave, art thou mad, 21. 194; Rauestow, *for* Rauest þou, b. 18. 186; Raued, 1 *pt. s.* I raved, b. 15. 10.

Raveyn, rapine, R. 2. 159. O.F. *ravine,* Lat. *rapina.*

Rauhte, *pt. s.* was stretched, was extended, 5. 179 ; raught, i.e. reached, got, a. pr. 72 ; reached, a. 9. 30. See **Rau3te, Raghte.** A.S. *rǽcan,* to reach, extend, pt. t. *ic rǽhte.*

Rauischede, *pt. s.* ravished, a. 4. 34; Rauisshed, b. 4. 49 ; Rauyschede, 5. 57 ; Rauysshed, plundered, b. 19. 52 ; Rauesshede, *pt. s.* harrowed, ravaged, 22. 52; charmed, 3. 16 ; Rauisshed, *pp.* carried away, b. 11. 6; Raueshed, 12. 168, 290. See Cath. Angl.

Raunceoun, *s.* ransom, b. 18. 350.
Raunson, 1 *pr. s.* ransom, redeem, 21. 398.
Rauȝte, *pt. s.* reached, b. 8. 35; got, b. pr. 57; was extended, b. 4. 185. See Rauhte, Raghte.
Ray, *s.* array, R. 3. 125. Short for *array.*
Ray, *adj.* made of striped cloth, a. 3. 277. See Rayes.
Rayed, *pp.* arrayed, R. 3. 120. Short for *arrayed.*
Rayes, *pl* striped cloths, 7. 217. Also called *cloths of raye;* from F. *raie,* a stripe, Lat. *radius.* See note. '*Hoc stragulum,* ray;' Wright's Vocab. i. 238.
Raymen, *pr. pl.* roam about, make royal progresses, a. 1. 93. To make a progress was esteemed a royal duty; the B. text has *riden.*
Reall, *adj.* royal, R. 3. 361. O.F. *real,* Lat. *regalis.*
Realles, *s. pl.* royal personages, R. 3. 301; *hence* Realles kynde, the kindred of men of royal blood, relatives to the blood royal, R. 1. 91.
Realte, *s.* pomp, royal state, a. 11. 224, R. 1. 53; Reaulte, 17. 52; Reaute, b. 10. 335. See above.
Reame, realm, kingdom, 1. 192, 4. 266; Reaum, a. 11. 259; Reames, *pl.* 2. 92; Reaumes, 11. 104; Realmes, a. 1. 93. See Reome, Reume, Rewme.
Reaute. See Realte.
Rebukie, *v.* rebuke, 1. 110; Rebuked, *pp.* blamed, R. 3. 221; abused, 17. 15.
Recche, *v.* reck, care, 5. 69; Reccheth, *pr. s.* cares, 21. 2, 22. 450; Recche, *pr. s. subj. as in* Haue þat recche, have him who cares, 9. 127; Recchep, *pr. pl.* 4. 391; Recchith, *pr. pl.* R. 3. 120; Recche, *imp. s.* reck, care, 5. 34, 12. 195; Recchep, *imp. pl.* 10. 101; Recching, *pres. part.* caring, recking, 4. 376. See note, p. 111. See Rouȝte.
Reccheles, *adj.* reckless, careless, b. 18. 2. See Recheles.
Recchelesly, *adv.* recklessly, b. 11. 125. See Rechelesliche.
Recetteþ, *pr. s.* harbours, 4. 501. Formed from the sb. *recet,* a place of refuge or resort, lit. receptacle.
Recettor, harbourer, 4. 501. See above.
Recheles, *adj.* careless, reckless, 13. 64, 21. 2. See Reccheles.
Recheles, *adj. as sb.* recklessness; But recheles hit make, unless recklessness cause it (to be otherwise), a. 10. 51. See above.
Rechelesliche, *adv.* recklessly, 14. 154. See Recchelesly.
Rechelesnesse, recklessness, carelessness, 9. 259; Rechelesnes, 12. 195; Recchelesnes, b. 11. 33. Misspelt *wretchlessness* in our prayer-books.
Rechen, *v.* reach, b. 11. 353; suffice, b. 14. 230; extend, 17. 73; Rechen, *pr. pl.* reach to, 20. 144; Reche, *imp. s.* reach, hand over, 21. 283.
Recheþ (*other MSS.* Richen), *pr. pl.* grow rich, a. 3. 74.
Reclayme, reclaim (in falconry), R. 2. 182. See Strutt, Sports and Pastimes, b. i. ch. 2, § 9.
Reclused, *pp.* shut up, withdrawn from the world, 5. 116.
Recomendeth, *pr. s.* recommends, b. 15. 228.
Reconforted, *pp.* comforted again, b. 5. 287.
Recordare, i.e. say *recordare,* b. 4. 120. See note to 5. 116.
Recorde, *s.* record, 4. 346; witness, b. 18. 85.
Recorde, *v.* record, set down, 4. 474, 5. 29; Recorden, *v.* remember (*or* declare), 18. 322, b. 15. 601; Recorde, 1 *pr. s.* witness, b. 18. 197; Recordeden, *pt. pl.* declared, 5. 151.
Recouer, *s.* recovery, 20. 67.
Recoure, *v.* recover, b. 18. 350; Recoeure, b. 19. 239.
Recourere, *s.* recovery, means of remedy, b. 17. 67.
Recrayed, *pp.* recreant, b. 3. 257. See below. *Recrayed* occurs in Dyce's Skelton, i. 189, l. 26; 207, l. 4; 210, l. 45.
Recreaunt, *adj.* recreant, defeated, 21. 105. See note. *Recreyande* = recreant, Roland and Otuel, l. 342.
Recreiȝede, *adj.* recreant, a. 3. 244. See Recrayed.
Rect, *adj.* direct, immediate (in relation), 4. 336, 344, 357.
Red, *s.* advice, 5. 29, 7. 270; Redis, *pl.* counsels, R. 3. 261. A S. *ræd.*
Reddere, means of restitution, 7. 322; *Reddite,* the commandment to make restitution, 7. 316; *Redde quod debes,* pay what you owe, 22. 187. See note, p. 88, last line.
Rede, *adj.* red, 3. 13, 18. 200.
Redeles, a riddle; Rede redeles, to read or explain a riddle, b. 13. 184; explanation, interpretation, b. 13. 167.

GLOSSARIAL INDEX. 423

A.S. *rǽdels*, a riddle ; from *rǽdan*, to interpret.
Redeles, *adj.* devoid of counsel, R. 1. 1. Cf. Ethelred the *Unready*.
Redelyche, *adv.* easily, readily, 5. 184; Redely, R. pr. 54 ; certainly, R. 2. 69. See **Rediliche**.
Redemptor, Redeemer, b. 11. 201.
Reden. *v.* talk about, give counsel about, b. 11. 98 ; Rede, *v.* advise, b. 4. 9, 29; Rede, 1 *pr. s.* advise, counsel. 2. 172 ; explain, 3. 14 ; Rede, *pr. s. subj.* advise, 5. 5 ; Red, *imp. s.* advise, counsel, 5. 108 ; Rede, *imp. s.* b. 4. 113; Redde, *pt. s.* instructed, bade, b. 5. 485. A.S. *rǽdan ;* see below.
Reden, *v.* read, a. 8. 90 ; Rede, *v.* 1. 205 ; read (with a punning reference to *counsel*), R. 3. 258 ; explain, b. 13. 184 ; Redyn, *pr. pl.* read, a. 12. 22 ; Reddestow, 2 *pt. s.* didst thou read, b. 3. 257 ; Redde, *pt. s.* b. 3. 334 ; Redeth, *imp. pl.* read, R. pr. 54; Red, *pp.* a. 11. 218. See above; and see **Radde**, **Rat**.
Reden, *pt. pl.* rode, R. 1. 53. See **Ryden**.
Redes, *pl.* reeds, b. 18. 50. See **Reodes**.
Redi, *adj.* ready, in readiness, a. 2. 130, a. 4. 155.
Rediliche, *adv.* readily, easily, a. 4. 153 ; Redilyche, willingly, 7. 91 ; Redili, R. 3. 347. See **Redelyche**.
Redyngkynge, a kind of feudal retainer, a lacquey, 7. 372 ; Redyngkynges, *pl.* retainers, 3. 112. They were also called *Rodknightes* (roadknights); see Minsheu's Dict. and Spelman. Cf. A.S. *rádcniht*, a roadservant, riding youth, soldier ; *rídend*, one who rides, chevalier.
Reed, *s.* plan, design, 1. 215 ; Reede, counsel, R. 3. 125. See **Red**.
Reed, *pt. s.* read, R. 3. 119. See **Reden**.
Reeue, bailiff, 22. 462. See **Reue**.
Reeuell, *s.* revel, R. 4. 20. See **Reuel**.
Reeue-rolles, *pl.* reeve-rolls, 22. 465. See note ; and see **Reeue**.
Refuse, *v.* reject, b. 17. 177 ; Refusy, *ger.* to reject, 4. 369 ; Refuseden, *pt. pl.* refused, 14. 142 ; Reffusynge, *pres. part.* rejecting, R. 1. 91.
Registre, *s.* list, 23. 271.
Registrer, registrar, agent, keeper of a register, 22. 259; Regystreres, *pl.* b. 2. 173.
Regnen, *v.* reign, rule, be king, be supreme, 21. 441 ; Regne, *v.* 1. 140; Regne, 1 *pr. s.* reign, 5. 171 ; Regnest, 2 *pr. s.* 14. 186 ; Regneþ, *pr. s* rules, 2. 117; extends, reaches, 23. 381 ; Regnen, *pr. pl.* rule, 15. 174; Regnede, *pt. s.* 22. 52 ; Regned, *pt. s.* became king, reigned, b. 19. 52 ; Regneden, *pt. pl.* reigned, a. 2. 35 ; Regnyd, R. 3. 345.
Regratour, retail-dealer, 7. 232 ; Regratere, b. 5 226 ; Regratours, *pl.* retailers, 4. 113, 118 ; Regrateres, b. 3. 90. F. *regrattier*, Ital. *rigattiere*, a huckster. Cf. Span. *regatear*, to wriggle, also to haggle, sell by retail. See note to 4. 82.
Regratrye, retail dealing, 4. 82. See above.
Regum, i. e. *liber Regum*, the Book of Kings, 4. 410. See note.
Rehercen, *v.* rehearse, repeat, enumerate, declare, 13. 35 ; Reherce, 5. 150, 10. 341 ; Rehersen, a. 8. 177 ; Reherseth, *pr. s.* rehearses, declares, b. 10. 293 ; Reherce, *pr. s. subj.* may declare, 10. 350; Rehercede, *pt. s.* repeated, 1. 198 ; Reherced, spoke, 7. 1 ; Rehersede, repeated, a. 4. 134 ; Rehersed, a. 5. 43 ; Rehersid, *pt. pl.* rehearsed, R. 3. 315 ; Reherced, *pp.* declared, 14. 225 ; declared (to), told, b. 11. 405 ; Reherce, *imper. s.* repeat, 2. 22, 7, 164. O.F. *rehercer*, lit. to harrow over again, hence, to repeat.
Reioysen, *v.* cheer, rejoice, 18. 198.
Reison, counsel, 1. 190. See **Resoun**.
Reken, **Rekene**. See **Rekne**.
Rekeouered, *pt. s.* arose, came to life again (lit. recovered), 22. 162. See **Rekeuere**.
Rekeuere, *v.* recover, regain, 22. 245. See **Rekeouered**.
Rekne, *v.* reckon, account, give account, 16. 285; reckon up, b. 1. 22 ; Rekene, *v.* reckon up, account, 5. 171 ; reckon, 2. 22 ; give account of, b. 14. 210; Reken, a. 2. 96.
Relacion, relation, 4. 344, 346, 363 ; Relacions, *pl.* forms of affinity, 4. 335.
Relatif, *s.* relative (in grammar), 4. 357.
Reles, *s.* release, a. 7. 83 ; Relees, forgiveness, 9. 99.
Relesed, *pp.* forgiven, 4. 62 ; Relessed, b. 3. 58. 'Relecyn, *relaxo ;*' Prompt. Parv.
Releuen, *v.* raise up again, 21. 393 ; Releue, *v.* relieve, 17. 314; give alms

to, 14. 70; assist, 10. 36; raise up again, restore, 21. 145; redeem, 18. 313; Releuede, *pt. s.* relieved, comforted, 14. 21.
Religion, a religious order, or religious orders generally, 10. 221, 11. 88, a. 5. 37. See note to 11. 88.
Religiouse, *adj. pl.* persons belonging to some religious order, 23. 59; Religious, 6. 148, 165; Religiouses, *pl.* religious men, b. 10. 317.
Rely, *ger.* to wind on a reel, 10. 81. 'Relyn. wythe a rele, *Alabriso*.' Prompt. Parv. See note.
Relyede, *pt. s.* rallied, took courage again, 23. 148. Cf. E. *rally;* and see Gloss. to Barbour's Bruce.
Remed, *pt. s.* stretched himself (?), 8. 7. Such is Stratmann's explanation; see Reyme. See *remen* in Stratmann, which, as he explains, is equivalent both to *ræmen*, to stretch, and *hremen*, to roar. Either will do.
Remenant, remnant, rest, remainder, 13. 48, 20. 204, 23. 292.
Remissioun, remission, forgiveness, 9. 99.
Renable, *adj.* eloquent, b. pr. 158. See note, p. 17.
Rendren, *v.* construe, translate, 18. 322; Rendreþ, *pr. s.* translates, 11. 88; Rendred, 1 *pt. s.* taught, gave, 7. 217; Rendred, *pp.* translated, b. 8. 90; Rendret, a. 9. 82. See note, p. 135.
Reneye, *v.* abandon, deny, reject, 13. 59, 60; Renye, b. 11. 121; Reneyed, *pp.* renegate, renegade, abject, 13. 64. O.F. *reneier* (F. *renier*); from Lat. *renegare*.
Renk, man, 8. 8, 11. 24; Renke, 15. 110, 16. 285; Renkes, *pl.* men, creatures, 10. 332, 14. 187, 192. A.S. *rinc*, a warrior, man.
Renne-aboute, i. e. Run-about, b. 6. 150.
Rennen, *v.* run, 4. 271, 17. 348; Renne, 13. 63, 19. 291; Rennen, *pr. pl.* run, 3. 193; Renne, *pr. pl.* hasten, 14. 32; Rennynge, *pr. pt.* running (his course), running, 21. 105, 169; moving, having reference, 4. 336; Rennyng, *pres. pt.* (while) running (his course), b. 18. 100: Rennenge, *pr. pt.* running, b. 15. 453. A.S. *rennan*. See Ron.
Rennere, *s.* runner, a. 11. 208; Renneris, *pl.* runners, roamers, a. 11. 199.
Rent, *s.* rent, revenue, R. 4. 12; Rentes, *pl.* rents, income, 15. 185, a. 3. 74.

Rental, rental, amount of property; Remission on that rental, a release from the dues recorded in the rental, 9. 99.
Renten, *v.* to provide with rents, endow, 10. 36.
Reodes, *pl.* reeds, 21. 50. A.S. *hréod*. See Redes.
Reome, realm, kingdom, 4. 191, 204, 255. See Reame.
Reot, *s.* riot, R. 4. 20.
Repe, *v.* reap, 6. 15; 1 *pr. s.* 7. 270; Repen, *pr. pl.* 7. 270. See Rope.
Repentestow þe, 2 *pr. s. refl.* repentest thou, b. 5. 449; Repentedestow, 2 *pt. s.* didst thou repent, b. 5. 232.
Repereyue, one employed to look after the reapers, a head - reaper (lit. reap-reeve), 6. 15. See Reyue, Reue.
Repreff, *s.* reproof, R. pr. 56. Spelt *repreef* in Prompt. Parv.
Repreue, *v.* prove wrong, disprove, b. 10. 345; reprove, R. 3. 197; Repreueth, *pr. s.* reproves, b. 10. 261; Reproueþ, *pr. s.* reproves, opposes, 4. 389; confutes, b. 18. 149; Repreued, *pt. pl.* blamed, b. 12. 138. 'Reprevyn, *reprehendo;'* Prompt. Parv.
Repugnen, *v.* deny, 1. 136.
Rerages, *pl.* arrears of debt, b. 5. 246. See Arerage.
Resceyte, *s.* receiving, R. 2. 98.
Reremys, *s. pl.* bats (which only come out *at night*), R. 3. 272. A.S. *hréremús*, a bat.
Residue, *s.* residue, rest, remainder, a. 5. 240, a. 7. 93.
Resonable, *adj.* proper, b. 13. 286; talkative, eloquent, 1. 176, 7. 33. From O.F. *reson* (F. *raison*), used in the sense of 'language' or 'discourse' as well as 'reason.'
Resonabliche, *adv.* reasonably, properly, according to reason, 13. 18.
Resoun, *s.* reason, b. 10. 112, b. 15. 28; respect, regard, 4. 376; Reson, 3. 50; talk, b. 14. 307; Resun, reason, a. 1. 22; To reson, (instructs men) unto reason, 15. 49 [it does not seem to be a gerund here]; Resones, *gen. sing.* of reason, 22. 88; Resones, *pl.* reasons, 12. 38. See Reison.
Reste, *v.* rest, remain, a. 4. 155; *ger.* a. 8. 126; Resteth, *pr. s. as fut.* shall remain, a. 4. 95; Rest, *pr. s.* (*short for* Resteth), resteth, rests, 1. 186; Reste me, 1 *pt. s.* I rested myself, b. 18. 7; Rest, *imp. s.* delay, stay, b. 10. 159.

GLOSSARIAL INDEX. 425

Restitue, *v.* make restitution, 7. 299, 344; Restitue, 1 *pr. pl.* make amends, 11. 54. F. *restituer.*
Restorie, *v.* restore, 13. 146; Restore, 1 *pr. s.* declare again, explain fully (to be taken in close connection with l. 3), R. 3. 1.
Retenauns, *s.* retinue, company, b. 2. 53; Retenaunce, a. 2. 35; Retynaunce, 3. 55. See note, p. 33.
Retribucion, repayment, 4. 340.
Reue, reeve, steward, farm-bailiff, agent, 3. 112, 4. 311; Reues, *pl.* 3. 180. A.S. *geréfa.* See Reyue, Reeue.
Reuel, revel (but used as the name of a place), 23. 181; Reueles, *pl.* feasts, entertainments, revels, 8. 102. See Reeuel.
Reuely, *pr. s. subj.* be rivelled, be wrinkled, 11. 265. Later *rivel.*
Reuen, *v.* deprive, rob, 21. 310; reave, take away, carry away, 17. 1, 19. 122; Reue, *pr. s. subj.* deprive, 21. 301; Reuede, *pt. s.* deprived, 4. 329; Reueþ, *imper. pl.* deprive, take away from, bereave of, 5. 180. A.S. *réafian.* See Rafte.
Reuerence, *v.* respect, honour, worship, 20. 259; Reuerenceþ, *pr. s.* salutes, shows respect to, 10. 123; Reuerencen, *pr. pl.* do reverence to, 21. 269; Reuerenceþ, *pr. pl.* honour, 15. 182; Reuerencede, 1 *pt. s.* worshipped, 19. 244; saluted, 14. 248; Reuerencede, *pt. pl.* did honour to, worshipped, 22. 73; Reuerenced, *pp.* honoured, b. 12. 260.
Reuerences, *pl.* obeisances, 10. 191.
Reuerentloker, *adv.* in a higher place, in a place of greater honour, 9. 44.
Reueres, *pl.* thieves, robbers, b. 14. 182; Reuers, 14. 58. See Reuen.
Reuers, *adj.* reverse, opposite, 13. 210.
Reuested, *pp.* dressed, attired, 6. 112. See Cath. Angl.
Reufol, *adj.* sad, miserable, 7. 237; Reuful, merciful, b. 14. 148.
Reufully, *adv.* pitiably, miserably, b. 12. 48.
Reule, *s.* rule, order, ordinance, 23. 247, 265. See Rewele, Rewle.
Reulen, *v.* govern, rule, 11. 104; Reule, *v.* 22. 468; Reulen, *pr. pl.* b. 7. 10; Reuleþ, *imp. pl.* 20. 225. See Reuwele, Rewele, Rewle.
Reume, realm, kingdom, b. 8. 105; Reumes, *pl.* b. 7. 10. See Reame.
Reumes, *pl.* rheums, colds, catarrhs, 23. 83. See Rewmes.

Reuthe, ruth, pity, mercy, compassion, 2. 172, 4. 118; Reuth, b. 15. 495. See Rewthe.
Reuwele, *v.* rule, govern, 17. 252. See Reulen.
Reward, *s.* regard, notice, heed, 5. 40, 20. 247; Rewarde, b. 17. 265.
Rewarden, *v.* recompense, b. 11. 129; Rewardy, reward, 22. 193; Rewarde. 2 *pr. pl.* regard, look after, b. 14. 145; Rewarded, *pt. s.* regarded, watched over, b. 11. 361. O.F. *rewarder*, to regard.
Rewe, *v.* rue, b. 16. 142; have pity on, R. 2. 118; Rewe, *pr. s. subj. impers.* it will grieve him, it makes him feel compassion, 21. 440; Rewe, *imp. s.* have pity, 7. 322; Reweth, *imp. pl.* have pity, R. 1. 1. A.S. *hréowaþ*, to grieve.
Rewe, row, 4. 107; By rewe, in order, 2. 22; Rewis, *pl.* rows, lines, R. pr. 54.
Rewele, *s.* rule, a. 11. 202. See Reule.
Rewele, *v.* rule, govern, 12. 214; Rewely, 1 *pr. s.* 5. 180; Rewelede, *pt. s.* ruled, governed, 14. 183. See Reulen.
Rewet, a small trumpet, 7. 400. See Ruwet, and see *Ruwet* in Halliwell.
Rewfullich, *adv.* compassionately, b. 14. 152. See Reufol.
Rewle, *v.* behave (lit. rule), R. 3. 272. See Reulen.
Rewlyche, *adj.* pitiable, miserable, a. 12. 78, *in the* Ingilby MS.
Rewme, realm, kingdom, b. pr. 177, b. 10. 76. See Reame, Reume.
Rewmes, *pl.* rheums, b. 20. 82. See Reumes.
Rewthe, *sb.* pity, R. pr. 21. See Reuthe.
Reyme, *v.* reach after, clutch, seize, 14. 96. See note. It is perhaps allied to O. H. G. *rámén*, to strive after, and the (doubtful) A.S. *ræman*, given in Leo's Glossar. In Wyclif's Works, ed. Matthew, p. 185, *raymeþ* perhaps means 'stretches' or 'tortures,' with reference to the false swearing then so common. In the Ancren Riwle, p. 72, l. 3, I explain *reame oðres* by 'grasp at that of another.' See *ræmen* in Stratmann.
Reyn, rain, 20. 315.
Reyne, *v.* rain, shed rain, 15. 24; Reyneþ, *pr. s.* 20. 315; Reyne, *pr. s. subj.* it rains, 6. 165 (see note); Reynede, *pt. s.* fell (as rain), 16. 270.
Reyne-bowe, *s.* rainbow, R. 3. 248.

Reynkes, *pl.* men, a. 4. 134. See **Renk**.
Reyue, reeve, bailiff, 8. 33, 12. 298. See **Reue**.
Rial, *s.* royal person, R. 3. 340. See below.
Riall, *adj.* royal, R. 3. 125.
Ribanes, *pl.* ribbons set with gold and gems, b. 2. 16.
Ribaud, *s.* villain, 19. 170, 21. 50; Ribaude, i.e. the Evil One, b. 14. 203; Ribaudes. *pl.* sinners, b. 5. 512; ribalds, worthless creatures (with reference to the seven sins), 17. 46. See note to 8. 150.
Ribaudour, *s.* profligate fellow, a. 7. 66. See **Rybaudour**, **Ribaud**.
Ribaudrie, ribaldry, sin, 1. 45.
Ribbe-bon, rib, b. 9. 34.
Ribbes, *s. pl.* ribs, a. 4. 149.
Ribibor, *s.* player on the *ribibe* or rebeck (a kind of fiddle), a. 5. 165. See **Rybibour**. The *ribibe* is said to have had three strings, to have been played with a bow, and to have been introduced into Spain by the Moors.
Riche, *adj.* rich, a. 1. 149; *pl.* rich (men), 6. 183. See **Ryche**.
Richesse, wealth, riches, 12. 109, a. 11. 224; Ricchesse, b. 2. 17; Richchesse, b. 14. 104; Richesses, *pl.* riches, a. 3. 24; Ricchesses, b. 3. 23. F. *richesse*, a sing. sb. See **Rychesse**.
Ride, *pp.* ridden, 6. 158. See **Ryden**.
Ridere, *s.* rider, horseman, a. 11. 208.
Riffleris, *s. pl.* riflers, R. 3. 197. See below, and see **Ryfie**.
Rifled, 1 *pt. s.* robbed, 7. 236; *pp.* robbed, plundered, 20. 90.
Rigge, *s.* back, R. 3. 287. See **Rugge**, **Ryg**. A.S. *hrycg*.
Rigge-bon, *gen.* back-bone's, b. 5. 349.
Right, *adv.* very, 21. 220.
Righte, *adv.* very, exact, 19. 291.
Riht, *adj.* right (hand), a. 3. 57. See **Righte**.
Riht, *adv.* rightly, exactly, a. 2. 172. See **Right**.
Rihtful, *adj.* righteous, a. 9. 17. See **Riʒtful**, **Ryghtful**.
Rihtfuliche, *adv.* righteously, a. 8. 10. See **Ryghtfulliche**.
Ringen; see **Rongen**.
Riott, *s.* riot, indulgence, R. 1. 6.
Ripe, *ger.* to ripen, b. 19. 314; Ripe, *pr. s. subj.* will ripen, 13. 232.
Ripen, *adj. pl.* ripe (ones), 19. 107. Cf. A.S. *-an*, as pl. adj. -ending in the definite declension. See **Rypen**.

Ritt (*for* Rideth), *pr. s.* rides, b. 4. 13; is moving about, running about, b pr. 171; Ritte (*better* Ritt), rides, b. 4. 24. See **Ryt**.
Rith moche, very much, R. pr. 16. See **Right**, **Riʒt**.
Rith, *s.* justice; þat rith wolde þei hadde, that which justice intended they should have, R. 2. 137; Rithis, *s. pl.* rights, R. 3. 269.
Rithfully, *adv.* justly, R. pr. 48.
Riʒt, *adv.* exactly, just, b. ·10. 297; directly, b. 12. 293; Riʒte, very, b. 11. 260. See **Ryʒt**.
Riʒt, *adj.* very, same, b. 17. 49; Riʒte, right, true, b. 10. 456.
Riʒte, *s.* right, claim, b. 10. 343.
Riʒtful, *adj.* righteous, just. true, b. pr. 127, b. 1. 54; regular, b. 14. 291; as sb. the righteous man, b. 8. 22; *pl.* righteous, b. 3. 241.
Riʒtfulliche, *adv.* rightly, honestly, justly, b. 11. 121.
Riʒthond, *s.* right-hand, a. 3. 234.
Riʒtyn, *v.* set right, R. pr. 13.
Robbour, *s.* robber, a. 5. 242; Robbours, *pl.* 14. 58.
Robbynge, *s.* robbery, being robbed, b. 14. 301.
Robeth, 2 *pr. pl.* robe. give clothes to, clothe, b. 15. 329; Robed, *pp.* dressed, 11. 1.
Roche, rock, 20. 12; Roches, *pl.* 21. 259. F. *roche*.
Rocke, *ger.* to rock, 10. 79.
Rod, *pt. s.* rode, 5. 14, 40; Rood, R. 3. 361. See **Ride**, **Ryden**.
Roddede, *pt. pl.* reddened, 16. 108.
Rode, *s.* rood, cross, b. 15. 506, a. 5. 145; *dat.* 3. 3, 5. 131.
Rody, *adj.* ruddy, red, 16. 108.
Roff, *s.* roof, R. 3. 248.
Rogged, *pt. s.* shook, b. 16. 78. Icel. *rugga*, to rock a cradle; see *ruggen* in Stratmann.
Rokked, *pt. s.* rocked, b. 15. 11.
Roileth, *pr. s.* roves, wanders about, b. 10. 297. See note to 6. 151. And cf.—' But ye *roile* abroade;' Ralph Roister Doister, A. ii. sc. 3.
Rolle, *pr. s. subj.* enrol, register, b. 5. 278.
Romares, *pl.* roamers, pilgrims, 4. 120.
Rome, *v.* roam, wander, wander abroad, walk, move about, 13. 48, 63; 16. 27; Romest, 2 *pr. s.* wanderest, 7. 331; Romeþ, *pr. s.* wanders, 10. 147; Romyþ. *pr. s.* 1. 186; Romede, 1 *pt. s.* roamed, wandered, 11. 1; Romed, wandered abroad, 16. 28; wandered,

GLOSSARIAL INDEX. 427

b. 8. 1, a. 9. 1; Romynge, *pres. part.* wandering, 6. 10. See **Rowme**.

Rome-renners, *pl.* Rome-seekers, lit. runners to Rome, 5. 125; Rome-renneres, b. 4. 128. See note. The right sense of the word appears to be 'an agent at the court of Rome.' See Wyclif's Works, ed. Matthew, pp. 23, 494.

Ron, *pt. s.* ran, a. 5. 43; Ronnen, *pp.* hurried, a. 9. 82; Ronne, *pp.* 11. 88. See **Rennen**.

Rone, *pt. s.* rained, b. 14. 66. The usual pt. t. of *reinen* is *reinede*, or *rainde*. See Stratmann.

Ronde, *adj.* round, a. 5. 193; Rounde, b. 5. 349.

Rongen, *pt. pl.* rang, 23. 59.

Ronges, *pl.* rungs, steps of a ladder, 19. 44. A.S. *hrung*. See Cath. Angl.

Roos, 1 *pt. s.* rose, arose, b. 5. 234. See Rys, Ros.

Rooten, *v.* take root, be firmly established, a. 10. 78.

Rop, rope, 19. 157. A.S. *ráp*.

Rope, 1 *pt. s.* reaped, b. 13. 374; Ropen, *pt. pl.* b. 13. 374. From the infin. *repen*, better spelt *ripen*; A.S. *rípan*. See **Repe**.

Ropere, rope-maker, or rope-seller, 7. 372, 387. See note, p. 91.

Rored, *pt. s.* roared, groaned, b. 5. 398; Rorid, R. 2. 119.

Ros, 1 *pt. s.* rose, 19. 244.

Rost, *s.* roast meat, a. pr. 108.

Roste, *v.* toast at the fire, 10. 144.

Rote, root, source, origin, foundation, 13. 247, 21. 324; Rotes, *pl.* roots, 9. 64; Rotis, b. 14. 44; Rotus, R. 2. 140.

Roten, rotten, 17. 253, b. 15. 99.

Roteþ, *pr. pl.* settle, establish, lit. root, 3. 55.

Rotey-time, the time of rutting, b. 11. 329. See **Ruteyed**.

Rotie, *v.* to rot, perish, die, 4. 360; Rotye, *v.* 19. 60; Roten, *v.* b. 10. 112; Roteþ, *pr. s.* rots away, 6. 151; Rotede, *pt. pl.* rotted, 14. 22.

Rouhte, *pt. s. subj. impers.* it would trouble (thee), i.e. thou wouldst reck, 13. 22. See **Rouȝte**.

Roume, *v.* make room for, avoid, 1. 181, 189.

Rouned. *pt. s.* whispered, 5. 14; Rounede, *pt. pl.* 7. 383; Rouneden, a. 5. 176; Rounyng, *pres. part.* whispering, 5. 25. A.S. *rúnian*, to whisper; from *rún*, a rune, mystery, whisper.

Rousti, *adj.* filthy, foul (lit. rusty), a. 7. 66. See **Rusty**.

Route, crowd, company, crew, 1. 165, 3. 62; Routus, *pl.* gangs, R. 1. 16. F. *rout*.

Route, *v.* slumber, settle down, a. 10. 78; Routte, *pt. s.* snored, 8. 7; Routten, *pt. pl.* 15. 95. A.S. *hrútan*, to snore. See **Rutte**.

Routhe, a pity, a sad thing, b. 15. 501.

Rouwe, *adj.* rough, a. 10. 120. A.S. *rúw*, rough.

Rouȝte, recked, cared, 2 *pt. pl.* b. 11. 73. See **Recche**.

Rowen, *v.* to row, 11. 52.

Roweþ, *pr. s.* beams, 2. 114; Rowed, *pt. s.* dawned, 21. 128. See note. Prob. from the sb. *row*, in the sense of beam or ray.

Rowme, *v.* wander about, roam, b. 11. 109, 124. See **Rome**.

Rowmer, roamer, wanderer, b. 10. 306. See **Romares**.

Rowneth, *pr. s.* whispers, b. 4. 13; Rownynge, *pres. pt.* b. 4. 24. See **Rouned**.

Roxed, *pt. s.* stretched himself, b. 5. 398. See note, p. 94.

Roynouse, *adj.* dirty, scabby, 23. 83. F. *roigneux*, 'scabbie, scurvie;' Cotgrave.

Ruel, space between the bed and the wall, lit. narrow lane, 10. 79. F. *ruelle*, dimin. of *rue*. See note. Compare: 'Ay, colonel, for such a woman! I had rather see her *ruelle* than the palace of Louis le Grand;' Farquhar, Constant Couple, i. 1.

Ruele, rule, religious rule or order, 4. 203; rule of life, 6. 144, 148; regulations, 10. 221. See **Ruwele**.

Ruelyng, *s.* rule, 1. 150.

Ruele, *v.* rule, govern, 2. 50; Ruelie, regulate, 1. 215; Ruelest, 2 *pr. s.* rulest, governest, 14. 187.

Rufulliche, sorrowfully, 20. 201.

Rugge, back, b. 14. 212, b. 19. 282. See **Rigge**.

Rugge-bones, *s.* back-bone's, a. 5. 193. See **Riggebon, Rygbones**.

Rulye, *v.* govern, 5. 9; Rulen, *pr. pl.* a. 8. 10. See **Ruele**.

Rusche, *s.* rush, 4. 179, b. 11. 420; Russhe, 14. 239; Russche, a. 3. 137; Russhes, *pl.* 10. 81. See **Ruysshe**.

Russet, reddish-brown cloth, 17. 298; Russett, 11. 1. See note, p. 132.

Rusty, *adj.* filthy, obscene, 9. 75, b. 6. 75. See Rousti. (Lit. 'rusty.') Cf. '*rustynes* of synne,' i.e. filthiness of

VOL. II.   D d

GLOSSARIAL INDEX.

sin; Coventry Mysteries, ed. Halliwell, p. 47.
Ruteyed, *pp.* rutted, copulated, 14. 146. See *Ruit, Ruité* in Cotgrave. And see Rotey-time.
Rutte, *pt. s.* snored, b. 5. 398; 1 *pt. s.* b. 18. 7; *pt. pl.* b. 12. 152. See Route.
Ruwele, *pr. s. subj.* rule, govern, 15. 36. See Ruele.
Ruwet, *s.* small horn, b. 5. 349. '*Ruett*, lituus, parvum cornu est;' Cath. Anglicum. See Rewet.
Ruysshe, *s.* rush, 13. 196. See Rusche.
Rybaud, ribald, wretch, rascal, 11. 215; Rybaudes, *pl.* 7. 435. See Ribaud.
Rybaudour, teller of loose stories, taleteller, 9. 75. See Ribaudour.
Rybaudrie, ribaldry, 12. 199; Rybaudrye, 7. 435. See Ribaudrie.
Rybibour, a player on the ribibe, 7. 371. See Ribibor.
Ryche, *s.* kingdom, b. 14. 179. A.S. *ríce.*
Rychen, *pr. pl.* grow rich, b. 3. 83. See Riche.
Rychesse, riches, 4. 327, 15. 19; Rychesses, *pl.* 10. 191. See Richesse.
Ryden, *v.* ride, ride about, 2. 91, 3. 184, 6. 74; Ryde, 22. 245; Ryde, *pr. pl.* copulate, 14. 154; Ryde, proceed, b. 10. 159; Rydeþ, *imp. pl.* ride, 3. 188; Ryde, *pp.* ridden, b. 11. 329. See Rod, Ride, Reden.
Ryff, *adj.* rife, numerous, R. 2. 5.
Ryfle, *v.* rifle, plunder, 5. 54; Ryffled, *pt. s.* R. 1. 16; Ryfled, *pp.* robbed, 11. 194. See Rifled.
Ryflynge, *s.* plunder, b. 5. 238.
Ryg, back, 10. 144; Rygge, 17. 55, 22. 287. See Rugge, Rigge.
Rygbones, *gen.* of the backbone, 7. 400. See Rugge-bones.
Ryghtful, *adj.* upright, good, 6. 148; righteous, 21. 95; good and just men, 5. 151. See Rihtful.
Ryghtfulliche, *adv.* justly, uprightly, 10. 10; rightly, 13. 60. See Rihtfuliche.
Ryghtfullokest, *adv.* most truly, 21. 476.
Ryghtwisnesse, righteousness, 20. 280, 21. 169. A.S. *rihtwisnes.*
Ryhtful, *adj.* just, right, 4. 377. See Ryghtful.
Ryhtfulliche, *adv.* justly, 2. 50.
Ryme, *s.* verse, 10. 82; Rymes, *pl.* rimes, ballads, 8. 11. A.S. *rim.*
Rynges, *pl.* rings, 1. 73.
Ryngynge, *s.* ringing of bells, 8. 5.

Rypen, *v.* ripen, b. 16. 39; Rypeþ, *pr. s.* 13. 223. See Ripe.
Rys, *imp. s.* rise, 21. 283; Rysen, *pt. pl.* arose, 7. 383.
Ryt, *pr. s.* rideth, rides, goes about, 1. 186. See Ritt.
Ry3t, *adv.* just, exactly, 2. 158, 15. 150; close, exactly side by side, 5. 25. See Ri3t.
Ry3tful, *adj.* righteous, upright, just, 1. 150. See Ryghtful.
Ry3tfulliche, *adv.* uprightly, honestly, 20. 233.

Saaf, *adj.* safe, a. 8. 38, 55; Saaf and sound, a. 9. 29, 44. See Sauf, Saf.
Sad, *adj.* grave, serious, steadfast, sober, firm, constant, 4. 337, 18. 264; Sadde, grave, religious, 11. 31; settled, sober, b. 15. 541; righteous, a. 9. 23, 39.
Sadde, *v.* establish, confirm, b. 10. 242.
Sadder, *adv.* more soundly (with reference to sleep), b. 5. 4.
Saddere, *adj. comp.* steadier, more steadfast, 12. 292.
Saddest, *adj.* steadiest, most resolute (for good), 11. 49.
Sadloker, *adv. compar.* more soundly, a. 5. 4. See Sadder.
Sadman, *s.* steady, upright man, b. 8. 28, 44.
Sadñesse, *s.* firm faith, confidence, b. 7. 150.
Saf, *adj.* safe, 15. 112; Saff, safe, saved, R. pr. 81; Saf and sounde, safe and sound, 11. 38, 40. See Saaf, Sauf.
Saf, *conj.* except, save, 7. 240, 9. 71.
Sage, *adj.* wise, b. 10. 379, b. 13. 444; Sages, *pl.* wise, b. 13. 423. In b. 13. 423, 444, the word is used ironically. Palsgrave has: 'Dissar, a scoffer, *saigefol.*' A *sage fool* was, doubtless, a licensed jester.
Sages, *s. pl.* sages, R. 3. 257; men of pretended wisdom, 8. 83.
Saih, *pt. s.* saw, a. 7. 222. See Sauh, Seigh.
Sailen, *v.* dance, 16. 208. F. *saillir,* Lat. *salire.* See note.
Sak, sack, 9. 8; Sakkes, *pl.* a. 7. 9
Salmes, *gen.* psalm's, b. 3. 247.
Salue, salve, ointment, remedy, 2. 140, 10. 263; cure, b. 13. 248; Salues, *pl.* salves, 23. 336. See notes on p. 127.
Salue, *v.* heal, anoint, 23. 305, b. 10. 271; Saluen, *v.* save, b. 11. 212; Saluede, *pt. s.* salved, treated, 23. 347; Salued, cured, healed, b. 16. 109.
Samen, *adv.* together, in company, 4. 27. A.S. *æt-somne,* together.

GLOSSARIAL INDEX. 429

Sam-rede, *adj.* half-red, half-ripe, 9. 311. A.S. *sám-*, half, Lat. *semi-*.
Sanz, *prep.* without, b. 13. 286. F. *sans*.
Sapheris, *pl.* sapphires, R. 1. 45.
Sapience, the book of Wisdom, 4. 487, 497; 12. 118; b. 6. 237.
Sapienter, correctly, b. 11. 304.
Sarasene, heathen, unbeliever, b. 11. 151; Sarasyn, b. 11. 159; Saracenes, *pl.* b. 3. 325.
Sarmon, sermon, discourse, 4. 121, 6. 201; Sarmoun, b. 3. 93; Sarmons, *pl.* 15. 201.
Sarrer, *adv.* more sorely, more, 1. 171, 16. 286.
Sauacion, salvation, saving, 4. 355, 6. 199; Sauacioun, b. 5. 126.
Sauce, *s.* sauce, 9. 274.
Saue, *prep.* except, save, 3. 250; *conj.* a. pr. 77.
Saue, *v.* save, keep, preserve, a. 3. 190, a. 8. 17, 27; Don sauen = cause to be saved, a. 8. 164; Saue, *pr. s. subj.* may (He) save, b. 8. 60. See **Sauye**.
Saueour, Saviour, 8. 145.
Sauerie, *v.* give a savour; To sauerie with thi lippes, to savour (please) thy lips with, 9. 274; Sauer, to give an appetite to, a. 7. 249; Sauereþ, *pr. s.* pleases, delights, 11. 107; Sauere, 2 *p. pl. pr. subj.* like, R. pr. 55. See **Sauoureth**. E. *savour*.
Saueriour, *adj.* more savoury, 19. 65.
Sauete, safety, salvation, 13. 55.
Sauf, *adj.* safe, b. 7. 51; saved, b. 10. 347. See **Saaf, Saf**.
Saufly, *adv.* safely, b. 10. 285.
Sauh, 1 *pt. s.* saw, 1. 231, 3. 9, 12. 51; *pt. s.* 1. 109. See **Seon, Seigh, Seih, Sei3, Seyh**.
Sauhtne, *v.* be reconciled, 5. 2. See note. See **Sau3tne**.
Saule, soul, 2. 35, 39.
Saulee, (*glossed* edulium), food, b. 16. 11. See note, p. 235.
Saumbury, a litter, 3. 178. See note. In the Romance of Sir Launfal, ed. Ritson, 950, we find: 'Her sadell was semyly sett, The *sambus* [trappings] wer grene felvet.' So also '*sambu* of silk,' various reading in King Alisaunder, ed. Weber, l. 176; see p. 373 of his edition. And again, in The Anturs of Arthur, ed. Robson, st. 2, l. 13, MSS. Douce has the reading '*sambutes* [for *sambuces*] of sylke,' where another MS. has *saumhellus* (perhaps a misprint for *saumbellus*).

Saumplarie, example, copy, *hence* instructor, 15. 47.
Saunest, *adv.* (*hardly* Sannest), soonest, 13. 223.
Sauour, *s.* savour, taste, 15. 187; Sauoure, inclination, b. 9. 150; delight, pleasure, b. 7. 148.
Sauoureth, *pr. s.* is satisfactory, is to my taste, b. 8. 108; To sauoure with thi lippes = to please thy lips with (by its nice taste), b. 6. 264. See **Sauerie**.
Saut, assault, attack, 23. 217.
Saute, *v.* leap, tumble, b. 13. 233. F. *sauter*, Lat. *saltare*.
Sauter, psalter, 4. 468, 6. 47; the Psalmist, b. 9. 121; *gen.* Sauter, b. 5. 282.
Sautrien, *v.* play on the psaltery, 16. 208.
Sauye, *v.* to save, protect, 11. 148; Sauy, save, preserve, 2. 80.
Sauyour, Saviour, 8. 121.
Sau3, 1 *p. s. pt.* saw, a. pr. 109. See **Sauh**.
Sau3tne, *v.* be reconciled, b. 4. 2; Sau3tene, a. 4. 2. Cf. A.S. *sahtlian*, to reconcile, from *saht*, peace. The ending *-ne* (Mœso-Goth. *-nan*) gives a passive meaning. See note, p. 54; and see **Sauhtne**.
Sawe, *v.* sow (seed), 10. 6. See **Sowen**.
Sawe, *s.* saying, proverb, 11. 107; Sawes, *pl.* b. 7. 137, b. 9. 93.
Sawt, assault, attack, 23. 300. See **Saut**.
Say, 1 *pt. s.* saw, 4. 128, b. 5. 10. See **Sauh, Seigh, Seih, Sei3, Seyh, Saih**.
Sayn, *v.* say, tell, 19. 262.
Saywel, Say-well, b. 9. 20.
Scalles, *pl.* scales, scabs, b. 20. 82.
Scalones, *pl.* scallions, onions, 9. 310. Cf. Ital. *scalogno*, a scallion, so named from Ascalon; the modern F. form is *échalote*.
Scape, *v.* escape, b. 3. 57.
Scape, hurt, injury, wound, 4. 61, 5. 75, 92, a. 4. 83; Scathe, b. 15. 58. See **Skaþe**.
Schabbede, *adj. pl.* scabby, a. 8. 17. See note, p. 127; and see **Shabbyd**.
Schafte, *s.* shape, make, form, b. 9. 31, b. 13. 297. See **Shafte**.
Schaltou, i. e. shalt thou, a. 8. 99.
Schap, *s.* form, shape, a. 10. 32. See **Shappe**.
Schapen, *v.* shape, a. 3. 17; build, prepare, a. 10. 160; Schapeþ, *pr. s.* causes, a. 8. 69. See **Shape**.

D d 2

GLOSSARIAL INDEX.

Schare, *s.* plough-share, b. 3. 306. See **Shar**.
Schedyng, *s.* scattering, dropping; For schedyng = to prevent scattering, a. 7. 9. See **Shedynge**.
Scheep, shepherd (rather than sheep), a. pr. 2. See note. See **Shep**.
Schelde, *v.* shield, protect, R. 2. 74. See **Shelden**.
Schelles, *s. pl.* shells, a. 6. 12. See **Shelle**.
Scheltroun, *s.* shelter, defence, b. 14. 81. See note.
Schende, *v.* harm, ruin, pillage, a. pr. 65; Schendep, *pr. s.* corrupts, a. 3. 151; spoils. a. 10. 213; *pr. pl.* hurt, spoil, a. 1. 39; disgrace, b. 6. 175; Schenden. *pr. pl.* ruin, spoil, 14. 115; Schent, *pp.* destroyed, ruined, undone, a. 3. 130. See **Shenden**. A.S. *scendan*.
Schendfulliche, *adv.* shamefully, miserably, a. 3. 261. See above.
Schenshepe, *s.* ruin, R. 3. 259. Put for *schend-ship*; see **Schende**.
Schep, *s.* sheep, a. 8. 17.
Schete, *s.* sheet, b. 5. 108 (here *broke* signifies 'torn'); see note, p. 75.
Schetes. *pl.* sheets, coverlets, b. 14. 233.
Schew, *v.* show, R. 4. 56.
Schewe, *v.* quote, a 3. 264; appear, R. 4. 30; Schewep, *pr. s.* shews, declares, b. 10. 36; Schewed, *pt. pl.* exhibited, R. 2. 33; *pp.* R. 4. 56. See **Shewe**.
Schides, *s. pl.* planks, boards, a. 10. 160. See **Shides**. 'Schyde of wode, *buche, moule de buches;*' Palsgrave.
Schire, *s.* shire, b. 5. 362.
Schire-knyȝtis, *s. pl.* knights of the shire, R. 4. 32.
Schirreues, *s. pl.* shire-reeves, sheriffs, a. 2. 130. 134. A.S. *scírgeréfa*, a shire-reeve.
Scholdest, 2 *pt. s.* shouldest, a. 1. 132. See **Sholde**.
Schome, *s.* shame, a. 4. 28.
Schomedest, 2 *pt. s.* didst disgrace, didst shame, a. 3. 183.
Schomeliche, *adv.* shamefully, a. 3. 45. But other MSS. have *shameles*.
Schon, *pt. s.* shone, b. 12. 153. See **Shon**.
Schop, 1 *pt. s.* put (lit. shaped); Schop me into a schroud = got me into a garment, a. pr. 2; Schopen hem to hermytes = made themselves hermits, a. pr. 54. See **Shop**.
Schoppe, *v.* chop, R. 3. 230.
Schoppe, shop, 15. 185; Schoppes, *pl.* a. 2. 189. See **Shoppes**.

Schore, score, twenty. R. 2. 42.
Schorned, *pt. pl.* scorned, R. 3. 236.
Schort, *adv.* lightly; Sette schort, think lightly, b. 12. 124.
Schrape, *pr. s. subj.* scrape, b. 5. 124; Schraped, *pt. s.* scratched, a. 5. 215; Schrapid, scraped up the ground, R. 3. 58. See **Shrapeth**.
Schreuys, *s. pl.* sheriffs R. 4. 28.
Schrewe, *s.* wretch, wicked one, evil person, villain, sinner, b. pr. 196, b. 4. 110; Schrewes, *pl.* wicked men, b. 19. 371. See **Shrewe, Screwe**.
Schrewed, *pp.* accursed, R. 3. 20. See **Shrewede**.
Schrift, *s.* shrift, confession, a. 3. 38. See **Shrifte**.
Schrine, *s.* shrine, a. 6. 48.
Schrippe, *s.* scrip, a. 6. 26. See **Scrippe**.
Schrof, *pt. s.* confessed, shrived, 12. 256. See **Shrof**.
Schroff, *s.* scruff, i.e. a poor kind of cheap fuel, R. 2. 154 See the note. '*Scroff*, bits of small wood;' Barnes, Dorset Poems.
Schroud, *s.* a garment, rough outer garment, a. pr. 2. A.S. *scrúd*. a garment. See **Shroudes**.
Schroup, *s.* (probably) rubbish; but really a covert allusion to Lord Scrope, R. 2. 154. See the note.
Schulde, *pt. s.* should, a. 9. 94.
Schulen, *pr. pl.* shall, must, a. 1. 117.
Schulle, 2 *pr. pl.* shall, must, a. 8. 37; Schullen, *pr. pl.* shall, 13. 206; shall (go), a. 1. 121.
Schup, *s.* ship, boat, a. 10. 160. See **Shippe**.
Schutte, *pt. s.* shut, closed, a. 6. 92.
Schynglede, *pp.* shingled, covered with shingles, a. 10. 170. See note to 11. 232; and see **Shyngled**.
Schyreue, sheriff, b. 2. 163. See **Schirreues**.
Scismatikes, *s. p¹* heretics, 13. 54, b. 11. 115.
Sclaundere, disgrace, slander, 4. 61; Sclaundres, *pl.* slanders, 3. 86. See **Sklaundre**.
Scleuthe, sloth, b. 14. 234. See **Sleuthe**.
Scoffyng, *s* scoffs, b. 12. 277.
Scolde, *s.* scold, b. 19. 279.
Scole, school, education, 6. 34, 10. 35, 14. 170. 16. 129, 23. 251; Scoles, *pl.* a. 10. 84.
Scole, *error for* Scele = Scile, i.e. skill, reason, a. 12. 34 (Ingilby MS.); see footnote.

GLOSSARIAL INDEX. 431

Score, *s.* score, twenty. 4. 159.
Scorne, *v.* to speak scornfully, b. 10. 332; Scornie, *v.* to scorn, 3. 86; Scorned, *pt. s.* looked scornfully at, b. 11. 1.
Scornere, mocker, 22. 284.
Scorte, *adj.* short; Scorte of hem telle, account but little of them, R. 3. 194.
Screwe, *s.* villain, cursed fellow, a. 7. 143. See Schrewe.
Scrippe, scrip, bag, 8. 180. See Schrippe.
Scripture, writing, b. 10. 150.
Scryuaynes, *pl.* scriveners, scribes, 12. 97; 'Escrivain, a notary, scribe, scrivener;' Cotgrave.
Se, *s.* sea, b. 18. 244. See See.
Se, *s.* throne, R. 1. 86. E. *see,* sb.
Se, *v.* see, 20. 11, b. 11. 9; *imp. s.* look, R. pr. 55. See Seest, Seigh, Seih, Sei3, Seyh, Sen, Seon, Seth; also Sauh, Sau3, Saih, Say.
Seal, *s.* seal, a. 3. 141.
Seche, *v.* seek, b. 7. 163, a. 5. 241, a. 8. 149; visit, 1. 48; Sech, *imp. s.* seek, a. 10. 96. See Seke.
Secre, *adj.* secret, private, 10. 37, 138.
Secte, *s.* sect, class. lit. following, 7. 38, 13. 132; suit, apparel, dress, b. 14. 258; suit, apparel, likeness, 8. 130, 141; retinue, train, following of people, set, 17. 98, 100; Sectes, *pl.* sects, classes of men, 16. 13. Lat. *secta,* E. *sect, suite, suit, set.* See notes, pp. 98, 212.
Sectoures, *pl.* executors, b. 15. 128. See Cath. Angl. p. 327, n. 4.
Seculer, *adj.* belonging to the secular clergy, 11. 284; *as sb.* one of the secular clergy, b. 9. 177.
Secutours, *pl.* executors, 17. 277.
Sed, *s.* seed, 13. 179, 22. 276; children, descendants, 11. 221, b. 10. 108.
See, *s.* sea, 5. 126. See Se, Seo.
See, *s.* seat. R. 3. 352. See Se.
Seeden, *v.* beget children, 11. 251.
Seel, seal, 3. 156, 4. 183.
Seeleþ, *pr. pl.* seal. 4. 185.
Seem, a load, horse-load, 4. 42. 'A sack of eight bushels is now called a *seam,* which was a horse load; hence, generally, a load, a burden;' Bosworth, A.S. Dict. s.v. *séam.* Borrowed from Low Lat. *salma, sagma,* Greek σάγμα; from σάττειν.
Seemes, *s pl.* seams, R. 3. 166.
Seende, *pr. s.* 1 *p.* send, a. 2. 178.
Seestow, *for* seest thou, b. 9. 150; *as fut.* shalt thou see, b. 15. 190.

Seet, 1 *pt. s.* I sat. b. 20. 198; Seeten, *pt. pl.* sat, were placed, a. 5. 190, a. 6. 11. See Sitten.
Seetes, *s. pl.* seats, places, a. 8. 39.
Seewel, See-well, 11. 145.
Seg, man, creature, 4. 67, 13. 150, 161; 14. 198, 16. 264. See Segge.
Sege, *s.* seat, i.e. abode, place, town, 23. 310, 313.
Segge, *s.* a man, person, b. 3. 63, b. 5. 127, b. 11. 237, 258; Segges, *s. pl.* men, 3. 172. A.S. *secg,* a warrior. See Seg.
Seggen, *v.* say, 4. 219, 13. 30; speak of, i.e. to be told of, 14. 175; Segge, *v.* say, tell, 4. 236; Seggeþ, *pr. s.* says, repeats, 8. 10; Seggeþ, 2 *pr pl.* say, 14. 243; Seggen, 2 *pr. pl.* b. 11. 425; Seggen, *pr. pl.* (they) say, 15. 201; Seggynge, *pres. part.* saying, repeating, 6. 107. A.S. *secgan.* See Seie, Seye.
Seggyng, *s.* saying, words, b. 8. 108.
Seie, *v.* say, R. 3. 292 (*in the same line* seie = seen); tell, shew, a 9. 22; Sei, *v.* 11. 30, b. 2. 67; Seie, 1 *pr s.* say, a. 4. 119; Seien, *pr. pl.* say, 18. 309; Seist, 2 *pr. s.* sayest, b. 6. 232; Seide, 1 *pt. s.* said, b. 8. 21.
Seigh, 1 *pt. s.* saw, b. pr. 50, b. 6. 237, b. 10. 454; saw, read, b. 10. 189; Seighe, 1 *pt. s.* saw, b. 7. 140; Seighe, *pt. s.* b. 5. 505; Seighen, *pt. pl.* saw, b. 12. 133; Seien, *pp.* seen, 12. 236; Seie, *pp.* seen, R. 3. 292 (*in the same line* seie = say). See Se, Seih, Sei3, Seyh, Sauh.
Seighed, *pt. s.* sighed, b 18. 89.
Seih, 1 *pt. s.* saw, 6. 125, 7. 57, 10. 294; *pt. s.* 3. 200; 2 *pt. s.* didst see, 11. 73. See Seigh, Seyh, Se.
Seilinge, *pr. pt.* sa ling, 21. 344. See note.
Seintis, *pl.* girdles, R. 3 140. [Both the word and the sense are somewhat doubtful.]
Seised, 1 *pt. s.* have been in possession, b. 18. 281. See Sese.
Seist, 2 *pr. s.* sayest, 7. 290, 9. 237; Seith, *pr. s.* says, 21. 28. See Seggen, Seie, Seye.
Seiwel, Speak-well, 11. 145.
Sei3, 1 *pt. s.* saw, b. pr. 230; *pt. s.* b. 2. 188; Sei3e, *pt. pl. subj* have seen, b. 19. 450; *pp.* seen, a. 11. 218. See Seih, Seyh, Se.
Sei3e, 1 *pr. s.* say, a. 1. 182.
Seke, *v.* find, seek for, 11. 2; Seke, 1 *pr. s.* 19. 269; Seketh, *imp. pl.* b 5. 58. See Seche.

Seke, *adj. pl.* sick, ill, a. 11. 187. A.S. *séoc*.
Seketoures, *pl.* executors, b. 15. 243.
Sekirly, *adv.* surely, R. 4. 92. '*Sekyr*, securus ;' Cath. Angl.
Selcouth, *adj.* various, b. 15. 579; *as sb.* wonderful (thing), 14. 175; wonderful (act), 19. 148; Selcouthe, *adj. pl.* strange, wonderful, 1. 5. A.S. *seldcúð*, lit. seldom known, hence, strange. See note, p. 3.
Selcouþes, *pl.* wonders, 15. 75, b. 11. 355. See above.
Selde, *adv.* seldom, 3. 26, 127; 7. 93, 8. 20; To selde, too seldom, R. 3. 58; Selden, seldom, b. 7. 137; Seldene, a. pr. 20; Seldom, a. 8. 124. A.S. *seldan*, rarely; G. *selten*, Du. *zelden*.
Sele, seal, 1. 77; Seles, *pl.* 1. 67. See Seel.
Sele, *v.* to seal; Seleth, *pr. pl.* seal, b. 3. 147; Seled, *pp.* sealed, certified (with reference to the sealing of measures which had been tested and found to be correct), 4. 88. See note to 4. 87.
Selk, *adj.* silken, 4. 451.
Selke, *s.* silk, 9. 10, b. pr. 210.
Selkouthes, *pl.* marvels, wonders, b. 12. 133. See Selcouth.
Sel ers, *pl.* dealers, 4. 116.
Selles, *pl.* cells, 18. 7.
Sellynge, *s.* selling, R. 4. 9.
Selue, *pron.* himself, b. 1. 102.
Selue, *pronom. adj.* very, 23. 43.
Seluer, silver, money, 1. 79, 14. 105; Spendyng seluer, money to spend, 14. 101; Seluers, *gen.* of money, 3. 68.
Seluerles, *adj.* moneyless, 10. 119.
Selynge, *s.* sealing, a. 2. 112.
Semblable, *adj.* similar, resembling, like, 4. 337. F. *semblable*, like.
Semblaunce, appearance, likeness, b. 18. 285. See below.
Semblaunt, *s.* looks, countenance, appearance, b. 8. 117, a. 9. 112; Semblant, 11. 117. F. *semblant*, appearance.
Semble, *s.* assembly, a. pr. 97.
Sembled, *pt. pl.* assembled, R. pr. 19; Semblid, *pp.* R. 4. 32.
Seme, Seem, *s.* load, b. 3. 40.
Semeliche, *adj.* suitable, becoming, proper, 16. 59; Semely, a. 8. 101. See Semly.
Semeþ, *pr. s.* appears (to be), 4. 386; Semen, *pr. pl.* appear, b. 15. 200; Semede, *pt. s.* seemed, appeared, 20. 55, 270.

Semiuyf, *adj.* half alive, b. 17. 55. See below.
Semiuiuus, adj. half alive, i.e. half dead, 20. 55. See Luke x. 30 (Vulgate).
Semliche, *adv.* becomingly, 20. 245.
Semly, *adj.* becoming, 4. 112.
Semynge, *pres. pt.* resembling, like, b. 15. 386; intimating, making as though, apparently, 12. 87.
Sen, 1 *pr. pl.* we see, b. 10. 362 ; *pr. pl.* look at, b. 9. 74. See Se.
Sende, *pt. s.* sent a message to, sent, 19. 262; Send, *pp.* given, 10. 55.
Sendel, a thin silken stuff, 9. 10. F. *sendal*.
Sense, *s.* incense, 21. 86, b. 19. 82. ' *Sence*, incensum, timiama, thus ;' Cath. Angl.
Sent, *pr. s.* (*for* Sendeth), sendeth, sends, 2. 179, 9. 348 ; *pt. s. subj.* (*for* Sente), should send, b. 13. 248.
Seo, sea, 21. 257. See Se, See.
Seod, seed, 22. 289. See Sed.
Seon, *v.* see, behold, 20. 199, a. 1. 146, a. 4. 73; Seo, *v.* 19. 192, 277; Seo, 1 *pr. s.* I see, 1. 206; Seost, 2 *pr. s.* seest, 22. 180 ; Seo, 10. 244 ; Seon, 2 *pr. pl.* 22. 252 ; Seon, 2 *pr. pl.* ye see, a. 3. 210, a. 8. 63 ; Seoþ, *pr. pl.* a. 1. 49 ; Seo, *imp. s.* a. 1. 39, a. 11. 145 ; read, a. 10. 145. *The* pt. t. *takes the forms* Saih, Say, Seigh, Seih, Sei3, Seyh, *also* Sauh, Sau3 ; *which see.* See also Se, Seest, Sen. A.S. *seón*.
Seowel, See-well, a. 10. 19.
Sepulcre, Holy Sepulchre, 8. 171.
Serelepes, *adv.* separately, b. 17. 164. See note. Extended from Icel. *sér*, several, separate, by help of the adverbial suffix *-lepes*. It occurs in the Ormulum. See Stratmann. As to the suffix, cf. A.S. *ánlépe*, which see in Grein.
Seriaunt, *s.* sergeant, officer, b. 3. 293, a. 3. 276 ; Seriaunte, 4. 451.
Serk, *s.* shirt, b. 5. 66. Icel. *serkr*, a sark, shirt.
Sertayn, *adj.* certain, fixed, 23. 255.
Sertes, *adv.* certainly, a. 8. 167.
Seruaunt, servant, 4. 370, 17. 98 ; Seruauntz, *pl.* b. 13. 392.
Seruen, *v.* serve, 6. 12, a. 1. 17; Serue, b. 9. 13, R. pr. 14; Serueth, *pr. s.* is of service, is of use, b. 11. 89 ; Serueþ, 13. 32 ; Serue, *pr. pl.* they serve, b. 9. 196 ; Serueþ, serve for, 20. 173 ; Serued, *pt. pl.* deserved, R. 4. 59 ; were useful (for), R. 2. 45 ; Seruid,

GLOSSARIAL INDEX.

pt. pl. deserved, R. 2. 28; Serueþ, *imp. pl.* serve, do your duty, a. 8. 63.
Seruice, service, 4. 274; service in church, 10. 231; serving, meal, b. 13. 51; Seruyce, service in church, 10. 227; duty, 4. 451.
Serwe, *s.* sorrow, woe, a. 2. 84, 89; Serw, a. 5. 104.
Sese, *v.* seize, steal, take, 7. 271; 1 *pr. s.* endow, a. 2. 69; Sesith, *pr. s.* seizes, R. 3. 49; Sesed, *pp.* seised, put in possession, 21. 311.
Sesen, *v.* cease, leave off; Sese of, cease from, a. 8. 102; Seseþ, *imp. pl.* cease, be silent, a. 4. 1.
Seson, *s.* season, time, 7. 184; Seyson, 1. 1.
Sestow, 2 *pr. s.* seest thou, b. 1. 5. See **Se, Seon, Seestow.**
Set, *pr. s.* (*for* Setteth), estimates, values, 13. 27; Seten, *pp.* set, put, 16. 42. A.S. *settan.*
Set, for *sed* (Latin), but, b. 10. 339.
Sete, *s.* seat, R. 3. 49.
Sete, 1 *pt. s.* sat, b. 13. 98; Seten, 1 *pt. pl.* b. 13. 36; Seten, *pt. pl.* sat, b. 6. 117, 195; sat down, 9. 122; Sete, *pt. s. subj.* might sit, might be, 7. 99; Seten, *pt. pl. subj.* should sit, might happen to sit, b. 12. 200.
Seth, 1 *pr. pl.* see, 1. 154, b. 3. 216. See **Se, Seon.**
Seþþe, *prep.* since, a. pr. 81.
Seþþen, *adv.* afterwards, then, a. 5. 151, a. 7. 59; after that, a. 10. 154; Seþþe, afterwards, a. 1. 134; then, a. 4. 15. A.S. *siððan.* See **Sithen.**
Setten, *pr. pl. as fut.* shall sit, a. 8. 19.
Setten, *v.* set, plant, 8. 186, 10. 6; Sette, *v.* set, place, a. 8. 34; plant, b. 7. 6; think, esteem, b. 12. 124; Sette, 1 *pr. s.* I set, place, reckon, b. 7. 194; Sette, *pr. pl.* set, b. 10. 392; Sette, 1 *pt. s.* put, placed, b. 10. 168; Sette, *pt. s.* set, placed, b. 6. 171; esteemed, thought, b. 11. 2; Sette, *pt. s. subj.* set, placed, b. 12. 198; Sette (*for* Set), *pp.* set, placed, b. 6. 48; Sette short, *v.* think little (of), 15. 65; Sette by, 1 *pr. s.* esteem, 10. 345; Setten by, *pr. pl.* esteem, 10. 302. '*Sette,* plantare, . . . locare;' Cath. Angl.
Setthen, *adv.* afterwards, 4. 50.
Seuene, *num.* seven, 2. 106; Seuen, a. 3. 141; Seue, 11. 73.
Seueneth, *num. adj.* seventh, b. 14. 306.
Seuenyght, a week, se'nnight, 8. 301; Seuenenyght, R. 3. 346.

Seuerid, *pt. pl.* severed, went in different directions, R. 2. 14.
Seueþe, *num. adj.* seventh, 17. 144.
Sew, 1 *pt. s.* sowed, 7. 271; Sewe, b. 13. 375; Sewe, *pt. s.* 22. 275; Sewe, *pt. pl.* sowed, planted, 18. 101. See **Sowen.**
Sewe, *v.* sew, R. 3. 166; Sewen, *pr. pl. subj.* 9. 10; Souweþ, *imp. pl.* a. 7. 19. See **Sowen.**
Sewel, See-well, b. 9. 20.
Seweþ, *pr. pl.* follow, accompany, 1. 46; Sewen, *pr. pl.* a. 11. 242; Sewede, *pt. s.* 23. 126.
Seweris, *s. pl.* sewers, people who sew, cobblers, a. 11. 301. See note, p. 163. cf. *sowers,* R. 3. 164. 'A *sewer,* filator, sutor, sutrix;' Cath. Angl.
Sewynge, *s.* regular order, 19. 63. See note.
Sexscore, six score, 4. 183.
Sexte, *num. adj.* sixth, b. 14. 399.
Sexty, *num.* sixty, 4. 234.
Seye, *v.* say, a. 3. 166; Seyne, *v.* declare, tell, b. 14. 278; Herde seyne, heard say, b. 16. 249; Sey, *v.* tell, show, b. 8. 27; Seye, 1 *pr. s.* I say, 20. 5, 19; Seȝe, 1. 118; Sey, b. 6. 286; Seyth, *pr. s.* says, declares, b. 10. 26; Seyen, 2 *pr. pl.* 12. 201; Seyne, b. 6. 131; *pr. pl.* say, preach, b. 10. 398.
Seyh, 1 *pt. s.* saw, 19. 242, 21. 117; Seygh, b. 5. 542; Sey, 8. 15; Sey, 2 *pt. s.* didst (thou) see, sawest (thou), b. 8. 75; Seȝe, sawest, a. 9. 66; Seyh, *pt. s.* saw, 8. 138; Sey, 21. 257; Seyen, *pt. pl.* saw, 15. 75; Seyen, *pp.* seen, 4. 104; Seyne, b. 11. 238; Seȝen, a. 3. 58. See **Se, Seon, Seih, Seigh.**
Seylde, *adv.* seldom, 1. 22. See **Selde.**
Seyned, *pt. s.* signed, crossed himself, b. 5. 456. O.F. *seigner* (Roquefort), Lat. *signare.*
Seynt, *adj.* holy, 12. 204; saint, b. 10. 46; Seyntes, *pl.* saints, 8. 133.
Seyntewarie, the sanctuary, 6. 79. O.F. *saintuaire,* a sanctuary, also a box for relics (Roquefort).
Seyson, season, time, 1. 1. See **Seson.**
Seywel, Say-well, Speak-well, a. 10. 19.
Seȝe, Seȝen. See **Seyh.**
Sh-. See also under **Sch-.**
Shabbyd, scabbed, scabby, 10. 264. See **Schabbede.**
Shadde, *pt. s.* shed, 20. 270. See **Schedyng.**
Shadeweþ, *pr. s.* throws its shadow, 21. 479; Shadweth, b. 18. 431.
Shaft, shaft of an arrow, 9. 351.

GLOSSARIAL INDEX.

Shafte, *s.* figure, form, b. 11. 387.
Shak, *imper. s.* shake, throw, 7. 13. See Shok.
Shale, *s.* shell, husk, 13. 145. See Scalles.
Shall, 1 *pr. s.* am to, R. 3. 170; *pr. s.* shall (remain), R. pr. 61; Shaltow, shalt thou, b. 5. 579; Schaltou, a. 8. 99; Shal, *pr. pl.* are bound to do, b. 11. 203. See Shult.
Shamedest, 2 *pt. s.* didst bring shame upon, b. 3. 189. See Schomedest.
Shameles, *adv.* shamelessly, 4. 46.
Shape, *v.* shape, R. 3. 161; make, construct, 11. 222; Shapeþ, *pr. s.* induces, sets, 10. 62; arranges, modifies, 2. 158; causes, disposes, b. 7. 67; determines, b. 1. 159; Shapte, *pt. s.* created, b. 17. 216; Shapen, *pp.* made, prepared, b. 14. 39. See Schapen, Schop, Shop.
Shappe, *v.* shape, fashion, 6. 18.
Shappe, *s.* shape, form, b. 11. 387. See Schap.
Shappesters, *gen.* tailor's, cutter's out, 7. 75. See Shepster; and see note.
Shar, plough-share, 4. 464. See Schare.
Sharpliche, *adv.* speedily, 7. 13; Sharply, 19. 107.
Shaue, *pp.* shaven, 17. 351.
Shawes, *s. pl.* woods, groves, 11. 159. A.S. *scaga.*
Shedynge, *s.* shedding, b. 12. 282; For shedynge=to prevent spilling, 9. 8. See Schedyng.
Sheene, *adj.* beautiful, glorious to behold, 21. 456. See Shene.
Shef, sheaf, 4. 482, 23. 225; Sheues, *pl.* sheaves, 6. 14.
Shelden, *pr. pl.* shield, defend, b. 10. 407. See Schelde.
Shelle, shell, b. 11. 252. See Schelles, Shilles.
Shenden, *v.* put to shame, b. 11. 416; Shende, *v.* destroy, ruin, 21. 339; Shendeþ, *pr. s.* ruins, corrupts, 4. 193; spoils, b. 9. 205; Shente, *pt. s.* ruined, killed, 23. 98; destroyed, b. 20. 97; ruined, 20. 270; Shent, *pt. s.* destroyed, b. 17. 288; Shente, *pt. pl.* spoilt, R. 2. 51; Shent, *pp.* ruined, disgraced, 4. 172, b. 3. 134, b. 4. 174. See Schende.
Shendfulliche, *adv.* shamefully, miserably, 4. 433; Shenfullich, b. 3. 275. See Schendfulliche.
Shene, *adj.* glorious to behold, b. 18. 409. See Sheene.
Shent, Shente. See Shenden.
Sheo, *pron.* she, 22. 120. A.S. *séo.*

Shep, *s.* shepherd; Shepe, b. pr. 2. See note.
Shepherde, shepherd, 1. 2; Shephurdes, 18. 98.
Shepper, creator, b. 17. 167. Lit. 'shaper.'
Shepster, *gen.* tailor's, b. 13. 331. See Shappesters.
Shere, scissors, shears, b. 13. 331; Sheres, 7. 75.
Shereyue, sheriff, 3. 177; Shereyues, *gen.* sheriff's, 5. 164; Shereyues, *pl.* sheriffs, 3. 59.
Sherte, shirt, 2. 99.
Shetep, *imper. pl.* shoot, 21. 294. A.S. *scéotan.* See Shotte.
Shette, *pt. s.* shut, b. 5. 611.
Sheues, *pl.* sheaves; see Shef.
Shewe, *v.* show itself, appear, 11. 159; Sheweth, *pr. s.* declares, b. 10. 252. See Schewe.
Shewere, *s.* indicator, revealer, 15. 96. See note.
Shewynge, *s.* showing; Hiegh clergye shewynge, exhibition of great erudition, b. 15. 76.
Shides, *pl.* planks, 11. 222, 12. 239. See Schides.
Shifte, *pt. s. refl.* moved, shifted himself aside, b. 20. 166.
Shilles, *pl.* shells, 8. 166. See Shelle.
Shipmen, *pl.* sailors, b. 15. 350, 354, 361.
Shippe, ship, ark, b. 10. 400. See Shupes, Schup.
Shireues, *pl.* sheriffs, b. 2. 58. See Schirreues, Shereyue.
Shiteþ, *pr. s.* evacuates, is surfeited with, 10. 264.
Shodde, *pp.* shod, b. 2. 163.
Shok, 1 *pt. s.* shook (so as to make the money fall out), emptied out, 7. 266. See Shak.
Sholde, *pt. s.* had to, b. 14. 105. See Scholdest, Shult.
Shon, *pt. s.* shone, 15. 96. See Schon.
Shon, *pl.* shoes, 6. 18.
Shonye, *v.* shun, avoid, b. pr. 174; Shonne, *v.* R. 3. 170; Shonye, 1 *pr. s.* I get out of the way, b. 5. 169; Shoneþ, *pr. s.* shuns, avoids, 14. 245.
Shop, 1 *pt. s.* shaped, i.e. put, 1. 2; Shope, set (myself), b. 17. 83; 2 *pt. s.* didst create, 7. 424; Shop, *pt. s.* shaped, made, 12. 239; got ready, set off, 14. 247; Shope, *pt. s.* arranged, 3. 177; prepared (himself), b. 11. 429; shaped, formed, b. 9. 65; built, b. 10. 400. See Schop, Shape, Schapen, and notes, pp. 2, 179.

GLOSSARIAL INDEX. 435

Shoppes, *pl.* shops, 3. 223. See **Schoppe**.
Shoriere, prop, 19. 119: Shoryere, 19. 50; Shoriers, *pl.* 19. 20; Shoryeres, 19. 25. From the verb *shore*, to prop up.
Shotte, *s.* shot, b. 20. 224.
Shotte, *pt. s.* aimed, threw, 21. 50; Shotten, *pl.* shot, discharged, 23. 225. See **Sheteþ**.
Shoue, *v.* prop, support, 19. 20.
Shoures, *pl.* storms, 21. 456.
Shrapeth, *pr. s.* scrapes, b. 11. 423; Shraped, *pt. s. subj.* should scrape, were to scrape, 7. 90. See **Schrape**.
Shref, *pt. s.* shrove, confessed, a. 11. 273.
Shrewe, rascal, wicked person, 5. 105, 7. 318; sinner, b. 5. 471; the wicked one, Satan, b. 1. 127; Shrewes, *pl.* wretches, cursed rascals, wicked men, 11. 164, 12. 26. See note to 2. 131.
Shrewede, 1 *pt. s.* cursed, 7. 75; Shrewede, *adj. pl.* cursed; 1. 122. See **Schrewed**.
Shrewednesse, *s.* sin, b. 3. 44.
Shrifte, confession, 7. 63. See **Shruft, Schrift**.
Shrobbis, shrubs, 1. 2. [But see the other texts.]
Shrof, *pt. s.* confessed, shrived, shrove, 4. 46, 7. 422. See **Shryue**.
Shroudes, *pl.* garments, rough outer clothes, b. pr. 2. A.S. *scrúd*, a garment, shroud. See **Schroud**.
Shruft, shrift, confession, 23. 306. See **Shrifte**.
Shryue, *v.* confess, shrive, 1. 62, 23. 280, 304; Shryuen, b. pr. 89; Shryueþ, *pr. s.* shrives, 23. 368; Shryuen, *pp.* b. 5. 309; Shref, *pt. s.* confessed, a. 11. 273; Shryf, *imp. s.* 7. 13. See **Shrof, Shryf, Shref**.
Shryuers, *pl.* confessors, 1. 64.
Shul, Shulde, Shullen; see **Shult**.
Shulle, *adv.* shrilly, clearly, 7. 46. See Cath. Angl. p. 336, *n.* 4.
Shullenges, *pl.* shillings, 4. 395.
Shult, 2 *pr. s.* shalt, 12. 113; Shulleþ, 1 *pr. pl.* shall (go), must (go), 13. 117; must, 10. 311; Shuln, ought to, a. 11. 237; Shullen, must, b. 7. 162; Shulleþ, 2 *pr. pl.* shall, 23. 248; Shulleþ, *pr. pl.* shall, must, have to, 4. 37, 53; shall, 11. 227; Shulde, 1 *pt. s.* I ought to go, I was bound, b. 15. 13; ought, b. 17. 293; Shulden, *pt. pl.* ought to be, b. 7. 13; Shulde, 2 *pr. s. subj.* oughtest, b. 6. 49. See **Shall**.

Shultrom, battalion, squadron, 21. 294. See **Scheltroun**.
Shupes, *pl.* ships, 9. 351. See **Shippe**. A.S. *scyp*.
Shupmen, *pl.* sailors, 18. 94. See **Shipmen**.
Shupte, *pt. s.* contrived, prepared, 23. 139, 306; created, formed, 20. 182.
Shynes, *pl.* shins, b. 11. 423.
Shyngled, *pp.* planked, b. 9. 141; Shynglede, 11. 232. See note.
Sib, *adj.* akin, related, 8. 280, a. 6. 113; Sibbe, 12. 198; *pl.* 13. 155, R. 3. 30. See **Sybbe**.
Side, *adj.* wide, large, R. 2. 51, R. 4. 28; long, R. 3. 170. A.S. *síd*.
Sigge, *v.* say, 1. 210; order, a. 2. 56; 1 *pr. s.* say, 1. 206; mean, a. 11. 13; Siggen, *pr. pl.* a. 8. 136. See **Seggen**.
Siggynge, *s.* saying, words, a. 9. 102.
Signe, *s.* sign, b. 13. 153; seal, 23. 272; badge, R. 2. 89; Signes, *pl.* signs, pilgrims' marks or signs, a. 6. 12, 15; signatures, a. 2. 82; badges, R. 2. 21.
Siht, *s.* sight, 20. 61; presence, a. 2. 82.
Sik, *adj.* sick, ill, 23. 305; *def. adj. sing.* sick man, 20. 61. See **Syke**.
Sike, *ger.* to sigh, grieve, 4. 403; *v.* a. 11. 190; Sikede, *pt. s.* a. 5. 229. Cf. Shropsh. *sike*, to sigh.
Siker, *adj.* certain, 15. 29; sure, b. 1. 130. G. *sicher*, Du. *zeker;* from Lat. *securus*.
Siker, *adv.* securely, a. 8. 55; assuredly, a. 11. 160.
Sikerere, *adv.* more securely, b. 5. 509. See **Sykerer**.
Sikerliche, *adv.* certainly, assuredly, 11. 26; Sikerlich, in safety, 5. 51; Sikerly, surely, b. 5. 547; Sikerli, a. 1. 123. See **Sykerliche**.
Sikul, *s.* sickle, b. 3. 306. See **Sykel**.
Siphre, *s.* cipher, R. 4. 53.
Sire, *s.* sire, i.e. our Lord, R. 3. 352; father, b. pr. 189; sir, a. 10. 1; Sir, sire, master, R. 1. 86; sir, a. 8. 140; Siris, sirs, lords, R. 1. 104. See **Syre**. See note to 7. 367, p. 90.
Sisour, *s.* juryman, juror, 22. 372; Sisoure, b. 2. 164; Sisours, *pl.* 3. 179; Sisoures, b. 2. 62. See **Sysour**; and see note, p. 34.
Sit, *pr. s.* sits, is seated, 15. 143.
Sith, *conj.* since, b. pr. 64.
Sithe, *s.* scythe, 4. 464.
Sithe, *s. pl.* times, 7. 40, 8. 37, 47; Sithes, *pl.* times, 10. 329, 11. 31. A.S. *síð*, a journey, turn, time; Goth. *sinth*, a journey, a time. See **Sythes**.
Sithen, *adv.* then, afterwards, b. 4. 14,

GLOSSARIAL INDEX.

b. 9. 132, b. 10. 365; *conj.* since, when, b. 10. 264; *prep.* since, b. 9. 164. See **Siþthen, Sitthen, Sythen.**

Siþhenes, *conj.* since, b. 10. 257, b. 19. 15; *adv.* afterwards, b. 7. 25; Sitthenes, b. 6. 65. See **Sytthenes.**

Siþþe, *adv.* afterwards, a. 2. 31; Sitthe, *adv.* afterwards, b. 7. 94; Siþþe, *conj.* since, a. 11. 265. See **Sith, Sithen.**

Siþthen, *conj.* since, 19. 193, 22. 15. See **Sithen, Sythþe.**

Sitten, *v.* reside, b. 14. 218; cost, b. 3. 48 (cf. the phr. 'to *stand* one in a large sum'); Sitte, *v.* press upon, oppress, beset, 3. 154 (see note); be situate, 10. 294; sit, i. e. situate, a. 8. 129; Sitt, *pr. s.* (*for* Sitteth), sits, is placed, is situated, 10. 108; Sitteþ, *pr. pl.* sit, are placed, a. 6. 20; Sitten, grow, are placed, 19. 64; Sittende, *pres. pt.* sitting, b. 17. 48. See **Sit, Setten.**

Sitthen, *adv.* afterwards, 11. 248, 19. 262, 22. 78; Sitthe, *adv.* 5. 15; *conj.* since, 19. 177; Sitthe, *prep.* since, 12. 55; Sitth, *adv.* afterwards, b. 14. 142. See **Sithen, Siththen, Sytthen.**

Sittinge, *s.* sitting-time, R. 3. 39.

Siuyle, *s.* a practitioner in Civil Law, a. 2. 57.

Sixt, 2 *pr. s.* seest, a. 1. 5. See **Syxt.**

Siȝte, *s.* sight, miracle, b. 16. 117; Siȝth, sight, R. 1. 28; Siȝtes, *pl.* sights, b. 12. 130. See **Siht, Syght.**

Skaþe, *s.* injury, harm, b. 3. 57. See **Scaþe.**

Skathed, *pt. s.* harmed, R. 2. 105.

Skil, *s.* reason, 7. 27, b. 12. 216; a reason, b. 11. 1; Skiles, *pl.* reasons, excuses, b. 17. 330; Skilles, reasons, grounds, b. 10. 301. See **Skyl.**

Skipte, *pt. s.* skipped, jumped, b. 11. 103. See **Skypte.**

Sklaundre, disgrace, shame, scandal, b. 3. 57, b. 12. 47.

Skleire, *s.* a veil, 9. 5; Sklayre, b. 6. 7. Cf. G. *schleier.*

Skyes, *pl.* skies, R. 2. 190.

Skyl, skill, b. 19. 279; Skyle, reason, 16. 136; excuse, 7. 22; Skylle, reason, R. 2. 105; Skyles, *pl.* reasons, proofs, arguments, 6. 154; excuses, 20. 312. See **Skil.**

Skynnes, *pl.* skins, R. 2. 32, 126.

Skypte, *pt. s.* skipped, jumped, 13. 40 See **Skipte.**

Slake, *v.* slake, b. 18. 366; *pr. s. subj* 21. 413.

Slaueyn, *s.* mantle (esp. one worn by a pilgrim), R. 3. 236. See Cath. Angl. p. 343, n. 2. '*Esclavine*, as *Esclamme*, a long and thick riding-cloake, to beare off the raine; a pilgrim's cloake or mantle, a cloak for a traveller;' Cotgrave.

Slayen, *pp.* slain, 1. 113. See **Sleen.**

Sleen, *v.* slay, b. 3. 385; Slee, 7. 107; Sle, 4. 443; Sleeth, *pr. s.* slays, kills, b. 14. 90; Sleeþ, *pr. pl.* slay, murder, kill, 20. 255; Slee, *imp. s.* b. 3. 264, b. 10. 367. See **Slen, Slayen, Sleye, Slouh.**

Slee-nat, *imper. s.* Slay-not (referring to the 6th commandment), 8. 224.

Slehliche, *adv.* by treachery, slily, 7. 107.

Sleithe, *s.* trick, craft, scheme, 21. 166; art, skill, cunning, 22. 98; Sleighte, *s.* cunning art, trick, b. 18. 160; Sleithes, *pl.* arts, tricks, deceits, frauds, 3. 91, 17. 274; Slehthes, 7. 107; Sleigthes, b. 15. 125; Sleightes, b. 13. 365. See **Sleythes, Slithes.**

Slen, *v.* slay, a. 3. 267; Sle, *imp. s.* a. 11. 247. See **Sleen.**

Sleope; A sleope, asleep, 23. 51.

Slepe, *v.* to sleep, to fall asleep, 1. 7; Slepestow, b. 1. 5; Slepte, 1 *pt. s.* slept, 1. 8, 21. 5; Slepe, b. 5. 382; Slepte, *pt. pl.* R. 4. 62; Slepen, *pt. pl.* 16. 272; Slepynge, *pres. part.* sleeping, 1. 13, 6. 125, 10. 298; Sleped, *pp.* b. 5. 4.

Sleuthe, sloth, 1. 46, 8. 1, 23. 158, 159, 163, 217; Sleuth, b. 2. 98; Sleuȝþe, a. pr. 45; Slewþe, 3. 102; Slouþe, a. 2. 69.

Sleye, *pp.* slain, 18. 275. See **Sleen.**

Sleyest, *adj.* most cunning, lit. sliest, b. 13. 298. See below.

Sleygh, *adj.* cunning, 23. 163.

Sleythes, *pl.* tricks, crafts, 20. 232; Sleyghthes, 7. 73.

Slilokeste, *adv.* most slily, most secretly, 12. 266.

Slithes, *pl.* cunning, skill, b. 13. 408. See **Sleithe, Sleythes.**

Slode, *pt. pl.* slid, R. 3. 234.

Sloh, *s.* slough, earth, 13. 179.

Slombred, 1 *pt. s.* slumbered, b. pr. 10; Slombrid, *pt. pl.* R. 4. 62. 'To *slomer,* soporare;' Cath. Angl.

Slouh, *pt. s.* slew, killed, 23. 150; Slowe, *pt. pl.* 12. 37; Slowen, a. 11. 40. See **Sleen, Slen.**

Slowe, *adj.* sluggish, 9. 244.

Slyken, *pr. pl.* render sleek, b. 2. 98. Cf. E. *sleek, slick.*

GLOSSARIAL INDEX. 437

Slymed, *adj.* slimy, dirty, 8. 1.
Slynge, *s.* sling, 23. 163, 217.
Slynge, *imp. s.* cast away, lit. sling, a. 8. 125.
Smaketh, *pr. s.* smells, a. 5. 207.
Smauhte, *pt. s.* smacked, tasted, 7. 414; Smauȝte, *pt. pl.* b. 5. 363.
Smerte, *adv.* smartly, severely, 14. 244.
Smerteþ, *pr. s.* smarts, is pained, 20. 305; Smerte, *pt. s. subj. impers.* it may grieve, cause to smart, a. 3. 161; Smerte, *pr. pl. subj.* smart, suffer, b. 3. 167.
Smit, *pr. s.* smiteth, b. 11. 426. See **Smyt**.
Smok, *s.* smock, chemise, 7. 6.
Smolder, *s.* smoke from smouldering wood, b. 17. 321. See below.
Smorþre, *s.* thick smoke, smother, 20. 303, 323. See *Smother* in my Etym. Dict.
Smylle, *v.* smell, 8. 50.
Smyt, *pr. s.* smites, strikes, 14. 244, 20. 303, 323; Smyte, *pp.* smitten, 4. 480. See **Smit**.
Smythie, *v.* to forge; Do hit smythie = cause it to be forged, 4. 463; Smytheth, *pr. s.* forges, b. 3. 322; Smythie, *pr. s. subj.* 4. 480.
So, *adv.* so, R. pr. 18; as, 8. 232; So ... so, so ... as, 14. 188; so that, b. 13. 64; *conj.* provided that, b. 13. 135; So the ik, so may I thrive, b. 5. 228.
Sobre, *adj.* sober, 16. 256.
Sobrete, sobriety, temperance, moderation, self-restraint, 16. 187, 17. 134, b. 10. 165.
Soche, *adj.* such, 1. 34.
Socour, *s.* help, succour, aid, 23. 170.
Sode, *pt. pl.* seethed, boiled, cooked, 18. 20; *pp.* boiled, sodden, 10. 149.
Sodenes, *pl.* sub-deans, 17. 277. See **Southdenes**, and note.
Sodeynliche, *adv.* suddenly, 22. 5; Sodeynlich, 16. 24.
Soeuereigne, *s.* prince, b. 19. 73.
Soffraunce, *s.* patience, a. 10. 115.
Soffre-boþe-weole-and-wo, suffer both weal and woe, a. 11. 113.
Soffren, *v.* suffer, be patient, a. 10. 114; Soffre, suffer, permit, allow, a. 9. 47; Soffren, 2 *pr. pl.* allow, permit, 1. 96; Soffrie, 2 *pr. s. subj.* allow, 2. 146; Soffrede, 1 *pt. s.* endured, underwent, 7. 57; *pt. s.* suffered, allowed, 4. 230; Soffredest, 2 *pt. s.* didst allow, suffer, 8. 125, 139; Soffre,

imp. s. suffer (thou), b. 3. 92; Soffreþ, *imp. pl.* a. 9. 84.
Softe, *adj.* mild, warm, 1. 1; fine, a. 7. 181. [*Soft* appears to mean mild, warm; not drizzly, as in Mod. E. dialects.]
Softeliche, *adv.* gently, 3. 165; quietly, gently, 16. 29.
Softere, *adv.* more gently, 23. 310.
Soiled, *pp.* soiled, dirtied, b. 14. 2.
Soiourneþ, *pr. s.* dwells, resides, 11. 18.
Sokne, district, soke, 3. 111. See note. Wright says—'a district held by tenure of socage.' A.S. *sóc, sócn,* allied to *sacan.*
Solas, *s.* consolation, 13. 208; amusement, 9. 22; encouragement, b. 12. 151; contentment, 10. 131.
Solasen, *v.* cheer, 20. 199; Solacen, cheer, amuse, b. 12. 22; Solaseth, *pr. pl.* cheer, comfort, b. 13. 453.
Solenliche, *adv.* solemnly, 4. 54.
Soleyne, *adj.* solitary, *hence* morose, sullen, R. 4. 66; *as sb.* a solitary person, b. 12. 205; Soleyn, 15. 45. See note. E. *sullen.*
Solfye, *v.* sing, sol-fa, 8. 31. To *sol-fa* is to sing by note, to call over the notes by their names, viz. ut, si, la, *sol, fa,* &c. See note.
Solitarie, *adj.* in solitude, 18. 7.
Somdel, *adv.* partly, somewhat, in some measure, 8. 44, 189; Somedele, b. 5. 438.
Somenour, *s.* apparitor, summoner, 22. 372; Somenours, *pl.* 3. 187; Someneres, *gen. pl.* 10. 263. See **Somnoures, Sompnoure.**
Someny, *v.* summon, call together, 22. 214.
Somer, *s.* summer, 7. 112; Somere, 9. 245; Somer, *as adj.* 11. 2; fit for summer, 10. 119; Somere, 1. 1.
Somer-game, a summer-game, b. 5. 413. See the note to 8. 22.
Somer-tyme, summer-time, b. 15. 94.
Somme, *adj.* some, b. 8. 120; *pl.* 19. 150; some of them, 4. 14 (see note); *dat. pl.* to some, 4. 442.
Somme, *s.* sum, number, b. 17. 29.
Somnoures, *pl.* summoners, apparitors, b. 15. 128; Somners, 3. 59, 4. 171. See **Somenour**, and note to 4. 171.
Sompne, *v.* to summon, 4. 472, b. 3. 314; Lete sompne = caused to be summoned, 3. 172; Sompned, *pp.* 13. 46.
Sompnoure, summoner, b. 4. 167;

Sompnoures, *pl.* b. 3. 133. See Somenour.
Som-what, something, 19. 265.
Sond, sand, 15. 40.
Sonday, Sunday, 7. 418.
Sonde, *s.* sending, message, visitation, 7. 111; b. 9. 126; gift, 17. 136; Sondis, *s. pl.* messages, R. 4. 28. *Sondis,* presents sent, occurs in Pecock's Repressor.
Sondrid, *pt. pl.* separated, R. 2. 154; dispersed, R. 2. 14.
Sondry, *adj.* sundry, divers, 19. 153, 23. 42; various, 19. 193.
Sone, *adv.* soon, 4. 50, 61; Sone so = so soon as, b. 10. 226; As sone so = as soon as, 20. 63.
Sone, son, 2. 164, 4. 370.
Soneday, Sunday, 8. 65, 19. 183. Sonendayes, *pl.* a. 2. 197. From A.S. gen. case *sunnan.*
Soner, *adv.* more easily, 4. 62.
Song, *pt. s.* sang, 21. 469; Songen, *pt. pl.* 8. 154, 15. 94.
Songewarie, interpretation of dreams, 10. 302. Lit. observation of dreams; from O.F. *songe,* Lat. *somnium,* a dream, and O.F. *warir,* to guard, keep.
Sonken, *pt. pl.* went down, b. 14. 80.
Sonne, sun, 1. 1, 2. 117; Sonnes, *pl.* 4. 482.
Sonnedayes, Sundays, 3. 231.
Sonnere, *adv.* sooner, 12. 257, 292; rather, 3. 141; Sonner, 19. 64. See Sone.
Sonne-rysynge, sunrise, 21. 70.
Sonnest, *adv.* the soonest, 2. 66; soonest, b. 1. 70.
Sonne-syde, sunny side, 19. 64.
Sope, soap, b. 14. 6.
Soper, supper, 7. 429, 9. 276.
Sopers, *pl.* soap-sellers, 6. 72.
Sophistre, professor, teacher, 18. 311.
Sophistrie, sophistry, 22. 349.
Soppe, *s.* morsel, piece of sopped bread, b. 15. 175; At a soppe = at the value of a sop of bread, at small value, b. 13. 124. 'A *soppe,* a *sope* in ale, offa, offella, offula;' Cath. Angl.
Sorceerie, magic, 19. 150.
Sore, *adj.* painful, b. 14. 96.
Sore, *adv.* sorely, b. 14. 106; much, deeply, b. 11. 219, sharply, strongly, painfully, 20. 272. Cf. G. *sehr,* very.
Sore, *s.* wound, hurt, 21. 388; Sores, *pl.* diseases, 18. 302.
Sorfait, *s.* surfeit, 9. 277; Sorfetes, *pl.* surfeiting, b. 13. 405.
Sorfeten, *v.* surfeit, 14. 188.

Sorghful, *adj.* in pain, 19. 15.
Sori, *adj.* sorry, repentant, grieved, miserable, b. pr. 45. See Sory.
Sorname, surname, 4. 369.
Sorquidours, *pl.* proud men, 22. 341. From O.F. *sorcuider,* to presume, think much of oneself; see *cuider* in Burguy.
Sorwe, sorrow, pain, 1. 113, 3. 126; lamentation, 4. 17; Sorwes, *pl.* griefs, troubles, 4. 90.
Sory, *adj.* 12. 58; wretched, unhappy, 4. 361, a. 11. 190; troubled (man), 20. 326. See Sori.
Soster, sister, 12. 98.
Sotel, *adj.* cunning, subtle, 5. 149, 11. 207. See Sotil, Sotyl.
Soteleþ, *pr. s.* cunningly devises, schemes, 22. 459; Sotelide, 1 *pt. s.* schemed, 21. 336. See Sotilen.
Soteltes, *pl.* subtleties, crafts, cleverness, 15. 76; Soteltees, deceits, 13. 240.
Soth, *adj.* true, 10. 62, 19. 194, b. 5. 282. A.S. *sóð.*
Soþ, *s.* truth, the truth, 20. 21, b. 9. 154: Soþe, 2. 82, 4. 287; Sothes, *pl.* truths, b. 3. 281, R. 2. 151.
Sothe, *pt. pl.* cooked, boiled, seethed, b. 15. 288. '*Sothen,* elixus, lixus, lixatus, coctus;' Cath. Angl.
Sothest, the truest, b. 10. 441.
Sothest, *adv.* most truly, 4. 439.
Sothfast, *adj.* true, real, 12. 132; steadfast, b. 13. 217.
Soþfastnesse, *s.* truth, steadfastness, b. 16. 186.
Sothliche, *adv.* truly, in truth, verily, 2. 47, 4. 332, 7. 240; Sothlich, 4. 54; Soþlyche, a. 11. 176; Sothly, 2. 116; Soþeliche, 23. 15; Sothelich, b. 3. 5.
Sothnesse, truthfulness, truth, right, 3. 24; Sothenesse, b. 11. 142.
Sotil, *adj.* subtle, cunning, b. 15. 392. See Sotel, Sotyl.
Sotilen, *v.* argue subtly, a. 11. 139; Sotileth, *pr. s.* devises cunningly, b. 19. 554: Sotiled, 1 *pt. s.* devised by skill, b. 10. 214; Sotiled, *pt. s.* schemed, 18. 169; Sotilede, 1 *pt. pl.* invented, 7. 189. See Sotyle, Soteleþ.
Sottes, *pl.* fools, sots, 10. 256.
Sotyl, *adj.* skilful, b. 13. 298; marvellous, b. 15. 12; Sotyle, clever, b. 15. 48. See Sotil, Sotel.
Sotyle, *v.* reason subtly, make use of cunning, b. 10. 183. See Sotilen.
Souchen, *v.* devise, 13. 240; Souche, *pr. s. subj.* 3. 26. See two quotations

GLOSSARIAL INDEX. 439

(in Halliwell) from Gower, where it is said to mean 'suspect.' But it is the F. *se soucier*, to be anxious about, from Lat. *sollicitare*.
Soudeþ, *pr. s.* pays, 22. 431. O.F. *souder*, Lat. *solidare*; see note.
Souel, *s.* anything eaten with bread as a relish, 9. 286, 18. 24. See Saulee. '*Sowle*, edulium, pulmentarium;' Cath. Angl.
Soueraynliche, *adv.* chiefly, above all things, best of all, 7. 92.
Souereyn, *adj.* excellent, chief, supreme, 7. 27, 16. 295; Souereyne, 2. 148.
Souereyn, *s.* master, a. 10. 72; lord,'22. 77; Souereyne, R. pr. 77; Souereynes, *pl.* lords, chief ones, princes, great men, 12. 269; Souereignes, principal guests, b. 12. 200.
Souereynliche, *adv.* as a conqueror, by force, 21. 397; especially, 14. 203; Souereyneliche, especially, 18. 278. See Soueraynliche.
Souhte, *pt. s.* went, retired, 18. 169; sought, applied to, a. 4. 49; Souhte, *pt. s. subj.* should seek, were to search, 4. 166; Souht, *pp.* sought, a. 6. 15.
Souken, *v.* suck, 13. 55.
Soule, *s.* soul, a. 8. 23; Soule, *gen.* soul's, b. 18. 365; Soule hele = soul's salvation, b. 5. 270; Soules, *pl.* souls, a. 1. 121.
Soule, *adj.* sole, single, R. 1. 62.
Sound, *adj.* sound, a. 9. 29.
Souneþ, *pr. s.* sounds like, hints at, reminds of, 10. 216: Soune, *pr. s. subj.* (*with* of), tend to, 12. 79; tend, 22. 455; Sounede, *pt. s.* tended, 7. 59. See note to 7. 59.
Sounye, *v.* swoon, faint, become insensible, 21. 58; Sounede, *pt. pl.* swooned, 23. 105.
Soupen, *v.* sup, b. 2. 96; Soupe, 9. 228; Soupeth, *pr. s.* sups, b. 15. 175; Soupen, *pr. pl.* have a meal, b. 14. 178.
Sourdid, *pt. s.* arose, R. pr. 5. From O.F. *sourdre*, Lat. *surgere*.
Soure, *adj.* sour, bitter, 21. 219, b. 11. 250; *pl.* bitter, sharp, 23. 47.
Soure, *adv.* bitterly, sourly, 3. 154.
Sourquidours. See Surquidous.
Souter, *s.* a cobbler, shoemaker, 7. 83; Souteres, *pl.* b. 5. 413; Souteris, a. 11. 181, 301; Souters, a. 5. 158. A.S. *sútere*, a shoemaker, borrowed from Lat. *sutor*.
Souteresse, *s.* female shoemaker or seller of shoes, b. 5. 315.

Souþ, *adv.* in the south, a. 8. 129.
Southdenes, sub-deans, 3. 187. See note. The Anglo-French form *south* is another spelling of *souz*, *soutz* (Lat. *subtus*), under. The *th* has here the force of *t*. See *South* in Gloss. to Liber Albus.
Souwe, *v.* sew up, mend, a. 7. 9; Souweþ, *imp. pl.* sew, a. 7. 19.
Souwen, *v.* sow (corn), a. 7. 59. See Sowen.
Souȝte, *pt. s.* went (lit. sought to go), b. 15. 392; *pt. pl.* sought, b. 7. 166. See Seche, Soȝt.
Sowe, *s.* sow, 14. 150.
Sowen, *v.* sow, a. 7. 28; Sowe, *v.* b. 7. 6; Sowen, *pp.* sown, 13. 186; sown seed in, 9. 3.
Sowen, *ger.* to sew, b. 14. 21. See Sewe.
Sowere, *s.* sower, 19. 227.
Sowers, *s. pl.* sewers, tailors, R. 3. 165.
Sowid, *pt. pl.* sowed, scattered, R. 2. 102.
Sowkid, *pt. s.* sucked, drew in, R. 4. 9. See Souken.
Sownede, *pt. s.* sounded, a. pr. 10.
Sowynge, *s.* sowing, a. 8. 102.
Soȝt, *pt. s. subj.* were to seek, 17. 293. See Souȝte.
Spac, *pt. s.* spake, uttered, a. 1. 47. See Spak, Speke.
Space, opportunity, 4. 217.
Spaklich, *adv.* quickly, b. 17. 81. See below.
Spakliche, *adv.* sprightly, lively, b. 18. 12. See note, p. 249.
Sparen, *pr. pl.* are sparing, save up, b. 12. 53; Spareþ, *imp. pl.* spare, a. 7. 11.
Sparwe, *s.* sparrow, b. 15. 119 *n.*
Speche, *s.* speech, a. 2. 23, a. 6. 43, a. 8. 50; word, a. 10. 34.
Specheles, *adj.* without speech, voiceless, 17. 198.
Spede, *v.* succeed, do any good, 4. 217; prosper, 8. 240, b. 3. 270; increase, b. 20. 54; Spede, *v.* succeed, fare, 4. 428; Spede if he myȝte, (hoping) to succeed if he could, b. 17. 81; Spede, *pr. s. subj.* prosper, 11. 107; Spedde, *pt. s.* prospered, 14. 24.
Spedelich, *adj.* profitable, a. 12. 95.
Spedily, *adv.* speedily, a. 7. 11.
Speke, *pr. pl.* speak, utter, b. 10. 40; Speke, 2 *pt. s.* spakest, saidst, b. 12. 192; Speke, *pt. pl.* spoke, 22. 130; Speeken, a. 2. 201. See Spac, Spak.
Speke, *v.* speak to, address, (but rather read *seke* or *seche*, seek out), b. 15. 183.

Spekes, *pl.* caves, b. 15. 270. From Lat. *specus.* See note.
Speke-vuel-by-hynde, Speak-evil-behind, i.e. behind one's back, 22. 342.
Spele, *v.* spare, save, 7. 432, 14. 77. See note, p. 94.
Spelle, *v.* spell, relate (*or* make out), 18. 321.
Spelonkes, *pl.* caverns, b. 15. 270. From Lat. *spelunca.* See note.
Spences, *pl.* expenses, spendings, 17. 40.
Spendeth, *pr. s.* spends, a. 8. 50. See **Spene.**
Spendour, spendthrift, 6. 28.
Spendyng, *adj.* to spend, for spending, b. 11. 278. See below.
Spendynge, *s.* spending, expenses, b. 14. 197.
Spene, *v.* spend, expend, 3. 101; Speneþ, *pr. s.* spends, expends, makes use of, 10. 46; Spenen, *pr. pl.* spend, expend, 10. 74, 18. 71; Spene, waste, b. 15. 322; Spene, *imper. s.* let him spend, b. 10. 87; Spene, 1 *p. pl. imper.* let us spend, b. 15. 139. See above.
Spere, spear, 21. 10; Sper, 21. 89.
Sperhauke, sparrow-hawk, b. 6. 199.
Spewen, *pr. pl.* spew, b. 10. 40.
Spicede, *pt. s.* spiced up, 22. 288; Spiced, b. 19. 283.
Spicerie, spices, 3. 101, R. 3. 273.
Spicers, spicers, grocers, 3. 235; Spiceres, b. 2. 225. (What we now call a *grocer* was formerly a *spicer.*)
Spices, *pl.* spices, 7. 358.
Spik, spike, ear, 13. 180.
Spille, *v.* destroy, waste, lose, 4. 427, 466; spend, b. 10. 100; ruin, b. 3. 308; punish, 22. 303; die, perish, 12. 43; correct, b. 19. 298; Spilleth, *pr. s.* spoils, b. 5. 41; Spillen, *pr. pl.* are ruined, b. 15. 131; Spilde, 1 *pt. s.* wasted, spilt, 7. 432; Spille, *imp. s.* destroy, b. 3. 270.
Spille-loue, Destroy-love, 22. 342.
Spille-tyme, a waster of time, 6. 28.
Spinne, *ger.* spin, a. 5. 130.
Spinsters, *pl.* women engaged in spinning, a. 5. 130. See **Spynnesters.**
Spire, *s.* shoot, scion, 19. 232; Spir, blade (of wheat), 13. 180. See **Spyre**; and see note, p. 172.
Spire, 1 *pr. s.* enquire, 20. 1. See **Spure**; and note. A.S. *spyrian.*
Spiritualte, spiritual possessions, or spiritual rank (opposed to *temporality*), 7. 125. See note.
Spiritus, *s. pl.* spirits, 1. 18.

Spise, *s.* species, kind, sort (of remedy for sin), b. 1. 147. The same word as *spice,* O.F. *espice,* from Lat. *species.*
Spitten, *pt. pl.* dug, weeded, 9. 184. A spade is sometimes called a *spit;* the same term also signifies the depth to which a spade goes in digging; see Halliwell.
Spitten, *pr. pl.* spit, b. 10. 40.
Spores, *pl.* spurs, 21. 10, 12.
Spottes, *pl.* spots, b. 13. 315.
Spouseden, *pt. pl.* married, a. 10. 173; Spoused, *pp.* a. 10. 154.
Spradde, *pt. pl.* spread, 9. 184. See **Sprede.**
Sprakliche, *adj.* sprightly, lively, 21. 10. See note. *Sprack,* lively, is noted as a Berkshire word, in a Glossary by Job Lousley.
Sprede, *v.* spread, b. 20. 54; Spredeþ, *pr. s.* 14. 24; Spradde, *pt. pl.* 9. 184.
Spring, *s.* a young shoot of a tree, a twig, rod, switch, 6. 139.
Springeþ, *pr. pl.* spring, issue, 19. 190; Spronge, *pp.* born, sprung, 11. 226, 19. 207; Spronge, *pt. s. subj.* dawned, 22. 150. See **Sprynge.**
Sprynge, *v.* spring up, 15. 27; take its rise, arise, b. 11. 194. See **Springeþ.**
Spure, *v.* enquire (Scottish *speir*), 4. 109. See **Spire.** A.S. *spyrian.*
Spye, scout, spy, 20. 1.
Spynnen, *v.* spin, 4. 466; Spynneth, *imp. pl.* a. 7. 11.
Spynnesters, female spinners, 7. 222. See **Spinsters.**
Spyre, *s.* shoot, germ, b. 9. 100. See **Spire.**
Squire, square (for measurement), 12. 127. Used by Spenser. Cf. *esquierre* in Cotgrave.
Stable, *adj.* steady, a. 10. 110.
Stable, *v.* be established, R. 3. 249; render firm *or* cause to rest, b. 1. 120; Stablithe, *pr. s.* stands firm, R. 1. 10. 'To stable, *stabilire;*' Cath. Angl.
Staf, staff, stick, 7. 106; Staffe, b. 12. 14.
Stal, 1 *pt. s.* stole, 7. 265; Stale, b. 13. 367; Stall, *pt. s.* R. 2. 164. See **Stele.**
Stalles, *pl.* booths, b. 16. 128.
Stalworth, *adj.* strong, b. 17. 96.
Stant, *pr. s.* (*for* Standeþ), stands, 21. 42; is, 18. 205; appears, b. 15. 505.
Stappe, *v.* step, walk, 7. 403. See **Steppe.**
Stare, *v.* stare, R. 3. 189; Stareden, *pt. pl.* a. 4. 143; Starynge, *pr. pt.* looking sternly, b. 10. 4.

GLOSSARIAL INDEX. 441

Statt, *s.* rank, R. 3. 174.
Statues, *s. pl.* statutes, a. 7. 305. See below.
Statute, statute, 9. 343.
Staues, *s. pl.* staves, sticks, 1. 51, 6. 131.
Steddeffaste, *s.* steadfast man, R. 3. 209.
Stede, *s.* stead, place, b. pr. 96; place, passage (in a book), b. 14. 131; In stede of, in place of, 1. 94; Stedes, *pl.* places, 6. 146.
Stede, a horse, steed, 7. 43; On stede, on horseback, b. 13. 294; Stedis, *pl.* R. 3. 21.
Steeris, *s. pʹ.* steers, oxen, R. 3. 251.
Stekye, *v.* stick fast, remain closed, b. 1. 121. Cf. Low. Scotch *steik, steek,* to fasten. See Stykeþ.
Stele, handle, 22. 279; see note. A.S. *stel.* Cf. Shropsh. *stail, stele,* a handle.
Stele, *v.* steal (slily), 7. 106; Steleth on, *pr. pl.* steal on, creep near, R. 3. 21; Stelyn, *pt. pl.* stole, 22. 156. See Stal.
Stel-net, *imper. s.* Steal-not, 8. 224.
Steorne, *s.* helm, a. 9. 30. 'Sterne of ye schype, *clauus*;' Cath. Angl.
Steorneliche, *adv.* sternly, a. 7. 305.
Steppe, *v.* walk, move, 20. 54, 87; R. 3. 54. See Stappe.
Stere, *v.* stir, move, 20. 54; Sterede, *pt. s.* stirred, 23. 103; R. 3. 269. See Stire.
Stereth, *pr. s.* steers, guides, b. 8. 47; Sterid, *pp.* R. 4. 80.
Sterlynge, sterling coin, b. 15. 342.
Sterne, *adv.* sternly, b. 15. 248.
Sterneliche, *adv.* sternly, angrily, 12. 4. See Steorneliche.
Sterre, star, 21. 243; Sterres, *pl.* stars, 10. 309; Seuene sterris, seven stars, i.e. the seven planets, R. 3. 352.
Sterte, *v.* start, run, 20. 297.
Sterue, *v.* die, perish, 7. 290, 11. 200; Sterueth, *pr. s.* perishes, dies, 6. 151; Steruen, *pr. pl.* perish, 10. 101; Sterue, *pr. s. subj.* die, 13. 179. A.S. *steorfan,* E. *starve.*
Sterynge, *s.* moving, stirring, motion, 11. 36.
Stewed, *pp.* bestowed, governed, 6. 146. See Stouwet.
Stewes, *pl.* stews, brothels, 23. 160. See Stuwes, Styues. See Cath. Angl. p. 363, n. 5.
Stiere, *s.* helm, b. 8. 35. See Steorne.
Stif, *adv.* stiffly, steadily, b. 8. 33.
Stihlede, *pt. s.* arranged, set in order, 16. 40. See note.

Stire, *v.* stir; Stirid, *pt. s.* instigated, lit. stirred, R. 1. 114; Stired, *pt. pl.* stirred, b. 20. 102. See Stere.
Stiwarde, steward, 22. 463; Stiward, a. 5. 39.
Stock, stock, 11. 207. See Stok.
Stockes, the stocks, 5. 103, 8. 223, 9. 163, 10. 34. See Stokkes.
Stode, *pt. pl.* stood, 21. 86; *pt. s. subj.* would stand, would exist, b. 14. 251. See Stant, Stonden.
Stodie, *s.* study, a. 12. 61.
Stodie, *ger.* to study, a. 12. 6; Stodieden, *pt. pl.* studied, consulted, 18. 307. See Studie.
Stok, stock, stem, 19. 30.
Stokkes, *pl.* the stocks, b. 4. 108, b. 5. 585; stocks, trunks, a. 6. 66; frames, b. 15. 445.
Stole, *pp.* stolen, 18. 40. See Stele.
Stole, *s.* stool, b. 5. 394.
Stomble, *v.* to stumble, fall, 11. 35; Stombleth, *pr. s.* b. 8. 33; Stombled, 2 *pt. pl.* stumbled, R. 1. 114.
Ston, stone, 7. 106. See Stoon.
Stonden, *v.* cost, 4. 51 (cf. the mod. phrase 'to *stand* one in so much money'); stand, remain, b. 1. 121; Stonde, *v.* stand, R. 3. 249; stand still, b. 6. 114; resist, b. 8. 47; Stondeþ, *pr. s.* stands, a. 2. 5; Stont, stands, exists, a. 10. 129; Stonde, *pr. s. subj.* though he stand, 11. 36; Stooden, *pt. pl.* stood, a. 4. 143.
Stone, *dat.* grave, b. 15. 584; Stones, *pl.* stones, b. 12. 77. See Ston.
Stone, *v.* to stone, b. 12. 77.
Stonyed, 2 *pt. pl.* didst astonish, didst amaze, R. 2. 125.
Stoon, stone, 15. 37, 42. See Ston.
Store, *s.* store, b. 3. 177.
Story, *s.* tale, R. pr. 82; Stories, *pl.* histories, b. 7. 73.
Stottes, *pl.* bullocks (*or perhaps* horses), 22. 267. See the note.
Stoule, a stool, 8. 3. See Stole.
Stounde, while, short time, 11. 64. A.S. *stund.*
Stoupe, *v.* to stoop, bend, 6. 24, 8. 3, 12. 197.
Stouttely, *adv.* proudly, R. 1. 114.
Stouwet, *pp.* ordered, arranged, a. 5. 39. See Stewed.
Strake, *s.* streak, narrow strip (apparently here used for a reef in a sail), R. 4. 80. See *Strake* (7) in Halliwell; and see Striked.
Strawe, straw for a bed, b. 14. 233; A strawe for = I would only give a straw for, 17. 93.

Strayues, *pl.* strays, 1. 92. The old sense of *stray* was property which was left behind by an alien at his death, and which went to the king for default of heirs. See *estrayeres* in Cotgrave, and *estrahere* in Roquefort. The form *strafe* is still in use in Shropshire in the sense of 'a stray animal'; see Shropsh. Wordbook.
Streche, *v. refl.* stretch, to stretch himself, b. 14. 233.
Strenede, *pt. s.* emitted, 14. 172. A.S. *streónan,* to procreate.
Strengest, *adj.* strongest, b. 13. 294.
Strengthe, strength, defence, a. 8. 83; Strengþe, strength, a. 5. 196; Strenthe, 4. 347; Strengthes, *pl.* strongholds, 4. 238.
Strengthe, *ger.* to strengthen, 4. 348; Strengþeþ, *pr. s.* a. 9. 42; Strengþe, *imp. s.* a. 10. 110.
Streyneth, *pr. s.* strains, exerts, 17. 76.
Streyte, *adv.* narrowly, strictly, b. pr. 26.
Streyues, *pl.* strays, b. pr. 94. See **Strayues.**
Strie, *v.* destroy, R. 3. 269; Stried, *pt. s.* destroyed, trampled on, R. 2. 26. Short for *destrie;* see **Stroied.**
Striked, *pp.* struck, let down (as in our 'struck sail'), R. 4. 80. 'I *stryke,* I let downe the crane, *Ie lache';* Palsgrave. See **Strake.**
Stroied, *pt. s.* destroyed, R. 2. 104. See **Strie.**
Strok, *pt. s.* moved, came quickly, 1. 197; Stroke, *pt. s.* b. pr. 183. A.S. *strícan,* to go, Du. *strijken,* to sweep rapidly over a surface, to graze. See **Stryke.**
Strompet, strumpet, 15. 42.
Stroute, *v.* strut, R. 3. 189.
Strouters, *pl.* strutters, R. 3. 269.
Stroutynge, *pres. pt.* strutting, 'swelling' about, R. 3. 121. See note.
Stroutynge, *s.* strutting, shewing off of dresses, R. 3. 134, 177.
Struyen, *v.* destroy, 18. 307; Stroyen, b. 15. 587; Stroyeth, *pr. s.* destroys, R. 3. 134; Struen, *pr. pl.* destroy, 9. 27; Struyeth, b. 6. 29; Struyeden, *pt. pl.* destroyed, 18. 307; Stroyden, b. 15. 287.
Stryke, *v.* strike, b. 12. 77; Stryk, *imper. s.* strike out a path, pass, proceed, take your way, 8. 224; Stryke, 2 *pr. s. subj.* mayst strike, b. 12. 14. See **Strok.**
Strykers, *pl.* wanderers, 10. 159. See above.

Stude, *s.* place, stead, a. 5. 39. See **Stede.**
Studefast, *adj.* steadfast, firm, a. 10. 110. See **Steddeffaste, Stydfast.**
Studie, *v.* muse, ponder, reflect, 10. 297; Studye, b. 7. 143; Studyest, 2 *pr. s.* studiest, b. 12. 223. See **Stodie.**
Studiing, *s.* studying, a. 4. 143.
Stues, *pl.* stews, b. 6. 72.
Stunte, *v.* stop, a. 11. 166; Stunt, *imp. s.* delay, a. 6. 66. See **Stynte.**
Stureþ, *pr. s.* steers, guides, a. 9. 42. See **Stiere.**
Sturne, *adv.* sternly, 9. 343.
Sturneliche, *adv.* boldly, 1. 197.
Stuwardes, *pl.* stewards, b. pr. 96, b. 5. 48. See **Stiwarde.**
Stuwes, *pl.* stews, brothels, 14. 75, 22. 437; Stuyues, a. 7. 65.
Stydfast, *adj.* enduring, b. 15. 573. See **Studefast.**
Styf, *adj.* loud, firm, b. 15. 584; Styffe, violent, R. 3. 104. See **Stif.**
Styffe, *pr. pl.* grow stiff, grow strong, R. 3. 54.
Styfliche, *adv.* stoutly, firmly, 13. 36.
Stykeþ, *pr. s.* is fixed, 4. 384. See **Stekye.**
Stykkes, *pl.* twigs, b. 11. 339.
Style, stile (in a hedge), 7. 145, 207.
Stynte, *v.* stop, leave off, 3. 166; halt, b. 10. 220; pause, b. 1. 120; Stynted, *pt. pl.* ceased, R. 2. 125; Stynt, *imper. pl.* stop, delay, 8. 223; Stynte, rest, b. 5. 585. See **Stunte.** A.S. *á-styntan,* orig. to blunt; see *stunten* in Stratmann.
Styueliche, *adv.* strongly, firmly (lit. stiffly), 4. 348.
Styues, *pl.* stews, 9. 71. See **Stewes,' Stuwes, Stywes.**
Styuest, *adj.* stiffest, sturdiest, 7. 43, b. 13. 294. See **Styf.**
Stywarde, steward, overseer, 16. 40, 22. 256. See **Stiwarde.**
Stywes, *pl.* stews, brothels, 17. 93. See **Stues, Stewes.**
Suddenes, *pl.* subdeans, b. 2. 172; Sudenes, b. 15. 128. See **Southdenes;** and note to 3. 187.
Suen, *v.* attend on, b. 11. 326; Sue, follow, b. 11. 414; Sueth, *pr. s.* persecutes, tempts, b. 1. 41; Sueth, *pr. pl.* follow, have adopted, b. 10. 202; Sued, *pp.* driven, b. 5. 550. See **Suwen.**
Suffraunce, allowance, tolerance, 1. 124, 4. 208; permission (due to negligence), a. 3. 93; patience, b.

GLOSSARIAL INDEX. 443

11. 370; Suffrance, long-suffering, patience, 14. 203, b. 6. 146. See note to 5. 189.
Suffren, v. endure, suffer, 22. 68; Suffre, 4. 403; allow to exist, b. 2. 174; Suffrye, v. suffer, 20. 322; Suffry, 21. 257; allow, 23. 322; Suffre, 1 p. s. pr. (I) allow, permit, a. 4. 1; Suffreþ, pr. s. suffers, allows, 22. 443; endures, b. 15. 169; Suffred, pp. had patience, been patient, b. 11. 403; Suffre, imp. s. suffer thou, a. 10. 96; Suffre, imp. 1 pl. be quiet, 21. 167; Suffreþ, imp. pl., suffer, allow, 19. 178.
Suget, s. subject, R. pr. 77.
Suggestion, cause, reason, excuse, 10. 62; Suggestioun, b. 7. 67.
Sullen, v. sell, a. 2. 189; Sulle, 4. 244; Sullen, pr. pl. sell, a. 7. 294. A.S. syllan.
Sullers, pl. sellers, tradesmen, a. 2. 46, a. 3. 79.
Suluer, silver, money, 4. 116, 7. 254.
Sum, adj. some, a. 8. 34. See Somme, Summe.
Sumdel, s. some deal, some part, in some measure, a. 3. 83. See Somdel.
Summe, pron. pl. some, a. 1. 114, a. 4. 97; dat. to some, a. 3. 266. See Sum, Somme.
Sumnors, s. pl. summoners, officers of the ecclesiastical courts (now called apparitors), a. 2. 46; Sumpnours, a. 3. 129.
Sunfol, adj. sinful, a. 5. 244.
Sunge, v. sin, a. 5. 151; Sungeþ, pr. s. sins, a. 9. 17; Sunget, pp. a. 8. 165.
Sunne, s. sin, offence, a. 3. 261; Sunnes, pl. sins, a. 1. 78. A.S. syn. See Synne.
Sunneles, adj. without sin, sinless, a. 7. 217. See Synneles.
Supersedeas, a writ so called, 3. 187, 10. 263. See note, p. 38. Cf. 'And litel or nought may helpen in this caas Saufcondit either supersedeas;' Lydgate, Siege of Thebes, ed. 1561, fol. 372, back, col. 1.
Suppriour, sub-prior, 7. 153.
Suren, v. plight one's troth to, give security to, b. 5. 547.
Surfait, s. surfeit, b. 6. 267.
Surgerye, surgery, surgical skill, powers of healing, 23. 178.
Surgien, surgeon, 23. 315; Surgeyn, 19. 140; Surgienes, pl. b. 14. 88.
Surlepes, adj. pl. distinct, separate, 19. 193. See Serelepes.
Surquydous, adj. arrogant man, b. 19.

335; Sourquidours, arrogant men, 22. 341. See note to 22. 341, p. 271. Cf. surquedrie, arrogance; described by Gower, C. A. 1. 105.
Suspecion, expectation, 18. 315.
Suster, sister, 4. 208, 21. 184; Sustre, 4. 54, 67; Sustres, pl. sisters, 7. 137; Susteres, 21. 207; Sustren, 17. 293.
Sustinaunce, livelihood, sustenance, food, maintenance, 6. 127, 23. 7.
Sute, retinue, train, suite, b. 14. 256; suit, clothing of human flesh, b. 5. 495. See note to 8. 130. 'A sute, secta; vt secta curie;' Cath. Angl.
Suþþen, adv. afterwards, 19. 18; Suþþe, conj. since, 21. 353; Suthþe, 10. 115; Suthen, conj. since, 20. 272; Sutthen, afterwards, 22. 143; conj. since, 21. 138; Sutthe, adv. afterwards, then, 12. 171.
Suwen, v. follow, attend, 14. 143; Suwe, attend to, b. 11. 21; Suwye forþ = keep, 3. 102; Suwe, 1 pr. s. sue, 4. 370; Suwest, 2 pr. s. followest, attendest, b. 11. 366; Suweþ, pr. s. follows, accompanies, 11. 161; pursues, b. 14. 323; Suweþ, pr. pl. follow, 6. 201; Suwen, b. 17. 101; Suwe, pr. s. subj. follow, practise, 23. 22; follow, 17. 95; may accompany, b. 14. 253; Suwede, 1 pt. s. followed, 20. 79; Suwed, b. 17. 84; Suwed, pt. s. 4. 328; pt. pl. b. 18. 190; Suwed, pp. followed, 11. 73; attended, b. 8. 75, a. 9. 66; Suwe, imp. s. follow, 13. 166. See Suen.
Suxt, 2 pr. s. seest, 11. 158, 20. 177. See Sixt.
Suynge, pr. pt. pursuing, 21. 361.
Swan, swan, R. 3. 28 (see note).
Swan-whit, adj. white as a swan, 21. 215.
Swelte, v. die, 7. 129; Swelte, pt. pl. died, 23. 105; Swelted, b. 20. 104. A.S. sweltan.
Swerd, s. sword, a. 1. 97; Swerde, 2. 103; Swerdis, pl. R. 3. 328.
Swere, v. be sworn (judicially), 6. 57; swear, 8. 200; Swerye, v. 2. 103, b. 14. 34; Swery, 1. 36; Swere, pr. pl. 10. 25. See Swor. A.S. swerian.
Sweten, v. sweat, toil, a. 7. 28; Swete, v. sweat, toil, labour hard, 1. 36, 6. 57; Swetynge, pres. pt. 9. 241.
Swettere, adj. comp. sweeter, 19. 60; Swettur, 15. 187; Swettour, 19. 65.
Swettere, adv. more pleasantly, 9. 228; Swettore, a. 7. 206.
Sweuene, s. dream, 10. 310, b. pr. 11, b. 7. 161. A.S. swefen.

GLOSSARIAL INDEX.

Sweyued, *pt. s.* flowed, rippled along (?), b. pr. 10. See **Sweyed.** This reading seems to be quite distinct from *sweyed*, i. e. sounded (in MS. W.), and to refer to the *motion* rather than to the *sound* of the stream. Cf. Dan. *svæve*, Swed. *zväfva*, to wave, hover, fluctuate.

Swich, *adj.* such, 1. 64 ; Swiche, R. 4. 2.

Swithe, *adv.* quickly, at once, 7. 422, 14. 53 ; Swithe, very, exceedingly, b. 5. 456, 470. From A.S. *swíð*, strong; Goth. *swinths;* cf. G. *geschwind.*

Swonken, *pt. pl.* laboured, toiled to get, 1. 23. See **Swynken.**

Swopen, *v.* sweep, cleanse, a. 5. 102.

Swor, 1 *pt. s.* swore, 7. 51 ; Sworen, *pt. pl.* 3. 181 ; Sworen, *pp.* 7. 427. See **Swere.**

Swot, *s.* sweat, 9. 241. A.S. *swát.*

Swote, *adj.* sweet, a. 10. 119.

Swouny, *v.* swoon, 7. 129 ; Swouned, 1 *pt. s.* I swooned, b. 16. 19.

Swowe, *v.* faint, swoon, b. 5. 154; Swowed, *pt. s.* b. 14. 326. A.S. *swógan*, to resound, sigh.

Swymmere, swimmer, b. 12. 167 ; Swymmers, *pl.* R. 3. 86.

Swynk, *s.* toil, a. 7. 220 ; Swynke, 9. 241, b. 6. 235. See below.

Swynken, *v.* labour, toil, 9. 263 ; Swynke, 1. 36, 6. 57. See **Swonken.** A.S. *swincan*, to toil.

Swynkeres, *pl.* labourers, 20. 173 ; Swynkers, 9. 260.

Swythe, *adv.* quickly, R. 3. 60. See **Swithe.**

Sybbe, *adj.* related, akin, 8. 278, 289 ; Syb, b. 5. 636. See **Sib.**

Sydbenche, a side-table, 10. 252.

Sydder, *adj.* (*or adv.*) longer, lower ; Wel sydder, even lower, 7. 200. See **Side.**

Syde-borde, a side-table, b. 13. 36. See below.

Syd-table, side-table, 15. 140, 16. 42.

Sygge, *v.* say, tell, 13. 233. See **Sigge.**

Syghede, *pt. s.* sighed, 21. 92. See **Sike, Syhede, Sykede.**

Syght, sight, permission, inspection, 3. 114 ; Syghte, sight, 22. 234. See **Siht.**

Sygne, stamp, lit. sign, mark, 5. 126 ; character, trace, 15. 40 (see note) ; Sygnes, *pl.* signatures, 3. 156 ; pilgrims' signs or tokens, 8. 169. See **Signe,** and note to 8. 166.

Syhede, *pt. s.* sighed, groaned, 21. 276. See **Syghede.**

Syke, *adj.* sick, ill, 9. 147, 272 ; sick (man), 20. 63 ; Syk, sick (man), 20. 326 ; Syke, *adj. as sb. pl.* sick men, 5. 122.

Sykede, 1 *pt. s.* sighed, 19. 16 ; Syked, *pt. s.* sighed, groaned, b. 14. 326. See **Syghede.**

Sykel, sickle, 4. 464, 6. 23.

Syker, *adj.* safe, sure, certain, fixed, 10. 331, 23. 255 ; secure, regular (thing), 4. 337. See **Siker.**

Sykeren, *v.* assure, give my sure word, promise faithfully, 8. 185. See above.

Sykerer, *adj. comp.* safer, in a safer position, b. 12. 162.

Sykerer, *adv.* more free from care, more securely, b. 11. 258. See **Sykerour.**

Sykerest, *adj.* safest, 6. 39.

Sykerliche. *adv.* surely, certainly, 9. 23. See **Sikerliche.**

Sykerloker, *adv. comp.* with more confidence, 8. 142.

Sykerour, *adv.* more securely, 13. 150. See **Sykerer.**

Sykinge, *pres. part.* sighing, lamenting, 6. 107.

Syknesse, illness, 9. 271, 20. 320 ; Syknesses, *pl.* 20. 316.

Syllynge, *s.* selling, 22. 235.

Symple, *adj.* meek, a. 9. 110.

Symplete, simplicity, b. 10. 165.

Synegen, *v.* sin, 13. 240, 20. 264 ; Synege, 21. 230 ; Synegeþ, *pr. s.* sins, 20. 161, 166 ; Syneweþ, does wrong, 23. 15 ; Synegy, *pr. s. subj.* sin, 15. 112 ; Syneged, *pp.* sinned, 20. 275. See **Syngen, Synwe.** A.S. *syngian.*

Synful, *adj. pl.* sinful (men), 22. 22 ; b. 7. 15, a. 12. 20.

Synge, *v.* sing, 21. 183 ; Syngen, *pr. pl.* sing, offer, 4. 313 ; celebrate, a. 3. 238.

Syngen, *v.* sin, do wrong, 1. 109 ; Syngeþ, 11. 23, 25, 26, 31 ; Synged, *pp.* sinned, 10. 329. See **Synegen;** and note, p. 13.

Synguler, *adj.* excelling all, 7. 36, b. 13. 283 ; sole, b. 16. 208 ; Synguler, alone, b. 9. 35.

Synne, *s.* sin, 4. 331, b. 10. 108.

Synneles, *adj.* sinless, free from sin, 15. 41 ; (*or adv.*) without committing sin, 9. 237.

Synne-ward, *adv.* with a wish to sin, 7. 179.

Synwe, *v.* sin, 7. 356.

GLOSSARIAL INDEX. 445

Syre, father, 1. 109, 19. 194; grown-up person, a. 11. 62; sir, 11. 126; Syres, *gen. sing.* sire's, father's, 4. 369; Syres, *pl.* elders, seniors, 1. 177. See **Sire**.

Syse, assize, 3. 178.

Sysour, jury-man, juror, 23. 161; Sysours, *pl.* 3. 59, 4. 171. See **Sisour**.

Sythe, scythe, 6. 23.

Sythen, *adv.* then, afterwards, b. 11. 354. See **Sithen**.

Sythes, *s. pl.* times, 1. 231, 11. 23, b. pr. 230. See **Sithe**.

Sythþe, *conj.* since, 3. 134. See **Siþthen**.

Sytthen, since, 6. 40. See **Sitthen**.

Sytthenes, *adv.* afterwards, then, b. 9. 115.

Sywestere, sempstress (lit. sew-ster), 7. 362.

Syxt, 2 *pr. s.* seest, 2. 5. See **Sixt**.

Syxte, sixth, 17. 139. Still pronounced *sixt* in Shropshire.

Syȝt, *s.* sight, b. pr. 32; Syȝte, b. 13. 283; look, glance, b. 14. 13; outward appearance, b. 10. 253. See **Siȝte**.

Tabarde, *s.* a short coat or mantle, with loose sleeves, or sometimes without sleeves, 7. 203; Tabart, a. 5. 111. See note. '*Hoc colobium*, a taberd;' Wright's Vocab. i. 238.

Taberes, *s. pl.* drummers, tabor-players, a. 2. 79.

Tabre, *s.* tabor, small drum, R. 1. 58.

Tabre, *v.* play on the tabour, 16. 205. See note. Cf. Shropsh. *tabor*, to drum.

Tacches, *pl.* stains, blemishes, faults, b. 9. 146. See *tache* in Halliwell and Stratmann. O.F. *tache, teche*; whence E. *tetchy*, and M.E. *tached*, tainted, stained. 'If he be *tachyd* with this inconuenyence' [defect]; Barclay, Ship of Fools, i. 58, l. 11.

Tache, tinder, touch-wood, 20. 211. Hence Mod. E. *touchwood = tachewood*.

Tail, tail, following, 3. 196; person, 4. 167; Taile, person, b. 3. 130; Taille, tail, b. 12. 242; tail, end, conclusion, b. 3. 347; train of followers, b. 2. 185; Tailles, *pl.* roots of trees, b. 5. 19. In 11. 80, 17. 258, *trewe of tail* (not *taile*), must mean 'true of person,' continent (cf. 4. 167), rather than 'true of reckoning.' See **Tayl**.

Taile, tally, a stick on which an amount of money is notched or scored, 5. 61; Taille, tally, b. 5. 252; Taille, b. 15. 103. See **Tayle**. O.F. *taille*, Lat. *talea*. See note, p. 56; and see below.

Tailende, *s.* reckoning by tally, b. 8. 82. (A false form for *tailynge*, by confusion of the sb.-ending *-ynge* with the pres. pt. suffix *-ende*). See above; and see **Taylende, Taile**.

Taillage, tribute, taxation, 22. 37. See **Tallage**.

Taille-ende, tail-end, wish to go to stool, b. 5. 395. See note to 8. 4.

Taillours, *pl.* tailors, 10. 204, a. pr. 100; Tailloures, *gen. pl.* tailors', b. 15. 447. See **Taylours**.

Take, *v.* (1) receive, b. 11. 282, b. 17. 245; (2) give, 2. 52, 4. 353, 14. 106, 23. 260; Take, 1 *pr. s.* I am taken, I am seized, b. 13. 334; Takeþ, *pr. s.* gives, pays, 5. 61; hands over, a. 2. 52; returns, a. 4. 45; Taken, *pr. pl.* accept, take, 4. 126; *refl.* collect, meet, consult, 7. 154; Taken on, *pr. pl.* continue to act, persevere, 14. 154; Take, *pr. pl. subj.* give, 4. 87; Take, *pp.* taken, 18. 289; Takeþ, *imper. pl.* take, receive, 21. 93. *Take* (= give) is common in M.E., and occurs in Chaucer. Cf. also Shropsh. *taking*, a sudden seizure of pain. See **Tok**.

Tale, *s.* tale, a. 2. 83; esp. a lying tale, b. 2. 114, b. 3. 45; account, 2. 9; enumeration, 4. 394; thing, matter, b. 11. 291; Holde þei no tale = they make no account, b. 1. 9; Gyue þei neuere tale = they make no account, b. 19. 451; A tale of nouht, a thing of no account, 14. 114.

Tale-tellours, *pl.* tale-bearers, 23. 299.

Talewys, *adj.* loquacious, slanderous, talebearing, 4. 167. See note.

Tallage, *s.* taxation, R. 1. 15. See **Taillage**.

Tapesters, *pl.* barmaids, a. 2. 79. The suffix *-ster* was orig. feminine.

Tarre, tar, salve, 10. 262.

Tarse, silken stuff, b. 15. 163. See note, p. 220.

Tartaryne, silk, cloth of Tartary, b. 15. 224. See note to b. 15. 163. In Mandeville's Travels, pp. 175, 247, we have mention of 'Clothes of Tartarye.' At p. 252 of the same, *Tartarine* means a Tartar; and at p. 255, we read of 'clothes of Gold and of Camakaas and *Tartarynes*.'

E e 2

GLOSSARIAL INDEX.

Taseles, *pl.* teasles, b. 15. 446. See note.
Tastes, *pl.* investigations, b. 12. 131.
Taste, *v.* feel, touch, b. 13. 346; venture to attack, b. 18. 84; kiss, 7. 179; Tasted, *pt. s.* felt, b. 17. 147. See note to 21. 87.
Tauerners, *pl.* innkeepers, 1. 228.
Tauernes, *pl.* inns, 3. 98, 7. 50.
Tauhte, *pt. s.* taught, 2. 71, 3. 8, 4. 440, 6. 131; directed, 23. 9; Tauhten, *pt. pl.* taught, 12. 216. See **Tauȝtest, Techen.**
Tauny, *adj.* tawny, of a dull orange or yellowish brown colour, b. 5. 196. See note, p. 82.
Tauȝtest, 2 *pt. s.* taughtest, b. 14. 183; Tauȝte, *pt. s.* taught, instructed, b. 3. 282, b. 6. 211; taught (us), b. 11. 222. See **Tauhte, Techen.**
Taxeþ, *pr. s.* taxes, lays a tax, 2. 159.
Taxour, assessor of a fine, 9. 37.
Tayl, *s.* tail, following, retinue, a. 2. 160; roots of trees, 6. 122; person, a. 3. 126. See **Tail.**
Tayle, *s.* tally, a stick (one of a pair) on which the amount of money is notched or scored, a. 4. 45. See **Taile.**
Taylende, *s.* reckoning of accounts, a. 9. 74; income, 4. 372. See **Tailende.**
Taylende, tail-end, tail, 8. 4. See b. 5. 395, and note. See **Taille-ende.**
Taylours, tailors, 1. 223, 5. 120.
Techen, *v.* teach, 1. 120; Teche, *imper. s.* shew the way, direct, 2. 79. See **Tauhte, Tauȝte.**
Teeme, team, 9. 141; Teme, b. 6. 136. See **Teome, Teme.**
Teeme, *s.* theme, subject, text, lesson, 9. 20, 10. 2. See **Teme.**
Teene, *s.* vexation, annoyance, 13. 49, 14. 7. See **Teone, Tene.**
Teenen, *v.* to vex, 15. 8; Teened, *pp.* annoyed, 12. 129. See **Teone, Tene.**
Teiȝen, *v.* tie, bind, a. 1. 94.
Tellen, *v.* tell, a. 3. 32; Herde telle, heard tell, a. 8. 1; Telle, 1 *pr. s.* 8. 17; Tellen, *pr. pl.* count, 1. 90; reckon up, b. pr. 92; Telle, *pr. s. subj.* may say, 8. 126; Telde, *pt. s.* told, R. 2. 151; Tellde, R. 3. 68; Telden, *pt. pl.* made account of, 16. 271; Telleþ, *imp. pl.* tell, 8. 298. See **Toide.**
Teme, team, b. 6. 136, b. 7. 2, b. 19. 256. See **Teome, Teeme.**
Teme, subject, theme, text, 7. 1, 13. 44, 16. 82. See **Teeme.**

Temperaltes, *pl.* temporalities, b. 20. 127.
Templers, *pl.* Knights Templars, 18. 209.
Temporalite, *s.* temporal power, 23. 128.
Tempre, *v.* temper, R. 3. 278; Tempreth, *pr. s.* moderates, restrains, 17. 146; Temprid, *pp.* tempered, R. 3. 202; Tempred, *pp.* fitted, attuned, b. pr. 51.
Tendeden, *pt. pl.* lighted, b. 18. 238; Tenden, 21. 250. Cf. A.S. *on-tendan,* to kindle. Allied to E. *tinder.*
Tene, pain, grief, vexation, 2. 166, 9. 124; annoyance, b. 11. 110; worry, trouble, b. 6. 135; sorrow, a. 10. 141; anger, b. 16. 86; Men to tene = as a vexation to men, a. 12. 9. See **Teene, Teone.** A.S. *téona,* vexation.
Tene, *v.* annoy, vex, trouble, 16. 160, b. 8. 97, b. 13. 163; 1 *pr. s.* injure, b. 5. 432; Teneþ, *pr. s.* annoys, troubles, 4. 160; Teneth, *pr. pl.* vex, b. 15. 412; Tene, 2 *pr. s. subj.* thou shouldst annoy, 4. 139; Tene, 2 *pr. pl. subj.* annoy, oppress, 9. 36; Tenede, *pt. s.* annoyed, troubled, 4. 478; Tened, injured, b. 3. 320; *refl.* was vexed, 3. 116; Tened, *pp.* vexed, annoyed, 8. 38; Tenyd, injured, R. 3. 79. A.S. *týnan,* to vex, from *téona,* injury. See **Teene, Teone.**
Teneful, *adj.* painful, annoying, harmful, 4. 498. See **Tene.**
Tente, *s.* intention, purpose, reason, R. 2. 92, 97. Short for *intente* or *entente.*
Teologye, *s.* theology, a. 2. 83.
Teome, team, 22. 261, 262; Teom, 22. 271. See **Teeme, Teme.**
Teone, *s.* vexation, a. 8. 100. See **Tene.**
Teone, *v.* injure, vex, trouble, a. 9. 89; Teoneþ, *pr. s.* injures, a. 3. 119; Teone, 2 *p. s. pr. subj.* injure, annoy, a. 7. 40; Teonede, *pt. s.* vexed, 23. 119; *refl.* was vexed, a. 2. 83; Teoned, *pp.* vexed, a. 11. 136. See **Teene, Tene.**
Tercian, *adj.* tertian, i.e. tertian fever, a. 12. 85.
Termes, *pl.* terms, similitudes, b. 12. 237.
Termysones, *pl.* terminations, 4. 409.
Testament, *s.* will, a. 7. 78.
Teþ, *pl.* teeth, 21. 84.
Þan (*dat. neut.*), that, 16. 295. A.S. *ðám.*
Þanne, *adv.* then, b. 6. 34, b. 8. 68,

GLOSSARIAL INDEX. 447

74; in that case, a. 11. 270; þanne
 . . . þanne, when . . . then, b. 16. 69.
þankus, *gen. s. as adv.*; Hus þankus,
 willingly, with his good will, 10. 66.
Thar, *adv.* where, 16. 289; þare,
 where, in which, 1. 114; there, 23.
 205.
That, *pron.* that which, whatever, 6.
 142, 17, 280; þat rith wolde þei
 hadde = that which justice intended
 they should have, R. 2. 137; he
 who, b. 15. 64; thou who, b. 18.
 362; him who, b. 12. 187; þat one
 = the one; þat other = the other, b.
 12. 163, 164; þat þat = that which,
 b. 3. 347; þat ilke = that very, b. 6.
 164.
Thauh, *conj.* though, even if, although,
 1. 199, 2. 10; þau3, a. 1. 132; þawe,
 11. 42. See þeigh.
Thaym, *pron.* those, 23. 110.
The, *pron. dat.* to thee, 2. 39, 14. 234;
 acc. thee, 2. 37.
þe bet, the better, b. 11. 169.
þe which, which, b. 10. 474.
The, 1 *pr. s. subj.* may I thrive, may I
 prosper, b. 5. 228. A.S. *þeón*, to
 thrive; cf. G. *gedeihen*.
þecchynge, *s.* thatching, 9. 199.
Theche, *v.* thatch, 22. 238. A.S.
 þeccan; Shropsh. *thetch*.
þedom, *s.* prosperity, thrift, 8. 53.
 From A.S. *þeón*, to thrive. We find:
 'That hit mai haue no *thedom*;'
 Seven Sages, ed. Weber, l. 587.
 'Now, sere, *evyl thedom* [i.e. ill luck]
 com to thi snowte!' Coventry Mys-
 teries, ed. Halliwell, p. 139, where
 the line is wrongly punctuated. See
 þeodam.
þeef, thief, 15. 132, 146; Thef, b. 12.
 192; þeeues, *pl.* 6. 17, 15. 130, 131;
 Theues, *pl.* b. 9. 118, b. 12. 191.
þeftis, *pl.* thefts, robberies, a. 11. 272.
 See þufþe.
Thei, *pron.* they, those, 22. 371.
þeigh, *conj.* although, though, b. 10.
 134; þei3, b. 1. 10; þei3e, b. 3. 148.
 See Thauh.
þen, *conj.* than, b. pr. 147.
þene, *adv.* then, thus, a. 10. 76.
þenken, *v.* think, reflect, a. 8. 152;
 þenke, b. 11. 153; þenke, 1 *pr. s.*
 intend, purpose, 2. 21; þenkeþ, *pr. s.*
 intends, 20. 314, 22. 195; þenkeþ,
 pr. s. intends (to go), 21. 234; þenche,
 2 *pr. s. subj.* intend, mean, a. 11.
 159; þenke, mean, a. 11. 143;
 þenke, *pr. s. subj.* is thinking, medi-
 tates, 19. 266; þenk, *imper. s.* re-

member, bethink, 9. 279. See
 þinketh, Thynke. A.S. *þencan*.
þenkeþ, *impers. pr. s.* it seems (to me),
 8. 99. See þynkeþ. A.S. *þyncan*.
 (þenkeþ *is an inferior spelling; read*
 þynkeþ.)
þenne, *adv.* then, 9. 23, 13. 14.
þennes, *adv.* thence, away, b. 1. 73;
 þennys, thence, 2. 70; Fro þennes =
 from thence, thence, 8. 136.
þeodam, *s.* prosperity, a. 10. 105.
 See þedom.
þeof, thief, 21. 427; ·þeoues, *pl.* 14.
 62, 20. 254. See þeef.
þeonne, *adv.* thence, a. 1. 71. See
 þennes.
þeos, *pron. pl.* these, 21. 126; þeose,
 22. 271, 317; a. 2. 97.
þeoues. See þeof.
Ther, *adv.* where, 1. 204, 2. 121, 13.
 234, 14. 56, 19. 214, 20. 250; R pr.
 1, R. 1. 87, R. 2. 134; þer, *adv.* then,
 a. 9. 32; whereas, 17. 88. See þere.
þer-after, *adv.* accordingly, 1. 25, 7.
 229, 9. 121, 12. 219; R. pr. 45;
 accordingly, with that intent, a. 3.
 180; afterwards, b. 11. 24; after
 them, towards them, 8. 225.
þer-amonge, *adv.* amongst it, R. pr.
 57.
þer-a3eyn, *adv.* against it, 21. 312.
þere, *adv.* there, b. 8. 67; thence, 21.
 382; where, b. 3. 14, b. 9. 41; when,
 b. 11. 237; þere þat, where that,
 wherever, b. 14. 302; þere as, there
 where, b. 4. 34; Fere . . . þere, where
 . . . there, b. 14. 99. See Ther.
þere-fro, *adv.* thence, b. 11. 345.
þere-inne, *adv.* therein, b. 1. 61;
 thereon, b. 10. 181.
þere-myde, *adv.* therewith, b. 7. 26, b.
 16. 262; þere-mydde, b. 6. 69, b. 15.
 311. See þer-myd.
þerf, *adj.* unleavened, a. 7. 269. A.S.
 þeorf, þerf, unleavened. See note;
 and Cath. Angl. p. 381.
þerfore, *adv.* for it, on account of it, b.
 4. 54, b. 5. 236.
þerlede, *pt. pl.* pierced, 2. 171. See
 þirled.
þer-myd, *adv.* therewith, thereby, with
 it, 4. 253, 6. 136; þermyde, b. 6.
 160. See þere-myde.
þerof, *adv.* thereof, of it, a. 3. 233;
 for them, 8. 148.
þeroute, *adv.* out of it, a. 6. 77.
þerste, thirst, 23. 19. See Thruste,
 þurst.
þer-þrow, *adv.* through that, thereby,
 21. 231.

GLOSSARIAL INDEX.

Þer-to, *adv.* to it, 21. 184; for that purpose, b. 15. 123.
Þer-vnder, under it, b. 19. 383; under (the form of) it, 22. 387.
Þer-while, *adv.* whilst that, b. pr. 173, b. 6. 165; Þere-whiles, in the mean time, b. 6. 8.
Þer-with, *adv.* therewith, with that, 11. 288, 20. 332.
Þer-ynne, *adv.* therein, 2. 12; into it, 8. 219.
Thesternesse, darkness, b. 16. 160. A.S. *þéosternes*.
Theuelich, *adv.* like a thief, b. 18. 336.
Þeues; see Thef.
Þewes, habits, manners, 7. 141. A.S. *þéaw*.
Þider, *adv.* thither, b. 2. 161.
Þikke, *adv.* thickly, profusely, b. 3. 156. See Thycke.
Thikkest, *adj.* thickest, b. 12. 228.
Þilke, *pron.* that, 19. 266; those, b. 10. 28. See Þulke.
Þing, *s.* thing, a. 1. 136; person, b. pr. 123; Þinge, *pl.* things, b. 6. 212. See Þyng.
Þinketh, *pr. s.* intends, b. 19. 190; Þinke, 2 *pr. s. subj.* intend, mean, b. 10. 213. See Þenken. A.S. *þencan*.
Þinketh, *impers. pr. s.* it seems; Me þinketh, it seems to me, b. 10. 182, b. 11. 399; Me thinkyȝ, a. 12. 5. See Þynkeþ. A.S. *þyncan*.
Þirled, *pt. pl.* pierced, 1. 172. A.S. *þyrlian*, to pierce; Shropsh. *thirl*. See Þerlede, Þurleden.
Þis, *pron. pl.* these, b. pr. 62, b. 2. 170, b. 5. 634; Þise, b. 1. 132.
Þi-seluen, *pron.* thyself, a. 1. 24, a. 5. 226; Þiselue, b. 8. 52.
Tho, *adv.* then, 1. 45, 3. 162, 5. 166, 11. 74; when, 10. 277, 14. 223, 15. 96, 21.243. A.S. *ðá*.
Þo, *pron.* they, those, 11. 110, 12. 27, 14. 6, 16. 90, 17. 46; those who, R. 3. 283, R. 4. 51.
Thole, *v.* suffer, endure, b. 18. 380, a. 4. 71; Tholie, 5. 80, 20. 105; Þoly, 21. 427; Þolye, b. 4. 84, b. 11. 390; Tholye, 1 *pr. s.* I suffer, b. 13. 263; Tholen, *pr. pl.* endure, 17. 33; Þoledest, 2 *pt. s.* didst suffer, 22. 174; Þolede, *pt. s.* suffered, 16. 72, 21. 139; Þoled, b. 13. 76; Þoleden, *pt. pl.* suffered, 13. 204. A.S. *þolian*.
Þombe, thumb, 8. 45, 20. 135.
Thonk, *s.* thanks, a. 8. 44; Thonkes, *pl.* a. 2. 119.
Þonken, *v.* thank, 20. 105; Þonke, 1 *pr. s.* 19. 17; Þonkeþ, 1 *pr. pl.* 9. 135; Þonked, 1 *pt. s.* I thanked, 11. 106.
Þonkynge, *s.* thanking, thanks, giving of thanks, 3. 162.
Þoo, *adv.* when, a. 2. 119. See Þo.
Þoo, *pron.* those, 19. 148. See Þo.
Þorgh, *prep.* through, 20. 280, 21. 155; by, 3. 43, 10. 182; by means of, 8. 88, 91; 11. 42; Þorough, through, 22. 357; Þorouȝ, by help of, a. 2. 123; Þorugh, through, b. 8. 43; by, b. 11. 317; by reason of, b. 9. 206; Þoruh, through, 4. 197; by means of, 4. 271; Þorw, through, 21. 88; by, b. 2. 41; by means of, 3. 138, 4. 104; in consequence of, b. 10. 107; Þorwe, by means of, 1. 106; Þorwgh, by, b. 10. 236.
Þorne, thorn-bush, b. 12. 228; Þornes, *pl.* thorns, 21. 47.
Þorsday, Thursday, b. 16. 140.
Þorst, 2 *pt. s.* durst, 7. 414. (Thorst = Tharst = Tharfest.)
Þoru-oute, *prep.* throughout, R. 1. 53, R. 2. 5.
Thought, *s.* reflection, b. 8. 74; Þouht, *s.* thought, 7. 100; Thouhte, 11. 72; Þouhtes, *pl.* thoughts, fancies, 3. 95.
Þouhte, *pt. s.* thought, intended, 21. 179; Þouht, *pp.* thought of, 7. 51.
Þouhte, *impers. pt. s.* it seemed (to me), 11. 68, 21. 118; it seemed (to them), 22. 139. See Þouȝte.
Thouȝt, *s.* thought, reflection, contemplation, b. 8. 107, b. 13. 4.
Þouȝte, *pt. s.* intended to go, b. 16. 175; *pp.* thought on, remembered, b. 13. 268. See Þouhte.
Þouȝte, *pt. s. impers.* seemed, 1. 196, b. pr. 6. 182; Thouȝthe, a. 12. 16; Hym good þouȝte, seemed good to him, b. 16. 194. See Þouhte.
Þow, *pron.* thou, 7. 138.
Þowgh, *conj.* although, b. 6. 40; Þowȝ, b. 6. 36; Þoȝ, 17. 293.
Þraldom, servitude, 21. 108; see note.
Þralles, *pl.* slaves, 22. 33.
Þrede-bare, thread-bare, 7. 305.
Thresche, 1 *pr. s.* I thrash, b. 5. 553. A.S. *þerscan*.
Þreshefold, threshold, 7. 408. See below. (*Thresh-fold* is a variant of the more usual *Thresh-wold*.)
Thresshewolde, *s.* threshold, b. 5. 357; Þrexwolde, a. 5. 201. A.S. *þerscwald*. See note to 7. 408.
Þresshynge, *s.* threshing, 9. 199.
Þrestes, *impers. pr. s.* thirst afflicts (me), b. 18. 365.

GLOSSARIAL INDEX. 449

Þrettene, *num.* thirteen, b. 5. 214.
Thretty, *num.* thirty, b. 13. 270.
Þretynge, *s.* threat, b. 18. 279.
Threve, (*lit.* bundle), number, b. 16. 55. Icel. þrefi, a number of sheaves; Shropsh. and Lowl. Sc. *thrave.*
Þrew. *pt. s.* threw himself, i.e. fell, 7. 408.
Þridde, *num. adj.* third, 8. 137, 11. 76, 19. 196. See Þrydde.
Þrift, *s.* prosperity, a. 7. 70.
Þritty, *num.* thirty, 20. 138.
Þriueþ, *pr. s.* prospers, a. 11. 154; Þriuen, *pp.* grown up, a. 8. 58. See Þroff.
Þrobbant, *pres. part.* throbbing, a. 12. 48.
Þroff, *pt. s.* throve, succeeded, R. 3. 137. See Þriueþ.
Þroly, *adv.* quickly, earnestly, a. 9. 107. See note to 11. 112. Icel. þrár, stubborn, obstinate; also, frequent.
Þrompelde, *pt. s.* stumbled, a. 5. 201. See Thrumbled. When Beryn was in a passion of misery, it is said of him: 'He *trampelid* fast with his feet & al to-tare his here;' l. 1350.
Þrongen, *pt. pl.* thronged, crowded, 8. 151. A.S. *þringan,* to press. See Þrungen.
Þropes, *pl.* towns, villages, a. 2. 47; Þroupes, 1. 219. 'Thrope, *idem quod* Thorpe, *supra; Oppidum.*' Prompt. Parv.
Þroweþ, *imper. pl.* throw, cast, 21. 295; Frowe, *pp.* thrown, R. 4. 82. See Þrew.
Þruft, *s.* success in life, a. 10. 105. See Þrift.
Thrumbled, *pt. s.* stumbled, 7. 408. See Þrompelde. (The word does not appear to occur elsewhere in English.)
Þrungen, *pt. pl.* thronged, pressed closely together, b. 5. 517. See Þrongen.
Thruste, *s.* thirst, b. 18. 366. See Þurst. Cf. Shropsh. *thrusty,* thirsty.
Þrydde, third, 22. 289.
Þu, *pron.* thou, 21. 363.
Thuder, *adv.* thither, 23. 285.
Þufþe, theft, thieving, dishonesty, 3. 92, 7. 349. A.S. þyfð, þeofð.
Þulke, *adj.* that, 2. 112; *pl.* those, a. 11. 13; those things, such things, a. 7. 286. See Þilke.
Thurgh, *prep.* through, a. 12. 60.
Þurleden, *pt. pl.* pierced, a. 1. 148. See Þirled.

Þurst, *s.* thirst, 21. 413; Þurste, 7. 438. See Thruste.
Þurste, *pt. s. subj.* might dare, 10. 257. (*Thurste* is a false form, put for *durste = dorste,* pt. t. of *dar.* The use of *th* for *d* is due to confusion with *tharf,* I need.)
Þus, *adv.* thus, as, 4. 181; thus, 9. 291, b. 9. 151.
Thuse, *pron. pl.* these, 4. 58, 6. 66, 8. 113; the following, 1. 198.
Þus-gate, *adj.* thus, in this way, 6. 51; Þus-gates, in this manner, 17. 306.
Thwytynge, *s.* cutting, whittling, 9. 199. A.S. þwítan, to cut; cf. mod. E. *whittle,* to pare, put for *thwittle.*
Þy, *pron. poss.* thy, 22. 480.
Þyderwarde, *adv.* thither, in that direction, 8. 205.
Þyn, *poss. pron.* thy, 2. 141; *pl.* thy friends, 4. 135.
Þyng, *s. pl.* things, 11. 155.
Thynke, 1 *pr. s.* I intend, b. 3. 95; Þynketh, *pr. s.* intends to go, b. 18. 222. See Þinketh, Þenken.
Þynkeþ, *pr. s. impers.* (it) seems, 1. 180, 4. 229, 6. 53, 12. 131. See Þinketh.
Þynne, *adj.* thin, poor, 22. 402.
Þy-self, thou thyself, 5. 187.
Tidy, *adj.* honest, respectable, b. 3. 320, b. 9. 104. See Tydy. 'Tydy, *Probus;*' Prompt. Parv.
Tikel, *adj.* frail, wanton, a. 3. 126; Tikil, b. 3. 130. See Tykel. Cf. E. *tickl-ish.*
Tikes, *pl.* country people, 22. 37. See Tykes. Lit. 'dogs'; cf. Icel. *tík,* a bitch.
Til, *prep.* to, 7. 188, 23. 134; towards, 19. 170. See Tyl. Icel. and Dan. *til,* Swed. *till.*
Til, *conj.* until, 7. 181, 185.
Tilde, *pt. s.* dwelt, lit. pitched his tent, b. 12. 210. See Tulde. From A.S. *teld,* a tilt, a tent; see note to 15. 150.
Tilie, *v.* till, cultivate, b. pr. 120, b. 19. 232; earn, a. 7. 220; Tilye, till, b. 6. 238; earn, b. 6. 235; see Tylie. A.S. *tilian.*
Tilieres, *pl.* husbandmen, farmers, b. 13. 239, b. 15. 357; Tilieris, a. 11. 181; Tiliers, R. 1. 54. See Tyliers.
Tilled, *pt. pl.* drew, reached, stretched, 7. 220. See *tillen, tullen,* to draw, entice, *tollen,* to entice, in Stratmann; also *tolle,* to entice, in Pecock's Repressor. Cf. A.S. *fortyllan,* to allure.

GLOSSARIAL INDEX.

Tilthe, *s.* tilth, produce, b. 19. 429; Tilþe, cultivated ground, a. 7. 128. See **Tulthe**.
Tilye, *v.* till, cultivate, a. 8. 2. See **Tilie**.
Timbrede, *pt. pl. subj.* would have built; Timbrede not so hye = would not have built such grand houses, a. 3. 76. A.S. *timbrian*, to build. See **Tymbre**.
Tinkere, *s.* tinker, a. 5. 160.
Tit, *pr. s. impers.* (*for* Tideth), betides, happens, 14. 213.
Tite; As tite, as quickly as possible, at once, b. 16. 61. See **Tyte**. Icel. *títt*, neut. of *tíðr*, frequent.
Titereres, *pl.* tattlers, 23. 299. See **Tyterers**. Cf. E. *tattle, titter*.
Tithe del, tenth part, tithe, b. 15. 480.
Tiþen, *pr. pl.* pay tithes, a. 8. 65. See **Tythen**.
Tituleris, *s. pl.* tatlers, talebearers, R. 4. 57. See **Titereres**.
Tixt, text, scripture, 2. 202, 3. 129, 4. 498; Tixte, b. 3. 342; saying, b. 10. 270; *pl.* Tixtes, a. 1. 182. See **Tyxt**.
Tiȝeþ, *pr. s.* ties, a. 3. 135. See **Tyen**.
To, *prep.* to; *but often used in other senses, as* after, b. 6. 30; against, a. 3. 274; as, b. 10. 47; as, in the person of, 7. 128; in, a. 11. 239; on, (confined) to, 7. 155; with reference to, by; To þe gospel, by the Gospel standard, a. 1. 88; for, b. 7. 125; upon, b. 5. 173; To body, so as to have a body, b. 1. 62; To gyfte, as a gift, 12. 104; To man, as a man, so as to become a man, b. 1. 82; To nonne, as a nun, who is a nun, b. 5. 153; To hepe, 11. 189 (see explanation in the notes, p. 142.)
To, *adv.* too, 2. 140, 14. 179; over, 9. 275. A.S. *tó*.
To, *num.* two, 7. 103.
To comynge, *gerund*, to come, 18. 313. Put for A.S. *tó cumanne*. See note on *to* as a sign of the gerund, in note to 2. 11.
To-, *prefix*, has two values: (1), intensive, answering to A.S. *tó-*, G. *zer-*, in twain, apart, in pieces, extremely, as in *to-bolle, to-broken, to-cleue, to-drowe, to-dryue, to-grynt, to-logged, to-quashte, to-rende, to-reueþ, to-rof, to-shullen, to-torn;* and (2) the prep. *to* in composition; answering to A.S. *tó*, G. *zu*, as in *to-comen, to-fore, to-forn, to-gederes, to morwe, tow-name, to-warde*. The former is still in use in the word *to-bost* (= to-burst); see Shropsh. Word-book.
To-bolle, *pp.* swollen extremely, swollen so as to be ready to burst, b. 5. 84. Cf. Dan. *bullen*, swollen, *bulne*, to swell; Swed. *bulna*, to swell. The intensive prefix is the A.S. *tó-*; see above.
To-broken, *pp.* broken in pieces, torn to pieces, b. 8. 87; To-broke, *pp.* broken to pieces, utterly broken, 1. 69, 10. 32, 11. 85, 22. 346. A.S. *tóbrecan*, pp. *tó-brocen*.
To-cleue, *v.* cleave asunder, 15. 84, b. 12. 141; fall to pieces, 21. 114; To-cleef, *pt. s.* was cleft asunder, 21. 62.
To-comen, *pt. pl.* came together, approached, 22. 343. (Here the prefix is simply A.S. *tó*, to, *prep.* in composition; not the intensive prefix.)
To-drowe, *pt. pl.* drew asunder, i. e. tortured, b. 10. 35, a. 11. 27. For the prefix, cf. To-broken.
To-dryue, *v.* drive quite away, 23. 174. The prefix is intensive.
Tofore, *prep.* before, a. 3. 110; in presence of, b. 5. 457; To-for, before, b. 13. 48. See **To-forn**.
To-forn, *prep.* before, b. 12. 132. A.S. *tó-foran*.
Toft, hillock, eminence, a slightly elevated and exposed site, 2. 12. Cf. O. Swed. *tomt*, a cleared space, site, Dan. *tomt*, a site, toft; orig. neut. of Icel. *tómr*, empty. See **Tome**.
To-gederes, *adv.* together, 1. 47, 61; 2. 38, 4. 282; To-geders, 4. 211; To-gederis, together, to close quarters, 17. 80; Togedere, together, a. pr. 60, a. 2. 23; Togideres, b. 1. 195, b. 2. 83; Togidere, a. 11. 226; To-gyderes, *adv.* together, 20. 198.
To-grynt, *pr. s.* grinds to pieces, 12. 62. For the prefix, cf. To-broken.
To-helle-ward, towards hell, b. 18. 114.
To-heuene-ward, *adv.* to heaven, b. 14. 211.
To-him-wardis, towards him, R. 3. 76.
Toille, *pr. pl.* toil, work, a. 11. 183.
Tok, *pt. s.* took, inflicted, 1. 117; gave, 14. 106; gave money to, bribed, 23. 137; Toke, *pt. s.* gave, b. 11. 164, 283; gave to, bribed, b. 20. 136; Toke, *pt. s. subj.* should take, 4. 296; Toke, 1 *pt. s.* took, 20. 14; Toke, 2 *pt. s.* didst take, accept, 4. 137, 23. 7; didst give, 10. 277; Toke, *pt. pl.* took,

GLOSSARIAL INDEX. 451

21. 307; Token, *pt. pl.* took, 21. 249; Toke þei on = if they added to their wealth, if they made profit, 4. 84.
Tokenynge, *s.* token, sign, 6. 122, 18. 33. See Toknynge.
To-kirke-ward, *adv.* to church-ward, towards the church, 7. 351. (*Kirk = church.*)
Tokkeris, *s. pl.* fullers, a. pr. 100. Prov. E. *tucker*, a fuller.
Toknynge, *s.* signification, b. 16. 204; Toknyng, token, a. 5. 19. See Tokenynge.
Tol, *s.* toll, 1. 98, 14. 73.
Tolde, 1 *pt. s.* counted out, reckoned, b. 5. 252; Tolden, *pt. pl.* counted, a. 5. 128; Tolde (*for* Told), *pp.* told, 4. 132; reckoned, considered, 20. 238. See Tellen.
Toles, *pl.* tools, instruments, b. 10. 177; Tooles, a. 11. 133.
Tolled, *pt. s.* drew, stretched, were drawn (out) to, b. 5. 214. See Tilled.
Tollen, *v.* to pay toll, 14. 51; Tolled, *pt. s.* taxed, R. 3. 81.
Tolleres, *s. pl.* takers of toll, b. pr. 220.
To-logged, *pp.* pulled about, dragged hither and thither, 3. 226 (*of* = by). Cf. Swed. *lugga*, to pull by the hair; and cf. To-broken. The verb *to lug* was esp. used of pulling by the ears or hair.
Tomblers, *pl.* tumblers, a. 2. 79.
Tomblest, *pr. s.* tumblest, a. 12. 91. See Tumbleth.
Tome, *s.* leisure, 3. 196. Icel. *tóm*, leisure, *tómr*, vacant, Sw. *tom*, Sc. *toom*, empty. See note; and see *toom* in Prompt. Parv.
To-morwe, *adv.* to-morrow, 3. 41.
Tondre, tinder, b. 17. 245. See Tunder.
Tonge, tongue, 3. 25, 4. 167, 7. 72; words, speech, 11. 199. See Tounge, Tunge.
Tonne, tun, cask, b. 15. 331.
Took, *pt. s.* gave, 4. 47; Tooke, 20. 2. See Tok.
Top, *s.* top, head, 4. 177; Toppe, b. 3. 139, b. 16. 22. Lit. a tuft of a hair on the head; cf. G. *zopf*, a pig-tail. See note, p. 46.
Topte, *adj.* at the top; Topte saile, topsail, R. 4. 72.
To-quashte, *pt. s.* shook (*or* shattered) asunder, dashed in pieces, 21. 259. Cf. E. *quash*. See note, p. 256.
Torche, torch, 20. 168.
Toren, *pp.* torn, 7. 205.

To-rende, *v.* be destroyed, b. 10. 112. Lit. 'become rent in twain.'
To-reueþ, *pr. s.* completely takes away, 4. 203. See To-rof.
Torne, *v.* turn, be converted, b. 3. 42, 325; change, b. 11. 44; Torned, *pt. s.* turned, b. 13. 319; Tornde, drove, a. 10. 139; Torned, *pt. pl.* b. 5. 19; *pp.* b. 3. 337. See Tourne, Turne.
To-rof, *pt. s.* was riven asunder, 21. 63. See To-reueþ.
Tortle, turtle-dove, 15. 162.
To-shullen, *pp.* peeled, with the skin stripped off, b. 17. 191. Ettmüller gives a theoretical A.S. verb *scelan*, pp. *scolen*, to peel; cf. *schellen*, to shell, in Stratmann.
To-synne-ward, *adv.* as if tempting to sin, b. 13. 346.
Toten, *v.* to look, gaze, b. 16. 22; Totide, 1 *pt. s.* looked, 19. 53. A.S. *tótian*: cf. E *tout*.
Top-aches, tooth-aches, 23. 82.
Top-drawers, drawers of teeth, 7. 370.
To-torne, *pp.* torn apart, much torn, b. 5. 197. Cf. To-broken.
To-treuthe-ward, towards the truth, 17. 146.
Toune, town, b. 13. 266, a. 11. 210; Tounes, *pl.* towns (*or rather* farms), a. 10. 134. *Town* = a farm, is still in use.
Toune-men, i. e. wise men, not countrymen, R. 2. 41.
Tounge, tongue, 20. 300; speech, 16. 256. See Tonge, Tunge.
Tour, *s.* tower, a. pr. 14; stronghold, a. 1. 54 (where some MSS. read *tutour*, i. e. guardian); Toure, tower, 1. 15. F. *tour*.
Tourne, *v.* turn, change their faith, b. 15. 509. See Torne.
To-ward, *prep.* towards; it occurs in *to-helle-ward*, *to-heuene-ward*, *to-kirke-ward*, *to-synne-ward*, and *to-treuthe-ward*. Cf. also *to-him-wardis*.
Towarde, *adj.* present, as a guard *or* protection, 1. 214.
Towe, tow, b. 17. 245.
Tower, *adj.* hardier, lit. tougher, 13. 187. A.S. *tóh*, tough.
Tow-name, nickname (lit. to-name), 13. 211.
Traillyng, *s.* trailing, dragging, b. 12. 242.
Transuerseþ, *pr. s.* transgresses, 4. 449; Transuersede, *pt. s.* transgressed, 15. 209. See note, p. 188.
Tras, *s.* trace, a. 12. 91. See note.
Trauaile, *s.* work, labour, trouble, 4.

GLOSSARIAL INDEX.

353, 375; Trauaille, b. 7. 43, b. 11, 189; trade, a. 11. 183; Trauail, 1. 195; Trauayl, 20. 212; Trauayle, 10. 152; Trauayles, *pl.* labours, necessary works, 10. 234.
Trauaille, *v.* work, toil, b. 6. 141; travel, b. 16. 10; Trauayle, work, 9. 252; Traueile, R. pr. 51; Trauely, *ger.* labour, work, 4. 297; Trauaileþ, *pr. s.* labours, 22. 440; Trauailleth, b. 13. 116; Traueileþ, 16. 126; Traueleþ, 13. 95; Trauaille, *pr. pl.* labour, b. 11. 279; Trauayle, 23. 260; Trauailed, *pp.* laboured, 21. 334.
Trauaillours, *pl.* workers, b. 13. 239.
Trauaylynge, *s.* labouring, a. 7. 235.
Traylid, *pp.* fenced round, entwined round about, R. 1. 47. Cf. E. *trellis.* '*Treiller*, to grate, or lattice, to support .. or hold in with crossbars;' Cotgrave.
Trecherie, treachery, deceit, 2. 194, 21. 321. See **Tricherye**.
Trede, *v.* tread, breed, 15. 162; Treden, *pr. pl.* walk on, tread, a. 10. 101; Treden, *pt. pl.* trod, engendered, 14. 166.
Treieth, *pr. s.* betrays, b. 3. 123. O.F. *trair*, Lat. *tradere.*
Treitour, traitor, 20. 238.
Treo, a tree, 21. 144, 200, 307, 401. See **Trowes**. A.S. *tréo.*
Trepget, *s.* trap, a. 12. 91. Put for *trepeget = trebuchet ;* see note; and see *trepeget*, Rom. Rose, 6279. '*Trebgot*, or *trepgette*, sly instrument to take brydys or beestys;' Prompt. Parv.; see Way's note.
Tresour, treasure, money, 2. 79, 10. 333, 11. 181, 15. 54; Tresore, b. 1. 45; Tresores, *pl.* b. 7. 54.
Trespas, *s.* trespass, crime, a. 1. 95.
Trespasseþ, *pr. s.* trespasses, sins, a. 3. 274; Trespassed, *pt. s.* did wrong, b. 12. 284.
Treste, *s.* trust, R. 1. 47.
Tretis, *s.* short poem, R. pr. 51.
Tretour, traitour, false man, 22. 440, b. 18. 378, b. 19. 435.
Treuliche, *adv.* justly, honestly, a. 8. 65; Treuly, truly, a. 8. 166.
Treuthe, truth, 21. 126, 146; Treuthes, *gen.* truth's, 4. 496.
Treuwes, *s.* a truce, 21. 463. E. *truce.* See **Trewe, s,**
Trewe, *adj.* true, just, 2. 84; loyal, b. 9. 104; upright, honest, 20. 238; a. 3. 228; *as sb.* true (men), 4. 177. See **Trywe**.
Trewe, *s.* (lit. fidelity, trust, *hence* agreement), truce. relief, respite, 9. 355; Trewes, *pl. (with sing. sense),* truce, b. 18. 416. See **Treuwes**.
Treweliche, *adv.* truly, in truth, 13. 202; justly, 2. 96; Trewlich, justly, b. 7. 63; Trewli, *adv.* assuredly, b. 9. 186; Trewely, *adv.* truly, 19. 26.
Trewes, *s.* a truce, b. 18. 416. See **Trewe, s.**
Trew-tunge, True-of-tongue (an imaginary name), 4. 478; Trewetonge, 5. 18.
Treys, three, 19. 240. O.F. *treis*, Lat. *tres.*
Triacle, *s.* a remedy, healing medicine, b. 1. 146, b. 5. 50, R. 2. 151. E. *treacle.* See **Tryacle**; and note to 2. 147.
Tricherye, treachery, deceit, 1. 12; Tricherie, a. 1. 172. See **Trecherie**.
Triedest, *adj. superl.* choicest, a. 1. 126. F. *trier*, to select; from Low. Lat. *tritare*, to triturate, from Lat. *terere*, to rub; cf. E. *trite.*
Trielich, *adv.* excellently, b. pr. 14. See above.
Triennels, *pl.* masses said for three years, 10. 330; Triennales, b. 7. 170, 179. See note to 10. 320.
Trieste, Tryest, *adj. sup.* most excellent, choicest, b. 1. 135. See **Tried**.
Trifflour, *s.* trifler, R. 3. 118.
Triste, *s.* dependence, 4. 160.
Tristen, *pr. pl.* trust, 14. 102; Trist, *imp. s.* 7. 333; Tristith, *imp. pl.* R. 3. 247. See **Trostiþ, Trustene, Trysten**.
Tristi, *adj.* trusty, R. 2. 103.
Tristilich, *adv.* trustily, certainly, 4. 498.
Triweliche, *adv.* justly, honestly, 84. See **Treweliche**.
Triȝede, *pp.* tried, proved, a. 1. 183. See **Triedest**.
Triȝely, *adv.* excellently, a. pr. 14. Lit. choicely; from F. *trier*, to pick, select. See above.
Troblid, *pt. pl.* troubled, R. pr. 15.
Troden, *pt. pl.* trod, b. 11. 347. See **Trede**; and note to 14. 171.
Troiledest, 2 *pt. s.* didst beguile, deceive, 21. 321; Troiled, *pp.* deceived, 21. 334. See note.
Trolled, *pp.* walked, wandered (lit. rolled), b. 18. 296. See note. '*Tryllyn, or Trollyn,* Volvo'; Prompt. Parv.
Trolly-lolly, *interj.* (the burden of a song), a. 7. 109; Troly-lolly, 9. 123. See note, p. 111.
Trompe, *v.* play the trumpet, 16. 205;

GLOSSARIAL INDEX. 453

Trompede, *pt. s.* blew a trumpet, 21. 469.
Trone, throne, 2. 134.
Troneþ, *pr. s.* enthrones, places upon thrones, b. 1. 131.
Trostiþ, *imp. pl.* trust, R. 1. 102. See Tristen.
Trotted, *pt. s.* trotted, b. 2. 164.
Trouþe, *s.* truth, a. 3. 274.
Trowe, 1 *pr. s.* trow, believe, think to be true, 2. 145, 4. 20; Trowest, 2 *pr. s.* believest, 22. 177; Trowestow, 2 *pr. s.* dost thou believe, b. 12. 165; Troweþ, *pr. s.* believes, 15. 123; Trowen, *pr. pl.* believe, b. 15. 470; Trowede, 1 *pt. s.* believed, 1. 15. A.S. *tréowian.*
Trowes, *pl.* trees, b. 15. 94. See Treo. Cf. A.S. *tréow,* a tree.
Trufle, trifle, insignificant thing, 15. 83; nonsense, absurd tale, 21. 151. E. *trifle,* O.F. *trufle.*
Trusse, *v.* to pack himself off, pack off, begone, 3. 228; R. 3. 228. O.F. *trosser, torser,* to pack up, lit. twist up; formed from Lat. *tortus,* pp. of *torquere.*
Trustene, *v.* to trust, a trusting, a. 8. 166. See Tristen.
Tryacle, sovereign remedy, 2. 147. See Triacle.
Trye, *adj.* excellent, choice, b. 15. 163, b. 16. 4. See Tried; and note, p. 220.
Tryennals, *pl.* masses said for three years, 10. 320; Tryennels, 10. 333. See Triennels.
Tryne, *v.* touch, 21. 87. See note. Possibly corrupted from A.S. *æthrínan,* to touch; but observe A.S. *tringan,* in the note.
Trysten, *v.* to trust, 10. 330; Tryst, *pr. pl.* trust, 2. 66. See Tristen.
Trywe, *adj.* true, 1. 100.
Tulde, *pt. s.* dwelt, had his abode, 15. 150. See Tilde.
Tulien, *v.* till, cultivate, 11. 199; Tulyen, b. 7. 2; Tulie, 1. 87; Tulye, 9. 244; Tuleþ, *pr. s.* tills, 22. 440; Tulyeden, *pt. pl.* laboured for, earned by tillage, b. 14. 67; Tulyeþ, *imper. pl.* till, cultivate, 22. 318. See Tilie, Tylie.
Tulthe, *s.* tilth, cultivation, 22. 434. See Tilthe.
Tulyinge, *s.* tilling, husbandry, b. 14. 63.
Tunder, tinder, 20. 211. See Tondre.
Tunge, tongue, 7. 426, 22. 172. See Tonge, Tounge.
Tunicle, jacket, tunic, b. 15. 163. 'A tunycle, *dalmatica, tunica, tunicula;*' Cath. Angl.

Turmentours, *gen.* tormentor's, R. 3. 118. See note.
Turne, *v.* turn, be converted, 4. 483; Turneþ, *pr. s.* turns, 20. 291; Turnede, *pt. s.* turned, 23. 137. See Torne.
Turpiloquio, evil-speaking, b. 13. 457.
Tutour, guardian, warden, keeper. 2. 52. From Lat. *tueri.*
Twei, two, a. 5. 109. See Tweye.
Tweis, twice, b. 13. 270. See Twyes. (*Perhaps a misprint for* Twies.)
Twelf-moneth, twelvemonth, year, b. 13. 337.
Tweye, *num.* two, twain, 6. 135, 7. 209. A.S. *twegen,* twain.
Tweye, *adv.* twice, b. 4. 22. Cf. A.S. *twýwa.*
Tweyne, *adj.* twain, two, b. 5. 32, 203, 317. See above.
Twiggis, *s. pl.* twigs, rods, R. 3. 79.
Two-tounged, *adj.* double-tongued, 23. 162.
Twyes, *adv.* twice, 8. 29.
Twyned, *pp.* twisted, 20. 169.
Twynned, *pt. pl.* separated, R. 3. 243. Lit. 'to divide in *two.*'
Twynte, *s.* jot; No twynte, not a jot, R. 3. 81. See note.
Tyde, *s.* time, a. 2. 42.
Tydy, *adj.* honest, upright, active, diligent, 4. 478, 21. 335, 22. 441. See Tidy.
Tydyour, *adj.* more seasonable, 13. 187. From A.S. *tíd,* season.
Tyen, *v.* bind, 2. 92. See Tiȝeþ.
Tykel, *adj.* unsteady, inconstant, frail, 4. 147. See Tikel.
Tykes, *pl.* low people, b. 19. 37. See Tikes.
Tyl, *prep.* to, 8. 127; towards, b. 15. 164. See Til.
Tyl, *conj.* until, till, 1. 211, 20. 306.
Tylie, *v.* till, cultivate, 21. 110; Tylye, b. 18. 105; Tylede, *pt. pl.* cultivated, tilled, 16. 267; Tyleden, 18. 100. See Tilie, Tulien.
Tyliers, *pl.* tillers, farmers, 1. 223, 18. 100. See Tilieres.
Tyllinge, *s.* tilling, R. 3. 247.
Tymber, timber, wood, 22. 321.
Tymbre, *v.* build (their nests), b. 11. 352; Tymbrid, *pt. pl. subj.* would have built, 4. 84. See Timbrede.
Tyme, due season, 11. 291 (see note); time, b. 10. 72; Tyme ynowe, soon enough, 12. 197; Tymes ynow, *pl.* times enough, i.e. often enough, b. 11. 35.
Tymed, *pt. s.* delayed, R. 3. 81. (Or an error for *tyned,* lost; see below.)

GLOSSARIAL INDEX.

Tyne, *v.* lose, 12. 197 (see note), 22. 344; waste, 15. 8; Tyneth, *pr.* as *fut. s.* shall lose, b. 10. 351; *pr. s.* loses, a. 11. 233; Tyne, *pr. pl.* lose, fail to win, 11. 278; Tynt, *pp.* lost, 6. 93, 21. 144. Icel. *týna,* to lose.

Tyrauns, *pl.* oppressors, 3. 211; Tyrauntis, tyrants, R. 1. 54.

Tyte, *adv.* soon, quickly, 23. 54; As tyte, as quickly as possible, b. 13. 319. See Tite.

Tyterers, *pl.* tattlers, b. 20. 297. See Titereres.

Tythe, tithe, 7. 300. See Tithe.

Tythen, *v.* pay tithes, 14. 73. See Tipen.

Tyxt, text, 20. 14. See Tixt.

Vaille, *v.* avail, be of advantage, 20. 81. Short for *availle = availe.*

Vale, *s.* vale, b. 18. 367.

Valeye, valley, R. 2. 150; Valeyes, *pl.* a. 6. 4.

Valle, *pr. s. subj.* fall, 21. 414. See Fallen.

Vanshie, *v.* consume, cause to disappear, 16. 8; Vanshede, *pt. s.* vanished, disappeared, 15. 217, 16. 24.

Vauntward, van, front, 6. 58; Vauntwarde, vanguard, 23. 95. Short for Avauntward; from O.F. *avant,* before, and *warde,* a guard.

Vche, each, every, b. 10. 94, b. 11. 188; Vch, b. 13. 415; Vche a, each, b. pr. 207; Vch a, every, a. 5. 96.

Vchone, each one, b. 1. 51, b. 2. 138; every one of us, a. 1. 49. For Vch one.

Vecche, 1 *pr. s.* produce, bring forward, 21. 156. Southern form of Fecche. See Vette.

Veen, *adj.* vain, idle, 3. 101. See Veine.

Veille, *s.* watcher, 8. 57. O.F. *veile,* Lat. *uigilia,* a vigil, a watch. MS. H.(A-text) has the reading *wakere.*

Veine glorie, vain-glory, 7. 35. See Veen.

Vendage, *s.* vintage, 21. 414. Cf. F. *vendange, vendenge,* in Cotgrave, from Lat. *uindemia,* vintage.

Venemoste, *s.* poison, poisonousness, 21. 161. Four syllables; lit. 'venemosity.'

Veneson, venison, 10. 93; Venesoun, b. pr. 194.

Venge, *v.* avenge, 20. 104; Venged, 1. *pt. s.* 7. 74. F. *venger,* Lat. *uindicare.*

Veniaunce, *s.* vengeance, punishment, 1. 115, 4. 413; Venyaunce, R. 3. 108.

Venkised, *pp.* vanquished, 21. 106.

Venym, *s.* poison, venom, 18. 223, 21. 156; Venim, a. 5. 70; Venymes, *pl.* poisons, 21. 158.

Venymouste, poison, b. 18. 156. See Venemoste.

Vernicle, *s.* vernicle, b. 5. 530. See the note, p. 101.

Vernisch, *s.* varnish, a. 5. 70. Another reading is *verious* or *vergeous,* verjuice.

Verray, *adj.* true, 20. 271; Verrai, 22. 421; Verrey charite, even Charity itself, b. 17. 289.

Vers, verse, b. 12. 290.

Verset, little verse, line, short text, 15. 129. See note.

Vertue, *s.* virtue, healing power; Vertu, 21. 161; Vertues, *pl.* virtues, 22. 313, 316, 318; power, b. 14. 37; Uertues, virtues, 22. 274.

Vesture, *s.* clothing, 2. 23.

Vetaile, *s.* victuals, R. 3. 371. See Vitaile.

Vette, *pt. s.* fetched, brought, 8. 57. See Vecche.

Vicari, *s.* vicar, b. 19. 417; Vicory, 22. 411, 421, 482; Vikery, deputy, 15. 70. See Vyker.

Vigilate, 'watch ye,' i. e. watching, vigilance, 8. 57. See note.

Vigilies, *pl.* vigils, fasts, 8. 25; Vigiles, 10. 232.

Vikery, vicar, deputy, 15. 70. See Vicari, Vyker.

Vil, *adj.* vile, shameful, 21. 97; Vyle, b. 10. 45.

Vilanye, *s.* outrage, 21. 97.

Visage, face, b. 18. 335.

Vitaile, *s.* food, 8. 49; Vitailes, *pl.* victuals, food, provisions, 3. 191, 16. 186; Vittailes, b. 13. 216.

Vitaillers, *pl.* victuallers, b. 2. 60. See Vytailers.

Uix, adv. scarcely, 15. 204, 16. 23. See notes.

Vm, as if for *um,* a mysterious symbol, 9. 351.

Vmbwhyle, *adv.* occasionally, sometimes, at intervals, 7. 396; Vmwhile, b. 5. 345. The prefix is A.S. *ymbe,* about; so that the lit. sense is 'about a while,' for a time; but it also means 'at times.'

Unblessed, *adj.* cursed, 22. 406.

Vnbokelede, *pt. s.* unbuckled, undid, 20. 68.

Vnboxome, *adj.* disobedient, 7. 16, 17; Vnbuxom, 3. 87; Vnbuxum, a. 9. 93. See Buxom.

Vnbynden, *v.* to loose, 1. 129.

GLOSSARIAL INDEX. 455

Vnchargeth, *pr. s.* discharges, frees, b. 15. 338.
Vnconnynge, *adj.* ignorant, stupid, 4. 244, 16. 16, b. 12. 185.
Vn-corteisliche, *adv.* uncourteously, 14. 172.
Vncoupled, *pp.* unfastened, loose, b. pr. 162, 206. See **Coupleþ.**
Vncristene, *adj.* unbelieving, unbaptised, heathen, 13. 77 ; as *sb.* heathen, unbeliever, b. 10. 350; as *pl. sb.* heathens, 2. 89.
Vncrouned, *pp.* who have not received tonsure, 6. 63. Here *croune* signifies the clerical tonsure.
Vnderfonge, *v.* receive, 10. 129, 17. 258 ; Vnderfongen, *pr. pl.* receive, 4. 272 ; accept, take, a. 3. 208 ; Vnderfeng, 1 *pt. s.* received, 2. 73 ; Vnderfonge, b. 1. 76 ; Vnderfong, *pt. s.* received, 13. 52 ; Vnder-fongen, *pp.* received, b. 7. 171 ; b. 10. 225 ; accepted, b. 11. 144 ; Vnderfonge, *pp.* received, admitted, 4. 111, 8. 279, 10. 322. A.S. *under-fón,* to receive.
Vnderling, *s.* servant, inferior, 9. 43.
Vndernymeth, *pr. s.* reproves, reprehends, b. 5. 115 ; Vnder-nym, 3. *imper. s.* reprove, b. 11. 209 ; Vndernome, *pp.* reproved, rebuked, corrected, 23. 51, b. 13. 282. ' Vnderneme, *Reprehendo, deprehendo, arguo, redarguo ;*' Prompt. Parv. See note to b. 5. 115, p. 75.
Vndernymynge, reproof, 7. 35. See above.
Vnder-piȝte, *pp.* propped up, lit. ' under-pitched,' b. 16. 23.
Vnder-shored, *pp.* propped up, 19. 47.
Vnderstonde, *ger.* to be understood, 20. 309 ; *pp.* understood, b. 12. 257.
Vnder-take, *ger.* receive, 1. 98 ; promise, assure, b. 10. 152 ; be surety, b. 13. 131 ; Vndertoke, *pt. s.* reproved, b. 11. 89 ; Vndertoke, *pt. s. subj.* would reprove, 13. 32 ; Vndertake, *pp.* undertaken, 21. 20. For the sense 'reprove,' cf. Vndernymeth, and A.S. *niman* = take.
Vndeuotlich, *adv.* without true devotion, 1. 126.
Vndir-writen, *pp.* underscored, marked for omission, a. 11. 255.
Vndon, *v.* undo, destroy, 21. 243 ; Vndoþ, *pr. s.* explains, 3. 40; Vndude, *pt. s.* disclosed, explained, 10. 305.
Vndoynge, *s.* ruin, overthrow, b. 15. 589. See above.
Vn-eisyliche, *adv.* uneasily, uncomfortably, 17. 75.

Vneth, *adv.* scarcely, b. 4. 60 ; Vnethe, b. 20. 189. From A.S. *éað,* easy.
Vnfeterye, *ger.* set free, unfetter, 4. 176.
Vnfolde, *v.* open, unclose, 20. 143 ; Vnfoldeþ, *pr. s.* unfolds, a. 8. 92 ; Vnfolded, *pt. s.* opened, 10. 284 ; Vnfeelde, *pt. pl.* unfolded, opened, 3. 73 ; Vnfolde, *pp.* open, 20. 150 ; Vn-foldyng, *pres. pt.* unfolding, a. 2. 58.
Vnglosed, without a 'glose' or comment, b. 4. 145. See **Glose.**
Vngraciouse, *adj.* ungracious, *hence,* without grace, untoward, 11. 299, 12. 229.
Vngraue, *pp.* unstamped, not engraved, 5. 127.
Vnhardy, *adj.* afraid, fearful, timid, cowardly, 21. 86, b. pr. 180.
Vnheled, *pp.* unroofed, uncovered, 17. 75, 20. 301 ; b. 14. 232 ; Vnhiled, b. 14. 252 *n,* b. 17. 319. From A.S. *helan,* to cover. See note, p. 212.
Vnhende, *adj.* unkind, uncourteous, ill-mannered, 20. 249 ; as *sb.* (*either*) ill-mannered people, (*or*) discourtesy, 23. 186. See note, p. 281.
Vnhiled, *pp.* uncovered ; see **Vnheled.**
Vnhonge, *pp.* unhung, R. 3. 293.
Vnioynen, *v.* disjoin, break, dissolve, destroy, 21. 268.
Vnite, *s.* unity, 6. 190, 22. 330 ; sanity, 6. 10 ; concord (in grammar), 4. 338.
Vnknowing, *adj.* ignorant, 19. 157.
Vnknytteþ, *pr. s.* undoes, dissolves, 21. 225.
Vnkonnynge, *adj.* ignorant, b. 13. 13.
Vnkouth, *adj.* strange, lit. unknown, b. 7. 155.
Vnkynde, *adj.* unnatural, 7. 296, 8. 43, 15. 19; wicked, 17. 273 ; unkind, uncharitable, 2. 190, 19. 157, 20. 215, 216, 21. 443 ; niggardly, b. 13. 379 ; Vnkuynde, *adj.* unnatural, a. 1. 166. See note to 15. 20.
Vnkyndely, *adv.* unkindly, 4. 264 ; Vnkyndeliche, unnaturally, b. 9. 155.
Vnkyndenesse, unkindness, 20. 221, 222, 230, 324 ; uncharitableness, b. 13. 219 ; Vnkyndnesse, unkindness, 16. 189 ; Vnkuyndenesse, unnatural conduct, a. 3. 280.
Vn-leek, *pt. s.* unlocked, opened, 8. 251 ; see note. A.S. *lúcan,* to lock ; pt. t. *ic léac.* See **Vnlouken.**
Vnleelle, *adj. pl.* false, 14. 69.
Vnlese, *pr. pl.* unloose, unclose, b. pr. 213. A.S. *lýsan.* Cf. Vnlose. (A bad reading ; read *vnlose.*)

456 GLOSSARIAL INDEX.

Vnlofsom, *adj.* hateful, unpleasing (lit. unlovesome), 11. 262.
Vnlose, *v.* open, unclose, 1. 162, 20. 114; Vnloseþ, *pr. pl.* a. pr. 87; Vnlosen, *ger.* to unloose, put forth, b. 17. 139. Cf. Vnlese.
Vnloueliche, *adj.* unpleasant, disagreeable, 11. 262, 15. 179; unseemly, b. 15. 114.
Vnloueliche, *adv.* nastily, unpleasantly, 7. 414.
Vnlouken, *v.* unlock, undo, open, 21. 268; Vnlouke, *v.* 15. 55, 21. 195, 362; Vnlouke, *pr. pl.* spread wide, spread out, 10. 143; Vnlouketh, *imp. pl.* unlock, b. 18. 261. A.S. *lúcan*, to lock. See **Vnleek**.
Vnlykynge, *adj.* unfit, improper, scandalous, 8. 23.
Vnmeeble, immoveable goods, lands, &c., 11. 186; Vnmebles, *pl.* 4. 425; Vnmoebles, b. 3. 267. See **Moebles**.
Vnnepe, *adv.* scarcely, hardly, 5. 63, 23. 190. A.S. *un-éaðe*, uneasily, hardly.
Vnpacient, *adj.* impatient, 7. 110.
Vnparfit, *adj.* imperfect in life, 7. 119.
Vnpiked, 1 *pt. s.* picked open, undid by picking, 7. 266.
Vnpossible, *adj.* impossible, a. 11. 225.
Vnpower, *s.* powerlessness, 20. 292 *n.*
Vnpynnede, *pt. s.* unbolted, opened, 13. 47, 23. 330; Vnpynneth, *imp. pl.* undo, open, b 18. 261. See Allit. Poems, A. 728.
Vnredy, *adj.* improvident, 13. 216.
Vnryghtful, *adj.* wicked, unrighteous, 11. 215, 13. 18.
Vnryghtfulliche, *adv.* wrongfully, 22. 245.
Vnsauerliche, *adv.* unpleasantly, with an ill taste, 16. 49.
Vn-semely, *adj.* hideous, 2. 55.
Vnskilful, *adj.* unreasonable, 7. 25; outrageous, b. 13. 277.
Vnsowen, *v.* unsew, slit open, 7. 6.
Vnsperre, *v.* unbar, 21. 272; Vnsperrede, *pt. s.* unbarred, opened, 21. 89. Lit. 'unspar.'
Vnstable, *adj.* unsteady, 11. 37.
Vnstedefast, *adj.* unsteady, 4. 390.
Vnstombled, *pp.* as *adj.* without stumbling, firm, R. 2. 82.
Vnsyttynge, *adj.* improper, unbecoming, 4. 208, 5. 189. See note. We find *sit* = befit, become, as late as the 16th century; cf. 'Before him *sits* [it becomes] the titmouse silent be;' Spenser, Shep. Kal. Nov. l. 26.
Vntempred, *pp.* untuned, b. 9. 102.

Vnthende, *adj.* small, out-of-season, b. 5. 177. Cf. A.S. *þéonde*, increasing, thriving, growing, powerful, pres. pt. of *þéon*, to thrive. So also in the Coventry Myst. p. 36, where it is unexplained.
Vntidy, *adj.* unseasonable, unfitting, 23. 119. See **Vntydy**. Cf. A.S. *tíd*, time, season.
Vntil, *prep.* to, b. pr. 227.
Vntiled, *pp.* untilled, b. 15. 451.
Vntydy, *adj.* unseasonable, vulgar, b. 20. 118; improperly prepared, illmade, 10. 262; dishonest, 4. 87. See **Vntidy**.
Vntyled, *pp.* unroofed, without tiles, b. 14. 252.
Vntyme, *s.* an unfit season, b. 9. 186. See note. Cf. 'a lombe that was borne in *vntyme* ;' Book of St. Alban's, fol. c. 7, back.
Vnwittylich, *adv.* foolishly, unwisely, 4. 133; Vnwittily, a. 3. 101.
Vnwrast, *adj.* base, deceitful, 21. 313. Cf. M.E. *wrast*, strong, Gawain and Grene Knight, 1423; A.S. *wrǽst*, firm, strong, good.
Vnwryten, *pp.* as *adj.* not entered, not written down, left out of the record, 12. 209.
Voideth, *pr. s.* clears out, gets rid of, b. 14. 94.
Vois, *s.* voice, R. 3. 56.
Vokates, *pl.* advocates, pleaders, b. 2. 60. '*Hic causidicus*, a vokyte;' Wright's Vocab. i. 209.
Vore, *s.* course, 7. 118; see *fore* in Stratmann. Der. from A.S. *faran*, to fare, go. See note.
Vorwes, *s. pl.* furrows, a. 7. 97.
Vouchen saf, *pr. pl.* guarantee, undertake, 6. 49.
Vowes, *pl.* vows, 8. 13; Vouwes, a. pr. 68.
Voys, voice, 21. 273, 363. See **Vois**.
Vp, *prep.* upon, b. 1. 12, b. 9. 99; on, 2. 159, 5. 128; in, 10. 333; as to, 11. 113; Vp gesse, at a guess, b. 5. 421.
Vp, *adv.* up, i.e. rife, R. 1. 29. See **Vppe**.
Vp-holders, *pl.* upholsterers, *or rather*, dealers in second-hand furniture, sellers by auction, 7. 374, 13. 218. Lit. 'holders up'; prob. from holding up things for auction. Also called *upholdsters*, whence mod. E. *upholsterers*, properly furniture-brokers. Palsgrave has: 'Upholstar, *frippier*.' An appraiser of goods is called *vpheldere ;* Riley, Memorials of London, p. 282.

GLOSSARIAL INDEX.

Vppe, *adv.* up, aloft, in the ascendant, b. 4. 72. Cf. mod. E. 'what's *up* now?'
Up-so-doun, *adv.* upside down, 23. 54. This is the orig. expression of which *upside down* is the corruption. Not uncommon; still pronounced *upsedown* [up·si'doun] in Shropshire.
Vr, *poss. pron.* our, a. 1. 78, a. 2. 154; Vre, a. pr. 32. A.S. *úre,* of us, our.
Vs, *pron.* us, 1. 175; Vs selue, ourselves, b. 7. 127.
Vsen, *v.* use, a. 5. 143; follow, practise, 20. 45; Vsen, *pr. pl.* follow, 11. 125, 19. 176; Vsyn, practise, R. 3. 491; Vsun, *pr. pl.* as *fut.* a. 4. 106; Vseth, *pr. pl.* use, make use of, b. 10. 129; Vse, 2 *pr. s. subj.* frequent, practise, art addicted to, 12. 112; Vsie, *pr. s. subj.* practise, 4. 469; Vsedestow, 2 *pt. s.* didst thou use, didst thou practise, b. 5. 240; Vsede, *pt. s.* used, a. 5. 139; Vsid, practised, R. 3. 220; Vseden, *pt. pl.* used, were accustomed, b. 12. 132; Vset, *pp.* used, customary, a. 10. 200.
Vsshere, usher, porter, 18. 112.
Vsure, *s.* (=usurè), usury, 7. 304, 21. 111; Vserie, 7. 239; Vserye, 3. 91.
Vsurer, usurer, 7. 307; Vsurers, *pl.* 4. 113; Vsureres, b. 11. 275.
Vttere, *adv.* outside, R. 3. 232.
Vuel, *adj.* ill, evil, difficult, 7. 87, 9. 45; ill, 19. 165. (Vuel=uvel.)
Vuel, *s.* evil, a. 8. 98; Vueles, *pl.* evils, 22. 46; pains, 23. 85.
Vuel-cloþed, *adj.* ill-clothed, 18. 196.
Vuele, *adv.* ill, wickedly, 11. 26, 14. 115; imperfectly, 8. 72; Vuel, ill, 6. 158, 10. 290. See **Vuel.**
Vuel-ytauht, *adj.* ill-taught, ill-mannered, 23. 186.
Vye, s. life, b. 14. 122. F. *vie.*
Vyker, vicar, b. 19. 477; Vycory, b. 19. 407. See **Vicari.**
Vylenye, *s.* (lit. villainy), wickedness, ill manners, disgraceful conduct, 7. 433, b. 18. 94.
Vytailers, *pl.* victuallers, providers of eatables, 3. 61. See **Vitaillers.**

Wacche, *s.* watch, guard, b. 9. 17, R. 3. 233.
Wade, *v.* wade, go, 15. 126; Wadeþ, *imper. pl.* wade, 8. 215.
Wafrere, a wafer-seller, seller of cakes, b. 13. 226, b. 14. 27; Waferer, a. 6. 120; Waffrer, 16. 199. See p. 199.
Wafres, *pl.* wafers, cakes, b. 13. 240, 264; Waffres, 16. 199.

Wafrestre, female wafer-seller, 8. 285. See **Wafrere.**
Wagen, *v.* give as security, pledge, 19. 285; Wage, *v.* engage, give surety, be security, 5. 93; Wage, *v.* pay wages to, 5. 192, 23. 269; Wage, *pr. pl.* pay wages, 23. 259; Waged, *pp.* given security, 5. 96; Waget, promised, a. 4. 87.
Waggeþ, *pr. s.* shakes violently, 19. 45; Waggede, 1 *pt. s.* shook, wagged, 13. 19; nudged, 22. 204; Waggede, *pt. s.* shook, 19. 109; Waggynge, *pr. pt.* shaking, rocking, b. 8. 31. See note to 11. 34.
Waggynge, *s.* shaking, 11. 34.
Waik, *adj.* weak, 6. 23. See **Wayke.**
Waite, *pr. s. subj.* examine, R. pr. 45; 2 *pr. s. subj.* take notice, R. 3. 128; Waitede, 1 *pt. s.* watched, observed, looked, 1. 16, 10. 293; Waite, *imp. s.* observe, R. 3. 129. O.F. *waiter, gaiter,* to watch. See **Wayten.**
Waitynge, *s.* watching, look, 7. 177; Waitynges, *pl.* watchings, glances, 3. 94. See note, p. 35. 'Waytynge, or a-spyynge wythe euyl menynge;' Prompt. Parv.
Wake, *v.* lie awake, 23. 369. See **Woken.**
Waker, *adj.* watchful, 10. 259. A.S. *wacor;* see Stratmann.
Walde, *pt. s.* would, wished, b. 13. 378. See **Wol.**
Walish, *adj.* as *sb.* Welshman, 7. 373. See **Walsche.**
Walishman, *s.* Welshman, 7. 309.
Walk, *s.* walk, a. 5. 113.
Walke, *v.* walk, walk about, 21. 32; Walketh, *pr. s.* walks, travels, b. 14. 210; Walken, *pr. pl.* walk, a. 6. 1; Walkynge, *pr. pt.* walking, 21. 119, 122; Walkid, *pp.* a. 11. 250.
Walkene, *s.* welkin, sky, b. 15. 355, b. 18. 236. See **Welkne.**
Walkers, *s. pl.* walkers, wanderers, a. 10. 102; fullers, 1. 222.
Walleþ, *pr. s.* wells, boils, turns about uneasily, *hence,* creates nausea, a. 5. 71. See note, p. 74; and see **Walwen.** A.S. *weallan.* Cf. Shropsh. *walled,* boiled, pp.
Walmed, *pt. s.* boiled up, R. 3. 114. See above. Cf. A.S. *wylm,* a boiling.
Walnote, walnut, 13. 144.
Walsche, *adj.* Welsh (lit. foreign); *hence as sb.* Welshman, a. 5. 167; Walshe, b. 5. 324; Walsshe scarlet, Welsh scarlet, i.e. red flannel, a. 5. 113 (in MS. T., instead of *walk*).

GLOSSARIAL INDEX.

Walterot, i. e. absurdity, 21. 146. See note.
Waltrid, *pt. pl.* fell grovelling, R. 2. 189. Cf. A.S. *wealtan*, to roll over; E. *welter*.
Walwen, *pr. pl.* roll, toss, 11. 46; Walweþ, fluctuate, roll, a. 9. 36; Walweth, b. 8. 41; Walwed, *pr. pl.* wallowed, R. 1. 27.
Wan, 1 *pt. s.* have earned, gained, 9. 105; *pt. s.* earned, gained, 10. 251, 18. 18; won, 12. 284; strove, disputed, b. 4. 67 (cf. A. S. *winnan*). See **Wonne**.
Wan, *adj.* pale, 7. 419.
Wandryng, *s.* wandering, 1. 7.
Wang-teþ, *pl.* cheek-teeth, molars, grinders, 23. 191.
Wanhope, *s.* despair, 3. 103, 8. 59, 8. 81, 12. 198, 15. 118, 20. 291, 23. 160, 166. Cf. Du. *wanhoop*, despair; where *wan-* is a privative prefix, allied to E. *wane*.
Wanteþ, *pr. s.* is wanting to, is absent from, 10. 106; *impers.* there is wanting, b. 14. 173. See **Wonte**.
Wantowen, *adj.* loose, wanton, wild, 4. 143, 8. 300.
Wantownesse, *s.* wantonness, profligacy, 4. 161; Wantounesse, a. 10. 67; recklessness, wildness, b. 12. 6.
Wantyng, *s.* want, lack, b. 14. 177.
Wanye, *v.* wane, b. 7. 55; Wanyeth, *pr. s.* wanes, decreases, ebbs, 11. 44; Wanyed, *pt. s.* decreased, b. 15. 3. See **Wonien**.
War, *adj.* cautious, careful, wary, 20. 224, b. 10. 270, b. 20. 162; careful, b. 13. 70; reluctant, 12. 81; assured, b. 13. 421; aware, b. 2. 8, b. 10. 142; Be war, beware, 1. 189. Cf. Shrops. *war*, adj. aware, conscious.
War, *imp. s.* be cautious; War þe, restrain thyself, keep thyself, 11. 285; beware, take care of thyself, keep thyself, a. 5. 225; *imper. s.* 3 *p.* (War hym), let him beware, 21. 300. A.S. *warian*, to be cautious.
Warde, 1 *pr. s.* guard, 19. 42.
Warde, gate-warden, guardian, 21. 368; Wardes, *pl.* wards, 1. 92; charges, 6. 186.
Wardemotes, *pl.* ward-meetings, meetings of the ward, 1. 92.
Wardeyn, *s.* guardian, 2. 51.
Ware, *adj.* cautious, 2. 40. See **War**.
Ware þe, *imp. s. refl.* guard thyself, b. 5. 452. See **War**.
Ware, *s.* wares, merchandise, 3. 223, 7. 95; a. 2. 189.

Wareine, *s.* warren, b. pr. 163.
Warie, *v.* curse, a. 7. 301, R. 3. 153. A.S. *wergian, wyrgian*, to curse; *wearh*, a wicked wretch. See **Waryen**.
Warinar, *s.* warrener, game-keeper, a. 5. 159. See **Warynere, Warner**.
Warisshe, *v.* cure, heal, b. 16. 105. O.F. *warir, garir, guarir*, F. *guérir*, to heal; pres. part. *waris-ant*.
Warmnesse, glow, R. 3. 288.
Warne, *v.* warn, a. 2. 178; Warnede, *pt. s.* warned, a. 5. 30; Warned, *pt. s.* prohibited, R. 3. 233; Warned, *pt. pl.* warned, R. 4. 77.
Warner, i. e. warrener, keeper of a warren, b. 5. 316.
Warp, *pt. s.* spoke, uttered, a. 10. 33; Warpe, b. 5. 87, 369.
Warpen, *v.* utter, speak, a. 4. 142.
Warroke, *v.* to girth, put a girth round, fasten with a girth, 5. 21; Warrok, b. 4. 20. Cf. M.E. *warlok*, a fetter, in Prompt. Parv. In Wright's Vocab. i. 154, a man is directed to tear up 'un warrok' of pease (i. e. as I suppose, a flexible piece of pease-stalk) wherewith to fasten up bundles of beans when cut. In Wright's Vocab., ed. Wülcker, col. 612, l. 23, we have: '*Sirentorium*, a warrok;' where possibly *cinctorium* is meant. In The Gent. Maga. Library (on Dialect), p. 158, there is a quotation from Blount's Tenures, p. 32, which mentions 'unum stimulum ferreum pro uno *warroke* super quoddam clothsack,' where the reference seems to be an iron peg for securing the cord drawn round the mouth of a bag.
Warth, *pt. s.* was, became, 6. 98. A.S. *wearð*, pt. t. of *weorðan*, to become.
Waryen, *v.* curse, 9. 337. See **Warie**.
Warynere, warrener, gamekeeper, 7. 363. See **Warinar, Warner**.
Wast, *s.* waste, extravagance, wastefulness, R. 1. 3, R. 2. 121.
Wast, *adj.* waste, 10. 225; vain, idle, 22. 286.
Wastell, *s.* a cake of bread of fine flour, 7. 341. O.F. *wastel, gastel*, mod. F. *gâteau*:
Wasten, *v.* waste, 22. 356; Wasteden, *pt. pl.* wasted, a. 5. 25; Wastynge, *pres. part.* 11. 300.
Wastour, a spendthrift, waster, 9. 149, 22. 437; Wastours, *pl.* spendthrifts, 6. 127, 9. 27, 139. See note to 1. 45.
Watel-ful, basket-ful, wallet-ful, 11. 269.
Watelide, *pt. s.* wattled, fenced, 22. 328. See **Watteled**.

GLOSSARIAL INDEX.

Waters, *pl.* urine (of patients), 3. 234.
Waterede, *pt. pl.* watered, 9. 172.
Watteled, *pt. s.* wattled, covered with hurdles, fenced, b. 19. 323. See **Watelide.**
Wattis, *s. pl.* wights, people, R. 4. 49. See note.
Wawes, *pl.* waves, 11. 45.
Wawe, *pr. s. subj.* walk, go about, b. 7. 79. A.S. *wagian,* to move.
Waxen, *v.* to increase, a. 8. 59; grow, become, b. 3. 300; Waxe, become, b. 11. 111; Wax, 1 *pt. s.* waxed, became, 21. 4; *pt. s.* became, 7. 422; Waxe, *pt. s.* 21. 135; Waxen, *pr. pl.* grow, are found, a. 11.12; Waxen, *pp.* grown, increased, b. 10. 75. See **Wexe.**
Wayke, *adj. pl.* weak, R. 2. 64. See **Waik.**
Wayten, *v.* watch for, 8. 187; Wayte, look after, b. 5. 202; Waytest, 2 *pr. s.* lookest at, regardest, 19. 275; Wayten, *pr. pl.* watch for, b. 8. 97; plan, a. 9. 89; watch, seek, 2. 124; lie in wait, a. 7. 149; Wayted, 1 *pt. s.* watched, examined, b. 13. 343; Wayted, *pp.* looked after, b. 5. 551; Waytid, *pp.* looked, examined, R. pr. 62; Wayte, *imp. s.* observe, R. 1. 82. See **Waite.**
Wayue, *v.* waive, move; Wayue vp = to open, b. 5. 611. Compare the entry '*wayne,* to raise, to lift up, to wind up, to rise, to rush, to gush, to strike; to lessen, to restrain,' with 7 references, in the Glossary to the Troy-Book; where I think we should read *wayue.* The same remark applies to *wayne* in the Gloss. to the Allit. Poems, ed. Morris. The MSS. can be read either way. See *wæven, waiven* in Stratmann, and *waff* in Jamieson; and see **Wayve** below.
Wayve, *v.* waive, set aside, remove, R. 1. 100; Wayueþ, *pr. s.* drives (away), 23. 168; Wayued, *pt. s.* drove, b. 20. 167. E. *waive.*
Wayues, *s. pl.* waifs, 1. 92. E. *waif.* See **Weyues.** See *guaive, guesve, guesver* in Cotgrave.
Webbe, *s.* the whole piece of woven cloth from which the coat was made, b. 5. 111. See note, p. 75.
Webbe, *s.* a female weaver, 7. 221. A.S. *webbe,* a female weaver, though the commoner form is *webbestre.* See below; and see note.
Webbes, *pl.* weavers (applied to males), 10. 204. A.S. *webba,* a (male) weaver.
Webbesters, *pl.* female weavers, 1. 222. A.S. *webbestre.* See **Webbe.**

Wecchis, *s. pl.* wakes, revels, R. 3. 364.
Wed, *s.* pledge, security, 7. 243, 14. 44, 19. 280, 285; Wedde, *dat., in phr.* To wedde, in pledge, as a pledge, 6. 73, 21. 30; Weddis, *pl.* pledges, R. 3. 309. See note, p. 85.
Wedde, *v.* pledge, wager, 3. 36, R. pr. 44; wed, a. 3. 113; 1 *pr. s.* wager, 5. 143; Wedde, *pr. pl.* wed, marry, 10. 167; Weddeþ, *pr. pl.* wed, a. 8. 74; Wedded, *pp.* b. 10. 149.
Wede, *s.* clothing, garment, 23. 211, R. 3. 118; Wedes, *pl.* clothes, dress, garments, 3. 95, 7. 177. A.S. *wǽd.* See **Wedis.**
Weden, *v.* to weed, 9. 66, 186.
Weder, *s.* weather, 21. 457; storm, R. 2. 131; Wederes, *pl.* storms, 9. 349, 11. 46. See **Wedir.** Cf. Shrops. *weather,* storms of rain, hail, or snow.
Wederes, *pl.* wether-sheep, 10. 269. See **Weperes.**
Wederwise, *adj.* weather-wise, 18. 94.
Wedes, *pl.* weeds, 9. 118. See **Weod.**
Wedewehode, widow-hood, 19. 88, 109.
Wedeweres, *pl.* widowers, 19. 76.
Wedir, weather, 7. 113, R. 3. 215. See **Weder.**
Wedir-side, *s.* weather-side, R. 4. 77.
Wedis, *s. pl.* weeds, garments, R. 3. 215. See **Wede.**
Weende, *v.* wend, go, a. 5. 144, a. 10. 171; *imp. s.* a. 3. 252. See **Wenden.**
Weene, 1 *pr. s.* think, a. 5. 251. See **Wene.**
Weer, *s.* doubt, 13. 50. See **Were.**
Weet, *adj.* wet, moist, b. 14. 41.
Weet, *s.* wet weather, b. 14. 171; Weete, wet, a. 6. 21. See **Wete.**
Weghtes, *pl.* weights, b. 14. 292.
Wehe, *s.* a neighing noise, b. 4. 22, b. 7. 91. See note to 5. 20.
Wei, *s.* road, way, a. 7. 1; A myle wei = the distance of a mile, a. 8. 131; Weye, *dat.* a. 7. 4.
Weie, *v.* to weigh, a. 5. 118; Weied, 1 *pt. s.* weighed, 7. 224.
Weile, 1 *p. s. pr.* bewail, a. 5. 94.
Weke, *s.* week, 10. 253. See **Wike, Woke.**
Weke, *s.* wick, 20. 169, 171, 178; Wicke, 20. 205. Spelt *weke* in the Cathol. Anglicum, *weyke* in Prompt. Parv.
Wel, *adj.* friendly, intimate, 4. 191, b. 3. 152; good, b. 3. 65.
Wel, *adv.* much, 1. 117, 122; very, 10. 244; quite, b. 13. 42; nearly, b. 15. 182; Wel sone, right soon, a. 12. 47; Wel worse, much worse, a. 5. 95;

GLOSSARIAL INDEX.

Wel worthe, well be to, 22. 432;
Wel be þow, well mayst thou be,
farewell, 9. 300; **Wel þe beo**, may it
be well with thee, a. 7. 264; **Wel
awey**, *adv. phr.* far and away, very
much, b. 12. 263. Cf. note to 14. 1.
Welawey *(for* Wel awey), far and
away, very much, b. 17. 42.
Wel-a-wey, *adv.* alas, a. 11. 215.
Welawo, *s.* wo, misery, b. 14. 235.
The A.S. *wálawá* is here turned into
welawo, and used as a sb.
Welch, *adj.* Welsh; *as sb.* Welsh cloth
or stuff, i. e. flannel (or some such
stuff), 7. 205. See **Walsche**. The
false reading *welthe* arose from misreading *welche*, for some scribes write
t and *c* almost exactly alike.
Wel-come, *v.* welcome, 21. 180; Welcometh, *pr. s.* b. 15. 21.
Welcomen, *adj.* welcome, a. 6. 114;
Welcome, a. 2. 208; *as interj.* a. 12. 62.
Wel-dedes, *pl.* good deeds, 4. 69.
Welden, *v.* receive, have (lit. wield),
R. 4. 52; have power over, b. 11. 72;
Weldeþ, *pr. s.* possesses, owns, 12. 10,
15. 18; Welldith, R. 3. 297; Weldeth,
pr. pl. b. 10. 29; Welden, *pr. pl.* b.
10. 24. And see **Welt**.
Wele, *s.* weal, happiness, 13. 326, 21.
210; wealth, b. 20. 37. See **Weole**,
Welle.
Wele-a-way, *interj. as sb.* wellaway!
alas! *hence*, misery, 21. 239. See
Welawo.
Welfare, *s.* good living, 22. 356.
Welkne, *s.* welkin, sky, b. 17. 160.
See **Walkene**, **Wolkene**.
Welldith, *pr. s.* possesses, R. 3. 297.
See **Welden**.
Welle, *s.* weal, prosperity, R. 3. 291;
Well, R. 3. 298. See **Wele**.
Welle, *s.* source, fount, 2. 161.
Welle-carses, *pl.* water-cresses, lit.
cresses of the well, 7. 292.
Wellede, *pt. s.* sprang out, welled up,
flowed, 22. 379.
Wel-libbynge, *adj.* living a good life,
b. 10. 431. (Here used to translate
Lat. *iusti*.)
Welnyegh, *adv.* almost, lit. well nigh,
b. 14. 113.
Welt, *pr. s.* (*for* Weldeth), possesses,
has power over, b. 10. 83. See
Welden; and note to 12. 68.
Welþe, *s.* wealth, riches, 1. 10, 2. 51,
10. 116; richness, 5. 158; success,
22. 285; good, benefit, 22. 452;
prosperity, R. 3. 288; Welthes, *pl.*
riches, b. 10. 83. See **Weolþe**.

Wem, *s.* stain, 21. 136. A.S. *wam*.
Wenche, *s.* damsel, maiden, girl, 13.
12, 19. 134; woman, 21. 118;
daughter, 7. 415; Wenches, *s. pl.*
wenches, mistresses, 1. 52.
Wenden, *v.* go, travel, 2. 130, 23. 381;
Wende, *v.* turn, 21. 210; Wende, 1
pr. s. proceed, b. 10. 156; Wendest,
2 *pr. s.* goest, 16. 161; Wendeth, *pr.
s.* b. 4. 105; Wenden, 2 *pr. pl.* 2.
175; Wendeþ, *pr. pl.* go, a. 6. 50;
Wenden, *pr. pl.* go (*or pt. pl.* went
about), b. pr. 162; Wende, 1 *pt. s.*
went, a. pr. 4; Wente, 1 *pt. s.* went,
wandered, 1. 4; Went me = turned
me, b. pr. 7 (see note); Wentest, 2
pt. s. shouldst depart, hast gone away,
9. 220; Wenten, *pt. pl.* went, b. 4.
76; Went, *pp.* gone, departed, 4.
438, 9. 24; changed, b. 3. 280;
Wende, *imp. s.* go, b. 3. 264; Wend,
a. 7. 264; Wendyng, *pr. pt.* going,
21. 131. See **Weende**. A.S. *wendan*, to turn, go; pt. t. *wende*; cf. E.
wend, *went*.
Wene, *v.* think, believe, suppose, ween,
imagine, 4. 458; Wene, 1 *pr. s.* 15.
167; Weneþ, *pr. s.* thinks, 23. 32;
Wenen, *pr. pl.* think, form their
opinions, b. 15. 470; 2 *pr. pl.* think,
suppose, b. 13. 308; Wende, 1 *pt. s.*
thought, b. 5. 238; Wendest, 2 *p. s.
pt.* didst ween, didst suppose, b. 3.
191; Wende, *pt. s.* believed, expected,
b. 13. 407; *pt. s. subj.* should suppose, 7. 32; *pt. pl. subj.* should
think, b. 13. 280, 292; Wene, *imp. s.*
think, believe, imagine, 21. 196. See
Weene. A.S. *wénan*, pt. t. *wénde*.
Wenge, wing, flight, b. 12. 263. 'A
wenge.' Cath. Angl. Icel. *vængr*.
Went, **Wente**. See **Wenden**.
Wentes, *pl.* ways, contrivances, 7. 263.
A.S. *wend*, a turn; from *wendan*.
Cf. Chaucer, Troilus, ii. 63, 815; iii.
788.
Wenynge, *s.* thinking, supposition,
supposing, 23. 33.
Weod, *s.* weed, a. 10. 122; Weodes,
pl. 13. 229. See **Wedes**.
Weole, *s.* weal, a. 11. 114. See **Wele**.
Weolþe, *s.* wealth, a. 1. 53; richness,
a. 4. 139. See **Welþe**.
Weorþe, 2 *p. s. pr. subj.* mayst become, a. 1. 26. See **Worthe**.
Wepe, *v.* weep, b. 5. 62; Wepeþ, *pr. s.*
weeps, a. 1. 154; Wepte, 1 *pt. s.* b.
11. 3; Wepe, *pt. s.* b. 5. 470. *Wep*
= wept, is still in use in Shropshire.
Wepne, weapon, 4. 462, 15. 50.

GLOSSARIAL INDEX. 461

Werche, *v.* work, act, do, b. 7. 198, b. 10. 209; Werche, *imp. s.* work, a. 7. 71; Wercheþ, *imp. pl.* do, b. 10. 413. See **Worchen.**
Werchinge, *s.* working, doing, R. 3. 114; endeavour, R. 1. 105.
Werdes, *pl.* fates, destiny, occurrences, 4. 241. A.S. *wyrd;* E. *weird.*
Were, *s.* doubt, perplexity, b. 11. 111, b. 16. 3. See **Weer.** Apparently the same word as E. *war;* see *werre* in Stratmann.
Were, *v.* to wear, 4. 451; Wered, *pt. s.* wore, a. 2. 12; Wered, *pp.* worn, 6. 81. See **Werie.**
Weren, *pt. pl.* were, a. 7. 102; Were, *pt. s. subj.* were, 6. 125, 161; would be, b. 3. 342; should be, b. 5. 167; would be, R. 3. 116.
Werie, *v.* wear, 20. 235.
Werkmanship, performance, virility, b. 2. 91; Werkmanshup, 3. 96; manipulation, 20. 141; Werkemanship, work, b. 10. 288.
Wernard, *s.* deceiver, liar, b. 3. 179; Wernardes, *pl.* deceivers, liars, 3. 142. '*Guernart,* trompeur;' Roquefort. Allied to the word below.
Werneþ, *pr. pl. (or s. with* Men), refuse. 23. 12. b. 20. 12. A.S. *wearnian,* to take heed; *wearn,* a refusal.
Werre, *s.* war, 4. 206, 14. 140.
Werren, *v.* war, make war, 18. 234; Werrid, *pt. s.* R. pr. 10.
Wers, *adv. comp.* worse, a. 11. 279, 280; þe werse = the less, 4. 221; Wel worse, much worse, a. 5. 95.
Wery, *adj.* weary, tired, 21. 4.
Wesche, 1 *pt. s.* I washed, b. 16. 228; Wesh, 19. 245; *pt. s.* Wessh, R. 2. 131; Wesshen, *pt. pl.* b. 2. 220, b. 13. 28.
Weschte, *pt. pl.* wished, a. 5. 195.
Wesp, *s.* wisp, bundle, a. 5. 195. See **Wips.**
Wete, *s.* wet, wet weather, 8. 176.
Wete, *v. (for* Wite), suppose, R. 3. 205.
Wetschod, *adj.* wetshod, with wet feet, 21. 1; Wet shood, 17. 14. Shropsh. *wetchet.* See the note, p. 247.
Weþebondes, *s. gen. sing.* of Weþebonde, woodbine, a. 6. 9. 'Woodbinde, binde-weede, or *withie-winde,* because it windes about other plants;' Minsheu. The Harl. MS. has *wodebyndes.* See **Weythwynde.**
Weueres, *pl.* weavers, b. pr. 219.
Wex, wax (much used for church-offerings), 1. 99. 11. 269.

Wexe, *v.* increase, grow, 3. 29, 13. 181; begin to be, 13. 50; become, 4. 458, 11. 195; Wexeth, *pr. s.* grows, b. 10. 12; increases, flows, b. 8. 39; waxes, 11. 44; Wexeþ, 2 *pr.-pl.* grow, increase, 23. 269; *pr. pl.* multiply, b. 15. 452; Wexe, *pr. s. subj.* grows, 15. 26; Wex, 1 *pt. s.* became, b. 11. 4; Wex, *pt. s.* increased, b. 15. 3; grew, arose, b. 14. 76; grew, b. 3. 328; Wexen, *pt. pl.* grew, sprang. b. 9. 32; were made, b. 14. 60; Wexe, became, R. 2. 64. See **Waxen, Wox.**
Wexed, *pp.* stopped up (lit. fastened up with wax), 7. 402. See note.
Wey, *s.* way, road, course, method, 2. 138; Weye, b. 13. 220; Weyes, *pl.* ways, 15. 196.
Weye, *s.* creature, person, wight, man, 8. 158, 14. 157. See **Wye.**
Weye, *v.* weigh, 7. 210; Weyede, *pt. s.* a. 5. 132; Weyȝed, b. 5. 218; Weyen, *pp.* 2. 175; Weye, *pp.* weighed, 10. 273. A.S. *wegan,* pp. *wegen.*
Weye, *s.* a wey, a weight so called, b. 5. 93. A *wey* of butter or cheese varies from 2 to 3 cwt.
Weyke, *s.* a wick, b. 17. 206. See **Weke.**
Weylawey, well a day! *hence,* wo, misery, 17. 78; Wele-a-way, 21. 239. See **Welawo, Weyllowey.**
Weyled, *pt. s.* bewailed, lamented, b. 14. 324; Weylyng, *pres. pt.* a. 5. 261.
Weyllowey, alas! i.e. sorrow, misery, b. 18. 227. See **Welawo.**
Weythwynde, *s.* wild convolvulus; In a weythwynde wyse, like a wild convolvulus, 8. 163. See note. See **Weþebondes.**
Weyues, *pl.* waifs, b. pr. 94. See **Wayues.**
Wham, *pron.* whom, 2. 43.
Whanne, *adv.* when, 2. 45.
Whas, *pron.* whose, 2. 46, 3. 17.
What, as to what is, partly, b. 13. 317; what sort of (being), b. 2. 19.
What so, whatsoever, whatever, b. 10. 128, R. pr. 36.
Wheder, *adv.* whither, in what way, 2. 138; whither, a. 12. 80.
Whederwarde, *adv.* whither, in what direction, 7. 354.
When *(for* Whenne), whence; Of when, (from) whence, a. 12. 80.
Whenne, *adv.* when, 2. 203, 19. 161.
Whennes; Fro whennes, from whence, 8. 170; When, a. 12. 80.

Wher, *adv.* where, 11. 123; Wyden wher = widely, astray, in different directions, a. 9. 53.
Wher, *conj.* (*contr. from* wheþer), whether, 1. 186, 4. 298, 17. 336, 20. 25; Where, 15. 213, 16. 281.
Wherby, *adv.* how, by what, b. 10. 436.
Wherforþ, *adv.* wherever forth, 17. 339.
Wher-of, *adv.* whereto, 17. 173; whereby, b. 14. 40; to what end, b. 11. 89.
Wherþorw, *adv.* whereby, a. 6. 79.
Wher-with, *adv.* wherewith, i.e. means, 7. 317.
Whete, wheat, 9. 8.
Whether, which of the two, b. 16. 96, a. 8. 59, a. 12. 37.
Whi, *adv.* why, 18. 204; *as sb.* why, reason, 19. 147.
Whi, *s.* neigh, a. 4. 21. See **Wehe**.
Which a, what sort of a, 5. 26, b. 7. 146; Whiche a, how great a, 21. 129; Whiche, *pl.* what sort of, how great, 12. 26, b. 10. 27.
Whider, *adv.* whither, 19. 293. See **Whyder**.
Whider-oute, from what root, whence, b. 16. 12. See **Whoder**.
Whil, *adv.* while, 11. 287; While, at times, whilom, 18. 99.
While, *s.* (short) time, 22. 357, b. *19. 351; þe while, *adv.* while, so long as, b. 10. 145. See **Whyle**.
While, *adj.* occasional, former, R. 3. 363.
Whiles, *adv.* whilst, b. 6. 320.
Whilum, *adv.* formerly, b. 15. 353.
Whistellynge, *s.* whistle, call, b. 15. 456; Whistlynge, b. 15. 466, 471. (In b. 15. 472, *whistlynge* is prob. an error for *techynge*.)
White, *pr. s. subj.* becomes white, 17. 332.
Whitel, *s.* blanket, covering, 17. 76. See note.
Whit-lymed, *adj.* white-washed, whitened, 17. 267.
Who; As who seith, as one who says, as if he should say, b. 9. 36.
Whoder, *adv.* whither, a. 5. 149; Whoder out, in which direction outwards, 8. 178. See **Whideroute**.
Whon, *conj.* when, a. 1. 124.
Whose, *pron.* whoso, whosoever, a. 4. 56. (*Here* who-se = who-so.)
Whuche, *pron.* of what sort, what kind, a. 2. 27; Whuch, what sort of, a. 8. 154. See note to 10. 300.

Whucche, *s.* trunk, chest, 5. 111, a. 4. 102. It seems to be due to a provincial pronunciation of F. *huche*, E. *hutch*. '*Whyche*, or *hutche*;' Prompt. Parv.
Why, *s.* the reason why, b. 15. 504; Whyes, *pl.* reasons why, reasons, b. 12. 217. See **Whi**.
Whyder, *adv.* whither, b. 15. 13. See **Whider, Whoder**.
Whyle, *s.* while, time, interval, 1. 16, 21. 169. See **While**.
Wicche, a sorcerer, a witch, 7. 81, b. 13. 338, b. 18. 46.
Wicchecrafte, *s.* sorcery, 21. 46.
Wicke, *s.* wick, 20. 205. See **Weke**.
Wicke, *adj. as sb.* ill, 12. 272. See **Wycke**.
Wickedliche, *adv.* wickedly, unfairly, 7. 210; Wickeliche, 9. 235.
Wickett, *s.* wicket-gate, R. 3. 233. See **Wiket**.
Wide-where, *adv.* widely wandering, b. 8. 62. See **Wher, Wydene**.
Widewe, *s.* widow, a. 10. 182; Widwe, b. 9. 162; Widewes, *pl.* widows, 8. 32. See **Wodewes**.
Wideyers, *s. pl.* widowers, a. 10. 194; Widwers, b. 9. 174.
Widwehode, widowhood, b. 16. 203.
Wif, wife, 4. 157, 12. 99.
Wight, *s.* creature, 20. 263, 21. 212. See **Wiȝt, Wiht, Wyght**.
Wight, *adj.* active, 11. 146. Cf. Swed. *vig*, agile. 'Wight, *alicer, acer, . . agilis*;' Cath. Angl.
Wightlich, *adv.* quickly, b. 16. 275. See **Wiȝtliche, Wihtliche**.
Wightnesse, *s.* quickness, b. 19. 240. '*Wightnesse, alacritas, . . . celeritas*;' Cath. Angl.
Wiht, *s.* wight, being, man, 11. 4. See **Wight, Wiȝt**.
Wihtliche, *adv.* vigorously, a. 7. 22; nimbly, quickly, a. 2. 184; Wihtly, strongly, well, a. 8. 29. See **Wightlich**.
Wike, *s.* week, a. 7. 243; Wikes, *pl.* a. 11. 105. See **Woke, Weke, Wyke**.
Wiket, *s.* wicket-gate, a small gate made within a large door, b. 5. 611. See **Wickett**.
Wiket-ȝat, *s.* wicket-gate, a. 6. 92.
Wikke, *adj.* wikked, b. 5. 229; *pl.* the wicked, b. 19. 193. See **Wykke**.
Wikke, *adv.* ill, wickedly, 17. 177.
Wikked, *adj.* bad, i.e. hard to find, b. 6. 1; Wikkede, a. 5. 217; Wikkede, *pl.* 15. 25; rough, bad, rotten (said of roads), 10. 31.

GLOSSARIAL INDEX. 463

Wikkedlokest, *adv.* most wickedly, b. 10. 427.
Wil, 1 *pr. s.* will, ordain, b. 9. 124; Wil, *pr. s.* wishes, b. 5. 40.
Wil, *s.* self-will, a. 6. 77, a. 10. 213.
Wile, *pr. s.* wills, wishes, 22. 396. See **Wil, Wol.**
Wiles, *pl.* wiles, crafts, tricks, sleights, 20. 240, 244.
Wilfulliche, *adv.* wilfully, wrongfully, 20. 267, 22. 373; voluntarily, 23. 49; Wilfullich, voluntarily, b. 20. 48; Wilffullich, wilfully, 5. 46. Cf. 'Wylfulle, *voluntarius, spontaneus;*' Prompt. Parv.
Willen, *pr. pl.* wish, desire, 2. 8; Willynge, *pres. pt. abs.* desiring, wishing, b. 13. 280 (see note to 7. 32). See **Wil, Wol.**
Wilnen, *v.* accept willingly, 22. 68; Wilne, *v.* wish for, desire, b. 5. 187, b. 10. 341; Wilne, 1 *pr. s.* will, desire, wish, 17. 184; Wilnest, 2 *pr. s.* wishest, a. 2. 30; Wilneþ, *pr. s.* desires, 4. 147, 13. 21; wishes, 2. 85; will have, a. 4. 139; Wilneþ, 2 *pr. pl.* wish for, desire, 18. 191; Wilnen, *pr. pl.* wish, 4. 387; Wilne, desire, b. 1. 8; Wilne, 2 *pr. s. subj.* desire, expect, a. 10. 88; Wilne, *pres. s. subj.* desire, a. 3. 106; Wilnede, *pt. s.* wished, desired, 4. 131, 7. 41; Wilned, prayed for, b. 11. 141; Wilnede, 1 *pt. pl.* wished, desired, 19. 261; Wilnynge, *pres. part.* (*absolute*), desiring, wishing, 7. 32; Wilneth, *imp. pl.* b. 10. 117. See **Wylnen.** A.S. *wilnian.*
Wiltow, wilt thou, b. 5. 310, b. 16. 25; Wiltow or neltow, whether thou wilt or no, b, 6. 158.
Wink, *s.* sleep, nap, a. 5. 3.
Winne, *v.* gain, win, a. 3. 230; Winneþ, *pr. pl.* win, a. 7. 22; Winne, 2 *pr. pl. subj.* gain your living, a. 1. 153. See **Wynnen.**
Winter, *s.* winter, a. 8. 114; Winter, *pl.* winters, years, a. 3. 40.
Wips, *s.* wisp, handful, 7. 402; Wispe, b. 5. 351.
Wis, *imp. s.* instruct, a. 12. 31. See **Wissen.**
Wise, *adj. pl.* wise (men), 21. 244.
Wisliche, *adv.* wisely, 4. 7, 9. 235; cautiously, carefully, 11. 285.
Wisloker, *adv. comp.* more carefully, b. 13. 343.
Wissen, *v.* point out, teach, shew, instruct, inform, direct, 6. 140, 8. 178, 15. 196, 22. 64; Wisse, *v.* 3. 199, 11. 6, 29, 74; To wisse, to be shewn the way, a. 9. 13; Wisse, 1 *pr. s.* b. 1. 42; Wisseth, *pr. s.* teaches, 2. 40; Wisse, 2 *pr. pl.* b. 11. 428; Wissen, *pr. pl.* 18. 84; Wissede, 1 *pt. s.* taught, 15. 4; *pt. s.* 2. 71, 9. 162; advised, a. 7. 151; Wissed, *pt. s.* taught, b. 6. 167; Wisside, a. 1. 72; Wissed, *pt. pl.* taught the way, directed, 12. 140. A.S. *wissian,* to guide, direct, instruct, shew the way. See **Wyssen.**
Wisshen, *pt. pl.* washed, 16. 32, 38. See **Wesche.**
Wissynge, *s.* teaching, 13. 12.
Wist, Wiste, knew; see **Wite.**
Wit, *s.* knowledge, understanding, 21. 244, 22. 82; mind, 2. 68; wit, a. 8. 56; wisdom (*but the line is corrupt*), a. 12. 72 *n*; Witt, knowledge, 10. 56; sense, wits, 10. 106; mind, 4. 458; Witte, wit, knowledge, b. 8. 9; sense, 1. 38; wisdom, R. pr. 69; trick, piece of skill, b. 13. 363; Wittis, *gen.* of knowledge, b. 10. 227; Wittes, *pl.* senses, 2. 15, b. 10. 6, b. 19. 211; wits, understanding, b. 15. 54; Wittis, senses, b. 14. 54. See **Wyt.**
Wit, *s.* blame, fault, a. 10. 75. MS. U. has the reading *wyte.* See **Wited.**
Wite, *v.* know, 1. 181, 4. 153, 5. 136; find out, b. 10. 117; Witen, *v.* ascertain, b. 6. 213; Witen, 2 *pr. pl.* a. 8. 62; Witen, *pr. pl.* know, 19. 147; Wite, 1 *pr. s. subj.* 5. 100; *pr. s. subj.* a. 4. 92; Wist, 1 *pt. s.* I knew, 16. 285; Wiste, *pt. s.* knew, b. 8. 4; learnt, 7. 70, 71; Wist, *pt. s.* knew, 11. 4; Wiste, *pt. pl.* R. 1. 76; Wisten, *pt. pl.* knew, recognised, b. 11. 230; Wist, knew, b. 15. 116; Wiste, *pt. pl. subj.* should know, b. 13. 312; Wist, *pp.* known, 21. 211; Wite, *imp. s.* know thou, a. 1. 162; Witeth, *imp. pl.* b. 2. 74; Witen, 3 *p. imp. pl.* let them know, a. 2. 60. See **Wuste, Wyte, Wot.** A.S. *witan,* to know, pt. t. *wiste;* pr. t. *wát.*
Wited, 1 *pt. s.* blamed, 7. 113; Wited, Witede, *pt. s.* laid the blame on (i. e. laid the blame of the deed on wine), 2. 30. A.S. *witan,* to blame, reprove.
Witen, *v.* preserve, keep, b. 7. 35; *ger.* guard, secure, b. 16. 25; *pr. pl.* guard, protect, a. 10. 67; Wite god = God protect (us), *a form of oath,* b. 5. 641; see note, p. 105. Goth. *witan,* to observe, pt. t. *witaida.*
Witerliche, *adv.* assuredly, for certain, verily, truly, 4. 222, 16. 89; Witerly, 10. 88, 23. 271. See **Witterly, Wy-**

GLOSSARIAL INDEX.

terliche. Cf. Dan. *vitterlig*, public, generally known.
With, *prep.* by means of, b. 3. 2; against, 13. 118, 192; like, a. 8. 71. *We should note the curious position of* with *in the sentence, in many instances, as, for example:* To amende with thy scaþe = to requite thy loss with, a. 4. 83; To bygge þe with a wastell = to buy thyself a cake with, 7. 341; To clanse with oure soules = to cleanse our souls with, 17. 25; To closye with heuene = to close heaven with, 1. 133; To fynde with hym-selue = to provide for himself with, 11. 181; To woke with themese = to wet the Thames with, b. 15. 332; &c. It follows the verb.
With-drow, *pt. s.* with-drew, 21. 61; With-drowe, b. 18. 60; With-drow, *pt. s. refl.* withdrew, 20. 62.
Withewyndes, *gen. sing.* of the wild convolvulus or bindweed, b. 5. 525. See **Weþe-bondes.**
With-halt, *pr. s.* (*for* With-haldeth), keeps back, withholds, 8. 195; With-helde, *pt. pl.* kept, detained, 3. 238.
Withinnen, *adv.* within (doors), a. 6. 37.
Withoute, *conj.* unless, 5. 176; Withoute, *prep.* besides, b. 14. 237.
Withouten, *adv.* without (doors), a. 6. 37; Withoute, on the outside, 13. 144.
With-sette; see **With-sitte.**
With-siggen, *v.* contradict, a. 4. 142.
With-sitte, *v.* oppose, contradict, 9. 202, 11. 97; With-sette, 1. 174; With-sat, 1 *pt. s.* 19. 251.
With þat, *conj.* provided that, 12. 92, b. 5. 74; moreover, b. 5. 307.
Witles, *adj.* out of my mind, b. 13. 1; Witlees, senseless, silly, 10. 111. See **Wittlees.**
Witt (*for* Wited), *pt. s.* blamed, laid the fault on, b. 1. 31. See **Wited.**
Witterly, *adv.* for certain, assuredly, truly, certainly, 2. 71, 4. 298, b. 3. 175, b. 5. 562, b. 9. 4.
Witti, *adj.* wise, a. 2. 1c7, a. 11. 5. See **Witty.**
Wittiliche, *adv.* skilfully, a. 10. 4.
Wittiman, Clever-man (as a name), 5. 31.
Wittlees, *adj.* out of (my) senses, 16. 1. See **Witles.**
Witty, *adj.* clever, learned, wise, 7. 24, 10. 51; clever (men), 12. 228. See **Witti, Wytty.**

Wittyliche, *adv.* craftily, skilfully, 11. 130.
Wittyour, *adj.* more learned, more clever, 6. 189.
Witynge, *adv.* knowingly, 22. 373. See **Wytynge.**
Wiȝt, *s.* man, creature, person, 14. 220, 221. See **Wight, Wyȝt.**
Wiȝte, *adj.* mighty, strong, b. 9. 21, b. 13. 173. See **Wight.**
Wiȝtliche, *adv.* actively, b. 2. 208, b. 6. 21; Wiȝtlich, b. 10. 219.
Wo, *s.* woe, trouble, 2. 166, b. 3. 152; hardship, 10. 78. See **Woo.**
Wo, *adj.* miserable, woful, b. 5. 3, R. 1. 67.
Wode, *s.* wood, 17. 180, a. 9. 54; Wodes, *pl.* 10. 196, 225.
Wode-syde, side of a wood, 11. 62.
Wodewes, *pl.* widows, 4. 161, 7. 143. See **Widewe.**
Woke, *s.* week, 13. 122, b. 5. 93; Of al a woke = during a whole week, 9. 270; Wokes, *pl.* weeks, 19. 134. See **Weke, Wike, Wyke.** Spelt *woke, wooke, wok* in Prompt. Parv. A.S. *wuce.*
Woken, *pt. pl.* awoke, b. 14. 69. See **Wake.**
Wokie, *v.* moisten, soften, 15. 25; Woke with themese = to moisten the Thames with, to add water to the Thames, b. 15. 332; Wokeþ, *pr. s.* moistens, 17. 332. See notes. A.S. *wácian,* to weaken, soften; hence to moisten; apparently confused with Icel. *vökr,* moist, Dan. *wak,* moist. '*Wokey,* moist, sappy; *Durham;*' Halliwell.
Wol, *pr. s.* will, 11. 19, b. 5. 250; desires, 15. 135; *pr. pl.* will, 12. 182; Wol þou, whether thou wilt, a. 7. 144; Wol he nul he, willynilly, whether he will or no, 22. 466, 23. 29; Wole, *pr. s.* will, 14. 44; wills, desires, wishes, 15. 217; Wole, *pr. pl.* will (so remain), 6. 81; Wolen, will, a. 5. 36; are ready to, b. 15. 151; Woldestow, if thou wouldst, b. 3. 49; Wolde, *pt. s.* would, 12. 65; intended, 19. 230; intended (to go), desired (to go), b. 13. 223; would have, required, b. 1. 13; meant, a. 2. 49; Wold, wished, was willing, 22. 239; Wolde, *pt. pl.* would, a. 8. 32; would have, b. 14. 173; Wolde. *pt. pl.* would like to do so, 1. 38; Wolden, would have, b. 16. 27. See **Wil, Wolle, Wolt.** A. S. *wile,* will.

GLOSSARIAL INDEX.   465

Wolhe nolhe, whether he will or no, willy nilly, b. 20. 29.
Wolkene, sky, welkin, 21. 248. See **Walkene, Welkne.**
Woll, *adv.* well, very, R. 1. 67. See **Wel.**
Wolle, *pr. s.* will, 11. 10; Woll, will do so, R. 3. 115; Wolle, 2 *pr. s. subj.* art willing, 12. 309; *pr. s. subj.* wish, a. 9. 44; Wolleþ, 1 *pr. pl.* will, are willing to, 9. 148; 2 *pr. pl.* will, wish, a. 6. 44; Wollen, *pr. pl.* will, 13. 8; Woll, will grant, R. 3. 240. See **Wol.**
Wolle, *s.* wool, 9. 12, b. 6. 13.
Wollen, *adj.* woollen, 2. 18, 7. 221, b. 5. 215; Wollene, employed in weaving wool, a pr. 99; Wollen, *s.* woollen stuff, b. 1. 18; Wollene, woollen things, 14. 103.
Wolleward, *adj.* having the skin next to a woollen garment, without linen, b. 18. 1. See note. (It should, however, be observed that the *literal* sense is 'with one's body *towards the wool,*' which comes to the same thing as 'with wool next one's body.' See it discussed in my Etym. Dict. s. v. *Woolward.*)
Wollewebsteres, *s. pl.* wool-weavers, b. pr. 219.
Wolt, 2 *pr. s.* wilt, 4. 154, b. 2. 44; Woltou, wilt thou, a. 3. 113.
Wolues, *pl.* wolves, 10. 226, 259.
Wolues kynnes, of the kin or nature of wolves, b. 6. 163.
Wombe, *s.* belly, stomach, 1. 57, 6. 52, 7. 439, 9. 172; womb, 8. 239; Wombe, *gen.* of the belly, of the appetite, a. 8. 111; Womben, *pl.* bellies, stomachs, 4. 83; Wombes, a. pr. 56; Wombis, R. 3. 4, 58. A.S. *wamb.*
Wombe-cloutes, *pl.* tripes, lit. belly-rags, b. 13. 63. '*Hoc omentum, Anglice,* a womclotte;' Wright's Vocab. i. 266. Mr. Wright adds the note—'The *womb-clout* was properly the caul which envelopes the intestines.'
Wommon, *s.* woman, lady, a. 1. 69, a. 8. 74; Womon, 10. 167; Wommen, *pl.* women, 12. 111.
Won, *s.* plenty; Good won, a good quantity, 23. 171. See note; and see **Woon.** For a proposed etymology from Icel. *ván,* expectation, see Guy of Warwick, ed. Zupitza, p. 444.
Wonde, *pt. pl.* wound, clothed, 3. 230; Wonden, b. 2. 220.

Wondeþ, *adj.* wounded, 21. 91. A.S. *wund;* Goth. *wunds* (Mk. xii. 4).
Wonder, *adv.* wonderfully, wondrously, 14. 5, 12. 219, 19. 55.
Wonderliche, *adv.* wonderfully, 7. 309, 12. 3, 167.
Wonderwyse, a wonderful manner, 2. 126.
Wonderwyse, *adj.* wonderfully wise, 18. 94 *n.*
Wondes, *pl.* wounds, 20. 65.
Wondir, *adj.* wonderful, R. 3. 343.
Wondrede, *pt. s. impers.* it surprised, 14. 153.
Wondringe, *pres. part.* wandering, a. pr. 19. Spelt *wandringe* in 4 other MSS.
Wone, *s.* dwelling, residence, 4. 141; Wones, *pl.* habitations, 1. 18, b. 3. 234. See **Wonen.**
Wone, *s.* custom, habit, 5. 22. 17. 321. A.S. *wuna, ge-wuna.*
Wonen, *v.* dwell, abide, live, a. 2. 74, a. 10. 140; Wone, a. 2. 30, 200; Woneþ, *pr. s.* lives, 16. 242; dwells, 22. 192, b. 2. 232; Woneth, 1 *pr. pl.* a. 8. 111; *pr. pl.* a. 2. 60; Wonede, *pt. s.* dwelt, 1. 18; (1 *p.*) 6. 1; Wonede, *pt. pl.* lived, 23. 39; Woneden, 18. 11; Woned, *pp.* accustomed, wont, 9. 164, 18. 89. A.S. *wunian,* G. *wohnen.* See **Wonye.**
Wonien, *v.* (*in this passage for* Wanien), to diminish, decrease, wane, a. 8. 59; Wonieþ, *pr. s.* wanes, a. 9. 34. See **Wanye.**
Wonne, *v.* dwell, R. 2. 149; Wonneth, *pr. pl.* dwell, R. 3. 282; Wonnynge, *pres. part.* dwelling, R. 2. 59. See **Wonen, Wonye.**
Wonte, *v.* be wanting, a. 5. 33.
Wonye, *v.* dwell, remain, 22. 198, b. 2. 106, 224; Wony, 3. 234; Wonyeþ, *pr. s.* dwells, lives, 2. 59, 8. 178; Wonieth, b. 1. 63; Wonyeþ, *pr. pl.* live, dwell, abide, 10. 83; Wonye, b. 10. 429. See **Wonen, Wonne.**
Woo, *s.* misfortune, trouble, 1. 10; Wilne to woo = wish for evil (to), R. 3. 30. See **Wo.**
Woolle, *s.* wool, 10. 264, 268.
Woon, *s.* plenty, b. 20. 170. See **Won,** *s.*
Wopen, *pt. pl.* wept, a. 8. 42.
Worchen, *v.* work, act, do, 6. 25, 12. 221; Worche, *v.* work, act, b. 6. 120, a. 1. 26; work, perform, 12. 91; do, b. 10. 145, a. 7. 8; make, b. 11. 337; *ger.* labour, 1. 38, 9. 18; accomplish, bring to pass, a. 2. 85; Worcheþ, *pr.*

GLOSSARIAL INDEX.

s. works, 20. 17; works, does, 11. 239; deals, a. 11. 154; Worche, *pr. s. subj.* act, 17. 219, 220; Worchen, *pr. pl.* work, 2. 125; do, 2. 130; act, a. 3. 226; Worcheþ, *pr. pl.* work, b. 3. 80; Worche, 2 *pr. s. subj.* work, act, a. 10. 93; Worche, *imp. s.* work, labour, b. 9. 81; Worcheþ, *imp. pl.* work, b. 2. 133; act, a. 2. 103; Worchinge, *pres. pt.* working, a. pr. 19. See **Werche, Wrouȝte.**

Worchewel, Work-well, 11. 146.

Worchyng, *s.* ordinance, ordaining, 9. 90; A worchyng = in making, i.e. being made, 4. 51.

Word (*for* World), world, a. 1. 37.

Worden, 2 *pr. pl.* talk, 14. 246; *pr. pl. subj.* may say, a. 10. 94; Wordeden, *pt. pl.* spoke, b. 10. 428; consulted, b. 4. 46; Worded, *pp.* spoken, 16. 149; Wordyng, *pres. pt.* talking, 20. 46.

Worlde-riche, *adj.* worldly-rich, 17. 16.

Worldliche, *adj.* worldly, earthly, 11. 90, 22. 285; Worldliche, earthly, as relates to this world, 4. 371.

Worm, *s.* worm, serpent, snake, a. 11. 66; Wormes, *pl.* snakes, 14. 137, b. 11. 320.

Worschipe, *s.* reverence, respect, honour, 13. 206.

Worshepen, *v.* worship, reverence, pay respect to, 1. 119, 2. 16; Worshupen, 19. 263; Worshiped, 1 *pt. s.* treated with respect, accosted with respect, b. 10. 222; Worshupde, *pt. pl.* reverenced, paid respect to, 4. 13; Worshupe, *imp. s.* 22. 210. See note to b. 15. 476, p. 231.

Worst, 2 *pr. as fut. s.* shalt be, 8. 265, 22. 408; Worstow, 2 *fut. s.* wilt thou be, b. 19. 404. See **Worthe.**

Wortes, *pl.* (prepared *or* boiled) vegetables, 9. 332.

Worth, *adj.* worth, 1. 76; esteemed, 12. 79; to the value or amount of, a. 8. 54.

Worthe, *v.* become, 12. 24, b. 8. 61, b. 10. 130, 143; be, 12. 89, b. 13. 147; dwell, a. 7. 75; Lete worthe, let be, let alone, 1. 201, 3. 49; Worth, *pr. s.* is, 14. 1; *as fut. s.* will be, 9. 160, 10. 238, 273, 322; will (*or* can) be, b. 12. 277; will, 13. 232; shall be, 2. 185, 3. 41, 248; Worþestou, shalt thou be, a. 6. 102; Worthen vppe, 2 *pr. pl.* get up, mount, b. 7. 91; Worth, 2 *pr. s. subj.* may be, b. 1. 26; *pr. s. subj.* may be, a. 3. 34; Worþ, *imp. s.* be done, a. 5. 248; Worth, 1 *pt. s.* became, fell, 12. 167. See **Worst.** A.S. *weorðan,* to become, be.

Worþly, *adj.* worthy, 9. 9.

Wose, *s.* ooze, slime, 13. 229. See note.

Woshe, *pt. pl.* washed, 3. 230; Wosshen, a. 2. 196. See **Wasshen, Wesche.**

Wot, 1 *pr. s.* know, 10. 88; Wote, 1 *pr. s.* know, 20. 9, b. 5. 180; Wost, 2 *pr. s.* knowest, 4. 226, 11. 71, b. 8. 73; Wot, *pr. s.* knows, 1. 44, 100; 7. 163, 21. 212; Wote, b. 2. 77, b. 5. 181, b. 6. 132; Wote, 1 *pr. pl.* we know of, are aware of, b. 10. 363; Wote, *pr. pl.* b. 3. 329; Wot god, God knows, b. 4. 37; god it wote, God knows it, b. pr. 43. See **Wite.**

Wouwere, *s.* wooer, 13. 20. See **Woweres.**

Wox, *pt. s.* grew, sprang, a. 2. 20; Woxen, *pt. pl.* grew, a. 10. 33; increased, 16. 264; Woxen, *pp.* grown, 4. 212. See **Wexe.**

Wowe, *s.* wall, a. 5. 136; Wowes, *pl.* 4. 65, b. 3. 61. A.S. *wah.*

Wowed, *pt. s.* wooed, coaxed, entreated, b. 4. 74.

Woweres, *pl.* wooers, b. 11. 71. See **Wouwere.**

Wo-werie, *adj.* wo-weary, worn out with sorrow, 21. 1.

Wrake, *s.* persecution, 21. 459; retaliation, R. 1. 43; destruction, 18. 85. A.S. *wræc,* exile, misery; from *wrecan.*

Wrang, *s.* injustice, 20. 232.

Wrang, *pt. s.* wrung (her hands), 3. 252; twisted, 9. 172. Pt. t. of *wringen.* See **Wrong.**

Wrastel, *pr. s. subj.* struggle, wrestle, b. 14. 224. See **Wraxle.**

Wratthe, *v.* enrage, b. 2. 116; Wrathe, 3. 118; Wrath, R. pr. 80; Wratthest, 2 *pr. s. reflex.* becomest angry, 4. 229; Wratthe, *pr. s. subj.* be angry, 1. 189; Wraþede, 1 *pt. s.* was angry, 12. 166; Wratthede, *pt. s.* enraged, 2. 26; Wraþþe, *imp. s.* be angry, a. 10. 94.

Wraxle, *v.* struggle, wrestle, 17. 67, 80. See **Wrastel.**

Wrecche, *adj.* wretched, 14. 95, 20. 326.

Wrecchednesse, misery, *or* (*perhaps*) wickedness, 13. 2.

Wreke, *v.* wreak, avenge, b. 5. 85;

GLOSSARIAL INDEX. 467

Wreken, *pp.* avenged, a. 2. 169;
Wreke, 3. 266; Wroke, b. 2. 194;
Wreke, *imper. s.* satisfy, b. 9. 181.
A.S. *wrecan.*
Wright, carpenter, wright, 12. 240;
pl. Wrightes, 12. 243. See Wriȝte.
Writ, *s.* writing, deed, a. 2. 49; Writt,
writ, scripture, 20. 286, 22. 329;
Write, writing, 20. 17; Writte, writ,
scripture, b. 10. 32; writing, R. pr.
31; Writtis, *pl.* writs, R. 4. 26.
Wriȝte, *s.* workman, b. 10. 401, b. 11.
340; Wriȝtes, *pl.* b. 10. 404, 412.
See Wright, Wryȝt.
Wroghte, *pt. s.* acted, 2. 26; Wroghten, *pt. pl.* 12. 270. See Wrouȝte.
Wroke; see Wreke.
Wrong, *pt. s.* wrung, twisted, pained,
a. 7. 162; wrung, a. 2. 212; Wronge,
pt. s. wrung (her hands), b. 2. 236;
Wrongen, *pt. pl.* wrung, wrung out
(said of clothes), a. 2. 196. See
Wryngen, Wrang.
Wroth, *adj.* wroth, angry, 4. 486;
Wroth as the wynde = angry (furious)
as the wind, R. 3. 153. This proverb
occurs twice in the Coventry Mysteries, ed. Halliwell, pp. 8. 351.
Wroth, *pt. s.* doubled (his fist), 7. 66.
Pt. t. of M.E. *writhen,* to writhe.
See Wrythen.
Wroþer, *adj.* more angry, 1. 117.
Wroþer-hele, evil fortune, bad luck,
16. 301. See note.
Wropliche, *adv.* wrathfully, a. 5. 68.
Wrouȝte, 1 *pt. s.* acted, b. 11. 58; *pt.
s.* acted, a. 11. 262; worked (as a
labourer), b. 6. 115; Wrouȝt, *pt. s.*
caused, inflicted, b. 10. 34; worked,
b. 10. 401; Wrouhte, *pt. s.* wrought
(miracles), 19. 150; created, 19. 215,
21. 248, a. 10. 40; Wrouhte me to
mon = fashioned me as a man, a. 1.
80; Wrouȝthe, *pt. s.* wrought, composed, a. 12. 101; Wrouȝte, 1 *pt. s.
subj.* should act, b. 10. 389; Wrouȝþ,
pt. s. subj. would work (*but read*
Worþe = may be, *or* Worþ = is), a. 12.
92; Wrouhte, 2 *pt. pl.* acted, did, 2.
13; Wrouȝte, acted, b. 10. 427;
made, b. 10. 404; Wrouȝt, *pt. pl.*
made, b. 9. 152; Wrouȝten, laboured,
worked, b. 6. 111; Wrouȝth, wrought,
did, R. 2. 192; Wroughte, *pt. pl. subj.*
should do, 8. 212; Wrouȝten, a. 6.
55; Wrouȝt, *pp.* created, 16. 301, b.
7. 98; Wrouht, wrought, done, 21.
356. See Wroghte, Werche.
Wrye, *v.* turn aside, decline, evade, R.
2. 84. From A.S. *wrigian,* orig. to
drive; cf. E. *wry.* See Iwrye,
Ywrye.
Wryngen, *v.* wring out, b. 14. 18.
See Wrang, Wrong.
Wrynge-lawe, Pervert-the-law (as a
name), 5. 31.
Wrythen, *pp.* tightly folded together,
closed, 20. 141. Pp. of M.E. *writhen,*
to writhe. See Wroth, Ywryþe.
Wryȝt, *s.* workman, 20. 137. See
Wright, Wriȝte.
Wullus, *pl.* wools, R. 4. 11.
Wusshen, *v.* wish, 20. 328; Wussche,
1 *pr. s.* a. 5. 92; Wusched, *pt. pl.*
wished, 7. 402. See Wisshen.
Wuste, 1 *pt. s.* knew, wist, a. pr. 12. a.
3. 52; Wustest, 2 *pt. s.* knowest (lit.
knewest), a. 7. 199; Wuste, *pt. s.*
wist, knew, a. 11. 172; Wusten, *pt.
pl.* a. 4. 67; Wuste, R. 1. 64; Wust,
pt. s. subj. knew, a. 6. 120; Wuste,
pt. pl. subj. should know, 7. 59. See
Wyte, Wite.
Wy, *s.* man, b. 5. 540, b. 17. 98, R. 3.
288. See Wye.
Wycke, *adv.* wickedly, a. 12. 37. See
Wicke.
Wydder, *adv.* more widely, 21. 403;
Wyddere, further, 3. 213.
Wydene, *adv.* wide, far, a. pr. 4;
Wyden wher, widely wandering, wandering here and there, a. 9. 53. See
Wide-where, Wyde-where.
Wydewe, widow, 5. 47; Wydwe, b.
16. 214. See Widewe.
Wydewers, *s. pl.* widowers, 11. 282.
See Widewers.
Wyde-where, *adv.* (wandering) here
and there, 11. 61; in places far
apart, 18. 271. See Wide-where,
Wydene.
Wydwehode, widowhood, b. 16. 76.
Wye, *s.* wight, creature, man, 7. 105,
19. 230, 280; Wyes, *pl.* men, 22.
166. See Wy. A.S. *wiga,* a warrior, man.
Wyght, *s.* creature, man, wight, b. 5.
116. See Wight, Wyȝt.
Wyghte, *adj.* strong, 16. 172. See
Wight.
Wyghtes, *pl.* weights, 17. 130. A.S.
ge-wiht.
Wyghtliche, *adv.* quickly, 19. 293;
Wyghtly, 9. 18. See Wightlich.
Wyghtnesse, *s.* strength, nimbleness,
activity, 12. 284, 22. 246. See
Wightnesse.
Wyht, *s.* whit, bit, 4. 130.
Wyke, *s.* week, b. 6. 258; Wykes, *pl.*
a. 2. 204. See Wike.

Wykke, *adj.* wicked, 22. 442; evil, painful, 8. 118. See **Wikke**.
Wykly, *adv.* wickedly, a. 12. 37 (Ingilby MS.). See **Wycke**.
Wyl, *pr. s.* wills (us to do), b. 19. 392. See **Wil**.
Wyles, *pl.* wiles, deceits, 5. 77; Wylis, tricks, R. 2. 121.
Wylnen, *v.* to desire, 20. 328; Wylneth, *pr. s.* b. 10. 355; Wylne, 2 *pr. s. subj.* 2. 33; mayst desire, desirest, a. 7. 246; Wylned, 1 *pt. s.* desired, b. 18. 4. See **Wilnen**.
Wyltow, wilt thou, b. 3. 110. See **Wiltow**.
Wyly-man, Crafty-man (as a name), 5. 27.
Wyn, *s.* wine, b. pr. 228.
Wynk, *s.* sleep, nap, a. 5. 212. See **Wink**.
Wynke, *v.* wink, make a sign by winking, 5. 148; Wynked, b. 13. 85; Wynkyng, *pres. part.* half asleep, 1. 11. It sometimes means to slumber; as in 'go to bedde bi tyme and *wynke*;' Babees Book, p. 80, l. 72.
Wynkyng, *adj.* sleepy, drowsy, b. 11. 4. See above.
Wynkynge, *s.* fit of sleepiness, slumber, 12. 167, b. 5. 3.
Wynlyche, *adv.* with pleasure, a. 12. 46 (Ingilby MS.). A.S. *wynlíce*.
Wynnen, *v.* win, gain, 12. 221; conquer, 16. 155, a. 10. 9; Wynne, earn, gain, 22. 230, 235; prosper, a. 5. 251; force, a. 6. 92; Wynneþ, *pr. s.* earns, gains, 23. 15; Wynneth, *imp. pl.* earn, b. 6. 332. See **Winne**.
Wynners, *pl.* men who earned their bread, bread-winners, 1. 222.
Wynnynge, *s.* gain, profit, 6. 98, 138; 10. 26, 207.
Wynse, *ger.* to wince, to kick, 5. 22. '*Regimber*, to winse, kick;' Cotgrave.
Wynt, *s.* wind, a. 5. 14.
Wynter, *s.* winter, 20. 192; Wynter, *pl.* years, 7. 203, 16. 267; Wyntres, *pl.* winters, b. 14. 112.
Wyrdes, *pl.* fates, destinies, 13. 209, 15. 32. 'Wyrdis, Wyrde systres, *parce*;' Cath. Angl.; and see Herrtage's note. E. *weird*; A.S. *wyrd*.
Wyrie, *ger.* worry, tear, 10. 268; Wyryeþ, *pr. pl.* worry, 10. 226. See *worry* in my Etym. Dict.
Wysdomes, *pl.* knowledge, science, b. 10. 5. See **Wisedome**.
Wyse, *adj. as sb. pl.* wise men, b. 11. 247, b. 18. 232.

Wyse, *s.* manner, fashion, a. 2. 148, a. 6. 54.
Wysen, *v.* to instruct, inform, a. 3. 17. (Better *wyssen*.) See **Wyssen**.
Wysman, Wiseman (as a name), 5. 27.
Wyssen, *v.* teach, 22. 232; Wysseþ, *pr. s.* 14. 204. See **Wissen**.
Wyst; see **Wyte,** *v.*
Wyt, *s.* learning, knowledge, 22. 122; sense, wisdom, a. 11. 269, 270; Wytte, wit, knowledge, understanding, b. pr. 114; Wyttis, wits, i.e. senses, a. 11. 285. See **Wit**.
Wyte, *v.* know, learn, ascertain, 19. 276, 21. 131, b. 3. 74; Wytene, *ger.* know, be informed, b. 8. 13; Wyten, 2 *pr. pl.* know, 3. 142; Wyten, *pr. pl.* 4. 287; Wyst, 1 *pt. s.* b. 5. 272. See **Wite, Wot, Wuste**.
Wyte, *imper. s.* defend, protect, preserve; Wyte god, God preserve us, 8. 285. See **Witen**.
Wyte, *v.* blame for, 21. 356; Wyteth, *imp. pl.* blame, R. 1. 80. See **Wited**.
Wyterliche, *adv.* assuredly, dearly, 6. 37; Wytterly, for a certainty, b. 5. 272. See **Witerliche**.
Wytty, *adj.* wise, clever, sensible, 3. 151, 21. 357. See **Witty**.
Wytynge, *pres. pt.* knowing (it), wittingly, b. 19. 368. See **Wyte, Witynge**.
Wyue, *dat. of* Wyf, wife; To wyue = for his wife, 4. 147, 4. 371; Wyues, *pl.* wives, b. 5. 570; Wyuen, *gen. pl.* of wives, women's, 6. 132.
Wyued, *pp.* married, b. 9. 184.
Wyuynge, *s.* marriage, lit. wiving, 11. 288.
Wyȝt, *s.* creature, wight, 2. 59, b. 13. 122; Wyȝte, b. 5. 520; Wyȝth, a. 12. 89. See **Wiȝt, Wight**.

Y, *pron.* I, 4. 370, 20. 102, a. 4. 119, a. 8. 126. See **Ich, Ik**.
Y-, *prefix,* answering to A.S. *ge-*. It is commonly used with past participles, but there are a few exceptions; thus we find the infinitives *yhure, ywende, ywite;* the past tenses *ychiueled, yrifled, ysauede, yspilte;* the imperative *yhere;* and the adjectives *ywar, yliche*. Also written **I-,** q. v.
Y-armed, *pp.* armed, 22. 144. 354.
Yasked, *pp.* asked, b. 18. 294.
Ybaken, *pp.* baked, b. 6. 184.
Ybarred, *pp.* barred, b. 19. 162.
Ybe, *pp.* been, 7. 16, b. 14. 95.

Ybedded, *pp.* furnished with a bed, b. 15. 498. See **Beddyd.**
Y-bente, *pp.* bent, R. 3. 214.
Ybete, *pp.* beaten, punished, 5. 89; Ybette (*ill spelt, for* Ybete), beaten, b. 4. 93.
Yblessed, 22. 178; Yblissed, blessed, i.e. holy, b. pr. 77.
Yblowe, *pp.* blown, b. 17. 212.
Y-bore, *pp.* born, 15. 20, 21. 138; Yborn, R. 1. 109.
Yborwed, *pp.* borrowed, taken, b. 15. 307.
Ybrent, *pp.* burnt, 4. 105. See **Brennen.**
Y-called, *pp.* wearing a cap or caul, 17. 351. See note.
Ycarped, *pp.* spoken, b. 15. 296. See **Carpen.**
Y-charchid, *pp.* charged, R. 3. 230. (For *y-charged.*) See **Charge.**
Ychiueled, *pt. pl.* shook, trembled, 7. 200. See **Chiueled.**
Ychoone, i.e. each one. a. 3. 98. See **Ichone.**
Ychose, *pp.* chosen, b. 5. 331.
Y-clepid, *pp.* called (to be heard), R. 3. 306. A.S. *geclipod,* pp. of *clipian* (or *cleopian*), to call.
Ycloped, *pp.* clothed, 21. 172.
Yclouted, *pp.* patched, b. 6. 61.
Yclyketed, *pp.* latched, fastened, 8. 266. See **I-kliketed, Cliket.**
Ycome, *pp.* come, 4. 459.
Y-coped, *adj.* dressed in a cope, 23. 344, b. 20. 342.
Ycoroned, *pp.* crowned, 4. 257.
Ycouped, *pp.* cut, slashed, slit, 21. 12. See note. F. *couper.*
Ycoupled, *pp.* joined (in marriage), b. 9. 125.
Ycrammyd, *pp.* crammed, stuffed, 1. 42.
Y-crouned, *pp.* crowned, 22. 41; Y-crounede, b. 2. 10.
Ycrymyled, *pp.* (?), 17. 351; Ycrimiled, b. 15. 223. The various readings give us *ycrymeled, ycrymaylid, crymailed,* and I think the word is of *French* origin, and means ' anointed with holy oil '; from the O.F. *cresmeler,* to anoint with holy oil (Godefroy, Roquefort), frequentative of the verb which Cotgrave spells *chresmer;* from Gk. χρίσμα.
Ycrystned, *pp.* baptised, 18. 165.
Ycullid, *pp.* killed, 1. 199.'
Ydampned, *pp.* damned, 13. 243.
Ydel, *adj.* idle, useless, vain, 3. 95, 6. 27; idle (people), b. 13. 225; In ydel = in vain, 17. 38.

Ydemed, *pp.* appointed, R. 3. 229.
Ydo, *pp.* done, finished, ended, 4. 305, 21. 106; put, 21. 160; done, R. 3. 10; Y-done, ended, b. 18. 53.
Ydoutid, *pp.* feared, R. 1. 42.
Ydrawe, *pp.* taken, 19. 218.
Ydronke, *pp.* drunk, 7. 419.
Y-dubbid, *pp.* dubbed, knighted, honoured by knighthood, R. 3. 363. (It is not ironical, as if it meant ' beaten.' The men were dubbed knights at one time, but afterwards the tables were turned.) See **Dubbede.**
Ye, *adv.* yea, a. 6. 46. See **3e.**
Yeme, *v.* take care of, R. 1. 89. See **3emen.**
Yendyd, *pp.* ended, 4. 305.
Y-entred, *pp.* entered, written down, 12. 205.
Yeten, (*for* y-eten), eaten, b. 1. 252.
Yf, *conj.* if, 19. 217. See **3if.**
Yfalle, *pp.* fallen, 10. 179.
Yffeyned, *pp.* feigned, R. pr. 58.
Yffoundid, *pp.* founded, appointed, R. 3. 265. See **I-founded.**
Yfolde, *pp.* closed, folded close, 20. 113, 130, 150.
Yfounde, *pp.* found, b. 10. 253, R. 1. 75; found out, 16. 137; Yfounden, provided for, 4. 41.
Y-fruited, *pp.* come to fruit, b. 16. 39.
Yfryed, *pp.* fried, b. 13. 63.
Yfulled, *pp.* baptised, 22. 40.
Ygete, *pp.* got, gained, 7. 343.
Ygeue, *pp.* given, 3. 126.
Yglobbed, *pp.* gulped down, 7. 397. See **Igloupet.**
Yglosed, *pp.* explained, b. 17. 11.
Ygo, *pp.* gone, b. 5. 207; Y-gon, *pp.* gone, gone on, R. 2. 94.
Y-graced, *pp.* thanked, b. 6. 126.
Ygraue, *pp.* engraved, cut, 18. 207, R. 1. 40; graven, b. 15. 507.
Y-habited, *pp.* dressed, b. 13. 285.
Yhasped, *pp.* fastened tightly, as with a hasp, b. 1. 195. See **Ihaspet, Hasped.**
Yheedid, *pp.* antlered, lit. ' headed,' R. 2. 11; Yheedyd, R. 2. 4.
Yhelid, *pp.* covered, R. 3. 212.
Yherborwed, *pp.* harboured, i.e. lodged, 7. 235. See **Herberghen.**
Yhere, *imper. s.* hear, listen, b. 17. 137; Yherde, *pp.* heard, b. 10. 101; listened to, b. 14. 209.
Yholden, *pp.* held, considered (to be), esteemed, 14. 120, b. 1. 84; Yholde, 2. 80; kept, 6. 158, b. 20. 277; kept up, practised, 7. 233; bound, R. 3. 355.

GLOSSARIAL INDEX.

Yholpe, *pp.* helped, b. 17. 60.
Yhote, *pp.* bidden, commanded, 3. 228, 14. 45; named, b. 1. 63. See **I-hoten, Hote, Hoten.**
Yhowted, *pp.* hooted at, b. 2. 218. See **Houted.**
Yhudde, *pp.* hid, b. 10. 431. See **Huden.**
Yhure, *v.* hear, 5. 157; Y-huyre, 2 *pr. s. subj.* 5. 187; Yhurde, *pp.* heard, listened to, 17. 52. See **Hure.**
Ykeuered, *pp.* covered, hidden, 10. 138. See **Keuery.**
Y-keyed, *pp.* locked, 8. 266. See **I-kei3et, Kayed, Keye.**
Yknowen, *pp.* known, learnt, b. 11. 397; Y-knowe, *pp.* known, 7. 26; found, b. 11. 225; known (to be), 12. 96.
Ykud, *pp.* known, recognised, 13. 196. See **Kidde.**
Y-lafte, *pp.* left, R. 4. 20.
Ylakked, *pp.* blamed, b. 2. 21.
Ylau3te, *pp.* caught, R. 2. 173; seized, R. 3. 336. See **Lacchen.**
Yleine, *pp.* lain, remained, b. 10. 419; Yleye, b. 5. 82.
Ylered, *pp.* taught, 12. 128; educated, b. 13. 213. See **Leren.**
Ylerned, *pp.* learnt, been taught, 11. 10. See **Lerne.**
Y-lete, *pp.* (with *by*), esteemed, thought of, 6. 3. See **Lete.**
Ylettred, *pp.* educated, b. 10. 397.
Yleye. See **Yleine.**
Yliche, *adj.* like, 14. 194; alike, b. 5. 494 (*see* l. 489); Ylike, 16. 30, 34. See **Ilyke.**
Yliche, *adv.* alike, equally, 15. 149; b. 14. 167; in like manner as, like, 20. 330.
Ylike, *adj.* like, 16. 30, 34.
Ylikned, *pp.* compared, 17. 265.
Ylle, *adv.* ill, badly, 9. 211.
Yloke, *pp.* locked, fastened, firmly attached, R. 1. 44.
Ylore, *pp.* lost, 1. 112, 13. 183. See **Lesen.**
Y-lost, *pp.* lost, 13. 94; ruined, damned, 21. 270, 22. 411.
Y-luggyd, *pp.* lugged, pulled about, R. 3. 336. See **Luggid.**
Ylyche, *adv.* alike, b. 13. 300.
Ylyfte, *pp.* lifted, removed, R. 1. 4.
Ylyke, *adj.* like, b. 18. 335.
Ymad, *pp.* made, 7. 297, 2. 255; written, 8. 140.
Ymaginatif, *adj. as sb.* the personification of Imagination, 15. 1, b. 10. 115.

Ymaked, *pp.* made, b. 2. 72; begotten, b. 9. 135; Ymakyd, made, R. 1. 48.
Ymanered, *adj.* mannered, conducted, 11. 260. See **Manered.**
Ymaymed, *pp.* deformed, 6. 34.
Ymet, *pp.* dreamt, 14. 217. See **Meten.**
Ymorþred, *pp.* murdered, 13. 242.
Ympe, *s.* graft, shoot, 19. 6; Ympes, *pl.* shoots grafted in, b. 5. 137.
Ymped, 1 *pt. s.* I engrafted, b. 5. 138. See **Impe.**
Y-mummyd, *pp.* silenced by blows on the mouth, R. 3. 337. See **Mom.**
Ynempned, *pp.* named, reckoned, b. 16. 203; called, b. 9. 53.
Ynne, *adv.* in, gathered in, R. 1. 79.
Ynne, *s. dat.* lodging; At ynne = in (his) lodging, at home, 11. 4.
Ynned, *pp.* garnered, R. 3. 135.
Ynome, *pp.* seized, taken, 23. 46; caught, b. 20. 45. See **Nymen.**
Ynow, *adj.* enough, 3. 35, 10. 43; Ynowh, 21. 294; Ynowh, *pl.* 23. 249; Ynowe, *pl.* enough, sufficient, 3. 157, 160.
Y-nowe, *adv.* enough, b. 2. 162.
Ynowh, *s.* a sufficiency, 21. 227.
Yparroked, *pp.* shut up, enclosed, 7. 144. A.S. *pearruc*, an enclosure.
Yperssshed, *pp.* pierced, wounded, b. 17. 189. See **Percen.**
Yplyght, *pp.* plighted, covenanted, 7. 207.; Ypli3te, *pp.* plighted, b. 5. 202. See **Plihte.**
Ypoudride, *pp.* powdered, i. e. besprinkled, R. 1. 46.
Ypreised, *pp.* esteemed, 11. 310.
Ypult, *pp.* thrust, 12. 208. From Lat. *pultare*, to strike. See **Pulte.**
Y-pynned, *pp.* furnished with quills, R. 2. 148. From Lat. *pinna = penna*. Cf. **Pynnes.**
Yrauisshed, *pp.* carried away, a. 11. 297. See **Rauischede.**
Y-raunsoned, *pp.* ransomed, redeemed, set free, 12. 260, 20. 283.
Yren, *s.* iron, 9. 143, 22. 57; Yre, 1. 97.; Yrens, *pl.* irons, chains, fetters, b. 4. 85, b. 8. 101; Yrenes, *pl.* 5. 81. See **Irens.**
Yren-bounde, *adj.* bound with iron, b. 14. 246, 248.
Yrented, *adj.* endowed with property, 11. 265. See **Renten.**
Yrifled, 1 *pt. s.* robbed, b. 5. 234.
Yrobed, *pp.* dressed, arrayed, b. 8. 1. See **I-robed, Robeth.**
Yrynged, *pp.* covered with rings, 3. 12.
Ys, *pron.* his, 14. 9.
Ysamme, *adv.* alike, like to like, to-

GLOSSARIAL INDEX. 471

gether, a. 10. 193. Cf. A.S. *ætsomne*, together. See **Samen**.

Ysauede, *pt. s.* saved, 20. 30.

Ysekeles, *pl.* icicles, b. 17. 227. See **Isykles**.

Y-serued, *pp.* (1) well served, content, 7. 391; treated, 4. 312; served, b. 19. 434; (2) deserved (*where* serue *is short for* deserue), b. 6. 89. Cf. 'I haue *serued* þe deth' = I have deserved death; Will. of Palerne, 4352.

Ysette, *pp.* set down as, considered, b. 15. 218. See **Iset, Setten**.

Yseye, *pp.* seen, 19. 140; Yseie, 1. 177; Yseyn, b. 14. 155; Yseiȝen, b. 5. 4. See **I-seye, I-seo, Se**.

Yshape, *pp.* created, made, 16. 301; prepared, 16. 240. See **Shape**.

Ysothe, *pp.* sodden, boiled, b. 15. 425. See **Sothe**.

Ysoupid, *pp.* supped, R. 4. 55. See **Soupen**.

Yspended, *pp.* spent, b. 14. 102.

Yspilte, 1 *pt. s.* wasted, b. 5. 380; Yspilte, *pp.* wasted, b. 5. 442; Yspilt many tymes = wasted many hours, 8. 48. See **Spille**.

Yspoused, *pp.* married, b. 9. 125. See **Spouseden**.

Yspronge, *pp.* descended, sprung, born, 11. 260.

Ysshue, *s.* issue, family, 13. 113; Ysue, b. 5. 265.

Ysynged, *pp.* sinned, 11. 213. See **Synegen**.

Ytailled, scored on a tally, b 5. 429; Ytayled, 8. 35. See **Taile**.

Ytake, *pp.* taken, R. 3. 143; accepted, endured, 13. 147, 17. 325, b. 11. 254. See **Take**.

Ytemprid, *pp.* tempered, R. 1. 19.

Ytented, *pp.* stretched on tenter-hooks, b. 15. 447. Cf. F. *tenture*, a stretching; Cotgrave.

Ytermyned, *pp.* determined, decided upon, b. 1. 97; Ytermenyd, 2. 93. See R. 2. 97.

Ytilied, *pp.* gained in husbandry, b. 15. 105. See **Tilie**.

Ytouked, *pp.* tucked, fulled, b. 15. 447. Cf. prov. E. *tucker*, a fuller (Halliwell). See **Tokkeris**.

Yuel, *adj.* evil, wicked, 7. 20, 21; b. 5. 121 (as an epithet of *wille*); unlucky, b. 9. 120; difficult, b. 5. 121, b. 15. 63. A.S. *yfel*.

Yuel, *adv.* ill, b. 5. 168; sinfully, wickedly, b. 8. 23. See **Vuel**.

Yuel, *s.* injury, 4. 453; Yueles, *pl.* evils, b. 15. 92; diseases, 4. 96.

Y-used, *pp.* used, followed, 13. 88, 21. 342. See **Vsen**.

Ywaged, *pp.* engaged, hired, 23. 261. See **Wagen**.

Ywar, *adj.* aware, 11. 114, 12. 84; wary, careful, 10. 51; cautioned, warned, 12. 63; Yware, careful, wary, 21. 357. A.S. *gewær*, wary; mod. E. *aware*.

Ywasshen, *pp.* washed, cleansed, b. 9. 134; Ywasshe, cleaned, b. 13. 315. See **Wasshen**.

Y-wende, *v.* wend, go, 9. 62.

Ywisse, *adv.* certainly, assuredly, b. 11. 401. See **Iwis, Ywys**.

Ywite, *v.* to know, 4. 76. See **I-witen, Ywyte, Wite**.

Ywittede. *adj. pl.* sensible, 12. 235.

Y-wonded, *pp.* wounded, 20. 80.

Ywoned, *pp.* accustomed, wont, 7. 143. See **Wonen**.

Ywonne, *pp.* won, gotten, earned, 13. 235; saved (by), recovered (by), b. 11. 195; Ywone, *pp.* recovered, b. 18. 351.

Yworewid, *pp.* worried, R. 3. 72. See **Wyrie**.

Yworthe, *v.* be, be left alone, 11. 163; b. 6. 228; Yworth, b. 6. 84. See note to 1. 201. See **Worthe**.

Ywounden, *pp.* bound round, b. 5. 525; Y-wounde, *pp.* wound, wrapped, R. 3. 215.

Ywroght, *pp.* created, 9. 337; acted, done, 2. 132. See **Ywrouȝt**.

Ywroken, *pp.* avenged, b. 20. 203; Ywroke, 9. 301. See **Wreke**.

Ywrouȝt, *pp.* formed, created, b. 9. 113; manufactured, b. 13. 263; Ywrouȝte, done, b. 4. 68, R. 1. 74. See **I-wrouȝt, Ywroght**.

Ywrye, *pp.* twisted, awry, 17. 75. See **Wrye**.

Ywryþe, *pp.* wound, wreathed, entwined, 8. 163. A.S. *gewriðen*, pp. of *wriðan*.

Y-wys, *adv.* verily, 14. 221; certainly, a. 3. 101. See **Ywisse**.

Ywyte, *v.* know, 21. 221; learn, b. 8. 124. See **Ywite**.

Y-yokyd, *pp.* yoked, R. 3. 251.

Ȝ. This symbol is almost invariably written for *y* before a vowel. The corresponding A.S. word commonly begins with *ge-* or *gi-*.

Ȝaf. See **Ȝiuen**.

Ȝarketh hym, *pr. s.* prepares himself, b. 7. 80. A.S. *gearcian*, to prepare.

Ȝarn. See **Ȝernen**.

Ȝat, *s.* gate, a. 6. 117; Ȝate, b. 11. 108; Atte Ȝate = at the gate, 12. 42; Ȝates,

GLOSSARIAL INDEX.

pl. gates, 1. 132, 8. 242; ȝatis, *pl.* b. pr. 104, R. 3. 238. See Gate. A.S. *geat.*

ȝate-ward, *s.* porter, gate-keeper, a. 6. 85. See Gateward.

ȝaue. See ȝiuen.

ȝe, *adv.* yea, 6. 104, 8. 292, 12. 156, 195, 310; ȝee, b. 11. 41; Ye, a. 6. 46. A.S. *géa.*

ȝe, *pron. pl.* ye, you, 4. 222; ȝee, b. 10. 465; ȝou, *acc.* a. 8. 37; ȝow, *dat.* 1. 9, b. 15. 81; *acc.* 2. 172, 11. 28. A.S. *ge,* dat. and acc. *éow.*

ȝedde, *v.* to play, sing, a. 1. 138. A.S. *giddian,* to sing, *gidd,* a song.

ȝede, *pt. s.* went about, went on foot, travelled, walked, 13. 127, 19. 170, 21. 340; ȝede, 1 *pt. s.* went, 7. 267, 8. 53; ȝedest, 2 *pt. s.* didst go, didst go about, 8. 137; ȝeden, 1 *pt. pl.* went, proceeded, 7. 181, b. 8. 112; *pt. pl.* 5. 162, 14. 136, 16. 264, 22. 4; ȝeode, 1 *pt. s.* went, 9. 108, 10. 296, 21. 3; walked, 23. 2; *pt. s.* 23. 183, b. 1. 73; ȝeodest, 2 *pt. s.* wentest, 21. 316; ȝeoden, 1 *pt. pl.* went, travelled, 11. 112; *pt. pl.* went, 18. 196; ȝoden, *pt. pl.* went, 1. 41. From A.S. *geeode,* occasionally used with the same sense as A.S. *eode,* i. e. as pt. t. of *gán.*

ȝee, (1) ye, (2) yea. See ȝe.

ȝeeme. See ȝeme.

ȝeeres. See ȝer.

ȝeeuen. See ȝiuen.

ȝeftis. See ȝift.

ȝelden, *v.* yield, return, repay, b. 7. 83, a. 5. 236; give, a. 8. 175; ȝelde, *v.* pay, 22. 393; give, render, 10. 339; repay, 17. 369; ȝulde, *v.* repay, 9. 41; ȝeldest, 2 *pr. s.* restorest, payest, 7. 343; ȝeldeþ, *pr. s.* yields, gives a return, 18. 88; ȝelt, *pr. s.* yields, 21. 105; ȝelde, *pt. s.* gave up, yielded, 15. 133; ȝelte, *pt. s.* yielded (himself), b. 12. 193; ȝelt, *pt. s.* b. 12. 214; ȝelde, *pr. s. subj.* yield, give, 9. 133; ȝeldynge, *pres. pt.* paying, a. 2. 72. A.S. *gildan,* to pay.

ȝeme, *s.* notice, 4. 488, b. 17. 12; care, heed, attention, b. 10. 195; ȝeeme, care, a. 7. 14. See below.

ȝemen, *v.* care for, protect, take care of, b. 9. 201; ȝeme, *ger.* 11. 307; keep, rule, govern, b. 8. 52. A.S. *gýman.* See Yeme.

ȝemen, *pl.* yeomen, 4. 271.

ȝemere, guardian, b. 13. 170. See ȝemen, *v.*

ȝeode. See ȝede.

ȝeorne. See ȝerne.

ȝǝp, *adj.* active, vigorous, 11. 287, 12.

179; ȝepe, b. 11. 17. A.S. *géap,* cunning.

ȝepliche, *adv.* eagerly, 17. 328, b. 15. 183. See above.

ȝer, *pl.* years, 1. 203, 7. 214; ȝere, *pl.* b. 5. 208; ȝere, *s.* year, R. 2. 17; Be ȝere = by the year, R. 2. 89; ȝeres, *gen. sing.* year's, 23. 286; ȝeeres, *gen. sing.* a. 7. 43; ȝeres, *pl.* years, 16. 3, b. 7. 18, b. 10. 419, a. pr. 62, a. 1. 99; ȝeris, *pl.* 12. 179. The phr. *seuen ȝer,* seven years, is often used to denote an indefinite time; see 7. 214, 11. 73.

ȝerde, *s.* rod, *dat.* b. 12. 14; ȝerdes, *pl.* rods, 5. 112; yards, b. 5. 214. A.S. *gyrd.*

ȝere, ȝeres. See ȝer.

ȝeres-ȝiue, *s.* new-year's gift, b. 10. 47; ȝeres-ȝyue, b. 8. 52; ȝeres-ȝyues, *pl.* b. 3. 99, b. 13. 184.

ȝerne, *adv.* eagerly, quickly, 9. 321, 23. 159; eagerly, b. 4. 74, b. 6. 299; closely, 5. 53; vigorously, a. 7. 302; As ȝerne = as soon, 8. 36; ȝeorne, eagerly, a. 4. 68; anxiously, 23. 286; ȝurne, zealously, 9. 116. A.S. *georne,* earnestly.

ȝernen, *v.* run; ȝerne, *v.* hasten, b. 15. 183 (see note, p. 221); ȝarn, 1 *pt. s.* ran, passed swiftly, b. 11. 59; ȝorn, 1 *pt. s.* 13. 13; *pt. pl.* arose, was busy (lit. ran), 19. 165; ȝernynge, *pres. pt.* running, 22. 380. A.S. *ge-yrnan,* pt. t. *ge-arn, ge-orn.*

ȝerneþ, *pr. s.* endeavours (to go), desires (to go), 17. 328; ȝernyth to wite, yearns to know, a. 12. 31 (Ingilby MS.); ȝernen, 2 *pr. pl.* yearn, desire, b. 13. 184; ȝerne, 2 *pr. s. subj.* desire, b. 1. 35; ȝeorne, 2 *pr. s. subj.* a. 1. 33; ȝerne, *pr. pl. subj.* yearn for, R. 2. 139. A.S. *geornian.*

ȝet, *conj. and adv.* yet, b. 1. 136; besides, b. 7. 83; ȝete, *adv.* yet, b. 8. 108.

ȝeue, ȝeueþ, give. See ȝiuen.

ȝif, *conj.* if, b. pr. 37, b. 8. 51.

ȝif, give. See ȝiuen.

ȝift, *s.* gift, a. 6. 106; b. 10. 47; To ȝifte = as a gift, b. 10. 154; ȝyfte, 22. 253; ȝiftes, *pl.* gifts, 10. 48, 14. 61; ȝiftis, *pl.* b. 6. 42; ȝeftis, *pl.* bribes, a. 3. 234; ȝiftus, *pl.* gifts, bribes, a. 1. 101; ȝyftes, *pl.* gifts, 3. 163; ȝyftus, *pl.* a. 2. 120. A.S. *gift.*

ȝit, *adv.* besides, moreover, a. 4. 46; *conj.* yet, a. 1. 143.

ȝiuen, *v.* give, b. 9. 201; ȝiue, *v.* b. 7. 71; ȝeuen, *v.* give, 10. 116; marry, a. 10. 181; ȝeue, *v.* a. 8. 181; ȝiue,

GLOSSARIAL INDEX. 473

ʒ pr. s. a. 2. 67 ; ʒif, 1 pr. s. as fut. will give, b. 12. 146 ; ʒiueth, pr. s. gives, b. 7. 80, b. 9. 90 ; ʒeueth, pr. s. b. 14. 249 ; ʒeueþ, 2 pr. pl. 1. 74 ; ʒeue, b. 4. 170 ; ʒiueth, pr. pl. b. 12. 17 ; ʒeueþ, 11. 256 ; ʒiue, pr. s. subj. give, grant, b. 8. 61, a. 9. 52 ; ʒeue, pr. s. subj. 21. 428, a. 10. 112 ; ʒaf, 1 pt. s. I gave, b. 13. 374 ; ʒaf me = gave myself up, 8. 53 ; ʒaf, pt. s. gave, 11. 178 ; ʒaue, pt. s. gave, 2. 15 ; ʒaf, 2 pt. pl. gave, R. 2. 3 ; ʒeeuen, pt. pl. a. 8. 43 ; ʒeue, pt. s. subj. were to give, b. 12. 198 ; should give, b. 18. 381 ; ʒiue, pp. given, b. 5. 390 ; ʒeue, pp. given, 7. 440 ; ʒouen, pp. distributed, a. 2. 119 ; ʒoue, pp. b. 2. 31 ; ʒif, pr. s. imp. 3 p. may (he) give, b. 3. 165, b. 5. 107 ; ʒeue, imp. s. give, 13. 164 ; ʒif, imp. s. 16. 145. See also ʒyuen, Gyue.

ʒiuere, s. giver, a. 8. 72.

ʒoden. See ʒede.

ʒokes, pl. yokes of oxen, 8. 295.

ʒon, adj. yonder, 21. 149 ; ʒone, b. 18. 145 ; ʒonde, b. 18. 187.

ʒonde, adv. yonder, 21. 263.

ʒong, adj. young, 6. 35 ; ʒonge, b. 9. 161, b. 11. 17 ; ʒonge, pl. 1. 214.

ʒor, pron. your, a. 5. 38.

ʒorn. See ʒernen.

ʒoten, pp. poured, 2. 151. A.S. goten, pp. of géotan, to pour.

ʒou, ʒow. See ʒe.

ʒowre, poss. pron. your, yours, b. 8. 57, b. 13. 110.

ʒow-seluen, pron. yourselves, b. 10. 273 ; ʒow-selue, 9. 14.

ʒowthe, youth, 2. 140.

ʒulde. See ʒelden.

ʒurne, adv. ; see ʒerne.

ʒus, adv. yes, 8. 287, 20. 279. (It answers questions that involve a negative or statements expressive of much doubt, and is far stronger than the particle ʒe, which merely assents.)

ʒut, adv. yet, nevertheless, 4. 455, 7. 36, 9. 258 ; still, b. 12. 274 ; moreover, 1. 218. See ʒit.

ʒyuan ʒeld-aʒeyn (as a proper name), Evan Yield-again, 7. 310.

ʒyuen, v. give, b. 9. 161 ; ʒyue, v. give, b. 10. 47 ; give away, b. 10. 312 ; ʒyue nauht of = care nothing about, be reckless of, 23. 155 ; ʒyueþ, pr. s. gives, 4. 341, 15. 138 ; ʒyue, pr. s. subj. may give, give, 3. 126. See ʒiuen.

INDEX TO PROPER NAMES,

AND TO SOME OF THE PRINCIPAL SUBJECTS IN PIERS PLOWMAN AND RICHARD THE REDELESS.

⁎* The numbers refer, in general, to the Passus and Line of the C-text; when the reference is to the A-text or B-text, the letter "a" or "b" is prefixed to the numbers denoting the Passus and Line. References to Richard the Redeless are similarly denoted by prefixing the letter "R."

This index includes all the proper names, including those of the allegorical personages mentioned in these poems, together with some of the principal subjects.

For proverbs, see under "Proverbs"; for similes, see under "Similes"; and see "Parable."

Abbot of Abingdon; see Abingdon.
Abbot of England, 6. 177.
Abel, 11. 247, 19. 219, 231.
Abingdon, abbot of, b. 10. 326.
Abraam, Abraham, 14. 5, &c.; 19. 113, 184, 242, 267; 20. 97, 21. 147.
Abraham's lap, 9. 283.
Absolon, Absalom, 4. 411.
Abstinence, 7. 440, 8. 272; b. 7. 132.
Actif, Active, 8. 299.
Active Life, 19. 83; Activa-Vita, 16. 194, 19. 80.
Adam, 2. 61, 8. 250, 11. 213, 12. 258; 19. 68, 113, 220, 231; 21. 201, 400; in Paradise, 14. 227.
Adam and Eve, 13. 113, 15. 163, 17. 224; 21. 147, 157, 182, 305; 22. 54.
Agag, 4. 418, 442.
Alberdes, Albert's, i. e. Albertus Magnus, a. 11. 157; b. 10. 212.
Alchemy, b. 10. 212.
Alexander, b. 12. 45.
Alisaundre, Alexandria, 8. 173; *spelt* Alisaundrie, 18. 272.
Alsace (*Oseye*), 1. 229.
Alters conse rated, 18. 279.
Altoun, Alton (in Hampshire), 17. 139.
Amalek, 4. 418, 422.
Ambrosie, St. Ambrose, 16. 45, 22. 267.
Amends, mother of Meed, 3. 120.
Amend-you, 8. 244.
Amor, 17. 196.
Anchorites, 1. 30, 4. 141, 9. 146.
Andrew, St., 18. 18.
Angel, b. pr. 128.

Angels, fall of the, 2. 110, 21. 349.
Anima, 17. 183.
Anima, Lady, 11. 133, 148, 171.
Animus, 17. 184.
Antecrist, Antichrist, 22. 219, 226; 23. 53, 64; his banner, 23. 69.
Antony, St. Anthony, 18. 12; b. 15. 267, 278, 413.
Apocalypsis (Goliæ), 16. 99.
Apostles, the, 10. 118; 12. 32.
April, the dry, b. 13. 269.
Arches, court of, 3. 61, 186; 23. 136.
Aristotle, 12. 122, 216; 13. 274, 15. 194; b. 12. 44, 266.
Ark, Noah's, described, 11. 222.
Armenia, 8. 173, 18. 272.
Arsenius, St., 18. 12.
Arts, Seven, 12. 98; 13. 93.
Ascension, 22. 191.
Assye, Assisi, a. 6. 19. *See* Syse.
Astrology, 15. 30.
Astronomy, 18. 105; b. 10. 207.
Astrot, Astaroth, 21. 282, 449.
Avarice; *see* Covetise.
Auenoun, Avignon, 22. 424.
Averay, St., 16. 99.
Augustine; *see* Austin below.
Avinet, b. 12. 257.
Avise-thee-before, 4. 21.
Austin, St. Augustine (of Canterbury), b. 15. 437.
Austin, St. Augustine, 12. 149, 152, 287; 16. 45, 17. 199, 22. 269; b. 10. 116.
Author, the, is habited as a hermit, 1. 3; falls asleep, 1. 7; is called

INDEX TO PROPER NAMES AND SUBJECTS. 475

Will, 2. 5; is left asleep by Holychurch, 3. 53; dreams of Meed's marriage, 3. 54; awakes on Cornhill, 6. 1; his wife Kit, 6. 2; is clothed as a loller, 6. 3; his youth, how spent, 6. 35; falls asleep, 6. 108; awakes, 10. 293; wanders on Malvern hills, 10. 295; is robed in russet, 11. 1; his stature, 11. 68; his name, 11. 69, 71; falls asleep, 12. 167; sees the Mirror of the World, 14. 134; sees Imaginative, 14. 220; his age, 15. 3; awakes, 16. 1; he is like a 'mendinaunt,' 16. 3; falls asleep, 16. 25; talks with Freewill, 17. 165; awakes, 20. 332; sleeps, 21. 4; awakes, 21. 472; sleeps, 22. 5; attacked by Old Age, 23. 183; is advised by Nature, 23. 208; awakes, 22. 483; is at Bristol, R. prol. 2; advises the king, R. prol. 31.

Babilonie, Babylon, 8. 172; *spelt* Babiloigne, b. 15. 538.
Badges, R. 2. 21, 78.
Bagot, R. 2. 164.
Banbury, 3. 111.
Baptism, 15. 207; b. 14. 183; by whom to be performed, b. 10. 350.
Bayard (a bay horse), 5. 56; Bayarde, 9. 178, 192; 20. 70.
Bear, the, R. 3. 29, 94.
Beasts ruled by Reason, 14. 143.
Bedlehem, Bethlehem, 15. 93; Bedleem, b. 15. 538; Bethleem, a. 6. 18. See Bethleem.
Beggars, 1. 41; 9. 128, 210; 10. 61, 98, 166; 14. 95.
Belial, 21. 284; Beliales, Belial's, 23. 79.
Benit, St. Benedict, 5. 117; Benet, b. 15. 414.
Bernard, St., 12. 38; 17. 221; b. 4. 121, b. 15. 414.
Bet (Bat), Bartholomew, 7. 379; Bette, 6. 135; the beadle, 3. 111.
Bethleem, Bethlehem, 8. 172, 21. 245, 22. 71; b. 17. 122. *See* Bedlehem.
Beton, 6. 136; the brewster, 7. 353.
Bible, the, 9. 238, 10. 304; referred to, 1. 205; translated, 11. 88.
Birds, 11. 63; b. 7. 128; 14. 137, 15. 170, 18. 33; their nests, 14. 156; are called by whistling, b. 15. 466.
Bishop, 1. 76, 85; Bishops, 10. 13, 11. 191, 14. 124, 17. 203, 18. 283.
Book, 21. 241.
Bread from Stratford, b. 13. 267; for horses, 9. 192, 225; for dogs, 9. 225.

Brewer, the wicked, 22. 398.
Bristow, Bristol, R. prol. 2.
Britoner, a man of Brittany, 9. 152, 173.
Bromholm, rood of, b. 5. 231.
Bruges, 7. 278 (b. 13. 392).
Brutenere, Brytonere; *see* Britoner.
Buckinghamshire, b. 2. 109.
Bulls, 1. 67, b. 13. 249.
Bushy, R. 1. 99, R. 2. 152, R. 3. 75.
But, Johan, a. 12. 101 *n*.

Cain; *see* Caym.
Calabre, Calabrian fur, 9. 293.
Caleys, Calais, b. 3. 195.
Caluarye, Calvary, 7. 319 (b. 5. 472); 13. 108, 22. 142; b. 16. 164.
Cana, feast at, 22. 115.
Cardinal virtues, 1. 132; 22. 274, 339; 23. 22.
Cardinals, 1. 134, 22. 419.
Caro, Castle of, b. 9. 48.
Caro, the horse so called, b. 17. 107.
Castle of Care, 2. 57.
Castle made by Kind (Nature), 11. 128.
Cato, 5. 17, 8. 34, 9. 338, 10. 69, 10. 303, 14. 214; b. 10. 189, b. 12. 21.
Caton, Cato, 22. 296.
Caunterbury, Canterbury, 18. 274; b. 15. 437.
Cayfas, Caiaphas, 22. 140.
Caym, Cain, 11. 212, 218; Cain's seed, 11. 221; *spelt* Cayme, 2. 62, b. 10. 329.
Cesar, Cæsar, 2. 48; Cesares, Cæsar's, 2. 47.
Cesse (Cis); *see* Sesse.
Chancery, 1. 91.
Chaplains, 2. 187.
Charity, 2. 185, 8. 273, 16. 163, 16. 279, 17. 284, 18. 61; tree of, 19. 14.
Charter, when challengeable, 14. 117; not to be made by a churl, 14. 61; how to be made, 13. 61.
Charter of endowment, 3. 69.
Chastity, 7. 273.
Chepe, Cheapside, b. 5. 322, R. 3. 139.
Cherubin, 2. 106.
Cheste (Chiding), castle of, 3. 89.
Chester, R. 3. 317; rood of, b. 5. 467, R. prol. 56; earl of, 8. 11.
Chichester, mayor of London, b. 13. 271.
Chimney, room with a, b. 10. 98.
Christ (always written *crist*), 1. 148, 2. 78, 3. 51, &c.; the conqueror, 22. 15, 22. 24, 22. 53; His clothes, 11. 93.
Christ Church, Bristol, R. prol. 4.
Christendom, cart of, 22. 332.

VOL. II.   G g

INDEX TO PROPER NAMES AND SUBJECTS.

Christians (*cristine*), 2. 199; (*cristene*), 2. 89, 13. 57, &c.; duty of, b. 10. 161.
Chrysostom (*Iohannes crisostomus*), 17. 271.
Church services, 10. 228, 243.
Civil, *i.e.* Civil Law, 3. 63, 67, 72, 115, 155; 23. 137.
Clarice, dame, 7. 134, 366.
Clement, 7. 376, 390, 409, 412.
Cleophas, 13. 123.
Clergy (Learning), 1. 151, 12. 94, 12. 138, 12. 205, 15. 35, 15. 70, 16. 26, 16. 43, 16. 128, 16. 178.
Clergy, benefit of, 15. 129.
Clerks, 17. 255; 18. 68; duty of, 6. 56; life of, 12. 236; talk of, b. 10. 51.
Cloth, how prepared, b. 15. 444.
Cocklane, 7. 366.
Coin, bad, 18. 74.
Coltyng, the name of a fiend, 21. 290.
Commandments, Ten, 8. 204; 20. 13.
Concupiscentia-Carnis, 12. 174, 178, 308, 311.
Confessor, 4. 38, 13. 196; Confessors, 6. 195.
Confession, 17. 26; b. 14. 18, 89.
Conqueror, 22. 30.
Conscience, 1. 95, 151; 3. 152, 202; 4. 49, 146, &c.; 16. 26, 37, &c.; 17. 192; 22. 12, 207, 358; 23. 106, &c.; b. 7. 133.
Constantyn, Constantine, 6. 176, 18. 220.
Contemplation, 8. 305.
Contemplative life, 19. 77.
Contrition, 17. 25; 23. 316, 357, 369; b. 14. 16; b. 14. 82.
Corfe castle, 4. 140.
Cor-hominis, country of, 19. 4.
Cornehulle, Cornhill, 6. 1.
Corpus Christi feast, 18. 120.
Courtiers, R. 1. 25, 88.
Covetise (Avarice), 17. 80, 17. 364, 23. 121; confession of, 7. 196; county of, 3. 90.
Covetise-of-Eyen, 12. 175, 193; 13. 3.
Creed, 18. 317.
Creeping to the Cross, 21. 475.
Cries—'hot pies, hot!', 1. 226; 'good geese and pigs! go we dine, go we', 1. 227; 'a taste for nothing,' 1. 228; 'white wine of Osey,' &c., 1. 229.
Crisostomus; *see* Chrysostom.
Crist, Cristendome; *see* Christ, Christendom.
Cristene, Christians, 2. 89; Cristine, 2. 199; *see* Christians.
Cross, why honoured less than the noble, 18. 200; creeping to the, 21. 475.
Crown, the king's, R. 1. 33.
Crucifixion, the, 21. 51.

Damaske, Damascus, 18. 189, 261; *spelt* Damascle, 8. 173.
Daniel, 9. 72, 10. 305, 21. 113; b. 15. 589.
Dauid, David, 2. 102, 3. 39, 4. 415, 4. 444, 8. 154, 12. 265, 12. 281, 15. 69, 16. 310, 22. 134; b. 3. 236, b. 13. 433.
Dauwe (Daw, Davy), 7. 369; Dawe, 9. 354.
Dearth, 9. 353.
Death, 21. 28, 23. 100, a. 12. 63; deep vale of, 1. 17.
Degon, Diggon, R. 3. 362; *gen.* Degonys, R. 3. 351.
Degrees, too easily obtained, 18. 111.
Denote, Denot, 9. 72.
Despair, 20. 289.
Devil, the, 19. 43.
Dinner in hall, 16. 39.
Diseases, 23. 81.
Dismas, 7. 320 (b. 5. 473), 12. 254, 15. 132.
Dives, 9. 279, 16. 303, 20. 230, 20. 250.
Do-best, 11. 76, 11. 92, 16. 127, 22. 182; b. 14. 21.
Do-bet, 11. 76, 11. 82, 11. 138, 15. 15, 16. 126, 22. 129; b. 14. 19.
Dobyn, Dobbin, R. 3. 362.
Doctor; his dinner, 16. 46.
Doctors, the four, 22. 269; b. 9. 72; a. 11. 294.
Domenik, St. Dominick, 5. 117, 23. 252; b. 15. 413.
Donemowe, Dunmow; the flitch of bacon there, 11. 276.
Donet (Donatus), 7. 215.
Do-right-so, 9. 81.
Dove of Mahomet, 18. 181, 239; of Christ, 18. 246.
Dover, b. 4. 131.
Do-well, 11. 2, 11. 76, 11. 127, 14. 221, 16. 112, 22. 110; b. 14. 18; R. 4. 93.
Dread, 3. 217.
Dreams, 10. 302.
Dress, extravagant, R. 3. 120.
Duche, Dutch; Dutch coats, R. 3. 193.
Dungeon in a dale, 2. 57; b. pr. 15.
Dunmow; *see* Donemowe.

Eadmund, Edmund, 17. 345.
Eagle, the, R. 2. 9, 145, 176; 3. 74.
Ebrew, Hebrew, 20. 4.
Edmund (*Eadmund*), 17. 345.

INDEX TO PROPER NAMES AND SUBJECTS. 477

Edward, 17. 345.
Egidie, St. Egidius, 18. 9.
Egypt, 10. 314.
Elde (Old-age), 12. 189, 13. 1, 19. 106, 23. 93, 23. 167, &c.
Election, 13. 51.
Elements, the four, 2. 17, 10. 56, 11. 129, 21. 247.
Eleyne, b. 5. 110.
Eli (alluded to), 1. 109, 123; b. 10. 283.
Elias, b. 14. 65.
Ely, Eli, b. 10. 283.
Elyes, of Elias, 16. 269; b. 14. 65.
Emma, dame, b. 13. 340; Emme, 1. 225.
Emmaus, 13. 122.
Engelond, England, 1. 194, 6. 177, 18. 279; *spelt* Ingelond, b. 15. 435; abbot of, 6. 177.
English, 4. 435, 10. 214, 17. 120, 17. 188; b. 13. 71.
Englishmen, 17. 217.
Envy, 23. 273, 23. 294; confession of, 7. 63; earldom of, 3. 88.
Episcopus, 17. 205.
Ermanie, Armenia, 8. 173, 18. 272.
Erseny, St. Arsenius, 18. 12.
Essex cheese, b. 5. 93.
Estwarde, Eastward, 1. 133.
Evan, 7. 310.
Eve, 2. 61, 8. 250, 11. 213, 11. 292, 19. 218. *And see* Adam.
Eve, holy, 14. 86.
Eves of festivals, 7. 182.
Exchequer, 1. 91.

Fable—'belling the cat,' 1. 165; 'of the hart,' R. 3. 17.
Faith, 19. 186, 20. 57, 21. 96; merit of, 12. 159.
Fall of the angels, 2. 110.
False, *or* Falseness, 3. 6, 42, 70, 77, 82, &c.
Famine, 9. 347.
Fauntelet, *or* Faunteltee, 12. 310; b. 11. 41.
Favel (Flattery), 3. 6, 25, 43, 65, 77, 83, 157, &c.
Felice, Felicia, 6. 132; R. 3. 160; Felyce, b. 12. 47.
Felony, punishment of, 11. 240.
Fever, a. 12. 82.
Fickle-tongue, the Liar, 3. 6, 44, 69.
Field; the Fair Field of Folk, 1. 19, 2. 2, 6. 111.
Finees, Phineas, 1. 107, 123.
Fires in a town, 4. 102.
Five Wits, 16. 257; R. prol. 50.
Flaundres, Flanders, 7. 367.

Flesh, the, 19. 35.
Flood, the, 11. 222; 12. 240.
Floods, 9. 349.
Foleuyles, 22. 247. See note.
Food for beggars, 9. 224, 286, 327.
Food for the poor, 9. 304, 322.
Food of man, 16. 240; b. 14. 33.
Fortitude, 22. 289, 23. 25.
Fortune, 12. 168, 173, 185; 13. 14; 23. 110, 156.
Four evangelists, 22. 262; four doctors, 22. 271; four cardinal virtues, 22. 274; four orders of friars, 1. 56; b. 7. 192; a. 2. 48.
France, 1. 192, 4. 243, 4. 259, 5. 125, 11. 134, 16. 155.
Fraunceis, St. Francis, 5. 117, 17. 353, 23. 252; b. 15. 413.
Freedom of a city, 4. 108.
Free-will; *see* Liberum-Arbitrium.
French language, b. 5. 239.
Friars, 1. 56, 3. 220, 7. 118, 10. 246, 16. 9, 17. 230, 17. 356, 23. 58, 23. 230, &c.; false brethren, 16. 75; five orders of, 9. 191, 10. 343, 16. 81; how they give to the poor, b. 15. 322; two, 11. 8; Friar at dinner, 16. 30; Friar confessor, 13. 16; Friar Flatterer, 23. 315.
Friday, 7. 352, 7. 439, 11. 8, 19. 168, 22. 142, 23. 312; b. 1. 99; Fridays, 6. 30, 7. 155, 7. 182. *See* Good Friday.
Fynes, Phineas, b. 10. 282; *see* Finees.

Gabrielis, Gabriel's, 19. 124.
Galile, Galilee, 22. 147, 158.
Galys, Gallicia, 5. 124, 8. 166; a. 6. 12.
Garlick-hithe, b. 5. 324.
Gascoyne, Gascony, 1. 229.
Geffray, Sir, b. 15. 120.
Genesis, 9. 240.
Gentiles, 18. 132.
Giles, St.; *see* Gyle.
Gluttony, 17. 72; confession of, 7. 350, 423.
Gobelyn, a demon, 21. 325, 330.
Godfathers, b. 9. 74.
Godfrey, 7. 373.
Godfrey Go-well, b. 9. 22.
Goliardeys, b. prol. 139.
Goodfaith Go-well, 11. 147.
Good Friday, 8. 107, 8. 131, 12. 254, 15. 132; b. 5. 496, b. 13. 447.
Grace, 22. 213, 22. 262; porter of Truth, b. 243.
Green, R. 2. 153, R. 3. 101.
Gregorie *or* Gregori, St. Gregory, 6. 147 (b. 10. 292, a. 11. 201), 13. 77,

13. 80, 22. 270; b. 5. 166, b. 7. 76, b. 11. 223, b. 15. 436.
Grekis, Greeks, b. 15. 594.
Greyhound, the, R. 2. 113.
Griffin, 7. 373.
Guile, 3. 69, 126, 158, 198, 213, 221.
Gybbe, Gib, i.e. Gilbert, b. 5. 92.
Gygas, the Giant, b. 18. 250.
Gyle, St. Giles, 9. 54; seint gyles doune, St. Giles' down, 5. 51. (See note to 7. 211.)

Hall for dining, b. 10. 98.
Hand, a symbol of the Trinity, 20. 110.
Hanging to be only *once* performed, 21. 424.
Hart, the White, R. 2. 4, 42; fable of the, R. 3. 17.
Haukyn, b. 13. 273; b. 14. 1, 25, 320; his wife, b. 14. 27, 97.
Heart of man, the garden of the, b. 16. 15.
Hear-well, 11. 145.
Heathen, etymology of, 15. 451.
Hebrew, 20. 4.
Hell, Descent into, 21. 272.
Hende-speche (Fair-speech), 23. 348.
Henrri, Henry, R. prol. 11.
Hermits, 1. 30, 51; 9. 146, 183; 10 187; Paul the hermit, 18. 13.
Herodes, Herod, 11. 177.
Hertfordshire, 7. 413.
Heruy, Harvey, 7. 197.
Heyne, a. 5. 91.
Hick, 7. 365, 378, 389.
Hick Heavy-head, R. 3. 66.
Holidays, 14. 86.
Holychurch, Lady, 2. 3, 72; 3. 30.
Holy Ghost, descent of the, 22. 201.
Hope, 8. 152; 20. 1, 98.
Hophni (*ophni*), 1. 107, 123; b. 10. 282.
Horse, the, R. 3. 27, 106.
Horses, 3. 176.
Houwe, Hugh, 7. 365.
Hugh; *see* Houwe.
Humility, 8. 272.
Hunger, 9. 171, 223, 345; a. 12. 63.
Hurlewaynis, Hurlewayn's, R. 1. 90. (See note, p 290.)
Hypocrisy, 17. 264, 23. 300.

Iack the Iogelour, Jack Juggler, 9. 71.
Iacob, Jacob, 10. 310, 316.
Iame, St. James of Spain, 1. 48, 5. 122, 6. 198, 22. 164; b. 6. 57; Iamys, 2. 182.
Ierico, Jericho, 20. 49.
Ierom, Jerome, 22. 270.
Ierusalem, Jerusalem, 20. 50, 77; 21. 15.
Jesters, 8. 82, 90, 115; b. 10. 38.
Jesus, birth of, 19. 126; His miracles, 19. 140; betrayal, 19. 167; entry into Jerusalem, &c., 21. 6; as a conqueror, 22. 15; name of, 22. 19, 70; burial of, 22. 143; resurrection of, 22. 152; by Jesus, 1. 180, 4. 193.
Iewene, i.e. of Jews, 2. 63. (Genitive plural.) *See* Iuwene.
Iewes, Jews, 4. 458, 483; 5. 194, 7. 241, 13. 54, 15. 201, 18. 252, 21. 96; b. 10. 348. *See* Iuwes.
Jews can teach Christians, b. 9. 84.
Imaginative, 15. 1, 15. 203, 16. 17, b. 10. 115.
Imago-dei, tree of, 19. 7.
Inde, India, 18. 272; Ynde, 22. 165.
Ingelond, England, b. 15. 435; *see* Yngelonde.
Inwit, Sir, 11. 143, 170.
Iob, Job, 12. 23, 14. 5, 14. 15, 14. 20, 14. 25, 21. 153; b. 12. 43.
Iohan But, a. 12. 101 *n*.
Iohan, St. John the Evangelist, 8. 24, 8. 101 (b. 13. 441), 13. 98, 15. 137, 15. 143, 22. 164, 22. 265.
Iohan, St. John the Baptist, 11. 179, 12. 257, 19. 114, 19. 269, 21. 370.
Iohan (John), a common fellow, b. 7. 44; Sir Iohan, b. 15. 120; Master Iohan, 22. 288.
Iohane, dame Joanna, 7. 133.
Ionette, Janet, 9. 71.
Iosaphat, Vale of, 21. 414.
Ioseph, Joseph, 10. 308, 310.
Iosue, Joshua, 20. 23.
Ire, earldom of, 3. 88.
Isaac, 19. 249.
Isaiah, 12. 258, 19. 113.
Isidore, St. (*Ysidorus*), 17. 199.
Israel, children of, 1. 105, 111.
Iuda, Judah, 22. 138.
Iudas, Judas, 2. 63, 19. 167, 19. 172; b. 9. 84, b. 9. 90, b. 15. 259; Judas' children, b. pr. 35.
Iudas makabeus, Judas Maccabeus, 20. 23.
Iude, Jude, St., 15. 143.
Iudith, Judith, 20. 23.
Justice, 22. 298, 23. 29.
Iuwene, Jews', 22. 108. *See* Iewene.
Iuwes, Jews, 22. 34, 44. *See* Iewes.

Kalote, the author's daughter, 21. 473.
Keep-well-thy-tongue, b. 10. 163.
Kind (Nature), 11. 128, 131, 149; 23. 80, 97, 109.
Kind Wit (Common Sense), 1. 141; 2. 51; a. 12. 41.
King, the, 1. 90, 1. 139, 3. 204, 3. 245, 4. 2, 4. 9, &c.; 5. 1, 22, 467; abandons France, 4. 243; address to the, 4. 210; gives gifts, 4. 251; is killed,

INDEX TO PROPER NAMES AND SUBJECTS. 479

4. 233; his court, 3. 202; his father, 4. 163, 233; his mark, 5. 126; his pardon of felons, 21. 426; his son, 5. 43; Kings, 2. 90.
Kingdom, clerks a harm to the, 3. 247; is sold, 4. 244; strength of a, R. 3. 248.
Kings, book of, 4. 410, 416; the three, 22. 75.
Kit, the author's wife; *see* Kytte.
Knight, coming to be dubbed, 21. 11.
Knights, 2. 90, 97, 108; 14. 110; duty of, 9. 26, 10. 9, 10. 223.
Kytte, Kit, the author's wife, 6. 2, 21. 473; a woman's name, 8. 304.

Ladies, duties of, 9. 8.
Lammas, 9. 314.
Largeness, Liberality, 8. 275.
La Reole (*ruele*), 1. 230.
Latyn, Latin, 2. 140, 4. 124, 4. 490, 10. 164, 10. 212, 11. 91, 12. 165, 16. 78, 18. 53, 20. 4; b. 13. 151, b. 15. 116.
Lauacrum, probably the baptismal font, 20. 71.
Laurens, St. Lawrence, 3. 130; *spelt* Laurence, 18. 64.
Law, 18. 136, 139; the Jewish, 18. 299; maxim of, 13. 61.
Lawyers, 10. 44.
Lazar, Lazarus, 9. 280, 18. 304, 19. 144, 19. 273, 21. 277, 21. 280.
Learning, use of, 15. 111, 127.
Lecherye, lechery, 4. 57, 7. 170, 11. 286, 17. 91, 22. 355, 23. 71, 23. 90, 23. 114; lordship of, 3. 93; laund of, b. 10. 161.
Leeches, i. e. doctors, 3. 233, 9. 296.
Legenda Sanctorum, 18. 157; b. 11. 145, 214.
Lenten, Lent, 1. 89, 7. 183, 14. 81, 21. 5, 23. 361; b. 14. 5.
Letice-at-the-stile, 7. 145.
Leuites, Levites, 15. 58.
Leuitici, *gen. of* Leviticus, 6. 55.
Lex-dei, 20. 71.
Liar, 3. 6, 44, 69, 77, 204, 215, 225.
Liberum-Arbitrium, 17. 158, 162, 165, 173, 182; 19. 1.
Liberum dei arbitrium, 21. 20.
Life, 21. 30, 23. 143, 23. 152; a. 12. 44.
Life-to-live-in-lechery, Sir, 23. 311.
Liveries and badges, R. 2. 2.
Lollers, 10. 137.
Lombards, 5. 194, 7. 241, 7. 246.
London, 1. 83, 89; 3. 148, 169; 6. 4, 44; 7. 96, 17. 286; b. 13. 264.
Longeus, Longinus, 21. 82. See note.
Longing, land of, 12. 169.
Lord's Supper, 22. 387.

Lot, 11. 177; *spelt* Loth, 2. 25, 31.
Love, 2. 149, 156, 200; 5. 156; 12. 134, 18. 131; song of, 21. 470.
Loyalty, 5. 156, 13. 24, 18. 126.
Luc, St. Luke, 22. 263; Lucas, 8. 24, 140; Luk, 22. 448.
Lucifer, 1. 40, 2. 107, 2. 112, 2. 128, 3. 107, 6. 188, 8. 135, 12. 259, 20. 10; 21. 33, 142, 273, 297, 348, 363, 396, 447; b. 12. 41; Luciferes, Lucifer's, 8. 116, 22. 55; Lucifer's aunt, 7. 330; his feast, 8. 116; his fiddle, 8. 117 (b. 13. 456).
Lukes, Lucca, 5. 194, 9. 109.
Lukys, Luke's, 2. 87. *See* Luc.
Lumbardes, Lombards, 5. 194, 7. 241.
Lunatics, 10. 107, 137; 11. 182; a lunatic, b. pr. 123.
Lussheborue, Luxembourg, 18. 72, 82; Lussheborgh, 18. 168.
Lydfford, Lidford, the law of, R. 3. 145.

Magdalen, b. 13. 194. *See* Marye *and* Maudeleyn.
Magi, the, 15. 88, 22. 85; their offerings, 22. 86.
Mahon, Mahomet, 19. 151; 21. 295; Mahoun, b. 13. 82. *See* below.
Makamed, Mahomet, 4. 485; Makamede, 18. 159, 165, 239, 316; Makemede, 18. 314; Mahomet and the dove, 18. 171.
Malkin, 2. 181. See note.
Malvern hills, 1. 6, 163; 6. 110, 10. 295.
Mammonaes, Mammon's, 11. 87.
Man not ruled by Reason, 14. 182.
Marche, March, R. 4. 7.
Margaret, 5. 48.
Maria Egyptiaca, 18. 23.
Mark, St., 8. 24, 8. 140, 22. 264, b. 10. 276.
Marriages; *see* Wedlock.
Marshal, the Earl, R. 3. 105.
Martha, 13. 135.
Mary (the annunciation to), 19. 125. *See* below.
Marye, Marie, the Virgin Mary, 3. 2, 3. 51, 4. 152, 4. 209, 4. 257, 8. 138, 8. 149, 10. 347, 12. 145, 13. 133, 21. 133.
Marye, by, by St. Mary, 4. 257, 5. 139, 5. 173.
Marye, i. e. Mary Magdalen, 8. 138, 12. 263, 13. 135, 18. 21, 22. 157; b. 13. 194.
Matheu, St. Matthew, 4. 314, 8. 24, 8. 140, 9. 247, 13. 133, 22. 264.
Matrimony, 19. 86.
Maudeleyn, Magdalen, a. 11. 279. *See* Magdalen.
May, 17. 10; b. 14. 158; May morning, 1. 6.

INDEX TO PROPER NAMES AND SUBJECTS.

Mayor, 2. 157; 4. 77, 108, 117.
Measures, false, 4. 88, 7. 231.
Meed, Lady, 3. 9–5, 163.
Memoria, 17. 186.
Merchants, 4. 282; 7. 212, 278; 10. 22.
Mercy, 8. 288; 21. 120, 171, 189.
Messias, 4. 460; Messie, 18. 298; Messye, 18. 159.
Metropolitanus, 17. 204, 18. 267.
Michael, St., 10. 37.
Michaelmas, 16. 216.
Mid-lent Sunday, 19. 183.
Midsomer, Midsummer, b. 14. 160; Mydsomer, 17. 13.
Minors, friars, 11. 9.
Minstrels, 1. 35, 3. 237, 4. 277, 8. 97, 10. 128, b. 9. 102; their habits, 16. 194.
Miracles, 1. 99.
Mirror of the World, 12. 170, 12. 181, 14. 132.
Missionaries, 11. 198, 18. 191; b. 15. 431.
Monks keep not their rule, 6. 157; their fare, 7. 159; their fixed numbers, 23. 264.
Moses; *see* Moyses.
Moubray, Mowbray, R. 4. 7.
Mountain of the World, b. 11. 315.
Moyses, Moses, 4. 460, 15. 37, 18. 298, 18. 314, 21. 183, 23. 278; Moises, b. 1. 149.
Munde the Miller, 3. 113; b. 10. 44.

Nabugodonosor, Nebuchadnezzar, 10. 306.
Nazareth, 18. 189, 22. 137.
Need, 23. 10, 232.
Neptalym, Nephtali, 18. 189, 261.
New fair. 7. 377.
Noe, Noah, 11. 177, 11. 221, 12. 241; Noes, Noah's, 12. 238.
Norfolk, b. 5. 239.
Normandy, b. 3. 188.
North side of heaven, 2. 113, 118.
Northern men, 2. 115.
Nynyve, Niniveh, 18. 189, 261.

Offyn, Hophni, b. 10. 282; Ophni, 1. 107, 123.
Omnia-probate, a. 12. 50.
Ophni; *see* Offyn.
Orders, five, 10. 343 (four, b. 7. 192) *See* Friars *and* Four.
Oseye, i. e. Alsace, 1. 229.
Ovid, 13. 174.
Oxen, the four, 22. 262.

Palm Sunday, 21. 6.
Palmers, 1. 47; one described, 8. 161.

Parable—adding water to Thames, 18. 331; adding trees to a forest, b. 15. 327; apple grafted on an elder, b. 9. 147; briar bears no grapes, 3. 28; of a calf, b. 15. 458; drunken man in a ditch, 14. 236; figs grow not on thorns, 3. 29; fishes die on dry ground, 6. 149; hart and adder, R. 3. 13; lark and peacock, 15. 173, 186; like a blind man in battle, 15. 50; like a spark in the Thames, 7. 335; the lord that lacked parchment and pen, b. 9. 38; marriage-feast, 13. 46; merchant and messenger, 14. 33; mote and the beam, b. 10. 263; the partridge, R. 3. 38; peacock, 15. 175; pearl of price, 6. 94; red rose on a briar, a. 10. 119; slothful servant, 9. 247; one staff better than two, b. 17. 36; two men thrown into Thames, 15. 104; wagging boat, 11. 32; wheat from a weed, a. 10. 122; white and black, b. 10. 436; wolf in sheep's clothing, 17. 270.
Paradys, Paradise, 14. 227; Paradis, 21. 381, 22. 61.
Pardon, 10. 3; b. 15. 246; Pardons, 10. 330.
Pardoner, 1. 66; Pardoners, 3. 229.
Parliament, 5. 45; R. 4. 14; described, R. 4. 53.
Paske, Passover, 19. 168; b. 16. 139.
Pastor, 17. 205.
Patent, 20. 12.
Pater-noster, 8. 10, 12. 295, 16. 249, 17. 320.
Patience, 16. 33, 41, 63, 186, 248, 252; horse of Soothness, 3. 201; a maiden, 8. 274; tree of, b. 16. 8.
Paul, St., 1. 39, 9. 298, 10. 112, 11. 89, 12. 268, 16. 72, 17. 169, 17. 289, 18. 17, 20. 317; b. 10. 200.
Paul the hermit, 18. 13.
Paul's, St. (church), 12. 56, 16. 70; dean of, b. 13. 65; canon of, b. 10. 46.
Paulines, 3. 110, b. 2. 177. *See* notes.
Paumpelon, Pampeluna, 20. 218.
Paynym, a pagan, 8. 161; Paynymes, pagans, 18. 255. (A false form; *Paynim* meant originally the land of pagans.)
Peers Plouhman, 8. 287, 10. 42, 21. 8, 21. 24, 21. 32, 22. 6, 22. 11, 22. 432; Peerses, *gen. case*, 9. 182. *See* Piers.
Pees, Peace, 5. 45, 74, 94; 8. 274; 21. 172, 180, 192, 209; 23. 298, 330; song of, 21. 453.
Penance, 23. 306.
Penetrans-domos, Sir, 23. 340.
Perkyn, a familiar diminutive of Piers,

INDEX TO PROPER NAMES AND SUBJECTS. 481

9. 56, 112, 115, 118; 10. 292; b. 6. 25; Perken Plouhman, 9. 1.
Pernel, Purnele (from Lat. Petronilla), a common female name, esp. for an overdressed vulgar woman, 6. 129, 7. 135, 367, 18. 71; Pernel Proud-heart, 7. 3, a. 5. 45; Pernelles, *gen.* b. 4. 116; Purneles, 5. 111.
Pernell, R. 3. 156; Peronelle, b. 5. 26. *See* above.
Persecution, 13. 205.
Pestilence time, 1. 82, 11. 272; Pestilences, 6. 115, 9. 350, 11. 272, 12. 55.
Peter, 1. 128, 136; 10. 112, 16. 225, 17. 169, 18. 18, 21. 253, 22. 163; b. 10. 346, b. 13. 354; by Saint Peter, an exclamation, 8. 182, 9. 1, 10. 288; St. Peter's church, b. 7. 172.
Peter Comestor alluded to, b. 7. 73.
Pharaoes, *gen.* Pharoah's, 10. 313.
Pharasewes, Pharisees, b. 15. 594.
Philip the sparrow, b. 15. 119 (*footnote*).
Phineas (*finees*), 1. 107, 123.
Phip (*fyppe*), 12. 310.
Physic, 9. 292, 23. 169.
Piers, (*peers*), 8. 199, 287; 10. 300, &c.; Peres the pardoner, 3. 110.
Piers, Sir, 7. 367.
Piers the pardoner, 3. 110.
Piers Plowman (*or* Plouhman), 8. 287; 16. 34, 131, 138, 150, 195; 22. 187, 213, 258, 360, 388, 392, 432, 436, 439; 23. 77, 320, 382, 385; first appears, 8. 182; testament of, 9. 95; pardon of, 10. 282; his wife, daughter, and son, 9. 80-82; *Petrus est Christus*, b. 15. 206; cf. b. 16. 17; as the name of the work, a. 12. 102.
Pilat, Pilate, 21. 83; b. 10. 34; Pilatus, 21. 35, 39, 83.
Pilgrim described, 8. 161; Pilgrims, 1. 47.
Pillory, 4. 79.
Plato, 12. 121, 12. 304, 13. 173, 15. 190, 21. 212, 23. 275.
Pleasure and Pain, 21. 212.
Pontifex, 17. 204.
Poor, the, 2. 172, 4. 83, 17. 50; described, 10. 71, 178; duties of the, 14. 80; little cared for, 12. 42; reach heaven, 12. 293; reward of the, 16. 289; should be fed, 13. 103, 164.
Pope, 1. 135, 3. 23, 3. 244; 4. 164, 184, 317, 332; 6. 192, 22. 444; his enemies, 16. 173; teaches men war, 18. 233; Popes poisoned, 4. 164.
Porphyry, 13. 173, 15. 190.
Poverty, 13. 141, 13. 150, 17. 116; praise of, 14. 1, 14. 99, 17. 117.
Predestination, 12. 207.

Presul, Lat. *præsul*, 17. 204.
Pride, 17. 58, 22. 337, 23. 70; confession of, 7. 8, 7. 14.
Pride-of-perfect-living, 12. 176, 194.
Priests, 14. 101, 17. 268; a slothful priest, 7. 30.
Privy-payment, plaster of, 23. 364.
Prophecies, 4. 443; 9. 346.
Proverbs and proverbial phrases: a blind buzzard, b. 10. 266; a glass hood, 23. 172; as bold as blind Bayard, 5. 120; as common as the cart-way, 4. 168; as courteous as a dog in a kitchen, b. 5. 261; as dead as a door-nail, 2. 184; as dead as a door-tree, b. 1. 185; as fain as fowl of a fair morrow, 12. 103; as it becomes a cow to hop in a cage, R. 3. 262; as lean as a lantern, 9. 174; as light as a leaf on a linden, 2. 152; as much pity as a pedlar has of cats, b. 5. 258; as naked as a needle, 15. 105, 20. 56; as useless (lewd) as a lamp unlighted, 2. 186; as wrath as the wind, 4. 486; as you brew, so drink, 21. 404; at their wits' end, 18. 105; *bele vertue est suffraunce*, 14. 205; calm after a storm, 21. 454; cast not pearls before swine, 12. 7; cast water into Thames, b. 15. 332; farewell, Phip! 12. 310; for all the realm of France, 1. 192; *homo proponit*, 12. 304, 23. 34; in the corner of a cart-wheel, 16. 162; lay there a bean, 13. 92; let go the cup, 7. 394; like a cipher in augrim, R. 4. 53; lyues and lokynge, 22. 159; Malkin's maidenhood, 2. 181; measure is a merry mean, R. 2. 139; measure is medicine, 2. 33; *melius est mori quam male uiuere*, 18. 40; much honey cloys the maw, 17. 218; no good apple on a sour stock, 11. 206; not worth a cress, 12. 14; on fat land grow foulest weeds, 13. 224; *patientes uincunt*, 16. 138; *quant oportet, &c.*, b. 10. 439; seldom mosseth the marble-stone, &c., a. 10. 101; sweet liquor lasts not long, 13. 220; that that rathest ripeth, soonest rotteth, 13. 222; the wolf s—ts wool, 10. 265; the leuere childe, &c., b. 5. 38; three things drive a man from home, smoke, rain, and a scolding wife, 20. 297; to beguile the guiler, 21. 166, 385, b. 10. 192; to cast the crock amid the coals, R. 2. 52; to catch a hare with a tabor, R. 1. 58; to drink with the duck, 7. 174; to have pepper in the nose, b. 15. 197; to live and look,

INDEX TO PROPER NAMES AND SUBJECTS.

11. 57, 22. 159; to mete the mist, 1. 163; unless a louse could leap, it could not walk on his coat, 7. 204; venom expels venom, 21. 156; where all are equal, wo!, R. 1. 66; where the cat is a kitten, 1. 295; whoso spareth the spring (rod), 6. 139; whoso stretcheth in the whitel, 17. 76; worth both his ears, 1. 76. *See also* Similes.
Prudence, 22. 276; 23. 31.
Prus, Prussia, 7. 279; Pruslond, b. 13. 393.
Prydie, 7. 367. See note.
Psalter, the, 4. 289, 6. 47, 7. 303, 9. 260, 12. 25, 12. 51, 12. 118, 13. 29, b. 2. 38.
Ptolemy, 13. 175.
Puns :—to *bear* children, b. 9. 163; *cross* (on money), the *cross*, 18. 200; *fratres* (friars, brethren), 16. 75, b. 11. 87; *good, goods*, 11. 254; *grace, grass*, 15. 23; *heart, hart*, R. 2. 36; *life* (man), *life*, 21. 389, 23. 92; *naughty*, b. 6. 226; *prouendre* (prebend, provender), b. 13. 243, 245; *quean, queen*, 9. 46; *Robert, robber*, 7. 316; *worts, words*, b. 5. 162.
Purnel's finery, 5. 111. *See* Pernel.

Ragamoffyn, the name of a demon, 21. 283.
Rain, 20. 301; signification of, 20. 315.
Randolf, earl of Chester, 8. 11; see note.
Ratio, 17. 188.
Reason, 5. 14–194, 14. 143, 14. 197, 16. 27, 16. 40, 16. 151, R. 2. 69; talks with the author, 6. 11; his sermon, 6. 114.
Recklessness, 12. 195, 199, 274, 283; 13. 4, 14. 129.
Reginald, b. 4. 49.
Regrating, 4. 82, 113, 118.
Regum, i. e. *liber Regum*, the book of Kings, 4. 410, 416.
Religious men, proud conduct of, 6. 157.
Repentance, 7. 1, 12, 62, 91, 164, 234, &c.
Resurrection, 22. 152.
Revel, a place so called, 23. 181.
Reynald the reeve, 3. 112.
Rhine, the (þe *ryne*), b. pr. 229.
Rich, the, 2. 172, 10. 134, 11. 165, 12. 63, b. 10. 96; doom of, 13. 210, 15. 18, 16. 285; duty of, 14. 66.
Richard, king, R. pr. 9, 1. 1, 3. 110, 3. 338, 4. 3.
Riches, 17. 1, 46; poison the church, 18. 220.
Righteousness, 21. 177, 194, 467.
Roberd's knaves, i. e. robbers, outlaws, 1. 45; see note.

Robert the robber, 7. 316, 322.
Robert Run-about, b. 6. 150.
Robin, 7. 387, 9. 75.
Robin Hood, 8. 11.
Rochel, Rochelle, 1. 230.
Rochemadore, Roquemadour, b. 12. 37. See note, p. 179.
Romanye, Roman territory, b. 15. 559.
Romaynes, the Romans, 18. 281.
Rome, 1. 48, 3. 243, 5. 123, 6. 198, 7. 246, 8. 167, 9. 1, 10. 323, 22. 425; b. 5. 468, b. 12. 37, b. 14. 196.
Rome-runners, 5. 125.
Rondulf, Randolph, a. 2. 78.
Rosamonde, fair Rosamond, b. 12. 48.
Rose, a widow, 5. 47; a dish-seller, 7. 372; a regrater, 7. 232.
Ruele, i. e. La Reole, 1. 230. See note, p. 20.
Ruth, 4. 416.
Rutland, b. 2. 110.

Sacrament, the Holy, 20. 88; once a month, 22. 390.
St. Giles; *see* Gyle.
Salamon, Solomon; *see* Solomon.
Samaritan, 20. 47, 63, 106, 279.
Sampson, 19. 114; b. 12. 42.
Samuel, 4. 417, 420, 432, 442; 19. 114.
Sapience, book of, 12. 118, b. 6. 237. *See* Wisdom.
Saracens; *see* Sarasyns.
Sarah (alluded to), 14. 9.
Sarasyns, Saracens, 4. 484; Sarrasyns, 13. 54, 15. 201; Saracenes, b. 10. 348; Saresyns, 18. 123; Sarrasines, 18. 132, 150; Sarasenes, b. 13. 209; Sarrasyn, a Saracen, 13. 87.
Sathan, Satan, 8. 106, 19. 152; Satan, 21. 276, 353; b. 2. 105, b. 10. 118, b. 13. 446; referred to, 2. 59.
Satisfaction, 17. 27; b. 14. 21, 94.
Saturday, 7. 418; b. 13. 153; wind on a, 6. 117; Saturdays, 7. 173.
Saturnus, the planet Saturn, 9. 348.
Saul, 4. 412, 414, 417, 420, 432, 443; 15. 61.
Say-well, 11. 145.
Scripture, 12. 97, 101, 163; 13. 40; 14. 130; a. 12. 12.
Scrope, Lord, R. 2. 154.
Seeds, 13. 179–192.
Seem, Shem (*but meant for* Seth), b. 9. 123.
See-well, 11. 145.
Seneca, 17. 143, 23. 275.
Sensus, 17. 189.
Sepulchre, the, 8. 171.
Seraphin, 2. 106.
Serjeants-at-law, 1. 160; 4. 451.

INDEX TO PROPER NAMES AND SUBJECTS. 483

Services of the Church, 10. 228, 243; ill said, 14. 123.
Sesse, Cis, Cicely, 7. 362.
Seth, 11. 248, 252. *See* Seem.
Seven Arts, 12. 98, 13. 93, 18. 114.
Seven Psalms, 4. 468, 6. 47.
Seven (Deadly) Sins, 7. 1-8, 119; 17. 44-98; b. 15. 72.
Seven Sleepers, 16. 272.
Seven stars, i. e. the planets, 18. 98; R. 3. 352.
Seven times a day, the just man sins, 11. 21.
Seven Virtues, 8. 270.
Shame brings amendment, 14. 241.
Shepherds, the angels appear to, 15. 92.
Ship in a storm, R. 4. 72.
Shoreditch, b. 13. 340.
Shrift, 23. 306.
Sim-at the-stile, 7. 207.
Similes; an apple-tree, 19. 61; 'ark is Christ's church,' 12. 246; 'as a bride leaves her kindred,' 17. 106; 'as a spark of fire in the Thames,' 7. 336; 'as clothiers comb wool,' 12. 15; 'as clouds hide the sun,' 11. 158; 'as I a shepherd were,' 1. 2; 'as the hen cherishes her chickens,' &c., R. 2. 143; 'clerks are carpenters of the ark,' 12. 249; coped as a friar, 4. 38; 'dumb dogs,' b. 10. 287; 'foul weeds,' &c., 13. 224; 'good man like a taper,' 20. 258; 'in habit as a hermit,' 1. 3; 'like a beggar on the hall-floor,' 15. 138; 'like a dog that eats grass,' 7. 431; 'like a fowler laying lines,' 7. 406; 'like a gleeman's bitch,' 7. 404; 'like a snow-covered dung-heap,' 17. 265; 'like a stake as a land-mark,' 4. 384; 'like a whited wall,' 17. 267; 'like bad coin,' 18. 73; 'like growing grain,' 14. 23; 'like the widow's wooer,' 13. 20; 'like wood on fire,' 17. 180; 'the death of seeds like that of men,' 13. 179; 'the soap of sickness,' b. 14. 6; 'the walnut and kernel,' 13. 144; 'trees with rotten roots,' 17. 247, 271; 'with manners like a hawk,' 8. 44. *See also* Proverbs.
Simon, i. e. Peter, 10. 257.
Simon, St. (apostle), 15. 143.
Simon's son, 6. 79. (Here the 'son of Simon' means one guilty of simony; see note, p. 63.)
Simony, 3. 63, 67, 72, 115, 117, 155; 4. 185, 10. 55; 23. 126, 137; cf. 6. 79.
Simplicity-of-speech, b. 10. 165.
Sin, b. 14. 323.
Sin against the Holy Ghost, 20. 276.

Sinai, 8. 171; 20. 2; b. 5. 528.
Sloth, 17. 95; 23. 159, 163, 217, 373; confession of, 8. 1-81.
Smoke, 20. 305; signification of, 20. 323.
Sobriety, b. 10. 165.
Sodomye, Sodom, 16. 232; Sodome, b. 14. 75.
Solomon (*salamon*), 4. 121, 326, 487; 9. 243; 12. 211, 271; 14. 198, 15. 193; b. 12. 42; in hell, 4. 331, 12. 220.
Song—*Deux saue dame emme*, 1. 225.
Soothness (Truth), 3. 200.
Sortes, Socrates, 15. 193. See note.
Southwerk, Southwark, 7. 83.
Southwest wind, 6. 117.
Spayne, Spain, 18. 272.
Spes (Hope), 20. 1, 44, 51, 78, 95.
Spicers (grocers), 3. 235.
Spirit, gifts of the, 22. 229.
Spiritus, 17. 198.
Star in the East, 15. 97; 21. 243, 249. *See* Seven stars.
Stories, clerk of the, i. e. Peter Comestor, b. 7. 73. See note, p. 121.
Storms, 9. 349; ship in a storm, R. 4. 72.
Stots, the four, 22. 267.
Stowe, Thomme, 6. 131.
Stretforth, Stratford, b. 13. 267.
Study, Dame, 12. 1, 84.
Suffer-both-weal-and-wo, 12. 107.
Suffer-thy-sovereigns-to-have-their-will, 9. 82.
Suffer-till-I see-my-time, 4. 20.
Suicide, 11. 162.
Sunday, 7. 418, 8. 65; Sundays, 3. 231, 10. 227, 242, 244.
Surname, not to be given up, 4. 369.
Surrye, Syria, 18. 169, 240; Surre, b. 13. 209.
Swan, the, R. 3. 28, 86.
Symond, Simon, R. 4. 55; Symondes, Simon's, 6. 79 (see note, p. 63); Simeon's, 21. 261 (see note, p. 256).
Synay, Sinai, 20. 2. *See* Sinai.
Syse, Assisi, 8. 166.

Taddee, Thaddeus, 22. 165.
Tarse, b. 15. 163. See note.
Tartaryne, b. 15. 224. See Tarse.
Taxes, R. 4. 15, 49.
Temese, the Thames, 7. 335, 15. 104.
Temperance, 22. 281; 23. 23.
Templers, Templars, 18. 209.
Thames; *see* Temese.
Theft, borough of, 3. 92.
Theology, 3. 116, 129; 12. 129; b. 10. 195; a. 12. 9.
Thobie, Tobit, 18. 37; b. 10. 85, 87. *See* Tobie.

Tholomeus, Ptolemy, 13. 175.
Thomas, St., 8. 201, 22. 165, 170;—of Canterbury, 18. 274.
Thomme. *See* Tom.
Thorsday, Thursday, i. e. Maundy Thursday, b. 16. 140, 160.
Thought, 11. 72, 110, 112.
Three things that drive a man out of doors, 20. 297; see note.
Tobie, Tobias, i. e. Tobit, 12. 70, b. 10. 33. *See* Thobie.
Tom the tinker, 7. 364 (Tim the tinker, b. 5. 317).
Tom Stow, 6. 131.
Tom True-tongue, 5. 18.
Tom Two-tongued, 23. 162.
Tonsure, clerical, 1. 86; 4. 59.
Torch, a symbol of the Trinity, 20. 168.
Tournament of Christ, 21. 17.
Trades, 12. 125.
Tradesmen, 1. 221; fraudulent, 4. 80.
Trajan, 13. 75, 90; 15. 150, 205.
Tree of knowledge, 21. 307; opposed to the tree of the cross, 21. 400; of charity, 19. 9; of Patience, b. 16. 8.
Trinity, 12. 37, 152; 20. 96; b. 9. 35; symbols of, 19. 26, 189, 211, 216; 20. 110, 177.
Troianus, Trajan, 13. 75, 90; Traianus, 15. 150, 205.
True-love, tree of, 19. 9.
Truth, 9. 137, 141; 10. 1; 21. 124, 167, 271, 463; St. Truth, 6. 199; tower of, 1. 15, 2. 12, 2. 134, 8. 232; Truth is a treasure, 2. 81, 136, 203.
Tullius, 13. 175.
Tyburn, 7. 368, 15. 130.

Versification, 18. 109.
Vicar, the careless, 22. 411.
Vigilate, 8. 57.
Virgil, b. 12. 44.
Virginity, 19. 89.
Vncristene, men who are not Christians, 2. 89.
Unity, house of, 22. 330, 359; 23. 75, 204, 227, 245, 297.
Uriah, 12. 265, b. 10. 423, a. 11. 280.
Usury, isle of, a. 2. 66.

Wafers, b. 13. 263.
Wages, 4. 267, 292, 310; 9. 336; 17. 3.
Wales, b. 15. 435; Walis, R. prol. 23.
Walish, Welshman, 7. 373.
Walishman, Welshman, 7. 309.
Walsingham, 1. 52; b. 5. 230.
Walterot, 21. 146. See note, p. 254.

Wanhope, 23. 160; Sir, 12. 198.
Waryn Wiseman, 5. 27.
Waryn Wring-law, 5. 31.
Washing clothes, 17. 330; b, 14. 5.
Waster, 9. 149, 326.
Watkyn, 7. 70, 71 (Wat, b. 13. 326).
Watte, Wat, 6. 133, 7. 363.
Weather-wisdom, 18. 94.
Wedlock, 11. 203, 256.
Wednesday, b. 13. 154.
Westminster, 3. 174, 4. 13, 23. 284, a 5. 129; Westminster hall, 23. 133; Westminster law, 11. 239.
Weyhill, 7. 211. See note.
Whistling, b. 15. 466.
Widowhood, 19. 88.
Widow's mite, b. 13. 196.
Wife, scolding, 20. 299; signification of, 20. 310.
Will (self-will), 4. 22.
Wille, Will (for William), 7. 2. 70, 71; a. 8. 43; the author's name, 2. 5, 11. 71, a. 12. 99, 103; Long Will (the same), b. 15. 148.
Wily-man, 4. 27, 31.
Winchester, 7. 211; fair, 14. 52.
Wind, great, 6. 117.
Windows, glazing of, 4. 51, 65, 69; 17. 41.
Wisdom, book of, 4. 487, 497; 12. 118, 211. *See* Sapience.
Wit, 5. 77, 87; 11. 110, 114, 127; 12. 5. 84; R. 3. 211.
Witchcraft, 7. 85.
Wits, five, 2. 15, 11. 144.
Witty-man, 4. 31.
Witty-word, b. 4. 20.
Wolves, 10. 259.
Workmen, 1. 22; 2. 124; 4. 310, 350; 6. 66, 9. 197, 337.
Work-well, 11. 146.
Work-when-time-is, 9. 80.
World, the, 19. 31; mirror of, 12. 170, 14. 132.
Wrath, 8. 261, 17. 67; confession of, 7. 103.
Wrong, 5. 46, 65, 80, 100.
Wy, Weyhill, 7. 211.

Ynde, India, 22. 165; Inde, 18. 272.
Yngelonde, England, 23. 279.
Ypocras, Hippocrates, b. 12. 44.
Yrelonde, Ireland, 23. 221.
Yrisshe, Irish, R. prol. 10.
Ysaye, Isaiah, 19. 113, b. 10. 418, a. 11. 275; Ysaie, 12. 258.

Zaccheus, Zacchæus, b. 13. 195.
3yuan, Evan, 7. 310.

OTHER TITLES IN THIS HARDBACK REPRINT PROGRAMME FROM SANDPIPER BOOKS LTD (LONDON) AND POWELLS BOOKS (CHICAGO)

ISBN 0-19-	Author	Title
8264011	ALEXANDER Paul J.	The Patriarch Nicephorus of Constantinople
8143567	ALFÖLDI A.	The Conversion of Constantine and Pagan Rome
9241775	ALLEN T.W.	Homeri Ilias (3 volumes)
6286409	ANDERSON George K.	The Literature of the Anglo-Saxons
8219601	ARNOLD Benjamin	German Knighthood
8208618	ARNOLD T.W.	The Caliphate
8144059	BAILEY Cyril	Lucretius: De Rerum Natura (3 volumes)
814167X	BARRETT W.S.	Euripides: Hippolytos
8228813	BARTLETT & MacKAY	Medieval Frontier Societies
8219733	BARTLETT Robert	Trial by Fire and Water
8118856	BENTLEY G.E.	William Blake's Writings (2 volumes)
8111010	BETHURUM Dorothy	Homilies of Wulfstan
8142765	BOLLING G. M.	External Evidence for Interpolation in Homer
814332X	BOLTON J.D.P.	Aristeas of Proconnesus
9240132	BOYLAN Patrick	Thoth, the Hermes of Egypt
8114222	BROOKS Kenneth R.	Andreas and the Fates of the Apostles
8214715	BUCKLER Georgina	Anna Comnena
8203543	BULL Marcus	Knightly Piety & Lay Response to the First Crusade
8216785	BUTLER Alfred J.	Arab Conquest of Egypt
8148046	CAMERON Alan	Circus Factions
8148054	CAMERON Alan	Porphyrius the Charioteer
8148348	CAMPBELL J.B.	The Emperor and the Roman Army 31 AD to 235
826643X	CHADWICK Henry	Priscillian of Avila
826447X	CHADWICK Henry	Boethius
8222025	COLGRAVE B. & MYNORS R.A.B.	Bede's Ecclesiastical History of the English People
8131658	COOK J.M.	The Troad
8219393	COWDREY H.E.J.	The Age of Abbot Desiderius
8644043	CRUM W.E.	Coptic Dictionary
8148992	DAVIES M.	Sophocles: Trachiniae
814153X	DODDS E.R.	Plato: Gorgias
825301X	DOWNER L.	Leges Henrici Primi
814346X	DRONKE Peter	Medieval Latin and the Rise of European Love-Lyric
8142749	DUNBABIN T.J.	The Western Greeks
8154372	FAULKNER R.O.	The Ancient Egyptian Pyramid Texts
8221541	FLANAGAN Marie Therese	Irish Society, Anglo-Norman Settlers, Angevin Kingship
8143109	FRAENKEL Edward	Horace
8142781	FRASER P.M.	Ptolemaic Alexandria (3 volumes)
8201540	GOLDBERG P.J.P.	Women, Work and Life Cycle in a Medieval Economy
8140215	GOTTSCHALK H.B.	Heraclides of Pontus
8266162	HANSON R.P.C.	Saint Patrick
8581351	HARRIS C.R.S	The Heart and Vascular System in Ancient Greek Medicine
8224354	HARRISS G.L.	King, Parliament and Public Finance in Medieval England to 1369
8581114	HEATH Sir Thomas	Aristarchus of Samos
8140444	HOLLIS A.S.	Callimachus: Hecale
8212968	HOLLISTER C. Warren	Anglo-Saxon Military Institutions
9244944	HOPKIN-JAMES L.J.	The Celtic Gospels
8226470	HOULDING J.A.	Fit for Service
2115480	HENRY Blanche	British Botanical and Horticultural Literature before 1800
8219523	HOUSLEY Norman	The Italian Crusades
8223129	HURNARD Naomi	The King's Pardon for Homicide – before AD 1307
9241783	HURRY Jamieson B.	Imhotep
8140401	HUTCHINSON G.O.	Hellenistic Poetry
9240140	JOACHIM H.H.	Aristotle: On Coming-to-be and Passing-away
9240094	JONES A.H.M	Cities of the Eastern Roman Provinces
8142560	JONES A.H.M.	The Greek City
8218354	JONES Michael	Ducal Brittany 1364–1399
8271484	KNOX & PELCZYNSKI	Hegel's Political Writings
8212755	LAWRENCE C.H.	St Edmund of Abingdon
8225253	LE PATOUREL John	The Norman Empire
8212720	LENNARD Reginald	Rural England 1086–1135
8212321	LEVISON W.	England and the Continent in the 8th century
8148224	LIEBESCHUETZ J.H.W.G.	Continuity and Change in Roman Religion
8143486	LINDSAY W.M.	Early Latin Verse
8141378	LOBEL Edgar & PAGE Sir Denys	Poetarum Lesbiorum Fragmenta
9240159	LOEW E.A.	The Beneventan Script
8115881	LOOMIS Roger Sherman	Arthurian Literature in the Middle Ages
8241445	LUKASIEWICZ, Jan	Aristotle's Syllogistic
8152442	MAAS P. & TRYPANIS C.A.	Sancti Romani Melodi Cantica
8113692	MANDEVILLE Bernard	The Fable of the Bees (2 volumes)
8142684	MARSDEN E.W.	Greek and Roman Artillery—Historical
8142692	MARSDEN E.W.	Greek and Roman Artillery—Technical
8148178	MATTHEWS John	Western Aristocracies and Imperial Court AD 364–425

9240205	MAVROGORDATO John	Digenes Akrites
8223447	McFARLANE K.B.	Lancastrian Kings and Lollard Knights
8226578	McFARLANE K.B.	The Nobility of Later Medieval England
814296X	MEIGGS Russell	The Athenian Empire
8148100	MEIGGS Russell	Roman Ostia
8148402	MEIGGS Russell	Trees and Timber in the Ancient Mediterranean World
8141718	MERKELBACH R. & WEST M.L.	Fragmenta Hesiodea
8143362	MILLAR F.G.B.	Cassius Dio
8142641	MILLER J. Innes	The Spice Trade of the Roman Empire
8147813	MOORHEAD John	Theoderic in Italy
8264259	MOORMAN John	A History of the Franciscan Order
8181469	MORISON Stanley	Politics and Script
9240582	MUSURILLO H.	Acts of the Pagan Martyrs & Christian Martyrs (2 volumes)
9240213	MYRES J.L.	Herodotus The Father of History
9241791	NEWMAN W.L.	The Politics of Aristotle (4 volumes)
8219512	OBOLENSKY Dimitri	Six Byzantine Portraits
8270259	O'DONNELL J.J.	Augustine: Confessions (3 volumes)
263268X	OSLER Sir William	Bibliotheca Osleriana
8116020	OWEN A.L.	The Famous Druids
8131445	PALMER, L.R.	The Interpretation of Mycenaean Greek Texts
8143427	PFEIFFER R.	History of Classical Scholarship (volume 1)
8143648	PFEIFFER Rudolf	History of Classical Scholarship 1300–1850
8111649	PHEIFER J.D.	Old English Glosses in the Epinal-Erfurt Glossary
8142277	PICKARD–CAMBRIDGE A.W.	Dithyramb Tragedy and Comedy
8269765	PLATER & WHITE	Grammar of the Vulgate
8213891	PLUMMER Charles	Lives of Irish Saints (2 volumes)
820695X	POWICKE Michael	Military Obligation in Medieval England
8269684	POWICKE Sir Maurice	Stephen Langton
821460X	POWICKE Sir Maurice	The Christian Life in the Middle Ages
8225369	PRAWER Joshua	Crusader Institutions
8225571	PRAWER Joshua	The History of The Jews in the Latin Kingdom of Jerusalem
8143249	RABY F.J.E.	A History of Christian Latin Poetry
8143257	RABY F.J.E.	A History of Secular Latin Poetry in the Middle Ages (2 volumes)
8214316	RASHDALL & POWICKE	The Universities of Europe in the Middle Ages (3 volumes)
8154488	REYMOND E.A.E & BARNS J.W.B.	Four Martyrdoms from the Pierpont Morgan Coptic Codices
8148380	RICKMAN Geoffrey	The Corn Supply of Ancient Rome
8141556	ROSS Sir David	Aristotle: De Anima
8141076	ROSS Sir David	Aristotle: Metaphysics (2 volumes)
8141084	ROSS Sir David	Aristotle: Parva Naturalia
8141092	ROSS Sir David	Aristotle: Physics
9244952	ROSS Sir David	Aristotle: Prior and Posterior Analytics
8142307	ROSTOVTZEFF M.	Social and Economic History of the Hellenistic World (3 volumes)
8142315	ROSTOVTZEFF M.	Social and Economic History of the Roman Empire (2 volumes)
8264178	RUNCIMAN Sir Steven	The Eastern Schism
814833X	SALMON J.B.	Wealthy Corinth
8171587	SALZMAN L.F.	Building in England Down to 1540
8218362	SAYERS Jane E.	Papal Judges Delegate in the Province of Canterbury 1198–1254
8221657	SCHEIN Sylvia	Fideles Crucis
8148135	SHERWIN WHITE A.N.	The Roman Citizenship
825153X	SHERWIN WHITE A.N.	Roman Society and Roman Law in the New Testament
9240167	SINGER Charles	Galen: On Anatomical Procedures
8113927	SISAM, Kenneth	Studies in the History of Old English Literature
8113668	SKEAT Walter	Langland: The Vision of William Concerning Piers the Plowman (2 volumes)
8642040	SOUTER Alexander	A Glossary of Later Latin to 600 AD
8270011	SOUTER Alexander	Earliest Latin Commentaries on the Epistles of St Paul
8222254	SOUTHERN R.W.	Eadmer: Life of St. Anselm
8251408	SQUIBB G.	The High Court of Chivalry
8212011	STEVENSON & WHITELOCK	Asser's Life of King Alfred
8212011	SWEET Henry	A Second Anglo-Saxon Reader—Archaic and Dialectical
8143443	SYME Sir Ronald	Ammianus and the Historia Augusta
8148259	SYME Sir Ronald	History in Ovid
8143273	SYME Sir Ronald	Tacitus (2 volumes)
8142714	THOMPSON E.A.	The Goths in Spain
8200951	THOMPSON Sally	Women Religious
8142625	TURNER E.G.	Greek Papyri: An Introduction
924023X	WALBANK F.W.	Historical Commentary on Polybius (3 volumes)
8201745	WALKER Simon	The Lancastrian Affinity 1361–1399
8161115	WELLESZ Egon	A History of Byzantine Music and Hymnography
8140185	WEST M.L.	Greek Metre
8141696	WEST M.L.	Hesiod: Theogony
8148542	WEST M.L.	The Orphic Poems
8140053	WEST M.L.	Hesiod: Works & Days
8152663	WEST M.L.	Iambi et Elegi Graeci
9240221	WHEELWRIGHT Philip	Heraclitus
822799X	WHITBY M. & M.	The History of Theophylact Simocatta
8206186	WILLIAMSON, E.W.	Letters of Osbert of Clare
8208103	WILSON F.P.	Plague in Shakespeare's London
8247672	WOODHOUSE C.M.	Gemistos Plethon
8114877	WOOLF Rosemary	The English Religious Lyric in the Middle Ages
8119224	WRIGHT Joseph	Grammar of the Gothic Language